THE BOY PIRATE;

OR,

LIFE ON THE OCEAN.

A NOVEL.

ILLUSTRATED WITH NUMEROUS ENGRAVINGS.

LONDON:
NEWSAGENTS' PUBLISHING COMPANY, 147, FLEET STREET, E.C.,
1865.

THE BOY PIRATE;

OR,

LIFE ON THE OCEAN.

BY CAPTAIN IRVING LYONS.

THE CONTEST.

OFFICE:

NEWS AGENTS' PUBLISHING COMPANY, 147, FLEET STREET, E.C.

SPECIAL NOTICE.

A New Tale, of startling and thrilling interest, called

IVAN THE TERRIBLE;

OR,

DARK DEEDS OF NIGHT!

Will be published on Tuesday, December 5.

The purchasers of this astonishing Story, written by one of the most deeply interesting Authors of the day, will be entitled to the Grand Gift of

A SERIES OF SPLENDID ENGRAVINGS!

The first of the series will be given away (Gratis) with Nos. 1 and 2 of the Story of "Ivan the Terrible," and will prove the largest and most beautiful picture ever presented with any work in any part of the world, the production of which has cost hundreds of pounds. Remember, "Ivan the Terrible," in Weekly Numbers, price One Penny, of all booksellers.

With No. 3 of this work will be published and given away (Gratis) an Illustrated Story, entitled,

THE GHOST'S HOUSE IN THE LONELY ROAD!

———

ORDER AT ONCE OF YOUR BOOKSELLERS

IVAN THE TERRIBLE.

THE BOY PIRATE;

OR,

LIFE ON THE OCEAN.

[THE ABDUCTION OF THE YOUNG HEIR.]

PROLOGUE.

THE SILENT SHIP—THE MAIDEN PRISONER—
A STRANGE SAIL—THE BLACK FLAG—A TER-
RIBLE RUMOUR—THE BOY PIRATE OF THE
SEAS.

MIDNIGHT on the dark waters of the Indian Sea.
The stars glimmered from a sky of blackness—the
moon shone on inky waves. A steady breeze was

blowing, but beyond the noise of the beating billows there was not a sound pervading the scene of
quiet interest.

A gallant ship speeds silently over the sea. Her
sails are set to every stitch, and she glides before
the wind in easy speed.

A few sailors are grouped about the deck; others

No. 1.

are sleeping by the bows. The man at the wheel stands motionless at his post.

No one speaks. The ship journeys as silently as if it were the vessel of the dead.

One would believe it were almost, if he could but glance to the interior of the principal cabin. Here, lying on a couch, was a female form—a lady, young and charming fair, but lying so still, and with features so white, that she seemed to have passed from life.

She was so young as to be almost childlike in looks. Her hair lay grouped about her face and shoulders in rich auburn masses. Her arms, white and cold, lay rigid by her side; her limbs were extended, and her little feet peeped lifelessly from the hem of a rich robe.

There was something singularly interesting in the appearance of this passive young creature, lying alone in that speeding vessel. The mind wondered why she was there, in her beauty and loneliness. What fate had been hers, or was to be? whether she yet lived, or if she were dead? by what means she had met with her doom?

If she had been undisturbed for some time she was not destined to remain long so. The door of the cabin was opened, and a gentleman entered, who, after gazing a moment at the silent lady, closed the door and advanced.

He was dressed in the uniform of a naval captain. His figure was tall and his limbs powerful, but there was an expression about his features that would have warned the gaze to avoid and beware of him.

As he stepped to the couch a satisfied leer gleamed from his cunning eyes. He clenched his hands, as if in triumph, and bending over the pale girl, muttered—

"Pale enough now; quiet, too. She begins to grow tame. It is well. I have trifled too long, and she has more than once tempted me to violence."

He sat beside her, and took her hand. It was as cold as marble, and he let it fall again. A look of alarm spread itself over his features, and he leaned forward to look at her more closely.

"Not dead!" he cried, "I have not gone too far. God! if it were so, and all my plans scattered like this, I could die in madness."

He touched her face, it was icy to his hand; her lips seemed breathless; her heart throbless; his looks grew wilder at every fresh indication of what he feared."

"Oh, God!" he cried, "I have killed her in my mad folly. Lilia, Lilia, wake; speak to me. Oh, do not die; it is I—Harwolf. Forgive me, and wake to life again."

A slight murmur came from the young girl's lips. Harwolf seized her in his arms, and lifted her from the couch.

"Lilia," he cried, "living still; mine, mine only, and for ever."

The pale girl unclosed her eyes; a shiver passed through her, as if with returning life some painful remembrance came to her mind; but when Harwolf again repeated her name, and pressed his lips passionately to hers, a look of horror passed across her face, and, with a shriek of anguish, she forced herself away.

A muttered oath escaped Harwolf's lips.

"If I had doubted you," he cried, "this would give me proof. Will you never end this? Am I to find in you only the same perverse, haughty being of snow?"

"Till you release me," came vividly from Lilia's lips. "Oh, God! would that in my trance I had died; it would have been better than coming back to life and you."

A second oath was Harwolf's answer.

"Girl!" he said, sternly, "I have risked my soul to gain you! I have dared all that man can dare, and, now that you are in my power, beyond *his* aid, I swear by the demons of hell nothing shall deprive me of you! I will make you mine for ever!"

"It shall never be!" she answered him, her beautiful face flushed in its excitement. "Sooner will I die in the cruel ocean!"

"You will have to die, then!" was his brutal answer. "And now, since I have you back to life, it shall be as you have said—back to me!"

He stepped towards her as he spoke.

She receded as he advanced.

Shrinking, shuddering, the light of passion was in his eyes; his cheeks were pale with frenzy; a sensual smile was about his lips. It was evident that he had her in his power, and intended to use that power.

When she had reached the end of the cabin he thought he had her at his mercy, but, as he laughed in scorn, her little hand struck hard at him, and the next instant she had glided from him, and was out of the cabin.

Harwolf leaped swiftly after her; his lips were foaming in his rage, but she was out upon the deck before he had time to seize her by the skirt.

That it was her intention to leap overboard was plainly perceivable. She sprang lightly to the bulwarks, and, resting there, fixed her startled gaze on her persecutor, and cried—

"God will pardon me! I take this leap only in self-defence, and because I prefer death to dishonour! Harwolf, thus will I baffle you! You shall never have it to say to *him* that I was your victim!"

It was very pitiful to see her standing there on the brink of destruction, looking so beautiful in her distress. Her danger was most imminent, for a lurch of the vessel would have sent her to the deep waters.

Harwolf hurried to the bulwarks, followed by the sailors, whom the unexpected crisis had brought to the scene.

But before any of them could have touched her, she would have committed herself to the deep; and every one fully expected that she would do so; but all in a moment a pleased light shone from her eye, she clasped her little hands to her breast, and leaped to the deck.

"I can defy you now," she said: "your power will have an end; it is in the air that *he* is near me. See yonder; they're speeding to my aid!"

The sailors followed the direction of her glance; the shadowing sails and masts of a vessel gleamed in the moon's rays, but little of the ship could be defined, and yet an instinctive dread fell upon the men, and even their callous leader quailed.

There was a silence of a few moments, during which all eyes were fixed on the coming vessel; it was speeding so swiftly that it appeared to be flying over the surface of the sea, and each moment brought it so close that its size and build were quickly seen.

A savage light gleamed from Harwolf's eyes.

"It is wrong," he cried, "for once, proud bird, you are mistaken; it is not he who comes; you are mine still; surround her, men."

The sailors surrounded the pale maiden, but she undauntedly regarded them; presently, her glance again swept to the approaching vessel, and her beautiful arm was raised, pointing towards it.

"See!" she cried, "that is an ensign that will lie like a pall about your hearts!"

They gazed across the sea; the coming ship had risen above the waves, and towered high with its mass of canvass; a shadowing light fell upon it, and with the speed at which it flew towards them, it seemed as if it were a spectral ship of doom.

It had as great an influence of dread on the hearts of those seamen, when suddenly a black mass fell from the top of the advancing ship and hung about it like a pall.

In a moment after it lay in the air, and the seamen and their leader gazed with awe on the signal of death—the black flag of piracy.

Every face went pale: paler still when a red spot shone on the flag of death—a red spot which, as the vessels neared, was made out to be a blood-red raven, with outspread wings and claws distended to fasten on its prey.

There was wildness in Lilia's look as she—the only one on board that vessel unnerved by the sight of that ominous flag of doom—gazed upon her persecutors.

It seemed strange that this pirate ship should excite so much dread in the minds of the seamen and yet seem so welcome to that pallid girl; her little hands were clutched wildly, and her features lighted up in triumph.

"It is so!" she exclaimed, "he is near, and I am saved."

A devilish look passed across Harwolf's features, and with a deep imprecation, he strode towards her.

"Not saved yet!" he cried, "by Heavens! I have dared too much to let you escape me now: let your hope leave, for sooner would I give you to the arms of hell's demons than lose you to him; let him come, he may take his stand upon my ship, but where he seeks for you, he shall find only a streak of blood upon the deck."

Lilla drew back, not in fear, but to oppose her foe; he had drawn his sword, and rushing upon her, drew her from the bulwarks. There was murder in his looks as he forced her to the deck; at that moment a sullen crash came from the approaching ship, and a red flame shot through the air.

The seamen shrank back, and Harwolf glared round in rage as a murmur ran from man to man, breathing the name of

"THE BOY PIRATE!"

CHAPTER I.

DEEDS OF CRIME.

The circumstances of our hero's birth were, to a great extent, enwrapped in a mystery—a mystery that aided the commission of a crafty and wicked scheme, the result of which was to place him in a position and chain him to a destiny far different to those to which otherwise he had been born.

His father, Lord Edgeforth, was the only scion of an illustrious house, inheriting estates that formed no inconsiderable part of one of the principal portions of Sussex. The young lord, left at an early age in possession of vast wealth and power, had not remained much in England to enjoy either.

He was fond of travel, and to distant countries he journeyed, leaving his affairs in the hands of his late father's steward, Andrew Harwolf, a man believed to be possessed of much integrity, and who had for years had the management of the fine estates that formed the property of the family.

After three years' absence, Lord Edgeforth returned unexpectedly to Frontemore Hall — the ancestral mansion of his father—but he came not, as had been expected, alone. He brought with him a wife whom he had, as it seemed, privately married, for no one had heard of the marriage, and no one knew anything respecting the lady's family connections, or even nationality.

Curiosity was, of course, on the *qui vive* to know all about her, but in this case the gossips were baffled, for the young wife was never seen abroad; and Lord Edgeforth neither sought nor admitted intercourse with society.

Arriving privately and at night, he had shut himself up in the hall with his bride, and his domestics were strictly forbidden to answer any questions respecting her, or their mode of life apart from society.

Rumours of all kinds soon got abroad: it was said that the lady was a young creature of surpassing beauty, whom Lord Edgeforth —ever noted for his rashness and impetuosity—had rescued from a convent; and whom he now kept in seclusion from the fear that discovery might result in her being taken from him.

This was only one of many reports, but it was the one that gained the most ground, the first part being especially confirmed by some who declared they had caught a glimpse of her face at one of the old-fashioned windows of the Hall.

The face they had seen was that of a pale, weak lady—a face that haunted those who saw it long after.

The next rumour that gained ground was that the lady had been taken ill, and had given birth to a son; but, as the same secrecy attended this event nothing certain was known respecting it.

But we will now take our readers behind the scenes, and let them know the real truth of things so mysterious to the people of the country.

Andrew Harwolf, the steward, was one of those sordid, cunning men who, worming their way by fawning slavishness into the confidence of their employers, scruple at nothing likely to serve their ultimate interest.

This man, when Lord Edgeforth went abroad, knowing that there was no heir to succeed to the estate if Lord Edgeforth died childless, conceived the ambitious project of making himself the possessor of Frontemore Hall, and inheriting the wealth of his master.

He had already, from the fact of having had things so long under his control, the possession of no inconsiderable sums of money.

This he had gained by, in the first instance, robbing his master, and also imposing fresh exactions upon the tenants of the estate, such as raising their rents and compelling them to render up a tithe of their stock—exactions which, had his lordship known, would have resulted in his steward's dismissal, but which he was enabled to indulge in with impunity.

It would have been well for the young nobleman if he had given more attention to his affairs and less trust to his false serving man: the catastrophe by which he was deprived of wife, wealth, and life, would not then have occurred.

Andrew Harwolf waited with the expectant anxiety of villany for news of some calamity befalling his young master—news which, however, never arrived; meanwhile he continued his fraudulent system of robbery, his nightly prayer being that Lord Edgeforth might never return alive.

The sudden coming back of his master put to flight his long established ease; but what were his sentiments when he found that his master had not returned alone, but had brought with him a young wife—a wife whom he appeared rapturously fond of, and who seemed to promise to rear children to perpetuate her husband's race.

Andrew Harwolf's chagrin was so great that he could scarcely control himself. He concealed it, however, and greeted the lady with the most slavish subservience; but at the same time his crafty brain was set to work revolving how he might get for himself the estates he had actually begun to look upon as his own.

Lady Edgeforth was a fair, timid young creature, full of trust and love for her husband. The story about her having been taken from a convent was true; he had rescued her from one, and she was indeed grateful to him for it.

The seclusion of the Hall accorded well with her feelings, so long as she could have Lord Edgeforth with her. She loved to walk with him through the antique building, to study its old paintings and statuary, its books and objects of interest.

She only had one antipathy, and that was to the steward.

She did not like his fawning slavishness; and his sullen brows and subtle looks gave her at times an alarm that she did not attempt to conceal from her husband.

Lord Edgeforth placed too much trust in Andrew Harwolf to think his wife's fancies had any foundation in truth; and so continued in that blind security which ultimately culminated in his and her ruin.

A new purpose had taken hold of the steward's mind; a purpose that he had matured long in secret, since he had made one discovery.

Lady Edgeforth was about to become a mother.

He had before fixed his avaricious eyes on his master's estate; he now desired also to become possessed of his master's wife.

And this was the plan—a diabolical plan, indeed, that Satan must well have assisted him to mature.

For some time he had carried on a connection with a young lady whom he had treacherously seduced; and he discovered that she was in the same interesting condition as his mistress, and likely to become a mother at the same time.

He resolved, then, that this child should take the place of the one born to his master;—that, to make himself secure in all his plans, he would put his master out of the way, and then compel the unfortunate lady to become his.

A terrible scheme, but his mind never shrank from it; he matured it subtley; and often when looking his young master in the face, was thinking how best to dispose of him.

At such times a murderous gleam must have shone from his eyes, and yet Lord Edgeforth failed to perceive anything.

The time came for which he was prepared; Lady Edgeforth gave birth to a son; the secrecy with which his lordship enshrouded its birth affording Harwolf full scope for his plans.

A doctor came at night and remained there till the young wife was out of danger, when he went out as secretly as he had come. The nurse engaged was a creature of the steward's, who would have suffocated either mother or child if it had been desired.

Lord Edgeforth was proud, indeed, of his firstborn. His love for his young wife seemed to increase each day as she grew better; and there was every prospect of a happy future for them both.

There would have been but for the malevolent designs of the steward.

Within two days after his mistress's confinement, the lady whom he had made his victim gave birth to a child—also a son; and everything being accordingly ripe for the consummation of his scheme, he engaged the services of an unscrupulous tramp—a London bully—who, for a sum of money, agreed to carry off the child, and bury it alive where it would never be discovered.

It was a clear, beautiful night when the steward admitted his confederate to assist him in his deeds of violence and crime.

Lady Edgeforth was recovering, and had gone with her husband to sit in his library. They had left their child in its crib, in the charge of the nurse.

The young nobleman leaving the library for a moment, heard, as he thought, strange sounds in the house, and hastened up the stairs on hearing that they came from the room where his child lay.

He entered to behold a spectacle that, while it recalled all the suspicions of his wife, amazed and confounded him.

A man whose looks and attire were enough to bespeak his character, was lifting the child from its cot—the steward assisting him to take it forth.

Astounded at the perfidy of his steward, the unfortunate lord had scarcely time to utter a word before he was violently assailed by the murderous Harwolf, who, springing upon him, armed with a life preserver, beat him about the head with it so swiftly and heavily, that he fell to the floor almost without uttering a cry.

"Away!" the steward cried to his vile confederate; "come back in four hours: I will dispose of him."

His lordship, though stunned, heard this speech; but the steward's attack had so prostrated him, that he could only utter the name of his beloved wife.

This only further incensed his treacherous servant, who, again attacking him, beat him mercilessly about the head till he had ceased to move, and, indeed, to exist.

His assassin was yet at his unholy work when her ladyship came up the stairs.

What a fearful sight met her gaze!

Her husband lying lifeless on the floor; his murderer standing over him covered with blood, and looking like a fiend.

The hapless creature could only gaze in speechless horror on the scene, and then fell senseless in the pool of her husband's blood.

Harwolf put down the pistol, and bent over his lifeless master.

He saw that he had beaten his skull in; and he smiled grimly when he found that he was quite dead.

His next care was directed to his unconscious mistress, whom he lifted in his arms and carried to a room whence no sound would come forth.

When he had locked her in, he repaired to the room where he had left the body of his young master, whom, now that he had destroyed, he wished to get out of the way.

He knew it was very likely that there would be a search instituted, on his disappearance becoming known, and he did not want any proof of his foul death to remain.

His first care then was to wrap the body in a thick rug to prevent any further stains of blood, and drag it away to a large apartment with a floor of stone, and containing an immense fireplace.

There he kindled a fire, and left it to burn up while he returned to the scene of the murder.

The floor and the furniture bore tokens of the deed, and he carefully went to work to obliterate every spot of blood, scraping them assiduously away, and hiding the marks by rubbing dirt into them, till the place bore no evidence of the sanguinary deed.

Having accomplished this, he retraced his steps to the apartment where the destroyed nobleman lay, and shut himself in to a deed that exceeded in horror almost the actual murder.

He first stripped the body of its clothes, and, having taken away the jewellery from the dress, and the money out of the pockets, cutting off even the buttons from the clothes; he threw the latter on the fire, which was now burning fiercely, and watched till every shred was consumed to gas and dust.

His next proceeding was to dissect the unfortunate man limb from limb, cutting the body into small portions, which he threw gradually on the fire, continuing his frightful task till all that remained of his victim was a heap of charred and burnt through and through.

These he took from the heart of the fire, and as soon as they were cold commenced hammering them on the stones with a heavy weight, till they were reduced to an impalpable powder, which he placed in a vessel and set aside.

This horrible procedure had taken him some time, and with the exertion and the heat he looked like a very fiend, as he bent over the fire to see whether any betraying trace yet remained of his hellish deed.

He had been half stifled by the fume of the consuming body, yet he had not dared to open the window for fear of discovery; but he now went and carefully washed the stains of blood from his hands, casting the water into the fire after he had used it.

The life preserver was next thrown there, and as soon as the woodwork had burnt away he removed the rest, and while it was red hot, hammered into an undistinguishable mass.

This he left to cool, that he might ——— pool, so that it might become co———

He had little fear of that leading ———

Any one might have thought ——— were com——— but he was not yet ———

He ha—— precious regard f——— not wish the hempen ——————

He took the button and jewe——— murder——— a———r and ——— them down jar wi—— som——— took place till th—— moved ——— It had cool——— shapeless ——— of at the first ———

His wolfish eyes ——— a glare of savage ——— accomplished the d——— no traces of ——— the next room in ——— little vessel of calcined ———

There was a brutal savagery in ——— when he passed his fingers through ——— dust; he seemed to be gloating over the ——— which mortals held over life ———

Four hours since and that dust was giving ——— port and strength to a living, throbbing frame now———

He rose chuckling, and walking to the ——— opened it, and ——— d the dust to the ——

All was over ——— nds bore away the ——— of his master.

When he had satisfied himself ——— nothing mained to bear testimony to the ——— mitted there, he left the apartmen——— ——— in his hand, and proceeded up to the ro——— had left his hapless mistress.

He had left her in total darkness ——— softly, and with caution, fearing ——— would be the signal of some outcry ———

But all was silent.

He closed the door, and looked round. His second victim was standing in the middle of the room, her glance was fixed full upon him, and it gave him alarm to meet her intense gaze.

He was much surprised that she should regard him with silence; but when he discovered the reason, a gleam of exultant malice lit up his brutal features.

She had gone mad.

She took no notice of him when he spoke, and Harwolf, with the same sinister light in his eyes, went to the door and fastened it.

He was then alone with her in her madness, at his mercy.

Deep as his villany had been, he yet meditated a fearful crime—a crime that only his blackhearted wickedness had suggested, but which his mistress's helpless position failed to turn him from.

It was a fitting seal to the deed that yet clung about him.

CHAPTER II.

IN WHICH OUR HERO PUTS TO SEA, AND IS THE OCCASION OF A MUTINY; IN WHICH ALSO THE FIRST THOUGHTS OF BEING A PIRATE ENTER HIS MIND.

THE mystery of Frontemore Hall was increased when it was reported that its owner had again departed, leaving his wife and child behind him.

People shook their heads when they heard the news, and said that some day strange things would come about.

And so it happened: the steward, who had never been liked, on account of his cruel exactions and his evil ways, now went about with such repulsive looks that people almost feared to meet his gaze.

He was much seen, too, in the company of a low-looking man, who usually dressed in a most flash style, sported very fine jewellery, and was very free of his money.

This was the ruffian who had taken our hero away to bury, and who now held the steward in some sort of terror, through being acquainted with his crimes.

Many a time did Harwolf regret that he had taken another into his confidence, and that he had not destroyed the child in the same manner as he had destroyed his master's body. He would have taken means to rid himself of his accomplice, if it had not been that he thought he might still make him of use, a fancy for which the other made him pay.

The mystery of the young nobleman's absence at such a time was hardly cooled down, when news arrived of his death, and within two months after the steward, much to the scandal of every body, led to the altar a lady whom he styled his lordship's wife, and with whom he returned to the Hall to enjoy the estates he had so long coveted.

The reader will have guessed that it was not the widow of his murdered master whom he had espoused; it was, indeed, the young being whom he had formerly seduced, and whom, to keep up appearances, he had married as the lady of the Hall.

This marriage of course enabled him to gain possession of the estates, and to rear as heir to them his child, which he spuriously passed off as the son of his late master.

In all this what had become of the hapless lady, so lately the victim of his wickedness.

There had been seen a poor demented creature walking about the Hall, dressed in the garb of a domestic.

This was her ladyship, whom he had attired thus to conceal her rank, and who, poor creature, wandered away one day, and was seen no more.

Thus far, Harwolf had prospered in his villany. He had got rid of his master without fear or chance of detection; the estates were his, and he saw his own son growing up as their heir.

If these ends had been attained by honest means, he might have been happy in the enjoyment of his wealth, but there is an unceasing sting to the evil doer, and Harwolf seldom laid his guilty head on his pillow, without the demons of his crime haunting his burdened conscience.

He had christened his son Daniel Harwolf, and this name he made him retain as he grew in years; he was a sullen, rebellious boy, the idol of his mother, who knew little of her husband's crimes—but a source of vexation to his father, who saw that he regarded him with neither love nor gratitude.

In the meantime what had become of our hero—the babe whom Harwolf had ordered his accomplice to dispose of—the rightful heir to the family estates.

He had not been put out of the way: Silas Rye, the ruffian who had been commissioned to bury him alive, left him to a different fate; he placed him at the door of a cottager's dwelling, where in the morning he was found, taken in, and adopted. Christopher Foundling they christened him, and under that name he was reared. Very often he encountered the proud boy of Frontemore Hall; they met in the woods seldom without a quarrel, for the steward's son was one of those wilful obstinate boys who covet everything they see, and as Christopher was not disposed to give way in anything, they had many squabbles, squabbles in which Daniel Harwolf invariably got the worst of it.

The steward often saw the frank looking, spirited boy, whom his son so often quarrelled with; he never suspected the truth, and yet he never met him without experiencing an indescribable feeling that almost amounted to hate creeping over him.

It was strange, too, that there should be such antipathy between the boys, so that one should slink, as if feeling his inferiority, from the other, who was by comparison the humblest of the poor.

Yet so it was, and while Daniel Harwolf slunk about his father's estates as if he were a thief, his head down-bent and his gait slouching, Christopher walked the woods bold as a lion, and hurled Daniel from his path if ever he came before him.

Once he gave him a sound thrashing for insulting Miss Lilia, the squire's daughter, a pretty little girl, who loved to wander in the woods alone, but whom Master Daniel took it upon himself once to insult most grossly, and would have gone further in his baseness if Christopher had not come to the rescue, and leaping over a hedge, his face glowing with noble excitement, struck the dastard boy to the ground, giving him a good beating when he got up.

The steward, now the lord of the manor, was nearly mad when he heard what had occurred; he watched the bold boy with wolf-like eagerness, and did not rest till, on some frivolous pretence, he had got him taken up and condemned to punishment.

The dauntless boy was galled at this, but he was repaid by Miss Lilia, who ever afterwards loved to be with him; and though it was against her parents' wish that she should have much to say to the penniless boy, they were too well assured of his uprightness to fear for their child.

Besides, they were grateful to him for having defended her from Master Daniel, whose character was well known.

They are trivial things that decide a man's destiny; and it is very likely our hero might never have entered upon the course that has gained for him such celebrity if it had not been for little Miss Lilia, for whose sake he longed to do something that should make him better than the poor boy whose dependence was on others.

He was very fond of talking to her of what he had heard about little boys who had become great men; and more especially would his handsome features glow when he spoke of our brave admirals, whose deeds have been our glory from time immemorial.

"If I could be great like them," he used to say, "I would not care what I endured."

Then little Miss Lilia would tell him how she would like him to be a great hero, with men and ships under his command; and how she would be true to him; and if her parents would not let her marry him, how he should come with his ships and carry her off.

All this she said in the earnestness of childhood, and Christopher listened eagerly, little thinking, either of them, that it would so happen exactly as they had said; that he would gain command on the seas, and come and take her from her friends to link her to a terrible destiny.

Miss Lilia did not believe anything else but that he was cut out for a great man; and Christopher listened to her till he made up his mind to stay no longer idle on shore, but to take passage on board a ship as the first step, that he might learn navigation and the duties of a sea commander, and rise till he gained a ship of his own.

So he took the first opportunity and went to sea, little Miss Lilia bidding him a tender good bye, and crying all day long after he had gone.

Once on the deck of a ship our hero was as happy as if it were already his own. He did not even mind the captain's surly orders nor the men's rough ways, but went about his work in a willing manner, that went home to the fearless seamen's hearts, and soon gained him their favour and admiration.

Sailors like a brave, willing boy; and they soon found out that Christopher was made of the right metal.

Smooth enough the first few days passed; and on the evening of the sixth Christopher was standing by the bulwarks looking over the expanse of foaming sea, and indulging in those wild dreams that live in the mind of a daring boy, when the first cloud was given to his hopes by discovering that his old foe, Daniel Harwolf, was on board with him.

He saw him standing aft by the captain, and knew that he was pointing him out in a way that was gaining for him the ill-will of the ship's commander.

Galled at the spiteful thoughts depicted in Daniel's features, the proud boy moved away, but was soon called back by the rough voice of the captain.

"I have just heard," said that gentleman, "a very bad account of you: I hope we shall have none of your vile capers on board here: this is the wrong sort of craft for such pranks, I can tell you; and if I hear of your vagabondising tricks with Master Harwolf, I'll flog you with a rope's end."

The boy's proud heart swelled at this undeserved and unkind speech; but he said nothing, only he fixed his bold, unquailing glance on the sallow face of Daniel Harwolf.

The latter slunk from his gaze; and for a few moments those two boys—the one a baseborn impostor, occupying a position to which nature had never adapted him; the other, whom he had dispossessed, proudly noble, even in his humble calling—stood face to face.

And as they stand there, we will draw their likeness.

There was but little difference in the age of the two boys. Not the slightest resemblance or similarity, however, existed between them in any other respect.

The sailor-boy was large for his years, with a figure that gave promise of symmetry, grace, and an early maturity; his head, in keeping with his body, was admirably developed, well balanced, and covered with a profusion of rich, dark brown hair; his forehead, broad and intellectual, lent additional beauty to his full, deep brown eyes; and with his ruddy cheeks, giving evidence of vigorous health, he was just such a boy as a nobleman might desire his only son and heir to be.

The other boy was slight and rather undersized, with a sickly look, produced apparently more by improper indulgences than natural infirmity; shining black eyes, black hair, and regular features, added to a well-shaped head and heavy brow, would have rendered him good-looking in spite of his sallow complexion, had it not been for a peevish, discontented, and rather malignant expression that was habitual to him.

The _physique_ of the lads did not differ more than their dress. The one was clothed in a suit of the most costly broadcloth, elegantly made, with well-shaped boots upon his feet, and a gold chain around his neck to secure the gold watch in his pocket. The other, bare-footed, bare-necked, jacketless, was under no obligations to the tailor for adding to the gentility of his appearance. Yet any one would at once have acknowledged that the roughest clad bore indelibly impressed upon him the insignia of nature's nobility.

By degrees, as the titled boy brought his furtive glance to meet the open look of the other, the difference of their mien showed to full advantage, and the captain, had he been honestly impartial, must have given the palm of conscious superiority to the sailor-boy.

But unfortunately he was biassed in favour of the sickly boy by his side, whom he regarded as the heir of Frontemore Hall, and who had been given in his care with his mother the steward's wife, who was then on board, they being on a trip to see a relative of the steward's.

Till this evening Master Daniel had been so sick, that he had not dared to move from his berth, and he was now anything but at home as he stood uneasily rocked by the roll of the ship, his limbs shaking, while Christopher stood, bold and firm, his bearing as cool and easy as if he strode the smooth pavе.

"Well, you young brat," was the captain's next address, "you heard what I said. Go now; but remember there are plenty of ropes' ends in the ship."

"I shall not want them," the brave boy said, for he was too indignant to be silent at this injustice; "I never did wish to interfere with Master Daniel, and I always strive to do my duty."

The captain was astonished at this outspoken speech. "You strive," he cried, looking round for a bit of rope, "go to the devil, you dirty-faced scamp, or I'll give you a dressing round the ship that will make your shirt stick to your back for a week."

Christopher saw that the lips of Daniel Harwolf curled in ill-concealed scorn; his proud breast rose, and his eye sparkled angrily, but a thought of his inability to encounter the hostility of the tyrannical captain caused him to subdue the hot words with which he would have replied, and with a sorrowful heart he walked away and went about the duties to which the harsh voice of the captain directed him.

He worked hard for some time; but at length his feelings found vent, and he murmured unconsciously, while his lips quivered in sorrow,

"Why did he come here to make my life hard? I could have persevered if it had not been for him; but now he is here I must put up with all he does to me, for if I speak I shall be flogged."

He controlled the tears that came to his eyes, and went once more to his duties.

"Don't mind him, my cheery," a manly voice said, near him. "We know what sort of a kidney the likes of him belong to, and shiver me if we'll see you put upon for such a whipper snapper; so rouse up, my hearty, we're all of a mess this side the funnel, and, demme, we'll take your part through thick and thin."

Christopher turned to find himself addressed by a fine-looking ruddy-faced sailor, whose honest heart was beaming from his eyes.

He put out his hand when the boy turned, and grasping his in a true sailor's grip, continued:

"It don't take two squints of a blind man to see how the wind is with that tallow-faced lubber; but if you get into deep water with him, you may count on one messmate to help you out, and his name's Jack Brierly."

He gave the boy's hand a parting squeeze, and with an encouraging look posted off to his work; and Christopher's spirits revived as he found that he had one friend at least on board the "Flying Dolphin."

And that night, when he turned into his bunk, his mind was happy in boyhood's hope.

"Hilloa there! now then, rouse up, rouse up, my hearty! Bear a hand and be lively, for that little devil-skin abaft has been hailing for you this five minutes."

Thus spoke, with a rough voice, but in a kind tone, a tall and powerfully-built sailor (the same who had before addressed our hero), as he descended the forecastle-ladder, to Christopher, who, lying stretched upon his back on a mess-chest, was fast asleep. Loud as were the tones of the speaker, they made no impression upon the boy. Wrapped in the deep slumber of boyhood, his body fatigued, his conscience clear, and his mind calm, he was enjoying one of those refreshing rests that are only permitted to the young and contented—the sleep that manhood longs after but seldom experiences.

Christopher's troubles were forgotten, as he lay there dreaming calmly of the future, a future that placed him high indeed above the sickly boy, who tossed uneasily in his soft berth in the cabin, in the hours that the sailor-boy slept easily and happily.

That forecastle and its inmates would have made a beautiful picture, could they have been transferred to canvas. The boy, as he reposed with closed eye-lids and upturned face, over which bright smiles were flitting—the reflection of pleasant, hopeful dreams—seemed an embodiment of intelligence and innocence, notwithstanding the coarse canvas trousers and striped cotton-shirt which formed his only attire. The man, with his muscular and strongly-knit figure, his bronzed cheeks, huge whiskers, brightly gleaming eyes, and determined expression of countenance, was the personification of bodily strength, physical perfection and perfect self-reliance. The one looked as if he were a spirit from a higher sphere, who had by chance become an inmate of that dark, confined, triangular-shaped and murky apartment, and appeared all out of place amidst its mess-chests, bedding, and other nautical dunnage, and its atmosphere reeking with the odours of bilge-water, tar, and lamp-smoke. The other was in keeping with the surrounding objects, his bright red flannel shirt, his horny hands, his very attitude, showed him one unaccustomed to ease and comfort, whose only home was a forecastle, whose chief abiding place the heaving ocean.

Jack Brierly seemed a little rejoiced with the picture, for his good humoured face softened as he gazed upon the soft, pleasing features of the boy, and something that would not have been comfortable for the pampered inmate of the cabin to hear escaped his lips. Presently, however, he became wearied with awaiting the result of his verbal summons, and stooped down to awaken his companion with a shake, and as he did so, a beam of affection so redeemed the expression of his countenance, and lent so much tenderness to his eye, that with all his roughness and uncouthness, the weather-beaten tar became really handsome. Though undisturbed by noise, no sooner was the sailor-boy touched, than true to the instinct of his calling, he sprang from

[CHRISTOPHER RESCUES LILIA FROM THE STEWARD'S SON.]

his resting-place, as wide awake, and with his faculties as much about him, as if he had always been a stranger to sleep, and exclaimed, "Is it eight bells already, Brierly? I thought I had just closed my peepers."

"Just closed your peepers, my little lark!" exclaimed the sailor, "I began to think your eye-lids were battened down, it seemed such a hard pull to heave them up. You haven't had much of a snooze though, for it is only four bells; but that young scaramouch astern wants you to take him in tow. So you had better up anchor and make sail, Chris, for the cabin, or the she-commodore will be sending

No. 2.

the boatswain after you with the cat. And there isn't any back would ache more than Jack Brierly's to see you come to that."

Gratefully rewarding the honest fellow with a murmured return of thanks, but scarcely waiting to hear the completion of the sentence, Christopher hurried up the ladder to the deck, and in a few seconds was at the door of the cabin. Standing just inside the entrance, a drizzling rain preventing him from coming further, stood the youth to whom Brierly had referred by the not very flattering appellations of devil-skin and scaramouch; he was shivering in the chill, and seemed the very essence of ill temper as he saw the ruddy looks of the hardy boy.

"Why don't you come on," he said sharply, "how dare you keep me waiting here in the cold, mamma shall have you whipped for being so lazy; you know you're to come with me and be my servant, while I do my exercises."

Christopher's brow crimsoned, but he said nothing, and inclining his haughty head, followed his petty tyrant into the cabin.

How great was the difference between the apartment in which the lads now were, and the one which Christopher had left but a few minutes before. It was the difference between wealth and poverty.

The vessel though a small one, was well fitted up in every respect; her accommodation was complete, and her cabin, a poop one, was fitted up in the most luxurious style. Everything that the skill of the upholsterer, and the art of the painter, aided by the taste and experience of the captain, could do to make it elegant, beautiful, and comfortable, had been done. Extending nearly to the main-mast, the distance from the cabin-door to the transom was full fifty feet. This space was divided into two apartments of unequal size, one of twenty, the other of thirty feet, by a sliding bulkhead of highly polished rosewood and superbly stained glass, the appearance of which was dazzlingly pretty.

Very conveniently the after-cabin was fitted up as a sleeping-room, with two mahogany bedsteads, and all the appurtenances found in the chambers of the wealthy on shore. The forward cabin was used as a sitting and eating-room. On the floor was a carpet of whose fabric the looms of Persia might be proud—so rich, so thick, so magnificent was it—and deep cushioned ottomans, lounges, and rocking chairs were scattered along the sides, and placed in the corners of the apartment in easy confusion.

But we have more to do with our *dramatis personae*. Not far from the door, reclining on a lounge, with a book in her hand, was Lady Edgeforth, as she was styled, the mother of Master Daniel, a handsome woman, but one who had ever permitted her fancies and her feelings to be the guides of her actions: her heart, which by nature was a kind one, was often severely wrung by the pangs of remorse, caused by the recollection of deeds committed from impulse, which her pride would not permit her to apologise or atone for, even after she was convinced of her error; but her faults were not of a nature to admit of comparison with the odious crimes of her husband, the guilty steward. Indolently, as the two boys entered the cabin, she looked at them, but, without making any remark, continued the perusal of her book, whilst they proceeded to the after-cabin, and, getting behind the bulkhead, were out of her sight and hearing.

Her attention was soon absorbed, and for some fifteen minutes the stillness of the cabin was undisturbed; but then the mother's attention was attracted by the loud, angry tones of her son's voice, apparently abusing Christopher. Hardly had she commenced listening, to ascertain what was the matter, ere the sound of a blow, followed by a shriek

and the fall of something heavy upon the floor, reached her ear. Alarmed, she rushed into the after-cabin, and there, upon the floor, his face covered with blood, she saw the idol of her heart, the one absorbing object of her existence—her darling son.

Her excitement at this sight was so extreme that it was a few moments before she could speak.

"You base creature," she cried, when she had raised her darling from the floor and in some measure soothed his groans, "How dare you lift your hand against my dear son?"

"Because he insulted me," the bold boy answered proudly.

"Insulted you," almost shrieked the mother, "Why, you vulgar brute, you good-for-nothing thief, you little *pirate*, I will have you flogged——"

"I am no thief or pirate," Christopher answered, and you have no right to call me such.

Before she could again speak Captain Simons entered; and being as much incensed as Daniel's mother, that a sailor-boy, a thing he had always looked upon as little better than a block or rope's end, had had the audacity to strike her son, he was furious. Taking hold of Christopher with a rough grasp, he pushed him out on deck, and called for the boatswain. That functionary, however, was slow in making his appearance; and again, in louder and more angry tones, the captain called for him. Still he came not, and, spite of his passion, the captain could but gather from the lowering expressions of the sailors' countenances, that something was wrong in the relations between the ship's crew and their commander.

From his youth accustomed to have his commands always promptly obeyed, the wrath of Captain Simons waxed high and furious at the dilatoriness of the boatswain. Without any other exciting cause, this apparent insubordination on the part of one of his officers was enough to arouse all the evil passions of his heart. Educated under the strict discipline of the navy, he had been taught that the first and most important duty of a seaman was obedience. "Obey orders, if you ruin owners," was the doctrine he inculcated; and to be thus, as it were, bearded on his own quarter-deck by one of his own men, was something entirely new, and most insulting to his pride. Three times had he called for the boatswain without receiving any reply, or causing that functionary to appear, and his face grew red in excitement as he found himself set at nought.

Enraged by Christopher's audacity, as he termed it, when he first came out of the cabin, his only thought was to punish the sailor-boy for striking his passenger's son; but his anger now took another course, and his desire to visit the boatswain's contumacy with a heavy penalty was so great, that he forgot entirely the object for which he had first called him, and was now only intent upon punishing the others.

He stepped towards the forecastle where the boatswain stood, and when within a few feet of him, he addressed him in that low husky voice, that more than any other proves the depth of a person's feeling, with, " Why have you so long delayed obeying my summons, Mr. Barker?"

" Accident, I was asleep in the forecastle, sir, and came as soon as I heard Mr. Hart call," replied Barker.

But the tone in which he spoke, the look of his eye, the expression of his countenance, would at once have convinced a less observant person than Captain Simons that the excuse offered was one got up for the occasion, and not the real cause of the man's dilatoriness.

" Fast asleep, sir! Attend now to the duty I wish you to perform—and be awake, sir, about it—and you may, perhaps, get off easier for your own dereliction afterwards, for your conduct shall not remain unpunished," answered the captain, angrily.

" If you please, sir, boy and man I have been going to sea now these twenty-five years, and no one ever charged Ned Barker with not knowing or doing his duty before, sir!" rejoined the boatswain, evidently labouring under as much mental excitement as his officer.

" Silence, none of your impertinence, sir! Not a word more, or I will teach you a lesson of duty you ought to have been taught when a boy. Where's your cat, sir?"

" Don't know, sir," replied the boatswain.

" Hell curse you!" ejaculated the captain, almost beside himself at this reply, yet striving to maintain his self-possession; " one more insolent word, and I will have you triced up. Strip that boy, and make a spread eagle of him; then get your cat and give him forty instantly."

The boatswain never moved; the crew during this conversation had been quietly gathering on the lee-side of the quarter-deck, until at this juncture every seaman in the ship, except the man at the wheel, was within twenty feet of the excited speakers. Not a word had been spoken amongst them; but it was evident, from the determination imprinted upon their countenances, from their attitudes, and from the extraordinary interest they took in the scene then transpiring, that there was something more in the boatswain's resistance of the captain that was not altogether spontaneous. It had, indeed, come to an actual mutiny, but the captain's only thought was to punish the mutinous conduct of his crew, never thinking of the possibility of failure; he gave one of his pistols to the chief mate, and telling the steward to take a capstan-bar, the captain and his two assistants boldly advanced to compel fifteen sailors to return to their duty and obey orders.

But the case was not so simple, for whilst the captain, mate, and steward were making their brief preparation for a most hazardous undertaking, the men of the " Flying Dolphin," with that promptness and resolution so common amongst seamen when they think at all, had determined upon the course they would adopt in the impending struggle of death.

Notwithstanding that the numerical discrepancy between the two parties seemed so great, the actual difference in their relative strength was not so considerable as it appeared. The sailors, it is true, had the physical force—they were five to one—but the captain's small band felt more confidence from the moral influence that they knew was on their side, than if their numbers had been trebled without it. Habit ever exercises a controlling influence, unless overcome by some powerful exciting principle, and men never fly in the face of authority to which they have always been accustomed to yield implicit obedience, but from one of two causes—either a hasty impulse, conceived in a moment, and abandoned by actors frightened at their own audacity, or a sense of wrong and injustice so keen and poignant, as to make death preferable to further submission to tyranny.

Captain Simons, aware of custom's nearly invincible power, having often seen seamen rebel, and then at the first warning gladly skulk back to their duty, unhesitatingly advanced up to the weather-gangway to the break of the forecastle, and confronted his mutinous crew. The men, who were huddled around the end of the windlass, some sitting, others standing, talking together in low tones, only showed they were aware of the captain's presence by suddenly ceasing their conversation—but not a man of them moved, nor was a hand raised for violence.

It was certain that they were resolved.

Captain Simons though quick-tempered, was a man of judgment and experience; and he saw by the calmness and quietness of his men, that their insubordination was the result of premeditation—a thing he had not before thought—and he became aware of the difficulties of his position. He could not, for his life, think of yielding; to give up to a sailor would, in his estimation, be the deepest degradation. And moral influence was all he could rely upon with which to compel obedience—feeling that if an actual strife commenced, it could but result in his discomfiture. His tone, therefore, was low and determined, as, with cocked pistol in hand, he addressed his crew calmly, " My men, do you know that you are, every one of you, guilty of mutiny? Do you know that the punishment for mutiny on the high seas is death? Do you know this? Have you thought of it? Are you prepared?"

Having spoken the captain paused for an instant, as if waiting for a reply; and a voice from the group around the windlass answered, " We have!"

Evidently surprised at the boldness of the reply, but still retaining his presence of mind, the captain continued, " What is it, then, that has induced you to brave this penalty; have you been maltreated? Step out, one of you, and state your grievances. You know I am not a tyrant, nor exacting.

Boldly one man stepped from the rest; this man was Jack Brierly.

" Cap'n," he said, " you can't beat to win'ard against a head sea without a ship's pitching, no more than you can reef a to's'-sail without going aloft." Brierly went on, without change of manner, though his voice became more concise and firm in its tone. " And I can't tell you, like some of them shore chaps, what you don't want to hear without heaving you aback. We ain't got anything agin you, if you was let alone; all we wants is for you to give your own orders, and to keep Harwolf from bedevilling Christopher. The boy's as good a boy as ever furled a royal, and never skulks below when he's wanted on deck; but he stands his regular watches, and then, when he ought to sleep, he's everlastingly kept in the cabin, and whipped and knocked about for the amusement of young master, and that's just the whole of it. We've stood it long enough, and won't return to duty until you promise that he is not to be made————"

"Hold," shouted the captain, as he levelled a pistol at Brierly's breast, "not another word: return to your duty, men; and you, Brierly, if before I count five you have not gone aft I will shoot you dead."

Silence reigned.

Jack Brierly stood like a statue.

The captain began to count.

"One!"

"Two!"

"Three!"

"Four!"

Every eye was fixed on the weapon pointed at Brierly's breast.

A movement among the men took place: Christopher's face grew red at the danger of his friend, but none seemed to know how to serve him.

And now the captain's finger rested on the trigger; his lips moved to pronounce the word "Five," but before it had sounded Christopher flung a piece of rope at the captain's arm, and struck the pistol from his hand.

Then he leaped forward, and picking it up flung it into the sea, and stood nobly fronting the ship's commander.

A spell had hitherto kept the men motionless, but now the captain and those who were on his side made a stir, and the charm that held the men in check was broken by the first movement towards action, and they made a rush towards the captain and his two supporters. Bravely, though, they stood their ground; and the boatswain received the ball from the mate's pistol in the fleshy part of his shoulder, as he was about to strike that worthy with a handspike. Gallantly assisted by the steward, the captain and mate made as much resistance as three men could against fifteen. The odds were, however, too great; spite of their bravery, the three were soon overpowered and the contest was nearly ended, when a temporary change was made in favour of the weaker party by the appearance in the fray of the second mate, a powerful and cool sailor, well used to dealing with the men.

This gentleman, during the whole colloquy, had been at the wheel, forgotten by both parties. His sudden arrival, therefore, as with lusty blows he laid about him, astonished the seamen, who gave back for an instant, and allowed their opponents to regain their feet. They did not allow them much time, however, to profit by this respite, for in a few seconds, understanding the source from whence assistance had come, they renewed the attack with increased vigour, and soon again obtained the mastery. But it was no easy matter to confine the three officers and the steward, who resisted with their utmost power, particularly as the men were anxious to do them no more bodily injury than they were compelled to in securing them.

And now an incident occurred which proves how true are the hearts of our gallant tars. So absorbed had been all hands in the strife in which they were engaged, that not one of them noticed the fact that what had been the weather-side of the barque at the commencement of the affray, was now the lee; nor did any of the men—all seamen as they were—observe that the vessel was heeling over tremendously, her lee-scuppers nearly level with the water. A report, loud as a cannon, high in the air, first startled the combatants; then, with a rushing sound, three large, heavy bodies, fell from aloft, one of which striking the deck near the combatants, threatened all with instant destruction, whilst the other two fell with a loud splash into the sea to leeward, and disappeared.

Before, they had been struggling against each other; but in this new danger both the victors and vanquished were equally interested, and at the same instant looked aloft to discover the cause. The first glance convinced every one of the necessity for prompt and vigorous action. Their position was, indeed, fraught with imminent danger. Left without a helmsman, by the second mate going to the assistance of the captain, the barque, close-hauled with a stiff breeze blowing, had come up in the wind, and was now flat aback; that is, the wind, instead of blowing against the sails from behind, was before them. The fore and main-royal, and top-gallant masts, with all their gear, had been carried away, and the ship was gathering sternway at a rate that would soon run her under, and make of her a complete wreck.

At this imminent peril, the natural desire for self-preservation combined with the instincts and habits of both officers and men to cause them entirely to forget the fierce contest in which they had just been engaged—their thoughts were changed from each other to the ship and its situation, and the officers were at once permitted to regain their authority.

The honest hearts of the sailors were actuated by the noblest feelings; and no sooner did Captain Simons find himself at liberty, than he at once assumed command, and issued his orders as loud and clear as if nothing had interrupted his authority for an instant.

"To the wheel! to the wheel, Silas! All hands wear ship!" were his first words; and the men with alacrity hurried to their stations, whilst the mate ran to the helm to steady her.

Daniel and his mother had been in the cabin, anxiously awaiting the result of the controversy on the forecastle, but alarmed by the falling spars, they had hurried on deck and were now on the poop. In the hurry and confusion consequent upon the ship's hazardous position, all hands were so engrossed that nobody noticed their danger, and all at once the swoop of a spar carried Daniel into the sea.

The shrieks of the mother first drew attention to the accident; but the lubberly boy, a very coward in danger, had not even the nerve to steady himself, and would never have stood a chance of coming on deck again, if he had not found a friend in one in whom he might have looked to find a bitter foe instead.

Christopher, with a nobleness that put to shame the petty spite of the steward's boy, leaped into the sea, reached him as he was sinking, and, holding him up above water, waited till a rope was thrown out, and climbing it with his burden, laid him on the deck.

A ringing cheer from the sailors showed their appreciation of Christopher's daring, and even the captain looked humbled : but what was the surprise of all when Daniel, recovering his consciousness, which the sea water had nearly carried away, basely accused his preserver of having thrust him into the sea.

So glaring was this act, that a murmur of disgust rose from the sailors, while Christopher stood gazing, confounded, at the white-cheeked liar.

Monstrous as the charge was, there was no one who could *prove* that it was not true; and the captain, who had a wish to exercise his authority on some one, and regarded Christopher as the cause of the recent mutiny, was not sorry to get occasion against him, and accordingly had him put into irons and confined below.

"If I find you incorrigible," were the captain's words, as Christopher was taken away, "I'll thrash the last inch of life out of you, and hang you up at the yard arm, you cussed young pirate."

"Pirate!" It grated on the boy's ears as he sat —there was no room to stand—in his dark place of captivity. "Pirate!" If he were that, instead of being a common sailor-boy, the spite of Daniel Harwolf would have no power over him; nay, more, the power would be his; he might even compel the tyrannical captain to bow the knee to him.

"Pirate!" "A Boy Pirate!" A red spot glowed on his cheek and flushed to his brow : wild fancies surged through his brain : he saw through that dark, loathsome hold out into the blessed light. He saw a vessel, glorious and swift, her sails spread to the gale, her prow cutting the golden waves: a brave, death-daring crew gathered on her decks, obedient to *him*, who stood proud in his boyhood rule of all, his scimetar of death in his hand, while above his head floated the black banner of fate,—the flag of piracy.

"Such a lot shall be mine," the bold boy cried, "rather than I will be the sport of tyrants. I will not stoop where I should soar. I was not born to serve, and never more will give obedience to any of earth. I will be king; others shall be my slaves. They have forced me to it : and now let all who cross my path beware; for my star shall rise, and the conquered shall quiver at my feet. The seas shall be my home and my empire, and every flag shall lower before the banner that shall wave above my head."

CHAPTER III.
THE TRIAL OF OUR HERO, AND WHAT OCCURRED THEREAT.

CHRISTOPHER went to sleep in his dark prison-hole; the sailors returned to their duty, the captain to his cabin.

Daniel Harwolf and his mother went back to their apartment.

The ship had been put in order after her recent straining, and was now gallantly continuing her way.

To some extent it was strange that the men, who had before resisted the captain's tyranny over their favourite, should now quietly allow Christopher to be placed in confinement on a charge which they knew was false.

It was that habit of instinctive obedience for which our gallant tars are noted, and also the collapse after the cessation of their late rebellion.

If Captain Simons had tried to imprison Christopher while the men were enraged against him, the mutiny would not have terminated as it did ; but now that it was over it required some very strong influence to excite the men once more openly against their commander.

Still there were sullen looks amongst them as they went below to turn in; none seemed inclined for sleep; and after they had sat quietly for some minutes, Jack Brierly opened the subject that was uppermost in their thoughts by saying—

"Messmates, you've seen how that poor lad's been set on by that numskull aft; damme! he'd only have done right to have let the young varmint sink, like the lubber he was, damn him !—and then to turn round and accuse him of pitching him overboard, messmates ! If it should fall out that that young devilskin *does* somehow tumble overboard when he doesn't expect it, I hope none of you will be near enough to lend a hand to bear him out."

The sailors looked very much as if they would rather have lent a hand to keep him under than one to bring him out, and Brierly continued—

"Howsomdever, that ain't neither larboard nor starboard; the question is, what shall we do about our young messmate ? Is he to stick all night in that black hole where they've put him ? I say, no ! Mates, I was glad to see as how none of you would have anything to do in putting him there, even when the skipper ordered it; but that ain't no reason why you shouldn't take a hand in getting him out ! "

"Ay, ay," was the response, proving the readiness of the men to join in any deed that would get their favourite out.

"Now what I propose," Jack resumed, " is that two on us wait on the young lad, that we get him out of the hole where they've put him, and that in the morning, when the skipper wants him, we bring him up safe and like a man "

The proposition met with instant approval, and although they knew that they were again acting against the captain's orders, and indeed against the rules of the service, not one of them had the least fear in what he was doing.

This conclusion arrived at, Jack Brierly and two of his mates went to the hole under the forecastle where Christopher was confined and groped their way in, having first of all given the fellow on guard a hint that if he did not want to be thrown overboard he had better be quiet.

When the light of their lantern showed Christopher lying asleep on a coil of cable, an honest tear glistened in the eyes of Jack Brierly, and he said, tenderly—

"There he is, brave lad, as sound asleep as if the

ship were his own, but as sorrowful in mind as any love-lorn landsman. It's just the way always with these motherless bairns; they hav'nt no one to care for 'em, and so they meet things like a rock : that'll be a great man some of these days, or I'm all abroad in my reckoning."

Stooping over the sleeping lad he shook him lightly by the shoulder, and roused him with a gentle "Hilloa !"

Christopher opened his eyes and stared at his visitors.

"Rouse up, my hearty," said Jack; "we have come to give you a better snoozing place than here with the rats, so open your peepers and screw your eyes into use."

"Has the captain ordered my release?" asked Christopher, his face brightening; a subdued oath passed Jack Brierly's lips.

"No, lad; he ain't come to that right pitch yet; but don't upset yourself about that, you're set free by your messmates' orders, and there isn't one of them but would sooner take your place here than go to his hammock."

Christopher's face clouded; he comprehended the honest kindness of the sailors, but knew what risks they ran.

"Thank you kindly," he said. "I will stay here till morning; I don't mind it now I've been here once, and I won't get you into trouble."

"Avast there !" cried Jack; "don't be palavering like a methody parson, but come along at once. You can go aft in the morning as cheerful as a lark, and then we'll hear what that scaramouch yonder has to say, damn him !"

"No, Brierly," Christopher answered. "I am not afraid to bear what they've put upon me; I won't be punished any more for what I have not done, but now I'm here I'll stay till they fetch me away. I'm not afraid to bear my own load."

"That's a cheery speech, my hearty, and I like you for it, but we must be skipper here. We're not going to our hammocks and let you lie here like a dog, so we'll have to carry you off; heave ahead, mates; we'll take him off like a rocket."

Christopher drew back proudly.

"Brierly, if you don't think me a coward let me stay here; if I am here till the morning with these irons eating into my wrists, I shall be better able to stand before Captain Simons and that base Daniel Harwolf; if you take me out of here I shall feel like a coward when I stand before them. They thrust me here," he continued, his eye sparkling and a glow reddening his cheek, "and if I am to stay here till I fall piecemeal, I will not stir till they fetch me away."

Jack Brierly could not help gazing admiringly at the dauntless boy.

"You are a trump," he said; "and damn you, shall have your own way, but Jack Brierly's not the one to leave such a mate in his trouble, so since you won't come with us I'll stay here with you. Clear away, mates, while I make the young lad comfortable, and then go back to the fo'castle and say I'm going to stay with Chris all night."

Christopher would have objected, but the sturdy seaman would take no heed of what he urged; he made as soft a bed as he could for his young friend to lie upon, and then, bidding his messmates good night, lay down to share this self-imposed imprisonment.

Christopher was deeply touched at this act of true nobility ; and when he closed his eyes in sleep, it was with the sweet belief that in Jack Brierly he had indeed a friend, steadfast and true.

So they lay down together; the proud, dauntless boy, and the rough-spoken hardy sailor, with his giant strength and heart of gentleness : and in the morning, when the captain ordered Christopher aft, he was surprised, and to some extent dismayed, to learn that his stoutest hearted sailor had been the sharer of his confinement.

It was an unpleasant discovery, inasmuch as it proved that he had to deal with a crew of stubborn men, who, though willing to work the ship and obey his orders so long as he treated them justly, were alienated into foes when any wrong existed.

Had he wisely regarded these symptoms he would have refrained from carrying out his animus against Christopher; but his disposition was soured by the previous day's events, and now that the power was in his hands he was determined to make the most of it.

Thus, without a shadow of substantiation of the charge, he had made up his mind to have the proud boy flogged.

Christopher came upon deck with resolute bearing and dauntless stride. His features were pale from his night's confinement; but his lips were firm and his eyes flashing. He shook his wrists as he came aft, as if the manacles galled him ; and then his cheek flushed when he saw that Daniel had come out to witness his degradation and punishment.

In that moment he registered a bitter vow—a vow that he promised to keep if years intervened before he had the opportunity—a vow that would have made his white-livered boy enemy quail and tremble had he known its existence.

For an instant, as Christopher saw the cold glance of the captain fixed upon him, his emotion made him falter ; but the next moment he was dauntless as before.

Captain Simons, confident now in his authority, looked sternly at his youthful prisoner, and after glancing round the ship to see if he could read in the men's faces any opposition to his rule, commenced his harangue by pointing out the heinousness of Christopher's crime.

"You, first of all," he said, in conclusion, "throw that young gentleman overboard, and then, for fear that your action may have been observed, leap in after him, and make a pretence of his rescue—a trick that only adds to your crime, for you know well enough that if you did not rescue him some one else would. There is no doubt that you are a very wicked boy, and that this young gentleman's life is not safe so long as you go unpunished."

This unjust speech fired the bold boy's breast.

"Captain Simons," he cried, "you know, and so does he, that I was not near him when he fell in, and that if I hadn't jumped in and got him out, he might have gone to the bottom ; it would have been right if he had gone there ; a boy who is base enough to accuse his preserver of such an act is not fit to live. The men know what he is, and if he's allowed to have his own way he'll make another disturbance——"

"Silence! you mutinous young dog!" cried the captain. "Another word and I'll flog you from head to foot."

"I won't be silent, and I won't be punished for what I have not done!" exclaimed the impetuous boy. "I am not afraid of death, and I will meet it sooner than give in; but I warn you and him that you will rue the hour when you trampled me under foot like this."

The captain's rage at this excited speech was so excessive that he could scarcely speak.

"Take hold of the young devil," he cried; "tie him up, and let him be flogged till I give the word for him to be taken down."

Silently the men heard him; no one moved to execute his command, and the mate and steward alone did not feel disposed to act in opposition to the crew.

They knew that every mutiny did not end so bloodlessly as the one of yesterday.

Captain Simons began to grow uneasy, but he had gone too far to retreat without, as he believed, lowering himself in the eyes of the crew, and he shouted loudly,

"Tie him up instantly, or I will shoot some of you down like dogs."

Jack Brierly stepped forward from his mates, and spoke,

"Capt'n, I don't wish to touch on things that ought to be bygones, but me and my mates can't stand by and see Chris tied up for that liver-faced devilskin 'there; and we'd sooner cut off our right hands than have anything to do except in preventing it."

"Mutiny again!" exclaimed Captain Simons, turning deadly pale; "I thought as much; but, my men, I am prepared for you."

He took a pistol from his coat pocket, and turning to the chief mate, said,

"Take that man into your charge; shoot him, if he attempts to resist. Now, Brierly, will you tie up that young thief?"

"No, captain," responded the true-hearted tar.

"It is mutiny, if you refuse."

"It must be then, capt'n, but I must speak: its tyranny for you to act as you do, that's what me and my messmates all think; and there would not be a more comfortable vessel than this if things didn't go wrong aft: we aren't more than flesh and blood, and can't stand to be put on like blocks. Capt'n, I gives myself into custody—to keep out of more mischief—for I am not able to judge of my acts when my blood is up; take me, and try me for what I've done. I won't resist; but, first I'll give Chris here a better chance than he has now."

Jack Brierly took a small hammer from his pocket, and walking up to Christopher, by one smart blow snapped the handcuffs that bound his wrists.

"There, lad," he said, "you'll be better without them bracelets than with 'em."

He walked to the chief mate and allowed himself to be made a prisoner.

It is probable that, but for this last act, his own life would have paid the penalty of his audacious deed, for the excited captain pointed his pistol at his head, and would have discharged it if Jack had not given himself into the hands of the mate.

As it was, he was almost beside himself with fury, and his lips were thick with foam, as he cried,

"Put him in irons; when I have settled with this boy pirate I will have him made an example of."

Brierly folded his arms, but said nothing; then Christopher stepped boldly towards the captain.

"Coward and tyrant!" he cried, "you have used your authority to oppress a friendless boy, but you shall not have the privilege again. You have called me *pirate*; it will be bad for you if I am driven to be one; I will hunt you over the seas. And as for *him*, there, I will make him know a thousandfold the bitterness that has been my food. I call you both cowards; and, by this act, will prove how little I fear death or danger."

Before the captain could do more than level the pistol at his breast he sprung full upon Daniel and bore him to the deck.

"As I triumph now," he said, trampling him under foot, "so I will again. I go, captain! when next we meet the black flag shall be over my head, and my hand shall be crimson with blood. Go on your course; but when you hear that *The Red Raven* is on your track prepare for the vengeance of THE BOY PIRATE."

He sprang to the taffrail, and, proudly glancing at his quailing foe, raised his hand in menace, and leapt into the sea.

The sailors rushed to the side; they lowered ropes and then buoys into the water, without the captain's order; they stopped the ship, and had the boats out.

But the brave boy was not to be seen.

He had disappeared—was drowned, as it seemed; and yet, as the ship reluctantly made way without him, Daniel Harwolf, the usurper of the rightful heir's property, grew pale as death, and shivered icely as he thought of the last words of him whom he was henceforth to meet as THE BOY PIRATE.

CHAPTER IV.

THE " FLYING DOLPHIN" PURSUED BY A MYSTERIOUS ENEMY—TERRIBLE TALES OF THE SEA: THE DEMON SHIP, WITH ITS BLACK WINGS AND RAVEN OF BLOOD. — THE BOY PIRATE MAKES AN APPEARANCE AT AN OPPORTUNE MOMENT.—THE DOVE IS RESCUED FROM THE HAWK'S CLAWS.

THREE years had passed since our last incidents: during that time no tidings had been gleaned of the daring boy who had thrown himself into the sea.

Old Harwolf, the ex-steward of Lord Edgeforth's estate, was very glad to hear that the boy had gone to the bottom of the sea; for his confederate in villany had let him learn enough to make him tremble for himself and his pet child, if Christopher Foundling lived, and were indeed his master's boy.

Christopher's foster parents were deeply grieved at his loss: they had predicted great things of him, and were besides much attached to the fearless youth.

But she who most deeply grieved was little Lilia: the child had grown deeply attached to Christopher, whose daring nobility, and proud, handsome features more than compensated for his humble rank.

True, she could not at times bring herself to believe that he was indeed dead; but as those long years went by, and she gathered no tidings of him, she began to fear that it was true that he had perished.

But it was not so: it was not destined that our hero should die, with the death of his father and the outrage of his mother unavenged; that he should be cut off early, when so brilliant a destiny and such rich love awaited him.

No. He lived, and had begun his wonderful career.

The ship on which we first saw him put into port; it was still commanded by Captain Simons: he had changed in these three years; his looks were much altered, his hair had grown grey, and his temper was not so furious as of old.

He, too, had learned something from Harwolf's accomplice, that made him feel more acutely the remorse that had haunted him since Christopher's supposed death.

I said the ship had put into port; but at one time during their voyage it had seemed very probable that they would never reach land again.

They had been caught in a storm, and, when freed from this danger, a singular event had occurred.

A vessel had suddenly appeared on their lee.

A smart rakish vessel it was; but it did not seem to move through the water, but, on the contrary, it appeared to come on by the roll of the sea.

The sails were of a dusky hue, and a long black streak streamed from the mizen peak, a curious white insignia in its centre, with underneath something that looked like a deep stain of red blood.

This ship had appeared so suddenly, and came on so mysteriously that the seamen, though not very superstitious, were held in some sort of awe by the presence of the stranger, and did their best to make way from it.

But, in spite of their greatest speed, it still hung on their lee—never gaining upon them, never being left behind, but gliding on like a shadow in their wake.

The sailors were appalled at the singular thing.

They kept together in gangs, and spoke fearingly of the mystic vessel on their lee.

Nor were their fears confined to themselves.

The captain walked the deck agitated at the unwonted sight: his eyes continually wandering across the waves, where the gloomy stranger loomed.

Day after day it kept the same position; at night, when darkness hid the scene it failed from sight at exactly the same distance, and the men felt that it was on their track, though they saw it not.

In the morning, with the first break of day, its dark hull and dusky sails showed in the same place.

This silent visitant filled the minds of the men with as much dread as if they had been followed by an actual spectre of doom.

The captain grew disturbed, and every now and then he tried the dodge of bringing his ship to lie under, that the other might gain upon it.

But not an inch nearer did it come. Then he would spread every stitch of canvas, but the strange vessel still maintained its equal distance.

Even the captain grew unmanned. As for the men, they only prayed that they might soon get into port—a thing they scarcely looked for without first suffering some calamity.

They believed the presence of the mystic ship betokened some dread fate, but what this fate was they could not divine.

Some thought that the plague was about to break out on board; others that they were doomed to be wrecked.

Some believed that they had some one on board who, like Jonah, was the cause of their destruction.

But no one knew whom it was, and the captain was as much mystified as his crew; till one day something occurred to revive fears that had slept for many years.

The sun was shining brightly, and the atmosphere was so clear that the dusky ship was more plainly visible than it had been hitherto.

Captain Simons was looking at the vessel through his glass, but he had not observed any movement in it, till suddenly one of the men cried,

"Look, captain; the flag!"

Captain Simons started as he saw the long black streak that had hitherto baffled his penetration fall in loose, but many, folds from the mast.

It was a flag—a black flag—marked with a white skull and crossbones!

Underneath these was a large crimson spot!

"A pirate," Captain Simons muttered, turning ghastly white; "a black flag! but what is that red spot beneath it?"

"It looks," said the first mate, "*like a blood red raven!*"

The telescope fell from Captain Simons' hands.

"*The Red Raven!*" he gasped; O God! it is he!"

And the captain fell senseless to the deck.

The attention of every one was at once bestowed upon him, and so, for a short period, the ship of death remained unregarded.

Now, when the captain was carried below, the seamen looked again towards the strange vessel.

But, to their unutterable amazement, it was not there!

Not a sign—not a vestige of its presence!

It had disappeared as entirely from view as if it had gone to the bottom; nor did they see it again.

Often, indeed, as they travelled homeward, did they fancy they could see the dusky shape towering above the waves, and following them like a monitor of doom; but it came not again in sight.

It was as if it had hung on their track just long enough to speak its mystic character, and then had gone, till it should come again at their hour of doom.

[CHRISTOPHER QUELLING THE MUTINY.]

From that time Captain Simons was an altered man. His face shrunk—his body wasted—his eyes lost their lustre—his commands were no longer peremptorily given. He seemed a wreck of what he once had been.

So the "Flying Dolphin" put into port. Her crew had their strange story to add to the rumours that were already afloat—rumours that made the blood of strong men curdle as they confirmed the statements.

A mysterious ship, it was said, with a daring crew scoured the main; their leader a youth, almost a boy, but so invincible that no contest saw him defeated.

Always coming at the moment of some wrong, this ship and its crew gained a notoriety that was a terror and a scourge to those whose deeds rendered them fearful of retaliation, for in their securest moments this mystic vessel was sure to hang upon them.

No. 3.

More than one helpless damsel, rescued from a terrible fate, had cause to bless the daring commander of this vessel; but against the record of his nobility and prowess there were reports of a merciless cruelty that shocked the most vindictive: he never gave quarter.

When he left a vessel, its crew, to the last man, lay in their blood on the deck.

Wherever his course lay, his track was always marked with the burning wrecks of blood-stained ships; his path was slaughter, and like a fiend he seemed to glory in scenting out any crime in order that he might cut to pieces those who were guilty.

From the fact that he invariably attacked vessels belonging to government he was called a pirate. The name of his vessel was unknown, but the mention of the blood red raven on his flag was enough to excite the direst consternation.

Such, briefly told, was some part of the history of the most daring boy of the world—the leader of the fearless—the champion of the brave—Red Raven, THE BOY PIRATE.

We take the reader to a fine old house in Sussex, a house not many miles from the mansion to which our hero was the rightful heir, but to which his boy-enemy, the mendacious steward's son, was brought up.

It is a stately, rambling structure, substantial without and luxurious within, the residence of Squire Meredith, the father of Lilia, and owner of property for miles around.

At a window of one of these apartments a young girl stood looking sadly across the golden expanse of mead and vale that spread between her and the distant sea.

A beautiful, graceful young creature, girlishly simple in her looks, but with a world of love beaming from her eyes. Her skin was delicately fair and soft, her lips were beautifully shaped and delicate in their colour, her bosom was fair as tinted snow. Her dress was very magnificent, and jewels sparkled from her arms and blazed around her brow.

Queenly in her beauty and surrounded by every evidence of luxurious comfort, it did not seem that she had much cause to be sad, and yet as she glanced down to her gold bracelets, her tears fell to the shining metal.

Lilia, the proud squire's daughter, was unhappy.

Her parents had given the old steward promises that she should be married to his son, and that evening a party was to take place in the long hall of the squire's house in honour of the event.

This was why Lilia was looking sorrowful and wishing she had been born a poor girl rather than what she was.

It was not alone that she disliked Daniel, but Lilia was true to the memory of her childhood's lover; in her own heart she had treasured his image, and had vowed that she would never marry unless she met some one like him, and as her fancy had exalted him above all the rest of mankind, it was likely that if she had her own way she would keep single all her life.

Her parents, who were very fond of her, nevertheless considered Daniel a good match, and as they could not understand why she should want to keep single on account of a dead sailor-boy, they had made up their minds that she should marry the supposed heir of Frontemore Hall.

Daniel was in the great room when she went down looking so lovely that all the gentlemen envied him for having her promised to him, and even the ladies acknowledged her radiant beauty.

As might have been expected Daniel Harwolf had grown to be a surly-looking, ill-disposed youth—tall for his age, and even strong for his years—but with his heavy features rendered almost disagreeable by the sullenness of his deep set eyes, and the cunning smile that so often played sneeringly about his lips.

He advanced towards her as she entered, and with a show of gallantry led her to a seat: distasteful as were his attentions, Lilia was forced to endure them on account of her parents, but her mind wandered away from thoughts of him.

Her memory was occupied by the image of that heroic youth who had been her champion in early days, and was to have been her husband when they grew up.

She was very sad during the whole of the evening, paying no heed whatever to the wooing words of her suitor, but only wishing that she might be able to escape from the contemplated marriage.

In the midst of the evening gaiety a visitor was announced by the name of Captain Paul, and was ushered into the room.

He was a stalwart young fellow, quite a boy in years, but with a powerful frame, and a countenance expressive of the sternest resolve, at the same time that its fairness redeemed and softened it.

He was attired in a naval uniform that displayed the shape of his graceful limbs; his sword hung by his side, and he carried his naval hat in his hand.

When he bowed to the assembly it was with the well-bred ease of a polished gentleman, and when he spoke his lips parted in a very pleasing smile.

By a quick but comprehensive survey he took note of all the company; he saw the sallow face of Daniel Harwolf, and his eyes took a troubled expression; he saw the low-browed visage of his father's murderer, the ex-steward, and the lines about his lofty brow grew hard, and his lips compressed.

He saw Lilia as she sat apart from the others, and a bright beam sparkled in his eyes, and his sun-bronzed features flushed with a genial glow.

The eyes of all the company followed the first movements of the handsome stranger, and many were the conjectures as to who he was, for nobody seemed to know why he was there, or who had invited him.

When Daniel Harwolf first caught his piercing eye fixed upon him an uneasy feeling stole over him.

Where had he seen that face? Where and when had he encountered that searching glance?

He could not tell, and yet it haunted him. It was familiar, and seemed to give him cause for dread.

Nor did the ex-steward behold with less disquiet the noble stranger; he, too, strove hard to discover whose face it so much resembled, but memory was at fault, and he had only his fears to guide him.

The young officer, after he had been in the room for a few minutes, found himself next to Lilia; a casual display of gallantry towards an elderly lady caused her to introduce him to the young girl.

The hearts of both seemed to throb with unwonted fervour as their hands rested a moment in contact: Lilia's troubled eyes wandered dreamily over the beautiful face of the stranger, and then, with a sigh, she let her arms fall to her side.

The sound of his voice had awakened singular emotions in her breast, and she withdrew into a curtained alcove to hide her tears.

"O God!" she murmured, "would that I were released; O Christopher, Christopher, why did you leave me?"

A graceful form glided beside her; a stout arm slid round her waist; the face of the young naval officer was bent down to hers.

"Lilia," he murmured, "dear Lilia."

The young girl started, then looked strangely in his face, her own cheeks going pale as the lily, and then blushing a faint crimson.

"Christopher," she said, lightly; and the tears started to her eyes.

"Hush!" he said, softly kissing away her tears; "Lilia, no one must know I am here; I have heard that you are to be married to him, and I have come to save you if you will—to-night I can bear you away: speak, the sails of my noble ship flutter in the wind, and ere daybreak, leagues of sea shall roll between you and him. Answer me, Lilia; say you will be mine and this arm shall scatter our oppressors like reeds; be mine, Lilia—share a destiny that, though terrible, is brilliant—and when the last cloud falls upon my career and my star burns out, I shall have had you to be my better angel: in deeds that have made my very name a terror I have mingled since I left you; but I dare not tell you all till you are mine."

"O Christopher, that cannot be, though I would as lief become the bride of the grave as the wife of this man, whom I cannot help loathing; yet for my father's sake I dare not listen to your promptings."

"Your father, if he knew how vile this creature is, would be the last to sanction your union with him: fly with me, dearest; the course I follow has been cruelly forced upon me, and wild and lawless as my career may seem, stormy and terrible as the destiny before me must be, as I have said, you will be near me, ever my good angel, and your influence will restrain me in hours of passion and deeds of crime; it is your mission to save me from the worst of evils.

Oh, love! were I otherwise than I am I could not cherish you so tenderly, adore you so madly; stern fate has placed me in a position where I dare not suffer one spot of softness to remain in my heart, where pity is weakness; humanity, folly; remorse, cowardice; and where these foibles are death to their possessor: my heart is hardened to a stone; my hand is stained; but I can love with an intensity of fervour that those born to a less dazzling and less guilty career know nothing of. Lilia! my own! cherished and sought so long, do not doom my soul to destruction by refusing to accede to my entreaties. Here you will languish through the pangs of outraged affection and quailing repulsion, and sink at last into the apathy of heartless indifference to your wretched condition as a slave sold for gold—a victim sacrificed to the Moloch of social *prestige*. Ah! death were preferable to such a horrible fate; the heaviest fetters would be links of roses compared to the galling chain that must bind you to a man whom you could never endure as a husband. With me how different your prospects! The idol of my burning devotion; the sharer of my brilliant triumphs; you would be the mistress of me and mine, the queen of the sea, the pride of the pirates' hearts. Oh! by all you hold dearest, my soul, hear me! and say that you will be mine."

"You tempt me strongly, Christopher. I have mourned for you as for the dead; I have tried to school my heart to duty and affection, but love would not revive in my soul, and I have suffered myself to be led like a victim to the altar: but I cannot resist my womanly impulses; they yearn to you only the more because you are following out your awful destiny through a thousand deadly perils: I will share them; and if I cannot divert you from the course you are pursuing, I can yet solace and support you in the darkest trials here. I should degenerate into all I most despise—but, ah, Christopher! we are talking too rashly: what hope, what chance have I of escape? What fearful dangers may not threaten you at this moment should you be recognised!"

"Fear nothing, joy of my soul! Your noble resolution has exalted my heart and fired my spirit, so that I could court the fiercest dangers only to show you how well I can afford to scorn them; but we must separate for awhile, love! for we may be observed; the length and earnestness of our conversation may cause surprise and provoke remark: you will fly with me to love and happiness—and tonight."

"Yes, if it must be so," replied the girl, turning a little pale.

"There is an old beacon beneath the cliffs," said Christopher, "near the ruin of the fisherman's hut; it is a lonely spot, but you must learn to live without fear, dear Lilia; I will be there with a boat to waft you away from every association of distress and thraldom. You will not fail me, dearest?"

"I will come," replied the girl. "But, Christopher, you have not told me at what hour?"

"It must be at midnight, dearest; and now let us part."

They were alone—the curtains of the alcove completely shielded them from observation.

Christopher clasped his beloved in a fervent embrace, and their lips met in a clinging kiss.

Another moment and he was gone.

Lilia stood for an instant as one in a dream, a wild light glowing in her eyes, a crimson flush burning on her fair cheek—she could not realise the events of the last hour.

Surely she was sleeping, and she would wake to find that her wild romance was but "the baseless fabric of a vision," and that her lost lover was still slumbering in death in the still cold depths of the changeful ocean—that she was still doomed to become the wife of one against whom the deepest instincts of her pure nature revolted.

She lightly pushed aside the curtain, and emerged into the gay and brilliant throng that crowded the splendid apartment, so handsomely furnished and so brightly illuminated.

He was there—the proud and noble youth—with his eagle eye and form of faultless symmetry. He was gaily conversing with some ladies of the party, who listened admiringly to his easy, bantering talk, and smiled bewitchingly at his well-turned compliments. He appeared to be the lion of the party, without seeking such a distinction; in fact, by an unaffected inobtrusiveness, he strove to resist the attempts made to "lionise" him, and with as much carelessness as courtesy permitted, evaded all questions as to himself and his experiences.

"Yes; I will be his. Misguided, unhappy as he may be, he is a hero worthy of a woman's devotion. He was my companion and protector as a boy; in his youth he is the most constant and fervent of all my suitors; and in his manhood he shall be my lord and my king. I will be by his side in peace and in war, in triumph and defeat, in joy and sorrow. I will live with him and die with him; for I am his chosen love and not his judge. Let the world war with him—the odds are on its side. Surely, then, I—a weak woman—may be true to my earliest and purest impulses without sin. From this hour is he mine and I am his. In interest, sympathy, destiny, henceforth and for ever, for good or for evil, we are one!"

In the heat of her excitement, the romantic girl murmured these words half aloud.

Emerging from the alcove, she was a little startled at perceiving one of the serving-men, who stood near the curtain that draped the alcove.

This man, whose name was Andrew Moss, had never been a favourite with his young mistress; there was an air of cringing servility in his demeanour that was particularly distasteful to Lilia's frank and confiding disposition.

A thrill of alarm shot through her heart.

Had this man overheard her conversation with Christopher!

If so, what might be the consequence!

How could she advise her love of his danger!

Perhaps her alarm was groundless.

It seemed so, for the man, with a hurried but profound bow and slavish smirk, passed her, and busied himself in obsequious attendance upon the guests.

Some pretty, laughing girls surrounded Lilia, and drew her away to the piano.

Andrew Moss slipped out of the room.

This zealous servitor instantly made his way to the library, whither Daniel Harwolf had retired to write some letters of importance.

He knocked gently at the door, with a sneaking, hesitating rap.

"Come in," said Harwolf. "What now?"

"Are you alone, sir?" asked the flunkey, in a dramatic whisper, at the same time looking up at the family portraits, as if he were apprehensive that even they were prone to eavesdropping; "I has something most pertickler to communicate, sir; most pertickler indeed."

"But can't you find some time more opportune for your communication than the present?" said his master, testily. "Do you not perceive that I am busily engaged, and that the house is full of company?"

"Sorry, I'm sure, sir—pertickler sorry; but as this business is most important, which nobody can help when one 'as a feelin' 'art, and whose bounded duty is to communicate—Yes, sir," he went on, hurriedly seeking to appease his master's impatience by bowing like a toy mandarin, "I'm going to, sir; —which is a officer, and as calls himself a gentleman; and a guest in a gentleman's house, sich conduct is peculiar, sir, and any one as 'as lived in noblemen's families——"

"What on earth, fellow, are you garbling about?" asked Harwolf, angrily.

"Werry sorry, I'm sure, sir—and a young lady, and sich loveliness; I'm sure cook and Maria was a-saying only yesterday——"

"Confound cook and Maria, and you too; get out of the room, you impudent rascal," cried Harwolf, passionately. "Did I not tell you that I am engaged. What do you mean by your pertinacious insolence?"

"Well, sir, in course I stands corrected, sir,—your obedient, humble servant to command; and it aint no business of mine, which I said to the coachman—a servant as knows his place——"

"Will know better than to play the fool in his master's presence. What the devil do you want, fellow?"

"I'm perfect satisfied, sir, and I wants nothing," returned Andrew, with sublime dignity; "Only when a gentleman, leastways as calls himself as sich—and a officer into the bargain—and a sea officer above all things—makes proposals to a young lady, which is keeping respectful company with a gentleman as 'as the honour to be my respected master, makes proposals to elope in a ship, and meet at midnight at a lonely place on the beach, in course, as a servant, with the best of characters from the first of families, and having a feeling 'art——"

"An *officer*—ha!" exclaimed Harwolf, turning white, and growing interested—"do you allude to our new guest, Captain Paul?"

"Yes, sir; in course that's the individ'al, sir,—leastways as calls himself the gentleman—which is going to carry off Miss Lilia in ships, and 'share his destiny,' and other sich things as are not fit language for one gentleman to use to another gentleman's young wom—future bride as is to be, I *should* say:—and, last of all, sir, I don't like to wound your sentiments, sir; for, as I say myself, having a feeling 'art,——"

"Will you drive me mad, fool?" shouted Harwolf, distractedly. "Go on with your story; and if I have any more of your insane digressions, I'll knock you down!"

"It is only natural that you would feel insensified at sich goings on, sir. Well, the young lady promised as she would meet him, time and place as agreed on; and, when they parted—I don't like to mention it, sir, having a feeling 'art—werry good, sir, I am a-going on—when they parted, sir, *they kissed one another!*"

"My God, can this be true?" cried Harwolf, in a voice of astonishment and terror. "And where is Captain Paul at this moment?"

"I left him in the drawing room, sir, a-deluding of the female 'art, which is the Dowager Lady Meagrely and her five daughters."

"Does he know or suspect that you overheard his conversation with Miss Lilia?" Harwolf inquired.

"O lor, no, sir; I wasn't a listening at all, but seeing of 'em in the alcove that leads to the conservatory, and feeling my bounded duty——"

"Enough—enough!" said Harwolf, impatiently; "look you, Moss, if you are prudent, and will keep your fool's tongue between your teeth, and carry out my directions without blundering, I will give you ten guineas; if there is any winking or whispering—aye, or any blundering, I will turn you off my service head and heels."

Andrew did not think proper to make any further reply to this delicate hint than the performance of a profound and well-studied bow that bore gratifying testimony to his zeal and humility.

Harwolf, who, since his engagement with Lilia had taken such a definite aspect, had used the apartment in which he was now sitting as if it were his own, rose, and drawing out a small bunch of keys, opened the drawer of the *secretaire* and brought out a polished rosewood case.

This he placed on the table, and opening it with a small key, disclosed its contents—a brace of gleaming revolver pistols.

These he placed in the breast pockets of his coat, and with a fierce injunction, accompanied by a threat to his faithful servant of silence and discretion, marched off to the drawing room.

Closely followed by the trusty Andrew, he mingled in the brilliant crowd that thronged the apartment. His search was futile.

Captain Paul was not to be found. One of the ladies informed Harwolf that he had departed some ten minutes before.

Upon the plea that she was suffering from a violent headache, Miss Lilia had stolen away to the seclusion of her own room.

Daniel was pale with baffled rage; Andrew looked sheepish and disconcerted.

"Infernal curses seize him!" muttered the sullen Harwolf, bitterly; "he has slipped through my fingers for once, and it is not policy to expose my humiliation to this idle assembly; the villain's handsome face and fearless daring will sure to gain him sympathy among the women, but I will bring such a posse to their rendezvous that the pirate thief shall not escape me—and then for Lilia—hottest love makes bitterest haste. Let the scorner beware! She has fooled and deceived me, and she shall dearly rue it."

CHAPTER V.

HOW THE BOY PIRATE QUELLED THE MUTINY.

THE night was dark and cloudy; the moon had not yet risen.

The sea raced fiercely up the shelving beach, and was tossed back in showers of foamy spray from the pointed rocklets.

The wind moaned dismally through the leafless branches of a few gaunt trees that grew on the summit of the cliffs.

The sea assumed those grey and black tints so portentous of coming tempests.

A few dim and weird stars, at long intervals, could be discerned distilling their feeble rays among the struggling clouds.

The hoarse roar of the breakers, and the speaking tones of the angry waters that lashed the sides of dark creeks and hollows, conveyed to the mind a sense of loneliness and awe.

It was a dull and dreary night, and the prospect was aught but exhilarating; yet, with a light and bounding step, our hero traversed the stony sands.

His eye glowed with proud delight, and his heart leaped with exulting joy.

She was won!

Without this consummation of his dear-bought triumphs, all his labour had been thrown away; all his victories would have been barren successes that he could not have prized; all his future would have stretched before him in a perspective gloomy and profitless; and only the stern joy of battle could have roused him from his numbing apathy; and when the fiery excitement of the engagement was over, the pall of listless despair would have fallen upon his heart, which would have been eaten away by gnawing regrets.

As it was, he had a gentle companion, who would share the pangs and the pleasures of his troublous existence—kind eyes from which to drink exhaustlessly rich draughts of tenderest love; a snowy bosom on which to rest his care-worn brow; a voice of sweetest music to still the conflicting passion-demons in his soul. Lilia! what ravishing melody is there in the sound of the heart-imprinted name of the beloved: the prematurely stern and commanding Boy Pirate, whose iron temperament seemed unassailable by fear or remorse, melted into happy tears as, in a tone of ineffable tenderness, he whispered to the soughing night-winds the loved name—Lilia!

He looked across the seething ocean.

The tumbling billows pounced and scattered at his feet, and receded, to gather strength for their eternal assault upon the rock-banded shore, with a hiss and a raging murmur.

He could not discern his vessel, though he knew she lay far out in the offing.

Like a troop of shadowy spirits, the mists were

sweeping landward, veiling the far far horizon in an obscurity.

Christopher had expected to find the boat ready to receive him.

Long accustomed to command, his impatient spirit chafed at this tardiness to do his bidding in those whom he ruled with a sway so strangely despotic.

At last the regular and steady plash of oars broke on his ear.

He started.

He had given strict orders that the boat should be well manned.

His trained ear could detect by the sound that but one man was rowing.

Could it be a stranger?

In any case, why were his orders disobeyed? What could have happened?

He was lost in conjecturing.

Was it possible that the crew had mutinied?

It might be so: he knew too well how frail are the bonds that unite lawless and crime-stained men. As he thought of Lilia his heart quailed.

As he thought of himself, his eye flashed fiercely, his hands clenched instinctively, while stern and indignant thoughts rushed to his mind.

The grating of the boat stranding on the beach arrested his attention.

From it stepped forth the tall and gallant figure of the lieutenant of the Boy Pirate—our old friend Jack Brierly.

"Avast there—what cheer?" shouted the old salt, in his ringing, manly tones. "Ah!—is it you, cap'en? You're as welcome as the first breeze in a dead calm. Shiver me, but this is a black day in our log: might as well have tried to steer without a compass as to manage the cursed unruly lubbers that have been sucking the monkey till they're drunk as blazes. Peter Gannon, the bo'swain, and that infernal bully Tom Bannister are playing the skippers, and the skunks are leading the crew by the nose to open mutiny. I tried the persuasion of the rope's end to some of the sneaking lubbers, but all the hide I got for my paternal correction was a pitch over the bulwarks, and I should be rolling about in Davy Jones's locker this blessed minute if I had not managed to crawl into the boat that was towing astarn."

"In open mutiny, are they?" said the Boy Pirate, sternly, "we will see whether they will dare to brave me to the teeth."

With imperturbable coolness Christopher stepped into the boat.

Jack Brierly seized the oars, and, plying his strong arms, sent the light barque speeding away from the shore through the dank and sweeping mists, and scattering the cold spray from its bows.

The dark hulk of the pirate ship looms through the haze.

The sounds of drunken shouts and inane laughter mingled with brutal and blasphemous oaths broke the solemn stillness of the night, so that the ship appeared to be a floating pandemonium of malignant fiends.

Throwing off his coat, and trembling with passion, the dauntless young pirate clambered the dark side of the vessel, unperceived by the riotous sailors on board, and sprang upon deck in the midst of the mutineers.

Stunned and sobered by the sudden appearance of their feared and respected commander they slunk back.

His eyes rolled round upon the clustering group with an expression of rigid sternness and resistless authority.

The true-blue, Jack Brierly, stood firmly by his side.

For a moment there was dead silence.

The blear-eyed drunkards looked one another in the face as if to draw resolution from mutual encouragement, and then turned their faces towards him who had hitherto been their idol with a general scowl of threat and defiance.

But the Boy Pirate quailed not.

His cheek was blanched, not by fear, but only with intense excitement.

His fine clear eye glowed like fire.

His teeth were close compressed.

"So," he said, with withering scorn, "this is the implicit obedience and unwavering fidelity you swore to me by oaths the most terrible that the mind could conceive, when of your own free will you raised me to the unsought honours of the thankless office I hold as your chief and your commander! This is my return for all the victories that I have won for you—the rich spoils I have shared with you—the fearful dangers from which I have saved you! But mark me, comrades, you swore an oath of fealty to me; on my part, I, too, pledged myself, and it was to hold my own, though every man aboard should mutiny, firm in the consciousness of having done my duty as your leader. I will not brook the slightest show of resistance. I am your captain, freely elected, and while I have breath will remain so. Let every man return to his duty; let this drunken brawl, which threatens us all with destruction, be stopped at once. Clear the decks—every man to his post—or by the God that made me I will shoot dead the first man who dares to disobey!"

"Hark ye, messmates," said Peter Gannon, a brutal-looking ruffian, advancing a step. "Have we put ourselves free of the rules of the sarvice, and made ourselves liable to be swung from the yard-arm by the skipper of the first man-of-war that can manage to overhaul us, just for the pleasure of hearing this vaunting young skip-jack cajole us with his land-lubber cackle, and bully his betters? Who is he any more than the rest on us? Do we all row in the same boat, or don't we? Don't we all share alike? What's the good of flying the rover's flag if it ain't to be *free?*—to do as we like and take what we can?—to drink grog while we've a keg aboard, and to elect whoever we likes, and as often as we likes? Is it bein' free or jolly, either, to be cowed by this boy-pirate, as if he were a lord high admiral of the blue? Shiver my tops'ils if I stands it for one!" With this the wretch gave a vicious grip on the hilt of a huge knife that dangled from his belt.

His wolfish eye lowered upon the young chief, and he was sidling along to get near to our hero, in order to cut short his brilliant career by a dig with his huge dagger.

Coolly, and with a strange, faint smile, Christopher drew a pistol from his belt, and, examining his victim critically for a moment, then levelled his pistol and shot him dead!

There was a cry of indignation among the crew.

"There is one traitor the less amongst us—let his body be removed and thrown into the sea; and now, my men, remember your oaths and return to 'your duty—the first who hesitates to obey me shall share the fate of him who lies a corpse at my feet—this regimen is painful, but it is necessary—you see my threats are not idle."

"My God—that shall be seen!" cried Bannister—an evil-eyed, swart, but attenuated wretch, who possessed great strength of body, and dogged courage.

He flew upon our hero, fastened himself upon his throat, and tried to drag him to the ground.

Christopher seized him by the neck, and by sheer strength lifted him from the deck: the fellow struggled in the pangs of strangulation, but the Boy Pirate did not relax his remorseless grip; at length the mutineer struggled more faintly, and the captain hurled him to the ground with stunning force.

There he lay limp and motionless, his face livid, and the purple stain of that iron grasp encircling his bull neck.

The youthful despot once more looked round upon the crew with a stern unquailing glance.

The men were sobered and awe struck.

Jack Brierly addressed them: he expatiated on the courage and conduct of their youthful leader—averted to the certainty of destruction from which there could be no escape if once order and discipline were banished from amongst them: he spoke in rough and homely terms, but not without eloquence, of the baseness and ingratitude, the folly and madness, of the ringleaders of the late demonstration, and in his own quaint way, without for one instant compromising the assumption or authority of Christopher, lectured the drunken pirates into good humour, so that when, in conclusion, he called upon them to give three cheers for their captain, and to return to their duty, they obeyed him in the first respect with uproarious zeal, and in the latter with perfect cheerfulness.

Thus the Boy Pirate and his lieutenant quelled the mutiny.

He had but little time to stay on board.

It was not so surprising as at first it may seem—the sudden restitution of order and comparative quiet on board that ship of crime. Scenes of slaughter and terror were of almost daily occurrence, and the summary punishment of the mutineers was only incidental to the common course of things.

When the body of Gannon had been consigned to the waves, and Bannister, more dead than alive, had been conveyed to the hold, and all on board was quiet and orderly, the Boy Pirate leaped into the boat and pulled landward, through the thick darkness of midnight.

CHAPTER VI.

THE RENDEZVOUS—THE AMBUSH—DESPERATE ENCOUNTER—ESCAPED.

WITHOUT communicating the discovery of the identity of Captain Paul with the famous and dread-inspiring Boy Pirate, or of the perfidy of his affianced bride, Daniel Harwolf resolved to take the most extreme precautions for ensuring the capture of the desperate criminal and the exposure of the fickle maid.

The mansion where dwelt the county magistrate was situated at some distance from the Squire's: the night was somewhat advanced, and there was no time to be lost; besides, it was impolitic to create a great sensation in the immediate neighbourhood, as that would only serve to drive the birds from the trap.

Attended by the faithful and zealous follower Andrew Moss, Harwolf went round to the cottages of some of his father's tenants, and telling them that the redoubtable Boy Pirate was in his power, and that with his direction and their own strength it would be an easy thing to secure the villain, he reminded them that, if they succeeded, there was a heavy sum offered by the government as a reward for his apprehension.

Fired by these representations, the patriotic villagers mustered in considerable numbers, and arming themselves with hay-forks, scythes, sickles and bludgeons, with a sprinkling of two blunderbusses, and some fowling pieces and horse pistols.

They reached the shore.

It was a wild and rocky coast; huge masses of chalkstone, that had gone down "white and thundering" upon the sounding beach, when the sea had stolen a march upon the land, lay scattered about in picturesque irregularity, offering famous places for an ambush even in the day time, and now it was midnight.

Harwolf, as well as the darkness would permit, marshalled his forces and placed them in ambush.

He patrolled round and among the rocks, to confirm himself in the assurance that all had been well arranged, and then took his own post upon a sort of table of chalkstone, from which he might the more readily catch sight of the pirate.

In his hand he held a highly-finished rifle, richly chased and beautifully mounted.

He had given strict orders for the profoundest silence.

Nothing was heard but the wild moan of the wind and the pitiless dashing of the restless waves.

The darkness was almost palpable.

The party had been watching about half-an-hour when the light and sylph-like form of Lilia glided, like a spirit, beneath the dark and lowering crags—and she stood, her heart wildly beating and her clasped hands trembling, and tried to pierce with her glance the shroud of darkness that was on "the face of the waters."

One of the farmers, distressed by his cramped position, in attempting to adjust his proportions to the size of the narrow crevice assigned to their accommodation, let fall his musket, and did not mend the matter by the utterance of a hearty oath as he picked it up again.

The girl gave a little scream, and started back.

But all was still; she listened breathlessly—she stole along the rocks, but it was too dark to see the ambush they concealed, and her womanish terror did not permit her to approach too near them.

At one moment she stood hesitating, and seemed inclined to leave the spot and fly homeward.

The crafty sportsman took no heed of the decoy bird, but only waited with intense suspense for the arrival of the mate.

Soon a red flame appeared flickering far out in the dark waters: it grew nearer and nearer, and glared more brightly as it approached.

Presently it waved in the murky night air, disclosed itself to be a torch, and its light fell on the forms of two men in naval uniforms.

One of these who held the torch stood back, and seemed to find some particular interest in contemplating the steep sides of the gloomy cliffs—whilst the lovers exchanged a rapturous salute.

The young officer immediately placed his arm around the girl's waist and led her towards the sea.

Scarcely had he advanced a dozen steps with his fair companion, their attendant carrying the torch before them, when a shot was fired.

Lilia gave a piercing shriek, and sank into her lover's arms in a deep swoon.

Christopher had felt the breath of a bullet as it whistled past his ear.

From crag and rock and from the ground sprang dusky forms; guns were levelled, steel-arms brandished, and the party were surrounded in an instant.

There was but one hope for the pirates and Lilia; the darkness might serve to veil them from the eyes of their assailants, and under its friendly wing they might escape.

The sea roared and chafed behind them, the rugged and steep cliffs were before them.

The flare of the torch fell upon the pale faces of the farmers and cotters who had volunteered in this dangerous service.

Harwolf hung back.

Lilia had fainted with shame and terror.

The drooping form of the lovely girl as she lay in passive lifelessness upon our hero's shoulder proved his safest shield.

The men were afraid to fire lest their bullets should strike the girl.

Jack Brierly perceived their hesitation and at once took advantage of it.

He pulled a brace of revolvers from his belt, and incontinently blazed away into the crowd.

One man—a strapping fellow in a smock frock—a farm labourer, was struck in the shoulder; two others were wounded.

The clodhopper first mentioned fell upon the beach and rolled over uttering a bellow of terror and pain so prolonged and so fearful that the others rushed back helter-skelter, and several guns were accidentally discharged.

"Hurrah, my lads," roared Jack Brierly from his stentorian lungs, turning his back to the enemy, and his face to the sea, and addressing an imaginary reinforcement, "Cheerily, ho! ho! shake out full sails, ye swabs, to the rescue. Tony, lend us your handspike and be damned to you; let's show the landcrabs what stuff we're made on."

There was such a heartiness in the glee with which the lieutenant hailed the creatures of his fertile imagination that the countrymen were completely taken in, and scattered in all directions. It was impossible in the darkness, and amid the din of the breakers, to determine the truth or the falsity of this implied turn in events, at least for a moment.

Even Christopher looked round expectantly.

"Fools and dastards, are you not ashamed of yourselves?" cried Harwolf. "Don't you see that the cursed rascal is playing a trick? Will you see your young mistress carried off before your eyes, when you are twenty to two? Seize the felons at once."

The valorous sons of the soil, at this re-assurance, returned to the charge.

One fellow, more bold than the rest, flung himself upon Jack Brierly.

The sturdy salt hugged him in his grappling arms and with a swing hurled him backwards against his advancing fellow-patriots, and the concussion caused a striking repulse of the enemy.

Christopher was not idle; drawing his sword, he slashed away through the darkness at every one who was rash enough to approach him, at the same time backing towards the water's edge in order to reach the boat.

The villagers were extremely cautious of firing, for in the mist and gloom they knew well enough that the chances were that they would kill the young lady, or shoot one another.

Harwolf was getting weary of this protracted scene, and resolved to end it by a *coup de main*.

With this intent, the currish fellow prowled round our hero, and sneaking behind him, and while his attention was diverted in keeping the others at bay, presented his gleaming barrel straight at Christopher.

But for the presence of mind and prompt action of Jack Brierly our hero would have been at once deprived of life, and our readers of this recital of his exciting adventures.

The quick eye of the old sailor at once discerned the deadly peril which menaced his beloved young chief. In the twinkling of an eye he whirled round his torch and struck it blazing full in the dastard's face.

Harwolf's eyebrows and lashes were burnt off, and his cheeks fearfully scorched.

"Run, cap'en," said Jack Brierly, in a hoarse whisper, "now's the time."

Harwolf, who had staggered back, stunned by the sudden and acute agony of the burn, fell on his knees with a howl of pain.

He was immediately surrounded by his clients and retainers.

They raised their defeated landlord with many expressions of indignation and sympathy; and then hurried to take summary vengeance upon the pirates.

But they were gone.

A general rush was made in the direction they were supposed to have taken.

The pirate chief and his trusty officer slipped behind a rock.

The whole party, with valour's better part inspiring them, kept close together, and with withering threats flew past the spot.

When the last man had gone by, Christopher, still bearing his lovely burden,—his lieutenant, who had thrown away the flambeau that had done such good service, keeping fast by his side—ran off in the opposite direction.

As they were rushing along they simultaneously struck against a dark mass that cumbered the ground, and were wellnigh precipitated on their faces.

"May I be keelhauled, cap'en, if we ain't struck upon the infarnal landshark himself; cuss me, if I don't scuttle his hull with my cutlass; it won't do to be too loud with the speaking trumpet."

So saying, he replaced his pistol and drew his sword with fell intent.

"Not for your life, Brierly," exclaimed the Boy Pirate, in a thrilling tone of command; "it were an act of cowardice to take his life in that way; let him alone—I reserve him for a terrible but open vengeance; I will spare him for this time."

"And by the rolling thunder, cap'en, you'll be infarnal sorry for it arterwards."

With a look of ill-restrained malignance, the sturdy pirate contented himself by administering a hearty thump with the flat side of his sabre upon the prostrate foe, and hurried along with his companion.

"Where are we steering, cap'en—do we make for port?"

"Yes, Jack," replied Christopher. "There is a ruined hut near this place, and thither we will convey my dear and hard-won prize: poor girl, terror and vexation have almost killed her; can we but outlive this night of danger and obstruction, and once more stand secure on the deck of our own gallant vessel, to scour the broad seas beneath our free-waving banner of death, I shall meet the wildest perils with a thirsty relish, and welcome the thunder of guns and the war-shouts of enemies as sounds that are sweetest; but I am sick of this foolish adventure, and wish I were clear of it."

"I ain't got much fancy for the cruise myself, cap'en," returned Brierly, "and I don't see the fun of being chased by such lubberly skunks as the swabs and chawbacons we had in our wake just now; but, hold hard, isn't this the bunk you were speaking on?"

Grey streaks seamed the east, palely flushing the heaving sea.

Before them was the rude and storm-battered hut, long untenanted.

In the dim twilight there was something weird and strange in its appearance.

It was formed partly of an old hulk—the remains of some dreary wreck—and partly with blocks of chalk, stone and sea-slimed timber.

Door, it had none—and the entrance was partly blocked by little hillocks of sand and heaps of stones; an old brine-stiffened sou'-wester lay near—some rotten net-strings and shrivelled bung-floats.

They entered.

The interior was in better preservation than they could have expected, judging from the dilapidated exterior of this squalid abode.

In one part the roof was splintered and rent, and the cold and pale rays of the grey dawn struggled feebly through holes and slits in the walls.

Into this lonely cabin they bore the fainted Lilia.

They formed a rude couch with moss and sea-weed, which they covered with their pea-jackets, and on this primitive bed they placed the beautiful unconscious girl.

Quiet and motionless she lay as they watched her delicately-moulded form, rounded in womanly beauty, and yet so tenderly frail; her face had lost all expression of waking interest, yet its absence was well atoned for by that seraphic "rapture of repose" that adorns the light slumbers of the young and guileless.

Even the rough pirate, Brierly, was moved to tenderness and admiration, and for a moment the native kindness of his untutored and misguided nature sympathised with the proud triumph and passionate love that glowed in the speaking eyes of the young pirate-chief as he gazed on her transcendent loveliness and exulted in the blissful thought that, sweet and beautiful as she appeared, she was devotedly and irrevocably his own.

"I ain't much judge of a figure-head, cap'en, and a lovely female is a sort of craft I never could understand," said Brierly, in a whisper; "but, shiver me, if there's any mistake to be made about young madam—she is a real, true beauty as ever made sunshine on a cloudy day; and I'll be bound she'll prove a noble consort for the finest and bravest youth in the 'varsal world. Douse my daylights, if I ain't proud of you both—if I aint making too free in saying so, your honour."

Unconsciously the stout-hearted salt lowered his

voice into a tone of respect, and pulled his forelock.

Could he have paid a fairer compliment to truth and beauty than this intuitive homage?

Christopher smiled happily.

"She is indeed a lovely, a true and noble bride." he said, "and woe to this head if the searing influence of my wild career should ever so transform me that I could, though but for an instant, forget the great and gentle sacrifice she has made for me. But I tremble, Brierly, to see her cheek so pale, to feel her hand so cold; what can we do to wake her from this lethargy? Ah me! this is but an ominous beginning to the new, strange existence, so adverse to her gentleness. Will she bear the fiery ordeal—will she forget her early training—will she despise the society's ban and the world's hostility—will she, who now lies so still and death-like, preserve a firm and steady countenance, a calm and reliant heart, when the quick-leaping lightning flashes and the thunder volleys from our guns—when the deck runs red with slaughter—when the air is tortured with yells and shrieks—when the black flag floats grimly above the scene of fury, and the Red Raven gloats upon its prey;—will she when I grasp her exultingly in arms that are weary with slaying, and proudly narrate my triumphs and victories—will she shrink from me with loathing, and hold herself polluted by my unhallowed touch? Brierly, I am mad when I think it! But, no, no; she has sacrificed all to love. I am her chosen, and she asks not what besides. Body and soul she devotes herself to me, and with me she shall reign! Not as a mild, subservient spouse; but as my glorious sultana—my queen of the sea! And dire woe to that rash being that shall not do homage to the rover's bride. See, Brierly, the rich blood tinges her fair cheek—her lids unclose—her sweet lips part—she revives to bless me with her smiles! Dear, dear Lilia, wake—look on him for whom you have cast away all—for whom you have braved scorn and dishonour — your own, your fervent lover!"

With wild and passionate tenderness, the strange, misguided but noble youth clasped his betrothed to his bounding heart.

She smiled, faintly, but with an expression of infinite sweetness; and she said, softly—

"It is all over now, Christopher—at least, the worst is past. I will be with you to the end; I am your own and you are mine, and I will not thwart you even where I cannot approve. But what place is this? Ah! my brain whirls. I thought I had seen Harwolf; others were with him. It must be fancy, for I thought they had killed you. But this is the place where we appointed to meet. Shall we go away soon, Christopher, to the ship which is to be our home? I long now to quit these shores, which I once thought I could never bear to leave. I want to be far away—far out in the wide seas; alone with you in your ship of battle, and then you will see that there is more of the old Norse blood in my veins than you think for."

The Boy Pirate did not reply, but only clasped her more rigidly to his breast.

"Hush!" cried Brierley, suddenly, approaching and listening intently.

"The cursed lubbers have made out our gibs and are giving chase. Look, cap'en, two on 'em are following up the wake we have left in the sand."

Christopher sprang to his side, and looked in the direction indicated by his subordinate.

Sure enough, at the distance of two or three roods, he descried by the increasing light the forms of two or three of the rustic *posse comitatus*, with guns in their hands, who were picking their way about the rude and scattered stairways of the cliffs, evidently following their trail upon the treacherous sand, and momentarily drawing nearer to their refuge.

"Lilia, dearest, we must leave you for a little while; we are in danger of being taken; you will not be afraid to be left alone."

"I must forget the taste of fear," replied the poor girl, with a smile. "I must learn to look on danger as my familiar companion. Dear Christopher, do not be apprehensive of my weakness; I am changed now."

"Spoken like my own brave girl," said the Boy Pirate, warmly. "Conceal yourself beneath the gloomy shadow of yonder wall; remain quite still and silent; I will not be far away. Come, Brierly."

With this, the two men left the hut; and as they did so they examined the primings of their pistols, and were by their looks evidently preparing themselves for a desperate contest.

The moments dragged away slowly and wearily with poor Lilia, as she crouched listening shudderingly to the hoarse murmuring of the restless sea. The shriek of a sea-fowl, or the rush of the wind through the ruin, caused her to start and tremble violently.

In spite of the confidence she assumed in the presence of her lover, the natural timidity of her gentle feminine nature would not stand the shock of the sudden and severe trial of her nervous energies.

A thousand nameless terrors thronged to her startled imagination.

For a moment a wild pang of remorse and regret sprang up in her heart, and she bitterly repented the rashness of the step she had taken.

Her father——

She stifled the thought—she crushed the suggestions of conscience by recalling for one moment the image of her dauntless, passionate lover—so wild and lawless, yet so handsome and true.

Still she listened.

No sound but the harmonious monotony of the dashing breakers. Cautiously she crept to the door and looked out.

The pursuers whom Brierly had discerned in the distance were not in sight.

The sea breeze caught her massy tresses, and broke their bonds; and her glossy hair floated and streamed lightly in the wind.

The flush of excitement glowed on her cheek, and her snowy breast rose and fell quickly.

She stood in an attitude of unconscious grace, with the lightness and the timidity of a startled fawn.

She heard the report of a pistol fired in the distance.

It struck a thousand dread echoes in her trembling heart.

What did that sound import?

Was it a signal shot, or was there death on its wing?

She could not tell.

A faint shout travelled to her; it sounded like a cheer.

Were the followers of the man from whom she was so eagerly fleeing—for whom she felt such a deep-rooted antipathy—exulting over the body of the gallant and beloved adventurer who had risked so much to rescue her from the misery of an uncongenial marriage?

She rushed back into the little cabin, and flinging herself upon her knees, sobbed bitterly in a paroxysm of suspense and nervous excitement.

Should her brave deliverer be indeed killed what would become of her?

The bitter, the overwhelming shame of being dragged back, and forced into a marriage with the man for whom she felt such repulsion, the idea was unbearable. There was the lesser misery that he would publicly discard her, and that she would thereby become a thing for scorn to point its slow unmoving finger at. Either of these alternatives were too terrible to bear reflection. She would never return: she would prefer death in its most horrible form.

The sound of a step! She turned her head and stood transfixed with horror!

A face, brutal and sullen in its expression, though handsome in its contour—a form, weak and degenerate, though straight and well-moulded—a

[HARWOLF CAPTURES LILIA.]

voice, harsh and querulous, though full-toned and manly—a heart, corroded by vice and indulgence, and steeled by its own intrinsic badness. It was Daniel Harwolf.

He had crawled to the spot, and supporting himself on one knee, while his left hand grasped the side of the door, he glanced into the interior of the cabin with malicious delight.

His features had been seriously scarred by the torch that Brierly dashed in his face.

Fascinated by the cold glitter of his malignant eye, Lilia stood shuddering, as the dove that flutters powerless under the eye of the deadly snake.

He rose; his clothes were disordered and covered with sand—his dark elf locks were strewn wildly upon his pallid forehead.

His teeth chattered, and his eyes glared with rage, while his fingers turned round the butt of his pistol with a murderous clutch.

No. 4.

His words came hissing through his teeth, and it was very evident that he had to struggle hard with the fiend that possessed him, and who seemed eager to throw his mortal agent of mischief upon the defenceless girl, and to rend her to pieces.

As it was, he seized her by the arm, and his fingers left their brutal imprints upon her soft, fair flesh.

"I meet you under circumstances that are creditable to us both, Miss Lilia," he began, with an ironical chuckle; and then, as she tried to break away, he shook her savagely. "Nay, do not struggle; you are as powerless in my grip as a dove in the claws of an eagle. The position you have taken does you infinite honour, and will doubtless be a source of congratulation to your fond and aged father, and to your affianced husband. Naïve and romantic your startling adventure with the dashing buccaneer; charming and edifying the story of your elopement with one who is nothing better than a thief and assassin of the worst order, outlawed and sentenced by the common law of nations to hang by the neck and to clank in chains till he swings a bare skeleton, a scarecrow to other bloody vultures of his kind. Worthy the object and the conduct of your love —a midnight elopement, a pursuit, a recapture, and the shame and ignominy of being dragged back to the scoffs and the reproaches of all who knew you as the affianced wife of an honest man. Come—time passes." He tried to drag her away.

"Never with my life! Villain and coward!" she cried, distractedly. "I never could school my heart to endure you, and your treatment of me now shows how just was my instinctive antipathy to you. Let me go, lest my cries should bring him to my rescue before whom you would quail like a hound. Let me go!"

With a brutal growl the ruffian, in his ungovernable passion, flung the frail and gentle girl violently against the wall, still holding her wrists in his spiteful grip, and shaking her brutally.

"No, by the Lord!" he said, in the intense calmness of concentrated fury. "I am not one to be tamely fooled and jilted within a few steps of the altar. And for him, too, whom of all men I most hate and——"

"Fear!" rejoined the girl, her beautiful eyes flashing with ineffable scorn. "Oh! that he were here to save me."

"Come, Miss Lilia, your friends are growing anxious at your protracted absence," he went on, sneeringly: "Aye, my spinsters and unmarriageable daughters are yearning to bask in your conscious blushes, and to treat your little *piquante* foibles with the tenderest charity; hundred-tongued Fame will not be free with your name, and the village-scolds will be jealously watchful of your unsullied reputation."

"You are the meanest villain that breathes the free air of heaven!" cried the girl, passionately: "Your vile taunts are unworthy of the basest wretch that vents his cowardly malice on the defenceless. I could have pitied, respected you, sorrowed for you; you might have had reparation of the involuntary wrong I have done you by many an hour's bitter remorse that I should have spent with your memory; but now you have shown me your black heart in all its deformity, and weak as I am, and brutal as you are, I tell you, now, while my wrists bleed with your torture, that I hate, and spurn, and defy you!"

Harwolf turned ashy white with passion.

"Be it so. Since you have thrown down the gauntlet I accept your challenge, and we will see which is the stronger; but first, to bring you back to the village: do not attempt to struggle—resistance is hopeless."

With this, the scoundrel flung his arms around the lovely form of the girl, and lifting her bodily from the ground, in spite of her shrieks and entreaties, carried her out of the ruined cabin.

As he emerged from the hut he was not a little delighted at perceiving that his band of villagers were approaching. With grave looks they surrounded her; burning blushes scorched her fair cheek, her brain whirled, and again she fainted.

Just as the miscreant, Harwolf, was about to carry off his recovered treasure in insolent triumph the advance of the party was suddenly arrested by a shout from behind. Turning, the villagers perceived a large boat put into shore. From it disembarked a score or so of determined looking seamen, armed with cutlass, pikes, and firearms.

At their head was the Boy Pirate, and his lieutenant, Briery.

"Stand!" shouted Christopher, in a loud and authoritative tone; "the first man who stirs steps to his grave. We have no intention of doing harm to any one of you, only at once release the lady."

"Are you such ingrate curs," cried Harwolf to the villagers, "as to let the daughter of your kind and worthy squire, and the betrothed wife of myself —your landlord—be snatched out of your hands and carried off by a gang of desperate felons and pirates —every one of them doomed to the gallows? Stand by me, if you are men—the odds are on our side! Surely you will not return to the squire and tell him that you gave up the young lady without striking a blow?"

"Darn un, noa! we'll fight for un," shouted the clownish partizans, at the same time putting themselves in battle array in a gallant style.

"My lads! let us avoid bloodshed, if possible," said Christopher, manfully. "I should be sorry indeed to do injury to any one of you for your praiseworthy devotion to the good squire's service; but believe me, lads, you could not do a better service for the worthy father than lending me your assistance to rescue Miss Lilia from that man, whom she abhors, and whom you all know—if you had the courage to stick by the truth—for a brute and a bully. There is a not a face among you that I do not remember; and it is strange if some of you do not recognise in me young Kit Foundling you were all so kind to when a boy."

The rustics stared at each other with extraordinary sagacity of expression, and then gaped at our hero in Bœotian amazement.

"Aye, but that be all guff, young muster," said one of the gentlemen of the smock frock, "for poor Kit Foundling were drowned in voreign parts, ye see."

"Nevertheless, I am he," said the Boy Pirate, with a smile; "and you will remember that I and Miss Lilia were playmates in childhood: we have loved each other since then; and of her own free will she came hither to meet me, and to flee with me from a marriage with one she can never love. Say, lads, would you bring shame and sorrow upon Miss Lilia, by leaving her in the power of one whose character is well known to you, when she has elected me to protect her from his persecutions?"

"Let un have her; he be better mon," said one of the peasants, in his broad dialect.

"I will kill her first," cried Harwolf, and he placed the pistol to her heart as he spoke. "Sheer off, you infernal thief and outlaw: rather than she shall be polluted by your vile touch, I will shoot her dead! I will, by God!"

He was about to put his threat into execution, for several of the pirates had instinctively stepped forward.

One of the seamen, however, with a sudden and dexterous whirl of his handspike, brought down the weapon with such impetus upon Harwolf's head as nearly to fracture his skull. He dropped like lead and the pistol exploded: there was a moment of dreadful suspense.

The blood from his forehead ran down on her snowy breast, and they thought he had killed her.

Christopher snatched her from the relaxed grasp of Harwolf; and, before the boorish spectators recovered their presence of mind, dashed off to the boat.

A movement was made on the part of the peasants, as if to follow and assail them; but the pirates levelled their firearms, and threatened a volley if they dared to oppose their movements.

The boat left the shore with a heart-stirring cheer, and thus was won Lilia, the Rover's Bride!

Won by a deed as daring as any of those of the olden freebooters, men like the renowned Morgan, the bloodthirsty Sawkins, or the dashing Sharp— pirates whose actions will stand out for ever in the records of desperate enterprises, a sample of which we lay before our readers.

A TALE OF OLDEN PIRATES.

Andrew Sharp, perhaps one of the most daring of the buccaneers, led his fierce crews from the coast of Guayaquil. That island had received its name from the illustrious navigator Drake, who put in there, and divided among his comrades the booty which they had taken from the Spaniards.

At this division they did not take the trouble to enumerate the pieces of valuable metal, but filled large pitchers with silver, and distributed them among the parties entitled to shares. At the period when Sharp appeared in these latitudes—viz., towards the close of the seventeenth century, the Spaniards still spoke with astonishment of the famous expedition of the English, the result of which had been transmitted to them, though greatly exaggerated by tradition.

They pretended that Drake's ship, notwithstanding it was of great size and burthen, could not carry away the prodigious quantity of silver with which she was laden, and that he was obliged to throw a considerable part of it into the sea.

The following was the plan proposed to be carried into execution by Sharp, under the conduct of an old negro, who was acquainted with the coast. he was to go to Arica, a city of Peru, situated in the eighth degree of southern latitude, and which served as an emporium for all the silver dug out of the mines of Potosi, Chuquisaca, and other mines contained in the neighbouring mountains.

From the island De La Plata, whither he had put in, the very opulent city of Guayaquil, containing about five hundred houses, was perceived; it was was the port of the great city of Quito.

The freebooters commenced their operations by seizing several Spanish ships, whence they took out everything of value, and afterwards left their prisoners the liberty of going wheresoever they pleased, detaining, however, the nobles and naval officers that fell into their hands, and treating them with much lenity.

They had with them, constantly guarded, Captain Peralta, who had been taken prisoner at the battle of Panama. Wherever the pirates went they compelled their prisoners to accompany them, and to share their fatigue and dangers, and without doubt extorted useful information from them. In the meantime the weather became bad, and water began to be scarce.

Tempests arose, in consequence of which the ship was obliged to keep off the land, and when they did attempt to approach it the steepness of the shore prevented them from landing.

To crown all their misfortunes, the whole country was prepared for the freebooters' arrival; the canoes were in danger of breaking to pieces against the storm-beaten rocks, and the least inconvenience they had to experience was that they could not possibly prevent their arms and ammunition from being wetted.

At length the scarcity of water increased to such a degree that every man was allowed only two cups of tea per day.

The crew now became very tumultuous and mutinous, and could not without great difficulty be managed.

Notwithstanding they were only six marine leagues from Arica, it was utterly impracticable for them to effect a landing there.

They succeeded, however, in entering the bay of Ylo, which lies to the north-west of Arica, about the seventeenth degree of southern latitude, where they disembarked, and carried by assault and pillaged the city of that name.

But they would not expose themselves to the danger of removing from the coast in order to penetrate further in the country, for they saw that all the neighbouring shores were occupied by the Spaniards, who had assembled there from the provinces, and whose number continued incessantly to increase.

In this dilemma, it only remained for them to avoid an engagement from which the most fatal consequences must result, and avail themselves of this hasty landing to procure what they most wanted.

This was accordingly effected; they filled their barrels with water, collected great supplies of sugar, oil, fruits, and pulse, re-embarked during the night, and immediately set sail.

Their design was next to land at Serena, a city containing eight churches and four convents, and from which they might form some hopes of procuring some booty.

But this plan of the pirates was in great measure frustrated: the inhabitants, who had been opportunely informed of it, had fled away with all their valuables.

The freebooters pillaged the little that remained, without experiencing the slightest resistance. The Spaniards, however, apprehensive lest their city should be reduced to ashes, sent a trumpeter to the pirates to offer them a ransom. This was soon granted; the sum required was fixed at ninety-five thousand piastres, but the payment of it experienced some delays.

The Spaniards, having regained their courage, flattered themselves with the hope of saving the ransom to which they had agreed, and endeavoured to gain time: with this view they discharged a sluice upon the freebooters, in order to drown them; the attempt failed altogether, and only provoked their resentment. They instantly set the place on fire.

At the same time they encountered a danger of much greater consequence, and which they escaped only by their uncommon activity. The Spaniards had conceived the idea of burning the pirates' ship: during the night one of them placed himself on a horse's hide stuffed with straw, and thus floated to the vessel. He forced sulphur and other combustibles into the joints and pieces of the helm, which he then set on fire. The ship was immediately filled with smoke, and the helm began to burn, when the freebooters that had continued on board discovered the cause of the fire, and succeeded in extinguishing the flames before they made much progress.

This circumstance, which might have hurried on the freebooters to the commission of new violences, produced an effect altogether contrary. They were apprehensive lest the unfortunate Captain Peralta, whose temper became daily more gloomy and morose, and the other prisoners should, in a fit of despair, attempt with more success what their fellow countrymen had so unfortunately endeavoured to effect; they thought it, therefore, the safest way to get rid of such dangerous guests, and set them all at liberty.

From the bay of Ylo the pirates afterwards sailed to the island of Juan Fernandez, which has since become celebrated from Admiral Anson's voyage. The discontent which had so long prevailed among them now burst forth; a complete insurrection ensued: they positively declared to their chieftain Sharp, that they would no longer obey him, and chose a new commander of the name of Watling.

At length, after wandering in various directions, at a greater or less distance from the South American coasts, they landed at Arica in the month of June, 1680. That city was garrisoned by nine hundred soldiers, who had just been joined by four thousand men sent from Lima, the metropolis of Peru, which is about one hundred and fifty leagues distant from Arica.

From this auxiliary body, three hundred men had been selected and placed in the fort. Watling left part of his men on board his ship, and taking only ninety-two with him, marched towards the place.

The Spaniards advanced to meet him, and a bloody battle ensued, which terminated in the ordinary manner.

Notwithstanding the inferiority of their number, the freebooters gained the victory and rushed into the city; and notwithstanding the care of preserving and guarding their prisoners demanded all the vigilance, they had the temerity to attack the fort: but they had reason to repent their audacity; they experienced a most vigorous resistance.

In the meantime the defeated Spaniards had rallied themselves; and penetrating into the town in a body, they attacked the pirates in the rear, and compelled them to relinquish their attack upon the fort, and sustain a new engagement within the very walls. But the number of their adversaries increased every minute, and they fought with the utmost desperation.

The freebooters had already lost several of their

comrades. Among the dead were their new captain, Watling, and some of their principal seamen. Others had been taken prisoners.

The Spaniards breathed nothing but vengeance against the cruel enemies of their nation.

The freebooters were too inferior in numbers to entertain any hope of success. They replaced themselves under the orders of their former commander, Sharp, whom they entreated to superintend their retreat. This measure was the more urgent, as they suffered extremely from thirst, and had not taken any sustenance throughout the day, so that their strength was exhausted. Sharp yielded to their entreaties with much difficulty.

Unawed by any danger, he revolted from the very idea of leaving his companions in arms in a state of captivity.

His aversion to resuming the command originated neither from the excessive desire of plunder or vain glory nor from any exalted sentiment of honour, but it was produced solely by that devotion to his brethren which was to each member of the association the most imperious of all duties. It was, however, absolutely necessary that he should determine to save the remainder of the combatants.

At length they retired from the city, though not until they had, by dint of valour, cut a bloody passage through their infuriated enemies. They had lost twenty-eight of their men—slain and taken prisoners—and they carried along with themselves eighteen who were most severely wounded. At the same time they experienced a loss which they could not but feel most sensibly. They were obliged to separate from their three ship's surgeons, who were so intoxicated with wine that it was impossible to bring them to their assistance.

During their retreat they were pursued by the Spaniards into the open country, where, being free in their movements, they formed themselves into a body, and took such defensive measures as disposed the enemy by no means to renew the engagement.

Towards the approach of night they regained their ships, and set sail for the gulf of Keoya.

Here their body experienced a fresh diminution, forty-seven men separating themselves from it, in order to disembark and attempt by land journeys to reach the shores of the opposite sea. The remainder of their troop continued to exercise their piracies; but before they took any further measures, they, in order to secure success to their future enterprises, solemnly engaged to remain united together. Shortly after they captured a Spanish ship that was sailing towards Panama, and which, besides a vast quantity of merchandise, also contained thirty thousand piastres. A second vessel of greater value, though less rich in cash, afterwards fell into their hands. This prize satisfied one of their ruling tastes: they found on board six hundred and twenty tuns of wine and brandy. At first her crew—which consisted of forty men—were disposed to defend the ship; but in order to disqualify her for battle, the freebooters had recourse to a terrible expedient, which, with their dexterity, never failed to be effectual.

They pointed their shot against the officers; the captain and pilot were killed, and the remainder instantly surrendered. The prisoners were immediately set at liberty by the pirates, whom they informed that such of their comrades as had quitted them were obliged to force their way arms in hand across the country they had traversed, and that the viceroy of Peru had beheaded the Spanish Admiral Ponce for not having found out and exterminated the freebooters during their residence in the island of Gorgona.

Such of the freebooters as continued their cruises were now hopeless of obtaining rich prizes by effecting disembarkations on the Spanish dominions. They were too inferior in point of number, and the whole coast was strictly guarded; it was therefore unanimously agreed to relinquish all further attempts; and after passing the straits of Magellan, to sail either for England, or towards the English

islands in the West Indies. This voyage was most unfortunate; the pirates had to contend with the most violent tempests, and not being able to find the entrance of the straits, they were driven towards the pole into unknown seas, where they were every moment apprehensive of being dashed against the rocks, or of foundering on sandbanks. In this perilous situation, their sole consolation consisted in the sight of their rich booty, in contemplating and dividing which they spent their time. At first they shared among themselves the gold and silver, both in cash and ingots; then the jewels and other portable articles that were of any value: the division of the remainder was deferred to a more happy moment.

The portion of each man, consisting of gold, silver, jewels, and other articles, was from this time valued at five hundred and forty eight piastres (about £100). But this small fortune, which they enjoyed only in expectancy, could not relieve or remedy the extreme want which they experienced in other respects. Being altogether destitute of fresh meat they were reduced to the most wretched food; one hog yet remained on board, which was kept for some months for a festival; at length it was eaten on Christmas day, 1680, and was, indeed, a repast, after such long privations. Ennui afterwards obliged these robbers to seek for some amusement in gaming, in which several of them lost the whole of what they had acquired with such infinite trouble and danger. At length, towards the close of January, 1681, they arrived, to their great satisfaction, in the latitudes of Barbadoes. They durst not, however, venture to land immediately on that island, as an English frigate was moored in its port, and they were apprehensive of being detained for cruising without letters of marque, and consequently of being treated as pirates; they determined, therefore, to sail towards Antigua, whither a canoe was dispatched to purchase provisions. They were not allowed to land, and only obtained what was absolutely necessary for them.

Thus it became impracticable to dispose of their ship, as well as of any part of their effects, whether of greater or of less value. Such of them as had lost their all in gaming had to congratulate themselves on these adverse occurrences. To them was given up the ship, with suitable provisions, in order that they might go in quest of other adventures. The remainder, who constituted by far the greatest number, separated from their comrades who were forced again to seek their fortunes, and embarked as passengers for England, where they arrived after a prosperous passage.

Having given this brief instance of the hardihood of the pirates of old, we now take up the thread of our hero's adventures.

CHAPTER VII.

THE INSTRUMENT OF VILLANY NAMES HIS PRICE.

NOTHING could be more elegant or luxurious than the reception room at Frontemore Hall; the croisée windows opened upon terraces adorned with marble statues and bronze vases, and overlooked a wide-spreading landscape of rich sylvan beauty, through which the broad and gleaming river lazily meandered, sometimes shooting under the quaint span of a rustic bridge, sometimes lapping the flowery sides of green and willowy isles, or gushing in diamond spray down little weirs and water-breaks—sometimes crossed by the straying herd. The deep brown woods, glowingly tinged with the hues of autumn, stand firmly and grandly together in their compact phalanxes of giant oaks and elms. The shrill chirrup of the grasshopper, the twitting call of the hedge-finch, the melodious revelling of the joyous thrush, all the thousand sounds, sights and scents that make the country so calmly and purely delightful combined in vain to sooth the dark broodings of that evil man who, like the fiend in paradise, took an aspect sterner, more guilty and abhorrent when contrasted by the beauty and innocence of surrounding objects.

In an easy chair at the window, where the cool breeze with perfume-laden wings fanned his hot and clammy forehead, sat old Andrew Harwolf: by his side, on a buhl table of masterly workmanship, was a cut crystal decanter of strong brandy; he held a glass listlessly between his fingers, from which a rich bead of the ardent stimulant was slowly straining.

Of late Andrew Harwolf had taken much to drinking.

He was not exactly a drunkard, for upon his strong nerves the ardent and intoxicating fluid as yet produced but little apparent impression.

After a day of sottish indulgence his voice might become somewhat thick and husky; the cruel sparkle in his deep-sunk eyes might dilate with a wilder, more intense ferocity of suspicion; his firm hands might tremble just a little, but that was all.

On this particular evening on which the reader again meets this atrocious villain, he was affected more than usual: there were glowing patches of hectic scarlet on his cheeks and forehead; there was a watery brilliance in his eye—a languid stoop of the shoulders and feverish catching of the breath.

It was one of his dark hours: the furies of unrepentant and involuntary remorse were clawing at his very heartstrings; red spots floated before his eyes—the river seemed to take a lurid hue: a vague sense filled his mind that the glorious sun, then setting so peacefully behind the clear blue hills, firing the gilt vane of the village church, and throwing long wavering shadows across the wide and velvet meads, was but the eye of the universe, and that its smallest ray was penetrating into the abyss of his guilty soul; and as the little songsters hushed their glad notes and came silently skimming by, he remembered the words he had heard at the church with such a thrill of qualmish suspicion—"A bird will carry the matter." For him there was no beauty in the universe, or if there was, the world's loveliness only mocked him as he walked forth, wrapped in his black pall of horrible remembrances, his every sense assailed by imaginary horrors; and the sweet fresh flower cups, breathing not the fragrance they wafted to others, but to him the foul stench of a horrible burning.

"The wages of sin is death." A living death to this false steward was the bitter fruit of his diabolical crimes.

Andrew Harwolf had been carefully trained in religious truths and doctrines during his boyhood, but he had paid no heed to such teachings; and the moral effect they produced upon his depraved nature was only to torment and not to reform.

Avarice was his ruling passion, but he would have given the better half of all the vast possessions for which he had paid such a terrible price to have excluded his belief in the existence of the Deity and in a state of future punishment for the guilty. At times he felt that there was no hope for him beyond the grave, and when this gloomy thought was upon him, he would cling to existence with the eagerest tenacity, and would attach importance to the slightest or remotest indication of failing strength. He knew almost every grey hair in his own head and every wrinkle in his forehead; and he would sit abstracted for hours in calculating the probabilities of his reaching a green old age.

A dark shadow fell between him and the sun.

A man appeared standing in the balcony without the window.

He advanced and laid his hand familiarly on Andrew's shoulder.

"Ha! You are doing a little day dreaming, Master Harwolf," said the man, with a gruff laugh; "I'm given to castle building myself, sometimes; but I don't suppose I can always conjure such pleasant reflections as you can."

Andrew shuddered.

"And how are things looking at Frontemore?" the fellow went on, coolly drawing a chair up to the window, and pouring out a brimming glass of the brandy.

"Ah! very good," he said, smacking his lips; "would put life into a stone image if it could but swallow. And what a delicious prospect there is from this terrace; the world, seen from this point of view, is a very Eden."

The ex-steward looked up with a malicious scowl at his companion, and exclaimed—

"I thought I had seen the last of you for some time to come."

"Oh, by no means; I cannot forbear availing myself of your generous hospitality as often as possible. True friends are so scarce—and we two are bound together by such charming ties of mutual interest and confidence; yet, I will confess, I should not have been here again so soon but for the heavy loss I have sustained by my unfortunate speculations at book-making."

"What!" cried Andrew, surlily; "money, I suppose—money. There is no satisfying your cursed greed for money; you have no more consideration, no more pity, for me than a vampire. Do you suppose, because I have inherited a tolerably large income, that my coffers are inexhaustible? Why will you be such a fool as to kill the goose for its golden eggs?—it is not to your interest to ruin me."

"I know that well enough, my good Andrew," replied the fellow, "and I am sure that you are doing me grievous injustice by supposing me capable of wishing to do a dirty trick by a partner who, it must be owned, though given to wince a little when the screw's put on, does certainly come down handsome. Now, I was a-thinking that you would not be sorry to see the back of me, Mr. Harwolf, and not be reminded by my presence of the little private affairs we have been engaged in in former times. Suppose, now, you were to make some neat little settlement upon me, and I were to take my departure to the new world or some of the colonies, and bind myself never to return to England."

"Aye, but what security should I have that you would not break your agreement?"

"What security can you have that I mayn't peach upon you at last?"

"Do you think, Silas," said Harwolf, in a dry, cold voice, "that I am so much in your power as to be afraid of your machinations? The worst you can do is to attempt an exposé, which would raise all sorts of surmises in the inquisitive minds of meddlesome neighbours; but you can prove nothing, and, excepting the unpleasantness of village scandal, I have nothing to fear. Silas, do not be ungrateful; you served me in a trifling matter, and I have ever treated you liberally."

"I don't say anything against that," returned the fellow; "but I want to make a fresh start in the world, so, should you really be more desirous of my absence than my company, I will not only give you my promise to keep out of your way henceforth and for ever, but, for a consideration, I will give into your hands certain documents that would, if kept in my possession, give me the power—I say the power—of demanding whatever sums I needed."

"And what documents are these?" asked Harwolf, suppressing his anxiety, and throwing himself back in his chair with an air of easy indifference.

"There are not only documents in my possession," returned the other, with a triumphant leer, "but proofs of another kind—facts, existing facts, which prove the identity of the child I stole for you, and of the disposal that was made of the mother."

"Ha!" cried Andrew Harwolf, "she did not then destroy herself; she did not: but, God! you are fooling me, and I will tear your lying tongue from your throat, I will—I will——"

The horrible terror that fastened upon the soul of this guilty wretch, as he felt himself to be thrown upon the mercy of his tool and parasite, threw him into convulsions.

We have already seen the ungovernable temper that characterized his son—it was a family failing. Harwolf was peculiarly an ill-tempered man, a man of ungovernable passions; his heart was all blackness and baseness. The conception of such a character may be declared by worthy and pure-minded philanthropics as strained and unnatural; but is there one of us who has not encountered, in the course of our existence, one at least whose base and selfish nature is impervious to every impression of extraneous interest and sympathy?

After what was narrated of the atrocious Andrew Harwolf in the opening chapters, the utter villany of his nature cannot be a matter of question.

Silas Rye looked at his patron and employer with a grim smile of gratified malice.

" Harkee, squire, what I told you is sober truth. I know enough, and what is much more to the purpose I can *prove* enough, to bring you to the felon's dock and the gallows drop—to make your wide estates sink under your feet, and to dissolve your fine mansion like a pile of snow—to give you bitterness for luxury—the condemned cell for the gilded saloon—the Newgate mattress for the eiderdown. And why shouldn't I? What, in the devil's name, do you care for *me*? What would you give me to save me from the cruel pangs of pinching hunger? Not a cursed crust; not a fleshless bone!—and why should I scruple to see you swing because you give me hush-money—blood money; because you buy my " eternal jewel," as the players call it, for a paltry roll of bank notes? Whew! I'm crucified if I don't see you hung like a cat—if I don't put the true heir in his right place—if I have any infernal humbug when I ask you for such a piper's share of your rich gleanings. Look ye! it is such cursed hounds as you that hunt the souls of the poverty-bitten and hapless to eternal ruin. I was once simple and honest; my heart was tender and my conscience clean; but you made me a villain, that I might tie your boot. I am sick of you—I'm sick of my present way of life; and I tell you, with truth, that I am eager to make a new chalk in the new sphere on the other side the wide sea; but if you refuse to accede to my fair terms, by Heaven's mercy in the extreme hour, I will bring home all your villany! I will crush you under the load of your own black guilt—I will have triple vengeance upon you! That I do not threaten idly, I will tell you something you little dream of. I can, within a day, produce the most damning proofs against you—and I will, unless you consent at once to my demands."

Harwolf was deadly pale; but his was no weak nature; he shrank from nothing—neither from crime nor fear; and after preserving a crafty and self-conquering silence for a few moments, he replied—

" You rave and threaten, Silas, as if I had refused you anything that you have asked me. You plead fair-play : you think of a desire to quit your present mode of life—and yet you bully and try to enrage me when I have always done my best to keep you in competence and ease; but boundless extravagance must destroy itself. If I gave you all I possess it would avail you nothing; soon you would be a crawling beggar—penniless and desperate. Come, we are friends! We can none of us control our destinies, and fate has made us what we are. We ought to be triumphant, for the devil does not always reward his victims. Simply to be guilty is not to be fortunate. What do you want? Make a demand within the extremest bounds of reason and it shall be gratified as far as I have power; but you see that I have sacrificed all—far more than you have; and upon your own principles of fair-play it is only right that I should have my share in the returns. Don't let's quarrel, then—cool yourself. I remember that you used to like my prime long-bottled Madeira; I will go and fetch a bottle of the choicest. Come in, Silas—let us sit at the table. I will ring for lights, and we can smoke away our broodings with a choice Manilla, and drown our guilty cares in a sparkling bumper of rich wine! Name your terms, Silas, and I will accede to them."

With this, Andrew Harwolf rose and entered the magnificent apartment. The sky had darkened, and the gleaming stars stood out of the lurid purple: the grand woodland scene was bleared and indistinct—the glancing river was mist-wreathed.

Andrew Harwolf rang the bell; the liveried servant entered.

The squire ordered the lights, and taking out a little bunch of keys, walked from the room, selecting one of them, with which, having entered the adjoining chamber, he opened an *armoire*, drew therefrom a sealed bottle of Madeira and something else,—a small phial.

What were its contents?

Let the sequel show.

Returning to the drawing-room, Harwolf invited his confederate in guilt to approach the table. The servant had drawn the blinds, a brilliant lamp had been placed by him on the table, the rich light flooded the room and lighted up the gilding and splendid ornaments of the luxurious apartment.

A silver salver was brought up upon which were some chased baskets of fruit and biscuits.

Andrew Harwolf seated himself at the table and folding his arms bent his eyes abstractedly to the floor.

There were cigars in a stand upon the table : Silas Rye carefully selected one, and having rolled it round in his fingers, lighted it, and puffed the blue smoke in light eddies as he flung himself back languidly upon the velvet couch, and looked from beneath his shaggy brows with intent scrutiny into the rigid face at his fellow-criminal.

" Silas," Harwolf began, " you are not telling me what you demand, and I am anxious to gratify your desires. Believe me, I am not mean or selfish, though you think me so : the past is gone by. Men do not live for the past, or the greatest and best would not so soon be forgotten. If you know my secrets, I know yours; and mutual interest is the strongest bond. Speak out, man; what do you want? An income; a little estate,—anything in reason."

The rascal looked at him suspiciously, as if doubting the motive that prompted his fair speech.

" I don't want much," he replied; " curse it all, if a man cannot have a home to cover him he might as well seek shelter in the grave. Yet I don't want land here in England—I hate the place. I am too well known, as I said; I wish to make a fresh chalk, and I intend emigrating, and to do that successfully one must have money. Now my chief capital consists in a knowledge I possess of your secrets, as you say, and the fact of having done you certain services for which I have a lasting claim upon you. You are very rich; let me have a small share of the swag that I helped you to win and I shall be satisfied, and willing to leave you in quiet possession of the rest. Come, suppose we say ten thousand pounds."

" Make it twelve, Silas—make it twelve," rejoined his companion, rubbing his hands; only I must insist upon your swearing, by all you hold sacred, never again to make a claim upon me on the score of old services—never again to show your face in this island."

" I will agree to that," replied Silas. " Twelve thousand is not too much, considering that you are a millionaire, and that you owe, in some measure, your present position to my unscrupulous endeavours in your behalf."

" Services for which I shall ever be indebted, Silas; but I think you said just now, when you were a little tiffed about my disapproval of your frequent visits to Frontemore—they are not safe, Silas, they are not safe—that you knew something about the supposed wife of my late master. Is it so?"

" And you know nothing of her?"

" Only this—that on the night when I discovered —that is, when his lordship absconded, she went mad—her brain was turned by the culmination of horrors—the loss of her child—the—the departure of her husband; but we need not speak of these things——"

The cold sweat hung on Harwolf's brow as he seized the wine bottle. He poured out a glass—he was about to raise it hastily to his lips, when he suddenly paused, turned ghastly white, and filled another glass with brandy.

Silas Rye had noticed this action, and his dark face went red with suppressed rage; nevertheless, he smiled blandly, and replied—

"Don't recal the past, squire. Let us look to the present and the future. Anyhow, you haven't much cause for complaint; and as for myself, why I'm not going to be a martyr to either side."

"Quite right, Silas," rejoined Harwolf, with a sinister smile. "It's a man's first duty to look to himself; but you were saying that Lady Edgeforth, who went mad, strayed from this house, and disappeared so strangely——"

"Well, I was going to say," replied Silas, bluntly, "that she is supposed to be dead."

"And is rightly supposed to be so," cried Andrew, excitedly. "No doubt the poor creature drowned herself in the lake."

"It was dragged—why wasn't her body discovered?" asked Silas, in a hard, dry tone.

"Well, well, she might have thrown herself down the Fox Leap!"

"Where is her body, then?"

"What has become of her I don't know; but no doubt the poor lady is no more."

"Let us suppose," said Silas, "just by way of argument, that she had been found by some person or persons unknown, and that they had taken care of her, and that she was still alive in their charge; what would you give for the surrender of her person to your keeping? Answer this question, squire."

Silas blew a long whiff from his cigar, and looked furtively at his employer.

"In that case—why I don't know exactly what course I should take," said Harwolf, hesitating, while his voice grew husky and tremulous.

"You would not mind paying pretty stiff, I suppose, to get her into your power?"

"Why, no," returned Andrew; "it would be worth a considerable sacrifice to do so. But you—you don't know anything of what has become of her?"

Silas grinned.

"I! what should I know? But if I did, and you could buy all my knowledge and power of me, would you not say twenty, instead of twelve, thousand?"

"Well, Silas, if I could depend on you, I might do so."

"Ha! then the secret is worth something to whomsoever owns it?"

"But why do you talk of things that are mere suppositions?"

"Simply for amusement and for information," said Silas, with a smile.

There was a pause.

A determined and dangerous look settled on Harwolf's face. Silas watched him silently.

At this moment a large bloodhound, an especial favourite of Harwolf, although the noble brute had never shown much preference for his master, but rather a dislike, wandered into the room.

He laid his head upon the knee of Silas.

"And when do you intend to set sail for America?" asked Harwolf of his companion.

"As soon as I have settled my affairs," rejoined the other. "I long to put the wide seas between myself and a country where till I became imbrued in guilt I knew nothing of sorrow."

"And where are you living, Silas?"

"At the Hedger's Arms," returned the other, carelessly.

"And you keep your papers with you?"

"Always!"

"I must employ you, Silas, upon an important service once more before you leave England."

"Indeed!"

"Yes. You must discover for me the facts of Lady Edgeforth's death: that she is dead I feel certain."

"And should I discover that she is still alive, and that those who hold her in charge are acquainted with

her name and rank, how much would you give me for my information?"

"If everything should turn out well, and I should be secured in my possessions," returned Harwolf, cautiously, "I would give an ample reward to any one who should be the means of bringing about such a desirable result."

"Look you, then, squire; I will—as I can—confirm your present position, and remove all dread from the future, but I must make my own terms; you have offered me twelve thousand pounds—I will take twenty!"

"You are extortionate," returned Andrew Harwolf, "but I suppose it is useless to oppose you. Well, be it so; only you must keep out of my path."

"You mean it, then. I am to have my tithe of what I helped you to win."

"It is only just—but you do not drink. You will excuse my drinking with you this Madeira; it does not agree with me."

So saying, Harwolf filled up his glass with brandy. "Come, let us drink success to the future, and let us drown the past."

"Well said," replied Silas, with a sneer.

"Hi! Bruno, old boy, what do you want, eh? A biscuit, dog, is that it?" said Silas Rye, patting the bloodhound's broad head, as the noble brute fawned upon him.

He dipped a biscuit in the wine, and held it aloft for the dog to catch at.

Harwolf sat with his cold, cruel eyes lighted by a gleam of evil: his face wore an inane look of rigid abstraction—his arms were tightly folded.

The dog leaped up and snatched at the bait.

Andrew Harwolf started, and turned towards his companion.

"Why don't you drink," he said, hurriedly. "Let us have your toast—drink success to me, plodding the miry lane of my ventures at home, while you will be bounding free over the wide prairie, in a young and lawless land, where you may follow the bent of your aspiring imagination. Drink—drink."

Silas Rye was about to obey this injunction, when suddenly he put down the glass, exclaiming, "Good heaven! what is the matter with the dog?"

With a piteous howl the poor brute had staggered backwards; his limbs trembled convulsively, his smooth coat was rugged with sweat, his muscles were shrunken, his eyes leaden-coloured, and the frothy foam dripped from his mouth; presently he tottered over on his side, and fell with a dull thud—stone dead.

"Villain and murderer!" cried Silas, starting to his feet, and dashing the contents of the wine-glass into Harwolf's face. "And so you thought to poison me in cold blood. I have it in my heart to take my revenge at once, but you shall see I will abide my time, and when you least dream that I am near you—when you have forgotten my name, or remember me but faintly—I will return, and then you will rue this day!" So saying, he left the room, with a look of unspeakable hate.

CHAPTER VIII.

DANIEL HARWOLF PURSUES THE RED RAVEN.

A SHIP is speeding swiftly over the leaping billows, her snowy sails outspread, bellying before the breeze that blows from larboard. The sea-gulls whirl their white wings in the glad sunshine that dances so glisteningly upon the lucid waters.

No other vessels appear in sight; the horizon is unspecked by a single sail.

In her beauty and her loneliness the pretty rakish craft forges rapidly through the skimmering spray that spurts up from her well-curved bows.

Its deck is paced by Daniel Harwolf. He is captain of the vessel which has been armed and manned to pursue the daring Boy Pirate.

After the escape of Lilia, stunned, scorched, and bleeding, the luckless Harwolf had been carried to his father's house.

For several days he was in a dangerous state.

He was feverishly hot; his eye gleamed with unearthly lustre, and his lips were dry and white.

He was tortured with a burning thirst. Sometimes he raved madly.

The excitement, consternation, and scandal that prevailed throughout the village, in consequence of the abduction of Lilia, may be easily imagined.

Upon his recovery he hastened to London.

Representing his case in proper quarters, he not only secured the service of a small war-steamer, but was himself appointed its captain.

For many days he had been at sea, but as yet he had seen no signs of the terrible Red Raven.

Whatever his faults in private life, considering the great disadvantages he laboured under—as having never applied himself to books; having injured his constitution by various excesses, and being of such an ungovernable temper—he was by no means an unskilful officer.

He was no favourite with the sailors; but in the service subordinates are obliged to succumb to much petty tyranny, which they must endure without resistance, as their first and all imperative law seems to have been framed upon the principle of passive obedience.

One day, as he was hastily and nervously pacing the deck, his attention was all at once arrested by the cry—

"Sail on the starboard bow."

He ran to the bulwarks.

Peering through the telescope he discerned the light form of a splendid vessel speeding full sail before the wind.

He called to the second lieutenant, and putting his own glass into his hand asked his opinion of the ship in the offing.

"Indeed, captain, but she seems a rakish craft, and is scudding along with the wind in her sails in the most graceful style."

"What nation, think you?" he asked of his officer.

"That is a question not easily solved at present."

"It seems to me that she carries no flag."

"She is speeding so swiftly, and is at such a distance, that it is hard to say," replied the young officer.

Harwolf shaded his weak eyes from the sun.

The first lieutenant now approached.

"I begin to think that the vessel yonder that is making such way before the rising gale is no other than the ship of the Red Raven, at last."

"What makes you think so?"

"Why, captain, she is of rakish build, keeps close to the wind, and seems to be doing everything to avoid us."

"And she is wise in that," returned Captain Harwolf, with a smile of hate, "for, by Heaven! if we can but overtake her we will slaughter every man on board that resists, and the others we will put in irons till we can see them tried and hanged—the infernal pirates."

Soon after Harwolf retired to his cabin news was brought him that they were gaining upon the strange ship.

He rushed upon deck.

The barque appeared much larger, and her light spars stood out clearly defined against the pure blue sky.

Every moment it was plainly seen that they were gaining upon the ship they had been so long chasing.

It was evident that it was not from any merit of superior speed that they were making this advantage.

As the evening approached, they came to closer quarters.

Now they could plainly discern the flag, floating in the gentle breeze that scarcely rippled the surface of the lightly lifting waters.

It was the black flag of piracy, and beneath its ghastly insignia was the Red Raven.

Upon perceiving their proximity with the vessel they had pursued so long, the gallant tars gave three hearty cheers. All on board was bustle, but not confusion.

The command having been given, the deck was cleared, and every thing prepared for action.

Night had now come on, and a stiff breeze was blowing.

A council of war was called.

The expediency of an immediate attack was deliberated upon; but the opinion prevailed that it would be better to defer the attack till the morning.

A double watch was set; and every precaution was taken to prevent the possibility of their being taken by surprise, should the daring pirates venture upon an attempt at boarding from their boats.

When everything had been arranged to his satisfaction, Harwolf summoned the officers together in the state cabin. In a few words he reminded them of the object of the expedition—to capture and exterminate the pirates, and to rescue a young lady who had fallen into their hands. Now, but for this last part of their mission there would have been no need to have recourse to strategy, but as the gang of desperate men would doubtless protract the struggle to the last, and would, perhaps, fire their ship rather than surrender, the lady was in deadly peril, and therefore it would be impossible to effect her rescue without the assistance of some ruse; and he called upon them to say whether they did not think with him that a night attack from the boats would be the most advisable means for effecting the purpose of the expedition.

The officers concurred in this opinion.

It was resolved that, when night should have fairly set in, the long boat, with the captain's pinnace and the smaller craft, should be manned by a boarding party; and, as the mists were sweeping up from the dark waters, it was thought the darkness of the night, which happened to be moonless, would serve to pall them from the vigilant eyes of the watch, and that under its veiling shadows they might be able to creep alongside the pirate vessel without causing alarm or even exciting attention. If any of the party could gain the deck and beat back its defenders, their first care would be to rush to the state cabin to the rescue of Lilia, whom the officers inferred, from the manner in which Harwolf spoke of her, was an involuntary captive in the hands of a set of lawless miscreants.

[LILIA RESCUED BY THE BOY PIRATE.]

The crew now bustled about energetically to get the boat afloat.

When it was safely under the quarter Harwolf selected three men upon whom he could depend, and, clambering down the side of his vessel, leaped into the boat.

It was a murky night; the fog was thick and stifling.

The wind had fallen, and the silence was oppressive.

No. 5.

Nothing was heard through the darkness but the sullen plash of the waves against the bows of the boat till the oars dropped into the water, and the little barque, cleaving the black waves, stole on through the gloomy night.

No one spoke.

Not only prudence but a feeling of breathless excitement caused the party to restrain their speech.

After they had rowed in this way for some time a marked change took place in the weather. The thick veil or rather mantle of vapour slowly ascended, and the moon, dim and watery, shimmered down her cold rays; yet they scarcely reached the dull dark and turgid waters but only faintly silvered the clinging mist.

At last the boat's crew were suddenly startled by the appearance of a light. It was the lantern in the stern sheets of an anchored vessel. Lazily it rose and fell as the ship rocked upon the gently heaving breast of the sea.

Harwolf and his sailors paused; they had stolen so near the vessel that they were for a moment taken aback at the effects of their own temerity.

It was evident the fog concealed them effectually.

They were not perceived by those on board, although a vigilant watch was set.

But how could they hope to approach near enough to enable them to effect their purpose? Before starting on this dangerous expedition Harwolf had prepared himself for every emergency he could think of as likely to arise. Under the cover of the fog, which was yet dense, though fast clearing away, the boat crept with muffled oars under the dark bows of the vessel.

The men kept breathless silence; they could distinctly hear the measured tramp of the officer of the watch as he went his round; and, at intervals, the long-drawled gruff " All's well " of the challenged.

Daniel Harwolf could scarcely restrain his impatience. The men looked at him inquiringly.

What was to be done?

Was the ship to be boarded by a handful of men, who would be out-numbered and cut down at the first moment of their setting foot on board?

Even an exasperated lover robbed of his affianced bride could not be suspected of entertaining such an insane design.

At last the mist cleared away and rolled off towards the horizon.

The night was still dark and cloudy, but the moon was faintly struggling with the envious vapours that strove to dim her glories.

Harwolf, who sat in the stern of the boat watching the tapering masts and web-like shrouds with intent suspense, momentarily expecting that he would be discovered, suddenly perceived something white and sylph-like gliding along by the bulwarks; it was she—it was Lilia, he could not doubt.

A storm of savage passion raged in his heart. That she should be so near him and that he should be so powerless to snatch her from his hated rival. The thought was distraction. As he watched, he perceived that she had ascended the quarter-deck, and stood looking over the side of the vessel.

Her face was buried in her handkerchief, and her luxuriant tresses floated backwards in the cold night wind.

Perhaps she was weeping.

Harwolf smiled grimly as he recollected how well he had prepared for such an emergency.

He drew from his breast a little case, and extracting therefrom a small phial he poured part of the contents upon some prepared fabric which he held in his hand. " Now, my men," he whispered to the crew, " I am about to make a desperate venture. All I ask of you is silence and prudence and ready hands when I have snatched my prize. I will give every man a sovereign and a double allowance of grog if I come out of this adventure unscathed. Silence! Now, cautiously—row me under the lee-quarter."

The men obeyed in an orderly manner.

So stealthily did the little craft glide along beneath the frowning bulwarks, that Lilia, who stood leaning over the side of the vessel, did not perceive it.

Certainly at the moment she was deeply absorbed in her own sweet and bitter fancies.

Very quietly, and with true seaman-like agility—for of late he had greatly improved in physical strength and energy—Harwolf clambered up the side of the ship; he sprang on board, taking advantage of an instant when a black cloud darkly curtained the moon.

The man who walked the deck in his pensive watch was approaching.

Harwolf crouched down beside a gun. .

The man passed on unconscious of his presence.

Stealthily as a panther crawling on his prey, Harwolf crossed the deck, and stood behind Lilia.

It was a thrilling moment.

She did not turn—she had not observed him. The sound of the footsteps died away; then they grew louder, as the sailor on guard once more slowly approached.

The fog still clung about the ship, and rendered it impossible for the eye to sweep the length of the vessel.

Harwolf stole close behind Lilia; she shuddered as if instinctively conscious of the presence of something evil. She turned, her face grew ashy white, the cry died from her lips with the suddenness of the shock; before she could recover her paralysed resources Harwolf had placed his hand upon her mouth.

The eyes of the poor girl grew glassy and expressionless, her lips trembled, and, her lids closing as in a mesmeric sleep, she sank passively into the arms of Harwolf.

All this passed in a moment's space.

The sailor of the watch was within a few yards of the spot, and was pacing slowly with his eyes bent thoughtfully upon the deck.

In a moment Harwolf had scrambled over the bulwarks.

The sailors in the boat below stood ready to receive him.

They got him into the boat.

The girl was wrapped in their rough pea-jackets and carefully concealed, lest the white colour of her dress might render her visible. Almost noiselessly they plied the oar, and the boat sped away lightly with its lovely burden.

The man on deck had not perceived what had happened.

For a moment he thought something had loomingly started through the mist, but he was upon reflection convinced that it could be but a freak of his imagination.

As he passed by the bulwark where Lilia had been standing, he turned his head to see if she were still there, but he perceived that she had departed, and reasonably concluded that she had returned to her own cabin.

Harwolf reached his ship just as the fog had cleared off and the moon had shone out in her fullest splendour.

His men received him with cheers.

Harwolf had never been popular with the crew, but his daring act had created a great impression in his favour.

When he leaped upon deck his officers gathered around him, and congratulated him upon the successful result of his bold adventure; yet, as they looked upon the pale unconscious form of the apparently lifeless girl, they could not suppress an exclamation of horror.

There was a fixedness of feature and a rigidity of body that resembled rather the effect of death than of mere temporary suspension of animation.

The doctor was sent for; he knelt by her side, and feeling her pulse, looked long and earnestly into her pale face.

" Captain Harwolf," he said, rather gravely, " it is evident that some such means as the application of chloroform have been used to induce this stupor which has overwhelmed the lady. If you ever again should think it needful to have recourse to such a dangerous expedient, Captain Harwolf, permit me, sir, to remind you that the greatest care should be used in administering."

The officers stared at each other in surprise, and then looked disapprovingly upon their sullen-visaged captain; but respect for discipline, and reverence of his post as their commander, prevented them from uttering their thoughts.

" But all is well, doctor, I hope," said Harwolf.

"You must consider the danger and difficulty of the enterprise that has resulted so successfully. I had no other means of reducing the poor romantic child to reason; but I trust her life is not endangered."

"Aye, but is, Captain Harwolf," returned the doctor. "Let me assure you that only care can save her: let her at once be removed to the saloon, and send my assistant to me at once."

Very carefully and tenderly Lilia was removed. The officers lingered about the deck for a few moments and then retired below.

Somewhat crest-fallen, Harwolf remained in his handsome cabin, listening anxiously for the sound of approaching steps, for he had ordered that the doctor should send a messenger to report progress.

At last, out-worn with aching solicitude, he rose and betook himself to the saloon.

He listened at the door.

The thought that he had perhaps caused the death of the beautiful Lilia was insupportable.

He could bear the suspense no longer.

He softly opened the door.

Upon a couch she was extended, her head thrown back, and her long waving hair falling around her marble shoulders and sweeping to the ground; her eyes were still closed, and her cheek was yet colourless. By her side sat the doctor, his hand upon her breast, listening to catch the faintest breath from her small and rosy mouth.

The assistant stood looking on, with an expression of interest and pity on his face, holding in his hands a glass containing some restorative he had just prepared.

"Does she still sleep?" asked Harwolf, in a hollow whisper.

"Hush!" returned the doctor, in an undertone, "the crisis is at hand. Her sleep, as you term it, Captain Harwolf, will break at once, or it will last for ever."

The assistant handed the potion to the doctor, who touched the lips of the entranced girl with the edge of the glass. Scarcely had a drop of the liquid moistened her lips, when she shuddered and opened her eyes, but their expression was vacant and void of intelligence.

She closed them again, and presently she trembled slightly, her bosom lifting and falling slowly and painfully.

Harwolf clasped his hands with a smile of triumph at this slight sign of returning animation. He gloated for a moment over the prospect before him of a sweet revenge.

"You will please to retire, Captain Harwolf," said the doctor, "it is not desirable that you should present yourself to Miss Lilia at the first moment of her return to waking life; let me tell you she has been to the very confines that lie between life and death, and her state is still dangerous; the slightest excitement might produce a relapse, and then the case is hopeless."

"Doctor, to your skill I shall owe more than I can ever repay," returned Harwolf, bowing as he turned to leave the room. "You have saved me from life-long regret and misery, and restored to my love one who is my affianced wife and the erring but beloved child of a worthy father."

"I trust she, too, will have cause to thank me for the service I render in bringing her back to life," returned the doctor, a little acrimoniously, at the same time somewhat impatiently waving the captain from the saloon.

When he was gone Lilia stirred, and even lifted her hand to her head.

"Christopher," she murmured, "we are on the wild sea now—for ever and ever; but I thought I heard his voice. Would he, think you—would he dare pursue us? I am sure I saw him. He looked on me with his cold, hated eyes, and—I died."

Languidly in her delirium poor Lilia turned upon the couch, burying her cheek, which now glowed scarlet with fever, among the tangling locks of her sunny hair.

At last she raised herself upon the couch and looked around her with a strange wild light gleaming in her eyes.

"Where am I? Tell me, what place is this? This is not our cabin. Oh! I fear my dream comes true," she murmured, sinking back exhausted. "I fear that I am lost for ever to every chance of happiness."

The doctor took her hand and remonstrated soothingly.

"Do not, Miss Lilia, for your life's sake, talk now. In an hour you will be sufficiently strong to converse, but now you must, as far as possible, close up every inlet to the mind, which must be kept perfectly quiet."

"Oh! if you would not have me die in torments of agonised suspense, tell me, have they reached him? Is he slain? Is he a prisoner?"

"Be calm, dear Miss Lilia; he whom you love with such misguided but heroic affection is safe; not only so, but is rather to be dreaded than pitied at this moment. But ask me no more questions, for I must not answer them; in your present state the least excitement may be dangerous."

The poor girl threw her snowy arm beneath her head and closed her eyes resignedly; a deep sigh seemed to rend her breast and then she lay quite still and motionless: presently she slept.

She slept—a sweet and balmy sleep; how different from the death-like trance from which she had been with such difficulty aroused. The fervid glow upon her cheek became less vivid; she breathed lightly, and the doctor stole to her side once more, laid his finger on her wrist, and fixed his eye upon the dial of his heavy gold chronometer.

He did not perceive that Captain Harwolf had re-entered the cabin.

With folded arms the triumphant lover looked upon the face of her whom he had so cleverly and so happily recovered, and he murmured to himself unconsciously, while his eye flashed, and his lip worked with passion—

"Yes, my destiny is to foil him in every way. When he was a boy I drove him to sea; when he was embarked I made the ship a hell for him; and what is he now?—a felon and an outcast. Good; he thought to make amends for past defeats by a crowning triumph at last; he thought to rob me of my bride; but how sweet is my retribution. And she; it will tame her pride, too, and I may now hope to find a very paragon of obedience and humility. Oh, I could hug myself for this last bold stroke, and its fortunate issue."

At this moment the door was softly opened, and a midshipman entered.

"There is a sail, sir, on the starboard bow."

"Indeed; what sort of craft does she appear, Mr. Lacy?"

"A heavy-built brigantine, seemingly a fishing smack of the largest kind.

"And which way is she steering."

"Beside the wind, nor' by nor' east."

"Has she just discovered herself?"

"Yes, sir, within five minutes."

"We will have a look at her. Doctor Horton, you send me word should there be any change in your patient."

With this Harwolf and the midshipman left the cabin.

CHAPTER IX.

THE HAWK AND THE DOVE.

UPON reaching the deck Harwolf scanned the horizon with a glance to descry the craft that had been announced to him.

A heavy lugger-rigged vessel stood out to sea.

Captain Harwolf watched it for a moment through his glass, and seemed satisfied with the scrutiny.

An eagle look-out had been kept for the "Red Raven," but as yet no signs of the rover's ship had been seen.

The men were gathered in little knots on the deck, and anxiously gazed over the billowy surface of the ocean, half in fear and half in hope of descrying the pirate ship. Nothing but the heavy-rigged fisherman, however, showed on the sky-line.

The men conversed in whispers; the conduct of the captain was pretty freely commented upon, and more than one fellow declared his opinion that though the lady's favourite did happen to sail under the "Jolly Oliver" he was probably a much more suitable match for a lovely girl than the sallow and morose-looking personage to whom they did honour as their skipper.

The officers, too, conversed in an undertone, and remarked severely on the trick by which he had entrapped the girl, thinking that half the glory of his daring feat was tarnished by his having used chloroform to subdue his victim, an expedient which they looked upon with no little abhorence, as being both un-English and unmanly.

Unconscious of these disparaging remarks that were passing among the crew, Harwolf paced the quarter-deck moodily, when the steward approached him.

"Captain," said this man, bowing, "Miss Lilia is so far recovered as to be able to converse, and she expresses a wish to see you."

Harwolf started.

"And what does the doctor say to this?"

"He has given his permission, sir, but desires to speak with you before you see Miss Lilia."

"Very well, I will attend him."

With this Harwolf went down into the state cabin and sent for Doctor Horton.

This worthy gentleman entered with a grave look on his broad and comely face.

"And what do you think of the patient? Is she in a fair way of recovery?" asked Harwolf.

The doctor shook his head and slightly shrugged his shoulders.

"You see, Captain Harwolf, the young lady enjoys the great advantages of youth and health, but corroding sorrows will, in a literal sense, prey upon the heart and sap away the vital energies: you have it in your power to do a great deal for her, and I am sure nothing would give you more after-peace than a little present self-sacrifice. I am very bold to tell you this, but mine is a privileged class, and I hold it my duty to stretch a point in order to save what unhappiness I can. It is useless—worse than useless—to attempt to control the affections; there is no forcing attachment; and, from the poor girl's ravings, I have discovered that her heart is entirely devoted to the unfortunate and desperate youth with whom she eloped, and from whom she has been so happily rescued. Now, that being the case, I think it proper to suggest, Captain Harwolf, that in her present state of mind you should deal with her tenderly and indulgently; that you should reassure her upon the subject of her proposed marriage—also with respect to her being forced to return home, a thing she cannot bear to dream of. But I leave her to you, Captain Harwolf, with many apologies for these hints, but I know that you are greatly and reasonably incensed by conduct which, tried by the common standard, is heartless and most censurable."

The good doctor bowed, as if a little nervous at his own boldness, and left the cabin.

Harwolf found Lilia reclining on the couch, looking very pale, and, within the short space of time that had elapsed since he had carried her exultingly to the deck of his own vessel, she was sadly changed. The fresh buoyancy of girlhood was gone for ever; the charm of childish recklessness and dreamy obliviousness of the cares and exactions of the hard rough world was broken and dispelled. Lilia, young as she was, was a woman now; her heart swelled with womanly passion or quailed with womanly fears. As Captain Harwolf drew nearer to her side she closed her eyes, and her cheeks mantled with blushes. It was some time before she could speak; when she did, however, her voice was firm—she was self-possessed and calm.

"Daniel," she said, "I have sent for you to have a little conversation with you, to implore your for-giveness for the wrong I have done you—to entreat you to spare yourself and me the bitterest griefs, and to throw myself fully and freely upon your generosity."

"Lilia," said Harwolf, "there is no wish that you can express that I will not do my best to gratify, if it do not clash with our engagement; for, remember, you are affianced to me, and if you have any respect for your own promise you can never be the bride of another."

"Of another!" exclaimed Lilia, starting. "No, I cannot blame you, Daniel; it is but right—it is but just. Even if my heart were not dead, as it is—even if time and change could wear away the remembrance of the past, which I know they never can, I should have no right to give myself to another. If you will be kind and indulgent with me now, Daniel, you shall have all my best and tenderest friendship—more is not mine to give you."

"And am I to understand, Lilia, that you really love the desperate felon from whose power you have been snatched so providentially?"

"You ask me but a fair question, Daniel, and one that, perhaps, you have a right to ask. I do love him! with all the fervour of my woman's love. He was my playmate and my protector—do not forget that, Daniel—in my girlhood, and for years I mourned for him as for one dead, and for years I detested you as the author of his death, for all was told me by one of the officers who commanded upon the vessel of Captain Simons. But all this is long past; doubtless I exaggerated your enmity and ill-doings. I tell you these things frankly now, and I trust you will forgive me, dear Daniel. I do not blame you, even though you have torn me from him whom I would have followed joyfully through all his dark career. Your action may be well meant; my conduct may be very—I know it is—very blameable; but I beseech you do not persecute me with your suit for my hand—do not force me to return to the village. I have some fortune; I am not without accomplishments. Worthless as I am, let me go free. Upon the continent I may begin a new career, and I may carry my remorseful heart into a strange land, where I may hide my shame."

"Dear Lilia, you talk idly," returned Harwolf, restraining his passion; "what you propose is not feasible. You are mine, Lilia; dearly bought, hard won, trothed and surrendered—and mine you shall ever be while I draw breath. I will not be robbed of my prize by all the fleets that ever swept the sea, not to speak of a beggarly boy-pirate and his rapscallion crew. I will not be repelled by your coldness nor your anger. You are mine, Lilia, till death you are mine, and the moon shall not wane before the village bells clash joyously at our wedding. You will forget this pirate thief. You will remember your duty to your father, and your promise to me: the past will be gone by like a dark and terrible dream, and the future will lie before us in radiant happiness."

"No, no! dismiss such a hope from your mind, Daniel; pity my weakness, pity my shame. If I am forced to return home I shall die—I shall never again look the sun in the face. Our marriage is impossible; I am quite unworthy of you; seek one who will cherish and make you happy. I will write to my father—I will explain all; perhaps he may forgive me."

Lilia burst into tears: presently she raised her eyes; they flashed with a wild and joyful gleam."

"But oh! if he would come; if the Red Raven would deliver me from my bondage. For I am his; it is my destiny to save him! Oh! that I could hear the cheers of his devoted crew—that I could see the black pennon with its ghastly insignia. For once I should bless the hated flag: for he is good and true to me; he is willing to shed his life-blood in my service. And you pretend to be his rival—you who refuse common mercy to me as a woman, when I crave it so humbly. Shame upon you: I am your prisoner, and you use your power cruelly and meanly."

"Lilia," said Harwolf, sternly, "you are my prisoner, and I do not forget what conduct compelled me to put a restraint upon your actions. What you ask of me, while loving you, it would not be possible for me to grant. You are my affianced wife, and as such I cleave to you, and will do so, by heaven, in spite of man or devil. Listen to reason; we will return to the village, and your creditable adventure will soon be forgotten: our marriage will take place at once; a long tour on the continent, and if you wish it even a settlement in a distant part—and then where will be the scandal? I will forgive you all. Say, Lilia, say that the past is forgotten, my forgiveness and my love accepted, and that you will be mine."

"Never, never! I have been torn from him," cried Lilia, wringing her hands: "The only bond that bound him to the common sympathies of his kind is broken, and he must perish alone and unsolaced: but at least I will be true to him—I will be true to my own heart. I cannot love you, Daniel Harwolf, and rather than you should drag me to the altar, I will kill myself before your eyes. I have begun a new life. I am a woman now, and I will not be trifled with. I charge you to let me go—I charge you by your love and by your manly pity to have mercy on me. If you will not listen to such appeals I *defy* you to detain me!"

"And you defy me—ha!" cried Harwolf. "Have you noticed—you who charge me with meanness—in what different strain I speak to you now that you are entirely in my power from that in which I talked to you when we met in the ruined cottage on the beach. Then you were to some extent free; you were protected by your respectable lover. Now I have sought to reason with you. I have freely proposed you forgiveness for the cruel wrong you have done me, and lo! my reward for these gentle measures. Mark me, Lilia! as you know I am not one to be fooled by an arrogant woman, as I told you but just now—by your father's consent, by your own assent, and by my deep and honest affection, you are mine, and, therefore, I will never part with you; and for your pirate paramour—let him look to himself. His dark career, as you rightly term it, will soon be illuminated by the blaze of his ark of refuge for the scum of society. Yes, Lilia; his doom is sealed, and your Byronic corsair will swing to the kites and the carrion crows."

"It is a lie," cried Lilia, fiercely. "Never! never shall the Red Raven die the death of a dog! He may be struck down in his high flight—he may burn, like a phœnix, in his own nest; but the death you so brutally taunt me with on his behalf is reserved only for such curs as yourself, who dare not face death in its nobler forms—whose best valour is to use your brutal strength against a weak and wretched woman. Oh! Daniel, I am mad with grief and remorse when I think of home. I am with Christopher only to warn him from his terrible associates; but when I think how basely and how undeservedly you insult and degrade me, I spurn you, and hate you; and I look upon the constant and high-souled Red Raven as infinitely your superior as the heavens are high above the earth. Leave me, oh! leave me."

The girl burst into a flood of passionate tears.

Harwolf shook with passion, but he replied in a hoarse, yet calm voice—

"Be it so, Lilia; I leave you for the present. I leave you to reflect. You have defied me. When we meet again, Lilia, I hope, for your own sake, I shall find you in a gentler mood."

With this Harwolf left the cabin.

CHAPTER X.

THE SUSPICIOUS BRIGANTINE—LILIA'S RESCUE.

THE large fishing barque still stood out to sea, and one day some of the sailors of Harwolf's crew stood lazily watching its heavy rig, and wondering why it stood out there so motionless and inert.

A steady breeze had been blowing for some days, not briskly, but with sufficient impetus to spread out the sails of the gallant ship, and move her with the slow and majestic pace of a gliding swan through the frothy billows.

"I'll tell you what it be, Tom," said a thorough old salt to another, as he squirted the tobacco juice through one of the port holes, and rubbed the back of his head knowingly. "There be more in that sluggish craft than you think for; don't you observe that we may be running any number o' knots a hour, and yet that sly brigantine seems allers asleep and at anchor and is sure to be in the same place at the same time next morning. I ain't a goin' to say as I knows more nor my betters, but it strikes me as that blessed barge is given to doin' a night run, just by way of keepin' in our wake; 'cos vy—when there's a ship which carries the 'Jolly Oliver' on the cruise, it ain't at all 'stronary as she should like to keep near sich a escort as our own pretty little craft, for there ain't a more rakish thing on the high seas than the "Ham-a-drying."

"Hamadryad, Bill," suggested a thin pale fellow, with a smile of contemptuous pity.

"Dried or drying be all one," returned the old tar, with a growl. "You may be a good scholard, Jem, but douse my daylights if you bean't a nation bad shipsman, and nothin' better nor a landlubber swab."

"Go on with your remarks, Bill, go on with your remarks," interrupted William, the peacemaker, nudging his companion and winking tremendously. You were offering your humble opinions about that queer-looking barque out yonder."

"Yes, and I was a-saying—only these landlubbers allers will put in with their jawing-tackle, and consequently by putting in themselves be putting out their betters—I was a-saying that there's more in the 'nœuvreing of that old hulk than some on you thinks for: you've all heard o' the Flying Dutchman, in course."

"Aye, aye, Bill!" said the others in chorus, "but let us have your experience."

"Well; perhaps you thinks as I've seen the Flying Dutchman?"

"Very like, Bill, we all knows you've seen the sarpint."

"The sea-sarpint I has seen," returned Bill, sententiously; "but the Flying Dutchman I has not seen."

There was a groan of disappointment.

"But if I hasn't seen the real Flying Dutchman it ain't because I never seed a phantom ship; 'cos everybody knows that they're as plentiful as porpoises; leastways, they used to be."

"Ah; and you've seen some of them?"

"Yes, some as was real and some as was only Fanny Morgans."

"Fata Morgana," supplemented the "scholard" with a grin, "which is the name of a peculiar phenomenon visible chiefly in the straits of Messina, where ships are, as it were, reflected upon the sky, and appear to be sailing along."

The sailors did not receive this proof of the erudition of their comrade with any appreciative pleasure, but looked upon him with a little awe, and a good deal of displeasure.

"You hear him; don't you, messmates," said the worthy Bill, with ineffable disdain, "that's the cove that goes aloft like a bear on a tight-rope. Well, as I was a-saying, when I first went into the service, and used to lie on the soft side of a plank, I saw several of them phantom ships. One on 'em was werry near, for when we fired at her she busted and flew away like a water spirit. Now its my opinion with respect to yonder barque that she's a phantom, and though we don't see her making way during the daylight, at night she creeps on us, and you may depend upon it, mates, neither sharks nor phantoms don't hang in our wake for any good. I say she's a phantom."

This sage opinion was received with blank looks and great deference by the auditors.

Every eye was turned in the direction of the object of their conversation.

Her sails half furled, listless she lay on the buoyant sea, just in the same position which she had held for many days.

To the surprise of the watchers she was seen to put off a boat, and their astonishment was not decreased when it became evident that the boat was steering its course for their ship.

Old Bill looked rather chagrined, as this fact tended to overset his theory of the spiritual nature of the palpable spectacle before them.

There stood the heavy-rigged brigantine, thither sailed the boat, in which there appeared to be two passengers.

With a few steady strokes of the oar the boat floated under the stern-sheets.

"Boat ahoy! what cheer?" shouted Bill the boatswain, for that was his degree.

"Cheerily, my hearties," returned the young fisherman, who stood erect in the boat, "if I may come aboard I can show you some cod and salmon that might grace the table of an alderman; and mates, I have, besides, a little barrel of sauce that you will find a dainty relish."

With this the fisherman twirled a little keg of rum in the air, and caught it deftly between his fingers.

The sailors laughed heartily.

One of the midshipmen on duty came aft. "What is this?" he asked; "who is this fellow?"

"Second mate of yonder fishing craft, your honour," said the young fisherman, touching his forehead with his thumb. "The skipper has sent me to know whether you would like some bait—some cod fresh from Newfoundland—some mackerel not an hour out of water—or some salmon that is crying to be eaten. We trade in all parts. Our fisheries are not confined to these seas; and sometimes we make a good haul." A peculiar smile flitted over the young fisherman's face as he said this.

"And I'll tell you what, mate; I'll give you a bit of my mind as you won't hurt by attending to," said Bill the boatswain. "There's a certain craft a-cruising in this latitude that's tolerable well known as the 'Red Raven.' Now, I don't suppose you've got much to lose; but you've a pretty hulk, though your rig is so infernal lumbering. Well, all I've got to tell you is—all is fish as comes to his net."

"Thank ye; I'll keep out of his way," returned the young fisherman. "But come, mates, won't you let me board you? I've got all sorts of pretty wares to show you besides the fish, which would make the Pope wish Lent might last for ever. Say the word, my hearties, and I'll be with ye."

"All right, mate; I'll ask his honour."

The middy, however, weary of this conversation, had walked away. The boatswain enquired whether the man might not be allowed to come aboard to exhibit his curiosities, and the young officer consented, and paced his beat with indifference.

The fisherman sprang on the deck.

The man in the boat passed up to him several large and heavy fish. These he laid carefully on the deck, and then leaned over for the "dainty sauce" he had spoken of.

Three barrels were passed to him from the boat. These he arranged upon the deck.

The middy passed at this moment. He examined the fish with affected indifference.

"Not so bad, master fisherman," he said, leaning against the capstan with an indolent swagger.

"Bad! Upon my soul, lieutenant," returned the fisherman, with a sly glance at the men as he bestowed this premature title upon his questioner; "if you were to throw them into the sea you would see them wriggle their silver tails and dart off laughing."

"I have more than half a mind to take you at your word, you lying rascal—try the experiment and pitch them overboard," returned the young officer, with a smile. "But what is in those barrels?"

"Oysters, your honour, the finest you ever saw. I shouldn't like you to taste them; they are so tempt-ing that if I opened one you would die of a surfeit, for you would never have heart to stop till you had devoured every barrelfull, shells and all."

"Open one."

The sailors looked at each other with a blank stare.

But the fisherman, without further hesitation, drew out a knife, and battering in the top of one of the barrels, poured its contents rattling upon the deck. He was about to open them.

"Put them back, you skunk, there are plenty in the cuddy," said the middy, with a laugh; "but what is your name, young fellow, and what sort of craft do you call that lugger of yours, that's always dogging in our wake?"

"My name, sir—I ain't ashamed of it—is Jem Brace, and as for our craft—which is a brigantine, and not a lugger—she is the prettiest craft in these waters, and a terrible shark for the other fishes, I can tell you."

"And the sooner you get back to your spanking brigantine the better for your skin, youngster," replied the middy, turning on his heel and marching off.

"You scampish swab," said the boatswain, in dudgeon, "you told us that you had brought some rum on board."

"Yes," replied the fisherman, with a grin, "and may be you'd like me to offer his honour a taste of its quality."

"He's a deep un; eh, Jem?" said the boatswain, with a wink at his companion, and a blow in the ribs with his elbow that only equalled in emphasis the swing of the piston of a steam-engine.

The fisherman now thrust the barrel between the capstan and the chain-box in order to conceal it from the vigilant eyes of the officer of the watch; he then inserted a straw.

"Would any gentleman like to taste the quality of the brine I pickle my oysters in?" said the fisherman; "you'll find it nice and fresh, my masters?"

"I told you as that craft was never a fishing smack, didn't I, hearties?" said Bill, eyeing the barrel desiringly.

"Yes," returned the other, "but you said she was a phantom."

"Well, mate," returned his comrade, with a leer, "at least there's plenty of spirits on board, I take it."

With this he stooped down and took a long pull at the straw; his eye twinkled, and he smacked his lips approvingly as he remarked—

"That ain't a bad sustainer on a long watch in a stiff breeze and a wet night. How much for your cordial, young mister physicianer?"

"We won't quarrel about the price, mate," replied the fisherman; "but what sort of a skipper have you got aboard—if it ain't a rude question?"

"An infernal queer sort, my nab; and you'd better make yourself scarce, little cheery, for if he lays hands on you he'll be asking too many questions for one of your resarve to answer 'em: he's got his eye on your old brigantine, I can tell you, and though he don't exactly belong to the preventive sarvice, he's a regler Commodore Legality, I can tell you."

"They say he is a man of pith and mettle."

"A man of lath and plaster—more like," returned the boatswain, with a rough chuckle; "a very Nelson agin poor girls as don't want to be taken in tow by him: but I say, my flounder, don't you sometimes take fish with poisoned bait?"

"Every member of my company would scorn such a mean trick——"

"Avast, there! and learn of your betters," replied the boatswain, with immense irony. "How do you think he takes young women?"

"Can't surmise."

"Why he chloroforms 'em till they're quite 'sensible."

"My God!" cried the young fisherman, starting to his feet with unwarrantable excitement.

"Fact, aint it, Tom?—and now he's below, a diverting hisself by bullying of the poor young creetur he captured so gallantly, like a real gentleman as he is!"

Scarcely were these words uttered, than a pealing shriek rang up the gangway.

Wild and disordered—her rich tresses flying in the air—her soft, blue eyes sparkling with terror and indignation—Lilia flew to the deck.

"Oh, men!" she cried, distractedly, "if you have sisters or lovers who are dear to you, save me from that remorseless wretch who calls himself your captain, but is not worthy to be the leader of a gang of robbers. Is there none that will save me from death?—for I will fling myself into the sea, rather than be prisoned at the villain's mercy another instant—is there none here will save me?"

"There is one here whose right is to protect you, and who will shield you with his heart," returned a calm, stern voice.

The sailors gaped at the fisherman—it was he that had spoken.

Lilia gazed at him for a moment in bewilderment, and then, with a joyful cry, flung herself into his arms.

Harwolf rushed upon deck, foaming with passion. Like one possessed by fiends, he appeared to be the prey of his peculiarly vile and ungovernable temper.

For an instant he stood checked, glaring upon his youthful opponent.

His drawn sword flashed in his hand.

The fisherman calmly loosened the clasp of his rough jacket, which he flung off; and suddenly extracting a flag he shook out its folds, and as he reared it, with a derisive laugh, the sable-hued banner surged and rippled in the wind. Ghastly defined upon the silken black field was embroidered his ruthless cognizance—the skull and bones, beneath which floated grimly the Red Raven.

"It is he—the wolf-cub is in the trap—lay hands on him, men," shouted Harwolf, hoarse with rage; "it is the Red Raven."

Words cannot express the astonishment caused by this announcement, and by this sudden, unlooked-for turn in affairs.

"Captain Harwolf, you performed a gallant feat; in the dead of the night, in a boat manned with picked men, yourself armed to the teeth, you contrived to board my vessel, and by means of a base subtle chemical deprived of animation and bore off her whom you came to seek. It is my turn to make reprisals. I think you will own that my act equals yours in daring. Alone, save for one unarmed youth who rowed my boat—unarmed myself, save for this cutlass I pick up from your own deck, not under the cover of a dense fog of a dark night, but under the cloudless sky of a sunny day, I stand before you and your whole crew and tell you that I have come to rescue my bride from your power. The time for revenging what she has suffered at your hands, though not yet arrived, is near at hand; save yourself if you can, for the Red Raven has marked you for his prey."

"Rash fool!" said Harwolf, gnawing his lips with rage. This is the difference of the daring feats between which you draw such biting contrast—I brought mine to a successful issue; you have entrapped yourself beyond all hope of escape. Lay hands upon the pirate thief at once, I command you!" he shouted, turning to his crew.

One man stepped forward to obey this order.

It had been well for him had he been less obsequious. With a whirl of his cutlass and a downright blow the Boy Pirate struck him to the earth, and then placed his foot lightly upon his prostrate body.

"Farewell till we meet again, Captain Harwolf," said the youthful but dauntless adventurer, coolly. "Our next meeting may take place broadside to broadside—flag flying to flag. You need not doubt that I shall nail mine to the mast."

Before one of the astounded men could interpose, the gallant stripling sprang agilely to the bulwark, and clasping his bride to his heart, leaped into the sea!

The next moment he was pulled into the boat with his beloved Lilia, whom he still clasped in his protecting arms.

A score of faces leaned over the side of the vessel, and several pistol-shots were fired as the boat shot along through the clear and glassy waves.

"Not a scar," cried the Boy Pirate, triumphantly, "and I am glad of it. To my shame, the villain bearded me in my own vessel, and went off scatheless, but I have not a scratch to lessen his dishonour,—Hurrah for the 'Red Raven.'"

In the buoyant exultation of youth, he flung up his cap, and his shout was echoed in his boat and from his gallant ship, that was swiftly disencumbering herself of the clumsy tackle that disguised her and assuming her own beautiful gear—which became her light and well-built hull so well and gracefully.

"Man the boats, all hands," roared the irate captain of the "Hamadryad." "Where is the armourer? Man the boats, my lads, and give chase, if you have one grain of British metal in ye!"

The order was obeyed, but not with such promptness nor ardour as might have been expected after this energetic appeal.

It was some time before all was arranged; at length three boats were manned, and pulled towards the pirates' vessel. As they approached, the last clink of the windlass was heard, the anchor was weighed, and the stately vessel floated free; the deck was thronged with swarthy pirates, and the yards were manned. In the hands of each of the freebooters swords were glancing, and guns were half poised, while the "Red Raven" poured a thundering broadside into the boats: one of these was swamped, another hopelessly damaged, rendering further pursuit impossible; and it was with the greatest difficulty that the crew were saved from a watery grave, and that the discomfited Harwolf could effect his return to his ship.

CHAPTER XI.

THE BOY PIRATE RELATES HIS HISTORY.

WE are on board the "Red Raven," and in the state cabin which Christopher had prepared with such perfect taste and lavish expense for the reception of his bride.

The sides were richly panelled, and inlaid at intervals with clear and glancing mirrors, and adorned with the richest trophies of the pirate's victories. The floor was thickly carpeted with rugs from Cairo; and sofas of gilt and velvet and low seats of costliest damask were arranged about this boudoir. Every means and appliance for luxurious ease and comfort that wealth could purchase or ingenuity produce; every grace that art could fling about man's dwelling was there; nothing was wanting. The most fastidious wish of satiated affluence was there: pictures, books, music, articles of vertu, even flowers, were not absent from this little cabinet of delights.

Upon embroidered damask cushions Lilia was sitting, her finely moulded bust encased in a boddice of blu silk, her flowing ringlets intertwined with emeralds and pearls, which she wore only to please the young pirate chief, for her taste, though chaste, was ever simple.

Christopher reclined at her feet; his warm and sun-bronzed cheek rested on her lap, and his crisp and glossy curls, sable as the silk of his own fatal banner, strayed negligently upon his square, determined but intellectual forehead.

His eyes wandered from a book of poems that lay before him on the ground, and ever and anon they met the soft, tender light of those orbs in whose blue depths he could have watched his reflected image for ever.

He seemed listless and weary, and he smiled faintly yet gratefully, as she bathed his heated brow with cooling perfumes.

"And now, dear Christopher, if you are not weary, let us resume your story," said Lilia, gently.

The Boy Pirate smiled.

"It is not all men that have so strange a tale to tell; and assuredly there are few men who, thrust into a position so distasteful to them as that in which I began this wild career, have reached to such a height as I have. I do not say this boastingly. I have seen too much not to be aware of the frail tenure on which I hold my honours—my very life; but when I look back, I can but wonder at the strange freaks that fortune has played me. My years are few, but my vicissitudes have been many. You remember, dearest Lilia, that I told you how, maddened by the cruelty and injustice of the captain of the "Flying Dolphin," the ship in which I first embarked as apprentice, and especially exasperted by an act of the blackest ingratitude on the part of Daniel Harwolf, who seemed to be a natural enemy to me from the earliest days of my boyhood, in a fit of despair I threw myself into the sea—not exactly with the intent of destroying myself, but in a reckless venture to escape from the insufferable miseries of my condition—to find some refuge from my tormentors, though I should have to seek the cold sanctuary of the ocean caves—though I should slumber for eternity in the still depths, where the wildest storms are unfelt. Upon diving into the turgid waters, I sank deep and was borne away by the current. Boats were put out to search for me; but I did not hail them. I was so stultified by the stormy scene I had passed through—so numbed and paralysed by the chill of the cold sea, for it was in winter that this happened—so eager to escape to land, for in my madness I deemed that possible, though we were nearly a league from shore. Upon rising, I struck out manfully. The ship was receding from my view, and the boats had gone back. I was in terrible danger; but I murmured not, even in the midst of death. But yet I was free, and nothing but the influence of that animal instinct for self-preservation which is so strong in all of us mortal beings, sustained me; for so far as any motive or inducement was concerned that might bind me to life I knew of none, but should have welcomed death as a relief to my protracted and heart-sickening sufferings.

"Onward I wrestled with the buffeting waves. At last, oh, joy! just as my resources were about to fail me—just as my energies were giving way—I descried some dark object floating towards me. I struggled desperately to reach it; how powerless I was in the treacherous element! More than once I sank; but at last I caught hold of the floating spar—clambered upon it, and enjoyed a certain security, and, above all, rest. But, except that I might hope for some short respite from annihilation, there I had the option of choosing between the lingering pangs of starvation and the shorter throes of drowning. For what had I to console me but hope—to which I clung with rigid tenacity, when it seemed most futile. A heavy, endless day ended at last! A dark, unwaning night had waned at length into morning; the sun soared to the zenith—his meridian beams fell full on my devoted head—defenceless against his ardours; I was alone on the heaving ocean—sea and sky—sky and sea. I was parched with raging thirst; my eyes became bloodshot, and I prayed for rain. I cooled myself as best I could by dipping myself in the water, but the expedient was practised too late—for there was a fire raging within me—the fever fiend was burning my very heart. I maundered out foolish and feeble words; I shed maudling tears; my memory became impaired; at times I forgot the horrors of my position and spoke familiarly to fancied companions—the offspring of my seething brain; I suffered all that death has made most terrible; I was smitten with a sun-stroke. How long I remained in this state I never knew. It might have been for many hours, perhaps for several days; for at last so intense were my sufferings that I became simply delirious, and knew not how the time went by. Then came a blank—a sort of boundary sleep which passed between my old existence and my new. When I awoke from it I was lying in the cabin of a strange ship and was watched by a strange man. Looking around I perceived the place to be much disordered; I was lying in a hammock, and I looked down upon the floor of the cabin, which I found to be strewn with a miscellaneous spread of arms, clothes, fine linen, chests and caskets, implements of agriculture, and even jewelry; against the wall were hung a succession of the flags of all nations, and my eye ran along them with confused surprise. Presently I noticed something in one corner—probably a cask of brandy, or a barrel of gunpowder; it was covered with a trailing flag of black silk, on which grinned the scull and bones.

"I started, and tried to rise; but I was too feeble. A tawny, black-browed fellow, with eyes dark as midnight and teeth of ivory whiteness—the watcher I told you of—jumped up and poured me out a cup of some cool and refreshing beverage, which I drank with an ecstacy of pleasure. He reseated himself. He was employed in carving some wooden beads, which he was stringing for a rosary. Little pictures, brightly coloured but execrably drawn, caricatured the martyrdom or beatification of some of the thousand and one saints of the Roman calendar.

"This man was a Mestizo—a Spanish half-breed—whose name was Lopez.

"I spoke to him. I asked him where I was.

"His only answer was to show his white teeth in a broad grin.

"I repeated my question.

"This time he replied in a strange jargon of bad Spanish and worse English—so vile, in fact, that I could not understand a single word.

"With this I gave up my hope of gaining information for the present—at least from him. I had recourse to the evidence of my own senses, and to the conclusions that might be drawn from the aspect of surrounding objects.

"The conviction forced itself upon me that I was on board a piratical vessel, and that the black flag which lay in the corner was its banner of death; that the confused mass of property that cumbered the floor was the plunder of rich-laden merchants and Indiamen; and that the colours that hung around the cabin were the sheeps' clothing on which the ravenous wolves crept upon their prey.

"Presently a man came down the gangway. As he advanced, Lopez rose, and stood back respectfully.

"This person looked what he was—one of the most remarkable men that I ever knew, amongst all the thousands with whom I have had dealings in peace or in war.

"His skin was tanned to a chesnut hue; his dark eyes shone with penetrating lustre. He was tall and meagre, and his hair was grey. For his dress he did not wear the usual naval uniform, but was attired in a long loose dressing-gown of cashmere, tied at the belt with a silken sash, through which were thrust a sort of crooked yataghan, such as that used by the Belokees and Marattahs, some richly chased and silver-mounted pistols, and a green silk cord. Upon his head he wore a scarlet fez with a gold tassel. If this were the pirate chief, his appearance completely disconcerted all my preconceived notions of such a character.

"Excepting for his bristling zone of arms, this lean and slippered pantaloon might have been some Indian nabob, bilious and enfeebled from the effects of a twenty years' residence in the Punjaub.

"He approached me, and desired me, in an accent slightly foreign, to hold out my hand.

"I did so.

"His long, thin and smooth fingers, upon which several brilliants of fabulous value were glittering, met upon my wrist, as with delicate touch he felt my pulse.

"'How long has he been awake, Lopez?' asked the captain, of the Mestizo.

"'About an hour, senor,' replied the half-breed, with a bow.

"'Hum; and was his last sleep less feverish—he did not rave so much?'

[THE BOY PIRATE BOARDING THE "HAMADRYAD."]

" 'No, senor, he slept like a healthy child.'

" The captain then held out his hand, which I touched with some degree of awe.

" 'Congratulate me,' he said curtly, with a smile.

" 'If sir, you think it a matter for congratulation, your having saved a life so little prized as mine,' I answered, 'I am very grateful, and thank you most sincerely.'

" 'No, no; I did not speak of that; I allude to my skill as a physician. I flatter myself that could you have been carried at once from your scorching raft into the best hospital in England or France you would never have left it a living man: medicine is my study and practice, sometimes surgery.' As he said this, he turned his eye carelessly, and with a quaint smile, upon a pile of arms that stood near.

No. 6.

" 'And may I ask to whom I owe my deliverance?' I enquired.

" 'Yes, I am Don Miguel Vasquez, a Spanish merchant; I deal in sundries, and am a freetrader —but I need not ask you who you are, I know your story.'

" 'Indeed, sir, and who could have supplied you with such information?'

" 'Yourself,' he replied. I looked at him in great surprise. 'Myself,' I answered; 'how can that be possible?'

" 'A bed of fever is the best confessional. A raging man pours forth from the most secret fountain of his soul. You have been badly treated by the world; take your revenge upon the world.'

" 'In what way?' I asked him.

" 'By accepting the challenge that the world

threw out against you from the hour you were born. You are a noble boy; nature's impress of worth and dignity is set upon your forehead, but you are nameless and poor; you might as well have been born a pariah in the land of Brahmins, a serf on the Russian soil, a slave on a Virginian plantation, as to come into the word nameless and portionless in the great centre of christian civilization, under those word-humble and ' deed-arrogant successors of the simple and loving early brotherhoods, amongst whom who would be the greatest was the least—who shared all things in common.' ' But, sir,' I said, wondering at hearing such strange discourse from one in this man's position; ' At least, there is this advantage in being born in a free country; a poor man can rise by his merits.' ' If he be a colossus to carry the world on his shoulders,' interrupted Don Miguel, ' What chance have you, at least, to rise above the condition of a favoured slave? What better can Kit Foundling hope for than to be patronized? Ha—but the word is galling the most unselfish heart, which is jealous of nothing, but quails at the taint of shame and dishonour: and is it not a curse that society should build its dignities upon old Gothic, rotten foundations; that it should honour itself for its sleek condescension towards those whom God and destiny alike proclaim as equals, although they be not descendants from the pander and minion of some unconstitutional tyrant! Master Christopher, I will teach you better doctrine than you have learned before; I will teach you how to make a pride of what you have counted a shame—how to bid defiance to the laws you have suffered from, and yet in your folly have obeyed. In fact, I like the look of you, Christopher, and I mean to make a pirate of you.' "

" So he said, Lilia, and he kept his word."

" But dearest Christopher, one moment; let me speak boldly before you go on with your story. You will answer me truly; you will not chide me, dearest?"

" Chide you, Lilia!" returned the pirate, with a smile of reproach; " Speak, dearest."

" This man—this tempter," she began, timidly, " you were not impressed by his shallow, inconsistent arguments?"

" Perhaps it would be well for my peace of mind if I had been," returned Christopher, thoughtfully, unconsciously sighing as he spoke, " but I knew too well how absurd and false those arguments must be by which the desperate and dishonest seek to justify their practices—as if they were not running full tilt against the idol of public probity which they set up for others to worship—as if one should say, because the world is bad I will be villanous—because the laws are imperfect I will be lawless. No! I am a pirate, Lilia, because it has been my destiny to become one. I was forced into my present position, and now I have no alternative but to keep it, and certainly, if ever a poor wretch was unjustly hunted and persecuted by the world—at least, by his own world—it is I; but we must not think of these things; the skeleton in my house is hideous indeed. To go on with my story——"

But here the narrative was abruptly interrupted by the entry of a young sailor.

" Captain," he said, touching his hat respectfully, " there is a sail in the offing: by the rig I should take it to be the ' Hamadryad.' "

" By all the furies I hope it may be," returned Christopher, slinging round his sword-belt as he leaped up; " I long to meet my old enemy foot to foot; I warrant he shall rue the day when he ventured to give chase to the ' Red Raven.' "

With this, and a smile and nod to Lilia, the Boy Pirate rushed upon deck.

The pirates stood in little clusters, intently watching the distant sail.

Christopher looked at it through his glass for an instant and then turned away.

" We have yet an hour's watching," he said, " and then, my lads, we will try whether we cannot float a Raven on the mainmast of yon craft that carries my bitterest enemy. In the meanwhile, let me be called

if anything new transpires. Let everything be prepared for the assault, and the decks cleared."

" Aye, aye, sir," returned the pirates, readily, as if the youthful commander had been a commissioned officer of the British service.

Christopher, with his alert step, took one stride round the deck, gave one parting glance of mingled scorn and pleasure at the ship of the enraged Harwolf, that was training every stitch of canvas in the pursuit.

This done, once more he descended to the cabin.

Lilia looked a little pale with anxiety, but restrained every indication of her emotion for the sake of Christopher.

The Boy Pirate reseated himself gaily.

" We shall have the villain soon," he cried, gleetally, " his ship bears down upon us, and the distance between us is lessened every instant: I carry as little canvas as possible to give the scoundrel every chance."

" O Christopher, let me ask this first and earnest favour: he was my plighted husband, however unwillingly I allowed myself to be drawn into an engagement with him; spare him for my sake—save his life. He has treated me basely and cruelly, but I forgive him in consideration of the involuntary wrong I have done him. You will not slay him, at least, dear Christopher?"

There was a stern look on the face of the Boy Pirate, but he answered with an affectionate smile.

" Dearest Lilia, I will grant you anything you ask. I cannot resist you; but I fear you will some day have cause to regret that you pleaded for that life which I once saved to my sorrow: but we have yet an hour's repose."

" And you will go on with your story?" said Lilia, eagerly.

" If you will, my own! But I will be brief, for I find little pleasure in retrospection. Well then, we were discussing the arguments of Don Miguel Vasquez. I should tell you that for an hour at least he declaimed with no little power and eloquence against the injustice and partiality of existing laws; of the roguery and chicanery that were countenanced in high places; the insurmountable obstacles that obstructed the path of the honest poor in their aspiring; in fact he took every pains to convince me that though society might put its ban upon me, and hunt and persecute me to the death, yet I was no worse than my fellows, but only more bold: he put it to me that had I received a commission from the Admiralty I should consider it my duty to pay unquestioning obedience to orders, and that I should aid in the carrying on the most ruthless war against any nation that my government might choose to send me against, quite irrespective of the justice of my cause. Why would that course be right? Because I should earn honour and rewards for my victories. Why is my career of piracy wrong? Because it entails upon me the danger of a shameful death for those same crimes for which another man, in other circumstances, receives a coronet. Of course I could see the fallacy of all this false logic, for, deny it who dare, there is an instinctive sense of right and wrong in the hearts of the worst of us. But what could I do, Lilia? Lonely was I, desolate indeed: bitterly and undeservedly I had suffered, and what could I do against him in whose power I found myself? I could but succumb to my fate. Stung and maddened as I was by my wrongs, I did so the more readily. He took me into every part of the ship, except the state cabin, into which no one ever ventured save his servant, the Mestizo Lopez, and his old coxswain, another Spaniard, named Fernandez: everything was prim and in admirable order; his crew were a fine set of fellows, mostly Spaniards of South America, but there was more than one Englishman amongst them. His ship was well served, and we made a successful cruise in the Spanish Main: we took several West Indiamen, and a craft laden with silver ingots from the mines of Potosi, having first riddled the escort brig, and burnt her to the water's edge. Many wild scenes I saw of lust and slaughter, but Don Miguel could always restrain his men in their moments of fiercest licence and excess. He was, besides, averse to bloodshed; he protected the honour of women, and seldom robbed passengers at all, his principal design being the stores, the cargo, and the appointments of the luckless vessels that happened to come within his track. There was a strange story told to account for his having taken to the wild and lawless life of a pirate of the seas. It seems he was of very noble family, and possessed a large plantation near the great city of Rio Janiero; he was married to a woman of surpassing loveliness, with whom he lived in great happiness for many years, and by whom he had one child—a beautiful girl—whom I have seen, and whose name was Aurora. Now, it appears that the wife of Don Miguel had a cousin, Don Diego, by whom she was said to have been wooed before her marriage with Don Miguel, and whom, as the sequel shows, she secretly loved. This man, who had been absent from Brazil for many years, returned unexpectedly; he was introduced to Don Miguel, who received him with the frankest cordiality: he invited his new friend to pay a visit to the plantation, and, upon the acceptance of the offer, earnestly entreated him to remain an inmate of the house as long as he pleased. As Don Miguel held some post in the government which greatly monopolised his time and attention, he was frequently absent from the plantation for days and even weeks, during which time Donna Inez and her old lover were left together. The sequel is not difficult to guess; this treacherous Paris prevailed upon this second Helen to flee with him. It would be impossible to describe the rage and anguish of the sensitive and proud Spaniard upon receiving information of his wife's perfidy: he at once applied to the government of Rio Janeiro, but he received no better retribution than insulting condolence and the vague promise of justice upon the adulteress and her paramour. Tired at last with his wrongs and insults, and learning that Don Diego had borne away the Donna Inez to a plantation near the sea-coast, Miguel secretly freighted and armed a sloop, which he manned with devoted servants who, themselves and their ancestors before them, had served in his family for generations. They came down in the night upon the plantation: every one slept—the place was unguarded; silently they stole through the groves till they reached the verandah house; it was summer time, excessively hot, and the doors and windows were all open. With flaming torches, like the fiends let loose, the avenging band broke into the house, which they fired as they passed along. Reaching the boudoir of the faithless Donna Inez, they found her paramour there, with a drawn sword in one hand and a pistol in the other: as soon as he saw Don Miguel he fired at him; the bullet struck off one of the fingers of his right hand; the next instant a dozen swords were struck into the traitor's heart by the infuriate followers of the outraged husband. Donna Inez was dragged from the room, and Don Miguel placed a pistol to her breast: wildly she shrieked for life. He remained pitiless, and sternly bade her spend the few moments of life remaining to her in prayer: she reminded him of all the happiness and love they had known together; it only embittered him the more; at last she spoke of the child Aurora, and reminded him how she would in after years curse him as the murderer of her mother. This last appeal was in part successful, for he spared her life, but consigned her to the convent of a sisterhood of the severest order; and there she atoned for the misery and crime her faithlessness had induced by a life-long penance of wearying masses, cruel fasts and scourgings. The little girl, the daughter, was removed to a distant plantation and left in the charge of an old and faithful steward of the family; and afterwards she was removed for her education to a convent-school in Seville, the prioress being a relation of Don Miguel, and there I believe she is now."

"And pray what became of the wretched husband?"

"Don Diego was a man of influence, and had many friends, and a great clamour was made for vengeance upon the perpetrator of the ruthless murder. The estates of Don Miguel were confiscated, and his person outlawed; he had, however, sold everything he could, and had invested his capital in European banks. From that time forward he turned buccaneer, and many and brilliant were his adventures."

"I think you told me that he would not suffer any one to enter his state cabin."

"No; but the reason of his reserve during the first cruise I had with him, was this—he had his daughter on board; he had taken her to Rio Janeiro for some purpose, and was now bringing her back to the convent in Seville."

"Did you never see her, then?'

"Once only, when she disembarked."

"Was she pretty?"

"There was an angelic sweetness and adolescent purity in her fair face that I have seldom seen equalled, never surpassed, in the ideal portraiture of the richest of the old master-pieces."

"And what was the ultimate fate of Don Miguel, or is he still living?"

"No; he is dead. One day we had overhauled a lumbering Indiaman, and were ransacking her almost lazily, for it was very hot, so breezeless that the black flag we had carelessly tied to the shrouds in token of victory did not even stir—and of late we had taken plenty of booty—when we were run down by a Brazilian frigate: we had a hard and bloody fight; the flower of our crew were killed, but by disabling her masts we managed to escape. I never saw the captain to such advantage; he fought like a lion: three times we were boarded, and three times we cleared the deck; but our escape was dearly paid for—a bullet struck the head of Don Miguel and fractured his skull. From that moment he who had taken such credit to himself for having saved me from my fever delirium was himself a raving maniac, beyond hope of recovery."

"How terrible."

"It was a dreadful time—our best men slain—dissatisfaction broken out among the rest into mutiny and quarrels. For the captain, sometimes he was moody and silent, but too often we were forced to lash him to a gun to save him from the effects of his madness.

"I know not how it was, but, by a tacit understanding, the command devolved upon me.

"After we had suffered a great deal from weakness, for fever broke out amongst us, and there were left, after our engagement with the Brazilian frigate, only half sufficient hands to work the ship, everything that could happen for the worst did happen; and, last of all, our ill luck was consummated by our being run down by two armed steamers, and we were all taken prisoners. Then I thought that my sins and my sorrows were ended for ever. We were put into irons, and stowed away into the hold. But it has always been my misfortune to have enemies ready made, and always was my fortune to find friends when I need them. Through the assistance of a kind fellow, who pitied my youth and my ill luck, I managed to escape. But I have not finished with poor Don Miguel. On the day when our ship was taken there was a dead calm, and the poor wretch was possessed with the notion that a furious gale was blowing. It was ludicrous, yet very pitiful, to hear him, in his stern, sharp tones, ringing out his orders to meet imaginary dangers, and it was strange and sorrowful to see the swarthy, ill-looking fellows, moving about with grave faces, pretending to obey his mandates. On the day the ship was taken he had a gleam of consciousness, and the few brief, coherent orders he gave were followed with blind faith; but nothing could avail us against an overwhelming force. The crew of the government vessels swarmed our deck. Then we thought of our last alternative; a rush was made to the hatchway, where the powder was kept. We found it closed, and we could not open it, so tightly was it battened down. We were immediately seized, and hurried into the boats. With a cheer the men pulled off, leaving a number of their comrades and the captain of one of the steamers on board. Just as we were reaching our prison-ship, a tremendous explosion burst upon our ears. The sea, as it were, shook with the concussion—a glare and a dazzling blaze for one moment eclipsed the light of day—and the waves were strewn with the mangled bodies, broken spars, and floating ship-stores. Mad Don Miguel had fired the gunpowder, and had perished, like Samson, together with his foes."

As Christopher finished this recital, the young officer entered.

"Captain," he said, "the 'Hamadryad,' almost within hail, has lowered her main-top; and, from the bustle on board, I take it that they are going to attempt to board."

"By heaven! but I will forestall them;" cried the Boy Pirate, hurriedly.

He pressed Lili fervently to his heart.

"Fear nothing for me, love," he said; "I lead a charmed life, and it is not by the hand of such a dastard as Daniel Harwolf I am doomed to fall."

His bride made no reply: she was so agitated that words failed her; but still she clung lingeringly to her adored and gallant lover.

He gently disengaged himself, and hastened out of the cabin.

Dreadful sounds of preparation were heard above —the trampling of heavy feet, the rattle and lumbering of the heavy guns that were being breeched and loaded.

She looked from the cabin-window, and she fell upon her knees with a sob of intense anxiety. The boats were putting off, manned by the sturdy pirates.

The Boy Pirate stood erect, brandishing his sword, and giving his orders in a loud, firm voice; whilst the black silk folds of the banner of death swept down from the tiller of his boat, and trailed along in the water.

They had sped across the expanse of sea till they looked no larger than insects. She watched them with all the eagerness of suspense and the solicitude of affection. She perceived that they were nearing the vessel. A puff of white smoke and leaping jets of flame ran along the side of the distant vessel, and the pounders came bounding and spanking along the face of the deep, till they sank with a dull plash and a fountain of spray.

Lilia gave a little scream. It was the first broadside she had ever witnessed, and her womanly terror overcame her for an instant; but she resolved to school herself to the endurance of such a spectacle as that before her.

Presently there was another roll of thundering guns and another plash, and hissing flight of heavy shot. This time the discharge was not so harmless; for a shot struck the bowsprit of the vessel, causing it to quiver and roll over, and bring such a qualm of fear to the untried heart of Lilia, that she almost fainted.

Now from a-far came the shouts of battle—the rattle of musketry—the clashing of weapons. Boats were putting off from the "Red Raven," and were received with loud shouts by the combatants. Louder and louder grew the contest—shots were fired from the rover's ship, and it shook with the recoil of its own guns.

Lilia was learning a terrible lesson. But with the heroic fortitude of her sex, she watched calmly in the midst of her dismay.

The mizen of the "Red Raven" was struck, but her well-mounted and well-served guns had made sad havoc in the rigging of her adversary.

Now came the tug of war: the "Hamadryad" steamed like a caldron, and belched fire like a fiery dragon, crashing through her fragile masts, tattering her loosened sails.

Still flew the remorseless shots with deadly impetus from the fiery mouths of the rover's guns.

A roar came over the waters.

The men in the boats raised their oars, and those of the pirates who remained on deck cheered vociferously.

Ghastly and grim, the black flag was run up, and the Red Raven hovered in the smoke and the flame.

A final roar of exultation from the pirates—the "Hamadryad" was their prize.

CHAPTER XII.

THE ACTION BETWEEN THE "RED RAVEN" AND THE "HAMADRYAD."

BUT it is necessary that the reader should have a more detailed knowledge of the manner in which this engagement was fought.

Upon reaching the deck, the Boy Pirate had ordered his men aft, and thus addressed them—

"Comrades, I should not think it needful to make a speech to you just upon the point of a battle; it is an implied insult to suppose that true and tried hearts like yours need the incentive of a fiery harangue: your own sterling mettle will be the best stimulus to a daring assault—but there is one thing to which I wish to call your attention, and which I am proud to hope will urge you to surpass yourselves on this occasion—remember, lads, this battle you fight for *me*: the man against whom we are about to contend is my personal enemy. For his paltry craft we, who have swept the seas of their richest spoils, could well afford to despise such a capture, but for once your interest concentrates in me; and as I have ever striven my hardest to deserve your loyalty and approbation, I know there is not one of you who will not take to himself the insults that have been heaped upon one who has the honour to be your captain. Hurrah! comrades; it is time we stirred for a short and merry cruise: our arms are getting nerveless, and we have almost forgotten the voice of our own guns. Hurrah for the 'Red Raven!'"

Three stern and hearty cheers rang round, and with steady alacrity the men jumped into the boats.

"Belay," shouted our hero, "now we shall see how long yon tawdry yard of silk shall fly from the mainmast."

Through the glancing waves speed the burdened boats, heavily manned and drawn deep; there is a stern silence reigning.

They near the "Hamadryad."

Every preparation is being made on deck to give the assailants a warm reception.

The excitement grows intense.

The silence more impressive.

Nearer and nearer they approach.

There is no quailing.

"Stand to your guns—make ready—fire," roars a harsh voice on the deck of the fated vessel.

A thundering volley followed, the ship was veiled in smoke, and the heavy shots ploughed the wave.

"Now, comrades, let us show what stuff we are made of, and let these audacious meddlers know what it costs to follow the track of the 'Red Raven,'" shouted the Boy Pirate. "Hurrah for the 'Jolly Oliver.' Quick, lads, the grapnels; let every man clamber like a squirrel to the bulwarks, and the first one that sets foot on the quarter deck shall have a double share of the plunder."

Warily the boatsmen feathered their oars, and cautiously they glided beneath the guns.

Another broadside was fired, but too high; the shot flew over the boats and skimmed along the brine.

The boat was close alongside, and under the lee quarter.

The men cheered.

The stunning boom and the burst of a flash from the port-hole over their heads caused the vessel to shudder, and the boats to rock desperately.

"Now's the time, hearties," cried the Boy Pirate; "who is the first to follow the Red Raven?"

Grasping a cutlass in his teeth the dauntless boy seizes the ledge of the port-hole, and firmly fixing his feet against the side of the ship, nimbly clambers towards the deck.

Faces now appeared looking over the bulwark; pistol shots were fired, both from the ship and from the boats; furiously pikes and swords are thrust at the men as they mount in the rear of their gallant boy-leader. The man who guides the boat is struck in the right arm; instinctively he snatches at the wound with his left hand; he drops the oar, and the boat vears away from the side of the vessel, making the ascent more perilous.

Several men are shot dead before they can secure their hold upon the bulwarks, and the life of the Boy Pirate himself is only saved by a doughty seaman, who fires his pistol full in the face of a man who threatens our hero with a handspike.

It is a wild and thrilling scene.

But in spite a most furious resistance, in the face of a volley of musketry—a hailstorm of missiles—a perfect whirlwind of sweeping and flashing cutlasses—

The deck is won!

Desperate and exciting the hand-to-hand struggle between the pirates and the crew of Harwolf's ship. Men wrestle in the throes of death, and force each other alternately to the side of the vessel, with intent to hurl one another into the sea. And more than one body, gashed and stabbed by a fellow creature, staggers and falls prone, or is hurled brutally into the foaming waves, whose white manes are blood-smeared already.

The first to set his foot upon the deck is the Boy Pirate.

Harwolf is there to meet him. The eyes of these ancient enemies glow with hungry hate; and for the moment Christopher forgets that he has pledged his word to Lilia to save the ruffian's life.

Like infuriate panthers they leap upon each other. This is the very tug of war, indeed. No man stands upon authority—no man looks for directions. Every man singles his enemy, and fights with desperate fury on his own account. No one has eyes for his brother's fate, except it be coincident with his own struggle; and in that case many a cherished life is saved by staunch comrades.

Oh! but the roar—the curses—the yells—the cheers—the crackling of the guns—the fumes of those hellish ingredients that man has combined to blast and to shatter God's own image—the sharp clinking of striking hand-weapons!

Harwolf has fired a pistol at the Boy Pirate. The bullet has grazed his temple.

This is but the latest of a thousand hair-breadth escapes he has had within half an hour.

Now they are fighting hand to hand and foot to foot—their swords clashing, and their eyes darting lightnings of fiendish battle passion. Presently, with a dexterous twist of his wrist, Christopher strikes Harwolf's weapon out of his hand, and sends it whizzing over his shoulder.

He then leaps upon the ruffian, and, with the strength of a young giant, hurls him to the ground.

Several of the pirates rush to his side.

All flushed and breathless, the gallant Boy Pirate points to his prostrate foe.

His obedient followers at once understand the signal, and Daniel Harwolf, cursing blasphemously and fiercely struggling, is dragged to the mainmast of his own vessel, and, amid the derisive cheers of the victorious crew, is securely lashed to it.

But the fight is not over.

Quarter is neither asked nor given.

The deck runs red with blood, and has become slippery with gore.

An interchange of firing has passed between the two vessels, even during the desperate struggle on deck.

The crew of the "Hamadryad" had some faint hope that if they could do some material damage to the "Red Raven" it might create a diversion in their favour.

But the gallant fellows at last give up resistance in despair.

A final broadside is fired; there is a final discharge of small arms; and, with loud, heart-thrilling, ringing shouts of triumph, the black flag floats through the white smoke that is soaring slowly aloft.

The men who have been working the guns below are dragged upon deck with sullen passiveness as of lion hearts. At length subdued, they tamely submit to the indignity; they are hurled to the ground, over-powered by numbers; muskets and pistols are levelled at them, knives already at their throats.

Christopher stands erect, panting with exertion, but seeing all with his quick discerning eye.

He feels a gentle touch on his shoulder. The beautiful Lilia is in his arms.

Softly she breathes one word—

"Mercy!"

"It is enough, comrades," says Christopher, in his clear ringing tone. "Let those men be spared; they have done their duty well, and I can afford to give them quarter. Thanks, brave lads; you have vindicated the honour of your elected commander; and now let us give three cheers for the 'Red Raven!'"

CHAPTER XIII.

SCHEMES OF VIOLENCE FRUSTRATED.

THE Hedgers' Arms was one of those dilapidated, yet picturesque resting places, that are frequently found upon lonely spots on the high roads that lead from city to city, winding across many miles of the rich and beautiful scenery of our green and lovely island.

It was a low thatched dwelling, built of wood dark and splintering, that contrasted strangely in its black decay with the viscid dew-glistening leaves, and the conscious-blushing petals of the luxuriant but ill-trained wall-roses that partly trellised it: before the door were some painted rustic settles, patched and sun-scorched; and a long table rudely constructed of a warped plank and knarled stanchions. On one side of the house stood a tall and rickety sign-post, but the device on the harsh-grating tabard had been long defaced, beyond recognition, by the wind and rain.

On the other side was a dung heap, the empire of a grunting sow and a few strutting partlets.

There was an air of vagabondism and indolence about the place that extended even to the lazy curling of the clear blue smoke of the wood fire, that wandered listlessly from the broken chimney, and hung lingeringly in the air.

The pure and bracing atmosphere of the sylvan and hilly locality redeemed it from dirt or squalor, and the country calm and freshness gave it a charm of its own.

Upon the settle Silas Rye was seated, a pot of ale before him, his hat upon the ground, and his shaggy elf-locks waved by the speaking breezes, as his bloodshot eye drank refreshment from the quiet loveliness of the wide and chequered prospect fading away soft and blue in the receding distance.

But if the hallowing influence of surrounding peace and beauty soothed to some extent his fiery passions of remorse and anger, there was something in its tenderness that gave a thrill of acute pain to a heart that was not quite unsusceptible of worthy impressions.

His eye fired; he drank a deep draught of the ale, blew a long whiff from the cigar he was smoking, and smote the table with his clenched fist.

"By God!" he exclaimed in his reverie, unconsciously speaking aloud. "But that scene with my infernal partner has done me more good than all the cant and rant of a hundred tabernacles.—I have been a beast—I have been a rogue: it is not often that the fact gives me much vexation, but curse me if I like to think myself a *fool*; and I am nothing better than a bleared idiot to fancy that any good can come of the price of blood. What the better am I for the infernal swag that has given me the means of wrecking my health and prospects? I have scarcely a mag left. I live in town and see life. Life—or death! By the Lord, it is hard to say which name it may better bear. I am not like a poor thief, without education; nor a blind owl, that can see no pleasure except through the gleam of strong brandy at some drunken sing-song. I like the country; I like living in the square; and in some of my dirty black jobs I have worked devilish hard. I've a precious good mind to bring poor little Charley down here; the country air might fetch the colour back to the poor chap's sunken cheeks. I know he would like to creep about the hedges and learn the names of the trees and the flowers; he would like to hear the little birds sing and the village bells chime; he would like to hear the sheep bleat, and have a sniff at the new mown hay or a bunch of wet violets. Perhaps I'm a bit mawkish with this new fad, but a man may be a scamp without being a brute, and its cursed murder to let the poor little fellow pine and die in the ugly stinking cesspool of drink and villany when there are such nice hospitals of nature's own building. The silly little covey is the only one there ever was or ever will be that loves or believes in me; he was my dead mother's pet, we were happy enough in the old innocent days. There is no blood on my hands, and I mayn't be such a very black one after all; anyhow, its never too late to mend, and I can't afford to lose little Charley."

A tear sparkled in the wild grey eye of the adventurer, and in his softened mood he rose and listlessly sauntered towards a green lane that opened from the road before him.

As he crossed the little paddock before the house two men passed him.

They were both tall fellows, and seemed to be tramps.

One was dressed in a long shabby blue coat, wore a battered wide-awake, and held a heavy stick in his grasp; his lineaments clearly testified his nationality as an Irishman.

His companion was a wild cut-throat looking gipsy, with a basket of flash song-books, tapes, pins and trashy trinkets on his arm.

They looked at Silas with a sullen scrutiny, and then passed heavily over the threshold of the inn.

Silas Rye started as they went by, and with affected carelessness strolled up the lane: soon, however, he returned, and cautiously skirting the little green stealthily drew near the open window of the tap-room, and ensconsed himself in a little arbour that was built by the side of the casement. Leaving him ensconsed in his ambuscade we will follow the wayfarers into the inn.

Striking the brick floor with his heavy stick the Irishman bawled out for the tapster of the lonely hostel.

"Wisha! there—house, house! And bedad, are ye all aslape whin its the gintry that's dry as fishes with the thirst and the hate? Come out of it, ye lazy spalpeens, or we'll be after helping ourselves, bad cess to ye."

A neat-handed Phillis stepped from the garden, where she was spreading the snowy linen upon the gooseberry bushes, and, with a stare on her rosy face, entered the bar.

"What do you please to want?" she asked.

"Jist a trifle that I'll make bould to take, darlin'," returned the rough-looking fellow, chucking her under the chin, and impressing a smacking kiss upon her lips, which caused her immediately to raise the corner of her apron to her mouth, and to recoil with a giggle and a crimson flush of virtuous indignation, "and another little blessing in the way of a drop o' whisky and a stopper of baccy: and how's the world at Frontemore, mavourneen? What's come of the father, bad luck to him."

"He bean't home," returned the girl; "since that affair about the squire's grey horse as was sold, he be gone up to London; but it's many a long day since we seen you, Oiny."

The Irishman laughed.

"Isn't it the birds, and the honeybees, and the

flowers, that come back in the summer, Bridget, and why shouldn't Black Oiny? Sure it's yourself that's the loadstone would draw a railway train of purty fellows to Frontemore. But, botheration! where's the whiskey?"

The girl laughed, and brought a dusty bottle and some glasses, pipes, and tobacco, and placed them on the table by the window.

The two men seated themselves, and, lighting their pipes, soon diminished the contents of the bottle by an ample moiety.

For some time they smoked in silence; then the gipsy rose and walked to the back door to see if Bridget had returned to her work.

He perceived her at the bottom of the garden, under a little shed, her buxom arms plunged above the elbow in the frothy wash-tub; he gently closed the door. He then went to the front, and looked out.

Silas Rye kept close in his arbour.

No living creature appeared, save that at some distance down the road was heard the slow rumble of a waggon, laden with fragrant hay, the highest truss of which appeared slowly moving behind the leafy hedges.

"We'd better shut the window, Oiny," said the gipsy.

"Arrah! but you'll do no such thing. Be asy, if you can, with your botherin'—you're as fidgety as a wasp in a bottle. Isn't it the fresh air we're breathin', and there's divil a cratur' within a mile uv us? Well then, this squire's son, that the pirate boy's in love with, and run away, so she says, with his sister—Och, but I'm murtherin' the coincidence: it's the purty Miss Lilia's brother that's coming home to the manor, and he thinks it illegant to walk the road this fine summer weather; and, sure, he'll find his journey longer than he looks for, unless the gossoon has rayson enough in him to submit to the force of circumstances, and to stand and deliver like a gentleman."

"You brawling fool," said the gipsy, with a scowl; "do you want a job at crow-scaring, that you raise your voice to such a view-holla?"

"You ugly baste!" cried the vivacious Irishman; "is it Oiny Macarne that he's the boy to put up wid your black insults? It's yourself that can do the holler when you're wanted to kape quiet, and will you be afther bullying me for airing my throat, when there's never a sowl within a mile uv us? Faix, I've a mind to lave you out of the job entirely—you big blusthering thafe."

"Well, there's no need for a split between us, my pal," returned the gipsy, sullenly. "I know that you can do a job of this sort as well as any one, and always share fairish, but you must be discreet if you don't want to be jagged; there's no knowing who's who, nowhere."

"Sure then, and aint I discreet, you haythen?" returned Black Oiny, still in dudgeon; "but whin is the time and where is the place we must make acquaintance with his honour?"

"Behind the home spinney there is a dull walk that leads up to the manor house—it passes over a bit of rough common, where my tribe have lit their camp fires many an autumn night," replied the gipsy; "he will take that path, and there is a gap in the hedge where we can hide till he passes."

"Och! but you're a jewel, Esau," returned the Hibernian, as he drained his glass and refilled it with the whisky. "And when we've done the thing nately we'll just get back to London, and I'll buy myself a new coat, and I'll get a power of poteen and wax candles for my third cousin, Dan Reily's wake; the ould women were keening when I came away, so betimes we get back we will have a splendid funeral."

The girl now entered the room; the gipsy spoke to her.

"You ar'nt above doing us a favour, Bridget, for a bob or two, are you?"

"No, I bean't! Leastways, if its nothing bad nor dangersome, and if I can do it."

"Bedad! and it's right for you, my girleen, that same 'if I *can* do it,' for there's divil a harder thing you could have to do, for its to keep a sacrat, and that's past the power of most wo men entirely."

"Are you going to tell me something?" she asked, nervously. "I don't want to know none of your business, Oiny, nor more I won't," she exclaimed emphatically.

"We only want you to keep in that mind, Bridget," said the gipsy. "If anybody asks whether you've seen me or Black Oiny, of course you ain't, that's all."

"And that's easy. I ain't to know who comes into the tap or who goes out on't; the father threatened me with a hiding awhile gone for answering of a bothering question as the squire put to me, and so never no more I don't mean to know nothing, and I wont!"

There could be no doubt of the sincerity of a promise confirmed by such a long string of negatives, and the worthy confederates seemed satisfied.

The evening was advancing, the twilight deepening, and the night winds began to blow freshly through the casement.

They paid for the whisky and tobacco, and gave the girl a couple of shillings as a token of their confidence in her discretion, and together they sallied out of the inn.

Silas slipped from his hiding place, and crouched behind an angle of the house.

"Oiny," cried the gipsy, suddenly, "I swear I saw some one flit from that arbour."

The Irishman looked round him with a savage frown and then he burst into a laugh, as he said—

"Look at that now; sure, you're as easily scared as an old crone that has seen the banshee; sure, for seeing ghost sights you've never been equalled. But come on, bad luck to ye, or we shall be too late to pay our respects to his honour."

So saying the fellows crossed the high road, and carefully wended their way down the shadowy lane.

From time to time they peered over the hedge or looked behind them, and it was only by keeping under the deep shadow of the high banks that Silas could elude their vigilance, while he followed them as closely as he dared.

At length the road became wilder and more lonely. On one side the hedgerow ended abruptly at a little brook that flowed under a wooden bridge.

On the other side appeared an enclosed plantation of stumpy firs, whose trunks were half buried among the tall dancing fern and rough brushwood.

Opposite the spinney was the rising ground of a piece of waste land or common, tufted in places with the dark green and bristling broom, from which peeped forth the yellow blossom.

The little ascent lay dark against the deep red glare of the molten west. Amid the purple of the clear zenith a few brilliant stars sparkled forth.

Black Oiny and the gipsy suddenly stopped.

They stood listening.

The croak of the landrail still grated harshly among the furze. The leather-winged bats fluttered and trembled through the air, ever and anon whizzing with their tiny shriek past the faces of the night watchers.

The men spoke in low, hoarse whispers.

"He might be armed, Oiny, eh?" said the gipsy, looking about him with trepidation. He was evidently a craven.

The Irishman did not answer.

"Rather than lose the swag I'll sneak behind and knife while you fall on."

"Be asy," returned Black Oiny: "my shillelah will do the business. But, by the holy saints, it's quare you're looking, Esau. If your heart's milky, kape out of the way, and I'll attind to the gintleman myself."

"No, no; I'm game," returned the other, with forced manfulness. "Only do be careful, Oiny, not to make a row. Those infernal gamekeepers walk the preserves all night to watch the young pheasants."

"You're mighty civil, Esau," replied the more determined ruffian; "but I think it's myself that's received the careful education. Bad luck to you, kape out of the way, you shivering spalpeen. Go back to your basket in the hedge, and wait till I come to ye, for by the blazes I hear the sound of a step. He's coming; nobody else would walk so jauntily. Faix, I'm ready for him! Kape off, you lily-livered naygur!"

The gipsy, nothing loth, kept close beneath the hedge.

The Irishman also receded. A tall young man, wearing a heavy cloak, and carrying a small portmanteau in one hand and a walking stick in the other, turned the corner of the lane, crossed the wooden bridge, and emerged upon the open roadway. He walked with a firm, free step, but his eyes were bent thoughtfully on the ground.

He drew near the spot were the robbers were awaiting him.

At this moment the gipsy crept nervously behind his comrade, and touched him with quivering arm.

The Irishman in his hot impatience threw back his elbow with such impetus as might belong to the recoil of the piston of a steam-engine. Esau caught the blow full in his ribs, and was knocked backwards, crashing among the crisp bushes.

The young man was startled. He looked up, took a step backward, and instinctively raised his walking stick.

Black Oiny came out of the gloom, and stood full in the middle of his path.

"Good evening to your honour—the saints protect you," said Black Oiny, in a whining tone. "Sure its your honour's self that has the good heart that can never deny a bit of silver for a poor Irish boy that's not done a stroke of work since he hurt his leg, last harvest. By my faith, it's Captain Meredith you'll be, and it's myself that will pray for your honour's soul, if you'll take pity on me."

"My good fellow," said Meredith, quietly, "if you are deserving of such help as I can give you, come over to-morrow by daylight to the manor, and I will do something for you; but I tell you at once that you will get nothing from me at such a time and place as you've chosen to make your petition. Let me pass, please; good night to you."

With great coolness the young man attempted to pass on.

Black Oiny stood in his way.

"Arrah, now! it's not your honour that's the gintleman to drive a poor lad to desperation."

"If you imply a threat by that speech," returned Meredith, with undisturbed serenity, "I can tell you it is an idle one. I have a pistol under my cloak, and I shall not scruple to shoot you dead if you presume to intercept me; for your own sake, I warn you to get out of my way."

"Och and is that it; then, by the powers, we'll see whose threats are idle entirely."

With this the ruffian flung himself upon Meredith. The latter was a slight-built man, but supple and powerful withal, and he struggled with great determination; but the Irishman was almost a giant in stature, and certainly a giant in strength; he had folded his arms tightly about the young man, and together they swayed backwards and forwards, like contending athletes.

Meredith wrestled to get a purchase; a pistol was in his breast pocket.

The Irishman had no intention of allowing him to carry out this purpose, at least as far as his own strength and fury could avail to prevent.

In the tussle the pistol was drawn; it passed from hand to hand, and exploded in the air.

The gipsy was stealthily creeping behind the combatants; he held a long sharp knife in his hand.

Just as he was about to plunge the knife into the body of his victim, he was felled by a heavy blow, and lay upon the ground doubled-up and motionless.

The next instant Black Oiny felt a brace of iron arms about his neck, and felt himself strangling, while he was hustled and shaken away from his grip upon the young officer. At last by dodging his head under the arm of his new antagonist, he contrived to stagger across the path half choked, with a thousand sparks dancing before his strained eyes.

He stumbled against the bank. For a moment he gathered himself together for another round with his new foe, but when he saw the stalwart figure and resolute bearing of Silas Rye—for it was he—he took into consideration that his comrade being disabled the odds were now turned against him, and that an honourable retreat was next to a creditable victory; therefore he broke through the bushes, and plunged into the depth of the spinney.

Captain Meredith turned towards his deliverer.

"In cases of this kind," he said, with manly frankness, "on the spur of the moment it is hard to find words sufficiently apt to express one's gratitude; and I doubt whether there is any need of the exchange of mere wordy thanks and deprecations between honest men. You have won my friendship, and though that is not of much value, I am eager to know to whom I owe my safety."

"Do not speak of this business as if it brought any credit to me," said Silas Rye. "I am not much used to listening to compliments I don't like, for I find the worst rogues are the best flatterers. I'll bid you good night, sir, as I see your friends approaching. I suppose it was the pistol-shot alarmed them and brought them to the rescue. I should of course have wished to see you safely to the manor, but it seems it is needless. Good night, sir; may you never again be assailed by such a peril."

"Stay, stay. By Jove, you shall not run off incontinently and in that fashion."

At this moment a carriage rattled quickly along the road, and the clattering of several horses' hoofs was heard.

Squire Meredith, a white-haired but firm and stately-looking man, lenped from the barouche, and seized his son by both hands.

A number of mounted gentlemen and servants rode up with a sort of cheer at perceiving the young man uninjured.

"Dear Ned, I thank God that you are safe!" exclaimed the old man, fervently; "one of the hunting party that crossed the road before you, early this morning, recognised you as he passed, so we knew you were coming; we are aware of your penchant for walking, and were prepared to give you an unexpected pleasure by holding a general assembly for your welcome. Just now we were all startled by the report of a pistol; we thought of you, and rushed off to see if aught was the matter."

"But where the deuce is the fellow gone to?"

"What fellow, Ned?"

"Why the fellow who saved my life. I was attacked by a couple of footpads—there lies one of them, and well-nigh garotted—when a stranger came to my assistance, and I scarcely recovered breath to thank him, when, evasit, erupit—he sloped, he skedaddled. Do ride after him, one of you, please; he cannot have got far on the road."

"How was he dressed?" asked one of the mounted gentlemen, shaking his reins for a start.

"Faith, I never noticed; I only looked at his face."

"And his features?"

"I did not notice them; I only observed the expression."

"And what sort of expression was it, sage physiognomist?" asked the gentleman, laughing.

"Well, he looked like an artificial rogue; there were lines of cunning in his face, but they were drawn on a substratum of natural frankness."

The whole party laughed heartily at this remark.

"Faith, Ned, if you're not the man that warmed his cold hands with a live bomb-shell, you're his first cousin," said one of them. "You must have found a quiet moment to study his physiognomy while the thief was putting the hug on you. Well, let him go; I dare say he will turn up some day as a poor relation; let us go back to the manor, squire."

"Aye, but I think with Ned, some exertion should be made to recall one to whom we are so much indebted," replied the elder Meredith, with seriousness. "If any of you have a mind for a gallop, give him chase—bring him back—take no denial; he may be some poor fellow to whom we may do a service; if not, at least we can ease our hearts by thanking him."

Several of the party dashed off in pursuit.

"Get into the carriage, my dear boy," the squire resumed, addressing his son; "this is a joyful day in my calendar. Oh, how glad they will all be to see you, lad, up at the old manor."

"And little Lily?"

"She is dead," returned the old man, sternly.

"Dead!" cried Edward Meredith, turning very pale.

"At least, she is dead to us; don't talk about her, Ned—don't talk about her. I wish to be as cheerful as I can on the first night of your return. Get into the carriage, lad—you needn't fear for a beggarly tramp now; for we're strong enough for a scrimmage with a gang of high toby-men, though that's a glorious piece of fun that is quite dead since the rare old coaching days."

The little band laughed merrily at the tone of plaintive regret with which the old squire spoke the last words.

CHAPTER XIV.

THE MEETING OF SILAS RYE AND ANDREW HARWOLF—THE ACCIDENT.

ON the dull platform of a lonely little station on a branch line of the Brighton railway Silas Rye is moodily pacing; he has walked from the scene of his gallant exploit.

He has walked over "the long grey fields at night," and down the sombre by-ways of the country lanes, and has arrived an hour too early for the up-train.

His dark and solitary walk has not tended to raise his spirits.

We all know that there are repulsive scenes and loathsome sights that will not be swept from the mirror of the eye.

Awhile the reflections may be clouded or may fade away, but from time to time they will return with enhanced vividness.

The dressing-room in Frontemore Hall obtrudes itself upon the mental vision of Silas Rye.

His own participation—though not in the fearful deed, yet in the schemes that led to its perpetration—presents itself in all its force to his aching brain, and gnaw at his heart with bitterest, though subdued agony.

He revolves a thousand plans for his future. He pictures himself a settler in some distant colony, but even there he dreads the shadow of his guilty knowledge will hang over him go where he will: for him that gloomy shadow spans the earth, and he cannot escape from its gloom and its chill.

He seeks to shake off the weight from his heart—he curses the lagging moments and looks about in search of something to divert his thoughts.

The long railway stretches on either side of him. The association does not cheer him, for it runs from one side out of the lovely bordering of fruit-burdened orchards into the grim black charnel of a dark tunnel. The lamps of the signal-posts are blood-red, and they remind him of the "damned spot" that lies upon a hand that has tainted his own by its clasp. He is very moody, very heavy-hearted that night. The appearance of the sky is changed—the misty clouds waft over the deep blue sky like shadowy spirits hovering on the shores of the blue ocean of eternity. He feels nervous and excited: the strong and peaceful thoughts that exalted and softened him when he sat at the door of the Hedgers' Arms but a few hours before have left him, and he burns now for the change and excitement of "life in London."

[THE FIGHT IN THE MAIN-TOP.]

Then the fact forces itself upon him that he has in his possession but a few sovereigns—that he had come down to Frontemore expressly to raise the sinking funds; and now he left for town poorer than he came—all his trouble and anxiety thrown away.

Why had he not dissembled? or why had he not threatened his employer into another instalment of the great debt that he owed him?—a debt that all the money coined since the world began could never repay.

He was half resolved to return to Frontemore, and risk another interview with the murderous and remorseless villain on whom he depended for bread. He felt the more inclined to do this, as a strange terror and foreboding were creeping over him—sensations he had never before experienced, and which he could by no means account for.

He was weighing in his mind the expediency of this measure when the rattle of carriage wheels struck on his ear.

No. 7.

He looked over the wooden barrier or the platform and saw that the carriage had stopped.

A man, closely muffled, jumped out, and hurriedly strode into the station, and presently appeared on the platform advancing towards him.

The man, upon drawing quite near, stood still. The red light of the signal lamp threw its lurid glare on his face.

Silas Rye at once recognised him. It was Andrew Harwolf.

"I'm glad I have been able to overtake you, Silas," said the old steward. "The fact is, you left me under a false impression. I will confess to you a shameful weakness; the Madeira I offered you was indeed poisoned. I own it; but remember, there was *other* wine on the table, and *that* I had prepared for myself. Sometimes the fiend will get into my heart, Silas, and he goads me on to think of seeing my quietus in death; for wealth is not happiness, though the poor man thinks so." Visibly the wretch shuddered at his own lie. To no man was the exit from the " warm precincts of the genial day " more horrible. Yet he was not a coward. No; his nerves were strong, and he had the faith of fatalism in the success of his own villany, though at times this confidence terribly wavered. " But we must not let our little differences interfere with matters of business," he went on. " You came to me for money, in order to enable yourself to emigrate. We were about to clinch a bargain, by which a competence would be guaranteed to you, which your own exertions might develop into affluence. Now, Silas, you promised, for twenty thousand pounds, to give into my possession certain important documents, and to afford me the knowledge of certain facts which it is essential I should know. Will you do this, if I secure to you the sum you mentioned ? "

" No! by the heaven above our heads," cried Silas, fiercely; " I told you honest truth when I said that I wished to change my way of life, and to leave for ever the scenes of my sorrow and villany. I offered, for a poor share of your rich booty, to act square and to trouble you no more; and what was my return for this attempt to serve you? You tried to kill me; to poison me like a mad dog! Look you, Andrew Harwolf, I have no time now for talk, the train is due within a few moments, and this is all I have to propose—give me ten thousand, and I will give you time to live and enjoy your ill-gotten treasures; but, mark me! your fall shall not depend upon my frail life alone, for could you cut my throat where I stand —a thing, devil! you would be glad enough to do—you would not escape my vengeance! I have constructed a machine that must eventually crush you; it may twine and twirl for some time, and look harmless, but it will do its work at last. Curse you! you will find that you could not escape the effect of your old crime though you were licensed to shed a sea of blood to wash away its traces! Let me whisper a word in your ear—'Go away for four hours; I will dispose of him.' Was I bound to obey ? "

White and aghast, the foam springing to his lips, his eye-balls wildly starting, the guilty wretch looked with a mad look of horror and subjection upon that sullen face lighted by a sardonic leer.

The panting of the steam-engine was heard far away.

" Come; there is no time to be wasted. Time and tide wait for no man, squire, neither does the train. Here," he went on in the same tone, producing a pocket-book, " write me a cheque for a thousand. Post a letter as soon as you return home to your banker, and let me receive the balance by the end of the week. Hitherto you have ruled and curbed me: I served you faithfully. Now the tables are turned, and it is my part to bully and threaten. See that you play your part of tool and pander as well as I played mine. Look to yourself, Andrew Harwolf. I will be more just to you than you were to me—but not more merciful. You will not be poisoned by me, but you shall be fairly tried by twelve of your fellow countrymen, and hung, Andrew, hung! But look sharp; the train is bowling in—write at once."

" I have a cheque for the amount here in my letter case," returned Harwolf, feeble and faint with despair.

He drew it out with trembling fingers as he spoke.

With a leer of triumph, Silas transferred it to his own pocket-book.

As he did so the porter clanged the bell, and with a shriek the fiery engine and its long train bowled into the station.

Silas jumped into a first-class carriage.

" Good night, Squire Harwolf," he cried aloud, in a conventional tone, " my compliments at home. I trust you will reap a rich crop in the coming harvest."

He looked into the deadly pale face of his foiled accomplice with a malicious grin.

Through the darkness of the night on its wing of fire sped the rattling train.

Away—ever away! the rushing wind lingering in its tardiness behind them.

Silas Rye gazed abstractedly out from the carriage window upon the wild, gliding landscape, so sombre and shadowy in the night. The stars flew by, the dark trees rushed passed and seemed to catch each other.

" The hound ! " he muttered bitterly, grinding his teeth; " but I hug myself for this triumph; it is very seldom that revenge is profitable."

So absorbed was he that he had not noticed as anything unusual the extraordinary speed at which they were spinning along, nor the rocking and bouncing from side to side which shook the carriages.

" The train is very late to-night," remarked one of his fellow passengers, a lady, to another lady who sat opposite.

" Yes, much behind time."

" But they seem determined to make up for the loss, at any risk," returned the other.

" Indeed, we do seem to be going at a fearful rate; this fast travelling must be dangerous."

At this moment they plunged into the blackness of a gloomy tunnel with a shrill scream.

The speed seemed to be redoubled, and still the whistle kept up its piercing alarm.

The passengers began to look frightened, and several rose, and, pulling down the sashes, tried to peer out into the dark night, but they gained very little by this proceeding.

At last the steam seemed to be turned off, and the train to be progressing less rapidly; at last, slower and slower, the pace gradually to diminish till at length the train was only floating along in accordance with the laws of motion and inertia.

Then again there was a shrill shrieking of the whistle, and the guards, with pale faces, lanterns in hand, rushed by the carriages.

All within was horror and consternation. It were useless to attempt to describe the scene, or to depict the thousand forms in which the deadly terror displayed itself.

Such a scene has often been described, but never yet, as it never can be, with adequate effect.

By the side of the line, shading their eyes with their hands, and peering back through the gloom with white, wild faces, stand two men: they are the engine driver and his assistant.

The screams, sobs and prayers in the carriages are heartrending.

A prolonged shriek, as of some fiend in torture, from behind, increasing in compound ratio—a fearful panting and fluttering sound.

CRASH ! CRASH !!

Oh! the wild mingling of every sound of fearful agony and awe: the horrible raging of the iron giant broke forth like the image of Frankenstein from the feeble and profane hand of its puny architect. A few moments and the worst is over; but the worst is not known !

A terrible vision dances before the inward eyes of Silas: he is bound, bruised and bleeding, to a fiery wheel, on which he revolves amid the crashing of elements and a fair world bleared back into chaos. Sounds, ear-deafening and soul-piercing, torture his ears. He opens his eyes—he is in a small neat chamber, from the window of which he can see the long line, and a train lazily gliding along, flinging back its cloudy wreath of snowy steam, and ringing over the Golgotha of its fellows: he can see no more —his eyes seem blinded—his sense paralyzed—he falls back in his bed in a dull swoon.

CHAPTER XV.

THE BOY PIRATE'S GENEROUS REVENGE.

THE "Hamadryad " was taken; Daniel Harwolf was a prisoner; the triumphant pirates commenced the work of pillaging the ship.

The deck was in confusion.

The mizen-mast had fallen, and beneath the rigging lay the crushed bodies of the dead and dying.

It was impossible to clear the cabins until the deck was ready to receive the treasure, in order that it could be removed to the boats.

The crew of the "Red Raven" spent many hours in labour; the dead bodies were thrown into the deep without compunction, and the mast and tackle were cut away, and such of it as was useless, or not capable of removal, was flung overboard.

During these operations the prisoners were bound and secured.

Daniel Harwolf, lashed to the mast, glared on the work in impotent fury. His ungovernable temper increased his torments; he ground his teeth like a caged hyena, while his brow became swollen and knotted by his excessive passion.

Lilia had returned to Christopher's ship and to her own cabin.

The Boy Pirate stood on the deck of the "Hamadryad" giving out his orders in his quick, stern way, and his slightest commands were obeyed with cheerful alacrity. It was strange to see what strict discipline was observed among these lawless men. But they had learned the value, and, indeed, the pre-eminent necessity for the observance, of order and subordination. As the miscellaneous burthen of the ship was being rummaged and Christopher stood at the gangway watching the proceedings, there arose on deck a sudden cry—

"Sail on the larboard bow."

The Boy Pirate turned his seaman-like glance in the direction indicated.

A splendid frigate—plainly a man-of-war—was bearing down upon them.

There was no time to be lost in hesitation. Lose what they might by the expedient, there was no other hope of safety for the daring buccaneers but an instant return to their ship, of their putting on every stitch of canvas in order to elude their swift pursuer, for there could be no doubt that the vessel they were watching was one which had put to sea on their special behalf.

As they had no wish to walk the plank they accepted the alternative of returning to the "Red Raven" and using their best endeavours to outspeed the government vessel.

Christopher immediately ordered the boats to be filled with as much of the stores of the ill-fated ship as they would hold, and they were put off to the pirate-vessel.

The Boy Pirate was not a little chagrined at being forced to relinquish his prize, as he had already formed many designs for using it as a store-ship and a consort to his own.

Daniel Harwolf's eyes flashed with savage delight as he watched the magnificent three decker sailing like a swan before the wind.

No notice, however, was taken of his exultation or depression; and the fate of the "Red Raven" would have been a subject of little importance to him if the crew could have had their own way. Many a time they looked at him with menacing glances.

The Boy Pirate hastened the men into the boats, and taking a bundle of fine silk and a casket of pearls in his arms, drew a mark upon them with the point of his dirk and passed them over into the boat; then he took a lighted torch, and gazing round the deck for an instant to see that all was clear, sprang down into the hold. The swart faces of the pirates in the boats were turned anxiously in the direction of the swift-coming avenger, and they gave a cheer of satisfaction as their youthful captain appeared once more upon the deck and, catching hold of a rope, slung himself lightly into the boat. He had thrown the flaming torch into the sea, and as he left the ship thin wreaths of smoke were seen to emerge from the interstices of the deck and from the portholes.

Presently these eddies of fume increased in volume, and sharp tongues of bright flame glared out at intervals.

The Boy Pirate had fired the ship!

Harwolf, who sat bound and helpless, and surrounded by his wild-looking captors, in one of the boats, scowled back with baleful eye at his brave vessel whose "last sea fight was o'er," for the "Hamadryad" was in flames.

Nearer and nearer came the frigate.

Darker and sterner grew the anxious looks of the men.

Their boats floated beneath the hull of the "Red Raven."

Hastily they clambered the side, hauling Harwolf with them in the most unceremonious style.

Once on deck the Boy Pirate ordered the instant clearance of the field of action. Hastily the plunder was stowed away, and the men gathered round their young commander with ready and eager looks.

He gave his orders; sails were set till the tall, graceful masts bent like pine-saplings bowing before the wind.

A stiff gale had risen, and keeping close to the wind they skimmed along through the parting water, that leaped in foam as it rushed beneath their bows, in gallant sport.

When their beautiful ship was fully under way the pirates greeted their pursuers with a derisive cheer. They flew before the stinging blast; and the quickness of the motion, the recency of their triumph, the little spice of danger so charming to the daring and adventurous, excited the men; they wore bold faces, their steps were firm and elastic, their hands steady, and their eyes twinkling with a keen sense of enjoyment.

Daniel Harwolf had been put into the hold, and left to his reflections.

Intense became the excitement as the frigate was perceived to be gaining upon them.

It was useless to attempt to put on another yard of canvas; the ship was already in danger from being over-strained.

The gale was gaining power.

In the strong wind the superior size and strength of build of the frigate began to tell, and she seemed bearing down upon the "Red Raven" like an eagle upon some bird as swift of wing but not possessing the same strength of endurance.

A handsome young officer came to the side of Christopher.

"Do you think she will overhaul us, Captain," said this youth; "if she should come within a long shot I suppose there will be nothing left for it but to die as desperately as we can."

"Yes, Walter, I am thinking that if it comes to be broadside to broadside there is little chance for us, but if the wind should chop round I have a brave scheme for eluding her; but we have been in worse perils than this."

"And the ship is overladen, Captain?"

"Clearly; but a little risk no brave man cares for but rather enjoys; it is the price we pay for our commodities," replied the Boy Pirate, with a smile; and I tell you truth, Walter, I would rather fling overboard the richest cargo of the wealthiest Indiaman that ever we encountered than relinquish a yard of ribbon or a half-dollar that we have taken from the 'Hamadryad.'"

"And what is to be done with the prisoner?"

"We may make use of him if we come to close quarters."

"I do not think so, Captain, with pardon; the cursed skunk is so unpopular that the blues wont buy his life with a cat's. But you spoke of a scheme by which you expect to get clear out of this dilemma; may I ask for an explanation?"

"We are not far from land. For the frigate, she is of many more tons burthen than we and where we can run safely she cannot follow; there is a shallow creek not many knots from hence, that slices off a piece of the continent; we will run round this. I know its soundings, and we may manage it with ease and safety; but see, they are almost within range."

The men clustered the deck and watched the advancing frigate with redoubled eagerness.

The masts were straining terribly, the sails almost bursting from the yards.

The vessel bowed and shuddered as she forged through the waves.

A racing sea surged by them and every now and then a header would leap over the bulwarks with heavy plash, and swamp the deck.

The Boy Pirate was forced to order the top-sails to be reefed. They were nearly overset by a series of bouncing waves that poured in from landward and successively smote the taut sides of the gallant vessel with violent percussion.

The Boy Pirate gave orders for silence; a dead stillness prevailed.

The breechings of the guns were secured: they were manned; the watch was changed; the greatest order and discipline prevailed.

The Boy Pirate looked round upon his steady men and his well-ordered ship with a glow of pride and self-respect.

He then turned, with the wild battle-light shining in his clear eye at their beautiful but terrible enemy, as she gradually made way in their track.

A qualm passed over him and his lip trembled with regret. Great as was his courage—skilful his seamanship—thorough his power of command—what was he but a branded pirate, hunted for his life like the vermin of the field, or the wild beast of the forest? The ship he was looking upon was not one which would bring fame and honour on its hot breath of destruction. Fight as he would; display whatever qualities he might that belong to the conventional conception of a hero, his desperate valour, his cool prudence and foresight, his masterly discipline, would bring him no triumph. If he conquered it would be to his shame; if he fell it would be without pity; and his death would be hailed by mankind as a triumph of order and justice, a victory of right over wrong.

And mankind were just in so using him. He had thrown himself out of the pale of society and had taken up arms against his race; he had ignored the claims of law and probity and openly rebelled against the lives and liberties of banded man; and it was but right that he should be looked upon as a scourge and a pest, to be hunted down and extermi-nated.

His clear intelligence, his generous heart, recog-nised the force of this truth; he was no vulgar soul who could find glory in the madman's triumph of world-conquerors, or the daring exploits of famous robbers by land or sea, whose subtlety, dexterity, valour, and magnanimity were only the sources of a double dye in their shame, because they were rich gifts abused; the dashing highwayman was but a brutal thief, the bold rover but a cut-throat mu-tineer.

Young Christopher felt this and he murmured bitterly—

"Why—why was I forced to this? Oh, that I were some admiral, to strike one glorious blow for the helpless or oppressed, though I were cut to pieces in my first battle!"

The men gave a slight cheer; the Boy Pirate turned to see the reason. He found the wind had veered, and that they were running with increased speed, while the frigate seemed to have met with a momen-tary check.

As they watched the man-of-war they perceived a white puff of smoke shoot out from the side, tongued with a bright flash: a dull boom travelled slowly to the ear, and a heavy shot came bouncing and splashing from wave to wave, and sunk at a few yards before their bowsprit.

Christopher flew to the helm; he turned the ship, and soon they were making for the land.

With every stitch of canvas set the frigate pur-sued them; with all the skill of a pilot young Chris-topher contrived to run the headland that stretched out beyond the little creek, of which he had spoken to the young officer.

The night had come on; it was dark and misty, and though the wind had somewhat fallen, the sea still ran very high. The "Red Raven" had safely eluded the hostile frigate; very cautiously they were crawling along the coast, taking the soundings at every yard in their progress.

Christopher was all activity; he displayed an anxiety he had not shown when pursued by the man-of-war; perfect caution alone could enable them to navigate the dangerous channel; sunken rocks and treacherous shoals were on all sides. But at length the morning came. As the grey light suffused the eastern sky they were rounding the last promontory of the island, and soon their sails were bellying before the speeding breeze, the golden sunlight flashing the water into a sea of glory. The sea-mews and petrels swerved and dipped on their long wings, or, on their strong pinions, darted in their throbbing flight through the higher air.

Weary, but satisfied with the successful issue of his manœuvre, Christopher had retired to the saloon.

His head was reposing on its true pillow of rest, that pure and faithful bosom that suffered so many a cruel, though hidden, pang for him whom nature had made so noble, but whom fate and ungovern-able ambition had led so far away from the path of rectitude. He slumbered deeply, and his dreams were happy; the beam of genius flickered on his fine countenance, his mobile lip curled in a light sweet smile, his arched brows knit proudly.

Lilia bent over her pirate husband and kissed his lips passionately. He opened wide his dark full eyes, and looked up into her face with a soft smile.

"What is it, dearest," he murmured, "have I slept very long?"

"No, love!" she answered, "but you have slept very deeply; you must be terribly weary."

"Weary," cried the youthful adventurer, rising to his knee, and clasping his bride fervently to his heart; "can I be weary when you are with me? I drink fresh strength from the magic depths of your dear eyes, a strength that makes me invincible; but I was dreaming, Lilia," he said, with a languid sigh, "and I almost regret awaking, for I had not lost you, you were with me in my dreams, and you seemed nearer to me in my visions than in my waking moments. The Lilia of my dreams is no brighter nor dearer than my real beloved, for that is impos-sible; but I am not, there, the Red Raven or a pirate. But I must go on deck, there is much to be done. I mean to cruise once more on the Spanish Main, and it may be, darling, the time is coming when I shall have finished my career as a rover, and shall be able to bear you to a lovely island that I know of, a spot that, in its beauties, eclipses my conception of the islands of the blessed: but you told me awhile ago that you had a favour to ask of me. What is it?"

"Christopher, this man Harwolf; he is in your power. I know you are incapable of using your advantage ungenerously."

"And you wish me to set him free?"

"What do you think, Christopher? I feel myself bound to make him some reparation for the wrong I have done him, even though he has used me so cruelly."

"I was myself thinking of setting him free," re-turned the Boy Pirate, musingly, "but his base nature would not understand, far less appreciate, my motive in granting him his liberty; but that is nothing; his approbation is the last thing we care to secure; but it is a dangerous thing to do. Enough, that settles the thing, Lilia; I will let him go scatheless for this time, and then he and I are quits; and I can afford to brave his machinations."

"O Christopher, you are so good—so noble!"

"Do not flatter me, dearest, I am neither; but meanness and baseness are not of my faults."

With this the youth rose, and kissing Lilia tenderly, left the cabin.

When he stood on the deck he called his officers about him and sent for the prisoner.

With the bravery that despair lent him, the pallid ruffian advanced between his custodians, and con-fronted the Boy Pirate with swaggering boldness.

Brierly and Walter Mervyn, his favourite as-sistants, stood beside the young buccaneer.

Christopher, with careless dignity, seated himself upon the carriage of one of the guns, over which the black banner, with its death's head and red raven, happened to be thrown.

"Daniel Harwolf, what have you to say as a man who has outraged the laws of common humanity in having insulted and maltreated a noble and lovely being whom you affected to love?—for having driven an honest lad to the desperate life he is now leading? Had you been victorious—as you would have been if the devil had been sufficiently powerful to have assisted his votary—you would no doubt have been still further acquainted with sin. What have you to say why you should not pay the penalty due to a false and detestable villain?"

"Do what you will with me, pirate thief!" cried Harwolf, recklessly. "This is my comfort—you and your gang of felons will be hunted to the death. I pray that you may escape the English frigates, for hanging is too gentle a death for such miscreants. I beseech fortune that she may throw you into the hands of some uncivilized nation who may burn you to death at slow fires."

"Give him a taste from his own prescription, the infarnal rip," growled one of the savage pirates.

"No more words, cap'en, no more words!" cried Brierly. "Let the cussed skunk walk the plank at once."

"My men, I have promised, and I will not break my word; if you love me do not complain to each other of the order which I give you now: put him in a boat, cast him off, and let him use his worst influence against us; we can laugh at his malice, and the day is coming when we shall have ample and terrible vengeance."

"Douce my daylights, cap'en, I'll mutiny if it comes to that," roared Brierley; "do you think we're going to let off the infernal skunk every time we has him in our power? This shall settle that question, by Jehoshaphat!"

With this the old salt drew his dirk, and would have flung himself upon Harwolf, but Christopher caught him in his strong arms.

"If you do, Brierley," he exclaimed, "I swear you shall answer for the act with your own life; some of you put down the boat and send him adrift."

Harwolf sprang to the bulwarks. Two of the youngest sailors put down the boat; he scrambled down and got into it; he was cast off: all the authority of the Boy Pirate could not prevent the men from assailing him with a whirlwind of missiles, some of which struck him down in the boat.

CHAPTER XVI.
HOW SILAS RYE TURNED TO ACCOUNT THE RAILWAY ACCIDENT.

SILAS RYE was not so much injured as was at first supposed; the violent shock had stunned him, his face was scarred, his arm sprained, and his nerves unstrung, but towards the evening of the second day he was able to rise.

He had been removed from the scene of the catastrophe to a newly-built hotel close by the nearest station.

The papers contained thrilling accounts of the "appalling accident." A score of unfortunate beings had been killed and as many injured, more or less severely.

As he sat in the coffee room, his face bandaged, and his arm in a sling, as usual smoking and meditating, a strange scheme presented itself to his mind by which he might accomplish his vengeance upon his treacherous employer, in a manner unprecedented in its craftiness.

He knew that in spite of the appearance of quailing and subservience which Andrew Harwolf had worn during their last interview, the squire was a formidable antagonist, and that he had reason enough to act without conscientious scruples. Even were he not the man he was, he was one who would stick at nothing to carry out his villanous plans,

and to secure himself in the quiet and fearless possession of the riches for which he had bartered his soul.

Besides all this, Silas Rye had greatly exaggerated his knowledge of Andrew's secrets; as, for instance, he really knew nothing of the horrible manner in which the atrocious monster had disposed of the body of his murdered master.

He was struck by the novelty of the plan he proposed to himself, even in its crudity; and, as far as he was personally concerned, almost congratulated himself on the mishap which was the means of suggesting it.

But there were very many obstacles in the way, and he had but little time to lose—indeed, he feared it was already too late to carry out his design.

It was not an easy thing to get a cheque for so large a sum as a thousand pounds cashed in any place, and here he was at a little outlandish station, in a place where he knew no one, and was alike unknown to any.

While he was perplexing himself with these thoughts, he happened to stray towards the window.

Looking out, he perceived that the door of the hotel was thronged by carriages, cabs, and other vehicles, besides a motley crowd of foot passengers—relations and friends of those killed and wounded by the iron Juggernaut.

He sallied forth.

He passed through a group of persons who were conversing in low tones, and looking up furtively to the drawn blinds of the room in which the dead were awaiting recognition, and the arrival of the coroner. Some of them were silently weeping, others were making extravagant demonstrations of inconsolable grief.

Among the latter was a slatternly looking woman, dressed in a faded black dress—her bonnet half off her head, her face swollen with weeping, her eyes blood-shot, and her nose rather red—who was wringing her hands in maudlin desolation.

A bright idea sparkled in the eyes of Silas as he recognised this creature; he approached her, and touched her on the arm.

The little crowd followed him with greedy eyes, as being one of those who had suffered in the catastrophe, and almost envied him his wounds and bandages.

Such is the irrational taste for sensationalism in this enlightened age—a taste, of course by no means akin to that feeling which, with righteous indignation, we deprecate so warmly—that feeling, or rather, that want of feeling, which induced tender women to be witnesses of the horrors of the bloody arena, or the cruelties of the Spanish bull-fight.

Silas Rye had no wish to gratify the morbid curiosity of the rude starers, and therefore drew the woman out of the throng, and led her away into a deserted parlour in the hotel.

"And you recognise me, then, Mrs. Mulciber?" said Silas, painfully smiling.

The woman looked at his battered face, and answered, holding up her hands, with a melodramatic wail—

"Oh, dearie, dearie me! Mr. Silas Rye, can it be you; why your blessed mother as ever bore you would not recognise you—your poor face, and your poor bones! It must have been dreadful; it is a 'stronary thing that you're alive to tell—which your poor mother, if she was here to see, would downright agree to; but there, there," she went on, bursting into a flood of violent weeping, "anyhow, you are a living object, which I do say is something; and a dead dog is better than a living lion. But, poor Jonathan, look at him, a mangled corpse, with never so much as a widow to put on the weeds for him. Ah! Jonathan, Jonathan! why did you venture your precious neck all along of a week's wages—fifteen shillings a week, Mr. Rye, nothing more nor less, sir; he was a-working at the bricklayerin' up a new house at Mudborough, and the poor unfortnit creetur, you see what he's come to. He came home every week on a Friday; if he'd only taken my advice—I says to him, Jonathan, I says, come home every night, and don't stay a-spending your money with your mates, Jonathan, says I, its only tenpence by return ticket, and then you'll get used to the trains, which he wasn't used to 'em, and you see the consequence."

"But who is Jonathan?"

"My only brother as ever was, and I suppose ever will be, seein' that my parents is departed, poor creeturs!"

"And he had no wife, you say?"

"Never a one, sir."

"And you, are you married? for I forget, Mrs. Mulciber; besides, it is so long since we met."

"Sir, sir;" and the interesting creature hid her blushing cheek in her ample and tear-bedewed handkerchief.

"What's the matter, woman?" said Silas, rather snappishly.

"Well, you did take me so sudden like," she went on, with a simper. "I *ain't* married, sir. Not as it's my fault; for there's lots of young men as would give untold gold and their two blessed ears if I would only look at them, which a gentleman friend of mine —a corporal officer in the militia, sir, which is occupied at the ladies' boot-binding——."

"Yes, yes; I dare say you have many suitors, my dear madam; but——"

"And if any gentleman with a separate income and a 'art to dispose, which didn't drink and is fond of his home—which a poor lone woman wants perfection we all knows, 'specially when she has lost a only brother with fifteen shillings a week; and who only last month as ever was had a present from a gentleman as takes care of barges, and a gold locket with hair and 'In memory'——"

"This woman is too great a fool for my purpose," said Silas, vacantly, and speaking aloud.

"Fool yourself, sir, and many on 'em! Fool, indeed! Yes, fool enough to listen to the nasty deceitful promises of a set of false, designing creatures that calls themselves men, not to say individuals," cried the woman, with an extraordinary burst of scorn and anger. "You ought to be ashamed of yourself to hurt the sensible feelings of a poor, lone woman, which 'as just lost a brother as was a bricklayer in work—which we ain't all perfect, and you ought to be exposed, that's what you ought."

"Why, my dear woman, what have I done to offend you?" asked Silas, in amazement.

"Oh, I ain't offended, not at all, sir—not at all, at all," she went on, with a giggling sneer. "You didn't ask me whether I was married; those were not your words—of course not. You ain't above denying on 'em, of course."

"Oh, now I see," rejoined Silas, with a smile. "But how do you know I'm not married myself?"

"How *should* I know?" replied the irate fair one, with withering sarcasm. "I dare say you are brute enough for anything; its just like 'em!"

"I'm not married, Miss Mulciber," returned Silas Rye; "and pray don't let's quarrel. We were acquainted long ago; and latterly I find it in my power to do good for many people who were kind to me in old times."

"Really, sir; well I never did!" exclaimed the woman, suddenly changing her voice. "I hope you'll excuse me, I'm sure, sir; but my feelings is upset by the train and the accident and poor Jonathan; and you ain't forgetful of them as had a parential interest in you at the time of your little difficulties? It's very good of you, I do declare. Well, if you should feel any call to help a poor, lone, young woman, twenty-eight last birthday, which is a clear-starcher——"

"I have thought of a plan, Miss Mulciber, by which you can help me very much; and I will give you a hundred pounds for your services."

"Lor, sir!" cried the woman, opening her eyes wide with astonishment, "pray what is it to do? I hope it wont get me into trouble; for my landlady as had twins twice in two years."

"It is the simplest thing in the world, but I am afraid I can't trust you, Miss Mulciber; you are too apt to confide in others, and to tell your secrets."

"What, don't you think I can hold my tongue for a hundred pounds? I *must* hold my tongue, or that gossiping Mrs. Tattleby as lives at the coalshed would——"

"Will you do what I ask you?"

"Well, sir, if you think as no harm will come on it, for the consideration you mention I will do it."

"Have you yet seen your poor brother's body?"

"No, sir; I was a-waiting for the doors to open when you came."

"Does anyone know that he has met with an accident?"

"Not a soul, sir; I happened to be a-passing by the station and I seed a list of things found on the corpeses of the unfort'nate victims; it was exhibited so as people might be helped to recognise their friends. Among other things I saw one respectably dressed man—Jonathan had on his Sunday best, sir, 'cos he was going to his club, you know, and there was some sort of description of the poor fellow, but not much of it, he was so terrible massacreed—among other things was 'a snuff-box marked with the initials S. R.' I knew the snuff-box directly; for why—it was that slut Selina Rawlings as gave it him afore she run off with the greengrocer."

"S. R.—how strange and yet how fortunate!" exclaimed Silas Rye, "my own initials; fate seems to have cleared the road for me.". And he went on mentally—"This woman, she has a long tongue, but she is gifted with low cunning and will be involved in the conspiracy; for her own sake she will be quiet; it all works together to my wishes. Well, Miss Mulciber, now to business—a gentleman has given me a cheque for a heavy sum; now, for reasons it is needless to explain I wish this gentleman to believe I am dead; but your penetration will at once discover the impossibility of my drawing this money after my death: now, you can personate my sister, and if we return to London at once by the express you can draw the money as my sister, not saying anything about the accident, lest there might be some demur—go simply as my messenger."

"But how will you make the gentleman believe you are dead?"

"There you must help me—what is your Christian name?"

"Aminta Jane, sir, which my mother used to say common names is odious."

"Well, will you call yourself Aminta Rye, and call poor Jonathan Silas Rye, and say he is your brother; few questions will be asked and in the list of the killed in to-morrow's papers my name will appear: of course the gentleman will look down the list in the hope, I mean the fear, of seeing my name included amongst others; he will think me dead, and my design will be accomplished; but we must to-night hasten to London, and draw the money before he has time to cancel the cheque."

"But wont they put your name down twice," exclaimed the woman, warily, "first killed and then injured?"

"That's good for you, Miss Mulciber, you are a prudent girl and I can trust you," said Silas, blandly; "I will take care for that—I am not much hurt, and will request that my name should not be published; but come, the people are crowding into the room were the poor creatures are lying, get in as soon as you can, for we are greatly pressed for time."

"A hundred guineas?"

"Yes, guineas if you like, only make haste."

"And my expenses?"

"Do pray look sharp."

"My expenses, I stands upon my expenses."

"Yes, yes, anything you like, but make haste."

"I'm a-going, sir. Aminta Rye, Aminta Rye" she murmured, tapping her teeth with her parasol, "that may be my real name by-and-by—he's evidently smitten. A hundred guineas! That's five pounds more to the good, and my expenses. Oh! Jonathan—Silas, I must say—I don't know how you'll look with it all, poor fellow;" and with the silent throng she stole into the room where the dead were lying.

Impatiently Silas Rye walked about the station.

Every now and then he pulled out his gold watch to observe the progress of the hands.

Never had they seemed to steal so fast round the dial.

He began to feel feverishly anxious; having once matured his schemes he was one who followed them up with dogged perseverance. If this should fail, he would be exactly in the same position as before.

He knew enough to terrify his murderous associate into paying him liberally.

He looked at the door of the hotel. Several fainting women were borne out; whoever emerged from that doom-shadowed threshold was more or less stricken by horror or troubled by grief.

Presently Aminta Mulciber came to his side; all trace of her natural foolishness and levity had faded from her pale face.

"I have done it," she said, in a hoarse tone, "there was nothing in it to do, sir,—it was easy enough, they believes all as I told 'em, but, oh! sir, the heart-breaking sight!"

Silas Rye made no answer; he got into the special express train, which ran up and down every hour to bring fresh mourners to the platform of death; Silas took a ticket, helped his fair companion into a first-class carriage, and reached London.

As Andrew Harwolf had expected that from prudential motives Silas would abstain from applying to the agent personally, the cheque was cashed in the usual way; Aminta Jane was liberally paid and complimented, and returned home in chastened exstacy. This design worked out, the adventurer's thoughts turned from their dark channel, and with a light step, he walked towards his home, looking in the splendid shops in the aristocratic districts to find some present for his little sick brother Charles.

CHAPTER XVII.

THE BOY PIRATE ON SHORE—THE PRIEST'S DILEMMA.

Our scene is a little hostel on the French coast.

It is situated on a barren plain that stretches away far inland; it is surrounded by a few tall and ragged poplars. A quaint little fishing town scrambles among the cliffs and rocks.

A band of merry Frenchmen are gaily gabbling about the door of the long, low, and many windowed auberge, with a number of pretty girls dressed in short blue petticoats, high white caps, with little crosses about their necks, and gold rings in their ears.

The host is a fine fat personage, with a face like sunshine, the very impersonation of mirth and good humour.

Upon a table a young dark fellow is sitting, a cloak thrown lightly over his graceful shoulders: by his side stand two swarthy, manly-looking English sailors, one an elderly man, the other a handsome young man with dark eyes and hair, apparently about nineteen years old, with a strange resemblance to his companion.

The youth who is seated on the table appears the "observed of all observers," and discourses fluently in French with the landlord.

"Monsieur has reason," said the host, in his French idiom, "it is not often that one sees so large a vessel off this coast. The sloop has a rich cargo, and I know Monsieur the Captain; he is a timid little bourgeois of Havre, and knows not much of sea affairs. His wife is altogether beautiful; she is aboard with their son Emil and their daughter Celestine. The ship is laden with silks from Lyons, which all the world knows are magnificent."

"And you have not many ships of war cruising in the channel?" the young man asked, carelessly.

"Not at all," replied the host, "we have not seen a single sail since the splendid vessel 'Le Roi Fainéant' was wrecked on the accursed rocks out yonder."

"How long is that ago?"

"A few months after the English frigate chased the pirate they call the 'Red Raven.'"

"A great scoundrel, that fellow, I've heard?"

"Yes, Monsieur, a thorough good-for-nothing; but the women—ah, the women, they have no sense, and he is certainly a gallant man."

"Have you ever seen him?"

"Seen him! Perhaps yes. One dark night the 'Red Raven' was winged, and she put into our quiet little harbour for repairs——"

"And the captain?"

"He is a tall dark youth, not unlike Monsieur, not to imply any bad comparisons."

"I should like to see him."

"Monsieur has reason; he is altogether an extraordinary personage, though, as every one knows, a bad subject. But, as I was saying, he is an immense favourite with the women; my good daughter, Fanchante, was enamoured of him. He is entirely perfect—manners, French; pay, English."

"Does he speak your language well?"

"As well as yourself, sir, and that is saying a great deal, for you speak French like a native."

"Ah! you flatter me; but let us have more bottles, perhaps your guests will do me the honour of drinking with me. Allons, let us have more bottles."

"Monsieur is too generous," replied the host, nevertheless hurrying off to execute the order.

The young Englishman chatted with the company till M. Dodu returned with the wine.

He filled up glasses all round, and the health of the Monsieur Anglais was drunk with great good will.

After a while the little crowd dispersed, and the youth drew his companions aside.

"I'll tell you what I mean to do, Brierly," he said; "I shall stay here till morning: the weather has been threatening some time, and the barque of the Lyons' mercer is safe on its moorings. To-morrow I have it in my head to set out for a cruise to reconnoitre; I know of a famous magazine some miles hence, down the shore, where all sorts of contraband goods are kept by a French smuggler, by name Ferrole—I have done business with that fellow before. As the world goes, he is fair dealing, and we are sadly in want of ammunition and other things, for we did not have much of a haul in the powder and shot way from the 'Hamadryad.' Now, I mean to stay here to-night; to-morrow the gale will burst, the 'Red Raven' will not suffer, she will ride securely at anchor, every mast shipped. At nightfall, if the weather is clear, we will put in with the extra lumber of our vessel, for she is wellnigh over-laden with cargo, and quite unfit for swift sailing. Ferrole is at the old caboose, and has some fine fellows in his crew, and I think of borrowing from him a man who is the best pilot in the channel. We will have a merry night of it, Jack, in his cavern. What say you? You are ready?"

"Aye, aye, cap'en," returned Brierly; "but I ain't got a over amount of faith in these frog-eating Frenchmen. Johnny Crapaud has sleek smiles, but devilish little true-blue in him. I knows a thing or two which I have learnt in my experience of these parsley-broth feeding 'parley-vous,' as is only fit for grinning through a horse-collar: they hates us English, and is always ready to do a sly turn of the wrong sort for a boy that sails under the union-jack. They hates us like pison."

"All vulgar prejudice, Jack," answered the Boy Pirate; "you don't suspect our jolly, good-humoured landlord, for instance?"

"Blow me if I trust him; they're all alike."

"But then his daughter, Fanchante, she is true-blue, I suppose?" said Christopher, with a smile.

"Well, sartain—women is females, and females is women, all over the world," returned the old sailor, sagely; "and with such a pretty figure-head as yourn, cap'en, 'taint at all 'stronary if she mightn't strain a point to get you off the rocks. But don't make her jealous, for mercy's sake, or it'll be all up with us. I saw you looking at the pretty fishing lass just now—it ain't prudent, cap'en, they are so precious wide-awake."

Christopher laughed.

"You are a good fellow, Brierly," he replied; "but you don't quite understand my motive in showing necessary attentions to these girls—but about the little *bourgeois* of Lyons, we must overhaul him in some way."

"Aye, cap'en, but we must first lighten our ship, afore we think of re-freighting," returned the lieutenant; "and we have to get out of this rat-trap, and to see your free-trader. But here comes the girl you were speaking on, and for a Frencher she is a tight little craft, and no mistake. We'd better sheer off, while you exchange signals. Come, Harry," he went on, plucking by the arm the young sailor standing at our hero's side, "let us go on a cruise into some other latitude; cap'en wants us to part company."

The young man smiled, and went off with Jack Brierly.

Fanchante approached: she was a pretty, dark girl, neatly and becomingly dressed in the picturesque costume peculiar to the French peasantry of that district; her air was naive and engaging; she had fine eyes, large, and intelligent; and there was something very fascinating in the general charm and tact of her manner.

Christopher caught her by both hands, and kissed her on either cheek.

She did not resist this gallant salute, but only blushed a little, as she said—

"Monsieur is a stranger: there are more than six months that we have not seen him."

"It seems six years since I had the delight of looking into your eyes, beautiful Fanchante, that outrival in their lustre and eloquence the eyes of all other maidens whom I have met in all my voyages—but I have been here all day, and have not seen you before."

"I have been carrying chaplets to my mother's grave," said the French girl, with a little sigh; "it is the anniversary of her death. And how has Monsieur borne himself this terrible long time; all the maids of Vieuxchalet have been grieving for your return. We all thought you were drowned or killed."

"No, my dear Fanchante, I have escaped every wound but those inflicted by the piercing arrows of your adorable eyes; such wounds are incurable."

"Ah, Monsieur! that depends. Is there no physician who can treat them?"

"But one, charming Fanchante; it is she who gave them. But let us go into the house, your father calls you; and we can there chat at our ease till it is time—too soon time—for me once more to leave you."

A gay scene—the ample public room of the inn, crowded by sailors and peasant girls merrily laughing and prattling.

In the midst of mirth and music—for several songs were sung, and more than one of the company was a good violinist—the hours rolled rapidly past.

There was a dance. Christopher gracefully opened the ball with the pretty Fanchante. She was danced with in turn by Dick Caffyn, the young man whom we have before described as bearing so strong a resemblance to our hero.

Even old Brierly was melted—though by no means friendly disposed—towards the "parley-vous." There was something refreshing and innocent withal, in the exhilaration of the gay-spirited French peasants that the old salt, who was genial and good-humoured, for the time ignored his national antipathies and heartily joined in the fun.

So the evening passed.

The guests parted as merrily as they had met, exchanging all sorts of pleasantries, and humourous, but harmless practical jokes; no one of them was "drunk or disorderly."

Christopher and Fanchante kissed a "good night," and, somewhat flushed with exertion after the long dances and the sports of the evening, the Boy Pirate retired to the room where he was to sleep.

It was a pretty little apartment, exquisitely clean and pleasantly situated; from the window he could see the waves gently lifting and sinking, spanned by a wide pathway of glittering silver, where the moon threw down her flood of argent radiance. It was a lovely night, and the lights from anchored ships far out at sea twinkled like tiny glow-worms; but heavy clouds were slowly piling far away to windward.

The young outlaw seated himself on the snowy coverlid of his little bed, and, folding his arms, fell into a reverie.

The glow at his heart cooled, the smile on his face faded away, and was succeeded by a deep shade of remorseful depression.

It was after the enjoyment of such hours of innocent gaity and pleasure that the evil of his reckless life obtruded itself before the clear sight of conscience in all its deformity. With a half suppressed sigh he rose and drew out a pair of beautifully mounted gleaming revolvers, and laid them by the side of his pillow of quiet. He had thrown off his pea-jacket and unbuckled his sword. He wandered to the little diamond-paned window.

Lost in thought he looked out on the billowy waters; the sheen of the moonlit pathway was dotted by the dark form of a long boat fast making for shore.

Presently the steady stroke of the oars was plainly heard.

Christopher started, a strange presentiment overpowered him.

He rushed back to the bedside—replaced his pistols, threw on his coat, and re-buckled his sword-belt.

He returned to the window: a band of men disembarked, at their head walked three officers, all seemed well accoutred, the moonlight flashed on their side-arms.

The Boy Pirate drew a long breath, his eye flashed and his teeth were close shut; even at the distance he thought he could recognise one of the officers.

It was Harwolf.

A sense of his danger caused him to spring to the door, which he secured as well as he could by its inadequate fastenings, and by placing the table against it.

He then went back to the little casement, the men had rounded the house and had disappeared.

Christopher opened the window, but the outlet was too narrow, and the descent too steep and too high to offer any chance of escape.

What was to be done.

He had no doubt that his apprehensions were well-founded.

The house was very quiet.

The inmates had all retired for the night.

He listened.

There was a breathless silence.

The Boy Pirate craved to end his career upon the burning deck of his own vessel, in a hand-to-hand encounter with the avengers of the law, and he scarce dared to hope for a better fate, for he felt that a violent end must result to his career of lawlessness and crime; but his soul shrunk with instinctive loathing from the felon's doom, the degrading death of a fettered culprit who swings upon the gallows as an edifying warning to fellow criminals.

A loud knocking reverberated through the silent house.

Doors were opened—windows unclosed, faint streams of light flowing from them into the night air.

But as yet there was no other answer to the peremptory summons.

The knocking was redoubled.

Christopher heard the sound of footsteps descending the stairs.

His first impulse was to open the door, to rush down into the lower part of the house and make his exit by some back way.

[THE CONFLICT ON THE RAFT.]

But he was deferred from this expedient by reflecting that there was little doubt that such a measure on his part would have been provided for.

He had no doubt that the house was surrounded.

Presently he heard the voice of the host cursing and protesting at a third and yet more noisy summons, and opening the door softly, and peeping over the ballusters, he spied the worthy Maitre Dodu hurrying down the stairs.

The old man had wrapped a loose dressing gown about his obese person ; he had a light in one hand, a blunderbuss in the other, and his head was topped by a tall and cone-shaped night cap.

The light died away in the dark passages.

Christopher heard the slow unbarring of the door amid the impatient rappings of those without.

There was a rush of heavy feet, and he caught the sound of voices in his own tongue, blaspheming and calling him by name. Amongst the others, there

was no difficulty in recognising the harsh accents of one of his deadliest foes.

It was the voice of Daniel Harwolf.

Whither should he fly—where hide himself? Separated from his followers, what would his single strength avail against the combined force of numbers?

But as is the case with all brave men, his spirits rose with the occasion. Eagerly he searched the room to find some other mode of egress than the door.

His search was futile.

He could hear them rushing about below.

Some were even mounting the stairs.

He again looked over the ballusters—he felt himself all but lost.

With stern pleasure he gripped his revolvers.

Now they would stand him in good stead.

If he must perish, at least he could fall among half a hecatomb of his enemies.

While he was hesitating Fanchante rushed into
the room.

She was half undressed. Her dark hair flowed
luxuriantly on her finely-moulded shoulders; her
fine eyes shone with terror and excitement.

She flew to his side.

She spoke in a hurried whisper.

"Ah! mon Dieu!" she cried, "it is Monsieur
that they are seeking. Do not disguise the truth.
You have done something dreadful, and they hunt
you for your blood. I will not betray you; I will
save you! But how? that is —— Saint Vierge!
they are coming!"

With difficulty she repressed a shriek.

"Monsieur, there is but one way. Follow me;
follow me. The père abbé—the priest of the little
village of St. Omer—is in the next room. All the
thunder in Heaven would not wake him. Perhaps
I can steal his clothes. You must take orders and
become canonical. Come—come."

She led him along the little passage on either side
of which were the numbered doors of various sleeping apartments.

She bade him pause.

She softly opened the door of one of the rooms
and peeped in.

The musical cadences of a deep-toned snore thrill
forth.

The abbé had not been as yet awakened by the
fracas in the house.

She glided in.

Presently she emerged with a bundle of clothes
under her arm.

She hurried the Boy Pirate along into an empty
room at the end of the passage.

Here she threw down her plunder.

She had not spared the unfortunate ecclesiastic.
His robe, his band, his hat, even his nether garments,
were there.

Even in her terror and excitement the lively
French girl blushed and laughed almost gaily. However, she repressed her merriment, and, with a nod
to the young adventurer, hurried from the room.

She waited outside the door while Christopher
effected his "translation."

Presently he came forth arrayed in a long black
gown, white band, curly-brim hat, buckled shoes,
and sable unmentionables.

Fanchante snatched up the sailor's clothes that our
hero had rejected and, flinging them into the abbé's
room, closed the door upon the worthy and somno-
lent pillar of the church.

They rushed down stairs.

They were stopped midway by a party of rough-
looking fellows, armed with cutlasses and firearms.

"Hillo! Avast there! Stop, my pretty wench!
Who's this you've got here in such loose tackle?
Stop the parson swab, Tom. Give him a soother
with your marlinspike if he won't stand;" roared
one of the sailors to another.

"Ah! mon Dieu! English scélérats; you sall no
touch le bon prêtre. Do you not respect a priest?
Ah! ciel! you sall no touch him," screamed Fanchante, in her shrillest soprano, while she shielded
the young "clergyman" with extended arms.

"My eyes and limbs! Ain't she just a screecher?"
cried one of the tars, with a rough laugh.

"Rather a queer time for confessing, eh, Jack!"
said another, with a leer.

"Let the lubber bide, will ye," cried another, "if
you don't want to be keel-hauled. Women and
priests! You might as well meddle with lawyers or
devils. Let the young paternoster bide, I tell you;
while you're overhauling the reverend gentleman,
the infernal Red Raven will take wing out of some
hole or cranny in this cussed old rackety pigeon-
house. Come along, ye swabs; hell take the hind-
most."

Up stairs they tumbled, and were presently
battering at the door of the room where the real
abbé was crouching in deadly terror at the unusual
clamour that disturbed the quietude of the peaceful
auberge.

It need not be told that Fanchante and the Boy
Pirate darted down the stairs, and quickly passed
out of the house. A little crowd of the peasantry
had assembled, and stared on in silent wonder.

The girl and her companion were not noticed in
the crowd.

In the meanwhile, with bitter oaths the sailors
were assaulting the thin barrier that parted them
from the wretched ecclesiastic. Even his somnolency
had not been proof against the frightful uproar. He
had started from his bed. Trembling with horror and
amazement, he had examined the room for a mode
of egress, but all in vain. He opened the door: the
fierce faces of the English seamen, eager and scowling, appeared through the gloom; lighted by the
flickering glare of their lanterns, pistol barrels shone
coldly, cutlasses flashed threateningly. He could
see no more; the good father clapped to the door,
fixed the bolts, and, dropping on his knees, invoked
all the saints in the Roman calendar for mercy and
protection.

The cold draught began "to feelingly persuade
him what he was;" his aboriginal condition occurred to him. Greatly shocked at the idea of being
caught in a state of semi-nudity, with shaking hands
he proceeded to strike a light: after several unsuccessful efforts he managed to illumine a little
lamp; he looked round him in search of his canonicals and et ceteras—the feeble gleam burnished the
brass buttons of a naval uniform that lay scattered on
the floor.

But where were his ecclesiastical robe and the rest
of his habiliments?

Echo would have answered where? had she not
been too busy in recrimination with the rough cries
and bitter oaths of the beleaguers. Driven at length
to desperation, he seized the unmentionables and
thrusting his legs into them, he glanced upon the
wreck he had made with rueful gaze; they were
much too short for him.

By a providential freak of fashion sailors wear
proverbially loose brogues, but even this advantage
was scarcely sufficient to compensate for the utter
disproportion betwixt his lower members and the
"lendings" that were to encase them. Several dire
rents and splittings, a general strain and wrinkle, had
rendered the appearance of the wearer most painful
to himself and diverting to the spectator.

He tried to put on the pea-jacket; he might as
well have hoped to float leviathan in a water-butt.
He threw the garment with graceful negligence
over his sturdy shoulders and flew once more to the
door.

It was burst open.

The worthy abbé was struck backwards, and
rolled, groaning, into a corner.

"Hurrah!" shouted the first sailor, who rushed
in, brandishing his cutlass. "There he lies. Come,
mates, who's the first man to clip the wings of the
'Red Raven'?"

The abbé turned over, and slowly raised himself
on his knees.

"Ah, Messieurs Anglais! if it you please, have
pity—I have not speak verra much English—but I
again imp ore—Ah, misericorde!—one poor priest—
I will give absolution to all the world."

"Do you call that the great Boy Pirate," roared
one of the salts, indignantly.

"Well, he be great enough, anyhow, mate," rejoined another.

"I reckon his must be a ship of heavy burthen
when he's aboard," cried another.

"Ah, Messieurs! I am not nobody vat you may
t'nk. My name is Père Matthew, and I not do bad
to anybody—but you see, Messieurs—Ah, quelle
horreur!—my pantaloons—my culottes. I beg you
tousand excuse. Some voleur, some tief, some
forçat, has stolen my—vat you call—my everyting."

"His ducks," supplemented one of the tars.

"Shiver me, mates," exclaimed another, "but
I'm thinking we're all in a fog; and the cunning
pirate devil has bilked us after all. Don't ye see it;
he has stolen this gentleman's toggery, and he was the

lubberly parson chap we met on the stairs; we might as well reef sails at once, and cast the sheet anchor, for we shan't take our prize-money on this cruise, my hearties."

Harwolf rushed into the room.

"Ye blind fools and dastards," he shouted, giving way to his characteristic furiousness, "do you see what you have done? The felon has escaped—he passed through the midst of you. All hands to the chase—don't stand gaping here. Ha! sir, you there —what insubordination do you call this? laughing to my very teeth. Is this good gentleman the object of your insolent tomfoolery?"

"Monsieur le Capitaine, I look to you for the protection. These are your men, they will attend to vat you shall say," cried the poor priest, in piteous accents. "Look vat is arrived to me: I wear somebody's clothes. I sleep altogether quietly, and these gamins vill kill me—they vill kill me for never and never no more, if you do not save me; but Monsieur is too generous to let me expire for these canaille."

"Calm yourself, reverend sir," replied Harwolf, in French, "this is a stupid mistake; we come hither in pursuit of the greatest villain on earth; he has eluded us, but we shall catch him yet. My men," he went on, addressing his crew, "the place is surrounded, the wretch cannot finally escape; be vigilant, and don't spare exertion for the capture of the thief, and I will see that you are well rewarded."

The men answered promptly, several being greatly chagrined by the miscarriage of the assault.

They left the room, and took no heed of the unspeakable misery of the fat abbé, who was still lamenting the loss of his "properties."

CHAPTER XVIII.

THE PURSUIT.

IN the meantime, conducted by Fanchante, the Boy Pirate had escaped to the sea shore.

They wandered along for some distance, at times pausing to listen.

Christopher smiled, as the poor girl would ever and anon pause and utter some muttered expression of anxiety and excitement.

At length they reached a wild and lonely spot, distant a mile from the inn.

Here the French girl stood still for a moment.

"What can we do?" she said, "you will be lost if you stay here; you can go nowhere without a passport, and a description of you will be forwarded to every office of government. Ha! good—I know what can be done: my cousin Gustave is the captain of a little ship that trades in the channel; I will get you on board—he will do anything for me—and thus you may escape. Let Monsieur trust to me."

"Dear Fanchante," replied the Boy Pirate, "how can I ever repay your tender devotion. I cannot quit these shores without my companions; I will not leave them in danger. Besides, I have business to do that must be done before I leave France. Is there nowhere I can hide."

"Monsieur is too reasonable to run into needless danger. His comrades shall be cared for: I think they have escaped. At all events, Monsieur can render them no service by returning to Vieuxchalet. If my cousin Gustave is honoured by the presence of Monsieur on board his ship they can pick up the friends now absent and put off to sea."

"Come, then; let it be so; but where is the ship of your cousin, dear Fanchante?"

"In the little creek behind that hill," replied the girl. "The clouds are drifting over the moor, and the wind is rising."

"You are right, Fanchante," returned the Boy Pirate, looking across the turgid and swelling waters; "we shall have a stiff gale to night."

"Ah! but this is terrible," said the girl. "What have you done, Monsieur, that you should be pursued in this fashion?"

"I have been hunted down till nothing was left me but to turn at bay," returned Christopher, bitterly; "but having used my teeth as well as shown them there is no forgiveness."

"Ah, ciel! they are upon us, Monsieur," suddenly screamed the girl. "Fly here, between the rocks, I will keep the way. I am a woman; they will not kill me, and if they do, ça ne fait rien, it is no matter, fly."

Christopher turned quickly, and drew the girl towards him. He was touched by her devotion, and embraced her warmly. Beneath the loose robe he was wearing was his sword belt, the cutlass, and pistols.

Four fierce-looking sailors, shouting and cursing, appeared leaping from rock to rock, and fast approaching them.

In a moment they were round him.

He levelled his revolver with steady aim at the first who came within range.

"Knock him down, blow his brains out—the infernal shark," cried the fellows severally.

Christopher stood firmly opposing them, his eye beaming with calm intrepidity, his lips locked in a smile of placid fortitude.

A shot was fired at him.

The bullet struck off his hat.

Another man blazed away at him; there was a sort of cheer from the assailants as the effect of the shot was seen.

The bullet grazed the temples of the bold young outlaw, and a little red trickled down his cheek.

Fanchante gave a scream, for Christopher staggered a little under the force of the blow.

She thought he was killed.

As he slipped backward against a rock, she wrenched the pistol from his hand and fired at the man who had aimed at him; the bullet struck the man in the shoulder and knocked him over. When the girl saw the seaman drop heavily, she shrieked and fainted. The fire of passion flashed in the eyes of the Boy Pirate as he lifted her on his strong arm.

Whirling round his cutlass he flew suddenly upon the first man, and hewed him to the ground.

Another shot was fired at him, but it flew wide of its mark.

The young pirate then struck fiercely yet skilfully at the others.

They fought manfully.

But the Boy Pirate was younger than either of them, and more agile; his courage was indomitable, his coolness imperturbable.

One man was wounded in the sword arm, and put quite *hors de combat*; but one opponent remained: the Boy Pirate surveyed him with a look of contempt, and waved him away with his blood-stained weapon; but the fellow was not inclined to relinquish the fray so readily; he flew upon Christopher, prepared to take him or die.

The Boy Pirate, cumbered as he was by the fainted girl, fought desperately, and the result of the contest was doubtful.

The man was a good swordsman, and dealt furious blows with his weapon.

Christopher had several narrow escapes.

At length he found it needful to content himself by simply acting on the defensive till an occasion might offer for a bolder display of his prowess.

With much science he parried the blows the other rained upon him, husbanding his strength.

The fellow's arms began to weary; he soon perceived that his only chance was to force the fighting. This he did gallantly.

At length the moment came.

Christopher feigned a stroke at the shoulder of his antagonist.

The man raised his sword to parry the blow.

The Boy Pirate, by a dexterous turn of the wrist, cleared the way for a down-right blow.

It fell full on the fellow's head.

His stout, leather hat and his thick hair were cut through. The blood flowed freely.

The sword fell from his relaxing grasp; the man

stumbled forward, sunk on his knees, and then fell prone on his face.

Christopher flung Fanchante on his strong shoulders, and dashed away towards the cliff.

He had not advanced far when he heard the loud shouts of a strong party behind him.

Turning, he beheld the whole crew—Harwolf and the officers at their head, in hot pursuit.

He sprang up the cliff.

It was precipitous, almost perpendicular, but Christopher was nimble as a mountain goat.

Seizing the ragged points of projecting rocks and protruding tendrils of creeping plants, he bravely struggled forward and upwards. He had nearly reached the summit, when a fierce shout arose from below; bullets scudded past his head and sunk deep into the chalk. He turned his head; several of the most daring of his pursuers were climbing after him. He coolly drew a revolver and fired down upon them : the foremost man fell backwards, oversetting his followers. Christopher sprang to the top of the cliff; the beach lay far below; the roar of the sea sounded like a hoarse murmur. The Boy Pirate paused not to look at his partner but flew along as if his feet were feathered by the wings of Mercury.

CHAPTER XIX.

SILAS RYE VISITS LADY EDGEFORTH.

SILAS RYE was slowly walking through one of the eastern suburbs of London. He was lost in thought, and moved on unconscious of the passing crowd.

At length he reached the utmost bounds of the monster city, and came to a neat stuccoed cottage that stood back from the road. Before it was a trim little garden, with bright green palings, and a miniature grotto, with a plaything fountain in the centre plat. The pure, white blinds were closely drawn, and the sunlight glowed on the white walls and flashed from the bright brass knocker and bell-handles.

Silas threw open the little gate, and, walking up the prim and narrow gravelled path, knocked at the door.

It was opened by a stout, respectable-looking woman, who smirked and curtsied upon recognising her visitor.

"Dear me, Mr. Rye," she began, "why, sure to goodness it is months since I had the pleasure of seeing you. Come in, sir; pray come in. And is business prosperous? And your health? I do say, sir, that health is the greatest of all blessings."

"Thank you, Mrs. Wilton; I am well enough. And it is indeed a long time since I paid you a visit," returned Silas, following his conductress into a neat and pretty little front parlour, adorned with well-chosen pictures, flowers, and several birdcages. "But how is the patient?"

"Well, sir, sometimes better—sometimes worse. At times she will talk most awful. I couldn't tell you what she says; and when her better moments come, she is so woful—so pitifully woful—that we're almost glad to see her back in the old fits again."

"Ha! So she talks in her fits, does she, Mrs. Wilton. Well, well; you know people in such circumstances say all sorts of wild things. But is she well in health? Does the doctor think she will ever recover her reason?"

"You see, sir, this is what it is," replied the woman. "When she is better—that is, when she is conscious like—she seems to have something on her mind so dreadful that the thought of it drives her back, and she is worse than ever."

"I should like to see her."

"Lor, sir! but the poor lady is in one of her worst fits. Hadn't you better defer your interview till she is more sensible?"

"No," said Silas; "I will see her at once, if you please."

"Well, sir, in course I have no objection at all; only I thought it best to mention that she is quite astray, poor dear, just at present, and even a few hours may bring a change."

With these words Mrs. Wilton led the way up the stairs, and opening the door, ushered Silas Rye in a tolerably large room, light and cheerful, and very neatly furnished; there was a piano; books and needlework were scattered about. Upon a low couch was seated the inmate of the chamber, her eyes fixed abstractedly on the prospect without the window, her hands playing listlessly with the leaves of a book that lay upon her lap.

It was Lady Edgeforth.

The woman left the room.

There was something ineffably sad in the brain-sick-hopeless insanity of her terrible affliction.

She was singing.

A pretty little spaniel was crouching at her feet; he rose and barked sharply as Silas entered, but the lady rebuked him languidly and with a low growl he replaced himself at her feet.

She went on with her singing.

Silas softly approached her.

The lady took the little dog into her arms and looked at her visitor with a startled air.

"Lady Edgeforth," said Silas Rye, in a hoarse, low voice, "are you better? Are you happy?"

"Happy!" cried the poor lady, and she laughed long and strangely, but the music of her laughter was "like sweet bells jingled harsh and out of tune." "We are very happy, Lionel, are we not?" she said, caressing the little spaniel. "We have all we want, poor creatures that we are. We have the sunlight, and the free air, and rich company—angels very often, and he comes at times. But, do you know, doctor, I cannot bear to look on him, he is so deadly pale; he must be ill—he must be very ill. What o'clock is it?"

Silas did not reply to this sudden question, but shaded his eyes with his hands and turned very white.

"I know what time it was," she went on "time has stood still since then—they stop the clocks when people die, as if time would stand still for every wretched mortal that breathes away his life on the chance wind. How many hours are there in a day? That is not hard to reckon, though some days are months. But how many days are there in a life? That depends—all the flowers come in spring, but they do not all live through the summer; some wither with frosts, some are poisoned by adders. Did you know Andrew Harwolf?"

Silas started and shuddered.

"I did!" the poor lady continued. "He is the fiend—the fiend; but the angels tell me sweet, comforting things: he shall be bound, and my bird shall fly free. He did not kill my child. But who are you?"

"One, madam, who pities your great grief, and will risk his life to bring you peace."

"Peace!" said the lady, musingly, "Peace—I wonder what it is!"

"God send you may soon know and enjoy it," replied Silas Rye, much affected.

"Perhaps you mean well; there are many counterfeits, but there are some true. He looks very pale; there is blood on his forehead; he does not embrace me—he does not even speak to me when he comes, but he was true. You are quite sure that you are not the servant of a noble and confiding master; let me look at your hands."

She took the hand of Silas Rye and gazed on it a moment with strange scrutiny.

"There are always red spots floating before my eyes; perhaps it is the strong light; it is a strange question, doctor, but do you believe in God?"

"It is a fearful question, lady, yet it admits of but one answer—there is an Eternal Being who marks our lightest words and actions."

"As we sow, so shall we reap!" she interrupted. "You see how well I remember; but when I think of Andrew Harwolf, I almost pity him; his punishment will be so terrible, so very terrible. Is he dead yet?"

Silas did not reply.

The poor lady looked at him expectantly, as if awaiting his answer; presently she turned her head with a vacant stare, as though she had quite forgotten the question. Again she sang; presently she paused, and said, abruptly—

"I remember the name of the place; there is the long avenue of pine trees, and there, the painted window of the grand hall. Some folks think I am mad; are they not foolish?"

She arose and approached the piano; she opened it and deftly ran up the scale, sounded some of the higher notes, tuned her voice to them, and burst into a rich and plaintive melody, accompanying herself with exquisite taste and perfect accuracy as she did so.

At length she paused suddenly, leaned her head on the piano, and wept quietly.

Silas Rye drew near her cautiously, and laid his hand on her arm.

"Lady Edgeforth," he began, softly.

"Why do you call me so?" returned the lady, with petulance; "that is not now my name; in Heaven there is a new language, there are new titles; do not let me forget that I died with him. I would that my child had died too," she went on, with a heavy sigh, "for then he would have been with us."

Silas drew from his pocket a little portrait which he placed in her hands. She did not look at it, but held it in her hand listlessly, and looked about her with an air of restlessness and weariness.

"Do you know, doctor," she said, "that I am getting tired of this place, it is so dull and dungeon-like. I pant for the open country, I long to gather fresh flowers—to see if the turf on the graves of the beloved is verdant, and the trees that weep over them leaf-mantled. I am better than I was; have I been long ill? Yes, I know it has been a long and weary time with me; but I was not mad. No! no!—I remember it well."

She sat for some time in a vacant reverie, and at last her eyes wandered to the little portrait: she raised it and started; she looked at it long and eagerly, violently trembling. At last she sank down upon the floor, and burst into a passion of weeping.

She raised her head.

Silas Rye was watching her silently.

"My babe! my child! what have they done with him? I remember it all—all. My husband is murdered, and the child is gone. Oh! pity me, tell me where is my boy, and I will forgive you all the rest. Pity me! pity me! I am going mad."

The poor lady fell into convulsions.

Mrs. Wilton rushed into the room.

Silas Rye quietly picked up the little portrait.

The woman signed for him to leave the room; the adventurer gave one glance of deep commiseration at the unfortunate lady, and stole from the chamber.

He sat moodily in a chair in the parlour, when the landlady entered.

"You see, sir, how violent the poor thing seems; but she will be better after this. She is sobbing like a child; it would break a heart of millstone to see her as she is now, lying so meek and patient like in her little bed—her poor hands folded and her lips murmuring. I never did ask any questions, sir, and you have always behaved extremely liberal—but who ever it was that wrecked this poor lady's mind must have been a very black villain, and I would not have his load on my conscience for all the money in the Bank of England."

"No, nor I," returned Silas, huskily. "But Mrs. Wilton, you will, I know, take care of the poor thing—there is one thing I must warn you of."

"Indeed, sir!"

"Yes, it is not impossible that the base and wicked wretch who has been the cause of the poor lady's terrible sufferings will try to get her into his power. He is very cunning, knows the law, and can easily back his assumptions by a show of authority. You will not give her up?"

"Not if he burns the house down!" cried Mrs. Wilton, with vehemence.

"That is well; but you are no match for him. Will you be guided by me?"

"In course, sir; you have always acted the gentleman, and you are my rightful employer."

"Well, then, in dealing with such a customer, we can't afford to be too scrupulous as to the means we use to deceive him. If he should come——"

"He had better not," cried the woman, briskly. "I warrant he will rue the day, the scoundrel!"

"Oh, these women, they mar everything!" cried Silas. "Why you are going the right way to put the poor lady in this enemy's hands, and you will, no doubt, have her death to answer for. I tell you this man is not only as cruel as a hyæna, but he is cunning as a fox. I thought you had more tact and cleverness; can't you fight him with his own weapons? If at any time he should come—as, may be, he soon will—for though I have done all that can be done for concealment, a thousand chances may bring him the information he would give half his wealth to procure—if he comes you must act as I direct you."

"Very well, sir; I shall be very happy to do my part, and he must be deep indeed if he gets over me."

"Mark me, then; his name is Andrew Harwolf."

"Sure enough, the lady has mentioned him a thousand times in her ravings; and if it be not all madness, he is not only the wretch who persecutes the poor dear creature, but is guilty of mur——"

"Hush!" cried Silas, starting, "that is all idle raving, indeed; yet he is villain enough for anything; but please do not interrupt me. Should he come, affect a pleasure at meeting him; tell him that I am dead,—killed in an accident on the Brighton line; he thinks that is the fact. I have so far deceived him. I am obliged to trust you very deeply, Mrs. Wilton. Say that a month before the accident I took away the lady one night, and that you know whither. Affect great indignation against me for having removed your boarder so abruptly, and show him some trifling articles left by the lady—a scarf, some books, or aught you please. Mislead him if you can, and when he departs send me word immediately."

"I understand you perfectly, sir," replied Mrs. Wilton, approvingly; "it is an excellent plan, and leave me alone to throw dust in his eyes, the villain—you shall see how I'll tweedle him round my little finger. But hark! my lady is stirring; I will return soon."

"No, I will be off at once, thank you, Mrs. Wilton," returned Silas Rye; "but take this, it is a trifle I think I owe you, and a little bonus for your great care and kindness to the patient."

"Really, sir," replied Mrs. Wilton, with a curtsey, "you are very good; but pray let me bring you some refresh——"

"Thank ye, no—I cannot stay," replied Silas, moving to the door. "Pray remember my caution."

"Do not fear, sir; good bye—I will let you know if anything new transpires—good evening."

Silas walked out into the road.

It was late in the summer afternoon; there were fields before the house, and it stood in the midst of its little garden, for it was detached; he could hear the mowers whetting their scythes. Instinctively, he turned to take a last look at the cottage where he had left the unhappy lady.

She was at the window, her lovely face turned upwards to the calm, blue sky, over which the little fairy gold clouds were sailing afar.

There was a pathos of sorrow and despairing self-abandonment in her eloquent features that was ineffably touching.

Silas stood in the road.

The poor lady saw him and faintly smiled, and waved her lace handkerchief to him in token of farewell.

Silas Rye sprang away, and did not abate his pace till he had entered a dark and winding lane.

Here he paused.

His cheek was flushed; beads of sweat stood on his clammy forehead.

He grasped his stick, and struck it fiercely on the ground.

"Damn him! Villain, pitiless and godless. I will—though I swing from the same drop—I will track him to the death; and I will wash these hands—infected though not stained—clear in his blood!"

CHAPTER XX.

THE FIGHT IN THE MAIN-TOP.

CHRISTOPHER is pacing the deck of a smart-looking little craft, with Gustave Devigne, the cousin of Fanchante.

The fair deliverer of our hero had not entered into particulars as to the offences which had provoked the hostility of the government and had brought the officers of the law upon the track of her admirer; but merely stated that Monsieur was in danger, that he had committed himself by some political indiscretion, and that she relied upon her cousin's good-heartedness to defend, or, at least to conceal, a fellow sailor.

Gustave, with native kindness, undertook to do his best for the friend of his sweetheart's father, and was much impressed by the frank and *débonnaire* bearing of the Boy Pirate.

They were now on board the smart little vessel, which was called the "Heloise;" it was a small trading ship, well appointed and well manned.

"Monsieur, perhaps, is suspected of some connection with a conspiracy," said the Frenchman, with natural curiosity. "The eyes of the police are very vigilant; I was myself among the proscribed after the revolution in '48; I narrowly escaped being sent to Cayenne.

"The nature of my crime is this," returned Christopher, rather sternly. "I was goaded by the oppression of one set of persecutors, and forced by the power of another into whose hands I had fallen, into a position that I have filled with some *éclat*, and one from which they will give me no chance of escaping. But yours is a pretty barque; your men seem able and well disposed; have you been long a sailor?"

"Monsieur, my father and my brothers are all seafaring people; but, sometimes, I get tired of this life; this vessel is not my own, and the merchant who owns her is a harsh and exacting man, and I am weary of his service."

The Boy Pirate was about to reply when a man came up and announced the fact that a large ship was bearing down upon them.

The captain and the young pirate hurried to the bulwarks; they perceived that a large frigate in full sail was majestically forging through the waves, every moment lessening the distance between them.

Gustave looked at our hero with a blank face.

Christopher smiled calmly.

"What does Monsieur think?" said the French captain, "is there no way for him to escape? They are in chase, and it is no use for us to shift our anchorage. Suppose Monsieur took the boat; we are not far from shore."

"It would be useless, my kind friend, to try to escape in that way; their boats are already out and they are signalling for us to lay to."

He was right. Several boats, well manned, appeared rowing towards the "Heloise."

Christopher seized the glass. He could plainly discern the savage and exultant features of the inveterate Harwolf.

Besides this worthy there were several French officials, whose mission was to legalise the arrest of an English subject on a French ship.

"Would you be recognised among the crew?" asked Gustave, anxiously.

"I fear so," returned the Boy Pirate. "My head is bound from the wound I have received; and though you have kindly dressed me in this fashion, my face is too well known to my enemy for me to hope to escape detection."

"At all events, we will make an effort," replied Gustave.

"But I know the marine laws of France are very severe, and you will seriously compromise yourself."

"I do not care for that," returned the young Frenchman, generously. "I will save you if I can."

"You shall make no sacrifice for me. These weapons are my own, and I will use them to effect; for I will never be taken alive."

"You shall not be taken at all," returned Gustave, greatly excited, as the boats lifted steadily through the surf, and the oar-blades flashed in the morning sun, which was struggling among wild and threatening clouds.

"Go below, Monsieur; they are almost alongside."

"Perish the thought!" cried the Boy Pirate, manfully. "You shall not sacrifice yourself for me. If I cannot escape, at least I can brave my fate."

With this the heroic boy leaped upon the quarter deck, and tossed up his cap with a derisive laugh at his frantic pursuers.

They gave a grim cheer of anticipated vengeance, and dashed roughly under the lee-quarter.

In a few seconds, Harwolf, a French official, and other officers were on deck. Behind them were a party of sturdy men, armed with pikes and cutlasses.

Gustave stepped forward.

The Boy Pirate leaned carelessly against the mainmast.

The French police official advanced.

He held a document in his hands.

"Captain Devigne," he begun, "we have come aboard your vessel, by the authority of the law, to arrest a convicted pirate, known as the Red Raven. Of course you will not shelter the atrocious ruffian for one moment now that his true character is known to you. I hope, for your own sake, you have not attempted to conceal him."

"I am here," cried the Boy Pirate, stepping boldly forward; "look on me; I am the man you think to hunt down; take care for yourselves, since you have brought me to bay. My soul shall not leave my body without company; you may kill me, but to take me is more than the best of you can do."

With this he levelled his revolvers at the French official and at Harwolf.

But several of the sailors had levelled their guns.

The Boy Pirate saw the imminence of his peril.

Like a squirrel he flew up the mainmast, swinging from rope to rope with wondrous agility.

He reached the main-top.

Several shots were fired at him. The bullets lodged in the rigging; but he made good his foothold on the main-top, and waved his cutlass derisively.

"By the fiends! I will bring the cursed Raven down from his perch!" cried Harwolf, in an agony of rage. "The villain seems backed by the devil, his master, to fool us all."

Harwolf seized a rope, and, with great fury but some clumsiness, managed to reach the Boy Pirate.

Terrible and exciting was their struggle at that giddy height. Both were armed with cutlasses, and they first exchanged a few thrusts; but, with the scorn of his native magnanimity, the Boy Pirate suffered his antagonist to make good his footing on the yards.

The men below watched the thrilling contest with great excitement.

They dared not fire, for fear of endangering the life of Harwolf.

When the vicious and ill-conditioned ingrate who thirsted so eagerly for the blood of one from whom he had experienced such generous forebearance had righted himself to some extent on his precarious footing, he flew upon the Boy Pirate, his eyes flaming with malice. Christopher coolly sheathed his cutlass; and, suddenly catching the miscreant by the throat, pitched him down.

Down, down he rolled, gasping, and clutching at the mast.

There was a cry from the deck below!

The rigging, however, broke his fall. Bruised and senseless he reached the deck.

Then there was the crackle of musketry.

But Christopher was too high, and the mark too difficult, for any harm to result from the volley.

With a shout of defiance, the intrepid Boy Pirate ran along the yard-arm, and, as the ship lurched, from his dizzy height he leaped into the sea!

The boats were manned. All on board was rage and confusion; but the morning was wild and gloomy—the sun hidden by clouds—the billows were racing landward frothy and malignant.

Christopher could not be found. Once more he had foiled his bitter foes!—once more the Red Raven was free!

CHAPTER XXI.

THE EXAMINATION OF THE GIPSY.

WE are once again at Frontemore Hall. Andrew Harwolf is seated at his table in a large library, a young man, who acted as his secretary, writing by his side. The husband of the reputed Lady Edgeforth was lord of the manor and county magistrate.

A little crowd of villagers and the rural police stood before the table. They had in charge Esau, the gipsy, who, it will be remembered had been stunned by Silas Rye, and left insensible, on the occasion of his attempt, with Black Oiny, to rob young Edward Meredith, the brother of Lilia, the rover's bride.

The gallant young officer had just given his evidence, which was corroborated by the further account given by old Squire Meredith and one or two of the gentlemen who were present immediately after the acts on the occasion in question.

The gipsy listened to the bitter censures of the magistrate with sullen obduracy, and Harwolf was about to commit him to gaol, when, as a matter of form, he asked the fellow if he had any defence to make.

"No, your honour, said the gipsy, coolly, "only there is a little matter I has to communicate to yourself alone which is pretty likely to alter your decision."

"Well, sir, let us have it at once," said the magistrate, turning to the assembly, with a shrug and a deprecatory smile. "There is nothing that you can have to say that may not be spoken openly. What is it, my man?"

"It concerns the Lady Edgeforth," returned the gipsy quietly, lifting a sly glance at his judge to note the effect of this speech.

Andrew Harwolf's face, which had before worn an expression of truculent authority, suddenly changed to a livid hue, as he replied—

"Of Lady Edgeforth, eh, you insolent dog! Do you mean my wife?"

"No, I don't mean your wife," returned the fellow, doggedly. "I means what I says: I have got something to tell you about Lady Edgeforth."

With a miserable attempt at a smile, the magistrate waved his hand with affected carelessness.

"Well, well, I suppose it is formal to hear what the rogue has to say. Squire Meredith, I congratulate you on your son's most fortunate escape, may I hope that you will honour me by staying to dinner. I will detain this fellow for awhile and listen to his communication. I hope you will not refuse to stay."

"I am extremely sorry to be obliged to deny myself the pleasure of accepting your kind invitation, Mr. Harwolf," returned the old squire, "but I am forced to do so; my son's stay at Frontemore will soon terminate, and to-night we have a tenants' dinner at home. If you could honour our little reunion with your presence we should be heartily glad to see you."

With many courteous expressions Andrew Harwolf declined the invitation, and shaking hands with the old man and his son ordered the room to be cleared.

The villagers gaped at each other in Bœotian wonder at this mandate; one of the rural constables ventured to protest against the danger incidental to such a measure, and cautioned the magistrate to beware of trusting himself alone with such a desperate ruffian.

Considering that the fellow was handcuffed, and that his face was remarkable for an expression of currish cowardice, the caution was somewhat superfluous.

However, it was "with many a lingering look behind" that the rustics slouched and lumbered from the room.

The secretary seemed inclined to thinking, perhaps, there were some depositions to be taken, but Andrew Harwolf waved him away impatiently.

When the young man had left the room the squire turned his guilt-stricken face towards the gipsy, and, controlling himself as well as he could, he said sternly—

"Well, sir, you have some communication to make with respect to Lady Edgeforth—my wife. What can you have to tell that can have anything in common with her ladyship's affairs."

"I told you once," said the man, roughly, "as I don't know nothing about your wife nor her pretensions. I have got something to tell you, if you like to make a bargain with me for my being let off and bagging a quid or two, information as has allusion to the real Lady Edgeforth."

"For God's sake, fellow," cried Harwolf, starting up in great alarm, " keep your lying tongue between your teeth, don't speak so loud—these fools——"

"It ain't no mortal consarn to me," cried the gipsy, raising his voice in defiance of this request. "I don't care a cussed straw who's the rightful Lady Edgeforth, and who may be a-acting of her part. Moll's as good as my lady in the dark, only all I says is that I never attackted no gentle'm, but only came up to help him and got floored for my pains."

There was something terrible in the fiendish flash that sparkled in the eyes of Andrew Harwolf as he flung himself upon the gipsy, and clutched him by the throat.

"So you heard me, hell-hound," he hissed through his teeth. "Do you think I am to be bayed at by a starved jackal—eh! eh! By the skies above us, I have a mind to strangle you, and swear you assaulted me. Still your gibbing tongue, will you, baboon!"

He emphasised every sentence by a vice-like grip at the throat of the struggling gipsy.

There was something of demoniac sublimity in the ease with which the greater villain trampled upon the less. Andrew Harwolf flung the meaner rogue from him with infinite contempt.

It was strange—while the gipsy, who had stumbled to his knees on the carpet, was recovering himself, Andrew Harwolf found time to soliloquise—

"No, no," he murmured, folding his arms, and pressing them closely against his panting breast, "though he his dead, though my confederate is a battered corpse to the devil's honour, evidence springs up like rank weeds in foul places. Circumstantial evidence—it has hanged many a man, but it shall not hang me. I will burn out wounds I cannot heal; I will spare no one, and it is a virtue to kill this wild beast."

He turned suddenly on the gipsy.

"Look ye, friend, when a servant, however high his degree, marries his master's wife, and enjoys his master's honours, envy and scandal will be busy with his name—so I don't want your lying tale told. Though none would credit it, many might abuse it to my disadvantage. You see your power. Now for mine. I know you, do you comprehend? There are charges I can substantiate against you, charges that will bring you to the gallows—you may well look pale, for you know that I speak truth—but I do not wish to threaten you; only understand, I am not to be dictated to. You must go to prison; I will take care that you shall soon be liberated, and I will pay you well if you serve me faithfully. If you serve me false, or seek to do so, you might as well seek to play with the devil. But come, fellow, now I have shown you that I am not to be brow-beaten, let us to business. What do you know of this person whom you call Lady Edgeforth?"

"You think I am goin' to tell you all you wish to know afore you fulfil the compact atwixt us," returned the gipsy, suddenly, "I ain't a-goin' to be no such fool; no, not if you hangs me."

"My friend, I am not unreasonable, I only want to be convinced that you really possess the information you wish to sell, and which must ransom your captivity."

"And when you've got all the information you requires you'll send me across the herring pond. Catch a weasel asleep; I'm fly to that sort of thing. No; what I say is this, just knock off the darbies and dub up the shiners, and you shall know all I knows, and there's a end of all negotiations atwixt us."

"You shall have no cause to complain of me; I am accounted liberal in business, though I am a little exacting. Speak, then, this person whom you call Lady Edgeforth——"

"As went mad and rushed out of the house, and was going for to kill herself if it hadn't been for a friend of mine——"

"Silas Rye!" exclaimed Harwolf, clenching his hands, and listening attentively.

"Well, it might be or it might not be; anyhow, I ain't a-goin' to mention no names; she went to a public with him—in course, he led her like a lamb. I seed it all; I knew as it was her, 'cos vy?—didn't I see her come out the house. My tribe had got a camp on the common, down along the brook, and I was a-roaming about these here plantations to, leastways, admiring of the place, for I'm uncommon fond of buildings and stables, or any sort of natur, when, who should I see rush out of the folding windows on the balcony but her ladyship. I knowed as it were her by the fine clothes and jewels and the rest of it. Down the balcony she comes. She stops—she holds her head. She flies—she rushes clean into the plantation, her silk dress a-fluttering and a-rustling, her long hair a-flying and a-waving, her fingers a-twisting and a-twining, and her lips a-muttering all sorts of rubbige. Hillo! What's up, says I—a row with the old man or a fit of delirious tremblems. 'Cos I know as these gentle folks likes a drop as well as the lower classes, which they can get it when the others can't.

"Go on, you devil!" shouted Harwolf, "this woman rushed into the plantation and——"

"Well, then," said the fellow, "all I've got to say is as somebody caught her just as she was a-going to spring over the Fox Leap, this very Sil—leastways, a party as I knows—caught hold on her just as she reached the brink. Where he took her to, what he did with another little party, and all the rest on it, I ain't a-goin' to tell you till you pays me."

"Your wild story is incredible," said Harwolf, with a ghastly smile; "they say this house is haunted; perhaps you have seen the pale lady."

"Or the pale gentle'm as they say walks," returned the gipsy, looking round in some little terror, for it was a grim and gloomy chamber, the massive shelves cumbered with heavy volumes, the narrow window faced by a frowning wall.

The conscience-stricken wretch turned ashy white.

"What is your name, fellow?" he asked, trying to recover the equilibrium of his tottering dignity. "I must dismiss you now; I shall remand you, but I shall not fail to use my influence on your behalf."

"Thank ye, your honour," returned the gipsy with a sly grin, "but you has already been told my name."

"True," said Andrew Harwolf, taking up the charge sheet from the table. "Esau Cooper; you are a hawker?"

"Yes, your honour, and a honest man, though I am put upon. But I leaves my case in your hands, you're a worthy gentle'm, and advocates the cause of the poor, and won't see me put down by any haristocrat in the country."

The gipsy chuckled.

Harwolf rang the bell.

The constables bustled into the room.

"This man is remanded," said Harwolf, addressing them, "let him be removed."

The gipsy bowed humbly to the magistrate, and was led away by the police.

Harwolf was alone.

He paced up and down the library in an agony of conflicting passion. At last he flung himself into a chair.

"This is ill and this is well," he muttered.; "ill, because it proves upon what slight chances the fatal issues depend; well, because I can now learn what I most wished to know. As for this fool, when I have done with him he must be cleared off—he must die! The hound is not worth a thought. But are there others in the secret?—shall I be outmatched every time?" he whispered, hoarsely. "My peril increases in compound ratio. But I am like a drunkard or a gamester—I must go on. It is the worst curse of guilt that it compels continuance. A man may be virtuous for a generation—may fall suddenly and fall for ever; but he who is once sunk in the quagmire of guilt may struggle his hardest and struggle in vain, for there is no deliverance. For me there could be none; therefore, squeamishness would be idiocy. The worst I can do now is immaculate innocence compared to the deeds of the past. Well, I will live while I may; a few years and I shall have surmounted all obstacles, and shall rest. Daniel is little better than a villain—he cares nothing for me; his base and selfish nature is incapable of love. All the better; all the better. Were he a pure and noble youth, the very sight of him would burn my eyes in their sockets; as his father, I should dread to touch him. O God! O God! what have I won and what have I lost. Oh, for the whips and knotted scourges of the old penitents! Oh, for atonement! I have lost the game. I looked on conscience as an idle fable—I looked upon self-aggrandisement as all in all. Lo! my reward for all my soul-bought possessions—care, miserable uncertainty, a son that has not humanity enough to despise me, but, wrapped in the boorish stolidity of his selfishness, ignores my very existence. Blood! the fiends cry still for blood! When I have removed this hydra's head another will spring forth. The miserable, love-blighted, poverty-frozen wretch can die. At least he can die—and death is rest. But die—hereafter! Oh, horror, horror, horror!"

The guilty wretch flung himself at the table, and buried his face in his hands.

His eternal torments had begun on earth—"the wages of sin is death." A living death was the punishment of his diabolical wickedness.

CHAPTER XXII.

LILIA'S DANGER.

IT is a wild night, the waves heave mountain-high, the night is black as a velvet pall, the wind rages and bellows over the rocking and tortured waters, the sky seems lowering to the ocean's breast. A solitary being clings to a rifted rock that rises from the surging waters.

The roar of the tempest is around him, the foaming breakers dash over him, drenching him to the skin; the wind hisses cuttingly past his ears, and tosses and twists his rich curls savagely—his eyes are strained, his ears intent: he is listening through the storm for the sound of voices or the boom of guns. This drenched and jaded watcher is the Boy Pirate. Wilder than the storm is the turmoil in his heart.

A thousand perils ring their alarm in the hoarse roar of the tempest. Lilia! The anguish is too great; he dare not think of her.

After his escape from the "Heloise," he had with great difficulty reached a long reef of straggling rocks that stretched from the shore, and at low tide were connected with it, but when the waves were swollen, and in stormy weather, were separated at

THE ESCAPE OF BRIERLY AND DICK CAFFYN.

intervals, when the lower links of the stony chain were hidden by the seething breakers.

Even here the Boy Pirate was in fearful peril; at measured intervals the huge mass of a swelling head-wave would dash against and over him, leaving him half suffocated, bruised and stunned against the rock to which he was clinging. There was not only a furious gale, but a fearful thunderstorm; the vivid lightning flashed, leaped along, or quivered over all the dark expanse of the darkened heavens.

Oh! the horrors of that fearful night! The revolving light of a distant lighthouse glimmered out amid the driving blasts that were almost visible in their keen impetuosity. But it was vain to hearken for signals of distress, for the heavy roll of the rattling thunder grew louder and louder, crashed, and died away in a sullen growl. Then was heard nothing but the boil of the maddened waters, or the wild

No. 9.

shriek of a terrified petrel, turned round and about on her powerless wings by the rushing tempest.

The dauntless young pirate felt the agony of love's solicitude. It is a bitter curse to be alone in the world, but there are moments when it would be worth any sacrifice to be spared the anguish of anxiety for those we love and cannot save from pain or peril: the ills that we bear or pangs that we suffer on account of those we love are so much keener, so much more agonizing, than the cares and sufferings we have to support on our own account.

The night lagged fearfully, but there must be an end to everything, though the durance seem an eternity to the impatient or suffering.

Morning came at last; the grey light seamed the east, the sky became mottled, and the night gradually wore away before the waxing light. The gale lulled, but the waves had been too much agitated to subside at once. With heavy plash they continued to leap over the reef where Christopher was clinging. Gradually they subsided.

The sun rose from the sea—his glowing rays flashed along the heaving surface of the waters. At last all was quiet: there was a great calm. The Boy Pirate looked seaward. Something broke the sun-flashed smoothness of the water at a little distance. It floated alongside of the rock.

Christopher almost sank into the waves with horror; it was the body of one of his own men. Some heavy spars, webbed with tangling cordage, came lifting through the water. At once the Boy Pirate recognised them as belonging to his own vessel.

What had happened!

His gallant "Red Raven" was a wreck; his beloved Lilia slept in the caverns of the sea.

He was ready to plunge into the cold Lethe that surged around his narrow domain.

When he reflected upon his helpless and hapless condition, after all the wonderful escapes he had had, he was quite unnerved.

He looked over the sea; far away in the distance he could discern a hull heavily lurching, almost mastless, and evidently water-logged.

The Boy Pirate smiled grimly, for he knew well enough that it was the frigate whose crew had chased him on shore, and whose boats had overhauled the "Heloise" in order to capture him.

Where was Brierly? Where was his devoted foster-brother, Dick Caffyn?

Had they fallen into the hands of the enemy?

For awhile anxiety on their account would monopolize his thoughts, then again they were all absorbed in solicitude for Lilia.

Like most men of his class and character the Boy Pirate was something of a fatalist, a little inclined to superstitious belief in predestination; he could not bring his mind to think that his career was to end so abruptly and so wretchedly. And Lilia, so good, and true; she who was with him from such pure motives; his wife—his queen! Should she perish in his absence in the ship which had weathered so many gales? Should he have saved her from so many and such imminent dangers to perish at the very commencement of her wedded life? It could not be.

The Boy Pirate gazed yearningly over the sinking waters.

He was startled by the appearance of something which seemed to be a raft, on which three figures were moving.

What could it be?

He strained his eyes, shading them from the sun with his hand.

There was no mistaking the object, it was a raft; upon it were three persons.

Two of them men, the third a woman.

She seemed to be on her knees in an agony of prayer. Christopher could plainly perceive that her hands were clasped and uplifted.

He watched for a moment.

The men were evidently guiding the raft with a broken spar, and making for land.

He collected his strength, stretched his cramped limbs, and plunged into the sea.

His cutlass was in its sheath by his side when he leaped from the main-top of the "Heloise;" he had now drawn it, and held it firmly between his teeth.

With great power and fortitude he struggled through the waters; as he neared the raft he perceived that one of the men had dragged the woman down, for she had made an attempt to fling herself into the waters. Dauntlessly he struggled on.

He reached the raft. Neither of the men had perceived him till he was within a few strokes of the goal of his hopes.

His amazement may be imagined when it is told that the two men were desperate ruffians of his crew. The woman on the lonely raft was Lilia!

One of the men turned and saw him. For a moment he staggered back with astonishment and dread. He then whirled round the spar to strike the dauntless youth back into the waters; but Christopher eluded the blow of the unwieldy weapon, and scrambled upon the raft.

The other man at this moment was struggling with Lilia, breaking forth in blasphemous oaths and imprecations. With a single blow of his cutlass the Boy Pirate cleaved down the man who was steering, and then kicked his body overboard. He next turned his attention to the other.

The fellow was thunderstruck by this sudden apparition of his captain; and before he could recover his resources, the Boy Pirate seized him by the throat, and, after a desperate struggle, hurled him overboard.

He then seized the spar, and guided the raft away as quickly as possible. The men were borne off by the swell: one was drowned; the other buffeted his way to the shore.

Christopher caught the sobbing Lilia to his arms.

She clasped him convulsively, weeping and murmuring.

Christopher gently raised her.

They were alone on the raft on the wild and heaving sea.

"Lilia, my own, my dearest one! What a wretch I have been to drag you into the midst of perils so horrible! What has happened? You need not tell me that my brave vessel is a dreary wreck. But how did you fall into the hands of these traitorous villains?"

"O Christopher! it is a long, sad story! Why did you leave me?—why did you leave the ship? Yet all went well till this fearful gale struck a panic into the stoutest hearts among your crew. Then all was confusion. The ship broke away from its moorings—every sail was reefed—the masts went by the board—the head waves leaped over the deck, and at every dash swept away its victims!

"I remained in my cabin engaged in prayer. When things were at the worst on board—when the storm had wrought a very chaos on the deck, those two scoundrels came below, and told me that water was in the hold, and that the ship was sinking. I went with them on deck; part of their story was true, the boats were being manned, rafts were being constructed; and I know not how it was, but in the pell mell of dismay and exertion I was not noticed. They got me over the bulwarks on to their raft, just as there was a cry that the ship was going down; she lurched and veered, but righted herself, and while I was clinging to the planks of the raft I was borne away by the lifting billows into the palpable darkness. Then I guessed the fell design of these ruffians. I heard them speaking together; it might be they wished to take me back to Frontemore in hopes of receiving a reward from my father. With the morn came the calm; the 'Red Raven' was not in sight; either she had sailed into some harbour of refuge, or had gone down with all hands on board. About an hour ago, one of the villains insulted me; I appealed to the other, but he only laughed in my face. Had you not come to my rescue nothing should have prevented me from flinging myself into the depths: but you are here, dear Christopher; once more we are united, and I am safe and happy!"

CHAPTER XXIII.

HARWOLF'S AGENTS SET OUT ON A SEARCH.

JOE MILES was the landlord of the Hedgers' Arms —the little roadside inn where Silas Rye had overheard the gipsy and Black Oiny planning their highway robbery.

He was a wiry man, in the decline of life, but still supple and powerful. His skin was bronzed with the sun, and his eyes were clear and piercing. There was a look of low cunning and ruffianism in his face that gave him the air of a poacher or a smuggler.

In truth, with his ordinary calling he combined several by-way professions that were more lucrative than respectable.

Though he was a hard drinker he was a miserly

man, and generally reputed to have a "power of money."

He was seated on the settle outside his door, and was smoking his long pipe and sipping a glass of strong brandy, but slightly diluted.

At his feet reclined a large and disreputable looking mongrel of the lurcher kind.

As the old man sat lazily watching the smoke that curled from the bowl of his pipe and jetted from the corners of his mouth, some one came down the little lane and advanced towards him.

It was the squire.

Upon perceiving Andrew Harwolf, the landlord of the Hedgers' Arms rose, and, shuffling awkwardly forward, lifted his slouch-hat with a sort of boorish courtesy.

"Mornin', squire; fine weather for the crops. How is your honour: quite well?"

"Thank you, Miles, I am well enough," returned Harwolf, rather distantly; "but I have come to have a chat with you. Let me have a glass of brandy. I will sit with you here in the shade; I have something to ask you."

"Always at your honour's sarvice," returned Miles. He hobbled away towards the house, and then, turning his head, eyed the squire suspiciously.

He fetched the brandy, and offered the lord of the manor a choice cigar, none the less well-flavoured for being contraband.

The squire took it listlessly, and lighting it, puffed away for a few moments in silence.

"Miles," he said, at length; "I want to ask you a question."

"Very good, your honour. If it be anent the night lines az be laid in the preserves, I doan't know nothin' on 'em, I azzure ye; and az for the snares along the home vield, durn me if I doan't think I can find the scamp for 'ee az zets 'em. I ain't a-goin' to bear the blame for other people's misdoings. I be a poor man, your honour, and no better nor my neighbours, but I be honest, I be entirely honest, I azzure ye."

"I am not going to question your probity," Harwolf replied. "I tell you I came to ask you a question; if you answer it to my satisfaction I will reward you."

"Your honour may depend on Joe Miles for speaking truth; he be about az bad az another mortal, but he be no liar."

"Well, then; do you remember the night of the 10th of August, this day nineteen years ago."

"God zooks, squire, that be a 'nation long while to look back to."

"But you have a good memory, I suppose."

"Well, your honour, no better nor another, but I doan't forget much as is worth recollecting, I doan't."

"Do you remember anything 'worth recollecting' that happened on the night in question."

"Yez! Zure, your honour, Tom Weatherfield's barn were burnt down."

"Nothing else?"

"Well, noa; unless, may be, it was the same day when the news came from town about the election."

"Nothing else?"

"Not az I can think on just at this moment, your honour."

"Shall I remind you of something."

"Ah, zure, your honour."

"A poor woman, ill and distracted, was brought to the Hedgers' Arms, but a man who is now dead—killed——"

"Good Loard! Your honour doan't zay so? Silas Rye killed! Well, that is a sad joke."

In his surprise he had unconsciously betrayed himself.

The next moment he perceived his error, and looked down convicted and foolish.

Harwolf smiled artfully at the advantage he had gained, and passed an old newspaper to the host of the Hedgers' Arms.

The old man looked at a little paragraph that was marked with a pen, and among the rest, in the list of the killed, he perceived the name—

"Silas Rye—address unknown—apparent age about 30."

"Poor fellow!" cried Miles, holding up his hand pityingly. "Well, now I think on't, my darter Bridget told me az he were here, sittin' at this very table, on the day az he wur killed. Poor fellow! Well, railway accidents is the way of all flesh, as the zaying is. But he had a good heart, zur; he wur a wild lad, but he had a good heart, zur!"

"Perhaps so," returned Harwolf, coolly. But come; you remember the incident I spoke of? You know that a poor girl was brought to this house—and a babe?"

The humbler rascal looked at the other warily.

"Well, yer honour, it arn't likely I should remember much about things that happened such a 'farnal long while agone. But I'll zee what information I can collect for yer honour; but as it will take me some time—and time is money and bread to poor hard-working men as I be—and it may cost summut in the way—well, in many ways—zo ——"

"Yes; you are not rich, Miles."

"'Farnal poor I be, yer honour," returned Miles, with emphasis.

"Well, how would you like the Brookley Farm at a rack rent, and the post of overseer on my new place at Glenleaf?"

"Your honour!" cried the grasping fellow, his eyes and mouth wide open with breathless astonishment. "But you be jesting?"

"No; I don't jest—I never jest," returned the squire. "You will earn your reward by vigilance and fidelity. You must tell me all you know about this woman and this child. Where are they?"

"Faith, squire, I don't zee what a curse I should care to let you know all as you axes, but there be one thing I must bargain for—you mustn't zuppose that I have got more knowledge than I really do possess, for durn my wig if ever there were a cuter zort of chap than that zame Silas Rye; but he had a good heart, poor fellow."

"Then you don't know where this woman is?"

"Upon my soul I don't, squire. There be no good in deceiving of you."

"And you cannot discover her whereabouts now?"

"Zounds! but that be a mighty different sort of thing, squire. I'll undertake to find her wherever she be, if you will stand the damage."

"And the child—you know something of him?"

"In course," Miles was beginning, for his mind was quite preoccupied in the contemplation of the good things in store for him. But all at once he checked himself, and looking furtively at the squire, he went on—"that is, I would zay, squire, excuse me, that I knows 'nation little about him."

"But you know that the child is not dead?"

"Aye, zure, I'm sartain of that, squire, though, if I make bold to zay zo you wouldn't be quite inconsolable, eh, squire?"

"What do you mean, fellow? What has the fate of this child to do with me, except that I choose to take an interest in his fortunes?" cried Harwolf, fiercely. "Mark me, Miles, I must have none of these hints and meaningless suggestions. I am married to Lady Edgeforth, and by her right am master of these estates. As you know, if you will venture to serve me—for mind, they call me a hard man, which is only another way of saying I am a just man—if you serve me faithfully you will have good cause to congratulate yourself on having struck a bargain with me. But come, you must collect all the information you can glean about the child. Till you can tell me something definite of him you must expect no bonus from me. When you can give me proof that you have discovered his present location and condition I will give you a hundred pounds."

"All right, your honour, I'll discover all, but I must go up to Lunnon to find out what you want to know as to Lady Edge—leastways, of the young woman you are zo good as to take a interest in."

"Yes, you must do so at once."

The squire pulled out his gold watch.

"A train starts from Frontemore two hours hence," he said, "you must be ready to leave home at once. I will give you money to defray your expenses, and will come up to-morrow by the first express."

The squire pulled out his portemonnaie, and presented the landlord of the Hedgers' Arms with a little roll of notes.

His eyes sparkled as he clutched them in his greedy fingers.

"Your honour is a real gentleman," he exclaimed "and you may depend on seeing the lady safe in an asylum, poor thing. I think I has a clue."

"At the station you will find the gipsy, Esau Cooper, the man who was charged with highway robbery; it seems he was not guilty; his presence at the scene has been accounted for; at all events I have procured his release. Take him with you, he knows my wishes and may be depended upon."

"I'd rather a gone alone, squire; but it ain't for me to argy. All square, sir; I'll go and tell Bridget as I be going up to town a' out some hosses, and I'll be off in a giffey. Mornin', zur."

With this they parted.

Two hours after, the host of the Hedgers' Arms was at the little platform of the quiet station; there he encountered the sullen-looking gipsy; they eyed each other for some time in silence and distrust.

Miles held out his hand.

The gipsy touched it coldly.

"Look here, mate; afore we starts on this precious business, I want just a word or zo."

"What is it?" asked the gipsy, rather sulkily.

"If we're to row in the zame boat, Esau, I'm thinking we must pull together."

"I'm square," said the gipsy, bluntly.

"Zo be I. It's plain we shall get this squire fellow into our hands, so as we can play the 'tarnal devil with him. We mus'nt let him know too much."

"He pays for all I tells him," said the gipsy.

"And I doan't tell him all he pays for," rejoined the worthy publican.

"Does he know what's come of the heir?"

"Not he; nor I doan't mean he should," returned Miles.

As they spoke the train bowled into the station.

The two took their places

The guard blew the whistle.

With a jar and rattle the heavy up-train was already on the move when the door of the carriage in which the gipsy and Joe Miles were seated was suddenly burst open.

A dark, burly fellow burst in, and took his seat opposite.

Esau started up with an oath on recognising the new passenger.

It was Black Oiny.

"Faid, and its raal glad I am to see you, darlin'," cried the garotter, gleefully, to his old associate. "I thought that you had yet a government appointment, and that you would be going to foreign parts for a long tower. Good luck to ye, but what's the news; there's nobody in the carriage but our blessed selves. Ah, sure, and is it your reverence, Master Miles. I'm the most fortunate craytur this same lucky day. Arrah, but it's fortunate I am, for a divil a stiver has this boy in his pocket; and, except for the matter of a raw turnip, it's little that has passed his lips in the way of a meal since the black day whin the infernal spalpeen well nigh chated the hangman of his purty job! Och, but I have a blue necklace round my throat!"

"You're a precious fly pal, you are—much to be depended on," said the gipsy, with a sneer, "to leave a chum, as you did me, with the crusher dead on him."

"Sure, now, it's a big liar you'll be, Esau," returned the Irishman, hastily; "for it's myself that's the boy to stick to an old pal in trouble. Haven't I been a-sneaking about the hedges, you dirty spalpeen, a-slaving and a-quaking this week, to see

if I might help you out of your ugly scrape, bad luck to ye; but now I'm wid you once more, bedad, it's not Oiny Macarne that'll leave ye till he knows all the perticulars of your purty little game."

CHAPTER XXIV.
AN UNEXPECTED MEETING.

IN one of the back streets of a London suburb, and in a neat and comfortable room, a pale-faced boy was lying upon a sofa: his eyes were large and luminous in their deep thoughtfulness, his features were regular, and the general expression of his face particularly engaging and amiable.

He was about fourteen years of age; on the table were books, maps, engravings, models, drawings, pencils and colours. The walls were hung with many well-drawn sketchings and paintings, his own work, and in the windows were an aquarium of fish and water plants, flowers and bird cages.

On one side of the room hung a portrait.

It was a fine picture, painted by an eminent artist, who had been an intimate friend of the pale boy's father in former and happier days. It was the portrait of the boy's mother.

She was very lovely, her loveliness emanating from the beauty of expression, not from the mere perfectness of figural outline—all that was kind and noble was expressed in that look which the painter had copied so faithfully. The reader will have readily divined that the pale boy was Charlie Rye, the brother of Silas.

Charlie was neither affected nor precocious, he was a thorough boy. His heart was bold and romantic, his brain clear and imaginative, the gentle affection which formed the redeeming characteristic of his brother's passion-ruled and faulty nature had surrounded him by everything that could alleviate his sufferings.

Charlie suffered keenly: his free adventurous soul was caged in a feeble, nervous, pain-withered body; he who would have joyously faced the stinging blast on the tempest-raving sea shrank and faded beneath the weak and stealthy draught that invaded the chamber. He who would have clambered the Andes and gazed in the blazing disc of the sun, like the eagle who builds his eyry on their heights, was wearied and exhausted by parading his little room, and dozed by the poor sunbeams that could creep down the abyss of the towering street, piercing the vale of smoke and fog.

He was much to be pitied, but his case was not so pitiable at this epoch of his life as it had formerly been.

However ill obtained, Silas managed to get money now, and his first care was to provide his sick brother with everything desirable that lay within the stretch of his utmost means.

The affection of Silas Rye for his sick brother was a fine trait in his character, and poor little Charlie deserved all the affection and solicitude of his sole relation. But because Silas Rye was not destitute of good qualities he was only by so much the less a rogue; hitherto he had been the mere catspaw of a more fortunate villain, and now he was a sharer in a prize won by means the most diabolical. His kindness to his little brother arose from natural goodness so fatally perverted. It was a natural instinct and not a principle, and on the other hand the weakness, nervousness, and delicacy of poor Charlie Rye rendered him none the less a true, brave fellow than the disabling wound renders the hero less honourable.

The boy turned wearily on the sofa, and throwing his thin arm behind his head looked languidly through the window. He saw a little bird start upward from the eaves of the opposite house, and wheeling round and round in the air dart upward and vanish in the lucid sky. Poor Charlie sighed and opened his book of "Wild Sports," and was soon mentally following the tract of the moose, or breathlessly crouching near the lair of the tiger. There was a light tap at the door.

Charlie raised himself on his arm with a bright smile.

"Come in, come in," he cried, delighted; "I know it is you, Milly."

The door was opened; a girl about the same age as the invalid came in.

She was very pretty and gentle; she had sweet blue eyes, and her hair was golden and luxuriant, though modestly bound beneath her little hat.

She softly drew near to Charlie and held out her hand. The boy drew her to him and kissed her affectionately.

"Oh, Milly; what a dear, good girl you are," he said, "how kind you are to me: how lonely, how discontented I should be if it were not for you. Oh! I wish I knew how to tell you how much—how very much I love you; how thankful I am to you."

"Don't talk nonsense, Charlie," said the girl, with a pretty blush, sitting at his side; "see what a treasure I've brought you, real cowslips; come from the real country, Charlie; not such half-town places as Clapham common and that sort, you know, but from little dells and dingles, right away, miles and miles from this noisy smoky place where there is no room for children to play, and where there's nothing but sparrows and rats and mice. Don't you like the country, Charlie? Shouldn't you like to live in a pretty quiet village, with fields and woods and farms and brooks all round it; with hills in the distance, and birds and flowers everywhere. I often dream about the country; don't you?"

"Very often, Milly," replied the boy, with a slight sigh, "But there, there, what would be the use of my going into the country! I could not climb a tree, I could not breast a river, I could scarce clamber a hill. But then, I might lie under the spreading trees in some deep wood when the March winds were blowing, and fancy the lions were roaring in the jungle; I might watch the blue moonlight quiver among the green leaves and throw queer shadows on the grass, and fancy the fairies were dancing before me. Yes, Milly, I do like the country; I should like to die there."

"Don't talk about dying, Charlie, you will live to be a hale old man; because you're poorly now, do you think you'll be ill all your life; not a bit of it, see how much better you are lately?"

"Am I," said Charlie, with a quaint smile.

"Of course you are—ever so well—look how merry and contented you are to what you used to be."

"I should be very ungrateful to my kind brother, poor Silas, if I were not merry and contented; but somehow, you girls don't think of yourselves as we boys do; you never seem to think at all of your own troubles, and you don't have such a bright life of it with your drunken grandfather."

"Hush!" cried Emily, deprecatingly, "don't call him drunken, that's such a hard word. He does take a little too much, but not so often as many do; and he has great trouble. But, Charlie, I have such brave news to tell you, and yet it's not brave, neither, for I shall have to leave you for awhile. I am actually going to be apprenticed, Charlie; what do you think of that?"

"Apprenticed? Oh, Milly! I'm so sorry! Are you going away?"

"Yes, dear; but not for ever, you know. Madame Delacour is going to take me in; and I shall learn to be a milliner and dressmaker, and then I shall have a little business of my own."

"Oh, Milly! I don't like the idea at all!" returned the boy. "I should like to work hard—I don't care how much; I could sit up for nights to study; I could spend long days in the hardest toil; but women and girls are so different, and I cannot help thinking that they get desperate, and sometimes wicked, when they are tasked so much. I remember the funny, mournful song, Milly—'Stitch—stitch—stitch'—and I think the song of the 'Ball-dress' may be sung to the same tune as the 'Song of the Shirt.'"

"But, Charlie, I must do something, you know; and by-and-by, it will be very sweet to work for myself, to be independent; it is so nice to earn one's own living when one is well and strong."

"And even when one is neither well nor strong it is so pleasant to earn one's bread," cried Charlie, with a sudden gleam in his eyes. "There are lots of things I can do; if I cannot be a soldier, nor a sailor, nor even an architect, nor engineer, at least I can paint and write; I can win fame by some means, can't I?"

"Yes, dear Charlie, and be an engineer or architect, or anything you like, by-and-by, if you get on so well as you do now; you are always better and better, and will soon be well; but you shan't be a soldier nor a sailor—I won't let you."

Charlie smiled and pressed her hand.

"I would rather be a hunter than a soldier, after all," said the sick boy, thoughtfully. "One man is little stronger than another, and even with this weak hand I could shoot Goliath; but a tiger or an elephant is something to contend with."

"Oh, Charlie, what a good thing it is you are not quite strong," rejoined Emily, "if you were you would be always in danger—you are so brave!"

"I, brave!" replied the sick boy, a shade of anguish sweeping over his expressive face, "I am so nervous and cowardly that sometimes I shudder when a cur barks."

While they were thus discoursing Silas Rye suddenly entered the room.

His face was white and care-stricken: he nodded kindly to Charlie and his companion, and passed into the adjoining room.

The jingling of keys was heard, and presently he returned with a small strong box in his hand, and seating himself near the window extracted therefrom a number of parchment documents, from which he seemed to select certain important ones.

Emily looked at him with a little awe, and clasping Charlie's hand, whispered that she would be gone.

"Stay, Emily," said the boy, earnestly, "I know your grandfather is away, and there is no reason why you should leave me so soon, and if you are really going to be apprenticed we must make the most of the little time we can be together. I want you to promise me to write, and I want to build all sorts of castles in the air; so don't go, there's a dear."

Emily reseated herself, but looked furtively at Silas.

The elder brother rose, and carefully placing the documents he had selected in a large letter case, replaced the strong box, and approached the boy and girl with a pleasant smile.

"Well, Milly," he said, "and how is your patient; but I need not ask, the young scapegrace is always well enough when you are here. There is something healthful in your cheerful smile, it does him more good than all the doctor's stuff."

"That's right enough, Silas," replied the boy, "Milly does me more good than all the doctors. But you look tired and jaded, Silas—what's the matter?"

"Nothing, Charlie, nothing!" returned Silas, in a hollow tone; "but now you're beginning to look so hearty, young chap, I shall want you to help me——"

"To work?" cried Charlie, eagerly. "Oh, I shall be so glad. What am I to do."

"Well, youngster, I'll tell you; I'm going to take a bit of a cottage out of London, and you must be my head gardener. I have ordered rakes, and hoes, and garden roller, and seeds enough to plant an acre. But I was forgetting; Milly, I've brought you a little present."

With this, Silas Rye produced a little reticule—one of those exquisite trifles, the produce of modern taste and ingenuity—furnished with every requisite for needlework.

While Emily was thanking him, and both the children were admiring the completeness and prettiness of the gift, they were startled by the loud crack of a whip without the door. A man burst suddenly into the room. He was a short rubicund fellow, with red hair, red face and red waistcoat; he wore a white hat and a light grey coat with a peony in the button-hole; the pattern of his nether garments was very "loud," and the sable brilliance of his highly-polished boots was quite transcendant. He had a long whip in his hand, at the top of which was a little knot of mauve ribbon.

He spoke with a jerking sort of vehemence that brought the blood to his ever florid face, till it assumed the hue of a poppy.

"Thomas Chipkins—your humble servant," he began, almost fiercely, "Mr. Silas Rye—respected and esteemed friend—I'm here, sir—I'm here. You will naturally inquire *why* I am here."

"I shall make no such inquiry, Mr. Chipkins; but only thank my good fortune for your visit," said Silas, holding out his hand with a smile. "You are very welcome—pray sit down."

Both the young people turned with eager pleasure, and laughed rejoicingly at the entrance of the visitor.

"Always willing to oblige Mr. Silas—always willing; but I am a man of impulses, and I have a mission to perform. Yes, sir, I say I have a mission——"

"Indeed, Mr. Chipkins; and what may it be?"

"This morning when I opened my eyes, Mr. Silas, the sunshine reminded me of the country. My lark sang of the country. When I went into the shop, the fruit smelt of the country; the man brought me strawberries—luscious, blushing, fresh and fascinating; beneath them, bright green leaves, broad and dew-gemmed. They almost settled the point, but the matter was clinched in this way: strolling after my cat, who wandered out for a bask in the morning sun, I encountered the postman, sir; he had brought me a letter—directed post-haste and immediate, prepaid and Mr. T. Chipkins, Esquire, fruiterer and seedsman. It was from a female friend, and it commenced 'Tom, dear,'—the party, sir, is privileged to call me Tom. The letter was conceived in affectionate terms, and contained three post-scripts. The first was an intimation that the old gentleman was gone down to his shooting-box for the season; the second, that the said female friend —party afore-mentioned—had got a day's holiday; the third had reference to a miraculous veal pie. as also to several bottles of superfine contents. Now the thought struck me, Mr. Silas, so forcibly that I was almost prostrated. Chipkins, it is expedient for manifold reasons that you should have a change. I don't refer to the female party, Mr. Rye, though there is a change contemplated in that direction—a change that will transform me from a lonesome single-handed tradesman—I do say a *single-handed* tradesman—to a married family man—settled, and I won't say done for. But that's a digression—let us return to the subject: in short, I mean to make a day of it—I intend to ruralise, and my present mission is to announce the startling fact that I am unalterably resolved to carry you all off bodily to do honour to the occasion by your presence. My chariot—that is, a four-wheeler—waits without. A friend of mine—a lawyer's clerk—who has also determined to make a day of it, is the Jehu who will drive us. Ladies and gentleman, I have but one word to say in conclusion—Come!"

"Really, Mr. Chipkins," began Silas, "we are much obliged by your kind invitation, but——"

"Sir, I admit of no 'buts,' no 'ifs,' no apologies. I have but one word—Come!" You are looking as grave as a Turk, and as yellow as a Tartar; while your poor brother is as pale as a Swede—I use this epithet in a vegetable sense. Opposition to my laudable design will be unavailing: the carriage waits, and I am firmly resolved to take no denial."

"But business——"

"Cannot be properly conducted by a man whose blood is clogged with the dust of cities; whose body is mummified by confinement in the pent and polluted atmosphere of this metropolitan black hole of Calcutta. I appeal, Mr. Silas, to your fraternal feelings; you are not quite inhuman. Look, sir, upon Master Charlie; consider how much he will benefit by a day's dosing of pure oxygen, and refuse me if you dare!"

"Should you like to go, Charlie?" asked his brother, kindly.

"Very much, Silas; that is, if you would go with us."

"But I don't see how I can," returned Silas, hesitating.

"Don't you?" rejoined the lively Chipkins; "then I will show you. But I must go and report the success of my mission to my learned friend the lawyer's clerk, and to the adorable, in fact the charming, female party above-mentioned."

With a profound bow, and a satisfied glance at his dapper person and elegant attire, which were reflected in the pier-glass, Mr. Chipkins darted out of the room.

A little while after, Silas, his brother, and Emily Mervyn emerged from the house and joined their vivacious acquaintance.

The door of the vehicle was opened and a buxom, fresh-complexioned, good-looking young woman peered out:

With great glee and good nature she assisted Charlie and Emily into the carriage.

With much fuss and bustle, Mr. Chipkins urged Silas to get on the box. He did so, and a radiant smile of immense satisfaction beamed on the honest greengrocer's face as he surrendered the whip and leaped into the cab. Silas had not noticed the charioteer, neither had the young clerk noticed him.

The driver whipped up the horse, and they were soon "a-trot."

"Glorious day, sir, for our excursion," said the young clerk, by way of opening a conversation.

As he spoke, Silas started and turned a quick look of surprise upon his companion.

All the colour faded from the young clerk's face— he nearly tumbled off the box—he suddenly released the reins, and the horse shied against a lamp-post. Silas caught the reins, biting his lip with vexation.

"Sir," cried the clerk, in a hoarse whisper, "are you—in fact—are you a gho—ost?"

"No, nor a dead man neither," returned Silas.

"Nor a vampire?"

"Look here, Sibly; if you are not in a fit state to drive, you had better give the reins to me."

"Why—didn't I see your name advertised in the list of those killed in the Brighton accident? Didn't I hear Squire Harwolf tell the governor that you were dead?"

"Sibly, I'm forced to make a confidant of you by the unlucky coincidence of this chance meeting; but I believe you are a good fellow, and I will make it worth your while to keep my secret. For certain reasons I wished the gentleman you mention to think that I have made my exit from the world's great stage; so I took advantage of several fortuitous circumstances that favoured my plan, and got my name inserted in the paper, as you saw."

"I can scarcely believe my eyes, Mr. Rye; but there is no getting over the fact that, whether or not you were run over by the train, you are here *in propria persona*, and don't look much the worse for the catastrophe, except that you still carry a few scars, I perceive. Well, this is the most wonderful thing that ever happened in my experience: and to think how you hoaxed old Harwolf and the governor —it is beautiful!"

"I could not have done it so well but for two or three lucky coincidences that helped me."

"What a pity, what a dreadful pity?" murmured Sibly, abstractedly.

"What's a pity?" inquired Silas.

"Don't you perceive what a good thing you lost, seeing how nicely everything went off; if you had only insured your life, eh? That would have been sublime."

Silas laughed.

Soon after, they pulled up at a little inn for rest and refreshment.

Like a butterfly bursting from its cocoon, Chipkins sprang out of the cab, his grey coat flying, his red waistcoat glowing, and his bouquet flaunting; he handed out his " bonnie Mary;" Charlie, too, and Emily alighted.

The party adjourned to the little green behind the house, and here they regaled themselves with the miraculous veal pie, and the bottles of superfine contents.

While Emily and Charlie wandered about the grounds, admiring the freshness and richness of the trees and flowers, the worthy Chipkins made love to his fair. Silas Rye and the lawyer's clerk sat secluded in one of the little green-painted arbours, deeply absorbed in earnest conversation.

" Well, you see, Mr. Rye," said Sibly, reflectively, "old Skinner is a wary sort of fellow, and not easy to deal with; he has the law at his fingers' ends, and knows all its twinings and twistings. Squire Harwolf is also a 'cute man, and either one of them is more than a match for both of us; besides, I don't see much good, after all, that can accrue to us, if, as you say, the true heir to the Edgeforth estates is gone so far to the bad; and then, I suppose, you would find it difficult to lay hands on him."

" I have thought of all these things," replied Silas; " but I am not to be deterred from my plans by worse obstacles. I am not without money—at least, I have sufficient for my present wants,—and I am resolved to have this man in my power. You don't know, Sibly, how much cause I have to hate him."

" Well, I'm not so fond of him, myself; for I overheard him tell the governor to give me the sack as genteelly as might be, because I had by accident caught a glimpse of some of his papers. Look, there are already some substantial proofs of the child's identity in your possession."

" Yes, it may be so, but I must have them all. I suppose Mr. Skinner keeps some of them, don't he?"

" Yes, and I'll get them for you; though it is a dangerous job." He looked round suspiciously as he spoke, and lowered his voice. " But I say, you must act square, Rye; for you were watched by those you little knew of up to the time of the accident. But look up man; you are as pale as a sheet."

" It's nothing, Sibly," returned Silas, smiling faintly; " but that cursed break down did give me a terrible shaking."

At this moment Charlie and Emily advanced, their eyes beaming with innocent pleasure, their hands laden with wild flowers.

Chipkins stood gesticulating and shouting vociferously, as he pointed to the vehicle that had been brought round to the gate; his *inamorata* had already got in, and the greengrocer was as impatient as Gilpin himself for a fresh start.

" What makes you look so dull? Is there anything on your mind now, Silas?" whispered Charlie to his brother.

" No, lad; come along; let us be off; the day is waning, and we can't afford to lose an hour of it, for our little jaunt seems to be doing you a power of good already."

The party were once more agog, to dash through thick and thin; and Silas and the lawyer's clerk, seated on the box, renewed their grave discourse.

CHAPTER XXV.

HOW JACK BRIERLY AND DICK CAFFYN ESCAPED THEIR PURSUERS.

It is necessary that the reader should be made acquainted with the circumstances that led to the separation of Jack Brierly and Dick Caffyn from the Boy Pirate, on the eventful night when he so narrowly escaped being captured by his insatiable enemies.

Upon the breaking-up of the carousing party, Jack and his comrade had been ushered into a small, but neat and pretty chamber, on the opposite side of the house to that in which Christopher's bed-room was situated.

The casement looked out upon a wide and windy plain, studded at intervals by rough bushes; there were a few long, low walls of stone, that parted little incorrigible patches of arid land that had been raked and ploughed into a sickly attempt at raising some sparse and feeble blades of poor wheat, and rows of tall poplars stood away in regimental order and stiffness at regular distances in several directions from the house.

Dick Caffyn was in excellent humour, and, as he flung off his pea-jacket, and arranged his pistols, &c. by his pillow, he whistled and sang in the glee of his heart.

Brierly was more taciturn; the old pirate sat down on his little bed, and musingly tapped the broad palm of his left hand with the bright barrel of a revolver.

" What's in the wind to make the sky so cloudy, Jack?" asked Dick Caffyn, with a laugh.

" I'll tell you what, messmate," replied the other; " I'm thinking that it's queer policy of the cap'en grounding among these land-sharks when we're likely to have dirty weather at sea. He's as fine a fellow as ever walked the quarter-deck, but he's a younker, and having always had plenty of sea-room, he doesn't see the danger of running on these cussed shallows; but I do; darn me if I wouldn't rather be caught in a white squall, with every sail set, than I'd be battened under hatches with such land-rats as these French lubbers; 'cos vy? they're as poor as Job, and not half so vartuous; they would no more mind selling us up to the 'reg'lars' than they would cutting a toad's throat to make a ragout. I can confide my sentiments to you, Dick, 'cos I knows you're as true as the compass. Ever since young madam came aboard, the cap'en has been playing the devil's divarsions. In the first place, he gets logged up in the channel, in the wake of that infarnal Harwolf; then he lets the infarnal skunk go; and, last of all, he leaves the ship at its moorings, as if there were never such a thing as a man-of-war on the high seas."

" But then, you know, it's time he got rid of the cargo, Jack; and this French smuggler, Ferrole, is about the safest man along the coast. And as for Harwolf, why, Jack, you havn't got such a devilish low opinion of human nature as to fancy he would be black enough to betray the captain within a day of his release."

" Shiver me, if I'm fool enough to trust him the length of a marlinspike. But there never came no good of women anywhere, and a woman aboard the ' Red Raven ' is rather a dangerous ornament to our society."

" But is she not kind and beautiful?—is she not brave and true? Why, Jack, I gave you more credit for chivalry."

" Chivalry or devilry, I may have a power on it for all I knows, never having heard on it," replied Brierly, rather testily. " All I got to say is this—there aren't a hand among the crew as would be more ready and willing to lay down his life for ' the gals we leaves behind us,' but the leaving 'em behind us is the thing I sticks to—they're no good aboard, and only a hindrance; but as soon as the captain gets out on the high seas, where it won't make so much difference, I shall be on for a hornpipe. But let's close our peepers, Dick, for we must be out of our hammocks, or whatever else they call these landlubber fixings, by first watch. I shall sleep with one eye open, mate, so you can strike your flag to Morpus and sleep like a seal on a rock."

Dick Caffyn laughed, and divesting himself merely of his boots and cravat, threw himself upon his pallet.

Brierly pulled out a short pipe, which he lighted, and seating himself on his little bed, folded his arms and gave himself up to profound rumination.

An hour passed away. Jack Brierly began to feel drowsy, and kicked off his shoes with intent to afford himself the luxury of a few hours watchful rest, when he was startled by the sound of voices.

He rose.

He was startled by the fact that the few rough words that he could distinguish were uttered in English.

He softly rose.

His companion was sleeping deeply.

He went to the window, and looked out.

The prospect was unbroken by the shadow of any living thing.

Again he heard voices.

They came from the other side of the house, from the direction of the sea.

He cautiously drew near Dick Caffyn, and touched him on the arm.

The youth sprang up and stared about in semi-unconsciousness.

"Get up, Dick," whispered Brierly, "I'm afeard as there's some suspicious craft a-hailing in Queen's English. Don't ye hear 'em?"

"Ay, Jack," replied Caffyn, in a whisper, listening intently.

A voice was plainly heard giving directions in an imperious tone.

"There's another fellow on our quarter."

"It is Harwolf, by Heaven!" returned Caffyn, seizing his pistols.

Loud and continuous knocking now echoed through the house.

"Humph! that's their first broadside," muttered Brierly. "Its about time we sheered off, my hearty."

"But the captain?"

"We can help him better when we've freed ourselves. It'll be poor comfort for him to see us in irons, I take it. Where shall we steer to, Dick?"

"We can get out of the window," Caffyn rejoined, as he tried to open the casement.

"No, no, Dick, we'll get into daylight some other way; the window isn't bigger than a bull's eye, and if it were as wide as a harbour mouth, the hull's too high to think of leaping overboard. We must go aloft."

With this Brierly went to the chimney, which he examined with great care.

Another tremendous peal of knocking threatened to shake the house down.

Oaths, curses, and shrill whistling were heard without.

"Shiver me, if the noisy skunks don't think they're piping our death watch, but, cuss them, we'll skulk the muster," cried Brierly, securing his arms, and beginning to scramble up the chimney. "Come along, Dick," he continued, as he made his way up the narrow outlet, which, fortunately, was not clogged with soot, a stove being used in lieu of a hearth in the winter.

Caffyn listened awhile at the door. He found that the sailors sent to arrest the Boy Pirate and his companions had broken into the house.

He opened the door, and, hiding himself in a dark corner on the staircase, was witness of the scene detailed in a former chapter—the encounter of the Boy Pirate, when disguised as the priest, with the sailors on the stairs. He beheld with great satisfaction how, by the intervention of Fanchante, the captain had escaped; and then, and not till then, he thought of himself, and prepared to follow Brierly.

He sprang nimbly up the chimney, which was oblique, and not hard to climb; and soon emerged on the roof.

"Curse 'em, they've driven him on the shoals; but we will get him off, Dick, in spite of a whole navy on 'em. But how are we to get down from the mast-head, my hearty?"

They were looking over the balustrade, and their glance was thrown upon a very cheerless prospect.

Sentinels had been posted all round the house, and stood with guns and small arms, ready to shoot down any whom they might suspect.

Brierly turned to Caffyn, and waved him to crouch down.

He did so.

"Dick, you get down the chimney that gives on yonder balcony; if the room is empty, and you can pass through and so manage to reach the ground—but, blow me, if they aren't all off in hot pursuit."

"Ay, but I'll warrant they'll find it hotter work to take him," cried Dick, with gleaming eyes. "Oh, Jack, I am on burning stones; I can't stay here, we must be off to the rescue."

"Steadily ho, my cheery; strikes me they'll have a long chase after that bit of bunting. Anyhow, we'll be on their lee. Hist! down with you; here comes another half crew of the skunks."

Again they crouched down.

"Who goes there?" cried a voice below.

"Friends."

"Give the word."

"Hunted down!"

"Pass."

"Did you hear that, Brierly?" whispered Dick Caffyn to his mate.

"Ay, ay, that little bit of book larning is worth a month's grog. But come on, mate, now's the time."

They crept towards a trap-door that gave admittance to the roof.

Very carefully they opened it.

It gave upon a small loft, bare and untenanted.

Assisting each other—for there was no ladder—the two fugitives reached the floor.

But here was a new dilemma.

The door was locked!

They looked at each other in consternation.

"What's to be done now, Jack?" whispered Caffyn.

"Well, mate, if we breaks the door we shall make a row, and bring the sharks on us at once. But then, if we lay close, the cap'en will be cut to pieces by the cuss and his backers, and that sha'nt be while this old hulk's seaworthy. Lend a hand, mate, and the devil take the consequence."

Without more ado the gallant old salt charged at the door, which yielded to his efforts, and burst open.

But the noise and its reverberation was tremendous.

Like lightning, Brierly flew downstairs.

Dick Caffyn followed close at his heels.

In the midst of their descent they were suddenly stopped.

A number of men rushed out from a narrow passage and blocked up the way.

"Hillo! hillo! my hearties. Come along, ye swabs, they've just broken the door open, and are out on the roof," roared Brierly, so suddenly and so loudly that conviction was hammered into the astounded ears of the crew, and they ran up the stairs, tumbling over each other in their haste.

It must be remembered that the only light which tempered the darkness was emitted by the candle of a lantern in the hands of one of the sailors.

"Who's that aloft, you lubbers?" shouted a man from behind.

"I think it's Jack Ridley, bo'swain," replied the other, "but it's so infarnal dark there's no knowing one hand from another."

"Stop the fellow—make him give the word."

"Give the word, man; don't you hear the bo'swain?" cried one of the sailors, trying to lay hands on Brierly.

"*Hunted down!* and be hanged to ye," shouted the lieutenant of the "Red Raven." "While you're a-hindering with your jaw the devilskins are clambering the roofs like cats, and will be out of your reach before you can get in full way."

The men rushed past him, and were soon darting, with their cutlasses gleaming in the moonlight, through the trap-door.

Jack Brierly and his comrade gained the lower part of the house safely.

They met with no obstruction till they reached the door; but that was guarded.

A number of men were stationed there armed to the teeth.

"Stand," they shouted.

Brierly and Caffyn halted, at the same time clutching their pistols.

THE APPARITION IN THE DRESSING-ROOM.

"Hunted down," cried Brierly. "Let us out, mates, according to our orders."

"I'll be cursed if anyone leaves the house," was the gruff reply. "I'm not a-goin' to be bilked a second time, my hearties; hand over the lantern, let's have a squint at the cut of this fellow's gib."

A light was thrust in Brierly's face.

"Hillo! knock him down; lay hands on him; he's one of them; seize the infernal thief," shouted the man who held the lantern.

In the hurry of the rush to the door several of the men got jammed in the entrance. Brierly levelled his revolver, the report shook the whole house, and was followed by pealing shrieks from the women who had concealed themselves in their rooms in deadly terror of the invaders. The men uttered fierce and bitter curses, and were about to fly into the passage, but a gap was made in the phalanx by the fall of the man whom Brierly had shot.

No. 10.

Over his prostrate body the two men leaped, lashing on either side of them with their cutlasses.

Way was made for them, or rather they hewed a way for themselves.

When they had fought on to the distance of a few steps from the door, they were forced to turn to defend themselves from the furious assaults of their assailants.

They fought long and desperately, backing inch by inch and reserving their fire.

They would have been shot at once by their outnumbering foes but the men were ashamed to kill them, as they had strict orders to take them alive.

The motive that prompted this mandate will be easily divined.

It was very desirable that some of the terrible gang should be secured in order that they might betray their associates.

Fighting like tigers, dealing despairing and wild

blows at their pursuers, the two men reached the low wall at the end of the little green.

As if by a mutual though tacit understanding they made one last dashing charge at the crew.

The men were beaten back.

The lieutenant and his comrade once more presented their revolvers. The fired their barrels successively, and in the confusion that followed upon the discharge leaped over the low wall, and fled towards the shore.

As they rushed onwards, without casting a look behind them, they came upon the bodies of the men slain in self-defence by the heroic Boy Pirate.

The two stern men looked in each other's faces and smiled grimly.

The shouts of their followers was heard in the rear.

Soon they perceived that the attention of the party was directed to the Boy Pirate himself, who was hastening to the cliff with Fanchante in his arms.

With pride and joy they saw their gallant young leader gain the summit of the precipice, and by his wondrous daring make his escape. They lay close beneath the beetling rocks till the exasperated and baffled party reluctantly returned.

Then they came forth; they were half dead with fatigue, hot and flushed with excitement.

"And whither away now, Jack," cried Dick Caffyn, laughing merrily, and shaking the blood from his sword. "I thought it was a dead case with us, mate, but there's many a merry cruise for us yet. Long life to Captain Kit, and hurrah for the 'Red Raven;' but whither away, mate?"

"To the cavern of Ferrole, the smuggler."

CHAPTER XXVI.

SQUIRE HARWOLF SEES AN APPARITION.

THE clock has struck twelve.

Andrew Harwolf sits in his wide and splendid chamber wrapt in thought. As usual a gloomy mood was upon him.

He was alone at Frontemore.

He had sent his wife away. The reputed Lady Edgeforth was passing the season amongst the gay society of London.

He sits listening to the ticking of the ormolu clock on the marble mantel. The wind rustled and surged through the splendid trees about the noble mansion; all the servants had retired.

As usual the strong brandy stood within his reach, and he drank deeply and repeatedly of the burning stimulant.

In his hand he held several letters; one which he had been reading had fallen upon the floor.

It was written in an execrable scrawl, and it was the bulletin from the respectable agents he had sent to London to track out the ——.

But it is needless to detail the contents of this letter, as a subsequent chapter will give full information of the progress made by Esau and Miles in their virtuous mission.

Andrew Harwolf's face glowed red with the fire of the drink, and his fiendish eyes twinkled with venomous passion.

He happened to turn his eyes upon the *Times*, which lay upon the table.

His glance fell upon an article headed, "The Last of the Brighton Accident." He smiled maliciously, and passed his fingers through his shaggy elf locks—untimely grey with care and crime—and muttered, chuckling,

"Yes, he is gone; he is swept from my path. Well, well, I did not do that! I have not *his* blood on my head; his ghost will not haunt me. Ghosts! Pish! that sort of thing is all miserable fudge; the world is over-crowded as it is; the dead have no inducement to bring them back from their restful graves to this theatre of farce and tragedy. The spectres and apparitions of old gossips' tales are but the fumes of an over-heated brain, fevered by mental excitement or by ardent drink. Ah! drink—can it

be that my only nepenthe should be the spume to breed goblins: that I cannot even drown my guilty agonies in the bottle but must run the risk of conjuring hideous phantoms to my imagination. I should not care for a pale face and a little blood, but, as he was—as I disposed of him—Ah, God! it is too horrible! too horrible!"

The nights were chill, and the room was large and somewhat draughty. The fire had flickered out, its last embers were dying in the grate.

Yet he rose, and opened the *croisée* windows for air.

There was a hideous fume of burning. He knew that it was not real, but would gladly have exchanged the hideous fancy for the stench of material conflagration in his own house.

He looked out into the night.

It was black as his own thoughts.

He re-entered the room.

Having closed the window, he took up the heavy silver candlestick, and, having struck a light, was about to retire to his restless bed.

A slight noise was heard in the dressing-chamber—which the reader will remember was the scene of the hideous murder which had put him in possession of his present affluence, and had coupled that with an intensity of misery the world's wealth could not compensate.

Again a faint rustling sound!

In the silence and gloom of the vast and shadowy chamber—he had blown out the flame of the ormolu lamp—Andrew Harwolf stood alone, transfixed with horror.

The blood crept freezingly through his shrinking veins.

A qualm of deathly terror rose to his throat, his lips grew livid in their hue, his eyes started from their sockets, his knees trembled as if he were smitten with a sudden ague, and his lips quivered with fearful agony.

Again that ghostly sound.

Harwolf scowled; his cheek grew hectic red.

He was a matchless villain, but constitutionally, a brave, a very brave man. He seized the candle.

"Ghost or devil, I will face thee!" he cried, bitterly. "If I killed thee it will be part of my eternal punishment to have thee ever in my sight in thy direst and most revolting aspect, for I am lost—lost for ever. I will look on thee now, dead thing. I brave thee, dread mystery—do thy worst."

So saying, he rushed into the dressing-room.

He held aloft the candle.

At the far end of the room he perceived the figure of a man standing, his arms folded, and his cold grey eyes fixed calmly and searchingly upon the horror-stricken wretch.

"Ha, ha! so it is you. You cannot rest, then, in the grave? You have come back from the very charnel to brave me and to thwart! Maybe your death was a lie. You have escaped after all! By the eternal furies, I will know of what metal you are made."

But the figure made him no answer, but only smiled calmly and mockingly.

Two pistols hung by the wall. Harwolf tore them down and presented one full at the breast of the figure.

But it quailed not.

Exasperated, though trembling, Andrew advanced a step.

He was within a foot of the vision.

"Die, burglar and thief!"

As he uttered this, he pulled the trigger. A loud report rung through the house.

He peered curiously at his intended victim.

As the smoke cleared off, he perceived the figure still standing before him, unmoved—the same light smile beaming mockingly on his pale face.

Harwolf could bear no more: he uttered a cry of horror, and fell on his face insensible.

Silas Rye quietly stepped over his body; and, stooping, picked up the pistol that had not been fired.

"By Heaven, I did well to take out the kernels," he murmured, with a triumphant smile; "but I may want one loaded, for I expect I shall have worse foes than ghosts to spend powder on."

He put his fingers into his waistcoat pocket, and pulled out a bullet and slipped it down the barrel.

He turned an evil eye on the prostrate man.

His fingers played spitefully with the lock of the pistol.

"Shall I kill him now?" he muttered, in a hoarse whisper. "No, no—I will not be so merciful: the bitter villain shall not make so easy an exit from the earth which he has so long polluted. He shall hang. I have sworn it. Ha! they are coming. But, victory! I am triumphant!"

As he said this, he struck his heavy foot on the body of his hated foe, and flourished a packet of papers with exultant glee.

Light poured through the keyhole and the crack of the door. A rush of steps and a sound of voices was heard without.

"A good thought," said Silas to himself; "if I leave this pistol loaded, he will think there was no trick. And, better still—the other bullet shall lie there."

He placed the ball just on the spot where he had been standing, threw the pistol down by the side of the squire, and just as a crowd of men-servants, half dressed and well-armed, were rushing into the room, leaped out of the window, which was *croisée* and near the ground.

Hurrying across the lawn and breaking through the shrubbery, he joined a man who was anxiously awaiting his coming.

With pale features and frightened looks, this person advanced towards Silas Rye.

It was Sibly, the lawyer's clerk.

"My God!" he cried, as Silas joined him, "what's up, I thought murder had been done."

"It would have been, and to my cost, if I had not drawn the teeth of the barkers," replied Silas, with a gleeful laugh, "but I opened the bureau with the skeleton key, and closed it again so skilfully that none would ever believe it had been broken into, and here are the certificates, with a bundle of priceless letters, envelopes, postmarks and all; but come along, man, or we shall be seen and pursued. Oh, this is a brave night's work."

With these words Silas Rye hurried his companion away; they increased there speed, and in a short time a long mile lay between them and Frontemore Hall.

CHAPTER XXVII.

THE PIRATE AND THE SMUGGLER.

THE cavern of Ferrole, the French smuggler, was situated a few miles from the fishing town of Vieux-chalet.

It was very extensive and spread far and wide beneath the cliff, either in chambers, or long passages cut in the solid rock.

For several centuries it had been the magazine and stronghold of successive traders in contraband goods.

The father of the present occupant had amassed an immense fortune by illicit commerce, a wealth which, in after years, he had squandered in the gratification of his inveterate passion for gaming.

Ferrole was a man who for a long time had kept up a fallacious appearance of respectability, and had lived in the most luxuriant style, both in Paris and in the country, as a wine merchant; his nefarious practices were at length discovered, and, becoming an object of suspicion to the vigilant police, he had sold up all the possession he could secure and embarked in a defiant enterprise of illegal trading.

His retreat was supplied with every means and appliance for security, convenience and defence; a long covered gallery of rock stretched along the side of the cliff for a very long distance, in which there were cunningly concealed loopholes for the admission of light and air, and for surveying the wide expanse of sea and coast that the view commanded.

A little creek swept in from the bay, and shot under the dark brow of a cavernous hollow; and it was in this place that the boats which brought off the contraband goods from the ships of the free-trader were used to put in, a heavy stone, turning on a pivot on one side of this secret landing-place, giving admittance to its penetralia; from thence a wide passage led into several chambers hewn in the heart of the rock, many of them stores and magazines of the smuggled booty, others, apartments for the use of Ferrole and his gang.

In one of these a number of rough fellows were carousing.

Some were seated on barrels and boxes, others on rude benches about a long rough table.

It was a wild and picturesque scene.

The lurid blaze of a log fire, and the greasy flare of a swinging iron lamp, illumined the stern and weather-beaten faces of the band.

There were men of many nations among them—French, English, Scotch, Irish, Germans, and Spaniards.

There was a large assembly on this particular occasion, as several of the crews were met.

There were cans of grog and dusty bottles upon the table, besides trays of meat and bread.

The men had been regaling, and were now laughing and chatting in picturesque clusters, as they reclined in every attitude of indolent abandonment.

They seemed to be in high spirits, and appeared to have no fear for their security, except that the lamplight glinted on the bristling blades of their knives, or down the barrels of their firearms.

Presently a rough sail which covered the doorway that led into this den of desperadoes was pulled open, and a young officer, in the naval uniform of the merchant service, appeared.

"Messieurs," he said, addressing the party collectively, "Monsieur Ferrole is coming."

At this intimation the men rose, and gathered themselves in a large group at one end of the room.

Two youths cleared the table.

Presently a young man entered; he was dressed in a fashionable style; his hair was luxuriantly curled; he had rings on his fingers, and wore a heavy gold chain.

The smugglers did not take much notice of him, though they acknowledged the courtesy of his slight bow with nods and smiles.

Two seats had been placed at the end of the table; one was a large arm-chair, the other a low stool, on which the young man seated himself, producing pen and ink, and laying before him a huge and massive ledger.

The noise of conversation was suddenly hushed.

Ferrole appeared at the door.

He was about the middle height, dark, and keen-eyed; he was neatly dressed in dark private clothes, but as the flaps of a large great coat he wore opened and folded back, the handles of two long pistols were disclosed.

There was a deep silence, when, after a graceful wave of his hand to invite attention, he addressed the assembly.

His words were few and manly; he thanked the crews of the different vessels for their zeal and good faith, and praised them for their prudence and diligence: he asked the men if they had any complaints to make against their officers, and expressed his satisfaction upon learning that all was well. At this point a coffer was brought in by one of the men, from which Ferrole pulled out a number of money-bags and arranged them on the table.

He then proceeded to pay the men their wages and prize-money, judiciously adding little bonuses to the share of those who had particularly distinguished themselves.

After this he filled up a bumper of wine, and holding it aloft, proposed the toast—

"Unity in our band!"

The toast was drunk with hearty pleasure, for the rough fellows were in rare good humour.

Ferrole filled up his glass once more.

"Success to Free Trade!"

This was drunk with great applause; and when Ferrole set down the glass and left his chair, the men took off their hats and gave three hearty cheers for their liberal and clever chieftain.

His vacating the chair was taken as a signal that business proceedings were at an end, and the men resumed their former ease, and abandoned themselves to the pleasures of drinking, singing, games of chance, and similar amusements.

Ferrole drew near the fire-place and conversed with the officers of his little fleet, and many a strange adventure they had to tell, and many a hair-breadth escape to laugh over: the hours passed rapidly—the mirth was at its maddest, when suddenly a shrill whistle sounded without.

In an instant every man started to his feet.

The officers advanced from the hearth, and the men drew their knives and pistols and listened.

In the sudden stillness that pervaded the cavern, the roar of the breakers and the rush of the wind were plainly heard.

Again the whistle sounded—once, twice, thrice—with a peculiar modification of tone.

A bright smile broke on the clouded face of Ferrole.

"Hurrah, boys!" he cried; "open locks,—for that signal tells of the approach of one whom you will all be glad to see—the gallant Red Raven!"

"Hurrah for the Red Raven," responded the men, with a boisterous cheer.

Several of them left the room.

All eyes were turned expectantly towards the door.

The Red Raven entered. Upon his arm, clinging to him timidly yet confidingly, her sea-washed tresses hanging upon her shoulders, was his beautiful bride.

The men received the heroic pair with a furore of cheering.

Ferrole caught the pirate captain's hand and addressed him in excellent English, and with the faintest accent—

"Ha, Master Christopher, if ever an old comrade were welcome to our smuggler cave it is yourself. When you were but a stripling, we were partners in toil and danger, and now, though you are still but a youth, you have attained to the summit of your ambition—are a free rover, with a gallant ship, a devoted crew, and the fairest bride under heaven. I, too, must not rail at fortune; she has not been unkind to me: I, too, have been successful! But you look pale and your dress is disordered, and this gentle lady doubtless judges us by appearances, and thinks this but a rough asylum for her tenderness."

"You were congratulating me, just now, on being fortunate," said Christopher, with a smile, "if you were informed of all that has happened to me lately you would change your opinion entirely. The tide of ill-luck has set in strong against me, but I am no weak fool to murmur at the caprices of so fickle a jade as Fortune—yet all but the worst has happened to me, Ferrole. I have narrowly escaped with my life; I am quite alone and almost defenceless, and the gallant 'Red Raven' is lost to me for ever."

"There you overrate your misfortunes, Christopher, I am right glad to say," rejoined Ferrole. "Your gallant ship is safely harboured in a little bay along the coast, and she has been refitted under my own supervision. She was saved——"

"Saved! Can it be possible! By whom?"

"By an old friend of yours, Mark Brand."

"What, Brand, the Pilot! I shall be his debtor for ever—but how did he effect her rescue, for I am told that she was wellnigh foundering."

"It is impossible to exaggerate the danger of her position. She drifted from her moorings, and when she stood out in the offing she threw up a rocket, and changing lights, she stood to sea in a direct line from our refuge. She was descried by our look-out, her signals answered, and Mark Brand put out in the pilots' boat, boarded her, and floated her safely into the little creek where I tell you she is lying."

"And what of Brierly, my mate, and young Caffyn, my foster-brother; have you no news of them?"

"Yes, captain, I have; the faithful fellows made their escape from the village inn, and hurried to assist you in that daring encounter you had with the bloodhounds on the beach; but the Red Raven needed not the arms of his followers to save him from a host of such enemies."

"And Brierly and Caffyn are now on board?"

"Yes, captain, and all is quiet and orderly as you could wish."

"Ferrole, to you I shall owe the future triumphs of my wild career," cried Christopher, heartily; "but now I will further encroach upon your kindness by requesting to be permitted to remove this lady to more quiet and secluded quarters."

Ferrole, with great politeness, apologised to Lilia for having, in his eagerness to communicate the good news to the Red Raven, forgotten for a moment what was due to courtesy, and now gallantly escorted the young pirate and his bride into an adjoining chamber in the rock.

The smugglers separated to make way for them as they passed along, and many eyes were bent upon them with looks of intense admiration, and when our hero and his lovely partner turned to acknowledge their murmured expressions of goodwill with a graceful salute, hats were thrown up, arms brandished, glasses clinked, and the hollow caverns rang long and loud to the stirring shout—

"Long life and a bright career to the Red Raven!"

CHAPTER XXVIII.

LADY EDGEFORTH.

WE must now follow the course of Esau, the gipsy, and Joe Miles, who, the reader will remember, had been sent to London to find out the retreat of Lady Edgeforth, and, if possible, to get her away from her guardians.

About noon, on the third day after their arrival in London, Joe Miles and his companion betook themselves to a public house situated in the far east.

It was a large, glaring gin palace, with much tawdry gilding and florid ornamentation, that contrasted miserably with the dirty, sawdust-sprinkled floor, and Miles entered, and, after an appeal to Esau, called for a pot of "cooper."

The pot-boy drew it, and Miles leaned over the bar and nodded to the host in the parlour.

He was a tall, wiry fellow, with little of the jovial Boniface about him, and as he shambled out of the parlour he cast a glance of mingled discomfort and affected pleasure at the recognition.

"Ha, Master Miles!" he said, "it is many a long day since I've seen you, sir; and how are things getting on down in the country; beautiful harvest weather, sure-ly?"

"There be fine weather, Master Nipps; tidy sight, too dry though; and how's business in Lunnon?"

"Mustn't grumble; might be better, might be worse. What will you take, though, and your friend? What shall I offer you, sir?"

"Thank'ee," said the gipsy, "I'll take a glass of summut short for the sake of old times. You don't remember me, I s'pose, Mr. Nipps?"

"Well, sir; really, but I don't."

"In course not, how should you," said the ill-conditioned tramp, with a sneer; "but I remember you though; werry well I recollects you."

"Indeed; 'pon my word I don't know where or how you could have been acquainted with me."

"Oh, you don't; well, perhaps you may call it to mind."

"Hold thy tongue, dolt, will'ee," murmured Miles; "do you think we can draw him out if you be goin' to scare him with what you recollects and what he don't want to remember. Hold your tongue, I tell ye."

The landlord had turned away to wait upon a customer.

The man for whom he was drawing a "go of gin" was a dirty, sottish-looking fellow, short and bloated, his face stained and scarred from the effect of his alcoholic libations. He was dressed in an old and ragged coat, such as is worn by cabmen in rough weather; in his hand was the stump of a whip that for age might have belonged to the original Jehu.

He tossed off the glass, and then lighted his short black pipe, and veiled his face in a cloud, through which his red-rimmed, piercing eyes peered curiously at the two men.

"Now I want to ask ye a question, landlord," said Miles to the host, "and bein' a friend, and in the line like, I thought as you wouldn't mind answering of it to the best of your ability, 'specially as we be coom up to Lunnon on a little business—at least I be—and shouldn't at all mind paying for the information as we requires."

The landlord looked from one to the other of his guests with suspicious eye, and then answered, with a forced smile,

"Well, sir, I'm sure if it's anything I can tell you, I shall be most happy to do so. What's it about?"

"Well, it's about a sartain ewent as took place say eighteen year ago."

"That's a precious long time for a chap to look back upon," rejoined the landlord, with a laugh. "It must have been something very partic'lar for me to keep in my head so long."

"It were something werry pertickler," returned Miles, gravely; "and it were a thing you wouldn't be very likely to forget in a hurry. It be along of a sartain lady."

"A lady—a friend of yours?" asked the landlord, with a laugh.

"Why no, not dizactly," said Miles, shaking his head. "She were a raal born lady as ever were, and she coomed up to Lunnon in the train, and was druv to your old house—the little beer-shop as you used to keep afore you come it out in this style."

"Ah, indeed!" said the landlord, ensconcing himself in the citadel of his extremest caution, and leaning, with well-feigned carelessness upon the bar; "and so she were a real lady, were she? I ought to remember her, 'cos I didn't have many of sich sort at my place. What were she like?"

"Durn it all! I can't tell ye much about her; for, though she sartainly were brought into my house, the fellow as cotched the poor young thing when she were running wild among the fields, and was nigh upon killing of herself, kept her close up, and I did never see her till she was getting into the drag that carried 'em over to Frontemore station."

"Well, Mr. Miles, I can soon tell you all I knows about the party—just nothing, and that's all."

"But I say, what are you skeared on?" cried the country publican; "that fellow you know, Silas Rye—you bean't afeard of him, be ye—doan't ye know as he be dead?"

"You don't say so!"

"E'es, but I do; look 'ere," cried Miles, and he pulled out a pocket-book and showed a little slip of paper cut from the *Times*, and containing an account of the accident.

"Sure-ly!" cried the landlord; "I couldn't have believed it; a fine young fellow as ever stepped in shoe-leather, no meanness in him; he was always ready to stand to any tune. Ah, well-a-day! what does happen!"

"So ye see, Master Nipps, you ain't got no cause to be afeard of he; and a gemman as I knows would give 'ee whatever you like to ask of him if so be as you could supply this said information."

"Well, I should only be too happy, Mr. Miles; but what I don't know I can't tell, can I?"

"And what I do know I can tell," Esau put in, with a coarse grin.

The landlord looked him full in his face.

"If you think you know anything about me, you may do what you like with your knowledge, Esau Cooper, and mind that too much is not known of you in certain quarters. Good morning, gents."

With this the landlord returned to the parlour and shut the door behind him.

"That's no go," remarked Esau, sententiously.

"Darn his carcase, I'd like to rip it out of his liver!" cried Miles, rolling his eyes maliciously, "but come on, we must seek farther, Esau."

Just as they were about to leave the public-house the man who has been described approached and touched his hat.

"'Scuse me, gents," he said in a thick, husky voice, "but I heard a little of your most hinteresting conversation, and I thinks, altho' you doesn't know me, I believe's as I'm the individ'al as can supply you with just the werry information as you're a-seeking on."

"I doan't think you be, maister," returned Miles, suspiciously regarding him, "I doan't see what you've got to do a-meddling with other people's business."

"Oh, werry well, werry well, gents, werry well," returned the little fellow, in a thick voice, shrugging his shoulders deprecatingly, "I begs your humble pardin; I ain't no ways dispodged myself to poke my nose into other people's business; I knows what I knows, and if you don't think it vorth your vile to give a cove a hearin' you must be the losers, that's all as I got to say."

With this the little man turned to re-light his pipe, and was about to depart altogether.

"Stop a minute, my pal," said the gipsy, interposing, "you pretends to know something as we want to larn, what proof can you give that you knows anything at all about it."

"Werry well, let me ax you a few questions."

"Go on."

"Didn't Nipps once keep a beershop down the City Road as was called 'The Recruit.'"

"Yes, I s'pose any of his customers might know that."

"Wait a bit; weren't there a man as used to come there named Esau Cooper, as was lagged for trying to pass flimsies?"

"Thou'rt right. By the lord Harry, he had thee there, Esau!" roared Miles, with a hoarse laugh.

"Wait a bit, I tell ye; wasn't there a pale man as used to come often and sit and write and sich like, as looked too clever to be so poor; and wasn't there another gemman, a reglar country swell, as used to come in and talk to the pale young man?"

"Darnation! this be our man," cried Miles; "he knows what he be talking on, safe enough. Well, neighbour, go on wi' your story."

"I ain't come to my story; I'm ony a asking you warn't it so? Afore I comes to my story I must wet up. I'm a quiet man, and given to observing, but I aint't used to talking—it makes me dry."

"In course," replied Miles, "What's it to be?"

"Another go of rum."

The cordial was drawn and paid for. The little man tossed it off, and recommenced his discourse.

"Well, you must know, I were in better circumstances in those times. I had a 'ansom of my own, and two osses and a four-wheeler, and one night I were ordered by the poor fellow as was killed by accidental death—Silas Rye, I means—to call and take up hisself and another gent at a house in D—— square. I goes and takes 'em up and they went off by the train. Afore they started he took me aside—Silas Rye, I mean—and says he to me—'Tupper,' says he, 'I shall want you to wait at this station for me to-morrow night, and don't mind if I shouldn't arrive by a train or two so early as you expects me.' Well, I waits; he comes; I had two on 'em in the cab, hisself and a lady—werry good fares they was, for Silas Rye always paid like a lord. *Now* do you think I knows anythink?"

"Yes, that may be all very well, and I don't say as it isn't," returned Miles, "but what you did know and what you does know be very different things.

You don't mean to say you know where she be at this identical time."

"Yes, but I do though, and if you likes to come to terms with me, I'll drive you over at once."

"All right, we'll pay you liberal if you can do as you says," returned Miles; "but when do you propose going?"

"Whenever you likes, gents."

"Well, there's no time like the present."

"But what do you mean to do when you finds her?" asked Esau.

Miles smiled grimly.

"You don't mean anything in the settling way?" muttered Esau, in a low voice, pulling his companion aside, and speaking in a low and hurried tone. "If you've got to settle her off, I washes my hands on it. I ain't goin' to run my head in a noose for a bit of a puling woman. Why the devil can't the fellow let her bide where she is?—she don't thwart him no ways, do she?"

"Keep your tongue still, fool," returned Miles, "and let's be off. Comfort your squeamishness, durn yer; we ain't got to do nothing but to get hold on her, and when we've managed that just to write to the governor."

"Well, gents, when do you think you shall require my services? I am usually engaged during sich hours of the day as this; for though I've been unfortnit, I'm of a industrious turn. But when do you think of making a start? I knows where I can get a cab for the day, which I can drive myself; and, as we goes along, gentlemen, we can settle about terms, and I looks to you to act liberal."

With this the party started off.

Their further proceedings may be thus described: On their road to the bait stables, whither they were bound for a cab, they entered several public houses, and, after an animated debate, managed to agree to terms.

Tupper pulled out a dirty pocket-book, in which he wrote out a sort of impromptu agreement, which he made the others sign. He then positively refused to proceed further in the affair till he had been paid five sovereigns down. After this the three worthies selected a cab, and drove off in the direction of the suburb in which Lady Edgeforth was secluded in the wayside cottage of her kind nurse and protectress.

The cab was pulled up at a contiguous inn, and after some consultation it was determined that Miles, as being the most respectable, or rather the least disreputable looking of the party, should go to the house to reconnoitre, and, if possible, to ascertain whether Lady Edgeforth was, under any circumstances, accessible.

Miles started off on this errand, and having reached the house, walked past with a careless air, casting up a glance at the curtained windows in hopes of catching a glimpse of the poor lady. In this, however, he failed; but he was not to be easily beaten. He passed round the houses to some fields at the back, and approaching the house from behind concealed himself behind a little clump of trees and looked up eagerly at the upper windows. One of them was open. Presently a lady came to the window; she plucked the head of one of the roses, and shaking the rich petals apart watched them as they floated down on the still evening air.

Presently the face of a staid and elderly woman was seen. The lady started up and threw her arms about the new comer, who gently smoothed her patient's hair and quietly drew her from the window, which she closed abruptly.

CHAPTER XXIX.

THE "RED RAVEN" TO THE RESCUE!

ONCE more at sea.

Once more the Boy Pirate treads the deck of his gallant vessel.

Once more he is reunited to his lovely bride; and the world is before him!

A steady breeze is blowing, and the splendid craft spreads her wings full before the wind, and glides over the heaving billows with the majestic grace of a swan.

Light clouds stream across the pearly sky and the sunbeams shine clear in the mid-heavens.

Proudly the Boy Pirate walks the quarter-deck, surrounded by his officers.

It may be well to give a brief description of some of the chief amongst them.

The first-lieutenant—for it is ever the custom with the officers of such a crew as that of the "Red Raven" to assume the sounding titles of the Royal Navy—was Jack Brierly; he was a simple old salt, brave as a lion, and honest, so far as the corrupting influence of evil associations would permit—and though, as far as learning was concerned, he was but an ignorant man, he was, nevertheless, a thorough seaman and an able officer. He was a fine handsome old man, and deserved to command in a better service.

Next in degree to our old friend Brierly was Gomez, a dark, fierce-looking Spaniard, the last of the crew of mad Don Miguel Vasquez who had followed the fortunes of the Boy Pirate throughout his career; he was a proud, taciturn and sombre man, somewhat imperious, but a most excellent leader; he was liked and respected by all on board, and, having from his earliest boyhood served in Brazilian privateers and other licensed piratical vessels, seemed to have no compunction for the life he was now leading, and seemed to think his calling perfectly legitimate, and infused a certain sort of chivalry into his most ruthless exploits that partly redeemed them from detestation.

The third-lieutenant or mate of the "Red Raven" was Dick Caffyn; he was remarkable for his great resemblance to our hero in form and features, with whom he had been brought up at Frontemore; in fact, he was Christopher's foster-brother, and in their boyish days these two playmates and schoolfellows had vowed an eternal friendship, and they had well kept their mutual promise, for though the Boy Pirate far excelled his youthful friend in mental and even in physical acquirements, yet he ever preserved a warm attachment towards his young friend, and Dick Caffyn's devotion to his adored superior was extremely noble and touching.

Tom Garrod, the boatswain, was a dashing, rollicking fellow, with lank sandy hair and freckled complexion, nimble as a squirrel, and strong as a lion; fear was unknown to him, and in the worst of perils he always preserved his constitutional gaiety and joyousness.

There were others with whom the reader will become acquainted in the course of this history. But to return to our story: the Boy Pirate walked the quarter-deck, and was conversing merrily with his staff.

Suddenly the man aloft called out—

"Boat ahoy!"

The officers glanced to the larboard. At about a cable's length from the ship appeared a boat containing a solitary passenger. It was a man, who stood up in the stern waving a handkerchief bound to the blade of an oar.

"Heave to," cried the Boy Pirate. "Gomez, that fellow is one of the crew of the young French captain's vessel, the 'Heloise.' Bring him aboard, bo'swain."

"Ay, ay, cap'en!" returned Tom, cheerfully.

A few moments after a good-looking young fellow got over the bulwarks, and pulling off his cap as if he were on a man-of-war, walked aft to the little knot of officers.

"Gules Delorme, you are right welcome," exclaimed the Boy Pirate, shaking the young man heartily by the hand.

"Ah, Monsieur, I am so glad that I have been able to come aboard of your good ship. My captain, Monsieur, is lost."

"Lost; what do you mean, wrecked?"

"Worse than that, he is taken."

"Taken!"

"Yes, Monsieur, taken prisoner."

"For what offence?"

"For no offence, Monsieur, but for a gallant action."

"What do you mean?"

"Monsieur was suspected; my captain took him on board and would have defended him to the last if it had been possible, when Monsieur made such a daring leap from the main-top and disappeared, and before he could be pursued had reached land. Everybody spoke against my captain, and the English officer, M. Harwolf, persuaded the commissaire to put him in irons, and he is now a prisoner on board the 'Astyanax.'"

"Is it possible; the dastards!" cried the Boy Pirate, hotly. "Gentlemen," he continued, hastily turning to the others, "our long cruise in the channel is not yet over. By Lady Fortune, we will leave such a terrible name behind us when we quit these waters, that the cursed blood-hunters shall think the days of Van der Wit and De Reule have come. Garrod, send up Mr. Brand."

The officers looked at their captain with surprise and awe.

"Surely, sir, you don't mean to run on to the teeth of a ship of the line," they asked.

"I will attack the whole fleet rather than my kind friend should come to grief for his noble defence of one who was a mere stranger to him!" cried Christopher, passionately.

The pilot came on deck.

"Mr. Brand, we must have on every stitch of canvas," he said, authoritatively, "we must 'bout ship and retrace our course, for there is a vessel I must overhaul before sunset."

"Must it be so, captain," said the pilot, evidently taken aback by this order. "There is just a capful of favourable wind; but the breeze may chop round, and these are ugly waters; let me entreat you to change your purpose."

"When once I resolve upon a course of action, Mr. Brand, I never allow any consideration to stand in the way of the execution of my resolution."

Brand bowed and walked away; presently his clear voice was heard to sing out—

"Wear ship!"

The men looked rather surprised at this unexpected mandate, and glanced in the fine, earnest face of their heroic young commander.

There was a power in his unquailing eye that the stoutest of them dared not disobey. With a stirring cheer, they hastened to carry out their orders.

"Put the helm up," shouted the pilot.

"And whither are they steering with the prisoner, Gules?" asked Christopher.

"To Cherbourg, Monsieur."

"Helm's a-lee," cried the man at the wheel.

"And what would be the fate of M. Gustave if we could not succeed in overhauling the 'Astyanax?'"

"He would be sent to Cayenne, or possibly they would shoot him as an accomplice and abettor in what they call piracy on the high seas."

Christopher's eyes flashed fire.

"Let go the after bowlines," cried the pilot.

"I hope this will be our last adventure in these waters, captain," said Gomez.

"For the present," rejoined the Boy Pirate, dryly.

The little knot of officers watched with great admiration the evolutions so smartly executed, and so well directed.

"Hillo! aloft; let the boom brace and tack bear an equal strain," cried the pilot.

"Ay, ay, sir," answered the men in the shrouds and on the yards.

Soon was the speeding ship beside the wind, scudding along on her backward track.

"Clear deck," said Christopher "for action; man the guns and serve out the weapons."

"How do you mean to get alongside of our consort, cap'en," asked Brierly, with a dry smile; "do you mean to crawl on her with a decoy, or do you mean to hoist the 'Jolly Oliver' for a battle royal."

"Thanks to my friend Ferrole," answered the Boy Pirate, "our beautiful piece of handicraft is in fine sailing trim and fit for any service; run up the 'Red Raven!'"

The men caught his enthusiasm and gave a deafening cheer.

The banner of death rippled its sable folds as it floated up the stu'nsail and flowed fiercely in the rushing air.

They were now flying along at a terrible rate, and the splendid craft scattered the hissing foam from her graceful bows.

The quickness of her motions caused an exhilaration of spirit to exalt the hearts of these indomitable sea dogs above all thoughts of fear.

The pilot still gave his orders, which were implicitly and deftly obeyed by those aloft.

On deck all was bustle. It was an exciting scene.

Christopher walked from the quarter-deck to the forecastle, directing every movement, and with his quick eye discerning everything. His cheek glowed, and his breast swelled with pride. He had lately passed through so many vexatious adventures, and had encountered so many thwartings from petty sources, as he deemed, that he was overjoyed at the prospect of performing a feat that should throw all past achievements into the shade.

His exertions were ably seconded by those of his officers.

All at once the look-out shouted—

"Sail ho!—sail on the starboard quarter."

The "Astyanax" hove in sight.

Every stitch of canvas was put on, and the vessel sped along through the frothing billows like a lightning flash.

The enthusiasm and excitement among the pirate crew was intense.

"Hurrah for the 'Red Raven!'" shouted Christopher; "we fight here under our own colours."

This speech was eagerly reiterated by the crew. As they got nearer and nearer to the man-of-war, they became almost wild with the eagerness of their daring.

Gomez stood—his hand on the bulwark—his keen eye flashing, and his Spanish face beaming with repressed agitation.

Dick Caffyn had drawn his sword, and lifted his eyes from its flashing blade towards the ship they were so eagerly pursuing.

Brierly stood, with his arms folded, carelessly leaning against the foremast.

The "Astyanax" was now almost within range.

Christopher walked from the quarter-deck to the forecastle, to see if all was in order.

The men, arranged at their posts, received him with a cheer.

An eager look-out from aloft was kept.

It was not impossible that the frigate had a consort.

As it was nothing could be more desperate than the venture they were about to make.

Why was it made?

If anything could palliate the reckless crime of the young pirate's career it was the nobleness of his better moods, and the generosity of his spirit.

Gustave Devigne had served him, and for that service he was now a prisoner and in danger of losing his life.

Christopher would have faced the most appalling dangers, would have matched the wildest odds, rather than allow his friend to suffer harm for him.

As the "Red Raven" flew upon her enemy, skilfully piloted by Brand, the "Astyanax" veered round, seemingly astonished and enraged by the audacity of her pursuer.

A boom from the portholes of the frigate, as the light cloud of smoke floated away in the sunlight, came along the heaving bosom of the sea.

It was the first shot.

It flew wide of its mark.

Still the dauntless "Red Raven" held her course.

The men cheered defiantly as a second shot whistled past their bows.

Christopher conferred with the pilot.

The vessel performed several evolutions.

This manœuvre was so sudden and so boldly managed, that the crew of the Government vessel seemed paralysed with astonishment.

Christopher's clear, ringing voice commanded the men to fire.

For one instant the side of the pirate vessel seemed in flames, the next it belched out dense volumes of light smoke.

The cry that rose from the deck of the "Astyanax" was terrible in its power and fury.

The next moment the effects of the first broadside was apparent: the hull of the "Astyanax" was terribly shattered.

They answered with a dreadful volley.

But it was too late.

The pilot seized the helm, thrusting aside the man who held it.

A light of pride gleamed in his eyes as the stately vessel swayed aside with graceful ease and wondrous swiftness, and shot right athwart the bows of the monster enemy.

It poured in another broadside.

The cannon of the upper gun-deck had been pointed skyward.

Flying with deadly force through the rigging and the sails, the well-directed shot left the tackle of the "Astyanax" in hopeless ruin and wreck.

The crew of the man-of-war were English.

"When Greek fights Greek then comes the tug of war."

This misquoted sentence, set down as the writing of the mad Nat Lee, was very applicable in this case.

The English of the old Norse blood, true descendants of the "Vikings" of Norway, have ever "ruled the waves."

Now, English were matched with English.

Let us ignore the evil courses of the Boy Pirate at this exciting moment; let us deplore that his matchless prowess and wild valour were not bestowed in a better cause; do not let us forget the stainless name, Gustave Devigne, for whose rescue, the gallant outlaw had braved such desperate odds; his generosity in befriending one so warmly favoured by his own betrothed sweetheart.

The ships are side to side.

Nothing but the most untiring celerity and deftest skill can save the pirate crew from destruction.

The guns are well-served—the hostile crafts exchange a raking fire.

The flag of a single rover floats defiantly, with its ghastly symbols, in the very teeth of the guns and the field of the standard of the mightiest empire.

"Now is the time!" cried the Boy Pirate, waving his cutlass. "The grapnels! Let us leap on their deck. Gomez—Caffyn—Brierly, my old and tried friend, do not leave the protection of your devoted leader. If we can take the 'Astyanax,' we will be —not Ravens, but Eagles!"

Christopher turned his eye to the helm.

As with wondrous sea-craft Brand steered the little vessel out of the range of her opponent's guns, he cried,

"Gentlemen, remember that your own superhuman exertions would be nothing but for the skill of our matchless pilot, Mr. Brand. Is all ready? Good. Now for our deathless fame—a grand assault that shall dwarf all our antecedents into playful sport, and raise us to the height of glory's wildest achievements. Hurrah for the 'Red Raven!'"

With this the Boy Pirate rushed to the bulwarks.

No sooner were the grapnels of the robber-ship thrown, than the enemy responded by flinging a double number of their own men upon the sides of the Boy Pirate's vessel.

His men rushed to cut them away. In stern loud tones the desperate young hero forbade them to do so.

With one look of scorn and confidence at his foes, one wild appeal to his followers, he leaped off the deck and boarded the "Astyanax."

He was closely followed by his shouting crew.

Fierce and furious was the conflict; hand-to-hand encounters prevailed all over the deck.

The cannons roared—cutlasses clashed—pistol shots, oaths, cries, shouts, and the "hurly burly" of battle made the wrekin quail—it was a fearful scene, the deck was loaded with the dead and dying, and ran with warm blood, which rushed in rapid channels to the purpling sea.

The pirates were out-numbered. Christopher and his dauntless band were driven back.

Men fell into the water, others fell struggling to the deck.

Harwolf and the officers of the ship fought with the courage of shame and desperation.

Inch by inch the deck was won. Some of the crew of the "Astyanax" clambered the rigging and and poured a deadly fire on their enemies.

This volley, however, was stopped by the command of their own officers, for they fired so recklessly that they killed their own comrades in the melée.

Was it never to end!

The pilot had turned the "Red Raven," and as he still pulled over at the spokes of the wheel, he shouted his orders to the few men aloft, who watched with wild enthralment and impatient regret at their own non-participation in the terrible affray.

Christopher singled out Harwolf. The ruffian, as we have seen, was not a coward.

Their eyes exchanged lightnings of fury; their swords struck sparks in the fierce conflict.

Harwolf's gaze scanned the person of the Boy Pirate, yearning for his blood. The mean villain roared for assistance, believing that if the chieftain of the pirate gang could be slain the battle would be over.

No one answered his appeal; every one was engaged in the settlement of his own quarrel.

The ships were now sufficiently separated to exchange a fearful firing.

It was broadside to broadside.

The Boy Pirate had struck the sword of Harwolf from his hand; and as the dastard flew upon him he knocked him down with a blow of his fist.

Before the villain could rise Brierly and a seaman caught hold of him. At a sign from the Rover Chief they dragged him away.

Christopher then sent word to Brand by one of his midshipman to cease his racking cannonade, because he looked upon the "Astyanax" as vanquished, and wished his prize to be as little damaged as possible.

One more desperate charge of the man-of-war's men—one more deadly fire of the marines—one more furious response on the part of the pirates—and all was over.

The officers were seized—the men were almost all slain—the rest were made prisoners.

The captain, who had fought with unexceptionable courage, lay dead upon the gory deck. Brierly had killed him.

The royal standard was hauled down—the black flag of piracy floated in its place!

Christopher stood exulting on the quarter-deck.

He ordered the ship to be cleared.

He sent for Brand.

The pilot came aboard the "Astyanax," and was warmly praised for his skill and zeal.

Brierly and Caffyn, with others of the crew, rushed below to find Gustave Devigne.

They struck off his irons and brought him on deck.

He embraced our hero, and thanked him with awe and fervour.

"Comrades," cried the Boy Pirate, "whatever be our future chance—even if we die the death of shame—we can look back to this day with the proudest exultation. This grand ship is our own. Henceforth we will embrace higher aims. The

THE ABDUCTION OF LADY EDGEFORTH.

trusty "Red Raven" shall be our consort. This frigate shall be re-named—we will call her the "Fortune of War!"

A thundering shout rent the heavens.

"Hurrah for the ' Fortune of War !' "

CHAPTER XXX.

THE ABDUCTION OF LADY EDGEFORTH.

IT is night—dark and gusty ! The wind sweeps from the open country, down the wide, bare road in which the cottage of Mrs. Wilton, the sanctuary of the poor demented Lady Edgeforth, is situated.

Not a sound breaks the silence; not a star-beam modifies the blackness of the sky.

There has been rain.

Beneath a high, frowning hedge that crowns a steep and rugged bank, two men are crouching.

No. 11.

They remain quite motionless.

A man appears far down the road.

Slowly he tramps by.

He has a lantern hanging at his belt.

He peers curiously along the dark road.

He pries into suspicious glooms and hollows.

He passes close to the hedge beneath which the ruffians are crouching.

They lie quite close and cunningly avert their faces.

He pauses an instant.

The bright ray of his "bull's eye," turned on, dances in a glittering patch upon the wet leaves.

He seems satisfied with his scrutiny, and moves on.

Gradually his footsteps die off in the quiet distance.

Miles and the gipsy emerge from their ambush.

The wind comes blustering past them, howling around the gables and chimneys of the cottage, and bearing in its chill breath the first missiles of the cloudy heavens.

Late as it is, there is a pale red seam in the far west.

After listening awhile the men came forth into the road.

Behind the bushes was a sort of path, just wide enough to admit of the passage of a light vehicle.

Such a carriage came travelling along as stealthily as possible.

A man was on the box closely muffled.

The wind suddenly fell, and the air seemed suddenly close and oppressive. There was a flash of lightning.

"Durn me, Esau, but we'll have a 'nation black night on it."

"A black night and a black job, I think," replied the gipsy, who was looking about him in ill-repressed alarm. "I'm thinking as there's no need for so many on us. You'd better get in, Miles, and I'll keep watch outside; 'cos vy?—didn't we see a peeler on the scent this werry minute?"

"Zo be it, Esau, I'm willin', only look ye, neighbour, if you shirks the wust part of the job, in course you must expect to be paid accordin'."

"Well, what do you want on me, then?" said the gipsy, surlily.

"Why, just to do what I zays, not to funk, and not to make a row. What's there to be afeard on? There's nobody in the house but women, and the wust they can do is to squall, and I s'pose you ain't afeard of a woman's tongue—not but many a better man is mortial scared at it: all az is, Esau, we must gag—but do'ee come on."

There was another flash of lurid lightning. As yet it had not begun to thunder.

"Whew, how the lightning whizzes!" said the cabman, in his thick, dram-harshened voice.

"Zo it do—better to light us to work, my mates," returned Miles.

"Well, come on; let's get the infernal thing over!" cried the gipsy.

"Zoft and zure, neighbour," replied Miles. "If you can bring your purty vehicle a bit nearer the house all the better," he went on, addressing the cabby, "but for marcy's sake don't 'ee make a blazing rowdy-dow with your bandbox."

The cabman gave a chuckle, and softly "tcheking" and shaking the reins, made the horse advance to an opening in the hedge.

"In the devil's name, look out for the crusher," cried Esau.

"Now mate, be ye screwed up and dead on for this lay?" asked the landlord of the Hedgers' Arms, in a dubious whisper.

"Yes; more nor you are, if I ain't sich a brag. Go on, without any more palaver," cried Esau, in a hollow tone, but with blustering fierceness.

There was yet another flash of lightning, this time more dazzling and prolonged. There was a distant murmur, gradually increasing to a sullen roar.

It was the first thunder-clap.

Miles took the lead in the expedition; he was closely followed and promptly obeyed by the gipsy.

The man of many vocations turned to the gipsy and pointed silently to a feeble light that streamed from one of the windows.

There was a rush in the air—a pelting shower poured down upon the thirsty earth.

The trusty agents of the black villany of the blackest of villains stole under the wall.

Before the house was a row of low iron rails.

Miles cautiously clambered over these and crossed the little bed of flowers, and crept round the house, keeping well within the dark shadows.

Esau carefully followed his example.

When they arrived at the back of the house, they stood for a moment irresolute, doubtful as to what course it would be advisable to take.

There was a little outhouse that stretched from the cottage into the garden; it contained gardening tools, bags of seeds, flowers, &c.; the door was fastened by a padlock.

If possible, the night was darker than ever; a drenching shower fell.

"Shall I try my jemmy on this here piece of panel!" whispered Esau, laying his hands on the back door.

"No; do'ee leave the generalship to me, my pal," said Miles, curtly.

A blue glare of lightning blazed and quivered across the heavens, and lighted up every little object with appalling vividness, turning the blackness of midnight to the blaze of noonday!

It was followed by a crashing volley of the celestial artillery.

"I wish she warn't a mad 'un," whispered the gipsy, hoarsely. "I allus hated mad 'uns; they say there's devils in um. I'd rather have to do with ghostes or spectators!"

"Durn 'ee, keep your blabbing tongue still, wull 'ee?" returned the other, in a fierce whisper.

Miles placed his foot on the window-sill.

"Give us thy shoulder, Esau," he said.

With the gipsy's assistance he clambered to the top of the outhouse.

He leant over from the parapet, drenched slippy from the washing rain, and helped his trembling comrade to the roof.

"Gad zooks! yer be but a poor craven, and not a mossel a use at this business; better have kept to your basket, area-sneaking, or kinchin lays; but come on, we mun get in at the staircase window," muttered the sturdier rogue.

Again the fierce lightning dazzled and glared. A little above them was the window of Lady Edgeforth's sleeping apartment.

The cowering gipsy was looking upwards.

In the wild glare of the light that once more brilliantly brought into relief every object in its intense blaze, a female form was discovered at the window.

Dressed in snowy white, with her blue eyes abstractedly and fearlessly upturned to the lurid sky, stood Lady Edgeforth.

She looked so unearthly and spirit-like that Esau gave vent to an irrepressible cry and stumbled backwards.

The thick darkness fell down upon them as if they had been smitten with sudden and utter blindness. Had not the resolute Miles roughly caught his craven mate by the arm, the latter would doubtless have fallen from the house-top.

Even he was so terrified by the suddenness and weirdness of this unexpected apparition, that he felt the pallor that the darkness concealed and trembled violently.

For the moment Esau was quite unnerved.

There was a silence of some duration. Then came the vivid glare of another flash, and by its light the two worthies approached the wall.

Instinctively they looked up at the window—the face was gone.

Miles then clambered up to the casement.

It was a dangerous feat.

The darkness was so intense and the foothold so precarious, that it was only by a miracle that he escaped falling.

Miles having managed to clamber to the window-sill, proceeded to place a piece of prepared material upon the window-pane; he grasped this adhesive covering tightly, and drew a plumber's diamond round the edge of it—he drew back the glass quite noiselessly, and then, inserting his hand, undid the bolt of the sash, and, with extreme caution, opened the window.

The vivid lightning-flash once more broke in a bluish glare upon the white walls,—it discovered the rascal stealthily entering the window.

The deafening bellow of the raging elements growled away, followed by a wild rush of torrents of heavy rain.

Miles carefully lighted a dark lantern, and turning its ray upon his pale and craven fellow-ruffian, assisted him to mount the window.

He stood upon the little landing on the stairs.

There was darkness within, and a comparative hush of the rain-storm without.

The silence was broken only by the patter of the drops and the sluice of the sweeping waters outside, and the jarring tick-tack of a noisy, old clock on the gloomy staircase.

"You knows her room, mate?" whispered Esau, in a thick voice.

"Knows everything; take off your shoes."

"I say, Miles," muttered the gipsy, as he obeyed this order.

"Well; what do you say?"

"*No blood!* Cuss it all, Miles—no blood!"

"You knows our orders is to avoid it. What a cur you be!" returned the other, in the same tone, and in great contempt.

"That's right," replied the gipsy, with a gasp of relief; "mad 'uns and girls as is drownded always walks."

As they passed quietly up the stairs—their boots slung at their sides, treading with the most delicate caution—the fearful anger-lights of heaven burst again through the window, lighting the stairs, silver-gleaming the brass rods, and displaying the white face of the clock.

The hands were meeting at one.

"It's a hawful night!" groaned the gipsy, flinching and shuddering.

"The werry best for our purpose," rejoined the resolute Miles.

They stood before the bedroom door.

It was partly opened.

A faint light streamed from within.

"There's somebody with her," said the gipsy.

"Never mind—it's only another female. We can settle 'em; and you see, Esau, as they may squall till all's blue, and nobody won't hear 'em in this infarnal storm. Look sharp! Where's the crape and the barker?"

"Better not the barker," replied the gipsy, nervously, "it might lead you into mischief."

"You idiot!—give it here! Now, tie up your pretty peepers, and let's make an end of this infarnal job."

"Dear me, who's there? Did any one speak?—is any one outside?" cried a woman's voice from within.

The steps of some one crossing the apartment towards the door were heard.

"Stand by, in the shade; that's the old 'ooman; we'll settle her first," whispered Miles.

The sharp and furious barking of a dog was heard, and a little spaniel flew towards the door. He struggled to get out.

Mrs. Wilton, however, held the door half closed.

She thrust out her head.

"Goodness gracious! I shall go into fits—*is* anybody there?" she cried, in a voice of extreme terror.

Miles, whose face was covered by the black crape mask, suddenly threw his arms about the old lady, and dragged her out.

In an instant he pressed the cold, shining barrel of the formidable-looking horse pistol to her buxom cheek.

The gipsy stood holding the lantern turned fully on—his teeth chattering, and his knees knocking together in abject fear.

All the while the storm raged wildly around the cottage.

Mrs. Wilton struggled for a few moments, and then fell heavily in a dead swoon.

"Humph, that's convanient," said Miles, gruffly. "Now, you lily-livered cove, give us the light, and we'll have a little conversation with the lady."

"Mind—for God's sake, mind—these here mad 'uns is the wust of all sorts to deal with."

Miles placed the landlady as gently as he could upon the ground.

He drew out a strap, and bound her securely to the ballusters.

The precaution was needless, her swoon was deep and lasting.

The two ruffians entered the room of Lady Edgeforth.

The little dog had crouched back, fiercely yelping.

The faithful animal was no little hindrance. He sprang to the side of his mistress.

The rough countryman stooped down and struck the poor little spaniel on his flossy head with the butt of the pistol.

Lady Edgeforth, who was dressed in a long white dressing-gown—her blue eyes wildly flashing—her beautiful, snowy teeth clenched, and her hands extended, rushed upon the countryman, and caught him by the shoulders.

With great coolness, Miles caught her wrist, and disengaging her soft round arms, held her tightly.

She struggled wildly—shrieking and laughing in awe-stricken madness.

The gipsy looked on this scene; he looked a picture of terror.

The lightning all this time was whizzing and seething, the thunder crashing, the wind blustering, and the rain dashing.

The candle had been overturned, and nothing illumined the dread darkness that succeeded every lightning flash but the struggling ray of the dark lantern.

Miles threw the lady back on his left arm and pressed his thumb tightly upon her throat, in such a fashion that she soon fainted.

He threw her over his shoulders.

He was leaving the room; just as they reached the door a vivid blaze shone through the room.

Miles turned his head.

"Esau, there be three on 'em—the young 'un we ain't seen. P'raps she don't sleep in the house. Howsomever, just look round the room, and if you catches her, tie her up to the postes of the bed. I do zay this job will be managed. Come on, mate, the old gal won't recover in a hurry I reckon."

Esau nervously walked round the bedroom.

As he passed the bed he thought he saw the curtains rustle. He started back, and then nervously snatched at the curtain, but found his fears unverified.

Just at this moment, Miles called out to the gipsy to follow him.

The latter obeyed with alacrity.

The storm had somewhat subsided when they reached the door.

They opened it cautiously.

They emerged upon the little green before the house, forced the little gate, and carried their unconscious burden to the gap in the hedge behind which the cab was awaiting them.

They placed the unfortunate Lady Edgeforth inside, and Miles took his seat by her side, drawing down the blind.

Esau leaned on the box, and telling the cabman to drive fast they rolled off at a rapid pace.

They had scarcely departed when a young girl sprang from behind the curtains of Lady Edgeforth's bed, and flew wildly to the window.

She lighted a candle.

Returning to her mistress she found her still insensible.

She rushed madly down the stairs, and issuing by the front door flew through the drenching rain towards the neighbouring house to seek assistance.

CHAPTER XXXI.

THE RESCUE OF THE YOUNG SPANIARD.

AFTER the capture of the splendid frigate, and the refitting of his own rakish craft, the Red Raven, our hero, sailed out of the channel.

After a few days sail he arrived at the mouth of the Mediterranean.

All was well, for all had ended well.

The Boy Pirate had reason enough to congratulate himself on the successful issue of his late perilous adventures.

Gomez, on whom the command of the "Red Raven" devolved, had counselled the Boy Pirate to try his fortune in a cruise in the Mediterranean.

The magnificent frigate and the swift and elegant sloop had assumed a complete disguise: they had mounted the tricolour of Sardinia, and assumed to be trading vessels from that power; and this assumption lent consistency to their half-warlike appearance, as many vessels of the smaller maritime states follow the double vocation of trade and war.

It was a glorious evening.

The Boy Pirate had signalled Gomez to heave to. Through the purple haze of the rich sunset the high majestic cliff of Gibraltar the impregnable rose from the gold-green waves, sublime in the distance.

The sea was dotted with ships of all nations, from the huge broad-sailed frigate to the little swallow-winged felucca.

The hardy pirates—many of them Spaniards—were gathered around their saturnine leader; their eyes glowed with glee and satisfaction at having once more returned homeward.

A boat was put down from the "Fortune of War," and the Boy Pirate was seen to enter it, accompanied by several of his officers.

With their sweeping oar-blades glancing in the red oblique rays of the departing sun, the little bark danced over the long rolling head-waves, and neared the consort ship.

The "Red Raven" fired a salute.

The redoubtable young pirate chief was received with "all honours."

Gracefully bowing and radiantly smiling at the crew he passed aft and ascended the quarter-deck; here he was joined by Gomez and the officers of the "Red Raven."

The men stood about the deck with folded arms, looking on with eager and curious glances upon their young chief and his seconds, who were slowly pacing the quarter-deck and conversing in a low tone.

What were to be their new adventures? What was to be the result of their present cruise?

Who should say? Dangerous and toilsome the wild service in which they were engaged, as in a desperate game of hazard, in which there were a few extravagant prizes to counterbalance the risk of almost certain and most fatal losses.

The officers did not seem to be disposed to reveal the subject of their conversation to the men.

All eyes were on them.

The hardy crew noticed with satisfaction that the handsome, bold face of the young captain beamed with hope and confidence, that his hand clutched firmly at the hilt of his dirk, and that his step was light and free.

After awhile the officers descended to the lower deck, and adjourned to the gunnery. Christopher, Gomez, and the pilot, Brand, examined the condition of the cannon and their mountings, and found everything in excellent order.

They then adjourned to the state cabin.

Several groups of men were gathered in different parts of the vessel exchanging their conjectures and opinions in a whisper of excitement.

"I'll tell ye what, my hearties," said Tom Garrod, a thorough old salt, to a messmate, "my eyes is as good to see through a fog, my ears as quick to hear breakers a-head, as any on you; not as I goes to boast, far from it, but what brings us into these seas?—what is the cap'en's idea in making this little cruise? Ain't that the question, my mates?"

"Ay, we knows what coorse we're steering on, don't we?" asked another, interrupting.

"On course we does, for we're all making full sail, and going to blazes; but what does the young Raven think we're made on? Does he think we're composed of some sort of material as is gun-proof, and that we've got nerves like the links of the sheet-chains. Shiver me! but I think he means taking Gibraltar."

"Avast there, ye lubbers," growled a villanous looking fellow, whose intense black eyes were set in a face that bore the look of mahogany, "why don't ye listen to your betters; let us hear what Tom Garrod has to say of this cruise."

"No, no, I knows manners; any gentlemen ready to offer a opinion let him rig his jawing-tackle and sing out 'What is the cap'en's notion in making this little cruise, my hearties?'"

"A-going to set fire to Constantinople, and carry off all the pretty girls from the Harem," suggested one.

"A-going to put a stopper on Mount Vesuvius, and put its pipe out," added another.

"Hush! ye swabs, here they comes; parade the decks, and be hanged to ye!"

When Christopher appeared on board with his gallant, jaunty air, his grave companions by his side, the men received him with an irresistible cheer.

"My boys," cried the young chief, with a smile and a wave of his hand, "the 'Red Raven' now sails in the wake of the 'Fortune of War,' and from the mainmast of our 'Fortune' we can plant the standard under which we have served so gloriously. I have no doubt that you are all in a state of excitement. True sea-dogs eager for the chase, all in wonder as to the cause and the conduct of our present enterprise. Comrades, I have no secrets from you. I am no crafty diplomatist to concoct plots and carry them out by using my faithful followers as blind agents. We feel all—we know all—we shine with all—we share all—together! In the present instance my schemes are not yet quite matured. I shall have to call upon you for your unquestioning aid in several ventures, but I am confident in my assurance of your devotion. Comrades, you can trust me?"

"To the death, cap'en! to the death! Hurrah for the Red Raven!"

The men shouted enthusiastically.

The Boy Pirate smiled proudly at the responsive cry.

It was getting dusk; the stars gleamed out, sprinkling the blue vault, and glimmering on the foamy crests of the heaving billows.

A man had stepped to the side of Christopher.

"Cap'en, there's summut alongside, under the lee quarter, and a sort of a parlez-vous — I fancy, though, as he's a Spanisher—a-roaring to come aboard."

"Ha! we must beware of treachery; we are venturing into its veriest stronghold," said the Boy Pirate, cautiously. "What sort of fellow is he, Williams?"

"Not much of a fellow, anyhow, cap'en," replied the man; "he's a dark, slight-built young chap, with ragged ducks and a guernsey as never was worn out by soap."

"Is he armed?" asked Gomez.

"Yes, senor, armed and handed, but devil a weapon has he got except a spar with a piece of rotten board tied to the end of it to make a oar on. Seems to me, cap'en, he's some chap as has slipped the darbies, and is doing a night run to escape from some prison hulk; there's loads on 'em along this coast—some for females, leastways, as they calls nunneries——"

"And what sort of boat has he?" Gomez enquired.

"Never a boat at all, senor, he is clinging to a few planks bound together for a raft—he looks wild-like and gabbers away for a wager."

"Bring him on board," said the Boy Pirate.

This order was at once obeyed.

A thin, haggard-looking youth, with handsome though worn features and long unkempt hair of raven blackness came on deck.

He was dressed in the manner the sailor had described, and presented an appearance of piteous distress and exhaustion.

With instinctive sympathy Christopher stepped forward and caught him as he staggered against the bulwarks.

"Thanks, senor, many thanks," said the Spaniard, in a hoarse voice and with a feeble smile.

"Good heavens! what cruel sufferings have reduced so fine a youth to such a grievous condition," exclaimed the Boy Pirate.

"Senor, they were harder than the chains they bound me with. I will tell you all if you will give me some food. I faint with hunger—I have passed three days on the sea without eating—but you will not give me up, senor ?"

He went on nervously starting and looking doubt-ingly in the faces of the stern pirates, who looked on with countenances expressive of rough but genuine pity.

"We are true men: neither the spies nor the agents of the law: we are neither judges nor execu-tioners. But what is your crime ?"

"An insane but ungovernable passion for the most beautiful woman on earth."

The pirates laughed.

"Rather a light offence to warrant so heavy a punishment," remarked the Boy Pirate.

"Alas! senor, my offence is heinous in the eyes of all good catholics."

"Indeed, I never thought that love was a crime with any sect."

"But, senor, this lady for whose sake I have suffered so much is a bride of the Church."

"If you were in better condition, I think you would make the better husband," replied Christopher, with a laugh.

"Senor speaks Spanish well, but he is an Italian ?" said the stranger.

The Boy Pirate waved his hand towards the banner of green, white, and red that streamed from the stu'nsail, but did not answer the question in any other way.

"I see, senor; it was your tricolour that attracted me, and the hope that, as the subject of a free and gallant kingdom, ever the sworn foe of bigotry and oppression, you would aid and protect me, which urged me to the most terrible exertions to reach this ship. I am here, senor; I throw myself upon your mercy, and claim your generous sympathy."

The Boy Pirate took his hand.

"You will find me ever glad to succour the unfor-tunate, and you have paid me a high compliment by the free and perfect confidence you have placed in my honour and humanity. Be assured, if I can help you I will. Maybe I can even help you in your love affair. The lady, I presume, is a novice in some convent ?"

"She is, senor; but, ah! so eager to escape. She is very rich, and the abbess and the priests are so enraged against her, for they have discovered that she loves me, and are in terror of loosing their prize. She has now a weary life of it; nothing but chiding and penance—punishment and tears."

"We will carry her off, by the furies!" cried Christopher, his eyes sparkling. "'Twill be a gallant feat; but tell me, what is her name ?"

"Senor, her beloved name is Aurora Vasquez."

"Can it be possible!" cried the Boy Pirate and Gomez in a breath.

"She is the daughter of a South American planter long since dead, and of late she has inherited a rich legacy from a relation at Madrid."

"It is the daughter of Don Miguel, my preserver and your old commander. Gomez, what do you say to this ?"

"What is the name of the convent?" asked Gomez, with suppressed eagerness, his cheek glow-ing, and his eyes gleaming with a strange light.

"St. Esperanza," replied the youth; "but I beseech you ask me no more questions—let me have food and rest and I will tell you all; but first be kind enough to strike off this shackle—through my unwonted exertion my leg has chafed against the stricture till it has swollen: the iron eats into my flesh."

As he spoke, he advanced his half-bare leg which, with his shoeless foot, was terribly swollen.

A heavy iron ring surrounded the ancle, and seemed embedded in the discoloured flesh.

On the other leg there was also a purple rim which betokened that that member had also been subject to the same cruel ligature though the shackle was gone.

The fierce pirates gave a groan of indignation.

By the Boy Pirate's orders the man was led away, and after his cruel bond had been removed was care-fully tended by the surgeon of the vessel; he was then refreshed by a moderate but substantial repast, and lay down for an hour in the hammock slung for him in the cabin.

CHAPTER XXXII.
THE YOUNG SPANIARD'S STORY.

AFTER his sleep he rose much invigorated, and in obedience to a summons from a young officer, made his way to the state cabin.

Here he found our hero and his bold companions seated around a table, on which were decanters and bottles of wine and spirits and little baskets of choice fruits.

The young Spaniard had received a change of clothes from the sailors, and now that he was refreshed by food and rest appeared a very graceful and comely youth.

He seated himself at the bottom of the table; the wine was passed to him.

An excited and merry interchange of banter and jest was going on round the table.

Christopher called the young Spaniard to his side, and placed him between himself and Gomez, and they carried on a conversation in an under tone.

"What is your name, my young friend," asked the Boy Pirate; "let us be well acquainted with each other's affairs. I will trust you as far as is con-sistent with the responsibility I am burdened with; do not hesitate to confide in me."

"I trust you freely and thankfully, noble senor. My name is Manuel Perez; I am of good parentage, and am a student apprenticed to an eminent physician. I am of warm and enthusiastic tempera-ment. I heard awhile ago that the aunt of a poor novice in the Convent of St. Esperanza had left her a large fortune—for it was the talk of the whole town—and that the young lady was surpassingly beautiful and very anxious to make her escape from the nunnery, which belonged to an avaricious and very severe order. Of course the young novice's wish to return to the world was strenuously opposed by the priests and the sisterhood, and every inducement was held out to her to remain and to confirm her vows by the irrevocable act of taking the black veil; how-ever, being still under age, they could not compel her to this fatal deed, and the superiors of the order were not appointed executors or guardians by her aunt's will, for she had left the charge of the vast property to the care of a certain notary in Madrid, who had been her own lawyer and confidential adviser, and who, though an astute and worldly person, and one certain to oppose any suit, is nevertheless a practically just and worthy man. Under these circumstances every one expressed their commiseration for the poor young thing, whose bright prospects were to be quenched in the gloom of the cloister, and who, so well fitted to charm and to enjoy the world, was to be buried alive in the dungeon of a dreary nunnery. Now having much leisure time, being of a romantic and adventurous spirit, and having taken a fancy to Quixotic adventures through my love for reading works of fiction, I took it into my head that I would devote myself to this lady's service, and that I would leave no means untried to effect her release. Now it chanced that I had a certain friend who was a lay brother of a religious order, and he lived in a house adjacent to that occupied by my master, the doctor. I prevailed upon this young man, who is not a priest by choice, but is forced to the selection of the ecclesiastical profession by the influence of rich relations, on whom he is entirely dependent for sup-port, to lend me a suit of canonicals and some papers, with a breviary and the like, in order that I might personate a lay brother, and obtain admittance to a certain house—as I told him—where a young heiress was watched by a lynx-eyed duenna. He gave credence to my statements as to the motive of my request and "got me up" with great care and pre-cision. It cost me a luxuriant moustache and whiskers, and I narrowly escaped having my head shaved; but when my disguise was complete I started off to the convent. I fabricated a plausible tale, conciliated the abbess by some well-timed compliments, and by telling her that I was a relation of Aurora Vasquez, and had come to use my eloquence to induce her to stay. As I played my part well, I prevailed upon the abbess to admit me to the presence of the beautiful young novice. I was taken into a little cell, Aurora was summoned, and the abbess, who seemed to be fully deceived by my plausibility, left us together. We recognised each other at once."

"How so?" cried the Boy Pirate, quickly. "When or where could you have met before?"

"I ought to have told you, senor, that it was a conviction I felt of having at some time seen the lovely Aurora that chiefly led me to think of risking such a feat as obtaining a meeting with her."

"But you have not answered my question," said Christopher.

"No, no, senor Perez, you forget that Aurora has been shut up in the convent since her girlhood. When and where could you have seen her?" rejoined Gomez.

"Have patience, senors; you all know that it is the custom for the nuns to walk in procession at certain festivals of the Church; you also know that they assemble within the grating in the cathedral when any of the sisters take the veil. On several such occasions I had been greatly touched by the sweetness and beauty of the face of one among the novices. We had exchanged glances; her delicate cheek glowed, and her soft eyes fell; she was evidently pleased, in spite of her maiden bashfulness, with the hearty admiration and tender sympathy my features must have expressed at such moments. We met in this way several times. The sweet, lovable, and saintly face haunted my sleeping and waking dreams; it was with me everywhere; I yearned with intense longing to hold one woman's communion with the beautiful unknown, to tell her how deeply I loved her, for love is an impulse prolonged."

"That's true. 'Who loved at all that loved not at first sight?'" interrupted Christopher, smiling.

"Good, captain, but let him go on with his story," rejoined Gomez, with impatience.

"Well, senors, I told you the worthy abbess left me alone with the fair creature whom I had risked so much to serve, and for whom I would have dared a thousand far more terrible dangers."

"Though torture and rat-dungeons are not unknown in your precious country, Senor Perez," rejoined Christopher.

"Nay, captain, let him go on. Don Miguel's daughter—I must know all that concerns my master's child. Go on, senor."

"I took her hand," pursued the young Spaniard, "and I spoke to her as tenderly and respectfully as I could. She turned deathly pale, and wrung her little hands in breathless terror. Then the rose-tint on her cheek deepened to the richest red, and in sweet tones she pleaded, with a voice broken by sobs and with soft eyes beaming with gratitude and timid affection, that I would be gone. I drew her to me—I clasped her in my arms. She shuddered and half fainted, but I pressed my fervid lips to hers, and I wildly fancied that they received just the faintest returning pressure. We were all alone, within those grey stone walls, but we were in heaven—we were intensely happy. With childlike artlessness and pure simplicity, she told me that she loved me, and that in spite of all her efforts she could not exclude me from her thoughts. Yet every instant she would look around her, like a startled gazelle, and entreat me, in a frightened whisper, to fly. I reassured her, and then she told me her story. She had not much to tell. In her earliest childhood she had been placed in the convent school. At times her father came to see her, and would sometimes carry her with him on a voyage, for he was the captain of a stately vessel, but whether a ship of trade or war she could not remember. In fact, she never knew,

for she said that, with strange care, her father kept her out of all collision with his crew, making her a petted prisoner in the state cabin, and only allowing her to take exercise on deck when the men were as far as possible removed. At her father's death—he was killed in some naval engagement, the particulars of which never reached her—at her father's death, a marked change took place in the demeanour of the lady abbess. She became suddenly sour and authoritative. She had never shown much liking for Aurora. It was rumoured that the lady superior had formerly been betrothed to Aurora's father, and that she had lost him through her indomitable pride and arrogance; and that he had, after the last of their long series of quarrels, incontinently married another lady, who became the mother of our fair young novice, and this might account for the dislike the abbess manifested towards her rival's child. Aurora was now sixteen years old, and was removed from the school and associated with the sisterhood as a novice; then her trials commenced. The lady abbess treated her with the most vindictive harshness and cruellest severity. Her childlike spirit was not broken, but was subdued to a mild submissiveness that was void of all meanness, for it arose from her isolation from the world, her early training, her respect for the abbess, her native gentleness and devotional fervour. With touching meekness she submitted to every affliction. She told me that for two years her life had been one continual round of exhausting fastings, wearisome rituals, painful prostrations on the cold stones in dank cloisters, and severe penitential floggings, inflicted by malicious hands on her nude flesh for the most trifling omissions or merely in the way of general discipline. She seemed so tender and sorrowful, so saintly, yet so simply and lovingly feminine, that I could scarcely tear myself away from her. However, I was forced to go. We hurriedly planned, or rather I eagerly found, a stratagem for her abduction. She listened, shook her head, and wept. I left her, telling her that I would return soon in the same disguise, and that I would find means to bribe the porter of the convent, or that I would find some other means of rescuing her from her purgatory of restraint and misery. I also impressed upon her that she must affect resignation to her fate.

"The lady abbess eagerly questioned me. I told her I had met with unexpected success, and counselled her to render Aurora's life at the convent as pleasant as possible, and assured her that I would return and use my best influence with the young novice to confirm her half-given promise to take the black veil."

"And after this I suppose you made an attempt to carry her off," said Christopher.

"I did, senor, and it failed,—miserably failed."

"What was the result?"

"We were taken, both disguised as priests, just as we had reached the outer gate of the convent, having passed all obstacles. Then the gentle penitent seemed suddenly transformed; her lovely form seemed to dilate with passion when I was roughly seized by the sturdy priests and lay brothers and was dashed to the ground. She threw herself between us, and with the resistless power of her beautiful weakness, that even those rude bigots and tyrants could not but intuitively respect, she withheld them from harming me. The rage of the abbess was boundless, and she gave free scope to it; for she had just received a letter from the notary I spoke of, whom she had, through a correspondence, cajoled into the belief that Aurora wished to stay at the convent, that gave a sanction to his young ward being devoted as a bride of the church. I was bound, and, before my eyes,—but let me not think of it, senors!"

The fierce young Spaniard leaped to his feet, gnashing his teeth, and clutching his hands together in ungovernable and unspeakable rage.

The stern pirates, who had not listened to the former part of the story, had for several moments begun to lend attention, attracted by the evident excitement of the narrator.

"Nay, tell us all: let us know the worst of your wrong, for you shall have ample revenge. I, the Boy Pirate, tell you so; and I should keep my word, were I not, as I am, bound, for other reasons bound, to aid your beautiful novice, under whose father I first served."

"Go on, you hear the captain," said Gomez, in a hoarse, thick voice, his eyes searingly bright and motionless with eager rage. "You were bound, and she, Aurora Vasquez——"

"Was stripped of her disguise by the abbess, and mercilessly scourged in my maddened sight; after which I was borne away, placed in a boat, and carried across the little bay, where I was taken to a sort of monastery—a college for priests—and was placed in a deep, dark cellar, loaded with chains. I was left so long in the stench and darkness, that I began to think that it was the intent of my captors to leave me to perish by the lingering pangs of starvation; but at last a surly fellow brought me some hard, stale bread, and a pitcher of filthy water. I implored him to leave me a light, but he refused; and I was left alone in the gloom to my bitter reflections.

"You may imagine my sensations. I could see the ravishing form of my own loveliest and adored one writhing beneath the pitiless lash, so cruelly plied by the hands of her venomous tormentor. I could hear her sweet and plaintive wail—I could grind my teeth in the madness of my impotence. Then I recalled my present position; then the truth forced itself upon me, that I was doomed to remain a wretched, hopeless prisoner in the vilest of dungeons for life. As I sat, one weary hour, in the solitude and darkness, I noticed that the washing of the sea at high tide or in rough weather was distinctly audible in my prison, and I fancied I could hear the sound of water trickling down the walls. But I was heavily shackled, alone, and in the dark. In my confusion in being brought to the place I had noticed positively nothing, and I dared not move. At length I bethought me that I had a box of lucifers in my vest. I opened it and struck a light. For a moment the place was lighted up with a feeble glare, that shone on the damp and slimy walls and along the puddles on the floor, in the black waters of which hideous rats were splashing. Then, again, all was darkness, as the weak and momentary flame expired, and threw me back into my fearful night of horror. I lighted another stick of wood, and grudgingly watched the greedy flame devour each precious inch that gave me eyesight. Quickly I looked round. A steady flow of water streamed down the wall opposite in a trickling streak; and it was plain that my terrible cell was built beneath the level of the sea, and that the water oozed in through some crevice in the stone.

"Again I struck a light. This time I made a fresh and important discovery: above my head swung a rusty iron lamp, suspended by a rotten chain. By standing on the stone settle on which I was sitting, I could just reach this lamp. To my unutterable content, I found it yet contained a modicum of oil and a piece of wick. With great difficulty, and after breathless anxiety, I contrived to fire the thread. The flame spluttered and flared, and every corner of my prison was made visible. The place was octagonal; there were four pillars by the walls and two in the centre, and it was plain that the water-level must be high, in fact, close beneath the ceiling.

"The rats, alarmed by the sudden breaking of light upon their darkness, dashed off in all directions, their little dark bodies and whisking, fleshy tails showing hideously as they rolled over each other in crawling masses.

"What wretch could be farther removed from hope than I was? To whom could despair have seemed more reasonable than to me? Yet I dared to hope. I thought of Aurora—I drew courage from her sweet name, as I lovingly and pityingly murmured Aurora! Sweet spirit of morning freshness and purity, she arose in all her brightness to herald the sun that should disperse the thick clouds and darkness of this loathsome night. Besides, wondrous escapes had been made by captives under circumstances as desperate as my own. I recalled the adventures of Trenk and of De La Tude, and I resolved to make one bold effort for emancipation. But while I was thus shackled my movements were so much impeded as to render any hopes of my being able to work my deliverance impossible. I looked about for some means to unfetter myself. I found a pair of rusty nails and a piece of an old ring, probably the remains of the shackles of some unfortunate predecessor, that had been knocked off before his leaving that prison to seek his liberty through the dark portals of the grave. With incredible labour and a power of endurance a sense of my fearful peril alone could give, I contrived to file and shatter away every link but the iron ring you saw upon my leg when I came on board; this I could not remove. Every now and then I paused in my work breathlessly to listen, but I heard no sound save the sullen plash of the water as it lapped against the stones of my prison, and the rustle of the scampering rats; all was deathly still. Perhaps I was only mocking myself; perhaps I should only render my state more intolerable by this futile attempt at an escape; yet I quelled doubt. I could not suffer more than I had already borne.

"I steadily worked at my task, and I was comparatively free, so far as my bodily movements within my confined space were concerned. I walked round and round my cell. Arming myself with the nails, I scrambled up the wall, by placing my fingers and toes in the interstices of the rugged blocks of which it was built, and I listened intently to see if I could judge by the flow of the waters how high the tide reached. I could only judge by the stream of water pouring down. I reflected that it did not always run; consequently the little aperture through which it came must be above water at low tide. With intense anxiety I sat watching the stream for hours, till it subsided, and the green smeared line it had tracked down the wall remained clearly defined in its moss-like viridity. Then once more I clambered to my hold. Eagerly I worked away, driving at the stone with lunges, and boring, and scratching, and chipping, till I became so faint I almost fell prone from my feeble tenure. At length a stone gave way. Through the chink I looked out. Though it was low tide I could perceive that there was a good depth of water. However, no time was to be lost—the hour when the gaoler generally visited me was close at hand. I worked away for dear life! I had made a pretty large aperture. Anguish and privation had wasted me to a skeleton.

"After a few more strokes I was able to emerge, but it was a terrible feat, and I threw myself into the sea with a qualm of despair. However, I struck out. It was evening. In my lonely prison I had no means of judging whether it was day or night. I knew too well that there was eternal night within; and in such cases people soon lose their reckoning with respect to times and seasons. But as I breasted the waves, I felt to some extent free. But whither should I direct my course? Should I turn towards the shore of the creek? No doubt I should be taken if I ventured within miles of the convent. The boundless ocean was before me; a long reef ran far out into the sea. At the end of it was a high sandbank, the summit of which was never completely covered, even at the highest tides. Thither I swam! I reached it with great toil, for I was faint and weak. On this islet I remained for the rest of the night, shielded by the rocks. And during the next day I could see that the shore was covered with peasants, called out to arrest the profane wretch who had dared to carry off a bride of the Church. What could I do?—I was at my wits' end. Some broken spars of a wreck washed up to the reef; I secured them, and formed a kind of raft, by binding them together with some rope that I found attached to them. I saw your vessels standing out to sea, and at once I recognised the Sardinian tricolour. The rest you know; and, in concluding my long story, I am bound to express my ardent thanks for your kind and noble protection."

"You have nothing yet to thank me for. But have you anything to add respecting Donna Aurora?" said Christopher.

"Alas! nothing; but I fear that she will be made the object of the cruellest tyranny."

"She must be rescued," said Gomez, firmly.

"She shall be," rejoined the Boy Pirate.

"I'll tell you what it be, cap'en," said Brierly; "it strikes me that the sooner this bit of business is cleared off the better it'll be for all parties, specially for the poor young lady herself; for though my experience of monstrosities ain't so wery limited such an infernal black piece of cruelty I never heard on. And as for this here lady abbess, which I s'pose is captain of yonder great ugly hulk, she out-Jezebels Jezebel, and ought to be flayed with her own cat-o'-nine tails."

"Let us run in to-night when all's quiet, captain," said Dick Caffyn. "We can take the place by assault and carry off our prize."

"No, no; that's folly, Dick," returned the Boy Pirate. "Our late successful escape from foolishly incurred perils ought to teach us caution and not rashness; besides, the wretches would most likely remove the lady or even murder her before we could effect an entry; the place is strong and jealously watched. What do you say, Gomez?"

"I say you are right, captain," returned the Spaniard, thus appealed to. "Let us get out the pinnace and run her close in shore; we will then disembark with Señor Perez for our guide, and will contrive by some means to get into the convent and effect her deliverance."

"I approve of the scheme," returned the Boy Pirate, "and I am sure that Senor Perez will lend us his assistance."

"Oh, senor," cried the young Spaniard, starting up and catching his hand. "I bless my captivity, I am pleased with my suffering, since they have led me to so noble a person as yourself. I shall yet be united with the hapless and lovely Aurora; I shall yet have to serve out a life of gratitude to the bravest and most chivalrous of—of——"

"Professed adventurers," Christopher joined in, with a smile of bitterness.

"To the most generous of men," Perez went on, with a blush. "And there will be sweet lips to breathe a prayer for you, senor, that will not be unavailing, for the saints will protect you in your darkest peril when invoked by one so little removed from them in purity and goodness."

The pirate captain smiled.

"Comrades," he said "let all who choose to volunteer for this dangerous service fill a cup with me. Who will follow me?"

Every hand eagerly filled or raised a glass.

"All, captain! all!" cried the pirates, in stern and hearty tones.

"I thank you heartily for your zeal, and will leave it to Gomez to make a selection, and doubtless for many obvious reasons he will choose the Spaniards of the crew. In the meanwhile let us fill to the success of our gallant enterprise, and let us drink all happiness to the beautiful Aurora, the rover's daughter!"

Glasses clinked, and with a cheer the toast went round—"Aurora, the Rover's Daughter."

CHAPTER XXXIII.

THE ABBESS AND THE CANON.

OUR scene is a large and comfortable apartment in the convent, with stained windows and Gothic but rich and commodious furniture. On the walls were several splendidly gilded and illuminated pictures, illustrative of saintly legends, with crucifixes and little statues of the Virgin and the saints in niches. The windows were of stained glass, through which the moonbeams stole with mellowed radiance. High candles in heavy stands were placed upon a little devotional table, at the foot of which were piled some splendid cushions of crimson velvet, richly embroidered in gold threads. Before the genial fire that blazed on the ample hearth the abbess was pacing up and down with haughty and excited mien. She was a superb woman, not past the meridian of life; she was tall and commanding, her face ascetic and cruel in its expression, her thin lips tight-drawn, with remorseless primness; her cheek was aglow with exultant gratification, and her eyes with the fire of insatiate spite. As she paced up and down like some majestic Nemesis her long, lithe fingers firmly clutched a little "discipline," or knotted scourge, such, as it is well known, is used even to this day as a means of inflicting penance in many religious establishments by the hapless and credulous enthusiasts, who cling to the false and cruel traditions of the darkest of dark ages. The Nemesis was thinking of her fancied wrongs, and was gloating over her imagined triumph, forgetting that good is stronger than evil, and that if virtue is its own reward (and it need be as the world goes) vice is its own punishment. She thought how she had been jilted by a lover whom she thought her slave; she exulted over the shame her rival had wrought him, and the fatal termination of his career; and now that he was gone her insatiate lust of vengeance craved to vent itself upon his pure and lovely child. She played, with the fiendish pleasure that characterises a thoroughly bad-hearted woman, with the sceptre of her cruel sway, and then flinging it into a corner, seated herself luxuriantly before the blazing fire.

There was a knock at the door.

A priest entered.

"Peace be with you, my sister!" he said, inclining his head.

"And with you, reverend father!" replied the abbess.

"I have come, my sister, to have a little serious converse with you concerning your rebellious novice Aurora Vasquez."

With this the dignitary—he was the prior of a neighbouring monastery—seated himself and looked searchingly at the abbess.

The haughty lady bit her lip and answered coldly.

"Indeed, father, there is no subject I have more at heart, and I am almost in despair about her. She is incorrigible."

"What means have you used to bring her to reason?"

"I have used means of every kind."

"Persuasion?"

"Yes, father; I have exhausted my eloquence in vain."

"Indulgence?"

"She has been more indulged in every idle wish than the strict rules of our holy order warrant."

"And have you tried coercion?"

"As a last resource."

"Indeed! yet you have ever been faithful in the discharge of your maternal duties, and have been rigidly strict, even to severity."

"Young girls require severe regimen; they are impulsive, and the heart of youth is ever prone to evil instincts, which must be uprooted with a strong hand; but since she has been a novice, at least, of late, I have held a gentle course—you see the fatal consequence."

"And how do you treat her now?"

"Severely—according to the rules of our order; her stubborn spirit must be tamed by penitence and stripes."

A dark shade passed over the features of the priest, and he said, somewhat sternly—

"I question the prudence of the course you are taking, and must warn you that you do not drive the poor child to desperation. Let me see her."

"Nay, father, not now," said the abbess, reddening and hesitating. "Pray, find some apter season. The foolish child has just refused the responses to the anathemas I thought it expedient should be read in

THE FIGHT ON BOARD THE PIRATE SHIP.

the oratory against the profane heretic who dared to perpetrate an act of sacrilege that is unparalleled in its boldness and atrocity. She refused to join in the responses, and, of course, I was in duty bound to punish."

The frown on the priest's face darkened; he gasped for breath, but answered calmly.

"You did wrong, my sister; inordinate zeal is a fault rather than a virtue, and when we forget humanity we slight divinity. Let me see this wronged and unhappy girl."

"Father, I am not used to be dictated to in matters of conventual discipline, especially in an establishment of which, by the saints' favour, I am the
No. 12.

head," returned the fierce abbess, with burning brow.

"My sister," returned the priest, "we, whose passions are dead, should resist the Devil when he stirs up in our hearts the leaven of the old Adam. Pride and self-esteem are sad stumbling-blocks in the Christian's path, and He who carries the young lambs in his bosom would never give his divine sanction to the cruel punishment of a natural feeling. I must see the poor girl at once."

"By whose order, father?"

"If by my own desire, why refuse me?"

"In this case, father, I must be firm. The girl has retired—I have given orders that she should be left to her own reflections. Pray do not interfere with my arrangements," returned the abbess, in a haughty tone of determination.

"But, my sister, my orders are peremptory, and must be obeyed."

"Orders! from whom?"

The priest drew a packet from the breast of his robe, and replied, with a sinister smile—

"From his eminence the Cardinal Gonsalvez."

The abbess turned very pale and then crimsoned as she read the contents—and cried with animation—

"Why, father, what does this mean? 'Instant removal from the convent!'—do I read aright? 'Under charge of his Reverence the Prior of St. Juan,' and 'to-night!' Really this is very sudden. I must protest against such a measure; the girl is not in a fit state to leave the convent at this late hour; she has excited herself—is unwell. The cardinal has ever manifested a tender interest in this unworthy sister, and he cannot wish at such an hour—the nights are chill—besides—

"Hesitation is needless, my sister," rejoined the priest with a sneer. "I fully appreciate your solicitude for the frail and foolish child, but your maternal anxiety must not lead you into a useless and vexatious opposition of the express commands of his eminence. Conduct me at once to the sister Aurora."

Without waiting for a reply the priest moved from the apartment, and was proceeding up the corridor when the abbess, flushed and greatly alarmed, flew after him.

He walked on swiftly.

A nun met him.

"Sister Agnes, show me the cell of the novice Aurora."

The recluse gave a glance of surprise and pleasure—bowed her head, and then led the way.

The abbess had joined them.

They stood by the door of a solitary cell.

Convulsive sobbings and piteous wailing were heard from within.

"The evil and ungovernable temper of the heretical creature has rendered her fairly hysterical," said the abbess, in a hollow voice of stifled rage and mortification.

The priest bowed coldly, and signed for her to open the door.

Sister Agnes took up a lamp from a stone slab in the wall.

The abbess with trembling fingers applied the key.

The heavy door flew open with a harsh jar, and the nun held the lamp aloft, and its light illumined the small stone chamber.

A sad sight met their eyes. Crouched down by the side of her bare hard pallet, Aurora was reclining.

Her rich hair streamed dishevelled on her shoulders. She was half undressed, but had thrown her robe loosely around her frail, beautifully moulded form.

Her hot cheek was pressed against the coverlid of her pillowless couch—her hands were clasped in listless despair.

She was weeping passionately.

The priest bent over her, and gently raised her.

"My daughter," he said, softly, at the same time regarding the abbess with a look of indignation, "what means this violent emotion? Calm yourself! Look up, and reply with confidence."

"Oh, father," cried the poor girl, "kill me! Let me not bear this maddening load of shame. Kill me—but torture me no more! Leave me to Heaven's mercy, since there is none for me on earth."

"Come, my daughter, be of good cheer. I have come to take you away from the scene of your tribulation. Will you go with me?"

"Anywhere—anywhere—only take me away—take me from her! If I have done wrong inflict some penance that I can endure, but do not drive me to despair lest I turn rebellious—maddened by wrong."

"You see, father," said the abbess, wild with fury and chagrin; "you see she is incorrigible."

"Peace!" returned the prior, sternly; "let the

doors be unlocked. We must be gone! A boat awaits by the order of his eminence. Sister Agnes, see that this poor child is well protected from the chill. Let her have some refreshment, and use all speed."

"Father, before she leaves the convent, I must speak with her. Let us be alone for a few moments."

"I am sorry to disoblige you, but it is against my orders," replied the priest, with firmness.

He took the abbess by the hand, and leading her from the cell, and softly closing the door, left sister Agnes to attend upon the unhappy novice.

The superior gnashed her teeth with anger.

When they were alone the nun threw her arms about Aurora, and mingling tears with hers, kissed her with womanly tenderness.

"My beloved sister, sad shall we be to lose you, but glad enough for your sake, since we are all powerless to shield you from the cruel persecution of our mother, or superior. But, oh! beware of the temptations of this wicked world—its lures will be so sweet to you after your long and bitter sufferings; but, remember, better the chastening scourge of the severest directress than the stings of remorse—better the cruel prison-house of our strict order than the gilded palaces of splendid infamy. Be strong, my poor, weak child—be brave, my frail one. Shall I tell you why you are sent for by the cardinal?"

"Dear, kind sister Agnes, tell me anything that it is needful I should know, if such knowledge may save me from sin."

"But can I trust your discretion?"

"You may, indeed."

"Well then, the saints protect me from uncharitableness or irreverence, but it is said that the cardinal has ruined himself by his ambitious speculations, and that it is his intention to redeem his fortunes by giving your dear hand and rich fortune to his nephew Don Carlos—a man of high birth but evil character, one who is said—but I must not tell you——"

"Nay do, dear sister Agnes, I will be very prudent."

"I know not whether I am doing right, but I feel impelled to tell you. He is a man who is said to have gained immense wealth by dealings with African slavers and—and with murderous wretches—sea robbers that are called pirates."

"Pirates!" cried poor Aurora. "Oh, you do not know what horror there is in that name. Oh, I will not go. I will claim sanctuary and stay here."

"No, darling; you must go. The abbess would kill you by her cruelty; there is no peace for you here. Besides, idle rumours must not be too far trusted; only, I warn you, do not wed this man."

"I would not if he were king of Spain!"

"That is well—but you must be very cautious. You are powerless against the force of circumstances and the strength of men. But you do not love that rash and profane youth who tried to bear you away from us?"

"I do; I do with all my heart and soul; I love him as my only friend, my brave preserver. Ah, what have they done with him?—have they not killed him?"

Sister Agnes sighed, but did not reply to the question.

"Come," she said, "the good father is waiting."

Aurora having re-arranged her dress, and thrown a cloak around her, leant on her companion's shoulder, and left the cell.

The abbess and the prior awaited them.

The face of the lady superior was very pale, and her eyes glared with baffled malice.

The prior looked sad and thoughtful.

When they reached the landing steps the abbess bade Aurora kneel to receive her blessing.

The poor girl shrank away from her cruel superior, but instinctively obeyed her.

In a hard, dry voice the abbess pronounced the customary benediction.

At this moment a boat swept over the lifting

waves, and glided to the steps; it was rowed by a cowled monk.

The night was wild and the wind blew in fitful gusts, cold and fresh from the sea.

The prior and the novice got into the boat, the man pushed off with his oar, and they were soon rocking on the frothy billows.

Like a cruel enchantress of some Castle of Despair the tall figure of the abbess stood in her long sweeping, black dress and her white hood, beneath the lowering dungeon-like arch that gave upon the water.

Aurora turned her head away and listened to the rippling of the fresh and rushing waters as they leaped along under the bows of the boat.

She looked towards the convent; the tall cone-shaped minarets, surmounted with crosses, were growing dim in the distance.

Aurora addressed the prior—

"Whither are we going, dear father?"

"My daughter, I scarce can tell you. I received a letter from the Cardinal Gonsalvez, in which he commanded me to remove you from the convent: I believe you are to be taken on board a ship belonging to Don Carlos, the nephew of his eminence."

"Oh, father, I have heard, at least I fear, there may be some sinister motive for my removal."

"Daughter, what have you to fear—rich, lovely, pure and young, you are not a mark for evil usage—the worst that can befall you is a fate that happens to almost every ward of gentle birth or great possessions throughout Spain—a marriage of interests; and as you have never seen, or rather have never spoken to any layman, except the audacious wretch that polluted the sanctuary to effect your removal from your childhood's stern but sinless home,—as you are quite strange in the world, your destiny will not be a hard one."

"Do you mean, father, that it is hoped, that it is expected, I should marry Don Carlos?" asked Aurora, in alarm.

"It may be so; I have no certain information," replied the priest; "but he is a gallant man—handsome, wealthy, and has been admired by the noblest and fairest."

"Father, I will never marry him!" cried Aurora, with abrupt energy.

The priest looked at her with surprise and displeasure, and replied sternly—

"I fear, my daughter, that there is a waywardness and stubbornness in your disposition that partly warrants the severe measures the lady abbess thought needful to use for the correction of your lamentable fault. Weigh your strength against the power of society, and learn your own weakness. Surely you have some common sense, let it teach you the folly of sacrificing all your future prospects for the sake of one whom you ought to abhor as a profane tempter—one whom you saw but for a few moments, and whom most certainly you will never see again."

Aurora made no reply, but wrung her hands despairingly, and murmured—

"Oh, Holy Virgin, will my sorrows never end; shall I never know one day, one hour of gladness!"

The blue line of coast rimmed the foamy sea far to their left; the convent was just visible by its pointed spires; before them a large, heavy-built Spanish galleon was lazily rocking at anchor.

A boat was put down from this vessel.

With throbbing speed it pulled strongly through the brine and neared them.

Another boat, seemingly a large one, with a light spanker flying, appeared at the same time in the opposite direction; it seemed steering its course towards the little creek, in the curve of which the convent was built.

Far out in the offing two vessels were at anchor: one appeared to be a fine frigate, the other a rakishly-built sloop.

The men in the boat that was advancing from the Spanish galleon seemed to be surprised by the apparition of the other boat, and several of them rose and glanced over the blue expanse in its direction. But the object of their examination seemed to pay no heed to them, but moved steadily on its course.

The Spanish boat was now alongside.

It was manned by a crew of well-dressed and well-armed, but cut-throat looking fellows. An officer was with them, who stood erect at the prow. A hideous-looking negro was steering.

The prior rose and gently lifted Aurora.

With grave courtesy the officer extended his arm from the other boat.

"You are welcome, holy father," said this man, respectfully, "the wind is freshening, and we must heave anchor. Donna Aurora, permit me to offer you my arm."

The girl gave a frightened look at the fierce, brigandish seaman, and instinctively clung to the priest.

"You must go with him, my daughter," answered the prior; "it is the cardinal's express command."

Aurora looked around her timidly and appealingly, and then lightly touching the sailor's arm passed into the other boat.

"Farewell, my daughter: bend before the wind and you shall rise when it has passed. The Virgin and the Holy Saints protect you."

"Your blessing, father," cried the rough and evil-looking sailors.

The old man stood up in the boat and held up a cross in his right hand.

In a solemn and impressive manner he pronounced his benediction.

The men knelt down in the boat and devoutly crossed themselves, and kissed the little pictures and relics they wore about their necks.

Then they pulled away towards the dark ship.

The priest stood watching the boat as it glided over the rough heavings of the restless sea, and saw the novice waving him a farewell.

CHAPTER XXXIV.

THE ASSAULT ON THE CONVENT.

LET us follow the course of the other boat.

Our readers will have divined that it was the boat from the "Red Raven."

It was manned by the Boy Pirate, Gomez, Brierly, Dick Caffyn, Manuel Perez, and a number of picked men, mostly Spaniards.

Cautiously they rounded the headland that ran out on one side of the creek.

It was a wild and gusty night, and the men rowed in silence.

The leaders were moody and thoughtful. They were on a dangerous mission. For the feat itself—the attack upon a religious house, tenanted almost exclusively by women—there was nothing particularly daring in such an adventure.

But the consequences might prove terrible.

The profanity and audacity of their deed would rouse the hottest vengeance against them. They might be hunted from sea to sea—placed under the ban of all catholic nations.

As they were steering round the headland, they descried the heavy Spanish galleon.

They watched, curiously, the boat which put off from it, and were witnesses of the meeting between the two barques, and they could just discern that some one was passed from the one to the other.

"Cap'en," cried Brierly, "it strikes me that yonder boat has taken some notice on us, and that it be sheering off with a supercargo as we might want to overhaul."

The Boy Pirate looked through his glass.

"Yes; by Heaven! it is a woman; should it be Aurora!"

"Nay," cried Perez; "they will never let her leave the convent. For the love of all that is good do not draw back now. I know a secret way to the place, by which we can make our entry safely. Go on, I implore you."

"Yes; he is right, captain," said Gomez. "They

would never uncage so sweet a bird when it is so much to their advantage to detain her.　Pull away, comrades; we are nearing the shore."

In silence the men obeyed the order.

The boat was run up on the strand.

The men disembarked.

A hasty consultation was held.

Perez leading the way, the whole party clambered the rocks, and made for the landward side of the nunnery.

There was a high wall at the back of the building, enclosing a little orchard.

Beneath this they halted.

All was silent, save the hoarse roar of the sea and the rustle of the night wind through the waving trees.

There was a sort of dry ditch or moat around the convent.

Into this they descended.

In whispers, the Boy Pirate admonished his crew.

He bade them remember that they were bent upon a mission that required the greatest tact and prudence, that all their future glory would be tarnished if it could be charged against them that they took advantage of the defenceless condition of a few weak women to perpetrate outrages that would show the blacker if wrought under the present circumstances.　As they were entering upon the hazardous adventure for the most disinterested and chivalrous motives, he exhorted them to extreme caution, and assured them of his eternal gratitude if they would avoid everything that could be stigmatized as unmanly, and would confine themselves simply to the end they had in view—the rescue of the wronged and gentle Donna Aurora Vasquez.

The men promised prudence and strict obedience, and the impatient Perez led the way to a part of the wall which was joined by the roof of one of the offices.　Here again they halted.　Christopher motioned them to conceal their arms and to render their appearance as little menacing as possible, and, once more urging them to promptness and firmness qualified by discretion and moderation, seized a long rope-ladder, attached to iron grapnels, and with a sure and strong arm sent it whirling through the air.

It caught securely on the top of the wall.

Perez mounted.

The Boy Pirate and Gomez closely followed.

The crew stood silent below.

When Perez had reached the roof of the house, he peered in at a barred window.

The bare stone corridor was plainly visible.

A lamp was burning in a niche in the wall.

Perez proceeded to shake one of the iron bars.

With very little trouble he tore it away from the stone, and, with a smile, passed it over to our hero.

He then extracted another.

When he had thus made a passage sufficiently large for the intrusion of his body, he gently opened the lattice.

It was plain that the bars had been previously loosened.

Perez had formerly worked at them for many anxious hours.

He crept in, and dropped softly into the corridor below.

Gomez and Christopher followed him.

They noiselessly stole along the stone passage.

They passed many cells.

They stood and listened.

No sound was heard.

The nuns were soundly sleeping.

They passed on.

In the meanwhile others of the crew had mounted the ladder, and had forced an entrance.

These also moved stealthily along in the opposite direction.

They reached a large door, before which was a curtain; this they pulled aside, and opening the door, found themselves in the little chapel.

An air of solemnity pervaded the place.

The walls were covered with paintings, and on all sides were niches containing images of saints; the moonlight streamed in through painted windows; and at the chancel end was a large altar, on which three candles were burning before a Madonna.

They stole quietly over the chequered floor, the slabs of which were engraved with the names of many deceased superiors and sisters of the order.

At the further end was the door of the sacristy.

Somewhat sacrilegiously, one of the pirates seized a candle from the altar, and lighted the way to this little chamber.　It was small and vaulted, but the walls were richly ornamented with fretwork and carving, and the place was quite a treasury of costly embroidery and glancing symbols, cups, and vessels of gold and silver.

Several of the men cast greedy looks at these treasures, but they remembered the Boy Pirate's warning, and forebore to touch them.

Passing through this chamber they came upon a narrow passage, and when they reached the end of it perceived a flight of steps leading to another door. They were about to mount them when they were startled by the sudden appearance of a tall, commanding woman, dressed in a long, loose robe, who stood at the top of the steps.

It was the abbess.

When she caught sight of the party she gave a pealing scream, and fell upon her knees.

Two of the men rushed up the steps, and seizing her, placed their hard hands over her mouth.

"Eh, Tom, but she will raise the roof with her caterwauling."

"Shiver me, if I don't think we'd best gag her!" cried another.

"Phew! she fights like a tigress.　Look out, mates, she'll be having some of you tied up and flogged as she does her poor lasses," cried another. "Don't you perceive, my mates, as she's the precious martinet of a abbess as used the old Rover's gal so cruelly?"

"All the wuss for her," growled another, "haul her along."

The abbess was dragged off to her own apartment.

Another nun, an old woman, was there, and upon their entry rose, and shrieking, tried to leave the room.

"Stop her, give chase, you lubbers, she'll alarm the house with a vengeance," cried one of the ruffians.

The nun was brought back.

The abbess had recovered her presence of mind, and breaking from the arms of the seamen, stood erect with the mien of an empress, her dark eyes flashing as much with rage and disdain as with terror.

"Who are ye—thieves and assassins, who respect not the sanctuary of Heaven—what do you seek? Gold, take your fill; there are costly vessels here, but they are not ours, they are dedicated to the service of the Virgin and the Saints, touch them if you dare. Heaven and earth will join to avenge the sacrilegious outrage.　For us poor frail women, we brave your outrages; our trust is in a high power, who is all able to protect us."

"Now, mates, she's what I call a genuine Tartar," said one of the pirates, with a coarse laugh.

"Reg'lar Billingsgate."

"What shall we do with her."

"Carry her on board and make her bo'swain."

"Sartain, she has got a fine woice for a speaking trumpet."

"And there's a arm, my hearties—there's a arm to wield a cat."

"Out upon the old rip, see if we can't show her the pretty knack of taming a Tartar."

"Look! here's her sweet little instrument with which she fillips the sins out of the tender limbs of delicate girls," cried another fellow, picking up the scourge the abbess had used so pitilessly.

"By the blazes," shouted another, hoarse with indignation, "but the cords are tinged quite red."

"Yah, the devil's dam, give her a taste of her own physic," roared half-a-dozen furious voices.

"Ay, ay! seize her, mates, and I'll lay on; may I be keelhauled if I spare her."

"Sarve her right, sarve her right; she gives no quarter, don't let her expect none."

The abbess was seized, her hands were tightly bound, and she was being dragged screaming to the wall when suddenly the Boy Pirate and Gomez entered the room.

Christopher stepped forward and held up his hand with an authoritative gesture.

The men slunk back, cowed by his fierce look.

The abbess was instantly unbound, and, throwing her robe about her, turned with an imploring glance towards the Boy Pirate.

"Am I your commander? Are you men or fools?" cried the captain, sternly. "Did I not imperatively forbid any outrage?"

"Well, cap'en," began one, "look here, sir: we found this infernal hag's cat, and when we thought of her cruel usage of the poor young creatures committed to her charge it was more than flesh and blood could stand."

"And we shouldn't have laid a finger on the rip, if she hadn't a sauced us," said another.

"And we never put a hand on the gold and silver, though there's a little mine of it in the other chamber," said a third.

"Enough!" cried the Boy Pirate. "Redeem your error by a hasty return to the boats; we have been informed the young lady has been carried off to the ship of a gang of Spanish pirates; it was she whom we saw transferred to their boat. All hands aboard; up with the anchor, shake out the sails; I will follow directly. Send me the pinnace."

"Ay, ay! cap'en," returned the men, humbly. "We're ready to a man to die for the Red Raven."

With this they hurried from the room.

"Will these marauders plunder the sacristy?" cried the abbess, with animation.

"Madam, you see how readily they obeyed my orders in one instance. They will not fail to do so in respect of your valuables," replied Christopher, sternly; "indeed, it is needful to enforce obedience, but I find mild means and tempered justice even with these rude men to be the best for insuring their submission to my will—profit by that lesson. Madam, farewell! You will find no further damage has been done than the destruction of the iron grating of the window by which we entered. Apologising for this intrusion, forced upon us, I am sorry to say, by your own inhumanity to an innocent and lovely girl, I leave you. Do not forget that more mercy than you extended to one of your own sex who had never given you offence has been shown you by ruthless men who serve under the ghastly symbols of the blood-stained flag of piracy—for they who have spared you are my crew, and I am feared and detested as the 'Red Raven!'"

The abbess fell on her knees, and shudderingly hid her face in her robe.

The fame of the Boy Pirate was world-wide— even the sequestered inmates of the quiet seagirt nunnery had often trembled at the wild tales told of the dauntless and remorseless scourge of the seas.

Christopher haughtily bent his head, and passed from the chamber.

As he and Gomez were passing along the corridor they encountered Dick Caffyn, whose cheek was flushed, while his eyes glowed with anxiety.

"Captain, I have a request to make," he said, dropping his hat to his foster-brother.

"This is rather an odd time to prefer your suit, Dick," replied the Boy Pirate, smiling; "but what is it?"

Dick Caffyn reddened with some bashfulness, and hesitated.

"Speak out, man," said Christopher, with a laugh; "I shall begin to think you want to carry off one of the nuns."

"Excuse me, captain," replied Dick, looking down, "but you have hit the right mark."

"It must not be," replied the Boy Pirate, gravely. "No one of the inmates must be removed from this place unless by her own consent—by her own request."

"Right, captain," cried Dick, briskly; "I'm the lady's advocate. She wishes to leave the convent in order to join Donna Aurora, who is her bosom friend."

Sister Agnes approached the speakers.

"Do I understand rightly, senorita," said the Boy Pirate, "you wish to leave the convent, in order to share the perils that beset your friend?"

"Oh! senor, you should be generous. You have not abused your power; and whatever your motive for wishing to rescue sister Aurora from this place, you have not wronged any one. My wish, I know, is a wicked one—my request, perhaps, lacks modesty —but, I implore you, restore me to my dearest, only friend, and I will bless you! I shall be so useful to her, and she is unspeakably dear to me."

"But do you know by what name the world calls me and my followers?"

"Men are often unjust. I know not and I care not," returned the devoted girl. "If Aurora be in evil hands it is the more desirable that I should be with her."

"Senorita, I shall be proud to accede to your wish," returned the gallant rover; "and be assured you will not be less safe from injury or insult on board my lawless ship than you would be within the sacred walls of this convent."

Gomez smiled.

"It is well, captain; I am glad that the daughter of Don Miguel Vasquez should have a female companion while she is on board with us."

"Come, then," cried the Boy Pirate. "Dick Caffyn, I leave the young lady to your chivalrous protection. Let us afloat. We shall have a gay chase for the richest prize for which we have ever set a skysail or thrown a grapnel. Once more let us trust to the 'Fortune of War!'"

CHAPTER XXXV.

THE DESTRUCTION OF THE SPANISH GALLEON.

"Haul aft all sheets."

"Ay, ay, sir."

"'Bout ship."

"Ready, a' ready."

"Tack and sheet."

"Well done, Mr. Brand. Now haul over the boom. Capital! Now we are fairly under weigh," cried the Boy Pirate, exultingly.

All was bustle on board the "Fortune of War." The splendid frigate raced forward, scarcely lifting on the rolling waves, but gliding along like a swallow.

The Boy Pirate stood on the quarter-deck. By his side were Brierly, Dick Caffyn, and Walter Mervyn.

"We shall have a short cruise and a merry one," said the young rover captain, laughing gleefully as he scanned the horizon with his glass.

The "Red Raven" was making way, but not so swiftly as the frigate, for she was not so well to the wind.

Every instant they were gaining upon the heavy galleon, though in her own clumsy fashion she was rocking and tumbling on with commendable speed.

The hardy pirates stood with gleaming eyes, grasping their cutlasses and marlinspikes, and eagerly noting the advance of their splendid vessel.

They were like lions in the slip, eager and thirsty for the fray.

"'When Greek fights Greek—' eh, Walter?" cried the Boy Pirate to the young mate at his side. "Oh, that they would run up the 'Jolly Oliver,' and then we would hoist the 'Red Raven.' This is my first fight with a fellow-rover. We must do our best, comrades, for the honour of England; let even her robbers carry the palm for pluck and endurance. Bah! these Spanish buccaneers, what are they? Bloody and brutal monsters, who defile the sinister glory that attaches to such deeds as ours by rapine and ruthless butchery. They howl to their saints in a storm, and trust to their canvas when they have to match a worthy foe; and they are very Hectors and Pa'adins when they can board some lubberly merchantman, to torture the men and insult the women. Don Carlos has a great name, but he follows a dirty calling—he is an owner of slave ships. When we have finished our cruise in these waters, I mean to have a crusade against those heathens the slavers; and that's a service the most squeamish amongst us will be glad to engage in. What say you, Walter? Since we do so much mischief, we can afford an occasional spell at worthier work."

"I wish you constant victory and mighty prizes, brave captain," returned the youth, with a faint smile, "but I shall never share your glory."

"Why not? What, 'all in the downs!' By our fortune, you look as pale and as melancholy as a young girl who has lost her sweetheart! What is the matter?"

"Nothing," returned Walter, quietly; "as well now as hereafter, I am ready."

"Ah! you have faith in presentiments, but that is folly, Walter," said the Boy Pirate, gently.

"It is not a mere fanciful presentiment, it is an unerring conviction."

"You have dreamed!"

"I dreamed of my mother, captain, and she has warned me that my wild career is ended."

"Dreams are delusive, Walter."

The youth only answered with a sad but brave smile.

"The same dark fate threatens me equally with you and with all; yet I am bold and confident, and you are as brave as I. Courage is our mutual stock-in-trade, and no one has a larger share of the commodity than yourself, Walter."

"You flatter me," returned the handsome young pirate, now smiling brightly; "but you shall see, captain, that I am not afraid to die."

"No; by Heaven, Walter, while you are in this gloomy mood your sword shall rest in its sheath," said the Boy Pirate, in a kind tone.

"Rather a thousand deaths than such dishonour," cried Walter, fiercely; "if this be my last battle, it is, at least, not dishonourable; our foes are pirates—wretches worse than ourselves, and the cause for which we engage with them is a generous and a holy one."

"You shall not fight, I tell you; you shall not fight," cried the Boy Pirate, impetuously.

"'Way aloft; reef topsails," shouted the pilot at this moment.

"Cap'en, we are within hail; shall I give the order to lower the boats?"

"At once, Brierly; see, Gomez has got beside the wind, we shall have finished our work before he can get within gunshot."

The first to leap into the boat was Walter Mervyn.

The crew soon hurried over the bulwarks, and were afloat cheering and brandishing their cutlasses.

The dark hull of the lumbering galleon belched fire and flame, and the deafening report of the guns shook her strong timbers; but the cannon had not been well served, and the volleys did but little damage.

"Hurrah for the ' Red Raven!' "

"Hurrah for the ' Fortune of War!' "

Like clustering bees the dauntless English out-laws scrambled up the dark sides of the enemy's vessel.

Soon many a foot was on the bulwark, and many a rash assailant was hurled headlong into the waves.

More boats came from the " Fortune of War."

The " Red Raven " was approaching.

The Spanish galleon was a ship of heavier burden than the Boy Pirate's frigate, and possessed more guns, and its deck was thronged by a numerous crew of desperadoes.

Christopher, who remained awhile in the boat to give orders, sent off word to signal the " Red Raven " to keep off as he wanted to take the galleon in an equal fight.

The " Red Raven " was run up.

The Spaniards gave a roar of astonishment and fury, and hoisted their own flag of piracy.

The battle on the deck raged furiously.

Amid the smoke and fire, and the roar and din of raging combatants, one fellow of the Spanish crew showed conspicuously by his strange, half-mad demeanour—he seemed to rage and thirst for blood.

He was a huge negro, with all the lineaments of his race hideously exaggerated. His big woolly head was black as a coal; his cunning and cruel eyes flamed with brutal and demoniac passion; his large splay feet spread on the deck or trampled on the fallen bodies of his fellows and foes with blind indiscrimination; he had a huge sabre in his hand, with which he hewed and slashed away with irresistible fury.

The fight raged long and furiously. The tide of battle ebbed and flowed—now victory seemed to smile on her favourites the followers of the Boy Pirate—now she turned fickle, and the fierce Spaniards prevailed.

The crew of the galleon far outnumbered that of the " Fortune of War," and in his reckless daring, Christopher had resolved to fight the battle to the last without the aid of his consort ship.

In the wildest moment of the terrible fight—when hand to hand men were madly struggling, while the deafening roar of the guns and their blinding flash rendered the scene a chaos of horror and confusion —a wild cry was heard.

The officers of the " San Trinidad," such was the name of their vessel, were fighting with the desperate resolve to perish at the direst cost to their enemies.

The lieutenant, who was the chief officer on board, commanding as he did for Don Carlos, of whom we shall hear more hereafter, and who was at the time absent from the vessel, was engaged in a hand-to-hand struggle with our hero.

Brierly was leading an attack upon the forecastle.

Dick Caffyn was fighting his way to the hatches in order to get below deck.

Walter Mervyn, who fought with a desperation almost superhuman, was struggling on the ground with three of the crew, one of whom he had fatally wounded; the other two were striving to avenge their comrade's death, and were dealing fearful lunges at his head with their cutlasses; but the victory was his—one he knocked down with his sword, cleaving his skull; the other he pistolled.

He now sprang to the side of the Boy Pirate.

The Red Raven was still wildly contending with the chief officer.

The prowess and the acts of one we have not yet chronicled. If he had shown some inaptitude in clambering the vessel's hull—if his foothold on the shifting and slippery deck were not of the firmness of his companions—if his unpractised eyes and ears were deafened and dazed by the thunder and lightning of the terrible conflict—his heart was not only void of fear, but leaped with wild exultation. Love fired him to deeds which in his calmer moments he would have thought beyond his strength or resolution. This man who battled so heroically was he for whose happiness the generous Boy Pirate was risking his life so dauntlessly—Manuel Perez.

A wild scream rang over the deck.

The hatches had been forced; there was another and a lower circle in these infernal regions of contending furies: a fearful battle was being fought between decks.

Liberated from the cabin in which she had been secured, the beautiful Aurora flew upon deck.

She flew among the whirling weapons and crackling musketry like some frightened wood-bird along the line of flashing barrels at some grand *battue*. She reached the mainmast. She beheld her lover fighting side by side with the Boy Pirate.

With a sobbing cry she flew between them and their antagonists.

The Spanish officer seized her by the arm, and fiercely raising his sword, with a malicious grin at Perez, was about to cleave her in two. Our hero rushed forward to snatch her from his grip.

The hideous negro we have before described, who had mowed his way to the spot, drew a pistol and levelled it at the head of the Red Raven.

Another instant and all would have been over—the crisis of the battle was reached: the death of the gallant young English rover would have decided the contest.

Christopher felt himself pulled roughly back. He turned round furiously—he was in the strong hands of the faithful Brierly. The pistol exploded close to his ear, and the bullet whizzed close to his head.

Some one fell heavily, prone on the deck.

It was Walter Mervyn.

"Yah—yah—yah!" yelled the hideous black, in fiendish laughter.

Brierly rushed after him.

But the monstrous negro raised both his massive fists and brought them down with such stunning force upon the sturdy pirate's forehead, that he smote him to his knee. At the same instant the Red Raven had run the commander of the "San Trinidad" through the body.

Aurora was in her lover's arms.

The Boy Pirate was tenderly supporting Walter Mervyn; the gallant young seaman looked up into our hero's face with glazed eyes, and softly murmured—

"My dream is verified. Fortune crowns your life, and be your death as easy as mine. Mother!"

He fell back—dead.

All at once was perceived a stifling fume; long tongues of flame shot up through the crevices of the planks, volumes of smoke burst from the port holes.

Several of the desperate Spaniards were seen flinging barrels of gunpowder down into the fired hold.

With his cannibalic laugh, the huge negro once more leaped upon deck, a flambeau blazing in his hand.

Shots were fired at him, thrusts made, but he seemed invulnerable; like a hunted deer he bounded over the bulwarks and plunged into the sea.

The scene of confusion and horror is indescribable, red fiery gusts of smoke and blaze curl along the deck.

The ship reels, guns explode with tremendous concussion, the ship is in flames, and the roaring element leaps up among the rigging; it flies, leaping wildly and dazzlingly, from shrouds to tackle, the taut ropes wither and break like burnt threads, the fields of canvas are shrivelled, and pass away like a burning scroll.

In the dreadful dismay that prevailed, men are reckless of everything but their own safety.

They leap into the boats pell mell and simultaneously.

In the hopeless confusion and horror, friends and foes scramble into the same arks of refuge.

But the heroic Boy Pirate is imperturbably calm.

His first care is for Aurora.

She and her lover are first safely placed in the pinnace under the charge of Brierly.

Loud cries of consternation and yells of excitement and horror resounded from the decks of the "Fortune of War," and her consort, the "Red Raven."

Boom—bang—boom—still thunder the exploding guns.

The tottering masts and swaying spars crash down, killing and crushing the few who still remain alive on deck; the suffocating smoke enshrouds the doomed ship.

Heavily and staggeringly she heaves over on one side.

It is a fearful scene.

The sea is strewn with bodies and spars, and all sorts of ship fittings.

The "San Trinidad" is fast sinking.

Why does she not burst and be scattered to the elements?

The fire has not yet touched the centre hold, where the magazine is situated.

The Boy Pirate calmly walks the deck, not storming, not hectoring, but in cool, quick, and discerning words uttering his orders. All is cleared; the dead and the dying are left, but the able are saved; men are picked up; the boats are steadily rowed.

The moment has come—a sudden and tremendous roar and blast.

The red and smoking *débris* of the gallant ship flutters and skims along the sky like seething rockets.

Then all is silence, and the seas are strewn with ruin.

Who had been the last to leave the burning deck?—The Red Raven—The Boy Pirate!

CHAPTER XXXVI.

HOW THE BLOODHOUND TRACKED THE GHOST.

OUR readers will remember to what advantage Silas Rye had turned the railway accident.

He had so thoroughly misled his detested fellow-criminal that the latter was fully persuaded of the veracity of the newspaper account of his partner's death, even though he had seen Silas in the body.

After Silas Rye had made his exit from the window to the balcony he closed the window after him, and cautiously stole down the stone steps, sprang along the top of the marble terrace-way, leaving no mark of a footstep, no trace behind him.

Upon the recovery of Daniel Harwolf from his horror-induced trance, he looked round upon the bewildered servants with bloodshot eyes and a face white and aghast with terrible and deadly awe.

They thought that he had lost his reason.

His lips turned livid, and his teeth chattered together.

In a passion of horrible fear he muttered incoherent words, and called upon his master and accomplice by their names.

The servants exchanged intelligent glances.

But the instinct of caution so deeply implanted in the nature of the atrocious steward was startled from its numbing lethargy by the whisper that went round—"He is talking of Lord Edgeforth."

With a mighty effort he choked down the qualms of terror, and sought to hush the loud beating of his guilt-smitten heart.

"Andrew Moss," he said, with as much firmness as he could assume, addressing that worthy and devoted follower, who, it will be remembered, had showed his zeal by reporting the purport of the Boy Pirate's conversation with Lilia on the night of her abduction. Andrew Moss had risen from the ranks, and was now in the full blush of his new-bought honours—the most dignified of "upper servants," being butler at Frontemore.

"I am at my post, sir," said the butler, with a bow, which almost prostrated him, for he had not, when bending so profoundly, made due allowance for the convulsive weakness of his tottering limbs.

"If you had been at your post, sir, when the house was closed for the night I should have been spared the pain of the assault, and may be a heavy loss by the ——"

"With pardon, sir, but which robbery?"

"Why, fool, do you suppose I am given to firing off pistols in the dead of the night merely for amusement?"

"Not at all, sir; I am sure, sir, I should scorn sich a thought, sir," returned the butler, with cringing suavity; "but really I do most humbly assure you, sir, with pardon, as I did most carefully examine all the bolts and fastenings throughout the 'ouse, and they was all secure, I do most humbly assure you."

"And yet within ten minutes there was a burglar in this room."

"A burglar!" cried all the servants, huddling together like a flock of sheep in a storm.

"Yes; I tell you the fellow struck me down. I fired at him, but he was gone before I could aim for another shot. Look about ye, will you, ye craven curs! See to the windows—search for footmarks—examine the chiffonnier—the cases. See to what extent I have been robbed!"

The servants flew about with assumed alacrity, but took special care to keep well together. No trace was found that could lead to the supposition that any intruder had invaded the quiet of the well-ordered household. Everything was in its place; there was no print of a step on the carpet, though, as the floor covering was of thick-piled Brussels, it would not show the trace of a footstep.

Harwolf's next care was to examine the desks, the armoire, the drawers that contained his papers and valuables.

But they were all securely locked; he did not think it needful to open them.

Perhaps it would be well to inform the reader by what means Silas Rye had contrived to open the armoire and extract the proofs of the lost heir's identity, and other important documents, and yet had re-closed the panels and re-locked them.

The reason was simple enough—he had another key.

The way in which he obtained it shows another trait of the deep cunning of his artful nature.

Only for an instant, on a former occasion, Harwolf himself being in the room, had Silas been trusted with the key, which was of wondrously complicated workmanship; while crossing the room he drew out a little box of prepared wax and took a mould of the key, and had subsequently had one made from the impression by a skilful locksmith.

"See, sir, here's the bullet; it seems to have been stopped by summit or other," said the butler, "for it lies in the middle of the floor, and it could not have rebounded, 'cos if it had struck the wall it would have smashed the pier-glass, and there ain't no dent in the ceiling."

Harwolf became deadly pale.

"Robert," he said, to one of the footmen, "pass me over the other pistol—perhaps the villain has played me a trick, and has drawn the bullets."

He took the weapon in his hand, and tried it with the ramrod.

It was charged.

Our readers will not have forgotten that Silas Rye had replaced the ball in the pistol that had not been fired, and had placed the bullet he had previously extracted from the other on the ground.

The squire flung the pistols away from him with an exclamation of impatience, and, seating himself at the table, covered his face with his fear-palsied hands.

The servants stood gaping about him.

"What do you here, fools and meddlers! Search the grounds, and then go to bed."

"Well, sir, beg pardon, but I don't think as the burglars is now on the premises, but I will have a strict search made," said Andrew Moss.

"Stay! I will retire to my own bed-chamber—when you have gone round the place get to bed. Let me be called early to-morrow."

With this the squire took a candle from one of the servants, and retired.

"Well, did you ever see the like of this here!" cried one of the men to the others, "there ain't not the least signs of nobody, and the house ain't been robbed of a pin's worth, and yet there's been a burglary."

"I don't like sich going's on. There's summut supernat'ral in it, you may be bound," said another.

"Excuse me, gentlemen, but what sort of gaolbird do you think the culprit was?" asked the coachman, who had run over from the stables at the sound of the pistol shot.

"My humble opinion is as he is nothing but a spirit on a ticket of leave," said the groom.

"Ah!" groaned the chorus, looking around with knocking knees.

"There's strange tales going about," said the first footman.

"And queer sights is seen," rejoined the second.

"The house is most indecidedly haunted," exclaimed the last.

"Ah!" re-echoed the chorus.

"Have you seen anything?" whispered the groom to the coachman, with breathless anxiety.

"A many things!" returned that worthy, shaking his head with awful solemnity.

"Ah!" shuddered the chorus.

"I've seen heyes!" exclaimed the page.

"And as for rustlings, and bell-ringing, and clanking like chains, it's like the 'Castle of Otranto, or the Bleeding Nun.'"

"Well, I ain't a-going to injure my character by sich disgraceful proceedings," cried a footman.

"No, nor I either; I leaves it my month."

"Come, come, gentlemen, this is not attending to orders, no how; the grounds is to be searched—that's the coachman's place, and the gardener's," said the butler, interfering with bland dignity. "Come, can't some of you percede to investigate this mysterious affair? Coachman, lead the way."

"Not if I knows it, Mr. Moss; I wern't engaged to lag ghosteses."

"Nor I neither," rejoined the groom.

"In that case," said the butler, shrugging his shoulders and whisking his silk handkerchief, "I'm sorry to say as I shall be in duty bound to report you for disobedience of orders."

"Why, we has looked at the grounds, Mr. Moss; it ain't two hours ago since the gardener went his rounds."

"Werry well, I s'pose that is quite satisfactory," replied the butler; "you may all go to bed, and if anything happens remember your places, and do what is required. Good night, gentlemen; I wish you good night."

With astounding dignity the butler bowed his fellow-servants from the room.

He returned to the scene of the night's adventures. He seated himself by the table.

"Lor, how frightened I feels," he muttered; "but spite of it all I should dearly like to know whether it was really a spirit or not—a spirit as was here. I has my head on and I knows a thing or two: as for the squire, what's he: ain't he nothing but a former servant—and mayn't I become a master as well as he? I has rose to the top of the ranks, and with my address and discretion there's no knowing what I mayn't come to."

He rose and walked about reflecting.

"Ha, I has it!" he cried, suddenly. "In course, don't they track the niggers in Uncle Tom with bloodhounds. Well, that's a good idea; I gives you credit for it, Andrew Moss. The devil's in it if a dog would run after a ghost. There's poor Bruno's whelp: I'll fetch him up, he can always scent a stranger, though he is a young 'un, and if any bodily creetur as been here he'll sure to tell."

With this the butler left the room, and proceeding to the court-yard, unchained a young, fierce-looking hound, and brought him upstairs.

When he had the hound in the dressing-room he cheered him to the scent.

The dog walked round and round the apartment, swaying his dew-lapped head from side to side and smelling about.

"Ha—fetch him out; seize him, good dog; tear him, Towler, tear him," cried Andrew, clapping his hands in great excitement.

The dog paused in the middle of the room, gave a prolonged growl, and then with a sharp bark, flew to the window pawing and whining; he seemed to request it should be opened.

Andrew threw wide the folding casement.

The hound darted out, leaped the parapet of the terrace, and scampered across the lawn.

At a respectful distance, and with no little dread, Andrew followed over the wet grass by the shadowy trees and shrubs.

The dog was out in the carriage road, squatted on his hind legs, howling and evidently at fault. There were fresh marks of carriage wheels.

THE DEATH STRUGGLE ON THE CLIFF.

The slight ruts wound along the pathway and merged into the lane.

At the point where the dog had stopped they were more deeply indented, as if the carriage had stopped there to await some one's arrival.

Andrew followed the tracks down the miry lane to the high road.

Here it diverged.

Andrew perceived that it went off townward.

He called the dog to his side and thoughtfully re-traced his steps.

As he returned, he noticed the lines marked by the carriage wheel were narrow and near together; by this he judged that the vehicle must be a small one, probably a fly or a small brougham.

The morning was breaking with a ghostly light in the wild and cloudy east.

He re-chained the bloodhound in the courtyard.

Softly entering the house he crept upstairs.

No. 13.

As he passed the servants' rooms, he perceived that their lights were still burning

He listened at each as he passed along.

The universal topic of their conversation was the strange events that had occurred.

He heard Lady Edgeforth's name mentioned more than once, but in such low tones, that he could not catch the purport of what was said.

At last he reached his own comfortable bed-chamber.

He sat on the side of his bed for some time in deep rumination.

"Any ways, whatever he were, he wern't no ghost, and he didn't come here for nothing. Well, I'll worm it out, and in the meanwhile these inferior creatures may form their own conclusions. I knows a man as can keep his own counsel, and his name is Andrew Moss."

CHAPTER XXXVII.

SILAS RYE RECEIVES NEWS OF LADY EDGE-FORTH'S ABDUCTION.

SILAS RYE and Sibly, the lawyer's clerk, were seated at the window of the lodging of the former, which has been already described.

They were smoking at a little table, on which were a bottle and glasses, and a packet of papers.

"And you don't know what has become of the true heir," said the clerk, blowing a long whiff from his pipe, and shaking his head meditatively.

"I am sorry to say I do not," replied Silas, "all I can be sure of is that he follows the sea, and if what I conjecture is right we shall gain but little by finding him."

"How so?"

"You have heard, Sibly, of an audacious felon who has twice escaped from the hands of justice, who has committed all sorts of outrages, and who is the scourge of the high seas."

"Do you mean the Boy Pirate?"

"Yes."

"But what can he have to do with what we are talking of."

"Why only this, that we are venturing guesses as to the present occupation and pursuits of the lost son of the unfortunate Lord Edgeforth."

"But surely he is not the Red Raven?"

"I have no doubt of it; I will tell you why: you know that the child was placed in the charge of some poor, but respectable, villagers at Frontemore."

"I remember you told me so."

"And when he grew towards manhood he was apprenticed to the sea, and to his misfortune served in the same ship as that detestable scapegrace, Andrew Harwolf's son, at whose instigation he was so harassed and persecuted by the ship's captain, that in a fit of frenzy and passion he threw himself overboard."

"Why, then, he must be dead."

"Have patience, every one on board believed that he was drowned, but, wonderful to tell, a few months after he reappeared as the captain of the 'Red Raven', confessedly the most daring robber and pirate that ever mounted the black flag; since then his terrible deeds have excited universal awe and involuntary admiration, for the black part of his character is relieved by the most dazzling qualities of courage and generosity."

"But how can you be sure of his identity with the lost heir of Frontemore?"

"I have no doubt of it. You must know that in his boyhood he conceived a strong attachment for Lilia Meredith, the daughter of Squire Meredith, a fine old gentleman, who, next to the Edgeforth's, possesses the largest estates in the county. After the alleged death of her youthful and humble lover, Miss Meredith was affianced to Daniel Harwolf. Just before the time when the marriage was appointed to take place, a young naval officer came down to Frontemore, and was introduced at the squire's, and as he was very handsome and gallant was petted and *fêted* by everybody. One night, however, a conversation betwixt Captain Paul and the fair Lilia, who had retired into the conservatory, was overheard by an officious lacquey, who rushed, in his dismay, to this fellow Daniel, and informed him that Miss Lilia had agreed to elope with the captain that very night, and that a lonely spot on the beach had been appointed for their place of rendezvous. The fiery Daniel collected a large force of his tenants and servants, and allowing the lady to keep her appointment, laid an ambush at the trysting place, in order to seize the romantic young couple. However, he failed in capturing them; with desperate courage the Boy Pirate and a single companion, said to be his lieutenant, carried off the girl in spite of the opposition of Daniel's force. Since then young Harwolf is said to have made several attempts, as desperate as abortive, for the capture of the 'Red Raven.'"

"This is a wonderful story!"

"Is it not?"

"But what a fearful tragedy!" exclaimed Sibly, thoughtfully. "And in spite of his sad misguidance, and his wild and terrible career, this pirate may be possessed of many great and good qualities."

"I have heard that he is one of the finest fellows in the world—and I warrant is as conscious of his own degradation as any man can be."

"Then why does he not give up his abominable way of life?"

"You see he was, in a manner, forced into it, and now he is bound like Prometheus to the rock—and the conscience-vulture that gnaws his liver does not strike at his chains."

"But surely there is some alternative!"

"Yes. An ugly one—the gallows."

"Ah!" exclaimed Sibly, with a shudder.

"But what an unheard of, unspeakably black villain is this Andrew Harwolf," cried Silas Rye, striking the table fiercely. "How fearful are the effects of his awful crime—Lord Edgeforth murdered, his lady a maniac, their son a slaughtering thief, a pirate on the high seas."

"And yet this villain flourishes," said Sibly, bitterly. "His wealth, his *prestige*, his influence are objects of envy to the highest and proudest of the land, and there is a talk of his being returned a member for Frontemore."

"Yet honoured, envied, pampered as he is," returned Rye, "he is the same white-faced, horror-stricken wretch that, in the superstition of his tortured conscience, fell into convulsions at my feet, thinking me a ghost. Whew! The smell of blood has poisoned his brain. Swathe him in ermine, cover him with diamonds and rubies, enthrone him king of the universe, and, Sibly, the vilest beggar that drags his mangled limbs through the mire of pitiless cities is a happy angel of heaven in comparison with him."

"Yes, yes. It is indeed terrible to contemplate his state of mind," returned Sibly, with deep seriousness.

"That man has done me good as well as evil," returned Silas Rye. "My weakness, my poverty, my want of fixed principles would have rendered me wellnigh as great a rascal as his innate badness has made him, but for the horrible spectacle of his depraved condition. Now, please God, I am changed—for, Sibly, I will use him as my tool; money is the *sine qua non* of my existence, and I will rob from the robber; but only to serve the rightful owners of the rich fruits with which the devil has rewarded him for the surrender of his soul."

"And I will help you, Silas, as heaven may help me!" returned the lawyer's clerk, with heartiness.

"You can assist me materially, and I am glad to have a friend I can depend on," replied the other. "How now, Charlie boy, what's the matter now?"

As Silas asked this question, little Charlie rushed into the room and came to his side.

"Oh, Silas!" he said, "there is a girl below who wishes to speak with you—she looks so strange and wild-like, and seems in such a hurry to speak with you."

"Did she mention her name?"

"Yes. She called herself Lucy Blake."

"Indeed, I don't think I know her, at least, by name," said his brother, consideringly. "Did she say where she came from?"

"Yes, from a Mrs. Wilton. She said she wants to tell you something about a lady you know."

"Ha! the servant at the cottage, no doubt," returned Silas, with animation.

"Perhaps Lady Edge——", began Sibly.

"Hush. Send her up, Charlie; and go for a walk, lad, you don't look so well this morning."

Charlie left the room.

"What can she want, Sibly?"

"Perhaps the lady is worse; perhaps better, and wishes to see you," said the clerk.

"Perhaps she is dead!" exclaimed Silas.

"Or Harwolf may have found her," suggested the other.

"I don't think that likely," said Silas Rye; "but

here comes the girl, and we shall know. I will put away these papers."

The door opened, and a girl, with a bright, intelligent face, apparently about sixteen years of age, entered.

Silas Rye placed her a chair.

"Well, my girl; what news? How is the lady at the cottage, and Mrs. Wilton? Nothing has happened, I trust?"

"Oh dear, sir, it's most dreadful," cried the girl, wringing her hands.

"Ah! you alarm me," cried Silas. "Is the lady worse?"

"Oh no, sir."

"What, then, is the matter?"

"She's gone, sir: she is gone."

"Gone?" cried Silas, starting up in amazement.

"Yes, sir; in the middle of the night, in a most awful thunderstorm, two men, sir—at least, two burglars, with blackened faces, broke into the house, sir, and tied the missis up to the ballusters, and carried the poor lady off in a cab."

"Good God."

"It's true, indeed, sir; and the missis is terribly ill—almost as insane as the poor, dear lady was, sir, with the fright and all the rest of it."

"But you—how did you escape?"

"I hid myself, sir. I couldn't do anything against the ruffians, sir, and I hid in the curtains of the lady's bed till they were gone."

"But didn't you alarm the neighbours? Did you not try to find out what direction the villains had taken?"

"I did the best I could, sir; but it was such a bad night. Our house, you know, is detached, and as we keep ourselves to ourselves, why, you know, sir, it is not easy to get people out of their beds in such weather who are not interested."

"Did you ever hear the like, Sibly?"

"It makes me almost doubt the over-ruling of Providence. Poor lady, she will be murdered."

"And she shall be avenged," cried Silas Rye, with a bitter oath.

"But surely, girl, you tried to find out which way they went?"

"Oh, yes, sir. I found the wheel ruts of the cab, and I tracked them over a rough cart road round the brickfield, and after a while walk, just as the morning began to break, I came to a lonely little wayside public house, and there I stopped for a moment. The place was shut up, but there were lights in the upper windows, and I thought, sir, whether she might be taken there, as the wheel marks swerved to the door, but as the marks went on down a dark lane, sir, I thought I had better follow. After a time I came to a place where they seem to have stopped again, and there was a number of foot-prints, sir."

"Just Heaven! there she was murdered?" cried Sibly, in great excitement.

"No, sir; I don't think so. There were the prints of little naked feet which I am sure were the lady's, and heavy tramplings of great boots; a piece of the lady's dressing gown which I have here, sir, was fluttering from the bushes."

"She must be murdered!" cried Sibly.

"No, sir," replied the girl; "from the marks I should think she had managed to open the cab door and jump out, had run up the lane, and all the scuffling, you know, sir, was to get her back; this is not unlikely, sir, for she is very cunning in her fits, as I have reason to know."

"You are a brave, good and clever girl, Miss Lucy Blake, and deserve to be well recompensed for your devotion to this hapless and friendless lady. I am inclined to take your view of the case—if the villains had murdered the poor lady they would have done it in the cab. But did you follow the traces any farther?"

"I should, sir, only I was stopped by a man."

"Indeed, what sort of a fellow did he seem?"

"He was a great rough, trampish-looking fellow, sir, an Irishman; and when I saw him I was very frightened, and shrieked out, and begged for mercy, for I feared he would rob me or insult me."

"And what did he say?"

"He is a very queer person, sir; he got into a towering passion and asked me what was my meaning for insulting him. And I thought he looked like a man that would take advantage of a poor young thing alone in the black night. I did not answer him, sir, for to tell the truth he looked savage enough for any villany, but he asked me whether I was following the cab."

"Did you tell him the truth?"

"No, sir, I thought it best not. I made no answer but turned to run away; he caught hold of me, and held me back, and, after swearing most dreadfully, called upon somebody by the name of Esau, and questioned and abused him as if he had been there. After this he took my arm, and, telling me to come along, almost dragged me back to the cottage. It was full daylight when we arrived; we found a little crowd round the door; the neighbours had moved the missis on to her bed. The Irishman went to her and presently came downstairs with a piece of paper, on which your address was written, and with a purse of money; he called to me to follow him, and I did; he took a cab which brought us to the corner of your street, where the Irishman is now waiting."

"Can you doubt the over-ruling of Providence in this case, Sibly?" asked Silas Rye, with a smile.

"No; but I doubt the Irishman."

"Well, we will call him over. But Tom, I have some knowledge of the rascal," he went on, approaching the window and beckoning; "I believe he is the very rogue I had such a tough tussle with at Frontemore. If so, we must use great caution."

Presently the door opened, and the subject of these remarks made his appearance.

He looked round with a bashful sort of stare, and then bowed to Sibly and Rye severally.

"Sure, I hope your hanners are quite well; and its sorry I'd be to intrude upon ye—but I'm come to make the enquiry consarning Misther Silas Rye, who is the guardian of a blessed lady that has been most confoundedly ill-used by a set of dirty blackguards that have carried her off, poor darlin', but——och! the divil!" he cried, suddenly recognising his former opponent, and instinctively raising his hands to his own throat, as if he feelingly remembered the iron grip of the sturdy adventurer.

"I see you remember me, my man," said Silas, with a dry smile.

"Faith! I'll not be afther forgetting ye at all for a very long time; it's the fist of a fighting man, is your hanner's, entirely. But ye'r the true gentleman, and ye'll not go to take the mane advantage of a poor boy that was mighty hard up, and fell into botherin' bad company."

"Your mate was a sneak as well as a garotter?" asked Silas, with a smile.

"Whew! garother is it? Divil better than the 'kinchin lay' for sich a milk-livered spalpeen; and it's true for your hanner, for a dirty snake is Esau Cooper, and all the likes of him; he's the jewel for a clane speech and a dirty action, the haythen—bad cess to him! If your hanner will overlook the little mistake I made, it's myself that will put ye in the way of recovering the poor crayther the infernal nagers have got into their black hands."

"I desire no more. But I suppose you are convinced that I'm not one to be played the fool with," replied Silas, with sternness.

"The divil burn me if I care a rapee about the affair at all—at all," returned the Irishman, fiercely. "And if your hanner can't trust me ye's may just carry your fish to another market."

"What is your name?"

"Oiny Macarne, at yer sarvice; they calls me Black Oiny."

"Ha! I recollect."

"It's botheration little good yer hanner can recollect of my mother's son. But faix! I'm above staling poor demented crayters, and cracking sich cribs as the owld woman's cottage down yonder. And if ye'll trust me I'll put yer hanner in the way of recovering the poor darlin', and defating the black skames of one of the infarnellest blackguards un-hung."

"Well, we will trust you, with a caution—if you play any tricks, I will give you into charge for high-way robbery."

"And sure, I could establish a counter-charge against yer hanner for assault and battery. Divil little work ye'd have left to Jack Ketch if you'd hugged me so affectionately another moment. Och! it's the steel and whalebone is your hanner's fingers, that niver were equalled for cracking chestnuts."

"What have they done with the lady?"

"Sure, they have just taken her away."

"Well; but whither?"

"That's more than I can tell, yer hanner. I concaive that I can inform ye where they tuk her at first, and I heard that they meant to take the poor thing to France, and put her in an asylum there; but divil a bit will I be bound for the truth of it."

"Then what use are you, fellow?" said Sibly, angrily. "You can tell us no more than we know already."

"Be aisy. I know very well where they took her to first; and by the holy saints, I'll engage to track her to Australy, if so be as they've carried her there."

"We must at once determine on what course is to be taken, Sibly," said Silas Rye. "I imagine it will be best to send the girl back to her mistress, and at once to set out in search of the lady. We will first discover whether the villains have conveyed her, and then we must take such measures as expe-diency may suggest to get her out of her enemy's power."

"I'm with you," cried Sibly, readily; "let us be off without delay."

In a few minutes everything had been arranged.

Lucy Blake was dismissed with a liberal present and the warmest expressions of approval.

A cab was fetched. Black Oiny was about to mount with the driver when Silas objected, as the Irishman might be recognised by some of his dis-reputable companions, whose curiosity would be excited.

Sibly took his place on the box, having received full directions as to the locality of their destination, which, for motives of caution, they resolved to reach by a circuitous route.

The evening was darkening apace when they started on their mission.

After a long and tedious ride they drew up at the corner of a long street of unfinished or untenanted houses, and here Black Oiny signified his wish that they should get out.

The cabman was sent away, with directions to re-main at a certain spot till wanted.

A part of the case was revealed to the man, and as there was something very persuasive in Sibly's enthusiastic eloquence and in Silas Rye's liberal pay, the man testified with some sincerity his interest in the lady's cause, and assured his fare that he would "stick to 'em till the last!"

He drove off.

Black Oiny advised his employers to beguile a few hours in the spacious and gaudy tavern that glared out in all the splendour of its brilliant gas jets and the newness of its gilding. While he went to re-connoitre, Sibly proposed a game of billiards, to kill the tedious time that must intervene before the re-turn of Black Oiny.

CHAPTER XXXVIII.

PIRATES AND BRIGANDS.

AFTER his splendid victory over the Mediterranean pirates, the "Red Raven" and the "Fortune of War" repaired the damage they had sustained in their late encounter, and, resuming their former disguise, anchored in a little creek on the Spanish coast.

The Boy Pirate and a number of his most trusty officers put on shore in the long boat.

They had modified their warlike appearance, and had dressed themselves as Sardinian mariners.

The beautiful Aurora had been removed to the "Fortune of War."

She remained in the cabin with Lilia, the Rover's bride.

The two girls, though very different in appearance, were nearly of the same age, and soon conceived for each other the warmest attachment.

Surrounded by a set of fierce and desperate ad-venturers of the opposite sex, a witness of constantly recurring scenes of battle and bloodshed, Lilia re-ceived the young Spanish maiden with heartfelt delight, and spent many happy hours in her society.

The Boy Pirate, who was in every sense a genius, had made himself, by study and intercourse, a perfect linguist, and had taught his bride Spanish, which she now spoke with considerable fluency.

Nothing could be more touching than the vivid affection of these delicately-nurtured young crea-tures, cast by their strange fate among scenes so alien from their gentle nature.

It may be well now to mention that as soon as the Boy Pirate had carried off his beloved sweetheart from her home at Frontemore, his first care had been to sanction their mutual loves by marriage. He had not the opportunity to do this till after the rescue of Lilia from the indomitable Harwolf; but as soon as he had recovered possession of his gallant "Red Raven" he landed with his bride on the English coast, and consummated his wedding at a village church near the shore.

Lilia confided to Aurora her anguish of mind at the sad fortune which had driven her wild but noble husband to take to his present lawless, wicked, and degrading way of life.

Aurora timidly questioned her new friend as to the pirate's state of mind, and eagerly enquired whether Christopher was reconciled to his terrible and perilous career, or whether he suffered the pangs of remorse.

With floods of tears, Lilia informed her that, in spite of his dashing and heroic bearing, in spite of the remorseless firmness with which he carried out his desperate schemes, that the Boy Pirate was a prey to the blackest despair, and at times gave way in secret to the most crushing agony of mind. His case seemed hopeless, but from the beginning he had been opposed to the hardest side of a hard-dealing world, and that, as in the bitterness of his soul, he had embarked in all the mad ventures of the pirate who had saved him, and as he had not preferred the only alternative—death, he was now powerless against his destiny, and must follow it out to the end.

Aurora listened with breathless attention.

Lilia with native delicacy, avoided any allusion to the fact that the pirate alluded to as Christopher's first tempter was Don Miguel—Aurora's own father.

But to return from this digression. We have stated that the Boy Pirate, with the flower of his crew, had landed on the coast, disguised as Sardinian sailors.

For some days they remained at a little seaport.

In this place was a wine shop which was much fre-quented by the inhabitants.

This inn was the rendezvous of the crew of the "Fortune of War" and her consort.

Christopher had been very busy during the week.

Bales of plunder were hourly brought from his ships, and as they were parted with at low prices, or exchanged for ship stores and ammunition, they found unquestioning purchasers.

One day Christopher strayed in thoughtful mood through the sunny little town.

He was alone.

There was something to his inward disquiet in the picturesque beauty of the surrounding scene.

Grotesque and quaint the curious and elaborately ornamented wooden houses that straggled along either side of the hilly and pebbly streets.

Such a scene has been the exhaustless theme of many an artist.

Under the heavy gables moved along a bright and motley crowd—dark-eyed, olive-skinned peasant girls in their gay dresses, black-robed priests, tawdry soldiers, vagabond muleteers, ox carts laden with luscious smelling fruits.

The sky was pure and intensely blue, and the clear and sparkling waters of the bay melted away at the hazy sky-line in fading tints of rich sapphire—its liquid mirror specked at intervals by the broad sails of some heavy merchantman, or the curved white wing of a swift-sailing felucca.

Our hero wandered towards the flower market.

Placed in the centre of the quaint, little maritime town, and on the precipitous side of a rugged hill, it was a beautiful spot.

It commanded a wide, ranging prospect of the indented sea coast, whose meanderings were marked out by a snowy rim of foam.

A cool and grateful air stole forth from the place, and met the heated traveller as he toiled up the white and dusty road.

Awnings were stretched across the little square to protect the beautiful and luxurious flower-clusters from the hot and blazing rays of the meridian sun.

In the centre, a fresh and melodious fountain flung up its crystal spray, scattering it about like dew-beads on the green foliage of the scented laurels and myrtles by which it was surrounded.

A number of peasants and inhabitants were gathered here.

Oriental-looking peasants, half clad with heavy gold ear and finger rings; lazy lazars, stretched in a luxurious indolence upon the ground, or upon benches; tittering black-veiled senoras, who furtively eyed the healthy, handsome young seaman as he passed.

As Christopher looked around his lip curved with irrepressible scorn; he contemplated the stalwart proportions of the dirty vagabondish idlers, and the lascivious girls that languished by the side of the flower stalls, or languidly swept past, attended by their sour-visaged, lynx-eyed duennas, and his hot action-loving spirit thrilled with reminiscenses of the haughty and chivalrous Spain of Ferdinand and Charles, and he looked upon the proud, yet sanctimonious, monks in the crowd with a glance of bitter scorn.

Musingly he seated himself beside the fountain.

The battle-roar still rung in his ears; the laughter and the exultant cheers of his desperate crew. The black pall of his death-flag fluttered before his eyes and darkened the glory of the sun.

An anguish of regret swept along his heart-strings as he contrasted the dark fame he had won by his feats of lawless daring, and the bright renown that might have been his, had cruel fortune been more propitious.

He was a brave man, but a thief; a renowned sea-captain, but a pirate never ceasing his remorse, never-failing the poignancy of his untold regrets.

A humid and refreshing breeze swept coolness from the fountain, balm from the flowers, to his heated brow. A thought of love, memory of Lilia and Aurora, infused a softer influence upon his hard thoughts.

As he sat, pensively listening to the leaping and plashing bound of the fountain, his attention was suddenly arrested by the approach of two fierce and tawny fellows, dressed in a style half-military, half-peasant-like. They were armed with pistol, sabre, and carbine; they wore high hats, with scarf and feather, and adorned with little trashy colourings of patron saints; they were cross-gartered, and their breasts were refulgent with a number of ribbons and crosses.

"Jesu Maria! do you see that caballero, Inez?" asked one of the flower girls of another, in a loud and eager whisper.

"Not I; do you think I pay heed to every hidalgo that passes through the flower-market," returned the girl addressed, tossing her head contemptuously.

"Nay; do but look at him?"

"So I do."

"But don't you know him?"

"Not I; who is he?"

"You will tremble if I tell you."

"A man! I tremble at a man."

"Well, shall I tell you who he is?"

"If you like."

"Look at him. My father is contrabandista, and has dealings with him. That man, Inez, is Juan Lopez, the captain of the brigands of the Sierra, and the other is his lieutenant. He burned down a village, and murdered two Englishmen—the heretics that were staying at the hotel."

"Ah, the fine man!" cried the other, looking at the villanous robber with wonder and admiration.

The Boy Pirate started at these words, and gave a glance at the brigand.

The fellow was chatting with one of the flower girls, his eagle-eyes beaming, and his white teeth flashing.

He pulled out a large silver piece, paid for a bouquet of flowers and put them in his buttonhole.

The lieutenant followed the example of his superior, and purchased another bunch of fresh and bright-hued flowers.

Then after kissing the girls, with a sweeping *congé*, the two scamps departed.

The Boy Pirate rose, lingered a moment, and then followed them.

The men moved along side by side, talking in low tones, but with animated gestures.

Averting his glance, and seemingly preoccupied with his own reflections, the Boy Pirate cautiously kept pace with the objects.

They made their way by devious paths through tortuous streets to a distant and less frequented part of the city.

As they advanced the aspect of the scene was changed; stately houses were succeeded by squalid hovels. Every grade of penury and infamy seemed to find an abode in the cut-throat suburb.

The Red Raven pulled round his belt, flung his Spanish mantle gracefully over his broad shoulders, and laid a firm hold on his pistols.

At length they reached a dirty, low wine shop. Several rascally-looking fellows made way with profound respect, as the two brigands approached. Like haughty barons walking through a rank of serfs and menials the grandiose bravoes passed along with supercilious majesty of mien, without deigning to take the slightest notice of the humble salutations of the little crowd.

They passed into the wine shop.

The Boy Pirate, keeping as much as possible in the shade, walked round the house, and having made his observations through a little window on one side of it, entered by the back door.

A wild, ill-conditioned youth stepped before him.

"This part of the house, senor, is reserved and private," he said, scanning our hero with no favourable eye.

"Send your father to me," said the Red Raven, sternly.

There was something so authoritative in the tone in which these words were spoken that the boy quailed, and dived down a narrow and dark passage to obey the order.

A growl and succession of terrible oaths was heard from within a little chamber at the end of the passage, and through the half-opened door a man was seen rolling heavily from a squalid bed.

Presently a short, fat fellow, with his leg swollen with gout, and bandaged, limped, groaning and cursing, towards the guest.

He raised his eyes impatiently towards our hero.

Recognizing him, he started backwards with a cringing bow.

"Ah, senor, is it you? Ten thousand pardons; but my affliction, senor—the gout—is a bad teacher of patience. What can I do for you?"

"A bottle of your best vintage," returned the Boy Pirate, with a smile. "Show me to the old room."

"But, senor——"

"I know what you would say."

"But you mean no harm to the contrabandista?"

"That's not your business."

"With pardon, senor," returned the innkeeper, speaking in whispers, and shuddering with fear, "but it is my business."

"In what way?"

"Only this," returned the man, drawing his forefinger across his throat, and shrugging his shoulders with a frightened look.

"Bring me the wine, give me a light, and keep quiet; you know I hate to threaten," returned the Boy Pirate.

With a bland smile and a muttered curse, the innkeeper hastened to do his bidding.

He fetched a lantern from the room, descended into the cellar, and returned with a sealed bottle.

"Who are your best customers?" asked the desperate young pirate, with a smile, as he took the bottle and the light.

"English guineas are better than Spanish maravedis."

"Very well, then; tread softly."

With trembling steps, the innkeeper noiselessly led the way down the passage.

He carefully opened a door, and ushered our hero in a large, dark and dusty chamber; the shutters of the windows were closed.

No sooner had he left Christopher in this place than the latter looked about him, and peered into every corner.

Satisfied with the search, he returned to the partition that separated him from the brigands.

He passed his hand along the wall, and drew a piece of wood from a crevice it concealed, and looked through.

The two miscreants were seated at a table, drinking from large and brimming glasses.

Christopher could see and hear all that was passing.

"And so the villanous priest ordered our comrade Jose to be shot!" cried the chief brigand, with flashing eyes.

"He did, senor captain."

"And knew him to be of my troop?"

"Even so."

"And how did the people take it?"

"They were awe-stricken. One man, a miller, tried to get poor Jose out of the hut where he was confined the night before his execution, but the picket saw him, and fired at him; he was badly wounded. He was taken, and is now in gaol."

The brigand leader gave vent to a savage oath.

"And what is worse, senor, when Jose had been shot the cardinal thief proclaimed you an outlaw, and vilified your name in the most abominable terms —the mildest of which were brigand and murderer."

"So much for the specious Cardinal Gonsalvez, who has paid me to do his dirty work a score of times; but I'll be even with him, the precious Cardinal Gonsalvez."

Christopher started at the name. He recollected that the dignitary mentioned was the guardian of Aurora Vasquez, and that at his instigation she had been removed from the convent.

He listened eagerly.

"And excepting this miller, none of the peasantry interfered to save our comrade."

"Not one, senor."

"Then, by my patron, I'll burn every homestead in the cursed village, and give up the whole brood of dastardly traitors to the sword and flames. I swear it, by the Virgin, Zambullo!" cried the infuriate robber.

"One woman gave information against us."

"I'll rend her tongue out!"

"And a man declared he overheard the conspiracy for the ambuscade that failed so miserably."

"I'll slice his ears off and make him eat them," cried the chivalrous Don Juan Lopez.

"Just so!" returned the lieutenant, coolly tossing off a brimmer of wine.

"I was ever counted a man of my word," cried the brigand, fiercely grounding his carbine. "And by the smoke of the infernal pit, I will make this meddling priest dearly rue the hour he braved me— and that would I if he wore the tiara instead of his cardinal's hat!"

"I would not wear his scarlet robe for the mines of Mexico, senor captain, since he has offended you," returned the other, with a grin.

"Zambullo, I am not a man to be offended with impunity—that you know. I choke with wrath. The barefaced audacity of this miserable priest, to prate of law and justice too—the unconscionable villain!" The ruffian burst into a rough, contemptuous laugh. "Well, we shall see."

"He will never succeed to the Popedom," returned the obsequious lieutenant, with a leer.

"You may take your oath of it," returned the captain of the brigands; "but what of the other affair?—did Almanzo follow out my orders with respect to the safe custody and speedy concealment of the rich novice, Aurora Vasquez?"

"No; that's what galled the cardinal, depend on it," returned the other.

"So she is safely housed? She shall pay for her uncle's impudence."

"What, captain, you have not heard the disaster that has befallen Almanzo?" asked the lieutenant, aghast.

"How should I? Have I not just returned from the Sierra?"

"By St. Janiero! then, you have evil news to hear. Scarcely was the senorita secured on board, when the vessel was run down by two immense ships, a sloop and a frigate; after a desperate conflict the vessel was burnt to the water's edge, and our crew, almost to a man, exterminated."

The brigand, as he said this, shrugged his shoulders with a heavy sigh, and crossed himself devoutly.

The brigand chief smote his forehead, and starting to his feet, paced the room in a paroxysm of fury.

"A sloop—a frigate? Of what country?"

"They carried Sardinian colours, but were plainly English."

The captain uttered a blasphemous cry.

"English! But where was our flotilla—twenty barques? Why did they not give chase?"

"They were better where they were, safe at their moorings. We might have suffered worse shame and loss, considering who was our opponent," returned the other, with a grim smile.

"By the thunder! and you dare——Who was he?"

"The Red Raven—the Boy Pirate," replied the man.

The brigand chief sank back in his chair with a gasp of consternation.

"Is it possible? Is that sea-dragon in our waters again?"

"Truth he is, captain, and, as of old, he seems to direct all his vengeance against those of his own calling. There is not a worse foe of brigands and pirates than this king of freebooters."

"If you give him such fair names, Zambullo, I'll strangle you; I served under his master, Don Miguel, in Chili and La Plata. Well, his is a heavy reckoning, and he shall pay it in full."

"The sooner you bring him to his account the better, senor captain," Zambullo rejoined, with a grin, "for he has played the devil long enough."

"Enough! his term is wellnigh run out; but, Zambullo, all this comes of our impious neglect! We brought no gifts to the Virgin's shrine at the Assumption festival; we have neglected our offerings to St. Janiero; no masses were paid for the men we lost in our last victory! what can be expected? But this cardinal, have you no news of him?"

"Yes, senor, news that will do your heart good;

to-night, carried in his sedan—for he is sick—he crosses the Sierra close to our fastness; he is on his road to Cordova."

"May I linger ten thousand ages in purgatory if ever he reaches his destination," cried the ferocious Lopez, rising and poising his carbine.

"We will lay a brave ambush for him; he has no escort but a few shavelings and a mounted servant or two; they don't muster six firearms among them."

"Good! Let it be near the Holy Well in the dark valley beyond the Sierra."

"I know the place, captain; to make the thing secure I will march over fifty men and place them in concealment."

"I leave the management of that part of the affair to you, Zambullo; I will join you at the place."

"We cannot fail, captain," returned the other brigand, rising and finishing off the wine.

"And Almanzo is killed—his ship burnt and sunk! but why did they let Aurora be taken?" growled Don Juan.

"True, senor; but what could they do?"

"They should have cut her throat! But come, I will hasten to conciliate the saints; I will go at once and pay masses for poor Jose; you proceed to muster the band at the appointed place. We will do justice upon the spiteful old priest, and then for the Red Raven!"

With this the two worthies slung their carbines on their shoulders, and tramped out of the room.

The Boy Pirate laughed bitterly—paused for a moment—adjusted his weapons, and cautiously left the wine-shop.

CHAPTER XXXIX.
THE BATTLE.

THE Sierra was a long range of lofty hills that bounded the table land on which the little sea town was built.

Our scene is wild and picturesque; the hour lends additional grandeur to its weird majesty. It was a dark night, the moon struggling feebly among the heavy masses of cloud that pile upon each other to obscure her argent brilliancy.

On one side of the rough and rocky pathway stood one of those wooden pent-houses so common in this country, erected to protect from the effects of inclement weather the crumbling image of some apocryphal saint.

Beneath this little shrine, from the living rock, a pure and limpid spring of water poured forth its crystal stream, which fell gushing into a basin, rough hewn in the stone.

The rocks on either side the ravine were fringed with firs and dark cypresses.

The south wind fanned its soft wing, waving the arms of the spectre-like pines, and rustling the heavy and luxuriant foliage of the rich chestnuts.

On one side of the road was a precipitous descent that shot prone down in a long and dark valley, through which a little mountain brooklet, a foamy torrent in the rainy seasons, whispered hoarsely over its pebbly channel, under a tangling covert of briary underwood.

Through this gloomy hollow a band of men were stealthily creeping, every now and then pausing at at a sign from their leader, and then advancing in the same cautious manner.

As they stole round an open part of the dell the faint moonbeams gleamed on their weapons, and discovered them to be a party of seamen.

They were the Boy Pirate and his crew stealing upon the ambush of brigands.

They reached the rocky wall that bound the declining road.

Here they halted.

Our hero, Dick Caffyn, and the young Spaniard crept forward.

Presently Christopher paused and held up his hand.

"Hist!"

A branch broke and crackled.

A sentinel, with his peaked hat and gleaming carbine, sprang to the side of the road, and swaying round his piece, peered down into the gloomy hollow.

"Who goes there?"

There was no reply to this challenge. No sound was heard but the fitful moan of the night breeze, the restless murmur of the bubbling stream, the shrill, sweet trill of a lovelorn nightingale from the distant surging mass of shadowy trees.

The brigand listened acutely for a moment.

He shouldered his carbine, and whistling in a low tone a national air paced his beat with measured tramp.

Christopher crawled into the midst of his crew.

"Now, mates," he whispered, "all depends on the next move. We must scale these rocks as quietly as yon mist-wreaths steal from the hill-tops."

"Ay, ay, sir," responded the men, in the same low voice.

"Are you ready?"

"Ready, sir."

"Softly then."

With cat-like stealthiness the gallant band clambered the height.

A long and straggling line of trees and bushes appeared.

Another brigand at this moment appeared descending the narrow pass between the mountains.

The sentinel walked away to meet him.

Taking advantage of his removal, the crew pushed forward and reached the bushy screen.

With all their caution a loosened stone was displaced beneath some careless foot, and rattled down into the valley, bouncing from rock to rock.

Both the brigands started, and ran to the side of the road, pointing their arms.

"'Tis a second time within a moment," said the sentinel. "Some one is there!"

They listened.

All was still.

"'Tis a fox or a polecat creeping into its burrow," whispered the other, "the earth is loose here."

"By the Virgin, that I will discover?" replied the brigand.

He leaped into the bushes, and clambered along the steep side of the bank.

He passed so near our hero and Dick Caffyn as almost to touch them.

As he re-passed, the young sailor whispered to the Boy Pirate—

"Captain, shall I shiver his costard with my pistol-butt; we can easily settle the other fellow."

"Idiot! lie close!" returned our hero, with fierce impatience.

As the man passed very near to them they must have been seen but for a lucky coincidence.

A heavy black cloud at this moment floated over the moon, and deep darkness closed around them like a pall.

The brigand scrambled on to the road.

"Are you satisfied?" asked the other.

"No. Come with me, I will try again," the other rejoined, sharply.

They were about to plunge together into the cover, when Christopher gave a low bark, flinging back the sound with ventriloquial skill, and imitating the cry of a fox so naturally, that even his companions started.

"I told you so," said the second brigand to the sentinel. "Give up your fool's chase, 'tis nothing but a straying fox."

The man seemed convinced and returned to his post.

"Where did you learn that fine trick, captain?" asked Dick Caffyn, softly.

"Among the Chippeways," returned our hero, with a smile.

And now from the other side of the road came forth a large party of brigands.

The feeble moonbeams again half-illumined the scene.

Zambullo, the lieutenant, was easily distinguishable by the extra number of feathers in his high-crowned hat, and the lavish display of tinsel medals and trumpery orders on his breast.

The band conferred together in low and excited whispers.

The tableaux would have been a fine study for a masterly artist.

The romantic beauty of the dark, lone hills, the wild and tortured sky, the solemn firs, the rocky path, and the group of swarthy contrabandists in their picturesque garb."

"By George! they muster strong," muttered Dick Caffyn.

"Tush! we have the odds. Three groats are but one shilling," replied the reckless Boy Pirate.

"This melodrama is to my liking," said Dick Caffyn, with a chuckle.

"And to mine," returned his foster-brother; "but it's not the first time I've played in Fra Diavolo."

The band of brigands now dispersed, and melted away among the rocks and bushes on the opposite side of the road.

Zambullo stood alone in the middle of the path.

He looked in the direction of the mountains.

Far away in the sombre distance was heard the faint jingling of bells, and a number of lanterns were seen dancing along like so many fire-flies.

"They are coming, captain," whispered Dick Caffyn, excitedly. "This is glorious fun——"

"Hush!"

Stooping low and trailing his gun, the brigand officer sneaked into the thicket to his companions.

"Manuel Perez!"

"Here, captain."

"You must more immediately attend to the cardinal. For your own sake and Donna Aurora's you must win his favour."

"Thanks, noble captain."

"Dick, pass the word to Brierly—he is the oldest and steadiest of our crew—to keep back part of our force for reserve; he can best restrain their impatience. You stick by me."

"Ay, captain, with a will."

The jingling of the bells grew louder, and now, as the travelling party drew near, it was seen to consist of a number of monks and muleteers, some mounted, some on foot, with long staves and lanterns. There were a few armed attendants on horses, and in the centre of the little caravan was a gaudy litter swaying between two led mules; this was occupied by the old Cardinal Gonsalvez.

The procession moved slowly along the road.

A moment of breathless excitement ensued.

The cavalcade was passing between the two ambuscades.

There was a shout from the robbers.

Don Juan Lopez and his worthy lieutenant, Zambullo, stood full in the face of the advancing travellers.

"Holy Saints! we are beset by brigands," cried one of the monks—a tall, cadaverous fellow, mounted on a mule, which stopped suddenly with advanced ears and legs—with a shriek of asinine terror."

"Ha, ha! your eminence," roared the robber-captain, with a hoarse laugh; "you will have cause to repent that your mercy spared one of my band—that you did not shoot us all with my trooper Jose."

"There's nothing I more regret, damnable thief and murderer, whom the saints anathemise!" squeaked the feeble but irate dignitary, as he struggled to alight from his litter.

"You shall deserve to be canonized, cardinal, for your eminence shall be honoured with a hotter martyrdom than your patron saint, who was roasted on a gridiron," shouted the ruffian.

"Do your worst, son of Satan, doomed to eternal perdition!" again screamed the doughty ecclesiastic.

"Down with the shavelings, down with the blood-hounds," shouted the gang. "Death for the death of Jose."

Several shots were fired on either side. A charge of the brigands followed.

"Perez, look to the cardinal," said the Boy Pirate, quickly, and then turning to the crew, he shouted in his cheery, manly tones, with a gleeful laugh—

"Now my champions of the church, to the rescue; we'll see who have the sharpest teeth, land-rats or water-rats."

"Heave ahead, my heroes, hurrah for the Red Raven."

The lone hills rung with the responding shout of the gallant crew, and, like dogs let loose from the leash, they burst from bush and tree, their pistols crackling and their swords flashing.

Nothing could exceed the consternation of the brigands at this sudden assault.

There was a wild _melée_.

Don Juan Lopez was stunned by surprise and dismay; but upon collecting his resources his first thought was to kill the cardinal.

He rushed up to the side of the litter, which had been overturned, and fired his pistol at the old man, who lay on the ground unable to rise.

He was hurled back and across the road by the Boy Pirate with such force that it was only by wildly clutching at the branches of the trees he could save himself from rolling headlong down the precipice.

Manuel Perez, who was on one knee disentangling the cardinal from the meshing harness and drapery of the litter with intent to raise him, paused and levelled his pistol with deadly aim at the brigand-chief, who at the moment was struggling to secure his foot-hold on the brink of the abyss.

"No," said the Boy Pirate, striking aside the weapon, "leave him to me." With this he strode across the path and encountered the brigand-captain, who was now standing on firm ground.

"_First I will settle the cardinal, then for the Red Raven_," said the Boy Pirate, grimly, making use of Don Juan's own words, which he had overheard at the wine-shop.

"Cursed spy and insolent braggart," shouted the brigand, "_now_ for the Red Raven. I commend your soul to the devil, who owns it."

For a moment they watched each other with fierce eyes, then they raised their swords, and a desperate fight began.

They were both skilful swordsmen, wary and determined. A few masterly passes, however, and Don Juan, who was maddened and unnerved by his sudden defeat, incautiously exposed his breast while attempting a thrust.

The Boy Pirate ran him through the breast.

The agonised ruffian grasped at the sharp blade with his naked hands, which were fearfully gashed, and in the fierce agony of the moment, wrenched it from the Boy Pirate's grasp.

They were too close for him to use it. He dropped the red weapon, and in the last throe of his dying strength seized Christopher by the throat.

A frightful struggle then took place on the brink of that cliff.

The Boy Pirate was so firmly held by his foe that his own fate seemed imminent.

But in an instant, when the death grip of his enemy was dragging him over the precipice to destruction, he shook him off by a mighty effort, and planting his knee on his breast, hurled him backwards.

Don Juan, with deadly glaring eyes and set teeth, grasped wildly at a branch growing from the side of the rugged cliff.

One moment he rested there, with the red stream gurgling from his breast; then, with a snap, the decayed stem gave way, and Don Juan fell.

Down, down the cliff he rolled, dashing from crag to crag, till he descended with a sickening crash to the rugged bottom of the appalling precipice.

The other combatants, who had been held in a state of breathless awe by the scene before them, now came hurrying forward.

They paused at the brink of death. Men whose hearts were drunken with the thirst for blood almost

THE BRITISH TAR TO THE RESCUE.

shivered as they gazed after the shattered, bleeding form lying at such a depth beneath them.

Even in that wild moment the indomitable youth found time for reflection.

" 'Tis ever so," he murmured, "one sort of vermin destroys another; now were I not an outlaw as well as he how this feat would blazon my honour throughout Europe."

Young Perez and a pirate had managed to extricate the cardinal from his encumbrances, and had raised the feeble old man in their arms.

"Ah! 'you are English—without doubt a Lutheran," cried the fiery old priest, addressing the sailor; "but if you will exterminate these beasts I will entreat St. Peter to grant you plenary indulgence for all your heresies. Look, look; by St. Michael they are running. If you let one of the fiends escape I will call you all cowards."

The brigands had indeed taken to flight, but they

No. 14.

were intercepted at a turn in the road by Jack Brierly and his reserve.

The sound of shots and shouts re-echoed from the distance.

The Boy Pirate and Dick Caffyn rushed to the scene of the renewed fight.

The conflict took place at a wild part of the road.

A wall of rocks rose on either side.

Hemmed in on all sides by the pirate crew the brigands' case was desperate.

Some of the more determined of the gang fought with all the fury of despair.

Others of meaner spirit shrieked for quarter.

Not a few flung themselves on their knees and invoked their saints and kissed their crosses and pictures.

The battle was degenerating from a fair though furious contest to a terrible slaughter.

The pirates shewed no mercy.

The ground was strewn with the bodies of the dead and dying.

Screams, cheers, yells, the rattle of muskets and the clashing of swords pierce the dull ear of night.

The bravest of the gang, the sturdy Zambullo, still kept his ground, or even managed to force his way through the phalanx of his enemies.

All at once the fast decreasing band of robbers gave a joyous cry.

A pealing scream was heard from the rocks above, and a wild dark woman appeared on the summit.

In one hand she held a flaming torch, in the other a gun.

She was accompanied by a score or so of brigands.

With wild gestures she pointed down to the scene of slaughter.

She stuck her torch in a crevice in the rock.

At the instant scream was one of the sailors was fiercely fighting with Zambullo—they were armed with daggers.

Zambullo was getting the worst of it, in fact was forced down upon his knee.

The brigand's wife raised the gun to her shoulder, it flashed, and the bullet struck the pirate full in the back; he fell dead upon his prostrate foe.

Zambullo pushed him off, leaped to his feet and wildly cutting his way to the side of the path, scrambled up the rocks.

He was fired at, but though slightly wounded reached the top in safety.

By his direction, the brigands from their heights poured a murderous fire upon the pirates.

At this juncture the Boy Pirate and Dick Caffyn appeared on the scene.

His quick eye at once discerned that the tide of battle was turning against them.

He called some of the stragglers about him, and in the face of a deadly volley scrambled up the cliff, in order to dislodge the reinforcement of brigands.

With but few to back him he gained the height at an incalculable risk of his own life.

After a most desperate conflict he drove the brigands backwards down the other side of the rock.

The brigand woman rushed upon him like a fury, at the same moment as a bloated, sensual-looking fellow, dressed as a priest, flung himself with maniac savageness upon Dick Caffyn, but who was speedily struck down and disabled.

When the brigandess saw this, she broke away from Christopher, who withstood her by clasping her in his arms, laughing and struggling—for he was too manly to harm a woman. With uplifted poignard she rushed upon the slayer of her confessor, bent to avenge him.

"Hi! Dick, look out for this flirt!" shouted the Boy Pirate, laughing. "She has jilted me, and means to make love to you. Don't hurt her, for your life, Dick."

"But what the devil shall I do with her," spluttered his foster-brother, for his sword was clenched in his teeth, and he tussled desperately with the virago.

The Boy Pirate stooped over the body of the hedge priest, and untied the rope at his waist.

Stealing behind the brigandess, he made a lasso of the cord, and, throwing it over, tightened it as it sank to her waist, and pulled her away with as little force as possible under the circumstances.

Aided by his foster-brother, the Boy Pirate managed, after a hot struggle, to bind her to a tree.

"That's the worst fight that ever I had in my life," panted Dick, wiping his face, which was bleeding from the scratches he had received in his encounter.

The Boy Pirate laughed.

But Dick had reckoned without his host, for a deadlier peril threatened him.

He felt himself seized by the throat, and was forcibly hurled to the ground.

The ferocious Zambullo had flung himself upon him, and the keen edge of the knife was at his throat.

Christopher's attention was diverted. With a few of his crew, who had managed to reach him, he was making a furious rush upon the reinforcement of brigands. The robbers seemed struck with a sudden panic and took to their heels, running like sheep down into the valley, and making their way towards a plank that bridged over the mountain torrent, at this place deep and rapid.

Christopher noticed that as they passed they cut loose the woman from the tree, and that she joined with the others in their flight.

The sailors, headed by Brierly, dashed over the top of the rock, and made off after the fugitives like hounds in full cry.

The Boy Pirate was about to follow, when he suddenly heard a shout behind him.

Turning his head, he perceived that Zambullo had dragged Dick Caffyn to the brink of the steep bank of rock, and was about to hurl him into the road.

They wrestled madly on the verge of the steep—the brigand above, dealing furious thrusts with his knife, which the pirate warded off with his arm.

Dick Caffyn was now pushed half-way into mid-air.

The Boy Pirate rushed to the spot.

Seizing Dick firmly by the shoulder, he coolly levelled his pistol at the brigand's head, and blew out his brains.

Zambullo rolled over, and crashed down into the road.

Christopher helped his foster-brother to his feet, and together they sped in the track of their flying foes.

Upon reaching the banks a strange scene appeared.

The pirates were firing a parting volley.

The bridge was crowded with the fleeing brigands.

Among them was the woman who had so doughtily engaged with Christopher and Dick Caffyn.

All at once, by some chance, she was pushed over the narrow plank; but she managed to cling to the side of the rude bridge.

Another instant the heavy boot of one of the robbers crushed her fingers, and with a piercing shriek she fell backwards into the stream, and was hurried away by the seething torrent.

Without hesitating a second, the gallant Boy Pirate threw off his jacket and kicked off his shoes, and plunged headlong into the wrathful waters, and seizing the woman round the waist, buoyed her up.

Thunderstruck and aghast with suspense, the crew ran along the banks, and watched their young commander struggling hopelessly in the furious torrent, still clinging to the woman, who, in her terror, was doing all that was possible to drown herself and him.

There was a pile of rocks in the midst of the stream; against this they drifted.

Brierly plunged into the water breast deep, and with much difficulty, helped him to land.

As he stood looking tenderly upon the woman who lay fainting on the turf, the stern seamen watched the noble and dauntless face of their youthful hero for some moments, in the impressive silence of mute, because intense, admiration.

Before he could protest or resist, the Boy Pirate found himself seated upon the broad shoulders, and hurried along amid the deafening cheers of his devoted crew.

CHAPTER XL.

OINY MACARNE'S EXPEDITION.

OUR readers will remember that Oiny Macarne left Rye and Sibly at the tavern, and proceeded to make his observations in the neighbourhood.

He passed through a strange outlandish quarter where the growing town was ruthlessly encroaching upon the country.

There yet remained tokens of the former rustic character of the locality—an ivied church, a clear brook, and an avenue of primeval elms.

But such relics were being fast swept away before

the mighty army of new houses that advanced from day to day further into "the bowels of the land."

Oiny passed a stately edifice dignified as the "Guelph Arms," which glared down, in all the majestic disdain of stuccoed front, portico, cornice work, fields of plate glass, and acres of brewers' blazonry and gilding, upon its lowly and bashful neighbour the little plain, brick literary institute, art school, and library.

As he was turning the corner of the imposing temple of Bacchus, he suddenly perceived his old companion the gipsy Esau on the other side of the street.

Oiny stopped abruptly, and dodged into one of the partitioned "departments" of the bar.

The gipsy had not perceived him, but came swaying along—his sullen and drink-flushed face bent towards the ground.

Black Oiny had called for a glass of whisky.

The gipsy stumbled into the next division, and sulkily ordered brandy.

The Irishman slunk back, and seated himself out of the other's sight, and coolly lighted his short pipe.

He knew his man, and guessed that it would be some time before he left the place.

Every now and then, when quite unobserved, Black Oiny stood on the settle and peeped over at the gipsy.

Esau had called for more brandy; and by the way he tottered from side to side, might seem to be getting more than "half seas over."

Presently a woman came in with a jug, and the gipsy lurched and fell against her.

"Oh! you drunken brute! keep your feet, do!" cried the slip-shod woman, in a shrill tone.

The gipsy looked at her with bent head from under his heavy brows—his eyes winking and glittering with the strong fumes of the stimulant.

"Brutsh! 'sult me? Employed by a gemman—perfect gemman!—paysh like a marquish! Ah! get along with ye. Look ye here! if supposh a woman's mad, and you there——"

The drunken fool was about to begin a rambling confession to the strange woman, but, briskly snatching away her shawl, which he had clutched, and bestowing on him a withering look, she bounced out of the tavern.

"Bedad! if I should'nt howld it the swatest bit of a job I ever did to crack this blethering thafe's empty brain-pan," growled Black Oiny. "Och, murder! to the divil wid a boy's hanging sacrets if he makes a pal of sich a gibbering monkey."

Esau put down the glass, and staggering from the bar, fell heavily against the thin partition.

Black Oiny rose, intending to follow the gipsy into the street, when he heard a deep gruff voice on the other side of the partition. He at once recognised it as Joe Miles's.

"This be purty, I zay; this be mortal purty. You be a vine vellow to be employed on 'ticklar business; no how you bean't fit. Look ye, if ye doan't stand on yer feet and come out on't, I'll split on ye to the squire—and be durned if I doan't!

"Whatsh use of—of—I shay, quarrelling. I ain't a-goin' to be bullied—hic! put upon; for if she's madsh, —I zay if there's cracking cribs—hic—and women-stealing—why the beaks and the crushers. I want more brandy."

The insensate drunkard was fumbling along the partition to return to the bar for more drink.

Oiny heard a short scuffle. He flew to the door; as he opened it, he saw Esau hurled across the pavement.

The gipsy fell in the road.

Miles emerged from the public house.

He stooped over his companion, and raised him.

He shook and bullied him for some moments; then making him sit down on the curb, returned several times into the public house, and plied him with soda water.

After awhile, Esau became more sobered.

Oiny was watching them among two or three idlers, who looked on with grinning faces.

Oiny heard Esau mutter in a hoarse, thick tone to his companion,

"I say, Joe, it's the cussed brandy. They couldn't hang a fellow, could they? O lord, my head! I didn't blab, eh?"

"Come on, ye infarnal fool, before you have ruined I and thou too.

The countryman dragged him away.

The little crowd laughed and hooted.

Black Oiny followed at a distance.

The two men passed down a dark alley of squalid houses belonging to the old village, which the new town was supplanting, and came into a wide road strewn with building materials, the very air seeming impregnated with brick-dust and mortar, and either side of the road being lined with gins and pitfalls in the abounding forests of scaffold poles and gulfs of foundations.

Through this gloomy region they passed on till they came to a large house standing at the bleak corner of an unfinished row.

The gas had not yet been put on in that dreary quarter of the "New Town."

Oiny stole along beneath the shade of a wall on the opposite side of the way.

The two men ascended the steps of the corner house, the only one in the unfinished street, or rather terrace, that appeared to be tenanted or, indeed, habitable.

Esau still shambled along unsteadily.

Miles applied the key, and taking his companion by the arm, pulled him into the house.

Oiny watched them, and glanced eagerly down the passage within.

There was nothing particular to reward his scrutiny.

He noticed that the passage and stairs were uncarpeted, and that the place was evidently but newly occupied, and incompletely furnished.

For half an hour Black Oiny walked about watching the lights in two of the windows. He walked to the back of the house; he saw that there was a light in the window of a little room—he could see it stream through the interstices of the folding shutters, for the room seemed to be cautiously closed up.

Oiny returned to the front of the house by passing through the dark and draughty building adjoining, which was not in a very advanced stage towards its completion.

A carriage rolled by.

Oiny kept himself concealed in the wide, black shadow of the wall, and noted the movements of this vehicle.

A man got off the box and knocked imperiously at the door.

It was opened.

An elderly man got out. As he looked at the house, Oiny, even where he stood, could see his eyes quail and his cheek turn ghastly white.

He recognised this person at once as Squire Harwolf.

The door slammed, the carriage rolled away.

The Irishman was perplexed.

He looked at the house, he could discover no way of ingress.

He looked at the dark, half-built house attached. He decided upon a plan, and without hesitation proceeded to carry it out.

Entering the house, he made his way by ladders and stairs from story to story, till he reached the roof.

He crawled along the parapet, and after some hesitation clambered down one of the chimneys.

He used great caution. It was autumn, and the weather, except during occasional blights, was sultry hot, and fires were disused.

Midway down the winding flue was a strong iron bar.

On this the fellow perched himself.

He looked down, he could see that there was a light in the room, he could hear that some one was singing.

CHAPTER XLI.

ANDREW HARWOLF FOILED.

WHEN Andrew Harwolf entered the house, he walked straight up the stairs and entered a large room on the first floor.

It was but partly furnished; but it was apparent some effort had been made to arrange it for the reception of a guest.

Harwolf seated himself and fanned himself with his handkerchief.

Miles stood at the door.

Harwolf rose and nervously paced to and fro.

" She is here ? "

" Yes, squire ; she is safely housed, and is tolerably quiet like."

" That's well," said the villain, with a gasp. " Had you much trouble to carry out my orders ? "

" Very little, yer honour, I must zay, considering. It was all well-managed, and it thundered and lightened like blazes, so, as there was no one abroad, we met with no opposition ; and as for the old woman as keeps the house, she fainted away, and we tied her to the stair-rails."

" Only one witness ? Then you didn't——"

Harwolf did not finish the sentence, but looked enquiringly, with an oblique glance of his sinister eyes, at his agent.

A scowl passed across the innkeeper's face, and he slightly shuddered.

" Durn it, squire ! that wasn't in the bargain," he said.

" No ! I do not wish what you surmise," returned Harwolf, quickly. " It is only desirable the woman should hold her tongue."

" It be durnation little she can tell ; she were as good as dead in a swoond when we left her, your honour."

" Good ! but the lady ? "

" I tell yer honour she can zay nothin', not she, poor cretur, vor she be madder than the March winds."

Harwolf clenched his teeth ; he took a stride forward, and pulled savagely at his cravat as if his throat were swelling, and muttered,

" If I should go mad ! "

He turned his pale face towards the innkeeper.

The keen-looking countryman was watching him stealthily.

" Such a malady is very terrible, Miles," he said, with forced calmness.

" Ay, to be zure, yer honour, such things do be ; but there must be a cause for 'em."

" A cause ? " said Harwolf, in a startled manner.

" Ay, zure ; I mean to make a zane man or woman mad, yer honour. I was a-zaying there must be a cause for everything. Zometimes it be nat'ral, and zometimes it be grief as does it."

" Yes, yes ; you are right—grief or guilt will make one mad. Where are you going ?—don't leave the room."

" Does yer honour mean to see the lady ? "

" Anon ; I'm tired, and somewhat faint."

" Will I get 'ee a mossel of summut, squire ? "

" No, I cannot eat ; but have you any brandy ? "

" I will get yer honour some."

" Do ; but make haste."

" All right, sir, I'll be back in a twinkling. This be a lonesome place, yer honour, but it be too new to be haunted. He, he, he ! "

And with a chuckling laugh the countryman dived downstairs, leaving his employer to his own reflections.

Harwolf walked about uneasily, and muttered to himself—

" I did not think that reflection followed actions that it dared not precede ; I did not estimate this subsequent terror. Houses, new or old, are not haunted ! Surely the spirits have no wish to revisit the scenes of their mortal miseries. I am not such a fool as to think it, but my brain is becoming ulcerated by the ever-puncturing sting of one aspic thought that works me to madness—to madness ! Ah, God ! mur-

der and madness ! Here and there, on my right hand and my left ; and I am the damned magician that has conjured up these fiends to plague and destroy my best and most confiding benefactors. Andrew Harwolf, fool, beast ! is it not enough that the law should sharpen its fangs for you, that the dead should rise up and gibber at you, but must you be your own tormentor ? Oh, no, it is not ; it is conscience, and conscience is not myself, it is the breath of some exterior awful power, else, why can I not check it ? Wandering again ! What have I to do with such thoughts, now—now, at the crisis, when I want such a clear head and hard heart ? Will that fellow never bring the drink ? "

The miserable wretch walked to the window.

He leant his hot brow against the cool glass, and eased his strained eyes by gazing out into the closing darkness.

A moment passed away ; the mind of the possessor of Frontemore Hall and the Edgeforth estates was deeply, very deeply absorbed in reverie.

The gloomy scene recalled some reminiscence of the past, and he was quite unconscious for the moment of surrounding objects.

He heard a deep sigh from behind him.

He stood marble still, a quick quiver of his muscles, and he remained as if suddenly paralysed.

He dared not turn his head, the qualm of fright was so strong.

Could anyone have seen his clammy, rigid face, his fixed and glassy eye, and his convulsion-clutched fingers, they would have thought that he had been struck dead.

Another sigh, and, then, with a wild bird-like warble thrilled forth a plaintive melody, some simple village love-dirge.

Harwolf controlled himself, and turned round.

In her long, white dress, her hair wildly streaming on her shoulders, the unfortunate lady stood satyr-like—her great, blue eyes glaring on him wild and expressionless, and her lips pouting. Time had indeed stood still with her, and it was wonderful how well she had preserved her youthful appearance.

" Lady Edgeforth ! " gasped Harwolf.

" Ah ! your grace can recognise me," said the poor lady, bending with fantastic grace. " I am not much changed, so they tell me. Why should I change ? I can get no news of my husband. If I knew that he was dead, I would, or I think I would, go to him. Yes ; there are many ways—and there is no occasion why I should stay here."

" Ha ! then she does not always think of his murder as I do," whispered Harwolf, hoarsely. " If she were sane she would never ignore it for an instant. Well, well, this guiltless madness is a blessing—sheerly a blessing ! "

The lady seemed listening attentively.

" You talk of blessing ! " she said. " Ah, you are holy. Cursing is fiendish—but there are fiends as well as angels ; I see many sometimes ; no others for a thousand and one days when I am in the wilderness. Blessing—did you say blessing ? Perhaps he will bless me—but he cannot, with that pale face and bloody brow. His eyes are glassy, and his tongue is stiff—he is speechless ; but I will curse for him, for he is the arch-fiend, and his name on earth is——I will speak low and tell you what it is—shall I ? "

She clutched the ex-steward by the wrist.

" No, lady, calm yourself."

" His name is—Andrew Harwolf," she hissed in his ear. " And the angels never speak that name—it is so foul—phew ! so foul. My husband wants me to go to court, but my brain is weak, and I might forget myself. I should think my clean, white gloves were all smeared with blood. How they would laugh at me."

She sobbed and laughed hysterically.

" This is horrible ! " murmured Harwolf, wiping the beads of sweat from his burning forehead. " I will get her back to her room."

He took hold of her arm, and said, soothingly,

" Come, Lady Edgeforth, let me lead you to your room."

She started back, and pushed him away.

"Hands off, rude fellow, for I know who you are; I knew there were three: three witches, three wizards. Not to-night, I will not ride with you to-night; there is no rain, no thunder, no lightning. A pretty chase through the black clouds, but they could scarcely keep me, and though they have put me in this enchanted place, I shall get home again; the angels will lend me wings."

"Where is that idiot Miles? Another moment, and I shall go raving mad. Curse her! I have had enough of it," he cried, his native savagery surmounting his weaker passions. "Come, lady, come; you must go with me," he said, with hectoring sternness; "you don't know who I am."

"If you treat me so," said the poor lady, in a voice of feminine yielding, "I shall be forced to think you are——but let me see you!"

She wrenched away her hands with the strength of mania, and placed them on his shoulders.

"Ah! no—yes—it is—it is the fiend, it is Andrew Harwolf. Husband—baby; murder! murder!"

The silent house rang horribly.

All the diabolic furies in Harwolf's evil nature were roused to the extremest pitch.

He wrestled violently with the poor lady. He dashed her to the ground, and setting his knee upon her delicate breast, clutched her lips in his iron fingers.

His eyes gleamed with a green scintillation, like a hyena's.

"It must be, it shall be; she shall follow him," he hissed out, in a husky whisper. "It matters not, one more or less to my account. Ah! minx; you can bite, eh! Down," cried the monster, as poor Lady Edgeforth struggled with him.

He put his hand in his pocket, and drew out his penknife.

"This little thing will do it. But, stop!—no blood, no blood. I know how it may be done; I will use one drop of my own panacea—my last resource; it will suffice. I will say she died in a frenzy."

With this the miscreant took from his pocket a little phial, from which he drew the stopper, and was about to pour the poison upon the lips of his victim.

He was struck stunned to the earth.

"Och hone! but the murdering baste has killed the poor darlin'," said Black Oiny, bending over the seemingly inanimate form of the lady. "But may be it's swooned, and not dead she be. Wisha! there's some one coming up the stairs; I must be off. Sure I can carry the colleen in my arms. It's along the top of the houses; and the divil take the cow that can't run."

With this the Irishman lifted the lady in his arms, and rushed up the stairs.

He managed to find the trap that gave egress to the roof; and, getting out, with the lady in his arms, he ran along the leads, through the wind and the darkness.

"I humbly ax yer pardon, squire, for being gone so long, but that darnation, drunken pig, Esau, the gipsy——" Miles was beginning, apologetically, as he entered.

He started with wonder and astonishment to perceive his master lying doubled-up on the ground, as if without life.

He ran to him, and lifted him up.

The squire's face was livid pale, and his temple was black and swollen.

Miles poured a few drops of the cordial into his mouth.

After a few moments, Harwolf opened his bloodshot eyes.

He reclosed them with a shudder of pain.

Once more he opened them, and he gasped, tried to speak, and to raise himself to his feet.

Miles helped him to stand, but he staggered with dizziness.

He sank in a chair.

The countryman pressed him to drink some brandy.

He did so, and appeared slightly to revive.

"Miles," he said, faintly, "in the devil's name look for her; if she has escaped we are ruined."

"Escaped! Who, your honour? How did all this happen? My lady—she is in her room, your honour."

"No," said Harwolf, still faintly; "no, I tell you, Miles, she broke from her room, came down here; trying to sooth her paroxysm, I was suddenly struck down by some unseen hand, and she is gone."

"Zounds! squire; we will search the house, and find the fellow who struck you, and where he be gone with the lady. That infernal sot, Esau; I'll be the death of him!"

With this he rushed out of the room.

The house was carefully searched, but in vain; neither Harwolf nor the innkeeper thought of tracking the Irishman to the roof.

Half frantic with rage, the squire left the house, and made enquiries in the neighbourhood.

As they were returning to the house after their fruitless search, the ruffianly Miles drew close to Harwolf.

He spoke in a deep, sullen tone.

"Squire, this be all along of that infarnal gipsy tramp, Esau; I was jackass enough to give him part of the money you zent us. He went on the lush at once, and twice this cussed night have I fetched him from the dram-shop, and when I went to vetch yer honour's brandy, there was the durned thief a-blowing on our wust secrets to a whole taproom of gaping busy-bodies. He were shouting like a ranter parson at a camp meetin', and I had the devil's own work to get him hoame. Tell ye what, squire," he went on, in a hoarse whisper, "that scamp be dangerous—mortal dangerous; he ought to be quieted."

"He shall be," returned Harwolf, with a fiendish smile: "he must take a drop too much for the last time."

"Or may be we shall have to take a drop too much; eh, squire?" Miles rejoined, grinning at his wretched joke. "I 'gree with yer honour; we mustn't break for such a beast as he be, seize him!"

"We will get him out of the way; when a dog goes mad it's time to physic him," said Harwolf, coolly.

"Ha! right, squire; better the dog should hang than his master."

They reached the house.

Closing the door, and bolting it, they exchanged meaning looks, and descended into the kitchen in search of the gipsy.

Their dismay may be imagined.

Esau Cooper had absconded.

CHAPTER XLII.

SAVED.

SIBLY and Silas Rye had played several games of billiards with little zest or pleasure.

Several times they paused and looked at their watches.

The time was rapidly fleeting, and the night hours advancing on their march.

The companions began to grow uneasy.

They sauntered to the door.

The street was deserted.

It drizzled rain.

They lighted their cigars and conversed in low whispers.

The time stole on.

They grew more and more alarmed.

Had Black Oiny been fooling them? Had a larger bribe caused him to transfer his allegiance, and go over to the enemy.

Each of these surmises was grounded upon strong foundations of probability.

Both Sibly and Rye vehemently reproached themselves that they had trusted the Irishman to go alone on this errand.

Just as their impatience had reached its climax

and they were about to set off in search of their agent, a man came running round the corner.

It was Black Oiny.

He dashed up to them.

He was hot and out of breath.

It was some moments before he could speak.

"Och hone! for a murthering job, yer honners," he said at length; "it's myself that have run as if I'd seen the divil's horns, or heard a banshee. The poor lady! Arrah! it's by the saints' blessing I'm here for the telling of it."

"How did you succeed? Where is she?" asked the confederates in a breath.

"Och! for a dhrop of the crayther to unlock my lips, for I'm as faint as a girleen in the theayter at a new pantomime."

Sibly brought the trusty Irishman a glass of whiskey.

Oiny swallowed it at a draught.

"Where is she?" asked Silas, excitedly.

"At the top of the houses, good luck to yer honner."

"The top of the houses?"

"The divil anywhere else."

"How came she there?"

"Sure I'll tell ye when I can yet breath. I found out the place, yer honner; I've not the time to tell ye now, but a mighty quare place it is, with a building house next door, into which I got, and so clambered to the roof of the nate little place where the spalpeens had taken her; and sure, as I could neither git in at the door nor the windy, I got down the chimney. After a bit I heard a screeching and a growling like a agle a-worriting of a dove, yer honner. Downstairs I slipped; there was that black thafe of a squire a-kneeling on the poor colleen, and a-going to murther her. I slid behind him, faix, and I guv him a Donnybrook favour wid the nubbly end of my shillelagh, which will kape him quiet for a long while. I caught hold of the colleen and carried her through the trap on to the roof, and rin away wid her to the end of the strate, and then I tied her to a chimney stack for better security, slid down the scaffold poles, and here I am, yer honners."

"This is incredible!" cried Sibly.

"Sure ye may well say so; it's the quarest thing that has happened in my gineration," returned Oiny.

"But why didn't you bring her here with you," asked Sibly.

"Sure, it's mighty fine this boy would have looked a-carrying a lady in a swoond through the public strate. Get away wid ye, and don't insult the police; I should have been taken in charge, and the lady returned to her friends, good luck to 'em."

"No, no, you were right; it was the only thing you could do, Oiny; but how shall we get her away."

"Faix, there's but one way of doing that same; yer honner must fetch the cab that brought us, and I'll climb the pigeon-house and bring down the bird, poor darlin'."

"A good plan; run Sibly, bring the cab and follow us. Oiny, tell him where the place is, and then come; you and I will go together."

Sibly started off to carry out the order. Silas and the Irishman hurried away towards the buildings.

When they reached the dark, gaunt houses, Oiny entered.

Silas waited below.

After awhile the Irishman re-appeared.

Poor Lady Edgeforth was still in a deep swoon.

She lay listless, and apparently lifeless in the rough fellow's arms.

The cab rolled up to the spot.

Sibly and Rye tenderly removed the lady and placed her in the cab, carefully drawing the blinds.

Sibly mounted the box.

Not a second elapsed after the completion of these arrangements, when a carriage dashed by them.

The head of a man was protruded from the window.

The street lamp threw its light upon the pale face of Andrew Harwolf.

Sibly held his breath with apprehension.

The carriage rattled past, and the sound of its wheels died away in the distance.

CHAPTER XLIII.

THE CARDINAL'S PLOT.

OUR scene changes to a large and stately room in a religious house in the little Spanish sea-town near which the Boy Pirate had fought such a desperate battle with the brigands.

The Cardinal Gonsalvez was seated in his pillowed chair.

The Boy Pirate and Manuel Perez stood before him.

"Well, sir Englishman," said the old cardinal, in continuation of their previous conversation, "I must own that you are an eloquent advocate; and you have strong claims upon my favour. And for this aspiring youth, it seems he is of gentle birth, though he is scarcely a match for my niece in other respects, for you may suppose that she would be a prize for the richest and noblest. Well, Senor Perez, I will make a bargain with you: if you love my niece you will gladly take her without a dower. The wealth bequeathed to her is wholly under my control—take her then, but take her as she is, poor or poorer than yourself. Come, senor, are you satisfied?"

"Never, your eminence," returned Perez. "I love Aurora too dearly to suffer her to make so great a sacrifice for me."

The old priest looked at the handsome young Spaniard with a searching glance.

"But if my niece loves you, she will not consider the loss of what she has never enjoyed as a sacrifice."

"Oh! if it were so. But do not tempt me, I pray you; do not teach me to be selfish. Aurora has seen so little of the world, and I should be worthless if I could let my selfish passion stand in the way of her brilliant prospects."

"Well, Perez, I must consider this matter; I may consent to your marrying my niece, but her fortune must not be bestowed upon one who has no fair claim to it; besides, she is already affianced to my nephew, Don Carlos."

"Who is a villain, your eminence, and in league with pirates and slave stealers," rejoined Christopher.

"That is a bold assertion, senor," said the cardinal, sternly. "What proof have you of this?"

"It is notorious. Common fame."

"Common fame is a common liar," returned the old man, peevishly. "My nephew has denied the imputation, and lying is not a Spanish vice."

"The worse for him who makes an exception to a national virtue," returned the Boy Pirate, haughtily. "What I tell your eminence is true."

"Proofs, senor, proofs!" cried the old cardinal, with rising anger.

"Since nothing but proofs will convince your eminence, I will show you these papers, which were found upon the piratical vessel from which I was so fortunate as to succeed in rescuing the lovely Donna Vasquez; they are letters from Don Carlos to the captain of that desperate gang that was long the terror of these seas; read them, and convince yourself."

With a deep frown and glittering eyes the ascetic old man tore open the packet. As he read, his thin lips quivered, and his feeble hands trembled with uncontrollable passion.

A priest entered, and bowing to the cardinal, said,

"Don Carlos is below, your eminence, and desires an audience."

"Well, I will see him," said the cardinal, sharply." The man left the room. "And now, senors, you will leave me. I will reflect upon the subject of our conference, and to-night you shall have a final answer—till then, adieu."

Christopher and the young Spaniard bowed to the haughty old priest, and left the apartment.

As they descended the stairs they passed the Spanish noble.

Don Carlos was elegantly dressed, and would have been extremely handsome, but for the villanous expression of his dark features.

He looked suspiciously at our hero and his companion, and bowed haughtily.

The old cardinal had perused the letters, and thrust them into a heavy casket on the table as his nephew entered.

Don Carlos saluted his uncle with stately grace, and at a sign, seated himself carelessly on an ottoman.

"I am glad to see you, Carlos," said his uncle. "I conjecture you have come to speak to me of your intended marriage with the enfranchised novice, Aurora Vasquez."

"Indeed, your eminence, the immediate occasion of my visit was to congratulate you on your fortunate escape from the atrocious brigands."

"I would rather they had killed me, and have paid the penalty on the gallows or at the hulks—their fate was not sufficiently ignominious to satisfy my sense of justice. They fell like soldiers in fair fight; they ought to have swung like felons, amid the execrations of their outraged fellow men," replied the fiery old man.

Don Carlos smiled and shrugged his shoulders.

"But to the business—my niece—Aurora Vasquez—I believe you are in love with her," the cardinal went on, in his rapid manner.

"I have seen her, your eminence, and to see her is to love her."

"Ha! then you really are enamoured of her?"

"She is irresistible."

"That's a pity."

"How so, your eminence?"

"You can have her, Carlos."

"You speak in enigmas."

"Not at all. You say you love my niece?"

"Indeed I do."

"Marry her, then."

"That will I—the saints guiding me."

"Are you sure you love her?"

"Your eminence, why this iteration?—my love for her is too ardent for expression."

"'Tis a very silly passion."

"And yet you bid me marry her!"

"Because you seem so deeply smitten that you cannot live without her."

"Life were death but for my strong hope of possessing her hand."

"What would you do to win or to deserve her, Carlos?"

"I would make any sacrifice."

"I'm glad to hear it—for a very heavy sacrifice must be made."

"Ha!"

"Note me, Carlos. I am the executor of my sister's will—do you think your aunt was very partial to you?"

"I don't think she was, your eminence. But what has that to do with me or Aurora?"

"It concerns you to the trifling extent of some square miles of land, and some thousand gold pieces."

"No; that cannot be."

"Aye, but it is so. I am glad you have come; I knew you were not acquainted with the facts of the case."

"Nor am I now."

"No; but you shall be at once, Carlos. You are not such a fool as to sacrifice everything to a foolish infatuation for a girl of whom you have seen so little."

"Your eminence, I hope not, if what you hint at is true, though I do not yet quite understand you."

"Yet Aurora is a match for a king?"

"Indeed she is. In beauty, grace, accomplishments, virtue, wealth——"

"Nay, Carlos, not in wealth."

"Uncle!"

"Now you have it. There is a clause in her aunt's will expressly forbidding her alliance with you, under forfeit of the whole of her bounteous legacy."

"Holy Saints!"

"'Tis true, Carlos. I do not understand these things—I am dead to the passions of this world; but I shall not blame you very much if, in consideration of the tender loveliness, the infantine purity, the numberless charms of your beautiful cousin, that you will be overjoyed to take her as she is, without a maravedi—without a change of dress from her conventual hood and robe; but, as a man of the world, I scarcely think you such a fool."

"You do me no wrong, uncle; I am not such a fool. I am sorry, but I am too poor to marry one who is dowerless."

"Very right. I mean to settle on you, Carlos—not at my death—now, whilst I live—my estates on the Guadiana, and my plantations in Brazil; and a rich man as you are, or will be, you must make an equal match."

"'Tis only just and prudent."

"And you'll reject this girl, seeing that she is as she is, and will not throw away your hopes of future advancement for the sake of a weak and idle fancy."

"Uncle, I have ever been dutiful to you, my only friend and guardian."

"I admit it. Then you reject Aurora because she is poor?"

"Because you wish it."

"No, no—I abhor subterfuge—I hate evasions. You reject her because she is poor?"

"Well, then, because—because——"

"She is poor?"

"Because I cannot afford to marry a woman unless she is wealthy."

"Not having good possession-right your ambition soars higher?"

"Just so."

"But do our family no dishonour. Aurora is lovely, virtuous, and accomplished."

"She has all these qualities."

"Yet, wise in the world's best wisdom, you resist the natural impulse of youthful and romantic love; you reject ——"

"I do. I reject her!"

"Enough. Leave me now, Carlos. I will write to you."

"But, your eminence ——"

"Ha! I have told you I am tired of talking. You have shown me the true side of your character, and I am satisfied. Please to leave me."

"But—your eminence does not misunderstand me?"

"Not in the least—except that you boasted yourself dutiful, and yet will persist in teasing me, when I told you I was tired with talking."

Don Carlos rose.

"Your eminence," he said, with a profound bow, "I take my leave with a thousand apologies. When may I hope to hear from you?"

"To-morrow."

"Farewell. Commend me to my fair cousin. Once more, your eminence, adieu."

With another and deeper bow the haughty Spaniard passed from the room.

"My uncle is breaking fast," he muttered, as he descended the stairs, stroking his long, black beard, musingly; "but shrewd—shrewd to the last. But to think of Aurora being without a maravedi! What a lucky escape I have made. The cursed English pirate has unwittingly done me a good turn."

The old cardinal's hands were palsied with concentrated passion.

When his attendant entered, he spoke in a thick voice—

"Father Ignatius, send my niece to me, and let some one fetch hither the youth Manuel Perez."

Presently the lovely Aurora entered.

It is impossible to do justice to her charms, enhanced as they were by her becoming dress.

For the first time since her childhood she had

donned a lay garb, and her beauty, no longer obscured by the disfigurement of the conventual habiliments, shone with tenfold lustre.

Her face and neck were free from swathings—her delicate rounded form, freed from the straight, stiff gown of hideous serge, and decked in graceful folds of whispering silk.

The old cardinal looked at his fair ward with a proud smile.

He spoke softly, and drew her to his side.

"Come hither, my dear one; I have grave words to speak to you. You owe a deep debt to the young student, Manuel Perez."

"Not more than I am willing to pay, your eminence, with a life service of love and duty," the fair girl replied, with a deep blush.

"But he is very poor, fair niece."

"But I am not!" returned the girl, smiling sweetly.

"But if you were?"

"I should be sorry for his sake."

"And for your own?"

"And for mine; because I do not think I should have means to make him so happy."

"And you would be such a loser, too, yourself."

"Never having had riches, I should not miss them," rejoined Aurora, simply. "In any case, I don't think I should prize them on my own account."

"But surely, Aurora, supposing yourself poor, without possessions, you would not marry this man whom I suppose I must call your lover?"

"Indeed I would, if he loved me as much as I love him, for then he would be thwarted by no worldly, sordid considerations; I am sure of that."

The cardinal pondered. Unconsciously he muttered,

"What have I lost! But such qualities are rare."

Father Ignatius entered.

"Manuel Perez attends your eminence."

"Admit him."

The young Spaniard reddened bashfully on seeing Aurora.

"Come hither, Manuel," said the cardinal. "Niece," he went on, addressing Aurora, "your aunt has left you her great riches on the condition that you marry your cousin, Don Carlos. You have given your heart to this youth—will you forego your brilliant prospects for his sake, and give him the hand he solicits so urgently?"

"Indeed I will," returned the simple girl, with a beaming smile.

"No, dearest Aurora, you shall make no such sacrifice for me," cried Manuel, in a tone of anguish, yet firmly.

"Do you hesitate at such a little sacrifice for me?" returned Aurora, in a tone of reproach.

"Ah, cruel! Can you doubt me?" said the student.

"I do not, Manuel. If thou art mine, I am thine."

Impulsively the young lover caught her to his heart.

The fiery old cardinal was much moved.

He rose tremblingly.

"Kneel, my children, and I will give you my blessing," he murmured.

They sank at his feet.

The old priest extended his hands over them.

"The Virgin Mother and all holy saints and angels make intercession with that God who is above to bless your noble affection. And now, my children, leave me; I have a letter to write to Don Carlos."

CHAPTER XLIV.

THE CHALLENGE.

THE Boy Pirate, Dick Caffyn, and Manuel Perez breakfasted together at a little hotel that looked upon the sea.

They were a merry party, everything conspiring to raise their spirits to the height of joyousness.

The windows, thrown wide open, framed a panorama of sea and land unmatched in Europe for its rich, romantic beauty.

On the sunny shore, among the grotesque wild rocks, were groves of chestnuts and elms, arcades of orange trees, and trellises of vines.

The sea flashed a thousand glowing hues of silver, green, and purple, with the changeful gloss of shot silk, with a delicate tint upon its pure, clear surface almost like the bloom of a peach.

The Boy Pirate and his young officer were greatly exhilarated by the triumphant success which had attended their partizanships of the lone and unhappy fugitive they had taken into favour.

Manuel Perez was intensely happy; he had reached the highest summit of his ambition; indeed, his wildest dreams had never promised him the bliss he realised through the generous aid of the noble Boy Pirate.

Noble, indeed, was poor Christopher Foundling, the outcast, the rover; but he had been forced into taking one false step, and his grand, heroic qualities only rendered his fall the more tragical.

Let the young and ardent, who look forward to high achievements in either service as soldiers or sailors, by land or sea, take warning by him who won such renown, not as the patriot, the liberator, the defender, but by the detestable titles of the "Red Raven" and the "Boy Pirate!" Fame that was dishonour!

Let them think of him with admiration, indeed, for his heroic courage and skill, but with pity and regret for his terrible misguidance.

Satan himself, the personification of all wickedness, "whose good is evil," was once not only an angel but an archangel, and not only so, but high among the highest.

In a fine wild, old Norse ballad a great enchantress, bewailing the fatal errors of a demi-god, exclaims, while invoking the deities of our idolatrous Saxon forefathers—

"Odin, Freya, all in Walhalla!
Oh, how low his fall will bring him!"

As we have seen, in his proudest moments of triumph Christopher suffered acutely from the pangs of undying remorse.

His mental sufferings were as bitter, and far more pitiable, than those of Andrew Harwolf.

The latter was the base perpetrator of a diabolical murder, which he committed for the meanest, most selfish motives, who only quailed because his coward-soul dreaded the terrible punishment that awaited him. The former a noble spirit, born for higher things, but fallen through one step, tortured by his own self-approach and contrition, whose exultation at his marvellous success was ever blighted by the constant thought, "I am but a successful thief. I am but a conquering pest and pirate!"

Let the utter worthlessness of crime-won victories be the stern moral of our romantic history.

With pardon for this long digression, needful that the end and aim of our record may never be lost sight of, let us return to our story.

It was one of the Boy Pirate's halcyon days.

He laughed and chatted with his gay companions, in the mirthfulness of youth and vigour.

There was a knock at the door.

A waiter entered.

"Senor Manuel Perez, a man below has brought a letter for you," he said.

"Bring him in," returned Perez.

The man left the room and soon returned, ushering a servant in handsome livery.

With a bow the new comer presented a letter to the young Spaniard.

Manuel broke the seal, and as he read his countenance changed.

His eyes flashed, but he looked grave.

"Ha! what is it: some ill tidings?" asked our hero, kindly."

"Not pleasant, any way," replied Manuel. "Don Carlos is Aurora's cousin."

THE RESCUE OF IDA.

With these words, he handed the letter to Christopher.

"By the great guns! a challenge," cried the Boy Pirate. "Be good enough to wait without," he went on, addressing the servant; "you shall have an answer presently."

The man left the room.

"He challenges you to a duel *à outrance*, with small swords."

"Even so."

"And will you meet him?"

"Of course I shall."

"But are you skilful with the sword?"

"Not particularly. Don Carlos is the most accomplished duellist in Spain."

No. 15.

"Then fight him with pistols."

"He does not give me the preference; he mentions swords."

"The miscreant! because he thinks he will have the advantage."

"It may be so."

"But don't you see that this is out of order. As the challenged, you have a right to the choice of weapons."

"I shall not avail myself of the privilege. I will use the arms he mentions."

"Are you resolved upon this course?"

"Unalterably."

"Will you accept me for your second?"

"With sincere thanks, and the greatest satisfaction."

"Very well, then. Caffyn, call in the fellow."

The servant was summoned.

"Tell your master," said our hero, addressing the messenger, "that Don Manuel Perez and myself will attend upon him at the time and place appointed, and that we are willing to accede to his desire in the matter of the choice of weapons."

"I will, senor," answered the man.

He bowed, and left the room.

"Keep up a plucky spirit, Manuel; trust to your good cause, and you will do well. If he gets off lightly, I will fight him myself."

CHAPTER XLV.

THE DUEL.

AT the distance of half a league from the little sea-town was a wood.

It was a beautiful and picturesque piece of land, wholly wild and sequestered.

The bells from the distant convents and churches had chimed nine.

It was a splendid morning, and the cool sea breezes blew inland and fanned the rich foliage of the little forest which was to be the scene of the duel between Don Carlos and Manuel Perez.

The young Spaniard, with the Boy Pirate and Dick Caffyn, were the first on the ground. They came in a coach.

They had not to wait long before the opposing party arrived.

Don Carlos was accompanied by a military officer, in an extravagantly elaborate uniform. He was a tall, stern personage; his name Don Guzman.

The principals and their seconds exchanged salutes with chill courtesy.

Preliminaries were arranged, the paces marked out, the choice of ground being left, according to etiquette, to Manuel Perez.

Christopher also had the first selection of weapons.

Each of the opponents threw off his coat, and they stood leaning on their weapons.

"Defend yourself till you have learned his tactics," whispered Christopher to his principal. "Do not attempt a thrust till he is heated. Be very cautious."

"Commend me to Aurora if I fall," said Manuel, with a smile.

"Not I; you will be your own apologiser."

"I will not kill him if I can help it; he is my love's kinsman."

"Stuff! If you try half measures you will never be your love's husband. Pink the mean scamp at the first opportunity, but don't be reckless," returned our hero, in his short, imperative manner.

"Now, senor, all is ready; we will withdraw," said Christopher to Don Guzman.

The latter bowed stiffly, and the seconds retired a few paces.

The antagonists gracefully saluted by measuring weapons above their heads.

They crossed swords!

Manuel Perez was just a little pale, but admirably cool and determined.

There was a cold, cruel smile of confidence and anticipated triumph playing about the lip of Don Carlos that caused the fiery Boy Pirate to shudder with suppressed indignation.

The fight commenced.

At first the combatants exchanged but a few harmless passes.

Then they feinted, thrust, and parried more rapidly.

It was evident they were testing each other's skill and prowess.

The seconds looked on in breathless silence!

In a few moments it became apparent that the young student was out-matched.

Don Carlos perceived his superiority, and his lip curved with an insulting smile.

Manuel Perez caught the look, and lost his temper, but not his presence of mind.

Some rapid passes ensued.

Don Carlos smiled, and grew careless.

Manuel took advantage of this change in his adversary's demeanour, and made such a sudden and deadly lunge at the breast of Don Carlos that the latter narrowly escaped its effects.

He turned his wrist, however, and parried with such marvellous dexterity that the seconds on both sides gave an involuntary gasp of admiration.

Don Carlos' dark face seemed to grow yet darker in its fierce expression.

He acted more warily, and seemed more vicious.

Manuel seemed to think that his only chance remaining was to finish the fight by a successful thrust, and he lunged away all recklessly.

Perhaps his want of caution saved his life.

Almost involuntarily Don Carlos made a thrust at advantage, which sent his thin sword seething through the shoulder of Manuel's sword-arm.

The blood gushed out, soaking the white shirt as it flowed down in free streams.

Manuel grew giddy and pale, reeled for a moment, and sank down.

Christopher bounded forward, and caught him in his arms.

Don Carlos looked on with ill-restrained malice and chagrin.

He saw that the duel could not be renewed, and was savage that it had not ended more fatally.

"Enough!" said the Boy Pirate. "Don Manuel is disabled. I trust, senor, that you are satisfied?"

"For the present," muttered the rascal, sullenly, as he turned on his heel.

Christopher carried the young Spaniard to a tree, and left him in charge of Dick Caffyn.

The sailor with some skill bandaged the wound and repressed the hemorrhage with handkerchiefs.

The Boy Pirate coolly walked up to Don Guzman and drew him apart.

They conferred together for a few moments in a low tone.

The Spaniard shrugged his shoulders and seemed to be protesting against something our hero proposed to him.

Presently, however, the Spaniard walked over to his principal, and Christopher carelessly sauntered to the tree where Caffyn was tending the patient.

"What were you saying to old Wormwood, captain?" asked his foster-brother, as he pressed a brandy flask to Manuel's lips.

"Why, only this, I have challenged our doughty champion of toasting-forks."

"Good God, captain," cried the other, leaping to his feet in boundless consternation, "what do you mean; such sword play I never beheld in my life. The crew will murder me if I suffer you to run into such unnecessary danger; you must be mad, plainly he is the better man."

"If you insult me by such an insinuation, Dick, I will challenge you," cried Christopher, laughing gaily.

Don Carlos and his second now approached.

"Senor, do I understand aright, you feel aggrieved by the issue of this affair and have challenged me."

"It is so, senor," replied the Boy Pirate, "I crave the honour of a few passes."

"But, senor, you must make arrangements with my second, and through some one who will negotiate for you."

"Let us waive formalities."

"Well, senor, I will meet you to-morrow."

"I'm sorry to seem importunate, but the duration of my stay at this place is so precarious that I must encroach upon your kind indulgence for the immediate settlement of our little dispute."

"Dispute, senor? I am not aware of having

given you cause of offence, but be it as you will, some other time."

"You said, senor, but now, when I asked you if you were satisfied with the issue of this passage at arms—'For the present,' implying that your thirst for life was not fully gratified. I am ready, senor, to give you instant satisfaction; besides, I am anxious to change my opinion of you."

"Ha! your opinion! What do you mean, senor?" cried the Spaniard, fiercely.

"I mean simply this: it is evident that you are a scientific manslayer, but I think for all that you are morally and constitutionally an infernal coward."

"Senor, this is not to be borne."

"I do not ask you to bear it," returned the Boy Pirate, coolly; "I ask you to vindicate yourself."

"You will find me more ready to do so than is consistent with your own safety," returned the Spaniard, glancing maliciously at young Perez, who lay, pale and faint, against the tree.

Don Carlos spoke aside to Don Guzman.

"You deserve a round dozen for that pitiful grimace, Dick," cried the reckless Christopher, with a laugh; "do you think I have passed scatheless through so many perils to die by the hand of such a harlequin skunk as that?"

Caffyn did not reply, but shook his head ruefully.

"Are you ready, senor?" said Don Carlos, selecting a sword.

"At your service, senor," returned the Boy Pirate, taking up a sword, and stepping to his place.

"By the Virgin! you shall pay dearly for your insolent braggadocia," cried Don Carlos.

"That remains to be seen," replied Christopher, with impassible coolness.

"Defend yourself, senor," cried the Spaniard.

The Boy Pirate bowed.

After saluting, they crossed swords.

They exchanged a few passes with great rapidity.

They were equally matched.

They fought with great determination and the most perfect skill.

The seconds looked on with intense interest.

It was soon noticeable that Don Carlos fought with less confidence than in his encounter with the young student.

He changed colour, and looked anxious, fought warily, and kept an eagle eye for the chance of a home thrust.

The Boy Pirate was cold, calm and cautious.

After a number of indecisive passes, Don Carlos made a furious lunge.

The Boy Pirate parried the thrust, but his sword was borne down, and the sharp steel entered his left arm, but not deeply.

The blood flowed.

"Are you satisfied now, senor?" asked the Spaniard, with a grin.

"Not finally," returned Christopher, with a provoking smile.

The Spaniard flew upon him, evidently bent to finish the fight.

Dick Caffyn turned away with a groan of disgust.

"After so many hair-breadth escapes," he muttered, "to fling away his life like a fool."

The sharp quick tinkling of the tempered steel caused him to turn round.

The combatants were fighting with mingled skill and swiftness.

One moment.

Christopher plunged the long, thin sword full to the hilt in the Spaniard's breast.

The weapon glided through his heart, and protruded from behind him.

As the Boy Pirate drew it back, Don Carlos threw up his arms, hissed out a curse, and dropped dead.

"He is satisfied now," whispered Caffyn, as they removed from the spot.

"I think so—'for the present,'" returned our hero, with a bitter smile; "the inexorable bloodsucker!"

CHAPTER XLVI.

THE HAWK AND THE PIGEON.

IT is necessary that the reader should be made acquainted with the circumstances attending the flight of Esau Cooper, the gipsy, who it will be remembered had eluded the vengeance of Miles and Harwolf on the eventful night of Lady Edgeforth's rescue.

Esau had been literally dragged from the tavern by Joe Miles, who found him, as he afterwards told his employer, haranguing a tap-room audience upon their worst secrets.

The gipsy was a man of peculiar temperament; when sober he was to the last degree sly, cautious and cowardly. Nor was he an habitual drunkard; the consciousness of his own weakness when under the influence of drink restrained him from frequent indulgence in stimulants, for when temptation had once surmounted his resolution no maniac could be more insane and desperate, no idiot more impotent and preposterous, than this wary, sneaking fellow in his drunken fits.

Miles had pushed him down the stairs and kicked him into the kitchen.

He lay for some time on his back growling and babbling in bestial intoxication.

Miles had reached down a glass, which he intended to take upstairs with the brandy bottle for the use of Squire Harwolf, whom he left, as he supposed, alone and in security waiting to see Lady Edgeforth.

Before leaving the kitchen the rustic drew a pailful of water, and dashed it viciously upon his besotted colleague.

Esau snarled and gasped for breath.

Miles took the brandy flask and the glass and slammed the kitchen door with a muttered curse.

The shock and sudden chill of the cold stream pouring upon his hot brow and his stained and flabby cheek served to rouse the brutal gipsy from his deep lethargy.

He stretched himself, and after several abortive attempts he managed to rise, and, by feeling his way along the wall, stumbled to the door, which he opened.

Winking his red eyes and feebly wringing the water from his straight black hair, he stood listening.

All was still.

The house was unfurnished except in those rooms which had been hastily arranged for the reception of the unfortunate lady.

He still listened.

Like Sindbad wrestling with the Old Man of the Sea did the gipsy struggle against the enervating sloth and maudlin inanity of the drink-fiend who had brought the whole weight of his dreadful and disgusting spell upon him.

He even struck himself fiercely on the forehead and the mouth, and clutched the stairs fiercely as he staggered in his attempt to stand without support.

He reclined against the wall, and still listened intently.

He was startled by a cry from Miles, whom he could hear rushing across the drawing-room above.

As quietly as his condition would allow he crawled up the stairs.

Distinctly in the echoing house could be heard every sound.

He heard Harwolf narrate to Miles how he had been attacked by some unknown, unseen person, stunned, and the lady carried off.

He heard Miles reply, and presently knew that the squire and he would search the house.

The deluge of cold water, his terror, his foreknowledge of the consequence of the catastrophe which resulted indirectly from his own drunken neglect and obstreperousness, in a great measure sobered the cunning rascal.

He crawled downstairs, and threw himself upon the kitchen floor in his former position.

Miles soon after burst open the door. The pale face of Harwolf peered over his shoulder.

They were on the search for Lady Edgeforth.

The innkeeper uttered a bitter curse, and shook his fist at the gipsy.

Esau lay motionless, snoring and feigning unconsciousness.

Soon the squire and his agent were heard noisily examining the premises.

Now, with a jar and quivering echo, the unused door of some empty apartment was pushed open; now their voices were heard in the yard at the back of the house in tones of rage and vexation.

Presently the front door slammed heavily.

They had left the house.

Esau lay quiet for some time.

He scarcely breathed.

He slowly raised himself to his hands and knees.

All was still.

He stumbled to his feet.

He drew a pail of water, and dashed the cold fluid upon his still burning forehead.

Then he blundered out of the room.

He reached the hall.

He quietly unbolted the door and peeped out.

The street was dark and deserted.

He shut to the door, and tried to walk along the pavement.

Excitement and the remedies applied had so far sobered him that he contrived to make way with only an occasional stumble.

When he was clear of the street he walked more slowly.

The houses seemed wheeling round him, the sky lifting and sinking, the cabs and vehicles appeared distorted and individually multiplied, and for every lamp the bleared vision of the sot beheld a score revolving in sickening confusion.

Still he kept his feet and pushed on.

As he progressed he walked more steadily.

He entered a public house, called for soda water, and rested awhile. Upon emerging once more into the cold, damp streets, for it had drizzled of rain, he felt much better, and kept his way without mishap.

He was advancing into the heart of the city.

Late as it was, and in spite of the bad weather, the streets in this populous part of the great metropolis were not entirely deserted.

Numbers of carriages and cabs rattled by.

The policemen paced their beat, and knots of debauched men and poor, painted girls made night hideous with their boisterous hilarity.

Slinking beggars shivered along through the dripping rain, cowering like guilty things beneath the stern, sharp eyes of the watchful constables.

As he became sober all the recklessness and obtrusiveness of his drunken bravado died from the gipsy's face. He kept close under the house, sidling along, his head bent on his chest, his arms awkwardly swaying, and his eyes deadened by a stony look of inward mortification, shame, and viciousness.

As he suddenly turned the corner of a street he struck against a thin, old gentleman, well muffled up, who was striding along at a rapid pace.

This personage was knocked backwards, and it was only by balancing his heavy stick and going through a number of gymnastic contortions he could preserve himself from a tumble into the gutter.

The old gentleman gave utterance to an oath and looked fiercely at the gipsy.

The polite Esau growled out something about people keeping their own side of the way, and was about to pass on when the stranger caught him by the arm.

"Excuse the question. Ain't you Esau Cooper?"

"What if I are—what's that to you—I don't know you—keep your own side!" said Esau, doggedly.

"Holy masses! You ain't a-going to pass me like that. Don't ye know me?" asked the stranger.

Esau turned quickly.

The speaker was a strange-looking old man, well, though somewhat shabbily dressed, wearing a gold chain and several rings. He was evidently a Jew; his large aquiline nose, his keen, restless, black eye, his crisp, curly hair bore unmistakeable testimony to the fact.

Esau looked at him sullenly.

"I don't suppose as you wants me, do you?" he said, uneasily.

"Yes but I do, my boy," said the old man, with a bland smile, slapping the other on the shoulder.

"What for? I paid your reckoning pretty stiff, didn't I? You used to be square," said the tinker thief, looking at the Hebrew with suspicion and ill will.

"No, no, no, dear boy!" said the Jew, with a smile of exquisite suavity; "there is nothing disagreeable between gentlemen of honour. I might find a leetle, just a leetle matter for complaint as to the way you managed our last bit of business; but I employed you and I payed you. Have you anything to object to my conduct in any way?"

"Not as I knows on," returned the gipsy, amicably.

"Very well, then; very well, then," returned the Jew, still blandly smirking. "How does Dame Fortune use you, time current, Mr. Esau Cooper? Sad coquette that same lady, isn't she? Does she smile or does she frown?"

"Don't know the party," said the gipsy, gruffly.

"Ah! I see; not poetical?—don't understand the figures?"

"Figures! what figures? I've given up smashing long ago."

"Very judicious of you, I'm sure, Mr. Esau—I mean dear boy. How does the *world* use you just now?"

"Blasted bad!" was the emphatic reply.

"Dear, dear! the ingratitude of human nature, to be sure. Well, dear boy, I think I can put you in the way of resenting its ill-usage or buying its favours. I want you, Esau; I really do want you to do a little business for me."

"Ha! what is it?"

"Never mind now. What's to be got by it?—that is the question, eh? Yes, dear boy, what's to be got by it? Well, well, something handsome."

"If you paid as stiff as you promises fair, you wouldn't be a bad customer, Mr. Nathan," returned the gipsy.

"Now that's too bad of you—much too bad of you, dear boy," returned the Jew, holding up his hand in tender remonstrance. "I might reply—if you did your work as well or as thoroughly as you charge for it, why you wouldn't be a bad journeyman. But come, dear boy, let us be off; my house is not far hence, and it is deucedly late, and the weather is bitter bad, and no mistake."

"I ain't a-going till you tell me what you wants of me," said Esau, with determination.

"Dear, how perplexing! Why are you so ridiculously suspicious?" said the Jew. "By the way, before we go, may I ask you a question?"

"You may ax as many as you thinks you will, but I ain't bound to answer if I don't choose," returned the gipsy, sullenly.

"Ah! I know you; I know you, Mr. Esau—your blunt way. Well, I'm not to be offended. Pray, do you know anything of an old client of mine, Daniel Harwolf, Esquire, of Frontemore Hall?—let me see, *Daniel*! yes, that's the name."

"Never heard on him."

"Strange! Nor of his father, Squire Harwolf?"

" Don't know nothin' about any of the cussed lot. Are you answered ?"

" Thank you, thank you ! Oh, dear, dear ! what a pity—what a thousand pities ; such a good thing ; delight me to serve an old friend !" exclaimed the Jew, shaking his head with a peculiar smile. " But, Esau," he said, drawing close to the gipsy, " good night ! and take care of Foxley ; he is after you, dear boy. A nod's as good as a wink, eh ?—a word to the wise—Ha !"

" Foxley ! what, *him* ?—the crusher—the detective ?" whispered Esau, hoarsely, staring aghast.

" You are the boy of penetration ; sly dog ; he, he, he ! Yes, dear boy, Foxley, the crusher—the detective—strange fellow, unreasonable. *He wants you !* Look at that now. Odd, isn't it, dear boy ? *He* thinks that you know something of Squire Harwolf, and of—of other parties connected with him. *He* thinks so, and he is a wonderful fellow, and *so* obstinate, Mr. Esau—so *very* obstinate ; you will find it hard to convince him. Do you remember Jem Sidler ? "

" Kite-flyer ? I knows him well."

" Met him the other day."

" What the devil has that to do with me ?"

" Met him in the train."

" What of that ?"

" He was downy, wasn't he ?"

" Yes ! the rum 'uns called him ' Jem o' Nine Lives.'"

" Foxley was with him."

" S'help me !" cried the gipsy, with a gasp.

" Jem looked all a cure in the darbies. Poor Jem ! he was 'cute, now, he *was* downy ! Poor Jem ! And so you really don't know anything about Squire Harwolf ? Good job. Very glad ! I do say, dear boy, I *am* glad. If you could have had any odd scraps about that client of mine I would have bought 'em of you ; besides, I could muzzle the crusher Foxley for you ! but it's better as it is. Good night ! A very good night ! Lagged for life ! dear boy. Well, you're clear of that. But mind Foxley, do, dear boy. Ah ! *good* night !" With a smile of ineffable sweetness and a bow of inimitable grace and profundity, the Jewish gentleman turned away.

Esau rushed after him.

" Stay, Mr. Nathan, don't be in such an infernal hurry," he cried. " Is it all a flam about Foxley ? Look ye here, if he's downy, so am I. Except when the cussed lush washes my brains out," he muttered. " I ain't no babe, I tell you," he went on aloud, " and you won't get any good by guffing me. S'pose I did know something of Squire Harwolf and the other parties. Mind I ain't a-saying as I do, but s'pose I did. What then ?"

" Why, dear boy, I should say that it was very fortunate for you, that's all. But, good night ! its so late, and the weather so unfavourable for promenading. But do take care of Foxley ; I do hate to see an old friend in trouble. Good night !"

With another bow he started off.

Esau ran after him.

" Stay ! I don't know what to think of all this."

" Very sorry, I'm sure," returned the Jew, shrugging his shoulders, and looking about him with impatience. " I did think you could assist me. My mistake ; no harm done ; goodnight ! I am horribly cold."

" Curse it all, if I swing for it !" cried the gipsy, sullenly, " I ain't nothing to do with it, Nathan, but I knows all about it, and if you'll clinch a fair bargain I'll tell you everything."

" Ha ! brave ; you are so eccentric, so very eccentric ; but a man of talent and discretion for all that. Yes, dear boy, that's my fixed opinion ; but come along, I know a night-house where we can get a drain of brandy."

" Not a cussed drop," exclaimed the gipsy, with emphasis.

The Jew looked him cunningly in the face. He turned his head with a sly leer ; he had detected the marks of recent intoxication.

After a short time they arrived in the neighbourhood of Houndsditch, and turning up a narrow, close street of lofty, black houses, Nathan opened the door with a latch-key, and taking a candle from a sideboard, lighted it, and closing and bolting the street-door, led the way up a roomy, but dilapidated and dingy staircase.

He opened the door and gave admittance to a room that was well though sparely furnished, and had the appearance of being a sort of office or reception-room for the money-lender's clients. A bright fire was blazing on a large hearth, the gas was burning, and the place looked sufficiently handsome and cheerful.

The Jew started back as he opened the door.

" This way, dear boy, this way. I find a client is awaiting me—rather a droll time to receive customers, eh ?" said the Jew, leading the gipsy up another flight of stairs, and rubbing his hands and chuckling as he did so. " But he's a well-feathered pigeon, and can stand a deal more plucking yet."

He ushered his companion into a large room, not so well furnished as the one they had avoided, and stocked with a number of iron safes and strong boxes, numbered and endorsed, and holding parchments which had been fatal as so many death-warrants to more than one reckless prodigal.

The Jew courteously presented a chair to the sullen gipsy, and telling him that he would return, left the room.

CHAPTER XLVII.

THE JEW AND HIS CLIENT.

WHEN Nathan returned to the reception-room he made a profound and reverential bow to the client of whom he had spoken.

Seated carelessly upon the table, tapping his lip thoughtfully with his gold-headed cane, was a young gentleman dressed in the extreme of fashion.

He was very handsome, his patrician features regular and refined. He had a glossy black moustache, a fine set of teeth, and his dark, curling hair waved back from a brow of marble whiteness.

The Jew stood looking at him with an obsequious air.

" Nathan, you are an infernal thief—a wolf—a vulture—a vampire—a ghoul !" cried this youth, suddenly leaping to his feet, his eyes flashing and his cheek glowing red with the heat of wine and passion.

The Jew did not reply, but raised his eyes, shrugged his shoulders, smiled with affectionate reproach, and stood with his head bent and his hands behind him.

The young nobleman, for such was his degree, paced the room furiously, not heeding his companion, his eyes glaring and fixed on the ground.

He stopped abruptly, threw himself into an arm-chair before the hearth, and poked the fire savagely.

The Jew said nothing, but stood watching, his intense bright, black eyes glittering cold and cruel, his mouth wreathed from an inward chuckle.

" What time is it, Nathan ?" asked the youth, suddenly, " I have broken my watch."

" It has struck two, my lord," replied the Jew.

" Ha ! then its early yet."

" My lord, with all humility may I enquire—you are upset to-night—unfortunate—cards—roulette—

billiards? Games of chance are exciting and pleasant, but so—so very expensive."

"Rather, Nathan; to-night I have lost ten thousand."

"Well, well, my lord, its useless to cry over spilt milk. Ten thousand?"

"Yes; and to think I should be in such a fire and fury for a paltry ten thousand" replied the young noble, laughing bitterly; "I who have played away thrice the sum in half the time without a headache. But money ' takes to itself wings.' *Wings*, egad! it melts like snow in the jaws of a volcano. My hands are too hot to hold such a soluble commodity. And I—I who hate play, who do not care a curse for cards or cues, and am no Tartar at horseflesh neither—well, let it go, 'twill be better for me when it is all gone." ·.

The Jew smiled dryly.

"My lord, you must not give way to desperation. You must consider my offer, and think better of your refusal of it."

"I *think* well enough. If thought were action with such as I, friend Nathan, your bags would not be so full, and your deed boxes would be empty."

"Look at that now. Ah! my lord, if there is one class of the community more abused, ill-used, and misrepresented than another, it's my class. Where would you have been had it not been for me? But, come, shall I have the pleasure of serving you in this instance? Your lordship shall have thirty thousand, hard cash, if you will but attach your name to the harmless document I spoke of."

"But to mortgage the last acre. Don't be a fool, Nathan. Don't you see that if I choose to retrench—and, hang it all! a man can reform if he please—if I sell my commission—and surely I am not to be driven to the devil by a little chaff—don't you see, if I reform you will barely get back the thirty and it's interest, whereas, if you lend me a few thousands now, I may be able to give you a good bonus. If you are a vulture don't be such a fool as to spoil a a life's feast through over greediness at a single meal."

"Ah! my lord, take my office, take my place. You call me a ghoul and a vulture; you would do more justice to your own discernment and my true character if you called me a silly dove, or a benevolent fairy godmother."

"What do you mean? Don't be an ass."

"I can't help it, my lord—I am an ass. Whenever you are concerned an indescribable tenderness over-rules all self-respect, all precaution; and my devotion to your lordship renders me, as you aptly express it, an ass."

"What do you mean?"

"What does your lordship mean?—to ruin one who has always tried to serve you? Haven't I, now?"

"Perhaps you have. After all, you hawks, and the fortune-tellers, spiritualists, lawyer sharks, and panders who prey upon the extravagance, the superstition, the malice, and the lechery of their fellow mortals, are not so vile as more respectable humbugs, who live upon the benevolence of the trusting, and ruin men by taking advantage of their best qualities. All right, all right, my good Samaritan, give us a taste of your loving kindness."

"Come, now, I'll lend your lordship ten thousand down on the Dashmere plate and effects, on the same terms as before, and we'll defer the mortgage."

"No? Why, Nathan, you are a deuced good fellow," cried the young nobleman, joyously.

Nathan smiled with paternal sweetness, and drew out papers, which he passed over to his client.

The young noble glanced at them carelessly and threw them down.

"I will give you five hundred pounds, ready cash, to-night, my lord, and to-morrow I will do myself the honour to call at you lordship's residence; I will bring a witness, and give you a cheque for the rest. Will that satisfy your lordship?"

"Admirably; you are no Shylock after all."

"And Shylock was no Jew if he could prefer a pound of flesh to three thousand ducats. A very poor conception that of Shakspeare's; not at all to nature. Ah! my lord, we lend our money, and risk it; we get interest sometimes, which compensates our losses, and buys us bread and cheese—that's all."

At this moment there was a rustling of silk without the door, which was opened, and a girl entered.

She was a superb creature—a Jewess, with all the dark glowing beauty of her voluptuous race; her complexion was clear, yet rich, her figure round and supple, her black hair, soft as silk and glossy as satin, was luxuriant to heaviness; she was tall of stature, and in every movement displayed an exquisite grace.

She was attired to perfection in a rich dress of black silk, and she wore costly jewellery.

"A thousand pardons, father," said the lovely Jewess, sweeping ·back; "I thought you were alone."

"Nay, Deborah, my child, do not hasten away, I want you to be witness in this little negotiation: 'tis my Lord Hawksbury, child."

"Miss Deborah," said the young noble, starting forward and taking her hand, with a respectful bow, "it is some time since I enjoyed the delight of seeing you; permit me to assure you that you are looking as charming as ever, and appear to be enjoying the best of health. One would think that you would feel the ill effects of solitude and confinement, for it appears you live, to the world's loss, quite a recluse."

"Indeed, my lord," replied the Jewess, lowering her eyes and richly blushing, "I find but little pleasure in society, and my father is so full of cares and business that he needs my presence in his leisure moments."

"Deborah, my dear, please read that paper," said the Jew; "we shall attach your signature as a witness."

The Jewess read it through carefully. She put it down with a slight, unconscious sigh.

Lord Hawksbury watched her for an instant, his eyes lighted with a beam of deep and respectful admiration.

"Now, my lord, if you will sign your name the little affair is concluded," said the Jew, leaning from his chair and opening a strong box on a shelf beside him; he drew out a roll of bank notes, closed and locked the box.

Lord Hawksbury stooped over the table, and carelessly took up the pen.

The Jew passed him over the notes, counting them as he did so.

Deborah was unobserved. She drew a little bottle from her breast, emptied its contents into the ink, and instantly concealed it.

"Now, my lord, your name; and Deborah, my love, yours."

Lord Hawksbury scrawled his name on the document.

Deborah wrote hers in a neat, clear style.

The young noble turned towards the Jewess, and extending his hand, said courteously,

"Miss Deborah, I thank you, and take my leave. Nathan, you will be at my place to-morrow."

"I will attend upon your lordship," returned the Jew, lighting the way downstairs.

"Nathan," said Lord Hawksbury, when they reached the door; "you have a priceless treasure in your daughter."

"Ah, my lord! you may well say so. She is as good as she is beautiful."

"By Jove, he were a lucky man who might possess such a treasure. Good night. To-morrow I shall see you."

No sooner had the Jew closed the door upon his visitor than he flew upstairs, and entered the room where Esau was sitting.

He beckoned the gipsy to the window.

"Look!" he said. "Do you see that gentleman just about to turn the corner of the street? After him, Esau; and follow him at a distance, and bring me word whither he goes; and when you return we can talk over other affairs."

The gipsy went down the stairs, opened the door quietly, and, slipping out, followed in the track of Lord Hawksbury.

"What are you doing, Deborah?" asked the Jew, pettishly, as he entered the reception-room.

"I have spilled the ink, father—that is all," returned the Jewess, with a smile.

"How stupid and careless, child," exclaimed the old man. "Deborah," he went on, drawing his daughter towards him; "do you know that young spendthrift was commending your beauty just now!"

"Indeed!" said Deborah, with a fiery blush.

"Yes, child. But the fool is no bad match for his own kitchen-maid. A few months and he will be a beggar."

CHAPTER XLVIII.

THE SLAVE OWNER AND HIS VICTIM.

MANUEL PEREZ married the beautiful Aurora; and the Boy Pirate, by whose instrumentality the happy consummation of their loves was brought about, had been offered a home for life in the house of the young couple.

The old Cardinal Gonsalvez bestowed many marks of his favour upon his young preserver; but the death of Don Carlos, the sensation caused by the destruction of the robber band, the appearance of the daring Red Raven at the Abbey Church, to honour the nuptials of his young friends, drew too much attention to him; and for this, and other reasons, he took "loving leave" of those whom he had served so well, and sailed from the Mediterranean.

After a long and prosperous voyage, the "Fortune of War" and the "Red Raven" arrived on the coast of America.

Here the ships were carefully disguised as merchantmen.

The "stars and stripes" were mounted, and for some time the outlaws carried on a legitimate trade.

And now we have other adventures to narrate of our chivalrous young hero, which will throw into strong relief the bright redeeming qualities of his generous and fearless character, and will give the reader an insight into the nature of that institution of which so much has been written and so little truly known—the slavery in the Southern States?

As the great championess of liberty to the slave has written so eloquently, speaking of America:

"Nothing of tragedy can be written, can be spoken, can be conceived, that equals the frightful reality of scenes daily and hourly acting on our shores, beneath the shadow of American law."

Let our readers imagine themselves in the state of Louisiana, on a lone plantation miles from any other; let them picture to themselves a large and handsome house, verandahed, and surrounded with China trees; a smooth lawn, out-buildings, conservatories, and everything that could testify to the wealth of the proprietor.

There was yet a lack of true beauty in the place, there was a hardness, a coldness in its very outlines; the trees were rigidly pruned, the house fastidiously clean, there was no tact, but all toil, in the arrangement of the flowers and mosquito blinds that adorned the windows; the neatness was the neatness of a barrack, the display that of a self-indulgent and exacting man.

Upon the lawn before the house two men were seated, smoking their pipes and drinking their 'eye-openers,' for it was in the cool of the evening, and in the press of the season.

These were the planter, Jonas Rashleigh, and his overseer, Tom Dillon.

"Wal, that were pretty stiff, I reckon," said the latter, squirting the tobacco juice from his yellow fangs, "after paying such an almighty price for the gal I guess you arn't a-gwine to stand any humbug from the creetur."

"No! I've had enough on it. I means breaking her in," returned the planter, viciously.

"Ha! it's all her fine education notions; the sort o' breedin' she's had allers spiles 'em. Bah! I've seen enough of it; what do sich want with larning?"

"Tell yer what, Tom. I don't care a cuss about the gals havin' accomplishments—about her singing and dancing and pianoforte. She's none the wuss for 'em, but all the better; she's a fancy piece and I meant her for ornament—but, damme, let her be as accomplished as a queen, she's my slave as I paid stiff for, never and above, I opine."

"That is the fact. Wal, you'll have some trouble with her yet, Mr. Rashleigh."

"Ugh! Aw! like enough," cried the planter, a cruel gleam in his eye. "But that kind is allers better when they is broke, and I tells you agin that I likes her superior ways, and I means to make the finiking cuss display 'em for my amusement. 'Cos why? I ain't a proud man, Tom, devil a bit. I was born on a plantation myself, and I've been a driver, a overseer, and last of all a owner a-gwine for thirty year. I ain't a book scholar; all I knows is 'cotton,' and there's many a capering professor, I calkilate, as writes books, and gives lectures, would be glad if he made as much of his larning as I do of mine."

"Wal, she's a bloomer, that's the kink of it," returned the other, swallowing his dram greedily, "and she's got a sperit."

"I'm pretty considerable sartin I'm 'ware of that fact," returned the other, flicking at the flies with his whip. "She has got a sperit, and that's where I means to begin. I means to tame her sperit."

"Ah, she wants 'cutting up' a bit you mean?"

"Wal, I ain't exactly speaking of that—'cause she's a bit of dainty ware I don't mean spiling. She ain't worth a quarter in the field."

"Then yer don't mean to fetch Satan out of her satin skin, eh?" asked the overseer, with a leer at his execrable pun.

"Wal, I might begin with a willow switch, but I don't mean trying the cowhide. The cuss, I 'ave had her a month come Thursday, and she's as wild as when I fust bought her!"

"You means to begin in private, I s'pose?" said the other.

"No flogging her that fashion, its no 'tarnal use—it's her spirit which I must break. Shall I tell you jest what I du mean?"

The overseer looked him in the face inquiringly.

"I jest means to send her off to work along of the gang—to give her a day's pickin' and a night at the niggers' quarters. That'll break her spirit, I guess; that'll teach her a lesson the schoolmaster's forgot to impress on her. I reckon that she's a nigger, and nothin' but a nigger, though her skin is whiter than other creeturs of her breed."

"Wal, for a man as knows the kind of cattle, you lick creation, Mr. Rashleigh."

"I'm tolerable sure I du," returned the other, firing a salute of tobacco juice; "one and all varieties of the critters—blacks, mulattos, quadroons, octoroons, mustaphas, and mustaphinas!"

"Wal! And for a well-managed, spry, and hard-working lot, give me the gang all the world over!" cried the overseer. "But it has been 'farnal hot to-day, and my arms ache."

"Yes; it's pretty stiff work with the critters—them fresh hands. Wal, you don't shirk your duty, Tom—you wake's em up; I must say you're a good disciplinarian. I du opine that I never seen a over-seer that could lay on so much without spiling the hands, and yet give so much punishment."

"Yes; guess I know the knack," returned Tom Dillon, with a gratified smile.

"'Spects I'll saunter in. I mean to talk to my little octoroon charmer. Its my last lecker, Tom; if she comes any blasted humbug to-morrow off she goes with the gang, and when she comes to the weighing machine I'll give her a dressing. Lor bless yer, natur's natur; arter a week with the gang she'll know the difference between hell and heaven, and she'll doat on me like a span'el."

With this the scoundrel rose, yawned, and flinging on his hat, strolled lazily into the house.

He entered an elegantly furnished room at the back of the building, and confronted his victim.

She was a "white slave!" Many a proud lady of the Circassian race would have given much for the rich and delicate complexion of the lovely octoroon.

Many creole ladies were not of purer blood, yet the taint of the African curse still clung to her. Her mother had been a quadroon.

She was reclining upon the sofa, her face hidden among the masses of her raven hair. She seemed to have abandoned herself to utter despair, and remained as motionless as a statue.

Rashleigh drew nigh.

He pulled a chair towards the sofa and seated himself, pulling out a cigar, which he lighted and began to smoke.

"Look you here, my good gal, I'm just a-gwine to have a little logic with you, and I calkilate you'd better pay some considerable attention to what I am about to suggest for your consideration; fust and foremost, my gal, who are you?"

The octoroon made no reply, no movement; she still remained with her head bent on the pillow of the sofa.

"You seem mighty bounceable about your lady-breeding, and slick span education, you du; is it ladylike not to answer a fair question when its put to you, eh! Speak, you minx!"

The octoroon raised her beautiful, intelligent face to her tormentor, and replied, with glowing eyes and imploring looks,

"Master, I am your slave; all my life they have deceived me. I thought myself free, but I was in error. Though many have told me that my skin is white; though right and reason confirm the truth that a white or black man's birth-right is freedom; yet I know I am your slave. I will not rebel; I will not resist; only let me work for you, and ask no more of me than I may do without sin and shame, and I will be your slave; I will toil with unremitting diligence at the severest tasks that you can assign me."

"Wal, I du say that's the fust wise speech of yours that I have heard. You're coming round, Ida, but I don't want yer to talk about slaves and masters. Nothin' out of reason. Look you here; you be a lucky gal, an infernal lucky gal. You see what my house is; very well. You see my gang and the hands 'bout the house; all straight. You may jest do what you please in the place, and I don't care a cuss if you spiles half the niggers. Look yere, I makes you queen over the lot, and you can cut 'em up right and left if they don't please you. There now, yours be a hard case, ain't it, jest? There, Ida, you're a reg'lar beauty, and I means to do well by you."

With this the planter threw himself beside the girl, and passing his arms around her waist, with hot, red face and glowing eyes, drew her towards him.

She pushed him away and sprang across the room.

She flung herself on her knees.

Raising her eyes and arms she muttered an inward prayer.

Rashleigh rose and stalked across the room.

His face was alight with rage and brutality.

"Master," cried the poor girl, "I implore you, as you are powerful be generous! Do not degrade and insult me, and I will do all in my power to please and to profit you. I can work in many ways: my music, my knowledge, my needlework are all so much stock in trade; I will go out and toil for you till sight and feeling fail me. Only as a poor, defenceless girl I throw myself upon your mercy! Spare, spare me!"

"Blast yer! I'll not spare you, you precious dainty callet; yer the ungratefullest—But there, I aint a-goin' to argy with yer; I've showed yer the outside of the pictur'—nothin' but fun and fine livin'—now I'll show you t'other. I means breaking yer in; if soft words won't do it, hard work and cowhide 'll take it out on yer. Your mine, yer know; fourteen hundred dollars, slick down, I paid for yer, and I ain't one to throw my money down the gutter for nothin'. Come here and give me a kiss, and beg pardon, or it'll be the wuss for yer."

The octoroon started to her feet.

"The sooner you kill me the better for me. I can give you my life since you claim my person, but if you attempt to wrong me, Jonas Rashleigh, you will have thrown away your fourteen hundred dollars indeed, for I assure you I shall kill myself."

"You will, will yer? I guess yer'll have no 'casion, for a nigger you are, for all your white skin, and I means to tame yer if it cost me twice the sum, I du."

With this the ruffian smacked his whip, which cracked like a pistol shot.

"Wal, which is it to be, Ida, war or peace? Come, look alive, I tell yer; speak!"

With this he gave another crack with his whip, which caused the girl to sink on her knees, quailing and terrified.

"To-morrow I sends yer off to the cotton field to work with the gang," he said, fiercely; "and if yer ain't done yer weight o' work I'll give yer a little of this stim'lant to make yer more lively."

"Do with me what you will, only kill me soon. I will work the flesh off my fingers if that will content you, but only let me leave the house, and be with my fellow slaves."

The brute gave vent to a bitter oath, and wielding

SILAS RYE WITNESSES A MURDER.

the heavy whip, brought down the lash upon her delicate white and quivering shoulders.

She writhed, and uttered a piercing shriek.

A red weal appeared where the cruel thong had lacerated her soft, naked flesh.

"Thar! I calkilate yer'll larn gratitude, yer thankless cuss. I'll bring yer down till yer ain't worth a picayune."

The girl made no reply, but remained kneeling, sobbing bitterly.

"I shall send word in the morning, and if yer ain't ready to come to terms, wal, I hope you'll take to the cotton pickin'. In the fields there's no shirking; I arn't got no favourites at the weighing-

No. 16.

house. There I pays all round, and I 'spects your thin skin'll get the cursedest dressing. Good night, *Miss* Ida; hopes you'll think better on it."

When he had left the room, the poor girl rose and looked around her with a wild glance of desperation.

She walked across the room and drew near to a little table, on which was a mahogany case. She touched the spring, the lid flew open.

The box contained a pair of pistols—she drew one of them out.

She placed it against her heart.

Suddenly she lowered the weapon with a shudder. "No! no!" she murmured. "Not till the last—I have borne nothing yet. I will endure till death shall come from other hands to give me peace, or till there will be no other means to save me from pollution!"

CHAPTER XLIX.

THE WHITE SLAVE IN THE COTTON FIELD.

TOM DILLON, the overseer, had blown the horn at day-break.

With heavy looks and listless movements the gang were assembling at the door of the weighing-house, preparatory to a start for the field.

Rashleigh appeared on the ground; he seemed in high dudgeon, and found fault with several of the hands and laid about him with his whip, savagely.

"Wal, I guess you'll be off before sundown," he said, with a growl to Tom Dillon. "Be smart—weather's fair; so, ye niggers, full weight or a licking."

The slave driver cracked his whip, and the negroes started off to the field.

"Wal, Mr. Rashleigh," said the overseer, lingering; "did the octoroon gal come to tarms, or did she cut a shine?"

"Cuss her. She'll have to be brought down a long stitch. I mean to send her to the field to-day. Hi! you thar, Dido?"

A clean, good-looking quadroon appeared at the door.

"The new gal—Ida—is she up yet?"

"Dunno, mas'r, I don't tink she gone to bed—neber see her since last night—hear her, though—sob, sob—I tink she break her heart."

"Cuss what you think—fetch her out of it. Come, look sharp—but stop, she's in bed, ain't she," he said, quickly, a sudden, sardonic gleam lighting his sensual face. "I'll go and ring the alarum for her drowsy ladyship."

With this he cracked his whip ferociously and strode to the door.

"O lor! won't she cotch it! Poor young missee; she soon wish she were dead."

"She's a fool to hold out, Di, I guess," said Dillon, with a leer.

Just at this moment the octoroon appeared at the door.

She was very pale; she had taken off the ornaments that adorned her ears and fingers, had neatly bound up her hair in the plainest fashion, and had put on a strong cotton dress.

She stood meekly, her eyes bent on the ground, her hands folded; she would have served as a good model for a statue of "Resignation."

Rashleigh stopped short and looked at her for a moment in speechless surprise; for a moment his brutality was rebuked by her tenderness and frail appearance.

The red seam appeared upon her neck, though she had carefully covered her shoulders with a blue kerchief.

"Master, I am here, ready to work my hardest to please you; I am willing to go to the cotton-field, or to do anything else that I can at your bidding."

"Look yer, Ida; I told yer as I didn't pay so devilish stiff to use you up in the fields; I mean better by yer; I'll make a reg'lar queen of yer, so no 'fernal humbug. Get along in, there's a good girl. If yer don't go at once cuss me if you shan't strip, and I'll flog yer till yer gives in."

"I am your slave, Jonas Rashleigh," returned the girl, firmly; "I will toil at the cruellest task you can set me at; I will bear your scourging and

tortures as long as life holds out, but though I am your slave, I will never be your—your——"

She did not finish the sentence, but hid her pretty face in her hands, her cheek burning with hot blushes.

"Wal! we've not much tu be thankful for, I don't think," said the savage planter, with a nasal drawl of sarcasm. "This is pretty considerable edifying. Wal; yer mind, yer shall be a slave, and nothing but a slave, till yer'll be 'nation glad and thankful to be anything I likes. Off with yer," he continued, slashing her shrinking body with his cowhide; "foller yer nigger brethren, and see as yer brings in full weight to the trying house, or you'll repent it."

The octoroon made no reply, but walked meekly towards the field.

"I leaves her to you, Tom; look after her," said the brutal and ignorant slave-owner. "Don't let her shirk, and to-night we'll lay the devil in her. Worse luck, I have to ride over to Sumpterville, and shan't be home afore ev'nin'. Look to her, I tell yer."

An hour later Tom Dillon crossed the cotton field where the long row of slaves were advancing on their weary march, picking toilingly under the scorching blaze of the noon-day sun.

With the energy of despair the poor octoroon was nimbly and cleanly plying her aching fingers.

A faint hope urged her to superhuman exertion.

She ventured to cherish a faint trust that if, unpractised as she was, she could only manage to make up the due weight in her slowly, so slowly, filling basket, she would appease the wrath of her savage master.

She knew that the overseer was looking over her, but she did not turn her head. With burning cheek she kept her eyes fixed on the work, and exerted herself breathlessly.

"I'll tell yer what, Ida, my good gal, I'm 'fernal sorry for yer. It ain't no mortal good for you to be a-killin' yourself in that yere fashion. You can't 'scape, no how, yer can't. It's all one—full basket or empty, ye'll see what ye'll catch. Why don't yer give in?"

The girl raised her head, her eyes beaming defiantly; but she did not speak—she dropped her gaze humbly, and went on picking.

"Wal, I'm sorry for yer, Ida; you're a purty girl, but slave-born, yer see. Niggers is niggers, however near they comes in shade to us whites. Look yere; it's all a matter of fancy; I likes the look on yer, Ida, and I'll do yer all the good I can."

"Thank you, master," returned the octoroon, quietly, drawing a heavy sigh.

"And you're getting awful tired of this work, I can see."

"It's the sun, master, and I'm unused to it," replied the girl, faintly; "but I shall be better presently."

"Wal, you consider of my offer," the overseer went on, squirting the tobacco juice from the corner of his mouth, and making a diabolical grimace, which he meant to be amatory and conciliatory; "if yer likes to trust me, and to be a good gal, as yer oughter, I can save yer something too dreadful to think on. You don't know Jonas Rashleigh. Pretty well, I opine, I du. How will yer like to lie down and be put in the vice, as they calls it, and be exposed and flogged afore all these grinning black cusses? That's what you'll get. Consider my offer; I can save yer. I tells yer I have got a feelin'. I likes yer! and if yer not a fool I'll do more for you nor you think on. There's many a octoroon walking as free as a raal born lady in Canada and in the North'n states. Wal, consider my offer."

With this the overseer shouldered his whip and stalked away.

Ida's brain whirled; a deadly sickness laid hold upon her heart.

Flogged! it was nothing to the acute anguish of her mental degradation, the scorpion stings wounding her heart and brain. The lead-knotted scourge that tore the flesh from its frame, it was a wisp of straw in comparison with those keener torments. But to be put in the " vice!" Exposed to the brutal gaze of slaves and the lowest of detestable blackguards! She knew too well what that meant. She covered her eyes, half blinded with the sun; she gave a convulsive sob, and sank to the ground in a deep swoon.

"O Gorra! look dar! New gal fainted right away. Dead, I tink," cried one of the blacks, running to her side.

"O Lord! She's delikit raised, no stand de sun," cried another fellow, looking on her pityingly, and shading her face with his palm-leaf.

"O Lor' hab mercy! she dead," cried a woman, lifting the poor girl in her arms.

"Boh! debblish grad, dis chile," said a huge negro, leaning on his basket and showing his white teeth in a sardonic grin, rolling his yellow blood-shot eyes and chuckling. " Dar's no use in dis kind; better never been born; niggers with hair worse nor niggers with wool, got more feelin'. I wish't were dead. Yah! let her bide, the poor crittur."

"You go 'long, Zampa; tell oberseer ob yer. Hi! you dar, run and fetch some water for missee," cried the woman.

"What the blazes are you all about! Hoity-toity; mutiny; reg'lar struck! Yer blasted skulks, get to yer work, will yer," cried the gruff voice of Tom Dillon, who had raced across the field to the spot.

Crack! crack! went the whip, and the negroes scampered in all directions.

"Oh, mas'r! please Mas'r Dil'n, dis yar white gal reg'lar die right away. 'Spects she faint, Mas'r," cried the gang, severally.

"Whew! the devil; seems she's soon done up. Wal, you get back to yer work, you black cusses, or there'll be a fine currying of yer black hides when the skipper comes home. You there, Zampa, take up the gal, and come 'long with me."

"Iss, mas'r," returned the stalwart negro, in his deep guttural intonation.

He lifted the girl as lightly as if she had been a child and held her in his iron arms, his red eyes blinking enquiringly.

"This way, you nigger, mind how you carries her, she arn't a cotton bale, and's wuth fourteen hundred dollars."

"Gorra, look dar!" cried Zampa, with an imbecile grin on his mighty countenance, as massive as the iron moulded head of some Indian pagod.

"Take her to the tool house up field."

"Iss, mas'r," responded the black, obsequiously.

"I'm just going to lay about the backs of some of those gossiping skulks, and I'll be with you. Where's Quasher?"

"Hi! you dar; you cussed nigger, don't you hear mas'r call," shouted Zampa.

A boy ran up.

"Send Dido over to the tool house; tell her the new gal is fainted; tell her to bring some salts and cold water, and things to bring the gal back to life; run, you imp."

He emphasised this order with a smart cut of his whip.

"Iss, mas'r, I run," returned the lad, dashing off at full speed.

Zampa went on with his light burden.

The hideous African glared on her face.

There was something picturesque and piteous to boot in the appearance of those two representatives of the extremes of that varied race of beings denied man's plainest right by a traditional ban, and an eternal subjection to stronger and oppressive races.

Zampa turned his eyes towards heaven, and strange to tell, the big tear drop rolled down his hard and black skin, and his full, broad chest and bull neck swelled with uncontrollable emotion of compassion and fury.

He looked at her with a sort of wistful tenderness, and then bore her into the tool house.

He laid her down on a bundle of straw, and, watched her for a moment.

She slightly stirred, and murmured as one speaking in sleep—

"Oh, papa, dear, I have had horrible dreams. I thought you were dead, and they had sold me down south for a slave, papa. Ah!" and with a profound sigh she relapsed into her former unconsciousness.

"Gorra 'Mighty," said Zampa, in his strange guttural accent, "I good min' kill dis buckra—wha' for she lib—dis buckra gal; she lily white? 'Spects she no die for all dat. Wal, not my 'fair."

"Wal, Zampa, you, how's the patient? Is the gal alive?"

"Iss, mas'r," returned Zampa, with a grin; "buckra missee no dead till she wish't it more."

"What do yer mean, yer black cuss?"

"Don't mean nothin', please mas'r; on'y it's kinder hard to this yere sort, the field work, mas'r; 'tain't their breedin'; weren't raised for it, no how."

The quadroon, Dido, entered the cabin.

She applied restoratives to the fainting girl, and after awhile she was able to set up and look about her.

She had murmured strangely in her unconsciousness, but now, though pale and ill, she had fully recovered her senses.

She did not speak, but sat numbed by bewilderment and despair, looking wildly about, raising from time to time her little hand to her beating brow, tortured by the agony of a slight sun-stroke.

"Wal, my purty gal, I calkilate this yer work don't no ways suit yer."

"Yes, yes, I'll go on. Must I fill the basket? Oh! pray let me go; master will exact full measure, and the day is wearing."

"No, no; yer stay where ye are. I'll come back to yer presently. You get back, Di; and you be off to the gang, Zampa."

When the overseer left the place, the gigantic negro lingered a moment.

He stooped down beside the octoroon.

"Missee, what you do to get free?"

"What I must do; kill myself."

"No, no; buckra missee run away soon. Tink now; de old debil no here—gone away. You see my back, missee?"

With this the huge negro turned his shoulder.

It presented a revolting spectacle, being scored and welted with crossing scars and knotty ridges.

Ida covered her eyes and shuddered.

"Hi! you go 'long; no spare you, missee—flog you dis berry night. You lie down; wal, he strip your clothes up 'fore 'em all, and cut you up wid de cowhide. You stan' dat?"

"My God! no, no. How—where shall I find death. Oh! Zampa, you are a good, kind, gentle fellow. Oh! if you would do me the great service to kill me."

"I great min' just now, when you no feel—when you faint away—better for you, missee, anyhow. Wal, you listen to dis chile. Massa do nothin' but cut dis nigger up—cuss him. Tink I not hab my revenge? Yah! I not raised, missee; I come from Guinea—sail in de buckra ship—cotch me. Wal, I hab my revenge! You look dar, young missee; can you swim?"

"Yes, yes, well. At home in Virginia swimming was my favourite diversion."

"Wal, you see dat open place dar, down de brake; you go down dar, den swim de riber. But, Gorra 'Mighty! tak care ob de dam alligator. When t'oder side you go run 'bout mile, den you find ship—'long de Sabine riber—dar Englis' sailor—North'n traders, eberybody. Yah! I go myself soon; but now I'm off. I reckon I'll cotch it. When you hear de cry ob fire—I go set de warehous burnee—burnee like a little hell.—He, he! yah, yah!—wal, missee, den you run. Next time I try de dam house——"

"You infernal lazy beast," cried Tom Dillon, springing into the cabin, and slashing the black furiously with his heavy cowhide round the head and on his scarred shoulders.

"Oh, mas'r! please mas'r! O lor'! O lor'! I run—dat's enough. I tink you tell me stay wid missee till you come. O lor' 'ave marcy!"

The negro yelled and writhed, but though with one blow of his massive fist the sable giant could have crushed his tyrant to the earth, his face betrayed no marks of honest indignation, but he only whined, writhed, and yelled like a flogged hound.

"Thar, yer black cuss; now get back to yer work, and if yer don't make up for this skulk you'll get it when yer comes to the weighing house, I reckon."

The overseer turned to the octoroon with a leer.

"Warm work—eh, my gal. Wal, yer see the way we does business down these yer parts—and that's what you'll get to-night if yer don't listen to me—but thar, I'm not a goin' to see it come upon yer, so don't begin fluttering and trembling in that fashion."

With that the scamp threw himself down beside the octoroon, and passing his arm round her waist, drew her towards him.

"Wal, if you ain't a reg'lar beauty and no mistake," he said. "I would'nt mind a degradin' myself to marry yer outright. Look at that now!"

"Oh, please sir, let me go," cried the poor girl, struggling with him. "I would rather go back to my work, I am better, I am well now. Let me try to save myself if I can. O Heaven! is there no mercy above nor below!"

Just as the ruffian had caught her in his arms and impressed a fervid kiss on her trembling lips, a wild cry was heard from without.

"Hi! he! oh!—yo! hi! he!—fire!—fire! Ho! yo!—fire!—fire!"

The overseer rushed out of the cabin.

Ida looked from the door.

The store-house was in flames.

It was situated in distant part of the plantation.

Nothing could equal the terror and consternation of the blacks.

The whole of the cotton crop of several seasons, and what had been got in during the present summer was in a blaze.

The negroes rushed off with uplifted arms and wild gesticulations, yelling like so many mad or demoniac beings.

Dillon, who was in a measure responsible for the accident, seemed to be in a state of the wildest excitement.

He appeared to have lost his presence of mind altogether.

As the inflammable material caught the quick-shooting, dazing fire-flakes, and burst into spontaneous gusts of fire and smoke, Tom Dillon yelled and wrung his hands.

The hoarse, hooting cry of the negroes died away across the fields.

The wide space about the cabin was comparatively silent. The house stood in its outlines, hard and bright in the sun. The flames from the cotton-house were struggling with the daylight, and the dense smoke from the close-packed bales rolled and drifted through the clear hot air.

The hoarse, savage baying of the bloodhounds, wrestling with their chains and howling at times in the excitement which they shared with their less-favoured fellow dependents was terrible to hear.

None of the negroes seemed more excited, more zealous to suppress the flames than the huge Zampa.

He flew hither and thither, discernable from his monstrous proportions.

No time could be more favourable for flight than the present.

The whole gang and their overseer were wholly preoccupied with the disastrous conflagration.

The fields were utterly deserted.

The planter himself was absent.

Ida stole from the door.

She crept round the house.

She had not been seen.

With a wild beating heart she plunged into the brake.

She shuddered as she trod.

A thousand dangers beset her. She knew not how soon she might be pursued; she well knew the dangers of the locality.

Swarms of mosquitoes and other noxious insects hurtled in the air.

She trod the hard, crisp, and heat-festered swamp with a shuddering consciousness that every moment she was in peril of setting foot on some venomous reptile.

And then she might lose herself in the brake!

The high leaves and reeds rose over her head, and formed a sort of arch.

She struggled on, tearing her delicate skin with thorns and stinging herself with thistles.

But she thought nothing of such sufferings.

She remembered the torments she should have to endure on the plantation, and most thankfully pursued her toilsome way.

At length, just as the day was drawing towards night, she came to the banks of a bend of the Sabine river.

It was very wide at this spot, and Ida knew that it was infested with alligators.

She sat to rest for awhile on the lonesome, but majestic, banks.

All was solitary around her.

The dark, deep forest—the gigantic fan-like leaves and tall fluted reeds that stood in flower-topped masses, like columns of some Moorish ruin—the green, deep, gliding waters warbling round the huge leaves of monster water lilies—the island-like promontory from the opposite shore—the undisturbed whirr of the myriad of insects—the plash of the fish —the trill of a mocking-bird—enhanced the solitude of this dense fastness and citadel of animated nature.

After a time, Ida took off her clothes, and holding them in a bundle above her head, with strong and graceful movement clove the glossy stream.

Just as she was about to reach the shore she heard a rush.

With huge, long head, hideous jaws, and glinting oblique eyes, an immense alligator flew through the seething stream.

She had scarcely scrambled the bank when he plunged at her, leaving a series of widening circles behind him.

She seized the branch of a tree and clambered the bank, and plunged into the bottom of a dense hollow. Here she sat for some time, panting and trembling; at length she rose and dressed herself. She then pursued her way, as Zampa had directed her, in hopes of reaching the other bend of the river, where it was navigable, and where she expected to find the ships of which the negro had spoken.

Towards evening she arrived at the place.

She found that the river was very wide at this part, and she judged that it must have held a serpentine course for many a mile from the spot where she had crossed it.

There was a block-house among some China trees on the bank. It was a long, low building, and there were several poles raised near, from which were streaming the flags of the United States, of Brazil, and of Canada.

At the widest part of the river, where it wound into the sea, were several vessels at their moorings.

Conspicuous by their superior size and their exquisite figure were two ships riding easily at anchor—a frigate and a sloop.

There was a little stone embankment along the side of the river, with a jetty here and there, close to which several heavy vessels were moored, from which goods were being unladen.

At the most remote of these landing places was a heavy-looking lugger, which, by its flag, appeared to be a companion craft to the frigate and sloop at anchor at the mouth of the river.

To this ship, as being placed farthest from the block-house, the octoroon made her way.

Her heart leaped with a qualm of terror and shame, but she had no resource but to push on. Would they have mercy on her? Would they succour her? Would they drag her back to her terrible oppressor?

She could but trust to fortune. She had yet one alternative. She could die!

Surely she was cunning enough to find a chance to avail herself of the ready means of self-destruction!

She went on.

She found the lugger had been unladen; the sails had been half shaken out, as if the craft were about to return to its consorts.

Upon turning her head, she perceived that a number of the sailors were walking together in a group towards the spirit stores attached to the block-house.

She thought that the circumstance seemed favourable to her purpose.

The men were gone to have a parting glass, after the accomplishment of their day's heavy work at unloading.

Some one must be left in charge of the barque.

It was better she should trust one or two than the whole crew.

She stepped on the gangway, and walked on to the deck. Bracing every nerve she walked towards the hatches.

She heard the tramp of some one's steps ascending the ladder from below.

She started back.

With mingled hope and fear she leaned against the mast, eager to catch a glimpse of the stranger's countenance; eager to discern whether it wore a hopeful or sinister expression.

A palm hat appeared above the hatchway.

A Yankee came on deck, a heavy whip in his hand.

With a pealing shriek the octoroon sank on her knees.

The stranger proved to be no other than the brutal and tyrannous Jonas Rashleigh.

The Yankee looked at her for a moment with an expression of wonder, which resolved itself into malignant exultation.

"Wal, I du think you air come round on a sudden, my dainty queen o' niggers. And so you sort a' pined for me, did yer? and must come a runnin' arter me. Wal, you're a good gal; and when we gets home I'll inquire as to who were responsible for lettin' of yer leave yer work in the cotton field. Come on! Yer see as Providence is agin yer. For why?—ain't yer mine, yer nigger? Ain't I paid for yer?"

He stepped forward to seize her.

She sprang towards the side of the barque, and would have plunged into the stream had not the scoundrel planter leaped forward and pulled her roughly back.

He uttered a tremendous oath, and seizing the octoroon by the arm lashed her cruelly with his whip.

Her screams rang along the deck.

A sailor leaped on board.

He was an elderly man, rough-looking, but well dressed as an officer; and with a hardy but kindly face.

He sprang forward.

Flinging out his arm with powerful impetus, he struck the Yankee planter such a violent blow in the face that he staggered backwards and fell against the bulwarks.

The octoroon still leaning, clung to the arm of her protector.

"Wal, yer coon—that's good breedin', I must say. This here gal's mine, stranger. I paid for her pretty considerable smart, sir, I did; and, the ungrateful cuss, I meant to make her my woman; but she must try running away, and yer see the mouse has run into the cat's claws; and the cat shall claw her, too—the minx," he went on, raising his whip.

"Damme, will you strike a woman—and a white woman—before my face? Be off, ye skunk!" cried the sailor. "You've paid, I s'pose, and there's a end to negotiations. Be off, or I'll give you as cursed a licking as ever you laid on one of yer poor victims—yer snivelling, man-stealing, woman-whipping, Yankee brute."

"Wal, stranger, this yere ain't the place to answer yer blasted insinuations. I shall take all this yere like a saint, and put up with any disawnings. I shan't jest go and lay this yere case afore the judge up town. I shan't seek perfection of the sworn constable. Oh, no! Come on, my precious mistress. I'll larn you to follow me—he! he!—come on with yer."

"Save me! Oh, for pity, save me!" shrieked the poor girl.

"Avast there, you cussed swab," cried the sailor, snatching her from the monster, and retreating towards the hatchway. "Go below, miss, go below," he went on, addressing the octoroon. "Now, my hearty, sheer off," he said to the planter, when the slave was fairly under hatches, "afore I lays hands on ye."

The planter foamed with passion.

"Give me the gal, cuss yer—she's mine; and look out for yourself, for I'll bring all the devils in Sumpterville upon yer. You won't pay for this yere—oh no!"

"Will you sheer off?"

"What, without the gal? you thieving Britisher rowdy. I knows yer, I knows yer; cuss me if I don't denounce yer, and yer whole gang."

"It shall be to yer fellow sharks then, ye swab," cried the sailor, as he seized the Yankee by the throat.

He dragged him to the bulwarks.

The planter drew a huge bowie knife.

Before he could use it the sailor flung his arms about him and hurled him into the river.

Leaving him struggling in the rapid stream he went below.

The octoroon was crouching between decks.

She flew towards him as he entered.

"Oh, sir, I implore you, as you have a mother, a wife, a sister, do not give me up to these wretches. Kill me, rather, I beseech you."

"Cheer up, miss; you ain't a-goin' to be ill-used, no ways, I'm bound for that; but sure-ly, miss, you're never a slave."

"Alas! but I am. You will tell me that my skin is light; true, but the taint of African blood is in my veins, and the sad curse cleaves to me. My father was a Virginian planter. He bought my mother, who was a fair quadroon, when she was quite young. He educated her, and then married her, in spite of the opposition of his friends. I am the child; but my mother had never been set free. My father was an extravagant man, and when he died, I was seized upon as a most valuable acquisition by his creditors. My mother had perished with grief within a week of my father's decease. The proofs of her marriage were not to be found, and though no one doubted, though many knew it for a fact, that it had taken place, I was sold, sir; sold to the inhuman wretch, Jonas Rashleigh, from whom you defended me so nobly; and I cannot tell you what I have suffered till I fled hither, little thinking to encounter him from whom I believed I had escaped. Oh! save me; do not let me fall into his hands. Give me some means to destroy myself, and I shall be content."

"You are quite safe, miss, have fallen into good hands, and don't mistrust us. But come you here, Miss—get into this cabin, and take the key in it, lock yourself in till you hear the windlass creak and know we're afloat."

"Generous friend! Oh, tell me by what name I shall bless you!"

"Well, miss, shiver me, if I knows how to tell you a lie about. My name's Jack Brierly, and I'm mate of the vessel yonder in the offing."

With this our old friend opened the door of the skipper's bunk, and giving the key to the octoroon handed her in.

She locked the little door and was alone.

She threw herself on her knees, and offered up a fervent prayer for her deliverance.

CHAPTER L.

THE SLAVE CHASE.

WHEN Ida rose to her feet she looked about her anxiously. The little cabin was packed with all sorts of lumber.

She saw arms, fishing tackle, bunting, small kegs, wearing apparel, colours, signals, lanterns, and rope coils.

She happened to turn her eyes to the window, beneath which was a sea chest. Between this and the ship's side she perceived a large piece of black silk, folded and crumpled, and thrust in as if hurriedly concealed.

She could not account for the instinctive feeling which caused her to draw this forth.

She spread the glossy black field on the floor.

With a cry she leaped to her feet.

The ghastly white skull and the charnelly cross-bones grin up into her face, thrown into horrible relief by the deep black sheen of the field in which they were emblazoned. Beneath them gloated fearfully the Red Raven.

The conviction shot like a convulsive throb to her heart's core.

The vessel in which she had taken refuge belonged to a wandering corsair; she was in the hands of pirates!

She sat down to collect her thoughts. She seemed stupified by the magnitude of her peril and the bitterness of her thwartings.

She knew not that the scourge of the rich and the proud was the chivalrous defender of the weak and oppressed. She knew not that the unhappy Boy Pirate vainly strove to balance the weight of his crimes by generous actions of the most daring and romantic type.

She could not realise the truth that she would be safe from dishonour in the vessel of an outlawed robber.

She only thought of escape.

Whither could she fly?

It mattered not; she dared not stay.

But was flight possible?

That had to be experimented.

She rose.

The door opened to her hand.

She crept out.

Cautiously she stole up the gangway.

A sailor was leaning over the bulwarks at the stern of the vessel, smoking, and holding a fishing line in his hand.

He seemed to be the only man aboard.

She crept to the bulwarks.

Unnoticed she sprang upon the jetty.

When she had crossed the road, crouching below the palisading of a little garden, she re-entered the brake.

She paused not, but fled back to the river side.

Here she stopped.

For awhile she reflected.

She recalled the hearty kindness of the seaman who had defended her so gallantly. She remembered how freely he had trusted her with the key of the cabin. She thought of the ease with which she had escaped from what might have proved a place of refuge rather than a prison; for, after all, the black flag and its symbols of death—were they of necessity the true colours of the stately vessels to which the little lugger belonged? Might they not be the trophies snatched by the conquering arms of such hearty fellows as him whom she had mistrusted.

She thought of her present terrible position, surrounded in the primeval forest with beasts of prey and venomous reptiles.

What alternative had she but to return and to conciliate her master by submission to his brutal will?

One she had yet, the one she had mentioned—she could die!

But why kill herself? She might save herself from the great wickedness of suicide. Doubtless her hour was near at hand; she would soon perish by a cruel but quick destruction from the desert monsters, or would expire from hunger and exhaustion.

She selected a large hollow tree; into this she crept. She had tasted some water at a gurgling spring; she had plucked some wild fruit.

She barricaded herself within the hollow of the trunk with branches and reeds.

Then she lay down to sleep, having fervently commended herself to the protection of heaven.

Weary hours moved heavily away; she could hear the terrific sounds that shake the forest by night.

The roar of the puma, the howl of the wolf and the jackal, the shrieks of their prey.

The wind, too, arose, and roared through the dense foliage like the wailings and threatenings of a troop of angry genii.

At last she slept.

Sweetly, profoundly.

She was at home.

Merrily she danced with her gay companions under the bananas, to the music of the sweet strained viol, with free, light laughter, the ripple and drip of fountains plashing on the bright flowers of the sunny south. A dark, weird cloud arose, and swept away this vision; it floated upwards and overhung frowningly all that was clear and beautiful and free in heaven or on earth.

She was at the weighing-house, surrounded by leering negroes, the sensual, brutal planter, and his overseer. She was dragged to the ground with the sickness of shame and agony; she felt her soft and delicate limbs uncovered, and then came the swift stinging cut of the cowhide across her quivering flesh.

She started from her slumbers with a wild scream.

She had, indeed, been awakened by the lash.

It was broad daylight.

The rascally planter stood before her whip in hand.

"He, he! so I've cotched yer, my purty fly, by night. Wal, I guess this is something like a Providence. A hunting the crow I ar trapped the pigeon! Wal, I could almost forgive the black cuss Zampa for all the mischief he has done me. Anyhow, I didn't have my chase arter him for nothin', and I guess I'll cotch that blasted nigger yet. Hi! you there! Juba! Sambo—you rascals! bring up the dogs. Look sharp, you there!"

The octoroon recoiled for a moment.

Her brain swam round, but she recovered herself.

The sting of the disgraceful blow seemed to nerve her. All the heat of her African blood was roused.

She rushed upon the planter.

He raised his whip.

With wondrous swiftness and agility she darted under his arm and snatched his bowie knife from its sheath.

As he tried to seize her she gashed his hands, uttering an appalling cry of fury and despair.

He staggered back, and she flew along like an arrow.

She darted into the brake.

The men and dogs came to the spot at this moment.

The planter shook his bleeding fingers, and stamped his foot, swore, and reviled in the most awful manner.

As well as he could he indicated the way the fugitive had taken, and the whole party started off in full chase, the dogs making the forest ring with their dread-inspiring bay.

The octoroon sped along at great speed, her hair wildly flying.

She doubled; and the underwood was so thick that she seemed to have baffled her pursuers, at least for a moment.

She reclined against a bank, overcome with fatigue and horror.

Through the leaves, at a little distance, she perceived the person of a man crawling towards her.

She seemed paralysed, like a bird under the fascination of a deadly snake.

She recognised the figure as it approached.

She knew it was Tom Dillon, the overseer.

Yet she could not move; she could not speak.

He came from his hiding place.

"Ida," he said, in a deep thick voice, "look here, I loves yer, gal, and I means to have yer. Hark! don't yer here those purty critturs givin' it mouth. Them's the sort, Ida; they'll tear you to ribbons. Come, gal, trust me and I'll pertect yer."

"Oh, sir, for God's sake pity me. Oh! whither shall I flee. From death to infamy? Never! Ah, why have I lost the chance of ending my wretched life?"

"You come along, then; cuss it all, there's no time to be lost," cried the overseer.

He threw his arms about the girl.

"No! no! no!" cried the octoroon, shuddering.

Just at this moment the shouts of the pursuers were borne on the evening breeze.

Just as, with triumphant yells, they were dashing up to the spot another cry was heard in the woods.

Jack Brierly and a party of a dozen resolute seamen came dashing through bush and briar to the rescue.

With a sob the girl threw herself into the seaman's arms, for she recognised him at once.

The overseer sprang after her, but Brierly received him with a downright blow.

He fell to the ground.

There was no fight, no skirmish.

The sailors appeared with their prize upon the side of the bank, and then with a derisive yell plunged into the forest.

The planter and his gang were so much taken aback by the sudden appearance of the opposing party, and so overawed by their apparent strength and determination, that they stood rooted to the spot without the power of action.

CHAPTER LI.

SLAVE AND MASTER.

THE rover merchants have sailed from the mouth of the Sabine river, but still cruise along the coast of Louisiana, and are steering for the Red River.

The Boy Pirate has assumed the Brazilian colours, and has donned the uniform of a privateer with a Government license.

He and his crew are gaily attired as Spaniards.

The ships still anchor off the coast.

One day, as Christopher was seated in his cabin, intent upon a chart, an officer knocked at the door. At the captain's bidding, Tom Garrod, the boatswain, entered.

"Pardon, cap'en," he said, touching his hat and grinning; "but the Yankee nigger-driver has come aboard—the fellow as we bilked of his pretty wictim, Miss Ida."

"Indeed," said the Boy Pirate, with a smile. "And does the rascal think we mean to give her up?"

"Well, cap'en, these Yankees has a tolerable share of brass; but, shiver my bowsprit, I don't think there's e'er a one on 'em, from the President to a potman, as would wenture aboard the ' Fortun' o' War' on sich a sarvice. No; I don't think as he know's she's aboard."

"No? What the deuce does he want, then?"

"P'raps he thinks, as we're likely boys, your honour might sell him some on us," returned the boatswain, with a grin.

He was a licensed wag.

"Well, you'd be among the last I should part with, Tom, and one I should expect most for," replied the Red Raven, with a laugh.

"It's kind of you, that same, cap'en; but I guess this Yankee skunk will find himself sold, if he thinks what I guess."

"Well, what do you guess?"

"Fact is, cap'en, we've hoisted Brazil buntin'."

"What then?"

"We parsonates the South American government."

"Well?"

"So we've got a kind of two identities; that's about the altitude on it."

"Tom, you amaze me! Your erudition is something unexpected; we have many identities."

"And yet we're identical—werry identical, and no 'dulteration," returned the transcendant wit, winking with immense unction. "Now this precious nigger-licking rowdy thinks as you're a Brazilian privateer—perhaps a African cattle dealer into the bargain, and that you'll give chase to the—the— why, in short, cap'en, to your own shadder."

"Faith, Tom, I think that's a sort of chase I have set many a sail for," returned the Boy Pirate, gravely; "and the shadow I have hunted is a deuced black one: but don't look so flabbergasted, Tom, and I won't moralise. Come! let us see this Uncle Sam."

"Who's no friend, anyhow, to Uncle Sambo," returned the facetious bo'swain.

"Stay—not here—send him down to me in the hold."

"Ay, ay, cap'en."

The Boy Pirate rose, run his eye once more over the chart, and left the cabin.

When he reached the hold he found the sailors arranging the boxes which they had taken on board in exchange for booty. An immense chest was as yet unstowed, and stood in the middle of the place.

"Cheerly, boys—hard at it?" said the pirate chief, with his peculiar and pleasant smile.

"Ay, cap'en," returned the men, doffing hats and pulling forelocks respectfully.

"Now, hearties, there's the Yankee nigger-driver coming down to set us in full chase for our own shadows, as Tom Garrod says. We're Brazilian privateers; keep up the ruse, lads. I trust ye to be as sober as Quakers."

"Never fear, cap'en, never fear."

"Ha! Brierly, he'll recognise you. Are there any here who were with Mr. Brierly when he went to rescue the octoroon?"

"I, cap'en."

"And I."

"And I, too."

"Well, lads, sheer off for a bit. What should be done to this inhuman villain, who does not respect the tenderness and helplessness of lovely and defence-less women?"

"Give him a round dozen."

"Keelhaul him."

"I hope he'll bring his own tools."

"Yes; I should like to flay him with his own cowhide."

"Well, mates, we're not in a convent now, but in our own stronghold."

"All the worse for him, the skunk."

"And he's not a woman."

"I guess he'll wish he was afore we've done with him."

"By the red retribution! I wish we'd a nigger aboard."

A strange scuffling and bumping was heard.

"What the deuce is that?" said the Boy Pirate, turning quickly.

"Perhaps it's the ghost of some of the niggers he's flogged to death, anxious to obleege ye by his presence and sarvices, cap'en," remarked Tom Garrod, with a grin.

"Or maybe it's the devil come to fight for his brother," said another.

"Hist! here he comes!" said the Boy Pirate, holding up his finger.

Brierly and the rest of the octoroon's champions stole away.

The men pretended to be busy stowing the boxes.

The Boy Pirate affected to be absorbed in the superintendence.

The planter lumbered down into the hold.

"Wal, stranger, here I ar at last," he said. "I calkilate I have had a tolerable long spell of huntin' afore I could come down on yer. Know me, stranger? I'm Jonas Rashleigh, of Rashleigh Penfold, cotton grower and nigger raiser; and I guess I ain't the most remarkable man in our parts—Oh no! That's my name and station, stranger; what's yourn?"

"My name is Don Cleofas, and I'm a Brazilian privateer."

"Wal, and I du say, sir, you're a likely lookin' man, and one as could whip a fleet of Britishers. Wal, 'spects we shall come to terms; I likes the looks on yer."

"You flatter me."

"Not a cuss! Chaw?"

"No, thank you; it's not my practice."

"Wal, stranger, we've all got our gifts. Chawing's mine, and cotton growin', and nigger raisin', and I considerably opine, nigger tamin'," he said, cracking his whip.

"Yes, stranger," he continued, "you see as I were allers used to 'em. I owns a gang as licks all Ameriky for subordination, stranger, but for all that sometimes I'm unfortnit. I have been very unfornit lately. I bought a gal, a octoroon, and she run away from me. Wal, stranger, it happened that this yer precious gal—for which I gave fourteen hundred dollars, stranger—fact, I assure ye—come down to the Sabine river, and ran on the very ship where I were settling off with the skipper's mate. In course I claimed her. Cuss me, if the blasted Britisher, for sich he were, and no mistake, did'nt pitch me overboard and sail off. Wal, stranger—this yer tale is rather 'stronary, I guess—same day as the octoroon run off everything seemed to go wrong. A nigger I had, an obstinate brute, stranger, tuk a almighty deal o' tamin', he did, stranger. Wal, as I were a-saying, a nigger named Zampa, one on his fingers

No. 17.

off—I wounded it with a slick of the cowhide—wal, he went on, spitting, "that yere nigger, I bought him off a ship, and he were a powerful piece of ebony and no mistake; he wern't raised, yer see, and so he were a hard sort to break in, but Lord love vou, I tamed him gentle as a dove, I did, stranger."

"You're a regular fire-quencher, a real down-south driver, I should fancy," said the Boy Pirate, his eyes darting a strange light; "your hand is as hard as your heart, and your heart is as hard as the devil's pitch-fork."

"Wal, stranger, yer may mean that speech for a compliment or yer may not, but of this yer ye may lie down easy—I'm a reg'lar hand with all kind of niggers; I brought this yer boy Zampa under; wal, he skeduddled same day as Ida, the octoroon I were speakin' on. Chaw?"

"No, thank you, never do."

"I forgot. Wal, stranger, so you see I lost 'em both."

"But, is this the subject you have to propound to me; has it any connection with what concerns the affair that is between us, for I suppose you didn't come aboard without some object?"

"Not so fast, stranger, not so fast; you say you are Don Cleofas and a privateer."

"At your service."

"Wal, I told you how a cuss of a Britisher—he were a Britisher, though he carried the stars and stripes—I told yer how this yer merchantman carried off my octoroon; leastways I was goin' to."

"I know, I know; I heard of it. You pursued the negro Zampa, and fell in with the fugitive octoroon. Exhausted with hunger and fatigue, the poor girl was sleeping; you roused her with the cowhide and was about to take her captive when she fled away, and was rescued by some English sailors."

"Just so, stranger; wal, it seems yer must be tarnation 'cute to know all this without the telling; 'spects yer knows the coon that were skipper of the ship."

"Yes, I do know him; don't you?"

"No; I guess I never seed him. I did all my business with his mate."

"Well, but what do you want of me? What can I do to serve you?"

"Seems yer knows the infernal owdacious British rowdy, for sich he were, in spite of all his respectable appearances. Wal, now, as I paid a little fortin' for the gal, and would give the worth of a dozen of his like to cotch that boy Zampa—I wants him 'pon principle, stranger; I ain't use to this breaking loose—I wants to cotch him and make an example on him."

"Ah! you're not one of those milksop planters that look upon their slaves as fellow-creatures and treat them accordingly."

"Feller critters; niggers!" exclaimed the planter, with infinite disgust. "Wal, dogs is our feller critters for that matter, but yer pretty tolerable 'cute, stranger; I'm not one of them yer milksops you speaks on; I never were for spilin' niggers. If I cotched this gal and boy I warrant I'd have no more runnin' away."

"No; I suppose you would make a pretty severe example."

"Rather!" the planter went on, with a fiendish grin, "for the gal, I should give her a pretty warm dressing, but I shouldn't cut her up just at present; but as for Zamp—wal, he's my own, yer know."

With this he spat and carelessly leaned against the bales and tea chest.

"Yes, and you'd use him accordingly."

"Stranger, I'd jest kill him. I mightily suspect that he fired my cotton store, and that's death to the beast by any 'spectable law; wal, I should kill him in my own way."

"Ha! I have heard of such things being done as roasting such fellows at slow fires; of driving them mad by pumping on their heads; tying them up naked by their wrists till all their bones are dislocated, and whipping them till life has exhausted endurance. Well, I suppose strong measures are needful; it's no use to try shilly-shally means to keep them down."

"Now, stranger, I du say that you air a man of reason and common sense; you've none of those infarnal North'n notions as is a disgrace to cultivated humanity; I honours yer, stranger, fact."

"And I suppose you've had all these means tried and found 'em successful."

"Wal, there's different modes of whippin' and pumpin'; I knows 'em all. And then there's by blocks and manacles; and for the burnin', 'cept it be with a brand—and I marks 'em all, stranger, the yaller gals as I wants for show and raisin'—I don't often practise the burnin'; I keeps it in reserve for sich cusses as this blasted Zamp, but it's very 'fectiv, stranger, awful 'lective."

"I suppose so; I dare say your negroes are well kept under, and submissive to a word."

"Rather, I guess. A word, stranger? they has to know without much tellin'. Lor bless yer, they're jest like dogs, they're as feared of this yer child, stranger, as rats of a terrier."

The planter emphasised his undisputed assertion with a loud crack of his whip.

"And what can I do for you, Mr. Rashleigh, for the recovery of your runaways?"

"Wal, you have port-holes to this yer ship, and I 'spects yer mouths arn't without teeth; you carries the Brazil flag. Now, it strikes me, stranger, as this same owdacious thief as harbours my lawful property is a feller not quite unknown in these yere ports, and if he's the man I take him for, there's no government in the Old World or the New as wouldn't pay pretty considerable for his carcase, dead or livin'; fact, stranger, I do assure yer."

"Who is he, then?"

The planter looked round on the faces of the crew, and then lowering his voice and speaking close in the captain's ear—

"Skipper, you may take yer oath he's the *Red Rover—The Boy Pirate.*"

"Never!"

"Fact!"

"And if we catch him?"

"Wal, I don't ax any share of your prize money; I ony wants to make a example of my runaways for the benefit of the rest of my nigger lot and that I'll pay lib'ral for. Ain't this a fair offer?"

"Look here, Mr. Rashleigh, I'm not a man of squeamish notions, but I've heard this octoroon is very pretty."

"So she air, there ain't a lovlier piece of alabaster in all the states."

"And that she is piously raised."

"So she air, sanctified as a sister of mercy."

"But that she is willing to work."

"So she a'r; worked like the devil at the cotton pickin'; 'bliged to give it up, though; too delicate, knew she'd come round."

"Well, then, excepting in the matter of her running away, what is her vice?"

"Her vice is her vartue, stranger," returned the planter, with a grin, "and that I means to lick out on her."

"I see, you want to marry her."

"Go to. Thunder! marry a nigger."

"But some octoroons are as fair as lilies."

"Not fairer than Ida, none on 'em. I meant to make her my woman; the gal was obstreperous, I sent her to the field to bring her down a stitch, and she broke loose and got away to the infernal pirate; now yer know."

"Well, I'll do my best to recover the girl for you on one condition, which is, that you'll give up the idea of making her your mistress and will promise to overlook this little error of hers—this running away."

"Are yer poking fun, stranger? I take yer; what did I buy her for? And as for not cuttin' her up, I don't mean spilin' my let goods, you may be sworn; I shall just take her to the calaboose and lay on pretty smart with the cowhide, but for that infarnal Zamp, I roasts him."

"You inhuman, unmitigated monster of tyranny and revolting cruelty," cried the Boy Pirate, with boiling passion, "you curs, you pest, and stain upon the surface of the earth; you festering canker of humanity, that would make one think the fiends can play false with our mothers; you detestable brute, what right have you to enslave your fellow-man, black or white? And for the beautiful, gentle octoroon—but the thought is insufferable. And how dare you, villain, to insult me, even me, with the offer of blood-money. Am I a pander and a man-stealer? And were I both, do you think me such a hell-born miscreant as to feed the blood-thirsty fangs of such an outrageous murdering hound as you?"

"Hulloa! stranger," cried the Yankee, flinching, dodging back and raising his arm as if to ward off a blow, though the Boy Pirate had stood with folded arms, his eyes glowing with searing fierceness. "Hulloa! what the devil? This is carrying a joke too far. Nothin' I hates like practical jokes; they're cussed unpleasant; let me get out of this."

"You will find this joke particularly practical and unpleasant. Stop him there!"

The Yankee, who was about to fly up the hatchway, was dragged back and dropped on his knees.

"Oh, lor! remember our sins. What are you going to do to me? I'll have law and justice; who are ye?"

"I am the Red Raven, and this is my crew," returned the Boy Pirate, sternly.

"My G d! Look you here, skipper; I'm a monied man; I'll give yer a bond for all I ar got in the varsal world; I'll leave all my farms and plants to yer, if you'll only spare my life. I'm an awful sinner, fact, I assure yer. Ain't prepared, I ain't no ways prepared, else I should'nt care. I heard as yer were allers a generous kind o' man, and I axes yer pardon for all offences. I ar on my knees, stranger; I hopes you'll remember mercy. As for Zamp and the octoroon, what I told yer's all flam; I would'nt hurt a tuft of the boy's wool nor a hair of the girl's head, 'pon my soul. It's all plain; I'll set the boy free and you shall have the gal yourself. Oh Lord! I'm not prepared. Mercy, only my life, only spare my life; anything else I'll bear like a lamb."

The Boy Pirate was half choked with a qualm of rage and revulsion; he turned away from the miserable craven with a look of the most perfect disdain.

"Had you been a tiger instead of a hyæna I mightn't have spared your life; as it is I cannot *kill* such a crawling snake, but I will teach you a lesson. If the unfortunates, your slaves, are not your equals, though children of the same great Father, you, at least, are their equals in the matter of bodily feeling and suffering, as you shall be practically shown. They're very effective—the cowhide, the pump, the brand, the slow fire; which shall we begin with?

"Demons! devils! mercy! mercy!" shrieked the planter, grovelling on his knees and looking pleadingly from one to another.

"We'll begin with the cowhide, and if you are perfectly satisfied with the efficacy of that gentle measure, we may dispense with the more severe part of your own prescription."

"Oh Lord! you are a brave man, stranger; the cursedest rip of a pirate as ever whipped a man-of-war or scuttled a Indiaman. It ain't a manly thing, skipper; I ain't strong, my constitution——" gasped and panted the terrified wretch.

"Delicate like Ida's," said the Boy Pirate, with a bitter sneer.

"I would for my life I had one of his own poor niggers on board, with a strong arm, nerved with African malice and vengeance," cried the rover captain, fiercely.

"Oh, Gorra Mighty! Yo ho! you dar. Why de debil you no let me out. I do dam job for you, yah! yah! yah! Ho, ho, it's so drefful hot I shall bust wid larfin."

These words were or rather this garble was uttered by some unseen being with the most guttural intonation, thickened by a diabolic chuckle, and made shrill by a scream of gleeful anticipation.

The sailors scattered in all directions, and seemed to think it an indubitable fact that the devil had broke loose amongst them.

So hastily did they retreat that they tumbled over each other in each corner of the hold.

"There's somebody in the chest," said the Boy Pirate.

A man touched the spring-lock of the huge box; it flew open

Then the ebony head and body of a ludicrously ugly, immense and powerful black appeared. His yellow eyes glared, his thick lips stretched from ear to ear, and his ivory teeth flashed in his irresistibly comic grin of mingled pleasure and spite.

"Oh mercy, Heavens! it's the black cuss, my nigger, Zamp," roared the planter, tumbling backwards.

"Yah! dat same gentle'n. Berry grad see yer all, buckra. You dar, mas'r, berry grad to see *you*. You come to 'quire arter this chile; berry 'fectionate."

The seamen held their sides with laughing, as they looked upon this strange apparition.

"And who are you, rascal?" said the Boy Pirate, turning to the negro with ill-assumed sternness.

"Me, gen'leman? Buckra cap'en, me no dam slave raised in Kentuck nor Ole Virginny, me serve in de cuddy—got cotch—Mas'r Rashleigh buy me—you see, den. Wal, de gal get off slick clar, and so I——"

"You scamp, how do you know I shant send you back?"

The nigger opened his eyes and then burst into a scream of mirth.

"Oh, mas'r! Yah! yah! yah! You please not make me bust o' larfin; you send me home along o' dat nigger—yah! yah! I shall die, you are drefful funny. Oh! please don't."

There was something infectious in the insane yell and chuckle of the negro's laugh, that the men in spite of themselves could not but join in until they fairly roared.

The craven planter thought it a good opportunity to put in a plea; he thought the indignant tars might be conciliated in this moment of general hilarity.

He pretended to laugh with them.

"He! Zamp," he said, with an abject attempt at a swagger, "you nigger, tell these yere gentlemen whether I didn't use yer well, yer coon; didn't I give yer many a warming of whiskey—many a holiday at a break down; speak out, and speak fair, you nigger."

"Berry much obliged to mas'r for past favours," returned the sooty gnome, ducking his head with ludicrous gravity, "grad to show dese gentle'n many marks ob him dam kindness."

"That's well Zampa, and you shall have the task of repaying them in kind," returned the Boy Pirate.

"Oh Lord! No! not him, the blood-thirsty devil is sure to kill me. Oh Lord! skipper, do take pity on a miserable wretch," shrieked the planter.

"Show us these marks of past favours," said the rover captain.

"Dar, mas'r," answered the African, holding out a hand minus a finger; "and dar," extending a foot minus a toe. "Yash, and dar," showing a deep cut in his head. "Still more dam favours mas'r," he went on—the upper flesh of one of his ears had been sliced off with a blow of the whip, but when he turned his back and showed it, literally a net-work of welts and scars, the men hissed and groaned and the tyrant well-nigh fainted.

"You see, mas'r berry kind, no spare de cowhide, 'spects it's good for dis chile."

"Well, you have shown right and title enough to be the instrument of the punishment I award to that inhuman wretch."

The negro rolled up the iron muscles of his mighty arm, and tapped them with a grin.

"Off with him—strip him and lash him to a gun, and leave him to the slave's mercy."

"Oh Lord! skipper, if you hope for salvation hear me. Murder! murder! Thieves—devils—pirates!"

Yelling and screaming the planter was dragged away.

The Boy Pirate coolly returned to his cabin, and seating himself, pored upon the chart.

After awhile Tom Garrod entered.

"Cap'en, the nigger has paid off a heavy score to the slaveholder cuss—the skunk has fainted."

"Well, throw him into the boat—cast her adrift; he will soon recover, or he will be picked up by some of the skiffs alongshore. I think he has learned a lesson that will feelingly convince him of his cruelty."

"That nigger's a character, cap'en," said the the boatswain, with a grin.

"Yes, I fear a dark and evil one," returned the Boy Pirate, rather seriously; "but he may have all the good qualities of his race. Anyway, he is a powerful fellow, and an acquisition to us; but turn the Yankee blackguard adrift. What does Mr. Brand think of the weather, Tom?"

"Most afeard of the weather's eye, cap'en—looks threatening."

"Ay; I fear so. We shall have a white squall."

"God help us, then, cap'en. Hadn't we better stand out to sea?"

"Send Mr. Brand to me."

"Ay, cap'en."

"The wind will be steady to-night, Tom, the squall will not come on for a day, perhaps two days. I know that by sure signs."

"'Tis log-book true, cap'en—any more orders, sir?"

"No," answered the Red Raven. "Turn the Yankee adrift."

CHAPTER LII.

LORD HAWKSBURY HEARS OF LADY EDGE-FORTH'S MADNESS.

OUR readers will not have forgotten that Esau, the gipsy, had been commissioned by Nathan, the Jew, to dog the steps of Lord Hawksbury, and to bring back intelligence of that nobleman's movements.

The morning was breaking palely, and the first beams of the grey dawn lighted the damp and deserted streets.

Lord Hawksbury walked heedlessly along, evidently lost in thought.

The gipsy came behind him, keeping at a distance, and dodging under porticoes and round corners to avoid being seen.

But the young noble did not turn his head; he kept right on his way, his steps bent westward.

The gipsy soon lost all interest in the task assigned him, and was terribly weary from the effects of the excess in which he had indulged, and the excitement and fatigue he had passed through on the preceding day.

Lord Hawksbury reached the corner of Regent-street.

He was suddenly stopped by a timid touch on the arm.

By his side stood a girl of some nineteen summers. She was ravishingly pretty; her pale cheeks were flushed for the moment; her eyes, swimming in tears, were bent on the ground. She was very plainly dressed, but though old and faded, the materials were of good quality, and her attire fitted her slight, but elegant figure to perfection.

"What is it, pretty one?" said the noble, with a smile. "Ah! well, give me a kiss and you shall have a guinea for it. My heart is heavy to-night; I feel I could curse the world as I stand," he muttered, impetuously, advancing a step. "So young, so lovely, and come to this already; but I wonder she looks so poor, and is so meanly dressed; with that sweet face, too; perhaps its a ruse," he thought.

"Sir, I am here to beg—to beg—for charity, for bread," exclaimed the girl, hiding her face in her hands with a choking sob.

"Calm yourself, my dear, good girl," said the young noble, with unfeigned kindliness. "God forgive me if I entertained a misconception of your character. Speak out, tell all; if I can help you, be assured I will. Come, come! what is it?"

"My mother, sir; it's not myself. I am young enough to bear anything; but poor mother, sir, she is suffering so quietly and patiently, it drives me mad. Oh, I will beg, I will steal, I will do anything but yield to a woman's worst shame to save her. Oh, pity me, sir, and help me if you can, and I will work myself to death to repay you."

"Is she so poor; can she get no relief?"

"She is too proud to ask it, sir, and so am I; indeed, indeed, I am," the girl went on, sobbing bitterly; "but I must not let her precious life be sacrificed. She must not starve to death because I cannot stoop to necessity."

"And what is your name; do not think I wish to question you from unworthy curiosity. I will help you if I can."

"My name is Jessie Vere, sir."

"And do you work?"

"Oh, yes, sir, at the embroidery, but work is slack, and so very badly paid for, and my brother lies at home in a fever. We are in debt for rent, and the people of the house wish to eject us; my poor brother cannot bear removal, and my mother, whither should she go?"

"With that lovely face and splendid form, with your evident good breeding, Jessie Vere, why, you know you are not compelled by anything but conventional prejudice to remain so poor."

"Sir!" exclaimed the girl, drawing back, her fine eyes a-glow with anguish and indignation. "But I am rightly served," she said, in a cold but quivering tone. "I ought not to have begged even to save my mother's life."

"Stay, Jessie, stay; by the God that made me, I spoke those words with a mean intent to try one whom I curse myself for doubting," cried the young noble, impetuously. "Stay, my dear young lady, I will ask you no more questions. You can do me a great favour, you are just the sort of person I wished to meet. I have some silk and damask furniture; I wish it to be handsomely embroidered. Will you allow me to send it to you?"

"Oh, sir!"

"But I will not ask you whither I must send it; as yet you have no right to trust me. Do you know Madame Delacour's, in Regent-street?"

"Oh, yes, sir, very well; I have worked for Madame, but not lately."

"Well, I will send them to her place, and you can fetch or send for them. Meanwhile, let me pay you something now. I may be gone into the country; you may want money for material, though I will leave word with Madame to supply all she may think of. Here, take this."

The young noble drew a ten-pound note from his pocket-book, and pressed it into her hand.

"Oh, sir! I must be dreaming," cried the girl, her eyes radiant with joy; "but not so much, it is impossible I can accept so much."

"Nonsense! I shall feel insulted. Depend upon it you will have to write for some more, you don't know how careless I am; there's a host of things Madame may forget."

"Oh, dear, sir! that's impossible, the thing is so simple."

"Is it? Well, good night, Jessie. But here, one word."

"Oh, sir! how greatly am I indebted to you."

"Not the least in the world, quite glad to have met you. But, look here, Jessie, now mind what I say; you think me kind, but you mustn't respect me."

"Sir!"

"No, 'pon my soul you mustn't. I respect you, Jessie, and people whom I do respect I wish them to take me at my proper worth, that is, a little less than nothing."

Jessie Vere looked at him wonderingly.

"Well, you don't understand the feeling. Now, what I want you to avoid is going to your mother and giving her a rhapsodical description of me, because I really can't bear it, Jessie; I want the embroidery, and I am positively the weakest transultimate fool in creation."

"Weak! A fool! Oh, sir! what can you mean?"

"You cannot tell, Jessie; I have given forty thousand pounds sterling for the chance of besting my neighbour, and never drew a penny, even from a wealthy staker, without an uncomfortable conviction that I cared nothing for the trash, and that I was sharping on my acquaintance, and yet—Well, I was born a fool. Good night, Miss Jessie."

"God bless you richly, sir! When can I have the silk and damask?"

"Why soon; I'll leave word at Madame's, yet remember, Jessie, there's plenty of time; I shall want it for a cottage ornée I am building. It will do six, nine, twelve months hence."

"Oh, sir! that's a long time, but I will take so much pains with the work."

"But, Jessie, don't work too hard at that or anything else, you are young and delicate. Have you accomplishments?"

"Indeed, sir, I am but half educated."

"Well, good night, you shall hear from me at Madame Delacour's. Stay, Jessie, let me come and see your mother and your brother. May I not?"

"Oh, sir! you are too good."

"Not at all. Where shall I find you?"

The girl blushed deeply.

"You hesitate. Well, I was not generous when we first met," replied the young noble, shrugging his shoulders with a smile, and turning to depart. "I admire your prudence, Jessie; so good night, my warmest wishes for your mother's health and your brother's recovery."

With this he turned away.

"Sir," said Jessie Vere, running after him, "did I not come to you—here, in this place of infamous notoriety? Did I not boldly prefer my suit for charity? Ah! I looked you in the face, and saw that you were good and noble. And do you think me base enough to mistrust the purity of your motives, when you have aided me so bounteously, so delicately, and so freely? Here is an envelope with our address; and oh! if you would do me a pleasure, give my mother or myself the slightest chance of proving our warm true gratitude for your deep, genuine goodness. Good night, sir."

"Not so fast, Jessie; stay."

But she was gone.

She sped across the road, and disappeared down a narrow street.

"Confound the girl! and curse myself for a fool. Either the cold wind or something else has brought the water to my eyes. Well, well, what a fool I have been; I must reform. I will, and no more resolutions; there's enough of it."

With this, his lordship sauntered to the corner of the street.

He waited awhile.

The clock chimed the half-hour. It was half-past three.

He lighted a cigar, and crossed the road.

He waited yet, stamping his foot impatiently.

Esau was still following at a distance.

The gipsy pretended to be bent on some other quest.

His assumption of indifference was needless, Lord Hawksbury had not seen him.

Suddenly a man walked towards the young noble and held out his hand.

Lord Hawksbury grasped it warmly.

"Oh! my lord, I am overjoyed to meet you."

"Well, what news?"

"Not so pleasant as might have been hoped, and yet more satisfactory under all circumstances than I for one anticipated."

"Then you have heard news of her?"

"Well, not exactly news; but there is a vague report at Ravenswold that she is not dead."

"I knew that long ago."

"And an old postmaster in the village—he is wellnigh in his dotage—remembers that a gentleman used to call for letters at his house years and years bygone; and that one day this gentleman, in his impatience to get at the contents of one of these letters, tore off the cover and flung it down. The old man happened to be writing at his desk; when the gentleman had departed from one of those unreasoning impulses that often induce us all to do odd things, he picked up the paper and flung it among his own papers."

"And this paper, where is it?" cried the young noble, impatiently.

"In my possession—even here," returned the other, presenting it.

"Lord Edgeforth! My God! Sidney, the fellow who disappeared so mysteriously, who is said to have died abroad, who married some poor unlettered wench he kept in close seclusion; whose steward, Squire Harwolf, has succeeded to all his property through a marriage with his master's widow."

"Your sister is that Lady Edgeforth."

"Quite a mistake. I have seen her; she is no sister of mine, I assure you, Sidney. I have met her in society."

"How strange!" exclaimed his friend. "Everybody knows that Squire Harwolf married Lady Edgeforth, and you seem confident that your sister eloped from home with his lordship!"

"I am sure of that."

"And are you sure that your sister and Lord Edgeforth were really married?"

"I do not question the fact for an instant."

"Then here is some deep plot, some infernal villany. The gay Lady Edgeforth, who plays so distinguished a *rôle* among the belles of London society while her husband broods away his life at Frontemore, or hurries about town on all sorts of strange missions, as it is darkly whispered—this distinguished lady is only a *parvenu* and a deceiver."

"It cannot be otherwise."

"Now I see it all; but, my lord, we are coming upon dark places—the veil which we are about to lift will disclose something too horrible to contemplate. You must be prepared for the worst, and you must be very careful. Should the guilty learn that we are on their track, the means are ready and easy to take us off. It is a great mistake to fancy that a large percentage of crimes find their way into the public newspapers. Ha! who is that fellow?"

As the gentleman spoke he turned sharply round.

Esau was leaning against one of the pillars that supported the portico of a large shop.

"Some poor night tramp, some houseless dog. I'll give the scamp a slight hint that his absence would be agreeable. What is it, my man?" he said, turning towards the gipsy, who in great confusion affected to be begging.

"'Scuse me, your honour, but if you've got any change about yer, I've a large fam'ly, nothin' has passed these yer lips 'cept a crust for more nor a day."

"Sorry for you, lad, wish you may get work. Here—now be off, like a good fellow," returned the young nobleman, as he drew some shillings from his pocket and gave them to the fellow.

Esau, in a sulky sort of way, muttered his thanks and sheered off.

"I don't like the look of that fellow."

"Pshaw! I daresay the feeling is mutual," returned Lord Hawksbury, with a smile, "he looks on you with envy; you look on him with repulsion—this is the precious interchange of mutual sympathy between man and man. But I am all at sea yet, Sidney, about the matter we have in hand."

"I told you I had a clue."

"Ah! let me know what that is."

"But, my lord, I repeat you must prepare yourself——"

"Enough, Sidney, is my sister dead?—is she murdered?"

"Worse."

"How is that possible?"

"If I be not mistaken in the identity of her person, your sister is mad—raving mad."

"My God! my God!" cried the young noble, wringing his hands in horror.

"And what think you became of her husband."

"It is hard to say—I have my opinion. But now, my lord, are you ready to place yourself in my hands, to go with me into strange neighbourhoods, to mingle with unusual company, in order to unravel the fearful mystery that overhangs your sister's fate?"

"Go on; I burn with impatience. Lead me whither you will, I will follow; and, Sidney, if your fears prove true I will compass Heaven and Earth to bring the diabolical members of this black conspiracy to condign punishment, for I am sure there is something terrible at the bottom of the strange events that have happened at Frontemore. But never fear, murder will out, and woe to the wretches if our suspicions are confirmed."

A cab was called.

The two gentlemen got into it.

It rattled away.

Esau, who had made a circuit of the houses by passing through a little dark entry at some distance from Lord Hawksbury and his friend, came down a street behind them in time to catch the last words and to see the cab hailed and driven off.

The cold sweat stood on the gipsy's forehead. He breathed hard and leaned against the wall, as he muttered, between his clenched teeth,

"I didn't do that black job; knows nothin' on it. But if the crushers was to nab me and that cussed Miles on the crib-cracking and kidnapping lay, durn me, if they mightn't swing the old lot on us, the infernal squire and all. Cos vy? Ain't she a lady born? and *he*—I wonder what the infernal mur—— Oh, Lord! how awful that 'ere word! I wonder what he did with him; buried him, most like. Well, self-preservatin fust nat'ral law; if I thought I were in any danger, why I'd split on the whole gang, blast 'em!"

He glanced with his sinister eyes after the cab that was just disappearing down the long street.

He then slunk back towards Houndsditch, to report progress to his worthy employer, the Jew, Nathan.

CHAPTER LIII.

THE WHITE SQUALL.

THERE was a thoughtful look upon the face of the pilot, Brand, as he entered the Boy Pirate's cabin, that caused the latter some uneasiness.

Christopher was in much doubt as to the prudence of having ventured his ship into a narrow passage between the continent and some small islands along the coast, for the weather was threatening and the "Fortune of War" was a vessel of heavy tonnage.

"Well, Mr. Brand, I've sent for you to learn your opinion as to what's in the weather's eye."

"I fancy, captain, our planks are exposed a trifle too much in such navigation as this. We've little water and a good deal of rock, and our soundings are uncertain."

"I'll come up, Brand; we must get out of this roadstead. Let's go on deck."

The Boy Pirate ran up the companion ladder, followed by the pilot.

It was a glorious day.

The dazzling sunlight flooded down on a sea of gorgeous beauty.

Land on either side; the islands mantled with brilliant wild flowers—wasted gifts of liberal nature in this floral clime, though costly exotics in our drearier latitude—and feathered with palmettos and cocoa trees.

Along the continent the wild sea shore, with its coral reefs and wave-worn archways, was crowned with the most luxuriant foliage, and from either side of the narrow, river-like channel that glanced and gloomed between the mainland and the islets came the distance-muffled sounds, the outpouring of the teeming vitality that peopled either shore with living creatures.

There was the short sharp bark of the wild dog, the scream of the paroquet, the chattering of the monkey, the hiss of the serpent, the growl of the puma, and the unceasing drone and murmur of myriads of insects.

Birds of bright plumage or of grotesque form flapped or glided across this narrow arm of the main, and beneath the pure, the crystal surface of the fresh green waters might be discerned waving forests of sea ferns and lichens.

Branching corals, flaming anemone, and glittering fish, which flash their silvery sides as they cleave the lucid stream.

There was but little wind stirring, and what breeze there was came in "caps full," bellying out the half-furled sails and lifting the Brazilian pennant, and then passing leaving the canvas and the bunting to collapse and hang feeble, as if heat-oppressed, among the tapering masts and complex spars.

What could the seamen have to fear? Why did they wear looks so grave and anxious? Why was the cheerfulness of the dauntless Boy Pirate too apparently assumed and hollow? Why was the steady eye of the masterly pilot watchful and full of solicitude?

In the serenity of the air, in the calm beauty of nature's wildest, most profuse, grandest display, in the lucidity of the water and the transparency of the purple sky and glowing atmosphere, lay the most portentous signs of the fiery tempest that would follow that brilliant calm.

A man was at the bulwarks throwing the lead.

"By the mark—six," said the sailor, in a gruff tone.

"Good!" said the pilot.

"Aloft there—which way the wind?" shouted the Boy Pirate, hailing the tops.

"There's a light cat's paw, now and again, from the land, cap'en."

"By the deep—seven," said the leadsman.

"Good!" re-echoed the laconic Brand.

Lilia came on board.

Our heroine is much changed—the sun has richened and deepened the tint of her lovely complexion, her form is fuller and more womanly, the advancing maturity of her beauty is even more enhancing than was her girlish prettiness and grace. Her large, soft eyes are deep in their expressiveness, and a light shade of pensiveness and melancholy give a pathetic interest to her eloquent features. She steals softly to her husband's side as he walks aft thoughtfully; she lays her tiny hand on his strong arm. He presses her fingers lovingly, and smiles with tenderness as she raises her love-lit countenance to his.

"You are looking anxious, Christopher," she said. "What is it, love? Can we not afford to rest awhile at anchor; are you so eager to begone from this lovely spot? I feel I could stay here for ever. In my school-days I read of these halcyon seas, of these golden islands, of these groves of spices with gardens of splendid flowers, their teeming life embodied in types the most beautiful and multiform; but I never dreamed, when fancy was in her wildest moods, of such a glorious fairyland as this. Do let us stay awhile upon this coast, the weather seems so settled and so calm, and you have worked hard lately. Can there be storms in such a climate?"

"Yes, Lilia, and the beauty of this calm is not more sublime than the terrific grandeur of the awful storms that occur at times on this region, times when the raging elements contend, wind and sea, fire and water. The surface of these islands is peculiarly volcanic, and the heat and stillness of the last few days presages an earthquake—while on the surf there are infallible signs of a coming squall or tornado."

"Oh, you alarm me, Christopher; I have heard of these white squalls—in narrow seas no ship can withstand their fury."

"Well, then, Lilia, as we are in narrow seas, and a storm is threatening, you cannot wonder if I am somewhat anxious."

"Here, captain," said the pilot Brand. "Look yonder, skyward of that long reef you may see a streak of foam rolling along in a line—'tis the meeting of the currents. Hands aloft! Reef topsails!"

"By the mark—five!" cried the leadsman.

"We are drifting, captain," said Dick Caffyn, coming from the side of the vessel.

Ida, the octoroon, who was still on board, came aft to Lilia.

The impression made by Christopher's warning seemed to have been faint, simply she could not realise the threatening danger. All was so cloudless, beautiful and calm in earth and sea and sky.

As Ida drew near Lilia smiled and pointed to the long ridge of creamy foam darting and curving along the glassy green ripple of the water, for the sea was like a mill-pond for smoothness.

"Ida, dear," said Lilia, "they say yon graceful curl in the water is an omen of danger. Would you think that there could be any fear of tempest when everything seems so sweetly calm?"

"And yet it is always so in this world—the storm succeeds the calm. This peaceful aspect of affairs, madame, may be ' the torrent's smoothness in its dash below,' as some poet said. I am afraid we shall have one of those hurricanes so terrible along this shore."

"Golly! dat ar am jest right, missee—yah! yah!" said the guttural-tongued Zampa, leaning over the capstan and addressing them. "Dis yere chile knows all de signs ob a dam white squall. 'Scusin' me, buckra missee, no swar before ladies—yah! but yer see as the birds is all flyin' to de land, and dat long white ridge of soapsuds. Gorra Mighty! dat 'ere, missee, its nuffin but de dam row ob tief of a big alligator which'll scrunch up de buckra ships and ebery nigger aboard. Yah! look dar, missee."

The negro pointed to the far sea-line.

Like a black screen a mass of cloud was slowly rising from the boundary of the sea inch by inch, totally and not partially quenching the brilliant sunshine which gleamed along its rolling edges as it rose, throwing a broad span of midnight shadow upon the face of the deep.

The gallant Boy Pirate had leaped on a gun; he stood over-looking the clear strong current which had set in with a resistless flow; he grasped one of shrouds of the ship to steady himself in the position he had taken.

Reversing the motion and supposing the curtain that quenches some brilliant fairy scene on the stage to rise instead of descend, the reader may form some faint idea of the solemn darkness of one half of the heavens, strongly contrasted by the brightness of the other, as grandly and awfully the black pall of clouds rose from the sea, with their under-current of leaden-coloured *cumuli* or scrolls of vapour.

A sullen hush suddenly took the place of the noisy mingling of the utterances of beast and bird. The lap of the quiet but mighty tide-lifts that heaved against the oozy banks of the mainland and the islets, the creak of the windlass, or the shrill whistle of the boatswain alone pierced the increasing silence.

"One of the anchors is adrift, shall we let go the bottom, Mr. Brand?" asked the Boy Pirate of the pilot, who stood beside the leadsman in the weather main-chains.

"Ay, ay, sir," returned Brand, "we will trip anchor."

"She shoaled, captain," whispered Dick Caffyn, in a voice strangely clear and thrilling in the anxious stillness.

"Yes, but now she travels; we will stand by our braces; is Tom Garrod aloft?"

"Ay, captain."

"Down from aloft! lower the booms!" cried the Red Raven.

The deck was now cleared, the bare and tapering masts were stripped to the yards. Brand came from the chains and walked towards the captain.

"Lilia, go below," said Christopher to his wife, "this is wild anchorage; but the current is strong and, due allowance for rocks and breakers, we may reach the open sea, and if we can once slip out of this confounded roadstead we may weather the roughest gale."

Lilia with Ida obeyed the order and retired to their cabin.

"Captain, what of the ' Red Raven?'" asked the pilot.

"She is an egg-shell that will caper over the reefs, like a dancing master. My own, my gallant ' Red Raven,' my first prize, my last ark of refuge—much as I value this splendid frigate, I would give her rig and hull for the figure-head of my saucy sloop," cried the rover, with animation; "she is safe enough; Gomez is a masterly seaman, and old Brierly is aboard."

"Good, captain! Now for it," cried the pilot. "Hold on everything," he roared through the speaking trumpet.

The rakish masts of the " Red Raven" were seen still carrying jib and royals, and swaying in the bright sky-line in that quarter upon which the door of darkness had not yet closed.

Another instant and the gloom of midnight fell down upon the " Fortune of War," which shuddered along the perilous coast.

Stealthily the ship drifted past the shore.

The intensity of excitement and suspense repressed every murmur among the crew.

The muffled sound of a distant gun came faintly booming down the narrow channel, answered by echoes from the rocks and jungles.

"Thank God!" cried the Boy Pirate, fervently. "'Tis a signal from Gomez that they have cleared these waters, and have plenty of sea-room. I wish we rode stern to stern."

"That's the first cat's paw," said Brand, as a breath of warm air swept past their faces.

"Ay; we shall have it tooth and nail presently. I'll take the helm," said Christopher.

Dick Caffyn walked aft, and encouraged the men.

The sea began to swell and surge, and the ship glided along at a rapid rate as the tide burst in from the open main.

The darkness might be felt.

Then there came a hoarse, dull sound, between a roar and a murmur, and a cloud of foam hurtled along the sea, visible by its frothy whiteness even through the depth of the awe-striking gloom.

It burst full against the bows of the ship.

There was a slight cry from the men as the seething head-waves dashed upon the deck, trouncing the creaking planks, straining the quailing masts, and sweeping with deadly rush over the forecastle.

The men reeled and staggered like drunkards, and clove to the bulwarks and hatches with the tenacious instinct of self-preservation.

One moment the tide-wave was heard rolling above its extremities, pouring along the echoing beach as it swept through the narrow roadstead.

The " Fortune of War" rocked and plunged upon the now agitated waters, and seemed to be drawing in the wake of the tremendous body of water that had passed like the giant herald of the rising tempest, dashing it gauntly in the teeth of the weak foe opposed to its horrible fury.

And now the black pall was rent into strips by the vivid sight-blasting zig-zag runs and flashes of the nimble and sulphurous lightning.

Afterwards, all was utterly dark and deadly still for an instant, and then, with a crash to which the heaviest thunder of our northern clime is but as an infant's whisper, burst and bellowed the stunning report of the first volley of the contending elements.

Every spark of courage and consciousness seemed for the moment to be extinguished in the hearts of the pirate crew.

Mutely they stood to their posts, clinging on to the slippery vessel for dear life.

The purling and writhing of the waves as they gurgled over the shallows were fearful in their significance.

With sublime heroism the Boy Pirate stood alone at the helm.

Brand, with wondrous daring, had clambered down the vessel's side, and was calmly seated in the chains, mantled in palpable darkness, taking the soundings.

A light was swung over to him, and he kept at his work, calling out his directions to the invincible rover who stood obedient to his command, his dark hair wildly flowing from his pale firm brow, and his eyes glowing with a calm light of self-conscious power.

Onwards they drifted—ever onwards.

On either hand, from either coast, two reefs of coral ran out into the sea, and there were treacherous quicksands, and a whirlpool of the meeting currents —dangerous in calm, but fatal in tempestuous weather.

Let us stand with the Red Raven at the helm.

Let us follow his train of thought.

He hears the cheery voice of Dick Caffyn giving orders to the men, though little now can be done.

A man brings information from the pilot, and his voice is a little husky with dread.

Christopher consults his own heart, as his iron muscles strain at the spokes of the wheel. A wild thrill of sickening terror runs like the blade of a stiletto through his heart—it is for Lilia. He thinks of himself; his breast throbs with a defiant feeling and he glares at the dark frown of the sombre sky with a calm exultation. He thinks of death. He shudders; a remembrance of his crimes renders the thought terrible; and then he thinks—but only to palliate, not to justify, his course—of his great provocation, and of the chivalrous way in which he has defended himself from his enemies, and has succoured his friends. But there is sweet peace and rest in the thought of death; he yearns to quit the scene of the humiliation of his proud high spirit, and he would rather die by the tempest-shock than fall a victim to the hot vengeance of the law-armed blood-seeker. He thinks how he may redeem the past, and then hope struggles in his dark soul. He thinks of his darling bride, of the poor octoroon whom he has saved from the bestiality and cruelty of a class of men whose names are a black stain on the muster-roll of humanity. He thinks of his brave and devoted crew, and strives to the uttermost to save the drifting vessel from the fate so imminent.

A long lurid glitter of lightning, with its blue and electric light, appears, and shows every halliard and every spar, glints in the eyes, glares on the cheek of every man, and sparkles on the polished brass-work of the compass-stand and barometer, throwing every thread of the shrouds, every knot and fold of the ropes and buntlines, into dazzling relief.

It quivers and wavers.

The ship is enveloped in a cloud of shimmering surf.

The flash has passed.

A dead and deep darkness.

A silence breathless and awful.

Then the raging crash, the maddening, stunning roar of the harsh and tremendous thunderclap.

Again the awful stillness and imminent jeopardy.

"When the tide falls all will be over, captain," murmured the pilot, who now stood by the side of the Boy Pirate.

"Till then we must do our duty, and leave no means untried to save the vessel," returned the Boy Pirate, calmly.

The wind came in gusts, not very heavily, the straining of the timbers being principally caused by the immense velocity of the tidal waves that chased each other along and around the headlands.

The "Fortune of War" was drifting towards the reef.

The pilot gave a few prompt, clear orders to the men, and the ship's course was somewhat changed, but still she flew on before the beating head-waves, and at length was lifted above the reef.

Now happened the most appalling catastrophe that had ever tried the brave heart of the pirate commander and his desperate crew.

They were drifted along through Egyptian darkness, ever and anon the bows of the stately vessel touching the points of the rock, causing a shudder to run through her well-knit timbers as if she were a live thing.

Zampa the negro came to the side of the thoughtful but unquailing Boy Pirate.

"Look yar, mas'r cap'n—please you listen to dis nigger. Thar am no signs ob de white squall for a few moments; let dis chile take de buckra ladies ashore. Dar is a ribber down dar — call him de Lotus ribber—could tak boat easy, mas'r."

"No, Zampa, thanks, neither my wife nor Ida will leave the ship to encounter worse perils than those that threaten us on board. This you may do —we are shoaling fast—the flow may settle us quietly on the reef, or a tide-wave may smash us to atoms— you are a strong swimmer?"

"Golly, mas'r—swim de 'Lantic give me nuff to eat."

"Well, if things come to the worst you can look to Ida the octoroon, while I will take care of my wife. Be off, Zampa—look to yourself. This is my post at such a time, but if she behaves well we are safe."

The vessel was implicitly obedient to the guidance of the heroic helmsman, and forged along on the swell, throwing the spray over her mighty yards.

The same solemn darkness and silence reigned, then there was a long quivering flash and choking blaze, which brilliantly illuminated everything within the range of sight—the rocks, the trees, and even the fields of gorgeous flowers, and the foamy brooks and cascades that rushed down the hill sides. The scenery of both the continent and islands was lit up with magic distinctness; the enormous head-waves rolled like snow-capped mountains far ahead, the ship drifting in the swell behind them. Hideously the savage breakers were plunging and tossing over the ridgy mole that the tiny coral insects had built so firmly. Above all was fire; the heavens showed like a chromotrope of weaving lightning shafts, crossing and darting like rockets, though so much swifter, upon a wide field of a twinkling bluish glare. On board the vessel the men—who crowded the deck, clinging to every tangible object, and showed their countenances pale and cadaverous and hideously distorted—looked like corpses resuscitated by the spells of some evil magician. All but the Boy Pirate. A corruscation of brilliant light played over his head, but with a calm, enduring look, his eyes watching the vessel's course as if she were sailing into harbour on a fair day, he stood like a martyr at the stake, the spray raging over him as he preserved his slippery foot-hold, manfully tugging at the wheel.

The lightning seemed as if it would never cease: a zig-zag shaft of forked lightning seethed through the air. There was a blue, electric scintillation at the mast-head, and a wild cry arose on board.

Captain and crew were smitten with the sudden blindness that followed each glare.

Then awfully broke thunder of thunders.

And now were seen the bodies of several men lying crushed on the deck; the main-top gallant mast had crashed down, struck by the lightning, and lay across the ship.

This sight of horror was visible, even between the lightning flashes, even in the Stygian darkness that prevailed. But what light illumined the scene of havoc? *A red tongue of fierce flame that shot up from the hold!*

THE SHIP WAS ON FIRE!

THE DESTRUCTION OF THE "FORTUNE OF WAR."

No tongue can express, no pen describe, fancy can but faintly picture the horror of that tremendous moment.

Now came the bustle and swell of the waves; the white squall was coming on swift wing like the angel of death, and the immense headers leaped before it and dashed against the yielding bows of the doomed ship as if they were maddened by terror.

The sky was one blaze, the crashing of the thunder was soul-quelling, death in every hideous form threatened his worst horrors – and the ship was in flames.

The Boy Pirate alone remained calm.

The men seemed panic-struck, stiffened and stulti-fied by deadly fear.

They gathered round their heroic commander like sheep about their watch-dog. He looked with pride and affection in their appealing faces.

No. 18.

"My brave hearts," he said, in a deep, firm voice, "if we are conquered by these raging elements, if we are stricken by the hand of justice or Providence —we were never yet beaten by mortal man; the Red Raven has been nailed to the mast; our wild sea-bird, our halcyon of victory! Who has ever dared to pluck her down from her eyry? None; then tell me, comrades and beloved friends, which one of you would not prefer this death to being killed like rats on our reeking deck, burnt to the waves by the minions of a law whose evil administration has made us what we are. Who would not rather die sub-limely in this free, wild tempest than walk the plank on a man-of-war?"

"All of us, cap'en."

"Surely, you who have lived like lions can die like men?"

"Ay, ay."

"And now we have looked to the worst, let us do our duty to the last. Every man to his post. Caffyn, we may quench the fire yet. Prepare the boats; but if ever you loved your chosen commander, do not put off till I give you the word. Silence, fore and aft! Mr. Brand, take the helm. Dick, follow me to the hold—cheery, my lad, we've a long cruise before us yet."

The men responded with much heartiness, and gravely ranged themselves obedient to orders, though each moment the tempest raged with increasing fury.

Every pump and bucket was put into requisition.

The magazine was instantly flooded, for the wind drove the fire towards it, and at any moment the lightning might strike it.

The ship's carpenter and his men were busy scuttling decks, barring in the ports, and seeing that the hoses led along the deck towards the fire.

Tom Garrod, with his riggers, were getting the gear in order for hoisting the boats.

The gunners were at work in the magazine.

Still the red flakes and the wreathing black smoke were belching out from the hold; still the dreadful raving of the breakers, the wild and blinding shoot of the lightning, the overwhelming crash of the thunder, render the awful calamity appalling beyond description.

All lumber was cleared away, windsails, tackle, and barrels were thrown into the raging sea.

Hammocks were unstowed and unlashed, beds and blankets were soaked to stifle the destructive element.

Brand leaped to the wheel and put up the helm, keeping the ship's head before the wind as well as he could, but still the flames wafted aft.

It was a moment of horrible agony.

Lilia and the octoroon were on their knees.

The first warnings of the dread shock of the coming white squall were heard in the strange howling of the wind through the trees, and the prolonged clatter of the shingle.

The men were at the boats.

They dared not let them down till the hurricane was past.

They knew the boats would be swamped beside the wreck of their doomed frigate.

The Boy Pirate came near to Lilia and the octoroon, who were cowering beneath the bulwarks.

"Come, Lilia, my darling, I must trust you to the wild waters," said the Boy Pirate, embracing his wife. "For me, I shall stay on my vessel till the last. Go, dearest, do not pain me by causing me to suffer on your account. Go, I implore you!"

"Christopher, never! I am your true wife—a rover's bride—and though Heaven and Earth conspire against you I will remain with you till death. Do not seek to move me, your entreaties will be vain. I live in you and I die with you. Better we sleep in each other's arms in the caves of the sea than that we should be separated. I will remain."

The Boy Pirate sighed, but made no reply. He drew his scarf from his waist, and bound his wife to the mast.

Then he hurried to the hold; the flames were still bursting forth, and were wafting to the quarter-deck.

At this moment Brand shrieked out from the wheel—

"Down, for your lives; hold on like limpets."

The crew flung themselves on the deck and clung to every available object.

Zampa threw one of his ebony arms about the octoroon, and caught an iron ring on the deck with the other.

"Hi! keep your purty face down, missee, or de dam wind blow all de daylight out of yer lubbly eyes; to say nuffin about the sparks here—yah!"

Fainting with terror the girl obeyed this injunction, and lay prone upon the deck. The black pulled a wet sail over her and crouched by her side, holding her in his vice-like grasp.

Down came the gale!

The sea was a very chaos of wrath and madness; the sky seemed to pass like a scroll, the flames hissed along the washed deck, the sparks roared up and scattered like chaff; the noise was deafening—horror culminated upon horror; the ship veered like a feather in a whirlpool, and spun onwards.

One dull grinding crash, one piercing cry; one wild dash of the foamy breakers, and the noble vessel was battered to pieces upon the teeth of the coral reef, and her *débris* was scattered far and wide upon the roaring waters. Then the white squall was passed, and flew in the wake of other ships, doomed victims to its fury, as if thirsting for fresh work of destruction.

CHAPTER LIV.
THE MURDER.

NATHAN, the Jew, was seated in his private office in conference with Silas Rye.

"Dear boy," he was saying, "all those little affairs of the past, we must not remember them; but you see I have found you out and have sent for you in order that you may give me a little information about certain parties in whom I take great interest. Nothing more than that, I do assure you. You have prospered, Mr. Rye; glad to see you look so well; in old times, now, it was different. Ha! do you remember the first time you ever came to me?"

"Too well!" returned Silas, bitterly.

"Eh! come, dear boy, no ingratitude; did not I introduce you to Squire Harwolf when he was land-steward to the late Lord Edgeforth. Didn't I, now?"

"You did, Nathan; and if you had any cause to hate me you have reason to be satisfied with the means you took to gratify your malice. You introduced me to the devil; look you, before I knew——" he was beginning, excitedly; then he suddenly broke off, and added, resignedly, "Yes, thanks; go on, count up the rest of the favours you have bestowed on me."

"Shocked and surprised, dear boy; positive fact. I'm hurt to the quick. Surely Squire Harwolf is a most desirable connection; one by which you have profited greatly. What more do you want?"

"What he nor you can ever give me," returned the adventurer, with a sigh.

"Father Abraham! but you are getting precious sentimental, dear boy."

"Devil a bit," returned the other, briskly. "But you sent for me, Nathan. Here I am; what do you want with me?"

"Well, you give me credit for real friendship towards you, eh, Silas? Really now, genuine regard? You don't know——"

"Curse the palaver! What is the use of throwing away your soft breath on me, unless it be to mock me? and mark, it is not arrogance, but something worse, that makes me so hot and spleenish lately. Go on, and curse the blarney."

"Tut, tut; you are too exacting; your temper has been greatly tried, I know it has, dear boy—I know it has; but you *must* keep cool. Well, I suppress my feelings, and we'll at once to business."

"Right."

"You know that Andrew Harwolf is a great scoundrel?"

"One of your aptest pupils."

"Now, pray, if you please, no sarcasm—and he is wofully in my debt."

"A bad debtor and a bad debt."

"Well, well, I am not without prudence—fore-thought; it is one of my little virtues, you know it is, dear boy. And as the young dog has signed a number of little affairs without thinking of the consequence——But, Silas, why is the young scamp so reckless?"

"Because, when he has squeezed you like a lime he will cut your throat."

"Holy Powers! But how do you know that?" exclaimed the Jew, in unfeigned alarm.

"I dreamed it," returned Silas Rye, grimly.

"Ah! dreams; all bosh; purest humbug, dear boy. No, no, no. Now I will tell you why the little rascal is so careless about penning the *carte blanche*—He is not the true heir of Frontemore! Eh, do you take now? Well, to be sure there is a deal of anxiety connected with my busness."

"Not the true heir! How can that be if Lady Edgeforth——" Silas checked himself, and repeated, "Not the true heir! How can that be?"

"Precisely what I want you to tell me."

"Precisely the information I should be the last to give."

"Why?—unkind and suspicious man—why?"

"For aught I know the true heir of Frontemore may be cast loose in the bleak world, without a guide or friend; he may be subject, for aught I know, to every curse of mind and body; he may be drifting, like a straw upon a cataract, on the stormy waves of the sea."

The speaker little knew how near to truth was his supposition; and the Jew interrupted, with a grin,

"Or he may be rotting in a debtors' prison, or most likely a gaol."

"I would rather he should be anywhere or anything than he should be in your clutches," cried Silas, bitterly.

"Pshaw! I only want to put the right man in the right place. Why do you abuse me, Silas? What am I, my boy, that the youth should not be entrusted to me? A really parental interest I feel in that unfortunate boy. I would be his friend."

"His friend—his fiend! What are you but the jackal of iniquity, the devil's provider?"

"Now, really, Mr. Rye, these invectives, this temper, is very preposterous."

"To hell with palaver, then," cried Silas, fiercely; "there is not a shade of necessity for it with me, and it makes me sick. If you want a babe strangled, any woman abducted, any church robbed, explain the job, name the terms, and I will tell you whether I will accept or decline it; but no infernal humbug."

"As you will, then." He drew near and whispered, softly, "Silas Rye, I have done as much with Andrew as I can, but it's not much; the sly old fox keeps his paw upon all he can. Now, dear boy, from my soul I like ye, Silas. Well, well; let us be a couple of Warwicks—earl-makers, anyhow. Let us set somebody on old Harwolf's perch—the right heir if we can find him, if not, any puppet. We'll have one made to order. He, he, he! And then there's a princely fortune for both of us."

"But, the papers?" said Silas, with a start at this proposal.

"Daniel Harwolf brings them to-night. I expect him almost immediately. He is to rob them from his father's bureau."

Silas Rye smiled quietly.

He had substituted false papers for those he had stolen so cleverly, having once made a rough draft of the documents in short hand, at which he was an adept.

"Well, Silas, what do you say? Shall we see virtue triumphant and vice punished. Shall we restore the true heir of Frontemore?"

"If you will. But if we find him a proscribed criminal? It might be so."

"Money will purify him. Gold is medicinal to the most sickly reputation. Well, Silas, are you with me?"

"I will think about the matter."

"Quite right, dear boy; like yourself. But hark, that's Harwolf! he must not find us together. That there might be no witness of his coming, I gave him a latchkey. Hide, for Heaven's sake! hide, Silas."

The adventurer sprung up with alacrity, and concealed himself in a cupboard.

Daniel Harwolf burst into the room.

He was richly, somewhat showily dressed, but his hair was dishevelled, and his eyes burnt with a strange evil light; his voice was hoarse, for, though not intoxicated, he had been drinking hard; the wrinkles in his forehead deepened and interlaced in portentous manner, and there was a look of eager and sinister purpose in his face and bearing which he strove in vain to conceal. At the moment he strongly resembled his father.

"Ha! my dear sir, my very dear sir, this is indeed an honour," said the Jew, bending and smirking; "always punctual, a great, I do say a great, quality in business."

"Yes," said Daniel, huskily. "Nathan."

"Well, dear sir?"

"Are we alone, Nathan?"

"Alone?"

"Yes! you would not be such a fool as to wish for listeners."

"Prudence is another great quality," returned the Jew, with a sigh of admiration. "No, indeed, my dear sir. Be seated, pray be seated; we are quite alone, there is no one in the house but my daughter Deborah, and she has retired to her room."

"Ha! that's right."

"These things cannot be managed too secretly."

"Quite impossible."

"And have you brought the papers."

"All. Among the rest a packet of love-letters that passed between the father and mother, that is Lord Edgeforth and his wife Lady Eleanor Lauriston of Hawksbury, who, it seems, eloped with him in defiance of her father's will; the old Lord Hawksbury seems to have been a rigid papist and had intended his daughter to be given to an old and wealthy gentlemen of the highest family. You will find all these details in the letters."

"My dear, my generous sir, you overwhelm me," returned the Jew, fawningly.

"And you will advance the money that you promised on this security."

"Surely yes, dear sir," returned the Jew, with infinite suavity; "and will add five hundred pounds for the additional security of these letters, and shall remain for ever a debtor to you for the honoured confidence you place in me."

He sat himself at the table, filled and signed a cheque, which he presented to Harwolf, who took the paper carelessly, almost abstractedly, and placed it in his pocket-book.

The Jew, seated at the table, drew the lamp closer, and was soon absorbed in reading the letters.

Harwolf looked around the room suspiciously.

He hemmed, and stirred.

The Jew looked up with his usual smile.

"Are you sure we are alone, Nathan?"

"Dear sir, you need be under no apprehension," replied the Jew.

"Are you not rather nervous at times in this strange, lonely house?"

"Indeed, no. Why should I be?"

"There is money in those strong boxes; notes and gold."

"Well, well, I must keep ready money in the place; so many gentlemen who apply to me are in want of change—ready cash, sir. Yes, but I am not afraid, not the least in the world. See here."

He touched a spring in the table, a lid flew open and disclosed a pair of pistols.

"He, he, he! not at all a bad scheme, eh! Mr. Harwolf. I have all sorts of strange customers. A fellow came one day and sat in the same chair you occupy; he tried to bully me, and even drew a knife. I touched this spring, and, presto, I was formidably armed, and the fellow was cowed in an instant. Rich, was it not? But you are so good, so indulgent, Mr. Harwolf, no doubt you will excuse me a very, very few moments; these documents are so interesting."

"In the meanwhile I will examine this piece—upon my soul, the workmanship is beautiful. Will you permit me?"

The Jew murmured a bland assent. His mind was entirely preoccupied; he was completely absorbed in the perusal of the correspondence of the unfortunate pair, who little thought their cherished effusions of tenderest affection would fall into such hands.

Daniel Harwolf rose carelessly and sauntered across the room.

The pistol was still in his hand.

He stood a few paces behind the Jew, who was reading on with thirsty eagerness.

He took a deadly aim from behind full at Jew's head.

His eye was fixed and his teeth close set, but the muscles of his arm did not tremble.

A sudden thought struck him.

He muttered hoarsely in his throat—

" No, no, better than that."

He placed the pistol in his bosom, and drew from his pocket a long clasp knife, which opened with a sharp snap.

" This," he muttered, " is surer and more silent."

He had scarcely given involuntary utterance to these words when the wily Jew rose from his chair.

Harwolf rushed upon him, and seizing him by the throat with one hand, with the other he drove the weapon to the very hilt in his victim's chest.

Nathan staggered giddily, tossed up his arms, and fell with a heavy thud on the floor.

This all passed so suddenly that Silas Rye was only apprised of what was happening by the noise of the Jew's fall.

He slipped from the cupboard into the room.

His first thought was to rush upon Harwolf, whose back was towards him.

But he reflected that such a movement would result in his immediate death. The pistol was still in the murderer's possession, and he did not doubt that Harwolf would have shot him dead.

The letters!

Quick as the thought flashed through his brain he snatched them from the table.

Harwolf still stood over his prostrate victim.

He spoke with thick utterance.

" 'Tis easy, very easy, and yet *murder!*"

He turned.

Silas had slunk behind a book-case.

" Ha, what was that?" gasped the murderer. " I am sure I heard something move."

He walked about the room for an instant, peering into the corners, and Silas Rye very narrowly escaped detection.

He passed the hiding-place of the single spectator of his horrible deed.

He then turned his attention to the strong boxes.

He stooped over the murdered man, and after some trouble managed to possess himself of the keys.

These he tried upon several of the iron safes.

Eventually he succeeded in opening several.

Silas Rye dared not move, as Daniel Harwolf had secured the other pistols from the table, and had thrust them both into his pockets.

Besides, there was no mistaking the desperation that his wild and scowling face expressed.

Rolls of bank notes, bills, several pieces of jewellery, and cash-boxes.

All these treasures he strewed upon the table, breaking open the cash-boxes, and pouring the rich gold in a mass upon the table.

This done, he went to the door and listened.

No one stirred.

He returned to his work at the table ; he arranged the gold as well as he could into little heaps. These he secreted about his clothes, he stowed the notes away in his pocket-book, and then advanced to the door.

Silence was still unbroken.

With a fiendish leer he stood over the body an instant in meditation, and then dragged it into the middle of the room.

Then, with the coolest deliberation, he took up the burning lamp, poured the seething oil down the window drapery and about the woodwork, and gathering together a quantity of waste paper and old letters, set them alight.

The flames sprang up the dry and crisp window-curtains, and blackened the ceiling.

They curled along the wainscot, and the room began to choke with smoke.

Just as Daniel Harwolf was about to leave the room, Silas Rye crept round by the wall, and threw his strong arms in a hugging clasp around the murderer.

The ruffian struggled with him a moment, and gave an irrepressible cry.

The conflict was terrible.

For a moment both men were wrestling fiercely to get possession of the pistol.

In the struggle it was discharged.

The bullet flew by the cheek of Silas Rye and left its bloody mark.

Silas recoiled, and the ruthless Harwolf was about to flee down the stairs when he was intercepted.

Deborah, the Jewess, stood full in his path.

She had thrown a loose mantle about her night dress, and held a candle in her hand.

She tried to oppose him.

He levelled the pistol at her ear.

Instinctively she flinched.

He dashed past her, rudely thrusting her aside, and flew down the stairs.

" The villain has escaped ; the devil has broken loose to do worse mischief," cried Silas Rye, in a faint voice, for he was exhausted from loss of blood.

" Oh, sir, my father? Did my eyes deceive me ?" shrieked the Jewess. " Where is my father, and whence is this horrible smell of fire ?"

" Young lady, this is a time when love must teach you fortitude—your father is murdered. Hasten for assistance ; the papers in his office have been fired by this demon ; I will try to extinguish the flames. Oh, run !"

But with a wild scream the Jewess rushed into the room where her father lay dead—killed by the first blow.

She threw herself upon his breast, regardless of the flames that were spreading around her.

Then she started to her feet.

With a grandeur of mien that was very imposing she thrust back her masses of raven hair.

" Not now to weep, first to revenge my father," she hissed out; " I saw the villain's face ; he shall not escape me."

In the meanwhile Silas Rye, with great presence of mind, had torn down the drapery, swept the paper to the hearth, and had, by throwing water and trampling out the fire, succeeded in extinguishing the flames to a great extent.

By this time loud knocking was heard at the door, which was opened by an old Jewess woman who slept in the lower part of the house and was the only servant in the place.

A number of people rushed upstairs, amongst them one or two policemen.

The state of affairs was soon revealed by Silas and Deborah. The latter declared she had come downstairs at the moment her father had fallen; she averred that she saw the murderer standing over his victim, but that she had controlled herself, perceiving that the ruffian was armed with a pistol, and, from the same motive which had kept Silas Rye from rushing upon the monster in the first instance, she had awaited her time, for she felt sure that had she attempted to give an immediate alarm her own life would have been sacrificed.

The body was removed ; the place cleared.

The policemen asked Silas Rye if he knew the man.

The latter hesitated whether he should answer the question truthfully, but skilfully evaded it by speaking of his struggle with the assassin, and of his weakness from loss of blood.

Several persons volunteered to remain in the house.

The police authorities took possession of the place, locking the doors and keeping watch.

Silas Rye was conducted to a chamber, where Deborah gave him some wine.

Pale as snow, and evidently suffering intensely, the beautiful Jewess sat as calm as a statue.

"You know this man," she said, suddenly.

"I do, I will not deceive you, but we must be very prudent—he will escape."

"Will he! If he does be my father's blood upon my head. He has burnt the papers, too."

"'Tis strange," muttered Rye, putting his hand into his breast; "last night I *dreamed of a fire at sea*, and I thought the ship was the BOY PIRATE'S!"

CHAPTER LV.

THE PLANTER'S LAST ACT OF CRUELTY.

TURNER alone could convey a faint conception of the beauty of the scenery that surrounded the Boy Pirate and the remnant of the crew of the "Fortune of War."

The calm returned after the storm; the bright-plumaged birds flitted among prostrate branches of the mighty trees that had been blown down by the furious hurricane. The insects, those creatures so easily crushed and yet so tenacious of life under inflictions that would be fatal to the mammoth of creation, fluttered their sheeny wings in the blaze of the cloudless sky. The waves heaved lightly, and warbled musically along the rocks they had broken in their fury. The air was fresher and less oppressive than it had been for a long time previous to the storm.

The Boy Pirate and his dejected crew were seated by the signal post which they had raised on the summit of a hill in the island on which they had been cast.

The "Red Raven" was not in sight, but the pilot, Brand, who had escaped with the others present, predicted that the light sloop was safe, and she would soon appear in the horizon on her mission of deliverance, for she had had plenty of sea-room, and her taut sides could withstand the utmost violence of the heaviest billows when out in the open main.

There was no want of the necessaries of life.

The woods teemed with animals suitable for food, and the ground was strewn with rich fruits like the turf in an orchard after a whirlwind.

Our hero, his devoted wife, and his foster-brother, who sat apart from the rest, would have formed the subject for a fine group for the sculptor or the painter.

The glowing face of the rover of the seas beamed with that cheerful confidence and hopefulness so needful and so powerful in a commander.

His wife hung on his shoulder, and looked up into his eyes with the yearning sympathy of love and reliance, while the foster-brother reclined on the turf, watching the pair with silent admiration.

One thing, beyond all others, hung heavily at the heart of Christopher. It was the fate of the beautiful octoroon and her sable guardian, Zampa.

He had seen these representatives of the extreme conditions of the enslaved race clinging to some drifting spars, and borne along upon the boiling waters.

The channel between the island on which the larger party had been cast and the continent of South America was narrow; the part of the reef on which the ship had struck was in the midst of the roadstead, and the chances were in favour of the strong swimming and great endurance of the negro. And Brand, who in such matters seemed to be possessed with the most keen perception, was of opinion that the lost ones had reached the opposite coast.

The natural restlessness and activity of the Boy Pirate soon rendered him impatient of the dull suspense and delay that might attend the coming of the "Red Raven"; and, after awhile, he kissed his lovely bride and, confiding her to the care of his foster-brother, conferred with Brand as to the practicability of constructing a raft that might convey them across the channel to the mainland on a search for the absentees.

Tom Garrod and a strong party of resolute seamen volunteered their services.

Selecting those on whom he could most depend the Boy Pirate went into the forest.

By his orders a number of bamboos and palm trunks were chosen for the purpose, and in a few hours a strong and buoyant raft was constructed, and once more the hardy sea-dogs committed themselves to the treacherous deep.

They found the passage easy enough.

On reaching land, however, they encountered not a few perils while exploring the jungle, for they had to pass through the lairs of the most ferocious wild beasts, and they trod upon the nests of the most venomous serpents and reptiles.

Their trouble and danger for a long time seemed to have been fruitlessly incurred.

There were no traces of man in the primeval forest.

The day was wasted in their vain endeavours, and they were about to give up the search and were inclined to believe that, notwithstanding their hopes to the contrary, the lovely Ida and the faithful black had indeed perished in the storm.

They ascended a high peak that overhung the sea and commanded an extensive view of the wave-indented coast.

The experienced eye of the Boy Pirate at once discerned a dark object lying at the extremity of a ridge of weedy rocks that ran out into the water at about a mile from the cliff.

By the aid of his glass Christopher's suspicions were confirmed.

The dark body proved to be the battered hull of a wreck that had been thrown upon this reef.

The whole party set off in the direction of the ship.

It was found on reaching the spot that the tide was on the turn, and was rising in such a manner as to render the position of the black hull very difficult of access.

But obstacles are only inducements to the bold and determined.

Not wishing to trust the large raft to the precarious navigation the Boy Pirate caused a smaller one to be made, on which, with Brand, Tom Garrod and several of the hardiest of the men, he ventured over the sunken rocks and insidious quickshoals.

They reached the ship.

The Red Raven was the first to clamber the deck.

On board a dreary spectacle was seen.

Several dead bodies of drowned men were lashed to the bulwarks and ports.

No living creature appeared on board.

The quarter-deck and stern were completely stove in, and the light spray leaped playfully over the ruin.

The Boy Pirate walked towards the hold.

He looked down.

All was gloomy and cheerless.

He thought that there was a slight taint of smoke in the close air of the place.

He descended.

Brave as he was he could not help starting as a wild and prolonged cry rang between decks.

"Hulloa dar! Oh, oh, oh! What de debil you stand staring like a 'possum? Don't yer see? If yer don't distinguish dat yar frizzling bit of tow we'se all go to glory togedder in a flip! O golly, mas'r, do put him out!"

The Boy Pirate stood for a moment petrified with astonishment.

The negro, Zampa, was tightly bound to the side of the hold.

In the middle of the deck a large barrel of gunpowder was placed.

A train had been laid from the negro's feet to the edge of the tub, which had a long piece of tow hanging from the edge, and communicating with the gunpowder.

It was already on fire, and the little flame had reached the top.

With wondrous presence of mind Christopher seized a rope, and fastening it to the stump of the mast, lowered himself to the spot, pushed away the barrel, and put out the lighted tow.

"Berry much 'blige, mas'r," said the negro, ducking his head. "Yah, yah! ye come at de right conjumption. By dis time I'd 'a been blown to glory."

"But what the deuce brought you into this plight, Zamp?" asked the Boy Pirate, who could not help laughing.

The negro grinned.

"Sarve me right, cap'en," he said.

The Boy Pirate cut his bonds, and as Brand and Tom Garrod descended into the hold the negro stumbled feebly against the bows and sat down.

"Nebber yo' min', mas'r; sarves me right. Yah, de dam cuss!"

"What 'dam cuss,' Zamp?"

"Mas'r Rashleigh, in course, cap'en. Cotch dis yar genwine nigger and de white nigger gal. Wal, sarves me right; 'scuse my 'pinion!"

"Serves you right, Zamp! Why—what have you done?"

"'Tain't what I done, buckra; it's what I didn't do."

"And what's that?"

"Bah! didn't I ort to ha' cut de libber out ob de cuss when I got de chance. Look yer, mas'r; I got on shore wid missee—yah! Den we come into de wood. Den Mas'r Rashleigh and dam crew came, and dey cotch us. Thought it was you, mas'r; nebber try to run. Wal, yo' see, mas'r, dey gib me lickin', and den dey carry off Miss Ida into de forest. What they do wid dis chile yo' see with yer own orbits. Dey tie me up yere; dey put de dam gunpowder under my nose, and light de train wid de slow match. Gorra Mighty! I sweat like a alligator; thought me done for, slick sartain. 'Spects they nebber tink mas'r come. But I'm berry cut up about de missee; she tuk on so."

"But what brought the brutal scoundrel here?"

"S'pose he come in Brazil ship; want to cotch yo', mas'r; wrecked here. Wal, they finds us in wood—Missee Ida ask me to kill her. Look you har, mas'r—I's not do that; thought you'd come—yah! yah! I's de sly coon; but wust on't is dey'se cotch de yaller gal."

"Can you tell which way they went?"

"No, mas'r. Can't see trou' dis yar plank, no how—hearn 'em say something 'bout de ribber. S'pose they'se got a boat, cap'en, and is a-going to row down de ribber to de plantation."

"Well, we will follow her, Zampa, and rescue her, wherever she is," said the Boy Pirate, furiously.

"You must get nigh to 'em, mas'r, like a snake a egg-hunting. 'Cos, if they see yer, 'spects they'll shoot her."

"Come, Brand," said the Boy Pirate, "here is a little adventure before us that will just keep us alive till the crew of the 'Red Raven' turns up."

"And how long since have they sheered off, nigger?" asked Tom Garrod.

"'Bout quarter'n hour. I tink dey gwine down ribber."

"Have they got a boat, then?" asked Brand.

"Iss, mas'r, dey brought me to dis dam hulk in her."

"Well, my hearties, let us be off, every moment we waste is a shame to ourselves and a peril to the pretty octoroon."

When the party reached land they found their companions had come upon the recent track of a body of men, and they only awaited the return of their captain before pursuing the marks which they knew must be left by the crew from the vessel that lay shattered on the reef.

After a hasty consultation they followed the traces into the wood.

At first they could not understand why the party had taken the overland route, but they came to the conclusion that the boat was scarcely large enough to contain the whole party, and that they had left some one in charge of it who could bring it round to some point down the river where the whole party were to reunite.

The gallant band, their captain leading the way, plunged through the brake, and it was not long before the freshness of the trail caused them to pause abruptly and then to fall on their hands and knees and proceed with the utmost caution.

The forest was very dense in this part of the country, and they had to make their way by fallen trees and over swampy places, for even the continent along the coast had suffered from the storm.

Soon they were crawling among the bushes, and they could hear the sound of a brutal cry from rough men and the shriek of a woman.

"Hi! mas'r, you hearn dat? Ole Rashleigh gwine to flog missee! Said he would. She got off once at de cotton pickin'; guess she cotch it now!"

The sound of piercing screams and appeals came ringing over the hill, mingled with the sweep of the lash, discernible even at that distance.

The Boy Pirate and his companion thought no more of prudence, but flew up the hill at full speed.

Upon reaching the top he found that the castaways, who, even from afar, appeared to be a set of rowdies—either pirates or slavers—had "camped down."

They were seated in a ring smoking, and drinking from a brandy cask.

The villains were remorseless spectators of an act that shamed humanity.

Rashleigh had stripped the octoroon nude, and bound her by the wrists to the branch of a tree in such a manner that her feet scarcely touched the ground.

He was inflicting the most cruel whipping with his heavy cowhide.

The Boy Pirate's cheek crimsoned with passion; he drew out a revolver, and, taking deadly aim, fired.

Rashleigh had raised his whip at the moment the bullet struck him. It went through his heart; he sprang into the air and fell prone on his face.

The rest of his brutal party leaped to their feet in an instant.

The Boy Pirate and his men blazed at them indiscriminately.

Several of them bit the dust.

The little band of deliverers rushed down the hill in full charge.

As they flew down into the valley at the top of their speed they made the woods ring with their shouts.

A very short scuffle took place, for though the pirates were outnumbered, the dastards who could unfeelingly witness the torment of a woman, and of such a beautiful and gentle girl as the octoroon, only acted consistently with the vileness of their character when they sought safety in a disgraceful flight.

Rashleigh lay dead.

The octoroon hung by her arms, her head fallen back, her eyes closed.

The blood marks covered her delicate and throbbing flesh.

She had fainted!

The Boy Pirate cut her bonds and covered her in a cloak.

He placed her gently on a bank.

His men brought boughs and made a litter, on which the girl was placed and very tenderly carried along.

The Boy Pirate turned with a dark frown towards the body of the atrocious planter.

Zampa, the negro, grinning, laughing, and singing, danced about his fallen tyrant, loading him with abuse and spurning him with his feet, with all the buffoonish savagery of the most barbarous tribes insulting a captive at the stake.

Christopher turned away with a qualm of disgust, but he could scarcely wonder at this display on the part of the ignorant black, who had suffered so cruelly from his more enlightened oppressor.

Upon reaching the coast the unfortunate white slave was committed to the care of Lilia.

She received every attention that the tenderest kindness could bestow, but she seemed suffering terribly.

She was in high fever, moaned feebly, and was quite unconscious.

Wearily the day passed.

A careful watch was kept during the night.

All the next day the castaways employed themselves in fishing turtle, hunting, or rambling the coast in search of drifts from the wreck.

Towards evening the look-out announced a sail.

A tiny mote appeared in the red glare of the gorgeous sunset.

The men watched it with unutterable anxiety.

It might be some hostile ship!

The crews of all nations were their sworn enemies.

There was but one ship on the high seas that could help them, and the last time they had seen her she was driving along, her masts shipped, before a terrific gale.

Hope grew into confidence and joy as the little mote assumed the form of a hull and masts.

All hands went to work with a will at the signal post.

Nearer and nearer the vessel approached, lightly lifting and sinking on the slumbering bosom of the main.

A flag fluttered up to the mast-head.

Brand and the captain glanced at it eagerly through their glasses.

The men strained their eyes to catch a view of it.

The flag rolled out.

That fearless rover-flag rippled out its black folds, showing the ghastly white scull and bones, with the blood-red crest of the Boy Pirate.

With flashing eyes and glowing cheeks the men brandished their weapons and once more shouted,

"Hurrah! Hurrah for the 'Red Raven!'"

CHAPTER LVI.

THE FLIGHT OF DANIEL HARWOLF.

ANDREW HARWOLF had returned to his magnificent seat at Frontemore.

His search for Lady Edgeforth had ended without any satisfactory result.

Tortured by every conceivable anxiety of fear and remorse, the squire had sought to distract his thoughts by alternate close application to business and utter abandonment to sensual pleasures.

As usual the unsocial man had dined alone, and sat sipping his wine and gloating upon the darkening sky through the open window.

Suddenly he perceived some one stealing along through the bushes; he started up, and was about to ring the bell for the servant, thinking it possible that some tramp or thief was prowling about the grounds.

The man stood out from the shrubs and held up his hand.

Andrew Harwolf at once recognised his son.

He stood in the middle of the little plat with his hand upraised appealingly; he then slunk to the window, and ascending the step of the balcony, entered.

His first proceeding was to draw the window-blinds, the next to lock the door.

He then confronted his father.

Andrew Harwolf looked upon him for awhile with speechless amazement.

Daniel's clothes were torn and weather-stained, his cheeks were pale and pinched with hunger; his eyes started from his head, and in his hand he clutched a ragged stick he had torn from a tree.

Andrew's first impression was that his son had gone mad, his next that his own mind was wander-ing, and that he beheld some creature of his own tortured imagination.

"Father!" said Daniel, sinking into the chair, "give me some food. I am nearly dead with hunger."

"Good God, son, what is it?—something fearful has occurred. Food? I will ring the bell."

The squire rose and moved to the wall.

With a cry of terror Daniel interposed.

"No! no! no!" he exclaimed. "No one must see me, better I should starve. O God! Be prudent, father!"

"Daniel," cried the old squire, with a frown, "what is the matter?—what have you done? Tell me quickly."

"I dare not, I dare not," groaned the wretched young man, burying his face in his hand.

A blank, wild look flitted across the old man's face, and the elder criminal looked at the younger with a glance of penetrating enquiry.

He could not speak but muttered out hoarsely,

"There is blood on your wrist, Daniel, red spots on your shirt. *Is the blood your own?*"

"Yes, yes; whose should it be?" cried Daniel, wildly.

"Tell me no lie, Daniel, I am your father. Your hands are stained with the blood of your first victim! It is destiny!"

"I will tell you all, father, but for God's sake, caution! Can I not hide. The blinds drawn, the door locked—should the servants come suspicion would be roused, and I shall be brought to the drop. But food, for mercy! I have walked all the way from London and have tasted nothing yet."

"Why not? You have money; you have jewellery about you. Are there no places of refreshment on all the road?"

"Do not speak of it," returned the wretch, faintly. "The first place into which I ventured was a lonely ale-house on a wide, bare moor. It was night!—hereafter my only season; I have nothing more to do with day. At night, and in a rain-storm, I ventured into this lonely house upon this desolate heath. Little did I look for company; but the bar was filled with boors—fellows who, it seems, had been cutting furze, and took shelter here from the rain. The topic of their conversation was the 'dreadful murder!' So, then, the news had travelled even to this lonely place. The fellows eyed me with vulgar curiosity; they asked me if I had read a description of the perpetrator of the horrible deed; they entered into details; they saw I was pale and haggard, and one, the wit of the party, asked me whether I was not a detective. I could stand it no longer; I made my escape, and never since have I dared to enter a house."

"But why did you not come down by train?"

"I feared that I should be arrested. Oh, father! once I was bold as a man; now, I am nothing but fear."

"A lily-liver should never go with a black heart," said the elder villain, with a contemptuous sneer. "Had it been my case—ha! Well, Daniel, you must be stowed away. Let me see, where were you the night before last?"

"Why, here at Frontemore."

"I did not know that you had left the house till this morning. That fellow Moss is just the fellow to swear anything. Perhaps we can prove an alibi at the worst pinch. But whom have you murdered?"

Daniel was surprised at the calmness with which his father spoke, but courage and tact in his self-defence was the bulwark of this ambitious and usurping steward, who, had he been of royal birth, would have been more remorseless than John and Richard in removing the living obstacles between himself and his glittering prize.

Daniel made no reply till his father repeated the question.

"A cursed money-lender, a Jew. I was trammeled in his nets, and I had no help for it but to let myself out of them through his life. My plan was a good one, but it is not the first good plan

that has failed through an accident not to be foreseen."

"Where did you kill this Jew?"

"In his own house. I went to him on business.
I knew him to be meddlesome; he wished to pry too
deeply into our family affairs; he wanted to scan
our title deeds for Frontemore."

"Ha!"

"Yes, and he showed me pistols that he kept to
overawe some of those clients whom, like myself, he
had stung to vindictive fury. I was tempted, and
while he was reading I struck him down with the
butt-end of the weapon."

"Has he a wife?"

"No; but a daughter."

"She will go mad; you should have killed her
too," muttered the old man, dreamily.

The guilty son looked at the guilty father with
surprise.

The squire sat moodily in his arm-chair, his eyes
fixed abstractedly on the door of his "chamber of
horrors," the dressing room.

"It is coming home at last," he groaned, bending
his care-greyed hairs upon the table.

He looked up, his face firm with satanic power.

"Did you take no measures to remove the traces
of your crime?"

"Yes, the best. I meant to purge the place with
fire."

"Fire!" hissed out Harwolf, his features livid and
distorted with sudden agony.

"Yes, it was common with the old man to sit
late in his office. We had been alone together, no
one had seen me enter. I gathered together all the
papers I could lay hands on and set them in flames."

"Well, and what prevented your escape?"

"I was seized by some one, who suddenly started,
I think, from the earth, for I thought I had carefully searched the room."

"And who was he?"

"Wonderful to say, a man I have seen with you."

"With me. Ha!"

"I think they call him Silas Rye."

The squire leaped up, and approached his son
with a threatening gesture.

"Hear me, boy. I understand you—you are
getting weary of me, you 'hunger for my empty
chair.' So do your worst, kill me if you choose,
but do not think to drive me mad. I am too strong
for you there; your cunning can never withstand an
intellect so strong as mine!"

"For God's sake, father; you will drive me mad.
What I have said is true—fatally true!" cried Daniel,
excitedly.

"It cannot be; Silas Rye is dead; he left me in-
sultingly, on a mission of vengeance, but the train
was smashed, and he was killed ere he reached his
destination. I have looked on his grave."

"And have you ever seen him since?"

Andrew did not reply.

"I have not told you. I fired at the villain."

"And did you kill him?" cried the old man,
quickly.

"No; the place was full of smoke. I do not
know even whether I wounded him; but for
Heaven's sake get me some food, I am dying with
hunger."

The old man rose and led the way to the dressing-
room. He locked his son in this room.

He then threw up the windows of the saloon, and
opened the door.

He rung the bell.

A servant entered.

He ordered some refreshment.

The man bowed and left the room.

He dismissed the servant, who was remaining to
wait on him.

He took his son from the dressing-room.

Young Harwolf devoured the viands with ravenous
appetite, and drank the wine with great relish.

Scarcely had he finished his repast when the
barking of dogs and the sound of carriage wheels
announced the arrival of guests or of intruders.

Daniel Harwolf jumped up in deadly terror.

With great presence of mind Andrew Harwolf
motioned him to the dressing room.

"You will find that the pier-glass let into the
wall turns on a pivot; the spring is under the fifth of
the gilt rosebuds on the lower edge of the frame—
press it hard. You will find a passage that has been
the burrow of many an attainted rebel in the civil
wars. Go. I'll take your place at this table. I
have settled Miles, of the 'Hedger's Arms,' in a
lonely shooting-box at Glenleaf. My butler shall
swear that you slept here last night, and Miles shall
swear that you came over this morning for a day's
shooting. Look sharp, only fools are ever found out;
the worse foe is one's own indiscretion; the best of us
want forethought."

With imperturbable calmness the squire pushed
his son into the dressing-room, closed and locked
the door after him, and seated himself quietly at the
table, and threw the *serviette* across his knees as if he
had been eating.

There was a knock at the door.

"Come in, Moss, come in," said the squire, irri-
tably. "Well now, what is it?"

"Oh, sir, the house is full of people, sir. The
whole neighbourhood is up in arms. There has been
a hawful murder, sir, of a Jew gentleman, or sich
like, up town, sir. And really its on'y a sense of
duty as makes me speak, sir."

"Well, what has the affair to do with me?"

"Mr. Daniel, sir—he isn't here? I humbly hopes
as he ain't here—it's him, sir, as they charges."

"My son is not here, Moss, as you know, and the
charge is simply absurd," returned the squire.

"They've got a warrant to search the house, and
there ain't a vulgarer set of men, sir, than the
perlice, ven they vonce gets authority. What's to be
done?"

"Nothing is to be done; let the law take its
course. Throw open the rooms, but see that the
rough fellows are careful with the ornaments and
valuables. If my son were guilty I would not
screen him. Get the thing over as quickly and
orderly as you can, and then let the officers have
some refreshment."

"Werry good, sir."

"Is there any of the murdered man's friends with
the party."

"Yes, sir, one on them—his daughter, I believe, a
kind of lady, in fact, a young person, sir, as looks
about as fierce as a crouching tigress."

"Poor girl. Let her be kindly treated; how I sympathise with her," said the rascal, with a sigh.
"Well, they'll be getting impatient."

"Werry good, sir. I'll do my best to see your
orders carried out."

"One thing, Moss."

"Yes, sir."

"My son, Daniel, slept here last night, rose very
early and started off to Glenleaf, to go shooting at
Miles's place."

"I humbly understands, sir," returned the obsequious Moss, lowering his eyes.

"And understand me humbly, please don't make
a parade of what you know, say nothing unless asked.
By the way, they might search Daniel's room; of
course they will find his favourite fowling-piece
removed from its place; don't point that out, let
them notice it of themselves. There might be some of
my son's papers about; see that they are not put
into inquisitive hands."

"I understands it all, sir. But here they is."

"Let them come in."

Four police officers, a lady, and one or two gentlemen entered the room.

The lady was dressed in deep mourning and closely
veiled.

"We are sorry, sir, to be forced to intrude upon
you in this manner," said the principal officer, addressing Harwolf, "but we are on the track of a
man charged with the dreadful crime of murder. I

FEARFUL POSITION OF ZAMPA.

trust that the suspicious circumstances which led to the charge being laid against your son will be cleared up. If he will surrender himself it is to be hopèd that the first examination will establish his innocence."

"As I am sure, sir, my son is innocent, so I am confident that, were he present, he would willingly commit himself to your charge till he had confirmed his guiltlessness in this matter. Unfortunately, he is not here; he slept at Frontemore last night, rose early, and went to a shooting-box of mine at Glenleaf to spend the day with one of my tenants, and little expecting the hunt now made for him. As the evening is now advancing he may presently return, though I cannot vouch that he will do so, as his stay at Glenleaf is of uncertain duration."

No. 19.

The officers were taken aback at the coolness with which these words were spoken.

Harwolf did not betray the slightest agitation.

However, the colour stole from his cheek when he caught a glance of the black eyes of the Jewess glittering upon him through her veil.

"I am sure he is here," said Deborah, firmly. "I grieve to say the young man bears a striking resemblance to this gentleman, and there is no doubt of his identity."

"It is cruel of you, madam, to say so, though I freely pardon your rashness on account of your natural and laudable desire to do justice upon one who has wrought such a detestable crime. If there is any way in which I can assist you I am entirely at your service."

" Then I am sure, sir, you will pardon the necessity of searching the house as a matter of form," said the officer. " We will be careful to disturb as little as possible domestic arrangements, and will take our leave as soon as possible."

" I wish you to do everything to satisfy yourselves that my son is not here. Mind! if you leave the place unconvinced it is your own fault."

Nothing could be more masterly than the wonderful self-possession of this accomplished villain.

" I am sure you will excuse me if I leave an officer in this room until my return."

" As you please, sir. Do not hurry; I wish you to be finally convinced of the truth of what I have told you."

The officers bowed and left the room with Deborah, whose presence was required that the prisoner might be identified.

Harwolf seated himself at the table carelessly, and took up the journal.

A few hours after the party left the house.

They rode over in a carriage to Glenleaf.

They found the place deserted.

Much puzzled they returned to Frontemore.

One of the officers had found a letter in the squire's own bedroom.

It was a brief and common-place note.

It was compared with another in the possession of Deborah which had been written by the alleged murderer to her father a few days previous to the terrible act which had excited this inquisition.

There were other proofs of very confirmatory nature, and Deborah clung to the assertion that she was able to swear that Daniel Harwolf was the guilty person, and none other.

The reader may wonder why the squire's former accomplice and actual enemy, Silas Rye, was not present, but for many reasons he wished to avoid notice in the present stage of affairs.

He had requested that for the present his name should be studiously suppressed, and the police authorities consented to this arrangement the more readily as they hoped to be materially assisted by their ally.

Andrew Harwolf was treated with the greatest respect and courtesy, and so well had he managed his son's escape that an opinion seemed to prevail that he was really himself deceived by his ruffianly son.

Soon after Harwolf retired to his bed-room.

His agony of soul can never be expressed.

" But why should I stay here? Why should I play about the hook till the barb strikes me? No, I am resolved! If they do not take Daniel, soon the reality of his crime will eclipse and wear out the suspicion of mine. Still I am always in danger here. There is a new world across the Atlantic; I will let Frontemore on lease; I will turn all I can into money, and then I will go. Surely neither his spirit, nor the ghost of Silas Rye, nor the devilish madness of his terrible wife, can follow me across the great ocean! No; I shall end my life in peace, and then I may repent. Repent! The price of blood in my hand; the curses of raging madness, induced by my crime, ringing in my ear; my only child a murderer, hunted by the bloodhounds of the law! Repent! Peace! No; but I will have no material furies to afflict me; no plagues but my own pangs of remorse."

CHAPTER LVII.

TOM GARROD'S YARN.

THE Boy Pirate was once more united with his crew on his first ship.

For some days all hands on board moved about their duty with mournful faces.

They had lost a splendid vessel and rich booty, and worse than all, many of their bravest and jolliest messmates.

But sailors are proverbial for their elasticity of mind.

A thorough sea-dog is almost as forgetful of the sorrows of yesterday as he is heedless of the cares of to-morrow.

The Boy Pirate had done all he could to raise their spirits.

As the weather was calm, and they had not yet fallen in with a worthy prize, he gave his well-disciplined crew as much liberty and as liberal an allowance of grog as expediency would permit, and all on board were very merry at times.

In the gorgeous evenings, when the sunset gilded the masts, and chequered the decks with a network of light and shadow; when the broad sails flapped lazily, and the ropes and tackle of the vessel seemed to be cords of pink silk woven with gold; when the white-winged gulls screamed and dipped about the ship; when the flying-fish darted in their oblique flight, and herds of swift porpoises gambled through the light billows, the crew would assemble for a dance and a song.

Seated on the quarter-deck, Lilia and the octoroon would look on the gay scene with pleasant faces.

Many a practical joke was played; many a frolic elicited roars of laughter; many a tender song from the octoroon, who had an exquisite voice, caused the crew to stand in rapt silence, grave and attentive.

Zampa, the negro, too, was the source of endless amusement.

His drolleries were so mirth-provoking, and his native gayness so infectious, that he was an immense favourite with all.

One day Tom Garrod and several of his cronies were standing or sitting about the capstan spinning yarns and drinking grog.

" Now, I'll tell yer what, my hearties, you've all on you got summut queer and unaccountable to crack on; but let it blow, if I can't tell you summut, messmates, as whips all as I ever did hear on."

" Aye, aye! let's have it, Tom," chorussed the others.

" Well, mates, fust I'll whet my whistle, and then I'll pipe all hands to attention. 'Cos vy?—this as I'm a-goin' to tell yer may be of sarvice to all on yer."

" Heave ahead, Jack; let us have it."

" Steady a bit, mates; this yere's solemn."

" Shiver it, then, Jack, we've had solemnity enough lately to please a meetin' of quaker-lubbers—summut jolly," said one of the men.

" Nothin' about eatin', messmates, on a raft—livin' without water."

" And no more sea serpents," said another.

" It's a stale fish, Jack, 'tirely out of season," exclaimed the coxswain.

" An', Gorra Mighty, no dam nigger skinnin'; I'se had 'nuff of that," cried Zampa.

" And as for the Flying Dutchman, he's gone to the ship-broker's, voted not sea-worthy," cried another.

" Summut jolly, Tom, summut jolly," rejoined the chorus.

" Well, gentleman and hearties, you're precious pertic'lar, I must say; well, you shall have something jolly—jolly solemn."

" Werry well, trip anchor, mate; all's ready."

" But the moral—don't forget the moral, hearties; there's no sense in a story without a moral."

" Blow me, but the moral's this—'the least said soonest mended,'" interrupted the coxswain.

" And a werry good moral when one's talking to Jews."

" We ain't no Jews, Jack."

" Well, anyhow, some on yer are unbelievers. Many a good yarn I could ha' told yer, but it's the swollering—there's the pinch, mates."

" We'll swoller anything, Jack; we're hungry for your yarn. Open your log-book. 'Nuff said."

" Fust I'll ask yer a question—whose the finest rover as ever mounted the ' Jolly Oliver?'"

" The Boy Pirate—the Red Raven!" shouted the rest.

"That's a true fact—ain't it? Well, what I'm goin' to tell you is just as true as that, my hearties."

"Well, let's have it."

"There's such things as sharks, I suppose—and whales and porpoises?"

"In course."

"And there's such things as mermaids?"

"Sartain."

"And there's not only mermaids, messmates, but there's mer-wives and mer-widders."

"I s'pose you're right, Jack."

"In course. Did any of yer know Jemmy Skyflyer?"

"Heard on him."

"A werry old messmate of mine were Jemmy, and a better seaman never handled a bunt-line. Well, ye know, hearties, he was a whaler, and once his ship were cruisin' off Labrador. Now, Jemmy was alike most on us. We're like life, purty much up and down; we has all our gifts and our failin's. Jemmy had a werry good failin'."

"What was it, Tom?"

"Grog."

"That's a very bad failing," said a sailor, grinning.

"How's that, ye swab?"

"Better junk and water failing than grog in a long cruise. Its better to stint water than spare spirits, any weather."

"Spare your jawing-tackle. Well, mates, if this baboon-behaved lubber as never larnt better manners than the cannibal islander teaches at their dinner parties——"

"Never mind him, Tom, work along."

"Well, mates, Jemmy was fond of his grog; the officers growled about that sometimes, but the monkey allers managed to steer clear of rough coasts. He had a fine figure-head, had Jemmy, and a woice as clear as a ship's bell. He were a respectful kind o' man; and as for the lasses—blow me, if they warn't puttin' on ducks, and trying to pass as A. B.'s, months arter he was off, in hopes to get a cruise with him. Bless yer sweet eyes, he nearly spliced the main-brace with a real admiral's only darter."

"Then they didn't sail consort arter all, Tom. What a pity!"

"A pity, not at all; he slipped his moorings, did Jemmy, and steered off. 'Cos vy; her father was a teetotaller, the lubber, and Jemmy thought it might run in the family."

"Well, but the mermaids, Tom."

"And the mer-wives and widders."

"They're a-coming; patience and a quid in a long watch, my souls. You should ha' seen Jemmy throw a harpoon, whether at a fin-back or raal oil-butt. But a whale was a whale to Jemmy. Six feet by the deep in the hanimal's blubber was nothing to Jemmy. I have heard that sometimes he would send the barb through the creatur from starboard to larboard; that I never did see. I hates to tell this, mates, it's allers a dead reckoning. Well, one day Jemmy was in the bows of the long boat, poising his harpoon at one of the biggest blubbers as ever sculled the ocean. 'Snub him, Jemmy,' says the cap'en. 'Ay, ay, sir,' says Jemmy. Away went the harpoon, messmates, and away went the boat arter, with a vengeance!"

"Starn off," cried the cap'en, "the creatur's in his flurry." The boat was dragged along, shipped water from stem to starn, and the fish were roaring little thunders. Away rolled the oil-butt, and away went the boat, cutting the surf in his wake, and the hanimal threw up a rainbow of blood and mist, like a waterspout.

"Here he comes in chase," sung out the strokesman in the boat. "Well, mates, the boat swamped, and the men were bobbin' about in the surf like corks; but Jemmy Skyflyer was not the man to give up his game so easily. He held on to the whale line for dear life and glory; the whale sank and towed Jemmy down alongside. I never heard how Jemmy settled him, but he did; I rather con-sider he gashed him with his cutlass; but, p'raps he hadn't one with him. Howsomdever, he pegged the life out of him somehow, and, nat'ral like, was awful hot and tired, so he sat down on a bed of oysters to cool himself and to get wind."

"What, at the bottom of the sea?"

"Well, the atmosphere is rather confined in sich latitudes," Tom went on, with a twinkling eye, "but if you'll have patience, hearties all, you'll come to the moral."

"And the mer-widder?"

"She's a-comin' to Jemmy instanter," said Tom. "Well, Jemmy began to think it were time to go aloft, and was just a-heavin' the whale with his harpoon to send him above deck to sarve as a mainstay till the brig sent to fetch 'em when all at once he heard a sort o' gurgling, which anyone might take for a wailin' and mournin' as were so disposed, and there riz up summut from among the perrywinkles which looked like a walking tangle of seaweed. Now, Jemmy was a perlite man, as respected his betters; I wish we all did that same; but people as interrupts a history of facts and says grog ain't a good failin', why all I've got to say——"

"Never mind, Tom; heave ahead—'Jemmy was a perlite man—'"

"He was so, messmates, and thought as this green object might be Neptune, or some of his family, so he took off his sou'wester and bowed like a gentleman. The green seaweed, which were raal hair, ye see, parted in two, and a purty face with sea-blue eyes, coral lips, and pearl teeth, spick and span from the manufactory, where the lover-swabs sends for 'em to put in their walentines, looks at him and speaks to him, passes the time of day, asks him what cheer, whither bound, and all the rest on't, as men and mermaids does on sich occasions. Well, she were a purty little craft, and Jem said the scales on her fish part were reg'lar beautiful, but then, as he sensibly remarked, arter refusin' a admiral's darter because her father were a teetotaller, to marry a mermaid as lived upon sea-water——"

"But did he marry her?"

"Did he! In course he did. Why shouldn't he? Howsomever, Jem was allers a rover; he soon got tired of his high-life-below-stairs, though I'm told he had several mer-babbies, so he axed his mer-wife's permission to go aboard again. Well, as Jemmy had set his eyes on another mer—widder I think—his wife was glad to see him outward bound for a spell. Well, he got on a Indiaman, but sometimes he sneaked overboard to wisit his wife and fam'ly, who followed in the wake, 'cos he had the power from his married connections of walking on the ocean; but he found it awful slippery work in rough weather. Well, one day the men had leave to go on shore to a sky-larking at Little Harbour Town, but Jemmy's leave was stopped."

"Why, Tom?"

"Grog."

"Oh."

"And so as Jemmy sat on the boom about dog-watch he could see the sport from the distance; they laid in so nigh alongshore he could almost hear the squeak of the fiddles. He couldn't stand it any longer; he slipped over the bulwarks and bowled along over the waves; he were gettin' use to 'em. Jolly he was. He danced, he sung, he grogged, and he winked at the pretty lasses, and set signals at 'em, till one on 'em, a sweet little cutter with red pennants flying at her peak, overhauled poor Jemmy, and took him in tow as her prize. Well, mates, Jemmy and she separated from the rest of the company and sailed away down the coast side by side. Jemmy, who was a good Christian, forgot all about his mer-woman, and made love to the purty land-woman in his most rakish style, when all at once, as they sat on the beach, a slobbering, a blubbering was heard, like a whale a-blowing; it was the mer-woman a floundrin' up the beach behind them. The mer-women finds their fish-tails most ockard on shore. 'Crikey, what female dog-fish is this,' cried the land-gal. 'Blow me, if it ain't my wife,' hollers

Jemmy; but the fish-woman sprang upon the flesh-woman's shoulders and banged her about the ears with her fins and the paddles of her fish-tales, that it was like the stormin' of Gibraltar. As for Jemmy, he set off full sail afore the wind; he run like any Frenchman."

"I say, though, Tom, that wasn't very seaman-like. Was he afeared?"

"Rather, he never stopped running till he fell down, having no more wind in his sails."

"But I didn't think Jemmy would turn coward."

"A coward! Jemmy Skyflyer a coward! Blow me, if he warn't a match for half the navy. But, my hearties, it's set down in the Articles of War as it's lawful for every man to be afeared of his own wife."

"But how did he get back to his ship?"

"Well, mates, I'll tell yer. He thought as he should run aground, and so he did; he tried to get a boat, but he couldn't. Besides, he dared not row alongside, for breakin' leave was cat and irons; so he thought he'd trust to his wife's dutiful feelin's. Now it was a dirty night, pitch dark, and the waves was looking ugly. After a spell he plucked up spirits and defied the devil; so he scrambled over the breakers and stood on the top o' the water. At first he swaggered like a landlubber aboard in his fust rough sea; but Jemmy was groggy and his conscience got into his knees and made 'em shake. Howsomever, he sprawled along, catchin' hold of the tops of the headers to steady himself, and feelin' just a little giddy and sea-sick. At last he slipped and rolled into the trough of the sea; when that lifted it rolled him into another, and so he travelled; but it was awful steerage. The night was as black as a gun's mouth, and every now and then he was overhauled by a clinging string of slimy weed or a clammy cold jelly-fish, which made him think the long corpse fingers of some of his dead messmates rollin' about in Davy's locker was put up to clutch him. At last he rolled under the black hull of the ship, and saw the lantern swinging in the chains; for that matter, p'raps a reg'lar 'lumination on 'em—Jemmy could allers see more when he was drunk than when he was sober. So he thought, mates, he would stand on his legs and clamber up the starn, and get on board afore the rest came back, and trust his luck to steer clear of the skipper. He gave one look back across the wild, dark, dreary sea, and then turned his eyes up the swaying ship's side, when—when——"

"Aye, Tom, aye! 'when—'"

"He felt a tight, spiteful, bony grip round the ancle of his left foot, and, screamin', strugglin', splutterin', suffocatin', he was lugged and tugged down through the cold black waters."

"Down! down! down! Blow me, my hearties, I sweat to think on it. Hand over the grog."

"But, Tom, how the devil could you know all this if they carried him off to Davy Jones in that sort of fashion?"

"Ben, I had it from his own lips! He was found next mornin' in the jolly boat that was towing astarn."

"And how did he come there?"

"One ignorant lubber tried to make out that he had swum ashore and back again, and he was still in the whaler and not a Indiaman, which sartainly puzzled him. But the thing's as straight as a marlin'-spike—the mer-woman deworced him for the sake of her connections, and so they put him back again. So much for my yarn. My moral is—You allers carries yer wife's eye on yer at the foremast-head if you goes a-cruisin' arter strange craft when your once consorted."

"Hi! mas'r, look dar; some one swim to de ship," suddenly cried the negro.

The Boy Pirate and his foster-brother were passing arm-in-arm at the moment.

They turned their eyes in the direction indicated.

A man appeared breasting the waves, swimming from shore.

Just as he drew near the ship a rush was heard, and a shark was seen gliding on its prey.

Christopher leaped on the bulwark.

Dick Caffyn tried to hold him but he broke away, and his foster-brother resolved to save or sink with him.

Almost simultaneously the Boy Pirate and Dick Caffyn leaped into the sea!

CHAPTER LVIII.

THE SEMINOLE CHIEF.—THE FIGHT WITH THE SHARK.

THE Boy Pirate and Dick Caffyn leaped into the sea.

Dashing aside the surf with their strong arms they forged through the clear waves towards the spot where the scuffle was going on between the swimmer and the shark.

The young man, for so he now appeared to be, with wondrous coolness and presence of mind, dashed down into the bosom of the green waters, diving under the belly of the fish each time that the creature turned to place himself in a line with his victim before making his deadly rush.

It is well known that the upper jaw of the animal is much longer than the lower, and on account of this arrangement the animal is forced to turn nearly half over when seizing his prey.

The swimmer was evidently becoming exhausted from the effect of his continuous plunges into the depths.

The shark was sculling backwards, turning his long body as he steered with his huge fin.

When the Boy Pirate and his foster-brother had swum up alongside, the animal, diverted from the former object of pursuit, rolled over on its side, showing his white, glistening belly, and winnowing the brine with his tail.

The Boy Pirate took his cutlass from between his teeth, and taking advantage of the shark's momentary powerlessness, struck him a downright blow with the keen edge of his glancing weapon.

Down into the profound sank the terrified and infuriated creature and his valiant assailant.

The sea churned and frothed, while its fleecy foam was tinged with streaks of blood.

There were wild cries and curses from the deck of the "Red Raven."

Lilia and the octoroon, who stood on the quarter-deck, shrieked their terror, while Tom Garrod and the seamen, late his edified audience, were excitedly pushing off in the long boat.

It was a terrible moment.

How much hung upon the life of the Boy Pirate.

The young man in whose defence our hero had risked his life in this terrific encounter threw himself on his back and rested for a moment.

Dick Caffyn swam round and round the whirlpool of foam and blood, desperately fighting with the lifting billows.

The shark rose.

But not the Boy Pirate.

There was a general cry of consternation.

Far away the gallant Christopher emerged from the trough of the sea, brandishing his cutlass and laughing.

There arose a heart-stirring shout of rejoicing.

The young man, with a gleaming knife, and Dick Caffyn with his cutlass, simultaneously attacked and after a desperate struggle dispatched the monster.

The boat pulled through the yielding waters, and arrived at the scene of action.

The three swimmers were picked up.

Upon getting into the boat the young man who had been so heroically saved from certain destruction displayed the lithe and graceful form and proportions and the copper-red skin of an American Indian.

With a smile of gratitude, and with remarkable calmness, he took his seat at the stern; and the boat was soon alongside the sloop, and was received with a ringing hurrah!

Lilia tenderly embraced her gallant husband, and warmly thanked his devoted and heroic foster-brother, while all hands crowded around the stranger.

He was tall, and peculiarly dignified, dressed in a hunting shirt of blue stuff beautifully embroidered with stained quill-work and glittering beads. He had wampum about his neck, a little deerskin pouch by his side, and in his girdle were placed his calumet or pipe, his tomahawk and scalping knife. A number of withered, ghastly scalps hung at his side.

He was a Seminole of Florida, and a splendid specimen of his handsome race.

Soon after the Boy Pirate, Gomez, Brierly and the rest of the officers received the young native on the quarter-deck.

"My brother is a young man of the Seminoles of Lake Macaco; he is welcome from the land of flowers!" said the Boy Pirate, addressing him in his native tongue, with which he was well acquainted.

"Caragungha is a great chief in the tribe of Macacoes," returned the young Indian; "the big waters cannot wash the stains from his tomahawk, which is red with the blood of the squaw warriors of Haffa. The heart of Adder-Fang is good to the white chief who has shown him such kindness; my brother shall call him "Bounding Elk," as he is called in his own lodges; my brother shall be safe on the war-path or the hunting trail, and shall not lack game or maize among the young men of the tribes that follow my father, the sachem of chiefs. I have spoken!"

The Indian bowed gracefully as he finished this grandiloquent speech.

"What does he say, Christopher?" asked Lilia.

The Boy Pirate interpreted.

"My red brother is welcome to the winged canoe of the pale-faces."

"My brother has the tongue of a Seminole. It is not unknown to the pale chief that the red children of the Manitou have their peculiar customs as the pale-faces have theirs. My father, whom his enemies call 'the Jaguar,' took the chief of the tribe of Haffa captive on the war-path, but the heart of my father was good towards the chief of the dog-hearted son of the river, and he spared his life. When the sachems of the council and the old squaws in the wigwam thirsted to bring Khahuahua to the stake of death my father spread his blanket over him, gave him to smoke the calumet of peace, and kept him in his own lodge. My father, 'the Jaguar,' brought the chief skins, and fire-food, and fire-water. My father loved the chief of the serpent tribe of Haffa. Then the sachem returned to his nation, but the first rains were not passed, five moons had not waned, before Khahuahua unburied the war-hatchet and smote the war-post, and his young men set out on the war-path, and burned many lodges, and took scalps of the sleepers of my father's nation; but a great warrior of Macaco, whom they called 'Sweeping Wind,' led his young men against Khahuahua. 'Bounding Elk' was of the party, but the Great Spirit hid his face, and Caragungha was taken prisoner."

"And has now escaped from his enemies, and has sought refuge in the big canoe of the Yengeese?" suggested the Boy Pirate.

"My brother's words are good," returned the Indian. "Khahuahua would have tied the 'Bounding Elk' to the death-stake, but the wise men of the council, though their hearts are doves' hearts, yet their tongues were not forked. The sachems gave the word that Caragungha should not die, but that he should fight the son of Khahuahua on the sea-shore. The hatchet of Adder-Fang is sharp as the fork of the serpent; his arm is as agile to strike the son of the chief. The soul of Haffa could not bear the lightning gleam of his eyes nor the thunder-stroke of his tomahawk, but fled, fled far off to the hunting-grounds of his fathers in the spirit-land of the Manitou. The scalp of the son of the chief of

Haffa is hanging in this girdle, and the squaws weep in their lodges for the young brave who shall return to them no more. I have said."

"But why was not my brother set at liberty?"

"Khahuahua is a dog," returned the Indian, fiercely, "his heart is like the yearling fawn's, but his tongue is subtle as the tongue of a mocking bird; his smiles are like the fog fires in the great swamps of the prairie; his thoughts are black as a wolf's mouth; he heeds not the traditions of his nation; he cares not that the great Master of Life is the hater of lies. He wished to slay Caragungha, who rested in peace in his wigwam, who had smoked the pipe with him, and whom the sachems had adopted as a son of their tribe; the young men were heedful of his dark words, but a maiden of the Seminoles whose name is Haieta, the 'Morning Dew,' showed to Caragungha all that was in their hearts to do against him; but Caragungha is the 'Bounding Elk' on the land, and in the waters he is a fish. Caragungha laughs at the snail-footed Haffas; they are day's trail behind him, and Caragungha is here. I have spoken."

The Indian gave a low, chuckling laugh, and glanced scornfully over the sun-gilt billows towards the distant shore.

"And where have the men of my brother's tribe built their wigwam," asked the Boy Pirate.

"The Seminoles have left Lake Macaco" returned the young Indian, "and are on the hunting trail, which has led them to the banks of the Indian river. The great chief, my father, has taken a white prisoner," said the Seminole, with a flush of triumph in his eye.

"And who is the pale-face?" asked our hero.

"A great chief—he is the 'Sea Eagle!'" answered the Indian.

"By my life, Gomez, another countryman of yours. Here's luck—a parallel adventure to the affair of Manuel Perez! A 'great chief' and the 'Sea Eagle,'" cried the Boy Pirate, briskly, "it is true he went by that title among the Seminoles, who, to tell you the truth, first suggested my name, the 'Red Raven'—a pest upon 'em for the shabby title; do you know who he is, Gomez?"

"Ombre de Dios!" cried the Spaniard, his dark, wild face lighting up with animation, "who but my old comrade Leon de Zamora! Why, captain, he commands a flotilla that would show fight to half the navy of these Southern States, and I understand that he has a treasure island in one of the mouths of the Mississippi that is worth the wealth of your Bank of England!"

"I mind him well, cap'en; a reg'lar tiger," rejoined old Brierly. "He was called the "Tiger," and shiver me, but he deserved the name. If we could only join company with him we might sweep the seas with a new broom; we should find the Pacific and the Atlantic reg'lar 'Tom Tiddler's ground.'"

"Right, old fellow!" cried the Boy Pirate, gleefully. "We must get him out of the hands of these redskins, but perhaps, like us, he has met with some disaster; I will interrogate our aboriginal friend."

The Boy Pirate addressed himself to the Indian.

"Is the prisoner of the great chief of the Seminoles a captive of the war-path? Is he doomed to die at the stake, or is he adopted in the tribe?"

"Sea Eagle was not taken on the war-path," returned the Seminole; "the pale chief was cast upon our shores when the Master of Evil had made the waters angry and had shattered the great canoe with his breath."

"He was wrecked in the white squall, Gomez," interrupted Christopher, "in the storm that proved so fatal to our gallant frigate."

"A cat has nine lives, but a 'tiger' has ninety, cap'en," said Brierly, laughing, "and, 'ceptin' your honourable self, blow me if ever I heard of sich a eel for slipping off the shoals as Don Zamora. He was took off North Carolina, put in irons, and shoved under hatches, but no hold could hold him. They put the 'Tiger' in a tolerable strong cage down

Maryland, but the banimal broke loose, and used his claws pretty freely, I was told."

"But, senor, let the captain question the Indian," said the grave Spaniard, impatiently.

"What will the great chief, my brother's father, do with his captive?" asked the Boy Pirate.

"The great sachems of the Yengeese, the chiefs of the pale-faces, have offered to give many blankets, fire-weapons, wampums and beeves to the tribe which shall give up the Sea Eagle into their hands, for he hates his white brothers, and though they are the children of the same Manitou, the Sea Eagle's beak is red with their blood. Yet tigers do not prey on their kind, and even the Seminole, whose life is war, takes not scalps from the brothers of his tribe!"

A pang shot through the Boy Pirate's heart as the Indian pronounced these words.

"And I stand reproved by this untaught savage!" he murmured.

His more callous companions looked at him inquiringly.

"The intention of the Indians is to sell him to the whites, who will hang him at once; he has been tried a dozen times," said the Red Raven, with a forced smile. "But what say you, comrades?—we will be first in the market; and if gold will not buy him, there is another medium of barter, other metals —lead and steel!"

"Hurrah!" shouted the men, who were heartily sick of the long calm, unbroken by any stirring incident, except that sad one—the wreck of the "Fortune of War," and panted for action.

"Let my brother come with me," said the Boy Pirate, leading the way to the cabin; "he shall be shown furs and blankets, fire-weapons and wampums. Perhaps the chief of the Seminoles will sell his prisoner to the Red Raven."

"It is good," said the Indian, bending his head, gravely, and following the Boy Pirate. "Caragungha does not forget that he owes his life to the white chief, but the sachems of his father's tribe are vultures that hunger for the spoil."

CHAPTER LIX.
THE DETECTIVES' VISIT TO THE THIEVES' DEN.

OUR scene is a loathsome den in one of those cesspools of ghastly infamy and squalid misery that are the canker-spots in the very heart of our queenly city.

Our scene is a thieves' ken.

It is a large square apartment, the plastered walls showing at intervals their ribs of lath, and everywhere defaced by the filthy material and the more filty emanations of sickening indecency and depravity scrawled upon the walls.

From the middle of the ceiling descended an iron bar, to which was attached a ring of leaden piping, from which flared spluttering jets of gas, illumining every corner and cranny of the bare and pitiless den with a fierce, coarse glare.

Around the walls were long tables, beer-stained and dirt-encrusted, to which, strange to tell, at intervals knives and forks were fastened by little chains.

The room was crowded with a motley crew— representatives of every grade of vice and misery.

Some were seated at the tables, laughing over a smoking meal, for the preparation of which Soyer had not been studied; while others, with lank cheeks and hungry eyes, look envyingly upon the gluttonous enjoyment of their heartless and more fortunate companions.

Some were stretched before a bright red fire that scorched all around, at one end of the room, though the place was as hot as the Black Hole of Calcutta. Perhaps there was something cheering in the bright red blaze; but be that as it may, around it were crouched many squalid forms of men and women in fœtid rags, smoking their short pipes, drinking strong drinks, and foully blaspheming.

Here and there were a few timid pretty girls, newly fallen, "fallen from their first estate" of innocence and purity, fallen, it may be, as victims to temptations against which they were almost powerless, and for transgressions that their own wounded pride and self-humiliation would have amply punished; but there they sat; they had taken their first plunge into the volcano of fiery debauch and evil companionship, driven to this pandemonium by the harshness of the police, or the roughness of parish officials; stray daisies trodden down in the miry streets; daughters and sisters become outcasts and pests. There they sat, in all their gentle, kind, impressionable womanhood, lambs among wolves, with the sot, the thief, the burglar, the brutal garotter, perhaps the murderer, the filching beggar, and the utterly lost and abandoned *pavée*.

Men were reclining or lying prone upon the floor, against the walls, or upon the settles, snoring in their deep slumbers.

The air rang with hootings, rough laughter, oaths, foul songs, cat-calls, and whistling, and every now and then the shrill harsh vituperation of a quarrelsome woman, or the deep growl of a sullen man, was put down by a general shout of "Stash that!" "Order there, order!"

In a corner, the most obscure one that he could find, sat an apparently middle-aged man; he was dressed in a shabby suit of corduroy, had a greasy fur cap pulled over his brow, from the edge of which hung down his grey hair upon his stooping shoulders; his head was bent upon his knees, his chin was unshaven, yet, despite his grey hair and bent gait, his unrazored chin and seeming dejection, there was something youthful in the expression of his countenance.

By his side, on the table, were strewn the ashes of a cigar he had been smoking, and a glass of brandy, but slightly diluted, stood within his grasp.

There was a large faced dial over the mantelpiece, and every now and then the young-looking old man would raise his eyes to watch the hands as they jerked along.

"Ware hawks," cried a thick voice across the room in a loud hoarse whisper.

There was a sudden hush.

Even the sleepers seemed to start in their deep sleep.

The sudden fall of silence seemed to waken them.

The women slipped from the knees of the rough scamps they were caressing with gin-inspired mawkishness; the burglars pulled down the ear-flaps of their hideous caps; there was a general hemming and coughing, and the young-looking old man drooped his head upon the table and affected to sleep.

The cowering crowd presented the appearance of a school-room of riotous boys on the appearance of a severe master.

The door opened.

Two tall, sharp-eyed, stern-faced men entered. They were dressed in plain clothes, but were easily recognisable as detectives.

Like butchers going the round of a cattle market; like hawks at an auction, or rowdy planters at a slave sale, the grave gentlemen walked along, looking into the coarse faces, which paled as they passed along.

Near the man of doubtful age whom we have more particularly described a young girl was cowering.

She was neatly dressed, and appeared to be quite unused to such scenes as the present.

The gentlemen stopped opposite to her.

A visible convulsive shudder shook the limbs of the young old man who was sleeping at the table. What could disturb his dreams?

The officer tapped the girl on the shoulder.

"What is your name?" he asked, curtly.

"My name, sir," repeated the poor girl, in a quivering voice.

She was evidently half fainting.

"Yes; your name; your *real* name. Mind, no

humbug—won't do," said the officer, in his searing way.

"Jane Lee. My name was Jane Lee," answered the poor girl, faintly, wringing her hands.

Too well she knew that she had "lost her name."

"Very well. Put on your bonnet, and come along. *Your wanted*," said the officer, in a freezing tone.

"Me, sir? Me wanted?" murmured the girl. "Why, what have I done. O God!" she went on, in a tone of utter despair. "To-night I stood on the dark steps; now I might be lying in the clear, calm waters. Ah! why didn't I go?" She burst into convulsive weeping.

"'Cos yer knowed a trick wuth two on it," said a sneaking thief, with a forced laugh, and a fawning grin at the " authorities." " Yer knowed that this yere good gemman was a-waitin' to take yer home in his carridge with the roy'l harms, to a werry large country 'ouse, where yer'll live like a lady. Lor, what luck!"

"Stand back, Chiffin," said the officer, pushing him aside.

"Lor, to see that creetur take on! I say, my covies, this yere genteel-bred gal wants us to believe this is the fust time. We takes, don't we?"

The scoundrel winked at his depraved companions, who laughed obsequiously.

The officer took the girl's arm.

She rose, and with a despairing look around, walked by his side to the door, through which she passed, followed by the other officer, who paused a moment, casting round him a thoughtful scrutinizing glance, and then followed his companion and the prisoner.

The departure of the unwelcome guests was announced by a loud derisive yell from the servile brutes that had quailed before the lynx-eyes of the detectives like hounds from the upraised lash.

The boisterous shout rung like heavenly music in the ears of the young-looking old man. He raised his head with a long sigh of relief, and set his cap on his grey locks, and once more turned his eye upon the clock; he drank off the brandy, and seeing the ill-conditioned fellow who served as potboy passing at the moment hailed him, and called for a fresh supply of the ardent stimulant.

He looked around boldly upon the surrounding crowd.

There was a sort of free-masonry existent among the thieves and vagabonds that precluded any outward display of suspicion or curiosity.

There was nothing in his appearance calculated to raise remark.

He presented the appearance of some lazy or unfortunate labourer out of work, or some sly cadger who had assumed the corduroys in hopes of raising compassion for a poor fellow without employment, and nothing more.

He must be well-known, his crime must be notorious and black indeed, to attract to him special attention among that circle of miserables, not one of whom but had almost forgotten the name of innocence.

The door opened, and a man appeared on the steps.

He was broad-chested, had a fierce-rolling black eye, and a large black beard; his skin was as dark as mahogany, he was wrapped close in a large blue cloak, and walked with a bold and careless air.

His appearance seemed to give cause of unusual interest.

There was a universal murmur of mingled awe and admiration as he sauntered down the room.

But as the new comer walked listlessly among the throng he quelled the inquisitive glances of the more curious with a glint of his authoritative, powerful face and flashing eye, and passed on with the coolest nonchalance.

The face of the distressed labourer flushed as he approached, and he extended his hand.

The stranger gripped it and then seated himself, without speaking.

"Curse it all, you're here at last!" said the other. "This infernal place! I'm almost choked."

"If you don't want to be quite choked don't abuse your harbour; its safe anchorage, and there is heavy weather outside, I can tell you, comrade," answered the other.

"My God! I suppose so," said the labourer, with a gasp; "but why have you been away so long?"

"My cruise was over a rough bottom and through shallow water, mate; I had to throw the plummet at every ship's length. But I've overhauled the prize, and all's well," said the stranger.

"That's well! I did not deceive you," said the labourer.

"Never do, or rather never try to do so; it's not to your interest to deceive me, even were it possible, which it is not," returned the man, coolly.

"I'll call for some more brandy," said the labourer.

"No, mate, not yet, this is so public and so vulgar; let us adjourn to the opera stalls."

With this he rose.

The potman bustled to his side.

"Joe, that Schiedam, is it all gone?"

"No, yer honour, there's a bottle or two in the cellarage."

"Bring one for me and some brandy for this gentleman. Show us to the stalls."

"Werry good, sir."

The man led the way.

He opened a little door in the wall, which the labourer had not before perceived, and ushered them into a small apartment, furnished with a couch, a square mahogany table, and a few fancy chairs.

From the ceiling hung a gas jet and lustres.

The walls were adorned with some tawdry tarnished giltwork, and several pictures that ought to have been burnt by the common hangman.

The stranger threw himself into a chair, and the labourer seated himself opposite.

He lighted a fragrant cigar and passed over the case for his companion to select another.

"And what do you think of my 'get-up,' Ralph?" asked the labourer, with a sickly smile.

"Hist!"

At this moment the potman entered with the drink.

When he had left the room the labourer repeated the question.

His companion looked at him critically.

"That's a good wig," he said, coolly.

"It ought to be. I paid stiff for it," said the other. "Then you think I shall do?"

"Yes. Very well for the crushers. You're nicely marked out for Foxley's newest novice."

"Why, when I looked in the glass I could scarcely recognise myself!" returned the labourer, briskly.

"Bah! How few people know themselves, mate."

"But what's the matter with me?"

"You dress too old."

"Ah, you know much about these things, no doubt."

"I do, some!" answered the other, dryly.

"Well, I have not been seen."

"As far as you know."

"I'm glad you've come," exclaimed the pretended labourer, with a deep sigh.

"I lost no time."

"That's true; but it seemed an eternity awaiting you in that hell-hole. Do you know what I thought about while I was there?"

"Something pleasant, I daresay."

"I thought of an old fable, a queer old fable I read when I was a boy. I forget the point of it, but Death convenes an assembly of all the vices, diseases, and miseries that scourge the slaves of earth. I thought that I was present in the court of Death, and that all those loathsome fellows and wenches were the evil agents described in the fable. I thought——"

"Curse such thoughts!" cried the other, fiercely. "Drink your brandy, mate, and while I run over these rolls of notes, and tell out this bag of shiners, here's something to amuse you. You're fond of reading, and this is no fable, but a summons from that very potent monarch you speak of, grim King Death."

With this, he threw a crumpled paper to his comrade.

The latter spread it out upon the table.

He recoiled, and sank back in the chair, with a faint groan, as his eye fell on the first words, printed in huge black letters—

"MURDER.

One Hundred Pounds Reward."

Then followed some details of the assassination of the Jew Nathan, and a minute description of the horrified reader, in whom, no doubt, the reader has recognised Daniel Harwolf.

The other sat telling over, with gleaming eyes, the notes and gold.

"That's pleasant sort of light reading," said the fellow, with a grin. "A nice way of being brought into notoriety. You see what a value your fellow-citizens set on you?"

"My God! I am lost! There is no escape for me," groaned Daniel.

"Good little piggy, do'ee come to have his throat cut," whined his companion, mockingly, and then burst into a gruff laugh. "Blood and thunder! Dan, you are not going to strike your flag when you are already dead afore the wind, and will soon leave these rocks and quick-shoals leagues in the wake?"

"I never was a coward till now."

"And now it's too late," said the other, sententiously.

"But what are your plans?"

"First, to invest the money."

"No, no! Let's keep it," said Harwolf, tremblingly. "It's always in some infernal negotiation of that sort that secrets come out. This man has money! Good! Where did he get it?—and, as a natural consequence—who is he?"

"I mean we should keep it, lad; but it must first be converted into something more profitable than itself, for kept in our pockets it will never give 'a breed of barren metal.' No dead money! I'm going to speculate. Nay, for that, it's all done but the stake down," said the man, with a laugh.

"And what do you mean to buy. Land?"

"Not land. In Newgate they find graves gratis."

"Curse your brutal jests," cried Harwolf, writhing.

"Keep down your dander, Danny, you're mine, ain't you? Come now!"

"And you're the devil," growled the other.

"Not so bad for a young one; I was called 'The Devil,' and a devilish good title too. 'Ralph the Devil,' a name, sir, that would make a penny-a-liner's fortune. Ralph the Devil, but I'm commonly known as 'Black Ralph.' And you, Harwolf, what cognomen shall be added to your patronymic. Harwolf the Jew-killer! Glorious! Glorious!"

"You brute, have done with that."

"Brandy's the best cure for conscience qualms; it's nothing but a throat disease that wants physicking according to the patient's taste! My dose is a nip of Schnapps."

"You don't believe in remorse?"

"What, for killing wolves and rats, bugs, fleas and money-lenders. A Jew, too! Ah, bah! You ought to be enrolled in the Legion of Honour as a public benefactor."

"You never feel remorse?"

"None but your whining half-saint whole-sinner ever does; fellows who are triple rogues for being half men, curs with not more grit than cucumbers. Phew! Remorse! what is it?"

"What should you think?"

"The hangman's shadow, nothing more. But to business, and a truce to philosophy, my learned Theban. I mean to invest the money."

"So you said. In what?"

"Hark ye, mate, in tight timbers and taut canvas, in iron and steel and saltpetre. Look here, this is the sign I mean to hang out."

The speaker drew out from his cloak the black banner of death, the flag of piracy, with its ghastly symbols dreadly embroidered on their sable and silken field."

"A pirate! Turn pirate!" cried Harwolf, aghast.

"Ay, mate; a pirate! Not an infernal snivelling, sentimental angel of mercy and retribution; not a dancing dandy of chivalry and gentility; not a Boy Pirate, a lady's duck that has the cheek to call himself a 'Rover'; not a lily-livered Boy Pirate; but a Man Pirate, sir! a real, roaring, ranting Rover! Black Ralph the Devil, the Rover of the Seas!"

> "The toby-man may praise his prads,
> The cracksman be the prince of pads,
> With fib well-lined and gleaming brads,
> All honour to all roving lads.
> I am what I am, and I don't care a d——,
> And I sail 'neath the Jolly Ol-iv-er!"

The scamp rattled his boots on the floor as he sang this doggrel, and throwing himself into a melo-dramatic attitude, shook out the black flag.

"But this is worse and worse," cried Harwolf. "We shall be run down sooner or later."

"Of course we shall," rejoined he; "but there's a long and merry cruise first."

"I won't go."

"Then stay and be hanged."

"But Talbot."

"Well?"

"You say you have made all arrangements."

"So I have."

"But for the crew?"

"'There's Adam Bell, and Clym of the Clough, and William of Cloudesley,'" sang the rover.

"Don't be an ass."

"No, I'll be a tiger, or a raven, or something of the sort. But all I have to say, Daniel Harwolf, is this—don't you disturb your weak mind about the affair at all, but follow whither I lead, and you'll find yourself in a comfortable berth, in a good ship of your own purchasing, with wide seas between your neck and the noose; enemies swearing at home, and friends awaiting ready to be plucked abroad. For we'll 'scour the seas for many a day'; and hark'ee, my soul, we'll begin with a fiery cruise in the Gulf of Mexico. And if I hear any more snivelling about a paltry Jew—pshaw!"

"There's one thing, Ralph—there's one thing."

"What is it?"

"You must help me in this."

"I will if I can, mate."

"I have an enemy."

"How extraordinary! I thought you had a hundred."

"I have a thousand in one."

"I take—a woman-enemy."

"Yes."

"Well, that's serious—I own that's serious. Samson had his Delilah, Hercules his Dejanira, Jack Shepherd his Edgeworth Bess, and Daniel Harwolf his Deborah the Jewess."

"Ah, you're right, 'tis she; the vindictive minx will hunt me like a Nemesis; 'tis indeed old Nathan's daughter; a good guess."

"Devil a bit a guess; look here;" Talbot pulled out a silk purse, the bulky sides of which were confined with a costly diamond ring. "That's a pretty present, isn't it?"

"Did she give it you?" asked Daniel Harwolf, turning deadly pale.

"I pretty considerably guess she did."

"But what for?"

"For my good looks."

"To betray me?"

"Something like it."

"Daniel Harwolf."

"Well?"

"We must look to that woman, mate."

"She's dangerous, is she not?"

"She will be fatal."

AN INTERRUPTION.

"Do you think so?"

"Women always are."

"It would seem so."

"They must be 'taken in time,' as the old nurses say with the Yellow Jack."

"Ha! do you mean taken off?" whispered Harwolf, leaning forward and clutching his companion's wrist.

"You ought to be taken off, for you are the most blood-congealing, muttering villain that ever thrilled the gallery in a New Cut theatre. You snivelling fool. There, there, I'll be civil; but it does rile me, Daniel. Just now you were whining about the old Jew, and now you're ready for settling his daughter."

"No, no, I don't exactly mean so," said Harwolf, with a sickly smile.

No. 20.

"No, my Luke the Labourer; but adjust your pretty cap on your fashionable wig."

"Curse the wig."

"Neither curse it nor dash it; you may well wear false grey hairs, for you'll never wear real ones."

"What bosh is this? We were talking——"

"About the Jew's daughter."

"She must be removed."

"Exactly so."

"But how?"

"A child may ask a simple question all the wise men of Goshen can't solve."

"Well, I'll pay anything; but take it out of my hands, as you say she must be removed."

"That's a *sine qua non*."

"When must it be done?"

"The sooner the better."

"Does that mean to-night."

"No; we'll first run up the river and have a look at the 'Albatross,' a nice little schooner that is anchored up Thames, and then we must pay a visit of condolence to the orphaned Jewess."

"You wretch," gasped Harwolf; "but what shall be done with her?"

"She must go a voyage."

"In Charon's boat," was the grim rejoinder.

"No, in our bonny 'Albatross.'"

"What, take her on board with us?"

"Even so."

"Talbot, you must be mad," cried Daniel, starting up from his chair. "But you are joking! What a fool you are!" he went on, sinking back again into his chair.

"Now, suppose I have fallen in love with the pretty Jewess."

"In love! You in love!"

"I don't believe in fear or conscience as you do, Master Daniel," said the rover, a darker shade sweeping over his dark face; "but I believe in love." His eyes softened. "I had a wife once, and if she had lived——" He suddenly paused, and then burst out boisterously—

"I am what I am, and I don't care a d——!
For I sail 'neath the Jolly O-li-ver!"

"But come, our conversation is getting long and wearisome; the night is waning," said Harwolf. "When, and where, and how, do you mean to dispose of the she-devil, Deborah the Jewess?"

"I mean to carry her off like a gay cavalier, and to take her on board to tame her down a bit, and make her a rover's bride."

"You cannot mean it?"

"I do mean it."

"Then we dissolve partnership at once."

"And I shall go over to my 'Poll and my partner Joe,' Tom Foxley the crusher, and Debby, the rich Jew's pretty daughter. Where's that paper? 'One Hundred Pounds!' 'Twill pay for the wedding breakfast, though, to be sure, Foxley will claim his per-centage."

The evil temper, so peculiarly the vice of the old steward and his reprobate son, rose and scintillated in the snake-like eyes of Daniel Harwolf.

His lips compressed and paled.

Black Ralph looked at him and saw he was venomous.

He respected him the more, however, as he thought the gleam of withering passion and ruthless malice betokened the power or quality he wanted his comrade to display.

"Come, come, mate, we yelping sea-dogs must have a snarl sometimes to cool our teeth. I meant no more than this—it is not policy to kill—call things by their proper names—to kill this woman, just now at any rate. Her death following her father's so quickly would excite suspicion, however delicately she was tripped over the border. Let her live, let her plot; let me help her. She has great faith in me, and I have great taste for her and her deep purse. I will cajole her to come aboard; you must disguise, or keep out of sight. She has gone on one hunt. Her father's murder will be the general cry, and when the nine-days-wonder has cooled down, there will be an end of it, and when we leave her 'far, far upon the sea,' why, you know we must consult the expediency of the case."

"I don't like the scheme."

"Why, man, would you rather have this tigress at liberty, raging up and down, seeking whom she may devour, or have the beautiful creature—and, curse me, if she is not a splendid piece of workmanship—securely chained and muzzled in the hold of our own vessel?"

"I wish she were dead," muttered Harwolf.

"Pish! she will die in good time—it's the worst thing she could do at present. But, have you heard the news about your father's leaving Frontemore?"

"No! He would never do that."

"But he will though. Perhaps there are associations connected with the place irksome to his sensitive mind. However, it's rumoured he will let the old place on lease and go abroad."

"Is it possible?"

"Possible and proper. He is a 'cute man, your father. Follow in his steps and you will go straight."

"To the gallows," muttered Harwolf, with a shudder.

"And now we'll away; but, ere we go, let's fill a bumper to our own success. Here's to Harwolf and Black Ralph, mates and brothers in exile—pirates—and real one's, black as their sable flag,—ruthless as their death's head and cross bones. And here's death and desolation to the mongrel Red Raven, and all such mawkish twaddlers. With a three-times-three—Hurrah for the Jolly Oliver!"

CHAPTER LX.

THE INDIAN'S TREACHERY.

IT should be explained that the date of the events recorded in our last chapter is anterior by a space of four months to the time when those we are about to narrate took place.

The "Red Raven" was anchored at the mouth of the Haffa river.

The crew of the pirate vessel had put down the boats, and the officers were mustered on deck, prepared for a run down the river on an expedition for the recovery of the celebrated corsair of Spanish America, the famous Don Leon de Zamora, from the Seminoles.

Among them, his earnest face turned impatiently to the shore, his arms folded, and his lithe body easily poised, stood Caragungha.

The Boy Pirate was below, about to ascend from his cabin. He had taken his farewell of Lilia, and had equipped himself in a handsome suit as a Spanish commander, wishing to render his appearance as imposing as possible to the savages.

Lilia advanced from her cabin and threw her arms about him.

"Oh! my husband," she said, "do not chide me, but I dread your absence more than ever."

"My darling, what folly," returned Christopher, laughing. "Our ship is manned from the luckless 'Fortune,' and carries an ample crew; and I mean to take only some thirty men with me—an army against the Seminoles. Besides, the tribe to whom we are bound are not hostile, and I have rigged my pinnace, and stowed in her a cargo of guns, spirits, and trinkery that would turn the heads of all the aborigines in Florida. Cheer up; these partings are to be regretted, but they can't be helped, you know; and oh! they make reunion so sweet."

The Boy Pirate tenderly embraced his wife.

"But I have such a strange foreboding, Christopher," murmured Lilia; "I know not of what, but of something terrible. Last night I dreamed of Harwolf."

The Boy Pirate started.

Lilia noticed this, and she looked up into his face inquiringly.

The rover laughed.

"I dreamed of Harwolf, too. But would you make such a bugbear of the miserable villain as to let him scare you in a dream? I dare say it was his ghost we saw, for I'll warrant the skunk was hanged long ago. Come, love, look up; I leave you with the better half of the best and bravest crew that ever reefed a sail. I have disguised my ship in the gear and have on board the papers of a Brazilian privateer, and my mission into the land is one of peace and purchase. So laugh at your fears and qualms, and amuse yourself with Ida till I return."

"Whom have you left in command?"

"Old Brierly, and Dick Caffyn."

"None could be better. But, my husband, listen to me."

"What is it, dearest?"

"Can you trust this youth?"

"Pshaw! the Seminoles are a brave and trustworthy people. Do not stay me, love; every moment I linger makes it harder to part. Good-by, my rover's bride. One more cruise, and then for our Happy Island!"

With a hasty embrace the Boy Pirate tore himself away and rushed upon deck.

He was received with a cheer.

The officers and men got into the boats.

They put off and soon reached the shore.

They found the land to consist of a wide plain, with an amphitheatre of volcanic hills; and a pool of mineral waters in the centre of the level glanced out like a mirror among a bouquet of flowers, for the whole plain was mantled with the most gorgeous blossoming.

They disembarked.

"Where are the lodges of the Seminoles of Macaco? Is the father of Caragungha in the wigwams of his nation, or does he dwell in the lodges of his own tribe on this side of the river?" asked Christopher of the Indian.

"This is the hunting ground of Khahuahua," returned the youth. "The chief of the Haffa dogs, of whom my brother has heard, lives far away, two suns on the straight path."

"Beyond the Charlotte river?"

"The Yengeese call it so."

"And must we pass the outpost of the Haffas?" asked Gomez.

"We have nothing to fear from them; we are too well armed to have the slightest cause for fear," replied the Boy Pirate. "The journey is a longer one than I looked for, but it is through a lovely country."

"Ugh," cried the Indian, suddenly clutching the rover's arm, and dragging him aside.

A deadly puff-adder was gliding along among the leaves and petals of the flowers at Christopher's feet.

"Werry lovely, cap'en," said Tom Garrod, the boatswain, "some werry purty specimens of hanimated natur."

The pirates laughed.

Christopher would have hacked the reptile with his cutlass, but the Indian intervened.

To the surprise and terror of the pirates, who shrank back, Caragungha stooped and took the venomous creature into the palm of his hand.

The serpent bristled, coiled, and raised erect his diamond-frosted head, his oblique eyes viciously glinting, his venom bags puffing out, and his long, black, forked tongue flipping round his hideous mouth; he gave a low hiss.

The young Indian fixed his eye with mesmeric steadiness and power upon the reptile, which immediately shrank down in closer coil.

Caragungha instantly ran to a flowery bank and deposited the serpent.

He returned smiling.

"An adder is the crest of the Seminoles of Macaco," he said, pointing to his breast, on which the picture of a serpent was tatooed. "The snake will not strike the Seminole children of the Great Spirit, though his bite is death to the Yengeese."

An incident parallel to the above is a fact, and the fearlessness of the Indians of Florida for creatures of the most terrible kind is truly wonderful.

The pirates lingered not many moments, but proceeded on their journey, a party of the men carrying the boats, for the pinnace had been left in the charge of the pilot Brand, who was commissioned to bring her along the coast to a certain place—a little creek among the Palm Islands, where the presents were to be unshipped.

No pen can describe the beauties of the country through which they passed; but in the thick forests were the lairs of ferocious wild beasts and the nests of venomous reptiles and insects.

There were pools infested by the alligator; boundless treacherous swamps and impenetrable fastnesses of brake and prickly cactus.

Towards the evening they reached the Charlotte river, which they forded with no little difficulty.

Here the goods were run down the river in the pinnace and brought ashore.

Christopher, who was well acquainted with the nature and the customs of the Indians, sent forward the youth Caragungha with a present to the wigwams.

He gave the young Indian full directions as to the purport and the conduct of the embassy, and then set about preparing for any emergency.

Huts were built of osiers and saplings, beneath which the blankets, arms, and trinkets were concealed.

Watch-fires were lighted and a flagstaff set up, from which the Brazilian banner floated grandiosely.

The officers were gathered together under a banana tree.

Some of the men strolled into the woods to search for fruits, others mounted guard or were at work in the little encampment.

"Look, senor; someone has come already from the Seminoles. It is strange Caragungha has not returned," said Gomez, pointing to a tall, feathered savage, who was advancing through the wood. "The lodges of his tribe must be nearer than he told us. The young villain is a traitor, I dare swear it."

"My life for his good faith," returned the Boy Pirate. "I know these people well, and even did I not, if there is anything in physiognomy our new ally is an honest fellow."

"I trust he may prove so," rejoined the Spaniard.

At this moment the Indian advanced and gracefully saluted our hero.

The Boy Pirate smiled frankly.

"Does my brother bring the words of counsel from the sachems of his tribe?" he asked, in the Indian tongue.

"My brother's thoughts pierce like the sunbeam into very deep waters: I am a chief among my people; my name is Haska, and I come from the lodges of Macaco."

"My brother is welcome. But why does he come alone? Where is the young chief, our guest, our friend? Why does he not return to his white brothers?"

"Bounding Elk is a great chief, he keeps his place at the council fire."

"Then no council has yet been held, and I am to wait for the answer?"

"My brother is right; the great fathers of the pale-faces have offered much treasure for the scalp or the body of the Sea Eagle, for it is to rescue him my brothers are come."

"Does my brother know that?" said the Boy Pirate, with a start, and casting a searching look upon the Indian, who answered calmly.

"The tongue of the pale chief is not forked, he will not deny it."

"Is this fellow a Macacoan or a Haffan?" asked Gomez.

"'Tis hard to say," returned Christopher, "though such bitter foes may be branches of the same tribe and speak the same language."

The Indian glanced keenly at the pirate.

His lips wreathed in an approving smile.

"The pale chief is subtle as a fox," he said, "he cannot be deceived."

"Not easily," returned the Boy Pirate, with a searching glance.

"Does not my brother know a chief of Macaco from a Haffan squaw?"

Christopher did not reply.

There was a pause.

"Let the pale chief look on this."

The Seminole shook back his blanket and laid his finger on his breast.

In blue punctures the figure of a puff-adder appeared branded upon the speaker's flesh.

"'Tis the crest of the tribe," said the Boy Pirate, turning to his companion, "these savage noblemen carry their arms and recognizances as well as the proud peers of Europe."

"Well, we have nothing to fear, senor," returned Gomez, "provided the men keep together, and do not wander from the fires."

"Let my brother sit by my side," said the Boy Pirate to the Indian, "let him smoke the calumet with me, let him tell me the words that the chiefs have spoken."

"Caragungha sent this tomahawk in token of faith," said the Indian.

"It is certainly his," said Christopher, "I know it by the quilled baldrick; I remarked its fine workmanship, and have handled it before."

"Good!" said Gomez, lighting a cigar, and leaning back against a tree as if he had dismissed his suspicions.

The Indian gravely lighted his pipe and handed it to Christopher.

The latter smiled, drew a long whiff, and passed it round the little circle.

The pirate officers gravely smoked in turn, and the pipe came back to Haska, who took it in his fingers and looked round with a quiet smile.

However, he did not raise the calumet to his own lips.

The men had staved in a cask of rum, preparatory to mixing their grog.

The Seminole pointed with the pipe to the little barrel and showed his white, gleaming teeth in a broad smile.

"Fire-water!" he said, curtly.

He rose and advanced to the little group round the cask.

One of the men poured out a horn of the stimulant and held it out to the Seminole.

The Indian took it and drank deep.

His eyes flashed and he turned towards the officers with a grin.

"Good!" he said, emphatically.

For a moment he leaned over the cask, and passed his fingers round the edge of it, as if admiring its construction.

He then rose to his feet, and reseated himself among the officers.

"How many will my white brothers give for the ransom of Sea Eagle?" he said, pointing to the kegs that were strewn on the ground.

"The chiefs of the Seminoles shall be contented," was the cautious reply.

"It is good," said the Indian.

"Senor, I do not like the looks of this fellow," said the Spaniard to our hero.

"Tush! We must be careful of treachery, but his united tribe would not dare to attack us boldly; and for him, why he is entirely in our power."

Cups were filled round, and the freebooters were soon in a jovial carouse.

But the Boy Pirate was not forgetful of the requirements of their position.

Gomez had not drunk with the others, but stood rather sullenly watching the proceedings.

Tom Garrod was entertaining a little knot of seamen with some of his amusing yarns.

One fellow was playing a fiddle as he sat on a cask, and some of the others were dancing hornpipes.

"All went merry as a marriage bell."

The Boy Pirate, at the head of a party of men, went the round of the encampment in order to see that every precaution for safety had been taken, and to relieve the pickets that had been placed at some distance from the watch-fires.

As Christopher moved along he was conscious of a sudden and unaccountable dizziness that caused the sky to appear whirling like a wheel above and the ground melting under his feet.

He and his subordinates were at the moment some distance from their companions.

The Boy Pirate turned his gaze upon his fellows.

Each was deadly pale, and seemed tottering under the effect of some instantaneous attack of paralysis.

Every object about our hero seemed revolving at a maddening rate. He could see but dimly the horror-stricken faces around. He thought that some of the men had fallen, that others had sunk on their knees; but he was not sure of the fact, for he doubted his own sanity.

For awhile the whirl continued to craze him, then all was bleared, then all dark. The Boy Pirate flung up his arms, and dropped like a stone to the ground.

Some of the men had fallen already; others, clutching their fevered brows, stumbled and reeled, and then sank down.

Not one retained his senses.

There was a wild cry from the watch-fires. The rest of the crew started up, and ran to aid their chieftain and comrades; but, stricken by the same plague, one by one they staggered and fell.

Gomez, who sat beneath the banana tree, leaped to his feet, and flew madly into the encampment.

He seemed stricken through with amazement.

He stood amongst his fallen companions as one among the dead!

Around him lay the forms of the gallant crew of the "Red Raven," in every conceivable position.

A hideous and prolonged yell broke the thrall of his transcendant horror.

He turned.

The keen edge of a flying tomahawk grazed the skin from his cheek.

The treacherous Haska stood before him.

He started back.

The villanous Indian had snatched up a musket. The long bright barrel, with its deadly muzzle, was level with the Spaniard's eye.

A fiendish grin of infernal malice sat on the countenance of the savage.

It was a fearful moment.

The Indian's long lithe fingers clutched the lock.

Bang!

With a chuckling laugh of demoniac triumph the red-skin had fired.

As the smoke cleared off and the treacherous savage lowered his piece, Gomez appeared stretched on the ground.

With another terrific yell, the savage drew his scalping-knife, and rushed upon the prostrate Spaniard.

What was his surprise when Gomez started up and flung himself upon him.

With marvellous presence of mind, the Boy Pirate's lieutenant had watched the instant when the Indian's finger contracted on the trigger, and had thrown himself upon the ground.

A desperate struggle ensued.

Gomez wrestled to draw his pistol from his belt.

Haska, seeing his intent, caught his arms, kicking, striking and writhing.

Gomez extricated the pistol from his leathern belt, and pointed it at the rascally Indian's head.

The latter, however, managed to clutch it by the barrel.

In the struggle it exploded.

The bullet flew through the long and straying hair of Gomez, tearing away an elf-lock.

The Indian was now on his knees, waving his tomahawk and shrieking his war-cry.

Gomez swerved back, rolled up the iron muscles of his arm, and brained the savage with the pistol-butt; and then snatching up the scalping-knife, plunged it through his throat.

Leaving his antagonist stretched in death, the Spaniard ran to the spot where the pirates had been carousing.

The rum-cask stood half-emptied.

Upon tilting it Gomez found that his suspicions were verified, for some narrow, whitish leaves were floating near the bottom.

What was to be done? Was the poison mortal, or was it but a trance-inducing narcotic?

Gomez had no time for conjecture.

The woods rung with furious and exultant yells.

Gomez was surrounded by feathered and painted savages.

On they came, a circle of terrible foes.

Whither should he fly?

Had he any chance of escape?

It would seem none.

Gomez was not a man to surrender his life without a struggle.

He seized a gun from a pile of arms and discharged it at that part of the living circle which was wavering down the rugged rocks.

He followed up this act by a daring assault, striking right and left with his gun.

He broke through the advancing crowd; shots were fired, missiles levelled at him, and blood-congealing yells rang round him.

But the savages were too intent upon the booty to think of giving chase to the solitary man who had escaped the effects of that treachery he had so well avenged.

They swept down upon the encampment, and with frightful cries were about to throw themselves upon the prostrate seamen, when a tall and handsome fellow stalked forward, trailing a gun in his left hand, while he held up his right in an authoritative manner.

The greedy Indians fell back at once, though rather sullenly.

"Let my brothers listen to Khahuahua," began the chief. "The Jaguar will run into the snare that is baited with flesh. My brothers have jaguars' hearts, but the beast has not their wisdom. My brothers know that the wide forests are full of game, so they will not chase one gazelle when they may kill the whole herd. My brothers will take the booty from the Yengeese, but they will not take a basket of wampums or a few lengths of blanket when they may have the great medicine-canoe of the pale-faces, and all its treasures. If my brothers kill the pale-faces they will lose their ransom; the Yengeese do not buy scalps. I have spoken."

"It is good!" cried the Seminoles, with general assent.

"Let the young men of my tribe," pursued the chief, "bind the pale-faces and take from them their fire-weapons, let them carry the Yengeese on their shoulders to the wigwams of Haffa; there are sumpter-mules and horses for the prey that the great warriors of the Seminoles have taken. I have said."

At this moment the Indians gave a yell of rage and execration.

A circle of them were gathered round the body of Haska.

They turned their fierce eyes from the dead spy to the apparently dead victims of his treachery and wielded their knives and axes with ferocious looks.

Khahuahua stood once more before them.

"Let not the eyes of my brothers be blinded with anger," he said, firmly; "the pale-face dog who slew Haska is in the bush; we shall find him and the spirit of our brother shall not cry in vain for his blood; he shall die at the stake of torment. I have spoken."

CHAPTER LXI.

BROTHER AND SISTER.

OUR readers will not have forgotten that Lord Hawksbury and his friend Sidney Manners had taken a cab and started off in quest of the unfortunate Lady Edgeforth. After an hour's ride the cabman, in accordance with his directions, pulled up at the corner of a street situated in an eastern suburb of London.

The gentlemen got out and, dismissing the driver, proceeded to a solitary house that stood secluded down a little lane on one side of the road.

The house was not large, but was neat and cheerful, though surrounded by a rather high wall.

The friends stood by the gate.

"My lord," said Manners, taking the nobleman's hand, and speaking in a voice of deep sympathy, "I fear that my worst suspicions are but too well-founded. I have no doubt that you will soon learn what you have so long desired to know. She whom I have traced to this house I doubt not is your sister, but you must be prepared to meet her terribly changed."

"Changed! I doubt not she has suffered much," returned the other.

"Oh, my lord! I cannot express to you my deep commiseration for this hapless lady."

"But are you sure that there is no mistake?"

"My lord, I think there can be none."

"Well, we shall not long suffer the misery of suspense."

With this his lordship rang the bell imperatively.

There was no immediate answer.

Impatiently he rang again.

Still no reply.

"Surely this is strange," said Lord Hawksbury. "There is a light in yon window; some one must be in the house. Why do they not give us admittance?"

"I do not wonder they should be cautious if all I have heard be true," returned his friend.

"Sidney," said the young noble, turning a pale face to his companion.

"Well, my lord."

"Is this a—a madhouse?"

"Why should you think so?"

"Speak! A strange idea wakes in my mind and tortures me. Sidney, my sister—she whom you think my sister—is she *mad*?"

"This house is not a madhouse," returned his friend, evasively.

"Confound the house! Sidney, if you love me speak honestly—is my sister mad?"

"Mad is a hard word, your lordship. I admit that great grief will often cause a temporary aberration of the intellect."

Lord Hawksbury struck his forehead, stamped his foot impatiently, and pulled the bell with impetuosity.

A step was heard crossing the courtyard.

The gate was cautiously unbarred.

A woman peeped out, holding the door tightly, and casting a scrutinizing, half terrified look upon the strangers.

"Is Mr. Silas Rye within; we wish to speak to him, we are friends?" said Manners, seeing the woman recoil.

"Mr. — leastways, Mr. Silas Rye, sir," said the woman, evidently with great unwillingness, "is at home, sir; leastways, he ain't exactly out, but he doesn't often receive visitors at this place, sir."

"Will you be good enough to give him that card?" said Lord Hawksbury, interrupting, "and tell him that my business is important."

"Please to walk in, sir," said the woman, curtseying.

They crossed a little garden.

The place seemed to be well protected from intrusion.

The walls were high, and bristling with broken glass. An immense mastiff crouched watchfully at the end of his chain, and several of the windows were barred.

Upon ascending the steps and entering the hall they encountered a thick-set man, decently dressed, but with a rather ill-conditioned air; he looked at them dubiously, as he said,

"Sure, yer honners, is it the masther you'd be afther seeing; faix, I'm thinking that he's jist gone out, for I've niver been near his room at all at all since this two hours, and as we're all alone in the ould place with niver so much as a female 'ceptin' Mrs. Martha ——"

"My good fellow, Mr. Silas Rye will be as glad to see us as we shall to meet him. Please give him my card at once."

The Irishman bowed awkwardly, and took the card from the woman.

"Och, murder, it a raal lord!" exclaimed the Irishman, in naive admiration, scanning the handsome young man as if he were a *rara avis* indeed.

"Sure, yer honner's lordship, I'll announce yer with all due riverence to the masther at once, good luck to ye."

The friends laughed.

"Thanks, there is no need to do so," returned Lord Hawksbury, "for here, as I conjecture, comes Mr. Rye himself."

Silas at that moment descended the stairs.

He bowed, and the young noble addressed him.

"Mr. Rye, I am sure you will pardon this intrusion when you learn the cause of it."

With a profound bow the Irishman had put the card into the hand of Silas Rye, who glanced at it for a moment with a flush of surprise and pleasure.

"Your lordship is most welcome," he said. "There is no one whom I have more desired to see."

He led the way upstairs, and ushered his guests into the drawing-room.

When they were seated Silas Rye looked penetratingly at the two strangers, and said,

"I think there is but one cause to which I can ascribe the honour of this visit," he began, hesitatingly, and pausing abruptly.

Lord Hawksbury looked at him, but did not speak.

"Mr. Rye," said Manners, "we have come to you, trusting by your means to unravel the mystery which surrounds the fate of a certain lady."

"Indeed, I thought so," said Silas; "but will you first inform me by what means you have acquired information which could induce you to seek out me. I thought I was unknown—indeed, I have lived so secluded of late that in some quarters I am even thought to be dead."

"It were long to tell, Mr. Rye," returned Manners. "Be assured you may trust us implicitly, and that I will not fail to give a particular account of the means by which I traced you out."

"Yes, yes," cried Lord Hawksbury, impatiently; "but at once to business. You know, at least you can divine, the object of our visit."

"My lord," said Silas Rye, a shade crossing his face, "I do not know what will be the result of this interview. I do not know in what light I shall be placed by the revelations you require of me."

"Whatever you tell us, Mr Rye, we will receive in strictest confidence," returned his lordship, "be in no fear that you have anything for apprehension. Speak freely."

"My lord," said the adventurer, bitterly, "I have been a great villain."

"Nonsense. I cannot believe it," replied the young noble. "If all that I surmise be correct, you have acted the part of a generous and honourable man."

"No, no; no, no," returned Silas, shaking his head, his cheek whitening with the horrors of recollection. You must not say so."

"Well, we are none of us perfect; few of us are better than worthless."

"But, my lord, I have more excuse than he, though very little, for my heinous guilt."

"Guilt!"

"Yes, guilt, my lord, guilt of the deepest dye."

"You begin to alarm me," said Lord Hawksbury, with excitement; "yet you may firmly rely upon the promise I have given you; whatever is in the past shall be forgotten, or at least forgiven, if forgiveness be required."

"You may forgive me," replied the adventurer, "but I can never forgive myself."

"For what?"

"For preferring crime to starvation."

"The offence is pardonable."

"Not so, my lord, yet there may be some palliation, for human nature is weak, and the temptations that lay in the path of utter poverty are almost insurmountable. God knows, I was very, very poor!"

"And who was your evil genius?"

"The Devil's chief agent on earth. I do believe him so, my lord," exclaimed Silas, vehemently.

"Andrew Harwolf!" said Manners, with emphasis.

"I often think that after all it is only the un-charitableness of the affluent that makes the needy dangerous," said Lord Hawksbury; "but you speak in enigmas, Mr. Rye. You know that my sister was courted by a man whom, through a family feud, my father deeply hated. The lovers met abroad, that is certain. My sister was then in a convent. Shortly after my sister disappeared, having, as it is now supposed, eloped with her lover."

"And he?"

"Was the unfortunate Lord Edgeforth, who left England so suddenly, and died in Germany—so it was reported—but I fear that report in this case is not worth much. I have spoken with many mutual friends of mine and Lord Edgeforth's, and they all assure me that he was never heard of on the continent throughout that fatal season."

"But, Lady Edgeforth," said Manners; "she remained in England, and, after the alleged decease of her husband, married his land-steward."

"Do you believe that story, sir?" asked Silas Rye.

"If we did should we be here on such a mission as the present?" rejoined Manners.

"Lady Edgeforth is not my sister," said Lord Hawksbury; "the person, I mean, who is Harwolf's wife, and passes in society as the widow of his late master."

"And we have reason enough to think that the real Lady Edgeforth is yet alive, and that she is in your keeping."

"You are not deceived," returned Silas Rye; "she is here."

"I thought so," cried Manners.

"My sister here!" exclaimed Lord Hawksbury. "My dear, kind Eleanor—my own sweet sister. O God, how strange, how cruel. But, sir—is she?—that is—I cannot speak what I surmise—has the great grief that fell upon her when her husband died passed without injury to her intellect. Can it be that her enemies have kept her in their power so long and she a sane woman."

"My lord," replied Silas Rye; "it is useless to deceive you. Ever since the day—well, I mean since the time of her husband's death—has Lady Edgeforth been in a state of delirium or of apathy."

"O Heaven! there is foul play here!" cried Lord Hawksbury. "My poor, poor sister! But this matter shall be well sifted—the guilty shall not escape."

"For my share in the crime I am willing to pay the penalty," returned Silas, sighing heavily; "but I would counsel your lordship to beware of hasty measures. This Harwolf is my sworn foe, and I am his bitterest enemy. Yet," he went on, smiling grimly, "by this time he has forgiven me, for he thinks that I am dead, and that I am alive he will find to his cost—alive to work his ruin."

"He shall be brought to justice," cried the young nobleman. "But, my sister; where—where is she?"

"I will take you to her, my lord."

"Oh, yes; at once."

"Mr. Rye," said Manners; "Lady Edgeforth's child? Is this Daniel Harwolf really the heir to the estates of Frontemore?"

"No; he is an impostor."

"I was sure of it; there is no trace, no shade of resemblance between him and the late Lord Edgeforth."

"But my sister; let me see her," said the young lord, eagerly.

Silas Rye led the way.

With sad faces his two guests followed him.

They ascended the staircase, and paused before the door.

Lord Hawksbury was deadly pale; his teeth were clinched, and he started as a long, low wail broke on his ear.

The mournful sound was followed by other utterances still more heart-breaking in their suggestiveness of the "poison of deep grief"—the snatch of a merry song, sung plaintively; a long, warbling, wild laugh.

Silas opened the door and they entered.

Everything that money could do to alleviate the sufferings of the helpless lady had been done.

The room was elegantly furnished, and with no little display of taste.

The windows were barred, but around each barrier weaved the tendrils of some creeping plant.

There were cheerful pictures, mirrors, and cool and pleasant drapery.

Lady Edgeforth was seated on a couch, her head leaned on her hand.

She was carefully and handsomely dressed.

Her favourite spaniel lay in her lap.

She raised her face.

There was something strange, weird, unearthly in that pale, wan face; those large, wild, and expressionless blue eyes; the meshes of that long yellow hair.

Lady Edgeforth rose gracefully and advanced with a quaint but sweet smile.

She leaned upon the arm of the adventurer and looked upon his strong, stern countenance with an air half confiding, half appealing.

"They have not come to take me away," she said, timidly, looking with a doubting glance upon the visitors; "I am quite well here; you are Greatheart and I am Mercy or Christiana. I have no fear of the lions when you are with me. Some people are mad and some people are thought to be mad. When one is considered mad one is shut up in a prison or carried off, sometimes through thunder and lightning, sometimes through the air and over town and tower. Who is that man?" she said, abruptly, pointing to her brother.

"My dear lady, a good friend; one who will cherish and protect you. You are not afraid of him?" said Silas Rye, gently.

"No, I am very brave," replied the poor lady, drawing herself up. "Sometimes they tell me that I am not dead, and that all the faces and all the voices I see and hear are only the chimeras of my fancy. If that is true I wish they would kill me. Kill me—kill me, as they killed him."

She lowered her voice gradually as she uttered the last sentence till it fell to a thrilling whisper.

Lord Hawksbury seemed stricken with horror.

"Killed him!" murmured Sidney Manners. "A strange fancy that, Mr. Rye. May there not be 'method in this madness?'"

The adventurer started.

"I cannot be answerable for the idle and wandering phases of delirium," he said, quickly, "but perhaps if your lordship spoke to the poor lady it might have some effect for good."

Lord Hawksbury advanced and gently took his sister's hand; she yielded it passively, but looked into his face intently and suspiciously.

"My sister, Eleanor," he began, in a broken voice, "do you not know me? Can it ever be that you have forgotten me? No—no. Look on me—I am your brother."

"My brother!" said the lady, after a pause, lifting her hair with her fingers, and fixing a steady look upon his face. She clapped her hands and broke into a laugh as she replied, "I know your riddle; 'all men are brothers.'"

"Sister, my sister!" cried the young lord, wringing his hands distractedly.

"Ah! sister again. No. Why—why should I have a brother? That he may be struck down at my feet as was my husband. Oh! I am so weary—so weary of that one remembrance. Why should I have a brother?" The poor lady paused for awhile, and then again gleefully laughed and clapped her hands.

"Yes, yes, I will have a brother; shall I tell you why? Come near, I will whisper."

She drew her brother to her side and whispered in his ear—

"Because—because I am mad." She drew back with a look of childish satisfaction. "Good; yes, you shall be my brother. Ophelia, whom I pitied so, was mad, and she had a brother; she had a father murdered, but not before her eyes."

Lady Edgeforth stood suddenly still, as if in deep thought.

Silas Rye would have spoken, but Manners held up his hand in token of silence.

"Yes," said Lady Edgeforth, with glowing eyes, and drawing herself up with the air of a tragedy queen, "she had, indeed, a brother; one who swore to avenge her upon the murderer, 'to cut his throat i' the church'; but that is profane. If my husband will not come to me I will go to him. Oh! soon, soon! Very, very soon!"

She laid her hand on her heart and sighed heavily.

Lord Hawksbury threw himself into a chair, in speechless agony of mind.

He started up.

"Since the world began," he cried, bitterly, "was there ever aught so wicked, so cruel, so damnable as this! But I will exceed all that went before in the world's history in the remorseless persistence of my plans of vengeance. Yes! I will hunt him down, the treacherous, murderous ingrate, for he is guilty of Lord Edgeforth's murder. I cannot doubt it."

"Calm yourself, my lord," said Manners, in a tone of deep sympathy, "there is little fear but that, with Mr. Rye's assistance, we shall be able to bring the wretch to justice; meanwhile, we must do all that we can for poor Lady Edgeforth."

Lord Hawksbury had walked to the piano.

"Sidney," he said, "I have read in a hundred novels and poems that associations of childhood will return and bring memory with them to the disordered mind at the sound of old familiar music. Let us try."

With great feeling and with masterly execution he touched the keys of the instrument and played the accompaniment of the beautiful Scotch song, "The Flowers of the Forest or A' Weed Awa'."

Lady Edgeforth seemed startled, and listened as if her soul hung upon the notes.

Lord Hawksbury sang.

With deep, clear, but quivering voice he poured forth the simple lament, the tears gleaming in his fine pleasant eye, his hearers standing thralled by the melody and deeply touched by the affecting scene.

Lady Edgeforth drew nearer and nearer to the side of the musician.

Silas and Manners remained quite motionless, watching her with intense interest.

She kneeled by her brother's side and looked up wistfully in his face.

Lord Hawksbury did not cease, but went on singing, fearing lest the charm should be broken.

He went on singing though he was almost choking with emotion.

At length he broke down.

Lady Edgeforth gave a scream and flung her arms about him.

"Home! home! home!" she cried, exultingy. "It is all past! You are indeed Arthur, my brother! It was all a long fearful dream!"

Lady Edgeforth fainted in her brother's arms.

Silas rang the bell.

A staid matronly woman entered.

She looked with surprise at the strangers, and then, with great devotion, applied the usual restoratives to the poor lady, but no signs of returning consciousness rewarded her efforts.

Oiny Macarne was summoned, and with his assistance Lady Edgeforth was borne tenderly to her own room.

"Mr. Rye, I shall return tomorrow; my sister must be removed to my seat in Norfolk, and then you must fulfil your promise and give me your assistance in hunting down this wolf."

"My lord, I am yours," returned Silas. "I have sworn to see justice done to this poor lady, whom I have protected at some risk to myself, and to whom I am at the best a most worthy keeper."

"But the child," said Manners.

"The son, he is no longer a child, but a man; a great man too—one who has gained a terrible renown."

"What do you mean?"

"All that your lordship has seen of this tragedy, black as it is, is noontide brightness to the gloom and horror of the rest."

"But my sister's child—who and what is he?"

"He is fallen, my lord; fallen beyond hope of redemption."

"Good Heavens! it cannot be that he is a felon."

Silas did not reply.

"Speak, man; tell me the worst."

"The rightful Lord Edgeforth," replied Silas, "is known and feared as the BOY PIRATE!"

CHAPTER LXII.

DEBORAH, THE JEWESS, ENTRAPPED BY BLACK RALPH.

ABOVE Woolwich, and where between the level and marshy plains the broadening Thames runs freely onward to the ocean, gathering breadth and strength the farther it bounds on its eternal way from the dense and polluted streets of the monster city, a strong taut ship lies quietly at anchor.

It is a vessel more remarkable for strength than beauty; its hull is heavy and broad, though its masts are taper and rakish.

A boat has put to land, manned by a number of fierce, determined-looking fellows, smart and well-dressed, but without exception sullen and ferocious looking.

In the stern of the boat are two officers.

The boat comes close beneath the hanging bank.

The two officers disembark.

They are both strong and manly in development.

One is tall, and has an intensity of darkness in his face that is almost shadowy; his skin is bronzed, his eyes are black as jet, and he has a long, silky, black beard.

His companion is an ungainly, ill-conditioned man, with a sinister expression and a subtle, cautious air that ill accords with his apparent youthfulness.

"And she will come, think you?" said the latter, as he and his fellow-officer got out of the boat.

"Come! Yes, as a she-bear that scents her cubs. I never saw such a venomous harridan since I learned to take things coolly, and to look upon slaughter as a thing at first painful, then exciting, and finally indifferent—which I do think it is. For murder—well, what would you have? Hunting and eating imply murder; so does the duellish honour and the warrior's heroism. Even religion in some countries, and supreme justice yet in our own, imply murder. Pooh! 'tis but cutting a very short string and saving patients a deal of needless suffering—this useful, ugly murder!"

"Why do you read me such a homily as this?" returned the other, with a visible shudder; "especially at this time."

"Well, such philosophy as I am preaching is acceptable at all seasons," returned the other. "Curse it all! what will you do when our merry barque is once at sea if you begin your career so squeamishly, Master Remorse?"

"Curse you for a fool!" growled the other. "No name could be less applicable than that to me. Remorse! No, Ralph, 'tis not remorse that torments me."

"What is it, then; cowardice?"

"Ha!"

"Because I hope it is not fear," the other went on, coolly; "for, let me tell you, fire in the hold or a leak in the bottom of the ship are less fatal than fear in the breast of one of our powder-monkeys. Remorse you will soon cure of, but fear's incurable."

"I am no more a coward than I am a braggart."

"Well, Master Harwolf, I have no reason to despise you for want of mettle. I have heard of your fierce encounters with our great rival the Red Raven, and though you have not always been vic-

torious, you have generally displayed great prowess. But come, my sage, let us shut the books and talk with our own tongues."

"But, why did you bring me ashore?" asked Harwolf. "Would it not have been better I should have stayed on board; when this Jewess comes—if she be fool enough to fall into such a trap—she will recognise me at once."

"And if she does?"

"Why, of course she will scream and denounce me."

"Well, I'm no beak, my crew are not crushers," returned Black Ralph. "This is a lonely spot. 'Twill all be managed admirably, and I don't care about leaving you on board till we have put many a league between these shores and ourselves. You might weigh anchor and slip off."

"You are a villain to suspect me."

"I should be a fool if I did not; by-and-by we shall be dependent on each other, and then I can be more confiding; meanwhile, prudence is prudence. But where's this woman?"

"What need is there to bring this infernal Jewess blood-hunter on board at all. Do you want to carry danger into our very midst, and make a pet of it; you might as well have a live shell in the magazine as a woman aboard. They say the Boy Pirate has been sheerly ruined since he took away my sweetheart; hell take him! He fights now only with brigands, pirates and slavers; he has become a redresser of woman's wrongs, and is a milksop altogether."

"Well, there's no fear of our degenerating," cried Ralph, laughing. "We'll tread our deck with light hearts, though it run as red as a slaughter-house—

"For this was for a wench,
And this was in a trench,
When fighting with the French,
To the sound of the drum."

"Hush! Here comes the lady," said Harwolf, nervously. "Well, I shall get into the boat, and I don't see what need——"

"Oh, question not the need," said Ralph. "But don't pull the white cap over your face with your own hands, though your cheeks want covering; they are as white as the foam in a header. Don't be an ass, Dan—

"Come what, come may,
Time and the hour run through the roughest day!"

The lady was now advancing, dressed in deep mourning; she held her way along the top of the bank, and glanced about her with looks expressive of alarm and distrust, for the appearance of the surrounding country was extremely desolate.

As she drew near, Ralph Talbot advanced to meet her.

"My dear madam," he said, with a grave bow, "you are come most opportunely. Mr. Foxley is aboad, with several detectives in plain clothes. Your presence is needed in order to identify the murderer, as it seems the rogue gives a very plausible account of himself."

"Indeed! I will be thwarted by no obstacle," returned Deborah, "for I am resolved to carry out my mission of vengeance against my father's murderer. But why did you appoint a rendezvous at such a dreary spot as this?"

"Because, my dear lady, the ship lies off this bank. By the road across the fields we are not far from the town. You are looked for impatiently on board. A man—one of the crew—is suspected, and as the time is due for the ship to sail, the skipper is anxious to get the man identified."

"Well, let us begone," said Deborah, nothing doubting when she saw the boat's crew resting on their oars.

Harwolf had slunk to the stern of the boat, and got behind one of the oarsmen, in such a manner as not to be visible to the Jewess, who sat with her back to him.

The boat pulled steadily through the tide, and Deborah was soon on deck.

THE BOY PIRATE ESCAPES WITH THE CAPTIVE MAIDEN.

She looked around her with some surprise.

Though disguised as a brigantine the ship was evidently armed; the deck was cleared, and the men drawn up along the forecastle.

The fellows received the boat party with a general grin.

Black Ralph turned a fierce look upon them, and then touching Deborah's arm, led her down into the state-cabin.

This saloon was very elegant, richly gilded, veneered, floored with sandal-wood, and panelled with mirrors. There was a rich, thick carpet on the floor; voluptuous but masterly pictures adorned the walls; there was a couch, a piano, and a book-case.

Deborah entered, expecting to meet the captain, and thinking it rather unmannerly that he had not come on deck to meet her.

No. 21.

"Dear Miss Deborah, I must beg a thousand pardons," said Ralph Talbot, with a dry smile. "But I am quite unable to account for the captain's want of gallantry. I thought to find him here, perhaps he is inspecting the work in the stowage. Pray be seated."

Deborah began to feel a little suspicious and terrified; she made no answer, but seated herself on the little couch, and looked about her with some admiration at the richness and elegance of the handsome cabin.

She started.

The clash of a strong lock into its bolt made her rush to the door. She was locked in the cabin.

In great dismay she flew round the walls and looked from the window, but she was hopelessly a prisoner.

With a sickening qualm of horror, and with dread anticipation, she sank down upon the couch.

The sound of deep voices, monotonously singing out, " Cheerily ho! Heave ho!" was heard, mingled with the cranking noise of the windlass. Presently the sluggish craft was freed from its moorings, and floated slowly and heavily through the strong rushing tide.

The anchor was weighed, and Deborah a prisoner.

CHAPTER LXIII.

THE BLACK PIRATE AND HIS CREW.

BLACK RALPH was seated on a gun.

Daniel Harwolf was standing gloomily by his side with folded arms.

The ship was sailing far out of sight of land, forging before the speeding breeze with full and fluttering sails.

Black Ralph was handsomely dressed in naval uniform, and certainly looked the pirate to perfection.

His sun-tanned skin, his long, glossy black hair and beard, his great, fierce, rolling eyes, his gruff laugh, his authoritative stride, his reckless devilry and evident fearlessness, rendered him a very fair specimen of a very foul class.

He was armed to the teeth, and in his hand he held a long, slender, ivory-mounted pistol, with which he was heedlessly toying.

His dark face beamed with an expression of exultation and savagery as he harangued the crew.

The fellows were the most repulsive-looking scamps imaginable. They were picked men, however, fierce as bull-dogs, and equally unyielding; they were outlaws for the most part, deserters from the service, and wretches who had been Talbot's companions on town and turf in better days.

The men stood, glass in hand, attentive for their leader's speech.

"Comrades and hearties," said Black Ralph, commencing with great pomposity; " unaccustomed as I am to public speaking I venture to address this honourable assembly, fully relying upon its kind indulgence for my want of eloquence, and its ready appreciation of the vast difficulty and disadvantage against which I labour, through being called upon to address an audience so distinguished for intelligence and high principles. My pals, I learned that at an election dinner; but I am going to speak plain words to plain men. I am going to put hard facts before hard men, for neither am I a soft-hearted, thin-skinned, methodistical Boy Pirate, nor are you a crew of twaddling, sentimental Quixotes, with white liver and soft hearts, fellows that are the worst abortions in nature, half saints, half devils, only I thought I'd better begin with a flourish, for I am not a man of one style; I can declaim like Demosthenes, exhort like Parson Leatherlungs, reason like Lawyer Shark, and talk dry truth and common sense like Ralph Talbot, who has the honour to be by free election your commander. Pass the grog, lad."

The men laughed and handed over the can.

"It matters not," he went on, " from what causes we have, each and all, been induced or compelled to take up this course of life, to throw down the gauntlet against the world, to set ourselves free from the bondage of a law that persecutes instead of protecting us when we happen to be without money, but, here we are, lads, pirates on board our rover-ship, knights of St. Olive, under our black banner, banded together for mutual aid and mutual strength, in harmony with each other but in open warfare with all the world; but let me tell you this, I will have no remorse, no regret, no piety, no infernal humbug aboard this ship; some of us were once tame dogs, whom the snubs and wrongs of our richer fellow-creatures have turned into tigers. But, mark ye, comrades, we are tigers, and as such we leave behind, with old times and old associations,

ruth and pity and every respect for humanity; except as regards each other. The softest of us will soon harden, and will soon think no more of cutting a throat than of squeezing an orange. Even the pious ordinary will lead us to the gallows. Why should we be less unfeeling than our foes? Enough of that, comrades. I have had some experience in this sort of life—the very jolliest a man can follow. But no happiness on earth is perfect. We have many perils and hardships to look in the face, but we are not to be stared out of countenance by shadows and fancies; we must be jolly! We must pack all the fun and self-indulgence we can into our short, merry cruise, but we must have no quarrelling; we must have no jealousies among ourselves, and I exact subordination. If any among you is better able to command than I, elect him in my place, and I will serve him. But, after this day, I will have my lightest order carried out by the most desperate among ye. I will never repeat a command; if my first word is not obeyed I shall at once give the mutineer his discharge—from the muzzle of my pistol. I don't speak this to threaten, but to show you that I am one you can depend upon, for your best interest and safety lies in my firmness; is it not so?"

"Right, cap'en, right; we will serve true," returned the men, and they cheered.

"Let us drink to our fortunes, mates; but remember in your toasts that I am Black Ralph, the Man Pirate, and that this ship is not the beggarly ' Red Crow,' but the ' VULTURE!' "

The pirate gang cheered vociferously.

"And now, hearties," continued Black Ralph, " I should not wonder if you are reckoning upon going at once into action. You shall not be disappointed. This ship, thanks to the master, is well-appointed; but we must refund the first outlay: and the real 'Tom Tiddler's Ground' for a gentleman-rover is the Spanish Main."

"And my hated rival, the cursed Boy Pirate, cruises on the Brazilian coasts," said Harwolf.

"Well, the Man Pirate shall thrash the Boy Pirate; and the ' Vulture' shall swoop on the ' Raven,' and leave him without a feather to fly with. And look ye, my hearties, we will find the raven's nest. This crow is a regular magpie for bringing home silver spoons. I think I have got a clue to the discovery of his hiding place—his treasure island; and, sirs, one cruise will make us or break us; for, as I have told you, I mean to adopt no half-measures. Not I! We will sweep all before us. And now, lads, give yourselves up to jollity. Don't get too drunk; don't play too deep; don't swear too loud, and don't quarrel too vindictively. Fill up! Thrice round ' Hurrah for the Jolly Oliver!' Up with the ' Black Vulture,' and down with the ' Red Raven!' Long live our worthy master Daniel Harwolf, and a scourge to flog all maudlin Boy Pirates from the sea. We, and we only, will be kings of the main! for,

' The Vohrking of old,
  Was as jolly as bold ;
His hand it was red, but so also his nose ;
  For his ship was his steed,
  And he quaffed his rich mead,
From the brewer's best vat, in the skulls of his foes!'

And now, lads, I leave ye for awhile; be merry and wise."

The men laughed, and responded with a cheer.

All on board gave themselves up to riotous merriment.

Black Ralph went below.

He opened the door of the cabin and stole in.

Deborah rose and encountered him.

"Sir, what does this mean?" she said to the pirate, with a piercing glance. "Am I a prisoner? Can it be possible that you are acting a treacherous part against an orphan girl, who is seeking to do justice to the memory of a murdered father? Are you an ally of my father's assassin? Is it your intention to kill me?"

"Really, Miss Deborah, I am horrified at the

insinuation," returned Black Ralph, with a hearty laugh. "My intentions towards yourself are most honourable. Murder you! for shame; unless, indeed, you might be the heroine of a new version of 'A woman killed by kindness.' Not so, my adorable Deborah—my warrior prophetess! I am your Baruch. You shall share all my triumphs; nay, monopolise them! A day—or a week, perhaps, if you are very cruel—and every trace of anger will have passed out of your own kind little woman's heart. In your eyes my slight peccadillo of having decoyed you into this golden cage will be overlooked; for faint heart never won fair lady, and all is fair in love and war. So 'Buss me, my bonnie bride,' and let's go on deck and see my fellows dance."

With the coolest nonchalance the ruffian approached the beautiful Jewess, took her soft hand, and placed his arm around her waist.

"You unparalleled villain," she cried. "Who and what are you?"

"A man that would turn the head of every romantic or sentimental girl that is in the kingdom. You are both, for you are a woman with a mission—a very pretty mission, too, I think. Phew! all balderdash! 'Your father lost a father, that father lost his.' The mission of 'Deborah the Avengeress!' There, leave that to the detectives, to the Chief Justice, and old Calcraft! Turn from a dead father to a living husband, and rejoice in the exchange."

"Oh! Heaven defend me," cried the girl. "Why was I born so weak that I cannot kill this monster?"

"Why were you born so strong that I am slain by the searching light of those glorious orbs, the soul-piercing thrill of that cherubic voice? But come, we'll talk prose for a bit, my darling; three words will explain your position—I came, I saw, I was conquered; you listened, you believed, you are kidnapped! Fact, Debby; don't be galled. I was too modest to hope you would listen to my suit, too desperate to risk a refusal, so I cut the Gordian knot I could not unravel; I enticed you to the shore and have carried you off triumphant."

"And the wretch who murdered my father? You villain, your story was all a black lie, and you knew nothing of him or his whereabouts."

"In that respect I did not deceive you; I have him on board, and we'll see him hanged every day for your special diversion; only do show your wisdom by submitting to your destiny and reconciling yourself to one whose worst fault is that his immense love makes him perfectly unscrupulous. You *must* love me, Debby; I shall make you love me, so be agreeable and let us go on deck, and suffer me to introduce to you my gallant crew, who will henceforth adore you as their queen."

"And what are you," said Deborah, fiercely, controlling her shame and passion, for she was a brave, high-spirited woman; "are you a merchant, or do you disgrace Her Majesty's service?"

"Well, I am a free-trader, and I am no disgrace to any service, for I am a thorough seaman, brave, handsome and good-natured, rich, potent and particularly prepossessing, only I'm a devil when I'm roused."

"But under what flag do you sail; is this an English ship?" asked the girl, with white lips but unquailing voice.

"I sail under flags of all nations, but I will show you my true colours."

With this the outlaw drew a folded banner from the wall and unrolled it.

It shook out, and he displayed it on the floor.

It was a pall of black silk emblazoned with the skull and bones, beneath which, on a yellow heraldic shield was displayed the Black Vulture with outspread wings.

Deborah gave a wild shriek, and buried her face in the pillow of the couch.

"Are you afraid of these symbols? Do not think, Deborah, that because I carry this flag at the masthead I am forced to carry black thoughts in my heart. We will have a jolly life, my bride; and

'you shall walk in silk attire,' and I shall keep a treasure island, whither we may resort at intervals, and we will draw deep from life's sweetest pleasures. Use, Debby, habit! You will soon learn to wonder that you could even have lived any other life than that from which there is now no escape. So, cheer up, my 'winsome lassie,' for the old times, they are by-gone—for the future, it glows brilliantly in prospect—for me, I am resolved to make you a happy and enviable woman, if you are not such a fool as to oppose me in my good designs."

"Oh, hush! hush!" cried the Jewess, pressing her forehead in an ecstacy of despair. "Will you do me a favour?" she asked, suddenly, in a calm, cold voice.

"I only live your slave; what is it, Debby?" asked Black Ralph.

"Leave me! Oh, leave me now!" said the poor girl, distractedly.

"It's the hardest task you could inflict upon me, my sweetheart—but I'll go. When I see you again, I trust I shall find you reasonable and reconciled—till then, my love and homage."

Black Ralph made a sweeping, theatrical bow, and passed out of the cabin, humming as he mounted the gangway—

"I am what I am, and I don't care a d——
For I sail 'neath the ' Jolly Ol-iv-er!' "

CHAPTER LXIV.

THE VILLAGE OF THE SEMINOLES.

The wigwams of the Seminoles of Haffa were built along the banks of the river, from the name of which they derived their distinctive cognomen.

The scenery about the little settlement was very grand. There was a sublimity impressed upon the snowy crests of the towering mountains, a tender beauty enshrined in the flowery crypts of the tree-aisled forests, a profundity of rich blue in the glassy waters of the broad river.

But in spite of the rich tints of the sky, the vivid gorgeous colouring of the foliage, the translucent purity of the ample stream, the wigwam was a pandemonium of chagrin and misery to the unfortunate Boy Pirate and his crew.

The herb which the villanous Haska had steeped in the rum-cask was a narcotic of miraculous potency, and it had such deadly effect upon some of the crew that they had died in the trance induced by it.

Christopher himself was pale and wan, and it was some days before he thoroughly recovered from the effects of the fatal potion.

The prisoners were separated.

Some of them were removed to a large hut in the centre of the wigwams, which was surrounded night and day by a crowd of Indians armed with muskets.

The chiefs had determined to keep the Red Raven in rigorous custody, but were all of opinion that it would be better to treat him with some leniency in case of his being able at some future time to retaliate present injuries.

Their object was to get a heavy ransom for him from the vessel, and for this purpose it was resolved in council that a considerable number of principal leaders and chosen warriors, armed with muskets and native weapons, should be sent to the shore to signal the "Red Raven," and to make proposals for the delivery of the prisoner, and the payment of the heavy price they intended to exact for him.

The Boy Pirate had been removed to a lodge near that occupied by the chief, and to his surprise and pleasure found that it was the prison of the captive privateer, for so, indeed, he was, as he bore papers from the government of one of those little independent republican states that are found along the coast of South America.

Our hero and the Spanish buccaneer fraternised at once.

Don Leon de Zamora was a tall, handsome, gentleman-like fellow, almost a mulatto as to complexion, with very dark eyes and long dark hair, soft and luxuriant as a woman's.

Khahuahua, the chief of the Haffans, came with his sachems to visit the Boy Pirate.

The rover was extremely cautious in his interviews with the astute savages; he evaded their questions and avoided any direct promises, implying, by careless allusion to the prowess and devotion of his crew, the most terrible threats, in case of their not keeping faith with him.

After this he was not troubled with further molestation, and was left to cultivate the acquaintance of his fellow-prisoner.

In a very short time the two adventurers had exchanged confidences; the generous impulsive disposition of Christopher felt a ready sympathy for the present irksome position of one who had been a terror on the seas, and who had performed feats of daring that struck the mind with wonder.

Their confinement was alleviated in some measure by the freedom of intercourse allowed them, and often the chiefs would send Christopher a bottle of spirits and a bundle of cigars from his own stores.

One evening Leon and the Boy Pirate were seated at the door of the hut smoking their fragrant Havannahs and sipping their drink, when the Spanish adventurer related the story of the events which had led to his capture by the savages. We will give the reader a short account of them in his own words.

CHAPTER LXV.

THE STORY OF DON LEON DE ZAMORA.

"I NEED not tell you, senor, that I am of noble parentage, descended, indeed, from the most ancient family among the Spanish emigrants in Brazil. I was born at Rio de Janeiro. I have been a sailor from earliest boyhood, and though I am not old I have seen much service. I am not, however, about to give you the history of my life, its principal facts being known to the world, with whom I have waged war for nearly twelve years. A long cruise, you will say, for a pirate; but you see, senor, that I have advantages, in being born in one of those maritime states that cannot afford to keep up large armaments and are indebted to the enterprise of private individuals to swell their fleets in times of danger, and these allies, when war is over, become pirates from being privateers, and their enormities, as the world would call such deeds as ours, are winked at by governments too feeble or too indolent to punish them. Some day I may tell you through what combination of circumstances I became a pirate—by what means I rose to the supreme command of a formidable flotilla; but now my object is to let you understand how I came to be made prisoner by the Indians. It is needless to speak of the motives which induced me to embark on a Demerara steamer, disguised as a Spanish planter. We were bound for New York. We had a prosperous voyage, for when the lightest sailing vessels were becalmed our engines sculled us through the wide seas with unabated speed. On board, I met with a lady of your country; she was lovely and amiable, and her beauty was perfect. But I will not weary you with the praise of Mona Lee, for praise is weak and harsh; language is but a crude and worthless medium in which to express the admiration I felt for the fair and gentle English beauty.

"I ought to have told you that it was through a fortunate accident that I was enabled to cultivate so close an acquaintance with this divine girl. Her father, who was a clergyman connected with the British Consulate, I think at Demerara, while on a voyage had been taken prisoner by a French ship. This happened during the war that was raging between that nation and the Mexicans.

"I was then serving on board a privateer commanded by my uncle, and it was my chance to be of the boarding party that attacked the French ship. I saved the life of Mona's father, who was nearly killed in the *melée*.

"She was then about ten years old, a little elfin creature, full of mirth and gentleness. I was at the time about nineteen.

"We were separated. Years passed, varied with me by the wildest vicissitudes, but I never forgot little Mona; I remembered her beautiful face in those softer moments that succeed our fiery hours of battle or revelry. I remembered her to love her.

"I would oftentimes fancy my lily-bud expanding to the full chaste flower—my little Mona a fair and gentle maiden and myself her lover, and then I would laugh at my own folly.

"As I told you, senor, I met this very Mona on board the steamer. She was accompanied by her father and her cousin.

"The latter was a low-minded fellow, who, as I thought, loved the fair Mona only for her beauty. It seems he had been guilty of some act of villany in England, for the consequences of which his parents were so apprehensive that they sent him to Demerara on a visit to Mona's father.

"The young man was wealthy; old Lee was very poor, and urged his daughter to accept the hand of her cousin, who wooed her urgently.

"But Mona, though she did not dare to disobey her father, received her suitor's vows but coldly. Yet she was looked upon as affianced to her cousin, and everyone was glad that Mona should make such a desirable alliance.

"You will think it strange, perhaps, that I could learn all this, but the undeserving fellow was too vain and purse-proud to be jealous. He did not appear to value the lovely girl, having, as he supposed, gained her affections. He talked but little with her, and for the most part spent his time in other company.

"The steamer was passing near the Bahamas when she was wrecked in a sudden squall. My first thought was for Mona.

"The ship went down. I knew that it was hopeless to trust to the boats, over-crowded as they were. I remained with Mona and her father on board the vessel as long as I dared; the boats had gone, but the storm was subsiding. I made a raft, and we contrived to reach an island; on this desert place we lived for nearly three months.

"Mona's father had been hurt by some accident during the wreck; every day he was declining, and at the end of the second month he died; but, by his own desire, he married us formally before his death, and bestowed on us his fervent blessings.

"It would be a story of no little interest, the story of our life upon that desert island. We were very happy—nay, I have known no such happiness in all my life as I knew there, alone with my beloved; we wanted for nothing, the woods teemed with game; fruit the most luscious hung within our reach. I had recovered many things from the wreck; best of all, a large sea-chest floated on shore—it was full of books.

"Oh! happy, happy was my sojourn on that lone, wild spot. I was desirous of no society but hers, and the companionship of others would have been intrusion to her—for I was all the world to Mona; but enough, senor, happiness, even on a desert island, is but transient; we cannot fly from our fate.

"A ship came in search of us, and at the head of the crew who disembarked was the young Englishman to whom Mona had been affianced. It would have seemed absurd to have remained upon the island, yet in our hearts we both should have preferred staying in our solitude to mingling once more in society that absence had made distasteful.

"Mona told her lover in as gentle terms as possible how she had thought him dead, and how she had married. She showed him her father's written testimony to the fact; but the brutal fellow only laughed at such nuptials—his vanity was deeply wounded. I saw how vindictively he glanced at us, but thought it prudent not to hazard a remark.

"The Englishman resolved to have his revenge, and to recover his bride. Such men as you and I, senor, can understand such motives; we see the blackest side of human nature, and know that some men's villany is unfathomable. He contrived to send me into the centre of the island on some errand. When I returned the ship had sailed, and I was left alone in my solitude.

"I was nearly mad. My loneliness was insupportable, my despair unutterable. Besides, senor, I am a Spaniard, and am naturally jealous and impassioned, for there is a world of fire beneath our grave, proud exterior, that the wits have laughed at. I was well-nigh frenzied; but I calmed myself, and sought means of redress.

"To the determined all things possible are probable. Hope was strong within me when I had once resolved upon a course of action.

"I constructed a raft. After incurring the most terrific dangers, I reached the main-land. I reached a lonely town on the coast. Strange and fortunate! The Englishman had disembarked here, and had joined in an expedition against some brigands in the mountains with a band of Mexican rangers.

"He had left Mona behind in the town.

"I found the house where she was living.

"I assumed the disguise of a wandering gitano, and sang beneath her window. She escaped with me.

"For many days we travelled across the Savannahs, pursued by the rangers. But at length, as we were about to cross the Haffa river, we fell in with the Seminoles.

"I was recognised by one scoundrel, to whom I had been kind enough in former times.

"Leon de Zamora was no mean prize. Ten thousand doubloons were offered for my head, and the villain Indians made me their prisoner; and Mona, too, is a captive in their wigwams!"

CHAPTER LXVI.

THE ESCAPE OF THE BOY PIRATE.

As Leon and Christopher were one morning discoursing in their prison, and seeking oblivion of their thraldom and its anxieties in an assumed cheerfulness, the Indian squaw who attended upon them entered the lodge.

The girl looked at the prisoners with a glance of mute compassion, which Christopher at once perceived and gently detained her.

"My sister," he said, in the tongue of the Seminoles. "Why are your eyes downcast?—why do you sigh? Is the heart of my sister good towards the Yengeese captives?—has she no word of warning for prisoners not taken on the war-path? Surely the Manitou is the spirit of the pale-faces as well as the father of the Seminoles, and it is his voice that whispers my sister to speak to her brothers?"

"The words of the pale chief are good," returned the girl, "and the chiefs of my nation have forked tongues; they look before them, but their eyes are behind."

"Ah! then there is danger hanging over us," cried Leon to Christopher, for, though not so well versed as our hero in the language of the natives, he was yet sufficiently skilled to understand the purport of what was said.

"The Yengeese are coming," returned the girl, looking around her and speaking low.

"What Yengeese? Are they of my tribe?" asked the Boy Pirate, eagerly.

"No, they are enemies to my brother; they live beyond Macaco, in the great wigwam of the pale-faces."

"And what evil do they intend to us?" asked Leon, speaking as well as he could in her own language.

"The sachems of Haffa have sold my brothers to their enemies, and the customs of the pale-faces are not as our customs; they will kill my brothers. But the braves of the Seminoles laugh at the malice of their enemies, sing at the death-stake the song of their deeds, and count the scalps they have taken. Are the pale-faces less brave?"

"Is the heart of my sister good towards her brothers?"

"Waiona's heart is good; yet she is but a squaw in the chief's lodge," returned the girl. "My brothers must be very subtle if they would escape from the Seminole; let the Sea Eagle listen to my words. Khahuahua and the great medicine-man of the tribe are coming to visit the captives; let my brothers tell them of treasures of blankets, of weapons, of fire-food and fire-water, of mirrors and wampums. It maybe the chief's will to let my brothers go."

"But where is the maiden of the pale-faces. Is she still in the lodges?"

"The Yengeese Lily is in the lodge of the head chief. But I must be gone; if my husband should know that I am speaking the words of the sachems he would kill me."

With this the Indian girl took up the calabash and left the spot.

The Boy Pirate folded his arms and pondered.

Leon walked up and down the room, his head bent and his eyes flashing.

"Senor," cried Christopher, suddenly, "nothing but a very bold stroke indeed can save us."

"I am ready for any venture so there is hope in it, senor," returned Leon.

"Well, what I am about to propose is indeed a desperate expedient, but I have had so many hair-breadth escapes that I look upon the worst position as admitting of hope. If we fail in this attempt we shall but die, and that by a sudden death. Even so we gain, for if we do not make some effort to escape they will sell us to the Mexican rangers and we shall be hanged, that is certain."

"What is your plan?"

"Khahuahua mostly comes alone."

"Always. He does not like the greedy chiefs to hear our promises."

"To-night he brings another with him."

"Well, we are two."

"Are they in the wigwam now?"

"I should suppose not."

"Just so; they have gone to meet the rangers," returned the Boy Pirate.

"I can partly guess," said Leon, "what is the object of this visit."

"What can it be?"

"We are a treasure to these rascals, and the wary thieves will make the most of us. It is not impossible they will propose to send for our ransom on security, and sell us after we have bought ourselves."

"It is growing dark."

"Every moment darker. What is your plan?"

"Let us conceal ourselves behind the deerskin coverings of the lodge, and when these Indian thieves have passed the curtain steal out upon them and settle them as quietly as possible; then we might don their savageries and in the disguise pass through the wigwams unmolested, for after sundown it's as dark as a wolf's throat."

"An excellent plan, senor, though difficult of execution; and I have a suggestion to propose. If we get free we can fire the lodge before leaving it, which will create a diversion after we have fled."

"Good!" said the Boy Pirate; "and we might find the lodge where they have imprisoned my men, and set them free."

"Hist!" said the Boy Pirate, crouching down by the fire.

"They are coming," said Leon, in a hoarse whisper. "But what for arms?"

"We will use those that nature gave us."

"Yes; but here is the headless shaft of a spear, and here a stone, which I will slip into this piece of net that lies so handy," said the Spaniard. "Now, senor, hide yourself."

Leon and Christopher concealed themselves behind the deerskin coverings of the wall.

The curtain before the door of the lodge was parted.

Khahuahua and another Indian, hideously smeared with paint, entered together.

The medicine-man had a torch in his hand.

The lodge was rather large, and the couches on which the prisoners slept were heaps of heather and buffalo skins, placed in the far corners of the room.

The two Indians advanced a step.

It was their last!

The Boy Pirate and his new colleague flung themselves upon their captors.

With a down-right blow of the stone in the net, Leon brought the medicine-man to the earth.

At the same moment, Christopher struck down the chief with the headless spear.

So suddenly was this manœuvre performed that in less time than it has taken in narration the two captives stood looking into each other's faces with some surprise at the sudden and effectual manner in which the bold stroke had been accomplished.

Leon stooped and picked up the fallen torch.

The pirates lost not an instant in tearing away the hunting shirts and blankets of the fallen Indians, and throwing them over their own persons.

They also took the gun which the chief had carried, his hatchet, and scalping-knife.

Leon stripped the medicine-man of his tomahawk and poisoned arrows, and then prepared to start.

During the work they had not spoken, but moved about the stunned and senseless bodies of the two chiefs as softly as possible, pausing at times to listen.

Now all was ready.

Their hearts beat loud, for they could hear the voices of the crowd of sentries outside the door.

Leon now took the torch, and, throwing the heather of their beds into a pyre, set light to it, flinging the rude seats and wooden cooking utensils on the top of the heap.

"Senor, the old fellow I personate is lame. Do not appear surprised at my limping; I will make good use of my legs, be sure of that."

His torch in one hand and his staff in the other, Leon hobbled out of the hut. He held the light aloft, and bent his head in such a manner that his face might not be seen, while the Indian head-dress quite disguised his rich black curls.

The Boy Pirate, who had smeared his bronzed cheek with some colouring he had found in the chief's paint-bag, was forced to preserve a more erect carriage.

He folded the blanket over his left shoulder in such a manner that he was completely disguised, and threw his gun across his arm in a style which he had noticed was habitual to the Seminole chief.

The crowd of Indians before the door fell back.

Leon and the Boy Pirate passed unmolested.

They crept through the narrow lanes between the closely-packed lodges; it was dark as pitch. The principal and the worst obstruction that they met was from the dogs which swarmed in these narrow lines of huts, and which were as ferocious as a pack of jackals.

Leon and the Boy Pirate kicked them in all directions, and after a time, escaped their pursuit.

Just as they came within sight of the large hut where the luckless crew of the "Red Raven" were in "durance vile," a wild yell pierced the dull ear of the night; a red glare, based with a forked blaze, shot up, like a pillow of red fire, against the deep black sky.

The lodge from which they had escaped was in flames.

Men, women, screaming children, and yelping curs rushed out promiscuously from their cabins, and flew towards the scene of the conflagration.

The greatest consternation seemed to prevail, as well it might, when the close propinquity of the buildings and the inflammable material of which they were constructed are considered. Even the picket of men stationed before the large hut which encaged the pirate-crew started, and excepting a few veteran warriors, who remained steadily at their posts, started, and ran off to the fire.

Now was the time.

Leon looked at his companion.

The Spaniard was struck by the hardy determination, the fiery enthusiasm, that lit up the fine dark face of the Boy Pirate. Disguised as he was in his picturesque Indian pageantry, he looked the very *beau ideal* of the "noble savage."

Leon laughed as the Indians shot by him in their leaping run towards the fire.

Yells and shouts, however, checked his mirthfulness.

It was plain the real state of the case was known in the wigwam.

The chiefs had been struck down, the hut fired, the prisoners had escaped.

But the pirate chief was battering the door of the hut that held his gallant crew, while Leon struggled with the sentinels.

Two of the Indians had been shot down by the desperate pirates.

Two others were now struggling with Leon de Zamora.

With a crash the door of the hut gave way.

A loud huzza rent the ear of night as the crew burst forth, tumbling over each other in their eagerness, and swarming from the door like bees from a hive.

"Halt! Steady, lads! Hold on!" shouted the Boy Pirate. "It is I, your favoured commander, the Red Raven. Stick together, hearties; don't scatter, or you destroy each other."

The men looked at the speaker.

When they saw how strangely he was dressed they could not resist laughing.

"Hurrah for the Red Raven!" they shouted heartily.

The fire had spread.

More than a dozen houses were in flames.

The confusion of the scene can scarcely be imagined.

Khahuahua having been put completely *hors de combat* by the blow he had received, there was now no legitimate head to direct the movements of the tribe in this emergency, for though in times of peace the chiefs are supposed to share an equality of power, yet a great war-chief is always an influential man and generally possesses the supreme authority.

With a party of the men he had so gallantly liberated, the Boy Pirate made his way to the house of the chief, for Leon, who from a longer residence had gleaned more information with respect to the topography of the wigwams, led the greater part of the men on a quest for weapons, and was engaged at intervals in fighting his way through crowds of the enraged savages, who wildly opposed his advance.

Christopher had a desperate struggle to get into the chief's lodge.

One hideous fellow fought desperately to keep the door, and when the Boy Pirate had pushed him back and struck him with a tomahawk he reeled round and fired his musket into the cabin.

Christopher rushed in with a qualm of horror, for a loud shriek thrilled through the lodge.

Crouched in one corner he perceived the lovely girl of whom Leon had told him.

Her shoulders were uncovered, and the long showering ringlets of golden hair flowed upon her bosom.

By her side the dry bamboos which formed the walls were splintered and perforated by the bullet, which the Boy Pirate feared had passed through her breast.

He lifted her gently.

She seemed to have swooned.

The noise without the lodge was terrific.

Divided between two purposes the Indians were nearly frenzied, contending with two enemies they were nearly stultified. On one hand the raging fire, on the other their revengeful enemies, so lately their helpless captives.

But just as Christopher had reached the door another shout arose.

It was the watchword of the Mexican rangers!

What was to be done.

The pirate-crew were scattered

Not one of them was near.

A chief of the Seminoles had mustered a strong party, who had come down to defend the lodge and to recover the lady.

The pirate-crew knew nothing of the hostility of the Mexicans.

The Boy Pirate stood for a moment unnerved.

His men were flying.

He was glad of that, for he then knew they were conscious that the new assailants were enemies.

Now he thought only of his beautiful charge.

He would die rather than she should fall into the hands of her dastardly lover.

But how to escape!

The Boy Pirate lifted the fainting girl in his arms and flew through the line of huts.

None had the audacity to oppose him.

Some, indeed, still supposed him to be an Indian.

He reached a little open place on the banks of the river.

He looked behind him; the dark and lofty forests were lighted weirdly by the red glare of the burning village.

A shout went up in the distance—he had been discovered.

A party of the Mexican rangers were in hot pursuit.

The Boy Pirate was on foot, his speed impeded by his lovely burden.

What could he do.

Another moment he would be captured.

The rangers were within a few yards.

He turned savagely at bay.

He levelled his musket.

It was charged.

But the pursuers showed no signs of any intent to pause, but came pouring on.

He fired.

As the report rolled away into the echoing depths of the wood and the smoke cleared away, the foremost rider, who had outstripped his companions, plainly being the best mounted, reeled in his saddle and dropped from his horse.

The frightened steed came bounding forward.

The Boy Pirate caught the rein.

In another instant he had leaped into the saddle, lifting the girl and placing her before him. With a shout of defiance, he dashed his heels into the horse's sides and flew forwards.

He reached the river's banks.

He paused not an instant, but, giving one backward glance, leaped the horse into the rapid stream.

Soon he was struggling across the wide expanse of water.

The current was strong, and the horse was drifted down the stream.

Still the Boy Pirate clung to his hold.

The clatter of the horses' hoofs, as they rang along the turf, struck his ear.

With a shout, the Mexicans galloped along the banks.

They saw the peril of the desperate Boy Pirate. For a moment they were paralysed with dread, and hesitated to incur the terrific danger which threatened the fugitives.

They fired at him, however, and their bullets skimmed along the surface of the water, or whistled close to him. Yet he still gallantly struggled to gain the opposite bank.

Several of the riders plunged into the stream.

Nothing could be more desperate than the position of our hero.

His horse drifted down the river, in spite of its desperate plunging and struggling.

It was evident that the animal was getting exhausted.

The river wound round a little neck of land.

To this spot the Boy Pirate guided the horse as well as he could.

After several fruitless attempts, the animal managed to struggle up the banks.

The Boy Pirate was, therefore, once more upon *terra firma*; the wide savannah lay before him. He disencumbered himself as quickly as possible of the blanket and the rest of the Indian attire, and, arranging himself and his charge upon the saddle, once more struck his heels into the horse's side, and sped along like a swift arrow.

He flew over the ground like an uncaged bird, but the cries of the Mexicans came rolling after him.

He turned, in his excitement, shook his fist at the pursuers, and laughed gleefully.

The wild night-ride was congenial to his fiery, adventurous spirit.

The pursuers gained upon him, but he cared not; he trusted by some turn in the chapter of accidents finally to elude them.

He breathed his horse.

As he reined and moved on more slowly the Mexicans thought him exhausted; their own steeds were well-nigh out-worn.

They came within a few paces of him, they fired, but the shots flew far wide of the mark.

The Boy Pirate turned in his saddle, took deliberate aim, fired and killed one of the men; he then once more urged his steed to the maddest speed, flew across the plain like a swallow, and plunged deep into the sanctuary of the dense forest.

CHAPTER LXVII.

HARWOLF'S WIFE—A NEW CLUE—A MESSEN-
GER OF EVIL.

ANDREW HARWOLF found that he was carefully avoided by his neighbours since the murder of the Jew Nathan.

The ex-steward perceived that, with all his wealth, and with all the *prestige* wealth gives to its possessor, he could not stand against the tide of his unpopularity.

Strange wild rumours were afloat; the servants were always leaving, for Harwolf gave way at times to the most ungovernable paroxysms of anger, and Frontemore had the reputation of being haunted. The pretended Lady Edgeforth was an intriguing, profligate woman, who caused much scandal by her dissolute career. In London she also was shunned by the higher circles, but found some equivalent for the loss of their esteem in the adulation she received from a clique of wealthy *parvenus* to whose level she descended, and who worshipped her for her title.

Andrew Harwolf had entertained serious thoughts of disposing of the whole of his land property, of turning all his possessions into hard cash, and retiring to some distant colony, or to some obscure foreign city.

But there were many obstacles to this course; the estates were entailed, and so far as Andrew's claim was concerned were forfeited.

Lady Edgeforth would be required to produce certificates of her birth, marriage with Lord Edgeforth, and to give her sign-manual to all documents referring to a transfer of the estates. All this would be productive of the worst consequences.

Lady Edgeforth and Andrew were at breakfast in their luxuriously furnished *boudoir*. The wife of the ex-steward was reclining languidly in a large arm-chair; Andrew Harwolf, with folded arms, was moodily watching the fire, for it was late in autumn, and the mornings and evenings were dark and chilly.

Lady Edgeforth was a handsome woman, with large voluptuous brown eyes and a wealth of rich brown hair; she was buxom and somewhat vulgar-looking, and the expression of her face was artful and depraved.

"Eleanor," said Andrew Harwolf, "I am resolved to leave England."

"The town is empty; this is a flat, stupid place. Let us go to Baden-Baden," returned his wife, laconically.

"Good God!" cried the husband, fiercely. "Can you be so insensible? Has contact with that infernal mob of heartless profligacy they call society brought you to this? Have you not even the maternal instinct left, that belongs to the fox and the wolf? Are we not the parents of an only child, branded with the mark of Cain, banned by the worst anathema, hunted as a murderer? And can you call a solitude where you may hide your shame 'flat, and stupid?' Do you talk of gay continental cities, and pant for the dissipation of a ball, or a scandal party, or the excitement of *roulette* or *ecarté*, when—when——"

"Tush! Andrew, I am a woman—better and worse as such than, as a man, you can ever be. You are an unreasonable reasoner. You would sell your 'eternal jewel' for a price the Devil seldom pays his votaries, and yet would preserve the sensibilities and the anxieties of innocence. They say my son is a murderer. While he is free and untried he is traduced by his enemies; for every man legally is held guiltless till he is found guilty by a jury of his peers. Shall I suspect my own son? Shall I respect the opinion of the world when I have ceased to respect myself?"

"Most unnatural!" groaned the criminal.

"What folly. There is truth in the old fancy that men who sought the Devil's aid to help them in their purposes of evil are always haunted by a familiar, an ever-present imp of hell. With some it is a bottle-imp; with others it is a painted ace in a pack of cards; with others, it lies in the painted blush of a courtesan. It hastens on our ruin, but it smooths the road of thorns, else we should be lacerated by the thistle we have sown to our own torment. Bless it, then, this imp that shortens a career of misery, that makes the biting chains wearable, that hides the crown of thorns with flowers."

"You can talk like this—yet women are scarcely reasonable beings," said Harwolf.

"Reasonable, but unreasoning," said Eleanor. "What is the use of boasted reason to you? Will it delete the foul blots on the past's records? Never, never!"

"But a mother."

"And a murderer's mother, and a murderer's wife—what would you have of her?" cried the hardened woman, with a scoffing laugh.

"Curse you!" cried Harwolf, clutching her wrists, his eyes green-sparkling. "Was it not for your sake?"

"Do not blast yourself blacker with the hideous lie, Andrew Harwolf," cried the woman, struggling to release herself. "Let go, brute as you are, I don't like jet bracelets. What!" she said, breaking from him; "Did you say for *my* sake, you mean villain, you ferret, you snake. For *my* sake. Had it been to your interest to cut my throat you would have done so as remorselessly as you killed *him*. Oh! bad as I am I love sincerity. Lost and abandoned as I feel, how I hate and loathe hypocrisy. I am a wanton, a gamester, an *intriguante*. Well, you made me so. A man gives tone to a woman's mind; you tuned my soul to the harmony of a witch's sabbath, and yet you talk of me as a mother, a wife. But don't let's quarrel, Andrew; it excites you and it wearies me. Besides you are so rough and brutal, and I am not so strong in endurance as the devoted wife of such a worthy husband ought to be. There, there; be calm, most reasonable creature. Every one of these fits is a turn of the cart's wheel that is carrying you to the gallows."

"Why, Eleanor, you must be mad!"

"I ought to be, but I am not. *She* is mad, who is pure and innocent; but I, who have lost all, am sane, quite sane, and mean to enjoy all rational pleasure; so, my black angel, stay at home and weave your webs for wasps, while I go to Baden-Baden and spin mine for butterflies."

Harwolf covered his face with his hands and groaned deeply.

"Come, come; be quiet, husband. You are right, we must begone; though "all the perfumes of Arabia will not cleanse these little hands," yet fresh air will sweeten them a little."

"I will not bear it—I will kill myself!" cried the wretched Harwolf, striking his brow.

"And go from worse to worst. No! Do not kill your whole body or mind, but put the caustic of searing pleasures and excitement to the black spot in your heart, for though you cannot pluck out the root you may soften what anguish lies on the surface."

"But should not you comfort me?" murmured the miserable villain, plaintively.

"Well, so I do. I am an able, clever woman and a practical comforter. I preach the most reasonable means of distracting your thoughts; but if you like I will give you other counsel."

"What is it?"

"Pray!"

"Ha! Would that give me peace?"

"Pray, but don't blaspheme. Do you know on what conditions prayer is possible?"

"Grace is free," said Harwolf, feebly.

"To those who can give up their wickedness."

"Were the thing to do again, I would not do it."

"You repeat the action every day."

"How so? The past is past!"

"But the fruits, the motive of the crime, remains. To kill a man by accident would be no crime; you stained your hands with blood that they might be filled with gold. Fling away the gold; denounce yourself to justice; restore Lady Edgeforth and her heir to their possessions; meekly submit to the capital punishment man will inflict, and make your peace with God."

"Then I cannot pray," gasped Harwolf.

"If you do this, you may; who shall measure out the mercy of Heaven?"

"I cannot pray," said Harwolf, emphatically.

"No? Then be merry while your short term lasts; enjoy to the uttermost the prize for which you paid so dearly; seek pleasure wherever she may be found; be charitable to my self-indulgences, and I will be so to yours. Let us spend and lavish the fortune we cannot transmit to our child. Let us go to Baden-Baden, or where else you will, but let us leave off talking of this skeleton in our house; let us leave him at home in this old mansion. I wonder you could have stayed here so long."

"Eleanor, you are my evil genius," said Harwolf, who was in one of those moods of weakness and despondency in which the most daring and impenetrable ruffians will fall at times.

"It is a base lie and a cruel," retorted Lady Edgeforth, with fire. "A woman is a man's genius to urge him on the path he chooses for himself; she cannot find one for him. Besides, I am no Lady Macbeth. I gave you no incitement to what you did, nor were you like the Thane, 'full of the milk of human kindness.' But no more. You are a puling wretch, and I am sick of your injustice."

With this the abandoned woman swept haughtily from the room.

Andrew Harwolf rose, put on his hat, and sauntered into the grounds.

It was a gloomy day. The sky was wrapped in leaden-coloured vapours; the woods were melancholy and drear, for the decaying leaves were fast falling.

Unconsciously, the man of guilt strayed across the lawn, and, passing the shrubberies, approached a large fish-pool.

Some men were in a punt, dredging the water, which had become stagnant during the droughts of summer.

Harwolf spoke to them.

He made some careless remarks about their occupation.

A NIGGER DUEL.

The men answered respectfully.

"They say you have been dredging the river lately?"

"Ay, squire. We were looking for the body of the poor lass that drownded herself, your honour. Poor crectur! we found her arterwards, though not at the time we were lookin' for her. She floated down stream, poor crectur! and was picked up above the falls, sir. She was on top of the water, for she began to dissolute," said the man, sagely, "and then they allus floats."

"Sometimes you find strange things that cannot float," said the squire, not heeding what he said, but upon recollection starting with a strange and sickening qualm.

"Aye, so, your honour's right," said the man. "Here be a rum sort of thing, now, we've just fished up."

No. 22.

"What is it?"

"A lump of lead, your honour."

The villain shuddered long and convulsively, his face went livid pale.

"Well, there's nothing extraordinary in that," said the squire, clearing his throat.

"Why, no, zur; p'raps not," returned the man. "Only its the queer shape of the thing."

Harwolf trembled violently.

"It looks as if some one had melted it, and had squeezed it with his fingers while it was cooling: here are the marks of the clutch as plain as ever, your honour."

Our readers have not forgotten that Harwolf had perpetrated the diabolic murder of his kind and noble master with a life-preserver loaded with lead, and that when removing the traces of his crime he had melted the metal, and had crushed it into a lump in the manner described by the man, and had afterwards thrown it into the pond.

It was some time before he could speak.

"Give it to me," he said, at length.

The man put it into his hand.

With a thrill of horror he looked at the impressions, and then slipped it into his breast pocket.

"You may leave your work awhile," he said; "you were at it early. Go, drink my health at the 'Hedgers' Arms.'"

With this he threw a half-crown to the men.

"Thank you, kindly, zur," cried the men, leaping out of the punt with alacrity.

Harwolf walked away.

As he approached the house, he was met by a brawny, fierce-looking man, who seemed in great haste, and whose looks testified that he came on some business of importance.

"Well, Miles," said Harwolf, as the man took off his hat upon drawing near. "What brings you from Glenleaf?"

"Lord, yer hanner!—bad news—infarnal bad news!"

"Something about Esau Cooper, I'll warrant."

"Your honour's not much out. The cab-driver brought the information, zur—Tupper, you know. But this arn't a werry good place for us to be talking."

"No; come in. Is the fellow with you?"

"Yes, squire. But are yer prepared for bad news?"

"I'm prepared for anything," returned Harwolf, as they entered the house.

CHAPTER LXVIII.

THE QUARREL—THE "BLACK VULTURE'S" FIRST QUARRY.

THE "Black Vulture" was driving before the freshening breeze all sail set.

The crew were clustered on the deck on the look-out for a prize.

They had now been at sea many days, and had not fallen in with any craft worthy of their attention. They were getting impatient; every man on board was eager to strike the first blow.

Daniel Harwolf was leaning against the bulwarks with folded arms, his sullen, sinister eye roving over the rolling waves, a look of discontent and peevishness on his face.

Black Ralph came from below; his dark cheek was flushed, and there was a savage gleam in his fierce black eye, but he was humming as usual with his characteristic *nonchalance*.

He approached Harwolf.

The latter received him with a slight sneer.

"So, and how prosper you in your love-making, my gentle Corydon?"

"Bravo!" cried Black Ralph, in his deep, gruff tone, laughing heartily.

"What do you mean by that ejaculation?" asked the other, starting at the suddenness and vehemence with which the word was uttered.

The broad open hand of Black Ralph clapped down on his comrade's shoulder with the force of a sledge-hammer.

"I am struck with admiration at the favourable change that has taken place in your deportment, Master Dan. So you are lively enough to be sarcastic, eh, my weeping philosopher. Forgotten the Jew? Thought you would. I was sure you could never continue to pull such a long countenance, or you would soon have been all face, like an old caricature. My love affair! Well, for my courtship, I make sufficient progress in my suit to suit myself, for all the zest of the chase consists in the difficulty of running down the game. A fig for your yielding beauties; they are as common as butterflies at Midsummer. This Jewess is one of the right sort; I like her all the better for her obduracy."

"But does she like you the better for your importunity?" asked Harwolf, with a leer; "think you she will yield at last?"

"She must!" returned Black Ralph, with a grim smile. "When I get tired of this pretty game of cross purposes, then will I woo her 'as the lion woos his bride'; till then her pleasant reluctance to be mine only amuses me."

"Look here, Ralph," said Harwolf, catching him by the arm, "every man is worse than a fool—because he becomes a slave—when he falls in love with a woman. Before you get too deeply enthralled with the fair Deborah let me advise you, for your own sake, for mine, for the sake of our crew, to get tired of your amusing warfare at once, to conquer or to quell."

"Pish! look you, too, Master Dan," returned Black Ralph, "there is no 'falling' in love or in anything else with the Black Vulture, whatever may be the case with that poor crow the Red Raven. I am no sentimental, snivelling Boy Pirate, to carry off my 'first and only.' I am a man-pirate, and she is a woman-captive. She is mine, won at some risks."

"To me as well as you," cried Harwolf, interrupting. "I am owner of this ship, and will be master of it."

"The devil you will," cried Black Ralph, fiercely; "then to hell with your ship, and you too. I am captain of it, and will be commander while I've a hand to my sword and a tongue to my throat. Thunder and devils! what's to prevent me striking our sweet little bunting to the first man-of-war in our wake, and giving you up as the cursed Jonas of our ship; or pitching you overboard, and posting you home in the whale's belly? Though it strikes me, mate, there isn't a fish dirty enough to stomach such carrion."

"Heyday, you're violent," returned Harwolf, wincing. "Is it policy that we should quarrel?"

"Curse policy! It's policy I should have my own way in my own ship."

"Your own ship!"

"Aye! my own ship; when it isn't mine it will be a luckless day for me, you skunk; meanwhile, be content to obey my orders, and gulp down your dignity, mighty master."

"You don't know me; you don't know the kith I come of," returned Harwolf, who, like his father, was no coward, his blood being up. "You have been useful and true to me thus far, but if——"

"True to you," cried Ralph, "you lily-livered cut-throat. Wear tallow cheeks, your true colours, for having killed a miserly fence. You have no more humanity in your composition than Herod that slew the yearling babes, only that you qualm at the white cap and the running noose. Your kith, forsooth! You would sell father and mother and all your progenitors from Japhet downwards for a pinch of salt, or a few minutes' respite from the gallows you're doomed to, though they were innocent as you are guilty. Truth! If I want to vomit, and the doctor's abroad, talk to me of truth, and I shall be as sick as a cat. Now, for my part, I am true. Don't kick up a row with me; don't bluster and brag about your mastership, and that you are my joint partner in command, my superior in sharings, for, by the big and little furies, if you presume to thwart me, Master Dan, you shall share neither in command nor booty; you shall neither give orders nor take swag."

"You villain, do you think that I can brook such language from a piratical braggart like Black Ralph, an escaped transport, a beggarly, haunted, penniless felon."

"I see, I see," returned the other, with suppressed fury, speaking in a dry, hoarse voice; "two suns cannot burn in the same firmament; we cannot have two skippers aboard."

"To match your own simile, dog," cried Harwolf, giving rein to his passion, "you will find me a comet that bodes sore plagues to you if you dare to come within my influence."

"A comet," cried Talbot, with a rough laugh,

what a long tail our cat has, to be sure. A comet! That's rich indeed. Well, we'll see if this great light is quenchless. There was a sage, I think, from Goshen, that promised to set the Thames on fire; we'll see if you cannot illumine the sea. Better six feet of water in the hold than such a spark of fire in the state cabin, so, out you go, my spark. I suppose you'll hiss this act of our melodrama. 'Put out the light,' says Othello; and 'put out the great light,' adds Black Ralph. It's time to quench a comet that bodes plagues to honest men."

Without more ado the ruffian flung his strong arms about Harwolf, swayed him round, and pitched him over the bulwark.

With a heavy plash Daniel fell prone into the sea!

The ship was travelling at a great rate, and when Harwolf rose to the surface of the water he was fast drifting aft.

With a desperate effort Daniel, who was an expert swimmer, flung himself against the hull of the vessel, and snatched at the sheet chains.

He managed to clutch them; the ship rolled over on her side, burying him in the trough of the surf.

Several of the pirates rushed to the side.

"Man overboard," cried one or two, who had not witnessed the dispute of their commanders, nor the summary manner in which it had been decided by Black Ralph.

Among others who rushed to the side of the ship were the first and second mates, and the boatswain.

The first mate, whose name was Cassidy, was a very fine fellow, tall and supple, yet full-chested and sinewy. He had a dark, stern face, a cold and abstracted manner, and a clear, low voice that was peculiarly thrilling and authoritative.

"This is a bad beginning, captain," said the pirate, with quiet gravity. "A house divided against itself can never stand; the same law holds good on sea as on land. Let me throw a rope."

"D—n your meddling, sir; about your duty!" cried Black Ralph, turning fiercely to the speaker.

He then leaned calmly over the bulwark and regarded his partner with a leer of malicious triumph.

"Ah, Master Dan, and how fares your fiery cometship in the uncongenial element where you find yourself. Acknowledge yourself beaten, Dan. Water versus fire is a case where the defendant is always nonsuited, although he may get the costs. Look up, man; he who was born to be hanged will never be drowned; profit by that wise dispensation; keep up, man. Ha! ha! you travel gaily. Comets' orbits are so eccentric!"

Harwolf made no reply to these brutal taunts, if, indeed, he heard them at all; he was sufficiently engaged in his battle with the waves that every moment dashed over him, and threatened to tear him from his hold.

Cassidy and the second mate, Wardlaw, now approached.

Cassidy had a coil of rope in his hand.

He fixed his pensive, yet piercing black eye upon his superior, and bent back his arm ready to fling the rope.

Black Ralph glared at him.

The expression in the fine melancholy face of the young seaman was one of profound respect, but his thin lips were close drawn with immovable determination.

"Look here, Cassidy?" cried Black Ralph, roughly, "am I captain on this ship, or are you?"

"I care not what I am on sea or on shore," returned Cassidy, in his clear, yet hollow tones. "I would as lief serve before the mast as bear command on this or any other plague-ship; but the man in the water is the owner of the craft, has paid down for every plank of her; and you'll be sorry if you let him drown—that's all."

"I'll be sorry, you infernal mutineer. What will make me sorry?"

"Your own good sense, captain. I wait your orders to throw the rope."

"Ho! ho! you wait my orders?"

"Yes, sir."

"Well, throw it, then, and be hanged," returned Talbot, turning away impatiently.

"Ay, sir," cried Cassidy, demurely, as if the command had come quite unsolicited.

He launched the rope.

Harwolf caught it convulsively; with much difficulty he was hauled on to the deck.

Black Ralph turned sharply upon Cassidy.

There was not the slightest taint of triumph in his placid face as he helped the half-fainting Harwolf over the bulwark.

It was well for him that it was so, for Talbot's finger was bent upon the trigger of his revolver, and there was a threatening glance in his intense black eyes.

Many men who are capable of the most atrocious crimes are not without some touch of good-feeling. As Ralph looked upon the quiet resolute countenance of young Cassidy, he laughed gruffly but not ill-humouredly.

"I like you better, mate," he said, "than those fawning toads that hang upon a skipper's smiles and frowns, and bend to his worst will in all things; but neither you nor this skunk must think that there is, or ever will be, any other man at the helm than Ralph Talbot." With this the pirate-captain turned away.

With a look of deadly hatred at his colleague Harwolf slunk below. Cassidy folded his arms, and walked moodily forward.

Suddenly a cry was heard from aloft, "Sail ho!"

The men started to the bulwarks, and flew up to the yard-arms.

"Let go the top bowlines," shouted the captain, seizing his glass, and eagerly scanning the horizon.

Far away, along the sky-line, a trim-built vessel was spreading her snowy sails in the sun, and forging along at a spanking rate.

The eager watcher could not repress a slight cheer.

"Now, lads," cried Black Ralph, cheerily to the crew, "the time has come at last; we can now flesh our maiden steel and hear the first lisping of those iron throats that shall hereafter shake the main with their thunderings—

' For the wind is in our sail,
And the prize is within hail,
We're men who never fail,
Quoth the bold buccaneer!'

Hurrah for the 'Black Vulture!'"

The men responded with a hearty cheer.

Harwolf at this moment rushed on board to learn the import of that shout, for he was sorely suspicious of treachery, and almost expected to find that the men had revolted from their allegiance to him, and had transferred it to his partner.

He had changed his dress and was armed to the teeth.

As with red cheek and glowing eyes he walked up to the crowd of pirates that were gathered about their captain, he looked inquiringly into their fierce countenances.

Black Ralph also looked round upon the faces of the gang, and read the import of the doubting looks they cast from him to his partner.

He approached Harwolf and drew him aft.

"Hark ye, Master Dan," he whispered, "yonder flits the first white wing of the 'Black Vulture's' quarry. We are about to enter upon our first action; we must be of one accord. Our honours are yet but green; till we have shown these men a right of mastership by our skill and success there is no safety for either of us. We mounted our pretty standard that we might be free, free to quarrel as often as we like, and to be reconciled as often as we quarrel; but there must be no rupture between the helm and the binnacle, or we shall be spared the trouble of pitching each other overboard, for the men will do that kind office impartially for us both if they see that we cannot consort amicably. I'm sorry for my share in the late piece of tomfoolery, but the girl below riled me. Curse her, she shall pay for it! And I am too hot-blooded to stand hectoring from Timour Bey. Don't be an ass, forget and forgive; there's no need to cut each other's throats; while the wolves fought the fox carried off the booty. Tip us your daddle, Dan, and don't forget we hunt in couple."

With this Black Ralph held out his hard, broad hand. Struck by the force of this reasoning, Harwolf took it sullenly, and the colleagues thus walked forward.

The reconciliation was timely, and had a good effect in restoring confidence among the men.

The crew testified their approval by a lusty shout.

"Now, lads; silence, fore and aft! I've a few words to say to you; a clean butcher and a pretty sportsman never mangle their game more than is needful. That frail barque that scuds along so gaily is a butterfly we could pound to smash with our first broadside; but she's a good sailer, like enough to give us a longer chase than such a prize is worth, so we will reserve our daring for a worthier occasion, and try a little strategy."

"Ay, ay, sir," responded the men, laughing.

"Cassidy, are the guns well masked?"

"Ay, captain."

"Good. Wardlaw, send the armourer aft with the surgicals."

"Ay, sir."

"And Mr. Harwolf, I'm sure you'll be good enough to see that the guns are manned and well-served. Aloft there, round in the weather braces! Bo'swain."

"Here, cap'en."

"Run up an inverted ensign for a signal of distress, fire the long minute-gun for assistance, and further to deceive the good Samaritans, all hands to the pumps, and when the swobs come within hail pump away like steam-engines, for ye see, hearties, we've sprung a leak, and are settling down an inch a second. Tell the purser to make a stiff jorum of grog to give us life in this disastrous emergency."

The men laughed and cheered, and hastened to carry out these orders.

Some went below with Harwolf, others ran to the stores. Arms were carefully concealed along the side of the bulwarks or under pieces of canvas and tarpaulin, while busy hands aloft were reefing the topsails. All on board was bustle.

The pumps were arranged and the men stood ready, at a signal, to begin their self-imposed labours.

"You might as well take full orders first as last," said Black Ralph. "When we get alongside throw the grapnels. Board, and, mark ye, make a fair beginning; no squeamishness—no quarter. Kill the last man and share forthwith the legacy."

"Is it understood, captain, that none are to be spared?" asked Wardlaw.

"Well, you can reserve the skipper; and don't hurt the women. Should there be any youngsters pitch them overboard, unless they can walk and talk; if they can, they'll be eligible for powder-monkeys, soon. We'll make pirates of the small fry, and bring 'em up on saltpetre. But, mark ye, no quarter! No lily-livers are permitted to tread the deck of a ship that carries our colours, mark that! You are Vultures, mark that! You must be vultures if you would be pirates."

"But the passengers, captain?" suggested Cassidy.

"Curse the passengers," cried the ruffian, ferociously; "cut their throats like pigs. More sea-dogs of our breed have swung through sparing passengers than from any other cause; there's no gratitude in the landlubbers. Spare passengers! What for? Ransom? Do you want to take blood-money for your own betrayal? Down with 'em, one and all! Now, gunner, fire away. That's brave. Set the vulture on the halliard trap; we'll fly him soon, and woe to the pigeons when he swoops! Now, lads, pull with a vengeance."

"So yo! ye ho! cheerily ho!" sung out the men, and they pull away at the pumps as if the ship were fast filling with water.

The ship which the ruthless miscreants had doomed to destruction was as pretty a little brigantine as ever had sailed on the high seas.

She was of graceful build, and her light gear was perfectly symmetrical, and admirably adapted to her taut and well-shaped hull; she carried all her canvas with rakish ease, and swept through the parting waters like a gliding swan.

She soon ran alongside.

She appeared to be a merchantman, was clean as a snowdrift, and bright with fresh paint and gilding. The lion of Scotland fluttered from her mainmast-head, and her name was wreathed about her carved prow—the "Highland Mary."

"Ship ahoy!" cried Black Ralph, through the speaking trumpet.

He was answered from the shrouds of the pretty and unsuspecting brigantine.

A number of well-looking, neatly-dressed seamen were crowding on the poop; among others appeared the captain, a speaking trumpet in one hand, a glass in the other.

"What cheer," cried this personage, in a loud and hearty tone, and with a broad Scotch accent.

He was a short, stout man, with a freckled face, a high forehead, and long sandy whiskers.

"Sprung a leak; help us, for God's sake!" roared Black Ralph, at the same time winking at his men, who pretended to be labouring at the pumps in utter dismay.

"Weel, mon, we'll just do a' that may be done to assist ye. But who are ye?"

"Spice merchants of Hull."

"Weel, and hoo do ye ca' the masters?"

"Messrs. Jolly and Oliver," roared Black Ralph.

"Weel, noo, I canna say I've heard of sic a firm. At Hull, say ye?" asked the wary Scot.

"At Hell if you don't help us. We're going down, sir; the water's amidship," shouted the treacherous pirate.

"Dinna fash, mon; I dunna think the water's rising sae vera fast, for you're steady in the surf as any limpet on a rock; but if ye'll just lower your jib-boom we'll board you in a winking. I've a canny carpenter below, and ye sall hae a' the help we can gie ye, and that wi' a will; but dinna blaspheme when you're in danger, it's nae worthy o' a Christian seaman."

"No offence, cap'en," shouted Talbot, "only, for Heaven's sake, be alert, whoever you are."

"I am Fergus Macallister of Leith, and my brigantine of the said port is bound to Barbadoes. But I'll be wi' ye. Alexander, tell Jock and Donald to board the vessel with a' the han's we can spare."

The ships were now stern to stem. Grapnels were thrown from either side, and a dozen smart fellows from the "Highland Mary" prepared to leap upon the fatal deck of the robber-ship.

"Have you any supercargo, cap'en?" asked Black Ralph.

"There's nae passenger aboard the brigantine but my ain daughter Mary."

At this moment a number of the pirates ran up the rigging as if to man the yards, others came from the pumps and surrounded the men who were treading the deck on their way to the hatches.

The carpenter was at the head of the little party so treacherously decoyed into this den of wolves; he had an axe in his hand.

"Friend, what may be the name o' your bonnie craft, and what's yer burthen?" asked the Scotch skipper, leaning over from the quarter.

"At present I'm not half freighted."

"And what do they ca' the ship?"

"The 'Black Vulture.'"

"And a mair awesome, ugly name I never heard on," cried the Scot, indignantly; "for sic a pretty bit o' workmanship, too. Weel, every man must gang his ain gait, and there's no accounting for taste; and you're spice merchants, say ye—what sort of spice may ye carry?"

"A very pungent spice indeed—chili and cayenne are cool to it. It's as hot as blazes, and burns and bites like the devil."

" I'm really sorry, friend, you hold sic language," said the Scot, evidently much scandalized, and at the moment he lifted his eye doubtingly to the flag that streamed down from the stu'nsail boom.

"Ha! ha! you're looking for my colours. Well, skipper, you shall see my true ones. I'm a free-trader, and fly my own flag—and there it floats. How do you like the look of it?"

As he spoke, the black banner, with its ghastly insignia of death, was run up.

The pirates gave a terrible shout, and, snatching up the cutlasses and fire-arms they had concealed, fell upon their victims.

Thunderstruck by the suddenness of the attack, the poor fellows stood paralysed, and unable to offer the slightest resistance.

Amidst the fearful hooting and cheers of the fiendish outlaws, shots crackled from all parts of the "Black Vulture's" rigging, and the horrified captain of the "Highland Mary" beheld his sailors dropping on all sides of him, for they had been severally picked out.

The scene on the deck of the pirate-vessel was appalling.

The deck was cumbered with the gashed and bleeding bodies of the "foremost slain," while the few unfortunates remaining struggled hopelessly to reach the bulwarks, but were pistolled or brained till the deck ran blood like a slaughter-house.

Maddened, as men will be by the sight of carnage, the half-drunk pirates exulted in their hellish work, spurning the bodies with their feet, and firing into them after life was extinct, and in mere wantonness.

As the crew of the "Highland Mary" happened to be all on the decks of the two ships, the ruthless slaughter of the whole party was the work of a few moments.

One man only had been able to make a desperate resistance. This was Donald, the carpenter, who inflicted some frightful wounds upon his assailants, till he was knocked down by Wardlaw and pistolled by Harwolf.

Macallister had not been fired at. The luckless captain leaped upon the quarter-deck; he threw up his arms, and cried, in a voice of intense anguish and fury—

"The curse of God and man be upon ye, heartless fiends! And maybe you're thinking that you'll take my guid ship, and ruin my daughter. But, by the vengeance of Heaven! you shall never set foot on my deck."

With this he turned the helm; the ship swerved round, and Macallister was frantically rushing to the hatchway, plainly with intent to fire the ship, when Black Ralph sprang nimbly from his own deck on to that of the merchantman, seized the Scotchman by the throat, and after a desperate struggle, stunned him with the haft of his cutlass.

Fresh grapnels were thrown.

Harwolf and a great part of the pirate-crew now leaped on board of the "Highland Mary."

In an instant the ship was crowded above and below deck by the greedy thieves, intent upon plunder. Sea-chests were broken open, stores rummaged, cabins ransacked.

With excellent tact, Black Ralph walked among the men, cheering them on to their felonious work, but taking good care to keep with them, and by his presence to prevent them from quarreling or running into excess.

He had stationed Cassidy, with half-a-dozen men with loaded pistols in their hands, at the door of the cuddy where the spirits were kept, and had given them the most imperative commands to shoot dead any man who should attempt to break into the stores.

The ship, though by no means large, was well-appointed; it was laden with bales of silk and other fabrics of inflammable nature, and it was evident that if Macallister could have reached the hatchway he would have had no difficulty in carrying out his desperate resolve, as there were several barrels of gunpowder in the hold.

When Black Ralph reached the door of the state-cabin he waved the men back; he tried the lock and found it fastened. Very coolly he placed the muzzle of his pistol against the lock; he fired, the report echoing loudly between decks; the lock was shattered and fell like broken glass. The report of the pistol was followed by a piercing shriek. Talbot burst open the door.

As he entered he perceived a very pretty girl, evidently a Scotch lassie, and the skipper's daughter crouching against the side of the cabin.

One of the men had passed into the cabin; he pointed to the girl.

"Shall we leave her there, cap'en, or take her aboard the 'Vulture?'"

"Bring her along, I want this ship cleared of all superficial encumbrance."

The girl rose to her knees, and held out her clasped hands imploringly.

"Oh, dinna tak me awa'! Kill me here, as ye killed my father, and I winna murmur!" she cried, frantically.

"Curse that catawauling! I had enough of such music this morning," growled Black Ralph; "haul her along, boys; don't hurt her, be hanged to ye, but if she squalls, gag the baggage."

The poor girl no sooner found herself in the arms of the brutal pirates than she fainted and was carried passively away.

Black Ralph examined the cabin, found it substantially and comfortably furnished with every appliance of ease and competence, and he was greatly elated with his gallant little prize.

When he reached the blood-stained deck, he was received with a stirring cheer from all hands.

He took off his hat, and with a theatrical salute thus harangued his crew—

"Comrades, we have just achieved the first and smallest of a series of victories that I am conscious will be ours. Have I managed this trifling affair to your satisfaction? I have. Have you proved yourselves the men I took you to be? You have. I see that you have cleared the decks; that you have thrown to the sharks the bodies of our foes—for all men are our foes that hold allegiance with the tyrannous government whose yoke we have thrown off—and for these red stains that paint and gild our victory, why, as Shakespeare has it—

' A little water clears us of this deed,
How easy is it, then!'

Thus, in a conjuror's *presto*, we have taken the smartest little thing that ever rode the waves. We have swept off her crew with a *coup de grace* worthy of a Spanish matador, so elegant and sudden in its execution. We have captured the 'Highland Mary' and all her wardrobe, for below there's 'silken store and gold galore,' and a cargo, hearties, that would have been worthy a great deal more trouble than was needed in its overhauling. So, hurrah for the Jolly Oliver! Good luck to free trade! A long cruise and a merry one to the 'Black Vulture!'"

The men answered with a wild huzza, and the black folds of the triumphant banner of death rippled up to the masthead.

Thus was won the first prize of the villanous Ralph Talbot, whose name was long a byword of terror on every sea.

Is the youthful reader dazzled by the bluster and the burlesque declamation of the miscreant pirate-chief; is he excited by the subtleness of the strategy and the violence of the assault? Do the riches of the wealthy merchantman glitter before his eyes? Let him not forget that the pirate-ship was a pandemonium of discord, selfishness, mistrust, and hideous debauch, that its crew were despised and detested felons and rogues, and meanest and basest of all, thieves; for how low must a man fall that will descend to such a paltry vice as theft! Our object is to show Vice in her own image. Would she might be appalled at her evil looks. Nothing can be more unreal, more false, to nature than the ideal portraiture of beings imbued with every virtue but common honesty, the test and basis of self-respect, without which no man *can* possess high and chivalrous qualities. Our reader will see both sides of a dark picture; he has beheld the melancholy remorse, the craving regret of the generous Boy Pirate forced into his evil courses, and not possessing sufficient good principle nor manly resolution to abandon them; he will now see the bloody-minded, ruthless pirate, Black Ralph, in all his enormity, a wolf or a shark, or worse than those monsters, inasmuch as he preys upon his own kind. Writers of fiction need never fear lest they should exaggerate in descriptions of acts of atrocity, for since the world began men have been guilty of diabolic cruelties, which they have not shuddered to perpetrate, yet cannot bear to see recorded. A corsair, or a Red Rover, a Captain Macheath, or a Cartouche, may be very pretty personages in a novel or a drama, but in real life they are pestilent rascals, and mean, miserable characters to boot.

CHAPTER LXIX.

CARAGUNGHA'S RETURN.

IT will be necessary for the clearer development of our story to return to Gomez, whom it may be remembered we left hidden in the forest, after having avenged the apparent death of his comrades upon the treacherous Seminole Haska.

He was so enraged at the perfidy of the Indian and so appalled at the fearful catastrophe that had befallen the Boy Pirate, that for some time he felt quite unnerved.

His first thought was to follow the trail of the Indians, and to watch their proceedings before returning to the ship with such fatal intelligence. His next plan was to seek the Seminoles of Macaco, and claim the assistance of the father of the young chief whom the gallant Boy Pirate had rescued from the waves.

But when he thought of the utter destruction of his noble leader and the flower of his devoted band, he could scarcely summon fortitude to contemplate the greatness of the sudden calamity.

But then came the promptings of revenge.

With pressed lips, and eyes that glowed with concentrated rage, he clutched the musket he had snatched from the ground, and stood trembling with the force of his emotion.

He listened to the swaying of the wind through the heavy-hanging foliage; it bore on its wing the sound of retiring feet; he knew that the Seminoles had started on their homeward march.

Noiselessly he glided through the flowery dingles, and wound among the roots and stems of enormous plants and trees.

He soon came upon the line of march.

It was plain that the Seminoles, either confident in their numbers, or robbed of the wonted prudence by the intoxicating power of the "fire-water," in which they had been freely indulging, did not perceive him, but held their way with careless indifference.

They were carrying the bodies of the Boy Pirate and his crew upon litters, and on the backs of their mules and horses.

A happy thought occurred to the enraptured mind of the Spaniard, which at once settled into conviction.

The brave Christopher was reserved for a happier or at least a worthier termination of his wild, but bright career.

He was not dead, neither he nor his companions. The object of the Indians in entrancing and bearing off the redoubtable Boy Pirate was obvious enough; they knew that if a high reward had been offered for the person of Leon de Zamora, something very enticing to their cupidity would be proffered for the English pirate and his desperate gang.

Crouching low among the long grass, Gomez suffered the cavalcade to pass on.

After a few moments' cogitation he decided upon what course to pursue, namely, to seek the wigwam of Caragungha, and, with the young chief and his braves to support him, to follow up the track of the Haffans, and, if possible, to recover his beloved young leader without the assistance of that part of the crew remaining on board the "Red Raven."

In execution of this plan he travelled for some distance, guiding his steps as well as he could by means of his pocket-compass, and the signs familiar to woodmen.

He crossed the little open spot which had been the scene of the late catastrophe, and plunged once more into the thicket.

As he stole quietly along, brooding upon the late misadventure, and anxiously forecasting the probability of his meeting with treachery among the natives with whom he was about to mingle, he was startled by a rustle among the bushes, accompanied by a guttural cry—

"Waugh!"

It was Caragungha himself, who sprang up and advanced towards the Spaniard.

Gomez looked into his fine eloquent face, and he saw in it no trace of guile; he extended his hand.

The Indian took it, and bent over it with grace and dignity.

"The clouds have darkened the sun that shone on the path of the great chief of the pale-faces when Bounding Elk left the watch-fires to seek the wigwam of his father; the dogs of Haffa employ witches and devils, and charm the enemies they dare not meet like men. How has my brother escaped?"

"I would not drink the fire-water that the hound had poisoned."

"It was Haska?"

"Yes."

"They call him the 'subtle.'"

"He is well-named."

"And where is the Seminole?" asked the young Indian, cautiously glancing around him.

"Where his subtlety will avail him nothing."

"Ugh!"

"You do not understand me; well, then, Caragungha, I have killed the viper, he is dead."

"It is good!" replied the Indian, with evident satisfaction.

"What is to be done. Shall we follow the trail of the Haffans?"

"The young men of Caragungha are few, and the dogs of Haffa are many," replied the Indian.

"Then you are not alone?"

Caragungha gave a low call like the cry of a whip-poor-will.

At the signal about a dozen Indians crawled stealthily from among the thickly-netted ground weeds.

They rose to their feet.

Their wild faces were smeared with war paint, and they trailed long muskets in their hands.

"These are not sufficient for our purpose; if we would recover the Red Raven, we must needs storm the wigwam of the Haffans," said the Spaniard.

"A hundred of my father's braves shall strike the trail of Khahuahna, shall burn his lodges, and bear off his scalp; my brother, the pale chief, shall be rescued from his enemies; but first Caragungha must return to Macaco."

"And that will cause a delay that may be fatal," said Gomez, impatiently.

The Indian did not understand these words, but evidently guessed their purport.

"Caragungha and his young men are ready to follow the trail of the Haffans—will my brother go, too?" he said, advancing some paces in the direction the captors had travelled.

"No, no—that would be madness. Let my brother lead the way to his father's wigwam, I will follow."

"It is good," returned the Indian, quietly.

He then addressed the Indians, who expressed their ready obedience by meaning looks. The young war-chief then beckoned the Spaniard, and walked forward into the thicket. He arranged the men in Indian file, that is to say, one by one, placing Gomez in the centre of the line, and, according to the native custom, himself bringing up the rear.

When they had passed through the denser part of the forest, and were nearing the savannah, they made a detour which brought them to a lovely and romantic spot on the banks of a wide and majestic river.

Under the frowning brow of a tree-covered cliff Gomez found they had concealed their horses. They had two extra mustangs of great power and speed, which they had brought with them in case of any similar emergency to that which had arisen.

On one of these Gomez mounted; and at a furious rate—still keeping the same order they had observed while on foot—the whole party dashed off across the wide, rolling savannahs.

CHAPTER LXX.

THE PIRATES ATTACKED BY THE MEXICAN RANGERS.

By the help of a series of strange accidents that are too complicated to be fully detailed, the Boy Pirate had managed to gather together his scattered crew. Some he had fortuitously met, and others had been searched for by those who had already rallied round their leader Don Leon de Zamora had also rejoined his new ally, and with Mona gave him unbounded thanks for his gallant devotion to their cause.

Little respite was allowed the fugitives by the Mexican rangers, who were enraged beyond expression at the escape of such important prisoners as Zamora and the Boy Pirate.

They followed up the pursuit with great ardour, and had now besieged our hero and his party, who had taken refuge in a cavern in some rocks that ran through the deepest part of the forest.

The Mexican soldiers so far outnumbered the pirate-crew that it would have been sheer madness on the part of the seamen to venture a battle; but the pirates had taken up a strong position, and as, with the forethought taught them by long and severe experience, they had provided themselves with what provisions they could obtain by sacking the wigwam of the treacherous Haffans, the siege promised to be protracted and bloody.

The Boy Pirate and his men had sworn never to surrender; and as they had a national contempt for their guerilla-like opponents, remembering their victories in Spain over a class of brigands but little worse in their characteristics than these Governmental bravoes, they were not hopeless of a felicitous result to their determined resistance.

It was night. The Mexicans, who had been worsted in several attempts to storm the Raven's eyry, were bivouacing at the foot of the rocks. They had lighted huge fires, and were keeping a vigilant watch, as many as half their number remaining on guard whilst the others slept.

A huge stone had been rolled before the mouth of the cave, the ascent to which was almost precipitous, and could never be clambered by the returning party after a sally except under cover of the guns of their companions.

A fire had been lighted in the cavern, and for some time the volatile seamen were amusingly employed in beating off the flocks of bats that were drawn from their crannies in the rocks by the heat and glare of the fire.

A man had killed some wild birds that he had caught in one of the outlets of the cave, and these were cooking by the log fire.

The Boy Pirate, Zamora, and Dick Caffyn, were gathered in a circle.

Mona Lee was reclining on a couch that the seamen had made with their pea-jackets.

She seemed to be deeply sleeping, worn out by fatigue and excitement.

An animated debate was going on among the leaders as to the expediency of a sudden attack being made upon the besiegers in an attempt to force a way through them.

This, though a most desperate venture, was considered to be the safest course to pursue, as, in all probability, a reinforcement of Indians and others might be expected to join the besieging party on the morrow, and, the longer the sally on which they depended for deliverance was delayed, the less able they would be, through the failing of their ammunition, to perform the daring act to which they were to trust for their safety.

The council was interrupted in its deliberations by the approach of Tom Garrod.

The seaman looked flushed and excited.

"Shiver me, cap'en," he gasped forth. "But this be no time for palavering, for, strike me, if the Mexican skunks haven't found the companion-ladder, and are coming aboard as bold as rear-admirals."

The men, who were assembled round the fire, stopped at their work, and looked on with animated faces.

The officers leaped to their feet.

"Comrades," said the Boy Pirate, looking round upon the serious and attentive faces of his devoted band, "perhaps this is well, for the devil's in it if we let them 'beard the lion in his den.' They will find that a nest of Ravens cannot be taken without the buffet of wings and the striking of beaks and claws. Huzza, lads! Stand together. Danger is fun to such desperates as we; and that man among ye who isn't a match for a dozen of these Mexican brigands is unworthy of his messmates. Keep together; plant yourselves at the mouth of the cave—don't waste a shot—kill every man that passes the edge of that boulder. Let that narrow path be as fatal as the gallows ladder; no man can pass it if you take steady aim. For my share in the work—which hark, is beginning——"

The shouts and firing without the mouth of the cave proclaimed that the men on guard were encountering their assailants, who were swarming up the rocks.

"My share of the work, comrades, is to create a diversion by leading an assaulting party right into the heart of the camp."

"No, no, cap'en, you shan't go," roared the men.

"Now, lads," cried the Boy Pirate, briskly, "this is no time for mutiny—it must be done. We may cut off the rear of their storming party and enclose them among the rocks. These skunks have no notion what British metal will do; but we know that many a more daring deed has been crowned with success. Who volunteers in this perilous service?"

"I'm one to the for'ard, cap'en," said Tom Garrod, settling his belt, with its murderous array of pistols and side-arms.

"And I'm another," cried the coxswain.

Others volunteered.

"Captain," said Dick Caffyn, "I go with you, of course."

"No, no, for Lilia's sake."

"For her sake. How would she receive me if I returned to her without you? She is in good hands, nowhere safer than with old Brierly. We are brothers, captain, and we will live or die together."

The Boy Pirate grasped the speaker's hand.

He then looked round to see that all was ready, gave up the command of those remaining in the cavern to the Spaniard Zamora, and then led the way to the mouth of the cave.

A furious combat was going on, although there was but one narrow footway by which the Mexicans could ascend in numbers. Several of the more desperate of the beleaguers were scrambling up the side of the wall-like rock.

Upon these the pirates were firing, while their shots were answered from below by the volleys of rattling musketry which the Mexicans were pouring, with very little effect, as the pirates were well protected by the nature of their position.

The Boy Pirate stayed not an instant, but, brandishing his sword and uttering his battle-cry, which was re-echoed along the sounding rocks as it blended with the cheers of his men, dashed down into the vale in the face of a heavy fire.

The Mexicans shouted and charged up the rock to meet the sallying party.

The Boy Pirate and his devoted little band rushed upon them with the bound and power of a mountain torrent, flinging them back on the slippery rocks, and fighting with maddening fury into the very heart of their phalanx.

Stunned and appalled by the suddenness and the irresistible fury of the charge, the Mexicans receded as fast as they could.

The gallant Boy Pirate hewed a way through their ranks, and reached even the tents they had pitched in the valley.

Although the soldiers outnumbered the pirates in triple measure, yet they fled before the invincible Red Raven and his followers, and wildly blew a call on their bugles to bring the storming party to their relief.

With prolonged huzzas the pirates made the most of their advantage, fired the tents, knocked down every one who attempted to oppose them, and carried off several barrels of gunpowder and boxes of ammunition. They were returning triumphantly to the cavern, when the storming party, retiring from the assault of the fastness held by Zamora and the rest, and crossing the little valley, came down upon the Boy Pirate in a dense body.

The gallant band was surrounded, and a most furious hand-to-hand contest ensued.

Hemmed in on all sides, the desperate outlaws fought with the fury of demons.

But nothing could avail against the overwhelming numbers of the Mexicans.

Yet inch by inch the pirates made way in a compact mass, few of them falling, and none dreaming of surrender.

Zamora was afraid to quit his position, lest the enemy should carry it during his absence; but he kept up a galling fire upon the Mexicans, while, to save their fast-failing ammunition, many of the seamen employed themselves in hurling huge stones down upon their opponents.

But every moment the case of the pirates grew more desperate. Spite of their matchless valour, the rovers began to give way. All but the Boy Pirate! He cheered his men, seemed to revel in the wild excitement of the furious fight, and dealt such terrific strokes on all sides with his sabre, that the arms of his antagonists sank nerveless at his approach.

Once he narrowly escaped a mortal wound.

Among the Mexicans was one to whom the battle seemed a pastime; who darted about inflicting the most terrible injuries, yet escaping unhurt.

He had stolen behind the Boy Pirate, and was about to bury a long knife in the rover's heart, when Dick Caffyn turned to attack him.

He perceived that the fellow was a hideous-looking black, and he at once recognised, to his extreme astonishment, that this was the same negro who had fought so desperately on board the pirate-ship in the Mediterranean, and had killed the favourite mate of the "Red Raven," poor Walter Mervyn.

Christopher, who looked round at the moment, breathless and weary with slaughter, perceived the ugly negro engaged with Dick Caffyn.

He also at once remembered the fellow's face, and in the midst of his peril and exertion, found time to wonder by what chance he had come to that part of the world.

The battle now raged with the utmost fury, yet all seemed lost with the pirates. They were so far outnumbered that they could hope for nothing better than a short respite, to be gained by a speedy return to their cave; and even that hope was almost precluded by the fact that they had wellnigh exhausted their ammunition, and were nearly outworn with fatigue.

Yet the dauntless, the indomitable Boy Pirate encouraged his men, and fought his way back to the cliff with the most unparalleled daring.

One by one the men reached the rocks, and sprang up from the boiling whirlpool of the battle.

They were severally fired at as they clambered the rocks, but Zamora and his men poured down a volley from their height that swept back the Mexicans and covered the pirates, enabling them to make good their ascent.

The brave band cheered vociferously on reaching their height.

The Mexicans cursed and growled, and vented their fury by discharging their muskets at the fugitives.

The returning party sank on the ground in the cavern, exhausted with heat, fatigue, and excitement. They were eagerly attended by their messmates, who bound up their wounds and poured cordials upon their lips.

Mona threw herself by the side of the rover-chief, and eagerly questioned him whether he was wounded.

The Boy Pirate answered smilingly. A few gashes in his right hand and arm were all the marks he bore of the desperate fray.

These Mona bandaged with her scarf, and the Red Raven rose once more to his feet, and seemed, like the earth-born giant, to have renewed his strength by his contact with the ground. So, freely and gracefully, he strode through the cavern, followed by the yearning glances of his despairing crew, who hoped against hope when they looked upon the gallant form of their noble and unconquerable commander.

"Dick," said Christopher to his foster-brother, "did you recognise that ebony monster, with a face like a Hindoo idol—the nigger you were thrashing below—do you remember him?"

"Surely, captain," returned Caffyn, "he is the same fellow that served on the 'San Trinidad,' the rascal who killed poor Walter Mervyn."

"I am certain he's the same fellow. Well, we must mark him, my hearty; I daresay some of the cussed Spanish buccaneers are in these waters."

"My God, cap'en, it's all up with us," cried Tom Garrod, rushing up to the spot; "that infernal nigger has wormed out a cave beneath this, and the imp of hell has set these Mexican cusses to mine us with gunpowder; we shall be blown up like bees in a hive."

Yells, shouts, and triumphant peals of laughter rang in the air.

The Boy Pirate and his crew rushed to the edge of the rock, and peered down from the entrance to the cavern.

A number of men were dragging a large barrel of gunpowder towards a little hollow below the cave, where the hideous black stood ready to receive it.

The Boy Pirate's presence of mind did not forsake him for an instant. Ever fertile in expedient, he had devised and executed a manœuvre to bring about a temporary check in less time than it takes to narrate.

Wrapping a piece of gun-wadding round a bullet, and wetting it with brandy from his flask, he lighted it, and fired it from his already charged gun full into the barrel.

The flaming bullet struck right through the wood, firing the powder.

The explosion was terrific. Several men were frightfully injured.

Those who could do so rushed off, scattering in all direction.

The Mexicans in the distance, who thought that the explosion came from the mine below the refuge of the pirates, set up a shout.

It was answered with savage fervour by the indignant and desperate crew, who prepared to risk all in a last desperate charge.

The Mexicans, however, were hastening to the foot of the precipice in great numbers.

The morning was now breaking on this terrible night.

With the darkness expired the last hope of the gallant band. At least they would die like men.

Mona clung to the breast of her Spanish lover.

THE DUNGEON IN THE CASTLE OF SAN SALVADOR.

Ross and Tom Garrod were employed in directing a party, who were alternately firing their last charges and flinging down missiles at that spot where the mean-spirited foemen were trying to force a way, in order to lodge the powder.

The triumphant yells and derisive cheers of the Mexican rangers might have struck terror to less tried hearts, but they only inflamed the pirates to the highest pitch of vengeful passion.

" Hu—hu—hu—hu !"

What is that strange wild cry that comes with a wailing yet fierce mellowness, grating up from the dense thickets of the primeval woodland ?

What causes the Mexicans to start and look behind them ?

Again the wild war-whoop rings its blood-congealing peal.

No. 23.

The tawny bodies of a hundred Indians start from all parts of the forest, their long rifles levelled with deadly aim upon the disconcerted rangers.

Then follows a rattling discharge.

As the white veil of smoke sails off, the ground appears strewn with the writhing or motionless bodies of two scores of the besiegers.

A man dashes out from among the trees mounted on a wild-looking mustang ; he has a long spear in his hand, from the top of which flutters a piece of black silk, bearing the rudely-painted device of the skull and bones and the terrible Raven.

In a moment he is recognised by the thunderstruck and now joy-distracted pirates.

There is no mistaking that sign ; no doubting the identity of the dark-skinned grave-looking cavalier.

It is Gomez !—to the rescue.

The pealing savage yell is music divine to the numb hearts and strained ears of the late desponding crew.

It is the war-whoop of the Seminoles of Macaco, and the dashing young chief who flies forward wielding his tomahawk or slinging his long rifle is the young chief Caragungha.

The Boy Pirate looks on with beaming face; he utters one word—vengeance!

He rushes down the rocks, followed closely by Caffyn, Ross, Tom Garrod, and the rest of the men.

Assailed on all sides, a sudden panic seizes the dastardly Mexicans, and they fly in all directions.

The Indians pursue them, and though their flight is fast and furious, yet more than one horseman bites the dust.

In a few moments the Boy Pirate and his allies are masters of the field.

A hasty council is convened; the leaders return to the cavern to exchange congratulations and to compare notes.

It may be imagined that the British tars cordially fraternised with their coloured deliverers.

The chiefs are assembled in the cave, gleefully explaining matters of mutual interest.

Their converse is interrupted by the entrance of three or four sailors dragging in the horrid-looking negro before described.

"Here's the infarnal Guy Faux, cap'en," cried Tom Garrod, who lead the party, "and he's a reg'lar guy, and no mistake. Give the word, sir, and we'll make a skyrocket on him. We'll just put him a top of his own mine and send him on a woyage of discovery to the moon in a tar-barrel. Only give the word, cap'en."

"No; let the fellow alone: stand away, but shoot him down if he attempts any deviltry," returned Christopher.

The men fell back, and our hero confronted the slayer of Walter Mervyn with a stern glance.

"What is your name, darkie?" he asked.

"What de debil dat got to do wid yo, dam tief?" returned the black, showing his yellow fangs in a malicious grin.

"You will gain nothing by insolence, my fine fellow, and your impudence may cost you dear," said Christopher, sternly.

"Don't care nuffin yo can do to dis chile, buckra; wish't I did just fire de powder, an' den should see de dam ravens fly. I bound dey find dere wings broke afore dey comes down into de dogs' mouths. Yah! you blow up de Trinidad: wal, yo see, my fine buckra, yo hab your day. Yah, go along!"

There was something so grotesque and ludicrous in the tone and gestures with which the sable ogre expressed his spleen and contempt of his captors that the rough sailors could not resist a hearty laugh.

This so enraged the savage black that he turned round upon Tom Garrod, and flew upon him with bent head, butting him in the chest and prostrating him upon the seat of honour.

Leaping over the recumbent form of the boatswain, the negro darted towards the outlet from the cavern.

He was, however, stopped and dragged down by the seamen, who menaced him with their pistols and knives.

"Do not hurt the rascal; let him be carried aboard, and we will then determine what's to be done with him," said Christopher, firmly.

"Ay, ay, cap'en," returned the sailors, dragging him away kicking, struggling, spitting, and uttering the most garbled expressions of boundless wrath and execration.

CHAPTER LXXI.

A DUEL BETWEEN THE NEGROES.

THE Boy Pirate's return to the "Red Raven" was the occasion of much relief to that part of the crew who had remained on board during his protracted absence.

Brierly's joy found expression in the most cordial welcomes, and the old salt seemed never to weary of following with his eye the gallant form of his beloved commander, who once more gaily and proudly trod the deck of his own vessel.

Mona was introduced to Lilia and the octoroon, and the three girls, each of them so gentle and beautiful, moved like the three graces about the ship, ever with arms entwined, and finding wonderful solace in each other's friendship, feeling almost reconciled to their strange and anomalous position.

Zamora remained on board with the English rover.

The gallant Seminole had been dismissed and sent home to his father with the warmest praises and sincerest expressions of the gratitude of those to whom he had rendered such important service, and not without more substantial marks of gratitude in the shape of abundant and costly presents.

Soon after the return of the rover to his ship—the ladies being below—Christopher called his officers and men about him, and sent for the negro, who had been confined in the hold.

It had happened that when the ferocious black had been brought aboard Zampa was away from the ship, turtle-hunting along the coast, so that though he had been told by some of the sailors that they had caught another "darkey," whom they had caged between decks, Zampa had never yet seen his compatriot, and the Boy Pirate was anxious to see how he would comport himself when confronted with him. Zampa was sent for.

"I've a friend to introduce to you—one of your own complexion, Zamp. I want you to tell me what you think of him," said Christopher, with a smile.

"Raal, genwine niggar, mas'r?" asked Zampa.

"Yes, black as the devil."

"Dat's de buckra's debil, mas'r, yo mean—our gen'leman's a white un," returned Zamp.

The seamen laughed.

"And dis chile reg'lar black—no sham 'bout him? Cross-breed, half-cast, dere de coons. Yah! not 'spectable—neider one ting nor t'oder—ain't worth a cuss!"

"Well, you will find this fellow black enough to please you, Zamp. But here he comes. Stand out of the way, for he's as savage as a mad dog at midsummer."

"Ah, dam! raal Guinea, dat chile," said Zampa, sententiously, grinning good-humouredly, as with his head buried in his chest, the scowling, sullen negro was marched along between two sailors.

"Hillo, Sambo; hi!—yah!—how you do?" cried Zampa, with a chuckling laugh, flinging his splay feet high into the air, performing a grotesque antic, and finally finishing off his gymnastic display with a trailing bow.

The sailors laughed heartily and turned their gaze upon the other Ethiop, who stood with his chin buried in his breast, glaring at his capering brother, and looking the very incarnation of brutal ferocity.

Zampa lifted up his broad face, aglow with a radiant smile of fun and good-humour; his eyes met those of the captive—the expression of his face underwent a change so marked, so sudden, that it caused the lookers-on to start with amazement.

Zampa crept near the savage negro who confronted him, and peered into his evil countenance with a searching look.

He then sprang back, dropped upon one knee, and raised his clenched hands to his broad breast, as if to beat down some rising thought or remembrance.

"Yo dar, at last. Dat yo! Oh, Gorra Mighty, dat Pluto! no mistake. Stand yo on one side, buckras. See yo how easy Zamp strangle de beast dat kill his wife and chil'en."

Before any of the seamen could interpose, the two blacks had rushed upon each other.

With a generosity that touched the rough seamen, Zampa tore his knife from his girdle and flung it across the deck, for his antagonist was unarmed.

"Part them," cried the Boy Pirate, authoritatively. "This is no place for such unseemly brawling."

But the command was easier to give than to execute; and it was only after a desperate struggle that the pirates could separate the two negroes.

And even when they had dragged them asunder, they had hard work to prevent them flying upon each other to renew the fight.

"Zamp! are you mad? If you are not a fool you need not fear but you shall have justice if you have been wronged," said Christopher; "but if you do not desist when I command, I will have you lashed up and flogged for your disobedience."

"Yas, he's dar. Yo let me go, dam buckra," screamed Zampa. "Flog! who debil cares about flog? Ole Rashleigh will tell yo—Missee Ida will tell yo—ebbery body down Louisiana tell yo how dis nigger, Pluto, cut up my wife till she die, and den de chil'en starve! Mas'r brand me cos I knife him. Yah! I no brand for nuffin dis time! Yo let bide, buckra cuss, or I kill yo too."

With amazing strength the furious black dashed the sailors away from him, and sent them reeling across the deck.

Once more the negroes closed, and wrestled furiously to throttle each other.

"Part them," cried the Boy Pirate.

The men were dragged asunder.

"Let 'em fight it out, cap'en," said Brierly.

"Such is my intention, but the duel must not be fought in this disorderly manner."

The Boy Pirate drew a pistol from his belt.

"Look you, Zamp; stand clear of the men, and keep away from your enemy. If you advance one step towards him I shoot you dead, and then you will never see your vengeance upon him whom you call the murderer of your wife and children. Pluto, keep back, too. If you are in earnest, off with your shirts and fight it out like men."

The negroes needed no further encouragement. They disrobed themselves in an instant, and stood ready to renew the battle.

Pluto snatched up a knife from the deck and leaped upon his adversary.

Zampa hurled him back with terrific force, recovered his own weapon, and stood ready to receive him.

The malicious foe, seeing his opponent armed in like manner with himself, became more wary.

The antagonists walked round each other with cat-like stealthiness, narrowly eyeing each other's movements, and watching for the right moment to make a spring.

Their left arms were doubled across their broad chests; their right hands lowered, vindictively clutching their weapons.

Intense silence reigned around.

Officers and men looked on with thrilling interest.

For some time the sable duellists observed extreme caution.

Then Pluto rushed in, and striking down his enemy's guard with his ponderous fist, attempted to thrust the knife into his lungs.

Zampa swerved back, narrowly escaping the thrust, which passed over his shoulder.

He slashed his knife across Pluto's naked breast, but the negro was springing back when the cut was made, and therefore escaped with a flesh wound; yet the blood flowed down in a flood, staining the deck.

There was a faint cry from the excited spectators.

Enraged by the smart and the flowing blood, Pluto flung himself desperately upon his adversary, and warding off a well-aimed blow, inflicted a deep cut on Zampa's brawny shoulders.

After this the men receded from each other for an instant, and then manœuvred for breath.

As Zampa was getting dizzy with loss of blood—for his wound was deeper, and the blood welled up in greater quantities than the stream from the gash which seamed the breast of his foe—as the wild, villanous face of Pluto floated before his eyes, grinning with demoniac spitefulness and passion—

Zampa could not restrain his fury, but, regardless of consequences, flung himself upon the other.

Pluto held up his right hand just as the blow was falling, and the knife was struck out of his hand, and rolled away along the deck.

With a wild guttural exclamation Zampa seized his foe by the throat and dashed him down; he then knelt upon his breast, his arm was raised for a moment, and the next would have brought the knife straight down into the heart of the struggling Pluto.

Calmly the Boy Pirate advanced, and caught Zampa's arm.

"Fair play," he said, "not thus."

Zampa rose.

Pluto was on his feet in an instant. He recovered his weapon, and the duel was renewed with redoubled fury.

So closely were the infuriate savages struggling, that it was almost impossible to see on which side victory smiled.

Blows were exchanged, and blood flowed freely.

Presently they parted, and Zampa stumbled back and fell.

As Pluto rushed upon him the seamen pressed forward.

But the Boy Pirate waved them back.

As Pluto neared his victim, he suddenly stopped, staggered, and threw up his arms.

The cause was obvious enough. The haft of Zampa's knife protruded from his side—the blade was deep in his heart.

The black gave one look round—a look unspeakably horrible in its fiendish meaning—reeled, and dropped like lead.

The men gathered round him, and lifted his head.

Life was extinct, but a grim smile sat on his hideous features.

Zampa had fainted.

CHAPTER LXXII.

HARWOLF'S DARK HOUR.

ANDREW Harwolf and his agents walked into Frontemore Hall, and betook themselves to the library.

The squire looked sternly upon his quondam instrument of villany, and seemed to be preparing himself for a contest of shrewdness against treachery; for he sorely doubted the motives that prompted the gipsy to seek him, after the notable failure of the designs upon Lady Edgeforth, through this very fellow's outrageous folly and bestial senselessness.

Esau stood with his sullen eyes downcast, shuffling from one foot to the other, and preserving a dogged silence.

"Esau Cooper, you have not come with the idea to blind or mislead me by any plausible lie you may have been schooled in," said the squire, in a cold, thrilling tone. "I have been too busy to attend to you, Esau Cooper, but do not presume upon the delay of a punishment which is assured to all whom I employ if they prove false to me."

"I never proved false to you; I never wanted to," said Esau, sulkily. "I know I'm too square by half to deal with sich as you, else why did I come down here to face you out over that cussed business of my getting so infarnal boozed at sich a bad time. But I'm a sober man in a general sort of way; a little drop takes effect on me; I confesses it. I'm sorry I were anyways to blame. There, ain't that enough?"

"And what have you come for now?"

"Money."

"You confounded rascal, have you the impudence?"

"Let 'un bide, squire," interrupted Miles; "do 'ee now. He has got somethin' to tell 'ee as may do 'ee good, and it ain't much harm to listen to the creetur, though, durn me, I have promised to beat his brains out a hun'red times. I have zo!"

"I arn't got nothin' to tell unless I'm paid for it."

Harwolf's face blazed with his native passionateness; but he gulped down his wrath, and a sinister, quiet smile curled his lip, and his voice assumed a tone of unnatural softness, as he replied—

"Well, Cooper, one indiscretion may be overlooked in a faithful servant; see that you don't offend again. If your information be worth the price you put upon it, you have reason to know that I am not one to treat you illiberally."

Miles stared at the speaker.

The countryman shuddered at the cold glitter of those serpent eyes, and the stealing mellowness of those bland words seemed to congeal the blood in his veins.

On the more stolid nature of the gipsy they had not the same effect; his eyes shone with insolent triumph.

"I s'pose your honour wouldn't be sorry to know what's come of Lady — the young person, leastways, you takes sich a hinterest in. Well, I knows where they've housed her and whose arter her."

"Ha! you're a jewel, Esau. Well, here's something to begin with," said Harwolf, with affected carelessness, drawing some sovereigns from a drawer and placing them in the fellow's hand.

The greedy eyes of the gipsy gleamed with pleasure as he clutched the bait in his claw-like hand.

"As for the 'ouse, yer honour, vy, there's two 'ouses; 'cos, fust of all they took her to a private lunatic asylum, and then her brother got her away from that crib and took her somewhere's else."

"Her brother!"

"Yes, yer honour; leastways, as calls himself as sich. Well, now, the way I found it all out. I was sent to dog that gemman, and who was I sent by, think ye?"

"Tell, don't question," said Harwolf, still suavely.

"Vy, by the werry Jew Nathan as your son Daniel Harwolf murdered." He the gipsy fairly broke down; he had made a *faux pas* that seemed irremediable.

Miles stared at him, at least expecting the squire to knock him down.

But after a moment, Harwolf replied, hurriedly,

"You mean the unfortunate gentleman whom my son is falsely charged with assassinating. He, then, set you on the watch, did he? What could have been his motive?"

"Hanged if I know," returned the gipsy; "but I followed him up, your honour, and I overheard him—the brother you know—a-conwersing with another gent, who informed him as he knew where Lady —well, you know who I means, sir—where she was. I were goin' to say nothin' would do for my lord —for it seems as he is a lord—but he must go there and then arter his poor sister, as he called her; and go they did. Well, I larned on the cab-rank where they druv to, and by the look of the place I should take it to be a sort of 'sylum place; but from what I made out, I discovered as Lord Hawksbury—that's the gent's name—took the poor 'sane creetur to his own house in Mayfair, and there she is now."

"Well, I shall sift this matter," said Harwolf, with imperturbable calmness; "and if I find there is truth in your statements, it will be well for you."

"Your honour's werry kind; but if I might give you a bit of advice, sir, I should advise you to take a trip to foreign parts, for I'm given to understand that this gemman's likely to institute inquiries and that sort of thing."

"Well, well, I shall act as I judge best," answered the squire, trying to assume a hauteur he had not strength to support. "I shall require your services again, Esau Cooper; meanwhile, you must lie close, and not let your tongue wag like a mill-clack in every pot-house at Frontemore. You must consider yourself a prisoner at Glenleaf until further notice; and I desire you should show yourself to strangers as little as possible. Leave me now. Miles, you may remain for a few moments; I wish to have a few words with you. Cooper, good morning."

The squire opened the library door.

The gipsy slunk out, muttering,

"Good mornin', your honour; you may rely upon me; I'm square, cos vy? I ain't got no hinterest to be otherways. Good mornin', sir."

Harwolf closed the door, and folding his arms, thoughtfully paced the room.

"Miles!" he said, suddenly.

"Well, yer honour?"

"What do think of that fellow?"

"Durn me, yer honour, if I knows what to think on him; but I do zay he be useful."

"We must use him while he is useful, and when he ceases to be so we must find some means to render him harmless."

"Right, squire."

"He remains with you at Glenleaf?"

"Aye, your honour."

"Take care of him."

"I will."

"Miles, have you any objection to travel?"

"None in the 'varsal world, your honour, if zo as it be made worth my while."

"I shall leave England."

"Better zo, squire; leastways, for the present. 'Scuse me, sir, but you're not lookin' at all well lately."

"No; a change will be good for me. But first, Miles, two things are to be done."

"Zure, if I can help your honour—What are they?"

"First, we must mislead—totally mislead—this meddler the gipsy speaks of, and then we must quiet the gipsy himself."

"Well, squire, I do zay, what must be must be. Has your honour heard the news about the Jew Nathan's darter?"

"No."

"Well, it's told as she be disappeared altogether mysterious, and zome there be as will have she be gone on the track of Master Dan'l."

"She had best not cross his path," said the squire, bitterly.

"I 'gree with your honour," said the countryman, smiling drily. "If she won't be convinced of his innocence, she'll have to larn the effects of her own obstinacy. But these women, if they once takes a notion——"

"Well, you may go now, Miles. When shall I see you again?"

"Always at your honour's zarvice."

"Let it be to-morrow, then—and early."

"Very good, squire. Here, or at Glenleaf?"

"I will come over to you."

"All right, zur."

"Good morning, Miles."

"Zame to you, squire."

"And Miles, look after the gipsy."

"I'll watch him with the eye of a weasel, zur."

"I know I can trust you."

"You may zo. Good mornin', squire."

The countryman bowed awkwardly, and left the library.

Harwolf remained for a few moments lost in thought.

He rang the bell.

Andrew Moss came into the room and smiled as he made an obsequious bow.

"Moss, where is your lady?"

"Really, sir, as I have a 'art it really gives me pain—but I beg your pardon, as in duty bound; only being a old, I must confess a werry favoured servant, I makes humbly bold to speak."

"Well, speak plainly—what do you mean?"

"Some things isn't pleasant to the feelin's, sir," returned the worthy domestic, "though I'm quite aware as a servant which knows will allers speak plain, even when his wishes is the other way; and though I knows my place is to 'see all and say nothin', yet, as I made humbly bold on one occasion to speak my mind to your most unfort'nit and respected son, so I will now, though I dies for it. Her ladyship, sir, is a hacting in a most peculiar, not to say hextronary manner. You know, sir, as the Honourable Captain Fitz-Osbert, of the Royal Muffs, pays werry great attentions to Lady Edgeforth—as is perfect nat'ral with all handsome young gents when there is sich beauty and breedin' and the like accomplishments; but there is no reason for him to hurt her ladyship's feelin's, which we're all men and women, even when we is ladies and gentlemen."

"Hurt her feelings!—what stuff you talk, Moss. Explain yourself."

"Well, sir, at this blessed identical minute her ladyship is down in the rosary a-sobbin' and a-sighin' in a really figurative manner, and the captain is down on his bended knees a-talking like a lovier at the theayter."

"Moss," said Harwolf, after a moment's silence—a moment of intense chagrin and bitterness to him—"do you make known the result of your observations to your fellow-servants?"

"To the lower servants? Lord, sir, I has a 'art—I beg your humblest parding—and dignity becomes all men. I have no connexion with the lower servants at all, sir, which may mean well, but is ignorant and inquisitive; but what I do see I am humbly bold to tell you, sir."

"Thanks; and now, Moss, leave me, and as I am about to retire to the dressing-room for an hour or so to write, don't suffer anyone to disturb me."

Moss was about to speak.

Harwolf waved him away impatiently.

The butler made his salaam, and glided out of the room.

Harwolf rose.

His face was fixed as the face of a statue, its workings were numbed. The chill hand of care seemed to have petrified that clammy, wrinkled brow, and frosted the thick, massy hair which hung so heavily upon those withered temples, and to have left no other life in that countenance but the intrinsic spark that glimmered ever and anon on the brink of a black abyss of guilt and misery.

Harwolf walked across the grounds towards the rosary.

His brain was so absorbed with its mental atmosphere of shadowy threatenings and fiery remembrances that he had no thought of jealousy—a passion too immediate: his mind brooded on the hovering darkness of the past and future.

Almost mechanically, then, but with a dull, stifled pang knawing at his heart's core, he stole across the lawn, and crept softly near the arbour of roses.

He heard a woman's voice—a voice that could once thrill his every nerve, that could bring the fresh warm blood welling up to his now arid heart.

"Edmund, why do you tempt me? What you urge is true," said Lady Edgeforth. "I do not, cannot, love my husband; but I must not forget that I am his wife, and he is my husband."

"But, Lady Edgeforth, he is not worthy to be so remembered."

"Oh, I beseech you not to judge me harshly! I am ineffably wretched, and the misery of my present condition renders temptation more luring. What have I to live for? How much reason have I to sigh for death! My husband treats me with the chillest politeness—entirely neglects me; my son is hunted about the world on a false and dreadful charge, and I have no one to protect me from such importunities as yours."

"But, Lady Edgeforth, did you ever love this man?"

"Oh, yes; I did, I did, with all my heart's affection," cried Lady Edgeforth, "till—till——"

"Till you found that his love for you was no more, and that you had nothing further to expect of him than indifference and neglect."

"Yes—yes! just so," returned the lady, in great confusion, "I meant no more than that."

"Then if you do not love him; if he has forfeited your esteem and confidence, as I know he must have done, being most palpably a villain, why will a woman of your judgment trammel herself with considerations of what the world will say? Indeed, the world is more charitable than your scruples, and will only commend you for escaping the wretch. And I—

Oh! Lady Edgeforth, if you could tell how passionately I adore you——"

"Hist! we are watched," said Lady Edgeforth; "some of the prying servants from the Hall are by the lodge of yon gate. They see us. Let us walk along the path."

"But I may hope?"

"You need not despair, Edmund. I cannot live in this wretched place much longer; there is a black cloud hangs over it that lies on my spirits like the sinking roof of the leaden dungeons of the Piombi; it descends every day nearer and nearer, and will crush me heart and mind if I do not fly from beneath it—but let us walk."

The voices died off along the shrubbery.

The wretched Harwolf stood behind the arbour with his hands and teeth clenched. His thoughts found utterance, and fluttered from his quivering lips in hoarse and broken accents—

"Let her go! What is she to me? There is nothing to me in this world—nothing—nothing—nothing! Then why not die? I have a strange thought—a quaint, strange thought. If I were to cut my own throat; if I were to offer my life's blood as a libation to the haunting manes of him I—I murdered, perhaps it might atone."

He started.

"Yet why should I be my own executioner?" he said, grimly; "where are the days that once I knew; where is my old self. Andrew—fool—be once more the hard, the imperturbable. I drink too much. I am getting old. Clues that lead the way to the blue-chamber in my house strew the earth like spring ground-weeds, and they tangle about my feet and weary me. I wish I had killed that woman—that I had not suffered her to live to lose her reason—that I had never seen her mad! Mad! Ugh—horrible. I have heard that madness is infectious. If I should go mad!"

With this constantly-recurring thought still torturing his brain, Harwolf returned to the house; he locked himself in the dressing-room.

He drank a dram of brandy, and then walked with a firmer step to the *armoire*.

He pulled out his keys as he muttered—

"Yes, like her ladyship, I weary of Frontemore, though I paid for it with my soul, and signed the contract in letters of blood. I weary of it, and I'll depart; she may go her way and I will go mine, but I'll take care to leave no trace of the past behind me; and first, I'll secure the papers that identify the true heir, whom I turned abroad like a houseless cur, to be bandied from foot to foot by the citizens of this great, heartless world. They shall find it hard to hunt me down. I will leave them little to find; I will destroy all proofs."

He opened the *armoire* as he spoke. He was rather surprised to find a few loose papers scattered without the drawers.

With some trepidation he touched the secret spring of one of the drawers: it flew open, but saving for a single leaf of paper it was empty.

Overwhelmed with dismay he started back.

He eagerly tore open the other drawers; they were alike empty—the papers were gone.

Harwolf sank in his chair in the most profound despair.

Presently he started up, and snatched the paper from the secret drawer. It contained these words—

"*The documents relating to the birth of Lord Edgeforth, and the proofs of his father's murder by the present usurper of the Frontemore estates—Andrew Harwolf—are in the hands of the protectors of Lady Edgeforth.*"

The terror and agony of Harwolf at reading these fatal words were too great for description.

He foamed with rage.

"Yet," he exclaimed, "this is well in one way. I am a maudlin idiot. Do I not know that half the world are worse than I, only they let 'I dare not wait upon I will,' and are too cowardly to snatch the prize they covet. Ha—ha! So they put me upon my mettle, do they. Well, I am roused at last. No more remorse; the furies shall not be more insatiate than I for the torment of this enemy. I will find him out, and I will have his life!—his life!

CHAPTER LXXIII.

THE BOY PIRATE'S NEW MISSION.

SOME months after the events recorded in our former chapters, Leon de Zamora and the Boy Pirate were walking in the streets of Rio de Janiero.

The Spaniard had resolved to visit certain quarters in the city, in which he knew that he should find many members of the numerous band of which he was the leader.

It was his intention to refit his vessels, some of which were already lying in the harbour, for several of the ships which belonged to his flotilla had escaped the effects of that storm which wrecked the vessel on which he had embarked, and these had been brought into the harbour by his lieutenants.

Leon de Zamora soon announced himself to the crews of these piratical craft, and was welcomed with great demonstrations of zeal, and at once re-installed in his post as commander.

Rio de Janiero is a strange, gay city, crowded at all times by mariners from every country. The Boy Pirate and his companion threaded the streets, and passed through the motley throngs that crowded them, absorbed in the interest of the subject of their conversation.

Before leaving this port Leon was anxious to accomplish a long-cherished design.

He confided to the Boy Pirate his intention of attempting to rescue a friend who was at the time a prisoner in one of the closest dungeons in the old castle of San Salvador, on the banks of the Rio Paranahyba. He related the story of the captive in these words—

"Although at present, senor, I have the honour to command the largest flotilla that is under the direction of a single privateer—at least along the coasts of South America—I was formerly but a mate on board the 'Montezuma,' and served under Don Giraldez, in whose cause I hope to enlist your sympathy and obtain your valuable assistance.

"You must have heard of my former master, senor. He was a man of learning, of pure descent, of a brave and chivalrous disposition; had followed the sea from his childhood, and had served in high command in the Brazilian fleet; and finally, invested his large fortune in fitting out a splendid flotilla. He received certificates from the Government, and cruised in the Pacific as a privateer. For several years he was the scourge of the seas; and then, worn out with age and infirmities, the venerable old man, who rivalled your much extolled Drake or Raleigh in his deeds of daring, and who had served his country so long and faithfully, relinquished to me the command of his vessels, and retired to his estates in Mexico, where he hoped to pass the remainder of his declining days in peace and honour. But he had many enemies. Friendship is evanescent, hatred is enduring. Many who were deeply indebted to him

for a thousand services ignored his very existence; but those who had incurred his resentment, or who envied his prosperity, were watchful for an opportunity to work his ruin.

"In a sweet and pastoral district Giraldez passed a life of rest and seclusion, surrounded by his family and neighbours, who treated him with the greatest reverence and tenderness.

"Some insult had been offered to the French flag; the Government of that empire demanded explanations. The enemies of Giraldez urged in the Senate that some one must be sacrificed to satisfy the French ambassador, who had threatened to leave the city.

"As the highest authorities in the state were implicated in the affair, which had given umbrage to the French, it was insisted by the enemies of Giraldez that it would be advisable to bring evidence against him, which some of the senators offered to produce, to convict him as a pirate and a traitor, and to transpose the onus of the late indignity the French had suffered to his aged shoulders, and to make him pay the penalty of his country's injustice. Giraldez was dragged from his farm, and after a mock trial was thrown into a dungeon at the Castle of San Salvador."

"And is the place impregnable?" asked the Boy Pirate.

"It is accounted so, and it could never be taken by any force that we could bring against it," replied Zamora; "but what we cannot do by strength we may effect by strategy."

"But how will you get into the place?"

"Ah! there's the question."

"Well, I think I have a key that will open the prison door."

"I do not understand you."

"You have no doubt of the service I was able to render to the celebrated Cardinal Gonsalvez, whom I rescued from the brigands in Spain?"

"I am acquainted with all the details of the case, as also of your subsequent duel with an old comrade of mine, Don Carlos."

"Well, this cardinal gave me letters of recommendation to several of the principal hidalgos in Rio de Janiero, and one of special importance to the governor himself. Could I not, think you, by making use of this interest, obtain permission to visit the captive Giraldez?"

"You could but try their efficacy, and I do not fear you would obtain our mutual wish, senor, and be enabled to ascertain whether Giraldez be still alive, or whether he has died in bonds; and if, indeed, he live there is little fear but occasion will offer some means of setting him free."

"Then I will go at once to the house of the governor," said the Boy Pirate, with animation.

"And I will accompany you as far as the wine-shop at the corner of the quay; for, though I am well disguised, I have bitter foes in the town, and may be recognised."

As the Spaniard said these words a gentleman-like, but sullen-looking man, wrapped in a long Spanish cloak, turned the corner.

"For my part," said the Boy Pirate, laughing,

" I was never born to walk the world in masquerade; I always despise myself when I am disguised, and feel thrice as aggressive and pugnacious as at other times. I like to look my foes in the face; but I have often fretted under false colours for weeks and months, and therefore should learn caution."

The stranger had passed them.

Neither of the pirates had observed him.

He turned round and fixed his eyes on the noble form of the youthful rover.

His face was lighted with a glare of hate and malicious pleasure.

Keeping out of sight as much as possible, he follows the steps of Christopher and his friend, never for an instant losing sight of them.

The Boy Pirate left Zamora at the wine-shop of which he had spoken, and hastened on towards the governor's house.

The stranger still followed him, and started with surprise at seeing him ascend the steps of the governor's palace.

He entered a wine-shop opposite the building, and, taking his position by the window in such a manner that he could see all who passed in or out of the house, called for some wine, and, lighting his cigar, settled himself down for a long and vigilant watch.

Meanwhile our hero had ascended the steps with graceful and dignified air, and entered the alcove, where a number of haughty-looking Spaniards in naval and military uniforms, bedizened with sashes and orders, were loitering, prior to their admission to the magnificent presence of His Excellency the Governor of Rio Janiero.

The Boy Pirate was very handsomely dressed, and created a great impression; a loud and enquiring whisper went round the gay crowd, who drew back as the daring outlaw passed along with as much self-possession as if he had been pacing the decks of his own vessel.

A chamberlain advanced to meet him.

In a few courteous words the Boy Pirate expressed his desire of being allowed a private interview with his excellency, and produced his credentials.

The chamberlain glanced at them, and then with much ceremony ushered the Boy Pirate into another apartment.

Christopher seated himself, and the officer left the room, telling our hero that he would return as soon as possible with an answer from his excellency.

Left alone, our hero coolly took up one of the newspapers that strewed the table, and was soon absorbed in the perusal of an article on the suppression of piracy in the high seas.

After some time the chamberlain returned and expressed his excellency's readiness to receive the youthful bearer of the cardinal's letters of credence

Upon entering the reception-room the Boy Pirate found himself in the presence of an elderly man, white-haired, but hale and stalwart, whose broad breast glittered with stars and ribbons, and whose left arm was fixed in a sling, apparently disabled by a wound received in battle.

The governor rose and extended his hand to our hero with a courteous smile.

" I feel more pleasure than I can express, senor," he said, " in the honour of this meeting. Captain Paul Manvers is one to whom I owe a debt of gratitude as the preserver of my only brother the aged Cardinal Gonsalvez."

" Your excellency's kindness exaggerates the merits of the little service I was fortunately the means of rendering to the cardinal," returned the Red Raven; " and I am, therefore, the more grateful for the good disposition you show towards one who is a stranger, with no other recommendation than these credentials."

" And they are all-sufficient, Captain Paul Manvers. I lived long in England; my happiest reminiscences are connected with your queenly island. I fancy that I have been acquainted with some of your relatives?"

Christopher Foundling started. *His* relations? Who could know aught of his relations; a parentless outcast in the harsh, cold world from the day of his birth.

" It may be possible," returned the Boy Pirate, calmly smiling, though with a quiver of pain on his thin, arched lip, but I myself know little of my kinsmen; I was brought up abroad."

" Indeed! You speak Spanish like a native."

" I fear you flatter me; but I am no stranger in these parts."

" I am glad to hear it—I hope you never will be. Captain Paul, I am most delighted to meet with you; but I was saying, that from the remarkable resemblance you bear to a cherished friend of my youth, I should almost take you for his son; but as that cannot be, you must be some near relation—his nephew, perhaps."

" And he, your excellency, who is he?"

The governor spoke half musingly—

" Poor fellow. Mysterious! I do not know what became of him. Left his home—never heard of after —killed most likely by brigands—lost in a storm or murdered by the hellish pirates. Well—well; he was my earliest friend."

" But, sir, your excellency has not told me his name," said the Boy Pirate, quelling his excitement, yet, in spite of himself, speaking with intense eagerness.

" Lord Edgeforth!"

The Boy Pirate recoiled, every vestige of colour stole from his cheek; he could scarcely keep himself from falling.

The life-long persecution of young Harwolf—the ill-will shown him by the reputed Lady Edgeforth when he was a boy; that taunt—that epithet " little pirate," which had envenomed his heart against his kind, and forced him into the belief that every " man's hand was against him," and that he had no alternative but to turn his hand against the world in his own defence—all—all was plain now; he could not doubt it—but, oh! the anguish, the shame that came with the knowledge he had so often in secret yearned to gain. He was not ignobly born—though had he been, he should not have despised his parentage—he had by right the precious advantages that high birth gives; position, wealth and honour. He might, he would have used them for the noblest ends, but now the long race of his knightly ancestors ended in a felon, a pirate. The breed of eagles had degenerated to a carrion crow, a miserable "Red Raven."

"You seem to be surprised at this little coincidence," said the governor, with much astonishment; "perhaps you were acquainted with Lord Edgeforth, and cannot think of him without emotion?"

A shade of anguish flitted across the pirate's face, and he answered evasively—

"No one, your excellency, can be so insensible as not to sympathise with a case so deplorable. I have heard of his lordship," he went on, sickening with disgust at his own duplicity, "but I had no idea that he bore any resemblance to me."

"You shall judge for yourself," replied the governor, "take a glance at yourself in that mirror, and I will produce the fac-simile of its reflection." With this the old gentleman opened a bureau and drew therefrom a velvet case.

This he opened with a spring, and disclosed the portrait of the last Lord Edgeforth.

The fine intelligent face, with its affectionate beam and its fearless manliness, seemed to start from the pearl-bordered case, and to wreathe in yearning smiles as the foundling looked on it.

The Boy Pirate turned away his head in silent agony.

"It's very like you, Captain Paul. Indeed, if you displayed this picture as your own portrait every one would praise its exactness; there is but one trait missing, as I perceive, and that may well be dispensed with."

"And what is that, your excellency?" asked the Boy Pirate, after a struggle for speech.

"That under-shade of melancholy, may I say regret, that throws the more active traits in your countenance into such bold relief. You will pardon these remarks, Captain Paul; I am fond of the arts—in fact, am something of a painter myself; but don't think I'm going to weary you by showing the paces of my hobby. And you like the miniature?"

"So much that I would give all I possess to call it mine!" cried the Boy Pirate, with vehemence.

"Well, then, as it has to be reproduced for me in the form of a full-length portrait by an eminent Italian painter, on one condition you shall have it."

"Name it; Oh, name it!"

"I learn from my brother, the Cardinal Gonsalvez, that you are a 'knight errant'—rather a *rara avis* now-a-days—that you are the rewarder of virtue and the redresser of wrong. If by any possibility you can find any clue to the mystery of Lord Edgeforth's disappearance, follow it up till it bring you to the scene of his death and the person of his assassin—for I feel sure he was murdered—and then revenge him."

"I will! So help me Heaven, as I keep my oath," cried the Boy Pirate, passionately.

"You seem greatly moved; no doubt there is real cause for this emotion. I cannot think your resemblance to my hapless friend can be the effect of mere coincidence. But now may I ask you what was the immediate cause of your seeking this interview?"

The Boy Pirate explained to the governor that certain friends in Spain were anxious to know whether the celebrated Giraldez was living; and he also stated that he himself had particular reasons for wishing to see him.

The governor looked grave, and told his visitor that he could scarcely grant him a pass without a stretch of his authority; that he had a great respect for Giraldez, and that it was through no fault of his that the worthy, patriotic old admiral was kept in such cruel bondage.

Christopher pressed his suit, made the most of the cardinal's influence, and after some time exacted a reluctant consent from the governor, accredited by his written order, of admission to the dungeons of San Salvador.

With many expressions of courtesy, Christopher took his leave.

The governor shook him warmly by the hand.

"Make my house your home during your stay at Rio Janeiro, Captain Paul," he said. "I claim your friendship, and so, for the present, adieu; and you will not forget the condition on which I have surrendered the portrait of my dear friend."

"Never, your excellency."

"And if your spirit of enterprise leads you to seek an adventure as glorious as perilous, I can recommend one that might engage all your youthful ardour and approved courage."

"And what enterprise is that, your excellency?"

"Why, if you like, I will fit you out a war-ship," returned the governor, with a smile, "with which you shall hunt down that outrageous rascal—that unconquerable corsair—that has baffled all our efforts to take him—the terrible Red Raven, the Boy Pirate!"

"Ah, your excellency, that is an enterprise beyond my humble capacity," returned the rover, with a dry smile; "let us hope that the redoubtable outlaw may some day mend his ways, and command one of your vessels himself, with credit to your state and glory to himself."

"That's an odd wish, Captain Paul; but you are so romantic. Well, personally, I owe the rogue no grudge, and we Brazilians cannot afford to be too squeamish as to those we employ, for our own maritime polity will not bear too nice scrutiny. Farewell till your next visit, which I hope will be early. I cannot but laugh at the honour you wish for the 'Raven,' but he's a dashing fellow. Well, adios, senor."

With much urbanity, the old gentleman once more shook hands with the rover, and they parted.

Christopher hurried through the streets in a state of bewilderment, eager to join his ally.

No sooner had he passed the window of the wineshop from which the strange man was watching him, than the latter emerged from the door, tracked the Boy Pirate for a little distance, and then returned to the governor's palace, and at once mounted the steps and entered by the porch.

When Christopher joined Zamora he told him the result of his interview with the governor, and showed him the official letter which gave him authority to pay two visits to the captive Giraldez.

Zamora was delighted, and after some consultation it was determined that the Boy Pirate should pay his first visit to the prison that night, and that he should make use of the occasion to convey to the captive an intimation of the attempts about to be made for his deliverance.

The companions started on their mission. They left the town, and as the evening approached the dark bastions of the tower of San Salvador appeared crowning the rocks by the side of the broad and glancing river.

Zamora remained in a little wayside inn, keeping himself close in a private apartment, while the Boy Pirate went forward to the castle.

It was not without much trouble that he gained admission into the grim fortress, which he found to be garrisoned with soldiers.

The provost-marshal, the chief officer of the place, examined his papers, and after a long delay ordered a heavy-browed brutal-looking gaoler to conduct the stranger to the dungeon of Giraldez.

This fellow led the way down long flights of stone stairs, along winding passages, and, last of all, made a final descent into a well-like cavity that brought them to a heavy, iron-bound door. This was opened by the morose-looking janitor.

The Boy Pirate entered, and found himself in a square stone room.

A lamp swung from the ceiling, faintly illumining the humid stones. On a pallet of straw an old man was reclining, chained by the leg to a staple in the ground.

He appeared sleeping, but started up as the visitor entered, and looked at him with a vacant stare.

DANIEL HARWOLF REVEALS THE SECRET OF CHRISTOPHER'S BIRTH.

The Boy Pirate eyed the captive for an instant with a look of compassion and indignation, and then, with a kindly impulse, threw himself down by his side.

The old man raised himself on one hand, and glared into the face of our hero with a wild, strange look.

His eyes shone with a beam of suspicion and semi-insanity.

His beard was matted and grisly, and his unkempt hair was strewn upon his bent shoulders.

"Ave Maria Purissima! have you come to kill me, hidalgo?" he said, in a voice hoarse and faint with disuse. "Be quick, then, amigo; I wish to be gone."

"Poor fellow; I have come to save you if I can, and if that prove to be impossible I will avenge you
No. 24.

with as much remorselessness as if you were my father."

"Aye que hombre, what a man," said the aged captive, with a discordant laugh. "Do you think you can move the Senate with your prayers? More probably you can break these shackles with your teeth—I have tried that. Go away; leave me alone."

The old man crouched down upon the dank stones and groaned deeply.

"O God! is it possible that man can be so cruel to his fellow-men?" cried the Red Raven, in a tone of sympathy. "I am a pirate, but the worst of my foes—could I treat them thus?"

"What do you want—to kill me?" cried Giraldez. "Well, then, here is my throat. I am half dead already."

"Do not mistake my mission; I am not come to harm but to save you," was Christopher's reply; "But hush! I will see that there are no listeners."

The Boy Pirate rose and approached the door.

He listened for a moment; all was still.

He mounted the steps.

A light burned in the passage above.

The savage gaoler was seated on the ground, with folded arms and closed eyes.

"Is he asleep?" muttered the Boy Pirate, clutching his poignard.

He cautiously advanced upon the janitor.

The man opened his eyes and stared at the Boy Pirate with a look of alarm.

"What is it, senor?" he growled out in his surly accents.

The Boy Pirate stepped back, feeling that prudence dictated that he should kill the gaoler, and possess himself of his keys, but such an act was revolting in its treachery to the mind of the generous Christopher, and he was glad it seemed impossible.

"Your captive dies with hunger. Can you get him some food!"

"Against orders," returned the surly keeper, curtly, and closing his eyes.

"But I will pay for it. Let it be something good."

"Do you take me for a *tortillera*? I am neither cook nor confectioner," the man replied, with an insolent leer.

The fiery Boy Pirate, upon the mirror of whose eyes still floated the sad spectacle of the loathsome dungeon and its misery-maddened occupant, felt an almost irresistible impulse to dash out the brains of the unfeeling scoundrel before him against the prison walls.

He restrained himself, however, with great difficulty, and replied suavely,

"My good fellow, I am from England——"

"You lie! You are a Spaniard," interrupted the ruffian, ferociously.

"I'll excuse the insult in behalf of the compliment to my efficiency in your language," replied Christopher, torturing his face into a smile. "My good fellow, here is gold—English gold; get me some food and a bottle of *pulque*."

"And while I am gone to fetch it you will be trying some cursed scheme to liberate the prisoner. Ha, Senor Heretico!"

"I am not such a fool; but if you are so insolent I will report you to the provost."

"And I will tell him you are an Englishman and a heretic, and he will applaud me," replied the gaoler, with a grin. "Go; your time will be up shortly, make the most of it; say what you have to say to the prisoner and be off—though you might as well go at once, for this air is unwholesome, and Giraldez will not understand you, he is *medio tonta* —half a fool!"

The Boy Pirate frowned darkly, and was returning to the dungeon, when the gaoler called out,

"Here, Senor Inglesa! What will you give me?"

The Boy Pirate drew out a gold piece.

"This to begin with. You shall have two others if you bring me something good."

The gaoler clutched the money greedily, laid it on the palm of his hand, examined it by the light of his lantern, and then rung it on the stones.

He rose, and looked doubtingly on our hero.

"You English are devils," he said, politely. "Well, you can't get out of this place, so there's no use in trying to do so. I'll go on one condition."

"What is it?"

"I must lock you up with Giraldez till I return."

"Be it so," returned the rover.

"Come along, then."

"Have you many captives in this place?"

"What, in San Salvador? Not so many as formerly," growled the gaoler.

"And for that you should be glad," said Christopher; "you have less work to do."

"I like my business," the ruffian answered, with a villanous scowl.

They reached the dungeon.

They entered.

"See that what you bring me is fit to eat; I shall pay you in accordance with its quality," said the Boy Pirate.

"You seem to think this place an hotel or a *pulque* shop," rejoined the man. "But I'll rummage the refectory, and see what I can get; in the meanwhile you are a prisoner."

With this he left the cell, and slammed the heavy door noisily.

The clash of the bolts shot through the rover's feeling heart, and he turned his eye pityingly upon the wretched prisoner.

"Is he gone?" said Giraldez, a sickly smile on his wan face. "And are you, too, a prisoner? You look gay and handsome enough now, hidalgo; but a little while, the dirt and the darkness, the rats and the vermin, loneliness, hunger, and misery will make you what I am. Hark!" he went on, striking his chains upon the echoing stones; "that is my music; I could play tunes with them once; but time died, and when time was dead my heart died too, and I had no soul for music."

The Boy Pirate raised him tenderly.

"Giraldez!" he whispered, softly; "nerve yourself; I have come to save you; I am a successful man, and mostly carry my wildest schemes to a successful issue. I am come to set you free."

"Free!" murmured the captive, dreamily. "What is it to be free? To revel in the light of broad day; to drink in the air of Heaven; to see woods of green, waters of crystal, and clouds of gold. Why are free men ever wretched?"

"As God shall help me once more, you shall taste these rich delights too little valued," returned the Boy Pirate, greatly moved. "I have come to rescue you; it cannot be done in a moment—but be of good cheer, it shall be done; he has sworn it who always keeps his word."

"But who are you, young senor?"

"I am an Englishman and a seaman."

"Ah, but I do not know you. You knew me, perhaps, in those bright days that seem so long gone by."

"This is the first time I have seen you of whom I have heard so much; but I come on behalf of my friend, your former lieutenant, Don Leon de Zamora."

"Zamora! Ha! did he send you? Cannot it be true, or are you a traitor?"

"It will matter little whether I be or no if you cannot muster strength to aid in the exertions needful for your own liberation. But hark, here is the gaoler."

The trampling of feet and the clanking of keys were heard without.

The door was opened; it grated harshly, and swung back on its rusty and massive hinges.

The gaoler entered, bearing a plate of bread and meat and a bottle of *pulque*.

He set them down and stood staring at the visitor.

"I will visit you once more, and will try to get my pass renewed. I was particularly requested by the governor to bring him a minute account of the nature of your treatment and the condition of your place of confinement," said the Boy Pirate, speaking in an even tone, in order to deceive the gaoler.

He then placed the bottle to the captive's lips.

Giraldez drank greedily.

"Thanks, senor," he murmured, with a long sigh. "Good angels keep you and the Virgin intercede with Heaven to bless you—that moment was ecstatic. Now I can eat, and then I shall be able to talk with you about the world without, which I shall never see again."

The Boy Pirate smiled; the last words of the old man sounded pleasantly in his ear, for they gave token of his returning consciousness and his natural shrewdness.

The Boy Pirate took a drink from the bottle and passed it to the gaoler.

He then drew out two gold pieces and gave them to the man.

"Drink," he said to the gaoler, "the rest of the *pulque* in the bottle; drink health to the captive and to me, for if you want to retire from your office I will give you a berth in my vessel, and reward you handsomely."

The gaoler gave a peculiar look at the Boy Pirate, and then quaffed off the remainder of the liquor at one draught.

He dashed down the bottle, and then sprang on to the step of the door.

"Look you, hidalgo, I hate you because you are an Englishman. I am an honest man, and you have tried to corrupt me. Well, I will go to the provost and tell him what you say; in the meantime you are my prisoner."

With a chuckling laugh the fellow was about to spring through the door, when, to our hero's amazement, Giraldez scrambled to the end of his chain and caught him by the leg.

Thus tripped, the fellow fell heavily, his temples striking against the stone step.

Christopher ran to him.

The man did not move.

The Boy Pirate turned him over on to his back; his upturned face was deadly pale, and he was evidently stunned by the fall.

"Senor, your presence of mind is admirable," said Christopher to the prisoner. "I see you are recovering your resources."

"The drink and food have revived the little spark of my old cunning, and that is sufficient to baffle such a mean brute as this," returned the captive, with a smile.

"He does not bleed, so he will remain insensible," observed the Red Raven. "But there is no time to be lost."

The Boy Pirate ran from the dungeon, once more ascended the stairs, and harkened intently. All was still as death.

He returned, and drew a file from his pouch.

He then set to work to sever the links of the chain that bound the unfortunate Giraldez to the staple in the ground.

The prisoner groaned once or twice, but suppressed his anguish, although the operation gave him great pain.

Christopher worked as carefully as he could, using all possible tenderness.

When he had disconnected the links, he gently drew the captive from the spot.

"And now, my good senor, what is to be done?" asked Giraldez.

"As I came down the passage that leads to your cell, I observed an arched doorway, and from its appearance and by the look of the pavement, I should fancy it leads into another corridor that may bring us to an outlet. I will go and try the lock, and will return to report progress."

With this, the Boy Pirate cut the keys from the gaoler's girdle, and, taking the lantern, once more left the dungeon.

Arrived before the door he had mentioned, the Boy Pirate tried several of the keys.

At last he found one that would fit the lock, but it was only by the exertion of great strength that he was able to turn the key.

The bolt flew back with the report of a pistol.

The blood flushed to Christopher's cheek, and his heart leapt. He stood thralled for an instant, harkening intently.

Still as the grave!

He pushed open the door. The damp, chill air wafted in his face.

He groped along, for it was very dark.

His lantern rendered him but little help, for its feeble ray struggled scarcely through a square yard of the surrounding gloom.

On one side he could distinguish a cell, with an open, broken door.

Into this he entered, and held aloft the lantern till his eyes became accustomed to the more than semi-obscurity.

There was a loud scampering of rats.

Something glittered like a diamond at his feet—it was the eye of a huge toad, ugly and venomous. He started back with a shudder from the loathsome reptile, on which he had wellnigh trodden.

He advanced a step.

A sad spectacle presented itself.

Against a pillar was chained a skeleton—the remains of some wretch; the skull—his own hated crest—seemed to glare at him with its eyeless cavities, and grin at him with its fleshless jaws, while the few squalid rags in which it was enveloped fluttered in the stealing draughts.

Christopher stepped quickly from the cell.

He thought it advisable, however, to pursue his way.

To his bitter disappointment, after travelling to the end of the passage he found himself stopped by a dead wall of solid stone blocks.

He was retracing his steps with much chagrin when his foot struck against an iron ring. He stumbled, and almost fell.

Upon applying the lantern, he found the object to be an iron hoop fixed into the stone by a staple.

He tried to raise it, but he could not effect his purpose. Carefully examining the slab, he found on one side of it a strong iron spring; upon pressing this with his heel the slab sank at one end, and with some difficulty, the Boy Pirate managed to lift it, and found it was a trap.

As he raised it, he was conscious that he was moving some hidden machinery.

But he heeded nothing except his eager curiosity to know whither the steps he could make out would conduct him.

Faintly stole down from the turret, its tone deadened by the obstacles through which it must vibrate, the rapid toll of a bell.

Could it be that the machinery was connected in some way with an alarm in the turret, and that the stone could not be raised without awaking the malicious utterances of its iron throat?

If so, what was to be done?

Christopher had gone too far to recede.

For a moment he wished he had deferred his attempt till the next visit his pass permitted, and that he had contented himself, according to agreement, simply with making his observations on the present occasion.

But no time could be spared for idle regret. All was lost if he could not make his escape at once.

He flew down the steps.

The place was so narrow and dark that he was above his knees in water before he perceived that the staircase led down to the river.

Upon groping about with his lantern he perceived a boat, while far ahead, like a pale star, could be discerned the blessed day-light without this aqueous tunnel.

The vibrations of the bell could still be faintly heard.

Would it not be well for him, now that he had a chance of securing personal safety, to leap into the boat and make off at his best speed?

What, to leave the old man whom he had come to save to a more rigorous confinement—to more cruel usage?

His generous heart spurned the thought.

He sprang back, flew wildly along the passage, and breathlessly rushed into the dungeon.

"Senor," he cried, "I have found a way of escape, but I fear I have raised an alarm. We must fly at once; not a moment's delay or all is lost."

"Alas, senor, but I cannot walk," returned the aged Giraldez, pointing to his swollen limbs.

"Then I must carry you," was the Boy Pirate's resolute reply.

With this he raised his venerable load to his brawny shoulders.

Giraldez took the lantern and the keys.

The Boy Pirate gripped his sword in his teeth, and grasped a revolver in his right hand.

He left the dungeon.

Scarcely had he reached the arched door of the stone corridor than a stream of red light flowed along the passage in which he stood, and the trampling of feet was heard racing down the stairs by which the gaoler had led him to the dungeon.

The Boy Pirate flew through the door of the corridor and slammed it after him.

With loud curses and cries, a number of soldiers, headed by the provost-marshal, arrived at the spot, and began furiously battering at the barrier that parted them from the fugitives.

The Boy Pirate dashed on to gain the trap and get off in the boat.

He was within a few yards of it, when, like fiends leaping up from the earth, a number of fierce Spaniards rushed up the steps from the water tunnel, with torches, bayonetted muskets, and swords.

At their head was a man dressed in the uniform of an English naval officer.

How great was the fury and astonishment of the Red Raven on recognising his old foe—Daniel Harwolf!

The Boy Pirate fired his revolver, but his aim was unsteadied by his burden, and, though the bullet struck off the miscreant's hat, it failed to harm him.

Christopher was surrounded in an instant, his revolver knocked out of his hand, and the poor old man whom we had so gallantly risked his life to save was torn from his arms.

Fiercely the Boy Pirate struggled with his captors but he was powerless against such numbers.

With triumphant cries the world-famed Boy Pirate was whirled and dragged along.

The provost-marshal's party had broken the door and advanced to meet their comrades as they were hauling along their redoubtable prize.

With curses and taunts and jeers the gallant rover was brought to the door of the dungeon from which he had rescued Giraldez.

"Senor," said the old man, who was by his side for a few moments, "the saints will shield you, but I am not worthy so great a sacrifice. But who are you, that the villains show such extraordinary malice?"

"Well they may," returned the Boy Pirate, grimly. "I am the Red Raven, but there are other birds in my eyry whose beaks and talons shall be red with the blood of these curs."

In a few moments the Boy Pirate lay chained to the ground on the same spot where Giraldez had languished so many years of anguish.

The door was closed, but Christopher was not alone.

Upon looking up he saw before him the form of his ungenerous enemy.

Harwolf looked down upon him with tightly-folded arms and demon-like eyes in gloating triumph.

The dauntless rover looked upon him with exquisite disdain, ineffable disgust, and haughtily waved him away.

Spite of himself the mean villain obeyed the movement, and receded a step.

"And have I reached you, scorner!" cried Harwolf, with a bitter laugh. "Fortune before this has snatched you out of my hands when your case seemed most desperate, but now I am sure of you; were it not so I would have shot you dead when I saw you first in the midst of your Quixotic adventure, when I cut off your last chance of escape. My gallant Red Rover, your career is past; the best thing you can do is to strangle yourself with your chains, or dash out your brains against the stones of your prison, for you are marked for the hangman. And your brave ship, by this time she is safely docked in the harbour, for the whole fleet will be on the wing to capture such a prize. And Lilia, she shall be mine; not my bride, but my slave. You thought you did a generous thing when you set me at liberty; I hate you for your generosity. I would rather you had killed me than fettered me with the loathsome obliga-

tion. Farewell sweet dreams and pleasant waking; this dungeon is dark, but the grave will be darker."

"Heaven is more powerful than your master, the devil," replied the Boy Pirate, with a calm, contemptuous smile; "and if, in his justice, he strike me down, I dare not murmur. But though I am chained and defenceless, with death doomed upon me, I am confident I shall yet escape. The thunderbolt my crimes may have called down will never pass through the hands of such a villain as you."

"'Despair your charm,'" returned the scoundrel, with a fiendish leer. "My family were born to plague yours. I will tell you now, because the knowledge can do me no injury and will be a bitter plague to you. You have been, since consciousness dawned into reason, a pauper in the great workhouse of the world—a foundling, at the tender mercy of the hardest-hearted guardians. Poor, friendless whelp, what could you do but bite the legs of those who kicked you; but why did you so? Why did you not sneak and fawn as other hounds that are houseless and masterless? Because you were thorough-bred—no cur by birth, though a cur in inheritance. You are the son of Lord Edgeforth, Christopher Foundling; you are descended from the Earls of Frontemore, Red Raven the Pirate! My father slew your father, my mother usurped your mother's fortunes, and I myself have brought you to the gallows."

"Villain," cried the Boy Pirate, in a voice of intense passion and anguish. "There is a sweetness in the very bitterness of your malice, for it is so inhuman that while this fair world is governed by the Essence of Good, it cannot prevail to you—even to you. I confess myself a wretched criminal, but I was driven into my courses by the 'whips and scorns' of the cruellest oppressors, and never has blood been shed by this hand except in my own defence, or in righting the wrongs of those whom I loved. When I was under the sway of others, I did my utmost to quench their cruel lusts, and to soften the strokes that fell upon their victims. Since I have fought under my own flag I have used all temperateness and mercy that were compatible with my sad calling. I am only the less a villain. I know it; but let Heaven punish me. You will never dare to harm a hair of this head, and I shall yet live to revenge my father's death and my mother's wrongs, chained and powerless as I am. Flee me, flee me, for I am your Nemesis, Daniel Harwolf; you may run a long course, but you cannot escape me!"

The miscreant's grey eye flashed with deadly malice.

"I will settle that question at once," he hissed forth, between his clenched teeth. "I will despatch you now, even though I lose the joyous spectacle of your ignominious execution. I will take 'a bond of fate' sealed with your blood!"

The ruffian, as he spoke, levelled his pistol at the rover's heart.

He pulled the trigger with a brutal laugh.

The pistol flashed in the pan.

Livid pale, the scoundrel let it fall from his hand.

The Boy Pirate stared at him with calm defiance.

At the same moment the door opened and a soldier entered and said, addressing Harwolf,

"Senor, His Excellency the Governor has come, and is now in conference with the provost-marshal. He desires you to come to the council-room at once."

Harwolf cast a look of deadly hate at the Boy Pirate and left the room.

The door clashed to.

The bolts jarred roughly in their sockets.

The light that streamed through the crevices died out, the sound of the retreating footsteps passed away.

The darkness fell like a black pall upon the eyes of the youthful captive.

He moved his limbs, his fetters clanked, the iron entered into his soul.

He laid his beating heart against his stony pallet and threw his arm under his head.

The fluttering in his breast stilled, his breath came softly from his parted lips, his eyelids closed.

THE BOY PIRATE'S DREAM.

Light, azure and dazzling, and proceeding from no visible source, permeated the dungeon.

The walls melted away like the dissolving castles of a phantasmagoria.

Green trees waved above him and around, and the larks' matin rippled down from the far, dazing sky.

He moved; he looked around him.

Among the lordly elms and down the chequered vistas of stately limes glinted the fretted gables of the hall of his fathers.

He rose, but not in the full height of his manhood. He was a boy, a bold, free, light-hearted child, and he roamed among the flowers, the arbours, the statues and the fountains.

He wandered to the brink of a glassy pool. He looked down into its pictured depths and he perceived a face looking thoughtfully up to him.

It was the face of a child, with rich, clustering locks, fresh-budding lips, arched and fearless; eyes clear, happy, and pleading for love; limbs rounded and lithesome.

His heart kept murmuring, like the sound in a sea-shell, a strange and indistinct echo of the poetry of the past mingled with the fairy whispers of the rainbowed future.

Presently in the mirror's depths floated another face.

Gold clustering locks showered down upon his own; soft blue, tender eyes yearned upon him; sweet rich lips dimpled and smiled, and soft white arms wound gently round his shoulders. The clustering curls showered more heavily, and covered his head with their golden meshes, sweet lips touched his smooth, clear forehead, and he knew that it was his mother who kissed him.

Hand in hand with her he wandered along the marble terrace. All was summer and beauty about him.

With her he entered into pleasant rooms and drew near the chair where a dark and noble-looking student was seated, poring over a chart on which were drawn ships and their courses.

The student embraced him, and he watched how his fingers traced out deviations of the sea and the land, and he knew 'twas his father that taught him.

He lifted his eyes from these pleasant surroundings.

At the door stood a strange, tall, and ill-looking man, haughty and subtle, cruel as a ghoul.

This he knew; but the tempter still smiled and still beckoned till he went forth to follow.

Onwards and onwards, while it ever grows darker, till the form he pursued was lost in the deep gloom.

Then he lay in the darkness to rest and to slumber, and soon lost all tracings of things he had seen.

But the light came again and he rose with its dawning.

Brighter glows it and clearer; azure and dazzling intrinsic.

Then stood out the carved pillars with fairy-like wreathings, and the aisle long, blue, and vaulted.

A priest and fair company, an altar and symbols, and the flow of the organ, with the chanting of singers, whose voices seemed blent with the hymning of angels.

And his mother was near him; the gold locks were silvered, the blue eyes glowed milder; but the smile was as happy and sweet as of yore.

Dark-eyed and manly, with glance brave and radiant, yet calm and time-softened, stood his father beside her.

But nearer and dearer was one kneeling by him, in her bridal dress, sylph-like—his pure, his proud Lilia; her wreath was snow-frosted, than her pale brow not whiter. He looked, and his passion grew "stronger than death."

Then the priest read the book with the words that should bind them in links that no sorrow, nor time, nor yet discord, could break or could sever.

And the ring, plain and golden, the pledge of their union, was placed on the bond of the holiest of mysteries.

Why does the bride shriek? and why shouts the bridegroom? Why cease the organ's soft peal and the choiring of singers?

The ring is an aspic, a green and gold serpent that writhes in a circle, and sparkles and burns.

A dark form has swept 'twixt the bride and the bridegroom; a red hand is laid on the page, which it stains.

And the scene fades away; it grows darker and darker, till the darkness is utter, and lost are the traces of all that has been.

But still through the gloom sounds the groan of the dying and the wild, gushing laughter of madness.

Ah! the sounds die away as if darkness had quenched them, and the sleep dews from Lethe drench all in oblivion.

Yet the light beamed once more, and he rose with its dawning.

Brighter glowed it and clearer, azure and dazzling, intrinsic.

His bride is beside him; he yearns, but in vain, to embrace her.

Rolling clouds sweep before him; they sunder far wide in their wreathings.

Glory eternal beams forth till the sun's blaze seems pallid; yet tempered the brilliance, sweet, calm and undazing, prisms angelic float mist-like and wavering.

He starts, and in vain holds his bride to his bosom; she flees from his clasp, and before him are spirits ethereal, yet warm with life's dear personation. His parents, his wife! Ah! they wave through the Heaven-light; they smile and their eyes beam the love of immortals!

Wild, wild in his ears ring the din and the shrieks and the cry of the battle. He rushes to clasp all his soul's-loved; in anguish he rushes to flee from the fiends his companions.

Wide rolls the dark pall, black-waving and solemn, as the thunder-cloud blots out the brightness of morning.

Ghastly displayed the grim skull and the bones, gaunt and foul, the vile badge of a pirate, a murderer, a felon.

He quails; the hot tears on his cheek, the hot brand in his true heart, are searing.

All is blackness, despair. His loved ones are lost, and for ever, for ever, for ever!

Whence the mingling of voices, wild, strange in their accent, yet joyous and kindly? Whence the crowd that surrounds him and cheers him with pitying affection?

Names sweet and familiar, Mona, Aurora, and Ida; faces glowing with joy as they look on their valiant deliverer; the ebon Ashantee, the ruddy and paint-'dizened Indian, the old captive, worn with the long years of iron and darkness; the youth, with the fresh blush of first love unblighted.

Ready hands rend the veil; the pall of his shame and perdition, the pirate's fierce banner, is strewn into shreds and wide-scattered, and the glory eternal glows forth, and the sun's blaze seems pallid, and the soul of the pirate soars up with his parents and Lilia his chosen; they have crowns on their foreheads, golden and starred with the nimbus; *his* head is ungemmed, but he craves not the jewels of angels; sweet his contrition and boundless his joy.

*　　*　　*　　*

The Boy Pirate started up. Was he in Heaven? No; for the close air seemed to strangle him; his chains clanked; all was darkness around him. Leaning his hand against the pillar, he rose, kneeled—and prayed.

He lay down again, and sank into a deep sleep, that was long and dreamless.

CHAPTER LXXIV.
THE FIRST MATCH BETWEEN THE "VULTURE" AND THE "RAVEN."

OUR scene changes to the state cabin of the "Black

Vulture," where Deborah, the Jewess, and Mary Macallister, the daughter of the unfortunate Scottish merchant, had been confined by the ruthless Black Ralph.

As our reader will readily divine, the pirate-ship was moored in the harbour of Rio de Janiero.

The persons in this scene of our romantic drama are the mate Cassidy, and the two luckless maidens.

"You see I am, as it were, bound by my oath and agreement to obey all the orders of the captain of this vessel," said Cassidy, gravely.

"Weel, but dinna ye ken that you're mair bound by your conscience, and it's tacit oath to your queen and country to preserve the peace, and to do nae injury to your fellow creatures," said the clever Scotch lassie, "than by the most awesome pledges to this wicked mon and the de'il his master? Noo I'm ashamed o' ye; I'm quite ashamed o' ye. A quiet, weel-spoken, proper young mon to talk aboot a league made wi' Satan as if it were a covenant wi' the Kirk. Dinna tell me, I'd rather hae never a conscience at a' than sic a conscience as that, whilk would gie me credit for oppressing the weak and for taking part wi' the wicked and the strong."

"But what can I do? As I have told you, I am an outcast, falsely charged with the crime of forgery. I have been compelled to flee my country."

"With forgery!" said Deborah. "How came you to be charged with such a crime?"

"My story is told in a very few words," returned Cassidy. "From my birth, for I was born on the sea, I have been a sailor. Awhile ago my ship was paid off; I was chief mate on board a merchantman, and I went on shore with a pocket-full of money. I made a number of acquaintances, all promiscuously; among others, I fell in with some young chaps who were clerks in a banker's office. After we had become very intimate. one of them asked me to get a cheque for £200 cashed at a certain bank in Lombard-street, and to bring the money to him at a coffee-house, saying that he had been commissioned to draw this money, but that, falling into company, he had lingered till the banks were closed; and that as he must be at his office by nine o'clock the next morning, there was no time to carry out his skipper's orders, and that he should be very grateful to me if I would cash it for him, and bring it to the coffee-house where he dined. Unsuspectingly I complied. The money was at once given me, and I placed it in his hands; he was very gracious, and asked me if I was hard up. I told him that I was, that being the truth, as I had lavished all my earnings with him and his companions; he offered to lend me ten pounds, which I accepted very gladly and gratefully. My ship was to sail within a month of this time, and I spent the interval in gaiety and pleasure; and one night, or rather one morning, on my return home, I found a strange man awaiting me. It turned out he was a detective; he charged me with having forged the cheque, and asked me if I had not gone shares with the clerks, my colleagues. I frankly owned that I had received ten pounds from one of them, and explained the manner in which I had been induced to cash the cheque. I was taken before the magistrate, committed, and at my trial one of the clerks, who turned queen's evidence, swore I had forged the cheque and had taken the greatest share of the money. I was sentenced to ten years' penal servitude, but I broke away, and here I am—an outcast and a pirate."

"You are none the less an innocent man," returned Deborah, the Jewess, "and it will be all the more creditable to you if you act as a worthy seaman should, and do your best for those who are defenceless. Jehovah will bless you richly for your disinterestedness, and I, his humblest hand-maiden, may be able to assist you to clear your character by legal proceedings, and will promise to give you means of living in competence, nay, I could say in affluence."

"But, lady, I am sworn."

"Sworn! Are ye sworn, tell me. But to what?" asked Mary.

"To take all I can lay my hands on, and to spare the life of no one whom my captain may choose to declare war against, and in that case to regard neither age nor sex."

"And ye're a real living man, and wad tak' sic an oath as that! But dinna ye fash, ye're nae booned to keep puir women in captivity to serve the lust of a monster like your maister, I'm thinking; that's not in your oath nor in your conscience neither, maybe," said the frank, bold, but innocent lassie.

Deborah blushed deeply, but added,

"Mr. Cassidy is too generous, too noble, to be capable of lending his aid to such villany."

"Well, noo, I'm sure of it; but I dinna want him to rin ony risks for sic as mysel'," returned Mary. "A' that I ask o' him is to lend me his knife, that I may plunge it into my breast rather than lose that which suld be mair than life to ony gude lassie in the world."

Cassidy looked at the Scotch girl long and fondly.

"Be assured," he said, "that I neither can nor will suffer you to be injured or insulted, and if I can effect your deliverance from this den of wolves I will."

"And the God of all power and mercy bless and protect ye, as I humbly pray for sic gude intents, and may ye croon 'em wi' performance, and then ye sall hae a' the affection and a' the gratitude o' my humble heart, and my father's blessing and prayers to boot; and 'the prayer o' a righteous mon availeth much' says the Holy Writ."

"But I am a pirate and a felon," said Cassidy, with a sigh.

"A man's a man for a' that, said Robbie Burns, and he learned in Nature's school, and could sing how men wad rue mony an act they were compelled to do under sair temptation."

"Oh, Miss Mary, you're an angel!"

"Dinna say that; I'm nae mair but a puir, frail, mortal creature like yoursel'. But rather than I'd hae a pirate for my gude mon, I'd hang mysel' like Judas. And you suld be o' the same min', and prefer death to piracy, ony day, simmer and winter and a'; sic a brave canny lad! Well, Mr. Cassidy, I'm loth to say it, but I'm heartily ashamed o' ye."

"And my promises are not vain ones. You have heard I am rich, you shall have all my earthly possessions if you will save my honour," rejoined Deborah. "I am sure that you will prove our champion; you have been so kind."

"I will do my best, but, though I have influence with the men, I am suspected by the officers and strictly watched by them. Well, if we are to match with the captain or the master we must fight them with their own chief weapons."

"What arms are they?"

"Duplicity and cunning."

"I am little used to either; but I will try my skill with both in the holy cause of saving my own honour and Mary's," returned Deborah.

"Harken, then. Let Miss Mary retire to her own cabin; put off the importunities of Black Ralph by seeming to yield to him; give him a half-promise that you will be his bride if he consent to marry you formally—he will agree to that; and as he is much occupied on shore at present, will give you time."

"My heart sickens with disgust."

"Nevertheless, you must do what I tell you; there is no other way of lulling his desire to possess your hand. Smile on him if you can; seem resigned; do not put on an over-strain of acquiescence, or he will be alive to the plot at once. He is craftier than a fox."

"But Harwolf?"

"He cares nothing for your presence, except that it threatens his safety. He would wish you to enrage the captain till he killed you."

"If I thought he would I would urge him on to the last act of fury. I would madden him till he struck me down. I have often thought of doing so," said the Jewess, "but no—no; then Harwolf would be safe, and I will never rest till I have avenged my father's murder."

"You will, then, accede to my request, and delude the captain with false seeming?"

"I will do my best."

"It is well. Come, Miss Mary, I must conduct you to your cabin, for, by the bustle overhead, I judge the captain's gig is returning from shore. I will go aloft, that he may not think I have been conversing with you; and, Miss Deborah, I trust to your skill totally to mislead your tyrant."

"Never fear me; I will blind the Philistine," returned Deborah, a fierce light glowing in her splendid black eyes.

"I will gang wi' ye, Mr. Cassidy," said Mary. "Deborah, you suld be worthy o' your name, and suld nae fear this Sisera. God bless ye, my dearie."

The Scotch girl threw her arms about the neck of the Jewess, and kissed her lovingly. She then left the cabin with the mate.

" 'Know ye what pulque is,
Liquor divine!
Angels in Heaven
Prefer it to wine '—

"We-we've taken the B-Boy Pirate!" roared Black Ralph, as he stumbled into the state-cabin, beastly drunk. "We-we've ca-caged the Re-Red Raven, my d-darling st-starling! Did I say—say starling? No! he's not a st-starling, but a cussed, croaking raven—a Red Raven! He'll soon be a white raven, and a black raven—black in the face, anyhow, as tight cravats occasion There's a shtorm blo-blowing and devil a fellow at the h-helm. The ship reels like—like a—a rolling porpoise; but never mind that—let the ship go to blazes—

' For to-night we'll merry merry be;
For to-night we'll merry merry be;
To-morrow we'll get sober!'

"Sober! Who says—who says I'm *not* sober?

' There's many a lad I know is dead,
And many a lass grown old;
And as the lesson strikes my head,
My weary heart grows cold.
But wine awhile drives off despair,
And bids a hope remain ;
Why that, I think 's a reason fair,
To fill my glass again!'

"So, my fair, fill up, fill my glash again."

The intoxicated ruffian stumbled against the couch on which Deborah was seated and fell prone.

The Jewess drew herself away with a shudder of horror and detestation.

"Who's cap'en aboard this vessel?" cried Black Ralph, furiously, "I am, of course; Ralph Talbot.

' For each immortal on the billows rode,
And I, myself, appeared the leading god.'

"And so I am, now the Red Raven's knocked off his perch.

' We all must die, said the Toby-man;
If the gallows gapes for me,
In hale full life die game I can,
With a leap from the leafless tree.'

"That's not so classic as the last, but its more to the purpose; did you know the Boy Pirate, my dear; he was a lady's man?"

Wardlaw rushed into the cabin.

"Captain," he said, hurriedly, "pray come aboard. There is a sail on the starboard bow, and from the best of our judgment it is the sloop of the Boy Pirate bearing down on us at a raking speed; we shall have a hot contest, for no doubt the crew of our rival is incensed beyond bounds at the capture of their leader. Shall we weigh anchor, sir?"

Black Ralph stared at him stupidly for a moment, and then pressed his forehead as if to concentrate his scattered and bewildered intellects. "I'll come aboard," he said; "so the sloop is going to fight us without a cap'en, ha! Well, if a black vulture is not a match for a screaming hen-raven that's lost her mate, wolves will run from sheep in the next generation." Again he burst into singing—

"The bugles are ringing for me, lassie,
The bugles are ringing for me,
And aye, full well may ye weep, lassie,
Full well ye may weep for me."

"But Deborah, you are the Rover's bride, and must weep for nothing till we play the Wreck Ashore. Lord, when I was stage-struck and a strolling player, walking a hungry cadger all day, and strutting a ranting tinselled monarch half the night! Well, we know what we are, but we know not what we may be.

' Where is the life that once I led.'

"But shiver all ravens and every other sort of poultry—

' I am what I am,
And I don't care a d——
For I sail 'neath the Jolly O-li-ver.' "

"Captain, you must be mad," cried Wardlaw, fiercely, "the 'Raven' is bearing down on us all sail set; Harwolf is ashore; the men are half boosed, and you are as drunk as a fool. Whose to command the ship? Say the word and we'll obey your deputy."

The pirate-leader looked at his subordinate for an instant with an ominous scowl, and laid his hand on the pistol in his belt.

His wine-flushed cheek went purple, and his fierce black eyes glittered with watery brilliance.

But the scowl passed off.

"Frank Wardlaw, you are right," he said, gloomily, "I am not in a fit state to command the ship at this moment; I have been drinking pulque-wine, and all sorts of swiney trash, but one nip of brandy, and 'Richard's himself again!' "

Wardlaw left the cabin.

As Black Ralph spoke, the clear, thrilling voice of the mate Cassidy was heard giving orders amidship.

"Let what land-lubbers there are among ye serve below, to hand up the round shot, wad, grape, and saltpetre. Let Teddy Macarthy, the bo'swain, station the steadiest on the forecastle. Send the chief gunner to the magazine. Whose captain of the after-guard?"

"Nat Ray, sir."

"Here, sir."

"Ray, I shall want you; keep near me. Where's the captain of the top?"

"Gone aloft, sir, with the men."

"Good! Now, my lads, be smart; all depends on your being alert; and no confusion—*silence!* mark that."

"Whose this infernal skunk that walks in my shoes before my toes are too stiff to wear 'em?" growled Black Ralph, drawing his pistol. "I'll teach the lubber who's who, and spoil his pretty jaw-tackle."

With this he raised the weapon, and aimed at Cassidy through the half-open door.

"Mr. Wardlaw commands in the action," Cassidy went on, unconscious of his danger. "I shall stand to the helm——"

Black Ralph's finger curled round the firelock.

"Till the captain comes on deck, and then we know who's commander."

The last words saved his life.

"He's a good man, and I'm an infernal dolt," cried Talbot, flinging down the pistol with an oath.

He rushed to a cabinet, drew out a bottle of strong brandy, poured out a brimmer, and swallowed it at a draught; he then bathed his temples, adjusted his dress, flung the black flag over his left arm, drew his sword, and walked on deck with a firm step.

By the exertions of the skillful and able Cassidy the strictest order prevailed; every man was at his post, and the look-outs were watching with eager eyes the advance of the dashing sloop, which was accompanied by a brig belonging to Zamora, and was racing with her consort through the parting waters at terrific speed.

The men looked at their leader with doubting glance when he first appeared, but upon seeing him pace along with head erect and dignified air, apparently cool, confident, and firm as a rock, their satisfaction found vent in a hearty cheer.

Black Ralph walked aft.

Cassidy stepped down from the helm, another man taking his place.

He advanced towards the captain with some feelings of apprehension, but they were at once dispelled when the latter gripped his fingers in his hard, broad hand, and said in a clear, deep tone,

"Mr. Cassidy, you have my hearty thanks for the able manner in which you have discharged your duty in these preparations. You are the best seaman on board, sir, and the first prize we take you shall command."

"Thanks, captain!" said Cassidy, quietly.

Again the men cheered.

"My hearties," said the pirate-leader, turning to his men; "this is the first time we have had real work before us. Our enemies are our rivals; they have had the advantage of forestalling us in their career as rovers, but let our deeds outblazon theirs as much as the prowess of the vulture should eclipse the poor strength of a beggarly raven. Now to your posts. Wardlaw, have you shipped all the anchors?"

"We have taken on board the stream-anchor and the best bower; we still ride by the little bower, captain," said the second mate.

"Cut it away, Wardlaw, at a whole cable, for there's no time to be lost; we will warp round to the south-east, and sail out into the open bay, and show our foes a dauntless front. No sneaking to harbour; we'll open the ball, and fling the first iron."

The ship was cut adrift; the sails were crowded on; they shook, flapped and bellied out before a head-wind.

All on deck was ready for the attack; the men stood to their guns, and Black Ralph mounted the quarter-deck.

Faint over the waters stole the furious shouts of the Boy Pirate's crew.

The sloop and the brig tacked round and bore down upon the "Black Vulture," with every sail set to catch the side wind.

Soon the hostile ships came within distance.

Black Ralph, whose courage and seamanship should have been allied with better qualities than his native ferocity and rascality, behaved with the most admirable presence of mind. His first care was for the guidance of the ship, for he knew that he was out-matched by his enemies, and that his only chance of victory, or even of safety, depended upon the skill of his manœuvres. Convinced of this, he picked out some of the strongest and most resolute of his men; some he placed to assist the helmsman, in order that each movement of the ship might be the quicker executed; others were to attend to the adjustment of the sails—to the replacement of any important gear that might be injured during the action; while the best marksmen were sent into the tops, that by their fire they might annoy and distract the attention of the Red Ravens.

Now the Spanish brig, commanded by the fiery Zamora, struggles round, and, catching the head-wind, soars grandly down upon the "Vulture."

But these birds of prey hovered about each other in their wheeling course for many minutes, without proceeding to actual hostilities.

As yet the only shot fired had hissed from the guns of Black Ralph's vessel; the "Red Raven's" voice had not been heard.

Now she opened fire.

Directed by the experienced Brierly the seething shot swept through the air with telling effect.

Crashing through the main-royals and tearing the rigging they smashed the mizen-tops, which rushed down with chaotic confusion, the cordage rattling like ribbons in the fierce, strong breeze.

Again came the roar of the guns, stunning in their blaze; the "Red Raven" had discharged another and heavier broadside.

This time the effect would have been fatal to the "Black Vulture" but for the skilful steering of the mate Cassidy, who turned the ship's head as she righted after her deep lurch from the first shot.

"Cut away the booms—clear decks!" roared Black Ralph, from stentorian lungs. "Port helm, Cassidy, and be hanged! Wardlaw, see to the men. Shift over the jib-sheet. Now, Cassidy, run her home; and the devil take the consequence! We must get to close quarters, and fight it out like furies. Now!"

"Aye, aye, cap'en!" responded Cassidy.

Truly like a huge bird of prey soared the "Vulture," cleaving the whelming brine. It was a thrilling moment.

The dark hull of the "Raven" seemed to expand, her taper masts to shoot up higher and higher into the clear air, her sails to broaden; and along her bulwarks, red, wild, and appearing to dance giddily, as the "Vulture" swept by them at terrific speed, were the forms of the Boy Pirate's crew.

The broadside had just been fired; the guns were run back on their breechings, and for a moment they were voiceless.

Quicker quicken the foamy and emerald-glancing seas, rushing and glinting and glooming and darkening with their snowy crests, as they flew along the dark and arrowy prow!

Brand was at the helm of the "Red Raven."

Gracefully swayed round the rover-barque, obedient to the will of the matchless pilot, whose keen eye at once comprehended the "Black Vulture's" intent, but the steersman was almost too late to avoid its execution.

Crash!

They have struck.

Flit and flash the long tongues of lurid, blinding flame; boom! bang! thunder the storm-voices of the guns.

The very sheathing boards of the "Black Vulture" seem to creak and sunder as both ships fire at once.

The taut sides of Talbot's vessel splinter and the bulwarks are staved in.

Away goes the "Red Raven's" bowsprit and part of her forecastle, with the red bird itself that grimly roosted at the prow.

Powerless the feeble hand of man to guide the beautiful craft moulded by his own skill.

Side to side dash the ships, as if they were imbued with the passions of their inmates, and rush to the encounter like furious and ungovernable steeds.

Grapnels are thrown.

"Hurrah for the 'Black Vulture!' Down with the rooks and ravens! Pirates and piracy, no snivelling hypocrisy! Huzza, lads! Women and boys are easy prey," frantically cried the ferocious Black Ralph, as he leaped up and down on a gun carriage, raving and cheering, while the grapnels were fixed.

Helter-skelter, pouring pell-mell upon the crowded deck of the "Red Raven," leaped Black Ralph and his band.

Their welcome was warm and cordial.

With the fierceness of untamable panthers the Boy Pirate's crew flew to the charge, while the muskets in the tops jetted and crackled with deadly effect.

Reckless each heart of aught but its thirst for wild slaughter.

Shrieks, yells, and shouts madly mingle together.

Hand to hand, foot to foot, throat to throat, no words can describe the hubbub and the hellish out-pourings of fury.

Oaths, curses and groans, the clicking and blasting of blazing muskets, and brandished steel blades in this whirlwind of demoniac and ruthless strife.

Over the clean decks the blood pools in a red tide of slaughter.

Murder rides rampant, and madness breaks loose in its cruellest frenzy.

And this is the glory, the manhood of war!

But as the sweeping simoon flings back the whirling flocks of passage birds that breast its power—as the dense tide drives hard against the strong but vainly struggling swimmer, so the crowding mass of the Boy Pirate's retainers forced, inch by inch, their obstinate and desperate foes to the bulwarks.

Caffyn and Garrod are fighting like fiends.

TAMPA RESCUES LILIA FROM THE ATTACK OF HARWELL.

Zampa is thoughtless of himself and only regardful of enemies, whom he hews down as in former times he scythed the canes in the brake.

The trusty old old seaman, Brierly, shouts himself hoarse through his trumpet as he runs up and down the bridge like a hungry lion in his narrow cage.

It cannot last long, yet, with a man left on either side, there seems no hope for cessation of brutal and profane butchery.

It is over awhile.

Black Ralph is the last to leap back on to his own deck.

The blood and perspiration bathe his face, and he pants and reels with exhaustion.

It is now their turn, and the "Ravens" prepare to take reprisals. Zamora's fleet ship runs down on the fated "Black Vulture."

Whence is that long, dull roar?

A heavy iron bolt flies sparking and splashing from wave to wave, and with a foamy spout sinks down through the green, glassy waters within a few yards of the stern of Zamora's vessel.

Another missile, that carries death on its wing, rushes fearfully over the "Raven's" quarter. Another, luckily spent, thuds fully against her bows and gracefully she lurches, and dips deep into the trough of the waves.

The ports and batteries on shore have opened their fire.

Brierly yells madly to the blood-thirsty and the insensate crew to hold, and to give up their intention of boarding, for the sea is white with suds floating out of the harbour to the succour of the "Black Vulture."

No. 25

Brand sees in a moment the imminence of the danger that threatens his own ship and Zamora's.

The whole of the Brazilian squadron are down upon them; they are full within full range of the guns of the forts of Rio de Janiero.

Nimbly the "Ravens" fly aloft; their quick, trained fingers are busily plied.

The forts are silenced for fear of injuring the American vessels.

Presently the sloop and the brig clear away with a cheer of defiance. The "Raven" and her mate have spread their wings, and fly fleet and far from their pursuers.

Ralph exults at their retreat as if he had won a victory, and leans against the taffrail waving his hat, hooting and bawling his derision at his retiring foes.

CHAPTER LXXV.

A LONG CONFERENCE—HARWOLF MATURES HIS PLANS.

IN a well-furnished room in the little farm at Glenleaf, which Andrew Harwolf had made over to his agent Miles, the squire and the countryman were seated in conference.

Harwolf has greatly altered in appearance since we last met him.

The villain had begun to feel the effects of long, wearying vigils, deep drinking, and ever-crowding anxieties. His face had worn the traces of decay and mental exhaustion; his bold, firm step had degenerated into a listless shamble, his clothes hung about his emaciating body loose and disordered, his hair strayed unkempt on his furrowed brow, his entire demeanour was indicative of the languor and heartless lassitude of a wretch conscience-haunted and self-abandoned; but now he presented an aspect widely different.

All the evil impulses of his vile nature, all the fiendish passions of his dark soul, were roused from the moment that he found the secret drawer in his cabinet had been ransacked, and he looked upon the letter that had been substituted for the documents as a challenge, and braced himself to meet it with all the remorselessness of self-defence. He knew that his life was staked against the lives of his enemies, for he was conscious that while living they would leave no means untried of hunting him down.

"I'm mortal glad you've come to the determination of getting out of this cussed country, zur; and I tell 'ee az I be not a little pleased to get off myself. For why? My darter, Bridget, be a-goin' to get wed, and I allers had a notion as I should like to die rich, and there's no gettin' rich in this infarnal island."

"I wish that it were possible to emigrate to another planet," grumbled Harwolf, thoughtfully; "but time is wanted, as well as space, to part me from my foes. Yet don't think I mean to run from my cover without leaving the mark of my fangs on the hands of those who drive me hence. What did the gipsy say about Lord Hawksbury?"

"Why, he said az how that gentle'm intends to institoot persecutions, and all that fal-de-lal: but the queerest part of all is about that fellow Zilas Rye."

"The dog that braved me is dead!" said Harwolf, turning pale; "dead, and by an accident that I am not accountable for. But, though I have seen him since, I do not fear him, for I have no cause. I am not a child, to be scared at 'a painted devil,' but why do they keep so quiet? Why do they not beat the cover at once?"

"Why, your honour, I'm not larn't, but I be nat'ral shrewd. Born zo—cos why? I never had nothin' to inherit but my wits, and constant use has sharpened 'em—but this Zilas Rye?"

"Let him rot in his grave! Why, think ye, have they left me so long in peaceable possession of my wealth and station?"

"My humble thought consarning that matter I'll tell your honour—but this 'cute fellow, Zilas Rye?"

"I can see no motive why they should not have commenced hostilities long ago," interrupted Harwolf. "Perhaps," he added, with a sneer, "as the land is entailed they have ceased to interest themselves in a matter which can be no source of profit; perhaps they have good reasons for silence; nay, maybe—for the devil often helps his votaries—the proofs may be lost or destroyed."

"Aye, zure, your honour, let us hope so. But this Zilas Rye, squire?"

"Why do you pester me about him? A few broken bones are all that is left of his mangled carcase. I fancy I see the bragging thief now, strutting the railway platform like a ranting actor, and hectoring me—me, that am half wolf in name and whole wolf in nature: but the cur met a cur's death, and I saw him no more."

"Once more, your honour," Miles remarked, dryly.

"You allude to the apparition in the dressing-room?"

"Yes, your honour, the ghost."

"I drank much at that time, I must own, and I might have been mistaken. I must have been m——."

The wretch paused; the word seemed to choke him.

"Mad!" supplemented Miles, with emphasis. "Well, now, in my humility, your honour wasn't mad; but really did see the creetur."

"Well, well, not in the flesh; the worms of the earth have claimed that."

"I wish a slug from your honour's pistol had claimed the infarnal burglar," said Miles, with a grin. "I warrant it wud a bitten him sharp as a leech."

"I fired at him, Miles," returned Harwolf, shaking his head, while his cheek went deadly pale.

"A trick, a trap, a blind; nothin' else in the 'varsal earth, your honour," returned the rustic, contemptuously; "them conjuring chaps that swallers pokers and spues fire at country fairs would do twice the trick, and if e'er a man was a 'cute man, Zilas Rye be a 'cuter."

"Then you believe he is alive?"

"Be zure on it, squire; he's all right, leave him alone for that, and the gipsy feller zays as he's seen him up Lunnon."

"Impossible!"

"Anyways, ghosteses as takes to stealing valuable dokiments ought to be looked arter about the zame as their fellow creeturs, which arn't got the knack of coming in by the keyhole, and flying off through the ceiling; that's my humble 'pinion."

Harwolf started up and paced the room in a frenzy of self-reproach and fury; repeatedly he shook his fists and struck his forehead.

"You're right, you're right, it must be so—it is so. Ghosts! Pish!—why should the dead visit this great stage of their mortal tragedy? Is there none will lash me, spurn me, brand me with thrice red-heated iron. Fool! Yes—yes; he is alive—the miserable villain has baffled me. I saw him, too. I saw him on the night when Lady Edgeforth was snatched from my grasp so mysteriously. I saw him standing by the unfinished house—saw him and the Irishman, Black Oiny. I would not trust my eyes at the time; I thought it all a mere coincidence of personal resemblance—but it was he. The villain lives to mock me. Ha!—ruined? Not yet!—not yet!—not yet! Hanged? Not yet! My account is not made up; the scroll shall be wet with his blood before the reckoning is settled! So, this has made me a man again! The crawling reptile, the beggarly whelp, whom I took out of the kennel to do the dog-service, and when his ribs were stuffed, and his skin sleekened, he showed his teeth—he bit me. So he arrays himself against me, does he? He pits his prowess and subtlely against mine! Well, the match shall be played out. Mine is the genius of remorseless villany, his the low cunning of a catspaw and a tool!"

The countryman looked at his atrocious employer with a thrill of awe.

"Well, your honour, I do say its plain that Zilas Rye has got the lady into his power, and with pardon, zur, I'll tell ye what I think is the reason they keeps from molestin' you."

"Aye!"

"There was a heir!"

"Yes. The Boy Pirate," said Harwolf, with a malicious grin.

"Werry good, squire. Well, he's a pretty sort of a heir, he is; a werry nice peer of the realm he'd make, the gallows-bird! Ha—ha—ha! Now in course they wants to get him patched up in some style afore they palms him off on the public."

"True, they *must* dress him up in some disguising fashion; his 'skull and bones' would make a very queer sort of escutcheon, and the 'Red Raven' would scarcely do as a substitute for his father's 'Eagle.'"

"Aye, zo; and as the cookery book zays, 'you mun cotch your hare afore you dress it,'" returned the countryman, with a leer.

"They *have* 'cotched' him, I believe," said Harwolf; "here is a scrap I cut from the newspaper. Listen! It is among the telegrams from the Southern States of America."

"A rumour prevails throughout Florida and the neighbouring states to the effect that the terrible outlaw who has won such transcendant renown as the 'Boy Pirate' and the 'Red Raven,' together with another desperado of the same class, called Leon de Zamora, had fallen into the hands of the Seminole Indians on the River Haffa, and that they are detained by the savages on account of the liberal reward offered for their capture. N.B. We place no reliance on this report, and, even if it be true, the matchless rascal has effected so many hairbreadth escapes, that, were he in Newgate, we should expect to hear of his breaking away, however closely watched and guarded."

"Well, zure, he's a roarer, and no mistake!" gasped Miles, holding up his hands in admiration.

"Yes; they'll find it hard to set him on the throne I abdicate," returned Harwolf, grimly. "But once more, where is Lord Hawksbury?"

"Why, that gipsy chap has a sharp scent; he's found it all out. My lord has gone a-towering in his yacht; bless yer, no doubt to look for the heir, and has taken Zilas's brother with him. Lord alive! I've nussed that hurchin when he was a sickly baby. I mind their mother when I were quite a lad myself; she wor a purty woman. Poor soul, she was a hopera dancer, and could do the 'hop rare,' too, as a certain cove as I knows would say. He's a larned chap, but the horfullest muff at word-twisting and punning, or Punch-ing I s'pose, as ever you heard on."

"Balderdash! I see my way clear. Hawksbury has gone on a fool's chase; Rye has sunk into confidence from long impunity; my wife—well, she may go, but she shall take some brand with her to mark that she was mine! Nothing could be better. Oh! brave new world, brave new life! Remorse, pity, conscience, remembrance, shall be left as far behind as the wide, wide Atlantic can part me from old sympathies!"

"And when do you think of making a start, squire?"

"To-morrow, to-night, this hour! I have been preparing for this measure for years. I have purchased, under a false name, a large plantation in Arkansas. Little by little, upon plea of speculation, I have removed my wealth from the English to the American funds. For Frontemore—may an earthquake swallow it! And now good night. A glass of brandy. Good! Here's health and success to all bold adventurers. You will see me no more at Glenleaf; meet me in town, at the old quarters, and bring Esau with you; we have not done with him yet."

"It's a wildish night, squire; the sky looks red and vicious over yonder, and its as dark as Tartars [probably Tartarus.] Shall I go a piece with yer honour?"

"No, thanks. I am myself, Miles; the devil will not harm me; he knows me to be too useful a servant to be spared from earth. As for any mortal I may meet—*I've a pistol in my pocket!*"

CHAPTER LXXVI.
HARWOLF'S WIFE.

THE wind soughs wailingly through the autumnal woods, black clouds roll and spread across the lurid face of the night sky.

Harwolf treads the ground with passion-given vigour.

His weight of years seems to have fallen from his shoulders, and he paces on, erect and bold; his wild, evil grey eyes shine through the darkness like the orbs of the kindred wolf or hyæna.

The monster, who is no caricature, no overdone personification of selfishness and villany—as fact and history sadly testifies, walks defiantly through the solemn gloom of the dread midnight hour, reckless of its suggestion of the "mere oblivion" into which the brightest and purest stars must sink, the eternal darkness in which the most destroying fire-brands must be quenched. Onwards he stalks, gloating like a beast of prey in the congenial blackness of the night, that harmonises with his dark thoughts and purposes.

There is even a sort of demoniac exultation in his heart as he looked forward with anticipated triumph to the victories he was about to gain over his enemies. Are Iago and Regan real or ideal characters? Search the annals of the Inquisition, read the history of Ivan the Terrible, or of a thousand of his kind. What is the moral to be drawn from the contemplation of such fathomless depravity, Tantalic thirst and lust for cruelty? This, the most solemn of morals—that once unchecked our passions run away with us. The boy that will wantonly torture a worm will be the clown that will mercilessly bruise and injure the faithful and devoted wife of his bosom, or the king that will preside with ghoul-like enjoyment at a feast of torture and blood. But not to moralise, the villain walked through the dark night with thoughts blacker than the gloom that surrounded himself, the first and sole object.

His heart did not revolt from crimes the most horrible, so that they tended to the sole purpose of his life—self-gratification. How he out-reached himself! How, in grasping the passing prize too greedily, he crushed it, and rendered it worthless. Oh! let us guard ourselves from being our own slaves. Oh! let us remember that worth and happiness lie deep in self-denial, and that he who can sacrifice most to the good of his fellows is he who will reap most of the truest comfort and happiness on earth. Let us hate the bad because it is bad; let us love the good because it is good. As our bodily eyes seek the beautiful and shun the loathsome, so let our inward vision contemplate the pure and unselfish, and shut out the selfish and impure.

The dark trees whispered mystically round him as he threaded the lonely, hushed, and gloomy lanes.

He reached the high road that led to Frontemore.

He had not proceeded far, when he heard the distant rattle of carriage wheels, and like fiery eyes the approaching carriage lamps dilated as they neared him.

Who could be travelling from Frontemore at this late hour?

He could not discern the dark pine woods, the myrtle shrubberies, nor the white gables of the mansion he was about to desert for ever, for, though the Hall was distant only about half a mile, the darkness was too intense for him to distinguish.

A rising mist swept along the earth; the nights were getting cold, and the sweat poured in steam from the sides of the horses, and their breath was condensed as it panted from their quivering nostrils; this he could discern from the halo round the lamps.

He shrank back, and hid himself in a gap in the hedge that happened to be facing the door of the carriage.

A tall and manly personage got out of the vehicle. The man that was driving jumped down from the box.

"Spinks; I am going a little way down the road to meet the lady. Keep a good watch, I shall be back in a moment."

"Yes, sir."

"Drive close to the hedge, and when we get in don't spare the horses, but drive hard and fast to the station; an express runs up to town at 1.40."

"Yes, sir."

"Possibly I may not find a better chance to give you full orders. When we arrive at the station we shall start at once; at our best speed we shall arrive there barely in time, so you must put up at the 'Railway Tavern,' and bring the horses down by the first train in the morning. One thing more."

"Yes, sir."

"Squire Harwolf is at Glenleaf; he is not expected to return to Frontemore to-night. If he does, he must of necessity pass this way; if he asks you any questions say you belong to the Merediths; he hates that family since Miss Lilia jilted his son, and he will go without further inquiry."

"Right, sir."

The gentleman left the carriage, and walked towards Frontemore.

His form was soon lost in the darkness.

The man got down from the box.

The night was dank and chilly, and the wind blew not brisk, but keen and drizzly.

The man struck a match and lighted his pipe.

The gusts blew out the tiny flame.

The man retired to a spot sheltered from the wind to "light up," whistling a popular air.

Harwolf crept forward.

He got close to the carriage.

The man had not seen him but was busy igniting his pipe.

Harwolf opened the door of the vehicle and got in.

He threw himself into one corner of the large and lumbering vehicle.

It was pitch dark, and he flung the edge of his cloak over his face.

"Oh, Edmund, what are you urging me to do? But why—why should I not confide myself to you, and if you keep faith with me only for a day, it is better than my being with a demon whom I cannot trust for an hour. In flying with you I am doing a shameful thing; but though I am lost to shame, I love you not less dearly, and I will be your slave, if you will be kind to me."

It was Lady Edgeforth who spoke.

"My darling, my kind Eleanor, do not fear; all will be well; once separated from that detestable man you will be happy, and I—Oh, the bliss of delivering you from that scoundrel, who neglects and maltreats you—the delight of claiming you as my own!"

"Ah, Edmund—I could weep, but the fountain of my tears is scorched up. Do, pray, be kind to me!"

"My dear one!"

The couple got into the carriage.

So dark was it they thought themselves alone.

The man drove on. The dark landscape swept past them.

"When we are once in London we are safe from pursuit."

"For *him*—he will not pursue me; he cares nothing for me."

"Insensate brute! Eleanor, did you ever love him?"

"Oh, yes, once, with all my soul."

"But not now?"

"I hate him!"

"That's well."

"You are jealous."

"Love and jealousy are sisters; they go hand in hand."

"But I shall be jealous of you?"

"You will never have cause to be so."

"Are you sure?"

"Quite, darling."

"I am not young."

"You are in the ripeness of your womanhood—in the richest maturity of your beauty."

"You flatter me."

"No—it is truth."

"It cannot be—my son is twenty-five."

"Time deals gently with some. With you he has been more than indulgent—he has given and not taken."

"But I shall change."

"My love will not."

"Oh, tell me so. I love to hear you say it."

"It is folly to repeat a truth so palpable."

"I am happy."

"Eleanor!"

"Well, Edmund?"

"Did you not say that you once loved this man?"

"I did. I told you truth. I loved him more purely but not so deeply as I love you."

"I'm glad of that."

"Oh, if you will always speak so."

"Were you afraid of him?"

"No; women seldom fear their chosen."

"I think you are right."

"I am; if they did, there would not be so many wife-murders. A woman will taunt a man she loves very hotly or hates very cruelly, and that to her own destruction."

"But you will not taunt me whom you love hotly, eh, darling?"

"If you make me jealous; but I shall not fear you."

"Oh, I am terrible!"

"If you said so in a tone of thunder instead of in a banter of tenderness I should not care for you; no, none other but him could harm."

"But him; whom?"

"He who was destined to kill me."

"And who is that?"

"Harwolf."

"Bad as he is he could not murder."

"His babe, if it stood in the way of his lust or ambition."

"Ha!"

"He has done all that is dreadful, more than I dare to reflect on."

"Indeed!"

"If I tell you a secret, will you trust me with another?"

"I will, but first, may I ask you a question?"

"A thousand."

"Do you love me?"

"I have told you so; if you make me repeat it you will make me think I am old."

"I once saved a miser's life, and he left me a large fortune; but I like my old calling."

"Is that your secret?"

"No; answer me my questions."

"Yes, dear."

"On your oath."

"If you please, on my oath."

"Well, then, do you hate Harwolf so much that you would destroy him?"

"I would pay the fees of his execution; but I shall not live to do it."

"Why not? What makes you think so?"

"I have a presentiment."

"That's nonsense; but now the main question, on your oath. Do you love me as Captain Fitz-Osbert, or for myself, my very own person."

"For yourself—yourself only."

"If I were poor?"

"If you were a beggar!"

"If I were Red Raven, the pirate, for instance?"

"Or Hopley, or Townley, or Yelverton."

"Then I am not what I seem. I am Foxley, the detective; I came to capture Harwolf, but you have captivated me; nevertheless, I love you, dearly, sincerely. I am rich by prize money and legacy, and if you will love me I will be yours for ever!"

"Good God!"

"Ha! do you repent?"

"Is your name Edmund?"

"Your own Edmund."

"Then Edmund Foxley, body and soul I am yours."

"But if Harwolf were here you would disown me and plead to him."

"I would cleave to you and spit on him, and defy him!"

A sudden light, like the storm glare, throws into vivid conspicuousness every corner of the carriage, every object in it, with intense vividness, the seats, the cushions, the panels, the embracing paramours.

BANG!

Darkness, utter darkness, a dull groan, a shriek of torture.

The horses rear and plunge violently.

Spinks throws himself from the box, and in the helpless recklessness of terror runs for many a yard down the road.

He returns—his arms shake like quivering reeds —his knees beat together—he tears the lamp from the side of the carriage—he staggers to the door.

It is open!

He holds aloft the light.

At the bottom of the carriage lie the forms of the man and the woman—arms entwined—dead—and weltering in one mingling pool of blood.

He looks around him.

Darkness—utter darkness!

CHAPTER LXXVII.

THE EXPEDITION AGAINST THE CASTLE OF SAN SALVADOR.

IN the blaze of the noon-day sun which flashes the emerald waters into intense splendour along the verdant coasts and beneath the shadow of the peaked and romantic headlands that are suffused with tints of carmine and amber, a light pinnace is gliding.

The coast is lonely, wild in grandeur and glowing in beauty, and the white felucca sails of the skiff brighten or gloom as they pass through the long spans of light and shadow that penetrate far down into the crystaline depths of the opal sea.

The barque skims along, scattering the frost-white foam like diamond dust before her cleaving prow; it rounds a dark and arched causeway, which looms out grandly in its awful hugeness and ruggedness, and might well, be imagined the cave of the Cyclopean Polypheme.

The boat is run up on a sandy flat at the mouth of a river that rolls placidly round its curving shores into the sea. A number of determined-looking seamen disembark. In a moment we recognise, in those robust and sinewy forms—those sun-bronzed, thoughtful faces, the persons of the flower of the Boy Pirate's gallant crew, about forty men.

Among them there is the thorough old salt, grey-haired, it is true, but broad, lithesome, and powerful, his brow almost without a wrinkle, his eye with a light clear and kindly, limbs as hard as iron and pliant as steel, only time has scattered a little snow on his head and his brain is the cooler; but the frost has not got into the core of that rare heart of English oak, to wither the sap or blight its strength or its toughness.

Old Brierly is the very ideal of a thorough British tar.

The two Spaniards, Leon and Gomez, the first all fire and animation—the latter stern and inscrutable. And there, the Boy Pirate's "double"—as the Germans have it—the tall, graceful, yet manly and thorough-bred seaman, Dick Caffyn, with his smiling face, firm, thin lips, and gentle mild eyes—differing from his foster-brother only that he lacks that Promethean quintessence of fire, stolen from the gods, that of yore warmed the dull clay into life, thought, and action—*genius*.

And there is the gigantic negro: the sun of kindness and prosperity has brightened up his ebon face, before so clouded and wrinkled, and has straightened and broadened his massive form, formerly toil-bent and scarred by the brandings of cruelty and slavery. Zampa rolls his thick lips and flashes his great white teeth, the very picture of African geniality, fun and animal power.

But who is the beautiful youth, the last to spring out of the boat, assisted by the droll-eyed Tom Garrod, who acts as the coxswain? Surely he is a stranger; his bright, golden hair is gathered in a Spanish net beneath his light shako, his smooth rounded limbs are set off in their perfection of symmetry by the graceful uniform of a Mexican soldier.

Those large love-pleading eyes so ethereal blue, those pouting, rose-red lips, that tint like the blush of the morning; surely there is but one face so sweet yet so animated, so kind, yet so exalted in its expression of queenly command and womanly fortitude— the fair face of Lilia the Rover's bride!

"What do you think, senor," said Caffyn to Zamora; "shall we set up our signal-post here, or shall we push on to San Salvador? Our party is not over strong."

"Shiver me, sir, but I think that the sooner we get off these shoals the better," said Tom Garrod. "My plan is to put our heads dead to the wind, and to pour a broadside right into that hulk yonder, and board and take her at once. What if there is a provost-marshal and a whole garrison of marines aboard her. Douse my daylights if I wouldn't smash the whole box of toy-soldiers, if we had but one of our long pounders ashore, and take the place without a lubber to back me."

"You look dar, Mas'r Brierly, you hear dis buckra. Mas'r Tom berry good woice. Hearn a whale beller? Don't tink him hab better lungs nor Mas'r Tom. Dis buckra berry well where dey can't hearn 'em; but, golly, yo bung up yer speakin' trumpet while your on shore, buckra; dis yere ole bush may be full ob de dam Spaniards. No 'fence to you, Mas'r Gomez, you arn't de *raal* niggar, you see; but de dam Spaniards, 'scuse me, are a kind o' cats and tigers; dey crouch down on dere bellies and spring out like Injuns, and fire yo dead 'fore yo can 'spress yer 'bjections; once cotch 'em out on de prairie, and dey run like dam possum. Yo just put your tongue down yer troat, and keep out de sun, Mas'r Tom, or we'll hab to set yo name down in log-book, 'died ob a strong woice.'"

The seamen laughed, and Tom Garrod reddened with wrath.

"Uncle Zamp is right," said Brierly; "we must act with caution, hearties, for if ever we had need to be prudent and watchful it is *now*, for, since young madam will have her way and will join her dear self in this adventure, why, bless her eyes, we must take care on her."

In every glance flashed a beam of enthusiasm, every hand was raised to a cap or a forelock; and if Brierly and Gomez had not held up their arms with the eager deprecation of alarm, there would have been a general and uproarious shout.

Lilia blushed deeply, rosily, and closely drew her ample mantle around her moulded form.

Her eyes sparkled with pride, hope, and grateful affection.

"Gentleman," she said, in a voice clear, though trembling, "you are pirates, but you are true men. My husband, your leader, is a hero well worthy of your noble devotion; I am a weak woman, not worthy to be the consort of him who is a king among strong men; but I am grateful with my heart's tenderest gratitude. I must *live* for my husband, but could *die* for you!"

It was hard to restrain the spontaneous burst of admiration and enthusiasm among the outlaws, as they looked on her who was, indeed, "the pride of the pirates' heart"; but the leader partially quelled it, it sank into a deep-toned murmur.

"Senors," said Zamora, after a pause, "let me claim your attention for a few moments. It was in an attempt, by the risk of his own life for a stranger, it was in seeking to save my friend Giraldez, that the noble Boy Pirate fell into this trap—to me, then, belongs the duty and honour of achieving his rescue. Is it not so?"

"Ay, ay, cap'en," responded the men.

"Well, then, let me take the lead in this enterprize. When arrived at San Salvador, I will scale the walls and get into his dungeon by some means that will present themselves, and I will set him free."

"No, senor, no; that is my office," cried Dick Caffyn, warmly; "the Boy Pirate is my own foster-brother, and I will not let any one usurp my right to shed my last drop of blood for him."

"Avast there, with your swagger. I was the first to show him the difference between a mast and a marlin-spike, and none desarves to be nearer to him than his old bo'swain, Jack Brierly," said the aged tar; "but I leaves the 'ropes to run through the glowing hands' of you young powder-monkeys. For why? My old hulk is not so taut as it was, and I don't go aloft so smart as I used to do; if there's any scaling to be done, I leaves it to Master Dick and Senor Zamora. I steadies the lads and leads the action. Now you knows your bearings."

"The best arrangement," said Gomez. "Brand has command of the "Raven;" I'll lead the storming party; Dick and Zamora shall get into the castle to reconnoitre, and Mr. Brierly——"

"Sticks to the fo'castle—the bo'swain's place when good seamanship is wanted," said Brierly.

"But whose to be our land pilot?"

"Dis chile," said Zampa. "Knows ebbery inch ob de dam country. Yo leab ebbery ting to ole Zamp; dis nigger consid'rable sharp."

"But, Madam Lilia stays here; we can make a snug calaboose under these palmettos," said Brierly. "And we mustn't let our wish to be obedient to orders bring her into peril."

"Brierly, I must, I will go with you. Why am I thus disguised? Merely to my own shame and your hindrance? Never believe it; I will be of use if I can, and will superintend all, for I am your chieftainess, and shall not flinch at danger."

"Young madam must be obeyed, though the orders is oncommon against my wish; but no one would expect the Boy Pirate's consort to act otherwise. Now, lads, for a start, let's make our way to the scene of action."

Twelve of the men were left behind to take care of the pinnace.

The pirates threaded the forest in Indian file, Zampa taking the lead, as guide and pioneer, Dick Caffyn and Zamora following close behind; Lilia in the centre, jealously guarded by the sturdy old Brierly; Tom Garrod and Ross, the third lieutenant, brought up the rear.

In this order they proceeded till they reached the woods near the old castle, and they halted and gathered together in a little dingle.

Upon looking around them they had reason to be satisfied with Zampa's pilotage, for the place was most admirably adapted both for concealment and observation.

The banks of one of the river's innumerable little confluents, which was wide but rocky, shallow, and easily fordable, were interposed between them and the castle like a screen.

To the top of this natural rampart Zampa had crawled, to take the first peep at the fortress, while Dick Caffyn clambered up a tall palmetto, and shading his eyes with his hand from the burning rays of the sun, looked back towards the sea.

"Aloft there, maintop watch, how's the wind?" cried old Brierly to the latter.

"South-by-south-east, Jack. And Brand has shaken out his canvas, and is sailing down the creek with the Brazilian pennant at his mast-head," said Caffyn, as he descended from the tree.

"Gemmen, dis nigger has made a most curiss discoberation," said Zampa, returning to the party. "Dar's a picket camp'd a piece down de brake, t'oder side ob de Jordan. Seems to dis child dese ar kind o' bad lot like ye'selves, dam seafarin' buckra. Dese no good, nohow."

"Shiver me, it's a watch from the crew of that infarnal Harwolf," said Brierly.

"All the better," cried Dick Caffyn, impetuously. "They had rather the best of it last time, through that cursed land-wind; but we shall have 'em hand to hand on the broad green deck yonder; there'll be no sheering off then, I'm thinking."

The men faintly cheered.

"Senor," said Gomez, his black, arched brows meeting in a look of quelling sternness, "if you have left your common sense and prudence aboard, you had better go back for them. Without extreme caution we shall do our captain more harm than good, and shall sacrifice Donna Lilia to a folly that would disgrace a powder-monkey."

"Don't look big. He's right, Dick," rejoined old Brierly. "Batten down. 'Nough said."

The party now proceeded to active operations. They chose a lonely and retired spot round one of the serpentine curvings of the river, and there forded the stream, springing from rock to rock.

Old Brierly would have assisted Lilia; but she only blushed brightly, and sprang away from him as light as a fawn.

They paused in great perplexity.

"In all my experience I never knew a cruise where such good seamanship is wanted. How shall we get past Harwolf's picket, my hearties?" said Brierly, with a wry smile.

The question was more easily asked than answered.

"Well, we shall have to fight 'em, after all—fool as I am," said Dick, testily.

"And they'll kill the captain at the sound of the first shot," exclaimed Ross.

Lilia pressed her hand to her heart, and turned pale as the flower from which she was so well named.

The negro had gone ahead to reconnoitre; he returned at this moment.

"Well, uncle Zamp," said Dick Caffyn, "what's your sage advice?"

"Chil'en," replied the nigger, with a chuckle, "can't 'spress my feelin' ober de honour you does me, but I'se de raal chile as conducts dis 'portant experdishun. So please yo sit down dar till I comes to ye, and p'raps, if yer behaves yerselves, I'll bring yer suffin as 'll do yer ole eyes good. Yah, yah!"

With this, Zampa threw a summersault, and then flew up the bank, flinging out his splay feet as if they were endued in Hop-o'-my-Thumb's Seven-League boots.

"What does the nigger skunk mean?" said Brierly.

"Hang the swab!" exclaimed Dick, petulantly, flinging himself down on the turf in great mortification. "You'll see we shall have to fight it out, after all."

Several of the others followed his example, and stretched themselves along by his side, and seemed to be lost in a quandary of doubt and perplexity.

Zamora, Brierly, Gomez, and Ross each in turn proposed some plan, which was abandoned as impracticable.

In the midst of their consultation, they were startled by a rush through the bushes.

The recumbents jumped up, grasping their weapons.

Zampa leaped in amongst them; in his brawny, black arms he carried the insensible body of a Spanish peasant, who seemed to have been stunned by a down-right blow.

This man he dropped to the ground, and performed an exultant dance around him, that was worthy of a cannibal at a grand roast.

"What the devil does this mean; who is this fellow?" cried Dick, while the rest stared on in astonishment.

"Yo—yo! yah—yah, gen'leman! look at dis chile; look at him, he'se de coon! Yah—yah!" And away he went round like a spindle.

"I'll break your thick skull, you black cuss, if you don't speak!" cried Dick.

"More'n I could do for dis one, you see; yah, damn him, got a tick skull for a buckra; most on 'em not ticker dan a egg-shell."

"Who is he, you scampish——"

"Listen, chil'en; dis yere man, berry sorry I'ze 'bliged to hurt him; gib him some rum and a picaroon dat 'll make him happy."

"Who is he?" roared the pirates, in chorus.

"Chil'en, I'm reg'lar 'shamed ob ye; de buckra's a 'spectable man ob dese parts, and him business war to carry yams and bananas into de old hulk yonder; him got a big waggin, wid two reg'lar fine bulls to it, chock full ob splendious fruit, wid a great piece ob canvas stretch ober 'em to keep off de sun and de 'skeetos. Most like him got a pass-paper; berry well. Yo get into de cart; I pack yo up one a top o' toder like bamboos, and den cober you ober wid de canvas; one ob you can do de job for dis poor buckra dat's met wid sich a dam bad accident; so yo can get into de berry hold ob de wessel and play

de debil—what tink 'o dat? Yah! look a' dis chile, he isn't de 'possum—oh, no."

Only with extreme difficulty the pirates could repress a hearty huzza at the proposal of this ingenious expedient.

A council of war settled the mode of proceedings in a very short time. As no hands could be well spared, Lilia was to remain hid in the woods, with Zampa as her guard. Ross and Tom Garrod, from a neighbouring hill, were to signal Brand to open fire on the castle from the "Raven." Two others were sent to fetch a reinforcement from the pinnace; the rest of the party to conceal themselves in the oxwain, and to get into the fortress by a strategy similar to that which brought about the fall of Troy.

There was some dispute as to who was best fit to personate the peasant, but the election fell upon Gomez, acknowledged to be the coolest man among them.

The Spaniard dressed himself in the clothes of the luckless driver, and the whole of the party set off to the spot where the waggon awaited them.

There was great fun at the "packing." The yams were thrown out, and Zampa arranged the men, who lay down in the broad, low vehicle closely grasping their weapons. The negro covered their feet and the lower part of the wain with bananas, covered it over with the canvas, and in a few minutes all was ready; the Spaniard goaded the oxen, and the heavy wain rumbled off.

An eternity was crowded into the weary, weary hour that Lilia spent watching in the forest, alone with the negro.

Zampa, with a pistol in his hand, tramped up and down, like a sentinel on guard.

No words passed between the rover's bride and her keeper. It was evident they had enough to occupy them in crushing their mutual qualms of excitement.

The hour had passed.

Suddenly, through the woods came a shout—the firing of muskets—the clangour of an alarum bell—the sullen boom of Brand's guns.

The negro quickened his pace up and down, evidently seeking to deafen himself to the sounds of the conflict. At last his feelings overmastered him, and, with a look at Lilia, "to mark he would return in haste," he rushed off to the top of a mound, and was lost among the thick-growing trees.

Lilia rose to follow him, when a stern voice cried—

"Stand!"

She turned; the blood welled to her heart and fled from her cheek—she almost fell with the suddenness of her terror.

She drew her pistol, but it felt awkward and repellent in her tender hand.

A man, dressed in a naval uniform, sprang towards her.

He looked her steadily in the face, as if he knew her at a glance. The recognition was mutual.

She confronted the villain Harwolf!

"Lilia, my hour of retribution is come," hissed forth the scoundrel, in a tone of gloating malice.

"Your Raven is red now with his own blood; and the dove that he mated with is safely netted. You thought I could never reach you? Down, minx, down, I say, and plead for pardon, and I may forgive you."

Lilia raised the pistol.

"If my husband is dead," she exclaimed, in a thrilling tone, "you shall never live to triumph in his fall. I can die; but to you I will yield never, Daniel Harwolf—never!"

Before she could fire, the scoundrel leaped towards her, and seized her soft arm in a vice-like clutch.

Lilia screamed, and the pistol exploded.

A down-right blow from a massive fist struck the dastard right between the eyes—he stumbled and fell.

"Run, Missee, run, de devil is arter us, dogs and all—I cotch you. Fust I cut de troat of dis buckra-cuss; den I foller yo."

"No—no!" screamed Lilia, "spare him, spare him; he is the greatest villain on earth, but he was once my lover!"

A party of soldiers appeared galloping over the brow of the hill, and pouring down into the dingle.

Lilia beheld them with dismay.

Harwolf raised himself on one hand, and then staggered up, waving and pointing to Zampa and the girl. The black stopped and caught Lilia's arm.

"Missee, ye no used to dis sort of ting. 'Scuse me; dar, dat's better. I 'se de ole hoss as wins de race—yah! yah!"

With this he caught the half-fainting Lilia, and placed her, blushing and trembling, on his brawny shoulders. Dashing right through the thick wood, he flew onward through places impracticable for mounted men, and soon doubling, eluded pursuit.

As he ran rapidly along the wide plain that stretched beyond the forest, a frightened horse came bounding towards them; it was a wild mustang, bridled and saddled, probably the horse of one of the soldiers killed in the affray with the pirates from the pinnace, of which we shall have more to tell hereafter.

The wild steed flew towards them. Zampa set down his lovely burden, and waited till the horse came near them; he then caught the rein.

"Mountch, missee," he cried, "and ride like de wind down 'long de ribber, through de trees thar; nebber min' de castle; dat yar's de nearest. Yo fin' de pinnace whar 'em lef' 'em. For yo look dar—de dam fellers are arter us."

True enough, Harwolf and a number of soldiers were galloping at a rattling speed from the far end of the branch of the forest through which they had forced a way.

"Oh! Uncle Zampa, you are a dear, kind fellow," cried Lilia, "can you not mount and save yourself with me."

"Yo go 'long. Dis yere hoss, he's half done now, he is. Fly, missee—tink dey cotch me? Lor bless yer picaninny heart, de blind man cotch a possum if dey cotch Zampa. Dat way. I'm kind o' used to tree-flying. I likes it. Cotch me! Yo go along!"

With this he placed his mistress securely in the saddle, and then, waving his hands, plunged into the dense wood.

Lilia urged her horse; the frightened animal sped along at a terrific rate.

Her pursuers dashed after her, the air ringing with their shouts.

More than one spent bullet grazed her horse's flanks, only to increase his speed.

At last she came upon the jungly border of one of those wild and deep fissures, those earth flaws, so common in volcanic regions.

It is a fearful gap; the edge of it is precipitous as a stone wall, and slippery as the crags of an iceberg. The horse's hoofs seem magnetically attracted to the ground, yet the creature, with outstretched head and wild, strained eye, slips and slides to the very verge of the darkness, Lilia grasping the rein, her face the picture of whelming horror!

But, at the very brink of ruin, the horse finds foothold, and, with the bound of a chamois, springs across the gulf. Lilia sees the dark precipice and the almost fathomless descent float under the flying feet of the mustang. She shudders, and almost faints; but she is roused from her sickening lethargy by the shake and rattle of her horse's feet as he tears along the level savannah, the long grass rushing by him with the roar of a rising tempest.

Away, away!—ever away, away—the horse seems maddened with fright and incapable of exhaustion.

Wildly up and down the long, rolling ridges that rise in parallel succession on the llanos; fiercely through the opposing barriers of the intricate forest, and now on fair ground, as after the circuit she has taken to elude her pursuers, Lilia arrives on the bank of the river.

The siege is raging in the distance. The "Raven" is firing from the creek, answered by the guns from the fortress. The castle is already in flames!

The horse, with undiminished speed, flies along the edge of the bank.

A file of Brazilian soldiers are marching, or rather running, down the road.

The mustang stands still in the midst of the way, not knowing whither to turn for escape, rearing and shaking his long shaggy mane, and seemingly regardless of his rider.

A broad-built, black-bearded fellow, dressed as a naval captain, is brandishing his sword and encouraging the soldiers to push forward.

They see the young Mexican ranger riding towards them, and surround him in a moment.

Black Ralph, for it is he who accompanies the reinforcement that is hastening to the relief of the fortress, seizes the rein.

"Stay, young senor; whither away so fast? What news from San Salvador? Is it true that they have wrung the foul bird's neck—is the Red Raven killed?"

But Lilia is dumb with terror.

"Malraya! He is a spy. Make the boy speak," shouts the officer of the file.

But Lilia only struggles to free herself; she draws her pistol and fires at random, with only this effect, that Black Ralph is forced back, exclaiming,

"Que demonio! are you tongue-tied, my pretty fellow? we'll make you answer."

With the strength of desperation Lilia urges her steed and flies past them.

"Alfuiera! he escapes," shout the Spaniards; "Matan le! Kill him; kill him!"

Forty guns are pointed instantly at the fugitive.

Lilia takes off her hat; rends away the fillet that confines her tresses.

Her sunny hair unbound ripples and glows along the wind like some fair meteor of golden light.

Black Ralph throws himself before the file of soldiers.

The muzzles of their guns almost touch his breast.

"Hold fire!" he roars. "Ye dastardly Spanish swabs, don't ye see 'tis a YOUNG AND PRETTY WOMAN!"

FEARFUL POSITION OF ZAMORA.

CHAPTER LXXVIII.

THE PROFESSIONAL DISGUISER.

HARWOLF and the gipsy Esau are threading the busy streets in one of the low quarters of London; they are both disguised, the squire having dressed himself in the clothes of a labouring man, and Esau also wearing a suit of corduroy.

They are on a strange mission, and discourse in a low tone as they walk along.

"And you think, Esau, that this Jew can really effect such a change in my appearance that I shan't be recognisable?"

"I don't think, I knows it," returned the gipsy, decisively; "when he's 'namelled yer, mounted yer nose, clapped on the wig, stained yer and all the rest

No. 26.

on it, why yer mother wouldn't know yer, let alone yer father."

"But is the effect permanent?"

"Well, I don't know the name of the stuff; they may call it 'permerant' for all I knows, but its a sort of dye he uses, but you'll have to pay down hard, I can tell yer, if yer wants it done well; why, his wigs is worth a little fortun', but there are sich as will cut it stiff to escape bein' hidentified. Any costume chap could make you hup jist for gas light, but this one alters yer for good, and in sich a style as makes yer start at yer own phiz in the glass and ax your new self where your old self is gone to."

"I wish the fellow's dye would sink into my heart and brain, and change me to a 'new self' without and within," murmured the villain, with a sigh. "But, Esau, have you ever seen it tried on any one."

"On a many," replied the gipsy; "one cove in perticklar, a reg'lar moocher he was, a man as was lagged for smashing; he cracked the Jug, though, he did, and 'cause he 'saulted the perlice they wos infernally riled agin him, they wos. Now this yere cove wos about the shady side of forty, but oh, crikey; the smart chap this Levy made on him. Afore he had been a spare man, with a low forehead and turn-up nose; arter the hoperation he wos a young swell about eight-and-twenty, with yaller hair, a hook nose, and brown cheeks; a reg'lar 'Donis. Them pads is good things; some chaps goes in for a training."

"Whats that?"

"Why, yer see there is a great deal in a walk. Me for one; why, if you was to shet me hup in a room and set all as ever I knew to walk one by one hup the stairs houtside, men, women, and young 'uns, I'd tell yer every Jack and Jill as true as the clock. Vell, there is a great deal, a werry great deal, in the way a cove puts foot to the ground. Some on 'em 'ud rattle hup as if they pattered on the devil's hoofs; others sidle and shovel away like the coves wot loose their legs and push along on their stumpses."

"Then he teaches a peculiar style of walk?"

"Dizactly, every indiwiddle chooses a perticklar kind o' step as he thinks is best for disguisin' on him. I've seen 'em like coves at the mill, walking round and round the room a practisin' all sorts of dodges; some are fly to anythink, from the kangaroo leap to the snail's quick march. And he stands in the middle, like the flash cove at a circus wot whips the clowns."

"And one man must practise these painful expedients to escape the vengeance of his fellows, maybe incurred by a scrawled signature to save a wife or child from famine; but while the hawk preys on the pigeon it will ever be so. Well, its my comfort I was not born a pigeon. Esau, I'll tell you what I'll do; I have not told Miles that I am going to be thus transformed; if I can deceive him I shall be satisfied."

"Vell, squire, I'll bet any lay on it."

"Don't call me squire, I am Michael Warren."

"Werry well, Mike," returned the gipsy, with a grin.

They had now passed down a narrow alley, and arrived at a little barren square of large but high houses.

"That's the 'ouse, squire—Mike; that 'ouse with them green werandahs. You ax for Mr. Levy; he's allers at 'ome at this time o' day. It'll cost yer three hundred quid, clothes and all, to do it proper."

"Never mind that. Esau, go to the 'Wassail Bowl,' and wait for me; Miles will return from the docks, where he has gone about the passage-money, and to ship our goods. We sail in a week; do you hear?"

"Werry good, Mr. Warren."

"Say nothing to Miles about the object of my present mission."

"I'm fly. Good morning, yer honour; good day, Mike."

Within a quarter of an hour the gipsy was seated in the tap-room of the "Wassail Bowl," with a pot of beer before him, smoking a long pipe and furtively counting some sovereigns into a dirty letter-bag.

"This is a good lay," he chuckled. "I thought as I'd sell this yere cove to the 'tectives; but I knows a trick worth two on it. I'll stick to him; 'cos vy? It's my hinterest."

Soon after Miles entered.

"Vell, Miles, vot's the noos?" asked Esau, looking up with a grin, for the sullen fellow was for once in high good humour.

"Where's the governor, Esau?" asked Miles.

"Vell, he's nowhere by this time," returned the gipsy, with a leer. "Leastvays, I means I ain't dogged him; I knows he'll be here presently, and that's all I do know."

"He's a deep 'un, I do zay," muttered Miles. "I zuppose ye'll choose to go with uz to Amerikey, Ezau?"

"Vell, I arn't made up my mind," said the gipsy, reflectively. "Leastvays, not quite. Do yer think as it wud be better for my hinterest to go?"

"I do zo," said the countryman, in a deep voice, and with a meaning grin.

"It's time he was gone," said the gipsy; "the crushers is dead arter him. But let us shift our quarters; I see some flash coves are coming out of the bar; we can talk more to ourselves here in the corner."

The two men ensconsed themselves at a table in an angle of the room near the fireplace, and carried on their conversation in whispers.

Several mechanics entered; they had just "knocked off" from their work.

It was about noon, and they had come into the tap-room to their dinners, which they produced from their pockets and tool-baskets, and cooked on the coals of the red and dusty fire.

They ordered some beer, and were soon conversing with animation.

The general theme of their discourse was the "horrible and mysterious tragedy at Frontemore;" and there was an animated discussion as to the guilt or innocence of Harwolf, though the general opinion was of course against him—his strange disappearance, his late fits of moodiness and strange despondency.

Some of the men seemed to pity him, as the father of the reputed murderer of the Jew Nathan, and the husband of the profligate Lady Edgeforth, and palliated the enormity of his crime on account of the greatness of his provocation.

Attentive listeners to this discourse were two respectably dressed men who had last entered, and who had seated themselves near the window and called for a bottle of "Bass" and some biscuits. One of these was a thin, wiry, pale-faced fellow, rather showily attired, with crisp black hair, a large aquiline nose, and a black beard.

The other was tall and tolerably good looking; his brow was clear and polished, his hair black and glossy as the raven's wing, and his cheek dark and sun-tanned.

He was dressed in a suit of black; his neck was banded with an old-fashioned stiff black-silk stock; he wore a heavy gold chronometer, and presented the appearance of one connected with the medical profession.

When the work-bell rang and the men shuffled out of the room to resume their labours, the gentleman in the black suit walked over to the table where Miles and the gipsy were sitting.

Both men stared at him with surprise and suspicion.

"Am I addressing Farmer Miles of Glenleaf?" asked the gentleman in a clear, full tone, and with a peculiar smile.

Esau peered from beneath his shaggy brows at the stranger; his craven heart leaped with fear and his cheek blanched.

"Be fly; he's a crusher," he muttered to his companion in the lowest of whispers.

Miles looked him boldly in the face; his broad rustic face reddened—that was all.

"Pray, sir, may I ask what's your business?"

"I know you, Mr. Joseph Miles," returned the gentleman, "you are of Frontemore."

"I am zo," cried the countryman, in a brisk firm tone. "I am zo, at your zarvice; what's your will."

"Excuse the liberty I take in asking you this question—were you not acquainted with Squire Harwolf, who is suspected of having murdered his wife and her seducer so horribly?"

"I know the villain well!" cried Miles, smiting the table with his fist, "he's the infarnallest scoundrel unhung!"

"You do know him—was he not at your house at Glenleaf on the night of the murder?"

Miles shook his head, and grinned maliciously.

"Lord, zur, I wish, I only wish he had a been; I'd a fixed him there; but he warn't, wuss luck."

There was something so spiteful and so hearty in the regret expressed in the tone with which these words were spoken, that the gentleman started.

"Then you think he could prove an alibi?"

"A halibi? Why I zeed him go off by the 9.30 up train a good two hours afore the horful event; and there's heaps as swears to his bein' in Lunnon at the time, zur."

"Then you think he couldn't have perpetrated the murder."

"I think quite the contrary; I am zure he did, zur; not by his own hand, 'cos he couldn't do it, bein' in Lunnon; but he got another cove to do the business for him."

"Ha! do you know whom?"

"My pal here thinks az he does, zur; what zay, William, didn't you tell me az there was a chap in the Peggy's Horse [Pegasus, perhaps.] up the Whitechapel road, which swore az he'd got a job to do for a flash gemman down the shires az would bring him in a hundred pounds."

"In course I did," replied the gipsy, but in a very weak voice.

"And you think you could trace his guilt home to the murderer?"

"I be zure, zur. I'm come to Lunnon for the 'spress purpose of huntin' him down—and doamned if I doan't do ut!" Again red with wrath he smote the table.

"Have you any personal reason for ill-will to this man?"

"Rayther, zur; you may zay rayther," cried Miles, with chuckling irony. "You might have heard down our parts az I held a little varm of him, called Glenleaf; I was his land-steward, horse-doctor, and a power of things beside, and I was to have this varm in conzideration of my zarvices. There never was any zigning nor lawyering, the thing seemed zo clear understood, but now he's bolted they tell me I can't lay claim to a stick on the place. What do you think of that for a villain? And a poor man I be, your honour. I only just wish az I could meet with one of them detective chaps; I'd zend him somewheres; durn 'un!"

"Whither would you send him, Mr. Miles?" asked the gentleman.

The countryman got up, looked around the room with a cautious scrutiny, and then dropped his voice into a thrilling whisper.

"I'd zend him down to the var end of Cornwall, zur, where this murdering blackguard's a-hidin' of hisself. He's dressed up as a sea-varin' man, and goes by the name of Walker, doan't he, Willum?"

"P'raps he does," responded his colleague, with a wink of the eye meant to be very knowing, but which rather failed in its effect.

Esau tried to gulp down his terror with a draught of the porter.

"Well, Mr. Miles, if I bring a gentleman from Scotland-yard to meet you here to-morrow, will you collect all the information that you can in the meanwhile?"

"Aye, zur, that will I," cried Miles, with rabid eagerness. "But why not zee about it to-night?—the villain may be goin' to voreign parts, and——"

"No, no; let it be to-morrow."

"Well, zur, I'll trust you'll do what you can for me about the varm, zur, for I'm a 'nation poor man."

"And he's in Cornwall, is he?"

"Yes, zur, at Land's End, and goes az Walker, but you'll not vail to come, zur."

"No; you will see me to-morrow. Good day!"

"Zame to you, zur, I'm zure. But do 'ee come."

The two gentleman left the room.

It would have made a strange picture for some character painter, that pair of villains, representatives of such different types of rascality.

The sturdy, crafty rustic stood, his broad chest heaved with a deep sigh of relief, his great brown hands clenched, and his face was scarlet with excitement.

The craven Esau, pale as a ghost, dropped his clammy brow upon the table, and whined forth,

"Lor'! O Lor'! O Lor'! Vy hever did I get on this yere infernal lay? I shall be lagged and scragged, and all along of a hundred quid and a few fair promises. I'll peach on you all, blow me if I don't! I'll peach on ye! I ain't a-goin' to be swung for any von!"

"Where the blazes is the governor all this while?" cried Miles, in a low, fierce whisper. "Is he mad? Why doan't he come?"

"He is here!" cried a familiar voice.

The countryman started round, and Esau leaped up in mortal terror.

The two gentlemen had returned.

"I am—am—Michael Warren," said Harwolf, who was identical with the gentleman in black, "and you are a trusty fellow, Miles, one whom I most want at this crisis. Here is a note for a hundred pounds, a small token of my gratitude for your devotion, for I can be grateful to my friends as well as terrible to my foes."

"Loard alive, yer honour!" cried Miles, grasping his hand with something of hearty fealty, "but I'm mortal glad of this. But that weren't a bad blind of mine, eh, Muster Walker, of Land's End?"

"And this is not a bad disguise."

The pale-faced, hook-nosed gentleman, whom our readers will no doubt have divined to be the "professional disguiser," looked at Harwolf with admiration, and declared with enthusiasm,

"Shtrike me dead, but your my mashterpiesh!"

CHAPTER LXXIX.
SAVED AND LOST.

OUR readers may have wondered why the indefatigable Silas Rye and the gallant Lord Hawksbury had as yet taken no means to procure a restitution of Lady Edgeforth's rights, and to avenge the death of her noble husband; but the motives of their forbearance were just what the cunning Miles had guessed.

It was less easy to bring the murder of Lord Edgeforth home to the culprit than might appear at first sight, for Silas knew well what precautions Harwolf had taken to get up seeming proofs that his lordship's death had taken place in some obscure little town in Germany.

For whom, on the other hand, was restitution to be made?

For a madwoman and a pirate!

Lord Hawksbury, the enthusiasm of whose warm and generous disposition was awakened by glowing accounts he was always reading of the nobility and chivalry of disposition that the unhappy Christopher displayed throughout his adventures, reflected that the Raven was not now, in the very worst sense, a pirate; for of late years the wealth he was said to have accumulated had been made, in many instances, by fair trading in his disguised vessels, or in engagements with the cruel oppressors of the defenceless; and at worst, in fair fight with foes who gave him no choice but to battle or die.

Moved by these considerations, the kind young nobleman had fitted up a large yacht, in which he might cruise after the lost heir, over the world's wide seas, in the hope of reclaiming him, and disguising his identity with the felon of the past, in order to restore him to his rights and honours, to be enjoyed through a worthier career in the future.

Lady Edgeforth, too, was steadily improving; her fits of madness were less frequent, though still very violent when they did occur; and in her calmer moments she seemed to be more resigned, and sometimes even cheerful.

One ingenious expedient had been adopted to soothe her tortured and disordered brain. As the returning light dawned on her reason it illumined the ghastly picture that was seared upon her brain—the awful night at Frontemore; her murdered husband; her stolen child; and her soul, horribly repulsed by the fearful remembrance, plunged back into the darkness of mania.

To counteract this every means were used to persuade the unfortunate lady that she had never fled with Lord Hawksbury from the French convent, but that she had suddenly lost her reason there, and had been removed to the home of her father at the first appearance of her terrible malady, and that the fearful interval between her flight from the convent and her restoration to her home and friends had existence only in her wild imagination.

This love-prompted fiction had some effect in soothing the poor lady's grief, for as it was constantly persisted in, belief and hope began to rise in her withered heart, which was freshened by the atmosphere of peace, tenderness, and sympathy that ever surrounded her.

Lord Hawksbury had conceived a cordial friendship for the reformed and worthy Silas Rye, and had taken the best means of giving him heartfelt pleasure by bestowing all his spare time in promoting the education and enjoyment of little Charley, whom our readers will soon again meet, to find him no longer the pale, sickly boy pining in the confinement of his chamber, but a smart, active, clever, enlightened lad, full of boyish fun and spirit—indeed, with high principles of courage and virtue—ever striving to accomplish the bravest feats in hard study and self-denial, in fact, we trust, a bright example to the youthful portion of our readers, who will find how much real courage and heroism may be shown in the maintenance of self-respect, and who will find his career a fair light running sweetly and brilliantly through the darkest pages of our wild, sad, and romantic history.

Silas Rye sat by the genial fire-side in his cosy study, intently perusing some letters that appeared in the daily papers, when the door was suddenly burst open and with a quick cheerful step a man entered the room.

"Sibly!" cried Silas Rye, starting up, throwing down the paper and catching his friend's hand; "This is indeed a pleasure—are you not ashamed to look me in the face, you perfidious deserter? Why, I haven't seen you these ages!"

"Since I have been manager in our firm, I've had the screw on awfully tight, and assure you have had no time to think of pleasure," replied Sibly, warmly returning the grasp.

"And how's Lucy?"

Sibly reddened and laughed.

"As well as ever, and prettier and better every day."

"Then she'll be perfection by-and-by."

"Perfection is zero on her thermometer; she has risen above that low mark long ago."

"Ah! I see your blarney-stone was a real Irish one; but sit down in your old place, that side of the fire, and while Mrs. Wilton prepares the tea I'll talk to you about a matter I have always at heart."

"But this horrible affair about Harwolf and his wife?"

"We'll talk of that afterwards; for the present let the topic be the one that is ever uppermost in my mind."

"What is that?"

"Poor Lady Edgeforth's lamentable malady."

"Ah! true, does the poor lady improve?"

"Steadily, thank God, and I think the fellow who writes these letters and articles could cure her altogether."

"Do you think so? Well, there's something in his 'new system' that sounds possible, but I dare say he is some quack or charlatan, whose only object is to ring money from the afflicted."

"Well, perhaps so, but as money is no great object to me, there would be no folly in my trying him; he could do no harm if he could do no good."

"Don't make too sure of that."

"Well, I don't see how he could."

"He pretends to be disinterested."

"That I admit looks bad."

"It does, and don't forget Aladdin's evil magician, with his 'old lamps for new ones.'"

"But our evil magician must be too much occupied with seeking his own safety, after this last of his fearful crimes, to find time to trouble us."

"I would not trust him."

"Of course at all times it behoves us to be careful."

Here the subject dropped.

A servant entered and lighted the lamps.

Mrs. Wilton presided at the tea-table, and a cheerful hour passed away in pleasant converse.

When the tea-things were removed, and the good old lady had left the room, Silas Rye paced up and down uneasily.

"Sibly," he said, suddenly, "I am almost ashamed to tell you what I have done."

The latter, who was engaged in reading a long epistle from Charley to his brother, in which he narrated his travels with boyish zest and enthusiasm, looked up.

"Make a clean breast of it."

"Well, then, I have written to this celebrated Dr. Morgan, and appointed an interview for a consultation, and if he is punctual he will be here in a few minutes."

"I'm sorry for that," cried Sibly, with briskness.

"Now I think, even in our case, there ought to be bounds to suspicion."

"Perhaps so," returned Sibly. "But I confess, like Iago, it is my forte to pry into abuses."

At this moment there was a startling rat-tat-tat at the front door.

"Here he is!" cried Silas, with animation. "And if he can do the poor lady any good, why we shall not repent relaxing the reins of our caution. I fervently hope he may help us."

"Amen!" rejoined Sibly, but doubtfully.

A tall gentleman in a black suit was ushered into the room.

His hair was dark and glossy, his skin olived as by travel; he had overhanging black eyebrows, beneath which shone with strange lustre, small but piercing grey eyes.

"Mr. Silas Rye," said this personage, in a deep, clear tone, "I cannot find words to express my gratification that you have enrolled yourself among those who have sufficient liberality to trust a stranger, and are not averse to giving a trial to a good system because it is new."

Silas looked at him long and searchingly, and then replied, with a smile,

"I trust, sir, to find you the herald of happiness to a most unfortunate lady. Seeing is believing, and if I am satisfied with your skill, and the efficacy of your new system, you will find me a warm and grateful advocate of it."

Sibly did not speak.

"Thanks, thanks! That will be my best reward. But as I have but a few moments to spare, I will see the lady at once if convenient. But I will consent to do so only on the condition of your granting me one favour."

"Pray what is that?"

"I have two other patients similarly affected, who live in the immediate neighbourhood. I visit them this evening. As I am most earnest to convince so sensible a man as yourself, I trust you will accompany me."

"With all my heart."

"And now let me be introduced to the lady."

Silas led the way.

Sibly followed the doctor, his face expressing annoyance.

They reached the drawing-room, and entered.

Lady Edgeforth rose from the sofa to meet them. It was one of her lucid moments, and she had a book in her hand.

"Oh! my dear friend," she said, sweetly, addressing her protector, "I am so much obliged to you for this pretty book, in which the heroine suffers so much in her long dream. That is so like me; I suffer horribly in dreams."

"My dear lady," said Silas, "I trust your sufferings are at an end for ever. I have brought you a gentleman whose skill will secure you refreshing sleep and bright waking. You must have faith in him; there is a great deal in faith."

The doctor noiselessly glided behind the speaker, seated himself by the side of Lady Edgeforth, grasped her wrist, and stared her full in the face.

A deathly pallor overspread the lady's cheek, her eyes dilated with a fearful glance, her lips quivered and she fell back entranced.

"My God! sir, she faints," cried Silas.

Sibly was speechless with doubt and surprise.

"Hush!" cried the doctor, without turning his eyes from the pale face; but holding up his finger, and speaking in a low thrilling tone. "It is only the effect of the mesmeric influence I exercise over my patients; softly, gently; that pillow, please; good. Now."

With this he walked on tip-toe across the room towards the buffet.

Sibly followed him.

Silas remained kneeling by the side of the hapless lady.

The doctor took a glass, which he half filled with water from a crystal bottle, and then poured into it a white powder; the water remained colourless.

At this instant Silas cried from the other side of the room—

"My God! she mutters a name she only mentions in her worst frenzies!"

The doctor set down the glass with a sudden start, and, as if upon involuntary impulse, advanced a few paces.

Quicker than it can be told Sibly thrust back the glass, threw his handkerchief over it, and substituted another glass, into which he had poured, as nearly as possible, the same quantity of water.

"She has mentioned that name for the last time!" said the doctor, huskily.

He returned for the glass; Sibly handed him the one into which he had poured the water.

The doctor took it and poured a little of it on the lady's lips.

A strange smile passed over his face as he opened the window and threw away what remained.

"When she wakes the past will be nothing to her," he said, solemnly; "and now, Mr. Rye, I claim your promise," he went on, calmly, "to accompany me in my visit to other patients."

"My dear fellow, with all the pleasure in life," cried Silas, stepping to the door.

The doctor was by his side.

"Silas, Silas!" cried Sibly, eagerly.

But it was too late.

In his pleasure and excitement the kind fellow had shot downstairs with the doctor.

Sibly flew after them, but ere he reached the hall the door slammed heavily; they were gone.

He rushed into the street, but they had turned some corner and was out of sight.

Sibly was fain to return to fetch his hat, resolved to go in pursuit of them.

When he returned he found a carriage at the door, and a portly, good-humoured gentleman on the steps.

"My dear fellow," said this person, "you are very imprudent to be running about in this chill night air without hat or overall; you will have to pay for these delinquencies when you grow older."

Sibly at once recognised Lady Edgeforth's regular physician.

"Oh, my dear Docter Wilmore, you were never more welcome!" cried Sibly, "come in, come in; Mr. Rye has foolishly admitted that 'new-system' fellow, and he has mesmerised the lady, or worse."

In an instant they were in the drawing-room.

Lady Edgeforth still lay insensible on the sofa, Mrs. Wilton and her maid attending her.

"Did this fellow administer any nostrum?" the physician asked of Sibly.

"He would have done so, but I substituted a glass of water," said Sibly, quickly, as he whipped off the handkerchief and placed the tumbler on the table.

The physician took it up, smelt it, and set it down again as he said with rigid calmness,

"Bring me a silver spoon."

The maid fetched one.

The physician coolly stirred the mixture for a moment; he then held the spoon towards Sibly.

Its bowl and stem were green with corrosion.

"My good sir," said the physician, "this lady owes her life to your prudence; this mixture is a deadly poison, the slightest taint of which, if it had touched her lips, would have rendered her a corpse in less than two hours."

"My God! and who was this villain?"

"Was it Harwolf?"

"I cannot think so, no disguise could be so complete; and yet I fancy I can identify with his, some traits of this fellow's repulsive countenance."

"Of course it was he."

"Just Heaven! and Silas has gone with him! Oh, doctor, what is to be done; can I not ride to the address mentioned in the paper?"

"Take the lady to her room. My carriage below is at your service; I will go with you, but we shall not find him there."

And so it proved.

The keeper of the chambers, which were situated in a fashionable quarter, stated that a gentleman had paid her liberally to take in letters for him, for which he called or sent occasionally; but where he resided she knew not.

CHAPTER LXXX.

THE TREACHERY OF THE DOCTOR.

SILAS RYE and the doctor walked at a brisk pace, discoursing upon the different symptoms and phases of mania, till they reached a large and dreary-looking street, down which they turned.

The doctor paused at a tall dark house, and rang the bell.

An ugly-looking fellow opened the door, and the doctor without speaking ushered Silas Rye up a wide staircase, and took him into a large ill-furnished room.

"You will see that my patients are not in good circumstances," he said, with a peculiar smile, placing an arm-chair for Silas before a curtain that screened a door leading to another apartment, "but this place, poor as it looks, is quiet and peaceful; the doors are wide enough for egress; and it is altogether preferable to the raving interior of a barred and guarded madhouse."

Silas looked at him in surprise, but nevertheless seated himself, though with a slight qualm of apprehension.

"I'll be with you in a moment; I am going to prepare your way. You will soon see enough of my mad patients and of the manner in which I tame the refractory. Meanwhile, read this, it will amuse you."

He threw a piece of paper towards him and hastily left the room.

Silas Rye picked it up, and read breathlessly, in his own hand-writing—

"The documents relating to the birth of Lord Edgeforth, and the proofs of his father's murder by the present usurper of the Frontemore estates, Andrew Harwolf, are in the hands of the protectors of Lady Edgeforth."

To which were added these words, in Harwolf's bold, fierce scrawl—

"No greater proof than the above words are needed of the writer's insanity; he is, therefore, committed to confinement as a dangerous lunatic during the pleasure of him whom he has dared to brand with a charge he can never substantiate."

Silas was starting up, but he felt himself drawn back; steel bands turning on springs clasped round him, and he struggled in vain in their cruel embrace.

The sweat stood on his brow; he opened his mouth to utter a fearful cry; but something struck harshly against his teeth—he was gagged. The curtain rustled behind him as if a man had passed through it.

The door opened and the doctor entered.

Silas Rye glared upon him with impotent fury.

With exquisite coolness the doctor took a chair, and seating himself across it, folded his arms on the back, leaned his chin on them, and gloated with his fiendish grey eyes upon his victim, as a fiend might be supposed to chuckle over a votary whose term had expired.

"Ha! is my ghost-trap so secure that such a mercurial spirit as the ghost of Silas Rye," cried the doctor, " cannot ooze through it as it did through the stone wall of my chamber at Frontemore. Ha! ha! I have the best of you; if you are a Mephistopheles or an Asmodeus I am Proteus, that can change my person. What, poor mute, you stare and don't know me? Be convinced that I am your old master, who raised you from beggary to serve him so well; be convinced of the fact, and behold me as you knew me of old." With this the doctor threw off his wig; his shaggy eye-brows were still black, but there was no difficulty now in recognising the diabolic villain by his square rugged forehead, his light and grizzled hair, and his fiendish grey eyes. Harwolf laughed long and gleefully; he pulled out a pistol and pointed it at the head of Silas Rye.

"I have a devilish good mind, my invulnerable goblin," he said, " to try whether you are still impervious to a pistol bullet, but painfully I deny myself the treat; I don't mean you such mercy. Now, mark me, Silas, listen to the last words you will hear from a sane man, except from your keepers. I owe you thanks, Silas Rye; you who would have given half your life to have tied the noose that should hang me have in all likelihood saved me from the gallows; for I was becoming a maundering, remorseful wretch, that weighed my choice between suicide and surrender. If I had had a tender wife; if good and well-timed words had been spoken to me, I might have chosen one course or the other and have atoned for the past with my blood. I might have repented, but you would say, if you could, that I was too far gone. Perhaps I was; therefore, let me revel in the little term the fiends vouchsafe me, ere I am lost for ever."

The wretched passion-maddened criminal gasped for breath, and paused on his awful words.

"I owe you much, Silas Rye, for you put me on my mettle; my dignity as a villain was injured, for there is a pride for evil and a pride for good, and an ambitious man's choice lies between them. You cozened me with a pitiful cheat; you openly defied me; you left me a daring challenge in the cabinet, which you had filched of the papers on which hung my life and my fortunes. I accepted it as soon as I found it; our duel of subtlety is fought out. Who is the conqueror? You would say it you could, that I am; but you know not yet how far. She whom you dared to snatch from me is dead; the potion I gave her was poison. Her son, who was your foundling, is a felon, hunted for his life by my own son, who will triumph over him as I have triumphed over you. I go hence; I go whither no English inquisitor can follow; and you, perhaps you think I mean to kill you. Oh, by no means; I reserve you for a revenge sweeter, far sweeter. My paladin of mad women, you shall have congenial company for the rest of your intolerable life; you will be removed hence and for ever, and shut up, hopelessly, eternally, as far as the unfortunate brevity of life can comprehend the eternity of anguish I have doomed you to, for I hate you, I con uer you, and I enjoy my revenge. You shall die too," the monster went on, rising and pouring chloroform from a phial on to a handkerchief, " but you shall be resuscitated in a tomb of the living-dead, which you would gladly exchange for the ghastliest sepulchre of the dead who are lifeless! Farewell—Farewell!"

With fiendish insanity gleaming in his eye, the wretch, whose vile passions had rendered him delirious, thrust the handkerchief in the face of his victim, who hailed the respite of temporary suspension of life as a boon in the midst of such horrors.

Silas Rye became insensible.

Harwolf stamped his foot; the curtain was torn down from the door, and flung over the victim, and two ferocious ruffians carried him bodily away.

CHAPTER LXXXI.

BROKE AWAY.

THERE were sad partings of friends and parents, who might never meet again; there was smiling through tears, and hopeful words from aching hearts; there were a thousand lingering looks and clinging embraces; there was the exchange of promises to write as early as possible; there was waving of handkerchiefs and kissing of hands, and the emigrant-ship sailed and steamed out of the dock on to the turgid highway of the broad river. The bewildering panorama of quays, wharves, factories, bales, cranes and piles; smoky chimneys, fleets of hulls and forests of tall, tapering masts, swept mistily by as the good ship, throwing up the slush of the filthiest of rivers from her black broad bows, moved onwards to the fresh, green and open sea.

Who is the traveller that stands on the deck with folded arms and lowering brow, and scans the dense dark mass of gliding buildings as one who looks upon them for the last time, as one who has no sympathy with his kind, and whose teeth grate and eyes scintillate because he cannot see some baleful effect accrue to the vast city as he breathes his impious curse upon it.

It is Harwolf—henceforward Michael Warren—who has started on his voyage.

The emigrant-ship which bore this pestilent villain to a bright new world bore an ominous name, "The Scourge."

The wide and dirty path by which Mammon pours his richest treasure into the little strong box of insular Britain from the cornucopias of all the wealthiest and fairest of nations broadens and broadens; the shores recede and become faint in the sunlight; the waves roll up with a heavier shock, and the breeze wafts over the crowded decks bluff and brackish from the free and open main, and, as the white and sunny cliffs of dear, dear Albion—never so dear as now—glow out, crowded with rich corn or vivid green sward, a tearful cheer goes up from the hearts of the emigrants, and the little band strikes up " Rule Britannia " and " Auld Lang Syne."

There was something transcendental and darkly grand in the stupendous villany of the wretched Harwolf.

Tears spring to his hard and cruel eyes, his soul melts, and he hoarsely murmurs,

"Aye, aye! farewell, England; farewell! For me you do not smile; nor do I sigh for you, den of ingratitude and perfidy. My wife, my son, for whom I trod in ways of darkness and sulphurous burning, for whom I snatched such rich prizes, fouling my hands with the bloody indelible stain that marks the souls of the fiend's bought bondsmen; my wife, my child, to whom I was ever indulgent, *they*, even *they* revolted against me. The wolf-cub sets not his fangs in the throat of his sire, but dark man might learn mercy of hyænas! Yet ah! my revenge is complete, it is glorious! I have silenced the mad woman; she can couple my name with her curses never more, never more! And now I go free, with all of my wealth but the earth that refused my master a grave, and is strewn with the dust of his ashes. I wash out the past with all the multitude of waters in the ocean. I triumph, but woe, woe! the joy of the wicked is a groan from the pit; precept and practice could never teach wisdom and virtue so well as the awful example of my corroded heart, where the worm that never dies fattens at the core. Oh! if there were a window in this breast, that the weak and the tempted might look in and behold the fiery darkness; if there were an echo of the past, that their ears might know how soft and how subtle are the first whisperings of the evil one, they would fly with horror from the death wages of sin, and find sweetness in the very pangs of famine if these could save them from such a doom as mine! What now, Miles?"

The countryman stepped up to his master.

His broad face wore a look of unfeigned alarm.

Harwolf did not notice this.

"Look, Miles," he said, "there fade the last outlines of the coast of Great Britain; all has gone well —to admiration! Bring me some brandy; we will sit here and listen to the music, and drink prosperity to ourselves in the future, and peace to the foes of the past, whom we have swept off so cleanly."

"Ay, zure, yer honour; but this cursed, infarnal Esau ——"

"Ha! what of him?" cried Harwolf, with a start.

"Did yer zend him below, Mr. Warren, to rummage the packings."

"No; what does the impudent scoundrel mean by so doing?"

"Zure, then its no use to cry over spilt milk; but the durned scamp has robbed us of our money," said Miles, dryly.

"Not so; I carry the heaviest part of my fortunes about me, in bonds and notes; it is best and safest. We don't know what may happen."

"Then there was no money with the luggage?"

"Yes; five hundred sovereigns in a leathern bag."

"Then they're gone!" said Miles, dryly.

"But Esau?"

"He's gone too."

"Thunder and devils!"

"Won't fetch him back," rejoined Miles, shrugging his shoulders.

"But he knows our whereabouts; our worst secrets are in his hands, to use them as he list."

"I suppose az he slipped off just as the ship was about to leave her moorings—howsomedever, gone he is."

"Fools, dolts, that we were to trust him!"

"I thought zo; we had meant to zettle 'un."

"Oh, that we had done so! Another specimen of the reward I get for forbearance, the treacherous scoundrel."

"I'm mortal zorry; more than once I thought o' scragging the cur myself."

"Why didn't you?"

"I was afeared to displease your honour."

"Never again will I spare anyone; on the first thought of suspicion I will act; even you I will not trust; so beware how you tempt me."

"Durn'ee, I've been true to 'ee," growled the countryman, doggedly. "If I takes to a course, I sticks to it, and I never yet peached on a pal; but dunna think one thing?"

"Ha!"

"Dunna think I be afeared on 'ee; if such a jelly-livered, snivelling whelp az Ezau can bilk ye, I be your match on any occasion."

"Fool, brute that I am. I was too, too secure. Well, this has taught me a lesson. I have locked up the door that bars me from my enemies, and have thrown them the key. Miles, what's to be done?"

"Nothin' as I knows on, yer honour."

"Well, I have heard that down Arkansas there is a large gang of bush-rangers; I'll band with 'em. I cannot live a square life now, I am past it. They shall be my body-guard, and I'll set the world at defiance!"

"Ay, zo; if they do not cut yer throat in a mutiny."

"Oh, how I could curse myself."

"Durn it, there be no need for that; the snivelling gipsy can do no more harm than to verret out Zilas Rye and set 'un at liberty. Hawksbury arn't in England, and Ezau, maybe, will be content to rest quiet with the booty he's taken."

"A slender hope."

"All we haz to hang by; zo we'd best make the most of it."

"I will send an agent to England, or I will return myself."

"Zure, Mr. Warren, I'll go for 'ee when all's zettled abroad. Meanwhile, why we muzn't think on't."

"Go below," said Harwolf, faintly; "look to the baggage."

"Ay, zur."

"But first, some brandy."

Harwolf took a look draught.

"I'll come to you directly," he said.

"Ay, zur."

Miles walked away; as he did so, he muttered,

"Maybe he's 'cuter than I be; but, durn 'un, not so steady; this infarnal blunder haz whetted his suspicion. Well, I'll look to 'un; I'm playin' a dangerous game, but, durn it, I'll make it profitable."

"But the mad women's silenced," whispered Harwol, huskily; "there's comfort in that, her wails cannot follow me over the seas. Maybe I shall meet the Boy Pirate, and then I can set my heel on the last of the adder's brood."

CHAPTER LXXXII.

THE STRATEGY OF GOMEZ.

THE ox-wain, with its unwonted and warlike load, rumbled on down the road and reached the low valley through which the river meandered, and on which, from its rocky eminence, frowned the gloomy Castle of San Salvador.

Beneath the shade of a clump of tall and graceful palmettos stood sternly a picket of seamen, with guns on their shoulders and belts bristling with pistols and knifes.

These were a portion of the crew of the "Black Vulture," who had volunteered to keep watch and ward over all the entrances of the castle that held such a famous and terrible captain.

The cunning Gomez, who acted the peasant to perfection, whistled a national tune, cheered the oxen, which tugged on, sweating and panting with their living burden under the scorching blaze of the sun.

The picket advanced as the huge wain heavily and wearily lagged down the hot and dusty path.

Wardlaw, the second mate of the pirate-ship, laid his hand on the pole of the wain.

"Where are you going, you swab?" he said, fiercely. "You don't pass without giving an account of yourself."

Gomez shook his head, and answered with well-feigned simplicity,

"No spek Yengliss."

"Who are you? Where are going?" repeated the seaman, in bad Spanish.

Gomez answered rapidly, and in a strange, unintelligible dialect.

Wardlaw could not understand him, but pointed to the castle and made signs that he must not pass.

He then tapped the butts of his pistols threateningly.

The artful Spaniard winced in sham terror, as if he were already shot.

He then pulled out what Zampa had called his "pass paper."

Wardlaw took it; he could not read it, but the boldly-written signature of the provost of San Salvador was unmistakeable.

He gave it back to the pretended peasant, but still looked at him sternly and suspiciously.

Gomez grinned with exquisite stupidity.

Wardlaw advanced to the edge of the wain, and threw back the covering.

Some of the yams and bananas tumbled out.

The Spaniard smirked and obsequiously replaced them.

He then took the head of the oxen, as if to turn them back.

"Let the lubber pass; we've overhauled his log— he carries true colours," said one of the men.

"Ay, ay! yams and bananas—rations for the pig-feeding garrison," said another.

Wardlaw made a sign that the waggon might go by.

Gomez made a grimace, shrugged his shoulders,

and urged his beasts to a trot, as if very glad of the permission.

The seamen laughed as the wain rattled down the road.

"The Spanish cur! how he quails at British bull-dogs," said one of them. "He's off like a shot."

"But you'd find his fangs pretty sharp between your shoulders, hearty, if he owed you a grudge, and caught you alone in the dark streets of Janiero," Wardlaw remarked, with a smile.

"Well, we're keeping a secure guard, I'm thinking," said another.

"Yes," said Wardlaw, with satisfaction; "the Boy Pirate's chance of a rescue is small indeed while we keep every way of access to his prison. I wouldn't have let that skunk pass but that I haven't the heart to rob the half-starved marines of the garrison of their dinner. I don't wonder the swabs have no more heart nor brains than jackasses when they feed on such donkey's provender."

"Aye, but his pass!" said one of the seamen.

"Shiver his pass! that shan't avail another;" returned Wardlaw. "The free list is closed as they say at the theatres. I admit no more orders."

As he spoke a man, seemingly a priest, came rushing down the road, his cassock flying behind him.

He had a pistol in his hand.

With extravagant gesticulation he told a long story in Spanish, pointing first backwards and then to the castle.

Finding he could not make the obtuse listeners understand, he tried to rush by.

They seized him and forced him back.

He stamped his foot impatiently and produced a passport.

"No, no, mate; no admittance on any business," said Wardlaw, with a grin.

Again the priest gesticulated furiously.

"Ask him who he is," said a pirate.

"Who are you, senor," asked Wardlaw, in his execrable Spanish.

The man seemed delighted at being addressed in his own language, and by an odd coincidence replied that his name was Gomez, a very common Spanish name.

"Gomez!" shouted the men. "The Boy Pirate's chief mate. Kill him! Knock him down!"

The priest raised the pistol to defend himself, but it was hurled out of his hand by a blow from the cutlass of one of the pirates, and a blow from Wardlaw laid him insensible on the ground.

"Look, mates," cried a man who picked up the pistol, "here's the figure of a raven carved on the stock. No doubt the scamp is really Gomez, and is trying to bamboozle us."

The fact was that the poor priest had seen the "Ravens" roost in the cart, and full of zeal for his country, and for the detention of the Boy Pirate, had rushed to the picket to warn them of the trick played upon them.

The pistol was one which he had found on the road; it had fallen from the cart.

"Moor his hulk to that tree," cried Wardlaw. "If he proves to be he whom we take him for, he shall swing, as a scarecrow to the rest of his flock."

Thus, by too much caution, Black Ralph's sentries overreached themselves.

Meanwhile the wain had arrived at the gates of the castle.

A number of Brazilian soldiers guarded the gate.

These presented arms and challenged the pretended peasant.

"Who goes there?"

"A friend!" returned Gomez, in Spanish.

"Ha! but you're not the right man. Where's Sancho?"

"Met with an accident—fallen from the cart and hurt his head. I'm his partner,"

"Ha—ha! the dog; a regular pulque-barrel, he," returned the soldier. "Well, amigo, show us your pass."

Gomez produced it.

A door in the heavy iron gate was opened and the lumbering wain passed through with its dangerous burden.

Gomez was in some perplexity, for he knew not in which tower Christopher was confined, and though the daring pirates had got into the court of the citadel their position was one fraught with the most terrific danger, and their force by no means adequate to the desperate enterprise.

However, he thought he would leave the guidance of his steps to the sagacity of the oxen, which had no doubt often gone the same journey before.

The weary animals dragged eagerly towards a large barn-like store-house.

As they approached the door a fierce and stout fellow, in white cap and blouse, apparently the head cook, rushed out and assailed Gomez.

He seized him by the neck, and poured upon him a torrent of abuse at his tardiness in bringing the provisions.

Gomez quailed, and earnestly excused himself by narrating a detailed account of the fictitious accident which he declared had befallen Sancho, and by vehemently anathematising the Yenglesa sentries, who in their jealousy had detained him.

The cook pointed fiercely to a little stone yard beneath the frowning walls of a high turret, and then rushed into the store.

Gomez took the hint and drove the cart beneath the wall.

A soldier tramped by, his musket on his shoulder.

"Amigo, if you put your ear to that wall you'll hear a lion roar," said the soldier, with a grin.

"Ha! is the prisoner there?"

"Yes—the Yenglesa pirate."

"I should like to see him."

"Well, he wouldn't bite you—he's heavily ironed. There's many would like to see him."

"You seem to be mortally afraid of his escaping."

"Dios! We don't give the poor devil much chance. One would think the place was besieged. I'm just going back to my post, and the provost himself mustn't pass me without giving the counter-sign."

"What have they done with old Giraldez?"

"The provost was for shooting him, but the governor came over and his excellency told another story. He has given the old man better quarters, up there in the bell-turret."

"Well, I say they ought to hang all these cursed pirates," returned Gomez, "as soon as they catch them."

"Oh, they'll throttle the Raven soon enough, never fear," returned the soldier. "But I say, amigo, do you know the word?"

"No."

"Then you might as well expect to walk without feet as to go a step through the garrison without it."

"What is it?"

"Our patron's name," returned the soldier, devoutly crossing himself; "San Salvador!"

"Thanks."

The soldier grinned, and passed on to his post.

Gomez cautiously lifted the canvas.

"Is all well done, senors?" he asked, in a low tone."

Dick Caffyn groaned and answered, dryly,

"I'm too well done, scorched on one side; I want turning."

"Look, senors, I am going into that bakehouse."

"And I'm coming out of this oven," said Dick, resolutely. "Make a move to jump out of the wain."

"Patience, senor; in yon bakehouse the fellows are at work who will come to unload the waggon. The waggon must unload itself while I amuse them. You have the rope and grapnel, and must scale the turret wall. This court-yard is deserted for the present; we have so far succeeded wonderfully; I leave the rest to your valour and prudence, I must begone."

"Better stay with us, they'll kill you," said Brierly, panting for breath.

"Well, I shall make as good a scape-goat as another; but, pray be careful, for the captain's sake."

THE RED RAVENS TO THE RESCUE.

With this Gomez hastened across the yard and entered the bakehouse. A number of men were busily employed kneading dough at long tables.

Several of the men desisted from their work and gathered round him.

"Ha! you're a new man; where's Sancho?" asked one of them.

"Cracked his head when he was drunk, and is laid up," replied Gomez, promptly.

"And how go things at the hacienda?" asked another.

"Oh, bravely."

"And how do Lopez and Inez get on?" said a third.

"A nice young couple that!" cried Gomez, warmly.

"Charming," returned the other, with a laugh; "do you think they'll make it up after their quarrel."
No. 27.

"Oh, they're going to be married soon."

"What, has there been a divorce?" cried the cooks, in a chorus.

Gomez was rather taken aback, for he had made sure that the persons to whom allusion was made were a couple of village lovers.

"No! no! I mean they are going to be reconciled —by the priest's persuasion."

The cooks laughed and winked at each other.

"Fra Gomez is the usual mediator between them," said one, with a grin.

The Spaniard started at hearing his own name mentioned; but recovered himself upon perceiving that the priest was his namesake.

What the title had cost the poor padre our readers have learned already.

"But, senors, I have brought you a keg of brandy;

don't start nor stare, there's no one here, I got it of a Yenglesa for some yams. I'm a poor fellow, perhaps you might as well put a few maravedis into my cap, and buy it of me."

"He's a bold rascal, now," said one of the cooks, looking around in alarm.

"If our head cook, Marillo, lays hands on you he'll flay you alive."

"Well, senors, don't let me be flayed for nothing; if you won't buy the stuff, I'll give it to you to drink health to our better acquaintance."

The men looked at each other as if mutually suspicious, and then one went off to keep watch at the door, while the others tapped the little cask, and passed around a glass of the stimulant.

Gomez drank in turn.

"And now," cried one of the men, "to unload the bananas. Let us make haste, for if Marillo catches us idling, the devil will be let loose."

"Senors, one or two of you will be sufficient, for they are all unpacked but a few."

"Well done; this is a better fellow than that lazy Sancho. Did you take them into the store-house opposite the bell-turret?"

"Yes, I did so. Sancho mentioned——"

"Run—run—run!" cried one of the cooks, from the door. "Here's Marillo, foaming at the mouth like a mad dog, or a wild bull in the arena. Get the yams out of the cart, and send the fellow off at once."

Gomez and two of the men rushed out.

To the inexpressible delight of the Spaniard the coast was clear.

The men filled some baskets with the few fruits that were in the cart, and ran across the pavement to the store-house.

"Why, how is this?" cried one of them. "The door is locked."

"It was open just now," returned Gomez, readily. "I dare say some of the fellows shut it and replaced the key; you know what a martinet we've got for our overseer."

The man went off, and presently returned with the key in his hand.

He quickly opened the door.

"In with them," he said, quickly.

Both the men carried the baskets into the store-room.

No sooner were the birds in the trap than Gomez clapped to the door, and turned the key twice in the lock.

With a smile of grim humour the wily Spaniard recrossed the yard, and leaping into the wain, goaded the oxen, and bounced and jingled along at a rattling rate.

"Halt!" cried the soldier on guard, the man to whom Gomez had spoken before.

"Don't stay me, senor, for the love of pity," cried Gomez, laughing. "I've offended Marillo, and if he lays hands on me he'll pitch me into one of his cauldrons."

"Give the word!"

"San Salvador!"

"Pass. Spare not your ox-hides, if you don't want your own to be spitted. Here comes the head-cook, rushing along as hot as a sky-rocket."

Gomez goaded and thrashed his poor beasts, who, now relieved of their fatal and heavy burden, thundered over the stones at a great rate.

Another sentinel challenged him; he was suffered to proceed on giving the word.

In a few moments he was free of the castle.

He swerved round at a point in the road which branched away along the river.

This he did in order to avoid Talbot's picket, from which he had escaped so narrowly.

He hurried the oxen and wain into a field by the road, and then hastened on to the boats and the signal post.

The sharp crackle of gunshots was heard in the distance, succeeded by loud and furious shouts.

It was plain that the Ravens had begun their work of havoc.

The white sails of the pirate-sloop were now visible, smoothly rounding the precipitous rocks at the mouth of the river, and gliding down upon the fortress like the poised wings of a swooping bird of prey.

CHAPTER LXXXIII.

THE STORMING OF SAN SALVADOR.

LET us return to the pirates concealed in the wain.

No sooner had Gomez crossed the court-yard and entered the baking-house than the impatient seamen raised the canvas, and after a hurried survey of the place, leaped out.

Not a second was to be lost.

The men's faces were scarlet with heat, and the perspiration stood in beads on their forehead.

"Shiver me, if that warn't a cruise in the tropics, my hearties; and it now seems to me we're a-going into high latitudes. Dick, throw the grapnel," said Brierly.

Two ropes spun up through the air at the same moment; the iron hooks fastened at the end of each of them caught on the top of the castellated wall, and two eager rivals ran up the ropes simultaneously, as swiftly and as nimbly as squirrels.

Dick Caffyn leaped upon the top of the tower.

Zamora came next, though almost within the same second of time.

The others clambered up. The tower was a heavy square structure, and was surrounded by other towers, with bastions on all sides, in such a manner that a person who could escape detection while climbing from the courtyard might remain concealed on the summit, screened from the eyes of the look-outs on the other towers.

From their height the pirates could command a wide prospect of land and sea, one of unparalleled grandeur and romantic sublimity. They peeped down into the courtyards mapped out below.

Several of these bristled with the gleaming bayonets of the soldiers, who mustered in great force, and were parading under the inspection of their officers.

In one part was the small but well-kept garden of the provost, with its pretty and refreshing fountain, and its bright china trees. A little girl was playing with her spaniel among the shrubs and flowers—she was the provost's daughter.

In another quarter were the long stables, before which the men were lazily grooming their horses.

One side of a triangular court-yard appeared to be formed by a little chapel, for a bell was tinkling from its fretted spire, and a number of priests and choristers were ascending the steps, followed reverently by several soldiers and a little crowd of men, women and children belonging to the castle.

The pirates laughed to see Gomez seated on the shaft of the ox-wain, which was tearing along at roaring speed, pursued by the furious head-cook, who was armed with a spit and seemed to be bursting with passion.

They saw Gomez pass successively every sentinel till he reached the gate; they saw the portal opened and the Spaniard go free. They could but compare his position with their own, as the rashness of their daring enterprize forced itself upon them. They were little better than prisoners; but not a heart quailed; every man was inured to peril and enjoyed it, and not one valued his own life at a "pin's fee" compared with the safety of their admired and beloved commander.

The cooks were running about the court-yards in search of their companions whom Gomez had locked up in the store-house.

It was evident that the strategy of the pirates would be instantly discovered.

"Now, mates," said Brierly, "strikes me that the sooner we try our soundings the better, and the sooner we get below deck the nearer we shall be to the hold where the cap'en is kept by these cursed land-sharks."

"But where's the hatch-way, Jack?" asked Dick Caffyn.

"Here, senors, though it's close battened down," said Zamora, as he stooped over a slab of stone and passed his hand through the iron ring in the centre of it.

After several vain attempts the pirates succeeded in raising the stone, and a flight of steps were discovered leading to the belfry.

Down this they cautiously made their way. The light was admitted by little loopholes in the wall; the staircase was a spiral one, the steps narrow and steep, and the place half in darkness.

Zamora led the way, Dick closely followed, Old Brierly brought up the rear.

After they had continued descending for a considerable time, they came upon a wooden floor or platform, which was reached by means of a ladder.

On this they stood, looking down through the wide interstices of the beams and planks upon a wheel, and heavy blocks, ropes, wooden framework, and a large rusty bell.

"You may be sure, senors, that this bell is in some way connected with the outlet that the captain is said to have found, and at the very threshold of which he was taken," said Zamora. "I heard the bell ring myself as I was awaiting the captain's return at the pulque-shop."

"True. These cowardly Spanish rascals do all they can to gag the mouth of rumour, but they can't stop all her hundred tongues; some of 'em will wag," said Dick. "And I learned that it was in moving a stone trap that the Raven roused the peal that brought the Philistines upon him."

"But Harwolf betrayed him."

"Yes," said Dick. "But if it had not been for this confounded bell, they would not have known at what outlet he had escaped."

"Hush!" said one of the pirates, holding up his finger. "Some one is praying or speaking in a measured tone."

Zamora walked over to the place where the man stood, and listened.

It was evident that there was an apartment just below, and level with the belfry, and that some one was speaking.

They opened a sort of hatch, and climbing down a ricketty and half-rotten ladder through a cloud of cobwebs, crawled along the immense beams between which the bell was hung.

It was a strange spectacle—the weird, dark, and dangerous belfry, a streak of light from a small loophole throwing into deep shadow the massive woodwork and the grim tocsin that was to give alarm at the escape of a prisoner, or the entrance of an enemy—the desperate outlaws, despite such terrible obstacles, so perseveringly bent on the rescue of their leader, perched along the beam, with contracted brows and fixed eyes, unconsciously laying their hands on their weapons as they listened for the sound of voices.

The talking could be plainly heard within a little niche that appeared to be bricked up.

Zamora carefully examined the wall at the back of it, which proved to be a false one; on trying the bricks he found one to be loose on the edge of the wall nearest the bottom of the niche. After turning it he discovered beneath it an iron bolt; this he was forced to shatter; it was too rusty to be withdrawn. The echoes rang down the dark and well-like turret most alarmingly, and in their vibrations waved over the bell till it murmured like an Æolian harp.

The men's hearts leapt, and their cheeks blanched —not from fear, but from the excitement attendant upon the strangeness of their position.

There was a hush within the adjoining apartment.

"There'll be no getting through this lubber's hole, my hearties," whispered Brierly. "We must go a shipman's tack, right down the rigging. It seems to me if we could follow this halliard-chain that runs below from the bell to the outlet, we might bring the boats under the water way——"

"Hist!" cried Zamora. "Your plan is good, if it prove practical. But now we must be unanimous, if ever. I lead this expedition, as Zampa says. Is it not so?"

"Ay! cap'en."

"I am confident that both the voices we hear are familiar to me; one of them is the voice of Giraldez, of that I am certain. Now, we are not in sufficient numbers to stand the merest chance of taking the place by assault; let us, then, divide, and if one part of our company fail, the other may be successful."

"Divide! Shiver me! this is an odd place in which to talk about parting company. Wait till we get off the rocks, anyhow; a little more sea-room, mate, and then we'll follow orders."

"And yet we should feel at home here, for where better should Ravens roost than in an old belfry?" said Dick, with a grin.

"'Nough said," rejoined Brierly, impatiently. "What's your plan, senor?"

"I will move this false wall, which is an entrance to the cell of Giraldez, or force it. I speak Spanish, and know my man. One of us will be enough for that part of the business. Brierly, you try if you can follow the chain; of course it will pass through several stages, perhaps some of them tenanted. That must be left to fate. Our risk cannot be more desperate than it is at present. If you can reach the outlet, which, perhaps, is not guarded, as it is so secret and secure, you can get off to the boats, and bring them under the water gate. Some of you will remain here while the others go aboard."

"Ay, ay! I don't leave San Salvador without the captain," said Dick.

"Nor I, neither, hearty," added old Brierly, quietly.

"I leave that part of the arrangement to yourselves," said Zamora; "And now, if you will assist me to open this door, we will part at once."

Several seamen clambered into the niche, and, by the united strength of three or four of them, the wall was forced back, and swayed open upon an iron frame on which it was constructed.

A short dark passage appeared.

"Now, mate, I wish you luck aloft, while we try our fortunes below," said Dick, as he swayed down the rusty chain.

The others followed his example.

Zamora looked after them till nothing but the glinting of their side-arms was discernible in the nether gloom.

The Spaniard walked to the end of the passage.

He found that it was closed in with a wooden panel.

Feeling about he laid his hand upon a handle; this he shook for some time without result, but, at last, pulled it out; as he did so, the heavy wooden screen rushed down.

Light flooded in upon him.

He leaped into a cell!

Upon looking about him he perceived that he was in a room built partly of stone and partly of wood, on one side of which was a grated window.

Giraldez was reclining upon a couch; he was not ironed.

A priest knelt beside him.

The old captive raised himself on his elbow.

The priest started to his feet with a cry of surprise and alarm.

Zamora rushed to the side of Giraldez, and, throwing himself on one knee, tenderly took his hand.

"Padron," he murmured, "I have come to save you and my friend the Boy Pirate. I must not look on you lest the blood in my heart turn to tears, and now I need more than my manhood. Speak! this is no time for wonder or questioning. Is this man true?" he pointed to the priest.

"Zamora!" cried the latter, flinging his arms about the pirate. "Thanks to the Mother of Heaven, it is you! Do you not know me? I am Fra Montez, your old tutor and friend!"

The pirate held the priest at arm's length for an

instant, eagerly scanning his features; he then warmly embraced him.

"Viva! a friend in need; we shall yet be successful. But lose no time in idle converse; what is to be done?"

"Oh! I will tell you," cried the priest, eagerly, "I came not here to save but to console my old friend Giraldez, but even I, perhaps, may assist you. I have one plan to suggest, terribly uncertain and dangerous indeed, but the only one I can think of. Have you a rope?"

"Yes," said Zamora, unwinding one from his body. "I prepared as well as I could for this enterprise."

"Good! I have an order to visit the Boy Pirate; you shall change dresses with me, and take my place. But if I am left here, the gaoler will return, and we shall be foiled; besides, there is a sentinel on the stairs. Fix your rope to the window, or better, fasten the grapnel on to the roof of the tower if you can, and let yourself down without the line of eyelets that range down the staircase. I will let you in by a little side door at the bottom of the steps; we will then change dresses; you shall visit the Raven, I will take my chance."

"Senors, I cannot speak my gratitude for your good-will," said Giraldez, "but if the meanest life were lost in my behalf it would be a shameful sacrifice for a worthless object; but spare nothing to save the gallant, the noble Boy Pirate."

Zamora flew to the window.

The bars were old and rusty, and soon gave way.

He stood on the narrow ledge without and dexterously threw the rope.

The grapnel caught on the edge of the high wall.

Zamora looked out.

No soul appeared.

High walls were about him, but they were for the most part windowless.

He nodded to Giraldez and the priest, glanced for an instant at the fearful descent, then, grasping the rope, he launched himself forth.

He was working his way cautiously down the cord when he felt it move; it swayed and turned round.

He looked up.

His position was truly horrible.

He swayed in mid-air by the slender rope over a frightful depth, down which he must inevitably fall and be dashed to atoms.

The fierce, sullen, exultant face of Daniel Harwolf projected over the battlements; a knife was in his hand, and the edge of it was already pressed upon the rope.

Zamora gripped the rope firmly with his left hand, with his right he drew his pistol; he aimed upwards; the knife was already dividing the strained hemp.

He fired.

The well-aimed bullet struck the knife from Harwolf's hand.

But it was too late, the rope was almost sundered it was giving way, it broke!

Down he had shot for a yard or two, when the cord fell upon him.

Blindly he had clutched the wall with one hand, and just as the rope fell he seized the staunchion of a window to which he had swung himself.

He hung by one arm, which was almost dislocated by the weight of his falling body.

He struggled desperately, and managed to cling to the window; he broke through and leaped upon the stairs.

As he did so a shout arose from below, followed by the report of muskets, and the pattering of many feet; then the alarum bell was rung; it was evident that either an attack had commenced from without, or that the pirates were baffled in their desperate enterprise.

He rushed down the stairs.

He was encountered by the sentinel.

He shouted the word.

The man paid no attention to this, but levelled his musket.

Before he could fire Zamora threw himself upon him.

A brief struggle took place, and Zamora rushed past.

Several other soldiers came running down the passage; they lifted their unlucky comrade.

"Me ha matado, he has killed me," said the soldier, feebly; "he has gone that way."

The men flew along the passage in the direction indicated.

Meanwhile Zamora had met the priest.

"Leon," said the latter, quickly, "it is useless for you, even in my robe, to seek the dungeon of the Raven—at such a juncture none would be admitted. Here, take my robe and pass, and this crucifix; by such means you will be able to cross the court-yard, perhaps get out of the castle altogether. Fly, the soldiers are coming."

"But you!"

"Heed me not; you must not perish for Giraldez's sake."

"Never; you shall not suffer for me."

"I shall not suffer, I have thought of a trick that will save me too; so, on with your cassock, your scapula, cover these unclerical adornings, take the church's weapon in your right hand; with the crucifix in your grasp you need not fear detention. Here is my pass; pull this cowl further over those tell-tale locks. Now you'll do; you're a perfect priest! Mark my part; I fling myself down and sham insensibility; they will think you have stunned me for the sake of my robe; if they catch you they'll hang you on the higher gallows, that's all, or if you escape 'tis no matter. Jesu Maria! they are upon us. Fly!"

With this the priest threw himself down.

Zamora let himself coolly out by the side door, and crossed the yard.

He was surrounded by the soldiers.

An officer advanced, and rudely laid his hand upon his shoulder.

"Benedicite, mi fili," said Zamora, in a stern, quiet tone, holding aloft the crucifix with one hand, while he extended the pass with the other, "it is said the profane heretic and murderer, the English Boy Pirate, has broken from his dungeon; there is absolution and indulgence for the man who takes or kills him."

"Thanks, father," returned the officer, and followed by some of the men, he rushed in at the door to find the other soldiers engaged in raising the priest from the ground.

They wasted no little time in trying to elicit some explanation from him; but the monk only groaned, and raised his hand to his head.

The provost himself, with several of his officers, now arrived upon the scene.

"Senor, 'tis Fra Montez," said a soldier to the governor of the fortress, "one of the pirate-villains has struck him down, I make no doubt to get clear under disguise of a priest."

"Follow him at once, I passed him myself," returned the provost; "by this time he is well-nigh clear of the gate. Giuseppe."

"Senor!"

"Detach ten of your carbineers, and descend at once to the Boy Pirate's dungeon and shoot the villain dead; cut off his right hand and bring it to me with his shackles, that I may know he is no more. Rinaldo, parade the guard in the court-yard; I myself will go the rounds, and we will soon take or kill all these outrageous desperadoes like so many rats."

The file of men that were told off to execute our hero marched into the court-yard.

The rest of the soldiers stood to their arms as the provost issued from the door.

A man was crouching low behind one of the bastions.

"Giuseppe, be quick!" cried the provost. "Stay not to unchain the wretch. Shoot him where he lies, and bring his red hand and his fetters at once to me. Your life for the due execution of my command. March!"

"Stay!" cried a voice from the deep shadow of one of the bastions; "the Boy Pirate dies not like a wolf in the snare. He is here! at least he will die in the open day."

It was the devoted foster-brother of our famous rover who leaped forth and stood, his form erect, his breast heaving, his eyes glowing with enthusiasm, his right hand clutching back his jacket, as if to expose his dauntless breast to the fire of his foes.

We have often mentioned the striking resemblance that existed between the foster-brothers; and Dick Caffyn, from motives of affection towards his noble commander, copied him as nearly as possible—with due regard, however, to their difference in station—in the matter of dress.

The Spaniards, who, with few exceptions, had never seen their prisoner in daylight, but only in the gloom of the vaults and dungeons of the fortress, were entirely deceived, and instantly and unanimously the shout went up—

"'Tis he! this is the Boy Pirate!"

The whole mass of the soldiers surged towards him. Every musket was levelled at his head.

The men, however, looked at the provost for his signal.

The word "Fire!" was arrested on the provost's lips by an unlooked-for accident that is not without parallel in the annals of war.

A seething rush, as of a rocket, was heard in the air.

A live shell dashed down into the centre of the court-yard.

It burst with a terrific explosion.

With a wild yell, mingled with fearful screams, the men bounded back. Many were maimed, and several killed.

Thus timely had Brand poured in his shot from the "Red Raven," which, under false colours, had crawled down the river, and was under the very walls of San Salvador.

Dick Caffyn saw his advantage. Smiting right and left with his cutlass, he bounded over the bodies of the fallen, and sped across the court-yard.

"Malraya! you will lose him. Strike him down," roared the provost, himself discharging a pistol at the flying seaman.

Guns crackled, but the pursuit was stayed by the crash of another shell, followed by the thunder of the distant guns.

"The castle is bombarded!" cried the provost, in great agitation. "Giuseppe, follow up the arch-villain; he cannot escape. Rinaldo, let every cannon that will command the ship of these transcendant scoundrels be manned and served. We will blow them from the face of the waters."

But the Brazilians seemed struck with a sudden panic. Confusion almost hopeless prevailed.

Officers were bawling their unheeded orders; soldiers were running about inanely, attempting to form; women were rushing out of doors wildly shrieking; priests were on their knees invoking the aid of every saint in the calendar; children were squalling; several oxen and horses had broken loose, and were racing about the buildings, lowing and neighing in the very madness of fright.

All the while sullenly roared the guns—bomb! bomb!—each hoarse detonation burdened with the warning of death and destruction; and, like a fierce winter shower of monstrous hail-stones, the grape and canister, shot and shell, poured down their hellish storm of blasting and crushing iron, crumbling the grey walls of the old fortress, long the scene of many a deed of horror, and killing or scattering its doomed inhabitants.

CHAPTER LXXXIV.
THE BOY PIRATE'S DEADLY PERIL—
EVER MAGNANIMOUS.

It becomes necessary for the reader's comprehension of the rather complicated details of the siege of San Salvador that we should recall the moment when Brierly and Dick Caffyn, with the rest of the dauntless party, clambered down the well-like tower by means of the chain which attached the stone trap that gave access to the sally-port on the river to the remorseless bell that told of the attempted escape of any wretched captive who might find it.

They met with fewer obstacles than they had anticipated, though, as predicted by Zamora, they found that they had to pass through several floors or stages before reaching the subterranean base of the turret.

Most of these stages consisted of stone rooms, in some of which were cannon and piles of shot, but most of them were quite empty, and all of them tenantless; and each successive stage gave on to a lower one by means of a trap, or some such contrivance; though a ladder or steps were not always found to connect them, and the pirates had to leap from considerable elevations in their passage downwards.

At length they reached the last stage. A flight of steps led them through midnight darkness into the long corridor, in which it will be remembered our gallant hero had been taken; and here, having lighted a lantern, they found the slab and ring-bolt.

They listened. The door at the end of the corridor—that beneath the archway which Christopher had discovered, and which was nearest to his present dungeon—was locked and had been repaired. A seaman, who crept on tip-toe along the stone passage, brought this news to his comrades, who were cutting away the bell-chain which they found to descend through a groove in the wall; and he added that two soldiers were stationed on guard on the other side of the door.

Upon descending the steps they found the water lower than our hero had done, for the tide had gone down. The boat, however, was not there; and, to their mortification, a grating or portcullis covered the entrance of the tunnel. Upon wading breast-deep in the water they found, to their surprise and delight, that the iron was so old and so rusted by contact with the water—for it was lowered at night, and also during the day, in times of danger—that it was easily broken away, although the bars were very massive.

Having made an aperture sufficiently large for the passage of a man's body, several of the men plunged into the water and swam across the river unobserved by the sentinels on the walls—for the walls were high—and kept close beneath them till they found a spot of which the sentinels could not command a view, and as soon as they reached the opposite shore they plunged into the thick brushwood which fringed it.

Old Brierly and the few remaining groped about in search of some way of ingress to the passage beyond the door. They found some steps, and, climbing over a stone apron, they got into a winding passage which ran in a cloister-like manner along the wall of the tower, but, to their vexation, found that it led them into the outer court of the structure that was curtained by the last and highest wall. They stole along beneath the high barrier, and, as the sentinel advanced to challenge the guard, they contrived to slip into a long, low wooden hut where some goats and sheep were stabled.

Dick Caffyn remained in the corridor of the water-gate; he claimed it as his post, clinging to the hope that he might yet find a way into the prison of his foster-brother. He, too, discovered another outlet, but to his chagrin it brought him out into the court-yard where, by so nobly and so boldly personating the Boy Pirate, he had saved that hero at least from immediate death, by preventing the shooting party at once proceeding to the dungeon on their mission of death, and by leading them to believe that the Raven had broken out the inmost coil of his net, though he might be still struggling in its wide meshes.

It may well be supposed that Dick Caffyn, upon perceiving himself in the very midst of his foes, would have at once retired to the outlet he had found and have returned to his subterranean sanctuary.

This, indeed, he would have done; but at the moment he was about to return to the passage, Zamora rushed out of the castle disguised as the priest.

Dick recognised the Spanish pirate at once by his voice.

He waited to see if the *ruse* were successful, resolving that if Zamora should be detected, that he himself would rush forward and die by his comrade's side.

The rest has been told.

Our readers will, no doubt, be glad to catch a glimpse of our hero—to mark how he has borne his captivity.

A few days' confinement in his loathesome dungeon have wrought a marked and sad change in our dashing rover.

His eye still shines with its wonted fire, but his cheek is wan and pale; his limbs have lost their roundness and much of their vigour; his lips are tight drawn, and the expression on his countenance is one of almost hopeless resignation; but there is a heroism of endurance in every line of his eloquent features.

There are times when hope will faintly whisper of his gallant band, of his devoted wife, of his numerous friends and admirers—there are times when he shudders over his father's murder, and gnashes his teeth in his impotent desire to wreak vengeance on the ingrate and atrocious Harwolf.

It has been announced to him that he must die, and he has just heard with a disdainful smile that to-morrow is the day fixed for his execution.

In the meanness of their malice his captors have told him that a priest will be sent to confess him and to give him absolution for that worst of all his crimes—his heresy; they add, that unless he enters the bosom of the church in this his dark, last hour, there will be no absolution here, nor salvation for him hereafter.

The Boy Pirate assures his tormentors that he seeks not a ghostly comforter in any member of their priesthood, that he is willing to leave himself to the mercy of the All-Merciful, and to endure the justly-incurred punishment of the All-Just.

Perceiving his unwillingness to receive the priest, they impress upon him the helplessness of his condition, and bid him remember that he must submit to whatever they please to inflict on him.

A strange thought crosses the rover's mind; the priest may be his friend.

Once possessed with this idea he is eager to see him, for many reasons. He has a parting message to his wife and crew—he has a story of his wrongs to be told to the governor of Rio Janeiro, his dead father's real friend.

The Boy Pirate is therefore fiercely urgent in his protest against the cruelty of his last hours being disturbed by a fanatical follower of an intolerant creed, knowing that by leading his keepers to believe that he does not wish to see the priest will be very way to make them concur in his secret wish.

But now he is alone in his dungeon.

No one has broken his solitude for hours. He wonders much that the threatened visit of the priest has not been forced upon him; perhaps the provost or the governor has interfered to prevent what he has so vehemently objected to; perhaps the poor priest has been discovered to be his friend, and is paying the penalty of his goodwill to a condemned felon without the pale of mercy.

The Boy Pirate smiles a grim smile, and the light flashes to his eye, and the blood throbs to his heart, as he hears the heavy tramp of the sentinels down the steps, and thinks how much caution is deemed necessary for the safe custody of a solitary prisoner in the deepest of dungeons, and languishing under the heaviest weight of shackles.

The time wears on.

Is that a shout that struggles through his prison's thick walls?

He starts to one knee.

Ha! yet again.

The populace are shouting as the men erect the scaffold on which he must die a death of all others to his soul most abhorrent.

He listlessly stretches his limbs, lays his burning brow against the cold, dank pillar to which he is chained, and wearily closes his eyelids.

A shout—the firing of muskets.

He starts once more to his knees, his eyes and ears wildly strained.

The roar of cannon!

He is not dreaming. The hard walls of his prison are before him; the sounds come faintly; his fetters are biting his swollen flesh.

The bursting of shells; the wild raving of fighting men.

It is no dream; it is a reality.

The castle is being stormed.

By his band?

It cannot be possible that the handful of men which comprises his crew could be so reckless of their lives—could brave so much!

Yet, what has he not dared for them? What will they not dare for him?

Oh, there is ecstatic melody in that subdued roar of the battle.

But why do not his enemies rush into his dungeon and put it out of the power of his friends to aid him by slaying him at once?

Christopher did not know the inestimable service that his foster-brother had done him. The Spaniards were fully persuaded that he had escaped, and never dreamed for an instant that he still lay chained in his cell.

The din increases.

The Boy Pirate fights with his chains.

Oh, to be once more with his gallant screw; to strike once more at the hearts of those who oppressed him without personal cause—those who were tyrants—the sons of the ruthless murderers of a whole people, generous, simple, and trusting as children; tyrants who had trafficked in human blood, and bartered in the sale of human liberty; pirates far worse than he had ever been—pirates from choice, pirates in taste, and dastards in all respects.

No; let him strike his flag to the justice of some free-handed, fair-dealing government. Let old England do justice upon his head; let them remember the old sea-kings, their forefathers; let them consider his acts of generosity, and let them allow him to die the death of a warrior—to bare his own breast to the bullets of soldiers; but to be hung like a whelp by the betrayal of such a brute as Harwolf, to die by the hands of Spanish guerillas and slaves; no, no; it could never be.

But whence is this horrible stench, as of fire?

The air grows close and suffocating.

The roar of the cannonading is louder and louder, the mingling of shrieks and war-cries more piercing.

A mist seems to creep into the dungeon through the very stones.

The air becomes hotter and hotter; the flame of the lamp burns lurid and dim.

Just Heaven! it is smoke that is wreathing in beneath the door, and through the little grating that gives light upon the stairs. The horrible truth breaks in on the agonized soul of the rover; the castle is in flames!

Presently a bright light glares through the grating, clouds of smoke roll densely and heavily in.

The Boy Pirate is strangling.

He wrestles madly with his chains.

And now long, insidious, serpent-tongues of dazzling flame creep in beneath the door, and lap snakishly around the dank walls of the vile abode of misery and anguish.

Their blaze is intense, their heat scorching.

Oh! how much more welcome the accursed darkness, how much more endurable the blackness of passive despair, than the blearing of this mortal agony, that glows like infernal lumination only to torment!

The long snakes of flame creep higher and higher up the horrible walls, licking off the green damp and vegetation of rankness, hissing fiercely as the go.

The Boy Pirate gazes round him, his heart turned into a stone by the Medusean horror. His hair rouses, his parched tongue withers on his blistering lips, his eyes straining and bursting.

Loathsome creatures gather about him, toads hop, and newts crawl towards him; a ball of huddling rats seek shelter behind him. Still vainly he raves and struggles with his fetters.

He is writhing in the contracting islet of an ever-spreading sea of fire.

Then the heroism of his nature returns.

Then memories of his misdeeds seem to run among the flames like fiends of the pit, and then the breath of his conscience-approved thoughts and actions seem to waft coolingly to his tortured brow.

He kneels, he raises his eyes and extends his hands, like a martyr who would be purified by fire; he blesses Lilia, and he calls upon his mother; he remembers his dream, and he dares to cling to the reverent hope that the mercy that tempers Almighty justice is measureless, and will reach the deeply and sincerely penitent, however guilty. He accepts the dreadful visitation with tears and resignation, but, oh! with sad shame and bitter, bitter remorse.

His resignation is not that of a holy saint who dies in a good and glorious cause, but that of a vile and terrible criminal, whose only hope is found in divine forbearance to the worst of sinners.

Will the flames come nearer and nearer till he can scarcely restrain a shriek of pain.

The hot and rarified air ascends and carries up the smoke, which hangs above his head like a pall.

And now he is closely edged in by the fearful element; the reptiles climb upon him, but he is too much paralysed to shake them off; all feeling of humanity's repulsion to crawling and slimy things seems deadened.

But what is that sound as of falling masses of stone. He must be maddening, for he fancies he can catch the shout of well-known voices.

Crash, and again crash; the walls must be falling about him.

But there are steady blows, as if from some iron implement.

His lips are parted, but no breath seems to leave them.

Louder and fiercer the sound of hammering, and the thunder of falling stones.

A wild, wild huzza!

A part of the wall tumbles in; a wide smoking gap is before him.

Excited faces glare red in the fire glow.

It is Caffyn and Brierly, Gomez and Zamora.

They have matchlocks and axes in their hands, and they bound through the flames to his rescue, shouting and sobbing like maniacs.

His limbs seemed numbed, as if they had been smashed on the wheel, when, with no gentle hands, his comrades shiver his chains with their hatchets, and, taking him on their broad shoulders, carry him, passive as a child amid their wild, glad cheers, from the stronghold of fire and torture.

He is borne as in a dream through the burning corridors.

He is carried out into the calm cold air.

He looks round.

The whole turret totters and falls in with a thundering roar, and the whole air is in a blaze with myriad sparks and flame-jets, and huge masses of smoke roll heavily upwards, and, like the sable flag of his vision, blot out the glory of day.

"Cap'en!" cried old Brierly, grasping his young chieftain's hand, while his eyes brimmed with tears, and his voice was hoarse with emotion; "humble thanks to One aloft, we have saved you, we have saved you; and old Jack Brierly was the first to discover where the Spanish devils had stowed ye."

"And Dick was not the last at your rescue," cried Caffyn, in a thick tone, as he affectionately grasped his foster-brother's hand.

"It would be hollow mockery to try to speak thanks that are too great for expression. My brave, my noble comrades, what can I do in return to bespeak my gratitude?" cried the Boy Pirate, with great feeling.

"Do as you *have* done, cap'en, and we are more than repaid for a sarvice that is nothing after all, for you would have done as much for the meanest man amongst us," cried old Brierly, with heartiness.

"And Giraldez; is he rescued?"

"Yes, noble senor, yes," returned Zamora, with a beaming smile. "I and Fra Montez got him down from his high perch. Your burrow we could not find."

"And is Lilia safe?"

"Cap'en, I trust so. She has a good pilot and a steady watch while Zampa is her convoy," said Brierly.

"But who fired the castle?"

"Who but that devil, Harwolf," cried Dick, fiercely; "whom we will run down if he seeks refuge in Portsmouth Harbour! They mistook me for yourself, and therefore did not overhaul your dungeon, thinking you had slipped cable and had sheered off."

"The infernal scoundrel! but his time will come. And now, hearties, if you don't think in these few days I have fallen into second childhood let me get on to my own pins."

"No, no, cap'en, you're weak. By leave, we will carry you."

"Thanks, hearties; but I'm seaworthy yet, as my friends and foes shall find."

"Cap'en, here's Tom Garrod come to say as young madam be safely shipped, and, odd to tell, that devil, Harwolf's partner, Black Ralph Talbot, saved her life when the Spanish swabs would have fired at her."

"That's strange, indeed. Well, he sha'nt lose by it."

The rover walked proudly and erect; excitement lent him strength, but he was still weak, and his limbs tottered.

"Come, cap'en, come, we must run for it, even now," cried Tom Garrod. "There's a whole fleet awaiting us in the creek, and Harwolf is bringing half the squad of Brazilian marines from Janiero. As for Brand, he has fired the minute-gun till it's hoarse with giving signals; and he'll go ramping mad if we're not aboard in the twinkle of a handspike."

"Aboard, then," cried the Boy Pirate.

The men gave a long and hearty cheer.

The castle was still roaring in flames behind them.

A man rushed frantically past.

He was immediately seized by the pirates.

"'Tis the Spanish skipper of this cussed hulk," cried one of them. "Shall I scuttle his figure-head, cap'en."

"Kill me," cried the provost, hoarsely; "it will be mercy. O God! my child—my little one! My youngest, best-beloved; Lucia—little Lucia! Oh! Virgin Mother! is Heaven inexorable, or do the fiends rule all? My Lucia! Oh, horrible! horrible!"

"Your child," cried the Boy Pirate, in a trembling voice. "Is she lost?—is she dead?"

"Yes, senor; she is yonder in my burning house. No mortal can save her; the villain in his reckless malice has destroyed all that was innocent, all that could make my old harsh life endurable."

"She is there?" cried the Boy Pirate, breathlessly.

Quick as thought he snatched up a hatchet, and sprang away like an antelope.

The men gave a shout of warning, but deprecation was unavailing, the rover dashed on.

The provost and the seamen flew after him.

As they scrambled over the walls of the garden we have already described, they perceived Christopher dashing wildly with his axe at the door.

He burst in.

Huge volumes of smoke bellied out.

The men gave a cry of horror.

Dick rushed in after him; the staircase had fallen down, and was a huge pyre of glowing ashes, while the walls looked like one of the tombs of fire in Dante's Inferno.

Dick was driven out by a burst of flame; his hair alight, and his eyebrows scorched off.

Presently the Boy Pirate appeared once more to the yearning eyes of his agonised crew. He stood on a high and flaming buttress, and carried a bundle in his arms.

"Now, hearties, throw me a rope," he cried, cheerily.

This was done.

Why did not he advance his hand to catch the rope?

His hand lay limp at his side!

"Now, mates, spread your jackets. I can't grapple the halliard; but never mind me, only look out for the child."

With this, the Boy Pirate with one hand tied the rope round the bundle, and swaying it out of the reach of the flames, let it fall as gently as possible into the arms of the men.

The provost snatched it from them. He threw back the covering; a little girl appeared wrapped in it. She looked as if she were in deep sleep, and though she did not otherwise move, her snowy breast heaved.

"Blessed Mary!" cried the old man, in an agony of joy. "She breathes, she lives; she is not even scarred!"

The pirate-crew yelled in their intense anxiety and terror.

Clutching by one hand to every point of vantage, the Boy Pirate was scrambling down the side of the house through the smoke and flames.

"Patience, my lads," he cried, in a bold and pleasant tone. "Don't ye see I've lost my sea-craft, and climb like a land-lubber?"

He reached the lawn, and advanced towards his men, who received him with a deafening cheer.

"Good God, captain! how palé you are. Are you injured?" exclaimed Caffyn.

"No, Dick," returned the pirate, but with a ghastly smile. "I've hurt my arm, nothing more."

The Boy Pirate as he spoke staggered a step, and sank down insensible.

———

CHAPTER LXXXV.

BLACK OINY AND THE DETECTIVE.

THE consternation that prevailed in the household of Silas Rye upon the sudden disappearance of its principal may be well imagined.

Sibly, after spending three days in fruitless search of his absent friend, wrote to Lord Hawksbury a detailed account of all that had happened, adding that Lady Edgeforth had suffered a severe relapse since the visit of the charlatan, who, he could not doubt, was Harwolf himself.

Black Oiny, the Irishman that had followed so faithfully the fortunes of his master, was inconsolable at his loss, and vowed, by all that was sacred and profane, that he would find him if he searched all over the world.

In the first instance he had made inquiry for his old confederate, Esau Cooper.

He called at all the usual haunts of the perfidious gipsy, but could hear no tidings of him.

One night, after a long and weary ramble through the slums of the City and the Borough, the Irishman returned homeward, acutely mortified at his want of success; and remembering that "when the heart of a man is depressed with care the gloom is dispelled if a woman be there," and many other saws to the same purpose, Oiny stopped as if struck by a sudden thought, and exclaimed, gleefully,

"Faix! I'll go and see the girleen."

The "girleen" was Lord Hawksbury's cook, a buxom and comely country lass, of whom the gallant Irishman was deeply enamoured, and with whom he

had "walked" and "kept company" ever since she had been in the service of the present family.

Lord Hawksbury's town-house was situated in Pimlico, and thither the Irishman bent his steps.

As our reader is aware, his lordship was out of town, in fact was now cruising in the Mediterranean in his yacht, and with Charley Rye for his companion.

Upon reaching the door of the house, Oiny was surprised to hear the sound of minstrelsy, and to behold—like the figures in a Fantoccini, or the Ombres Chinoises—floating across the bright field of the blind of the kitchen-window, dark shadows mingling in merry dance—Belgravia's beauty and her chivalry.

For a moment he gripped his stick with an impulse of jealous indignation.

Why had he not been invited?

Then he recollected that he had left home so early in the morning that in all probability the invite had arrived after his departure.

He therefore eagerly knocked at the door.

It was opened by his betrothed, who looked at him with a bright smile of glad surprise as she closed the door, and after a hearty embrace tripped away to the top of the kitchen-stairs and called out in a voice of exultation,

"He's come—he has—after all!"

She then turned to her lover, who held her in his arms, chucked her under the chin, and rolled his black eyes with an expression of the most fervent and romantic adoration.

"Shure, mavourneen, it's not the sun that can smile life into the withered flowers so brightly and so swately as your big beauties of orbs of eyes, good luck to 'em. Bring back the spring to my heart, darlin', that's froze up wid botheration entirely. And how are ye, my colleen ruad? Shure, that's a kiss that would make a pineapple or a pache taste as sour as a lemon after sich swateness. Och! but it's a magnificent Providence to have sich a purty bit of consolation after so much trouble and vexation as I've suffered lately. And shure, without ye, Katie, it's not a summer evening I'd live through at all, at all."

"Oh, I'm so glad you've come at last—but why didn't you come before?"

"Shure, I shouldn't have come at all if I'd known you'd invite me, darlin'; I'd ha' stopped at home for your bit of a letter quite proper and dutiful—but it's wandering about like a stray dog at Donnybrook I've bin since the blessed mornin'."

"And have you found poor Mr. Rye?"

"The divil a bit; faix, I'm bothered immensely; but shure, we'll talk of something more pleasant, my girleen. Och! now, ye never ware aqualled."

"Be quiet! don't, you false fellow. I know it's all blarney—but, gracious! I wish you'd known we've got a party; it's a dress party, Oiny, and white waistcoats are in—and Miss Truffle's young man, the baker, is dressed in his volunteer uniform, and looks elegant!"

"Illigant! Och, bad cess to the spalpeen; isn't this boy a rale descendant of the owld kings of Connemara, that drissed in ermine and purple, and wore crounds by the dozen, and thought no more of a armful of gowlden sceptres than just a bundle of faggots? Wisha! But come along—dancing is it? Faix, but we'll have a raal jig, Katie, that shall make yer military bakers and pert colleens look lame ever afterwards. Och! that's the fiddle, and we'll be to the fore."

With this, Oiny put his arm round his sweetheart's yielding waist, and, whisking his stick, with a shrill whoop danced down the stairs.

The guests assembled in the kitchen paused at their places, for the dance had begun; the music ceased and all eyes were turned to the new arrival, who was received with the most gratifying politeness.

Bows and compliments were exchanged, and Mr. Macarne was introduced to the company severally and collectively.

He then stood up to dance; he and Miss Cathe-

THE ESCAPE FROM THE BLACK VULTURE.

rine led the ball, Miss Truffles and the martial baker
vis-à-vis.

With much hilarity and some confusion the "first
set" was performed, and the ladies gallantly handed
to their seats.

Refreshments were passed round, the burly greengrocer told a merry tale, the comic man—a youth
who was looked upon with great awe by the whole
circle, and was continually addressed by the coachman as "Doctor," on the strength of his dispensing
medicines at the chemist's in the next street—performed several surprising feats of legerdemain with
handkerchiefs, watches, coins, and playing cards, to
the intense admiration and delectation of the company, and then made "night musical" by singing
how certain young ladies of great personal attractions and shocking moral delinquency victimised
No. 28.

certain inane but generous young men, chiefly "from
the country," by tricks of the most extravagant,
heartless, and, therefore, irresistibly comic description.

A tall, sallow-faced compositor, with a villanously
melodramatic scowl, who had a taste for the drama,
was a "distinguished amateur," and had even played
"first murderer" in Shakespeare's sublime Macbeth, as performed by the "Illustrious Buskins," at
the Theatre Royal, Tottlefields, for the benefit of the
Lancashire weavers, stood up, and placing his right
hand in the breast of his waistcoat, bowed his head
with infinite dignity and condescension, and after
the cries of "order!" chair!" "oblige with a recita-
tion," had subsided, threw himself into his part.

He personated the Swiss patriot, William Tell.

Doubtless in accordance with the native habit of

that celebrated hero, when contemplating the rugged beauty of his romantic mountain land, the "distinguished amateur" rolled round his eyes in the manner peculiar also to moving mandarins and wax-work images, and wreathed his lips into a smile of such aggravating benignity and boundless patronization as would fully account for the intensity of Gesler's spite against the great archer, and produced such effect upon the audience in the person of the Swiss hero's prototype, that they felt an almost convulsive impulse to hit him.

After leaving his "con damnable faces," he began by apostrophising the plates, dishes, soup-tureens, in fact, the dresser collectively, as "Ye crags and peaks!" and expressed his infinite self-gratulation at being "with them once again;" he made a slight *faux pas*, by alarming the ladies with an intimation "that he rushed to them as though he could embrace them;" he wound up, however, in practical taste—for he was in a violent perspiration—by bidding the wind "blow on—this is the land of liberty."

Immense relief was experienced by the auditors at the conclusion of this piece, which they kindly gave vent to in the form of prolonged and vociferous plaudits.

"Yes, sir; I played Shakespeare's murderer for the benefit of the Lancashire distress," reiterated the amateur, as he drained a glass to the comic man.

"And looked your part to perfection," returned the latter, cynically.

"I did, sir," said the amateur, with emphasis.

The martial baker then struck up a martial stave, and musically bade "the riflemen—riflemen form."

A cross-eyed postman, who had been crossed in love and was habitually cross in consequence, poured out from his broken heart a heart-breaking ditty, something to the effect that "he had sighed and suffered long," but couched a deliberate fib in a poetical licence by stating "yet he'd never told his grief," and the song had the desired effect, for a sudden depression of spirits seemed to weigh down all the congenial souls in the assembly.

To dispel this untimely seriousness Oiny was called upon for a "raal Irish melody."

With national bashfulness the modest Macarne long resisted every importunity, but was at length forced to yield to the pressing entreaties of his colleen.

With a droll twinkle in his black eye, Oiny trolled out a lugubrious ditty, anent "an Irish lad, that loved a cloistered nun; which made him very sad;" yet, as the minstrel most reasonably inquired, "Och! what was to be done?" The singer then feelingly expressed the indignation of the hero of this ballad; "he thought it was a big shame, a most confounded sin; that she could not git out at all, and he could not git in;" and how the hero added, rather sacrilegeously, "The divil take the iron boults; the divil burn the door," and, moreover, how he consoled himself, for the sufficient reason "that he could do nothing more" by "singing, swately, Smallalee, gramachree, and paddy-wack!"

The sequel of the Irish lad's illicit amour never transpired, for the whole party were suddenly startled by a short, imperative rat-tat at the front door.

The "girleen" went out of the room; the visitors exchanged glances, and sat in awkward silence awaiting her return.

Presently she rushed in.

"Well, Oiny, I never did—it's for you!"

"Sure, darlin', for me is it? Well, then, what is it?"

"It's a gentleman."

"Och, murder—a gintleman? And what sort of a gintleman, tell me?"

"No sort of a gentleman, or he wouldn't have snapped me up so sharp; he is a tall, hard-featured fellow—but there, go to him yourself."

"By jabbers, if he's a quack docther, it's Black Oiny 'll physic him," said the Irishman, snatching up his stick and bounding out of the room.

When he reached the door he found the stranger to be a tall, square-built man, with a stern, inscrutable face, and dark, searching eyes.

"Is your name Owen Macarne?" he said, in a quiet but authoritative tone.

"The divil a Macarne was iver ashamed of it."

"You are my man, then. Put on your hat and come with me; I want you."

"Arrah, thin, I'll likely be one o' the many things ye'll be afther wanting and won't git, bad cess to ye! Do you think to kidnap *me*? Is it the boy *I* am, to be docthered by quacks? Faix, but ye'll find, Mr. Spider, that Black Oiny's too big a blue-bottle to be caught in such a net as you can spin, bad luck to ye!"

The gentleman made no reply, but went out on to the step.

A policeman was passing.

"Richards!" said the stranger, in his curt, quick way.

The policeman advanced and touched his hat.

"Yes, sir."

"Fetch us a cab. You will see Adams of the force, dressed as a navvy, at the corner of the square; tell him to get in, and send the cab to this door."

"You want to know who I am, Owen Macarne? I am Foxley, the detective," said the stranger.

"And bedad, ye may tell that to your brother quacks. Foxley was killed by the same black villain that has murthered the master, poor Mr. Silas Rye."

"My name is Thomas Foxley. Edmund, whom you allude to, was my brother. I also am a detective; I am on the track of his murderer, and I mean to find him."

There was something deeply impressive in the cold tone of inflexibility with which these simple words were spoken.

"Och, glory to the Powers! I'm wid ye!" cried Oiny, with enthusiasm. "Do but stay till I've put on my coat and kissed the girleen, and it's myself that 'll follow ye to Australey or the Injies. We'll catch the wolf, sure, let him run as far as he will; I am convinced of that entirely."

"Macarne, where is Esau Cooper, the gipsy?"

"Sure, Mr. Foxley, it's the hare I've been hunting for a week and more; but, botheration, I can't strike the scent at all, at all."

"I think I know where to find him, but here's the cab. Are you ready to start?"

"Be aisy, Mr. Foxley; I'll be wid ye in a star-twinkle."

Black Oiny rushed downstairs.

There would have been no need for him to explain the nature of the business that called him away so suddenly even had he felt disposed to do so, for several of the girls had clustered on the stairs and had listened excitedly to all that had passed.

The party gathered round the Irishman and looked upon him with great veneration as his lady fair assisted him to put on his great coat.

"Ladies and gintlemen," said Oiny, with an elegant bow. "I wish ye all good-night. I hope that the young gintleman yonder will kape up his spirits and not be sighin' and sufferin' and tellin' his grafe; unless, maybe, he groans at my wake, for bedad, I'm goin' like a lamb among thaves; so I will just sip the poteen and wish myself a mighty grand funeral; and, once more, the top of a fine mornin' to ye all intirely."

CHAPTER LXXXVI.

THE ESCAPE OF THE PRISONERS.

It was not without a sharp exchange of broadsides that the "Red Raven" eluded the fleet of vessels that awaited her at the mouth of the river, but the swift-winged rover easily cleared away from her pursuers when she had reached the open main, and her tall masts dwindled away on the sky-line, and soon she faded from sight altogether.

The "Black Vulture" weighed anchor and sailed,

with its prize, out of the harbour of Rio Janiero a few days after the escape of the Boy Pirate, for a suspicion of the real character of the brigantine began to get afloat, and the provost had taken care to let it be known that Harwolf and his men fired the Castle of San Salvador for the purpose of destroying those against whom they waged war only for reasons of personal jealousy and hatred.

Daniel Harwolf and his colleague had made an arrangement by which it was agreed that they should, every month, exchange command of the "Black Vulture" and her prize, the "Highland Mary," which Talbot had renamed the "Cormorant."

It happened that the command of the "Cormorant" devolved upon Harwolf, and he was therefore not on board the "Black Vulture" when the events about to be narrated took place.

After several days' fair sailing the two vessels sighted the Cape Verd islands, and here they cast anchor, intending to rest at their moorings till some barque worth overhauling passed by.

Black Ralph had watched with a jealous eye the growing influence exercised among the crew by the quiet but fearless, inobtrusive but commanding and inscrutable Cassidy.

Talbot was seated on a gun-carriage when the first mate passed him; he called the seaman to his side and tapped him on the shoulder.

"My man," said the pirate-captain, "I want a few words with you."

Cassidy bowed respectfully, but made no other reply.

"Curse ye! why don't you speak?" cried Black Ralph, impatiently.

"Well, captain, what do you wish me to say?" returned the mate, lifting his clear, melancholy eyes unquailingly.

"I can't wish you to say less than you do," growled Ralph.

"And I am very willing to do more than I do if it's needed; I am always ready to work hard to do my duty. I hope you give me credit for that," said the mate.

"Look here, Sam, you're the last man I wish to quarrel with," said Black Ralph, uneasily, "for, always excepting myself, you're the best man aboard. But I'm afraid you are not to be depended on—I am afraid so."

"You believe that I am not to be trusted?" returned Cassidy, with imperturbable calmness.

"No; curse it all! I only think, and even that bodes you danger, for mark me, if I believed you treacherous or mutinous I'd cure your treason and mutiny with the contents of this."

He clapped his hand on his pistol.

"Is threatening a man the way to make him trustworthy?"

"I don't want to threaten you, Sam. The first prize we overhaul, if I can find hands enough to man it, you shall command. What I want you to understand is, simply, that I'm not to be tampered with."

"But can I trust you?"

"Ha! you dog! what do you mean by that?"

"Why this: you're captain, I'm mate; the first time there's a row aboard the men may get tired of both of us. What's to prevent them pitching us to the sharks and choosing their own leader?"

"Let them try it," said Talbot, grimly.

"I am ready to obey orders, but it would be a poor defence before a court-martial for me to plead that I acted under the orders of a pirate and an outlaw. If you cannot trust me, let me go."

"If I can't trust you to stay, I could not trust you to go. No, no, Sam; when you leave me you leave yourself. The next captain you serve under will be Davy Jones, trust that, Sam."

"Well, captain, there is one thing I cannot do for you or for any man."

"Ha! and what's that?"

"I cannot fear you."

"And yet I have means to try your courage," said Black Ralph, with a meaning smile.

"Use any means, fair or foul, and you will not make me a coward. I am inured to pain, and the worst is death, which none can escape, so there's nothing left to dread," said Cassidy, with his wonted pensive calmness.

"Well, we'll talk of something more pleasant. Look here, Sam; damme, I'm a pirate—I'm a Black Vulture. There's no soft place about me."

"Well, captain?"

"But no brave man likes ill using women. I would shoot down a whole flock of the plovers if it had got to be done, but I'd rather leave that dirty work to Harwolfs or hell-hounds, and when I've caged a dove I don't like to see it beating its poor little fluttering heart out against the bars of its cage."

"I understand you, captain," said Cassidy, with beaming eyes. "This Jewess and Mary, the Scotch girl. You mean to——" He checked himself suddenly; brave as he was, he feared for them. His cheek paled a little as he added, "to treat them well, that is——"

"I mean just that, if they'll let me; as for the Jewess, she's mine, but if she is wilful I cannot help the consequence. Now, I see you are smitten with the Highland lassie."

Cassidy reddened a little as he answered quietly, "Well, she's a good girl."

"What the devil have you to do with goodness?" cried Black Ralph, savagely.

"She's pretty, and I like her," rejoined the mate, unmoved.

"That's better; then you shall have her, Sam; but mind, no elopement. I bid you beware, for her sake, for there is no chance for you."

"Good, captain, I'll speak to her about it," said the mate, with a smile.

"Speak, all bosh! She's yours, I give her to you, take her; and now go about your duty."

Cassidy walked aft and Talbot went below.

About an hour after this Mary Macallister, who was weeping in her cabin, was aroused from her lethargy of grief and fear by the sound of a light springing step outside the door.

She raised her head, hastily dried her tears, and arranged her hair, while a pretty blush tinged her round cheek, as she dropped her eyes upon some work that lay in her lap and swiftly plied her needle.

Cassidy entered and sat down by her side.

His voice slightly trembled as he spoke.

"Mary," he said, quietly, "I cannot tell you how much I would risk to save you; but there is no chance of escape for us yet."

"Oh, dinna say that, dinna break my heart and bring the grey hairs o' my puir father wi' shame and wi' grief to the grave," cried the girl, distractedly; "I ask ye ony to let me get out o' this den of wolves. I dinna care for my life; the sea will tak' me into it's great open arms and shield me in it's cold heaving breast from the unholy fire that burns in the hearts of these villains to destroy me. Oh, let me die. Dinna fash aboot saving my life; I care na for that."

"Mary, I would save you if I could; and even now I can protect you from the worst if—if——"

"Weel, noo, I'm sure ye hae nae cause to vex me wi' ifs. Ye ken vera weel that I'll do a' that I can within bounds of virtue and honour; maybe, ye'll want me to tell the fiend that rules ye, silly mon that ye are, some wicked untruth, as ye counselled puir Miss Deborah to do. It's an awesome thing to lay a lee upon one's soul for any cause, but I'll tell him what you will if ye'll ony get me one chance o' fleeing fra' the cruel world a'together, e'en though I suld hae nae ither way o' escape but the single dark door opened to a' that are afflicted—death!"

"But, Mary, you are talking very rashly, and—do you care for me, Mary? would you endure to be my wife if, by becoming so, you could walk even the deck of this plague-ship in honour and safety."

"I dinna ken that I suld be ashamed to own that your kindness has touched my heart very deeply. I canna tell why I need shame to love ye, barring that ye're a pirate," said Mary, with native frankness.

"And you would marry me?" cried Cassidy, catching her hand.

"If my father would consent; and I would love ye dearly, Mr. Cassidy;" she answered, simply, "but I dinna see how that can be, sir; we canna get out o' the ship."

"Listen, Mary; the captain both suspects and values me; he wishes to bind me to his interest; he has therefore consented, in case you should accept me, to let me be lawfully united to you. Will you be a rover's bride?"

Mary rose, her bonnie face aglow with passion, her eyes flashing with indignation.

"I'd be the wife o' a beggar if I loved him, but I would die a thousand deaths, rather than be the bride o' a murdering pirate; and ye ken that, Mr. Cassidy, ye ken that! I thought ye a braw canny lad, that wad rather kill me than insult me; and noo I find that a body must suspect even the face o' kindness in this wicked world. Oh, but I'll brak my heart."

The poor girl buried her face in her hands and sobbed convulsively.

"Mary, dear Mary, for heaven's sake forgive me; I had no thought to wrong you; I will not remain a pirate one day longer than I can help—I will make my escape, and that soon, meanwhile be cheerful; I live to protect you."

"Oh, Mr. Cassidy, I canna help but trust ye; for my father and I ha' nae ither friend under heaven but yoursel. Oh, dinna, dinna deceive me."

The poor girl still sobbed in her lover's arms.

The cabin door was burst open and Deborah rushed wildly in.

"Mary! Mr. Cassidy, I am lost! The villain Talbot came to me just now with an ominous frown on his cowling face; I saw that my life hung by a thread; I am no coward, but I quailed before his fierce look; he spoke low and threateningly. At first I defied him, but he seemed so terrible, his manner was so different from his usual truculent, swaggering bearing, that when he offered to marry me formally, I remembered your advice—and I—I consented."

"But ye'll nae keep your promise?" cried Mary, quickly.

"Heaven forbid, I would rather be the bride of the grave. Oh, what—what is to be done? this mockery of marriage is fixed for the second day from now. And all the profane levity of this hardened reprobate broke out as, in his wild ranting style, he planned out the pomp and circumstances that should attend our wedding; the villain laughed, sang and scoffed at my prejudice in wishing to confirm our union by an idle ceremony. He filled my lap with bracelets, gems, and money bags; and then rushed on deck raving and singing in his mad mood."

Cassidy smiled.

"He would make a better husband than many a better man," he said dryly; "but since it is not to be a match, why the sooner you are gone the safer for your peace. Well, this is perplexing, there is nought but the ocean around us for leagues, unless we could make the Verde Islands in a boat; I know not how else we can escape. Stay, there will be a carousal on board the prize to night; if the sea were an ocean of pulque or brandy, Black Ralph would soon drown himself. I shall be left in charge of the 'Vulture.' I must get you through one of the ports into the pinnace towing astern, and we must get off in the gloom. One thing is in our favour, the nights are dark at this season, and I will take care to make the men too drunk to harm us. But now I must be gone."

"And my father! I'm sure ye winna leave him behind, for I wad never leave the ship without him. Oh, Mr. Cassidy, ye are sae guid and sae brave; but I winna praise ye, till ye've left miles and miles o' sea between yoursel and this your ark o' bondage and shame."

When Cassidy came on deck, Black Ralph advanced towards him, singing, with a jaunty air,

"Oh, I am a son o' Mars, and I've been in many wars,
And I show my wounds wherever I come;
For this was in a trench, and this was for a wench,
When fighting wi' the French, to the sound o' the drum."

"Weel noo, and how are ye, Master Sam? I canna say ye wear sic a braw face as ye suld, when ye have just been sunned by the smiles o' your ain bonnie Mary," cried Black Ralph, with a gleeful chuckle, slapping his mate on the back and laughing gruffly.

"Ah, captain, my love she's but a lassie yet; and I'm not such a killing gallant as you," returned the mate, with a dry smile.

"Maggie Court her head fu' high,
Looked at Duncan unco skye;
Ha, ha! the wooin' o' it."

"Cheerily, mate, you must persevere; for me, I am victorious, and soon the 'Vulture' will be mated; a precious brood ours will be, ha, ha! pirates every one of 'em! Why, this old barque shall sail among them like an old duck in the midst of her ducklings, and we shall be strong enough to whip the Red White and Blue—cocked hats and marines. Hurrah for the Jolly Olliver!"

A gun was fired from the "Cormorant."

"Hark! mate; our consort speaks, and she says on a servi—or, being a Scotch craft, 'come, the haggis is cookit;' but this is High Dutch to you, Sam, till your wife is purser. Well, mate, we're going to do a 'rouse on board the 'Cormorant' and to wash down our salt-junk with pulque and montillado. I'm sorry to leave you behind, but none but you must act skipper while I'm away; and I'd advise you, Sam, to improve the occasion in the state-cabin with the obstinate Miss that—

"Winna, canna, munna;
That winna buckle to."

"Phew! the Scotch nurse plays all her tunes on the bag-pipe."

At this moment the boat was put down.

Wardlaw and some of the other officers approached.

"Captain," said Cassidy, "the men have had a rough cruise lately, and they're looking sulky; would it not be well to pipe all hands to mischief?"

"Not when I'm away, mate," said Black Ralph, who appeared to be in a very placable humour.

"Then take some of them with you."

"Ha! Do you want to be left alone, then?"

"I'm not afraid of the men; they like me, and obey me," said Cassidy, with emphasis.

"But you might mean treason; eh! Sam?"

"If I did mean treason the men would be better removed from contamination. But there—before you accused me of being too silent, and now you start at my lightest suggestions. You're captious, Captain Talbot."

With this, Cassidy walked carelessly away.

"Put down the jolly boats," cried Talbot. "All hands for fun. Teddy Macarthy's watch, man the boats; the rest be as merry as Mother Cary's chickens. But mark, lads, a round dozen and two days in the hold for the man that gets drunk or disorderly. Keep a good watch, Cassidy; and good-night."

The men huzzaed.

With this, Black Ralph leaped into the boat that was rocking beneath her bows, and the men pulled off to the "Cormorant."

All was hubbub and merriment aboard.

Cassidy went below.

He seated himself in his cool and dogged style at a table, and wrote in a clear, bold hand, a letter to Black Ralph. He took it into the captain's berth, and placed it in the breast-pocket of a pea-jacket that hung over a chair.

He then took from the side some finely-mounted guns, boxes and pouches of ammunition, and gently let them down from a porthole into the pinnace that was towing alongside; he fetched out from the stores small barrels of provisions, which he disposed of in the same fashion, threw after them some kegs of rum, then some blankets and wearing apparel.

The noise on deck grew more and more boisterous.

When he went on board, the men were shouting, singing, dancing, and sky-larking, and the night air rung with laughter; while, spite of the captain's threat, not a few of the men were already helplessly drunk.

Cassidy was received with a unanimous cheer, and the men insisted on his remaining on deck while they drank his health with all honours.

This ceremony over, they let him go.

He rushed down the companion-ladder, and quickly made his way to the cabin where the luckless captain of the "Highland Mary" was confined.

He unlocked the door, and entered.

Mary, whom Black Ralph had permitted to see her father, had told the Scotchman of the kindness that had been shown her by Cassidy, and the unfortunate seaman recognised his friend immediately when he held up his hand to impress caution.

"Ye're tryin' to save us, lad," exclaimed the wary Scot, briskly, though in a low tone. "I'm glad, for ye're own sake, that there's ane true heart to be found in this ship of hell. Weel, what'll I do?"

"Follow me, quietly as you can," said Cassidy, coolly. "We're amidships, and there's the port; the pinnace lies alongside; get in. First put on this jacket. Good. Get into the pinnace, and till I bring the girls pretend you are sleeping. If the men on deck see you they'll think you're there by order. Now, sir."

The Scotch skipper got through the port, and softly let himself down into the pinnace.

Cassidy went into the state cabin.

Deborah and Mary had been apprised of the attempt that was to be made for their rescue.

They were prepared to depart.

They sat cowering at the noise and riot above.

They had donned their hats and mantles.

They started up with blanched faces as the mate entered.

"Hist!" he whispered. "You must not speak; all depends upon you caution. This is a most desperate adventure. We may be seen in the pinnace, and shot down in an instant."

The girls rose, and softly followed him.

As they passed along the berths, Cassidy suddenly stopped, and with a wild look, pointed to a dark corner.

The girls understood the signal, and at once crouched down.

Cassidy quickly threw a piece of bunting over them.

A man rushed noisily down the gangway.

He came up to the mate, pulling his forelock, and said, in a thick voice,

"Mishter Cassidy, you're skipper aboard; the men ain't scarcely we—wetted their whistles, and, damme, the g—grogs out."

"You're drunk, Deans; I'll have you put in irons."

"Drunk!—irons! I'm a shober mansh, shir, and I tell ye all the gr—grogsh out."

"Are the men steady?"

"Shteady!—shteady as the mainmasht, yer honour. There arn't a shwab among ush arn't ash shteady as I be—but, damme, I say the grogsh out."

Cassidy went to the stores and returned with a brimming can.

"Look ye, mate, I'll trust ye with this—but it's all you'll get, so make the most of it—and, remember, if you or any of your messmates are found the worst for liquor——"

"Worst for liquor!—who ever *was* worst for liquor? Your honoursh a pirates' man, the only gentleman offishler on board the infarnal crafish, and I do shay again that every man, fore and a'ts, ash steady as I be."

The fellow stumbled up the ladder, taking care, however, drunk as he was, not to spill the grog.

Violently trembling, the two girls rose from the corner.

They flew to Cassidy.

He took them by the hands and led them to the port.

He looked out.

The pinnacle had been towed close alongside.

The wary Scot, in his pirate's jacket, sat doubled up in the boat, his head on his knees nodding and apparently fast asleep.

He looked up.

Cassidy made a sign.

Macallister rose and steadied the boat.

Very tenderly and carefully, Cassidy lifted down first Deborah and then Mary.

The Scot caught them in his arms and placed them in the stern of the boat.

Strict silence was preserved.

Cassidy looked about him for a moment.

A man rushed down.

"Ain't ye coming on deck, Cassidy?" said this man, who was an officer. "There's rare fun forward—but the men are getting warm."

"I'll be with ye, mate, soon."

"But the men?"

"Tell them that I, Cassidy, have threatened to pipe to quarters if they don't moderate the racket they're keeping."

"Ay, ay, sir; but you're not well, Cassidy, you're looking pale."

"I am tired."

"As for myself, I am tired too."

"Of what?"

"Of things in general—and this life in particular."

"Are you sincere, Oakland?"

"I am indeed, Cassidy."

"But it's a dangerous confession to make."

"But I know I can trust you, you are true-blue."

"And so you are weary of being a pirate?"

"So weary, that I shall kill myself soon if no one is kind enough to spare me the trouble. My throat's at the service of any one."

"But why not escape?"

"It is impossible."

"If you had a chance to-night?"

"I would embrace it at all risks."

"Oakland, if I offered you one, you would betray me to curry favour with Talbot," said Cassidy, quietly.

"You are a villain to say so!" cried the other, hotly.

"Then you will declare on your oath that you are not deceiving me?"

"I swear by the mother who bore me—and she is in Heaven, thank God!"

"Get you out from this port then, and jump into the pinnace, you will find company; but first let me give them a signal to admit you. Good. Go, I follow you, not an instant is to be lost."

Oakland looked out; seeing the prisoners at liberty, he clutched Cassidy's hand and leaped into the pinnace.

A few moments after the boat was drifting away from the ship of riot, debauchery and murder.

Cassidy stood up and looked back with folded arms.

The Scot, his daughter, and Deborah threw themselves on their knees and poured out their thanks to the Most High.

Oakland murmured a fervent Amen!

CHAPTER LXXXVII.

THE MADHOUSE.

SILAS RYE awakened from his trance.

His brain seemed on fire, his bosom heavier than lead; his tongue was parched with raging thirst, and his eyes seemed seared as with a brand.

Feebly he lifted his arms.

The roof above him, and the walls about him, spun

round and round, and he sank back on the pillow
of the couch, to which he seemed bound, and gave
utterance to a groan of intense pain and horror.

Many minutes passed away before he could realise
the helplessness, the misery of his position.

He shut his heavy lids—he remained quite still;
his brain semed sickened as with the fumes of strong
drink.

He tried to recall the events of the past day.

In vain.

Like phantoms, forms swept around him, familiar
to his memory, but hideously distorted to his imagination.

At last, and by slow degrees, his thoughts concentrated into one dread point—the piercing conviction that the terrible scenes through which he
had passed were not the figurings of a dream, but
stern realities of waking life.

He was not in the grave, there he might have
rested in oblivious apathy; he was not in prison,
there he might hope for escape, or in some way support himself by the conciousness of rectitude, of
having atoned for the past by the sincerest devotion
to those whom he had once assisted to injure; but
he was confined in that den of horrors, to which the
grave is a refuge, the dungeon, a palace—the mad-
house!

There was a noise in the adjoining apartment.

He called out.

He received no answer.

The light was grey and sombre, for the evening
was dark and cloudy, and the sky lowered gloomily
through the bars of his cell window.

The room was square, white-washed, and bare of
all furniture, except the bed on which he was bound,
and a single arm-chair.

After a long and weary delay heavy steps sounded
without the door, and three men entered the
room.

The first was a tall, meagre, hard-featured man,
with a small, sharp eye, firm and repulsive mouth,
and a thin hooked nose.

His satellites were two sturdy, bullet-headed
fellows, with short necks, and low foreheads, rascals
that appeared to be capable of maintaining sway
over their luckless victims only by sheer brute force
and intimidation.

The principal of the asylum seated himself by the
side of the patient, took his hand, and pinched
his wrist between his claw-like fingers.

"Give me some water; I am dying with thirst,"
muttered Silas, in a dry, hoarse tone.

"Bad case, Rawson!" said the mad doctor, with
a leer, raising his eyes to one of his myrmidons.

"Werry bad, sir."

"If you mean to kill me, be quick; yet give me
one draught of cold water, I ask no more," Silas
again panted, from his white and cracked lips.

"Yes, Rawson, a very bad case," said the doctor.

"Symptoms is wiolent," responded the man.

"I am resigned to endure all if you will not pretend to think me mad," groaned Silas, feebly.

"Raging thirst, extreme restlessness, a constant
looking at the winder, and a werry hobstinate conviction of sanity; it's a hawful case, sir!"

"Yes; but there is cunning too. We must treat
him not as a raving maniac, but as one of those
criminal lunatics——"

"As is given to disguisin' of their feelins," the
man interrupted. "Werry good, sir; he ain't mad,
in course. Oh, no; don't look like it; he's almost
a foamin', sir."

"You villains, I am not mad!" shrieked Silas.
"Give me some water; I parch, I scorch with thirst
and fever; if I do but once break these bonds you
shall find that, mad or sane, the devil has got loose
among ye. Let me gut up; let me go hence.
Water! mad! Oh, God! Oh, God! where is the
justice of Heaven, the policy and protection of
society, if I am to be made the victim of such a
hellish villain as Andrew Harwolf. Mad, mad!
No—no—no! Give me some water; for charity,
one drop of water!"

The unfortunate fellow sank back upon the bed in
a swoon of exhaustion.

"Rawson, take him from the bed, put him into a
bath, give him the clothes, and when he recovers
turn him in the press-room with the others."

"I'll look after him, sir."

"Assist him, Marshall; I will go into the main
ward, and prepare the way for him."

About an hour after this Silas Rye was marched
into a large padded room with barred windows, and
without other furniture than long tables and benches,
stapled to the ground.

He walked dejectedly, though his eyes shone with a
fierce light.

His cheeks were very wan and haggard, and he
reeled a little.

A terrible spectacle was before him.

The room was thronged with a crowd of wretched
being in all stages of rampant madness or drivelling
idiotcy.

The hubbub and confusion was frightful.

Here a poor wretch stood on the table, a piece of
paper in his hand, vehemently haranguing the unheeding assembly.

Opposite him a large-headed idiot, with lolling
tongue, was crouched, watching his movements with
inane attention.

One man, whom madness had crowned, was seated
on the form with majestic air, giving preposterous
orders to his imaginary ministers and subjects;
while one, in a strange delusion that he was acting
as chief mourner at a funeral, paced round and round
the room, his face buried in his handkerchief, stopping at intervals to raise his streaming eyes and
wring his hands, as if in mute but poignant sorrow.

At a table a man sat with a number of pieces of
paper, buttons, and small coins, which he was
counting and arranging in heaps every now and
then, clutching the little piles and listening with
alarm, as a miser might be supposed to do when
counting out his cherished hoardings.

Some were singing, some weeping, while others
crouched on the ground with folded arms, buried
in the deepest dejection, and maintaining sullen
silence.

Silas Rye seated himself in one corner of the room.

His entrance caused but little notice in a general
way, but one or two individuals looked upon him
with staring eyes and open mouths, and pointed at
him with mutual gibberings.

"I must not close my eyes; I must learn to bear
this sight," muttered Silas. "I must not assimi-
late my condition with that of these poor creatures,
or I shall soon become as bad as the worst maniac
amongst them. No, no; I'll fancy myself their
keeper. This place cannot be impregnable; I can
get out. I must, I will hope. Yes; not to-day,
perhaps—not to-morrow, but sooner or later I shall
escape. Meanwhile, I will keep myself quiet, that
my brain may escape contamination."

With this resolve he looked about him, and tried
to accustom himself to the strange company into
which he had fallen.

A very tall and wretchedly spare fellow stood
before him with folded arms, and regarded him
intently.

Silas looked up at him, and smiled good-
humouredly.

The man gravely bowed his head and seated
himself.

He then smiled weirdly, and laying his long, bony
hands on the knees of Silas Rye, looked at them
curiously

"You see how it is?" he said, raising his palm,
and pointing to it with a deep sigh.

"You mean that you are worn with sorrow
and privation; but, poor fellow, it may be, like me,
you are not deranged."

"Does that mean mad?" asked the man, in a
strange, hollow voice.

Silas did not answer.

"Because, if it does, you make the same mistake
as the doctor. I am not mad; no, but I am afflicted

with a strange and awful affliction. Look at that, and tell me what you think of it."

Again he held up his hand.

Silas did not know what to say in reply, but clutched his own fingers together in mortal distress as he gazed into the wild eyes of his poor, insane companion.

"You do not perceive anything singular? Look here—and here," he pointed, as he spoke, to his body and his head.

Still Silas remained silent.

"You cannot all be blind!" cried the man, passionately.

"What would you have me see?"

"The effects of my frightful malady."

"You do not bear them in your person."

"No! Why do you tell me that lie now? We all know that you are a lunatic. It can do you no good to sham thinking the master's thoughts. No, not his thoughts—he knows I am what I am—he knows —bless you—he knows!"

"I dare say he does," returned Silas, raising his hand to his beating forehead and languidly smiling.

"You think he does. Ha! ha! Now you are sensible; of course, every one must see. Why do they seek to deceive me?"

"I cannot tell."

"Perhaps it's done to comfort me—don't you think so?"

"You must be comforted; soothe yourself with quiet thoughts. You understand what is said to you, and I will talk to you—sing with you if you like. I'm sure I'll do anything in my poor power to give you solace. I have comforted another far more terribly afflicted than you," said Silas, in a kind tone.

"Ha! what ails him?—you did not seek to comfort him by the trick they try upon me."

"What is that?"

"By telling him lies; by pretending to be blind to the ghastliness—the hideousness. Bah! what shocking treachery! Perhaps they think it kind; but I hate them for it, and some day I'll murder them all. They can do me no harm, you know, with knives or pistols—you know why?"

"No one wishes to harm you."

"But I'll tell you why—and you'll believe me, won't you?"

"What is it?"

"Because they cannot hack my flesh or shed my blood—it's plain why, eh?—isn't it?" he dropped his voice to a whisper as he said "because I have no flesh to hack, no blood to spill—I am fleshless and bloodless!"

"Perhaps you are a spirit," said Silas, gravely, to humour his conceit.

"No; I am a living, walking *skeleton!* Yes—it's strange—a *skeleton!*"

Silas started with horror.

The poor wretch took hold of his hands and kissed them, and cried in a tone of delirious gratulation,

"Don't mind my lipless gums; I'll not hurt you; I like you, I love you, because you believe me."

Silas drew himself away gently, but with awful loathing.

"Look you here now," cried the man, speaking rapidly, "I am not what you are—that is, mad. I have all my senses, my scull is not masked with a face, but I think the brains it holds are pure. I see you are mad; but I call 'myself an odd name, that I call myself Live Death—and Live Death shall sit beside you, and if any of these poor wretches seek to do you harm he will set his bony grip in his throat and strangle him."

"Stern, strange world! How dark, how appaling the shades of life; how pale and faint their modifying lights!" cried Silas, in a voice of agony. "And how weak are the strongest; I, whose heart has risen in every peril, have braved the most dreadful of villains, have been gnawed by the sharp tooth of scorn and famine, may call myself a strong man, and in a month, perhaps, I shall be as one of these!"

"Not if you *pray*—prayer will save you. If the world were all we could wish we should have no faith in the goodness of Providence; but this bitter life is but a brief phase of an existence immortal, eternal!"

These solemn words were spoken in an impressive tone by a pale man seated by the side of the captive.

Silas started and turned in breathless astonishment towards the speaker.

The latter looked him calmly yet beseechingly in the face.

"If you say I am not sane I may retort that you have no proof to give me that you are not really mad."

Silas would have grasped the speaker in his arms with a joyful cry, but the latter made an idiotic grimace, waved his hands, and frowned him back.

"For the love of all that is holy," he said, in a trembling whisper, "be quiet! make no demonstration. The eyes of cats are dull to the glance of the keeper yonder. See what you've forced me to do?"

With this, the speaker rose, and ran round the room like a lapwing, upsetting several orators and potentates, and trampling on several grovelling imbeciles.

With a fierce growl, the keeper collared him, and gave him a rough shaking.

The poor fellow crouched down as if cowed by this discipline, and slunk back to his place.

"That's your only chance of safety," he said, mouthing at the beginning and end of the sentence. "When I was first put into the main ward the accursed ruffians knew me to be as sane as you are. If I had given way to melancholy, I should soon have lost my reason. But I knew that though I am a prisoner now, I have a sweet wife and a darling daughter, and better still (as I am not an Atheist), that I had God! I was not foolish enough to think that the Divine Being would work my deliverance by a miracle, but I felt that if I trusted in Him, and did not give up to rebellious despair, He would sustain and preserve intact his precious gift of reason; so that at night I prayed constantly, and by day I beguiled my brutal keepers by affecting to be as mad as the rest of these unfortunates. I kept a keen watch to find among them one, like yourself, unjustly confined. Oh, pray be cautious! Seem to treat me as a lunatic, and to-morrow grow sullen, and refuse food, and they will see in your despondency the first symptoms of insanity. And now I'll leave you awhile, lest we should be detected. We will make our escape, and soon. I have devised means; but the risk is terrible. Good night. Think of me when you are alone in your cell. Be patient, and Heaven will protect us."

With this the man rose and walked about the room with rapid strides, mouthing and gesticulating.

"No. 15 is in one of his fits to-night. Look to him, Jem," said one keeper to another, as he passed him.

"All right, I'll look to him. Cuss the feller! he gives a devil of a deal of trouble. I'll chain him up to his bed to-night."

"No, hang it! we don't want to make a 'raver' of him, or we shall have a worse bother still."

"I don't see why they don't quiet sich like," said the other, regarding the patient with a scowl.

"When he stops of chatterin' his teeth the governor will stop chinking the shiners he gets for him, and that won't pay no how."

"Well, Bill, as things is, he's better'n than them as won't be conwinced," said the other, turning a vicious eye upon Silas.

"In coorse," returned his comrade. "But it don't take long with sich, arter all. It'll soon be all genuine with that cove."

"Think so?"

"In coorse. Don't ye see as he mopes a'ready?"

"*Ah!* yes, so he do; and when they mopes, Bill, it's a case decided."

"Certain sure. Well, it's all the better, 'cos examination-day's a comin' round, and he wants preparin'."

"They'll find a true werdict, don't be afeard. And

now I wotes we takes him straight off to his cell, and gives him a taste of the ' solitary,' whiles as he's in a good humour."

"' Treatment werry jndicious,' as Dr. Swearall says. Come along, my covey; you ain't at all wild, are ye? Never no need of a straight-jacket and low diet with sich a binnocent lamb. My eyes, you're reg'lar hintelligent! Bring him on, Bill."

Silas suffered himself to be lead passively away.

When he was locked up for the night in his narrow and dark cell, he poured out his fervent thanksgiving for the bright beam of hope that had risen in his dark night of despair, and carefully excluding all agitating reflections sank into a deep and refreshing slumber.

CHAPTER LXXXVIII.

BACK TO RIO JANIERO.

"My father's portrait; it is still in the hands of the Governor of Janiero," murmured the Boy Pirate, as he leaned meditatively against the capstan of the "Red Raven." "He promised I should have it, and, no doubt, if Harwolf's treachery had not brought on the long series of calamities, through which my gallant crew have sustained me, he would have kept his word. Why did I not press for immediate possession of it? I should have done so, although he told me that it had to be reproduced as a full-length picture, if I could have foreseen what followed. I have ventured my life for sordid plunder; I will not stint daring for such a sacred pledge."

The Boy Pirate walked aft and called to the boatswain, Tom Garrod.

The "Red Raven" was anchored in the roads between the little island, far out to sea.

"Tom," said Christopher, to the boatswain, "is the pinnace disguised?"

"Aye, cap'en; the shipwright as bolted her sheathing boards couldn't swear to his handicraft. She looks like the yacht of some Spanish cruiser. Want to go ashore, your honour?"

"Yes, Tom; send for my brother, and man the boat."

"Aye, cap'en; but why the pinnace? Shiver my top-lights, cap'en! but I think she'll hardly float over yon shallows. Souldn't we put down the gig—with pardon—or one of the jolly-boats?"

"I'm not going to the island, Tom; I'm going to the mainland."

"Back to the Brazilian coast?"

"Even so, Tom."

"Devil a bit!"

"I mean what I say, hearty, so down with the boats."

"But, cap'en——"

"Come, Tom, was I ever the man to be gainsaid?"

"Not if you meant going back to Janiero."

"That's just what I do mean."

"The Lord help us then!" cried the boatswain, holding up his hands; "for they'll take good care not to give us another chance of snatching you out of the fire, cap'en."

The Boy Pirate shook him by the hand with warmth and gratitude.

"Tom," he said, the tear rising to his bright, fierce eye, "you are all very good to me, and I strain your loyalty to its utmost stretch, but you believe me when I assure you of the necessity of a seeming piece of fool-hardiness?"

"Cap'en, I'll take my davy we're in at the galley fire, if so be as it were told by your honour."

"I know you would, though it were a yarn about Jemmy Skyflyer and the mermaids," said Christopher, with a smile.

"But that's true, cap'en, that yarn; true as the log-book," returned Tom Garrod, shaking his head with virtuous indignation.

"Who doubts it, Tom?" said the young pirate.

"But here comes Master Caffyn; rig the pinnace, and man it with picked men."

"Aye, cap'en."

Dick Caffyn at this moment approached.

"My brother," said Christopher to the young seaman, "I am called on shore."

"The vision of a day's shooting, captain?" asked Dick, with a grin. "Lord! there's nothing to pop at but monkeys or macaws, and apes are no luxuries and we don't want feathers. Zamp says, though, that it's a 'dam good coast, sar, for turtle and pulke-aloa.'"

"I'm going back to Janiero."

"Going back to blazes! We have had enough of that port, I fancy, captain; bees don't hive in the nest they've been burnt out of. The Ravens were wellnigh served up as roast fowl to the Brazilian epicures, who would have thought our blood savoury sauce for any fare. What's in the wind's eye, captain? I hope the breeze don't blow that way?"

"But it does, Dick, and it's a wind that blows me towards a prize that I must win. I shall not tell you all now, my foster-brother, but the time may come when you will be glad that you did not refuse to gratify my wish in this instance."

"Captain, of course your orders are paramount to everything, and I hope you believe the last man to turn mutineer is Dick Caffyn."

"Stay aboard then, Dick, and take care of Lilia."

"Lilia lives in your life, captain, and I'm with you wherever you are bound," returned Dick, heartily; "but I wish I could dissuade you from going back to Janiero."

"It can't be, Dick; what I return for is a trifle, but one more precious to me than all the galore I am likely to be master of for many a cruise. You remember when we left the shores of Brazil for North America, when we fell in with the Seminoles of Florida."

"Ay, captain."

"Well, long ere I resolved to embrace that adventure I had resolved to make inquiries in Rio Janiero for certain people whom I had heard of as being acquainted with my kinsfolk."

"And who were they, Christopher? I thought you were a foundling?"

"Time will show who and what I am, but the revelation will bring me disgrace and not honour, Dick," returned the rover with a heavy sigh; "but look, the pinnace is ready; will you go with me?"

"Aye, captain, where you will."

"Good, then; I will go below; I shall leave the ship in Brierly's command, and bid adieu to Lilia."

Tom Garrod took care to choose the hardiest and staunchest of the rover crew for the service, and, having manned the boat, sat at the stern waiting for his commander.

When the Boy Pirate and his foster-brother got into the pinnace the halliard was pulled by Tom, the sail swelled out before the fresh breeze, and the little barque flew on its course dancing over the head-waves light as a fairy, and soon neared the shore.

The place where they landed was a low and sandy beach in a little bay.

There was a large log-house, and a flagstaff from which the Brazilian standard was drooping in the sultry motionless air; a few palmettos and a string of barges and bumboats were moored along the side of a sort of quay built of piles and bamboos.

A large and formidable-looking Brazilian frigate was anchored in the bay with two or three armed steamers that had acted as convoys to some heavy barques whose masts could be seen above the trees, for they were docked in a little water-lock behind the station.

The Boy Pirate looked at the frigate with a smile, and turned to his men with a gesture of encouragement.

The pirates grinned.

As the pinnace glided along the side of the bay signals were run up on the frigate, and also on the flagstaff at the station.

The Boy Pirate readily replied by signalling that

THE FIGHT WITH THE BRIGAND.

he was the captain of a merchant vessel which lay out at sea, and that he was putting to land with intent of penetrating into the interior.

As the day was extremely hot and the people on shore for the most part blacks and mestizoes there was little further notice taken of the pirates' skiff from the station.

The frigate, however, showed a disposition a little more inquisitive, and put down a boat.

The pirates' hearts leaped as the heavy-oared boat tugged strongly through the surf.

The men were sallow-faced fellows, armed with cutlasses and side-arms; their officer, a slight, graceful youth of about twenty, somewhat showily dressed in uniform.

"Whither bound, senor?" he said, addressing the Boy Pirate.

The latter leaped up in the boat with a radiant smile.

Christopher was dressed in a Spanish jacket and trowsers; no waistcoat, but half-way up his shirt, which was embroidered and of the finest linen, was a cincture of rich coloured silk—a sash that bristled with pistols. He looked perfectly a Spaniard.

"I am bound to the station of South Maria on the Parahyba," returned the rover.

"Good, senor; I see you are wise."

"What proof do I show of wisdom?" returned Christopher.

"Why, senor, you are well armed and have a fine crew."

"Indeed, one need to be well defended now-a-days, when the seas are scourged by so many pirates."

"And have you seen anything of the audacious

'Red Raven?' Fancy a single ruffian and his band storming the fortress of San Salvador! But the pirate is a gallant fellow. Did you hear how he saved the child of the provost marshal?"

"Yes, I heard of that, but 'twas nothing; he would have been a great villain if he had left the child to perish without an attempt to save her," returned the rover carelessly.

"Well, I fancy his career is nearly at an end, he has had a long run for a pirate," said the young officer.

"You are on the look out for him?"

"Yes, and not our ship only, but a consort which is cruising off Cuba, for there is a report that he is in West Indian waters."

"You and your consort are widely parted."

"Yes, but we are sure to catch our man."

"Do not make too sure."

"And you have seen nothing of the sloop?"

"No; I hope he will give you a stiff chase," said the rover, with a smile; "you will not value your prize if you do not have some fun in its taking."

"Never fear; he will not surrender at discretion, the Yenglesa rascal," said the youth, with a laugh. "I hope we may be alone in his wake, that we may have the more sport in his capture."

"Better to be alone in his wake, than along side with half the corvettes in your navy," said the Red Raven, grimly, sternly flashing his eye.

"Muy ben, senor," laughed the youth, "I see you will not believe the villain is annihilated till you behold him thrown into the sea with a shot at his heels."

"I have no desire to see that sight, senor," said the pirate, smiling. "I leave his execution to you and look out for my own defence. When do you sail from the bay?"

"We cruise about, weighing anchor once in every forty-eight hours," returned the young officer. "We shall leave our moorings early to-morrow, so you had best not protract your stay, for it is known that the Boy Pirate has taken but few prizes lately and you fare not the worse for sailing under the shadow of our flag."

"Thanks, senor."

"Adious."

The officers of the pinnace and the gig exchanged salutes.

The pirates' skiff soon ran close upon the sandy beach.

The Boy Pirate and his men landed.

As had been pre-arranged, Christopher and his foster-brother were to cross the country and to enter Janiero from the landward side; and, as the small number of men would be sufficiently large to excite inquiry or suspicion, and too small to be of any use in the heart of a great city, it was resolved that the two principals should take with them no other companion than Zampa the negro.

This being settled, the bold and reckless adventurer and his unquestioning retainers started off to the city which had been the scene of such disastrous catastrophes to the indomitable rover who once more braved its dangers.

Before entering the town the Boy Pirate led his companions into the wood.

"Now, Zamp," said he; "unship your cargo, and let us rig in our new gear."

"Iss, sar. Dis chile him raised 'special for mas'r's sarvice. Dere ain't a better valet nor dis nigger gemman, from Kentuck to Louisiana. Make you up reg'lar buckra charmer; curl yer wool—'scuse, buckra, ought to say hair: brush yer coat, shine yer boots, do ebbery ting handsom'; make you raal genwine admiral, and no mistake."

Between each chuckling sentence the negro drew out from the parcel different articles of wearing apparel. There were in fact three suits; one, that of a South American planter; another of a mate in the merchant service; the third a rather showy livery.

The three pirates dressed themselves in accordance with the parts they were to assume: the Boy Pirate throwing on the light garments commonly worn by gentlemen of the Southern States; Dick Caffyn dressing in the mate's uniform; Zampa, bursting like a butterfly from its cocoon, in all the glory of a pretentious livery.

The pirates looked at each other; they could not resist a mutual hearty laugh.

"Iss, sar, dis niggar berry splendious," cried Zampa. "Don't tink yo find a nigger handsomer nor more becomin' to him libery-fashion dan dis same chile. Yah! dam buckra, what dey am for libery? Sar, dere nuffin. Yo look at ole Zamp—he's de Wenus."

Dick laughed.

"Well, captain," he said; "I don'tj know on what errand you have come; but I believe we run but little risk in these disguises."

"No, we incur no peril—at least, I think I have judgment enough to know the value of the hazard on which I cast the die," said the Boy Pirate, moodily; "but I seek that which—— Enough, Dick, it does not do to moralise—at least in our trade."

The foster-brothers and their attendant continued their way without exchanging many words, and soon arrived at the suburbs of Janiero.

Penetrating to the centre of the city, the pirates entered an inn as the evening was growing dark, and after having dined with great glee—the negro acting as waiter—Christopher left his foster-brother at the inn, and went alone on his mission.

He soon arrived at the entrance of the Governor's palace.

He had not come unprovided with credentials, and he contrived to delude the chamberlain, who looked at him with a peculiar interest and scrutiny; and after some delay he was ushered into the presence of the Governor of Janiero.

The old man rose, and received him with a courteous bow.

The rover looked around him.

They were alone.

"Your excellency," said the rover, calmly; "I have come to throw myself upon the mercy of a generous man."

"That voice! But no, it cannot be—it is impossible!" cried the governor, starting to his feet.

"You are not mistaken in your impression," said the other, simply; "I am not what I seem."

"But you are not Captain Paul——"

"No, truly; for I am the nameless Red Raven!"

"And you dare to stand there, villainous pirate, and tell me—the Governor of Janiero—this to the teeth! Your audacity is unparalleled; but it reflects you no dark credit, for you must be mad."

"Is it madness to trust your excellency's approved nobleness of character and disinterested friendship?"

"What do you mean?"

"Your excellence taught me to believe that I resemble your murdered friend."

"Sooth to say, pirate though you be, you are the very counterpart of him."

"Of Lord Edgeforth?"

"It is so."

"Nor is it wonderful, your excellency—for ——"

The Boy Pirate paused suddenly, as if over-powered with his rising emotion.

He paused, pressing his hand against his brow, and sighing heavily.

"I am his son!"

"No!—his son, and a pirate!"

"Alas! yes; the villian Harwolf, who has been my foe since boyhood, revealed all to me. When I lay hopelessly bound in the dungeons of San Salvador, the wretch confessed that his father, who was my father's steward, murdered his master; and that his mother assumed my mother's titles. It is more than probable, for Lady Edgeforth remained in seclusion till my father's sudden death, and then she appeared in public, to the scandal of the whole world, as the husband of this Andrew Harwolf."

The governor seated himself, and for a moment seemed lost in thought.

"I cannot tell how true this tale may be, but I do not doubt that you are Lord Edgeforth's son, much as I desire to think otherwise; you bear in your features confirmation too strong for doubt. Rash, misguided, lost, guilty youth, what do you want with me?"

"You promised to give me my father's portrait, your excellency," replied the rover, softly. "I am here to beseech you to redeem that promise."

"And is that all?"

"I ask no more, your excellency; I would entreat you to deal charitably with me, to believe that I was forced into my present condition in the first instance, and that, bad as I am, I am not lost to every sense of honour and virtue. But it is the worst part of my punishment that those whose esteem I most covet are those who have the greatest right to judge me severely. Accept my thanks, a rover's thanks, for your goodness. I shall never look upon the picture of my father without remembering how much I owe to the generosity of his friend."

"Can it be possible that you have risked so much for so little?"

"So little! The gift I claim of your excellency is a priceless talisman; and I have never been used to estimate the value of anything by the risk incurred in obtaining it. My life is one wild venture."

"Captain Paul, your feats are the most brilliant and fascinating; but you must not presume too far on my power to shield you; it is my duty to denounce you, but I waive that duty in consideration of your father's memory, and of those bright redeeming qualities that contrast so strangely with the dark shades of guilt that mark your character. But, begone from Rio de Janiero at once; I will not be responsible for what will befall you when you leave the palace."

The good-natured old man went from the room, and presently returned with the portrait, which he placed in the pirate's hands.

"Farewell, Captain Paul; I dare not wish that we may meet again. I trust you may speedily turn from the dreadful path you are pursuing, and atone for the past by a life spent in the service of humanity."

The Boy Pirate stretched forth his arms and murmured a fervent amen.

He held out his hand to the governor with a grateful smile.

The latter recoiled, however, and shook his head.

The red glow of shame fired the pirate's cheek, and he thrust his hand into his bosom, saying, rather proudly,

"Be it so; I cannot blame you; were I as you are, I might do the same. Well, my enemies are my own, and not my country's, that is true; but no blood stains my hand but was spilled in fair battle. I would pray for you—but, at least, I may bless you—farewell, your excellency; the day may come when the chance of returning this kindness, of giving some proof of his gratitude, may revert even to the Red Raven."

CHAPTER LXXXIX.

AN ADVENTURE WITH BRIGANDS.

ZAMPA and Dick Caffyn awaited the return of the Boy Pirate with no little uneasiness.

They had walked to the side of the quay and had made certain inquiries among the sailors and others in order to ascertain the latest news about the "Black Vulture," and to hear the sequel of their own rash but successful attack upon San Salvador.

Dick soon become acquainted with several facts which tended much to enhance his anxiety for the return of the captain.

The reward that had long been offered for the daring pirate was trebled; no less than three ships of war—the two frigates already mentioned and a corvette, had been sent in search of the "Raven," while the police authorities all along the coast were on the *qui vive* for his apprehension.

After a long hour of suspense the rover was seen walking among the stores with the most perfect nonchalence, turning every now and then to inspect the names and trade marks on the bales, or to examine the qualities of the different wares.

He joined Caffyn and the negro.

"Ah, captain, I am glad you are here. Is all well?"

"Quite well, Dick."

"We must get off these shoals, captain, without more ado. They are on a dead scent."

"Dead enough," said the Boy Pirate; "I've just made a bet with a planter named Hammond, whom I met in yon pulque-shop, that I would be the first to tread the deck of the 'Red Raven.' I am to send him word as soon as I have achieved this great feat, and——"

"But, captain, who is he? Are you sure there is no treachery?"

"There's no discovery, Dick, for this planter, Hammond, is the prefect of the police, and he had a dozen of his subordinates within call."

"You are too much the dare-devil, captain; you ought to think of your wife and crew."

"I did not run into needless danger, for it is all important we should know our enemies' plans if we mean to baffle them; but I am willing to leave these latitudes, Dick, as soon as maybe, for the weather is getting excessively hot."

"But you'll not get off without a skirmish."

"You're right, Dick, we shall have to fire a parting salute in mere courtesy."

The three pirates now lost no time in making their way from the city; the evening was advancing when they reached the suburbs, but the sky was still red with the short-lived glory of the sunset.

As they advanced nigh the open country they walked with lighter steps and lighter hearts, smoked, and beguiled the tedium of the way with a lively interchange of jest and laughter.

A rather wild piece of savannah lay between them and the little bay where they had left the boat. As they were crossing this, they were suddenly startled by a loud shriek for help.

"You hearn dat, mas'r, whar debil dat come from?" cried Zamp, halting, and opening wide his mouth and eyes.

"From that bit of bush by the swamp down yonder; there's some one in distress, let's go and see what is the matter."

"Gorramighty! no; dere's all sorts ob debils and kinder sperits in the llanos, mas'r; dis chile hearn 'em squealin' down long de ole plantations many a time. Don't yo go a runnin' arter sich, they'se blind yer eyes, they'se do that ar, mas'r, or p'raps flings yer down a land slip. I seen one on 'em on de swamps myself, mas'r, and the horfullest row as that ar goblum made war jest a caution. And I seen him too in de pitch dark, mas'r."

"Indeed! and what did he resemble?"

"Didn't zemble nuffin, mas'r, nor none on us; 'cos we all run like coons, and give de dam squealer no chance to 'semble us."

"I mean what was he like?"

"Look at dat! I thought ''semble' mean 'Obi,' one ob de dam witch things. Look yo, mas'r, dere was dis chile, and Uncle Glory—dey call him Glory, mas'r, 'cos him so dam black—and dere was ole Marius dat play de fiddle, and his yaller gal, Phœbe,—we'd all de ruck been to a break-down at de oder plantation 'long cross de ribber, and when we come home, oh, Golly! it was so dark, buckras, couldn't recumnise one anoder's woices : wal, yo understand, mas'r, we seed suffin—me, Uncle Glory, Phœbe, ole Marius and de fiddle, all on us, we seed suffin,—him got four legs, buckras, a pair ob eyes—dere was no sham, dey was real eyes, dey was—and a debil ob a tail, and, lor, de squealing'! Marius—dere's many about like dat yar niggar, mas'r—him tink him know why de black man's blood same colour as de white man's, when one's a born buckra and toder's a raised nigger? Yo go 'long, dat yar Marius, too cleber a good piece."

"And what was his opinion of the ghost?"

"Dam bad 'pinion, mas'r, him had ob de sperit—said it was nuffin but Mas'r Riley's vicious ole grey hoss; but I told him, mas'r, I says to dis nigger, 'Marius,'—I wish't Ise knew how to say it perlite—'you'se been tellin' the most infernallest lies; dat yar hoss is no hoss: it's a sperit.'"

"'Nothin' o' the kind, Uncle Zamp,' says he; 'if brains would grow under wool, you'd kinder consider dat hosses whinny in der most dismalonous manner; and warn't it night? and don't yer know Mas'r Riley's ole grey mare?' 'Bery well, nigger,' says I: 'didn't we seen her arter a dam heavy supper, so she couldn't be nuffin but a kinder sperit, if 'spose she war a quadruple.' 'And what kinder mare do yo tink her, Uncle Zamp?' says he, wid a smile dat was peculiar 'sullin—'Why,' says I, 'she wor a night-mare?' He wor shet up, and couldn't say nuffin, in course."

There was another cry for help.

"While we are laughing at this black scamp's nonsense, some poor fellow is wailing for assistance; perhaps in danger and agony. Come, Dick."

With this, the rover sped across the savannah, and entered the little wood that surrounded the swamp.

Dick and Zampa followed him.

The superstitious negro showed little of his wonted courage, but slunk behind, and was evidently ready to run at the first intimation of the supernatural.

They soon found the source from whence proceeded these cries of distress.

A Spaniard, half naked, and seemingly wounded, was tightly lashed to a palmetto.

"Ah! senors, come quickly. I am dying."

"What is it? Who has done this?" cried the Boy Pirate, fiercely, at the same time drawing his knife and severing the rope.

The man sank to the ground.

"Dios! I am perishing!" groaned the Spaniard.

The foster-brothers kneeled at his side, and gently raised him.

"Who has done this?" Christopher repeated.

"Ah! senor, I will tell you presently. Gently; you torture me. Thanks."

"You have been robbed?"

"Yes, senor; and, I think, murdered," returned the fellow, in a whining tone.

"By whom?"

"By the brigands, senor, that infest this neighbourhood."

"The scoundrels! Were you alone?"

"Yes, senor. They have robbed me of my mule, and of all I possessed."

"What shall we do with him, Dick?" said the Boy Pirate, drawing his brother aside.

"We have set him free. I don't think he is so much hurt as he pretends to be. These Spaniards are such skunks," returned Caffyn. "It won't do for us to linger here. Let us leave him, and tell the first native we meet of his distress. We'll give him the brandy-flask, that will console him."

"Out upon you for an inhuman counsellor, Dick!" returned the generous rover. "Can't a man be a pirate without being a monster? I would not abandon the poor wretch to be stung by a snake or torn by a puma for all the silver of Peru or gold of Mexico."

"Senor," cried the man, feebly, "did you not pass the hacienda on the river?"

"Within half an hour," returned Christopher.

"Well, senor, I am known here. Go, one of you, and tell the hidalgo, Don Ribiera, that Matias has been struck down by the robbers. He will send help, and will pay you well."

"I'll go," said the Boy Pirate, impetuously. "Stay with him."

"No, captain, this infernal delay may lead to the worst consequences."

"Do you mean to say you think I will leave him?" cried his foster-brother, impatiently.

"No, captain. By leave, we'll carry him."

"Very well."

"Senors, you are in haste?" asked the man.

"We are, indeed. Nothing but the sternest demand of common humanity could induce us to pause," replied the rover.

"Reflect, senor; if you carry me in to the hacienda it will delay you more than if you hasten thither encumbered and return with assistance; but, I beseech you, leave me not alone."

"He is right," said Christopher; "you must stay with him, Zamp, and you too, Dick; you may have to defend him from beasts of prey, either bipeds or 'quadruples,' as our obtruse Zamp calls them. Rest quiet; I'm off."

"But, captain, alone? The robbers——"

"Stuff! Have I not just bearded the Governor of Janiero in his own palace, and shall I quail to encounter a score of dirty brigands, that run from a pistol-shot like a flock of sheep from the bay of a hungry wolf? Look out for snakes, Dick; I'll be back in a trice."

With this the Boy Pirate walked off at a smart pace.

The shades were rising, for they could scarcely be said to be falling, as the darkness was creeping up the sides of a distant range of mountains, whose summits still faintly beamed with a roseate glow.

As he crossed a little plaitt, as it is called in America—a tuft of trees on a level plain—he was suddenly aware that some one was before him.

He grasped his belt with its armoury of side-arms, for he had resumed his former dress on leaving the city.

Upon looking ahead through the deepening gloom, he perceived a tall, cloaked figure.

It was one of the bandits.

With great presence of mind Christopher dropped on one knee.

Just in time, for a bullet whistled over his head, striking off his cap, and the report crackled along the savannah, and died away as he rose.

With a yell of disappointed rage the Spaniard flung himself upon our hero.

Christopher hurled him backwards.

He stumbled and fell.

The Boy Pirate pointed his pistol at his head.

But he would not fire till the fellow was once more fairly opposed to him.

The man jumped up and eyed our hero with a vindictive glare.

The hacienda was not far off.

The fellow seemed to have changed his mind as to the judiciousness of venturing a shot, or, may be, he thought he had no chance of forestalling his antagonist, whose revolver was directed towards him with steady, deadly aim.

He wrapped his mantle round his left arm, and, clutching his long dagger in his right hand, sidled along towards the rover.

Christopher watched this movement, and with a sinister smile imitated the movement, wrapped his cloak about his left arm, and drew his stiletto.

They drew nearer and nearer together.

The Spaniard feinted quickly, as if to strike the Boy Pirate in the face.

The rover instinctively raised his arm as the gleaming blade flashed close to his eyes.

With great skill the bandit turned his wrist, and brought the knife under the arm of his foe.

But not before the latter had managed to slip aside.

The knife glanced off, but Christopher stumbled.

Before he could right himself the fellow rushed upon him.

They closed.

There was a sharp, quick struggle.

The rover, who was a much slighter man than his

opponent, and was taken at such a disadvantage, fell under, and they both wrestled on the ground.

Christopher caught the Spaniard's wrist as it descended with the knife full at his throat.

The rover's dagger fell to the earth.

The Spaniard, seeing this, wrestled hard to disengage his wrist, but the pirate clutched it with native strength, increased by the power of desperation.

His right hand being free, he struck the Spaniard several blows in the face.

Exasperated by this, the bandit flung himself bodily upon Christopher, crushing him with his weight and struggling to draw his weapons.

But the Boy Pirate remained still and stretched himself out stiffly.

Thinking his victim lacked nerve, and was giving way, the Spaniard incautiously raised himself to get a purchase on the butt of his pistol, for his knife had been knocked out of his hand.

Christopher snatched up his stiletto; it glanced like a lightning flash, and struck true and deep right into the robber's heart.

The blood rushed over him, but the dying man grasped him by the throat and attempted to strangle him.

The Boy Pirate shook the man off.

He sprang to his feet.

The sound of threatening voices caused him to look about him.

On either hand bandits were approaching.

Six ferocious assassins stood around him.

He looked about him with a steady glance.

The men crouched back handling their long knives and awkward pieces in momentary hesitation.

"My men," cried the Boy Pirate, levelling both his revolvers right and left, "you think, perhaps, that I am alone, but you are mistaken; with one pipe of this shrill whistle I could bring my crew upon you. I have more than odds in my companions yonder, and I hold ten charges in my ten fingers."

The bandits looked at each other as if rebuking each other's cowardice, but, excepting that they darted dagger looks, they made no attempt to attack our hero.

One fellow, however, ran behind, and fired a heavy old carbine, which made as much noise as a piece of ordnance.

The Boy Pirate had thrown his back against a young tree, the trunk of which was not sufficiently large to protect his whole body—a shattered piece of lead struck him on the shoulder, inflicting a wound which, though not dangerous, was very painful, and caused him to drop his left arm, which was still weak on account of the hurt the gallant rover had sustained from a falling beam on the occasion of his noble rescue of little Lucia at San Salvador.

Thus encouraged, the bravoes set up a mighty shout, and fell upon the rover. He shot one dead, but his pistol was struck out of his hand—he kicked the fellow away who was stooping to pick it up, and striking at them indiscriminately, expressed his wrath in terse though not elegant extracts from his English vocabulary.

"Diavolos! he is Yenglesa! Down with him! Fight, comerados, fight! he is the devil!"

The others seemed to think this the fact, and therefore considered themselves sufficiently overmatched to excuse their extreme attention to the better part of valour.

Christopher soon found an opportunity of recovering his revolver.

No sooner did the bandits perceive this than they gave up the contest and took to their heels.

The Boy Pirate laughed and fired after them.

As he turned towards the swamp near which he had left his comrades he saw Dick Caffyn and Zampa.

They told him how they had escaped from a similar peril to that which had threatened their captain.

The wounded man had proved to be a treacherous villain used as a decoy by the bandits.

The rascals' object had been to separate the three companions that they might rob and despatch them singly.

Zampa had therefore been sent to a certain spot to find a spring from which he was to bring water for the alleged victim of the bandits.

He had not gone many steps from the spot when he was suddenly attacked by two of the gang.

Another, in conjunction with the villanous traitor, fell upon Dick; but the whole of the party took to flight after hearing the shots and cries that betokened that a battle was going on to their disadvantage between the Boy Pirate and their leader.

"Well, captain, if we had such skunks as these to deal with in every engagement," said Dick Caffyn, with a hearty laugh, "we might shut up the cock-pit and fight out our battle's with the rope's end."

They reached the boat without further accident, and the Boy Pirate returned to the "Red Raven."

Brand told them that she had been spoken with by the Brazilian frigate, but that the captain had been satisfied upon overhauling the papers and had sailed away on a phantom chase.

CHAPTER XC.

A STORM AT SEA.

THE pinnace of the "Black Vulture" was now sailing far out in the North Atlantic.

It was morning, breaking grey and cold; the light flushed the far east.

The clouds were rolling into wreathing masses that spread wide across the sky, and the wind came in capfuls over the long, heaving waves.

A stilly silence that was very impressive reigned between each gust of the gathering breeze, which noisily flapped the little sail, and the hush was only broken by the throb of a huge albatross gliding through the air, or the scream of a petrel tumbling along the crests of the waves on their landward flight.

Deborah and the Scotch girl sat in the stern of the pinnace—the Scotchman, Cassidy, and the young sailor Oakland steered the little barque. The seamen looked grave, and the girls sat mute and pale with suppressed terror, for the appearance of the weather was darkly ominous.

"What think ye of the weather, captain?" whispered Cassidy to Macallister.

"I care na to say; but the Lord will not desert us, I'm sure, after sic a special manifestation of his goodness as our free deliverance from yon ark of refuge for murder and infamy. I'd advise you to tighten that halyard, Meester Cassidy."

"There's something ugly in the wind's eye, cap'en," said Oakland. "What's our bearing?"

Cassidy consulted the compass and replied, when the Scotchman cried out sharply,

"Hold on!"

The Scotchman pulled at the tiller, and the sail was taken aback by a long rush of wind, and a heavy wave plashed over the little vessel.

Then she rose on the green, glassy back of a rolling mountain, and glided hissing down into the shifting valley below, once more up, up; once more down, and the headwaves had passed by and left the pinnace rocking on the smaller billows caused by the swell.

The morning was breaking fast; but the sky presented a wild and weird appearance. Huge dense blocks of clouds, dark and lowering, were piled along the horizon, behind which were substrata of yellowish sulphurous-looking vapours, while the eastern limits of the mighty expanse shone with a line of dull, fierce red.

Still the wind came, but in capfulls; but each successive gust stronger than the last, as if the gale were gathering power.

At a sign from the Scotchman, Cassidy took in the sail.

And Oakland began to bale out the water which had been shipped during the last few moments.

"'Tis no time to spread white duck," muttered Oakland.

"No, we may look for a tornado," returned Cassidy, quietly; "but this comfort remains, there is no chance of our being chased by the 'Black Vulture.'"

"Is our danger great, Captain Macallister?" asked Deborah of the Scotchman, in an under tone.

"Well, for that, our danger is na sae dark in its nature as that which threatened us body and soul among the awesome pirates. The sperit of death is ever slumbering in the great deeps, but whenever it may rise from these mighty waters to call us, we have our anchorage above, and it matters not through what stormy strait we pass sae long as it bring us safe to the haven, which knows no tempest. I wad na hae ye presume too much on safety; solemn thoughts are soothing, as well as proper company in sic hours as these; but dinna fash yourselves, for we've a taut bit fabric between us and the fury o' the waters, and canny seamen to guide her course."

As the old man spoke the sulphurous vapours that underlined the chain of black clouds suddenly glared and quivered with electric blaze, throwing the heavy masses below them into wild and startling relief, and giving them the appearance of monster rocks and castles.

Then came over the vast ocean the distant, sullen roar of the grand thunder.

A dead calm reigned about the little craft, and the water spread out in a smooth swell; but afar off rolled along in one foamy line a large tidal wave, that seemed to be rushing down upon the doomed barque to shatter it to pieces, that swept along like the black angel of discord, turning the calm surface of the level main into a maelstrom of seething, flashing billows.

Flocks of sea-foul shrieking and whirling tumbled away through the air in precipitous flight from the coming gale.

"Down with you!" cried Cassidy, in a loud, clear tone, but with inimitable coolness. "Now is the pinch; if she stands the shock of this header she'll make no more of the rest than the bubbles on a duck pond."

"Into thy, thy han's!" murmured the pious old Scot, rasing his eyes with a look of calm and manly resignation.

He placed Deborah and his daughter in the bottom of the boat and covered them over with a sail which was lashed to the belaying pins and bows of the pinnace.

"Now, Sam, hold your own," said Oakland.

"Aye, aye, mate; I wish we'd had time to ship our mast."

"Are ye hearty like, Miss Deborah? I dinna fear mysel', I can weel droon sin' we're escaped from sic' monsters."

Deborah pressed the hand of her warm-hearted companion, and they drew closer together.

It was a solemn moment.

The water hissed along beneath their bows.

The huge foam-crested tidal-wave grew nearer and nearer.

It came quicker—quicker!

It struck the frail barque!

For a moment the little skiff was engulphed; then she seemed tossed upwards to the fading stars, and then flew down the watery avalanche; her helm shifted, her mast strained, bent like a fishing-rod, and snapped like a dry reed; her very sheathing boards groaned and creaked; the boiling surf poured over her sides; the shouting billows leaped from stem to stern, drenching the mariners, and almost rending them from their convulsive clutch upon the bows and sides of the boat.

But soon the worst danger was passed; the enormous water-mountain rushed ahead, leaving the little barque dancing like a walnut-shell in its wrathful wake.

"The canny wee thing, she rights!" shouted the Scotchman, exultantly. "The Lord, our deliverer, be he thankit!"

"Bravely she weathered the shock. That heavy wave has carried away all the heaviness from my heart, which it nearly knocked through my ribs," cried the quiet Cassidy, with a low chuckling laugh of great delight. "How's the wind, Oakland?"

"Behind us, thank God!" returned the other, heaving a profound sigh of satisfaction. "Well, after that, we can stand anything!"

"I canna say I'm sae confidant; another sic a stroke and we suld be lost; and ye see that she let's in the water already."

"All hands to the pumps!" cried Cassidy. "We must bale out, hearties; we must work for dear life!"

"Aye, lads and lassies, we can afford no skulking the muster," cried the Scotchman, setting the example, and baling away with great energy.

The whole party worked very hard.

It was only by extreme exertion that they could keep the water down; it was plain that the pinnace had sprung a leak.

The men's faces grew anxious, but they laughed and cheered for the sake of the girls, and worked away with a good will.

Cassidy found the leak, and fastened a piece of the sail upon it, which he smeared with tar from a little barrel that chanced to be on board.

But still the water did not seem to be exhaustible, and unfortunately their powers were so.

"Land on the lee bow!" Oakland shouted, suddenly.

The party looked across the heaving waters.

A dusky line appeared looming beneath a red patch in the lowering sky.

It was illumined the next instant by a fierce lightning-flash that played with terrific brilliance among the clouds, and darted its arrowy forks against the surging bosom of the sea.

Then came the thunder-roll, deep, growling, and crashing, and rolling off in sublime and awful diapasons.

For some moments the men had been working at the oars while the girls baled.

Oakland had taken the tiller.

All at once he shrieked out,

"Breakers dead a-head!"

Quite powerless on the strong waters was the frail barque.

It floated upon the surges' waves, and rose high upon their crests.

The boat was now drifting rapidly towards the land.

The rugged tree-clustered cliffs of the long, low shore of an island appeared.

The breakers were lashing furiously upon the beach, raving, and wildly tossing their manes of foamy brine.

Dark, green and glossy the weed-cumbered rocklets shot up through the froth, and towards these the light skiff was wildly dashing.

Cassidy walked the swaying boat, preserving his foothold with the ease and agility of a practised seaman; he took his seat beside Mary, while Deborah was lifted into the forepart of the skiff by Oakland, where she reclined in a mist of cold skimmering spray.

Faintly the far lightning flashed sullenly; long and mutteringly rattled the thunder-roll in the distance!

Like the crash of the falling ice-bergs—like the roar and the rage of the battle—the rearing, the fall, and the pounding plash downwards of the seething scattering breakers.

At the top of the bursting burdens of the waters of eternal oceans leaps the frail and yielding barque, and while the hearts of its passengers are congealed as to ice by the awe and the dread of the terrible but sublime emotions of their intense peril, the racing waves run far up the shingly strand, floating the pinnace with them; then come the surly breakers, trouncing her stem, and breaking and splitting her bolts and timbers.

The party are submerged with water; then, as the rustling breakers draw back, Cassidy lifts Mary, Oakland, the half-fainted Jewess, and breast deep they plunge into the surf.

The stout Macallister seizes the painter, and with all his might strains and tugs at the boat to drag her up the shingly beach.

This he accomplishes, while his youthful companions carry the girls to shore.

They are safe on the island.

They look back over the immensity of warring waters.

Their eyes blink beneath the vivid gleams of the quick, forked lightning.

The frail barque that has carried them safely through so much danger lies high and dry upon the strand, but it is shattered and no longer seaworthy.

They clamber the rugged, shelving, weed-strewn beach, and reach a long bank fringed with palmettos.

Here once more they halt.

Here, in the awe of the moment, in the isolation of their position, the women cling trustingly to the men as by the natural instinct of feminine confidence and weakness.

The pious Scot stretches his arms heavenward, and pours out his soul in fervent thanksgiving.

Mary throws herself upon her knees and responds with the deepest and truest devotional enthusiasm.

The stern seamen take off their hats and lower their eyes, though the stinging blast whirls their dark locks and constrains them to fix firm their feet in the slippery sand.

The storm raves around them, but what a solemnity in the thunder's deep crash! what a majesty in the wild rush and rich glare of the lightning! declaring the omnipotence and omniscience of the Deity!

It is a thrilling scene; one to be long remembered. The grey-haired veteran, with hands and eyes uplifted; the kneeling girls; the sturdy seamen, their dark faces grave with a look of subdued devotional feeling; the wild, treacherous sea, roaring for its prey, just by their side, but the solid earth beneath their feet.

CHAPTER XCI.

PLAN FOR ESCAPE.

SILAS RYE was roused from his profound slumber by the harsh voice of one of the keepers.

He was scarcely able to realise his position, even on this second day of his captivity.

He looked around him with a wild stare.

Once more he remembered that he was a prisoner, and that his prison was a mad-house.

He rose.

As he dressed himself, he reflected that the words of the sane man who had lived so long among the maniacs were words of the truest wisdom. He felt that he had no chance, no hope, except what lay in the misguidance of the villains who held him in thraldom.

He assumed a sullen, abstracted demeanour.

A scanty meal was put before him alone.

The keepers exchanged knowing looks as their victim sat in his chair, his head buried in his shoulders, his eyes wandering.

He would not eat.

After the breakfast had been cleared away, he was conducted to the main ward, and looked around with suppressed anxiety for the sane prisoner.

The man walked up, murmuring and laughing, ever and anon stopping to gibber at one or other of the poor wretches, his comrades.

He took no notice of Silas, though he looked him straight in the face, as if utterly unconscious of his presence.

Yet at one moment, when the keepers' attention was directed towards the other unfortunates, the allies contrived to exchange meaning glances.

There was something so shrewd and intelligent in the look of the inmate, that Silas felt a joyful thrill run through his veins, and answered with a beaming smile.

The keepers walked away, and for awhile the two captives were together.

Silas Rye's colleague drew a piece of string from his pocket, and twisted it about his fingers in the manner designated by youngsters a "scratch-cradle;" with an imbecile cackle, he played with the string.

There was something truly terrible in the strange contrast of the sickly deceit with which he beguiled his jailers and the clear subtle tone in which he interjected his eager whispers to his companion.

"I have arranged all; let us exchange names."

"I am Silas Rye; I will tell you more of myself when occasion offers."

"And I am John Fawcett, of her Majesty's navy. But, whist! they are coming—the keepers. The man in the moon, and the Emperor of China, who, you understand, is the brother of the moon. But I've no connections now, except among the good people—they're Scotch and Irish fairies, you know—but the vampires and wehrwolves the Germans tell of are scarcer now than ever they were; there used to be witches, and many men possessed with devils are to be met with every day."

"Hush, for God's sake! They are gone by."

"Did you see the leer on the beast's face as he listened to my gibberish? Eternal Lance of Justice, is it wrong that I should feel this uncontrolable impulse to annihilate the unnatural monsters?" cried Fawcet, clutching his fists and raising his eyes, while his whole frame shivered with passion. "Are my tears shed into a bottle that may measure their quantity, not what shall test their bitterness? I am not mad—I am sane; I have thought of my darling wife—my sweet child, and just as my brain has reached boiling point, I have 'sprinkled cool pitch on it,' for reason, whom misery and associate madness were dragging her from me, has whispered: Die, and God will keep them; live, *you* are His agent. Keep, then, your senses: you have a will, you have a strong hand—a fearless heart. Live, oh, live! and hope for Janie and for Nelly—for your wife and your child! Why do we slight blessings because they are common? Oh! Mr. Rye, 'sweet are the uses of adversity;' this miserable sojourn in this hell on earth has done me good. I have learned to prize common blessings—reason, speech, sight, freedom, love! Rob a man of these—one of these—these common birth-right blessings, the very cadger's inheritance as well as the king's—rob a man of but one of these boons, and give him in exchange the universe—the solar system and all the unknown wealth of the mystic planets—what will it avail him? But, there, there, let me cease my rhapsodies, or you will think that I, too, am mad; and, indeed, if anything could touch my brain, it is this—my meeting with a sane companion when hope had almost died out of my soul. Oh! Mr. Rye, when once more we can walk forth free men how shall we prize that freedom which before we knew not how to estimate!"

Silas Rye grasped his new friend by the hand.

"Mine is the strangest story, Mr. Fawcett. I have seen something of the terrors of madness before I came here."

Fawcett looked up, and then went on incoherently, "And the Queen of Sheba visited King Solomon at the Great Exhibition, that she might behold his treasures; but she marvelled much at the three calendars—what was I saying? Oh, I was talking about the invention of the harp and how it drove the fiend out of the Israelite king in his hours of madness; but some say that the fiend will lurk in a trumpet or a drum, and blare or batter the world into a phrenzy that it shall call wholesale murder by the name of glory, and raise the costliest monument to him who destroys the most; but those devils are devils of madness—and the world is a great madhouse. The lover is a madman, the statesman a madman, but the poet is the worst madman of all!"

The principal of the asylum was standing before them, looking down on the pair with a sinister smile.

"Well, Mr. Rye, how like you your new life—your new abode?" he said. "I know that you are afflicted only with a monomania. Your companion is a maniac; how do you like him?"

"Poor creature, he is gentle enough," returned Silas, with a deep sigh. "And I feel too a strange sensation as if my brain were corrupt and the pure fount of my imagination were sullied with foul images; as if the devil had looked into it——"

"Did he bear resemblance to Mr. Harwolf?" asked the mad doctor, with a leer.

Silas felt inclined to seize the wretch by the throat and dash him to the ground, but he restrained himself, and replied with a well-assumed look of stupidity, "Harwolf—ah! true; I hate that man, but I almost forget who he is."

Silas Rye rubbed his forehead and parted his elf-locks from his eyes.

The principal looked at him with a smile of contempt and moved away.

"I dare say the fellow *was* mad," he muttered; "but I have my certificate, that is enough. If every real idiot who pretended to be sane were sent to me as a patient I should have to rebuild my house on a much larger scale. It is a dogma in law that it is better ten guilty men should escape than that one innocent should suffer; but that rule does not hold good in society, it is better that ten sane men should be incarcerated than that one madman should go free."

The principal retired to his private apartments to caress his wife and fondle his children, for he was an exemplary husband and father.

Is this inconsistent? By no means. Family love may take its rise from selfish instinct or taste. The principal of the asylum looked upon his patients as so many channels for the influx of prosperity to the plants in his own garden, which he delighted to water with the golden streams of his success in "business."

"When you are alone in your room, Mr. Rye, get up, put on your clothes, and expect me. I will not show you a piece of wire I have in my pocket, lest this poor, dreadful-looking fellow at our side—who, by the way, is detained during her Majesty's pleasure, for a deliberate, horrible murder—should snatch it away from me. But this wire I have bent in such a fashion as to make it serve as a key to open the door of your cell. I have obtained at different times some pieces of rag, which I have twisted together to form a rope. There is a loose bar in my window, we can extract it, and with little trouble get into the yard; an out-house joins the wall; by crawling along the roof, and again using our scaling ladder, we may contrive to make our exit from this tomb of spectres. What do you say?"

"It is an excellent plan, and I am prepared to run any risk to escape from this place."

"Very well, then. You will be wakeful and vigilant; for though I have contrived a way of getting out of my own cell, I cannot promise to join you till all is quiet; so you must be patient."

"Do not fear me."

"I do not; you seem a man of energy. But what we need so much, is prudence and caution."

"Exactly."

FEARFUL DEATH OF ESAU COOPER.

"Well, I can rely on you?"

"Believe me, yes—for prudence and discretion. You must try to appreciate the hazard of our enterprize, and must remember what an Argus watch they keep."

"I will."

"Presently we shall be paraded in the court-yard; I will then contrive to show you a spot where a withered tree almost joins the wall; there is a *chevaux de frise* on top of that. But I have prepared a piece of leather which I tore from the under part of a chair; besides this, awhile ago, there were some workmen here. I contrived to steal some chisels, a hammer, nails and other treasures from the basket of one of the fellows—and, for ropes——"

"Hush! we must not be seen so much together."

No. 30.

With this Silas Rye got up and walked across the room to the keeper, who had been watching them rather suspiciously.

"My good fellow, it is not by your fault that I am here; I know that," said Silas, "and I cannot blame you for doing what you consider your duty, by acting under the orders of the chief of this establishment, but surely I am only a prisoner because I am considered a lunatic——"

"Considered a lunatic! Vell, that's rather good, that is; a power of consideration is wanted to desarn that fact. You're what we calls here a 'incipient stager,' its a word we've got; and that von as you were talkin' to jest now, vy, he's a 'confirmed stager,' and all these yere others as is given to showin' there feelins in such 'stronary style is ''reg'lar stagers.'"

"Was your 'confirmed' lunatic formerly 'incipient?'"

"In course he were; musn't there be a beginin' to every think? they soon gets 'confirmed,' they does."

"That poor creature seems very bad."

"You're wuss than he were afore he gave up and carried on in the general vay; don't ye know that ere pleasant sayin', 'one must howl with the wolves?' They all soon gets as bad as one another."

"But, what villany! what monstrosity! Do you mean to say, then, that commonly men are kidnapped to this place while they are sane?"

"You don't seem to be up in your proverbs, or you'd know as 'perwention is better than cure.' We puts 'em in fust, and then they can go mad as soon as they likes."

"You scoundrel! you black-hearted wretch!"

"Come, I say—I say—if you is insane you must be civil, 'cos we've got a refractory ward, and every convenience in sich cases."

"And the examination, when does it take place?"

"Vy, in course, when you is in a proper condition to answer the questions they axes of you. Do you know exactly vot o'clock it vos when you vos born—vether it vos a cloudy mornin?' Do you know vere your great grandmother vos buried, and vich of your maiden aunts doesn't vere false teeth?"

"What do you mean?"

The provoking rascal shrugged his shoulders, made a lachrymose grimace, and addressed an imaginary examiner.

"Ah, sir, it's a werry sad case; the poor creetur's memory's quite gone, most awfullest confusion of intellects—queer all sorts of queer habits—moves his eyes about—opens his mouth—shakes his head—does all sorts of things as is quite uncommon. He's fits is melancholy. I interduced him to Rantin Rob, and the king of Simbuctoo, and all the most lively patients in the 'sylum. Lor, bless yer, he won't sort with none on 'em, but sits a droopin' of his head—poor creetur! You'll 'scuse me, sir, these yere tears—my 'art, sir, allers was a soft 'art, and—its—too affectin'—for he seemed to be a most intelligible gentleman as ever were."

The fellow rubbed his eyes, wining and snivelling. Silas found himself possessed with twenty fiends of disgust and passion, that almost drove reason and will from their seats in his "distracted globe." He champed his teeth, and quelled his almost irresistible desire to rend his tormentor to pieces.

"Poor creetur!" says docter Swearall, with a side wink at the governor," "if he were taken orf it would be a 'appy release."

Silas did not answer.

"P'raps, you think, some of these yere days, you'll find your cage-door ajar, or one of the bars loose—wery likely. I'd advise yer to run; the excitement will do yer good, and be money in my pocket, 'cos I gets a reward. I were honourable mentioned to the committee some while back, 'cos I popped at a creetur as tried to get off; the big mastiff over the wall broke one of his legs; I sent a slug into the bother. You see, it were needful, as a hexample, and the poor creetur's feelings was quieted since then; he don't show no inclination to run, though we've given him a 'reglar handsome pair o' crutches; but we likes to be liberal, we does, and we don't mind accomodatin' yourself, if so be——"

Silas could bear no more; entirely losing his presence of mind he leaped upon the truculent brute, gripping his throat and almost strangling him. Rye was a wonderfully powerful man, and the bully in spite of his heavy proportions and great strength, was a sneaking coward.

The tussle was brief, and the heavy body of the keeper rolled like a log on the floor, and Silas stamped upon him with clenched hands and glaring eyes. Then arose a fearful hubbub among the insane occupants of the ward.

Some shrieked, others howled, some waved their arms and shouted as over a victory.

It was a moment of fearful danger to the keeper, whose authority had received a deadly blow, and who was thrown at the mercy of those who had hitherto thought him invulnerable.

Not a few rushed upon him, intent upon rending him to pieces.

Fawcet rushed forward.

"For God's sake, Rye!" he muttered, "one grain of common sense—one drop of cold caution—be quiet. There will be murder done!"

A crowd of maniacs raged about their prostrate tyrant, who lay shuddering with terror; they howled like a taboon of jackals.

The door was burst open, the principal and some half dozen sturdy myrmidons rushed into the room.

They slashed about them indiscriminately with thongs of leather and life preservers, driving the cowering idiots in all directions.

"Johnson, what does this mean?" cried the principal, his face scarlet and his breast heaving with excitement.

"Its all a'long o' the new patient," growled the fellow, scrambling to his feet; "the vicious creetur took me unawares, when I were a soothin' of him. He means to get up a mutiny."

"Ah, Mr. Rye, is this so? Is there so much method in your madness?" cried the principal, bitterly.

"You will find, sir, that I have method enough to break from your infernal prison, where I am detained against every law of humanity, not to say of England, and to denounce your illegal proceedings throughout the kingdom."

"Indeed," said the man, with a peculiar smile. "Well, sir, I shall be happy to be rid of you, providing the board thinks you in a fit state to be set at liberty; meantime, I'm sorry you have compelled me to keep you under closer restraint. Put this unfortunate gentleman into a straight-jacket, and remove him at once to No. 16 cell."

The men rushed upon Silas to drag him away.

One of them was felled to the ground.

The tall, gaunt maniac, who had revealed to Silas Rye his singular delusion, leaped before him.

"Touch him if you dare!" he shouted, "I am Death! every wretch's friend. Don't you see the poor fellow is mad? But I—Live Death—I am his friend. My javelin is raised, advance at your peril!"

The maniac raised his gaunt arms, and poised a long stick which one of the keepers had dropped in the *melée.*

But he did not long preserve his imposing attitude; one of the keepers crept stealthily behind him, and, throwing his arms under his chin, forced him away.

"Bind him with chains! out with him! cast him out! He says he is not one of us; he brags of his connections. Out with him! I'll help; *do* let me help! cried Fawcet," dancing about Silas. "Ha! ha! mates, lash up the mutineer, and make him walk the plank. (Fight me; curse me; kick me; show disgust, and the spiteful devils will put us together." he muttered to Silas, as he busied about his head, pretending to be gaging him). Hurrah! mates, the pirate strikes his flag! haul him along."

"Hear me; I will bear any cruelty; but keep that wretched idiot away," cried Silas; "I shall go mad —mad—if he is near me."

"You are mad already," cried the principal, sternly; "the fellow is docile, and well, intentioned; he shall go with him."

"Bless you—bless you, I will take care of him. Ah, the wretch, he wants to bite me; give me a cutlass, I'll cut him down at the hatchway."

"No, no—take him away!" cried Silas.

"No, don't—pray don't—I'll keep him; let me go with him," cried Fawcet.

"You shall; I'll not be braved," cried the principal, fiercely.

"Beware what you do. If I am left alone with this fellow one hour, I shall go raving mad, and you will be responsible," cried Silas.

"I accept the responsibility. Take them off, my men," shouted the principal; "chain this fellow to the bed, and leave the other with him; he is quite harmless."

"O, bless you! bless you!" cried the crafty Fawcet, leaping about in childish delight. "Come along, you are my prisoner; escape if you can."

A little while after, Silas and his friend were alone in the cell.

Poor Rye groaned bitterly.

"I cannot bear much more of this; I am fast loosing my wits."

"There's not much more to bear; but, why don't you sham as I do; believe me, it is too often needful 'to howl with the wolves.'"

CHAPTER XCII.

THE DEATH OF ESAU THE GIPSY.

IN a former chapter we have described a flash ken at which Black Ralph and Daniel Harwolf had met for the purpose of making the final arrangements for their daring enterprise, and for the abduction of the Jewess, Deborah.

To this place suspicion pointed as a likely refuge for Esau Cooper; and Foxley, the detective, whose professional acumen was intensified by his natural eagerness to avenge the murder of his brother, had applied himself with unwearied diligence to obtain a clue to the whereabouts of the missing gipsy.

Upon getting into the cab, the arrival of which had broken in upon the delights of the social meeting of his girleen and her friends, Black Oiny found that Sibly, with another man, a stranger, and probably a detective, occupied the vehicle.

The cab stopped at a private house in a quiet street in an eastern suburb, and the party got out and were ushered into the dwelling by Foxley, who opened the door with a latch-key.

They entered a neat little parlour, and Foxley turned on the gas and lighted the little brass gaselier that depended from the ceiling.

The bright light flooded cheerfully the little room, and displayed a pretty parlour, furnished with taste, and possessing an air of neatness and comfort.

"This is my sanctum," said Foxley, with a smile. "I will leave you for an instant, for I must get the key of my wardrobe, to which I shall introduce you. You will find I have an extensive assortment of properties, and am able to accomplish some famous 'getting up.'"

Foxley went to a cheffioneer, and drew out a bottle and glasses, and handed round some cigars.

"You see," he said, with a quaint, yet sad smile, "I am obliged to undertake these expeditions in a matter-of-fact way; indeed, I have found it the best policy through life to take all things easy, and never to allow myself to be hurried in any emergency. Hurry is not haste, and haste is not quickness. If a man hurries himself he is sure to fall into confusion; if a man hastes he generally omits something important, or commits something undesirable, and one may take it easy and yet act with all due promptness. You will laugh at my reading you this homily, and at my sagely propounding such palpable truisms, but simple as the rule of 'take it easy' sounds in theory, nothing is more difficult in practice. One moment; I will advise you to dispense with your watches and jewellery on this expedition; before we start we will deposit such tell-tale ornaments in this box."

So saying, the detective took a little casket from the sideboard, and placed it on the table.

Oiny, who had been presented with a gold watch by the good-hearted, unfortunate Silas Rye for his gallant rescue of poor Lady Edgeforth, drew his treasured chronometer from his pocket with a twinkling eye, and placed it in the chest.

Sibly divested himself of his, and drew the ring from his finger.

The detective placed the watch he was wearing for use in the box, and drew another from his breast.

As he looked on it, his broad chest heaved and his brow bent with a frown of sorrow.

It was a gold watch, with a handsome Albert chain, to which was attached a *bullet*.

"I can appreciate your emotion at the sight of that watch, for I divine that it belonged to your unfortunate brother," said Sibly, seriously.

"You are right," said the detective, quietly.

"And shure, may I make bowld to ax yer hanner why you kape a leaden bullet as a charm on such a purty chain?" said the Irishman.

"I will tell you, Oiny," replied the detective. "It is the bullet that killed my poor brother. And this is why I keep it so sacredly, and so near me,—I fear the villain, whose deeds are almost unparalleled in the black calendar of crime, has escaped to some distant country, perhaps to America, where a strict law of extradition prevails, and whence it is not always easy to drag away a suspected criminal; besides, the backwoods afford an ample asylum to all sorts of miscreants. Should I discover that he has left England, I will follow for his track, and if I once strike it, I will pursue it though it lead me round the globe; and if I come across my man in some fastness beyond the reach of the law, I myself will be his executioner, and he shall die by the same bullet with which he slew my only brother, whom I am solemnly sworn to avenge!"

"I cannot blame you. I should do the same," rejoined Sibly. "And it is a holy act to drive such a bloody wolf from the face of the earth."

"And bedad, it's an act that would make yer hanner's friends wish to ensure the life of ye. For, be jabbers! I'm thinking that sich a wolf-hunt would not lack for the swate sasoning of danger that I'm towld is sauce to a true hunter's sport."

"There is one danger I incur that I confess is more repellant than the worst peril that I need dread from his cunning and remorselessness," returned Foxley.

"And what is that?" asked Sibly.

"The chance of losing him!" returned the detective, with bitter emphasis.

Foxley led the way up the staircase; they entered a pleasant little bedroom, and the detective shifted a panel on one side of the partition wall, and disclosed a tolerably large room, into which they entered.

Here also the detective lighted the gas.

It was a strange apartment. Around the walls were tiers of large drawers, numbered and labelled; a few chairs, and dressing-tables; wig-blocks, and stands, containing sticks and umbrellas of every quality and dimensions; large cheval glasses; while the walls were hung with photographs, costume pictures, and more than one brace of pistols.

"This is my sanctum sanctorum," said the detective, with a smile. "It is seldom I admit any one into this inner crypt; but I know you are all to be depended upon; but please don't speak of anything you see in my house, even to your intimates. One cannot be too cautious. 'A bird will carry the matter.'"

"We will not forget your caution, Mr. Foxley," said the lawyer's clerk.

Black Oiny looked round with an expression of awe and surprise, and gave a low whistle.

"Wisha! this is a nate little spect-a-cle, which would have caused my mother's son to trimble in his high-lows not so many a fine day gone. But faix, too, among these photygraphs I recognised more than one of my pals. Sure, now, I shouldn't wonder but yer hanner knew this boy in the good owld times."

Foxley answered with a dry smile, and drew from a drawer a little card."

He held it out to Oiny, who started back upon looking at it, and then let it fall from his hand.

Sibly took it up.

It was the sun-picture of a ragged, disreputable fellow, with a scowling brow, though a broad, humourous mouth, and a heavy bludgeon under his arm.

In his domesticated condition this "wild boy" dressed neatly, in a plain but good suit of cloth, his broad face kindly and honest, and even handsome in its manliness and drollery, presented a strange contrast with the portrait of his old and unreclaimed self.

Sibly laughed, and then clapped the worthy fellow on the shoulder.

"Oiny, I congratulate you on the admirable improvement that has taken place in your appearance."

"Sure, yer hanner, I trust that the good change has gone a little deeper than than my fine outside. Good luck to poor Mr. Silas Rye! may the praste pray for his sowl!" returned the Irishman, with a thoughtful look.

Genius of kindness, spirit of liberal trust and solid encouragement, thou art the truest, best reformer; thou art the Eolus that can'st bind the storm-winds of passion by the strong links of gratitude; thou, and thou only, can'st empty the prisons to fill the workshops, unfetter the felon gangs to swell the marching army of progres and civilization!

"And sure, I should be mighty plased to know where yer hanner got that purty picter of a raal, genwine Macarne, of Connemara?"

"I took it myself, Oiny, at Greenwich fair, and you paid for it with a pot of porter."

"The divil rin away wid me for a big fool! but shure, I allers thought yer hanner's profession could boast of some downy coves, but this bates Ballaragan."

The detective now proceeded to disguise his guests.

They assumed the dresses of navigators, and low, rough fellows, and left the house, this time proceeding towards their destination on foot.

"Are you armed, Mr. Foxley?" asked Sibly, in an undertone.

"Joe!" amended the detective, with emphasis.

"Well, Joe, may I repeat the question?"

"No need; I'll answer it—yes."

"With a revolver?"

"With a nobody-knows-how-many-pounder," returned the detective, laughing.

"That must be a long gun by its name," Sibly remarked, with a smile.

The detective showed in the palm of his hand a little silver whistle.

They reached the door of the "flash ken."

A dirty, ill-lighted lamp of ground glass displayed the scrawled and crudite legend, "Lodgins, 3d. and 4d. per nite."

The party bent their heads under the low-browed door, and descended by some steps into a narrow, sanded passage, and turned off into the "kitchen," which we have before had occasion to describe.

As ever, the filthy den was crowded with a motley crew of outcasts and arabs of all ages and both sexes, quarrelling or maudling, singing or brooding, feeding, swilling and smoking at the long, dirty tables.

Little attention was paid to the new arrivals, for they were well disguised.

At the far end of the room, and at a separate table, were seated three flashily-dressed men, resplendent with smash jewellery, drinking brandy, talking noisily, and puffing fiercely from huge cigars, which enveloped them in wreathing clouds of smoke.

The worthy who was seated in the middle was immediately recognised by the spy party as Esau, the gipsy.

Having been previously cautioned by the detective they took no heed of their man, but seated themselves at a table as near him as possible, and yet, as nearly as could be, screened from his observation.

It was plain that Esau was in an advanced stage of intoxication.

We have previously remarked that the gipsy was not an habitual drunkard, yet we have had occasion once before of introducing him in one of his inebriation fits, if they may be called so.

Some men can take the enemy into their mouths, and yet lose little of their brains; but in the case of the gipsy, Esau, the stronghold of reason was very accessible, and whenever mastered by temptation, he once admitted the drink fiend, he was lost to consciousness, and was little better than a maniac.

The detective gave a side glance at the companions of the man whom he sought, and a grim smile sat on his firm lips.

"Weally-aw-positively, you will be admitted to fust-wate so-ci-ety, and wide in Wotten-Wow," said one of Esau's flash companions, blowing a dense cloud from his Havannah.

"Yesh, a good lay, a infernal good lay. I assure you, gents, five pun', real p-pounds. You don't be-b'lieve me; well, I could show y-you the c-cash. Oh, lor, I'm on again!" groaned the infatuated Esau, raising his hand to his brow.

"Drink!" said the other mobs-man, pushing the glass towards, and speaking in a gruff tone, strangely differing from the voice of his supercilious confederate. "I never saw sich a wishy-washy, tea-swilling beggar as you are in my life; you drink like a pigeon. Here, pour it down. How can you get the steam up if you don't put fuel in the furnace? You were saying——"

"I wash sayin'; cuss me, if I knowsh what I was s——. Shant drinksh any m-more; I'm drunksh already, an-and blow me—it's no good to drugsh me, I-I don't keep the—the shwag about me—'cos vy, I knows my co-company, hic, and I knows my dan-danger, that ish. O, lor—O, lor, I'm as drunk as a fool!"

One of the flash-men looked at the other with a knowing wink.

"I'm not only drunksh, but may I never if—if I don't th-think I'm—I'm drugged!"

"That be hanged!" growled the "heavy-man" of these actors on this tragical farce.

"Aw, confound, this is a vewy peculia' pwace for owa wittle conversationer; but weally dwugged! Dam'me, widiculous. The Maitre d' hotel—the land-lowd, or whateva' you call the fellah, would never dare to dwug a fwiend of mine—it's weally pwe-postowous!"

"There's no s-swag!" groaned Esau, in hoarse tones; "it's all—all where not no von can git at it; but when I likes a drop too much, I splits on all 'some dever. I did it once afore, but this yere time I'm—I'm drugged! My tongue swells like a burning st-sting, my throat's in flames!"

"Shall we take you into the open air?" asked one of the mobs-men, excitedly.

"Yes, for one moment," panted the gipsy.

"Curse you, you gave him too much, you've poisoned him!" cried the heavy man to his comrade, in a loud fierce whisper.

"Aw, weally!"

"Into the a-nir," muttered the wretched Esau, faintly. "T-take me away."

His head fell like a lump of lead in a bag on the side of the tables.

The supercilious swell rose.

"Weally, he's vewy bad; I think it adwiseable—fact, I'll bwing assistance, I'll weturn diwectly."

With this, the fellow with a pale face and trembling limbs, hurried down the line of the tables.

The mingled buzz of oaths, laughter, songs and whispering continued.

"Stop that man!" cried Foxley, suddenly leaping to his feet.

A tall navvy, who was reclining upon the settle as if asleep, started up and attempted to seize the mobs-man.

The latter nimbly leaped over the table and reached the door.

He was gone.

The man followed him.

The other fellow, upon hearing Foxley's imperious mandate, had thrown himself against the wall—he drew a knife.

The intrepid officer leaped upon him; Sibly and Black Oiny flew to his aid, and soon the rascal was handcuffed; two men of the assembly stepping to his side.

The sensation that prevailed among the spectators is easily conceived.

Foxley took Esau by the arm and tried to lift him from the table.

With the assistance of Oiny he contrived to bring him a few paces forward.

"Esau Cooper," said the detective, "you are my prisoner on various charges, the chief of which is that you are an accomplice in the murder of Lady Edgeforth!"

"Mur-murder! Lady Edge-forth! she—she's mad—and I'm drunk! d-drugged! poisoned!"

"He is dying," cried Sibly. "Quick, Mr. Foxley! ask him if he knows what has become of Harwolf."

"Your employer; speak, where is he"

Esau did not answer.

"Don't hesitate; tell all; you shall have a free pardon."

"He—the devil—the Harwolf! I'll peach! he is in—in Ameriky—Ark-y—Ark-y—Arkansas!"

"Yes, yes! Ark-y-ansas!"

"And Mr. Rye?"

"O, Lord! I scorch! Poison! murder! police! murder!" shrieked the gipsy.

"And Silas Rye?"

"M—madhouse! Oh! God; p-poisoned! dead! not prepared! I'm a great sinner! Oh! pray—pray for me. The drink! the hellish drink! p-poisoned!"

The men who were holding the man looked in his face eagerly.

His eyes were starting from their sockets; the foam frothed to his lips; his cheek was stained with a lived, purple hue.

His supporters recoiled with instinctive horror.

He fell flat, with a leaden thud; rigid! dead!

"Look not on the cup when it is red!" "The wages of sin is death."

CHAPTER XCIII.

OLD FRIENDS WITH NEW FACES.

OUR scene changes once more to sunny Spain, and to the little sea-town near which the Boy Pirate had fought his battle with the brigands and his duel with Don Carlos.

It was a cloudless day in the middle of summer, yet the ardour of the meridian heat was modified by the freshest breezes from the blue, calm sea, which was just rippled by the light airs that wafted coolness to the beautiful shores.

In the harbour were moored a few boats in which some indolent Spanish seamen were lying or sitting dozing through the noon-tide; a few barques were lying along the sides of the quay, but they seemed to be deserted, if judged by the stillness that reigned aloft and on deck.

In a vine-trellised harbour by the side of the water two persons were seated, gaily laughing and chatting.

One was a slight, handsome young gentleman, the other a boy of about fifteen, with an intelligent face, supple and graceful form; he was not very robust, but by no means sickly.

Our readers will recognise Lord Hawksbury and young Charlie Rye.

"And do you mean to follow up the clue you have found, my lord, and seek the 'Red Raven' in America?"

"Indeed I do, Charlie; it is rather a dangerous enterprise, for the seas are infested with pirates and other water-rats, and my yacht, though sea-worthy, could not stand a broadside, you know."

"Well, when you can't fight, you must run," said Charlie.

"I do think, Charlie, my pretty 'Atalanta' is well named, for she has won me many a wager on her speed; but then, you know, even the swift-footed princess herself was caught at last, and my 'Atalanta' may be run down also."

"You can but fight, then," said Charlie, boldly.

"But I may be killed by the rogues."

"Well, there's the risk; but you must take care to kill them, and then you will escape that danger."

"And may be taken."

"Then you will have all the fun of escaping."

Lord Hawksbury laughed.

"Why, you saucy scamp, you are getting quite formidable. Who would think that my bellicose esquire is the pale-faced little invalid that used to lie on the sofa so languidly, and chafed under the confinement of ill-health like a wounded knight who hears the battle-cry? Oh, Charlie! yours is a happy age; and keep your boy's heart as long as you can, and don't let worldly wisemen laugh you out of your aspirations for good, your love of adventure and victory. Yes, be a boy as long as you can, and despise all monkeys with bob-tail coats, that smoke pipes, drink beer, and go sweethearting before they get into their 'teens.' Be a genuine, sky-larking, plucky boy, and if you must get into mischief, Charlie, rather be flogged for thrashing a bully who insults yourself or your friend than be 'lagged' for forging a check of your master's to buy shares in a sweepstake."

"Look, my lord," cried Charlie, quickly, "at that lovely, giddy little thing—the sweet little girl with the sun-golden hair, dressed so brightly, and flitting about the brink of the quays and over the bowers and cables as light as a butterfly. Isn't she a little dear?"

"Yes, Charlie; but the gay child is running a great danger; she will fall into the dock. Go and take care of her; be quick, my boy, she has strayed from her nurse."

Charlie ran off, intent to catch the little fairy-girl who was prattling and warblingly laughing as she bounded about in her glee.

A large vessel of heavy build was moored alongside of the quay; there was a space of about a yard between the dark hull and the green, slimy stone apron, the water stealthily glancing and gliding below in the dark, well-like interval.

The little girl came to the edge, and seemed suddenly impressed with seriousness, as she bent her large, thoughtful eyes down the gloomy moat, and stood looking at the dark water with childish awe and curiosity.

A flossy little spaniel, who seemed to have been sent in search of his straying mistress, came galloping along; he leaped upon her with a sharp bark.

The girl gave a little shriek, sprang forward, and fell into the lock.

Charlie rushed to the brink of the quay; he looked down.

The little girl was struggling in the waters, her sweet pale face upturned, her long golden ringlets rising and falling on the swell.

The boy slipped over the edge of the wall, holding by one hand, but he found that there was no purchase for his feet.

He recovered his former position, receded a step, and leaped boldly for the deck of the vessel.

No one seemed to be on board her.

Charlie had cleared the bulwark, but would not waste time by attempting to go below, though he thought he heard a noise in the after-hatchway.

He sprang into the water.

He had taken a header—the space was narrow, and as he rose he grazed against the bows of the vessel.

With a brave smile the gallant lad tossed back his hair and struck out boldly—for the men on the yacht, with whom Charlie was a favourite, had taken great pains to make him a fearless swimmer.

He darted through the surging waters, and caught the little girl's dress just as she was a third time sinking.

He held her above water, and contrived to get his left arm round her soft waist, while, with his right, he struck out and kept himself on the surface.

He raised his eyes at hearing a shout.

A line of eager faces appeared on the verge of the wall, while several men rushed on deck from the fore-peak of the vessel.

A wild scream was heard, and Charlie saw a lady—whom, even at that moment, he thought the fairest he had ever beheld—restrained from leaping into the water by a handsome, noble-looking Spanish gentleman.

Several ropes were thrown to the gallant boy—one

from the hand of Lord Hawksbury. This he caught, and contrived to scramble to the top of the wall.

The cheek of the happy boy flushed, and his eye brightened as he was received with an enthusiastic cheer.

The fair lady threw her arms about him, and her soft blue eyes beamed through their long tear-bedewed lashes, and her sweet, childlike lips smiled with a look of unspeakable gratitude.

"Maria Purissima! dear, brave boy! Teach me to thank you, for I am dying with thankful joy, yet I cannot speak!" she cried, her voice tremulous with deep emotion.

"Senora," said Charlie, with a bright blush, and speaking in fair Spanish, "it's nothing. Surely, there is no one who could have done otherwise than try to save this dear little girl. Excuse my awkward speech, senora, I am Yenglesa."

"English!" cried the young mother. "Ah, Virgin! how much I owe to you, brave English; but my child—darling—my life! Look, Manuel, and tell me quickly. Oh, does she live?"

The Spanish gentleman took the little one into his arms.

He raised his eyes to Heaven with a glance of fervent gratitude.

"Our Father in Heaven be thanked! we are not childless, Aurora," he cried, with deep emotion. "Our darling is ours still—yet His, who has made this noble boy the agent of her rescue, and he is English. What do we not owe to English friends?—but who are you my brave, young gentleman?"

"I am Silas Rye's brother," returned Charlie, naively.

"And *my* brother too," said Lord Hawksbury, with a smile. "Senor, may I be so bold as to inquire whether I am right in conjecturing that you are Don Manuel Perez?"

"Yes, senor, you are right; that is my name."

"Then this meeting is most fortunate, for I have for some weeks sought an interview."

"Is it possible? We have arrived here only this morning from our hacienda, near Madrid; but if you will kindly excuse me till I have taken our poor little daughter home, or will accompany me, I shall be proud and grateful to attend your commands."

"Oh, hasten!" returned Lord Hawksbury, warmly; "she is a little pale; but, see, her eyes are open—her lips part—she revives, thank Heaven! I will go with you, senor."

"Lilia, my poor little Lilia!" murmured Donna Aurora, taking the child from her husband.

"Lilia!" repeated Lord Hawksbury, in surprise. "It is a beautiful name, senora."

"And she for whose sake we called her so was beautiful and good, and to her husband we owe all our happiness."

"And who was he?"

"We call him the good knight-errant," returned the lady, with a smile, "but the world calls him the Boy Pirate."

"The Boy Pirate!" returned Lord Hawksbury, starting. "Ah, senora, do you know where your good knight-errant is gone? I seek him as a friend who would give my life to serve him."

"Is he a benefactor?"

"Why, no, not personally; at least, I mean he has other claims upon my affection than those of rendered services."

"Indeed! you are a relative?" asked Donna Aurora, with womanlike curiosity.

"He is my—but I have not introduced myself; Donna Aurora, I am your humble servant and Arthur Hawksbury."

"Lord Hawksbury?"

"Ever at your service. But come, let us take the sweet senorita home without delay. Here comes Jem Trafrail; so, Charlie, I leave you to his charge. Make haste to change your clothes, for though you are convalescent, my brave boy, we've scarce yet struck you off the sick-list."

"But you may, my lord, as soon as you please," returned Charlie, with a smile, "for I am as well now as I can ever wish to be."

The lad tripped away with the mate of Lord Hawksbury's yacht, while the rest of the party got into a splendid carriage which awaited the rich Donna Aurora and her husband at the end of the quay, and the little Lilia was delivered into the charge of the nurse.

Aurora left his lordship and her husband in a handsome apartment which gave out upon the sea, while she hurried with motherly solicitude to attend the child.

Lord Hawksbury and Manuel Perez were alone.

"I have sought you, Don Manuel," said his lordship, "to make inquiries respecting that strange youth whose deeds have startled, and whose character has puzzled, the boldest and the wisest."

"You allude to the Boy Pirate?"

"Even so."

"I tell you, senor," cried Manual," with enthusiasm, "that man is a hero."

Lord Hawksbury smiled.

"You are indulgent," he said. "The world calls him by other and darker names, and though the world is not always right in its estimates, yet a pirate can scarcely be a hero."

"I care not for the world, senor, or the world's title's, for good or evil, in reference to one who is a brave and noble man. A pirate! he is no common thief; no thief at all; for I am told that long since he has warred only with those who chase him, and such deeds as his rescue of the old Admiral Giraldez deserve a laurel wreath and not a hempen halter. I say he is a hero, and I can never change my faith."

"I do not wish to dispute it," returned Lord Hawksbury. "I am his friend. I intend far and wide to seek him, and I came to you, Don Manuel, in hopes of finding that you and he held some correspondence—secret, perhaps, from the necessity of the case—or, at least, that you could tell me where I may expect to find him."

"I would to Heaven I could! I have had thoughts of starting on an expedition similar to your lordship's; but I have been deterred from so doing by a consciousness of the almost absolute certainty of its failure, as well as for other reasons."

"And have you any other motive except your friendship for wishing to see him?"

"I have, senor, a very important motive; for I possess the means of saving him from the miserable catastrophe which will end his wild career."

"Is that possible?"

"Perhaps not, senor. But the impossibility will rest in his natural predilection for a lawless, adventurous life, for long habit must have rendered him unfit for ordinary modes of existence."

"But by what means do you intend endeavouring to reclaim him?"

"You have heard, perhaps, how the Red Raven and his band rescued Aurora's uncle, the old Cardinal Gonsalvez, from the brigands of the Sierra?"

"Europe rings with the fame of that brilliant adventure."

"You may have heard, too, that the Cardinal is dead."

"I have."

"When his eminence died he had appointed me his executor, and, excepting some handsome legacies bequeathed to myself and Aurora, he left the bulk of his immense wealth——"

"To the Boy Pirate?"

"Even so."

"You amaze me."

"The Cardinal was an eccentric man, and I am not much surprised at the bequest."

"Then the hunted Red Raven is a rich man?"

"A millionaire."

"Nominally. Well, well, I pity him. Wild and wicked as the course he has pursued, I cannot help thinking that these riches might have fallen into worse hands. But he must lose it, every maravedis."

"Why, my lord?"

"Is he not an outlaw—a felon?"

"Too true."

"Then he cannot inherit."

"There is a way."

"But not provided by the Cardinal?"

"Yes. The property was left in charge to me, and I am bound by oath and by ties of interest, as they affect my own possessions, to deliver up these estates and money to a certain Captain Paul Manvers—that, I should tell you, was the soubriquet assumed by the Red Raven."

"Well, Don Manuel, and what are your plans?"

"First, to find the missing heir."

"Aye, there's the rub," returned Lord Hawksbury, with a dry smile. "But supposing that accomplished?"

"I think we could reclaim him."

"I fear not. At least, it is doubtful."

"He could merge his identity into a clever assumption. He might take another name; or, for that matter, he speaks Spanish so well, and is so dark featured, that one might swear to him as a descendant of Don Roderic."

"But his band?"

"They are an obstacle."

"He would never desert them."

"They are devoted to him, and share many of his better qualities."

"What could be done with them?"

"It is hard to say."

"The rascals will not exchange their roving life for any inducement; besides, not one of them would be safe."

"I have been thinking, my lord," said Don Manuel suddenly, "that it would be possible to fit up an iron-plated steam sloop of war for—shall we say—our hero, and send him and his band off with a letter of marque on some dashing enterprise for the deliverance of the oppressed, or the liberation of some revolting people, whose cause is that of right and freedom."

"It would suit his temperament exactly; but before we train our poaching falcon to a worthier flight—why—we must catch him."

Don Manuel laughed; the conversation was changed. The Spaniard pressed his guest to stay to dinner, and requested permission to send a servant to fetch little Charlie Rye.

His lordship excused himself for that day on the plea of having letters to write, and with many mutual expressions of politeness they parted.

Lord Hawkesbury went on board his splendid yacht, and descended into the handsome cabin.

Charlie was there and received his lordship with a look of pleasure.

"I am glad you are come, my lord; here are letters from England; but none from Silas."

"Indeed, that's rather strange. I requested him to write at once."

"Oh, I hope it is all right," said Charlie: "but, do you know, I have a strange feeling as if something dreadful had happened."

"Nonsense; you're a muff; but here's a letter from Mr. Sibly; I dare say, from him, we shall get some 'good news from home.'"

Lord Hawkesbury carelessly seated himself, and broke the seal.

As he read he turned deadly pale—the paper fluttered from his hand, and he struck his brow, exclaiming,

"My God! and the accursed villain escaped!"

"What is it, my lord? Is Silas ill? is my lady dead?" asked Charlie.

"No, no! you must not ask a single question," returned his lordship, rising and pacing the cabin in great agitation; "but you must prepare to depart, for to-night we set sail for England."

CHAPTER XCIV.

THE ESCAPE FROM THE MADHOUSE.

WHEN Silas Rye had been removed to his cell he was bound upon the bed, and the ruffianly keeper took up his position by the patient's side.

Fawcett remained in the room, rendering assistance to the keeper with childish officiousness.

Presently the doctor and the madhouse-keeper entered.

The physician was a stout, burly fellow, with a fierce red face, and a bovine voice.

"Ha! humph!" he said, taking the patient's wrist, and looking him sternly in the face. "A—very b-ad case!—ve-ry bad, I do assure you! the diagnosis ——"

"You rascal!" shouted Silas, infuriate, "you walking lie, you disgrace to the noble profession of which you pretend to be a member; you dare not say I am mad; you dare not, in this advanced age, keep me in this horrible durance upon a shallow pretence. I will communicate with those who shall blow such a trumpet peal of indignation with the organs of publicity that shall shake your cursed hell-house about your ears."

"My account of this case was nowise exaggerated, Doctor Swearall," said the principal, with a shrug and a sly smile of derision.

"Not at all, sir—not at all!" thundered the bovine doctor; "it's a horrible case, one of those where a deluded wretch of a patient, wilder than whirlwinds, imposes upon the credulity of ignorant meddlers persuading them that he is not mad, and having been cast adrift by his exasperated protectors, cuts his own or his neighbour's throat, or sets his house in blazes. Poh! poh! I've no patience with the inquisitorial examinations, the caution and distrust that are advocated by some writers of the press; such fellows ought to be turned over to the tender mercies of raving maniacs; but I must go my rounds. I dine within half an hour, and there's time to spare."

"And what will you prescribe?"

"Low diet, bleeding and——"

"Morphine?"

"Decidedly; morphine."

"A strong dose?"

"Yes; the patient is excited, and must be quieted by a strong narcotic."

"Very well, Doctor Swearall."

"Hark you, rascal!" cried Silas.

"Poh! poh! don't talk, poor fellow; be quiet; nothing but 'cool patience' can allay the heat of your distemper. Give him the morphine at once."

"I will."

"And how is Master Fawcett? Eh! Hold up your head, sir, and reply like a sensible man."

"I've got to take care of him; the madman has to keep the sane," returned Fawcett, with an insane look from the patient to the doctor; "but I will keep watch upon him, for I was sane once—many, many years ago, you will say. Well, it's no wonder people get giddy and lose their wits, when the world is twirling and twirling from day to day and year to year; it makes me stagger to think of it."

The two mad doctors exchanged meaning glances.

The principal of the madhouse regarded Fawcett with an air of satisfaction, and asked him, with a dry smile,

"You are contented here?"

"Where—here? Yes, I am contented; but I am not so mad as this one."

The doctors left the room laughing.

The keeper accompanied them.

"Fawcett," groaned Silas Rye, when they were alone.

"Well."

"Are you really in your senses?"

"Yes; are you?"

"Why do you ask?"

"Why do you ask?"

"Because you appear so intensely foolish and mad. I can easily imagine a man shamming 'pious,' though when one considers how the awful name of God is impressed in all about us, it seems really dreadful, that shamming 'pious;' but mad! I could never sham mad."

"Unless you were drunk; but that would be no sham either. Look now, Mr. Rye, if here is 'method' in my madness there is madness in your method. Reason apparent is madness in a man who wants to escape from a lunatic asylum conducted on the principles that sway this place. If you are mad they have a right to you, and if you try to escape they will contract their clutch upon you. Whereas, if you sham idiot, as I do, they will relax in their vigilance, thinking that, should you break away, you would be gladly restored to them."

"You are right," said Silas; "but, for all that, I could die rather than contend with these rogues by dissimulation. Yet there was a time when I was crafty enough; but, immured in a madhouse, I am in a dilemma I never anticipated; and do you think there is any chance of escape?"

"Hist! I will seek that chance at once; but first create a diversion, for we are closely watched. When the attention of our tyrants is distracted we can get away."

"What means do you intend to take for withdrawing their attention from us?"

"You shall see, or rather you shall hear," returned Fawcett.

He stole to the door.

He opened it and listened.

He nodded at Silas and left the room.

Silas lay perfectly still, listening and trembling with suspense and anxiety.

He could not imagine by what means Fawcett intended to effect their deliverance, for the case seemed hopeless enough.

They were but two weak creatures opposed to a large number of strong and unscrupulous men.

The place was carefully guarded, and, for himself, he was bound in a cell.

Yet hope and confidence returned when he reflected how wonderfully he had been preserved by Providence from the worst effect of Harwolf's malice, and how much cause he had for thankfulness in respect of his having found so valuable a friend as Fawcett.

His reverie was broken by wild and discordant cries.

There was a horrible yell, loud shouting, and the hurried trampling of feet.

Fawcett returned.

As he entered the room he paused and harkened to the hubbub without.

He drew near the bed.

His face was very pale.

"Good God! what have you done?" cried Silas Rye.

Fawcett smiled.

"Nothing so horrible as you might imagine, judging from the horrid fracas you hear. I have liberated one of the most desperate 'cases'—a poor, mad fellow they keep in the last cell in this ward. There are two keys to that cell; one of them I stole."

"But will they not suspect you?"

"We'll not give them time to verify their suspicions. Nerve yourself, Mr. Rye, for you will want all your prudence and courage."

Fawcett drew from his sleeve a table-knife, and severed the thongs that bound Silas to the bed.

The latter jumped up.

"Give me the knife," said Rye, "I will murder the first man that opposes me."

"It's time you were gone," said Fawcett.

Silas looked him in the face inquiringly.

Fawcett touched his own forehead, and smiled.

Rye's voice was husky, as he replied,

"You may be jesting, but it is a fact, I am losing my wits; another day in this den of horrors, and I should be a maniac."

"Follow me, then; trust more to your heels than your arms. Oh, Mr. Rye," said the poor fellow, suddenly, and laying his hands on the shoulders of his fellow prisoner, while the tears sprang to his eyes, "if you could tell what I feel at this moment; the work of eternal months is accomplished; I am about to make one dash for liberty; in any case the result

will be happy, for my bondage and degradation are over. I will never be carried back to this pandemonium a living man!"

"Nor I; as God may help me in my need!" cried Silas, bitterly.

"Hark!" exclaimed Fawcett, raising his finger, "don't you hear them scampering like frightened rats? the garden door is open, I'll be bound the 'desperate case' has broken loose, they are all gone in pursuit; now's the time!"

He opened the door and beckoned his companion.

The cell gave out upon a long passage.

Silas Rye cautiously followed his companion.

They reached a barred window.

The grounds lay mapped out below; a number of keepers and servants, some with life-preservers and other arms, were panting among the bushes. Soon they cleared away, and went off to the other side of the house.

"I did not mean that fellow to get out of the house entirely," said Fawcett; "but if he could manage to make his escape we need not despair."

"But this window."

"My dear fellow, I have 'worked' it." As Fawcett said this he pulled two of the bars from their sockets, and, with a smile, laid them on the ground.

"And that door at the end of the passage," said Silas.

Fawcett drew from his breast a key, and then replaced it with a significant smile, as he said,

"I shall keep that for a trophy."

"You may find it useful as a weapon," returned Silas.

Fawcett walked across the passage, and stooping down pulled a loosened piece of board from the flooring. He drew from the cavity a bundle.

This he opened.

"See what treasures I have collected," said Fawcett, with a smile; "here is a rope of my own manufacture, and here's the corduroy jacket of the gardener, which I stole from the hedge one lucky morning, and here's the blouse they gave me to work in when I was promoted to be sluicer general of the yards and doorsteps; but now for our attempt."

Silas Rye kept a watch from a window at the end of the passage, which partially gave a view of the premises on the side of the house the keepers had taken in pursuit of the escaped maniac.

Fawcett tied the rope firmly to the iron bars, and then whistled to his companion.

"Now for it!" he exclaimed; "I think I have omitted nothing that can secure success, and of one thing I am certain, I will die, but never surrender; here goes."

With this he launched himself into the air, sliding swiftly down the rope.

Silas followed him.

There was a quiver in the limbs of Silas Rye as he touched the sod, and looked about him on the expanse of green fields and free sky; there was a determined expression on his face, and a fierce glance in his eye.

It would have been dangerous for a strong and bold man at that moment to attempt to "let or hinder" the escaping prisoners.

Fawcett led the way rapidly across the grass.

They were obliged to pass round the house; but they kept within the dark shadow of the high wall.

They heard a shout.

A pistol-shot was fired.

The maniac was seen racing along the top of the wall, the keepers and other pursuers running below.

The shot had probably been fired to intimidate the poor wretch.

The hunters and the hunted soon disappeared behind the shrubs and trees, and Fawcett led his companion to a little green-painted gate in the wall.

The lock of this was rusty and brittle and soon gave way to their united efforts.

The door was opened.

They were about to pass through when the way

ZAMPA'S UNEXPECTED BATH.

was blocked by the broad figure of the keeper who had aggravated Silas to such a pitch of fury.

"Halloa! that's your little game, is it? Just walk back, and see what you'll get for this yer relapse of the wust symptoms."

Silas made no reply; but threw himself upon the bully.

He fixed his knuckles tight in the fellow's throat and forced him down.

With admirable coolness and presence of mind Fawcett closed the garden-door.

The struggle did not last long.

The man's eyes appeared to start from their sockets, his swollen tongue protruded, his cheeks became livid—he showed every symptom of strangulation, and fell back on the sward.

"Have you killed him?" whispered Fawcett.

No. 31.

Rye's cheek flushed and his eyes glared, as he replied in a thick, fierce voice,

"I care not if I have!"

"I would rather you had not, friend Silas," returned the other, dryly. "And yet the act would be more than justifiable, it would be commendable; however, come on."

They passed across the field.

"Our sorrows are not complete," said Fawcett; "the madman has jumped the wall and has not broken his neck."

"Nor his legs either," rejoined Silas, "if one may judge from the rate at which he is running."

The hunted man was seen springing like a kangaroo over ditch and hedge, the pursuers shouting in his track.

"Stay here a moment, Mr. Rye," said Fawcett, quickly. "I will see what direction they take, that we may avoid them—ha! they are off the scent."

Silas was alone for a moment.

His heart swelled with mingled emotions of intense joy and anxiety.

He looked around him.

It was a lonely spot.

The blue smoke curled up from the roofs of some cottages; but they were embowered among a clump of trees, and at a good distance.

Silas heard a noise of panting and the crashing of boughs.

He hurried in the direction of the sound.

A tall, spare man, with a hideously formed head, with glaring eyes and frothing lips, jumped over a bush and confronted him.

By his tight dress and cropped hair, Silas could have recognised the madman, were not such distinctions rendered needless by the awful appearance of that face which rendered the soul's workings as a broken mirror might reflect the countenance in distortion.

Silas moved towards him, with a conciliating gesture, in hopes to pacify him.

The next moment he felt himself hurled backwards, and fell heavily; the trees, the sky, whirled swiftly round; a great darkness fell upon him, and he became unconscious.

Fawcett returned hastily.

His horror was boundless.

Silas lay motionless upon the earth. The maniac stood glaring, his foot set on the prostrate body of his victim.

With a despairing eye Fawcett glanced round him. A large party of the keepers were rushing towards them.

He felt inclined to court death from the madman's hands, when through the trees he heard voices whispering, and a posse of country fellows stole into the open space, and flung a lasso of ropes over the madman and hurled him to the ground, where he lay kicking and struggling, but only by his convulsions tightening his bonds.

In an instant Fawcett turned towards the countrymen.

"My friends," he said, "if you have one spark of human kindness amongst you, listen, and heed what I am going to tell you. I and my companion are detained in yon madhouse, though we are as much in possession of our senses as one of yourselves. In order to divert the attention of the keepers while we were attempting our escape, I let this poor maniac loose from his cell; but did not suppose he could get out of the house. Here come the villains that have entrapped us, and treated us with shameful cruelty. All I ask of you is to take us prisoners, and to keep us till fair inquiry is made as to whether or not we are sane. But if you would not have the crime of murder on your souls, protect us; for, rather than be dragged back to that abode of cruelty and misery, I will kill myself. Pray do not be deluded by these liars, who will tell you we are mad. Let unbiassed, honest physicians decide that question hereafter; and, till then, we will remain in your detention."

"Durn un! he talks like a book. He doan't talk like a mad'un," said one of the men.

"Noa. I b'lieve, neighbour," rejoined another, "there be a many on 'em as goes into yon 'sylum as is more sensible than their keepers. Howsumdever, we maun't interfere."

"You will not abandon me?" cried Fawcett.

"Noa, noa; durn it, noa! I'll not 'banden ye. But I maun't zet 'ee at large if ye be mad. But I'll 'zult the parson, and Doctor Biles. I'll not let 'ee go, neighbour, till I hears from your friends."

"That's all I ask. God bless you and reward you! for if ever man did his fellow a true service, your generous protection is a worthy act."

At this moment the principal and Doctor Swearall, with their forces, arrived at the spot.

"Humph! ha! Incorrigible case. Thought to escape, No. 40, did you? Humph! won't do, my friend. I thought you were improving; but the old fits of slyness and duplicity are returning, eh! Come along, sir; come along."

With this, the bovine man of medicines caught Fawcett by the collar.

The sturdy ploughman interposed.

"Durn'ee! hands of, wull ye? This gemmun's under my pertection, and ye shan't lay a finger on un."

"Hough! what—what!" cried the doctor. "Do you mean to say, sir, that you will aid and abet this poor wretch in his attempt to escape from necessary restraint? Don't you perceive, sir, that he's an idiot?"

"He may be a nat'ral, for aught I knows; but ye be durned un-nat'ral to treat a man of his years as a child, and to bully him like a cur. I tell ye I pertect him."

"You, sir! Who are you?"

"I be a better ploughman than thou'rt a physicioner, any mornin', measter; and I'm too much of a man to see ye put on a poor cre'tur, mad or zane, that asks me vor pertection; you notify that."

"This is insufferably absurd, unbearably preposterous," remonstrated the doctor, wrathfully. "And are you alone in your meddling rascality, or is there a conspiracy? Of course you will at once surrender the patients?"

"Noa, noa," returned the country lads.

Several of them had attended to Silas Rye, who was now sufficiently recovered to stand, with a little assistance.

"Tell'ee what we'll do," said the labourer; "we'll give'ee the raal mad'un, and keep these yere, rum-uns we'll call 'em, till we knows the raal true fac's, and I'll sult Doctor Biles."

"That practitioner is my personal enemy," roared the mad-doctor.

"Loard, if ye tell me that, I'll break in your ugly red face, and let the devil out," shouted the countryman. "Any man that's an enemy of our good doctor is allers open to a thrashing in our country parts. What say, neighbours?"

"Aye—aye, Luke; thou be'st right."

"My good, kind fellows," cried Silas; "if you will only protect us till we are examined by a proper person we will reward you; not that any recompense is adequate to the great service you will render us. Tell us, truly, do you think we're mad?"

"Durn'ee, noa. I doan't; what say, neighbours?"

"Noa, noa; doan't let'un have 'em."

"Then, may I tell you a short story that is as true as it's strange. If I tell you it I fear you will think me mad."

"Thou may'st be mad as thee likes, neighbour; old Rough-and-Tough shan't have'ee; leastwise, without Doctor Biles 'sents to ut."

"You Bœotian blockheads! you ignorant clodhoppers!!" screamed Doctor Swearall, spluttering with rage; "will you be led by a raving madman?"

"Darnation!—we won't be 'sulted and blackguarded by you, old Jowler. Durn'ee, let the poor cre'tur speak, or we'll souse'ee in the hoss-pond."

"Aye, aye; let us speak," chorused the others.

"You have all read or heard how a villain named Harwolf murdered his wife and a man in her company, and how he afterwards poisoned a lady and spirited away her guardian?"

"Thou'rt not right; he tried to poison her. I heard that larn'd chap, Jack Reader, tell about it down at 'The Three Turnuts.'"

"Then, Lady Edgeforth — the lady — is not dead?"

"Noa, neighbour; b'lieve not."

"Thank God!"

"Go on with thy speechification!"

"You heard, then, of Silas Rye?"

"Hulloa there, neighbour; seen him pasted up against the pound, down village, on a large print as they stuck there, offerin' a large reward to any lucky chap as might know what come on him."

"Well, then, I am he. Harwolf ensnared me, and had me carried off to these villains; and I have been detained in the mad-house on the pretence that I was insane. If you will waive the truth of what I tell you till Doctor Biles has inquired into my case, I will double the reward, and for life be grateful for your kindness."

"Thou'rt Zilas Rye!"

"I am; let these wretches disprove it, if they can."

"Abominable! You see he is mad; the whole story is ridiculous. Surrender him at once!" shouted the doctor, in great anger and consternation.

"Noa, stand clear, I tell ye!" cried the plough-man.

"You scoundrel! Men, assist me; we will take them by force."

A desperate rush was made at Silas and his companion.

"Doam the kidnappers, down wi' 'em!" cried the sturdy champion.

"Douse 'em in the hoss-pond—durn 'em, give 'em a bit of your crab-stick, my lads," cried the others.

"I'll have you all locked up!" shouted the doctor.

"In thy pretty mad-house wull 'ee? Hear that, neighbours—straight jackets and tickled feet all round; here's a Christ'an creetur for ye."

"Down wi' 'em, doamed men-stealers!" responded the chorus.

A furious fight would have ensued, but a short, stout gentleman, mounted on a sturdy nag, galloped across the field and joined the party.

"Hey-day; a riot! What does this mean, Luke? I always thought you a quiet fellow."

"Lord alive! noa, Dr. Biles, I be a desperate nat'ral and lun-at-ic. They're jest a-goin' to lock me up in the 'sylum for hidgiots!"

"And I shall think them right to do so, if you conduct yourself in this mad fashion. What is the matter?"

The man explained.

Doctor Biles jumped off his horse, and approached Silas and his companion, fixing on them a penetrating glance.

"Sir," he said, addressing the elder of the two, his voice trembling a little as he spoke, "may I ask your name?"

"My name is Fawcett; I was formerly the captain of a merchant-ship; I was entrapped by this brace of infamous rogues into yonder strong-hold of misery, and have been detained there for several years. It is true that I have affected to be idiotic for some time in order to increase my chance of escape; but both I and my companion, Mr. Silas Rye, whose name has been brought into notoriety in connection with the late horrible outrages of Andrew Harwolf, are sane men, no more tainted with mania than anyone amongst you."

The good doctor stood as if petrified with astonishment; he then seized the speaker by the hand.

"And do you not recognise me?" he said.

Fawcett looked him in the face, started, and then warmly embraced him.

"When I heard your name mentioned, I did not recall it in my confusion and terror at being taken back to that hellish prison, but I never dreamed that such a fortunate coincidence as this happy meeting could occur. But, dear doctor, my wife, my little one, there must be some evil news to damp this joy, I know. Well, I will endure it patiently in behalf of this great deliverance."

"There is no ill news, thank God," returned the worthy physician; "they are alive and well; but we have long mourned for you as dead; we thought you had been shipwrecked."

Fawcett raised his eyes to heaven in mute but fervent thankfulness; the worthy rustics gave a hearty "hurrah!"

"I suppose, Doctor Biles, that you will lend credence to this absurd story, and that you will illegally detain my unhappy patients?" said Swearall, evidently much cowed.

"Sir, you have rightly stated my intention," returned the physician, coldly, turning away in disgust.

"Very well, Sir, very well; there will be legal proceedings."

"Be assured of that."

"And I suppose you think you have a strong case? But you will see, sir, you will see; you will be sorry for this day's work."

"For your sake I am sorry already," returned the other.

"Hem! ah! and will you not surrender the third patient?"

"Not, sir, to your care, at least, until further proceedings have been taken. I will have charge of the poor creature, and, I trust, for the sake of humanity, you will soon cease to hold a position you have disgraced."

"Vastly fine, sir," rejoined Swearall, hurrying away with his party, "you will hear of this again."

The rustics set up a triumphant shout, and threw a shower of stones as the blushing doctor waddled off with his colleague at the head of his gang; they would have proceeded to extreme measures but for the intervention of the worthy physician.

CHAPTER XCV.

TOM GARROD'S YARN.

THE Boy Pirate's crew were assembled in the trip deck.

The rover and his officers had gone ashore.

The men were carousing, and, as the can went round, Tom Garrod, the boatswain, grew more and more loquacious.

"Aye, aye, shipmates, you may think its all galley yarns that I tell ye; but, look ye here now, I arn't one of those chaps as experiments with their mates, and tries how many and how big lies can be crammed down their winds'ls; but this here weather-beaten old hulk has been fitted for all services, and I've seen as queer sights as any foremast-man since."

"I thought it no use to repine at my lot,
  Or to bear with my perils ashore;
So I pack'd up the trifling remnants I'd got,
  And a trifle, alas! was my store."

"Well, if I hadn't taken to this service, and got braced to it for the sake of our gallant skipper, I might now be piping all hands on a man-of-war, or, for aught I know, putting on a gold scraper in the state cabin; but I was goin' to twist a yarn; give us the clue-line."

"You were saying, Tom, that you had seen as queer sights as any man that ever reefed a top-s'il on a cold night."

"Aye, messmate," said another; "but you forget Jemmy Skyflyer."

"Avast heaving, mate," exclaimed Tom, with a

twinkle in his eye, " I respects Jemmy; a better seaman never went aloft; but he hadn't my experience,
you know, and for sights, my toplights, why he was
but a fresh-water swab in comparison with me."

" Why, you never married a mer-woman, did
you ?"

Tom winked knowingly.

" Belay ! you don't think I'm a lubber to kiss and
tell—mermaids is common; but devils, at least,
devils in their own gear, is oncommon; but I've seen
'em, full rigged, horns as long as the jib-boom, eyes
like the red lamps in a light-house, and tails, mate,
as long and thick as the bower-cable, with a hook at
the end like the flukes of a stream-anchor and their
grappling irons. My eye, to be clapper-clawed with
talons, sharp as the head of a marlin-spike!"

" Do they smell of brimstone, Tom ?" asked one of
the men, with naive seriousness.

" Right you are; they chaw sulphur; they roll in
their cheek a quid of brimstone about as big as your
fist, and jets of smoke curl out from between their
teeth like the puffs from the ports after a broadside.
When they squirt out their sulphur-juice it fires
off like a streak of lightning, and an old quid will
smoulder and smoke like Mount Etna for a month
together."

" Golly ! dis child berry much like to see buckra
debil; seen 'nough of darkies' debils. Dey'se not so
form'able."

" What are they like, Zamp ? "

" Big buckra, wid him skin as white as de stun-
sil, and dam' long cowhide to cut up de sinners."

" But, how do they talk, Tom ? "

" Well, mate, various; sometimes they bluster like
a white squall, and thunder like big guns, but sometimes they pipe as soft as a flute; but, arter all, they
are mostly civil-spoken chaps."

And how did you happen to overhaul 'em ?—twist
the whole yarn."

" Aye, aye, Tom; twist it stiff."

" Well, I'll freshen hawse, re-charge my pipe, and
blaze away."

There was a long pause as Tom relit his pipe and
drained his grog very leisurely, for he loved to keep
his auditors in breathless expectance.

At length he spoke.

" I suppose you have heard of Betsy Warmer."

" No, Tom; can't say we have."

" What lubberly ignorance! she was my old
maiden aunt."

" Aye, aye; heave ahead."

" You know, mates, that I was born a horfan and
sarved apprentice under my martinet of a aunt.
Lor' bless your fine eyes, hearties, she was a she-
commodore that could wield the cat like a bo'swain's
mate. My starn-quarters were sometimes grooved
and fluted like a breech-loader. She'd a tongue as
long as a admiral's pennant, and would rattle away
from day-watch to 8 bells, and get no more tired of
grumbling than the breakers of roaring. Poor old
Aunt Betsy! here's her health, mates, and wishin' I
may be as taut on my pins at forty as she was trim
with her jawing tackle at ninety-five. In coorse, we
all know about perpet'al motion, but her clock,
though it never wanted winding, ran down at last.
Sich is life ! "

" But what the devil has she to do with Old
Nick ?"

" Steady, mates; we can't make way till we catch
the wind. I never heard when I were young
whether the growth of new skins is limited; I couldn't
count how many her cat had scratched off my starn-
end, but as they grew thinner and thinner every
time, and whenever I wasn't on my feet I was decidedly on hot coals, I thought I might as well be
right away at blazes at once, so I desarted and went
to sea. I met with many adventures, as you know,
and suffered many hardships. The fust skipper I

served under was a bullying tyrant, but, Lor love
you ! only a pocket-pistol arter a Armstrong. When
he swore at me, he was like soft sawder arter Aunt
Betsy's hullabaloo. I never cared when he kicked
up a Bob's-a-dying; I was an old gunner, and could
stand fire."

" And did you ever see the old girl again ?"

" Under werry peculiar circumstances. But you
shall hear, shipmates. I sailed in the ' Cocktaw,' a
werry fine craft, that came to grief in the South
Pacific; she sprang a leak, and foundered, in a heavy
sea. All hands perished except myself. I fitted a
raft with some spars and sheathing boards, on which
I bound myself, taking with me a little barrel of
stingo. I'm not agoin' to tell ye all I suffered on that
cruise, because I can't. But there's one thing I
learned while adrift, and that was the rumarkable
fact that rum is not a werry ' cool, refreshin' beverage,'
as the purser swabs ashore call the bilge-water they
sweeten with fine names to poison their wictims. Lor
bless yer ! there was the sun pouring down his blazes
on to my dewoted head, and showing me how he
makes the fruit grow, when I would have given a
whole year's pay and prize-money for half a peach;
and there was the surf laughing and flushing about
me, and throwing the salt in my face, when I would
have given the whole ocean, with big and little fishes,
for half a cupful of dirty water. I consoled myself
by making myself worse, and did nothing but suck
the monkey from morning till night. Well, what
with famine and thirst, I began to regret there was
no sail-maker to take my measure, for I felt myself
foreign-fitted; and so I lashed the helm, and gave
myself up for shark's meat. I took a long pull and a
strong pull at the stinger; I felt my windpipe bubble
into blisters, and nearly set my beard on fire with
my burning breath; and so I laid myself down on
the spars, not dead, because I hadn't strength
enough to die. It was night, with double-power
darkness, that seemed to crush one. All at once—
I had not closed my weather-eye—on the lee-quarter,
I spied a light; it looked as if one of those ' comic'
stars—I s'pose they calls 'em comic cos they waggles
their tails—had rushed straight down for a cooler,
and remained on the surface of the water, as if taking
soundings, not seeming to like it; or perhaps, like a
pretty girl—God bless her !—that sees her own reflection in the looking-glass, and can't help kissing
it——"

" Heave ahead, old shiver-the-mizen. We wan't
to get to the devil."

" You lubberly swab ! where's your manners ?
Ladies first. And you're running to your destination
afore a head-wind, no end o' knots an hour——Well,
as I was a saying, I saw this light, and said I to
myself, ' Tom, my hearty, bless your stars that you're
not of that ship's company;' for I thought it was a
ship on fire. It was good of me, though, to keep up
such a brave heart, for my own hulk was well nigh
scorching into a flame, and every moment I looked
out for its spontaneous 'bustin——"

" But, the devils, Tom."

"They're hard a port, messmates.——Well, the ship
on fire had scarcely hove in sight, when the officer of
the larboard watch—that's me — reported to the
skipper—that's me—that the craft was bearing down
at a devil of a rate. And well she might be, considering what sort of crew she carried. Afore I can
tell ye how many leagues she made in less than no
time, she ran alongside, and I had a full view of her.
My jib! was there ever such a sight seen ! Her hull
was of red-hot iron, her three masts were bright,
spark sprinkled, hissing, and red hot; and her tackle
looked like molten wires. But her sails—what do
you think her sails were made of ?"

" Can't say, Tom."

" Just sheets of pure flame; and the sky-s'ls and
jibs were really something pretty. And from the
foremast-head was a long pendant; and what do you
think it was like ?"

" What, Tom ? Go-ahead."

"Like a woman's tongue; and it kept a flipping and flapping in a most provoking manner, that was really femaline. And then, flying aft, was the Satanic ensign."

"As it arn't entered in the signal-book, p'raps you'll tell us the colours."

"Well, mates, it's a tri-colour—red, black, and yellow—which, as I takes it, means: red, blood; black, cloth—lawyers and parsons, perhaps, or else troubles; yellow, what we can't have too much of. But, the dewice—werry cur'ous, the dewice."

"Aye, Tom; what was it?"

"You've all seen Old Nick's trident—what the wulgar landswabs call a pitchfork?"

"Aye, Tom; in picters."

"Well, that's the dewice, only it's baited, you see—on the starboard prong, a laurel-wreath; on the larboard, a fat purse; and in the centre, full amid ships, a pretty little witch of a woman."

"Tom, that's werry cur'ous."

"Arn't it, messmates? Well, the skipper hailed me; he was black as Zamp, and werry much favours him, only for his long tail, his cow-horns, and bull's eyes—red ones, like red-hot stones in glass globes. Well, the skipper squirts his quid over the bulwark, just surging the froth off a big wave, and he asks me whither I was bound, and if he could do me a good turn. I told him the best turn he could do me would be just to turn his back and sheer off. At this he laughed; and shiver me, messmates, if the werry air didn't echo like a roll of thunder. He shovelled in another mouthful of sulphur, and the white smoke was some relief to his black face, for it hid all but his teeth and eyes. I thought it was best to be civil, and as he is such a werry old liar, I considered as I'd better tell him the truth. I overhauled the log, and told him all as had happened. I asked him if he could give me some water; he said that was the last thing to look for among his ship-stores. But he made me a liberal offer; he said he would restore me to England, home, and beauty, and make me as rich as Prester John himself, if I'd do him a favour. I axed him what it was. Says he, 'Mortal, it's a werry hard thing for flesh and blood, which is too much for the spirits.' I didn't quite understand him, so I axed his meaning. 'It's an old woman with an—the devil's, I mean—an old woman's own tongue; they've packed her off from the main ship and sent her over to our department; but we've been poor devils ever since she came, and though we're spirits, there's not a bit of spirit left among us. Now, I'll rig you out a four-decker, and make you a port-admiral, if you'll marry the old rip, and ship her off—not to Jericho or Blazes, or any of our ports, though; we've had too much of her. Will you do it?' 'Avast, Cap'en Nicholas,' says I (it's best to be civil) 'my four-decker, parade of marines, and gold scraper. Let me see my craft afore I comes to the clinch.'"

"The skipper makes no more ado, but poises his trident and flings it plump into the sea as you might throw a harpoon at a fin-back. A great cloud of steam rose from the place and rested like a fog-bank on the surf. It cleared slowly, and, as it faded away, the mighty spars and webbed rigging of an enormous frigate began to appear, and I heard the drums and fifes beating to quarters. I felt stiff about the starn, heavy on the figure-head and bows, and I looked at myself fore and aft, and, blow me, if I warn't togged out as a genwine port-admiral, sword, epaulets, scraper, full-rigged. 'Will you marry the old woman to be an admiral?' said the skipper, as if he thought I shouldn't like it. 'Marry?' says I, "I'll marry the dev—'scuse your reverence—I mean the old woman.' Says he, 'Midship imp, tell Mr. Belzebub to bring the old woman aft.' 'Aye, sir,' says the petty officer, in a devilishly seamanlike manner. I heard a voice; they were hauling the old girl aft, and she was clapper-clawing them starboard and port; her jawing-tackle was in full swing. My knees knocked together, I felt a chill at my heart, and a glow at my quarters, and, when the two gentle devils

'scorted their convoy alongside, 'Cap'en Nick,' says I, 'it's a werry great disappointment on both sides, but I really must decline your kind offer, as it is all agen regulations for me to marry the old gal. 'How so?' growls the black-'un. 'Why, you see, cap'en, I can't marry, for she's my own aunt, Betsy Warmer!'

"What happened immediately arter that I don't know, but I heard a roar like the howl of a pack of wolves, and I was seized by my beam-ends and hurled overboard; I fell plump on my raft and knocked my head against the rum-keg. On opening my eyes I saw a boat alongside, which had put off from a ship that had made out my signal and sent out the jolly-boat to my rescue. Now, dam'me! some book-larnt lubbers wanted to persuade me that the devils were sperits of rum, and sartain they were rum devils, but when once told that a desarving foremast man can't become a port-admiral by the devil's assistance and that a four-decker of the line is only the effects of 'delrious tremblings' I say, 'stopper over all!'"

After the yarn the jolly tars went on deck for mischief, and soon the merry scrape of the fiddle-string, and the brisk patter of naked feet, bore token to the hilarious glee of the adventurers.

The can passed round, and the expression of many a scowling face was softened by a pleasant smile.

Zampa performed several insane dances, and imbibed more than his quantum of rum.

In the midst of the sky-larking, the nigger jumped upon a cask that stood by the lee-bulwark, and harangued the crew.

"'Spected gentl'm, as de can am berry near dry, and de dam steward not gib us no more till ferder orders, it becomes un's duty to drink de helf ob all cap'en's cap'en. Pass to dis child de can—'bliged. Now, gemman, hats off—here's to de helf of Lilia, and three times three."

"Lilia!" shouted the men, but with a hungry, or rather thirsty look at the can, in which Zampa had immersed his thick lips, and hidden his black figure-head.

"De next toast it 'comes un' duty to perpose is de cap'en hisself—long life and glory to Cap'en Kit. Hoorah for de Red Raven!"

Zampa took another merciless pull at the grog, while the men looked on entreatingly.

"And, chil'en, dere's de ossifers, dam gallant buckra gem'mans as ebber spread dere foot on de quarter-deck; must drink dere helf considerable deep, berry 'portant to keep up proper respect for 'ems 'periors."

Zampa's head disappeared altogether; the men groaned.

"And de crew" (he drank about half-a-pint), "and de cap'en's friends" (a little less), "and de bo'swain" (another half-pint), "and ole Zamp "(the last drain). "And now, chil'en, I'm berry grad to see you so spectful; hi, I feel berry 'lated. I think I could sing, if I knew de song and hab a voice. But, de cap'ens a fine buckra, and ole Zamp, wal, yo go along; I'm not 'toxicated—I—m—"

> "Dis nigger him what go to sea,
>   Ho—high—yo!
> For de galley cook to be,
>   Ho—high—yo!"

"Why, you infernal scamp," roared the boatswain, taking up the can; "he's drank the last drain of the purser's allowance, and is as drunk as the devil."

Tom Garrod emphasised this dictum by throwing the can at Zampa's head.

The latter received it on the scull it could not fracture, and was knocked down like a nine-pin and pitched over the bulwark souse into the sea.

The pirates looked over the ship's side, and laughed as they perceived Zampa spluttering and floundering in the surf.

But the nigger was three sheets in the wind, as well as over head in water.

Tom Garrod launched a grapnel at the end of a line, and dexterously caught the barb in the nigger's unmentionables, and, sprawling like a crab at the end of a string, Zampa was hauled upon deck amid uproarious shouts of laughter.

CHAPTER XCVI.

THE CASTAWAYS.

THE island on which the prisoners escaped from the "Black Vulture" had landed was a beautiful spot, about four square miles in area, and clothed with the loveliest and most luxuriant vegetation.

There was something so balmy and peaceful in the aspect of the surroundings, something so exhilarating in the freshness of the sea-breezes, that the heart could not but recover something of that elasticity with which nature has mercifully endued, even in the most distressing trials.

How much had they to be thankful for! How fairly might they hope for eventual rescue, and what an escape was theirs : the girls and the worthy Scotch skipper, from death or worse evils ; the pirates, from a life of crime, and, doubtless, the catastrophe of a shameful execution.

Besides, the party were well assorted ; Deborah and the Scotch lassie were charming girls of equal attractions, though of the opposite type of beauty : one dark and queenly as a southern night in summer ; the other fresh, bright, and artless as the simple dawn blushing on the crest of her native mountains. The men were manly fellows ; they had been misguided, it is true, but had neither of them taken part in the ruthless slaughter of Macallister's crew, and had paused in the beginning of their black career ; while the old Scotch skipper was a sensible, pious man, yet withal "canty" and genial.

The castaways had found a delightful cave, or rather series of caves, connected by rocky passages, in the hills that ran along the coast.

These natural grottos, that might have served as the home of some island Calypso, were festooned with flowering creepers, carpeted with moss, and perfumed with aromatic herbs.

Almost gleefully the little party had shared a breakfast, the concomitants of which were not by any means despicable. The girls had gathered some bread-fruit, and other spontaneous luxuries of the bounteous soil ; while Cassidy and Oakland had killed some wild-fowl in the woods, which they found to be teeming with game.

The old Scotchman, with quiet reverence, breathed a hearty prayer and thanksgiving to Heaven for their deliverance, and asked a blessing on the repast that came so directly from His bounteous hand. The men listened with serious and respectful air, and the girls fervently responded.

"And now, Mr. Macallister," said Oakland, "we must do 'business. What about setting up our signals ?"

"Weel, noo, I'm sure I canna think, my gude lad, that it's in the power o' flesh and bluid to endure a langsome, lonely life on a desert island, when there are so many great duties to be performed before the time 'time sall come ' when no mon can work ;' but I am afeared to be too bold wi' the signals, foreby, this is a canny spot, with gude headlands, and a fine offing, might we not not signal our foes into our midst ? the villain pirates can see a flagstaff and read the meaning o' a flag o' distress as well as honest men."

"You are quiet right, Mr. Macallister, Black Ralph is a shrewd fellow, and I know that he has every motive that can influence such a man to track us while the least hope remains. Now, there are two plans which I have to suggest, each founded on an opposite theory. In the first place, the Black Vulture may have suffered much in last night's squall, and may not be able to follow us. Our happy escape was almost miraculous ; the Vultures may conclude we were swamped by a heavy sea, therefore we had better take to the pinnace at once, and cross from island to island in order to elude pursuit. My next plan is that we should find ourselves a fastness somewhere inland, and lay close, while, in order further to delude our wary enemies, we might put some broken spars of the pinnace on the end of the reef, which can be reached at low water ; they will then then think we have perished, and, perhaps, give up the chase."

"I approve o' your last plan, Measter Cassidy ; so it sall be, the pinnace is nae seaworthy, and I canna think we suld gain much by rinning from ane island to anither like hunted sea-gulls."

"Then we will be off to the beach, and do what we can to deceive the wretches," said Cassidy.

"And we maun stay at hame and attend to the house ; we'll have everything braw and canny, when the gude men come the night," said Mary, with a merry smile.

"There is no need we should suffer for the rust of idleness," Deborah rejoined ; "we shall find enough to do in making nets and other necessary implements for our island life."

Oakland had left the cave.

He returned hurriedly.

His face was very pale.

"Do not be alarmed," he said, as collectedly as he was able to speak ; "but there are two ships in the offing ; they are tacking to windward !"

"Just Heaven !" cried Deborah.

"O, I canna bear to think that they suld tae us noo, after sic a providential deliverance," rejoined Mary ; "but, at least, I am free to die, and I will never be theirs if I can find freedom under the waves ; but we mauna be dashed, 'gin they could be made believe we're wrecked and perished they would nae trouble us mair."

"Humph ! they will assuredly land," said Cassidy, calmly ; "the pinnace bows are staved in, and with a fair cast the waves might have thrown her as far up on the beach as she is lying now. Miss Deborah, and you, Miss Mary, must be stowed away like costly treasures in the deepest and most inaccessible cave we can find ; we must garrison your stronghold with Mr. Macallister, who is an army in himself. I and Oakland are destined for more active service. Where are you, Ned ?"

"My God ! the long boat has been run up the little creek to the west of the island, and the crew have lighted a fire on the beach," cried Oakland, rushing back into the cave. "Black Ralph and Harwolf are coming this way, and I doubt not will enter the cabin. Come ! hurry, this way into the inner cell ; he may not discover the little winding rockway from the main cave."

The men took the girls by the hand, and placing them behind them, stood at the entrance of the inner cavern.

A gruff laugh was heard without : the blustering tones of Black Ralph and the sullen voice of Harwolf.

The pirate captains seemed to be sauntering into the hollow of the rock, as if to rest awhile ; but did not appear very anxious to examine the place.

Black Ralph was singing and ranting in his peculiar strain, and either was, or assumed to be, in good spirits,

"The black flag was hoisted, the schooner bore down,
    And the merchantman yielded to fate."

"I tell ye, Daniel, we shall overhaul them yet."

"Most likely we shall see them washed ashore or floating in the surf," rejoined Harwolf, surlily.

"A canny sight I wish to see."

"Poor devils; but I don't think that you'll have the gratification of glutting your mental maw with the sight of their water-logged carcases."

"They are better out of the way."

"Especially the Jewess, you think."

"I do so. And if you had not been a fool in the first instance, we should not have been cumbered with such a dangerous supercargo."

"There is something we all strive for, even the feeblest and meanest. And my something——"

"Is what?"

"My own way, comrade."

"Irrespective of my safety or the crew's?"

"Don't be splenetic, Daniel; I'm in no mood for a quarrel."

"Nor I," returned Harwolf.

"Stay you here," said Harwolf. "This is a likely spot—our birds may have taken refuge in some of these crannies."

"And what do you mean to do with them if you catch them?"

"For Deborah—I have acted more like a saint than a pirate with regard to her, and I meant well by her—now it has come to this: I will either put a ring on her finger or send a bullet through her heart."

"And what will you do with Oakland and Cassidy?"

"It all depends—make them walk the plank, most likely."

"And the old skipper?"

"I shall leave him 'monarch of all he surveys.' He'll be picked up by some barque or another."

"Pshaw! And you call yourself a vulture?"

"Yes; but vultures prey upon carrion, not upon eagles. I'm not squeamish; I could swab the decks with the blood of an enemy; but I must kill him fairly. I don't see the pleasure nor the profit of cooping a man up like a poulterer's chicken—first fatten, and then wring his neck."

"Well, you are headstrong, and I fear we shall all suffer for your perversity."

"Time will show. I shall return directly. Hark, there's a shout, the fellows have found the trail."

Black Ralph ran out of the cavern.

Wardlow and several ruffianly-looking pirates entered the cave.

"Are you agreed, mates?" said Harwolf.

"We are, captain."

"That's good."

"Teddy Macarthy and the cormorants will stick to him."

"How many of them came ashore in the jolly-boat?"

"Seven."

"We are thrice that number."

"Ay, captain."

"Ours, then, are the odds?"

"Ay, captain."

"There will be no wavering among ye. If any one wishes to recede, let him return to the boats."

"We've made up our minds, captain."

"You do wisely. Do you think the fugitives are ashore?"

"No, captain, they went down in the squall."

"How do you know?"

"I am sure of it."

"Upon what grounds?"

"The pinnace was scarcely sea-worthy."

"May be they made for the main-land?"

"No, captain; Cassidy is too deep for that."

"If I catch them I will clear off the lot."

"Right."

A man entered the cave.

"They are on the island, captain!" he said.

"Ha! is there proof of that?"

"Why, we have found the clearest tracks; and, more than all, the pinnace."

"In what condition is she?"

"Stoved in, captain; she looks as if she had been swamped."

"Well, you are all convinced that we have no safety but in the death of this swaggering filibuster, who is a traitor to us all."

"He is."

"He cares for nothing but to use us all as slaves to carry out his most absurd caprices."

"That's right; we'll cut him off."

"Follow, then."

"Captain."

"Well."

"We must contrive to separate him from the 'Cormorant's' company."

"We must."

"Do you think he suspects?"

"No—not he."

"Follow me, then, and be resolute."

The pirates left the cavern.

Cassidy and the rest stole out from their hiding places.

They looked in each other's faces with some anxiety.

Cassidy folded his arms.

The blood tinged his cheek, and his eye flashed.

He spoke.

"Mr. Macallister, this rascal, Black Ralph, has treated you badly; but his conduct, considering his calling and his utter want of self-controul, might have been worse."

"I canna tell; I know that he killed my crew and took my braw ship; that he is a villain out of the pale of human mercy."

"Yet, Harwolf is a greater villain; you shall run no risk. I once swore fealty to this bad man; it was a free-will act, and I cannot see him murdered in cold blood without an effort to save him."

"Weel, I dinna ken, Meester Cassidy, what your ain sentiments may be, but I'm thinking that when sic rogues fa' oot, it's better that suld destroy each other than that honest folk suld suffer."

"Yet murder is murder; and I cannot bear to feel myself even an involuntary cognizant of Black Ralph's assassination. He now rules the devils, and, blood-thirsty as he is, he has some good qualities, which may stand between some victim and death or dishonour. Harwolf is a very devil; a remorseless, sullen reprobate, whose nature is darker than the arch-fiends."

"You maun act as yer conscience guides ye, for you're a gude lad, and I will be o' the last to gainsay ye."

"Do you, then, keep in the inner cave; the entrance is so narrow that but one man can enter at a time, and we are well off for fire-arms."

"Be it sae; God bless ye, laddie; for the sake o' us a' ye'se nae 'rin into needless danger."

"I will not."

"Cassidy," said Oakland, "I am of your mind, and I think you would find partisans among the crew."

"I am a quiet fellow," returned the ex-mate of the pirate ship; "but whence it springs I know not. Perhaps I am insensible, but I am never afraid, and I possess, not the art, nor the knack, but the 'gift.' I suppose it is, of leading people; if this blackguard thief, who would have murdered us all in cold blood, proves too strong for his fellow rascal, why I'll try my powers of persuasion; but we must be subtle as redskins, or ruin will accrue to us all."

Cassidy smiled in his melancholy quaint manner, and held out his hand to Deborah, which the Jewess clasped warmly in her own.

"You will yet live to be a great man, Mr. Cassidy," she said, warmly. "Oh, if we were but once more in England. Well, you must be gone. Oh, for Heaven's sake, be prudent."

Cassidy smiled.

He drew Mary to his side.

The ingenuous Scotch lassie looked up into his face with beaming tearful eyes, and murmured gently,

"Ah! Mr. Cassidy, ye are a proud mon; but I tremble for ye; swords are sharp, and bullets deadly. Oh, dinna be unco rash and daring, for——"

"Oh, say it, Mary."

"Weel, then, for my sake."

"Do you love me, then?"

"Aye, laddie, ye ken it vera weel; sin ye're nae langer an awesome pirate, I love ye wi' a' my heart."

Cassidy pressed the girl to his breast; a happy smile flitted over his pensive face, and he beckoned to Oakland.

The two seamen took one of the winding passages of the cave, crawling over heaps of fallen stones, and, making their way through darkness and danger, for there were many deep crevices, and not a few well-like water-springs, at last they emerged in the open air.

A screw of bushes fortunately shaded the entrance of the cavern.

They lay close.

They heard voices.

They cautiously raised their heads.

A number of seamen were crouched beneath the bush.

They were conversing in low whispers.

Cassidy crept forth.

Oakland followed him.

The quiet Cassidy raised himself on his knee.

He turned to Oakland, his eye shining with a cold, bright light.

They were plotting the murder of Black Ralph.

"I don't care a curse if I do the same job for both on 'em."

"Nor I, mate; our ship might be well officered, if there were but one skipper."

"Aye, mate, and of the two I should prefer Talbot."

"So should I."

"But we've overhauled no prizes lately, and the other skipper offers to draw money from England to pay us."

"But Talbot's the boy for a cruise."

"The petticoats is his ruin."

"Allers so."

"But here they come, mate; clinch your barkers and lay close."

The men crouched low among the fern and flowery shrubs.

"Cassidy," whispered Oakland.

"What is it now?"

"How many are they?"

"Three."

"We're over-matched; but I will stick to old Ralph."

"So will I."

"Did you never warn him of treachery?"

"Yes; I left a letter in his pocket."

"Why, then, does he trust himself ashore with the Vultures?"

"He scorns that skulk, Harwolf."

"He's a damnable villain."

"Hist!"

Wardlow was seen entering the valley, followed by Black Ralph and Harwolf.

"You see, our search has been fruitless," said the latter.

"No, mate, I see nothing of the kind; I see that our search has been a cruise without rudder or compass. This swab, Wardlow, has put me on the wrong scent."

"Come, I am sick of this gull's chase; I return at once to the 'Vulture.'"

"Au revoir, then, my friend," returned Black Ralph, waving his hand impatiently. "Leave the gig; two men will row you out in the jolly. Send it back for the rest."

"Look you, Master Ralph, what do you take me for?" cried Harwolf, making a sign towards the bushes, and speaking in a hectoring tone.

"Look you, master Daniel; I'll show ye, in the twirl of a marlin-spike, what I take you for, and what I know you to be. You are an infernal, double-tongued, treacherous, cowardly hunk, only fit to swab the deck or feed the cuddy fire. Do you think I don't know what you are? But the men are mine; can you deny that?"

"I can—I do. You and the crew are mine; I bought you both—dearly I paid for you."

"Dam'me! you infernal Jew-killing, bilge-drinking, tallow-skinned crimp! Brag and murderer, draw your toasting-fork, or I'll spit ye on my own, and then break it as something too foul to wear, once stained with such gutter-blood!" roared Black Ralph, drawing his sword.

Harwolf sprang back.

He drew a pistol and levelled it at his colleague's head.

The pirate captain flew upon him.

The pistol exploded.

The bullet grazed Talbot's cheek.

"Come," he whispered, hoarsely, wiping off the blood as he spoke, "I see we cannot agree, Master Dan, therefore, in spite of your cowardly attempt to take the advantage of lead over steel, I'll fight you like a gentleman. If I kill you, I am commander-in-chief; if you kill me, I leave you my blessing and all my property. Lay on, Macduff, for, dam'me! if Sam Cassidy riled me, and I lost a good man for being over haughty, I'll not be commodored by such a skip-jack as Dan Harwolf."

Harwolf made another sign towards the bushes.

The men rose and aimed their muskets at Black Ralph.

"Ah! treachery! mutiny! Wardlow, stand to my side, and we'll skim the earth of this dirty scum with one sweep of raw steel."

Wardlow replied by raising his arm, and pointing his own pistol at Black Ralph's head.

Harwolf laughed bitterly.

"Et tu, Brute!" cried Black Ralph, fixing a stern glance upon his officer. "Well, fortune, do thy worst; I never feared death, and I am content to know the hangman will avenge me, and I only pray that you may all be spared for his good offices. Dam'me! fire; but if you attempt to taunt me, Dan Harwolf, I'll brain ye. I see you have stolen the caps from my nipples. Well, blaze away, fools! I can't leave you a hotter plague than your new leader."

"Fire!" shouted Harwolf.

What was his amazement that the two executioners of his treacherous orders threw up their arms and sank down.

The report of a brace of pistols rattled off among the rocks.

Cassidy and Oakland leaped over the bushes, and stood by the side of Black Ralph.

THE ATTACK ON THE JEW

CHAPTER XCVII.

THE TRAPPER AND THE JEW—KEEPING UP HIS
SPIRITS — THE INDIAN FRIEND — IROQUOIS
AND YENGEESE—THE RANGERS' PLOT—THE
ROBBERS ON THE TRAIL.

IN the far west, under the low-hanging branches of
grand, interminable forests, two men are riding on
their little shaggy horses, and merrily conversing.

The first is a tall, wiry fellow, with a shock of grey
hair and a beard sweeping his breast, a hooked nose,
and a piercing grey eye.

His companion was also tall, but stouter and more
youthful, his cheek sun-tanned and ruddy, his blue
eyes clear and rolicking.

By the side of the horsemen trotted a couple of
large, shaggy hounds, who made the old woods ring

No. 32.

with their bayings as they gambolled and bounded
ahead of their masters.

The cover was very dense; the mighty arms of the
monster trees interlaced, and the leaves formed an
almost impenetrable mass of verdure, only to be
pierced by the long oblique rays of the western
sun, that brightened up little patches of sward with
their light, and left the main part of the surrounding
scenery buried in the darkest shadow.

The road was rough and the soil various.

Sometimes the horses' hoofs rattled along stony
ground; sometimes the creatures sank above their
fetlocks in miry swamps.

Yet they spurred on, staying not for any obstacle.

The riders could not find much time for conversation, for they had enough to do to keep their saddles.

Every now and then the elder of the two would

check his horse, and turn his head with a startled air, as if to catch some warning of danger on the breeze.

He was reassured, however, by the quietude of the dogs and the derisive laugh of his companion.

"Wall now, really, stranger, I du say that you seem purty considerable anxious for a row with the rangers, or a brush with the Injins," said the younger, heartily laughing. "You seem a snuffin' the air like a springbok when there's wolves to the wind'ard. Whar's the use of pulling up to wait for danger that follers behind yer? Better keep on your path; it'll be less likely to reach yer, I opine."

"Yesh; thatsh all very well for you, my dear boysh, but its my monish. Thesh wolves can shmell the monish ash quick ash their four-footed brothersh can schent a sick buffalo. Holy Mosesh! what's that?"

"An antelope the dogs have started; they're plentysome these parts. The Pawnee-Loups have a good huntin' ground; it ain't much worked nohow; what with the cussed Blackfeet, and the cusseder Black Rangers, they've found the weather rather too hot for 'em. Lord, the scenes as I has seen in these yere parts, Mr. Simeon Abrahams, it licks reportin'. I were one of the fust, I reckon, with a white skin and a thick beard, as ever came into these settlements. I were pioneering then; I was paid tol'ably slick for blazin' these old stumps for a emigrant party; but, bless your soul, stranger, they all perished, every one on 'em. Not as I didn't act pathfinder to satisfaction; I got 'em here safe enough—didn't lose above half-a-dozen on 'em, and that was on the grand prairie, but when they was comfortably camped down, and might have increased and multiplied till further orders, may I be whipped if they weren't allers a aggravatin' the aborigin's, which was then as numerous as 'squitos, till one full moon the Sioux and the Arkansas riz and butchered every mother, son, and darter on 'em, and you may see their scalps a dryin' in every wigwam 'twixt here and Texas."

"The devilsh! I never could undershtand what they were made for."

"Wal, that's a argument, stranger. Injins is Injins, and if there warn't summat to keep down the population there wouldn't be seen so much as a single head of elk or bison in all the North'n States. You may depend upon it, Mr. Abra'ms, there's a time comin' when there won't be left sich a thing as a bustard or a prairie-fowl, unless, maybe, in some poultry-yard. Lord, what I have seen in these yere parts, and not so many years ago neither; but it's all changed now. Then there was nothin' but Injins, and now you can't go forty miles in any direction without comin' to some squattin' or other."

"Shtrike me if I should care if there wash a settlement at every forty yardsh," exclaimed Simeon, with fervour.

"Wal, you see, stranger, my prey is buffaloes and bars; yourn is yer feller creetur's. See that stump, stranger?"

"Yesh; ish there anythingsh behind it?"

"No, 'spects not, unless its a grissly; bars ain't scarce in this purty spot. But, keep up your sperits, stranger; I was going to tell you a narration along of that old stump. I seed the Injins brile an old feller there; he cheated the devils in tradin' for hides—gave 'em barrels of swamp-slush instead of firewater, I b'lieve. Howsomever, they roasted him."

"Oh, Father Abrahamsh! the devilsh! are there Indiansh in thesesh partsh now, Mr. Weatherfield?"

"They are as plenteous as bees a swarmin'. Ottos, Saqaes, Snakes, Flat-heads, Nez Percé, Shoshoné, Grand Pawnees, Pawnee-Loups, and Blackfeet; one an all on 'em as subtle as sarpints, and as eager to take the scalp of a pale-face as you are to pouch a dollar, stranger."

"S'help me!"

"But the cur'ous part of this yere narration war that the poor varmint as the infarnal Snakes grilled at a slow fire was one of your people—he was a Jew, stranger."

"Shtrike me deadsh if I don't go back againsh!"

"Wall, considerin' as you air a man as is fixed for adventurin', p'raps you might get a shot at some of the redskin devils; there's heaps on 'em behind us; they allers strike a trail from the Mississippi banks at this yere time of year; but, then, if we had better hosses, the chances is we should reach Mike Warren's plant afore they cotched us; as it ar, why you've got your piece and I ar got mine, though I think, stranger, your rifle's summut out of tune, and won't stand more nor a couple o' charges, and I arn't got but a pinch in my powder horn, and can count my bullets on my fingers. Wall, life's a oncertainty at all times to Jew or Christian, and 'spect you won't die harder nor any other creetur; so, cheer up yer sperits, Mr. Abra'ms."

The Jew groaned and looked about him in hopeless dejection.

One of the hounds crouched down and growled.

"Hi, Wolf! here, sir! down! what is it, boy?" cried the trapper. "Cheer up, stranger; it's only a Snake," he whispered, consolingly, to his companion.

"A Snake! we shall all be killed!"

"Wall, considerable like, it's a Injin; one o' your tribes old admirers, I 'spects. Hi! down, you brute."

A tall, slim Indian stepped from between the trees.

He appeared to be quite young, and was fantastically dressed in a blue hunting shirt embroidered with beads and quills; his buffalo robe flowed from his shoulders; about his neck was clasped a necklace of the claws of grissly bears; the long fringes of his moccasins swept the ground; his hair was gathered up into a scalping lock and ornamented with eagle's feathers; his cheeks were stained with paint, and he carried a long rifle in his hand, from which depended a beautifully worked baldric of dyed leather.

Nat Weatherfield, for such was the trapper's name, started in his seat and poised his gun in his hand.

"My brother's steps are counted; the young men of the Shoshoné are on his trail; Catahaga loves the pale-face; will my brother trust him?" said the Indian, waving his hand towards the west with native dignity, and unaffected grace.

"Whatsh he shay? Holy Moshesh! why don't yer shoot him?" cried the Jew, fumbling at his firelock.

"Be quiet, stranger; he is a Pawnee-Loup, and my friend," said Nat Weatherfield, impatiently.

"Eagle-Wing has not gone with the young men of the chief, his father; they are on the war-path; why does my brother stay in the wigwam?" asked the trapper, scrutinising the fine face of the young redskin with a steady look.

The Indian hung his head, and murmured,

"Catahaga loves the pale-faces; the great chief, my father, disowns Eagle-Wing, and the maidens of his tribe scoff him in their songs."

"The great sachem of the Pawnees has hardened his heart against the Yengeese; the Master of Evil has blinded his eyes, and his thoughts are black," said the trapper, gravely.

"Wah! my father is wise; the pale-face must not speak evil of him to Eagle-Wing," replied the youth, fiercely.

"And has my brother come to warn us of our danger?"

The Indian bowed his head, and said, with a bitter smile.

"The pale-faces think themselves wiser than the Iroquois; they send us medicine-men to teach us words of life from the great book of the Manitou, but they are bloodier in heart than the cruellest of our tribes; their tongues are forked; the wind that stirs the leaves in these forests change not as easily as their minds. I think their thoughts, I speak their tongue; I have mingled with them till my heart is become soft as the wax in the bees'-nest; my hand is clean from the blood of my enemies; I have no scalps in my girdle; my hatchet is not red; the chiefs of my tribe have forgotten me, and the young men call me the Squaw of the Pale-faces. I know them well, these Yengeese, and yet I love them!"

The young Indian bent his head and remained silent a moment.

"It is said that the chief, your father, has burnt the lodges of the new settlers, and has murdered their wives and little ones; and this, when the Yengeese had smoked the calumet with him. Is this well, my brother?" asked the trapper, seriously.

"Ugh! The heart of Catahaga burns with fierceness; his eyes see red; he is choked as by the smoke of the prairie-fire. Does my brother *believe* these lies of the lying white dogs—that the great nations have taken into their wigwams to be bitten by them. Does my brother believe these words?" cried the Indian, in a tone of poignant grief and fury.

"The Yengeese say it is true, and the friendly Saques saw the braves of the Pawnee-Loups, mounted on their mustangs and smeared with war-paint, riding towards the Salt Lake beyond the Graftonville the night of the massacre," said the trapper.

"Had all the pale-faces that ever crossed the Great Salt Lake to blight the land of the Iroquois one throat, my father would slit it," cried the Indian, in fierce derision; "but Elkhorn has lived in my father's lodge, and if his tongue is single and not forked, he will confess that the chief of the Pawnee-Loups is no Shosoné dog, that will raise his tomahawk or feed his fire-weapon against those over whom he has spread his blanket, with whom he has smoked the pipe of peace."

The trapper shook his head and looked dubious.

"Has my brother ever mixed with a herd of live buffalos by dressing in the head and hide of one he has killed?" asked the Indian, suddenly.

"I have."

"Cannot the pale-face bear the weight of a blanket? Is a turbo of wampums too heavy for his neck? Would his brow carry a bundle of grosbeak's feathers? Would his cheek be scorched by the smear of war-paint? Wah! Let my brother answer!"

Nat Weatherfield started and turned deadly pale.

"Does Catahaga think, then, that the bloody wolves who burnt the lodges of the slumbering Yengeese were *pale-faces*, and not red-skins?" he asked, with a gasp of conviction, for he had lived long among the Indian tribes, and was well acquainted with their customs and prejudices, and knew that, though treacherous in many respects, they were ever strongly bound by the laws of hospitality and confederacy, and never violated them unless provoked by the bad example set by the whites. So astounded was he by the suggestion made thus naively by the young Indian, that he forgot his own danger, and stood lost in conjectures.

"The great sachems of my brother's nation in their big wigwam of the Mississippi were very bitter against the Pawnee-Loups when it was told that they had taken scalps of the settlers. And the war-chiefs sent many red-coats to the great valley with large and small fire-weapons; the prairie grass grows rich, for it is nurtured with the blood of my fathers, my brothers, and my sisters. Yet Catahaga remains in the lodges of the Yengeese; the squaw of the pale-faces loves this nation of serpents."

"Wal, its enough to rile a Jew! What say, Mr. Simeon, this yere cussed trick of the infernal rangers?" asked Nat, turning to his companion.

"Why, boysh! how should I know watsh you're talkin' about? Thinksh I understandsh your outlandish gibberish? Holy Moshesh! are we going to stopsh here till night? Didn't the Indiansh shay that the Schnakes were on our own trail? S'help me, they shall take my life, but I keepsh my monish."

"Tarnation, stranger; right you are. What can I be thinkin' on?" exclaimed the trapper. He then addressed the Indian in the Iroquois.

"Did not my brother warn me that the Snakes were on our trail?" he asked.

"*Snakes*, but not Shoshoné—serpents, but not red-skins," returned the other, contemptuously, and speaking throughout in the tongue of the more civilised tribes, the vocabulary of which was greatly

improved and elaborated by contact with the Europeans. "My skin is growing white," he added, with a quaint, sad smile.

He started.

His attitude was very graceful and striking, his appearance strangely picturesque, as his native instincts revived by the emergencies of the hour. He stood, his fine head slightly bent, his hand half raised, his wild, gamish eyes fixed, his body lightly poised, listening intently, like a startled deer.

"Ugh!"

As he gave vent to the guttural utterance he dropped on one knee, and laid his ear against the bank.

With a light bound he sprang to his feet.

"The dogs are many!" he said. "My brothers must fly; let them take the river; Eagle-Wing will remain to throw dust in the eyes of their pursuers."

"Oh, my monish! by the twelve tribesh, I shall loshe my monish!" cried the Jew, in great agony of soul.

"Let my brother give me his money," said Catahaga, in good English. "It shall be safe with me."

"Ah, thievesh, they will robsh me of my monish!" cried Simeon, folding his coat lightly over his breast. "No, my good young monsh, much obligesh; your intentionsh may be very goodsh, but nobody must protect my monish but myself; I cannot permitsh you to shuffer for me or my monish!"

"Look you here, stranger; if you ain't a fool, you'll take a good offer; in the red-skin's possession the money's as safe as it would be in the best bank in New York," said the trapper. "Take my advice; don't run the risk of losing it. No one would suspect a Pawnee of having a fortun' of dollars in his pouch; but a Jew, the very name reminds one of jewels; there's a richness in the sound of it. You know you can't fight!"

"Not for my monish! I can die for my monish!" cried the Jew, clutching his breast with his crossed hands, while his eyes sparkled with avarice.

The trapper laughed heartily.

"Eagle-Wing will not carry the money under his pinions, nor defend it with his beak," he said, merrily. "The old vulture has got it in his crop, and the rangers will cut his throat to get at it."

"It is good," said Catahaga, gravely bowing his head, a humorous smile playing on his lips.

"And now let my brother show us our path, and let him conceal our trail," said the trapper.

Catahaga took the bridle of the Jew's horse, and led them towards a river.

He pointed across the wide stream.

"My brother sees the oak against that red cloud?"

"On the bluff of the hill yonder? It is good. Eagle-Wing, is that the path to the squatting of Michael Warren!"

Catahaga started.

"Does my brother's path lead to the lair of that wolf?" he exclaimed, with emphasis.

"Wolf!" repeated Nat Weatherfield, in surprise.

"I call him the 'grey wolf,' but if his hair is frosted his teeth are not blunted. Let not my brothers go to his lodge, he will set his fangs in their throats while they sleep."

It was a strange coincidence that Andrew Harwolf, in his changed guise, should receive the soubriquet of the "Wolf" from a simple Indian in the back-woods of the Far West.

"But do not both the Yengeese and the red-skins speak good of this man? Is he not honoured by all who know him?"

"By all who do *not* know him."

"Eagle-wing, I have business with this man; I must see him," said the trapper.

"It is good," said Catahaga, quietly. "My brothers will swim their horses over the river; when they have reached the opposite bank they will direct their course by yon clump of firs. Wagh! my brothers must fly; the Snakes are upon them."

"Oh, my monish! I shall be a beggar—a misherable beggar. I shall loshesh my monish," cried the

Jew, in great terror, as he galloped his horse to the bank, and was the first to plunge into the stream.

The trapper leaped his horse after him.

He turned, and waved his hand to the Indian.

"I will follow my brother as soon as I have concealed the trail," said the Indian. "Let him not forget the words of the Pawnee; his path is before him."

Nat Weatherfield turned to speak once more to the Indian, but he had vanished.

The trapper urged his horse, and was soon breasting the stream by the side of the trembling Jew, while on either side the dogs were easily pushing their way through the wide, deep waters.

———

CHAPTER XCVIII.

THE RANGERS—THE INDIAN TO THE RESCUE—THE JEW LOSES BY HIS MISTRUST—AN OLD FRIEND IN A STRANGE GUISE.

IT was a wild spot where the fugitives landed.

The banks were covered with sedges as high as the canes in the brake, and almost as impenetrable as a stack of bamboos.

It was only by dint of breaking and cutting away through the tall reeds, which were scorched almost to dust by the ardent heat of the summer sun, and were therefore rendered brittle; it was only by the most fatiguing pioneering that the two men could drag their horses through the cover.

At length they reached the open plain.

They spurred their horses, and darted onwards towards the clump of trees the Indian had indicated.

The day was waning.

The shadows were lengthening before the declining sun.

The purple tint of the sky deepened.

A few bright stars broke out.

Still they urged on their horses.

Nat Weatherfield observed that the river made a bold curve into the plain.

He divined that the Pawnee-Loup would be able to cut off at least a league of the distance by crossing the river at a favourable point.

As yet they saw no signs of the Indian.

They reined their horses and began to breathe more freely.

The trapper had fallen into a reverie.

Few words were exchanged between the riders.

Nat Weatherfield began to speculate on the possibility of the Indian's assertion concerning the trick played by the blood-thirsty and marauding rangers being founded on national prejudice.

The Jew was counting the moments and quivering in every nerve lest something should happen to deprive him of his money.

They had reached the trees, and had plunged into the shade.

The dogs were running before them.

The animals suddenly stopped, yelped, and bayed deeply, and then came bounding back to their masters.

There was a crackle among the bushes.

The Jew gave a cry of horror.

The dark muzzle of a long rifle was directed full at his head.

He reined back his horse.

It reared and plunged.

The fellow who threatened the lives of the travellers appeared to be a ferocious-looking savage in all the bravery of blanket, feathers and war paint.

Two guns were fired simultaneously.

One from the savage in the bushes, the other from an invisible in a tree behind the travellers.

The savage in the bushes dropped his gun.

He bounded into the air, clutching at his forehead.

He fell upon his back.

Two other savages now appeared among the bushes.

Before either of them could raise their guns to

their shoulders Nat Weatherfield levelled his weapon and fired.

One of the men was hit and sank down.

The other took to his heels and fled.

The hounds shot after him.

The trapper followed them, loading as he went.

The Jew had slipped from his horse.

He was about to remount when he felt himself seized about the throat with a vice-like grip.

He struggled and was brought to the ground.

He wrestled for a moment, but found himself so firmly held that he could not move.

A knife was placed at his breast.

He snatched at it with his hands.

They were gashed.

He felt that a heavy pocket-book was cut away and torn from his pocket; had his heart been rent out with it he would have scarcely suffered more anguish.

A shot was fired at the savage just as he was about to draw his knife across the Jew's throat.

The bullet, however, did no more than graze his cheek.

The blood flowed freely.

He sprang to his feet.

He dodged among the trees.

The Jew raised himself on one hand.

He saw that two men were firing at the robber.

They were the trapper and Catahaga.

The darkness was deepening, and the brushwood was very thick.

None of the bullets appeared to reach their mark.

"Oh, my monish! the thiefsh! I will give you half my monish if—if you will shave me shome of it," shrieked the Jew. "What for should I loosh my monish? Here ish my horsh; oh, shave my monish!"

"Wal, it's tol'ably sartain, stranger, as ye'll never see your monish again; but if I were to cry over every 'possum I've fired at and never hit, or every coon I have hit and never cotched, my eyes would run like the source of Missouri. Cheer up, keep up your sperits; I told you as we hadn't come to the end of our pilgrimage, nor more we ain't, now; you arn't briled yet, so there's summut in store for you, any how; keep up your sperits."

"Ah, my monish! So poor ash I am, so dr-readful poorsh. Holy Abraham, I will die! Why should I live without my hard earnsh monish?"

"Come, mate, keep up your sperits," cried Nat, raising him.

But his "spirits" had apparently fled, for the Jew sank down in a "faint" that was not feigned.

Eagle-Wing touched the trapper's arm.

Nat Weatherfield followed him.

They stooped over the fallen body of one of the bandits.

He laid on his back and groaned.

A bullet had lodged in his shoulder.

The Indian poured some water from the little calabash hung at his side on the face of the wounded man, and wiped off the paint.

The face was that of a white man.

Eagle-Wing, with flashing eyes, raised his tomahawk.

Nat clutched his wrist.

"I do zay, yer hanner, the doamed gipsy be dead. I dreamed he were," cried the wounded man, in his delirium; "and I do zay az I be vit to hact real red Injun in Richardson's show at the country vairs."

The red Indian was our old friend Joe Miles.

———

CHAPTER XCIX.

A NEW LIFE — DEAD SECRETS — A STRANGE GUEST—AN IMPENDING DANGER.

LET the reader imagine himself in the interior of a large and comfortable apartment in a log-house, the new home of Andrew Harwolf, whom we must henceforth recognise under the name of Michael Warren, or, as he was called in the settlement, Judge Warren.

The room was decidedly handsome and imposing, for though the walls were not adorned with rich satin paper, brilliant gilding, or artistic mouldings, they were not without ornamentation.

Hangings of Indian gilt-work, and of richly-coloured blankets; heads of elks, with wide-branching horns; spears, boat-hooks, tomahawks, and trophies of arms, glittered in the light of clear-burning lamps that hung from the ceiling; while on an ample hearth blazed a mighty cheer-giving log-fire.

The ground was carpeted with rugs of skins and furs, and the furniture was of massive but finely-grained wood.

In a large easy-chair, before the blazing fire, Judge Warren was seated.

He was alone.

His cruel, grey eyes, reflected the red gleam of the spluttering flames.

His long fingers, twined together, rested upon his knees, and he seemed to be buried in deep reveries.

On one side of the room, in an old oak case, was a large clock.

The hammer loudly and discordantly struck nine.

A black fellow, very neatly dressed, entered the room.

"Massa Leighton wish to spek yo, sar," said the nigger, bowing his head.

"Tell him I am at his service," said Warren.

The servant left the room, and his voice was heard without.

"Massa Leighton, Judge Warren am at you sarvice, sar. Please, sar, yo walk dis way."

A tall, handsome young man, with a dark face, a glossy black moustache, and rich curly hair, entered the room.

He was dressed in a blouse of dark colour, braced at the waist with a belt fastened by a plain brass buckle, on either side of which were rests for a pair of revolvers, which he now wore; he carried his palm hat in his hand.

"Sit down, Mr. Leighton. Zip, bring us an eye-opener," cried Warren, to the negro.

"Iss, sar," replied the darkie, and hurried away.

"Mr. Warren, I beg to congratulate you," said Leighton, with a smile.

"Indeed! On what occasion?" said the judge.

"This is the anniversary of your arrival at the settlement."

"It is; a memorable day with me!" resumed Warren, smiling. "But it is kind of you to think of me."

"It was my uncle's intention to have given a feast, but this devilish affair of the Pawnee-Loups has spoiled all. My poor cousin Edward, among others, was shot by the bloodthirsty red devils, whom it is a Christian duty to exterminate."

The negro entered with the cordial, and Warren filled a glass, and passed it to his guest.

"Well, we will drink destruction to the destroyers, and peace to the peaceful," said Warren. "But are you sure the settlers are not to blame? It seldom happens that a fair inquiry fails to show that the natives have been exasperated by some act of injustice or aggression."

"In this case nothing of the kind can be charged against the whites," said Leighton, warmly; "they were apparently on the best of terms with the treacherous redskins. It is true that the Pawnee chief, Monotah, is an inveterate hater of the pale-faces, and wished the tribes to declare war to the knife against the whole settlement, and has discarded his son, Eagle-Wing, for marrying that foolish girl, Minna Wyotte, who is also abandoned by her friends, on the same grounds; so that they must be a lonely couple. But I was saying the Pawnee chief, Monotah, or the White Pine, as they call him so aptly, from his arrow-straight figure and his silvery hair, was over-ruled by the sachems of council, and signed the treaty with the rest. No, the Indians are a set of reptiles, that ought to be swept off the earth like other vermin; they are not men, but biped-beasts, and there ought to be a reward set on the head of

each of them, and an order of honour ought to be conferred upon the man who killed a hundred of them, and a pension be awarded to him who knotched a thousand."

"You are bitterly hostile to the poor creatures, Leighton," said Warren, shaking his head, deprecatingly. "I would urge you not to forget that they are our fellow-creatures."

"So are wolves, and pumas, and other brutes of prey; but we spare them none the more for that."

"But we have evil passions, as well as these poor wretches."

"So we have. But we have good ones, too. These painted fiends have nothing but evil qualities, our own, perhaps, but fearfully aggravated and quite unrestrained."

"I never heard any one speak so bitterly against the natives."

"I have reason enough to hate them. Poor Ned! shot down like a dog by these hellish rascals, in the dead of the night!—and on the night succeeding the day when my uncle received the ungrateful copper-skin cut-throats with boundless hospitality. Well, I'm glad to learn the troops made fine havoc among some of the branch tribes of the Grand Pawnees, and drove them almost to the foot of the Rocky Mountains."

"I will see to them; we must have a regularly organized corps in the village for checking the villanous thieves in their depredations, for repulsing the scouring parties of the Blackfeet, and for other useful service. If once the rascals are allowed to think they can perpetrate with impunity such atrocities as those they were guilty of on the night of the massacre at Graftonville we shall never be safe an instant; our lives will not be worthy a picayune. We must raise a corps of volunteers, and promptly."

"Well done, Mr. Warren," cried Leighton, in a laughing tone; "you will live to be President!"

A peculiar smile flitted faintly across the judge's face; he shook his head, and then said, suddenly,

"But there was a subject of interest, at least, I understood you so, on which you wished to ask my advice; if you remember, we found no time to discuss the matter then; suppose we undertake it now."

Leighton's cheek reddened a little.

"Well, Mr. Warren, you have always been kind to me, and I have the utmost confidence in your goodness of heart and your excellent judgment, so I will confide in you freely. You know that my father has from her childhood protected his sister's child, my cousin, Agnes Staunton. Now, my uncle Staunton had a friend to whom he was devotedly attached, and who died in defending him during the war; this friend had a son to whom my uncle promised to wed his daughter Agnes when she should be of marriage-able age; the boy and girl were affianced, and their betrothment was ratified by a mutual oath between the parents. Now, the young affianced husband turned out to be the veriest scamp in creation—a spendthrift, a duellist, a gambler, a libertine, and, at last, after trying my father's long-suffering patience to the last degree, he was turned out of the house as an incorrigible reprobate."

"And what was his name?"

"The scoundrel is of French extraction; I should think, of good family. I know his name is Oswald Lamond."

"Ha—ha! I have heard of him; he is a horrible rascal."

"Horrible——"

"He has been charged with forgery, has he not?"

"Tried and acquitted. He has been charged with every cardinal crime short of murder, and he might be held guilty of that, for he has used the bowie-knife most savagely on more than one occasion."

"Well, but he does not trouble you now."

"Not only have we lost sight of him, but we never hear of him now," returned Leighton.

"Well, then, how does he stand in your way?"

"Why, you see, the 'oath of betrothment,' if I must call it so, still remains uncancelled. My father is a man strangely punctilious, and will not suffer

Agnes to marry me, though I have won her affections, while this unheard of scamp is alive."

"But that is unreasonable. Surely her father did not contemplate her wedding such a villain; he has forfeited all right, and, with it, all claim to her hand, and it is only proper that she should be given to one more deserving."

"Ah, Mr. Warren, if my father possessed your keenness of apprehension and your liberality of principle, there would then be no obstacle to our complete happiness."

"Humph!—this is distressing. But I am sorry, my dear Mr. Leighton, that I must own I can see no way in which I can help you."

"Your influence with my father is very great. If you would make out a good case for me, you might prevail upon him to relax his scruples."

"I will see what can be done."

"You have my heartiest thanks, though thanks are an inadequate return for such great kindness," returned the young man, earnestly.

"But, perhaps, this young wretch is dead."

"I wish I could be as sure of that."

"Or he may be undergoing ignominious punishment for some of his rascalities."

"That is more than probable."

"In that case, I should think your father could not remain obdurate."

"But, how am I to ascertain?"

"Well, I will prosecute inquiries for you; but I will not be held responsible for their successful issue. Of course, they may, and probably will, fail in their purpose."

"Your kindness will not be diminished by their failure, Mr. Warren," returned Leighton.

"Well, you may depend on me for doing my utmost to find out all you require to know respecting him. But, are you sure the young lady loves you?"

"I have every reason to think so."

"Keep up a brave heart, for remember a faint one never won fair lady."

"I will be hopeful, and trust in you; so permit me once more to raise my glass in congratulating with you the anniversary of your welcome arrival, and to wish you a long life, that you may number many more returns of this day. Your health, Mr. Warren!"

"And yours, with all my heart, and a sincere wish that your 'course of true love may run smoothly,' in spite of the adage."

"Many, many thanks. And now, good night!"

"Good night, Mr. Leighton; we will renew this subject on your next visit, which, I hope, will be early. Good night! Steer clear of the rangers and the Pawnee."

"I wish I could meet with them; I'd chalk my few, I'll warrant," returned the young man, briskly, laying his hand on his revolvers.

"Where is that fool, Miles?" exclaimed Warren, when left alone.

He paced the floor impatiently.

"Why does he linger? Has he met with any misadventure? I trust not. A year, a brief year, and I am Judge Warren, the most respectable man in the little colony. And year may succeed year in this my place of refuge and regeneration, and the past may still remain a dead letter. Yet, why could I not give up my old habits? Why can I not restrain from mingling with criminals in their dark ventures? No; there is all that manliness can want, even to luxuries, in this new home; but there is the gipsy in England; he knows that I am here. I must begone, but not yet. I must prepare another refuge as before, and each of my nests shall have a thicker lining of gold than the last. Ah, I am chuckling as if I bore a charmed life, and were invulnerable! I hate these moods; a haughty spirit presages a speedy fall; and I notice always that when I have been hugging myself for general prudence, I am sure to have to curse myself for some particular folly or oversight. Why does not Miles return?"

Warren looked at the clock.

He started to see that it was getting late.

He returned to the fire, and stood before the blaze, his hands behind him, listening to the wind soughing dolefully among the grand and ancient trees that surrounded his house.

The negro servant entered the room.

"Strange gen'm, sar, wish spek to yo. Nebber seen him afore, sar. Him ruffle up in berry long cloak; him eyes under de brim ob his hat. Berry cur'ous parson. Dogs no like de look ob him; dey bark most fur'ous. Shall I tell him massa 'ceive him, sar?"

"Was he on horseback, Zip?"

"No, sar. Him got off him hoss."

"Bring him in."

The servant ducked his head, left the room a few minutes, returned, ushering in a tall, slight young fellow, with dark blue eyes, and yellow hair; he was pre-eminently handsome, and as he shook back the folds of his long black mantle, he displayed a fine and symmetrical form, that was perfect in every grace of manly beauty.

He walked forward with a jaunty air, his spurs jingling.

"Hi, Sambo!" he said, turning to the negro.

The darkie's real name was Sempronius, and he tossed up his woolly head with the indignant disdain that "Alfreda Matilda" might display on being addressed as "Sally."

The strange guest rattled the tumblers on the table.

"The glasses are out. Let us have brandy-smash, and some buffalo-hump, done to perfection, with a seasoning of yams and salmon-row. Be spry, you nigger."

The negro gasped with wrath at this scandalisation of his dignity, and shambled off on trembling legs to execute the orders.

"Warren," said the youth, stretching himself, languidly, "I'm as tired as a dog, and as hungry as a wolf. The cold air has swept me in an out, and I faminate."

"And what brings you to the 'Larches' to-night, Regan?" asked Michael Warren.

"A devil of an affair, I assure you. But here comes 'the feed.' I like Americanisms, they're so graceful, so expressive. Good-bye, for the present. My mind soars off with the exquisite aroma of the steam that curls up so coyly and invitingly—ha! soft as a woman's heart, white as a lily's petals! Are you a gourmond, Warren?" asked the young man, slicing away at the dainties before him.

"No. I hate sensuality."

Regan put down his knife and fork, threw himself back in his chair, and laughed long and heartily.

"Oh! Michael, for charity sake, don't, pray don't spoil my 'feed.' 'I hate sensuality!' In any shape, eh! Michael. You don't prize wealth, wine, or women. Stoic philosopher, you are impervious to the weakness that afflicts your fellow mortals."

"But what affair did you allude to, as being the cause of your visit to the 'Larches?' I thought it was agreed that you should not come here."

"Where's Thornton?" asked Regan, abruptly.

"He should be at home," replied Warren, "long ago. I cannot conceive the reason of his delay."

"How many of the band are with him?"

"Twelve, Regan. They are on an easy mission. I don't see how they can fail."

"An easy mission. What is it?"

"Simply to waylay a Jew and a trapper, who are travelling from Graftonville to the 'Larches.'"

"An easy mission!" cried Regan, bursting into a derisive laugh. "The Jew was coming here. Why not have 'spoiled' the Hebrew on your own ground? and, if it had been needful, why you could have cut his weasand here as well as elsewhere. None would have been the wiser. You could have led the people on the plant to suppose that he had left the house, and no more would have been said or thought of him."

"And what could I have done with his carcase?"

"Burnt it!"

"No. No skeleton in my home!" cried Warren,

with a visible shudder. "Do you think I could breath the air polluted by his corse? No, I will keep my floors clean, and my house unhaunted."

"Pish! there are ways to get clear of carrion; there's a furnace now, Master Warren!—why, you might give the old fellow a classic funeral, and burn him on that log pyre, then treasure his ashes in an urn, and keep it in your bedroom as the old Roman wives and doxies did the cinders of their husbands and fancy men."

Warren turned away his head; the lurid flames lighted a face distorted with horror; a cold creep of self-loathing and mortal dread caused him to recoil from the hearth-side with a sort of gurgle in his throat.

"You shudder, Master Warren," said Regan, with a laugh, and dipping a biscuit in his cordial, and eating it with *nonchalance.*

"Yes, with horrible disgust!" cried Warren, emphatically. "Your jests are not in good taste, Regan."

"It's considerable certain I'd rather you had cannibalised him, than given him the chance of escape; he 'wants his monish.' Pish! pluming and war-painting to filch a handful of dollars from a snipe of a Jew; all of the gang concerned in the silly business ought to be tarred and feathered!"

"What! has it miscarried?"

"No, it 'carried' well enough, it wasn't so heavy as all that, though it was a tolerably round sum; but he'll get it back, every stiver of it, for we shall have him reading lamentations Sunday and workday till he has it, for 'justice is his plea,' and, if he 'please,' his plea will be admitted; however, it will give you a chance of coming out strong; it will serve right well as a blind. Yes, so far so good; but it's provokingly annoying this mishap of of Thornton."

"What are you talking of, Regan?—has anything befallen Miles—I mean Thornton?" cried Warren.

"Miles Thornton is shot!"

"Humph!" muttered Warren, as if he were uncertain in his mind as to whether the news was or was not to be considered distasteful.

Regan's bright blue eye flashed keenly, and his pouting womanish lip curved with a satanic sneer.

"Shot, but not chalked; winged, but not bagged.'

"Then he lives, he lingers; there will be parsons and fools about him—there will be a death-bed. Con—— Regan, I will put on my hat and cloak; we must visit him at once; ruin is on the wing of every flying moment. Where is he? Was he taken in his Indian gear? Does he rave?—does he speak?—does he talk of me? Come, we'll be off! I will call Zip; he shall saddle horses on the instant!"

Warren seemed to have lost his presence of mind, and paced about in great excitement.

"Phew! what a hallabaloo about nothing; sit ye down, commander, while I read my dispatches. Miles Thornton was rescued by me, and is now lying in safe quarters.

"Why did you scare me then?"

"Scare you? I thought you had more nerve. I told you he was not 'bagged;' sit down and listen, while I light a manilla, and mix the brandy-smash."

Warren flung himself on a seat and tossed some logs on the fire.

"I suppose you know that though I have spent most of my time, for the last two years, either beyond the Rocky Mountains, or on the Yellowstone, where I had the pleasure of making your acquaintance, Mr. Warren, that I have connections here, at Larchville."

"Indeed, I was not aware of that."

"No! a fact, I assure you. I am connected with the Leighton family."

"Is it possible?" cried Warren, with a start. "I shall not wonder if you tell me you are—Oswald Lamond."

"The very 'Simon Pure,'" returned Regan, laughing.

"Oswald the reprobate! Oswald the out-cast!"

"Did you ever hear me spoken of?"

"Yes, and in the most gratifying terms," returned Warren, with a grin. "You seem to have created quite a sensation in the settlement. The hard name they give is always supplemented with 'unheard of,' 'unparelleled,' 'transcendant,' and the girls——"

"Ha! the sweet solaces of mortal care! Heart-shrined idols of man's adoration! What do the *girls* say of me?"

"Negatively they pay you the highest compliment."

"Indeed! Don't mind my blushes; what do they call me?"

"A perfidious monster!"

"Ha, ha, ha! adorable charmers. How refreshingly piquante is the manner in which they testify their admiration. I wish I could love; but there is something so awfully serious in your heavy loves, that it gives me the heart-burn to think of falling in this 'slough of despond.'"

"It is good for you that you cannot love, for you have a dangerous rival."

"Ah!"

"In Mark Leighton."

A beautiful carnation flush spread on the cheek and forehead of the handsome young villain, and he said with a subtle gleam of malice in his azure eyes,

"Let the fellow persecute my Agnes. She is mine! By the oath of the dead; by the betrothment of the living; and she loves me!"

"And you love her?"

"And, if I do! she is mine. But, as I said before, love is not for my market. Yet she adores me," he added, musingly.

"Do you think so?"

"How can she help it? Am I not an Adonis, an Apollo, or an Antinous—one of those A-one's that are so hard-worked by the scribblers? Look at me now; take my points, and tell me whether I am not a lover for a princess. To these grand qualifications I add a cool head, a false heart, a warm hand, and a silver tongue; I am brave as a lion, and a CAPTAIN OF BUSH-RANGERS! Am I not, *par excellence,* a lady's man?"

"But we are wandering from our business," said Warren, impatiently.

"Aye, true. Well, in this round-about fashion I have given you a hint of the notions that induced me to visit the 'Larches.' As I was crossing the prairie, this side the river, I heard the sound of shots among the trees. and, spurring forward, I soon encountered a couple of rascals running as fast as antelopes from the prairie-fire; they were dressed like Pawnee-Loups, but were more like scare-crows. I called to one of them to stop. I was not deceived in them for a moment. He would not halt. I blazed at him, not with the intention to pink him, but to bring him to a stand. He stopped; he told me that he and his comrade had attacked the Jew and the trapper, but that they had been driven off their prey by a party of real Pawnees. I swore at, and roasted, the skulking curs, till they gathered round me, determined to redeem the day. I had rallied the lot except two—one killed, the other winged: this Miles Thornton. Well, we charged into the bush; the war-party of Pawnees, like the old woman's ocean of cats, had dwindled into one brave, and that one the whity-brown, semi-civilised Pawnee, Catahaga the Eagle-Wing, the husband of Minna Wyotte. Miles Thornton lay on his back; the Pawnee-Loup, with a little of the old devil in him, had raised his hand to scalp your confidant, but the trapper gripped his wrist, seemingly amused by the poor scamp's mutterings. The Jew had fainted with anguish at the loss of the 'monish.' A couple of charges from my whistler spoilt the pretty tableau. The trapper and the red-skin carried off the Jew, and we recovered our wounded, whom we carried off to Ronald Holme's plant."

"Did the Indian recognise Miles Thornton?"

"I don't think so; his hair was thrust back, his face shaved, his cheeks ruddled with ochre. And yet it will be known that the Pawnee-Loups are counterfeited, and a rigid inquisition will be made for the culprits."

"Of course; but, who will conduct the inquiry?"

"Judge Warren, to be sure; and then what a field for your patriotism. You can produce the body of the poor devil that got his billet, swear that he was one of the assassins killed by yourself or your agents—the poor wretch is but a friendless rowdy, a recruit; you can restore the Jew his heavy bunch of dollars, and you will be voted into the Senate."

"A good plan, Regan, if the red-skin does not baulk us."

"Bah! We can settle him off at the expense of a leaden pill—a pinch of saltpetre."

At this moment the negro once more rushed into the room.

"Berry much 'sprised, sar; more company 'rive to-night, sar; two more gen'ms, both on 'em in a reg'lar fit of 'plexy; swar at dis niggar, sar, 'cos him say dat Massa War'en couldn't 'ceive 'em. Reg'lar mad, sar."

"Hi, you Sambo!" cried Regan.

"Sempronius, if you please, sar," amended the nigger, bowing stiffly, and then drawing himself up with sublime hauteur.

"Confound you, 'Sar!' who are these strangers?"

Before the negro could answer Nat Weatherfield and the Jew hurriedly entered the room.

Regan jumped up, turned his back upon the new comers, and, without looking round, walked with affected carelessness to the door of an adjoining room, which he opened and passed through.

The Jew threw himself on his knees at Warren's feet.

"You are Mishter Warrensh. I have heard of you; you vill give me justish. You are a good sharitable shentleman; I shee it in your fashe. I shall go madsh—raving madsh! I am a poor man—I am dr-dreadful poorsh; not a shtiver but I earn it hardsh, very hardsh. It is murdersh! treasonsh! felonysh! I am robbed—killed. Ah, my monish! two thousand dollarsh, Mishter Warrensh — my hard-earned monish! You offer to shell me shome peltries; they were not sheap, but I brought your monish, and now I am robsh. O, Father Abrahamsh! let me have justish on the thievesh and villainsh and I will sherve you with my lifesh."

"My good sir, this is a strange hour to make your complaint; but you shall have justice, never fear. I will head the regulators myself, and hunt down the thieves, if you think you can identify them."

"Ah, you are a fine mansh, a noble mansh. I am so poorsh; if you vill recover my monish I vill kish the shole of your shoe."

"And when and where did this robbery take place, and what was the appearance of the robbers?" asked Warren of the trapper.

"Wall, judge, I calkilate that the spot whar this infarnal business tuk place were chosen by considerable 'cute chaps; it war just the sort of spot for a ambush. As for the ranger-cusses, for sich they war, I reckon they were actin' Pawnee-Loups, feathered and painted for a war-party; but I'm too old a cock-o'-the-woods to be caught with sich beastly chaff. One on 'em we knocked off his perch."

"Could you swear to him?" asked Warren, rather eagerly.

"Wall, judge, I could swear *at* him, tol'able inclining, if sich were proper; but as to swearing *to* him, further than that he war no Pawnee, I couldn't kinder be convicticated about his indentification; but my mate, the Injin, says he could know him kinder anywhar."

"Indians will swear to anything," said Warren, quickly.

"Wall, the coon I war speakin' on is native 'cute, I guess."

"What is his name?"

"Wall, he ain't got a name in his tribe; they've reg'lar excommunicationed the red-skin, I calkilate, for marryin' a white gal, but he is the son of Monotah, and his name is Catahaga the Eagle-Wing."

"His evidence will be important."

"Ah, guess so."

"To-morrow I will summon the regulators; the rascals shall be tracked, and, if possible, the property restored."

"Wall, judge, cried the trapper, enthusiastically, "this yere is reg'lar kind, and I du say you're a ring-tail squealer, and no mistake, for the poor critter pines for his dollars as if every one on 'em was a babby Benjamin."

"And where do you 'camp down?'"

"Ain't no ways perticler; we ain't fixed on no reg'lar diggings."

"You must sleep here to-night, and to-morrow we will think what is to be done, and, rather than the money should not be restored, I will hunt these ranger thieves to their very stronghold."

CHAPTER C.

THE PAWNEE-LOUP'S DEFENCE.

IT was by the door of a lone log cabin, far sequestered in the mighty forest, that Minna Wyotte was sitting at her wheel.

She was a beautiful girl of eighteen, her long rippling hair sunny bright, her eyes soft and pensive, her gentle form slight and girl-like.

A solemn grandeur was impressed upon the features of the woodland scenery around her; behind the house were phalanxes of majestic pines which seemed to prop the clouds and quench the sunbeams in their deep, dark vistas.

Before the door stretched a clearing, strewn with the trunks of trees that had slowly succumbed before the toiling hand of man, or had crashed down in a moment under the quick-striking lightning-shaft from heaven.

Across the centre of the clearing purled along a broad, shallow brook, running at intervals into marshy pools, clustered with pollards and other willows.

Beyond, and dark against the ethereal pallor of the fading twilight, ranged the mighty army of firs and pines.

At Minna's feet a huge, gaunt deer-hound was sleeping, and by her side against the wall a pair of wood-doves in a wicker cage were low and plaintively cooing.

As the busy wheel whirred round, the Indian's wife kept time with a sweet half-murmured song.

From time to time the girl would raise her eyes and glance scanningly around the wide, grand sylvan amphitheatre in search for one who did not come.

A light shade of melancholy would then sweep over her soft and eloquent face, and she would pause in her work to ponder.

Then a light, yet vacant smile would pass over her lips, and with a little sigh she would continue her work.

At last the deer-hound stirred in his sleep, he threw back his watchful ears and sniffed the air, and then, with a deep bay, leaped to his feet and scampered noisily across the plain.

With a little chuckling laugh of joy, her sweet, blue eyes liquid-sparkling, the health-rose on her cheek crimson-deepening, Minna Wyotte tripped from her seat, lightly bounding forward to meet him whose approach had elicited the expression of delight on her face.

The deer-hound doubled and returned to her, and then darted off again.

Far away down the brook, his form dwarfed by the distance, a man was crossing a rude wooden bridge.

He was an Indian; his crested head was bowed, his buffalo robe swept behind him, his gun lay listlessly on his shoulder, and he seemed to walk absorbed in deep broodings.

When he had reached the end of the bridge he halted suddenly, flung his gun by the fringed bald-

THE RESCUE.

rick across his shoulders, and extending his arms walked quickly to meet his wife.

Minna threw her arms about her husband, and looked up into the young Indian's dark face with a look of yearning affection.

The deer-hound yelped and climbed upon the red-skin, placing his shaggy head on his master's shoulder.

"The eyes of my wife are deep waters, in which I see my face," murmured Catahaga, fondly; "my wife's voice is softer than the note of the mocking-bird when he sings his own song in the night. Eagle-Wing is happy; the Manitou has smiled on him; he mourns not for his father nor his nation; he heeds not the scorn of the pale-faces. The Yengeese lily is medicine at his heart, that heals all its wounds and sorrows."

No. 33.

Minna gave a little sob, and clung to her wild but noble husband.

"Why has Eagle-Wing lingered on the return path? Minna has listened for his footsteps these three suns."

The arched brows of the Indian met in a dark frown, his thin lip curved and quivered.

"Let us enter the lodge, my sunbeam; Catahaga will tell you what has happened."

The lonely but affectionate young couple wound their arms about each other, and entered the cabin.

The interior presented an appearance of rude but substantial comfort, and was remarkable for its neatness and tasteful arrangement.

Catahaga placed his gun in a corner, and seated himself at a table by the fire-side.

He sat moody and silent.

His wife prepared the supper.

Eagle-Wing partook of the meal frugally, and then turned towards the hearth, and, leaning his elbow on his knee, relapsed into his former abstraction.

Minna stole to his side, and placing herself upon a bear-skin rug on the ground, drew his arms about her.

The Indian slightly started.

He looked down upon his fair young wife with a tender smile.

"My husband's heart is darkened by a cloud," said Minna, softly. "But why is his tongue silent? Has he no words for his own wife, who yearns to know his thoughts, who has not heard the sound of his loved voice three lagging suns. Speak, Catahaga."

"Minna, I will speak with the tongue of a Yengeese," he began, in English.

A quaint pleasant smile flitted over Minna's face, as her husband rolled out these words in his clear thrilling tones, with the most charming tinge of native accent.

"I listen, husband," said Minna, sadly, for the smile faded off her lip as she watched the Indian's changing countenance.

"Minna, I have been listening to the words of a great medicine-man of your nation, a 'mission' whose heart is good towards the Pawnee; but his words are dark; they give me no light; my mind is blinded by them."

Minna looked grave.

"My husband's heart still turns to the lodges of the Pawnee. Catahaga cannot forget the customs and teachings of the sachems of his own tribe."

"No, Minna, I would not wash my skin white if I could, yet I love the pale-faces. I have adopted their ways, though I cannot always think their thoughts, Minna."

"My husband!"

"Many moons have waned since Eagle-Wing stood between the fawn of the pale-faces and the death-angel, to save her life. Minna gave that life to the brave that saved it; she left the lodges of her fathers; she chose the barren path of a poor hunter; when the frost had turned the rivers into beaten paths, and the air was darkened by the clouds of silent snow, she left her father's wigwam, where she was rich and happy, and bore with her the curse of those she loved, to become the squaw of a Pawnee-Loup, whose name was forgotten in his tribe. Does my wife repent? Does her soul whisper to her of the home she has abandoned?"

The tears sprang to Minna's eyes, and she answered, brokenly,

"Minna is your wife, Catahaga; you are her husband—we are one; but you are the dearer part of me. What are father, or mother, or brothers to a woman compared with the brave she has chosen? What are the rich wigwams of great nations to her whose heart lives only in the lodge of her elected master?"

The Indian pressed her to his heart with tender gallantry, and respectful, warm affection.

"Minna is a woman; the world is a wide stony prairie, where man is the path-finder! Minna, for your sake, Eagle-Wing loves your people; but his heart is often tempted to hate the proud, grasping, selfish, false, and destroying pale-faces, whose tongues are forked as adders and their paths as crooked, who boast themselves the Manitou's only favoured children, and destroy their brothers, whom the Great Spirit has made of other colour and customs than their own. The Master of Evil will sometimes stir the heart of Eagle-Wing to return to his own nation, to unbury the hatchet, to wage war against his oppressors, and to prize nothing so much as the scalps of these Yengeese dogs!"

Catahaga trembled with fierce emotion.

In a few fervent, graphic sentences he told his wife how the bush-rangers had perpetrated several diabolical outrages in the guise of Pawnee-Loups, and how the American government had sent out half a regiment of soldiers into Arkansas and the Jowa territory, in order to punish the supposed atrocities of the really innocent red-skins.

Minna listened with deep interest, her looks betokening her grief and indignation.

"They are the scourge of the Great Spirit, these pale-faces," added the Indian, with bitter emphasis; "they spread in all lands like the pestilence; they bring with them fire-powder to consume our bodies, fire-water to madden and destroy our spirits. I have heard your Yengeese books read, Minna, and I hear that in far islands, in a group like those from whence they first came in their big, winged canoes, they are waging exterminating war, only because they wish to steal from the 'Maori,' so they call the tribe, land and peltries; they say that they are better than their brothers whose skin the sun has darkened; they call us by Yengeese words of scorn, 'savage' and 'heathen,' and the forked-tongues preach a medicine doctrine of 'love,' yet they kill without hate, steal without need, because they war against the children of the Master of Life, who have skins of different colour. Wagh! they are serpents and dogs, who will have no colour but one, no customs but their own! They make profane havoc of the works of their great creator, yet, because the Iroquois cleaves to his traditions as they do to theirs, and bends low to the great sun-throne of the Manitou, from whence he scatters his light and his bounty upon the great hunting-grounds and maize-fields of his children, they insult the Iroquois with their pity, they send their 'missions' to win his spirit from the hunting-grounds of his fathers—their warriors to take his life, that the print of his moccasin may not be seen on his own land which they would rob from him. Yet Minna is of this tribe. Minna is very good, and Eagle-Wing loves the pale-faces for his wife's sake."

Nearly rendered are these too just accusations of the fiery Catahaga against the aggressive and oppressing whites.

"Let my husband remember that the Yengeese bring with them the knowledge of their wise nation, which is light."

"Is the Iroquois the better for this light? What does it show him? That there is no freedom in the pathless prairies, no beauty in the mighty forests; that he who lives in health and liberty, that robs his robe from the buffalo, that earns his food on the hunting-path, that draws his drink from the cold spring, that braves the winter's frost and the summer sun, is an outcast and a savage! Wagh! And their gifts — fire-weapons and fire-water! fire, fire, and burn—burn! Ugh!"

There was something demoniac in the fierce frown of the Pawnee-Loup as he clutched at his tomahawk, and rose from his seat.

A knock at the door caused Minna to start and tremble.

Eagle-Wing placidly moved across the room, and opened the door.

A man entered hastily, after looking behind him to the right and to the left.

He quickly shut the door, and threw himself into a chair, as if exhausted.

He was a fine manly fellow of middle age, dressed as a trapper.

"My brother is welcome," said the young Indian, calmly.

"Let Catahaga listen," said the man. "There are enemies on his track; his lodge will be attacked this night. My brother must not ask how I know this; he must not tell that I have warned him. Let Catahaga take his mustang and mount with his wife, and fly far across the prairie; let him with care conceal his trail; his life is in mortal danger."

"The heart of his brother is good towards the Pawnee. Catahaga is grateful. Can my brother tell me how many are the young men of this war-party?"

"Three are appointed to do this deed," returned the trapper; "three of the chosen braves, who are subtle as foxes, and bold as jaguars. Let not my brother neglect my warning. The Pawnee has been good to me, and his Yengeese wife is the love of the

whole settlement. I would not see my friends die·
You must fly at once, Catahaga ; the enemies are
already on the path ; they think to find my brother
sleeping. Let them find him flown."

"It is good !" said the Indian, with imperturbable
calmness.

"You will take something, Jonas ; you must need
refreshment after your long ride on this kind errand,"
said the girl, who, though very pale, preserved her
presence of mind and calmness with womanly fortitude.

"No, I thank you, Minna. No, no," returned
Jonas, quickly, "I must begone ; I was forced to
make a circuit lest the rascals should strike my trail.
They would kill me if they knew that I had given
you this warning ; I implore you not to neglect it.
Good night !"

The trapper darted through the door, and before
the Indian or his wife could detain him, had leaped
into his saddle and dashed away.

Catahaga stood with folded arms and glowing eyes.
"Three ! It is good."

A sinister smile rested on his lip.

"Husband, Catahaga, let us get out the horses and
fly ere it be too late."

"The heart of Eagle-Wing is happy. The Pawnee-
Loup will have scalps of the pale-faces ; he will not
remain a squaw ; his hatchet is too bright," muttered
the Indian, fiercely.

"My husband will not give his life to his enemies,
for the sake of his true wife, his own Minna," cried
the poor girl, excitedly.

Catahaga made no answer.

He motioned his wife to dress herself for a start.

Minna threw her cloak about her, and, gathering
as many articles as she thought possible to bear away
with her, she made a bundle of them, drew her hood
over her head, and gave her hand to her husband.

Catahaga flung his rifle on his shoulder, and,
taking his wife by the hand, led her from the cabin.

The night was very dark ; the clearing could be
but dimly distinguished, and the amphitheatre of
pines stretched round like a black screen ; yet the
stream shone with pale, silver light across the dark
and misty plain.

The dismal hooting of the owls in the forest
rendered the night-scene more awful and weird.

Catahaga led his wife to a log-built shed at the
back of the cabin.

The deer-hound ran by their side.

He brought out two horses, and quickly saddled
them.

He lifted his wife upon one of them. He drew from
his girdle a pistol, a powder-horn, and shot pouch ;
these he handed to Minna, who turned pale, but took
them without comment.

Catahaga then took the horses by their bridle, and
led them onwards through the black wood, under the
dark, frowning trees.

The sharp bark of a fox, or the hideous howl of a
stray wolf, pierces the deep intricacies of the gloomy
dells.

Catahaga, with his lovely wife, proceeded in silence
till they reached the banks of a brook.

Here they halted.

"Why does my husband not mount his mustang ?"
said Minna, in a trembling voice. "Surely he will
not leave his wife, alone, in the night, in the wild
forest ?"

"My wife must stay here," returned the Indian,
with quiet firmness. "Catahaga will return. Swift-
foot will guard the mustang. If Minna hear the
sound of shots let her not forget she is the squaw of a
chief. Eagle-Wing will not return without scalps of
his enemies."

"Catahaga !"

But he was gone !

The darkness was intense.

She listened.

No sound broke the stillness but the pawing of the
mustangs, and the panting of the deer-hound.

She could scarcely see the head of the horse on
which she was mounted.

With long, swift strides, the Indian glided between
the trees, and reached the cabin.

He stood before the door, poising his gun, and
listening.

There was a bright gleam in his splendid eyes ; but
his face was rigidly calm.

The Pawnee-Loup looked through the window into
the interior of his cabin.

The red glare of the smouldering logs illumined
every corner of the hut, and threw long black and
grotesque shadows from the quaint, rustic furniture.

Catahaga went into the cabin and fetched out a
beam of wood.

He closed the cabin door.

He took up an axe, and quickly and skilfully
chipped out a pair of sockets to receive the beam ; he
placed the piece of wood across the door, which opened
outwards, in such a manner as effectually to prevent
its being opened from within.

He tried the door ; it was firmly held by the
beam.

Catahaga removed the piece of wood, and concealed
it near at hand among the grass.

Again he entered the cottage.

He arranged the deer-skin curtain which concealed
the bed at the far end of the cabin, threw down a
hunting-shirt and a pair of moccassins, as if to intimate that he had retired to rest, took some of the
logs from the fire, and left the ashes to smoulder.

He looked around him, with a calm, stern face, but
brightened eye.

He took down another rifle, and examined the
primings.

The ramrod rattled down the bore.

The rifle was not charged.

The Indian deliberately loaded it.

He flung it across his shoulder, and once more
passed out of the cottage, carefully closing the door
behind him.

He went round the house, and securely fastened a
door at the back.

He walked to a clump of trees a few yards from
the house, and here he crouched, to wait in dogged
patience the arrival of the enemy.

He had not long been ambuscaded when his quick
ear detected the far distant sound of horses' hoofs.

Not a muscle of his face moved.

The wind soughed wailingly past.

Nearer and nearer rattled the sound of the galloping steeds.

The owls still hooted in the woods.

And now the sounds died away.

The darkness was unbroken by a single star-beam,
the silence by the lightest sound ; the very wind had
paused on the wing to listen.

The gallop, the gallop of hoofs grew louder and
nearer.

Perhaps the riders had rounded some bend of the
forest, but now they were rattling on direct towards
the cabin.

A plash was heard in the stream.

Catahaga started, and grasped his rifle.

Four dark objects were seen swimming the brook.

The Indian smiled grimly, and then his features
became fixed in their former rigidity.

Four mounted men drew up their horses upon the
near-side bank of the stream.

They dismounted, and stole softly across the
clearing.

Four sturdy ruffians, conversing in low whispers,
passed the Indian's ambush.

"No, I tell yer, let Abinidab stay here ; I and
Josh and Amariah are enough to do this bit of work,
I calkilate."

"We'll not kill Minna Wyotte ; she's luscious,
I reckon," said one of the brutal wretches, with a
grin.

"Wal, she air summut too admirational for a red-
skin cuss, I guess ; but we ain't a gwine to have any
rowdy-dow with a squealin' female. If she comes
the squeaker I shall spike her voice, I shall," said
the third, in nasal accents.

"I tell yer, Abinidab, you must keep picket here; keep near the hosses. You skeddadle."

The fellow seemed loth to remain alone in the darkness, and looked about with a frightened air.

The house was distant some yards.

The three men walked towards it.

They paused on the way and stood as if consulting on the plan of their proceedings.

They had turned the corner of a clump of firs.

The sentinel shouldered his rifle, and paced about in evident uneasiness.

Presently he grounded his piece, and stood leaning on the top of it, peering through the darkness, intent upon the faint lurid patch of red light from the distant cabin window.

Catahaga glided from his hiding place.

With lithe and cat-like motion he crawled along the ground.

The sentinel started, poised his gun, and turned quickly.

The Pawnee-Loup stretched himself flat on his face.

The whistling wind soughed wailingly; the owls still dismally hooted in the wood.

The sentinel seemed reassured.

He walked a few paces forward.

Again he grounded his musket, and watched intently the red patch of light that wavered on the sward before the cabin window.

His comrades were hidden behind the trees, or lost in the darkness that intervened between the spot where he stood and the cabin.

He anxiously awaited to see them emerge into the light from the dwelling of their intended victim.

The Pawnee-Loup crawled nearer and nearer.

He was within a foot of the sentinel.

The man started.

Catahaga bounded to his feet.

"Ugh!"

Down, straight down, driven with the iron nerve of the Indian's well-trained arm, flew the gleaming knife.

It struck deep through the bull-neck of the ranger.

The dying man convulsively grappled at the throat of the Pawnee.

Catahaga did not move a step, but lightly pushed the man away.

The ranger staggered, and dropped like a stone.

The Pawnee-Loup kneeled by his side.

Not a muscle of his stern face changed.

He drew out his scalping-knife, and with horrible dexterity drew round the head of his fallen foe.

The next instant he rose and placed the ghastly, reeking scalp at his girdle.

He then calmly glided forward towards the cabin.

The three rangers now appeared grouped in the fire-glow before the house.

The Indian had crept so near that he lurked behind the angle of the cabin.

"Wal, I think as we're tola'ble nigh slick sure of chalking the coon," whispered one of the fellows, "but though this yere Eagle-Wing cuss is a raal genwine son of Sachems, a reg'lar thoroughbred Pawnee, he ain't kinder used to Indian ways since he got drummed out of his father's wigwam for marrying the Wyotti's gal; but for all that he's considerable 'cute, so I suggestionate as one on yer moves round a piece to the other side of the lodge, 'cos if we miss him he'll try to run out from some back way, I reckon."

"'Taint no 'tarnal bit o' use, Abner, the Injen cuss will skedaddle afore one can reach the back settlements, and I opinionate as we shall lose him arter all, if we don't push on to haction without any more palavering."

"Wal, are yer primin's all slick? Are yer braced up for the pint, mates?"

"All right; go a-head!"

"Yer see that deer-skin hanging? the Pawnee devil's asleep behind that with his pale beauty. I'll jest send a bullet through the 'squeeter-curtain, and jest wake 'em up a bit. You be ready to foller suit with a clear aim, and no funkin' or flinchin'—now for it!"

The men softly opened the door.

Cautiously they stole in, shutting the door behind them.

They clustered together in a corner by the hearth.

Quick as thought and quite noiselessly, Catahaga placed the beam in its sockets, completely preventing the egress of the foes in the trap.

He drew to the window, unslung his double-barrelled gun, dropped a glance on the priming, and quietly drew back the lock.

All this passed in much less time than it occupies in the narration.

One of the fellows slowly and deliberately raised his piece to his shoulder.

A fork of flame, a puff of smoke, and the loud report shook the cabin.

The curtain fell down.

The bed was disclosed.

It was unoccupied!

A shot was fired from without.

The ranger who had fired at the curtain dropped his piece, clapped his hand to his side, and stumbled to the bed, on which he fell heavily.

Another turned quickly to the window, raising his rifle.

He advanced a step.

It was his last!

Once more a rifle crackled; the man sank on his knees, tossed up his arms, and then fell flat on his face.

The third ranger, mortally terrified, sprang to the door.

It was fastened without!

Uttering a prolonged and terrific war-whoop, and brandishing his glancing tomahawk, the Pawnee-Loup burst through the window and flew upon his last adversary.

The struggle was brief as desperate.

The Indian's hatchet crashed down, cleaving the ranger's skull to his shoulders.

The next instant the red-skin stood alone among the dead!

His calm, statuesque countenance remained immovable, but his wild dark eyes flared with exultation.

Very coolly he drew his scalping-knife, already smeared with blood.

The floor was washed with the red tide of life.

The Indian walked from one body to another and swiftly and deftly tore the scalp from each skull.

The ghastly scene failed to move his impassable heart.

He fixed his dripping trophies in his belt, and then calmly picked up the rifles and took the powder-flasks and shot-pouches from the fallen foes.

He had already secured the weapon of the sentinel.

He bound the straps of the cartouches together and buckled a thong round the rifles and threw the load upon his shoulder.

He then got out of the window.

He looked back into the cabin of death.

The smouldering flames of the burning logs hissed out horribly, extinguished by the rippling puddles of blood.

The fire flickered and winked as if eager to quench in darkness, the sight of such horrors.

The faintest sneering smile fluttered around the thin lips of the remorseless Indian as he plunged into the darkness of the forest.

He reached the banks of the brook.

Her cheeks whiter than the lily's petals, Minna sat on her horse tremblingly awaiting him.

The deer-hound ran to greet him, but smelt the blood and slunk away with a piteous howl.

Minna tried to speak—she tried to inquire what had happened, but the words froze on her lips.

Quietly and collectedly Catahaga arranged the load of rifles and shot-pouches across the pommel of his horse's saddle.

He mounted.

"My husband," said Minna, faintly, "let us leave a long trail behind us; the rising sun will find us on the banks of the Arkansas; let us cross the great river and seek a home in the far prairies of Oregon."

The Indian shook his rein and answered sententiously, " It is good !"

CHAPTER CI.

THE CAPTAIN OF THE BUSH-RANGERS AND HIS LOVE.

LEIGHTON HOE was a large and well-arranged log building, surrounded by offices and outhouses, and garrisoned with quite an army of guests and retainers of the worthy and long-established emigrant, Richard Leighton.

The house had long been hushed ; the whole household had long sank in sleep.

The watchful dogs were slumbering in their kennels.

In one chamber of the house a fair girl was sleeping, her parted lips softly breathing, her tangled tresses strewing the snowy pillow in meshes of gold.

A pensive look that rested on her perfect features betokened the nature of her youthful dreams.

At times, a quivering sigh would lift her pure, soft bosom, and her hand would move wearily upon the coverlet.

It was moonlight ; the august flood poured in through the little casement, and sweetly illumined with its calm light the chaste white drapery of the neat and pleasant chamber.

The room was situated in a part of the building that overlooked the garden.

Suddenly through the stillness of the night thrilled the full, sweeping tones of a manly voice, serenading in fine melody.

Agnes Staunton moved in her sleep ; she raised her hand to her head.

She started, and woke.

The rich blushes mantled her cheek and neck. She rose, and hastily dressed herself.

She sank on a chair, and turned deadly pale, and almost swooned.

Still the rich tenor trolled out, full and clear,

"My love she sleeps a dreamless sleep,
    The night wind whispers low ;
The moonbeams through her lattice peep,
Then 'neath the quivering jasmine creep,
    And 'mid her tresses golden glow.
O ! richly fair, my peerless one,
    And sweet it is to be
At vigils, while the stars alone
    Keep silent watch with me."

Agnes rose, and opened the window, which gave upon a balcony.

Wrapping a mantle loosely about her, she stole out into the night, or rather the daybreak, for the morn was palely dawning, though the moon still reigned supreme in the zenith.

She crept down the steps ; she reached the lawn. She never raised her eyes for an instant.

She felt herself snatched to a quick-beating heart, and she burst into a flood of bitter tears.

"Agnes, my own !" cried a silvery voice, in a tone of passionate fervor ; "my truly, dearly, deeply beloved ! I hold you in my arms again. It is gone ! The pain, and the shame, and the danger, and the sorrow ; the wild excitement, the cold revulsion, the ruthless guilt, the poignant remorse of my mad career ! It is past, all ! Elysium is come again ! I am in Heaven, for I am with you. O ! speak to me, my wife betrothed ! my bride, given by the dead, who are spirits now, and watch our diverging paths with more than mortal sorrow. Speak to your wild, bad affianced ! speak to your true, doating lover—your own, and only yours—Agnes, Agnes, my beautiful, my good !"

"Oswald, why, why have you returned ? Why, why have you come back to me, to mock me with protestations that are false and worthless ?" sobbed the poor girl ; "to make me feel my weakness, that I—I—love you, whom I ought to abhor."

"Abhor me !" cried the youth, in a tone of agonised reproach. "Is it needful that *you*, too, should be against me ? Have I not suffered enough ? True, I am a villain ; my passions are strong, my will is ungoverned. I am now ruthless. I have been scorned, and to my hot and sensitive temperament, scorn is unbearable. I must have money, for I love pleasure, and my hand is open ; I must have danger, for I cannot live without excitement ; and I must have love, for love is the richest of life's rich boons."

"You have no thought for me," murmured Agnes. "You would sacrifice me to your caprice. You would have me brand my brow, and peril, nay lose my soul for you, only to please the fierce, exacting fancy of a passing day ; and then you would discard me, and leave me to die, without pity or remorse. You are selfish, Oswald, intensely selfish."

"How much you wrong me, Agnes," cried the youth, impetuously. "I am here, over many a league of rolling prairie, through many a broad, deep river, among the wild, murderous Indians, along the skirts of deadly swamps, through the mazes of trackless forests ; I am here. Is this selfishness ? I have braved death, and detection, worse than death, to see you, and I am here, to be rated and frowned upon, and stigmatised as selfish, by her who is plighted my wife—by her whom I love with a fiery passion that consumes me !"

"Oh ! why did you come ?"

"You are not glad to see me ! I am not welcome ! I might have looked for this. I do not blame you. Well, Agnes, I will go."

"No, no. Be reasonable, dear Oswald. You know —you know I love you. Oh, God ! forgive me ! that I should confess so much !"

"Is it a crime to love me ?"

"Ask your own conscience."

"I do, and it replies—no ! It is not crime in Agnes that she should love Oswald. We are knit together by ties the most sacred. I have respected you, and though I have given free run to my wild passions, I have been constant to you."

"Are you sure, Oswald. I have heard——"

"You have heard !—Bah ! you have heard ! Who can help hearing scandal ? The air is impregnated with poisonous gases ; the moral atmosphere with noxious slanders. If I love women, Agnes, it is because you are a woman ; all that reminds me of you I love more fervently than others would love yourself. You I love far better than could a better man ; for, to me, virtue, reputation, reason, Heaven, are light dust in the balance compared with Agnes."

The girl trembled violently.

She raised her tear-streaming eyes to Heaven.

She cried, in a voice of exquisite anguish,

"Oh ! Thou who said'st to the waves, ' Peace be still !' and there was a great calm, quell in my heart my yearning for the love of this man, my own wild affection for him. He is a tempter, and I am weak. Oh ! shield me ; keep me that I may not obey the impulse of my soul, that I may not suffer myself to be swayed by an indomitable master-passion to my own destruction !"

Agnes threw herself at the feet of the handsome young villain, and sobbed bitterly.

"Oswald, do you love me ?" she cried, wildly.

"Are you so cruel as to ask me such a question ?"

"What would you sacrifice for me ?"

"I will not say my life, for that is nothing, Agnes. My soul ! aye, my soul !"

"What would you suffer for me ?"

"Dearest, I could die, but I could never cry ' cease !' to tortures endured for your sweet sake."

"Well then," returned Agnes, the tears drying on her hot cheek as she rose and drew herself up with womanly dignity, "Oswald Lamond, I conjure you, by the passion you profess, to leave me—never to see me again—leave me to the anguish of my love ; leave me to the love of my anguish. My heart is broken ; such grief as mine must kill, and with Heaven there is peace !" Agnes again burst into hysteric sobbing.

"But, why leave you, my gentlest?" said Regan, folding the yielding girl in his arms, and murmuring in his fondest accents. "Come love, cheer up; look into my face and sun me with one smile. Darling Agnes, beautiful Agnes, my bride from birth, we will be so happy, so very, very happy. What have I done to deserve this chill reception? What ought the world's opinion be to you? To *you* I am true—what have you to do with the rest?"

"Oswald, you are a felon, an ingrate, or a mur——"

"No, no; you err, dearest; call me not by such cruel names."

"I know all, Oswald. Oh, leave me—pray leave me!" cried the girl, passionately, withdrawing herself from his embrace.

A smile of triumph lighted the face of the robber, but he turned his head aside as if to conceal his emotion.

"Well, Agnes, be it so," he murmured. "I leave you—I go—I will recross the leagues of trackless prairie that I made light of as my path to you. Farewell! farewell! do not look at me lest my resolution fail; your wish shall be my law, the torture of this parting I will cheerfully endure for your sweet sake, only do not unman me by one look; leave me, quickly—I will begone."

He moved a few paces away.

"No, no, no, Oswald! my betrothed! a moment—I will see you again; the moon is paling, the sky is brightening, the lark is singing, do not let my cousin see you."

"Your cousin whom you love and who hates me—Mark Leighton, whom you will marry!" cried Regan, hotly.

"No, no, indeed, I do not love him; I love no one—I love you—I will marry no one."

"You will marry me?"

"Never! Oswald, never—never! but the day is breaking; our people rise early—begone."

"Shall I see you no more?—must I leave you for ever?" cried Regan, pressing the trembling girl to his heart.

"Once more; to-morrow, that is, to-day, for it is already morning; but for the last, last time. Oswald, one word."

"My soul's dearest!"

"Yesterday, there was restitution made to the Jew, who had been robbed; his money was restored to him by Michael Warren. Tell me, as you love me, were you concerned in the massacre at Graftonville, for which the poor Indians were made to suffer?—were you, your—your villains, were they concerned in that diabolical affair?"

"By the sun now breaking—the sun that sees so much wrong and guilt; by my mother's honour, Agnes, I swear no! I have dealings with that black gang; but my own band never cross the Arkansas. Do you believe me?"

"Yes, Oswald, I do; but, adieu. Where shall I send you word? I will see you again; but, indeed, for the last, last time!"

"You must send me word at Michael Warren's plant, for there I am staying."

The girl started.

"Does *he* know you—in your real character?"

"Don't ask me, Agnes, I cannot tell you his——"

"I thought he was a villain; he looks like one!"

"You must not form hasty conclusions. Well, good morrow, my treasure; we shall meet in a few hours."

"Yes, for the last time."

"You will come alone?"

"I will; meet me at our old trysting-place in the forest."

"I will be there, Agnes, my own, farewell!"

The girl did not answer; she clung to him, shudderingly, and then tore herself away.

There was a strange smile on the splendid face of the Captain of Bush-rangers, as he cooly walked away.

He clasped his hands.

"O God, I love this girl—I love her—I love her!" he cried, "as none but I can love her! She shall be mine, I will bear her away; she cannot resist me, and then!—well, and then? I will make no rash resolutions, or I shall be sure to break them."

He started back.

Mark Leighton stood before him.

The face of the cousin of Agnes was very white; his dress was disordered; he shook with passion.

"Scoundrel!" he cried, "destitute of every sense of honour and virtue. Monster! with every crime written in the recording books against you! tempter!"

"Phew! what old woman has donned man's attire to beshrew me for my sins and shortcomings?" rejoined Regan, with a light laugh. "Stand out of my way, squaw, my patience is rather short, and I don't wish to hurt you."

"And you have dared to return to Larchville."

"Yes, in spite of the dragons!"

"You measureless villain!"

"You immeasurable —— old woman! Let me go, pretty vixen. I beg your pardon, are you not my wife's cousin?"

"Your wife's?"

"Aye, my wife's! Is not Agnes my wife? Will the wind off your weak stomach blow away the solemn pledge that binds us, hand-fasts us? Well, this joke of mine is unseemly, but so is your conduct that provokes it. The morning is up, cousin Mark, and so are you; but you look as if you were still oppressed with a nightmare. Come, let's adjourn to the stores, and have an 'eye-opener,' and drink the forgetting of old grievances. I owe you no grudge, and if I did I shouldn't pay you, for I am a bad debtor; don't be a fool."

"A fool!—were I *not* a fool ——"

"Chaos were come again!—ha—ha—ha! Mark, you mistake your vocation. Don the buskins, turn actor, and your fortune is made."

"If——"

"Hard words were bullets, I would talk with you."

"I have bullets at your service——"

"You are very kind; your favours in that way will not be misplaced—I can reciprocate."

"You will fight?"

"Yes, Mark; but not quarrel."

"Follow me, then."

"To the death!—*yours*, of course, not mine."

"I could tear you to pieces."

"No, you couldn't; but, if you can blow me to pieces, I will give you the chance. Are you armed?"

"Yes," returned the other, drawing a pistol.

"Very good; lead on—I follow you," returned the Captain of Bush-rangers, with inimitable coolness. He suddenly paused, and laughed. "Poor Agnes, she is hard beset by two villains—a big one and a little one. The Fates direct her aright!"

"Will you come?" cried Leighton, impatiently stamping his foot.

"Assuredly—lead on."

The two young men walked quickly across the garden.

The dawn was fast waxing into day.

They emerged from the garden by a side door, and walked into the pine forest.

The birds were noisily chirruping; the morning mists seemed tangled among the higher branches of the black and mighty pines, and hung about them like the films of spiders' webs.

On the plant the cocks were crowing, and the deep baying hounds howling to be set at liberty.

The virgin pale rays of the rising sun slanted between the dark stems of the trees, and blazed upon the little windows of the building.

Mark Leighton's cheek was flushed with jealousy and rage; his rolling eyes darted lightnings of passion.

Oswald Lamond was as calm and cool as the morning air he seemed to drink in with such refreshment and pleasure; his clear blue eyes roamed about in search of familiar objects, but these seemed not to raise in his breast any feelings of pain or regret by their associations; he only softly smiled, and strolled on after Mark Leighton.

They paused when they had plunged sufficiently deep in the forest to be entirely screened from the house.

"Now, Mark," said the Captain of Bush-rangers, very coolly, "I have a brace of the most perfect revolvers you ever beheld—here they are. You see I trust them out of my hand; few such as I am would put their weapons into the grasp of an enemy, to leave themselves unarmed. Don't you admire the workmanship of these beautiful little engines? As for that old barker of yours, it is only fit to scare sparrows from cherry-trees!"

"I cannot kill you with your own weapon," murmured Mark Leighton, hoarsely.

"Of course you can't—you don't suppose that if I thought you *could*, I'd trust you so freely. Now! —but first shake hands. When my poorest foe stands on the narrow frontier-line that lies between this life and the next, I cannot bear malice. Let us shake hands. So, farewell—I fear we shall never meet again. You are a proper young man, and are not going my road."

With this the imperturbable rascal walked backwards.

"Now, Mark," he said; "one shot; I never need to fire more."

"You are a brag——"

"And a dead shot, I assure you. Should you hit me (earthquakes do happen) give me a quiet burial, and don't remove the golden tress that I wear at its place—my heart. Will you grant me that favour?"

"Yes, yes; are you ready?"

"Ready, but scarce prepared. One moment. If you do not hit me, and I choose to spare you, we part without firing again."

"No, no!"

"Yes, yes. Don't compel me to kill you!"

"You will not fire?"

"Won't I? Do you hate me?"

"Like venom."

"That's hard."

"Venom is precious balm to me compared with your detestable person."

"Don't be personal, Old Buskins. Ready! I'll give the word, as I am cooler, and more used to this kind of thing."

The two antagonists turned from each other, and simultaneously extended their right arms.

The gentle morning beams glinted on the finely-polished steel-barrels of the revolvers.

"One, two, THREE!" cried Regan, in full, clear tones.

One pistol exploded.

A bullet whizzed right past Regan's face, almost grazing his eye-brows.

"Ha, ha!—better than I anticipated. Very well done. You did not wheel quite steadily. Next time, pivot your heel firmly. However, it's my turn. Can you stand fire?"

"Yes, villain!" roared Mark Leighton, his cheek blanching, his knee trembling, yet keeping his ground with fortitude.

"I'll give you a lesson. You must measure the distance, mind the light, not fire too high, nor think too much of your man."

"Demon!"

"I will show you what difference the fraction of a hair's-breadth will make — too wide or too low—so!"

The pistol-shot crackled, and the smoke soared up through the branches.

Mark Leighton's hat rolled on the ground.

"And, now you're satisfied, you may keep the barker; and, when you have had more practice, we'll fight it out; and, as Norval says—lor, how I should like to see you play Norval—' When we contend again, our str-rife is MORTAL!'"

"Coward!"

"And villain," laughed Regan, stepping lightly away. "Au revoir, mon ami! Learn to turn firmly on your left heel, and you'll do."

"Rascal! there are more barrels to the revolver, and you shall have their contents. You are a bandit, and a pest, and deserve no ruth. Die! die!—the act is hallowed!"

Mark Leighton fired wildly.

The bullet grazed Regan's cheek, and the blood trickled down on to his dainty collar.

The Captain of Bush-rangers turned.

His cheeks burned; his eyes flamed with uncontrollable fury.

He hissed out his words in accents low and piercing in their concentrated passion.

"You are a beggarly dastard! *Now I will kill you!*"

Regan flung away his pistol, and, drawing his bowie-knife, rushed upon Mark Leighton.

The latter fired.

Too late; Regan's grip was already at his throat. The strong men tussled an instant.

Leighton was heavily thrown.

Regan planted his knee on his breast, and threw back his arm to strike a mortal blow with his flashing knife.

A pealing shriek rang through the wood, and soft arms were thrown about Regan, and drew him from his foe.

The bush-ranger clasped a girl to his heart, and murmured, in trembling accents,

"Agnes, you have saved the dastard's life; I am glad I have not killed him. He shall live awhile to rue his treachery. Love, we shall meet again. Mark Leighton, I gave you the chance of a fair fight; now you have no chance. The sword hangs by a hair over your head; at any moment it may fall. There is an ambush in every thicket to destroy you; there are viewless hands ever raised to strike you. You are condemned, Mark Leighton! and when the time comes, do not forget that you provoked your own fate. Farewell, Agnes; reject me if you will, it is only wise of you to do so; but, jealousy apart, I would rather see you mated with the Arch-fiend than married to this cowardly slave!"

The Captain of Bush-rangers turned, and walked disdainfully away.

CHAPTER CII.

REUNION—THE LOST RESTORED.

IN a comfortable and moderately well furnished parlour of a little cottage in one of the most rural of the suburban districts of London a mother was sitting amongst her children.

She was pale and careworn, but still bore the traces of beauty.

Her family consisted of three merry girls, and a bright-eyed, curly-haired little rogue—a boy, about six years old, who strutted the room at play with his sisters, over whom he seemed to domineer with the most despotic authority, and who treated him with the most lavish affection and forbearance.

The mother was dressed in mourning, and she sat looking on her children with motherly pride, saddened by anxiety.

The little fellow drew to his mother's side, and laying his hands on her lap, looked up into her face, and said, sagely,

"Ma, Willie knows what he will do when he is big."

The mother smiled, and kissed the little one.

"Well, and when my little boy becomes a tall man, what will he do?"

"Willie has seen pretty pictures, very pretty—a great 'frigate.' Janie *will* call it a boat. Ain't that silly? But she says it to tease. Old Jack Capstan, you know, ma, told Willie it is a frigate; and when Willie is a big man, he will have a great frigate, and carry ma, and Jessie, and Flossy, and Janie all round and round the world. Won't that be nice? For, you know, ma, Willie loves the sea, and the sands, and the big rocks, and the pebbles, and shells. Only, when ma goes to the sea, she cries, quiet, to herself, and then Willie is sad."

"Oh, no!—no, no!" cried the mother, pressing the child to her heart. "My Willie must not talk so; he must not be a sailor. It would break mamma's heart."

The little boy looked wistfully up into his mother's face.

"But papa was a sailor, ma—wasn't he now? If papa was a sailor, it must be good to be a sailor, for you often tell us all how good papa was."

The widow could not restrain her tears.

"Would not Willie like to build great houses, to grow beautiful corn, to see the big engines pant and twirl, and turn, or to make pretty pictures, or play pretty music?"

"Oh! yes, ma—drums! I can play the drum, mamma—can't I? And I should like to be a soldier, with red coat, and gold things on my shoulders, and a bright sword, and march, march away. I often play at captains; but Jessie can't march a bit; when I tell her to 'halt,' she laughs, ma. No, I shouldn't much like to be a soldier. Shall I tell you why, ma?"

"Yes, dear."

"Because soldiers don't go on the sea. And I do so love the sea—oh! so very, very much!"

The mother sighed, and a shade of terror swept over her face.

"Come, Willie, let's have a game at 'Puss,'" said one of his sisters, drawing him from his mother's side.

Soon the childrens' merry laughter rang round the room, and they sported about the floor in high glee.

Their romping was suddenly interrupted by a knock at the door.

The worthy Doctor Biles entered, hastily.

The widow rose, and shook hands with the physician, welcoming him with a genial smile.

The children crowded round him, and crowing and laughing, thrust their hands into his ample pockets.

Their mother chid them, and the good doctor pretended to make a desperate resistance.

Soon each of his little assailants had captured a box of toys, or a packet of "goodies," with which the kind old gentleman always stored his pockets when he visited the family.

When he had kissed them all round, and had finished his romp, he left the youngsters to divide their spoils, and seated himself by the side of their parent.

He figited in his chair, grew hot in the face, fanned himself, and showed other unmistakable signs of uneasiness.

At length he spoke.

"You are looking pale and a little downcast, my dear madam," he said, "and I see you are in mourning."

"It is the anniversary of our sad loss," was the mournful reply.

"Ah, yes; very true; sad, indeed. But, my dear madam, I'll ask you a question."

"What is it, doctor?"

"Don't you think, now, that fatal strokes of great calamities fall with less crushing force upon us than too great joys—too sudden turns of fortune? I mean, when we have given up a desirable thing as being out of the pale of the most expansive hope, and by some wondrous chance it happens——"

"What do you mean, doctor?"

"I scarcely know how to explain. I had a patient, Mrs. Fawcett, the tenderest of husbands, the best of fathers, a good man. He was laid low with a dreadful fever; I gave him up as one beyond hope of recovery. His distracted wife resigned herself as well as she could to the anticipated loss, but, to my wonder, the crisis passed favourably, the patient recovered, and is now restored to his wife and family, I trust to outlive me, who judged him at one time to be upon the verge of death. It was a great trial

to the wife, I assure you. The reaction—you know——"

"Doctor—O, if you knew—I am faint; I shall be myself directly. You speak so solemnly; you look so anxious. This wife—while there is life there is hope, but the dead cannot come from their graves!"

"The sea, madam——"

"The sea! Do you—do you allude to my husband?"

"Now, I implore you, calm yourself; th'nk quietly if you could bear to hear news of the manner of your husband's wreck; if you would find comfort in knowing his last words; if you would bear to know that severe sickness, and not death——"

"My husband is alive! Yes, doctor, I will pray to God, who has supported me through all my troubles, to sustain me in this great, this unlooked-for ecstacy of joy. I will be calm; I will be patient, I will. My husband, my dear husband!"

The wife burst into a flood of tears.

The doctor encouraged this flow of emotion, and spoke to her in touching words of sympathising delight.

The children grouped round with frightened looks.

The door was opened.

A pale, tall man glided in.

In an instant the woman sprang into his arms.

He locked her closely in his arms.

Softly they murmured each other's names.

"My loved ones, you are not fatherless! the sea has given you back your parent!" cried the weeping wife. "Kneel, my darling. You have a father in heaven, to him pour forth your praises, for he has restored your earthly parent. 'He was dead, and is alive again; was lost, and is found!'"

"Papa!" cried the children, clustering round.

Not the fond wife, who had wept out the long months of two dreary years, gave way under this sudden reversion of fate's decree, who found herself whelmed with joy, as no longer bereaved of her life's chief solace and support, but the weary husband, worn out with oppression and cruelty, at last restored to liberty, and love, and home, it was he who sank back in the chair and lost consciousness.

"Doctor, my husband dies!" cried the wife, distractedly. "Is he restored to me that I should lose him now? Dear doctor, speak; say, is he gone?"

"No, my dear madam; calm yourself, for his, for the children's, for your own sake," replied the physician, huskily. "He is conquered by an emotion, the whole cause of which you do not yet know. He has suffered cruelly, but all is well now. Be calm, be happy; he revives; he is well. There, there, God is too good to take him from you now."

CHAPTER CIII.

HARWOLF AND BLACK RALPH DISSOLVE PARTNERSHIP.

WHEN Sam Cassidy and Oakland sprang before Black Ralph, all the party receded in wonder.

"Look you, Mr. Talbot, we have won our liberty, and mean to keep it. We have a nest in the rocks from which you could never drive us, and we would turn our hands against each other to kill each other rather than be dragged back to the "Vulture;" but, for all that, Talbot, as Oakland and I have served under you, we won't see you murdered in cold blood by such a dastard as Harwolf."

"Now, my boys," cried the doughty pirate captain with a laugh, "this is rather a surprise to me, I must confess; you have turned up a colour that I never saw displayed by that camelion creature in all my days; but I'm afraid you have only rushed on your own destruction, Sam; however, your hand lad, and a couple of caps for my barkers."

"Fire on the spies! down with them!" cried Harwolf.

The men aimed their pieces.

THE CONSPIRACY ON THE ISLAND.

"Hear me speak a few words, my hearties," said the dauntless Cassidy, in his quiet, impressive manner, "and then, if you must butcher a messmate in cold blood because he wants to prevent you exchanging a bad skipper for a worse—I am more ready to go aloft now than I have been for some months, and you may do your worst—I'll not say 'hold fire.' But tell me, hearties, which is the man amongst ye that can say I have ever done him an injury? or which one of you that can say he wouldn't carry a sweetheart, a modest girl whom he loved, from a pirate ship where she would see nothing but blood and rapine? The bloodiest Moorish corsair had his home where his wife and little ones might be protected from the cannon-ball or the boarding-pike; and, for the old skipper, Fergus Macallister, are ye such snivelling crows that you have not sufficient

No. 34.

pluck to dare the consequence of leaving a solitary old man on a lone, uninhabited island, when you have robbed him of all but his life, and when you know him to be in the charge of two old messmates, who, though they have learned to abhor your calling and don't care a fico for your wrath and vengeance, are too true-blue to blow the gaff on ye; while that skunk you want to make your captain would see ye all walk the plank if it would save him half-an-hour's toothache? Fire, if you will; life's not worth much to me; but, if ye do, the act will be one of cowardly skunks and not free rovers!"

"Hear—hear! tremendous cheering! How I should like to report that speech—'The contested election.' Sam Cassidy for ever; let us come to the poll; hands, ye lubbers!" shouted the fearless Black Ralph, with genuine unction and enjoyment.

The men could not resist a laugh.

"No, no, Sam; we'll not kill *you*, mate," they answered, severally.

Cassidy stood with seaman-like grace, his arms folded, his head thrown back, and the wind dallying with his raven locks.

He looked around him with a quiet smile, and said, simply,

"I knew ye wouldn't, hearties."

At this moment Teddy Macarthy and a number of the Cormorants arrived at the spot.

They soon understood what had happened, and gathered round Talbot, towards whom they still retained their allegiance.

The two parties exchanged defiant glances.

Daniel Harwolf sprang forward and held up his hand.

"Let me speak," he said.

"Aye, mates, let us have Danny's oration; it will be an intellectual treat," said Black Ralph, laughing, and seating himself on a stone, laying his bared sword across his knee, and priming his pistol.

Harwolf thus harangued the crew.

"You all remember under what circumstances you were first mustered on the deck of the 'Black Vulture;' you all know on what sort of cruise you were bound when you set your names in the ship's books; you were made aware under what flag you were to serve, and you were willing to accept berths in the vessel as a place of refuge from your enemies of the law, or the wolf of poverty. Tell me, comrades, was it not so?"

"Aye, aye, captain," responded the "Vultures."

"Now, I ask you, mates, as sensible men, how can we hope to preserve ourselves from ruin if we pay no regard to that mainstay of safety—mutual trust and honour that should exist even 'among thieves?'"

"Hear, hear!" shouted Black Ralph, applaudingly.

"Can anyone deny that the schooner is in every respect well-appointed, in fact, that for build and gear, for action or swift-sailing, she is the prettiest craft on the high seas; her stands of arms are not unfurnished, her stores are not scanty? As a fair question, and on the principle my rival acknowledges so warmly, 'honour among thieves,' who fitted the craft?—who freighted her?—who received her crew and administered the oaths? Who has the best right to command her?"

"A Daniel come to judgment!" shouted Black Ralph. "Hear, hear, hear!"

"Answer the question fairly, hearties; if we are not to cut each other's throats, if we are to share equally all booty, has not the man who paid for every plank of the ship, and every stitch of her canvass, the man whom you all swore to obey, who is fitted for command by his interest as owner of the ship, and by his life-long experience as an officer in the royal service, is he not the 'right man in the right place' when he walks the quarter as your legitimate captain and commander?"

"Aye! aye! hurrah for Cap'en Harwolf; we'll have no other skipper!" roared the Vultures.

"One word more, and I conclude, hearties, and leave the decision of the respective merits of myself and my rival to your impartial decision. Who brought you mutiny, which is destruction? who brought the women aboard, who are worse then fire in the hold or a leak in the streakings? who fooled away a whole cruise with his fal-lal love-making, ranting, swaggering, swilling, and hectoring, to the utter ruin of all order, the utter obstruction of all prize-chasing, the danger of your lives and liberties, his equals in all, as if he were some Tartar cham, and you were his miserable slaves? Speak quickly, mates, you can have but one leader, is it to be Ralph Talbot or Daniel Harwolf?"

There was a shout of acclamation after this speech.

Ralph Talbot cooly rose and walked into the midst of the circle; his broad, dauntless face moved steadily round, and was lighted with a quaint humourous smile.

Many of the men scowled upon him, and some fingered their weapons.

"Let him speak; let us hear Black Ralph," shouted the 'Cormorants.'

"Hearties, my rival has told you that you are my equals, thereby inferring that I am your equal, and hinting that he is our superior. Superior! Bah! As captain by election we acknowledge a superior. But he, my rival, sets his claim upon his ownership of the vessel, as if a man could freight a rover-ship, and take bold fellows like merchant swabs or king's pressed men. The ship is ours! Dam'me, are we not pirates? Shall we draw our cutlasses to board and take our own vessel? The thing is absurd. He paid for it, he freighted it. Well, he sold it, too; he sold it to you for your strong arms and brave hearts, that might protect him from the minions of the law, which he had outraged by a crime of murdering a miserly old Jew, at the remembrance of which I have seen him shake like a top-sail in a squall. He says I have swilled. Are we to be bilge-drinking, tea-meeting lubbers? Our life is one cruise of fun and enjoyment. And when was my hand less steady at the helm? when was my voice less clear on the quarter for having drank about like a jolly good fellow? He says I am your equal. I am!—it is my pride and glory to remember it! He says I 'hector' you, and endanger your lives. I am freely given command of a ship. I have no Admiralty nor articles of war to assist me. I have one last argument to appeal to in cases of fatal insubordination, and that argument lies in the mouths of these pistols; and, by the great guns!—I look ye all in the face, though I stand here like William before the gold-scrapers—if any man dared to play the mutineer while I trod the deck as skipper, I would shoot him down if he were my twin-brother! He complains of my devotion to beauty. Bah! We will find an island, mates, and make it an 'agapemone,' an 'abode of love,' and every lad shall have his lass to cheer him when his cruise is over. He says that I have lost a cruise. Who was it that, to carry out his personal spleen, peached on that splendid fellow, our great rival, the Boy Pirate—peached on him to beaks, on shore, mark that? Who fired San Salvador, and almost burnt the old provost's little daughter—a deed too dirty for a pig's conscience? Who, wishing to put me out of the way, dared not challenge me like a man, but set an ambush to out-master me, and even stole the caps from my nipples? He, a pirate!—a pirate chief! a crimp! a pander! an area-sneak! a fence! but not a pirate! What man amongst us is respected more than my ex-mate, Sam Cassidy? Yet, though I hunt him as a deserter, with full intent to make him walk the plank, or dance upon nothing at the yard-arm, even he steps forward to defend me against that soulless whelp, that would bamboozle you into owning him your rightful master, and yourselves his purchased slaves! Sam defends me for this reason: he knows that our rich prize was taken by me, by my master-stroke; taken, without loss of a man, in less than twenty minutes. He knows that when the 'Red Raven' bore down on us in all her terrible fury, when her mighty warriors, whose deeds are Homeric, leaped on her deck, he who headed your brave charge, and swept them like dust from the deck, was *I!*—your equal, your elected—Black Ralph, the Rover!"

Thunders of applause both from the Vultures and the Cormorants followed this speech.

Then arose the hubbub of discussion which soon degenerated into dispute, warmed into contention, and nearly blazed into a pitched battle.

"Hearties! silence fore and aft! let me speak once more!" shouted Cassidy's clear-toned voice.

"Aye, aye, hear Sam, let him speak; heave a-head, Sam, we're all attention," cried the pirates, eagerly.

"In my life, hearties, I never heard so much speechification except at a court-martial or a council of war. I am not going to make a long speech; you are men of action; there is never much good in tacking too much to get over close to the wind; more time is lost than space gained by it. You are divided in your opinions. Well, divide; you are free rovers, you have two ships; if you can part company with numbers on each side sufficient to work each ship, let Captains Harwolf and Talbot dissolve partnership. Captain Talbot certainly took the 'Cormorant', Captain Harwolf certainly purchased the 'Vulture'; then let them command their respective vessels; let the crew split into two parties and select their separate commanders."

"Hurrah!" shouted the crew. "Sam for ever! it is a capital plan."

Soon the crew had separated into two divisions; they were pretty equal in numbers.

Talbot walked forth and grasped Cassidy by the hands.

"Sam," he said, in a hearty tone, "you have done me a service; while I was consorted with that skunk my genius never had fair play. Now, I shall be a rover in the bravest sense, and you will hear brave things of me. Cassidy, I envy you; if merit in this world could secure promotion, you would soon carry the admiral's pennant at your fore peak. Give my love to Deborah; remind her that I did not treat her very cruelly, pirate as I am, and assure her of my lasting devotion.

'I know not why at this, our parting,
My blood should flow so chilly through my veins.'

"But, I swear, Sam, that I feel as if half my heart with half my heart's cargo of resolution were rent away when I think I shall see that girl nevermore. Hearty, good-bye; here we part company; you may hear that I am blown up with my ship, but never that I swung like a dog; the devil is not so black as he is painted, and Black Ralph is not quite sable. A long and sunny cruise in peaceful waters to you, Sam; to-night I will send you the 'Cormorant's' pinnace with what stores I can spare, and I'm sure you will be the last to blow the gaff on me. Adieu—adieu, and don't forget me!"

With a grim smile and a hearty grip the rover parted from the castaway.

CHAPTER CIV.

A LECTURE ON DASHING CRIMINALS.

SILAS RYE is restored to his home.

Lord Hawksbury, who has returned to England, his friend Sidney Manners, Sibly, Doctors Wilmore and Biles, Captain Fawcett, Tom Foxley, the detective, and little Charlie have dined together to celebrate the happy rescue of the two prisoners from the madhouse.

A golden day has passed, and round the cheerful fire the happy, genial party are assembled.

How spirit-stirring and instructive was the converse of these men of the world—the lawyer, the doctor, the sailor, the adventurer, the detective, the boy, were met—there reigned amongst them the warmest geniality, the most perfect harmony.

Each, in turn, had some merry jest, some "sunny memories," some thrilling story to relate to the amusement of the others.

With great warmth and enthusiasm Lord Hawksbury had told the tale of young Charley's rescue of the pretty Lilia Vasquez, and not a little was said of the Boy Pirate.

Charley's eyes brightened as he listened to a narration of some of the deeds of daring for which the Red Raven was famous.

Lord Hawksbury looked at the boy rather gravely, and said,

"Charley, I fear you are too much amused, too much dazzled by the tales that you hear of the great pirate. Believe me, these stories are harmful because they mislead you."

"Mislead me!" cried the boy, with enthusiasm. "Oh, my lord, I have heard you admit that the Red Raven is a magnificent fellow."

"So he is, Charley—brave, noble, generous, able; but he is a pirate!"

"Well, my lord, if he has all these good qualities, I can't see what it can matter. A pirate! He might be a privateer, or a post-captain, and not do worse things than he does—he only robs the rich to help the poor, like Robin Hood."

"Charley, you are young, earning money is hard work. You enter an office, or, to put you down a step, young fellow, on life's ladder—but not morally to abuse you—you are an errand-boy, a bricklayer's lad, or something of that kind. Remember, a good man in corduroys is a king; a monarch in ermine and purple who is a bad man, is a despicable wretch, for, take off his crown, and rub his name out of the Herald's books—call him Harry Tompkins instead of Henry Tudor, we'll say—and to prison he would go as a bad man, and a pest to society—a wife murderer and a bully. Call him Charley Smith instead of Charles Stuart, and let him rob his master's till instead of the nation's exchequer, and he would get his six months in the House of Correction."

"Well, my lord?"

"Are you willing to suppose yourself an errand-boy?"

"Very willing, my lord; I am not ill now, I could carry a hundredweight."

"Well then, you work hard for your master—he is cross with you, he is exacting, he expects more of you than you can do; your father at home goes too often to the dram-shop, your mother is shrewish, your playmates call you 'old quaker,' and 'steady-bones,' or something of the kind, because you don't care for their company, and have no wish to be seen with a pipe in your mouth, or to be heard talking of the 'champion fight,' or the 'Derby favourites.' You are 'spooney,' you know, not 'fly,' not 'up to snuff,' [not 'downy,'—have no appreciation for 'cracking cribs' with Blueskin and Jack Sheppard, no wish to murder crews with mothers and wives yearning at home for their return with 'Red Rovers,' or 'Black Ralphs,' though you may love a tale of dashing adventure, and profit by the moral of a bad man's wild career, miserable, contemptible existence, and dreadful end—you may sorrow for his bluntness, his generosity, and say 'what a pity,' 'what a mistake,' he ought to have been something better. A thief!—a sneaking thief!—a pirate! a throat-cutting, robbing pirate!—pah!—better be a snubbed, persecuted, plucky errand boy, that rubs windows till his arms ache, thrashes bullies till he is half killed, brings home full change when he is hungry—for you are an errand-boy you, know, Charley."

The boy laughed merrily.

The men joined heartily.

"Well, since you have been steady in my shop, since you have been a jolly, sky-larking, generous, hearty, hard-working, honest, plucky English lad, I promote you. I'm the chandler, don't you see, and make you my shop-man. I'm a little given to the tap-room, rather fond of my dram. I look like such a one, you'll say. Well, well, you might rob me through thick and thin, and I shouldn't know it. Tom Turf stole a half-crown from his master's till, won a sweepstake of a sovereign, and put back the money, and 'where's the harm?' But you reflect that Tom might have lost, might have 'got the sack,' and have been found out; and though he was not, he still deserves a good hiding, or a week in gaol; and you'd be very sorry to trust him to take home your wages to your mother. Now, you wouldn't like any one to distrust you. But you're honest, Charley, and though you like to read how the Boy Pirate's men stormed the Spanish fort to save their leader, or even how cleverly Jack Sheppard broke out of Newgate, and you're not over sorry when the gallant rover beats the man-of-war, with thrice his number of guns, or eludes him by his skilful seamanship, yet, for ten thousand worlds, you would not be a pirate, or a highwayman; you have too much pluck. You can look even hunger, unjust punishment, and very hard work in the face like a Briton, and toil on, though you have to say, 'No one praises me!' Hang praise! The world did not spring out of nothing by chance. A benevolent, though awful Creator, made it, and he whispers you in the still, small voice of your conscience, perhaps when you go to bed supperless — 'Labouring boy, you outface what these dashing, false heroes slunk from like cowards! You are *true* and *honest!* and God, who speaketh to thee now, will reward thee with peace that passeth understanding.' But, I have promoted you, Charley; you save your money, and as I've a nice little marriageable daughter, I give her to you, and leave you my shop, or you set up business for yourself, with your savings. You get rich. There is a poor widow, with her children, starving; you take her clothes, food, money. You make no brag about it; you are rewarded in seeing them happy. You would do this, would you not, Charley?"

"I hope so," returned the boy, gravely.

"I'm sure of it. Now, a rich man may be a good man—what do you say?"

"I should think so!" cried Charley, with animation. "The more money he has, the more chance he has of doing kind things."

"That's it. Well, when Sixteen-String Jack meets a lonely horseman, at dead of night, on Hownslow Heath, and bids him 'stand, and deliver!' and robs him of all he has upon him, surely you're not muff enough to think he asks the question—'Are you a liberal, charitable rich man, or are you a mean, stingy, oppressive rich man?'"

"Of course not."

"Well, suppose yourself a BOY PIRATE, or a BOY HIGHWAYMAN. You go to the poor starving widow and children, and you say, 'Here, my good woman, is money; buy food, and be merry.' She flings herself on her knees; she calls down the blessing of that God who has said, 'Thou shalt not steal,' upon you; and you leave her. But you feel, 'These thanks and praises are not justly mine; I filched this money, by brute force or sneaking cunning, from one who had not the strength or the courage to prevent me. I am not like the hardworked errand-boy, who fought with labour, and won its prizes, and then freely gave his hard earnings. I am a humbug, purely a humbug. When I want money, I steal it; what matter what I do with it; the more I give away the more cause I shall have to commit fresh crime.' You wouldn't like to feel like that, Charley?"

"No, no, no! God forbid."

"What is the most contemptible character in the world?"

"A coward."

"Then, be assured, a highwayman or a pirate is a coward. Use, and a boldness of spirit, or constitutional 'nerve,' will brace a man to put his head in a cannon's mouth, who would not have pluck and endurance sufficient to carry him through half a year's troubles and temptations."

"I'll never forget that," said Charley. "And though I may like to read wild and stirring stories, I'll never cease to remember that a man who can murder and steal is a coward as well as a villain, and I will study dark characters only to find out what is most to be avoided, and if I find good and brave qualities in them, I will think how easily even a great and good man may be led astray, and will be the more watchful over my own conduct."

"Well said, Charlie. Do this and you will be happy."

"And now, apropos of this theme," said the detective, "I will tell you a story—perhaps, you will say, a sad one—which comes within my experience, and which I can therefore vouch for as a fact.

"A city banker—we will call him Barton—had in his office two junior clerks; they were young men as much opposed in every attribute as one can imagine, except only that they were about the same age. Adolphus Frail and Tom Strong, we'll call them—I don't wish to mention real names even amongst ourselves. Frail was an extremely fine young fellow, as bright and handsome as noonday, and quite as genial. He dressed with perfect taste and elegance,

was most easy and gentlemanlike in his deportment, was a skilful penman, had tact and address, and was everybody's favourite. Few could see faults in Adolphus Frail; he was gay, they admired him the more; occasionally tipsy, but he always 'stood Sam;' not over truthful, but he was such a jolly fellow; he did not know always what he said, and you might be sure that he would keep his promises if he only thought of them; he had a stake on the St. Ledger, of course he had, what 'man about town' that would 'cry off' on such an occasion? Everything that Adolphus Frail did was right; everything about him was handsome.

"Poor Tom Strong, he was a heavy-browed young chap, inclined to be serious, diffident, awkward, and even somewhat clownish. The women called him a quiet young man, and the servant girls admitted that he was a droll fellow, in his quiet way; that he was very kind and patient; and that, though he always carried his two shillings per week to the post office, he was never without a penny for the street musician or crossing sweeper; had a broad shoulder ever ready to lift a burden too heavy for another, and his stumpy legs were ever nimble on an errand of kindness. Tom seldom drank, never smoked, could not tell the name of the winner of the last Derby, and, when pressed to go to places of amusement, would shake his head and 'wish he could afford to.' Tom went to church, too; he would creep into a highbacked pew in a quiet corner; bashfulness was his worst fault, and it is a fault, and the congregation would wonder whence proceeded that fine clear baritone voice that sang in such good time and tune, and with such manly, Christianly fervour. Tom was not very happy! He was sensitive, and he shrank from society, where he was only 'tolerated,' and evidently not wanted. Bashfulness is a great plague, it is a sort of disorder, very painful to the afflicted, and very irksome to others. Barton could not bear Tom; he saw that he was ungainly; that whenever he was addressed he turned red in the face, and that he was by no means of 'good address;' yet, if any mistake occured, if any difficulty was met with in overlooking the books, Tom was immediately appealed to, and, in 'his quiet way,' always rectified the error, or cleared up the difficulty. Adolphus, on the contrary, though he wrote a clear fine hand, and had an excellent turn for business, when he chose to display it, was utterly untrustworthy, and always making blunders which he laughed off in his 'nonchalant' sort of way, or by artful insinuation lay the blame on his fellow clerks.

"But, to cut short a long story, and to come to the point of it. Some defalcations appeared in the banker's books; Adolphus Frail had for some time looked ill and anxious, had drank rather freely, and as it was reported, had lost a stiff sum on the last race. However, like the king, 'he could do no wrong,' and suspicion soon fell upon poor Tom Strong. In a fit of anger the banker indirectly charged him with robbery. There are some burning mountains, sluggish-looking mounds, for years emitting no sparks, and covered with snow, but when an eruption *does* occur, it is terrible.

"Earnestness is eloquence, and once put such a fellow as Tom sufficiently on his mettle, to leap him over the barriers of his native diffidence and bashfulness, and he bursts out a regular Boanerges. With manly pathos, with deepest indignation, he repelled the charge, and the banker, enraged, gave him at once a dismissal from the office. However, it happened that a large sum of hard cash was in the bank, and some repairs were going on which rendered the place rather liable to be broken into; for several nights Tom had slept on the premises with a brace of pistols at his side, and either from a lingering sense of the injustice of his treatment, or from some other cause, the banker requested Tom to sleep once more in the office—the good-natured fellow consented. By an odd coincidence that very night occurred a desperate burglary; four desperate ruffians broke into the place. Tom wounded one of them, two fled, but one, more resolute than the rest, secured a bag of sovereings, and flew up the stairs to make his escape. Tom had fired both his charges; the pistols were not revolvers; the thief was armed with a knife and a pistol, but Tom stuck to him with English pluck. The pursued and the pursuer reached the roof of the house; the man fired at Tom; the bullet flew wide of its mark; Tom closed with the burglar; they stepped down on the narrow parapet, and poor Tom was pushed off and fell some thirty feet, till he crashed upon a parapet with the bag of gold in his hand. The thief decamped, and poor Tom was carried home to his aged mother, whom I have not yet mentioned. He seldom spoke of her himself; she was very poor, and Tom was an excellent son to her. The burglar who had pushed him from the roof was taken, and at his examination the unmitigated scroundrel swore unblushingly that Tom was an accomplice in the robbery, that the pistols had been fired by accident, and that the clerk had fallen from the house-top in his attempt to escape with the plunder in his grip. Of course no one believed this tissue of lies; but, to the disgrace of humanity, Barton the banker maintained a strict reserve, and having gone down into the country, paid no regard to the sufferings of his clerk, who lingered for many months, his little savings being soon exhausted, in extreme poverty and anguish at his mother's lodgings.

"I went to see him when he was dying.

"The defalcations at Barton's bank proved more heavy than they were at first supposed to be, and I had been commissioned to discover the defaulters.

"Not for an instant did I suspect poor Tom Strong, but I went to him in order to obtain another link to add to those I had already connected in the chain of evidence.

"The poor fellow was fading away: his cheeks were sunken, and glowed with a hectic patch; his eyes were deathly brilliant, his lips were fever-festered. He took me by the hand; a bright, triumphant smile shone on his dying face—

"'Sir, I am told you are a police officer; but, thank God, sir, I can look you in the face, and so I could, sir, were I in the prison clothes serving out the term of an unjust sentence, for I am honest, sir; honesty was my only birth-right, and I have kept it unsullied, and can with humble trust leave my poor mother to God's good care.'

"He spoke but little after this; he died soon after; he passed away very gently; they thought he was asleep.

"Now, Charley, who is your hero, the clerk or the burglar?"

"But this inhuman, rascally banker!" cried the boy, hotly.

"I never saw a man more conscience-striken than he was when informed of the death of poor Tom. He was not a bad man, but he was narrow-minded, and swayed entirely by prejudices; he had taken a dislike against Tom and therefore was always ready to believe ill of him. You will meet many such folks as that old banker, Charley, as you carve your way through the world; getting through life is like sawing a plank, and these obstinate, prejudging people are knots in your plank, and precious tough ones. However, the banker did all in his power, by attention to the living, to make amends for the wrong he had done to the dead, and Tom's mother never wanted for any comfort while she lived; but her heart was broken, poor creature, and she soon followed her only and loved son to that land where the just and the rightly brave are richly rewarded."

"And what became of Mr. Adolphus?"

"He absconded. I was soon on his track; he was taken in a wretched condition in company with a gang of swell mobsmen and skittle sharpers. He was tried, convicted, and sentenced to seven years' penal servitude, but is now at large on a ticket of leave, and, I hope, will keep on the square."

After a few hours had passed away in genial conversation the party broke up.

Tom Foxley extended his hand to Silas Rye, and after congratulating both him and Fawcett on their fortunate escape from the madhouse, he shook hands all round.

"And now, gentlemen," he said, with a smile "it becomes needful to bid you farewell, and a long farewell, for it is probable we shall never again meet under circumstances similar to the present, for I am going a long journey on a perilous mission; the ship sails to-morrow, and, as this moment of parting has come, I request your good remembrances of me. It may be I shall return triumphant; it is possible I may be laid low; in any case, I shall never forget the happy hours spent in your society."

"And are you resolved, Mr. Foxley, to hunt your brother's murderer in the far prairies of America?" said Silas.

"Unalterably."

"You are taking out of my hands a work I had myself resolved to carry out," said Silas, grimly. "I had myself sworn to bring that villian Harwolf to the gallows."

"Believe me, he will die a very ignominious death. Here is the shot with which he killed my brother, and, as every 'bullet has its billet,' the destination of this bullet is the villain Harwolf's black heart!"

CHAPTER CV.

THE VULTURE CHASES THE PINNACE.

TRUE to his promise Black Ralph sent the pinnace ashore, towed by the jolly boat.

The men who brought it shook hands with Cassidy and Oakland, and left them with hearty expressions of good will and wishes for their prosperous navigation.

Upon examining the pinnace the castaways found it to contain provisons, arms, and ammunition; clothes, compass, and quadrant, and everything necessary for a long cruise.

Amongst other things, was found a small casket, labelled, "For Deborah, lost to me: a rover's and a lover's gift." The box contained some costly jewellery.

The castaways embarked the next day.

The sun shone with tropical splendour, the sea was calm and the wind fair.

They sped along through the scattering brine at a great rate.

Soon the land hazed and then disappeared.

They were rising and plunging in their little ship, far away in the Pacific.

Night fell.

The stars burst forth with wondrous brilliancy in strange galaxies.

A solemn watch passed slowly by.

The women retired to the cabin to sleep.

Cassidy and Oakland sat on deck.

Sea and sky, sky and sea.

Opal the water's hue, golden clear the stars beam. Like the winnowing of the wings of viewless angels the balmy breeze wafted fitfully past.

"Cassidy," said Oakland, "that scoundrel Harwolf cruises in these waters!"

"I did not think of that," said the other, with a start. "Do you think that we are in danger of being overhauled by the villain?"

"I cannot tell."

"Nor I."

"How soundly the girls sleep."

"Aye, and the skipper too!"

"He has been watchful—he is worn out with anxiety."

"Your sweetheart is a sweet, a charming girl, Sam!" said Oakland, warmly.

"Do you think so?" returned Cassidy, with a quiet smile.

"Can any one dispute it?"

"I think not. Tell me, Oakland—you love the Jewess?"

"How shall I answer?"

"Truthfully."

"I do!"

"Does she return your love?"

"I fear not—a deep impression has been made on her by another."

"Ha! do you know that?"

"I fear so."

"Have you told her your sentiments?"

"What!—when we were alone in the desert island?"

"Aye, mate."

"Could you think me so base?"

"Why base!"

"I am not worthy of her; she is my superior in all, and would I take advantage of her position to perse-cute her with addresses that most likely would be unwelcome?"

"If I loved a girl I should tell her so;" said Cassidy, cooly.

"You are a strange fellow, Sam."

"Am I?"

"Aye, mate; in all my experience I never met your equal."

"My equal! How's that?"

"You are so cool, so calm; what exasperates or delights another seems to have no effect on you."

"I cannot see the use of chafing against stone walls, and the more deliberately you set about climbing them the less likely you are to break your neck."

Oakland laughed.

"What do you think of that fellow Harwolf!"

"He will live till he's hanged."

"And Talbot."

"He will rant and sing till he's run down, and then he'll blow up his ship, himself and all hands."

"Cassidy!"

"Well, Oakland."

"When we reach the mainland what shall we do?"

"If we can't find a ship we must travel overland."

"That's evident; but how shall we carry the girls safely through all the dangers that beset the long, long path?"

"We must leave that to fate!"

"How solemn, how calm and holy seems this watch, Cassidy. Do you know, when I am in these seas, I always think of the first navigators? what men they must have been! what hearts of oak!"

"Aye, mate, I often think of what I learned at school in my Horace."

"The Mantuan poet; but I know no Latin, Cassidy. I always thought that you were a scholar; what does the poet say?"

"That triple brass must have banded the breast of that man who first trusted himself in a fragile bark to the treacherous main."

"Sail in the starboard-bow!" cried Oakland, suddenly."

The night was bright as day; the glowing moon, the dazzling starbeams, the pelucid air, the flashing waters render the atmosphere ablaze with silver light.

Snowy white as the wing of a sea-gull a large vessel loomed in the distance.

"My God, Cassidy, we are lost! it is the Black Vulture!" cried Oakland.

"Aye, mate."

"I will kill myself rather than be taken."

"Hist!"

"The villain! Oh that I had pistoled him when I had a chance—after all our dangers, Sam!"

"Hush, mate, you will wake the sleepers."

"Were they not best awakened?"

"Why? could they do better than remain uncon-scious? they could not help themselves, and would only hinder us."

"Set the gib, Cassidy."

"Aye, mate."

"The cursed 'Vulture' hugs the wind."

"She bears down on us."

"Aye, mate, our chance is small."

"Do you think she spies us?"

"It is to be questioned, as we lie."

"There is no question, Sam; see, she shakes out her royals, and the wind is freshening."

"As well for us as her."

As he said this, the Scotch captain came on board.

"I think ye maun be tired, Mr. Cassidy, and you, too, Mr. Oakland; its nae to be expected, and it is nae necessary that ye suld keep the dog-watches, my guid laddies, and leave an old seaman, like mysel, to sleep like a passenger in his ham-mock. Eh, but the wind's canny."

"But there's something driving before the wind that's not 'canny,' Mr. Macallister," said Oakland.

"Weel, noo, its the awesome 'Black Vulture.' We mauna fash, laddies, and aboon a' we mauna wake the puir lasses. If ye'll take my advice ye'll just luff, Meester Cassidy. Noo, dinna ye see our hope and comfort rising in a cloud aboot 'as big as a man's hand '—nor-by-nor-west?"

The men looked eagerly in the direction indicated.

A mass of cloud was seen rolling as if upon the surf itself.

"We maun try anither sail, sae—that's bonnie. I wish that we could get a wee bit nearer to the wind; but we maun aboot ship while we have sae much as an infant's breath to keep us running."

"Look, Cassidy," cried Oakland, suddenly. "She runs up a signal—this night is not less light than day—and we can see it distinctly."

"Aye, mate; 'heave to,' that's what it means—an order we are precious likely to obey. Slacken that hawser, mate, so we make way; the wind veers in our favour. Curse that hound! if I could but turn our little pinnace, by some mermaid's charm, into a barque half the 'Vulture's' burthen, I would run him down and swing him like a cat, for he is a coward at his heart, though he shams courage. Pah! did you ever conceive of such a skunk?"

A puff of smoke jetted from one of the larboard ports of the "Vulture."

A shot came spanking along the surface of the sea and sank at some distance in the wake of the pinnace.

The "Vulture," however, luffed, and fell off from the wind.

The girls rushed on deck.

When they saw from whence the shot was fired, they sank on their knees in intense agony and fear.

The pinnace, under every inch of canvas her strained masts would carry, shot along through the glossy billows.

They were distancing the "Vulture" every instant.

The mass of cloud still rolled towards them.

The "Vulture" fired several shots, but without effect.

An hour had passed away.

Again the wind veered.

The ship gained upon them fast.

The girls screamed, as one shot flashed down into the depths within a yard of their stern.

Just as their case was getting hopeless, when the frail mast bent like a sapling under its weight of canvas, the cloud reached them, and the next moment they found sanctuary from their deadly enemy behind a curtain of wreathing mist.

CHAPTER CVI.

THE CASTAWAYS ABOARD THE RAVEN.

THE Boy Pirate did not long remain cruising off the the coast of South America.

Being anxious to return to Europe he disguised his ship as a Spanish merchantman, removed the raven from the prow, and substituted the gilt glow-ing head of a Spanish saint, and called his ship the "Santa."

Leon de Zamora had disembarked at an island in the North Atlantic, where a complete flotilla of small ships awaited him.

Here the Spaniard feasted the crew of the pirate

vessel, and loaded our hero and his lovely wife with an abundance of the most costly treasures; for the lonely island was his magazine, and hither he had, from time to time, brought the booty he had won as a privateer and rover.

A happy month was passed on Leon's treasure-island by the Boy Pirate, and the rest, and here, when the time for sailing had arrived, were left the old Admiral Giraldez and the beautiful Mona, whom Zamora had married.

Ida, the octoroon, still remained on board with Lilia, to whom she was deeply attached; the rover's ship to her was an asylum of refuge; she was a slave, and in the world a slave can have no home.

The vessel had been under weigh for several days.

It was a glorious day, the stately ship slipped along through the glancing billows before a fair wind; the sky was pure opal, the ocean green gold, and at intervals a long line of porpoises would roll by, or a flight of flying fish take their oblique bound from billow to billow, the wide-winged albatross throbbed on his strong flight from aloft, or the screaming petrels swerved and skimmed with flashing wings along the glassy foam-rimmed waves.

Lilia and Ida reclined on the settee at the open windows of the state cabin.

The Boy Pirate lounged on a couch, while Gomez sat at the table with a map before him.

"My thoughts tend that way, Gomez," said the Boy Pirate, in pursuance of the subjects of their conversation. "I can depend on you, I am sure."

"Captain," returned the grave Spaniard, "I cannot say that I feel the same compunction in following our present calling as you do; but, as we have been so successful, and are enriched by means that are not revolting, though they are lawless, I believe that not only honour, but profit also, would accrue from such a course as that which you propose."

"Oh, Christopher! to be no more a pirate!—to rend the black flag, and mount the colours of a national deliverer!" cried Lilia, eagerly. "You are resolved on this?"

Gomez folded his arms, and bent his eyes on the ground.

Christopher sighed, and answered, sadly,

"Lilia, my own, what is done cannot be undone; my star that burns so brightly now may be eclipsed. When men have gone so far as I have gone there is but little safety in repentance."

"But there is dignity, self-solace, forgiveness from God and man; there is joy among the angels," cried Lilia, with enthusiasm.

"Captain," said the stern Spaniard, with a dry smile, "pirates we are, and pirates we must remain; whatever good we have done in the past, however we may better our best deeds in the future, the world will not condone the fact of our mounting the 'Rover,' although it has grinned ghastly death only on the oppressors of others, or our own natural enemies; we shall receive the same punishment as if we were the most ruthless of savages. No, captain, the 'Ceres' lays off the reef, and is richly laden; let us pursue our true prize; glory is bright, but unsubstantial."

Ida drew to the side of the Spaniard and touched him lightly on the arm.

"Senor," she said, with a beaming smile, "your promise—a sail in shore; the pinnace is ready."

"You are right, Gomez," said the pirate captain, moodily, without noticing the gentle interruption of the conversation made by Ida; "there is no chance for us but to stick to our colours to the last!"

"Are you coming, Senor," said Ida, with a light laugh, "or is Mr. Brierly to be my 'convoy?'"

The Spaniard smiled, bowed courteously, and left the room.

Ida kissed the pirate's wife, and whispered something in her ear.

Christopher sat in a fit of depression, his brow bent, and his lips compressed.

Ida left the cabin.

Lilia approached her husband; she threw herself beside him, wound her arms round him, and said, passionately,

"Oh, Christopher, hear me. I have followed you joyfully through all your changing fortunes; you have no cause to complain of me. There was a time—the dear old time—though I shudder to think of it now, when in my father's home I mourned for you, and only at times have vaguely hoped. I was your ideal then, your love; what would you not have done for me then?"

"'Tis easier to do some things than it is to leave others undone," returned her husband, a little coldly, a cloud of despondent care settling on his forehead.

"Ah, yes! then it was different; I was your love then," murmured Lilia, in a voice of tender reproach; "now I am but your wife, the every-day partner of your griefs and joys; use and constant communion beget indifference; my prayers are nothing to you now, when the slightest hints of my wildest wish would once nerve you as an all-powerful motive to the most daring ventures; but now——"

"Lilia, you are the solace of all my misery, the joy-light that gilds my dark mind-world, the fresh and strong tendril that clings round my seared heart to sustain it, to give it life; but you are an impulsive woman, and you expect me to accomplish impossible ends by inadequate means. What can I do, a branded outcast, a felon, a pirate? what hope is there for me?"

"Hope! There is hope of heaven," said Lilia, warmly.

"Heaven!" murmured the pirate, musingly.

"Lilia, I will tell you of a strange dream I had when I was chained in the dungeons of San Salvador."

One of the pirates hurriedly entered the cabin.

"Captain!" he said, "there is a sail to the leeward, and, by the look of it, I judge it to be the 'Vulture.'"

"Ross, that's brave news," cried the Boy Pirate, quickly; "should your conjecture prove true we will give chase."

"Is Harwolf on board?" asked Lilia.

"I hope so!" said Christopher, with bitter emphasis.

"But, husband, he has two ships."

"I wish he had twenty!"

"His consort, captain, seems to have parted company," said the officer, "at least she has not yet hove in sight."

"We'll not fire a shot till she bears up," cried Christopher, impetuously. "Mount our own bunting, my hearty, and give orders to make all sail. Aye, beat to quarters, and run up a signal for Gomez to bring back the pinnace. I'll come on deck directly; weigh anchor at once."

"Aye, captain," the officer returned up the hatchway.

"Christopher, what do you intend to do with that villain, if you overhaul his vessel?" asked the rover's wife, anxiously."

"Do not plead for him, my own. I will not be moved from my purpose, which is to have retribution for all the cruel wrongs I have suffered at that scoundrel's hands," cried the Boy Pirate, buckling on his sword, and selecting a couple of pistols from a stand of arms.

Lilia did not speak, but clung imploringly to her husband.

He kissed her, and pressing her for a moment to his heart, placed her upon the settee, and with a bright smile left the cabin.

He came on deck.

The men were clustered in the forecastle, in the rattlings, and on the quarter, eagerly watching the distant vessel.

"'Bout ship!" cried old Brierly, who was pacing the deck with his glass under his arm, and looking with a brightened eye towards the speeding ship.

"Way aloft!" cried the Boy Pirate.

"Ready, aye, ready?"

"Ready it is."

"Helm's a lee!"

"Cap'en, she hugs the wind," said Brierly, discontentedly.

"Aye, Jack, we shall lose her," returned our hero, with impatience.

This prediction proved true, greatly to the chagrin of the pirates; the rival ship was right ahead of the wind, and soon disappeared from view.

The Boy Pirate gave strict orders that a vigilant watch should be kept, and directed the officer of the watch to send him word if they should come within sight of the "Vulture."

As the pirate captain was about to return below, his intent was arrested by the cry from aloft.

"Sail on the starboard quarter!"

He turned.

Two little vessels were speeding along before a fresh breeze.

They were similar in size and build.

One was easily recognisable as the "Raven's" pinnace, the other appeared to be a little cutter.

The Boy Pirate was rather surprised at seeing the pinnace thus consorted, and awaited in some excitement the return of Gomez and Ida.

Dick Caffyn and Gomez came on deck.

"Captain," said Caffyn, eagerly addressing the Boy Pirate, "we have brought on board two of Black Ralph's gang. It seems that they have escaped with some prisoners."

"They are welcome, Dick," said Christopher; "but did you see the 'Black Vulture' to the starboard? Where is her consort?"

"Captain, they have parted company," returned Caffyn; "but our guests will tell you all about her."

Cassidy and Oakland jumped on board.

They handed the girls over the companion-way.

The old Scotchman followed.

The men moored the pinnace astern, and came on board.

The Boy Pirate received his guests with his wonted courtesy.

He fixed a searching eye upon Cassidy.

The ex-mate of the "Vulture" returned the glance with one of quiet self-possession, and scanned the noble form of the the Boy Pirate with an approving glance.

The two men seemed to conceive for each other a strong liking, even at first sight, and shook hands warmly.

After they had gone below, Jack Brierly walked aft, and spoke to Tom Garrod.

"Where did you find these supercargo, Tom?" he asked of the boatswain.

"Like turtles crawling along the beach, sir," returned the seaman, laughing. "They had run the pinnace up a shallow creek, and docked her in a place where the trees grew as thick as nests in Teneriffe. They were mightily skeared at the 'Vultue's' wing in the offing, and glad enough to have the Ravens for their escort. Two on 'em's reg'lar cherubs—one a angel with a broad Scotch dialect, the other a daughter of Judah, which, it seems, belongs to the family of the old chap as Dan Harwolf knifed or tomahawked afore he left England. But, what's the orders, sir? Are we to make all sail to chase the 'Vulture,' or are we to heave to?"

"Crowd on every stitch, Tom; the cabin passengers will know the 'Vulture's' bearings, and we must keep in her wake."

"Aye, sir."

When the old pirate had retired below Tom Garrod gave orders to the men aloft, took the wheel for awhile' and then, having left it in charge of another seaman, threw himself under the lee of the weather bulwark, and was in an instant surrounded by his shipmates.

"You told us, Tom," said one of the seamen, "as you'd twist us a yarn about a flood as you were a witness to."

"Well, if you weren't sich unbelieving lubbers—"

"Stopper all, Tom! we believe's yer as much as the compass. Heave ahead, mate."

"But, messmates, if so be as a indiwiddle is a seaman and a man of honour, dam'me, sich insinua-

tions as I've heard fall from some of you insulting swabs comes across his feelins like the first lash of the boatswain's cat. Now, spinning a lying galley yarn is a thing my principles are quite avarse to, and——"

"Avast, Tom; we knows as you are a reg'lar 'weracity.' I sailed in a craft of that name, and allers under false colours, but don't stop clapper-clawing till eight bells; heave and a weigh."

"Well, mates, I'm going to tell you a yarn about a inundation as swamped the decks of a whole French department. Aye, mates, and carried off everything from hull to trucks, and left the whole country reg'lar water-logged. You know what it is that I am going to discourse about, and, that you may be sure I ain't running the rig on ye, you may overhaul some of the land lubbers' log-books, and you'll find it set down in black and white. But this is my experience."

There was a profound silence for a few moments, when Tom thought proper to resume.

"You have heard on Mount Vesuvius, and how sometimes there's a 'blow up,' when the magazines get fired by some of those careless giant swabs that live in the hold of that nat'ral fire-ship, and will smoke their clay pipes agen all regulations?"

"But, Tom, your yarn's consarning of a flood, and not a 'ruption," cried one of the men.

"Hearties, you'll have to go through fire and water afore you come to the moral," rejoined the boatswain, dryly, "and as for you, Jem, why we all knows as you ought to be Fust Lord of the Admiralty, but, while you are only a foremast swab, have a little piteous compassion on ignorant sinners as don't quite know the way through lubber's hole; condescend not to put in your stroke oar."

"Belay! Stopper all! Lay by, ye swab!" roared and growled the indignant auditors at the irreverent interrupter.

Jem subsided.

"Heave ahead, Tom!" they cried encouragingly, to the boatswain; "we'll see as you steers a clear course, only ship anchor and make sail."

"Well, hearties, you all know as there's monkeys at that sea-wall, Gibraltar, with the most wicious disposition for making grimaces at their betters?"

"Werry true, Tom."

"But all grinning monkeys don't live at Gibraltar, and some on 'em goes aloft as if their legs were broken," the erratic boatswain continued, with a malicious leer at poor Jem.

"Axing pardon, Tom, and nothin' personal," remarked an old salt, very cautiously, "but our hintellects, you know, gets a little sea-fogged in the dog-watches these misty nights, and we don't quite see the connection between 'ruptions of a burning mountain, rock-apes, and French floods; but, howsomever, we axes pardon."

"And granted it is, hearties, 'cos you means respectful. Well, you know, when you pipes a tune or claps hands, these Gibraltar monkeys will fly up to the main-royal pints of the cliff like a flock of pigeons let out of a coop."

"That's right, Tom!"

"Well, mates, just as the barber's lather runs over the creature——"

"Avast!" groaned one of the erudite. "Burning lava runs over the crater, you mean."

Tom got red in the face, and, shrugging his shoulders, preserved for some time a dogged silence.

It was only at the most urgent entreaties, and after the black-balling of the imprudent commentator, that the boatswain continued.

"And swamps the whole country as it did when it buried them two ports, Hercules and Pompey."

"Know'd 'em, buckras," cried Zampa, eagerly; "both them niggers raised on ole Rashliegh's plantation. Hercules' gal stole one ob mas'rs shirts, and gave it the nigger; and, lor, he got most amazin' cut up for it. Wall, this Pomp had a drefful fight with a devil of a chap named Cæsar, at a break-down. Poor Pomp was forced to run; Cæsar gave him the orfullest licking. Know'd 'em all, buckras."

PREPARATIONS FOR THE TORTURE.

"Mates, is this confounded——"

"Heave ahead, Tom," cried the men, bestowing several admonitory kicks upon the negro.

"And as the monkeys fly up the rattlings so did the waters of the Garonne break over the bulwarks and swamp the land fore and aft, and so did the poor devils run from under hatches and scamper up the shrouds and man the cross-trees all over the fleet, or the town, rather—for, let me tell you, hearties, that I lay in dock at that harbour till I was launched like a pressed-man, quite agin my inclinations. But I have 'lost way,' through you, officious, meddling lubbers, and I must 'haul up.' I was a younker then, about sixteen years of age, and I was apprenticed on board a wessel as was owned by a skipper of free-trading principles, and I was left in

No. 35.

this little town. Blow me, if I don't forget the name of it, but it was Chatter something——"

"Chateau. Aye, Tom, never mind the name."

"It was a rum little wigwam, built of long, narrow houses, with six or eight decks, and more ports than a seventy-four; the roofs had a run as sharp as the forecastle, and on either side of the houses grew tall trees—popular, they calls 'em, and 'popular' they were, for everybody seemed to think as much on 'em as we do of the foremast; and werry much like the mast they were, 'specially when it's unrigged and a broom is mounted at the head. These trees, hearties, had a precious long run of stem, but deuced little leaves or branches at the top-peaks."

"Shiver the trees, Tom!"

"So we shall presently, for the devil of a breeze

is blowing up, I can tell ye, messmates; at any rate, the whole place had a bright-painted, wooden, hulky look, like a child's farm out of a Dutch toy-box, and the female cherubs wore tall white caps—aye, as white as the surf on the head-waves, and tall as sugar-loaves. Howsomever, it were a nice berth, and I was werry jolly on that land cruise; werry pleasant the soft tack which the lubbers call 'pain,' as if it were teeth-breaking sea-biscuit, and not soft tommy."

"'Pang,' Tom, 'pang,'" suggested the privileged amendator, with humility.

"Well, 'pangs' or 'pains,' it's about the same, I s'pose," returned Tom, impatiently. "Now, what was I——"

"You were taking 'pains,'" rejoined one of the salts, grinning.

"Right, Bill, I were, and 'hoofs' also."

"Œufs they call eggs, in French, Tom."

"Well, I dare say you know more about 'hoofs,' and long ears, too, than I do, my hearty, so I won't be personal. Now, I was aboard a provision-ship, kept by a purser as sold butter, which they call 'beer' out of contradiction, I s'pose, and 'freen and frummage'—that's flour and cheese—and other sich pursers' stores; and I ran alongside of the prettiest little craft as ever blessed my day-lights; she was the purser's darter, a reg'lar little beauty. Now, it was one night, about middle-watch, when we were having a bit of a sky-larking in old Mounseer Beauventre's state cabin—I believe it was at what they call 'Parks,' which means Easter, for they makes use of our signals, only they changes the numbers—and we were all as jolly as liberty-men after Trafalgar, when in rushes a chap, his jawing-tackle——"

"Sail-ho!" cried the man on the foretop.

"Stopper all, Tom," cried one of the men. "We must caulk seams, and keep the water out till next watch. We must have your flood some other time, for, blow me, here comes young Caffyn, with his face as red as a marine's jacket."

"Tom Garrod," cried Caffyn.

"Aye, aye, sir."

"Beat to quarters."

"Aye, sir."

"Forecastle, there!"

"Aye, sir."

"What sort of craft is that yonder?"

"A brig, sir. All sail set."

Dick snatched up a glass.

He looked eagerly at the craft.

Another sail loomed in sight.

In the offing there was a long high rock with a backbone of low hills and sandy islands.

Round the edge of this the brig steered off and disappeared.

The other sail was soon also lost to sight.

The Boy Pirate, Gomez, Brierly, and the rest of the officers came on deck, and eagerly scanned the receding masts as they moved along beyond the low bluffs.

Cassidy came up the hatchway in time to catch a glance at the sail of the ship that had last hove in sight and scudded away to behind the island.

"Captain," he said, with a gleam of subdued fierceness in his fine black eye, "that is some lubberly merchantman crawling inshore, perhaps, for water, perhaps——"

"And what do you make of the other stranger, Mr. Cassidy?" asked the Boy Pirate.

"Captain," returned the other, with a smile, "it is your rival, the 'Black Vulture.'"

"My rival no longer, but my prize!" cried the Red Raven, hotly. "At last my enemy and I will meet broadside to broadside, and the career of one or both of us must end at once!"

CHAPTER CVII.
THE RESCUE FROM DROWNING.

THE "Miranda" was a stately brig of many tons burden.

Her bows appeared high out of the water; her build was somewhat heavy, and her gear cumbersome; yet there was in her rig no trace of the slovenliness which too often characterises merchant craft.

Her captain was an elderly man, a thorough weather-beaten, impassable, keen-eyed seaman, his voice somewhat husky from the sea-damps which he had inhaled for years, his grey brows arched over a clear, calm, yet quick roving eye, his forehead lined and wrinkled by intense concentration of mental power, his hair bleached by anxieties and time.

His name was Fleming; he was greatly respected both by the masters and by his crew, and was responsible for a very costly freight of sundry articles of ornament, usefulness, and defence.

The red tompions of four guns projected from ports fore and aft of the ship.

The crew consisted of a number of fine, well-selected men, who seemed to be exceedingly alert, cheerful, and contented, and particularly steady and competent.

On board the vessel was a supercargo of four passengers.

An old man and his daughter, with her maiden aunt, and a young fellow, who had no connection with this family, and who spent but little time in converse with any one aboard, being either at study in his cabin or else aloft in the foretop, watching the rich and varied hues of the sky by day or night.

The first mentioned party comprised Mr. Eldridge, one of the firm who were owners of the ship, his maiden sister, Prudence, and his daughter, a sweet girl, of eighteen, whose name was Florence.

We must anticipate by a few hours the events recorded in the latter part of the last chapter.

Eldridge was sitting on the main-deck, his daughter on one side, and his sister on the other.

The girl and her aunt were at work, while the old man was deeply engaged in perusing the papers.

"La! aunt, I don't see what harm there can be," cried Florence, pettishly, "in my interest for a poor young gentleman who looks so sad, and seems so quiet and unassuming."

"My dear child, you are young, and unsophisticated. You know, my dear, that men are never to be trusted," returned Aunt Prudence, prudishly. "I am continually on my guard; I can appreciate courtesy, and even gallantry, but I am never so deluded as to think there is any lasting sincerity in any man; for remember, my dear, all men are—story-tellers."

"But when a man does not speak at all, he cannot be charged with telling falsehoods. Besides, aunt, what would be the use of his telling falsehoods to me? If men pride themselves on their powers of dissimulation, he would have very little credit, for I should be sure to believe him."

As Florence said this, with the most refreshing naïveté, her aunt shook her head, and remarked, with a deep sigh,

"Alas, child, if I had been as impressionable as you, or so little under the controul of discretion, I don't know what might have happened; it is even possible that I might have been deluded into matrimony by some smooth-spoken young gentleman, and there are—at least, perhaps, I should say there were—many who paid me great attention. My extreme caution, in two cases, my dear Florence, though it preserved me from compromising myself by incurring the anxieties, risks, and responsibilities of matrimony, was fatal to two of my most ardent admirers."

"Dear aunt, is it possible?"

"I don't know why it should not be possible, my dear," returned Miss Prudence, rather testily. "But it was so very shocking, the result, that had I not have been sufficiently strong-minded to have been able to support myself on the consciousness of having done my duty, I think I should have died too."

"Died! Why, aunt, did your poor rejected lovers kill themselves?"

"Indeed they did, my love; they committed suicide in the most determined manner. One of them threw himself from his horse while hunting, and the other, seeking to drown his sorrows in the cup——"

"Poisoned himself!"

"No, my dear; but approaching a window when he was in a state of inebriation, he fell out, and broke his neck. After these calamities, it was always my first care, on making a male acquaintance, to inform the gentleman of my positive determination to remain single. But, even then, I could not prevent much disappointment, and on more than one occasion, I think, if romantic delicacy had not restrained my admirers from broaching the subject of love, I might have been moved to pity by the fervent devotion I inspired."

"What are you talking about, sister Prue?" asked Eldridge, raising his eyes from the paper.

"About our fellow-passenger, papa," returned Florence; "the strange young man, who is so quiet and reserved."

"Well, what of him, Florry?"

"Oh! nothing, papa; but aunt wants to make me believe he is a dangerous character."

"Most probably your aunt is right, my dear. Still waters run deep."

"And deep waters are most dangerous, but they are more noble and more useful than shallow waters."

"What, have you fallen in love with the Childe Harold? See how he stands, with folded arms, looking over the tafrail, broodingly and romantically, as if he had all the sorrow or all the guilt of the world on his young shoulders."

"Papa, you are speaking rather unkindly."

"Not a whit. I should like to do him a service."

"Indeed! What service, papa?"

"I should like to give him a month's work at balancing the books of the firm."

"And I'll warrant he could do it better than the prosiest old clerk in your office," returned Florence, warmly.

Eldridge laughed at his daughter's vehemence.

Presently the subject of their canversation walked past them.

He smiled and bowed courteously, and then went below by the after hatchway.

The captain of the "Miranda" now approached, his dark, weather-beaten face beaming with cheerfulness.

"Well, Mr. Fleming," said Eldridge, with a smile, "and pray how does the ship progress? Have we not fallen to leeward?"

"Not a point, Mr. Eldridge," returned the captain, with a smile, "and now our only danger lurks along the coasts of these islands in the shape of pirate sloops and schooners."

"Pirates! But surely the 'Miranda' is a match for a pirate? We have four guns and a stern-chaser, besides a numerous crew of brave and well disposed fellows."

"For any ordinary rascal we are a match, most decidedly; but for the extraordinary fellow we are in some danger of running fowl of in these waters—but, there, I must not alarm you needlessly, and this rover I am told is not the worst rogue into whose hands we could fall; indeed, there are some generous acts recorded of him."

"To whom do you allude?"

"To the Boy Pirate—sometimes called the Red Raven!"

"The great Red Raven! Does he cruise in these waters, captain?" cried Florence.

"He did some time ago, but I should think the atmosphere is growing too warm for him."

"Oh, how much I should like to see him!" cried Florence, with animation.

"In an iron cage, disarmed and pinioned, my dear young lady, but not afloat in his craft of death; he is terrible then to the bravest men. Your preconceptions of a dashing rover would be sadly disconcerted, I assure you."

"Have you ever seen him, captain?"

"No, Miss Eldridge, and I have not the slightest wish to make his acquaintance."

"He is a fine fellow, nevertheless."

"So is a tiger or a leopard; and nowhere so fine as in his native forest, prowling free; but we could well dispense with a sight of his terrific beauty to be out of the reach of his terrific claws."

"Florence, I am positively ashamed of you," cried Aunt Prudence, much scandalised, "even to pollute your lips with the name of such a monster. If you or myself were to fall into his hands! I faint at the slightest thought of such a catastrophe."

Florence blushed and smiled at her aunt's tirade.

The captain looked to the leeward, and suddenly exclaimed,

"A pretty school of flying-fish yonder, Miss Florence."

The girl rose quickly, and ran to the side of the vessel.

Glancing like silver arrows in their oblique flight, a number of those beautiful creatures darted through the air from one billow to another at a great distance.

It was a very pretty sight, and the light-hearted daughter of the merchant laughed and exclaimed with delight.

More than once she recoiled with a slight cry when startled by the rush; she recoiled as one of the creatures flew past her and got enmeshed in the rattlings or thudded on to the deck.

She had leaped on the side of a carronade.

She peeped over the side of the vessel, and watched the rush of the benito, that deadly enemy of the flying-fish, as it skimmed along the surface of the water in pursuit of its prey.

The ship lurched.

The spray from one of the sea-boats that successively dashed against the bows of the vessel flew over the heedless girl, and, as she looked down into the creamy pool of foam beneath the dark hull, and felt the ship swerving over on its side, she was suddenly taken with a sensation of sickness, and, her foot slipping, she dropped from the open port plash into the sea.

As, with a thrilling shriek, she saw the dark vessel roll heavily over on the opposite side from herself, as if discarding and leaving her to perish, she threw back her arms and sank down, down through the cold and treacherous waters.

The scene on deck was very distressing.

So instantaneously had the catastrophe occurred, and so long was the ship in righting herself, that some moments had elapsed before Florence was seen drifting away on the surf.

Along the side of the vessel appeared a row of eager faces, expressing the utmost horror and commiseration.

Yet, though ropes were thrown and the men flew to the davits to lower away the boats, none ventured to plunge into the sea.

In fact, the currents in the roadstead between the islands among which they were sailing were particularly strong and dangerous.

The captain had thrown his brawny arms about the father of the girl, and forcibly restrained him from leaping overboard.

His eyes glaring distractedly, his teeth clenched, and his arms extended, the old merchant fought to the bulwark.

He must inevitably have leaped into the waves, and most probably drowned, but for the sturdy intervention of the captain.

Miss Prudence had fainted.

She lay prone on the deck, in a state of happy unconsciousness, and even no obstruction to the unheeding surrounders, who had no eyes but for the poor girl struggling in the waters.

The boat was just lowering; when a bitter cry burst from the lips of the unhappy father, and was involuntarily echoed by the seamen.

The girl had disappeared from the surface of the water.

Apparently she had sunk for the last time.

A man at this moment leaped upon the carronade from which poor Florence had taken her fatal step.

Again there was a cry from the deck.

Once more the girl appeared.

The next instant every eye was turned upon the youthful form that stood perched, light as a bird, beside the gun.

It was the mysterious passenger.

The captain would have interposed, but, regardless of his warning cry, the young man dashed off the side, and dived deep down into the surging billows.

In another moment he was striking boldly towards the sinking girl.

The sea rolled heavily.

He buffeted hard with the wilding brine.

He was lifted high upon the top of a " header," and then pitched down into the trough of the sea.

It seemed to the swimmer that instead of reaching his object he was only receding from it.

Encouraging shouts and cheers reached him from the ship.

A long line of foam and serf dashed over his face and head.

His arms seemed numb and powerless.

His legs sank and he felt the horror that comes with the sense of the utter incapability of the watery space to support its struggling burden.

Yet he was a fearless fellow, and as the milky arm of the poor girl was hopelessly thrown in the air, he battled on fiercely.

Florence sank.

Her deliverer plunged into the cold bosom of the sea.

He clutched her.

Feebly her supine arms drooped around him.

He grasped her with convulsive tenacity.

Her weight dragged him down.

The water hissed and grugled in his ears; the pangs of suffocation in his throat almost caused him to relinquish his hold, and the strong impulse of self-preservation impelled him to raise himself to the surface, and seek nothing but his own safety.

He resisted all these feelings, and clung to his prize.

They rose together.

Heavenly harmony to the ears of the drowning man was the steady stroke of the throbbing oars.

The captain himself was in the stern sheets of the boat.

A rope was thrown.

The youth managed to grasp it.

There was a kind of sob, a deep sigh of relief and gratification, which burst from the hearts of the sturdy seamen, as they lifted Florence and her preserver into the boat.

They placed the pair on the gratings along the bottom, and with a loud and joyous shout pulled towards the " Miranda."

The joy of all on board was very great.

Florence was removed to the cabin, and tended with the most tender and sedulous attention.

Soon the ship's doctor proclaimed her to be out of danger, and when the old merchant realised the truth of this bulletin, he rushed on deck almost frantically, and caught the youth by his hand.

" My dear sir," he exclaimed, " I should be ungrateful if my feelings could find expression in mere words of thankfulness; you have saved me from a life of intense and undying misery. My dear child owes you her life, and I owe you far more. What shall I do to give you some proof of my heartfelt gratitude and appreciation of your inestimable act?"

" You will let me sometimes listen to your conversation, when I cannot readily take my part in it. You will bear with my moody abstraction and taciturnity, which are the effects of the most appalling calamity that ever befel an unfortunate man," returned the youth, sadly. " No one detests the folly of taking a deep grief into ones bosom, to foster and increase its anguish, than I do; but that which has happened to me and mine is so terrible and so recent that I cannot think of aught else."

A deathly pallor overspread the youth's face, as he uttered these words, and he sank down upon a seat and covered his face with his hands.

" Mr. Edward Leighton, I am deeply concerned," said the old merchant, in a tone of sincerest sympathy; " but, let me trust your depression is in some measure accountable by the natural reaction that must follow your transcendant exertions in the noble rescue of my poor child. Let me persuade you to go below, and take a rest in your hammock. I will send my servant to you, and, while I and my sister are on board, you will never want for devoted attendance. I am sure your are ill."

" Oh, God! it is horrible!" murmured the youth, with a shudder.

" Mr. Leighton!"

" For three weeks I have lived almost a solitary on this ship; I have not told my dreadful story to a single creature; but, since you are so kind, I cannot refuse you my confidence."

" You will do me great wrong, Mr. Leighton, if you think there is anyone—I speak it defiantly—I say anyone who has a greater wish to serve you, or anyone to whom you have more right to confide your troubles, with the fullest assurance of sympathy, than myself, whom you have served so unspeakably. But let us go below, and talk matters over in my cabin, where we can converse more freely, for your late gallant action has made you ' the observed of all observers.'"

" Be it so, Mr. Eldridge, and when I have told you my tale of horror, I am sure you will not think that, because I wear pale cheeks and haggard looks, I am a mere morbid sentimentalist, or one who studies to preserve an air of misanthrophy from motives of ridiculous affectation."

" And, oh, if I can help you!"

" Even He who is omnipotent can give me back what I have lost only by a special miracle," returned the youth, solemnly. " But it will give me some relief to pour my sad story into the ears of a sympathising friend, and there yet remains to me the better consolation of seeking for my wrongs the vengeance accorded by the law upon the fiends who have robbed me of all, who have left me desolate indeed."

CHAPTER CVIII.

A CHAPTER OF HORRORS.

" As you know," began the youth, when he was alone with the old merchant in one of the after-cabins, " my name is Edward Leighton; my father was—oh, Heaven! that I should speak of him, of my mother, my brother, sisters, as if beings no more existing! Shall I ever be able to tell this tale of hellish butchery, of awful misery?"

" Your father, mother—your whole family murdered!" cried Eldridge, aghast with horror.

" You shall hear. My father was a wealthy planter, who many years ago settled on the Arkansas, at a place called Graftonville. He was very prosperous; a just, kind, and hospitable man; he was beloved both by his fellow settlers and by the native red-skins. He had, besides myself, a younger son and two daughters, and a happier family than ours, I believe, never enjoyed the comfort, the unity, and love of a sweet home. Oh, I must not recall these things or I shall go mad!"

Edward Leighton paused.

For several moments he sat, his head slightly averted, his hands tightly clasped.

The old merchant remained silent, his cheek blanched and evidently expecting a narration of some unparalleled atrocity.

In this expectation he was not deceived, as the sequel will show.

When he had sufficiently recovered calmness, he continued, hurriedly.

" I will not, as I dare not, trust myself to give you any account of those who are dead, nor of the happy days that are by-gone for ever; but I will speak at once of the great calamity. About three months have elapsed since the fatal day, when my father held a harvest feast, to which he invited a large party of Indians of the Shoshoné or Snake tribe, and also of the Grand Pawnee and the Pawnee-Loups. It was always his policy to keep on friendly terms with the natives, and the fiercest, most uncivilised of the Iroquois tribes respected Graftonville, even to its farthest and lonliest homestead, and when, in their war-parties, they passed by the village, they would often pause and refresh themselves at my father's house, and more than once they have been known even to relinquish their expedition of murder and plunder at his entreaties."

"And the black-hearted savages rose against their friend and benefactor at last!" cried Mr. Eldridge, with indignation.

"Patience, sir; you shall hear."

"The villains! Oh, the weakness—the madness of the false policy that spares the painted hell-hounds!" reiterated the merchant.

"Oh, sir, let me beseech you not to anticipate my wretched story; the catastrophe is more horrible even than what you are presaging."

"Humph! I beg your pardon, Mr. Leighton, but I have heard so much lately of the horrible raids and murderous doings of these uncivilised wretches in the Arkansas country, that I cannot contain myself at the inactivity and culpable neglect of a government that does not extirpate the hideous wretches. Pray go on."

"My father had a motive for inviting so many of the sachems to the harvest-feast. He had just achieved the purchase of a considerable tract of fine land from the Pawnees, and as he had paid for it most liberally, and had loaded the chiefs and their braves with presents, the redskins left the plant in great good humour. After the exertions of the long, exciting day, we—that is," he added, with a bitter sigh, "myself, and the whole of our family and household—were quite worn out with fatigue. My father sat by his ingle-side, and we were grouped about him, almost too listless and weary even to retire to our rooms. We chatted pleasantly for an hour, my father being much elated by the successful issue of his negociation with the natives, when an Indian entered hastily. We at once recognised him as Catahaga, the Eagle-Wing. He warned us that treachery was intended, but would not say from what quarter it was to be expected; he earnestly implored us to watch the night, to arm ourselves, and fortify the house. My father slighted the caution, and mistrusted the redskin, for this reason — Catahaga had married a white girl, and had been on that account discarded from his nation, his father, a chief of a branch tribe of the Pawnee-Loups, being an inveterate hater of the pale-faces, in fact, one of the few sachems who sullenly held themselves aloof from the harvest-feast, in spite of the allurement of free gifts, so powerful with Indians—and it seemed very feasible that motives of jealousy or avarice should prompt the young Indian to make us uncomfortable by a vague threat of impending treason and danger. My father tried to laugh down the bodings of him whom he mistrusted too rashly, and offered him a handsome blanket as a present and a compromise for his not having been invited to the feast. This gift the haughty young chief refused with the sternest contempt, and left Graftonville in high dudgeon. It was not without secret apprehensions that I retired to bed that night, but as I was very weary, I soon forgot my anxieties in the profoundest slumbers. Towards morning, I was awakened by a hideous yell; I started from my bed in great dismay; it was repeated. It seemed a war-whoop in imitation of the battle-cry of the Shoshoné; but it was but an imitation. I had lived too long among the redskins to be deluded, and no white man can utter the peculiar and terrific yell of these savages. I gained confidence, for I judged that it must be a part of a silly practical joke played upon us by our neighbours. I was soon

undeceived. First a red glare flashed on the windows then came the quick crackling of rifle-shots. I ran out upon the balcony. A horrible spectacle presented itself, when the veil that concealed it at first wafted away—that veil was the wreaths from the deadly muzzles of murderous guns, and that veil was pierced by deep groans and shrill shrieks, curses, shouts, and demoniac yells. Oh, horror! untold horror! Oh! that I had been struck blind on the instant that I rose from my bed to look upon that orgy of hellish carnage——"

Edward Leighton struck his forehead in agony.

His auditor sat with white face and quivering lips, in shuddering silence.

"Oh, sir, the yard ran like a slaughter-house with blood—the blood of the kind old servants, of guests, of dear friends, and then flames leaped up, and threw their black canopy of smoke over the face of Heaven, lest the lightning should be called down to arrest the wretches in their work of horror. The doors were burst open, screams rang through the house; they were crushed out and silenced by crashing blows of sharp tomahawks, and the roar of deadly barrels. I opened the door of my room and rushed out. The first object that I saw was my sister staggering on the steps. She was weltering in blood, struck by a shot from below.

"Every room was ransacked by the fiendish besiegers.

"In an instant it occurred to me to save myself, at least, so far as to get out of the house and fetch assistance from some neighbouring plant, though the nearest was distant more than two miles.

"Against the wall in my room hung a buffalo robe and a head-dress that formerly belonged to a great sachem whom my father knew. I donned these quickly, snatched up my rifle, and ran down into the court-yard.

"No notice was taken of me—I was looked upon as one of the gang, and in my disguise was permitted to pass whither I would. As I crossed an angle of one of the out-houses I saw my father struggling with half-a-dozen of these murderers. I set up a whoop and pointed towards the road, in hopes of decoying them from their victim. They all fled but one; he turned upon my father, and struck him to the earth with a hatchet. I fired upon him and killed him, but my father was dead. I then rushed back into the house. I found my little brother's body lying across the threshold; in my mother's bedroom I found my sister and her—my mother—dead! both dead! I rushed back into the yard; the house was blazing beside me; the ground was strewn with the slaughtered. I could endure no more—I sank to the earth, and all consciousness left me.

"When I recovered my senses I found myself half stifled, swathed in my buffalo robe, and wedged in between a couple of groaning ruffians who had been wounded in the fray, and after the massacre tossed into a jolting waggon. I suppose when I was found lying insensible upon the earth I had been mistaken for one of the bandits and had been placed in the cart with the rest. My first impulse on recovering my resources was to deal around death blows with a knife that I had thrust through my belt. Yet, at most, I could wreak my vengeance only on one or two of the villains, and those wounded, and perhaps dying, and though I did not value my life one straw for its own sake, yet I clung to it in the hope of reaping that revenge for which I thirsted so madly. I lay still, or, at least, I surrendered myself to the rumbling and jarring of the ox-wain. On either side of the torturing vehicle rode a strong party of the bush-rangers, for it was evident that the wretches belonged to that gang; they were mounted on little vicious, shaggy mustangs, and were hurrying along at a great rate.

"Other waggons, loaded with plunder, bumped and jingled over the stony road behind us. Brutal as they were, the wretches appeared somewhat awed by the frightful deed that they had just committed, and the forced laughter and beastly jests that occasionally broke in upon the conscious silence were only the effects of a strained and hollow mirth.

The waggon drew up in a bottom, near a plant belonging to a man of repute, one Roland Holmes; the wounded men were lifted out one by one, and I among them.

It was discovered that more than one was dead.

I was borne into the ample kitchen, and laid upon the floor.

Presently there entered a tall, grey-haired, grey-eyed rascal, who appeared to be the chief of the gang, and whom at once I recognised as being one of the most respected planters of the next squall from my own, which is called Lurch Ville. The name of this hypocrite is Michael Warren. He complimented the men on the admirable manner, as the villain termed it, in which they had carried out their enterprise, and, after an hour's discussion, concerning the best plan that could be adopted for completely lulling the suspicion of the settlers, in diverting it entirely from the real culprits, the wounded men were removed to the barn at the back of the house.

"I was carried away with the rest.

"Most of the fellows who had received gunshots or other wounds—they numbered about seven—were taken away severally. I, however, was left, as no one claimed me. Ronald Holmes came into the barn; he started back as I rose to my feet; we were alone. As I said, I was not quite unarmed; every passion of vindictiveness was stirred in my breast. The fellow levelled a revolver at my head, and I flew upon him. The pistol flashed in the pan, but he struck me with the butt, and I fell to the earth stunned.

"Again, upon recovery, I found myself cramped within a narrow space. I was imprisoned in a dark hole between the ceilings of the barn.

"Upon moving, I found the wall on either side was thick, and the trap, down which I had been thrown, firmly closed from above.

"I waited for hours in the solitude and darkness. A horror indescribable thrilled through me; the wretch Holmes had cast me down into this living tomb, fancying me already dead, or wishing to escape the immediate act of my murder by leaving me to die of starvation.

"All the horrible events of the past night recurred to my distracted mind.

"I raved, I tore my hair, I cursed my kind; I tried to pray, but it was useless to attempt collecting my thoughts, much less to embody them in words. I tried to rise; I struck my head against the beams so close above me. I groped around in the hideous darkness. Soon to my misery were added the pangs of thirst and hunger.

"I then thought of my knife.

"It was concealed beneath my cloak. The ruffians had not robbed me of it.

"I began to think of saving my life. Before I had no wish to live, except for revenge; now there was something so horrid in the form of death which threatened me, that I was as eager to extricate myself from my grave as if the world had not been despoiled of all that made it of value to me. Reflecting that any present cravings for food would be succeeded by languor and exhaustion, I resolved to tax the little strength I had remaining to the very utmost.

After hacking and hewing at the wood—stopping at intervals to listen—I contrived to make a hole in the wall, through which a feeble ray of light flickered.

"The heavy tramp of feet along the floor above my head caused me to pause in my work.

"Again concealing my knife beneath my cloak, I threw myself upon my face, and remained quite motionless.

"The trap was open.

"A lantern was partly lowered through the open trap.

"Holmes and another villain looked down upon me.

"'It's young Leighton,' muttered one.

"'Are you sure he's dead?' returned his companion.

"'Little fear of that, mate,' said the first speaker, 'I picked him up, stark and stiff, in the court-yard; the fellow tried to escape in the buffalo-robe, but was either shot or struck down; I took him at first for one of our own party, and threw him into the ox-wain with the rest of the disabled.'

"'I'll get down and have a look at him.'

"'There's no need, the fellow's as dead as a herring.'

"'But that's a fine skin that covers him; might as well secure that.'

"'Better not,' returned the other villain, 'the captain has removed every scrap of the booty beyond the frontier, and that hide may be recognised by some meddler or another.'

"'I thought I saw him move,' said the more suspicious of the rascals.

"'Fancy, mate; what chance would he have of escape if he were alive? you may depend upon it he would appeal for mercy, or defy us to kill him. If I thought there was a spark of life left in him I would draw my knife across his throat in very charity to save him from lingering agonies.'

"'Well, let him bide, then,' growled the other; 'as well buried here as elsewhere.'

"'Aye, mate,' returned his comrade, with a laugh, and the trap fell heavily, leaving me alone in the gloom and horror of my living tomb.

"But the little ray of hope still glimmered through the breach I had made, and I set to work with renewed vigour.

"After hours of toil I managed to carve out a hole sufficiently large to admit of the passage of my body.

"My dismay was great when, on looking out, I found myself at a sufficient distance from the ground to insure the fracture of a limb if I attempted to take a leap.

"What could I do?

"My buffalo robe! I cut it into strips which I bound together as tightly as possible.

"As the robe was ample I had plenty of tether, in fact enough to have let me down from the summit of the peak of Teneriffe, for I cut the robe in very thin strips, and, like Queen Dido's ox-hide, it extended beyond expectations.

"I looked out from the rent in the wall. No one was within sight.

"It is hard to imagine how many obstacles impede one in such a position as mine. No hard matter, you will say, to escape from a wooden barn, armed with a strong knife and a rope, or, at least, an excellent substitute for one, yet it was some moments before I could hit upon a plan for attaching my rope upon a hold firm enough to support me in my descent.

"A nail I found but it was rusty and rotten.

"I bored a hole in the wall; through this I passed the rope and tied it firmly.

"I caught hold of it; tried it by pulling my hardest; I then grasped it firmly, and flung myself out of the breach.

"As soon as my feet touched the ground I took to flight.

"I made my way through the bush and reached the river.

"I thought at first of going to Graftonville, but I reflected that he whom I had seen in the house of Ronald Holmes was the judge of the settlement, a man of great influence, and of whose hostility I might be well assured; besides the settlement was many a mile distant across the prairie, and I was too much exhausted by hunger and fatigue to think of undertaking so long a journey.

"I sat down in the forest and gave way to the hopelessness of one outbeaten by misfortune.

"I heard the stealthy rustle of moccasins.

"I started to my feet, and perceived among the bushes the lithe and crouching form of an Indian.

"Instinctively I drew my knife, but I replaced it in its sheath; I cared not what befell me, and, relinquishing myself to my pole, I resolved to surrender at discretion. The redskin proved to be Catahaga, he who warned my father of impending danger; by his assistance I reached the port, where I embarked on the 'Miranda;' money was supplied me by a friend of my father, who lives there, and now, as you know already, I am bound for New York, to seek justice for the massacre of my parents, and to denounce this gang of villains, for whose crimes the guiltless Indians have been made to suffer."

As Edward Leighton finished his sad and cruel story, a shot fired from the main-deck caused the ship to quail and shudder, and the two men rushing on deck, found the captain, his mate, and the rest of the crew scrutinizing a schooner that was rounding the point of an island, and sailing down with wind dead abaft her beam.

"What do you make of her, Griffiths?" asked the captain of his mate.

"Captain, I don't care to say. What do _you_ think of her?" returned the mate, his cheek paling.

The captain answered hoarsely,

"She's a pirate!"

CHAPTER CIX.

THE SALAMANDER — THE VULTURE — THE BOARDING OF THE MIRANDA — A FEARFUL CONTEST — THE BOY PIRATE.

"KEEP a close luff, sir," said the mate of the "Miranda," addressing the captain, and watching with anxious eye the advance of the "Black Vulture."

"No, no, Griffiths—it is useless to try to run; and though she is of rakish build, and has something disreputable about her rig, it is possible we are quite deceived in her character."

"I hope it may prove so," returned the mate, rather dubiously.

"At any rate, man the sides, and turn round the swivel amidships; yet don't make too much of a hostile display. Let him see that we're ready for any emergency."

"The ports are closed, captain; if she carries any guns they are well concealed. I see nothing but the chaser at her head."

"See! she signals!"

"She wants us to heave to."

"Ready about," shouted the captain of the merchantman, rather excitedly.

The pirate vessel hove to.

She carried South American colours. Her lower ports were closed, and her crew were stationed at their posts, or feigning to be asleep on the deck, and several stands of arms and shot-racks were covered with sail-cloth.

Nevertheless, there was little effectiveness in the disguise, for the "Black Vulture" was too grim and frightful to wear false feathers to any advantage.

There was a slight cry amongst the men on board the "Miranda," for they knew well that the seemingly inert sleepers who strewed the deck fore and aft were but crouching tigers, and that they waited but the word of their leader to start up and rush upon the deck of the doomed merchant-man like a pack of wolves breaking into a sheep-fold.

Harwolf, who had begun to lose what little refinement he had acquired by his connection with good society, and was become a blackguardly morose-looking ruffian, leaped upon the forecastle, and shouted through his speaking trumpet,

"Brig, ahoy!"

"Put the helm up," said Fleming to the man at the wheel.

"Aye, sir."

"Now, lads, steady," said the captain. "Stand to the guns when I whistle. Some of you go below and hand up the wads and grape-shot, and a bundle of cutlasses."

The men obeyed their orders with promptitude.

"Mr. Eldridge," said Fleming, calmly, "this fellow is a pirate; you must go below, and lock the ladies in their cabins. Keep below yourself, and Mr. Leighton."

"I am ready, sir," said the young man, his pale cheek brightening with a hectic flush, his eyes flashing. He had thrown off his coat, bared his right arm, and was selecting a cutlass from a heap that lay at the foot of the foremast.

"Mr. Leighton, as I can but hold myself responsible for your safety, let me entreat you to go below."

"When the battle is over," returned the youth, in a fierce hoarse voice. "These villians, as you say, are pirates, fiends of the kindred race with the devil against whom I will wage war to the last gasp of my life. Cheerly, Mr. Fleming, we are not taken yet, nor shall be till we have made half the dogs bite the dust."

"Be it as you will," returned the captain, "you might as well fight first as last, and you are a brave man. Mr. Peak."

"Aye, sir," responded the mate.

"See the hatches firmly battened down, and shoot anyone who attempts to go below without orders."

"Aye, sir."

"Now, lads, aloft; rise fore-tack, ease off fore-sheet."

"Ahoy! brig, ahoy!" roared Harwolf, savagely. "Have you no tongue to your trumpet? Heave to, and be hanged to you!"

"Who are you?" cried Fleming.

"Come alongside, and I'll tell you," laughed the pirate.

"You carry false bunting."

"Does that offend you? I'll pull off the mask—run up our own standard."

The black flag fluttered up to the fore-peak.

There was a sudden shout on the pirate's deck, and the pretended sleepers leaped up and waved their cutlasses and swords.

"Shift off the jib-sheet!" shouted Fleming.

Too late, a shot from an elevated gun in the midships of the "Black Vulture" carried away the fore-top-gallant, and with the fore-tackle it crashed down, striking two men from the yard-arms into the sea.

The pirates yelled and shouted.

"Strike your flag, old Blowhard, and you shall have benefit of clergy!" cried Harwolf, with a brutal laugh.

"No clergy could benefit you, you thief and murderer, doomed beyond salvation!" cried Edward Leighton, leaping on a carronade, and firing at the speaker.

The bullet tore away the flesh from the upper part of Harwolf's arm, and he was struck flat to the deck by the force of the blow.

With a cry of rage and dismay the pirates ran round their fallen leader.

"It's nothing, mates, nothing but what the skunks shall pay dearly for I'll shut them all down in the hold and set the ship a fire."

The "Miranda" fired two well-directed shots, and made a rare smash into the quarter and after part of the "Vulture;" two of the pirates were killed by a grenade fired from a long gun, or swivel, which Fleming pointed himself.

The "Vulture" poured a raking broadside, but, thanks to the steadiness of the man steering, who put the helm down and turned the ship "round on her heel," the damage was not so great as it would have been had the ships lain broadside to stern.

"Wardlaw, the boarding nettings; throw a grapnel, Macarthy. Hurrah, lads, for the Jolly Oliver! No quarter! board, and take all!"

The ruffians threw their grapnels.

Another shot had struck away the main-royals of the "Miranda" and the ship refused to answer to her helm, and was swayed round by the hawser till she lay stern to stern with the "Vulture."

"Board there!" cried Harwolf, springing on to the deck of the "Miranda," and firing at the man at the wheel.

Wardlaw and the rest of the villains poured upon the fore part of the ship.

They were soon engaged in a pell-mell conflict.

Edward Leighton ran aft, and threw himself before Harwolf.

The next instant the women even engaged in a desperate fight.

Their cutlasses clashed as they wildly hewed at each other, amidst the smoke from the guns, and the flashes of the small arms.

The captain of the "Miranda" was a brave and resolute seaman, and his crew were not men to surrender at discretion.

The pirates, however, were thirsting for plunder, as they had gained but few prizes during their present cruise, and the provisions and stores on board the "Vulture" were beginning to fail.

While Harwolf was eager to distinguish himself on this the first occasion upon which he had independently commanded.

The deck of the "Miranda" was the scene of a desperate fight, and the swaying ship re-echoed with the shouts of the contending crews.

When suddenly a man, who had rushed up the shrouds, and was looking out for the appearance of another ship, suddenly cried—

"Sail off the lee-shore!"

But no one on deck responded to the cry. Every one was engaged in the desperate fray, and had work enough in defending his own life.

The heavy boom of a gun, and a cry from the few men left aboard to manage the "Vulture," caused a mutual cessation of hostilities.

Both the pirates and their victims rushed to the side of the vessel.

Stately gliding round the points of the island, soared along, as if skimming the surface of the waters, the queenly barque of the Red Raven.

She had opened one of her after ports, and the shot had smashed in the cabin windows of the "Vulture," and splintered a bulkhead to pieces.

The Vultures, perceiving that it was likely the tables would be turned against them, scrambled on board their own ship.

Harwolf was wounded and bleeding.

He had made a very narrow escape from the hands of Edward Leighton, who seemed to be inspired with the fury of a demon.

The pirate reached the quarter-deck of the "Black Vulture," and seized the helm.

He looked round upon his men.

The great black banner, with the scull and red raven, floated aft of the Boy Pirate's ship.

Consternation sat on the faces of the "Vulture's" crew, and they listened to the spirited harangue of their leader with dogged silence.

Deep-toned and awe-striking came the shout of the Ravens over the restless sea.

A well-aimed shot cut through the weather-braces, and stove the main-stay.

Still louder as nearer grew the cheers of the Boy Pirate's men.

The crew of the "Black Vulture" seemed paralysed.

The "Red Raven" tacked, and tried to get to the windward of her enemy.

The "Miranda" weared round, and fired her two shotted guns into the hulk of the much-belaboured "Vulture," who seemed every moment less and less inclined to continue the battle.

Hands were busy aloft making all sail, and presently the sloop slunk off.

When Harwolf, whose ferocity and recklessness lent him an amount of daring and courage little in accordance with the treacherous vindictiveness of his general character, rated the men for their pusillanimity, and tried to keep them to their guns.

But as the "Raven" poured broadside after broadside with terrible effect, the wildest consternation prevailed on board the "Vulture."

Harwolf sprang to the wheel, and shouted in a piercing voice to his cowering fellow bandits,

"You dastardly, chicken-hearted rogues, will ye neither fight nor fly? Will ye crouch like mongrel curs before dogs of your own breed? Down, then,

with the black flag, you white-hearted thieves, and hoist my lady's scented 'kerchief at the foremast! Wardlaw, pitch some lighted oakum into the hold. Let us be blown to the devil rather than these traitorous milksops should give us up to a bragging powder-monkey, only fit to play the skipper in a harem. Because these lubbers are to be frightened by the croaking of a beggarly raven are we to walk the plank and be made sharks'-meat by the 'Boy' and his dainty boarding-school Miss? Stand to your guns, and you'll see the raven's feathers fly and hear the crow's scream for quarter. Funk, and you're all dead men, by a death that disgraces the name of a pirate. Way aloft! Rig-out, ye lubbers! Wardlaw, elevate that starboard gun, tauten the lashings, and blaze away!"

Stimulated by this strong appeal the Vultures fired a well-directed shot that splintered the jib-boom of their enemy's vessel, causing her to shudder and stop for an instant.

Only for an instant.

With deafening cheers the Boy Pirate's sloop bore grandly down, and swept right astern of the "Vulture."

The peril to the villanous crew of Harwolf was terrible.

A few of the braver men crowded together, and walked aft towards their commander.

"Sure now, Mr. Harwolf, its not to be kilt we are, like poulterer's pullets," said Teddy Macarthy, the boatswain; "whin we're vultur's, as ye say; though, be jabers, I never heard as them same vultures are sich good fighting birds as game-cocks, in spite of their red wattles and sharp beaks. Bad cess to 'em!—what will we do now, for it's not this boy that will strike his colours to a girleen in seaman's rig? By the powers, if there was any pluck among us we could wallop the gosoon with swabs and rope-ends! Sure, my hearties, now, let's make their hearts tremble to a divil's own cheer, and let the guns play a swate tune for thir idification!"

"Hurrah for the 'Black Vulture!'" shouted the men.

They flew to the guns.

They fired a heavy broadside.

The ship was enveloped in smoke.

With matchless seamanship Daniel Harwolf gave his orders.

The skulkers were animated by the example of their more resolute comrades.

The damaged spars and tackle were cut away, and flung overboard.

Every strain of canvass was clapped on.

The "Red Raven's" crew were busy getting the geer ready for hoisting out boats.

Too secure of their prey, the firing on the Boy Pirate's part had ceased.

He and his crew were swarming the ship's side, eager to push off to board the "Vulture."

Obedient to the helm, the pirate ship swayed round and forged ahead.

She made way.

The boats were steadily fired upon, and one of them was struck; her gunnel was smashed in, and she capsized.

The wind was freshening and heavy seas rolled into the roadstead between the islands.

As the "Vulture" sheered off, she kept up a constant firing, and a dense cloud seemed to rest on the sea.

This was done to disguise the ship, to cover her retreat and to make her a difficult mark for the shots of her antagonist.

Brand, the pilot to whom Christopher had entrusted the command of the "Raven," was making all sail to give chase.

Suddenly across the horizon appeared two long black streaks.

A brace of Brazilian steam-frigates were bearing down upon the contending rovers!

THE AMBUSH.

CHAPTER CX.

THE FLIGHT OF EAGLE-WING AND MINNA—
ALONE IN THE PRAIRIE—PRAIRIE SCENES—
THE VULTURES—A CHAIN OF HILLS—THE
INDIAN'S PLANS—A HALT—THE INDIAN'S
COMPLAINT—A TRUE WIFE—THE JOURNEY
RENEWED.

ALONE on the far prairie Eagle-Wing and his young
wife were swiftly riding.

It was day-break.

Glowing clouds seamed the horizon, and the bright
rays of the sun, which had not yet risen above the
blue line of the far lone hills, shot up into the purple
zenith, paling the glimmering stars.

Still onwards and onwards with unslackened speed.

The rolling prairie spread boundlessly before them.
No. 36.

Its wide expanse was dotted here and there with
clumps of trees that showed among the heaving and
waving long grass like islets in a billowy sea.

As the darkness paled into light the heavens
assumed a strange and majestic appearance.

Cloud-castles, sky-lakes, and mist-arabesques pile
high, spread wide, or flitted lightly across the blue
ocean of space.

The mustangs forged along with untiring speed.

Matchless the sagacity with which the half-wild
creatures avoided the numerous pitfalls, nests of
ants, and burrowing animals.

Far off were seen tumbling swiftly along in one
surging shaggy mass a herd of buffaloes.

It was evident that they were fleeing from some
enemy.

The cry of a pack of jackalls, and the pattering of

numberless feet, were heard very far away through the tangling underwood of a long strip of pine-forest.

As the day advanced they drew near the long line of hills.

Eagle-Wing reined his horse, and, stooping from his saddle, examined the ground.

He jumped from the mustang.

Minna caught the rein.

The Indian threw himself on his hands and knees, and crawled to a brake on the summit of a grassy mound.

He cautiously peeped over the thicket.

Minna watched him with anxiety.

So cunning was the Pawnee that even in this lonely spot on the trackless desert he practised the same caution he would have used though surrounded by an ambush of native enemies.

He snatched up some flags and long grass, and thrust them throught the fillet that bound his forehead.

As he stole along the ground, under cover of the bush, he swayed his head to the leeward, so as, when he peered over the brush, his feathers might be concealed, and his head-dress mistaken for a tuft of waving grass.

He crawled back to the foot of the mound.

He sprang with agility to his feet, and, shouldering his long rifle, walked nimbly towards the mustangs.

He mounted in silence.

His wife looked at him inquiringly.

He did not speak.

He appeared very thoughtful, but not sullen.

"My husband, are the enemy on our trail?" asked Minna, gently.

"No; there is a dog of the pale-faces riding towards the river; his trail lies beside ours. and we shall meet him," said Eagle-Wing, in English.

"And whither does our path lead, Catahaga?" asked his wife.

"To the wigwam of Wabiskoa, the great chief of the Dacotahs," returned the Indian.

"The Sioux, husband?"

"The pale-faces call the Dacotahs, Sioux," returned Eagle-Wing; "they are a great nation, and have sent many braves on the war-path to take scalps of the Chippowais."

"But my husband is an adopted son of the great Sachem Wabiskoa."

"It is true, my sister," returned the Indian, "the Bison-Hoof has promised Catahaga a hundred braves with fire-weapons."

"Wabiskoa is a cruel chief, husband," said Minna, with a shudder.

"The Manitou of the Iroquois loves the great Sachem; his lodges are full of meat and maize, his hunting grounds teem with game, and his rivers are alive with fish; the pale-faces do not send their red coats into his country, for he is above all the Sachems of the Shoshoné, the Pawnees, or the Chippowais, and the Yengeese fear him, and his heart is very hard; he hates the pale-faces."

"My husband's heart is changed, his thoughts have gone backward; because the wolves have broken into his lodge in the night he would lead his nation against his white friends," said Minna, timidly.

Eagle Wing did not appear to have heard these remarks.

His eyes were fixed upon the brightening sky.

A smile of triumph sat on his face.

Minna looked at him earnestly.

She raised her eyes from his face in search of the object which had fixed his attention.

Far above their heads, throbbing strongly through the clear air, their huge wings flapping, their raw and hideous necks stiffly out-stretched, four vultures were winging their way in the backward direction of the path the fugitives had traversed.

Minna lowered her eyes.

She shuddered and grasped the rein as if she were in danger of falling from her seat.

The Indian smiled grimly.

They pushed onwards and reached the hills.

As they ascended the air became purer and more rarefied; the scenery grew bleak, but the fresh air and cheerful sunlight gave a special beauty to the jagged and towering rocks, and the purple-heathed table-lands and grassy flower-spangled acclivities.

The merry shout and plash of a cascade that leaped, revelling in the sunbeams, from a table-rock prone down into a little green valley, the chirruping of insects in the grass, the charming spectacle of a graceful group of leaping antelopes, the quailing and whirring of monster flights of migratory birds from time to time passing through the air, all these sights and sounds combined to raise the drooping spirits of Minna Wyotti, and to smooth the rugged brow of her fiery husband.

As they ascended the hill the wide plains below them expanded more and more.

Grand beyond description was the majestic scenery; leagues of prairie and miles of waving forest, silver meandering rivers, blooming heaths, and grand eternal mountains.

The sun had just raised his dazzling shield above the purple hills and flooded the rich prospect with his glowing beams.

Eagle-Wing drew the rein on the summit of the hills, and, leaping from the saddle, lightly and gracefully lifted her to the ground.

She leaned affectionately on his shoulder and nestled close to his side, and together they gazed down upon the grand prospect that lay below.

"That land is now claimed by the Yengeese, which was my father's," cried Eagle-Wing, passionately. "Why?"

"They have bought it, my husband; they have paid for it with money, and with blankets and wampums, with weapons and fire food, with many other treasures."

"And who sold it to the kites?" asked the Indian, fiercely.

"The Iroquois themselves, husband; the father of Eagle-Wing sold it to the fathers of Minna," returned his wife, with a winning smile.

The Indian pressed her fondly in his arms, and looked into her eyes with a glance of ineffable love.

"If Eagle Wing were sachem of the great world on either side the big Salt Lake he would give it all for Minna," he said, fervently.

His wife looked at him fondly, and laughed low and musically; the grace of nature, the child-like simplicity of the aborigine, still clung to Catahaga, and yet he had learned in many respects "to think the thoughts," as he expressed it, of the pale-faces, and his generous, sensitive heart had earliest learned that lesson practically, which is too often only theoretically, or poetically acknowledged among the pretentious whites—a reverential, a chivalrous devotion to virtuous woman.

"And yet, Minna," said the Indian, "by what right did my fathers sell the earth given by the Great Spirits to their children? Can the birds sell the air, or the fish the streams? Will the cushat give the nest she has built for her fledglings?"

"We must not talk of these things, husband. Let Minna be a squaw in the lodges of the Pawnee; let her carry heavy burdens, toil in the maize-field, be set apart from the braves when she tastes food—be treated worse than dogs: give my brother the calumet of a great sachem—let him wear the chief's feather and carry the hatchet of his tribe, and when an enemy—perhaps a mere boy, who was taken sleeping—is brought into his wigwam, let him torture the great prisoner at the death stake, while Minna prepares the brands and the lighted splinters, tears the flesh of the victim, and gloats on his agony with all the cruel joy of the Master of Evil. Would my brother have it so?" asked Minna, looking bravely into her husband's face.

She quailed beneath the scowl that darkened his fine face.

It melted away, and was succeeded by a pleasant smile, and he answered, with a little national prejudice, but with more liberality than is common among the more civilised,

"My sister's words are good and wise; the Yengeese are evil, yet they are good; the Iroquois are good, yet they are evil."

Minna laughed gaily.

"My husband," she said, cheerfully, "we are like the birds—free; if the tree is blazed on which we build our nest we can flee away before it is felled, and seek another home. Minna will be happy among your people; we will teach them what is good of Yengeese customs, we will learn what is good of theirs."

"It is good," returned Catahaga, naively.

He brought the mustangs.

He lifted Minna to her saddle.

Once more he mounted, and interlaced the reins of the horses.

"The path before us is long, Minna; we must be-gone," said the Indian.

"Shall we meet the pale-face?" asked the girl.

"On the banks of the Arkansas," returned her husband.

CHAPTER CXI.

ON TOWARDS ARKANSAS — A REST IN THE FOREST — AN UNWELCOME VISITOR — THE INDIAN KILLS THE BEAR — MOUNTED ONCE MORE — THE PRIARIE FIRE — THE LANDSLIP — A FEARFUL PERIL — A TIMELY RESCUE.

THE Indian and his wife crossed the plain that stretched beneath the valley.

At nightfall they reached the forest beyond.

After they had ridden into the heart of the woods they paused to rest the horses and to refresh themselves.

The Indian seemed to think that they incurred no danger by lingering at this point in their journey.

Doubtless he was right, for they were in that part of the country which the Dacotahs, or Sioux, claimed as their territory.

The scenery was lovely and picturesque in the extreme.

They sat down on the enamelled sward in an open spot in the hoary forest.

Minna produced some provisions she had brought for the journey.

Eagle-Wing took his calabash and left Minna to go to the spring that warblingly told of its nearness.

The Indian's wife prepared their simple meal, and beguiled the time by singing to herself in a low, plaintive strain an Indian song her husband had taught her.

The hound was lying by her side, weary after his long run, and with luxurious indolence winking at the fitful flames of the wood fire Minna had lighted.

Without losing one trait of refinement, Minna had thoroughly accommodated herself to the simple, hardy habits of her husband, whom, as we have seen, she loved with wife-like devotion.

The dog suddenly roused himself, and, crouching back, snarled and cowered.

The horses which the Indian had tethered to a tree became restive and neighed shrilly.

Minna turned to discover the cause of these demonstrations of alarm on the part of the animals.

A few yards before her, between two low-hanging trees, stood the dread cause of their terror.

An immense bear, an old grizly, stood watching her with his small, red, deep-set eyes.

His massive head swayed heavily; his huge mouth yawned for prey, and his shaggy hide hung loosely on his gaunt, strong ribs.

His huge body remained motionless.

Minna started up.

She uttered a shriek.

She seemed rooted to the spot by terror.

She dared not fly.

Bruin uttered a terrific growl and lumbered towards her.

The dog flew forwards.

But the hound lacked courage necessary to tackle such a formidable enemy.

Minna screamed for help.

The dog barked furiously.

The bear paid not the slightest regard to him.

He still moved on, every instant drawing nearer.

Minna receded before him.

The bear gave another and yet fiercer growl.

Eagle-Wing had left a gun by the side of the fire.

The bear stood between the flaming pile of logs and the girl whom he had exclusively destined for his prey.

How could she reach the gun?

The dog, however, had been so well-trained by his master that, upon seeing Minna stretch her hands yearningly towards the weapon, he darted towards the bear, snarling and howling.

Neither the yelping of the hound nor the noise made by the horses, who were beating the sod with their hoofs and tugging at the halter in order to break away from the bonds that confined them and left them to the mercy of their ferocious foe, seemed to make the least impression upon the obtuse brute, who devoted his attention to no other object than that which he had marked for his prey.

The dog snapped at the strap of the gun and drew it towards his mistress.

She snatched it up and poised it in her hand.

Bruin seemed to disapprove of this manœuvre for he set up a roar that made the forest ring.

He trotted swiftly towards the girl.

She raised the gun to her shoulder.

Aiming as well as she could she fired at the brute.

The bullet struck him on the forehead.

He stood as if stunned by the blow.

His head drooped and a perceptible tremor shook his ponderous body.

The next moment he recovered his "somewhat blunted purpose," and dashed upon Minna, who fled wildly before.

Emitting a succession of growls, whines and deep-mouthed roarings the savage creature flew upon Minna.

He seized her dress.

In an instant she was down.

The brute leaped over her and moved round her.

He set his ponderous paw with crushing weight upon her breast.

He stooped down his dreadful head and was about to fix his huge fangs in her throat.

A musket crackled among the underwood.

A bullet struck the enraged beast in the flank.

With a frightful roar he turned towards his antagonist.

Eagle-Wing stepped lightly from among the bushes and walked steadily to meet him.

The animal trotted on a-pace and was within a couple of yards of his antagonist.

Very deliberately Catahaga aimed the second barrel and fired.

Again the bullet told.

The animal seemed too intent upon coming to close quarters with the Indian to pay much heed to his own wounds, though his hide began to be thick clotted with blood.

Just as the beast reared on his hind legs to crush the Indian in his savage embrace Catahaga swung round the rifle and brought the butt across the eyes of the monster.

He only growled faintly and seemed stunned or stupified.

Catahaga repeated the blow with redoubled energy.

The huge beast stumbled and seemed to have lost his senses.

The Indian uttered a wild whoop and threw himself upon the grizzly, and, in another instant, had struck his knife deep into the monster's heart.

Minna returned to her husband's side, when she beheld him bending over the animal and cutting away its claws to serve for ornaments.

Eagle-Wing seemed to deliberate whether it would be necessary to leave the skin untouched. The limbs of a large bear was no despicable prize, and after an instant's thought, the young Pawnee drew out his knife once more and skilfully took the skin from his prize, and arranged it under the pack saddle of the third horse they had brought with them to carry their baggage.

Once more they were upon the open prairie.

Flying along like the wind, for the day was already waning, they sped towards the Arkansas.

As they rode along, the immense plain stretching about them in all directions, they suddenly perceived large herds flying across the prairie.

Not merely, as before, a herd of buffaloes fleeing from the baying of wolves or wild dogs, but bisons, elks, stags, roebucks, and antelopes, with jackals and other beasts of prey, mingled together as if forgetful of their mutual enmity, and huddling together as if pursued by some enemy common to all.

The air was darkened by immense flights of birds.

Minna looked about her to discover the cause of this strange phenomenon.

Far away to the windward rolled up little spiral jets of smoke, which, after ascending some height in the air, mingled together till the whole cloud extended the whole length of the visible horizon, resembling in form the peristyle of some mighty temple, with its rows of majestic columns.

On the ground flashed along flames, red, glaring, or dazzling bright.

The sky grew dark, and from afar came a sound like a succession of reports, and a strange rumble such as is heard on the eve of an earthquake.

Near re-echoed the thud and trample of countless hoofs, while the air vibrated to the whizzing of countless wings.

The mustangs advanced their feet, and snorted in deadly terror.

"Catahaga!" whispered his wife, as she clung to his arm, and he was obliged to support her, or she would have sunk to the ground, "we are lost, the prairie is on fire!"

The Indian answered with his usual guttural exclamation.

He looked around him with an anxious glance.

Then he turned his face in the direction of the river.

He found it was impossible to continue their onward path.

To reach the river they would have to run the gauntlet of the line of fire.

Not an instant could be spared.

The air was already impregnated with the rank and stifling stench of burning vegetation.

The mustangs were getting unmanageable.

Minna turned a wild look to her side.

Nearer and nearer rolled the roaring sea of fire.

Catahaga turned the horses.

The reins were slackened, and the animals flew before the remorseless tide of flame.

The ground seemed swept by magic from beneath their feet.

The sky floated past above their heads; the darkness grew deeper as the face of the heavens were paled in one dense canopy of smoke.

The roar grew louder, the stench more suffocating, and the heat more scorching.

The horses shrieked and plunged.

The animals were exhausted after their long journey and were not fit to compete with the gliding and insidious element.

"Husband!" said Minna, looking back with affrighted glance, "to what haven are we fleeing? our mustangs will not bear up much longer—we shall perish."

"Minna's heart must not be clouded," exclaimed Catahaga, with a brave smile. "Before us is a landslip which the fire cannot pass."

"But is it too wide for our horses to leap?"

"If not, we must creep down into the fissure," replied the Indian, "and abandon the mustangs."

Again they urged their struggling horses.

The fire was close at their heels.

Minna shrieked, as the heat was so intense that she scarce dare draw a breath.

The ground was covered with snakes and reptiles which crept out of their holes, driven thence by the heat and the stench.

The ground began to incline gradually up to a certain point, along which appeared a low ridge—a natural wall or embankment.

Minna's rein had become detached from Eagle-Wing's.

Her horse, thus freed from restraint, dashed wildly up the steep.

The fire, for some reason, perhaps referable to the nature of the soil or the state of the wind, flowed round suddenly in a curve, the point of which scorched the horses' flanks.

Minna lost the rein, and clinging to the pummel of the saddle, turned towards her husband, waving him with imploring gestures.

Catahaga shouted, and pressed after her.

Every instant she was nearing the brink of the chasm.

Again Catahaga shouted wildly.

Minna could not answer with the faintest cry.

There was a sharp descent from the top of the ridge to the verge of the abyss.

They gained the brow almost together.

But Minna's was, under ordinary circumstances, the better horse, and now, maddened by fright and pain, the poor creature was blind to every danger but that which was threatened by the raving flames.

The mustang shot like an arrow down the steep incline.

It was within a yard from the edge of the gulf.

A shot was fired from the bushes.

The animal reared, and then fell over on its side.

A man, who, judged by his dress, was a trapper, ran towards the spot.

Eagle-Wing also dismounted.

They stooped over the fainting girl.

So eager were they in their desire to know whether she had been injured by the fall, that they did not exchange a word.

Minna soon showed signs of returning consciousness.

By a miracle she had escaped without being at all seriously hurt.

Eagle-Wing turned away, and, clasping his hands together, murmured his thanksgiving to the Great Spirit, who made his sun to shine on the evil and the good, and is no respecter of persons.

CHAPTER CXII.

THE DON JUAN OF BUSH RANGERS—CATAHAGA'S GRATITUDE—MINNA'S REPROACH—INDIANS IN AMBUSH — REGAN'S BRAVADO—A SKIRMISH—THE GREAT CHIEF OF THE DACOTAHS.

HIS eye beaming with liveliest gratitude, the Pawnee regarded the young deliverer.

Minna blushed as her glance fell on the stranger.

He was a youth, neatly and quaintly dresssd in a sort of Indianised garb, with hunting shirt and moccassins.

His eyes were blue as the sky, and his hair flaxen, and waving in rich ringlets. There was something sinister, nevertheless, in the expression of a face pre-eminently handsome. A native grace was in all his movements, and he stood leaning on his rifle, smiling good-humouredly.

"My brother has made Catahaga his captive by his kindness. Let my brother say what Eagle-Wing shall do to show that his heart is not stone, that he can be grateful?" said the Indian, in English.

"Why, chief, give me your hand; let the past be forgotten, and the future bring a large share of mutual good services."

Catahaga took his hand, gravely.

"My brother has saved my wife from death," said the Indian, gravely, "and Catahaga will not notch his 'fatal arrow' for the heart of him who has served him."

The Indian drew from his belt an arrow, red-feathered, and pointed with chalcedony.

The trapper laughed.

"A pretty sort of a gift that as a token of gratitude."

"You have done me a service, stranger, and so I won't cut your weasand, nor riddle your hide, nor skin your brain-cap."

"Is that your notion of gratitude?"

"My brother may command me," returned Catahaga, simply. "All that I have I will give him; and were it all the riches of Wabiskoa it would be little for the great service he has done me. But Catahaga had vowed to kill him."

"Then I have saved my funeral expenses in a very pleasant way," returned the youth, laughing, and taking the hand of Minna.

The girl did not like to repulse the man who had just saved her life, but she looked down, and gently withdrew her hand.

"Oswald Lamond," she said, "it would be un-gracious on my part to say that I would rather have owed my life to any one than to you. But when I remember who you are and what calling you follow——"

"Ah! do you know that?" cried Regan, with a start, for by that name he was known in all other parts except his native settlement.

"Do not ask me, Oswald Lamond, by what means I have gained this knowledge. Terrible as you are, I tell you boldly that I sought it."

"And wherefore?"

"For Agnes's sake; my earliest and dearest friend."

"And where did you get it from, charming Minna?"

"I must not tell you."

"But, are you sure that your information was correct?"

"I had proofs but too convincing of its truth," returned Minna, with a shudder.

"Proofs, proofs! Ha, ha! What a big word is that word proof! No distant relation of mine, the other day, was *proved* to be away down the Yellow-stone when he was at Larchville, I guess."

"Oh, if you could tell me, Oswald, that what I have heard of you is no longer true, how much I should rejoice."

"Why, to what on earth trade did they 'prentice me?" cried Lamond, laughing gaily.

"To one, Oswald, too congenial, I fear, to your character and inclinations."

"Oh, I see; a dancing-master!" he replied, laugh-ing; "or a gentleman usher of the white wand; her highness's pet page; a model for a sculptor, or an idol for the ladies!"

Minna turned away scornfully; yet her cheek softly glowed as she looked at the dashing young villain, and, spite of her common-sense, her love of right and abhorrence of wrong, something faintly whispered excuses for him in her heart.

"Come, come, Minna, you, at least, may be chari-table. I wonder what I have done that every pretty lass I meet beshrews me as if I were given to brow-beating babies, or had passed an act for the abolition of valentines. Now, don't pout your rosy lips so temptingly, Minna, nor don't take so much trouble to call attention to the perfect arching of those pencilled brows. You may call me a coxcomb, but you don't think me one, for a coxcomb's a coward, and that I am not; he is too frivolous for loving truly or deeply, and that, dear Minna, I would give my life to prove to you!"

The captain of the Bush-Rangers took the girl's hands.

She drew away from him indignantly, and, with a deep blush, turned towards her husband.

Catahaga was taking the harness from the dead horse, and did not pay attention to his wife or to the robber.

The fire had stopped on the summit of the ridge which bordered the land-slip, which was one of those deep fissures we have before described as being com-mon to all parts of America.

The air was still dense with smoke, but the wind had changed, and it had rolled off rapidly.

Minna moved towards Eagle-Wing, but this Don Juan of Bush-Rangers caught her hand.

"Minna, I have offended you. I am sorry," he said, in a tone of soft and manly seriousness, which contrasted strangely with his habitual levity. "Do not leave in anger one to whom you have no cause to show displeasure, who has done nothing to deserve it."

"I am not angry, Oswald Lamond; I am deeply grateful to you for your kindness, and there is one way in which I should like to show it, and that would be, if I had the power, the eloquence sufficient to persuade you to abandon your evil courses."

"Your influence with me! You can never over-estimate it, beautiful Minna Wyotti! For your sake—ah, you think me jesting!—you think I cannot love. Oh, have you forgotten how blissful were my dreams of happiness that I poured into your con-fiding ears, when I was a boy! dreams which raised me such towering castles on such sandy foundations! I loved Agnes then; but, you, perfidious as you are, you played traitor; you won me from my allegiance by your witching glances!"

"I see you are joking, Oswald Lamond; but you much choose your jests in better taste. My hus-band——"

"Your husband!—a Pawnee-Loup, and that's the French for a kind of wher-wolves! Your husband! Look at the scalps in his girdle, and call him your husband!"

Minna turned away in great indignation.

Her husband joined them.

"Does my brother follow our path?" he said.

"Whither does it lead?"

"To the wigwam of the Dacotah."

"Of the tribe of the Crested Snake?"

"Yes; the nation of the Great Sachems, Bison-Horn."

"Wabiskoa."

"Mount then, and let us be off."

The party were soon once more flying along on their mustangs.

They were riding under the low branching trees of a dense bush.

Suddenly Catahaga reined his horse, and touched the arm of the trapper who rode by him.

"Ugh."

"Iroquois, my brother?"

"A war-party in the woods."

"They are Chippowais."

"Yes."

Oswald Lamond leaped off his horse, tossing the rein to Eagle-Wing.

"Wait for me," he said, cooly throwing his gun over his arm; "there are two rogues behind yon tree; I want a word with them."

The Indian called to the bush-ranger to stay, but, reckless of the warning, he pushed on, and approached a huge pine, branching out over a thicket.

Behind the tall and dewy grass, and amid the flowers and creeping plants growing profusely on the spot, two red-skins were lurking; one lay upon the ground, his scalping-knife gleaming in his hand; the other, half hidden behind the trunk of the tree, grasped his tomahawk.

With the most perfect nonchalance the dauntless young captain of bush-rangers walked towards the tree.

He shouted to the Indians to show themselves.

The savages made no reply, but writhed like snakes away from the brake.

Regan levelled his gun at a piece of fringe which fluttered from the hunting shirt of one of the red-skins, as he glided through the bushes.

The ambuscader uttered the peculiar cry of these savages.

"Wagh!"

He leaped up.

His face was hideously smeared with war-paint.

A look of satanic malice and cruelty set on his thin and greenish face.

"Is my brother in the war path, that he crouches to throw his hatchet at one who is not an enemy?" said Oswald, with a severe smile, but in a clear firm voice, and carelessly playing with his fire-lock.

"The Chippowais are on the war-path of the Dacotahs, and their hatchets are raised against the pale-faces, who are his friends," returned the Indian, in a harsh guttural accent.

"But my brother knows that Wabiskoa hates the pale-faces, that he is allied with Monotah, the Sachem of the Pawnee-Loups, and that White Fox is no longer a Yengeese, that he lives among the great nations, and conforms to their customs; why, then, does my brother hunger for my scalp?"

"It is good; but my brother has with him the Eagle-Wing, the squaw of the pale-faces," cried the Indian, savagely; "he has thrown dirt on the lodge of his fathers, he has married a Yengeese woman, and has left his tribe. My brother must give this rabbit into our hands; he is a prisoner on the war-path."

"Let my brother catch his rabbit," returned the bush-ranger, with a sly laugh.

"The White Fox will not keep the dog and his squaw; he has smoked the calumet with the chief of Chippowais, and will not oppose his rights."

"Am I a brave of your party, Chippowais, that I should fight my own friends?" said the captain of bush-rangers, laughing.

He turned away carelessly.

He remounted his mustang.

"How many braves are on the path?" asked Eagle-Wing.

"I do not know, my brother," rejoined Oswald.

"Are they on the trail of the Dacotahs?"

"They look towards the sun, and have crossed the frontier of the hunting-grounds of the Sioux," replied Oswald.

Eagle-Wing gave a low and chuckling laugh.

"The doves will hurry the eagles," he said. "Had the dogs rifles?"

"No; but they had a tomahawk for your scalp, Eagle-Wing."

"They are crows without beaks," returned the Pawnee, chuckling.

Minna looked at her husband sadly and with painful misgivings.

She could not help perceiving that the Indian was fast returning to his old sympathies of his race, and his strange principles taught in his tribe.

The Indian had been scorned and deeply injured by the pale-faces, and was imbibing a disgust for those customs which he had once loved and admired.

"My brother will seek refuge in the wigwam of the Sioux."

"He is adopted of the Dacotahs."

"The pale-faces have wronged my brother."

"Catahaga is not a papouse; he knows how to find his revenge," returned the Indian, fiercely. "The young chief is banished from his tribe."

"It is true, the Pawnee-Loup is forgotten in Manotah's wigwam."

"Does my brother love those that hate him?"

"Eagle-Wing was deluded by dark words, and he would bury the hatchet for ever; but his heart is changed."

"Wabiskoa will give my brother young men and weapons."

"A hundred braves with rifles," returned Eagle-Wing, readily.

"The great chief shall sweep the prairies like the prairies' fire, and the earth shall be cleared of his enemies, and he will fill his belt with their scalping locks."

Eagle-Wing smiled.

Minna looked at the young bush-ranger with great indignation.

Oswald stroked his silky moustache.

"I do not fight with Iroquois," said the Eagle-Wing, in a tone of thrilling sternness; "but I war to the knife with the pale-face dogs!"

Both Minna and the bush-ranger started in their saddles at the vehemence with which this threat was uttered.

"Phew!" whistled Oswald. "Then Eagle-Wing will not tamely endure the cruelty and oppression that he has suffered at the hands of his enemies?"

"The pale-faces borrow the blankets and moccassins of the Shoshoné to murder each other; but I will join the braves of my father with the braves of the Dacotahs, and we will sweep away the traces of these tyrants from the soil. I will not be called the squaw, but the scourge of the pale-faces."

"Now that is talking like a Pawnee brave; the earth shall tremble when the name of Catahaga is whispered," rejoined Oswald, smiling exultingly.

"He is mine!" he whispered, "and four hundred Dacotahs armed to the teeth! Does my brother mean to make open war upon the pale-faces?"

"Till there is not one Yengeese left in Arkansas," returned the Indian, arrogantly. "It is spoken!"

Minna watched her husband's face; but it was inscrutable; she could scarcely believe that all at once he should have turned so bitterly hostile to the whites as to renounce all the teachings of civilization, and to play the part of a barbarous savage.

Oswald Lamond could only think of the anticipated alliance, and he muttered, in rapture,

"A real Sachem, and four hundred picked Dacotahs braves! My deeds will outrival those of Cortez or Pizarro!"

––––––

CHAPTER CXIII.

THE BOY PIRATE AND HIS CREW RESOLVE TO WITHSTAND THE BRAZILIAN MEN-OF-WAR—CHRISTOPHER AND CASSIDY NAILING THE COLOURS TO THE MAST—THE GUN-SHOT FROM THE "DOLOROSA"—A BATTLE ROYAL.

THE "Vulture," spread her wings and fled from the "Red Raven."

The timely appearance of the Brazilian frigates, and the desperate exertions made by Harwolf, saved her, at least, for the present, from the vengeance of the Boy Pirate.

Christopher sat on a carronade, panting with rage and excitement.

His eyes glared alternately from the clouds of smoke belching from the tiers of the receding "Vulture," and rolling in masses along the surface of the deep, to the long, low hulls, flaunting sky-sails, and smoking funnels of the steam-vessels.

An artist wishing to paint the portrait of our dashing young hero could not have chosen a more favourable moment to depict him in all the glowing characteristics of his wild and daring nature.

His black, shining eyes alight with the genius of heroism, his dark, glossy locks flowing on the breeze, his finely-cut lip arched in scorn and defiance, the graceful posé of his supple and symmetrical form, and the picturesque style of his rich dress.

His jacket was thrown aside.

He wore an embroidered shirt of the finest and snowiest linen, loosely tied at the neck with a fluttering kerchief of silk in brightest colours.

His trousers were ample and flowing, seamed and braided in the Spanish style, and his waist was swathed with an Indian shawl of great beauty and value, the material being of glowing scarlet and purple, magnificently interwoven with the most exquisite gold-thread work.

Through this were thrust a long, gleaming stiletto, and a brace of quaintly-shaped and silver-mounted pistols.

Grasped in his right hand, and lying across his knees, was a flashing, curved yataghan.

His officers were gathered about him, straining like dogs in the slips.

Catching the enthusiasm of their dauntless boy-leader, the hardy outlaws cast fiery glances at the swooping war-steamers, and seemed more disposed to give them the stern welcome of indomitable warriors than to fly like criminals before the ruthless avengers of justice.

Old Brierly stood jauntily, his arms lightly folded athwart his broad full chest, his grey hair streaming in the wind, his clear, grey eye fixed upon the taper masts and bellying sails of the terrible enemy bearing down upon them at race-horse speed.

Dick Caffyn, whose resemblance to his foster-brother was at such moments more than usually striking, was perched like a bird on the ratlings, shading his eyes from the sun, and gazing on the objects that excited such general and keen attention with a countenance betraying his eager desire to risk the perilous encounter.

The inflexible and taciturn Spaniard, Gomez, kept an eager look-out from the forecastle, and did not lower his glass from his coal-black eye, even for an instant.

The rollicking Tom Garrod, the oracle of his appreciative messmates, leaned against the capstan, a pistol in each hand, while the Ethiopian paladin, Uncle Zamp, showed his great teeth in the broadest of grins, and rubbed his huge hands, branded by old scars, and panted for the fun and excitement of the fray.

"Jack, my old Greek," cried the Boy Pirate, with a cheery laugh, "you're the nestor of our councils, and ought to teach us youngsters discretion. Shall we receive these Dons like gentlemen, or shall we, in accordance with the 'better part of valour,' pipe all hands to make sail and sheer off from the legals?"

"Cap'en" returned Brierley, with a grin, "the longest and the roughest cruise can't wear out the relish that every true British tar must feel for a brush with a foreign enemy. Howsomedever, if any sensible chap adwises you to skulk a fight when there's sich long odds agen' us, all I say is as he might give you much worse adwice who votes for clapping on skys'ls—but, dam'me, don't make me that counsellor, I shirks the duty."

The crew laughed and cheered.

Gomez and another officer came on to the main-deck and drew near the young commander.

The Spaniard's companion was a short, sharp-faced man with a keen, restless eye—Brand, the pilot.

"Well, amigo," said the Boy Pirate, addressing the Spaniard, "I hate this shilly-shally; besides, we can't afford to delay. Shall we stick to our colours, or shall we hug the wind for protection? Come, yours shall be the casting vote."

"Senor," returned the Spaniard, promptly, "let us fight."

"Don Gomez for ever! Hurrah for the Red Raven!" roared the dauntless pirates, with one accord, starting, alert for orders.

"Be it so," said Christopher. "Man the side."

At this moment a boat that had been put off to the merchantman, which struck her colours to the Boy Pirate after Harwolf had been driven off, returned to the "Raven."

Cassidy and Oakland came on board with those of the officers of the "Raven" who had been sent to take possession of the prize.

The Boy Pirate walked up to Cassidy and drew him aside.

"Hark ye, mate," he said, "you have struck the black flag, you have sailed your last cruise under the 'Oliver.'"

"Aye, sir," returned Cassidy, quietly.

"And you are no longer a—a pirate."

"No, sir," returned the ex-mate of the "Vulture," in the same calm tone.

"And you could not easily be induced to set your name on my ship's books though I offered you the command of the prize?"

"Never," replied Cassidy, softly, but in a tone of inexorable firmness.

"I am sorry."

"Captain, I would serve under you while I had an ounce of blood in my veins—if——"

"I were not a pirate?"

"Aye, sir."

The rich flush on the clear-bronzed cheek of the young buccaneer deepened; he bit his lip and frowned.

"Well," he said, a little fiercely; "man does not always make his own destiny."

"But he may defy it," replied Cassidy.

The Boy Pirate turned away with impatience, exclaiming,

"Cassidy, you may be brave and able; I think you both, but I shall doubt it if you brag."

"I never do."

"Ha! and yet you say a man can defy fate."

"So he may."

"I am your fate, Cassidy, do you defy me?" asked the Red Raven in a tone of indomitable authority.

"I defy not, as I fear not any man," replied the dauntless seaman, gently.

"You presume upon my character and forbearance," said Christopher.

"These are not words I should have expected to hear from the Boy Pirate," replied Cassidy, in an even tone. "Captain, I pity and respect you, but I will never be a pirate."

"But you are condemned, Cassidy," returned the rover, in a tone of poignant sadness, "the unrelenting laws of merciless men give no countenance to the most practical repentance; with human justice there is no absolution; once a felon ever a felon."

"The law may do its worst," returned the seaman,

firmly; "a man who is not true to himself is a pitiful coward. I am not bound by my own principles to surrender to the law; but, if they catch me, let them hang me; I suppose I can walk forward as firmly as another."

"Cassidy, you are a far greater man than I, though the world rings with my fame," returned our hero, with all the warmth of his generous soul. "You are the rarest, noblest brave!"

"You flatter me, sir; I am not so; I am not lofty-minded, large-hearted, open-hearted, chivalrous and great, as the Boy Pirate," returned the seaman, with fearless sincerity, "but I happen to have a certain amount of doggish tenacity to my own resolutions. If I had been a pirate I should have been quite ruthless; but I don't want to be a pirate, and if I wavered from my will for any threats or any inducements I should not be——Sam Cassidy."

"Well, mate, I respect your scruples, and will not ask you to command our prize for the nonce against these Brazilian thunderers; but, I warn you, if you are taken, you will swing with the rest of us."

"One word, captain," cried the seaman, with unusual briskness, detaining the Boy Pirate, who was turning away, "these Spanish skunks are not English jollies; I am not bound to yield to them; I will fight them to the last shot in the locker, if you will give me leave."

"Now, that's well said, hearty," responded the gallant rover, shaking his hand. "Dick, call the officers aft to me," he cried, addressing his foster brother.

The next instant the Red Raven stood on the quarter, surrounded by the attentive leaders of his daring band.

"Gentlemen," said Christopher, "amongst us there have never existed those feelings of petty jealousy which are common fore and aft on too many crafts that sail under the black banner. I am sure you will not think my confidence misplaced when I tell you that I intend to give the command of our prize, the merchantman, during this action, to Mr. Cassidy; if any one dissents from this arrangement let him hold up his hand."

The officers murmured approvingly.

"None, captain," cried Dick Caffyn, impetuously; "but if we don't want to leave all the fighting to the Spaniards, we must get to work at once."

"Right, Dick!"

"The steamers are hard a-port, sir," said a man, stepping up to Christopher.

"Good! Tom Garrod?"

"Here, sir."

"Get tackle ready for hoisting boats."

"Aye, aye, sir."

"Gomez? Brand?"

"Here, Senor."

"Aye, captain."

"I shall leave the 'Raven' to your charge."

"Do you mean to board, cap'en?" said Brierly with a start.

"Yes! Zamp?"

"Here am, buckra cap'en," cried the negro, springing on to the quarter.

"You shall be my coxswain, Zamp."

"Nebber fin' a better, sar," responded the nigger.

"Follow Tom Garrod."

"Dick."

But the impatient fellow was at the davits hurrying the men, who were putting down the boats.

"Who's at the signal halliards?"

"Pierce, sir."

"Right! pull down that bunting."

The men laughed.

The flag was lowered from the foremast.

As the Brazilian standard floated down a triumphant cheer echoed over the waters.

The war-steamers had borne down in gallant style, and were now running within a cable length of the pirate schooner.

"Run up the Red Raven."

"Hurrah!"

"Tell the carpenter to send aft a hammer and some nails."

"Aye, aye, sir."

All on board was bustle.

The decks were cleared.

Busy hands were reefing sail aloft.

Brand stood in the forecastle.

He was shouting his orders in firm and ringing tones to the men in the rigging.

The sides were manned.

The guns were run back.

There was haste, but not confusion.

Everything passed off as orderly as if the pirates had been long-trained seamen on board a man-of-war.

Dick Caffyn was chafing at the accommodation-ladder.

Tom Garrod was employed with some men sharpening the cutlasses and pike-heads.

Zamp turned the wheel of the grindstone, his brawny arms swaying the handle round and round as he kept true time with some doggerel nigger melody,

"We're de darkie boys to fight,
Oh!—yo—yo.
Jest could whip de world outright,
Oh!—ne—no.
Make de sparks fly I'm be bound,
While de ole wheel turn him round,
So—go—so."

Shots, bayonets, and canister-wads, powder-cans, and small arms were handed from below.

The boats were lowered.

Every man was at his station.

Cassidy had gone on board the merchant.

Captain Fleming and Leighton, who thought it prudent to decline active co-operation in the fight, though they had little sympathy with the Spaniards, and the girls, who were trembling with fright, were sent below.

The hatches on both ships were battened down.

Brierly, who had gone on board the merchantman with Cassidy, talked with him and Oakland on the main-deck as collected as if there were not such a thing as a raking broadside or a running noose in creation.

The Boy Pirate took the hammer and nails.

As he walked down the deck he looked about him with an air of pride and satisfaction.

"My hearties! comrades that have stood by me in weal or woe through many a cruise," he cried, exultingly, "nothing can be more needless than a long harangue to impel you to act as you only can—the bravest rover crew that ever served under the free flag. There floats the Raven, and never shall she be lowered from her lofty perch by any of this ship's company. While the mast-head remains above the engulphing surf, our gallant bird shall flap his red wings in the black cloud that is fraught with such crushing thunder to our foes. Comrades, we will fight while we have enough life and strength left in us to wield a blade or blaze a barker. Hurrah for the 'Red Raven!' We will nail our banner to the mast!"

The cheers were deafening.

The Boy Pirate flew like a squirrel up the rigging.

He struck the nails through the bunting, and from the masthead rolled out in the freshening breeze the dread banner of death, with its white, grinning skull and cross-bones, and its soaring, blood-red raven.

A cry of horror rang along the deck.

The sharp crackle of a gun was heard from the yard-arm of the Spanish steamer, and the Boy Pirate was seen to stagger and fall among the rigging.

THE BOY PIRATE SURPRISES HARWOLF.

Christopher, however, clung to the rigging.

He lowered himself to the main yard.

Here he dropped athwart the yard arm, and lay seemingly insensible, perhaps dead.

The rigging was at once swarmed with men.

The pirates were reckless of their own danger, for a heavy fire was opened upon them from the war-steamer.

The first who reached the Boy Pirate, as he lay extended on the yard arm, every lurch of the ship threatening to topple him overboard, or worse, to cast him down on deck, was his devoted foster brother.

The Boy Pirate was deadly pale; his eyes were closed, and he appeared quite inanimate.

He was carefully lifted from his hazardous position and brought on deck.

No. 37.

The crew flew round him.

His face was pale and rigid.

Blood flowed from his arm.

It was evident that he had been struck by a bullet.

Not fiercer the roar of the lioness robbed of her cubs than the yell of the pirates as they looked down upon the unconscious form of their heroic boy commander.

Cutlasses waved, a volley of muskets were fired, and by whose orders it was never known.

More than one gun blazed from the ports, and, strange to say, with telling effect.

As tenderly as a man would carry his sick mother the men bore the young hero to the cockpit.

Perceiving their advantage, the Spaniards poured a broadside into the " Raven."

It was respouded to by a roar of the infuriated outlaws.

Every man seemed to be nerved to the highest pitch of desperation.

Gomez, with his stern face yet sterner in its expression, walked the deck, and issued his orders in loud and piercing tones.

Brand took the helm.

Restoratives were quickly applied to the young chief, and he soon opened his eyes, to the great joy of the surrounders.

A cry of intense delight was emitted by the anxious spectators.

The first form on which the wandering glance of the Boy Pirate fixed was the gentle form of his devoted Lilia.

His wife hung over him with tenderest care, and sobbed with joy as she saw that the light of life once more broke upon the darkness of his torpor of anguish.

She placed his head on her lap, and kissing his pale brow, assisted the men to bind his wound.

But again he fainted, and lay as if dead.

It was at this juncture that the genius of Sam Cassidy displayed itself to the greatest advantage.

The Boy Pirate had been easily distinguished by those on board the merchantman by his light dress and glittering arms.

They had seen him fall.

They had joined their voices in the shout of dismay and fury which followed the catastrophe that threatened such fatal consequences to the band.

In a calm and collected manner the new commander of the merchantman gave his orders to tack round in such a way as to bring his vessel, which was a superb sailer, across the bows of the steam war-ships, which lay on the lee-side of the schooner, pouring their broadsides, the pirates returning the fire with desperate fury.

As Sam and Brierly walked forward Cassidy looked at the small four pounders and at the scant array of armed men aboard; the quiet fellow shrugged his shoulders and smiled.

Brierly looked thoughtful and turned a look of intense fierceness upon the steam-ships.

Cassidy's eye brightened, however, as it fell upon the long swivel chaser amidships.

"Oakland, take the helm."

"Aye, Sam."

"I mean to get the barque athwart hawse with the 'Dolorosa.' We stand much higher out of water, and can sweep her decks with the stern-chaser."

"Aye, Mr. Cassidy, but the blubber ribs of this heavy craft will have to stand fire without her being able to return a shot, except from these child's pop-guns, and they will command a part of the deck, and the most they can do is to knock some poor reefer off his perch."

"Put the helm up!" cried Cassidy.

"Aye, Sam."

"We must signal the 'Raven' to reserve her starboard broadside. The 'Dolorosa' will open all her larboard ports, not giving us the credit we deserve for pluck, and then we can run close alongside, elevate the guns, and cut away some of her pretty gear; Gomez will understand my manoeuvring. Tell the man at the signal-halyard to signal that we are going to board; she will run full into the wind's eye. These Spanish skipjacks lay like the log, and think that, like pressed men, we shall growl a little and give in. If we can get along the lee side of the 'Dolorosa,' we will jump on her deck like tigers leaping down from a cage, while the 'Raven' scuds round to windward and opens a rattling fire on her weather-quarters."

"Cassidy, you're a thorough seaman," returned Brierly, "but the other corvette is paddling round. See how she laughs at the wind. Blow me, hearty, if these steam-ships arn't built by some chaps which is got a most uncommon contempt for the clerk of the weather-office and all wind reg'lations. Dam'me,

with naked masts she glides full in the teeth of this nor'-wester, and she looks wicious, hearty."

"Hark! what a shout from the deck of the 'Raven,'" said Cassidy.

"Aye, mate, and I like the tune on it," rejoined old Brierly.

"What does she mean by that signal?"

"It's one as he larnt from mad Don Miguel—it means, 'all's well—go ahead!'" returned Brierly.

"Well, then, see to the men of the 'cutting out' party, Mr. Brierly, while I manage the ship. If she behaves we shall soon look over our high bulwarks on to the deck of our foes. See to the grapnels and boarding nets, and cheer up the lads. Lend me the speaking-trumpet."

Cassidy took it, and, putting it to his lips, shouted in a clear and ringing voice to the men in the rigging,

"Way aloft!"

"Ready, sir."

"Heave away!"

The deck sounded to the tramp of the men at the capstan.

Men were to be seen along the mighty spars, and hanging about high aloft in the rigging, like flies meshed in the spider's films.

"Ready the fore-royal!" cried a voice in one part of the rigging.

"Ready the main-yard!" responded another.

"All ready aft, sir!" cried a man from the mizen.

"Let fall!" cried Cassidy.

Grandly the immense vessel swept along before the wind, the spray founting before her steady gliding prow.

"We're away!" roared the pirates, brandishing their weapons in wild excitement. "Hurrah for the Boy Pirate!"

Meantime the scene in the cockpit of the "Red Raven" defies all description.

Well disciplined as they were, the lawless pirates, both officers and men, were only restrained by their enthusiastic admiration of their dauntless boy hero, and their blind faith in his good fortune.

Now he was to all seeming mortally wounded, the more steady among them had much ado to reassure their companions and keep the cockpit clear of intrusion.

It soon, however, was proved that Christopher's wound was not dangerous.

The bullet had struck into the fleshy part of the arm which he had injured at San Salvador, and which still occasionally gave him great pain.

He had lost his hold of the tackling, and in his fall had struck his head against the maintop-yard, and was stunned by the blow.

The roar of the cannons, the wild yells of his terrified, yet exasperated men, the shuddering of the ship, the floating of bright clouds of smoke above the hatchway, the yearning eyes and quivering, pallid lips of Lilia, the eager and excited faces of the men clustered round him—these were the sights and sounds that assailed the senses of the Boy Pirate on his return to consciousness.

"I have been wounded," he said, a little faintly; "but I am little hurt; I shall live yet, comrades, to lead you on to many a victory."

The men testified their intense satisfaction by the most fervent cheering.

"Carry me on deck," said the Boy Pirate.

The men did not hesitate to obey these orders, they did not attempt to remonstrate.

They were all in deadly peril; fearfully outmatched.

Their noble young chief in whom they had such blind faith was alive; he had spoken, and that was a victory in itself.

As Christopher was borne aft he waved his yataghan and laughed encouragingly.

He was laid down on a pile of sail cloth on the quarter-deck.

He raised himself on his arm and looked through the veil of smoke and the line of flashing flames;

he looked up at the rigging riddled with flying shots, above all floated with grim impregnability the black banner.

"Zamp," shouted Christopher, to the sable giant, "your shoulder. Dick, let down the boats; we will board them to the teeth, and I will lead the party!"

"Yes, mas'r, dis chile carry yo' to glory," chuckled Zampa; "berry glad to see mas'r so spry—yah! yah! Lor, I can't 'spress my feelin's; they's quite 'dic'lous; as if dey'se kill de Red Raven! dam bird much too cute for dat, I'se reckon. Mas'r like a elephant. Gib him hand, him ride on de shoulders of ole Zamp, like de Nabob in Injey—yah!"

The stalwart negro placed the slight, boyish form of the redoubtable young buccaneer on his shoulders.

Christopher was pale; the blood soaked through the bandages round his arm.

But the strength of genius and indomitable courage lent a power to that countenance; a fierceness to that unquailing eye, a rigid firmness to those tight drawn lips, that braced the spirits and fired the hearts of his crew as soon as the Boy stood proudly amongst them.

When Nelson was struck down at Trafalgar, and dying in the cockpit, his men fought just as bravely as if he had been on the quarter-deck commanding them, or rather should it be said with enthusiasm, they fought with redoubled valour; but the Boy Pirate, an outlaw, a felon, by his good qualities, allied with that good luck which had brought him rich prizes without compromising altogether his worth of nobleness, had no other claim upon his devoted followers than the love they bore him and the reliance they had on his approved skill and courage; he could not refer them to a higher motive than that of self-preservation; he could not remind them that their native country exacted their best service, for they were men who had been expatriated, and were at enmity with all the world.

The merchantman skillfully managed by Cassidy, veered round through the parting waters and was tacking to get alongside of the "Dolorosa."

The boats were put down.

They were manned by the sturdy sea-dogs, and pulled off to the corvette, amid the most terrific cheering.

A dreadful fire was opened upon them.

One of the boats was struck athwart the bows, and its living freight the next moment were struggling in the waves.

The others soon were dancing beneath the dark side of the "Dolorosa."

Her consort, the "Saratoga," steamed up, firing her swivel-guns at the merchantman.

Grapnels were thrown, and the desperate outlaws clambered her side, and in the face of the most furious opposition leaped on her deck.

Dick Caffyn on one side, Tom Garrod on the other, laughing and madly cheering, the Boy Pirate was borne on the stalwart shoulders of the gigantic negro.

He seemed to bear a charmed life.

Pale and faint as he was he yet struck about him with his yataghan, amid the smoke and din—the thunder and the lightning of the bloody fight.

The Spaniards were so paralyzed by the audacity of their opponents that they seemed quite beside themselves.

The officers bawled their orders; the men dashed themselves wildly but with ineffectual impetuosity against the serried ranks of the boarders as they swarmed over the bulwarks, and at the word of their boy leader formed into a dense mass as orderly as if they had been so many marines on parade.

A panic broke out among the crew of the "Dolorosa."

The slaughter was indiscriminate.

The decks pooled with blood, which ran along the scuppers and trickled into the sea.

The ship smoked like a furnace and rocked like a cradle; the thundering of exploding guns; the

yells of the battle-maddened savages; the keen slash; the heavy fall; the shriek and the groan of the unheeded wounded and dying; the trampling of feet on the slippery and swaying deck; the yells, curses, and shouts, combined to render the fray one of the most awful description.

The "Saratoga," seeing that the "Raven" was comparatively deserted, paddled round to get alongside.

The "Raven" tacked about, yet, in spite of the sea-craft of her matchless pilot Brand, she manoeuvered awkwardly, for the sufficient reason that there were not left aboard sufficient hands to manage her advantageously.

Sam Cassidy had changed his tactics.

Feigning to be bearing down upon the "Dolorosa," he contrived to get so near the "Saratoga" that his guns commanded her deck.

He opened a murderous fire with great and small arms, and catching the wind ran foul of the steamer.

The concussion was tremendous, and the Spanish vessel lost her bowsprit, and in spite of the advantage she possessed in the machinery, that rendered her independent of the wind, which fell suddenly and had to be so diligently courted by the merchantman, was nearly foundering.

With all the fury of hungry lions the Ravens, who were working the merchantman, swooped upon the deck of the "Saratoga."

It was hard to say which of the boarding parties was engaged in the deadliest work.

Meanwhile the "Raven" and her prize lay passively on the waters, their helms lashed and their sails feebly furled by the few men who were left aboard, rather to prevent a collision than for any other purpose.

On both sides the firing from the ports had ceased.

Now a pitch battle was raging—hand to hand between the pirates and their foes upon the gory decks.

The contest lasted long, and was fought on both sides with the utmost obstinacy.

At length the Spaniards hauled down their flag.

Wounded and bleeding, forced by his anguish and weakness to accept the support of the negro's shoulders, the Boy Pirate had won this surprising victory.

He stood on the deck of the "Dolorosa" and was hailed as the winner of two steamers of war and a rich-laden merchantman.

Cassidy approached him.

"Sam," said the Boy Pirate, "your feat has exceeded my best expectations."

"Captain," returned the seaman, with a smile, "I will not praise you, because I am not eloquent in flatteries, but were you the Boy Patriot instead of the Boy Pirate, the world would be proud of you."

"Sam," said Christopher, with a frown, "when men begin to exchange commendations they begin at the same time to despise one another. Now, Cassidy, I have two fine war-steamers: I can find hands, for there are many reckless fellows abroad who will gladly follow my fortunes. The world is a wide arena, and there is a higher game than that I have been playing. The world is selfish, Sam; states are governed much in the same way as individuals, by what Shakespeare calls 'commodity,' expediency, self-interest. You smile, Sam, at such a truism. Well, I don't state the fact as anything original, but I hate all humbug, and I hate it worst in lawn sleeves or senatorial scarlet. The best way that I can conceive of redeeming my self-respect is in devoting myself now that I have made my fortune, to the cause of right and liberty. Do you know what I shall do with myself and with these my hard-won prizes?"

"I don't know, captain, but your act will be generous, I'm sure of that."

"I have fought for myself; now I mean to devote myself with all my heart and energy to the cause of a gallant and suffering nation, most cruelly op pressed, slighted, and neglected by those who trumpet the loudest the glories of their own blood-bought freedom; slighted and neglected for the sake of 'this commodity', this self-interest."

"What nation is that, captain?"

"My fortunes are desperate; I lose nothing by the most insane Quixotism—I mean to fight for Poland!"

"And I will join you, captain, in such a cause," cried Cassidy.

"But first," said the Boy Pirate, "I will settle my reckoning with Daniel Harwolf.

CHAPTER CXIV.

HARWOLF'S PRIZE—THE WOLF SHOWS HIS TEETH—A CARNIVAL OF CRUELTY—DEATH OF THE LASCAR—A RACE IN CHAINS—HARWOLF STRUCK DOWN—THE CREW'S VENGEANCE—WARDLAW'S INTERCESSION—THE STEAM FRIGATES IN THE OFFING.

THE "Vulture" had run down a prize off the coasts of Mexico.

It was a brigantine of heavy burden, its cargo of great value, and its crew numerous.

The details of this capture are too horrible for narration.

Harwolf had long ceased to feel the least compunction for the blackest crimes, and the atrocities of pirates can scarcely be exaggerated.

Harwolf was one of the most ruthless.

Suffice it to say that the men on board the "Polly of Portsea," for that was the name of the vessel, were all murdered in cold blood.

To enhance the diabolical villany of this act of piracy, no resistance had been made; the captain offering to surrender the ship and the whole cargo, on condition that the women passengers should be spared.

Harwolf acted with the blackest treachery.

As a boy, this monster was morose, cruel and selfish; as a man, altogether abandoned to profligacy and villany.

Now his object was to establish himself in despotic authority by leading his men on to the perpetration of such desperate outrages that, being lost to hope, they might be united more closely in the bonds of mutual crime and mutual self-protection.

The pirate lounged against a carronade.

His eyes were fixed on the deck.

The gleam in them was cold and cruel as the spark that lights up the brilliant eye of a cobra.

The frown on his brow was black as the flag that hung at the mast-head of his vessel, and fiends seemed to crouch in the wrinkles of his passion-worn face.

He was drinking brandy and smoking.

"Bring hither the skipper of our prize, the three Lascars, and the mate," he said, addressing one of his fiercest ruffians.

The man grinned.

Heavily ironed, the men were dragged from below.

The captain was a pale-faced, weakly, unseamanlike looking old man, apparently of nervous and irritable temperament, starting and trembling at the cold malignant voice of the black pirate, looking reproachfully at his fellow prisoners, as if he considered them in some way responsible for the capture of the ship—yet by no means cowardly, and giving way to his temper, regardless of danger.

The Lascars were lathy fellows, callous and with faces betoking the subtlety and ferocity of their nature.

The mate was a simple, stolid-looking sailor, and seemed remarkable only for the dogged way in which he unfaced the wretched Harwolf.

"Well, captain," said the pirate, daintily twirling his cigar, and modulating his voice to that tone of mocking suavity that is peculiar to those who delight in acts of wanton cruelty, "I hope you like your berth. How did you sleep, my good sir? I hope your dreams were not disturbed by the phantoms that tread the rover's barque when the sun goes down in a wild sky, and the scuds of wind and rain rattle his black bunting as if to rend it to ribbons. You're a hardy man, spite of your tallow cheeks and lantern jaws, ha? you can sleep in a slaughter-house, and not be qualmed at the smell of blood."

"You bloody-minded wolf! I can sleep soundly, for I dare you to do your worst, knowing that *your* bed will be one of the hottest when Jack Ketch tucks you up, you infernal murderer! Your cruise won't last long, black thief! you are measured for the halter if the devil doesn't carry you off in a whirlwind before your time."

The captain of the "Polly" was bathed in cold sweat; he quivered and quaked in every limb, yet he shrieked forth his abuse with convulsive passion, in a tone so shrill and shrewish, that the ruffians around roared their brutal laughter.

"I admire your pluck."

"I curse your impudence."

"Well, you shall have a chance——"

"Of seeing you swing, yet, you infernal pirate."

"Here's a goodly companion, comrades; we'll make him bo'swain's mate; if he can wield the cat as well as he can use his jawing tackle we shall have better discipline for'ard and aft. You, sir, what is your name?" he went on, addressing the mate.

"William Thompson," returned the man sullenly.

"And a meddling fool!" shrieked the irascible captain. "If you had not advised me to put out of port when I wanted to wait till the 'Dolorosa' arrived to convoy us, we should never have fallen into the black hands of this wretch."

"I thought for the best, sir," returned the other, humbly.

"Pshaw! I suppose a captain is not to be master in his own ship. Rank mutiny! You deserve all you'll get, sir, for daring to oppose my wishes."

"I did not mean to oppose you, sir," replied the mate, humbly.

The skipper stamped and chuckled with a contemptuous disgust.

"I wish I'd put you all in irons, for your infernal interference," he cried, shrilly, his teeth chattering, and his limbs tottering with mingled fear and fury.

The pirates burst into shouts of mirth; there was something so ludicrous in the conduct of this man in rating his assistant at such a moment.

"I should think, mate, you'll be glad to exchange skippers," said Harwolf, with a leer. "What say you to entering on my ship's books? heaps of galore, and boundless liberty, fun, and glory, and gallons of grog."

"No, sir, it can do you no good to do me harm, and I hope you'll think better of your present intentions," returned the mate, with calm fortitude. "I will never be a pirate."

"You won't, ha! Well, you ungrateful beast, you know the alternative?" cried Harwolf, maliciously.

"Yes, sir."

"You'll walk the plank, and die game; is that it?"

"I hope not, sir; I hope you'll consider——"

"I *will* consider; I will deliberate the most fitting punishment for an audacious pig-head, that refuses a good offer. I'll have you know, sir, that aboard this schooner I am autocrat—here there is no other will than mine. Perhaps you've made up your mind that, as every squall brings the chance of your being swept over-board, that it's no such a great matter to be sent 'forty fathom down,' with a shot at your heels; but, remember, if I have any resistance, I shall make an example of you; another element besides water, my beauty, is—*fire!*"

"Well, sir," returned the mate, a sickening pallor overspreading his firm face, "I am in your hands, but God is above all."

The pirate looked at him with the scowl of a gloating demon.

"Excellent well, sir," he said, coldly; "I'll re-serve my answer—stand aside. And now, skipper, what have you to say why I shouldn't give you a dance from the yard-arm?"

"Devil! I have nothing to say but this: I defy you to do your worst! You smirk because I tremble; I'm a nervous man. But may I be roasted if I speak another word; what you mean to do, do at once."

Even the savage pirates murmured approvingly; the evident bodily anguish and physical terror of the heroic seaman only enhanced the true courage of his moral character.

Harwolf gnashed his teeth at this display of sympathy on the part of his villains.

He scowled round with a threatening frown.

"You say so *now*, my pretty martyr," he cried, savagely, "but we shall have you piping another tune presently, or it will go ve-ry hard!"

The merchant-captain made no answer, but quelled his mortal trepidation, straightened his shaking knees, and clenched his twitching fingers.

Harwolf looked at him with savage contempt.

The pirate drew a long, shining pistol.

He deliberately drew back the fire-lock.

The "click" seemed to shoot through the frame of the prisoner like an electric shock.

He winced and ducked his head.

The pirates laughed.

The glitter of icicles sparkled in Harwolf's wolfish, green-grey eyes, as he pointed the weapon at the skipper's head.

"Now, my doughty, will you sign articles, turn pirate, and cut throats, or will you take your billet from this barker? Sharp's the word—Yes or No?"

"N - n - no!" screamed the self-conqueror, in trembling accents, but with thorough fixedness of purpose.

Whether or not Harwolf would have shot the man dead can never be known.

A girl rushed up the after hatchway, and flew towards him.

Three fierce-looking wretches, armed with knives and pistols, followed her close.

The girl threw herself on her knees before the Vulture, and clasped her hands imploringly.

She was a frail and beautiful creature, with wavey golden hair, a sweet pensive face, slight, but finely moulded form, and had not yet reached her woman-hood.

"Oh, sir, spare my father!" she cried, distractedly. "Grief has driven him mad; he would not denounce you, he will forgive you everything—indeed, he will—spare him for his grey hairs—spare him, as you hope for heavenly pardon!"

"Who let this pigeon out of the coop?" cried Harwolf, turning savagely upon his men.

"Not I, cap'en. Nor I," responded the men, cowering with fright.

"Look you, my pretty lass. Come, what's your name?"

"Mabel, sir," answered the girl, faintly.

"Well, Mabel, you must be good and obedient, my love. Recollect, obedience is woman's first duty, is it not? Come, no sulking; answer."

"Yes, sir," answered the skipper's daughter, shuddering.

"Well, then, go below, and wait till I visit you, for I want to have a long chat with you. I shall make you a lady. Will you obey me, my dear, with-out constraining me to use coercion?"

"If you will spare my father, sir," returned the poor girl, feebly.

"I exact unquestioning obedience. Do you know I am king here and despot? It is not for you to pro-pose conditions. Go below at once, but first—no hesitating—give me your sweetest kiss."

The old skipper sank on his knees, and, raising his eyes to Heaven, cried in a tone of unwavering firmness,

"If you do, Mab, I will invoke from Heaven a father's bitterest curse upon you."

"Curse you! I will attend to you anon," shouted the tyrant, striking the poor old man in the face.

Harwolf was getting intoxicated with his power for wrong and his indulgence of a morbid passion for cruelty.

He was, as men will be who put no restraint upon their evil impulses, a mere madman in a phrenzy of hellish remorselessness.

Our passions are like wild horses; give them the rein, and they will dash us onward to condign ruin; stop the beginnings, the bitter end will find the self-indulgent wretch a brute, a sot, a swindler, or a desperate robber, though at first he may content himself with rough words, an extra glass, a small stake, or a trifling dishonesty.

"Come, my little angel," said the pirate, with a beastly leer, "one sweet little kiss. I command it; if you are refractory I shall have to bring you to reason."

"Is there no man kind enough to put a knife in my child's heart?" groaned the hapless father.

"Quick, or I shall punish you for the delay, for I must have *promptness*, as well as fullness of obedi-ence," said the insane monster, regardless of the scowling looks of his own ruffians.

"Never sir! Please kill me quickly," replied the girl, half dead with fear.

"You fellow! you copper skunk!" cried the pirate, turning towards one of the Lascars; "I shall want you. Untie his hands, Blacklock. Listen, my dear," said Harwolf to the trembling girl; "there once commanded a ship—he was a pirate, for he murdered a whole ship's crew except the captain and his daughter—his name was Black Ralph, and he had a face as fierce and a voice as loud as a lion's. He was a hectering, blustering fellow, and, to hear him talk, you might fancy that he had never heard the word pity, yet he had the heart of a chicken, and would let a woman play the devil with him. I am of a different disposition, my dear; I like soft words and a quiet life, but I *must* be obeyed, so give me a kiss, like a good girl, or you must suffer the penalty of your disobedience. I cannot be out-braved before the whole of my crew, not one of whom for his life dare gainsay me. Give me a kiss, and go below."

"Never, never!" sobbed the poor girl, firmly.

"God bless you, Mab! your mother in Heaven will bless you," murmured the old merchant captain, weeping like a child.

"Hi, you; I must know my friends. Your name, darkie?"

"Janée," replied the Lascar.

"Very well; strip that girl, lash her to the mast, and whip her till I cry hold," said the fiendish pirate, his eyes swimming with the intoxication of the lust of cruelty.

Be it observed this scene is only a parallel to many similar and even more diabolic carnivals of Satan, if even the great "Master of Evil" can be capable of such paltry malice as would disgrace the filthiest of his fiends.

"How, sir, did you hear me?" cried Harwolf, in a harsh and husky, lust-quenched voice. "Strip this girl, and flog her till she promises obedience."

"No, sar, me no do so, me no floggee young missee. See yo dam fust!" returned the savage-looking fellow, his face almost beautified by the heroism of his resistance against the tyrant.

Harwolf drew a pistol and shot the Lascar dead.

Mabel shrieked, and hid her eyes in her raining tresses of gold.

The wretched prisoner emitted a low and bitter moan.

"Pitch him overboard," said the monster, re-placing the smoking pistol, and drawing another, as he spurned the body with his foot.

The men obsequiously obeyed; they were cowed by his intense expression of maniacal ferocity.

The poor Lascar plashed into the sea.

"He's mad, Jack," whispered one pirate to another.

"Yes; but, by the blazes, he is armed, and we shall be killed, some on us," returned his comrade.

"I wish we had Black Ralph among us; he was a trump, for all his play-acting and bounce."

"Well, nothin' lasts for ever," responded his messmate, sapiently.

"Now, then, let us see if any among you wants to sail in the wake of that mutineer. Set 'em free, Blacklock. Who's for doing this duty?"

Harwolf cocked the second pistol.

The Lascars hurried forward.

In an instant the dress was torn from Mabel's fair, soft shoulders, and the Lascars with wild, starting eyes were dragging her eagerly to the mast.

Wardlaw stepped forward.

"Captain," he said, sternly, "you said just now that you were king aboard. So you shall be; but you must treat us as subjects, not as slaves. We can't afford to be over nice—granted; murder is our trade, we can't be burdened with useless lumber—granted also; but we kill men in fair fight or for preserving discipline—murder for fun and woman-torturing is not in our bargain."

It was a bold speech.

Like all bold actions, this interference carried with it the almost ever-sequent reward of hardihood—success.

The crew looked at their leader with frowning faces.

"Well, Gerald Wardlaw, I'll not refuse this favour, though I'll bring the girl to submission, be assured," returned Harwolf, with forced indifference. "Mabel, I shall have to give you a little lecture on your duty to him who is your master. Meanwhile, obey me."

"In all that I can, sir," replied the poor girl, half-fainting with fear.

"The ribbon in my slipper is loose; tauten it, my dear."

The girl bent over the shoe, and with quivering fingers tied the string.

Her father stamped with rage.

"A good girl. If you had been as submissive in the first instance, it would have been better for your father; but no matter, go below."

The girl obeyed without a murmur.

"Now, hearties, all hands for skylarking. I won't have you milksops. I must and will be obeyed, and the sooner you quash all fastidiousness the better. You're pirates; if you play the Boy Pirate, and fight for the slave, and act like philanthrophists, where's your recompense?—would they save the 'Red Raven?'—wouldn't he hang as high as the worst of us? Of course he would—once offending never pardoned. And yet a man—every man—the best of men—is a saint one moment and a grievous sinner the next. The doctrine of perpetual condemnation is emphatic; but it is paramount and will be paramount. Let a ticket-of-leave do more good when released from punishment than a saviour of nations, or a Sister of Mercy, he or she can never be such good people, for though they have eaten the bitter bread and done the hard work of penal slavery, though their term be served out to the last hour, they are felons, and respectable folk eschew their company, though the scorners themselves may be seducers, oppressors, or slanderers, clever enough to look out for number one and keep from the clutches of the law. I'm a villain, so are you; the world—curse the world! What did ever the world do for any man? Some say a man should live for his own pride and self-approval; very well, let such philosophers grow fat on their principles. We're villains; but we'll be jolly villains, and if making those we've won in hard battle tremble and obey us, if skinning our enemies gives us pleasure, we'll enjoy that pleasure. And as for these prisoner skunks, they're all alike—all spies, and the better you treat them the worse for you. I've known many a rover betrayed by those to whom he showed the most liberal mercy; we won't swing for such a failing. Tell our purser to serve out the grog, and a hip-hurrah for the 'Black Vulture,' and death and defiance to all 'Ravens' and cormorants and sharks of the law."

The men cheered, but not very heartily.

The grog-kid passed round.

The prisoners still stood before their tormentor.

The grog began to do its work, and as the men were awed by the savage daring of their leader, so their worst passions were roused by the drinking-fiend as they became intoxicated.

"Hold!" cried the despotic pirate-chief.

There was a subservient display of attention on the part of the men.

"We're in safe moorings; cast anchor, reef sail, and then once more for fun and jollity!"

"Hurrah for the 'Black Vulture!'"

"Well said, my hearties; fill my glass. Avast, no water; death to all ravens and other crows. Luck and glory to the 'Black Vulture!'"

"Hurrah!"

"And now, lads, be alert. Fore-top there, keep a good look out."

The captain of the merchant ship at this moment sank to the deck.

"Ha, ha! not used to the irons!" cried the brutal Harwolf. "Get used to them in time, as the chaw-bacon does to the mast-head. Its your own fault, you lubber; you're chained by your own stupid fads of honesty and other cowardly humbug. Get up, you swab, or you shall lie down by many a fathom. So—ho—lads, once more serve round, brim the grog-kid, and let's be jolly!"

The anchor was cast, the sails were furled, though in a slovenly manner.

All on deck was uproar.

"Now, hearties, let's have some sport with the Lascars," shouted Harwolf, in drunken glee.

"Hie, you Malay devils, let's see you run."

"No can run, sar; feet tied in irons, sar; run like debil if you take off de chains," said one of the men.

"Ha! ha! clear the gangway, you swabs!" shouted Daniel Harwolf to his crew, laughing brutally.

Two or three of the more sober of the ruffians rushed along the decks, pushing their comrades back to clear the way.

Like drunken bacchanals, the pirates were reeling, shouting, dancing, and quarrelling, or lay extended on the deck in a disgusting state of intoxication.

Again Harwolf drew his pistol.

"Silence fore and aft!" he shouted.

There was a partial hush, but nothing like silence could be obtained, the men were too far advanced in inebriation to attend to orders.

The line was cleared.

Harwolf levelled his pistols at the two Lascars.

"Now, my hearties, toe the scratch."

"O, lor a mercy, no can walk," groaned the poor fellows, limping in their fetters.

"We must have you run, my charmers," cried Harwolf, with a chuckling laugh. "Come, make ready for the start; the course extends to the fo'-castle, and back aft. Time, one minute, thirty seconds; a glass of grog for the first in, and an ounce of lead for the second. So be spry—once, twice, thrice and away!"

It was painfully ludicrous to see the poor, attenuated Lascars waddling and tottering along, impeded by their chains.

As they stumbled about groaning and panting, the sweat pouring from their brows, the ruffianly pirates became infected by the contagion of mischief, rallied and urged the unfortunate racers by oaths, yells, kicks and blows.

"Time! time!" roared Harwolf, as with thin, sallow faces, distorted by agony, their black eyes starting from their sockets, blood smearing their lips, the poor wretches toiled and wrestled with their weakness in the miserable selfishness of their ignoble contest, each trying to outrun the other.

Just as they reached the gun on which Harwolf was lounging he uttered a bitter laugh, and blazed at them with his pistol.

Both the poor wretches fell flat on their faces.

"A warning shot, my tawny cherubs," cried Harwolf, swilling off a brimmer of brandy. "Up! up! next time I shall take aim; you know the conditions; be, spry, time's up. Oh! oh! you won't, won't you?" he roared, reeling to his feet, for he was now mad drunk. "We shall see."

He clutched his pistol and blundered towards the poor fellows, who lay moaning and sobbing, unable to rise.

The old skipper, who had feebly risen, and was leaning on the bulwark, stepped before the unfortunates, and confronted the monster with a wild look.

"Who are you glaring at, old lantern-jaws?" shouted the drunken and passion-mad outlaw, dashing his glass full in the old man's face.

The next moment Daniel Harwolf fell to the ground like a stone.

The mate Thompson had stolen behind him, and raising his fettered wrists brought his clenched fists swiftly down upon the tyrant's skull.

The mate set his foot on the prostrate villain.

The next moment a fearful tragedy was enacted.

Pierced by a dozen cutlass blades, shattered by a volley of pistol shots, the brave seaman sank to the deck without a groan.

Maddened by the sight of blood the atrocious pirates flung themselves upon the old skipper.

Wardlaw, however, threw himself before the old man, and levelled his pistols right and left.

"Stand back, you blood-thirsty skunks! By thunder, I'll blow out his brains who advances a foot. If this slaughter-fever breaks out among you you will rend each other to pieces like a pack of mad dogs. I am commander now! Carry our precious captain below, and toss him into his cabin; batten the prisoners down in the hold, let the drunken go to sleep, and the sober, if any of you be sober, attend to their duty, or we shall go to blazes together."

"Sail ho! sail ho! sail on the starboard bow!" shouted a husky voice from the foretop.

"By the foul fiend, 'tis the 'Dolorosa,' and her consort steaming down on us like a flash of lightning!" cried Wardlaw. "To your duty men! all hands to make sail! heave and a weigh!"

With yells of consternation the pirates dispersed, some dashed to the capstan, others flew wildly into the rigging.

CHAPTER CXV.

THE WAR-STEAMERS STILL IN THE VULTURE'S WAKE—HARWOLF'S REVERIES—THE WOLF CAUGHT SLEEPING—THE ATTACK BY NIGHT.

WHILE Harwolf was sleeping he did not quite lose consciousness of passing events.

The rattle of feet, the grinding of the windlass, the voices of the men blended together, with the dull lashing of the fleeting waves kept him half conscious, even in his drunken stupor.

More than once he strove to rise.

The cabin-door had been opened by the officers of the ship several times, when the pirates had come below to ascertain the condition of their leader.

With a growl of disgust more than once the door had been sharply closed.

Harwolf was aware of these interruptions to his repose.

But his brain seemed aflame with the fire of strong drink, his heart was laden with the weight of his crimes, and the consciousness of his own insecurity.

He asked himself feebly whether the crew had not weighed anchor, regardless of his authority, and he thought of mutiny and shuddered.

The hours passed away, the night was fast falling, and still the pirate lay inert; so great seemed the bustle above his head, so shrill were the orders to make all sail, so near was the ship tacking to the land, as he could discover by the drawl of the leadsman in the main chains, that Harwolf felt convinced that something unusual had happened; he knew that the "Black Vulture" was chased.

He considered whether it would be safe for him to venture to the deck; it might be that his incapacity at such a moment had so greatly enraged his lawless gang that they would murder him.

Yet, perhaps his absence was more dangerous to himself than his presence.

The dogged courage which distinguished him, only in a less degree than his father, revolted at the idea of submission to those whom, in spite of the fact that a great crime equals all concerned in it, he looked upon as his inferiors, and, as he was the sole monarch to whom they owned fealty, as his subjects.

He began to ascend the hatchway.

He scarce reached the top of the gangway when he was sprinkled with the surf that drifted fiercely across the decks, while there was a sharp cry from aloft.

A trysail had broke from her stay, and was streaming and fluttering before the wind.

Wardlaw advanced to meet the captain.

"Sir, we're chased."

"Well, we must run," said Harwolf, sententiously.

"But our pursuers have got the advantage of us, captain, in their independence of wind or tide—they have ribs of iron instead of wood. We are chased by the war steam-frigates."

"What, the Brazilians?" cried Harwolf, eagerly.

"Aye, captain."

Harwolf seized his glass and jumped on to the quarter.

The men thronged the deck with excited faces.

"My God!" exclaimed Harwolf, starting.

Wardlaw drew to his side.

"See!" cried the pirate captain, with a gasp, pointing to the tapering masts of a sloop and a brigantine that hove heavily on the sea-line.

"Humph! I should never have believed it," said Wardlaw, his face a little pale.

"Nor I; but that's the 'Red Raven.' The fowlers have caught their bird, and she mopes with broken wings."

"There's no doubt of that being the Boy Pirate's sloop."

"So much for your great buccaneer; run down at last, you see, and towed like a skunk to the gratings."

"He was no match for the war frigates."

"Dam'me, you did not think he would suffer himself to be taken?"

"Perhaps he had no choice in the matter."

"Choice! He had the choice of blowing up his ship or leaping overboard—there's choice for a resolute man between self-dealt slaughter and a swing from the yard. Do you think I would be taken?"

"S'pose not, captain."

"Not while there exists in the world such agents of destruction as fire, water, lead, and steel. So much for the Boy Pirate."

"It's not the end one would expect for him after such a bright career."

"Bright! The lubber being but a stripling was made the pet of his crew; they liked the young braggart to play Tom Thumb and defy the thunder. I wonder they didn't let him off with a spread over a carronade, and the boatswain's cat at his starn-beams, like any other swab of a drummer-boy, powder-monkey, or a schoolboy horsed on playing truant. The pirates pet! Yah! And to give up his ship with all hands to the jollies when his magazine was full of powder. The treacherous skunk, I'll wager he went whining to the Spanish skipper, swabbing his eyes with his 'Oliver,' and blubbering that it 'wasn't his fault,' that the bad 'Ravens' had led the little innocent astray. His girl-wife aboard too; and she's a pretty lass, whom I myself once thought of marrying; this comes of having a silver tongue and a brazen face. The time is not far gone when 'Boy Pirate' meant 'Big Bogey,' and every body quivered and quailed at the sound of it, as though they had heard the devil roaring. Pish! I always knew him for a coward."

Wardlaw looked at the mean aspersion of the gallant young rover with a glance of dislike.

"Blow me, captain, if you must be too hard upon the young skip-jack. He was true-blue, for all you can say. Perhaps he was killed at the beginning of the fight, or it might be he was ashore when his sloop was run down, for he was a beggar for roaming."

"More shame, then," returned Harwolf, sullenly; "he ought to be roasted alive for deserting his colours when he knew that the frigates were on the look out for his craft. But let him alone for taking care of himself. This comes of able men trusting the command to a posse of boys and girls only fit to play at skipping-rope or thumb their primers. But, tack in shore, Wardlaw, and, if it comes to the worst, we'll blow up the 'Vulture' and trust to the boats; we will never be taken in tow, like the lubberly Boy yonder."

Little did the rascal think, while thus disparaging his dashing rival, that the Red Raven himself trod the deck of the gliding steamship bearing down so swiftly and surely upon his "Vulture."

"Here comes a friend, captain," cried Wardlaw, briskly, pointing to windward.

A heavy fog was rolling up and thickly spreading on the horizon, while the sky was darkening, and the masts of the "Raven" and her prize, whom the Vultures took for captives and not conquerors, were blotted out in the deepening gloom.

"You're right, Wardlaw," cried Harwolf, joyously; "when the fog reaches us we must forge along in spite of every danger. There is good anchorage in these waters, and I can feel my way like a blind man, for I know this coast well; when I was a mid on the 'Warlock,' and studying navigation, I cruised this coast with the pilots till I learnt every reef and shoal in the roadstead. We will tack round that headland. We must out to sea, lad. Bah! we shall never be run down by such a bumboat as that!"

Wardlaw laughed, and rubbed his hands.

The pirates cheered as the sweeping fog crept round the "Dolorosa" and concealed her from view.

With admirable skill Harwolf ran the ship through the darkness round the headland, closely hugging the wind, which was failing, every sail set.

In a few hours the ship had entered a narrow straight between the islands, and, as the navigation here became extremely perilous, Harwolf gave orders for reefing sail and casting anchor, and, after enjoining his men to keep a steady watch, and to call him if the wind changed or there were any fear of a surprise. Worn out with fatigue, yet gleeful at heart at having eluded the enemy, Harwolf went below.

He threw himself on the settee in his cabin, and, folding his arms, fell into a gloomy reverie.

As gently as a mother rocks the cradle of her sleeping child the heaving waters swayed the black hull of that plague-ship.

The lamp swung on its stand, lighting the grim cabin with its feeble glare.

Harwolf was half pleased, half dissatisfied, as he took a retrospect of all that had happened of late.

The Boy Pirate was either a prisoner or had fallen, of that he was certain, and with the certainty well content, though, in his malice, he fretted that he himself had not in some way been instrumental in the defeat and death of his hated rival.

He was dissatisfied with the spirit of distrust towards him that the crew had displayed in more than one instance, and he was no way pleased with the victory of Black Ralph, who had robbed him of the better of the ships and the flower of his crews.

Hideous fancies oppressed his brain, and he was sick with a dull, instinctive boding of approaching danger.

He reviewed his past career from the day when his betrothed had been snatched from his arms by him who had triumphed over him throughout his career; he reflected, with fiendish pleasure, that he had been the chief instrument in forcing Christopher into the evil course he had at length run out; but he could not help chafing that he failed so often in accomplishing his purpose of vengeance against one whom he had always looked upon as his natural enemy.

He thought of his first murder; he sneered as he recalled the agony of remorseful terror which he had suffered after the perpetration of that diabolical crime.

He thought of his mother; he remembered a fearful dream he had once had about her; he felt a conviction that she had been murdered, though he had never heard real news of the frightful catastrophe.

He speculated on the probability of his father's detection.

He grew fevered, and his limbs trembled like reeds in a strong wind, as his eye roamed back on the dark records of the past, stained with misery and blood, and he asked himself the question whether it would not have been better if he served before the mast as a common seaman or had followed the plough as a village clown, so that he had not rendered earth a hell by acting the part of a fiend.

A vision rose before him of a humble thatched cottage, a loving wife, and simple little ones; he thought of hard but careless labour in the free broad fallows, the sunlight sleeping about him, and the skylark revelling in his sun-gilt cloud; then the dullness of such an existence called up a sneer of disgust.

The hearts of many men are rotten to the core—it is a fact as sad as certain—and the devilish pirate longs for the burning excitement of the smoking deck, or the orgies of drunkenness and pastime of cruelty.

The pirate, worn out at length by the agitation caused by his conflicting thoughts, sank into a profound slumber.

Silence reigned on deck.

The fog was thickening, and the night intensely dark.

The pirates kept a careful watch; but the gloom was impenetrable, and no sound broke the stillness of the night.

In his sleep Harwolf was roaming, once more a boy, in the woods of Frontemore; the hall of the Earls of Edgeforth appeared through the rooving trees.

He started in his sleep.

He heard a sound as of the cautious dip of an oar in the rippling water without.

He started up.

He blundered half asleep across the cabin.

Stumbling on his hands and knees; he listened to the whistle of the sweeping wind, the lapping of the dreary waves.

Lightly plashed and plashed again the sound of oars.

The pirate was about to start up.

He heard a rattle at the cabin window.

He looked up, thinking himself to be in a dream.

The cabin window had been torn open.

The form of a man was shown by the wavering lamp.

The pirate felt himself lost.

Except his sword he had no weapons.

The "Dolorosa" had stolen upon the "Vulture."

He was attacked.

He heard a shout and yell on deck.

Turning towards the window, his blood congealed with horror, as he recognised the daring intruder, who had made his entry by the window into the cabin.

The Boy Pirate!

So convinced had Harwolf felt that the young buccaneer had been taken or killed that he scarcely believed the evidence of his own senses when he saw the young rover before him.

Harwolf was fully aroused.

He leaped to his feet.

A moment the two foes looked at each other with a terrible concentration of fury.

They grappled each other.

They looked in each other's eyes.

They mutually panted with hate and vindictiveness.

HARWOLF'S DREAM OF THE PAST.

The Vulture freed his arm; he threw himself against the side of the cabin and unsheathed his glistening sword.

"Once more we meet, Daniel Harwolf! This time you are the prisoner; yet I have not come to taunt you, nor to triumph in your fall; I pursue justice, and not vengeance. Your sword is drawn," cried the Boy Pirate, "defend yourself!"

"Christopher—Foundling—you will never boast a prouder name—Christopher Foundling, since I was old enough to be swayed by passions, I have hated you, and I have sworn, by all that binds, to slay you. I thought that my appointed work had been already accomplished by others; but you are doomed to fall by this hand, and your hour has come!"

Their swords clashed.

No. 38.

A wild shout was heard on deck.

While the enemies fought wildly the ship lurched and righted and lurched again.

The trampling of feet, the tinkling of weapons, the discharge of pistols, and the thunder of guns shook the ship.

Still the Raven and the Vulture fought fiercely.

They were both skilful swordsmen.

The noise of the fray on deck redoubled in fury.

The Boy Pirate's sword was broken by a blow from the heavier weapon of his antagonist.

With a yell of triumph Harwolf sprang upon him.

The Boy Pirate threw himself upon his foe.

The men were thrown to the ground by a lurch of the ship.

They fought with the fury of panthers.

The Red Raven drew his poignard.

Harwolf managed to extricate a pistol from the belt of his opponent.

The Boy Pirate was too generous to oppose his enemy with any advantage given by his being better armed.

His magnanimity nearly cost him his life.

The dastardly Harwolf fired his pistol.

The Boy Pirate, however, had grasped his wrist.

The bullet lodged in the bulkhead of the cabin.

The roar of the battle fought on deck grew louder.

The Boy Pirate, it must be remembered, was still weak from his wound.

He yet resisted with incredible valour.

The sound of steps descending the gangway was heard.

Striking aside his youthful foe the pirate darted through the door.

During the contest the lamp had been extinguished.

Harwolf blundered through the darkness along the mid-deck.

He seized a lantern which he found at the door of one of the bunks.

Dick Caffyn, old Brierly, and others of the Boy Pirate's men, rushed into the state-cabin.

They found their young leader reclining faintly against the side.

"Hearties! the scoundrel is off to the magazine; we were fighting together but now. I am none the more formidable for my ugly fall of yesterday. He drew my pistol when we had come to close quarters; but run, or we shall all be sent up to the stars like congreve rockets."

The men shouted and dashed off after the Vulture.

Meanwhile Harwolf with the lantern was, indeed, blundering along between decks towards the hold.

He passed an open port.

He looked out as he heard a plash.

A boat was pulling by.

"Ahoy!" shouted Harwolf.

He received no answer.

There was a lantern dimly burning in the stern-sheets.

He perceived that the boat was manned by as many of his crew as could escape into it.

"Hulloa! you treacherous scoundrels! Wardlaw, ahoy!" shouted the pirate.

The boat glided beneath the bows.

"Is that you, captain?" cried the mate.

"Who the devil else? You have surrendered the ship, you rascal!"

"Better to lose the ship than our lives."

"Let me get down!"

"Quick, then, captain; the devil is after us."

Harwolf scrambled into the boat.

The men pulled sturdily off.

There was a cry of disappointed fury from on board the Raven.

The Boy Pirate's men had discovered that the cunning wolf had eluded them — that they had "broken away."

Harwolf stood up in the boat, and, shaking his fist at the ship from which he had been compelled to retreat so ignominiously, poured out a volley of curses too awful to be recorded.

CHAPTER CXVI.

THE INDIAN COUNCIL—CUSTOMS OF THE RED-SKINS—EAGLE-WING'S ORATION—THE HEART OF FIRE — REGAN OFFERS THE AID OF HIS BUSHRANGERS—A CUNNING RUSE PROPOSED BY THE WILY CHIEF—SMOKING THE RED PIPE — WAR TO THE KNIFE DECLARED AGAINST THE WHITES.

OUR scene is one more striking and picturesque than mere words can depict.

We are in the large and densely populated wigwam of the great Dacotah Sachem, Wabiskoa.

On all sides, around an open space, are thickly crowded together the cone-shaped huts of the Red-Skins.

In the centre of the square the forum of the Indian town is erected, the tall war-post decorated with tawdry ornaments, scalps, and trophies of native weapons.

In a circle around a log fire are seated a council of the old men and braves of the powerful tribe.

On the side beneath the war-post, and separated by an interval from the rest, is seated the fine old chief Wabiskoa, with two supporters, the principal war-chief on his right, and a stunted, hump-backed fellow, whose dark skin is hideously smeared with blue and white streaks—the medicine man or conjuror of the tribe.

Outside of the circle, and standing in respectful silence, the youths who had not reached the age which entitles them to take their place among the councillors, Indians of other tribes, children and squaws, were grouped in a motley multitude.

The faces and attitude of the savages were grotesque and original in the extreme.

The profoundest silence and the most impressive gravity prevailed in the synod.

Wrapped in their skins the Dacotahs sat with respectful expectation, awaiting their chief's rising and the opening of the ceremony. Some were decorated with feathers; some wore blankets worked like a herald's tabard with the wearer's recognizances; most of them had rifles lying across their laps or slung upon their shoulders, and all were decked out with tufts of the buffalo's head, necklaces of the claws of wild beasts, wampums or glass beads, and crosses which they had obtained from the Catholic missionaries. Though not a man in the circle was without a rifle yet they were all armed with bows, many with clubs, for it was the will of their chief that they should preserve, as far as possible, their native weapons and all other marks of their nationalities as thorough-bred Iroquois, and true upholders of the customs and traditions of their fathers.

Diametrically opposite to the illustrious Bison Hoof sat, with careless grace, the Adonis of bush-rangers, Oswald Lamond, or, as he was generally called, Regan, and who, among his numerous soubriquets, was known among the Dacotahs as the White Fox.

By his side was seated the Pawnee-Loup Eagle-Wing, dressed in all his bravery as a war chief; the four scalps he had won with such ruthless daring and matchless cunning were dangling from his quill-wrought girdle.

A handsome youth, whose splendid figure was undisguised by the barbaric tawdry that adorned the rest, except as regarded a short skirt of feather work, preserved the naked simplicity of nature, advanced from the sacred tent in which were kept the symbols of the national religion, if the superstious observances of the untutored savages deserved the name.

He was the Benjamin of the old Sachem's very large family, for the King of the Dacotahs, as the whites styled him, had six wives, by all of whom he had children.

In his hand the youth carried the large calumet or pipe of peace.

It was lighted, and, with an air of solemnity, he presented it to his father.

Wabiskoa, who was a fine old fellow, "every inch a king" and a "noble savage," gravely took the pipe from his youthful esquire and blew a long whiff.

As usual, the calumet of peace was finely carved and ornamented with little strings of beads.

This pipe is of a sky blue colour, and is reverenced by the Iroquois as a Manitou or good spirit of peace, while the evil spirit of war is represented by a red pipe.

Wabiskoa gravely passed the calumet to the chief on his right hand, who, with perfect deliberation, passed it to the next, and he also having "blown a cloud," handed it on round the circle; each of the "conscript fathers" with their guest and ambassador smoked in turn.

Though it was a considerable time before the pipe reached the medicine man on the left of the great Sachem, there was no display of impatience among the assembly; each Dacotah with fixed and taciturn countenance sat immobile as a statue.

Then the medicine man rose slowly.

He made a strange and hideous figure, his stunted body was hideously disproportioned—his face broad, and, as far as could be discerned through its thick mask of filthy paint, anything but handsome or prepossessing. He was clothed in a shirt or tunic of tanned fawn skins, painted and worked with peculiar devices—devils with horns, coiled serpents, beetles, and mystic signs and characters; around his neck hung a necklace, from which depended snake-skins, teeth, and feathers, and to which was attached his medicine bag; round his waist was bound a leathern girdle hung round with long, swinging, tufted buffalo tails; in his hand he held a branch with leaves, the symbol of his tribe.

The Sioux or Dacotahs are divided into several bands—six or seven—each of them distinguished by their peculiar symbol. The tribe of which Wabiskoa was head chief were the "Wapecothee," or People of the Plucked Leaf.

We have entered into these details because we know that youthful readers take a strong and wholesome interest in the strange and picturesque appearance and customs of the wild people of the yet uncivilised countries of the globe.

The medicine man turned towards the setting sun, and, stretching forth his arms, breathed a solemn prayer.

The Indian warriors bowed their crested heads with simple and profound reverence.

The imagery used by the Indian in his supplication to the Great Master of Life were very poetic.

The prayer concluded, the medicine man turned to the assembly, and announced that their great father wished to address them.

At the more important of the Indian councils no chief is supposed to address the synod as first speaker until the usher of these primitive parliaments has requested for him permission to speak.

The taciturn chiefs grunted in chorous—"Uhoa!"

This word is equivalent to our "hear" or "bravo."

With real majesty of mien, the old sachem rose, and thus harangued his people, in words that may be thus translated: it began in the usual style, with a glorification of himself and his tribe:

"My children, let your ears be open. The sun-manitou is not more pure, more warm, than the heart of Wabiskoa towards his children. The Dacotahs are a great nation; there is no end to their trail on the great hunting grounds of their fathers; their war-chiefs are very brave and subtle, and their young men bring many scalps of their enemies. The Chippowais are curs; when they hear the name of the Dacotah, they tremble and die; but the Pawnee-Loups are the adopted brothers of my people. For them there is a place by the winter fires in our lodges; for them there is a share of our maize and our game; the Dacotahs have smoked the calumet with their brothers the Pawnee; the hatchet rusts in the earth, and the tree of peace flourishes green with bright leaves. Let my children hearken: a young chief of the Pawnee, Catahaga, the son of Monotah, is come amongst them, and wishes to speak his thoughts to the wise chiefs of the Dacotah; will my children hear his words?"

"Uhoa!" again grunted the assembled braves, as with one voice.

With dignity and grace the fine young Indian rose. He glanced round the circle, a calm light in his eye, and his thin lips set with respectful but imperturbable composure.

As Regan looked at his new ally his colour mounted and his eye sparkled with anxious interest.

"It is hard for the heron to come into the eyry of the eagles," the young Indian began, in a rich thrilling tone. "The bubble of the little river is lost amid the roar of great cataracts; the Eagle-Wing looks upon the great sachem, Wabiskoa, and his brave war chiefs, as a man looks at the sun and the stars, that shine so far that he cannot reach them; but the Great Lake receives the little rill, and the Dacotah have welcomed their lowly brother into their wigwam. The earth speaks when my fathers speak—when the Dacotah strikes, the gleam of his hatchet is like the flashing of lightning—he counts not his scalps, they are too many—the squaws of his tribe are braver than the chiefs of the Chippowais. Yet Eagle-Wing does not dread the anger of his fathers, for they will hear him speak."

"It is good," murmured the braves, much tickled by these fulsome flatteries.

Regan stroked his silky moustache to conceal the grin that wreathed his features.

Catahaga went on with impassable gravity.

"Let my fathers listen; Catahaga is a son of a sachem. His blood is pure as the veins of silver. Eagle-Wing knows no fear: his tomahawk will strike like the fang of the rattlesnake. My fathers may see that his girdle is heavy with scalps of the dog-hearted pale-faces."

"Uhoa!"

"Yet the son of Monotah has no name in his tribe," he went on, in a tone of exquisite feeling; "the young branch of the White Pine is rent away from the stem, and lies bruised and withered in the path of the Yengeese, who tread on it because they know it is severed and sapless; the branch cannot live torn from the tree—the Iroquois cannot dwell apart from his nation—the son cannot bear the curses of his father—the jaguar cannot hunt with the wolf—Catahaga will not breathe in the lodges of the white devils—he will not drink from the same spring as the Yengeese, whose lips are poisoned!"

"Uhoa—it is very good!" deeply grunted the Redskins in great approval.

"My brothers will listen. The heart of the Pawnee was good towards the pale-faces. He loved not the brightness of the sun more than their presence: he left his nation: he went no more in the war-path: his hatchet was thirsty, it had no blood of enemies to drink. Catahaga had forgotten that he was the son of Monotah; though the maidens scoffed him and the young men called him the squaw of the pale-faces, his heart loved the Yengees, and he bore all like a squaw."

The Eagle-Wing paused: there was intense silence.

"My fathers," he resumed, "Catahaga had taken to his heart a maiden of the Yengeese, and he loved her as the Yengeese love, who make the fair women their manitous, and the name of Minnie Wyotti was music in the ears of all who knew her. Her breath was as sweet as the south wind that brings the rain to the scorched prairies; but I will not speak of the bright spirit.

"It was in the month of yellow leaves; Catahaga returned to his lodge weary with hunting; he stood at the fire, and talked with the wife of many dark things that pressed on his heart. A man, who was a friend of the Pawnee, entered his lodge. He told Eagle-Wing that four dogs of the Long Knives were coming to kill the Pawnee, and to steal his wife. Yet Catahaga had smoked the pipe with those rabbit-hearts; they had sat by his fire, and he put food before them; and my brothers have heard the medicine men of the Black Robes say that children of their manitous would hate no man, but would love all; but these words are lies."

"Uhoa!" shouted the Dacotahs, with unwonted vehemence.

"But the pale-faces are dogs that bite the hand that feeds them, liars that speak of mercy when their hearts are thirsting for blood. My fathers want meat; if they find a bear they will kill him. It is good; but the bear will growl; he will show his strong claws, and use them. My fathers are wise, and will keep out of reach of his huge paws. The Yengeese want land; the hungry wolves would have all. They kill the Iroquois as the hunter kills the bear. But, are my brothers reeds and branches, that may be torn down without resistance? If they give all their hunting-fields to the Yengeese whither will they go?"

There was a tumult of applause; the native stoicism of the Red-Skins broke down before this home-thrust.

"But the Manitou has turned his face from his children," continued the young chief, in a plaintive tone; "they will sell their broad rivers for a draught of fire-water, their wide lands for a painted blanket or a string of wampum-beads. The Dacotah sharpens his hatchet against the Chippewais; the Pawnee bends his bow against the Shoshoné. The axes of the Yengeese frighten the game from the woods; their fire-canoes drive the fish from the rivers. While my fathers are taking each other's lives, step by step the feet of the Long Knives tread out the dull prints of the red man's moccassin. Let my fathers rouse from their sleep; let the woods sound with their terrible war-whoop. The wolf and the dog will band together when they are both hunted by the bear. Let the Dacotah, the Pawnee, the Shoshoné forget the evil that lies between them; let them unite like the streams that run into the Blue Earth, and let their united floods sweep away the wigwams of the cursed Long Knives, and fling back the hungry dogs to the far hunting-grounds from whence they first came, like a cloud of locusts, to devour the land of our fathers! I have spoken."

There was a deep groan of conviction, and a rolling murmur of applause.

Regan began to feel uncomfortable; visions of the death-stake, and slow-fire-sensation of burning splinters torturing his seething flesh, caused him to leap to his feet with a swift bound.

In a spirited harangue the young scoundrel called upon the war-chiefs to listen to the words of his Pawnee brother.

He praised, in the most glowing terms, the brave character of the Indians; he animadverted on the treachery of the whites; he instanced the case of the late massacre at Graftonville, which the villanous pale-faces had perpetrated, he said, only because the Leightons were kind and friendly to the Iroquois; reminded them how the false charge had been credited without inquiry, and spoke of the terrible slaughter that followed.

He came of the stock of these ruthless destroyers, he could not deny that; but they had hunted and persecuted him only because he loved his red brothers.

His face was pale, but the sun had tanned it till it was nearly as dark as their own; and with the colour of his skin the colour of his thoughts had changed.

He was now, in heart, an Indian, and, if his red brothers would adopt him in their tribe and accept his services, he would aid them in their resistance against their cruel oppressors with a hundred chosen braves well armed with rifles; he would give them guns, ammunition, and all things needful to carry on the struggle; and when all was done, when the earth had been swept clear of the scorpions, he would retire with his braves beyond the Rocky Mountains, or with his small numbers would settle among them, and would dwell with them in peace and brotherhood.

He urged Wabiskoa to give the Eagle-Wing a hundred of his bravest warriors, and wound up by assuring them that they were objects of the most dismal terror to the whites, who would flee like clouds before a hurricane, if the tribes would only unite in the common cause of freedom.

The excitement that prevailed as the daring young reprobate calmly reseated himself passes all conception.

Oil was poured on the flames, when a fine, wild-looking young brave, who was called by the expressive name Heart of Fire, burst into a stirring appeal, inveighing with great eloquence against the conduct of the whites in all their transactions, and imploring the chiefs to accede to the request of the Pawnee, and to detach as many braves as they could spare to exterminate the pale-faces throughout Arkansas.

Wabiskoa gravely rose; with much impressiveness the old chief assured the assembly that he concurred in the truth of all that had been said, but, as he added, pithily, "the dogs were many," and he thought that even with the assistance of White Fox and his pack, it would not be easy to hunt down the whole of the accursed foes at once; besides, it would take time to make up old quarrels with the various nations of the Iroquois, with whom they were at enmity, and who in many places were friendly to the whites. He suggested that they should trust to their native subtlety, and turn to good account the discovery that had been made that the bushrangers had assumed the disguise of Indians, and should use against the whites their own weapons, by assuming a spirit of conciliation and then attacking lonely plants, pretend that the outrages were committed by bushrangers in disguise, and even be the first to carry information against themselves.

This inimitable piece of Indian Machiavelism suited the young bushranger to his heart's content; he greatly applauded the wisdom and wariness of the wise old sachem, and declared that no plan conceivable could be better adapted for carrying out their purposes.

When he had reseated himself, Wabiskoa appealed to the decision of the assembled chiefs, whether they were willing to declare war against the pale-faces.

The reply was unanimous—

"It is good!"

Then strange ceremonies began.

The youth of whom we have mentioned retired into the sacred tent.

The medicine man followed him.

The braves in council still kept their seats.

They preserved the most solemn silence.

The crowd without the circle fell back.

A number of youths, with drums and castanets, entered the wide circle; they were armed, and adorned as for the war-path; to their feet were attached little bells, and several of them had tambourines in their hands.

The medicine man re-entered the circle. He carried in his hand a head-dress of the feathers of a rare bird, called by the Indians wamend-hi, and by the Canadians the quillion,—plumes which only warriors of the highest renown are permitted to wear; over the sorcerer's arm was a handsome buffalo-robe.

The medicine man approached the bushranger, who gravely rose.

He could not have preserved a more serious and respectful demeanour if he were about to be invested with the order of the garter.

The medicine man addressed him a set speech, telling him that he had been adopted by the tribe, and exhorting him in all things to conduct himself as became an adopted son of the great nation of the Dacotahs.

After he had concluded this address, he drew from his quiver an arrow with a party-coloured shaft.

The young bushranger did not flinch, though the Indian pressed the point of the barb against his forehead till the blood started.

The sorcerer turned towards the sun and muttered some mystic charm.

He then placed the head-dress on the bent head of the young outlaw, and threw the buffalo-robe about him.

As Oswald drew himself up to his full height, his nodding plumes and the free and graceful folds of his loose robe gave him an appearance not a little imposing.

The medicine man took his hand and led him to the old chief, who motioned him to seat himself on the right hand.

Oswald obeyed in silence.

This ceremony of adoption performed the rites of declaring war commenced.

The youth presented to his aged father a red pipe, which the old man took, and after smoking it for a moment in silence, passed it to his neighbour, and so it went round the circle.

Then began the dance.

First, the youths divided into two parties; they

then struck their drums and tabors, and with strange contortions performed a mystic dance.

The medicine man, who acted as master of the ceremonies, stood in the centre of the circle, keeping time to the wriggling motions of the terpsichoreans, by beating together two pieces of bark.

Gradually the dance became more animated.

Flinging aside their instruments of music, or rather noise, the young braves drew their tomahawks.

A mimic battle was fought.

So furiously did the two lines seem to charge each other, and with such seeming heartiness were blows struck and parried, that Regan began to think his hundred warriors would soon have shared the fate of those feline celebrities, the Kilkenny cats, who devoured each other, leaving nothing as a trophy of their contest but the tips of their tails.

However, at the moment when the war-dancers had worked themselves up to all the frenzy of the whirlwind gallopade, the old sachem held up his hand; the dancers suddenly paused, and then quickly formed in Indian file—that is, a single line. They deported, or rather contorted themselves in an edifying manner by writhing like snakes, mouthing like monkeys, and howling like cats, and then with a bound, like the recoil of an india-rubber ball, they leaped up and down, then, after wielding their bright tomahawks, and slashing in mincemeat an unlimited number of invisible enemies, as if seized by a sudden impulse, they broke through the surrounding circle, upsetting their adopted brother, and with a truly blood-freezing yell, or war-whoop, wheeled about the war-post, discharging at it their flashing hatchets with unerring aim, every one of them leaving his weapon quivering in the wood.

With a shout, the chiefs of council sprang to their feet and followed their leaders, trotting one after the other round the war-post.

Regan, upon whose forehead appeared an ugly bump, had seen quite enough of the improving spectacle, and at the risk of offending his new friends, walked straight off to the nearest hut, with his hands to his ears, and his teeth clenched in the manner peculiar to the poor wretch who chances to enter a workshop where files are being sharpened.

He rushed into the lodge.

He drew hastily back.

Her long, golden ringlets streaming down her shoulders, her hands clasped, her eyes up-raised, Minna Wyotti was fervently praying.

The Indian's wife rose as the bushranger entered, and with heightened colour and glowing eyes, darted such a look of bitter reproach on the intruder, that, in spite of his usually unquailing impudence, he dropped his glance and recoiled while Minna turned with disdainly anger, and passed through the deerskin curtain that divided the lodge into separate compartments.

CHAPTER CXVII.

THE BUSHRANGERS IN AMBUSH—THE SENTINEL—THE SHOSHONE—THE TRAVELLERS SAVED BY AN INDIAN—A SHOT IN THE WOODS—A HORRIBLE DISCOVERY.

"THERE'S Hiram Bly and Ronald Holmes with the Larchville fellow, and there's you and me and Joab; a pretty considerable quantity, Johine, for sich a job."

"I tell yer, Jerusher, as I'm just slick, swar I saw him."

"Who's him? What were the Snake about then, not to give us warning if any of the Dacotah cusses were on our trail? 'Tarnt no ways likely."

"I'll swear it. I knowed him by his slight figger."

"We're all astray, Asa, one yere and one there, like the stars which we can't see now, wuss luck;

you caught sight of the Injen, our pioneer, I guess. Wall, all as is, we must keep a pretty considerable 'cute look out, I calkilate; p'raps you could tell what tribe the Injen cuss belonged to, seein' as you have sich cat's eyes for the dark, Asa—how did he paint?"

"I knows a coon from a cockatoo; I tell yer, Jerusher, as it war that infarnal devil, Catahaga the Eagle; tell yer I'll swar it."

"This yere ain't jist a relief to my anxious feelin's, oh no; why, now, I'm sure that it wasn't nothin' but a ghost of your own raisin'; fust, because you swar about it, and then agen, because the Pawnee is gone t'other side of the 'Kansas to the wigwam of the Sioux; I hearn jest so down at our rendezvous, from Makalosh hisself; you're sewed up now, ain't yer?"

"Wall, p'raps so; it's 'farnal dark, and the movin' tree is awful deceivin', but if that war'nt a——"

"Shut up! don't ye hear the owls is hootin'? that's Ronald Holmes."

"Some one answer him."

"Yes, that's the 'farnal Britisher; he hoots more like a nox than a howl."

"He'll spile all!"

"'Taint onlikely."

"Sam Weatherfield's too old a cock-o'-the-woods to be caught with sich stupid chaff."

"Wall, I reckon he does know a screeching owl from a braying jackass."

"Jest so! Hark ye, Aza, you stay here; I'll jine the coons. Jist positionate so as the Hebrew can pass without touching yer; they must pass this way; they goes by the blazen's on the trees; they carries a torch or a lantern—it's time they were comin' I reckon."

The speakers were a couple of ruffians dressed as trappers. The time was about midnight, the scene, a wild spot in the thickest parts of the forests.

"Ugh!"

Both the men started, and poised their rifles.

"You narvous cuss, it's only the Shoshone," cried Jerusha.

The tall, lithe form of a red Indian rose among the bushes.

"No shoot, mustang; one, two," said the Snake.

"Which way, Makatoosh?" asked the bushranger, excitedly.

"On the moss side of the trees, mustang; go quick."

"Wall, I s'pose we're ready for 'em."

"I say, Jerusha?"

"Wall, what is it, you coon?"

"I'd agi'n half the shiners for a mossel of moonshine."

"'Spects I shouldn't object myself to a light on the subject."

"Wagh!"

"What's the matter with the Injen?"

"Don't yer parceptionate? that blasted Englisher's at it again."

"Jest like a turkey gobblin'."

"So it is; I'll be off and jine 'em, and calkilate I won't put my fist in his mouth, and spile his whislin'; there agen, he orter improve arter so much practice; me and the Injen will jest go and gag him, and I'll come back."

"I say, Jerusha?"

"Wall, what now, once more?"

"Don't be long."

"Yah! go home to bed, you precious rabbit."

"Come, Makatoosh."

The bushranger and the red skin glided softly through the bushes.

They reached a place where the trees grew less thickly.

Three men appeared dimly in the obscurity, peeping over a ferny bank.

The bushranger gave a low whistle, in imitation of the cry of some night bird.

It was immediately answered by a similar note, sounding stealthily in the night.

"Heard on 'em?" asked the bushranger, in a whisper.

"Wall, can't exactly say we has; but we shan't have to wait long, I reckon, they're over here already."

"The Injen says he has heard 'em."

"I do zay as them hottentot devils is nation 'cute. I shouldn't care to have a squad on 'em arter me. Zometimes I think az they must veel all az they hear, vor I've hearn um tell when the hosses was tired. Zort of instinct, I do zay, like my old lurcher at Greeat-Greenville, in course, I should zay," said Miles, checking himself.

"Ah, you warn't raised in these parts, stranger," said Hiram Bly quickly.

"Doam it man, why be ye zo cu'rous? I told you where I was raised."

"In England—I know. Green—summut."

"Green! Grenock, in coorse; but I do zay az this be no time for axin' of such darnation silly questions."

"Hist!"

"That's a hoss's hoof, zurelie!"

"Hush, you fool; you'll spile our game all over. Can't you be quieter?"

"Aye, zo, neighbour; but you best be civil. I had have you know he's a vule himself az dares to call a vule. I never were the man to take a insult from your biggers and betters, and be zartin sure—"

"Hist, you idiot!"

The pattering of hoofs sounded louder.

"Hiram, we'll let them pass on."

"Yes, further into the wood; this place is too open."

"Makatoosh can go back to Asa; or stop at half the distance," said Ronald Holmes.

Hiram Bly gave the redskin some directions in his own tongue.

Makatoosh glided swiftly away.

The crackling of branches was now plainly heard, and the thudding of horses' hoofs.

The bushrangers crouched low.

Mounted on stout, rugged little horses, two men rode by.

"Yesh, thatsh all pery welsh, Mr. Weatherfield, but, shwelp me, if ever Ish come into thish dam countrish any more!" said one of the riders to the other.

"Wal! I guess you won't be much missed; but how was it you didn't buy the land and crop?" returned the other. "As for the soil it was dirt cheap."

"Sheap! what do you call sheap. Sheap at a thoshand dollars!"

"Considering, you must allow; Mr. Abrahams, a clever man like you, I guess, could realize tremendous profits."

"Go along with your profitsh! Vot shall I profitsh with my money—ha! if they shall cut my throat?"

"Wall, 'taint too late for that, I reckon; and this is the most likely place for an ambush as I know."

"Sthrike me! you are a cruel brute to frighten mesh."

"La, stranger, arter your fight with the Zummerset Indian you ought to be a match for anything."

"I will not lose my monish any more. I will lose my life, but I will keep my monish."

The travellers had passed on.

The bushrangers stole softly from their hiding-place.

The trapper and the Jew had lanterns swung by the side of their horses.

Guided by the light, the murderous rascals followed close.

"Murdersh!—thieves!! there ish von devilish red Injen. I shall losh my monish and my lifesh!"

The cries of the terrified Jew rang through the silent woods.

The bushrangers laughed as eagerly they pushed on.

"Curse it all, Hiram," cried Ronald, who, in the dark, had struck his head against a tree, "let us have a light. The beggars can't escape us all, and we can't go on in this way."

Jerusha struck a light, and set fire to a torch; they held this aloft, and rushed on through the wood.

They heard the horses' hoofs clattering with increasing speed.

They hallooed to the man they had left on guard.

They received no answer.

Again the woods re-echoed their shouts.

Cursing with fury, they still forged their way through the tangling briars.

Just as they neared their prey, a figure was seen by the light of the torch, to leap over the bush.

A bright flash, and a loud report.

The bullet scudded past the cheek of Miles Thornton, and flew plump half a foot into the trunk of a tree.

When the smoke cleared off the man who had fired had vanished.

The bushrangers were smitten with a sudden panic.

The darkness was intense.

They hurried back.

They knew not on what side their foes might be.

No single man they thought would have had the courage to outbrave them.

The noise of the horses' feet had grown fainter and fainter, and was fast dying off in the distance.

What should they do?

They looked blankly into each other's faces.

The Indian, Makatoosh, ran up to the spot.

He pointed backwards.

"Dacotah!"

"It is Eagle-Wing!" cried Hiram.

"Durn'ee, let's follow un. That's the vine rascal that so well-nigh took my life, a while foregone. I owe him a chalk. Let's follow un!" cried the stout-hearted Miles, with true English wilfulness.

"Stay, you infarnal fool! The brave isn't alone. We'd better skedaddle, I s'pose," cried Hiram.

"Durn'ee! if ye talk of giving me the go-by till I've winged this feller, I'll stop your 'skedaddling' by breaking your legs," roared Miles.

"Where's Asa?"

"Fled; he'll be lost in the woods, and run a terrible risk."

"Come on, then!" cried Holmes, recklessly.

The men rushed through the woods.

They looked fearfully about them.

They fancied an ambush in every thicket; they saw a red Indian in every shadow.

At length they reached the spot where they had left Asa.

They entered the little dingle.

They looked at each other with pale features.

Hiram whistled.

Jerusha stamped his foot impatiently.

The Indian laid his ear against the bank, and listened.

"Be ye zure, neighbour, as t'ware here you left him?"

"Sure, Miles."

"Well, let us look for his track."

"Wagh!"

"The Ingen mutters something," cried Hiram, quickly.

Makatoosh rose, and beckoned the rest of the party to follow him.

"Let us go, my brothers," said the Indian.

"Let the Shoshone lead the way, his Yengeese brothers shall follow him!"

The Indian promptly obeyed.

He led the bushrangers deep into the heart of the forest.

Every now and then he would pause.

The woods now howled with the hideous yells of wild beasts.

A troop of wolves seemed to be pattering through the forest.

Still the Indian pressed on.

Closely the others followed him.

He stood and examined the ground like a dog at fault.

He crept stealthily on his hands and knees.

"I'll tell you what, Jerusha," said Hiram Bly, "I shouldn't wonder but the coon is following the trail of our travellers on his own account."

"Has not got the pluck. I guess we'll find him presently."

They passed between two majestic pines, and entered upon a little dell, covered with furze and brambles.

They lowered the torch, stood low under some hanging branches, and entered this thicket.

The place was swampish.

They were suddenly arrested by a strange sound.

It was the sobbing yelp of a greedy and half-famished wolf, to judge by the peculiarity of the noise he emitted.

Presently a great grey wolf, his fangs running with blood, rushed past them.

Jerusha cried out.

Miles flung himself upon the brute, but his hands were bitten by the savage animal, and, though he clove to him with the most audacious boldness, the brute contrived to break away.

The bushrangers continued their progres , every moment becoming more and more anxious.

They walked, as usual, in single file, the `hoshoné taking the lead ; Miles and Jerusha brought up the rear.

Suddenly the two men in the rear were startled by a cry of horror.

They rushed forward to learn what it might portend.

CHAPTER CXVIII.

THE EAGLE-WING ALONE ON HIS WAR-PATH—BESET ON ALL SIDES, YET BUT ONE IN AMBUSH—THE SNAKE AND THE PAWNEE—A FATAL ERROR—TERRIBLE REPRISAL—BUT ONE ESCAPED.

UPON rushing forward at the terrible alarm that echoed so hideously through the silent woods the two bushrangers were struck with horror and dismay.

Upon the ground, and in a pool of blood, lay the body of him they were seeking.

Jerusha threw himself by the corpse of his comrade, who was also a kinsman, and breathed the direst curses against the Indian who had slain him.

"This is the work of Eagle-Wing. Mad fool that I was not to listen to the poor fellow's caution ; but, I guess, I'll make the whole nation of red devils pay for it."

"What a fool is our captain, with the power he holds, not to put a stop to this kind of deviltry," rejoined Ronald Holmes, fiercely.

"If he does not undertake the job himself soon, I shall declare war on my own account, and with as many good fellows as I can muster to my aid, I will go on an expedition to kill every one of the cusses, without concerning myself about any nice scruples as to age or female sexes. I'll chalk every one I come within range of.

"I doan't blame thee, lad ; for I'll be hanged if ever I heard of such wretches," cried Miles.

And yet these very fellows were lurking in the woods, intent upon committing murder and robbery. Such is the consistency of human nature.

"What shall we do now ?"

"Beat the bush and run down the blasted savage, that's what we'll do, I reckon," cried Jerusha.

"No, no, mate ; we should only run ourselves into the same danger, and share the same fate as he did, poor chap," returned Ronald Holmes.

"Thou'rt about right, maester, roamin' about these woods in the night with some cussed devilskin in every thicket to pull a trigger or fling an axe at you. It minds me o' the old poachin' times in England ; it's like it used to be down along the spinnies and coppices in the old preserves, only, darn it all, a tidy sight worse."

"Wagh !" cried Makatoosh, leaping from the ground where he was kneeling.

"What now, old pointer, hast'ee started a fox ?" cried Miles.

"Dacotah !" muttered the Snake, bending down with a suppleness worthy of the reptile after which the tribe was named.

"Where ?" cried Jerusha, turning savagely.

The rest of the men drew together.

The Indian, who lay flat on his face, moved his finger only, and pointed to a bush before them.

Jerusha rushed forward and fired at random.

The bullet crashed through the branches ; there was a rustle among the leaves as they splintered and feel down.

Jerusha pointed his musket and stood listening.

With extreme rashness he snatched the gun from the hands of Hiram Bly, and flew into the bushes.

"Stay, you mad fool !" cried Hiram and Ronald in a breath.

But Jerusha neither answered nor heeded, he rushed straight on, reckless of every consequence.

The men stood paralysed with dismay.

The wary Shoshoné was crawling on his belly along the top of a bank, in the direction Jerusha had taken.

"Zounds! be this sticking together like true neighbours ? Durn'ee, pluck up a heart, weell'ee, and see if we can't have a shot at the doamed gamekeeper !" roared Miles.

Stimulated by the hearty courage of the Englishman, the bushrangers followed on his heels.

Yet they huddled close together as if to find protection by mutual contact.

True to his name and nature the wily Snake wriggled along swift and sure towards the brake.

A distant shot was heard through the forest.

"One on 'em has got his billet, anyways," said Hiram Bly.

"Jerusha, for every heap of dollars !" cried Ronald Holmes, flinching and trembling.

"Gad zooks ! it be time we put a stop to this purty game, I do say. Come on, then, weell'ee ?" shouted Miles, wildly ; "let's keep together, like men, and face the devil zimultan'ous ?"

"Stay, Miles, we shall be chalked, I know we shall. The Lor a mercy ! we're dead men, I reckon," cried Ronald, violently quaking.

"Where's the Shoshoné ?" asked Hiram.

"Durn'ee, let 'em bide. The haythen's the best man among ye, arter ; all and a mortal shame, I say, that you should let him zee what cowards ye are. Come on !"

The Englishman, without   king behind him, plunged into the bush.

Seeing him so resolute, his comrades thought that they should be safer in his company, and therefore followed him.

"Do you think we shall find him dead, Hiram ?" gasped Ronald, in the most abject trepidation.

"'Taint no question, I guess, mate ; this yere's a purty night's job—oh, no. And all along of one blasted devilskin."

"There's more than one, I do opine ?" returned Ronald. "I'm sartain there's more than one."

Miles rushed back."

His broad face was deadly pale, his thick lips quivered.

"Thou wert right, lad, he be dead as a salted herrin', and the blood-sucking thief has torn his brains out."

The men stumbled forward.

Their limbs shook under them.

Prone on his face, Jerusha was lying, the blood pooling round him.

His scalp had been torn from his head, and he looked an object terrible and ghastly indeed.

The men emitted their agony with a yell, and were rushing away, when the sturdy Miles caught their arms.

'· Not zo vast, lads, not zo vast. If zo be az ye have no care for your lives, I'm not going to throw away mine. Neither of these poor devils would have come to this zorry pass if they had only stuck together."

The men stood bewildered with terror.

"Thee hast no heart, Ronald; and thine, Hiram's, but a gizzard. I zee I mun do all the vighting vor'ee; but, doam it, lads, do'ee keep by me just for the vine zhow ye'll make; come on! I'll be bound we shall sight the wolf in a minute, for, durn me, if I *can* be afeard of devils that dress themselves up like mummers and wild men, be they black or red. Doan't 'ee be skeared, or its a done case. Put on a bold countenance, and doam your feelins; it's the only way to get through this wood, or this world, I do azzure ye."

Onward they crushed through the wild wood.

A loud and fearful yell—the voices of two men hooting in different notes an equally dismal warwhoop.

The two bushrangers turned on their heels and fled back.

Miles, the redoutable, stood his ground, roaring his anathemas.

Finding themselves again left to themselves, the currish rangers rejoined the Englishman.

Once more they forged forward.

Soon they came in sight of their quest.

Two Indians were furiously battling with their tomahawks.

Miles shouted triumphantly, and steadily aimed his rifle.

He was an old poacher, and a dead shot.

He only waited the slightest chance of getting a clear aim at the right man.

The night had been consumed in their protracted and eventful wanderings, and the morning light was waxing brighter every moment.

The Indians seemed well-matched, and fought with the utmost desperation and equal advantage.

The clash of their tomahawks, mingling with their soul-appalling war-cries, rendered the duel one of the most thrilling of encounters.

Plucking up a braggart's valour, now that he found himself comparatively safe, Ronald Holmes levelled his gun and fired.

One of the Indians leaped into the air and fell on his knees, then flat on his face.

The other stepped nimbly over him, and, swift as thought, tore off his scalp, leaped over the thicket, and disappeared.

The rangers rushed up to the spot.

They raised the Indian.

He was quite lifeless.

They sprang back with a bitter execration.

Ronald had shot the Snake; Eagle-Wing had escaped.

Miles foamed with rage.

He flew upon Ronald Holmes and would have strangled him, but for the intervention of the other bushranger.

When the passion of the sturdy Englishman had in some measure cooled down, which it did the more readily from the necessity of preserving coolness in their deadly peril, he looked around with apprehension, and then lowered his voice, and said, impatiently,

"If ye were men and not baa-lambs, I do zay there'd be nought to be skeared at; but as ye be but a couple of babbies in the wood the loard knows how I shall get ye out of this precious fix; but these Ingens are so mortial skittish, they've a zort of game that once zighted will run into any barrow or hole to keep out of the way, and, perhaps, this Spring-heeled Jack will keep in his box till future notice. Well, I'm blamed if this bean't the roughest brush, with the smallest 'varsal cause, as ever I heard on, all along of beggarly tramps and trappers with not more than twenty pounds between 'em; but the devil helps the Jews."

"Miles, I reckon you're a genuine game 'un," whispered Roland, faintly.

"No, I bean't, I'm nought but a blamed Britisher with a bit o' the nat'ral bull-dog, a sort of phillyhoss-feller, that knows better to run when its safest to stand still, and you zay you're a Yankee wot whips creation; the loard help'ee, poor soul."

The men stepped swiftly and cautiously through the wood.

"Go a piece faster, my good feller; when we're once on the prairie we shall be safe from the copper devil."

"Aye, zo; I wonder what Joab thinks on it all; we left him with the horses, I hope he ain't left them at hearing the gun shots."

"Oh lord, Miles, if——" Roland began, but he was stopped by the crackle of a shot in the forest.

In the twinkling of an eye Miles and Hiram blazed wildly at the spot where the thin blue smoke arose.

They then turned towards Ronald Holmes.

The bushranger had dropped dead with a bullet in his brain.

This was too much even for the stolid Englishman.

He uttered a fearful cry, and dashed madly through the wood.

His comrade followed.

They both ran at full speed.

Miles was somewhat in advance.

He did not pause to look behind.

Again a shot was fired by this Daniel of the forest.

The quick pattering of feet behind suddenly stopped.

He heard the crushing of bushes.

He looked back.

The screen of boughs concealed the view for within a few yards of the place where he stood.

He staggered against a tree.

His tongue clove to the roof of his mouth.

He became thirsty with horror.

He waited awhile.

His comrade did not come.

Again he flew onward with wildest speed.

At length the trees began to grow sparser.

The light that flooded the wide prairies broke in.

He reached the skirts of the forest.

He stood for a moment lost in perplexity.

Scarcely could he sufficiently collect his thoughts to enable him to remember at what place the horses had been left.

However, a dark object lying among the grass at some distance attracted his trembling steps.

His heart sank like lead.

He rushed on.

Scarcely did his astonishment equal his dismay.

Joab lay dead and scalped by the side of the tree to which the mustangs had been tethered.

The horses were gone!

He sank on the ground overwhelmed and stupefied.

What hope had he?

At least not here.

On the broad prairie, at least, he might face his foe.

The breaking of a branch, the soft fall of a cat-like step behind him, caused him to bound through a dense thicket as if he had been propelled from a cannon's mouth.

He recked not of the piercing briars, though they rent his cheeks and well-nigh tore his eyes from their sockets.

Madly he flew onwards.

He reached the prairie.

The gallopping of hoofs caused him to turn his head.

A wild mustang had got loose from a tree, and was tearing along, his broken bridle streaming behind.

With a desperate effort, Miles threw himself at the horse's head.

He stopped the frightened animal, and scrambled into the saddle.

Just in time; a last shot was fired from the wood.

The bullet struck into his arm, almost knocking him off the mustang, but he grasped at the mane, and frantically urged the horse forward.

And away and away over the skimming prairie he flew, as if death on his pale steed were pursuing him.

A DEADLY STRUGGLE.

CHAPTER CXIX.

CATAHAGA'S RETURN — THE TEMPTERS — THE
STRANGE CONDUCT OF THE YOUNG INDIAN
—A RECONCILIATION.

THE Dacotahs were assembled in great numbers in
the grand square of the wigwam.

The greatest excitement prevailed. Nothing had
been thought of for days but preparations for the
coming struggle with the whites.

The young men were exercising themselves at
rifle shooting, flinging the tomahawk, and hurling
the javelin.

It was morning, and the slanting sunbeams fired
every blade of grass with glittering diamond sparks
of dew.

No. 39.

The squalid and tawdry ornaments on the war post
swayed heavily in the wind.

The cone-shaped lodges threw long and darkly-
defined shadows on the sun-lit sward.

The old chief Wabiskoa stood leaning on his club.

He looked upon the shining scene with affected
imperturbability.

But with an animated gleam in his wild black
eyes, undimmed by age, that had bleached his long
hair white as the snow flake.

There was a loud shout.

The braves, the old chiefs, the young men, the
bright-eyed rich-tinted pretty maidens, the hideous
and malignant-looking old squaws; the boisterous,
impish children; even the ragged, vagabondish curs;
every living creature gathered around the stately
young Indian, who walked on to the green plat

with downcast eyes, abstracted air, and tight-drawn lips, but with a graceful springing step, full of ease and dignity. But what caused such a general cry of astonishment and admiration was the number of reeking scalps of the pale faces that hung from his belt.

Wabiskoa walked forward to greet the young chief.

"My son is welcome," said the old chief, with grave courtesy. "Whence does he come?"

"From the war-path," said Catahaga, carelessly, and with unchanging countenance.

"The Eagle-Wing is a great chief, and has brought many trophies of his prowess," said the sachem.

"They are but the tufts of the prairie wolves," returned Catahaga, with a sardonic smile.

"The name of Eagle-Wing will outshine the names of all his fathers," said the old man, with a burst of admiration that even his stoicism could not check.

Catahaga replied only by a faint smile, playing like the summer lightning in the cloud.

"My father, the heart of Catahaga is darkened; he will never see the sun till he has beheld the last of the Long Knives swept from Arkansas."

"The young chief has high thoughts and a proud heart. He shall see his wish. Who is so subtle as the White Fox? The wiser brave has said that before two suns are past he will bring his young men to join with the people of my tribe in the war party."

"And let my father hear my words. The Master of Life is just. The pale-faces oppress the Iroquois, and they will not suffer them to abide by their own customs; but we will not act so with the Yengeese, we will observe their customs, and we will give them warning—we will give them time; but if they will not leave Arkansas, we will crush them before they grow in numbers, and then beyond our strength."

"My son speaks wise words, they shall be told to the Sachems of Council," returned the old chief, cautiously.

Catahaga proudly bent his head and moved away towards the lodge that had been assigned him in the wigwam.

As he advanced Regan sprang out from the door of a lodge and led him aside.

The bushranger quelled a slight glance of disgust that passed across his handsome features as he looked upon the filthy tokens of the ruthless Indian's bloody victory.

He called up a look of intense admiration.

"My brother will be greater than the Manitou chiefs of the Dacotahs who came into the land of the Cypowais and won it all by their bravery."

Eagle-Wing started; a gleam shot from his eloquent eyes, and his intelligent face darkened with anxiety.

"It is true," he said, with a sigh, "my fathers conquered the Cypowais, but yet not as the accursed Yengeese would conquer all the red nations. We came with hatchets in our hands, and not with books that speak good things while the bearers are false as the changing winds. We were not double-tongued; we did not sweeten our lips to embitter our hands. Enough; Catahaga is weary, he will not speak of these things."

"Yet the squaws of the pale faces and the braves of his own tribe have mocked at the name of Catahaga; will he not let them see his deeds? will he not show himself the son of a great chief? There is a detested wolf that caused the blood of the Iroquois to flow like the torrents when the snow melts; will not my brother join with me against this enemy?"

The eyes of the young Indian flashed.

He drew a deep sigh.

"Minna is of the pale-faces," he murmured, "and Minna is the life of my heart."

"A great chief should not be swayed by his heart," cried the young villain, earnestly. "When my brother's tongue craves for water does he complain? When his body wastes for food does he weep? No, no! he remembers that he is a great chief, and that he is brave and can bear pain. My brother's heart,

is it not as his body and his tongue? does it not thirst and hunger and waste away? My brother must not listen too much to his heart; he must not love the bright star of the Yengeese too hotly. Does my brother remember the fable? the jaguar that lived with the fawns was killed by the roebuck."

"Catahaga would darken his heart from the light of the eyes of Minna, not to carpet the wide prairies with the scalps of his enemies to stretch his hand round the sun's pathway, and say all this is mine."

With unaffected pathos and romantic grace the young Indian unconsciously grounded his musket and raised his eyes fervently to the cloudless sky glowing so calmly above this stormy world of sin and sorrow.

Regan bit his lip.

He thought it best to say no more at present.

Catahaga entered his lodge.

Minna sprang forward to meet her husband.

He opened his arms to embrace her.

She was about to rush into their clasp when the grisly scalps touched her, and her light, half-Indianised dress, was flecked with blood.

She recoiled with a shriek.

The face of the young Indian darkened.

He walked to the side of the lodge, and, flinging his gun into the corner, folded his arms in a moody reverie, his face expressing his discontent.

White and trembling, his fair young wife stood before him.

She tried to speak.

He gave her no encouragement, but sat with his eyes fixed on the ground, as if unconscious of her presence.

Again she tried to address him soothingly.

But her eyes fell again on the matted, hideous scalps, swinging in his belt, and utterance failed her.

Catahaga looked up at her coldly.

With a spiteful gleam in his eye he loosened the belt from his waist, and held it out to her.

She drew back with a shudder.

"Let my sister hang the scalps Eagle-Wing has won from his enemies in the smoke of his lodge-fire; it shall not be said that no trophies hang in the lodge of the son of Monotah."

These words were uttered in freezing accents.

With a look of intense anguish Minna took the thong meekly from her husband, and threw it over a nail by the fire.

He sat still, his sombre face darkly clouded.

Minna drew softly to his side, and removed his weapons.

She treated him as she had seen the proud and haughty chiefs treated by their squaws, who looked upon them as their earthly gods, and had been taught to regard themselves as so infinitely the inferior of these lords paramount.

There was such a depth of melancholy in the expression of Eagle-Wing's face.

Minna could not ascribe it to that impulsiveness and waywardness of temper that still displayed itself at times in the untutored nature of her Indian husband.

She asked him some simple question.

He answered briefly and coldly.

He rose, and took down a couple of handsome rifles.

He soon became absorbed in polishing them.

Minna stole close to his side, and laid her hand carelessly on his shoulder.

"Will there be ever a cloud on my husband's heart?" she murmured, humbly. "Why has he turned away his face from his own wife? Why is he angry with me?"

"Eagle-Wing is not angry," returned the Indian, coldly. "His heart is on the war-path; he has no thoughts for a squaw, who would make that heart, which should be harder than the rock, softer than the wax in the bees'-nest."

"And must I be your squaw—your slave, Catahaga?" returned Minna, with tender reproach in her tone. "I that was once the wife of your pride."

"Why should you murmur? Shall I be neither Iroquois nor Yengeese?—what shall I be?" cried Catahaga, bitterly. "Shall I stay with your nation to be murdered in my sleep?—shall I return to my own people to be a mark for their scorn?"

"My husband's will is my law. I will be the squaw of the great chief Catahaga," returned Minna, tearfully. "I am his for worse or for better, and I will not weary him with complainings."

At this moment a girl entered. She was one of the daughters of a neighbouring chief, and was sent to attend upon the White Fawn, whom all the Indians regard with much reverence, though even the women despised Catahaga for the tenderness with which he treated a mere squaw, however beautiful she might be.

Very gently, but peremptorily, Minna dismissed the wondering girl.

She took up the earthen pitcher which the girl was about to carry to the river to fetch water.

Catahaga did not move or appear to notice her as she departed.

With saintly fortitude the noble-hearted girl who had sacrificed all to her wild passion, knelt by the river side. She raised her streaming eyes to heaven, and breathed a fervent prayer.

A light step sounding behind her sent a thrill through her heart.

She turned quickly.

Catahaga had resumed his arms and belt, and the hideous scalps still hung at his side.

The Indian stepped lightly forward, and snatching the pitcher from his wife's hands, dashed it to pieces.

She drew back quailing with terror; but the impulsive Indian snatched her to his heart, and bestowed upon her the tenderest caresses.

He then tore off his girdle with its burden of scalps.

He held it aloft, and flung it far away into the river.

With a sob of joy Minna sprung towards him; but, waving her back, he, turned sharply, and plunged into the forest.

CHAPTER CXX.

ON THE ISLAND—HARWOLF'S UNPOPULARITY—A ROAM ROUND THE ISLAND—THE SHIP-BOY.

IT was night when Daniel Harwolf made his escape to the island.

Upon reaching the shore with his boat's crew the little bark was run up under cover of the rocks, and carefully concealed above the water mark with stones and sea-weed.

The pirates ascended a hill that intersected the island.

They looked out to sea, but could not make out the "Dolorosa."

The vessel carried no lights.

This was a bad sign.

The pirates considered it to be a token that the captain of the steamship had an intention of sending her boats ashore in pursuit of them.

A panic of terror possessed them, and they pushed their way into the centre of the island.

Here they halted in a lonely dell.

Harwolf's face was white as ashes with concentrated fury.

Fear for his own safety was added to his chagrin at the loss of his ship.

The men wore sullen faces.

Among the crew was a man named Blake, a thorough ruffian.

This fellow was universally detested, even among the abandoned wretches who called themselves vultures, and made the end and aim of their lives to perpetrate such deeds as should be consistent with their self-chosen, atrocious title.

He was a huge, ugly fellow; his face had been much damaged by a ghastly wound made by the thrust of a boarding-pike in some piratical action.

His hair was red, his teeth long and fang-like; the expression of his countenance sheerly diabolic, and his voice gruff and surly as the growl of a bear.

He was, however, faithful in his allegiance to Harwolf, knowing that he was protected from the vengeance of several of his comrades, whom he had exasperated, by that monster with whom he was a favourite.

This murderous fellow was the executioner of, or the assistant in all the most fragrant outrages perpetrated by his captain.

Cold and dispirited the remnant of the Vulture's crew seated themselves in a circle to consult upon the best course to be pursued in the present emergency.

The spirit of Daniel Harwolf rose with the occasion.

As we have seen, he was not without some amount of dogged resolution.

He rose and addressed his men in a bold tone.

"My lads," he said, "when we first fitted the ship which we have lost by such an unlooked-for surprisal, not one of us with common-sense could be blind to this truth, that we were commencing a game of hazard in which great prizes were to be gained at great risks. Not one of us but had already rendered himself liable to be pounced upon by the talons of the law. Now, I must own, that our first cruise has not been so favourable as we could wish; in the first place, through the cursed folly and arrogance of my ex-partner, Black Ralph; in the second, by the weakness caused by that treacherous villain's desertion, which rendered us an easy prey to our triumphant rivals. But, as an old gamester, I am acquainted with the infallible rules of chance. As sure as the morning succeeds the night, so sure does good-fortune follow a run of bad luck, and, so sure as the brightest day must end in darkness, so certainly will a crushing calamity fall upon this haughty upstart, this invincible Boy Pirate. Though we have much to regret, we have also no little to rejoice in. Hitherto we have had fair success, merry life aboard, light work, and, above all, have eluded the bloodhounds of justice, who would long since have had their fangs in some of us if we had not had recourse to our ark of refuge. Every day brings its dangers, and every day its advantages; I think it scarcely likely that the "Red Raven" will land on this island, as it is not the nearest to the ship, from which we escaped so happily, to the confusion of our sneaking foe, who stole down on us in the dead of night, and dared not face us in the open day, even with superior numbers. He will have enough to do to secure his own safety, for you may be assured the Brazilian government will take amplest vengeance for his daring act. At all events, there is nothing to be done but to await the morning, keeping steady watch, and Fortune is so fickle there is little doubt she will desert her favourite and smile on us. Come what may, I am with you, to share your roughest trials, your deadliest perils. I have done nothing yet to forfeit your confidence; had you kept better watch, the worst might not have happened, though that is wrongly stated, for the worst has *not* happened. We are free; we have a boat load of arms, and a keg of stingo. Never hang your heads then, but let us show our pluck by laughing at Fortune's floutings, and, like a true woman, she will love us the better for our indifference. Hurrah, lads! there is yet arms in our hands, liquor in our tubs, and stout hearts in our breasts, and the sea-bird may be driven from her rock. The world is wide, and there will ever be found somewhere on its surface an eyry for the Black Vulture."

The men murmured a surly approval.

Disgusted by their want of enthusiasm, Harwolf walked away.

Wardlaw joined him.

"Captain," said the pirate, "the men are in an ill-humour.

"Curse them! the lily-livered curs!" cried Harwolf, savagely. "I would walk the plank with joy if it were to tread on the heel of the last of them!"

"Nevertheless we're at their mercy," returned Wardlaw, moodily.

"We! How many will stick by me? You, for one, I trust?"

"Every man for himself, captain."

"I'd advise you to be true to me, Wardlaw, for yourself, then," said Harwolf, with a sneer. "I have been leader from the first; if I am murdered by the traitorous skunks there is an end to all stability of government. You will suffer by the precedent of my downfall; they will make you captain one day and depose, or murder you, the next."

"Very likely; I'm not ambitious of imperial honour, but——"

"Depend on it, Wardlaw, my luck will change, and a happy issue of this ugly affair will restore me to their confidence for ever."

"I hope it may prove so, but——"

"But!" cried Harwolf, contemptuously. "What sapient ass was it, I wonder, that invented those conditional 'ifs' and 'buts'?—only found in a lubber's lexicon. If you mean mutiny, 'but me no buts.' I am alone; I have been unlucky, but Hannibal in retreat is Hannibal still, and à ram rampant is no more than a sheep, and the best of these knaves is nothing better. Ha! here's this fellow Blake. We three are a match for the whole herd of these cowardly jackals. What news, Tom?"

"Hark, cap'en, how the devils are hissing and yelling. They are boozing their jibs over the brandy cask, and swaggering like troopers; they are using your name pretty roughly, I can tell you. Will you listen to me?"

"Yes, if you talk wisdom."

"So I will, cap'en—wisest wisdom. We are in mortal danger; the best thing we can do is to part company from these drunken mutineers. I have seven good chaps as we can rely on; let us propose going out a reconnoitering the island, and they will be cooled down afore morning, and something may chance to restore us to their good graces; if not, they may be overhauled by the Ravens, and that's no matter."

"It's good advice, captain," said Wardlaw.

"I think so, too," said the leader. "We'll act upon it."

Laughter and shouts were heard from the trees, where the brainless pirates were revelling.

"The cursed fools!" hissed the pirate. "They will betray themselves."

"No matter, so we escape, cap'en," said Blake.

"And where are your men?"

Blake whistled.

"Here they are; some o' the right sort, as won't stick at nothin'," returned Blake.

"I wish I had poisoned the grog!" growled Harwolf."

Seven men cautiously stole up from among the bushes.

"Welcome, my lads," said Harwolf. "Do you mean to stick by me?"

"To the death, cap'en!"

"You are wise."

"I'm the most popular among ye, I think," said Wardlaw; "I'll go back to the rascals, and tell them that you have set off to reconnoitre the island."

"Do so."

"But they'll think there's some trick about the boats," said Blake.

"Hearty, that's a good thought," returned the pirate captain. "What do you say, Wardlaw?"

"I'll tell them to find some men to keep watch on them, and to give signals in case of their being discovered by the Ravens."

"That's your course; go at once."

"Better, they're getting vicious; hark at the night owls how they are screeching."

"I wish the Boy Pirate might land and cut all

their throats; I'd run the risk of the worst he could do to us," cried Harwolf."

"Well, I'm off," said Wardlaw; "stand to your arms till I come back."

"We will; don't doubt it."

Wardlaw returned to the men.

They were solacing their fears with strong drink.

They still sat in a circle carousing.

The fog had cleared off.

The moon was breaking through a bank of clouds.

Her pale beams rippled down through the waving branches of the tops of the trees.

Many of the men were intoxicated.

Some were stretched on the ground fast asleep.

They received Wardlaw with a shout.

"Hurrah! here comes our cap'en," roared the men. "Give him a bumper, and drink death to the tyrant; no more wolves, Harwolfs, or wher-wolves; no more on 'em—down with 'em all!"

"Cheerily, lads, keep your hearts; drink the go-by to care and sorrow," cried Wardlaw, with a false laugh. "But, some must watch, the cussed Ravens are hovering, and the boats may be seized. Who's in charge of them? No one? that's bad management with a vengeance. Come, be spry; some of you sheer off to look after the boats. I am going with our captain and his sturdy fellows to cruise round the island; he is going to make amends for skulking last night's watch; but if you sleep, sleep with your weather eye open. Au revoir, my lads, don't forget the boats."

Before the drunken fellows could reply he turned on his heel and vanished in the surrounding darkness.

After some dispute among the pirates as to which of their number should undertake the care of the boats, a few of the more sober of the desperate villains staggered off.

The rest stretched on the ground, gave themselves up to heedless repose, or succumbed to the enervating power of the strong drink.

Meanwhile, Wardlaw joined Harwolf, and the rest of the watchful party who were bent upon examining the island, and preparing for emergencies.

The island proved to be more extensive than they had expected.

The surface was much diversified, and a chain of low hills ran through the centre, terminating at one extremity of the island in a high, bold peak, gradually sinking at the other and dwindling off in a reef of sharp rocks.

Over these hills the pirates made their way.

Beyond, the country stretched out towards the sea.

The moon now shone forth in splendour, edging the mist that hung upon the blue sea-line with bright silver.

The pirates lingered for a moment, and scanned the circle of land and sea in the centre of which they stood.

They descended the hill.

As they were passing through the wood below, they were suddenly surprised by hearing a shout.

They paused, and listened breathlessly.

Still through the wood the voice rang long and loud.

The pirates crept into a thicket.

Harwolf motioned them to remain quite still.

They obeyed, and crouched low among the tall waving grass.

A boy passed, his hand to his mouth, still hallooing lustily.

The ruffians started up from their ambush.

They seized the boy.

One fellow thrust his hand over his mouth.

The other bound the boy's arms.

The boy, who was a lank and awkward-looking Spanish lad, trembled violently, and looked pleadingly in his assailants' faces.

"He's one of the Ravens!" cried Blake. "We'll tear his heart out."

"Ah! senor, mercy!" cried the boy, as the man removed his hand from his mouth.

"Leave him alone, Blake," said Harwolf to the ruffian, who had seized the boy by the throat, was shaking him violently, and dashing his head against the side of a tree.

The man released the lad, but still rowned upon him with brutal malice.

"Who are you? Speak the truth, or it will be the worse for you," said Harwolf, in a threatening tone, speaking in Spanish.

"Ah! good senor Yenglese, mercy, if you please. I am a boy from the "Mosquito." Some of my comrades are ashore; they have come for water; they are going over to the other side of the island, as I think."

"No lies, you little villain! Why have they gone there?"

"Senor, pardon! They are gone, I believe, to see the fight between the Brazilian steam-frigate and the pirates. We heard the guns."

"A spy! a Spanish whelp, belonging to some South American war-ship on the cruise for rovers," cried Blake.

"Be quiet," said Harwolf, impatiently. "How many are your comrades ashore?"

"Six, senor."

"If they are gone on the other side of the island, why were you shouting for them?"

"Senor, I expected them back more than an hour ago. The tide is rising. I was left with the boat. Hearing your steps in the wood, I took you for my comrades. That's why I shouted."

"Perhaps they have fallen into the hands of our fellows," said Wardlaw.

"Ah, senor, that would be dreadful!" returned the boy. "But I have no reason to regret my comrades, they are cruel enough to me!"

"And what sort of barque is she, your ship?" asked Wardlaw.

"A brig, senor; freighted with furs and tobacco."

"How many are now aboard?"

"The captain, senor, and about twelve men."

"Does she carry any guns?"

"Yes; she was once a privateer; but now she's brig-rigged. There are seven guns with the 'chaser.' The master finds them of use; these seas swarm with pirates."

"True. Ah! the men, then, came on shore for water?"

"Yes, senor; we were becalmed, and suffered greatly. All the food we had was mouldy; a biscuit, and little of that, with but a pint of water a-day; for me, they gave me nothing. I almost died of thirst; I stole a little junk and biscuit, now and then, and when it rained I caught water in a bucket, which I stored as if it were a treasure of gold."

"Then you bear your messmates no particular goodwill?"

"I hate them, senor! I have reason enough to hate them; they have often made me wish myself dead!"

"Well, then, you have a chance of revenging yourself upon them."

"I am willing to do that, senor."

"You shall have your wish."

"But, how?"

"Do you know who we are?"

"No; but I think you are Yenglese fighters."

The pirates laughed.

"You are right; we fight for prizes; and if you are true to us, you shall have a better time in our company than you had with your comrades."

"Senor, I am ready to do anything you wish."

"Where is the boat?"

"Just below, senor; under the rocks."

"We will go aboard your ship."

"Oh, senor, do not take me with you! they will kill me!" cried the boy, imploringly.

"You must go, my boy; and, mark me, if you attempt to play us any tricks, we shall kill you; and there are more ways than one of making death very terrible. We are men who can't be played with."

"Good senor, I will not deceive you."

"Lead the way, then."

The boy grinned, and walked towards the beach.

"Can we trust him?" said Wardlaw to the pirate captain.

"I think so," returned Harwolf. "The poor young wretch seems to have scarce enough flesh to cover his bones. Besides, he would never dare to brave us to the teeth."

"He's to be trusted, cap'en," said Blake. "Anyhow we'll gag him when we take him into the boat, and there'll be no fear of his giving any alarm."

"We'll adopt that precaution."

"If we can take this ship, what a triumph it will be. I would give my right hand if we could do without those mutinous thieves," cried Harwolf. "At any rate, they will not share in the glory of this capture, and I may yet find means to recruit my company."

"But for them we might be in a sorry strait, after all, captain," said Wardlaw, with a laugh. "The men ashore might be down on us before we should be ready to receive them."

"That's true; but we have the boat now, besides we outnumber them."

"Come on," cried Blake, "no quarter; mercy should be the last word in a rover's mouth; infernal squeamishness has almost been the ruin of us already; we'll steal aboard afore daybreak, and cut the throat of every one we lay hands on."

The boy went on to the beach.

True to his story he showed them the boat drawn up among the rocks.

The pirates drew the boat down to the verge of the water.

They embarked.

The boy was placed in the stern-sheets.

He was effectually gagged with a piece of wood and a cord; they also bound his hands.

He submitted with better grace, as his appearance in such a forlorn and helpless condition would exonerate him from blame if the pirates were unsuccessful, and he should again fall into the hands of his shipmates.

The boat put off.

The morning was faintly breaking.

Still on the surface of the water deep darkness sat.

The moon had gone down.

Dancing over the leaping billows the little boat sped on.

The pirates pulled steadily and stealthily.

Soon they floated alongside.

All was silent.

The ship rocked in the trough of the passing waves, rising and falling gently as the breast of a sleeping child.

"Is that you, Pedro?" said a voice from above.

"Yes; the water must be brought off to-morrow, we missed the tide."

"Malraya! curse the water. Come aboard quick, Pedro, they're all asleep; but I and my eyes are heavy with sleep, I've had a long watch."

"Right, camerado, throw us a rope," returned the artful pirate.

Harwolf seized the rope.

Nimbly he sprang aboard.

Two of the men closely followed him.

"Did you bring the fruit for the captain?" asked the man, for it was too dark to distinguish faces.

"Yes," returned the pirate, with a low, fiendish laugh, "you shall taste it."

In a second he had raised his pistol.

He brought the butt down on the poor fellow's head with stunning force.

The man dropped on the deck without a single utterance.

Blake took him in his arms and hurled him over the bulwark.

"Fool!" muttered Harwolf, as he heard the plash.

Startled by the noise, a boy, who was sleeping beneath some sail-cloth, started up.

Blake pounced upon him.

The boy sprang on to the bulwark.

Harwolf flashed a knife across his face.

The ship lurched.

The lad sprang backwards.

He fell into the sea, and was swept off by the strong current.

All was quiet fore and aft.

Harwolf stole cautiously along the deck.

He pointed to the hatchways.

The men gathered round them, grasping their pistols and cutlasses.

They stooped over the gratings and listened.

Still profoundest silence.

The men from the boat now clambered the side of the vessel.

They joined their fellows at the main and after hatchways.

Harwolf turned to his men and whispered one of them to bring a lantern.

The man obeyed.

A light was struck.

The faint gleams streamed along the cumbered deck of the brig.

Harwolf stood at the head of the companion watch.

Blake was by his side, lantern in hand.

With a hellish leer the pirate captain drew his forefinger across his throat and pointed below.

The men grinned and nodded.

Harwolf cocked his pistols, and clutching one in each hand, softly stole down the hatchway.

The pirates divided into two parties.

One moved towards the bunks where the men were sleeping.

Harwolf walked aft, stooping under the low deck, and making for the skipper's cabin.

Soon the darkness below was broken by the flashing of pistols.

The silence was disturbed by a wild yell and heavy groaning.

A savage shout proclaimed that the " Mosquito " was won by these tigers of the seas.

Not a man of the crew was spared.

The bodies were pitched overboard through the ports.

Harwolf rushed on deck.

He leaped upon the quarter.

With a roar of exultation, the pirates leaped on deck, and the still night air wafted landward the hideous howl of these remorseless demons as they waved their reeking swords, and tossed up their smoking pistols.

The boy, who sat bound in the boat, shuddered and sickened as the cry was borne past on the night wind,

" Hurrah for the Black Vultures !"

CHAPTER CXXI.

HARWOLF ON BOARD HIS PRIZE—THE FATE OF THE "MOSQUITO'S" CREW—HOW THE SPANIARD ESCAPED.

THE morning broke.

Harwolf had just ordered two of the men to put off in the boat to announce to those on shore the capture of the "Mosquito," when the long-boat saved from the "Vulture" was seen throbbing through the waters towards the brig.

When daylight dawned, the pirates had come in search of their leader and their comrades, and had seen the signal which Harwolf had hoisted.

The pirate captain received his men with a cheer.

The fellows looked rather sheepish as they came aboard, for they had not forgotten their conduct of the past night, and this fortunate stroke of Harwolf's skill and daring had re-established him in their confidence.

With well-timed dissimulation, the pirate captain received his men with bold nonchalance and hearty cheerfulness.

He lectured them upon the necessity of keeping better discipline, remarked upon the danger of giving way to drunkenness, and reproached himself as well as them for the late disaster, which was, in a great measure, attributable to a want of caution.

He then dismissed the men to their duties.

It was found difficult to work the ship with so few hands.

The anchor was raised, sails set, and the " Mosquito " got under weigh.

The fate of that part of the rightful crew which had gone on shore still remained doubtful.

Just as the brig, about noon, was rounding the last point of the island, a boat was seen putting from shore.

Harwolf consulted his glass, and was soon convinced that the boat was no other than the boat of the " Mosquito."

She was made out by the pirate and his mate to be crowded with a number of men, who were straining every nerve to get alongside.

" These Spanish scamps will accept any alternative from starving on the island. No doubt we shall find them willing to join our band," said Wardlaw.

" Yes, if we were as willing to receive them," Harwolf returned, " and that is not very likely."

" I do not know, captain, we are short of hands; they are used to the ship and would be entirely in our power."

" Until they found a chance of betraying us."

" Well, we might keep them as long as they were found useful," replied Wardlaw.

" It is not worth the risk. How was it, think you, that there was so few hands to work such a large ship ?"

" The boy says that the greater number of the crew deserted when the brig lay off the mainland."

" Humph ! that's a trick these fellows might find a chance of playing us to our cost."

" Well, it's just possible."

" And therefore must be prevented."

" And how do you mean to receive them ?"

" How should you think ?"

" Get them aboard, and then make them walk the plank."

" No ! there's an easier way ; they are armed most likely, and might give us trouble, and weak-handed as we are we can't afford to lose a man."

" That's true."

" This little affair is to be managed in a much clearer way."

" I guess what you mean."

" Nevertheless I will show you my plan at once."

Harwolf called the ruffianly Blake.

" Double shot two of the guns on the lee quarter," he said, " and when the boat comes alongside be ready to fire into her."

" Perhaps the rascals will be too wary for us."

" Not at all ; keep the ports half down, let the men who are to work the guns keep out of sight," said Harwolf, " and throw up a signal for a parley."

These treacherous orders were carried out.

After the lapse of a quarter of an hour the boat came alongside.

Harwolf stood on the hammocks and hailed her in Spanish.

" Ahoy, senor; let us come aboard," shouted the Spaniards.

As the men stood up in the boat they looked such ugly cut-throats that Harwolf was almost tempted to follow his mate's suggestion to take them on board, and swear them into his gang.

However they were well armed and desperate looking fellows, and the dastardly pirate could never endure to lose the least chance of gratifying his lust for wanton cruelty.

" What now, comerados; what do you want ?" cried Harwolf, through the speaking-trumpet.

" We want to come aboard the ' Mosquito ' to serve under its new, gallant captain," shouted one of the men, laughing.

" Do you know under what colours I sail, amigo ?"

"Yes, very well, senor Inglese; better to serve the devil than starve."

"But can I trust you?"

"Yes, yes, senor, we're safe enough; we know the trade!"

"Then you have fought under the rover's flag before this?"

"Many a time, brave senor; we know the coast and we know what ships are crossing these seas; we can tell you of a rich Indiaman that lays off the continent."

"Well, get under the lee-quarter, and I will give you your answer."

The boat floated under the shadow of the dark hull.

The pirate gave the word.

The ports were opened.

The guns run out.

The breaches raised, and then the ship shuddered with their roar.

Mingled cries of agony and execration were heard.

The next moment the sea was strewn with the fragments of the boat and the bodies of struggling seamen fighting with the heavy waves.

The water, in more than one place, was tinged with blood.

Several of the drowning men shrieked for mercy.

The fiendish pirates only laughed their derision.

The sails were hauled round to the freshening wind, and the brig sheered off.

Soon the heads that dotted the surface of the cruel waters disappeared.

One man, however, a strong swimmer, had contrived unseen by the pirates to reach the side of the vessel.

He crawled into the stern chains.

After remaining four hours lashed by the surf, he ventured to clamber up to the mouth of one of the ports.

He crept in.

He crouched down behind some bales.

He took some biscuits from a canister, and crept into an empty sea-chest and closed the lid softly.

He was just in time, for Harwolf and Wardlaw came below, laughing with brutal glee.

Towards night the sky began to lower with storm clouds.

The wind gathered power and swept wildly over the swelling ocean.

The gale struck the vessel.

The men found the greatest difficulty in working the ship.

Harwolf, however, exerted himself to the utmost. He took the helm, and cheered his men by words of encouragement. The sails were eventually furled, and the "Mosquito," with bare masts, drifted before the heavy gale, huge masses of surf leaping and raging over her creaking deck.

At night the brig stood off the main-land.

For several hours she remained in terrible danger.

Once she shoaled, but was got off the rocks by the superhuman exertions of Harwolf and the crew.

When the second night dating from her capture broke into morning, the "Mosquito" was riding at anchor at the mouth of a wide river, and the exhausted men, worn out with fatigue and excitement, threw themselves in their hammocks, and, regardless of any besetting peril, abandoned themselves to the sweets of toil-earned repose.

A heavy mist gathered over sea and sky.

The Spaniard crept from the chest, let himself down into a boat, cut away the seizings with his long knife, and drifted with the tide till the density of the fog and the distance he had made, encouraged him to dip his oars into the rolling waves.

In less than an hour he ran the boat high up on a sand-bank, and fled into the woods.

CHAPTER CXXII.

THE PIRATES EXHAUSTED — HARWOLF'S EAGERNESS TO RECRUIT HIS BAND—THE CASTAWAY—A DESPERATE RUFFIAN—THE CONVICT'S PLOT.

THE hours passed heavily with the pirate leader.

His men had worn themselves out with fatigue; it was evident that they could not be expected continuously to manage a vessel so large and heavy rigged, their numbers being so inadequate.

He walked the deck of the silent ship, Wardlaw by his side.

"We have not gained much in taking the brig, captain," said the mate, "unless we can find some means of increasing the number of our men."

"The furies sieze that cursed hunk that has stood a block in my path from boyhood!" cried Harwolf, darkly frowning. "I have great faith, as I told you, in the run of luck, and as I have won this prize so opportunely, something may turn up to strengthen our hands. I would sell my soul to have him within reach of my sword—that cursed Raven; but his time will come."

"Look, captain, is not that a boat to windward? It appears to me that we are hailed by some castaway from last night's storm."

"You are right," said Harwolf, applying his glass to his eye; "and a strange-looking fellow he seems to be. I make him out to be dressed in party-coloured clothes, and he holds aloft some rag of a shirt or blouse at the top of an oar."

"He appears to be shouting."

"Yes; though we don't hear him, he is raving his heart out."

"He walks backwards to the stern of the boat."

"And limps as if he were in chains."

"He does so."

"Now he sinks down."

"The poor devil seems quite spent."

"No wonder, if he had to weather out last night's gale in that cockle-shell."

"Especially if he's lame."

"Well, I am curious to know who he is, and I have an impression that he is an harbinger of good luck."

"Shall I have the boat put down?"

"Aye, directly. The fellow seems to have given us up in despair."

Wardlaw roused some of the sleepers.

The boat was let down, and Wardlaw and half a dozen of the pirates pulled off.

Harwolf paced the deck impatiently till they returned.

When they came alongside, towing with them the other boat, a man appeared lying almost senseless in the stern-sheets.

He was brought on board.

They laid him down against the binnacle.

He presented a strange spectacle.

He was a tall, bony fellow, as brown as mahogany, with a fearful expression of villany in his dark face; his hair was cut short, and covered by a sort of skull cap.

His dress was peculiar.

It was something in the style of the ancient motley, one side being red and the other yellow; on his leg was a heavy fetter; one he had struck off, the other had proved too much for his strength.

"What is he, think you, captain?"

A light of intelligence flashed in Harwolf's grey eyes.

"Good may come of this'" he said, quickly.

"How, captain?"

"We may find this fellow of service."

"In what way?"

He may help us to recruit our forces, with some of the right sort, genuine bloodhounds, that are pirates in soul."

"Why, what is he?"

"Don't you know?"

"Not I; though, by his dress, I should take him to be a Merry-Andrew."

"Let me tell you he wears a badge of great distinction."

"Indeed! that's odd. At all events, he wears the order of the garter," returned Wardlaw, laughing.

"An honour he would gladly dispense with."

"Rather! Look how the poor devil has wounded his lanky legs in trying to free himself from his darbies. I think I can guess what he is; he is some convict."

"Exactly so. Perhaps an old fellow-tradesman," returned Harwolf, laughing.

"Very likely. One half the mariners along this coast indulge in buccaneering."

"Very sensible, too, for there is no more classic sport on the world's surface for such work than the South Pacific. And were not your Raleighs and Frobishers as much pirates as we are?"

"But why do they dress him in this flaring style?"

"That he may be conspicuous, and easily detected if he attempts escape," returned Harwolf.

The pirate captain ordered the men to bring a flask of spirits.

He poured brandy on the convict's lips.

After awhile, the man unclosed his bloodshot eyes.

He moved his hand feebly, and pointed to his swollen leg.

His hand dropped heavily by his side, and he fell back into his former state of torpor.

"Where is the armourer?" asked the pirate.

The word was passed for the man to whom the charge of the arms was usually confided.

He brought his mallet and struck off the felon's chains.

The man uttered a piercing shriek.

Upon opening his eyes, and glancing about him, he found himself surrounded by faces as dark and savage as his own.

"Give me a cup of water," he said.

This was brought him.

"You are Yenglese pirates?" he said, aintly, but with a hideous leer.

"Yes, camerado, but we mean you no harm."

"If you will give me some food, I will teach you how to make your fortunes," murmured the fellow.

Harwolf ordered him to be carried below.

Food was brought him.

He ate voraciously.

His spirits revived with his strength.

He seemed to be delighted with his new position. He cursed and blasphemed his enemies in a brutal dialect, sang snatches of vulgar songs in the most lugubrious tones, and brandished the knife he was using with the chuckling triumph of a gloating demon.

Harwolf watched him in silence.

"Now, senor," cried the fellow, "Muy ben, I am restored; and—vengeance!"

With this, he attempted to leap up; but his swollen legs tottered beneath him, and he fell heavily.

He lay on his back, rolling his fierce black eyes, knashing his teeth, writhing, and cursing.

The pirates laughed, and raised the foaming brigand on to a hammock.

"Captain, I want a few words with you alone," said the Spaniard to Harwolf. "Pack off these ladrones."

When the men had left the deck the convict leaned on his elbow and bent a thoughtful glance upon the pirate.

"Senor, you are not the Boy Pirate?"

"No; I am his enemy!"

"All the better. They say that fellow is half a priest, and that he will have no dealings with such fellows as I."

"He is more than half a cur. He has some brave fellows among his crew, and shines, like the moon, by borrowed light," returned Harwolf, spitefully.

"'Tis the way of the world, senor. True merit is never appreciated. Some knave with an extra share of that grand quality impudence always carries off the palm."

"And what have you to communicate to me?"

"Not much to communicate, but a good deal to propose."

"Ha! Upon what subject?"

"You are weak-handed, senor. Either you have just begun business, or you have lost half your men by some cursed mischance."

"I want hands that I can trust, certainly," replied Harwolf.

"And I can tell you how you may get them."

"And who are you?"

"My name is Don Paulo Corderes," said the ruffian, with a brightening eye. "Diavolos! senor, like yourself, I have seen better days. I was a captain of Guerilleros."

"Ha! brigands!"

"In English, perhaps. But, senor, I have fought for my country, and have gained a dozen orders and medals by my bravery and conduct," returned the ruffian, with a grin.

"And deserved the further honour of a halter, I'll be bound," replied Harwolf.

"Well, senor, when we both get our deserts, no doubt we shall share that honour together,"

"And for which of your sins did you get condemned to the galleys?"

"For giving a handful of dollars to a poor padre," returned the man, with a scowl and a laugh.

"Well, that was curious."

"Not at all, senor; weakness is the source of failure. If I had not been so weak, if I had acted wisely, and slit his reverend throat when I cut his purse, all would have been well."

"You are right. There is no use to look for gratitude in this world," said the pirate, sagaciously.

"No, senor. Yet it is hard when a man has committed every crime in the calender, cardinals and peccadilos, that he should be made to suffer for a single good action. It chanced in this way. I and my band had passed through a successful campaign; we had taken off our booty into the mountains, and all was well. However, one unlucky day, we fell upon a party of travellers crossing the Llanos; we cut them to pieces all but this graceless dog of a priest. Malraya! if ever I catch him, he shall be canonised as a martyr. I'll roast him like St. Lawrence —may that good saint pray for me," the rascal crossed himself devoutly. "We found on this ingrate devil a bag of dollars; we spared his life for the sake of his cassock, and, at his earnest entreaty, I gave him a good handful of his own money, and yet the villain betrayed us! However, I'll do him this much justice, he knew that his offence was too enormous to escape punishment, so when all my poor fellows were strung up together like a bunch of grapes, he begged me off for the favour I had shown him, and with a consciousness that some day I should return to pay the reckoning between us."

"Go on with your story, amigo, we shall then come to the point which I wish to reach, for already I shrewdly guess in what way you can help me."

"True, senor, I was condemned to the galleys. I worked in the docks at San Salvador; escaped, was taken, tried to to get up a revolt, failed through the currishness of my confederates, was flogged, branded, and hung up by the cord till my arms were dislocated; soon after, I killed a keeper because he offered me a mouldy loaf, should have been hanged but had friends among the guerillas who threatened to shoot the judge if he condemned me to death. I was, however, condemned, but the judge sent Malvarez, my good fellow brigand, a purse of money and a handsome apology, which was the most he could do, poor fellow. I would let him off with a bullet, for he might have treated me worse. He commuted my sentence, senor, and I was shipped off with a cargo of other saints to a penal settlement established in one of these islands."

THE PUNISHMENT OF THE MUTINEER.

"And you managed to escape from the convict ship?"

Exactly so, senor, I managed to file off one of my irons, cut the throat of the keeper with his own knife, which I snatched from his girdle, got out of a port, cut adrift the boat, and here I am! I could have set all my comrades at liberty; we might have taken the ship, hoisted the free flag, and outrivalled the Boy Pirate by so much as I am the better man; but the affair at San Salvador had shaken my confidence; I dared not trust my fellow villains, for I was soon out of the reach of the protection of my friend—the worthy brigand I told you of—for the captain of the ship would not have hesitated one instant to swing the illustrious Don Corderes at the yard-arm, or make him walk the plank without benefit of clergy. I shall not attempt to describe

No. 40.

my sufferings of last night, the storm nearly capsized my boat; but I vowed a score of wax candles to my patron saint, a vow which I will keep religiously, but for his intercession I should have died without making my will."

"And do you think your comrades would mutiny if we gave them the chance?"

"That they would. They are ripe for revolt!" cried the convict. "If we can run alongside of the vessel we can mount the black flag, and open our broadside."

"Be it so," said Harwolf; "but we must act with extreme caution. Failure would cause our own destruction."

"Assuredly, senor. What is he name of your vessel?"

"We will call her the 'San Pedro,' and say we are merchants from Janiero; but do you know where we shall find her?"

"Yes, she is among the islands," replied the brigand; "we are sure to overhaul her. There is no doubt that she suffered terribly from last night's storm; perhaps she may be driven upon the rocks and wrecked."

"We will look for her."

"And now, senor, let me sleep."

CHAPTER CXXIII.

THE CONVICT TRANSPORT—HARWOLF DELUDES THE SPANIARDS—HARWOLF'S TREACHERY—THE FELON RELEASED—A CREW WORTHY OF THEIR LEADER.

HARWOLF came on deck.

He called Wardlaw.

The mate was rather dubious of the expediency of the plan proposed by his leader.

He thought it would be needlessly running in the face of danger.

It would be putting themselves in the power of a gang of foreign villains, who would probably overpower their deliverer, and cut all their throats, and elect their countryman, the worthy Don Corderes, to be their captain; for though he was a pirate himself, he believed foreigners to be considerably worse, and to be without the slightest sense of honour.

Harwolf overruled all these objections.

He perfectly understood Spanish; he knew how to humour his new confederates.

Vile as they were the Spaniards were very superstitious in religious matters; he would find out the name of the patron saint of each man, and swear each upon his several divinity; besides, though the convicts would be sufficiently ruthless and perhaps courageous for the honourable calling of sea-robbers, they were all landsmen who did not know the forepeak from the quarter; they would not dare to trust themselves to the mercy of the waves and the winds even with so many saints to back them.

Harwolf did not deceive himself nor his associate as to the nicety of judgment, the firmness of purpose, blent with conciliation of manners, and great caution, that would be required in dealing with their dangerous allies.

But he was confident that he should be able to subdue them to his will, and put the unanswerable question,

"Supposing their forces were not in some way recruited, inadequate as their numbers were for the management of the brig, what was to be done?"

Wardlaw deferred to the superior judgment of his commander, but with reluctance.

In a few hours the ship was under sail.

Harwolf took the helm.

The wind was favourable.

The next day the brig was scudding gaily along in the roadstead between the islands.

The convict-ship, an immense and heavily-rigged vessel, lay off-shore.

Her top-masts were much injured, her bowsprit and forecastle partly stove in by the storm of the preceding night.

As soon as the brig appeared entering the channel the convict-ship threw up a signal for her to heave-to.

The brig, however, bore on.

She answered the signal by one of inquiry.

The convict transport replied by hoisting an inverted standard as a flag of distress.

The pirates who had made every preparation for an encounter, stood clustered on the forecastle anxiously watching the movements of the other vessels.

They perceived two long-boats well manned by marines and sailors put off.

Wardlaw looked with some consternation into the face of his commander.

Harwolf only smiled.

The boat came alongside.

At the command of their captain, the men affected to be busy about their duty.

Not one of them but had weapons concealed about his person.

Those below stood ready at the guns.

The officer from the convict-transport bowed to Harwolf.

"Senor," he said with a smile, "you seem to have escaped well from the effects of the gale; perhaps you can render us some assistance, as you will perceive we have lost our top-masts; our rig is much damaged, perhaps you have some able men aboard, who can assist us in fitting jury masts? You will not, of course, be unrewarded for the service you render us."

"We have suffered more, sir," replied Harwolf, "than you suppose; though freighted from Janiero, we are English; but, we have plenty of spare tackle, and you shall have what help we can afford you. On our part we should be glad if you could spare a few hands to help us to put into the nearest harbour."

"What, are you short of men?"

"Yes, senor, the greatest part of our fellows put off in their dismay last night; they got into the boats, whether or not they have perished, I cannot say."

"I understand you, senor, the men were panic-stricken, and trusted themselves in a launch."

"That is the fact."

"More fools they; they had better have kept to their duty. No boat could live in such a storm as that of yesterday."

"Nevertheless, I could not induce them to remain; but I trust you will help, senor?"

"Then, you were not, as I perceive, entirely abandoned?"

"No, senor, a few true fellows remained with me."

"Well, I will do the best I can for you. You must run alongside, and send your men aboard; the fact is, being high tide now, we float securely; but, should the tide fall, we shall be grounded on the sand-bank."

"We are at your service, senor," returned the pirate.

"Thanks; I suppose you know what cargo we carry?"

"No, indeed, unless a transport of soldiers."

"Of devils rather. We are freighted with a super-cargo of felons—men who have committed horrible crimes—whom we are carrying to the new penal settlement on one of these islands."

"I do not envy you your work, senor."

"You have not cause. I wish the cruise were over."

"It will soon be over, thanks, with your kind assistance."

"We will do our best to shorten it; depend on that."

"Senor Yenglese, you are very kind."

"Are you not afraid of the rascals you have in charge?"

"Fear is a feeling we do not acknowledge, but we feel sufficient anxiety, senor. Last night we had trouble enough with the villains."

"I doubt it not. Well, senor, we will do our best to help you out of your dilemma."

"You are very good; your arrival is fortunate," replied the Spanish officer.

Harwolf invited the officers and men to drink.

They gladly accepted the invitation, and Harwolf took them into his cabin.

He plied them well with strong liquor, and they soon grew very merry.

They were much elated with the issue of their visit to the " San Pedro."

Harwolf saw them return into the boats with a joyous smile.

They returned to the transport.

The helm was put up; the yards swayed heavily and slowly round, and the brig was fast nearing the transport.

The two ships lay stern to stern.

Harwolf rushed below.

The convict started from his hammock.

He beckoned the pirate, and together they looked out of the port.

A villanous face appeared opposite them.

"San Pedro, be praised! that's Mendes," cried the brigand; he signalled the convict.

They exchanged rapid but intelligible signs with their hands.

Corderes turned to Harwolf with a grin of satisfaction.

The man disappeared from the opposite port.

"What does it mean?" asked the pirate.

"This, senor," returned the brigand, "my old comrade has the means of getting on deck with the rest."

"Well?"

"You will have to take spars for jury masts on board?"

"Yes."

"And sail cloth?"

"I suppose so."

"Very good. Listen to me——"

"But tell me, comerado, how is it that there is no spare tackle on board?"

"That is easily explained."

"But how?"

"It was all thrown overboard to lighten the ship during the storm."

"That is possible."

"There is no mistake. Senor?"

"Well."

"You are primed for any venture?"

"Yes, if your friends will be true."

"I will be bound for them."

"Never fear, treachery will not answer with me."

"It never answers, senor, among comrades especially."

"I am glad you are of that opinion."

"You have plenty of arms on the ' San Pedro,' I suppose?"

"We brought a boat load from—that is, we have a plentiful supply."

Harwolf had checked himself; he did not wish the brigand to know too much.

"Excellent. Now, senor, you must contrive to secure as many pistols and cutlasses in a sail as you can."

"That is easy."

"And when you have carried your covered arms aboard the transport; lay them down before the main-hatchway."

"And the convicts, springing on deck, will seize them?"

"Just so."

"But how will they know?"

"Mendes knows everything."

"Your secret language of signs must be comprehensive?"

"In our trade it is often needful to be dumb; dumb men with eyes can find tongues that can speak plain words."

"So I perceive."

"Are you ready to venture this trick, senor?"

"' Ready, aye, ready!'—it's always my motto."

"Promptness in this sort of service is the first requisite."

"I agree with you; but, amigo?"

"Well, senor?"

"We shall be outnumbered by the crew of the transport, and the convicts may fail in attempting their escape."

"No fear. You saw that fellow Mendes?"

"I had that pleasure."

"Does he look like one who would fail?"

"In no ordinary enterprise."

"Such an escapade is nothing to him."

"I am satisfied."

"And, senor, listen to me."

"I attend you."

"Do you know that Mendes is a sort of overlooker? He can let the men out of their coop if he pleases."

"That's an advantage."

"Of course; but as soon as the sail is fairly on board—the arms, you know, must be securely lashed up."

"That may be done by the reefing points."

"Yes."

"Well; but if securely lashed, as you say, how are the men to get at them?"

"With a knife."

"But what will the officers be doing to let them arm themselves in this way?"

"They must be partially disabled."

"But how can that be managed?"

"How many guns have you?"

"Four, and the chasers."

"Can you mount the larboard guns on this side?"

"Easily."

"Then you must elevate the chasers."

"A good plan; I see what you are aiming at."

"I am aiming at the masts, senor."

"Yes; if we bring them down with a fair shot from the chasers, all on board will be crushed or stupified."

"The very idea. And all will be on board, senor?"

"Yes, to help my men."

"Is it not a good plan?"

"The best. It shall be executed."

"And what, senor, do you propose to do after that?"

"When the convicts are on board to fire a broadside into the vessel."

"Just so; but there is one precaution must be taken."

"What is that?"

"Your own men, senor, they will be aboard, and will suffer when the rigging falls."

"Of course they can leave the vessel on the pretext of fetching more tackle."

"Another hint, senor—the last."

"What is it ?"

"You have not shown all your men?"

"No; most of them are below at the guns."

"Keep them there. Send as few aboard as possible."

"I will, be sure. I shall want them at their posts in case of failure."

"There will be no failure if you are bold and prudent."

"And now I must begone, our consort is getting impatient."

"Let me go on board with the men."

"How can you manage that?"

"You think I shall be recognised?"

"How can it be otherwise?"

"I will disguise myself."

"I doubt your ability to do that."

"If you doubt my ability to do anything you will insult me."

Harwolf laughed.

"Hark!" he said. "The men have ceased working, all is prepared—all the spare tackle is ready."

"Very good. I will go on board with your men."

"But, your disguise——"

"Is easily managed; the devil sometimes robes in white, being such a bright spirit. I must blacken a bit. Get me some grease and charcoal, and some sailor's clothes."

"Then you mean to smear your face and appear as a negro?"

"For once, Malraya; it's a degradation, but never mind."

"Is your presence necessary?"

"Essential; the men have faith in me."

"I must be off at once then, they are calling for me."

"Obey the call, I'll be with you in a few seconds."

Harwolf went on deck.

At his direction a number of arms were slipped into the folds of the canvas of the sail, and the men were preparing to carry them on board the transport.

The men on board the transport ship received the Vultures with many expressions of thanks and good will.

The treacherous rascals replied by grins, and testified their readiness and zeal to refit the injured vessel.

The lazy Spaniards started at the energy with which the English seamen laboured.

Corderes came aboard his former prison ship.

He passed unnoticed.

Indeed, so skilfully had he altered his appearance that it was impossible to recognise him.

He had rubbed the greased charcoal into his skin, and appeard a perfect black.

Harwolf soon found an excuse for sending him below.

He then discovered that there was need for more spars.

His men quietly returned to the boats.

He followed them.

The captain of the transport endeavoured to detain him.

Harwolf, however, eluded this intention, saying that he must choose the best of the spare tackle and oversee the men.

The sail was laid close by the gangway.

The pirates went back to their ship.

There were none now left on the deck of the transport but Spaniards.

No sooner was Harwolf once more on the brig than he gave the word to fire.

The scene that followed can be better imagined than described.

The chasers went off with a loud report, and the heavy shot flew up, and ripped through the rigging.

Both the main and foremasts were struck.

Another volley was fired from the brig.

The yards and cordage crashed down.

The deck presented one scene of ruin and confusion.

The "San Pedro" fired a raking broadside.

The ponderous metal dashed into the ribs of the close anchored vessel.

The pirates shouted, and, sword in hand, leaped on to the transport, and fiercely attacked the half-armed sailors and marines.

The officers, though surprised at this unexpected attack, acted as gallant sailors, and threw themselves upon the pirates, calling upon their men to follow.

At the same moment the convicts rushed from below.

They were headed by Corderes.

In an instant they had possessed themselves of the weapons.

They were not all ironed.

Even those that were had become, as far as possible, used to the encumbrance.

The ill-fated crew of the transport, stunned and confounded by the additional catastrophe, were powerless, and despairing of a successful resistance, threw away their arms and begged for mercy

But to the Vultures this word was unknown.

True to their piratical maxim, that "dead men tell no tales," they shot down and stabbed the unresisting crew.

Soon they were all slaughtered.

But some measure of justice was at hand.

The transport was found to be on fire!

Thick volumes of smoke were ascending from the hatchways, and a glimmering brightness was discerned below.

Harwolf gave orders to his men.

Wet blankets were brought and thrown down the hatchway, and buckets of water were cast in profusion over the interior of the ship.

But the fire had got a firm hold of the vessel, and was spreading with great rapidity.

And now a panic arose among the pirates and the convicts.

The first, trained to some kind of discipline under Harwolf's direction, made for their own boats, and, with some few exceptions, gained their vessel in safety.

But the convicts, a motley crowd, following only their own impulses, impeded each other in their endeavours to escape.

The boats would not hold half of their number, but they crowded in, panic-stricken.

Corderes implored them to be calm, and assured them that the boats of the "Vulture" would soon return to rescue them; but his voice was unheard, and soon shrieks and cries for help were heard from the vessel's quarter.

A boat had capsized!

The river was covered with struggling, striving beings—all anxious to save lives that up to the present had been so ill spent.

But few succeeded in reaching the shore.

On board the transport the fire was rapidly spreading.

The deck planks were scorching, and burning the feet of those who stood upon them.

The boats of the " Vulture " were now approaching the transport.

An explosion of a barrel of gunpowder completed the panic of the occupants of the doomed ship.

Many of the convicts leaped into the sea, and were sunk by the weight of their shackles.

The rest escaped in the Vulture's boats.

The accident was probably caused by the lighted shells and fire-bombs the pirates were firing.

As the Spaniards scrambled on to the deck of the " San Pedro " a loud explosion, followed by the roar of guns, was heard, then appeared a pillar of fire and smoke, the next instant the sea was strewn with the wreck of the transport.

CHAPTER CXXIV.

THE RETURN OF MILES—HIS DREADFUL STORY —WAR AGAINST THE INDIANS—HARWOLF'S REMORSE—A VILLAIN FOR EVER A VILLAIN.

WHEN Miles returned to Larchville his disordered appearance was the subject of general remark among all who were at at work on the plantation.

His broad face was pale with horror, his eyes seemed starting, he trembled in every limb.

His horse too was in a terrible condition of fright and exhaustion; the sweet exuded in streams from his flanks, his knees quivered like reeds, his eyes were bloodshot, and his mouth and neck covered with foam.

Miles leaped from the saddle.

The men crowded round, questioning him concerning the reason of his appearing in such woeful plight.

He faintly gasped one word,

" Injens!"

There was a general cry of rage on the part of the men, and a scream from the women.

Miles gave the horse into the charge of one of the servants.

He entered the house.

Michael Warren and young Mark Leighton were seated at a table.

Before them lay a map.

A lively dispute was going on between them as to the accuracy of the tracing of a confluent to the Mississippi.

They both started up with a cry of surprise at the abrupt entry of Miles Thornton.

" I do zay az long az there be one of the 'farnal savages left alive in Arkansas we might az well let the corn stand, for, durn me, if there be one of us az wull live to zee the reaping on it."

" What is the matter?" cried the men in one breath.

" This be the matter, zquire—judge, axing your pardon, az I should zay," returned Miles, his face flushing with wrath, and striking his gun vehemently on the floor. " I do zay, zur, as this zettlement be no more than a home presarve for raring game for these durned devilskins, and we be nothin' better, none on us, than zo many hares or pheasants, loike to be bagged when they goes sportin'—these zaid blanation Injuns."

" Indians! Tut, tut! Always the Indians."

" Dang it, zur, it may be ' allus,' for the Injuns, but it won't be ' allus' for us. They keep September all the year round, and make no more on us, I do zay agen, than if we was zo many grouse or partridges."

" Miles, you're right," cried Leighton : " there is no end to their devilry, and never will be till all true men in the settlement band together to extirpate the vermin."

" Easy, young man; deliberation——"

" Deliberation be ——! saving your presence, judge; but Job's patience would fail to see fellows who pretend to have pluck awaiting their turn to be slaughtered like so many sheep in the shambles. Confound such deliberation! it is madness as well as cowardice."

" You are hot——"

" Hot! I wish I were a ball of fire, to roll from wigwam to wigwam till there was not a dirty lodge standing in the prarie!"

" Well, something must be done at once, but big words won't annihilate the Shoshoné. What's the matter, Miles?"

" You know, zur, this mornin' I started with the men?"

" Ronald Holmes and the rest; well?" said Harwolf, slightly starting.

" I do zay, zur, it be 'farnal——"

" Fallen in with the Indians?"

" Aye, zur, and a pretty vall out moreover."

" Some of them killed, judge, you may depend upon it."

" Very safely, zur; but you have not come to the worst of it for all that, for I be the only one of the whole party az be zafe returned to Larchville!"

" What, are they taken?"

" Dead, zur! all dead, do azzure 'ee."

" Just Heaven! were you surprised at a bivouac, or fired at from an ambush?"

" Loard, zur! that's more than I can zay, and be faithful, for it were about the most artfullest piece of trickery az ever was practised, even by Injuns. We were picked off (leastways, the rest on us) afore we could open our mouths to warn each other. Az for me, the hoss saved me, but, as you zee, zur, I didn't get off without a wound. Durn the copper devils, but I'll mark 'em for it."

" And did you not see the wretches?"

" True to zay. zur, I did see but one—a single varlet, az I fired at, and might as well a turned my shootin' iron to whistle at the moon."

" Was he a Shoshoné?"

" No, be zure, zur; a doamed Pawnee! and I knows him; got so near him az to recognize him, but my barrel was empty."

" The reptile! did you not say you knew him?" asked Warren.

" Az well as I know this hand, zur; a black cuss on him!"

" Who was he?"

" The fellow as wed that silly Wyotti lass—Cat-or-hog, or some such beastly titles."

" Catalaga, the Eagle-Wing!"

" Durn him, I'll clip his wings for him!"

" However, he is not unaptly named, Miles," said Harwolf, " he must have had eagle wings to escape you all."

" It is unsupportable, judge; you ought to be deposed if you do not act with vigour."

" Fear not, I have been to blame for my long forbearance; it is dangerous while the settlement is still but thinly populated to rush into open and deadly war with the savages, but it is plain that we have no other alternative."

" None whatever, sir."

" And Ronald Holmes was killed too?"

" Stalked like an elk, zur."

" It's monstrous !"

" We are his murderers, judge !" cried Leighton, furiously, " and of all the rest of these poor fellows ; if we had hunted down these prairie wolves before, all this might have been prevented !"

" I cannot deny it. Well, this very day shall witness a grand battue."

" Right, bravely spoken, Mr. Warren," cried Leighton, with joyous ardour. "I claim your promise, I am to act as your lieutenant."

" You shall ; but how shall we muster a party sufficiently strong ?"

" All that is pre-arranged by me," said Leighton, " upon the principle of the old stories of the ' fiery cross ; ' every lad in every plant within a circuit of forty miles has sworn to attend my summons, though he rush to the call from the dying bed of his wife or child, from the side of his father's grave, or from the altar and his bride ; this will be the best day's sport I have seen for a long time."

" If zo be, I do say, Master Mark, zur, as we can get to the windward of the game, for, dang me, if these prairie gipsies ain't warier than your wild bulls."

" And how will you get them together, Mr. Leighton ; one man will scarce be able to get over forty miles in a few hours, and then there is the distance returning, and the time lost in hunting up the men."

" It shall be done according to my former arrangement, judge ; I have a hunting dirk of particular make, I have strung it with a red baldrick, and it is marked with our acknowledged sign upon it—this sword will be passed from hand to hand, and every one of the Regulators is bound by oath and forced by heavy penalties to obey the signal."

" I have my own troop, and can call them out at any moment," said Harwolf. " Summon as many as you can gather, that we may be ready to start before night fall ; our first point of attack shall be the large village of the Sioux, beyond the Arkansas."

" The wigwam of the Dacotah chief, they call Wabiskoa ?"

" Yes, the Indian renegade, Eagle-Wing, has gone over to that tribe ; the Dacotahs are more powerful than all the rest of the neighbouring nations, and if we can get one severe blow at them, we shall strike terror into all the others."

" I will go at once. Mr. Thornton, I suppose, has had enough of adventuring in the redskins' territory, besides, he must want rest."

" Durn'ee noa, it shan't be zaid ov Miles az he be afeard of all haythen critters ar this zide the Atlantic ; if zo be as I can get one crack at that Eagle-Wing feller, all az wull may have the honour and glory."

" Agreed, then ; where shall we meet, Judge Warren ?"

" Here, lad, on the lawn before my house," returned the other.

Leighton rushed from the room.

" Miles," said Warren, closing the door and stepping quickly towards his assistant, " is this deep play, or was your tale true ?"

" True, every 'varsal word, squire, do azzure'ee," returned Miles, gravely.

" Humph ! if the men are picked off in this way, they might as well be disbanded at once."

" Zo I do zay, squire. It's hawful, and all along of the blamed redskins."

" And did you manage the affair of the Jew and the trapper ?"

" No, yer honour, they got off slick free."

" That's bad."

" Mortal bad, I do zay. But I don't think az they recognized us."

" Perhaps they, too, were killed by the savages ?"

" Don't think zo, squire, for why—Sam Weatherfield is cheek by jowl with every smut of outlander on the prairies, 'specially az to the Zaws."

" Saws ! The Sioux ?"

" Ah ! 'zpose so. Zure I think, yer honour, there is not one of the brutes az would injure that zame trapper chap."

" And how many redskins attacked you ?"

" Mortal 'zhamed I be to zay so, yer honour, but I'm blamed if I think there was any other besides that Cat-and-hog feller."

" You are but a blockhead, Miles, to be bested by a single Indian."

" Your honour's about right there. Darn my voolish eyes, I be quite abroad in these vurrin lands, zurelie ! Now, squire, if zo be I were at Glenleaf or Frontemore——"

" Peace, fool !" cried Warren, glaring upon his subordinate. " Why do you dare to mention that accursed name in my presence ?"

" Stands corrected, squire, to command ; no offence. But I were a zaying, I do think az we can turn this little game to account."

" So do I. Our band will be mustered with the rest of the Regulators ; when we get beyond the river, my party can detach themselves from the rest, and, assuming the Indian disguise, we may find booty in some far away homestead or plantation, get up a pure alibi, even fall upon some straggling Indians, and show part of our plunder as having been re-snatched from them. That's a scheme to my liking."

" Your honour's the cleverest man az ever made a fortun by a strong hand and a steady brain. But I do zay az the man which could bilk that cute dead-alive feller, Zilas Rye——"

" Will you be hushed, or must I silence your blabbing tongue for ever ?" cried Warren, hoarsely, fiercely clenching his fists.

" I be a nation vool, I be ; stand conwicted," returned Miles, deprecating his master's wrath. " And zhall I zummon the men, your honour ?"

" Aye, do ; but let them be well armed. Tell them that I shall lead them in person."

" Hurray ! every one man on 'em be worthy twenty if your honour be wi' 'em," returned the sturdy rascal, waving his hat as he passed through the door.

" I cannot rest," muttered the arch-villain of our eventful story. " How can I rest ? No, no, no ; it is said, with a jeer, there is ' no rest for the wicked.' I wish I had the gift of second sight, that I could see what is passing in England ! Is the gipsy alive, and at work ? Is the enemy, Silas Rye, at liberty ? Where is my son ? To the fiends with them all ! What are they to me ? Surely at last I have found a secure haven, where I may rest in peace. To give the Evil One his due, he has been true to his compact. Like Faustus, during my term I have enjoyed one long run of almost uninterrupted success—enjoyed I said ! ah ! there it lies ; there is no enjoyment in the triumph of wrong—never, never ! Did my triumphs bring me kingdoms, and crown me with laurels ; were I a Buonaparte or a Clive, to win a world for my country, the purple would cover, but it would not wipe out the stain of blood on my soul ; though the selfish who profited by my villanies might encircle my neck with the glittering George and its insignia, instead of twisting my throat with a hempen halter, I should know no peace. ' The worm dieth not,' it dieth not !"

Judge Warren sat down by his costly table that shone with plate and was laden with luxuries.

" Oh ! if the young, whose bold hearts leap to a wild tale of adventure—whose morbid tastes, too grossly pampered, delight in narrations of the bloody and the foul—if they could see the issue of even triumphant wickedness—if some poor scribbler could make them learn this lesson, it might relieve his heart when it sank at the blackness of the story he was penning. When I was at Janiero a while ago, I remember the governor of the city told me how the great Red Raven had come back to him, in spite of every peril, to claim his father's portrait; the noble told me that the dashing pirate blushed and wept like a child when reproved for his courses. No, there is no peace!"

He rose, and walked up and down in a fever of restlessness.

"Here now are three villains. The Boy Pirate, so misguided, lofty-souled, full of high courage, warm generosity, a man of genius, a soul of kindness; but driven, through one false step, to become a criminal. The third, my sneaking son, a mere wolf—had I no sensitiveness, I could not dissimulate so well, my remorse would not be so keen. I murdered my master through ambition, I foully burnt his body to escape detection—the sulphur clung to my heart and soul, I was henceforth anointed for the pit! And oh! what a warning could youth know from what small sources arose such vast miseries. I remember at this moment what made me kill my master; it was the subservient homage of the servants when he first returned home. A cringing bow—I sold my soul for that beastly mockery—and they say it was a harsh word, or a blow, that made the Earl of Frontemore a 'Raven,' and what but a paltry debt impelled my son to become a murderer. Here have we three wretches—the great-hearted Boy Pirate, the strong-minded Harwolf, and his base-natured son—all alike unhappy. But why—why do I play with such thoughts, when I cannot endure them? Away! away remorse and human feeling! I am a devil, and there is nothing but a devil's work before me!"

He snatched up his hat and cloak, and rushed out upon the lawn.

A number of mounted men, daring-looking fellows, armed to the teeth, saluted him with a hearty hurrah.

Harwolf bowed calmly. There was no trace in his face of the ravage the "worm that dieth not" was making in his heart; but the poisoned tooth worked there none the less keenly, implacably.

CHAPTER CXXV.

HARWOLF AND THE REGULATORS IN PURSUIT OF THE INDIANS.

Upon the side of a hill that commanded a fine view of the wide prairie, the Regulators had halted on their march.

Fires were lighted at which the game they had killed was roasting, horses were tethered to the trees, arms piled.

Judge Warren, with his "staff," consisting of Mark Leighton, Miles Thornton, a broad-built, ugly, ruffianly fellow named Rolt, and several of the richest and most influential of the settlers.

They were smoking cigars, or eating and drinking, and lightly talked of the business in hand.

"Wall, I opine, that's more than any one among yer can show, and I thinks as I can claim the honour of 'fust blood,'" said Rolt, laughing discordantly.

The honour—the honour of "first blood!"

The ruffian held out a bunch of feathers, and a blood-dripping scalp of *white* hair."

"Not much honour in killing such an old crow as that, anyhow, mate," returned Leighton, quite disgusted, yet half ashamed to show sympathy for a murdered Indian with white hairs.

"Wall, now I guess as you can't jest objectionate to this yere. If so as there was no old'uns, there couldn't be no young'uns; that's right, judge?"

"Perhaps so, but for all that in your feat there's nothing to brag about," returned Harwolf, coldly.

"Who's a bragging?" cried the rowdy, in a grumbling tone. "A fac' either is or isn't, I guess, and, p'raps, I shall cotch a young un presently, and I'll jest make him eat it."

There was a faint laugh.

"If you are so charitably disposed that you want to afford a meal to the next poor scamp of a Sioux that comes in your way, perhaps you have charity enough not to spoil ours by disgusting remarks," said Warren, lifting his small but glancing grey eyes from the loaf and meat he was cutting with his hunting knife.

"That's right, judge; for my part show me the man that hates an Indian more than Mark Leighton and he'll engage to marry the filthiest squaw in all the wigwams; but, hang it! we go against them as executioners of stern justice, meaning to spare none, but not as beastly hogs to wallow in a slaughter-trough."

"I do zay'ee be'ast right, Master Mark; and I do zay as sech chaps as talk so big has got more wind in their bellows than fire in their sperits," said Miles.

"What! you 'farnal British clod-stumper, do yer mean for to insinuationize at this child? 'cos if yer intentions to rampationate, I'm your coon, stra-anger, o ya-as!"

With this intelligent defiance the rough fellow turned threateningly upon our sturdy though rascally countryman.

"Durn'ee! keep yer hands off, wull'ee!" shouted Miles, fiercely. "Thou'lt find, my boy, my lad, thee hast taken wrong zow by the ear, if thee touches me! I zee where thy owdacious imperance comes from, but dang me if I cares for your bowie knife more nor yer bluster."

"Be quiet, Miles," said Warren, in a tone of command; "there shall be no quarrelling; the first man who begins a brawl shall be lashed hand and foot to the next tree, and I'll put a bullet through his head who dares to release him till such is my pleasure!"

"And I'll uphold your authority, Judge Warren, while I've a foot to stand on," rejoined Mark Leighton, firmly.

"I ain't for concoctionating any rowdy dow," grumbled the Yankee, "but I ain't jest the boy as can stand any sort of 'farnal remarks. I would have yer note that, stra-anger."

A man rushed up the hill.

"Judge, it's incredible! A band of six bare-faced rascals from the Dacotahs' camp are coming with all the bounce in natur' to seek a parley."

"I guess we'll slice 'em into mossels!" said Rolt, starting up rather nervously, and seizing his long rifle.

"Stand to your arms, boys," said Judge Warren; "be prepared for some devilry, but give the chiefs a fair hearing."

"Of the bark of our shooting irons, that's all, judge, for heaven's sake," cried Leighton, impetuously.

"No; boys, form a line; port your arms; so, we're ready for them; keep your eyes open, but your hands still."

"Wall, judge, I du most decidedly protestionate," cried Rolt.

"Sir; you will either obey orders or be treated as a mutineer," returned Warren, in a tone of unquailing sternness.

The men drew up in a line and stood to their arms.

Rolt, Miles, with Mark Leighton and others of the principals, ranged by their leader's side.

Six fine-looking Indians slowly and gravely ascended the hill.

They were dressed in all the picturesque finery of their nation.

Nothing could be more imposing than the array of these warriors of the wilds decked as they were for the war-path.

The Indians were well armed.

They all carried long rifles.

"Let my brother speak; our ears are open," said Warren, in the Iroquois tongue, which he had learned to speak fluently.

A fine young warrior advanced a step.

"Heart of Fire is a great chief," he began, with the invariable preamble; "his enemies cannot breathe when they hear his name; his eye entrances them as the eye of a snake fascinates the cushet in its nest. The great chief of the Dacotahs can do all save one thing—he cannot count the scalps of his enemies; the hand of the great chief is as the falling oak that crushes the dried grass beneath it; the fallen oak rises not again, but Wakomini is like the black thunder-clouds whose fire-arrows are never spent."

After this extremely modest prefatory flourish the orator paused.

His followers uttered a gutteral exclamation of approval.

The Regulators made no observation, and he recommenced.

"The great father of the Dacotahs, whose hunting grounds spread under the whole span of the heavens, and bring forth game more numerous than the stars in the sky, or the flowers in the prairie; whose young men are swifter than the tides of the great river, stronger than the horns of the buffalo, and subtler than gliding snakes; the great chief of the Dacotahs has given words to Wakomini to speak to his pale-faced brothers. Is it good?"

"Let my brother speak."

"The great sachem of the Dacotahs would ask his brothers, the pale-faces, why they have double-tongues? why their hearts are false? whether the great nation shall endure that the Yengeese should seize upon their land, should kill their game, should send their braves with fire-weapons to consume the Iroquois, should send their black robes to speak lies in the ears of the Dacotahs, telling them that their chiefs bring the olive when they carry the hatchet, that they mean peace when they mean war? Let my brother answer; is this good?"

"The Yengeese have but this answer: the great Manitou has given the world to those who are best fit to inhabit it. The Iroquois are not men, but dogs that tear the prey that they find wounded, or can steal by night. The great father of the pale-faces has declared war against the serpent tribes of the Iroquois, and he will not silence the thunder of his fire-weapons unless the Iroquois shall depart beyond the source of the Arkansas, shall give his hunting-grounds to the pale-faces, and deliver Catahaga, the Pawnee-Loup, into their hands."

"Let my brother hear the words of Wakomini. The beavers build their lodges on the banks of the Mississippi; the great streams flow down from the mountains, and the beavers are swept away with their wigwams; the birds make their nest in the branches; the storm-wind rends the trees up by their roots; the racoons nestle in the hollows on the prairie: the fire roars and soares across the wide plains, and their burrows are swept away. The pale-faces are the beavers, the birds, the racoons of the prairie; the Dacotahs are the floods, the winds, and the prairie fires. The name of the Yengeese shall be forgotten when the last of their scalps has withered to dust in the lodges of Wakomini. I have spoken."

With a haughty stride the arrogant young chief strode away, followed by his companions.

Such of the Regulators as could understand the Iroquois laughed heartily.

"Did ever mortal hear such fustian?" cried Leighton, stamping his foot. "One would think these dirty ragamuffins were the true bearers of Jove's thunderbolts. March on, Judge Warren; let us show them who are beavers and who are the big floods. Let us give these squealing racoons a bit of a scorch they prescribe for us. Pah! the ridiculous bombast of these mongrel curs is exasperating. March on!"

"To your death!" said Warren, grimly. "You are too rash, Master Mark. In that wasp's nest, the bush yonder, a single Indian is a match for a score of us; be cautious before one half has fallen to cool with their blood the overheated brains of their fellows. Buy wisdom more cheaply; be prudent from the first, lads—rank and file—stealthily and watchful as creeping jaguars."

"I reckon I'll have another scalp to hang with the old 'un afore we've gone a piece."

"Do you hear, Rolt?"

"Wall, judge, I consider I du; but let me suggestionate."

"I suggestionate that you obey this order—no scalping; the practise is monstrously barbarous, and disgraces any civilized man."

"Wall, judge, I reckon I am as willen as most of 'em to do my partition to the presarvationing of order—oh, ya'as; but if I du get a crack at one of the coons, I shan't stand nice noways as to the way I chalks him, I guess; and as for scalping and tomahawking, there's nothing I likes better than getting to close quarters with the devils and shaking 'em to ribbonation."

"No more palaver," said Leighton, impatiently. "If we can pick our way through the forest we can push across the prairie towards the Arkansas, and we shall reach the river before nightfall."

The men formed in single file.

They wound down the hill.

They crept under the arching trees.

Rolt kept in the rear.

They maintained unbroken silence.

So thick was the wood that the sunbeams could scarce penetrate its fastnesses.

Every now and then a convulsive shudder passed electrically down the living chain as the first man halted.

By some chance Rolfe got behind, and was last in the file.

The blood smearing scalp had not dried; it left its hideous traces on the bushes around.

When the line had passed round a thick citadel of mighty oaks an Indian crawled like an adder from the brake.

He crept cat-like on the trail.

He heeded not the winding footprints, he only regarded the blood.

The line of Regulators crossed a wide brook.

Rolt was about to spring up the bank.

An Indian suddenly leaped into the water.

Rolt fired at random.

A short combat ensued.

Rolt was struck down into the gliding wave by a blow of the Indian's crashing tomahawk. The next instant the savage had leaped back into the thicket —it was Catahaga, the Eagle-Wing!

BLACK RALPH AND HIS VICTIM.

CHAPTER CXXVI.

EVENTS IN ENGLAND—SILAS RYE AND HIS BROTHER—TWO NEW AND IMPORTANT CHARACTERS—A DANGEROUS COMPANION—THE THEATRE—THE BALLET QUEEN—BEHIND THE SCENES—AN EXCITING INTERVIEW—THE ENCHANTRESS.

IT is time that our readers should be made acquainted with the events passing in England. Silas Rye, after his restoration to liberty, soon regained his strength; and having, through the interest of his staunch friend, Lord Hawksbury, obtained a lucrative post in a government office, applied himself steadily to business. Charley had been placed as clerk in a banker's firm.

No. 41.

The boy was now grown to be a fine and handsome youth. His clear dark eyes were bright with cheerfulness, and full of intelligence, and his step of graceful ease and firmness : altogether, a more gifted and promising youth than the former pallid and nervous little invalid could scarcely be found.

Among the numerous clerks in the office where Charles Rye was employed one had gained over him an influence too great to be without danger.

Richard Eagleton was a dashing, handsome, well-bred youth, with an excellent address, and an inestimable amount of self-possession.

With the ingenuousness peculiar to confiding youth, Charles had devoted himself to his artful friend, who, under his apparent frankness, concealed a heart of selfishness and duplicity.

He would often borrow money of his open-handed companion, which he would spend in the most lavish style, and carried off his want of honour in the non-repayment of his debts by an assumption of boundless liberality.

One afternoon, when the office had closed an hour earlier than usual, the two youths sauntered along the busy streets, carelessly talking, and listlessly looking in at shop windows, or inspecting the numerous new buildings in progress in all parts of the prosperous and improving city.

Eagleton looked pale and thoughtful in the intervals of their conversation, and was evidently abstracted, though he strove to be interesting; an effort in which he was never unsuccessful.

Charles noticed this.

"You seem to be under a cloud, Richard; you are not yourself to-day," he said, kindly.

"No," returned his companion, unconsciously sighing; "but a fellow's spirits cannot be always at the same level—they rise and fall like mercury in a weather-glass."

"But I hope there is no chill in the weather to sink them. Richard, you ought to confide in me; is there anything the matter?" said Charles, seriously.

A forced laugh was the only reply.

"Because I get a little anxious when I find you so suddenly changed."

"Charles, do you believe in falling in love?—did you ever fall in love?"

"No," returned the other, ingeniously, "unless it be with little Milly, who used to nurse me when I was such a sickly little chap. I often think that brotherly tenderness I felt for her then would break out into real love if I saw her again; but she has long left London."

"People make a great fuss about 'love.' Of course it is a 'divine passion,' and all that sort of thing; but I can tell you that none are so idiotic, so restless, so tortured as those who are 'smitten'—to be in love, is to be a fool; for if jealousy makes its own food, love brews its own poison!"

This was spoken with pretended carelessness, but with unmistakeable bitterness.

"I understand, Dick; you are enamoured of some one who has deceived you, or from whom you are parted by some barrier—it may even be, whose conduct gives you pain. Tell me all about it."

"No, no. I am so confoundedly disgusted with myself for being so weak. Charley, let this subject drop. I've been bothered lately, and must have some diversion. What do you say; let's make a night of it?"

"So we will," cried the other, with animation. "You shall go home with me, and we will gather in a party of jolly fellows and have some good sport. What say you?"

"No, I'm not sufficiently up to the mark for that. I want to be amused myself, and have no power to amuse others while this stupid fit is on me. Suppose we go to a place of entertainment?"

"If you like; to the opera, for instance," returned Charles, briskly.

"Or, by-the-bye, a good thought—can you play billiards?"

"No, and I don't care much to learn; to be a dexter at making a cannon requires much time; and in these go-a-head days, when so much must be learned by a fellow, if he wants to keep in the van of the marching regiment, there are better ways of spending one's leisure hours than in acquiring perfection in the art of knocking ivory balls about a table."

"You're a jolly fellow, Charley, but rather verdant—just a little soft."

"How's that?"

"Now, don't you think that we should make but poor cheer if our dishes were not rendered inciting and palatable by sauces and spices, and other such condiments?"

"Well, to what does this apply?"

"What is the spice of life?"

"Excitement, you will say."

"Sensation, that's the word; sensation," returned Eagleton.

"I don't like the word. Because thou art virtuous shall there be no more cakes and ale? I don't say there should be any misusing of life's few pleasures; but let us keep to our cakes and ale. Sensation is alcohol, it is possible to make the mind drunk as well as the body."

Eagleton yawned and shook his head.

"Have mercy," he said, laughing, "I am dying with ennui already. Don't bore me to death with your heavy moralities; you ought to give lectures at Exeter Hall. Bye-the-bye, like a fool, I changed my coat this morning, and left my purse behind me. Have you got a sovereign or two in your pocket you could spare till to-morrow?"

"Yes," returned Charles, readily, "as fortune favours I put twenty pounds in my purse, for I thought of buying some photographic apparatus; we will divide the spoil now, and I'll make the purchase some other time."

"You're a brick!" cried Richard, emphatically. "There isn't a kinder fellow in the universe; but now, whither shall we go?"

"Where you please."

"Have you seen Sylvia Volante?"

"What, the new dancer?"

"Yes."

"I have not seen her; they say she is very charming."

"And she loses none of her charms when she leaves the stage; I know her well."

"Is it possible? I have never met with any one connected with the theatrical world."

"That's strange. Shall we go and see her dance to-night, and when the performance is over I will introduce you?"

"I shall be delighted," returned Charles.

They called a cab and drove to the theatre; they occupied the omnibus box.

During the performance of the first piece, which was a trifling farce, Eagleton, with folded arms, his eyes bent vacantly on the stage, sat as inane and unheeding as one of the gilded Muses that adorned the proscenium.

When with the merry clapping of hands, and the stirring murmur of applauding voices, the magic curtain had rolled down upon the apotheosis of the scampish young hero, who had won such measureless bliss by such immeasurable impudence, Eagleton started as one aroused from a deep sleep.

"'How like you this our play?'" said Charles, with a fresh, light laugh.

"Aw, very fair; what do *you* think?" returned his companion, who had no more idea of it's plot than it's author's great grandfather.

"A little more humour in the dialogue, and a little less pantomime in the action would better it, methinks; but I'm no critic, and won't be so graceless as to disparage what has given me the pleasure of a hearty laugh," returned young Rye. "That's a pretty air, isn't it?"

"I hate the squeaking of the wry-necked pipe," cried the other peevishly, "fiddling and piping, and glaring and daubing and spangling. The world is indeed a stage, and life a drama of sensations and situations, where every man plays a false part; nothing is natural, nothing is genuine, or, at least, if ever it is, it soon gets incrusted with the mask or the daubing paint. Oh, I am sick of life altogether!"

With a look of great surprise, Charles turned towards the speaker.

Eagleton's face was haggard and worn by the intensity of the quenchless fire burning at his heart, his brows lowered low over his eyes, and his lip quivered into a curve of scorn.

Charles Rye laid his hand kindly on the shoulder of his friend.

"Richard, I am sure you are doing me a great injustice," he said, smiling, "I am not frightened at your misanthrophy, because I know you are ill-humoured only for the passing hour; but you ought to tell me if there is anything serious that causes your gloominess."

"Serious! nothing is serious—all is a farce!"

"Why, you must be concerned about something very important, or you would never give way to such gloomy thoughts."

"No, I am simply 'blasé.'"

"Say, rather, bilious," replied Charles, with a pleasant laugh. "Come, cheer up, the music has ceased, and our orbs will be blessed with your vision of beauty."

The play was one of those brilliant extravaganzas, which are less indebted for success to the writers than to the painters, costumiers and machinists.

The scene presented a glowing tableau of houris in their resplendent home in the gorgeous sun-land of imagination.

A picturesque and beautiful ballet commenced. When the fair satellites had thrown themselves into grotesque, gay and sparkling constellation, then arose the magnet star.

Simply dressed in her white and misty muslin, a lovely girl tripped from her prismatic car, the strong light flashing mellow on her golden locks, with their simple fillets of pure white rose buds, and the twinkling star shining in the centre of her pale forehead.

With inimitable agility and perfect grace she performed a piquante, swift, and fairy-like dance, and with infinite tact yet naiveté, she curtsied in acknowledgment of the thundrous plaudits which shook the gilded rafters.

Eagleton laid his hand on Charles's arm.

"Is she not very beautiful?" he asked, in a low whisper.

"Yes," gasped Charles; "but she looks a little pale, I think."

"Either confidence in her unaided beauty, or a fear of spoiling her complexion, influences her—she never paints."

The curtain having fallen for the last time, the two young men left the front, and made their way to the stage door of the theatre.

Eagleton entered; he seemed well known, and passed unchallenged.

He made his way through the winding, shabby, dusty, and gas-flaring passages to the green-room. Most of the actors had doffed their gay costumes, and stood in groups conversing in animated tones, or resting on sofas and chairs, haggard and jaded after their night's exertion.

Among those who were still attired in their stage dresses was Sylvia Volante, who was talking merrily with a short, hawk-eyed, Jewish gentleman, richly but showily dressed, and adorned with a heavy gold chain, brilliant scarf pin, and rings of value.

"Sylvia," whispered Eagleton, bowing to the fairy-queen, "I have presumed upon your goodness to introduce a gentleman, who is one of the most devoted of your numberless admirers; receive him kindly, for my sake."

The beauty cast a look of scrutiny from her glorious black eyes upon the young clerk, and held out her soft white hand with a dimply smile of infantile sweetness.

She spoke a few words in a gentle tone, with the most charming tinge of foreign accent.

Charles tried to answer, but his voice grew husky, his cheek flushed, and his heart beat almost audibly; he made a few common-place remarks in a confused and bashful manner.

As the siren looked upon his comely form, his fresh ingenuous face, she felt his palm quiver in her own, her eyes widened, and a little sigh of pleasure escaped her.

Eagleton, who was narrowly watching her, started, and bit his lip at this slight display of emotion.

Sylvia tripped from the room.

Charles was introduced to several of the leading actors. They seemed to him free-hearted, good-natured fellows, with a large share of vanity, and some affectation, which displayed itself in the studied distinctness, impressive emphasis, and rolling smoothness of their "delivery," yet withal most genial and pleasing companions.

Charles was so absorbed in an interesting colloquy with a dramatic author of note to whom he was presented, that he did not notice that his friend Eagleton had left the green-room directly after the departure of Sylvia Volante.

The dancer had retired to her dressing-room, in order to divest herself of her fanciful attire, and Eagleton awaited her return in one of the numerous little ante-rooms in the labyrinth of passages.

He paced about excitedly, muttering to himself, and continually passing his shaking fingers through his hair.

He drew a pocket-book from his breast, and stood beneath the bracket gas-lamp, nervously turning over a bundle of paper slips.

The door opened.

Sylvia Volante swept in.

She was very neatly dressed, and lost none of her loveliness by the change in her attire.

She stepped quickly to Eagleton's side, and laying her hand on his arm, said in a low eager whisper—

"Is it he?"

"Yes, Sylvia, yes," returned the other quickly. "You have a difficult part to play. He is one of those bigots who have 'principles' forsooth, 'principles' in this world of knaves. He is not exactly a fool; I wish he were, we could then manage him more easily. Well, you will sift him, I know. I have ample confidence in your keenness. I don't want him to suffer, if I can help it, but I must have a confederate, a partner to play his cards with me; and he is the best adapted to my purpose of all the clerks in our office. Things look dangerous! All is so calm now, so deadly calm! And it is the dead calm that presages the storm! Yes, we shall find him very useful."

Sylvia Volante gave a low wail, and raised her hand to her brow.

"What is the matter now? What woman's folly induces you to sigh over this young pigeon when you have shown yourself so heartless, so cruel to others?"

"Ah, Richard, he is such a youth; he is still a youth; so simple, so trusting, so happy. For him there is friendship. He has not yet seen his nearest and dearest eager to grasp all, to sacrifice his best interests to their own selfish ends, to clutch at that he would give them so freely; and he has not learned that love is a stormy passion without worth. He is young in heart, and he *believes!*"

"Pish, I've no patience! Where is the French artist that poisoned himself because you raised him to the highest pinnacle of hope, and pushed him down without remorse—laughed at his ruin—where is he?"

"He was a selfish knave! He destroyed a life embittered by the pangs of wounded vanity! He only loved me because he thought me beautiful, and likely to become rich! Did I not affect to love him? and when he believed that I was all his own how did he treat me? Slighted me, boasted of his triumph with a sneer of vain-glory. This youth ——"

"I see you are impressed with sympathy. You are inclined to love him."

"No, my heart is quite dead; if a spark of nature revives in it I will stamp it out, for I will be no more consumed by the fire of jealousy and anguish," cried Sylvia, with intense fierceness.

"Very good; well, you must charm him with your subtlest witcheries. I tell you, Sylvia, you must subdue him into abject obedience, you must ——"

"Oh, Richard, I have been a good girl to you," said the dancer, laying her hand on his, and looking pleadingly into his eyes, "grant me this little favour—spare this boy."

"My God! it is impossible!" he cried, in great excitement. "Look, Sylvia, here is a note that was sent from one of our depositors, who is about to draw twelve thousand pounds; our money is all out, the partners are wildly, or, at least, most extensively, speculating."

"Is there no one else will serve your purpose?"

"Heaven and earth! can you be such a fool, Sylvia? I repeat that this youth is patronised by Lord Hawksbury, is the cleverest and most confidential clerk in the office——"

"Well, do not talk to me of it now; only tell me, will he suffer much? loss of reputation? forfeiture of his appointment? Yes—but will he be punished by the law?—will he become a——I choke to think of it."

"There is the very strength of my argument. My own peril is imminent. Would you prefer my death to his temporary humiliation? for I should kill myself were a discovery to take place. He has influential friends; I have none but myself on whom to depend."

"And yet, I entreat you, Richard, choose another victim."

"Ten thousand hot curses! There is in the world no such thing as gratitude; be the name expunged from the dictionary!"

"I am not ungrateful, Richard, but——"

"But! Sylvia, I was travelling on a lone heath, in a rough and remote part of the country, amid villages little better than pahs or wigwams, among a population rude as savages. I found you; you were the child-slave of a couple of human brutes; daily exhibited, in the scantiest clothing, to the vilest audience, as a dancer, on a showman's caravan; you were starved and beaten; the softest words you heard were coupled with curses. I took pity on you because you were gifted and beautiful; I was influenced by a motive, then strong in my breast, but which I have since abjured for ever—disinterested kindness! I paid almost my last shilling to ensure your liberty. Of your own free will you swore on your knees to be mine, to love and to serve me till death. On my part, I vowed to shield, to respect, to advance you. I have well kept my promise—a queen might envy you—you are caressed and admired, the breath of applause rises like incense around you; I have exacted nothing from you. Fair and prosperous as you are, I have never looked for more than sisterly affection; I have always treated you with honour—"

"Not always, Richard;" she answered, blushing crimson.

"Pshaw! I am hot and you are cold. I thought you had forgiven."

"I have, indeed."

"Well, then, of what do you complain?"

"Of nothing; you are very good."

"And you are very false, and base, and ungrateful."

"No, no."

"You are so. Is it a light thing? My life hangs on this chance, for I tell you that rather than wear shackles, and eat the bread of penal slavery, I would burn myself alive! Why, it is monstrous! This young upstart—I like the fellow, I mean him no harm—a man can work the deliverance of another better than his own—take off another's chains when he cannot break his own; if the burden is bound on his back I can unbind it. So it must be, I tell you; he is a stranger, and I have heard him say that women are weak as water—that there is no spell in a bright eye that could charm him; heard him boast that he can affect ingenuous frankness to the life—can deceive the wariest woman that ever sought to conquer wayward man."

"Is that true, Richard?"

"True! Am I given to lying? There's a little girl who was kind to him when his brother was a beggared adventurer, and himself an invalid, almost a cripple. You have no penetration."

"I will have no mercy on him," said the girl, clenching her fingers together, and speaking hoarsely.

"Well said; he will have none for you; though I can't conceive it possible that you could be enamoured of such a shallow boy; you that have refused coronets."

"And this girl; does she love him, think you?"

"Yes, as you love him whose name I must not mention, and she pines like a withering flower whose stem is broken."

"The villain!"

"Well, I don't say so; I have nothing to do with men's love affairs. He has been tolerably fair with me; I like him; but will you prefer such a fellow to me, who have, and do, and will for ever serve you as truly as if you were my sister?"

"I will ruin him."

"There shall be no need; only don't ruin your best friend in me; be reasonable."

"I will; I will gain such power over this young ingrate that I shall be able to mould him to anything."

"I doubt it, Sylvia. His simpleness seems so genuine he will deceive you," returned the crafty rascal, smoothing his moustache, and assuming a thoughtful air.

"Deceive me!"

Sylvia laughed low and musically.

"I grant you are irresistible; but they are all gone, and the fireman is going his rounds to put out the lights. Let's go."

Sylvia touched his proffered arm, and he lead her into the corridor.

"Oh, Richard," she murmured, "if you were free!"

"And so I shall be if you will sway this fellow."

"Exclusive of that, I will play with him like a tigress. If he has been false, as you say, I will avenge her whom he slighted."

Charles Rye at this moment advanced.

"I thought you were lost, Eagleton," he said. "I have been roaming this maze, much to the disgust of the impatient attendants, who are anxious to get home."

"We have waited for you. I would not let Sylvia leave the theatre without allowing you the pleasure of saluting her."

"You, you are very kind," muttered the youth, blushing, and qualming at his awkwardness.

Sylvia did not speak.

She fixed her soft eyes on the ground and sighed as if unconsciously, started, and blushed.

"Well, there isn't room here for such a phalanx," said Eagleton, laughing. "I will be usher; do you take advantage of the length of the corridor to make your adieux, Master Charley."

With this he moved on before them.

The young clerk made several efforts to speak. At last he murmured, nervously,

"You—you are rather fatigued, mademoiselle."

"Very," returned Sylvia, in a languishing tone. "Weary at heart. I am sick of the world—of my profession. But—but why do I speak thus to you? Only that you don't belong to our world. From another sphere you can look on and sympathise with a poor girl who is bound to a life for which she has so much distaste."

"Yet, mademoiselle, such richly-deserved adulation——"

"Adulation is not—well—friendship," returned the girl. She paused and laughed gaily. "You must not judge us harshly. We actresses are children of nature, or we could not portray her so well."

She fixed her eyes upon him, and bit her lip to repress the curl of scorn that was arching it.

Charles did not know how to answer.

"But," he said, "when one's path is strewn with laurels——"

"Strew the stage with wreaths and it is not home!" returned the girl with naïve frankness; "and yet—but there are some things we cannot command."

They reached the door.

Sylvia drew her mantle around her fair shoulders as they passed into the cold air.

A small carriage awaited her.

Charles gallantly handed her in.

"I shall—shall have the delight, mademoiselle, I fervently trust, of seeing you again," stammered the poor youth, already deeply smitten.

"Perhaps," returned the girl languidly, and lightly pressing his hand.

As the brougham moved away she bent her head coldly, her cheek warmly glowing.

The youth stood rooted to the spot in strange bewilderment.

Eagleton clapped him on the shoulder.

"By Jove, how I envy your luck!" he exclaimed, in a tone of deep heartiness.

"Eh—why?" said Charles, starting.

"Is not Sylvia Volante a ravishing creature?"

"I never saw any other so lovely."

"And she is so discreet—so pure; it is notorious that there was never one in her position who has more completely disarmed all slander."

"I have always heard so."

"And imagine—why she has refused the most brilliant offers."

"So I have learned."

"Well, you are the luckiest dog."

"Why?"

"Are you so obtuse?—did you not perceive?"

"That she is most charming."

"True; 'ah, I suppose a little prejudice—she is a danseuse."

"Prejudice; I—do you mean—am I in love with her?"

"Yes."

"Oh, Richard, I never loved till now! I thought love a mere sentiment; I did not think that I could be so enthralled; but I can never express my new and powerful emotion. Do not laugh at me."

"By Jove, let them laugh that win. She has caused many a heart to ache, I can tell you, and there are not a few who would laugh—aye, with joy—to be in your place; the coldest Dian, and yet at your first meeting—well, love certainly springs at first sight."

"You think she does not despise me?"

"Despise you, how soft you are! But listen, Charley; I have known Sylvia since she was a child, I am, as it were, a brother to her, and unless your intent is honourable—"

"Honourable, there is no happiness I can dream of so great as the bliss of having one so good and beautiful for my wife; but I dare not dream of such joy."

"Well, I apologise, but I'm a man of the world."

"Confound the world!" cried the youth, impetuously."

Eagleton laughed.

"Now, Charley, if I had been born so fortunate I would stand on my good luck and lay double my wager on the coming event at the Derby."

He would have found that hard, as he had risked his last sixpence, and thrice the amount of his own fortune to boot.

CHAPTER CXXVII.

DANIEL HARWOLF AND HIS NEW GANG—THE PIRATES SUCCESSES — THE TREASURE CAVE —THE CONVICT'S BROTHER— THE VICTIMS ASHORE— THE HUNT— CAPTURE OF THE SKIPPER'S DAUGHTER—BOUND AND ALONE— A WRESTLE WITH THE CORDS—THE CAVERNOUS PASSAGE—DIEGO DETECTED—HIDEOUS CRUELTY — DIABOLIC CRIMES OF DASHING ROBBERS.

DANIEL HARWOLF once more walked the deck as commander of a pirate vessel.

Too horrible for relation are the numerous atrocities of this cruel and dastardly villain and his fiendish band.

The vessel he had taken on the island he had named the "Sea-Wolf;" the convict transport, he called the "Shark."

The "Sea-Wolf" he gave in command to Wardlaw, while he reigned the fell tyrant of the larger ship.

His first cruise under these new auspices had been very successful.

He had taken, burnt and sunk several small craft, and had overhauled a large and richly-laden Indiaman: the crews of all these vessels had been ruthlessly butchered.

Almost sinking beneath their costly freights, the pirate ships had put into a lonely creek in an uninhabited island, where they landed the greater part of their ill-gotten cargoes, which were stowed away in an immense cavern at the foot of a volcanic mountain that lifted its blue and smoking summit at a little distance from the shore, and upon the banks of a broad but shallow river.

Among the crew on board the Indiaman was one man who had been saved, and transferred to the "Shark."

He had been recognised by one of the escaped convicts as his brother, and had been spared by Harwolf at the urgent entreaty of his respectable relation.

His name was Diego; and, from the first, he had been looked upon with no favourable eye by his new master.

The oaths had been administered to him, and he appeared contented with his new mode of life.

He was a quiet, orderly fellow, a good seaman, who did his duty well and kept himself, as much as possible, aloof from the rest of the men.

He took no active part in the scenes of massacre, of such frequent occurence, and appeared to succumb to stern necessity, and to obey the orders of the pirate chief only from a conviction that it was useless to resist.

This man came in collision with the wretch whom he served, for an act of humanity, and brought upon himself a punishment so terrible, that he felt the effects of it for the remainder of his life, and dated from its infliction the long term during which he pursued, unwaveringly, and through deadly dangers and unutterable sufferings, his purpose of revenge.

The crew of the merchantman that the pirates had taken made their escape in a boat to the island.

Harwolf's gang had pursued them thither.

The boats from the "Shark" landed at dead of night.

Harwolf himself, Blake, the Spaniard Corderes, and ten men, formed the party.

The wretches were stealing along the beach.

They examined the rocks and the rifts in the side of the stony ridges that rose in tables along the shore.

These ridges were layers of petrified lava, which had been secreted in former ages.

It was a wild and gusty night.

At sundown the two ships had stood off to sea.

This manœuvre was effected in order to deceive the victims.

It had answered its purpose thus far.

The fugitives consisted of four men and a girl. One man as sentinel was considered as being guard sufficient. The remainder of the poor fellows went to sleep.

They had chosen as their refuge a large cave among the inland hills.

Their citadel was well fortified by nature.

The ascent was narrow and precipitous.

Only one man could mount at a time.

The entrance of the cavern was protected by a huge mass of rock.

The three slumberers lay stretched on the ground beside the smouldering logs of the fire they had kindled to cook the sea-fowl they had killed and to dry their clothes, which had been drenched by a heavy wave, which struck their boat as they were putting in shore.

The third man, who was on watch, stood alert at the mouth of the cave, a pistol in each hand.

They anticipated no immediate danger.

They had discovered that the island, which was small, was entirely without inhabitants.

Oppressed by care and terror, the poor girl, who was the skipper's daughter, had given way to her restlessness, and the sentinel complaining of thirst, she had offered to carry a small bowl, which they had used to bale the boat, to a spring near the beach for water.

The man at first refused his consent, but at length suffered her to go, having entreated her not to wander beyond the spring.

The vessel which they had deserted was employed at a station at one of the islands to carry provisions aboard the various ships that cruised among the islands. It was also the pilot-boat of the station, and her father, who was an Englishman, was accustomed to navigate large ships through the more difficult roadsteads.

The girl took the bowl in her hand, and walked boldly from the cave.

She was a pretty, healthy-looking, dark-eyed, fresh, and buxom lass; had been inured from her girlhood to hardships and danger.

She was her father's constant companion, and he, though a rough, was a kindly fellow, and deeply attached to Esther, who was his only child.

To return to the pirates.

"Cap'en," said Blake, as they crept under the shade of the rocks, "why did you bring that skunk, Diego?"

"I know he's a craven," returned Harwolf, "and I suspect he's disaffected—that's the reason I always keep him in tow."

"I thought we were all to be pirates aboard," grumbled the ill-conditioned fellow. "That milksop is only fit to nurse babies."

"I'll give him lessons in rougher work."

"That's right. Shiver me if it don't make me squeamish to see him slinking about the deck, like a rat in an owl's cage."

"Hi, sir—you!" cried Harwolf, harshly, addressing the subject of their conversation.

"Aye, senor," responded the young Spaniard, in an humble tone.

"Did you ever cut a throat?"

"In battle—yes, senor."

"In battle, dam'me, sir; but answer me: Are you a pirate or a cursed spy?"

"I'm not a spy, senor."

"Ha! You wouldn't betray us if you had the chance?"

"No, senor."

"And why not? Tell me why not."

"I respect my oath."

"As much as the devil did the fat friar; but come, sir, you would not betray us because you have sworn to be true to us?"

"Yes, senor."

"And that's your reason, is it?"

"It is."

"And look you, sir, what a love of a reason it is; of course, you owe me nothing."

"Yes, senor, fidelity."

"Fidelity, and what else?"

"Service."

"I'm glad you own that—obedience, I hope."

"Yes, senor, obedience."

"That's a charity; if I put you under orders to do distasteful work you must do it?"

The man did not reply.

"Well, I shall test your obedience, my hearty; when there's any butchering to be done, which must happen in our trade, I shall make you my executioner. That's a high office, in some states the highest; give thanks for promotion! And now, you snivelling varlet, I ask you, once more, do you owe me nothing? Shall I remind you of your debt by taking acquitance of the loan with this?"

The ruffian drew his pistol.

"You will not take my worthless life, senor, which you have promised to spare?"

"You ungrateful beast; is it nothing that you have fed with us, fought with us, shared with us?—tell me that?"

"Senor, I am for ever obliged to you; you have spared my life."

"Well, my beauty, I'd advise you to show your

gratitude by implicit obedience in carrying out my orders."

"You shall have no cause to complain of me."

"You are wise if you keep your word then, Diego; trust me, I don't like the look of you."

"Hist!"

"What now, Blake?"

"Back!" cried Corderes. "Diavolos, senor, the fun begins; there's the woman!"

"Has she seen us?"

"No."

"Silence, then!"

The villains lurked behind a rock.

"Hark! she is singing."

"The Mariner's hymn; she is Spanish," said Corderes, crossing himself.

Diego and the rest of the Spaniards imitated the motion.

Harwolf scowled on them with a sneer.

"There's an old fable of the Kite and the Nightingale," he said. "We shall have to stop the pretty bird's piping."

The girl now passed quite close.

She was singing a plaintive melody very popular among Spanish sailors.

She had lived so long upon the islands that she was quite as well acquainted with the language spoken among the few inhabitants who peopled them as with her own.

"Where are you, Diego?" said the chief of the pirates.

"At hand, sir," replied the man, timidly.

"Well, we shall have work for you presently."

Diego shuddered.

"She has gone to the spring for water, senor," whispered Corderes.

"Cap'en?"

"What do you want, Blake?"

"Do you mean to spare the wench?"

"I don't know yet; but she had better not be cantankerous. I shouldn't mind having one woman aboard, and she seems as bold as an hawk."

"That's a good sign, cap'en."

"Yes; it is plain the fools believed that the 'Shark' has sculled off."

"She returns," whispered Blake.

"Lie close, men."

The girl had drank from the fountain, and then filled the bowl.

She drew near.

"Not till she has passed. If she screams she will be heard by the rest who are, of course, not far away, they will then take to some hole or burrow, and give us a power of trouble."

"Right, cap'en."

"Let one of you—Corderes, you are most eligible—creep softly and silently along the rocks and rush out upon the girl. Gag her and hold her fast."

The bandit grinned, and tapped the top of his long knife.

"If she scream, not otherwise," said Harwolf, coolly.

The Spaniard stole off.

The girl walked on unconsciously.

She still kept wailing her plaintive strain.

"Now, sir, you follow him; your life depends upon your skill and discretion in managing this trifling affair," said Harwolf to Diego.

The man made no answer, but crept after the other.

He arrived in time to see Corderes spring upon the girl, and grip her round the throat.

He hurled her down.

She bit his hand and uttered a wild shriek.

In an instant the knife of the brutal rascal flashed in the pale moonlight.

Diego caught his wrist.

The girl lay quite still.

She was in a deep swoon.

"Malraya!" hissed the foiled assassin. "What do you mean?—why do you interfere?"

"The captain, Corderes—he may be angry if you kill her."

"But she screamed."

"It is too late to help that now, she is either dead or has fainted. She will give us no more trouble."

Harwolf and the men came up.

"Corderes, you managed this business clumsily."

"Pardon, senor, it was done quickly, and that is all you can expect, as you ordered me not to use my fang. Pretty and white as her teeth look, I can tell you they're sharp. Look out when she kisses you."

"Ha! I am glad you haven't knifed her. It's her own fault if she gets bad treatment; but put a gag in her mouth."

This was done.

"And now bring her along to the large cave we were exploring just now. I don't think she is dead."

The ruffians carried their unconscious victim to a large cave on the shore.

A torch was lighted and held aloft by one of the pirates.

"Corderes, you are a poor attendant for a fair lady," said Harwolf, leering. "You have tied the gag so tightly the lass will strangle."

Corderes removed it.

"Give me the brandy flask," said Harwolf.

A man presented one.

The pirate chief knelt down and raised the girl's drooping head upon his knee.

He placed the flask to her lips.

Soon she revived.

In an instant she understood her position.

It was not to be easily mistaken.

Several of the most atrocious-looking criminals stood about her in a circle.

The red torchlight flared through the surrounding vault of darkness, and fitfully lit up faces so diabolic in their evil expression that they could not be gazed on without a shudder.

She uttered a pealing shriek.

The hollow cavern rang horribly.

Harwolf placed his hand over her mouth.

He gagged her once more.

"Diego?" he called.

The young Spaniard approached, tremblingly.

Harwolf rose.

He had lifted the girl in his arms.

"Bring a rope," he said.

A long piece of cord was given him.

He handed it to the Spaniard.

"Now, Diego, I shall hold you responsible for this girl's safe custody. Bind her to that rock."

Diego did so.

The girl looked at him appealingly.

He bound her to the rock with stern calmness.

"And now let us away. We are not too many for the work in hand, for the fellows may be armed, and take us at disadvantage. Diego, is your prisoner safe?"

"Yes, senor."

"Then come with us. You will be wanted."

"First, senor, let me take a last look at the fastenings."

He drew close to the girl.

He doubled a knot.

He felt the strength of the cord.

"Senor," he said, "lest anything happen, better try the strength of the knots, and bear me witness that I have done my best."

"Go to the devil! if she escape, you won't, that's all," growled the brutal pirate.

"Senor, better not be too hard on Diego; his brother is a dangerous man, and the Spaniard will take offence."

Harwolf frowned.

Nevertheless, he strode across the cavern, and tried the strength of the bonds.

"Good!" he said, curtly. "You had better keep in my sight till we go on board."

"Muy ben, senor," replied the Spaniard.

He gave a last tug at the rope, and among the twistings where they crossed her wrists, he slipped *a knife!*

The pirates then left the cavern.

"Two of you stay here, and shoot any one who tries to make his exit or his entry. I have hitherto been unlucky with my beauty-prizes, but this one I am resolved to secure. Heave a-head, to unburrow these rabbits. An extra glass of grog all round, if they're taken before the tide falls, and a gold doubloon to him who first sights them."

Esther was left alone, bound, and in darkness.

She had heard the pirate's final orders to his men.

She knew that the entrance was guarded by vigilant sentinels.

And, even though the knife was within her grasp, she doubted whether she could use it.

At any moment the pirates on guard without might enter to see if she were still in safe keeping.

The gag in her mouth half stifled her.

Her heart throbbed wildly.

She writhed and struggled with the cords till the blood started from her wrists.

Agony of agonies! the knife was slipping from her hold!

She caught it on her knees.

With a terrible effort she managed to stoop low enough to clutch it.

The rope strained, and the blood checked in its passage through her veins caused her arms to swell almost to bursting.

A heavy tramp was heard.

The flare of a torch.

For the moment it was well that her utterance was stopped by the gag in her mouth, or she would have betrayed herself by an irrepressible scream.

It was one of the pirate sentinels.

The man held the torch at arm's length, and shaded its glare with his left hand.

He was a fierce and thick-bearded fellow.

His belt glittered with deadly weapons.

She closed her eyes, threw back her head, and feigned unconsciousness.

Through her fringing lashes she beheld the pirate looking in her pale face gloomily, as she thought, half pityingly.

After a dreadful moment had passed he turned away.

His heavy tramp roared through the dark hollow, and the echoes swam round with bell-like detonation for some moments after he had left the cave.

She renewed the battle with her bonds.

She contrived to get the knife's edge across the rope.

By pressing with her side against the rock she succeeded in cutting through the thick cord.

She was free.

She laid the knife down at the top of the stone, while she disentangled herself of the impeding but no longer restraining ropes.

She supported herself for a moment, for she was dizzy and faint from the exertion, upon the top of the stone.

She touched the knife.

It fell with a loud clatter.

She drooped against the rock.

She quickly gathered the ropes round her waist and arms.

The pirate in great alarm rushed into the cavern, torch in hand.

But the girl still remained motionless.

He turned his attention from her, and sought to discover some other source from whence the sound might proceed.

He walked round the cavern.

The sputtering blaze of the firebrand distinctly revealed every corner and crevice in the rock.

By a lucky chance he started a little animal of the rat species, but larger than the common sort.

As the frightened creature scampered along a ledge of the rock several loose pebbles rattled down.

Ascribing the former noise to the same cause as that which produced the present, the pirate was satisfied; and having cast a look at the seemingly insensible girl, he growled out a fearful oath in execration of Harwolf and his comrades for their delay, and once more stalked back to his post.

Once more the girl was alone.

She started away from the rock.

She was unbound, but not free.

What hope had she of freedom?

The entrance of the cave was guarded by inexorable villains.

They would kill her if she attempted to pass.

There might be another outlet.

It was unlikely.

The pirates had been long away on their mission of blood.

They would doubtless return directly.

She would assuredly be retaken.

The knife!

The generous fellow she could see, by the treatment he had received, was no favourite.

The knife would be found.

He would be ill-used.

Perhaps murdered!

He should not suffer for her.

Yet she would not part with the weapon.

It might be her last resource.

She might plunge it into her own heart, and by a speedy death, escape a worse horror.

She concealed it in the sleeve of her dress.

She moved swiftly and as noiselessly as possible round the cavern.

She was in utter darkness.

She felt along the rocky wall.

The support abruptly ceased, and she stumbled forward.

She was still in deepest darkness.

She cautiously pursued her way.

She was conscious that her course had diverged.

Was it not possible that she had lost her way, and would wander till overtaken by hunger and fatigue, she should sink hopelessly in those drear and dread subterranean abodes?

More than once she had trodden upon some slimy crawling things, and would have shrieked her terror, but that the gag in her mouth from time to time admonished her.

As she stumbled painfully along, every moment pausing to listen, her steps were stayed by the rising of a sudden, loud, and hideous moan.

Her heart froze in her bosom; her hair seemed to stir; her limbs were violently convulsed with terror.

She leaned against the rock to hearken.

Still down the dreary vaulted rockway was borne that awful sound, rising and falling—now fierce, now faint—a moaning or wailing, as if spirits in torment.

It seemed that she had entered the confines of Orcus; that she had passed the boundary of the nether world.

To the end of her life Esther never could come to any conclusion whence proceeded those awful sounds.

Probably it might be the wind driven down the hollow passages, as the tide insidiously swept from the sea, undermining the land's barriers that are not eternal.

Many wild legends of gnomes and mountain spirits have had their origin in such natural causes.

Be the cause of that wild and dismal wailing what it might—were it indeed, the groaning of some rock-bound demon, and not the rushing of wind or water—it could not have been more awful.

She sank down.

After awhile she gathered all her strength.

She rose and pushed forward.

She struck her foot against a stone.

On what slight accident depend the issues of life and death.

That slight circumstance saved her life.

The stone flew forward with a bound.

She heard a dull thudding plash.

She was on the brink of deep water.

Yet it was so dark, she could not see her hand when placed close to her eyes.

She moved along on her hands and knees.

She reached the verge of a deep pool.

This she knew, for she had touched the ground at every inch with her outstretched hand.

Her hand had plunged into ice-cold water.

Her way was stopped by the natural well which spanned the whole width of the passage.

She sat down, stupified with despair.

Still she heard the moaning sound, but now faint and far.

Were the island spirits singing her dirge?

She knew not how time passed.

She had torn the gag from her mouth.

She leaned her cheek on her hand, and burst into passionate weeping.

She seemed to become childish in her musings.

Moved by a strange instinct, she tied the knife to the end of the cord, and sounded the pool.

Though the rope was long, and she added to its length by tearing her scarf into ribbons, and tying the pieces together, she found that her plummet did not reach the bottom.

The pool seemed fathomless.

She resisted the seducement of this strange fascination, for her brain began to whirl.

Strange thoughts arose in her mind.

She felt she was getting crazed with solitude and horror.

Once more she got up, and groped her way along in the palpable gloom.

She paused with a cry of joy, for above her shone a ray of light as from a pale star.

The morning ray had penetrated her dungeon

She clambered up the sides of the slippery cavern, for at this part they sloped like steep banks.

She thrust her hand through the crevice.

She worked with the knife—the pirate's gift—which had already been of such unspeakable service.

To her infinite delight a few stones were loosened.

After an hour's work she contrived to make an opening sufficiently large to admit of her escape.

She found herself, upon emerging, on the side of the mountain.

She clambered to a high spot, which commanded a view of the island.

Taking care to creep among the masses of stone that lay in heaps on the summit of this peak, lest she might be discerned by enemies on land or sea.

The ocean spread around like a girdle.

No sail was in sight.

Every part of the island was visible, but no living thing appeared.

She rushed down into the valley.

As she passed a marshy place, covered with sedge and oziers, a huge vulture rose, flapping his mighty wings, and removed lazily to a spot a few yards hence, where he watched her with his gloating eyes.

His wattles were wet with blood, and his breast stained and smeared with the same mortal red.

The girl advanced a step to place her foot upon the dead body of a man recently and barbarously murdered.

She uttered no cry.

She seemed paralysed by this culmination of horrors.

A few steps further on she found another corpse.

The bodies were those of her father's men.

Wildly she searched all over the island to find her father.

She called, she signalled in vain.

At last she found on the sands the traces of a sharp struggle, and a few paces on her father's hat.

She concluded unhesitatingly that he had been carried off by the pirates.

Her agony was boundless.

Yet in the midst of her grief she felt a passionate yearning for revenge against the monsters who had wrought such fell work.

She ran to the little creek where the boat had been concealed.

THE BLACK NURSE.

To her supreme joy and surprise it had not been molested.

With great trouble she pushed it off into the river. She sprang in, and plying the oars with vigorous hands, the pilot's daughter struggled bravely through the heavy, dashing billows to reach the nearest island, where she hoped to find assistance, and whence she trusted to set the hawks on the flight after the gorged vultures of the sea.

CHAPTER CXXVIII.
A BRUTAL PUNISHMENT.

"I TELL you," cried Harwolf, fiercely stamping on the deck, "that I will not be braved to the teeth for
No. 42.

the good will of every Spanish skunk in South America; the villain shall walk the plank, after he has suffered tortures that shall be a warning to his fellow-mutineers. I defy you!"

"As you will, senor," returned Corderes; "but Diego is my countryman; it is his first offence; let him be tried and severely punished, that's but just; but I say he shall not die!"

"I say he shall not live!"

"Senor, let there be no division between us; we are the stronger, remember that."

"Ah! do you dare me, then? Look to yourself. Bring the scoundrel hither!"

The subject of dispute among the pirate leaders was the penalty that poor Diego should suffer for his humanity to the captive girl.

He had been detected as the conniver at her escape by Harwolf.

The pirate captain had at once discovered the empty sheath swinging by the side of the thoughtless young Spaniard, who, in his excitement, had forgotten to conceal it.

A knot of villanous-looking Spaniards were gathered around Corderes, and they eyed the captain of the " Shark " with no favourable glances.

Some of the Englishmen of the crew, among whom was Blake, a rascal ever foremost in any act of cruelty, dragged the trembling Diego aft to the tyrant.

" Bring here a brazier, some charcoal, and pincers," said Harwolf, his eyes scintillating with the lust of cruelty.

These scenes in the life of a " gallant rover " are every one of them parallels of real events in the lives of some of the most admired and renowned gentlemen freebooters of his gentle class.

The men stared at the monster, but no one ventured to carry out these orders till Blake moved off with a chuckling laugh.

" Aye, aye, cap'en," said the ruffian.

" Holy Maria, senor ! " shrieked the poor wretch, flinging himself on his knees, " as you fear God's vengeance ! "

" Hand him a cross, or one of those royal academies," said Harwolf, pointing to a tawdry picture of a patron saint that hung about the necks of the Spaniards, " for he is about to die."

The scandalised papists groaned, and crossed themselves with horror at the words of this blasphemer.

" Malraya ! " shouted Corderes, whipping out his knife; " Is this being rovers? Ha! Give me back, then, the chain and the hulks. I'd rather serve as convict in the infernal pit than be a slave to this profane villain."

Harwolf quailed; he saw in the faces of his fellow countrymen, that abandoned murderers, thieves, and pirates as they were, there was a limit even to their wickedness.

" Well, to please you, comerado, I will spare his life."

" Muy ben, senor ! " growled Corderes, sheathing his knife.

" Dam'me, cap'en, what do you intend to do with the fellow ? " asked Blake, ferociously.

" I suppose none of these tender-hearted gentlemen object to every seaman's admonisher, the cat-o'-nine-tails ? "

As silence implies consent, the men may be supposed to have consented to the brutal deed which followed.

" Blake, you are boatswain's mate," said Harwolf, with a leer.

He took a cigar from his case and lighted it in the coolest manner.

" And do your duty effectively,"

" Aye, aye, cap'en," said the huge and dastardly rascal, roughly seizing his victim. " How many dozen shall I lay on ? "

" Flog till I cry hold."

It is worse than needless to detail what followed.

Diego was stripped and lashed firmly to the mast.

Long after he had fainted the cruel lash tore the flesh from his livid back, and not till the groans of the Spaniard grew deeper and more menacing did the inhuman wretch command the insensible victim to be carried below and heavily ironed.

CHAPTER CXXIX.

BLACK RALPH THE ROVER.

ESTHER arrived at the island so worn and exhausted that she was not able to proceed on her journey to the station which was situated at the opposite extremity to that on which she had landed, until she had recruited her failing strength by sleep.

The island was large and the soil so rugged and tree-tangled that it was only by a long and toilful day's march that she could arrive at her destination.

She crept into a thick wood.

She lay down upon a bank.

Soon she slept deeply.

Her dreams were terrible; the scenes through which she had passed were presented to her mind with fearful vividness.

The strange moaning in the rocks, the murder of her father's men, the supposed capture of the old pilot himself, her narrow escape from drowning, and dull foreboding, weighed on her heart, and she was possessed, even in her sleep, with a deep conviction that her sorrows were not ended and that she would again fall into the hands of merciless pirates.

She was awakened from her slumbers by gruff laughter.

She started with a scream.

The worst part of her dream had come true.

She was once more in the hands of pirates.

She could not doubt of the character of the rough-looking fellows grouped round, armed as they were, their leader towering like a giant among them with his broad chest, rolling black eyes, and huge black beard.

Quick as thought the dauntless girl snatched the knife from her sleeve.

In another moment she would have driven the gleaming blade straight to her heart.

So tight was the grip fixed upon her wrist that her fingers extended and the knife fell to the ground.

" No, no, my fair Calista; not yet," cried the deep voice of the leader, in laughing tones; " your part has not yet ended; we haven't come to the fifth act yet, my charmer; the curtain has but just rung up; besides, you're not the sort of heroine for a tragedy—not tall enough; you've a sweet face, but not stagy; you're a child of Thalia, fit to play the maddest part in the merriest comedy—rosy, round, and roguish-eyed, with peachy cheeks and cherry lips. Come, my gentle Thisbe, let me keep the knife till you want it to cut off one of my love-locks, which I know you will wear in your breast as a talisman, for I am your true knight and bold corsair.

" ' Oh, fairest of maidens, I come from the sea,
I've a bark that flies swift, and a flag that flies free ;
My good trenchant blade flashes red in the air,
When it mows down the foes of yon gallant corsair.'

" That verse was made in the dog-days, and is, therefore, rank doggrel; the fellow was hanged that made it lest he should infect the community. But now, my love, ' Here on this mole-hill will we sit us down.'

" ' So give me your hand, my sweetest maid,
And tell me all your troubles.' "

With this the fellow threw himself on one knee beside the girl, and took her hand, which he touched with that part of his beard which overhung his mouth like a pent-house thatch.

" Oh, Heaven ! is there no mercy for me ? " cried the poor girl, shrinking from him and raising her eyes that were filling with bitter tears, " you too are —a pirate ! "

" Tut, tut, don't call hard names, it is'nt pretty. Comrades, introduce me."

" Hurrah for Black Ralph the Rover ! " shouted the men, with a boisterous laugh.

" There, my dear, there are no such persons as pirates or highwaymen; people who follow the noble vocation of filching and jugular surgery on land and shore are known among the refined as Rovers and Knights of the Road. For myself,

"'I am a jolly buccaneer——'

"But we'll come to *al fin* with that stave; its first cousin is a donkey-driver's bravura with an accompaniment whose chords are all whip-cords.

"'Clic-clac——'

"It was scored by a dentist with a poor practice, as his last resource; he made his fortune. But you think me mad, don't you? Well, genius and madness are near akin, so I suppose I must plead guilty to the gentle 'impeachment.' What is your name?"

"Oh, sir, I beseech you, release me! If you knew all that I have suffered, even though you sail under the accursed banner of slaughter——"

"Hey, my lass, but I must not have you speak treason against my standard. No, you shall drink health and merry cruising to your gallant rover beneath its black shadow. Ho! Macarthy, there, bring our pretty bunting, and the grog kid, that our sweet Hebe may fill a brimmer of nectar to us Argonauts— us Vultures of the sea!"

The men laughed heartily, and the order being obeyed, Black Ralph waved the sable folds around the girl, while a man proffered her a glass.

She shrunk down in deadly terror.

The fellow forced it into her hand.

"Come, my dear, your prettiest toast; I'm a dragon to be obeyed, but a lamb if you don't thwart me."

"May the pirates who yet possess humanity enough to shield a poor girl die like men on their own deck, and not be hung at the yard arm," said the girl, gravely, just sipping at the cup, and then setting it down with trembling fingers.

The men shouted with laughter.

"Small favour," said Ralph, pouting his lip; "but still a good toast; for could a ranting rover better desire than to fall on his own red deck, his gallant bark blazing to the water's edge, like a hero's funeral pyre, except it be a snug retirement, with rhino-bag well stocked, scatheless and scot free, to spend the rest of his days in peace with a charming bride, for whose admiration he might recount his past adventures, and colour them bright as he pleased.

'What does the rover reck?
Where should the rover fall?
On his own burning deck,
His black flag for his pall.'

"Hurrah! Death and glory! swag and security! And now, lads, let's aboard, for there's work to be done before daybreak to-morrow."

"Oh, sir! kill me, but do not force me away," cried Esther.

"My child, you must learn that obedience is woman's best virtue, and I may add her rarest. Come, don't faint, you have the eye of a hawk, and surely not the heart of a pigeon; you are a fit mate even for the Black Vulture, and we will live as happy as birds in my eyry; but I tell you one puling woman was almost the ruin of me, and you must make amends to me by your kindness."

With this he took Esther's hand, and led her towards the boat.

The girl saw how useless it was to resist, and raising her thoughts heavenward, and resolving that she would take the first opportunity to free herself by death from man's cruelty and persecution, walked quietly by the rover's side, her eyes downcast and streaming with tears.

"Pull off, my jolly hearts!" cried the swaggering Ralph, as he lifted Esther into the stern of the boat, and threw himself at her side.

"To day we shall run down the 'Shark!' or tonight we shall sup with Pluto!"

CHAPTER CXXX.

OSWALD LAMOND'S SUDDEN APPEARANCE AT LEIGHTON HOE — HIS INTERVIEW WITH AGNES STAUNTON, HIS BETROTHED, AND ITS RESULT.

THE Regulators had not yet come in active contact with the redskins.

They had made their camp along the sheltering brow of a long range of hills.

They had learned from a renegade Indian that all the neighbouring bands had consented to accommodate their mutual differences, and band together to make a stout defence against the common enemy.

It was vaguely rumoured that Regan the captain of the Trans-Arcansar Bush-rangers, had joined the savages; it was said that he had even sent a messenger to his gang in order to bring them to the scene of action.

Plunder might be his motive for thus joining the Indians; yet the settlers could scarcely credit that he could be so black a villain as to lead the ruthless savages against his home and family.

The name of Catahaga had become, indeed, a byeword of terror.

It was said that he was now reconciled to his father, the White Pine, and the old chief had sent him fifty Pawnee-Loups to augment the large band of Chippowais braves whom the young chief already commanded.

On both sides an engagement was looked forward to with eagerest expectation.

In the Indians' council there was a strong division of opinion.

The fierce, but noble young chief called Heart of Fire, showed that his name was not inappropriate, for, with burning eloquence, he exhorted the braves to join *en masse*, and by their superior numbers and unequalled valour to crush the accursed pale-faces at one blow.

Catahaga far more discretely advised that they should make victory certain, by having recourse to their native arts of matchless subtlety, and before attempting to crush the enemy, that they should weaken him by cutting off as many of his braves as possible by ambuscade.

He instanced, as an example of what might be done by using Indian guile, his own extraordinary feats.

He counted up the number that had fallen by his hand, and implored the Indians to wage the war according to their native customs, and not to venture a pitched battle in the open field, where they were sure to be worsted.

It was much against the subtle young brave—who well deserved the high post among the allies—it was much against him that he was not a Chippowais.

Heart of Fire was very popular in his own tribe, and neither himself nor his partizans could bear that he should be checked and humbled by one of another and formerly hostile nation.

But many of the old sachems, who had seen much of warfare between the white and the red races, and were greatly impressed by the young Indian's arguments, opposed the violent measures of the Chippowais; so that the parties were divided, the more sensible being on the side of Eagle-Wing; but as the wiser are ever the minority, the Pawnee was much troubled to keep a post from which so many of his colleagues were ever ready to oust him.

Things were in this state beyond the Arkansas.

Larchville, and most of the other villages, were drained of their able men, and the settlers' homes left in an almost defenceless state.

Mark Leighton had returned to Larchville to enroll a fresh band of volunteers, who were expected to join him from a settlement beyond the Red River, which had suffered terribly from the marauding Blackfeet.

Old Leighton, his daughter Agnes, and Mark were seated at supper in a large and handsome room in the spacious comfortable building which had been formed of the spoils of the forest by the settlers' strong arms.

A cheerful fire was burning, and a dapper little negro was attending them, with a tact and agility that would not have dishonoured a Jeames of St. James.

The loud barking of the dogs without, and the merry twang of a bugle were heard.

The party started up from the supper table.

"Strangers at this hour!" cried Ambrose Leighton, starting up. "Perhaps it is an aid-de-camp from our general's head quarters," he added, with a smile, re-seating himself, and edging his chair towards the fire. "Run to the window, Cato, and tell me what sort of customers they seem."

"Iss, mas'r," returned the negro, ducking his woolly head, and then, straight as an arrow, and quite as stiff, he strutted quickly to the window; he started back with a cry such as a nigger alone could give utterance to, and his broad mouth wide open, and his eyes staring wildly, he exclaimed,

"Gorra mighty, massa, berry much 'spec suffin dreffel! 'bout tree tousand darn ranger fellows mounted on all sorts o' horses, they'se jist standing in a row like Jumbo's teef, with no end o' guns neither, massa."

"My volunteers!" cried Mark, with glee.

He was advancing towards the window when the door was opened, and a handsome young fellow, richly dressed, with the neatest and most beautiful moccassins, and a coat of brown velvet, entered the room.

A sword hung by his side, and a pair of pistols gleamed in his broad belt.

"Oswald Lamond!" cried the father, son, and niece, in a single breath.

"Yes, uncle, it's I. I trust that as I so seldom do myself the pleasure of paying you a visit you will not receive me too harshly on such a rare occasion. I have come to you on business,"

"To the devil with this insolent brigand!" roared Mark, snatching his gun from the wall, and rushing towards the bush-ranger.

Agnes threw her arms about her cousin and entreated his forbearance.

The young bush-ranger tapped his bugle, pointed out of the window, and drew his finger several times across his throat to indicate what they might all expect if they attempted to offer him violence.

Old Leighton rose, and fixed a stern glance on his graceless nephew.

He was a fine old man, with all the gracefulness and dignity, ennobled and softened by benevolence, which marked the gentleman of the old school.

The bush-ranger held up his hand and started to his feet.

"Uncle," he said, in a tone not unrespectful, "I anticipate your reproaches, I acknowledge their justice, but at present I cannot spare time to listen to them, for my business brooks of no delay, and I will stand no thwarting."

"Father," cried the fiery Mark, struggling with Agnes for the gun, "stand out of the way, and let me rid the house of this ruffian—the world of this monster."

"Bow-wow! Lay down, Cæsar! Be quiet, Norval!" cried Oswald, with a laugh of contempt. "You call me a ruffian! You are exquisitely chivalrous in making this brutal display of frothy fury before a lady. If your intents are really valorous, I left you my best pair of revolvers, and gave you ample time to learn to use them. I shall feel the greatest pleasure in giving you a chance of demonstrating your improvement, but never again the chance of blazing at me like a pitiful sneak, after I have spared you. A l'outrance our next encounter.

Meanwhile, be quiet, and let me get through my mission."

"Your mission!" said the old man, sadly and sternly. "What has been the dark mission of your detestable life? To bring misery and shame to the hearth where you were fostered—to bring down a blight and a curse on those who have loved and cared for you like true kinsmen. Put down the gun, Mark. I command you," he added, addressing his son. "I trust I shall not have to add to my grief the rebellion of my own children."

Mark threw the gun over his arm, and turned away with a bitter execration, scowling darkly on the bush-ranger.

"And now, Oswald, let our interview be as brief as possible. Are you here to rob the house?"

"Yes, uncle," returned Oswald, "of its fairest ornament. But yet my fixed purpose does not imply robbery, for the treasure I claim is my own, bequeathed me by the dead—irrevocably sworn away to me, and I am sure one who will never dispute my right to the dear possession."

The young bush-ranger rose, and advanced to the side of his cousin Agnes.

Mark Leighton levelled the gun, and would have shot the daring bandit had not the old man interposed.

"I must dispute your claim upon the firmest grounds of right and justice," said the old man, calmly. "When the father of Agnes Staunton betrothed her to you, you were a child, and it was fondly hoped would grow up a worthy man, one who might fulfil the duties of a husband and a father. But it would be an act, not only of grossest inhumanity to your victim, but of wrong to the dead, who would be revolted if he knew what had resulted from a vow made too rashly, and would be the most vehement of opposers to this cruel match if I were to place this pure hand in that hand which is stained with every smear of blood and infamy."

"An oath is an oath," said Oswald, hoarsely. "Your sophistries, uncle, can never cancel its binding power."

"You have cancelled it yourself. You have degraded yourself by your villanies to the level of a wild beast of the forest, whom man thinks it a virtue to hunt to the death. You are excommunicated from the society of honest men—a banned outlaw; you have forfeited every claim to respect or tolerance, and I would rather see my neice and ward in her coffin than united with yourself. I know that you have surrounded the house where you were fostered with your band of brigands. I know that my people being away on the expedition against the Indians, your fiendish 'confederates, I am quite powerless against your worst malice, but I tell you, nephew, that never will my neice accept your vile hand by the consent of Everard Leighton."

The young robber's glance fell.

Something like a sigh escaped him.

He looked up quickly.

"Nevertheless, uncle," he said, "Agnes is of age—she is her own mistress; if she consents to go with me you cannot fairly object to her doing what she pleases."

"If she consents, she is free to go with you; but I have more confidence in her good sense and good feeling than to suppose she would be guilty of anything so criminal," replied the old man, with sternness.

"May I speak with Agnes?" asked Oswald, mildly.

"She is here; you can receive an answer to your suit from her own lips."

"Father, will you endure this insufferable insolence?" cried Mark, in an agony of jealousy and rage.

"Calm yourself, my son; we are wholly in the power of this young serpent. We are beleaguered by his murderous gang, and it will be a satisfaction to me to know how my neice will act in this emergency."

"But she will sacrifice herself for us," muttered the lover, in a tone of anguish.

"Not so. She knows me better. She would rather see me slaughtered before her eyes than break my heart by dishonouring her family," returned Leighton, firmly.

Oswald Lamond advanced respectfully to the side of his lost betrothed.

"Agnes," he said, in a trembling tone, "irrespective of your purpose of accepting or rejecting me, answer me truly—do you love me?"

"Oswald," returned the poor girl, "can I love such a villain?"

"Then you are false!" said the young bush-ranger, drawing himself up with pride and disdain; "false to your own vows, false to the oath of our parents. You have told me that you loved me. Whatever I have been to others, I have been unswervingly true to you; and whatever I have been forced to do by evil impulse or bad usage, you should not change. But my cousin, who is a dastardly hound, and would have drained my heart's blood when I saved his craven life, for your dear sake, he is a more eligible match. He carries on his miserable rascalities in private life, while I defy the world that has used me so vilely. Oh! Agnes, every hour my life is in peril, on every hand I encounter cares, and toils, and dangers, yet amid them all my heart dances buoyantly; but that icy look freezes my very soul."

"Oswald, tell me," said Agnes, in great agitation, "you—do you love me?"

"Can you question my devotion? Oh! Agnes, dearest, that I had a tongue that could utter the emotions of my yearning heart—that I could tell you how dearly, deeply, madly I adore you!"

"And I love you!" replied his cousin with simplicity, placing her hand in his, and looking tenderly with her frank eyes into his handsome face, though her lip quivered with suppressed anguish.

"Do I dream, Agnes? Ah! but you will reject me!"

"No, not if you love me."

"If I love you!"

"Better than all."

"What is there in life comparable with you, my good angel?"

"Are you sure, then, that you prize my love beyond all beside?"

"Everything else is worthless."

"Then take me, Oswald; I am your own, and we shall be so happy."

"Agnes, my beloved, I am wild with joy!"

"And the condition. It is easy, and is in itself a blessing."

"Condition!"

"You will give up all for my love?"

"Humph! yes, indeed my love is boundless; but Agnes——"

"And we shall be so poor, shall suffer so much; but what matters? The cold winds of adversity will only make us cleave closer to each other. I will strive so hard to make you forget the sad past, to incite you to look forward to the happy future with zeal and courage. Oswald, you shall have a wife who will devote herself to your love as an enthusiast to a religion, who will look on you as her lord and her king, and will serve you in all the humility and fervour of love's loyalty."

"And what do you demand of me?"

"Love for love, sacrifice for sacrifice, tenderness for submission, purity for passion."

"Purity! ha, you mean——"

"I mean! Oswald, you know what I mean."

"I am a bush-ranger!"

"Oh, no, no! you were, but you are so no longer; you are my husband, and the husband of Agnes can never be a robber."

"And therefore a—a robber can never be Agnes's husband."

"But the past is past; I have washed out its record with many bitter tears.

"But the present, love; and the future?"

"Your band are without the house; go to them,

resign your command, abjure your wild and wicked life for evermore, and return to us; we will receive you as a dear lost one, happily restored. Or, if these will not open their arms to you, your own wife, Agnes, will go forth and do battle with the world, and will reconcile you to every suffering by intense love."

The young bush-ranger started back.

He looked upon the eager, loving girl with mingled admiration and chagrin.

He struck his breast.

"Agnes," he murmured, "it is impossible; bye and bye it may be practicable, but not now."

"It must be now; there is no time but now; life is now; to-morrow is a myth and a dream. I tell you, Oswald, I love you fondly. I do not blush to own this frankly; we were betrothed in childhood; even had I not loved you by predilection I should have schooled my heart to be faithful to my father's oath; but, so truly as I tell you this, so truly do I swear that unless you at once consent to abandon yon vile gang, surrender your ill-gotten plunder, forsake your base and lawless courses, every link that binds us is shivered—I am lost to you for evermore."

"Pshaw! hear me. Now, are you not a silly unreasonable girl?"

"Are you not a false and heartless villain?" cried Agnes, with passionate disdain. "Oh, Oswald," she added, throwing herself at his feet, "do not cast me off; you will not, you cannot be so cruel."

"Tut, tut, this is vexatious. Agnes, do you know that I should be murdered?"

Agnes rose.

She gazed on her lover with dilated eyes, and a face angelic in its glow of enthusiasm.

"Die!" she exclaimed, "die, Oswald! and I will perish with you; our death may atone for the shameful past. Heaven's mercy is measureless, and in Heaven, dearest, there is no parting!"

"This is romantic, impracticable, darling Agnes," returned the young bush-ranger, averting his glance, his full chest swelling with great emotion.

"Is it romantic to forego the life of a murderous cut-purse?—is it impracticable to live in common honesty?" she cried, with vehemence.

"Agnes, I have reflected; I will not deceive you; it cannot be!"

"Go, then, vile and cruel," sobbed Agnes; "in rending myself from you I cut asunder my heartstrings; but by Him whose justice is as inexorable as his mercy is bounteous, I swear that from henceforth for ever you are nothing to me but a dark memory, that I am lost to you for evermore."

The girl sank into a chair and dropped her forehead on the table, wildly and bitterly weeping.

Mark and her father rushed to her side.

"Uncle, my betrothed has rejected me," said the young bush-ranger, in husky tones, "I therefore resign my claim, but not her hand to Mark Leighton, whom I warn how he forces his attentions upon my lost love, for he shall never lead her to the altar. Mark, look to yourself; I repeat the caution I gave you at our last meeting, your life hangs on a thread that may be snapped at any moment, and in the hour you presume to speak of marriage to Agnes Staunton in that hour you die!"

Oswald bowed haughtily, and turned to leave the room.

"Stay, infernal bandit, coward, assassin!" shouted Mark Leighton; "if you are not a cur, stay till I join you—to-night! this instant!—let me have the chance you offered of proving that, though raging passion once caused me to fail in striking, deep and steady hate will now nerve this hand to kill you; that eternal justice will wing the bullet. Away! you shall not live another hour."

"Yours to command, Bombastes," sneered the bush-ranger, "if shame outface your cowardice, follow me to the wood. Take your last look at these familiars, for, by the hot thunderbolts, Mark Leighton, this time I will kill you!"

Oswald Lamond passed from the room. Mark

would have rushed after him, but the old man stood before the door.

"Stand back, rash boy!" he said sternly. "Do you imagine that if you succeeded in vanquishing this rascal that his band would spare you? can you doubt that yourself and all in this house would be butchered on the instant? Outlaw as he is, Oswald Lamond is our only protector from the violence of his ruthless gang. Shall Agnes be sacrificed to your senseless fury?"

"Let me pass, father, for I am mad, and shall not respect even you," gasped Mark, foaming with passion.

"Agnes, touch the bell, and then come hither," said the old man calmly.

Agnes obeyed.

A number of men, with frightened looks, rushed into the room.

"Can you look on this poor child, and not blush when you think of the danger into which you would recklessly plunge her?" said the old man gravely.

But Mark recked not this rebuke.

He tore down a pair of pistols from the walls, and would have forced his way through the little group.

At a sign from the old man, the whole party quickly left the room.

The door was at once clapped to and doubly locked.

"Maurice," said Leighton to one of his retainers, "you have a gun in your hand; keep watch upon the door. If my son break through and attempt to pass you, shoot him dead; I cannot bring destruction upon you all to gratify his madness."

CHAPTER CXXXI.

THE BUSH-RANGERS.

WHEN Oswald Lamond left the house he mounted a fine black horse that a man was holding at the door, and rode back to his gang.

His band consisted of a number of well-armed and well-mounted ruffians— desperadoes, the scum of every grade of society.

Alike in respect to the sinister expression of countenance which so generally mark men of this sort, they differed very much in dress, statue, and appearance.

Some had even an air of refinement—these were the sons of planters and other wealthy people; they had gamed away or lavished their last dollar, and now sought to recruit their fortunes by robbery— others were the roughest and most brutal-looking rowdies that ever did justice to their evil deeds by evil looks and foul language.

Of course there were few among the wretches who had not at some time or other undergone various sentences of the law, or if not, had only escaped its rigours by flight.

The man second in command to Oswald Lamond offered a strange contrast to the handsome young reprobate.

He was an extremely ugly fellow; tall, lank, his face scarred with a dreadful wound, the gash of a bowie-knife, which he had received in one of his numerous encounters.

He was tall and lank, ungainly and shambling in his motions.

His eyes were small, and deep-set; his hair was matted, and of a dull red colour.

His whole appearance was frightfully repulsive.

Nevertheless, he was a man of some education, had a smooth address, had seen much of life in all its phases, and was well versed in human nature, shrewd, cautious, and brave.

He had been imprisoned for forgery, but had made his escape, and was one of the oldest members of the ferocious gang.

Regan—for by that name Oswald Lamond passed among the men—reined his horse by the side of his lieutenant.

His cheek was hotly flushed, and his beautiful blue eyes sparkled, while his feminine lips were tight-drawn.

"What luck, Captain Regan?" asked the lieutenant, with a smirk. "Where is the bride?"

"In some of the palaces at Washington or New York, comrade," returned the young chief of the bandits, with a constrained laugh, smoothing his moustache. "Fortune is so kind that she will not suffer me to make a fool of myself by throwing myself away on this wench. But we must ride on to the bivouac. I partly expected to meet a rival here—a cursed raff whom I hate worse than a Regulator; though, for that matter, he adds the fact of his being an officer of Harwolf's sham corps to the rest of his offences. Well, I swore to kill him to-night, and I suppose I shall have to be as good as my word."

"And has he challenged you?"

"Yes. But, depend upon it, they will not let him leave the house."

"I see; they think we should take vengeance, if the duel ended in his favour."

"I think that is their notion."

"Not a bad one. And how do you mean to get hold of the fellow?"

"I have not yet determined. But I will make him pay for the injuries I have suffered at his hands."

"Are any of the servants in the house to be trusted?"

"By us, you mean?"

"Yes; are any in your pay?"

"Yes, two."

"Was the swag for them?"

"It was. I paid them a hundred dollars a-piece for doing nothing, and the unconscionable scamps had the impudence to grumble."

"The spies are always bad to deal with."

"The very worst."

"Captain?"

"I listen, Wyld."

"That judge chap, Harwolf."

"Is he to be depended upon? you would ask."

"Just so."

"Poison is poison."

"And would kill the poisoner as soon as his victim."

"You have this man in that speech."

"We shall make our fortunes, captain."

"I hope so; we have a good chance of doing so; plenty of work before us."

"And plenty of risk."

"From what quarter?"

"From head-quarters at New York."

"Stuff! The government is too much absorbed in its own dilemmas to trouble themselves about us."

"Do you think so?"

"I am sure of it."

"Do not make too sure."

"Why what bugbear do you see now?"

"A real bear, and a grizzly, captain."

"You think that a regiment will be sent out to stop our little game."

"I am convinced they will."

"Pshaw! Don't you know that they have legalized the enrolment of those lynching chaps, and that the Regulators are now a part of the police force of America?"

"But this war with the Indians?"

"What has that to do with the matter?"

"The first victory gained by the scamps will spread terror through the state."

"Humph! that's a shrewd thought."

"What shall we do, then? We must use such chances as these—make the Indians a decoy to draw off the strength from the villages, and make the most of the opportunities afforded by their absence."

"So it must be; but I am sorry for the Eagle-Wing, I promised to help him, heart and hand; and he has such a pretty wife!"

Upon the banks of the stream the men had

camped down, gipsy-fashion, and were roasting some heathcocks which they had shot.

They were in number about equal to those with Wyld and Regan.

The bush-rangers got off their horses, which they tied to the trees.

They joined their comrades round the fires, noisily laughing and talking.

They seemed quite at their ease, and did not appear in the least apprehensive of a surprise.

Regan sat himself down beneath a tree, and folding his arms gazed dreamingly before him into vacancy, and seemed to be quite unconscious of all surrounding things.

The lights and shades of many and various emotions swept across his eloquent features.

Wyld had thrown himself down by the side of the youth with a can of drink and some edibles.

He watched his young leader's face with a grim smile.

"Under a cloud, captain?"

"A dark one, one in whose bosom a fiery storm is brewing," returned the captain of bush-rangers, gloomily.

"Time to look scared when it bursts," said Wyld, with a grin, hideously distorted by the gash; "but I know what is the matter, there is but one trouble in the world, captain, that could make you pull such a face as that—it is love."

"Wyld, of all the curses that can befal a man there is none so great and bitter as to be parted from the object of one's first deep love. The worst of us can love, must love; it is an exigence of nature that a man should love. Then, why should not I be in the fashion?"

Wyld laughed heartily.

"Why, indeed; with that pretty face you are the very man that should set the fashion; but how did you fare in your wooing?"

"Rejected."

"Ha! that's wonderful; does not the lady love you then?"

"Doats on me."

"Then what is the matter—parents, friends?"

"She is of age, without parents; what fortune she has is firmly settled upon her."

"She refused you because you are a bush-ranger."

"Exactly so."

"And what did you do?"

"What could I do?"

"That is no answer."

"You know what I did, I left her."

"And I suppose you left as usual with lovers—for ever?"

"Yes."

"Ha! ha!

'I vow he courts me all in vain,
Because—I know he'll come again,
And if I thought he'd take my Never!
I'd run and scream—Oh, yes, for ever!'

"Will you have any more of it?—I'm a dabster at it sometimes."

Regan pitched the can at his head.

Wyld ducked his head and laughed.

"Look you here, captain, I am old in the ways of the world, and I know that a lovelorn swain is not fit for business of any kind much less to play out our high bold game; his mind is always reverting to the 'object.' You must be cured at once."

"How?"

"There is but one cure."

"You think possession."

"Of course. Now, are you sure Miss Leighton loves you?"

"Most passionately."

"Very well, carry her off."

"Ha! but she would never be reconciled to me."

"She never will be if you leave her now."

"She loves me dearly; I could take her to our fastness, keep her from all contact with my rascals, never speak of business, provide her with every comfort, sooth and caress. I love the girl, Wyld, and

you are right, I am but half myself till she is by my side."

Regan started up, and paced about excitedly.

"Yes, it shall be done; I have been a maudlin fool, and I dare say she would love me none the less for the bold stroke."

"She would love you all the better."

"I almost think so; at all events I am determined to do as you say; but there is one thing."

"What is it?"

"She must never come in collision with these fellows."

"Decidedly not; we can manage it without their assistance."

"Yes, I know every inch of the grounds; two of the fellows, as I told you, are in my pay. We will set about it at once."

"Right, you have little time to lose."

"And, therefore, will not waste a minute."

"Now you speak like a man."

"Come, then. I will tell the hands to follow as far as the range of the plantation."

Regan gave his orders.

The men received them in silence.

The captain of the bush-rangers and his assistant returned to Leighton Hoe.

All was still.

The inmates had barricaded themselves in the house.

All was silent around.

It was a bright night, the moon sailed supreme amid the waves of snowy cloudlets, and the wind lingered toying among the leaves of the whispering china trees.

The bush-rangers clambered the fence.

They stole softly into the garden.

They paused beneath a little clump of cedars.

A light was still burning in a little chamber above them.

A flight of steps lead up to a verandah on which the window opened.

Bidding his comrade conceal himself behind the cedars, Oswald Lamond stole softly to the little stair which led to the chamber of his beloved.

CHAPTER CXXXII.

THE ABDUCTION OF AGNES STAUNTON.

AGNES retired to her room immediately after the departure of the captain of the bush-rangers.

She threw herself upon her little bed, and gave way to an uncontrollable flood of grief.

Then she rose, and wearily paced the chamber, wringing her hands in all the agony of utter despair.

She kneeled by the bedside and prayed fervently.

She became more calm.

Seating herself by the window, she watched the star-spangled heavens.

Her thoughts soared upwards, and a sweet peace dawned upon the darkness of her mind.

Her heart was softened by the influence of holy thoughts, and she knew that though she was sowing in such bitterness, she might, nevertheless, reap in abundant joy.

Then she strengthened herself by reflecting on the character of her lover.

She blushed and hated herself that she could spend a moment's thoughts on one so worthless.

Then she recalled his handsome face, his soft tones.

She reflected that he was lawless, but not ruthless, and that with all his faults he had cloven to his love for her.

He was nobler than her cousin Mark, whose violent temper terrified her gentle nature. Terrible as he was, Oswald Lamond was always gentle with her. He had spared the life of Mark, and had met such a base return; he had surrounded the house with his brigands, and yet had parted at a word.

With the inconsistency of love, at one moment she murmured his name almost caressingly, the next wildly reviled it.

She had the book to read, and as she read, the chord of piety was again touched, and her face grew heavenly sweet in its tender resignation.

The night was at its noon, and the moon shone down in all her argent glory from skies that were liquid clear.

She put down the book, drew the curtain across the casement, and was about to retire to rest.

She started, and raised her hand to her snowy, rounded neck with a sudden motion of alarm.

She paused.

She heard the sound of a light step on the path.

She listened.

All was quiet.

The same songster of the night was thrilling the silence with his rich and mellow warbling.

She unbound her hair.

Her heart beat quickly.

She turned her eyes upon the bed with a weary glance.

She knew that sleep would be denied her.

She shuddered at the thoughts that would agonise the long, dead night.

Again the same sound.

Surely it was a step.

She lifted the curtain, and peered through the lattice.

The garden, with its rustling trees and closed flowers, slept peacefully below.

She thought she saw a shadow flitting along the path.

Her nerves were unstrung by her late and violent excitement.

At last the shadow was no longer visible.

It had mingled with the deep shades of the cedar trees.

As she turned from the window she heard a step on the stairs of the verandah.

She moved towards the door of her chamber.

The casement was open.

The young bush-ranger appeared.

He stepped lightly into the room.

He motioned her to be silent.

"Agnes," he said, in a hoarse whisper, so intense that it seemed to tear into her soul, "Agnes, I cannot bear this; I have repented."

The girl flew towards him, but paused and looked searchingly in his face.

"Do not raise an alarm," said the bandit, softly; "or, if you will, I care not, for though I shall be captured, or killed, it matters not, for you have rendered my life worthless by your falseness."

"Falseness!"

"Aye; you are insatiably cruel—you wish to have my life. None ever dared to call me coward; but I am young, and I would live for you, yet nothing but my death will satisfy you."

"Your death! Oswald—your death!"

"I tell you, Agnes, my death!" whispered the young bush-ranger, impatiently. "Will you not believe? Is it not palpable? My comrades have sworn to kill every deserter."

"Just heaven!"

"It was their only resource for preserving the unity of the band. Shall I go to them, and tell them that I am suddenly reformed; that I resign my post as their chieftain, and desert them for ever? What would be my answer? The bullets from a score of rifles—the blades of a dozen bowies! Yet I will go and tell them this, if you command it."

"I—no, no, no!—I am distract! Oh, Oswald, why—why did you come? I hoped and prayed that you might be gone for ever!"

"I will never leave your side, sweet Agnes."

"But you will reform?"

"Yes; if you will give me time."

"Oh, yes; indeed I will," cried the girl, eagerly. "I will resist all importunities of Mark Leighton. I will not listen to my uncle's discouragements. I will wait and wait, so patiently, and you will return soon, and will say, 'Now, Agnes, I am free from all

enmeshing thraldom, let us fly together,' and I will go with you; I will shield you, disguise you; you shall not suffer for past offences; I will be so cunning to conceal you, and we will go to England, and spend together a life of such dear happiness."

"Yes, Agnes; but, meanwhile, you must remain with me."

"With you? Oh, where?"

"I will find you a sanctuary that shall never be polluted by the tread of any of my band. I will cherish you as dear as my eyesight, and soon I shall, as you say, be free from my engagements with these robbers, and we will leave this wretched country for ever."

"No, Oswald, I cannot go with you; but I will pray night and day that you may be strengthened from on high in your hard work of undoing what is done. God bless you! Go at once. In my wild excitement I forget that you are here—here in my chamber. You have ever treated me respectfully, and think of your great peril. Go, fly at once."

"Agnes, I will; but you must go with me."

Oswald Lamond wound his arm round her soft bosom, and drew her towards the window.

"Can you be such a villain?" she exclaimed, with flashing eyes.

"If this be villany, I can; for I cannot live a day unless you are with me."

"Then, miscreant as you are, I spurn, hate and defy you!" cried Agnes, frantically; "I will call assistance, and leave you to your fate without remorse!"

The frightened girl would have uttered a piercing scream but the bush-ranger placed his hand above her mouth.

"You are lovely in your anger, darling Agnes; but we must begone; my future devotion shall make amends for this needful violence."

A face appeared at the window.

So hideous were the features, and wild their expression, that Agnes, who still struggled to drag away the hand of Oswald, cowered down in his arms.

"Captain," said Wyld, in a loud whisper, "haste, haste! we have been seen by the cursed negroes on the plantation; one of them has brought the news to the house. Come, or we shall have the Philistines upon us before we can get to the horses."

The face disappeared.

A loud shout and the clattering of feet were heard within the house.

The door was thrown open.

A gun was fired.

The flash lit the room an instant, and the report shook it to the rafters.

The bullet sped past Oswald's shoulder, passing through the streaming tresses of the fainted Agnes.

It was Mark Leighton who had fired the shot.

Clubbing his musket he rushed upon the bush-ranger with intent to dash him to the ground.

Oswald, however, had levelled a pistol in his face.

Mark Leighton, suddenly seized by a pang of terror, for death seemed to stare him in the face with all its clammy horror, leaped backwards.

"You have had another trial, Master Mark," said Oswald Lamond, in a dry tone, but with glittering eyes, "you have had time to make more improvement, but, as you are incorrigibly a bad shot, you must take the consequence. I told you that this time I would kill you, and I always keep faith with friend or with foe."

Deliberately firing the pistol he leaped out of the window.

Mark Leighton threw up his arms and fell heavily on his face.

A wild chase now began.

A number of negroes intercepted the two robbers, trying to prevent them reaching the horses.

Oswald and Wyld struck right and left with their knives, and the butts of their pistols.

A negro boy had untied one of the horses, and was quickly leading him away.

Oswald aimed at him with his revolver.

He fired.

A PERILOUS POSITION.

The boy gave a hideous scream, clapped his hands to his posterial development, and fell on his back, and then rolled over and over like an india-rubber ball to an indefinite distance.

Wyld ran like the wind till he got within some yards of the horses.

He gave a whistle, and the sagacious creatures trotted to his side.

The captain of the bush-rangers got into the saddle, gently lifting Agnes in his arms.

And now old Leighton and a number of sturdy fellows came rushing from the distant house, armed with firearms.

No. 43.

The plantations rung with a deafening shout, and the bush-rangers dashed out from their covert to cut off the pursuers of their leaders.

They fired a volley, though from random distance, and drove the servants back into the house.

They would have rushed upon the dwelling. have razed it to the ground, and murdered every inmate, but Oswald Lamond blew a short imperative note on his bugle, and the mounted bandits wheeled round, and, with a shout of disappointed rage directed against the planter's house, dashed after their leader through the close-growing trees of the plantation.

CHAPTER CXXXIII.

THE BOY PIRATE DETERMINES UPON OFFERING
HIS SERVICES TO THE HEROIC POLES.

THE Boy Pirate, in accordance with his custom, had renamed, and, as far as possible, disguised the two splendid steam-ships which he had taken so valiantly.

The "Defiance" and the "Avenger," as our hero had respectively called his prizes, were still moored in the narrow roadstead between the islands.

The Boy Pirate was now master of four fine vessels—the two Spanish steam frigates, the "Vulture" and the invincible "Red Raven."

He had surrounded himself by numerous staunch and devoted friends, and had acheived the most unparalleled triumphs by a rare combination of courage and conduct.

Our indulgent readers who have thus far followed the fortunes of our hero will perceive that by the marvellous "good luck" to which some folks are said to be born, Christopher Foundling had won prizes rather from those who had thrown themselves into his way as aggressors than those who were defenceless or unoffending.

What became of the Indiaman?

With a generosity that caused some displeasure amongst his crew, the Boy Pirate restored her to her captain intact, and with all her crew complete, except two desperate fellows who volunteered to join the Ravens and could be induced by no entreaties to change their resolution.

Determined to commence a new and yet more brilliant career, our dashing hero was much elated at the great advantages which he now possessed, and which would enable him to carry out his desperate, yet long cherished design of espousing a righteous cause, abandoned by the great powers for reasons of narrow and selfish policy; the cause of a gallant and oppressed people, to whose hero, John Sobieski, Europe perhaps is indebted for all the blessings of peace and civilization, as that doughty soldier stemmed the advancing torrents of conquering Turks, which then threatened to over-run those countries which now refuse to assist their former champions.

The Boy Pirate beyond hope an outlaw, with no chance of escaping from the death of shame but that which lay in maintaining his independence of the law, resolved that he would offer his sword to the national government of Poland, at that time secretly organizing another, but, alas! ineffectual struggle to free themselves from the hateful yoke of the Cossack.

Who does not sympathise with unhappy Poland? Who that recollects her numerous efforts, her immense sacrifices, the torrents of youthful blood that have been shed, the martyrs to the cause of freedom that have been led to the scaffold or driven in hordes, like cattle, to the dreary, frozen land of Siberia, can withhold their regret that so much of heroism should have been ineffectually expended?

The leading incidents of the last struggle must be fresh in the minds of all our readers; how the design of recruiting the ranks of the Russian army by the forcible abduction of the youth of Poland, precipitated a conflict for which the Polish preparations were scarcely begun; how bands numbering in most instances but a few score of men, for many months successfully held at bay all the available power of their oppressors, often defeating them, when the advantages of arms, discipline and numbers were immensely against them; and at last only succumbing when the other parties to the original unjust partition of the kingdom threw their moral weight into the scale against them.

These are now matters of history. Hereafter

Poland may again exist as a nation, and the Muscovite be driven from the land. Even she, with her immense military power, her ever grasping acquisitiveness, may fall before her internal and almost incurable disorders, and thus expedite the time. May it not be far distant!

But to return to our story.

The crew who had in the first instance taken umbrage at the surrender of the Indiaman had been restored to perfect good humour by their Boy commander, who commented upon the impossibility of manning that vessel, and the expediency of leaving behind them a good name, for they were at present so popular among the inhabitants along the coasts, who had lost but little, and had gained so much by the chivalrous deeds of the fortunate young rover; and they were "shut up," of course, in "measureless content," by a judicious distribution of costly presents on the part of the shrewd old skipper of the Indiaman.

Christopher had convened a grand council of war to determine upon the measures to be taken before venturing on his new expedition, to make a distribution of the crew, and to elect a captain and officers for the several ships.

The council was held in a large tent pitched on the sunny shore of the lovely island off which the pirate fleet was anchored.

At the top of a long camp table our hero sat throned on a barrel, over which the Raven was thrown.

On his right hand sat Old Brierly, Gomez on his left, below them Dick Caffyn, Ross, and the rest of the officers, including Tom Garrod, the loquacious boatswain.

Cassidy, Oakland, Old Macallister, and Edward Leighton, with several others, occupied the end of the table, while near the door, in a graceful group, were four lovely girls, who anxiously watched the proceedings.

Upon a sofa sat the fair and queenly Lilia. The beautiful Ida was reclining at her feet with all the charming negligence that marks the glowing creole, her head pillowed upon Lilia's breast; while the dark-eyed, noble-looking Jewess stood lightly embracing the bonnie Scotch lassie.

Christopher was speaking.

"Comrades, it joys my heart that you should receive so cordially my humble suggestions," he said, cheerily, "and now, since Mr. Brierly resolves to support me on board the 'Avenger' and you have so warmly elected Don Gomez to the command of her consort the 'Defiance,' to whom shall we confide the brave old 'Raven?'"

"Dick Caffyn for ever! Let him skipper the 'Raven!'" shouted the pirates.

The foster-brother of our dauntless hero rose—his face shone with a light of devoted enthusiasm.

"Hearties, it can never be. I am deeply grateful for, exultantly proud of, the honour you confer upon me by these acclamations; but my post is by the side of him whom I glory to regard as my brother, and while Captain Kit astounds the world by his bold deeds I will claim my share in the glory, not as a confederate commander, but as his foster-brother, ever eager to fling away my life for him, to whom, in all manly friendship, I am devoted. You have my answer, hearties, with my deep thanks. Old Brierly and I are the Boy Pirate's rightful retainers, and we will live or die on the same deck with him."

The men huzzaed with heartiest approval.

Lilia rewarded the speaker with a beaming smile, and the Boy Pirate looked on his foster-brother with a glance of mingled affection and remorse.

"Well, comrades, since such is the determination of my brother," he said, "whom I will not attempt by words to thank for his noble devotion, I will propose another candidate, yet not a candidate, for I fear that Cassidy has foresworn our rover life, and that though I assure him that henceforth I remain lawless because I am outlawed—that I will fight for the injured and oppressed, will gain what I can in a good cause, since man must live by bread—yet he will refuse to command the Raven."

Cassidy looked round upon the pirates with a quiet smile, as he calmly rose to address them.

"Messmates, I am a man of few words," he began. "Some fellows make this avowal as a claim to a certain character of bluntness, which I detest, because it is humbug in the guise of sincerity. I am of few words, because I am not eloquent, and so I will put my case to you in a ship-shape, seaman-like style. I am an outlaw, like yourselves; I might tell you by what injustice I was driven to this course; but it is hard to obtain belief in this world of lies, and for a man, whom the law has condemned to plead innocence, is only to expose himself to contempt. I am a pirate, like the rest of you, though I have for ever abjured the black flag, and during the short time I served under it did my best to mitigate the horrors that were perpetrated by that incarnate devil, Daniel Harwolf; yet I am a pirate—it is useless for the fox to plead repentance, he will not be spared —if I am taken I shall be hanged. Now, messmates, I am so happy as to have won the love of a good girl, who will marry me on the simple condition that I abandon the rover's life; but if she will not withdraw this consent I will sail this cruise with you, I will fight the surly barbarians of the north for the sake of these brave Polish girls, who suffer even to the cruel lash that their lovers and husbands may be encouraged by their example to risk all for freedom. Pirates as we are, we will sell our swords cheaply to the insurrectionists, and like British bull-dogs we'll have one wring at the muzzle of the savage and surly Russian bear; but I can never sacrifice my love to ambition; yet I will not disguise the truth, I should exult to command the rare old, old Raven!"

"Hurrah! Cassidy's the man!" shouted the pirates.

Old Macallister now rose, for his daughter had bounded to his side, and looked up into his face appealingly.

"I ken weel, Muster Cassidy, cap'en, and lads, that ye'll be thinking that I canna gie my consent for my puir lassie to wed a mon who is resolved upon sic a desperate venture; but sin' I am sae deeply indebted to gude Muster Cassidy, and canna deny that in luve these young things maun e'en gang their ain gait. I am willing to gie my child to the cap'en of the 'Raven,' if he'll but swear that his purpose in this cruise is but to atone by a noble act for the black fau'ts o' the past, and that never, sae help him mercy, will he follow the uncanny trade o' plunder and murder. Oh! but I never think o' bonnie Poland and her big oppressors, but I'm minded o' my ain auld Scotia and Wight Wallace— and wad that some Robert or Christopher the Bruce might spring up to do that act o' chivalry which great and boastful powers that wage war for base greed wi' the weak and uncivilised are too mean and selfish to perform in the gude cause o' humanity!"

"Hurrah for Poland!—hurrah for the avengers!" shouted the men with great enthusiasm.

Mary drew to the side of Cassidy, and with a bright blush, laid her hand in his.

He clutched her in his arms, and then drawing his sword, raised his arm.

His quiet handsome countenance shone with heroism.

"Comrades!" he said, "we have but a handful of swords, but they are at the service of the gallant nation so basely oppressed, and better men will blush that there is more disinterestedness and courage to be found among a gang of sea-robbers than reigns in the imperial senates of liberal France and philanthropic England."

"And I'll gang wi' ye, husband," said Mary, "through every danger; for I canna think that a great people should wage war for greedy commerce —a people sae gude and devoted to their ain mithers and sisters and swee hearts—and yet suffer the puir lasses of a brave nation in the very centre of Europe to be scourged for wearing a black dress and weeping o'er the wrongs o' their country. It's nae for me to speak, perhaps, but I am a woman, and I cannot help pleading for my sex."

The gallant pirates responded to this speech with wild enthusiasm.

The Boy Pirate laughed heartily, as their boisterous shoutings rung along the shore.

"Hurrah, my hearties! you are in noble mood, and I rejoice that you resolve to support me in this noble enterprise. And now, Tom, pass the grog kid, and, lads, I'll sing you a rough stave to the tune our hearts are beating.

' The premier may nod,
    Like the old pagan god.
        And the senate may shake with a shout of applause,
    When he sagely declares,
    That in foreign affairs,
        We must stick to old treaties and tyrannous laws.
    But though he pretends,
    That the poor have no friends,
    That non-interference will serve his own ends,
    We wolves of the sea, more human than he,
    Will die for the fair maids of Poland!'

"Chorus, my lads; and shame to the tongue that is silent!

' Then fill to Poland, hapless maid;
    Fill high the brimming flagon;
    We'll break the chains that tyrants forge,
    And, right or wrong, by brave St. George,
    We'll wrest her from the dragon!'"

"Again, captain; the grog's not out!"

"' Aye, aye, good lads, we'll drain the cup,
    And drain our hearts as free, I swear it,
In woman's cause. Why, damn the laws;
    When woman's wronged, what man can bear it?'"

In the midst of the tumultuous plaudits that follow the Boy Pirate's song, Zampa rushed into the tent, displaying great agitation.

"Gorra, buckras, dis chile seen suffen da 'em eyes good; dars a black hull wid a heavy rig, and a false buntin' to de no'thard ob dis island; what um tink on it?"

"Perhaps it's the 'Cormorant,' I know that Black Ralph is cruising off this shore," said Cassidy.

"What flag, Zamp?" asked the Boy Pirate.

"I tell yo, sar, dat I berry much respect dat dis yere's no Mexicum," returned the negro, "um carry de Mexicum flag yo see; but I tell berry well by the draught, and by de build ob de wessel what sort o' cargo 'em hab on board."

"What do you suppose it to be, then?" asked our hero.

Zamp showed his ivories in a broad grin.

"Ingin'-rubber, sar."

"What do you mean?"

"Jess so, sar; freight ob black cattle, sar; 'pend on it dat ship a dam slaver!"

"Hurrah, my hearties," cried the Boy Pirate, joyously, "much as I have wished to overhaul one of those respectable gentlemen in all my long cruising I have never yet had the luck to run one down. Let's aboard, messmates, clap on all sail, and give chase to the brute!"

"Yo not do that, buckra cap'en!" cried Zamp, eagerly. "What for you want kill de poor darkies? de cap'en see ye gib chase; berry well, what him do, yo tink? Him pipe up all de niggers, tie dere necks to one dam long pole, and pitch 'em into de sea."

"He's right there, I've seen it done myself," said Brierly; "these infarnal villains are capable of any devilry; I have seen a slaver run down by an English frigate, and when the officer has gone aboard not a single nigger could be found, though there were signs showed that below deck the poor devils had been packed like pigs in a box."

"And in such a case how did the officer act?" asked the Boy Pirate.

"Why, cap'en, he could do nothing; upon mere suspicion he had no right to interfere with a foreign craft, he would have risked his commission."

"By Heaven! I would have risked my soul rather than let one of these hell-hounds escape!" cried the Raven, hotly; "but let's get aboard by prowess or by strategy; I'll take that hulk, and if I find that Zamp is right in his conjecture I'll batten down the skipper and his crew in the dungeon-hold of their cursed plague-ship, and set the craft on fire."

Soon the two steamers were forging their way through the narrow roadstead, and stood out to the open sea.

The "Vulture" was left at anchor alongside of the "Raven," and Cassidy assumed his command of the latter, taking the girls and the prisoners on board with him.

The slaver appeared like a dark speck in the sky line.

The pirates watched her eagerly.

Christopher and his officers stood on their hammocks and applied their glasses.

Zampa stood in the rattlings, in a state of inconceiveable excitement,

"Haul the weather braces," cried the rover captain. "Now she's easier."

The command was well timed, for a ga'e was blowing, and the speeding ship was almost taken by the passing squall.

"I beg to spress my 'pinion, sar; please gib dis chile de glass, him want to see de signal—berry good, sar; my 'pinion dizactly—you please observe dey have trown up a litty bit bunting, white wid a black spot in the centrums; do yo know what dat signifies?"

"No, Zamp."

"Berry good, sar; allers grad to 'form de 'quiry dat means, sar. Niggers aboard, do you 'ject to our trade? berry good, yo must answer—tink 'em de most 'spectable calling, want to buy some darkies for raising; yo know how to say all dat?"

"No, indeed, Zamp."

"Dat berry pretty 'kerchief yo hab dar, berry fine bit ob white buntin', yo please gib 'em to dis chile; and now, yo sar, yo mas'r Tom Garrod, hand over dat pair ob ducks and de needle yo am sewin'—I gib yo dem back direct."

Tom, who was seated on one of the carronades, mending a pair of blue cloth unmentionables, tossed them to the negro, with a laugh,

"None of your larks, old ebony," he cried, "or I'll shiver your figure-head. What does he want with 'em, cap'en?"

"I'll not be bail for him, Tom," answered Christopher, laughing.

Very carefully Zamp spread the garments out on the deck, and in an instant had cut a large triangular piece of the cloth out of the broadest part of them.

In great wrath, Tom sprang up; he advanced towards the negro with a roar of indignation. Zamp flung the breeks in his face.

"I tell yo I gib yo dem direct. Not want no more. Only take berry lilly piece from berry large part."

"You black baboon!"

"Let him alone, Tom," cried the Boy Pirate, with a smile. "You know that you are bound to make any sacrifice in the course of duty; even your head must go for the public good."

"Aye, cap'en; my figure-head, that's all very well. But, dam'me, my chaps——"

"Avast! let's observe our sable instructor, who is teaching us a new set of signals."

Zamp had stitched the triangle of cloth in the midst of the white handkerchief, which he held by the corners.

The stiff wind caught it, and Zampa laughed and chuckled as it fluttered fiercely in the breeze.

He jumped up and ran to the signal halliard; attaching the handkerchief to the line, he ran it up to the fore peak.

He then returned to the captain.

"You see, sar, dat ole uncle Zamp knows how to talk to dat kinder gemmen."

"And how did you learn their language?"

"Sarved aboard a ship, sar, as used to hab dealins wid de dam slavers—dey catch me, you know; dis yer nigger nebber was raised, him free man as any buckra."

"A slave cannot be 'raised,' except by a fiction of injustice," returned Christopher, "all men are free by right, Zamp."

"Dunno dat, sar; hab slave in my country; yo know, sar, dat I be great prince in my country, hab many slaves, sar."

A sneer of scorn flitted over the Pirate's fine face; a pang of that discontent which often afflicts the great-hearted shot through his breast; yet, as he looked the simple negro in his kindly grinning face, he laughed good humouredly.

"Well, Zamp, you don't pretend to philosophy."

"What dat, sar?"

"The essence of humbug," returned the Boy Pirate, a little fiercely.

"Nebber hearn on him; but you not see de signal from de ship, sar!"

"Why, Zamp, you're a jewel; true, they have answered the signal."

"Berry good, sar; yo tink I take de pains wid Mas'r Tom's ting-um-bobs and your fine silk banana for notink? Shall I tal you what him say?"

"Aye, Zamp."

"Well, sar, him say dat him heave to, and let yo come aboard."

"He can't say more fairly," returned Christopher, laughing.

The officers gathered about our hero.

"Captain," said Dick Caffyn, "supposing we take the slaver, what's to be done with the blacks?"

"A standing question, Dick, and one unanswerable," replied our hero, with a smile.

"We can't ship them back to their own country."

"No; but we can give the mawworms at home a chance for sending out a special mission—for we can set the poor fellows upon one of the islands that belongs to the English, and every black mother's sable son will be petted by some serious patron in old England. It's all very well to pay for soft soap when money is abundant, but if some of our fetishes were themselves set to the dirty work of washing a blackamoor white, I doubt if even their zeal would not fail. Well, Dick, sing out to let go the head bowlines."

The steam ship now ran along-side of the slaver.

The guns were masked.

The Brazilian flag floated from the mast-head.

The pirates concealed their arms.

As many of them were really Spaniards, and the

rest had long learned cunning, the slaver was completely deceived.

A savage-looking fellow, with a whip under his arm, stood on the hammocks, and hailed through the speaking-trumpet,

"What ship's that?"

"The ' Dolorosa,' war-frigate, of Rio Janiero."

"But where's Don Matias?"

"Disabled. I've succeeded to the command," responded our hero, with startling promptness.

"Wal, I du opine that you air a remarkable man, if you can stand in his shoes. Don Matias were a screamer, I reckon."

"What have you aboard—a cargo of cripples?"

"The primest lot that were ever transported from the coast of Guinea, stranger."

"That's well, for I want to buy a few stout fellows to help in working the ship."

"I opine I've some raal genwines as will suit you, stranger."

"How many have you on board?"

"Wal, 'taint for the quantity as for the quality. I have at present jist one hundred and fifty. I bought 'em of King Toby, as the sailor chaps call him. Many on 'em is Ashantee; there's a few gals, and a likely picaninny among 'em."

"I'll come aboard and look at them," said the Boy Pirate, grinding his teeth, to repress his rising passion.

"Now, lads," he said, turning to his crew, "with this infernal villain there need be no palavering. I will go aboard. I shall go below with him, to view the negroes. When I come on deck again, board the vessel, and take every man aboard her alive, if possible. Do not man the guns; by firing a broadside you will only injure those we wish to preserve."

The Boy Pirate went on board the slaver.

He was accompanied by his foster-brother, Brand the pilot, and old Brierly.

"And what sort of discipline do you keep among the darkies?"

The slaver gave a grim smile, and pointed to his pistols, and cracked his whip, laughing.

"Wal, stranger, I opine that I don't spile the niggers by half measures. I'm skipper here, I reckon, but they aren't bruk yer see, and I must confess the devils give me pretty considerable trouble, they du so; but come into the hold, and I'll show yer how I contrives to keep 'em under a bit."

The Boy Pirate and his officers followed the slaver to the lower decks.

He led them to the hold.

A spectacle of squalid horror—a stench that was sickening—a gloom that was infernal.

A large number of miserable naked wretches, crouching in every attitude of listless despair, bound and handcuffed, were crowded into the narrow confines of their filthy prison.

Several were writhing in the embrace of some devilish instrument of torture that cramped their head and limbs close together.

But the great horror consisted in the hideous, livid corpse of a huge negro the slaver had brutally murdered for attempting to escape, which was chained to the bulkhead as a warning to the other wretches, his companions in misery.

"There—that's my work—a caution, I opine, to the infernal black cusses as presumes to show their teeth to me. Yah! There, rouse up, you niggers. Where's Cora?"

"Here, massa; here, massa," whimpered a pretty-looking mulatto girl about sixteen years of age, but a woman in appearance.

She was almost entirely nude; but as if in strange contrast to the wretchedness of her present condition, she wore heavy gold bangles and ear-rings.

Both she and these ornaments were the property of the savage slaver, and he did not trouble himself about either, knowing them to be safe in his power.

The girl carried a little black ball of humanity in her arms; it was a sleeping negro child.

"How's the picaninny—you? Why don't yer speak? Be spry!"

The brute lashed the writhing girl across her naked shoulders.

The Boy Pirate clutched his hand.

The slaver laughed.

"Wall, it ain't bus'ness to spile the wench, no ways, stranger," he said, with a beastly leer; "that gals walable, fetch a heap o' dollars down Louisiana. But, laws, trade's nothing to what it was. Lost one of my best customers in old Rashleigh, that was killed by the pirates when hunting arter a runaway yaller gal as they say were worth a fortin'. Wall, stranger, thar's the lot. Shall I call some on 'em forard for you to examine?"

"No, not now," muttered the Boy Pirate.

"Leave the choice to me, stranger."

"There are men among them who are used to the sea?"

"Yaas, I opine thar's three or four boys among us as afe reg'lar amphibious. On their own coasts swimming is as nat'ral as walking to 'em, and they can manage a long boat as well as a war-canoe, I reckon."

The Boy Pirate turned away in silence.

"And how's the picaninny, once more, you gal?"

"Tink him sick—tink him die, massa."

"You'd better die with him, my charmer, if he does, for I'll kill you if you let him go, that's all," returned the brute, with a frown.

He followed the Boy Pirate on deck.

Then all the concentrated fury that raged in the rover's heart burst forth in a whelming torrent.

Seizing the ruffian by the throat, he hurled him down upon the deck.

Placing his foot upon his breast for a few moments, he bitterly anathematised his brutality, and then turned sternly away.

The miscreant rose to his knees in deadly terror.

The pirates had leaped upon the deck, and overmastered the crew, in all a dozen men.

The slaver shrieked for mercy.

But, with a calm face, the Boy Pirate gave a curt order to Zampa and Tom Garrod, and then quietly returned to his own ship.

Lilia and Ida stood by the companion-hatch.

The Boy Pirate took a hand of each, and quietly led them below.

In a few moments the sullen boom of a gun was heard.

Twelve writhing bodies were dangling from the yards of the slaver.

The wretched Africans, for once, at least, were terribly avenged.

CHAPTER CXXXIV.

A TRAPPER'S HUT ON THE MISSISSIPPI.—THE NATURAL HISTORY OF THE BEAVER.

ON the banks of the Red River, and under the shelter of a high and woody hill, stood the log cabin of Nat Weatherfield the trapper.

It was a snug little dwelling, though built entirely of pine logs.

The interior was cosy, and well furnished with benches and tables of fine-grained and aromatic woods.

The walls were covered with deer-skin hangings, and adorned with trophies of the chase, Indian weapons, calumets and bead work, and one or two gaudy and trashy-looking pictures.

Nat Weatherfield was seated at the door of his cabin, smoking his pipe, and watching the sprightly gambollings of the castors that were plashing shoreward through the water from their little mud huts, or chasing about the green and shadowy banks of the river.

The beaver is, perhaps, the most remarkable animal of North America, and, perhaps, a quaint account of it, as given by Beltrami, an Italian, who professes to have discovered the sources of the Mississippi and the Red River, may not be unacceptable to the youthful reader.

Some of the statements made must be received with a reservation, but, upon the whole, the account given by the traveller of the habits of these extraordinary creatures is strictly correct.

He is speaking of a large piece of water which he found on a lake near the source of the queen of rivers.

"A small river flows into the lake on the western side. The beavers have barricaded the mouth of it by a dike, completed in a manner which would not disgrace a corps of engineers; the water is thus kept back and forms a pond, in which they have erected their habitations.

"It is proper to notice that the river in question is never dried up, as, otherwise, they would not have fixed upon it for their purpose.

"The stakes fixed in the earth, and the trunks of trees which are laid across them are of considerable thickness and length.

"It is difficult to conceive how such small animals are enabled to transport such bulky articles. But what is more astonishing is, that they never make use of trees blown down by the wind, or levelled by the strength of man, but select them themselves, cutting down such as are peculiarly adapted for the intended buildings, and doing this always on the banks of lakes or large rivers, in order to avail themselves of the opportunity of conveying them by water to the place intended.

"While five or six are occupied in cutting or sawing with their teeth the bottom of the trunk, another stations himself in the middle of the river, and indicate by a hissing sound, or by striking the water with his tail, which way the top inclines towards the fall, that the operators, without interrupting their labour, may conduct it with proper caution and preclude all danger.

"It is worthy of remark that they never gnaw the tree on the land side, but always on that of the lake or river, in order to ensure its falling into it.

"The whole tribe then combine their exertions and float the trunk to the place where it is wanted.

"Here, with their teeth, they point the stakes, with their claws dig deep holes for them in the earth, and with their paws introduce and drive them in.

"They then place branches against them, and fill up the interstices with mortar, which some prepare while the others are cutting down the trees or engaged in different departments of labour; for the tax of labour is carefully distributed and no individual remains unemployed.

"The mortar used by the wonderful animals becomes more hard and solid than the finest Roman cement.

"When the dike is completed, and has been proved fit for the purpose designed, they effect an opening at the bottom of it by way of a flood-gate, which they open or close as may be required, that the stream may not be too much impeded.

"They then commence building their habitation in the midst of the mass constituting the dike.

"They never begin to erect the habitation previously to forming the dike, lest the operation should fail of success, and they should consequently lose their valuable time and labour.

"Their mansion, formed equally of wood and mortar, consists of two stories, and is double; its length is in proportion to the number of the tribe for whom it is intended.

"The first stage, or story, is a magazine in common for provisions, and is under water; the second is divided into sleeping-places, each family having its distinct chamber. This part of the building is above water.

"Under the foundation of the buildings they form a number of avenues, by means of which they enter and quit subterraneously, so as not to be perceived by the most keen and watchful Indian.

"These all terminate at a distance from their dwelling, and in a part of the mound constituting their dike, or in lakes or rivers near which they usually form their establishments, that they may have it in their power to select that direction which may be most convenient and least dangerous in the various incidents and exigences of their lives.

"Beavers are divided into tribes, and sometimes merely into small bands, each of which has its chief, and order and discipline exist in these distinct societies to a greater extent probably than among the Indians, or even among some civilised and polished nations.

"Their magazines are invariably fully stored with provisions in summer, and no one is allowed to break in upon this stock until the scarcity of winter begins to be experienced, unless circumstances render it imperatively necessary to violate this rule.

"In no case, however, is any one permitted to enter without the express authority, and, indeed, the presence of their chief.

"Their provisions consist in general of the bark of trees, principally of the willow and poplar species. On some occasions when bark is not to be found in sufficient quantities, they collect also the wood of those trees, which they divide into distinct parcels with their teeth.

"Each tribe has its peculiar territory.

"If any foreigner be taken in the act of marauding

he is delivered over to the chief who, on the first offence, chastises him with a view to correction; but for the second deprives him of his tail, which is considered the greatest disgrace to which a beaver can be exposed, for the tail is the carriage on which he conveys stones, mortar, provisions, &c. and it is also the trowel (the figure of which it represents exactly) which he uses in building.

"This violation of international rights, however, is considered among them so great an outrage that the whole tribe of the mutilated culprit take up arms in his cause, and proceed immediately to obtain vengeance.

"In this conflict the victors, availing themselves of the customary rights of war, expel the conquered from their home, take possession of it themselves, appoint a provisional garrison for the occupation, and eventually establish in it a colony of young beavers.

"In this connection, another circumstance relating to these truly wonderful creatures will appear not less astonishing.

"The female beaver whelps usually in the month of April, and produces as many as four young ones.

"She sustains, and carefully instructs them for a year, that is, till the family are on the eve of a new increase, and then these young beavers, compelled thus to make room for others, build a new house by the side of the paternal mansion, if they are not too numerous; but if there should be too many to admit of this, they are obliged to go with others to a new spot, forming a new tribe and a new establishment.

"If, then, about this season the enemy should happen to be driven from his quarters, the conquerors instal in them their own young ones of the current year, provided they are capable of managing for themselves.

"The Indians have related to me, as a positive fact, another circumstance respecting the conduct of these animals; but it is so extraordinary that I leave you to credit it or not, as you may think proper.

"They allege, and some will even assert themselves eye-witnesses of such a fact, that the two chiefs of hostile tribes sometimes terminate the quarrel by a single combat, in presence of the two opposing armies.

"Beavers practise the usage of matrimony, and death alone separates the parties.

"In cases of sickness they mutually and anxiously take care of each other, and the sick express their pain by plaintive sounds and tones, like the human race.

"The Indians hunt the beaver in the same way as they hunt the musk rat; indeed, the latter animal may be considered a beaver of a secondary order. It is of the same shape, only smaller, and resembles it in many of its qualities, but its fur is very inferior in beauty and fineness.

"In winter the Indians make holes in the ice which covers the ponds surrounding the habitations of the beavers, and, carefully watching for the moment when they lift their heads up to take breath, instantly shoot them.

"A chief at Bloody Lake, called 'Great Hare,' confidently assured me, that on reaching the spot where two tribes of beavers had just been engaged in battle with each other, he had found upon the field fifteen dead or dying, and other Indians, both Sioux and Chippowais, have equally declared that they have occasionally obtained capital prizes on like occasions.

"It is perfectly correct that they are sometimes taken without a tail. I have seen one in that state myself, which corroborates the history of the punishment inflicted by them upon obstinate offenders.

"In short, these animals are deemed so very extraordinary, even by Indians, that they consider them as men metamorphosed into beavers, and killing them is regarded as conferring upon them an essential service, as it is considered to be a restoration of them to their original state of being."

Trusting that this long digression will not have been found uninteresting, we return to the trapper.

Nat Weatherfield appeared to be in a thoughtful mood, and sat long by his cabin door, as if unconscious of the flight of time.

CHAPTER CXXXV.

CATAHAGA AND HIS WIFE CONTINUE THEIR FLIGHT — THEY REACH NAT WEATHERFIELD'S HUT IN SAFETY.

THE shadows in the woods grew broader and darker, and the trees themselves were becoming blent in a purple haze, while the sky above the cottage was draped with black clouds, though still, through the sombre pine branches, a red, bright bar of sunset glowed along the heavens.

A large and shaggy deer-hound lay beside the trapper.

The animal suddenly raised his head.

He shook himself, gave a low growl, and then a sharp bark, leaped up, and bounded down the bank on which the cabin was erected.

Weatherfield rose, snatched up his rifle instinctively, glanced at the priming, and then moved down the bank after the dog.

He called the hound to his side, and chid him into silence.

He stooped down, and laid his ear against the side of the bank.

The far-off click of a horse's hoof was borne to his ear.

He rose, and walked moodily back to his cabin.

He walked to the back of its single apartment, and fixed a bar across the door.

He took a couple of pistols from the wall above the mantel, and thrust them into his belt.

A cloud of anxiety rested on his brow as he stood before his door, leaning on his long rifle, and hearkening breathlessly to the pattering of hoofs, which grew louder and louder every moment.

His quick eye soon detected the rider among the leaves of the gloomy wood.

For a moment the single red bar of fire in the

western sky shone on the stern face of a p ain Indian.

With a convulsive start Weatherfield grasped the barrel of his gun, and stood ready to take instant aim.

The rider now appeared, his horse walking slowly and panting with exertion.

He proved to be an Indian.

Weatherfield knew him at once for a Pawnee-Loup by his war-paint and trappings.

He was not alone.

Before him, on the pummel of the saddle, a slight girl was mounted; her arm was about the Indian's neck, and her pale cheek leant against his shoulder.

"It is Catahaga and Minna Wyotti!"

As Weatherfield pronounced these words aloud, with a deep sigh of relief he ran down the bank to greet his visitors.

"My brother and sister are very welcome to my lodge," he said; "but the eyes of my sister have lost their light, and her cheek seems stiff and frozen. The Eagle-Wing has left a long trail behind him."

"The backward path would lead you to the great Assineboin—the Yengeese are on the war-path against the tribes of the Iroquois; the Dacotahs have left their wigwams, and have built new lodges by the river of the Blue Earth; has my brother seen the young men of my tribe who are with Heart of Fire on this side the Arkansas?"

"They came to my lodge three suns ago," returned the trapper, "I know not if they have crossed the river."

"My father, the White Pine, promised to send a party of braves to join them. How many were the young men?"

"Twenty, beside their war chief."

"It is good."

Weatherfield assisted Minna to dismount.

He led her to his cabin.

Catahaga followed them.

The face of the young Indian wore an expression of gloom and abstraction.

He seated himself upon a couch, and drew his wife to his side.

Weatherfield looked upon the weary girl with pity and interest.

He prepared a frugal, but substantial repast for the fugitives.

After they had finished their repast, Catahaga rose, he walked towards Weatherfield, held out his hand, and said with a soft smile—

"The Yengeese and the Iroquois are each a mixture of good and evil men; my brother is as true as the sun to its rising. Eagle-Wing has brought his wife that she may remain in my brother's lodge till the war is ended."

"My sister is welcome, and will be safe in my cabin," returned Weatherfield; "but why does the Pawnee start?"

"Ugh!" cried Eagle-Wing, suddenly crouching by the door.

He smiled quietly, and then his face resumed its impassibility.

"They are my brothers," he said, with confidence. "I will go."

He held up his hand in token that he would not be gainsaid.

He then walked quickly across the room, and locked his wife in his arms.

She murmured endearingly and shed a few tears.

"Oh! Catahaga, will the past come no more?" she exclaimed, sadly. "And is there nothing in the future like the sweet peace that is gone? Will my brother never again bury the war hatchet? Will he mingle no more with the people of Minna's nation?"

"When he has slain his enemies!" he answered curtly.

He glided towards the door and passed out.

Minna and Weatherfield were alone.

The trapper led the girl to a seat.

"Oh, whither has he gone, Nathaniel?" she asked, distractedly.

"Wal now, I hope, Minna Wyotti, as ye haven't any good cause to dread that any evil can threaten the Eagle-Wing; he is gone to meet his father's braves, and you know that he is subtle as the lynx, and brave as the panther; rest assured that he will be able to save himself from his foes. And how came the Eagle-Wing to forswear his connection with the whites?"

Minna narrated to the trapper how their house had been attacked by the bush-rangers, how craftily the Eagle-Wing had trapped and slain them, how they had travelled across the prairies, and had at length, through many dangers, reached the wigwams of the Dacotahs.

CHAPTER CXXXVI.

THE TRAPPER'S ADVICE TO MINNA WYOTTI.

WEATHERFIELD listened with wonderment to this story, for he had been far away up the Mississippi trapping beavers when the greater number of these events took place.

"And now let me ask you," said Minna Wyotti, eagerly, "do you think that Regan, the captain of the Oregon bush-rangers, means fairly to the Indians, whose cause he has espoused?"

"Fairness, Minna, is a kinder quality as he never keeps in stock. I reckon he is one of those creatures that can never walk straight, but must first run to one hand and then to t'other like a wriggling snake. It arn't much I knows on him, but I thought that Catahaga hated him, and now I think on't, I guess I saw him notch the death-arrow a purpose to kill the warmint."

"He saved my life—he shot the horse on which I was riding before the prairie fire, on the very brink of a landslip."

"And it's for that the Eagle-Wing has broken the arrow—curious the ways of these Injuns. Catahaga is the finest chief among all the nations of the Iroquois, and he is strong affectionate towards yerself, Minna, I calkilate."

"Oh, no, his hate is stronger than his love," cried Minna, bitterly; "he hates my nation more than he loves me, and that is selfish, and O how hateful is selfishness when seen in the nearest and dearest. Oh, I am not selfish with him. I would suffer torments for his sake."

"I rather opine you have suffered enough for him already, Minna," returned the trapper.

"Oh no, it's not that," cried the girl, very earnestly, "for what woman takes any count of the sacrifices she makes for the man whom she loves; but I am so terribly anxious for the influence this Regan holds upon his impressionable mind."

"Beware of him! beware of him, Minna!" returned the trapper, seriously. "He is one to be dreaded, I can swar that; but, hark! Down, dogs. Don't cower away, Minna; they're too noisy for Injens, and thars no other sort o' critters as we need be feared on."

The sounds thus referred to proceeded from a party of mounted men, who rushed along the valley below the house.

Minna and Weatherfield watched them, with pale faces, as they laughed and caracoled over the tender grass, leaving deep prints behind them.

A FEARFUL POSITION.

Nat Weatherfield opened the door, and looked out.

He re-entered the room, glanced quickly towards Minna, and motioned her to conceal herself behind a curtain of painted canvas.

Behind this the girl quickly passed.

It was now quite dark, and Weatherfield snatched up a blazing pine-branch from the ingle, and rushed out of the cabin.

At the foot of the bank a number of evil-looking fellows, formidably armed and well mounted, were clustered.

Two had dismounted.

These were the captain of the bush-rangers, and Wyld, his lieutenant.

No. 44.

They were bending over the drooping form of Agnes Staunton, who still remained insensible.

The trapper advanced with the torch in his hand.

As its light fell upon the face of young Regan the backwoodsman grasped his gun.

"Ha, Nat Weatherfield!" cried the bandit, quickly, "lend us a hand to bear this lady to your lodge. What, you unmannerly hound, do you refuse your assistance to a poor girl, perhaps dying?"

These words were spoken fiercely, as Regan caught the look of hesitation with which the trapper regarded him.

"Wal, stranger, I guess that I am always at the service of the ladies, and there air, in these parts, no man more willing to do the best to shield Miss

Staunton from her enemies than I am; but, as you've the advantage of me in most ways, I reckon there's no use in trying to oppose you."

"Curse you for a fool. Do you not see the girl is on the verge of death?" shouted the robber, in great rage and excitement.

"And I opine, master Oswald, that should she slip to the darker side of that verge, she would be saved many a dark hour of a tarnation dark life that she could well dispense with. Stranger, it's no use glaring at me, I ain't no ways afeard of that lightning. Lend a hand and I'll help ye; but fair play among thieves, I've a few peltries, the fruit of a long year's 'farnal hard work, besides some little ammunition; you're welcome to a luscious buffalo hump, and maize cakes you'll find in the lodge, even to a taste of the stingo, but I hope you won't rob me of the earnings of the past, nor the provisions for the future."

"What the devil do you suppose we want with your beastly coon skins and paltry pinch of powder?" cried Regan, hotly. "Agnes, God's mercy! I think, Wyld, she must be dead. Oh, no, no, no, I will *not* have it so; I am villain enough, but not so. She is deadly white; bear her very tenderly. Now, old Beaverskin, will you lead the way?"

When Agnes was borne into the cabin and laid on the little bed, Minna who had concealed herself as before narrated, peeped through the curtain.

The pale and rigid face of the kind and lovely companion of her girlhood banished every thought of danger, every scruple of caution. With a piercing cry she rushed forward, and threw herself beside the girl.

She eagerly looked upon her lids so coldly closed, and wrung her hands which lay so passive on the bed.

The trapper held the torch aloft, and the handsome villain stood with tight clenched fingers gazing upon the pale, still face with breathless suspense and poignant contrition.

"Oswald Lamond, you are a monster with a heart, or this sight would strike you as dead as this sweet and gentle girl whom you have murdered."

This burst of indignation on the part of the fearless Minna Wyotti, caused the bush-ranger to start back with starting eyes and blanched cheek.

"Is she dead?" gasped Regan. "It was that cursed hound, her cousin: it was he that killed her. He maddened me till I forgot his kinship."

"And you murdered your cousin, Regan?" exclaimed the trapper, in great horror.

"Is self-defence murder? Had I not fired at him I should have been killed myself. Once I spared his life; a second chance I gave him of a fair fight, but the dastard had not the courage to embrace it, or rather sneaked off after he had himself challenged me; but why should I explain? who dares to dictate to Regan the Bush-ranger? Ha! By the spirit of Thunder, if Agnes is slain, I will have the blood of all her false-hearted kindred, but for whom we should be happy—they are her real murderers."

"Oh, she breathes—a little, just a little. I think —I hope she lives yet," murmured Minna, as with feminine aptness she used the readiest means of restoring the inanimate. "Oh, yes, she is muttering. Hark! I can catch her words."

Very faintly, as from some one in the distance, came a subdued plaintive wail of deepest agony.

"Mark! O, and I dare not forgive him—dead!— by his hand. Oh, do not wake me! kill me! let me die!"

"Agnes, my own, speak to me," muttered the robber, in a tremulous voice, laying his hand upon hers.

She drew away her hand instinctively, and gazed wildly, yet dreamily, upon him.

"Oswald, do not talk to me. I implore you, if you dare hope for the mercy of Heaven, if you have

ever loved me, go hence! I know not where I am; I care not. I have done with the world. Thought is too horrible for endurance. Go from me; let me hear your voice no more. It is all I ask."

"But, Agnes, dearest Agnes——"

"Do not speak to her now, unless you would bereave her of her senses!" cried Minna.

The poor girl whom she was tending looked wistfully in her face as she spoke, and clasped her hand with affection.

"Do you know me, dear Agnes?"

"You are Minna Wyotti. Your husband——But then he is an Indian, and has shed no blood of your kindred."

The girl sank back on the pillow, with a low, quivering moan.

Minna did not offer any vapid phrase of consolation, but bowed her head over the patient, and kissed her with sisterly tenderness.

Agnes threw her arms about her companion's neck, and murmured, beseechingly,

"You will not—oh! you will not leave!"

"Not till I have restored you to your home, dear Agnes."

A man entered the room.

He was about to speak.

Regan waved him back impatiently.

"Not here!" he said.

"Captain, there are Indians returning——"

"Silence, I say!"

The man, cowed by the stern look fixed upon him by the leader, withdrew from the room.

"Nat, I need scarce ask you to take care of my poor, suffering Agnes. She shall return home, if she please, but only with my knowledge and concurrence. Minna, I trust her to your kindness. Well, Wyld, what is it?"

"The Indians, captain!" returned the lieutenant of the gang, in an eager tone, as he stepped back towards the door.

"I will come."

When Regan left the house he found his men, impatient of his long absence, were chafing to start.

The young bush-ranger stood listening, leaning on his gun.

"I hear the steps."

"They are a strong party."

"How many should you guess, captain?"

"Between twenty or thirty."

"Of what tribe do you suppose them to be?"

"Pawnees or Dacotahs."

"Perhaps they are of Catahaga's party?"

"It may be so."

"Hush!"

"Look to your arms; it may be some cursed stratagem of the Regulators," said Wyld.

"It is not so."

"How can you be sure of that, captain?"

"The babes in the wood might know the light tread of a true Indian, which is never to be acquired by the pale-face."

"That is just. They are Pawnees of the Eagle-Wing's party."

At this moment a terrific war-whoop re-echoed in the slumbering forest.

"Let us go hence," said the bush-ranger, jumping on his horse, and spurring down the declivity. "Come, let us go and meet our red brothers, for I know by that shout that they have obtained some advantage, or made some important capture. Let us go out to meet the victorious with a pœan of victory!"

CHAPTER CXXXVIII.

CATAHAGA AND HIS BAND IN PURSUIT OF THE SETTLERS—THE ATTACK—THE DEFEAT OF HARWOLF.

CATAHAGA had joined Heart of Fire; the two war-chiefs were supported by a band of thirty men.

They were all picked braves.

The tall supple forms were smeared with war-paint.

Their faces streaked and barred in hideous fashion.

They were all armed with rifles.

Catahaga, who had been so long looked upon by the Iroquois as an incorrigible renegade, had now, apparently resumed his national habits and instincts, and was in all respects a red-skin.

It was strange that he made so little use of the valuable knowledge he had gained during his long intercourse with the whites, but probably he had more faith in Indian guile than in Yengeese tactics.

The Indians were threading a mighty forest, one by one in silence, and stepping so lightly that their trail was scarce perceptible even before it had been carefully obliterated.

The Indians glided through the mazy wood.

According to their custom, the two chiefs came last.

In one of these parties, the point of honour, justly, because the point of danger is in the rear and not in the van.

Their object was to surprise a party of the settlers who were bivouacing in the woods.

The spot where the Indians halted was very grand.

On either side it was walled in by precipitous banks of rock rising in gradations.

Here a short consultation took place between the chiefs.

The course of proceeding was at once decided upon.

The party separated into two divisions of equal number.

Heart of Fire was selected for the reconnoitring division.

The others were to remain concealed in ambush.

Catahaga motioned to his braves that they should conceal themselves.

As when some wizard waves his magic wand and the attendant spirits melt off into air, so did the subtle Indians sink and vanish when Eagle-Wing waved his hand.

Catahaga moved about the spot, and with a skill truly marvellous — forethought and apprehension really astonishing—he removed every trace of their presence.

He then concealed himself.

More than two hours moved heavily away.

The wind hurtled through the myriad-armed forests.

Heavy drops of rain slowly and at intervals began to patter down upon the dry, clicking leaves.

Not one of the Indians stirred.

Motionless as the trees around them they stood, or, firm as the gnarled roots that arched from the ground, they crouched and lurked.

No amount of weariness or pain produced by their cramping posture elicited a murmur.

Catahaga stood in the hollow of a decayed oak.

His position was not so painful as that of some of his less fortunate companions.

It was the more dangerous.

The fatigues through which he had passed were simply terrific, and now he was snugly ensconced from the rain and the cold.

But not for an instant was he lured by comparative ease and great weariness to relax in watchfulness.

He slightly started when he had passed nearly three hours in silence and immobility.

"Waugh!"

The guttural exclamation proceeded from Heart of Fire, who had crawled even to the foot of the tree.

As the Indians exchanged a look Eagle-Wing reddened at being so far outdone in cunning by his colleague, for he had not been aware of his being so near.

"My brother has the foot of a lurking panther," said Catahaga, with a smile. "Has he seen the fires of these pale-face dogs?"

The Dacotah answered only by a faint smile, and beckoned the Eagle-Wing to follow him.

One by one the Indian braves again wended their way through the woods.

They paused at length on the summit of a grassy knoll, up which they had writhed on their bellies, their knives concealed in their bosoms, and their guns cautiously trailed.

Through the interlacing branches glowed red and weird the watch-fires of a detachment of Regulators.

Harwolf had won a great victory over the combined forces of the Pawnees and Dacotahs.

His men were very tired for they had made a long and rapid march.

They lay stretched before the fires soundly sleeping.

A picket of four men guarded the bivouac.

They, however, stood wearily leaning on their rifles, or reclined, half asleep, against the trees.

Harwolf alone was awake among the sleepers.

His body, which was much strengthened since he had come to America, seemed impervious to fatigue; his mind, ever racked by torturing thoughts, incapable of repose.

There seemed to exist among the party of whites not the slightest fear of surprisal.

They had just won a victory over their enemies, and it was confidently reported that the Eagle-Wing had been killed.

The Indians slunk behind the covert of the trees and bushes.

Harwolf was walking, his eyes fixed on the ground in a moody fit of abstraction.

He wandered away from the fire and plunged alone into the dense forest.

The sentinel stared at him in sleepy surprise, but allowed him to pass without remark.

He advanced some distance through the trees.

He stood at the brow of a shadowy dingle.

He seemed to be refreshed by the deep darkness and the solemn stillness around.

With muttering lips and distorted features he crossed the little dell.

His ear had been attracted by the rippling fall of a little cataract.

Wishing to slake his thirst and to bathe his passion-fevered forehead in the cold stream, he moved cautiously among the gloomy trees and thickets.

He was quietly advancing, when suddenly the guttural exclamation of a savage concealed close by his side—a sound so like the pant of a wild beast, caused him to start back.

He leaped up.

His gun was wrenched from his hand.

He fixed his grip on his assailant's throat.

From the other side he was attacked by another savage, who struck at him fiercely with a tomahawk.

Against this new antagonist he defended himself as well as he could, by raising his arm to parry the blow.

He would have shouted, but one of the Indians threw his arm around his head and stopped his utterance.

His arms were then seized from behind, and he was forced down upon his knee.

Before him stood a tall, lithe Pawnee, his perfect features gleaming with subtle triumph, and his gun levelled at his prisoner's head.

At the same moment that he was thus secured, the sound of strife, the blaze and crackle of musketry, betokened that an attack was being made upon the others of Harwolf's party.

Then the Indians expressed their triumph in a long and fearful war-whoop.

CHAPTER CXXXIX.

THE TEMPTER AND THE TEMPTED—CHARLIE RYE'S FIRST MISTAKE—SYLVIA VOLANTE—THE DERBY DAY.

It will not have been forgotten that Charles Rye had been introduced by his friend, Eagleton, to the charming *premiere danseuse* at her Majesty's, Sylvia Volante.

Since the fatal hour when the young clerk had become acquainted with the siren, whose mission it was to lure him to destruction, he had become an altered youth.

To the piece of mind, the light-heartedness and buoyant hopefulness of his disposition, succeeded a restlessness and alternating gloom and exhilaration, equally false and exhausting.

Sylvia tortured him by her caprices; at one time she was warm and genial as a southern summer, at other's cold and pitiless as a northern winter.

Eagleton affected to sympathise with him in all his varied emotions, and obtained the most perfect controul over his implicitly confiding friend.

In one respect, however, Charles had preserved his firmness.

He had steadily refused joining with his friend in any betting transactions, and had not suffered himself to be drawn into those excesses which the other indulged in.

During more than a week before the great race day Eagleton had been in a fever of excitement.

It grieved Charles Rye to remark this, for it convinced him that the young clerk had staked some heavy sum on the event of the Derby.

He did not like to press him with any inquiries that might be obtrusive, and yet in the anxiety of friendship he was eager to know how far his friend had compromised himself.

The two clerks were returning home on the evening preceding the Derby.

"Richard, you seem strangely possessed with some spirits of gloom. What is the matter with you?"

"Nothing, Charley, nothing at all. We have all our moments of depression, and you are the most melancholy of hypochondriacs sometimes."

"I am certainly not half so jolly as I used to be," returned his companion, thoughtfully.

"That's because you're in love."

"I wish I was not."

"How, you traitor. Would you like that repeated to Sylvia?"

"I have told her so. I have told her that she fools me, and that I am conscious of her heartlessness."

"And what does she say?"

"Why, of course, we quarrel."

"Quarrel—pshaw! Now be a little less presumptuous, Master Charles."

"Presumptuous. Am I so?"

"Rather! Quarrel! Do you think you can afford to quarrel with a girl who has refused a duke, and more than one marquis?"

"If she despises me, let her tell me so. As long as I love her as I do I am more than her equal, for sometimes,—there, don't let us talk of her."

"Sometimes she is as arrogant as Semiramis; and at another as humble as Griselda.'"

"Are all women of that mood?"

"Yes, simpleton! from grandmother Eve successively."

"I don't believe it."

"Well, blind people are often incredulous. And you don't think I am her equal."

"In station?"

"Yes."

"What is she after all? A bayadere! a nautch girl! that gains her livelihood by throwing herself into graceful postures for the idle amusement of the broad public. Her equal! of course you are! I admit she is invested with the despotic nobility of beauty and genius. But of all things in the world don't affect humility; it's the last virtue a woman can appreciate."

"How well you know the world.'"

"I have paid for my knowledge; and so you quarrel already?"

"Quarrel, that's a strong word; I mean we disagree."

"Never quarrel, even with your enemies."

"But honest indignation—"

"Is virtuous madness: if a man wrongs me ever so much I never quarrel with him."

"No; are you so forbearing, so forgiving?"

"I never forgive; I quietly revenge myself."

"That's very bad, Richard," said Charles Rye, gravely, "and what do you mean by *quietly* revenging yourself?"

"In the jolly old days men fought with swords and shields, did they not?"

"Well."

"So do they now, my boy, with the shield of dissimulation, and the sword of scandal."

"But would *you* slander a man?"

"Not unless he wronged me, and I could do it very skilfully."

"Why, you must be a villain."

"I am not a fool; besides, truth will often form the best scandal, and if you hate a man, where's the compunction?"

"Oh, Richard, I wake as from a dream; I wake to hate the world I thought so loveable; I would have staked my life that you were true and generous."

"So I am; but when I am wronged, you know, I am no lion. Nature gives horns to the bull and fangs to the tiger. What does she give to the 'poor worm,' a soft and 'tender fork,' a weapon more deadly than those she bestows on her seeming favourites."

"Why, this is horrible!"

"It's all natural."

"You will teach me to hate nature!'"

"I would teach you not to strive after supernatural goodness; you must fight people on their own ground, however dirty that ground may be, with their own weapons, however base those weapons are."

"Rather let them sheath all their swords in my heart, rather let them despise me, and trample me into the mire!" cried Charles, with great warmth.

"Well, the fellow do despise you a little, Master Charlie," returned the tempter, with a dry smile.

"And why?"

"You don't care for betting and gaming, and 'seeing life,' you know."

"But I really abstain from these things because they do not take my fancy."

"But you *must* fancy them, or be thought a muff."

"That's very hard."

"So it is—but you must howl with the wolves—at Rome you must be a Roman—so let me advise you to stake a few sovs. on the favourite, it's a safe card."

"I won't; but I should like to go to the Derby."

"Have you never been?"

"No."

"Good gracious, how absurd; lived all your life in town—never make that confession elsewhere—of course you'll go to-morrow, seeing that we've a holiday."

"I will."

"And Sylvia will go too."

"That will be delightful."

"My uncle will lend me his chaise; you must come out strong for once, Charlie; have you any money?"

"I can get some."

"That's the style of talk!—a royal lark!—green veils and wooden dolls—champagne and charmers."

"I shall enjoy it beyond measure."

"Of course you will, and I will promise you Sylvia shall be in her sweetest mood; she is vexed with you only because you are such a muff—not at all 'fast' enough for a girl in her profession—which shows a mean feeling."

"How so?"

"Of course I speak only of appearances."

"But how do I appear ungracious?"

"Why, living such a 'serious,' slow, quaker-like sort of life; never coming out, never cutting a dash; it seems to throw a slight upon the gay life that Sylvia leads, and women are so sensitive. She looks upon you as a sort of 'Johnny Goodchild,' that never played truant, and is his granny's pet; besides, good or bad, the world is the world, and only a coward keeps out of it. Look at Sylvia, she keeps her good name in the midst of all the gaiety and levity of a vortex of the most witless and virtueless profligates; they dare not impeach her; now that's brave."

"So it is, I agree with you; well, I'll go to the Derby, there's no harm in that."

"And you won't sip your sparkling moselle as if it was prussic acid? Sometimes I am ashamed of you, Old Slowboy; but, here's our drum, we shall meet a lot of jolly fellows; be jolly too, and try your skill at billiards, it's a charming and scientific game, I do assure you."

They had reached the door of a brilliantly-lighted tavern.

A splendid cortége drew up at the door.

A stout and sullen-looking gentleman issued from a side door of the tavern. His eye caught Eagleton's; he smiled coldly, and with a slight bow entered the carriage.

The powdered footman slammed to the door, and leaped on to the box.

The greys were turned, and the equipage rattled out of the triangle in which the side entrance of the house was placed.

As the carriage rattled off, Charles Rye looked at his companion in surprise.

Eagleton's dark brows met in a gloomy frown, and his black eyes sparkled with hate.

"Have you seen a ghost, that you look so startled?" said Charles Rye.

"That man made me a——"

"A what?"

"A man of the world!" returned Eagleton, first drawing a heavy sigh, and then laughing harshly.

They entered the tavern.

A number of dapper waiters made way for them, with inane smiles and obsequious bows.

Followed by Charles Rye, Eagleton ran up the wide staircase, and entered a large room.

The bright yet mellowed light of the gas jets was thrown down upon several green-baize-covered tables, on which white, black and red balls were rolling.

A few young fellows were gathered around two of the tables.

"They are not arrived — we are early," said Eagleton; "let us adjourn to the smoking-room, where we may enjoy a little seclusion."

The friends went below and entered a large and noble room, with several tables, at one of which they sat down.

There were but few persons in the room, and they occupied the farther end of it.

The friends called for wine and lighted their cigars.

"And now you must tell me of your connection with that big-wig," said Rye.

"Thank ye, no; we'll talk about something more pleasant. Yet—let me ask you a question."

"At your service."

"You have heard of Redpath, and Robson, and Roupell——"

"What of them?"

"Those fellows made a deal of money."

"Yes; made money!"

"What's the matter?"

"Every person who aims at seeming *à la mode* expresses himself in that way. It is impolite to ask a man how much he *earns* in a year; we *make* money now-a-days."

"What a confounded bore you are with your sagacious remarks and moral reflections!"

"*Peccavi!* Go on; you were saying—"

"That these unfortunates made a power of money, and lived in a glorious style—"

"While their usurped reign lasted."

"Well, now, don't you think that a man might begin life by 'raising the wind' in a rather questionable manner, and yet live happy and glorious up till the day of his death?"

"Glorious, perhaps, but not happy. Richard, depend upon it, boy or man, whoever does a wrong thing is always inwardly miserable, however outwardly prosperous."

"Pish! You ought to be a missionary, or a parson in a little ranter's chapel."

"I might be worse than either, Dick, or rather should never be good enough for any such posts. Let's be jolly, as you say; but, Heaven helping us, let us be commonly honest."

"Well, the man you saw just now is a living example of my philosophy that roguery is no roguery, when not found out. That man has made an immense fortune by the most unscrupulous means, and yet he is firm as a rock."

"His sin will find him out."

"Thanks for the text, but spare the sermon, and drink, man."

Eagleton drew out his pocket-book, and played with some papers which he drew from it.

"Of course you know, Charlie," he said, with a nervous laugh, "when I see the wicked man flourish like the green bay tree, and all that kind of thing, it riles me; but for all that I love right as much as you do, and think much of honesty."

"I know you do—you are the best fellow alive. I have cause to say so," returned Charles Rye," "but you shouldn't talk such shallow nonsense quite so seriously."

"By the way, Charlie, what a good writer you are, and what an odd resemblance there is betwixt your style and old Bullion's," he said, cautiously; "here is one of the governor's signatures; for a wonder he writes as round and neat as a lawyer's clerk."

"Ah! mine will never be worth so much," returned Charles, scribbling his name on a piece of paper.

"Write the governor's name, and let us see how near it comes to the original."

Young Rye complied, and wrote "John Bullion" under the autograph.

"Try again."

The young clerk did so, this time imitating the form of the characters as from a copy.

"That's better, but not quite identical," said Eagleton, disguising his excitement by a horse-laugh.

"Ha, ha! why, you are gifted, Charlie, with a power of imitation I never saw equalled."

A third time young Rye scribbled his master's name on the paper.

"By Jove! it's perfect."

At this moment five or six dashing-looking youths entered the smoking-room.

"That's Mortimer, Jessop, and the other fellows. Welcome them, Charlie. Be jolly now for once in a way."

Young Rye sprang forward to greet the new comers.

He left the scrap of paper on the table.

With eager fingers, Eagleton snatched it, cautiously folded it, and slipped it into one of the pockets of the case, which he immediately returned to his pocket.

He jumped up, and advanced towards his companions.

He cordially shook hands with them.

Another bottle of wine was brought.

After a while the party adjourned to the billiard-room.

Several games were played with varying success.

At first awkward, but warmly encouraged by the others, Charlie found himself after awhile getting more skilful, and began to conceive a liking for the game.

During the play Eagleton took care to pass the wine frequently to the young clerk.

In the heat and excitement of the game Charles drank without caution.

At length they desisted.

"Come, old fellow, let's off to see the Peris."

"No; I think I have had enough fun for once. I enjoyed that game vastly, and now I shall go home, especially as I want to be up betimes for the start to the Derby," replied Charlie, whose cheek was flushed and his eye glittering from his unusual indulgence in wine.

His companions laughed, and bantered him.

"I say, you must come with us, and see the Peris."

"What Peris, eh? Oh! I'll go. But, confound it, who are the Peris?"

"The belles of the new ballet, to be sure. The Peris, Sylvia Volante, is queen of the genii, and they say she has the most exquisite dance arranged for her that she ever performed."

"Oh! yes, yes, I'll go and see the Peris. But there is something so exciting in the game of—what you may call—billiards——"

"You like it?" cried the fellows, in chorus.

"Vastly. Only I'm so particularly stupid and unskilful."

"You show great promise, my boy," cried Eagleton, clapping him on the shoulder. "I appeal to you, gentlemen?"

"We must not teach him too much. We shall stand no chance against him after a little more such practice," responded the others, laughing.

"Well, then, as you are so kind as to say that, why I'll go to the ballet," replied young Rye," rather hazily.

The fast men looked at the neophite, and smiled at each other.

Two of them took his arm, and led the way from the house.

The others followed.

Eagleton lingered.

A tall, dark fellow, with a handsome face, and splendid figure, drew to his side.

"What luck?" he asked.

"Don't you see?"

"Yes—he's coming round."

Eagleton drew his glove round and round his hand, significantly.

"Yes, Mortimer, he's mine."

"I think so."

"Can you doubt us?"

"No. He seems a quiet one, a fellow without any strength of character."

"Hardly so—he has principles."

"We all begin in that way."

"And he's free now."

"Well, he'll soon find himself in a mess."

"Yes; but I don't dislike him."

"Number one is the first number."

"First and last with me, just now. I am so mad about that Mowbray; the thief has bamboozled me entirely. But, come on, or we shall lose our freshman."

The worthies left the tavern, and followed their comrades.

"And how did you get on about the signatures—the 'trial' sheets, or rather the 'charge' sheet?" said the other, with a grin.

" I won't use them if I can help it."

" But I understand the checks you got cashed are not in the care of your department of the office, but in his."

" That's where my safety lies. If there should be a smash, he will be charged. I will slip these pretty little specimens, these amateur attempts, into his desk at home; and when his place is searched, the crushers will nab them at once. 'Ho! ho!' cries the detective. 'A man does not practice so carefully to imitate another's hand for nothing. Master Rye is no tyro, but an adept, he is the accomplished forger, and these are his rough studies. Penal servitude as sure as fate.' "

" And yet the fellow seems to have great regard for you."

" So he has. And I shall be sorry, very sorry, if I have to sacrifice him, but, as you say, it is one and all in the game in this world."

" Well his fate rides on the back of the favorite—that's some hope."

" And will Electra win, think you ?"

" I am not a prophet !"

——

CHAPTER CXL.

THE INDIANS AND THEIR PRISONERS—HAR-
WOLF IN BONDS—THE FEAR OF DEATH—
CATAHAGA HIS OWN AVENGER.

THE trapper, the captain of the Bush-rangers, and Wyld, answered the whoop of the Indians with a loud shout.

Emerging from the grand primeval trees, the war-party approached.

The youngest led the way.

In the midst of the line walked four men, tightly bound by the strips of a bark which serves the red-skins so well for cordage.

The last of these prisoners was Daniel Harwolf.

Catahaga and the Heart of Fire followed the train.

Every Indian's belt was heavy with scalps, excepting the Eagle-Wing's.

Since the day when he had so deeply wounded his gentle wife by his national arrogance and harshness, and had made amends by casting from him the hideous trophies which caused her such disgust, Catahaga had taken no scalps.

They therefore reverted to his less scrupulous associates.

Those who were so fortunate as to obtain these, were held in great honour, for one who lived long among these strange people gives the following account of their observance relating to their peculiar and most horrible custom of " scalping."

" If the enemy has been killed by discharges of fire-arms, or by cutting weapons, the glory is adjudged to him who presents the 'scalps.' "

This is the hair and skin which cover that part of the skull called the " occiput," as the hair on that part of the head forms a circle.

" Even though the enemy may have been knocked down by any other person than the man who exhibits his scalp, the honour always belongs to the latter, for the following reason. The enemy who falls might, as the Indians say, merely pretend to be dead, in order to destroy with more ease and security his pursuer; and upon this principle they decide that the person who scalped the fallen foe, by being the first to come in close contact with him, incurred the greatest danger, and consequently has a fair title to the honours of the triumph.

" There is no enemy, whether killed or only wounded, who, on falling into the hands of the Indians, escapes this terrible operation of scalping; and all Indians are so firmly convinced of the fate awaiting this part of the head, that they constantly keep on it a lock of hair which they preserve, as it were, ever ready for presentation to the scalping-knife of the foe. This assertion I make after very particular attention, and I have found it confirmed in every part of the Indian territories in which I have travelled."

" My brother's trail is like the track of the prairie-fire," said Regan, with a smile; " and what does my brother intend as the fate of his prisoners ?"

" Only one of them is mine," returned the Pawnee chief, " the rest belong to my brothers, the Dacotahs."

Regan was vexed and astonished at perceiving the man to whom the Indian pointed was Michael Warren.

" My brother has taken a great chief of the Yengeese," he said, " he will sell him for many wampums, muskets and fire-food."

" Catahaga will not sell his prisoner; he will kill him," returned the inexorable Pawnee, in a firm tone.

" My brother's eyes are darkened by the evil manitous; if my brother will use the advantage he has gained, he may put an end to the war; if my brother sends his prisoner to the death-stake, the pale-faces will have the life of every Iroquois they can hunt down; let my brother remember the teaching of his white friends; let him remember mercy."

" Does the hunter show mercy to the wolves of the prairie? The grey wolf shall not live. I have spoken."

" And what does my brother intend to do with the rest ?"

" To send them to the wigwam of the Dacotahs, that they may be sacrificed to the spirits of the children of that tribe whose blood has been drunk by the earth that these pale-face serpents have torn from the fathers of the Iroquois."

Catahaga turned and spoke a few words to his braves.

At his command, three of the men were borne away to a little clearing, where some of the braves were lighting a fire.

They were bound hand and foot, and thrown on to the ground.

Two ferocious-looking Dacotahs paced beside them on guard, their long guns upon their shoulder.

"Curse it all, captain, but these fellows belong to another gang that we're in league with. How can we let them perish?" said Wyld to Regan.

The latter shrugged his shoulders.

"We cannot save them."

"Why not?"

"A rupture with the Indians would be bad policy."

"And this Judge Warren—he is too high a quarry to be struck down by a kite of a red-skin."

"I will save him, if I can."

"If you can. Where is the difficulty?"

"I tell you that the safety of the band depends upon our discretion."

"But shall we see a comrade murdered before our eyes?"

"One must go, or there will be death for us all."

"I think this league with the Indians is all cursed folly."

"As it was made at my suggestion, then you imply that I am a cursed fool; thanks for the compliment. But would you seriously advise me, Wyld, to bring the vengeance of all the Indian tribes upon my shoulders for the sake of saving this old villain?"

"Well, perhaps not; but you must do what you can to save him."

"That is my intention."

Regan looked round for the Pawnee.

The young chief stood calmly beneath a tree.

Three or four Indians of his own tribe were standing about him.

"Will my brother torture his prisoner?" asked the bush-ranger, awed, in spite of himself, by the imperturbable malignity expressed in the young chief's countenance.

"Catahaga has learned to kill his enemies at once. His heart is thirsty for the blood of the whole race of the pale-faces; but he takes no pleasure in useless tortures."

"Then my brother will spare the great father of the Yengeese wigwam?"

Catahaga made no other reply than to drop a bullet down the rattling bore of his musket, and drive home the charge with a graceful dash of the long ramrod.

The Pawnee threw his long rifle across his left arm, and waved his hands to his braves.

Two of them immediately seized the prisoner, and led him into the wood.

Two others followed.

And then, slowly and gracefully sweeping along, his long, bright-stained robe sweeping the ground, his long plumes of the "quaillon"—which none but hereditary sachems are allowed to wear—fluttering in the night breeze, went the indomitable chief, weapon in hand, the executioner of his own vengeance.

As the villanous murderer walked along, his eyes bent on the ground, his heart, so firm by nature, but so shaken by the cowardice of guilt, beat almost audibly.

"And is it to end thus?" he muttered, inwardly. "Have I escaped the dread justice of the first government in the world—have I run through such a long career of successful crime to die by the hands of a savage in the lone back-woods, whither I fled for covert and security? To die! Why have the lying priests and morbid poets made death seem so hideous? This awful change! Shall I see him? Will she rove the dark shores, mad and distracted, her great wild eyes freezing my soul, her dishevelled hair wreathing like a crest of snakes? And he! the fire consumed him, and was quenched. Me it will not consume—

never, never! The torture may be of the mind; worse and worse, for one might wallow in fire, and hope that all stain may be scorched off in the ample space of eternity, for punishment must be some atonement. To see that pair—to be mocked by the gibbering Rye, who, may be, died in the mad-house—to see my wife, with the blood staining the breast which suckled my only son! Villains! Murderers! Let me go! Let me go! I dare not, I will not, die!"

He made a rush to escape.

The two Indians laid their iron grip on his shoulders.

He was as powerless as a fox in the claws of eagles.

He was dragged along.

He raved at the horrible spectres conjured to his guilty soul by the demon of remorse.

He felt himself thrown against a tree.

The hard, cutting thongs were tight compressed about his swelling arms.

A few paces before him stood Catahaga, as calmly as if he were about to stretch himself upon a bed of rest.

In his hand he lightly poised his glancing rifle.

He was drawing back the fire-lock.

*　　　*　　　*　　　*　　　*

"There is but one chance for him," said the captain of the bush-rangers to his lieutenant, as he looked after the retreating figures of the Indians and their prisoner, as they were lost in the gloom.

"What, that we make a rush to his rescue?"

"A rush to the place whither yon poor rogue is bound? No, no; stay here. There is but one whose voice can move that stubborn heart—the voice of Minna Wyotti."

With this, Regan rushed back to the trapper's cabin.

Weatherfield, who had not interfered in behalf of the captive, for whom he had a great aversion, as believing him to be implicated in the attempt at robbing and murdering himself and the Jew, now followed the bandit, in order to see the issue.

Minna still sat by the side of Agnes.

She flew across the room, and waved him to leave it.

Agnes was deeply sleeping.

"I am here, Minna, only for your good," said the bush-ranger, impatiently, yet instinctively lowering his voice to a whisper; "your husband has gone mad! His blood-thirsty Indianism has burst every barrier of prudence, and you must both perish."

"Just Heaven, what has he done?"

"He has taken prisoner Michael Warren the Judge of Larchville."

"Well, well."

"At this moment he has carried his captive into the wood to murder him."

Minna could not repress a shriek.

"This is all very well on the war-path, but a cold-blooded murder will bring condign vengeance on you both."

"Oh! where is he? where is my husband? Lead me to him," cried Minna distractedly.

"Softly, he knows your influence, and you must steal close upon him, for if he sees you coming, he will forestall you by the death-shot."

"As you will; but quick, O quick!" exclaimed Minna, violently trembling.

The young bush-ranger took her soft hand, pressed it encouragingly, and placing it under his left arm led her with a manly step rapidly into the wood.

Great excitement prevailed among the bush-rangers.

Several of the Dacotahs yelled malignantly, and even threatened to throw their hatchets.

THE STARTLING APPEARANCE.

But, heedless of these demonstrations, the dauntless young bush-ranger stalked firmly and swiftly
on, Minna tripping lightly by his side.

They passed between the sombre trees till they
came upon the objects of their chase.

Very carefully they drew near.

Catahaga had raised his gun to his shoulder.

He was taking deliberate aim at Harwolf.

Conquered by guilt, the man of courage hung as
if dead by the thongs that bound him.

In an instant Minna had thrown her soft white
arms around her husband.

She looked tenderly and pleadingly into his dark
yet noble face.

"For Minna's sake!"

Catahaga turned away, his lip quivering, a gloomy
light in his dark eyes.

No. 45.

He held out the gun, and she took it from his
hands.

He waved his hand to his braves to set the captive
free, and then walked sullenly into the forest.

Minna followed him.

She threw her arms about him.

He thrust her away.

She sank on her knees, sobbing bitterly at this repulse.

"Catahaga is the slave of a pale-face squaw," said
the Indian, bitterly. "His enemies laugh at him;
his heart is not hard. His wife has broken his war-
hatchet and his notched arrows. The Yengeese may
well scorn the son of Monotah, for he is a serpent
that has no sting."

CHAPTER CXLI.

THE RACE—LOST AND WON—EAGLETON'S AGONY
—CHARLES RYE'S KINDNESS—THE RETURN
HOME—ARRESTED FOR FORGERY.

THE Derby day.

The sun blazes in a cloudless sky.

The road is thronged with an endless line of vehicles of every kind jostling together in mad emulation.

Four-in-hands, dog-carts, tilburies, barouches, wagonettes, carts, and trucks, whirled along by bloods, hacks, and donkeys, and carrying nobles, millionaires, city men, shopkeepers, clerks, costermongers, actors, artists and authors, publishers, and wild boys.

With a glorious fracas, with a heart-stirring buzz, and thrilling shouts of mirth, with an occasional blast of wrath, or scream of terror, away and away, and onward and onward, pour the living stream, throwing up its blinding clouds of dust.

Among the thousands that swell the mighty phalanx are our two clerks and the *premiere dansente*.

Sylvia is dressed with simplicity, yet extreme elegance.

The two young men are attired in the height of fashion, and seem determined to enjoy themselves.

They are riding in a pretty little phaeton, drawn by a pair of ponies.

Eagleton effects a boisterous gaiety to conceal his restlessness of mind.

Sylvia uses all her blandishments to allure young Rye to the most perfect confidence in herself and her colleague in treachery.

In a few hours they have reached the course.

The scene is animated beyond description, for the liveliest word-picture the pen ever drew cannot give an adequate idea of the stupendous gathering of London's millions on the green level—a "Goodwin's Sands" to many, "Tom Tiddler's ground" to Fortune's favoured few.

Eagleton soon left the chaise, promising an immediate return, and excusing himself on the plea of an appointment he had made with some of his companions with whom he had bets.

He forced his way through the flocks of hawks and pigeons that had met respectively to cheat and be cheated, through the crowds assembled round a band of "niggers," or a company of strolling acrobats, and reaches the grand stand, near which a party of fast men, with books in their hands, were eagerly disputing with a tall, keen-eyed Jew.

He touched one of them on the shoulder.

The young man turned and shook hands with him. Both the friends looked pale and careworn.

"I have left him with Sylvia; I know he has money, and that he will stake the last penny for me; he is one one of that rare sort who stick at nothing that implies self-respect in the service of those he looks upon as friends."

"And how did you manage about the signatures?"

"Oh, the matter was easy; I went home with him, and by pretending that I had an important letter to write, which I had hitherto forgotten, I induced him to open his desk, and very soon contrived to slip the paper into it."

"Of course, when his place is searched, they will be found, and he will suffer."

"It's a pity; but, perhaps, we may have no occasion to injure him."

"But, even if Electra wins the race you will find it hard to restore the money without creating suspicion."

"It can be done; we can even get him out of the way for awhile by some means, or, through Sylvia, we may even persuade him to throw up his engagement at the office."

"I wish it were decided."

"So it will be in ten minutes."

"I shall not return to the chaise till the race is run."

"No, or you will betray yourself."

The bell now rang to prepare for the start.

Then the dense mass of beings swayed and rolled into a long, compact, and broad line along the course.

The sleek, slender, glossy, and gamish-looking race-horses, on whose long backs were jauntily perched the small and agile jockeys, with their skull-caps, and yellow, blue, red and striped jackets, and their flexile riding whips.

Mortimer and Eagleton occupied an advantageous position near the winning-post, and commanded a view of the whole course.

The signal given the slim and beautiful coursers made a start.

They were recalled.

It was a false start.

Eagleton groaned and cursed.

Again the master of the course gave the signal.

This time it was all fair and free, and away flew the fleet steeds swifter than wind.

They had passed the critical "corner," and close together came tearing back.

The crowd held deep, impressive silence, every breath hushed, every eye strained.

Eagleton panted in an agony of dire suspense.

Electra was ahead of his competitors by many a length, and was making fast for the winning-post.

The air was rent with loud and thrilling shouts.

Just as success seemed certain a strap gave way, the gallant racer stumbled and fell.

The other horses swept past in a straight line.

The deafening cheers told that the race was won.

Eagleton staggered back.

His face was livid white, his teeth close set, and he murmured some broken words of intense despair.

Mortimer caught him in his arms.

When the crowd had broken up once more, into smaller or larger masses, Mortimer led his friend apart.

He poured him out a glass of strong brandy.

Eagleton drank eagerly.

Then he walked away towards the chaise, his brow wrinkled into a frown of anguish.

Sylvia's cheek was very pale, and Charles Rye caught his hand with a grasp of sympathy.

"There is no sport in these great risks, Dick, after all; but Sylvia has told me that you have lost heavily, and, as far as my means allow, I will help you. Cheer up, old fellow, and let this be a lesson for life, and so, remembering that fortune is fickle, and much better jilted when she plays the gamester, forget your loss, which is not irreparable, and be as jolly as you can."

Eagleton answered vacantly.

In the evening as they drove home he seemed to have recoved his elasticity of spirits.

He laughed and jested, and appeared rather as one who had obtained a great success than as a heavy loser.

Sylvia grew thoughtful, and looked wistfully into the face of her young adorer.

Charley was the soul of good-humour, and exerted himself to the utmost to distract his companion's thoughts from unpleasant subjects.

When they parted Rye assured his friend that he would draw his last penny and place all his fortune at his disposal, and thus they separated with mutual expressions of regard.

Little did Charles Rye suspect the scoundrelism of him whom he esteemed with such romantic friendship, or her falseness whom he loved with all the fervour of a warm and affectionate nature.

It happened that Silas Rye had gone down to Frontemore with Lord Hawksbury.

The generous young noble had resolved to secure to his unfortunate sister the possession of her estates, and then to set out on his long-projected search for the Boy Pirate.

As Charles Rye placed the key in the lock to open the door, a strange tremor ran through his veins, an unaccountable forboding of approaching trouble.

A man wrapped in a cloak swept round the corner.

He beckoned to the young man to stop.

Charles, who had not observed him, entered the hall and mounted the stairs.

He had reached the drawing-room, when he heard a short, quick knock at the front door.

His impulse was to return and receive the visitor, whoever he might be.

But seeing, through the open door, the shadows of two men seated, and apparently awaiting his coming, he changed his mind and entered the room.

A tall, stern-faced man rose from a chair, and approached him.

Another inscrutable-looking personage stood up at the same moment.

He had some papers in his hand.

"Gentlemen, may I inquire——" Charles was beginning in some amazement.

"Young man, you are wanted," said one of the strangers, tapping him on the shoulder.

"Wanted?"

"Yes."

"And by whom?"

"By me—by the police authorities. I am Inspector Williams, and am commissioned to take you into custody."

"Nonsense; upon what charge?"

"Upon the charge of forgery. And as we have examined the house, and have found in these papers the most conclusive evidence against you, resistance is perfectly useless."

Charles Rye could not realise his position; he stood stupified and bewildered, while one of the officers snapped the handcuffs on his wrists.

CHAPTER CXLII.

THE BOY PIRATE'S HUMANITY TO THE POOR SLAVES—HIS REVERIE—ZAMPA'S BLACK FOUNDLING—A VISIT TO THE ISLAND HOME OF THE SPANISH PIRATE IS RESOLVED ON—ZAMPA IN A NEW CHARACTER.

WHEN the bodies of the slaver and his crew had been cut down and thrown into the deep the Boy Pirate went on board.

With a number of his men he went below, and did what was possible for bettering the condition of the poor Africans.

When the pirates first presented themselves, the negroes imagined that some dreadful danger threatened them, and expressed their fright by the most heart-rending groans and gesticulations.

But Zampa stood by the side of our hero, and addressing his fellow-countrymen in their own language, soon restored them to confidence and quiet.

The dead body was cut away from the wall, and was, at Christopher's command, committed to the sea with some attention to seriousness and propriety.

The poor wretches who were locked in the cruel embrace of the iron instruments of diabolic torture were released.

Under the direction of Zamp the negroes set hard to work and cleansed the decks, which were in a frightful state.

Windsails were then strung in such a manner that a rapid draught of purifying air swept through the ship, and waited on its breezy wing health and cheerfulness. The gratings above were disencumbered of the heavy spare booms and sail-cloth with which they were covered, and the darkness was dispelled.

What fresh provisions could be spared from the steam-frigates was served out in moderate rations to the half-famished wretches, and they were encouraged to celebrate their happy deliverance by mirth and jollity.

As our hero stood leaning against the taffrail, his ear soothed by the merry, chuckling laughter of the volatile blacks—who were now as happy as sandboys, whatever they may be—and his eye brightened by the sight of the splendid flotilla that he had won by his own strong arm, aided by the few faithful followers whom, by his merit and genius, he had gathered around him, his mood was softened, hope whispered in his heart; he did not seek to justify to himself the crimes of his long, eventful and desperate career; but, sincerely penitent for the past, deep shamed by the consciousness of his guilt, yet he could not but remember that he was compelled, in the first place, to serve as a pirate, and that he had fought almost solely with his enemies, or with those who were the oppressors of others, and he murmured, half sad, half comforted,

"It may be that my bright star is on the wane; my career, perhaps, draws to an end; whoever may record my story might be better employed, but, like myself, perhaps, he will be forced by some incentive, too strong to be resisted, to do that work which his heart does not sanction; but, perhaps, he will find this excuse, that his hero is not proud of his shame, takes no delight in even the most brilliant deeds that are lawless, that he repents and would atone, that the moral of his life is that a man, good or bad, who breaks the laws of society, is to be despised and punished. Out of the blackness my historian may evoke a germ of brightness; some of the young and ardent lovers of bold romance may learn better where to find ideals of bravery and nobleness than in the records of crime. Some may shudder at the little temptings which seem so easily resisted, and yet are *not* resisted, and which lead to such fearful results. Well, if the boy who exults in reading the dashing adventures of a bold buccaneer, could be brought to feel the sweetness of good actions and the bitter fruits of robbery and murder, even when God reserves to himself their punishment, he would have no heart for a canting song about "The Road," and no interest in the fate of such villains as are made heroes by foolish or unscrupulous romances, unless to rejoice when he found that they all came to the same respectable end, and, like pests and vermin as they were, died on the gallows. Oh! that I had not been a pirate. With half the skill and courage that only make me more to be dreaded and pursued, I should have been a *real* hero; now, make the best of me, I am but a pirate, a little less hardened than others."

Lilia at this moment came on board the slaver with Ida; she wished to have a look at the negroes now that they were made comfortable and presentable by the humanity of the rover-chief.

She at once saw the look, which told of unhappiness and remorse, darkening the face of her beloved husband.

She hurried to his side.

She wound her arms about him, and cheered him with a merry smile.

He pressed her fondly to his heart, and spoke cheerfully of the future.

When they had returned to the "Avenger" Zampa came aft, and doffed his hat to the captain.

"Buckra, cap'en, I'se beg yo pardon, I ab something to 'quest, which hope yo not refuse."

"Nothing in reason to you, uncle Zamp," said Christopher, smiling.

"It not nuffin to do wid me, sar'; yo see dat buckra's werry curiss, 'speck see eberybody wear—'scuse me, sar—not mentionables!"

"Well, you scamp, go to Tom Garrod and ask him if he has another pair for the signal halliard. Why, you rogue, do you want to reduce us all to our aboriginal condition?"

"Not know, what dat, sir; but it's de yaller gal, Cora, sar, she berry much like to 'pear like——"

"Where is she?" asked Lilia, who could not help laughing, in spite of her blushes.

"Nuss de baby, missus, in de after cabin ob de slaver; berry fin' gal, do beautiful for missus's maid; ole Zamp de major-domo. Lor, missus, when in Ashantee, Meajanée hab devil of lot of wives."

"And who is that worthy?"

"Dat's me, sar, dat's raal name in Ashantee; some buckra call me Zamp. Dunnow nuffin what 'em mean; berry fine name, Meajance. When I'se in my country—much palaver many battles—I drink out ob de skulls ob my enemies, and the seafarin' buckras call me King Johnny."

"You are a terrible rascal, Zamp, and don't deserve your high fortune in falling into my hands; but go, Lilia, and look after this poor mulatto girl."

When Lilia had left him Christopher walked up to Gomez, who was standing by the forecastle, for he had come aboard for stores and ammunition, which were being removed in boats to the "Defiance."

"And what are we to do with the negroes, Senor Gomez?"

I have been thinking, captain, that it will be a good plan to set them down on the island I told you of; there is plenty of fruit and game, the soil is fertile, they will be under the shade of the British flag."

"But will it not be better if we take them to the plantation of Leon de Zamora; his island is also under British protection, and since he has given up our trade I hear he has prospered rarely on his new estates."

"Yes, senor, and the old admiral Giraldez is with him, and Leon's beautiful wife, Mona. I should be glad to see them all before we leave these waters."

"And so should I. Well, we will land our supercargo on a lonely part of the island. Many of them can speak English; they may tell the truth if they please, for we have now the speed of the ' Fiery Dragon,' as well as of the 'Flying Fairy'—we can elude pursuit."

"Yes, senor! We can land the blacks on the night preceding our departure. The station on the island is but small, and the governor of it, for aught I know, may be Zamora himself."

"Agreed then!" returned the Boy Pirate. "And for transporting arms and stores for the brave nation we have adopted—then for a land cruise and a wild and dashing career in Poland."

The sailors now crowded to the bulwarks, shouting and laughing.

Zampa came on board.

In his arms he carried a fat black baby, which was kicking and squalling most lustily.

He walked aft, and presented it to Lilia.

The rover's wife took it tenderly, but not without a slight quiver of repulsion.

As soon as the child looked up into her bright and beautiful face he began to leap and crow with pleasure.

When Lilia had thus soothed him, she gave him back to Zampa.

The negro had seated himself on a barrel. A basin of some steaming mess which he had concocted by Cora's prescription, stood by his side, and he held an immense spoon in his hand.

With a solemnity that was truly ludicrous he fed the child, from time to time raising his head and looking at the Boy Pirate and Lilia, who stood laughing, and grinned with infinite drollery.

CHAPTER CXLIII.

DON LEON DE ZAMORA AT HOME—A GRAND BALL—THE TWO STRANGE CAPTAINS.

LEON DE ZAMORA had built one of the most fairy-like edifices ever erected by mortal hands upon the sunny island of which Gomez had spoken.

It was a long, low building, shaded on every side by a deep, depending roof of verandah supported by fretted pillars, round which were twined long tendrils with drooping blossoms of some exotic plant.

The roof, which was flat, was a parterre of flowers;

it was the evening resort of the inmates of the house, who repaired thither to enjoy the cool and freshful breezes from the blue ocean.

Around the house were groves of palm and bowers of aromatic shrubs and flowers of the most gorgeous hues, sparkling fountains and beautiful statues.

Before the door was a large and smooth plat of grass kept verdant by the spray which was scattered from a rippling fountain in the centre.

Leon de Zamora was a man of exquisite taste, and applied the treasures which he had collected, both as a privateer in the Mexican service, and as a rover on his own account, to the adornment of his splendid mansion.

Pictures of great value and high merit, often the rarest works of the greatest masters; costly plate, and ornaments of the choicest and most charming description; books in all languages, and arms of every kind and quality. These rich spoils enriched his palatial home, and rendered it a paradise of beauty.

Now, it happened that Zamora, who had been elected governor of this and of several of the adjacent islands, had invited a number of officers, both naval and military, and the few ladies—their wives and daughters—who could be collected, to a grand ball which he gave on the anniversary of his election to the governorship of the islands.

His ball room presented a scene of splendour little to be expected in such remote latitudes.

The walls were draped airily with white silk richly worked with gold, and ornamented with the banners of the British and other powers who divided the islands amongst them.

The room was lighted by the mellow glow of wax-lights in golden sconces, and in boundless number; all the windows, which were folding, were thrown wide open, showing the exquisite scenery without,—the bowing gardens, in whose green glades, so solemn and quiet, glimmered the little globe lamps like glow-worms.

Beyond, the high peak which shot up from the ocean, and then the sea of silver jewelled with illuminated islands, and the heaven's one blaze of brilliant southern stars.

At one end of the room, on a platform, a military band were playing a stirring tune, while the guests were saunteringly promenading the room, for a dance had concluded, and the music which was now performing was a march played by request to the admiring company.

Among the bevies of officers in their bright uniforms, and ladies in their beauty and rich dresses, a number of black servants in purple and silver liveries were swiftly gliding with silver trays presenting tiny cups of coffee.

Don Leon de Zamora, dressed in a stately uniform, his breast blazing with stars and orders, moved with the ease and self-possession of experience among his guests, delighting each in turn by his urbanity.

Though there were a few creole girls present who were of surpassing beauty, Mona de Zamora was by far the loveliest woman there, yet neither her beauty, wealth, nor happiness appeared to excite feelings of envy in the hearts of any of the ladies, her friends.

Near the band Admiral Giraldez, whom our hero had rescued so gallantly from the castle of San Salvador, was seated conversing and chatting with a little girl upon his knee.

His mild blue eyes and long sweeping beard gave him a gentle and amiable appearance that contrasted strangely with the breadth and hardness of his forehead, which was scanned by a long scar as from a sabre-cut.

A number of the officers, before mentioned as belonging to detachments stationed in the different islands, and to vessels moored in the bays or off shore, were gathered around Don Leon.

"I assure your excellency that I have no doubt of the fact. I should not be surprised to hear that the Boy Pirate had run down the entire Brazilian fleet," said the captain of an English frigate that lay off at anchor in the little harbour of the island.

"He is indeed a formidable man, Captain Roland,"

answered Don Leon, gravely; "but he is the most generous of the brave."

"That character will not save him if he falls into our hands; but I have this much respect for the fellow, that I will give him every chance of dying like a warrior on his own deck, for I will not attempt to take him alive, and lest he chooses to surrender, which of course he will never do, he may escape a swing at the yard-arm by dying in battle."

"Captain Kit, the Boy Pirate would, doubtless, express his thanks for your kindness and consideration were he present," said Don Leon, with a dry smile.

"Now, I like the dog; for what are Brazilian frigates to us?" said a dapper little lieutenant of a corvette, on the cruise for slavers. "I should not care, as my friend says he should not wonder, if he took the whole fleet; but there was another craft of suspicious appearance to which we gave chase, but she got before a head-wind, and we lost her."

"Do you think she was a pirate?"

"Yes, a schooner-rigged vessel; she answered in all respects the description given of a craft commanded by another extraordinary fellow, also an Englishman, who is known as Black Ralph."

A broad-built, handsomely-dressed officer, with a dark, swarthy face, rolling black eyes, long raven elf-locks, and a large black beard, who was enchanting a possy of pretty girls by his bantering compliments, started at this name.

"I think you will pardon my intruding so abruptly upon the conversation; but a name was mentioned which I have not as yet heard spoken, the name of a man with whom I have come in contact."

"What! have you seen Black Ralph?" cried the officers in one voice.

"Indeed I have, on more than one occasion," returned the other, with a smile. "In fact, I once served in the same ship with him."

"Is it possible?"

"Yes. He once commanded an American privateer."

"I never heard so," returned Don Leon, looking hard at the speaker.

"Oh, yes; but, of course, you all know from report what sort of a fellow he is?"

"A tall, powerful man, with a fierce, dark face, and a black beard. No offence, Captain Oliver, but not unlike yourself."

"Thus does report deceive people. Reports are seldom quite correct, and, in this case, report is all in the wrong. Black Ralph is so called because he is always dressed in deep mourning. An affair of the heart, you know; he was the most exemplary fellow in the world, everything good and proper; but his wife ran away with a French purser, and from that hour he turned desperate, and having killed his rival, which caused his wife to commit suicide, he went into deep black, and to escape the law he defied the law and turned rover."

"Poor rogue!"

"He is a little fellow, not much higher than my sword. He is fair, with a freckled face, and a brush of red hair."

"Then he's no beauty."

"His hair was not always red."

"No! that's something new," said Captain Roland. "I've heard of people's hair turning white, and I know of its getting black again with the assistance of the barber; but for turning red——"

"Well its stated that when he heard that his faithless spouse had eloped with the purser, he turned so scarlet with wrath that the colour of his face conveyed itself to his hair, which turned flaming red, and has remained so ever since."

"That's rather stiff, Captain Oliver."

"His hair, or my story? Well, I'll not vouch for the veracity of this part of his history, all the rest you may rely upon."

"I wish I could overhaul the rascal."

"There are many say so; but none have outmatched him yet."

"His time will come."

"With the 'good time,' or doomsday," returned Captain Oliver, laughing. "You men-of-war's men must be fast asleep; you let the wolf bark under your noses, and suffer him to escape, when you have him by the ears."

"Well, we shall run him down at last," said Captain Roland, viciously.

The little group now dispersed, for the band had struck up a quadrille.

Captain Oliver gallantly offered his arm to Donna Zamora. She accepted him as a partner, and every one admitted that, in spite of his burly figure, Captain Oliver danced with the most perfect grace.

A servant approached Don Zamora.

"A stranger, your excellency. Shall I admit him?"

"Does he appear to be a gentleman?"

"A noble, I should think."

"Indeed! What name did he give?"

"Captain Paul."

Zamora started.

"Shall I usher him into the ball-room, your excellency?"

"We have a Roland for an Oliver, and now we are to have a Captain Paul. There is but one I know who bears that soubriquet."

These reflections on the part of the governor of the island were interrupted by the servant, who repeated his former question.

"By no means admit him; but lead me to him."

The servant bowed, and preceding his master, crossed the room towards one of the open windows.

He started back as the stranger stepped in from the balcony, and stared confidently at him, and taking off his cap, made a low bow.

He was a tall and graceful youth, with large and lustrous eyes, and a mass of glossy dark curls.

He was very richly dressed, in the picturesque costume peculiar to the Spaniards of America.

A large Spanish mantle was wrapped round him, one side being thrown with graceful negligence across his left shoulder.

He extended his hand.

Zamora grasped it warmly.

"My friend! my benefactor——"

"Hush!"

"You are right; by such names you will at once be discovered."

"Do not flatter me; but introduce me to your friends."

"Oh, senor! why this needless risk?"

"It is not without purpose. Pray introduce me."

"Consider for one moment——"

"It is too late to consider now."

"Do not blame me for what may follow."

"Do but oblige me by what must precede an introduction."

The dance at this moment concluded.

Again the company broke up into brilliant groups.

Don Leon de Zamora led the strange guest by the hand into the centre of the room.

"Ladies and gentlemen," he said, "with the most heartfelt pleasure, I introduce to you Captain Paul, of the, the——"

"Audacious!" quickly prompted the visitor.

"Of the 'Audacious;' a very valued friend."

In a few moments Captain Paul was lionized by the ladies, envied by the gentlemen, stared at by the servants, and admired by all.

Amid that gay and bright assembly, when the gorgeous apartment rang with music and revelry, two of the guests stood watching each other with curious glances.

They were the Red Raven and the Black Vulture, the Boy Pirate and Black Ralph.

———

CHAPTER CXLIV.

A JEALOUS DON—CROSS PURPOSES—THE DUEL—THE BOY PIRATE DENOUNCED—SAVED BY BLACK RALPH.

THE ball proceeded with unflagging spirit, the mirth grew fast and furious.

Captain Paul caused quite a furore of excitement amongst the ladies, and more than one of the gentlemen began to be possessed with the "green-eyed monster," that imp of mischief yclept jealousy.

One there was present who keenly watched our hero.

In the recklessness of his bold nature, in the impunity of his long and firm success, the Boy Pirate suffered himself to be carried away by the ecstacies of the moment, and in the company of the gentle girls, who leaned upon his manliness and delicate tact, and were rejoiced by the homage paid them by one so handsome and brave, the Boy Pirate recked nothing of the danger he incurred by incensing the many rivals in their favours, who were now discountenanced on his behalf.

The man who noted every look and movement of our hero with such intense scrutiny was a dark and haughty-looking Spaniard, who rejoiced in the sounding title of Don Philip Alonzo Maria Terralvarez.

It is narrated of a Spaniard who boasted a name as long or longer than that of the distinguished person thus introduced that he knocked at the door of an inn late at night and asked for a bed; being asked who he was he replied by enumerating about a dozen names. "What," cried the landlord, who had popped his head and nightcap out from an upper window, "are there *twelve* of you? Well, I have not accommodation for half that number, you must go elsewhere."

To resume our story.

Don Philip happened to be one of those nobles who had visited our hero, from motives of curiosity, when the latter lay chained in the dungeons of San Salvador; in fact he was the brother of the governor of that fortress.

He recognised our hero at once.

Respect for his host had prevented him from denouncing the Boy Pirate on the instant.

He was in great perplexity.

What could he do?

Should he create a disturbance in the midst of such harmony, break up a reunion where every one was so happy? should he offend his host by an affront the most deadly?

He thought of a better plan.

He would kill the pirate first, and denounce him afterwards.

To achieve this, he must first pick a quarrel with him, then challenge him. Being skilful as a swordsman, and, moreover, particularly vain and self-confident, he believed that nothing could be easier than to vanquish a sailor, who, however well he might wield a cutlass or sabre, was no adept with the small-sword.

Our hero was seated by the side of a charming young creole, affianced to the gentleman above mentioned.

He had not the slightest idea that any one in the company was plotting such deadly ill to him.

Captain Oliver, who had, despite his sinister countenance, made a very favourable impression upon the company, was crossing the room to join a party in the ante-chamber, when his glance fell on the face of the Spanish noble, who had so doughtily resolved to win world-fame by vanquishing the Boy Pirate.

In a moment he guessed the great danger which threatened our hero.

He intercepted the Spaniard, and touched him on the shoulder.

"Senor, I crave the favour of a few words," he said.

"At your service, captain, in a few moments. I have a little business in hand, which will not brook delay."

"Senor, I must settle my affair first."

"You *must!* Ha! do you dictate to me?"

"If you please to think my request dictation, you may."

"Ha! then you mean to insult me?"

"Exactly so—to get up a quarrel, senor."

"But you amaze and enrage me. Why should you quarrel with me?"

"Because a quarrel is a necessary prelude to a duel."

"Then you wish to cross swords with me?"

"Just so."

"But what cause have you, senor, for enmity against one whom you never saw before?"

"I am not bound to give a reason for my antipathies. Will you fight, or are you a coward?"

"It would be well for you if I were, insolent!" returned the Spaniard, gnashing his teeth. "Lead on; I will follow you close."

Captain Oliver bowed, and passed through one of the open windows into the moonlit garden.

He walked into the shrubbery, and here he paused.

The two men stood facing each other, with frowning looks.

"It appears to me, Senor Inglesa, that you are a confederate of the wolf in sheep's clothing that it was my intention to denounce—that you are one of the gang of the Boy Pirate."

"Senor, you are mistaken; I have not the honour to belong to that gallant band," returned Captain Oliver.

"Perhaps, then, you are a pirate on your own account."

"Senor, you have not come hither to risk vague conjectures with regard to my affairs, but to defend your own honour and life."

"You will find me ready and able to do both, senor," replied the Spaniard, drawing his sword.

The two antagonists now crossed swords.

In a few moments it was apparent that Captain Oliver was a good swordsman.

The duel was fought with desperate fury, it being apparent that each had resolved to kill the other.

In parrying a lunge of Don Philip's sword, Captain Oliver received a slight wound in the arm.

The blood flowed.

Enraged by this, the Englishman threw himself recklessly upon the Spaniard.

Their swords seemed to cling together with magnetic force, and separated with a recoil that caused sparks to be emitted by their slim and highly-tempered blades.

In the midst of the fray, when hot and flushed and passion-maddened, the duellists were fiercely fighting, two or three gentlemen hastily entered the shrubbery.

Among them were Don Leon and our hero.

They beat down the swords of the combatants, and tore them asunder.

"Is my authority to be repeatedly mocked in this way, Don Philip?" said Don Leon, in a stern tone. "Have I not been already censured for want of firmness in putting down these disgraceful proceedings?"

"I will kill him; my honour demands it," panted the Spaniard. "He insulted me without the least provocation, and one of us must die."

"Malraya!" cried the governor, the sleeping passion rousing in his heart. "I will have you both tried by court martial, and shot for mutiny."

"Senor, I am beside myself with fury at this wrong; but I will waive this quarrel for the hour, for I have a duty to perform which all will allow to be paramount to every other consideration."

"Indeed, senor; and what may it be?" asked the governor, uneasily.

"I call upon you, Don Leon, to arrest this man," he said, pointing to our hero. "I charge him with every crime commitable under the head of piracy."

"Piracy!"

"Yes, gentlemen, draw your swords and surround him, for he is the Boy Pirate."

"The Boy Pirate!" cried the Spaniards, starting back as if a shell had burst amongst them.

"The man is mad," cried Captain Oliver, quickly; "it was but now that he charged *me* with being a pirate. This insult shall not go unpunished. I defy the authority of these estates of Britain to deprive me of satisfaction for the gross outrages of this insolent mar-peace. Come on, senor, if you are not a coward as well as mischief-maker."

Nothing loth, Don Philip, thus challenged, made another lunge at Captain Oliver.

The latter eluded the thrust, and drove his sword home to the hilt through his antagonist's shoulder.

Don Philip reeled, and, flinging up his arms, dropped on his face.

The bystanders lifted him with looks of consternation.

"Arrest him! I tell you, senors, he is the Boy Pirate!" muttered the luckless duellist.

"You had better retire as quickly as possible," whispered Zamora, to our hero.

"I am sorry, sir, that I must put you under arrest," said the governor, to Captain Oliver; "but I should be neglectful of my duty if I did not. Give up your sword!"

"Obey him; I will procure your release," whispered the Boy Pirate.

"Well, gentlemen, I yield myself a martyr to my own honour; this gentleman, whom I have placed for the present *hors de combat*, was either drunk or insane; he charged me with being the Boy Pirate, and, when Captain Paul appeared upon the scene, he transferred the charge to him. Gentlemen, I appeal to you if our young friend, Captain Paul, has in any respect the appearance of a desperate criminal."

"I second your appeal to the good sense of the company," said Don Leon; "I have known Captain Paul for several years; do you think I could be mistaken in his identity?"

"No, your excellency; Don Philip is too punctilious—too meddlesome," answered more than one of the guests."

"My friend is silent, he scorns to exonerate himself. Has he the air of a pirate?"

"No, no; absurd, preposterous. Viva los Yengleros! Viva Senor Paul!" laughed the others.

The Boy Pirate bowed his acknowledgements, but he did not speak.

A surgeon was summoned.

He declared the wound to be serious but not dangerous, as the sword had passed through the fleshy part of the arm.

"Nevertheless, Captain Oliver, you must remain my prisoner, till this affair is blown over."

"Upon parole?" said the duellist, with a dry smile.

"Your word must be your bond."

"May I never wear more binding chains," muttered the sea-captain.

"And now, gentlemen, let us quickly return to the ball-room before the ladies become alarmed and this unfortunate affair becomes known among them and mars all the sports of the festival."

"You have done me a service, Ralph Talbot," whispered the Boy Pirate; "what can I do for you?"

"Help me to hunt down that infernal Harwolf," replied Black Ralph, and together they sauntered into the ball-room.

CHAPTER CXLV.

WARREN SET AT LIBERTY—HE RETURNS TO THE REGULATORS—THE CAPTIVE SPY—ARRIVAL OF A STRANGER.

CATAHAGA walked on into the forest, leaving Minna in tears.

She did not attempt to follow him; she knew his strange and inconsistent nature, and was well aware how useless it was to oppose him when he was in what she called his "Indian" moods.

The character of the red skins is a strange mixture of the most contradictory qualities.

Abandoning his vengeance, he abandoned his prisoner, and Andrew Harwolf was set at liberty.

He expressed to Minna his gratitude in the warmest terms, and as soon as the sudden terror of immediate death had passed away he resumed all his natural callousness and presence of mind.

Minna received his thanks with some reserve, thinking that if her husband returned he might express some displeasure at her communing with his enemy.

Harwolf's horse was restored to him.

He mounted and rode away.

The Indians looked after him with sullen faces.

He rode across the prairie and made for the camp of the Regulators.

It was night before he reached the camp.

The news which he brought was received with a shout of execration against the Indians.

In the camp Harwolf found Mark Leighton.

The young settler's wound had proved less serious than had been anticipated.

He was now so far recovered that he could walk abroad, though feebly.

His cheek was very pale, and his left arm was bound in a sling.

His fury was great when Harwolf told him of the catastrophe of his own defeat.

He rated himself that he had not shot the captain of bush-rangers dead when he had the chance, and vowed that he would hunt him to the end of the world.

Among the settlers assembled round the watch-fire was a man named Rahab Bryan.

He was a huge and burly fellow, with an immense beard, broad chest, and a pair of arms that would have done credit to a Cyclops.

They were speaking of some fresh recruits who had joined the volunteer army from the settlements far and near throughout Oregon, Texas, and Arkansas, for the squatters had joined with great unanimity and zeal in the general enlistment.

"And among other fellers, judge, as we may reckon on, is a cute chap that jined us last night. We ain't noways sartain as to what part this 'ere coon was raised in, and he has that sort way with him as 'cute chaps requires when a wide mouth don't quite suit their interests; but I take it he's a Britisher."

"An Englishman!" cried Warren, with a start. "What sort of fellow was he?"

"I reckon, judge, that you'll say, when you see him, that he be a remarkable man, tall, pale and a devil of a shot."

"A good shot, is he?"

"Aye, judge."

"And pale you say? Did he tell you his name?"

"Yes, judge; He calls himself Walter Reynard."

"Ha! I don't know him."

"Reynard—Fox——" Warren gasped, as he muttered these broken words to himself, "but no, no!" he muttered, "he would not be such a fool!"

He rose and watched the log fire meditatively.

"Why, judge, you seem perplexed; air ye thinking of the Injun cusses? Wal, we'll soon settle them, I opine, with such a reinforcement as our friend Mark has brought from Larchville."

"I was not thinking of the Indians!" said Warren, abstractedly.

A tall and pale stern-faced man now stepped up to the group.

He bowed to Harwolf.

They exchanged a rapid glance.

The pride of villany was awakened in the heart of Warren, and he returned the fixed look of the stranger with one of stern determination.

The stranger smiled a sickly smile, as a hangman might at the defiance of a poor criminal adjudged to death by the fiats of a nation.

From that moment the disguise between them, the mask of hollow courtesy, was assumed to deceive others, but not themselves.

Harwolf did not extend his hand.

He thrust it into his breast and bowed haughtily.

The stranger did not on his part evince more cordiality; he only moved his hand with a slight wave, and then, perhaps unconsciously, laid it on the top of his pistol-butt.

There was a shout at this movement, which was re-echoed in the camp.

A bois-bruté, or demi-Indian, was brought into the camp, bound hand and foot.

The bois-brutés, are half-castes, the sons of white fathers by Indian mothers.

He was brought before Judge Warren.

It was explained that the fellow was an Indian spy, and that he had been taken in one of the wigwams of the Dacotahs.

Harwolf sternly questioned him.

The poor wretch testified the greatest terror.

The infusion of Yengeese blood in his veins seemed to have washed from his heart that indomitable fortitude which marks the red-skin.

He answered with craven terror, telling the inquisitors that he had been entrapped by the Dacotahs and compelled by them to betray the outpost of the Yengeese troops.

He told the Regulators that Eagle-Wing had conceived a design of crossing the prairies and attacking the settlement of Larchville.

Great surprise was testified by the Regulators at this audacious design of the fearless young chief.

But they did not question the truth of his statement, for they knew how insatiable was the hatred of the young Pawnee against the whites, and how indomitable was his courage.

The Indian was removed and carefully guarded.

A council of war was called, and it was unanimously determined that Warren should intercept the Indians on their march to Larchville.

The demi-Indian also informed them that a meeting had been appointed between the Eagle-Wing and the chief of the Shoshone, who had also resolved to join the general league against the Yengeese.

It was late in the evening when Harwolf sat brooding in his tent.

A man entered.

It was one who had always seemed faithful to the villain.

Harwolf grasped his hand with something of sincerity.

Selfishness lies at the bottom of such men.

"You be looking zadly zquire."

"Will you never drop that title?"

"Master Warren, zur, I do humbly beg thy pardon. But, dang it, it be that pale anxious look that reminds me of the old times, yer honour."

"I'm afraid we shall yet have cause to remember them."

"How zo, your honour?"

"Miles, we have enemies."

"Zo have all, zur, but I reckon we've left 'em all behind uz."

"But they may follow."

"Durn 'em—but they shall be welcome!" cried the sturdy countryman.

"There's the gipsy."

"He bean't nowt to be afeard on. The craven chap, thou may'st swear that he'll never cross the herring-pond, unless it be at the Government expense."

Harwolf paced about the tent impatiently.

He paused and struck his forehead.

"It is impossible to live, and it is horrible to die!"

"Zquire, I do zay that I be zorry to zee thee in this mood," said the trusty retainer, in a grave tone.

"Can I be otherwise? I have learned that which I could never have believed of myself."

"And what is that, Master Warren?"

"A coward!"

"A coward! You be not, zquire. Durn 'ee, it gives me a cold convulsion to hear 'ee talk zo."

"Miles, how weak a thing is a man! I know I am lost; I know that my best safety lies in resolution, and yet I am turned coward again."

"Why, dang it, zur, I trust there be no bad news from England."

"You remember, Miles, the immediate cause of my flight?"

"I do zo, zur."

"You remember that I had a wife, whom I raised from the lowest station, and for whose sake I risked my soul. She brought the darkest shame upon me, and I took a husband's revenge."

"Durn'ee, zquire, I be the last man that would blame thee vor't. It makes a man's blood boil to think on't."

"Well, Miles, the paramour died at the same moment with my wife."

"Right, zquire."

"But he had a brother, who was sworn to avenge him, and has tracked me hither."

"Durnation! thee bee'st jesting, zquire!"

"It's no jest, Miles; I have seen him to-day. We have scarce spoken a word; we have exchanged false names, but by our eyes we have mutually challenged each other to a mortal combat."

"But who does your honour mean—not Foxley?"

"The same."

"Phew! that be bad. I'd rather have met Catahaga and a regiment of his braves, and that's a bold word, too. Well, zur, there be but one thing az I knows on to be done in this case. We knows our gentleman, we knows that he bean't noways particular az to the betraying on us, and we knows az he bean't come across the Atlantic for nought. We must jest put a bullet into un, and that be made easy by this fortinate war. But, durn'ee, I do zay az it must be done at once."

"You are right, Miles—at once! Can I trust this matter to you?"

"I believe you may, zquire. It be the fust time az I have tackled this kind of business; but, durn'ee, az it be vor the zake of both of us, it must be done."

"When?"

"What zay to-night, zquire?"

"He cannot be removed too soon."

"Thou mayst look upon't as bein' done, zur."

"But how will you manage?"

"I tell'ee, zquire, the thing be az eazy az lying to lawyers."

"I am glad you think so; but I don't see in what way."

"Well, zur, I'll inform ye. Maybe you haven't heard that this zame feller be zet to do duty as picket to-night?"

"Ha! that's brave."

"Plain it be, I do zay."

"I will go with you."

"Az ye please, yer honour."

"We will kill him on his post!"

"That's the idea. Well, yer honour, there'll be no blamed trouble come of that."

"No, I should think not."

"Zartain zure, yer honour. It'll all be zet down to the blamed Injens."

"Perhaps they might save us the trouble."

"Doant'ee trust to that, yer honour. There be a good old zaying, 'Dost'ee want aught done, do it thyself.'"

THE DUEL.

"He will be well armed, and we must be cautious."

"Thou'rt right, zur, but I do zay that it be no more than jest stalking an elk, vor we can creep on the warmint unawares."

"But the report of a gun, Miles?"

"True for yer honour; but we arn't forced to use lead if steel will do the job more quiet-like."

"That's true."

"Well, yer honour, it's but to zay if you're agreeable."

"Miles, he must die!"

"'Greed on afore your honour. Do'ee zay to-night on guard?"

"No better time."

"And we can scalp him—ha!"

"Yes—that's a good thought."

No. 46.

"In course, yer honour, Injens is like the sarvant's cat,—they has to bear the blame of all the mischief that happens."

"Loaded both the guns. Do you think you could shoot with a poisoned arrow?"

"Like Adam Bell or Robin Hood, yer honour. When I were a lad I shot many a bird with arrows, zo az not to make a row to disturb the durned game-keepers who be zo fond of peace and quietness that they can't abide even the snap of a rabbit-trap—he! he! Loard, yer honour, I've half a liking for this work—a sinivatin' conceited peeler to fancy az he could bilk Joe Miles and Zquire Harwolf; but sich imperence is onheard on. Well, yer honour, the chaps are stretching themselves out for a snooze; you and I can go round and inspect the sentinels, and maybe I'll be able to bring home news of the haccident ourselves, for I do zay, zur, it be a good plan, and the zooner carried out why all the better for both on us."

"Yes, I will do what you advise; and now for awhile we must separate."

"All right, yer honour. Don't 'ee be afeard of the foes at home; they may come one and all, and we can give him a zettler's welcome, and give 'em a zettlement too, yer honour, that no man az don't deal in old bones will want to take from 'em—eh, Master Foxley! I hope ye made your will afore you left the old island. I do zo."

The worthies parted.

Harwolf walked to the largest of the watch fires burning in the midst of the camp.

He walked firmly, and assumed an air of easy nonchalance little according with the uneasiness that sat at his heart.

"You are foolish, Master Leighton, to expose yourself so much. Your wound was thought dangerous but a little while ago," he said, with calm gravity.

"Judge, my wound is nothing; but my impatience at the shilly-shallying style in which this campaign is managed is consuming me."

"My dear young man you are far too headstrong; you must be patient."

"Patient! with my cousin—my betrothed in the brutal hands of blood-thirsty robbers."

"She shall be rescued, never fear."

"When there is nothing to save but her lifeless body."

"Have we not lost enough already by our recklessness?"

"I grant this. Catahaga has played the very devil with us; but we shall trap the rogue at last."

"I hope so; but let us keep watchful guard to-night."

"That's sense and reason. Our sentinels are all picked men."

"And where is our friend the Englishman?"

"Lots were drawn who should go on guard, and the lot fell to him."

"He seems a trusty fellow."

"'Cute as a 'possum. For a Britisher I consider him a remarkable man."

"Where is that fellow, Miles Thornton?"

"Haven't seen him since he was chatting with you."

"Here I be, zur," said the man in question, coming up, with a couple of guns under his arm; "I have loaded the rifles, zur, and am at your zarvice."

"Thank you; you must be tired, I know, as you kept guard last night. But we'll soon take our rounds, and then you can enjoy a few hours of rest."

"Why, what do you mean to do, judge?"

"Thornton and I will just go round and have a look at the pickets, and then we will camp down for a few hours till morning."

"I will go with you."

"No, I insist upon you remaining in the camp, and I must advise you to get as much rest as possible; for, I assure you, if you do not mend in looks, I shall vote you unfit for service, and invalid you."

Leighton smiled faintly, and stretched himself on his rug, with a sigh of pain and weariness.

Miles and his master left the camp on their dark mission.

CHAPTER CXLVI.

A CHAPTER OF WILD ADVENTURES—THE LONE PICKET—HARWOLF AND MILES IN AMBUSH—THE SHOT—THE STRUGGLE—THE BOWIE KNIVES—THE DETECTIVE STABBED BY HARWOLF—THE FATAL BULLET—INDIANS—THE FLIGHT—THE REGULATORS ALARMED—THE PICKETS—THE PURSUIT OF THE INDIANS—AN UNEXPECTED REPULSE—A RACE FOR LIFE.

FOXLEY was alone in the forest.

Alive to the dangers of his position he kept a steady watch.

The dark shadows of night enveloped him.

The wind soughed through the branches of the trees, and roared down the grand avenues of the mighty woods.

Ever and anon he would start and poise his gun, which he kept at half-cock.

Danger threatened him on every hand.

He felt sure that Harwolf had recognised him.

He could not doubt that the villain would take the readiest means to remove him.

Why had not Foxley denounced the murderer at once?

He could give no proof of his identity.

Michael Warren had won the confidence of the settlers, a man of wealth, influence, and unimpeached character. Foxley himself was a stranger, of whom nothing was known.

The sentinel began to feel more secure as the night wore on.

He stood leaning on his gun and deeply ruminating.

He recalled the events of the years during which he had pursued the undeviating path to his vengeance.

Many temptations he had met with that would have been too strong for an ordinary man, temptations which at times almost induced him to give up the hopeless chase; hopeless, for day by day brought him fresh disappointments.

More than once he had, in fact, abandoned the idea of searching for his brother's murderer, but the death of his only relative remaining unavenged, there was no rest for him, and again and again he embarked in fruitless expeditions.

And now at last he had overtaken the wretch whom he had hunted so remorselessly.

But would he triumph even now?

The wind that moaned so weirdly, the darkness that lowered so appallingly, seemed to mock the hope.

Alone in the wild wood, on a service so dangerous, that those who fulfilled it were chosen by lot.

Night after night the terrible Eagle-Wing had swept past with his murderous braves, and killed every picket on his station.

And he had other foes to fear.

From which of the bushes, from behind which tree might not a fatal bullet speed from Harwolf's weapon winged with death?

These thoughts kept him wakeful and watchful. So confident he felt that Harwolf would take advantage of this occasion that he was half inclined to load his gun with the bullet he wore attached to his watch chain, the bullet which had killed his brother and Harwolf's wife.

He tried to shake off thought.

He whistled a tune.

Paced up and down, counting his steps.

Ever on the alert he was constantly startled.

A sear leaf fluttered whispering past.

His heart leaped and he shuddered violently.

A branch broke before the wind.

He was ready to rush in the direction whence came the sound, to do battle with some hidden foe.

His fears were not groundless.

Harwolf and Miles were stealing softly through the wood.

They had visited each sentinel.

Harwolf affected not to know where Foxley was stationed.

The sentinel offered to accompany him.

Harwolf would not suffer him to leave his post.

Noiselessly the two assassins glided through the wood.

"I do zay the night be fit for the job," whispered Miles.

"Yes, it is dark enough."

"Do'ee think I'll be able to get close to him?"

"You must tread softly."

"The durned bush be so 'farnal thick."

"Well; we must use our guns."

"Better not, I do zay."

"You may be right; but we can charge it to the Indians."

"And how can ye aim in the dark, zquire?"

"Well, we must get to close quarters."

"Aye; zo."

"Hush!"

"I heard nothing, yer honour."

"Listen again."

"Loard, you might listen to such a wind as this and fancy it were talking to yer."

"Hark! fool. The bark of a fox."

"Or the cry of an Injen?"

"Which think you?"

"Dang it, zquire, but the Injens are reg'ler zo'logicals; they knows every kind o' wood-music, from the growl of a bear to the whistle of a pie-finch."

They stood harkening in the darkness.

Convinced at length that they had been mistaken, they moved on.

They reached the spot on which the picket was pacing out his lonely watch.

They were forced to use extreme caution.

Do all they could to avoid making the slightest noise, every now and then they would tread on a snapping stick, or brush against a crackling furze bush.

After many minutes of intense anxiety, they stood beneath the black and blending shadows of two large trees.

They peered forth into the gloom, almost as palpable, which lay beyond.

The pale face of the vigilant sentry stood dimly out against the field of darkness, like the faces in some of the time-darkened portraits by old masters.

He seemed to be wide awake to every peril.

He stood in a startled attitude.

He firmly gripped his gun.

"Now, Miles," whispered Harwolf, in his companion's ear, "we must get closer yet."

"Dang it, zur, but I'm blamed if I see how'st to be done."

"I fear we shall have to use the guns."

"I zaid zo."

"Hush!"

"Aye, zur."

They crept close down below the bushes.

They scarce breathed.

They did not stir hand nor foot.

The sentinel came to the place where they were lurking.

He seemed to be half conscious of the nearness of his danger.

Miles looked up.

Through the darkness they could just discern his face, and the gleaming barrel of his gun.

Again they sank down.

Miles lifted his musket from the earth.

His right hand slid down the gun-stock.

His thumb carefully drew back the muffled lock.

His forefinger curled round the trigger.

Harwolf laid his hand heavily on his arm.

"Don't fire," he muttered, faintly; "it can be done without that. We shall be discovered."

"Aye, zquire," returned the other, trembling with excitement.

"When he turns, leap from the bush, and strike him with your knife.

The sentinel started.

He seemed to have heard voices.

"Who goes there?" he cried, his voice trembling.

The echoes of the forest mocked him.

A jackal bayed.

A night bird, startled by the loud challenge, whirred out of a thicket, hideously shrieking.

"Who goes? Speak, or I fire!"

Still no answer.

The sentinel levelled his gun at the bush behind which the two men were crouching.

Miles would have risen.

Harwolf held him fast.

"You will be killed if you expose yourself; lie close, let him fire, all the better; his charge spent, we can tackle him, and his bullet will not pierce this bush."

Convinced that he heard voices, although the speakers had lowered their tones to the lowest pitch audible; moved by that instinct which often apprises us of the presence of the obnoxious, even when it is not visible; the sentinel levelled and fired point blank into the thicket.

"Durn'ee, zquire, thy prophesy bean't true; I be mortal stung if I bean't wounded," whispered Miles. "Blame the crusher, now for un."

With this, the doughty fellow leaped the thicket and threw himself upon Foxley.

They struggled fiercely for a moment, and then Miles was violently thrown.

Foxley's pistol was drawn from his belt in an instant.

Miles had risen to his knee.

Foxley thrust the cold muzzle against his cheek.

Another instant Miles would have been sent to his account.

Harwolf, that old murderer, unsheathed his knife, whirled it in the air, and brought it down to the hilt on the detective's shoulder.

Foxley fell with a groan.

The men stooped over him.

They panted in the dark, but neither spoke.

As a hunter would take the paw of a beast he had slain, so coolly did Andrew lift up the limp hand of his victim and laid his finger on the pulse.

"He has gone to tell his brother that I had the 'charmed life,' and that my faithful spouse must wait awhile for my coming; perhaps I shall send another courier before me."

As he made this beastly jest with a ghastly grin, the monster rose.

"Durn'ee, zquire, here be a bullet stuck in his watch-chain."

"Ha! give it me," cried Harwolf.

Miles drew his knife and hacked at the chain, to disengage it.

"Hu-hu-hu-hu-hu! bang! bang!"

"Run, zquire. Injen! I do zay, run," shouted Miles. He set the example, and sprang like mad through briar and bramble.

Harwolf followed him close.

As they neared the camp shouts were heard.

The flare of torches streamed afar through the darkness.

All the camp was roused.

"This is well, Miles. Your arm bleeds; you have been shot by the Indians. Do you understand?"

"Aye, zure, yer honour, very well. I do zay this be fort'nit."

Leighton and the Regulators now swarmed about them.

"Keep together, my lads; have care. Don't get too near the woods; we are beset," cried Harwolf.

"The redskin devils! Are there many of them?" asked Leighton. "Is it a grand attack, or is it only the Pawnee thief and his braves shooting?"

"I don't know, Mark, but this I am sure of, the pickets have suffered mortally. Come on; keep together, I say, and let us go round."

"The faithful fellows keep to their posts," said Leighton.

"We will recall them," returned Harwolf.

He unstrung a bugle from his side.

He blew a long, cheery blast.

There was an anxious pause.

Again he sounded his bugle.

Another pause.

One man was seen running.

He reached them.

He stumbled to his knees.

His face was bathed with blood.

The top of his head was bare; the hair had been torn off by the scalping-knife.

It sometimes happens that the operation of scalping is not fatal.

When an Indian strikes down a foe, he scalps him; that done, if the man should recover, he is at liberty to go where he will. Once having secured the coveted trophy, the most inexorable savage is satisfied.

The Regulators uttered a furious yell.

However their alarm quite equalled their wrath.

They huddled together like sheep when the wolf appears.

Forming a phalanx they moved along, skirting the forest on the search for the sentinels.

"Miles," whispered Harwolf, "where is your knife?"

"I'm blamed if I arn't left it by the side of our man."

"Fool!"

"Yer honour; tell me, zur."

"What now?"

"Where be yer knife?"

"By all the furies, it sticks in Foxley's heart!"

"Mortal bad, yer honour, I do zay."

"We are lost."

"Not till he be vound, anyway, zo, zquire."

"What's to be done?"

"I'll go ahead, zur, and see to master."

"Aye, Miles, do so; be prudent."

"I shall, depend on't; these blamed Ingens have done us harm instead of good, when it comes to all."

Miles led the way.

He stumbled over something that lay doubled up in the long prairie grass.

He jumped back and uttered a yell.

It was the body of one of the luckless sentinels.

The fury of the Regulators knew no bounds. They visited the posts of the pickets one by one, and at each spot they found the mangled corpse of the sentry.

At last they sought the spot where they supposed they should find the body of Reynard, the Englishman, who, they naturally concluded, had suffered the same fate as his comrades.

Miles seized a torch.

He hastened forward.

The men called out to him, reproving his rashness.

He heeded them not.

He was intent upon recovering the bowie-knives.

He entered the lonely dell.

He rushed to the spot where Harwolf had struck down the detective.

To his amasement Foxley was gone!

The others arrived at the spot the next instant.

The sod showed the marks of a struggle.

There was a pool of blood.

Foxley's pistol was found under a bush.

Harwolf would not suffer them to make too close scrutiny; but it was not difficult to conjecture what had happened.

"It is plain," said Harwolf, "that our new acquaintance has had a terrible contest with the savages; he has been struck down by one of them, that is evident from these indentations. He was possibly found to be still alive, and was carried off by the wretches."

"Horrible! he will be tortured at the stake!" cried Leighton.

"Had you seen him in your rounds?" asked one of the Regulators, of Harwolf.

"We had."

"Yes, you must have done so," cried another settler. "Here are your foot-prints."

"We left him all right. We had not got many yards when we heard the noise of the guns and the whooping of the Pawnees; and, as we were but two, we fled."

"And we must suffer another victim to be dragged to the shambles by these hellish butchers!" cried Mark Leighton, with fierceness.

"Never be it said!" cried Harwolf, stoutly. "Follow me, comrades; we are a strong party, and if we can drive them out of the woods, may notch every one of them. Come along! Honour to the foremost!"

The men uttered a deep, stern shout.

They pressed boldly on into the wild, dark wood.

They held their guns poised, ready to fire.

Their excitement was breathless.

They quickened their speed.

"Halt!" cried Harwolf.

The men rushed back.

They were brave enough to have attacked twentyfold their number on open ground, but to be struck down by hidden hands, as so many of their comrades had been, was something more than they could bear.

The dauntless Mark Lieghton upbraided them with their want of courage, and pushed forward.

The rest kept close behind him.

A sudden blaze lighted the wood.

A sudden crackling roar burst with thundrous echoes.

A dozen sturdy fellows dropped where they stood.

The rest fled in all directions.

Their panic was so strong that they thought nothing of their comrades.

Still, at intervals, to the ears of the several fugitives came far or near the sound of shots, ringing the death-note of one or more of their comrades; and their speed increased as much as possible by the warning, they fled pell mell, dashing through thorns and thickets till they tore the very clothes from their limbs.

CHAPTER CXLVII.

EAGLETON'S TREACHERY — EMILY MERVYN'S INTERVIEW WITH SYLVIA VOLANTE.

CHARLES RYE was taken into custody by the officers and conveyed to the nearest station.

His first paroxysm of amazement and indignation past, he calmed himself sufficiently to write to his brother and to Eagleton.

The next morning the treacherous and ungrateful banker's clerk walked down to the office with the coolest effrontery.

He was received with a buzz of excitement by the other clerks who considerd him, as being an intimate of young Rye, best able to give them the latest and most authentic account of the culprit.

Eagleton looked very grave, shrugged his shoulders, and smiled pityingly.

"It is very sad," he said, in a tone of deep seriousness; "it's given me a shock I shall not speedily recover. Who could have thought it possible? Well, poor fellow, you may be sure he yielded only to some very great temptation."

"But what could it be, Eagleton? He has good friends, has some money, and is a steady file; and then he never bets."

"I'm afraid there lies the 'error in the bill.' In making up the accounts 'pro and con' for poor Charley you must not leave out that great item. He was very careful, very reserved, displayed great tact in concealment, but for all that he did bet, and largely too!"

"Is it possible?" cried the others in chorus.

"Yes; it's the fact, I assure you."

"Of course, you know, I speak freely now, as I am among friends, for Charley is certainly a good fellow; is he not?"

"We all thought him the jolliest of fellows; but, do you think he will plead guilty?"

"Well, I can't say; I should rather think he will not. Of course, he will obtain the best of counsel, and, I am afraid——. Well, Charley is my friend, and we will say nothing about it."

"What are you afraid of?" asked the clerks in one voice, for their curiosity was whetted by his hesitation.

"Then I'll tell you what I fear. Remember, I am not judging him from my own estimate of his character, but by his own words—and a man in his position will do desperate things in self-defence—he will try to implicate some of you!"

"Never! he could never be so base!" cried the clerks, exchanging looks of fright.

"No, I should trust not; but what he said——. Well, if I tell you much more about him you will think him a consummate hypocrite; and I don't want you to form that opinion of him, for I have faith in Charley, even yet."

"You are a good fellow, Eagleton," said one of the clerks; "I never in my life saw you looking so pale and wretched; you seem to feel this very deeply."

"He was my friend, and I am truly grieved at what has happened," replied the treacherous rascal, with a seeming frankness altogether deceiving.

The door was opened at the moment.

The clerks hurried off to their work as a stout old gentleman entered the office.

This was Mr. John Bullion, one of the chief partners, and the gentleman whose name had been so often forged by Eagleton.

He beckoned Charley's false friend to follow him into a private room adjoining the office.

He offered him a seat, and then threw himself into a large arm-chair by the fire.

He seemed to be deeply chagrined.

His red face glowed hotly, and his fine blue eyes seemed fixed with a look of vexation; and he passed his silk handkerchief over his bald forehead with the nervousness of irritation.

"This is a lamentable affair, this disgrace of young Rye's—truly abominable. A young man whom I would have trusted with the wealth of the world. I thought him firm as the rocks as to integrity; so honourably recommended, too. His brother a most worthy man; tut—tut—I am grieved beyond expression."

"It is very sad."

"Sad! it is monstrous—atrocious—preposterous!" cried the old gentleman, vehemently. "But business must be attended to, and duty is business, sometimes unpleasant and always imperative; and I shall be forced to ask you a few questions, Mr. Eagleton, to which, as a man of honour, I am sure you will give me direct and faithful answers."

"Mr. Bullion, I trust you will not press me too far. I hope that you will not forget that it becomes me, as poor Charles Rye's friend, to cleave to him to the last; and as it is not the province of friendship to censure or punish, but to support and to solace, I hope I shall not be called upon to give evidence against him."

"Ha! indeed. Then you *can* give evidence? you are acquainted with facts that tend to criminate your friend?"

"I have not said so; I beg that you will not misunderstand me. I wish to do my duty to you, but I will not be false to my friend."

"Humph! then you are not prepared to give us any information respecting this misguided youth?"

"No, sir, I am not."

"You cannot?"

"I *will* not."

"But you will be subpœned."

"Very well, sir, I must take the consequences."

"It is said, Mr. Eagleton, that the young fellow was acquainted with the celebrated dancer, Sylvia Volante. Is it not possible that he might have been ambitious to vie with richer rivals, in making her presents and in giving her other substantial tokens of his adoration, and that he has ruined himself by his generosity?"

"Well, she had letters—but I implore you not to press me on this subject."

"I cannot stay the course of justice; the foolish and guilty fellow is now a prisoner, and will soon be brought to trial. Neither I nor my partners are personally willing to prosecute him, but we have a duty to perform we cannot shrink from; and I am about to visit Mademoiselle Volante, and you must accompany me."

"Sir!"

"It must be so, Mr. Eagleton. I hope you will not pain me by a refusal."

"No sir, I will go with you; but I entreat that you will respect the relationship in which I stand to the unfortunate young man."

"Every consideration shall be allowed to your feelings, which I duly honor, Mr. Eagleton," replied the old gentleman with emotion, at the same time shaking hands with the clerk.

Eagleton shuddered, and the blood rushed to his heart, and left his cheek white as marble.

The banker and the clerk left the office, they got into a cab and drove off to the quiet suburb in which the *premiere danseuse* lived in retirement.

It was a neat and pleasant house covered with jessamine, and adorned with a pretty plat and parterre of flowers.

Upon knocking, they were admitted by a neatly dressed servant girl, and ushered into a chastely-furnished drawing-room.

Sylvia entered soon afterwards.

Eagleton grasped her hand, and gave her a look half exacting half entreating.

She bent her eyes to the ground, and blushed deeply.

With delicacy and caution Mr. Bullion unfolded the object of his visit.

The girl listened with beating heart.

She sat mute, a deadly pallor overspreading her cheek.

With a subtleness and heartless ingenuity that struck her with horror and disgust, she heard Eagleton throwing out hints and suggestions as to the motives which had influenced Charles Rye in his alleged crime, and blackening his character by the craftiest allusions to the most innocent transactions.

The interview grew so painful, that the banker, who was really kind-hearted and much moved by the agitation of the lovely girl, broke it off suddenly, expressing his sympathy with Sylvia and Eagleton that they would be constrained to appear against their mutual friend.

The clerk had alluded to certain letters that Sylvia could produce, in which reference was made by young Rye to matters which had an important bearing on the case.

As Sylvia made no offer of showing these letters, Mr. Bullion waived the subject, and with many kind expressions, hastily took his leave.

When they had re-entered the cab, Mr. Bullion addressed Eagleton.

"Mademoiselle Volante is a very sensible, and very charming young lady, and I can deeply sympathise with her in the painful position in which she is placed."

"I fear my poor friend was too devotedly attached to her, however. Such a *liason* is always expensive."

"Ha, I suppose so."

"But you may be sure that Mademoiselle is quite guiltless of any connivance in the affair."

"I would wage my life on that fact," returned the old gentleman.

"You might safely," returned Eagleton.

He sighed wearily.

"Mr. Eagleton, you are looking wretched. Of course, till something decisive puts the case of young Rye either beyond hope or beyond fear, your suspense and agitation of mind will quite unfit you for business, so I propose that you should absent yourself from the office for a few days till you have recovered your equanimity."

"You are very kind, and I shall be much relieved by availing myself of your indulgence," returned Eagleton.

He left the cab, pretending that he was about to return home.

He walked back to the house of Sylvia Volante.

She rushed into the room where he was sitting, and threw herself on her knees before him.

"Oh, Richard, you have imposed on me a task beyond my strength," she exclaimed, wringing her hands, while her cheek streamed with tears. "I cannot stand in a court of justice, and perjure myself for the ruin of one who is innocent, and loves me sincerely. Oh, do not urge me too far, Richard; I am sure I shall fail."

A dark frown gathered on Eagleton's brow.

Fierce words rose to his lips.

His cunning and presence of mind prevailed, however, and he murmured gloomily,

"It is a black business, I acknowledge; but it is not for him I feel."

"For whom then?" asked Sylvia.

"For her."

"And who is she?"

"How absurd you are! His *fiancée*—the girl he was engaged to before he became smitten by your resistless charms."

"If you will tell one lie you will tell a thousand," said Sylvia, with passion.

"I wish to say no more than this, that the girl of whom I speak is well nigh broken-hearted. She has visited him in prison—they have become reconciled, and if he escapes, will be united. Of course your favouring was all feigning, and therefore that is of no consequence; but this *is* of consequence, that if he does not pay the penalty I must—I, who have been more than a brother in kindness to you, Sylvia."

"Visited him in prison?"

"Yes; Emily Mervyn—that's the name, and a pretty girl, I admit, with that quiet, unassuming gentleness, that makes such a lasting impression on some fellows."

"And he is false to me!"

"Ha! ha! I am in no mood to laugh, but when you have made such a fool of him. Well, woman's vanity is insatiable!"

"Engaged to marry her!"

"Why not? But he is a pitiful fellow to speak of you with such disrespect; but of course it would never do to praise one woman to another."

"I will convince myself of the truth of all you say, and if—"

"Well, you will find it hard to get full conviction. He is artful enough—he knows himself to be entirely in your power, and will not spare dissimulation."

"What a perfidious villain! Well, I'll have my revenge!"

"Revenge is all nonsense; only a girl who has queened it in the highest circles ought not to suffer herself to be set down by a milliner wench, nor sneered at by a miserable fellow who would be too highly honoured to come into your presence as your hired servant. Hang revenge! Think of me, Sylvia—think of your own old friend Richard Eagleton, and don't feel too much compunction in the ruin of this fawning puppy; for I more than suspect—in fact, am almost certain—that he has tampered with the books as well as I—"

"Henceforth, I am remorseless!" said Sylvia, drawing herself up, her lips set, her eyes glowing, her face very white.

Eagleton kissed her.

"You are a dear, kind girl, Sylvia, and I know I may depend upon you."

He left the house soon after, and spent the night in a debauch with several of his profligate companions.

Sylvia had thrown herself on the sofa, and was sobbing with excitement and jealous passion, when the maid entered the room, and announced a visitor.

Sylvia asked the girl if she knew the person.

"No, Mademoiselle," replied the maid, "but it is a young lady, and her name is Emily Mervyn."

"Indeed," replied Sylvia, coldly; "admit Miss Mervyn, and let me be disturbed by no other visitors while she is here."

"Very well, Mademoiselle."

Emily, little Emily, who had been the kind nurse and gentle companion of Charley Rye, when he lay pining on his bed of sickness and pain, in the old happy times of his free boyhood—bygone for ever—Emily, his little playmate, was now grown a tall and graceful girl, as innocent and as sunny as ever, but prettier and even richer in goodness.

She showed some natural bashfulness at being introduced so suddenly into the presence of one so celebrated as Sylvia Volante.

The opera-dancer rose with infinite grace and slight hauteur, and extended her hand to her guest.

"Mademoiselle, I am so ashamed of this intrusion," said Emily, with fluttering heart and lip, "but the importance of the sad business on which I have come, I am sure will excuse me."

"There is no need of excuses, Miss Mervyn," returned Sylvia, quietly, "I have much wished to see you."

"To see *me*, Mademoiselle?" asked the girl in unfeigned surprise, "has he ever spoken then of me?"

"You allude to your intended husband, to Mr. Charles Rye?"

Emily blushed brightly.

"My intended husband!" she gasped, "indeed, Mademoiselle, you are greatly deceived. Oh, I did not estimate the difficulty of what lay before me, when I took the resolution to come boldly to you."

"You may trust me freely, Miss Mervyn," returned Sylvia, her lip arching with scorn. "I cannot be suspected of enmity to Mr. Rye."

"Indeed, no, for he loves you," cried Emily, warmly. "It was thought by every one that knew you both, that you favoured his suit, and I am here, Miss Sylvia, to implore you not to mistrust him, not to lend an ear to the absurd accusations raised against him, for he is innocent, you know; you cannot doubt that he is innocent. He has a secret enemy who is striving to work his ruin, and I have heard that you will be brought as a witness against him. I know you will speak nothing but truth, but let me intreat you to be cautious, for the lawyers are so cunning and often so unprincipled, and so many innocent have suffered when the guilty escaped. It may not accord with strict notions of propriety that I should intrude upon you thus, but I have been his friend from my girlhood, and love him as if he were my own brother, and would as soon doubt my existence as his innocence of the crime he is charged with."

"Neither you nor I can be deceived in Mr. Rye," returned Sylvia, still very coldly; "but it is strange that you should plead to me for him; it is mean and unworthy. Do you insult me by supposing that I cannot penetrate your shallow pretence? You feel that Charles Rye is in my power, and you are therefore induced to mislead me with respect to the position in which you stand to each other."

Emily's cheek grew crimson with shame and indignation.

"I have told you the truth, Mademoiselle," she said, her voice quivering as she rose proudly. "I know that my conduct is questionable in allowing my sisterly friendship for Mr. Charles Rye to lead me so far; but I judged you from my own heart, and thought that, conscious as you must be of possessing his fervent love, you would be joyed to receive one who can claim his friendship, and who came to advise you on his behalf. I see I have committed an error, and I will hasten to repair it by leaving you at once, Mademoiselle."

Emily moved towards the door.

Sylvia rose and drew her back.

"Stay, there is some error," she said, in a hoarse tone, "you are not deceiving me?"

"How, Mademoiselle?"

"You do not love Charles Rye?"

Emily blushed, and a shade of sadness crossed her face.

"Mademoiselle, you have been told that there is something more tender than friendship in the sentiments with which Mr. Rye regards me?"

"I have been told so."

"It is false."

"And you are sorry—you love this youth?"

Emily blushed indignantly, and once more tried to leave the room.

Sylvia detained her.

"Well, well, I am much to blame, I know that; but I am frank, *impressé*; I speak my thoughts fearlessly, it is my nature to do so; but if you would not have me despise you utterly tell me the truth. Did he ever try to persuade you that he loved you?"

"Never, never, Mademoiselle! I am his friend, his sister; as children we were playmates, and, I believe, that I possess his warm regard. I hope so; but he has never spoken to me of love, unless, when he has spoken of you; he is confiding, and we are old friends. I confess that he has told me often that you were dearer to him than words would express, that he loved you sincerely."

"He told *you* so? How base and selfish are all men!"

"He is neither."

"Not in your eyes. Love is blind."

"Then, you, Mademoiselle, do not love him?"

"If I say no, it will give you pleasure?"

"It ought to give me pleasure, if you can talk so unworthily. Mademoiselle, if I have done wrong in seeking this interview, let it end at once."

"Do not be hasty. I believe you, and even did I not, I would not be so wicked as to pretend for an instant that I know anything to his disparagement. What do you wish me to do?"

"To tell me that you believe him innocent."

"I know that he is not guilty."

"Now you speak like yourself; and you will not suffer yourself to be misled by his enemies?"

"No; I will not."

"And, oh, Mademoiselle, he is in fearful danger! They have found many seeming proofs against him!"

"I will save him if I can."

"And may I assure him that you are firm in your belief of his innocence?"

"You may tell him that I have wronged him, that I have injured him; but, tell him that I will not let him suffer by the treachery of a false friend. Do not ask me whom I allude to; do not seek any explanation; tell him what I have said, without addition. And now I must leave you, for I must start at once for the theatre, as there is a new ballet to be rehearsed."

With this Sylvia caught Emily in her arms, kissed her, and burst into tears.

"I am very wretched," she said. "If I save him I must sacrifice one to whom I am indebted for every triumph, every comfort in life. But, I will reflect; there may be some middle course by which I can save both the real offender and the falsely accused. Adieu, then, for the present, dear Emily; but come again to me, and very soon."

CHAPTER CXLVIII.

DON ZAMORA'S BALL—BLACK RALPH ON PAROLE—DON GARCIA CHALLENGES THE BOY PIRATE—THE PIRATES DENOUNCED—A TUMULT ENSUES—THE LADIES DEFEND OUR HERO—THE RAVENS TO THE RESCUE—RICH GIFTS AND BRAVE WORDS.

UPON returning to the ball-room the Boy Pirate and Black Ralph found themselves in a position less agreeable than that which they had occupied in the first instance.

Though the majority of the guests were not disposed to credit any evil reports concerning two such gallant-looking fellows as our hero and the dashing Black Ralph, yet there was a strong minority who suspected that all was not right.

Don Leon was known at one time to have been a privateer, which was only another name for a pirate, at least in those waters.

Old Giraldez was known to have been rescued from San Salvador by the Boy Pirate.

Our hero's appearance was so handsome and heroic that not a few could not help identifying him with the hero of so many wonderful and thrilling adventures.

The Donna Catarina, the beautiful affianced of the haughty and meddlesome Don Philip Maria and everything else Torralvezez, was, of course, with all the rest of the ladies, ignorant of the mishap her lover had met with.

It must not be supposed that because Don Philip has been mentioned as her lover, and was her affianced, that Donna Catarina had the slightest affection for him.

On the contrary, she felt a secret aversion to him, which, though she strove hard, she could not entirely conquer.

She was a lovely, lively girl, much younger than the morose fellow to whom she had been betrothed by her friends before she was old enough to speak her own name.

Being very affectionate and sensitive, she was certainly doomed to lead an unhappy life, unless propitious fates should decree that she should be released from her engagement by some unlooked-for contingency.

In gentleness and beauty none surpassed the peerless Lilia, but, had it been otherwise, the Boy Pirate was too high-souled and too warm-hearted to be false to the wife of his bosom; but, as he loved everything good and beautiful, he could not help feeling strongly attracted by the splendid Spanish girl.

He stood by her side at the piano, as she played some brilliant airs and sung some ravishing songs, during an interval in the dancing.

But the relations of the fair girl looked on with disapproval, and soon there came upon the stage one who was destined to bring a very sudden change in the spirit of their dream.

This was a Don Garcia, a tall and lathy fellow, with very black eyes and very lank hair; minus the etherial expression of chivalrous enthusiasm which we may suppose to have lighted the "sorrowful countenance" of Don Quixote, he would have given a good idea of the appearance and attributes of that illustrious knight errant.

Now, Don Garcia happened to be a cousin of Don Philip, and being a man "jealous of honour, ready and quick in quarrel," when that noble had been brought home seriously wounded by an audacious Englishman, he happening to be at the house at the time, burst into a torrent of wrath, and swore by every saint in the Romish calender that he would take immediate vengeance for the injury and insult.

Fired by this resolve, he hastened to the governor's house, and entered the ball-room with anything but a festal face.

He looked around, or rather over the company, for he was taller by the head and shoulders than any there present, and frowned in a most portentous manner.

The ladies looked vexed and frightened, and the gentlemen wore grave faces.

He walked straight up to Captain Oliver, who, as the reader will remember, was indentical with the worthy Black Ralph, and tapped him on the shoulder.

"Senor, I have to demand the favour of your company for a little while; there is a slight affair of honour which requires immediate settlement." He knocked the top of his long, thin sword with his long, thin finger, and moved a step towards the door. "Will you come?"

Black Ralph stared at him with his fierce, black eyes, and laughed gruffly beneath his great black beard, and then shrugged his shoulders with a dry smile.

"Senor, you would pity me if you knew how truly sorry I am to be forced to decline this honour; but see, my scabbard is empty, and I am a prisoner under arrest."

"For the murder of my cousin," said the Spaniard, sternly.

"Senor, by St. Lazarus, your patron, you have the soul of a beggar, or you would not taunt a man whose hands are tied," hissed the fiery Ralph, from between his clenched teeth.

"We may find some time when it will be convenient for you to settle this little difference."

"We shall, senor; comfort your impatience by this assurance, I am not the man to let an insult pass."

"Senor, if that be the case, I will content myself with the prospect of meeting you under more favourable circumstances, and at an early date."

The haughty Spaniard bowed with stately air, and stepped away.

Disappointed in his laudable desire of avenging his cousin's wound upon the inflicter of it, he now turned his attention to our hero.

The wrath of Don Garcia being now at boiling point, he determined to give Captain Paul no chance of escape.

Seeing our hero in dalliance with the lovely Donna Catarina, he strode up to him, and with the greatest rudeness, pushed the lady aside, and struck our hero in the face.

Christopher returned the blow by catching the aggressor by the collar, and swinging him right across the room.

In a moment there was a tumult.

Ladies screaming.

Gallants gathering round our hero and his assailant.

Don Garcia scrambled to his feet, and, drawing his long toledo, flew upon the Boy Pirate.

Our hero advanced with glaring eyes, but did not draw his sword.

"Senor, you must be mad so to forget yourself!" he cried, in a tone of piercing sternness. "We are in the presence of ladies. You attack me like a brutal ruffian——"

"Malraya! cursed Yenglesa, I will have your heart!" roared Don Garcia, all his dignity giving way before the tide of his fury.

He flew once more upon our hero, brandishing his long sword.

The Boy Pirate did not even now lay a finger on his weapon.

He rushed at the tall Spaniard, and, bare-handed as he was, wrenched the sword from his antagonist's grasp, broke it in half, and tossed it contemptuously over the Spaniard's head.

Then a terrible *fracas* arose.

Some of the cavaliers sided with our hero, others with the Spaniard.

Swords were drawn on both sides.

"What, gentlemen, is it possible that you will draw a blade against your own friend and kinsman in the defence of that arch-villain, that scourge of the sea—the Boy Pirate?"

At this announcement of our hero's fearful title general consternation prevailed.

The ladies shrieked and recoiled from him as if he had been some dread creature.

But a handsome face and a dashing demeanour, like charity, cover a multitude of sins.

They soon gathered around him.

A sudden turn in the wheel of favour brought Christopher down to the lowest, as he had been at the highest, point of popularity.

The gentlemen set up a shout of triumph at the prospect of capturing the redoubtable Captain Kit.

The Boy Pirate stood and eyed them calmly.

Black Ralph had snatched up a sword, and stood by our hero's side.

"Down with him! Down with the Pirate!" shouted the nobles.

They made a rush to seize him; the ladies threw themselves between and shielded him with their soft bosoms.

"Senors, if you would not bring destruction on yourselves, if you would not dishonour your host, listen to reason."

"What can the villain say? Down with him!"

"Hark ye, messmate! this comes of thrusting one's paw into the cur's kennel," cried Black Ralph, throwing off at once all his assumption of dignity and refinement. "For my part, simply as an Englishman, I am a match for this swarm of Spanish hornets; but, as Black Ralph, why, dam'me, I feel insulted that each man here has not a regiment to back him.

'Come one, come all, this rock shall fly
    From its firm base as soon as I!'

That's Scott for you, you slaves by tailor's blocks! You blushing swabs, stuffed full of pride and pomposity! You padded supers of a paltry burlesque! Where's your Cid? Where's your Pizarro? Where your Don Cæsar? Come on,

'I am Hamlet the Dane!'

And a famous rat-catcher; and so here goes to spit a mouldy cheese on my toasting fork."

With this torrent of ribaldry, Black Ralph charged at a fat and fiery Spanish grandee, who menaced him with a large sabre.

The old warrior darted back, wielding his great sword round and round till it looked like one of the traditional scythes turned on the axles of our ancient British war-cars.

"Ha, ha! Three up, three down! Sparks for the gods! Now, under the arm-pits! Hicks for ever?"

Christopher caught the desperate fellow by the arm, and pulled him back so suddenly that he stumbled, and soon found his seat on the cold ground.

"Once more, senor, I entreat you to hear me! I am here as the guest of Don Leon; if I am the pirate you call me, I can look you in the face, and say truly, that no one present has been injured by me or mine. I would bid you notice that, though I do not wish to take the initiative in violence, I can summons in a moment an overwhelming force. If my presence is so distasteful, I will leave the island at once."

"So will not I," roared Black Ralph. "The tallow-faced threepennies have put me on my metal, and I'll not budge till I've cooled my passion with some of their 'libbard's,' or lubber's blood. This is the sweetest bit of sensation that I have known since I killed three carpenters and two ballet-girls at the siege of Ascalon, on the boards of the royal Vic! Let me go, you Boy Raven, remember I'm a Man Vulture; and, dam'me, I'll flutter these hinds like an eagle in a dove-cote!"

"Deavolos! fetch the padre; the devil has got amongst us!" cried one of the Spaniards, falling back upon the others, who, little inclined to advance themselves, were pushing him on to the point of Talbot's sword.

"Silence all!" cried Don Leon.

"Your excellency shall not protect these ruffians," shouted the throng.

"They are my guests; no man shall do them harm!" cried Don Leon.

"It's a pity your excellency keeps such bad company. These men must be taken!"

"Muy ben, the business shall be settled at once!" cried Don Garcia, coming forward, and aiming at Christopher with an immense horse-pistol.

Donna Catarina, who, with several other ladies, had thrown themselves before our hero to protect him from his furious enemies, now flung herself into his arms, crying in a loud and thrilling tone,

"Don Garcia, if you fire your bullet must pass through my heart before it strikes this gallant young stranger!"

THE GHOST REPEATS ITS VISIT.

Seeing that his danger was getting so great as not to admit of hesitation, Christopher drew from his neck a little silver whistle attached to a small gold chain.

He blew a long and shrill call.

A roar of many voices was heard without.

The Spaniards fled away to the other end of the room, and gathering together, drew their long rapiers, and stood defiantly.

Through doors and windows thronged in the Boy Pirate's men.

Old Brierly, Gomez, Dick Caffyn, Brand the pilot, Ross, Cassidy, Oakland, Tom Garrod, Black Zampa, and almost the whole of the Boy Pirate's crews.

"These are Clan Alpin's warriors true!" shouted Black Ralph. "Now, you Spanish swabs, will you take us? the thieves outnumber the honest men in

No. 47.

this world. Submit to your fate, then, and walk the plank like heroes."

"Hearties, disarm these dastardly swabs, drive them all into yon ante-room, and batten the doors, using all courtesy to these kind ladies."

The Spaniards needed little driving.

Like rats escaping into their holes, they rushed into the ante-room.

The pirates set up a wild cheer, and dashed after them.

While they were disarming the vanquished, and binding them together, the Boy Pirate called to Zampa, and gave a hurried order in a low tone.

In beautiful groups the ladies crouched on the floor or on sofas, trembling and sobbing in their terror.

Zampa returned with a heavy box on his shoulder.

This the Boy Pirate opened.

He drew from it a sparkling necklace of diamonds, and placed it round the neck of Donna Aurora; in a few well-chosen gallant words he expressed his fervent thanks to her for her brave and generous partizanship. He then presented costly jewels, bracelets, and brooches of rubies, emeralds and pearls.

The ladies received them with rapturous ecstacy.

Partly moved by dread, and partly by admiration.

The men now returned from the ante-room with bundles of swords under their arms; they locked and double-locked the door, cheering and laughing.

They gathered round the Boy Pirate, and waved their swords with prolonged huzzaings.

"Dam'me, Captain Kit, give me your hand," cried Black Ralph, "and if there's a berth for a powder-monkey aboard the 'Avenger,' I will accept it freely, and every swab aboard my schooner is of the same mind."

"But I am a pirate no longer!" returned our hero; "except in the name which has rendered me so famous."

"Then, in the name of the Fates, what are you?"

"My flag-ship bears the name of my new calling. Henceforth I am the Avenger!"

"And what do you mean to avenge?"

"Woman's wrongs!" returned Christopher, laughing.

"Phew! by the shades of Munchausen, you have undertaken more than all the nine worthies and seven champions united would ever dare to dream of. Where do you mean to begin? By the abolition of latch-keys, the stopping of pipes and the flogging of pretty bar-maids. Hurrah for the girls! Pirate! Long live the Ladies' Avenger."

"And will you help me? I mean to fight for Poland."

"I'm with you, captain. I once learned how some deuced handsome fellow, with a devilish ugly name, made Miss Freedom scream, by an unlucky tumble; and I've always been anxious to set that gallant little country that fell with him once more on its legs, and if we can be of any use to the strugglers —why, we can fight as long as we live, and die when we can fight no longer!"

"Bravely spoken! and, lads, hats off. Three cheers for the dear ladies, who have defended me so generously, and three cheers for the women all the world over. A wave of your swords, in silence and seriousness, to express that, by deeds and not words, we will do honour to the fair maids of Poland!"

CHAPTER CXLIX.

AGNES AWAKES FROM HER SWOON—GOOD NEWS OF HER COUSIN—RETURN OF THE INDIANS —MORE SCALPS AND MORE PRISONERS— THE PAWNEE'S CAPTIVE—WYLD DISCOVERS MINNA'S PLOT FOR THE RESCUE OF AGNES —CATAHAGA GOES ALONE TO WORSHIP HIS MANITOU — THE BUSH-RANGERS RESOLVE UPON A DEED OF BLOOD.

WEARILY Agnes Staunton opened her eyes as she awoke from a long and deep slumber.

She found herself still in the cabin of Nat Weatherfield, the beaver trapper.

The first object which met her gaze was the handsome form of her wild and lawless lover.

Oswald Lamond stood with his arms folded, his fine face pale and anxious, looking tenderly upon her.

He started as her soft, sad blue eyes fixed on him with a wistful look of reproach and grief.

Agnes shuddered as he seated himself by her side and gently took her hand.

"Dearest," he said, soothingly, "I have news to tell you, which will give you pleasure."

"Nothing on earth can give me joy henceforth," wailed Agnes. "Oh, that one might die when life is insufferable!"

She turned on the pillow and buried her head in the tangling meshes of her hair.

She raised herself on her white, rounded arm, and raising her hand to her head with an air of distraction, she murmured wildly,

"Oswald, I implore you to leave me; you would not have me curse you! Can I look on your calm face—can I listen to your cold and heartless tones, and not be mad with indignation when I think of your fearful guilt which you bear so lightly? Tempter, avoid me! Oswald, mad as I was, I believed till the last that you loved me!"

"I am weary, Agnes, of pleading a passion which you so ill requite," returned the young bush-ranger, with a sigh. "You know that I am all truth and devotion to you; and you are never weary of upbraiding me. Come, Agnes, quarrel with me no more; submit to your fate; I can die contentedly, but live without you it is impossible. I will abjure my present course of life as soon as circumstances will permit me to do so with safety, and then we will live so happily."

"What, with my kinsman's blood upon your head?"

"His blood, Agnes, yes, but not his life," rejoined the bush-ranger.

"Not dead? He is not dead?" Agnes almost screamed in her eagerness.

"By the fiends, it would not concern me much if he were; the dastardly hound was my deadliest enemy!" cried the bandit, with a scowl.

"But, indeed, you have not killed him?"

"No; he is with the Regulators, on the hunt for me," returned her lover.

"Thank God!" cried the girl, with deepest fervour.

The sound of approaching steps caused the bush-ranger to move towards the door.

Nat Weatherfield entered.

His face was blank with alarm.

The bush-ranger signalled him not to speak before Agnes, and passed through the door with him.

Wyld and several of the bush-rangers stood around, expressing their consternation in their wild faces.

"Well, what has bleached your hatchet face? have you seen the devil?" asked the captain, angrily, looking into the countenances of those about him, with a disdainful frown.

"Wal, I reckon his fust cousin, if ain't the old 'un hisself," returned Nathaniel, shrugging his shoulders; "blood hounds is all werry well, but they're none the wuss for a muzzle."

"Hark ye, captain, how do you like this wild beast show business? Curse it, I say."

The most awful yelling and whooping shook the woods.

"Humph! the Eagle-Wing has gained another victory?" asked Regan, biting his lip with some vexation.

"Yes, and if he arn't quickly stopped, I opine, there won't be a white face seen on the prairie, unless it be spiked on a pole in some devil's den of a wigwam," said one of the rangers.

"But Harwolf stormed the lodges on the Blue Earth, and butchered every mother's son and daughter of the tribe; isn't it so?"

"Scotching one swarm of hornets isn't quite a hextermination of stinging insex," remarked Nat sententiously.

Young Regan's glance fell on his belt, glistening with arms.

He looked up with a faint smile.

"Such brilliant stars are only meteors, they fall soon," he said, with a grin.

The trapper started.

"You just look here, Master Regan," he said, firmly, "this Catahaga is my friend, and up to this yere time has acted all fair and square accordin' to contract, and those as are his enemies are mine, I guess."

"Who but you talked of muzzling the bloodhound?" said Regan, fiercely.

"A muzzle isn't a halter. We can put a stopper in the Ingen without cutting his throat, I opine."

"Where is he?"

"By the fires. His men are camped down in the valley; they've been feasting like hogs, and are now sleeping like squirrels in winter."

"Very good. I'll speak to the Eagle-Wing."

With this, the captain of the bush-rangers descended the hill.

A strange scene presented itself.

The Indians, who were thoroughly exhausted after their long raid, gave way to their weariness, and having feasted sumptuously on some provisions they had foraged on their way, lay stretched on the ground as motionless as if they had been inanimate.

Against a tree several unfortunates were bound by thongs of bark.

They were white prisoners taken on the war-path.

Between two splendid oaks, which knit their huge arms in a grand leafy arch, was seen a rough bier of branches and oziers.

On this lay the body of a man wrapped in a buffalo robe.

Whether alive or dead, it would have been difficult to determine at a glance.

His features were rigidly set, and his cheeks lividly pale, his pulseless forehead smeared with clotted blood.

As Regan walked into the circle formed by the blazing log-fires, the Dacotah chief, Heart of Fire, rose from the ground to meet him.

The Indian's eyes gleamed with triumph.

His belt was full of scalps.

He held out his hand.

Not without a qualm, Regan grasped it, as he said,

"The Great Spirit has smiled upon my brothers. The Dacotahs have taught the Yengeese that they live only by the forbearance of the Iroquois, and that the rising of the red nations is like a rise of the great winds, that sweep down old forests and shake the very mountains to their base."

To this grandiloquent compliment the Dacotah vouchsafed no further reply than to bow his crested head with assent.

"And has the great chief of the Pawnees returned from the war-path?"

"Catahaga has gone to the river alone, to pray to his Manitou."

"And what is the Manitou of the Eagle-Wing?" asked Regan, with a faint sneer.

Every Indian has his own Manitou, or special divinity. Sometimes the skin of a deer, or the teeth and claws of a bear; sometimes a peculiarly coloured stone, or a carved calumet; at others, a living animal is the Indian's Manitou, a wolf, or a snake, no creature of which species will he, on any account, kill.

"Catahaga has no other Manitou but the great sun-spirit, whom he worships when he rises and when he sets."

"Like a Persian, or a Peruvian," said Regan, smiling.

"Waugh!" returned the Indian, with a scowl, scandalised by the levity with which the words were spoken, though, of course, he had no knowledge of their application.

"And where is the great chief?"

"The Yengeese have thrown the log of a tree across the chasm of the mountain torrent that flows into the Arkansas," replied the Indian. "The Pawnee chief is there."

"It is good!" returned Regan.

He then glanced at the prisoners.

"Are these the prisoners of the Dacotah, or do they belong to the Eagle-Wing?"

"The Pawnee takes neither scalps nor prisoners;

he only kills," returned the Indian. "Yet he has brought one of the braves whom we found wounded on the war-path, and by the knives of his own people, which we found by his side."

Regan started.

A sudden thought seemed to strike him.

He left the Indian bivouac.

Wyld joined him.

"Captain," said the bush-ranger to his leader, "this red cuss is getting dangerous."

"What is the matter now?—anything new?"

"His prisoner is the Britisher chap."

"What have we to do with him?"

"Why, I hear that he was murdered—for I think he is dead—by some of Harwolf's gang, and the Pawnee has found the knives of two of them, which have names carved on the handles."

"Ha! the fellow is getting too meddlesome."

"And, captain, a fellow has just ridden over the frontier with news that the Government have sent out a regiment to subdue or exterminate the Indians."

"Phew! then we must make hay while the sun, or rather, the moon shines, for we must be over the borders before the Light Horse are on our track."

"But this cursed Eagle-Wing is drunk with success; he is getting enthusiastic. He thinks himself ordained to deliver the wolves from the watchdogs!"

"And will the tribes support him?"

"He claims no honours—takes neither scalps nor prisoners, and therefore rouses no jealousy. Besides, his long residence among the whites, coupled with his native and insatiable bloodthirstiness, makes him a terrible foe, and where was his match in ambush? Wabiskoa has risked several battles in the fair field, and lost them all; Eagle-Wing is too wary to do that, but he will fill the woods with sharpshooters till they are impenetrable to the very armies of the States. Do you think he will respect us?"

"I don't think it would be safe to trust him."

"It would be madness, captain."

"Well, we must look to him."

"And, captain, there's another cursed traitor amongst us."

"Ha! the trapper, Weatherfield?"

"You're right, I guess. What do you think the whelp has been plotting with that Wyotti gal?"

"What, with Minna?"

"Exactly."

"Plotting! ha, the minx! And what is the gist of their plot?"

"To rob you."

"Rob me!"

"Of your pretty sweetheart. They have concocted a plan for carrying off Agnes, and delivering her up to her uncle and cousin."

The handsome face of the young chief of the bush-rangers assumed a look of demoniac savageness.

"And she—does she consent to this precious conspiracy?"

"That I don't know, captain."

Regan's voice trembled a little, as he cried, wildly,

"If it be so, let her go. I remember the song of the old cavalier—

'Quit, quit for shame,
This cannot move—
This cannot take her,
If of herself she do not love,
Nothing can make her,
The devil take her!'

And so say I."

Regan drew a deep sigh, and then laughed, harshly.

"I love this girl, Wyld," he said, rather sadly; "and, barring that, I could not withstand the temptation of carrying her off, upon your persuasion and my own passion-promptings. I have treated her with honour. Now all blights and curses fall on that fool's head who places his trust in false and heartless woman. They are all alike worthless and faithless!"

Wyld laughed.

"Why, captain, I thought you a very Don Juan —that you could see beauty in every fair woman, and prize all alike that were lovely."

"Not all alike, Wyld," returned the bush-ranger, in a tone of seriousness. "My love for Agnes is a thing apart from every other attribute in my nature. I am as jealous of her honour, strange as it may seem, as I am covetous to possess the favour of every other fair one. Let her go."

"Then you are to be bilked of your prize by this infernal trapper, and the big bashaw of the Pawnees, with his saucy wench. Your betrothed is to fly to her cousin's arms for protection, marry him, with your uncle's blessing, and the whole of the interesting family, who have treated you so graciously, are to give thanks for her deliverance, and curse you in chorus. Is it to be so?"

"Rather a gibbet as high as Haman's!" cried the bush-ranger, fiercely. "No, I have boldly won her, and I will keep her. Not all the chariots and horses shall drag her away from me!"

"Good! then we must kill the Pawnee!"

"True. On the first fitting occasion I will chalk the prowling jaguar."

"And when can there be a more fitting occasion than the present? Another such may never offer."

"What do you mean?"

"Are not his braves drowned in sleep, and is he not alone?"

"And praying——"

"Like a heathen, to the sun."

"Well, we will settle him. I know the Panther's Pass; it is a lone spot, and we may creep on him unawares."

"And, captain, remember the doughty rascal will be unarmed."

"How's that?"

"Don't you know that it is a custom with these heathenish savages, when paying their devotions to their Manitous to lay aside their arms?"

"It is so."

"Good. And we can kill him without a shot."

"So much the better. So, the Pawnee dog thought to play the part of Tecumseh or Oceola, of the Seminoles. Humph! it's time he was cut off."

"And it's time we cut off, if we mean business. The sun is already sinking; when it dips behind the lakes, he will return to the war party, and our opportunity will be lost."

"Good. Tell Lawrence to surround the hut with the steadiest of the band; give him orders to shoot the trapper, and to pinion the Wyotti girl if they attempt to rescue Agnes. Yourself and four other fellows shall go with me to the Panther's Pass, and Catahaga may pay his devoirs to the setting sun, and bid him adieu for ever, for, by the oath of a ranger, he shall never behold another rise!"

———

CHAPTER CL.,

FOXLEY IN THE HANDS OF THE INDIANS— CATAHAGA'S PRAYER TO THE GREAT SUN- MANITOU—HE IS ATTACKED BY THE BUSH- RANGERS.

LET us return to the scene of the attempted murder of Foxley the detective.

It will be remembered that the whoop of the savages had driven off the villains Harwolf and Miles at the moment when the latter was cutting away the fatal bullet from the detective's watch chain.

The Indians surrounded the prostrate body of the unfortunate sentinel.

Catahaga's keen eye at once perceived the bowie-knife lying on the grass.

It should be borne in mind that the Pawnee not only spoke English fluently but could read tolerably well.

It was Minna's labour of love to teach him to read and write in those days when he had lived among the pale-faces and had striven so hard to win their respect and confidence.

He at once knew by the letters carved on the handle that the knife was the property of Miles Thornton.

The other, though not marked with a name, was as palpably Harwolf's, for it was of very curious workmanship, it was much admired, and Catahaga himself had seen it often.

The chief gave orders that his braves should construct a litter of branches and boughs on which to carry the body of the pale-face.

The attack of the Indians upon the pickets—the volley they poured upon the advancing foes—these are details with which the reader is acquainted.

The battle over, the Indians had started back to their quarters around the hut of Weatherfield the trapper.

Hither they brought the insensible Foxley.

It should be mentioned that on their way, by applying brandy to his lips and dashing cold water on his brow, the detective had been partially restored to consciousness; but he soon after relapsed into his former lifeless condition.

Upon the return of the war party, which took place in the evening, Catahaga had passed a few words with his wife, and then retired from the vicinity of the bivouac in order to reflect upon his plans for future enterprises and to pay his devotions to the great Sun-Manitou, his deity.

He partook but sparingly of the food his companions devoured with the voracity of vultures, and then, after a few moments' rest, he rose, and placing his long rifle on his shoulder, set out for the Panther's Pass.

The glowing sunset red-blazoned the western sky and reflected its coloured rays upon the mirroring breast of the broad Arkansas. The purple hills, the trees, enhanced in height and grandeur by their lengthening shadows, and the magnifying effects so noticable in the soft and solemn air of twilight, seemed to smooth the brow and to soften the fire-flaming eyes of the wild Indian chief.

With stately tread he glided through the grand old forests, his eyes bent on the sward, his long robe trailing, his moccasins swept by the waving grass and heather.

He reached the banks of the grand river, and clambering the rocks that bordered it, arrived at length at a place where the white-frothed rushing torrent poured its brawling stream into the deep, calm gliding waters of the mighty Arkansas.

Woods of fir and pine crowned the rocks, and fringed their rugged sides.

Through the wood the Pawnee wended his way.

He emerged at length upon an open, elevated plain.

This he crossed.

Once more he reached the fir-fringed rocks.

A fearful precipice shot down.

The light was midway choked in the bluish darkness.

On the side of the cliff he left his arms—his rifle, his tomahawk, and scalping-knife.

A single log, tapering at one end—the split trunk of a tall pine-tree—spanned the fearful chasm.

With fearless tread, the Indian walked the narrow path, with yawning horror and the death-void on either side.

He paused in the middle of the dreadful bridge.

He folded his arms, and looked towards the broad, strait-like river.

The wind fluttered his blanket, and streamed the

THE BOY PIRATE; OR, LIFE ON THE OCEAN. 373

long tassels of his moccassins, and waved the long plumes of the quaillou on his brow.

Beyond the silver flood, and behind the far, lone and misty hills, the red sun, like a molten ball, was sinking.

Perched like an eagle, the Indian watched the crimson-glowing orb descending through clouds of ruby and amber tints, and the brilliant stars shoot out singly, then in groups, in the deepening opal.

His lips murmured.

Over the frightful abyss, from which rose far, sullen, and subdued, the hoarse roar of the foamy mountain torrent.

He breathed a prayer to his deity, now parting to gild other lands with his bright and fostering rays.

"Great Sun, throne of the Master of Life, home of the Father of Good and Evil! the son of Manotah bends to thee in humblest reverence. Great Manitou, thy simple red children adore thee through all the maize-fields and hunting-grounds of the Iroquois! Why hast thou given power to the hand of Catahaga that he is able to strike the wise pale-faces on the war-path; to sting them subtly, as the ground-snake strikes the heel of the passer that treads upon his nest? Why hast thou made the flash of his tomahawk like the gleam of thy blue lightning arrows winged with swift death, and yet hast darkened his heart that he walks in blindness—that there is ever a cloud before his eyes, so that he may not see thee throughout the wide prairies, nor in the wigwams of thy red or white children? The Black Robes of the Pale-faces pretend to know thy mysteries; but their tongues are forked, and they know thee not. Source of Light, pour thy beams into the soul of the simple Pawnee, that he may see plain, that he may know why thou hast given the lands of his fathers into the hands of the blood-thirsty, proud, and grasping Yengeese; why thou favourest them so much that thou hast given them power and subtlety to conquer thy red children; why they speak so many false words; why they bring with them charms and spells to make the Iroquois drunk with their fire-water, and to destroy them with their fire-weapons. Great Manitou, thy son of clay hath dwelt in the lodges of the mighty Yengeese, and he hath a prize of them—his wife, thy richest gift; he has learned their ways, he has spoken with their tongue, he has learned much good of them, for they are wise; he hath seen much evil in them, for they are wicked. Why hast thou given them wisdom to beguile thy red children? Why dost thou permit them to sweep away thy works, to crowd these banks with their stone wigwams, and to sully these waters with their fire-canoes? Is all given into the hands of the long-knives? Is nothing preserved to thy children of the Iroquois, whose fathers hunted on these grounds when the moon and stars were young? Give us strength, great Sun-Manitou, to strike our enemies, to quell the dog-hearted pale-faces, and to win back the land of our fathers!"

The Indian murmured these words in a fervent tone of devotion, and stretched his arms above the deep abyss, and yearning towards the setting sun, whose broad, lurid disc was now half eclipsed by the rugged mountain peaks, and whose broad path of red gold shimmered across the wavy river.

He was not unobserved.

Oswald Lamond, Wyld, and four of the bush-rangers, like prowling foxes, were crouching along behind the bushes that skirted the precipices.

The captain of the bandits raised his head above the thicket.

As he looked on the heroic form of the splendid young chief, who stood so fearlessly on the narrow plank that crossed the airy and profound ravine, he could not repress an utterance of admiration.

"Captain. 'fore Heaven, don't let's have any mawkishness," muttered Wyld, emphatically. "The redskin devil will see us, and in an instant detect our little scheme, and then, if we spare him, woe to the strongest of us. You may depend on it he's a

party in the plot for taking Agnes out of your hands."

"Enough, Wyld, I am neither a child nor a fool," he answered, curtly. "Look at the red fiend, how he stretches his arms out to his sun-god, imploring him, I dare say, to infect the air, and poison all pale-face dogs and Yengeese squaws. The man is mad; he takes no scalps, he is less than Indian in beastliness, but he's more than a hell-hound in remorseless vindictiveness. Do but watch him."

"I can pick him off from behind this sloe-thorn, and notch him for a wager."

"Hold! it is not safe to fire so near the camp."

"True."

"Look, Wyld, I don't want to break with the Indians. The pine bridge is known to be rotten; we can chop it down, and with a little rending and trimming of the stakes that fasten it, we can make it appear that it had broken under his feet."

"Good! but our pious friend seems to have finished his evening orizons. Now we'll settle him."

"Quick; just now his spirit had left his copper carcase, and he was deaf to all but his own mutterings; now he's himself again, so be wary."

"How shall we prevent him from springing to the other side of the gulf?" asked Wyld.

"You aim at him with your revolver, while I hew the bridge," said Regan, quickly, as he drew his hatchet from his belt. "Come the worst, you must fire; you have four charges, and the other side of the gulf is as rough and bare as the back of an alligator, so the devil's in it if you can't pink him before he reaches the bush."

"Right, captain; but look sharp, for he turns, and is coming this way."

In an instant the treacherous assassins had leaped from their covert.

"Ugh!" exclaimed Catahaga, suddenly recoiling.

He stood midway on the narrow bridge, scarce wide enough for a cat to run upon.

The terrific gulf lay dark below him.

Crash!

It was the first blow of the glancing axe falling upon the frail and rotten timber.

A dreadful group hung on the shelving rocks on one side of the gulf.

With one hand grasping the arm of a tree, Wyld reclined among the stones and furze; his other arm was extended, with deadly directness, his pistol pointing at the Indian's head.

The rotten plank shuddered and creaked beneath his feet.

Some loosened stones clattered down, but the noise they made was soon choked in the far depths of the fearful abyss.

Instinctively, Catahaga clutched at his girdle.

It was empty.

He stood defenceless, facing his deadly foes, a bending, cracking plank between his feet and the dark gulf of eternity.

His hope died, but his heroism could not perish but with his life.

With the stoic fortitude of his strange race, he drew himself up, laying his right hand on his breast, and tossing back his plumed head with ineffable disdain and daring defiance.

The last time the hatchet of the villanous chief of the robbers glinted in the fading red beam of the rich sunset.

Crash!

Down went the bridge crackling into the gloom.

Wyld blazed his revolver madly.

A wild shriek had caused him to start back.

In a half of the time it occupies in narration, the Indian had made a terrific leap, and with the strong bound had reached the edge of the gulf.

In a second he had grappled with the treacherous Regan.

Fiercely they battled for the axe, which had fallen to the ground, and was slipping to the edge of the rocks.

Over and over they rolled in their mad tussle;

down and down they shot stones and decayed fern leaves, showering about them.

The death-whoop of the warlike Pawnee-Loup, the agonised yell of the well-requited traitor.

Gloom and silence.

The distant snarl and roar of the frothy torrent amid the rifted rocks.

The shriek of a brace of mated owls, which startled from their cranny in the black gulf, soared up into the clear twilight, as if bearing on their wings the souls of the ruthless wretches.

"My God! so much for our gallant captain!" gasped Wyld.

"They are both killed!" said one of the men.

"Have their bodies reached the torrent?"

"Ask the owls, who see in darkness," muttered the awe-struck Wyld.

"Hush! Listen!"

The dull, steady roar of the ever-raving torrent, but no sound of human voices.

"Give me a rope, some of you," cried Wyld, in trembling accents.

A coil of rope was produced.

A hatchet and a coil of rope is always to be found among a party of three or four backwoodsmen travelling together.

Wyld fixed one end of the line round a tree, and wound the other about his body.

"Now, my lads—hold tight," said Wyld to the two rangers. "I mean to launch myself into the gulf, and if I can recover the body of our captain, I will, if not, at least, we may be satisfied as to his fate."

"Best not venture, Wyld," said one of the bushrangers, whose knees trembled so violently that he was in imminent peril of a fall.

But the sturdy ranger made no reply.

Tightly gripping the rope, he flung himself off the rocky ledge of the abyss, and swiftly lowered himself into the gloom.

The rangers listened breathlessly.

There was a sudden jerk of the rope.

The echoes roared along the rugged steeps reverberating.

They had been dreadfully awakened by a wild and piercing cry!

CHAPTER CLI.

THE BOY PIRATE PREPARES FOR HIS GRAND ENTERPRISE—THE PROUD SPANIARD—THE DUEL ON DECK—THE GENEROUS CONDUCT OF THE BOY PIRATE.

AFTER the bold deed, by which the Boy Pirate had extricated himself and Black Ralph from their awkward dilemma, the pirates had steamed away in the "Avenger" and the "Defiance," towing along the sailing vessels.

They anchored off another of the myriad green islets that gem the southern seas.

Here they lay for several days.

During this time they were joined by many daring spirits from amongst the settlers—English, French, and Spanish.

The Boy Pirate and the rest of the commanders of the now formidable fleet had been busily employed in freighting and manning their various craft and making extensive preparations for their grand enterprise.

The blacks still remained on board the slaver.

After what had happened at Don Zamora's ball, it was out of the question that they should be disembarked on the island of which he was the governor.

The course to be pursued in regard to them had not yet been decided upon.

The Boy Pirate and his officers were in the state-cabin engaged in the perusal of letters, and arranging of plans, when Zampa entered.

"Beg yo pardon, sar," said the negro, ducking his head; "but hab to report a piece ob de orfullest imperance as neber was heard on. Mas'r cap'en know de Spanish feller what want to fight you on de island?"

"Don Garcia?" cried the Boy Pirate, in great surprise.

"Yas, sar, Don Starcher, dat's the gemman, and berry good name for de dam buckra, for I believe de nuss gib him starch instead ob sop when him picaninny. Dar him stand midships stiff as de fo'mast."

"Is he alone?"

"No, sar; berry lilly chap, sar, in de boat wid him."

"And what on earth does he want?"

"Notin on de earth, sar, but summat on de sea, which gib him great satisfaxion."

"And what's that?"

"De satisfaxion, sar?"

"Yes."

"Yo gib him, sar, de choice ob walk de plank or cut de throat—dat ought to gib him perfee satisfaxion, sar."

"Is he armed?"

"Iss, sar. Berry fine brace ob pistols and two swords, 'bout as long as de bowsprit, and not so tick as de sailmaker's needle.

"By Jupiter! I should not wonder if the fiery Spaniard has come to challenge me!" cried the Boy Pirate.

The officers laughed heartily.

"Well, I like the confidence he places in my honour. I cannot hate the man who trusts me," returned our hero, smiling. "I will see if I cannot doctor his wounded honour without having recourse to surgery."

The Boy Pirate came on deck.

The haughty Spaniard awaited him.

Drawn up to his full height, his dark brows knit, and his lip compressed, he stood as Zampa had expressed it—"stiff as de fo'mast."

He bowed haughtily as the Red Raven approached him.

The first impulse of the generous young pirate was to stretch forth his hand; but he restrained himself, fearing a result.

"May I inquire to what happy circumstance I owe the pleasure of Don Garcia's visit?" said our hero, with a smile and a bow.

"Senor Paul, I am aware that you are a man of courage, and though you have defied national law you are not ungoverned by law which binds all men of pride or feeling—the law of honour."

Our hero bowed assent.

"You must be aware, Senor Paul, that the affront you offered to myself and kinsman on a late occasion leaves me no alternative but that of seeking you to demand that satisfaction which one gentleman has a right to exact from another."

"And you have come, senor, to challenge me?"

"Even so, and in full confidence that you will not refuse to meet me."

"Senor, are you inexorable?"

"Unless——But, indeed, I can see no way of compromise, the offence being so deadly."

"Then you wish me to accept your challenge?"

"I am certain that a brave man would not dishonour himself by refusal in such a case."

"But I assure you, Don Garcia, that under existing circumstances it will be quite impossible for me to leave the vessel."

"An objection I anticipated, Captain Paul; as you will see I am not without weapons. I have no second, for I was resolved to waive ceremony."

"And would you have this duel fought on the deck of my own ship?" asked our hero, with a smile.

"As it is not convenient for you to return to shore, Captain Paul, I suppose it must even be so."

"But, senor, have you considered the rashness of such a course?"

"I have, senor, but when I came on board the vessel of the Boy Pirate I felt that this little affair was confided to a man of honour."

"By George! that doctrine may hold good while my influence and my life co-exist, Don Garcia;" returned our hero, dryly; "but I cannot be responsible for what my crew may please to do if you should chance to kill me."

"Captain Paul, I come prepared to run every risk if I may be permitted to remove the stain that rests upon the honour of my family."

"Family? Pshaw! what was my offence, Don Garcia? You denounced myself and my colleague as pirates—nay, if you remember (I am apt to forgive such offences, unless I avenge them at the time) you treated me with insane rudeness. Well, I must confess, senor, I feel highly flattered at the great mark of confidence you have given me, pirate as I am, in this visit to my prize. I hope you will ignore past difficulties over a cup of pulque wine, and blow to the winds all unpleasant memories with a whiff of a choice cigar."

The Spaniard frowned darkly.

"Senor, if you are inclined to treat the matter with such levity, I shall be forced to conclude that fame has given you too much credit for certain high qualities."

"Ha! you imply that I am a coward?" said our hero, with a calm smile.

"Captain Paul, when I return home, I confess that I shall bear with me a regretful conviction that you are not the man I took you for."

"If you thought me one who could not afford to refuse to fight upon such shallow argument for fear of being stigmatised by the name of coward, you did me wrong. I think, without vaunting, I may say the time is far past when I should have been eager to vindicate a character which is now too firmly established to be so easily shaken."

"Captain Paul, you have doubled the injury for which I seek satisfaction. There is only one view of the case in which I can console myself, my sword will be unstained by the base blood of a pirate!"

With this he turned away, and was stepping towards the side.

The blood tinged our hero's face, and his brow grew dark.

"Stay, sir!" he cried, a little fiercely. "If you are not too anxious to keep your steel unstained by blood which would dishonour it, I am ready to give you such satisfaction as lies in my poor power to bestow; at the same time warning you that I cannot be responsible for the actions of my crew if you should chance to slay me."

At this moment a number of the pirates gathered round.

The Boy Pirate explained to them the case as it stood, and exhorted them to respect the person of Don Garcia if the Don should be victorious.

The men made but little answer.

The fiery Spaniard had divested himself of his cloak and coat.

The Boy Pirate did the same.

They drew their swords, and saluted.

They fought warily for some time.

They were very equally matched.

They seemed to be watching each other's tactics narrowly.

The bystanders, of whom there were not many immediately near the spot—for the Boy Pirate had given strict orders that the men should not desist from their duty—could perceive that our hero was doing his best to guard against the necessity of injuring his foe.

This Don Garcia became soon aware of.

The fact only increased his eagerness in the attack.

He was doing his best, or, rather, his worst, to provoke his antagonist.

The Boy Pirate had narrow escapes from several well-meant lunges.

A scream was heard.

Lilia had rushed from the quarter-deck, and would have flown between the combatants.

Zampa, laughing and chuckling at the skill displayed by the Boy Pirate, threw his black arms about her, and drew her back.

She struggled to be released.

To her infinite joy she beheld the Spaniard's sword whirl through the air, and fall splash into the sea.

The Boy Pirate stoo looking steadily at his opponent.

His face displayed no vulgar exultation nor affected indifference.

Don Garcia was pale with baffled fury.

"Senor, may I trust that, as a man of temper and reason, you are satisfied with my conduct?"

The Spaniard held out his hand.

The Boy Pirate grasped it with some warmth, and bowed with a look of mingled pride, vexation, and good feeling.

"Senor, since this little affair of honour is happily settled," he said, with a smile, "perhaps you would like to inspect my rover ship, and see what good-fellowship, order, and discipline reigns among men who are governed by no law but the law of mutual interest and friendship, for friendship is not unknown even on board the 'Avenger.'"

"Senor, for a pirate, you are the most wonderful man that ever existed," cried the Spaniard, with great admiration.

"Don Garcia, I became a pirate through being forced, when a boy, to serve under a pirate; it has been my fortune to have bitter, aye, and rich and powerful enemies."

"Your misfortune, you would say, Captain Paul."

"Not in the worldly sense," replied the Boy Pirate, with a smile, "for these rich and powerful enemies have hunted me long, but when I turned at bay no one of them has been able to stand before me, and you know that the hunter who falls before the tiger or the wolf becomes in his turn the prey of that creature whom he hunted. My prey has been as valuable and serviceable when conquered as it was terrible when on the chase for my life. Come, senor, let us go below; but first let me introduce you to my wife, Lilia."

With this the gallant rover presented his bride to the Spaniard.

Don Garcia started with surprise at the supreme loveliness of our heroine.

He spoke a few smooth phrases in compliment to herself and husband and followed them below.

The Boy Pirate showed the Spaniard through every part of the vessel.

Don Garcia was greatly surprised at the perfection of neatness and order that everywhere prevailed, he could scarcely persuade himself that he was not on board a man-of-war.

The Boy Pirate took him into the saloon where he introduced him to Ida, Deborah, and Mary, who chanced to be aboard with several others of those remaining willing captives on board the pirate's ship; lovely girls whom, as we have seen, our young hero had delivered from darkest perils.

Don Garcia could scarce believe that all he saw was not the picturings of some brilliant dream.

From time to time he looked at our hero.

Christopher might well be known as the presiding genius of the scene.

His face of perfect beauty, full of the fine expression of a warm heart and a liberal mind, his genius-lighted eyes, his flashing cheek, and his lips firmly arched, tender yet resolute, while the ruddy glow of health which tinged his sun-bronzed cheek spoke of youth and untiring vigour.

The Boy Pirate led his guest into a cabin, adjoining the handsome saloon sacred to himself and his bride.

It was fastened by a strong door.

This our hero opened by a key, and displayed a number of costly articles, carefully stowed.

He drew down a pair of beautiful small-swords.

"Don Garcia," he said, "these weapons I purchased years ago of the captain of a Turkish vessel. They were not won in battle from my foes, and I have not now in my possession a shred that has been taken in the ordinary manner of pirates. Let me entreat you to accept this trifling gift as a slight token of my deep sense of the honour you did me by trusting yourself so fearlessly on board my pirate vessel."

The Spaniard refused at first, but as our hero pressed him to accept the gift, he finally consented.

After saluting the ladies, Don Garcia accompanied our hero on deck.

"You have showed me many costly treasures, Captain Paul," said the Spaniard, musingly, "but they are all as worthless as dross compared with your rich prize, the adorable senora, your wife."

"If every nation could heap its riches into one mass, the pyramid of wealth could not equal in value the lightest of her smiles," said our hero, with enthusiasm. "I owe all to her. She has followed my fortunes with more than womanly love and devotion, more than martyr-like heroism and endurance; she has been my better angel. But for her, I could never have found the energy which has enabled me to struggle against the devil, the world, and—worst foe of all—my own heart; but for the sunshine of her smile, poor trampled weed, how could I have raised my head through the fierce blasts of war, the cold slights of ignominy, the hot drought of remorse? But it is useless to speak of her. My love for my wife is unspeakable, and I am not inclined to touch too freely on a theme so sacred."

"You are a noble fellow, senor," said Don Garcia, warmly. "And what is your object in the next cruise?"

Our hero answered, quietly,

"To fight for Poland!"

CHAPTER CLII.

THE LANDING OF THE SLAVES—THE GOOD MISSIONARY—THE MARRIAGE OF CASSIDY AND MARY—THE NEGROES OF THE ISLAND—THE ALARM—THE ATTACK—FLIGHT OF THE NEGROES—MARY ONCE MORE IN THE HANDS OF THE VULTURES—CASSIDY BOUND—HIS FORTITUDE—SCENES OF HORROR—A FEARFUL POSITION—ARRIVAL OF HARWOLF.

BEFORE accompanying our hero on his long-designed cruise to aid the Poles, we must narrate a startling adventure, of which Sam Cassidy was hero.

The slaves were landed on a pleasant island, of large size and fruitful soil, where dwelt a certain missionary, surrounded by a little colony of the converted natives from different islands, who had betaken themselves to this sanctuary, under the charge of their good pastor, to escape the persecution of their idolatrous fellow countrymen.

The worthy missionary had undertaken the difficult task of providing for the poor slaves, and finding them employment, with great willingness; and he and his native subjects, for he reigned in patriarchal fashion among them, built a number of huts for their involuntary emigrants, and allotted to each a piece of land to till for his own use.

The Boy Pirate, his officers, and Lilia visited the kind old man.

The missionary was over-joyed to see our hero, of whom he had heard so much, and in whom he perceived so many good qualities.

He had too much tact to intrude exhortations and admonishings upon a wild gang of terrible pirates; but with simple dignity and hearty frankness, he showed them the power of goodness by the force of example, and so won the hearts of the sea-robbers that there were not any of them who did not listen to him with profound respect.

When the rest of the crews of the Boy Pirate's fleet had gone on board, Cassidy and Mary lingered ashore.

They had been pressed by the good missionary to spend another evening on his plantation.

On the previous day the good old man had united the hands of the seaman and the Scotch girl in the bonds of marriage, and the old skipper had bestowed on them a pious and hearty blessing.

The evening passed pleasantly.

The old missionary was a very entertaining companion, and full of anecdote and pleasant wit. The young pair were much delighted with his kindly interest in them.

He had not attempted to dissuade Cassidy from joining our hero in his bold enterprise, but had looked upon the Scotch lassie with a glance of admiring sympathy when she had rapturously expressed her high hopes for the success of the Avengers.

Night came.

Cassidy and his wife rose hastily.

A party of the negroes were to row them in the boat.

These were assembled without, and when the young seaman and his wife appeared they welcomed them with a shout.

The plantation was situated at some distance from the shore.

The house was built in a valley.

The sea was not visible from the spot.

A party of six negroes, who were to man the boat, accompanied Cassidy and Mary.

It was a dark night.

The negroes carried torches.

They made their way through the aromatic groves of cedar, till they reached an open plain beyond the plantations, and came upon a rocky bank on either side of a narrow and rapid river.

Along this bank they walked quickly, till the country began to appear more level, and the river to widen.

One of the negroes spoke to the seaman.

"Yo see, massa Cass'dy, down yar is de boat-house. None can come up de ribber all de way 'cept in canoe. Yo know why mas'r got him house built down de walley, right in middle of de island?"

"No, Quashee; why does he not live nearer to the shore?"

"Jest tell yo, massa; dar's berry sinful creeturs in dis world, as don't jest know nuffin about New Jerubalem, neber sing nuffin but wicked songs, and swar de orfullest words, poor sinners, does a many on 'em."

"Well, what has that to do with it?"

"Yo see, massa, dey're like yo'self."

"Do I sing bad songs and swear, Quashee?"

"No mean dat, massa; yo berry nice buckra, and missee reg'lar converted, sing de hymns and spirt'al songs most as well as Aunt 'Rora."

"And who's Aunt Aurora?"

"A reg'lar roarer, and no mistake. Yah, yah! Golly, massa!"

"Golly! Oh, Uncle Quashee, yo hab not fought de fight wid de debil if you let him tempt you to talk sech!" cried a lathy, sanctimonious-looking nigger, his red eyes rolling with deprecation.

"Yo go 'long, Elijah; tink yo better 'n a good many, I s'pose. Yah! Berry grad yo tink so; but I tell yo what, yo nigger, yo go and do likewise, and don't be findin' fault wid dis chile, 'tain't noways becomin'."

"Don't quarrel, my boys. And who is Aunt Aurora?"

"I tell yo, massa; she sing in de church. But, massa, no let her sing afore de sermon."

"How's that?"

THE DISCOVERY IN THE SHIP'S HOLD.

"'Cos, massa, berry good reason; when she begin to sing no can stop her; and her woice is so beautiful strong no can hear massa preacher for it!"

"But when the sermon is ended the service is over, I should think, so you don't get much of her music?"

"Gol—de gal, I mean, sar—she sing and sing, and we leab her dar, sar, till next day meetin'."

"And do you find her still at it?"

"Iss, sar; but she not got so much woice; she get so tired, yo see."

"But why am I like those wicked fellows?"

"Yo come in ship, sar; dey'se come in ship, too, and sometimes dey want hands for workee de wessel, yo see."

No. 48.

"Well?"

"Iss, massa, and dey catch some poor nigger and take him on board for sailor."

"The rascals!"

"Iss, mas'r; de debil get sich, and no mistake."

"And you seem to have cut a canal here."

"Dat's for freight de ships, massa."

Before them stood a log hut, open on the side facing the canal.

Several boats were moored upon the river.

Some heavy barges there were, laden with bales.

A sort of launch lay out in the middle of the river.

"Hi! yo, what yo doin'? Yo not come out to meet de buckra gemman, yo nigger?" cried Quashee, stepping forward.

There was no answer.

"To whom are you calling, darkie?" asked the seaman.

"Callin' Sambo, sar, what mind de boat."

"Ha! then he's coming," said Cassidy.

Mary started and clung to his arm.

"What is it, dear? you seem startled," said her husband.

"I canna but think that there's some awesome danger hanging over us," returned his wife.

"Nonsense," replied Cassidy, "these black fellows are scared at their own shadows."

The negroes had crouched back.

With uplifted torches they stood listening and trembling.

With a rough shout and a volley of coarse oaths a number of ruffians in seamen's clothes rushed from behind the boat-house.

The negroes uttered a yell of terror, and dropping their torches fled in all directions.

Mary screamed.

Her husband wound his arm about her waist.

She clung to him in a convulsion of fright.

The next moment a number of savage fellows, with glancing cutlasses and pistols, surrounded them.

Cassidy fired at them.

They recoiled.

He flung his wife across his strong arm.

He drew a second pistol, retreating step by step.

The men seemed baffled for an instant.

He was soon lost in the darkness.

He fled towards the rocky banks of the river.

He was swiftly pursued.

He turned at bay.

He was seized by three or four dreadful-looking villains.

They dragged him to the ground.

Mary was torn from his arms.

She shrieked.

She struggled with the man who held her.

He drew a knife.

In her mad wrestling she caught hold of the bare blade.

Her hands were gashed.

She shrieked again and fainted.

Frantic with agony and rage Cassidy fought fiercely to rise.

His efforts were vain.

Half-a-dozen pistols were pressed to his throbbing brow.

As many cutlasses to his throat.

A fellow, if possible, more brutal-looking than his comrades, stepped forward.

"Hold, messmates, don't knife the skunk, or the captain will curse you all for doing the good turn; it's the peaching Cassidy. Harwolf will tear his liver out with hot pincers. Catch hold of the wench!"

There was a stake by the river side to which boats were sometimes moored.

To this the ruffians bound the unfortunate Cassidy.

A guard of four men was left in charge of him.

"And what's to be done now, Blacklock?"

"We are to storm the parson's plant, cut every throat our knives will fit, and seize everything we can lay hands on."

"This will be a good night's work."

"A bad night for somebody, I reckon."

"Shall some one run to Harwolf?"

"Where is he?"

"With Wardlaw, ransacking the barges."

"And where's the 'Sea Wolf' now?"

"At the river's mouth."

"Ay! he will thank the bearer for his news."

"And now let us carry off the girl, and do you look well to the prisoner."

"Never fear! Come, hearty."

The imperturbable Cassidy, finding his case hopeless, remained perfectly still.

Not that he endured tamely to see his wife torn from his hands and in the arms of those whom he looked upon as in no degree better than fiends.

But he was a man, as we have seen, remarkable for that highest of high qualities—self-controul.

Aware of the utter uselessness of resistance he endured his torments like a hero.

How fearfully the time dragged away.

He listened intently.

His keepers seemed to share his excitement.

The night advanced.

And now from afar came the sounds of a fearful attack made on the plantation.

The air was laden with shrieks and cries.

Cassidy bit his lip and breathed hard.

It was more than man could bear.

He tried to tear himself from his cords.

The attempt was quite useless and only increased his fearful torture.

The very pirates looked pale.

The grey dawn broke.

But that part of the sky where night had not yet lost her empire was aglow with a red wild glare.

A number of pirates rushed by carrying their spoils.

A party of the villains came towards him.

At the head of them was Blake, the atrocious rascal whose real name was Blacklock, and whose story will form a dark chapter of itself.

The ruffian placed a pistol to the captive's head.

Cassidy turned upon him a glance so cold and indomitable that the fellow's fingers relaxed on the trigger as Harwolf and the remainder of the fiendish gang appeared upon the scene.

———

CHAPTER CLIII.

THE PIRATES ON THE ISLAND — HARWOLF GLOATS OVER HIS VICTIM—ATTACK ON THE BARGES — THE PIRATES CARRY OFF THE SCOTCH GIRL—BLACK RALPH AND ZAMPA TO THE RESCUE—ENCOUNTER OF THE BOATS' CREWS—TERRIFIC STRUGGLE—MARY SAVED —DIEGO'S ARTIFICE.

MARY had been carried to the quay, on which Harwolf landed from the "Sea Wolf's" boats.

Wardlaw and Corderes were with him.

"This is rather a dangerous service, captain," said Wardlaw, gloomily; "we might as well have left the job till we had made sure of the 'Raven's' departure."

"I tell you he is gone; I heard the last gun fire from the other side of the island as a signal for all aboard, and the Spanish fellow, who was too much a craven to dare to tell us a lie, said that the steamers and other craft had sheered off hours ago."

"Captain, captain," cried several men, at this moment rushing to the spot, "we have made a glorious beginning to this night's work."

"What, have you taken the Big Boy, or his mincing girl?" asked Harwolf, with a gruff laugh; "I expect nothing less after such a hullabaloo."

"Almost as good," returned one of the men, "the Scotch girl is in our hands, and Sam Cassidy, that deserted from the 'Cormorant' and took Black Ralph's part against us."

"That's brave. I've an old book in black letter—'The Secrets of the Inquisition,' which treats of racks and tortures; I'll warrant I will find some novel means of torturing that skunk," cried the brutal villain, with a leer. "And the girl, too; you have taken the bonnie Mary, eh?"

"Aye, cap'en."

"Well, she must look to herself; she must be very sweet indeed, or she will find me bitter, I'm thinking. If it had been the other girl, now."

"What, Deborah the Jewess?"

"Yes," returned Harwolf, with a gasp, "I hear she is still with St. Christopher."

"Aye, cap'en, but she seems to have forgotten her wrongs," returned Wardlaw. "I should have thought that such a vixen would have spent her life in a chase for yours."

"She knows better," returned Harwolf, fiercely. "I killed her father; that deed may be followed by another—her own murder."

"Murder!" exclaimed Wardlaw, starting and turning pale.

"Did you never hear that pretty word? did you never see the pretty deed done, that you rolled up your eyes, and changed colour like a dying dolphin? But come, my hearties, show me this princess."

As senseless as the cold stones on which she lay was the poor girl to all that was passing around her.

Harwolf lifted her in his arms.

"At least *she* shall not escape me," he said, with a dark frown. "It seems as though some invisible power exist whose mission it is to snatch every woman out of my hands."

"Santa Maria, I tell you how it is, senor," said the Spaniard, "the saints are mighty fond of pretty women and always do them a good turn when they can."

"Well, carry her off to the boats; and, look you, Corderes, a thousand chances may happen to-night to compel our hurried return to the 'Sea-Wolf,' see her safe aboard, and remain with her. Should I fall to-night she is yours; do you understand?"

"Very well, senor," returned the Spaniard, with a grin.

Five or six of the ruffians carried Mary to the boat.

They placed her on the hatches.

Corderes jumped in and the boat was pulled off.

Pale and feeble from his terrible punishment, but so far recovered that he was able to do the fell work which was exacted of him, sat the youth Diego, who had so generously risked the danger of a terrible death for the sake of preserving Esther, the pilot's daughter.

"Now is the time, Panolo," muttered Diego, "the Spaniards aboard are ripe for it."

"Good! But I shall have to send you back when we have taken the senorita on board."

"I desire no more!"

"Ha, Diego, but if we sail off and leave the infernal Yenglese on the island, what will become of you?"

"What can become of any of us?"

"Muy ben, there is no need to seek death when he is always on our track. Besides, Diego, it would not do now!"

"Why not?"

"How long since you confessed and got absolution, and who's to pay masses, comerado?"

"No priest can give absolution for such dreadful sins as ours."

"Out, *heretico!* I grant you it will cost a heavy sum, but some priests work cheaper than others. You had best take care."

"It is as dark as a wolf's mouth," said Corderes, "I hope that there will be no misadventure in store which will compel the captain to re-embark before we can get out of the roads."

"Do you think the Boy Pirate has really sheered off?"

"I do not think so," returned Corderes. "How came this girl ashore?"

"Perhaps she and her gallant Cassidy have left the pirates."

"Malraya! she had better have stopped with them."

"Harwolf will kill Cassidy."

"Kill him! not so long as he can keep him alive by torture."

"He is getting fiercer and falser every day."

"There it lies, amigo; he may be as fierce as the arch-fiend if he pleases to our foes, but, as you say, there is no trusting him among ourselves."

"And do you think I could ever forget his cruelties?"

"Well, Diego; disobedience to orders, you know——"

"And you would forgive him?"

"I? I should have strangled him long ago, but when we get clear off with the ship, I have a plan for sending the Brazilians to arrest the whole gang."

"I have no spite against any but him," replied Diego."

"Every cursed Yenglese is my enemy; I hate them all! Besides, as an ambitious man, I must command a ship of my own," said his brother.

"I care not how soon I am killed, if I can but wreak my revenge upon that monster," returned Diego."

"That's nonsense, amigo. We shall have a fine life of it, when we are our own masters; and the Yenglese girl is beautiful, 'tis a pity she's a heretic."

"Hush! hold water!" cried Diego, suddenly.

A boat was heard plashing through the waves before them, dipping with muffled oars.

"What ho, what cheer?" cried the Spaniard, leaping up in the boat, and seizing their weapons.

"Gorra! yo dar? What yo got in de dam boat, sar? Yo stop, I tell yo; I'm de Boy Pirate's aid-de-scamps, tell yo dat, sar!" cried a voice through the darkness, in a guttural chuckle.

"Heave to, you lubbers; I am Black Ralph the Rover. So tremble in your tawny hides, you tiger-cats! for here's a sea-lion will smash you into mince-meat, if you attempt another turn in the rollocks. Hold water, and hang to ye!"

"Malraya! it is the 'Raven's' men," cried the Spaniard.

The boats rocked side by side.

A terrific encounter took place between the crews of either of them.

The Spaniards fought with intense fury.

Zamp and Black Ralph whirled round their cutlasses, hewing the Spaniards down in the long boat.

The noise of the fray was borne to the shore.

A gun was fired from the "Sea Wolf."

The Spaniards answered by their shouts.

Black Ralph leaped into the boat and seized the girl.

Corderes tried to wrench her from his grasp.

Black Zamp slashed him down with his sabre.

Bleeding and faint he rose to his knees.

His brother Diego warded off a deadly blow aimed at him as he rose by one of the Avengers.

The "Sea Wolf" now threw up lights.

The ship was illuminated by the phosphorescent glare.

The ghastly light shone on the waves, and lividly brightened the faces and the forms of the contending seamen.

Black Ralph had secured Mary, and seated himself in the stern of the boat.

Corderes had leaped into the sea.

Diego followed his example.

The "Sea Wolf" fired three or four guns from her bows.

The pounders spanked past the prow of the boat; one passed over her.

"Gorra! what for yo not pull, yo lubberly buckra, want young missee killed now yo cotch her?" cried Zamp, in great wrath. "Mas'r Ralph, better 'n as we get off to de vessels, thar's no good in being sent to de bottom just to cool our big courage; fight 'em noder day, yo know, sar."

Another cannon burst forth into roar and flash and cloud, and another round shot whizzed right past the stern of the boat.

The boats were now separated.

Corderes swam to the "Sea Wolf;" he seized the main-chains and clambered on deck.

Diego made for shore.

The other men were either drowned or yet clung to the boat, which was swamped with water and fast sinking under them.

Black Ralph and his men pulled lustily, for they heard the enemy scrambling over the bulwarks, and leaping into the boat.

They had left the "Shark" at sunset, in consequence of the appearance in the offing of a suspicious craft, which, though disguised, they were almost certain was the "Sea-Wolf."

Their suspicions were confirmed when a long boat

was discerned making for the shore evidently well manned.

Zampa, who happened to be on board the "Shark," suddenly remembered that Cassidy and Mary Mac-allister were on shore.

Black Ralph ordered the boats to be put off, and was steering to the island, when the encounter which we have described took place.

Meantime Diego had swam to the island.

As with much difficulty he managed to reach the mouth of the river and clambered on to the quay, the firing from the "Sea-Wolf" suddenly ceased.

Harwolf and Wardlaw, with a number of the other pirates, had been busy lading the barges with cotton-bales.

They had, however, paused in their work.

Half drenched, the crafty Spaniard hurried up to Harwolf.

"What croaking song have *you* to sing?" asked the pirate captain, fiercely. "What is the meaning of all this bobs-a-dying? Has Corderes lost his poor remains of top-hamper, or is there an attack of the Boy Pirate's blood-hounds?"

"The firing, captain; but, for Heaven's sake, let me get breath."

"The firing. Well?"

"A boat!—I faint with exhaustion."

"Speak, and faint afterwards, and be hanged to ye," cried the pirate savagely, "A boat! what boat?"

"A crew of—"

"Of the 'Raven's' men?"

"No, no! my breath."

"I'll stop it for ever, you Spanish spy, if you don't use it to better purpose," growled Harwolf, "what crew?"

"Poor devils, senor,—escaped—Ah! senor, my life is passing away."

"Escaped? Speak! do you allude to your mess-mates? Has the infernal Raven taken my ship?'

"No, no, captain,—poor wretches escaped from the barges—that's all—drowned every man of them."

Harwolf looked searchingly at the speaker.

His villanous countenance was distorted in an expression of fiendish malice.

He seized the Spaniard by the throat.

"Look you, Senor Sanctimony," he growled, "if your pious tongue has spoken a lie, I will tear it out by the roots."

"Senor, you may prove me by sending off to the 'Shark', at once."

"If the 'Raven' is cruising in the roads, we must make sail at once, my men, for it will not be prudent to meet when the odds are so hard against us."

"They cannot be in the roads, captain," remarked one of the seamen, "or they would have heard the firing on the plantation and from the 'Sea-Wolf.'

"They say that Black Ralph's vessel is left behind to pick up the liberty chaps, but that the Boy himself has steamed off to Black Beard's Land, as the rovers call the long bank out no'th'ard."

"Well, then, I suppose we must believe the skunk, but look to him some of you. Blacklock, I leave him to your care."

"I does my duty in sich cases," returned the ruffian, with a grin.

"And now, lads, as morning breaks, we will go and pay our respects to Captain Cassidy," said Harwolf, with a laugh.

The villains followed their commander with many a brutal threat against the luckless prisoner.

Blacklock went before.

They arrived just at the moment when that pirate menaced poor Sam with his pistols.

Harwolf interposed.

"Not so, Blacklock, we must play with this mouse before we kill him," he said; "bring him away."

Cassidy was cut loose.

Harwolf folded his arms, and peered in his victim's face, with a look of infernal triumph.

"So, Master Deserter, you have fallen into the hands of your ship's captain. Sorry for you; but you shall have a fair trial and a merciful punishment if

we are forced, as an example of justice, to put you to death. We will do so by slow degrees. Ha! there is another mutineer, an arch-traitor, we must apprehend, a roystering cavalier, called Black Ralph. Know him?"

"Fool!" said Cassidy, with supreme contempt.

Harwolf raised his hand to strike him.

There was something so imperative in the cold, calm gleam of the dauntless seaman's bright, dark eye, that Harwolf's arm fell powerless at his side, and he drew back instinctively.

"You are not wise in braving me, but perhaps you think that I shall be tempted to strike you dead upon the spot," he said. "Bring him away."

Cassidy was dragged to the shore.

Diego came to his side.

He seized him by the arm, and bullied him in terrific style.

The seaman looked at him in wonder.

Harwolf thought this display of needless violence on the part of the young Spaniard was the effect of a craven desire to conciliate.

Diego seized a rope.

Harwolf started.

"*You* mean to bind the prisoner, eh? Remember how you do the job, my beauty; reflect on what your want of skill cost you last time."

"I shall never forget that debt, senor."

"Debt! ha! What do you mean?"

"That I mean to pay out every prisoner for what my kindness to that cursed wench cost me."

"Ha, ha! You will have plenty of chance to take acquittance in full, lad."

Diego wound the ropes round the prisoner's arms.

"Ah, you scamp! desert, will you?" he bawled. "*There's a loose plank in the boat,*" he whispered. "Malraya! you will be keelhauled," he shouted. "*There's a knot in your hand; you have but to pull it, the ropes will loosen,*" he whispered. "Wait till we get you on deck!—*Strike the plank with your heel when I give the signal.* So, so; break these fastenings, and you may break my neck in a noose.—*And jump into the water, and make for the island.* He is properly trussed for roasting now, senor capitano."

The pirate laughed.

The officious custodian was left in immediate charge of the prisoner.

They hurried to the boat.

Cassidy was placed in the centre.

Diego sat at his side.

A long knife was in his hand.

He waved this weapon before the prisoner's eyes, and even pricked him with it.

The brutal pirates laughed at this excellent jesting.

Before the prisoner, and with a huge pistol grasped in each hand, sat Blacklock.

Harwolf sat in the stern.

The boat was over-crowded.

They neared the mouth of the river.

Diego gave the signal to the prisoner.

At the same moment a Spaniard at the prow of the boat started up.

"Diavolos! senor, what has become of the ship?" he cried, in a tone of consternation.

Blacklock started up.

He shaded his eyes from the strengthening beams of the rising sun, and glanced over the sparkling waters.

The horizon stretched its arc afar, undotted by the sail or mast of any vessel.

"Captain, the ship is gone!" he cried. "There is some treachery!"

The words were his last.

Lithely springing upon his former torturer, the young Spaniard struck the knife to the hilt in his heart.

Cassidy sprang up.

He leaped upon the loosened plank.

It yielded, and shattered.

Diego sprang upon Harwolf.

The next instant, the boat was swamped, and such as could swim were struggling to the shore.

The Spaniard and the atrocious Harwolf wrestled amid the foaming waves.

It seemed that it was not the destiny of this wretch to fall by the hands of our hero, so certainly imminent was his death.

CHAPTER CLIV.

THE SANDY ISLAND—THE TRUE STORY OF A CELEBRATED PIRATE.

THE man who told Harwolf that the Boy Pirate had steamed away with his consort vessels, to the long, barren reef and bank, called by the sailors Black Beard's Land—in association with the terrible pirate of that name—had stated the fact.

Impatient of the delay of Cassidy and Mary, our hero, who was impatient to get out of the roads into the open main, had weighed anchor, leaving his colleague, Black Ralph, to pick up any who might still be straggling on shore.

Perhaps a short account of this celebrated pirate, who has figured as the hero of so many romances and melodramas, may interest our readers.

They will perceive how utterly abandoned are those monsters, who have sometimes been presented in an attractive light as corsairs and dashing rovers, and will have a good specimen of their general character, in the following brief narrative, drawn from authentic sources, of the

LIFE OF BLACK BEARD, THE PIRATE.

Edward Teach was born at Bristol, and, having emigrated to Jamaica, sailed from that place as one of the crew of a privateer, during the war with France.

In his new position he gained distinction by his boldness and personal courage.

At length Captain Benjamin Hornigold gave him the command of one of the prizes that he had captured.

Hornigold and Teach set sail from Providence for America, in the spring of the year 1717. In their passage they took a small ship freighted with one hundred and twenty barrels of flour.

Soon after they captured two other vessels, from one of which they took some gallons of wine, and from the other plunder of great value.

Coasting Virginia, they took a large French Guineaman, bound to Martinique.

The command of her was given to Teach, who separated from his colleague and went upon a cruize.

As for Hornigold, he returned to Providence, with the two vessels, and surrendered to the king's clemency.

Teach was now left to act independently. He mounted his vessel with forty guns, and named her "The Queen Anne's Revenge."

Near the island of St. Vincent he took a very large vessel called the "Great Allan," and, after taking as much plunder as he could stow away, set her on fire.

A man-of-war, called the "Scarborough," was sent in pursuit of the pirate. The ships encountered and were engaged for some hours; but the man-of-war, seeing the resolution of her adversary, sheered off.

He was now joined by Major Bounet. They cooperated for some length of time, but Teach, finding his partner quite ignorant of naval affairs, entrusted the command of the sloop to one of his own crew, a man named Richards, and received Bounet on board his own vessel.

While watering at Teneriffe, where they remained a week, they discovered a sail.

And Richards, with the "Revenge," slipped her cable, and ran out to meet her.

Upon seeing the black flag she tacked and came to under the stern of Teach's vessel.

This ship was the "Adventure," outward-bound from Jamaica.

They put the captain on board the large ship, and manned his sloop for their own service.

From Teneriffe they sailed to the Bay, where they found a ship and four sloops.

Teach hoisted the black flag, and began to fire at them, whereupon the captain and his men left their ship, and fled to the shore.

Teach burned two of these sloops, the others he allowed to depart.

Teach and Richards sailed to different places in company, and, having taken two small vessels, they anchored for a few days off the bar of Charleston.

Here they captured a ship bound for England, as she was coming out of harbour.

Another vessel, coming out of harbour, was seized by the pirates, and two pinks coming into the port, together with a brigantine with fourteen negroes aboard her.

The audacity of these transactions, performed in the sight of the town, filled the inhabitants with great consternation, especially as they had been visited by other notorious pirates within a short time.

There were eight sail in the harbour, not one of which durst set out to sea for fear of falling into the hands of Teach.

The trade of this place was totally interrupted, and the inhabitants thrown into the depths of despair.

Their calamity was greatly augmented by the fact that a long and terrible war with the natives had just terminated, and they began to be infested by those robbers.

Teach having detained all the persons he had taken in these ships as prisoners, he had the audacity to demand a chest of medicines from the governor.

A fever had broken out amongst his crew and captives.

Teach sent Richards, the captain of the "Revenge," with Mr. Marks, one of the prisoners, and several others, to present their request.

Richards informed the governor that, unless the demand was granted, and he and his companions returned in safety, every prisoner on board the captured ships should instantly be slain, and the vessels consumed to ashes.

During the time that Mr. Marks was negociating with the governor, Richards and his companions walked the streets at pleasure, while every eye flamed with indignation against them, as the robbers of their property and the terror of their country.

Though the affront thus offered to the Government was great and most audacious, yet, to preserve the lives of so many men, they granted their request, and sent on board a chest valued at three or four hundred pounds.

Teach, as soon as he received the medicines and his fellow pirates, pillaged the ships of gold and provisions, and then sent the prisoners away with their vessels.

From the bar of Charleston they sailed away, and made for North Carolina.

The audacious pirate now began to reflect upon the means of securing his booty.

He determined only to preserve such of his crew as were his favourites.

Under pretence of cleaning he ran his vessel on shore and grounded; he then ordered the men in Richard's sloop to come to his assistance, which they endeavoured to do, but ran aground and were both lost.

Teach then went into the tender with forty hands, and upon a sandy island, about a league from shore, where there was neither bird nor beast, nor herb for their subsistence, he left seventeen of his crew, who must have perished if Major Bounet had not received intelligence of their miserable position, and sent a long boat to rescue them.

After this treacherous deed, Teach with the rest of the crew surrendered themselves to the governor of North Carolina, retaining the whole of the booty he had taken.

By the influence of Black Beard's gold, the governor was bribed to obtain for the pirate a legal right to the ship called "The Queen Ann's Revenge."

A court of vice-admiralty held at Bath Town, condemned the vessel as a lawful prize taken from the Spaniards, though it was universally known that she belonged to the English.

About this time he married a young woman, only sixteen years of age, the governor himself being present at the wedding.

Though this woman was so young, and of a gentle and amiable disposition, he treated her most brutally, and in a manner so revolting to decency, that even his abandoned crew were disgusted.

Black Beard now directed his course to the Bermudas, and met with several English ships.

He plundered these of their stores, and left them to proceed.

Soon after this he met with two French vessels, bound for Martinique; one of light, the other of heavy burden. One of them was laden with sugar and cocoa; he put the men on board the latter into the former, and suffered her to depart.

He brought the freighted vessel into North Carolina.

Here Black Beard shared the prizes with the Governor.

Their audacious villany was carried still further.

Black Beard, and some rascals of his crew, waited upon the Governor, and swore that they had seized the French ship at sea, without a soul on board; a court was called, and his excellency received sixty hogsheads of sugar for his share, his secretary twenty, and the pirates the remainder. Lest their roguery might be detected, they burnt the vessel.

For some time Black Beard, being in the province of Friendship, traded with such ships as came into the river, sometimes in fair commerce, but oftener in his own fashion—robbing them at pleasure.

The captains of the vessels who frequented the river, and had been so often harrassed and plundered by Black Beard, consulted with the planters what measures to pursue in order to drive such a miscreant from their coasts, and to bring him to justice.

Knowing that they could get no redress from their own Governor, they applied to the Governor of Virginia, and besought him to send an armed force, the men-of-war lying there, either to take or to destroy the pirates who infested their coasts.

The Governor consulted with the captains of the two men-of-war.

It was determined that two small vessels should be hired which could pursue Black Beard into all his inlets and creeks, and that they should be manned from the men-of-war, and the command given to Lieutenant Maynard, an experienced and resolute officer.

When all was ready, the Governor called an assembly, in which it was resolved to issue a proclamation offering a large reward to any, who, within the space of a year, should take or destroy any pirate.

Maynard left James's River in quest of Black Beard upon the 17th of November, 1717, and came in sight of the pirate on the evening of the 21st of that month.

This expedition had been fitted out with all possible secresy, no boat being suffered to pass that might convey any intelligence, while care was taken to discover where the pirates were lurking.

However, his excellency the Governor of Bermuda and his secretary having obtained information of the intended expedition, the latter wrote a letter to Black Beard, and sent him four of his men, who were all he could meet with in or about the town, and so bade him be upon his guard.

These men were sent from Bath Town to the place where Black Beard lay, about the distance of twenty leagues.

Having often been deceived by false intelligence,

the hardened pirate was not convinced of its accuracy till he beheld the sloops sent to apprehend him.

Though he had only twenty men on board, he prepared to give battle.

It was evening when Lieutenant Maynard arrived with his sloops and anchored, as he could not venture under cloud of night to go to the place where Black Beard lay.

The latter spent the night in drinking with the master of a trading vessel, with the same indifference as if no danger had been near. Nay, such was the desperate wickedness of this villain, that, it is reported, during the carousals of that night, one of his men asked him: "In case anything should happen to him during the engagement with the two sloops who were waiting to attack him in the morning, whether his wife knew where he had buried his money;" when he impiously replied, "That nobody but himself and the devil knew where it was, and the longest liver should take all."

In the morning Maynard weighed, and sent his boat to sound, which coming near the pirate, received her fire; Maynard then hoisted the royal colours, and made for Black Beard.

Soon after the pirate ran aground, so also did the King's ships.

Maynard lightened his vessel of the ballast and water, and made towards Black Beard. Upon this the pirate hailed him in his own rude style.

"Who are you, and whence come you?"

The lieutenant answered, "You may see from our colours we are no pirates."

Black Beard bade him send his boat aboard that he might see who he was.

Maynard replied, "I cannot spare my boat, but I will come aboard you as soon as I can with my sloop."

Black Beard took a glass of liquor, and drank to him, saying, "I'll give no quarter, nor take any from you." Maynard replied, "that he expected no quarter from him, nor should he give him any."

During this dialogue the pirate's ship floated, and the sloops were rowing towards him.

As she came near the pirate fired a broadside, charged with all manner of small shot, which killed or wounded twenty men.

Black Beard's ship a little after fell broadside to the shore, and one of the sloops also fell astern.

Maynard finding that his sloop had weighed, and would soon be on board of Teach, ordered all his men down, while himself and the man at the helm, whom he commanded to be concealed, were the only persons remaining on deck.

He at the same time desired them to take their pistols, cutlasses, and swords, and be ready for action upon his call; and, for greater expedition, two ladders were placed in the hatchway.

When the King's sloop boarded, the pirate's caseboxes, filled with powder, small shot, slugs, and pieces of lead and iron, with a quick match in the mouth of them, were thrown into Maynard's sloop.

Fortunately, however, the men being in the hold, they did but little injury on the present occasion, though they are usually very destructive.

Black Beard, seeing few or no hands on deck, cried that they were all knocked on the head, except three or four, "and therefore," said he, "let us jump on board, and cut to pieces those that are alive!"

Upon this, during the smoke occasioned by one of these case-boxes, Black Beard, with fourteen of his men, entered, and were not perceived until the smoke had dispelled. The signal was given to Maynard's men, who rushed up in an instant.

Black Beard and the lieutenant exchanged shots, and the pirate was wounded.

They then engaged sword in hand until the sword of the lieutenant broke, but fortunately, at that instant one of his men gave Black Beard a terrible wound in the neck and throat.

The most desperate and bloody conflict ensued—Maynard with twelve men, and Black Beard with fourteen.

The deck was profusely stained with blood, and uncommon bravery was displayed on both sides.

Though the pirate was wounded by the first shot from Maynard, though he had received many cuts and as many shots, he fought with desperate valour, but at length, quite exhausted, fell down when in the act of cocking his pistol.

By this time eight of his men had fallen, and many of the rest being wounded, cried out for quarter, which was granted, as the ringleader was slain.

The other sloop also attacked those who were left in the pirate vessels, until they cried out for quarter.

And such was the desperation of Black Beard, that having small hope of escape, he had placed a negro at the gunpowder door, to blow up the ship the moment that he should have been boarded by the King's men, in order to involve the whole in general ruin.

That destructive broadside at the commencement of the action, which at first seemed so very unlucky, was, however, the means of their preservation from the intended destruction.

Maynard severed the pirate's head from his body, suspended it upon his bowsprit end, and sailed to Bath Town to obtain medical aid for his wounded men.

In the pirate sloop several letters and papers were found, which Black Beard would certainly have destroyed previous to the engagement, had he not determined to blow her up upon his being taken, which disclosed the whole villany between the honourable Governor of Bermuda and his honest secretary on the one hand, and the notorious pirate on the other.

Scarcely was Maynard returned to Bath Town, when he boldly made free with the sixty hogsheads of sugar, in the possession of the governor, and the twenty in that of the secretary.

After his men had been healed at Bath Town, the lieutenant proceeded to Virginia with the head of Black Beard still suspended on his bowsprit end as a trophy of his victory, to the great joy of all the inhabitants. The prisoners were tried, condemned, and executed.

"And thus," adds the interesting narrative, from which we have drawn this account of the notorious pirate, "thus all the crew of that infernal miscreant, Black Beard, were destroyed, except two."

One of these was taken out of a trading vessel, only the day after the engagement, in which he received no less than seventy wounds, of all which he was cured.

The other was Israel Hands, who was master of the "Queen Anne's Revenge." He was taken at Bath Town, being wounded in one of Black Beard's savage humours.

The appearance of the ruffianly pirate, has been thus described—

"Let the youthful reader contemplate the following picture of a dashing criminal. He derived this name from his long black beard, which, like a frightful meteor, covered his whole face, and terrified all America more than any comet that had ever appeared. He was accustomed to twist it with ribbon in small quantities and turn them about his ears. In time of action he wore a sling over his shoulder with three brace of pistols. He stuck lighted matches under his hat, which appearing on both sides of his face and eyes, naturally fierce and wild, made him such a figure, that the human imagination cannot form a conception of a fury more terrible and alarming; and if he had the appearance and look of a fury, his actions corresponded with that character."

The biographer of this celebrated outlaw has made the following comment upon the general character of those desperate wretches—pirates on the high seas.

"In the commonwealth of pirates, he who goes the greatest length in wickedness is looked upon with a kind of envy amongst them, as a person of most extraordinary gallantry; he is therefore entitled to be distinguished by some post, and if such a one has but courage, he must certainly become a great man. The hero of whom we are writing was thoroughly accomplished in this way, and some of his frolics of wickedness were as extravagant as if he aimed at

making his men believe he was a devil incarnate. Being one day at sea, and a little flushed with drink, 'Come,' said he, 'let us make a hell of our own, and try how long we can bear it.' Accordingly, he, with two or three others, went down into the hold, and closing up all the hatches, filled several pots full of brimstone, and other combustible matter; they then set it on fire, and so continued till they were almost suffocated, when some of the men called out for air; at length he opened the hatches, not a little pleased that he had held out the longest."

CHAPTER CLV.

CHARLES RYE'S FRIENDS PREPARE FOR HIS DEFENCE—THEIR INTERVIEW WITH EAGLETON—LORD HAWKSBURY OFFERS EAGLETON A THOUSAND POUNDS NOT TO APPEAR AT THE TRIAL.

LORD HAWKSBURY, Silas Rye, and Sibly were assembled in conclave to determine upon measures to be taken for the defence of young Charles, who was soon to be brought to trial on the charge of forgery.

Neither Silas nor his patron believed the young man to be guilty.

Sibly, both by natural disposition and professional prejudice, was inclined to be more suspicious.

He had now risen to distinction as a lawyer, and had undertaken to defend young Rye.

"I am sure that Charles is as guiltless of the alleged forgery as I am," said his lordship, with great warmth, "it is some piece of scoundrelism on the part of his fellow clerks, some treacherous conspiracy to ruin the poor fellow."

"That is a grave charge to make against any one, my lord," said Sibly, with a shrewd smile. "We are friends of the defendant, but we must not be partial morally."

"That fellow, Eagleton, who, I suppose, will be the chief witness against him, seems well intentioned," said Silas Rye. "I do not think that there can be any mistake about his non-connection with the plot for ruining my brother; he looks quite ill, and is evidently much distressed at the unfortunate position in which his friend is placed."

"The young reprobate!" cried Lord Hawksbury. "If Charles's guilt were possible, it might be ascribed to his connection with that 'fast' fellow, who has been living too fast, you may be sure. I heard that he had a heavy bet on Electra."

"Ha, do you know that?" said Sibly, quickly.

"Yes; the report rests on very good authority."

Sibly made a note in his pocket-book.

"My lord, we must find out what sum this Eagleton waged, and under what circumstances his bets were made; it will have an important bearing on the case.

"We will do so; we can employ a detective."

"I wish poor Foxley were here," said Silas Rye, with a faint smile.

"I wonder how he has succeeded in his mission of vengeance," said Lord Hawksbury, "it was a mad expedition altogether, but if he can hunt down the inhuman monster he will deserve a monument. I fear that he has not yet succeeded, for we have heard no news of him. Perhaps he may have fallen a victim to the transcendant villain."

"Well, my lord, you may be sure that the wretch will not finally escape the vengeance due to his awful crimes," said Sibly. "In the meantime, I think you have been fortunate in having secured to Lady Edgeforth the estates of Frontemore."

"Yes, and the worthy Squire Meredith, who is, I believe, the father of the silly romantic girl who eloped with the Boy Pirate, has offered to rent the house."

"A very eligible tenant, my lord," returned Sibly.

"And there should be some one in charge of the old place, for it has the reputation of being haunted."

"It may well be so," said Silas Rye, the colour fleeing from his cheek.

There was a pause.

Sibly broke the silence.

"Let us return to the subject of which we were speaking," he said. "At what time, my lord, are we to expect this Eagleton?"

There was a loud knock at the door.

"By my life, there's truth in the old saying!" said Lord Hawksbury, with a smile.

Eagleton was ushered into the room.

His calm, handsome face was very pale.

He was dressed with studious care and perfect neatness.

His address was gentleman-like, and his easy self-possession not without its power.

He bowed to the friends, and at their invitation seated himself.

He fixed his eyes on the ground and assumed a look of profound melancholy.

Sibly looked keenly at him.

"We have sent for you, Mr. Eagleton," said Lord Hawksbury, "in order to know your mind with respect to Charles Rye. Is he, think you, guilty or not? You are his friend; as an honest man you owe this duty to the laws that you must speak the truth, and the whole truth, we desire you to do no less. But now, as to a friend of Charles Rye, we appeal to you; apart from all circumstantial evidences, do you believe that Charles Rye is a forger?"

"I do not know, my lord, I cannot judge; I must entreat you not to press the question," returned Eagleton, evasively. "Charles, as you say so truly, is my friend, and I have every faith in his honesty; but while such proofs of his misguidance are in my hands, I cannot but feel bewildered when I try to reconcile them with his innocence."

Lord Hawksbury's eyes flashed.

Silas Rye watched the clerk with lynx-eyed scrutiny.

Sibly gave a slight sigh, and his face expressed a conviction of the rogue's sincerity.

Lord Hawksbury looked at Silas Rye and then at Sibly.

"Now, gentlemen," he said, "I mean at once to break the ice with Mr. Eagleton, and boldly to make to him the proposal I mentioned."

Sibly and Silas Rye bowed gravely.

Eagleton looked up with a crafty and penetrating glance.

"We are aware, Mr. Eagleton, that your warm regard for Charles Rye renders the duty you owe to society very painful," said Lord Hawksbury.

Eagleton answered only by a downcast look, and a faint sigh.

"And you have expressed your conviction of his innocence."

"Conviction! my lord; a hope, a trust that he is not guilty of this offence."

"But not conviction of his innocence: very well, Mr. Eagleton. Now. I dare say that you are acquainted with many of young Charles's secrets; for instance, neither I nor his brother knew anything about his betting transactions; in fact, we were under the impression that he never staked a shilling, while you, I suppose, as his confidant, were well aware of the risk he was running?"

"Indeed, my lord! I knew nothing about that," returned Eagleton, briskly, "I knew that he had staked heavily on Electra, but was not aware either of the real sum nor the odds."

"Nor even that the money had been placed in his name, in the hands of the stake-holder, Mr. Kites," said his lordship, very quietly.

Eagleton started—the blood rushed to his cheek and then died away.

His voice was calm and firm, but just a little husky as he answered,

"I was not aware of that—at least I did not know it for the fact, though now I recollect having heard some mention of it."

"Inspector Falcon has made some very strange discoveries, since he undertook to elicit the facts in this case. Do you know Falcon? Perhaps not; he is a very able detective officer."

Eagleton showed no other sign of emotion than a slight twitching of the lips.

Sibly watched him narrowly.

"I am very glad that you have engaged the services of so shrewd and indefatigable a man. He may be able to discover something important in Charles's favour," said Eagleton.

"He has his eye upon a young man of fashion, with whom you are acquainted."

"My lord, is it possible?"

"A young fellow in some government office."

"Indeed! Who can it be?"

"His name is, Mortimer."

Eagleton could not hold the colour in his cheek, though he steadied the gleam in his eye, and kept his lips compressed.

Lord Hawksbury did not look at him, but said carelessly.

"Of course these detectives make the most to their employers of any little discoveries they can make. Falcon seems quite sanguine of getting up a good case for the defence."

"I wish him every success, my lord," said Eagleton, faintly.

"I am sure you do; and would do all in your power to aid in the cause of friendship."

"I wish, my lord——" said Eagleton, suddenly— he paused.

"Go on, Mr. Eagleton, we are friends; you may speak freely."

"Well, then, I tell you boldly I wish it were possible that I could avoid appearing at the trial."

"Well, I cannot blame you for the wish; and though you owe obedience to the law, there is no slight virtue in self-sacrifice for friendship's sake— suppose you keep out of the way?"

"My lord, think of me what you please; say that I have not a proper sense of duty; that my principles are unstable; I care not; such repulsion do I feel at the idea of giving evidence against my friend, that were it possible, I would flee the country, rather than appear against him."

"It is not possible, because you would be forced to throw up your appointment, and would be put to great expense."

"My lord; I will return to the office no more. The associations connected with it are so painful, that I could not endure the place. I will seek employment elsewhere."

"And if you had the means of leaving England till this affair had blown over, you would go?"

"Right joyfully!"

"Well, suppose, Mr. Eagleton, you were to honour me by the acceptance, say of a thousand pounds, just to enable you to escape the torture to your kind nature of standing in the witness-box to blast the prospects, and to stab the moral life of your friend by every word of accusation wrung from you by uncompromising justice. It would be a very venial fault, I think, if you were to accept the means I offer you to escape this ordeal."

"My lord, you must be careful," said Sibly, gravely, "to compound a felony—"

"Yes! But confound your law terms; for we will 'to do a great right, do a little wrong.' What do you say, Mr. Eagleton?"

"But, my lord, a bribe."

"A bribe, man! do you not say that you must relinquish your appointment? You must have money to travel."

"And yet, what might be said?"

"That you had acted sensibly under all circumstances."

"My lord, I accept your offer," said Eagleton.

"Well said; then I will write you a cheque at once."

"And when may I begone?"

"The sooner the better!"

"And I will communicate with your lordship."

THE SHIPWRECK.

"Do so."

"But, my lord."

"Well, Mr. Eagleton."

"The detective, Falcon, it may be that he may mistake the motive which induces me to abscond; he may hunt me down, and circumstantial evidence, which, you know, is sometimes apparently conclusive, may bring suspicion upon me."

"I cannot be responsible for that; you must make good your escape, losing no time and keeping out of the way of the police."

Lord Hawksbury wrote him a cheque.

He took it with restrained eagerness.

He took a hurried leave, and rushed from the house.

He got the cheque cashed.

No. 49.

His brow throbbed with excitement.

"It is all a dream," he muttered. "Escaped, and no one suffers! For my appointment let that go, with this and what other sums I can draw, a bonus from Sylvia!—Ha, I shall make a fortune, and cut this cursed country for ever!"

When Eagleton had left the house, Sibly looked very grave.

"My lord," he said, "I fear you have compromised yourself."

"Not a whit. I am acting partly according to the advice of Inspector Falcon. This treacherous rascal is the real forger," said Lord Hawksbury. "Charles is evidently afraid of saying anything which would inculpate this dastardly scoundrel, and he will not even tell me how he came to scribble those copies of Mr. Bullion's name, which he does not deny were written by himself. I think such Quixotic regard for such a traitor is altogether ridiculous and unworthy."

"Perhaps so, but my brother is evidently under the influence of Sylvia Volante."

"Who is a good girl, and will see him righted," said Lord Hawksbury; "and now I am bound with Sibly to a certain haunt, where I expect to hear more of this precious young hypocrite. Oiny Macarne shall go with us."

CHAPTER CLVI.

THE BOY PIRATE COMPLETES HIS PREPARATIONS FOR HIS ENTERPRIZE—CASSIDY MISSING—A WIFE'S DEVOTION—THE BOY PIRATE VISITS THE MISSIONARY—NEWS OF HARWOLF AND HIS GANG—CASSIDY AND DIEGO RETURN—THE "SEA-WOLF" IN HARWOLF'S FORT—WAR TO THE KNIFE.

THE Boy Pirate had now made every preparation for his grand enterprize.

But one thing remained.

Before leaving the Southern Seas, he and Black Ralph had sworn to take condign vengeance upon Daniel Harwolf.

They were the more exasperated with the villain that he had been so successful in his daring attack upon the island.

The good old missionary had been left for dead, and his house had been fired by these dreadful miscreants.

Some of the negroes, however, had broken into the burning house, and rescued their beloved pastor.

The next day after the attack upon the plantation the Boy Pirate had returned to the island in the "Avenger."

Upon perceiving the state of things, he had repeated his vow of vengeance against Harwolf, and had afforded what succour he could to the unfortunate planter and his dependents.

In a council of war held on board the "Defiance," it was resolved that our hero and Black Ralph should chase the "Vulture" in the rare old "Raven."

It was also chivalrously determined that they should take with them only as many men as were considered to be equal in number with the enemy.

The officers appointed to assist the two commodores, were Dick Caffyn, Brierly, the pilot Brand, Tom Garrod the boatswain, and the black Zampa.

The greatest anxiety prevailed among the crews of the pirate ships on behalf of Cassidy.

Mary had been rescued by Black Ralph, and the boat's crew from the "Shark," but of Cassidy, as yet, there had been no tidings.

The Boy Pirate therefore knew nothing of the terrible disaster which had befallen Harwolf.

He knew nothing of the desertion of the treacherous Spaniard Corderes, with Harwolf's vessel.

The Boy Pirate weighed anchor in the "Raven," and sailed towards the island.

Mary had entreated our hero to be allowed to accompany him.

He at first refused, but moved by her urgent pleading, at length consented.

The avengers landed on the island, and made their way to the missionary's plant.

Their hearts were saddened by the appearance of the fair country, which had been ravaged by the fell sea-wolves.

On every side were signs of their infamous villany.

Sheds containing grain or sheltering cattle had been fired by these demons, and now mouldered to the soil in charred and blackened ashes.

Horses, sheep, and oxen, strewed the ground, and presented a grand banquet to the vultures and other vile carrion birds which hovered round them.

Bales of cotton had been torn to pieces or set in flames, rich sheafs of corn and maize were scattered about, as if a hurricane had devastated the fields.

And, greater horror than all the rest, the dead bodies of the simple defenceless negroes, many of them women, were strewn about in dreadful numbers.

The Boy Pirate paused at some distance from the half-burnt house, and contemplated the scene with quivering lip and towering brow.

His partner and his followers looked up in his face with saddened air.

"It seems as if this man were spared to show me what a pirate should be; he is my Nemesis, my evil angel. Thank Heaven, my good angel has hitherto been too strong for him, but though he has not conquered, has not matched me, yet he has eluded me on every occasion."

The Boy Pirate uttered these words in a tone somewhat depressed, and then raising his head, shook his clenched fist with a bitter curse against his ancient enemy.

"Spared, say you, my brother in arms," replied Black Ralph, "aye, but we have given him a long tether, and he will hang himself at last; to think he should be such an infatuate fool as to perpetrate this hideous outrage almost within gunshot of such an armament as ours; but every dog will have his day, and it's time this rabid wolf-cur should be dosed with a leaden pill, or choked with a hempen necklace, for he's midsummer mad for a certainty."

"Well, Ralph, be sure I shall chase him while I've an inch of canvas left in the yards, a shot in the rack, or a single cutlass; but let us go into the house, though it is like entering a charnel. Such a home of peace and goodness, of plenty and security, as it seemed, too; it is a strange dispensation that wrong should be so triumphant."

"Heave ahead, hearty, and if you would go lightly, don't moralise," laughed Black Ralph; "those who live in glass houses must not throw stones—

' For lads we're ranting rovers all,
    We drink, we fight together;
  We win or lose, we rise or fall,
    According to the weather.'

But just now we're certainly saints, Captain Kit, for we are patriots and liberators, so let us visit good Father Peter's."

As they approached the house a number of negroes ran forth to greet them.

The poor fellows seemed beside themselves with joy at the appearance of the young rover and his companions.

They gave a shout and ushered the adventurers into the house with every demonstration of affection.

The simple negroes had conceived a great liking for our hero, and with good cause, for he had been a great benefactor to them in their distress.

The pirates entered the house.

They were received by the grave yet gentle-mannered overseer of the plantation, whose name was Baptiste.

Father Peters, the good missionary, was a Catholic priest; he was born and educated in France, although of English parentage.

At an early age he had been placed in a college, where he received the highest training. He eventually became a priest, and receiving from the English government a grant of land in the island, had emigrated thither, and had spent his life in the works of the most devoted philanthrophy.

"Ah! Monsieur; how glad that I am to see you," said the Frenchman, with a smile, extending his hand to our hero. "The good father, he is so sick and so sad, he will be charmed to see Monsieur."

The servant led the way into a large room.

The scene presented was very affecting.

The walls of his apartment, before so prettily ornamented—for Father Peters was a man of strong common sense, and could see nothing objectionable in mirth and beauty—were now blackened with smoke and flame, and in some places broken away.

The roof was charred and black, and in more than one part destroyed.

Father Peters lay upon a sofa.

His kind, yet shrewd and intelligent countenance was deadly pale.

Upon an ottoman, at his side, was a large, open book of devotions.

In a feeble voice he had been exhorting and encouraging his flock of "black sheep," who knelt around him sobbing and murmuring.

There was a sudden hush as the Boy Pirate and his comrades entered.

The good old man held out his hand with a smile of cordial welcome.

"Captain Christopher," he said. "You are most welcome. Your aid and protection are entreated. Perhaps you have not heard of a new danger which threatens us?"

"A new danger!"

"Yes; but from the old source. That infamous pirate, Daniel Harwolf, was seen with a number of his wretches, wandering along the beach."

"Ha! then he is on the island!" said the Boy Pirate, with animation.

"He was this morning; Baptiste, with several that are present, went in search of a poor boy whom these villains had left half-dying on the beach beyond the hills. They were very cautious, and, thank Heaven! were not seen, though they descried this wretched criminal, and about a score of his men. They say too that retribution has been rendered, for many dead bodies of this villain's crew are daily washed on shore —his boats, it seems, were swamped."

"But, father, is the 'Sea-Wolf' in the offing?"

"Strange to say, she is gone."

"Can anything have befallen her?"

"She was all right—at least, to judge by her voice, captain," said Black Ralph, "when I rowed under her hulk, and was nearly smashed in with her broadside. Perhaps she is behind one of the headlands; if so, the better for us, though Harwolf might have been on the island this morning, it does not follow that he is here now."

CHAPTER CLVII.

THE AVENGERS RESOLVE TO ATTACK HARWOLF'S STRONGHOLD — THE SCOUTS — THE REMORSELESS SPANIARD DIEGO OVERHEARS HARWOLF'S PLOT—THE SIEGE—THE PARLEY.

THE Boy Pirate and his crew, having armed themselves, set out on an expedition against the Vultures.

The report still held good that the atrocious pirates yet remained on the island.

Our hero stood without the ruined house of the worthy missionary.

His gallant men were ranged around him.

Our hero thus addressed them.

"Hearties, the time is coming when, for awhile at least, most of us will have to prove our prowess on shore, as we have established it on sea. We must be soldiers as well as sailors in the struggle to come! When we fight for the Poles we cannot hope to do more than to add our small force to swell the army of patriots. We have not had much land-cruising to prepare us for this work, but an action that many of you were engaged in proves that you are no mean warriors, even on this ungenial element the land. I allude to your noble rescue of your loving leader, at the storming of San Salvador!"

"A glorious piece; I wish it were to be played again," laughed Caffyn.

"Many thanks, brother Dick," said our hero, dryly; "but in that drama I played a part that I am very willing to leave to better actors. A fine soliloquy, amid red fire and blazes, may be a telling point; but I like a quieter part and cooler accessories."

"Stopper all, Dick; let the cap'en speak," said Old Brierly.

"Then, my lads, I will finish my harangue with the wit of brevity. A little practice in land-service will be acceptable. Our ancient enemies the Vultures are ashore. Look on this scene of ruin, and— even forgetting past wrongs—this sight will fire your hearts for vengeance against the most hellish miscreants that ever disgraced the human form. Let us hunt these wretches from the earth; if we find them strongly intrenched, or if the story we hear, that they have taken possession of a fort containing arms and ammunition should prove true, why, all the better! We shall learn a lesson in tactics that will stand us in good stead, when we have occasion to storm some Russian fortress. We will fight to the death, and will give no quarter!"

"Hurrah! Down with Harwolf and his gang! Death to the Black Vultures!" shouted the sturdy Avengers.

The Boy Pirate turned to his colleague.

"Captain Ralph and his brave crew will assist?"

"Until my eyelids can no longer wag!" cried the ranting rover.

"That's well; and so, hearties—march on!"

It was at the end of an hour, when they had traversed the breadth of the island and had come to a wild and rocky region near the shore, that they halted.

Our hero called a council.

It was resolved that some of the steadiest of the party should be selected to go forth to reconnoitre.

Black Ralph volunteered for this service.

The other scouts were Cassidy, Old Brierly and Black Zampa, and the Spaniard, Diego.

They were well armed.

They made but slow progress.

The spies took every precaution to conceal their track.

They kept close under rocks and banks.

They maintained perfect silence.

At length they paused.

"Senor," said Diego; "by your leave I will creep nearer to the fortress."

"Is it at hand?" asked Cassidy.

"Within sight, senor, when you have turned the corner of yonder cliff."

"And how did the rascals gain possession of this stronghold?"

"By the strong hand, senor. It was known to contain a quantity of arms, and to be poorly guarded, in fact the garrison numbered no more than twenty men; these were overmastered by the Vultures and all slain."

"I suppose the place is a sort of arsenal for warships cruising among the islands?"

"It is so, senor; but I will creep on ahead, I know the ground better than you do."

"You seem to have a mighty grudge against this Harwolf," said Cassidy.

"And yet I can only kill him once," returned the Spaniard, through his clenched teeth.

"Dam'me! you ought to have some good reason for such bitter spite," said Black Ralph.

"Reason enough, senor," returned the Spaniard. I bear on me the scars of his cruelty, and I will balm them with his blood!"

"Well, hearty, we'll await you here, but make haste," said Cassidy, "for I'm impatient to finish this part of the business, which is not to my fancy, I assure ye."

"Shiver my tops'ls, nor to mine, messmate!" returned old Brierly. "Let us get back to the cap'en and the rest as soon as may be. I see no need of all this 'farnal sounding in sea-room; what's in it, but to march up to the walls and shake 'em about their ears? Heave ahead, mate."

Diego crawled on.

He emerged from the clustering rocks.

He walked behind a long water-break that ran out into the calm sea.

It was a glorious day.

The heavens blazed with sparkling sunbeams, and the far sea was purest blue.

Diego walked upon the yellow sands.

The breeze, sweet with rich odours from the balmy shore, seemed to be rushing forth to greet the dancing sea, and kissed and toyed with the gentle wavelets as they chased each other on that pearly margin.

Birds of gorgeous plumage came out from the woods and floated along on their crimson, gold, and azure wings, keeping in shore, while the pirate shags and kittewakes flapped the white sails buoyantly as they dipped with a saucy scream into the limpid breast of the morning sea.

Yet upon the halcyon shore lay the water-logged carcases of several of the rover gang who had perished in the swamping of the boats by the ruthless self-avenger.

A grim martello tower rose on a rifted rock.

By day and night it served as a warning beacon, and it contained the cruel bolts and sulphurous elements men brew for mutual destruction, as if industrious Death could not be left to do his own work.

Diego was insensible to the peaceful beauty of the scene.

He thought of nothing but his mission of vengeance.

He scrambled on to the top of the water-break.

He lay flat on his face, lest he might be discerned by the bandit sentinels.

He had now a good opportunity of viewing the fort.

It stood erect like a tall monument, surrounded by quaint-roofed outbuildings, and curtained by an outer wall.

The rocky bank on which it was built was separated from the rest of the shoals by a sort of moat, partly worn by the ceaseless lapping tide, and partly hewn by the hand of man.

This moat was crossed by a drawbridge, now raised.

The place appeared impregnable.

A part of the wall had been battered down, or rather blown up.

In the boats that were not swamped were several barrels of gunpowder.

Finding a deep fissure in the rocks on the castle side of the chasm, Harwolf had worked it till he had penetrated beneath the foundations of this stone barrier.

In the mine thus made he had lodged the powder, fired it, and had thus made a breach in the wall.

He had crossed the rocky ditch by means of ropes, and rushing in, had taken the place.

He slaughtered every man in the garrison.

A number of the pirates were hard at work repairing the breach by piling huge stones.

Others were raising and lowering the drawbridge, which had been injured.

They had mended the chains and strengthened the planks.

A sort of anvil, made of a piece of rock, and a roaring fire of dried wood, sea-coal, and weeds, enclosed by stones, was tended by those who were doing duty as smiths, and reforging the broken links of the chains.

Harwolf and Wardlaw looked on.

The bridge was lowered.

Harwolf and his companion passed on to it.

They stood half way over, looking down into the dark chasm.

The tide was rising.

The moat was half full of water.

The pirate and his lieutenant passed over the bridge, and reached the off side of the gulf.

Diego, seeing them approaching, dropped from the top of the water-break.

He concealed himself among the rocks below.

Harwolf and Wardlaw walked along the beach.

They were conversing with some appearance of eagerness.

They reached the groin.

They climbed to the top of it.

Diego was concealed just below them.

"If we can take some barque, and that can't be impossible. If we watch the station we shall do well enough; we can hold our own in the tower until we can board some ship and take it, captain," said Wardlaw.

"Aye; and if what they say is true of Corderes we shall yet be able to keep our presence on this island a secret."

"What is said of him, captain?"

"Did you not see the poor devil who escaped from the 'Shark?'"

"No, captain"

"I remember; you were away with the men in the woods, hewing timber for the work."

"Aye, captain."

"Well, this fellow, it seems, escaped from the Spanish thieves in this way. He was forced to walk the plank; he fell into the sea; the infernal traitors laughed and scouted him as he attempted swimming—the 'Shark' being at least three leagues from shore—but he struggled on. A spar from some wreck was floating in the surf; he reached it, his strength failing him as he grasped it; he clung to this stay till he was picked up by some fishermen. He told them that he was a prisoner who had escaped from the pirate schooner. They believed his story, and soon after they learned from the skipper of a Mexican vessel, which happened to pass, that Corderes had taken a large well-armed brig, which tried to overhaul the 'Shark' and that he had transferred his men to the prize."

"But what became of the old ship, captain?"

"She was abandoned, her masts having been struck in the fight."

"We will put off some launch to see if we can retake her."

"Aye, Wardlaw, but I did not ask the fellow whether they had left her at her moorings."

"Perhaps they scuttled her."

"No, they were in too great haste to escape, a steam-frigate being on the cruise for her."

"Then perhaps she has been found."

"It may be so."

"But, captain, is it your intention to remain here long?"

"Only so long as I am forced to do so," returned the pirate. "This refuge must be temporary at the best, and as yet we are not safe from the infernal Ravens.

"It was rumoured that the Boy Pirate was about to leave these waters for good."

"For good! I'faith, 'and will be for the good of some of us. How I hate that skunk. How I should exult to meet him throat to throat; but the devil has fought on his side, and has deserted me."

"And that's ungrateful," returned the other, with a grin.

"Well, let's return to the works. I will have a wall built on this side the moat; no part of our fastness shall be accessible."

"Right, captain. We may make some sly runs, and take rich prizes, and then, perchance, we shall be able to clear away from this coast, which is getting too hot for us."

"Avast! I shall not leave these waters till I have paid my reckoning to that traitor."

"You mean to Don Pavolo Corderes," returned his associate, with a laugh.

"Aye; and if I lay hold of his kinsman——"

"What, Diego?"

"Yes; if I can catch that cursed thief, I will burn him alive."

"Is he on the island, think ye?"

"If he is, I would advise him to find some hole in the heart of the earth, for no place above ground shall hide him from me."

The pirates returned to the fort.

Diego crept back to the place where he had left Cassidy and the rest."

He told them all that had transpired.

They then set off to join the rest of their force.

When they reached the Boy Pirate and his men, they told him all they had learned.

"We must put off a boat and see if it may not be possible to overhaul the 'Shark,'" said the Boy Pirate. "It is plain that these villains left her hurriedly. You say that they did not scuttle her; there may be some poor wretches left aboard, and, at least, we can make free with the ship stores, which we shall find acceptable."

"Harkye, Captain Kit. If you are Agamemnon I am Achilles," said Black Ralph. And if so, as it is important to save time, suppose I lead the army to the Trojan walls, while you return to the fleet. I will be your herald, and find a more soul-quelling trumpeter if you can. Aye, my comrade in honour—

'Thou'art the Mars of Malcontents: I second thee. Troop on!'"

"Hold! not so fast, Ralph; you will want all our powers to match those foes of Ilion," returned our hero, laughing. "Let Troy fall first, and then we'll come for this galley."

"Troy falls not in a day," returned Black Ralph. "These hornets must be smoked out of their nests. I tell you, Captain Kit. I am your challenger, your pursuivant, your courier of vengeance. I will see if I cannot shake these walls with the thunder of my lion-like roar. There was once a little fellow, who played Macduff to my leading business, and so impressive was my delivery that I withered the poor wretch into a roeless herring, when I gave him the celebrated

'Lay on Macduff.'

"What d'ye think he did?"

"Can't say."

"He 'laid down'—his basket-hilt. I mean,—an! ran off, and I stood at the wing ten consecutive minutes before I could induce him to come and kill me."

"But Harwolf is not to be scared by Bombastes: the villain knows that his time is come, and that there is no surrender."

"Tell you what, Kit, I am as good at the persuasive as I am at the abusive, and I'll so wheedle his crew with my melting eloquence that they'll march out of their fortress with ropes round their necks, like Jack Cade's rebels, and throw themselves upon my royal clemency.

'What say ye, countrymen, will ye relent,
    And yield to mercy, whilst 'tis offered you,
    Or let a rabble lead you to your deaths?'

"Let me try the virtue of blank verse."

"You'll find it a very blank virtue; but you and Ulysses—that's Sam Cassidy—shall march against this citadel, while I and black Othello—that's Zamp—"

"Aye, a moor and a good deal more—

'The blacker nigger he, and you the brighter angel,'

Being a re-version. Well, go thy ways, Captain Kit; do thou look after the salt junk, biscuits, and bilge water, for I'll warrant they've left no drain of grog aboard, while I and my valiant soldiers advance our waving colours on these walls!"

"Fight! When I return I shall expect to see them there, and Zamp, if you like, shall make you a standard!" returned the Boy Pirate, with a sly glance at Tom Garrod, who had supplemented the excision made in his unmentionables with a red patch.

"Golly, buckra, cap'en want 'em all to make a reg'lar jack," said Zamp, with a grin.

With one hand Tom instinctively gripped his nethers, shaking his other fist in the nigger's face.

"Well, Tom, I see you want protection, come with me. Dick, you're my Pylades—my shadow, we always travel in couples—about twelve of the others will suffice for our ' bloodless purpose,' and we will find the 'Shark,' if we can, and bring what we find in her maw; as Corderes transferred his men so quickly, I'll be bound that he left the greater part of his stores behind him. We will return as soon as may be, and hope to find you warm at work, Ralph."

"Reeking! gallant captain; speed you, fair sir, and now—

'Once more unto the breach, dear friends,
    March on, to find this danger out!'"

"Massa Ralph, berry fine palaver; make him berry great king in Ashantee, gib him a big house, all raal sculls," said Zamp, in great admiration, as the Boy Pirate's party moved away.

"His own being as thick, yet empty as any brick in his palace walls," laughed our hero. "I should like to have heard this parley, we've lost a treat; but heave a-head, for if it comes to an assault they will want our assistance, for Harwolf knows the time of Ralph's thunder, and won't be scared at it."

Meantime the rest of the Avengers and their deputy-commander, ranting Ralph, marched on in martial array to the foot of the castle.

They were somewhat taken a-back at the apparent strength of the Vultures' fastness, and a little dismayed at the width and depth of the moat.

By some means or other Harwolf had obtained an intimation of their approach, and was well prepared to receive them.

The walls were manned by his savage gang.

He himself, supported by Wardlaw and Blacklock, stood on one of the buttresses of the lower wall.

No sooner had the Avengers spread in a line along the side of the moat than a heavy cloud of smoke wafted from a loop-hole in the wall, followed by a tremendous explosion, and a massive shell came leaping through the air, and burst at a little distance from the besiegers.

Black Ralph drew his sword from its sheath, and a dainty white cambric from his pocket.

He tied the white handkerchief on to the blade of his sword, and held it aloft, as a token for truce and parley.

The Vultures gave a derisive laugh.

Harwolf, however, signed them to lower their weapons.

Black Ralph threw himself into a dramatic posture, and raised his right hand.

"Captain Dan Harwolf, right royal and most rascally king of cut-throats, I, Black Ralph, formerly captain of the 'Vulture,' and late your equally rascally ally, now most commendably reformed, and colleague of the big Boy Pirate—that staff of Poles, that champion of woman's rights, and righter of all the wrongs of outraged humanity—do bid you surrender at discretion, to lay down your arms, item your necks, and to receive the gracious award of my boundless clemency and favour to yourself and followers, to wit—the franchise of a general gibbet together, an unlimited supply of good rope-yarn halters, and the courteous attendance of an accomplished strangulator in ordinary, with all naval, military, and gallows honours."

"Braying ass! beggarly mountebank! scum of a penny gaff!" snarled Harwolf.

"None of your gaff. Your answer!"

"Take it from a throat not louder than your own; hear it, in a voice that carries weightier matter!"

Another gun was fired.

The massive pounder fanned the cheek of the bold rover, and ploughed up the sand at a great distance beyond him.

"Prince of politicians, that is not coming to the point!" returned Ralph, with a sweeping bow. "If the parley is to be carried on thus by proxy, we, on our part, may find such agents as this iron-tongued orator, who will bring the force of our claims home to your very hearts. I shall be with you presently, and no doubt, after a little sharp debating, I may give you such a home-thrust that you will be fain to come to terms."

"Mark me!" cried Harwolf, fiercely.

"I will!" responded Ralph, promptly, as he levelled a musket.

He blazed at him.

The bullet grazed his cheek.

He fell back on the rampart.

"Alas, poor ghost!" ejaculated Ralph, coolly recharging his piece.

Then there burst forth the roar of cannon; then fell there a perfect hailstorm of small shot.

Exposed to this deadly fire, the Ravens were forced to choose valour's better part, and take to their heels.

However, they rallied behind the bank of the rocky moat.

"Now, lads," said Black Ralph, "it's plain the swabs have got some advantage. We must devise some means for getting 'over the water to Charley.' I propose that a furious demonstration be made here, while some of the hardiest of you come with me to a part of the crag which is not so well protected, and where the water is shallow enough to be waded, for though this 'castle's strength might laugh a siege to scorn,' yet a little leak will sink a great ship, and——"

"A gimblet hole will empty a hogshead of grog, Cap'en Ralph," laughed a sailor.

"Avaunt! Such a simile is too painful, such a truth too horrible for contemplation!"

"Well, cap'en, but if you are missed they will guess that you are gone to reconnoitre, and will double their vigilance."

"A good thought. I must follow the example of the great Falstaff at Shrewsbury, I must 'feign!'"

Waving his sword, Black Ralph rushed to the top of the bank.

He was exposed to a deadly fire from the walls.

Several pistols, aimed at him, exploded.

He immediately dropped on his face, and rolled back off the bank.

The Ravens gave a shout of consternation.

The Vultures yelled their triumph.

"Is he hurt?"

"Is he dead?"

"As a door-nail," shouted Black Ralph. "You flint-hearted swabs, can't you afford one howl to my memory?"

The men took the hint, and set up a tremendous roar.

"Revenge, revenge Black Ralph!"

The Vultures, assured that they had slain such a formidable foe, renewed their wild cheering.

As if in desperation, the Ravens rushed to the open ground, and discharged a rattling volley at the tower.

"He who dies pays all debts," said Ralph, sententiously; "so in the next world one may shake hands with one's tailor. Dead men are beyond suspicion, therefore I shall not be mistrusted; my absence will be reasonably accounted for. Sam Cassidy, I, and Oakland, with Brand and five or six other choice spirits, will sneak off and find some means of scaling the fortress, while you and the rest must assail like Saracens! If they take me for a ghost they'll get pepper! Now, lads, imitate the action of the tiger, which is precisely similar to the movements of 'an harmless, necessary cat,' and glide along the bank like sea-serpents, as you are, till we get beyond these ramparts, and then, 'Up guards and at 'em!'"

Black Ralph crawled round and among the rocks, eight stern-faced fellows, with weapons in their hands, creeping after him.

CHAPTER CLVIII.

A FREIGHT OF CORPSES.

THE Boy Pirate, with Dick Caffyn, Zampa, Tom Garrod, and the rest, had put off in the long-boat.

They coasted the islands for some time without finding the object of their search.

"And did this fellow say that all the English seamen who were upon the 'Shark' had been murdered in cold blood by the Spaniards?"

"Yes, captain; he said that he was forced to walk the plank with those remaining."

"Those remaining? What did he mean?"

"Why, captain, as I take it, the hell-hounds had killed the greater number previously to their forcing him overboard."

The Boy Pirate mused.

"It seems, Dick, that my long cruise in these seas is not to end yet."

"It is but to capture Harwolf, and I should think he cannot escape you now."

"It will go hard with him!" said our hero, grimly.

"Thar she is, yo see; shipped her mastes, and heel ober. Yo can swar as that bark's de 'Shark,' sar."

Dick and the Boy Pirate looked in the direction indicated by their dark satellite.

A long, low hull, with the remains of two masts, was seen at a great distance upon the burnished waters.

"You are right, Zamp, in your conjecture."

"Right in my 'jecture, sar; I told yo dat, sar! my 'jecture allers right, ebberywhere else," returned the negro.

"Hold water, lads; look to your arms, it's as well to be cautious, if only for practice in a good habit. Now run her under the starboard beam."

This order was obeyed.

Our hero and his companions came aboard.

They found everything in confusion.

There was every indication that the Spanish gang had made their escape very hurriedly.

Upon the whole the pirate ship proved a prize of considerable value.

There appeared to be not a creature on board.

While ransacking the state-cabin our hero found many papers belonging to Harwolf which had a reference to the estate of Frontemore, and the conditions of succession to them.

These papers our hero secured.

"And now, Dick," said the Boy Pirate, "let us go to the hold."

Followed by Zampa our hero rushed down into the hold.

What a frightful spectacle was before them!

The floor was strewn with half-putrid corpses!

The pirates looked on them with overwhelming horror.

They started electrically.

They could scarcely credit their senses as they heard a faint and agonised moan.

They found that it proceeded from a poor, emaciated wretch, who crouched in a dark corner.

They raised him.

"If you have come to kill me, be quick," he hissed out, in a tone as of one in scorching agony! "I burn to death! O, pity, pity; a cup, a drain of heavenly water!"

This was brought him.

Having drank he remained still some time.

Closing his eys and extending his limbs he moaned faintly.

There was a blazing red flush on his sunken cheek; his eyes were unearthly bright.

"I am dying, dying! I should like to tell something before I followed these poor messmates; but I am so hoarse, my words cannot be heard."

"How came these poor wretches by their death?"

"Who are you?"

"I am the Boy Pirate."

"Ah, captain, then I can trust you. When the Spaniards returned from shore we knew nothing of the swamping of the boats; Corderes invited us to carouse and broached the grog. A few refused to drink, fearing they might take too much, and bring themselves under Harwolf's savagery. Those poor wretches were afterwards murdered; those who partook of the drink were all poisoned!"

"Just heaven!" cried our hero, greatly moved.

He tried to wring a few more words of explanation from the poor fellow.

He could elicit nothing.

The guilty wretch seemed to be losing his senses.

He foamed at the mouth.

His convulsions were horrible.

At length he grew more calm.

He opened his dying eyes.

"Mother is in heaven," he murmured. "Daisies are coming in again, Nellie. I shall not always be so poor. Oh, Mary, do not scorn me. Ha! they lower the flag, captain. Heaven! a pirate!"

Black Zamp's eyes were full of tears.

And our hero's were not unmoistened, while the pang at his heart grew keener and keener, and his cheeks grew as pale as the faces of the corpses around him.

They raised the young sailor, his lips moved, then set rigidly.

His head sank back, his soul had fled.

———

CHAPTER CLIX.

DOWN THE ABYSS—SCENES OF GRANDEUR AND AWE—THE INDIAN'S LEAP—WYLD STRUCK DOWN—THE GLARE OF A PISTOL SHOT—ANOTHER RANGER VENTURES HIS LIFE FOR HIS CHIEF—WYLD BROUGHT TO THE BRINK OF THE CHASM—NEWS FROM THE CAMP—FLIGHT OF THE BUSH-RANGERS—AGNES STILL A PRISONER—HER INTERCESSION FOR THE EAGLE-WING—THE ASSASSINS ON THE TRACK—THE MIGHTY CATARACT—THE FRAIL CANOE—THE RIFLE SHOT—THE WAR-WHOOP OF THE PAWNEES.

WYLD having launched himself into the gulf in search of the bodies of Catahaga and Regan, steadied himself in his descent as well as he could by placing his feet against projections in the rock.

He was now in utter darkness.

The last tinge of rose had died out of the west.

He seemed to be passing through a black cloud.

Above him the intense purple and the sparkling stars, below the misty brawling mountain stream.

He clutched the rope convulsively, for it swayed and then caught against one of the sharp points of the rugged steep.

He reached a kind of ledge.

On this he rested one foot.

He still clung to the rope.

He panted with excitement and awe.

He cursed himself for his folly in having so rashly ventured his life for nothing, for he was now certain that both the Indian and the Ranger were lost.

"Halloo! Wyld there—Wyld!"

Wyld—Wyld—Wyld! roared a thousand echoes.

"What is it?" cried the ranger boldly.

His words were repeated as if mocking, in a thousand reverberations.

"Have you found 'em?"

"No."

"Quick, then."

"What's the matter now?"

"Some fellows are riding from the camp!"

"Indians?"

"The devil knows what they are. Have you found the Pawnee?"

"No."

"Give up the search."

"Not yet, mates," returned the ranger firmly. "Slacken the rope a little—right!"

Twining his arms about the cord, the sturdy lieutenant of the bush-rangers shot down.

The roar of the rushing torrent waxed louder and louder.

Now the sound was almost deafening.

Scuds of cold spray leaped and swept over the reckless climber.

He had reached a shelving rocky bank.

It lined the stream on either side.

On this slippery footing the ranger alighted.

He shouted his captain's name.

He received no answer.

Groping on his hands and knees as far as he could, for he dared not relinquish his hold on the rope, the ranger found that there was at some distance a little hollow.

As he was about to turn the edge of the rock to enter it, he was suddenly startled.

A grip was at his throat.

He uttered a fearful cry.

He struggled.

He received a heavy blow on the forehead as if from a stone.

He fell on his knee.

A fringed dress rustled past him.

He heard a plash.

The next moment a pistol was fired over him.

Its instantaneous, transient flash illumined the awful chasm—the rifted rocks, the brawling torrent.

He who had fired the pistol now stooped in the darkness and caught hold of the ranger.

"Wyld, speak! has the Pawnee killed him?"

These words were muttered huskily.

It was Regan himself who spoke.

Receiving no reply, he groped about for the rope.

It had swung away.

The men, finding it loose, and being moreover startled by the cry, were shouting uproariously.

"Such cursed ban dogs always run counter," he grumbled. "Ahoa! Aloft, there! Come, some of you, and lend a hand. It's I, Regan."

"Huzzah!" shouted the men above.

Another rope was fixed, and a man descended.

"Bravo, captain! we thought you'd cheated the hangman," he said, buoyantly.

"A dishonesty you'll never be guilty of, Walters."

"And how is it, captain? Hold my hand. Have you killed the Pawnee?"

"Killed him! he is invulnerable. Look to yourself, or the thickness of your skull may be tested. But what a dolt must you be to pitch into this pit of Ackron without a light."

"In the hurry, captain——"

"Hurry! who but old women or marriageable maids are ever in a hurry? Give me hold of the rope; there. Steady! keep your grip on this stone, and find as much foothold as 'nothing' affords, and I'll bring a torch. Above, there! steady, lads; I'm coming."

Regan seized the rope, and flew up with admirable agility.

He stepped on to the brink of the ravine.

The men testified their satisfaction at his re-appearance by a hearty cheer.

"And the Pawnee, captain?"

"Curse the thief! he has gone. Turned into a fish, and leaped into the torrent—vanished like the air-bubbles! But, look sharp, he has struck Wyld, who lies below on the brink of destruction, said brink two feet by nothing. Cut your stick, and cut me one from that fir yonder. Let it be sappy, I want it for a torch."

The man hastened to obey this order.

"And how does the redskin think to escape? He can never climb this perpendicular," said one of the rangers, looking down the chasm with paling cheek.

"No," returned Regan, thoughtfully, "these subtle snakes are prepared for everything. Before the bridge was made some of the savages used to venture down the falls in their canoes. Perhaps the rogue has one concealed beyond the gap; if the ledge below runs as far as the falls which pour into the Arkansas we'll see to that. He shall not escape if I can chalk him."

"This is a devil's own business, captain!"

"Yes, and the devil has it all his own way. Give me the torch, Dan, and lend me your pistol."

Regan once more threw himself over the edge of the rock.

He shot down, and as he descended waved the flambeau.

No artist, no poet, but would have risked the danger for the sake of the sublime emotion occasioned by that wild, grand scene.

Tartarean rocks and stream, lit by the flaring torch, and rendered more stupendous to the eye by the mingled light and gloom.

"I'm glad you've come, captain; a moment spent here is longer than a month on *terra firma*."

"This is *terra infirma* and *inferna*, too," shouted Regan, gaily. "By my life, I swear I enjoy it; but let us see if our comrade has any life left to swear by."

Wyld lay quite still.

They raised him.

His face was covered with blood.

The sharp flint with which the ubiquitous and invincible Pawnee had struck him had inflicted a severe gash.

Perhaps, however, the flow of blood was the means of saving his life.

He gazed wildly into the faces of the bush-rangers as they raised him, as well as they could, allowing for the insecurity of their own position.

The two bandits, stern and callous as they were, could not repress a shudder.

The reader will remember the description already given of Regan's lieutenant.

His red elf-locks, his scarred face, his deep-set eyes, his ungainly form, his general hideousness.

Let him imagine the wild scene, the huge mountains of rock, the deep black trough of the chasm, the raving torrent, the flaring torch, the wild-looking rangers clinging to the rope with one hand, while with the other they raise the ghastly, blood-smeared face of their ill-looking comrade.

"I've had enough of this region of the Inferno. Let's get into a higher sphere, Walter. Ah, that's right; our ropes hang parallel! Now we can raise him."

"But, how, captain?"

"I'll take one arm, you the other. Stop; let his body fall over here! Now knit your fingers in mine; grasp firmly the rope with your right hand, and clamber by the rocks!"

The bandits swung the limp and passive body of their comrade over their left arms, and, gripping the rope with their right hands, began swiftly to ascend.

Every moment threatened death.

The ropes strained.

One of them had been chafed almost to a fringe against the sharp projection.

The men above looked shudderingly over the awful brink, and watched the red, blazing torch, rising like some fiendish light from the black abyss.

The summit was gained.

The men tried to shout, but they suffered their voices to faint into a heavy sigh of relief.

Wyld was borne forward.

"I fear we have had our trouble for nothing; we have but carried so much carrion," said Regan, moodily. "But still it shall be a meal to those legitimate consumers of kings and cobblers, the earth-worms; it shall not gorge vultures!"

"Better cheer yet, captain," said one of the men; "his pulse beats. Look how his breast is heaving! He will live to knotch Catahaga!"

"Then there'll be nothing gained by insuring his life, for he'll outlive us all; that Pawnee is not to be scotched."

"Why, captain, I thought we were to pursue him to the falls?"

"And so we will; we will line the banks, and if he escapes rocks and bullets, fire and water, he may go till we catch a rainbow. But, who said there was a row at the camp, and that horses were at hand?"

"I did, captain. I am the sentinel you left in the wood."

THE ALARM.

"Then, why the deuce did you leave the wood?"

"I left my post, captain, to tell you that I heard the sound of shots afar off, and the click of horses' hoofs."

At this moment the sound of voices and the thudding of hoofs became distinctly audible.

Regan and the bush-rangers ran to the top of a bank.

Galloping in a disorderly manner all the rest of the gang of bush-rangers were seen fast advancing.

Among them rode a girl.

She was mounted on a small but fleet mustang.

A long thong attached to her bridle was held by a tall fellow somewhat better dressed than the others, and evidently taking the lead.

This man was third in command.

When the troop galloped up the girl proved to be Agnes Staunton.

Her face still deathly pale, her form drooping, her dress hurriedly thrown on, and much disordered.

She was bound by scarves to the saddle, and seemed in such a condition that nothing but the support of her bonds prevented her from slipping off her steed.

The rider who held her in charge appeared breathless and exhausted.

"What does this mean, Lawrence? What's amiss?" cried Regan.

"A miss is as good as a mile, captain," returned the bandit with a grin; "thar's a pitched battle being fought down yonder; the camp has been attacked."

"Attacked! by whom?"

"By Judge Harwolf, Mark Leighton, and the other reg'lators, I reckon."

"And you decamped."

"We decamped when the camp became too hot to hold us. We thought, captain, that you were not in the mind to forget the old saw about self-preservation; we could have gained no good by whipping the reg'lators, and, as for the Injens, why we warn't a gwine to spill the ruby for sich half-humans, 'specially arter what you told us consarning the Eagle-Wing; so here we are. I calkilate we've had a rough ride, cap'en."

"Ha! and you have brought Agnes," said the bush-ranger, quickly. "My own, this is rough usage; these are bitter times. O life, it is not my fault; I will see you safely lodged. Once beyond the Rocky Mountains I will foster and attend you as a votary would the being of his worship."

These words were whispered to the girl, whom, spite of his strange conduct, and practical fickleness, and evil character, he dearly loved.

"Untie these bands, you villains!" he cried, fiercely to his men. "Which of you dared to bind this lady as a prisoner?"

The men quailed before the intense fierceness that gleamed in the sparkling blue eyes of their handsome and fiery leader.

The scarves were unbound.

"I reckon it jest were necessary, I du," said Lawrence; "the lady were just nigh faintin', I guess, and if we had not tuk possession, she would have been seized on by Mark Leighton; to say nothin' of the trapper cuss and that designin' cutest feminine—the Wyotti gal—who was for carryin' the lady slick off, oh, yes!"

"The minx!"

"It's a extraordinary fac', but that gal and Nat Weatherfield bilked us in one case, and pretty nearly in another."

"For that beaverskin thief, I'll mark him, be assured; and for Minna, I'll kiss her!"

"She be 'nation 'cute, without any kinder disputationizing; she got the feller slick off, she did du so."

"What fellow?"

"The 'farnal Britisher, cap'en."

"Ha, Reynard?"

"Jest so; I heard as Harwolf and the other British boor——"

"Miles Thornton?"

"I opine, *the* same! Wall, they were most awful riled."

"And Minna carried off her husband's prisoner?"

"She and the trapper and the Pawnee-Loups atwixt 'em."

"Now, that girl is what I call a help-mate!" said Regan, laughing. "I wish——but no, I do not wish it, Minna; it would be a lie to say so!"

"The Eagle-Wing wars with his national enemies; Oswald Lamond with those who have loved him!" said the poor girl, bitterly.

The bush-ranger gnawed his lip.

"The girl is true to her lover; she cares for none but him," he answered, sternly.

"Because he is worthy of her devotion," rejoined Agnes.

"He is a ruthless murderer!"

"Of those who would murder him, and all of his race!" said the girl.

A fierce imprecation rose to the robber's lips, but he checked it, lowered his eyes, and said, curtly,

"Women differ; yet mostly when a man treats a woman with slight and coldness she cares for him, when he blindly adores her——But why do I talk thus?"

"And before these!" rejoined Agnes, in a low, provoking calmness.

Regan turned away with heightened colour.

"But what is the cursed Britisher to me? Let the squaw look to the Pawnee's captive, I have a long score to settle with the confounded devilskin himself."

"Oswald, you can deny me nothing?"

"In reason, no, dearest."

"Save Catahaga, for my sake."

"For my own sake, and for yours in mine, I cannot do so, either he or I must die; but come, this is not the place for bandying words. Lawrence, I leave you here in charge of this lady and poor Wyld yonder, who has been half killed by that copper cutthroat, who prides himself on being the scourge of the pale-faces. I shall leave you twenty men of your own lot; I and the rest are going to the falls below the Panthers' Pass to settle that infernal Pawnee."

Agnes turned to speak.

The bush-ranger shook his head, covered his ears with his hands, and glancing at his men in token that he wished them to follow him, hurried away.

When they had proceeded some distance he turned to them.

He explained how he had failed in his attempt to assassinate the Pawnee.

"Look ye, comrades, there's no safety for us while the chief lives. You might say that he has acted fair and square with us hitherto; well and good; but he is getting too dangerous and too meddlesome. His very wife, who, as a white girl, opposed all her love and persuasion to bring him back to his old condition of a friendly native, even she has turned against us, and with more than a woman's courage lends herself to his schemes. Now old death finds this copper rascal such a zealous and successful assistant that he will not throw a dart at him unless he is obliged; we will give him no chance. I feel convinced that he has a canoe hidden among the rushes somewhere up the river; of course, his first wish will be to return to his braves, and to do that he must risk the falls to reach the Arkansas. We have but to stand at the head of the cataract and blaze at him; if there is not a telling shot amongst us, it will not matter, he will be confused, and the turn of a straw capsize his canoe, and dash him among the rocks. You are prepared to use your best cunning and skill?"

"Aye, captain, push on," responded the bush-rangers.

"The moon is rising," said Walters.

"All the better; we want light," was the answer.

When the bush-rangers had reached the falls, a great change had taken place in the aspect of the heavens.

The sky was thick-spangled with glittering stars, and the moon glowed down in all her argent refulgence.

The falls were very grand.

At no time could they be seen to better effect.

On either side rose huge precipices of rock.

The scene being richly wooded.

Calm-gliding, then smooth-sweeping, then down and still down gliding swift and fleecy white, rolled the mighty torrent; then, with continuous thunder, it dashed deep into the foamy bosom of the depths below, throwing up clouds of beaded steam; then on again swifter, glancing, and rocking, and tossing; then glossy, clear, and deathly-smooth, then finely curving over, foamy-white again, and then crashing, and tossing, and streaming amid the wave-worn rocklets of the lower fall.

A pale-hued lunar rainbow spanned the lovely cascade, while the river at its foot shot along tinged in blinding silver brightness, under the moon's flooding splendour.

The bush-rangers stopped and gazed at the magnificent scene with some emotions of awe and admiration.

"Can it be possible, captain, that any man could be foolhardy enough to trust himself in a frail canoe over that sliding fall into that frothy gulf? It has never been done."

"It has been done, and if it had not, this Eagle-Wing would venture it : but the feat is common among the true-bred redskins," returned his leader.

"But we may have lost him ; he may be gone?"

"No ; for he could never breast the stream below the falls unless the tide were running out, and it is only just on the turn," was Regan's answer.

"Well, it looks flat suicide, and it seems but a waste of powder to fire at the fool," said Walters, in a tone of incredulity.

"Now, lads, to your ambush !" cried Regan. "I shall take my place at the head of the cataract, as I am allowed to be the best shot amongst ye; for the rest, crouch behind the bushes, and among the osiers, and fire in succession."

The rangers disposed themselves in this manner.

Forty of them there were in all.

This formidable party lined the bank.

They were stationed at irregular intervals.

Each in succession occupied the most advantageous position he could find.

They crouched behind bushes, rocks, and reeds.

Still the eternal river rushed on, still the equally eternal but changeful planet of night beamed along her heavenly pathway.

All was solemn, silent. The quiet was enhanced by the stilly noise of the ever-rushing torrent, and the sighing of the gentle night gales—the rustling of the reeds and the whisper of the myriad leaves of the green old forests.

An hour passed away.

One who knew not of the ambush might have passed listlessly along the silver-glowing banks, muttering half aloud his sacred love-fancies to the conscious night, secure of solitude.

And yet two score gleaming barrels, charged with death-bolts, were concealed along that bright and peaceful shore, for the murder of a poor, untutored native, exposed already to the deadliest perils among the treacherous rocks and raging waters.

At last a dark object appeared, dotting the blazing sheen of the molten silver that sheeted the top of the fall.

It was an Indian, deftly guiding with his busy paddle a light and frail canoe.

The bark just trembled on the verge of the frightful fall.

A flash, a sharp crackle from the bush nearest the head of the fall.

A white soaring cloudlet of smoke.

Too late !

The rushing cataract swept down the bark as if it were a waif of thistle down.

The branch of a stunted tree growing midway across the fall, on a jagged and moss-wreathed rock, snapped and toppled into the current, which rent away the leaves from its boughs.

Rapidly along the smooth current, that flew towards the lower fall, sped the canoe.

But its steersman—where?

To all appearance not in the canoe.

And yet the paddle worked deftly, as if moved by invisible hands.

On, swiftly on, to the head of the second fall.

It seemed as if the boat and its occupant were identical ; that, like the armadillo, which folds itself together in a ball and is rendered impervious to the missiles of his adversaries, it had incased its living part. Like a weed, a fragment of bark, or a floating feather, it sped on through the leaping, lashing, raging waters.

Crackle !—bang ! Bang !—crackle !

Forty rifles emitted their flitting flame, and belched forth their puffs of smoke.

But far down the stream shot the light bark, uninjured.

A last shot was fired.

The canoe was pierced.

Yet still it danced onward buoyantly.

Slower now, and nearer and nearer sinking to the waters edge.

The rangers utter an eager shout, and run into a cluster.

The boat sinks, but close to the opposite shore.

A man is seen swimming.

The next moment he appears, standing erect, on the opposite shore.

His hands are upcast in mocking triumph.

The dim woods shudder at a prolonged, terrific war-whoop.

The rangers grasp their guns.

They gnash their teeth in impotent fury.

Every barrel is empty.

Full well they know that long ere they can reload, their mark will be far away in the deepest intricacies of the woods, and far beyond their reach.

Oswald Lamond utters a fearful oath, and dashes his rifle to the ground.

Once more the Eagle-Wing escapes his deadly foes !

CHAPTER CLX.

THE TAKING OF THE FORTRESS—BLACK RALPH SCALES THE WALL—TERRIFIC FIGHT ON THE BATTLEMENTS—THE BOY PIRATE AND ZAMPA APPEAR ON THE SCENE—FLIGHT OF HARWOLF AND WARDLAW—ZAMPA THROWS HIS COMRADES OVER THE WALL—THE POWDER MINE —AWFUL DESTRUCTION OF THE MEN.

BLACK RALPH and the officers he had selected for the attacking party, stole quietly away.

They passed along the edge of the moat till they had reached the opposite side of the tower.

Here they halted.

Meanwhile, to create a diversion from the true point of attack, the main body of the pirates made a furious assault.

They were driven back with shot and shell.

The besieged seemed confident in their position, and yelled their triumph.

The enemy responded as heartily as they could.

Black Ralph, with Brand, Gomez, and Cassidy, descended into the moat.

The place was very ill defended from attack in this part.

The pirates threw a rope with a grapnell.

It caught against the iron bars of a grated window.

Black Ralph placed his sword in his teeth.

He firmly gripped the rope, and began nimbly to ascend.

"Dam'me, this is not the first time I have scaled a fortress," he laughed. "And this wall is something better as a mainstay than the tottering canvas turrets at the Vic !"

He reached the window.

He set to work with a bar of iron he had brought for the purpose.

Soon he wrenched the iron staunchings from their sockets.

He leaped in.

He was quickly followed by his daring comrades.

He waved his sword, and, in a theatrical manner, shouted his threats and defiance against the enemy.

"Yield, villains! Yield or die!"

"Calmly, Ralph," said the more quiet Cassidy, who had joined himself to the party on purpose to moderate the hectering violence of his ranting companion.

"That drop of blood, that's calm!" he raved, "Well, well, we will reserve the thunder of our wrath till a more fitting occasion. We seem to have it pretty much to ourselves just here."

And this was the fact.

Not in sufficient numbers effectually to defend the place at every vantage, Harwolf's gang found plenty of work in repulsing the furious attacks made upon the other side of the fortress.

A gun had been brought ashore from one of the steam frigates.

This was pointed at the tower, and did much damage.

Its effects would have been ruinous if the besieged had not kept up such a deadly fire that it was hard for the Avengers to stand their ground.

But to return to Black Ralph's party.

They rushed along the stone corridor till they came to an arched door at the summit of a low flight of steps.

This barrier they broke through by shattering the locks with their pistols, and battering the woodwork with their hatchets.

When the door yielded to their efforts, they rushed up another flight of steps. They found another at the top of this.

It was ajar.

Stumbling over each other in their eagerness the rashly venturous pirates dashed on to the roof.

They threw themselves right and left upon their opponents.

The fight on the summit of the castle was terrific.

Harwolf fastened himself upon Black Ralph.

The two outlaws contended with all the fury of demons.

Harwolf was dragged to the brink of the tower.

His head already projected over the dismal depth.

He would have been dashed down, but his life was saved through the intervention of his deadliest enemy.

The Boy Pirate, Zampa, and the rest of the Avengers who had gone in search of the Sea-Wolf now returned, and, with others, had clambered by the rope which had been left hanging.

"Hold, Ralph! he is my mark, by your leave," said the Boy Pirate, intervening; "you and he have been partners; between myself and Daniel Harwolf there has been warfare from our boyhood, and now the end has come."

"For one or both of us," shouted Harwolf, the strength of his dogged nature roused by hate.

He was rescued.

In warding a blow his foot stumbled and he fell.

The generous Boy Pirate disdained to take advantage of his helpless position.

His bright sword flashing in his right hand he stepped back, regarding his foe with a haughty glance.

A rush was made at the Boy Pirate.

He was surrounded, and, but for the timely assistance of Zamp, who slashed about him with a great axe, he must inevitably have perished.

"Come, Wardlaw, now's the time!" shouted Harwolf to his lieutenant.

The latter, who was hotly engaged, with Dick Caffyn, who had defended his foster-brother with amazing heroism, followed his leader and jumped down the trap.

Cassidy and several others of the men had strangely disappeared.

The departure of the wily seaman, as may be supposed, was not the effect of treachery.

He had beckoned the negro to follow him.

As soon as Zamp had cleared the road for the Boy Pirate, he darted before our hero, and rushed fiercely laughing towards an open trap.

The Avengers sought to tear up the trap.

There were now only left Dick, Black Ralph, and the Raven.

It was firmly fastened below.

"What does this mean, captain," asked Dick.

Before the other could reply they were startled by a wild shriek from below.

"Ah, yah! ah, yah! yo dar! what yo do in dis dam tower, yo sar, yo buckra?"

"Cap'en, lor' bless yer!" cried Zampa, rushing up through the door by which the first party had reached the roof.

"What do you mean, you black rascal?" cried our hero, turning fiercely upon the negro.

"What yo mean yo'self, sar? Tell yo must not stop here, sar!"

With this, he threw his ebony arms around the waist of the youthful rover, and lightly tilting him over the brink, dropped him plash into the moat.

Black Ralph rushed upon him, with a roar, as of a wild bull just turned into the arena.

"Yo, sar, yo no cause to be here, sar. 'Stay one more minute, blow yo up where yo never go by yo'self, sar!"

With this, the gigantic black tossed even the sturdy Ralph over the battlements.

Dick stared at him in amazement.

He was so stunned by the events of the last few moments, that he had presence of mind only to jump back, lest the negro should rush upon him as he had upon the others.

He stared aghast at him.

The negro, wild with excitement, dropped on his knees.

He pointed downward, and then upward.

He sprang to his feet, and leaped over the parapet, far down into the deep moat.

Dick Caffyn now began to perceive the nature of the peril which threatened them.

He hesitated no longer.

He followed the example of Zampa.

It was well for him that his obedience to the worthy negro's signal did not come too late.

A blaze was before his eyes.

His ears started blood at a roar as of the crack of doom.

Down, down he shot through the quivering waves.

When he rose to the surface of the now raging waters, he quickly dived again; he forged his way beneath the stream to the opposite bank.

Here he rose once more to the top of the water.

He clambered on to the bank.

He found himself surrounded by the Boy Pirate, Black Ralph, Cassidy, Zampa, and the rest of the Avengers.

Every eye was strained with awe upon the terrific spectacle.

The tall tower, which had for centuries been a beacon at sea and on shore, had crashed down into a pyre of smouldering ashes, while many of its heaviest blocks and rafters had been hurled far and wide, at immense distances over land and sea.

The Boy Pirate drew a deep breath.

"I wonder if the infernal miscreant saw me escape?" he exclaimed.

"I hope so, captain," returned Cassidy. "Well, the devil has lost his chief agent on earth."

"No so; there is a villain yet greater than this, still living."

"It must be his father then, comrade," growled Black Ralph.

"You are right; it is he of whom I speak. And so this wretch is swept off at last! There have been no means found for escape, and he thought to have involved us all in his own ruin; but failed in carrying out his charitable design, thanks to our worthy Zampa!" said the Boy Pirate.

"The castle is surrounded on every side by water —the sea and the moat," said Cassidy, thoughtfully. "Well," he added, after a pause, "every man of the garrison has perished, without doubt."

"Well, as the villains have been their own executioners, we have nothing now to do but to re-embark. and to carry our avenging swords where they will find harder employment," returned our hero, glancing with some emotion at the smouldering ruins, which were scattered here and there with mangled corpses.

"So end the works of darkness!" grunted Black Ralph. "You may say now that the devil has committed suicide."

"What dat, sar?" asked Zamp.

"Killed himself, Ebony."

"No be too sure o' dat, sar; the debil kill hisself like de 'possum."

"How's that?"

"Why, sar, 'possum sham dead, yo know; pick him up, sar, pull him tail, not move a mossel; put de 'possum in de bag, sar. Berry well, de 'coon bite a hole at the bottom, fust ob de bag, and den, sar, ob de feller as cotched him. Soon as trapper turns round to 'spress his feelins'—

"'Possum up a gum-tree high,
Racoon in a hollow, yo!

Ah, yah! shouldn't be 'sprised at nuffin'; sure to 'pear, sar; ghost of ole Mas'r Dan sure walk afore long."

"He must walk on something stronger than his mortal legs then, I fancy, or he'll want crutches," said Dick.

"I have half a mind to dig his body out of the ruins and give it a fair burial," said the Boy Pirate. "I had no immediate hand in his death, yet he was to me such an ungrateful, such a bitter foe, and such a black villain, that I wish I could have had the satisfaction of cutting him down with my own sword, but at death all malice dies. Come, hearties, let's aboard and trim sails, for the wind has veered a point."

The men took a last, lingering look of mingled awe and satisfaction at the mouldering ruins, and then, uttering their hearty hurrahs, sheathed their swords, re-belted their pistols, and returned to the ship.

There were many wounded, and several killed, of the Avengers, but, comparatively, their loss had been trifling.

CHAPTER CLXI.

A DOUBLE DELUSION.

THE morning breaks palely upon the desert of waters.

The island is silent as a sepulchre.

A tomb, indeed, it has proved to many who have set their fated step upon it.

A golgotha from far times, this lovely island in the Spanish main.

In the days when the first explorers had appeared as the murderers of innocent and happy races which peopled the continents and islands of the New World, a massacre of special cruelty had been perpetrated upon the unhappy natives.

At a distance little short of a mile below the point at which the moated tower had stood, was a strangely-formed boulder in the cliff, which stood out like a watch-tower, and had been pierced with holes.

It was the look-out from a long series of subterranean passages, being at the top of a flight of rude steps, which shot far down into the bowels of the earth.

A number of ruffians stood watching from this position.

The red ray of the rising sun shot in through the cranny, and gleamed in their intensely strained eyes.

Their glance was fixed upon the distant sails of a stout little fleet, which was making free way before a fair wind.

"It is done at last!" grumbled that one of them who was nearest the opening; "but it was not so well done as it might have been."

"I don't know, cap'en, we have no particular spite against the crews," returned the other.

"No; did they not fight us like demons?"

"Well, we can't complain, the three chiefs have fallen—Captain Kit himself, ranting Ralph, and that crafty commodore Sam Cassidy!"

"'Twas a bold stroke. Ha! how malicious is pleasure!"

"What do you mean?"

"She just gives us a sip from her sweet cup, and then snatches it from our lips; always, it is always the same. Look you now, Wardlaw; all my life I have hated that fellow; we have hunted each other in turn, and when it comes to the last behold the sweets of my revenge upon the man who robbed me of my bride, stood between me and the titles and states of Frontemore, the man whose name I loathed. I can have no better revenge on him than this, a tingling in the ears, a flash before the eye, the choke of sulphurous vapours, a crash, dead!"

"And a death horrid enough to satisfy Nero!" returned the other, rather fiercely.

"A twinge of toothache."

"Why, what would you have done with the great Red Raven had you taken him?"

"You ask a question it would take me long to answer, for my revenge should have equalled my hate, and that is boundless!"

"Captain, you are vindictive."

"So is every man. What would not any man do to his faithless wife or sweetheart, his false friend, or his bitter opponent, if he dared?"

Wardlaw did not reply.

"This a bad business after all, for I should have taken Lilia, got off in a launch, and armed the whole government of South America against the successors of Mahomet. Ha! ha! how I chuckle when I remember the taunts he heaped on me; but it was a lucky discovery this secret mine, we can still live like gnomes or ghouls in the earth, and hold our own against all comers!"

A few words of explanation are necessary to account for the reappearance of Harwolf and his gang after their seeming destruction.

A number of secret corridors had been discovered lying below the tower.

They had been contrived and executed by pirate's of former days—Spanish adventurers, who had not the wrath of justice to fear, but the envy and greed of mightier pirates than themselves, the good kings and queens of Spain and England, who sent them out to plunder for their "country's good."

It had been resolved to fire the magazine when a large number of the Avengers should have gained the fort by storm, and have already taken possession.

However the three chiefs being together on the tower, the tide of battle turning so strong against Harwolf, he determined to fire the mine at once, and make his escape by the secret passages.

Cassidy had perceived his object and had sent Zampa to warn our hero, while himself and his men escaped.

"And beneath the water, too, captain," said Wardlaw, "runs this secret gallery. It was a clever work."

"Aye, but the passage was cut first, and the moat made afterwards," returned Harwolf. "On one side of the tower it is natural, on the other artificial. But it will serve us for a burrow till we can find a launch."

"Captain, captain!" cried a man, rushing up the steps. "There is a whole regiment of Brazilian Rifles landing on the island to destroy us."

"Ha! We must resolve whether we can best meet them like lions, or trick them like foxes. Let us adjourn to the cavern below the cliff, Wardlaw. I care for no enemy, now; let all Europe and America unite against me in the grand contest. I am conqueror! Victory! He is dead! I have killed the Boy Pirate!"

*　　　*　　　*　　　*　　　*

As our hero leans against the taffrail and thoughtfully watches the fading of the island, he murmurs,

"Some atonement is made for the past; yonder rot the bones of the usurper of Frontemore!"

CHAPTER CLXII.

OLD BRIERLY'S ADVENTURE.

"DID I ever tell you, mates, the adventures of my first voyage?" asked old Brierly.

"No," replied Garrod, on behalf of his companions. "We should like to hear it."

It was a beautiful calm evening; the ship was gliding lazily through the water, for the light air was scarcely sufficient to belly out the sails.

The work of the day was over, and all, except the regular watch, were enjoying themselves in the forecastle, with the great all of a seaman's happiness, full pipes and plenty of grog.

"Well," said Old Brierly, refilling his pipe, "you must know that I was very young when I first went to sea, little more than ten years old. I shipped on board the 'Sarah Jane,' as cabin boy, bound for Canton, and a first-rate voyage we had going out, doing our passage in a remarkably short time, and I was very comfortable with all; the captain was kind to me, and the men made me a bit of a pet, because I was so little.

"After we had discharged our cargo, as we found we had about two months to wait before our lading of tea would be ready, our captain, with the consent of the ship's agents, determined upon making a voyage to Macao, in order partly to get rid of some surplus ship's stores, and partly to accommodate a Chinese mandarin, who, with a large suite, wished to make the passage there by an English ship, their junks being very slow and uncertain.

"Accordingly, we weighed anchor and stood out of the river, and then headed for our port, and the weather still continuing fine, we made rapid progress. The Chinamen, especially, seemed highly delighted with their trip.

"Two days soon passed away, and on the third we expected to arrive at our destination.

"It was just growing dusk when I observed a movement among the Chinese that I did not like. They had hitherto appeared unarmed, and had wandered freely about the ship, in groups of three or four (for I should tell you that there was about forty of

them in all). Now they appeared to be all congregating together, and I saw plainly the gleam of their long knives as they moved their arms about, while talking earnestly, and they pointed frequently to the crew, who were listlessly pacing the deck.

"All at once, while I was debating whether it would not be better for me to inform the captain of my suspicions, the Chinese raised a loud shout, and flung themselves upon the astonished crew.

"Stabbing and yelling, these pirates soon covered the deck with blood.

"The helmsman was almost the first to fall a victim to their fury, and the few on deck soon shared his fate.

"Alarmed by the cries of their companions, the remainder of the crew rushed upon deck. Some seeing the state of things, and comprehending it, at once ran below for arms, and among them the captain; but the others were seized by the Chinese, and murdered instantly.

"They then battened down the hatches on those below, and steered the ship towards the shore, then about four miles distant.

"As for me, my insignificance saved me at first, and as soon as I had recovered from my terror, I flew aloft, and hid myself among the ample folds of the mainsail, keeping, however, a good look out on deck.

"Shortly the crew below made an attempt to recover possession of the ship. By the aid of some spars they shivered the battens to atoms, and strove to fight their way on deck.

"They fired their pistols up the hatchways at the crowd, who were trying to confine them, and by a fierce charge succeeded in gaining a footing; but they were fearfully out-numbered. Though several of the Chinamen fell, the English sailors fell also, till at last the captain, a man of immense strength, was the only one left alive of the whole crew, myself excepted.

"Familiar with the blood-thirsty character of these wretches he knew that he had only one desperate chance of life, and that he availed himself of; cutting his way by his sword, he reached the gunwale of the ship, and, without a pause, threw himself overboard, and so the Chinese had the ship to themselves.

"They did not linger long over their victory, leaving a few to attend to the ship, the others went to their work of plunder, and in a short time the deck was covered with various articles they had taken fancy to. A signal was then made to the shore, upon which several boats put off, and the plunder was stowed away in them.

"During this time I had kept my eyes on the captain, whose head I could see every now and then rising on the top of the waves. He was a good swimmer, and often used to boast that he could pass a day in the water, and I had great hopes that he would reach the shore in safety. The last I saw of him was when he was within about a half a mile of the land, when the increasing darkness shut him from my view.

"The pirates now made preparations for quitting the vessel; they had stowed all their booty in the boats, and many of them had left the ship's side, taking with them many of the actors in the late tragedy, so that there was not more than a dozen left on the 'Sarah Jane.'

"These, after one more visit below, which was prolonged for some time, as though giving a final search for valuables, at last got into the boats and took their departure; and I, much relieved by their absence, descended to the deck, the sole tenant of the ship.

"I turned towards the hatchway, intending to get some food, for I was faint and hungry, when, to my dismay, I saw dense volumes of smoke roll up, lighted here and there by flames.

"They had set fire to the ship!

"Here was a predicament. I had escaped their knives, but only to perish by fire.

"Quickly the fire spread; but, before I could make up my mind what course to adopt for safety, the flames were circling the whole ship, and running like serpents about the rigging.

"The boats were too heavy for my strength to lower, and I gave myself up for lost.

"The ship meanwhile had been drifting slowly towards the shore, which, on this part of the coast of China, is very rocky, and shoals very abruptly. It was still about two miles distant.

"I looked about the deck to see if I could find anything that would float me ashore, but the ship's battens were, as I have said, shivered to fragments, and in the struggle, the hen-coops and casks had rolled overboard. Nothing lay on the deck but the dead bodies of the slain and a few weapons, even the very oars in the boats were smashed.

"Fiercer and fiercer raged the fire; the devils had been well used to their work, and had fired it fore and aft before leaving. The boards of the deck blistered my feet, and the pitch was boiling in the seams, and I now knew that only a choice of death was left me, fire or water. I determined on the latter as the least painful.

"I clambered over the bulwarks, and dropped into the water. I could not swim, but I possessed a coolness and a confidence at which I have often since been surprised.

"I struck out, and my first awkward efforts soon became a system.

"I saw a few hundred yards ahead of me a black mass rising out of the water. This I knew to be a rock I had seen some hours before, and I thought that if I could reach it, I might hold on till succour came.

"Slowly I progressed, and was certainly lessening the distance between myself and the rock, when the measured sound of oars attracted my attention. At the same moment my feet touched the ground, and I waded for some distance quite easily.

"Then hearing the oars more distinctly, I shouted at the top of my voice, and my heart leaped within me for joy when I was answered by a cheerful English voice, demanding,

"'Where away!'

"It was a boat belonging to the 'Scorpion' sloop-of-war, which was anchored up an inlet near by, and I can assure you, mates, I was not sorry when I found myself safe on board of her.''

CHAPTER CLXIII.

TOM GARROD'S GHOST STORY.

THE Boy Pirate's fleet had weighed anchor.

The foremast men of the "Avenger" were seated round the galley fire.

They were sipping their grog and talking over the romantic adventures of the last few days.

Tom Garrod listened very sagely.

He pursed his lips.

His brows darkened with an ominous frown.

He preserved the most profound silence; as a dead calm is supposed often to come before a strong storm, so did these silent moods precede his stiffest yarns.

He pressed his finger in his pipe, passed his hand over his head, and took a deep pull at the grog-kid.

"What do you think, Tom, of this black rascal? He says that Dan Harwolf's ghost will haunt us."

Tom looked at Zampa with profound solemnity, shook his head, and began to smoke.

"There are some chaps as say too much, and

some as say too little, and believin' is a thing there's no accounting for.''

With this very clear expression of his sentiments, Tom once more relapsed into deep abstraction.

His mates were deeply impressed, and looked at him with much awe.

They winked at each other, and kept silence.

They hemmed and fidgetted.

"Well, hearties, as to ghosts, I have seen a many wonders, but ghosts is things as I never could believe in," said one of the seamen.

The speaker was frowned down in an instant.

"And there are some lubbers whose eyes are weiled with a mist as thick as a channel fog, so as they can't see the cat-heads when they leans over the fo'castle. There be some lubbers, sich hogs in harness, that they can't get at the masthead 'cept through lubber's hole, and is, therefore, firmly convinced that that's the only passage. As for ghosts, we're all ghosts; we gives up the ghost, and as for apparitions and spectators, they has been seen by almost every man of experience that keeps his eyes open. The fust ghost as I had the honour of making acquaintance with——"

"A ghost! Have you seen a ghost?"

"Have I never seen the hocean?" cried Tom, indignantly.

"Aye, aye, hearty; heave ahead!"

"And the hocean's a ghost too. I can tell ye, my hearties, I've been favoured with sights.''

"I should think so; mermaids, devils, ghosts!"

"Stopper all!"

"Aye, haul in your talking-gear, you lubber; let Tom speak!"

"Aye, twist us a stiff yarn."

"A yarn? Humph!—that's a tarm which is as common as lying," returned the boatswain. "But my histories is true weracity.''

"No one doubts that, Tom. But what about the flood? You remember, the water was just rising when you broke off that last 'weracity?'"

"Some other time; there's too much water in the hold already," said Tom, turning up his nose at the grog-kid.

One of the obsequious audience poured in another half-pint of hissing stingo from a kettle that boiled on the galley fire.

"Ah, mate! that will fetch up the sperits, and it's sperits we're talking on; ghostes, leastways. But, lor, the unbelieving lubbers there are on this varsal arth! If there's one sort of insult I can forgive, it's when an honest man tells me to the teeth, 'Tom, you lie!' 'Cos vy? No honest man would do sich a thing, so I forgives him. But for those know-all lubbers that jeers out of their eyes as much as to say, 'I'm afeard you're a labourin' under a slight mistake!' For sich, or for any man as calls himself a humanity, to doubt my weracity because he hasn't had my experience, why let him choke in his ignorance, I say! But, about the ghost!"

"Aye, aye, Tom."

The boatswain looked about him with a solemn air.

"It's a hawful subject, messmates! But pass round the kid."

"You must know that when I fust left the patarnal sarvice under my aunt, Betsy Warner——"

"You served aboard a Indiaman."

"Well, this was my second cruise, messmates; there was a sartain London marchant as traded in the South Pacific, and this feller was a man of prejudice as was full of his own opinions, and would never listen to his betters; so what do you think he did, jest to spite the skipper of his wessel?"

"Can't say, Tom."

"Had the ship refitted, gave her a fresh name, and what do you think he called her?"

"Summat queer."

"Queer! it was jest a temptin' o' providence; he called her the 'Friday,' and made her hoist the blue peter on a Friday, and set sail.''

The men groaned.

"They was all lost, poor souls! eh, Tom?"

"Wuss! a great deal wuss!"

"Cast adrift, and dewoured each other?"

"Wuss!"

"Well, tell us all about it."

"But why did the men sail in her?"

"He had 'em all afore a sort of lawyer-shark as sat up in a box with a wig on his figure-head, and they was all bound over to sarve their tarm."

"Oh!"

"Well, this cruise the skipper took his wife with him; fust they was becalmed and used up a'most all the ship-stores; then they was taken in a fur'ous chop wind, and lost their main-tops, fore and aft; arter that they was boarded by savages, and half on 'em murdered; then the cat got shoved overboard; then they sighted the 'Flying Dutchman,' gave chase, and lost their reckonin' by a hundred leagues; then the lightnin' struck her, and she werry narrowly escaped being burnt; then she ran aground off Cape Horn; then they was obliged to throw over all their cargo to get her off; then the water failed and the rum-casks sprung a leak; then the captain went ravin' mad, cut his wife's throat, and jumped overboard; and, last of all, the wessel was taken by a privateer, and old Blowhard, the marchant, had to lay down three times her wally afore he could ransom her, which he did out of werry perwerseness."

"And, Tom, did he—did he tell the truth for once? would he, could he send her to sea again?"

"Yes! he had the figure-head repainted and fresh lettered 'Friday,' and she sailed on a Friday too."

"But how could he get another crew?"

"Most on 'em was no better than landswabs, and he got 'em kinder inweigled with the lawyer-shark, and sail they did. I was but a younker then, and I went with 'em."

"And a most awful voyage you must have had."

"You shall hear."

"But who was the new skipper?"

"As good a seaman as ever walked the deck of a better vessel, a Cornish man, brought up to the coastin', a jolly dog; but he had been inweigled, too."

"And foul weather all the way?"

"Avast, hearties, let me twist the yarn. The clerk o' the weather office seemed all right."

"Oh!"

"Yes! we made a spanking passage at fust."

"Ah!"

"Prowisions as might make you almost respect the purser, and grog——"

"Plenty of grog, Tom?"

"'Nough to have sunk the ship if it had broke loose."

"And privateers?"

"One gave chase; a man-of-war blew her off the water."

"Savages?"

"Caught two-dozen, and pulled the gold rings out of their noses."

"Yellow Jack?"

"Not so much as a chaw-bacon sea-sick."

"Run aground?"

"Plenty o' sea-room, and sheets full of fair wind."

"Then what was the matter?"

Tom lowered his voice to a thrilling whisper.

"The ghosteses!"

"A-ah!"

"It was a werry dark night; the wind had fallen, a sort of curious sensation perwaded the breasts of of our crew. The cap'en went below, and sat overhauling the log and sipping his glass, afore tumbling into his hammock for the night, when, all at once, as he looked out through the cabin-winders, he spied somethin' white!—somethin' white sweeping along full sail over the waters! Presently it reached the stern of the wessel. It sprang up to the winder, and sat there a gibberin', or rather, a trying to gibber, at him, for it's cheeks was bone."

"What was it? What was it, Tom?"

"That's just what the cap'en axed hisself, as he took his hanger and pistol-belt from the bulk-head."

"Did he fire at it?"

"Point blank, and soon made a blank in the window-frames, though that was still stoppered by the white shroud."

"It was a ghost."

"Well, I'll give you its description, and then re-far you to the nat'ralists. Fust for its eyes: there was on'y one objection to them, which was, they had desarted their posts—their look-outs was quite hollow and empty, 'ceptin' for a sort of little balls of rollin' fiery mist, which didn't seem to know their places, and kept going up and down, and in and out. And then for its nose; well, that had gone from the 'arthly tiniment, and left the two doors wide open. Its teeth was all right, only rather sulphury; its hands was small, and white as ivory, and jest as hard and bony; its white sheet was all in a pale blaze of blue phosphorous."

"Did it wanish?"

"The men on deck heard the pistol-shot, and they rushed below, for they thought that the cap'en had shot himself. But no, there he stood, rolling his eyes like a dying dolphin, and trembling like a jelly-fish, with his pistol in one hand, and his cutlass in the other.

"'Ben,' says he, to the mate, 'look at that winder; do you see anything?'

"'If I look at the winder I sees the winder, cap'en,' says he.

"'Aye! aye!' returns the skipper, in a trembling voice.

"'Bob,' says he to the bo'swain, 'do you see anything?'

"'I see you've broken the glass, yer honour.'

"'Aye, aye; but do you see nothing else?'

"'Summut watery in the moon's eye,' says the bo'swain.

"'It's at the full,' says the mate, with a kinder wink, which showed his ignorance.

"'Do you see anything, Tom?' say he to me.

"'Summit white, yer honour,' says I (it was a gull).

"'Tom,' says he, 'I'm your friend for life; you're a good lad, you shall be well reported to the owners. Gentlemen, good-night; call me if the wind changes.'

"We went on deck.

"Bo'swain shook his head, and said to the mate,

"'It's beginning to work on him this black——'

"'Black what?'

"'Black draught?' snapped the mate. 'A regular too-good, as blind as the barnacle.'

"'No, sir, the black Friday.'

"'Why not black Monday, Tuesday, Wednesday, Thursday? Pooh! pooh! a thorough seaman, a family man, you ought to know better than to dishearten the crew with such old women's rubbish,' says Master Sapience, in a 'sinivatin, provoking manner. It was on'y mercy that kept me out of irons; I could have kicked him overboard.

"'All old women arn't fools, nor all young men arn't wiseacres, and if Friday isn't what it used to be, its werry much altered.'

"You ought to treasure them words, messmates; that bo'swain said some werry good things in his time, for which I forgives him many a larruping he bestowed on me.

"Well, it was my watch aloft.

"So I perched myself on the maintop cross-trees, and tried to whistle myself to sleep.

"I think I told you it was a dark night."

"And yet the moon was shining, eh, Tom?"

"Well, she showed a werry dirty face, hearty, for the clouds were scudding over her, and she could only be seen through her weil like a Terkish beauty, just on the sly."

"It was rather cold."

THE FLOGGER FLOGGED.

"Just cold enough for convenience. You know what that means; it made one's breath wisible, and they say one can allers get a nap by watching ones breath flowing out of ones lips.

"I began to jerk up my knees, throw back my elbows round my neck, and grip at the yard, for I began to nod, feeling rather inclined to fall into the lap of Morpus, when all at once I saw sich an 'orrible sight that I was a'most taken off in convulsions.

"Afore me on the fore-yard was seated a figger."

"The ghost?"

"My timbers creaked; my woice wanished; I tried to call out, but couldn't whistle up a catspaw of wind to tell my feelin's. The ghost looked at me
No. 51.

and nodded it's skull; both its misty, fiery eyeballs got into one port-hole, and it winked furious; then, up went both its fins, and its bony fingers spread out as if it wanted 'em counted—there was five on one hand, but on'y three on the other—cos vy? When the late skipper scuttled his wife's hull, he chopped off two of her fingers. Now, I knew my customer. Arter the most dreffl struggling, I managed to find enough woice to hail the wision."

"And what did you say, Tom?"

"Well, hearties, I began werry solemn.

"'Mrs. Binnacle!' says I (the old skipper's name was Binnacle) 'Why, marm, do you haunt this wessel, arter the sail-maker's done his part by you and your bones has been canonized, a cannon-shot bein' tied to your heels and you has been duly committed to the deep? Are you so deep yourself, marm, as Davy Jones can't keep you in his locker? What on 'arth, or in sea, marm, can we do for you?'

"You couldn't ha' said anything more to the purpose, Tom."

"She made no other reply, messmates, than jist to hold up the two fingers of her left hand, and point at the stumps of the other two with her other hand.

"' Werry well, marm,' says I."

"Did you understand what she wanted?"

"I guessed it was summat consarning the fingers she'd lost, so I thought it was best to show hintelligence—bein' all sperit themselves they like to see a mortial show a sperit.

"' Aye, aye, marm,' says I, 'it shall be attended to.'"

"And did she make any answer?"

"She nodded her skull, and then bolted upright. She stood on the fore-yard as straight as a marlinspike, though the wessel heeled over and shipped a heavy sea."

"And how long did she stay?"

"She held up her two-fingered hand, gave a kinder blind wink, bobbed a werry respectful curtsey, and wanished!"

"And did you tell the captain?"

"Avast heaving, messmates! you shall hear.

"When I came on deck, I walked straight up to the mate.

"' Mr. Tackle,' says I, 'excuse me, sir, but I've had a communication.'

"' From whom, you lubber?' says he.

"' From Mrs. Binnacle. Her mind is disturbed, sir.'

"' And so is yours. The spirits is too strong for you.'

"He grinned.

"I likes discipline; even as a rover I respects my betters. Howsomever, I demonstrated with him.

"' Sir,' says I; 'excuse me, for I axes pardon, but do you 'sinivate that I'm groggy?'

"' I say that the spirits have got into your head, and the parson himself won't drive 'em out,' says he.

"' And you haven't been favoured,' says I. 'Well, sir, its werry responsible to be a lady's man, but, having seen Mrs. Binnacle up on the fore-yard, which acted in a very ladylike manner, and held up her fingers——'

"' To her nose?'

"I was fearful disgusted.

"' When a party, especially a lady, has the misfortin' to have lost a prominent featur' of her figgerhead, sich 'sinivations——'

"' What are you talking about you swab?' he roared at me. 'Do you mean to look me in the face and tell me you've seen the ghost?'

"' I do not mean to do nothin' to displease yer honour,' says I, werry cautious; 'but if you wants me to look you in the face and say, I have not seen the ghost, I'm werry willin' even to tell a lie to oblige my betters.'

"I was humble and wartuous, messmates, afore I fell into your company.

"Pass the kid, and don't mind my sighin.'

"' And what sort of creetur did she appear?' says he.

"And I was werry glad to see him exact a little common sense, for he was getting awful pale as become a Christian.

"' Sir,' says I, 'I once seed a notice writ up in a show at Greenwich Fair, "Must be seen to be believed!"'

"' Werry good,' says he; 'when I sees her, I'll believe in her.'

"' Hopes you'll enjoy the honour of a wisit, sir,' says I, 'and will be able to oblige the lady about her fingers.'

"' Her fingers?' says he.

"' The fact is, sir' when Captain Binnacle was so

misfortunate as to go mad, and kill the wife of his bosom with the carpenter's chopper, he cut off her fingers—two on 'em.'

"' Tom!' says he.

"' Well?' says I.

"' I've a good thought.'

"' Yes, yer honour.'

"' Perhaps,' says he.

"' Just so,' says I.

"But, how so, Tom, how so?"

"Why, messmates, the mate he winked.

"I winked.

"And we came to a decision."

"Which was?"

"That we wouldn't say no more on the subjec', on the condition that I should have a hextra glass of grog."

"Oh!"

"Well, the next night the mate was on watch. It was glorious weather; the moon was shining like a silver sun, and the wind was just curling the sarface of the water, when the mate was walking on the larboard side. All at once he started back, as if he smelt fire in the hold. It was a great night-raven that caused his alarm. The cre'tur had flown over the deck, and, resting on its black flappers, set up a most dismal croak, rolled its red eyes, and snapped its beak.

"Mr. Tackle was about to knock down the unlucky raven when his attention was diwarted to another objec'.

"There stood the ghost.

"Mrs. Binnacle, though demised, was werry evident not without her feelin's. She had been greatly scandalized by bein' doubted by the mate. She shook her skull at him, and her jaws clattered truly femaline; but the marcy was, she had no ghost of a woice. She pointed with one hand to the deck, and with the other to the hocean, and then held up her three fingers, as much as to say,

"' You know what is my rights, you willin, and if you takes adwantage of a poor, lone woman—a respectable married woman, too—you'll suffer for it!'

"Once more she wanished.

"' Oh lor!' says the mate to me; 'I'm dyin'!'

"' Then, don't forget poor Tom, yer honour; a little corner in your will,' says I, 'might be filled with a more undesarvin' name.'

"' I'm mad!' says he.

"' So is the cap'en,' says I.

"' But, I've seen it!' says he.

"' Oh lor!—oh lor! Send for a parson!' cries the bo'swain, running up at the moment.

"' It's no use, we sailed on a Friday! We're all lost men!'

"' What's the matter, Bob, my jib? Oh! what's the matter?' says the mate, werry feeble and faintin'.

"' I've seen it, sir; I've seen it!'

"' What have you seen?'

"' The two-fingered ghost, sir; the restless spirit of poor Mrs. Binnacle!'

"Arter that there was no peace.

"Mrs. Binnacle got really quite tremendjus.

"She seemed quite out of all patience.

"All sorts of misfortins happened.

"Weather turned bad, and we was all in the downs.

"When I was on watch, she would suddenly appear and run gibbering alongside, and hold out her two fingers. Then she would pint at the hocean and at her bosom; then she would make a grab at me which froze all my blood, and left me standing like a man of snow, till the ship lurched and carried me off my pins.

"Well, we put into port.

"A lot of chaps desarted, swearin' as they'd rather be strung up like salting pilchards at Execution Dock than sarve in a 'fernal haunted ship, with the name of 'Friday.'

"We was perfect wretched.

"The captain and the mate was almost redooced to the same condition as poor Mrs. Binnacle.

"I got a letter from Poll Wapping.

"One sentence in the tenth postscript shot through my tophamper like lightning through the stays:—

"'My ducky Tom, don't forget what you promised about the *wedding ring* and our *marriage lines.*'

"Down into the cabin I shot as if Mrs. Binnacle had leaped on my back.

"'Cap'en,' says I.

"'Tom,' says he, werry sad-like, 'Are you mad? cos if you are, I envies you.'

"'What'll you give me,' says I, 'if I lays the ghost?'

"'Fifty pounds,' says he, 'and a double allowance of grog every day for the rest of the woyage.'

"'And I'll be a sovereign and half a dozen old shirts,' groaned the mate, lifting his nose above the rim of his hammock.

"'Then,' says I, 'cap'en, I've found out what Mrs. Binnacle wants.'

"'Do you think she knows herself? Women in flesh or sperit is so perwerse,' moans the skipper.

"'Look here,' cap'en; she's lost two fingers of her left hand.'

"'Werry good, Tom, but I don't know where to find 'em.'

"'Now, how is she to keep up her respectability, yer honour, eh?' says I, and he shut one eye werry tight and stared most awful with the other.

"'What has her respectability to do with her fingers? you don't 'sinivate as she was light-fingered, Tom?'

"'No, yer honour,' says I (messmates, it was nothin' but hinspiration!), 'but, havin' lost her fourth finger, larboard fin, how can she perduce her weddin' ring? Perhaps it's in the cabin along with her marriage lines.'

"And so it turned out to be, hearties. The cap'en found the weddin' ring and certificate in an old desk. We packed 'em up and directed 'em, with the cap'en's respectful duties, to the late Mrs. Binnacle, and lowered 'em into the sea. The ghost appeared only once more; she had the ring on the third finger of her right hand, which, as the other wasn't left, made it all right. She flourished the paper in her other hand, bobbed us a most respectful curtsey, and wanished, with a bony smile, which was hidjeously well-meant, and we saw no more of her.

"Arter that, there was a reg'lar mutiny agen the owners, and they consented to call the ship by a Chris'n name, and she sailed no more on a Friday."

CHAPTER CLXIV.

EAGLETON AND MORTIMER—THE MASTER PAS-
SION—A SIREN AND HER VICTIM—CREMORNE
—THE DANCE—LOST IN THE CROWD—HEART-
LESSNESS AND PASSION — THE DAGGER
RAISED—EAGLETON'S DESPAIR.

EAGLETON walked rapidly through the busy streets. More than once he paused at the glaring entrance of some noisy, garish, gilded, gassy temple of Bacchus.

He entered several, apparently in the search for some one.

At last he found his comrade Mortimer sitting moodily in one of the compartments of a large "palace," reading *Bell's Life,* and sipping his "brandy hot."

The handsome young fellow looked up anxiously.

"What news?" he half-muttered. "Ha! you seem elated."

"Elated! inflated rather. I feel like a balloon; this low atmosphere is too gross a medium for my 'mounting spirit.' I could vault, I could fly, such a burden is taken off my heart, such an ecstacy infused into my brain by the most brilliant triumph that ever I experienced."

"What! and young Charlie Rye? I suppose you have cleared yourself immaculately, and have fixed him beyond hope."

"No, no, no! better and best of all; Charlie will be freed. I am to abscond."

"But you are bound over as witness."

"Only by chains of gold; they are to be slipped, and handed over to the gaolers."

"And who stands the damage?"

"Lord Hawks—— But why have you no more respect for my temporary weakness induced by such unwonted excitement? Why are you such a blabbing fool, and in this public place, too? Enough! Come, what is to be the elixer—Montilado or Champagne? To-night I mean to sacrifice to joy and Angeline — my sweet, my charming Angeline; although we quarrel so, and though thou art but—nothing. Why, Mortimer, I love that girl, and may——"

"May live till she hangs you, and live a hang-dog life the while," returned Mortimer, sneeringly.

Eagleton raised his hand to his head.

"Who can resist her?" he said, hoarsely. "What is there in life—sport, wine, pleasure—compared with one smile of hers? 'Tis true I am her slave, but I love my bondage; sometimes, indeed, I fret under it, but when could I dare to wish myself free?"

"You are sentimental to-night."

"I am happy, that is, I am triumphant. 'All's well that ends well;' when I get abroad I will begin a new career."

"But, Angeline; you will find it hard to leave her," returned Mortimer, with a thoughtful look.

"I shall see her to-night; she will not refuse to go with me. Who can tell but that I may redeem the past?"

"But will *she?*"

"Is she fallen so low that she cannot rise again?" Mortimer laughed.

"You had best go home, or spend an hour with me at bowls or billiards; you are sentimental and maudlin, not half yourself; this sudden stroke of good fortune has upset you."

"No, no; I am well enough; a little agitated naturally, but I am bound to start hence to-morrow, and to-night I must see her."

"Where?"

"At Cremorne."

"My God! Is it possible?" cried Mortimer, impatiently.

"What is the matter?"

"Well, well, it is useless to advise; you are possessed by that winged imp of the devil."

"Hush! You must not blaspheme the power of love!" returned Eagleton, with a false laugh.

"They say there were more Cupids than one. They paint them in bevies. Some may be angels of light; but most are but imps of darkness," cried Mortimer.

"What are you raving about?"

"To think——There, it will not bear reflection!"

"To think that I am such a fool?"

"If you were consistently a fool it would be so natural; but cold, self-possessed, practical and plucky, with an address perfect, a heart without weakness, a brain that is ever in working order. Yet, as soon as all is done, and all is won, down, down you sink to the level of a drivelling idiot, and tremble at the feet of a poor, painted puppet, who has sold her soul, and has nothing of the woman left, but her frailty and her venomous beauty! Bah! Is there no philanthrophist will found an asylum for such unhappy maniacs?"

"Come, come, you jest too roughly," said Eagleton, in a hoarse tone. "The girl has fallen; but she is not morally more degraded than those who were her destroyers."

"A curse upon such cant!"

"I never 'cant' unless in business, and in the game of life it will not do to show one's 'hand.' But Angeline loves me; with all her faults, caprices, devilries, the girl loves me!"

"Slights you, mocks you, fools you! Look you

here, Richard, this concerns me as well as you. I have been your partner in many little schemes that we have been forced to carry out for our own benefit. 'Dangerous!' Ah! when I see you on the ice, skating full tilt into a fissure, as a friend I would holloa or rush to save you. But when I stand before the danger-sign, and you and your pretty paramour are about to dash me before you in your headlong course, I think it time to clear out of your company."

"But, Mortimer, you exaggerate. I am not so weak as you fancy. To-night I will come to a definite understanding with this coquette, for to-morrow I leave England for ever."

"Well, shall we begone?"

"Yes, we will call a Hansom; it is getting late. You will see that I am not such a child as you have supposed me hitherto if I find her as sordid and heartless——"

"As ever."

"No, no; sometimes she has been so tender, so generous."

"There lies the danger. Folks with no principles follow their impulses, and win esteem and gratitude for some passing kindness, and from that vantage-ground shoot their arrows of after injuries. But I am talking stuff."

"I wish," murmured Eagleton, with a profound sigh.

"What do you wish?"

"Hang it; life is a farce! Work is thankless, pleasure is poisonous, love is frenzy, speculation is fever, death is rest!"

"Worse and worse! 'Ye sweet little cherubs that sit up aloft' throw down a spare chimney-pot on this devoted head the first moment that you perceive poor Jack Mortimer to be struck with incipient love-mania! Hi, Cabby! Colney Hatch!"

"Where, sir?"

"Cremorne, and be hanged to ye! Mortimer, you will drive me mad."

"I leave that work of charity to gentle Angeline."

The companions reached Cremorne.

It was a lovely night.

The scene was one of fairy beauty. Amid the dark green leaves twinkled the myriad coloured lamplets of the illuminated gardens. The quiet of the calm, star-sprinkled heavens was contrasted by the gay bustle of the merry crowd of revellers who wound in couples or groups down the green arcades, or gathered before the illuminated orchestra for the dance.

Eagleton and his companion walked to the open space for the dancing, and seated themselves in one of the gilded and frescoed arbours that surround the open lawn.

They called for wine and cigars.

They sat watching the dancers.

A laugh like the merry peal of little silver bells struck on their ears.

Eagleton quailed and turned ashy white.

His comrade looked at him with moody sympathy, largely blended with contempt.

A party of gaily-dressed girls and stylish-looking fellows sauntered past the arbour.

Somewhat in advance of the rest two youths of distinguished appearance, and of the "inane" type of patrician manhood, walked on either side of an exquisitely piquante and lovely blonde, dressed with extreme elegance and perfect taste.

She was sweetly laughing and gaily prattling, with child-like glee.

"You see her—now, you see her—or are you stone blind?" said Mortimer, querulously, and pushing his glass across the table with an air of petulant disgust.

Eagleton's eyes glared fiercely, and he hissed out a bitter word.

"Well, then, why linger near the siren? Depend upon it, this foolish infatuation is easily broken off."

"Easily!"

"Look at her."

"Ah, if she were always so! Then, indeed, it would be easy, but sometimes she is so witching

sweet that St. Anthony himself could not withstand her. Well, well, well, I don't care—not I—it's all fancy. If everybody else did not think her so pretty, I shouldn't."

"Oh, you miserable, miserable fool!" growled Mortimer. "Women are the prime movers of all mischief; sure as fate she will be the ruin of you, Dick."

"Ruin!" returned the young reprobate, in a tone of bitterness. "When I first knew that girl—but, there, she has turned all the milk of human kindness in my heart to verjuice. Sometimes I feel so full of malice that I can get no relief except in cursing my kind. Look you, Mortimer, remember what I am, think how remorselessly I have sacrificed that poor fellow, Charley Rye, who clove to me like a Corsican brother; think how roughly I have treated poor Sylvia Volante—it was all for her. Money, money, money, and I can be satisfied with smiles that are sold for dirty trash, with favours she sets up to sell by auction. Ugh!—but you may well call me a miserable fool. But I will show you how cavalierly I can treat her. I will prove to you that I am not quite the dolt I appear. The music strikes up. I will secure her hand for this waltz."

"Dick, one word."

"Well?"

"Don't let her know that you are flush with chink."

"No!" gasped Eagleton, once more turning his haggard face towards his enchantress, who was lightly bantering with her two dashing admirers.

He advanced and spoke to his mistress.

She received him rather coldly.

There was something so fierce in the wild, black eyes of the manly, handsome youth that she seemed subdued beneath their intensity.

Mortimer watched him with interest.

The two young aristocrats, who were diverting themselves by a loose, but sparkling dialogue with the lovely Angeline, fixed their eye-glasses and regarded the young clerk with a supercilious stare.

However, they soon walked away.

The girl cast a look of teasing indifference upon them, and took the arm of her lover for the waltz.

As she and Eagleton stood awaiting the signal for commencing the dance Mortimer observed that, while she clung to his friend's arm and tapped him pettingly with her tiny gloved hand, her great, cold, blue eyes wandered restlessly about, and her dimpled lips wreathed into passing smiles as she recognised in the crowd one or other of her numerous admirers.

She spoke a few honeyed words from time to time, with her gold-fringed lids down-bent, and her face wearing a look of pensive tenderness; then once more her great cold, blue eyes would wide dilate, and wander around with an air of pre-occupation that showed how pitilessly unmindful she was of the nearness of her passionate lover.

Eagleton trembled with emotion.

His eyes grew bright and his cheek flushed.

The music rose on the calm night air, brisk and soul-stirring.

Angeline danced like a fairy, and she and Eagleton were soon whirling swiftly and gracefully in the exciting round.

Mortimer sought a partner.

He found one of the same class as Angeline, nearly as pretty, and far more ingenuous.

When he had danced with her for some time he led her to one of the arbours, and, leaving her for a moment, went to seek his companion.

Neither Eagleton nor his charmer appeared among the dancers.

Not without some feeling of distrust he passed down several of the green arcades, and along the illuminated parterres.

He reached a sequestered bowery spot, adorned with an artificial cascade and grotto and several statues.

He checked his steps.

He heard the sound of voices raised as in dispute.

He concealed himself behind the pedestal of one of the images.

"Angeline, do not make me curse you," he heard Eagleton say, in a voice so harsh and discordant that it was scarcely recognisable. "It may be superstition, but I feel that there is something really blighting in the curse that springs from the tortured heart of an injured lover. I do not wish to harm you. I love you. I will leave you, though it is death to be away from you; but I will go; only do not talk to me so heartlessly, say something kind before we part; do not let us separate in anger."

"Why should we? La, there is no one I am less disposed to quarrel with than yourself, Richard. You know I feel a great regard for you."

"You love me— you told me that you loved me?"

"Did I?" returned the girl, languidly. "You must not teaze me with every light speech I make."

"Then you do not care for me?"

"No. I care for no one—at least, I am not responsible to you for the bent of my affections; besides what is the use of your preaching love to me?"

"Do you distrust it?"

"No. I believe you are sincere; but, then, you see, Richard, I am practical."

"What do you mean?"

"Why how dull you are! Then you worry me so, Richard; it makes me hate you. Now, as a sensible man, I appeal to you. Are you in a position—have you ever been in a position, to marry me?"

"Angeline, I have striven hard. I obtained a good post and a fair salary; you said—you promised that you would share the humblest home with me— you were so submissive, so loving, so gentle; and when you were sick and poor, I worked so hard for you, did I not? And did I not rise to a post of trust? Did I not?"

"Oh, dear! Oh, dear! What a brute you are, Richard, to teaze me so. You seem to think a woman can live in beggary. What was your paltry salary?"

"Did I pause at anything? Was I content with what I earned so hard? Did I not dare all to get you gold? Did I not do a deed which it is not safe to whisper in the night? Did I not risk all in the event last Derby? Did I not sacrifice my two dearest friends? All for you; all to bring you money."

"But, then, you see, my dear, good Richard, why, you weren't *successful*, you know," returned the girl, with provoking suavity.

"And I can look at you and love you!"

"I dare say you do nothing of the kind. Men! I detest the whole race, except—— Oh, isn't that a pretty waltz? Now, don't be a brute; come, let us dance and part friends. I shall always think of you as a brother, indeed I shall. Come, Richard, this is the last waltz. I will walk with you, talk with you, dance with you, and so forth; but marry a man who is forced to flee the country or confess love to one who is not 'eligible,' I'm not so absurd. Yesterday I refused a young country squire, with an immense estate. I am not young and beautiful for nothing; I must make the most of my only patrimony. Well, I have been frank with you. You brag a great deal of what you have done, but if you had loved me half as much as you pretend, you would have done a great deal more!"

"Angeline, you are false, and cold, and cruel."

"Oh, of course! And every thing else that is bad; but, I am practical. I know you have been unfortunate, very; I know I am selfish, and all that; but I am perfectly sick of your troubles, and tired of you too. There, now, I am plain with you; what can you complain of?"

"And you, who have looked into my eyes, your face radiant with love; you who have told me that if you thought I should change you would kill yourself!"

"If you please, my dear, good, indulgent Richard, do leave off abusing me. And pray excuse me. Yonder is young Bullion, your master's nephew. He dances almost as well as you, and is a much pleasanter companion. Bye, bye! I shall always think of you as a brother, dear Richard."

The young clerk threw himself before her, and wildly clutched her wrists, and muttered, fiercely,

"Woman! to call you a murderess is to bestow on you a title of honour! Worse, far worse, than the most ruthless wretch that ever embrewed her hands in blood; you have killed my soul, you have fed on my heart, you have exulted in degrading, ruining one who would have coined his last drop of blood to buy you the lightest pleasure! But there is justice —justice! By the living fiends, your life shall answer for the wreck of mine!"

The girl shrieked, and cowered down.

Merrily the music flourished, and soothingly the fountains plashed; gaily the revellers laughed and jested; calmly the moon looked down.

In the cold, quiet beams flashed the blade of a dagger.

Foaming with passion, Eagleton raised the gleaming weapon.

The girl tried to scream again; but her breath seemed frozen with terror, and she almost felt the keen steel already riving her soft, fair bosom.

Mortimer leaped from his hiding-place.

He caught Eagleton's arm.

"Fool! is she worth the sacrifice of your life? Madman, calm yourself, or I will call for help!" he cried, in a loud and thrilling whisper.

Angeline sprang to her feet.

Deathly white, and violently trembling, Eagleton stood passive.

With one hand Mortimer tightly gripped his arm, in the other he held the dagger he had wrested from him.

"Begone!" said Mortimer, sternly, to the girl, whose face wore a look satanic in its fury.

"And so, this is your love, Richard Eagleton! these are the friends you sacrifice for me! Who are you, sir, that dare to talk to me so imperiously? 'Begone!'—is that a word for a lady?"

"Your beauty covers all," returned Mortimer, with mingled scorn and admiration.

"All!" returned the girl, with a sneer. "Surely I owe this murderous villain nothing. And you——. Well, you are too snobbish to quarrel with."

"An ignorant, common-place, abandoned woman. And yet, bright eyes, golden hair, damask flesh, statuesque form," murmured Mortimer, half abstractedly.

"You insulting fellow! what do you mean?"

"Insulting! I am thinking of your power, miss —of the glamour of your glowing charms," returned Mortimer, with a slight bow.

"Thank you."

"But I am thinking, too, how transient are these powers. It seems but yesterday that I was an innocent boy; it is but to-morrow, and your reign is over."

Angeline spat on the ground, tossed her head, and swept away.

"Does not that comfort you?" said Mortimer, with a contemptuous smile, addressing his companion. "A Dame aux Camelias, a soiled dove! Come, there is cant in all garbs; there's the cant of piety, and the cant of false charity. The man who feels pity for that power of heartlessness is not the man who would have respect for the simple and confiding girl he has wronged. I like life, it is jolly, it is existence; but when I think of the humbug in the world, and in myself, I wish there were a powder-mine at the centre of gravity, and I held the slow match!"

Eagleton made no reply.

He sank upon a seat.

Mortimer looked in his paling face with solicitude.

"And it is for this that I have become a forger, a felon, an ingrate, a traitor, a perjurer! But you must acknowledge her loveliness. Well, I am cured; but henceforth I foreswear all faith in women!"

Mortimer smiled grimly.

Eagleton feebly rose.

"Let us get away from this cursed place," he said. "To-morrow I must start from England, and to-night I want rest."

"And how came you to carry a dagger in your pocket?" asked Mortimer, gravely. "Surely you did not meditate murder?"

"No," returned the young profligate, in a tone of shame and chagrin; "I kept it for my own heart! I have sworn not to be taken, and a dagger is more convenient than a pistol!"

"You must not entertain such dark thoughts."

"I have done with the world!" returned Eagleton, in a strange and altered tone; "I have found it too hard for me! I surrender at discretion!"

"You would never commit the crime of self-murder, Richard?"

"I fear I have not sufficient courage," returned the other, moodily.

At this moment they passed the orchestra.

Whirling gaily round among the dancers moved the sylph-like form of Angeline.

CHAPTER CLXV.

THE REGULATORS' ATTACK UPON THE INDIANS' BIVOUAC—THE TRAPPER AND THE INDIAN'S WIFE—THE PLOT TO RESCUE AGNES—THE BUSH-RANGERS BESIEGE THE TRAPPER'S CABIN—MINNA DEFENDS HER FRIEND—THE CAPTURE OF AGNES—THE FLIGHT OF THE BUSH-RANGERS—MINNA RESOLVES TO SECURE HER HUSBAND'S PRISONER — THE HEART OF FIRE.

IT is necessary to the due elucidation of our story, that some account should be given of Harwolf's attack upon the camp of the bush-rangers and redskins, of the carrying off of Agnes Staunton, and the escape of Minna Wyotti with her husband's prisoner.

Mark Leighton and Harwolf had fought a sharp skirmish with the Dacotahs and Pawnees, in which the latter had come off victorious.

Their assault upon the camp was well-timed.

Catahaga and Regan, with the flower of the bush-rangers, were away.

The Indians were exhausted from a long and weary march, and, having gorged themselves with their usual gluttony, lay supine around the fires, utterly unmindful of danger.

Their resistance, however, was resolute.

They were surrounded, and fought with the fury of despair.

Upon the first alarm the bush-rangers prepared for flight.

They did not wish to take part with the Indians against whom they had been conspiring on their own account, and were unwilling to face Harwolf's party in the open field.

Their first care, however, was to secure Agnes Staunton.

The boldest amongst them would not have dared to confront their fiery leader if she had escaped from their hands.

Minna formed a design to carry off her friend, which she communicated to the good-natured trapper.

Nat Weatherfield had fortified himself in his cabin.

He listened with patience as the wife of the Pawnee chief unfolded her plan.

He shook his head when she had concluded.

"I du opine, Minna, that the ways of women is like the tides of some of these Arkansan rivers, there be no accountin' for 'em; sometimes you finds 'em overflowin' the banks in dry weather, and then agen, arter heavy rains, they'll ebb so low as a'most to leave dry channels."

"And how does this apply to Agnes Staunton's case, Nathaniel?"

"Wall, Minna, it's most affectin' to hear the poor gal a pleadin' and prayin' to that graceless dog, her cousin here; but, for all that, if she was suddenly restored to the Leighton folks she would hardly be thankful to her deliverers, I reckon."

"Why, you never can suppose she wishes to remain with this brigand?" cried Minna, with great warmth.

The trapper looked at her with a dry smile.

"Wall, I must repeat as I opinionate that women's ways is onaccountable; nothin' personal, in course, but look at yerself, Minna; wall, no one can deny as the Eagle-Wing is a king of a Injen, but then, fancy is everything."

The girl blushed brightly.

"Catahaga is my husband," she answered, with an unconscious sigh; "he fights his national enemies—too ruthlessly, I own, but Oswald is not the husband of Agnes, and she is sincere in her wish to return to her friends. But hark at the shots; the Indians' war-whoop sounds fainter, the shouts of the cruel Yengeese grow prouder and louder. Where, where is my husband?"

A grave and thoughtful look rested on the trapper's face.

He fixed another bar across the door.

"And Regan is not here!" he said, "nor Wyld; there is some treachery. Nay, don't look so pale, we are safe enough, the settlers will do us no harm; but where is Catahaga?"

"At the Panther's Pass."

"What does he there?"

"He is gone—gone to pray to his Manitou," gasped Minna.

"I thought he had turned Christian?"

"Yes, yes; but all is changed with him now; the injustice of the whites have retransformed him, he is now but a Pawnee-Loup."

"Humph! was he armed?"

"Yes, but he lays his arms aside when he prays, and in his fervour forgets all but the object of his devotion."

"Ha! but the Eagle-Wing will out-match the double-faced scoundrel yet!"

"Oh, what do you mean? You do not think that Oswald Lamond would turn traitor?"

"No, for he must become somethin' werry different to that if he turns at all, I guess; for he's confirmed in treachery since his tongue grew strong enough to tell lies."

Minna clasped her hands.

Her brave and beautiful face was pale and rigid.

She raised her soft blue eyes with a resigned look.

"His will be done!" she murmured. "But I will have justice for my husband if he has fallen by treachery; for his people are my people, and his cause is just!"

"But what's to be done with Agnes?" asked the trapper, hurriedly.

Sounds of the conflict grew nearer, the mustering of horses, and shouting of the bush-rangers, rang round the cabin.

Agnes herself at this moment rushed from behind the screen of painted deer-skin.

Alarmed by the noise without, she had risen and thrown her dress loosely about her.

Her face was wild and haggard.

She seemed very ill.

Minna Wyotti clasped her tenderly in her arms, kissed her pale, cold cheek, and reassured her with kind words.

Agnes trembled convulsively, and almost sank to the floor.

"Speak, Agnes dear, quick? Will you return home to Leighton Hoe? Will you abandon the wretched criminal who has snatched you from your friends?"

"Yes, yes," murmured Agnes, in a hoarse faint tone; "but Oswald, have they killed him? Oh! have mercy on me, speak! have they killed him?"

"He is far from hence, on a mission of treachery,"

returned Minna, in a tone of indignation; "you are unworthy if you bestow one thought on such a villain!"

"Then he is not dead! Thank Heaven for that! He is not fit to die. Oh, there is hope while life remains that he may repent. What is the meaning of this dreadful firing? these shrieks and yells?"

"My tribe are attacked by the false Yengeese," returned the Indian's wife fiercely.

"Open the door, Nat Weatherfield! We'll have your blood, I reckon, if you dare to oppose our entrance. Bring out the Leighton's gal, or by the devil we'll burn the lodge over your head!" shouted Wyld, crashing at the door with his hatchet.

"By Jehoshaphat, I'll hold my own agen yer whole pack, ye beastly prairie wolves!" cried Nat Weatherfield, in a passion, and snatching up his rifle. "Hide yourselves, gals, the bullets will soon riddle these timbers; but I'll scorch some of the coons, I reckon. We can keep it up till the Reg'lators raise the siege. Ye forked-tongued vipers, arn't we smoked the pipe together? ain't I a leg'lator? Clear off, you ungrateful ruffs!"

With this the sturdy trapper aimed and fired through a hole in the shutters that closed the window.

Agnes shrieked and clung to Minna.

A furious yell from without preceded a desperate attack upon the door.

Pistols were fired through the fastenings.

Hatchets thundered and crashed through the splintering logs and planks.

Agnes remained on her knees.

She uplifted her arms, and poured forth a fervent prayer fot heavenly protection.

Minna resolutely crossed the room.

She took down a rifle.

Gracefully her pretty white arm wayes back as she rattled the ramrod down the barrel of the gun.

She threw the rifle across her arm, and looked sternly towards the door.

The door crashed down.

Nat Weatherfield fired, and leaped back.

Wyld and the gang rushed in.

Minna levelled her rifle.

Wyld sprang upon her.

A tussle ensued.

The gun went off.

The bullet sped through the roof.

Agnes lay prone and lifeless on the flo

The shouts of the Regulators were heard without.

Not an instant was to be lost.

A rush was made to secure Agnes.

In an instant she was in the arms of the bush-rangers.

Wyld had hurled Minna across the room.

She leaped to her feet.

She snatched up a hatchet.

In her fury, and her eagerness to protect Agnes, she would have rushed upon Wyld.

Nat Weatherfield seized her by the waist.

He flung her over his shoulder, and striking right and left with the butt of his rifle, reached and cleared the door.

He fled into the wood.

He leaped into a hollow.

He lay against the bank, panting with exhaustion.

Minna rose.

She paused, with a shudder.

A horse was leaped across the gap, and over her head.

The rider was Wyld.

Agnes Staunton was bound on the saddle before him.

The rest of the Regulators dashed after him in wild pursuit.

"The cusses are escaped. Shall we jine the Reg'lators?" said the trapper.

"No," returned Minna, curtly. "At least, I speak for myself, Nathaniel. My duty is not to desert my people. I am the wife of their chief, and I will look to his captive."

"Wall, you air a wonder, Minna Wyotti," re-

turned the trapper, with a stare of admiration. "But I can't blame yer. A wife should stand by her husband; it's on'y nat'ral."

"And you, Nathaniel, you will not betray me, I know?"

"Minna, if I leaves you afore I sees you safe in the wigwam of the Dacotah, may I never take another beaver-skin. But wait a moment, I'll fetch the rifles."

With this, he ran back to the cabin.

Presently he returned with a couple of rifles and some ammunition.

Minna slung the shot-pouch across her shoulder, and took the rifle into her hands.

By this time the murderous fusillade was silenced.

Both Minna and the trapper started, and levelled their rifles at the same instant.

A tall, lithe figure had started up before them, as if springing from the bosom of the ground.

It was an Indian.

The pair lowered their rifles as he glided to their side.

"Let the White Fawn speak! Where is the Eagle-Wing?" said the Indian, quickly.

"The Heart of Fire asks me what I cannot answer," replied Minna, sadly. "Catahaga has not returned from the Panther's Pass; and the White Fox is on his trail, to slay him!"

CHAPTER CLXVI.

THE INDIAN'S WIFE—IN AMBUSH—MILES AND HIS MASTER STILL IN PURSUIT OF THE DETECTIVE—THE RAGE OF MARK LEIGHTON AT THE FLIGHT OF AGNES—INDIANS ON THE TRIAL—THE SWAMP—THE BATTLE—EAGLE-WING'S CAPTIVE—THE DISGUISE—THE ESCAPE.

"My brother has lost many braves?" asked the trapper.

"Heart of Fire has brought his young men across the river; they are in ambush; he was not here when the Yengeese found the Pawnee sleeping," the Indian answered.

"They have ceased firing. What does my brother intend to do? Will he strike the trail of his enemies?"

"The Heart of Fire will lend me his braves that I may keep my husband's prisoner?" said Minna.

"It is good," returned the Decotah.

Minna now took the lead.

She passed from the covert.

She threaded the dark forest.

Several times she shudderingly paused as her foot struck against the stiffened corpse of some painted brave lying deep in the waving fern.

She seemed to be alone, for so cautiously did the trapper and the Dacotahs glide after her that she could scarcely perceive them among the underwood.

Suddenly she held up her hand as a signal to her followers.

She concealed herself behind a tree.

Two men, excitedly conversing, passed close to her.

They looked eagerly about them.

"I do zay, zur, that the cat-and-hog feller be gone vor zure if he had been in the camp we shouldn't ha' taken it so easy loike. He be gone, zur, and has taken the blamed crusher along, depend on't."

"I fear you're right, Miles," returned the other, gloomily; "but we will not give up the search. If we do not find him this action ends in a defeat, and not a victory."

"Hast'ee knocked many o' these blamed heath-cocks off their perch? Lourd! but it were better sportin' than we had the night I went stalking the Jew chap and the trapper; but as we arn't killed the eagle feller, I do zay we arn't done nothin' to brag on."

"We have neither killed him, nor taken Foxley. A curse upon my ill luck, I am becoming no better than a dotard; everything goes wrong !"

"May be, yer honour, they've roasted and eaten him already; vor I be zure these hottentots are reg'lar camels !"

"Cannibals! No; but there is some sense in what you say, they may have brought him to the death-stake, or, perhaps, have given him the *coup de grace* with their tomahawks, for he was half dead when they took him."

"Aye, zure, yer honour."

"But I am alarmed about the Pawnee."

"Durn it, zquire, it be no disgrace to 'varsal natur' to be alarmed along of that warmint, vor, by token, I never remember havin' sich a cold sweatin' az when he notched off all the Yankee fellers and the snake into the durned bad bargain, and, lor, if I hadn't reached the open vield and cotched that ragged grey mare, I'm blamed if my wig wouldn't be dryin' to dust in a chimbly corner of zome of their dirty skin tents, the durned gipsys !"

"Well, we shall trap him at last," returned Judge Warren; "but, look, here comes Mark Leighton, in a towering passion, as usual. This victory's fruits are rather crabbed, I think."

"Ho, ho! that be good for 'ee too, Zquire. If Maester Mark has tasted any vruit it must be some blamed crab-apple, for he looks az zour as Lunnon cream."

"Is not this rascally, Judge Warren?" cried Mark Leighton, rushing up, his face red with wrath. "You see the fruit of all our labour."

"Ho, ho! I zee that the vruit doan't 'gree with none of uz," cried Miles, with a horse laugh. "Zquire—leastways the Judge, were zaying az the fruits of this vict'ry was zummat tart, and I do zay as losin' the prisoner be mortal vexin'."

"Yes. But how did you know she was gone ?"

"She! I'm blamed, but it was *he* I was thinkin' on."

"He! Whom do you mean ?"

"Voxley, zure."

"And who is he ?"

"Why, Reynard. This idiot does not know what he is talking of," cried Harwolf. "The poor Englishman we thought to rescue. He will certainly be murdered by the savages."

"Let him go to ——. Well, Judge, how *can* a man have patience under such exasperating circumstances? My poor cousin, Agnes, is torn from her home by brigands and bushmen, carried off into the forests, a grand expedition sent against the cut-throats, the villains are overtaken, and then suffered a second time to bear her off before our eyes !"

"It can't be helped, Mark."

"No! because these dastardly, unmanly curs—it chokes me to call them comrades—refuse to join me in the pursuit until they have found the cursed Britisher, who deserves the worst he'll get for his insular impudence."

"We cannot suffer him to be killed by these savages without making some attempt to rescue him. But, never fear, we will hunt these thieves to their mountains," returned Harwolf, "and will rescue Agnes Staunton at any cost."

A man ran up to the spot where they were conversing.

"Judge Warren! Mark Leighton! the devils are carrying off the Britisher on a litter. They are wading across the swamp a piece below the long windfall. They seem to be Pawnee-Loups, Eagle-Wing's picked braves; the Dacotahs are all fled."

"Judge Warren, I'll throw all my best energy into this effort. We'll retake your fellow-country-man from these hell-hounds; but, that done, if any man deserts me till we have rescued Agnes, he becomes my enemy, and by this hand I'll have his life !" cried Mark, with fierceness.

"Good! One thing must be done at a time.

Secure our comrade, and then to follow the bush-rangers."

"Quick, then. I'll call the men together, and we'll mount and follow to the verge of the swamp. Then we'll have 'em on open ground and tackle 'em at close quarters."

"Miles," said Warren, when the hot-headed young planter had gone some distance, "there will be a skirmish. You know what must be done ?"

"Aye, zure, zur. The Injens maybe 'll brain the crusher, if they vind az they're loike to lose 'un. If not, in coorse a stray shot there be no accountin' vor."

"Come, then, I trust to you."

"For Heaven's sake, Nathaniel, save them if you can," whispered Minna, wildly.

The trapper shook his head.

"This be a tarnation black business, Minna; if we're seen with the Injens, they'll lynch us if we're caught."

The Heart of Fire and his braves seemed quite to disregard the presence or authority of Minna or the trapper.

They crawled on lithely in swift pursuit of the Regulators.

The wood was very dense.

They were lost to view in a moment.

The next shots were fired at little distance.

The war-whoop rung in its prolonged and terrible peal of death.

The Indians came rushing back, they were driven off by the heavy fire of the Regulators, who were now collected in a body.

Heart of Fire appeared crouching backwards, his long rifle gleaming in his hand.

"My brother," exclaimed Minna, flying to his side. "Catahaga would sooner lose his scalp to the pale-face than his prisoner; let us save him."

"It is good; the Eagle-Wing is a great chief; the Dacotah will not let the Yengeese dogs take his brother's captive. If Catahaga has fallen, the prisoner shall die on his grave !"

Minna and the trapper, with four or five Indians, now made for the swamp.

They found that the Pawnees had carried their captive to a sort of island in the midst of the morass.

This bank was covered with stunted pollards.

The Indians were firing from among the trees.

The Regulators had stationed themselves on the firmest ground they could find, and were firing in their turn, and with desperate fury.

It would have been an act of madness for them to venture upon the slimy marsh, as they must have sunk to their knees in the mire, and would have been so impeded in their movements that they must inevitably have perished under the dreadful discharge of musketry from the bank where the Pawnees had entrenched themselves.

Their object was to drive the red-skins from their post of vantage.

While the Heart of Fire and the Dacotah braves started up in the rear, and opened a deadly blaze upon the whites, Minna fled across the swamp, leaping from stone to stone, and, clinging to the rank and thick-growing osiers and wild canes, she reached the island.

"Ugh !" cried a Pawnee brave, painted and feathered, and wearing the quaillou plume of native nobility.

"Where is the Eagle-Wing ?" asked this brave, a very handsome youth, and one of Catahaga's numerous brothers.

"My husband has not returned from the Panther's Pass," returned Minna, hurriedly. "Let Akantoosh and his braves keep this post with their fire-weapons while Minna carries off the white chief, her husband's prisoner."

"It is good; my sister will reach the wigwams of the Dacotah before the sun rises," replied the chief.

He gave the usual call.

Seven braves crawled out of the bush.

RUSSIAN TREATMENT OF POLISH PEASANTS.

Akantoosh gave them some directions in the Iro-quois language, and gravely bowing their crested heads, they followed the girl, trailing their long rifles, and covering her from the shots in the most devoted manner.

"Minna," cried a voice by her side.

The Indian's wife started.

The faithful trapper, Nat Weatherfield, started up from among the bushes.

"Still no news of my husband?" asked the girl, faintly.

"Not yet, Minna," replied the trapper, "but I have crossed the swamp unseen by the Regulators. One of the Pawnees must lend me his blanket that I may not be known on the open ground."

No. 52.

"Let my brothers lead me to my husband's prisoner," said Minna, to the Pawnees.

A desperate battle was being fought.

Heart of Fire and the Dacotahs were firing from the other side of the swamp.

The Pawnees kept blazing from the bank.

Minna was conducted to a sheltered spot in the midst of the swamp islet.

Here Reynard lay groaning upon the litter.

The girl knelt by his side.

He looked wildly into her face.

"You are not an Indian," he said, in a feeble tone. "Surely you do not intend to murder me?"

"No, to save you. My husband means you no ill, or he would have killed you in the first instance.

The Judge Warren seeks your life; you are safe with us; be calm."

"I calkilate the Pawnee takes neither scalps nor prisoners, stranger," added the trapper. "You may just tranquilise yer mind, and trust to me and Minna. The Reg'lators makes a tarnal rowdydow about protectionising yer, but they don't mean good by it, for they've a forked tongue set no better nor the Rangers themselves, I guess."

"My eyes are dim with my weakness. I have lost much blood; I am quite powerless," murmured the captive, "but if I am not deceived, you are Minna Wyotti, the wife of the fine young Indian that lived at Larchville?"

"And I remember you too," replied Minna, with a smile. "You spent an evening in my husband's lodge?"

"God bless you! I would rather trust the falsest, cruelest of the red men than that hellish ruffian who calls himself Michael Warren."

"Fear no harm, you shall be protected. I fear that some harm must have befallen the brave chief, my husband, but I have influence in the tribes, and will protect you," replied the girl.

"And now, stranger, you must liquor up, and then try your understandings; if we can get you on horseback you will do very well."

Saying this, Nat applied the brandy flask to the captive's lips.

Revived by the stimulant, by the assistance of Minna and the backwoodsman, the detective contrived to struggle through the wood, and reached the other side of the islet.

There was a long and narrow ridge of dryer ground which extended to the forest beyond.

Horses were awaiting them.

Reynard was placed on one of them.

An Indian robe was thrown over him, a fillet of feathers placed round his forehead.

Similarly disguised, Minna and the trapper mounted and rode close beside him.

Six Indians followed on foot.

It was growing dark.

The shots now sounded fainter, as in the far distance.

The Regulators were evidently retreating.

Spurring their horses they rushed on.

They gained the wood.

With a whoop a number of the Regulators surrounded them.

They had foreseen that this would be the direction the Indians would take in order to make their escape.

One of the foremost seized the captive's arm.

Minna levelled her rifle.

She fired.

The man fell, and the horse bounded over him.

Minna shrieked at perceiving the effect of her own shot.

The trapper, the girl, and their charge, dashed wildly on.

The Indian escort attacked the Regulators and a furious contest ensued, to cover the retreat of the fugitives.

CHAPTER CLXVII.

PIRATES ASHORE—THE TREASURE-ISLAND— THE ROVER-CAVE—OPEN SESAME—THE BOY PIRATE'S BOUNTY—A CAROUSE ON SHORE— BLACK RALPH'S SONG—THE BOY PIRATE AND HIS BRIDE LEAVE THE REVELLERS.

BEFORE setting sail from the sunny isles of the south sea, our hero resolved to visit his treasure-island.

On a lonely rocky piece of land, which terminated a grand but dangerous coral-reef, was the deep caverns in which the Ravens stored the rich booty they had taken from their enemies.

Much of this wealth had been inherited by Gomez and our hero from mad Don Miguel, who, as our readers doubtless remember, was the man who was the cause of the moral ruin of the noble-hearted foundling; the man who forced him into that career of piracy which had rendered his name so famous and so terrible.

Never before had our hero ventured to visit this place with the whole of his crews; but so fortunate had he been in securing the aid and fealty of men, who, despite their lawless character, were devoted to himself, and true to the interest of the band, that the reckless young rover did not scruple to trust them to the uttermost.

People who are dauntless, seldom lose by this sort of confidence, which is quite compatible with the most perfect caution and foresight; it is often as dangerous to trust too little as to trust too much.

Behold our pirates! Yet it is hard to call our gallant hero still by the name he has practically abjured; behold our Avengers, then, on shore.

The island was an earthly paradise of fertility and beauty.

Its surface was covered with rich parterres of the most gorgeous and lovely flowers, of clear, pearly rivers, of shady groves of palms, cocoa-trees, and mangroves, with cedar glades redolent of the most grateful perfumes, and colonised by rich-plumaged birds and numberless animals of every variety, of every degree of strangeness or beauty.

It seemed a spot where one might wish to linger for ever in listless abandonment to the sweet delight and holy calm that spring from contemplating the transcendant loveliness of nature, and the goodness and bounty of the all-giving, all-beautifying creative power, which, beholding all things in their kind, pronounced them "very good."

The fair girls who, fleeing from wrong and oppression, or of their own love and choice, had placed themselves under the protection of the noble young chieftain and his chivalrous band, were in ecstacies as they roamed through this Eden, well worthy of being the fairy home of the sea-nymphs.

Lilia and her husband stood alone beneath the shade of a banana tree, which, with its many trunks and arching branches, formed of itself quite a plantation.

"My husband," she murmured, "would it not be possible that our toils and labours might end here; that we might build ourselves a cedar cabin in these balmy forests, and live together, sequestered from the troublous world, and grow old in peace and prayer, in the enjoyment of our mutual, unfettered love? Oh, Christopher! have you not suffered and dared enough?"

"My darling, what I have lost, what I have gained, has been under the cursed banner of piracy," returned our hero, sadly. "My whole life, short as it must be, is not sufficient space in which to make reparation for the unhappy past. I am rich and powerful. By good fortune I have been saved from the most revolting acts of an outlaw's career. My enemies, who have hunted me often without cause, and often with black ingratitude, have been my prey. But, now that I might rest if my former course had been honourable, I must atone, even with my life. Out of the pale of the law I can find no cause to uphold so worthy as that of a poor, struggling people, bleeding beneath the thongs and shackles of a great bullying power, and neglected by the cold and selfish policy of those who would be the loudest in their praises if the unhappy one would work their own freedom without their aid. Oh, Lilia! if I were guiltless, might I not be happy?"

"Who is guiltless, Christopher? And how many dark villanies may be perpetrated by those who never break the laws of nations?"

"My love, do not you flatter me. Do not you seek to excuse my conduct. I have been true to you. Love me on that account, and for the rest be silent."

"Dear, brave Christopher, you are a hero!" cried Lilia, with fond enthusiasm.

"Dear, charitable Lilia, you can see no faults in him you love."

They now joined their companions.

"Come, Ali Baba, show us to your cave of treasures. But, though I am your brother, and have somewhat of an 'itching palm,' I don't want to be *quartered* there," cried Black Ralph, laughing. "Oh! Fates and Destinies! When I played the captain of the Forty Thieves, how little did I think I should ever be a bandit in earnest. But 'Kismet,' it is destiny, and I'm now a veritable brigand."

He swayed round his gun, and strumming at the stock as if it were a guitar, burst forth,

"'To your light footstep let terror add wings,
For 'tis Massaroni himself who now sings.'"

"But, don't run away, nevertheless, Mrs.Christopher, for though deep-mouthed, I am but a harmless poor dog, as you shall find me. Lead on, Ali Baba. 'Accursed hunger of gold!' I feel an appetite already."

"Come then, Midas, no more braying," laughed the Boy Pirate, "and we'll lead you to a manger of gilded oats."

"Golly, Cap'en Ralph, most berry fine palaver!" exclaimed Zamp, rolling his eyes with unutterable admiration.

The merry rovers travelled on till they reached a stream, on the banks of which were piled rugged rocks, covered with thick, umbrageous trees.

It was a wild and gloomy place.

They embarked in two light canoes, which the seamen carried on their shoulders.

A launch was at the time making its way round the coast, in order to enter the mouth of the stream, to ship off that portion of the booty which our hero might wish to convey to his fleet.

They shot under a dark, frowning arch of the living rock.

For some time they travelled under a kind of tunnel.

Torches were lit.

It was a weird and awful passage.

They reached a rough flight of steps hewn in the rock.

These they mounted, and found themselves blocked by a heavy mass of stone.

"Exquisite! a scene for a melodrama!" said Black Ralph, staring about him with the air of a connoiseur. "This is assisting nature with a vengeance. What miser could contrive such an admirable strongbox wherein to keep his hoardings? But how are we to effect an entry?"

"By a spell with which I alone am acquainted," replied the Boy Pirate.

He knelt down; then rising on one foot, he pressed the stone with his hands.

"Open Sesamo!" shouted Black Ralph.

The stone rolled back.

A wide and darksome cavern appeared.

It was densely packed with every kind of wealth —spoils from rich barques of all nations.

Ship stores, mess-chests, plate, jewels, ingots of gold and silver, bags of coin, ship tackle, cannon, weapons of every kind and quality, pictures, mirrors, flags, and *et ceteras* countless, and almost priceless.

Black Ralph and the pirates gave a shout of ecstacy.

The Boy Pirate looked on with a saddened glance.

Lilia clung to him, and looked with sympathy into his grave face.

The Boy Pirate soon shook off his melancholy, and distributed some costly prizes amongst the men.

To Ida, Deborah and Mary Cassidy he made costly presents.

To his wife he brought a small casket.

It opened with a spring.

Within was a necklace of diamonds, each of great value.

"You may wear it, Lilia," said the young rover,

with a tender smile; "it was given me by a rich planter, whose daughter I saved from a wreck."

He now gave orders for the removal of a very large sum of money, and of arms and ammunition, for his grand enterprise.

For hours the pirates were at work removing the stores.

At length, in the cool of the evening, they gathered on the shore, to celebrate by a carouse their embarkation for Russia.

No pencil could paint the glowing beauty of the gorgeous sunset. The sky was a-blaze with crimson, amber, and golden light; the sea was intensely purple, flecked with snowy white; the shadowy groves seemed to be sprinkled with floating and shooting stars; the fire-flies were on the wing, and illumined the green glades like showers of bright sparks.

The pirates were seated on the silver sands, their launch lying lazily on the shore, its sail, half furled, toying with the passing wind; the steamers smoked, and the sailers rocked far out in the offing.

Black Zamp carried round the grog kid.

"A song! a song! Black Ralph for a song!" shouted the pirates.

"A toast, hearties, first a toast!" returned the ranting rover.

"Lilia, the Queen of the Sea!"

"Hurrah! Lilia, the Rovers' Queen!" shouted the others. "Lilia, the Queen of the Sea!"

When this toast had been drunk with due honour, the officers and crews once more called on Black Ralph for a song.

"Well, hearties, my muse is rather husky, but grog, if it spoils a good voice and impairs a fine memory, cheers a lone heart and drowneth much misery. Here goes, then; fill cups, and join chorus in—

THE SONG OF BLACK RALPH THE ROVER.

O wild, wild sea! the triton's shell,
  The naiad's harp and mermaid's song,
The ripple's plash and billows swell,
  The foamy breakers thund'ring long,
The gull's glad scream, the whistling wind,
  The rattling sail, the keel's keen rush,
The furrowy wake that rolls behind,
  The solemn night and morn's sweet blush,
All, all proclaim the rovers' choice
  Is worthier of the bold and free.
In gold and grain let boors rejoice,
  The rover ploughs the wild, salt sea!

CHORUS.
Hurrah for the rovers' flag!
  Hurrah for the old deep wave!
We lack no store, o' the land's galore,
  We reap with the pike and glave!

O wild, wild sea! with far, white wings,
  The rovers' prize the sky-line flecks,
Vain to the breeze her sail she flings—
  The rover sweeps her fated decks,
Or should the war-hawk, beak to beak,
  The wild sea-eagle rashly dare,
He bids his bolts of thunder speak,
  He spreads his storm-cloud in the air,
He recks not foeman great or small,
  He knows not fear or flight, not he!
Though on his own red deck he fall,
  O he sleeps in the wild, salt sea!

CHORUS.
Hurrah for the rovers' flag!
  Hurrah for the old deep wave!
We lack no store o' the land's galore,
  While we reap with the pike and glave!

The excited outlaws prolonged the chorus vociferously.

Our hero rose, and leaving them in the midst of their carousals, sauntered thoughtfully along the sands.

Lilia followed him. She timidly laid her hand on his arm.

He kissed her fondly, and they moved on together by the silver waters, beneath the purple night sky.

CHAPTER CLXVIII.

REGRETS AND FOREBODINGS—CHRISTOPHER'S
ISLAND—THE YOUNG CASTAWAY—THE VISIT
TO THE ISLAND—TOKENS OF EARLY LOVE—
THE RE-EMBARKATION—THE CHANNEL TIDES
—SUDDEN DARKNESS—THE WHITE SQUALL—
THE WRECK—THE RAFT—HOURS OF AGONY—
SAVED.

THE young rover and his wife seated themselves
beneath the towering cliffs, and, hand in hand, remained in conscious silence, their eyes wandering
across the wide-spreading waters.

"Husband, it seems to me that this western world
is younger than the old world; nature seems here to
show herself in all the vigour and stateliness of youth;
the forests, the mountains, the wide prairies, the
rivers, the lakes, all seem·grander and mightier,
and the very stars look brighter!"

The girl sighed as she raised her eyes to the glowing hosts of Heaven. Amongst their myriad phalanxes
was one constellation, the most brilliant and beautiful of all their combinations, the glittering Southern
Cross.

"We have been happy here," said Lilia, with a
sigh. "You have had great triumphs, and, though
a rover, have won a proud renown. I shrink from
the thought of returning to Europe; but I will not
murmur."

"You must not, Lilia; I need all the solace of
your love; but I am neglecting what should be the
chief aim of my life."

"And what is that?"

"My oath! I have sworn to avenge my father's
murder, to learn the fate of my hapless mother."

"Do not think of that now; your enemy, Daniel
Harwolf, is swept off."

"But his father lives—my father's murderer."

"Vengeance is slow but sure; he will not escape."

"No; but, as you say, we will not think of these
things now. Harken to my gay fellows; it joys me
much to hear their buoyant shouts and laughter as
they listen to the ranting of wild Ralph, or the
comicalities of Black Zamp. I envy them their light
hearts; like yours, my own is heavy."

"What is that island yonder? It looks like a bank
of snow or an iceberg in this dazzling starlight. Is it
associated with any memories of the past?"

"Strange, Lilia, on that island I lived a castaway
for many a month after my escape from the man of
war, which destroyed the schooner of my old master,
Don Miguel."

"And did you think of me, then?"

"Ah, then you were my dream, love; then, for
hours I would sit by the lone beach, and dream of
the green woods of Frontemore, and the dear little
fairy that haunted their mossy glades. I´carved
your name on the rocky walls of my solitary cave,
and even tried to sketch your loved features on the
stone. I remembered one bright day in June that
it was your birthday; I thought of Paul and Virginia, over whose sad story we have wept together
in the old, old times, and I planted two palmettos.
I wonder if they flourished?"

"Oh, Christopher, you never told me this before.
How much I should like to visit the island."

"Well, dearest, we will go ashore to-morrow."

"But alone, husband; let us go alone. We will
visit your Crusoe's isle, and we will sit beneath your
palmettos, and revel in old memories."

The impulsive young rover started up.

"Lilia, when could it be seen to better advantage
than at this glorious hour? The moon and stars give
us a silver day; the night hush harmonises with our
soothing thoughts; the sea is calm; the strait not
more than a league across. I will push off the
felucca; the merest catspaw will waft us over."

Lilia did not oppose her husband's wish.

The night seemed so placid, the waters smooth as
a mill-pool.

"Draw your cloak around you, love. I will call
yonder boy, and we will float the skiff. Do you

follow. The men will carouse till morning, and to-
night we will visit the island of my solitude, in
which, like Selkirk, I found few of her boasted
charms."

He walked down to the shore.

He called one of the boys belonging to his flag-
ship.

The lad saluted his captain and helped him to
push off the light bark.

The Boy Pirate handed his wife into the boat.

"Shall I attend you, Senor Captain?" said the
boy.

"Thanks, Jose, we shall not want you. You
need say nothing about our sail unless we're asked
for; then you may say we shall return before daybreak; that we have gone to visit yon island."

"Muy ben, Senor," replied the Spanish youth.

He threw off the rope.

The breeze blowing from land caught the curved
sail, and the light skiff sprung away, scattering the
drops of molten silver before her cleaving prow.

After a fair and pleasant sail they reached the
island.

The Boy Pirate hauled the skiff high up on the
beach.

They visited the signal post which our hero had
erected. They sought the cave within which were
the rude table and settle which he had made. The
walls were carved with many sentences.

"I thought to make them speak to me," he said.

And there, also, were the youthful features of
Lilia, sketched with a masterly touch, for our hero
was essentially a genius and did all things well.

After they had fully inspected the cave, they wandered to the elevated spot on which the young castaway had planted the palmettos.

They were touched with quick emotion upon perceiving the tall, stately trees, which had grown to a
good height, side by side, and blending their fan-like
leaves.

Our hero and his wife stood beneath them, locked
in each other's arms for a few happy moments, and
then returned to the shore.

Christopher was so deeply enthralled by the gentle
talk of his young wife, that he did not notice the
freshening puffs of wind which blew cold and keen
at intervals.

They stood upon the sands. The Boy Pirate had
already advanced to push the skiff off, when, looking
towards the horizon, he started.

A small black cloud was slowly rising from the
bed of the sea.

It looked in the distance like a far, lone peak or
dark mountain.

"You look grave, husband; is there threatening
in the appearance of the sky?"

"Yes, we shall have a tornado," returned the
Boy Pirate.

"Then we had best remain on the island till it is
past; they will send the pinnace to fetch us."

"No; I do not wish to be away from the fleet
when the storm breaks. These omens come very suddenly; there has been no indication of a squall. Well,
it will not come down before the dawn, and we can
reach the shore or steer for the fleet at our leisure."

"I would I were safe either on the island or on
board the 'Avenger,'" said Lilia.

"Courage; your wish will soon be gratified; the
felucca, though not strong as might be, is a swift
sailer, and we shall make this passage in half-an-
hour."

Lilia got into the skiff.

Our hero ran her off and leaped in.

His cheek grew cold as he looked at his beloved
wife, and felt the bouncing tide-waves roll slowly
but ponderously beneath the frail skiff.

He shortened sail.

He grasped the halliard tightly, and sat at the
helm.

Sometimes the skiff forged ahead at a spanking
rate, then she would suddenly stop, and even be
driven backwards as the fitful wind, which seemed to

dart from every quarter in succession, smote her light sail and slender mast.

Slowly and grandly the curtain of cloud rose in the horizon, quenching the bright stars, and palling the clear sky in awful gloom.

They had now reached the middle of the channel.

They had not exchanged a word.

Our hero sat calmly steering.

Lilia remained pale but patient.

Christopher now begun to evince symptoms of intense anxiety.

He raised his hand to his brow with a haggard look.

His worst fears were verified.

In the midst of the channel was a confluence of the tides that ran between the islands.

The power of the waves was terrific.

The little vessel quailed before the massy dash of the billows.

Higher and higher rose the black pall.

Darker and darker grew the night.

Heavier and fiercer dashed the waves against the frail skiff.

"My husband, we are in mortal danger; do not disguise the truth from me," said Lilia, quietly.

"It may be, Lilia, that having ended my course as a pirate, I shall not be permitted to live to better aims," said our hero, moodily. "But I am selfish, darling; death has lain down and has risen up with us, and we must be prepared for his summons; yet, though we are in danger, think for a moment of the great perils through which we have passed scathless, and hope will be stronger than fear. If we can but breast this under-low of the current and get out of its reach before the squall comes, all will be well."

Now the whole disc of the heavens was eclipsed with darkness.

Then the nimble lightning forked and flashed, and ran in lurid stream or blazed in a blue glare.

Then burst the awful thunder. It seemed as if the palaces of heaven had fallen upon their adamantine base with one dread crash. Hurtling, and shrieking, and whirling, lashing the circling pyramids of foam till they rose and writhed, stung to fury, raved along the dreadful White Squall.

It struck the felucca.

Her mast snapped like a reed; her graceful sail was rent like tinder; her timbers crushed like a dried husk.

In a moment the Boy Pirate was in the boiling waves.

But not parted from his constant Lilia.

Suddenly as the squall had struck the little bark, our hero yet had time to spring to his wife's side and bind her to his arm with his sash.

The fearful gale flew on to work fresh destruction.

The sea heaved and rocked behind it.

Our hero seized some drifting spars.

To these he clung.

A barrel was floating near with its lashings.

It touched the rover.

Our hero grasped it.

Wild as the waters raged, dark as the night lowered, he managed to fix the barrel to the spars.

On this rude raft he dragged his wife.

She was quite insensible.

An endless night of darkest horrors!

Morning came at last.

The Boy Pirate was now in the open main.

Still drifting on the spars.

Around spreads the circle of sea and sky.

Lilia remained unconscious.

No hopeful signs appear on either hand.

The islands have disappeared!

No sail dots the glittering main.

Now all is calm.

The morning beams with redoubled splendour.

Still our hero drifts drearily; his lovely bride lies in his arms insensible.

With ineffable anguish he watches her.

Despair takes possession of his heart.

His crews may search the island, and waste the precious hours of a long day.

They may conclude that he has been lost in the gale of the last night.

He is consumed by burning thirst.

But he thinks not of himself.

He shades with his hands the lifeless face of his fair bride from the scorching sun.

He murmurs her name; he seeks to restore her to animation.

He knows not whether she is alive or dead.

His brain reels; he will become frantic with his great agony.

He would be patient but for her, his Lilia, who is perhaps dead, she is so motionless.

He curses himself for his folly in trusting her on their sentimental voyage, alone in the frail felucca.

He abandons himself to speechless despair.

Suddenly he turns his glance to the leeward.

His heart stands still.

He almost faints for joy.

A sail!

He signals with his scarf.

He raves, as if he could be heard.

A smile of scorn lights on his lip at his own eagerness for preservation, but when he looks at Lilia he raves again, more madly than ever.

He has been seen.

It is the pinnace that has been sent in search of him.

A gun is fired.

Soon over the waters came the joyous cheers of his crew.

The pinnace is close beside the raft.

The Boy Pirate takes the hand of his foster-brother, and leaps boldly into the vessel.

Lilia is lifted on board.

The Boy Pirate hangs over her with intense anxiety.

The faithful Ida has volunteered to accompany the men in their search for their chief and chieftainess.

Zealously she applies the readiest restoratives.

Lilia opens her blue eyes languidly, and smiles fondly on her husband.

A look of intense joy brightens the handsome face of the Boy Pirate.

He tries to speak, but his voice fails.

CHAPTER CLXIX.

THE BILLIARD-ROOMS—THE CONFESSIONS OF RICHARD EAGLETON—THE DETECTIVE ON THE WATCH—THE BAR—THE ARREST—THE STRUGGLE—LORD HAWKSBURY STRICKEN DOWN—EAGLETON ESCAPES.

WHEN Eagleton and his friend left Cremorne, the former rushed into a public-house, dragging Mortimer with him.

"Come, come, I talked of going home to rest," he said, "but there is only one bed into which I can sleep now. There, I'll not talk like a death's head; I said I would be jolly, and so I will, in spite of all the fair women that nature ever made minus hearts, for to-morrow I shall be off the shore, and the next day 'far, far upon the sea!'"

They called for brandy.

Eagleton made a wretched though boisterous attempt to appear joyous.

He laughed and sang snatches of songs.

"And, now," he said, after a while, "let's be off to the old drum, and challenge all comers at billiards."

They started off to some large and fashionable billiard-rooms.

It was the same house where the artful scoundrel had induced Charles Rye to imitate his employer's signature.

After playing several games, Mortimer, finding his companion was growing excited, pursuaded him to descend to the coffee-room.

They took their seats in one of the compartments.

Mortimer looked into the box on either side of the one they had chosen.

They were empty.

When he had returned to his seat, however, a man in the next box to theirs raised his head from beneath the table.

Very carefully he rose, and seated himself on the side nearest to them.

"You are better now, you must keep yourself quiet, Dick," said Mortimer.

"Oh, quiet. Yes, I shall soon be quiet enough."

"What do you mean by these hints? You don't say you are quite such a contemptible idiot as to think of killing yourself for such a drab as that?"

"Killing!—what makes you talk of killing?"

"Faith, Dick, you put the notions into my head with a very practical demonstration this evening."

"I wish you had not stayed my arm. Hanged! Pshaw! they should never hang me if I had struck her. Well, perhaps it's best as it is."

"Dick, you're appalling. It's time you left the country, or were detained at Bethlehem during her Majesty's pleasure."

"Yes, I feel mad—raving mad, sometimes; but I'm all right now. Angeline! A blighting curse on her! It's a pretty name, and a man might as well hope to swim on the verge of Niagara without being swept down the falls, as to hope to escape torment if he meets with an enchanting false woman. I won't tell a lie, I have suffered horribly for her; but it's astonishing how suddenly one recovers from such maladies. I'm all right now—all right—quite jolly. I wish you had put some brandy in this coffee."

"You have swallowed enough of that poison, Dick; it only heats the brain."

"Well, perhaps so. I wish there were laudanum in the cup. That opium smoking must be a rare enjoyment. If it shortens life it eases it, and we all commit suicide one way or another—either we work ourselves to death, excite ourselves mortally, drink ourselves, indulge ourselves, or afflict ourselves to death; but, I say, what have you done with the—the dagger?"

"I have it safe."

"Give it me."

"I will give you as much of it as I can trust you with," replied Mortimer.

He slipped the dagger under the table, snapped it across his knee, and presented the handle to his companion.

"What the devil——"

"Do you want with a trenchant blade? Come, Dick, we're not New York rowdies, nor Spanish assassins. If you play with edged tools you will certainly cut your fingers."

"As you please. Well, 'Richard's himself again!' But now let us square up."

"Whist! a minute, I thought I heard some one in the next box; we want no eaves-droppers."

The head had just disappeared beneath the table, when Mortimer peered round the screen.

"How much do I owe you, Jack?"

"Fifty."

"Was it fifty? I thought not so much. Well, we were, in a manner, partners. Here's the soft."

"And did Lord—Tilbury give you a good round sum?"

"A thousand shillings, which is, of course, fifty pounds."

"Humph, that wasn't much of a bonus."

"Oh! but, my dear Jack, I shall get more; that was only down, you know. I shall get more, and I'll act liberally."

"I've always been square with you."

"Dam'me, it's true, Jack," cried the miserable profligate, with sudden vehemence, and stretching out his hand to grasp his companion's. "I've been a double-faced sneak, a most infernal rascal. I'm sorry I compromised Charley, he was a trump. Well,

it's all over now; and that girl, she exacted so much of me. I did my best; but money—money—money. Well, I'm glad I didn't let her know my purse was so well lined. Hark ye, Jack, I'll tell ye the truth, for I've done with all. Your ear, and I'll whisper to you how much he gave me."

He whispered something.

Mortimer sprang up with a stare of surprise.

"Phew! you may well be jolly."

"Jolly! who says I'm not jolly?—

'Midnight shouts and revelry,
    Tipsy dance and joll—i—ty.'

"Huzza! but there's no brandy in the cursed coffee."

"Business first."

Several notes changed hands.

"And about the other affair?" said Mortimer, in a low eager tone, looking nervously round.

"The bills were honoured all right. It's time I was off, it's getting late. I should like to have stayed over the spring meetings; but what the fiends care I for money now? I talk thus only from habit, I'll stick to some of this; but you shall share fair. I'm only drunk enough to tell free truth. I talk not meaningless when I tell you I cared only for the gold for her sake."

"Is it true, Dick; did she tempt you so?"

"Yes, indirectly. Look, Jack, I knew her first when she was turned out of the house where I lodged because she was too poor, through illness, to pay the rent; she was on the square then. I was good to her, aye, and honourable; I brought her round, she got employment in some business, and made a deal of money."

"Humph!"

"Yes, she turned pious—though she dressed like a queen, and was always at plays and operas—she turned pious and looked upon me as one of the ungodly. She would not reject me; I was a mouse this cat liked to play with; she loved the sport too well to kill me quite."

"What a fool you must have been!"

"I was a fool, a bitter fool to myself. I fell ill and lost employment. I suffered fearfully."

"But where was Sylvia?"

"She was dancing at Vienna; I was alone in London."

"And did this Angeline—bright angel—did she consent to meet you?"

"Yes, we had many assignations at dusk, at night; I was too mean-looking to meet her by day. I fancy that she had some little care for me; it is hard to think there was nothing in it but sheer cruelty, though she is but a vain woman. Yes, we met; she saw me sick and striving, and how, think you, she consoled me?"

"Coldly, I'll warrant."

"Coldly, indeed! Reviled me with my lack of perseverance, rated me for my starved looks and shabby coat, and oftentimes would leave me for hours awaiting her in drenching rain, where my very pride, the very dignity of my love, kept me watching. I was true to my troth, and, as I had not strength to break the chain that bound me, I suffered patiently."

"Can a man be such a fool?"

"A man who is passion-ridden is fool enough for the wildest extravagance. Oh, I could tell you—— But let it rest. With my prosperity smiles came again; then she became what she is now; but still I could not resist her fascinations. She urged me to get money; I staked some with which I had been entrusted by old Bullion on the Newmarket; I lost. I forged a cheque to pay back the cash which I had filched before, what remained I staked and lost again. At last a smash was at hand; the sums I had drawn were too heavy for Sylvia to pay, for she herself had lost half her fortune through a luckless speculation, besides it was impossible to refund the money without involving a discovery that it had been first purloined. Some one, then, must suffer. I victimised Charles Rye; and now behold the poetical justice of life. Angeline, whom I loved with romantic fervour, who treated me so basely, is petted and enriched; I am rewarded handsomely for my villany, and yet you wonder that I should growl at a world where all things are awry."

"You have small cause to growl. Let them laugh that win. But, come, let me take you to your lodgings."

"Aye, come home with me. We'll be jolly; and I shall not be alone. If I were lagged, I wonder if they would shut me in alone in my cell. I should go mad. Company is jollity—hic! But you're not steady, Jack; I shay you're not quite steady. There seems a good many more lamps here than usual. But just a nipper of br-randy, and I shall be ash firm ash a rock."

As Mortimer led him hurriedly across the room he began to show stronger symptoms of intoxication.

He tried to walk firmly, and fixed his glaring eyes on the ground. But he reeled a little, and Mortimer had to check him more than once.

A man glided out from the box next to that which they had occupied.

He was a tall, gaunt, stern-faced man, wrapped in a large coat.

He followed them down to the bar.

A number of persons were drinking; among the rest were three who cautiously watched the two clerks.

One of this party was a gentlemanly man, with pure patrician features, and a noble form; the other was a black-haired, sturdy fellow, with a roguishly curled lip, and twinkling black eyes, and a physique decidedly Irish; the third was a pale man, with a thoughtful face, and keen grey eyes.

Our readers will recognise in these portraits, Lord Hawksbury, Oiny Macarne, and Silas Rye.

Eagleton called for a glass of neat brandy.

He drank it off.

He seemed for the time somewhat steadied by the dram.

In spite of the remonstrance of Mortimer, Eagleton bought a bottle of brandy for home consumption.

He held the bottle in his hand.

The pair moved to leave the house.

Before they could reach the door, the man who had followed them from the coffee-room, leaped forward, and shouted,

"Now, gentlemen, lay hands on them both!"

Lord Hawksbury sprang upon Eagleton.

Silas and Oiny secured the amazed Mortimer.

With a glare of drink-madness and innate fierceness, Eagleton drew back.

Grasping the neck of the bottle, he swayed his arm round, and brought it down with a heavy blow, and smashed it on the young noble's temple.

Lord Hawksbury fell on his face.

With a shout of defiance, Eagleton hurled the remains of the bottle at the detective, Falcon, who rushed to seize him.

Bounding over the body of the young nobleman, he darted through the door, and fled.

"It's murther, and not forgery, bad luck to him!" cried Oiny. "Och hone! but he's kilt my lord entirely."

CHAPTER CLXX.

THE BOY PIRATE'S FLEET IN THE BALTIC—DEBORAH ON BOARD THE RAVEN — HER REVERIES DISTURBED—A REFUGEE FROM CRUELTY AND OPPRESSION—PROTECTION FOR THE POLISH PRISONER.

FOR several months our hero has been voyaging.

With great difficulty and terrible danger he has reached the Baltic sea.

Mounting the Brazilian colours on both the steamers, he represents them as the convoy of a number of trading vessels.

It would be long and tedious, and would not afford the reader much entertainment, to narrate the various escapes the Boy Pirate has had, from the effects of the keen scrutiny of maritime authorities.

At last his vessels are safely moored in the Baltic.

They are off Riga Bay.

The greatest excitement prevails among the crew.

The Boy Pirate preserves his calmness; Cassidy seems unmoved as ever, except that there is an under-current of stern delight, that shows through the calm of his placid exterior.

Tom Garrod is as loquacious as ever; Black Ralph as reckless.

It is night.

The clear dark waters of the Baltic mirror the stars.

Deborah the Jewess is located on board the "Raven," Cassidy's vessel.

She is sitting in the state cabin, at work.

The captain and his wife are on board the "Avenger," our hero's flag-ship.

There is a deep silence.

The only sounds are stilly noises that make the quiet seem more profound.

The dull lapping of the passing wave.

The sighing of the night-wind.

The slow and measured tramp of the watch on deck.

Deborah is pondering on her strange destiny.

Years have now passed since she left England on her mission of vengeance.

That mission was now accomplished.

She had seen the blackened ruin of the tower, beneath which, she had been assured, the body of her father's ruthless murderer lay, crushed.

After her escape from the schooner of Black Ralph, she had communicated with her friends in England.

She gave them a brief account of her disasters, how she had been entrapped by the pirates and persecuted by Black Ralph, and finally, how she had escaped from them by the assistance of Sam Cassidy, and requested them to send her supplies from her bankers.

Oakland she had not mentioned in her letters.

She tried to disguise even from herself that the young seaman had made so deep an impression upon her heart.

Oakland himself had never spoken to her of love. He was in his bearing towards her timid and even reserved; but he watched her with tender glances as she swept the deck with queenly march, by the side of the fair Lilia, contrasting with the bright queen of the rovers, in her dark beauty, her heavy tresses of silken black, her large black eyes, her noble profile, her full yet delicate form.

Deborah the Jewess sat dreamily watching the bright stars glittering coldly in the dark sky, pondering upon the past and future, and wondering what spell could bind her to her present strange, wild, and perilous way of life, among a band of lawless men, in hourly anticipation of their defeat and general slaughter.

A head appeared at the window.

She started up, a thrill of terror chilling her blood.

A pistol lay upon a table on one side of the cabin.

She laid her hand upon it.

She turned her head towards the window.

It had been forced open.

A man was clinging there.

So pale and wan he looked that he appeared like one of the drowned from the deep wave, resuscitated by some magic spell.

He was very aged.

Long white hair and a ragged white beard fluttered in the night breeze.

His blue eyes were glazed and fixed, and he seemed half fainting.

His wasted arm scarcely had force to support him.

She ran to his assistance.

She lifted him into the cabin.

He sank on a seat.

The water streamed from his quaking limbs.

He was a wretched object.

His dress was but a *schoub*, or coat of dirty sheep-skin, the wool side outwards.

His legs were bare below the knee.

Around his ankles were two heavy rings, with broken links, that had eaten into his flesh, which was festered, and his feet were blood-smeared.

Deborah saw at a glance that he was an escaped captive.

Had he been the murderer of all her kin she could not have refused to succour him. There was an air of nobility and a trace of refinement yet lingering in his misery-worn features.

He touched his blue lips with his palsied hand, in token that he was too faint to speak.

The Jewess gave him some wine, and spoke to him in a soothing, cheering tone.

He looked wistfully in her face, pointed to his white locks, and then to the remains of his cruel shackles, and smiled grimly.

She spoke to him again.

Tears brimming to her eyes, she sat down at his side, and took his hand in hers.

"No Russ, Ingliss," he said, with a look of pleasure.

She spoke to him in French.

He said a few words in answer.

It was plain that he thoroughly understood the language, but had so long disused his voice that he found it difficult in uttering anything.

"And are you a Russian?" asked Deborah.

"No, Mademoiselle, I am a Pole, of Wilna, taken by the Russians; you will not surrender me?"

"Never; we are bound in an expedition to aid your gallant nation; we are volunteers in the cause of freedom and justice, and we care not who laughs at our enthusiasm; we dare the mightiest who may oppose us with their power, for the Lord of Hosts will fight for us!"

Deborah spoke these words in a tone so thrilling and prophetic one might have supposed that the mantle of her namesake, the great Prophetess of Israel, had fallen upon her.

"Ah, Mademoiselle, restlessness is better than despair; but while selfish powers refuse their aid, Poland is without hope of Freedom!" returned the old man, in a desponding tone.

Cassidy and Mary entered the cabin.

They were greatly surprised at beholding their strange guest.

Deborah explained.

The captain of the "Raven" and his wife testified their sympathy.

They sent for Oakland and old Macallister, who still remained with the pirates.

The old man looked into the rough but kindly faces of the men, and the tearful eyes of the two girls, and gasped his thanks, speaking in French.

He implored them not to deliver him up to the Russians; he said he had escaped from a fortress at Wilna, where he had been confined for years, how many he could not tell, as he had been chained in a solitary dungeon, and had long lost all reckoning of time.

Cassidy at once gave orders that his fetters should be struck off, that he should be carefully tended and clothed, and that immediate information should be sent to the chief captain that an escaped Polish prisoner had found refuge in the "Red Raven."

"And whose vessel is this, Monsieur le Captaine?" asked the old man of Cassidy.

"Your safety is secure while bravery and devotion can defend you," returned the seaman. "You are on board the "Raven," and under the protection of the renowned BOY PIRATE!"

CHAPTER CLXXI.

THE FLIGHT OF MINNA WYOTTI—THE REST IN THE MOUNTAIN DEFILE — MINNA RE-ASSURES HER CAPTIVE—THE ARRIVAL OF THE PAWNEE-LOUPS—MINNA'S AGITATION— A RAMBLE BY THE RIVER—THE RETURN OF THE EAGLE-WING—MINNA'S JOY—ON THE TRACK OF THE BUSH-RANGERS.

AFTER galloping till their horses were nearly exhausted, Minna Wyotti, the trapper, and the Pawnee's captive reached a long chain of high rocky hills.

They drew rein in a mountainous defile, which sloped down to the banks of the Arkansas.

Here they lighted their wood fires.

The detective was lifted from his horse.

They placed him on a heap of heather and leaves, which they covered with their Indian blankets.

Minna sat by his side, her gun resting on her lap.

She was pale and thoughtful.

Heartsick with anxiety, from time to time she would clutch her restless fingers and breathe her husband's name.

Yet she strove to appear cheerful.

The trapper took his rifle, and started off to the prairie, in hopes of killing game.

It was a wildly grand scene.

Minna sat watching lone and thoughtful by the fitful blaze of the red log-fire.

The detective lay motionless and sound asleep on his primitive couch.

The dark hills shot up on either side.

The mighty river plashed on under the silver moonlight, its broad span broken by aits of willow and dark firs.

The tears chased each other down the white, soft cheek of the devoted Minna, as she thought of the sad change in her fortunes.

She thought of the peaceful times at Larchville, and of her handsome, brave, and intelligent husband, an Indian only in romantic beauty and simplicity of character; a civilised man in every other respect.

Now how altered.

Yet, when she thought of his loss, she was nearly frantic with grief, for she loved her wild husband dearly.

Nat Weatherfield soon returned with a brace of heathcocks and a hare.

These they dressed at the fire.

With the biscuit the trapper carried in his pouch, and a draught of water from the spring, warmed by a little fire-water from the precious flask, they made a very fair repast.

The detective was roused, and shared the meal with them.

He seemed much recovered.

He warmly thanked Minna for her kindness, and joined with her in a hearty wish that her husband was safe and would soon return, and declared his willingness to remain with the Pawnees.

Then through the gloom came gliding the dark, tall forms and tufted heads of Indian braves.

Their war-chief advanced to the fire, and held out his hand to the trapper.

Nat Weatherfield grasped it with heartiness, and looked at the fine young brave inquiringly.

"Akantoosh has returned from the war-path," said the Indian. "The Yengeese dogs are fled; the son of Monotah has taken many scalps."

He pointed to his belt, which was reeking with the hideous trophies.

"And where is the Heart of Fire?"

"The Dacotah has gone to the Panther's Pass, to seek for my brother the Eagle-Wing.

"Are there no tidings of my husband?" asked Minna, sorrowfully.

"Wakomini is on his trail. My sister must shut her heart for three suns; the Dacotah will join me at the wigwam of my father, on the Osage river."

RESCUE OF THE COUNTESS.

"I will be patient. Three days! Well, it is near morning, and the sun soon goes down," sighed Minna. "Three days! It seems an endless space to endure this racking anxiety. I wish I had gone myself to the falls."

"I reckon you must take the Pawnee's advice, Minna," said the trapper. "You jest 'shet up your heart' till you can expect to hear news of Catahaga."

"Is Judge Warren killed? Ask him that," said the detective to the trapper.

Nat Weatherfield repeated the question to the Indian in the Iroquois language.

"The Grey Wolf escaped, but the Dacotahs are on his trail," said the young brave.

No. 53.

"I shall leave Minna in the care of the Pawnee, and shall return to my lodge; perhaps the Eagle-Wing has been taken by the White Fox."

"Another Indian?" asked the detective, who could make out the general purport of this speech, though he had not lived long enough among the red-skins to speak their tongue with any fluency.

"No; a captain of bush-rangers, who calls himself Regan, but whose real name is Oswald Lamond, the most treacherous villain under the four corners of Heaven, I guess. Well, if he has killed the Eagle-Wing I shall make it my affair, stranger, for though the Pawnee-Loup did play the devil's own game with his enemies, that was kind o' natural, I guess, and he was as true as steel to his friends and his nation."

"Oh, do not speak of my husband as if he were dead!" said Minna.

"Wal, Minna, in this yere universal world a man may come to grief at any moment unexpected, so you must keep up your sperits."

With this consolatory speech the trapper passed his brandy-flask to the Indians.

He had a little keg of spirits at his belt, and, being glad at the arrival of the Pawnees, felt generously disposed.

The red-skins took the flask, and passed it round with glistening eyes.

They then prepared their supper.

They had killed a roe-buck, which they skinned and cooked at the log fire.

They ravenously devoured huge pieces of the half raw flesh, and then stretched themselves in the heat of the fire to sleep.

Three of them, with young Akantoosh, remained on watch.

Minna looked at the captive.

Once more he had sunk into a profound slumber.

She rose, and, taking up her rifle, walked down the slope of the ravine towards the river.

The watchful Indians looked at her as she passed.

Their paint-smeared features, and their wild black eyes lit up with admiration as the lovely Pale-face moved past them.

She reached the banks.

She stood looking sadly across the wide stream.

The misty distance, the awesome, shadowy, pine-crowned islands; the broad moon, half veiled in a shaggy cloud.

These sights thrilled her soul, and a thousand fearful fancies sprung up in her brain.

She pictured the mangled body of her husband, rotting in the prairie grass, torn by the hovering vultures.

She could have shrieked at the fearful visions imagination conjured.

A canoe swept swiftly to the shore from the veil of silvery mist which hung on the middle of the river.

It ran ashore.

The steersman leaped on shore.

With stately tread he paced along the bank.

His mocassins streaming, his long blanket idly moving, the tall quaillou crest fluttering on his forehead, his long tasselled rifle upon his shoulder.

Minna stepped behind a patch of willow trees.

Her heart leaped wildly with mingled hope and dread.

The Indian paused.

"Waugh!"

His rifle was poised, and the sharp click of the lock drawn back struck on the silence.

Minna sprang from her covert.

She gave a wild cry of joy.

The Indian stretched out his arms.

Minna flung herself into his embrace, and, winding his arms tightly about him, sobbed with delight.

Catahaga, for it was he, pressed her to his heart.

She looked anxiously and fondly in his face to see if he were wounded.

There was a scar on his forehead, but his eye was piercing bright; he showed not weakness except in his voice when, in tones of infantile softness and feminine sweetness, he murmured his endearments.

His wife pressed his arm.

She nestled her head on his shoulder.

With a smile of great happiness she walked close by his side.

When he arrived at the watch fire and stood, slight yet stately, the red blaze glaring on his fine garish form and his picturesque trappings, the Indians sprang up.

They gave vent to their satisfaction with a terrific "Ugh!"

And then stood round like passionless statues, their features quite expressionless, but their eyes sparkling with pleasure.

Akantoosh took his brother's hand.

"The great chief Catahaga is very welcome," he said, "there has been a cloud on our hearts, but the sun rises and the cloud melts away. How did my brother escape the Yengeese adders?"

"By the help of his Manitou," answered the Pawnee, simply.

"Akantoosh has saved his brother's prisoner of the war-path from the fangs of the pale-face dogs."

"It is good! My brother is a great chief," replied Eagle-Wing with a gratified smile.

Nat Weatherfield caught the Indian's hand with a joyous shout.

"Wal, now, thar's a hand, chief, that never gave a false grip, and here's a tongue as never told a lie, 'cept p'raps a little stretcher about a brush with the Shoshoné, or bar hunting—and here's a heart as is tough but true; hand and heart I'm your's, chief, and, if I ain't tarnation glad to see ye, say I'm a 'farnal ranger and no man !"

Catahaga warmly returned the honest grasp of the good-natured trapper.

"Husband, he has been so good to me," murmured Minna.

"Light of my heart, if he were a serpent in my path I would love him for that; but let my brothers listen," he added, quickly, addressing the Indians.

Akantoosh and the rest gathered round him.

"My brothers, the White Fox and his snakes, are fled to the wolf's glen; they have built themselves lodges, and have thrown up entrenchments. Heart of Fire and the Dacotah braves await me beyond the prairie lakes; we will return to our brothers, and strike the war-trail; for my captive, my wife and my white brother will guard him; let us go."

The Indians responded with a yell, and brandished their tomahawks and rifles.

Nat Weatherfield undertook the charge of the prisoner, and two of the Indians were left as an escort.

When morning broke, Catahaga and his wife were once more parted; he was stealing on the trail of his enemies, she journeying to the wigwams of his tribe.

CHAPTER CLXXII.

THE BOY PIRATE AT RIGA—SCENES IN A RUSSIAN CITY—THE INN—THE INN-KEEPER'S CHARMING DAUGHTER—A PLEASANT GOSSIP—ARRIVAL OF THE MILITARY—THE HUNT FOR THE POLISH COUNTESS—A BRUTAL OFFICER—THE BOY PIRATE GETS IN A PASSION—THE PIRATES UNDER ARREST—A FIENDISH MISCREANT—THE LASH—THE BOY PIRATE REVENGES THE COUNTESS.

CASSIDY and his wife had taken care that the Polish refugee should be made as comfortable as possible.

When Oakland arrived on board the "Avenger," he found that our hero had gone on shore with Dick Caffyn and Edward Leighton.

The young American was so charmed with the society of the dashing young buccaneer and his band, that he resolved to remain amongt them, at least, till they had ended their cruise in the Baltic.

The Boy Pirate and his two companions landed at Riga.

The party, all of whom found themselves for the first time in Russia, were much amused by the strangeness of the scene.

The streets were thronged with people of all nations.

The winter was setting in, and they wrapped in furs.

There were officers, naval and military, in their handsome uniforms; sailors of different nations from the ships in the harbour; tradespeople and citizens in their muffling dress and tall hats; moujiks in the schoub, or coat of sheep's-wool, their round caps and heavy wooden shoes or bark sandals; and pretty fresh-complexioned girls in their fur pelisses, and little velvet head tiers, their long fair hair streaming down their shoulders. All were chattering and laughing with great glee, for with all they have to suffer from despotism and misgovernment, the Russians are a lively people.

The Boy Pirate walked boldly into the custom-house.

He had a long interview with the harbour-master.

His papers were accredited.

And having bestowed a judicious present upon the man in office, the bold pirate was free to walk the streets without fear of molestation.

He and his comrades called a drosky, a vehicle which consists of a bench with springs under it and cushions upon it, running on four wheels; the horses tastefully trapped, and adorned with little jingling bells.

The driver, a stout, shaggy-browed, but broad-faced, simple-looking fellow, sat on a low seat just behind the horse, and on a level with the shafts.

He was wrapped in a long coat, had a fur cap with lappets covering his ears and tied under his chin, and on his back a square plate of tin, on which was inscribed his number and the quarter of the city to which he belonged.

The seamen mounted this carriage, and started for a ride round the city.

The drosky dashed off at a furious rate.

It is astonishing at what a reckless pace the public conveyances are allowed to drive, and more astonishing still that so few accidents occur.

The driver made a circuit of the city.

Our hero told the driver to make an excursion into the country.

The man urged on his horses.

In a very short time they were tearing along a bleak and dreary road.

Autumn was far advanced.

The air was piercing cold.

The few trees that skirted the road were red and sear, and dripped with moisture.

They were for the most part birches and gloomy firs.

The driver kept haranguing his horses, sometimes in a tone of reproach, and sometimes in a soothing voice of coaxing, addressing them as his "little mothers," and other odd terms of endearment, in which the Russian language is so copious.

He seemed fully convinced that they understood every word he said.

At last the travellers crossed a wide, barren plain, and finding nothing interesting in the aspect of the country, our hero was about to bid the man turn his steeds, when in the distance appeared a large wooden structure.

The man, being questioned, told our hero in bad French that it was a large inn.

Christopher bade him drive on.

They stopped at the door of the tavern.

The host, a stout, short fellow, with a very sallow face, and bloated appearance, shuffled out.

He saw that they were well dressed, and above all, Englishmen—at least two of them, for our hero was generally mistaken for a Spaniard, his cheek had become pure olive in its hue, and his eyes and hair were raven black.

With great obsequiousness, with profoundest bows, and suavest smiles, the host ushered the party into a large apartment.

It was a great room, built of wood, the walls in some parts covered with dirty, stained, and rotting hangings; round the wall ran a wide seat, before which were tables, and in the centre was an immense square stove, the fire in which was never extinguished, and which was hissing red hot.

Several Russians were playing dice and cards at one of the tables, and drinking "quass," a strong liquor, which is in great demand in their cold climate.

They appeared to be farmers. They were talking with great rapidity, and from time to time joined in hearty laughter.

These guests looked at the new arrivals with much curiosity and deference.

The educated Russians are the best linguists in the world, and even the commonest people in large towns and more civilized districts, speak bad French, and make themselves understood with ease.

Our hero entered into conversation with the Russians, and drank with them.

They appeared simple, good-natured fellows, and fraternized with the English seamen very readily.

A girl of about nineteen years of age entered and prepared a repast at another table.

Our hero crossed the room and chatted with her.

She was extremely pretty; her figure buxom but well-shaped, her complexion pure, her face round, and her eyes bright blue, while her expression was frank and winning. She was very neatly dressed, and wore her yellow hair in long braids, flowing down her back.

She blushed and laughed gaily at our hero's compliments.

She was very confiding, and entertained our hero with much family gossip.

She told him that her name was Catherine, and that she was the daughter of the inn-keeper.

"I am married," she added, with a pleasant smile. "My husband is a moujik—a serf; he belongs to the estate of Count ——" (we will spare our readers his unpronounceable name). "And Ivan is so handsome and good, and I love him so dearly," she added, naïvely. "He is now away in attendance on his lord, who has gone bear-hunting, but I expect him to return in a few days. I long so much to see him."

"He must be very happy," said our hero, smiling.

"Oh yes, indeed he is, and so am I," rejoined the girl, with sparkling eyes. "He brings me such nice presents, for my lord is very generous to him; he loves me so much, is so kind, and beats me only when I vex him."

The Russian wives appear to take in very good part the marital correction their husbands bestow on them pretty liberally, and are even said to despise their partners if they do not administer occasional castigation; many stories are told in proof of this, and there is a proverb in the mouth of every Russian peasant,—

"I beat you as I beat my coat.
I love you as I love my heart."

"But I am sure you never vex your husband," said our hero, smiling at the girl's artlessness.

"Only just to keep his love, you know," she said, archly. "Men so soon get tired of one if they are not teased a little."

Christopher laughed, and the girl tripped lightly away.

She brought some bottles of wine, and our hero invited the farmers to drink with him.

The men seemed much gratified at his attentions, and drank his health cordially.

There was a sudden start amongst them.

The girl shrank, and then walked quickly to the door.

Without sounded the heavy tramp of soldiers.

A file of tall, gaunt fellows marched past the window.

They wore long grey coats and spiked helmets, and shouldered guns with fixed bayonets.

Two mounted officers rode in their rear.

The officers leaped off their horses, and, with clinking spurs and creaking tramp, strode into the room.

To the Boy Pirate's surprise, on turning round he found that the farmers had vanished, and that none but his own party remained in the room.

As soon as the soldiers had passed the window they slunk through a side door, and hid themselves in the stables which adjoined the room.

Catherine was deathly pale, and looked as if she would faint with terror.

The officers were very fine fellows, as to form and feature, but they wore that cold, iron look peculiar to the agents of despotic power.

They stared with some surprise at the Englishmen. They bowed.

With graceful ease and self-possession our noble young hero returned the salute.

The principal officer fixed a stern look upon the girl.

She quailed and trembled.

"The Polish Countess Isidora Zorinski is in this house," he said, in a cold tone; "we have come to arrest her. You have dared to entertain the wife of an insurgent Pole. Speak, on the instant. Where shall we find her?"

"Oh, mercy! I—I know nothing. My father cannot be accountable for our guests. I will bring you to the room that is occupied by a lady who came here last night; she seemed ill, and we gave her a private room. Oh have mercy on us, indeed we are innocent of treason."

"You will be fortunate if you escape punishment," replied the officer, coldly. "Lead the way," he added to the girl.

He turned to his fellow officer.

"We shall catch this cursed woman at last," he said, roughly. "She managed her husband's escape skilfully, but it shall go hard if I do not make her smart for the trouble she has given us."

"You must show some example, to strike terror into the hearts of the disaffected who dare to harbour these rebels. That girl ought to be flogged."

"I will attend to her; but let me catch this pretty countess, and if she does not get a taste of the lash—"

"Lash!" shouted the Boy Pirate, in a tone so fierce, that the brutal Russian started back. "Are you a man and a soldier, and can talk of lashing women—of lashing a heroine, who has devoted herself for her husband?"

"How, sir, do you presume to question my actions? Do you dare to advocate the cause of traitors against his Imperial Majesty the Czar? Ho, there, sergeant! set a guard before this door, and shoot dead any one of these men who attempt to leave this room."

"Sir, I am an Englishman!"

"In Russia," returned the officer, with a sneer.

"In heaven, in earth, in hell, sir, I am not the man to bear this insult tamely," roared the Boy Pirate, in a towering rage, "nor to hear a villain talk of lashing women, and hold my peace."

"Your language, sir, you will answer for anon; but I know you are a Briton, and have your national prejudices. In Russia, sir, submission to the Czar is the whole duty of man, and I would flog my own wife or daughter, I would suffer the lash myself, in the course of duty to my august father."

"You lying craven!" returned our hero, in a tone of bitter contempt. "I see too, by the orders on your honourable breast, that you are a noble. By the Lord! sir, I could hack off your knightly spurs, and make you swallow them!"

"The Englishman is mad!" said the second officer. "If you stay to quarrel, we shall lose this countess. Clap to the door and call the sentry, we will teach these fellows to respect our authority; but one thing at a time."

He drew his companion through the door.

"Captain, you have destroyed us all," said Leighton, gravely.

"Would you have me unsay one word that I said?"

"Dam'me! no," cried Dick, hotly. "I could rave for a week at the very thought that such an infernal dastard should walk in broad day with a star on his breast, and epaulettes on his shoulder. Captain, if ever we did a bold, rash thing let's escape, carry that Prince Croakanstorff aboard the 'Avenger,' and make him valet to Black Zampa."

"Still, I was a fool. If we are to kick and plunge everytime we are galled by such scenes as this, we shall never run our course, or reach the winning goal. A pest on my hot temper."

A trap was opened in the ceiling.

A girl's face appeared.

A ladder was lowered.

Catherine descended.

She threw herself at the feet of the Boy Pirate.

"Oh, sir, all his lost!" she sobbed. "The poor countess is taken, the officers have dragged her off. The captain means to flog her with his own hand—the beast, it gives him pleasure, this cruelty. I am lost, I shall be carried to the police-office, stripped and flogged with willow-rods, or, perhaps, even knouted. I heard them say they would shoot the meddling Englishmen. Oh! what, what is to be done to save us?"

"What is to be done?—but one thing," returned the Boy Pirate, in his sharp and determined manner. "As good to die and go, as die and stay. Will you trust yourself to me?"

"Oh, yes, sir, if I could escape for awhile, the good count, my husband's master, would protect me; but this villain, it is known, takes a vile delight in lashing poor girls on whom he can lay his clutches—cruelty is his pastime. They say his serfs have twice revolted, and that he was reprimanded at court, and you know they are not very merciful there."

"Enough, is there an axe, or a mattock at hand?" said the Boy Pirate, in a cold, clear tone.

Dick Caffyn brought an immense axe from the wall.

"Now, comrades, stand together. We will break through the door, knock down the sentinel, and trust to Providence for our escape. Do not blush, pretty Catherine, if I take you in my arms; rather than you shall be knouted, I will be cut into ten-thousand pieces!"

"Ah, sir, you are brave as that fine man the sailor's talk of—THE BOY PIRATE!"

The reckless outlaws laughed.

Our hero took the girl in his arms.

He grasped a revolver in his right hand.

Dick Caffyn stood close beside him; his drawn sword in one hand, a pistol in the other.

Edward Leighton swung the mighty axe.

The door crashed down.

The sentinel leaped back and made a thrust with his bayonet, while his finger curled on the lock.

Down came Leighton's axe, cleaving his helmet, and splitting his head to the shoulder.

They bounded on.

Two or three men, only, opposed them, the rest were away with the officers.

At these the daring pirates fired, and rushed on.

They had gone some distance and concealed themselves behind a bank.

The soldiers were seen marching along the road, bearing the countess in their arms.

The officer caught the poor lady by the wrist and dragged her away into a little copse of trees.

In his right hand he held a cat-o'-nine-tails, with which he waved them back.

"My jib, captain! Do the cocked hats in this country, do the work of the drummer's and the bo'-swain's mate? Why does he drag her away from the rest?" panted Dick.

"Because," gasped the Boy Pirate, with red cheeks and choking voice, "he means to subject her to a brutal exposure, and to gloat in a devil's feast of carnal cruelty! Look to this girl and yourselves; this fellow shall find the truth of the old proverb, 'the biter gets bit,' on the word of the Boy Pirate!"

"Captain, it is death and destruction—mere madness!" shouted the others.

He was gone.

He skirted the bank and entered the copse unperceived by the soldiers.

He found that the villain had already bound the countess, a beautiful and refined lady, to a tree.

He gripped the whip, and was about to remove some of the clothing of his victim.

With the growl of a springing panther, the Boy Pirate leaped the bush, and fell upon him.

The Red Raven lost all consciousness. He was for the moment, a maniac. Sparks were before his eyes—he knew only that his left hand clasped the collar of the dastardly Russian—that his right wildly wielded the heavy cat-o'-nine-tails, and that he was lashing the miscreant with the fury of a demon.

CHAPTER CLXXIII.

THE RUSSIAN GUARD AWAIT THEIR COMMANDER—THE SWEEP OF THE LASH—A SLIGHT MISTAKE—THE AVENGER'S PUNISHMENT OF A MISCREANT—COUNT BRUTOFF RECOVERS HIS SENSES AND EXERTS HIS COMMON SENSE—THE CAPTIVES ESCAPED.

EXHAUSTED at length, the furious avenger threw down the scourge with which he had inflicted such a merciless chastisement on the miscreant Russian.

He found that the object of his wrath was quite senseless.

The poor countess, with instinctive gentleness of her kindly sex, had thrown herself at the side of the enraged pirate, and implored mercy for the culprit. Christopher heard her not, or if he did, her sweet soft tones were as oil upon fire, exasperating him more terribly against the tyrant.

The countess shrieked with terror.

The file of soldiers were still standing at arms in the road without the covert.

They heard the sweep of the lash.

They smiled faintly at the screams of the lady.

They little guessed what caused her cries.

They knew not that the biter had been bitten, the flogger flogged.

At last the screams died away.

"She has fainted," said the mounted officer to the sergeant, who stood beside his horse.

"My lord has no mercy on the rebels," returned the soldier, smiling grimly.

"Mercy to the enemies of his imperial majesty is treason to his august person," returned the officer.

"And what will become of this mad Englishman and his companions?"

"If I am not deceived in my lord's temper, the Englishman will fare roughly; the knout is not always inflicted in public, and there are some foreigners among the exiles that crowd the roads to Siberia."

"His rashness is appaling!" returned the sergeant, "his bold words makes me shudder; but in his country, men do not use the whip to women."

"No, but their fists sometimes, and if a woman sorely ill treated by her husband, has wifely patience to endure his torments and his worse abuse, till her patience is at last outworn, the husband gets off, and the wife is bound to live with him, to honour and obey, and all the rest of it, because, by her patience after frequent outrages, she has condoned the offence."

"No English jury would give such a verdict."

"Yes, they would, and did in the case of a man, who had already, with a heavy walking stick, thrashed the life out of a weakly boy, and in this free-spoken, woman-loving nation of Britons, who never, never will be slaves, this monster—perhaps, indeed palpably, he was mad—received a high compliment from the judge for his high principles and exalted schemes for making model wives."

"That judge was hen-picked, and did it for spite?"

"I think so."

"Or bribed!"

"No, soothed with a flourish of shawms, the volley of texts and pious ejaculations, he could see in the ruffian no worse character than that of a saintly martyr to domestic rebellion."

"Then England can't be much better than Russia."

"Better! Can you talk such treason? What empire in the world is to be compared with our sublime country, and our paternal government?"

"Our august father is a good parent, he does not 'spare the rod,' either with his sons or daughters," returned the sergeant, grimly.

"All the more reason we should honour him."

"But the prisoner is silent, and we hear nothing of my lord," said the sergeant, starting.

Many minutes had elapsed since the last sound of the falling lash had ceased.

"We will venture to peep through the bushes, sergeant," said the officer, getting down from his saddle.

He passed into the thicket.

He ran back with a yell of horror.

"Stand to your arms!—treason! murder! Count Brutoff lies dead!—the countess has escaped!" shouted the officer, aghast.

There was a general rush into the copse.

A piece of rope still swayed from the trunk of a tree, beneath which, stunned and bleeding, lay the form of the brutal officer.

His epaulettes were torn from his shoulders; his spurs had been hacked off with his own sword, which lay broken by his side; his orders had been rent from his breast, but by a strange caprice of the extraordinary youth, who is the hero of our story, were neatly folded in their ribbons, and laid carefully aside, while in that stony breast from which they had been rent, was laid a paper, on which was scrawled with pencil, this inscription, in French:—

"Not the common hangman, but a deservedly outlawed felon has inflicted this chastisement upon a miscreant. Count Brutoff's degradation is the more complete, and none the less just."

"Who could have done this?" cried the sergeant.

"By St. Nicholas," gasped the officer, "it was the Englishman."

"And who can he be?"

"He calls himself a felon."

"Yes, captain, and deservedly outlawed. Unusual candour in such a villain."

"There is but one man who would be guilty of so daring a crime. Only one who would have perpetrated the outrage in this remarkable manner."

"And who is he?"

"The Red Raven—the Boy Pirate."

"Ha—but, captain, he cannot be in Russia."

"I am not so sure of that. It was reported that he had left the coasts of South America, and was on his way to Europe. Several war-ships have been sent to capture him, but the rascal is certainly invincible."

"But shall we not start in instant pursuit?"

"I fear it will be useless. Let us first return to the inn with our luckless commander."

"Had I not better tear this insolent paper to pieces?"

"Give it to me."

"The innkeeper and his daughter are in the plot."

"If they are it will be the worst for them."

"I tremble to think of the count's vengeance."

The ignoble nobleman was borne in the arms of the soldiers.

He groaned deeply.

They carried him carefully to the inn.

Their rage and horror were great when they found the sentinel lying dead, the house broken open, the innkeeper gone, and the prisoners escaped.

They carried Count Brutoff into the house.

They placed him on a low bed in one of the rooms, and did what they could to restore him to animation.

Meanwhile the soldiers were searching the inn, and scouring the country around it.

When the count had in some measure recovered his senses, he turned heavily, and feebly raising himself on one arm gazed into the face of his companion.

"Has she escaped?" he muttered, hoarsely.

"Yes, my lord; but the men are in pursuit of the tremendous ruffian who attacked you."

"He is the arch-fiend himself."

" In the shape of the Englishman ?"

" Yes, the villain who braved me to the face, whom I put under arrest."

" He will be captured."

" It is well; but I am thinking that we must hush this matter up. I went too far; I was enraged at this woman's audacity and cunning; but her punishment should have been left to the secret police; a man killed, too, and all our prisoners broken away. We must be cautious how we make up our dispatches; but how came I thus? My epaulettes are gone, my star of St. Michael, my sword; what does it mean? The villain was a thief, and has robbed me as well as beaten me almost to death."

" Not a thief, my lord; the extraordinary rascal has taken nothing. He had even spared the diamond clasp of your ribbon; but he left, pinned on your breast, an insolent inscription, which I dare not show you."

" Let me see it."

The officer shrugged his shoulders, laughed, and presented the paper.

The count burst into a torrent of oaths.

Exhausted with fury, and groaning with pain, he sank back on the pillow.

The sergeant returned.

They had scoured the country round for many a mile, and had sent messengers into the city. A droska had been seen driving rapidly towards the port; but no certain intelligence had been gained of the direction taken by the English pirates.

___

CHAPTER CLXXIV.

THE DROSKA—THE FLIGHT—A HOT PURSUIT—
THE DROSKA OVERTURNED — THE BOY
PIRATE'S MISHAP—SAVED BY HIS FOSTER-
BROTHER—A DESPERATE BATTLE—A CART
LOAD OF CUTLASSES—A WILD DRIVE.

OUR hero and his men carried the unfortunate Polish lady to the road.

The droska which had lingered behind the trees, the driver not having received his fare, now dashed up.

The man's face was pale with alarm.

The Boy Pirate spoke a few words of encouragement, and slipped some gold pieces into his hand.

• The vehicle was somewhat crowded, the horses, too, were jaded.

Christopher urged the man to drive fast.

They were now within sight of the city.

The driver exhorted his horses to display their power and speed to the illustrious foreigners, and cheered them on with many droll words of encouragement.

All at once the countess gave a cry.

The pirates looked behind them.

A number of soldiers were seen running down the road in wild pursuit.

The officer was mounted, the sergeant and two or three of the men were also riding some rough pads which they had taken from the innkeeper's stables.

They hallooed to the fugitives to stop, and threatened them with their guns and pistols.

The driver of the droska, either by accident or design, threw over the droska.

The Boy Pirate was thrown out, and striking his head against a mass of stone in the bank, lay motionless, as if stunned by the blow.

At the instant of the oversetting of the droska one of the mounted soldiers had fired.

The driver ran to meet the advancing prisoners.

He threw himself on his knees, grovelling and yelling for mercy.

The officer buffeted him with his fist, and the soldiers seized and bound him.

Then a rush was made at the Englishmen.

Their case seemed desperate indeed.

Their gallant young leader was struck down.

The barrels of a file of soldiers were levelled at their heads.

Quick as thought Leighton had fired at the officer's horse.

The animal staggered and fell.

The Russian rolled out of the saddle.

Dick Caffyn leaped upon him, and presenting the pistol at his head, defied the soldiers to draw their triggers, swearing, at the first hostile movement, to shoot him dead.

A large carriage came dashing along the road.

The driver, who was closely muffled in a large fur cloak, did not seem to be a very skilful charioteer.

The horses dashed from one side of the road to the other.

No one appeared in the carriage—it seemed to be packed with goods covered by a large bearskin.

The sergeant hallooed for the driver to halt in the midst of the road.

The order was obeyed.

To the dismay of the soldiers and the delight of the seamen, a hearty hurrah uttered by English throats was heard from beneath the bearskin.

A number of fierce, well-armed outlaws leaped from the carriage.

Throwing off his robe of skins, the driver disclosed himself as a thorough specimen of the British tar. In one hand he brandished a cutlass, in the other a large pistol.

He was no less a personage than the great recounter of " weracities "—Tom Garrod, the boatswain of the " Raven."

Then from the carriage leaped in succession the blustering Ralph, the jovial Zampa, grave Cassidy, dark, stern-eyed Gomez, and half a dozen others, leal fellows of our hero's band.

Dick held the lifeless form of his foster-brother in his arms.

He fired at the officer. The officer returned the shot. He had scrambled to his knees.

The bullet whizzed past Dick's cheek, but did no harm.

The officer seized the lady. She fainted with terror.

The sergeant came to his assistance.

The lady was lifted on to a horse.

A mounted soldier clasped her in his arms, another rode by him. The pair dashed off.

The pirates were fain to leap on one side into the hedge as the soldiers discharged their muskets.

Sam Cassidy and Gomez both received wounds.

A hot skirmish ensued.

The pirates crowded into the droska, carrying our hero with them.

They fired point blank at the soldiers. Two fell.

The pirates lashed the mettlesome horses, and sped along like the wind.

There now remained but two mounted men of the Russian party, and pursuit was therefore useless.

Darkness fell before they reached the city.

The pirates betook themselves to their ships.

Our hero, recovered from the effects of his fall, declared he would not leave Riga till he made some effort to rescue the countess.

Black Ralph still remained with Zampa and Cassidy in the city, in spite of the fearful risk which they ran; but fear was unknown in the band of the Avengers!

___

CHAPTER CLXXV.

THE ROVERS AT THE TAVERN—CASSIDY'S FORE-
BODINGS—BLACK RALPH MORALISES—THE
MORAL OF THE BOY PIRATE'S LIFE—BLACK
RALPH LOSES SIGHT OF HIS COMRADES—
THE RUSSIAN GUARD—THE FAIR CAPTIVE—
THE VULTURE'S SWOOP—BIG WORDS AND
BOLD DEEDS—BLACK RALPH RESCUES THE
COUNTESS.

THE rovers who remained on shore were seated together in a small tavern at one of the most secluded quarters of the town.

They appeared rather anxious and depressed, and for some time drank their wine in silence.

At every sound without they turned their eyes suspiciously towards the door, and grasped their weapons.

"And what became of the innkeeper's daughter, Captain Ralph?" asked Cassidy.

"She escaped," returned the other, She hid herself in the wood, and made her way to a place where the road winds through an avenue of firs. Here she caught the droska and implored our protection. As it is the duty of the brave to protect the fair, and the little artless creature is the most winsome of the children of nature, we complied with her request. I am going to write her a sonnet, in which I shall call her 'Ursina,' after the Polar Bear, beneath whose chaste rays this Diana—this Lucretia of the North——"

"Avast! Captain Ralph; confound it, keep to the point."

"O most stoical Cassidy, has this frigid climate congealed your veins to icicles? or are you in wholesome dread of bonnie Mistress Mary's Highland 'burr?' I tell you, sir, this little Catherine is worthy to be the Czarina of Muscovy. A Muscovy duck she is, in truth! I offered to kiss her; the little huzzy screamed like a parroquet. I apologised, in the gallant manner peculiarly my own; she said she never could keep a secret from her husband, and that, if she told him, he would beat her. And when I threatened to annihilate the Scythian Quilp, she fell to praising him and abusing me in a style that would have brought down the house at the Royal Vic. I was quite vanquished."

"You are not lucky with the ladies, Ralph."

"No, since I kept such confounded low company. I am become brutified, barbarised," went on the rollicking rover, stroking his sleek black beard, "but if that mate of yours—Oakland—dares to marry Deborah the Jewess, there will be performed the tragedy of Black Ralph's Revenge, in which I shall take the leading business, and it will prove a black business to both. Shiver my figure-head (though it's a pretty one)! I've been jilted on three consecutive occasions during a twelvemonth!"

"I am afraid, Captain Ralph, that Fortune has jilted us all. Our new enterprise is fraught with fearful danger."

"Danger without profit, but the king wills it, and Captain Kit won't be gainsaid."

"It's little good that we can do for the poor Poles, I fear," added Cassidy, rather moodily.

"We will show them how Britons can run upon instinct; yet, jemini! the larruping our great Alcides bestowed upon that Russian bear, my bones ache to think on't. Old Grizzly will scarce dance so gracefully as he was wont. I should think he has not a beam in his hull unshivered. But what does the captain intend? Surely he is not going to cruise in the Baltic, in the face of the Czar's fleet! Is the 'Red Raven,' poor crow, a match for the 'Black Eagle,' royal bird, with two necks and beaks? Well, of all mad matches——!"

"You will see nothing will make the captain relinquish his enterprise; he will go on."

"Till he gets to the end of the plank, or the last inch of his halter. This is being 'thieves of mercy' with a vengeance; but while we are at Rome, we must do as the Romans, which means we must drink sperm oil, and whop our female relations; but, curse it! I am not a Roman yet. If I had found that brute flogging the pretty countess, do you think I would have left him with a spark of life in his ugly carcase? Away with such philanthropy, I say."

"The Raven inflicted a fearful punishment, nevertheless, Captain Ralph."

"What would you do to these women-flayers, Uncle Zamp?"

"Dunno, cap'en, 'spects I'd make him fall in lub wid some gal, and then set his wife at him. Lor, sar, I tell yo, men is berry good sometimes. Look at dat buckra, Captain Kit; there's a Nero."

"A what, Zamp?"

"A Nero, sar; a parfec' Nero!"

"A hero, you lubber!"

"Lubber yoself, sar; well, sar, men is good, but, laws! what women will do when they takes it into their heads, and their sufferin's; it's awful to tink on it, they'se so good; but when they is wicious! There was a planter's wife down Old Virginny, sar, and her husband get in lub wid a quadroon gal; wall, wife catch de gal, whip her a'most to deff, and how tink she bring her to life?"

"How?"

"Poured wit'rol on her, sar. Man would flog de yaller gal to deff, sar, lick all de life quite out ob her, but he not tink of de wit'rol."

"And is human nature so vile?" said Cassidy, with a shudder.

"Old Ebony's story is a fact," returned Black Ralph, his eyes glooming. "The great Catherine of Russia made it a pastime to set one slave to whip another most cruelly, for sport, sir, for sport. When I was a boy, I served under a bullying tyrant of a schoolmaster. I have seen that wretch walk into a room full of quailing children, with a thunderous frown, and lash about him with his cane, as if the exercise afforded him an exquisite pleasure."

"The angels must be very unhappy; they must find cause enough to weep," murmured Cassidy.

"Yes," said Black Ralph, tossing off a tumbler of wine. "Now, I could never see the fun of cruelty; I'm a rover—well and good. If I take a prize and can't ship off the hands, I must follow the example of many generals whose fame is spotless, I must cut off my incumbrances. But if they take me, if I walk the plank, or stand under the leafless tree, do I grumble, bully Rook?—not I. 'All's fair in war,' but these northerners are half barbarians."

"And we're a fine set of missionaries, vultures and ravens forsooth!" cried Cassidy, laughing bitterly.

"And a finer set of moralizers than the Boy Pirate's band, find if you can."

"Demoralizers, Ralph."

"That be hanged! If the tempting fiend must sometimes assume the form of an angel, it is sometimes needful for the reformer to guise himself in the garb most pleasing to those he deals with. If you sent me as missionary to the Fejees (a mission to which I have a special vocation), do you think I'd wear a long black coat cut to fit a lamp post, with an insipid white tie, a pair of tight black nethers, and a broad-brimmed hat? Not I, I'd assume their fetishes. I'd offer on their altars, and then, having authority, I'd show them the worthlessness and humbug of their institutions."

"They would be more disposed to listen to you."

"'It's a Temperance Tract,' says Boozy, and straightway lights his pipe with it. I knew an honest fellow, and this is a fact—I would I had time to devote myself to literature, though I don't say that to cause a commotion among Poet Laureate's and sensation stars; but if I had time I would write an ode to his memory—this man, comrade, would go into a flaming gin palace, and would fasten himself like a leech on his man, some wretched married sot; he left the bachelors to their own discretion. He would entertain him as few others could. He was the jolliest company, and while his man was getting drunk, he himself would drink nothing but spruce and lemonade. The man would feel abashed at the self-denial of this practical missionary, and would sometimes try to shake him off; but it wouldn't do, the fellow's society was so bewitching. Well, after awhile, he would entice his man home to his own pretty place, and when he had stroked the cat, whistled to the bird, kissed his wife, and exhibited a prize baby, 'Boozy,' says he, ' my home's humble, but it's pleasant and happy, isn't it? Lor, while I drank I lived in a hovel, my wife was a poor creature always in sickness and poverty—little Will died—but see what a change.' ' Yes,' grumbles Boozy, ' but spruce and lemonade cost as much as beer, and more too.' ' But, then, you know, Boozy, we can't talk in the streets, and coffee-shops, if more quiet, are rather dull.'

If I were at the head of the Temperance League, I'd set 'em all ablaze with gilt and gas jets, and have a concert and a comic singer, and even a drama of the Black Pirates, but what I'd bring in my men—but don't think I care much for spruce! Only I like your company (Boozy hadn't much to say for himself, and was a surly chap on most occasions), and if you'll come and smoke a pipe under my fig-tree, we'll have a prime cup of something hot (he didn't venture to say coffee), and I'll tell you how Bill Betterboys gets on, that used to get mad drunk before his accident with his wife—who has made it up, and they're quite sweethearts again. Confound that fellow, he's making a fortune—cut me out entirely—but two of a trade, you know—and so he would physic the jam for his patients.'"

"But what good could arise from the study of such records as the life of Daniel Harwolf?"

"His darkest deeds are not chronicled, and the worst that may be read are light indeed to the atrocities and blasphemies found in the lives of pirates. Besides, would the young and romantic be attracted by such a character? Are they not rather repelled and disgusted at the ugliness of vice? No; its the sentimental, dashing robber that does the mischief, your fellow with every virtue but common honesty."

"And such a one is the Boy Pirate!"

"Avast; did you ever see him alone? did you ever see his dark face with its look of speechless regret and hidden anguish? did you never note the blush on his cheek, and the sad gleam in his eye in the midst of his most brilliant triumphs? He is high-souled and noble-hearted; but what would a long chronicle of the life of a black villain be? and is there no moral in his restlessness and despair? Besides, he is now atoning for the past—he is now the avenger of a poor friendly people."

"If you hadn't a command we would make you ship's chaplain, Ralph," laughed Cassidy. "But what of yourself now?"

"Oh, I'm the best fellow amongst ye, a wild dog, but a jolly one, a beacon to show that the Blackest Ralphs have a brighter side, and to roar in the ears of the poor readers who are nodding themselves to sleep over your prosy histories. But for OUR HERO—OUR BOY! I won't hear any treason spoken of him. If he wasn't a pirate or a highwayman, a bandit of some sort to do desperate deeds, no one would read about him. He can't help the conditions of his sheer existence, and, on the whole, has borne his dark honours meekly. I'll hear nothing against him, I'm his firm ally—

'Hannibal!
With Hannibal I cleft yon Alpine rocks,
With Hannibal choked Thrasymene with slaughter;
But, oh, the raging night of Cannæ's field,
When half the Roman senate lay in blood,
And groaned without our huts while we caroused!
Another such a night, immortal gods!
Then throw my carcase to the dogs of Rome!'

Ha, Zamp, isn't *that* fine palaver?"

"Reg'lar screaming; most as good as dat niggar's ole uncle Cicero, what got dat poor darkie Cataline sich a awful licking' down de Ole Dominion. Yah, dat nigga had a woice most as good as any lion."

"And now, hearties, you're for sea, heave-a-head, and, having paid the reckoning, I'll follow you," said Black Ralph.

Zamp and Cassidy left the inn.

Black Ralph lingered for a moment, and paid the score.

When he emerged from the low door of the tavern, he looked in vain for his companions.

The house stood in the centre of a circle, round which there were many streets diverging.

He knew not by which of these he had come.

He resolved, however, to make his way to the harbour, and knew in which direction it lay.

It was dusk, but the streets were thronged.

Ralph Talbot threw his cloak over his shoulder, concealing part of his face.

He drew his hat over his brows.

He had no wish to be scrutinised, and was not very well pleased at having lost sight of his companions.

As he passed along a low wall, he heard the measured tramp of feet.

He drew back into the shadow.

A file of soldiers were conducting a prisoner to the police-office.

The captive was a lady.

Her eyes bent on the ground, her face deadly pale, her hands bound, she walked sadly along, knowing the shameful fate that awaited her.

This was too much for the daring Black Ralph.

He drew his sword.

With a torrent of ribaldry, which he uttered in a tone of thunder, he leapt from his hiding-place.

The soldiers, amazed by this sudden assault, broke their rank.

The pirate spoke to the lady in French, swearing that he would defend her from all the armies of the Russian empire; threw his strong arm round her waist, and placing his back against the wall, waved his sword among their presented bayonets.

As he appeared to have no chance of escape, the men were loth to fire.

"Oh! sir, do not attempt my rescue. You cannot save me, gallant Englishman. Do not throw away your life to no end! Oh! fight your way through, and fly!" gasped the poor lady, who was no other than the Countess Zorinski herself.

"Madam, your words inspire me with the strength of Ajax! Now then, you blubber-swilling, woman-beating bruins, brush! I am about to charge! Look out for your moon-faces, you Chams of Tartary! I am Black Ralph, the rover!"

With a desperate rush, the reckless outlaw slashed his way through them, and leaping across the narrow street, darted under a dark archway.

The officer swore at the soldiers, and used his cane freely.

One had fired.

The only effect of his shot was the breaking of several panes of glass in a neighbouring window, and the provoking of a general peal of shrieks from all the female inhabitants in the street.

However, the file was soon marshalled once more, and dashed after the rover.

Midway down the dark and narrow lane, the reckless rover paused. His left arm still encircled the waist of the trembling lady; his right held a pistol, while his sword swung from his wrist.

The ranting Ralph was whistling in a low tone the overture to "Lodoiska."

The lady looked up into his dark, manly face, and, despite her terror, could not repress a smile.

She lowered her eyes. There was a depth of fierce and ungovernable passion under that frank look, a world of cunning lurked in the lines of those sensual lips; but the great black eyes, though wild, and fiercely glaring, shone with a magnanimity and kindly impulsiveness which contrasted so strangely with the dark shades of his desperate character.

"You seem to know no sense of fear," murmured the countess.

"I fear nothing, madam, but the power of your irresistible charms," returned Black Ralph, with a profound bow.

"Oh, they are coming! There is no outlet at the end of this street! What is to be done? Can we find no refuge?"

"Aye, that we will, fair lady, though the walls be of adamant, and these doors of brass."

"Oh, do not make such a noise."

"Madam, I am dumb, my voice is in my sword."

With this he rushed up the steps of a house.

The door was partly open.

He led the trembling countess into the house just as the soldiers rushed past.

EAGLETON COMMITS SUICIDE.

CHAPTER CLXXVI.

BLACK RALPH AND THE COUNTESS TAKE RE-
FUGE IN A STRANGE HOUSE—A SCENE OF
RUIN—PROSCRIBED POLES—A MOURNFUL
STORY—A BROTHER'S SHROUD—A FATHER'S
DEATH BED.

THEY found the house dark and silent.

They moved along a wide and creaking wooden
corridor.

Black Ralph took care to lock and bar the outer
door from within.

They entered a large room, the door of which was
open.

The grey twilight streamed in through the broken
panes of a large embrasured window; they dimly
showed a scene of ruin.

No. 54.

The floor was strewn with broken furniture.

To all appearance, some desperate struggle had
taken place.

They looked about them with much surprise.

The countess clung to her protector's arm, and
shuddered as the glittering bayonets of the soldiers
flashed past the window. The guard, however, went
past without knocking at the door.

Black Ralph and the countess left the room.

They passed up the staircase.

They reached the first flight.

The strange house seemed quite deserted.

They looked at each other in great surprise.

It was now almost dark, and in the sombre passages the black shadows assumed weird and grotesque
forms.

A noise was heard without.

The soldiers were searching some of the houses.

The countess and her defender still remained breathless, listening on the staircase.

The sounds without at length died off.

They were about to ascend a higher flight of the steps.

Like a star twinkling in a murky sky, a light appeared above.

A fair-haired girl, her hair glanced brightly in the struggling light, leaned over the oaken balustrade.

She saw the form of Black Ralph—his fierce face, black beard, long cloak and murderous pistol.

She gave a scream.

The ready-witted countess sprang up the stairs and kneeling down, extended her arms as if imploring protection.

The girl, who now appeared, dressed in white, with a shawl thrown loosely round her shoulders, held the lamp aloft, and drew near the countess.

She knew by the costume which the fugitive lady wore, that she was a Pole.

"Oh, heavens! you are Polish; you are fleeing from the police. Are you pursued? Oh, my poor father, if he should be discovered," cried the girl, violently trembling.

"And you are my country-woman! Oh, you will protect me! I was being dragged to the police office, when a brave Englishman rescued me, he snatched me from a guard of soldiers."

"The police office! Oh, the shame and horror there! I have suffered there; but, oh, what ruin at home. This insurrection—what madness! This hope—what despair! But how many were the Englishmen? Did they get up a brawl, and snatch you away in the tumult?"

"No, no, there was but one, a stern, forbidding-looking man—but so brave. It seems a dream. He rushed into the midst of the soldiers, tore me from their grasp, beat down their pointed bayonets, and I am here."

"I heard them in the street; I thought we had been discovered; but surely Heaven will have mercy now, we have been so cruelly chastened."

"What place is this? Are you hiding too?" asked the countess.

"Our own home, our ruined home!" cried the girl, bursting into bitter sobbing. "My father was a rich Polish goldsmith, in league with the National Government of our unhappy country. We were discovered. My brother Thaddeus madly resisted, he was shot dead in the room below; we, that is myself and an old servant, carried my aged father from his sick bed, and concealed him in a secret strong room, where the ingots were kept. He is still there; dying, alas! He knows not that Thaddeus is dead; we dare not tell him."

"And are you permitted to remain here?"

"No, no, no! Did you not see the seal upon the door?"

"It was half open; besides, it was dark, and we heeded nothing."

"I was carried to the police office, whipped with rods and banished. But I am hiding here with my father."

"And will they not think of us, those great powers? will they not remember that frail women are lashed?"

"They will not believe it, though they know that the knout and stick are the dispensers of justice here, and that political offenders are looked upon as the worst of criminals. It is not for their interest to believe it. Russians are nether Hindoos, Maoris, nor Japanese, and the great selfish powers would have all to lose and naught to gain in succouring us poor and defenceless people. But where is the good, brave Englishman who saved you?"

Black Ralph drew near, and bowed in the most gallant manner.

He addressed the girl in French.

She answered him, blushing.

"I wish, sir, we could give you a better welcome," she said in a quivering voice, "but you will stay and drink a cup of wine, and partake of some refreshment, the best that our misery affords is yours."

The rover thanked the girl in a becoming manner, and she led the way up the stairs.

They passed into a large empty room. She lifted a sliding panel.

Before they entered the secret passage the countess warmly embraced the young hostess.

"And now let us exchange names, my sister in sorrow; I'm the Countess Isadore Zorinski."

"And I, Christine Lenska; my father knew your husband, my lord the count."

"My husband is not dead; I have saved him," returned the countess.

"Come softly, my father sleeps," said the girl, holding up her finger.

She led them into a small apartment crowded with many articles of costly furniture.

"We have saved some spoils from the wreck," said the poor girl, with tearful eyes. "Hush! my father is there; our old and faithful Melchior is watching him."

She pointed to an arch circled with a curtain.

The girl then bade them be seated, and placed wine on the table.

She then removed some work from a small inlaid table at one side of the room.

The countess turned very pale, and put back her rich tresses with a heavy sigh, as she looked upon the long white robe which the girl threw over her arm as she stepped across the room to place it in a press.

The girl caught the look.

She said, simply, but in a low and agitated voice, "It is my brother's shroud!"

A dark scowl swept over the pirate's face.

He thought of his ruthless deeds on the high seas, and a pang of bitter remorse struck his wild heart.

A moan was heard from within the curtained alcove.

"Is that Thaddeus?" asked a feeble voice.

"Not yet, dear master."

"Ah, he is with Langewicz, with the army of Poland! May his arms prosper! Have you heard any news of him, Melchior?"

"No, master, as yet we hear nothing."

"Why did he not take leave of me? He will be killed on the field, or murdered on the scaffold. Could he not so much as bid me farewell? But I am old, and they neglect me, these children."

"Say not that, master; your daughter——"

"Is not here to give me a cup of wine when I wake from my fevered sleep. Where is Christine?"

The daughter quickly rose.

She passed through the curtain.

An old and white-haired man stepped from the alcove into the room.

He bowed respectfully, and seated himself near the entrance of the little bed-chamber.

He looked at the countess, shading his eyes with his hand.

"You know me, Melchior; you served the count, my father?" said the lady, in a whisper, sweeping across the room, and seating herself quietly at his side.

The old man rose, and bowed reverently, and then kissed the lady's hand.

"And, my lord, your husband?" he asked, doubtingly, as he looked into her face. "Has the count fallen?"

"No, no."

"Siberia?"

"I trust, I hope, he is still free! I was so happy as to be able to rescue him from the Russians. This is a horrible affair, your young master murdered on his own hearth!"

The old man sighed, and looked wistfully at the shroud.

"His body will be given up to the Poles of Riga. We have a friend at the police office, a spy of Langewicz. He cannot do all; but this is much, Thaddeus will sleep in the grave of his fathers. My old master, I fear, will soon be placed at his side."

Christine at this moment rushed into the room.
She threw herself on her knees, sobbing bitterly.
"Oh, my father, he is dying!" she cried.
The countess, Melchoir and Talbot rose together.
The girl beckoned them.
She drew aside the curtain.
A bed was disclosed on which lay an aged man, struggling in the agonies of death.
They ranged themselves around him.
The countess knelt, and taking from her side a rosary of ivory beads began telling them, praying with deep fervour.
Black Ralph and Melchior raised the sufferer, while Christine moistened his seared lips with wine and water.
He talked deliriously, and gasped for breath.
The old man sank back on the pillow.
He clutched at the coverlit, opened his fainting eyes, and spread his hands to touch his daughter.
She threw herself upon his breast.
"Christine, my child, do not break your heart for me. Where is Melchior? Cherish him in this faithless world; I have found him faithful. I have left all to your brother and yourself; give my blessing to Thaddeus; if he had been here, but no murmurs—ha, he comes! His step, so light, so free; my own brave boy, come quickly—oh, come quickly; I cannot see, I cannot hear; I am dying fast, but 'tis he—there—there—why does he not speak? Nearer, dearest, do not leave me—Thaddeus—my children!"
The old man struggled to raise himself in the bed.
He fell heavily back, his lips fluttered.
There was deep silence.
Melchior and the two women were on their knees, weeping and praying.
The vision of a blazing ship, the sounds of slaughter, oaths, curses, and shrieks, rang in the ears of Black Ralph; the mortal pang of the death-shot rived his heart, as he thought of his own death-hour; he looked upon the loving child and faithful servant of the dying patriot with dimmed eyes.
The last struggling spark of life flickered out; a hallowed smile lit the old man's features; its brightness fled, but its impress remained on the rigid, white face.
Sorrow and suffering were over, the calm of death had succeeded the storms of life—Christine, the exile, was fatherless.

CHAPTER CLXXVII.

THE SEQUEL OF COUNT BRUTOFF'S MISADVENTURE—THE BOY PIRATE VISITS BLACK RALPH—AN ARDENT LOVER—THE COUNTESS AND CHRISTINE CONFIDE THEMSELVES TO THE ROVER—THE BOY PIRATE AND HIS FRIEND IN OFFICE.

OUR hero made all haste to leave the port of Riga.
By sending Gomez and his Spaniards ashore with messages to certain merchants with whom he had dealings by means of his false papers, the man in office to whom he had acted so liberally had his suspicions that our hero was in some way connected with the late disgrace of Count Brutoff and his troop.
The officers had been tried by court-martial; they had made the best of the affair, greatly exaggerating the number of their assailants and not stating that they were seamen, for they had no wish to be confronted with the fiery Boy Pirate, of whose scornful reproaches they had a wholesome dread.
The sergeant swore that the men who had robbed them of their prisoner were Poles in disguise; they made much of the valour which they had displayed in the recapture of the countess, and they could not be held responsible for the negligence of the police,

into whose hands the countess had been committed, prior to her rescue by Black Ralph.
Count Brutoff, being acquitted, was sent at the head of a regiment of Cossacks to Cracow to repress the insurrection of the Poles in that city.
Black Ralph received our hero on board his vessel after the latter had had an interview with the man in office.
"We must weigh anchor without delay, comrade," said the Boy Pirate, smiling; "my friend ashore is getting nervous; he will not, faith, he dare not, protect us any longer."
Black Ralph laughed, and struck up, in his ranting style,

"'And the provost, douce mon,
Says he, "e'en let it be,
The port is well rid o' this de'il o' the sea!"'"

"And your galleys, brave vi-king; what will you do with 'em?" asked the ex-tragedian. "Shakespeare gives us a sea in Bohemia, but your confounded maps won't show us one port in Poland. What will you do?"
"I've arranged it all, Ralph, and I've come aboard to ask you if you mean to remain with the fleet, or whether you will stick to your good resolutions?"
"Aye, though they pave the way to a certain place they are said to macadamise. I'm with you, brother in arms, to fight for pretty Lodoiska—Miss Poland. Captain Kit, were you ever in love?"
"Do you know Lilia, and can you ask?"
"Well, I've been in love myself, over head, but now I'm forty fathom down, never to rise again!"
"And into what sea of stormy passion have you fallen?"
"In love, I tell you; I am deep down in the blue depths of Christine's azure eyes. You have not yet seen her, captain? Blind, blind! you have not yet beheld a complete woman, she is the only perfect specimen."
"Thanks, for Lilia!"
"Oh, other men's wives, you know, always excepted; this girl is truly divine."
"Indeed, I must see her. What is she like?"
"Like! herself, and so beyond comparison."
"Fair or dark; short or tall?"
"Well, she has the perfection of every type of beauty, the grace of every stature; she is a Pandora where every goddess sets her seal to give the world assurance of a woman."
"But business, man. I have arranged that Gomez is to be left in command of the sailors. It's an ill wind that blows no one good, and an ill wind, a nor-wester, has wrecked two large merchantmen off Faro; I mean to steam up the Oder in some disguise."
"But the good your ill-wind has blown, senor capitano?"
"Two crews of good seamen who are willing to enter their names in the Spaniard's ships' books."
"What, for fair trading?"
"Aye! I'm the Boy Pirate while I live, but for all that I'm a pirate no longer."
"Your tether will be the shorter."
"Give me what length of rope you will, I don't mean to hang myself. I mean to fight for the Poles and there is no knowing but success may await me."
"Humph!"
"Once more, do you mean to give up piracy?"
"It's understood, captain, you've washed the blackamoor; I'm Black Ralph only in name, in intent I'm lily-white, without and within, all but my liver, and lily-livered these bruins will not find me; though, if I discover that Christine is in love with some sentimental Thaddeus of Warsaw, I'll not let fall my blade on any more crests, vulnerable or otherwise; I will make a black cassock of my black flag, and live merely monastic."
"And I will visit you in your cell."
"Cell! Phew! that word is condemned—it smells of Newgate; but a jolly monk leads a brave life, and

hears many pretty confessions from many pretty lips, for—

' It was a friar of orders grey
  Walked forth to tell his beads,
  And he met with a maiden fair,
  All clad in a palmer's weeds.'

"Sweet hearts ! Could I ever deny them absolution ? No, by St. Valentine !"

"Then, thus it is settled : you will accompany me, Gomez will command the flotilla."

"And are you in communication with the insurgents ?"

"Yes, through the agency of the poor fellow who took refuge in the ' Raven.' He has written to some of the chiefs, and we shall be received with open arms."

"And to whom do you intend to offer your sword ?"

"To a fine old warrior—a Count Josika. Well, Dick, what news ?"

Caffyn had come over from the side while our hero was speaking."

"Captain, the Countess Zorinski is aboard ; the innkeeper's daughter has been filched away by Ivan, her husband, and news has arrived that the Polish count has reached in safety the insurgents' camp."

"And has Gomez secured the seamen ?"

"Aye, captain, they're all aboard."

"Then he shall hoist the blue peter, and sail to-night."

"Friend Richard, have you seen the princess with the golden locks ?" asked Black Ralph.

"Came aboard with the countess."

"I thank thee, Richard, for that word, ' It nerves my heart and steels my sword !' Prithee was she weeping ?"

"Bitterly."

"If I live I will dry those pearly tears. Christine Leuska, thou hast lost a good father, but thou hast found a better husband. Captain, you shall dance at our wedding ; but first sound alarums, flourish, and excursions."

"We shall have hot work ashore, captain," said Dick ; "I hear that Count Josika has routed the Russians near Cracow. My heart burns to be at it."

"One thing vexes me," said Christopher.

"What's that, my co-mate ?"

"Why, Ralph, that faithful old Brierley—I want him to stay with our merchantmen, but he will not leave my side."

"Ah, the old sea-dog ! he will go hunting while he has a tooth. You must find another hound to watch the house ; that old lurcher will a-field till he's shot. Chains and muzzles wont hold him."

"And yet, what have I done to deserve such devotion, when I behold the best men deserted by those they have served, and I a pirate ?"

"Tilly-valley ! wait till you're solus, Captain Kit, before you deliver that dismal soliloquy. Sentimental morality is all cant ; the practical are of few words."

"I am practical, I trust, Ralph. I think I can make some atonement for the past. The cause of these poor Poles is righteous ; I will die to sustain it !"

"Bah ! Live to see it prosper. Nil desperandum, desperadoes ! Never say die while you've ranting Ralph to teach you courage. Victoria ! No more words ; let us ram our thunders into the throats of our guns and let them speak for us !"

"Well said, Ralph. At once we will weigh anchor."

"And then cry, havoc ! And let slip the dogs of war to bait this rugged Russian bear."

Our hero laughed, and followed Dick over the side.

The man in office awaited our hero on board the "Avenger."

It was dusk when that excellent magistrate was put on shore. He walked home without attendance, and reaching his chamber, threw off a heavy cloak, and relieved himself of a load of canvas bags that had made his arms ache in their portage.

As they fell on the table they sounded with a peculiar chink which is by some considered the most exquisite of all musical sounds.

But of course the officer in question would have fainted at the mention of a bribe—of course he was "incorruptible."

CHAPTER CLXXVIII.

THE AVENGERS ARRIVE AT THE SEAT OF WAR—THE YOUNG POLISH PEASANT—AN ANXIOUS WIFE—FEODOR'S RETURN WITH GREAT NEWS—THE HAPPY PAIR—A WIFE'S TENDERNESS—THE COSSACKS—THE COTTAGE ATTACKED—RUSSIAN TREATMENT OF POLES—THE FATAL SHOT—A HUSBAND'S PRAYER FOR JUSTICE—ORDERED FOR EXECUTION—THE FIRING PARTY—THE AVENGERS TO THE RESCUE.

THE Boy Pirate parted company with Gomez, who steered for Sweden with his new crews, his ships freighted with hides and furs.

Our hero and the rest of the band steamed up the river Oder, as far as Posen.

Near this town he found a quiet dock in which he moored his vessels.

After this, his band breaking up into small parties travelling separately, arrived at a lonely spot in that part of the country, near Cracow, of which the insurrectionists had made themselves masters.

The Boy Pirate and his immediate followers were hospitably entertained for several days by an interesting young couple—Polish peasants.

Their host, whose name was Feodor Polowski, had recently married a beautiful girl, and though his sympathies were strongly enlisted in his country's cause, he had not joined the insurgents, feeling that their enterprise was quite hopeless.

Our hero tried to persuade this youth to join his band.

Polowski, moved by the fiery eloquence of our young enthusiast, almost consented.

Alexina, his wife, however, pleaded so earnestly to the Boy Pirate, that at her entreaties he desisted, and even advised his young host to remain neutral till the prospects of the rash adventurers for freedom should become less gloomy.

After the departure of his guests, young Polowski became restless and fretful, and Alexina trembled lest their exhortations should have made such an impression on his mind as would lead him to embark in the perilous extremes of the patriots.

It was some days after our hero's visit to the hospitable home of the peasant's that Alexina sat at her wheel.

She was pensive, and oppressed with a feeling of alarm.

She had set upon the table the frugal evening meal and had waited for more than an hour after the usual time of his return from labour.

She left her work, and was crossing the room with the intention of watching at the door, when her heart leaped at the joyous baying of a large hound chained without, and springing forward was caught in her husband's arms.

"Oh, Feodor, you are come at last !" she murmured. "Ah ! if you knew what torments of anxiety I have suffered, you could not have lingered a moment. What has happened ? Ah ! but you look happy."

"Can my wife's husband look otherwise ?" returned the young Pole, gallantly, and he seated himself, gaily laughing. "Oh, it is glorious ! What a slavish craven must I be to have taken no part in such a deed of heroism."

"Have the rebels won a battle, then ?"

"Rebels ! Fie on you, little Russian. The patriots

have achieved a glorious victory; but you look as pale as if I had told you of a defeat."

"Ah, Feodor, you know my prayers are for the good cause. Indeed, I would sacrifice my life freely for the wrongs of my poor country; but when there's no hope! Oh, Feodor, to see you perish, not as a victor dies, but as one more victim to glut the malice of our triumphant oppressors; if there can be any merit in a chained man flinging himself into the lion's den, suicide must be a virtue."

"Suicide would have been a virtue in Count Brutoff this morning, it would have saved him this evening's disgrace," replied her husband, his face radiant with exultation. "Count Josika, with a force far inferior, drove him from his entrenchments, and we are now masters of the fort."

"We are! Oh! Feodor, your promise, your vow to me. Have you broken it?"

"No, to my shame I was not in the battle."

"To your shame! Then it is a shame to keep your promises to me?"

"No, no; but I should like to have struck one blow by the side of my brave and generous fellow-countrymen."

"You might as well seek to cleave the mountains with your sabre—to scare back the rolling waves with your threats as to contend with our mighty masters."

"Masters, you little traitress. I shall smother you —with kisses; but sit—sit down. This piece of bread is the last I eat in bondage. I'll be free, my Alexina. There, do not look so scared, think of the bride of Kosciusko—of the lady aide-de-camp of gallant Langewicz—of the maids of Warsaw, who stood by their champion's side in the fiercest heat of the battle. There, there, I say all this to tease you. Do not wring your hands, you see me safe and well. I fill this cup and drink health to myself, and may I long live to enjoy your love, which is dearer than fame or fortune. I shall keep quiet, never fear; but let me look at the hammer of yon blunderbuss, I think it wants repairing."

Feodor began his supper laughing joyously, and from time to time singing snatches of patriotic songs.

Alexina sat watching him with terrible anxiety.

"Feodor, tell me truly; you have not joined the insurgents?" she asked, faintly.

"Truly I have not, but the greater is my shame; the arm that can hew down an oak can cleave the helmet of a tyrant. Such laggards as I mar the good cause; we stand by the river, waiting for the stream to run past before we attempt to cross it, instead of plunging into the tide to sink or swim. We seek no foreign aid, we want but unity amongst ourselves, and Poland shall be free or depopulated!"

Alexina threw her arms about her husband, murmuring brokenly,

"Oh, wretched wife that I am, to see my husband perish in a hopeless cause! Do not leave me, Feodor; kill me rather! I cannot bear the agony of this parting; it may be that I am not brave, that I am not patriotic, but what is freedom—glory—Poland—compared with you who are more than all the world to me?"

The young peasant embraced his wife, and spoke cheeringly.

She seated herself by his side at the table.

She dried her tears, smiled, and tried to seem cheerful.

Feodor laughed and bantered her, and reassured her that he would not suffer anything to induce him to join the rebels, till she was willing to part with him.

Nevertheless he displayed uncommon interest in the examination of his blunderbuss and an old fowling-piece.

Alexina rose; she kneeled at her husband's side, and, nestling her head on his breast, talked to him affectionately of byepast times, and sought to draw his attention from the subject she knew to be uppermost in his thoughts.

He answered her caressingly.

Very quietly she took the weapons from his hands, and replaced them on the wall.

Seating herself once more by his side, she smiled archly.

Feodor shrugged his shoulders and laughed.

"Ah me! poor serf! what can I do against the will of my little tyrant? But, surely, my love, you will like to hear all about this glorious battle?"

"Oh, yes, dear Feodor. You must not think my heart is insensible to our country's wrongs, or that I cannot exult in the triumph of the good cause, only I confess I am not strong-minded. I am a poor, little, weak creature, neither good nor great enough to spare you, dearest."

But it was doomed the gentle wife should never hear her husband's story, should never know the valiant part he had taken in the noble deed.

The hound without bayed deeply.

The measured but quick tramp of many feet was heard approaching.

Before the young Pole could reach the wall to seize his gun the door was burst open.

With a pealing shriek Alexina flung herself into the arms of her husband.

In an instant the room was filled with Cossack soldiers.

Barbarous-looking ruffians, with sallow, Asiatic faces, heavy brows—made darker by their rough bearskin shakos—broad built, and ungainly, bearded like the pard, and quite as ferocious as that beast of prey.

They were armed with sabre and pistol, and brandished long lances in their hands. Some had muskets.

They seemed rather bent upon pillage and murder than upon a legal arrest.

A pistol was fired, and at the same instant the young wife was torn from her husband's arms, and dragged across the room.

She saw her husband stagger and fall.

She clutched her brow with a plaintive cry, and sank back into the ruffian's arms, swooning.

But Feodor was not killed.

The bullet had struck him in the shoulder.

He staggered to his feet.

He beheld his wife dragged from the cottage.

The greedy Cossacks were eagerly plundering what simple articles of furniture the humble cottage contained.

Feodor snatched a bill hook, and slashing right and left, cut his way through the throng, and passed through the door.

A mounted officer was pointing to a horse, directing his men to bind the girl on its back.

They were obeying obsequiously, uttering savage execrations, and hauling their innocent prisoner along.

She recovered from her fainting fit, and feebly struggled to release herself.

She perceived her husband.

She held out her white arms appealingly, and uttered a piteous cry.

Feodor leaped upon her miscreant captors, and smote them down with the bill-hook.

He clutched his wife to his heart.

The officer had presented his pistol, intending to shoot the youth.

The weapon exploded.

Alexina gave a shrill scream, and fell to the earth.

The bullet had pierced her heart.

The officer turned deadly pale, and let the pistol fall from his hand.

Feodor stood as one stricken by lightning, looking down on his murdered wife with a face that was awful in its distortion.

With a heart-rending moan he sank down.

His head drooped upon the cold breast, whose every pulse had throbbed for him, now pulseless for ever.

His glossy black locks mingled with the girl's fair hair; his hand wandered to hers, he clasped it, still warm, but lifeless.

The officer jumped from the saddle.

He advanced to the spot where the fearful tragedy had been enacted.

The Cossacks had raised the half-conscious Feodor from the bleeding body of his lovely and beloved young wife.

The officer could not repress a shudder as he looked upon his cruel work.

He threw his cloak over the body of the girl.

" Bear her into the cottage," he said, in a hoarse tone, " and secure the other prisoner."

The order was obeyed.

" Let him be removed at once," said the officer, sullenly, scarce raising his eyes from beneath his thick black brows to look at the young Pole.

The swelling torrent of passion, boiling in the heart of the bereaved husband, overflowed his lips in a swift, wild stream of bitterly invoked curses on the murderers.

The officer looked at him sombrely.

" The sooner a man so deeply injured is put out of the way of doing mischief the safer for the offender," thought Count Brutoff, for he was the same villanous and unlucky rascal who had been so roughly handled by the fierce Boy Pirate.

The noble drew out his gold watch.

" Your insolence is mistimed, you should be engaged in prayers not curses, for you have but ten minutes to live," said the Count, in a low, sullen tone ; " your wife has fallen a victim to your own treason against your sovereign. Compose your thoughts, and prepare for instant death."

Feodor sank on his knees, and stretched his hands to heaven.

His lips moved in prayer ; but his wild, passion-lit face betrayed the nature of his supplication.

There was something so awful in the silent invocation of Heaven's vengeance upon these wretches that even they, hardened to the most merciless acts of atrocities, could not help being moved.

Feodor rose and stood firm and erect.

His face was now calm ; he turned one wild glance at his home. The fire in his eyes died out, the wrinkles in his knitted brow relaxed, his look was fixed upon vacancy, he seemed unconscious of all surrounding objects. When he spoke it was in a steady, though hollow tone.

" I am ready," he said ; " there is no need to bind me."

The soldiers, however, paid no attention to this remark, but tied his hands behind him.

The firing party was told off.

They formed, and the prisoner was placed in the midst.

At some distance from the cottage stood a large elm tree.

Count Brutoff himself walked his horse to the spot where the young martyr stood like a statue, so marble firm.

His air was neither resigned nor defiant ; he stood abstractedly like one entranced, his burning eyes fixed on the distant hills, his lips apart, the red blood from his wounded shoulder soaking his shirt.

Two men approached from the cottage.

They had a mattock and spade, and commenced deliberately to dig the martyr's grave.

The firing party formed in double line at a few paces distance, and stood leaning on their guns.

One of the rugged Cossacks held a cross to the lips of the young Pole.

The young man started, like one startled from sleep.

He slightly bent his head, with downcast eyes, and reverently kissed the holy emblem.

A short, stern word of command levelled six shining barrels at the young patriot's breast.

Count Brutoff held the handkerchief at the point of his sword.

The word " fire " was on his lip.

Why does he start in his saddle ?

Why does the platoon of soldiers break from their rank ?

Because the air throbs with a furious shout.

Count Brutoff turns his horse and dashes off in wild flight.

If anything could excuse this act of cowardice it was the terrible appearance of our doughty hero, who in one hand grasped that memorable scourge, and with the other levelled a gleaming pistol.

Our hero knew not the worst that had happened, and in the scorn of his heart forbore to fire at his flying foe.

Black Ralph, Black Zamp, Sam Cassidy, and Dick, threw themselves desperately into the midst of the Cossacks.

The ruffians were glad to profit by the example of their valorous commander, and made a rush for their horses.

Never did equestrians vault more nimbly to the saddles, and never did jockeys better contend in speed, than these valiant warriors fleeing from a handful of British seamen.

The gallant avengers huzzaed lustily.

Our hero ran to the young Pole, and grasped his hand.

" What, man, are you so unnerved ? You seem paralysed. Sure Death's face should not look terrible to your brave eyes. How one may be deceived ! I thought you could have outfaced the grizzly skeleton."

" Noble Englishman !" returned Feodor, in a tone of fearful anguish, " do not think me ungracious when I tell you that you have unconsciously done a deed of cruelty and not of mercy. By this time I should have been with her !"

" With her ? With whom ?" gasped our hero, his cheek paling at the dreadful suspicion that arose in his mind.

" Yes. I cannot bear, no man with a pulse in his heart or brain could bear it. They have only left me to be my own executioner."

" Speak, for the love of Heaven ! What fatal chance has happened ?" cried our hero.

" Come, and I will show you a sight that will make your generous hearts bleed with mine," said Feodor, quietly, " but which at least will convince you that you have espoused a cause which may well enlist your sympathies. Come," he added, in a tone of that bitter mockery often expressive of exquisite mental torture, " I will lead you to my wife. She will give you cold welcome ; we have had other guests to-night. What am I saying ? I know not. I walk as in a sleep ; yet, no, for then I should be unconscious. But, follow me !"

CHAPTER CLXXIX.

THE MURDERED WIFE—THE HUSBAND'S VOW—THE BOY PIRATE AND HIS BAND SWEAR TO AVENGE THE DEATH OF ALEXINA—BURIAL OF THE POLISH MARTYR.

FEODOR POLOWSKI led the way to his cottage.

The stern Avengers followed him in profound silence.

They walked as reverently as if they were attending a funeral.

Every heart was chilled, every cheek bloodless.

The pretty little nest where this innocent and happy couple had nestled in their love and simplicity apart from the brawling city, unattracted by the garish pomps and vanities of heartless society, was now a dreary ruin.

The trained roses, so neatly tended by gentle hands, had been crushed beneath the heel of the barbarian hussar.

The windows were all broken, and the splintered door swung loose on its battered hinges.

They entered the still chamber, those remorseless men ; they entered the late happy home shudderingly.

The tables and chairs were overturned and broken, the cupboards open, and ransacked of their poor stores.

On the ground lay a large black cloak.

Yet now there was mortal clay beneath that dark pall—a human form rigidly defined through the mantle.

Feodor stooped on his knee, and softly lifted the covering.

Golden hair, idly strewn; features of sweetest beauty, but fixed and tintless; budding lips, but closed and rigid; a soft, white bosom, but throbless, and smeared with the clotted crimson stain.

The Avengers drew a deep breath, which echoed like a groan.

Feodor touched the smooth, white brow.

He lifted a long tress of yellow floss.

Stealing startlingly through the deep hush, and striking a quick, keen chord on every strained heart-string, broke the wail of the bereaved husband.

"Wife!"

He uttered but that one word.

"Oh that Lilia were near to draw tears from their bursting fount!" muttered our hero, his own dauntless eyes glittering with moisture.

The stern seamen turned aside; they who had looked on the mangled bodies of their slaughtered comrades heaped upon the poignant deck, now hid their faces from the agonising spectacle of that human face, stricken with mortal anguish.

"You must not think me cowardly, generous Englishmen," said Feodor, rising. "No, nor faithless. I cannot believe that God, whose goodness shines in every sunbeam, has rent my wife from me for ever! No, we shall meet again; I will look for that; I will order my steps in patience for that! I will not murmur; He works by general laws. There is no need of saving miracles when life is so very short. Oh, bear with me! bear with me! I blush for my manhood; but it is so sudden, so cruelly sudden! Oh, poor fools, how weak, how weak are we!"

It was but a few hours before that our hero had beheld the young patriot rushing upon the blazing mouths of the cannon, shouting in the stern exultant delight of the fearless who make war a pastime.

Now the stricken man leaned on his shoulder sobbing like a little child.

Our hero did not scorn those honourable tears; his own eyes were brimming in keen sympathy.

Still the upraised face lay so saintly sweet, so humanly lovely. Oh! it was distraction!

"And now, Feodor," said our hero, in a low, stern accent, "revenge!"

"Shame; shame for that word!" cried the husband, his face aglare with wild fervour. "Say she is not my wife; I know her not but as a sister-mortal, and I see her thus—so pure, so good, so lovely, yet so ruthlessly, wantonly stricken down, and where is your ideal saint or angel that will bid me bear it tamely? What man with one drop of living blood but will hoot and scorn me, thrice Christian though he be, if I can behold this black act, and not seek justice. Justice, not revenge. Call the off-sweeping of these hell-hounds by no worse name than justice, else I am her murderer."

"Justice! it is nothing but justice, and you shall have it amply," cried the pirates in one breath.

"I'll not insult you by thanks; you cannot, as men, say otherwise; you cannot refuse me your aid."

He took a sword from the mantel and drew it from its sheath.

"My father wielded this sword against our country's oppressors in the fatal battle of Warsaw, when Poland fell with Kosciusko. I have it now, and while my arm has strength to raise it, I will not sheath it, except in the hearts of these inhuman tyrants; and first it shall carve my way to the breast of the savage monster who has murdered Alexina. And if there is one amongst you who will swear with me to hunt out this bloodiest wolf from the rest of the ravenous pack, in manhood's name let him speak!"

"My sword is not unsullied with the guilty stain," said our hero, with great emotion, as he drew his flashing blade; "I have been banned and braved from my youth, but blood, spilled in such a holy cause will purify its spots; and, Feodor, I swear by my mother's love, I will hallow it to this service, and it shall second your's against this wretch, though he sat on the throne of Russia!"

"And ours, captain; ours! There shall be justice done for this cruel deed!" cried the others, each unsheathing his weapon.

"And now I will be calm," said Feodor, in a harsh, but steady voice; "and we will lay her to rest; she shall sleep beneath our old trysting tree, and we will raise a cross above the spot. Should I fall, lay me by her side, if it be possible. When justice is satisfied by the death of her murderer I may claim the only rest that I can hope for."

Very tenderly the rough outlaws raised the frail, inanimate form of the murdered wife.

Beneath a huge, whispering tree they buried her.

The passionless moon rose and glowed, pale and calm, through the dark branches.

Her silver flood fell on a group of sincere mourners gathered around the little mound which enshrined the kindest and gentlest of Poland's martyrs.

CHAPTER CLXXX.

MORTIMER A PRISONER—THE CAPTIVE REMOVED TO LORD HAWKSBURY'S CHAMBER—A CONSULTATION—MORTIMER'S DEFENCE OF EAGLETON — LORD HAWKSBURY'S INTERCESSION ON THE PRISONER'S BEHALF—THE GENEROUS NOBLEMAN GIVES THE CULPRIT A CHANCE OF RETRIEVING HIS CHARACTER.

WHEN Eagleton rushed from the tavern he was hotly pursued by the detectives' assistants.

He eluded them, however.

They were forced to return breathless and defeated.

Mortimer had been handcuffed.

He stood as if petrified by the suddenness of his capture and the scene of violence he had just witnessed.

Lord Hawksbury was raised, and placed in a chair.

A surgeon was sent for.

He examined the wound.

The hurt proved not so dangerous as Oiny had supposed.

Yet there was a dreadful gash in the young nobleman's high, pale forehead, and it was long before he returned to consciousness.

When he had fully recovered his senses, his wound being bandaged, and a stimulant forced through his clenched teeth, he looked round for the detective.

"The rascal has well-nigh made his crimes capital," he said, with a faint smile. "I was quite insensible, and I feel as if I had been roused from death."

"He will be taken, my lord; I will put some of my best men on his track. Meanwhile, the other man is in our hands."

"Upon what charge I can't surmise, sir," cried Mortimer, boldly, "I am eager for information, and I trust, sir, that you are acting under substantial authority in this rough treatment, or you shall rue it."

"Young man, you shall have full satisfaction on both points," returned the detective, grimly, "only have patience for a few moments."

"Is this fellow an accomplice?"

"Yes, my lord."

"Not in the forgery. I am run down, and I must submit—I don't care much. I have been fleeing from what I knew must come, and now I am overtaken at last I am out of suspense," said Mortimer, firmly; "but if you don't want to have a fellow-creature's life to answer for, you will beware how you deal too hardly with Dick Eagleton. The fellow is desperate. He had been wronged by a near friend. Although, perhaps, he deserves no pity—of course, he does not for his treachery—nevertheless I repeat, his blood will be on your head if you force him to extremity."

"What, will the rascal commit suicide?"

"I am sure he will, my lord."

"And so much the better for the ratepayers. He will save the Government some expense and responsibility."

"Your lordship seems to treat the matter lightly, and the life of a misguided man is not to be valued very highly."

"Misguided! the serpent! Well, he struck me, and you'll think I speak out of malice. In his case I should have acted as he did as far as making a bold dash for liberty; but such a double-faced, venomed scoundrel deserves no commiseration."

"Well, my lord, I will say no more, only it is a terrible thing to drive a bad man down the dark gulf of suicide."

"You're not a bad advocate, Mr. Mortimer."

"A fellow-feeling, my lord," said the inspector, grinning.

Mortimer sneered contemptuously, but made no answer.

"You say you knew nothing of the forgery?"

"I did not, till after it was committed, and if I had known anything, I am not called upon to criminate myself. It is plain enough I had no hand in it."

"And you did not know, I suppose, that poor Charles Rye was to be made the scapegoat for your precious friend?"

"I knew that from the first."

"Then, sir, you are a confounded rascal!"

"I know your lordship is at liberty to insult me, and I perceive that you are determined to avail yourself of that licence."

"Perhaps you are right in blaming me for my rough language, but any honest heart must revolt against such a dastardly trick as you plotted together for the ruin of a generous and worthy young gentleman."

"Your lordship's honesty has not been put to the test by poverty and temptation."

"Neither of which excuses you can plead, and, even though you might urge them as excuses for stealing a loaf of bread, and that you could not fairly, there can be no palliation for such vile treachery as that you have been guilty of."

"Guilty, only because I did not peach upon my friend Richard Eagleton. If I had informed against him, you would have called me treacherous for abusing his confidence; and, as for Charles Rye, he was almost a stranger to me, and his affairs were no concern of mine."

"Very plausible, sir, and confoundedly sneakish."

"Come, let's have no more of this, my man. Shall remove him at once, my lord?"

"One word, Mr. Falcon," whispered the young nobleman.

"At your service, my lord."

"Are you bound at once to remove this young blackleg to the station?"

"Well, my lord, such is the proper course."

"But couldn't you take him first to my chambers?"

"Out of order, my lord."

"But to oblige me."

"If your lordship thinks it desirable, why, perhaps——"

"You can manage it—do. If blame attaches to any one, I shall take care that it rests on my shoulders."

"Well, my lord, as you please, but——"

"As I please implies no 'buts.' I'll take care that you shall not be implicated in my illegal proceedings. Call my carriage, Oiny."

"And, bedad! I thought it was the ostrich vahical with the six black horses and the toine outsiders, I thought yer lordship'd be afther wanting for the next ride," returned Oiny; "and it's mighty plased

I am, sure, to hear your lordship spaking yer own wishes, though whin they has to be read for ye, I hope ye'll not forgit yer lordship's faithful Oiny Macarne."

"Be off, you saucy scamp!"

"Sure, Mr. Rye, but every man has his falings, and in this fray country, hasn't a poor boy the right to spake what he thinks now?"

The Irishman called the carriage.

Lord Hawksbury, Silas Rye, the detective, and the prisoner got in; Oiny jumped on to the box, and the carriage rattled away westward.

Arrived at the house, Lord Hawksbury ushered his companions and their captive into the library.

He gave directions to Oiny to prevent any interruption, and carefully closed the door.

He whispered the detective.

The officer removed the handcuffs from the prisoner's wrists.

When they were seated, his lordship addressed the prisoner.

"Now, Mr. Mortimer, I want you to tell us how far you have committed yourself in this sad business, and whether you can assist us in clearing up the doubts that hang upon the case for Charles Rye. It seems that the imitations of Mr. Bullion's name which were found in his desk were his work; and he maintains an obstinae and absurd silence about them."

"Because he will not compromise his destroyer—Eagleton!" cried Silas, indignantly. "The boy is a fool! I have no patience with him. But his spirit seems so broken by this first deep wound to his youthful confidence, that he appears reckless of everything."

"Well, Mr. Rye, we must make allowance for his want of experience, and the rashness of his hot youth. But I will again request Mr. Mortimer to tell me how it was that the writing before mentioned was found in Charles's desk?"

"My lord, first, I trust, you will permit me to ask a question," said Mortimer, fixing his dark eyes steadily upon the young nobleman. "Upon what authority do you act in this proceeding? Is this an age of secret tribunal, and are you a legal inquisitor?"

"Let me advise you, Mr. Mortimer, for your own sake, not to question my authority. Surely my brougham is a pleasanter conveyance than a police-van, and you're not worse located here than you would be in the station-house cells. The question I ask is one you may answer without injuring your friend, Eagleton; and you, by acting straightforwardly, may release yourself from a very unpleasant dilemma."

"In that case, my lord, I will tell you all I know. But I trust you will not set me up as a witness against Eagleton."

"You think much of that rascal. You have no consideration for my ill-used brother," said Silas Rye.

"Indeed I have. I am very sorry for him. And now the thing has gone so far, I believe that Eagleton himself is sorry, too. In fact, we did not think that Charles Rye would be convicted. I trusted that his lordship's influence would——"

"Be used to shield a thief and trust-breaker. Not if he were my only son!"

"Well, my lord, I will confess at once that Charles Rye was tricked into writing those signatures."

Mortimer then narrated the artful ruse by which the treacherous Eagleton had induced his simple and confiding friend to imitate the signature of his master, by way of sport, and as a test of his skill in penmanship; and how he had afterwards contrived to slip them into young Rye's desk.

There was a loud and general burst of indignation as Mortimer concluded.

"And now, my lord," he said, "am I permitted to say a few words as counsel for the defence, in palliation of Eagleton's fault?"

A NEW-FASHIONED BARROW.

"You must be an able advocate indeed, Mr. Mortimer, if you can lessen the blackness of such an act of treachery, even by the faintest shade."

"I will try, my lord, to show you that the faultiest men have their points of goodness, which, I believe, should be respected when their faults are punished."

"The best that can be done, is done," said the detective, curtly.

"Temptation or poverty, or natural disposition make rogues; they are punished, perhaps too lightly, but the ban of society confirms them in their crime."

"But surely you wouldn't have a man employ a liberated thief, to be always in danger of having his goods stolen?"

"I think I would rather be robbed by a man whom I had trusted, than bar the road to a poor wretch

No. 55.

striving to return to the path of rectitude," returned Mortimer.

"And a fellow who is in league with such a sneakish scoundrel as Eagleton to ruin a generous, affectionate boy, can express such sentiments."

"And yet I am not a hypocrite ; I speak now by the light of reason, but I act generally from the force of impulse ; but I will give you some account of Eagleton."

Not without eloquence, this strange youth told the story of his friend's life.

He stated that Eagleton had been his schoolfellow, had always been remarkable for his artfulness, that, as a boy, he was a confirmed and ingenious liar.

On the other hand, he was extremely intelligent.

and though morally sneakish and cowardly, physically bold and assuming, that he was generous to profusion, and that where he conceived an attachment he was constant and fervent in his devotion.

Mortimer spoke of his friend's kindness to Sylvia and to himself in better times, of his industry and perseverance in the face of many difficulties, for, from a very early age, he had been a friendless orphan.

He then spoke of Angeline, the siren who had lured him on to the pitiless rocks, where his bark, with all its freight of virtue, health, prudence, faith and honesty, had been miserably wrecked.

The detective confirmed this part of the story, and repeated what he had overheard at the hotel, and mentioned with some feeling the tone of despair in which Eagleton had said in speaking of the slights put upon him by the worthless object of his infatuation.

"I was true to my troth, and as I had not strength to break the chain that bound me, I suffered patiently."

Mortimer concluded by expressing his firm conviction that if driven to desperation by pursuit, Eagleton would assuredly commit suicide.

Lord Hawksbury rose with a grave face, and beckoned the detective.

The officer followed him into the embrasure of the window.

They talked together for some time in low, earnest tones.

The detective seemed remonstrating, but after some time seemed to yield to his lordship's importunity.

"Mr. Mortimer," said the young noble, reseating himself, "you are in a very unhappy position, you have drawn money of your employers for gambling purposes."

Mortimer's cheek reddened.

He looked at the detective.

"You don't suppose that what you say here will be brought against you in court?" said Falcon.

"I have replaced it all, my lord," said Mortimer, in a low voice. "I made a lucky bet on Goselle, which enabled me to do so."

"But you must not remain with your present employer."

"My lord!" cried the culprit, starting, a flush of hope rising to his cheek. "Why, no, I suppose not," he added, looking at the detective with a sickly smile.

"You have been guilty of a breach of trust. Now, as I am in want of a secretary, suppose that I act upon your axiom that it is worthier to trust a man whose character is doubtful, than to bar the way against a poor sinner striving to regain the straight path from which he has stumbled, should I have cause to repent of my rash experiment?"

A torrent of thanks rose to Mortimer's lips; but he repressed them, and answered, quietly,

"My future conduct will be the best answer."

"Well, I like you the better for making no parade of good resolutions which I know are sincere. God give you strength to keep them. Mr. Falcon and I have entered into a conspiracy to cheat the law. You are free, Mr. Mortimer."

"But we will not let Eagleton escape?" said the detective.

"No; but we must be cautious in the capture, and must not entirely forget Mr. Mortimer's able defence when we bring the rascal to judgment."

CHAPTER CLXXXI.

EARLY MORNING IN THE LONDON STREETS— THE DESPAIRING WANDERER—DRIFTING TO THE LOADSTONE ROCK—THE SIREN AND HER SLAVE—EAGLETON'S LOVE-PHRENZY.

EAGLETON had wandered the streets all night. He had made his way to a distant part of the town,

and, as morning broke, was slowly and wearily retracing his steps.

Whither was he going? He knew, and shuddered as he thought of his own weakness; but he could not resist the magnetic spell, he was drawn on by a power it was vain to strive against.

"I will see her once more!" he muttered. "If we part friends it will make remembrance softer, less painful; if this interview is to be as torturing as the last, why, then I shall only regret her the less, and be more joyous in freedom. Free! when shall I be free? Fly, whither and from what? I will do it! I will end it all; I will die, die! The word is as sweet as a breath of spring air, and I cannot escape; the deer may run through brake and thicket, but the arrow quivers in his heart. Pshaw! how I maunder. What sluggards are these dronish shopkeepers! Why don't they open their eyes and their windows, the eyes of the streets, and look alive?"

The morning was frosty.

The grey light drowsily streaking above the chimney-stacks.

Eagleton stood shivering at the corner of a wide but deserted thoroughfare, beating his feet upon the cold pavement.

"Ha! There's another policeman," he went on musingly. "Confound them! I think they've doubled their numbers on purpose to plague me. Once I could never find one if I lost my way or wanted a cab, but now they start up like sprites, in unexpected places, and every moment I expect to feel a fist at my collar. If I do, I shall feel the steel at my heart at the same time; they shall never take me alive. Oh, what a wretch I am! What a beast! A treacherous, fawning, dissimulating, pitiless hound! And the slave of a——well, a lady of pleasure. Pleasure! poison! Oh, how I hate her; how I could kill her! I wonder if cursing affects the object? If I thought so, she should be anathematised by bell, book, and candle! Will I see her? I'll see her hanged! No! I won't go near the witch; she is lost to me, and a blessed escape for me; but oh, she was kind to me once; she spoke so gently, and when I was poor she soothed me with promises of better fortune—it was but a caprice. The next day she left me almost fainting with hunger, on the streets, and laughed and shook her earrings, and spanned her hand with her new canary gloves, while she taunted me for looking such a scarecrow. Now, if this were another's case, shouldn't I enjoy it? Shouldn't I think the victim a drivelling dolt? Well, I can laugh at myself. Ha, that's right! The sluggards begin to stretch themselves; we shall have the streets alive presently."

A barman was lazily taking down the shutters of a large public-house.

Eagleton entered the bar.

He called for brandy.

He took up the evening edition of the yesterday's paper.

With an oath he pushed it back.

An advertisement caught his eye, in which Bullion, Brothers & Co., Bankers, offered the reward of £100, for the apprehension of Richard Eagleton, &c.

He rushed from the public-house.

"My life hangs upon a thread," he thought. "I know not whether I shall embrace the chance of escape, or whether I shall put an end to my wretched existence; but I will see her; I must not tell her that I have so much money, though I would give her all if she would let me die off in her arms. I love her! I can't help it! It's a malady that *will* cling to me."

The sunlight flashed on the window panes, the streets began to bustle with vehicles and passengers, when Eagleton reached a dull retired street in Bloomsbury, in which his mistress dwelt.

He sauntered about for two more weary hours; he thought it too early for his visit.

At length he knocked at the door.

It was courteously opened by a pretty, but slatternly girl, who inquired whether he wished to see the mistress.

He pushed the door open impatiently, and entered.

He felt inclined to get into an unreasonable passion, but as he thought of the cold sneer of that curled lip, the steady blaze of those blue eyes, which he dreaded so much, his courage failed, and he began to instruct the girl in a rambling message to her mistress.

She smiled, and looked at him rather contemptuously.

"Stay, Susy, I'll give you a note," he said; "take this to your mistress."

He tore a leaf from his pocket-book, and hastily scrawled with his pencil a few frantic words, imploring pardon for his violence on the previous evening, and stating that he had good news to tell her.

As the girl went upstairs, he stood blaming himself for having written so humbly, but had not the resolution to call her back.

The girl returned and told him that her mistress would see him.

With burning cheek and loud beating heart, he flew up the stairs.

Tremblingly he opened the door.

Angeline was reclining on a couch.

She looked calm and collected, and received him with frigid courtesy.

He threw himself at her side, and burst into a passionate tirade of endearments and self-reproach.

She listened with a light of triumph in her eyes, but with an expression of rigid indifference upon her lip.

It is useless to dwell upon this scene of human degradation, of wretched weakness and heartlessness.

He told her that he had money, that he was about to leave the country; but if she would consent to marry him, he vowed he would stay at all risks, or would take her with him; he had enough to buy land in a colony and to pay for labour; he could work hard himself, in fact, he would fear no kind of labour; that she should be the object of his worship; that he would cherish, too, his loved Angeline more dearly than words could express.

Marry him! Could she marry a man who had drawn a dagger to kill her? who, when she was only practical, and reasonable, and considerate, when she had treated him with kind regard, could bully and abuse her as he had done. No, never!

He urged that they were morally married already; that they had sworn eternal love to each other; that he had cloven to her through slight and scorn and misery; that he had shed rivers of bitter tears, had suffered a martyrdom of restless anguish through his unquenchable love for her; he had known sweet thoughts inspired by her smiles, he had felt his heart glow with sympathy to every sorrowing fellow-man, he had found his nerves strung to the bitterest trial when she was good to him. Oh, if she would be but kind! If her love would sun up the dark places of his soul, and purify their loathsomeness, he would make restitution for all his past bad acts, he would be a regenerate man! and life would pass like a dream of bliss, for he should have all that his soul craved for, in possessing her love. Oh, if she would be herself once more—be once more kind.

Still he raved on pitifully; still she laughed in spirit, and remained unmoved as the stone against which the storm-wind is chafing.

With perfect self-possession she gradually softened; at length, with a burst of tenderness, she threw her arms from him, and implored his forgiveness.

Then the poor wretch became delirious with joy; he exhausted himself in protestations of affection, and poured a heap of sovereigns into her lap.

She chid him for his folly and mistrust. What was money to her? Had she ever cared for gold? Had she not kept to him when he was poor? If she had upbraided him it was only for his good. Why did he not persevere in business? He had no need to suffer.

She was right; he was the veriest demon that ever polluted the earth, and she the brightest angel that ever had come to illumine its darkness.

Angeline rang for breakfast.

She pressed him to partake of food.

He could not eat; he was haggard, excited, pale, palsied. His throat ached with the violence of his passion, his heart beat faint with exhaustion.

She said he looked wretchedly ill; she parted the hair, rich, glossy hair, that strewed his pale forehead; she kissed his handsome face, and blushed; she soothed him with murmured endearments.

He was exhausted; he said he had not slept for several nights; the last he had spent in the open streets.

He thought that his heart being now at rest he could slumber for awhile.

Angeline brought him soft pillows.

He sank back in the couch with a deep sigh of intense weariness.

Once more she kissed him, and was about to leave the room.

Would she sit by his side till he sank to sleep?

She pressed his hand, and seated herself in a low stool at the head of the couch.

Like the shadows of clouds that sweep the calm sea, shades of waking emotion swept over his features as they became settled in repose.

Softly Angeline stole away.

She looked at her sleeping victim.

A pang of wild love sprang up in her false heart; it died away in a sneer of selfishness as the thought of the rich fool who had promised to make her a lady.

Quietly she closed the door.

"I had better turn the key," she said, with a peculiar smile.

She stood listening an instant, and then stole downstairs.

CHAPTER CLXXXII.

ANGELINE'S TREACHERY — TOM GOES IN SEARCH OF THE DETECTIVE—SELFISHNESS AND REMORSE—A BREATHLESS LISTENER—THE FOOTSTEP — ANGELINE'S LOVER — A DEEP GROAN—ARRIVAL OF THE DETECTIVES—THE OPEN WINDOW — BAFFLED —A LOVER'S QUARREL AND A DAY'S PLEASURE.

ANGELINE softly descended the stairs.

She entered the parlour.

She looked pale and excited.

Her heart twinged with a pang of remorse and pity, but her lip curled with arrogance and disdain.

A dissolute, vulgar-looking man, showily dressed, but evidently a low-bred fellow rose from the sofa on which he was reclining, stared at the Traviata and grinned.

He was crunching in his teeth the stem of a flower.

He had a bunch of showy blossoms in the front of his Newmarket coat.

"Here I am, you see, not exactly dancin' attendance, for I began to be tired, and thought I might as well take it easy."

"And what do you want, Tom," said the girl, pettishly, her great blue eyes beamed into the pier glass, while she hammered the mantel-piece with the key of the unconscious Eagleton's prison.

Now she looked herself; she had laid aside her glittering armour. She had stepped out of the magic circle of her enchantments, and appeared as much relieved as an actress coming off the stage after the performance of an arduous part.

"Blow me! Here's a question! Wasn't you engaged to go with me to the 'Scrubbs,' to see the volunteers?"

"Was I?" asked the girl, inanely. "La, I remember something about it."

"Well, that's cool!—humph, it don't pay to be

jealous; though as I've done pretty well at the races and with the booths, I can't see why you shouldn't put a stop to this game."

Angeline sneered, then seated herself gaily by his side.

She pouted her lip with infantile peevishness, and rapped him pretty hard on the knuckles.

"Oh!" cried Tom, snatching away his fingers and thrusting them into his wide mouth. "Come, I say, Angeliner, that's too bad, you wixen. What did you do that for?"

"Because I hate you."

"Ah, we know what that means," returned Tom, with a honied smile, and moving his arms nearer to her waist.

She started away from him.

"Let me be; it's a fact, I hate you."

"Why?"

"Because you are such a stingy fellow."

"Stingy! Well I never! That's the werry last. A gold watch, a muslin gound, not to say anything about the emerald ear-drops——"

"But, Tom, Tom, you're anything but a Tom Tiddler; there's nothing like this to be picked up on your premises."

She drew from her pocket quite a handful of gold pieces, and piled them in her lap.

"Oh, crikey! here's a sweep; where did you get 'em?"

"Tellings."

"Well, tell me."

"Why you?"

"Who else but me loves ye to distraction, Angeliner?"

"You poor, miserable, pot-house snob, you live in a palace, don't you? a gin-palace. You associate in fine company, don't ye? bruisers and sharps. A Whitechapel rat-catcher and bull-dog trainer! Don't say I don't hate you."

"Leastways, you're a werry fine lady yourself, Angeliner; your conduct and language is most becomin'," returned Tom, with cutting sarcasm.

"I might be a fine lady if I liked."

"What is that cove, a heavy swell?"

"A lover, Tom, oh, such a lover, handsome and gentlemanly; and talk about passionate devotion, he worships, he adores me. His love is twenty thousand times hotter than Romeo's."

"P'raps you'll find him an Otheller, if ye don't look out," said Tom, sagely.

Angeline turned a little pale.

"Well, Tom, I hate treachery, don't you?"

"Of course, peaching don't never pay, not among your own set, leastways."

"Can I trust you, Tom?"

"With your precious own self," replied Tom, gallantly.

"No, Tom, not quite so confiding as all that, but a secret, Tom."

"Let's have it."

"You know that perjury case in the paper, don't ye?"

"Ah, yes, about the clerk as swore agin' another about a forgery at old Bullion's. I knows the feller, too, Dick Eagleton—him and young Bullion, the nephew, and another cove, Jack Mortimer—trumps, all on 'em, done business with 'em."

"Did they act fairly?"

"Werry square, 'specially Dandy Dick, as we used to call this cove. I wasn't well up in the world then. The old buffer hadn't turned up his toes, and I didn't live in 'a palace,' as you says, leastways, not in one of my own. Well, there was a row, and I swear I was the victim. The gents collared my sticks and the Aunt Sally which they'd been shying at, beat me, and somebody gave me in charge. Dandy Dick paid my fine. Awful good-natured chap, but precious unlucky."

"Poor fellow! Ah, Tom, now, if I were like some selfish wretches of girls—I hate such heartless ways—but it is a temptation, heigho! We won't talk about it."

"What's a temptation, eh? Why, there's a hun-

dred pounds offered for Dick. I heard as Falcon was arter him."

"You never mean to say that you would peach on him? You wouldn't be such a sneak," said the girl, indignantly.

"No, would you?" he paused, and grumbled, "I wish I had the chance."

"Would I? What do you think of me, with this in my hands?"

"Well, anyhow, Angeliner, for all as I'm so stingy, what little presents I makes is paid for with my honest winnin's and earnin's. It all comes in the book or over the bar. If I might have the run of the Bank, I'd keep a cart, and send it round here every mornin' chock full of swag. It's werry easy to be generous with other people's money."

"Well, now, there's truth in that."

"In coorse there is; and they say as Dick's quite desperit'; goes a'most anywheres. They say he's reg'lar broken-hearted, along of a gal, or more likes a race-hoss. Of course, a big poster, with 'Reward, One Hundred Pounds,' will make the crushers shet their eyes and shake their 'eds. Oh no! they couldn't think o' such a thing!"

"It's very certain somebody will get the reward."

"Slick sure, and why shouldn't we be 'somebody,' eh? If a certain swell's so awful fond of you, he'd rather you should draw the prize than anybody else, I should think so."

"What!" gasped the girl, turning deadly pale, in spite of her hypocrisy, "what are you about? Where are you going?"

Tom had arisen, put on his hat, and was moving towards the door.

"You are not——"

"Oh, no, in course; don't I tell you so? Can't you believe me? You haven't told me nothin' what you don't know. Good-bye, my angel; you'll see me agen to-day."

"If you do——"

"You'll give me another rap on the knuckles, eh?" cried Tom, with a chuckle. "Werry well; on'y stick to the key till I comes back, and you may break 'em if you likes."

"Here, Tom, I swear I'll let him out. Stay, one word."

Mr. Tom, however, had reached the street, and rushed past the window.

"Oh, Richard, my darling, this is too much. No, no, I am not so vile as this. I will warn him, and send him away."

She rushed out of the room.

She did not, however, act according to her resolve.

She stole softly upstairs, and listened at the door.

"How deeply he sleeps," she muttered.

She crouched down, and looked through the keyhole.

She could not see him; the couch was not within the line of view.

"I had best not; after all what Tom says may be true: my Romeo may prove an Othello. How I tremble; I never knew before how weak I am."

A step was heard within.

Eagleton pulled fiercely at the handle of the door.

Scarcely repressing a scream, Angeline bounded swiftly towards the door.

The "dagger-scene" at Cremorne recurred vividly to her imagination.

At the foot of the stairs she stood violently trembling.

As if drawn by an irresistible fascination, this thousand and first Dalilah remounted the stairs quite noiselessly.

She draws her breath, and lurks at the door, listening eagerly.

She hears a deep groan.

"He has stabbed himself!" she thought.

Did she rush in to ascertain the truth of this surmise?

No; once more she softly descended the stairs.

"If they find him alive, out of revenge he will say I did it."

Now she screamed.

A startling knock at the door made her quail.

She nervously opened it.

Three men stood on the step.

One of them was Mr. Tom, the other two were rating him for his indiscretion in knocking so loud.

"What is your pleasure, gentlemen?" she asks, innocently.

"We understand that Richard Eagleton, who is charged with perjury and forgery, is in this house."

"He is; but I fear he has destroyed himself. Acting from a sense of duty, I locked him in the room above; as I listened at the door just now, I heard a deep groan. He has a dagger in his possession, with which he attempted my life. Pray gentlemen, be careful."

Thus admonished, the two policemen drew their truncheons, and, followed by Tom, went up stairs.

They opened the door, and entered.

Their man was gone!

Between the front and back rooms were folding-doors that were always kept locked.

Eagleton had forced them.

The window of the back-room was wide open.

It was by this outlet the prisoner had escaped.

Under the window was a buttress.

Just below that the garden wall.

The descent was easy to a bold climber.

The detectives and Mr. Tom were loud in their expressions of disappointment at the prisoner's escape.

"I thought he would have suffered himself to be taken, and then have upbraided me—not he!" muttered Angeline, with charming consistency; "he knew how to take care of himself. What selfish brutes men are."

The detectives left the house.

"Well, Angeliner, as the hunt's up, it's no good a frettin'."

"I'm glad! You are a mean, pitiful villain; he was kind to you, and he loved me dearly. I would rather suffer myself than that he should be taken," cried Angeline; "if I hadn't thought he was desperate with despair, and would kill me when I heard him at the door, I would have let him out. Why do you tempt me? You peach, you mean scoundrel; as if I were so ungrateful, so heartless—because—because—I know you like to take mean advantages to insult and degrade me. Poor Richard, I'm so glad he got off."

She threw herself on the sofa, and burst into hysteric sobs.

"Well I never; didn't you your own self set me on?"

"Vile reptile! beast!" shrieked Angeline. "And you'll lay the blame on me. Oh! you gallant chevalier—you champion of the fair. Get out of my sight. I only hope you may come in poor Richard's way. I warrant you will suffer for your treachery."

Tom was stoical; too used to these "summerflaws" to be daunted by them. He pretended that he was anxious to be gone, and only lingered in hope of conciliating his offended angel.

How Tom pleaded, and Angeline relented, it were tedious to tell.

So after all they went in perfect harmony to the Volunteer Review.

The weather was very fine; and on their return Angeline vowed in all her life she had never enjoyed herself so much.

CHAPTER CLXXXIII.
THE SUICIDE OF RICHARD EAGLETON.

RICHARD EAGLETON has escaped to his lodging.

He has written a long letter which he seals with black and throws down upon the table beside his bed.

He now seats himself before the hearth.

By the side of his chair he has piled a heap of papers.

For awhile he glares abstractedly into the blazing fire; his face is wan and wild with passionate grief and anguishing despair.

A sneer of contempt flitters across his eyes and wreathes his lip.

With the calm of self-abandonment he picks up one by one the letters from the heap and tosses them on to the fire.

He sees the greedy flame devour, letter by letter, the delicately traced vows of love and endearment; he sees the dainty pink, glazed leaves flare and blacken and then strew the hearth with sickly tinder and ashes.

He laughs in the very scorn and rancour of his bitter despair.

The last is burned.

His jewels are destroyed, and their dust scattered to the winds; the casket lies broken and trampled under foot; his heart's wealth is all lost; he is a beggar and a bankrupt; the light that was within him is quenched, and how great is his darkness!

He rises and saunters across the room.

It is gay and pretty; a batchelor's bed-chamber; the walls are hung with sporting pictures, there is a portrait of Sylvia Volante dancing as Giselle, and the walls are trophied with foils, boxing-gloves, single-sticks, fishing-rods, and other tokens of the manly pastimes in which the unhappy youth had indulged.

He threw off his coat.

He closed the window shutters and stopped every crevice in the room with pieces of clothing and linen, and placed the rug against the door.

He raked the fire from the grate and closed up the chimney place with a screen.

Having completed these arrangements he fetched from the cupboard a chafing-dish on which he lighted a pan of charcoal.

His face remained unmoved; the utter callousness of extreme misery had settled upon his handsome features. He poured some wine from a bottle and drank it with a ghastly smile. He took from the shelf a brightly bound novel, the last emanation of some licentious French author.

The air of the room became close and oppressive.

A choking sensation caused him to loosen his collar and open the breast of his shirt.

He began to read.

The air became hotter and more suffocating.

Eagleton, however, did not feel more pain than a slight heaviness at the chest.

A heavy drowsiness fell upon his eyelids.

The room seemed swimming about him; a thousand confused memories took dreamy forms before his closing eyes.

The book slipped from his fingers.

He drew a long deep breath.

He slept!

The chimney clock kept up its measured tick-tack.

From the street arose the dulled noise of passing vehicles, the murmur of passing voices, the drone of a distant organ.

Tick-tack, tick-tack!

Eagleton slept on deeply.

The air became more stifling.

The charcoal glowed a fiercer red.

A change took place in the expression of the sleeper's face.

The hectic flush fainted off. The lips quivered and parted.

More rigid grew the features, fainter heaved the swelling breast, profounder grew the sleep, till at last sleep herself fled the pillow, and death reigned in her stead!

* * * * *

"Richard, it is I! Sylvia! Open the door! Ah, ciel! he will die. Richard, très cher, speak but one word."

"Which if it isn't done, Miss, the house will be

burned down; which it's not insured. Murder!
Thieves! Fire!"

There was a violent pushing at the door.

"Tick-tack," clacked the mantel-clock, as if in
mockery.

The door gave way.

Two women burst into the room.

They were driven back for an instant by the
strangling fumes.

Sylvia Volante, with a muffled shriek, threw herself by the side of the bed.

Before the landlady could tear open the shutters
and pull down the screen, Sylvia had sunk on the
ground, senseless.

CHAPTER CLXXXIV.

THE BOY PIRATE'S AID TO THE POLES RE-JECTED BY COUNT JOSIKA.

It was early morning.

The Avengers had pitched their tents at some
distance from the fort where the insurrectionists were
entrenched. Our hero and his officers held a council
of war, in which it was determined that the Boy
Pirate, attended by his principal officers, should ride
over to the entrenchments of Count Josika, and offer
their services to the insurgents.

Christopher, however, made up his mind to ride
over to the Polish lines with no other attendant than
Black Zampa.

It was a bright and fresh morning when he started
on his mission, with a light heart.

Our hero was very richly dressed, and was mounted
on a fiery black barb, which he had bought of a
Russian noble at Wilna.

Christopher rode with perfect grace and fearlessness. During his boyhood at Frontemore, he had
spent much time with the grooms, and in those
stables belonging to the mansion, by rights his own,
he had performed many very daring feats of horsemanship. Since commencing his career he had had
good practice in Mexico.

Black Zampa presented a very imposing spectacle.
He, too, was a good rider, and, on a milk-white
horse, looked very imposing. He was dressed in the
Zouave fashion, wore a turban and plume, a heavy
sabre, and a pair of silver-mounted pistols in his
holsters.

Zampa had assumed a very grand but graciously
patronising air, styling himself "Cap'en Kit's aid-
der-kong," and looking down from a vast elevation
upon the foremast-men.

The waggish Tom Garrod and his clique pretended
to be deeply impressed and awe-struck at the distinguished figure cut by the magnificent Zampa, and
treated him with the profoundest homage, somewhat
profanely inciting him to tell the most astounding
lies in support of his dignity.

As our hero cantered out of the camp, Black Ralph
ran from his tent, laughing.

When the merry rover caught sight of Zamp, in his
"pomp barbaric," curvetting behind our hero, he
started back, and performed a low salaam.

"May the king live for ever!" he exclaimed, addressing our hero; and then again, bowing to Zampa,
he added, "O, great Vizier, may thy shadow never
be less!"

"Not use to dis kinder ting, buckra Ralph," said
Zamp, majestically waving his jewelled hand. "See
me in my own country. Berry great prince, dar;
when go out to ride, hab a string ob elephans like a
shoal of porpoises."

"There is no sultan but Kit Khan, and Zampa is
his prophet!" cried Ralph, with humble fervour.

"Tink so? Use to dis kinder ting. Buckra
cap'en profit much if him listen to dis chile. Yo
know, cap'en berry well 'board ship, but on shore
yah want some one kinder used to it."

"Zampa ackbar! Our nigger is great!"

"Oh, that our slaves were wise!" cried our hero,
laughing. "For heaven's sake come down from the
clouds, Ralph, and let's have plain dealing, and words
comprehensible."

"Who can look upon the sun and not be dazed by
its sublime brilliance?"

"Who can listen to a showman's gong and not be
deafened by its harmless thunders?" returned our
hero, rather viciously.

"Harmless thunders! Exquisite! But, captain,
let not your thunders be harmless when you are before
the Polish chiefs. Do justice to our gallant band.
Let those we are to befriend learn the inestimable
value of our assistance; let them burn incense for
having gained such allies as the Boy Pirate, Black
Ralph, and their band of Avengers. Let me go with
you, brother; I am an orator."

"Stay at home then and lecture the men into good
behavior during my absence. No, Ralph, the magnificent Zampa is escort sufficient on such an errand."

"To hear is to obey," returned Ralph, again
salaming.

As the rover returned to his tent, he muttered,

"Here's a change! I could have made that
cursed Harwolf my football; but, somehow, before
this big Boy Pirate my spirit is rebuked."

The entrenchments which had been thrown up by
Count Josika were sentinelled by a number of well-
armed fellows, who seemed much excited at beholding our hero and his attendant.

Several horsemen spurred across the plain to meet
them.

When the Avenger explained his errand the Poles
shouted with exultation.

Our hero was passed into the fort.

He stood in an open space, surrounded on either
side by bastions, over which huge cannon projected
grimly.

It was a stirring scene.

A crowd of men were busy at the works, raising
or pointing the guns, carrying up ammunition, and
repairing breaches in the walls.

These were superintended by several handsome but
delicate-looking youths of noble birth.

A number of peasant recruits were at drill.

A band was performing a wild, soul-stirring
Magyar waltz.

An old man, soldierly and dignified in his mein,
benevolent, yet somewhat haughty in countenance,
and dressed in a costly furred cloak, was conversing
with a little knot of officers.

He advanced towards our hero with a grave step.

The workmen ceased from their employment, and
looked on the stately young adventurer with awe
and admiration.

The soldiers and officers smiled at each other, and
spoke in whispers.

Count Josika courteously saluted our hero, and
invited him to follow into the interior of the fort.

The Ravens left Zampa in his glory, surrounded
by the eager patriots, who questioned him as to the
nature and number of the Boy Pirate's band.

Zampa glorified his chief, who was "a parfec' Nero,"
and "Cap'en Ralph, most amazin' palaver," and
"Tom Garrod, most suspectful gem'man; travel all
round dis world, and many oders."

Meanwhile our hero found himself in a large and
pleasantly situated stone room, overlooking a wide
and richly-wooded landscape.

The floor was heaped with small-arms and sabres,
and along the walls hung a row of cloaks and
helmets.

"I need not ask your purpose, brave Englishman,"
said the count, looking upon our hero with something of soldierly admiration, but more of pity and
pride. "You come to offer your sword in aid of no
ignoble cause; the cause of a suffering and struggling people is always holy. I give you warmest
thanks, for your generous intent; it is consistent
with many traits in your strangely-mingled character."

"You know me then ?" said our hero, lowering his glance before the stern, bright look of the soldier.

"I know you for a chivalrous man, for one who has performed many heroic actions that are beyond all praise."

"Oh, do not flatter me, your excellency! Neither mock me," replied the youth, in a tone of subdued anguish and shame. "You know me also——"

"As the Red Raven, as the Boy Pirate—aye, the pirate! The scourge of the seas; the breaker of bonds which bind societies; the braver of authorities that protect humanity; the enemy of law and order. We are not rebels, sir, but patriots. Our little force is not a rabble of licentious traitors, but an army of martyrs. We war not against the senate of our country, but against her tyrants!"

The Boy Pirate averted his face; his strong and noble form quivered convulsively.

"If there are men in these latter days (and base is he who doubts it) that do not value life as the chief good, but who are willing to risk for their wronged and oppressed brother men, we open our arms wide to them, we give them the meed of a nation's gratitude; we love—we honour them; their swords are treasured and their aid implored. The Boy Pirate has no sword but the steel of an assassin, no life but what he witholds from justice. We fight for human law, and no law-breaker must be our champion!"

A cloud of stormy passions swept over our hero's noble face.

He gnashed his teeth; his dark, wild eyes suffused with sorrow wrung from his tortured heart.

"You are harsh, pitiless, unjust!" he cried, with fire. "From my childhood I was subjected to the vilest persecutions; while a mere boy I was captured by a pirate, who forced me to serve him. Since then the brand has been upon me. Fortune has favoured me beyond all others of my class; I have been stronger than my enemies, and those that wilfully hunted me have become my prey, and in such fair fighting I have won riches. In one sense, I am not a felon."

"Englishman, I do not look upon you as one of those ruthless wretches who take to a life of robbery from wicked and selfish motives. I will grant that at first you may have been forced to become a pirate, but if you had not valued life more than honour, if your repentance had been sincere——"

"My life!" cried our hero, with unmeasureless disdain, "now you are base indeed. Who is there of my worst enemies who dared to say that the Boy Pirate ever blanched at death in its most dreadful forms? My life!"

"Do not misunderstand me."

"I will not; you grudge me my life! life that is forfeit to the law. Your Shylocks of the law must have their pound of flesh; there is no railing the seal from off their bond. But, tell me, what atonement is there in death? What do your judges gain? They hasten on the end that must come, Oh, Heaven eternal! how soon, how very soon! Where the tree falls there must it lie, but will the barren grave bear fruits of repentance?"

The colour rose to the cheek of the old soldier, and his eyes melted with pity.

"My life!" continued the pirate vehemently, "it is that I would give them. Oh that I could live out a vigorous century, that they might have it all, but not to crush it out—not to whelm the whole 'to come' in powerless oblivion. Oh, I would toil and hope and suffer, and since through one false step my fall is so great that had I the success of a Tell or a Washington I could not deserve the world's thanks, at least I would earn this consolation : the more charitable of my kind shall say of me, 'Let him sleep in peace; he sinned, he atoned, and man forgives him.'"

"You deserve forgiveness, Englishman. The better part of your conduct inspires the highest admiration."

"But my life! they shall not have it. It is far, far too precious to me ; as I cannot wipe out the black stains of the past I will set against them an array of bright deeds that shall partly outshine their darkness. If they take me they must hang me; it is well, I'll not complain—they have won and I have lost ; but while I have cunning to elude them I will live to do a little good if the All-merciful permit me."

"I believe your contrition is sincere. In such a false, frail world it is strange that sterling repentance is not more respected ; but this real reformation is so unusual."

"I think because it is next to impossible. Increase a felon's punishment a thousandfold, but, when he is once enfranchised, let him be looked upon as a leper cleansed, and received on equal terms by his fellowmen. Bad as human nature is, I cannot, I will not believe that the worst are not capable of some touch of pride and gratitude. Well, Count Josika, I take my leave ; but, since you refuse my aid, at least, for the sake of your comrades, you will accept a word of warning, even from the Boy Pirate."

"Ha! you have some knowledge of the enemy's tactics ?"

"Yes. The Prince Aronsow has joined Count Brutoff with a large reinforcement, and a night attack upon your position is intended."

"Heaven's will be done! and we will do our best to give them a warm reception. Your hand, Captain Christopher; there is no animosity, I trust, between us."

Our hero grasped the extended hand.

"I trust not, your excellency, and I hope to do some good for your cause, in spite of this discouragement. If I can win a victory over these licensed pirates, these imperial brigands, the toil of its achievement shall be mine, yours the honour and profit. Farewell, and do not judge me too harshly."

"I judge you not ; the just Judge forgive the sins of both of us, and may He bless you! Pray be careful; I should grieve much to hear of your capture. Farewell !"

When the Boy Pirate emerged from the fort, the Poles shouted and waved their hats; the soldiers presented their arms.

With a flaming cheek, our hero vaulted on his fiery black horse, and, gracefully bowing, dashed off at hot speed.

Zamp stared after him, and then got into his saddle. Smiling regally, and waving his hand with the condescension of the Grand Bashaw, the aide-de-camp rattled off in pursuit of his superior.

CHAPTER CLXXXV.

THE STEPPING-STONE TO THE ALTAR.

CHARLES RYE was set at liberty.

He returned to the office of Messrs. Bullion, the bankers, and resumed his duties.

Every one who knew him heartily rejoiced at his exculpation, and received him with endless congratulations.

And what became of Sylvia Volante and the fair enchantress Angeline ?

Of the former we have more to relate, the latter we will dismiss in a few words.

It was on the evening of the day of Eagleton's suicide that she received a letter by post.

Angeline had made a new and important conquest.

At the volunteer review she had met with a young gentleman of large fortune and small intellect, who had fallen passionately in love with her at first sight.

The distinguished personage was not a roué ; if his brain was soft, his heart was yet softer, and he paid his addresses to the heartless and abandoned woman with honourable intent.

That same night she was to meet him at a ball.

She was dressed, and stood before the glass contemplating her charms with exquisite pleasure and triumph.

She turned a little pale as she recognised the hand-writing.

She tore the seal and read it eagerly.

She quailed with horror as she read the few calm, yet touching words that her lover had written in his mortal despair.

The thought flashed like a stroke of lightning through her brain.

"Before God and my conscience he was my husband, and I am his murderess!"

For a long time she sat trembling and ashy pale; at last, she rose, and, tearing the letter to pieces, burnt them and forgot it.

Forget! Who can forget! She laid the weight of her selfishness upon the venomed wound remorse had struck in her heart, but the wound throbbed, it bled, and no cold arrogance could assuage its burning, no power of selfishness could compress its gushing lips. She spoke of it never; she would hold no commune with the memories it recalled, in that sense she forgot it.

After she had sat staring long into vacancy as if she had been petrified by this sudden stroke, she rose mechanically.

She wrestled hard with the snake in her bosom; she soothed it for awhile. Her new lover was greatly struck by her enhanced loveliness, for now she could display her beauty to the best advantage in her lady-like ball dress and amid the halo of the brilliant gaslight; her manner too was more subdued and gentle. Little did her admirer know the cause of this favourable change in her demeanour; he was all devotion.

As they were returning in a cab to her house, the new lover spoke casually of the old, saying that he had known him at school, that he was much grieved at the sad catastrophe of his suicide, adding that the matter had been hushed up through the interest of Lord Hawksbury, the coroner's jury having brought in a verdict of temporary insanity.

It was too dark for the speaker to see the face of his companion, but he felt her hand quivering and became alarmed.

"This story distresses you, dear Angeline," he said. "I am thoughtless to pain one so gentle and sensitive, by mentioning such a sad affair; but what is uppermost in my thoughts I cannot conceal from you, and it seems a coincidence that this poor fellow should be buried at his own request by his mother's side in our village church; I feel almost as if I were implicated in the affair."

"Indeed! Then did Richard—" gasped Angeline, "your friend, I mean, poor Eagleton—did he write anything? did he state the motives that drove him to his dreadful act? Perhaps he had been disappointed in some affair of the heart."

"It is possible; but a letter which he left sealed by his bed was addressed to Lord Hawksbury; it contained a confession of his guilt, and implored the forgiveness of his injured friend, Charles Rye; he said that his treachery had been justly punished by the perfidy he himself had met from one to whom he had been ever true; but he mentioned no names. I had this from Charles Rye himself, with whom I am well acquainted."

Angeline did not reply, and her lover changed the subject of conversation.

Soon after this, much to the rage of her devoted Tom, the fickle beauty made her new lover the happiest of men, and became the mistress of a mansion.

Did she die soon? Did numberless misfortunes overtake her? Did she elope? Was she divorced? Not at all. Angeline was purely selfish. She knew too well what was required of her in the position she had gained so cleverly. Besides, she had taste, and when it was her interest to observe the proprieties of life her conduct was strictly in accordance with her predilection.

On the day of her marriage she received a shock, from the inward effects of which she never recovered.

At the bridegroom's side, she was passing up the aisle, her eyes bent on the ground.

Just as she reached the altar, her fairy foot tapped a sculptured slab in the floor; it bore no other inscription than the simple name, "RICHARD EAGLETON."

Thus she had passed to the altar over the grave of the fond lover whose heart she had broken, whom she had tortured to frenzy and death; thus the reward of treachery seemed to have followed the perjured witness and false friend even to his grave!

Angeline lived rich, respected—not liked overmuch—for there must always be found some genuine merit in the faultiest people who are loveable. She became thoroughly reformed in manners, though not in heart; she lived a prosperous life and was—unhappy.

CHAPTER CLXXXVI.

THE BOY PIRATE AND BLACK RALPH—THE MARCH—THE PLUNDERED VILLAGE—THE WOUNDED SPY—THE OPENING OF A BATTLE ROYAL.

BLACK Ralph and Sam Cassidy were summoned to the tent of the commander-in-chief of the band of Avengers.

Zampa was stationed at the door with orders to prevent intrusion.

A settled expression of sadness marked our hero's face.

This was at once noticed by his comrades.

"What cheer, captain; anything ugly in the wind's eye that your brow is so cloudy?" said Ralph. "Bad news from the fort?"

"The Russians, captain? Are we too late? Have they forestalled us by an attack?" asked Cassidy.

"No, hearties. You will scarcely anticipate the news I bring."

"Humph! The poor beggars begin to show the white feather, eh?" grumbled Ralph. "They have struck; they have disbanded?"

"They remain true to their cause; they will hold out to the last; but they are patriots," returned Christopher, "and we are pirates!"

"Not I, for one, I disown the name," cried Cassidy. "We are the Avengers of Poland's wrongs."

"Sam is right. We are no longer on the 'grand account,' we have taken to privateering; we have letters of marque," rejoined Ralph, "and we are henceforth gentlemen of spotless reputation."

"I would it were so, Ralph, but the world is not so willing to let bygones be bygones, as we could wish."

"Who dares impeach the character of the Boy Pirate?"

"Who can rightly defend it, Ralph? But, no more. Dispel that black frown, and hear with patience that Count Josika has refused our offer; his cause, he says, is too holy to be sustained by gentlemen of our class."

Cassidy looked greatly vexed and surprised.

There was an explosion of wrath on the part of Black Ralph.

"The snivelling, slavish, chain-dragging, sanctified spaniels! Born to fawn and be kicked," he roared high dudgeon. "There shall be no need to cart them off to Siberia; we'll make a desert of their own pitiful country. Refuse our aid! They shall know the want of it to their loss; and shiver the mizen, but I, for one, will join the Muscovites, and make these tall Poles bow their high heads beneath our conquering feet; for if there's one thing I hate more than a barrel-organ, it's these psalm-singing, canting, quaker-swabs, that stand upon smash principles. Won't have us! They *shall* have us, whether they will or no; if not as avengers of their own wrongs, as champions of our own honour."

"Be quiet, Ralph!"

"Long live his august Majesty, the Czar!"

A STRUGGLE FOR LIBERTY.

"Don't be a fool,!"

"Not I. If we had not been idiots, we should have known better than to prop a falling house. Now, Captain Kit, you see what comes of tilting at windmills, of fostering these ungrateful, snarlish curs, that bite the hand which caresses them. I declare myself liegeman to the Dane, or rather to the Russ, and if I don't smite this sledded Polack on the ice, may I be court-martialed!"

"Why, Ralph, you would never be so base as to be a slave; you would never be a tyrant's minion, and aid in the works of oppression!" said Cassidy, laughing. "Would you shoot the brave soldier, and knout the fair heroine?"

"I'd have nought to do with that, I grant ye; but as I couldn't whack 'em, I'd kiss 'em instead.

No. 56.

But for the men, they should sigh for King Log; aye, or King Stork, for a Vulture's a bird that is not to be ruffled."

"But it is a rascally insult, without joking," said Cassidy. "Pirates! Hang it, we're good enough to cut throats in any cause, I fancy, and worse men than we are have fought under fair banners."

"Well, comrades, we will not give up our enterprize because one punctilious old fellow will not give us countenance—we'll fight the Russians yet."

"Aye, captain, ● our own account. I shouldn't mind being a Robin Hood in these forests, and waring with the tyrants for the sake of the slaves."

"Our cousin is Will Scarlet, I think, Sam," returned Christopher, merrily, as he looked at Black Ralph's flushing face and starting eyes.

"Such a red sky bodes thunder," replied the other, in the same tone of banter.

The prediction was worthy of old Moore.

Like a roaring thunder-clap a terrific oath burst from Ralph's lips, and he struck the table with his heavy fist.

"Come, hearties, let us sit down and overhaul this chart," said the Boy Pirate, seating himself at the table, and drawing from his breast a rough map of the surrounding country. "The Prince Aronzow and our old friend, Count Brutoff, will lead their detachment through this defile; and here we'll intercept them."

With a wrathful growl Black Ralph stalked away from the table.

"Achilles is sulky," laughed Sam Cassidy.

Our hero rose and laid his hand on his colleague's shoulder.

"Ralph, you are angry," he said; "you think we have been insulted by these high-minded Poles, and ought to abandon them."

"I do," replied Ralph, emphatically.

"And you and your Vultures will have nothing to do with the affair we have in hand?"

"We will not."

"And why not?"

"Why! Shall I support a canaille of beggarly, polka-dancing——" he suddenly paused. "There, I am vanquished!"

"Where?"

"At the very name of polkas. What do we not owe to these Poles, we who love the bright ball-room, and the gay casino? I've a happy thought!"

"Let us share the happiness."

"At every ball-room in London, when any of these pretty Polish dances are performed, polka, waltz, or crakovienne, the M. C's. should go round with the salver for a subscription to the Polish Fund."

"Bravo! you're coming round."

"I wish I were with a Parisian grisette, or a London charmer on my arm; but as the old saying is, my dancing days are over; nevertheless 'memory lingers,' and I may add, 'yes, 'tis a spell.' The very word polka, seems to reconcile me even to Count Joskins. So I dismiss him with a wish that he may soon dance without music."

"He will never live to be hanged for all your good wishes. They say he is as rash under his white hairs, as he was when they curled in glossy lovelocks. I am sorry the old man will have none of us, for he is a splendid fellow, though too headstrong to be a good general."

"Enough of him," said Ralph, impatiently.

He whistled a polka tune as if to keep himself in good humour.

In strange contrast with his usual swaggering nonsensical talk, were his shrewd suggestions, as he and the other chiefs of the Avengers bent over the map, planning the mode of operation.

When all had been arranged, they left the tent together.

Soon the camp rung with the notes of the warbling bugles.

Drums rattled, and fifes squeaked.

The Avengers mustered and formed in line.

They were a formidable party.

Our hero glanced at them with brightened eye but heavy heart.

He addressed them.

He did not disguise the danger of the daring deed he was about to venture, but he exhorted them to show themselves worthy of the fame they had won.

His band responded in the hearty manner with which they were accustomed to answer his appeals.

Leaving as few of his men as he could safely, to guard the camp, he marched boldly forth.

The Avengers kept steadily on their way for several hours, led by a Polish guide.

Among the officers in the van, rode Feodor Polowski.

It was scarcely possible to believe that the stricken, stern-faced man, who rode in silence and buried in such profound apathy, could be the light-hearted, simple peasant, who had received the Avengers with humble but cordial hospitality.

They were passing through a fertile and beautiful country, but on all sides appeared the fatal tokens of war and disaster.

Here in the plain were the long mounds which had been thrown up by the retreating army of the Poles.

There was the rent in the green mantle of the woods, where the trees had been cut down to form stockades; yonder the broken bridge, where the progress of the pursuers had been stopped by the deep river.

They passed through a ruined village, which had been sacked by the Russians.

On either side of the long street the straggling cottages were now but black, smouldering heaps.

Little clouds of smoke soared up from the charred beams and timbers.

The gardens were trampled, the hedges beaten down beneath the hoofs of the prancing horses.

More hideous than all beside, were the festering heaps of dead bodies; men, women, and children, massacred in common.

In more than one place a whole family lay strewn in death before the door of their peaceful cottage. The wolves had grown so bold from impunity that as our Avengers passed they only snarled and ran off to a little distance from their dreadful repasts, waiting till the troop had gone by, and then leisurely sniffing back their way to their feast of blood.

At the sight of all these horrors, Feodor grew pale and faint and looked his agony; he said nothing, however, but rode on with a fierce frown and gnashing teeth.

Our hero would have halted at this village and have detached a burying party; but this was impossible, as no time could be spared.

The Avengers contented themselves by firing a few shots at the wolves and ravens and hurried on their march.

Our hero, Dick Caffyn, and Edward Leighton were riding some distance in advance of the rest. A man suddenly leaped the hedge, and, staggering towards the horsemen, sank on his knees.

A gun fell from his hand.

His head drooped on his breast and his arms hung limp at his side.

Dick and our hero leaped from their horses.

They supported the man in their arms and led him to the bank.

It was some moments before he could speak.

The band of Avengers now halted and gathered round him.

He rolled his blood-shot eyes round about him.

He opened his fur coat.

A gush of blood welled from his breast, which was torn by a frightful bayonet wound.

Our hero gave him some brandy; he drank it eagerly and sat erect. He even rose to his feet.

But the fever that parched his lips and glittered in his eyes, the changing colour on his sunken cheeks, gave evidence of his mortal agonies.

He fell heavily backwards.

He looked with suspicious glance at our hero.

The Boy Pirate pointed to the colours which the gorgeous Zampa carried so proudly.

On the pure white field was embroidered a crown, supported by eight flowers, the crest of Poland.

The man smiled radiantly.

He pulled a packet from his breast and gave it to our hero.

"Ah, Poland!" he moaned, and sank dead.

Our hero opened the packet.

It was written over in strange and secret characters.

Feodor read it hurriedly.

He looked at the fallen peasant sternly and sorrowfully, and then addressed our hero.

"We have been discovered," he said. "This poor fellow bears a despatch from Cracow addressed to Count Josika; the Russians have made this detour only to deceive us."

"But did not the scout say that the attack was to be made after dark?" asked Cassidy.

"Yes; but it seems he was misinformed, or the Russians have changed their plans."

"And this poor fellow?"

"I should think he was found in the village, and mistaken for one of the people."

"Do you know him?"

"Yes; he is a Polish spy—a daring fellow! I wonder he was overtaken."

"What is to be done, then?"

"We must march at once to the fort."

"Be it so. I am ready," returned our hero, firmly.

"But, captain, we can't oppose the Russians with our small company!"

"Why not?"

"Well, we may oppose them, as the cat may spring at the eagle."

"As the raven may pounce on the wolf!" returned our hero, sternly. "Besides, these rugged Cossacks are semi-savages, and will run at the ring of our English voices."

"Well, this is a desperate deed, but adventures less daring would not be worthy of the Avengers," said Dick Caffyn.

"Death cannot come too early," murmured Feodor, bitterly. "But I speak for myself," he added, smiling faintly. "A week ago I should not have said so."

"Dick, tell Black Ralph to bring up the rear. We will make our way through the forest, and we may yet be in time to save the Count Josika and his gallant followers."

They had not penetrated the wood for a mile, when the distant roar of cannon travelled to their ears, and the wild shouts of the distant battle urged them to redouble their speed.

———

Lest our readers should think that we have been guilty of exaggeration in the account we have given of the brutal manner in which the unfortunate Polish patriots have been treated by their oppressors, we insert the following extract from a letter, appearing in one of the leading daily papers, which will give some idea of

"THE ATROCITIES OF THE RUSSIANS IN POLAND.

"This place (Kowno), usually so peaceful, has, during the past few weeks, assumed quite a different aspect.

"Here, you see prisoners in chains; there, dead or wounded brought in carts; from distant woods thunders the dull boom of cannon or the sharp crack of the rifle, and the nearer you come to the frontier of the government of Kowno, the oftener do you meet troops of flying or pursuing insurgents, who hasten to enter Courland, where, hitherto, no state of siege has as yet been proclaimed. The appearance of the usually pleasant country of the governments of Kowno, Wilna, Mohieu, and Witepsk, which, at the beginning of last week, I had carefully explored, made a sad impression upon me.

"Besides daily occurences of arrests, imprisonments, battles, &c., I have made some unexpected experiences from which I infer that *nothing will be left of all Poland but a heap of ashes!*

"Already you must travel for miles before you come upon an estate or a village. I passed innumerable towns entirely devoid of inhabitants, and where estates and villages had been razed to the ground by the Russian troops.

"What a sad fate has met many a Prussian colonist here!

"In the Wilkowiski district I was myself a witness of the cruel and lawless conduct of the Russians.

"The day before three hundred insurgents had entered the estate of a German resident here, and by threats of instant death obtained provisions.

"This was betrayed to the Russians, who immediately arrested the resident and burnt his estate to the ground, after having plundered it.

"It was on the 25th August, at 10 a.m., when I arrived here and witnessed this deed.

"The landowner, in chains, was being taken with his family in his own carriage to the nearest town.

"Behind was a cartful of furniture, &c., escorted by a sotnia of Cossacks and a detachment of infantry.

"Officers and soldiers had already taken what was best; a Russian officer offered me a gold watch for sale, saying it was his own property, but, as immediately after, Cossacks, loaded with *German* books came crowding in upon me, offering them for a trifle, I saw what people I had to deal with.

"Who will blame the national government for forbidding, under severe penalties, any one from buying anything from these lawless troops?

"Truly they must be in great need; how can a soldier live upon four roubles a year?

"Another terrible sight is the burning woods, set on fire by the order of Mouravieff.

"In many, many places you see hundreds of workmen felling the trees; but this having been found too expensive, or not sufficiently expeditious, they have begun to burn the woods.

"In Courland, and still more in Kowno, and Wilna, you may see everywhere the smoke rising from them, and near the railway and elsewhere, the black ground where the fire has been.

"In Kowno and Wilna there is an execution every day, usually of from one to four persons.

"On the 26th and 27th August, I was residing at Kowno, near the place where the executions took place.

"At mid-day the execution was heralded by the sound of the trumpet, and masses of people came out of the town to be present, while the prisoner was taken strongly guarded in a cart to the spot.

"The newly appointed governor of Kowno, a son of the known Mouravieff of Wilna, a young man about thirty, conducted the execution in person.

"After the sentence was read, the prisoner turned once more for pardon to the governor.

"'Away, away,' was the only reply, muttered in Russian.

"Twelve soldiers then came forward and fired at the victim, who was tied to a post, and as he did not fall immediately Mouravieff ordered twelve more to fire, upon which he fell.

"It appeared that one bullet struck a stone, it ricochetted and hit Mouravieff in the leg.

"The governor was carried to his house, but it appeared by a bulletin published next day, that the wound was not a dangerous one.

"It is a striking fact that the Russian press says nothing of all this, nor of the weekly execution of ladies.

"I have myself seen two ladies shot in Wilna, and three hanged at Kowno.

"I can appeal to thousands of witnesses to prove the truth of what I say.

"The process of executing these ladies is truly disgusting.

"A long white shirt, with a thick woollen cape covering the head is the only dress, and the halter is placed round the neck just below the cape.

"Before the body, already half dead, is strung up, six Russian soldiers pull with all their strength at the feet, in order to prevent the crowd seeing the convulsions of the victim, who is left hanging twenty-four hours."

When will such horrors end?

———

CHAPTER CLXXXVII.

A TERRIFIC SIEGE—A BATTLE ROYAL—THE PIRATES IN AMBUSH — CHARGE OF THE AVENGERS—HEROISM OF THE POLISH MAIDS — DEATH OF COUNT JOSIKA — OUR HERO CHOSEN CHIEF OF THE INSURGENTS.

WHEN the Boy Pirate and his band came within sight of the fort, they beheld the Russians wildly assailing the walls.

With loud cheers the gallant Poles defended themselves.

They had been forced to abandon the out-works.

Far outnumbered by the Cossacks, they had retired within the walls after a furious resistance.

They spiked their own guns rather than the enemy should take them. Some they even tore from their carriages and rolled them down the hill.

Others they crammed to the muzzle and so caused them to explode.

Now in their numbers they manned the walls.

Both the Polish officers and men were not a little sullen at the count's rejection of the pirates' aid, but they fought with all the fury of despair.

Perfectly confident of victory the Russians fought with grim persistence.

The Polish banner rent by the hurtling shot, streamed desperately in the wind.

Around the walls rolled the white clouds of smoke.

The thundrous, ear-splitting roar of the cannon resounded on all sides.

It was a terrific scene.

The Avengers remained crouching in the wood.

A wild cry arose from the fort.

A furious conflict raged more and more savagely in the bastions and curtain-walls of the fortress.

The Poles were giving way, disputing their ground inch by inch.

There is not in the world, as history well testifies, a braver nation than the Poles.

So desperate had been their resistance that the walls of the fortress were almost cleared of the assaulters, but the Poles were terribly reduced in numbers and seemingly quite powerless to resist another attack.

A body of Russians and Cossacks were marching steadily up to the wall.

They dragged with them some heavy guns, and uttered a furious shout.

Count Josika was seen on the walls from time to time, when the clouds of smoke wafted away; his white hair streaming, his sword flashing in the glare of flames and the flitting blaze of musketry; his dauntless breast exposed to the volleys of bullets, which rained in leaden showers.

The old man cheered his men to incredible efforts.

Exhausted by the steady assaults of their terrible foes, who bore them down by their mere numerical strength, the weary Poles would retire before the enemy.

Then the clear, firm voice of the gallant old soldier roused the fainting spirits and nerved the sinking arms of his followers.

Again and again the patriots rushed upon their beleaguers, and cleared the walls, for the charge of fresh and increasing masses.

To cut away the scaling ladders was impossible; they had enough to do to dispute possession of the ramparts.

Then a touching spectacle was seen. The wives, sisters, and daughters of the insurgents had been brought into the fort.

They now appeared mingling with the men.

Among these Polish maids not one but was a heroine; no screams, no appeals for mercy.

In silent fortitude these noble women aided their relations and protectors.

Not a few armed themselves with muskets, and kept up a fire that was admirably steady and effective.

Yet there was nothing of the Amazon in their manner, nothing unfeminine in their pale faces, many very lovely, and all beautified by a lofty expression of womanly heroism.

The ruffian Cossacks had no respect for age or sex.

They fired indiscriminately at men and women, or rather, they vented their fury more particularly upon the women, several of whom were shot down by the miscreants.

The Poles are rigid Catholics, and a number of priests and women on a tower that overhung the ramparts, and was now silenced for want of ammunition, sank on their knees, and blended their voices like Christian martyrs, as they were, in a holy hymn.

The Russians yelled their vindictive joy.

With the last dread effort of heroic despair, the gallant patriots made a furious charge, and scores of Russians, whirling round and round, pelted down from the walls.

Of course we have given a description including a large portion of time before the arrival of our glorious Avengers on the scene of action.

Count Brutoff and his detachment of cavalry were rushing up to a breach that had been made in the outer walls.

"My lads," cried the Avenger to his band, "look at yonder scene of brutal carnage, yonder grand display of true heroism. Behold those tender women shielding their loved ones with their own gentle bosoms. Think of your vow to avenge the murdered Alexina; remember your names, your fame, your country, and then there will be no need to exhort you to do your doughtiest. God for the Right! Vengeance for Poland!"

The English are not a demonstrative nation. It is said they are cold and phlegmatic.

Any one naturally modest may blush for the national vain-glory of our race, but well may the most callous feel proud of the deep fervour, the genuine lion-heartedness of a British cheer.

"Vengeance for Poland!"

From the depths of their sympathising hearts arose the deep cry.

Over the plain, not in a serried rank, but in pell-mell fury, rushed the gallant band.

They formed in double line at the twang of Zamp's bugle.

The sharp crack of their muskets, the lightning gleam of their brandished cutlasses, caused the Cossacks to rein their horses instinctively, and halt.

They had no time to get into order, the riders spurring behind jostled against those in front.

In voices of thunder the Boy Pirate and Black Ralph roared for their men to keep in line.

The impetuosity of Dick Caffyn, and the hungry hate of Feodor, caused this order to be totally disregarded.

These two rushed upon the Cossacks, pistolling the horses, and slashing at their riders as they fell.

The rest of the Avengers, incited by this example, flew to the attack en masse.

The consequences to the rash seamen might have been fatal, but for the steady Cassidy.

The captain of the rare Old Raven had, with the veteran Jack Brierley, been stationed behind the thickets, with a strong reserve, whose impatience they had much ado to restrain.

Seeing that his comrades would be trampled down by the very impetus of the charging body of cavalry, he left his covert, marched his men, orderly but swiftly, to the rear of the Cossacks, and opened a brisk and telling fire.

Huddled together, like sheep surrounded by wolves, the Russians had no room for action.

Only those in the front and rear could resist the violent shock of the Avengers, who kept shooting down the horses till the Cossacks rolled in heaps on the beaten ground.

The shouts of joy and encouragement, the tearful cries of women, and the sturdy cheers of men from the walls were more inspiring to the Avengers even than the terror and confusion they had struck to the hearts of the tyrants.

Black Ralph was in ecstacies.

Zampa blew the most appalling blasts on the war-trumpet, and positively routed his foes without striking except the drums of their ears.

Count Brutoff, enraged beyond measure, when he perceived by whom the charge was made, tore up and down on his fine blood horse, smiting his own men, and pouring out torrents of execration on their cowardice.

Black Ralph flung himself before the count's horse.

He seized the bridle.

"Turn, hell-hound, turn!" roared the ranting rover, shaking the rein so savagely that the horse reared and plunged, and almost threw the rider from the saddle. "More sanguinary coward than terms can give thee out, yield, and we'll have thee painted to please the Poles——"

The declaimer narrowly escaped a fearful slash of the count's keen sabre.

Ralph threw his arms round the count's body and dragged him to the ground.

His head was struck by the horse's hoof, and he sank insensible.

Black Ralph stamped on his breast.

"Now kiss the ground before young Malcolm's feet."

Count Brutoff made no reply to the insult, for he heard it not.

A number of the Cossacks dashed madly past.

Black Ralph was knocked over the prostrate count.

Before he could rise Dick Caffyn rushed to his side waving a reeking cutlass.

"They fly!" he shouted.

Like General Wolfe at Quebec, Ralph raised himself on one arm, and asked feebly,

"Who fly?"

"The Russians, general," answered Dick, with a laugh.

"Then I shall die contented—at ninety-five," responded Ralph, sinking back in a dramatically dying manner.

"The whole fleet is sheering off," cried old Brierley running up, "but, if there's any manhood among ye, crowd sail, the cap'en's in distress."

"Where is he?" cried Ralph, leaping up.

"He is in the old hulk yonder with Sam Cassidy and Zamp; they are broadsides with a squadron of these blubber-drinking swabs. Heave ahead, hearties, or it will be too late."

Our hero, who had fought as became his prowess in the charge against the Cossacks, when he saw that easy victory was in the hands of the Avengers, turned his attention to the fort.

With Leighton, Cassidy, Zamp, Tom Garrod and a dozen other picked men of his crews, and Feodor Polowski, he cut his way to the walls.

The Poles were still engaged in a terrific conflict with the Russians.

They were signalled by one of the ladies on the wall.

A sallyport was opened and the Avengers rushed into the fortress.

They threw themselves beside the struggling patriots and fought like lions.

Wilder grew the melée.

The Russians had such immense advantage, as their numbers more than tripled those of the Poles.

Our hero narrowly escaped death.

He was struck down by a huge Cossack who felled him from behind with a blow from his gun-stock.

Our hero was saved by a woman.

A pretty, brave-looking girl, dressed as a vivandiere, threw herself before him, and fired a pistol at a soldier who was about to thrust his bayonet into our hero's heart. The man fell.

Count Josika looked at our hero, who rose—for he was not stunned—with a strange glance.

"You have not kept your promise or you would have escaped this danger," he said,

"I promised I would serve you against your will," cried our hero. "I have kept my word, though I fear that we must rally these poor fellows once more if we dare hope for triumph."

Count Josika harangued the weary Poles in their own language.

Once more they made a desperate charge upon the enemy.

The cannons' roar seemed dumbed by the shouts of the victorious patriots.

Dashing down headlong from the walls, the Russians swept back from their furious opponents.

Our hero hewed his way to the side of the chief commander.

A parting volley of shots.

Count Josika staggered backwards.

Our hero caught him as he fell.

The Russian bugles sounded a retreat.

The battle was for once to the weak.

The patriots shouted their joy.

Black Ralph, Brierley, and Dick Caffyn now appeared on the scene.

They were startled by the shrieks of the women and the groans of the men.

A sad wail smote thrillingly on their heart.

Why this mournful cry at the moment of victory?

Its cause was soon apparent.

The Avenger on one knee, was supporting the bleeding body of the gallant old warrior.

A bullet had pierced the breast of the noble Count Josika.

The guns were silent.

The battle was over.

The banner of Poland still floated over the citadel of the patriots so heroically defended.

Our hero looked with tenderness upon the dying face of the old soldier.

Count Josika smiled faintly.

He pressed our hero's hand.

There was deep silence, broken only by the sobbing of the women.

A priest came forward.

His eyes were wet with tears.

He kneeled, and placed the cross to the dying soldier's lips.

The count kissed it, and, though he could not speak, pointed feebly to his sword, which lay near him.

It was placed in his hand.

He held it towards our hero.

A radiant look of joy lighted the face of the sensitive, high-souled youth as he took the sacred pledge in his hand.

He looked at the count with eager inquiry.

He held the sword aloft, and then pointed to the Poles surrounding him.

The dying leader bowed his head, and smiled.

He then made an effort to speak; the words passed off into a long, deep sigh.

Count Josika fell back—dead!

Our hero rose, somewhat bewildered.

He still grasped the sword in his hand.

The Poles saluted him with a loud cheer.

They all sank on their knees, and lifted off their caps.

Our hero found himself at this eventful moment of his strange history elected chief of this gallant band of insurgents.

He was about to decline the honour they had conferred upon him, and to propose the election of Feodor Polowski in his place.

The latter drew him aside.

"Noble Englishman, retain, for Poland's good, the command thus freely bestowed on you," he said.

"It must not be," our hero began.

"Yet, listen to me. Whatever you may hereafter resolve, do not raise obstacles now to this arrangement. Much is to be done. This advantage must be seized upon. We must pursue the Cossacks, we must repair the breaches in these walls, and we must," he added, with a gasp, "we must bury our dead!"

"But why not accept this post yourself, Feodor? Who so well fitted to fill it as yourself?"

"None so ill-fitted. I have one consuming desire—I must avenge Alexina. While Brutoff lives I have no heart even to serve my country; besides, who am I?—a peasant, unknown, and without ambition. The command has not been offered me; if it had, under the most favourable circumstances, I should steadily refuse it; and if I held it, I would joyfully transfer it to you."

"You honour me too much."

"You honour yourself by your noble conduct, brave Englishman; but do not let us waste precious time in idle words. I must away, it will be as well to chase these panic-stricken miscreants, and I shall know no peace till I have stained my sword in the blood of the accursed Brutoff."

"Rest easy on this score," said Black Ralph, pointing with his sword to the plain before the fortress. "Behold where lies the tyrant's cursed head!"

"You have killed him?"

"To speak modestly, I was more than a match for him—he lies dead on the field."

"Oh! can I ever forgive you! Ah! you should have left that to me," said Feodor, bitterly; "but I will not believe that he has escaped, even though to perish by another's sword. I am his fate! He lives only till we meet."

"I tell you he is dead—stark and stiff, and down among the dead men. Follow me, and I will show you his carcase."

But though they searched the dreadful field, they could not find the body.

It was concluded that the count had been wounded not killed, and had been carried off the field by his comrades.

It was strange how welcome this news was to him who thirsted for the blood of his wife's murderer.

CHAPTER CLXXXVIII.

NO TRACE OF HARWOLF'S GANG—THE BRAZILIAN WAR-SHIPS IN PURSUIT OF OUR HERO—A FRUITLESS CHASE.

DANIEL HARWOLF and his gang remained concealed in the subterranean passages, which they had found so opportunely.

The Brazilian soldiers hunted for them in vain.

The good old missionary, who was slowly recovering from the effects of the brutal treatment he had received at the hands of the pirates, informed the commanding officer of the troop that the Boy Pirate had besieged the fort, and had exterminated the band.

The soldiers had been conveyed to the island in a transport ship which was consorted with a man-of-war.

The captain of this ship was one Don Rodriguez, a keen-eyed, dark-faced Spaniard of a haughty and reserved demeanour, a man of great ability, valour and ambition.

He started at the mention of our hero's name.

"Is it possible that the great pirate has been cruising near this island? We were told that he had sailed to La Plata," said Rodriguez, quickly. "Do you know, father, whither he is bound?"

"I do not, my son, and if I did I should not betray the man to whom I am so deeply obliged for such generous services; but for him those wretches would have murdered every soul on the island, and have taken possession of the place."

"It appears they are not here at present," said the military officer.

"It is possible that they are hiding away in some of the lonely creeks on the main land, or among the islands."

"We will find them if they have not perished; but I am anxious to put a stop to these dreadful outrages of the pirates at one blow," said Don Rodriguez.

"Oh that it were possible!" sighed the old man. "My poor flock scattered and destroyed by these fiendish wolves; it is horrible!"

"But, the Boy Pirate——"

"Is hated beyond the rest."

"And without good cause."

"Father, is he not the most terrible scourge of them all?"

"To his enemies."

"And are not all men his enemies?"

"There are some who would be ungrateful if they were not his zealous friends."

"It is strange that he should be so popular along the coasts."

"It is well known that for years the Red Raven is but in name a pirate."

"How can that be? Whence are his prizes, his great treasures, his fleets, his crews?"

"For his wealth, it is said that he inherited much of it from the pirate Don Miguel Vasquez, under whom he served when a boy."

"And whose daughter he saved from a Spanish convent?"

"Yes; and for his prizes, they are the vessels sent in pursuit of him."

"He is a wonderful rascal. Well, it will be a proud day when I see him strike his flag," said the sea-captain.

"And it will be a day far distant, my son," returned the missionary. "The Red Raven will strike his colours to no living man."

"That remains to be seen, good father," answered the sea-captain, with a stern smile. "If I can overhaul him either he or I shall perish."

"Others have said so," rejoined the missionary, quietly.

"Ha, ha! and others have perished. Well, if anything could reconcile me to the fate of falling before a cursed pirate, it would be that I had one tussel with this king of the high seas."

"But, senor, the Raven has acted so nobly, has run such a terrible risk for the sake of my poor people, that he deserves some grace even from his bitterest foes. The sportsman gives the fox 'law;' do not be less generous to this splendid adventurer, let him have a day's sail."

"And lose him. No, father; besides, he will have 'law' enough, for I must wait for three warships that have been promised me; they will leave San Salvador this evening."

"Have you, then, already despatched a messenger?"

"I have."

"I cannot say that I wish you success. I believe this man will reform, and nobly retrieve the past; he told me himself that he was bound for Poland, and that he was resolved to spend his last breath in aiding the patriots."

"The leopard will keep his spots," replied Rodriguez.

"But the wildest beasts have been tamed by kindness."

"But they seldom change their natures, father; they are never to be trusted."

Here the topic of conversation was changed, and soon after Don Rodriguez left the house without informing the missionary of his intention.

It was night.

He returned to his vessel.

He sent for the officer commanding the troop.

These valiant fellows resolved upon a very rash adventure.

They agreed to fetch the soldiers from shore, to arm the transport with some guns which were to be found in a magazine near the shore, to divide the hands, and to man the transport, and with their two ships to go in pursuit of the pirate's fleet.

They hoped that they might fall in with some of his prizes, and engage them till the other pirate vessels came to the assistance of their consorts.

By this desperate ruse they intended to detain our hero's ships till the arrival of the war-ships from San Salvador.

All these well-planned schemes, however, were doomed to fail, for the excellent reason that the Boy Pirate's fleet was never overtaken.

We should not have narrated this episode but that it leads to a series of adventures which befel Daniel Harwolf and his desperate gang.

CHAPTER CLXXXIX.

HARWOLF AND HIS GANG ON THE WATCH—
THE LONG BOAT OF THE MAN-OF-WAR—
BLACKLOCK'S PRIZE—A DESERTER FROM
CORDERES—HARWOLF RESOLVES TO HAVE
HIS REVENGE UPON THE TRAITOR — HIS
STRATAGEM—TRAITS OF PIRATE LIFE.

NIGHT and silence reign on the island where Daniel
Harwolf and his gang are still lurking.

The pirate and his lieutenant are watching at the
mouth of a cavern which opens from the subterranean passages below the fallen tower.

The heavens are once more spangled over with the
glowing hosts; the moon once more trails her robe
of silver along the ever restless breast of the grand,
open sea.

The night is calm.

The billows wash the silver sands at Harwolf's
feet.

Wardlaw is seated on a ridge of the rocks, and
scans the sea and sky through his night-glass.

Three or four of the pirates are lurking in the
darkness.

Their eyes are ever turning towards two steam-
vessels anchored off the harbour.

These are the transport and her convoy, the
"Cortez," a fine war ship, commanded, as we have
seen, by Don Rodriguez, who is so ambitious to capture the "Red Raven."

There is a sort of bay or creek, running deeply
into the land, the cliff under which the passages are
dug forming one extremity.

The spot does not command a view of this bay.

The pirates rise.

Harwolf walks from the mouth of the cavern towards a huge mass of stone, which obstructs the
view of the bay.

Wardlaw followed him.

Harwolf stops and holds up his hand.

"Avast!" he whispered; "this is the sound of
oars, but the boat is not ours."

"I think not," replied the other. "They pull too
steadily, too slowly. Has Blacklock failed?"

"I have been so cursedly unlucky that I almost
doubt. Hush!"

Harwolf very cautiously raised his head above the
rock.

"Down!" he muttered fiercely to Wardlaw.

They hid themselves in the cavern.

"One of the 'Cortez' boats?"

"Aye!"

"I thought so."

"How manned?"

"An officer, the coxswain and eight oarsmen."

"What are they doing here?"

"Still on the look out for us," returned Harwolf.

"Won't they believe their eyes?"

"It seems not."

"Yet the tower is proof enough."

"A perfect wreck."

"The 'Raven's' men thought we had perished."

"Aye! They did not stay long to inquire."

"Now Captain Kit, Sam Cassidy and blustering
bully Ralph are gone, whom will they make commodore, I wonder?"

"Dick Caffyn was on the tower when the explosion took place, was he not?"

"And Zampa, the infernal nigger."

"I wonder who will wear the Boy Pirate's shoes?"

"Brand, or the Spaniard."

"Perhaps so."

"It will be a hard lot for Lilia."

"Pshaw! she will soon find consolation."

"She will mate with her husband's successor."

"Aye, Gerald; and, as novelty is charming, for
awhile she will be pleased with the exchange."

"Well, since the Boy Pirate is gone, they sail in
a helmless ship, I take it."

"Their cruise will be the shorter."

"They will soon land at the gallows-foot, all the
cursed lot of them."

"It eats my heart!"

"What does?"

"The gnawing regret that I did not take the
scornful harridan."

"Humph! I think it as well as it is."

"In these things a man is ever crossed; I loved
this girl, and, though soft feelings are forgotten with
me, I yet crave to possess her; she shall be mine
yet if there is any chance of overhauling the cursed
craft that bears her."

"Well we must wait the issue of Blacklock's adventure."

"Cap'en, a sail in the bay!" a man whispered,
crawling down from a hollow in the cliff, where he
had been on the watch.

"What sort of bark?"

"A small brigantine."

"Good news, Captain Harwolf," said Wardlaw.
"I'll wager she's the 'Alert,' and all has gone well."

"Blacklock is no fool."

"If we can once more get to sea there will be
hope."

"Aye, of capturing Lilia and clearing scores with
Corderes."

The man, who had returned to his post, once more
descended.

"Look, cap'en," he said; "smoke rises from the
funnels, yonder; boats have taken the shoresmen
aboard; they are shaking out their canvas."

The pirates looked in the direction of the vessels
indicated.

The sails were being trimmed, the anchor weighed.

A quarter of an hour passed, and the ships were
seen sailing and steaming away.

They passed the mouth of the cove at a great distance in the offing.

"Perhaps they are off on a cruise after the
Ravens," said Wardlaw.

"All the better for us," was Harwolf's reply.

"If they make out the brigantine perhaps they
will run in shore."

"No, folks who hunt for eagles will not take heed
of sparrow-hawks," returned Harwolf.

"Cap'en, a boat puts off from the brigantine,"
said the man.

The pirates were too eager to ascertain the result
of Blacklock's adventure to pay much regard to
caution.

They walked out upon the open strand.

A boat was run up.

The crew landed.

It consisted of Blacklock and a dozen other fiend-
ish-looking fellows.

They brought with them an ill-featured, half-
starved Spaniard, as dark as a mulatto.

"Well, hearty, what cheer?" asked Harwolf.

"All's well, cap'en," answered the fellow, with
gruff satisfaction.

"And whom have we here?"

"Avast! one thing at a time."

"Very good. I see you have captured the craft."

"And she's a good prize, I can tell ye, cap'en;
trim-built, and a fair sailer."

"You have done well. Was the job easily
managed?"

"Aye, aye."

"And the crew?"

"You shall hear."

"Is this one of them?"

"No, no. I don't do nothing agen orders."

"Then you cleared them off?"

Blacklock drew his finger across his throat.

"Ha! there's no danger, then; mercy is a pirate's
ruin," Harwolf remarked, with a sneer of malice.

"Well, cap'en, we found the brigantine lying a
anchor in the roads. She had been watering and
clearing, and the men were dead asleep. The night
was as black as the devil could wish it. We stole
alongside of the brigantine, and found but one man
on watch, and he was more than half asleep. We
got over the side, cut that fellow's throat, and the
rest we overpowered,"

"And put them out of harm's way?"

"Aye, aye; they all walked the plank."

"And swam ashore, you fool!"

"They walked the plank, I said, cap'en; and if you had given me time to tell you, you would know as it was impossible they should swim a stroke; a weight was tied to the heels of each."

"And the skipper?"

"Skipped overboard with the rest."

"This does you credit, Blacklock. And who is this swab?"

"One of Corderes' Spaniards?"

"Ha!" cried Harwolf, his eyes sparkling cruelly, "he's welcome."

"We found him on the island half starved."

"How came he there?"

"Avast, cap'en, let the lubber speak for himself."

"I escaped from the ship, senor," said the Spaniard. "I was beaten and ill-used, and we were chased by a sloop. I took advantage of the evening's dusk, got through a port and swam to the island; the ship was under weigh, and I was not missed."

"And how long did you stay ashore?"

"A wretched week, senor, during all which time, except a sea bird and a few shell-fish, I could get nothing to eat."

"I remember, you know, you cursed mutineer!"

"I have trusted myself to your mercy, senor."

"Mercy! Do you hear, I'll not be insulted, you villain! Mercy is a woman's virtue, and Harwolf disclaims it."

"Well, senor, I was taken, I was starving, and I don't care what becomes of me; but if I could have my revenge on Corderes I would be satisfied."

"And what sort of cruise has the Spanish thief made?"

"He has taken several prizes, rich ones, and he stormed a little village, burnt the houses, and robbed the people. He has been chased more than once."

"And where is he now?"

"Moored in a little river that runs into the La Plata."

"Will he remain long at his anchorages?"

"Yes, senor, they have taken a good prize, and when they have shared the bounty will disguise the ship, and send her into dock while they hurry to the towns to squander their booty."

"That is likely, captain," said Wardlaw.

"Yes, I heard myself that Corderes had been seen even in Mexico."

"It is true, senor, quite true, and Don Rodriguez was sent to capture him; but your affair in this island saved Corderes, for the steamers were ordered to this harbour that very night to set things in order and capture you."

"And you know where to find him, eh?"

"Yes, senor, I will stake my life that I can bring you within gunshot of the haven where he is moored."

"Blacklock, are you sure that none of the crew of the 'Alert' escaped?"

"Aye, cap'en, may I be served as they were when I goes agen orders."

"You would not be treated so mercifully," returned Harwolf with a sneer. "But what think you, Wardlaw, I have a scheme to pay this traitor a shrewd turn? We will disguise ourselves, and set the carpenter and painter to work with the craft, and then throw ourselves in the way of this Don Rodriguez."

"To what end?"

"That I may give information against the hound. Thus it may be done: we will personate the crew of the 'Alert,' and this fellow shall be our pilot."

This plan was adopted.

Harwolf, and as many men as he could take without exciting suspicion, went on board the vessel.

They found the brigantine to be a trim, fast-sailing craft, as Blacklock had reported.

She was amply stored with everything needful, besides containing several heavy chests of money.

The pirates cruised about in this disguise till they met with the vessels of Don Rodriguez, who was returning dispirited from his hawking for the Ravens.

The Spaniard was completely deceived in the character of his informers, but found from other sources that the account they gave him of the whereabouts of the crafty Corderes were perfectly correct.

They steamed for the "Plate river," as the sailors call the Rio de La Plata.

On their voyage they met with several fishing boats, aboard of which were men belonging to the village which had been sacked by the pirates.

These men gave a fearful account of the atrocities that had been committed by this murderous gang.

Our readers will remark that on board piratical vessels nothing is more common than murderous quarrels, treachery, and all kinds of villany; the principle of "honour among thieves" is never observed, and no one can trust his fellow; such is the rover's life.

The terrible crimes that have been perpetrated by this class of criminals can never be outdone by the most sensational and horrible pictures of romance.

A pirate of the "Corderes" type, a Spaniard named Benito de Soto is the chief actor in the following tragedy.

This pirate and his crew plundered many vessels, amongst others was an American brig, the treatment of which forms the masterpiece of their atrocity.

Having taken out of this brig all the valuables they could find, they hatched down all hands to the hold, except a black man, who was allowed to stay upon deck for the special purpose of affording in his torture an amusing exhibition to Soto and his gang.

The crew being hatched down, and the negro being left in the shrouds, they began their hellish work.

They set fire to the brig.

They lay to, to observe the progress of the flames.

The miserable African, scorched by the flames, bounded from rope to rope.

He climbed to the masthead.

Now he clung to the shrouds.

Now leapt to one part of the vessel and then to another.

Their enjoyment seemed raised to its highest pitch.

At length the hatches opened to the devouring element.

The tortured victim of their fiendish cruelty fell exhausted into the flames.

The horrid and revolting scene closed, amid the shouts of the miscreants who had caused it.

Another pleasing picture of life on board a dashing rover is that afforded in the following anecdote of Teach, or Black Beard, the principal events of whose life, drawn from an authentic source, have been laid before our readers.

The biography of this famous buccaneer makes the following just remark:—

"In the commonwealth of pirates he who goes the greatest length of wickedness is looked upon with a kind of envy amongst them, as a person of a most extraordinary gallantry."

Some of the frolics of Black Beard were as extravagant in wickedness as if he wished to make his men believe that he was a devil incarnate.

Being one day at sea, and a little flushed with drink,

"Come," said he, "let us make a hell of our own, and try how long we can bear it."

Accordingly, he, with two or three others, went down into the hold, and, closing up all the hatches, filled several pots full of brimstone and other combustible matter.

They then set it on fire.

They so continued till they were almost suffocated, when some of the men cried out for air. At length he opened the hatches, not a little pleased that he had held out the longest.

LILIAN, THE QUEEN OF THE AVENGERS.

CHAPTER CXC.

OUR HERO AN INSURGENT CHIEF—A REIN-
FORCEMENT — THE AMBUSH — TOM GARROD
SPINNING YARNS—THE POLISH VIVANDIERE
—THE PIRATES ENTRAPPED—THE CAPTURE
OF EDWARD LEIGHTON AND KATINKA.

OUR hero had now assumed the command of a large
body of the Polish insurgents.

His deeds of heroism soon became the subject of
general comment.

The hopes of the rebels revived, and the fears of
the Russians increased, as, almost daily, our gallant
hero obtained some victory over his enemies.

His numbers daily increased.

A proud, happy, yet grave look on the pirate's
features, showed how much more congenial to his
noble heart was his new labour of devoted heroism
than his wretched and degrading employment as
prig and pirate.

A thief, a miserable thief, that filches from his
fellows the trash that the honest prize only because it
buys them independence !

No. 57.

Let our youthful reader suppose himself (as,
perhaps, he does) a very fine fellow; let him relinquish the idea of work, honest, hard work; let him
live upon what he can borrow or beg from others,
and if he can get enough to spare, let him bestow
gifts upon others. Would his gifts be those of real
charity ? They cost him nothing but fawning,
cringing, and endurance of insult ! Would one of
our young readers take a gift from another which
he knew was borrowed from a third person ?

No !

Then, what can be said of the generosity of thieves
who are said, in romances, to give freely (which they
never do) from what they steal from others ?

The Boy Pirate could not redeem the past, but
his misguided nature was so noble, as well as faulty,
that he was intensely happy in the new mode of life
which he had so generously embraced.

Our readers have seen, in a previous chapter, an
extract from the reports of the correspondent of a
leading daily paper, that no exaggeration has been
made use of in describing the atrocities practised by
the Russians upon the poor brave Poles.

Our hero was shocked and enraged by the continuous accounts he received of the barbarous treatment of these people in whose cause he had drawn his sword.

With his great genius and high courage, our hero might have been the deliverer of the oppressed nation, might have won for himself a name which would have descended to the latest times. But he was a felon, and many of the Polish nobles, like Count Josika, were unwilling to receive aid from such a character.

The Boy Pirate, having certain affairs to arrange with some of the agents of the National Government at Warsaw, despatched three of his trustiest followers to carry out his wishes.

He selected Black Ralph, Caffyn, and Sam Cassidy.

These worthies met with a notable adventure, which we will hereafter chronicle; but, first, we must relate what befell Edward Leighton, and how he was captured and captivated.

Our hero had entrusted him with the command of a troop of the Avengers.

His orders were to intercept a reinforcement of Cossacks, who were marching to join the regiment of Prince Aronzow and Count Brutoff.

Tom Garrod, and Zampa, were with this party.

In the evening, Leighton and his men arrived near the village where the Russians were posted.

Tom Garrod and Edward, had consulted the chart, and found that they were occupying a narrow pass, through which the Russians would be compelled to march.

Finding that they had time for repose, as the enemy were not expected to arrive before evening, they posted the pickets, and having found a large cavern in the side of the hill, they entered it, carrying with them the provisions that had been sent them from a neighbouring village by some of the peasants who favoured the good cause.

They lighted a fire in a hollow of the rocks, taking care not to betray themselves by letting the smoke escape through any aperture that would cause it to be seen from the winding road which passed through the defile.

Edward Leighton who was much amused by the conversation of Black Zamp, and the loquacious boatswain, Tom Garrod, called those worthies to his side, and gave them an extra share from the keg of brandy that he carried.

With these remarkable personages, and five or six others of a similar stamp, he seated himself by the burning logs, and passed round the kid.

The men lighted their pipes or rolled their quids, and gave themselves up to enjoyment.

"I should think, Tom, you have seen a deal of service at sea, but little on shore," prompted Leighton.

"Avast, yer honour! I've seen as much sarvice on land as any shore-going swab among 'em."

"Tell that to the marines!" grunted Bill Brail, an old and surly-seeming tar, who grumbled his disbelief of Tom's choicest yarns, but enjoyed them as much as the rest did.

"And what people do you think are the queerest in their manners and customs?"

"You see, yer honour, they'se so warious, it's hard to say which is the most 'stronary people in the world, but about as rum a lot as any on 'em is the Chinese."

"Did you ever serve in China, Tom?"

"Seen a deal o' sarvice, there, yer honour. I were at the storming of Canton."

"In what service?"

"I sarved aboard a man-o'-war, yer honour, and helped to spike the guns. The poor devils was tied to 'em for fear of their running away. There was about thirty thousand of 'em in Canton, and we opposed them with a force of about seven hundred and fifty men; sepoys, marines and all.

"You saw some strange sights there, Tom!"

"Rayther so. Not as you're called on to believe what I tells you about 'em, for there's some things in natur' as no one can believe in unless they sees 'em. It's quite another affair about mermaids, sea sarpints, and sich, which every seaman of experience has a parfect right to discoorse about."

"Nevertheless, tell us some of the sights you saw in China."

"Well, once I saw five hundred rebels beheaded in one mornin'. It was two hours' werry hard work, but the poor crim'nals seemed to enjoy the hoperation. Nobody would believe that."

"And yet they run like sheep before a file of English red-coats."

"Dizactly. They're like women—fact they wears petticoats, and shaves off every bit of beard! They are all contrariwise. Now, you've heard as they are werry ingenious?"

"I've heard that they imitate the most difficult work, and make watches from pattern."

"They will so. Our cap'en wanted a new coat; the old 'un was worn—it was seamed and patched as an old mainsail. He sent for John Chinaman. He asked him if he could make a coat like that.

"Johnny looked at it, grinned, nodded his head, and sang out,

"'Ah! yah! me can do,'

"In two days, he brought his work aboard.

"He spread it out on the table in the after cabin.

"There were the seams, creases, patches, the skipper knew so well.

"'Did you ever know of such a bare-faced rascal?' asked the cap'en of the first lieutenant.

"'Never.'

"'He has the imperance to think that I don't know the old coat from a new one.'

"The officers laughed, and Johnny was much delighted.

"'How much, Johnny?' asked the captain.

"The Chinaman opened his hands and spread his fingers, then closed them and opened them again.

"'Twenty rupees,' said the lieutenant; 'a pretty round sum to give for one's own old coat.'

"'All right,' says the cap'en, beckoning the boatswain. 'Come here, purser, pay this man his twenty.'

"The cap'en winked.

"'Aye, aye, sir,' answered bo'swain, and poor Johnny was dragged to the gratings.

"He yelled most piteously.

"They pulled off his tunic, when out fell the werry identical old coat.

"The bo'swain snatched it up, and run off with it to the skipper.

"'My eyes and limbs, yer honour!' says he, gasping like a porpoise.

"'Don't swear, sir,' says the cap'en, sharply.

"'Beg pardon, sir, but was there ever sich a imperant warmint?—here's the werry old coat! The thief has stolen it afore yer honour's face!'

"'No, no; you're mistaken,' says the cap'en; 'here's the coat still on the table!'

"The cap'en bought the coat for a cu'rosity, ordered another, and got one good enough for any hadmiral."

"That's a good yarn, Tom," said Leighton.

"Well, sir, you ain't called on to believe it, but it's a fac', sir."

"And your own adventures, Tom? I heard that a heavy number of your company lost their mess in that cruise."

"Sartain; with cholera. Fifty on 'em died in one night."

"And yet you escaped."

"Made a werry narrow escape, yer honour. Fourteen on us was laid under a shed; thirteen died, and I fainted. So the rest of the crew sheered off, 'cos the enemy didn't give 'em time to bury us."

"And how long did you remain before you were picked up?"

"Twelve days and nights, sir; at the latter end of which time one of our officers peeped into the shed. I hailed him; he came alongside, and lifted me on to his back, and carried me off to the boats."

"And did you take much booty, Tom?" asked his messmates.

"Well, hearties, our commodore was a bit of a martinet; but I a'most bilked him once. We were a stormin' a part of the town, and I were sent with ten men to knock down a pawn-shop—there's as many in China as well as elsewheres—when I found a parfec' mine of rupees and ingots."

"They are in bars, ain't they, Tom?"

"No, mate; they're shaped like penny buns—round at the top and flat at the bottom. I tied a fortun' of 'em in a blue 'kerchief as Sal gave me; when I found a very cur'ous piece of workmanship—it was a little clock; this I concealed in the pockets of my ducks. Well, I was brought afore a court-martial. I got off about the ingots; said as I'd no intentions of sticking to 'em. When, just as I were about to be acquitted, 'ting-ting' goes summut in the pocket of my ducks. It was the clock a-striking.

"Even the cap'en hisself could not help laughing. Howsomedever, I got out of the scrape pretty easy like, and no more was said about it."

As Tom Garrod concluded this yarn, a girl entered the cavern.

It was Katinka, the Polish vivandiere who had saved our hero's life.

She was extremely pretty and merry; her complexion pure and rosy, and her bright eyes twinkled with animation. A true daughter of the regiment, she had something of martial pride in her walk; yet she was perfectly feminine and graceful.

Edward Leighton, who was a dark, tall, handsome fellow, started up to receive her.

His eyes flashed and his cheeks flushed as he took her hand.

She blushed rosily, and lowered her glance.

She then looked up with some excitement.

"Monsieur," she said, speaking in fluent French, "I bring you bad news."

"Even bad news is welcome when it comes by such a charming messenger," returned Edward, gallantly.

"I trust the messenger is more welcome than the news, however," replied the girl, laughing sweetly; "but this is no time for jesting, monsieur. You are all betrayed."

"Betrayed!"

"Indeed it is so; there is yet time to save yourselves."

"But, fair Katinka, how are we betrayed?"

"You are in ambush to surprise the Russians, are you not?"

"Yes; and in good hopes of cutting off Prince Aronzow's detachment."

"And you are yourselves in the power of the enemy. Your guide was a Russian spy; he brought you hither to deliver you into the hands of your foes."

"And where is the enemy posted?"

"On every side of you. Every pass has been blocked; your only chance is to climb the hills and to pour down upon the enemy in the valley."

"But how did you escape falling into the hands of the Russians?"

"I got the start of them, and being dressed as a vivandiere they thought I belonged to their army; but fly at once, there is no safety here."

The pirates left the cavern.

They climbed the hill.

The night was coming on, and the sky shone red and lurid in the west.

Below them was a long line of Russians, each standing with his musket poised, and eagerly scanning the side of the hill.

They heard the sound of bugles in the vale behind them.

Edward Leighton and the vivandiere alone were mounted.

With a wild shout the rovers poured down the side of the hill.

They made a desperate attack upon the Russian troop.

They broke through their line.

Edward's horse was shot.

It staggered and dropped.

The young American was stunned by the fall.

Katinka shrieked.

She then threw herself from her horse, and bent over the fallen Avenger.

She had no thoughts for her own safety.

Wildly the pirates poured past, cleaving their way at the point of the cutlass.

They looked at Leighton; but thought he had been killed by a bullet.

They fled on.

Katinka would not leave the side of Leighton.

She loosened the fastenings of his Polish jacket, and bathed his temples from the little keg of water slung at her side.

She started at the wild yells of the savage Cossacks, and looking up found herself surrounded and a prisoner.

CHAPTER XCI.

THE REGULATORS AND THE PAWNEE-LOUPS—CATAHAGA'S TACTICS—THE PLANTER AND HIS SISTER—A BRUSH WITH THE REDSKINS—ARRIVAL OF THE TRAVELLERS—A BACKWOOD'S CHARMER—THE HALF-BREED—FOXLEY A PRISONER OF THE RANGERS—HARWOLF'S PROPOSAL TO OSWALD LAMOND—A MURDEROUS PLOT—IMPATIENCE OF MA K LEIGHTON.

ANDREW HARWOLF and the Regulators had been apprised of the advance of the Pawnees.

They received the Indians with a furious discharge of their muskets.

The Indians attacked their entrenchments but were repulsed with slaughter.

However, they took some scalps, and the wily young chief finding that he had no chance of succeeding in taking the fort by an open attack, thought it would be better to abandon his design and to entice his foes from their strong position by a pretended flight.

He carried out this manœuvre so well that the Regulators pursued him and his braves far into the woods, and many fell under the deadly rifle-shots of these native foresters.

Catahaga continued his flight.

It was now winter, and the ground was covered with snow.

The Pawnees on their march fell in with a party of travellers.

It consisted of a wealthy planter, his sister, and a number of mounted servants.

There were two sledges.

One of them was driven by the planter, the other was laden with household property.

Catahaga kept out of sight.

He had caused a report to be spread among the Indians that he had fallen.

This news was carried to the Regulators, who believing it, and knowing that the hopes of the natives would cease with the death of the cunning young war-chief, left the fort, and returned to Larchville.

The artful Pawnees showed themselves on the banks that skirted the road.

The planter and his men fired upon them.

The Indians set up a yell, and beat a hasty retreat.

The planter laughed heartily.

"Wall, I opine that Judge Warren is a raal sublime screamer. Never in my life did I see the devils run in sich electric quick notice. They seem slick skeared, they du. I conjecture as the judge, for a Britisher, is a most remarkable cha-rack-tur."

The lady, who had slunk cowering under the bearskin rug, now looked up, and joined in the laugh.

She was a buxom, pretty woman, about thirty.

"It may be a feint though, Joab," she said. "I guess we'd best not spare hoss-flesh."

With this ladylike remark she handed over the whip to her brother.

Joab lashed the horses.

The party dashed on, the horses' hoofs ringing along the frozen ground, and the bells jingling.

Towards evening they came upon a large party of the Regulators bivouacked in a clearing, and, as usual, were cooking or reposing by their wood fires.

As the sledges and the riders approached the Regulators started up, surprised at seeing such visitors.

Warren and Miles Thornton came forward.

The jolly-looking planter jumped out of the sledge.

He caught Warren by the hand and gave him a terrific grip.

"I offer you extr'on'ary congratulation, Judge, on the amazin' whippin' you have given the infarnal screechers who have been making sich a excruciating smash in these yere colonial settlements."

"Ah! the Pawnees are tamed at last, are they?" returned the other, smiling; "we've had tough work with them."

"Wall, I du say that you air a military screamer. We sighted a pack of the scalping devil-skins and they run like quicksilver at the first shot."

"What were they, stranger, Pawnee or Daco-tahs?" asked Mark Leighton.

"I conjecture they were Loups," answered the planter. "What say, Abiram?"

The man thus appealed to was a tall, lanky fellow, with a thin face, and high cheek-bones, black eyes, and long-hanging hair.

He was mounted on a small, rough horse, and his feet nearly touched the ground.

"I reckon they was Pawnee-Loups from the Blue Earth," he answered.

"And did you see a tall young chief with them?"

"Wall, I can't say as I did."

"And they ran, you say?"

"Like 'possums."

"Then it must be true, the Eagle-Wing is killed," said Mark.

"And that's a victory in itself," said Warren.

"It might be had we caught and flayed the reptile," grumbled Mark. "It's all very well to blow shawms and trumpets over our miserable retreat, but if we had won what I should call a victory we should have exterminated the last of the infernal savages."

"Like all other wild beasts they shrink and die out before the advancing steps of civilization," returned Warren. "It's hard to catch them in their own woods."

"Durn'ee, I do zay as we've sometimes cotched a tartar," Miles joined in with a gruff laugh.

"Well, it's true, then, that Catahaga is dead."

"Aye, Judge, a Shoshoné showed me the chief's broken calumet."

"And, meanwhile, who suffers for my poor cousin Ned's brutal murder? Where is Agnes Staunton?" growled Mark.

"I am not the man to break my promise," returned the Judge. "Curb your impatience, Mark; since we have quieted the redskins we will now attend to the rangers."

"Now or never!" muttered Mark.

"Wall, Judge Warren, I think as the correc' thing is to introduce myself and my sister—I'm Joab Jackson, of Jackson Pint, down Arkansas, and this yere fine gal is Rebecca Jackson, my only and single sister; bakes, brews, spins, sews, darns, churns, and looks out for a husband."

Warren bowed.

Rebecca admonished her brother with a tremendous slap on the shoulder.

"Laws, shut up," she simpered.

"My gal, I reckon as whot I states is veracity—you air a reg'lar buster at making butter-cakes, and if a prime gal at thirty doesn't look out for a smart coon to be her marital husband, it's for the reason that she's got one already."

"Now, can't yer talk about yerself?" cried Rebecca.

"Wall, I opine that I'm as distinguished a man as any in these yere parts, and have got as many dollars and as pretty a plant as any planter in 'Kansas. There's my hand, Judge Warren, and I am most extr'o'nary glad, I am so, to make yer acquaintance."

"And may I ask you what is the happy occasion of this meeting?" asked Warren. "Are you travelling in business or for pleasure?"

"Wall, Judge, the coincidence is this—my sister Rebecca was tarnation skeared about the Pawnees, and as we had a brush with some of the tribes down by Jackson Pint, I thought as I would bring the gal over to Larchville and leave her under your il-lus'trous pertectioning."

"You honour me much, sir, by such confidence," returned Warren.

He handed the lady from the sledge.

"If such is your intent, it would be wise for you to remain under our escort till we reach the settlement; besides, you must require rest. Miss Jackson, I'm sure, must be very much fatigued."

"And so hungry. Laws, I could eat a painter!"

The lady meant but a panther.

Miles laughed and stared, and suggested in a whisper to Mark Leighton that there was a Pawnee boy they had taken who was in prime condition.

"She will be satisfied with a buffalo," grumbled the sulky youth.

He was still chafing with jealous rage at the delay in the pursuit of Agnes.

He answered sharply every question that was put to him, and walked with downcast eye and moody brow.

An awning of deerskins was stretched from the branches of the trees, and under this rude tent the lady and her brother retired to regale themselves.

Warren conversed with Abiram, who said he was overseer of Jackson's plantation, which he described as a magnificent piece of property.

The men who accompanied Jackson, feasted themselves on the roasted game, and drank plentifully from the barrel of spirits which Warren had opened for them.

The Judge beckoned his confidant, Miles Thornton, and walked away for some distance from the fire.

He sat down on a log.

"Miles," he said, abstractedly.

"What zays yer honour?"

"This war has been an unlucky business."

"I zay zo, too; thought as we were a band of merrymen. Zince that mortal bad scrape with the Jew and the bee-hunter we haven't taken the valley of a handful of oats."

"No, I have lost money—lost! Ha, I have lost the reward I sold my soul for!" muttered the villain, fiercely. "I am banished from Frontemore, another reigns in my stead."

"Aye, zure, and durn'ee, this Injen huntin' brings varsal small profits to Joe Miles!" returned the countryman.

"No, we must make money; the richer we are the safer we shall be."

"Zo zay I; and we musn't be over nice as to the means to be used, your honour."

"Wisely spoken. I am restless at heart; I burst in ignorance. I want to know who is at Frontemore; what has become of my son Daniel; whether *they* live, those enemies whom I spared, the gipsy and Silas Rye?"

"Dead, zur, all on 'em."

"You think so? And Foxley?"

"The blamed crusher, the Injens have skinned 'un."

"Well, then, we *must* be safe!"

"But, as you zay, yer honour, riches brings safety, and money be mighty desirable."

"You saw this planter's sister?"

"Az eats 'painters?' Durn'ee, perhaps she

wouldn't mind devourin' a ploughman. Ho, ho! I'll look out vor'un."

"I will marry her."

"How? Zure, squire, but that's a good 'un."

"Why shouldn't I marry her?"

"Dang it, squire, but she bean't much of the lady neither."

"Lady! What's a lady? A refined woman; treachery and frivolity distilled to the essence!"

"Zure, yer honour, I never heard a lady called that afore, and don't much understand what character that may be; but, I'm blamed if I can zee why you should prefer this dowdy lass, az wouldn't have been taken at home for a scullery-maid, when there be many zo much purtier and genteeler in the settlement."

"A woman's a woman, and an estate is an estate."

"Zure, squire; but, dang it, I doan't see it now!"

"Her brother is owner of the largest plant in Arkansas."

"And do'ee think az he'll give it your honour for his zister's dower? That would be a good joke."

"When Jackson dies his sister inherits all."

"Zartain, squire; but he's a hale man, and, maybe, will wed some lass, and have a score of children."

"He will never marry," answered the villain, in a cold, calm tone.

Miles turned pale.

"Maybe he'll die before his sister," he muttered, hoarsely.

"He will," said his master.

"Judge Warren, here's an Indian half-breed, one of the friendly Shoshoné's. I think he brings news of the Leighton girl and the rangers," said a man, running up to the leader. "Shall I call Mark?"

"Wait; where is Mark?"

"Hob-and-nobbing with Jackson in the tent."

"Let him stay where he is; the men must rest to-night or they won't be prepared for a brush in the morning."

"Very well, Judge; shall I fetch the half-breed?"

"Yes; and, unless I tell you to do so, say nothing to Mark, or he will rouse you all, and start you on some fool's chase or other."

"I'll warrant that's a prospect that would frighten even a gossiping woman to hold her tongue. Confound that fellow, he's mad himself, and wants to drive us mad too. The Leighton girl wouldn't thank him for his meddling, after all."

"Well, send the half-breed to me."

The Shoshoné drew near.

He was muffled in an Indian blanket, and his face was smeared with alternate stripes of white and blue paint.

He wore a cap of the fur of the martin.

In spite of this muffling and disfigurement his walk was lithe and graceful and his features supremely handsome.

"My brother is welcome," said Warren, extending his hand.

The Shoshoné grasped it, and replied in a silvery tone,

"The Grey Wolf is a great chief, his name is written red in the war-path."

"What mummery is this? No, you are in truth Oswold Lamond."

"The same, my lord, and your poor servant ever."

"But are you frantic? Why have you come?"

"Why should not the White Fox visit the lodge of his brother the Grey Wolf," returned the other, with a low laugh.

"But your cousin——"

"Old Buskins? Pshaw! he had better keep out of the range of my barkers. I always pay my shot, and I owe him one.

"You are a fool!"

"A man; of course I am. But, brother fool, let me ask you how you came possessed of so much wisdom as you have shown in this last affair?"

"What affair?"

"Why, are you not on your way to Larchville?"

"What then?"

"And did you not mean to pay a visit at the half-way house, my stronghold, on the mountains?"

"Faith, Regan, I don't see how I could help making some show of opposition against you. You have exasperated the whole colony by the abduction of that puling wench, Agnes Staunton."

"I cry their mercy, and shall do as I like."

"But what brings you here?"

"An ill wind."

"I should think so. Well, your precious folly will ruin all my plans."

"It will, I trust."

"You brave me, then?"

"Do you brave me?"

"You think I mean treachery?"

"I am not ignorant of your estimable character."

"What stuff is all this? What is to prevent me from seizing you on the spot?"

"Your sense of honour."

"Is that all, eh?"

"And a little precaution I took before venturing here."

"What precaution?"

"If I do not return to my fellows scathless and satisfied, there will be made an exposure of yourself and your band."

"You villain! Do you think you have it in your power to prove anything against me?"

"Who is Reynard?"

"How should I know?" returned Warren, coolly, though with a slight start.

"Your countryman, and yet you know him not, eh?"

"I know that he joined the Regulators, and was either shot or carried off by the redskins."

"Well, he knows you."

"Durnee, zur, do'ee speak. Be the blamed crusher a living man?" Miles broke in, with great excitement.

"Yes, my friend, and in possession of all his crushing faculties, among which he numbers a clear memory and a glib tongue."

"I woan't believe 'un," growled Miles, turning a blank face on his master.

"But where is the beast?" asked Warren, with glinting eyes.

"With my pack, away down by the River Mountains, Mr. Harwolf."

Warren sank down on the log as if the word had stunned him.

"He sent you this token," said Oswald, holding out a knife.

Harwolf made a snatch at it.

Oswald smiled, and placed it in his bosom.

"Your pardon, Judge Warren, this is for Harwolf when he comes to terms with me."

The elder villain looked upon the younger with a glare of deadly hate, and laid his hand on his pistol.

The captain of the Bushrangers smiled through his war-paint, and tapped his revolvers, which were concealed under his blanket.

"They say you're a good shot, well practised at home, squire, ha? You once killed a brace of beauties, I believe, with one shot?"

"My wife was false—all have been false to me," groaned the wretched Harwolf.

"And you were the faithful steward to—ha! ha! Well, let the past go, for it is gone."

"What do you want?" asked Harwolf, in a thick voice.

"Not to betray you to the bloodhounds, captain, that's a fact."

"You say you have the fellow in your stronghold?"

"Yes."

"How did you take him?" asked Harwolf, very eagerly.

"He has gone from hand to hand like a penny piece. First he was picked up by the Dacotahs, then the Eagle-Wing claimed him, then he was carried off by Minna Wyotti and the Pawnee-Loups,

454 THE BOY PIRATE; OR, LIFE ON THE OCEAN.

last of all he was captured by me, he and pretty Minna were both taken."

" And you say he is still your prisoner ?"

" He is."

" Well, Oswald, is there to be a breach between our bands ?"

" No. 'When rogues fall out,' is the old saying. It is for our interest to remain friends."

" Right. Oswald, what shall I do for you ?—what shall I give in ransom for your prisoner ?"

" He is not for sale."

" Well, if you are not a fool, you may now make your fortune."

" And live on the square ?"

" Yes."

" I should not mind that, I am almost weary of my present way of life."

" Jackson's Pint is far from Larchville."

" And what is the point of that remark ?"

" An immense estate which may be yours."

" On what conditions ?"

" The easiest."

" Aye man, but name them."

" You must surrender that fellow to me."

" Sell the calf to the butcher. Furthermore ?"

" You must marry the planter's sister."

" But how will that bring me to the holding of her brother's land ?"

" Why, is she not his heiress ?"

" Well, but he is not dead."

" No, but he is mortal."

" Ha !"

" It is easy—you can give him his share of the land."

" How much ?"

The villain of Frontemore answered with a ghastly leer,

" *About six feet !*"

" Humph !"

" Do you like the scheme ?"

" I should like the estate."

" And you don't feel much compunction for the swaggering Yankee ?"

" Perhaps not ; but, yet, my wife's brother——"

" Hark ye, Oswald, you can't be responsible for my actions."

" Heaven forbid !"

" A bargain, then ; let me arrange my own affairs with your prisoner, and in return, I will manage yours with your future brother-in-law."

" Well, the colony is in such a wild and unsettled state, I am known only in Larchville, and there the folks like me better than old Buskins. I'll consider of it."

" No, resolve upon it. Let us make the match ; I will contrive to get you married to this woman."

" But Agnes——"

" Pshaw, she has given you trouble enough already ; do you wan't to make her your plague for life ?"

" She would be a sweet torment, nevertheless. I love her, I hold myself to be her husband."

" Even that can be managed."

" How ?"

" Your wife will be older than yourself, and it is only natural to suppose that you will survive her."

" A consummation easy to be brought about."

" In these cases there must be no drawing back ; the ambitious throw aside all obstacles, come in what shape they may."

" Now may I never want a precious counsellor ! And you'll be responsible for that too ?"

" Aye, aye ; remorse is past with me. I cannot afford to feel one human sympathy. You smile ; well, the bond between us is only one of interest."

" And thus we have it then ; I give you my prisoner's life that you may take my wife's and her brother's."

" You use crude words ; we do more than we dare name," muttered Harwolf.

Was the man insane when he made these horrible proposals, or could he be really such a villain as to carry them out ?

Alas, the monsters of romance are, after all, but puny villains compared with the monsters of reality, as the political histories and criminal annals of all nations can testify. Was Oswald Lamond seriously inclined to join in this dreadful plot ? He was not. With all his dissimulation and roguery the young bushranger had hitherto stopped short of the crime of actual murder, except in the case of his attempt to assassinate Catahaga ; and even in that affair, so black and dastardly, he was influenced by a feeling which has disgraced better men, that there was a very great difference between the murder of a painted savage and that of a white man.

Oswald Lamond did not tell Harwolf that he had really married Agnes. Subdued by her fears and entirely in his power, the poor girl at last consented to marry the youthful miscreant.

" And now you must go," said Harwolf. " I will feign that news has come of your removal from your present position in the mountains, and draw the Regulators from your track."

" This done, I will send you an answer to your proposal. I will take time to consider of it."

" Do, and then we will to work in earnest."

" Adieu, then."

" Stay, I will pass you out of the camp."

As they walked by the tent they heard the sounds of coarse laughter.

The loudest among the voices was that of Miss Rebecca.

" Oh let me linger on those dulcet accents, that clear ring of silver bells," chuckled Oswald ; " for life will they murmur sweetly in my ears, when, happiest of mortals, I can claim that angel as my bride !"

" Ho ! ho ! I'm blamed zur," laughed Miles, " but the young lady do want vinishin' off."

" Good night, Oswald Lamond," whispered Harwolf, when they had passed the last of the men on guard.

" The bloodhound's throat cut, Jackson Point shall be Lamondville."

" And Beccy Jackson shall be Mrs. Regan," laughed the bushranger.

As Harwolf walked moodily to the fire Mark Leighton came to his side.

" Who was that fellow you were talking with just now, Judge Warren ?" he asked.

" A Shoshoné spy, Mark ; a half-breed I employ, a very trusty fellow."

" And what news did he bring ?"

" Bad enough."

" Ten dollars but I guess it. That cat-o'-nine-lives, Catahaga the Pawnee, is not dead after all ?"

" He said nothing about the Pawnee, we were speaking of the rangers."

" Then why on earth did you not call me ? What news, what news ?"

" It seems that the Rangers have left their position in the mountains."

" And where are they ?"

" Not far from hence."

" The burning thieves, let us rouse and give 'em chase."

" And lose them altogether."

" But where is the half-breed."

" Gone scouting ; we shall meet him to-morrow if he strikes the right trail."

" To-morrow ! wait, wait ! Hang me, Judge Warren, but I'll leave you and your Regulators to crawl home to Larchville, and singly I'll hunt down the brigands, and, if I fall, my blood be on your head. I believe you're all in league with the wretches, and I know that there's neither honour nor courage among ye."

Mark rushed off in a towering rage in the direction the Shoshoné had taken.

In sullen mood he returned having made a fruitless search and flung himself down by the wood-fire in deep dudgeon.

CHAPTER CXCII.

THE SOLDIER'S STORY.

WHILE the conversation as narrated in our last chapter was being carried on between the villanous plotters, a knot of the woodsmen who were disinclined to sleep or were awaiting their turn to mount guard, one of their number told the following tale, which we can assure our readers is one fact.

The hero of this adventure was a tall, smart fellow, an Englishman by birth, but long a resident in the back woods.

"Aye, comrades," he began, "you're right in your guess, I was once in the British army, saw much service, and was all through the Burmese war.

"At one part of the campaign we took a strongly fortified city which was for days fiercely defended.

"But, before I go farther, let me ask you did you ever get a real fright? I don't mean did you ever feel nervous, or qualmish, were you ever daunted or startled; but did you ever have a paroxysm of deadly terror?"

"Guess that's an odd question for a soldier to ask, and a Britisher, too. Were you ever so mortal skeard?" said one of the settlers.

"I was once, comrade, and I'm going to tell you all about it. Don't imagine I'm going to confess myself a coward. As a lad and a youth I was as bold as a hawk; I was promoted for a daring act, but got broke for some devilry, and broke my heart at the same time. I never liked the service after I was reduced, so I took leg bail and deserted."

"But your fright?"

"It happened in this way: Numbers of our poor fellows were struck down by the fever; they died by dozens; on one occasion eight of them laid in the dead-house.

"Now, this place was a long narrow shed, and the corpses after being opened and examined by the surgeons, were laid in a row upon a long table, and were covered with one large water-proof sheet.

"It was at the noon of night that I mounted guard at the door of the dead-house.

"My orders were from time to time to rap the door with the butt of my fire-lock.

"This was to frighten the rats from the dead bodies.

"It was a wonderful night, the broad calm moon blazed like a silver sun in the profoundly blue and speckless sky.

"The ground and the walls of the dead-house were aglare with one white sheen, and looked as if sparkling with hoar frost.

The air was still and sultry.

"I leaned on my fire-lock, and fell into deep thought.

"I was, as a fellow will be at such times, a little home-sick, and recalled the old times, and the pranks and pleasures of bygone days, and wondered whether I should ever see my native land again, or whether, like so many of my comrades, I should leave my bones in India.

"A sudden recollection of my orders broke my reveries.

"I went close to the door of the dead-house, and struck its planks with my gun-stock.

"Rat-tat-tat-tat.

"I paused and listened with a bit of a shudder to the scattering of the rats.

"I then shouldered my musket, intending to stretch my legs by a few paces.

"I heard a sound from within the dead-house.

"I felt a thrill as if bubbles of ice were trickling through my veins.

"My limbs trembled, and my knees shook.

"I felt certain that I had heard the sound.

"Again the faint, hollow cough.

"'Who's there?' I called.

"I received no answer.

"I began to think that perhaps one of the poor fellows was not really dead.

"With my firelock at half-charge, I rushed fiercely into the dead-house.

"I saw no living being.

"There over the table lay the white sheet, the forms of the eight poor fellows showing stiff and rigid through their ghastly pall.

"I felt their feet, one by one.

"All stiff, hard, chill.

"I raised the sheet.

"On every breast were the seams of the surgeon's lancet.

"I gave one look around me.

"I left the dead-house.

"It must, I thought, be all a morbid fancy.

"I shouldered my musket again.

"I moved a few paces from the door.

"I faced about.

"The moon still stood steady in the zenith, flooding the earth with a blaze of bright silver.

"I became more calm.

"Once more I began to be thoughtful.

"Visions of home once more rose to my mind.

"But not so vividly as before.

"My waking dreams were disturbed by a vague sense of awe.

"A slight tremor caused the cold sweat to exude from my forehead.

"I felt terribly, terribly lonely.

"Never did a watch seem so wretchedly long.

"Never had time lagged so wearily.

"Again I went to the door.

"Rat-tat-tat-tat.

"Once more I listened.

"This time there was no sound.

"The rats seemed to have been frightened away by my rude entry before, and had not returned.

"I retired a few paces.

"By a strange fascination my eyes seemed fixed upon the door.

"Every line and knot of the wood was clearly defined in the blazing moonlight.

"My God! the door was moving.

"No mistake; it was opened a little way.

"Every drop of blood seemed to rush to my heart.

"The top of my head seemed lifting.

"My hair seemed to stir and rise.

"I was choked by a qualm of thirst.

"My eyes burned with straining.

"My knees tottered.

"Yes! a hand was slowly passed through the opening of the door.

"Five fingers were clutching the sidebeam.

"A figure glided out, wrapped in white.

"I started backwards.

"My firelock slipped out of my palsied fingers.

"The very palsy of my fear kept me convulsively rooted to the spot.

"But for this, I own I should have run off my post.

"The figure glided towards me.

"It cowed down, and the white robe swayed back.

"It was a woman!

"She looked as frightened as myself.

"The thing is easily explained. The Burmese girl had been chatting with the sentinel who preceded me on that post.

"The picket coming round to relieve the guard, the sentry, to save himself from getting into trouble, had shut the girl in the dead-house.

"When I rushed in, she was afraid that, in my excitement, I should fire upon her.

"So she shrank down in a gloomy corner.

"Thus she had remained with the corpses and the rats in total darkness for more than half an hour.

"Before this adventure, I thought myself fearless, but the awful agony I suffered during the eternal moments of that paroxysm of terror have at least had the effect of making me more modest in respect of my courage and fortitude."

CHAPTER CXCIII.

CAPTURED AND CAPTIVATED—THE PEERLESS PRINCESS—A VISION OF BEAUTY—A WILD ROMANCE—PERSIAN TALES—ONCE MORE IN THE DUNGEON—AGAIN RELEASED—RAGE OF THE PRINCESS — UNGOVERNED PASSION— HOW EDWARD LEIGHTON TURNED A DESPOT.

WHEN Edward Leighton recovered from his insensibility he found himself couched on a soft bed, and in a small but neatly furnished stone chamber.

The room was of strange form, the ceiling shelving, the walls full of strange angles and recesses.

Upon a chair by his bed a girl was sitting.

Edward looked at her through his half-closed lids.

She was a ravishingly lovely and haughty beauty of about sixteen or seventeen.

Her hair was in its flashing hue as bright and radiant as burnished gold; her eyes were of sparkling blue, liquid and voluptuous; her lips were arched with great hauteur and pride, and there was a vindictiveness in the meeting of her finely-arched brows when they knit from time to time, which contrasted strangely with the infantine sweetness of her pearly smile.

She was wrapped in a long black dress, as of some conventional order, but beneath, a rich satin, gem-embroidered dress discovered itself.

She had a rosary of beads and a Greek cross round her neck.

She was reading.

As Leighton watched the swell and fall of her rounded bosom, and saw the peachy bloom-tints sweeping over her snow-white cheek, he could not believe that he was really awake.

He moved, and raised his hand to his brow.

"I must be dreaming," he muttered. "This being is an angel."

The girl started, and turned a quick look upon him.

Her glorious blue eyes were dilated, the dimples deepened in her crimsoning cheek, her tiny teeth glittered bright white between her scarlet lips, and she laid her hand to her side.

"Mon dieu! how you made me tremble," she said, with a mellow laugh.

"Mademoiselle, a thousand, thousand pardons," Edward stammered. "I know not where I am."

"Nor who I am. *Tais-toi*; you mustn't talk," returned the fair one, with an arch look.

She then demurely dropped her glance upon the book, and pretended to read.

"But, charming, honoured demoiselle, one word. Where am I? How came I hither?"

"You are a prisoner and I am your keeper. Monsieur the prisoner, no more for half an hour; the doctor has said you must not talk."

She held up her finger, and shook her pretty head.

"Oh, happy captivity!" sighed Edward.

"So you are rebellious. Well, I shall leave you to the punishment of solitude for half an hour," cried the beauty, pettishly.

With this she rose, and swept across the room towards the door.

"No, have mercy! Dear mademoiselle, devise some other punishment; this is more than I can bear," cried Leighton, stretching out his arm. "Only stay with me, and I will forswear the use of speech for evermore."

The girl's eyes flashed, the colour mounted her rich cheek; she bit her lip to repress a smile.

"Well, be good, then; in half an hour I will tell you all."

She reseated herself, and took up her book once more.

Leighton kept silence for a few moments, and looked at the lovely watcher with a wild-beating heart.

His impatience overmastered him.

He raised himself on his elbow.

"But——"

"What, again!" cried the girl, with an air of haughtiness that became her to perfection, as she started up, her face glowing with something of real anger.

A sharp pang shot through Edward's side, and he sank back with an irrepressible moan of pain.

In an instant the girl threw herself by his side.

She looked into his eyes, her countenance full of melting tenderness and infinite sympathy.

"Ah ciel! how cruel and thoughtless am I! And you are wounded, my poor knight," she murmured, in tones of warbling sweetness.

"Slightly, I think, dear, kind mademoiselle. I remember now, my horse was shot by the Russians, I was thrown, and stunned by the fall, and, I suppose, am now a prisoner; and you, beautiful lady, are a Russian."

"And, by consequence, your enemy," rejoined the girl, pouting.

"Ah, mademoiselle. I trust it is not so; such enemies as you would make me a good Christian, for were the worst foes like you I know I should love them."

"Well, then, love me," said the girl, bluntly.

"I am your slave."

"My slave! then I can't love you," returned the girl, fiercely. "Are you not an Englishman?"

"Yes; that is, I am of a Saxon race."

"And Britons never can be slaves."

"A king would be yours, mademoiselle."

"I hate slaves and serfs; Helots of all kinds I hate; none worse than those Polish pigs. How can you fight for them? How low-minded you must be."

"I believe in slaves of love, mademoiselle; but not in political serfdom."

"Then you're not a bit wise; life is all slavery, every toiling man is a slave, we are all slaves when we are others' masters; we are slaves to ourselves."

"Yet, hear me, mademoiselle."

"I won't, you vex me; be quiet!" returned the girl, pevishly.

Edward did not speak for some time.

"You are wondering who I am," she said, with a smile.

"I can but wonder, dear mademoiselle."

"Well, you must judge me by my dress, and not by my manner."

"You are of some religious order?"

"A nun."

"Ah! what a shame!"

"A shame to be a nun?"

"So much beauty to be immured in a convent, such a rich source of happiness to be lost to a joyless world," returned Edward, half earnestly, half banteringly."

"There, I am only a novice."

"Then there is hope?"

"I hope so," returned the girl, with a strange laugh.

"And by what name may I address you, my kind nurse?" Edward stammered, rather astonished at her naive frankness.

"Sister Sophia," replied the girl, with a smile.

"It is sweet to call you sister."

"And it will be sweet to call you brother," replied the girl, tenderly.

Edward was not a little startled at the fire which shone in those proud blue eyes.

But there was purity on that sunny brow—the frankness of bold affection in that face, which proved that the girl was ingenuous, though so full of caprice and arrogance.

"And is this a convent?" asked Edward.

"Fie; it is a dungeon."

"Well, the Russians must be much belied if they treat their prisoners so well."

"I will show you what your treatment would be if Sister Sophia were not of the Order of Mercy."

She opened a strong door, and showed a narrow and dark cell.

She tripped into it.

RUSSIAN TREATMENT OF POLISH PRISONERS.

She stooped, and picked up something from the ground.

She clashed together a pair of shackles.

Then her sweet laugh echoed merrily through the dusky vault.

"It is not very pleasant music," she said, turning to the prisoner.

"All this is very strange," returned Edward. "I cannot understand it."

"And isn't it charming—delicious!" returned the girl, as she bounded back to the couch. "Are you spiritual—romantic? Do you ever dream of enchanter's wondrous castles and the glamours of magic?"

No. 58.

"Certainly, this adventure is so wonderful, that I feel as if I were one of the three Calenders, or a prince in some Persian fable."

"Fable! If you'll listen, I'll tell you a true story. 'Once upon a time there lived a certain prince, who had but one daughter. This princess surpassed all the maidens of the world by her beauty and goodness.'"

"You are telling your own story."

"If you know it, then, continue."

"I will. 'And for some reason, unknown to historians, the prince confined his daughter in a lonely castle. A certain oppressed people of his dominions rising against the Sultan, the prince's master, were aided by an Emir, who travelled from a far country to assist the rebels in their struggle for liberty.' "

" 'Yes, yes. 'And as the princess, though but sixteen years of age, far outshone in beauty and amiability all the women, so did the Emir as far exceed in manliness and handsomeness the finest men in the universe, and his name was——.'

" ' 'Oh, horror—Ned Leighton!'

" ' 'Being of the giaours and barbarians, whose speech is iron and not silver—go on.'

" ' 'And this Emir, being taken captive by the prince, was thrown into a deep dungeon.'

" 'Right—capital!' "

" ' 'But the kind princess, taking pity on his misfortune, had him privately removed from his dungeon to a secret apartment, where he was treated with that benevolence which ever marked the character of——'

" ' 'Her Excellency the Princess Sophia Catherine Aronzow, of the Romanoffs and the blood royal!' ' "

This announcement so startled this hero of his own romance that, despite his wound, he leaped from the couch.

He sank on one knee.

" Your excellency, if I have carried this jest too far, it was in ignorance of your name and quality," he said, in a tone of deep respect. " I beseech you to let me be taken back to my prison, and do not degrade me by forcing me, by accepting your kindness, to be the means of your incurring your father's displeasure."

The princess threw back her mantle, and drew herself up with a majestic air, and looked proudly down on poor Leighton, who bit his lip with vexation.

She smiled graciously, then clapping her little hands and bursting into her sweet, girlish laugh, she cried,

" Oh, was there ever anything so beautifully romantic? Not since the days of the genii. But there, you must not presume upon my favour. You may kiss my hand, and I will leave you. I will not fail to send you some fruit and sherbet for your refreshment."

With an oriental obeisance the princess left the apartment.

The door was locked and barred.

" Well, if this is not the most extraordinary adventure that ever befell a traveller," cried Edward, as he stood alone in the cell. " I dare say, after all, I'm aboard the Avenger, or under canvas at Kowno. I must be dreaming; I shall awaken presently. At all events, I won't compromise my beauteous princess. It may be the little despot is the darling daughter of a doating father, and the imperious mistress of obsequious serfs, and having nothing in the world to do, has taken it into her sweet, silly little head to divert herself in this way. Well, I'll get into my cage, and I'll even put on the shackles myself, rather than her exquisite little excellency should get into trouble on my account. But what a lovely creature!"

Edward entered the dark cell, seated himself on a stone seat attached to a pillar, and looked wistfully back at the soft couch and neatly-carpeted room he had left.

The gloom of the dungeon was a great contrast.

He was in great pain.

His shoulder had been severely bruised by his fall.

He took up a heavy pair of irons, and then let them fall with a clash.

His arms were too weak to bear them.

He rose, and walked feebly about his prison.

His brows knit, but his lips writhed a quaint smile of amusement at the oddity which blended with the peril of his position.

He heard a noise, as of some one opening the door of the apartment.

A girl passed the door of his prison.

She looked alarmed, and seemed to be unwillingly enacting an allotted part.

She carried on a tray a bottle of champagne, and other more substantial luxuries.

She placed the tray on a little side-table.

She looked round in fear and surprise at the absence of the captive.

Edward Leighton stepped out of the dungeon, and spoke to her.

She made no answer, but recoiled from him and stood at the far end of the apartment.

As she looked in his pale face, for he was giddy with pain, she smiled encouragingly, pointed to the refreshments, and fled out of the room.

He followed her to the door.

It was locked from the outer side.

He stamped his foot with a bitter feeling of annoyance.

He then re-entered his dungeon.

Here he found a pitcher of water and a loaf of nauseous black bread.

With the fortitude of a stoic, he seated himself on his stone seat, and looking on the delicacies spread upon the table in the other apartment, began to munch at his hard fare.

" No, she may be a princess; she is entrancingly lovely, one of those beings whom one must adore with unreasoning devotion on account of their attractions, but one who would be a cruel torment to the poor fool who trusted her wretched capriciousness. She shall not make me her slave, though I am her father's prisoner, and it would be an act of great baseness to take advantage of her kindness."

But the black bread was very hard, and the champagne and silver-mounted sweets on the side table looked very inviting.

The pain of his shoulder increased, and the soft couch seemed to spread its arms to receive him in a luxurious embrace.

" Look not on the wine when it is red," muttered Leighton, with a mocking laugh. " How soon may a man be caught and vanquished by the most sordid sensual baits; but I'll not sell my birth-right for a mess of pottage, Princess Sophia Catherine Aronzow, though you be of the Romanoffs and blood royal."

He got up and dashed to the door.

He was now in darkness.

A very feeble ray of moonlight streamed in from an eyelet in the wall.

He felt his way to the stone bench and sat down on it with folded arms.

His heart still thrilled with the stirring emotions of strong sympathetic love. His ears rang with the sweet laughing of the wilful enchantress, and he forgot everything but her loveliness.

He heard the sound of quick steps.

His door was opened.

Two men entered his dungeon.

A girl stood at the door holding a lamp.

One of the men was a grey-bearded old man, the other younger.

" You said her excellency had taken the prisoner out of the dungeon, but you were mistaken. See, Anna, here he is."

" But now he was lying on the couch in the next cell. Her excellency had the place furnished and lighted to receive him."

" Perhaps he has displeased the princess and she has sent him back to his dungeon."

Edward addressed the old man in French.

" You are mistaken, sir. I was carried into yonder room in a state of insensibility, at the command of her excellency. I recovered from my trance and had the honour of conversing a few moments with the princess, who then left me; but I prefer remaining in my cell, to allowing her excellency to run the risk of her father's displeasure for my sake."

The serfs did not seem to understand the Englishman's scruples; they stared at him, and shrugged their shoulders.

"You see, monsieur the Englishman is the Czar's prisoner, and not the prince's. His excellency is responsible for your safe custody," said the old man. "I am the prince's seneschal, and therefore must do my duty."

"Well, sir, I am at your mercy, but don't forget that I am wounded."

"The princess will punish us severely for this," said the younger man, who carried a mallet in his hand.

"And the prince would hang us," said Anna. "He will return to-morrow early, and the princess will not come here again to-night."

"In that case, I'll rivet his chains at once," said the young serf.

Edward Leighton was shackled and chained to the pillar.

"And now I've got you out of this scrape," said Anna to the seneschal, "I trust to your gratitude not to tell the princess, or she will whip me like a demon."

"I hope she will not ask me," returned the seneschal.

"Good night, monsieur the prisoner," said the old steward. "But stay, bring hither the wine from the next room, Petroff."

The other serf obeyed.

"We are sorry to subject you to this rough usage, monsieur," said the old serf, "but it is more than we dare to treat you otherwise; it might cost us our lives. However, drink a glass of this wine, and eat something."

Mark Leighton was faint, and did not refuse to accept from the servants what he had refused from their mistress.

He felt greatly refreshed and his strength seemed renewed.

They then left him in the darkness.

He remained sitting on the stone seat, aching with pain, and weighed down by the heavy weight of iron, and the massive shackles began to gall his limbs.

An hour lagged wearily away.

A voice struck a quick chord in his heart, caused the blood to burn in his cheek, and checked the breath that flowed from his lips.

It was the voice of the princess.

"Has the traitor fled, then!"

He could not reach the door, but he clanked his chains.

"Fair princess, your knight is no traitor; he is here," replied Edward, trying to be jocular, but speaking in a tone that strangely quivered.

"And how came you here?" she asked.

"Of my own free will, beautiful princess," he answered.

"Come forth, then."

"I cannot, your excellency. I am bound, and the door is barred against me. I will not let you compromise yourself for me, but not to see you when you are so near me, that I could not bear, except perforce."

"And they have dared to disobey——" gasped the princess.

She became speechless with passion.

Edward heard her rush from the room.

Presently there was heard the sound of many voices.

The princess was pouring forth a torrent of abuse, and the servants were pleading for pardon as if they had been mere children.

Shortly the doors were unlocked, and, with fear depicted on their countenances, the serfs re-entered his dungeon.

With trembling hands the young serf again used his mallet, and in a brief space Leighton was again unshackled.

They carried him into the next apartment.

He did not oppose his deliverers now.

His giddiness increased; his pain had been rendered so excruciating by the weight of his chains that he was unable to walk without assistance.

He was borne to the couch.

"And who informed you of what I had done, Petroff?" she asked of the gaoler. "Pig! will you speak?"

"It was Anna, your excellency; but——"

"Ha!" cried the princess, with an emphasis worthy of Hal the Eighth. "She thinks I am a slight, frail girl, and that I cannot, or dare not exert my authority; she shall see—she shall see. Where is she?"

"Your excellency will be ill if you give way to this frightful excitement," said the old steward, with some show of spirit. "The prince will teach the serfs to respect their mistress; but——"

"Beast! where is she?" shrieked the lovely termagant.

"In the next room, your excellency," murmured one of the maids.

"Good, you shall see her punished. Follow me all of you."

The princess rushed from the room, followed by her retinue.

Soon Leighton heard her voice in angry tones.

Fierce denunciations flowed from her lips, and stern commands were issued.

There were bitter sobs and earnest pleadings for mercy, followed by the sound of rending garments and screams.

There was dead silence for a moment, and Edward hoped the haughty beauty had relented.

But no. Soon there came the wild, swift sweep of the lash upon nude flesh, and the piercing shrieks of a human being in agony.

Nerving himself to a desperate effort Edward staggered across the room and burst into the next apartment.

The scene for a moment rendered him breathless with horror.

Anna lay stretched on the floor, her arms and legs held firmly by the male serfs.

Her garments had been roughly torn from her back, while the princess stood over her, flogging her mercilessly with a huge whip.

"For the love of Heaven, stay this horrible scene!" exclaimed Leighton.

The princess made him no answer, but continued the punishment with, if possible, greater rigour.

The blood was streaming down the back of the poor girl.

Ned rushed upon the princess; all his strength seemed to return, and with a steady countenance and admirable firmness he tightly gripped her wrists.

The whip dropped from her hand.

He stooped, picked it up, and flung it across the room.

He then released her.

She leaped up, and struck him fiercely on the cheek.

Not a muscle of his face moved; he fixed a stern yet sorrowful look upon her eyes.

Again she raised her hands to strike him.

He made no offer of resistance.

She dropped her arm, and tried to terrify him by a fierce frown.

Still he looked her steadily in the eyes.

She stretched out her snow-white arms as if appealing tenderly for forgiveness.

He looked at her still firmly, and without betraying emotion.

The passionate, spoilt despot gave an hysteric shriek, and fell fainting in the arms of her attendants.

They bore her away.

Anna, who had fainted, was lifted up, and carried to the women's apartment.

Edward Leighton then sauntered back into his chamber.

He sank on the couch, muttering bitterly,

"So much for my peerless princess. Who would believe her to be such a demon?"

CHAPTER CXCIV.

THE AVENGERS AT WARSAW — GRIEF OF POLOWSKI—RALPH'S SUSPICIONS—THE LONE HOUSE—THE DESPATCHES—THE SPY AND TRAITOR—BETRAYED—IN PRISON—DARING ESCAPE OF THE DAUNTLESS AVENGERS.

BLACK RALPH, Dick Caffyn, and Zampa were lodging at a small tavern in a secluded suburb of the city of Warsaw.

Feodor Polowski, who had been stirring up the peasantry to revolt, travelling from village to village, and telling the story of his wrongs, joined the pirates a few weeks after their arrival.

He still continued in a state of utter dejection.

His handsome face grew wan and pale, and his eyes lost their brilliance; his cheek was rigid, and his lips close set; an air of apathy, of self-abandonment betokened the despair which had taken possession of his heart.

When he was alone he thought of his beloved Alexina, his darling wife, in whom he had found all the happiness of life.

At such times his agony was heart-rending.

He would clench his hands, and gnash his teeth, and weave his twined fingers about his throbbing brow.

The fretting moth of grief was wearing away the bloom of his manly beauty; chilling affliction had laid its hand on his head, and the black silky locks were turning grey.

When, at rare intervals, he spoke of his grief, he would pour out such a torrent of passionate anguish that his hearers, however callous, were struck with pity and reverence.

Among the peasants whom the exhortations of the brave young Pole had induced to join the standard of the patriots was a tall and shrewd-looking fellow, in whom Feodor seemed to place great dependance.

This man's name was Ivanovitch; he was of Russian descent.

He was commissioned to bring the pirates certain important papers from the secret office of the war department of the shadowy National Government.

The pirates and Polowski appointed to meet him at a certain house belonging to one of the patriots.

Hitherward they bent their steps, towards the close of an autumnal evening.

The streets through which they passed were almost deserted, and presented many indications of the terrible state of the wretched inhabitants.

Indeed, but for the measured tread of the Russian sentinels, who were posted in almost every direction about the city, the constant rumble of military carts, and the occasional advent of the picket, Warsaw might have been taken for a city without inhabitants.

In the centre of the public square were several gibbets, on which more than one of the rebels were hanging; and but few days passed without some unfortunate victim being added to the number.

A carriage rattled by.

It was surrounded by a troop of heavy-browed, sullen-looking soldiers.

It stopped.

An officer wearing a number of stars on his breast got in.

The blinds had been drawn previously.

When the officer entered the carriage, the door being opened, a lady appeared reclining on the seat.

She appeared to be in a state of perfect unconsciousness.

"She has been flogged, and sentenced to transportation. She will never see Siberia, poor creature," said Polowski, with bitterness. "They have banished her, but to Heaven."

"And people will know that these things are going on, and yet not band together to avenge their own cause," said Caffyn.

"They can't trust each other, Dick," returned Black Ralph. "Suspicion breeds more plagues than over-confidence; it's the source of all disunion. But while we know ourselves to be such rogues we can't help mistrusting each other. And as the world still contains a few spies, peachers, and hypocrites, I shall take the liberty of keeping a watchful eye upon a friend of yours, Feodor."

"Of mine! Which of my friends do you suspect?"

"Ivanovitch."

"No! you cannot suspect him. Of all the others I think him the most trustworthy."

"He has a Judas look," said Dick.

"I believe he's a traitor!" added Ralph, with fierceness.

"I do not think so; we shall get the despatches to-night, and to-morrow I hope we shall rejoin the Avengers."

They had, by this time, gained the outskirts of the city, and shortly after they arrived at the gate of a mansion that stood far apart from others, and presented a lonely and dilapidated appearance.

They rang a bell.

A small grating was opened.

A face appeared.

The pirates gave a pass word.

The gate was cautiously opened.

The pirates and Feodor entered.

The man, who looked pale and frightened and spoke in a breathless whisper, led the way across a stone-yard.

They mounted the steps, and went into the house through an arched door.

Here they were received by the master of the mansion.

He was a Polish Jew, one of a class that are generally treated by the Russians with great contumely, and who are subjected by them to continued exactions and tyranny.

He treated them with great courtesy, and begged them to be seated.

He told them that several of the government officials would attend upon them soon.

The pirates seemed a little suspicious at hearing this announcement.

"Is it not dangerous that such a number of our party should meet at one time?" asked Caffyn.

"It is for the preservation of our country," said the Jew, with a bland smile. "And so, gentlemen, we must be patient."

Ivanovitch entered hastily.

He carried the despatches in his hand which trembled excessively.

He gave them to Black Ralph.

"Is all well, Ivan?" asked Feodor, looking at him keenly.

The man looked down, and turned rather pale.

"All is well, Feodor," was the answer.

"Ivanovitch, it is suspected that we have a traitor among us," said Feodor, gravely. "Do you entertain doubts of anyone's fidelity?"

"A traitor! I—tl at is. No, I believe that our troop are all staunch men," returned the man, in some confusion.

"It is well; if you are suspected, you will have to clear yourself, or you must perish."

"Do you charge me with treason?"

"No, no; but your strange manner makes me half suspect that you are not true."

"Then I must defend myself," he answered, suddenly springing towards the door. "Long live the Czar!"

"Seize the traitor!" exclaimed Caffyn. "He has betrayed us!"

Black Ralph pointed a pistol at him, but a file of soldiers and officials bursting into the room, levelled their carbines at the pirates.

An officer advanced.

"Gentlemen, you are my prisoners," he said, bowing. "Resistance is useless; I have a powerful force to aid me."

"Sir, we are Englishmen!" cried the pirates in a breath.

"I warn you that our liberties are not to be lightly trifled with," said Black Ralph.

"True; you may be Englishmen, but you are taken in arms against his Imperial Majesty."

The despatches were taken from the hands of Black Ralph.

They were passed from one official to another with great formality.

The guard, who had by this time entered the room, formed in line.

The pirates' swords and fire-arms were taken from them.

They were delivered over to the military.

Black Ralph gave such a withering look upon the Jew and Ivanovitch, that they hung their heads and slunk away.

"Traitors," he exclaimed, "ere long you will bitterly rue this!"

They were carried off to the police office.

A crowd of people followed them as they were hurried through the streets.

Many of the women were silently weeping; all followed the captives with pitying looks, but they dared not give their sympathy expression by words. It might have carried them to Siberia.

It was piteous, too, when one of the police officers, with a mocking smile on his lips, turned towards them and lifting off his hat incited them to cheer for the emperor.

They very faintly rose their trembling voices.

No curse could have been more ominous than forced and mocking cheers.

The Avengers were kept long waiting in the lower offices of the prison.

The charge was entered against them, and they were delivered over to the governor of the prison.

They were then escorted up a flight of steps, and motioned to seat themselves on a long stone settle by the wall.

The guards then left them.

The prisoners for some few minutes remained silent, looking at each other.

Their capture had been so sudden and unexpected,

and accomplished by an act of treachery so foul that they hardly yet realised their position.

Of their ultimate fate they could have but little doubt.

The merciless treatment of their prisoners by the Russians was so well known that it drove every ray of hope from their hearts.

A form of military trial, a short march to the ramparts, a volley from a company of soldiers, and all would be over.

Black Ralph was the first to make any movement. On his light, devil-may-care disposition the event seemed to have made less impression than on his companions.

"Now, hearties," he said, "a bold stroke for liberty. We shall be hanged if we stay; we can but be killed if we venture to break away, so it's an even balance, and, for my part, I'd rather die fighting than be led out like a mangy dog."

These words were whispered to Dick Caffyn, who sat beside him.

There were at that time but two or three of the soldiers at the end of the passage.

As yet the prisoners had not been ironed.

The soldiers were chatting together, and seemed to be highly delighted with their capture.

Black Ralph was the first to spring up.

He threw himself violently upon one of the soldiers.

The man was taken by surprise, and his fire-lock was wrenched from his grasp.

The others threw themselves upon his comrades.

A desperate struggle ensued between the Avengers and the Russians.

Zampa and Dick Caffyn laid about them with their fists.

Dick was a famous boxer; he struck out right and left, and, possessing himself of a sword, cut the way down stairs.

Rushing along the corridor which led to the entrance they knocked down the men on guard and gained the street.

Here the crowd was still thronging, and, though they knew not what had taken place within the prison, they guessed that our friends were endeavouring to escape.

Way was made for the fugitives.

The Poles closed around them.

Cloaks were thrown over them, and, while pretending to be eager to retake them, the Poles urged them on.

There was a cart under a piazza in the market-place.

They blundered into this.

A cloth was thrown over them.

The driver whipped his horses.

The cart rolled heavily away.

The vehicle into which the fugitives had thrown themselves was an old Russian commissariat waggon, and bore on it the distinguishing mark of the regiment of Wladimir.

It was partly filled with articles destined for an outpost of the regiment which was stationed about a league from Warsaw.

The driver was dressed in the Polish costume.

But, as he turned into a by-street, he threw off his outward dress, and appeared dressed as a Russian soldier.

The fears of the fugitives rose as, through the cloaks that covered them, they saw the extraordinary metamorphosis of their driver.

A few words reassured them.

"Lie close," said the driver, "and cover yourselves well up. I am a Russian soldier, but I am also a Pole."

And now behind them rose a tumult of sounds, like to a roaring sea.

There was a heavy roll of the drum, the short, quick blasts of the bugle calling the garrison to arms. There were loud cries of men, and the screams of women.

Presently came the sounds of dropping shots, then the reverberations of musketry; there was a moment's lull, and then again uprose a loud roar, as though of many thousand voices.

"Let us get out of this," said Caffyn, "there is fighting going on, and we shall stand a better chance in the *melée* than we are like to do by remaining cooped up in these close quarters."

"Stay where you are," growled Ralph; "this is only a diversion to assist our escape. We shall do more service to Poland in getting clear now, than by taking a part in a street-fight that will be over in a few minutes."

At this moment a number of soldiers rode up.

They looked closely at the vehicle, but, appearing to recognise it, rode swiftly past.

The driver called out to them to stop.

The Avengers thought there was treachery.

But the man only pointed up a street with his whip and declared that the fugitives had taken that direction.

This is one of the most daring escapes on record !

CHAPTER CXCV.

SILAS RYE STILL BROODS OVER THE PAST—LADY EDGEFORTH'S SICKNESS—LORD HAWKSBURY RESOLVES TO REUNITE THE BOY PIRATE AND HIS MOTHER—SILAS PREPARES TO GO ON FOXLEY'S TRACK—MARRIAGE OF CHARLEY RYE.

SOON after the death of the unfortunate Richard Eagleton, the opera dancer, Sylvia Volante, left England, and started on a tour through Italy.

She never forgave herself the share she had taken in disgracing Charles Rye; and the suicide of Eagleton, whom she had ever remembered with sincere gratitude for his kindness to her in her times of distress, made a deep impression upon her kind and sensitive heart.

Charles Rye had pleaded for her love.

Sylvia estranged herself from him by degrees; she had never felt for him that passionate affection which she was capable of showing to one whom she really loved, but she regarded him with sisterly tenderness and respect.

Mortimer continued to act as secretary to Lord Hawksbury, and gave practical proof of the sincerity of his reformation.

For many months he seemed grave and unhappy, and was humble and reserved in his manner, but the steady kindness of the young nobleman re-assured him, and as the past was never alluded to, he began to gain confidence, and became cheerful and industrious.

Lord Hawksbury possessed a richly stored library, and Mortimer devoted himself with great ardour to study.

Milly Mervyn, who had been so true to Charles Rye in the hard times, was now his affianced sweetheart.

Lady Edgeforth, the hapless mother of our redoubtable hero, had now recovered her reason.

At least her relapses were few and far between.

No one dared to breathe to her that the events of which she would sometimes speak were really facts, but every one did his best to persuade her that they were but the hideous fancies of mania.

Silas Rye was very successful in his business transactions, and was frequently visited by Sibly, the managing clerk, who was now the father of several children.

All things had gone on in a smooth and ordinary way.

Yet Silas was restless in mind; he could never forget that he had been an accomplice in the abduction of the heir of Frontemore.

The news of the Boy Pirate's adventures in the South Seas and in Poland had reached England, and had caused a great deal of national interest.

The opinion of most people was favourable to the young buccaneer, who had abstained from deeds of murder and plunder, and had warred only to defend his life from his pursuers.

When Foxley, the detective, left his native country to hunt down his brother's murderer, he had promised Silas Rye that he would send him word if he succeeded in his object. There had been no intelligence from him.

With Silas a hatred against the murderous Harwolf was a blind passion; and as he had been the instrument of villany in the onset, he could not help thinking that in the end he should become the instrument of justice against the murderer.

It was a beautiful summer evening and Silas was sitting thoughtfully by the window of the pretty suburban villa of which he was now master.

He was brooding over the events of the past.

Lady Edgeforth was not with him now.

Lord Hawksbury had removed her to a country mansion.

She was in delicate health, and the physicians declared her to be in a rapid decline.

After a long and tedious lawsuit, Lady Edgeforth's title to the Frontemore estates was clearly proved, and the property was taken possession of in her behalf.

The terrible scenes of her early life had given Lady Edgeforth a repugnance to the old home, and Lord Hawksbury feared that a return to it would cause a return of the affliction that had darkened so many years of his sister's life.

The mansion was, therefore, given up to the care of some old servants, and was never visited either by Lord Hawksbury or his sister.

The estimable butler, Andrew Moss, had been discharged upon short notice by Lord Hawksbury, in consequence of his having been detected by his lordship in some act of petty tyranny upon the tenants of the estate.

As Silas was chewing the cud of sweet and bitter fancy in his quiet and pleasant drawing-room, he was pleasantly surprised to see his noble friend cantering up the road on his thorough-bred.

Lord Hawksbury leaped off his horse, and Silas Rye ran out to greet him.

"You are very welcome, my lord," he said. "I was at this moment thinking of you, and wishing for your return."

"Has anything new transpired, Silas?" asked his lordship.

"Nothing, lately, my lord; events keep an even course."

"That's well—and my sister? How fares it with her?"

"Her ladyship, I grieve to say, improves but little in health," answered Silas, " though her mind is still clear."

"Well, let us go in and talk awhile."

"And you have but lately returned from Paris, my lord?"

"Arrived in London last night."

When the friends were seated in the conservatory, smoking their cigars, Lord Hawksbury drew out a

French newspaper and read a report of the Boy Pirate's adventures in Poland."

"It is strange, my lord; but I was about to speak of the extraordinary fellow."

"And in connection with him there are many things of importance that must be determined on at once," rejoined Lord Hawksbury. "Have you heard from Foxley?"

"Not a word."

"I wonder at that."

"Perhaps he is far away in the backwoods in quest of the wolf."

"Or, which is more likely, his bones rot in the wolf's den."

"Let us trust not."

"But why does he not write? He promised to keep us informed of his movements."

"He may have been shipwrecked."

"He was at New York when he wrote the last letter."

"I would give my life to know that the wretch who murdered Lord Edgeforth, and brought such dreadful miseries upon my sister and her child would be brought to the gallows at last."

"He shall not escape."

"And my sister's health is failing too, you say; she may die and never behold her gallant though wild son."

"I cannot bear the thought of such a sad thing happening; but can you suggest what is to be done, my lord?"

"I'll tell you what is to be done, Silas: you and I shall set out in my yacht on a second voyage of discovery, as the first proved a failure. We will take the Irishman, Oiny, with us—he is a faithful and valuable fellow—and we will put into some port on the Oder, and seek out the 'Avengers.' So, I believe this extraordinary band of free-lances call themselves. Perhaps we may be fortunate enough to bring the lost heir of Frontemore to his mother's side."

"I could not, I dare not, be a witness of their meeting," Silas returned, with great emotion. "Besides, I have another mission of quite as much importance."

"Indeed! what is it?"

"To follow Foxley, and to track Andrew Harwolf."

"Then I will leave Oiny to you; you will have more need of him than I. But I think it is a wild scheme, Silas."

"Nothing shall induce me to abandon it," was the answer.

"Then we will put affairs in train for carrying out these plans. But, Silas, I must provide for your brother."

"My lord, he is well enough."

"Not so; we will see him fairly settled. He loves little Milly, and shall marry her, and when the wedding is over, we will leave him to his bliss, and while I and Mortimer go in search of the Boy Pirate, you and Black Oiny can set out in the hunt for the wretch Harwolf."

"A good arrangement," my lord, "I cannot imagine a better."

"I drink to our success."

"But my lady, your sister?"

"She shall go with me in the yacht. I will take the old doctor with me; you know he has given up his practice, and would no doubt enjoy the trip amazingly."

Here the subject of the conversation was changed, and as the evening grew darker, they re-entered the drawing-room, where they found Charles Rye busy at his books.

"Come here, my boy," said Lord Hawksbury. "I want a little chat with you."

Charles rose, and seated himself opposite his lordship, and listened respectfully.

"I am going away, Charley, on the old errand—to seek out the rover."

"Oh, my lord, if I might accompany you!" exclaimed the youth.

He paused, and his cheek reddened.

"Come, don't be a hypocrite; this time you would not take your heart with you."

"But at least, my lord, I could leave it at home in safe keeping."

"I think so; but business must not be set aside. You are rising with that tide in the affairs of man, which, neglected, leaves you all astrand, you know. But, tell me, how do you feel disposed with respect to marriage? Are you, like myself, a confirmed old bachelor?"

Charles laughed, and answered, bashfully,

"It is a subject of which I seldom think."

"I'll tell that to Emily, and she will jilt you to-morrow."

"Even your lordship must not scandalise her; but, indeed, if Emily would consent, and if early marriages were not so very imprudent, I should be supremely happy."

"Well said, and boldly. Now-a-days, I know, women are not often found who are willing to help a man to fame or a position; when a fellow has made a fortune they are eager to join him in enjoying it, but, until all is won, they are very prudently cautious."

"That may be true, my lord, but every honourable man wishes to secure his position before he ventures to take a partner."

"You are the chivalrous gentleman—you always defend the ladies, but I am the surly cynic, and have an eye to spy into abuses. I must say that girls are getting mercenary."

"But I musn't believe it for all that, my lord," replied Charles, gaily."

"Well, then," said Lord Hawksbury, "if that is your opinion, you had better put the question to Emily at once, and if she is not mercenary, why—perhaps you had better marry her at once."

"I will try her, my lord," said Charles, his eyes beaming with pleasure; "and as I feel certain of her answer, I will follow your lordship's advice as quickly as possible."

Lord Hawksbury laughed and wished him success, and then rising he again sought Silas Rye, with whom he had a long and interesting conversation, and then departed to make the preparations that were necessary for his journey to Poland.

A few weeks after this conversation, Charles Rye led his young bride to the altar. It was a quiet wedding, but Lord Hawksbury gave the young couple some substantial tokens of his regard, and Silas was much gratified at beholding the happiness of his favourite brother.

It was a quiet but a happy wedding.

CHAPTER CXCVI.

THE PRINCESS AND THE PRISONER.

EDWARD LEIGHTON spent a restless night in his confinement.

The next day he was visited by the old steward, who brought him something to eat.

The servant gave him a note, and said, in a tone of anxiety,

"Please destroy this; you see what a wretched position mine is? In obeying the princess I run the risk of being arrested for favouring the rebels, and might, perhaps, be knouted or hanged, and if I disobey her—well, you see how little she will brook thwarting."

"I assure you, friend, I am deeply grieved that any of this household should be subjected to her excellency's displeasure, or incur peril on my account. I am a prisoner, utterly powerless to resist whatever treatment I may receive at her hands. I am deeply grateful to the princess for the kindness she has shown me, but should be better pleased with harsher usage, for I am her father's prisoner, and——"

"Oh, sir, it is quite useless, quite! The princess will have her own way; she knows not how to put the least restraint upon her capricious passions. She is an angel one hour and a fury the next; her lightest whim deferred to by her father; every wish anticipated; every creature about her an abject slave. What can you expect of a being so young and beautiful, a descendant from such a haughty overbearing race, and of such an impetuous and imperious temper?",

"This is one of the curses of despotism. The princess spoke feelingly when she said that the master of slaves is always a slave to himself, but I am surprised to hear you talk so liberally, my friend; perhaps, though, the dawn of liberty has opened your eyes. Soon I trust serfdom in Russia, as long since elsewhere in Europe, will be abolished."

A bright smile lighted the face of the old steward, as he answered,

"Yes, sir. The act of emancipation will receive the Czar's sanction, and then every man in Russia will be free, in so far as he will not be bound to the soil."

"I trust that the serfs will make good use of their liberty, having once obtained it. It is a dangerous gift in ignorant hands."

"I hope so, sir, and I hope, too, that his excellency will, at his daughter's entreaty, set you at liberty."

"Thank you, friend; and now, as I mean to be master of my own actions so far as I can, take back this letter to the princess, and assure her of my humblest devotion and respect, but say that I petition her to hold no communication with me until she has obtained permission from the prince. She shall not herself be brought to disgrace, nor shall her servants suffer for me."

"Oh, no, she would kill me or you, or both of us, if I took her such a message," said the steward, in a great fright.

"I can give you no other," replied Edward, firmly.

He seated himself on the couch, and shrugged his shoulders with an air of determination that would not be gainsayed.

The old man shrugged his shoulders, and left the room.

Left to his own reflections, Edward felt heavy at heart.

Spite of her fiendish temper, and the scene he had witnessed the previous evening, there was something so fascinating in the beauteous young tyranness that Edward felt he could love her madly.

He considered his position, and was provoked at his own folly.

But some men cannot but feel a consciousness of their superiority in their intercourse with women of any station, and such heroes are mostly the favourites of the fair, for women love to be ruled even better than they love to rule.

Edward Leighton, though warmly affectionate by nature, was also a man as hard and unyielding as a granite rock when resisting attempts at enslaving him.

He was not such a fool as to wish to leap at the moon.

If he had been a king he would have sought no prouder consort than the uncultured but lovely princess, but as the matter stood, he determined that he would not suffer himself to be enslaved by her charms.

While he was deeply ruminating, the door of the chamber was quietly opened, and the princess herself entered.

She had now discarded her conventual dress, and appeared attired in white, with a cross of brilliants heaving on her snowy bosom.

She wore no other gems; her dress was simple, and her golden hair neatly braided.

She looked very proud and angry, and her cheek was richly tinted with deep rose.

Edward made a very profound bow, and received her with the most respectful courtesy.

"And so, monsieur, you have no more gratitude or politeness than to insult me by returning me my letter unread; you are a chivalrous gentleman, I must say.'"

"Your excellency would not think me wanting in respect or devotion if you knew my heart," returned Edward. "What I have done I did from a conviction that my honour required me to resist your kind attempt to serve me at your own peril, for well I know that even your high station will not protect you from the malice of the authorities, who persecute the friends of the insurgents even more vindictively than they punish the rebels themselves."

"Acknowledge that you were piqued, that I disgusted you by my violence."

"I confess that I think your excellency might find some gentler mode of teaching your dependants their duty than having recourse to the torture of the lash."

The princess blushed, and winced at the cold tone in which Edward spoke.

"Monsieur, you are ungrateful," she said; "but you don't know what a set of wretches these serfs are; we can do nothing with them without severity, they are like fools, or children, only to be ruled by the whip."

"A better sort of discipline may be found even for fools and children, your excellency."

"I don't want to hate you; you are the most provoking of men!" cried the girl, tossing her head, and pouting; "but as I will not quarrel with you, I will leave you at once."

She moved towards the door, and then looked back at him with a haughty smile.

Edward made a very reverential bow.

The princess bit her lip, and stamped her fairy foot with impatience.

She advanced a step towards him, and held out her hand.

Edward sank on one knee, and respectfully touched the little hand with his lips.

Again the princess moved, but with some hesitation, to the door.

She turned impulsively, came to his side, and laid her hands on his shoulder.

She murmured in a tone of bewitching sweetness.

"Monsieur Edward, de grace, forgive me."

Leighton stepped back and bowed low.

He felt a qualm at his throat and violently trembled.

"Your excellency, I——. Forgiveness is not a word to be used by you to me," he said, rather huskily. "I owe you devotion and gratitude, and would repay——."

Petroff ran into the room.

"Your excellency, the prince has returned," he said.

"I will go to him at once," returned the girl, impetuously. "I will save you, monsieur, though it cost me my life."

"Meanwhile, your excellency," said Petroff, "would it not be better for monsieur to return to the——"

The princess silenced him with a fierce look.

He cowered back.

"Pardon, excellency," he muttered.

"My father has influence, monsieur. He can deny me nothing, and you shall be set free."

Edward would have protested.

The princess, however, passed through the door.

Petroff followed her closing and locking it without.

Once more Edward paced the room in solitude.

ZAMPA ASTONISHED BY A BEAR.

CHAPTER CXCVII.

THE PRINCE AND HIS CAPTIVE—A STRANGE
RECOGNITION—ARRIVAL OF COUNT BRUTOFF
—THE PRINCESS IN THE SULKS—A TREA-
CHEROUS MAID—BRUTOFF'S DISSIMULA-
TION.

EDWARD LEIGHTON remained in confinement for
several days.

The time passed very wearily.

He was visited at intervals by the seneschal and
Petroff.

They brought him food, as Shakspeare says so
touchingly, "to make misfortune live."

A woman that could lash another frail fair woman
so cruelly!

An arrogant, haughty, capricious siren, without
one spark of true devotion, or one particle of
real principle!

No. 59.

That is too hard; if she loved, she would love with
all the fervour, all the self-sacrifice of woman's
fullest passion.

But why? Not upon reason, but upon mere impulse; by the same governing frenzy that maddened her to that pitch of fury that she could
flog her poor maid till the blood spots stained her
flesh.

And he to love such a woman!

But love has nothing to do with reason; she was
very, very witching.

She was kind to him, and selfishness is the canker-
worm of all Nature's beauty.

He could not help loving her.

The more he loved the imperious princess, the
more he hated and despised the submissive slave—
and that was himself.

Still he was true to the worthier part of his
nature, thus far: if he yielded to the yearning of

ungovernable affection he successfully resisted the merely sensual allurements she threw in his way.

He chose the plainest fare, touched neither wine nor delicacies, but eat his bread and meat, and blessed her for it.

Princess Sophia Catherine Aronzow, of the Romanoffs and blood royal !

Edward Leighton, son of an emigrant to the backwoods of America, whose grandfather had been an English carpenter, emigrating with a young wife on the capital of forty pounds, a strong will, and a taste for hard labour !

Yet Leighton was too sensible to care for social distinctions.

He thought so well of himself that, morally, he held himself superior to the princess.

Had he an enemy ? He felt strong enough to forgive him.

Had he a slanderer ? Slander is ever wounding, but he could despise it.

Had he a love whom he could not respect ? Women are lovely still, and he could but love her.

There lay his weakness.

His weakness was not demonstrative.

Out of the fullness of his heart his lips were silent.

Some men are of this disposition, happily.

Edward Leighton was so absorbed, by reflecting on the charms of his enchantress, that he quite forgot his own position of dependence and danger.

He was wretched.

His mind was distracted, his heart tossed by conflicting thoughts and passions.

On the evening of the fourth day he was visited in his captivity by the prince himself.

When his excellency entered the apartment Leighton was surprised to find his visitor a man of such reverend and benevolent deportment.

Prince Aronzow, despite his broad Asiatic face, and features slightly coarse and irregular, had a refinement and dignity of manner very impressive.

He bowed imperially.

Edward rose, and returned the salutation very respectfully.

Prince Aronzow approached him.

Looking in the prisoner's face, the prince started back, exclaiming,

"How strange, and yet I cannot be deceived !"

"Does your excellency recognise me then ?" said Leighton, with a smile.

"I do."

"And I your excellency."

"You have a good memory, Master Edward," replied the prince, in English.

"I was but a mere child when my father had the honour to entertain you, prince, but I remember all the circumstances of your visit as well as if they had occurred but yesterday."

"I am astounded, and most delighted to see you," returned the Russian noble, taking the young prisoner by the hand. "I was proscribed for advocating the emancipation of the serfs."

"And yet you permit——"

Leighton paused.

His cheek burnt red at the boldness and presumption of the speech he was about to make.

"And yet I permit my daughter to treat them so imperiously," said the prince, with a smile and a shrug. "Well, Mr. Leighton, you can't understand these things; at the risk of giving you a strange impression of my character, I will confess thus much, I love my daughter so dearly, that I cannot help leaving the serfs to her discretion, and I do assure you that ages of slavery render them so provoking, so dull their intellects, that only brutal discipline will have any effect on them; but if the princess misuses them, it is much against my will; but the little shrew, I am as much her slave as the humblest of them."

"The dear and honoured princess has been very kind to me," returned Leighton ; "but let me assure your excellency, that I did not wish for such good treatment. I know your position with respect to the Court, and would willingly have submitted to the harshest usage rather than have allowed the princess to compromise herself through her generosity towards me."

"I am sure of that, Mr. Leighton; but now that I know who you are, let me rejoice with you that you have fallen into good hands, though that don't sound modest, for you were claimed by Count Brutoff, whose Cossacks took you, and he—well he is affianced to my daughter, and I am sorry for it."

Prince Aronzow was evidently a weak-minded man but kind at heart.

The prince conducted our hero to his splendidly-furnished apartments.

Here he met the princess.

Her excellency received him with some haughtiness.

Leighton, in his bearing towards her, was very courteous and respectful, but proud and cold.

The prince and his daughter dined with their prisoner.

When the dishes were removed the princess retired from the room.

Wine, and a luscious dessert being set on the table, the prince pointed to an easy chair, gave Leighton a cigar, and lighting one himself, said, with a smile,

"Well, indeed, Mr. Leighton, do I remember your happy, hospitable, sylvan home ; and dearly do I cherish the recollection of your father's kindness to the poor exile Aronzow."

A dark shade passed over Edward's face, and in a tone of agitation he told the sad story of the massacre at Leighton Hoe.

The prince expressed his sympathy, and inquired the news of Larchville.

Edward informed him that his cousins were well.

"And that bold, graceless boy, who was so handsome, and so mischievous ?"

"Oswald Lamond ?"

"Yes; I will wage that he has joined the army."

"Of free lances," returned Edward, gravely. "He was a wild, bad fellow."

"I remember that a bitter enmity existed between him and his cousin Mark when they were children; but what do you mean by free lances ?"

"The last I heard of him was to the effect that he had joined a gang of robbers."

"Is it possible ?"

"Yes; after my escape from the massacre I myself joined a party of outlaws."

"Upon compulsion, I suppose ?"

"No, of my own free will."

"Then the report is true ?"

"What report, your excellency ?"

"That these English volunteers, who are fighting for the Poles, are a band of pirates commanded by the famous Red Raven ?"

Leighton laughed.

"The sturdy rascal, he must be desperate, indeed. Well, I hope he will fall in fair fight, for he deserves a more honourable fate than commoner villains."

"He is no villain, he is a very noble fellow," rejoined Edward, with warmth.

"For a pirate, I admit; but still he is a pirate."

At this moment the old steward entered the apartment, and announced Count Brutoff.

The prince started up, and gave a look of uneasiness at the door.

"I fear, Mr. Leighton," he said, "that it will be scarcely advisable for you to meet the count at present."

"It is an honour I can well dispense with, your excellency," was Edward's reply.

"Pass through that door, then ; the passage leads into my library, you will find there some curious manuscripts, which will amuse you until he takes his departure."

Edward bowed, and left the room.

He had scarcely disappeared when Count Brutoff entered.

He looked pale and ill, and wore his arm in a sling.

"You are welcome, count," said the prince, with a smile, "What news of the rebels ?"

"Under that cursed ruffian, the English adventurer, they are still successful. They say, prince, that you have taken some prisoners?"

"Merely a volunteer and a girl, a camp follower of some sort."

"You will now have a chance of striking terror into the hearts of these Polish dogs by making a terrible example."

"Only to provoke more horrible retaliations."

"At least, the girl should be knouted, and the fellow shot or hanged."

"There is time enough to decide upon this matter," said the prince, nervously; "meanwhile, let us talk of something more interesting."

"Apropos, I have not seen her excellency these three days."

The prince shrugged his shoulders, and smiled dryly.

"Her little sublimity is out of temper."

"Ha! she is captious," the count replied, in a rather ungallant manner, stroking his thick moustache and bending his black brows.

The prince looked uncomfortably at his companion.

"It is time that I should be relieved from the anxiety her capriciousness causes me," replied Brutoff. "Your excellency must be indulgent to my impatience, but I must entreat you to hasten the consummation of my happiness."

"My daughter is very young, count, and though she is your betrothed, I do not think we have a right to expect her to give her hand away, at least for a year or so."

"A year! my dear prince, the thought is not endurable."

"Well, I will send for her. Last time she saw you, it appears you gave her some offence, and she swears she will see you no more."

"She is of a high temper, and will not love me the more for yielding to her imperiousnes," returned the count, haughtily.

"If she is quick-tempered, pampered and wilful, she is also high-souled and sensitive," returned the prince, fondly.

He rang the bell.

A servant entered.

"Tell the princess that I wish to speak with her," said the noble.

The servant bowed, and left the room.

The prince reseated himself, and busied himself in overlooking some letters and despatches, which he had not before opened.

Count Brutoff paced about the room in abstracted mood.

Anna the maid, whom the princess had so cruelly punished, came into the room.

"Her excellency begs to be excused from presenting herself; she is indisposed," faltered the girl.

Count Brutoff turned a dark look upon the speaker.

The prince showed his annoyance by an impatient gesture.

"Where is the princess?"

"In her apartments, excellency."

"Lead me to her. Brutoff, I will bring the wayward girl directly; but, for Heaven's sake, wear a less cloudy brow, or there will be a storm."

With a forced laugh the old man left the room.

Anna presently returned.

She was about to cross the room.

Count Brutoff beckoned her.

She paused and curtsied.

"Listen to me, girl, I have a question to ask, which you must answer truthfully; you say the princess is indisposed?"

"Yes, my lord."

"Indisposed to see me, that is."

"Her excellency is not in good spirits."

"That is to say, her excellency is in bad humour."

The girl made no answer, but again curtsying, was about to quit the room.

"Stay!" cried Count Brutoff.

The girl arrested her steps.

"She will not see me; hump. Anna, there were two prisoners, Polish traitors; where are they?"

"In—in the dungeons, my lord," gasped the girl. She turned pale, but a spiteful gleam shone in her eyes.

"Are you sure of that?" he said, fixing a steady look upon her countenance.

"Ah, my lord, if you knew how severely I suffered before."

"Suffered what?"

"The princess whipped me till the blood came."

"Ho, ho!"

"I dare not, indeed, I dare not tell you the truth."

"You may trust me safely, girl, and I must, will know what the princess has done with the prisoners."

"There were two, my lord."

"Right; an Englishman, and a young Polish woman."

"The woman is still confined in a cell, but is not harshly treated; the Englishman—oh, heavens! I beseech you, my lord, do not make me pass judgment on myself. The princess will be so enraged."

"Continue, I command you. This rascally Englishman?"

"Her excellency removed him from his dungeon."

"Ha! escaped then?"

"No, my lord, he is still here, but treated more as a guest than as a prisoner."

"And is he permitted to converse with the princess?"

"Yes—yes, my lord," stammered the girl, starting back at the savage glare of the count's black eyes.

"And she shows him favours?"

"The greatest tenderness."

"St. Michael!"

"In fact, I think—that is, I'm sure she would not have flogged me so cruelly for causing him to be taken back to his dungeon if——"

"If—if what?"

"If she did not love him."

The count's face blazed with wrath.

He fiercely and brutally clutched the girl's arm.

She shrank down, and looked at him beseechingly.

He roughly flung her aside.

"Men or women are all alike. A serf is by nature a liar!" he gasped, in a hoarse tone.

The girl made no answer, but rising timidly, tried to slink from the room.

He dragged her back.

He seemed wild with passion.

For a long time he struggled in vain for words.

"His excellency is coming," cried the girl, breathlessly. "Oh, that my tongue had been cut out before I had told you this. The prince has released the Englishman from his prison, received him with great kindness. The man even dined to-day with their excellencies; but let me entreat you, my lord, do not betray me!"

"No, I will not," muttered Count Brutoff, gnashing his teeth. "I will dissemble till time serves, and then I will take my revenge in my own way."

Prince Aronzow now re-entered the room. He looked much vexed and humiliated.

"The girl is utterly ruined; she has been so petted and spoiled, so flattered and fawned upon, that she is quite ungovernable," he said, in tones of chagrin. "I have coaxed and threatened her, but all in vain, she remains in her apartments, count, and steadily refuses to see you."

The count frowned darkly.

He then laughed and replied with a false smile.

"Perhaps submission will best avail with my lovely tyrant; make my devoted remembrances to her excellency, and entreat her on my part not to protract a punishment which is insupportable. The next time I come she may relent so far as to give me a chance of seeking pardon for my unknown offence."

"You see that she is but a wilful child, in person, in heart, and temper."

"Time will remove her slight defects, and then she will be perfection," laughed the count.

"From my heart I'm glad to hear you talk so kindly and moderately," said the prince, with genuine pleasure.

"And now, your excellency, about the prisoners?"

"Ah! true; but we will speak of them some other time."

"I am not afraid to speak frankly to you, prince, I suspect——"

"Suspect! what?"

"That for some sufficient reason you are disposed to save them."

"The enemies of the Czar are irreconcilably my foes!" returned the prince, with animation.

"Of course, of course; but it sometimes happens that we are under personal obligation to those whom we are opposed to by public duty."

"My dear count, that is just my—at least I was about to put the question. How would you act with respect to a prisoner to whom you owed a deep debt of gratitude?"

"That depends on circumstances. We can trust each other?"

"Of course, fearlessly."

"Then, my dear prince, between ourselves, if I could do so safely, I would consult my own inclination and pass them over the border. It would be madness to set them at liberty in Poland, unless, indeed, you could get up an escape."

"Count, you delight me; you talk now like a kind-hearted man."

"And a seditious subject."

"Well, I'll tell the truth; the princess has set her little romantic heart upon gaining a release for the Englishman, and by a strange chance he proves to be the son of an American planter who treated me with the most cordial hospitality and kindness during my exile from Russia."

"How strange!"

"No words can express the generous sympathy and genuine kindness I received at his father's hands. What can I do?"

"Certainly not see the son of your benefactor shot like a dog, or driven like a beast to Siberia."

"Count Brutoff, I shall be proud of you as my son-in-law."

"Well, your excellency must let this fellow go; and if I can assist you in the matter I will."

"A thousand thanks."

The prince shook hands with his daughter's affianced, and they parted.

*   *   *   *   *

In the deep recesses of a forest about twenty miles from Warsaw an exciting scene took place some days after the escape of the Avengers.

A space of about an acre had been cleared of its wild, luxuriant growth.

A crowd of excited men were gathered there.

All were armed; some with the old muskets, others with pikes.

A few had simple implements of husbandry, turned for the nonce into weapons of formidable power.

Among these was the scythe—a weapon that, in the hands of Polish patriots, had proved more formidable than the bayonet, and had shown itself irresistable in many a deadly encounter with the hated Russian foe.

The men were grouped in a circle.

Near the centre stood a rude wooden bench used as a table; on it were materials for writing.

A few low stools were around it.

At the head of the table sat a man about fifty years of age, and of tall, commanding aspect.

He was dressed in the national uniform, and known as Colonel Korinski, chief of the patriots in the district.

Our hero, Dick Caffyn, Brierly, Feodor, and others of the Avengers, stood behind him.

Other seats at the table were occupied by officers of the National army.

Low murmuring sounds of voices buzzed round the circle.

Fierce, stern faces pervaded the assembly.

The chief rose from his seat.

All was hushed as if by magic.

He said in a clear, loud tone that echoed through the forest,

"Bring forth the prisoners."

From a hut that stood close by armed men issued conducting two men whose arms were tightly bound behind them.

They placed them in front of the president, and returned a short distance.

They were the two spies, Ivanovich and the Jew.

"Prisoners," said the president, "you are accused of having betrayed members of the National army into the power of the Russians. What say you, can you disprove the charge?"

The Jew was the first to answer.

"Mercy! my lord chief; I am a Polish Jew, but no traitor. By the bones of Abraham, I did not betray them!"

"Be careful how you speak, old man," said the president, with cold and bitter irony. "We can substantiate the charge."

The face of Ivanovich was deathly pale.

His eye scanned the features of the many there assembled, and in their stern determination he read the fate that awaited him.

After ineffectual efforts to choke his rising feelings, he said, whiningly,

"The charge is partly true; I was forced by threats and torture to betray these men, but had not the Russians been before the time appointed, I should have effected their escape, as was my intention."

"Did you not accompany the Russian troops to the house?" asked the president.

Ivanovich returned no answer.

"Did you not receive five hundred roubles for the information you gave?" again asked the president.

Still no reply. The president continued,

"And did you not both, traitors as you are, divide the wages of guilt between you within a few minutes after the capture of our friends?"

"Mercy! mercy!" cried the Jew.

"Mercy!" re-echoed the judge, in a stern, contemptuous tone; "mercy to you, a whining, cringing cur, who, dead to all feelings of honour or patriotism, would first espouse our cause, and then betray it."

"If I have erred, forgive me. Do not, I beg, in the name of Moses, do not consign me unprepared to an early grave."

A murmur of disgust ran through the assembly of rough, determined patriots, and many a sword or dagger was angrily drawn, which, at but a single token of assent from the judge, would have consigned the trembling traitor to eternity on the instant.

"Stand not there, trembling like a cur—you that had no temptations of poverty or want to prompt cupidity for a paltry reward, can hope for little at the hands of this assembly. Up from your knees, craving, cowardly hypocrite. Death is your portion."

"Mercy! I beg. Kind, good, powerful judge, do not condemn me!" screamed the Israelite, in despair. "Anything that I can do, anything that you command I will accomplish; but spare my life. I carry on my person valuable diamonds which I will willingly give for freedom's cause; but spare me!"

"Diamonds!" said the judge, ironically. "Produce them."

"There they are, most impartial and just judge. Their worth is great thousands of silver—roubles could not buy them. They have been coveted by all the rich and fashionable nobles in Petersburgh and Moscow. I throw them into the coffers of the patriot army; but spare my life."

The diamonds were delivered to the judge, who gazed upon their beauty and brightness with evident pleasure.

"Think you that money can buy justice, Jew," said the judge, with scorn. "Away with him. At sunset hang him to the nearest tree; his worthless body shall be food for carrion crows."

Willing hands were roughly laid upon the Jew.

Pale and trembling with fear, he was led from the assembly amid shouts and jeers.

"Bring forth Ivanovitch," said the judge.

The culprit approached with downcast eyes.

His attitude was lofty, unflinching and resolute.

He raised his head proudly, and gazed around him with supreme indifference as he calmly listened to the accusation.

"I need not trial at your hands," he said, with a calm firm tone. "I know my fate—my crime, for such it is in the eyes of all here, was not committed for filthy lucre; I did what I did for revenge, and from loyal duty."

"If you disclose your plans, Ivanovitch——"

"Do you take me for a craven, like that paltry trembling Jew? You mistake your man. My secrets and plans die with me! You may torture me, you may coax and promise—Ivanovitch is proof to all."

Dark frowns and menacing words were heard on all sides.

Some hot-blooded youths would have dispatched him where he stood, and flourished their weapons in unpleasant proximity to the culprit, but he turned his head aside and gazed on the infuriated multitude with a lip of scorn.

"Away with him," said the judge; "hang him beside the Jew."

Loud plaudits rent the air as the judge rose from his seat.

The prisoner was led away under guard, and the assembly dispersed.

At sunset all the patriots were astir.

Ropes were attached to lofty boughs of neighbouring trees.

Around the scene of execution a guard was placed.

The throng assembled were laughing and joking.

Drums rolled.

The crowd gave way.

Ivanovitch and the Jew appeared with hands firmly pinioned behind them.

Ivanovitch walked proudly and erect.

He gazed with a calmness that took the whole assembly by surprise.

Not so the Jew.

He trembled in every limb, and had to be supported on either hand by a stalwart peasant to keep him in an erect posture.

His face was deathly pale, his lips trembled, and he glared on those around him with the fierceness and bitterness of a powerless beast doomed to un-looked-for slaughter.

The prisoners were placed upon strong tables immediately beneath halters, which dangled above them, and a few feet apart.

Ropes were fastened about their necks, but their eyes were not bandaged, neither were caps drawn over their faces.

Thus they stood, between life and death.

"Has the Jew aught to say?" asked the judge. "Has he anything to reveal?"

The Jew gnashed his teeth, and hysterically laughed and sobbed by turns.

His mouth was all a-foam.

He grinned hideously on all around him, and essayed to speak; but utterance was choked.

At last he gasped out,

"My curses and maledictions follow you! I have not been fairly tried; I am innocent. My blood be on your heads. May the limbs, of one and all be mangled by hungry wolves, and may your souls be consigned to——"

He did not finish the sentence.

A signal was given.

The table was tilted from under him.

He fell.

A loud snap was heard.

His neck was broken.

He was launched into eternity.

Rounds of applause followed.

The judge motioned for silence.

"Ivanovitch! Have you any secrets to disclose? It is not yet too late to purchase life."

"Ask me no questions. I am ready," he replied, with thrilling calmness.

The table was pushed from under him.

He fell several feet.

A violent tremour passed through his frame, and Ivanovitch was no more.

The assembly dispersed.

Night closed in. The moon slowly rose, and shed its light upon the traitors who, side by side, dangled from boughs of a lofty beech tree.

Patriot camp fires glanced.

All was still, and the sentinel, noiselessly walking his lonely post, looked up at the dead men, around whom the night winds sighed, as if in tones of triumph for their doom.

CHAPTER CXCVIII.

WHILE the vindictive maid was so ungratefully endangering his life by her information against him, Edward Leighton was comfortably reclining on a couch in the library, for his wound was still painful, reading some of the rare books that enriched the prince's library; among others he found an old German manuscript, which contained the following story, which perhaps will interest our readers.

It was by some unknown author, and was entitled:—

HANS HERMANN; OR, THE WISHING ROSE.

Some centuries ago there lived in the heart of the Black Forest an honest, handsome, and clever youth, whose name was Hans Hermann.

His mother was the widow of a wood-cutter and charcoal-burner, who died while Hans was an infant.

Besides her own child, the widow Hermann had to support a little girl, whose name was Anchen, her sister's orphaned daughter.

Hans and Anchen were very fond of each other, and dwelt together in the log cottage in great content and perfect harmony.

The gliding years passed by.

The bitter winter blasts howled through the branched woods, stripping every bough of its leafy ornaments; the snow fell, frosting the dark firs and hoary oaks, and filling up many a sylvan glen and mossy dingle.

The spring returned; the languid sun from day to day gained power, the breath of Heaven was sweet and softened, and the snow melted before its genial wafting.

Then blushing summer came, and every dell was strewed with forest blossoms, and every bird tuned its wildest, gladdest notes, and the proud and conscious trees donned their rich mantles of green.

Then sober autumn succeeded, and the berries became ripe, and the woods rich russet tinted; the evenings calm, and silence hallowed.

And so calmly died the year.

Thus time moved on, and each successive year added to the strength and stature, and as yet took nothing away from the innocence and beauty of Hans and his cousin Anchen.

The boy was a powerful and industrious fellow, and though he was not able to gain luxuries for his mother and cousin, yet he contrived to keep them in comparative competence.

Hans and Anchen dearly loved each other, and the good widow watched their growing affection with joy and pride.

They had always lived in the old forests, and were so used to their simple, calm mode of life that they envied not the rich and proud who dwelt in the towers and towns scattered over the face of the fine woodland country.

Hans was not without learning; he had been placed at a village school, conducted by a very able teacher, and after he had learned all that his master could teach him, he formed an acquaintance with some worthy monks, who invited him to spend a few hours every day in the library of their monastery, and took great pains to instruct him in the higher branches of knowledge.

Besides his daily occupation as a wood-cutter, Hans had other sources of gain.

He practised the art of carving in wood, and acquired great skill in this kind of work.

He was employed in some elaborate carving at the monastery, and made many little models and the like, which he sold for considerable sums.

Altogether the Hermann family were prosperous and happy.

Now, it happened one unlucky day, that a regiment of hussars halted at a village not far distant from the wood-cutter's cottage.

Hans mingled with these men.

The brigadier of the troop, who was a fine, dashing fellow, and looked very imposing in his showy uniform, took a mighty fancy to the young forester.

He laughed and bantered at his quiet and country-like ways, and mimicked his strong dialect.

Hans, at first bashful, gained confidence after awhile, and took a great delight in the society of the troopers.

"And pray, Master Hans, tell me one thing," said the brigadier, as he and the youth were drinking beer together in the arbour of a road-side inn.

"And what is that, meinheer?"

"Do you think that you are a coward?"

"I have had more than one tussle with a bear or an izzard; I once had a skirmish with a robber band," replied Hans, "and I must say I did not feel afraid."

"Ah! Then you say you have valour?"

"I don't say so; but I don't want to confess myself to be a coward, for I am not," replied the youth, "for cowardice is to my mind the most disgraceful fault a man can have."

"You are right there, Master Hans, and you can read like a clerk."

"I am ignorant, alas; but still I can read and write, and cast accounts."

"And carve wood and kill bears, climb, shoot, and throw a lance."

"Yes, I think I can do so much."

"And your so much is a great deal. Well, Hans, answer this one question; to what purpose do you put these accomplishments?"

"Well, I use them in my trade, or for my amusement," returned Hans, blushing.

"And do you think that you could not put them to a better purpose?"

"If there were need I would."

"There is need. History wants heroes; its pages are getting dull and tedious. The King wants soldiers to defend his kingdom, or to secure his rights. Then why is Hans a peasant in a lonely wood, when perhaps he might be a courtier in a kingly palace, or a commander in a mighty camp?"

"Because Hans is content with his lot, for he finds his humble position a very happy one."

"Then he is without ambition?"

"Yes."

"Then he lacks the best and highest of all qualities. What animal is that which prefers acorns to pearls? What sort of mind is his who can content himself with sharing the pleasures of the beasts of the forests, the mere pleasures of eating, drinking, and sleeping, and forgets the triumphs of wealth, fame, and power? Still, as you say, you are happy, Master Hans; long may you remain so. I drink health, Master Hans!"

This sort of conversation fired the youth's mind with new emotions, new aspirations.

His heart, before so light, became heavy with discontent.

His brow, before so clear, became darkened with the clouds of gloomy broodings.

In this mood he returned home one day to his cottage in the forest.

Never before the arrival of the soldiery had he passed along the trim path of his neat and blooming garden without casting around him a glance of pride and pleasure.

Now he looked upon his treasures with a sneer of contempt, and his quaint, low-eaved cottage seemed hatefully mean and ugly.

The hum of the bees, and the sweet plash of the water-spring were now but dronish sounds unworthy of attention.

He entered the cottage.

His mother received him with a smile.

His betrothed embraced him tenderly.

He looked upon her.

She was still beautiful, but so artless, and so plainly dressed.

He returned her embrace, but so coldly that the tears sprang to her kind and pretty blue eyes when she looked into his altered face.

He sat himself down at the table.

His supper was neatly spread on a snowy cloth.

The ham, the beer, the bread,—mere husks they seemed.

He drank from a horn.

He put it back in disgust.

Not the murmuring hum of bees, not the leap and ripple of tinkling waters, but the loud flourish of silver trumpets, the brisk thunder of brazen drums, for him. Yes, he would be high-souled, he would soar upon the wings of endeavour, and would not crawl on the legs of passive contentment. Not for him the low-thatched cot, but the resplendent palace and the proud pavilion; not the plain fare, the mere bread and meat of his peasant life, but the delicacies of the banquet served on salvers and in chalices of gold and silver. Yes, and for his love, Anchen, still, but not in a simple blue kirtle and snowy kerchief, but in purple pall, ermine, and rich gems. He would be ambitious, he would be high-souled; others had risen to dizzy heights from depths as low as that in which he found himself; he would rise indomitable energy to carry out an untiring purpose, would win all.

"What is the matter with Hans to-night? He looks so fierce, and seems to have lost all his cheerfulness," said the widow Hermann, looking anxiously at her son.

"He is tired, poor fellow; the weather is sultry, and the wood so hard and heavy," said Anchen, sitting down at the feet of her lover, and looking sweetly in his face.

Hans tried to shake off his moodiness.

"Anchen, what shall we talk about?" he asked.

"What you please; we are not often at a loss for a subject to converse on. Let us arrange about the feast at the sheep-shearing."

"Pshaw!"

Anchen seemed surprised at her lover's unusual impatience, but kept meek silence.

"Anchen, do you ever build castles in the air?"

"Oh, yes; very, very often."

"And of what style of architecture are they?"

"They are rather cottages than castles," answered Anchen, with a blush; "but I must not tell you my day-dreams."

"Oh, yes."

"Well, then, Hans, I picture our happiness when I am your wife, and live in our pretty home, and watch for my husband's returning footsteps every night, and waking him with a kiss every morning."

Anchen blushed brightly, and laughed gaily as she said this.

"Aye, but if our home were a stately castle; if my returning steps were announced by the fanfare of the clarion and the ring of polished armour?"

"Then I should be so miserable."

"I suppose so. Women are strange beings; they resign themselves to whatever circumstance they are born in. They have no ambition."

"Ambition! What are the good fruits of ambition?"

"What fruitfulness is there in barren contentment?"

"Oh, Hans, listen to me,—

" The eagle that cleaveth the stormy sky,
    Exults in his pride that he soars so high ;
    Looks down in disdain on each lowlier thing,
    But soon he must stoop to his tiring wing.
    Ambition that mounts on wings of the morn,
    Looks back on his source with a smile of scorn ;
    But soon he descends with a fallen crest,
    For he finds no place for his foot to rest."

Hans got up in a very ill temper.

"The Mussulmen say women have no souls, and I believe the doctrine."

With this ungracious speech he bounced out of the room.

He threw himself in a seat in the garden, and folding his arms, fixed his eyes upon a large and beauteous rose tree, which he had planted there on his birthday.

He had reared this lovely bush of rich, red blossoms from a scion he had cut from a rose-bush growing beside a certain well said to be haunted by a fairy.

Many averred that the flower was magic, and that if the owner gathered three of the buds at a certain hour of the evening, and under certain conditions for each, he would have a wish granted ; but that, as with every rose there is a thorn, with each gratification of the desires of the owner of the talisman some sad calamity would fall upon one or other of his relatives or friends.

Hans Hermann placed no reliance upon this legend ; but still he could not help casting a wistful look upon the wishing rose.

As he sat there, dreamily, a strange spell rose to his lips, and he thus addressed the flower,

" Fay of the wishing rose,
    O say what joys are those
        That mortals gain,
    When for the golden prize,
    Boldly the brave uprise
        Through toil and pain."

A sweet, low voice, as if of the soft wind whispering to him, replied,

" Just one exultant thought,
    By many a bitter bought ;
        And one day's reign,
    By years of trouble won—
    Vain toil when all is done—
        Such prize they gain."

" Be such my prize, fay of the wishing rose, for I am restless now. I've eaten of the fruit of knowledge and the wood is no longer an Eden."

As Hans said this he snatched three rose-buds which grew upon one stalk of the tree.

He separated one from the rest.

" I would be a leader of warriors," he said.

He looked about him expecting to see mailed men start from every bush and tree.

But still he stood in the quiet garden, the stars gleaming mildly down, the wishing rose-bush lightly quivering, the water-spring rippling, and the nightingale singing his vespers.

He looked with some contempt upon the flower.

It was suddenly seared, as if passed through a white heat.

The thorns remained in his hand.

He thought they were sharper than any others that he had ever clutched, and the stem seemed to sting his fingers like a nettle.

Still no sign of the mailed men, no prancing horses, waving banners, flaunting plumes, and flashing swords and spears.

He wandered back into the cottage.

Just as he was about to take up his tools to carve an image, at which he had long been working, he was startled by a bugle sound.

Then came the tramp of the mailed men.

The door was open.

The man who entered first, and who seemed to be an officer, he recognised at once as his friend the brigadier.

But now he was dressed in complete steel.

The soldiers seemed to have ridden hard and fast, and were hot and breathless.

They told Hans that a number of the enemy were lying in ambush in a distant and lonely part of the Black Forest, and that they had come to seek his assistance as guide.

Hans joyously proffered his services. With his ambitious aspirations he was so engrossed, that he did not even stop to bid farewell to his pleading mother, but, seizing his hatchet and cross-bow, led the way through the dark woods.

A horse was given him, and as soon as he touched the back of the fiery charger, he seemed to be suddenly infused with the strongest spirit of martial pride and ardour.

He reached the spot where the enemy lay concealed.

He made a furious attack upon them.

There was a fierce and bloody battle.

The brigadier was killed, and but for Hans, the rest must either have fled, or suffered the same fate.

He, however, cheered them by his example, and cleaving his way through the foes, killed the captain and secured the standard.

The enemy were utterly routed.

The soldiers were so delighted with the valour of the young woodman, that they elected him to be their captain, and vowed they would obey no other.

Hans donned a suit of armour, which he wore as easily as if it were a doublet of silk.

In triumph he returned home, attended by his new comrades, shouting and chanting their victory.

What was his horror and amazement upon reaching his cottage to find it a smouldering shell of charred wood ! The garden was trampled into a chaos, the pale was broken down, the wishing rose nearly destroyed.

Yet the cold water-spring sang on as gaily as ever.

In great fear and agony, Hans flew into the cottage.

His mother lay dead at his feet, killed by a sword thrust !

And he had left her defenceless to the murderers ; had not so much as said farewell.

A party of the enemy, in full flight, had halted at the cottage, and finding that it was the home of the man who had defeated them so completely, vented their exasperation upon the poor old woman, whom they killed, and then they fired the house.

Anchen was not to be found.

Hans ran as one frantic into the most intricate parts of the wood, calling upon her name.

At last, to his great joy, his call was answered from the distance.

Anchen, who had concealed herself in the wood, threw herself into his arms and fainted.

He bore her away from the dreadful scene.

He was shortly after joined by the rest of the army.

In another battle he so greatly distinguished himself that he obtained the chief command.

He had been presented to the king at his capital, and from that moment became the reigning favourite in court and camp.

He was now a very great man.

He had many friends, and thrice as many enemies.

He was courted and cringed to, flattered, admired, obeyed, but the blandest smiles were often the masks of treachery, and he was puzzled to know which of his friends were true, and which were traitors.

His life passed in one exciting, wearying round of court intrigue, or toil and danger in the field of battle.

And where was Anchen all this time ?

In a convent.

In the great capital the simple country maid was quite out of her element.

For her the glittering pomp and parade of the Court was not only uncared for, but was painful in the extreme.

Envied for her beauty, despised for simple country manners, she found but small favour from those of her own sex.

Did Hans marry his betrothed?

No, he did not.

He had fallen in love with the king's daughter, and she returned his passion.

Another of the court favourites, however, was eager to secure the hand of the princess, and used all his influence to bring Hans into disgrace.

Anchen pined away in seclusion, and Hans could not help feeling that his neglect was the cause of her decline of health and spirits.

But in his heart ambition was stronger than love.

Yet he grew colder in his wooing of the king's daughter, and was not a little surprised when suddenly informed that the king had consented to her marriage with the other suitor.

Should the king die, and he was very old, the princess would succeed him on the throne, and, in that case, would be an enemy to him for her husband's sake, who hated him with all a courtier's vindictiveness.

He was loth to have recourse to the talismanic wishing rose, as he dreaded the sting of its cruel thorns.

However, growing desperate, he rushed home, and taking one of the two remaining buds in his hand, murmured,

"I would have the princess for my bride."

In an hour's time a messenger came running from the palace with the news that the king had discovered a plot against himself in which Hans Hermann's rival was concerned, and that all proceedings for the nuptials had been stopped.

When Hans arrived at the palace he experienced a very gracious reception both from the monarch and his daughter.

The friends of his rival raised an insurrection in the kingdom but Hans marched against the rebels and soon restored order.

All had gone well; the thorn of the second rose had not stung quite so sharply as the first.

Yet Anchen died; he stopped at the convent, where she was secluded, and she died in his arms.

But then she had long been ailing; at least she died happily, with a blessing on her lips, and now he was free to follow the bent of his ambition.

These bereavements are sorrowful, but then they are so inevitable, it is useless to take them too much to heart.

So Hans Hermann married the princess.

But he soon found that his beauteous bride was haughty and imperious, and not quite disposed to treat her husband as her equal.

This conduct he resisted fiercely.

He found, too, that his enemies at Court were doing all they could to poison the king's mind against him.

His position grew more and more painful, his cares and dangers day by day increased.

About this time the princess gave birth to a son.

All the thwarted love in Hans Hermann's heart gushed forth, and flowed to this new object.

He had sacrificed much for his own advancement, but for his child he would do and suffer far more.

The king had been ungrateful, he thought, or he would not have listened to the charges brought against him by his enemies.

He retired into his secret chamber, and took up the third and last of the fatal wishing roses.

"I would be king!" he gasped.

He sat trembling with horror.

He could not be king unless he turned traitor; he could not fill the throne till he had removed its present occupant.

If the talisman should rob the king of life, Hans would be in effect the murderer of his sovereign.

But all went well.

Again summoned to his master's presence, he found that the aged monarch was so outworn with the cares of state that he was anxious to lay them aside for ever; and in a short time he abdicated the throne in favour of the bold and successful soldier.

Now Hans was at the very pinnacle of greatness; a feared and powerful monarch, and the father of a beautiful child, who would succeed to his dominions.

This rose had been thornless.

But no! the king's son began to grow pale and weak; and though the most fabulous rewards were offered to the physician who could restore him to health, he gradually sickened and died.

From that moment the king lost heart; he took no further pleasure in the fruits of ambition; he became stern and reserved, and soon became unpopular.

After the death of her son, the queen became more estranged than ever from her husband.

They lived at separate palaces, and kept up rival courts.

The king had no more children.

Seated in his purple robes upon his jewelled throne, the golden burden of royalty pressing on his brow, he listened heedlessly to the fulsome flatteries of traitorous parasites; and he thought of the old, old times, of the sweet, yet manly life in the rare old Bohemian forests, of well-spent days, and peaceful nights.

After some time a number of the queen's partisans rebelled against him, and the queen herself opposed him in the field.

But his high heart was now bowed down by grief, and his arm nerveless with the apathy of disappointment.

He fought not with the same energy with which he warred in former days.

He lost the battle, and was forced to flee on horseback from his pursuers.

He took refuge in the Black Forest.

Becoming separated from his attendants, he rode moodily on till his horse almost fell beneath him from exhaustion.

He found himself in an open part of the wood.

Before him were the charred and blackened ruins of an old cottage.

He dismounted, and stood looking upon them with tearful eyes.

It was his native, humble home.

A few stems of the wishing-rose still flourished, bearing rich red blossoms.

"Fay of the wishing-rose, dearly have I paid for not heeding your warning. Vain toil, when all is done," he murmured, shedding bitter tears of anguish and remorse. "Honest toil brings peace; love brings joy, integrity, manly pride, and self-respect."

And he added, as he thought of some old rhyme he had learned when a boy,

Sweet home joys and home affections,
What can match your dear delight?
Not for me the world's infections,
Blood-stained laurels, despot might.

"But my mother, and my bride, sweet Anchen, ye are no more, and Hans is transformed; it is too late for hope!"

A silvery voice was wafted to his ear by the evening breeze.

"Mortal, the fay of the wishing-rose pities your distress! She will give you one more wish, and, if you choose, will restore you to your crown and kingdom!"

"My crown is my clustering locks, without one silver hair; my kingdom is my home, my own, my humble home!" cried Hans, with great fervour.

A merry laugh caused him to start.

He was reclining against a bank, the wishing-rose bloom before him.

The water spring sang the old, old song, the nightingale revelled as richly as ever.

There stood the old cottage, nothing changed, and there stood Anchen, blushing and laughing.

"My home, my humble home! They say folks tell truth in sleep," she cried; "but I am sorry to break your dreaming, for just now you looked as glumpy and discontented round the old place as if it were a hovel, and not the prettiest, happiest homestead in Bohemia."

THE PRINCESS ACCUSED OF THE MURDER.

Hans leaped up and caught her hands.

"Why, how you stare!" she cried. "Depend upon it, Hans, the pixies have bewitched you."

"And I am really at home? I have lost nothing but my crown and kingdom, and am restored to what no imperial power or wealth can bring."

"It's a gnome or a pixy that has bewitched you. But come in, and tell us your dream."

Hans Hermann complied.

Hans and Anchen soon after married, and in the bride's sunny hair there lurked slyly three pretty blossoms of the wishing-rose.

CHAPTER CXCIX.

LEIGHTON AND HIS NOBLE PUPIL—HARMONY AND DISCORD—A SCENE—IGNOMINIOUS EXIT OF COUNT BRUTOFF—A STORM BREWING.

EDWARD LEIGHTON found his position was by no means one of discomfort. Although he was a prisoner on parole, he enjoyed perfect liberty within the house, and was permitted to range the grounds about it.

He saw that the household was conducted on a

scale of rude magnificence, the prince being a man of vast wealth.

The princess tyrannised over her dependents in the most despotic fashion; but she was, in her turn, robbed, victimised and neglected to a wonderful extent.

Every branch of the domestic economy was mismanaged; no one seemed to be in his right position, or to have any clear notion of his duties.

The princess was a mere child in moral advancement, and though she had a smattering of languages, and spoke French purely, she was not a good musician, had but little skill in drawing; and, in fact, her learning was very superficial.

Her education had not been neglected.

The prince had spent great sums to procure the services of foreign teachers, but the wilful and passionate girl had profited little by their instructions.

Leighton, who was no mean scholar, offered to teach her drawing.

The princess applied herself with great diligence to study.

The prince was constantly employed with harassing affairs.

The dauntless Red Raven proved a terrible avenger.

Defeated once or twice by an overwhelming force he had made good his retreat to the fortress, which he still held out in spite of Count Brutoff's strong detachment.

The princess, under the care of Edward, seemed an altered being.

Subdued by his calm self-possession and great firmness of character she became as gentle and submissive as she had before been passionate and overbearing.

In truth, the princess was deeply in love.

Sometimes, as he sat by her side and pored over the same book with her, he would shudder; his voice grew thick, and a dread that was almost appalling settled upon his heart; for he felt himself gradually drawn into the fatal vortex of an insane passion.

At such moments his cheek went deadly pale.

The princess would look at him with yearning affection for an instant, and then demurely resume her studies.

After these slight displays of emotion on his part Edward always became colder and sterner than ever; the cunning princess more gentle and humble.

She had found her master.

Still she was subject to fits of temper at intervals, and often tried to pick a quarrel with her tutor.

He was impassable; calm and grave, never trusting himself to breathe one word of reproach.

The princess constantly refused to see Count Brutoff.

Her father stormed and entreated in vain.

As soon as the count entered the house she would lock herself in her room, and remain there till he departed.

One day Brutoff rode over to the palace from the camp.

He got off his horse, and, entering the garden, passed under the window of the library.

He suddenly stopped.

A storm of fury was depicted on his changing countenance.

The chords of the piano were struck, and the voices of a man and woman blended in clear harmony.

Giving the rein to his passion, he rushed up the steps of the balcony and burst into the room.

The princess rose, and repelled him with flashing eyes.

Edward Leighton remained calm, but frowned his indignation.

"Madam, as my affianced wife, I demand an explanation of your strange conduct; of late you have slighted me most grossly, and now I find you——"

"Singing a duet with another gentleman," returned the princess, with a mocking laugh; "you are a good bass, suppose we have a concerto."

"This levity——"

"Does not suit your growling gravity! You pitiful wretch, how dare you scowl on Sophia Aronzow as if she were one of your fawning serfs!" she cried, losing her dignity and sweeping into a terrific passion. "Look less ferocious, gallant count; do not forget that though I am a woman I am not without a protector. A man is here, be careful; perhaps he will beat you!"

"Traitress! you harbour a rebel and a pirate. I remember this villain, I know——"

"The weight of his arm, perhaps."

"Princess, you must be mad! But I will have my revenge for this insult."

"And so will I," replied the princess, in the tone of a virago.

"You are in league with the Poles."

"To drag you through a horsepond."

"This rascal is a spy of the National Government, a thief, a rogue, an adventurer."

"And the other rascal is a miscreant, a womanqueller, a hound, a coward (and a great many other bad things in good and strong Russian)."

In spite of his wrath and disgust, Edward could hardly refrain from laughing at the true Billingsgate style of this encounter, and he felt half amused, half piqued, at beholding the utter fruitlessness of his labour to train and subdue his lovely pupil.

The count stamped and swore, and the princess raved and shrieked.

This scene is only a parallel of one enacted in the presence of a distinguished author, by a Russian gentleman and lady, equal in grade to Count Brutoff and the princess.

But we must separate the belligerents at once, before mischief arises.

Edward was so stunned and confused by this vulgar and violent display of blind passion on either side, that he stood petrified with amazement.

At last the brutal noble seized the princess by the arm, leaving the prints of his hard fingers livid in the fair and delicate flesh.

Edward was roused in a moment.

Flinging himself upon the count, he seized him by the back of the neck, and dragging him to the balcony kicked him down the steps.

The princess bounded to the side of her champion.

Poor Brutoff was sprawling on the ground.

"Ah, the cursed wretch! but you should have broken his neck," cried the princess.

The count sprang up, drew his sword, and was about to rush up the steps; he seemed to change his mind on the instant, sheathed his sword, and rushed away.

Edward led the princess back to her chamber.

He bowed gravely, and seemed inclined to leave the room.

She threw herself down by a couch and burst into a passion of weeping.

"You hate me! you despise me! I am a coarse fish-wife, a Huron squaw! What am I?" she cried, in accents of bitter self-reproach; "but the man is such a brute, and I cannot restrain my temper. I have never learned to control myself; have kept no company, except with my slaves; ha! find excuses for me, cher monsieur; pardon!"

Edward Leighton raised her with trembling hands.

"Generous to me, kindest, most gracious princess, I would give my life to see you truer to yourself."

The princess wept like a child.

She then seated herself on the couch.

"Ah, I am so agitated; now my fit of temper—brief madness—is passed, I see the fatal folly of what I have done. The Count Brutoff is a ruthless villain, who will not fail to ruin us."

"Oh, Heaven! how unfortunate am I—I that would give a thousand lives rather than you should incur danger for my sake."

"Do not speak of that," returned the princess. "Ah, mon Dieu! mon Dieu! that I should be so heedless!"

"But where is the prince? We must consult his excellency."

"My father is absent, but will return soon. Meantime——. "Oh, wretched me!"

"My dear, my gracious princess——"

"You must fly! Yes, you must leave me; leave me, to laugh me to scorn, to hate me as a Goth, a savage! Well, I shall give you less cause to despise me if I say less about what is past, and cannot be recalled."

The princess wept passionately.

"Oh, what a beast I am! What fiend possessed me," she cried, wringing her hands, "to provoke this savage brute to rend us? Well, it cannot be helped; and I am so hot-tempered. But you must fly; and, I fear, on the instant, for it is not improbable that the count will go at once to my father, who is in the camp, and insist upon your surrender to the governor of Kowno."

"I will not leave this house, your excellency, without the consent of the prince, to whom I have given parole."

The princess looked at him searchingly.

She saw that he was immovably fixed in his resolution.

She swept about the room in great excitement.

"The foibles of honour which govern men, how stupid they are! I should not respect them! why should you? Besides, my father would rather lose his own head than a hair of yours should be harmed."

"And therefore, my desertion would be the more base," returned Edward, firmly. "No, your excellency, I will stay till the prince's return."

The old steward entered the room.

A handsomely-accoutred soldier accompanied him.

"I have brought monsieur a letter from his excellency the prince, who requests that monsieur will read it at once, and act upon it."

The man bowed, and presented the letter to Edward.

It contained these words:—

Fly! Count Brutoff, with a file of men, are on their way to arrest you. If you neglect this warning you are lost!

Urged by the princess, Edward Leighton prepared to leave the house.

"You will want a guide," said the princess. "Well, I will be generous; the vivandiere, Katinka, shall go with you. You must disguise yourselves."

Edward Leighton thanked the princess, and expressed his gratitude for her kindness.

The girl was brought from her cell.

She was dressed as a peasant.

As she stood beside the princess, the contrast between the two beauties was favourable to each.

Edward looked at them critically.

The refinement of the princess was somewhat superficial.

Katinka's grace and naivete were perfectly natural.

Edward retired to his room to change his dress.

Petroff and the old steward assisted him.

He put on a blue blouse and a fur cap.

Something heavy struck against his breast.

A parcel of gold coins had been sewed in the breast pocket of his jacket.

But the servants gave him no time to remonstrate.

He hurried on the blouse, banded his waist with the heavy belt, and thrust through it a large hatchet, such as is constantly carried by Russian peasants.

He was alone.

She rose to meet him.

He sank on one knee.

She tenderly clasped his hands between her own.

He sank on one knee, and reverently kissed her hand.

She spoke timidly.

"You are leaving me now, mon cher ami, and we may meet no more on earth! Think of me sometimes; forgive my wretched faults, for, bad as I am,

there may be found some excuses for me, and it is cruel to hate those that love us."

The princess spoke these words with great emotion.

Before Edward could reply, the steward entered the room with Katinka, and announced the approach of the prince and Count Brutoff, with a strong force of military.

Edward Leighton and his fair companion hastened to take their leave of the princess.

They mounted their horses, and galloped off towards the village where they were to find rest and shelter for the night.

The princess retired to her chamber.

The prince and Brutoff entered.

The former looked pale and excited; the latter frowned darkly, and seemed bursting with brutish fury.

The princess was summoned.

The prince asked his daughter what had become of the prisoners.

She replied that they had escaped.

Count Brutoff burst into a storm of rage.

He was, however, soon overawed by a stern look from the prince.

He maintained sullen silence while the house was being searched.

Soon after he left with his soldiers.

That very night the governor of Kowno sent a detachment of soldiers and two officers to arrest the Prince Aronzow and his daughter.

Their excellencies were removed in their own coach, and were lodged in the prison at Kowno to await examination.

———

CHAPTER CC.

ONCE MORE IN THE FAR WEST—THE BUSH-RANGERS' STRONGHOLD — THE FORAGING PARTY—THE TETON CHIEF—THE FEAST—OSWALD LAMOND AT HOME—MINNA'S NEW SUITOR—THE INDIAN'S MISSION — STRUCK DOWN — SPARED — FOXLEY ONCE MORE ON HARWOLF'S TRACK.

ONCE more the shifting scene of our wild romance changes; once more, with the swift glance of the mind, we sweep over continents and seas, and contemplate a group of robbers of Regan's band, who are carrying provisions up the rugged pathway which led to their cavern in the Rocky Mountains.

They are wild-looking fellows, ferocious and reckless in their mien, and dressed in a picturesque style half-Indianised.

Upon the back of one of them was a sack containing articles of value.

Another carried a bundle of various stuffs, linen, cloths, and even silk.

Several others followed burdened with baskets of bread, butter, cheese, hams, fruit and eggs.

Another carried a killed pig, another a heavy barrel of spirits.

They appeared very jovial, and the woods and rocks rang with their boisterous laughter.

They had been foraging at a distant homestead and had made a very successful raid.

One of them was mounted.

This was Wyld, the lieutenant, whose repulsive ugliness we have before noticed as contrasting so strangely with the unusual beauty of the young Captain Lamond.

By his side walked a burly, black-browed ruffian whose name was Morgan Lee.

Behind, leading a laden mule, walked a tall Indian brave.

He seemed to be a Teton chief, and was very strangely and savagely dressed.

He wore a heavy head-dress of raven's feathers, intermingled with wampums and a pair of buffalo horns.

Across his breast and depending behind from his left shoulder was a panther's hide.

At his waist were the scalp-locks of several native enemies.

His arms were heavier and ruder in construction than those in use among the Pawnees or Dacotahs, and consisted of a tomahawk, a small bow and a quiver of flint-pointed arrows.

On his shoulder he carried a long, clumsy, old-fashioned fire-lock.

Round his neck was a fillet with bears' claws and wolves' teeth.

He wore no mocassins on his legs.

His skin was of a darker colour than usual among the tribes, and his face looked like a painter's pallet; so much was it daubed with war-paint, while round his legs and arms were painted bars of blue and white.

Altogether his appearance was terrific.

It was not very easy to judge of his age considering the strange guise in which he appeared, but, if he had reached manhood's prime, he had lost nothing of the grace and suppleness of youth.

To this respectable company of travellers there was an advance and rear guard, each consisting of four men with muskets.

They entered the cavern.

It was a large and sombre hollow in the mountain side.

At the back were a number of compartments formed partly by nature and partly hewn out by the hand of man.

These recesses were veiled by curtains of skins.

A fire burnt under a cauldron in the middle of the cave, and around it a group of the bandits were seated.

They were all busily employed in sharpening their knives and hatchets, or in moulding bullets and shot.

The men in the cavern welcomed their comrades with a lusty shout.

With much jesting and laughter the stores were examined and distributed, and soon the grateful fumes pervading the cavern, proclaimed that the preparations for a luxurious feast were commencing.

The wild and barbarous-looking Teton chief stood gravely apart, leaning upon his long fire-lock.

Wyld, and the others of the foraging party narrated their adventures, which were listened to with much interest by their comrades.

At length the curtain of one of the recesses of the cavern was raised, and the captain of the bush-rangers appeared.

Oswald Lamond looked very handsome and gallant in his picturesque attire.

He wore a richly worked hunting shirt and quilled mocassins, his bugle and dirk on one side, and a bright-barrelled pistol in his belt.

He had on a slouch hat with an eagle's feather, and carried in his hand a fine rifle with a baldrick of bead-work.

" So, you have returned, Wyld, and have brought your welcome with you," he said, with a laugh, as he looked on the provisions strewn on the ground. " Well, my co-mates and brothers in exile, I reckon to-night we'll feast like aldermen."

" Catahaga is killed, captain," said Wyld.

" I've heard that report so often that I begin to doubt the truth of it," returned Oswald, impatiently. " If he is dead, rest his bones in peace, and let's say no more about him."

" But, captain, you gave me particular orders to find out the truth of this story; the Eagle-Wing 'ell in an action with the Regulators."

" And who comes in such a questionable shape ?" said the captain of the bush-rangers, looking at the Indian who was approaching the spot with a slow and stately step.

" An Indian of a wandering tribe ; we picked him up on the prairie," was Wyld's answer. " He wants to trade with you for arms and ammunition, he has a drove of beeves, and some of the finest peltries you

ever beheld ; besides, he offers his services, and has a splendid set of braves."

" Humph ! he is horned like the devil, and looks just as fierce and hideous," returned Oswald, in a tone of dissatisfaction. " Of what tribe is he ?"

" He is a Teton."

" Well, I must have a word with him."

So saying, the captain advanced towards the Teton, and held out his hand.

The Indian touched it, and bowed his head with much dignity.

Oswald looked at him very curiously.

The Indian steadily returned the glance.

The Teton's features were so disfigured by paint that it was not easy to recognise them.

On the stage he would have made a most appalling fiend or ghoul, so horrid were his looks.

" My brother is welcome ; why has he sought me ?" asked Oswald.

The reply was given in a strange and harsh dialect.

" Minowaka is the greatest of warriors ; the braves of his tribe are like the birds in the woods, which cannot be numbered," replied the Indian. " The Teton dwells not in settled wigwams, the earth is all his, and the prairies are his hunting grounds ; he wanders over far and wide, and the Iroquois dogs flee before him like hinds from the panther. His eyes give light like stars, and he follows his enemy's trail even through darkness ; his heart is harder than rocks, and his arm more terrible than the thunderbolt."

Oswald listened very gravely to this modest announcement.

" The great chief will smoke the calumet with his white brothers, and will sit down with them at the feast fires," said the Bush-ranger, smiling.

" It is good," grunted the greatest of warriors, with a hungry look at the provender.

A place was given to the Teton chief.

The bush-rangers then regaled themselves with great good-will and appetite.

They were joined by Reynard, still a prisoner among the bush-rangers.

He seeemed tolerably resigned to his captivity, and though still weak and emaciated from the effects of the terrible loss of blood he had suffered after his wound.

Oswald sat on one side of the Teton.

Reynard on the other.

The captain of the bush-rangers entered into a long conversation with the red-skin.

The men listened with interest.

Oswald asked him many questions as to his tribe, his place of abode, his resources.

To all these questions the Teton gave prompt and direct answers.

" My brother's belt is heavy with scalps ; the war-chief has just returned from the trail ?" hinted Oswald.

" Minowaka has won the scalps of the Pawnee Loups," said the chief, grimly, " but the pale-faces have taken the scalp of their chief the Eagle-Wing."

" You see, captain, what I told you was true," said Wyld.

" All the better ; but quite enough of a good thing."

" Have the young men of the pale-faces crossed my brother's trail ?" asked Oswald.

" The Grey Wolf and his braves have crossed the Arkansas and are returning to their wigwams."

" He is right," said Wyld.

" So pretty Minna Wyotti is a widow," said Oswald, musingly.

" Aye, captain, and her only consolation will be that she can take another husband."

" Yourself, for instance."

The ugly ruffian grinned.

" And why not me ?"

Oswald was about to make some answer but looking in his comrade's face burst into a laugh.

There is something in grandeur akin to beauty ; and nothing is nearer the sublime than the genuine flash of intense passion; for a moment one might have forgotten Wyld's deformity and ugliness in the haughty glare of his intelligent face.

It passed off and left a sneer on the gashed lips.

"You have been useful and faithful, mate," said Oswald, with a laugh. "If you think that you can play King Dick with my pretty prisoner, take your chance; at least you did not murder her husband."

Wyld's eyes sparkled.

"Now, captain, you speak like a man. I *will* take my chance."

There was a roar of laughter among the rough bandits.

The Indian fixed a steady, cold look on the face of the bush-ranger Wyld; the chief's features remained calm, but there was a fatal glitter in his cold black eyes.

"The first thing to be done," said Wyld, without heeding the derisive cheer of his comrades, "is to convince the girl that her husband is really dead."

"That's easy; you know what she said."

"No, captain."

"She said she would not believe unless she heard it from the lips of an Indian."

"The Teton here, captain; he might convince her."

The Indian chief sat with his eyes fixed vacantly, his face quite changeless.

"A good thought," said Oswald, laughing.

He turned to the Indian.

"My brother has seen the white fawn of the Yengeese, who was the squaw of the Pawnee chief?"

"It is good," returned the Teton, coldly.

"The girl is a pale-face; she is a prisoner in thy tribe; a chief wishes to marry her."

"Waugh!"

"My brother does not know that, by the customs of our nation, a maiden cannot marry a second husband till the first is dead."

"It is good."

"Well, perhaps it is," laughed Oswald.

He added, speaking in the Teton's language,

"The tongues of the pale-faces are forked; the words of the Iroquois are clear as light. Minna will believe those of her husband's nation. Catahaga is dead; but Minna's eyes are darkened, she will not believe this truth."

"Minowaka will tell this to his sister," returned the chief.

"That's brave," cried Wyld. "Let the Teton go to her at once; she will believe what he says."

"It is good," returned Oswald. "Will my brother follow me?"

The savage-looking chief bowed his head gravely, and rose.

Before doing so, his hand, as if unconsciously, touched that of the detective.

Foxley started.

For an instant his eyes met those of the Teton.

He was as cunning as a fox this rogue-catcher.

"Captain Regan, let me be present; the girl was kind to me. I am a fellow prisoner, and may have influence in soothing her grief."

Oswald Lamond, in his wild way, was tender with women.

He liked the suggestion.

"So be it," he said, curtly. "She will not listen to me, she fears me; I am her gaoler. Come, then, Master Reynard!"

The lieutenant of the gang scowled blackly.

This only confirmed the young captain in his purpose.

He loved mischief, and Wyld's jealousy was prime pastime.

"Good King Dick, his Grace of Buckingham shall plead for you," he said, laughing.

"Come, Reynard; will the chief follow?"

He rose, and led the way through the deer-skin curtain.

Passing down a passage in the rock, the bush-ranger, the detective, and the Teton chief entered another cavern.

It was carpeted with bear-skin rugs, and furnished with rude tables and stools of rough hewn oak.

"I will fetch her hither," said Oswald; and he left the cavern by a side entry, which led to the part of the caves where Agnes and Minna resided.

The moment he was gone the Teton whispered hurriedly in the detective's ear.

Reynard went to the wall.

He pushed back a stone. A narrow passage appeared. The Teton smiled grimly.

Oswald Lamond led Minna into the room.

"Even despair, Minna, is better than suspense," he said, pressing the girl's hand, "you will not believe that your husband has fallen; here is an Indian chief who can assure you of the fact."

Minna with a sobbing cry, sprang forward.

"Oh, let my brother speak!" she cried, bitterly, "though his words wither my heart as the lightning blasts the tree. Catahaga, my chief, my husband——"

"Is here!" returned the Teton, drawing himself up to his full height, and striking off his crest of horns and ravens' feathers.

Minna shrieked.

"Ha, treachery!" cried Oswald, springing forward.

The Indian struck him across the temples with the back of his tomahawk, and he fell senseless.

"It is he—it is Catahaga—it is my own, my brave!" cried Minna, clinging to her husband.

But the Eagle-Wing put her away calmly.

He looked down upon the fallen bush-ranger with an exultant smile.

He drew his scalping-knife.

He dropped with his knee on the breast of his enemy.

He fastened a tight grip on the rich, clustering curls.

Minna flung her arms about him.

"Catahaga, for Agnes's sake!" gasped Minna, clutching his upraised hand of the infuriate chief, at the risk of gashing her spotless hand.

Foxley, when he looked on the beautiful face of the insensible youth, could not help feeling touched with pity.

It was hard to hate Oswald Lamond, despite his dissimmulation; there were some pleasing traits in his character that were very fascinating.

"Let my brother spare his enemy till he meet him on the war path," he said, in Iroquois.

But Catahaga heard him not.

His soul was subdued by the melting love-light and tender entreaty of Minna's soft, sweet eyes of blue.

He sheathed his scalping-knife, and rose.

"And now let us fly while there is a chance; the men are carousing; the sentinel, who guards the passage I have shown you, is off his post; we can easily escape."

As the detective said this he once more rolled back the stone.

"Let my heart seek her sister, the Yengeese lily, she shall go with us," said Catahaga, to his wife.

"No, no," repled Minna, "Agnes has married the robber; she will not leave him."

"It is good," replied the Indian, quietly.

"Hasten! and hush!" cried the detective, excitedly.

They passed through the passage, rolling back the stone behind them.

Oswald Lamond still lay as if dead!

———

CHAPTER CCI.

ADVENTURES OF LEIGHTON AND THE POLISH
MAID—A MERRY CALVACADE—THE VOW OF
SILENCE—A HOT PURSUIT—THE INN—THE
SEARCH — THE ARREST — CHAINS AND
SLAVERY—THE SCOURGE.

ONCE out of the domains of the castle of Aronzow, Edward Leighton and his fair companion urged their horses to the utmost speed.

The animals were not of the best breed in the prince's stables, for if the fugitives had been too well mounted they would have become objects of suspicion at once.

Nor was it prudent when they reached the open road to let their haste be such as would draw upon them observation.

Edward therefore reined in his horse.

They met a number of peasants in carts and on horseback travelling towards the village, for it was early morning of the market-day.

These merry folk called out jestingly to Leighton and the girl.

The former, whose knowledge of the Polish tongue was very limited, preserved a discrete silence.

"My husband is under a vow of silence," said Katinka, with a cheerful laugh.

One of the penances imposed by the priests upon those whom they absolve is this "vow of silence" by which the penitent is bound to abstain from speaking for some length of time.

"Your little husband is good, he bears your burdens," cried a market-girl, saucily.

"Yes; the good father knows that she could not keep the vow, and so her husband has undertaken to perform it for her," cried another. "Well, and right, there's no quarrelling with the dumb."

"Anything for a quiet life."

"I'll warrant he speaks before night."

"No need; she has tongue enough for twenty."

"I warrant her husband never gets a word in edgeways."

"Oh, he's a good subject for a 'vow of silence,' poor man."

"With such a well-spoken spouse, he can afford to be tongue-tied."

With much more of this sort of banter, the cavalcade rattled past them, all the market folk laughing cheerily.

It did not excite much surprise that the young couple seemed abashed, and slunk to the rear.

"Pretty Katinka, you are as clever as you are kind," said Leighton, when the others were out of hearing.

"A woman is never without an expedient," replied the vivandiere, archly.

A road turned off from the highway, which led to the village.

The fugitives took this path.

They rode for some time without conversing.

Edward had left his heart in his house of bondage; he was dreaming of his beauteous princess.

Katinka watched him affectionately.

"Monsieur is anxious," she said, softly.

He started from his reverie, and it was some moments before he could form a reply.

"Only for your sake," he answered, with a smile.

"Do not trouble for me, I am so used to danger that I think nothing of it;" said the vivandiere.

"And have you always been exposed to such dangers and hardships?" he asked.

"Since I can remember," was her reply. "I am a daughter of the regiment; my father served in the French army. I followed him through many a campaign in Algiers and elsewhere. He was killed at last," she added, with a sigh, "and since then I have been friendless."

"Pray do not say so. Look upon me as the humblest, but most devoted of your friends," said Edward, warmly.

"Monsieur is very kind," she replied, with a radiant smile; "I trust I shall not long need protection; the war must soon be over."

"And will the good cause triumph, think you?"

"It may at last, monsieur, but Poland must suffer much."

"She must yield, I fear; she cannot without aid resist the great powers; but we will fight till the last breath of hope has expired."

"Ah, if all were as generous as the gallant Avengers!"

"But whither are we going, Katinka?"

"To an old hostelry a little way from the village; it is kept by a Pole who is in secret league with our party."

"Can we trust him?"

"We have no choice; there is no other place of refuge," replied the girl.

From time to time the fugitives cast anxious glances behind them.

The morning was now advancing.

The tops of the distant hills were now hallowed with golden light.

A cloud of dust appeared far behind them rolling along the road.

"Ah, heavens! you are lost!" said Katinka, reining her horse and drawing a pistol.

She did not seem to think of herself or her own danger.

"I will not be taken, I will die first!" said Edward, firmly.

"And I, monsieur, will die with you; but stay, you can leave the horse here; get through the hedge and clamber over the walls of yonder house, where, perhaps, you may find refuge."

"And meanwhile, yourself?"

"They are still at a good distance, and I can keep them in chase of me for a long time."

"But you must be taken at last."

"If so, monsieur will have ample time to get away."

"And you would thus sacrifice yourself for me?"

"Why not? Better one should escape than neither."

"Dear, good Katinka, I have no words to thank you! Come, we will live or die together; we are well screened by this clump of trees, I do not think they have seen us yet."

"Monsieur, be advised——"

Edward would hear no more.

He seized her rein.

Together they leaped over the thickets, and sped across the plains to a thick wood in the distance.

Count Brutoff and his Cossacks were pursuing them at a terrific speed.

They bounded across the fields, and reaching the wood plunged into the thickest part of it.

They urged their horses to a reckless pace.

Every instant their dangers multiplied.

The wood became wilder, more intricate, the ground rose or sank in more rugged ascents or steeper declivities.

They came to a brook.

They leaped their horses over it.

As it is ever, with good evil, with evil good, the very dangers and impediments they met with were their best protectors.

At last, their horses growing more and more exhausted, they abandoned them and pursued their way on foot.

The sounds of horses' tramplings, of shouts and calls, bugle notes, and stern mandates wore out.

For awhile at least they had eluded pursuit.

Still they pushed on.

They emerged from the forest.

Well nigh exhausted, breathless, and faint, they leaned against the trees, these hunted ones, and listened with their heart's anxiety quickening their senses.

No more sounds.

At least no sounds boding them danger.

A deep and solemn hush.

They smiled in each other's faces, and pressed each other's hands.

Then again they moved onwards.

There was a heath before them.

The scenery was very wild and grand.

The morning was calm and sunny.

Leighton stood supporting the weary girl.

Dressed in his simple blue blouse, with the hatchet gleaming in his belt, he looked the Russian Moujik to ideality.

Poor Katinka was very weary, but she had such a stout little heart that no amount of suffering could wring from it one moan.

Again they pressed onwards.

About noon they reached their destination.

They found themselves standing under the porch of a long and low thatched inn.

The host came forth to meet them.

"Is it possible?" he cried. "You are Katinka, the daughter of my old friend, Zaska; I thought you had followed the rebels."

"Rebels!"

"Well, well, not a word. Come in, come in," said the old man, in a tremulous voice; "and, pray, who is this gentleman?"

"One of the brave English volunteers, who have ventured their lives for our poor country," replied the girl, with much feeling.

The old man received Leighton with enthusiastic courtesy.

He conducted them into a sequestered apartment. He spread before them the best that his humble means afforded.

An old priest who was present inquired of them whence they had come, and what was the cause of their agitation.

They told him their adventures.

He turned pale.

He struck his forehead and groaned bitterly.

"Ah, it is utterly useless. It is madness; mere cruel suicide!" he exclaimed. "There is no hope for Poland; time was when our gallant country was the barrier that dashed back the tide of barbarism; it was our brave king, John Sobieski, who preserved Europe from, perhaps, an utter fall; but, now it is not the interest of the great powers to support us, we may die, we may be lashed to death, frozen, burnt, man, woman and child, for aught the liberal Frenchman or freedom-loving Briton cares."

"Let us hope, father, that the holiness of our cause will draw brave men to our standard. We shall conquer yet," returned Leighton.

The old priest shook his head despondingly.

The host of the tavern seemed very greatly alarmed but did what he could to render his guests comfortable.

When they had partaken of some refreshment he drew near to the table where they were sitting, and said,

"If you remain here you will be found, for the Cossacks will burn down the house rather than lose you; if you fly you will be pursued and caught."

"What is to be done?"

"May I advise you?"

"We are in your hands and grateful for your goodness."

"Listen, then; Katinka is not known to——"

"No, he has not seen me," said the girl.

"Good, then you shall dress yourself as one of the maids and work about the house and the dairy,

while Monsieur the Englishman, in the guise of one of the labourers, goes to work in the barn."

"It is a good plan," said Katinka.

"And we must put it into execution at once."

"But Brutoff knows me well," said Edward Leighton.

"I will disguise you as completely as I can," said the inn-keeper.

The fugitives had scarcely been dressed in their disguises when the troop of Cossacks galloped up to the porch.

Katinka, who was carrying a can of milk across the little courtyard before the house, was at once surrounded by the soldiers.

"Come, wench, you are a Pole, and so, of course, a rebel."

"All Poles are not rebels," she said, stoutly; "and all soldiers are not brave men."

"She insults us!"

"You insult me! How dare you call me a rebel?"

The men laughed.

"Well, we may fairly call you a vixen. Now, girl, show us where the precious insurgents are hiding; we know they are in this house."

"Find them, then; if I am a rebel, you don't suppose I shall betray them."

Count Brutoff galloped up to the spot.

"What does this mean? Why are you wasting time in talk with this wench?" he asked, fiercely.

"This girl, my lord count, can lead us to the hiding-place of the escaped prisoners."

"My lord, the rude fellow called me a rebel," cried the girl, indignantly.

"You are Pole, and that's enough," returned the count, brutally. "If we cannot find the traitors, it will be plain you have aided in their escape, and you shall suffer for it. Bring her along!"

They now entered the house.

They seized the old man, and questioned him.

Of course he professed his ignorance of the affair.

The Katinka spoke.

"There has been no one here this morning, my lord count," she said, "but a peasant and his wife; they were both mounted, and they stayed here for refreshment."

The old man looked thunderstruck at this bold stroke on the part of Katinka.

"Yes, my lord, I remember now," he stammered. "It is true; they have left the house about half an hour. But, with pardon, I don't think they are the persons you seek. The man was plainly a peasant, and the girl, his wife, is one I have myself seen at the village."

"Describe his appearance."

"He was a handsome youth."

"No, no!"

"It was not he, then."

"Go on with his description."

"This man was dark, had fine black eyes, and a moustache."

"The same, count; it's he!" cried the soldiers. "Where is he?"

"My servant knows better than I which road he took," said the old man.

"Yes, follow; I'll show you," cried Katinka, running to the door.

She pointed down the path which skirted the wood.

"To horse!" cried Count Brutoff. "We shall have them now!"

The Cossacks leaped into their saddles, and, with a gruff cheer, dashed after the count.

"Katinka, this is wonderful!" cried the old inn-keeper. "But they will return presently from their fruitless chase, enraged and disappointed."

"We will fly then at once."

"Yes, I will give you the swiftest horse in my stables."

"And you."

"I must fly too, there is no resting here; if I remain I shall certainly be murdered."

"You ruin yourself for our sakes."

"I should ruin my peace of conscience if I did not my best to help you," said the old man.

Edward Leighton, who had remained concealed in the barn, now came forward.

The horses were brought from the stables.

The two men mounted.

As there were but two good horses Edward took the girl in his saddle, and away they sped without turning a look behind them.

Soon after their departure the Cossacks returned foaming with rage and vowing deadliest vengeance for the trick they had been played.

They broke into the house.

Seized such of the labourers in the farm as had not escaped.

They examined the road for the fugitives' track, and determined to follow the freshest hoof prints they found.

But first in wanton vindictiveness they set fire to the inn.

The house was in flames.

The cattle-pens had been broken open, and sheep and oxen, scared by the lurid blaze, ran wildly about the fold-yard.

The Cossacks were on the right track, and soon sighted the objects of their chase.

When Edward Leighton saw that they were so closely pursued, he leaped his horse over the thickets by the road side and plunged down into a woody dingle.

The old man was about to leap after him.

There was the sharp crack of a pistol shot in the distance.

The old man's horse reared, and the rider was thrown upon the ground stunned and bleeding.

The bullet had pierced his arm, and had mortally wounded the horse.

The Cossacks, waving their long spears or brandishing their swords, sprang over the bank and were soon crowding after Leighton and Katinka.

The young American dismounted.

The wood had become too dense to be penetrated on horseback.

Throwing his arms round Katinka, Edward climbed to a ledge of rock midway up a steep bank.

Here he concealed himself behind a bush.

The Cossacks, however, had discovered his retreat.

They fired blank into the thicket.

Edward was slightly wounded.

He returned the shot by firing from his revolver.

He noticed that Count Brutoff took particular care to keep to the rear.

A second shot struck the luckless Leighton in the shoulder.

He sank and became insensible.

When, in great agony, his senses slowly returned, he found himself in darkness.

He tried to move.

Chains clanked.

He was fettered to a cold damp wall.

As his sight became accustomed to the gloom he could distinguish objects plainly.

Against the wall a girl was chained.

She was bitterly weeping.

"Dear Katinka, are you the partner of my sorrows?" he said, with a sickly smile. "I know not how we came here; it seems that I have awakened from a deep dead sleep, but to what anguish! My wound bleeds; is there a cup of water near?"

A piece of black bread and a pitcher stood within reach of Katinka.

She took it up, for her hands were not bound.

She tried to reach Edward.

She could not, for her chain, which was fastened to an iron zone passed round her waist, was too short to allow her more than a yard or so for motion.

She pushed the pitcher towards him with her feet.

He feebly reached it.

He drank of the dirty water deep and gratefully, as if it had been nectar. Still he felt very feeble, and was in great pain.

The contusions he had received when he fell from his horse, and was taken prisoner to the castle of the charming Princess Sophia, had been very severe.

He had not recovered from their effects when he started from the castle, and now he was wounded in two places by pistol bullets.

Katinka had bound his arm, but the blood still welled up and soaked the bandages.

"And where are we, dear Katinka?"

"Dear monsieur, I thought you were dead. With life there is hope. We may be sent to Siberia, and may even then escape."

"I will not discourage your kind hopes, but we had better seek consolation in patience than hope," murmured Edward, faintly. "But what fortress is this?"

"You are in our old dungeon in the Castle Aronzow, of which Count Brutoff has taken possession."

"The cursed villain!" Edward gasped faintly.

Again the sickening dizziness caused Edward to sink back.

He thought he heard the tramping of steps and the clashing of keys.

He knew not whether it was the effect of his fevered imagination or whether the sounds were real.

But he was at length roused from his torpor by a piercing shriek.

He was bound to the wall by a collar of iron clasped round his throat.

He struggled so hard to escape from this bond that his face became scarlet, his tongue blackened, and his eyes started.

A villainous-looking goaler had stripped the clothes from the back of the prisoner Katinka, and was lashing the poor girl most pitilessly as she writhed against a beam to which she was bound.

The brutal wretch took no heed of the struggling of the maddened Leighton, who raved like a maniac.

He went on coolly wielding the sweeping lash.

At last Edward Leighton fainted, and became unconscious to his own misery and of the torture of his kind and gentle companion.

CHAPTER CCII.

RENEWAL OF THE WAR BETWEEN ANDREW HARWOLF AND SILAS RYE.

Soon after the marriage of Charles Rye and Emily, Silas Rye started on his mission of vengeance.

He felt sure that some disaster had befallen Foxley, the detective.

He was determined to find out whether the wretch who had murdered the good Lord Edgeforth, had been the cause of the Lady Edgeforth's madness, and of our dauntless hero's dreadful fall from his high position to a condition of infamy as a pirate and bandit.

THE APPARITION.

He could have forgotten his own wrongs, but he could not rest till he knew that the murder of Lord Edgeforth had been avenged.

With Oiny Macaire he embarked on board a merchant ship bound for America.

The captain of this vessel was an old friend of Silas Rye, in fact, John Fawcett, whom our readers will remember as having been unjustly confined in the mad-house, from which, with the aid of Silas, he had so skilfully escaped.

As time was not much an object with Silas in this case, he preferred a long cruise with his friend, Fawcett, to a rapid passage by the ordinary steamship.

John Fawcett and Silas Rye had conceived for each other a firm and manly friendship.

No. 61.

Their companionship was mutually pleasing; they were both men of common-sense and great experience, and entertained each other with the most interesting stories of their past life.

Silas could never forget his deep obligation to the man who had supported him through all the horrors at the asylum, and had so subtlely worked their escape.

The honest, genial skipper was a thorough seaman, and a great favourite among the crew.

A West Indian plan'er, his young daughter, and her nurse, a Creole girl, sailed with them.

The vessel, which was called the "Samphire," was a well-built ship, and a fast sailer.

The weather was favourable, and they made a very prosperous voyage.

On board was a carpenter, by name Ben Bruce, a very droll fellow, a good dancer and skilful violinist, and one who could twist a yarn almost as stiff as the renowned Tom Garrod.

It was the custom on board the "Samphire" when the weather was fine and the sea calm to pipe all hands for fun.

The deck presented a pleasing picture on these occasions.

The captain, Silas Rye, and the first mate would seat themselves on the hammocks and smoke their cigars, while the old planter reclined on the quarter-deck by the side of his daughter's chair, clasping her hand, and, from time to time, looking tenderly into her face, for he was a widower, and she, his only child, was an invalid fast sinking into a decline. The ever-watchful Creole kept close to her young and gentle mistress, to whom she was devotedly attached.

Amidships the men danced a reel or hornpipe round Ben Bruce, who untiringly scraped the strings of his brisk violin.

On one of these occasions the merry-making of the light-hearted sailors was suddenly interrupted by a cry from the man on watch.

"Sail on the starboard bow!"

Upon looking through the glasses at the object thus indicated they found it to be a raft on which several figures were moving.

"It seems a strange craft, captain," said Silas.

"Yes, it is a raft; I take it."

"Sure enough; and there are three persons upon it, one appears to be a woman."

"Castaways."

"Yet, is not that strange?" asked Silas. "Such fair winds as we have had."

"Fair winds fill foul sails; these waters are infested with pirate sharks," returned Fawcett.

"Pray Heaven we may escape them."

"Well, the long gun would not be of much use if we came to a broadside with a rover."

"But what brought these poor wretches to this condition?"

"I should say they have been overhauled by some pirate villains, and have either escaped by a miracle, or have been left to perish," replied the captain of the "Samphire."

The captain ordered his men to put down the boats.

This command was obeyed, and the second mate and eight or ten men got into them and put off.

The officers, passengers, and seamen leaned over the bulwarks, or stood swaying in the rattlings watching the progress of the boats.

They reached the raft.

A faint shout was borne over the heaving waters.

The sailors were seen to lift the castaways from their raft, and place them in the boats.

Soon the boats came alongside.

Three persons were brought upon deck.

They were two men and a woman.

They appeared to be in the last stage of exhaustion.

They were brought aft, and seemed to be in a fainting state.

One of the men, too feeble to speak, pointed to the sun and then to the sea, and held up four fingers as if to indicate that they had been four days exposed on the raft.

The captain of the "Samphire" ordered them to be carried below and placed in hammocks.

He sent the ship surgeon to attend them.

They were almost dying with hunger.

They were nurtured very carefully, and at the end of two or three hours the doctor reported that the men were sufficiently recovered to converse with the captain, and were anxious to see him.

With Silas and Mr. Leyden, the planter, Captain Fawcett went below.

One of the men raised himself in the hammock, and received the visitors with a faint painful smile.

He was a Frenchman, an old man with a grey beard, and pale, wan cheeks; his eyes were glazed

and his voice thick and quivering; he had a scar on his cheek, as if made by a sword thrust.

"My poor fellow, you have suffered terribly, I perceive," said the skipper, in a tone of sympathy.

"Ah, monsieur, you may well say so," murmured the sailor.

"And your messmates?"

"All perished."

"Just Heaven!—and by what accident?"

"By no accident—by cruel murder!"

"By pirates?"

"Yes; a gang of Spanish wretches under the command of one Corderes, overhauled our vessel which was a brigantine of Marseilles, "La Perouse" she was called, and her captain was ensnared by these treacherous villains who invited him to come aboard their schooner."

"And he never returned, I suppose?"

"No; the first mate went with him; the boatswain, and several of the crew, all were murdered and thrown overboard."

"And did he overhaul the ship?"

"Yes; he took all he could transfer to his own ship, and scuttled ours."

"And how did you escape?"

"I was wounded, and feigned death. They left me in the hold down which I had fallen."

"And the rest?"

"Concealed themselves between decks; they were not seen by the fiends who butchered every man aboard."

"And did the ship go down immediately?"

"Yes; holes had been bored through her sheathing boards. We had scarce time to save ourselves. The villains had taken all the ship's stores, and we could find nothing but a small barrel of sea-biscuits."

"The atrocious scoundrels! and have they been buccaneering for any considerable time?"

"They were at first consorted with a monster named Harwolf."

"Harwolf!" cried Silas, with a start.

"Yes; he is an Englishman, a most bloodthirsty, barbarous wretch. They say he fled his country after having committed some dreadful crime—murder it is reported."

"A murderer—fled from England—Harwolf—a pirate! This is wonderful!" cried Silas, much amazed. "Have you ever heard him described? Is he an old man, say sixty, grey-haired, and cunning-looking, with shaggy brows, and lynx-eyes, bold as a tiger, and subtle as a fox——"

"No, no; the pirate I speak of is a young man, he cannot be thirty."

"And his Christian name?"

"I think it is Daniel—yes, Daniel Harwolf."

"The miscreant!" cried Silas, his eyes flashing, and his face lighting up with a glare of deadly hatred. "But at last I shall reach them both. The old wolf and the cursed whelp! I will yet see them hanged."

"Can this be the fellow of whom you have told me so much?" asked Captain Fawcett, in wonder.

"It is; the younger of a brace of the blackest monsters that ever made humanity shudder at crime!"

"Then, the sooner we are safe in port, Master Rye, the better I shall be pleased, I assure you. It will be an awkward scrape if we are run down by a pirate schooner, and such a shock as this will not be likely to better our treatment on the score of old acquaintance."

"Oh, let the hound come!" cried Silas, with unusual vehemence. "Only let me tear him, let me rend him to pieces, and I care not for myself."

"Yet you may afford a little consideration for your less valiant shipmates," laughed the captain. "And I tell you, friend Silas, I feel more anxiety than ardour; if this brig were a sloop of war and those bales shot-racks, I grant you the case would be different."

"There is a Brazilian war-ship cruising on these coasts," said the patient, "commanded by a very brave officer—Don Rodriguez."

"I wish we may fall in with her," said the captain of the "Samphire," in a tone which showed that he did not relish the thought of an encounter with the pirates.

Silas Rye went on deck.

He called Oiny Macaire to his side.

The Irishman skipped jauntily up to him, his broad, dark face beaming with animation.

Oiny enjoyed his voyage immensely.

He was of a bold and restless temperament, full of native humour, and had rendered himself very popular among the crew.

"Oiny, I have made a strange discovery," said Silas, in a serious tone.

"And sure, Misther Rye, what for else did we sail on a voyage of diskivery? Belikes ye mane that you've heard what's become of the poor detective gintleman, and whether his bullet has rached its billet."

"No, that remains to be unriddled," answered his master, "but I have learned that Daniel Harwolf, the son of the villain we are tracking, is cruising in these waters under the black flag."

"Horoo! sure its meself that would like to mate the spalpeen under his black flag—black death to the blackgu-ard!"

"And its myself, Oiny, and all the rest aboard, who are very willing to keep out of the shadow of his black bunting, for we are no match for a pirate, and have ladies aboard."

"Och, murther, but the coincidence is quare intirely; but does your honour mane to hunt him, too?"

"No; my affair is with the murderer of Lord Edgeforth," replied Silas, "him I will find at any risk of life or liberty."

"Faix, but it will cost us some throuble to lay hands on that same thafe; faix, the divil himself is scarcely a match for him."

At this moment the man aloft sang out,

"Sail ho!"

Fawcett, who had just come up the main-hatch, applied his glass, and said in a tone of satisfaction,

"A welcome sight, Mr. Rye."

"Yes, a couple of war-steamers; they carry Brazilian colours."

"I have no doubt they will convoy us; see, they signal us to lie to."

"But what craft is that they have in tow?"

"As pretty a little thing as ever ran before the wind," returned Fawcett, with admiration, "she is an English vessel, too, that I am sure of by her build and rig."

"Perhaps it is the pirate ship which they have taken?"

"That cannot be, there is an English Jack flying at the peak."

"A merchantman they are convoying?"

"Perhaps so."

"Well, we shall know presently, for they are lowering the boats."

"Yes, and there are two officers in each."

The boats came alongside.

The officers were received by Captain Fawcett with great respect.

They appeared to be commanders from different vessels. Such was the case.

Don Rodriguez was accompanied by the captain of the consort steamer.

The other men belonged to the merchant ship under convoy.

They were strange-looking fellows.

Silas Rye stood at some distance from his friend, who received his guests with much ceremony.

He started with surprise, but repressed his emotion.

The face of the skipper of the merchantman was sullen and evil.

He had a shock of rusty, dark hair, and a rough beard.

There were many wrinkles on his frown-knit forehead, and his eyes, which were grey and deep-set, glittered under the shadow of his shaggy eye-brows; his skin was sun-burnt to the hue of mahogany.

His companion, who appeared to be first mate of his vessel, was a tall, black-haired, manly fellow, with a saturnine, savage expression, but by no means unhandsome.

Captain Fawcett spoke Spanish fluently.

"Your presence is the more welcome," he said to Rodriguez, after some ordinary compliments had passed between them, "as we are in great dread of falling into the hands of a pirate rascal, one Daniel Harwolf, who, we understand, infests these waters."

"I am glad to tell you, senor, that the miscreant and all his band have perished."

Silas Rye looked at the man whose face had so much attracted him by its seeming resemblance to some one he had formerly known, and he met the steady glance that was returned with a feeling of awkwardness.

"I am heartily glad to hear this news," said Captain Fawcett, "but are you sure it is trustworthy?"

"There is no doubt of its correctness."

"Did the wretch fall into the hands of justice?"

"He did not."

"Perished in a storm perhaps?"

"No, senor. It sometimes happens that beasts of prey destroy each other; in this case, the tiger has killed the wolf that the hunter could not overtake. Harwolf, and the whole of his gang had taken refuge in a tower on one of the islands. They were besieged by the renowned Boy Pirate, who fired a mine, blew up the fortress, and brought destruction upon all within it."

"The deeds of that dashing adventurer are almost incredible!" said Fawcett, "but let me welcome you severally; dinner is served in my cabin, and I trust you will honour me by your presence."

The officers bowed and accepted the invitation.

"I have not introduced you to Captain Morton of the 'Alert,' to whom we are all much indebted; he has given information against a horrible criminal."

The captains of the "Samphire" and of the "Alert," exchanged salutes.

When the party were assembled in the state-cabin Fawcett told his guests of the castaways he had picked up a few hours before the war-steamers hove in sight.

Don Rodriguez had an interview with the escaped men and resolved to return at once to his ship to make all speed in chase of the rovers.

During the time that the Spaniards and their companions remained on board the vessel Silas Rye narrowly watched the captain of the "Alert."

But the seaman was reserved and taciturn, though he spoke much of Corderes, and described the manner in which he escaped from him so graphically that the Brazilian officer and the captain of the "Samphire" were both quite deluded.

The officers having returned to their respective ships all sail was made, and the ships steered to the Rio de la Plata.

They had been coasting along the continent for several days when a sail was discerned.

It was the pirate schooner.

An exciting chase commenced.

The Brazilian steam-ships signalled for the pirate to lay-to.

Dauntlessly the black flag fluttered up to the mast-head.

A gun was fired from the schooner.

The shot came ricochetting from wave to wave and fell astern of the "Samphire."

The wind suddenly changing the schooner was forced to tack.

The steamers bore down on her in dreadful array.

The daring Corderes opened fire.

A stiff breeze suddenly sprang up.

The chase was renewed.

Soon, however, the schooner was forced to lower her top-sails, and the steamers ran alongside her.

CHAPTER CCIII.

STERN TO STERN—A GANG OF DESPERADOES
—THE CAPTAIN OF THE "ALERT" ENTRAPS
SILAS RYE—THE STEAM-FRIGATE IN FLAMES
—THE BOARDING PARTY—THE EXPLOSION—
A TERRIBLE CATASTROPHE—A STRANGE RE-
VELATION.

WHEN the vessels lay alongside of the pirate
schooner, it was expected that the wretches on board
her would haul down their black flag, and surrender
at discretion.

But the desperate villains were too bold and determined to yield so readily.

Corderes leaped upon the quarter, and hailed Don
Rodriguez in Spanish.

"What cheer, camarado? What do you want?"
he shouted, with a gruff laugh.

"Lay to and surrender, vagabond!" returned Don
Rodriguez in a stern voice.

"Hear my answer," laughed the pirate.

There was a crackle of musketry among the rigging
of the pirate vessel.

Don Rodriguez fell on his face.

The Brazilians fired a broadside.

But in a calm sea and light winds small schooner-
rigged vessels have a great advantage over others of
heavier burden.

The pirate ship forged ahead so quickly that,
though the guns were served with great promptness,
the only effect that the broadside had upon the pirate
was that her bowsprit was damaged.

The captain of the steam-frigate was raised.

The bullet had pierced his breast.

The wound appeared to be mortal.

The crew uttered cries of fury.

The fiendish pirates yelled their triumph.

The lieutenant immediately assumed the command.

Rodriguez was borne off to the cockpit.

The other steamer fired at the pirates.

The shot did great damage.

The stern windows were smashed in.

With a shout the pirates discharged two mortars
that stood in the middle of the deck.

The next instant the air seemed blazing with fiery
meteors.

The frigate which had fired the last broadside was
struck by live shells and other combustibles, and
fairly deluged with a shower of fire.

She was forced to sheer off.

Flames broke out in various parts of her.

The triumphant pirates raised a terrific shout.

The schooner was now bearing down upon the
"Alert."

As she passed she opened fire.

The "Alert" returned her shot for shot.

A boat was put off from the merchant ship.

A savage-looking man came aboard the "Samphire."

Fawcett, Silas Rye, and Oiny Macaire, with the
rest of the passengers, were watching the fight with
great excitement.

"Well, my man, I suppose you want assistance,"
said Fawcett to the seaman from the "Alert."

"Aye, yer honour," answered the man; "will any
man of valour wolunteer for this sarvice? we're short
of hands, yer honour."

"And, bedad, it's this boy that will fight the
black thaves for the glory of Oireland," cried Oiny,
much elated at the thought.

"Do you mean to board her, then?" asked Fawcett.

"Yes, yer honour."

"Well, one of the frigates is on fire, and the other
has enough to do to aid her consort. The chase is
slipping away, and the wind is freshening," said the
captain of the "Samphire." "We will help you all
we can by trying to wing this high-flyer. A shot
through her rigging will bring her to."

"That's the way, an't please yer honour, and
meanwhile Cap'en Morton sends to ax if any gentleman feels inclined to wolunteer to board her."

"Sure, Mr. Rye, ye'll give permission for me to go
wid the gossoon; be jabbers, but I'll tache the black
thaves to riverence St. Patrick, bad cess to 'em!"
cried the Irishman.

"Well, Oiny, if you are so valourous, I won't
prevent you from following the bent of your inclination. Stay, Captain Fawcett, give me your
hand; I will go with him; if they kill me send word
to Lord Hawksbury."

"You shall not go, Mr. Rye."

"Nonsense, we are more than a match for the
cut-throats; it is a mortal disgrace to us that they
are not already in irons."

Several of the men belonging to the "Samphire"
offered their services.

The man from the "Alert" did not seem so eager
to secure the assistance of these as he was to get the
aid of Silas and Oiny.

However, he could make no objection.

They got over the side and manned two boats.

The man from the "Alert" contrived to get Silas
and Oiny into his boat, and thus separate them from
the rest.

A brisk exchange of broadsides was raging between
the "Alert" and the pirate ship, which were running
before the wind almost alongside of each other.

The steam frigate and the "Samphire" hung
back.

One of the steamers was burning; the other was
aiding in picking up the men and in extinguishing
the flames.

The fire was being brought into subjection.

The "Samphire" was a vessel of heavy tonnage,
and could not keep up with the other ships, which
were of lighter gear.

Still Captain Fawcett kept up a well-directed
fire.

Silas and Oiny, with the man from the "Alert,"
pulled stoutly towards the vessel which was pursuing the pirate.

The other boat also throbbed swiftly through the
glittering waters.

The pirates fired upon them.

The shots, however, spanked pass their bows, and
sank far astern of them.

The boat floated under the "Alert."

The two landsmen went on board.

The captain stood ready to receive them.

His arms were folded, and he fixed a strange look
on the face of Silas Rye.

"You are welcome, sir," he said, in a low and
sullen tone. "I thank you for your good will and
brave help in this emergency; we shall board the
cursed pirate in a few moments, and, with your help,
shall no doubt be victorious."

Silas Rye looked sternly in the speaker's face.

"We have met before!" he said.

The captain of the "Alert" sneered and walked
forward, as if to give some command.

"Oiny," whispered Silas.

"Sure and what's your honour's will?"

"This rogue will betray us."

"The divil rin away wid him. What, for your
honour?"

"Don't you know him?"

"The divil a bit, sir."

"Look at him."

"Sure I do, sir, but furder than I don't like the
ugly phiz of him. I don't know him at all."

"He is—Daniel Harwolf!"

"Och, murther!"

"He will shoot or stab us, and the pirates will
bear the blame."

"Arrah [now, I'd as lief board one pirate as
another; let's attack the blackguard."

The crew of the other boat came crowding over
the side.

The captain of the "Alert" seemed rather annoyed
than pleased at this reinforcement.

He scowled darkly at the man who had brought
them.

Silas set his back against the captain.

He held a pistol in one hand, and a cutlass in the
other.

He assumed an air of defiant calmness.

The captain of the vessel appeared not to notice him.

He stood bawling his orders to the men aloft.

The ships now lay broadside to broadside.

Smoke and flame belched from the ports of each.

They mutually inflicted fearful damage.

Nothing could be wilder and more terrific than the appearance of the pirates.

Many of them were half naked.

Their dark faces were demoniac in their villanous expression.

Corderes himself had stripped off his jacket.

His arms were bared as for slaughter.

Around his waist was tied a showy scarf of parti-coloured silk, which was bristled with knives and pistols.

He had a cutlass in his hand, which he brandished frantically.

He seemed crazed with passion.

His men seemed possessed with the fury of demons.

They fired their guns and pistols, recklessly exposing themselves.

The fire on board the Brazilian steamer had been got under, and her consort was once more swiftly paddling down upon the pirates.

"Now, hearties, if you would not have your laurels snatched by these foreigners, let us board the hell-ship before they come up," said Harwolf, for it was he who commanded the "Alert."

The "Samphire" men answered with a hearty cheer.

They manned the boats.

Harwolf contrived that Silas and Oiny should be placed in the same boat with himself.

They would have resisted this manœuvre, but it was very skilfully managed.

In fact, they did not know that Harwolf intended to join the boarding party, but got into the boat to which the mate of the "Alert" pointed.

Harwolf leaped in after.

In the rush and confusion there was no chance for them to protest against this arrangement.

The boats pulled off towards the pirate ship.

Harwolf's boat, not being so strongly manned as the other, did not make weigh so fast, so that it was the first to float under the bows of the schooner.

The pirates received them with a yell.

The steamers were now close alongside, firing broadside after broadside.

The men in the first boat from the "Alert" scrambled up the side of the schooner.

They battled fiercely on deck with the pirate gang.

Then came a tremendous explosion.

The air was filled with the *debris* of the ghastly wreck.

The shell of the pirate vessel was fast settling down, the flames hissing out as she sank.

The water was strewn with spars and the mangled bodies of the desperate wretches who had involved themselves and their foes in one common ruin.

At the moment the explosion took place Harwolf was seated at the stern of the boat, a pistol resting on his knee, and his eyes fixed, with a hungry glare of hate, upon the face of his intended victim.

Silas, also, was preparing for a treacherous blow, and had whispered Oiny to keep a sharp watch for an attack from behind.

The startling burst and roar of the exploding vessel, however, petrified them all for an instant.

The next, they were struggling in the water.

A falling spar had struck the boat, and capsized her.

Silas Rye received a blow on the head which stunned him.

He sank in the raging waves.

He rose, to sink again.

Oiny, who could swim well, seeing his master's danger, dived after him.

Seizing him by the arm, he brought him to the surface.

He struck out boldly, and reached a floating cask.

To this he clung, still supporting his insensible master.

The waves dashed over him.

Often they flew over his head with such force that he was almost wrested from his hold on the barrel.

At length he grew fainter and fainter, and became unconscious.

He and Silas were picked up by a boat from the "Samphire," just as they were sinking for the last time.

With great difficulty they were restored to animation.

Silas was removed to his hammock.

He had received a frightful bruise on the head, and awakened from his trance in a paroxysm of dreadful pain.

Oiny, who had received no injury, speedily recovered.

It was several days before Silas could distinguish the face that bent over him so kindly.

At length, however, he recognised the watcher as his old friend, Captain Fawcett.

The latter expressed the sincerest pleasure at finding that the danger was past, and cheered Silas by hopeful predictions, but forbade him to speak till he was entirely recovered.

He then left the cabin.

Oiny, who had acted as nurse in the most devoted manner, was beside himself with joy at the favourable issue of this disastrous adventure.

When Captain Fawcett paid a second visit to the patient he found him able to sit up and converse.

"And now tell me," said Silas, with a faint smile, "what has become of the captain of the 'Alert?'"

"Well, your question is a strange one, and will receive a strange answer."

"He is hanged I hope."

"Hanged! he must first be caught; but a man who has done such good service as he deserves a better fate than hanging."

"Well, I trust he is drowned, then."

"What do you mean? In what way has he offended you?"

"That were too long a story to tell you now, though I think you have heard part of it already."

"Indeed! Who is he, then?"

"First tell me what has become of him?"

"I wish I could. After the fight he was picked up and carried on board his own ship; at night we anchored in the road; there was a dense fog, when it cleared off the next morning, the 'Alert' was gone! We almost feared that she had received some damage, had sprung a leak and sunk at her moorings."

"I trust it might prove so."

"I did not. We found that she had stolen off under cover of the darkness, for a vessel we fell in with reported that she had been seen lying off one of the islands."

"And what of Don Rodriguez?"

"His wound, though so severe as to render him quite unfit for further service, does not prove mortal; the steamers are now under the command of the first lieutenant, and have put into harbour for repairs."

"I wish we were safely moored beside them."

"Why, what have we to fear since this cursed vagabond, Corderes, has met such a terrible fate?"

"We have a worse foe to dread in another villain."

"In whom?"

"In the captain of the 'Alert.'"

"In wonder's name, man, who is he?"

"The most monstrous of these bloodthirsty monsters; that fellow is no other than Captain Harwolf of the Black Vulture!"

CHAPTER CCIV.

THE CAPTAIN'S LOG — THE WRECK OF THE "NAUTILUS" — A TRUE STORY.

DURING the time that Silas Rye was confined to his cabin the captain and the crew of the "Samphire" treated him with the utmost kindness.

For many days after the dreadful catastrophe which had befallen the brave fellows who had volunteered to board the pirate, a gloom hung upon the spirit of all on board.

But as the sailor's eventful life is full of dire accidents by fire and flood, the shade soon passed from their faces, and they worked and whistled as merrily as ever.

Silas Rye beguiled the weary hours of sickness by reading the log-book of Captain Fawcett, a huge volume of manuscript and extracts from various newspapers which the seaman had collected during the course of his naval career.

Among others he found the following interesting account of the wreck of the "Nautilus."

"The sloop 'Nautilus,' under the command of Captain Palmer, charged with important despatches for England, was sailing under a fresh north-west wind through the Grecian Archipelago, on the 4th January, 1807, when the pilot that had charge of her declared himself ignorant of the coast they were approaching, and resigned his care of the vessel.

"The captain determined to proceed with his despatches, as the delay would be attended with very serious consequences.

"He accordingly shaped his course towards Cerigotto.

"The wind rapidly increased during the evening.

"At midnight it had risen to a gale.

"Thunder, lightning, and torrents of hail added all the accessories of a tempest.

"Through the midst of all the sloop held bravely on.

"The island of Cerigotto was discovered to them right a-head by a vivid flash of lightning at about three o'clock in the morning.

"The officers were congratulating themselves on their happy escape from all the perils of the night.

"The captain himself was just turning to examine a chart in his cabin, when suddenly the men were thrown out of their hammocks, and all was confusion and alarm.

"The vessel had struck!

"The sea was every moment lifting her up and dashing her down again with great violence upon the rocks.

"As soon as the first emotion of consternation had subsided everything was done that prudence could suggest in such an emergency.

"The crew attended to the orders of their officers with admirable coolness and alacrity.

"It was too late to think of saving the vessel, or even of holding her together for any length of time.

"An instant had scarcely elapsed before the main-deck was burst in.

"In a few moments the lee bulwark was entirely overwhelmed, and a heavy sea breaking entirely over the devoted crew.

"To abandon the sloop and take to the boats was the only course that presented a chance of safety.

"Unfortunately only one of these, a small whale-boat, was got clear, the others being either stove in or washed away and dashed to pieces on the rock.

"The boat that escaped, with as many men as it could contain, pulled towards the island of Pauri, being unable to render any assistance to the poor fellows who were left behind.

"The wreck continued to strike with great violence, and threatened, in the course of a few minutes, to go to pieces.

"At length a portion of the rock was perceived to be above water.

"A desire was eagerly manifested to reach this, as affording a refuge at all events safer than the frail timbers to which they were clinging.

"They were happily enabled to effect a passage from the devoted ship to the rock by means of the main-mast which fell over the side and served as a gangway, along which they could crawl through the surf to the little uncovered spot of coral rock.

"They accomplished the task in safety, though with great difficulty, and found themselves, almost a hundred in number, in the midst of the angry sea, standing without food and almost without clothing, on a bit of rock, measuring some three or four hundred yards long, and some two hundred wide.

"Had they delayed leaving the wreck a few minutes longer their destruction would have been certain.

"She was almost instantly dashed to pieces and her timbers were swallowed up in the waves.

"They were at least twelve miles from the nearest island, and their only chance of escape was in the possibility of a ship passing near and coming to their relief.

"Day dawned.

"The weather was bitterly cold.

"Contriving to kindle a fire from a knife and flint one of the sailors chanced to have in his pocket, and a small barrel of damp powder that had been washed ashore, they spent the day in vain efforts to distinguish a sail in the offing, and in the construction, out of such pieces of the wreck as they could collect, of a kind of tent for shelter, whilst they tried to dry their wet clothes, during the cold, dreary night.

"In the meantime the coxswain and crew of the whale boat had reached the island of Pauri.

"Observing the watch-fire in the middle of the night, a party of six of them pulled to the rocks, in order to ascertain how many of their comrades had escaped the sad fate, they feared, until now, had befallen them all.

"They were greatly surprised to find that so large a number still survived, and told them what sort of a refuge they had found for themselves.

"The island of Pauri was only a mile in circumference and without inhabitants or provisions of any kind, with the exception of a few sheep and goats kept there by the people of Cerigo, and a little rain-water, preserved by chance in a hole of the rock.

"The arrival of the boat was an event of considerable importance to the poor fugitives, but it brought nothing to appease their hunger.

"Captain Palmer resisted all the entreaties of the coxswain, saying,

"'Never mind me, save your unfortunate comrades.'

"He ordered him, after some consultation, to take ten of the men from the rock and make the best of his way to Cerigotto, whence he might return with assistance to rescue the rest.

"The boat accordingly departed on this errand, but quickly afterwards the wind increased to a gale, and the unfortunate men who were left were deluged by heavy seas, which extinguished their light and rendered it extremely difficult for them to maintain their footing, or to prevent themselves from being washed away.

"So terrible were the sufferings of the second night that several of the people died before morning, and many became delirious.

"The next day they were subjected to a bitter disappointment.

"As they lay down, the dead and the dying, huddled together on the wet rock, a ship with all sail set hove in sight.

"With hope beating high, they hastily hoisted signals of distress, and the vessel, perceiving them, was brought to, and sent out her boat.

"Deliverance now seemed certain, and the utmost excitement prevailed amongst the survivors of the party, who hurriedly exchanged congratulations.

"As many as were able began to make preparations for getting on board the strange ship, when, as they were thus busily engaged, the boat stopped, its crew rested for a moment on their oars, contemplating the unhappy sufferers, and then, from some unexplained and mysterious cause, pulled back again to the ship, and left the crew of the 'Nautilus' to their miserable fate.

"Inhumanity to a comrade is so rare a feature in a

sailor, and a refusal to succour a shipwrecked crew by those who know not how soon they themselves may be reduced to the same condition, so extremely uncommon an occurrence, that we would fain hope some sad misapprehension or accident must have occasioned this seemingly cruel desertion.

"However this may be, the poor fellows on the rock had to experience the terrible transition of hope to despair, at seeing this prospect of deliverance rudely snatched away.

"They could do nothing now but watch in miserable suspense for the return of the whale boat.

"Hour after hour passed without any result.

"The expectation of relief from that source became of course more and more feeble.

"During this period of terrible suspense they suffered the pangs of extreme hunger and thirst.

"Some of the men, unable to endure the want of moisture, yielded to the temptation of drinking the salt water of the ocean, the consequences of which were that they were shortly afterwards seized with hysteria and madness, under the combined influence of which several of them died.

"They prepared for another night, now rapidly approaching, by huddling as closely as they could together, and making the most of their scanty clothing, to keep some warmth in their poor benumbed limbs.

"They were utterly unable, worn out as they were, to find any refuge in sleep.

"The ravings of the mad were fearful to hear.

"Although the weather had somewhat moderated, it seemed impossible that they should get through the night.

"Suddenly, at midnight, they heard a hail from the crew of the whale-boat, who had returned to tell them that a vessel was coming next morning to their relief.

"Encouraged by this hope, they prepared themselves to sustain their sufferings with renewed fortitude.

"Unfortunately, the boat's crew had been unable to obtain anything but earthen vessels to bring a supply of water in, and these were destroyed in being carried through the surf.

"The morning at length broke.

"The morning to which they had looked with anxious expectation through so many hours of endurance.

"But no boat was visible!

"No vessel appeared to rescue them!

"It was the fourth day they had been without food.

"The expedients they resorted to, to satisfy the ravings of hunger were too horrible to be described.

"Many died before evening.

"Amongst the number Captain Palmer and the first lieutenant.

"The next day, the little body of survivors determined to construct a raft out of the bits of wreck they had heaped together, and trust themselves to the mercy of the boisterous sea rather than perish with famine.

"Alas! a singular fatality seemed to attend all the proceedings of these devoted men.

"No sooner was their labour finished, and the moment arrived for launching the raft, than it was dashed to pieces in a few seconds, and its fragments scattered on the sea.

"Seeing the last chance of escape thus snatched away from them, some of the men, rendered frantic by disappointment, dashed into the sea to catch at the floating pieces of wood, and were carried away by the waves.

"The fifth day passed.

"During the night death still further reduced their numbers.

"The survivors sank into a state of complete insensibility.

"But deliverance came at last to the remnant that still lived to welcome it, of the once numerous and gallant crew of the 'Nautilus.'

"The sixth morning brought the cheering sight of four fishing-boats and the the whale-boat approaching the rock.

"The half-dying mariners were refreshed by a small supply of food.

"They were then removed, and carried to Cerigotto.

"The inhabitants received and treated them kindly.

"Fifty-eight men, who parted with light hearts from the British fleet in the Hellespont, but a week before, had perished.

"Many of them might doubtless have been saved, if the Greek fishermen and sailors had possessed the sterling qualities of the English seaman.

"If the news were brought to our boatmen at Deal, or any other British port, that a few miles off, on a bit of rock washed by the raging waves, were a hundred men, naked, a-hungered, and a-thirst, not many hours would elapse ere a band of gallant fellows, braving all dangers in a generous, self-devoted humanity, would be buffeting the waves on their mission of relief.

"An incident, as honourable to the fishing population of our coast as it is deeply affecting, occurred at Worthing, on the 26th November, 1850, and may be cited as an illustration of the readiness of the English seaman to encounter any peril for the chance of saving a shipwrecked crew.

"The wind had blown a perfect hurricane during the night from south and south-west; and at daylight in the morning a large dismantled bark—the 'Lalla Rookh' East-Indiaman, homeward bound, with a valuable cargo, was descried at anchor, about two miles from the shore, riding heavily, with two anchors ahead, and signals of distress flying.

"A gallant crew of eleven men, the most experienced fishermen in the town, nobly volunteered to put off to her assistance; and, although the sea was running mountains high at the time, by eight o'clock A.M. they were fairly afloat, dashing through the breakers of this most dangerous coast.

"Their progress towards the bark was watched with the most intense interest from the shore.

"Their noble object seemed on the point of being accomplished, when a heavy sea struck their boat, and in an instant she disappeared, engulphing all hands in a watery grave.

"About noon a second effort was made, with a larger and decked boat, manned by upwards of twenty stout hands, to reach the distressed ship, and to ascertain with certainty the fate of the first boat's crew.

"With much difficulty the bark was reached, and fifteen of their hands put on-board her.

"The remaining five returned to the shore with the heart-rending intelligence that the former boat's crew had all perished.

"When a little to windward of the bark, she was distinctly seen to be struck, and the unfortunate men, struggling with the waves, and vainly clinging to the frail, water-logged boat, floated by, without the bark's crew being able to render them the slightest assistance.

"The bark rode out of the storm in safety, and was brought round into the river.

"So much interest was excited by the gallantry of the unfortunate men and their disastrous fate that a handsome subscription was raised for their widows and orphans, nearly sixty in number.

"The Greek fishermen of the islands were men of a different stamp.

"All the entreaties of the coxswain, and all his representations of the dreadful situation of the crew of the 'Nautilus,' could not induce them to put to sea whilst the gale continued.

"Their subsequent conduct proved that they were not without humanity, but they feared to encounter the element in its rougher moods, and this fear was stronger than their humanity."

CHAPTER CCV.

ZAMPA AND THE BEAR.

OUR hero had kept possession of the castle which the brave Count Josika had defended so gallantly till the last gasp, and the Russians had raised the siege.

Numbers of the peasantry had joined his standard.

The name of the great Avenger had become a byeword of terror to the enemy, and his feats of daring startled the government into the most stringent measures for repressing the rebellion in that part of the country, in which he was now in a great degree the master.

Count Brutoff had taken possession of the Castle Aronzow.

The prince and princess had been removed to prison, as we have seen, and were now imprisoned at Kowno awaiting their trial.

Our hero knew nothing of the misfortunes which had befallen Edward Leighton.

It was commonly reported that the young American had been killed in the battle-field, or had been borne off by the Russians, only to die in durance.

Our hero held a council of war, in which it was unanimously determined that a sufficient number of men being left to defend the fortress, the daring Avengers should make an attack upon the Castle Aronzow, and, if possible, take it by storm.

Acting upon this resolve, a strong party of the dauntless adventurers marched from the fortress with drums beating, and colours flying, and set off in the direction of the castle.

They were led by their gallant young chief in person, supported by a staff of chosen officers.

At night they encamped in a rocky valley, at the entrance of which our hero had been raising entrenchments and other fortifications.

It was during the halt of the patriot army at this place that a strange adventure occurred to Zampa, which will be narrated in his own words.

Tom Garrod and his cronies were seated in a circle, drinking their grog, and listening to their boatswain's tough yarns, of which they seemed never to grow weary, when suddenly they were interrupted by a terrific yell, and Zampa sprang over Tom's head, and came down on all fours in the midst of the circle.

His black face was almost pale, his very knotty and closely combined locks were almost parted, his lips were very widely extended, while his eyes were upturned with an expression of dismay quite indescribable.

It was not till he had received sundry kicks from the irate tars that he sufficiently recovered his senses to give an explanation of the cause of his terror.

"Hulloa! you ebony swab; what's all this?" roared Tom. "Do you call this shoregoing manners to distarb my discoorse in sich a fashion?"

"Oh, gorra, buckras, yo nebber seen! Oh!"

"Have you seen the devil?"

"I'se 'clined to tink I'm a gone coon! Oh!"

"What is it, Zamp?"

"Gib ober de grog kid."

"No! no! hold on, Bill; the nigger cuss has got a maw like the caves of Kentucky!" shouted the men.

Zamp, however, managed to seize the can.

Before they could wrest it from him he had considerably diminished its contents.

The men looked savage, and groaned their disgust.

But Zamp out-roared them, for he set up another terrific yell.

"Oh, gorra, yo tink I feared o' nuffin'; but sich would scare de cap'en?"

"What have you seen, Zamp?"

"Russians?"

"Berry grad to meet dem gen'lemen any time; yo tink I'se afeard of nuffin'. O lors!"

"Was it a ghost?"

"A kinder ghost."

"What 'kinder' ghost, you lubber?"

"Behave respectful, buckras; it's reg'lar solemn!"

"Was it a devil?"

"A kinder debil!"

"What was it like?"

"Berry like a bar!"

"A bear?"

"A kinder bar; but a most 'stronary animal as neber consisted. I's tell yo how him happen."

"Heave a-head, nigger!"

"Yo see, buckras, I'se berry fond ob contemplatin'; I'se 'tickler given to what Mas'r Ralph calls 'chewing de cud.'"

"The 'quid,' you lubber!"

"'Ob sweet and bitter'n fancy'"

"What's that, Tom, I've heard ranting Ralph say so? What's the quid of fancy?"

"Well, hearty, there's a kinder 'chew' as the land swabs uses, called 'fancy tobacco;' I s'pose it's that."

"Oh!"

"Yo don't know nuffin' about it, sar; berry good, I was a kinder meditatin', and felt 'clined to take a walk to de ole tree down yonder; to tell de truff, buckras, I had a lilly affair ob de 'fections."

"What 'lilly' affair was that?"

"My jib! here's a rascal," cried Tom, with a horse-laugh and winking at his mess-mates. "Don't you know, hearties, the Tartar chap we caught, the Cossack lubber; he had two women with him, his wife and daughter? Zamp is going to splice the main-brace with the young lass. Well, it's a werry good match; he's as black as night, and her face is jest like the moon."

"Avast heaving, Tom, let him tell his own story."

"Yo listen, buckras," continued the darkie, "I'd made a kinder assassination to meet dis yere yaller charmer at de ole tree down by de ribber, and I was walking in a werry majestic and sillymental kinder way jest to provoke her respects, 'cos dar's nuffin women likes so much as dignity, when I found myself 'rived alongside ob de tree werry sudden, 'cos I hadn't counted my footsteps. My mind was in a state of substraction; wall, yo see, as de gal warn't 'rived I sat down under de tree to wait for her; I looked at de lilly stars, and kinder wisht I was near one on 'em, 'cos I hadn't my tinder box wid me, and couldn't light my pipe, and I fell into a revelry. I thought ob a many tings."

"Never mind what you thought, Zamp; heave ahead with your yarn."

"All at once, buckras, I hearn a rustlin' and a scramblin' in de bushes. 'Dar's de gal,' says I, and thought I'd hab a bit ob a skylarking wid her, so I hid myself behind de ole tree, jest as I hearn her come along. I gib a kinder jump. High! Oh, golly!"

Zamp sank back faintly.

"What skeared you, Zamp?"

"Why, dis yere gal. Oh, lors!"

"Well, what of her?"

"Dis yere gal—— Pass de grog."

"What about the girl, you lubber?"

"Oh, gorra, buckras, dis yere gal she was a— BAR!"

The men burst into a roar of mirth.

"Did you run?"

"I was reg'lar strick! Couldn't move a step; de bar stood up on her hind legs and looked tremendjous."

"And did she attack you?"

"She stood as firm as the fo'-mast, her mouth wide open, and her eyes a starin'. I slipped backwards and backwards towards de tree; de bar was reg'lar 'mazed, she stood so long on her hind legs, she seemed as if she'd forgot her way down again. I run up de tree, and sat on one ob de boughs; de bar dropped on all fours, she trotted up to de tree and looked up at me wid a cur'ous sort ob expression. I hearn as dese like music and dancing, dese bars, so I sung her a song. De bar seemed a funny kinder creetur, and werry much 'mused wid de nigger

SAVED FROM DEATH.

melody; when I stopped she growled, and moved up to de ole stump. At last she jumped up de tree. Dere was one branch dat stretched ober de ribber, I climb to de end ob it, it bent like de main-top-gallant in a squall; de bar began to climb arter me, de bough bruk, and I fell souse into de ribber. I swum to de oder side, de bar stood shaking her head at me on de oder bank; I made her a polite bow and walked off wid dignity; bars like dignity as well as women do. But, when I'd got a few steps, I run like de debbil, and got so hot dat my clothes was dry when I reach de camp. And so pass de grog, chil'en, and, if ever yo goes to meet a yaller gal mind as yo don't fall in wid a black bar."

"This yere adwenture reminds me of summat that happened to my old messmate, Jemmy Sky-flyer," said Tom, reflectively.

No. 62.

"Let's have the yarn, Tom."

"It's a weracity. Well, Jemmy went ashore in Java, and he and some of his shipmates penetrated into the heart of the woods. Now Jemmy was fond of snuff, and always carried a box of rappee which was so strong, that once when he opened it down in the hold, a poor mid as was up at the mast-head fell into conwulsions and then on to the main-deck and broke his neck. But that happened arter what I'm a goin' to tell ye. Jemmy was brought afore a court martial, and the box was perdooced in evidence, but when it was opened all the court fell a sneezin' so fur'ous that it was impossible to pass sentence, and Jemmy got off easy."

"But about his land cruise in Java?"

"You shall hear, my hearties. As they were cutting their way through the jungling, suddenly a monstrous leopard made a spring from a bush and pounced on poor Jemmy; but my old messmate's presence of mind was mirac'lous; he pulled out his snuff - box and threw the contents into the leopard's face. The f'rocious animal immediately began sneezing so wiolent that he broke all his blood wessels and perished. I've met many men in my time, but, for a stronary character, give me my old mate, Jemmy Skyflyer."

CHAPTER CCVI.

HARWOLF AT LARCHVILLE—A CONSUMMATE HYPOCRITE—THE VILLAIN BLESSED BY THE GOOD—HARWOLF EVER IN TORMENT—ARRIVAL OF THE BUSHRANGERS—FATAL NEWS—THE CRISIS IMPENDING.

ANDREW HARWOLF has returned to Larchville.

He has resumed his duties as judge or chief magistrate in the little community.

The settlement rings with his praises.

This arch-villain was pre-eminently a man of talents and great force of character.

It was his interest to assume the character of a humane, just man; and it was surprising how well he played his part.

And, oh! the exquisite anguish he endured while enacting it.

Everyone spoke well of him but Mark Leighton.

The fiery young settler considered himself greatly aggrieved.

After the meeting of Judge Warren and Oswald Lamond, the whole design of the former was to deceive Mark, and to draw him off the trail of the allied gang of robbers.

Harwolf did not now engage in deeds of murder and plunder.

He bided his time.

Above all things, he was anxious for his own safety.

His chief anxiety was how to remove from his path the remorseless man who had crossed the wide Atlantic, with the sole intent of avenging the murder of his brother.

Lamond had failed to keep his promise.

He had not sought the judge as he had promised to do, in order to clench the bargain by which he was to deliver his captive over to the cruel mercies of his deadly foe.

Harwolf awaited the coming of the young bandit in a torture of suspense.

One day he sat in the library of his wealthy and comfortable home at Larchville.

There had lately happened a deplorable accident, which involved many families in ruin.

An inundation from the river Arkansas had whelmed a whole village.

The hypocritical magistrate of Larchville had set a-foot a subscription for the relief of the suffering survivors of this dreadful catastrophe.

An old man, the patriarch of the destroyed village, had waited on the magistrate, and with tearful eyes had thanked and blesssed him for his bounty.

He had gone.

Harwolf was alone, alone with his ever-haunting demon of remorse.

He paced the room brooding deeply of the past, and achingly reflecting on the dread results of his miserable mistake of his life.

A sneer swept over his lips.

"If this act were mine," he muttered, in a hollow tone; "if this deed, which invokes blessings from yonder simple, white-haired old man, were pure; if it were not, as it is, a damnable hypocrisy, oh, what would be my reward? What! Peace, sweet peace of the soul, that calm which is the only boon desirable, for joy itself is restless—it clogs on the mental appetite, like luscious honey on the tongue. Why do I shun death? Why do I not face this

bloodhound, and bid him do his worst? Why can I not dispel my hell-born charm and throw the warlike shield of my tried valour before my tortured heart, and damn myself rather than consent to yield to his clemency? Aye, but guilt is the parent of cowardice. The weak, the timid, who shrink from small pains, can endure torments when their spirits are roused by enthusiasm in a good cause; but the guilty are shrinking dastards, naked though locked up in steel. There is no overruling Providence! there is no divine justice to punish crime and reward virtue. No? Then why does the criminal murderer pine upon his throne? and why does the just man suffer all the sorrows of poverty and scorn with placid fortitude? There is nothing that can wound the good but the sordidness of their fellows, the smile that hails their prosperity, and poisons it with sweet venom, which breaks out in leprous spots of arrogance and selfishness upon him who is influenced by it—on the frown that gives the sting to adversity, and cankers and hardens the heart. But these are not great sorrows; they are gnat bites, stinging, irritating; but for the suffering good there is God to adore, and eventually to love. But for me! vengeance in heaven and earth; desolation, remorse, utter—utter desolation!"

The wretched man groaned, and hid his face in his hands.

"Ah! who but fools would murmur that the wicked flourish as the green bay tree? Their prosperity is their curse; it is their robe of scarlet, their crown of thorns, their 'Hail King,' when they are doomed to a death of torture. Punishment! Welcome, welcome, sweet rest in the burning graves of the inferno, so they would burn away the fault; but the blot stands, it will not leave it. Such villains as I cannot repent, at least, not practically. There is the despair, there the hell! Then who would envy them the cruel mockery of charmless prosperity? Who would not rather perish honest than flourish in crime? Heaven is just, and I am a villain!"

Could such a wretch entertain such sentiments?

After death comes judgment. No man commits moral suicide upon reason but by evil impulse. Then comes the reaction; then come the fruitless good reflections, when too late, too late!

Miles entered the room, to find his master overwhelmed with grief.

"Durn it, zquire! thou'st looking but poorly."

"Aye, Miles, my heart is ill at ease."

"Zure, zir, but I'm thinking az all be goin' tidy loike. I do zay zo, there bean't a man in the colony zo much respected in the colony as yer honour."

"Miles, tell me, man, do ye think that we cannot atone for past bad actions?"

The countryman stared.

"I have tasted stolen fruits of virtue. They are sweet. Do you think the blood that was shed in the past has so poisoned the soil that it will not bear one little tree of life for my hungry soul to feed on?"

Miles bent his black brows.

"I do zay, zur," said the less sensitive, though somewhat less villanous confederate, "that the priest be right, zo to speak, it iz honest for once—the atonement is by blood."

A bright gleam broke on the face of the tormented sinner.

A holy thought sprang up in his heart.

It passed off in a sceptical sneer.

He groaned bitterly.

"Yet," he said, after a pause, "I could die. It would make some difference. I think I shall confess at last, Miles."

He gave a weary sigh.

The man thought his master must be mad.

He looked at him furtively and uneasily.

"Depend on't, zquire, sich feelins is all narvousness. You should tak: some stim'lant. Brandy's as good as aught. Well, I'll tell the fellow you can't zee him, zur, for the vits on yer honour, and ye bean't in no mood to transac' business."

Miles turned to leave the room.

"Hold! Speak, Miles, what do you mean?"

"Why, zur, here's one of the rangers come over to tell ye zome news of the blamed crusher.'

With this announcement Harwolf's better angel fled, and the evil spirit resumed dominion in his black heart.

"Is it Regan?" he asked, quickly.

"No, yer honour, it's t'other chap—Wyld."

"Why does not the captain come himself?"

"Can't zay, yer honour."

"Well, Miles, admit the fellow and keep the door, that we have no intruders."

"Yes, zquire."

The man left the room.

Presently he returned with Wyld.

The ugly fellow, whom we have before described, was dressed in the ordinary style of the back-woods-men.

He bowed to Harwolf.

The latter pointed him to be seated.

"I did not expect to see you," he said. "Regan promised to come himself."

"And would be glad enough to keep his promise," returned the other, with a grim smile.

"What, has he been taken?" asked Harwolf, his cheek paling.

"Not so bad as that, though not much better," replied the ranger. "He has been wounded."

"By whom?"

"By that redskin thief who appears to be invulnerable."

"What, Catahaga?"

"Even so."

"Then the Pawnee is not killed after all!"

"Nor will be till he has done more mischief."

"A blight on him! How did this happen?"

"The Pawnee got into our strong hold in the disguise of a Teton chief, and struck down the captain with a blow from his hatchet."

"The cursed hound!"

"But the worst remains to be told."

"Speak quickly, then."

"He carried off his wife, Minna Wyotti."

"Well, let her go. Your partners will be the safer for her absence," returned Harwolf, impatiently. "Is this the worst?"

"Not quite."

"Speak, man, speak."

"The Britisher that the captain took prisoner—that fellow Reynard."

"Never say escaped?"

"Not to displease you, judge, yet such is the fact."

Harwolf uttered a fearful oath.

"And what makes the thing more provoking is this, the scamp knows all the secrets of our stronghold, and, in a measure, we are at his mercy."

"And so am I; he knows my secrets, too," said Harwolf, feebly. "But I am not to be crushed by such a worm as that. Where is he? Can you tell me? Do you not know whither the Pawnee has carried him?"

"I think to his father's wigwam."

"Monotah's, the White Pine? Their lodges are on the banks of the Blue Earth river."

"So I guess."

"I know it. Well, we must act promptly."

"You are right, judge, it is half the battle to be first in the field."

"How many men have you in your gang?"

"About sixty."

"More than sufficient to blast the wasp's nest."

"Yet, to make assurance sure, a hundred sturdy settlers from Larchville would do no harm."

"I don't see how I can meddle with it. I don't know on what plea I can renew the war with the Indians. The Eagle-Wing fought so well, and our successes were so small, that the settlers are heartily sick of it."

"I will give you a plea, Judge Warren."

"It will assist me."

"You have amongst you a planter and his sister?"

"Aye! Joab and Rebecca Jackson."

"Of Jackson Point?"

"True."

"You spoke of them to the captain."

"I did."

"Well, having heard of the riches of this Yankee fellow, Regan thought he should like to take a slice of the wedding-cake to taste its quality."

"He told you, then, that I proposed a match between himself and the planter's sister."

"He spoke of the happiness in store for him."

"Did he tell you more?"

"He reserves few secrets from me."

"Did he tell you mine?"

"He told me sufficient to convince me that you have good reason to wish the Pawnee and the Britisher both cleared off."

"Humph!"

"To continue my story: Regan determined to take advantage of the absence of the owner to make a descent on the plant, so he disguised the gang as Pawnee-Loups. We made a good sweep."

"Aye! and killed all the hands you found on the premises."

"Not at all; the captain is squeamish of bloodshed. We went in such force that both whites and niggers fled at our screeching, and left us in full possession of all we could lay hands on."

"And were Jackson's folk deceived, think you?"

"Entirely; they took us for Pawnees, and are running about the country thrilling all hearts with terror, and inciting them to fury against the treacherous redskins."

"This will be a good plea for renewing the war."

"And I have even a better."

"That can scarcely be."

"Listen; you know how mad the result of this campaign has made Mark Leighton?"

"Yes, he hates me like venom."

"Because he thinks, justly, perhaps, that you thwarted him in his expedition for the recapture of Agnes Staunton."

"He does."

"Well, has the fellow any influence in the colony?"

"Next to myself the son and heir of the rich Leighton is the most influential person at Larchville."

"And what will be his sentiments when he finds that you have scotched but not killed these snakes?"

"He will laugh at my peaceful policy and triumph in my confusion."

"He does already."

"The swaggering scoundrel!"

"He swears that if the red-skins attacked Larchville, aye, or his own plant at Leighton Hoe, he would not, for fear of offending your excellency, so much as raise a hand against them."

"The coxcomb shall die for his impudence."

"Not till he has rendered you service in this action."

"But if he will not fight I cannot force him into the field; and, secure at home, these selfish drones will not venture another war with the Indians."

"Then we must secure his aid."

"But how?'

"I will make him believe that Regan has carried Agnes into Monotah's wigwam, and to carry off his precious Helen he will fight like a Greek, though it were to storm pandemonium."

"An excellent thought."

"I will go to him at once and urge him on. You call a council of the chief settlers, before which I will appear with a well-studied oration, descriptive of the cruelties of the blood-thirsty Pawnees; and I fear not but every man, woman, and child in the settlement will band together to exterminate the wretches."

"It is good. Monotah's tribe will suspect nothing of the storm that is brewing; we can steal upon them in the night and kill them all, of course including the British renegade."

"When will you convene the assembly?"

"Within the hour."

"I and Mark will be present. I will speak of Reynard's desertion to the Indians, and throw stains upon his character till it is so black that nothing he can say against you will have the effect of convincing even the most disaffected."

"It shall be done."

Such was the diabolic plot of this brace of fiendish villains. Whether or not it was frustrated the sequel must show.

CHAPTER CCVII.

MEETING OF THE ASSEMBLY AT LARCHVILLE —MARK LEIGHTON'S HARANGUE — JUDGE WARREN'S REPLY—SUDDEN ARRIVAL OF FOXLEY AND CATAHAGA — FOXLEY DENOUNCES WARREN.

THE Assembly House in Larchville was a large and pleasant structure, built of pine logs.

The stars and stripes of the States floated from a long staff above the house, as a signal that the little parliament was met.

At one end of the hall was a dais, or raised platform.

On this were tables, with writing materials, at which the secretaries, clerks, wardens, and other officers of the little state were seated.

A guard of Regulators paraded before the door.

Judge Warren occupied a chair of state in the centre of the platform.

The hall was densely crowded by the excited settlers.

A mob of women and children, and youths whose age did not entitle them to join in the deliberations, stood without the door, or were jammed in corners of the hall, into which they had thrust themselves, and where they remained upon sufferance.

Upon the platform, and near the judge, sat the planter—Joab Jackson, and his sister Rebecca.

Both the planter and the lady looked very pale and agitated.

In the centre of the room, mounted upon a kind of rostrum, stood Mark Leighton.

Wyld stood beneath him.

As Mark was very much in earnest, he was not ineloquent in his harangue, for he was vehemently addressing the assembly.

From time to time he scowled upon Judge Warren, though in addressing him, or speaking of him, he confined himself to the most respectful terms.

He recalled the events of the Indian campaign.

He inveighed, with bitterest energy, against the weakness and baseness of the policy pursued throughout the war.

He touched, with some pathos, on the cruel massacre that had given rise to it, and spoke of the ruthless murder of his uncle and family, and especially of the gallant Ned Leighton, who had been beloved throughout the colony for his goodness of heart and manly graces.

Little did he think that at that very time his cousin was chained in a Russian dungeon.

He spoke of the bush-rangers, who were in league with the murderous red-men.; he spoke of the abduction of Agnes Staunton from her peaceful home, and he called aloud on fathers to protect their daughters, husbands their wives, brothers their sisters, lovers their sweethearts, from these audacious wretches, who, he said, at any time might set up the carrying off of Agnes as a precedent of the impunity with which deeds of rapine might be perpetrated upon a people who would not fight with any spirit, even to protect their homes and families. He then touched upon the atrocities at Jackson's Point, and spoke so feelingly of the immense booty carried thence by the unhunted robbers, that poor Joab and his sister shed tears at their loss.

When he got down from the rostrum, with flushed cheeks and panting breast, he was greeted with a startling cheer of applause.

Then the subtle Harwolf rose.

He spoke in a stern tone, with mingled fire and calmness.

"Brothers and fellow colonists—you have heard the charges laid against me by my young friend Mr. Leighton," he began. "Hear my reply. I stand rebuked, and acknowledge the weakness and impolicy of the system of pacification I have hitherto pursued; but those who know me best will be the readiest to give me credit for the motives which influenced my conduct in this matter. Though you have done me the great honour to elect me to the high and responsible post of chief magistrate in this settlement, the honour came to me unsought, and you took me, I may fairly say, with every aspiration of my heart wedded to your general interest, but you took me also with my imperfections on my head. I am an Englishman, and my national prejudice in favour of peaceful policy clove to me. I could not realise the boundless treachery of these miscreant Indian races; but now, though somewhat late for my own honour and your welfare, I perceive the fatal folly of crying peace when there is no peace, and I am convinced that there is no safety for one amongst us till these human wolves of the prairie are exterminated as remorsely as the less ferocious wild beasts themselves. Henceforth I disclaim all thoughts of treaty, all sentiments of mercy, and declare war to the death with all the surrounding tribes of bloodthirsty savages—redskins or whites!"

This declaration was received with tremendous cheering.

In the midst of this exciting scene two men stole into the hall, and glided through the crowd towards the platform.

They were both wrapped in long black cloaks.

They walked among the people with such bold confidence that the crowd instinctively made way for them.

They mounted the steps and stood on the platform.

Judge Warren started up in amazement.

The taller of the men stepped forward.

His cloak fell from his shoulder.

He appeared arrayed in all the picturesque costume of an Indian sachem.

It was Catahaga, the Eagle-Wing.

There was a roar of execration.

"Down with him! kill him! tear him to pieces! Arms, arms!" was shrieked from all parts of the house.

Catahaga raised his hand with stoic dignity and said in a calm, thrilling tone, and in good, though pleasingly accented English,

"First, let my white brothers hear me speak."

"The infernal wretch! Burn him! Lynch him! Some one knock him down!" shouted the assembly.

Still the Indian stood unmoved as a rock in the tempest.

"For God's sake beware what you do!" cried a voice in the crowd. "The house is surrounded by redskins!"

"Hu-hu-hu-hu!"

It was the yell of a dense crowd of braves, who now appeared at the doors and windows.

"There are at least five hundred of the wretches."

"We are lost!" cried another voice.

Harwolf sat as one who had looked on the face of Medusa, and had been turned into stone.

His glazing eyes were fixed upon the cold, stern face of the Indian's companion.

Before the assembly over which he was judge and president he sat like a murderer in the dock, confronting the detective, Foxley.

His trusty confederate was at his side.

"Miles," he whispered, hoarsely, "his power lies in the charm that hangs from his watch-chain—that bullet. Have it, Miles; it shall be a nugget of breeding gold to ye."

Miles started forward.

"Dang it! do'ee stand back!" he cried, "the judge wants air, he is faintin'."

With this he pushed swiftly past the detective.

He had drawn a small clasp knife, it snapped to, and the bullet was in the countryman's hand.

Foxley was so excited, and so absorbed in gloating contemplation of his victim that he did not perceive his loss.

There was a deep silence.

"My white brothers, I come not into your lodges as a brave on the war-path," said the Indian, calmly, "I bring the plaintain of peace in my hand; I come to show you the faces which are adorned with the emblems of your tribe, but which are the faces of poisonous enemies; I have come to open to your gaze a nest of adders which have subtly glided amongst you to plague and destroy you; I am come to teach you that there is goodness in the Iroquois as well as in the Pale-face, that mercy is not all Yengeese. Let my brother speak to his people."

These words were addressed to Foxley.

He turned to the assembly.

"Fellow men, I have come many thousands of miles across the perilous seas, through boundless forests, over trackless prairies; I have come to unmask a demon who has stolen in amongst ye, a wolf in the sheepfold; then hear me patiently while I speak a few words."

There was little need to invoke silence.

The assembly remained mute, and paralysed with awe and dismay, as if spell entranced.

"I have come to seek your aid in avenging a series of the foulest, most hideous murders perpetrated, both at home and in this colony, by the blackest criminal that ever lived the curse of his kind. I am an officer of justice, my name is Richard Foxley, and these papers are my warrants and credentials of authority."

At this moment it would have been hard not to feel some awe and respect for the wily and satanic villain Harwolf; even in wickedness, self-controul seems so admirable.

The wretch sat as mute as a statue, his face expressing only astonishment and guiltless indignation.

Foxley then proceeded with his explanation, commencing at the story of the villain's life at Frontemore; he told how Lord Edgeforth had suddenly and mysteriously disappeared, and how every circumstance combined to show that Harwolf had been the murderer of his kind and too confiding master; he told of the imposition Harwolf had practised in passing off his wife as the real Lady Edgeforth, and gave an account of the assassination of Mrs. Harwolf and Edmund Foxley, the attempted murder of Lady Edgeforth, the treacherous abduction of Silas Rye, and the flight of the miscreant who had committed such black crimes, and had brought such awful misery upon innocent people; and finished by announcing himself as the brother of the murdered Edmund Foxley, and declaring that he had crossed the Atlantic with the fixed intention of dragging the monster to justice.

The audience listened with breathless excitement to this extraordinary story.

Catahaga produced the knives of Harwolf and Miles Thornton, and told how he had found the detective lying in the wood stunned and bleeding, the knives beside him.

The story seemed so wild, strange and improbable, the prejudice against the Indians was so great, and the respect for Judge Warren seemingly so well founded, that the settlers were bewildered and knew not what to think.

Besides, many present belonged to Harwolf's secret gang, and feared lest they should be compromised if he were condemned.

There was something that commanded admiration in the demeanour of this matchless villain, at this fearful crisis in his black career.

He fixed upon Foxley a glance of fiery indignation and disdain, and with supreme dignity walked to the front of the platform.

Amid the most solemn silence he spoke.

His voice was calm and clear.

The wolf was at bay. Desperation nerved him, despair had rendered him reckless of life; innate craft and fiendish passion steeled his conscience.

"Forgive me, brother citizens, if this strange and extraordinary charge, brought against me by such persons under such circumstances and with such suddenness, confuses me, stuns me! For the story itself, I can easily refute it; and it would be insulting you to suppose you could, as men of common sense, give the slightest credence to such a tissue of lies; lies so black and so palpable that they cannot deceive the most credulous. You all know me, you all know whence I came; you all know in what manner I have conducted myself since I have been among you. This is only a deep-laid, bloody plot to destroy you all. As ever, in such conspiracies, the first blow is struck at him who is at the head of the government. The shepherd destroyed, the flock are at the mercy of the ravening wolves. Who are my accusers? A pack of murderous redskins, who have perpetrated such outrages that one's blood runs cold to think of, and an unknown Englishman who, by his own account, has come amongst us under false colours. He called himself Reynard, and now he says his name is Foxley; he joined my troop of Regulators, and conformed in all respects to my wishes and commands, breathing no hint of the purpose for which he had emigrated; he fought against the Indians with as much remorselessness as the most experienced backwoodsman amongst you, and now he comes hand in hand with the atrocious Pawnee chief, who may well be called the scourge of the Pale-faces. Brother citizens, believe him if you will.? If you can be so base, I am willing to surrender myself to your worst treatment : but if you are sane and not mad, true men and not villains, judges impartially between us—am I, think you, what this rogue represents? and can he be, even accepting his story as true, while in league with these fiendish savages against his fellow citizens, aught else but an accursed regenade, traitor, and perjurer?"

Spite of the presence of the overnumbering Indians, the audience received this cunning and dauntless speech with a storm of applause and approval.

Even the detective himself seemed confounded.

The Eagle-Wing looked on with a calm yet watchful countenance.

"All who are lovers of fair play give me permission to speak," said Foxley, addressing the assembly.

"Hear him, hear him !" cried some.

"Down with the treacherous villain !" cried others.

"A spy ! A regenade !"

"Hear him, hear him !"

A volley of cheers.

A storm of hisses.

Again cheers.

Catahaga advanced and upheld his hand.

"Are my brothers wise braves, or are they quarrelling squaws ?" he said, in that soft yet self-possessed tone which ever commands attention. "My brother's tongue is not forked, and the Grey Wolf is before the council; let them both speak. The wise sachems can weigh their words, and tell which are the heavier. I have spoken."

"Fellow citizens," cried Harwolf, "I implore you not to believe the lying tale told against me, but I also charge you not to make me the cause of bloodshed. Let me die; I am old, I am prepar——" (he could not utter the word; it died on his lips.) "Let me die; surrender me if you think by so doing you can save yourselves. I willingly give my life for you !"

"No, no !' cried Mark Leighton. "We'll all die first! Long live the good Judge Warren! Down with his malicious enemies!"

"Hurrah !"

"My brothers' hearts are darkened. The great Manitou of the Iroquis has blinded their eyes," cried the Pawnee chief, in a tone of scorn. "If they would listen to the words of Catahaga, they would know their friends from their enemies; but they are like men who are drunken with fire-water and cut their brothers' throats."

"Silence, all!" cried Harwolf. "I desire no more than that on either side there should be a fair hearing."

"You are guilty of suicide, Judge Warren," cried Wyld; "the wretches will destroy you, and there are not half-a-dozen present who have pluck to stand up for you."

There was another uproar.

Foxley came forward once more.

"A single word!" he shouted. "I challenge him to the death!"

Harwolf leaped up with a sparkle of valour and demoniac malice in his deep-set grey eyes.

"I accept the challenge, and whoever thwarts me is a coward!" he shouted.

There was instantaneous silence.

"All his other crimes set apart—though I have ample proof to give you of each and all of them, if you would hear me—I will cleave to him till I have satisfaction for the murder of my brother," said Foxley. "I have brought with me the very bullet with which he killed my brother and his own wife, that bullet's billet is his own black heart. That what I say is true; behold the token!"

He lifted his watch-chain. The bullet was gone!

Foxley stood aghast.

Miles, who had it in his pocket, clutched it in his hard hand and chuckled.

There was a roar of derision at Foxley's expense.

"You see the fellow is stark mad," said Harwolf, with a cutting sneer.

"You shan't fight him!"

"It's sheer murder!" cried voices in the crowd.

"But I will!" shouted Harwolf, fiercely. "No one shall prevent me. I am challenged, and I claim a man's right to respond to the impudent brave!"

"You shall, Judge Warren," cried Mark Leighton; "and I will be your second."

The loss of his talisman seemed to have unnerved the detective.

"I had the bullet when I came hither."

Groans of derision.

"But a shot fired by a sick girl would strike that venomed heart. I will fight him with his own weapons, with pistol or bowie-knife. May God defend the right!" cried the detective.

"Is this good? Let my brothers hold up their hands," said Catahaga.

Every hand was upheld in an instant.

Miles came to his master's side.

"I'm blamed, zur, but ye shall kill the doomed crusher with his own bullet."

"No, no, no!" whispered Harwolf, eagerly; "it would recoil on me. Keep it, Miles, till all is over; if I am the victor, I shall be safe for ever!"

The assembly rose.

There was a general rush from the meeting-house.

A party of his own confederates and those of the settlers, who were persuaded of his innocence, kept close around Harwolf, while the Indians and those who wished to conciliate them remained with Foxley the detective.

The whole party, English and Indians, gathered upon a wide lawn which stretched before the meeting-house.

"Durn it, zquire, if ye can pink the crusher our fortun' be made; do'ee be game, zur."

"It is not for him to kill me," returned the wretch in a hollow tone. "His brother was the paramour of my wife, to whom I was never false or unkind; others have deeper wrongs to avenge, and they alone can destroy me."

The man who had travelled from the old world to the new to avenge the death of his brother now confronted his deadly foe.

Harwolf, by his strange faith in destiny, had nerved himself to perfect calmness.

Now that the moment of his triumph was arrived, detective seemed to lose confidence.

His talisman was lost!

CHAPTER CCVIII.

THE CRISIS—FACE TO FACE—THE FATAL DUEL—THE DEATH OF FOXLEY THE DETECTIVE—HARWOLF WOUNDED—THE PACKET OF LETTERS.

ANDREW HARWOLF stood calm and collected beneath the primeval oaks that spread their wide, leafy arms above himself and the clustering sympathizers, who cheered this arch-villain with encouraging words.

Catahaga leaned on his long rifle, and looked at the wretched criminal with an eye of scrutiny.

As he watched the cool manner in which Harwolf examined the pistols, which were handed to him by a man who acted as Foxley's second, a smile of stern pleasure rested on his face.

The war-loving Indian saw that the match was equal: courage and desperation on the one side, revenge and enthusiasm on the other.

Mark Leighton, whose hatred of the red-skins was so intense, looked upon Harwolf as the champion of his own race, and felt sure that he would come off victoriously.

"If you fall, Judge Warren," he whispered, "I shall look upon your cutting off as an act of foul murder, and will avenge you! Now you perceive that I was right; now you see what is the result of your pacific measures. If you had been persuaded by me you would never have come to this pass. The Indians are fiends in cunning as well as in cruelty. But you will notch this rowdy, never fear; only be cool, and take fair aim."

"I don't want to have his blood on my head, Mark," said the hypocrite, lowering his eyes, and breathing a deep sigh.

"Then you must be content to perish, and to have your memory held in abhorrence as the miscreant he describes you."

"That shall never be, Mark!" returned Harwolf.

"Well said. Don't spare him."

"I will not."

Meanwhile, one of the settlers, who had espoused the cause of Foxley, cheered him in his turn.

This man was Nat Weatherfield, the beaver-hunter.

"Stranger, I have known ye since ye came into these yere parts. And when you was Minna Wyotti's prisoner you revealed to us a secret, the truth of which I never had no doubt on. I have had some experience in the prairies and in the forests, and I'm slick sure that this coon is a most infarnal humbug. The Eagle-Wing is a great chief, and he sticks by the right on all and every occasion."

"But the charmed bullet, Nat; I've lost it, and lost my courage with it."

"Wall, I guess as one pellet of lead is as good as another," answered the trapper; "and the pistols are Regan's, the bush-ranger, and so there bean't no oncartainty about their being genwine."

"God bless ye, Nat! This is an awful moment with me. I have been a sinner; but none can measure His mercy. But the vengeance long coming is heaviest at last; and if, as I think it will be, I must die by this murderer's hand, there are others who have sworn to track him, and they will avenge me!"

"I calkilate you must jist take a steady aim, not think too much of yer man; and if he chalks yer, wall and good, you'll have yer satisfaction. So keep up your sperits."

Foxley smiled a ghastly smile at this piece of well-meant consolation.

"Let me shake hands with the Indian," said the detective.

Catahaga caught the words.

He advanced with graceful step, and grasped the extended hand.

"My brother has been kind to his captive," said Foxley, speaking in the Iroquois language. "Let the name of Reynard live in his heart."

"Catahaga will not forget; the wise manitou will

do what is good," returned the Pawnee, with an encouraging smile.

Joab Jackson, who had been chosen as umpire, now tossed for choice of ground.

The selection fell to Foxley.

The advantage was not great.

The sun was shaded by a cloud, and the light was subdued.

The settlers moved back.

The ground was measured back.

The crowd of Indians stood on Foxley's side, leaning on their long rifles, and intently watching the combatants.

The excitement among the settlers was intense.

The duellists faced each other at their posts.

Joab Jackson held in his hand a white handkerchief.

He stepped a few paces backwards.

Not a sound was heard, every voice was hushed.

He counted,

"One—two—three!"

He dropped the handkerchief.

The duellists turned round, and away from each other.

Their right arms were extended, the calm sunbeams glinting on the shining barrels of their pistols.

There was a double report.

Harwolf sank on his knees, and then, tossing up his arms, fell heavily on his face.

Foxley made a bound in the air, and dropped.

Some of the settlers ran to the detective.

Others crowded round Harwolf.

"He has killed the judge!" cried several voices.

"He is killed himself!" answered others.

Nat Weatherfield lifted Foxley in his arms.

"How goes it, stranger?" he asked, in a pitying tone.

The only answer was a deep sob of agony.

The bullet had entered the detective's side.

His shirt dripped blood.

"Have I killed him?" muttered the poor fellow.

Nat glanced towards Harwolf.

The judge was now erect, supported by Mark Leighton and Miles Thornton.

The unfortunate detective cast a languid look at the villain.

"No; he moves, he speaks, he is reserved for a more dreadful doom!" he uttered faintly.

"Aye, mate, the hotter for him hereafter," said Nat Weatherfield, with bitter emphasis.

Catahaga stood beside the dying man.

Foxley took off the gold chain from his pocket with the heavy gold repeater. He held them out towards the Indian.

"Let my brother give these to his wife, she was kind to the pa'e-face who crossed the great salt lakes to avenge his brother," he said in a feeble tone. "The medicine bullet is gone," he added, with a ghastly smile; "he who finds it will have the murderer's life in his hands."

Catahaga gravely took the proffered gift.

He rose.

He spread his arms to the setting sun.

He bowed his crested head.

The simple Indian was praying to his manitou for the struggling soul of the dying pale-face.

"Nat Weatherfield, my rifle is yours; you will live to see the dread doom that will overtake yon assassin. Farewell! Heaven's will be done, and my sins be forgiven!"

He closed his eyes.

A twinge of mortal agony writhed his face. He grew paler and paler.

The life-tide welled more and more copiously.

Then the blood ceased flowing, and became clotted on the riven breast. The wanderer's head sank, his jaw fell, his limbs became rigid—his soul passed!

The Indian gazed sternly on the face of the dead.

The Pawnee chief now stalked over to the spot where the settlers were gathered with frightened looks around the fainting Harwolf.

A surgeon held his drooping hand, and touched his pulse.

"His wound is dangerous, perhaps mortal," said the surgeon; "but he may recover."

The ball had penetrated Harwolf's shoulder, inflicting a ghastly wound.

Catahaga looked curiously in the pale face of the wretch, and tured aside with a gloomy brow.

Miles Thornton had thrown off his jacket.

It lay on the ground.

A bullet, with a link of gold attached to it, had rolled from his pocket.

The Indian stooped very quietly and picked it up.

Unseen by the bystanders, he slipped it into his pocket.

Harwolf muttered brokenly,

"At last! I am struck at last! It is true—I —I am——"

"Most 'farnally ill-used, measter," cried Miles, greatly alarmed lest the criminal was about to confess. "An old man to be pitted agen a young spark az is a dead shot. I'm blamed, but thee'st done better than I thought vor."

Harwolf fainted with pain.

"We are in the power of the burning red thieves, and must hold the candle to the infernals!" growled Mark Leighton. "This is a cursed chance!"

"Wall, stranger, I du opine that we'd better remove the judge to the fust house, and then expostulate with the devilskins," rejoined Joab Jackson.

"Aye, its no use being cantankerous now, I reckon," added Wyld, the bush-ranger.

"Well, the copper cusses have taught us how to break treaties, that's one comfort," grumbled Mark. "We can promise fair, that won't cost much."

Harwolf was borne away, and carried into a cabin close at hand.

"And who is to act as your spokesman now, mates?" asked Mark Leighton.

"Yourself, none but yourself!" cried the settlers, in one voice.

"Be it so," said Mark, shrugging his shoulders. "Believe me, I don't like the office."

He approached the Indian.

"Let the great chief, Catahaga, be satisfied," he said, in a tone which he meant to be conciliating; "the Eagle-Wing is very wise; he will not close his eyes against the light; he has been beguiled by the false words of the Yengeese spy who has fallen. Let the chief come with his brother into the council lodge, and there a treaty can be made by which the pale-faces and the Iroquois may henceforth live in peace together."

"My brother's words are good," replied the Pawnee, gravely; "but he is very young. None but the old men of his tribe should sit at the head of the council."

"It is good," grunted the Indians.

Mark Leighton suppressed an oath of impatience which rose to his lips.

"Don't oppose him, our position is critical," said Wyld.

"Whom does the great chief of the Pawnees chose to be head chief at the council?" asked Mark, biting his lips.

"Let my brother send for the great chief, his father," answered the Indian, coldly.

Miles now returned from the cabin.

He put on the jacket which he had thrown off the better to support his wounded master.

"Well, Thornton, how is the judge?"

"Mortal queer, yer honour; the blamed crusher—that is, I mean, zur, the other chap—has winged his honour. I be deadly feared az his right arm be shattered."

"The poor old man! and we younger skulks to look on passively! Well, there'll come a change some day, I think. Go to him; you won't be wanted, Thornton. Is the doctor with him?"

"Zure, zur, he be; he's probing on the bullet, and

he zays az how there's hopes vor his honour's recovery."

"Well, see to him."

"I do zay, yer honour, I'm much obleeged, vor I be mortal cunsarned at this doamed avair!"

"Not more so than I am, mate; but the wheel will turn—our time will come yet."

"I do zay you be right, zur, and we woan't vorget to pay zcore for zcore."

"No, but skedaddle at once; we are going into the council, to buy our own scalps from these wretches. We shall have to pay pretty stiff, I reckon."

Miles nodded, and rushed back to the cabin.

"Mr. Jackson, you must act as ambassador to my father; tell him what has happened, and entreat him to come at once to the meeting-house."

The planter, with two or three others, mounted swift horses, and rode off to Leighton Hoe.

"I must give the beasts some provender, I suppose," growled Mark to Wyld. "I wish we could season it with ratsbane!"

"For Heaven's sake, give them no spirits!" replied the bush-ranger, earnestly. "They will drink themselves mad, and butcher every mother's son of us!"

"I will take care for that," returned Mark Leighton, "though I doubt that the cursed chief would suffer them to drink a drain of the fire-water!"

Once more the young magnate advanced towards the Pawnee.

"Let my brother's young men eat meat; they are way-worn and hungry."

The chief replied with the invariable phrase of assent.

"It is good!" he added, with a frown. "The braves of Catahaga shall not be poisoned with fire-water."

Leighton bowed his head.

"Let the chief speak to his warriors. Nothing can be done till the council is assembled."

The Eagle-Wing gave a few words of command to the Pawnees.

They seated themselves in a circle.

Provisions were brought out and distributed amongst them.

In silence they partook sparingly of the food set before them.

Mark walked over to the spot where lay the dead body of the ill-starred Foxley.

He looked grimly down upon the corpse.

The Indians were preparing it for burial.

They had removed the coat and waistcoat and shirt, and were making a kind of shroud with their blankets.

In the pocket of the vest was a small packet.

From this the brother of Catahaga, the young chief who was called Akantoosh, drew forth a small packet.

"Waugh!"

As he gave vent to this guttural note of surprise he opened the little bundle.

It contained letters.

These he threw aside.

He took up a little case, and opened it by a spring.

He stared at it with naive pleasure.

Throwing it to Mark, he said, with a smile,

"It is a medicine bag; the pale-face will take it with him to the far hunting-grounds of the Great Spirit!"

It proved to be the miniature of a gentle-looking girl.

There was also a silken tress of fair hair.

Mark picked up the letters, and glanced at them.

They proved to be love-lines from the dead man's sweetheart.

The last of the papers was written in another hand.

It was edged with black, and announced her death.

CHAPTER CCIX.

OSWALD LAMOND AND AGNES STAUNTON.

THE elder Leighton occupied the chair in which Harwolf had so lately been seated.

He was a very reverend old man, and his demeanour was marked by the grace and dignity which characterised the gentleman of the old school.

The place was even more densely crowded than before.

Mark Leighton, Wyld, Joab Jackson, Catahaga, and Akantoosh, were on the platform.

The body of the building was thronged by the settlers and Indians.

On this occasion the women were excluded in courtesy to the Indians, who never suffer females to be present at their own councils.

Catahaga was the first to speak.

He declared that his sole motive in coming thither with his braves was the desire he felt to establish a good understanding between the whites and the Indian tribes. He spoke of his long residence among them, of his marriage with Minna Wyotti, of the cruel wrongs which had driven him from amongst his pale-face brothers and had enraged his heart against them; he spoke of the war, and declared that it was only the aggravation of deep injury which had rendered him so bitterly hostile to the whites. Now, he added, he had discovered his mistake. He had with unreasoning rancour hated all his white brethren on account of the villanies practised by a few. He denounced Harwolf as one in league with the bush-rangers, and expressed his entire belief in the account given by the luckless Foxley of the antecedents of him, who, at the same time that he was acting as Judge over the colonists, was their most bloodthirsty and treacherous foe. He was willing, however, to abide by the result of the duel, and only claimed a treaty of peace and protection for the surrounding tribes of Indians.

Of course, we have given merely the substance of the chief's long speech, divested of its national imagery.

Leighton answered in a conciliating tone, expressed his regret that any misunderstanding should have led to the late cruel and disastrous campaign, and concluded by assuring the Indians that the whites were most willing to make a league with them upon certain conditions.

The Pawnee bade him name them.

"For Heaven's sake, father, do not forget my claim," cried Mark, with animation.

"What claim have you upon Catahaga, son?" asked the elder Leighton.

"He is in league with the bush-rangers. Let it be a condition of the truce that your neice and my cousin and affianced, Agnes Staunton, shall be given up to her rightful protectors."

"I cannot see what right we have to exact this from the chief," answered his father. "Heaven knows how much I love the poor child, and how anxious I am to rescue her from the hands of the abandoned wretches amongst whom she is a captive; but as the Pawnees had no hand in her abduction, I cannot see what claim you have upon them for her restoration."

"The Yengeese maiden shall return to the lodges of her fathers, if she be so disposed," said the Eagle-Wing, firmly.

"Now I will believe the judge was a traitor!" cried the impetuous Mark. "And, henceforth, I will say there is, at least, one honest redskin on the prairies."

"The White Fox has taken many blankets, fire-weapons, with money and corn from the wigwam of the pale chief on the Arkansas."

"Wall, I calkilate he did so," sang out Joab Jackson, "from my plant of Jackson Pint, I opine, to the tune of ten hundred dollars."

"The White Fox shall give back these spoils to my brother," said the noble young chief, in a tone of authority.

ANDREW HARWOLF ATTEMPTS TO KILL SILAS RYE.

"Wal, this Ingin is a mirac'lous squealer of probity and justice, I rather guess," cried the Yankee, in great delight.

"But can he do this?" asked Mark, doubtfully.

"If he does less, we might well be satisfied; we are at his mercy, remember," whispered the president.

"My brothers shall mark upon the earth-picture the boundaries of the hunting-grounds of the Iroquois, and shall not invade them," said Catahaga.

The president expressed his willingness to comply with this demand.

A debate ensued, and it was determined that there should be held a grand meeting of the sachems and war-chiefs of the various neighbouring tribes to settle this matter by agreement.

"And now let me ask the great chief of the

No. 63.

Pawnees when he can fulfil his promise, and restore the Yengeese maiden to her father's lodge?" said Mark.

"Catahaga will not compel the maiden to return unless she be willing," said the chief.

"It is good," rejoined Mark, impatiently. "But she must speak to her brothers, and must tell what is in her heart by her own lips."

"My brother shall have his wish," said Catahaga.

He turned to Akantoosh.

He gave him a command in the Iroquois tongue.

The young Indian glided from the room.

"Father, I suspect treachery!" whispered Mark.

"Do not show suspicion in your looks, or you will ruin all!" returned the old man, sharply.

There was a murmur of surprise among the settlers

when the Indian returned, ushering in the captain of the bush-rangers and Agnes Staunton.

Wyld started up as if he had been shot.

Oswald and Agnes were followed by Minna Wyotti and Nat Weatherfield.

The handsome young robber was very pale.

He rested his arm in a sling.

He walked with something of humiliation but more of drollery in his face.

His step was free and jaunty as ever.

Agnes kept her eyes fixed on the ground, and blushed deeply.

Mark leaped up with a cry of joy, and bounded to meet Agnes as she ascended the platform.

"My dear coz, welcome, welcome! What will you think of me that I have not long since borne you by force from the arms of this ruffian?"

He flung his arms about her, and was about to lead her to his father.

"Dear Mark, how happy am I that we may meet once more!" she exclaimed.

The fervent youth kissed his cousin's cheek.

Oswald Lamond seized him by the shoulder, and pushed him back.

He stepped between Agnes and her admirer.

"Buskins! fortunately I am not jealous. Nevertheless, I can't allow any man to kiss my wife!"

"Wife! His wife!" cried the settlers, in one breath.

"Wife! you monstrous villain!" gasped Mark, with hot, glowing cheek.

"Even so," said the bush-ranger, with a bow. "Your humble servant, and Agnes's husband."

He pulled a paper from his pocket.

"The curious or incredulous may convince themselves of my right of possession to earth's richest treasure by glancing at this document. Our marriage-lines, uncle. Hard lines to her, perhaps," he added, with a touch of genuine shame. "But, at least, they vindicate her spotless honour, and show that I, like another gentleman, I trust not present in such good company, am not quite so black as I have been painted."

"Niece, is this true?"

"Dear uncle, it is. Forgive us!" murmured Agnes.

The old man struck his forehead.

"Oh, my child!" he said, brokenly. "Shame itself would have seemed the better alternative, at least, you might have escaped from this miscreant, now you are bound to him for ever. Yet, still, you cannot, would not, remain with him—a bandit, a felon!"

"I am his wife, uncle," said the girl, quietly, and with a radiant smile, as she nestled to the side of the wild young outlaw.

Poor Mark threw himself down at the table, covered his face with his hands and groaned bitterly.

Catahaga looked admiringly upon the devoted girl, who stood fighting with her shame by the side of him she had chosen.

"Let my sister speak," said the Pawnee chief. "Will the Yengeese lily return to the wigwam of her fathers, or will she stay in the lodge of her husband?"

"Agnes—speak—answer, this is not marriage, you are betrayed! A thousand priests, all the solemnity of every rite of religion, cannot bind you to that villain!" cried Mark, with great bitterness; "you are free, do but think so, for by all that's just you are free. Come home, then; shun that leper, lest he taint you with the contagion of his guilt!"

"Oh, shade of Roscius! What a loss to the profession! That such a flower should be born to blush unseen, and waste its dramatic fragrance on the desert air of Arkansan backwoods. Mars and Bellona! that such a war-denouncing trumpet r should have no higher mission than to frighten the buffaloes of the prairie!"

"Oswald!"

"I am dumb, love."

"Were you not shameless you would indeed be

dumb in this presence," said the elder Leighton, sternly. "You have destroyed this innocent girl; but to you evil is good, you make a triumph of your heartless villany."

"Uncle, it is too cruel to chide a married man; but hear me speak a few words: I am not shameless, I stand here before you all, not to cry your mercy, but to acknowledge my past errors, or, if you will, as I suppose you must have it, my past crimes; to surrender myself to your judgment. I have been a great rogue, but in your treatment of me, you have not been altogether blameless. I was driven from home on account of sundry youthful follies of which I was guilty. What could I do? Whither could I go? I could not dig, and was too proud to become a beggar. One evil day I fell in with a band of robbers; they made me their captain; I found them worse than I left them, for there is no blood on my hands, and some restitution may be made for the wrong I have done society. I do not justify myself; I don't want to find excuses for my rascality; but here is Agnes, let her say if she will put herself under the honourable protection of cousin Buskins, or whether she will remain with her reformed, but ever unworthy husband, Oswald Lamond."

Agnes clung to him, her cheek flushing crimson.

"You are the prisoner of the chief Catahaga; it is not for us to dispose of you," said his uncle, coldly.

"Then I am free to go whither I will, and to bear my bride with me?"

"I have no controul over your actions, nephew; do as you will," replied Leighton.

"Say am I pardoned? Owning my guilt, promising amendment, and submitting to your decree."

"It is safe to say so; you are the Indian's captive," said Leighton, scornfully.

"Catahaga has given his prisoner to his father, the head-chief of the council," said the Pawnee.

"Be it so," rejoined Oswald. "Do with me what you please; hang me or pardon me."

"Go free, for Agnes's sake," cried the settlers, unanimously.

Oswald made no other answer than to thank the speakers by a beaming look, and bowed his head with deep reverence.

Agnes threw herself at her uncle's feet.

"Your blessing, uncle, let me bear your blessing with me."

The old man laid his hand on her head.

"God bless you, child; rash and misguided as you are, you have shown the true spirit of womanly devotion. Go with him whom you have saved from eternal infamy, and use that strong influence you have exerted so happily to complete the good work you have begun, and when you can tell me that your husband has given proof sufficient of his repentance, come back, Agnes; I should not die happy if I saw you no more."

Agnes rose.

She placed her hand in her husband's.

With downcast eyes they descended from the platform.

The crowd made way for them to pass.

Not a few invoked a blessing on Agnes's head, and even murmured their admiration at the manly beauty of her wild, lawless, but not ungenerous, husband.

They were gone, and the council resumed its deliberations.

CHAPTER CCX.

THE STORY OF THE FATAL BULLET.

ANDREW Harwolf lay writhing on his bed of pain.

His wound had been bandaged.

He had taken an opiate, which procured him a profound but unrefreshing sleep, from which he had just awakened.

He stared wildly at Miles, who sat watching by his side.

"I'm glad to zee yer honour looking so cheery," said the countryman with a grin.

"Aye, Miles, it won't come yet; I shall live to do more mischief."

"Zo long as you do live, zquire, it's zummut; you did a mortal vine bit o' mischief, howsomdever, when you pinked the crusher, Voxley."

"If he had had the fatal bullet I should have been spared a few years of crime and anguish," moaned Harwolf. "Miles, that bullet is charmed. I have a mind to tell ye how and of what it was made."

"Durn it, zquire, 'ee doant zay az it be majic like," said Miles, agape. "I've heard tell that there be zecret dark ways of making zome az never miss the mark."

"It is an unerring bullet."

"'Ee don't zay zo," said the superstitious fellow.

"Aye; are there any eaves-droppers at the door?"

"Noa, we be all t'ourzelves, zquire."

"Look round before you say so."

Miles stared about him as if he expected to behold a ghost or a goblin.

He rose and went to the door.

He looked out.

Returning to the bed-side on tiptoe he reseated himself.

"Noa, zur, the ro-ad be clear; but, I'm blamed, but should like to know how yer honour made the blamed thing."

"You know, that is, you think, that I killed Lord Edgeforth?"

"Dang it, zquire, it bean't vor I to think o' other people's business at all."

"I did kill him!" said the wretch, "and now I'll tell ye how I prepared with my own hands the instrument which is to avenge him."

"Do, zur."

"I struck him down with a life preserver, a heavy staff loaded with lead. When I was removing the traces of my guilt, which I did well—water is good but fire is better than all—I burnt the handle of the staff, and melted the lead into a lump, which I threw into the brook."

"Zure, zur, I remember it well, down by the vold yard, and the old smithy."

"Aye; but don't interrupt me."

"Very good, zur."

"I threw the lump of lead into the brook."

"Zo yer honour zaid."

"The first time I discovered my wife's perfidy I was walking in the grounds at Frontemore; coming suddenly upon a rosary I overheard a conversation between my wife and her precious paramour."

"Aye, zure, Edmund Foxley, this last man's brother."

"Yes. Maddened with jealousy I resolved to kill her. In the anger and despair of my heart I wandered listlessly down to the river banks; I found some men in a boat dragging for the body of a girl who had drowned herself that morning; the men fished up this piece of lead which had formed a part of the instrument with which I had taken the life of my master. I had squeezed it in my hand while it was cooling, and left the prints of my clutching fingers deep in it; these the men showed to me; I snatched the token, and brought it home with me. That night I quarrelled with my wife, and as she was ever taunting me with Edgeforth's murder, I vowed I would kill her with a bullet made from the instrument that did the deed; the impulse was either one of madness, or it was prompted by the fiend that haunts and tortures me; I moulded a bullet from the fatal lead, and with that bullet I killed my wife and the brother of this fool! this brainless fool!"

"Brainless now, I do zay," laughed Miles, with brutal glee.

"This Richard Foxley found the bullet in the carriage, and brought it hither to do the work of vengeance; but strange as it seems, even to me, after having kept it safe till the moment when he intended to have sent it through my heart, he lost it."

"And I vound it. Ho, ho, blamed good, 'zquire! Pity I vasn't a faker. I zeised it az neatly az ever a Lunnon pick-pocket could nail a diamond pin. He zeemed quite constarnated when he lifted the chain, and vound his pretty charm vas lost."

"Aye, I knew from that moment I should triumph."

"And it be good too that we've got the damnation unlucky thing; vor, now, zquire, I do zay az I should destroy it."

"I mean to do so. Give it me, Miles; you shall melt it in the fire, and then break it to pieces, while I lie here and watch you break the last link that fetters me to the hideous past."

"Zo be it, yer honour," returned the countryman, readily.

He plunged his hand into his pocket.

He started.

He searched again and again.

He sank in a chair with a look of dismay.

The charmed bullet was gone!

CHAPTER CCXI.

THE EXILES OF SIBERIA—THE COSSACK GUARD—THE SNOW STORM—KATINKA'S DEVOTION—THE HALT—THE RUSE—THE VIVANDIERE—THE SLEEPER'S POTION—THE SLEDGE—ESCAPED.

OVER the weary wastes of glittering snow a dreary cavalcade was slowly wending along.

It consisted of a long train of waggons, escorted by a detachment of Cossacks.

These wains were filled by wretched exiles on their way to Siberia.

Blinding sheets of snow were falling.

The fur-enveloped travellers were drenched with the heavy moisture.

Their hair and beards were masses of rattling icicles; their breath congealed upon their blue, drawn lips.

With bowed heads, the rugged-looking soldiers forged onward through the snow storm.

They were mounted on small, rough, and wretched horses; they carried long spears, which bent and quivered in the keen blast.

The unfortunates in the wains were huddled together shivering with the bitter cold.

From time to time a subdued moan gave vent to their sufferings.

Still the weary plains swept past them, the interminable steppes, their monotonous expanse broken only by the long dark fringings of gloomy pine forest.

For many days had the exiles been on the march.

More than one of them had died before reaching the first stage of their journey.

They were now crowded in their waggons, but it must not be supposed that they were allowed to ride from station to station; for a long wintry day they had been tramping on foot and in chains.

The ruffianly escort goaded the poor half-fainting women on the march by lashing them with their heavy whips upon their shrinking shoulders, and even striking them with the backs of their swords.

The night was advancing, the exiles were too much exhausted to keep pace with the escort.

They were therefore ordered to get into the waggons.

The horses were urged to greater speed, and the cavalcade blundered on through the scuds of wind and snow, and through the increasing gloom of the dreary evening.

As the night grew darker the perils that beset the travellers became greater; for heavy drifts of snow filled up the crevices and gaps in the wretched road, and in some places where the way wound through a wood or between steep banks, fairly blocked the passage. Several times there had been a halt when such an obstruction lay across the path.

The weary exiles were roused from their trance of exhaustion—for none of them could be said to sleep—by the curses and brutalities of their masters; men and women, old and young, were compelled to get out of the waggons to clear away the snow.

Then they were forced to walk, sometimes for miles, to lighten the waggons and to rest the quivering, steaming horses.

From time to time the howling of wolves fell on the startled ear hideously breaking the awful silence of the night.

The men and women were separated, but they mingled together when working to clear away the snow-drifts.

One of the officers of the troop was more humane than the rest, and as far as he dared, tried to relieve the hardships of his Polish prisoners.

Among the unfortunates were Edward and Katinka, who had been tried at Kowno, knouted and banished.

There had been some delay previous to the start of the cavalcade from the Polish city, and during this time Edward and the brave Polish girl had been kindly treated by the inn-keeper, in whose house they were quartered.

The sergeant to whom reference has been made was a cunning fellow.

He frowned as darkly and growled an oath as savagely as the most ruffianly of his comrades.

He even slashed his whip in a most ferocious manner, nevertheless, he took advantage of every occasion which offered of doing something to mitigate the miseries of the unhappy patriots.

He stood overlooking the men who were toiling at a block of snow frozen almost as hard as granite barring their path.

"Shall we reach the stage to-night?" asked Edward Leighton, in a tone of weakness and suffering.

He stood apart from the rest of his companions in misfortune, and was making a feeble attempt to strike a heavy pickaxe into the seemingly impenetrable mass.

"No," replied the officer, curtly, "but do not be discouraged, you will meet with better treatment at Tobolsk than you expect. You will have to work in the mines for some months, and then you will be set at liberty conditionally; and if you don't attempt to escape from your place of banishment, may live with some degree of comfort."

"But I have heard such terrible stories of the sufferings of the Siberian exiles."

"They are either false or greatly exaggerated. You will eat the bread of slavery for some months, and then, if you are wise enough to remain patient, you will be liberated from the chain."

Edward thanked the officer for his encouragement, and applied himself once more to work.

The soldier left his side.

Katinka stole up to him.

It was dark.

She was muffled in a coat of sheep-skin, and had drawn a furred hood over her head.

"Dear monsieur, my heart breaks to see you reduced to this condition," she whispered tenderly.

Edward had suffered so dreadfully from the effects of his wounds and his cruel ill-usage, that he was almost overpowered.

He could scarcely stand.

He supported himself against the bank, however, and smiled feebly.

"Dear, kind friend, you never think of yourself," he said.

"Indeed, but I do, monsieur. I wish we could make our escape."

"You have had more than once a chance of doing so, Katinka."

"If so, monsieur knows that I would not leave him who has defended me so gallantly, and whom I love as a brother," said the girl, simply.

"Every hour brings us nearer to misery and further from hope," said Edward.

"But, is there no chance of escape?"

"How is escape possible?"

"I have thought of a plan—a wild one, but it might succeed," said the girl.

"What is it?"

"You know that I nursed you, monsieur, while we were awaiting our removal from Kowno?"

"Yes, dear Katinka, with all the patience and tenderness of an angel."

"The doctor gave me a sleeping potion for you. I did not use it all."

"I begin to see the drift of your scheme."

"Yes, monsieur; we might drug the sentinels."

"I do not like the expedient."

"Well, monsieur, we cannot, in our position, afford to be too nice as to the means we use to make an escape."

"We are watched! Ah! Katinka, you have roused a wild hope in my heart, but one which, I fear, will only end in bitter disappointment," said Edward. "Oh! let us be resigned; and do not let us aggravate our miseries by any rash venture."

Katinka looked at him with tenderness and keen sympathy.

He appeared so wan and worn that she doubted much whether he would have sufficient energy to carry out the bold design she had formed for their escape.

She held out her hands.

He grasped them warmly.

"Do not sleep too deeply," said Katinka, with a meaning look.

One of the ruffianly escort now rushed up, and lashed the quailing girl with his heavy whip, and ordered her, in a hectoring tone, to return to the waggons.

Poor Katinka's cheek went deadly white, and she almost sank to the earth.

However, she meekly obeyed.

The soldier then turned fiercely upon Edward.

The youth looked so unearthly as he stood glaring upon the fellow, his pale face corpse-like in the ghastly light reflected from the snow, that the man started back.

Leighton passed him with a wild look.

His eyes flashed fire.

He breathed a bitter curse upon the savage Russian.

The man suffered him to pass without opposition.

He seemed to think it needless to quarrel with one so near his last hour, for the soldier fully believed that Leighton could not live through that bitter night.

Leighton walked back to the waggon.

He clambered in, and crouched among his fellow-miserables.

It was a wild and dreary scene.

The panting oxen which drew the wains buried almost to their breasts in snow; the fur-cloaked soldiers on their rugged horses; the huge dark, lumbering vehicles, the steep banks, and the black, waving pines.

Once more the waggons rumbled and jolted on their dreary road.

At last the snow ceased falling.

It was drawing near midnight.

Sleep to the tired exiles was rendered impossible by the violent shaking of the carriages.

At length the officers gave orders that the cavalcade should halt.

They bivouacked for the night.

The place they chose for the purpose was a narrow defile between some low hills, or rather mounds.

They were sheltered in some measure from the cutting wind by a wood and a high bank.

They lighted fires.

The men partook of some preserved meat, and a fiery stimulant called quass.

Some of the female exiles were allowed to prepare food for their friends and relatives.

Among the others was the Polish girl, Katinka.

We have described her as being pretty and lively, and though she had suffered so much, she still retained her courage, and assumed a vivacity which pleased those of the soldiers who were not quite brutalised.

The captain of the troop was seated on a barrel before the fire, smoking his pipe and humming a march.

He looked at the girl as she passed.

He held up his fur-gloved hand, and beckoned her to approach.

Katinka stepped smartly up, and saluted in military fashion.

"What is your name, girl?" asked the officer.

"Katinka; I am the daughter of Zaska, the Pole."

The officer laughed grimly.

"You have less cause to be proud of your parentage than of your personal charms," he said. "And how came you to be amongst these felons?"

"By the power of might over right I have been made to suffer innocently," replied the girl.

"Ah! then you were not taken in arms against the Government?—you were not in league with the rebels?"

"I am the daughter of a patriot, and have served my country. I was a sutler in the National army!"

"Well, you are a brave girl, too pretty, and too interesting to be a rebel," laughed the officer, "I will take care of you, Katinka; I must teach you more loyal sentiments."

Another officer now approached.

"This is a provoking misadventure," he said, "the clouds are rolling up westward, and we shall have a heavy fall of snow before morning."

"Meanwhile, comrade, let us make the best of our position. Where are you going, Katinka?"

The girl, who had turned away, paused and looked back.

"Stay, my good wench. Do you know this girl, Demetrius?"

"A Polish vivandiere, was she not?"

"Yes; an Amazon whom Count Brutoff captured."

"The girl who sings so well."

"Does she? I have a good thought; the jade shall be our vivandiere, our Hebe; her songs and jests shall cheer us on the march."

Katinka's eyes sparkled, and she showed her bright teeth in a pleasant smile.

"Let us have a song at once," said Demetrius.

"So we will, comrade, and as I have promised to reclaim this pretty wild bird she shall sing us the national anthem of Russia."

"But first let her fill, and drink health from her pretty lips."

The officers laughed, and a keg being brought Katinka slung it across her shoulder.

Opening the valve she secretly poured into it the strong sleeping potion she had in her possession.

The soldiers stood round the fire, and one by one she filled their cups, beginning with the captain, and serving the others in succession according to their rank.

She then filled her own glass.

Holding it aloft she sang in a bold and fine tone a stirring national air.

With beaming faces the soldiers joined in the war-like chorus.

She took good care not to drink, but quietly threw away the contents of her glass.

The song ended, the captain kissed her, and proclaimed her vivandiere of the regiment.

She was then allowed to return to the waggons.

Meanwhile Edward Leighton had taken care to place himself in such a position that he could creep out of the waggon, if summoned by Katinka, without disturbing his fellows.

He could not help feeling humiliated that the devoted girl should take the lead in this escapade.

He was, however, too weak and sick to undertake the responsibility of the attempt, and he knew that the chances would be more in the favour of a frail girl, who would not be suspected of having sufficient courage for such a bold stroke.

He lay shivering with cold and racked by pain.

An hour lagged by.

It was intensely cold.

The stars glittered brilliantly in the deep blue sky.

A light step fell on the silence of the night.

Edward raised himself cautiously.

Katinka stood beside the waggon.

"Come," she whispered; "it is done—they are asleep."

Edward crept softly from the waggon.

The soldiers were stretched around the fire, wrapped in their fur cloaks.

The sentinels stood leaning on their fire-locks.

They seemed oppressed with a drowsiness which half stupified them.

It was very dark.

"We shall be tracked by our footprints in the snow," whispered Edward.

"Courage, monsieur; I will show you how we can get such a start of them that our escape will be certain."

The girl walked softly behind the waggons, and then crept up the bank and entered the wood.

Edward Leighton followed her as quietly as possible.

The pines were closely clustered.

The girl passed between them.

They were issuing out from the wood at a point where the road curved.

Katinka stopped suddenly, and held up her hand.

"Hist!"

Edward drew back.

"Is it the picket?"

"Yes."

"Can we not elude his vigilance?"

"If we keep quiet it will be easy."

"How?"

"He is nodding to sleep."

"It is the cruel frost."

"And the sleeping draught I gave him," returned the vivandiere, smiling.

They peeped over the bank.

The sentinel sat on a rock below them.

He was leaning on his musket, his brow resting on his hands.

Presently he started.

He drowsily opened his eyes.

He looked curiously around.

The fugitives kept breathless silence.

Convinced, as it seemed, that no one was near, the weary soldier threw himself against the bank, his musket lying at his side.

Katinka again beckoned to Edward.

Together they stole down the road.

They stood looking at the sleeping man.

His slumber seemed profound.

Katinka bent over him.

She gently lifted the musket.

She passed it to Leighton.

Then quietly she turned and walked through the deep snow towards a dark mass that was sheltered in a hollow of the opposite bank.

It was a sledge.

A horse was tethered to a tree near at hand.

"It is the Captain's sledge," said Katinka; "it was left here when the waggons were driven into the defile."

"Can anything be more fortunate, dear Katinka? I feel my strength renewed at this sight. Ah! I am not half myself or you should not have been the chief actor in this adventure."

"Monsieur is ill and weak; if we can escape to some cottage we may find shelter and protection; and if there is another fall of snow before the morning, our trail will be covered, and it will not be easy to follow us."

Edward brought the horse from the tree.

He harnessed it to the sledge.

Within the sledge they found numerous treasures; a valise containing money and clothes, six pistols, and side arms, besides a box of preserved meat and another of biscuits, with several flasks of spirits.

Edward Leighton left the valise on the bank.

Katinka tried to persuade him to keep it.

"It was only spoil taken from the enemy," she said, "and all was fair in war."

But Edward would not do violence to his scruples of honour, and retained only the arms and provisions which could not be dispensed with.

Edward lifted his fair companion into the sledge, and wrapped the bearskin rugs around her.

He seated himself by her side.

He whipped the horse.

It was a fine creature, glossy black, and thoroughbred, with a broad deep chest, fiery eye, and thin nostril; its action was superb, and it seemed to be very powerful.

Away they dashed.

The horse tossed his head and neighed shrilly.

The sentinel was roused.

He leaped to his feet.

He looked about him in stupid bewilderment.

He stumbled about like a drunken man; he searched for his fire-lock.

It had been stolen.

Shaking his fist at the fast retreating fugitives, he leaped up the bank.

He rushed wildly to the bivouac, his heart shuddering with terror.

Not a little to his delight, he found officers and soldiers all deep in slumber.

He awakened them.

With a cry of alarm they started up.

They rushed to the trees where they had tethered their horses.

Katinka had cut the thongs, and the animals had scattered far and wide through the pine wood!

CHAPTER CCXII.

STILL IN FLIGHT—THE STEPPES—THE PINE-FOREST—A STRANGE LEGEND—PURSUED BY WOLVES—TRUE AND THRILLING WOLF STORY.

AWAY flew the sliding car over the frozen ground, scattering the snow-like spray on either hand.

Onward and still onward it swayed and rattled.

The dark pine forests shot past, and the white plains flew away beneath the swift-beating hoofs of the bounding steed.

The keen, rushing wind brought the glow upon Edward's pale cheeks.

Katinka laughed in the exhilaration of spirits caused by the rapid motion.

The horse's bells jangled and he snorted and tossed his trailing mane.

Greyly and wildly the morning rose in the east.

Clouds still piled up from the horizon, leaden-hued and boding a snow storm.

The fugitives turned many a glance behind them.

They were not pursued.

The Russian soldiers had been forced to chase their horses through the woods for several hours before they could catch them.

Too much time had been lost, and it was now impossible to overtake the escaped prisoners.

Still the fugitives dashed on, Katinka narrating gleefully the manner in which she had tricked the captain and his troop.

They rested for some time in a pine-forest.

It was about noon.

They dined upon the biscuit and preserved meat with great zest and contentment.

The sun was shining with some degree of cheerfulness.

The snow was melting on the branches of the firs and trickling down in rippling streams.

As they sat contemplating the peculiar beauty of the sun-prismed icicles that hung in quaint festoons from the branches of the trees they heard a strange wailing sound.

The woods are ever filled with strange and unaccountable noises.

Perhaps the cry was that of some animal borne from afar on the frosty air or the rustle of the wind through some hollow tree.

Katinka seemed frightened.

She listened with an air of dread and clasped her hands.

"It is a wood spirit," she said in tones of unaffected awe; "he gives us warning of some impending danger."

"Can you believe in the existence of such beings?"

"Why not? The world is full of wonders, and wise men have averred that they have seen these spirits. Do you know what befell my own father?"

"Let me hear the story."

"Well, monsieur, my father, who, as you know, was a leader of insurgents, had been routed by the Russians in a fight near Wilna; he fled alone through the forests for two days. At last he came to the banks of a stream, where he found a ruined hut; as he was very tired, and the sky threatened a violent storm of hail and thunder, he took refuge in the deserted cabin."

Katinka paused in her story.

Again the strange sound was heard.

"Ah, monsieur, let us begone," she said, rising.

Leighton seemed puzzled to account for the strange noise.

"It sounds like the far distant baying of wolves or wild dogs," he said.

"Ah no, monsieur, it is the spirit of the woods warning us of coming danger."

"Well, we will not linger long," replied Leighton; "but finish your story, dear Katinka."

"It is soon told. My father sat sheltered in the hut, when the sky became darkened, the thunder roared, and the lightning fiercely flashed; then came the dashing hail, tearing down from the thunder-clouds, and ripping up the flooded ground around the hut, and lashing the river into a current of foam. My father sat waiting for the storm to subside. When the tempest was near its height, he heard a shriek from some bushes by the river. At first, like yourself, monsieur, he was inclined to ascribe the warning sound to some natural cause, as the howling of the wind or of the wolves. He disregarded the omen. The thunderstorm grew more and more dreadful. Again my father heard that wild and piteous shriek; this time he thought it must be the cry of some human being in distress. He rose, and rushed through the drenching showers; he reached the bushes; he called aloud, but received no answer. He ran along the river side, and looked out upon its storm-riven breast; he could see no one. Then came the blinding glare and arrowy dart of forked lightning, followed by the appalling crash of the awful thunder. He fled back to the hut for shelter. It stood a blackened ruin! It had been struck by the lightning, and, but for the luring cry of the good spirit, my father would have been killed!"

"The good spirit was the All-Merciful who, by small means, so often works great deliverance, both to nations and to individuals," said Leighton, reverently. "You must not ascribe this noise your father heard to any other supernatural cause, but must think of it as providential accident."

"Monsieur is wiser than I, but those who live in great cities do not know the secrets of nature," returned the girl, simply.

Leighton smiled.

He could have told her of scenes of wild grandeur, of vast prairies, of lakes and forests in his own far West that dwarfed even the mighty woods, lakes, and steppes of the great desert land through which they were travelling.

"At all events, dear Katinka, we will not neglect this warning, nor yonder surer portent," he said, pointing to the dark snow-laden clouds rising behind them. "Let us get into the sledge and drive on to Tobolsk, as you proposed, for I heard one of the soldiers say that the great annual fair is held in that city about this time."

"Yes, monsieur, and on our way we shall pass through some villages where we can obtain a change of clothes, and we shall be safer in disguise."

"It is a good plan, dear Katinka. Thanks to the good souls in whose house we were quartered before our removal from Kowno, I have been able to keep the sum of money the Princess Aronzow gave me."

"Ah, the poor princess, she is in the same case as ourselves."

"Oh that I had a thousand lives, and could suffer a thousand cruel deaths to save her!" cried Leighton, with great fervour.

Katinka blushed and lowered her eyes, then her cheek paled, and she pressed her hand to her side and said, with a gasp,

"Monsieur has a warm heart; with all her faults the princess is generous, noble, and beautiful."

Edward did not reply to this remark, but cast an affectionate look upon his companion.

Rather faithlessly he pressed her hand and murmured,

"Katinka has all these good qualities without the faults which in her excellency's disposition accompany them; nevertheless the princess is a noble lady, has devoted herself for us, and we owe her more than we can ever repay."

"True, monsieur, and we are neither of us ungrateful," said Katinka.

They were once more whirled along over the dazzling waste of snow.

The sky grew dark with heavy clouds, and the snow began to descend in heavy flakes.

Leighton drew the fur mantle closer round his fair companion.

They did not converse much; the storm was blinding.

Their breath congealed on their lips.

The horse began to show signs of fatigue.

Much against his will, Leighton urged the poor animal to increase his speed.

It was late in the afternoon.

They were galloping over a wide frozen plain.

Far on their right stretched another of the apparently interminable line of pine forests.

Suddenly the horse stopped.

He stretched out his fore legs and tossed back his head.

He pricked up his ears and quivered with terror.

"Hush!" said Katinka, laying her hand on Leighton's.

Far over the snowy plain, far from the interior of the pine wood was wafted a stithy sound.

Pit-pat; pit-pat.

"Wolves!" cried Katinka, wildly. "There is a whole pack of them. Hark how the underwood crackles before them!"

"Courage, we have arms!"

"Ah, monsieur, they will not avail us much, the savage creatures hunt in immense taboons, sometimes by hundreds."

"We are more exposed to their attack on the open plain than we should be if we could reach the forest."

"It is our only hope!" cried the girl, wringing her hands.

Leighton shook the reins and cheered the frightened horse by a shout of encouragement.

He dashed off at terrific speed.

Katinka busied herself in extracting a rifle and the pistol-case from the back part of the sledge.

She loaded them and passed them to Leighton, who had enough to do to manage the horse, which appeared to be frantic with terror.

They reached the wood.

They were soon dashing through winding glades along a narrow bridle path at imminent risk of being dashed against the rock or banks.

A hideous howl rose behind them.

Still the untiring pit-pat was heard.

Nearer and nearer.

"You will load while I fire," said Leighton, leaping up in the sledge.

"Yes, monsieur; I am not afraid," replied the girl, bravely.

Again there arose that dismal yell.

Then, like a galaxy of stars, appeared the green-flashing, oblique eyes of innumerable wolves among the trees and bushes, and down the narrow path.

One by one, snapping and snorting, they leaped from the bank, and flew upon the sledge.

Leighton took steady aim at a monstrous fellow, who appeared to be the leader of the pack.

With a fearful howl he snapped at the wound.

He leaped round and round.

He fell over on his side.

His tongue protruded from between his white, fell fangs.

In an instant a dozen of his ravenous fellows had his body, and were rending it to pieces.

The rest rushed upon the traveller.

Leighton cheered the horse, and clubbing his musket knocked one of the ferocious beasts off the poor animal's haunches.

The horse's flanks were covered with blood.

He then fired both pistols at the savage creatures.

Those who were killed or wounded were immediately torn to pieces by the rest.

A terrific battle ensued after each shot that was fired.

The brutes were driven back by the blaze of the gun, and the loud bellowing reports which reverberated through the dark woods.

The ammunition began to fail.

Hope waned.

All at once, for some inexplicable cause, the wolves paused, and, setting up a terrific howl, fled.

It might be that they were attracted by the scent of some easier prey.

Exhausted by excitement and fatigue Leighton and the Polish girl were ready to expire with joy when, emerging from the forest, they found themselves drawing to a little homestead, through the windows of which shone the lurid, cheerful light of the stoves and lamps within, and the sound of merry voices fell like heavenly music on their ears, which were still singing with the hideous howling of the wolves.

An old man and woman ran out to meet them.

The next moment they were surrounded by rough but kindly faces, and were borne gently into a large and warm apartment.

Perhaps some account of the nature and habits of wolves, drawn from an authentic source, may be interesting to our youthful readers.

Wolves are still found in many countries of Europe.

What renders them so terrible a foe to both men and cattle is their insatiate appetite for blood, and the extreme delicacy of scent which enables them to track their victims with unerring accuracy.

The wolf is a beast of great ferocity of appearance, and of immense muscular power, with fiery eyes, a large mouth, and jaws and teeth of prodigious strength.

He usually measures about three feet in length, and two feet and a half in height.

The aversion of the wolf to vegetable food (except grapes, which he will gorge until he becomes intoxicated, in the hot summer months), and the ingenuity and perseverance of his pursuit after flesh, render him the inveterate enemy of the traveller and farmer in neighbourhoods infested with his presence, whilst his boldness and ferocity make him a favourite object of pursuit with the more adventurous and daring class of sportsmen.

His character altogether excludes him from our sympathy.

Terrible as are the ravages of the huge lions against whom Jules Gerard declared war in the forests of Africa, there is withal a dignity, and, under many circumstances, a magnanimity, about these kingly beasts, that elicits our respect.

They appear to belong to a class of nobles in the brute creation.

But the wolf is a dastard.

He steals upon his unwary victim with the cunning of the serpent.

If the opportunity lies in his way, he will rather carry off the infant from his cradle than attack the strong man, or the cattle whom Nature has furnished with the means of defence.

Where wolves are numerous, as in the forests of Burgundy, plans for destroying them are projected on a very extensive scale.

At fixed seasons of the year large parties of huntsmen assemble, pits are dug, traps set, and poison laid near their haunts.

But in addition to this wholesale slaughter, in which the farmers and peasants seek by every means in their power to exterminate the common enemy, the wolf is hunted with dogs by parties of gentlemen, chiefly for the sport itself.

The dogs generally made use of for this purpose are large greyhounds and bloodhounds.

The former worry the brute by flying at his haunches, and so impede his flight till the bloodhound comes up and brings him to bay, when he contends with great obstinacy for his life, biting with his tremendous fangs every assailant that comes within reach, and continuing to sustain the struggle at great odds for a length of time that sufficiently attests his muscular vigour and astonishing powers of endurance.

He is generally despatched by a pistol-shot from the huntsman.

Another mode of carrying on warfare against these beasts is for a party to lie in wait along their accustomed track, armed with fowling-pieces, whilst others hunt them out from their lair.

The sportsman loves the excitement of the chase, but, as we have said, the husbandman and peasant—who are kept in constant terror, and obliged to fortify their homes against the midnight depredations of the wolf with as much care, and to watch with as constant a vigilance as a besieged city against the enemy that beleaguers it—care for little but the brute's destruction, and will adopt any and every means to secure his wholesale slaughter.

A farmer of La Madeleine, on the borders of Burgundy, who was surrounded in all directions by wolves, chancing to have a young colt die, thought it a good opportunity to lay a bait for some of his savage enemies, and accordingly, at nightfall, placed it on a truss of straw in the midst of his farm-yard, surrounded on all sides by high walls.

To the folding-gates which led into the yard he had attached ropes, communicating with the interior of the house.

Having muzzled the dogs, to prevent their barking, the farmer and his family took up their post of observation within doors, to watch the events of the night.

It was not long before they heard the sound of wolves advancing, and could presently perceive them, by the light of the moon, sniffing the air at the entrance of the yard.

They were evidently attracted powerfully by the tempting aroma of horse-flesh on the one hand, and apprehensive of some peril to themselves on the other, they entered in.

They moved about restlessly.

Now apparently yielding to the power of appetite, and then again stopped by fear.

At last one great monster, whose hunger was keener, or whose courage greater than that of the rest, bounded onward, seized a portion of the prey, and quickly made his retreat, with the piece of flesh in his mouth.

Emboldened by his impunity, the rest of the pack entered, and greedily seized upon the carrion (which, it must be mentioned, the farmer had heavily weighted, to prevent its being carried away.)

As soon as they had fairly commenced their feast the signal was given, the ropes drawn, the gates suddenly closed, and the wolves, eight in number, found themselves captives.

They were encompassed by walls too lofty for them to leap, and without a hole through which they could find an exit.

Walls, in fact, built for the express purpose of serving as a barrier against their incursions, and, therefore, equally capable of serving as their prison.

Seeing their foes thus secured, the party in the house retired for the night, deferring further operations till morning.

At break of day, they looked upon the scene.

Their captives were restless and uneasy.

Their sagacity told them that they had been trapped.

They were running round and round like rats in a cage, perpetually searching for some mode of escape.

The farmer and his men took their fire arms, and stationed themselves some on the top of the wall, and others at windows, and opened their fire.

They succeeded but slowly in their work of destruction.

The wolf is tenacious of life.

The men were indifferent marksmen, and the difficulty of hitting the creatures was rendered greater by their incessant motion.

Irritated by such wounds as they received, they ran hither and thither with mad impetuosity.

They bounded with immense agility in their efforts either to get at their assailants, or to overleap the walls by which they were imprisoned.

At length, one of the party, a mere youth, in order to take steadier aim, bestrode the top of the wall, his feet hanging down on either side.

A large and powerful wolf, making a desperate spring, brought his jaws fearfully near the young man's foot.

Attempting, hurriedly, to lift his leg out of danger, he lost his balance, and fell headlong into the courtyard beneath.

The wolves were immediately upon him, eager to avenge the act by which they were ensnared, and the wounds from which they were smarting.

For a moment, consternation seized the companions of the poor lad.

The fearful shriek he uttered as he fell, and the sight of the wolves fastening on his throat paralysed them.

Their first instinct was to cease firing, for they saw that their bullets might hit the young man.

The farmer was the first to recover his presence of mind.

With gallant self-devotion, he leaped into the yard to the rescue, and found himself in the midst of eight furious wolves.

His example was followed by the rest of the party. A terrific conflict ensued.

Each side fought with the energy of desperation. The victim whose mischance had brought about this terrible scene lay bleeding and groaning in the midst.

Man's strength, unaided by arms, is of little avail against monsters so powerful.

The wolves were rapidly getting the upper hand of their enfeebled combatants.

The farmer's wife, who was a terrified witness of the scene, remembered the dogs that were muzzled and shut up in the house.

She immediately unbound their mouths and threw them from a window into the yard.

This incident changed the fortune of the day.

The struggle was sustained with renewed vigour, and, at the end of half-an-hour, the eight wolves lay dead upon the ground.

One half of the dogs of the farm lay at their side.

The lad who had fallen from the wall, too, was a mangled corpse, and not a man had escaped without serious wounds.

Numerous are the tragedies of this nature recounted by the fire-sides of Burgundy, where the presence of these fierce creatures, in numbers scarcely diminished by all the efforts annually made to extirpate them, occasions a constant feeling of terror.

LEIGHTON AND HIS COMPANIONS ATTACKED BY WOLVES.

CHAPTER CCXIII.

THE NOBLE EXILE—AN HOSPITABLE RECEP-
TION—TOBOLSK—THE FAIR—THE CAVALCADE
—THE PRISON—THE YOUNG MOUJIK—LEIGH-
TON RECOGNISES THE PRINCESS.

EDWARD LEIGHTON and Katinka found themselves
comfortably couched upon piles of skins in the genial
glow of the square stove, built of bricks, which stood
in the centre of the apartment.

The master of the house, who was a charcoal
burner and wood-cutter working in the neighbouring
forests, treated his guests with the most cordial hospitality.

It was not till after they had partaken of some
food that the old man questioned them.

No. 64.

They answered evasively.

They said they were travelling to Tobolsk but did
not mention from what place they had come.

The old man looked at them sorrowfully and shook
his head.

"My honoured guests," he said, with a benevolent
smile, "it is useless to attempt to deceive me."

"You are, I am sure, too kind to betray us," said
Leighton, eagerly.

"God forbid!" cried the old man, "you are right
welcome; but you must not leave us in your present
guise, you must not use the sledge which brought you
hither, or you will be betrayed at once and arrested,
for I know you are Polish exiles."

"I will throw myself upon your mercy, and for
the sake of my dear companion, will implore your

protection," said Leighton ; " I have money and will pay you liberally for your good services."

" I am not offended with your proffer, young gentleman, for I see by your frank face that you do not lack that humanity you give others so little credit for possessing, but I refuse your offer because I am sufficiently rewarded in being able to serve you."

Leighton was struck by the refinement of this old peasant.

He was a very handsome, hale old man, with an eagle eye and fine features ; though his hair was snowy white, his form was erect, his eyes clear, and his voice firm.

He now inquired by what means the young couple had escaped from the Russians.

They told him how they had effected their escape, and how they had been pursued by the wolves through the forest.

For several hours the old man entertained them with old-world stories.

They were astonished at the extent of his information, and listened with the greatest interest to his conversation.

" It is possible," he said, at length, " that you are wondering that I, who have travelled so much, who has seen so much of men and manners, could be found sequestered in this dreary spot. I am Count Menkoff!"

" Your name is hallowed among the Polish patriots," cried Leighton, warmly. " Often I have heard you spoken of as the noblest and most liberal of men. It was you who advocated so strongly the emancipation of the serfs and the liberation of Poland."

" For which capital offences I was banished to Siberia," returned the old man, with a smile.

He drew a lovely girl of ten years to his side, and smoothed her golden hair.

A handsome but rather hirsute man and a gentle and graceful woman watched the patriarch.

The child looked on with a tender solicitude.

" Yes," said the count, " Menkoff, the charcoal-burner, is happier in this hut, than he was when he dwelt in his palace at Moscow. Considering we are exiles, Teckla, we are not so very wretched, are we ?"

" No, grandfather, I am sure we are very happy, especially at fair time," said the girl, as she laid her finger as if unconsciously upon the little silver brooch on her breast.

A shade swept over, and then a quaint smile lit upon the reverend face of the aged man, as he said,

" I feel it for their sakes, sometimes. Men were not born for solitude, and even the home circle is not wide enough for the young, to whom change and amusement are essential ; but Teckla is a good child, and I think I shall send her to St. Petersburgh."

" You will not make her go, grandfather, she will always, always stay with you," replied the child, throwing her arms round the old man's neck, and kissing his cheek.

The old man answered pleasantly, and then took the hand of the kind-looking old dame, who sat by his side.

" I have the honour, Mr. Leighton," he said, " to introduce you to her Excellency the Countess Menkoff."

The aged and homely-looking woman drew herself up just a little stiffly, and bowed with an air of conscious dignity.

Leighton returned the salute with as much reverence as if she had been the czarina of all the Russians.

The evening passed very pleasantly, and the weary fugitives slept deeply.

They rose early.

After resting several days they resolved upon setting out on their journey.

The old man dressed them in suitable fashion as peasants, for the clothes they had worn were those in which the Russian government attires the criminals who are banished to Siberia.

The old man took care to burn the tell-tale garments ; he also broke up the sledge and buried it.

He lent them another with which to travel to Tobolsk.

He then offered them some articles, such as platters in carved wood, and pieces of warm cloth to sell at the fair.

He exhorted them to mingle with the poorer class, and to pretend that they had travelled to Tobolsk to sell their wares at the market.

Leighton insisted upon paying for these articles.

The old man consented at last to receive a fair price for them, but he would not accept a rouble for aught else.

Edward and Katinka left the happy home of the banished count with many expressions of regret, and with the most heartfelt thanks for his kindness.

It was a bright and bracing day when they started on their journey.

What perils, what labours were before them !

But Edward and Katinka felt no care, no apprehensions ; their happy escape, the count's hopeful predictions cheered them, and the rest they had enjoyed sufficiently recovered their strength to enable them to face their future with boldness and confidence.

They reached Tobolsk.

We will give the reader some description of this strange and wretched city as it appeared to a distinguished traveller.

The streets of Tobolsk are paved, or rather planked, with timber.

This pavement is far cleaner and much more agreeable than pebbles.

The market place is very spacious.

It is here the annual fair is held.

In this market, besides provisions and articles of the first necessity, large quantities of Chinese and European goods are exposed for sale.

Fish of all kinds are in great abundance here.

But the place in some respects is squalid and filthy beyond description. In the neighbourhood of the town, the peasants are too indolent to cleanse their cow-houses and stables, and it is a fact that they are frequently obliged to pull down their houses and take the materials to another place, where they erect them again, it being considered a task much less difficult to rebuild their houses than remove the enormous dunghills, which, in time, accumulate about them.

In tl is miserable place, Edward and Katinka remained for nearly a week.

They escaped scrutiny.

They sold their wares to advantage.

At night they were obliged to put up with the most wretched accommodation, and to herd with the roughest and vilest of characters.

After a few days they obtained a sledge, and started on their homeward journey.

They drove to a village at the distance of some leagues from Tobolsk.

In the centre of this little hamlet was a large building, which seemed to have been formerly the palace or castle of one of the nobles.

It was occupied by a garrison of soldiers. The guard was drawn up on the lawn before this fortress.

The two-necked Eagle of Russia soared in his white field above the roof of the castle.

Along the sides of the road were stretched a long line of the peasants belonging to the village, who had assembled to see the cavalcade which was conducting exiles from Southern Russia to the inclement region to which they were banished.

Edward had left Katinka at the inn, while he wandered out to gain information as to the state of the roads, and to take a survey of the scenes around him.

He addressed one of the bystanders, a handsome, but simple-looking young fellow.

"I am a stranger from Kungan. What is the cause of this gathering of people?"

"Don't you know that this is the last great stage on the road to the mines?" returned the man with a smile. "We are waiting to see the exiles brought in."

"Is there a large batch of them?"

"Yes. Our father, the Czar, has many troublesome children," replied the man, "though these are chiefly Polish rebels."

"The rebellion will soon be repressed?"

"Yes; the wretched dogs will find it no use to gnaw their chains while the good master stands by with the scourge in his hand," laughed the young man; "but you speak with a strange accent."

"My father is a foreigner," returned Leighton.

"That is evident."

"I trade in furs for the European markets."

"Well, the winter has been bad for the hunters."

"It has, indeed."

A gun was fired from the tower.

There was a stir among the crowd.

"They are coming," said the peasant.

Edward looked down the road.

A troop of ill-mounted, but well-armed soldiers were riding in advance.

Behind them came a long train of waggons drawn by oxen.

On either side of these rode the mounted guard.

In the rear was another troop of soldiers, with their officers.

"The poor wretches seem to have little chance of escape," Edward remarked.

"And yet they get off sometimes."

"Is it possible?"

"Yes; witness this last astounding affair—but, there, the English are devils, and there is no accounting for their mad actions."

"What affair do you allude to?"

"Why, you must have heard of the escape of the Englishman and the Polish girl from the escort."

"I have heard some mention of it."

"It is wonderful! But the fiend had a hand in it, you may depend. The Polish jade is a witch; she conjured the guard to sleep, and even made them drink with her."

"What, in their sleep?"

"No, but under the spell of her evil eye. They carried off the captain's sledge, though I fancy that was more out of malice against him than for their own benefit."

"How so? how could they travel without a sledge?"

"Ha! how can witches fly without wings? A broomstick is not hard to be got, and those long streaks of black cloud that you so often see driving along before a storm, they are sometimes full of witches and their accursed familiars."

Leighton reflected that he and Katinka would have been in evil case if they had had no better conveyance than a black cloud or a broomstick to assist them in their wild flight from the wolves.

However, he made no remark.

The peasant with whom he had entered into conversation, seemed a talkative fellow.

"Come, friend," he said, "let us clamber on to the top of this wall, so that we can overlook the waggons and see the prisoners."

Leighton made no objection.

The two men got on to a long low wall, which ran for some distance along the top of the bank.

From this commanding position they could obtain a very good view of the procession, which was now at hand.

The peasants preserved deep silence as the cavalcade clattered past.

It was terrible to see the ferocious-looking guard, with their fur busbies and long, bright-tipped lances, and two of them with a heavy whip hanging from their saddles.

"I understand we have some illustrious emigrants among them," said the peasant, rubbing his hands and chuckling, in a gleeful whisper.

"Do you know their names?"

"Not yet; but I can learn them, friend. I am acquainted with the head warder of the dungeons, or rather, between ourselves, his daughter is in love with me."

The young fellow smoothed his moustache, and smiled with an air of self-esteem, and added,

"If I have luck this winter, I shall be able to manage this little affair. But look, here come the last of the waggons, and in them are always to be seen the most distinguished of the exiles. Look out for the old man and the girl."

"Who are they?"

"A prince and princess, I am told. Ah! there

they are. Fie! what a shame! such reverend grey hairs, and such a noble face. And pray observe the lovely girl. Well, it is odd that traitors look so much like other people!"

Leighton turned his head aside to conceal his emotion.

Before him, borne passively along, was the object of his romantic devotion—the wild, ill-disciplined, but beautiful and generous Princess Aronzow.

She was attired in a loose blue dress, of coarse material, bound around her delicate waist with a leathern girdle.

Her soft cheek, which once glowed with the rich flush of health, was now paler than marble; she pillowed it languidly upon her left hand.

She gazed dreamily upon the crowd, as if her thoughts were far away, as if she looked upon all objects, animate or inanimate, as so many figures on a painted panorama.

Her father was reading.

The prince was allowed the privilege of thus diverting his thoughts.

Edward Leighton could scarce repress a groan of agony when he beheld his generous benefactors brought to this dreadful strait through their humanity to him.

At the same moment he thought of Katinka.

He was almost stung to madness by reflecting upon the misery and suffering he had innocently caused to others.

Slipping from the wall, he advanced to the front of the line of peasants.

He gave a look of yearning adoration and ineffable sympathy at the princess.

Her eyes met his.

In an instant her trance was broken.

She glared upon him with a wild look.

She feebly extended her arms, at the same time uttering a faint shriek.

It was only by the exertion of his utmost power of self-controul that Leighton could restrain himself from dashing through the crowd of peasants and soldiers and throwing himself at her feet.

Once more he looked towards her.

Now her head was pillowed on her father's breast.

The old man held her hand, and soothed her grief with tender words.

The princess wept silently.

It did not seem that she had really recognised Edward Leighton.

She had been struck by the resemblance the pretended peasant bore to him; but did not think that it was Edward himself who had looked at her so earnestly.

The train of waggons stopped before the portals of the fortress.

One by one the unfortunate exiles descended from the waggons.

Many of them were heavily ironed.

They were marched into the fort.

Last of all, the prince and princess were conducted into the prison.

As the lovely girl, leaning on her father's arm,

passed under the dark archway, the bystanders uttered a faint and timid murmur of compassion.

A mounted officer frowned darkly, and waved them back.

Several of the ruffianly troopers took the hint.

They rode among the people, and lashed them with their heavy whips.

The crowd neither offered resistance nor remonstrance, but dispersed, running off like a bevy of frightened children.

Edward Leighton returned to the young peasant.

"Ah, friend, what bad hearts we have, even the best of us," said the youth, with a sigh.

"What do you mean?" asked Edward.

"To tell you the truth, for you look like an honest fellow one may trust, I feel quite sorry for that old rebel and his daughter. I know it's bad of me, but I can't help it."

The tears stood in the mild blue eyes of the simple youth as he spoke.

"It is a feeling that does you credit."

"Oh, no. A good subject will always hate the enemies of his sovereign; but farewell friend, I wish you success in trade."

"Stay, you have been kind in giving me, a stranger, so much information, you must not refuse to drink a glass with me at the inn where I am lodging, before we part."

"Well friend, he's a fool who refuses a good offer, I will drink a glass with you, but first I must have just one peep at my pretty sweetheart, she will give me a smile through the bars of her cage, and that must last me for a week. Heigho! Her father is such a hard-fisted old miser that he will not hear of our marriage, unless I can afford to buy a piece of land, or a drove of rein-deer. Well, we must hope and have patience."

They now stood at the back of the fortress.

A pretty, confiding child-like face peered between the bars of a window.

"There she is; that is my Lisa," cried the youth, joyously.

He threw her a volley of frantic kisses.

Her little fingers also went often to her rosy lips, and she waved her hands and her kerchief.

After a few moments had passed in this pleasant pantomime, the youth turned sadly away.

He walked by the side of Edward Leighton, preserving unusual silence.

"Why are you so quiet, my friend?" asked Edward with a smile.

"Because, when my heart is sad," returned the youth, simply, "my tongue is silent."

"But that's not very often."

"No," replied the youth, bursting into a laugh; "they call me Michael the chatterer, but any fool can keep silence."

"I am not of that opinion, friend; but tell me what would you do to gain possession of your pretty sweetheart?"

"Do? I'd jump down a bear's throat and tear his heart out!"

"Then you would be willing to face any danger for the reward of her hand?"

"I'd kiss a Lapland witch, or go to bed with a vampire!"

"Well, come with me to the inn and I think I can put you in the way of something which will enable you to win your bride; but I must tell you it is a hazardous expedient."

"I am prepared to do anything to gain such a prize, so let us have no more words about it till we reach the inn where we can talk the matter over in security."

The young peasant assented to this arrangement, and they proceeded at once to the house, or rather hovel, where Katinka impatiently awaited the return of Edward Leighton.

The girl blushed deeply when Edward introduced her as his wife to the young peasant.

"And now, my dear Katinka," he said, "I have some business to settle with this gentleman; we will retire to the little room beyond, and you must take care to give us notice of the approach of strangers, for we must have no listeners."

Katinka looked surprised, but expressed her willing obedience.

Edward Leighton took a bottle and glasses and led the way into the adjoining room.

The young peasant followed him.

Katinka seated herself at the table, and looked towards the door of the little room with a glance of dismay, for she was convinced by their serious faces that the men were met on business of deep importance.

CHAPTER CCXIV.

THE INN AT TOBOLSK—KATINKA'S ANXIETY —RETURN OF LEIGHTON WITH A STRANGER —THE VIVANDIERE OVERHEARS THE PLOT TO SAVE THE PRINCESS — TERROR AND DESPAIR—A BRAVE RESOLVE.

KATINKA sat long and expectantly.

From time to time she cast a wistful look at the door of the little room where Leighton and the young Russian were consulting.

Her heart beat with excitement and suspense.

She could no longer restrain her anxiety.

She rose and crept to the door.

She crouched down and placed her ear to the keyhole.

The men were conversing in a low tone, but she could distinctly hear what they said.

"And I have little doubt, Michael, that the prince himself will find means of rewarding you."

"But yourself, monsieur, you will be seized and shot."

"I care nothing for myself, there will be a chance for me to escape. I will put on double clothing; the princess can wrap herself in my choubi; with the assistance of your sweetheart the thing will be quite easy."

"The princess!" gasped Katinka. "Yes, it must be the Princess Aronzow!"

"Well, monsieur, the scheme is most desperate, and I fear that Lisa will get into trouble."

"I will take care for that; I will say that I found some means of gaining admission without her aid."

"It shall be done, monsieur; I will undertake it. If you could obtain a pass from the governor of Tobolsk to visit the prisoners it would be better; but I cannot bear the thought of suffering you to throw away your life so rashly."

"I am an Englishman; and even if I am taken they will not dare to kill me."

"Do not be too sure of that; remember where you are, in Siberia."

"Well, I shall not be taken then. If she can but escape I will find some way of getting out of bondage; if not I am content to die if only I can make this attempt for her deliverance."

"But she will not leave her father."

"We can save him too."

"But how?"

"I will take arms with me, and we can overawe the gaoler, perhaps."

"But you will be searched."

"Not if your sweetheart admits me secretly."

"I'll tell you how it may be managed. Lisa sometimes leaves the castle by a little postern gate, when she goes to the market at Tobolsk. She is a great favourite with all the men of the garrison, and one of the guard is her cousin, a loutish fellow and my rival in love; she can coax him to admit you in the disguise of a priest, for there are always some of the meddlesome shavelings applying for admission to the prisoners. While you are gone into the fortress she can hold him in conversation. The princess must wrap your priest's robe about her, and the prince can put on a suit of clothes belonging to Lisa's father; and as he is an old man, white-haired, and about the same height as the gaoler, he will pass muster in the darkness. You must remain in the cell till Lisa returns, when she can get you off by some strategy, and by breaking the bars of the window and disordering the furniture in the cell, you can make it appear that an escape has been made from the window; but before we can mature this plan I must have a talk with Lisa."

"But you cannot obtain sight of her."

"If you will give me sufficient money to buy a flask of spirits, I can bribe the gate-keeper. I am well known and have managed to get into the fortress pretty often by bribing the porter."

"Go at once, then, my good fellow. Be assured if you can save the prince and his daughter you will be well rewarded. His excellency has wealth invested in English banks, of which the Russian government have not been able to deprive him."

"Rely upon my devotion, monsieur," said the young peasant. "I am a serf myself, and I cannot help feeling pity for the noble prince who has suffered so much for the good of my oppressed class, though I dare not openly confess so much."

"Fortune favours the bold, my good Michael, and

ly this daring action you will deserve her best favours."

Hearing the footsteps of the men approaching the door, Katinka darted back to the table.

She snatched up some work, and pretended to be sewing.

Her cheek was deathly pale, and her fingers trembled violently.

Leighton, however, did not observe her emotion.

He crossed the room with the young peasant, still absorbed in conversation.

He affected to be inquiring the prices in the market, and of the best route for travelling to St. Petersburgh.

The youth bowed to Katinka, and with Edward Leighton left the room.

When they were gone the Polish girl rose and paced the room in an agony of deadly terror.

She thought not of herself; all her fears were for the safety of him whom, in her simplicity, she loved with such fervent devotion.

Time passed.

Her anxiety became distracting.

At last she heard the well-known step to which her heart ever leaped so joyously.

Edward Leighton entered the room.

He threw himself in a chair.

His pale, haggard brow was wrinkled with care.

Katinka threw herself by his side, and burst into tears.

"Oh, monsieur," she sobbed, bitterly, "tell me, tell me, what have I done to deserve this?"

"My dear Katinka, what is it? You amaze me!" stammered Leighton.

"Can you not trust me? Ah, monsieur, I know I am a woman, but courage is not wanting to my sex. I think I have acted so far bravely, why, why then could you not trust me?"

Leighton started up.

"Katinka, you have overheard my conversation with the young moujik?"

"I have; I have learned how you mean to throw away your life for the Princess Aronzow."

"Dear Katinka, should I not be less than a man if I abstained, from dastardly motives, to do as much for her as she has done for us?"

"Oh, yes, yes; but nothing can be more rash, more absurd, than the attempt you are about to make. You will certainly perish."

"Be it so; I would rather die than live to remember that I had lost the chance of saving my noble benefactor and his daughter."

"But do you not perceive how much more easily I might obtain admission to the fortress than you could? I am a woman; women have more cunning than men, and yet are not so liable to be suspected. I could take some articles for sale, and the gaoler's daughter could easily get me into the fortress; I could then remain in the place of the princess, she could join you, and the worst they could do to me would not lessen the joy and pride I should feel at having proved my gratitude to yourself and the noble lady whom—you love."

"Love! you do not imagine that I could be so mad as to fall in love with one so high above me in station? My dear, devoted girl, you must not oppose me in this matter; if you can help me you shall, Katinka. Meantime, we must dismiss this subject from our thoughts; it may be that the young moujik will not succeed in gaining his sweetheart's aid and then we have lost our labour."

Leighton threw on his cloak.

"I must leave you again," he said, "but only for an hour. Do not distress yourself with evil forebodings; think how fortunate we have been hitherto, and found good hopes for the future on the pleasant experience of the past."

With a cheeful smile, he warmly pressed Katinka's soft hand and took his departure.

The girl stood for a moment lost in thought.

Her face brightened as if she had formed a sudden resolve.

Acting upon it, she started up and quietly left the house.

CHAPTER CCXV.

SILAS RYE IN ARKANSAS.

IT was fully a month after the arrival of Silas Rye at New York before he could obtain any satisfactory account of Foxley the detective.

At last he found a clue to the mystery.

He fell in with some traders, who told him that a man named Reynard, in every way answering the description Silas gave of the object of his search, had joined a party of hunters, who were going into the backwoods of Arkansas, for the purpose of obtaining a supply of furs and peltries for a certain company by whom they were employed.

Silas Rye immediately determined upon following up the track, whithersoever it might lead him.

The sturdy Irishman declared his willingness to follow his master through all his adventures.

They steamed up the Arkansas river, and landed at a spot not far distant from Larchville.

Here they had appointed to meet a party of trappers whom Silas Rye had promised to join in an excursion to the Oregon territory in search of game.

To the adventurous soul of the restless Oiny nothing could be more pleasant than this expedition.

Silas, too, felt that it was most probable he should meet either his friend Foxley, or his enemy Harwolf, among the half-lawless colonists of the Indian territories.

The place where the trappers met was at a store, built of pine logs, and perched on the rocky banks of the river.

It was the general rendezvous of the path-finders, hunters, trappers, and fur-traders, and the station from which the skins of the beasts slain in the chase were shipped in barques that were towed up the river.

Silas and Oiny were cordially received.

The former was known to be in possession of a good fortune; both were well armed, and provided; were manly, genial, and, though not skill d in wood-craft, were good shots.

The jovial foresters soon fraternized with their new companions, and at the end of an evening spent in revelry, Silas adjourned to the hut of one of the trappers, upon whom he was quartered.

The adventurer was not a little pleased with the novelty of the scene.

The hut was rudely furnished and roughly constructed, but looked, withal, cosy and comfortable in the blaze of a splendid fire of peat and furze.

The walls were covered with implements for hunting, fishing, and trapping, and not a few Indian curiosities of excellant workmanship, such as quill-worked hunting-shirts, blankets, quivers of poisoned arrows, tomahawks, calumets, and Indian clubs.

The trapper pushed a stool before the blazing hearth, and seated himself on a hewn log.

"Wal, stranger, I must confess I am tarnation glad to see yer," said the trapper heartily.. "And as we air about to retire for the night, suppose we have an eye-opener?"

"It must be something extra strong that will keep my eyes open to-night," replied Silas, yawning.

"Wal, you see that's a kinder figger of speech, for the effect of this sublime decoction is quite contrariwise," answered the backwoodsman, with a laugh; "but sometimes it be necessary to sleep with one eye open in these yere parts for the Injens makes no more of scalpin' a Britisher than I do of notching an elk; but there are some emigrants as comes to these parts that never gets tomahawked, but dies in the nat'ral way by the swamp fever, so you must keep up your sperits."

The trapper took a kettle of hot water from the fire, and began with great solemnity to prepare the grog.

"And have you lived all your life in these forests?"

"Wal, I may say so, considerin' I was born here, and have never crossed the borders more than once or twice, and during my tarm I've seen some queer things. I may say I've lived generations, for the settlers dies off like rotten sheep at certain times in the year; but I've seen some of 'em last out for more than half a dozen summers, in spite of the Injens or the swamps, so it's no use of letting your sperits go down, stranger."

"And now let us exchange names. I am Silas Rye."

The trapper started, stared, and gave a low whistle.

"Wall, this yere is the most remarkable coincidence, I reckon! Were you ever acquainted with a chap as was called Reynard, but who's raal designation was Richard Foxley?"

"Great Heavens! do you know him? It is to find him that I have come hither!"

"Wal, I guess you'll have to go further before you meet the poor feller."

"What has happened to him?"

"Wall, he has had satisfaction, so it's no use complainin'."

"Has he killed the infernal wolf?"

"No, stranger; the warmint were too strong for him, I guess; but he had a fair fight, and though he got chalked, as I said afore, there was a kinder satisfaction about it."

"Was there a duel, then?"

"Wal, I guess so; but Judge Warren hasn't got much to boast on, I reckon, for he was wound d most infarnally. However, I hear that he improves in health, not in morality, I opine; but, Catahago, the Eagle Wing is a great sachem, and accordin' to his natural gifts, a precious 'cute one, he will see as all is squared up afore long; his pretty wife, Minna, told me so."

"You speak in riddles," cried Silas, in a tone of astonishment. "Who is this Judge Warren?"

"Wal, I suppose I can confide in you, stranger, and since all Larchville rings with it, and as poor Reynard's got his billet, it can't signify over and above—"

"Well, who is this Warren?"

"I've hearn tell, stranger, in his own country he bears another name. Maybe, yer knows the 'coon, though it ain't much to your credit to have such connections."

"What is the name he is known by in England? Is it——"

"Wal, I'll tell yer, stranger. Liquor up, and drink confusion to the infarnallest rascal that lives in spite of Lynch law, and drink in the name of ANDREW HARWOLF!"

A smile of stern joy lighted on the face of Silas Rye at this announcement, and he drank the toast with bitter emphasis.

"Stranger, I must say, that I am tarnation glad that you've come among us," cried the trapper, "and as I believe that you air a most remarkable man, and the individual who is destined to bring this wretch to justice, I give you my hand, and promise to use my influence with the Pawnee chief to get his assistance. At all events, you can jist rely upon possessin' a sure friend in Nat Weatherfield, bee-hunter and beaver-trapper."

Silas returned the grasp.

For some hours the men sat conversing.

The trapper promised to take Silas and Oiny into the forests, and to give them their first lesson in wood-craft on the next morning.

At last, the beaver-hunter threw himself upon a pallet, in one corner of the room.

He had slung a hammock for Silas.

But it was not till the last log on the hearth had burnt out that the excited adventurer thought of retiring to rest.

When he had got into the hammock he lay long gazing at the moon, which shone brightly through the window.

He could scarcely realise his strange position.

After his long hunt he had almost brought the wolf to bay.

"Foxley had fallen; should he be victorious?"

The light was breaking before sleep fell upon his eyelids.

His dreams were disturbed, and he awakened in a few hours, fevered and unrefreshed.

CHAPTER CCXVI.

SILAS IS CAUGHT NAPPING.

ACCORDING to his promise, Nat Weatherfield took Silas and Oiny into the woods to initiate them into the mysteries of beaver trapping.

It was early morning.

The pale golden sunbeams filtered through the leafy trellis of the forest leaves.

With feelings of awe the two strangers wandered beneath leagues of luxuriant foliage, or over the rolling grass of the vast and ocean-like prairie.

Silas Rye looked long upon the bright, placid face of the glowing sun, rising so grandly from behind the far, lone hills.

"You are happy, mate," he said, with a deep sigh.

"Wal, I opine I manage to keep up my sperits," returned honest Nat, with a smile.

"Thrice happy!" murmured the man of guilty and sorrowful memories. "Oh! what a curse is it to be born in pent and pestilent cities! Here, all is peace and pleasantness; here there is food, on the hunting-grounds or the maize fields, for all who are willing to earn rest and content by labour; here there cannot be felt that cursed thirst of gold; here a man's heart may enlarge, his brain clear, his sympathies deepen; here, at least, he might live in concord with his fellows."

"Wal, I calkilate that there's truth in what you air propoundin'. And there's no negationing as Columbia whips the rest of creation to alm'ghty squash; and for remarkable objects it ain't peculiar—oh, no! Wal now, for instance, look yonder, stranger; yer see that mound with a tall tree standing all solitary atop of it? Now, that's a interesting object, I guess. What do you think it is remarkable for?"

"Perhaps it marks the spot where some pilgrim father first rested with his amily, to take a view of his promised land."

"I cannot jest say as that were the case, stranger. That air tree——Look at it."

"There is peace in the murmur of its leaves," said Silas, with a half smile at his own rhapsody.

"P'r'aps so; but its leaves were pretty well scorched, I reckon, when the Injens tied a young gal and her infant to its stem, and roasted 'em alive with a slow fire. They've called it ever since the Bloody Cedar."

"Och, the blazes! What a foine whorld we should all live in if there were no paple in it!" cried Oiny. "Even Oireland would be better without the Oirish,

though they're the foinest nation in the whorld, entirely."

"Oh, God! what a wretch is man!" cried Silas, bitterly.

"Faix, but sometimes I'm so botheration disgusted, even with my precious self, Misther Rye, that I fale incloined to cut my own company," said Oiny, with a sentimental sigh.

"I guess it's all nat'ral natur'. There's a kinder use even in sich things as misery and wickedness, I opine," said the trapper. "There's storms in the air and fires in the prairie; there's wild beasts in the woods; it's all one continual fermentin' which keeps things a-goin'. A man might sleep for ever if there were no hunger nor 'skeeters, as I heard a red-skin say. But it's on'y for life, so you must keep up your sperits."

They had now arrived on the banks of the Arkansas.

Nat Weatherfield dragged a canoe from under the reedy banks, and the three men got into it.

They paddled up the river.

Wild scenes of romantic grandeur floated past them on either side.

Nat Weatherfield showed his companions the beaver dams and villages.

Silas and Oiny were much astonished at the sagacity and skill of the wise little animals of whose nature and habits the trapper had much to tell.

They landed at a beautiful spot on the side of the river nearest the little town of Larchville.

"Now, stranger, I shall introduce you to the Pawnee chief, Catahaga," said the trapper. "He is going with me on the hunting path to-morrow; we shall have a buffalo-hunt, which you will find screamin' sport, I calkilate. You stay here till I return with the chief."

"I will, and meantime Oiny shall go into the woods and see if he cannot find some game for our long row has wearied me. I had but little sleep last night, and shall take a rest."

With this Silas stretched himself languidly upon a mossy bank.

"And be jabbers, but it's a foine country where there are no game laws," said Oiny, unslinging his rifle."

"Look out for the snakes," said Nat, "and, if a bar comes sniffing at yer mouth, don't move till he lays his paw on yer, and then set up a shout, and he'll run off for a yard or so, and, if you don't miss fire, you may kill him."

With this pleasant bit of advice the trapper went off with Oiny.

Silas, who was very weary, soon sank into a deep slumber.

There was a rustle among the bushes.

A tall, grey-haired, pale-faced old man came sauntering from the bush.

He carried a rifle in his hand.

Seeing the sleeper he approached.

With a chuckling cry he sprang back.

Andrew Harwolf had his deadliest enemy at his cruel mercy.

He took deadly aim with his rifle.

THE MYSTERIOUS SACK.

CHAPTER CCXVII.

THE SLEEPER AWAKENED—RECRIMINATIONS
—A NARROW ESCAPE—THE WOLF'S TEETH
ARE SHARP—OINY STABBED—ARRIVAL OF
THE TRAPPER AND THE INDIAN — THE
CHARMED BULLET FALLS INTO THE HANDS
OF SILAS RYE.

ANDREW HARWOLF, with deadly aim, had levelled
his gun at the head of the sleeping man.

For a moment his finger lingered on the trigger.
His hate was so intense that he could not help wishing his enemy might awaken.

To kill him while unconscious!

That was but poor revenge.

No. 65.

Was not his foe at his mercy, and should he not
make the most of his triumph?

Silas stirred. He opened his eyes.

"Once more we are face to face!" cried Harwolf.
"Rash fool, have I not ever been your master? Has
not the victory ever fallen to me?"

Silas was so bewildered at this sudden appearance
of his deadly foe, that he could not for some moments
speak a word.

"You may exult in your triumph, monster, but
with every crime you render your punishment more
heavy," he said, at length, and in a tone of wonderful
calmness. "Kill me as you killed the good Lord
Edgeforth, as you killed your wife; but the act will
live for ever to your perdition!"

"Canting dog!" sneered Harwolf; "did you not aid me in my first crime? Did you not share the fruits of it? Whence came your repentance? From self-interest, you found that you could gain more in the service of my enemies than in mine; and while your fangs were still red in the blood of Lord Edgeforth, you fed like a fawning cur from the hand of his brother-in-law."

"I did not murder Lord Edgeforth," muttered the adventurer. "You know how you misled me; but for the past I have regretted, and with my life am willing to atone for you. There will come a dread hour when Heaven's fiercest vengeance will overtake you; therefore, do your worst, I am prepared to die."

Harwolf uttered a fiendish laugh.

Once more he raised the gun.

It went off.

But the bullet flew through the branches of the tree beneath which Silas had been sleeping.

Harwolf was struggling with Oiny Macarne.

The Irishman had returned from the prairie with a brace of heath-cocks which he had shot for dinner.

He arrived upon the scene just in time to save the life of Silas Rye.

He hurled his heavy shillelagh at Harwolf's gun, for his own rifle was not charged.

Then rushing upon the murderous villain, he seized him by the throat.

They wrestled and fell.

Of course the men were unequally matched. Oiny was much more powerful than Harwolf.

Besides, the old ruffian had been wounded, and was still feeble from the effects of his hurt.

Silas Rye leaped up.

He approached the combatants.

His intention was to secure Harwolf as his prisoner.

Not a little to his surprise, Andrew jumped lightly on his feet, eluding the Irishman's grasp and sprang over the thicket into the wood.

Oiny grovelled on his face.

Silas ran to his side.

He lifted him.

"Och, murther, he's kilt me entirely," panted Oiny.

"The miscreant has stabbed you!"

"And, bedad, ye'se right, Misther Rye. Och hone, but I'm blading like a pig; bad luck to him!"

Silas Rye staunched the wide gash which Oiny had received in the fleshy part of the shoulder.

"If ever the fiend assisted his votaries he helps that villain!" cried Silas, bitterly. "It is useless to hunt him, he always escapes."

A cheerful halloo now rang through the wood.

Nat Weatherfield and Catahaga approached.

Seeing Silas bending over the prostrate Oiny, they ran to the spot.

"A bar, stranger? Hope it's not a snake, but I've heard as some fellers has been known to recover, though I never knew 'em to live long arter a bite from a black snake; but keep up your spirits."

"Yes, friend; we have been attacked by a snake, a serpent that would have stung me sleeping," rejoined Silas.

"Arrah, now, Misther Rye, give us yer hand, for it's not myself that will be kilt by the murthering villain without paying him off, the blackguard!"

"Wall, the cretur must have had sharp teeth, I guess," Nathaniel remarked, looking at the crimson-reeking shirt of poor Oiny.

The Indian was bending over the traces which the ground showed of the late struggle.

"Waugh!" he exclaimed, in his guttural tone.

Oiny stared at the Indian with much curiosity and awe.

Catahaga rose.

"It was the Grey Wolf," he said. "My brother is on his track."

The trapper explained to Silas that Judge Warren was known among the redskins as the Grey Wolf.

Upon being formally introduced to the fine young Indian, Silas Rye shook hands with him and thanked him for the the kindness he had shown to Foxley.

"He is gone to the great spirit-land of the pale faces," said Catahaga, simply. "The Grey Wolf is a devil, and can be killed only by charms. The pale-face lost his medicine-bullet, and his heart failed."

"Is it possible?" cried Silas, eagerly. "Then the fatal bullet fell into the possession of this murderer?"

"Catahaga found it," returned the Indian with a smile of almost childish pleasure. "He has the life of the Grey Wolf in his hands!"

"Will you give it to me?" asked Silas, earnestly. "For this one bullet I will give you a hundred rounds of shot, a horn of powder, and a rifle besides."

The Indian smiled.

"Catahaga has fire-weapons to spare. It is the will of the great Manitou that the wolf of the pale-faces should die by the hand of one of his own tribe."

Catahaga held out the bullet.

To it was still attached the little link of gold.

It was not without a slight feeling of awe that Silas Rye took the missile which had already proved so fatal.

He grasped it with an eager grasp, as if it had been a touchstone, which would change everything to gold.

The insatiable fire of remorseless hate and quenchless vengeance burnt fiercely in his heart.

He muttered sternly,

"His career is almost at an end; his term has almost expired. I was unconsciously an accomplice in the murder of Lord Edgeforth; I will be the chief agent in avenging his blood!"

- - - -

CHAPTER CCXVIII.

IN THE CAMP OF THE AVENGERS—BLACK RALPH GETS TIRED OF WAR'S ALARMS—THE RUSSIANS SEEK TO CONCILIATE OUR HERO—THE BOY PIRATE'S GENEROUS CONFIDENCE—THE BLACK BARB—THE RUSSIAN LINES—AN ACT OF TREACHERY—OUR HERO SAVED BY HIS HORSE.

OUR hero, and his little army of insurgents were posted in their entrenchments on the side of a hill, near the Castle Aronzow.

There had been some hot skirmishing with the enemy.

The Avengers had gained several victories, but they had also suffered some defeats.

The enthusiasm of the Poles was cooling.

Several of their leaders had given up the contest, and had taken advantage of the amnesty proclaimed at Wilna, to return to their allegiance to the Czar.

Finding that there was no hope of restoring confidence among the unfortunate patriots, after the crushing defeats they had sustained from the mighty forces of their oppressors, the gallant Avenger and his valiant comrades contented themselves by keep-up a harrassing warfare with the Russians, and, by the most daring assaults upon their prisons, rescued many captive patriots, who were under sentence of death, the knout, or banishment.

The name of the English adventurer became a terror to the Russians, and heavy rewards were offered for his head.

Black Ralph began to grow weary of this land cruising.

One day he sauntered into our hero's tent.

He was humming the "Rogues' March."

"Well, Ralph, what now?" said Christopher, starting up from a couch on which he reclined, smoking his cigar. "You look angrily."

"Have I not cause? I am tired of playing Thaddeus of Warsaw; I mean to hoist the blue Peter, and steer off, and

"If ever I go for a soldier again,
The devil may be my sergeant!"

"Have patience yet, comrade; we must not end this campaign so scurvily. Count Brutoff's castle must first be stormed, and then, as I find the patriots are engaged in a hopeless struggle, and are only increasing their miseries by a useless resistance, I shall once more put to sea in search of adventures."

"A brave resolve! Once more we'll mount the black flag, and sail on the grand account!"

"Never, Ralph; but I shall not be sorry again to pace my own deck, free. After all there is no life so sweet as a merry rover's. How soon one gets weary of the unchanging shore, how soon a sailor's heart begins to yearn for the wide tossing main."

"True for you, commodore."

"In gold and grain let boors rejoice,
The rover ploughs the wild, salt sea!"

Cassidy entered the tent.

"An aide-de-camp has brought you a despatch, captain,' from the new General Molowitz," he said, presenting some letters.

Our hero opened the packet.

He threw it down with a laugh.

"Do they offer you fair terms, captain?" asked Cassidy.

"Aye, comrade, and a bribe to boot, a commission in the Russian navy!"

"A good chance, captain, of making your name immortal," said Cassidy, with a smile. "You can obtain a free pardon for all that's past, and begin the world afresh in a fair character."

Our hero looked grave.

"No, Sam; not in the service of a despot."

"Then you will refuse this offer?"

"I must," replied Christopher; "but I shall, for all that, temporise with the new general, and as he invites me to ride over to his camp, promising me safe conduct, I will pay him a visit."

"But not alone, captain!" cried Cassidy, in a tone of alarm.

"Why not, Sam?" rejoined the Boy Pirate. "Do you think that I cannot take the word of a soldier and a gentleman?"

"A liar and a vagabond! I should have supposed the 'Raven' a bird decidedly too old to be caught with chaff," cried Ralph; "but the Russian fox is crafty, and the poor English crow is confiding; but remember, that there is more at stake than a lump of cheese. If you fall into this trap, captain, your chance of escape is small indeed. Be advised, then, make one sweep at the castle Aronzow, hang Brutoff, avenge Alexina, satisfy Feodor that the Avengers are true to their name, and then abandon this madcap enterprize."

To this advice our hero made no answer.

He changed the subject of conversation, and soon after his companions left the tent.

Our hero, when left alone, paced about, his eyes musingly fixed on the ground.

"Enough blood has been shed already," he murmured. "I hear that this general has taken half the population of a village prisoners of war, and will deal with them most barbarously. My intercession may save them. As to Count Brutoff, I can find means to bring him to justice for his fiendish crime without wasting the blood of my devoted band. It cannot be possible that a noble and a soldier could break faith with me; at least, I will run the risk. I have trusted in my destiny so far, and I do not think that I have erred; it can never be that after my successful career I should fall by such abject treachery."

Our hero threw his Spanish mantle across his shoulder, and bound his richly-coloured scarf about his waist.

He summoned Zampa.

He ordered the negro to bring his horse.

This charger was a magnificent creature, a black barb, fiery, and high-mettled, which our hero had trained to admirable docility.

He mounted.

Zampa asked whether his attendance would be required.

The Boy Pirate replied that he would ride forth alone, and bade the negro keep silence as to his departure.

Christopher shook the rein.

He galloped from the camp, and, after a long ride, arrived at an elevated spot where he could obtain an extensive view of the surrounding country.

Below him, the lines and entrenchments of the camp were mapped out.

He dismounted.

He led his horse down a rocky pathway.

He was now so near the camp—though screened from view by the masses of grand trees which grew by the side of the road—that he could hear the rattle of the muskets, and the stern challenge of the sentinels changing guard.

"I will retain no weapon but my sword," he said, inwardly. "There shall be no excuse for treachery, I will act with the boldest confidence."

He unslung his pistol-sash, and placed it under the horse's saddle.

He reconnoitred the camp.

Within a few yards of the spot where he stood was a paling, edging a square flat used as a parade ground.

On this a file of grey-coated soldiers were drawn up.

Their bayonets and brass helmets glittered brightly in the sun.

The general and his staff were clustered in a knot on the summit of a mound at one side of the parade-ground.

Our hero led his horse into a little dingle which was completely covered with briars and brambles.

The sagacious animal, at a sign from his master, laid down.

The Boy Pirate concealed him with ferns and boughs.

Christopher then emerged from the little dell.

In his hand he carried a white sash.

He walked erect and proud, and, without quailing, entered the parade-ground.

Even the well-disciplined soldiers could not help starting.

More than one levelled his fire-lock.

Still our hero walked proudly on, the white sash trailing from his hand.

The officers galloped up.

They surrounded our hero.

They seemed much amazed at his effrontery.

A smile of exultation swept across the face of the general.

He was a broad-built, savage looking man, with long, straight, fair hair, and shaggy eyebrows.

Our hero bowed gracefully.

"I do not doubt, general, that you are somewhat astonished at my boldness in venturing thus to visit your camp, unarmed and unattended," said the Boy Pirate, smiling, and speaking in the calmest tones, "but I know my confidence is not misplaced."

"It is the Boy Pirate!"

There was a gloating triumph in that shout.

Our hero's heart rose with suspicion and indignation.

Yet he bit his lip, and inwardly cursed his own folly and rashness.

"Your act is a bold one," said the general, his eyes flashing and his brow contracting."

"Not so; I am well protected."

"Stand to your arms, men! The pirate thief has

laid an ambush—he is accompanied by his gang!" shouted the general, backing his horse in trepidation.

"General, as I told you, I am alone; but not unprotected," returned our hero, calmly. "Here is that which, as you are honourable men and true soldiers, must be my safeguard."

So saying our hero drew from his breast the letter of safe conduct which the general had sent him.

"A shield of paper!" said the Russian officer, with a scoffing laugh.

A black frown darkened the noble brow of the Boy Pirate.

"Tell me, robber, by what right do you claim such treatment as can only be allowed to an honourable enemy? Have you not violated all law?—have you not lived in open defiance of every principle of order and justice?" cried the Russian, chuckling with malice. "And have you not fallen into this snare by that infatuation which possesses all great criminals, and brings them to ruin? You are my prisoner, illustrious captain of buccaneers! Prepare to die, for in ten minutes the crackle of muskets will proclaim that the world has been rid of one of the most atrocious scoundrels that ever lived to be its curse!"

A smile of ineffable disdain curled the calm lips of the indomitable rover.

"I will not argue with you; you are steeled against conviction," he said, with a bitter laugh. "You are a traitor to your own honour! Let me be thrice banned as a fiend in villainy, I came hither in free trust of your plighted word, and your breach of faith is just as black as if I were a heavenly saint. But, hark ye, slave—for slave you are, a fawning parasite of a barbarous despot—it is not in destiny that the Boy Pirate shall die by your hands. He will live to set his heel upon your neck!"

"Live!" cried the Russian, fiercely, his face flushing scarlet with mingled shame and passion. "He shall live, so long as life will hold out under torment. Soldiers, arrest the cursed outlaw, and bring hither the knout. Let him be paid with interest for his cruel usage of my friend, Count Brutoff!"

A sergeant of the guard sprang upon the Rover.

Trembling with ungovernable fury, the Boy Pirate fixed a grip upon the fellow's throat, and then hurled him to a great distance.

He drew his sword.

He set his back against the palisade and with defiant glare challenged the treacherous enemies to the attack.

They seemed awe-struck by his wondrous valour, and hung back irresolutely.

Christopher gave a long and peculiar call.

"Down with him! he is aided by his gang!" cried the officers.

A man presented a musket at the rover's head.

Our hero leaped at the fellow.

The gun was discharged.

The bullet flew wide of its mark.

Wrenching the weapon from the man's relaxing grasp, our hero clubbed it, and smote right and left.

A swift rush was heard among the bushes.

There was a wild cry from the men.

A splendid black steed leaped over the palisade, and curvetting and plunging among the Russians cleared a circle around his master.

In an instant the rover vaulted into the saddle.

He snatched a short carbine from under the saddle.

He presented it at the head of the general.

The officer spurred his horse.

He dashed against the pirate's charger.

The barb bit savagely at its opponent.

The general's horse reared.

Our hero caught the treacherous leader by the throat and dragged him from the saddle.

Nothing but the violent plunging of his gallant barb saved the pirate's life.

Not wishing to kill him without orders, the Russian soldiers strove to seize our hero.

The general was on his feet.

He pointed a pistol at the rover's head.

The Boy Pirate fired at him.

He fell dead.

The Russians, with a terrific shout, made a dash to secure the daring out-law.

Several bullets whizzed about his head.

One grazed the horse's flanks.

The animal took a mad bound.

He cleared the palisade.

A shower of leaves and branches rattled about the rover's head as he plunged through the forest, followed by a volley of shots.

After a wild and dangerous ride, he reached the open country.

In the distance was the Castle Aronzow, beyond it his own camp.

Our hero turned his head.

A large number of well-mounted troopers were pursuing him.

But his splendid barb out-stripped them in the race, and he soon left them far behind.

He was now galloping through a mountain defile at a fearful speed.

Gradually he slackened the rein, and turned with a scornful laugh to listen to the dying notes of the bugles which were ringing a recall.

CHAPTER CCXIX.

CAPTURE AND RESCUE OF THE BOY PIRATE.

OUR hero passed the castle.

His perils increased every moment.

The country was everywhere occupied by troops of soldiers.

As the daring rover galloped down the broad road he encountered a troop of light cavalry.

He reined back his horse.

He had no alternative but to turn and flee.

Once more he was in full flight, hotly pursued by the shouting Russians.

His horse was weary to exhaustion.

Not without compunction our hero urged on his brave enduring creature. Yet the swift motion, and the wildness of the adventure, roused the heart of the reckless rover.

He waved his sword mockingly at his pursuers, and shouted in the stern battle joy that the brave will feel in spite of reason.

War is a bitter curse, but the love of battle is deeply implanted in human nature.

It is the hazard and excitement of the fray or the pursuit which renders the dread pastime of war delicious to the daring.

Nearer and nearer.

A shot.

The noble barb reared and plunged.

Still he forged on with tottering limbs.

Our hero dismounted.

He caught the generous animal by the rein.

The beautiful creature fixed his blood-shot, eloquent eyes upon the face, and leaned his sleek head on the shoulder of his master.

He quivered through his sleek skin and sank heavily on one side.

With a yell of exultation the troopers dashed up.

Our hero bestriding his fallen steed fired both his pistols at them.

Two of them fell from their horses.

Several dismounted and attacked the rover.

The Boy Pirate drew his sword.

With masterly skill he parried the strokes and thrusts of his foes.

The conflict was terrific.

But the transcendant valour of the great Boy Pirate could avail but little against such overwhelming numbers.

He was felled from behind by a heavy stroke with the butt end of a musket.

He dropped senseless upon his fallen steed.

But for the interference of an officer a score of swords and lances would have pierced the passive body of the heroic rover.

At the command of their superior the troopers raised the pirate.

They bound him securely to a horse.

Two men with loaded carbines rode on either side.

The cavalcade rattled off and travelled at a great rate towards the nearest encampment.

But they were not destined to reach their destination without opposition.

At a wild and romantic point on the road they were suddenly assaulted by a crowd of the Avengers.

This troop was headed by Black Ralph, Dick Caffyn, and Sam Cassidy.

A desperate battle was fought.

With the fury of tigers the gallant Avengers fought for their leader's rescue.

Dick Caffyn seized the horse on which the young chief was bound.

Black Ralph threw himself upon the mounted escort.

The air rung with shouts, the clash of steel, the sharp crack of pistol shots, and the yells of the wounded.

The Russians fought with the utmost desperation.

They seemed determined not to relinquish their prisoner.

While Dick Caffyn and Black Ralph were struggling to drag the horse on which Christopher was bound out of the press of the conflict, our hero's life was put into jeopardy by a savage-looking Muscovite.

The fellow, thinking to gain favour with his commanders, resolved upon killing the Boy Pirate.

With a huge and clumsy horse-pistol in one hand, and a sabre in the other, he hewed his way to the side of the horse.

He pressed the muzzle against our hero's forehead.

The pistol actually exploded, but without effect, for Zampa had struck the fellow down with his cutlass at the moment he pulled the trigger.

Now the fury of the contest was redoubled.

The bullet had pierced the horse's side.

He fell over, crushing the rover beneath his weight.

While Dick and Black Ralph kept the enemy at bay, Zampa and Tom Garrod dragged the senseless form of their chief from beneath the horse.

Dick Caffyn took his foster-brother into his arms, and, fighting his way through the throng, reached the field which skirted the wood.

Here he remained by the side of his chief till the battle had ended in favour of the Avengers.

Fully one half of the Russian troop had been cut to pieces.

The remainder took to flight.

Black Ralph and the other pirates gave chase.

After awhile they returned.

They gathered about our hero, their faces blank with anxiety.

To all appearance he was lifeless.

He was placed on a bier formed of crossed pikes, and covered with cloaks and jackets.

When the rovers reached their camp, the pirate chief was carried to his tent.

He still remained motionless, his features rigidly set.

He showed no signs of life for many hours.

The distracted Lilia tended him with wifely devotion.

Their stern and swarthy faces overcast with gloom and suspense, the Avengers spoke in whispers and moved about the camp as softly as women in a sick chamber.

CHAPTER CCXX.

SILAS RYE MAKES ACQUAINTANCE WITH THE OLD SETTLER—STRANGE STORIES OF INDIAN LIFE.

OINY MACARNE's wound did not prove dangerous, yet he suffered much from exhaustion through loss of blood.

He remained in the cabin of Nat Weatherfield the trapper.

The reverend old Leighton was a frequent visitor at the cabin.

He was one of the principal partners of the fur company by whom the trapper was employed.

The old gentleman conceived a great attachment for Silas Rye, whom he found to be a man of intelligence and experience, and with whom he frequently held long conversations upon topics of interest, and the affairs of the "old country," as the settler fondly termed the land of his birth.

Silas Rye was reticent with regard to the object for which he had travelled to Arkansas, and spoke little of Harwolf.

He had cautioned the trapper against saying anything about Oiny's encounter with Harwolf.

Leighton supposed that the Irishman had wounded himself with his hatchet.

Finding, however, that Leighton was a man in whom he could safely confide, Silas Rye told him the whole truth, and, furthermore, narrated the history of Harwolf's crimes, and revealed the secret of his own mission.

Leighton was greatly astonished at this unexpected confirmation of the strange story told by the unfortunate detective; but agreed, with Silas, that it would be necessary to use extreme caution in carrying out his plans for bringing the criminal to justice.

"He strongly suspected," he said, "that the judge was, in some way, connected with a desperate but secret band of wretches, who, from time to time, appeared in various disguises to perpetrate the worst atrocities."

He gave his opinion of Harwolf's character, describing him as a crafty and dangerous man, and strongly advising Silas to conceal himself till such times as he should be in a position openly to confront him.

He added that the young chief of the Pawnees had discovered a clue to certain mysterious proceedings of the judge, and a number of the settlers, who were accustomed to hold secret meetings, at stated intervals, on a lonely island in the river Arkansas.

Mention being made of the late campaign, and of the adventures of the subtle and war-like Indian chief, Silas expressed his admiration of the splendid young warrior, and inquired for some information respecting Minna Wyotti, whom he had seen, and with whose beauty and goodness he had been much impressed.

"The story of Minna Wyotti is a strange one," said the old settler, "and one of great interest, for it involves some curious traits of Indian character."

"Is it not rather strange that one so lovely and refined should have consented to marry a redskin, a wild man of the woods, a savage, and a scalp hunter," rejoined Silas, smiling, "for such he is, though a very favorable specimen of his race?"

" The story is very romantic, and if you would like to know the details of it, I will tell you how it came about that the daughter of the wealthy Nicholas Wyotti married the Pawnee-Loup."

" Nothing would better please me, for I am very curious on this subject. To me it seems incomprehensible how a girl of such a character as Minna seems to possess could ever be induced to leave her kinsfolk to dwell in the wigwams of these terrible savages."

" Poor girl! she lost but little by the change, and for her kinsfolk, she had none, save her father, and he, poor man, was ruined by losses and luckless speculation, and died of a broken heart."

" Was he a man of influence in the settlement ?"

" Indeed he was ; but I will tell his history, or, at least, so much of it as refers to the kind and interesting girl who made the love-match with the Pawnee chief."

Old Leighton thus narrated

THE STORY OF MINNA WYOTTI.

Nicholas Wyotte, or Wyotti, was a man of ancient family.

His ancestors were royalists, who emigrated from England to Virginia during the civil wars which ended in the expulsion of the Stuarts.

Nicholas was a man of liberal principles, and tried his utmost to ameliorate the condition of the negroes on his plantation, but finding that all his measures were rendered futile by the character of the blacks themselves, and the ridicule and opposition he met with from the other planters, in a fit of disgust he sold off his immense estates, and joining a fur company removed from the old dominion to the new colony then forming in these backwoods.

He was a widower; his wife, who is said to have been a very beautiful and amiable woman, to whom he was fervently attached, had died in giving birth to Minna.

The voluntary exile came hither with his little girl, and was soon elected chief magistrate in the settlement.

The reign of the good Judge Wyotti is still remembered as a golden age by the older colonists.

He was a man in all respects adapted for the responsible post he filled, benevolent yet firm. He worked a great many reforms, protecting the settlers from the effects of their own rashness, for they were often mad enough to exasperate the Indian tribes, who at that time were very numerous and powerful.

His little girl became the pride and the pet of the whole colony, and grew from day to day more lovely and engaging.

The bereaved husband doted upon his only child, and his great affection for her throws a heroism round an act of patriotism I am about to mention which is rare indeed.

Some ruffianly backwoodsmen had attacked a wigwam of friendly natives, killed one of their men, ill-used others, and grossly treated their women.

The news of this outrage swept like wild fire across the prairies, and spread among the tribes.

The consequences would have been terrible, but for the energy and courage displayed by Judge Wyotti.

The settlers were paralysed with terror, and hourly expected an attack of the fiendish red men.

The sachems of the Dacotahs and the Sioux swore that they would exterminate every pale-face in the colony, and were already on the war-path, marching down upon the settlement, athirst for slaughter.

Judge Wyotti captured the ruffians who had been the cause of all this trouble.

One he hanged, the rest he flogged and imprisoned. Then, with matchless daring and devotion, he went alone into the wigwam of the principal Dacotah tribe.

He convinced the chiefs that the outrage had been perpetrated by a few individuals, who had been severely punished for their crime, and left no means untried to conciliate the savage warriors.

For a long time they remained impenetrable, and treated him with great indignity.

At last, he prevailed upon them to consent to hold a meeting with the pale-faces, and by distributing presents on the one hand, and on the other putting on as formidable an appearance as possible, he induced the chiefs to sign a treaty of peace.

The Indians departed quietly, and appeared to be well satisfied.

Judge Wyotti, however, was far from being easy in his mind with respect to the sincerity of the redskins, in whom, he had learned from experience, that little confidence could be placed.

One cause which conduced to his uneasiness was the obstinate refusal of Monotah the White Pine, an old sachem of great influence among the tribes, to attend the meeting of the chiefs and settlers.

This old fellow was the head chief of the Pawnee-Loups, and the father of Catabaga the Eagle Wing.

While he refused to sanction the treaty, the good judge was aware that there was no real safety for the little colony.

He had sent the old man some costly presents, which were furnished at his own expense.

An Indian will never refuse a gift under any circumstances.

Monotah, accordingly, took the presents, but made none in return, and maintained a sullen reserve.

Things were in this state, and, day by day, the good judge grew paler and more anxious.

It was in autumn, and Wyotti sat smoking at the door of his lodge at sunset.

On the lawn before the house, his people were disporting themselves after the labours of the day, for it was harvest time, and they were merry-making.

Little Minna had been crowned harvest queen, and was carried on a sheaf of golden grain by two reapers, while the girls and their swains marched in procession, led by the black fiddler, who was scraping the fiddle-strings right merrily.

All at once there was a sudden hush among the revellers.

The judge turned, to discover the cause of it.

A tall, gaunt figure emerged from the dark pines, and slowly advanced.

You may suppose how the judge's heart leaped, when he recognized the great sachem of the Pawnees.

The old man must now be nearly a hundred years of age, and, therefore, though this happened about twenty years ago, he was still very old.

He was then a meagre but sinewy old savage, with a scowling look, and a skin somewhat darker than is usual among the Pawnees.

He was as tall and straight as the tree whose name he bore; his long hair white as snow.

He was hideously smeared with paint, and carried a long tufted spear in his right hand.

The judge rose, and received him respectfully.

The old Pawnee looked round upon the company with a scowling glance.

Judge Wyotti ordered them to leave him alone with the chief.

The old sachem squatted himself on the ground at the door of the house.

Little Minna drew timidly to her father's side.

She looked at the Indian with fear, and clung to her father's arm.

Judge Wyotti sent her into the house to fetch his calumet, a pipe which had formally been presented to him by a chief of the Dacotahs on the occasion of a great meeting of the chiefs for the settlement of a purchase of land by the whites.

He gravely lighted this pipe, and then presented it to the chief.

The old sachem took it rather sullenly, and having blown a whiff, handed it back to the judge.

I will give you some idea of the way in which a conference is carried on with the redskins.

For some time they smoked in silence.

Then Judge Wyotti spoke. I give you the conversation as nearly as I can remember it, for I had the story from this old man himself.

"The heart of the pale-face chief is very glad, because the father of the Pawnee-Loups has visited his lodge; his heart is good towards his red brothers and he would joyfully live with them as if the Iroquois and the Yengeese were but one tribe," said the judge.

"The Yengeese chief is wise; his words are good, the roots of his tongue are not fixed in his heart like the Pawnee's," returned the Indian. "Monotah smoked the calumet with the pale-face, and gave him part of his hunting-grounds in exchange for fire-weapons and blankets, and he gave him food, and received him in his lodges. But the pale-face is a dog which cannot be trusted. The heart of the Iroquois is hard; his lips are thirsty to drink blood when he is on the war-trail, but in peace he is true to his friend, and has respect to the customs of his nation."

"Yet all in the tribes of Monotah are not good alike, there are many whose tongues are forked and their hearts double," said the judge, quietly. "The Yengeese also have bad men amongst them, and the wolves who injured their red brothers are hated by the Yengeese; they are punished and despised."

The chief answered with native frankness,

"It is good; there are evil manitous who are saved by the Iroquois and the Yengeese, they darken men's eyes and teach them evil; but the good who can be trusted are willing to trust others."

"The great chief of the Pawnees has spoken well; he is worthy to be trusted by his white brothers," replied the judge, little thinking to what all this palaver was to lead.

The old chief smiled and held out his hand to little Minna.

She gazed at him with some dread, but when her father took her hand and placed it in the sachem's she looked up into the face of the wild redskin with a smile of child-like confidence.

"My brother loves his daughter?" said the Indian, coolly.

To this remark the judge warmly assented.

"It is good," said Monotah, in the same cold tone. "Let the child come with the White Pine; she shall stay in his lodge three days, and then she shall return to her father."

The agony of poor Wyotti at this proposal may be easily imagined.

His darling child entrusted to the care of a barbarous savage!

He could not speak.

"Will my little daughter go with the chief of the Pawnees?" asked the sachem of the child.

The girl looked appealingly at her father.

She understood his silence, and read rightly his anxious look.

"Minna will go," she said, simply.

The old sachem got up and held out his hand to the judge.

"Let my brother ask his own heart whether the Iroquois can trust their children to the pale-faces."

A sad story of the barbarous ill-treatment by the whites of an Indian hostage recurred to the mind of the judge.

He was silent with anguish.

The girl threw herself into her father's arms.

She burst into tears.

She would not leave him, she said, and sobbed most bitterly.

Her father soothed her by caresses, and bade her go with the Indian, reminding her that she had often wished to visit the wigwams, and telling her that she would s e all sorts of strange and pleasant sights, and would very soon be restored to him.

Minna obeyed meekly.

The old sachem took the child's hand.

Proudly bowing his hoary head he walked away with a grave step, still leading little Minna.

The torture of mind endured by the fond father during the absence of his darling child surpasses description.

Every one blamed him for trusting the treacherous Indians, and few gave him credit for the noble motive which prompted the act.

On the second day after the departure of little Minna some lying trapper brought in a report that she had been cruelly murdered.

The good judge treated this idle tale with scorn.

Still his agony and suspense were extreme.

The sun seemed stationary in the heavens, the day seemed to be without end.

At length the third morning dawned.

From sunrise, throughout that weary day, the judge paced before the door of his house, and every moment glanced wistfully at the dark firs through which the little white dress had fluttered and disappeared.

The hours wore on slowly and heavily.

With a sickness of the soul, the good judge watched the shadows of the pines lengthen before the declining sun.

It was now evening.

Still the Indian did not come.

The torture suffered by the impatient father was intolerable.

He strove to controul his excitement; but in vain.

The broad disc of the setting sun was now half-hidden by the distant hills.

He had ordered the crowd which had gathered before his door to disperse.

He assumed a calm and collected demeanour.

With the last ray of the sun faded the lingering light of hope in his mind.

He sat down on a settle before his door.

He covered his face with his hands and groaned.

His lethargy was dispelled by a silvery laugh.

He started up.

With grave steps the Pawnee sachem was approaching from the forest.

Little Minna gambolled and prattled at his side.

The Indian squaws had dressed her in their native bravery.

She wore a little frock of Indian cloth, richly ornamented with quills and bead work.

There was a fillet round her head, in which was placed a quaillou's feather, to indicate that she was the daughter of a chief.

In an instant she was clasped in her father's arms.

The old sachem looked on with a kind smile.

The judge grasped his hand with warmth, and ushered him into the house.

From that day till the death of the worthy judge, which happened about five years after, there was continuous peace between the settlers and the natives.

During Minna's stay in the Indian's wigwam, she had made acquaintance with Catahaga, who was then a boy.

The children conceived a warm affection for each other.

From that time they became playmates.

Judge Wyotti took a great fancy to the little Pawnee-Loup, and taught him to speak English and to read and write, both which he can do pretty well.

As I have already told you, the virtues of the worthy judge of Larchville could not bring him immunity from those misfortunes which may befall the best of men.

The banks in which he had invested his fortune broke, and several promising speculations proved utter failures.

When he died Minna was left very poor.

She had several offers of marriage from wealthy planters.

She refused them all.

She gave herself to the young chief of the Pawnees, whom she loved from her girlhood, and, if love is happiness, I believe she has no reason to regret her choice, for the Indian worships her with all the fervour of his impassioned nature.

They remained at Larchville after their marriage, but they were despised and neglected, both by the natives and the whites.

The father of Catahaga, who had taken offence against the pale-faces, was much enraged with his son, and tried to persuade him to take another wife from his own tribe, but Catahaga refused to do this, for he had entirely adopted the civilisation and customs of the whites.

Monotah was so provoked at this conduct, that he expelled him from the tribe and disowned him.

The poor young brave, therefore, was hated and spurned by both parties, but he found compensation for all his losses in the rich prize he had won—his charming and devoted wife.

We have broken off at this point in the history of the young Indian and his wife, because the remainder of it is already known to our readers.

"I thought that the Indians despised women, and treated them with contempt and brutality?" Silas remarked.

"Catahaga, as I told you, lived long among the whites, and acquired their mode of thought; besides, like all people in a state of nature, the Indians are impulsive and susceptible of lively emotions; they can love hotly, as well as hate fiercely, and, amongst them, a pretty woman is more esteemed than is generally supposed by those who have not studied the Indian characters with attention."

"I should not have supposed that."

"Do you know what caused the great split between the Assinobins and the Sioux, kindred tribes, and Dacotahs?"

"I should like to know. They say there is a woman at the bottom of all mischief."

"Yes; and there are Helens to be found everywhere. The Dacotahs had theirs, and she was the cause of as great evils as the beautiful Greek."

"And pray what was the name of your Indian beauty?"

"Indian names are never very short or very pronounceable. The name of Ozolapaïda is renowned throughout all the tribes of Dacotahs."

"Of course, she was the wife of a chief."

"Yes, of the great Winahopa. Before her marriage with this great sachem she had been betrothed to a terrible brave who had almost as many scalplocks of his enemies hanging at his lodge and at his girdle as he had hairs on his own head."

"I suppose he carried her off from the husband?"

"Yes, he killed him, and bore away the fair and faithless one. He was pursued by her two brothers; he killed them also."

"And so this private quarrel gave rise to a national war?"

"It did; discord and vengeance arose between these two tribes, the most powerful of the nation. The relations, friends, and partizans of each took up the quarrel."

"And how did it end?"

"One act of revenge begat another until the whole nation was drawn into a bloody civil war, which at length divided the tribe into two portions, the Assinobins, who were the partizans of the offenders' family, and the Sioux those of the offended."

"And was the girl reclaimed by her tribe?"

"No; she lived with her lover to the end of her life, and he was buried by her side."

"And did the war end with the death of the precious pair who had been the cause of it?"

"The Assinobins and the Sioux are still implacable enemies. But now I must be going, Mr. Rye, for the stars are breaking out. I should advise you to take up your quarters in the Indian lodges, for you will need the protection of the Eagle Wing if you intend to pursue your plan of vengeance against Andrew Harwolf, alias Judge Warren, whom I sincerely hope you will succeed in bringing to the gallows."

Silas shook hands with the planter, and they parted.

CHAPTER CCXXI.

AT TOBOLSK — KATINKA'S RUSE—RETURN OF EDWARD LEIGHTON—THE SLEEPING POTION —A LITTLE FLIRTATION—THE MARKET GIRL —GALLANTRY AND JEALOUSY—KATINKA OBTAINS ADMISSION TO THE CASTLE.

THE shifting scene of our eventful drama once more changes to the little village in Siberia, where stood the grim fortress in which the Prince and Princess Aronzow were confined.

Our readers will remember that Michael, the young moujik, and Edward Leighton, had plotted to rescue the prisoners.

The devoted Katinka, however, had determined that Edward should not endanger his life and liberty in this rash attempt, but had made up her mind to sacrifice herself for the sake of the princess.

She left the house, and made her way to the market-place.

Here she purchased a quantity of ribbons and some articles of cheap jewellery.

She returned to the inn.

Seating herself at the table she resumed her work.

After an hour had passed, Edward Leighton returned.

He looked thoughtful, and seemed duly impressed with the danger and difficulty of the task he had undertaken.

Katinka shook her head.

"Monsieur is not wise," she said, "or he would remember that it is wrong and foolish to attempt impossibilities."

"There is nothing impossible, my dear Katinka, to the resolute and persevering," returned Edward, with a cheerful smile. "You must not let your little, anxious, woman's heart overrate the danger of this attempt. I have seen the young Russian, and he tells me that the thing can be managed, but Lisa seems to think that she would be better able to gain an entrance for a woman than for a man—but I am so tall!"

"A woman!" cried Katinka, in breathless eagerness. "Yes, yes, monsieur, she is right in that; there could be no suspicion, and the disguise could be so well managed. Did you tell him that I would come in your place?"

"Is that likely? Beshrew me for an idiot for telling you of this. Of course I told him that I would not consent to any arrangement that could bring any one but myself into trouble," Edward replied. "Now you are a dear, good child, and must be obedient. I am about to impose upon you a strict command," he added, banteringly.

"What is it, monsieur?"

"Only that you shall not tease me with any more remonstrances, for I have made up my mind on this point, and am a very obstinate fellow."

Katinka sighed.

"But, monsieur——"

"I would not seem ungracious. Well, if you will not obey me, you will not refuse to listen to my humble entreaty. Pray, my good Katinka, do not let us have another word upon this subject," said Edward, in a coaxing tone.

THE AMBUSH.

"I will be silent, if you wish it; but I am so grieved that you will not permit me to share this peril with you. Will you not listen to reason?"

Edward laughed.

"Is this your promise?" he said, reproachfully.

"I am a woman, you know; you must not exact too much from me. But do you not see how wretched my position will become if you should be taken? You say you are obstinate; I will confess myself selfish; for my own sake let me implore you not to run into this danger."

"Would you have me abandon my benefactors to their fate without one effort to save them?"

"No, no, no; not for all the world! but if the young peasant tells you that it would be safer and

more easy for me to gain an entry into the fortress why will you not consent to my engaging in this affair? You are not heeding me, monsieur; I will speak a little longer."

Edward shrugged his shoulders, and, smiling drolly, listened with mock gravity.

Katinka paused.

She blushed and laughed.

A bright beam lighted her eyes for a moment and then she said, with a half-sigh,

"Well, monsieur, I am silenced. At what time do you join the young moujik?"

"At sunset we are to meet at the gate of the castle."

"And it is now a little past noon; let me advise

you to rest awhile, monsieur, for you look jaded with over-watching."

"Thanks for the suggestion, kind Katinka, I am weary indeed; a little sleep would refresh me, and to-night I shall want all the energy and strength I possess for carrying out our well-planned scheme, so I will take a draught of wine and then a snatch of sleep, but have a care to call me at dusk."

With a peculiar smile Katinka took up a flask of wine.

She fetched a glass.

Unseen by Edward she put something into it.

She filled the glass and presented it to Edward.

He pledged her and drained it.

He then retired to the little inner chamber.

Katinka waited some moments.

She rose and stole to the door.

She peeped in.

Edward had already sunk into a profound slumber.

Towards evening she rose from her work.

Having arranged her dress and thrown around her a large, thick cloak such as is commonly worn by the Siberian peasant women, and taking up her basket of wares, she left the inn and proceeded through the deepening twilight to the gates of the fortress.

Here she met the young Russian.

"Bravo! monsieur has reason. This is as it should be," said Michael, rubbing his hands with pleasure; "you will be able to get into the castle now without any trouble."

"The princess can change clothes with me."

"Yes, and the prince can wear a priest's robe. We have arranged it thus: there is an old shaveling that visits the prisoners, he will pass the guard just before I smuggle you into the castle; if the prince puts on a priest's robe he can return, and, in the gloom, the sentry will take him for the chaplain I told you of."

"It is all well arranged."

"And where is monsieur? I suppose he will not be far off?"

"To tell you the truth these Englishmen are more brave than cunning. I am glad to say he is at the inn, for he is so daring that he might do something desperate and thereby betray himself."

"Ah! I am right glad you are here in his stead; now the difficulty will be to get you off after the prisoners have escaped."

"Oh! that's of no consequence," returned the girl, with an unconscious sigh; "if the princess is saved Monsieur the Englishman will be so delighted."

"Well, I am astonished that he does not come himself. When I proposed employing you in this affair he was so decidedly against it that I thought nothing could move him; but you are his wife, it seems, and women will have their own way; even Lisa has a will of her own, and I believe the reason we never quarrel is because I never venture to oppose her. But now is the time; there she is in her own sweet person. You see how she becks and smiles at the lubberly sentry, confound him! I suppose it's necessary to wheedle him a bit, but, by the great St. Nicholas, I don't see why she need look so *very* sweet."

"She does it to tease you and make you jealous. If she didn't love you she would not take so much trouble," said Katinka, archly.

"Humph! I would sacrifice a little love if she would act with a little more propriety. Life of my heart! she is pinching his arm!"

"Then perhaps I had better interrupt their conversation."

"Do, for the love of prudence. Phew! another pinch! Her fingers are like nutcrackers. How dare she pinch any one but me? The Tartar dog! I'll beat his brains out with his own gun-stock!"

Seeing that the green-eyed monster had begun to sting young Michael to desperation, Katinka thought it was time for her to make the venture.

"Carelessly lay your hand twice on your breast—

it's the signal. She will know you," said Michael. "Go; for St. Peter's sake, who carries the keys, make haste, for if there's any more pinching I shall shriek!"

Michael's simple face blazed scarlet, and he wiped the perspiration from his brow.

Katinka crossed over to the gate where the gaoler's pretty daughter was laughing and chatting merrily with her tall, rough-bearded admirer, who seemed much elated at the favour showed him.

Katinka approached with her basket, and made a timid courtsey, at the same time twice touching her breast with her right hand.

Lisa turned a little pale, and then burst into a silvery laugh.

"Now, my dear Claus, the golden opportunity of showing your devotion occurs in the shape of a gold ring or a bracelet. Buy for me, my good cousin Claus."

Lisa inflicted another pinch.

"Ho, you little vixen! you give me a pair of black bracelets, and expect a gold one in return. My arm is so sore I can scarcely carry my musket," cried the soldier, with a gruff laugh.

"You are like the Jews—money must be tortured out of you. *You* have a wife! Why, you starve your horse, and that is the only creature you care for. Come, now, if you mean one half of what you said just now, you would buy one half of the contents in this basket. Oh, this silver buckle! was there ever anything so beautiful?"

"A poor soldier can't afford to make presents," grumbled her cousin. "Michael, the carpenter, is a richer man than I."

"And a kinder, handsomer, braver man than the best of your kin, Master Claus; he wouldn't refuse me such a paltry request—a trumpery silver buckle! It's not the value of the thing, but to be refused, there's the vexation."

"You know that we have not received our pay. When I get some money I will buy you something fine," returned the sentinel.

"Oh, I don't care for gifts; but you never will oblige me in any way."

"Now, don't be so peevish, Lisa; you know I am always ready to do anything I can for you; only try me."

"I will, Claus, I will put you to the proof at once. You know the poor princess we have in prison is in great want of several articles which this girl has to sell, and she promised to reward me if I could bring such a person to her——"

"Against orders?"

"Orders! Oh, you mean, pitiful hypocrite! and to call yourself a lover!" cried Lisa, in a passion. "I suppose it is not against orders for me to be here chatting with you? I suppose I am not running the risk of a thrashing if my father catches me here? Well, I'll take care to run no more risks for your selfish sake; I'll be very attentive to 'orders' for the future, so good evening, most chivalrous cousin Claus."

"Halt there, you minx! I never said I wouldn't admit the girl; take her in with you, but be quick on your errand. Remember, the risk I run is greater than yours; but stop, let me look at the girl. Now, Lisa, I can tell you that she looks prettier and more amiable than you do. My little love, you cannot pass the gate without paying toll."

With this the gallant soldier gave the shrinking girl a kiss.

"Well, this passes all!" cried Lisa, with flaming eyes. "If the saucy wench is so fascinating you had better talk your nonsense in her ears; but let me tell you she must take her wares to another market, for I have no dealings with such traders as she!"

"Very well, all the better for me; I shall not get into trouble by disobeying orders. You hear what the mistress says, you must march off, my dear one."

"No, she shall not do so; I will have her come in, if it's only to spite you!" cried Lisa, pettishly.

She seized the girl's arm, and hurried her through the gate.

The sentinel laughed.

"Be quick!" he cried after them. "If you do not return within a quarter of an hour I shall send a comrade to seek you."

He shouldered his musket, and paced up and down.

Katinka followed her guide across a large courtyard.

They passed through an archway, and began mounting a flight of stone stairs.

They paused.

Lisa looked very pale and frightened.

Katinka remembered the sameful exposure, and the brutal torture she had endured under the lash when a prisoner, and she shuddered with fear.

However she nerved herself, and called up a brave smile.

"If we are discovered the consequence will be terrible," whispered the gaoler's daughter. "You must be very courageous, or we shall fail."

"Do not fear for me, I am prepared to suffer anything, however horrid, if I can but save the princess."

"Hush!" cried Lisa, holding up her finger.

The action was sudden, and Katinka was so startled she could scarcely help screaming.

"It is a step!" she whispered, tremblingly.

"Yes. Go into that embrasure of the wall; it is dark, you will not be seen," whispered Lisa.

The footsteps of a man were heard ascending the echoing staircase.

A priest appeared.

He was an old man, tall, and with a white beard.

"Peace with you, my daughter. Can I see the Princess Aronzow?"

"Not now, father, she has retired to bed."

"And the prince?"

"Is also retired."

"Well, I must visit them to-morrow night; I can see the other prisoners now."

"There is one of them very sick; he wished me to mention his case to you, father."

"Indeed! Where is he?"

"In the farthest ward from this."

"I will go to him at once."

The old man passed down a long corridor, on either side of which were rows of cells.

Lisa then beckoned Katinka to come forth from the dark corner where she was lurking.

Taking her hand she hurried her through all sorts of stone passages, and brought her to an arch door which she opened.

She found herself in a narrow and darksome cell, and in the presence of the Princess Sophia Aronzow.

CHAPTER CCXXII.

WITHIN THE CASTLE—THE PRINCESS IN CAPTIVITY—THE USES OF ADVERSITY—HEROISM OF THE POLISH MAID—THE DISGUISE—THE CORPORAL OF THE GUARD—THE LAST BELL.—THE ESCAPE.

THE princess looked very lovely, even in her disfiguring garb.

She wore a long dress of blue serge, open at the breast, and fastened at the waist with a piece of rope.

Her hair was plainly braided, and neatly tied up under a coif of the same colour and material as her robe.

Around her neck was a small cross, attached to a rosary.

Against the wall there was a niche containing a crucifix.

Upon the ground, in one corner of the room, stood a pitcher and a loaf, in another, a low, hard pallet, on which those delicate limbs were racked which had formerly been couched on beds of down.

She looked so tenderly frail, so patient and saintlike that it was hard to realise in her the fiery and tyrannic mistress of the Castle Aronzow.

She resembled, rather, some saintly penitent, hallowed by sorrow and suffering, and meekly bearing her cross.

Yet it was not by the power and cruelty of man she had been subdued; her proud heart beat as high as ever, the indignant fire would flash from her eyes, and the flush would mount to her cheek under the sense of her humiliation.

But she was subdued by the bitter lesson she had learned—that to inflict is easy, to endure is hard.

Till now she had never known how much she had caused others to suffer by her savageness and pitiless harshness.

She sprang forward and embraced Katinka.

"My brave, my noble girl, why have you endangered yourself for one so worthless as I?" she said, bursting into tears. "Let me entreat you to go at once; save yourself and the generous Englishman, and leave me to a fate which is almost deserved."

Katinka threw herself upon her knees, and kissed the hand of the princess.

She expressed her determination to remain in the prison to die rather than leave her side with such vehemence and evident sincerity that the princess at length yielded to her entreaties.

Lisa appeared distracted at the delay caused by the reluctance of the princess to compromise the devoted Polish maid.

At last, however, with the assistance of Lisa, she changed dresses with the vivandiere.

"I must hide you in a cell which is disused till I return, and then I can find some way of getting you out of the castle. But now I will bring hither the prince, and you must not lose an instant, for the bell will toll directly which warns the porters to close the gate, and then it will be impossible to get out of the castle."

The girl fled from the cell.

She returned with the prince.

He had wrapped a priest's robe loosely about him.

He wore the high and peculiarly-shaped hat which distinguishes the Russian priests.

The princess tearfully embraced her father.

The old man kissed her forehead, and taking her hand, smiled benignly.

The pretty peasant dress became the princess charmingly.

Lisa now lighted a torch.

She led the way to the stairs.

Tramp, tramp, tramp!

A file of soldiers clattered up the steps.

The corporal of the file carried a lantern.

The prince took care to keep out of the range of its light.

"Good-night, father," mumbled the corporal, as he passed.

"Peace with you, my son!" returned the prince, in a low tone.

"Who is this girl?" asked the corporal, fiercely, turning towards the princess, but addressing himself to Lisa.

"A friend of mine, Peter; at least, a market-girl with whom I have business. You will excuse me this time, know."

"You will never be satisfied till you have got the whole garrison into some devilish scrape," grumbled the soldier. "Mark ye, Lisa, send off that girl at once, or your father shall know how you set the rules at defiance, and your dainty skin will suffer for your foolhardiness."

"Now, Peter, don't talk like a savage. I know you are too good to betray me for such a trifling offence; but if you won't frighten me with your threats, I really will promise you that this shall be the last time."

"Bah! Well, look that you keep your word for your own sake," growled the soldier.

The girl trembled and passed on.

She ushered the prince and princess down the steps.

They stood at a little postern door that gave upon the court-yard.

Clang! boom!

It was the castle bell thundering in iron tones its signal to the warders.

The prince crossed the court-yard hurriedly, the princess and Lisa following him at some distance.

He passed beneath the portal.

The cousin of Lisa was still on guard.

He saluted the supposed priest as he passed.

"Your blessing, father," he murmured.

The priest mumbled a response and passed on.

Boom! clang! boom!

It was the last warning stroke of the bell.

The sentinel turned towards the two girls who had purposely lingered in order that he might be the more in haste to dismiss them.

"Why are you loitering, mad wenches? Do you desire to see me hanged, Lisa, that you take advantage of my stupid good-nature? Come out, I say. Come, lass, be off, you and your trinkets, or I will hand you over to the seneschal."

The princess hurried past him.

He caught hold of her dress.

"Stay, my girl, now you are clear of the gate there is not so much need for haste but you may take a friendly farewell. You have sold your wares, so let me have a kiss by way of interest."

He tried to put his arms round the waist of the princess.

The haughty lady recoiled from the rough soldier with a quiver of loathing.

Lisa rushed up to him and administered a hearty box on the ears.

She whispered to the princess in what direction they were to go in order to reach the inn where Leighton was staying, and then entered the court-yard just as the warders were closing the heavy gates.

CHAPTER CCXXII.

LISA AND KATINKA'S WILD ADVENTURES IN THE DUNGEONS OF THE FORTRESS.

LISA rushed back into the castle.

Her heart beat wildly.

She stole up the stairs and sought the unused cell in which she had locked Katinka.

She found the poor girl sitting trembling in one corner.

Although the room was no longer used as a place of confinement, it was made to serve as the receptacle of various instruments of the torture which the cruel laws of Russia inflict upon offenders.

On one side stood a kind of rack on which the wretch condemned to suffer the knout is stretched with iron rings, in corners were the bagottes or rods used in the military punishment called "running the gauntlet," in which the poor sufferer receives thousands of strokes from his comrades, each of whom is armed with a rod, while on the walls hung knouts and whips of different sizes and power.

Lisa put down her lantern, and stood harkening with a startled air.

"I dare not stay here now," she said, breathlessly. "I should be flogged and sent to the mines, for even women are forced to work in them. The prince has been seen with me, and the princess also; I shall be detected at once. Oh! what is to be done?"

"Can you not escape with us? The prince, will, no doubt, reward you handsomely, and your lover will protect you."

"It is my only chance," she said.

At this moment the rattling of keys was heard.

Katinka had barely time to conceal herself, when a stern-looking old man entered.

"What are you doing here, Lisa?" he said, with a scowl. "Are you rummaging amongst these pretty implements for something you require? I hear that you admitted a strange girl to-night," he added, taking up a scourge from the ground. "I suppose your guilty conscience brought you here? Well, you shall have your deserts."

With this he seized her by the wrist, and swung round the heavy thong.

"Mercy, father!" shrieked the girl.

"Get you to bed, we will talk over this affair to-morrow."

So saying he threw down the scourge, and roughly pushed his daughter from the cell.

The door was closed.

Katinka was left in darkness.

She clasped her hands, and resigned herself to suffering.

She felt almost certain that something would happen to prevent her escape; but she was resolved to brave her fate with womanly fortitude.

She remained quite still.

Nearly an hour had passed.

She heard the tramp of one of the warders, whose duty it was to watch the corridor by night.

He passed from time to time.

She heard a harsh, jangling sound, and then a loud jar.

The noise proceeded from the wall beside her.

"Who goes there?" shouted the sentinel, rushing across the corridor, and opening the cell.

Katinka slunk down behind the rack.

The soldier entered the cell.

He groped about in the profound darkness with his bayonet.

With a presence of mind which astounded her when, in after times, she recalled the adventure, Katinka rattled her fingers swiftly along the wooden rack.

Pi-ti-pi-ti-pat!

"A rat!" growled the soldier. "Who would think the cursed little vermin could make so much noise?"

He left the cell.

Again the jarring sound.

But very faint now.

"Katinka!"

"Lisa!"

"Come! Give me your hand."

"Where are you? It is so dark."

"For heaven's mercy, quietly!"

"Yes, I can reach you by the sound; I only fear stumbling."

"Hush, hush!"

"Hold your hand far through the door."

Clatter-bash!

"Curse the infernal rats, how they startle me!"

A long rest.

"I-I-knew it would be so," quivered the poor Polish girl; "it was this hideous rack. I-I-tremble. I am not nerved. I feel the cut of the lash. It has eaten into my very heart. I grow nervous. Don't care for me, dear Lisa! I-I-am willing to die, but I have over-rated my strength. I totter and grow faint."

The cruel scourging in the dungeons of Aronzow had fearfully injured the constitution of the noble Polish girl.

She was in darkness, well she knew, surrounded by those instruments of brutal torture, the cruelty of which she had experienced.

She was hysteric, and lost her presence of mind. In the deep dungeon gloom she fancied she could see the gloating eyes of incarnate fiends, whose delight is to gratify demoniac lust of cruelty.

She felt herself encircled in a warm embrace.

"If you do not strengthen yourself I shall be lost!" whispered an anguished voice in her ear. "I shall suffer all that you have suffered."

"No, no, dear Lisa; no, it is only for myself that I am a coward. I can be brave for you who have been so noble and so good."

"Oh pray do not speak, even in whispers," muttered Lisa, in tones scarcely audible.

She drew Katinka through the door in the cell, the opening of which had so startled the sentinel.

She closed it very softly.

Katinka, who had recovered her self-controul, mounted the steep steps which rose near this door.

When they had reached the top of the flight they found themselves on a stone landing. Before them was a spiral stone staircase, such as gives access to belfries in the small circular towers.

These they mounted.

At the top they found themselves in another stone passage.

There was a door on one side.

It was open.

Within appeared a neatly furnished bed-chamber with a high narrow window, through which the moon was brightly shining.

Into this room the girls entered.

They rested awhile to recover from the terrors they had passed through.

Greater dangers were before them.

"There is but one chance of escape left us," said the gaoler's daughter. "It is by this window; but it is better that we should fall and be crushed than that we should suffer worse things at the hands of the police. Speaking for myself, I can truly say I would rather die a hundred deaths than be subjected to the shame of such punishment as we shall be made to suffer if we were caught. Are you daring enough to try to get down by means of a rope?"

"Oh, yes; I'm not the least afraid," returned the vivandiere, with a brave smile. I think that in this feat I shall be more than your equal. I am not by nature a coward, Lisa, but my powers of endurance were once sorely over-taxed. After being taken prisoner by Count Brutoff, I was stripped and flogged till I fainted; I suffered, surely, the cruellest pangs of death. But give me the rope; the sooner we are away the better."

Lisa brought a coil of ropes from the cupboard.

Katinka bound them to the staunchions of the window.

"But, stay," she said, "I wear the prison dress which the princess wore. I must have other clothes."

This difficulty was soon surmounted.

Lisa produced some clothes, which Katinka put on.

Then the brave Polish girl launched herself into mid air.

She held the rope below while Lisa descended.

The moon shone down cold and calm and clear upon the slumbering village, the dark, reposing castle.

The girls were free!

They hurried towards the inn.

Scarcely had they reached the door when the harsh, loud and imperious clang of the castle bell proclaimed that the escape of the prisoners had been discovered.

CHAPTER CCXXIV.

FLIGHT OF THE ESCAPED EXILES OF SIBERIA.

MEANWHILE, the prince and princess made their way towards the village.

They met the young peasant, Michael, at the entrance of the village.

He recognised them at once by their dresses.

He approached the prince.

"Pardon, excellency," he said, bowing; "I am the moujik Lisa has told you of. I beg to offer you my humble services."

"They are very acceptible, my brave fellow," said the prince. "But you must remember that I have forfeited my title, and must call me simply father."

The princess who had followed now joined her father.

"The excellent princess——" began Michael, with a profound obeisance.

"Is now simply a peasant girl, and you must address her as such."

"A real bayard! a live prince! and a sublime princess! To call them Ivan and Teckla—it is monstrous!" stammered Michael, colouring, and bowing like a mandarin.

"You will betray us, friend. If you have any respect for our safety, pay less respect to our person."

"I will obey your excellency, but I am not one of the 'black people,' the ruffs. I know my duty to my superiors, and whenever I call your excellencies by familiar names, you must condescend to imagine yourselves addressed with proper courtesy."

"Hang the fellow, one would think he had been a courtier rather than a carpenter!" said the prince, impatiently.

"The man is quite right," said the princess, coldly. "He only shows his sense in recognising the vast gulf that lies between a bayard and moujik."

The prince sighed and shrugged his shoulders at this haughty and rather ungracious remark.

"And may I ask your excellent father what has become of the pretty little wife of monsieur the Englishman?" said Michael.

"Wife!" gasped the princess. "Impossible!"

"I trust not, my love. Edward Leighton is a sensible man, and knows the value of such a noble woman."

"Why, she is but a foolish camp-follower!"

"And Catherine the Great was but the wife of a sergeant before she became the czarina of Russia."

The princess was silenced.

She took her father's arm.

The prince feeling her press heavily on his arm looked at her inquiringly.

Her face was deadly pale, her eyes half closed.

"You are ill, my child," said the parent, in a tone of affectionate sympathy.

"A little," said the princess. "Is it far to the inn?"

"At hand, madam," returned Michael. "It is strange we do not meet monsieur. They say these Englishmen are good husbands, but he seems not to care much for his wife."

"She will join us soon, I trust; the gaoler's daughter promised to get her out of the prison."

"Lisa is the best and the most beautiful (that is for her station, excellency), the most beautiful girl in the world. But this is the inn."

The tavern was a large but rude building, frequented only by the lower orders.

"Stay here, father. I will go and speak to the innkeeper; he is a friend of mine and has promised to get us a sledge and some horses, and then I will call this laggard, the Englishman."

Michael entered the inn.

He spoke to the master of the house.

He then proceeded to the little room which Edward occupied.

Much to his surprise upon opening the door he found Edward lying upon the bed in a deep sleep.

Without awakening him he returned to the prince and princess and told them in what conditon he had found the Englishman; and added, with awe, that he could not help thinking that he was spellbound.

A strange suspicion rose in the mind of the princess.

With her father she hurried into the room.

She then went to the door of Edward's room, and looked in.

He stirred, and stretching his arms, started up.

It was night.

A lamp was burning.

"Great heavens! you have not failed in your promise to awaken me at sunset!" he cried, wildly, and casting a blank look at the princess, whom it was plain he mistook for Katinka; "you have not been so cruel; the princees is lost!"

He started from the bed and rushed forward.

"Your wife has devoted herself for you, monsieur," said the princess. "I am rescued from my dungeon by her noble self-sacrifice."

"Can I believe that it is yourself, dear princess?

Ah, your excellency, what a luckless wretch am I, ever robbed of the means of showing my devotion. I am but a puppet of fortune, who seems, in her strange freaks, to delight in placing me in a position of degrading dependence upon the goodness of those whom I should protect and serve. My heart is too full to permit of my expressing my joy at this meeting!"

He sank on one knee, and with reverence kissed the hand of the princess.

"Sir," said the princess, coldly withdrawing her hand, "your wife——"

"My wife! Surely I am still sleeping; this must be a dream."

Now was heard the distant sound of an alarm bell.

Then the boom of a cannon.

Lisa and Katinka darted into the room.

"Not a moment must be lost! You must fly at once!" cried Lisa. "Your escape has been discovered, and we shall be pursued. We are all in equal danger. Michael is preparing the sledges. Come, come!"

She rushed from the room.

The prince then entered it.

He shook hands with Edward Leighton.

He led his daughter out from the room.

Edward followed.

They found Michael at the door with the sledges.

He had harnessed the horses.

All was prepared for the flight.

The landlord, whom Edward Leighton had paid liberally, brought them each a cup of wine.

He wished them success, and bade them farewell.

There were three sledges.

In the first, the prince and princess; in the second, Edward and Katinka; in the third, Michael and Lisa.

They drove madly.

The fields, the village, the fir woods, the wastes of snow, the ice-bound rivers fled past them.

They journied on to Tobolsk.

The innkeeper at the village from whence they had started on their adventurous journed was, himself, a Pole, the son of a patriot who had been banished to Siberia, and had died in exile.

Leighton had promised him a sum of money from his store of cash, and had promised him that he would forward a bonus as soon as he reached England, whither the fugitives resolved to make their way.

They did not stay long at Tobolsk.

They separated.

Their number according with that which was mentioned in the proclamation which was placarded on the gates and walls of the city, would have ensured their recapture.

The prince assumed the disguise of a merchant, travelling with his daughter; Michael and Lisa pretended to be their servants.

Edward and the Polish girl retained their character of fur traders, but described themselves as brother and sister.

They took a relay of horses at Tobolsk, and travelled onwards into the interior of the country.

We must leave them for the present, as the exigencies of our discursive story require that we should take a far flight to another division of the globe, that we may follow the fortunes of that villain, Harwolf, who indirectly had been the cause of all the strange misfortunes which had befallen Edward Leighton and his friends in Russia.

CHAPTER CCXXV.

SILAS AND OINY ACCOMPANY THE INDIANS IN THE HUNTING PATH. — PICTURES OF INDIAN LIFE.

SILAS RYE and Oiny Macarne fraternised with the Indians.

They were greatly interested in all they saw in the wigwams of Catahaga.

That noble young chief had become a very powerful and influential personage among the tribes.

His sterling good sense, his nobleness of spirit, his early education among the whites, and far above all, his pure and exalting love for the kind and beautiful Miuna Wyotti, inspired him with a benevolence which was strangely contrasted by the darker parts of his mingled character.

As youthful readers delight in descriptions of aboriginal people, their manners and customs, we will give some account of the way in which an Indian village is constructed, drawn from the most accurate and trustworthy authorities.

Their houses are sometimes huts and sometimes tents.

They differ in shape according to the different tribes.

Some of them are shaped like bee-hives, others are cone-shaped.

The Canadians call them lodges.

Each of them contains a family, sometimes two, with or without their relations.

They sleep in a circle upon skins, mats, or dried grass.

The fire is made in the centre.

In the Indian huts the smoke passes through the round opening in the centre of the roof by which the light is admitted.

A copper, or tin boiler, which they get in exchange from the traders, often supported only by a wooden fork stuck in the ground, pieces of wood hollowed into spoons, bits of bark of trees formed into plates and dishes, the horns of buffaloes or other animals cut into cups, constitute the whole of their table service.

A stake supplies the place of a spit, their fingers serve for forks, and a skin or the beautiful carpet of nature for their table-cloth.

The dress of many of the tribes is very picturesque.

Their blanket of wool or skin is often richly stained or beautifully embroidered in quill work.

They throw it about them with extraordinary grace and dexterity.

The coverings for the feet and legs are called moccassins.

They are made of the skin of the roebuck, buffalo, or elk.

In summer, however, the Indians mostly go bare-foot.

Their offensive weapons are the bow and arrow, the pike, the lance, the club, the dagger, the casse-léte or tomahawk, and the guns and rifles, of which they have obtained a too abundant supply from the Europeans.

The shield is their only defensive weapon; like that of the old Romans, it is made of leather, and is either round or oval.

Strange to say, like the knights in the middle ages, the Indians paint their crests or armorial bearings upon their shields.

They paint them on their tents and elsewhere.

Catahaga's crest was an eagle's wing, which was embroidered upon his blanket.

The women wear a petticoat, fitting close to the body, and reaching to the knees.

Their legs are covered with a kind of gaiter.

In summer, however, their feet and legs are always uncovered.

During the period of youth their forms and faces are very attractive.

But their flowers soon fade.

These poor women are merely slaves to the men.

There is, indeed, no slavery more abject than that of the Indian women.

The greatest insult you can offer to an Indian is to say to him, "Go! you are a squaw (a woman)!"

They have very luxuriant hair, which they tie into a coronal.

Both men and women daub their faces with red, yellow, white or blue.

When they are in mourning they paint the whole face, or even the whole body black during a year.

The second year they paint only half, and at last only streak themselves with it in various patterns.

Men and women wear ornaments on the neck and arms.

Some wear what are called in French "marqueteries," which we will translate, "small glass beads," or composition trinkets, which the traders sell them in exchange; others the teeth or claws of wild beasts.

Their canoes are formed of the hollowed trunk of a tree.

Their oars or paddles resemble those of our ancestors, the ancient Britons.

The ease with which they manage their canoes is astonishing, and considering how narrow they are, how unsteady in the water, and how heavily they are laden, it is surprising they are so seldom overset.

When a tribe break up their tents to go in quest of a new abode or forest, all the equipage, utensils, &c., occupy the centre of the canoe; the house, that is to say the mats and skins for the tent, serve to cover them.

The children, the dogs, the bears (for there is generally one or more pet bears in a wigwam) are placed opposite the men on either side, and the women the two extremities, who row and steer.

Silas Rye and Oiny Macarne were present at a meeting held at Leighton Hoe, over which the old planter presided as chief agent of the fur company, and also of the Government, who is called the "Savage Agent."

These meetings are called councils.

The Indians came to offer or renew their assurances of peace and unity to the United States.

They likewise came to treat of affairs peculiar to each band or tribe.

Presents of gunpowder, lead, tobacco, and other articles of necessity or ornament were distributed.

Monotah, the father of Catahaga, was present on this occasion.

He formed a strong contrast in appearance with his noble son the Eagle-Wing.

He was an old man of hideous aspect, bent under the weight of years and atrocities.

But still the scars with which his naked body was covered, the dignity with which he wore his buffalo robe hung on his shoulder, his bow and quiver slung at his back, a long rifle, which added to the imposing appearance, in his right hand, gave him more majesty than is possessed by many sceptered kings.

He spoke in a frank tone.

"My father," said he, to the elder Leighton, "I thank the Great Spirit that he has granted me another year to behold you once more, for you see that I am very old, and expecting every year to go to inhabit another earth. I again repeat that I have been the fierce enemy to your nation because I have had bad advisers, who made me believe that you were coming to deprive us of the liberty of hunting and to kill our wives and children. But from the time we promised you our friendship our hearts have been as white as this (pointing to Leighton's shirt). Be our friends—smoke with us, and let the war-hatchet rust in the earth where it is buried! I have spoken."

The White Pine, though he had lived through nearly a hundred winters, was still much respected and even feared in the tribe.

Oiny Macarne tried to obtain the old fellow's bow and arrows.

He told him that he would show them to everybody in his own country beyond the great salt lakes, and would tell how great a chief was Monotah, the father of the Pawnee-Loups.

But this sort of blarney had no effect upon the cunning old chief.

Oiny offered him in exchange some tobacco and gunpowder.

Upon this he immediately grew generous, and gave them to him.

Red people, in general, give nothing for nothing, any more than white ones.

The council-hall was a great room built of trunks of trees.

The flag of the United States waved in the centre, surrounded by medals which are presented by the Indians. Calumets, arms, blankets, and other Indian presents, offered by the various tribes as pledges of friendship, decorated the walls, and gave a remarkable and characteristic air to the room. A table without an inkstand—for it would be a breach of politeness to write in the presence of those who are ignorant of the art—three or four seats for the agents, the interpreter and any spectator who might not choose to sit on the ground with the savages, composed the whole furniture.

The council opened by a speech from Wabiskoa, the great sachem of the mighty Dacotahs, who took precedence of all the other chiefs.

This king of kings addressed the agent.

He began in the usual way with the "Great Spirit," or the sun or the moon, whose purity is equalled by that of his own heart, &c., &c., and finished, as ever, with a petition for presents; firewater (whisky) finding honourable mention.

The agent replied.

He began by an acknowledgment of their friendly sentiments; he expounded to them the policy it behoved them to follow; gave them a little paternal advice, and ended with a flourish about the power, the valour and glory of his great nation.

Here the first act closed.

The second began with ceremony of the sky-blue pipe or calumet, which the Indians venerate as a manitou, or good spirit of peace; they, however, pay it much less respect than they do to the evil spirit of war, represented by a red pipe.

This calumet is always presented by one of the bravest of warriors, and by a war-chief, who on this occasion acts as aide-de-camp to the chief sachem in his right.

Catahaga was pipe-bearer on this occasion.

Leighton smoked first, he passed it to one of the partners of the fur company, who passed it to Silas Rye.

The other whites followed in succession.

The pipe was then passed on to all the red men, beginning with the chiefs in their order of precedence, till it had gone through every mouth.

There was another pause between the acts.

During this the agent and his assistants were busied in the store-house preparing for the third and last act.

This opened with the ceremony of bringing the presents which the "father" gave them.

The chiefs received them without speaking a word, or making any sign of gratitude, or even of the slightest satisfaction.

They delivered them to their savages, who departed still more silently than they came.

Those who remained in the hall of council maintained the same air of indifference.

The chiefs afterwards shook hands with the agent and the other pale-faces, and then every one went his own way.

As soon as the tribes returned to their homes in the woods, the chiefs distributed the presents, and those who had killed the greatest number of enemies during the year, those who had given other proofs of valour, those who had proved themselves most unwearied and skilful in the chase, are proportionately rewarded.

The chief himself is always the last, whatever be his merits, and if nothing remains for him he utters no complaint.

The chiefs, among these people, think only of their subjects, and they and their families are often the poorest in the tribe.

On the war-path, or on great occasions, the chiefs are extravagant in bravery; at any other time, if you see a savage simple in his deportment, sober in his habits, and distinguished by a certain Spartan plainness in his attire, you may conclude that he is a chief, or a chief's son.

One day, Silas Rye told Wabiskoa, the head sachem of the Sioux, that it was not quite usual among our chiefs to give all to their subjects, and leave nothing to themselves; that, indeed, the very reverse often happened.

"How!" replied the Dacotah chief, perfectly astonished. "You are, then, more barbarous than those you call barbarians, if your civilization teaches you only to be either stupid slaves or unjust chiefs. We are right in thinking you inferior to ourselves."

Silas could find no reply.

The travellers enjoyed themselves exceedingly among the Indians, and Silas Rye studied their language so diligently that he was soon a fluent speaker of several dialects of the Iroquois tongue.

He found the Indians very superstitious.

They all believe in a Great Spirit; but there is not an individual among them who has not his particular manitou, or god, of his own choice, either an animal, a tree, a plant, or a root, and it rarely happens that two in a tribe have the same.

Whether this arises from difference of taste, or whether they think it discreet that every man should have his own god, that he may not be distracted and bored with the prayers of others, it is hard to decide.

One day as Silas Rye and Oiny were fishing they greatly offended one of the Pawnees of Catahaga's tribe, by asking him to get them some frogs for bait.

The frog, it appeared, was his manitou!

The others of his tribe roasted and ate frogs.

An Indian will never fire at an animal which has the honour of being his god or manitou, even if it is a wild beast coming to devour him.

Nat Weatherfield showed Silas a magnificent skin of a yellow bear.

This creature had attacked an Indian whose manitou he happened to be.

He was on the point of making a dinner of his faithful worshipper, when Nathaniel came up and shot him.

The Indian was well armed but had made no resistance, and did not so much as thank the trapper for his interference.

If ever an Indian does kill his manitou by accident, he begs for pardon, and says,

"It is better that you should have been killed by me than by another man, for he would sell your skin, whereas I should keep it with the greatest devotion."

And accordingly it takes its station among the divinities in the medicine-bag.

The buffalo is the only animal that is spared by nobody.

They all argue that he is the Great Spirit who presents himself under this shape, to provide for all their wants.

Indeed every part of the buffalo is useful to them.

The horns serve them for a thousand purposes and even the fibres of the hide for thread.

During the sojourn of Silas Rye among the Pawnees, news was brought to Catahaga that the brave war-chief Wakomini, or Heart of Fire, had been killed while hunting bears.

The Eagle-Wing went over to the Dacotah wigwam, in order to attend the funeral of his late companion in arms.

Silas Rye accompanied him.

The deceased dressed, or to speak more correctly, covered as he generally was during life, was placed, in a sitting attitude, upon a mat or skin, in the middle of the hut, with all his weapons, his scalps, and his calumets placed at his side.

His face was turned towards the east and decked and ornamented most elaborately.

All his relations were seated round him.

For a certain time they maintained a profound silence.

Their countenances indicated at once seriousness and grief.

Each person then addressed him.

Some in pathetic tones but without tears, others more emphatically but still calmly, all uttering praises of his virtues and expressions of regret for his loss.

His widow delivered an address with a wild expression of grief that was very touching.

"Where are you, my beloved husband?" she wailed. "You are present, indeed, but you speak not to me. You are now entirely in the society of the spirits, and can no longer care for your wife, but your wife will never cease to care for you; look on me once more, if only for a moment! But your eyes are employed in looking upon something much more handsome and pleasing than your wife. Perhaps you will not even have it in your power to remember me; your wife, however, will remember you. The sun and moon and stars will ever see me deploring your loss, and I will not delay in joining you."

Catahaga with graceful stride reverently advanced.

He addressed the dead chief in these terms,

"You are still amongst us, my brother; your person still has its usual appearance like our own—not the slightest change, nothing wanting but action. But where is that heaving breast? Wafted to the Great Spirit! Why is there silence now on those lips that once spoke the language so strong to the braves on the war-path? Why are now motionless those valiant arms which discharged the farthest-flying arrows—arms which were the terror of our enemies? You are gone to the place where you were before you came into these countries, but your glory will remain with us for ever."

"Whoa, whoa!" murmured the assembly.

Catahaga continued,

"But, our brother, you will not be lost to us for ever; we will go and rejoin you in the grand region of spirits; again we will unite in the chase, again we will march together against the enemy. In the mean time we come to offer you a tribute of kindness; your body shall not be exposed in the fields as the prey of beasts, but we will take care that it, like yourself, shall be united to your predecessors."

All the friends of the deceased as they arrived moved on by his side, each expressing his regret and the praises of the departed.

When these funeral addresses were concluded, the body of the deceased was wrapped in his rug or skin, and enclosed in the bark of trees, which serves for a coffin.

All the arms of the deceased were placed in his coffin.

On the following morning at sunrise the body was placed outside the tent, and raised upon two supporters.

Then the scene changed.

All the relations began to cry and yell as if they were frantic, till they lost their voices, when they set up a low bellowing.

His *relations* threw away whatever they were in possession of, without exception, from their ornaments, with which they begin, to their very cooking vessels.

One would imagine that they wished to survive the deceased merely to lament him.

His *friends* exhibiting at the same time every appearance of grief, collect together the various articles, and take possession of them in order to do honour to him.

They prepared a feast of all their provisions.

When they have none, which is frequently the case when they are not engaged in hunting, the feast consists of a dog.

They sacrifice it to the names of their kinsman, and only *friends* eat; all the liquors, also, which they possess outside the tent, the friends drink.

Sunset now arrived, when the screams and bellowings of the morning must be renewed.

The friends then left the relatives to cry and bellow to themselves, and retired to sleep.

The corpse remained in this situation for three or four days till it had received the customary attentions, and the adieus of all who passed it.

The due period being completed, the friends again made their appearance, and conducted the coffin to the burying place.

The coffin was raised on four stakes, about ten feet high, fixed in the earth.

HARWOLF LASHED TO THE WHEEL.

The face of the corpse is always turned towards the east.

The deceased, being a distinguished person, a large piece of wood painted, or rather daubed, with red was fixed on the side of the coffin with hieroglyphics attached to it, recording his name, glory, and achievements.

The relatives, on returning to the camp, recommenced their lamentations at the appointed hour.

They pierced their arms and legs, some with thorns and pointed pieces of wood, others with knives and arrows.

A few days after witnessing this ceremony, Silas

No. 67.

Rye, Oiny, and the trapper set out on the hunting path.

The same day the buffaloes made their appearance.

Silas Rye's mustang gave notice of their approach.

He was the finest horse of the party, and as Silas had often dismounted and walked a little to rest him, he was in the best condition, and the most spirited in this extraordinary chase.

Following the traces of Catahaga, who was as renowned as a hunter as he was as a warrior, Silas gave his horse the reins, and let him go in pursuit of the first buffalo they saw.

They soon came up with and passed him, though

he was two miles off, and having turned him they drove him towards the rest.

At the same time, Nat Weatherfield killed another at a distance.

In the evening, Black Oiny and Akantoosh, the Eagle-Wing's younger brother, brought in a third.

Plenty reigned in the camp.

The following day they travelled to the prairie s near the Sioux river, which serves as an outlet to Lake Travers.

Silas Rye begged Catahaga to give him a sight of a buffalo hunt with bows and arrows.

The young chief consented to gratify his curiosity. They galloped out on to the prairie.

Wherever they turned their eyes they saw innumerable herds of buffalo.

They urged their horses on to a meadow that was black with them.

The mustang of Silas Rye plunged into the centre of the herd, dividing it into halves, and turned several of them.

The chief, who followed with Nat Weatherfield, let fly his arrow, and shot a female buffalo.

She still endeavoured to escape, but the motion of her body in running caused the arrow to sink deeper in the wound, and when she fell the whole barb had entered.

Never had Silas seen attitudes so graceful as those of the splendid young Pawnee chief.

His quiver, his plume, his prancing horse, and prone and shaggy victim, formed a group worthy the pencil or the chisel of the highest genius in painting or sculpture.

CHAPTER CCXXVI.

SAM CASSIDY, TOM GARROD, AND BLACK RALPH RELATE MARVELLOUS TALES.

IT was some weeks before our hero recovered from his wound.

During the time that he lay upon his bed of pain, he was attended with tenderest devotedness by his faithful wife.

At length he was sufficiently recovered to rise from his couch.

When he presented himself to his followers with his arm in a sling, and his face pale and haggard, though still lighted by the brave smile which inspired them with such confidence and valour, he was received with enthusiasm.

He addressed them in a long and eloquent speech.

Reverting to the motives which had induced him to undertake his present enterprise, he said that they were those of commonest humanity ; that a gallant nation, once the bulwark of Europe against the inroads of barbarism, had been suffered to struggle without aid, and almost without sympathy, against their cruel oppressors ; had been neglected by the great powers who swayed Europe. It was no shame to him, a private adventurer, nor to them, his generous-hearted followers, to confess that they had totally failed in obtaining their object ; they had not over-rated their own prowess, as their success in the campaign had well proved ; but they had placed too much reliance upon the natural hope that all who were inspired with chivalrous feelings would join them, and that such volunteers would start up by thousands ; as, however, the thunders of outraged humanity had been confined within the walls of Exeter Hall, and had resounded from the war-lips of mild-eyed young men, of a serious turn, but with no serious purpose of running personal risk in the cause they advocated so impressively ; as it was

useless to protract the struggle, he had resolved, at least for the present, to abandon the enterprize ; first, however, accomplishing his vow to avenge the murder of Alexina Polowski, and then he would return to his ships with the intention of making a last and glorious cruise before retiring for ever from his career as a rover.

The men, who were weary of their long land cruise, and yearned to be once more on the free main, received this announcement with a hearty cheer. Preparations for the attack upon Brutoff's castle were vigorously commenced.

While these were being carried out, as many of the men as could be spared were placed under the command of Black Ralph and Sam Cassidy, with orders to take up their position in a gorge at the mouth of the valley in which the camp was pitched, as an advance guard to defend their comrades from a surprisal by the enemy.

The winter had now set in.

The nights were intensely cold.

Water thrown in the air fell to earth with a crash congealed into a sheet of ice.

The ground was deeply covered with snow.

The days passed very drearily.

Long nights of cruel frost were passed by the gallant tars around the blazing log fire, with the grog-kid passing freely from hand to hand.

Black Ralph and Sam Cassidy mingled with the men, sharing in common with them the most terrible hardships.

One night—colder, if possible, than any that the rovers had yet known—the men sat wrapped in furs and huddling close round a roaring fire which they had lighted at the mouth of the valley.

One of the pickets had been brought in frozen almost to death.

It was long before his messmates could restore him to animation.

As it was he lost all the toes of one foot, and one of the fingers of his left hand, while his limbs for a long time were paralysed and powerless.

He had fallen fast asleep on his post, overpowered by the intensity of the frost.

"They may well say that sleep and death are sisters," said Cassidy, as he looked at the limp and languid body of the patient as it was carried away into a hut built on the hill side.

"Aye, I have heard strange tales of men who have been frozen at the wheel or in the shrouds," rejoined Black Ralph. "Winter is the wizard by whom many a poor wretch has been spellbound. When I was in the whaling service I remember to have found the bodies of men who had been dead for months, and even years, in perfect preservation."

"And I, too," replied Sam Cassidy. "Hand the flip, boys, and I will tell ye a true story."

"Aye, aye, sir," responded the men.

Tom Garrod folded his arms.

In spite of his reverence for his superior a slight smile of contempt curled his lip, and he listened in an indulgent sort of way to the narration of the quiet Cassidy.

He seemed to feel himself aggrieved that anyone should compete with him in twisting yarns.

"I once sailed under Captain Warrens, the master of a Greenland whaler—"

"That's odd," interrupted Ralph. "I sailed a cruise with him myself, and perhaps I can twist you a tough yarn about him ; but your story first."

"'Tis short and simple, yet a tragedy unparalleled."

"Humph !" grunted Tom, "there's nothin' as can parallel what happened to my old messmate, Jemmy Sky——"

"Avast! stash your gammon, Tom," growled the men.

Tom mumbled something and then remained silent.

"We were becalmed in the midst of an immense number of icebergs," resumed Cassidy.

"Same as Jemmy," muttered Tom.

"At length we discovered a canal of open sea, winding its way for an immense distance among them."

"A rum coincidence; Jemmy——"

"Stopper all, you swab!"

"Pursuing our course through this channel Captain Warrens perceived, at a distance of two miles from its mouth, a strange ship."

"In course."

"At first intervening icebergs prevented anything being seen but the masts, which presented a singularly dismantled aspect."

"Crushed between two ice-bergs, same as Jemmy's case."

"On nearer approach it was found that the hull was miserably weather-beaten.

"Not a living creature was to be seen on board.

"However, through an open port-hole was perceived the figure of a man reclining in a chair with writing materials before him."

"Werry good, the skipper. Heave ahead, sir."

"Captain Warrens and a party of the men went on deck and proceeded to explore the mysterious vessel.

"Entering the apartment into which they had already glanced, they found the occupant of the chair a corpse."

"I told ye so!"

"His flesh was covered with a green, damp mould, his hand still holding his pen, and the log-book before him."

"Which, of course, you overhauled?"

"We did, and, as nearly as I can remember, the following lines were the last entry:—

"'November 11th, 18—.—We have now been enclosed in the ice seventeen days. The fire went out yesterday, and our master has been trying to kindle it again without success. His wife died this morning. There is no relief.'

"Then how long had he been dead, judging from the entry in the log-book?" asked Ralph.

"No less than thirteen years!"* was Cassidy's reply.

"In the principal cabin the dead body of a female reclined upon a bed, with a countenance still bearing the look of life.

"On the floor was seated the corpse of a man, holding in his hand a flint and steel, as if in the act of striking fire on some tinder that lay beside him.

"Several other corpses were found lying in their berths.

"No fuel, and no food of any description could be discovered.

"Captain Warrens did not, however, make a more minute search."

"And why, hearty?"

"The superstitious feeling of his crew prevented him, but he brought the log-book to England; he was enabled by various inquiries to ascertain the name and history of the imprisoned ship, which he found, as I have already told you, had been frozen in thirteen years previous to his discovery."

"Ha! that's a stiff yarn, but perfectly ins'nificant to what I'm goin' to tell ye," cried Tom, eagerly. "Pass the grog, mess-mates, and open you port-holes."

After an unconscionable pull at the toddy, Tom resumed with less hesitation than usual.

"This yere veracious history occurred to my ship-mate, Jemmy Skyflyer, about ten years ago.

"It was durin' the autumn of one of the severest winters ever known even in those parts.

"There was an attack made upon the ship when she was frozen in by some Indians as was prowling arter seal-skins.

"Now, there wasn't a shot in the cannister, either for the great guns or small arms, so the crew had to load their pistols with frozen sea-biscuits, and their guns with dried salt-junk. The effec' was tremendjous! and no sort of leaden missiles could ha' been half so hard or so penetratin'. But that arn't what I'm goin' to tell ye—no, nor yet how the men had to hold the cap'en's hair on durin' a tarnation squall, but the subjec' of this weracity is Jemmy Skyflyer himself.

"Well, as Mr. Cassidy (my humble sarwice to yer honour) has said, Jemmy's ship lay becalmed and jammed up by the meetin' of two ice-floes. However, the cap'en contrived in a werry seaman-like manner to keep up the spirits of the crew (he never stinted the grog, Cap'en Ralph), and they managed to cut their way out into the open main.

"Arter they had sailed for some days, the man on the look-out reported as a couple of icebergs were rushing down on 'em at a terrific rate.

"It was all in vain that the cap'en tacked to windward; they were run down, and with an awful crash the ice-bergs dashed together.

"The vessel was struck and jammed between 'em.

"They parted and she went down.

"I needn't tell ye, messmates, as Jemmy was a wide-awake chap; he had bought a child's caul of an old girl at Portsmouth, and so in consequence it was quite onpossible for him to be drowned.

"He floated like a cork for several days.

"At last he made a mountain of ice that was soaring along the top of surf like a floatin' castle.

"Now, it's the opinion of some as if a man goes to sleep in open air without a fire in these frozen regions, he never more hears the bo'swain pipe all hands; but that's all accordin' to circumstances and exposure.

"I dare say there's not one among ye as hasn't seen a pipe of Maderia opened and a lot of flies found drowned in it, which as everybody knows philosophers have restored to life by lying 'em in the sun; sim'lar with Jemmy, he climbed on the iceberg, and as he could climb above a yard up the side, he laid himself down on a shelf of ice and soon fell fast asleep. Admire the action of natur'. Every dash of spray as flew over him turned into icicles, and arter awhile, quite unconscious, Jemmy was covered all over; and arter awhile, bedded in the ice like a fly in a lump of amber.

"So Jemmy sailed many a cruise along the undiskivered coasts in his snug berth in the iceberg.

"At last the summer came, the ice-fields broke up, and the iceberg broke into several divisions, the block which contained Jemmy being thrown up on to the shore.

"How many months or years poor Jemmy was sleepin' as sound as a seal on a rock in his snug berth, it would be werry hard to say, but at last he opened his eyes, and found himself enclosed on all sides by the ice. It chanced as Jemmy had brought with him his pipe and tinder-box; so, as the nat'ral heat of his body had melted away the ice about him sufficient to allow of his rummaging the hold of his pea-jacket, he pulled them out and struck a light. Now, Jemmy was rather flabbergastered at his position, for he could see by the light which shone through the ice that the summer were at its height, and that the winter would soon return; so, as there appeared werry little chance of the ice melting, he was rather in stays as to what course to take; howsomever, he smoked and reflected.

"Shouldn't wonder if some of ye ain't heard as toads have been found in trees and rocks and couldn't give a werry satisfactory account of theirselves; but though its the nat'ral instinct of sich animals to be on suction, ice-water to human creeturs is not a werry nutrative diet, so poor Jemmy beg—to——

hungry; the more he reflected the more wisions of prowisions rose up in his excited imagination, and Jemmy got so onpatient and so narvous that he pulled out his snuff-box (I think I told ye the yarn of the scrape he got into about the unfortunit middy as fell a wictim to Jemmy's perpensity for snuff). Well, messmates, he pulled out his box o' raperee, and he took a fist full in his excitement. He fell into such a wolcanic conwulsion of sneezin' that the block of ice in which he were embedded, though it were as broad and as deep as a three-decker, busted into splinters, and left poor Jemmy on the broad of his back agazing up at the blue sky, and listening to the roll of the breakers. It was some time afore Jemmy could manage to get himself into trim for sailing, but at last he made weigh, and falling in with the crew of a ship which was likewise frozen in, he joined them and so returned to Old England. Mr. Cassidy's yarn, with all reverence, is not unbelieveable, but this is a weracity."

After the men had enjoyed a laugh at Tom's story, Black Ralph followed suit with the following story of the "Mysterious Sack":—

"Messmates, I sailed under the same Captain Warrens of whom Mr. Cassidy has spoken.

"We were lying off Naples.

"I was first mate of our merchant ship.

"I went ashore with some messmates, and we boosed our jibs at a wine shop in the Strada de Toledo.

"Now it happened that we were provisioning, and several sacks of potatoes and other vegetables had been taken aboard.

"One sack was left at the wine shop.

"I and the bo'swain remained ashore after all the men had gone aboard.

"We had promised to bring the sack aboard with us, intending to get a porter to carry it to the boat, and then to row it ourselves to the ship.

"We sat spinning yarns and freshening hawse in the parlour of the wine shop.

"Two carriages rolled up to the door.

"Four men and two women got out of them.

"Three of the men were priests, the other one of the police.

"One of the women was dressed as a nun; the other was cloaked and closely veiled.

"The latter seemed much distressed.

"She was bitterly weeping.

"She appeared to be a prisoner to the rest.

"They passed through the room in which we were sitting.

"They were conducted by the inn-keeper to a chamber above.

"I could not get a glint of the girl's eye.

"She appeared not to notice us, but seemed quite overpowered with grief.

"Said Joe to me—for the bo'swain's name was Joe,

"'Shiver my top-gallant, Mr. Talbot, if that isn't a case for manly interference, I'm no seaman!'

"'I think so too, Joe,' said I, 'but unfortunately I can see no way in which we can help the little cherub.'

"'Dam'me, sir, there's always a way to do a good action!' says Joe.

"'But the way is sometimes difficult to find out, and you must remember, hearty, that we have not many hours to remain on shore,' said I.

"'You notify, sir,' said Joe, 'this little beauty has run away from some convent. Perhaps she has taken the veil, perhaps she hasn't, but all's as one. When they get her back to the dungeon they will treat her with most unmerciful cruelty. Dam'me, sir! will ye stand that?'

"Joe began to get red in the face.

"I kept as cool as a codfish.

"'It don't concern us, Joe,' said I, 'and we're bound to respect the laws of the land.'

"Joe started up.

"'Mr. Talbot,' says he, 'if the ship's chaplain had told it, I wouldn't have believed it on ye.'

"'Come on, bo'swain,' said I, 'it's time we went aboard; we sail at six bells.'

"This was more than Joe could stand.

"'Split my binnacle, Mr. Talbot,' he spluttered, 'you're never going to leave that tight little brig to be overhauled by the enemy without one effort to cut her out? Blow me hard, if I can believe it on ye!'

"'Belay your jawing-tackle, hearty,' said I; and I added in one of my fine couplets—

"''Twas for Helen they fought, those big bruisers of Troy,
So, my limbs! here's a broadside for Sally!'

"'Huzzay!' cried Joe, 'this will be a jolly lark.'

"'And may end in a flight from the forecastle with a string round the lark's neck,' said I.

"'I'm not to be bamboozled by that sort of gammon,' said he, laughing; 'but why do ye waste time in palavering?'

"'For our mutual diversion,' said I, 'and to pass time till the three parsons and the marine have finished their supper.'

"'Aye, aye, sir,' he answered, with a wink.

"He pulled out his watch.

"'And how about going aboard, sir?' he asked.

"'The skipper told me to stay ashore till I had finished my business with the agent, and though that's all settled, we can take advantage of this permission to carry out our scheme for carrying off the little renegade.'

"'Aye, sir,' answered Joe, 'and would it not be better if we could get a berth alongside of her? Suppose we ask the skipper of this bunk to let us have a hammock to lay by in for an hour or so.'

"'A good thought,' I replied, 'it's getting dark and the priests and the marine will be on the alert.'

"'But the old abigail?'

"'Well, perhaps we can catch the dragon asleep.'

"I got up and called the landlord.

"He was all smirks and suavity.

"He hoped that our excellencies were satisfied with the accommodation afforded at his poor albergo.

"We told him that we were entirely satisfied, and asked him to show us to a chamber.

"'Pardon, Signor Inglese,' said the old chap, with a cringing bow; 'I have no place convenable to such exalted guests; the best room in my poor inn is occupied by a young lady, a novice who has violated her holy vows by running away from her convent; the lady abbess is with her.'

"'Too bad—much too bad, this irreligion,' said I, with a severe look. 'A young novice to elope from the scourge, and the cell, and the oratory—monstrous!' I winked hard at Joe.

"Joe grumbled assent, and seemed as much scandalised as myself at the awful impiety of the pretty apostate.

"I sighed, and rolled up my eyes.

"I have played the Tartuffe and the priest in Hamlet.

"'Since the Holy order of the Inquisition was suppressed, the Church has been going to ——.'

"I blew out the 'blazes' with another sigh.

"Giacopo was in ecstasies.

"'Ah! Maria beata!' he cried, raising his hands and eyes. 'The signori Inglese are catholics and not heretics!'

"I would have crossed myself, but I have some respect for signs and symbols.

"However, the landlord was quite convinced of our orthodoxy, and was ready to kiss our feet.

"'Ah, miserable wretch that I am!' he exclamed, 'not to be able to give better accomodation to such virtuous and illustrious guests. But, you see, signori, this is the eve of the carnival, and every room is crowded. There is, certainly, a sort of store-room adjoining the apartment in which are the abbess and the novice, and there, by-the-bye, is the sack of potatoes which should have been taken to your ship, signori.'

"'That room will do well enough,' said I; 'we want only to turn in for an hour or so, as we're tired.'

"'I will order servants to make up a bed for the signori on the instant.'

"'Pshaw! just a mattress, or even a pile of sacks will suffice.'

"'Ebene, signori,' said the landlord, and away he went.

"The priests and the police officer now rose.
"The latter was armed with a musket.
"He took his post at the door.
"The others retired to rest.
"We followed them.
"They entered an apartment nearly opposite to that in which the pretty truant was caged.

"As we passed her door we heard the old abbess rating her, and threatening her with all the pangs of purgatory, which were to commence from that hour.

"The poor girl was sobbing and pleading like a child under correction.

"If we had yielded to the impulse that possessed us, we should have kicked in the door and carried her off by the strong hand.

"However, we restrained ourselves and entered our chamber.

"Here we reconnoitred.

"It was a slip of a place, crammed with trunks and bags and barrels, our potato sack amongst the rest of the lumber.

"Two mattresses with a blanket and counterpane a-piece were placed on the floor on one side of the room.

"Opposite, and on the side nearest to the ladies' apartment, was a door.

"It was locked, and had evidently remained unopened for a very long time.

"The partition was not sufficiently thick to obstruct the trasmission of sound. We could still hear the abbess rating the unfortunate girl.

"She compelled her to repeat an endless number of penitential psalms.

"She then ordered her to sleep on the ground by way of penance, while she herself got into bed.

"I tried to get a peep at the pretty culprit through the keyhole, but a curtain hung before the door on the inner side.

"During many hours we were nearly mad with impatience.

"The abbess, even after she had got to bed, could not cease bullying her victim.
"The girl still sobbed fitfully.
"At last the old crone gave us a musical intimation that she was asleep.

"I put my lips to the key-hole and said in a whisper,
"'Litto! Signorina!'
"The girl screamed.
"The abbess was awakened.

"'What is it, you abandoned and malignant creature? Why do you disturb my slumbers?' she cried in a passion at being thus aroused.

"'Ah, mother, my dream was so horrible!' answered the novice.

"'Profane wretch, can you wonder? The horrors of your dream will become realities if you do not repent betimes! Let me sleep, and, to dispel your bad thoughts, I enjoin you inwardly to repeat aves and paters till the morning.'
"The girl did not reply.

"Soon the mellifluous music softly breathed from the nasal organ of the saintly abbess, proclaiming that sleep had laid his leaden wand upon her eyelids. The old gal was snoring like a porpoise.

"Once more I applied my mouth to the key-hole.
"'Signora!'
"'Litto! Speak lower.'
"'Do you wish to escape?'
"'Shall I?'
"'Like a bird!'
"'How?'
"'We must see for that!'
"'You are not Italian.'
"'No, I'm English?'
"'Ever brave English!'
"'Ever charming Italians!'
"'But I'm French.'
"'Tant mieux.'
"'How can I get out?'
"'You must have patience, mademoiselle.'
"'I must indeed!'
"'I shall burst the door.'
"'O no—no—no; I implore you!'
"'It will be easy; the bolts are rotten.'
"'The mother superior will wake.'
"'Let her go to her father inferior!' I answered with a push at her door.

"'I shall scream.'
"'Exactly so; the nightmare.'
"Bang went the door.
"The girl, terribly frightened, uttered a terrific shriek.
"The lady abbess once more leaped out of bed.
"She gave her victim several hearty slaps.

"''Tis on purpose, you malicious heretic!' she cried. 'You will never get peace for your evil conscience till you have suffered a month's sharp discipline, and you shall have it. Prepare yourself for the morning's penance.'

"I thought it best not to interfere, as such a course would only make matters worse for the poor girl by destroying every chance of her escape.

"Yet I boiled with wrath.
"The abbess slapped the girl till she was out of breath, and then once more got into bed.

"The girl remained on her knees, sobbing bitterly.
"At last the abbess was once more asleep.
"The door was open!
"'Now, mademoiselle.'
"'Attendez!'
"'What is the matter?'
"'I must fetch my cloak.'
"'Make haste.'
"'I come.'

"With her cloak wrapped round her shoulders the girl glided into the room.

"She was a diminutive creature, thoroughly French, about twenty years of age, with glossy and wavy black hair, sparkling black eyes, rose-tinted cheeks, and teeth of snowy whiteness; she was ravishingly pretty and did not look the least like a nun.

"'Ah, messieurs, you are so good, so brave, I cannot thank you.'

"'I wish, mam'selle, you had better cause to thank us; we have not yet escaped.'

"'Ah, no, the thing is impossible.'

"'With courage and care it can be managed. You are eager to escape?'

"'Yes, oh, yes! What am I for a nun? I am a grisette of the Sorbonne, a milliner; a relation died and left me a considerable fortune, and my wicked uncle has conspired with that wretched abbess to rob me of my property and my liberty together.'

"'You shall lose neither, while we can defend you.'
"'Ah, mais mon dieu! how to get away?'
"'What's in the wind, Joe?' said I, to the

bo'swain, who had been listening at the door, and come up with a blank face.

"'That marine swab keeps the passage, with his fire-lock at half charge, and the four jackdaws are beginning to shake their feathers; I heard 'em cawing their matins in chorus.'

"'Yes, and after prayers they will call the abbess. Ah, what folly! Generous Englishmen, you cannot save me; I will go back to my room, and endure the worst with patience.'

"'Douse my day-lights if you do!'" muttered Joe, interposing his burly form between the girl and the door. "'I told old Blow-hard that we should be off before daylight.'"

"'Do not heed for me, kind gentlemen. Ah, why do I weep? Poor me!—poor Marguerite! What have I done to be made to suffer so much?'

"'Is your name Marguerite, dear mademoiselle?' I asked.

"'Yes. Remember me sometimes. I will return now. A thousand thanks and adieux!'

"But I detained her.

"'Ain't Marguerite the French for a daisy?'" whispered Joe.

"'So I thought,' said he. 'Now the thing's easy enough.'

"'How so?'

"'Why, one pretty daisy is easier to carry than a sack of potatoes.'

"'Capital!' I answered. 'Out with the pommes de terre, and in with the Marguerite.'

"At first the girl would not consent to this arrangement.

"She yielded at last.

"We cautiously emptied the sack of the potatoes.

"Wrapping the girl in her cloak, we placed her in the sack.

"We then opened the door, and carried the sack on our shoulders into the room below.

"'Did the signori sleep well, last night?' asked the landlord, who was up, though morning was just breaking.

"'Pretty well. Did you hear a noise in the night?'

"'Yes, a sort of bang, and then a scream. I believe the abbess was exorcising the spirit of Luther which possesses all these profane runaways. That novice will suffer for her impiety; she belongs to a strict order. Shall I call the porter to carry your sack, sir?'

"'Thank ye,' I answered, 'there's no need.'

"I slipped some money into his hand.

"We were stopped by the sentinel.

"He insisted upon knowing what was in the sack.

"I told him it was full of potatoes.

"I was rather taken aback, but I thrust my hand into the mouth.

"Two or three had been left at the bottom.

"Mademoiselle carefully handed them to me.

"She was a girl of spirit that, for she pinched my finger.

"The sentinel was satisfied.

"We lifted the bag on to our shoulders.

"We carried it through the street.

"We reached the boat, and pulled off to our vessel.

"The captain laughed heartily when we told him the story.

"The girl said we should not get into the least trouble, if we could but escape the Neapolitans, for that she had been carried off by a stratagem, and that her detention was illegal.

"The alarm was soon given at the inn.

"Boats were put off, and a gun fired to warn us to lay to, for we were getting under weigh.

"However, our captain slipped anchor, and we sheered off.

"We hailed a French man-o'-war, and her captain took charge of the Marguerite.

"She sent me a handsome present to share with Joe; but you would scarcely credit it, messmates, that though I offered her my hand and my heart, she threw herself away upon a beggarly medical student, her sweetheart, at Paris."

CHAPTER CCXXVII.

THE CAREER OF CAPTAIN HARWOLF—THE PANDEMONIUM OF A PIRATE SHIP—FIENDISH CRUELTY AND BESTIAL DEBAUCH—THE DRUNKEN CAPTAIN AND HIS MATE—PLOTS AND COUNTER-PLOTS — HARWOLF'S DISSIMULATION—A DARK CONSPIRACY.

HARWOLF, the villanous son of a villanous father, after having gratified his vengeance upon the Spaniard, Corderes, and within so little having destroyed Silas Rye, the inveterate foe of himself and of his father, the pirate escaped to the coasts of Cuba.

Here he perpetrated such diabolical cruelties, that even his crew, hardened in crime, and fiendish in atrocities, were revolted at his conduct.

Gerald Wardlaw, his lieutenant, though nothing better than a brutal ruffian, was still less demoniac than his commander.

Harwolf became confirmed in his habits of drunkenness and debauch.

His vessel was a very pandemonium of vice and blasphemy.

More than once he had exterminated the whole crew of the hapless merchantmen which fell into his power, by tortures the most cruel.

I think our youthful readers have seen enough to disgust them with the falseness of those pictures of criminal life which represent pirates and robbers as noble and chivalrous gentlemen.

Can black be white? Can crime be virtue? Can there be anything honourable or admirable in the daring of ruffians, whose life is forfeited by their crimes, and whose interest it is rather to die in fight, than to be dragged to the shameful death on the scaffold which they have deserved by their crimes?

And as for their robbing the rich to give to the poor, they only thereby implicate the poor in their crime, for the receiver is as bad as the thief, and, for the most part, thieves are too selfish and mean-spirited to relinquish any part of their booty.

The character of the Boy Pirate is altogether exceptional.

The object of its portrayal is to show that, even under the most favourable circumstances, the position of a felon at large is most miserable; if he is victorious for awhile and enjoys in his gang almost regal authority; if a chain of circumstances place it in his power to do good to many, and to compel him to harm but few, still he is a rebel against the best and justest laws, and the brand and the stigma can never be removed, until he repent and deliver himself up, for punishment or pardon, to the society he has outraged.

The Spaniard, Diego, had now another cause for vengeance in the death of his brother, Corderes.

He abandoned the Brazilian war ships, and, serving upon merchant ships for short voyages along the coast and among the islands, he always contrived to remain in those parts where Harwolf was said to be cruising.

Several times he had deserted his ship rather than be carried off the track of the man he hunted with hatred so implacable.

To return to the pirate schooner.

Every day the power of the tyrant Harwolf waned and was superseded by the growing authority of his lieutenant, Wardlaw.

Daniel Harwolf began to perceive this, and he re-solved, as all tyrants do under such circumstances, to maintain his power by rendering himself terrible to all around him.

Several times he had been guilty of the most dreadful outrages against his own men.

One poor fellow he had brained with an axe only for expressing sympathy for a wretched prisoner under the torture.

Another he had pistoled for advising him to go below when he had made himself half-delirious with drink.

On one occasion they gave chase to a small craft laden with wine and tobacco.

Being a vessel of light burden she took refuge in one of the creeks.

It chanced that Harwolf was so drunk that he was quite incapable of commanding the vessel.

The command therefore devolved upon Wardlaw. The pirate resolved to cut her out with the boats.

The crew of the little vessel, finding that resistance was hopeless, deserted the ship and escaped to the shore.

The pirates, satiate, for awhile, at least, with scenes of blood and slaughter, suffered them to escape.

They seized whatever they found on board, and conveyed it to the ship.

It was a splendid evening.

The sun was sinking like a ball of glowing red flame through a sky of molten gold and vermillion.

The sea was calm, as lightly rippled as a pool kissed by the evening wind.

The wild and savage-looking pirates were engaged in hauling up the last of the bales and barrels from the boats alongside.

Wardlaw stood leaning against the capstan.

His bronzed face wore a dark and thoughtful look.

He gazed along the lumbered and dirty deck with an air of contempt and discontent.

Daniel Harwolf came up the main-hatch. He approached his lieutenant.

The latter glanced at the intoxicated ruffian with a black frown and a bitter sneer.

Harwolf's dress was disordered, his rusty hair unkempt, his grey eyes bloodshot and staring, and his cruel, sensual lips drivelling and distorted.

His belt was unbound, and he trailed his sheathed sword in his left hand.

He hiccuped, and he reeled in his walk.

"Where—where the dev— the craft, the cursed brig? Haul over the main-sheet; a blight on ye!"

"Go back to your berth, the job's finished," said Wardlaw, turning away in disgust.

"Fin—finised? watsh finish? Who dares to take the—the command of the sh-ship whilsh I'm aboardsh? Wheresh the brig, I shay, ye lubbers?"

The dashing rover dashed against the capstan, and was forced to lay hold of the sides to support himself.

"Taken, I tell ye."

"Taken? Who dares to take? I shay, Master Gerald, allow me to speak a word in your ear. Curse ye, sir, who are ye?"

"One step above a beast, as you are infinitely below one. Get to your cabin, my pretty captain; I'm not treacherous, and I don't want to take advantage of your drunken impotence."

Daniel spluttered an oath. Resting on his heels, he stretched out both his arms as if to clutch the other by the throat.

He swayed backwards and forwards.

"Off, beast!" said Wardlaw, passing him with a look of loathing.

He laid his hand upon Wardlaw's shoulder.

The seaman pushed him back with his open hand, and passed on.

Harwolf scrambled on to his knees.

He struck at Wardlaw with his sword.

The pirate turned and hurled him backward.

Taking no further notice of him he walked forward.

The men had looked on with sullen faces.

They left their officers to settle the quarrel between themselves.

"Devils and darkness!" shrieked Harwolf, snatching up his sword. "Mutiny! mutiny!"

He stumbled on brandishing his sword.

His foot struck against the combings of the main hatch.

He was precipitated below.

He lay on his back bruised and powerless.

The pirates exchanged glances of mutual disgust and suspicion.

Blacklock, and another, a mulatto called Kumba, went below.

They raised the groaning drunkard, and bore him to his cabin.

They left him to sleep.

"That cursed madman will bring us to ruin!" growled Blacklock.

"Iss; and yo and me we far' wuss when him dead. De crew hate us most as bad as de skipper; guess dey cut ebery troat we'se got among us."

"Aye, there'll soon come a smash, I can see," returned Blacklock; "this cruise won't last long."

"Guess we better speck to him 'bout dis lilly affair. Yo hear what dat feller Wardlaw tell de oder feller, Ramsay—'Neber no luck till we've settled 'em all tree; de skipper, Blacklock, and de mullatto cuss—dat's me."

"Who's there," shouted Harwolf, with a dreadful oath.

"It's I, cap'en, Will Blacklock," answered the second mate, for such was this ruffian's degree.

With another oath, the pirate bade them come in. They entered the cabin.

Harwolf sat up in his hammock.

His eyes glared with suspicious terror.

He had bound a sash round his waist, which he had crammed to an extent which seemed ridiculous with swords, daggers, and fire-arms.

In each hand he held a pistol.

"What cheer, cap'en?" asked Blacklock, in a conciliating tone.

At the same instant he flinched back.

The pirate captain levelled the brace of pistols at his head.

"Clear out, you infernal skunks! I smell treachery!" he roared, and added, with a volley of frightful execrations, that he would set fire to the powder magazine, and blow them off the face of the waters.

Blacklock swore frightfully in turn, calling his superior a fool, who did not know his friends from his enemies.

"If there's a mutiny, shan't I suffer with you?" cried Blacklock. "Is there to be no unity amongst any on us? Are we to cut each other's throats as if there were no such thing as a man-o'-war in the high seas? What hope have we of a merry cruise or a safe landin', if we're to eat each other alive in this fashion? Hang it, cap'en, cool down, and hearken to reason."

"It's the cursed drink!" hissed the pirate. "That sabre wound and the drink together, have made me mad, I own it!"

"Well, cap'en, as you're coming round a bit, suppose we put our heads together, and consart some means of defending ourselves from Wardlaw's lot, who, as I'm sartain, mean mischief."

"Blacklock, I'm getting tired of the grand account."

"Blow me, cap'en! and so am I."

"Gorra! dat's my 'pinion. Cussed bad spec'lation!" added the mulatto. "S'pose we get hold ob all de gelore, and den set fire to de cussed ship, and blow all de mutineers out to de debil!"

"Go into the trip-deck, and see if there's any one listening," said Harwolf.

Blacklock obeyed this order.

He returned.

"The coast's clear, cap'en."

"Good. Shut the door."

The mulatto closed it.

"I suppose I can depend on ye?"

"Aye, aye, cap'en—our interest's one."

"It is."

"In course; the crew have sworn to have my life as well as yours."

"Ha! then there is treason!"

"So Kumba says."

"How do you know that, you black thief?"

"Yo listen, cap'en. I was on fo'castle fast asleep; hearn voices, open my eyes, seen as dar war dat Wardlaw and Ramsey. 'He's mad,' says Ramsey. 'Aye, mate,' says Wardlaw, 'and are we gwine to suffer for this swine that will neither command himself, nor leave the working of the ship to abler hands?'"

"He said that, did he?"

"Dat I swar, cap'en."

Harwolf growled a fearful oath.

"Go on."

"Berry good. I hearn Ramsey say, 'You do all de work, you hab sabe de ship many a time when we were 'bliged to tie dis cuss to de fo'mast to prevent him doin' us some mischief to de crew. What for yo not skipper yo'self?'"

"And what did Wardlaw answer?" asked the pirate, fiercely.

"He say dat him not stand much more'n ob sich humbug. He swar as him do fo' yo and Mas'r Blacklock, and de cussed Malay mulatto—dat's me."

"Well, it's plain, hearties, that we must do something energetic at once," said Harwolf. "Now, listen to me. How many think ye, Blacklock, may be depended on?"

"The fewer we trusts the better," grumbled the fellow, in a surly tone; "first tell us what you propose, cap'en."

"I mean to stick at nothing, however desperate, mind that."

"Aye, I think you've given proof enough of that already, cap'en," returned the other, grimly.

"Well, then, suppose we confine this plot to ourselves; let us have no confederates."

"Heave ahead, sir."

"We have stored most of our plunder in the cavern of our treasure-island."

"Aye, aye."

"And I have agents along the coast who will puchase it."

"Right, cap'en."

"I and you, Blacklock, will go ashore and send the boat's crew back on some excuse. Kumba shall stay aboard; I will lay a train to the magazine and leave the slow match for him to fire."

"Yo do so, mas'r, but if I hab de large share ob de danger, I hab too a berry large share ob de reward."

"Aye, that's but fair," said Blacklock, with a strange look at the captain.

"I agree to that; I deal fairly with friend as well as foe," said Harwolf, with a grin.

"And when's this pretty plot to be carried out, cap'en?"

"Why not to-night?"

"Why not, cap'en?"

"But how yo lay de train, sar, widout let de oders know what yo mean to do?"

"Leave that to me."

"Well, cap'en, we'll go on deck, now."

"Aye, do. When I order the boat to be put down, stand by the davits and give the sign to Kumba."

"Aye, sir."

"And now leave me."

The seamen left the cabin.

Harwolf leaped from his hammock.

He washed himself, and dressed with care.

He removed from his sash some of the steel weapons, but retained all the fire-arms.

Not to look aggressive he concealed them with a very handsome shawl which he threw loosely over his shoulder.

He came on deck.

Wardlaw had called all hands aft.

He had just commenced an harangue.

The pirates were not a little surprised when they saw their drunken skipper dressed neatly and walking with steady step towards them.

They fell back and looked rather sheepish and sullen.

The pirate leader's cheek waned pale.

Harwolf was not without a certain sort of courage.

Nor did he entirely lack the power of dissimulation which his father possessed.

He held out his hand to Wardlaw.

After a moment's hesitation the lieutenant touched it coldly.

Harwolf did not appear to take the least notice of the fact that the men had been assembled, nor did he ask the reason why Wardlaw had summoned them.

"Wardlaw," he said, with a faint and sickly smile, "a frank confession is better than a lame excuse. You have all, both officers and men, had some cause to be dissatisfied with my conduct of late; but the fact is, hearties, I have indulged too freely in the flowing bowl, and that cursed wound in my head has somewhat unsettled my brain, I think.; but, as you know I would never stand insubordination from the boldest of my men, so I am not too proud to acknowledge my misconduct, nor so ungenerous not to thank my colleague for the gallant manner in which he has acted for me during my temporary aberration. So let us forgive and forget, like true comrades, and while I set you an example of moderation do ye all give rein to your spirits and let's have a bout. Hurrah for the 'Jolly Oliver!' Bo'swain, pipe all hands for fun."

The men were so startled by the effrontery of this speech, that, despite their dislike of their leader, they uttered a loud cheer.

There wanted not some among them who clung to him with superstitious tenacity, as their first and most legitimate leader.

If they commenced the game of deposing their commanders, they knew not where it might stop, and justly feared that all order and discipline would be at an end.

There was something fiendish in the glance which the treacherous villain cast upon his crew, as leaving them to their merriment he walked aft, and entered the state cabin.

Blacklock joined him.

The mulatto kept watch in the trip-deck.

He had orders to give an alarm if anything transpired to indicate that the crew had got scent of the conspiracy.

THE BOY PIRATE RESCUES HIS WIFE FROM THE RUSSIANS.

CHAPTER CCXXVIII.

THE TRAIN—HARWOLF SUSPECTED—THE SIG-
NAL SHOTS—THE MINUTE GUNS—THE TREA-
SURE CAVERN—FOILED—HARWOLF A PRI-
SONER—LASHED TO THE HELM.

THE treacherous Harwolf and his willing agent left
the cabin together.

The men on deck were indulging in every sort of
licentious buffoonery.

Wardaw did his best to restrain them.

His efforts were utterly useless.

They drank, they danced, they sang, they swore,
they quarrelled, they fought.

No. 68.

Harwolf stood below gazing up at the thundering
deck above, with the concentred malice of every
fiend.   The man had gone mad with vindictive
spleen, quite ungovernable, because, from the first
ungoverned; his passions had overmastered his prudence and instict of self-preservation.

He shook his fist.

His face became distorted with hideous passion.

He breathed curses which would have been too
horrible for the ears of the most inveterate
blasphemer.

So much for your gallant rover! This picture is
but too true.

A man who will fly the grizzly emblem of death,

the horrid death's head and cross bones on its black pall, at his mast head as his banner, who will run down the unarmed merchantman, murder the innocent, hard-working crew, widowing their wives, and orphaning their children, murder the crew, ravish the women, and plunder the stores which would bring pleasure and comfort to the rich and the poor. Can such a man be accounted a hero? Can he be anything but a monster?

The lives of pirates and highwaymen, if truly told, would do more good among a certain class of readers than the most moral essays of the best intentioned.

Fancy Dick Turpin the bold, Dick Turpin the hero, the rider of bonnie Black Bess, taking a poor, decrepit old lady and placing her on the fire to burn, because she was too frightened at his cowardly threats to tell him where she kept her savings.

Fancy the gallant Jack Sheppard taken prisoner dead drunk at a pie-shop, a confessed informer, and peach who laid all the blame of his failures upon his comrade Blueskin, who was at least quite as gallant as himself.

A poor little fellow, perhaps, worse than those orphaned by having parents who teach him all that is vile, and train him sedulously in wickedness, steals a loaf or a sum of money because he is hungry. Pity him, reform him, teach him how brave it is to resist dishonesty; let him feel the sweet satisfaction that self-denying honesty affords. Do not be harsh with him, do not transport him, nor flog him, nor degrade him, teach him to hate his own fault, and feel ashamed of himself; but the man who has courage and skill and talents that will descend so low as to traffic in filching, let him be looked upon as a contemptible wretch, and a snob without a grain of the real metal of English pluck and endurance in his composition.

One of our youthful readers has earned by his honest labour a sum of money which he is bringing home, perhaps, to a widowed mother.

Suddenly he is stopped and robbed of every farthing by a dashing, handsome gentleman in a red rug coat, cocked hat, and gilt spurs, with a pair of gleaming pistols in his belt, and a sword by his side.

Penniless he returns to his home.

"Never mind, mother," says he, "I was robbed by a dashing highwayman, who could sing,

          "'To the road, boys.'

Who had a fine black steed (stolen), and was handsome and well-dressed."

Is such a speech natural or possible?

Would not the poor boy thus robbed call for the police, and bless them if they could restore the money of which he had been deprived, and punish the mean, sneakish rogue who robbed him?

Of course he would.

But to return to our story.

The gallant pirate proceeded to put in practice the murderous design he had formed for the destruction of the men who had cloven to him through all his tyranny and rascality.

He walked to the magazine.

He opened it with a key which he always kept in his possession.

Staving in one of the barrels of gunpowder, he strewed a train of the combustible to an outlet in the trip-deck.

Here he placed the slow match.

He called to the mulatto.

"When I am ashore," he said, "I will fire two shots as a signal for you to follow in the boat. Come alone."

"Iss, mas'r," returned the mulatto, with a grin; "me understand vera well. Yo tell de crew dat you send for me; I set fire to de slow match afore I get ober de side."

"Right, Kumba; all depends on your care and courage."

Harwolf went on deck.

The men were in the midst of their enjoyment.

The captain held up his hand for attention.

There was a sudden hush.

"I am going ashore, lads," he said, "to visit the treasure-cave. Bo'swain, man the boat. I shall not keep you from your sky-larking, I and Blacklock will stay ashore till we wish to return, when we will signal you by a pistol-shot."

The men, who were half-drunk, huzzaed, and busied themselves in putting down the boat.

Wardlaw called Ramsey aside.

"The skunk means treachery," he whispered. "Tell the bo'swain to make a feint of returning to the ship, but to row round the headland and land with the men, and if I fire the long gun let them seize the wretch and bring him aboard as prisoner."

"I will!" returned Ramsey. "I share your suspicions."

Ramsey sent one of the men to call the boatswain.

The boatswain went below.

The mate gave him his directions.

"Where is Kumba? Some of you fetch the mulatto,' said Harwolf.

The man was brought.

"What yo want, sar?" asked the half-caste, with a well-affected look of surprise.

"I may want you, Kumba, but only you. I don't want to mar sport; when I require your services I shall fire two pistol shots."

"Berry good, sar. When he'm hearn de pistols go off, Kumba come."

Harwolf and Blacklock got into the boat.

They were pulled ashore.

Harwolf and Blacklock leaped out of the boat.

"My lads, you can pull back; we shall weigh anchor to-morrow, and there are some jewels and money-bags in the cavern, which I wish to take with us; we can find them and bring them to the beach without your help. Go aboard and enjoy yourselves."

The men saluted their captain and pulled off.

The night was so dark that it was impossible to watch their progress as far as the vessel's side.

However, the two villains waited until they thought the boat had reached the ship.

Then, with the laugh of a gloating fiend, Harwolf drew his pistol.

He motioned his companion to do the same.

He fired in the air.

Blacklock seconded the shot.

They stood for a moment gazing as if by fascination upon the dark sea.

The night was hazy, and they could not see the vessel.

"Come," said the pirate captain, "let us go to the cavern and await the result."

"Had we not better remain where we are?"

"No; we can blockade ourselves in the cavern. There is an outlet which I alone know of, it opens upon the river; we can seek it. There is a boat hidden there, and if there should be any mishap we can escape to another island."

Blacklock followed the captain.

As they were nearing the cave they both started. Boom!

It was the signal gun from the schooner.

They exchanged looks of mutual horror.

"All is lost!" cried Harwolf, "let us hasten to the cavern before it is too late; we must take to the boat and fly for our lives."

They ran at the top of their speed towards the rocks where the cavern was situated.

They reached it.

Just as they entered a number of fierce-looking men rushed out.

They were the crew whom the villains supposed to have returned to the ship.

Before they could resist the men dashed upon them.

They were disarmed.

After a brief struggle they were securely bound.

They were dragged back to the boat and thrown down upon the grating.

With vigorous strokes the men pulled out to sea. Soon they floated under the dark hull.

Harwolf and Blacklock were received on deck by a roar of execration by the infuriate crew.

"Traitor and monster!" hissed Wardlaw, "you have taught us many a lesson of refined cruelty, you shall learn how well we have profited by your instructions. Away with him, let him be lashed to the helm!"

In an instant this order was obeyed.

"And now, boys," cried Wardlaw, "till the morning let us continue our revelry. We cannot within an hour devise a torture sufficiently cruel for such a miscreant; let him remain with all the horrors of anticipation till to-morrow shall break to realise worse than his worst fears!"

Lashed to the helm, Harwolf raved at his captors.

Their only answer was to fling at his feet the mangled corpse of the mulatto whom they had barbarously butchered.

For Blacklock they covered him with irons and pitched him down into the hold where he lay, half-stunned, and copiously bleeding.

Many of the men ranged themselves around the murderous traitor and amused themselves at his expense by assailing him with the vilest abuse and the most exasperating taunts.

The wretches seemed to gloat in his misery and exulted about him like Indians round the stake of their prisoner condemned to the torture.

What happened when morning broke remains to be told in a subsequent chapter.

CHAPTER CCXXIX.

LADY EDGEFORTH AT MADRID—DON MANUEL AND DONNA AURORA—DESTRUCTION OF THE INQUISITION—THE ASSAULT—ARTIFICE OF THE INQUISITORS—THE SEARCH—THE TORTURE CHAMBER—MEASURE FOR MEASURE—THE EXPLOSION.

THE health of Lady Edgeforth, the hapless mother of our hero, was failing fast.

She was no longer subject to such violent fits of insanity as she had formerly suffered, for her sad malady had resolved itself into a settled melancholy.

It was not easy to tell how far the unfortunate lady was conscious of the horrors of the dreadful past.

The subject of her marriage, of the murder of her husband, and the carrying off of the new-born heir of Frontemore were never alluded to in her presence.

Lord Hawksbury became so alarmed at his sister's illness that he seriously consulted the worthy Doctor Morton as to the expediency of trying a tour on the continent.

The worthy physician strongly recommended such a change.

Lord Hawksbury could not endure the thought of his sister's passing away without once beholding her faulty but noble-hearted son.

He had gained information from various sources with respect to the proceedings of the Avenger.

It was so long since the pirate had renounced his evil courses, and had become the champion of distress and the avenger of the wronged, that people began to pity him worse than they blamed him, and could not help according him some measure of admiration.

Had he never been a pirate this admiration would have been boundless, but the brand was upon him; by his false step he had, as he deserved to do, lost almost all the honour that would have been won by his high achievements.

Lord Hawksbury was resolved to leave no means untried for the reuniting the mother and her son.

To this end he travelled to Spain, resolving to seek the advice and assistance of our hero's former friends, Don Manuel Perez and his wife, the beautiful Donna Aurora, the daughter of Don Miguel Vasquez, the man who had made our hero a pirate, and thereby ruined him for ever.

The doctor and Mrs. Wilton accompanied Lady Edgeforth, and attended her with great tenderness.

Don Manuel received Lord Hawksbury and his sister with the most cordial hospitality.

The young couple were now blessed with several other children besides the little girl whom it will be remembered Charles Rye had rescued so gallantly from a watery grave.

Donna Aurora was never weary of sounding our hero's praises.

Lord Hawksbury listened with great interest to the interesting story told him by Don Manuel.

The young student's visit to the convent in disguise of a monk, the cruel treatment of the lovely novice by the abbess, her attempted rescue by the young student, the terrible persecution she suffered in common with her lover, the noble conduct of the Boy Pirate and his band, the battle with the brigands for the protection of Cardinal Gonzalez, and the consummation of the happiness of the youthful pair were narrated in fullest details by Manuel and Aurora.

Lord Hawksbury rejoiced to learn that the history of the unhappy outlaw was not one of mere brutal murder and rapine; and he felt half inclined to pardon one who had acted with such noble generosity, and had not scrupled to shed his own blood in the defence of the very laws of humanity which he seemed to outrage.

"But for that villain, Harwolf, what might not our rover have proved?" he exclaimed, bitterly. "O that so much nobility of character should have been marred so fatally; that one who, had he but kept honest, might have been a hero, but at best can be looked upon only as a chivalrous robber. Robber! the word is detestable, but it must cleave to the avenger to the very last, and it is his just punishment that he should bear it to his shame."

"Perhaps it is," returned Don Manuel; "but he was a benefactor to me; at least, I ought to be silent upon the faults of one to whom I owe all my sum of happiness."

"But to leave this painful subject," said Lord Hawksbury. "Can it be possible that in this enlightened age so much barbarism and superstition can exist, that there can be convents were poor girls are subject to such treatment as you describe, and which Donna Aurora suffered?"

"It is too true," returned Don Manuel. "And it is strange to think what horrible cruelties have been perpetrated in this our city of Madrid in the name of religion; but, as you know, this was the chief seat of that infernal tribunal, the secret inquisition."

"And they say it flourished till very lately," said Lord Hawksbury.

"It did. I will read you an account of the demolition of the Palace of the Inquisition in the year 1809, by the orders of Marshal Soult, as narrated by the officer commanding the division by which it was destroyed."

"And what was his name?"

"Col. De Lile, of the 117th regiment, under Soult. This is his narrative."

Don Manuel fetched a manuscript from a shelf, and read the following interesting account of the destruction of the prisons and torture-chambers of the Inquisition.

"In the year 1809, I was attached to that part of Napoleon's army which was stationed at Madrid.

"Soult was commander-in-chief and governor of the city.

"My regiment was the 9th Polish Lancers.

"One night, about ten or eleven o'clock, as I was walking alone in one of the streets of Madrid, two armed men sprang upon me from an archway.

"I instantly drew my sword, and defended myself as best I could from their furious attack.

"When struggling with them, I saw at a distance, crossing the top of the street, the lights of the mounted patrols.

"French soldiers, on guard, with lanterns, rode through the streets of the city at all hours of the night to preserve order.

"I called to them in French.

"As they hastened to my help, my assailants took to their heels, not, however, before I saw by their dress that they belonged to the guards of the Inquisition.

"Having been in the habit of speaking freely among the people what I thought of the priests and Jesuits, and the Inquisition, I have no doubt these men were set to watch for me, and to assassinate me.

"It had been decreed by Napoleon that the Inquisition and the monasteries should be suppressed.

"Months, however, had passed away without the decree being executed.

"I went that night directly to Marshal Soult, told him what had taken place, and reminded him of the emperor's decree.

"He said I might go the next morning, and destroy the Inquisition, giving me charge at the same time to take care of the pictures, library, and other things of value.

"I replied that my regiment was not sufficient for such a service, but if he would give me the 117th of the line, I would undertake the work.

"The colonel of this regiment was an intimate friend of mine.

"Marshal Soult gave me the troops required.

"That night the expedition was arranged.

"We proceeded at break of day to the Inquisition, which was about five miles distant from the city.

"A wall of great strength surrounded the buildings.

"I went forward with a company of soldiers, and addressing one of the sentinels on the walls, summoned those within to surrender, and to open the gates to the Imperial army.

"The man withdrew.

"After a conversation apparently with some one within, he re-appeared, presented his musket and shot one of my men.

"This was the signal to attack.

"Returning to my troops, who had halted at a distance out of sight, I ordered them to advance, and to fire upon those who appeared on the walls.

"It was soon obvious that it was an unequal warfare.

"The garrison was numerous, and on the walls there was a strong breast-work, from behind which they kept up a destructive fire upon our men in the open plain.

"We had no cannon, our scaling ladders were insufficient, the walls being higher than we had expected, and the gates resisted all attempts at forcing them.

"Wishing to get through the work as quietly as well as quickly as possible, I directed some trees to be cut down and trimmed to be used as battering-rams.

"Selecting a place where the ground sloped a little towards the wall, and so gave advantage to my men to cover with their fire those engaged in the assault, two of these battering rams were brought to bear upon the walls.

"Presently the walls began to tremble, a breach was made, and the imperial troops rushed into the Inquisition.

"Here we met with a scene which nothing but Jesuitical effrontery could equal.

The Inquisitor-General, followed by the fathers in their robes, all presented themselves as we were making our way into the interior of the place, with their arms across their breasts, their fingers resting on their shoulders, as though they had been deaf to all the noise of the attack and defence, and had just learned that it was going on.

"They addressed themselves in the language of rebuke to their own soldiers, saying—

"'Why do you fight our friends the French?'

"Their intention, no doubt, was to make us think that the defence was wholly unauthorized by them, hoping that if they could make us believe they were friendly they should have a better chance of escaping.

"Their shallow artifice did not succeed.

"I ordered them to be placed under guard, and all the soldiers of the Inquisition, who had not escaped in the confusion, to be secured as prisoners.

"We then proceeded to explore the rooms of the stately edifice.

"We passed through hall after hall.

"They were richly furnished; we found splendid paintings, a rich and extensive library.

"Everywhere beauty, splendour and order, such as I had never seen in any palace. The architecture, the furniture, the ornaments were such as pleased the eye and gratified the cultivated taste.

"But where were the gloomy cells and horrid instruments of torture which one had been taught to expect to find in an Inquisition?

"We looked for them in vain.

"The holy fathers seemed to be surprised at our expecting to find any such things.

"They assured us that they had been belied, and that the holy Catholic church, in this, as in other things, was grossly misrepresented.

"Although I saw through the cunning villany of the fathers in these remarks, and knew how the Romish church always affects to deny its crimes and cruelties, when it cannot carry them into execution, I was ready to believe, after our careful search, that this Inquisition was different from others of which I had heard.

"My friend was not, however, so easily convinced.

"'Colonel,' said he to me, 'you are commander to-day; and, as you say, so it must be; but if you will be advised by me, let us have another search; I do not believe we have seen everything yet.'

"We accordingly went again to explore especially in the parts under ground.

"By marking well what portions of the building we were beneath, we found that we had been in every part except the great chapel of the Inquisition and the buildings adjoining.

"The door of this chapel was formed of vast slabs of marble.

"The floors of the other part of the Inquisition were also either of marble or of highly polished wood.

"We could find no entrance to vaults or other indication of anything being below the chapel.

"We were now ready to give up the search.

"A thought struck my fellow-officer, who was still sanguine of discovery.

"'Let us get water,' he said, 'and pour it over this floor, and see if there is any place where it passes through more freely than others.'

"Water was immediately brought.

"A careful examination was made of every seam.

"Presently one of the soldiers cried out that he had found it!

"By the side of one of the slabs the water was passing through fast, as though there were an opening beneath.

"All hands were now at work for further discovery.

"The officers with their swords, and the men with their bayonets, were trying to clear out the stream and raise the slab.

"Others began to strike the slab with all their might with the butts of their muskets, in order to break it.

"The fathers, who had been looking on in great dismay, now broke into loud remonstrance against our desecration of their holy and beautiful house.

"As they were thus engaged, one of the soldiers who was busy with the butt of his musket, struck a part of the marble under which was a spring, and the slab partly flew up.

"Then the faces of the Inquisitors grew pale, and they trembled as Belshazzer when the hand-writing appeared on the wall.

"The marble slab being raised, the top of a staircase appeared.

"I stepped to the altar and took one of the long candles which were burning, some of my men doing the same, that we might see to explore what was below.

"One of the Inquisitors here came up to me, and laying his hand gently upon my arm, said, with a demure look,

"'My son, you must not take those lights with your bloody hands; they are holy.'

"'Well,' said I, pushing him back, 'I will take a holy thing to shed light on iniquity! I will bear the responsibility.'

"We proceeded down the staircase.

"On reaching the floor, the first room we entered was a large square hall, on one side of which was a raised platform with seats, the centre one being elevated considerably, being the throne of the Inquisitor-General.

"In the centre of the hall was a large block, with a chain fastened to it, where the accused was chained during the examination.

"On leaving the Hall of Judgment, we proceeded along a passage with numerous doors.

"These were the cells of solitary imprisonment, from which the miserable victims were never brought out except it were for torture.

"On opening the doors we witnessed such sights as I wish never to see again, the details of which are too horrible to relate.

"In some cells we found bodies, apparently but a short time dead; others were in various stages of decay, and we saw some of which little but the bones remained, still fixed by chains to the floor of the dungeon.

"To prevent this corruption being offensive to the occupants of the Inquisition, there were flues extending along the roofs of the cells and carrying the odours off to the open air.

"Among the living prisoners we found aged men and women, three-score and ten years; youths and girls of fourteen and fifteen, and others, in the prime of life.

"Some of them had been there for many years and lost count of the time since they entered.

"The soldiers went to work to release them from their chains, and took from their knapsacks their over-coats and other clothing to cover their nakedness.

"They were eager to be taken to the light of day; but, having heard of the danger of this, I caused food to be given them and then directed them to be gradually brought out to the light as they were able to bear it.

"We then proceeded to explore another room where were the instruments of torture.

"One of these was a machine on which the victim was stretched, and every joint of the body, beginning with the fingers, was racked until the sufferer swooned away or died.

Another engine consisted of a box in which the head and neck were immovably confined by a screw, and over this box was a vessel from which, drop by drop, water fell upon the head.

"This perpetual drop falling on the same spot caused excruciating agony, ending, ere long, in raving madness.

Another infernal machine lay along horizontally, to which the sufferer was bound, and then was placed between two beams on which scores of knives were fixed, so that by turning the machine by a crank the flesh was torn from the limbs in small pieces.

A fourth machine surpassed the others in fiendish ingenuity.

Its exterior was a beautiful woman, richly dressed with arms extended to embrace the victim; around her feet a semicircle was drawn.

Whoever stepped over this line touched a spring which caused the diabolical engine to open and a thousand knives pierced him with deadly force.

The sight of these engines of infernal cruelty kindled the fury of the soldiers, already enraged with the resistance they had met with when assaulting the walls.

"They declared they would put their prisoners to the torture.

"I could not stem their fury.

"They began with the holy fathers.

"They put one in the machine for racking the joints.

"Another was put under the dropping water, and terrible was the agony he seemed to suffer.

"The Inquisitor-General was brought before the machine called "the virgin," and commenced to kiss it.

"'You have caused others to do it,' said the infuriated soldiers, 'now you must do it.'

"They pointed their bayonets, and pushed him over the fatal circle.

"The beautiful image instantly prepared for the embrace, clasped him in its arms, and he was cut to pieces.

"My heart sickened at this awful scene, and I know no more.

"In the meantime the report had reached Madrid that the prisons of the Inquisition had been broken open.

"Multitudes already were hastening to the place.

"Fathers there were who found long-lost daughters, mothers their sons; wives were restored to their husbands, sisters and brothers met once more.

"Some were friendless and unrecognised.

"The scene of mingled joy, surprise and anguish no tongue can describe.

"While this was going on I gave orders that the library, paintings, and furniture should be carefully removed, and I sent to the city for a large quantity of gunpowder.

"This was placed in the vaults and subterranean places of the building, a slow match being set.

"We all withdrew to a distance, and waited the result in silence.

"Presently loud cheers rent the air, the walls and turrets of the massive structure rose majestically towards the heavens, impelled by the tremendous explosion.

"They fell back to the earth a vast heap of ruins.

"The inquisition was no more."

CHAPTER CCXXX.

ANDREW HARWOLF'S DESPAIR—HE RESOLVES OPENLY TO JOIN THE BUSH-RANGERS—HIS CAPTURE BY INDIANS.

ANDREW HARWOLF returned home after his encounter with Black Oiny.

He rushed into the house.

Miles was awaiting him in the library.

"Zound, zquire, why do 'ee look zo wild loike? Hast 'ee zeen summat az skeared ye?"

Harwolf sank on a chair.

His face was livid.

His eyes were starting.

He seemed choked with emotion.

He started up.

He hurriedly paced the floor.

"It must be a dream!" he exclaimed. "Yet no, here is the blood on my hands now!"

"Dang it, zur, how come it zo? What's happened? Hast 'ee had a brush with the Hottentots?"

But Harwolf made no answer.

With glaring eyes and trembling limbs he chafed about the room.

"Blame it, zquire, do 'ee but zpeak, zur!" cried Miles, in great dismay, "what is ut all about, zur?"

His master did not seem to have heard his words.

He paced about in the wildest excitement.

"Could no place hide me?" he muttered, fiercely. "No; though I buried myself in the earth's firm centre, or betook myself to the uttermost parts of the sea, my sin would find me out!"

Miles stared aghast.

Finding it useless to speak to Harwolf in his present state of excitement, he watched him anxiously till he once more sank down on the seat, and said in a tone of despair,

"The true avenger has come at last, Miles; my fate is sealed!"

"And who be he, zquire?"

"He, whom, like a fool, I spurned in my hour of pride and triumph, has returned to take advantage of my old age and impotence."

"Silas Rye!" cried Miles, breathlessly.

"Aye, Miles," returned Harwolf, faintly, "he is here. As I was strolling through the forest I found him sleeping on a bank."

"Egad, zur! then why did ye let 'un wake any more?"

"I must have been mad!" returned Harwolf, striking his brow with his clenched fist. "Some power restrained me; I overreached myself. I felt an impulse to waken him, to taunt him, and to exult in my final victory. He woke; I fired, but

the gun was dashed from my hand by the burly Irishman, his servant."

"Black Oiny Macarne, vor a wager!"

"The fellow who assisted Esau the gipsy."

"Then ye may depend on't, zquire, as the blamed gipsy be livin' still, and has peached on us!"

"It must be so."

"Hark ye, zur; this be in one way a mortal bad avair; in t'other light it bean't zo bad neither. You have zettled one of the cursed bloodhounds already, and if zo be az ye can outwit this 'cute chap, Zilas, why then I do zay we must be zafe for ever."

"Well, Miles, at least I will not be less in courage than I am in crime; I will be great in both. Must I give up my own neck to the hangman? Is that expected of me by even the law itself? No, let them catch me if they can; so long as the wolf can keep the hounds at bay he will use his fangs to their cost, I reckon!"

"Zounds, zquire, doan't 'ee talk o' hanging! The hemp was never zown that is to make a rope for the necks of either on us. We zhall live long and merrily vor all that twenty Zilas's can do ag'en us!"

"I am in danger here," said Harwolf, half musingly. "At any moment my connection with the bush-rangers and the river pirates may be discovered, and I may be denounced. Since the affair with Foxley, the settlers' confidence in me has been shaken, and I dare not brave my accusers in public again. Miles, I have resolved to throw off the mask and join the bush-rangers openly."

"I'm a'most zorry it be come to that, zquire; but if zo be az we can get away the property, and are lucky in our new spec'lations, I should zay it would be best."

"It would, Miles; and I will proceed at once to put my plan into operation," said Harwolf, rising from his chair and walking with a firm step.

He went to the wall and took down a brace of pistols.

He slung his rifle over his shoulder.

"If we meet the hound on our path, we are prepared," he said, grimly.

Miles also armed himself.

"And where be ye goin' then, zquire?" he asked.

"To the willow island in Arkansas. There is a hut there, cunningly concealed in the brake, and thither I mean to transport the chief part of my valuables."

"Ha—zo—I zuppose, zquire, you will take um thither by degrees?"

"Yes, I have a box of Frontemore deeds, and a chest containing notes, gold, and jewels; these I will take."

"But when, zquire?"

"Now, man, now."

"Very well, zur, I'll vetch the horses and we'll ride over to the river at once."

To this proposal Harwolf gave his assent.

Miles brought the horses and awaited a summons from his master.

Harwolf threw open the window of his library and beckoned him to enter.

Upon the table stood two caskets.

These the men carried with them, slinging one on each of the horses.

They galloped off.

After a long ride they arrived on the banks of the Arkansas River.

They dismounted and led their tired horses along the side of the broad stream.

In the centre of the river appeared the willowy islet.

There was but a small canoe by which they could cross the stream.

This had been concealed by Harwolf among the reeds by the river banks.

Miles, at his master's direction, got into the canoe, taking with him one of the chests.

He rowed over to the island.

Harwolf watched him till he and his little bark had dwindled to the dimensions of a tiny black speck upon the glittering surface of the changeful waters.

Then he entered the brake again, and prepared to carry the box to the returning boat.

As he bore his chest of treasure in his arms, his eyes intently fixed on the distant island, he was suddenly startled by hearing a deep and guttural sound.

"Indians!" he gasped aloud, letting fall the box.

A swift-flying tomahawk grazed his cheek.

He poised his gun.

He felt lithe arms twined round his neck.

A couple of Indians stood before him.

Their rifles were pointed at his head.

He wrestled to disengage himself from the grasp of the Indian who had assailed him from behind.

He was hurled to the ground.

He lay powerless.

In a moment he was gagged, disarmed, and bound hand and foot.

The next, he was lifted on the shoulders of his captors, and carried into the heart of the forest.

CHAPTER CCXXXI.

THE BOY PIRATE VISITS HIS FLEET—NARROW ESCAPE OF THE "RED RAVEN" FROM SHIP-WRECK — HORRIBLE SUFFERINGS OF HER CREW—DEVOURED BY SHARKS!

PENDING the preparations for the siege of the Castle Aronzow, our hero set out in company with Black Ralph and Dick Caffyn, for the little port in the river Oder, where a part of his fleet were moored.

Only the day before the arrival of our hero, Gomez and Brant had returned in the "Red Raven" and another sailing vessel.

It will be remembered that they were engaged in fair trading.

As merchants they found that they prospered far better than as pirates; and they were enabled to send heavy sums of money to our hero and his gallant Avengers, in order to carry on their noble enterprize.

The meeting of the Boy Pirate and his old comrade was very cordial.

It was long since our hero had passed a day so happily.

The evening was spent by the merry Rovers in a balcony, which overlooked the river.

Gomez and Brant narrated all that had befallen them since their parting with their comrades.

Our hero expressed his impatience to behold the "Red Raven" once more.

Gomez smiled, and narrated how nearly the rare old ship had escaped wreck.

The Spaniard, after mentioning the latitude in which the ship was sailing, he continued,

"The wind sprang up, senor, from the westward, about eight bells, and shortly afterwards shifted to the south, whilst a small black cloud, hovering overhead, warned the look-out of an approaching squall.

"Whilst all hands were being turned up, and making preparations for the threatened danger, the cloud rapidly increased in size and density, the breeze died away, and an ominous calm reigned around.

"This, however, did not continue.

"The water, whose surface was one moment almost without a ripple, became in the next a wide sheet of foam.

"A rushing, roaring sound fell suddenly on the ear, and, although I instantly gave the command to cut away the mast, there was no time to obey it before the full force of the hurricane fell on the devoted vessel, and in less than three minutes from the first burst of the quall we were shoaled on a sand-bank.

"A heavy sea had completely swept the decks.

"A bright flash of lightning for a moment illumined the scene.

"The 'Raven' herself had heeled over, and was almost entirely covered by the water.

"The darkness was profound.

"One of the crew, a new hand, but a thorough seaman, named Barnes, when the vessel struck, had succeeded in seizing a pair of oars which were floating near him.

"He told me that he gazed long and anxiously around him in the endeavour to ascertain if any but himself had survived the sudden catastrophe.

"He could not penetrate the deep gloom, nor, for a time, distinguish any sound to relieve his fear that of all the crew who but a few moments before had trod the deck of the 'Raven' without a thought of death, he alone was left alive.

"His terrible suspense seemed already to have lasted hours, when he heard a voice not far off, calling out to inquire if there were anyone near.

"It was a welcome and cheering sound to the poor fellow.

"He immediately pushed out in the direction from which the voice came.

"It was I who had hailed.

"I and six others were clinging to a boat.

"The boat was large enough to have saved us all if the fellows would only have been guided by me.

"But I lost all controul over them.

"In consequence of the frantic efforts of the men to scramble in it became half filled with water, and then turned keel uppermost.

"I appealed to them to endeavour to right the boat, however, and this time I was listened to with as much deference as would have been shown on board the ship before the wreck.

"Order being thus restored the boat was righted.

"Two of the men commenced baling her out.

"The rest remained in the water supporting themselves by the gunwale.

"The hopes of safety we now began to cherish soon met a fearful check.

"The cry of 'a shark!' was raised.

"Such was the effect upon the minds of the men that they again capsized the boat in their endeavour to enter it.

"Once more I managed to restore tranquility and discipline, and the night was spent in baling out the boat.

"This task was just completed, and the crew were on the point of getting into it, when the alarm of 'sharks!' was again raised.

"The boat was, in the confusion, a third time capsized, and the poor castaways found themselves in the midst of a shoal of these hungry monsters.

"For a few moments the crew remained uninjured.

"The sharks actually rubbed against them, frequently passing over the boat and between them that hung by the gunwale.

"This, however, was soon over.

"A terrible shriek then proclaimed that one victim was seized.

"Then another, and a second man disappeared beneath the waves.

"The sea became dyed with blood.

"I kept up the spirits of the surviving men as best I could, and we applied ourselves to clearing out the boat.

"One of the most gallant of the fellows was seized by one of his legs, which was torn from his body.

"But in the midst of his torture he uttered no cry, lest he might spread a new alarm among the crew.

"But his second leg was torn away!

"As uttering a deep groan he could no longer suppress, he was falling back into the sea, two of the men seized him, and laid him in the stern-sheets.

"He was still self-possessed.

"He spoke a few words to the men.

"He even shook hands all round.

"He bade them farewell, and was rapidly sinking when the boat gave a lurch, and the heroic fellow found an end to his sufferings in a watery grave.

"Gradually the number of our men decreased, one after another falling victims to the sharks, which continued to hover about them, until I and Barnes alone were left.

"The boat was, by this time, baled, and we found ourselves, after a night of deep slumber, afloat on the open sea, without sails or oars, or provisions of any kind, whilst no sight of land or ship could be distinguished on the boundless expanse of waters.

"Hope did not, however, desert us."

"For hours we remained motionless looking for a sail.

"After a long and weary watching a small white speck was dimly seen in the distant horizon.

"Presently it advanced nearer.

"It was a sail.

"So she continued to lessen the distance between her and our boat.

"We had tried to return to the rover, but we found that she had heeled over on the other side, and was covered with water.

"We had no means of attracting the attention of those on board.

"Imagine, senor, our bitter disappointment when we saw the brig, for such she turned out to be, suddenly alter her course and bear away!

"Weak as he was in body, Barnes, the brave fellow I told you of at first, conceived the spirited project of swimming after the brig in the forlorn hope of overtaking her.

"I had wounded my arm so severely that I could not swim myself.

"He took a kind leave of me, and cast himself into the sea.

"I resisted my impulse to follow him, for, as I told you, my arm was sorely hurt.

"I remained in fearful solicitude and suspense.

"Away Barnes swam.

"He had overrated his strength, or had miscalculated the distance to be traversed, and when he had succeeded in accomplishing two-thirds of the task his strength began to fail him.

"The poor fellow turned his dying eyes towards the brig, and summoning all his remaining strength, he gave a loud shout.

"The cry saved him.

"It was heard on board the brig, and a boat was lowered in sufficient time to rescue him from drowning.

"'Thus,' concluded Gomez, 'after passing through incredible sufferings, we alone were finally saved of all the gallant merchant crew of our rare old pirate bird!'"

"Just Heaven! this adventure surpasses all that ever befell me in all my career!" cried our hero; "and how was the invincible schooner got off the shoals?"

"When the storm subsided, her hull appeared above water. She was found to be less damaged than had been at first imagined; she was tugged off by a steamer after she had been cleared, and Brant's vessel bore down soon after."

The evening passed rapidly in the interchange of such wild narratives.

Our hero gave the history of his campaign in Poland.

The Spaniard and the rest were heartily pleased that he intended to wind up this act of the eventful drama of his life by the storming of Castle Aronzow, for each and all of the rovers sighed for sea-room.

Merrily the hours glided by.

Black Ralph was in exuberant spirits.

He ranted and sang.

The rafters rang to their laughter and their snatches of melody.

At length Christopher retired to his chamber.

He felt excited and could not sleep.

He threw himself on the bed without undressing.

His mind was full of the wild yet truthful story told him by Gomez.

He reflected how much more extraordinary is fact than fiction.

It was long ere he could sleep.

At last he closed his eyes in a gentle slumber.

He was awakened by a pealing shriek.

He started up, and grasping his arms, rushed to the window.

"A number of ruffianly soldiers were trailing along a woman.

"They seemed to be bearing her off towards the harbour.

"Without a moment's hesitation the Boy Pirate arranged his weapons, and scrambled out of the window.

"It was a great height from the ground; but our hero made a desperate leap on to the roof of a lower building adjoining, and so scrambled down into the street.

"He rushed off in the direction the soldiers had taken.

"He reached the quay.

"The long boat of a Russian man-of-war was seen pulling off towards a large vessel anchored in the middle of the river.

"Our hero looked about for a boat.

"With the coolest nonchalance he unmoored a very light craft, and pulled lustily in pursuit of it.

"He reached the ship.

"The men had carried their prisoner aboard.

"He could hear the voice of a woman sobbing and pleading.

"The voices of men responded with unmanly harshness.

"The Boy Pirate, reckless of all consequences, scrambled up the side.

"He leaped over the bulwark on to the deck.

"A number of marines and sailors were drawn up.

"The captain and officers were present.

"The girl was still pleading on her knees.

"There was a shout of astonishment when the dashing pirate leaped on to the deck.

"The girl sprang up, and with a scream rushed into his arms.

"It was Lilia, his bride!"

THE STRUGGLE ON THE RAFT.

CHAPTER CCXXXII.

THE BOY PIRATE RESCUES LILIA FROM THE RUSSIANS—THE LEAP INTO THE SEA—THE STUGGLE—PERILOUS POSITION OF THE BOY PIRATE AND LILIA.

THE consternation which prevailed among the Russian sailors at the sudden appearance of the terrible Boy Pirate, may be more easily imagined than described.

They drew back, overawed by his dauntless bearing.

With a stern, cold look, he regarded them as fearlessly as though he had been backed by every man of his crew.

No. 69.

He took immediate advantage of this panic, and leaped on to the bulwark.

Lilia still clung to him half dead with terror.

The Boy Pirate drew a pistol from his belt and fired at the officer who attacked him.

The Russian staggered back.

He dropped heavily on the deck.

The daring pirate, still clasping his bride, leaped into the sea.

The night was profoundly dark.

The sea was running high.

For an instant the pair were separated.

The surging waters rent Lilia from her husband's arms.

He succeeded, however, in clutching her dress.

He drew her towards him.

Boldly dashing beneath the dark hull, Christopher clambered into the chains.

Lanterns were lowered.

The drums beat to quarters.

The men had heard Lilia's wild shriek.

By the light of the lanterns could be seen the glittering uniforms and flashing bayonets of the mariners in the boat.

They rowed along under the side.

It was a terrible moment for our hero.

Fortunately Lilia was unconscious of the horror of it ; she was still in a deep swoon.

Our hero sprang in the raging waves.

He swam strongly, still supporting Lilia by the waist.

"He is there !"

This shout proceeded from the coxswain of the boat.

The lantern held aloft streamed brightly along the surf.

It shone upon Lilia's white dress and golden hair.

"Steady men, steady," cried one of the officers ; "make ready to fire upon him."

"No, no, lieutenant," cried another in a very eager tone, "you will kill the woman."

"That cannot be helped ; she has drawn her doom upon herself. Now !"

Half exhausted, Christopher was floating on the crest of the waves.

"Now ; take steady aim, men."

"Lieutenant, I beseech you."

"Silence, sir ; fire !"

Four guns were discharged.

The bullets flashed into the waves.

One of them grazed the forehead of the insensible Lilia.

Our hero uttered a yell of fury.

But he had enough to do in battling with the monstrous billows which, tumbling over each other, carried him in the direction of the vessel in spite of all his efforts to force his way towards the shore.

Again the captain ordered the men to fire.

They were unable to take fair aim in such a rough sea.

Our hero struggled on.

More than once he had almost lost his hold on Lilia.

The officer in the the boat, in nowise moved by the gallantry of the outlaw, commanded the men to pull stoutly towards the floating pair, and to seize them and drag them into the boat.

But the Boy Pirate, with all the fortitude of his wondrously brave nature, was wearily but undauntedly plying his quivering limbs through the boiling surf.

Every inch of progression caused him pangs of keen agony.

Lilia was still stark and cold.

Was she dead ?

The buffetting of the waves with which he was toilfully waring, the threatening shriek of the passing gale, the shots and shouts of the chasing boats were but so many incentives to the proud and high spirit of this extraordinary man.

Lilia was dead !

The thought was paralysing.

As he realised the seeming truth of this conviction, he felt as if tons of lead were dragging him down, self-abandoned and powerless, through the surging gulf below.

His heart lifted as his clear brain pictured his mourning and leaderless crew.

What was Lilia ? His own, himself.

What were they ? The stern, savage, guilty men, who, through all their criminality, had been so true to him.

Still with fainting force he struggled fiercely on.

The waves tossed their white manes far up the distant barriers of the stone quays of the harbour.

He reached the wall.

He seized an iron bolt.

Soon he had clambered up the steep and slimy wall.

He knelt on the spray-drenched stones.

Lilia lay motionless across his knees.

The wind and the shower hurtled past.

He put back her golden locks, and gazed with steadfastness upon her calm and rigid face.

His blood seemed frozen in his veins ; his heart sank colder than ice ; he shuddered convulsively.

He looked back wildly and vengefully over the foamy space he had traversed.

The lanterns were dancing towards shore.

He again glanced into Lilia's face.

"What cheer, noble captain !"

He smiled faintly as these words fell on his ear.

He looked up.

Black Ralph was leaning over him.

"She is dead !"

As he moaned this with dreary despair, his colleague knelt down and took the girl's hand.

"No, no ! Have courage, captain ! She is not dead yet ; but how came she here ?"

"I have carried her off from the frigate in the offing," replied our hero, wildly. "I was in my chamber, about to retire to rest, when I heard a loud shriek without. I opened my window and looked out. A number of Russian soldiers were haling along a woman ; they were dragging her towards the harbour. I followed. They carried her off in a boat. I flung myself into the sea. I reached the ship, and tore her from their arms. I sprang into the sea, and the boat was put down. She has been wounded by a musket shot. I fear the terror has killed her."

"And see, captain, the boat is nearing shore," cried Ralph, pointing towards it, "we must consider only the better part of valour and hold off as soon as possible."

"Where are the others ? Did you rouse them ?"

"Yes ; and as the wind blows landward, the sound of the shots was plainly heard ashore. Run, captain, we shall meet them."

The pirates started into the city.

At the entry of a little street which led into the town they encountered a soldier on guard.

"Stand !" he cried, "Who goes there ?"

"We can't both go and stand," mumbled Black Ralph. "We're friends !" he shouted, "and we are on business of life and death ! For Heaven's sake, don't stop us."

The Russian, who had before spoken in French, now grumbled something in his own tongue.

He then bawled out, fixing his bayonet at half charge,

"Advance, friends, and give the word."

"A leap from a hedge is better than a priest's prayer," grunted the rover to his comrade, in the axiom of Sancho Panza.

"The word, or I fire !" cried the soldier.

"One for his nob ! That's the word !" cried Ralph, with a forward bound which brought his fist full between the poor fellow's eyes.

The sentinel fell.

The pirates leaped over his body.

They rushed in.

The man-of-warsmen were now on land, and in a long file were steadily advancing.

No time was to be lost.

Away sped the pirates in the direction of a long and dreary flat in one quarter of the city.

They were still chased by the Russians.

Several of the enemy were fleet runners, who gained rapidly upon them.

Once they turned at bay.

They fought their way through the crowd of well-armed assailants.

After a brisk contest they made good their escape.

They gathered on the plain.

They then, by passing through a low and wretched suburb, reached the open country.

They hastened on towards the camp.

Their minds were filled with alarm and anxiety. They could not conceive by what accident Lilia had fallen into the hands of the Russians.

It might be that the camp had been attacked in the absence of the leaders, and that the gallant band of Avengers had perished or been taken prisoners.

CHAPTER CCXXXIII.

SAFETY OF LILIA—JACK TYRRILL'S STORY.

AT the distance of about a league from the city was a little inn, which was kept by a Pole, who favoured the good cause, and was in league with the Avengers.

The morning was already breaking when our hero and his comrades left the city.

It was now quite light.

The pirates were fain to pause at this inn in order to snatch some share of rest and refreshment before pursuing their journey.

The Pole entertained them very hospitably.

The brave fellow seemed to be altogether regardless of his own risk.

He told them that he had heard no authentic news from the camp; but that strange, wild, contradictory reports were spread about the capture of the rover chief's wife.

Lilia had been removed to a bed-room; an old priest, who had some skill in medicine and surgery, examined her wound, and pronounced it to be but slight, though the fearful scene through which the poor girl had passed had almost exhausted the vital powers.

It was long before she recovered her senses.

Longer still before she was conscious of her position, or able to recognise those about her.

Our hero tended her with the tenderest devotion.

The pirates were gathered around the table in the largest room of the house, drinking or stretching their weary limbs upon the rude forms when a man rushed into the room.

He was an old salt, white-haired, and weather-beaten.

His looks betrayed his grief and anger.

"Messmates!" he cried. "Speak! Where is the captain? I have black news for him."

"Out with it, then," said our hero, at the moment stepping in from the room where his wife was lying, "I am not a coward that you should hesitate to tell me the worst."

"This news might well make even our brave captain a coward," replied the man, with emotion.

"Speak then, man, and see if I shall blench."

"Your wife, captain——"

"The band is all well in the camp?"

"All's well."

"Then what of my wife?"

"Riding through the gorge, with Zampa and three others of the crew for her escort, she was attacked and captured. One of the men was killed, the other three wounded so severely that they fell after having run some distance; Zampa escaped with a slight wound, though the men say he fought like a dragon while there was any chance of a rescue."

"So she was taken?"

"She was."

"It matters only for her fright and a slight wound; but she shall be dearly avenged."

"Why, captain, what do you mean?" cried the sailor, staring at our hero with the utmost astonishment. "I should have supposed that you would have been struck down by this loss."

"There is one thing which consoles me," returned our hero, smiling. "Lilia was lost, but is found; dead, and is alive again."

"You have saved her, captain," cried the old man, in trembling accents.

"Yes, Jack, she is in yon room."

The sailor gave a shout of delight.

Reassured as to the safety of his crews, and thrilled with intense satisfaction at the rapid recovery of his beloved wife, who was now able to speak to him, and was pronounced by the priestly physician to be quite out of danger, our hero's spirits rose buoyantly.

His comrades shared their captain's glee, and the rovers seating themselves round the fire entered into a long and animated conversation.

The grog passed freely round.

"Jack Tyrrill," said our hero, addressing the aged seaman who had brought the news of Lilia's capture, "you are the oldest man amongst us all, and have served under the black flag before you enrolled yourself on my ship's books."

"Aye, aye, cap'en, many a cruise have I sailed in what are called the good old times," returned the old sailor, with gleaming eye; "the times when piracy was common; when Tyburn tree was in full bloom; when brutal ruffians infested roads, and thieves were hanged in batches and swung in irons; when women were flogged at the cart-tail, and ladies were carried off by force from their homes by titled villains. Egad, they were stirring times!" he laughed, rather bitterly, and added: "I think if I had been born a few years later, I should never have been a rover; but how I came to sail in the grand account I will tell ye, messmates."

The old tar drank off his glass of spirits.

For awhile he smoothed the white locks down on to his forehead, and seemed to be lost in reverie.

His audience maintained respectful silence, and in these words were told

THE OLD PIRATE'S STORY.

"I know not, messmates, who my parents were. I was found, when an infant, wrapped in rags in a cobbler's bulk, in Westminster.

"The parish officers sent me to the poor-house; and, when I was capable of instruction, they sent me to the charity-school.

"When I had learned to read and write, I was bound for a servant to Mr. Skinner, a neighbouring attorney.

"My mistress grew very fond of me.

"She was a religious woman, and took great pains to instruct me.

"As my master used to send me on many errands, and to entrust me with little matters of money on such occasions, on finding me always honest, he began to have almost as much regard for me as my good mistress had.

"But now came on my first falling away from all goodness.

"I was about twelve years old.

"In a cursed hour my master sent me to a distant part of the town with a bill to pay some money, and to bring him back the change.

"The change amounted to about four pounds in glittering gold and silver.

"It appeared to me a mint of money.

"I had never been in possession of so large a heap.

"I sighed and said to myself,

"'What luck to become the owner of so much money!'

"Then some one seemed to whisper me that I was the owner, and again some one seemed to whisper me that I was not the owner.

"Then I would go forward towards my master's; and again I would stop and turn aside.

"Then I would thrust my hand into my pocket, and feel the greatness of my treasure; then turn to the wall and spread its brightness before my hungry eyes.

"Then I would run a piece off; and again I would stop and turn and strive to force myself homeward.

"Till, what with doubting and delaying and going backward and forward, I considered that I should get nothing but blame, so I heaved a-head, and ran into the country as fast as my legs would carry me.

"I ran myself out of breath.

"From time to time I would look back and look back, and run on and run on, in the thought that my master, or some one from him, was at my heels.

"Often since I have reflected, and was persuaded in my mind, that my kind master and mistress had not the least suspicion of me, but rather inquired and sorrowed after me, as being kidnapped from them, and this was at times a great grief of heart to me.

"When I was quite tired and night came on, I turned into a sorry kind of inn which happened to be near.

"As I feared everything, I had the cunning to conceal my treasure.

"I took a penny from my pocket.

"I begged the woman for that, and charity's sake, to give me some milk and a little bread, and some hole to lie in.

"Having finished my supper, I was shown to a kind of hovel under the stairs.

"I threw myself on some straw with a piece of blanket over me.

"I fell as fast asleep as a rock.

"Awakening, however, about midnight, or somewhat after, and seeing all dark about me, and no creature near hand, I began to tremble greatly.

"I dared not pray.

"I lay sweating and trembling, and trembling and sweating till the dawn of day brought some relief to my spirits.

"Having breakfasted at the cost of another penny, I set out, though not with my former speed, for, reflecting that I had not my livery on, but a small frock coat, I was under the less fear of being known.

"However, I pushed on as well as I was able, wanting still to get as far from danger as possible.

"Indeed, I hoped by going on still farther and farther to get away from my fears and from my conscience.

"On the fifth morning of my travels, having expended what half-pence and small silver I had, I took out a half-crown and offered it to the man of the house, desiring him to return what was over the reckoning.

"As he took it he gave me a look that I thought went through me.

"He continued to stare in my face.

"He shamed me so that I was constrained to turn aside.

"He gave me the change, however, and I set forward on my journey all trembling and apprehending I knew not what.

"I had not gone over a mile, when, meeting a dirty road, I turned over a stile that led across the fields.

"Here I walked on a little way, when, turning, I saw my landlord making long strides after me.

"My heart beat, my knees grew so weak under me that I stood as still as a stone.

"He came quickly up with me.

"He seized me by the neck and cast me on my back.

"'Ha! you young rogue,' says he, 'let me see what money you have got.'

"Then, diving into my pockets, he pulled out the whole stock in which I trusted for happiness.

"'Oh, you little villain,' he cried, 'from whom have you stolen all this treasure? But I must go and restore it to the owner.'

"'Oh, good sir, good sir!' I roared out, 'will you not leave me a little, ever so little, dear sir, to keep me from starving?'

"He was deaf to my cries, and away he went.

"Hope, the last comfort of the miserable, now forsook me.

"I lay a long time as one who had no use for his limbs, nor any further way to travel on earth.

"At length I broke out in a great gush of tears.

"I got some ease by giving vent to my sorrow.

"I rose.

"I went I know not whither.

"I grew hungry after noon.

"I would willingly have begged the charity of passengers.

"This I did not dare to do lest they should ask me whence I came and whither I was going.

"I bore my hunger as well as I could, till, coming at night to a hovel where a farmer kept his pigs, I made way for myself amongst them, and slept on the straw till the morning.

"The day following, as I passed slowly and half-famished through the village, my eye caught at a penny loaf that lay on a little shop window which jutted into the street.

"I looked here and there, and peered into the shop.

"I was just going to seize it when something whispered,

"'Do not touch it for you life. Starve, starve, rather than steal any more.'

"I tore myself away.

"I ran as fast as I could for fear of turning back.

"I, at last, got clear off from the reach of temptation.

"When I had travelled something farther, I got into an enclosed country where there were hedges on every side.

"On every bush there was plenty of haws and bramble berries.

"Here I filled my belly with berries to serve me for a dinner.

"I stuffed my pocket with haws against I should want.

"Upon this I grew wondrous glad that I had not taken the loaf.

"Peace began to dawn upon my mind.

"About nightfall, having reached one side of the road, I crept, like a hare, under the shelter of the bushes.

"I supped upon my haws.

"I kneeled down.

"Half venturing a prayer, and gathering up in my form, I slept happily till morning.

"I lived thus for several days.

"I came into an open country, where there was scarce any path, nor any haws or berries within many a mile.

"I now began to grow sick with hunger.

"My sickness went off.

"I became so ravenous that I was ready to eat my flesh off my bones.

"Soon after this I spied at a distance a confused heap of something at the root of a great tree that grew in the open fields.

"I made up to it in expectation of I know not what.

"I found an old beggarman fast asleep under his patched cloak.

"A bundle was lying beside him.

"Instantly I opened his little baggage.

"To my transport a large luncheon of brown bread, with some half-pence, struck my eyes.

"I did not hesitate one moment about seizing the bread, for I could no more withstand the cravings of my appetite at the time than I could withstand a torrent rushing down a hill.

"Having appeased my stomach, I began to demur about what I should do with the remainder of the bread.

"I felt a notion to leave it behind me.

"'No,' said I, to myself, 'this is all the bread that

I have, or may ever have during my life; I know not where to get a bit in the whole world. Besides, I leave this man money enough to buy more.'

"So I put the bread into my pocket, and went on my way.

"I left behind me about four or five pence in the wrapper.

"That night I took up my lodgings in a waste hut that lay but a little way off from the road.

"But though, as I thought, I had plenty of bread, yet I found myself heavy at heart.

"I was not able to sleep so sweetly as I had done on the foregoing nights.

"During all this time I knew neither where I was or whither I was going, nor anything more in my travels than that I came from London.

"When I was walking, slow and melancholy, in a by-path that led through some woody lawns, I heard the voice of merriment.

"Quickly after I perceived a group of gipsies that came from behind some trees.

"As I could not escape them, I gathered courage, and went forward; when coming up, they stopped, and eyed me with much attention and made a ring about me.

"'Where are you going, my child?' asked a man with a broad girdle, and a very formidable beard.

"'Indeed, sir,' said I, 'I cannot tell.'

"'And where do you come from, then?'

"'From London, so please you.'

"'From London, child! Why, that is a great way off! And, pray, what made you leave London?'

"'To get away from my master.'

"'But I hope you did not come away empty?'

"Hereupon this venerable regent smiled, and, turning to his dependents,

"'As far as I see,' said he, 'this chap will answer our purpose to a hair.'

"Here one of the females asked if I was hungry, and, on my answer in the affirmative, they all invited me with a jovial air to dinner.

"We then turned to a distance off from the path in which we had met, and gradually descended into one of the pleasantest spots in the world.

"It was a dell, surrounded with hills, some of which were slanting, some headlong and impending and all covered or spotted with groups of trees of different heights, sorts, and colours, through which there descended a gurgling rivulet, which, having rolled over stones and pebbles, grew silent in a small lake, and reflected the circling objects from the hills around.

"Immediately Nature's carpet was covered with a large cloth.

"Before I could well observe what they were about, there was spread, as if by magic, before my eyes, a various banquet.

"Down instantly sank the guests, some sitting like Turks, crossed-legged, while others lolled like the Romans, beside each other.

"As they had travelled far that day, they all eat in silence.

"In a short space the burden of the luggage carriers was very much lightened.

"In the meantime, some arose and unladened two asses of the creels which they carried.

"The cloth then was quickly emptied of the cold fowls and baked meats, with the loins of beef and mutton, and leather jacks that contained plenty of the best of wines, were set before us.

"These again were decanted into clean japanned pitchers, and a japanned cup of equal measure was given into every hand.

"Then began mirth and jollity to flow round with the cups.

"Never did I see so pleasant, so gleeful a company.

"Joke and banter, without offence, were bandied from side to side.

"Bursts of laughter were echoed from the answering hills.

"As soon as I was warmed, and my heart opened by what I ate and drank, they conceived a liking for me, and requested that I would tell them my story without disguise.

"Accordingly, I made an ingenuous confession of all the matters related.

"Instead of meeting those reproofs which I expected, for my wickedness, they jointly began to ridicule my scruples and put to flight the little shame that I had of my evil courses.

"I continued among these people nearly the space of three years.

"During this time they initiated me into all the arts and mysteries of their manifold iniquities.

"Hitherto they had not proceeded to blood.

"On the night wherein I left them we were overtaken by a sudden and violent tempest, whereupon we took shelter in a waste barn.

"We had struck a light. We set together what combustibles we could find in the barn, and had just kindled a fire, when one of the company came and whispered that there was a man asleep in the far corner.

"Hereupon they took the candle and found a pedlar stretched along, with his head on a whisp of straw, and his box close beside him.

"They immediately lifted the box and brought it away in silence, to the place where I was sitting.

"On opening it, with as little noise as possible, they found therein a large quantity of silks, linens, and laces, with a rich variety of hardwares; and, at the bottom, a little padlock chest full of English and Spanish pieces of gold; in all likelihood, the whole amount of the labours of his life.

"Immediately all was in a kind of bustle and commotion.

The great question was, how to possess themselves of such a prey with safety to their persons.

"It was objected that the man might awake; they were unluckily seen coming that way, and it may be entering into that house; the country might be alarmed, and rise upon them; they might be overtaken, and they might be seized in the very act.

"At length a bold villain proposed to cut his throat, and that then there could be no witness to testify againt them.

"To this, it was objected that the blood itself would be the surest of all witnesses.

"Whereupon, another proposed to strangle him, and bury his corpse on the spot; to which scheme, though many were silent, yet no one expressly objected.

"During this deadly consultation, notwithstanding my long course of evil habits, my blood curdled throughout my body; and fear, horror, and detestation arose in my bosom, when they went, as I supposed, to put the deed of death into execution.

"I crouched and slunk inwards, and crept out at the door.

"The dread of being also seized and murdered gave me strength to get off my feet.

"I felt along by the wall; I got clear off from the house.

"I made off.

"I neither knew nor cared whither.

"The tempest still continued.

"The driving of the clouds added to the natural horrors of the night.

"I could scarcely descern that I had a road under my foot.

"But though I could not see my pursuers, I yet feared their eyes were better than mine.

"I still turned and listened, to try if the step of a murderer was behind me.

" All night I travelled as fast and as far as I could.

" On the rising of the day, I saw a large town before me.

" For the first time in three years I lifted my eyes, and inwardly blessed God for his mercy in my escape.

" I then walked leisurely.

" My fatigue went from me.

" I felt quite lightsome.

" I entered the suburb.

" I met a gentleman taking his morning's walk.

" I stopped and looked wistfully in the face; whereupon he also stopped, and eyed me with much attention.'

" ' Who are you, my pretty lad ?' says he.

" ' An unhappy stranger, sir,' I answered, ' who wants a service or any means of earning a little honest bread.'

" ' And pray what service can you do ?'

" ' Not much, sir, I fear ; but my goodwill shall strive hard to make up for my lack of ability.'

" ' Then,' said he, ' you shall be my servant; all the servants I ever had promised everything, but did little. I will now try what may be done by one who promises nothing. What is your name, my boy ?'

" ' David Doubtful, sir.'

" ' And what wages must I give you, David ?'

" ' Just as much, sir, or as little as you shall think I deserve.'

" Here he took me to a handsome house, where he kept a mercer's shop, in Plymouth.

" His name was Felton.

" He had been a widower of some years, and had an only son who was then at Westminster school.

" My master, at first, set me to the most servile offices, such as cleaning his own and his servant's shoes, and sweeping the store rooms ; but all this I did with willingness, and even with pleasure, as som little penance for my long course of evil deeds.

" On my separating from the gipsies, as I told you, I was proprietor of one hundred and seventy odd pounds, which were locked up in the common chest, being my allotted dividend of the fruits of our knavery.

" But in my present turn of mind, I would no more have accepted them than I would have taken a red-hot bar in my hand.

" I had in my pocket a few crowns, with some small silver, but these I secretly distributed among the poor that no part of the accursed thing might remain about me.

" In about three weeks my master changed the whole manner of my service.

" He set me to brush his clothes, dress his wigs, whet the knives, lay the cloth, and attend at table.

" These were matters in which I was quite expert as I had not yet forgotten my employment with my first master.

" In some time after, Mr. Felton asked me if I could read.

" ' A little, sir,' said I.

" ' And can you write too, David ?'

" ' If you please I will try, sir.'

" He brought me pen and paper.

" ' Why, David, this beats the hand of my clerk ! Where in the world did you come by this learning ? '

" ' From a very good master to a very bad servant; but, pray, sir, do not inquire the particulars of my history, the reproach of my conscience for all that is past is severe enough to me.'

" ' Well, lad,' said the gentleman, ' I will not give you pain.'

" He gave me a squeeze by the hand, and went out with glistening eye.

" From this time my master showed me an uncommon respect.

" He discharged me from all the menial offices of his household ; he gave me his burdens of silk and other wares to carry to his customers; and he desired me to take particular notice of the nature and value of what I carried.

" On this encouragement I became vastly more assiduous than he looked for.

" I attended the shop closely and took private notes of all that was estimated or transacted in it.

" My master looked quite amazed on asking me some questions with respect to his private affairs.

" His eldest apprentice soon after set up for himself.

" He then placed me behind the counter, and over his junior apprentice and in joint authority with his journeymen.

" Soon after he gave me the key of his till and the trust of all his treasure.

" I now dined with him at the same table, and consulted and conversed with him as his friend and companion.

" He frequently gave me pocket-money which he said he would not charge to the account of my wages.

" I was now very happy, and looking upon my master as my friend and benefactor, was altogether devoted to his service.

" Peace lay under my pillow ; my happiness seemed as a ship, that, after a long and desperate voyage, had anchored in a calm and secure haven.

" I had now been something upwards of a year in the service of Mr. Felton.

" One day I heard a bustling noise in the street.

" I stepped to the door.

" I looked to the left and perceived a great crowd about a cart, in which were five criminals going to execution.

" I stayed till they came just opposite to me.

" To my utter astonishment, I saw five of my old acquaintances, the gipsies.

" In front of them was the bloody villain who had proposed cutting the throat of the unfortunate pedlar.

" He saw me.

" We exchanged looks.

" I glanced at him imploringly.

" He answered with a malicious grin.

" He stooped and whispered one of his companions.

" This man also looked towards me.

" He then addressed the clergyman who was walking by the side of the cart.

" The reverend gentleman, who was a great friend of my master's, turned round with a strange look at me.

" Instantly I turned as pale as my shirt.

" I shrunk in.

" Dreading that the villains had accused me of being an accomplice in the murder and convinced that they had claimed acquaintance with me, my agony was extreme.

" I threw myself half-fainting into a chair.

" I now reflected that it was happy for me no one was in the shop to notice my confusion.

" I endeavoured to assume some courage.

" On the entrance of our journeyman I put on the most unconcerned countenance I could assume.

" He told me that one of the gipsies had denounced a man who had been seen by him in the crowd.

" I asked if he knew the person accused.

" He replied that he did not, and that it was kept quiet lest the culprit should make his escape.

" This was quite enough.

" I rushed into my room.

" I tied in a bundle some articles of clothing.

" I took my savings from a box, and, leaving the house by a back way, I made off as fast as I could.

" I fled to London.

" I embarked on board a ship bound for Cadiz.

"Amongst others who had entered themselves in the ship's books was a big villain whose name was Pat MacDouel.

"Having changed his mind and wishing to remain ashore, he deserted when we were on the point of sailing.

"The captain applied to the police authorities, and MacDouel was captured and forced to abide by the articles he had signed.

"The captain's conduct in the affair seemed to be the reverse of prudent, for MacDouel was a very undesirable addition to the crew; but the captain was an obstinate, overbearing man, who soon rendered himself very unpopular.

"The first sight of McDouel gave me a thrill of horror.

"His countenance was of that cast in which any one would place implicit confidence who wanted an associate for any dark, traitorous, or bloody purpose.

"From Cadiz we sailed to the Canaries, and when we were nearing the islands, Pat McDouel prevailed on most of the crew to enter into a conspiracy for making themselves masters of the ship, and to reap a fortune on the 'grand account' as pirates.

"Whereupon they barbarously murdered the master, the officers, and all who were not of their own gang, except myself, whom they spared on account of my being a good cook.

"Still I was in instant expectation of being put to death by the miscreants.

"They took several small vessels, which they plundered, cruelly despatching the entire crews.

"But they did not prosper long.

"We were held in chase.

"Then they wished for the help of the hands they had cut off.

"After a bloody battle we were taken by a Spanish privateer, commanded by one Don Pedro Paolo.

"We were given up to the authorities.

"Several of the crew were hanged.

"The rest escaped the capital sentence, and were condemned to work in the galleys, being chained to the oar.

"At every meal, which consisted of bread and water, we received ten lashes.

"I was somewhat better treated than the rest.

"On one occasion I was lucky enough to save the life of the officer who had charge of us.

"I should have told you McDouel had escaped death in this way.

"Being desperately wounded, he was not brought to trial with the rest, but left in prison, as it appeared, in a dying state.

"Here he was constantly visited by a Catholic priest.

"The cunning villain, whose parents had been Romanists, pretended to be much impressed by the good father's exhortations, and the priest used his interest to obtain a reprieve for his respectable convert.

"The brutal ruffian was not tamed by the severe treatment he received in the galleys.

"He vowed to wreak his vengeance upon the officer.

"He contrived to secure a weapon, half knife half dagger, and threw himself upon the officer, catching him by the throat, and making use of the most blasphemous threats.

"But at the same moment I seized his hand, and throwing up his heels, I wrenched the weapon from him.

"He received a hundred lashes for this attempt, and was thereafter loaded with double irons.

"Nevertheless, he made another attempt at murder, and was shot down.

"After this I was in hourly peril of being killed by my exasperated companions.

"I effected my escape, as I think, by the connivance of our guards, who were not a little intimidated by their ruffianly prisoners, and thinking that they could not protect me from the malice of the rest suffered me to escape.

"After this, I embarked on board of an English ship.

"One of the crew happened to have been on board of Don Pedro's vessel when he had captured us.

"He recognised and denounced me.

"I was put in irons, and confined in the hold.

"However, I had rendered myself popular among the crew, and they planned a means of getting me off.

"My irons were filed by one of them.

"And as we were lying close in shore, I got out of the port, and swam to the island.

"Here I was picked up by Don Miguel, our great 'Raven's' first commander.

"That rover was always anxious to secure the services of English sailors, whom he held to be the finest sailors in the world.

"After the death of Don Miguel, I was among the few who had escaped from the wreck of his ship.

"I afterwards fell in with my present gallant messmates, and so you have my story."

CHAPTER CCXXXIV.

HARWOLF'S INFURIATED CREW — WARDLAW ELECTED CAPTAIN.

HARWOLF writhed like Ixion at the wheel.

And like the infernals and furies, his crew raged about him.

Nothing is more terrible than the retaliation of slaves who become masters of their tyrants.

No cruelty had been too revolting to be perpetrated by the bloodthirsty Daniel Harwolf. Mercy itself would have been merciless in punishing such an atrocious monster.

He had lessoned his crew in deeds of the most dastardly cruelty, and they had "bettered their instruction."

Still they abstained from actual violence.

Their saturnalia was disgusting; they seemed to be mad with delirious pleasure at the opportunity afforded by the detection of their captain's treason for punishing his tyranny.

They circled about him, hooting, and howling, and gibing.

They reminded him of the tortures he had inflicted upon his victims, and, with gloating malice, dwelt in detail upon the torments that were preparing for himself.

It was a scene of horror.

Wardlaw was sufficiently alarmed at finding how little controul he had over his new subjects.

To the reign of tyranny succeeds the reign of anarchy.

Wardlaw walked aft with Ramsey.

"What shall we do with these devils?" he asked. "If we give the traitor up to them, and let them glut their fury upon him, perhaps they will return to order and quiet."

"I fear not, captain," answered Ramsey. "Blood does not make a cooling draught, it is the most fiery, intoxicating stimulent. Give them a taste of it as they are now, and they will drink themselves drunk."

Wardlaw sighed.

As his eyes fell on the deck, which was stained in many a place with dull crimson of past butcheries, a look of remorse passed over his dark face, and the colour fainted from his cheek.

"Did you hear what they said of Parker and Jose, and the rest of that clique?" said Ramsey.

"No."

"They said they were of Blacklock's gang, and that they would cut them all off together."

"And we are so weak of hands already."

"And is it likely that Johnson's clique will suffer him and half-a-dozen more to be murdered without banding together for mutual protection?"

"No; this cursed discord will be our destruction," returned Wardlaw, thoughtfully. "What, then, do you propose?"

"That everything should be managed dispassionately with respect to Harwolf."

"The cursed tyrant and traitor, he shall be roasted alive!" cried Wardlaw, fiercely.

"His groans would be music to me, but the treat is too expensive; this death by torture would bring about its own retribution."

"Why, hang it, Ramsey, you would spare the dog?"

"Spare him! Not to buy my own life and life-long happiness."

"What do you propose then?"

"Simply this, that we should use our utmost influence with the steadiest of the men to maintain discipline, and have this wretch tried by the crew in an orderly manner; of course, he will be condemned. Let him be hanged at the yard-arm with all the solemnity of an execution in the royal navy."

"Hanging is a death too easy for this scorpion."

"Tear him to pieces with hot pincers, if you choose, I should enjoy the spectacle; but vengeance, I tell you, is not justice, and justice will be our only guarantee for safety."

"It is a cursed business altogether, messmate."

"A clear head and a cold heart are indespensable to him who would govern."

"Good, then, I see the wisdom of this course; I'll put him in irons, and he shall await his trial with Blacklock in the hold."

"No, it would not be safe to unbind him now. The men are mere fiends; the drink has made them furious; they would kill him on the spot; some one would set up a yell for the blood of Johnson, Jose, and the rest of his favourites. These would fight for their lives, and by the morning there would be no work left for the hangman."

"Be it so, Ramsey, you are a prudent fellow; he shall remain at the helm till daybreak."

"Aye, and if you think these drunken swabs have had enough of this devil's dance for one occasion, clear the deck of the lubbers, and let us have silence fore and aft."

"Keep by me, then; I'm well armed, and we'll see whether we can command the dogs, or whether they are beyond our controul."

With this Wardlaw walked towards the forecastle.

The deck was strewn with the forms of seamen, lying and reeling in every attitude of beastly intoxication.

Others had joined hands, and were dancing and jumping in a ring, a black fiddler scraping away in the centre.

Wardlaw gave the word for silence fore and aft.

Very little notice was taken of this order by the half mad carousers.

They whooped and sang and whistled, and performed all manner of grotesque contortions.

"Cheerily, my hearties!" cried Wardlaw, in a firm but jovial tone. "A health to your captain."

The men seized their cans.

"Horoo! huzza! Long live our only captain. Long live Captain Wardlaw!"

"Well said, messmates," cried Ramsey, "I will drink that toast!"

"Hurrah! Long live Lieutenant Ramsey!"

"Consider hearties, there are better men among ye. Choose your captain; but, for your own sakes, obey his orders. There are some fine seamen among ye."

"No, no!" shouted the pirates. "Captain Ward-

law and Lieutenant Ramsey for ever and ever! Huzza!"

"Well, then, silence fore and aft!" cried Wardlaw, in a thrilling tone of kindly command.

A ruffianly, barefooted man jumped up from the deck.

"Aye; but no marring sport; let's finish our bout first," he shouted.

"Down, you cursed mutineer. Will there never be order?" growled another, leaping upon the speaker, and hurling him across the deck.

He struck his head such a violent blow against a carronade, that he was stunned, and sank as lifeless.

"We're all of one mind; we want a skipper, and you're elected, and shall be obeyed. We don't eat our own words, eh, messmates?"

"No. Long live Cap'en Wardlaw!"

"Thanks, hearties, I've no need to repeat my order, I am sure. I *must* have silence."

"Aye, aye, sir!" roared the seamen.

"Silence, ye drunken lubbers, silence—fore and aft!"

The men became comparatively quiet.

"My hearties, you are all men of sense and courage, and, as such, know well enough that our common safety depends upon our coolness and self-controul."

"Aye, aye, sir," responded three or four of the more rational of the men.

The rest responded.

"To-morrow we must weigh anchor, to-night you must have rest. Let the traitorous villain who would have destroyed us all remain lashed where he is till daybreak; meanwhile, let us have perfect quiet, and that all may be done according to regulation. To-morrow, your ex-captain shall be tried by court-martial."

The men assented by a general murmur of approval.

Some were alarmed at the fearful disorder that of late had reigned in the ship.

Others were too drunken to know what was passing.

The rest were overawed.

"Bo'swain, pipe the side!"

The few who were sober promptly obeyed the whistle.

"Let everything be drawn up, let every boat be firmly lashed to the davits!"

This order was obeyed with alacrity.

"And now let all hands get below, and be ready for the morning's duty."

Soon the deck was cleared.

Those who could not walk were carried down the hatchways.

Wardlaw and Ramsey paced the silent deck.

Flushed and excited, at length they went into the state-cabin, resolving to take turns for sleep.

There was darkness and silence.

CHAPTER CCXXXV.

ESCAPE OF HARWOLF.

HARWOLF looked along the deserted deck, and gnashed his teeth in impotent rage.

The larboard and starboard watches tramped about in moody silence.

The wind soughed through the dark rigging of the anchored vessel.

The breeze was freshening.

The ship rocked from side to side.

The peace without contrasted with the storm that raged in Harwolf's heart.

He struggled with his bonds.

He was firmly secured.

Wildly he looked towards the east.

A faint, red light was dawning.

The bloody hue reminded him of the terrible deed of blood that was to be perpetrated in the morning.

MEETING OF LADY EDGEFORTH AND HER SON.

And he who had so often been the torturer was now to be the victim.

He groaned.

"Hist!"

It was the voice of a man, creeping towards him.

"Who's there?" muttered Harwolf, trembling in every limb.

"A friend."

"Ha!"

"Johnson."

"Have you come to cheat the villains; to put me out of my misery?"

"Harkye, cap'en!"

"Speak low, the watch will hear you."

"Aye, but I'm one of the larboard men."

No. 70.

"What do you want?"

"To make you a present."

"Of what?"

"Of a knife."

"To cut my throat!"

"No; to cut your bonds."

"I am too firmly bound; I can't move."

"Hush!"

"Will you do it for me then?"

"Aye; but be quick."

"Quick, then. Give me one moment's freedom, and I will avenge a life of baffling and injury!"

Almost every rogue considers himself an injured man.

Johnson walked off.

"Here — stay — a word!" whispered Harwolf, eagerly.

But the man was now at a distance.

"It was but to taunt me!" groaned Harwolf. "Oh, if my hands were free!"

Johnson returned.

"Cap'en!"

"Aye."

"What would you do if I gave you your liberty?"

"You would find you had set the devil loose."

"You would be as treacherous as ever."

"No, no, Johnson; they hate you. They will murder you as they did Kumba."

"I'll cut your bonds on one condition."

"What is it?"

"That you will swear to obey me."

"I will!"

"But what is an oath to you?"

"It is not my interest to injure my friends."

"Hush, then!"

Again Johnson walked forward and again returned aft.

"Is there a boat at the treasure cave?" he asked.

"Yes—no!" hesitated Harwolf, who did not wish to compromise himself by insincerity to one who could render him such good service.

"Yes or no?"

"There is no boat, but there is a raft."

"That will do."

"Are you fooling me?"

"No, cap'en; we two will load the raft with treasure and make for the mainland."

"You may trust me; with your aid I can escape and live to work woe to these mutineers."

"Get softly over the side. I will drop astern, and together we will swim to land."

Still doubtful whether the man was mocking him Harwolf made no reply.

Johnson walked up to the wheel.

He drew the keen blade across the ropes.

Harwolf was free!

From being so long cramped by the taut cords he was so feeble that he could scarce stand.

He sank on the deck.

Johnson raised him.

It was still dark, though the light was faintly dawning in the far, far east.

Johnson helped him to the side.

He crouched behind a carronade and stretched his numbed limbs.

"I can move now," he said.

"Over with you, then; better to die by water than by fire. They have sworn to burn you alive!"

Harwolf crept over the bulwark, and, by a rope which the other had prepared, he lowered himself into the sea.

He forged on through the scattering waters.

Morning was now breaking fast.

He heard a voice shouting.

Looking over his shoulder he perceived Johnson at a little distance.

"Cap'en, help me! I drown!" cried the luckless adventurer.

He had overrated his strength and skill as a swimmer and was sinking exhausted.

Harwolf floated on his side and was about to turn to assist his comrade when he heard a noise from the distant ship.

The drowning man uttered another gurgling cry.

But the selfish villain heeded him not.

He reached the shore.

He paused and listened.

The haze prevented the movements on the ship from being seen.

Harwolf dashed on towards the cave of treasure.

He rolled back a stone and entered long and vaulted passages hewn or formed by nature in the heart of the rock.

He threaded them till he reached a square chamber which contained the rich plunder, the costly price of blood.

He selected a small chest, some bags of money and

articles of clothing, and, from among the stores, he rummaged a barrel of biscuit, a keg of rum and another of water.

As quickly as possible he got these articles down to the brink of some steps that descended to the water's edge.

Here a raft was floating.

On this he placed his cargo.

Guiding the bark with a long pole, he made for the mouth of the inlet and rounding the coast towards the opposite side of the island.

Meanwhile the man on the starboard watch had heard the splash caused by the unfortunate Johnson's plunge into the waves.

He rushed to the helm.

The prisoner had escaped!

Instantly he gave the alarm.

Wardlaw rushed on deck.

He piped all hands.

Immediate search was made for the criminal.

Johnson was missing.

The pirates were afraid lest their treacherous tyrant might still be aboard working for their destruction.

Wardlaw, however, encouraged them by the assurance that the powder magazine was strongly guarded.

Nevertheless, a wild rush was made down the gangway.

The men remaining on deck expended much time in lowering the boats.

They had been tightly lashed to the davits.

This precaution was the cause of the present delay.

The boats were got down at last.

The men below examined the ship from stem to stern.

With a yell of fury they rushed into the hold.

Though heavily ironed, Blacklock sprang to his feet.

He thought they had come to butcher him.

With a fearful oath he sprang into the midst of them, and struck right and left with his manacled wrists.

A seaman smote him down with a pike.

Another placed a pistol to his ear and blew his brains out.

The others stamped upon the gory body, and yelled their detestations.

Thus miserably perished a miscreant.

CHAPTER CCXXXVI.

THE STRUGGLE ON THE RAFT.

FOR several days the escaped Harwolf was tossed on the eternal waves.

He had made a rude sail by means of a spar and some canvas.

Morn dawned, noon glowed, eve darkened.

Still like some demon of the sea he crouched brooding.

His loneliness was terrible.

At times he felt almost a desire to exchange his solitude for the torments of his prison-ship.

Like a wolf baffled of his prey, he would howl out his fiendish malice.

When he raised his eyes to the brilliant host of stars, or saw the bright sun rise from the distant wave, strange thoughts arose in his mind, visions of peace and virtue; he dismissed them with a sneer.

He restrained himself from drinking.

His store of water was small, and the effect of the spirits was not to quench but to excite his thirst.

He passed near an island.

He would fain have landed here.

It appeared, however, to be inhabited, for, from a flag-staff on a hill, a Spanish flag was floating.

He resolved, therefore, to continue his course.

He sat steering the raft by the halliard.

Soon the island was fading in the distance.

As he gazed intently at the shore he thought he could distinguish the form of a man running along the beach.

Soon this figure disappeared.

He watched long and anxiously to see whether a boat might be put off to reach him.

But no.

Still quiet in the golden strand, the emerald leaves twinkled in the sun, and waved gracefully in the light, freshening gale.

Harwolf had passed nights of agony.

The peril and misery of his position; the fires of his vindictive passion; the gnawing of his remorse-wrung conscience banished sleep.

For the first time since he had been sailing alone he felt inclined to sleep.

He lay down upon the spars and fell into a profound slumber.

His dreams were horrible.

His brow wrinkled and his lips writhed.

His hands stretched out, and convulsively clasped each other.

He was aroused by a sudden and violent shock against the raft.

Lifting himself on his arm, he glared half awake and half asleep at a man who had crawled over from the landward side of the raft.

He was a dark, wild-looking youth, sunburnt, and dressed as a sailor.

A knife was between his teeth.

Harwolf could scarcely believe his eyes or collect his thoughts; the apparition came so unexpected.

Before he could clutch the pistol which lay beside him, the seaman sprang at him.

"Accursed monster, you are mine at last!" he shouted, in a voice of stern joy.

It was the young Spaniard Diego.

Harwolf grappled with him.

He swore a fearful oath, and, twining his arms round his youthful antagonist, tried to hurl him into the sea.

But the youth held his own.

Once his lithe right arm was free.

His dagger glanced in the sun.

Then Harwolf parried the blow with his hand.

Then, locked in a terrible close, they writhed and stumbled, and rolled on to the rocking raft.

The surf leaped over them.

Like dogs that worry each other, they growled and fought in mad passion.

Sometimes victory seemed to decide for Harwolf, and sometimes for the young Spaniard.

At length they both appeared exhausted.

There was a lull in the contest.

They lay side by side watching each other with cat-like heedfulness, but panting with exhaustion.

Harwolf, seeing a chance, grasped the pistol which still lay beside him.

It went off.

But Diego had been too quick for the enemy.

He had nimbly sprung at Harwolf's throat, dashing the weapon aside.

Now the knife was in Harwolf's hands.

Now in Diego's.

At last the struggles of the men grew fainter and fainter.

Blood was streaming from a wound in each breast.

Harwolf had stabbed the Spaniard.

The Spaniard had returned the blow when he had gained possession of the knife.

The revengeful antagonists had now quite forgotten their mutual hatred, and lay quietly side by side.

Their senses had fled, and motionless as the dead they lay upon the raft.

The sun blazed down upon them.

They wind wafted over them.

They were drenched by the dancing spray.

Still they stirred not.

Day set, and darkness fell upon the face of the deep.

Still they lay unconscious.

Then the breeze freshened.

It struck the sail.

The raft was hurried strongly and swiftly on before the rising storm-wind.

The billows threatened each moment to sweep the bodies from the raft.

The gale increased in power.

Away, away through the boiling and tossing main, through the drear mist and deep darkness sped the raft, its heavy sail stretched almost to bursting, Harwolf and Diego lying side by side bleeding and senseless.

CHAPTER CCXXXVII.

A TOKEN OF DEATH.

OUR hero returned with his wife and his comrades to the camp.

He was received with the wonted enthusiasm by his devoted band.

The most stirring prepartions were going on for an attack on Count Brutoff's castle.

The camp was removed and pitched in the ravine, on the steep side of which the castle was reared.

Our hero had sounded a parley.

The enemy had treated him with derision.

Our hero had mustered his men, was just finishing a letter which he had been writing in his tent, when Feodor Polowski, the young Pole whose gentle and lovely wife had been so ruthlessly murdered, entered.

His handsome face looked rather less sad than usual.

He held out his hand to our hero.

The Avenger grasped it cordially.

"I am glad to see you looking more cheery this morning," said our hero, kindly. "It is the anticipation of to-day's victory and vengeance that has raised your spirits."

"Yes, my friend, it is only natural I should rejoice that there will be some retribution made for an act so cruel as the murder of my poor Alexina; but I am happier because my sorrows draw near to a close!"

"You surely will not act that craven's part? You will not wantonly throw away your life in the battle?" said our hero, reproachfully.

"I shall not need to seek death," returned Feodor, smiling sadly. "I have been warned that my term of life will expire this day!"

"And whence have you received this warning?"

"From a strange source," replied Feodor. "Last night, as I was alone in my tent, and about to retire to sleep, I was conscious that some one was standing in the middle of the room. I looked up; it was Alexina!"

"Strange; you must have been dreaming."

"No, captain, I was wide awake."

"Some delusion of the mind."

"It may be so, but I feel conscious that I am not deluded by the warning that she gave me."

"She spoke, then?"

"Yes, I called to her in all the agony of my soul; I would have caught her in my arms, but she bade me not to touch her. I receded, imploring her to speak to me again, for she was long silent. She told me that to-morrow I should die—that I should join her!"

"And she vanished then?"

"I know not how or when she disappeared; only, after a long pause I became conscious that I was alone."

"Your brain was overwrought by anticipating this day's work," said our hero, "and imagination, dwelling ever upon one object, presented it more vividly than usual to the mind's eye."

"It may be so," answered Feodor, but not in a tone of conviction.

"These things are, indeed, 'passing strange,'"

said Christopher, reflectively. "It would seem irrational to suppose that the spirits of the dead really revisit us in their mortal forms; but it is impossible not to attach some importance to the numberless stories of apparitions seen by the most trustworthy persons. Many of the tales may be easily explained, many may be mere fabrications; but some of them must be true."

"You English are less imaginative than we, you are more practical and stolid; perhaps more enlightened," said Feodor, "and yet you, too, have your ghost stories."

"Many, and well authenticated. I heard a story of a lady and gentleman who had risen from bed, their child, who usually slept in a crib beside them, suddenly exclaimed, 'Mamma, grand-papa stands at the foot of the bed!' Both the father and the mother of the child turned towards the spot, and saw distinctly the appearance of the father of the former; the figure was the more remarkable from his being accustomed to dress in the costume of the last age. The phantom was visible only for a short time, and then disappeared. The gentleman, fearing that his father was no more, and that they had seen his spirit, despatched a messenger to his father's house. The old gentleman had expired on that very morning, and about the time when his shade had appeared to his son, his wife, and their child."

Black Ralph interrupted this discourse by bustling into the tent.

He was dashingly accoutred, and armed to the teeth.

"Once more unto the breach, dear friends," he shouted, waving his sword. "Brutoff has ranged his supers on the walls. Your friends are up, and buckle on their armour (one shirt amongst 'em), our banners float the sky. Ole Zampa rages——."

"Enough, Sir Ralph, we follow you."

"Come, sisters three—

> For, more perdie, I love to see
> The tented field afar ;
> And steed and knight, arrayed for fight,
> In panoply of war !

"What cheer, my worthy Feodor ?"

The young Pole smiled faintly.

A loud shout rang through the camp.

The sharp twanging of a bugle was heard from the heights.

Then came the bursting roar of a cannon.

"Come, gentlemen, to arms!" cried Ralph, rushing out of the tent. "Let us be first a-field."

Our hero followed ranting Ralph.

The Pole stood for a moment dreamily gazing upon vacancy.

He started, and a wild light flashed from his eyes, his colour mounted, and his limbs stiffened.

He drew his sword, the sword of his father's, the sword he had hallowed to avenge his murdered love.

He raised his eyes to heaven, kissed the blade, and having crossed himself, and muttered a prayer, rushed after the Avengers, who were crowding to the guns or forming for an assault on the Castle Aronzow.

CHAPTER CCXXXVIII.

THE CHALLENGE.

It is needless to give an account of the storming of the Castle Aronzow.

Our readers have seen already so much of the prowess and daring of our remarkable hero, that they will not be surprised to find that his singular good fortune did not desert him in this emergency.

A few shots from the heavy pounders which had been brought to bear upon the gates shivered them

to pieces, and left the ancient castle at the mercy of the Avengers.

So terrific was the shout set up by the indomitable rover band that the Russians were terrified.

They hauled down their flag in token of surrender.

Then the Boy Pirate sounded a note on his bugle, which had the effect of bringing his men to his side.

They formed in the square court-yard within the walls of the fortress.

Our hero summoned the Russians to lay down their arms.

They piled their weapons.

The battle was lost and won.

Brutoff had disgraced himself by his cowardice.

After the first charge of the daring rovers, he had recalled his troops and retreated within the walls.

With the most ordinary share of courage and skill he could have held the place against thrice the number of assailants for any length of time.

But losing all self-controul, and dreading the vengeance of the fiery English, he blockaded himself in a room in the inner part of the castle.

The door was burst by the Avengers.

He defended himself desperately from their attack.

Desperation makes a coward fight.

He was dragged from the room.

The shouting seamen carried him down into the court-yard.

Here, even his own men, who were prisoners, received him with a terrific yell.

The Boy Pirate and his staff stood on one side of the court-yard, discoursing.

"Now, Feodor, what of your dream?" said our hero, with a smile.

"Ask me that when the sun has gone down," replied the young Pole, with a smile.

Count Brutoff was brought to the Boy Pirate.

"Ruffian and adventurer!" panted the coward, putting on an air of defiance, while he trembled with fear. "We know that it is a necessary evil to pay black mail to brigands; name my ransom and let me be as liberal as my importance demands."

"And how much, think you, the Czar would pay to ransom such a subject," said the rover, in a tone of disdain, "a cur and coward, who has disgraced the profession of arms by atrocities that call aloud for vengeance, by a cowardice that dishonours his corps and his nation?"

"Do not taunt him," said Feodor, quietly. "I see death in his eye; his hour and mine are one. I will fight him and kill him with my father's sword."

"It must not be so," returned our hero, firmly. "He shall be tried by court-martial, and hanged for a brute and a recreant."

"Captain, you have deceived me."

"How so?"

"Remember your promise."

"Why should you run this risk? Probably he is the better swordsman, and we do not place much faith in the ordeal of battle. Let the man be tried and dispatched, and then justice will be fairly done."

"No; no. I claim him. Your promise! He is my prisoner."

"Be it so. I am sorry that I cannot persuade you to leave him in our hands."

The Boy Pirate gave a command to the soldiers that guarded the count.

They fell back.

CHAPTER CCXXXIX.

THE DUEL TO THE DEATH.

"Count Brutoff, you have been guilty of a base and cruel deed, and my time is come to avenge it," said Feodor, sternly.

"You mean, then, to assassinate me, Polish dog!" gasped the craven.

"I am no assassin; if with this knife I struck you dead on the spot, the deed would be one of justice; but I give you a chance, one or both of us must die within this hour."

"You intend to fight me, then?"

"I do."

"And with what weapons?"

"I leave the choice to you."

"Be it so."

"No, it shall not be so," said the Boy Pirate, interfering, "this man is skilled in the science of slaughter."

"And I am armed with the holiness of my cause. He is my prisoner, captain; I will do what I please with him," said Feodor.

Our hero shrugged his shoulders.

He took a step backwards, and folded his arms.

He fixed a stern glance on the count's face.

"Should your excellency be victorious in this contest you will have a chance of giving a second proof of your skill, for I shall then challenge you," said our hero, with a cold smile.

Count Brutoff did not receive this intimation with particular satisfaction.

"It is your intention to murder me, robbers!" he muttered.

The pirates scowled on him.

"Captain," said Feodor, "a last request; you are too kind to refuse me; if Heaven spares this criminal in his contest with me, do you spare him too?"

"Never! never!"

"This is to intimidate me, and to render my energy futile, you dastard!" cried the count.

"You fight for your life, fight well for a prize you know so well how to value," said the pirate, fiercely. "I am sworn, we are all sworn, to avenge the innocent blood of the murdered Alexina; but we will give you liberty to return to the camp of the Russian army, and we will take our time to bring about your just chastisement."

Count Brutoff's eyes gleamed with hope.

Feodor asked him to select the weapons.

He declared for swords.

"Then," said the villain, "there can be no tampering, no treachery. Give me my own sword."

The hero handed it to him.

The men now formed a ring.

The two men stripped to their shirts.

They stepped into the ring.

Our hero looked thoughtful and anxious.

His officers and crew seemed to share in his doubts as to the favourable issue of the conflict.

A sneer was on Count Brutoff's lips.

He was a famous swordsman.

From his boyhood he had been a mean and cruel dastard.

He had devoted almost all his leisure time to the art of fencing.

He saluted with graceful formality.

Feodor did not respond.

He stood leaning upon his sword.

His eyes were fixed upon his antagonist.

Not a muscle of his face moved.

He seemed to be unconscious of the presence of all but the murderer of his beloved wife.

There was deep and breathless silence.

Each of the duellists advanced his left foot.

Their swords crossed.

Count Brutoff's face was flushed.

Feodor's pale, but changeless as a statue's.

The clink and the clitter and twang of the entwining blades was now heard.

The men were fighting desperately.

A deep and involuntary sigh burst from the breasts of the pirate and his crew.

There was no comparison to be made between the combatants.

Feodor was fearfully outmatched.

He seemed to be conscious of this.

Yet the gallant young Pole was in nowise daunted, and remained as calm and as confident as if secure of victory.

Wildly they parried and thrust.

Had Brutoff been less a coward he might have finished the fight in a few moments.

He dared not venture a lunge at his opponent, lest he should expose himself to a counter-thrust.

So he feinted, and warded watchfully.

He awaited an opportunity of piercing his foe without running risk.

This chance occurred.

Feodor seemed to grow furious.

Hungry for revenge he fought savagely.

Clink! clash!

The excitement of the by-standers increased.

They uttered a cry.

Feodor sank back.

The blood poured from his arm.

With a yell of triumph, and eyes flashing with brutal glee, Brutoff sprang at the Pole.

He stood his ground, and parried with unusual skill.

Count Brutoff jumped backwards.

"Sa!" he exclaimed, and trembled like a craven.

Had Feodor possessed more skill it would have gone hard with the Russian.

As it was he tottered back, and leaned upon his sword.

Count Brutoff panted for breath.

Our hero ran to Feodor's side.

"This is insane—it is abominable!" said he, indignantly. "This man has had long practice in the art of butchery. He will kill you, as he killed your wife, and so escape justice. Give over this contest!"

"My wound is nothing," said Feodor, in a voice of faintness. "My left arm only is disabled; my right arm is free."

"And this clumsy sword, too!"

"Do not abuse it; in its day it has done good service for poor Poland," said Feodor. "It is my father's sword, and I will not throw it aside while I have life to wield it."

"You are too romantic; it is mere madness."

"Grief is romantic and mad; as you pity my grief, indulge it."

Count Brutoff now stepped up.

"You see, my good fellow, that you have no chance in this contest. I do not wish to take your life; I will even make amends for the fatal deed which you choose to regard as a crime, though it was but an accident. You shall not want for money or protection during your whole life; be satisfied, then, and name your reward."

"Give me——"

"Yes, speak."

"Give me my wife!"

"Well, I will pay you a ransome that will buy you a fairer one. A man is no man who takes so deeply to heart a loss that may be so well repaired. These sad mischances are a part of the curse of war."

"You shall pay me a ransome for my wife's blood."

"Name it."

"Every drop of your own that now freezes in your craven heart!"

Brutoff turned pale.

He looked at our hero.

"You see, monsieur," he said, "the man is implacable; there is no alternative left to me but to defend my life against his assault. Do not blame me if the issue is fatal to him, whom I would willingly spare."

"I shall not blame you, sir," replied our hero, coldly.

Unconsciously his hand trembled on the hilt of his sword, and he glared at the count with eyes that sparkled with his native warmth of passion and constitutional petulance.

"Come, let us finish," said Feodor, impatiently.

"We will finish!" said the count, with a sneer upon the last word.

The contest was renewed.

The combatants fought very warily.

The spectators evinced the intensest interest.

A sneer of mingled scorn and shame curved the lips of Feodor.

From that instant he discarded all prudence.

He struck wildly at the count.

Brutoff saw that his adversary had lost all presence of mind, and was insensate with impatience and fury.

He leaped back.

His face beamed with fiendish delight.

He even laughed.

Feodor sprang after him.

He threw his whole body open to attack, uprearing his ponderous sword.

Clash!

Thrust, thrust!

A yell from the Avengers.

Our hero up-lifts his hand and waves them back.

Feodor is tottering backwards.

He is literally bathed in blood.

Brutoff follows him close.

He staggers forward.

The men close.

Down, down they go, locked in tight embrace.

A scream—a groan !

Feodor crawls away.

Numbers rush to support him.

Count Brutoff lies stone dead, the broken sword driven to the hilt in his bosom.

Our hero raises Feodor tenderly in his arms.

As he looks on the heroic countenance of the brave young warrior, his eyes suffuse with tears.

"It is over," murmured Feodor, with a radiant smile, "what now do you think of my dream ?"

"Be it realised, brave friend ! Be you reunited to her whom you have loved so dearly, and have avenged so justly and so bravely !"

"I shall be with her ; we shall not forget you."

The hand that pressed our hero's grew cold.

The keen dark eye dimmed.

The cheeks paled, and the head fell.

The soul of the young patriot smiled an eternal joy and freedom, and left the brightness of its parting beam upon the calm dead face.

Our hero was deeply moved.

He gave orders that the body of the noble youth should be buried with all possible solemnity.

Feodor was placed on a bier.

He was wrapped in the Polish colours, and the sword of his fathers was laid by his side.

In this manner he was borne to his wife's grave that had been opened to receive him.

Before him walked the advanced guard of the Avengers, trailing their pikes or carrying their guns reversed.

The Boy Pirate, Caffyn, Old Brierly, Black Ralph, Cassidy, and the rest of our heroes, followed in the sad procession.

Every face bore the aspect of sincere and manly regret.

They laid him gently down by the side of his beloved.

A file of marines fired three volleys over the grave.

The grave was then covered in.

They raised a pile of stones upon the spot, and erected a strong wooden cross, on which they placed a laurel wreath.

Ever since the grave has been hallowed by the simple peasantry, who still weep for the memory of the amiable and noble pair.

Even the enemy has respected this touching memorial.

The flowers bloom around the spot, the sere leaves fall on it, the snow enshrouds it, and the little children, roaming the woods, deck it with festoons of fresh-gathered spring blossoms.

The hoary wood-cutter, returning from his toil in autumn, leans on his staff and gazes, with dim eyes, on the spot where the two noble hearts, in death united, sleep peacefully together, insensible to the stings and arrows of outrageous fortune, the whips and scorns of life.

*   *   *   *   *

Our hero returned to the Castle Aronzow.

He who dies pays all debts.

Our generous hero buried the body of the recreant count quietly and obscurely, but not without some show of respect.

The pirates did not pillage the Castle Aronzow.

They treated their prisoners with humanity.

Our hero did not venture to go in person to the Russian camp.

He dispatched a suitable messenger with a very strong escort.

When the Russians found that the redoubtable pirates had captured the castle and a whole regiment of soldiers they were glad to accede to our hero's very reasonable terms.

These were that the Avengers should be allowed to part in peace and unmolested from the unfortunate country which all their bravery and heroism had failed to liberate from the cruel and disgraceful oppression of its powerful and semi-barbarous victors.

Our hero delivered up his prisoners.

Many of the Russian nobles, attracted by his great renown and chivalrous character, visited our hero.

They treated him with much courtesy.

They were disposed to make him many rich gifts.

The Boy Pirate would accept nothing.

He went on board his fleet at the little port on the Oder.

He set sail.

For many days he was depressed and taciturn.

Remorse gnawed his heart-strings.

Regret clouded his brow.

He felt saddened at heart.

The liberation of Poland was not to be wrought by one who sailed beneath the black banner.

The holy cause could not prosper in the hands of a felon and pirate, however bright many parts of his character might seem.

———

CHAPTER CCXL.

THE LAST SICKNESS OF LADY EDGEFORTH.

LADY EDGEFORTH's health declined fast.

As we have before stated, the doctors recommended that the hapless lady should travel in the south of Europe.

Finding that she did not improve in health during their residence at Madrid, Lord Hawksbury removed her to his yacht.

Don Manuel and Donna Aurora accompanied the English nobleman.

All were tenderly assiduous in their care of the dying lady.

As her health declined reason resumed her sway.

Lady Edgeforth was sad but resigned.

One day her brother was summoned to her cabin.

He found her on her bed pale and exhausted.

She raised herself and looked him tenderly in the face.

He embraced her with tears in his eyes.

She leaned her head on his shoulder.

She wept silently.

He was greatly moved.

When she spoke her voice was faint and weak.

"Brother, you have been very kind to me," she said.

Lord Hawksbury pressed her hand.

He could not speak.

They both maintained silence.

Lady Edgeforth's changing countenance showed the traces of many conflicting emotions.

"I am dying at last!" she said, with a smile.

"Do not say so, sister," returned Lord Hawksbury; "you will live to see many happy days."

She shook her head sadly.

"No, brother; why should I wish to live? I have done with life. Surely I have borne its weary burden long enough."

"Your course has been one of bitter sorrow," murmured Lord Hawksbury, half unconsciously.

"Has it not?" replied his sister, in a hollow tone. "My life has been not only of sorrow, but of terror, of horror!"

The brother turned his head aside.

He did not wish her to see his deep emotion.

He cheered her with hopeful words.

She received his encouragement with a wistful smile.

"I have one request to make before I die," she whispered; "grant it, dear brother!"

Lord Hawksbury pressed her hand.

"My child!—I have a son."

He pressed her hand.

His face grew deathly white.

"It seems all a hideous dream! My whole life has passed as one long and terrible vision, but I am recovering my senses."

Very earnestly her brother besought her not to think of the past.

He tried to impress upon her that she was too weak at present to enter upon the subject.

She listened patiently.

"I know I have been mad!" she said, wringing her hands in agony, "but I am sane now, I know; at least, I think I know and remember all."

"You must banish the past from your thoughts, dear sister."

"I shall, I shall forget it," she said, with a radiant smile. "The darkness will be dispelled by light eternal, and all the past's record of misery will be swept away by the well-spring of joy in heaven. Brother?"

"What is it?"

"You are all I have; you are my only friend."

Lord Hawksbury smiled.

"On earth, but that is nothing; those who are above are conscious of your sufferings, and there will be a blissful reunion in His good time."

Lady Edgeforth laughed a low laugh of strange delight.

"Oh, I am so glad—so glad!" she said, clapping together her small, white hands.

"Of what?" my sister?"

"That he is dead."

"Dead! Who is dead?"

"My son, my dear child. We shall meet soon."

Lord Hawksbury wrung his hands.

He was silent.

He dared not tell his sister that the heir of Frontemore, the true Lord Edgeforth, the child of her love, was an oucast and a pirate.

"And now tell me ——Ah, but it is strange that I should wish to have seen him in the body; but he would have been so handsome and so noble had he lived. Tell me how he died; I have but confused memories."

"Another time, sister dearest," said Lord Hawksbury, shuddering violently.

"No, I will know now. Let me reflect. Stay, I will tell you the story."

Her brother waited in fear and agitation.

Her eyes fixed, she seemed to be struggling to remember something far byegone.

Suddenly her face grew blank with awful agony.

She uttered a wailing shriek.

She sank back on the pillow in a deep swoon.

CHAPTER CCXLI.

LORD HAWKSBURY AT LAST OBTAINS TIDINGS OF THE BOY PIRATE.

LORD HAWKSBURY summoned the physician.

Overpowered by emotion he came on deck.

He walked about in great agitation.

The light and beautiful craft was sailing swiftly along the mirror of waters.

There was scarcely a ripple on the sea.

The sapphire sky glowed with Italian brilliancy.

Far away in the distance were seen two steamers, leaving behind them their snowy wakes and black-wreathing clouds of smoke.

Soon the white sails of their heavier and slower moving consorts appeared on the horizon.

The blue intermediate space was flecked with quaint winged felluccas.

The scene was glorious.

The glassy sea flashed back the sun's brightness.

The glad gulls swerved and floated in the warm, clear air, their white breasts and long wings dazing white in the flooding sunbeams.

To distract his careworn thoughts, Lord Hawksbury glanced through his glass at the distant flotilla.

Don Manuel and the physician came from below.

"Well, doctor, and how fares your patient?"

The physician looked grave.

He shook his head.

"It is useless to disguise the truth, my lord, which will too soon be apparent."

"The truth that my sister cannot live long?"

"Even so."

"Well, doctor, you will give me credit for the natural affection I bear to her. I can desire nothing better for her than this, that death may come to her softly and speedily."

"She appears to be suffering from great anguish of mind."

Lord Hawksbury raised his hand to his forehead.

"Is she not calmer now than when I left her?"

"She sleeps peacefully, my lord. I administered

an opiate, and, perhaps, when she awakens she may be in some measure strengthened and pacified."

" But there is no hope of her recovery?"

" I grieve to say but very little, my lord."

" My poor sister !"

The nurse now approached.

" My lady is awake," she said," addressing the physician.

" I will come."

Lord Hawksbury and Don Manuel were alone.

" The mother and son will meet no more on earth," said the Spaniard, mournfully.

" I fear not," replied the other. " Perhaps, under all circumstances, it is better so."

" You are pale, my lord; you afflict yourself too much."

" If you knew all you would not think that possible."

" We must think of death, my lord, not as a curse, for One has changed that curse into a blessing, but as a beautiful dispensation, which, as your poet says, ' Makes these odds all even.' "

" It does; the martyrs knew it," said the young noble, with a look of happy conviction. " For the worst tortures we can suffer of mind or body are but transient when we reflect that the soul is immortal—eternity is a gulf in which time dwindles into nothingness, and in that sense death is life."

" I did not think, my lord, that you could believe in these theories; I have heard you talk as a sceptic."

" A sceptic !—not I. I care nought about theories. If there is any truth that is demonstrative, it is that matter cannot perish, that something cannot spring out of nothing, and that " nothing " cannot absorb something. If matter, then, cannot perish, I am humbly convinced that the life, the soul, or whatever that essence be which animates matter, is also imperishable—that is quite enough for me, I am sufficiently religious to leave all the rest to the Creator (not to speak this profanely). What do you think yourself, Don Manuel ?"

" Well, my lord, I think that this unhappy lady's unhappiness draws to a climax and a close."

" She told me so herself; she feels that she is about to die."

" How extraordinary !" said Don Manuel, putting down his telescope.

" What is extraordinary ?"

" You see that ship, the last to appear on the sky line ?"

" What then ?"

" She has exactly the rig and build of a certain schooner which I would give my fortune to see heave in sight."

" And the name of your ship of promise ?"

" THE RED RAVEN !"

Lord Hawksbury looked at the distant vessel.

" That is the name of the Boy Pirate's vessel, and such the odious title by which he was long known."

" It was."

" But that cannot be."

" I suppose not."

" It is impossible, the Boy Pirate is now fighting in Poland."

" What we most wish is most easy to believe," said Don Manuel, smiling. " Do you know that I could swear to that vessel ? I feel convinced that she is the veritable ' Raven.' "

" I hope not, in such company."

" No; for she must be a prize."

" I should think so ; there are two war-steamers convoying her and the rest of the trading vessels."

" Nevertheless, I can't help feeling a presentiment that Lady Edgeforth will not die without beholding her son."

" I hope your presentiment may prove a true one."

" I hope so ; but yet it seems improbable."

" Perhaps this meeting is scarcely one to be desired after all," said his lordship, reflectively; " but let us leave this gloomy subject. Shall we put down the boat and go ashore ?"

" With all my heart," returned Don Manuel.

The two gentlemen got into the gig and were pulled ashore.

They sauntered along the sunny strand till they came to a wine-shop.

Under an arbour of trellised vine a number of hardy-looking seamen were carousing.

They appeared to be men of many different nations, but the greater part were English.

The two gentlemen stopped, and regarded them with curiosity.

They were somewhat fierce-looking, but a splendid crew in respect to their manly bearing, and there was no lack of a kindly spirit in the expression of their faces.

Don Manuel drew his friend aside.

" These men belong to the Avenger's band."

" Impossible !"

" They are the Boy Pirate's men."

" Pirates ! they can never be pirates, they have not the sneakish, lurking look of thieves."

" Nevertheless, I tell you they are the ' Ravens,' and I make no doubt that their chief is here."

A tall and grave-looking Spaniard strode past at this moment.

He was dressed in the costume of a merchant captain.

He entered the wine-shop.

He was greeted with a gruff laugh by the men within.

" That is Gomez, the Spaniard, who served under Don Miguel Vasquez, my wife's father; now I am thoroughly convinced."

" What is to be done ?"

" I cannot perceive."

" We may betray them unwittingly."

" The daring rascals, they seem to know neither fear nor caution."

" I'll tell you how we may manage this affair; do you return to the yacht, my lord, and I, who am personally known to the Boy Pirate, will obtain a private interview with him."

" Yes; for he may think this but a trap to betray him."

" Yes, perhaps even you will find it difficult to gain his confidence."

" Do not think that; he is but too confiding, relies, I think, too much on his own discernment, and has more than once suffered for this rash confidence."

" Have you no token to give me of the truth of the strange, sad story I shall have to tell him ?"

" Well thought of. I have in this case a miniature; it is, you see, reversible; on one side is the portrait of poor Lord Edgeforth, on the other my sister's. The resemblance between the father and son, you have told me, is very striking."

" Return, then, at once to the yacht," said Don Manuel, " while I beard the lion in his den."

Lord Hawksbury nodded and stepped off.

Don Manuel entered the wine-shop.

He found the sailors carousing.

At a table, and surrounded by admiring auditors, a large, handsome fellow, with a fierce, yet rollicking black eye, and an immense and bushy black beard, trolled out in deep bass some merry sea-song.

Don Manuel waited till the singer had finished his ditty.

Then he walked across the room and addressed the seamen, speaking in English.

" Pray, my friends, will you tell me where I may find your captain ?"

" Which captain, senor ?" asked he of the black beard; " we have several captains, as we belong to several ships; there are captains Johnson, Tomson, Robson, and Richardson."

At this moment the Spaniard whom Don Manuel had noticed before rose and gripped his hand, and inquired after Donna Aurora.

Don Manuel made no answer to this question, but said, in a low and eager tone,

" Lead me to the Red Raven."

THE SENTINEL SURPRISED.—*See No.* 73.

CHAPTER CCXLII.

TOO LATE!

DON MANUEL PEREZ was conducted by Gomez into the presence of our hero.

The Boy Pirate and Lilia were alone in a little chamber which overhung the sea and commanded an extensive and lonely prospect of the winding shores and wide arching expanse of deep blue sea.

The young pair rose with looks of surprise and pleasure at seeing Don Manuel and welcomed him with hearty affection.

Observing that the Spaniard's brow was clouded and that he cast a wistful glance at them, the Boy Pirate and his wife pressed him to explain the cause of his emotion.

No. 71.

"Truly, Don Manuel, you look as gloomy as the Knight of the Sorrowful Countenance. Has anything happened to disturb your peace?"

"Donna Aurora? your dear little one?" suggested Lilia, turning pale.

The young Spaniard replied that his wife and child were well.

"We are in danger, perhaps?" said Lilia.

"If that be all, don't beetle your brows, Manuel; there is but one place in which I can be out of danger," rejoined our hero with a smile.

"I know of no danger that is imminent, and, as you have long given up your evil courses, and now are engaged in fair traffic, folks are not over curious to ask questions about your past career; of course you will know how to keep yourself out of the grip of the law. I trust you will be able to distinguish yourself in some good cause and thereby obtain a free pardon."

"And yet you look sad."

Our hero saw by the perplexed look of his friend that the latter was unwilling to speak before Lilia.

Our hero smiled and drew the young Spaniard aside.

They seated themselves without the window upon a vine-shaded balcony.

Now that they were alone Manuel's agitation increased.

"I must ask you some questions, senor, which may seem impertinent, but which you will answer freely when you know my motive for asking them. Your parents——"

"My parents!" said the Boy Pirate, starting up with blanched cheek and quivering lip.

"You do not know who they were! you do not know the sad story of your infancy! you do not know what honours you have lost!"

"I know it all!" gasped the Boy Pirate; "at least I know that I am the degenerate representative of a noble house, the vile descendant of noble ancestors, that the last of the Earls of Edgeforth is a pirate and an outcast!"

The Boy Pirate covered his face with his hands and groaned bitterly.

"Is it possible that you know this?"

"Aye, Manuel, and I will tell you how I came to this knowledge."

Our hero drew a little case from his breast and held it towards Manuel.

It was the miniature of Lord Edgeforth.

"This is strange! How did this come into your possession?" exclaimed the young Spaniard, in amazement.

Our hero narrated his adventure at Rio de Janiero, where, it will be remembered, he was recognised by the governor of the city as the son of Lord Edgeforth, by the striking resemblance he bore to that unfortunate nobleman.

"I know that they are dead, my parents both," sighed our hero, "and that my father was murdered. This was told me by the son of the villanous assassin. He taunted me with fiendish malice, as I lay bound in the dungeons at Rio de Janiero."

With much feeling and friendly cautiousness, Don Manuel gradually unfolded to the excited pirate the truth of the case regarding Lady Edgeforth.

The agony of the generous-hearted rover was extreme.

Mastering his emotion as well as he could, the Boy Pirate explained to Lilia the strange revelation made by the Spaniard.

"Oh, my brave, my dear husband," cried Lilia, flinging her arms about him, "do not look so downcast, there is comfort, even with this sorrow; we have a mother! And though she is found so late, we can know that she loves and forgives us, we can cherish her memory, we can implore her last blessing."

But our hero's cheek was hot and red.

His eyes were full of tears.

He gnashed his teeth in shame and bitterness of spirits.

"My mother!" he muttered, hoarsely. "and now it is too late!"

"Oh not too late, you are no longer a pirate, you have admiring friends, who, though they may justly decry your lawless conduct, are willing to screen one so brave and noble. Come, my husband, let us go alone, and at once to Lady Edgeforth."

Manuel approved of this purpose.

So without letting their purpose be known to the rest, they stole quickly from the inn, and embarked in the boat, which awaited to convey them to Lord Hawksbury's yacht.

CHAPTER CCXLIII.

TOUGH YARNS AND TRUE ONES.

UNCONSCIOUS of the grief and agitation into which Don Manuel's strange revelation had plunged their leader, the light-hearted seamen were still carousing in the wine-shop.

Black Ralph and Tom Garrod amused the company by their astounding yarns.

Ralph was in high humour and outlied Tom till the latter began to tremble for his own reputation as the most daring improviser in the crew.

Not all their gunpowder stories, however, were without foundation in truth, and as there is something curious and interesting in the wild lives of those desperate wretches, the buccaneers of old, the substance of Black Ralph's account of one of the most renowned of them will be acceptable to our readers; we, therefore, place before them the following interesting account of

CAPTAIN KIDD.

In old times, just after the territory of the New Netherlands had been wrested from their High Mightinesses the Lords State General of Holland by King Charles the Second, and while it was yet in an unquiet state, the province was a great resort of random adventurers, loose livers, and all that class of haphazard fellows who live by their wits and dislike the old fashioned restraint of law and gospel.

Among these the foremost were the buccaneers.

These were the rovers of the deep, who, perhaps, in time of war, had been educated in those schools of piracy—the privateers, and, having once tasted the sweets of plunder, had ever retained a hankering for it.

There is but a slight step from the the privateersman to the pirate; both fight for the love of plunder, only that the latter is the bravest, as he dares both the enemy and the gallows.

But in whatever school they had been taught the buccaneers, who kept about the English colonies, were daring fellows, and made sad work at times of peace among the Spanish settlements and Spanish merchantmen.

The easy access to the harbour of the Manhattoes, the number of hiding-places about its waters, and the laxity of its scarcely-organised government, made it a great rendezvous for the pirates, where they might dispose of their booty and concert new depredations.

As they brought home with them wealth of all kinds, the luxuries of the tropics, and the sumptuous spoils of the Spanish provinces, and disposed of them with the proverbial carelessness of freebooters, they were welcome visitors to the thrifty traders of the Manhattoes.

Crews of these desperadoes, therefore, the runagates of every country and every clime, might be seen swaggering in open day through the streets of the little burgh, elbowing its quiet mynheers, trafficking away their rich outlandish plunder at half or quarter price to the wary merchant, and then squandering in taverns, drinking, gambling, singing, swearing, shouting, and astounding the neighbourhood with midnight brawl and ruffian revelry.

At length these excesses rose to such a height as to become a scandal to the provinces, and to call loudly for the interposition of government.

Measures were accordingly taken to put a stop to the widely-extended evil, and to ferret this vermin brood out of the colonies.

Among the agents employed to execute this purpose was the notorious Captain Kidd.

He had long been an equivocal character, one of those nondescript animals of the ocean that are neither fish, flesh nor fowl.

He was somewhat of a trader, something more of the smuggler, with a considerable dash of the pickeroon.

He had traded for many years among the pirates in a little rakish, musquito-built vessel that could run into all kinds of waters.

He knew all their haunts and lurking-places, and was always hooking about on mysterious voyages, and as busy as a Mother Carey's chicken in a storm.

This nondescript personage was pitched upon by government as the very man to hunt pirates by sea upon the good old maxim of " setting a rogue to catch a rogue ;" or, as otters are sometimes employed to catch their cousins-german, the fish.

Kidd accordingly sailed for New York in 1695, in a gallant vessel called the " Adventure Galley," well armed, and duly commissioned.

On arriving at his old haunts, however, he shipped his crew on new terms, enlisted a number of his old comrades, lads of the knife and pistol, and then set sail for the east, steered up to Madeiras to Bonavista and Madagascar, and cruised about the entrance of the Red Sea.

Here, among other maritime robberies, he captured a rich Quedah merchantman, manned by Moors, though commanded by an Englishman.

Kidd would fain have passed this off for a worthy exploit, as being a crusade against the infidels ; but government had long since lost all relish for such Christian triumphs.

After roaming the seas and trafficking his prizes and changing from ship to ship, Kidd had the hardihood to return to Boston, laden with booty, with a crew of swaggering companions at his heels.

Times, however, had changed.

The buccaneers could no longer show a whisker in the colony with impunity.

The new governor, Lord Bellamont, had signalised himself by his zeal in extirpating these offenders, and was doubly exasperated against Kidd, having been instrumental in appointing him to the trust which he had betrayed.

No sooner, therefore, did he show himself in Boston than the alarm was given of his reappearance, and measures were taken to arrest this cutpurse of the ocean.

The daring character which Kidd had acquired, however, and the desperate fellows who followed like bull-dogs at his heels, caused a little delay in his arrest.

He took advantage of this, it is said, to bury the greater part of his treasures, and then carried a high head in the streets of Boston.

He even attempted to defend himself, when arrested, but was secured and thrown into prison with his followers.

Such was the formidable character of this pira'e and his crew, that it was thought advisable to despatch a frigate to bring them to England.

Great exertions were made to screen him from justice, but in vain.

He and his comrades were tried, condemned and hanged at Execution Dock in London.

Kidd died hard, for the rope with which he was first tied up broke with his weight, and he tumbled to the ground.

He was tied up a second time, and more effectually. From hence came, doubtless, the story of Kidd's having a charmed life, and that he had to be twice hanged.

Such is the main outline of Kidd's history, but it has given birth to an innumerable progeny of traditions.

The report of his having buried great treasures of gold and jewels before his arrest set the brains of all the good people along the coast in a ferment.

There were rumours of great sums of money found here and there, sometimes in one part of the country and sometimes in another ; of coins with Moorish inscriptions, doubtless the spoils of his eastern prizes, but which the common people looked upon with superstitious awe, regarding the Moorish letters as diabolical or magical characters.

Some reported the treasure to have been buried in solitary unsettled places about Plymouth and Cape Cod, but by degrees various other parts, not only on the eastern coast, but along the shores of the Sound, and even of Manhattan and Long Island were gilded by these rumours.

In fact, the vigorous measures of Lord Bellamont had spread a sudden consternation among the buccaneers in every part of the provinces.

They had secreted their money and jewels in lonely, out of the way places, about the wild shores of the rivers and the sea coast, and dispersed themseves over the face of the country. .

The hand of justice prevented many of them from ever returning to regain their buried treasure, which remained, and remains probably to this day, objects of enterprise to the money-digger.

This is the cause of those frequent reports of trees and rocks bearing mysterious marks, supposed to indicate the spot where the treasures lay hidden.

Many have been the ransackings after the pirates' booty.

In all the stories which once abounded of these enterprises the devil played a conspicuous part.

Either he was conciliated by ceremonies and invocations, or some solemn compact was made with him.

Still he was ever prone to play the money-digger some slippery trick.

Some would dig so far as to come to an iron chest, when some baffling circumstance was sure to take place.

Either the earth would fall in and fill up the pit, or some direful noise or apparition would frighten the party from the place, and sometimes the devil himself would appear and bear off the prize when within their very grasp, and if they revisited the place the next day, not a trace would be found of their labours of the preceding night.

All these rumours, however, were extremely vague and for a long time tantalised me, without gratifying my curiosity.

There's nothing in this world so hard to get at as truth, and there is nothing in this world but truth that I care for.

I sought among all my favourite sources of authentic information, the oldest inhabitants, and particularly the old Dutch wives of the province, yet for a long time my inquiries were unattended with any substantial result.

At length it happened that, one calm day in the latter part of the summer, I was relaxing myself from the toils of severe study by a day's amusement in fishing in those waters which had been my favourite resort.

I was in company with several burghers of the little city.

Our sport was indifferent.

The fish did not bite freely, and we frequently changed our fishing-ground without bettering our luck.

We were at length anchored close under a ledge of rocky coast, on the eastern side of the island of Manhatta.

It was a still, warm day.

The stream whirled and dimpled by us, without a wave or even a ripple ; and everything was so calm and quiet that it was almost startling when the kingfisher would pitch himself from the branch of some dry tree, and after suspending himself for a moment in the air to take his aim, would souse into the smooth water after his prey.

While we were lolling in our boat, half drowsy with the warm stillness of the day and the dullness of our sport, one of our party, a worthy alderman, was overtaken by slumber, and as he dozed suffered the sinker of his drop-line to lie at the bottom of the river.

On waking he found he had caught something of importance, from the weight.

On drawing it to the surface we were much surprised to find it a long pistol, of very curious and outlandish fashion, which, from its rusted condition, and its stock being worm-eaten and covered with barnacles, appeared to have laid a long time under water.

The unexpected appearance of this implement of warfare occasioned much speculation among my pacific companions.

One supposed it to have fallen there during the revolutionary war.

Another, from the peculiarity of its fashion, attributed it to the voyagers in the earliest days of the settlement; perchance to the renowned Adrian Black, who explored the Sound, and discovered Black Island, since so noted for its cheese.

But a third, after regarding it for some time, pronounced it to be of veritable Spanish workmanship.

"I'll warrant," said he, "if this pistol could talk, it would tell strange stories of hard fights among the Spanish dons. I've no doubt but it is a relic of the buccaneers of old times. Who knows but it belonged to Kidd himself?"

"Ah! that Kidd was a resolute fellow," cried an old, iron-faced Cape Cod whaler. "There's a fine old song about him, all to the tune of—

"My name is Captain Kidd,
As I sailed, as I sailed——

And then it tells all about how he gained the devil's good graces by burying the bible—

"I had the bible in my hand
As I sailed, as I sailed;
And I buried it in the sand
As I sailed——"

"Odsfish! if I thought this pistol had belonged to Kidd I should set great store by it. By the way, I recollect a story about a fellow who once dug up Kidd's buried treasure. As the fish don't bite just now I'll tell you the yarn."

But as the yarn is a long one, we must reserve it for a subsequent chapter.

CHAPTER CCXLIV.

THE BURIED TREASURE.

BLACK RALPH resumed his story, which was to the following purport :—

A few miles from Boston, in Massachusetts, there is a deep inlet, winding miles into the interior of the country from Charles Bay.

It terminates in a thickly-wooded swamp, or morass.

On one side of this inlet is a dark grove.

On the opposite side the land rises abruptly from the water's edge, into a high ridge, on which grew a few scattered oaks of great age and immense size.

Under one of these trees, according to old stories, there was a great amount of treasure buried by Kidd the pirate.

The inlet allowed a facility to bring the money in a boat, secretly, and at night, to the very foot of the hill.

The elevation of the place permitted a good look-out to be kept that no one was at hand.

The remarkable trees formed good land marks by which the place might easily be found again.

The old stories add, moreover, that the devil presided at the hiding of the money, and took it under his guardianship; but this is well-known he always does with buried treasure, particularly when it has been ill-gotten.

Be that as it may, Kidd never returned to recover his wealth, being, shortly after, seized at Boston, sent out to England, and then hanged as a pirate.

About the year 1727, just at the time that earthquakes were prevalent in New England, and shook many tall sinners down upon their knees, there lived near this place a meagre, miserly fellow of the name of Tom Walker.

He had a wife as miserly as himself.

They were so miserly that they even contrived to cheat each other.

Whatever the woman could lay hands on she hid away.

A hen could not cackle but she was on the alert to secure the new-laid egg.

Her husband was continually prying about to detect her secret hoards, and many and fierce were the conflicts that took place about what ought to have been common property.

They lived in a forlorn-looking house, that stood alone, and had an air of starvation.

A few straggling savin trees, emblems of sterility, grew near it.

No smoke ever curled from its chimney.

No traveller ever stopped at its door.

A miserable horse, whose ribs were as articulate as the bars of a gridiron, stalked about a field where a thin carpet of moss, scarcely covering the ragged beds of pudding stone tantalized and balked his hunger, and sometimes he would lean his head over the fence, and seemed to petition deliverance in this land of famine.

The house and its inmates had altogether a bad name.

Tom's wife was a tall termagant, fierce of temper, loud of tongue, and strong of arm.

Her voice was often heard in wordy warfare with her husband.

His face sometimes showed signs that their conflicts were not confined to words.

No one ventured to interfere between them.

The lonely wayfarer shrank within himself at the horrid clamour and clapper-clawing, eyed the den of discord askance, and hurried on his way rejoicing, if a bachelor, in his celibacy.

One day that Tom Walker had been to a distant part of the neighbourhood, he took a short cut homewards through the swamp.

Like most short cuts it was an ill-chosen route.

The swamp was thickly grown with great gloomy pines and hemlocks, some of them ninety feet high, which made it dark at noon day, and a retreat for all the owls of the neighbourhood.

It was full of pits and quagmires, partly covered with weeds and mosses, where the green surface often betrayed the traveller into a gulf of black, smothering mud. There were also dark and stagnant pools, the abodes of the tadpoles, the bull-frog and the water-snake; where the trunks of pines and hemlocks lay half-drowned, half-rotting, looking like alligators sleeping in the mire.

Tom had long been picking his way cautiously through the treacherous forest, stepping from tuft to tuft of rushes and roots which afforded precarious footholds among deep sloughs; or pacing carefully like a cat, along the prostrate trunks of trees; startled now and then by the sudden screaming of the bittern or the quacking of a wild duck, rising on the wing from some solitary pool.

At length he arrived at a piece of firm ground which ran out like a peninsular in the bosom of the swamp.

It had been one of the strongholds of the Indians during their wars with the first colonists.

Here they had thrown up a kind of fort which they had looked upon as almost impregnable, and had used as a place of refuge for their squaws and children.

Nothing remained of the old Indian fort but a few embankments gradually sinking to the level of the surrounding earth and already overgrown by oaks and other forest trees, the foliage of which formed a contrast to the dark pines and hemlocks of the swamp.

It was late in the dusk of evening when Tom Walker reached the old fort, and he paused, therefore, to rest himself.

Any one but he would have felt unwilling to linger in this lonely, melancholy place, for the common people had a bad opinion of it from the stories handed down from the time of the Indian wars, when it was asserted that the Indians held incantations here and made sacrifices to the evil spirit.

Tom Walker, however, was not a man to be troubled with any fears of the kind.

He reposed himself for some time on the trunk of a fallen hemlock, listening to the boding cry of the tree-toad, and delving with his walking-stick into a mound of black mould at his feet.

As he turned up the soil unconsciously, his staff struck against something hard.

Lo! a cloven skull, with an Indian tomahawk buried deep in it, lay before him.

The rust on the weapon showed the time that had elapsed since this death-blow had been given.

It was a dreary memento of the fierce struggle that had taken place in this last foothold of the Indian warriors.

"Humph!" said Tom Walker.

He gave the skull a kick to shake the dust from it.

"Let that skull alone!" said a gruff voice.

Tom lifted up his eyes, and beheld a great black man seated directly opposite him on the stump of a tree.

He was exceedingly surprised, having neither heard nor seen any one approach; and he was still more perplexed on observing, as well as the gathering gloom would permit, that the stranger was neither negro nor Indian.

It is true he was dressed in a rude, half-Indian garb, and had a red belt or sash swathed round his body.

His face was neither black nor copper-colour, but swarthy and dingy and begrimed with soot, as if he had been accustomed to toil among fires and forges.

He had a shock of coarse black hair that stood out from his head in all directions, and bore an axe on his shoulder.

He scowled for a moment at Tom with a pair of glaring eyes.

"What are you doing on my grounds?" said the black man, with a hoarse, growling voice.

"Your grounds?" said Tom, with a sneer. "No more your grounds than mine; they belong to Deacon Peabody."

"Deacon Peabody be hanged! Let him look more to his own sins, and less to those of his neighbours. Look yonder, and see how Deacon Peabody is faring."

Tom looked in the direction that the stranger pointed.

He beheld one of the great trees, fair and flourishing without, but rotten at the core, and saw that it had been nearly hewn through, so that the first high wind was likely to blow it down.

On the bark of the tree was scored the name of Deacon Peabody, an eminent man who had waxed wealthy by driving shrewd bargains with the Indians.

The one on which he had been seated, and which had evidently just been hewn down, bore the name of Crowninshield, and he recollected a mighty rich man of that name, who made a vulgar display of wealth, which it was whispered he had acquired by buccaneering.

"He's just ready for burning," said the black man, with a growl of triumph. "You see I am likely to have a good stock of firewood for winter."

"But what right have you," said Tom, "to cut down Deacon Peabody's timber?"

"The right of a prior claim," said the other. "This woodland belonged to me before one of your white-faced race put foot upon the soil."

"And, pray, who are you, if I may be so bold?" said Tom.

"Oh, I go by various names. I am the wild huntsman in some countries, the black miner in others. In this neighbourhood I am known by the name of the black woodman. I am he to whom the red men consecrated this spot, and in honour of whom they now and then roasted a white man by way of sacrifice. Since the red men have been exterminated by your white savages, I amuse myself by presiding at the persecutions of Quakers and Anabaptists. I am the great patron and prompter of slave-dealers, and the grand master of the Salem witches."

"The upshot of all which is, that, if I mistake not," said Tom, sturdily, "you are he, commonly called Old Scratch."

"The same, at your service!" replied the black man, with a half-civil nod.

Such was the opening of this interview according to the old story, though it has almost too familiar an air to be credited. One would think that to meet with such a singular personage, in that wild, lonely place, would have shaken any man's nerves; but Tom was a hard-minded fellow, not easy daunted, and he had lived so long with a termagant wife that he did not even fear the devil.

It is said that after this commencement they had a long and earnest conversation together as Tom returned homewards.

The black man told him of great sums of money which had been buried by Kidd the pirate, under the oak-trees on the high ridge not far from the morass.

All these were under his command and protected by his power, so that none could find them but such as propitiated his favour.

These he offered to place within Tom Walker's reach, having conceived an especial kindness for him; but they were to be had only on certain conditions.

What these conditons were may easily be surmised, though Tom never disclosed them publicly.

They must have been very hard, for he required time to think of them.

When they had reached the end of the swamp, the stranger paused.

"What proof have I that all you have been telling me is true?"

"There is my signature," said the black man.

He pressed his finger on Tom's forehead.

So saying, he turned off among the thickets of the swamp.

He seemed, as Tom said, to go down, down, down into the earth, until nothing but his head and shoulders could be seen, and so on until he totally disappeared.

When Tom reached home he found the black print of a finger, burnt, as it were, upon his forehead, which nothing could obliterate.

The first news his wife had to tell him, was the

death of Absolom Crowninshield, the rich buccaneer.

It was announced in the papers with the usual flourish,

"A great man has fallen in Israel."

Tom recollected the tree which his black friend had just hewn down, and was ready for burning.

"Let the freebooter roast!" said Tom. "Who cares?"

He now felt convinced that what he had seen was no illusion.

He was not prone to let his wife into his confidence, but as this was an uneasy secret, he willingly shared it with her.

All her avarice was awakened at the mention of the hidden gold.

She urged her husband to comply with the black man's terms, and secure what would make them wealthy for life.

However Tom might have felt disposed to sell himself to the devil, he was determined not to do so to please his wife.

He flatly refused, out of the mere spirit of contradiction.

Many and bitter were the quarrels they had upon this subject, but the more she talked, the more resolute Tom was not to be eternally ruined for her.

At length she determined to drive the bargain on her own account, and, if she succeeded, to keep all the gain to herself.

Being of the same fearless temper as her husband, she set off for the old Indian fort towards the close of a summer's day.

She was many hours absent.

When she came back she was reserved and sullen in her replies.

She spoke something of a black man whom she had met in the twilight, hewing at the root of a tall tree.

He was sulky, however, and would not come to terms.

She was to go again with a propitiatory, but what it was she forbore to say.

The next evening she set off again for the swamp, with her apron heavily laden.

Tom waited and waited for her, but in vain.

Midnight came.

She did not make her appearance.

Morning—noon—night returned.

Tom now grew uneasy for her safety.

Especially so as she had carried off in her apron the silver tea-pot and spoons, and every portable article of value.

Another night elapsed.

Another morning came, but no wife.

In a word, she was never heard of more.

What was her real fate nobody knows, in consequence of so many pretending to know.

It is one of those facts which have become confounded by a variety of historians.

Some asserted that she lost her way among the tangled mazes of the swamp, and sank into some pit or slough.

Others, more uncharitable, hinted that she had eloped with the household booty, and made off to some other province.

While others assert that the tempter had decoyed her into a dismal quagmire, on top of which her hat was found lying.

In confirmation of this, it was said a great black man, with an axe on his shoulder, was seen late that very evening coming out of the swamp, carrying a bundle tied in a check apron, with a surly air of triumph.

The most current and probable story, however, observes that Tom Walker grew so anxious about the fate of his wife and his property, that he set out at length to seek them both at the Indian fort.

During a long summer afternoon he searched about the gloomy place, but no wife was to be seen.

He called her name repeatedly.

She was nowhere to be heard.

The bittern alone responded to his voice as he flew screaming by.

The bull-frog croaked dismally from the neighbouring pool.

At length, it is said, just in the brown hour of twilight, when the owls began to hoot, and the bats to flit about, his attention was attracted by the clamour of the carrion crows.

He looked up.

He beheld a bundle tied in a check apron, and hanging to the branches of a tree, with a great vulture perched hard by, as if keeping watch by it.

He leaped with joy.

He recognised his wife's apron, and supposed it to contain the household valuables.

"Let us get hold of the property," said he, "and we will endeavour to do without the woman."

As he scrambled up the tree the vulture spread its wide wings and sailed off into the deep shadows of the forest.

Tom seized the check apron.

Woful sight!

He found nothing but a heart and liver tied up in it.

Such, according to the most authentic old story, was all that was to be found of Tom's wife.

She had probably attempted to deal with the black man as she had been accustomed to deal with her husband.

But though a female scold is generally considered to be a match for the devil, yet, in this instance, she appears to have got the worst of it.

She must have died game, however.

It is said Tom noticed many prints of cloven feet deeply stamped about the tree and found handfulls of hair that looked as if they had been plucked from the coarse black shock of the woodman.

Tom knew his wife's prowess by experience.

He shrugged his shoulders as he looked at the signs of a fierce clapper-clawing.

"Egad!" said he to himself, "Old Scratch must have had a tough time of it."

Tom consoled himself for the loss of his property by the loss of his wife.

He even felt something like gratitude towards the black woodman, who, he considered, had done him a kindness.

He sought, therefore, to cultivate a further acquaintance with him, but for some time without success.

The old black-legs played shy.

Whatever people may think he is not always to be had for the calling for; he knows how to play his cards when pretty sure of his game.

At length, it is said, delay had whetted Tom's eagerness to the quick and prepared him to agree to anything rather than not gain the promised treasure.

He met the black man one evening in his usual woodman's dress.

He carried his axe on his shoulder, was sauntering along the edge of the swamp and humming a tune.

He affected to receive Tom's advances with great indifference, made brief replies and went on humming his tune.

By degrees, however, Tom brought him to business.

They began to haggle about the terms on which the former was to have the pirate's treasure.

There was one condition which need not be mentioned, being generally understood in all cases where the devil grants favours.

But there were others about which, though of less importance, he was inflexible, obstinate.

He insisted that the money found through his means should be employed in his service.

He proposed, therefore, that Tom should employ it in the black traffic—that is to say that he should fit out a slave ship.

This, however, Tom absolutely refused.

He was bad enough, in all conscience, but the devil himself could not tempt him to turn slave-dealer.

Finding Tom so squeamish on this point, he did not insist upon it, but proposed instead that he should turn usurer, the devil being extremely anxious for the increase of usurers, looking upon them as his peculiar people.

To this no objections were made.

It was just to Tom's taste.

"You shall open a broker's shop in Boston next month," said the black man.

"I'll do it to-morrow, if you wish," said Tom Walker.

"You shall lend me money at two per cent. a month."

"Egad, I'll charge four!" replied Tom Walker.

"You shall extort bonds, foreclose mortgages, drive the merchant to bankruptcy——"

"I'll drive him to the devil!" cried Tom Walker, eagerly.

"You are the usurer for my money!" said the black-legs, with delight. "When will you want the rhino?"

"This very night."

"Done!" said the devil.

"Done!" said Tom Walker.

So they shook hands and struck a bargain.

A few days' time saw Tom Walker seated behind his desk in a counting-house in Boston.

His reputation for a ready-moneyed man who would lend money for a good consideration soon spread abroad.

Everybody remembers the time of Governor Belcher when money was particularly scarce.

It was a time of paper credit.

The country had been deluged by government bills.

The famous Land Bank had been established.

There had been a rage for speculating.

The people had run mad with schemes for new settlements—for building cities in the wilderness.

Land-jobbers went about with maps of grants and townships and El Dorados, lying nobody knew where, but which everybody was ready to purchase.

In a word, the great speculating fever which breaks out every now and then in the country, had raged to an alarming degree, and everybody was dreaming of making sudden fortunes for nothing.

As usual, the fever had subsided.

The dream had gone off, and the imaginary fortunes with it.

The patients were left in doleful plight, and the whole country responded with the consequent cry of "hard times."

At this propitious time of public distress did Tom Walker set up as usurer at Boston.

His door was soon thronged by customers.

The needy, the adventurous, the gambling speculator, the dreaming land-jobber, the thriftless tradesman, the merchant with cracked credit—in short, every one driven to raise money by desperate means and desperate sacrifices turned to Tom Walker.

Thus Tom was the universal friend of the needy, and he acted like a "friend in need."

That is to say, he always exacted good pay and good security.

In proportion to the distress of the applicants was the hardness of his terms.

He accumulated bonds and mortgages, gradually squeezed his customers closer and closer, and sent them home as dry as a sponge from his door.

In this way he made money hand over hand.

He became a rich and mighty man, and exalted his cocked hat on 'Change.

He built himself, as usual, a vast house out of ostentation, but left the greater part of it unfinished and unfurnished out of parsimony.

He even set up a carriage in the fullness of his vain-glory, though he nearly starved the horses which drew it, and as the ungreased wheels groaned and screeched on their axletrees, you would have thought that you heard the howls of the poor debtors he was squeezing.

As Tom waxed old, however, he grew thoughtful.

Having secured the good things of this world, he began to feel anxious about those of the next.

He thought with regret on the bargain he had made with his black friend, and set his wits to work to cheat him out of the conditions.

He became, therefore, all of a sudden a violent church-goer.

Tom was as rigid in religious as in money matters.

He was a stern supervisor and censorer of his neighbours.

He seemed to think that every sin entered up to their account became a credit on his side of the page.

He even talked of the expediency of reviving the persecution of Quakers and Anabaptists.

Still, in spite of all this strenuous attention to forms, Tom had a lurking dread that the devil, after all, would have his dues.

That he might not be taken unawares, he carried a prayer-book in his pocket.

He had also a great folio prayer-book on his counting-house desk, and would frequently be found reading it when people came on business.

On such occasions he would lay his green spectacles in the book to mark the place while he turned round to drive some usurious bargain.

Some say that Tom grew a little crack-brained in his old days, and that, fancying his end approaching, he had his horse new shod, saddled and bridled, because he supposed that at the last the world would be turned up-side down, and he was determined at the worst to give his old friend a run for it.

This, however, is probably a mere wives' fable.

If he really did take such a measure, it was totally superfluous; at least, so says the authentic old legend, which closes the story in the following manner:—

On one hot afternoon in the dog-days, just as a terrible black thunder-gust was coming up, Tom sat in his counting-house in his white linen cap and Indian silk gown.

He was on the point of fore-closing a mortgage by which he would complete the ruin of an unlucky land-speculator, for whom he had professed the greatest friendship.

The poor land-jobber begged him to grant a few months' indulgence.

Tom had grown testy and irritated, and refused another day.

"My family will be ruined and brought upon the parish," said the land-jobber.

"Charity begins at home," replied Tom. "I must take care of myself in these hard times."

"You have made so much money out of me," said the speculator.

Tom lost his patience and his piety.

"The devil take me!" he said, "if I have made a farthing."

Just then there were three loud knocks at the street door.

He stepped out to see who was there.

A black man was holding a black horse, which neighed and stamped with impatience.

"Tom, you are come for," said the black fellow, gruffly.

Tom shrunk back, but too late.

He left his little prayer-book on the desk, buried in the mortgage he was about to fore-close.

Never was sinner taken more unawares.

The black man whisked him like a child into the saddle.

He gave the horse a lash, and away he galloped with Tom on his back in the midst of the thunder-storm.

When the clerks, who had rushed out, turned to look for the black man, he had disappeared.

Such was the end of Tom Walker and his ill-gotten wealth.

Let all grasping money-lenders lay it to heart.

CHAPTER CCXLV.

ANOTHER YARN.

"WELL," said an old salt, who had been listening in silence to the yarns just related, "I have heard some strange stories in my time, most of 'em too tough to be swallowed whole, but none of 'em comes up to what I seed when I was a younker."

"What was that, Stephens?" asked Black Ralph.

"Why, it was the adventure of my first voyage," returned the seaman.

"Well, out with it then," said Garrod; "you may as well take your turn as any other, so take a pull at the can, and make sail."

"Aye, aye; order for Bill Stephens's yarn!" cried several voices.

The old sailor renewed his quid, and after a hearty drink of grog, commenced his story of the—

FEMALE PRIVATEER.

"In the year —— But I forget what year it was, so never mind the date; I was a boy then, and, like a good many others, had a strong desire to go to sea.

"As my parents were very poor, and glad to get me off their hands, they made no opposition to my wishes, and I soon got a berth as cabin-boy, on board a ship, called the 'Wehrwolf,' then lying in Bristol harbour.

"She was fitted out as a privateer, and mounted ten guns, and was to carry a complement of seventy men.

"At the time I joined her she was undergoing a thorough overhaul.

"Ship carpenters, caulkers and riggers were busy about her; a part only of her guns had been shipped and but very few of her crew were on board.

"What her destination was, was unknown. Nobody knew even who was to command her.

"A large firm had the job of preparing her for sea, and of providing everything necessary for the voyage, but they denied all property in her, or a knowledge even of her owners.

"At last she was reported ready for sea, and all hands were ordered to be on board of her by a certain day.

"Accordingly, on the evening of that day, the crew, who had nearly all joined, were mustered on the quarter deck to be drilled into something like order before being presented to the captain, who, we afterwards found, had come on board privately during the previous night.

"The first lieutenant, who inspected us and told us off for the various watches, was evidently an old seaman who had seen some service.

"He was a tall, stout man, with limbs like an elephant; but he had a good-humoured look with him that seemed to take with the crew.

"You know, messmates, what brutes some privateer officers are—and so are some crews, too, for the matter of that. But still, at the commencement of a voyage, a sailor likes to see something like good-temper in the officers under whom he is to serve for perhaps a year or two.

"At last the lieutenant goes below, and presently returns and calls us to the salute for the reception of the captain, and at the same moment the skipper came on deck.

"I shall never forget how we all stared at him.

"He looked a mere boy.

"But he was one of those boys that are men ere some other men have got over the habits of their boyhood.

"He was slightly built, and of about the middle height.

"His dress, which was of the richest description, fitted him closely, and showed off a form that a woman might have envied.

"His face was as handsome a one as I ever looked on; the complexion, though very white, was as clear as a woman's, the mouth small and the chin without a particle of down upon it; a thin, golden moustache covered the upper lip, his eyes were a light blue, and his hair, like his moustache, of a golden colour, hung down his back in ringlets.

"After gazing at us for a few moments he spoke, and his voice, clear and musical, had a tone of sadness in it.

"'My lads,' said he, 'I like your appearance much, and I do not doubt we shall get on well together. We are going on a voyage the duration of which I cannot tell; I have an object to accomplish, a mission to fulfil, and, until that is done, I shall not leave the vessel. We have dangers to go through, privations, perhaps, to suffer, and while I shall not shun the first, I will endeavour to soften the rigours of the other. All I ask of you is cheerful obedience, and in return, besides my care to render you happy and contented, I will divide among you my own share of all prizes we may take.'

"And then turning to the lieutenant, he said,

"'Mr. Belling, you can splice the main brace, and then pipe down.'

"Well, next day we set sail, and once out at sea, began to look out for prizes.

"The first we took was laden with wine, silk goods, and other articles, and was very valuable.

"We came upon her during a fog, and captured her before she had the slightest idea of our vicinity.

"The next day we sighted another vessel, who gave us a long chase, and attempted to keep us off by a couple of light guns.

"But one broadside was sufficient for her, and she was soon taken possession of.

"Of course, being a boy, and as it were in a strange world, I was all eyes, and if the opportunity had been given me would have been all ears also; but although I could make use of my sight, I gained no wisdom through my hearing that could satisfy the curiosity felt by the whole crew as to what the object was upon which our captain was bent on accomplishing.

"I saw that as often as a prize was taken every newspaper that could be found on board was taken into the cabin, and eagerly scanned by the captain, and after a short time thrown aside with an exclamation of disappointment.

"Then the master of the captured ship was taken into the cabin, and an interview, sometimes short, sometimes longer, took place between him and our skipper; but the nature of it did not transpire.

"Regularly every day the crew were turned up to drill; exercise at the long guns, with the boarding pike and sword, was persevered in constantly, and often just before the watch was turning in of a night the sound of the drum would summons all hands to quarters. Orders would be given to clear the decks for action, bulkheads would be knocked down, the guns run out, cartridges served, the very lanterns lighted, and then the retreat sounded.

THE PRINCESS ARONZOW.

"All this rather worried the crew, but as the captain invariably took his share in the bustle, and as they knew that in the event of our going into action this drill would not be lost upon them, they refrained from murmuring or showing any sign of discontent.

"We cruised about for some weeks, and at last entered the Mediterranean.

"We had been very fortunate with prizes, and the ship's company were well satisfied, both with themselves and their captain.

"My duties were principally confined to the cabin, though when there was a chase, or a bit of a brush expected, I always took my place on deck.

"One beautiful, calm night, not feeling disposed for sleep, I went on deck and joined the middle watch.

No. 72.

"I fancied—for it must have been fancy—that I heard my name called by the captain.

"He had always been very kind to me, and I would have flown anywhere to oblige him.

"I darted down the hatchway, and knocked softly at the door.

"There was no response, but there was the sound of deep hysterical sobs within.

"Alarmed, and fearing some mishap, I pushed open the door, and entered the cabin.

"I started back with astonishment!

"The captain was not there.

"But seated on a settee beside the table, with her back towards me, crying and sobbing as though her heart would break, was a lady.

"She was dressed in pure white, as though for a bridal.

"A long veil of a light tissue was fastened to the back of her head, and falling in folds down her back, trailed on the carpetted floor.

"Just facing her was a large mirror.

"By its reflection I saw that she held in one hand a miniature, and in the other a letter, and in the intervals of her paroxysms she kissed them alternately with great fervour.

"I felt bewildered.

"I had been daily, nay, hourly in the cabin, I had explored every part of the ship, but until this moment not a female form had met my eye.

"My glance at last fell on the table.

"There lay the silken moustache of gold that had adorned the upper lip of Captain Evans.

"On the head of the lady was the same sunny curls.

"I had penetrated a secret.

"The commander of the 'Wehr Wolf' was a woman.

"I don't know whether, in my surprise, I uttered any sound; but the lady started up, and suddenly flew towards me, and dragged me with some violence into the cabin.

"Her eyes flashed with the fire of passion.

"'Boy,' exclaimed she, in tones that I instantly recognised as those belonging to Captain Evans, 'what idle curiosity has brought you here? Speak, quickly!'

"'I thought I heard you call me, madam—sir, I mean,' answered I, in a trembling voice.

"For I was afraid that the possession of the secret might cost me dear.

"'Is it not your watch below?'

"'Yes,' I answered; 'but not feeling inclined for slep, I returned on deck.'

"'Did you not tap at the door as usual?' asked she.

"'I did,' I answered, 'and hearing you cry so bitterly made me imagine that there was something wrong, and so I opened the door to see what was the matter.'

"The lady captain eyed me searchingly for a few minutes, and then said,

"'I believe you; but listen. I am a woman, but for reasons that I will not now tell you, I have assumed the attire of a man. You alone in this ship know the secret. Can you keep it? I would not have the crew know my sex for a world's ransom. Answer me!'

"'I can,' I replied. 'I will try even to forget what I have seen.'

"'Enough,' said she; 'I will trust you. You may now go.'

"From this time, until the event to which I shall presently come, took place, no farther allusion was made to the subject, either by the captain or myself.

"On deck, in the presence of the men, if it was necessary to give me any order, it was given, perhaps, in a sterner or more decided tone than before; but when in the cabin attending to my usual duties, the tones were softened to those of her sex in kindness; and, boy as I was, I could have worshipped the beautiful and daring being whom I served as a humble cabin-boy.

"She often conversed with me freely; made inquiries as to my parents, and as to whether I intended to adopt the sea as a profession.

"But she never in any way alluded to the subject of her disguise.

"Storms, as you know, messmates, are of rare occurrence in the Mediterranean; but when it does blow, it is time for skilful mariners to look out lest they find themselves wrecked on an iron-bound shore.

"The sun, one morning, rose red and threatening, clouds of a deep purple spread out like feathers, floated in various directions rapidly across the sky.

"The air was murky and oppressive, and it was rather difficult to breathe.

"The sea birds flew towards the land with loud discordant cries.

"The sea seemed to moan like a man in pain, and the ship, riding on the short and chopping waves, creaked as though her timbers were starting.

"Lieutenant Belling looked grave, and frequently consulted the barometer.

"The older seamen cast their looks to windward, and strove to read in the disturbed elements the direction of the coming storm.

"Captain Evans alone looked around with a calm and confident look.

"'Mr. Belling,' he said, in a quiet manner, 'you had better shorten sail, and make all snug, we shall shortly have a hurricane.'

"And at last it burst.

"I have been in many storms during my life at sea, but never have I seen one equal to that in the Mediterranean.

"Darkness, as though the sun had departed from us, as though an enormous pall had been thrown over the ship, fell upon us, we could feel but not see each other.

The sea rose, wave upon wave, higher and higher, till, as we descended the side of one we seemed surrounded by walls of water.

"The wind came not in fitful gusts, but in one steady, awful roar.

"It cut off the summits of the sea, as with a knife, and heaped the water on our decks by tons.

"The ship shivered with the violence of the repeated shocks, and I thought each wave, as it fell upon us, would bear us to the bottom.

"The men were scared.

"Obedient to orders, they yet moved as though they thought each movement was but a step nearer death.

"Then came the lightning, flashing almost constantly—the thunder that deadened every other sound.

"With one sail only to steady the ship, we flew along.

"We knew that we were well off the land, but at the rate we were now going, there was no telling how soon a crash might warn us that all hope was gone.

"Moreover, we believed we were in the vicinity of a cluster of small rocky islands, upon which we might be cast.

"It was immediately after one of those vivid sheets of lightning that the whole crew were roused by the sudden voice of the captain.

"'Hard a starboard—hard; larboard watch, stand by with grapnells!'

"Another flash showed us, a few yards ahead, a vessel dismasted and apparently unmanageable, into whose stern we were driving.

"A few figures were to be seen on her decks, who, by their gestures, seemed to be asking for assistance.

"In the heavy sea no boat could have lived for a minute.

"It was doubtful if we could avoid running her down, but by great exertions on the part of the helmsmen, we avoided the shock.

"As it was, we ran alongside so closely that the two ships grated their sides together; the grapnells were thrown, and in a few seconds the stranger was made fast.

"She turned out, however, to be a complete wreck, and was rapidly sinking.

"Her crew were therefore taken from her, and she was cast loose.

"The storm soon passed away, doing us but little damage.

"As soon as we were once more in trim, Captain Evans turned his attention to those we had rescued from the wreck.
f

"Contrary to his usual custom, the captain questioned these persons on deck.

"We found that she was an English ship, from Constantinople to London, very heavily laden, and had been captured three days previously by a French privateer.

"The master and most of the crew had been transferred to the French ship, and a prize crew having been put on board with two or three of the English prisoners to assist them, she was on her way to Toulon.

"She had been struck by the lightning, which, having shivered the mainmast, passed through the bottom of the vessel.

"The wind and heavy seas had completely dismasted her.

"'What is the name of your ship?' inquired Captain Evans of the officer in charge.

"'Le Triomphe,' was the answer.

"A flush of deep red suffused the face of our lady captain for a few seconds, and then dying away, left her pale as a marble statue.

"Her features wore an expression of fierceness that was terrible to look upon, and a glare of passionate fire streamed from her eyes.

"'And your captain's name?' demanded she.

"'Paul le Grand.'

"'Where is his cruising ground?'

"'A few leagues from the mouth of the Bosphorus.'

"Captain Evans stood for a time like one entranced, her features worked convulsively, her lips slightly apart showed the teeth tightly set, and her small white hand clenched the sword she held with a tenacity that showed a deep resolve.

"'At last—at last!' exclaimed she, turning from the Frenchman, and then addressing the Lieutenant, said,

"'Mr. Belling, you will make all sail at once and search out this French ship. See everything prepared for action, and as soon as you make her out, let me know.'

"Captain Evans then went below, and did not appear again on deck during the day.

"We were now all bustle on board.

"There was tough work before us.

"From the men we had recaptured we learnt that the Frenchman carried sixteen guns, and was manned by a crew of upwards of a hundred.

"She was a very swift sailer, and had been extremely fortunate as a privateer, having done a great deal of damage to our commerce.

"The captain was a man of undoubted courage, but he cared but little for fighting, unless there was either a profit to be made of it, or he considered that the advantages were so greatly in his favor as to ensure him the victory.

"There were many stories circulated as to his cruel treatment of the prisoners captured by him, who it was stated he treated according to the trouble and expense their capture had caused him.

"Thus those who surrendered at his first summons, had little beyond the loss of their property and liberty to complain of.

"Those who sought to evade him by flight, were sometimes punished by blows, but invariably put upon the smallest possible amount that could keep life in the body.

"If resistance was offered, where the chances were against its being successful, and it resulted in loss of life to his own crew, he would allow no quarter to be shown to the prisoners captured.

"So that the name of Paul Le Grand was dreaded by all seamen whose duties were carried on in trading vessels.

"The next day we arrived at the Frenchman's cruising ground, and a good look out was kept to sight him.

"Captain Evan promised a handsome reward to whoever should give the first notice as to his whereabouts.

"That evening I was summoned by the captain to her cabin.

"I was desired to close the door.

"She was still in the attire of a naval officer, but the hat being thrown on one side, the long golden curls had floated round her face, giving her more the appearance of her proper sex.

"On the table beside her lay the miniature of a handsome man dressed in the uniform of a mate in the East India Company's service.

"A small packet of letters also lay on the table.

"She motioned me to take a seat opposite to her, and after a few minutes' pause, as though in thought, said,

"'My lad, I have sent for you to do me a service. Ere this time to-morrow I shall have bade farewell to the scenes of this world, and you must promise me that you attend to this my last request. It is a simple one. In a few days you will be on your return to England, you will then proceed to London, and deliver this packet into the hands of the person to whom it is addressed. This purse will pay your expenses, and leave you something to reward your trouble. Do you promise?'

"I answered that, if I was spared in the coming battle, I would fulfil her wishes."

"'Enough,' replied she, 'and now that you know what I am, you shall hear the reason why I, a woman, have thrown aside the safer duties of my sex to mingle in scenes of war and blood.'

"She was, she told me, the daughter of an officer of rank in the British army, who had held for many years a high and lucrative position in the Government of India.

"The unexpected death of a relative to whose estates he succeeded, induced her father to resign his appointment, and return to India, bringing with him his daughter, Miranda, then about nineteen years of age.

"The ship in which they took their passage was attacked during a calm by the Malay pirates, in the Straits of Madagascar, who, after a severe conflict, forced themselves on board, and penetrated to the cabin in which she had sought shelter.

"She was in great danger, and gave herself up for lost.

"A huge Malay chief had seized her in his arms, and was bearing her towards a large proa that lay alongside.

"It was not difficult to guess the fate in store for her.

"The passionate fire that flowed from the eyes of the savage, told of his purpose.

"Her knowledge of their cruel and remorseless nature was sufficient to assure her that dishonour would be followed by a cruel death.

"But help was at hand.

"The mate of the ship, a gallant young man, had succeeded in rallying a few of the crew, and animating them by his example, made a fierce attack on the savages.

"Believing their victory gained, most of them had dispersed about the ship in search for plunder.

"Those on deck were speedily dispatched.

"The savage who was fleeing with Miranda was intercepted and cut down, and the rescued lady placed in safety.

"The others, dismayed by the fresh attack, were driven to their proas, and pulled off to reorganise a fresh attack.

"A breeze springing up at the same time, they were ultimately enabled to escape from their enemies.

"From this an attachment, that grew warmer every day, sprang up between them, and soon after their arrival in England, listening only to their love, they were privately married.

This marriage was to be kept secret, until after Henry Masterman, that was the mate's name, returned from another voyage to India, where he was this time going as captain.

"His ship was well advanced on her journey when one morning it was discovered that they were pursued by a strange sail, which was afterwards made out to be the French privateer, "Le Triomphe.'

"Captain Masterman, like a true British tar, determined to escape if possible, and having a long eighteen on board, he thought he should be able to keep the enemy off till some lucky accident should fiee him from her altogether.

"He therefore disregarded the signals made him to surrender, and as soon as the Frenchman came within range he opened on him with such effect that he was soon glad to shorten sail and fall behind.

"But Captain Le Grand was not a man to be easily balked.

"He knew that merchant ships did not carry any great quantity of ammunition, and that if he could compel them to keep up their fire it must soon be exhausted.

"He, therefore, by his superior sailing managed so as to be ever near them, taking care to expose his men and spars as little as possible.

"Hour by hour he would creep up to them near enough to give them a broadside, less with the belief that it would prove effective than with the hope that a lucky ball might damage the powerful piece opposed to him.

"He had thought to weary out his opponents.

"His numerous crew enabled him to take every advantage of the change of the wind without distressing his men, and he knew that all on board the Indiaman were compelled to be constantly on the alert.

"Day after day the privateer pursued.

"Captain Masterman still endeavoured to evade him.

"He changed his course often, in the hopes of falling in with an English ship of war.

"In the darkness of the night he would run back for many leagues, but the morning's light found the privateer still on the track.

"The chase lasted for five days.

"At that time the result happened that he had calculated upon.

"The ammunition of the Indiaman was gone.

"But its expenditure had entailed the loss of many of Le Grand's men, and Le Grand was furious about it.

"On the evening of the fifth day he took possession of the prize, and then after foully abusing Masterman for his resistance, had him *cruelly flogged to death!*

"But one person escaped out of the entire crew—a poor cabin-boy, who, frightened at the butchery he saw going on, jumped into a boat that lay alongside, and got away unnoticed.

"He was picked up some days afterwards, and brought to England, where he soon made the story known.

"Mrs. Masterman felt the blow as few women do, she shed no tears at the tidings, but determined on revenge.

"Having an ample fortune of her own, she was not long in devising a scheme to achieve her object.

"By means of the Bristol firm, and under the name of Captain Evans, she purchased the 'Wehr Wolf,' and confining the secret of her sex to her own bosom, she, as I have told you, went forth to hunt out the murderer of her husband.

"Well, mates, I am drawing my yarn to a close.

"The next morning saw us within a mile of the Frenchman, who, thinking us a easy prey, did not decline our challenge for the battle, and we were soon busy exchanging broadsides.

"The enemy was heavier in metal than ourselves, and his shot came crashing through our bulwarks, knocking down some men and sending splinters in all directions.

"But our drilling had not been thrown away upon us.

"His decks were crowded with men, and our guns, rapidly and well served, caused great havoc among them.

"Mrs. Masterman was everywhere among us, her cheering cries were heard above the din of the guns, and she gave the orders as coolly as though in her own drawing-room.

"Lieutenant Belling, too, played his part well.

"He was no skulker.

"The men, too, had the old bull-dog spirit in them, and fought with the determination of victory.

"We were now drawing closer together, and the Frenchman, finding our fire so hot, sent some of his jollies into the tops, that they might pick off the men at the guns.

"And soon our chaps began to fall about the deck.

"Aim at the foremast!" sang out Belling. 'Knock it over, and the battle's our own!'

"Obedient to the word, one of the guns was directed against it.

"A loud huzza rose from us.

"The mast, struck full in the centre, toppled over, and fell, with the men on it, into the sea.

"We poured our broadsides into her, and soon all was confusion on board the Frenchman.

"Captain Le Grand, however, was not to be so easily beaten.

"The wreck of the mast was soon cut away, and, with its still living freight, drifted off.

"Both sides were too busy just now to send boats to their rescue.

"We desired to complete our victory.

"The Frenchman hoped to retrieve his fortune.

"His exertions soon restored order among his crew.

"His men returned to their guns, and again their shots came ploughing up our decks.

"But his intention now was evidently to close with us, and, relying on his more numerous crew, to carry us by boarding.

"This was in accordance with the wish of the Female Privateer, and, while the din of the guns still continued, the two vessels drew towards each other.

"Crash the two vessels came together, and to the cry of 'Boarders, away!' we left our guns, and flew to the quarter.

"But the Frenchman was before us.

"Hardly had the vessels touched than, at the head of a strong party of his crew, he threw himself on board of us, and then steel and pistols came into play.

"Mrs. Masterman uttered a cry of pleasure, and, with the glare of the tigress in her eyes, rushed into the midst of the fray.

"I was close behind her.

"Her light sword flashed in the beams of the sun, and passed through the bodies of two or three of those who intervened between her and the French captain.

"'Down, Wolves!' shouted Bellamy.

"And as we flocked to each side of the vessel, or threw ourselves on our faces on the deck, a stream of fire, from a gun he had turned, went right into the thick of the French boarders, and, before they could recover from their confusion, we again fiercely charged them.

"And now we could see that the victory was ours.

"The Frenchmen sought to regain their own

vessel, but the fastenings not having been properly secured, she had broken loose, and had drifted some distance from us, and their retreat being thus cut off, they again advanced to the attack.

"But now came the time to which the Female Privateer had so long looked forward.

"She was face to face with the murderer of her husband.

"'Ah, Monsieur le Anglais capitaine!' shouted the Frenchman, as he saw the slight form opposed to him. 'Bien, you sall die.'

"But the excitement that had given Mrs. Masterman courage had also given her strength.

"The furious blow aimed at her was parried with a firmness that caused the sword of the Frenchman to start from his grasp, and as he fell back to recover himself she followed to sate her vengeance in his blood.

"What followed passed in a second of time.

"Le Grand raised a pistol that was in his left hand and fired.

"The ball had hardly sped on its mission ere I had buried my dirk in his body.

"There was a cry from our crew.

"I turned, and saw Mrs. Masterman lying on the deck.

"The bullet had done its work.

"With the fall of the French captain the fighting ceased.

"We had gained the victory, but had paid dearly for it.

"More than half of our crew were badly wounded.

"Many had been killed outright, and but very few on board could boast that they had gone through the engagement without a scratch.

"I have seen a few decks after a battle since then, but I never saw such a shambles as those on board the French sloop.

"The dead and the dying were lying in every direction, and the deck was running with blood.

"Mrs. Masterman lived about two hours after the battle.

"She had the satisfaction of knowing that her husband had been avenged, and with a sweet smile on her features, and saying, gently, 'Dear Harry, I come,' she died."

CHAPTER CCXLVI.

MOTHER AND SON—THE DEATH OF LADY EDGEFORTH.

LORD HAWKSBURY walked the deck of the yacht in deep thought.

He felt much perplexed as to the coming meeting between Lady Edgeforth and her son.

Could he inform her that the son she had so long yearned after, that she had mourned as dead, was one whose name had been rendered infamous to all who were lovers of law and order?

It was true that the lapse of time had somewhat deprived most of his crimes of their sharp sting.

And that he had performed so many generous actions as might fairly entitle him to the clemency of justice.

But crime has no justification.

"Once a thief, always a thief," is a maxim of the law, though a knowledge of our own weakness, and of the influence of sudden temptation, should teach us to deny its truth.

Many a crime concealed for years has met with its just punishment at last; and many a criminal lulled into a fancied security by long absence from the scene of his crime, has returned to find, too late, that the arms of the law were still extended to receive him.

Our criminal records are full of such instances.

Lord Hawksbury, therefore, did not expect that justice would look with leniency on the misdemeanours of the Boy Pirate.

No; in the meeting he hoped was about to take place, Lady Edgeforth must know nothing of his past career, she must know him as her son only; and when the event that was now so fast approaching was over, he trusted that his influence over his nephew would be strong enough to withdraw him from his present associations, and in some quiet and secure spot let time cast an oblivion over the past.

Anxiously as he paced the deck, he ever and anon turned his glances towards the shore.

Then, sending for the physician, he would inquire of him the state of his sister.

He was informed that she was still sinking, though she might last several hours.

It was now getting towards sunset, and Lord Hawksbury began to think that Don Manuel must have been deceived as to the identity of the Avengers, when he saw a boat put off from the shore and make for the yacht.

Soon the distance lessened between them, and Lord Hawksbury could recognise the form of Manuel, and saw that he was accompanied by two persons, a male and a female.

His heart told him at once that his nephew was approaching.

"Tell me," said a feeble voice beside him, "is my son coming?"

Lord Hawksbury turned with surprise on his features.

Lady Edgeforth stood beside him.

There was the hue of death on her brow.

The poor frame, attenuated by disease, and worn by her early sufferings, seemed scarcely able to support itself.

But that mysterious principle of a mother's nature had warned her that her son was near, and had endowed her with strength to rise and meet him.

Lord Hawksbury did not answer, for the voice of the coxswain told him that the boat was alongside, and the next moment the Boy Pirate stood on the deck of the yacht.

Lilia followed, and stood by his side.

There was a pause.

Mother and son gazed silently at each other.

Their hearts were so full of deep feeling that words could not find utterance.

Lady Edgeforth peered earnestly at the face before her.

She seemed to drink in each feature, and compare it with those impressed on her memory by her early love—by her dreams of one whom her boy should resemble.

Our hero, too, stood like one entranced.

He had also had his dreams of a mother—of one whose form and mind were worthy of his father's love—but he could hardly realise in the frail form that swayed to and fro before him that he stood in the presence of her who had given him birth.

But the end was come.

The pair had thus met, but only to part.

A cry like that proceeding from a broken heart burst from the lips of Lady Edgeforth, and as the words, "My son!" "My mother!" fell on the ears of the listeners, she sank into those extended arms—a corpse!

* * * * *

"What are you grinning at, you lump of midnight?" demanded Black Ralph, of Zampa.

The scene was the officers' cabin on board the "Avenger."

The officers were at breakfast, and relating various anecdotes of their recent campaign.

Zampa was attending on them, and replenishing the table with eatables as fast as the previous supplies disappeared under the influence of good appetites.

"At t'oughts, Massa Ralp," answered Zampa.

"Thoughts be d——d!" returned Ralph. "What business has a nigger with thoughts?"

"De poet say dat t'ought is free," replied Zampa, with some dignity; "an' a nigger has as much right to t'ink as a white man."

"Stuff!" said Ralph. "When you was a slave down south they didn't give you time to think. But come, if your thoughts make you laugh, let's have them, and see if we can't laugh too."

"I laugh to t'ink how I frightened de dam Russian sentinel," said Zampa, "up at de castle of Aronzow."

"You frighten him!" returned Ralph. "Well, perhaps you did; you're ugly enough to frighten a whole regiment. But tell us how it was."

"Well, you see," began Zampa, "de captain went to find out de best way to storm de castle, and to know where de guns were, and how de place was guarded, and so he send for old Zamp, and ask him to go and see for him.

"Well, dis nigger no want a hole in him skin, and so he consider how he might best manage it, for dese Russians would fire at an old cow if he came near their camp, and t'ink it was an enemy come to spy their weakness.

"So I sets off, and takes with me my old nightcap and a piece of white sailcloth, and tying 'em closely round me, crawls through de bushes right up to de walls of de castle.

"Den dere was de dam ditch to cross, and, golly, it was full of water.

"But ole Zamp swam across, and looked for a place to climb up de walls.

"He hears de sentinel walking up and down, and singing some song to keep hisself warm.

"De walls were berry high, but old Zamp find de stones were laid anyhow, and that dere was room for him to get his hands and feet upon 'em.

"So he climbs up, and when he just at de top he puts on de old nightcap, and throws de white sailcloth on his shoulders, and suddenly pops him head over de battlements.

"Golly, you should have seen de dam Russian!

"Him no cry—him too frightened.

"He tink de debil came to fly away wid him.

"He drop his musket, and fall back like a dead man, while I count de guns and look about me for information.

"Den I go back to de sentinel, and seize him by de throat, when he set up a scream dat wake up all de guard, and den old Zamp have to run hisself."

The officers, who remembered that there had been a great commotion at the castle one night, that guns had been fired, and every symptom of alarm exhibited, though they did not know the cause till now, laughed heartily at Zampa's exploit.

"Bye the bye," said Ralph, "I will tell you a story of how I outwitted a Yankee, who, as you all know, are not very easily taken in.

"It was during the time that I followed the stage as a profession, and before I thought of turning either pirate or sailor.

"The London season had been very slack, and always roving after adventure, I determined to try my fortunes in America.

"I played in New York for some time, but at last, having a quarrel with the manager, I left him, and having become tired of the stage, I determined for a while to try something else.

"One night in a drunken frolic I was induced by some sharp customer to purchase three waggon loads of lanterns, and when I awoke the next morning the question arose in my mind how I was to get rid of them.

"My acquaintances bantered me exceedingly on my bargain, and so roused my metal that I swore I would travel all over America till I got rid of them.

"With this view, and with a firm intention to make money out of my drunken venture, I left New York the next morning, and took the road to Washington.

"On my road I stopped for a couple of days in the pleasant city of New Brunswick. On the afternoon of my arrival, six or eight of the townsmen were congregated in an hotel, discussing the character and animadverting upon the habits of one of their citizens, a Mr. Dunn, who was notorious for his cunning at a bargain and close-fistedness in money matters.

"I sat and listened to the talk with some vague hope that I might make something out of it.

"'Close, did you say?' said one; 'why, you might as well try to fish for a dollar out of the ocean as to get fairness out of him in a bargain. He would cheat you out of the hair on your head.'

"'A perfect skinflint!' exclaimed a little dissatisfied-looking fellow; 'I knew him when he wasn't worth a dollar, and now he counts thousands where I do hundreds, and all made by shaving and taking advantage of the necessities of others. He exacts more interest and demands greater security than any money-lender in the city. Oh, he is a sharper!'

"'True,' said another; 'he's the keenest fellow I ever knew. Look how he did Smith in that bargain; and a man should rise early to trade with Smith, I can tell you. I always thought Smith the sharpest fellow out, but old Dunn beats him.'

"'There's no mistake about Dunn's being a sharper,' said a third.

"'He would out-Yankee Yankeedom, and not half try,' put in a plethoric individual, who seemed to be determined to add his testimony.

"Others joined in, and I soon found that old Dunn was bitterly disliked by them all, and that they would all feel pleased if they could find some one sharp enough to outwit him.

"'I would give ten dollars to have him handsomely taken in,' said another of the party.

"'So would I,' repeated two or three.

"I thought this was a good chance for me, and as I had already formed a scheme to entrap somebody, and so get rid of my lanterns, I rose up, and assuming a strong Yankee twang and manner, I said,

"'Gentlemen, I don't know that ere individooal about who you are speaking—I say, I don't know him—but if you've a mind to subscribe a little grain of something, just to pay the ventur' like, why, I shouldn't mind tryin' it. I calculate it might be done. I've hearn of sich people afore, and I don't know but what I might be able to fetch him. I'm most in the trading line, and it's all in the way of trade.'

"The party eyed me for a few seconds in silence. They were evidently suspicious, and I saw that a feeling was growing over them that their scandal stood a very good chance of being repeated to Mr. Dunn.

"But I had not been on the stage for some years for nothing. I had learnt the art of preserving an identity of character, and bore their scrutiny very firmly.

"'Just the dandy, gentlemen,' exclaimed one of the party, at last, 'just the ticket for soup.'

"This was a verdict in my favour.

"'You're in the trading line, are you?' exclaimed another.

"'Yes, gentlemen, tradin's my occupation. I'm clean from Bangor, way down in the State of Maine. I can do a leetle of most anything. In the summer

I stay at hum and help the old folks ; in the fall and winter I peddle tin-ware, mostly lanterns.'

" 'You don't sell lanterns ?" said the plethoric citizen, inquiringly.

" ' I'd like to know if I ain't got three hundred of 'em in my waggons in the yard.'

" ' Oh, you have, eh ? Well, you're the very man we want.'

" 'Yes,' said the Yankee.

" ' We will make a purse of twenty dollars for you if you will bamboozle our friend Dunn. I shouldn't wonder if you could strike a trade with him. When will you do it ?'

" ' I calculate it can be done to-morrow.'

" 'Very well. If you succeed, the money is yours.'

" Twenty dollars were immediately collected and given to the landlord as an earnest of their seriousness, and the party broke up, promising to meet the next evening. On the day after I put on a genteel suit, for I had my theatrical wardrobe with me, and after having made a good many inquiries respecting the habits, manners, and appearance, and residence of Mr. Dunn, mounted a horse, and took a roundabout course for his house, with the intention of stopping there on my return, as if just from Philadelphia. As good luck would have it, old Dunn was standing in front of his house as I approached.

" ' Sir,' said I, ' will you be good enough to inform me how far it is to New Brunswick ?'

" 'Two miles, sir,' said Dunn.

" ' And how far is it to New York ?'

" ' About forty miles by stage.'

" ' Can you tell me if there are any tin-smiths in New Brunswick ?" continued I.

" ' Why, yes, there are two or three small affairs.'

" ' I am sorry they are so small,' returned I. ' I was in hopes of being able to fill an order there which our house has recived for lanterns.'

" ' Lanterns ?" said the old fellow, quickly taking the bait, for he had seen my three waggons loaded with them only the day before.

" ' Yes,' added I, in a careless tone, ' we have a heavy order to deliver, and I was told that the article could be had in New Brunswick.'

" ' You are from Philadelphia, then ?"

" 'Yes, we do business there. You have most probably heard of our firm, Hyde, Cook, Sage, Donnelly and Co ?'

" ' I can't say that I ever heard of that firm ; but there appears to be a good many of you.'

" ' Oh, yes, it is a large house.'

" ' How many lanterns do you want ?' inquired old Dunn.

" 'Three hundred will do.'

" ' What do you pay a hundred ?'

" I stated the sum considerably over the marketable value of the article, and which, if the bait took, allowing for the price he would pay me, would leave a handsome profit on my bargain.

" ' Do you wish them delivered in Philadelphia ?' he inquired.

" ' No,' said I, ' I will attend to that.'

" ' Add another dollar to the hundred and I will furnish them to you," said the sharper, eagerly.

" ' Agreed,' said I. ' Now, when can you procure them, for I have but little time to lose ?'

" ' In two days.'

" ' All right,' returned I, ' I must go some ten miles further ; I will pay you for them on my return.'

" After some further conversation about the size, make, and quality of the article, all of which served to impress Dunn with the legitimacy of the transaction, I returned to town, put on my old clothes, and otherwise altered my appearance, so that I was fully prepared to superintend the sale of my own

lanterns when the old skinflint arrived. In due time old Dunn arrived at the tavern, and, after much dallying, the bargain was struck, the money paid down, and the tin-ware delivered.

" I shall not soon forget the grin of satisfaction that was playing all this time on the faces of six or eight of the bystanders, but, of course, they said nothing.

" As for myself I was eager to see the end of the joke and went no farther than the next town, where I made myself up in the character of an Irishman, and then returned to New Brunswick.

" I did not make myself known to any of the conspirators, nor did they recognise me, but I found that old Dunn, after waiting for several days, had made urgent inquiries after the Philadelphia merchant, and, when he found that no one had seen him, he began to suspect that he had been victimised.

" His chagrin at being taken in was so marked that everybody noticed it, and the joke leaked out.

" Old Dunn was furious, and threatened to prosecute the persons for conspiracy, but he found the laugh so against him that he abandoned the idea, and, before I left the town he had the name of Old Lantern given to him.

" About three years afterwards I saw a notice of the sale of his effects in consequence of his decease, and among the catalogue was three hundred lanterns, almost as good as new, to be sold a bargain."

CHAPTER CCXLVII.

ANDREW HARWOLF IN THE HANDS OF THE INDIANS — OPEN AIR PARLIAMENT — SENTENCE OF DEATH—STRANGE CONDUCT OF THE PRISONER AT THE SCAFFOLD.

GREAT was the surprise of Andrew Harwolf when he found himself so suddenly and strangely carried off by the Indian band who had been lying in wait for him on the banks of the river.

The redskins were silent and taciturn.

Not a word could he extort from them.

And yet, from the looks they occasionally gave each other, Harwolf could not help fancying that the English tongue was not an unknown one to them.

Whither where they hurrying him, and for what purpose ?

He could hardly suppose their object to be a friendly one, for, if so, why should they gag and bind him ?

Some of those dark faces he felt certain he had seen before, and tried in vain to follow this slight clue.

Where he had seen them was a point which he was totally unable to decide.

Still his captors hurried him onwards into the depths of the forest, till at length all knowledge of his whereabouts was lost to the unhappy man.

He had long since ceased to struggle, being well able to see the inutility of any such proceedings.

The Indians had brought with them the treasure chest which Andrew Harwolf had been engaged in watching at the moment when he was surprised, and though they had not opened it, it was evident from their faces that they looked upon it as a rich booty.

At length the cavalcade stopped in an open glade, in the midst of which stood a collection of huts, or wigwams.

Towards these wigwams the whole party advanced,

and finally halted before the largest of the rude buildings.

Andrew Harwolf was dragged into this hut, which was perfectly empty, and after having his limbs rebound, was strapped up in a sitting posture, with his back to a post.

Presently the warriors entered the wigwam one by one, and solemnly took their seats upon the ground.

The last to enter was Catahaga!

He it was whose orders had caused Harwolf to be arrested, and he it was who now was to be his judge.

The pipe was lighted, and passed solemnly from lip to lip, each warrior in turn inhaling a huge mouthful of the smoke.

Then arose one of the old men, and wrapping his robe around him, prepared to address the assembly.

"The Great Spirit," he said, "had given all things for the use of the red man, before the pale-faced tribes came in their big canoes. Why should the pale-face come with his fire-bow, and occupy the hunting-grounds of the red warrior, as well as take his gold? The pale-face is a dog, and as a dog let him die!"

Low guttural murmurs of applause followed this speech, and many a tomahawk and scalping-knife was fiercely clutched.

Another greybeard of the tribe arose and signified his wish to speak.

"Many scalps," said the new orator, "hang in our wigwams. Our warriors are brave and valiant. Our land is large, and the white men are few in number. Let the whiteman live. I have spoken?"

No applause followed this speech, and Catahaga rose to address the meeting.

"My brethren, the wise men of our tribe have spoken, but with you rests the fate of the pale-face. He is in your hands. Decide, then, brave warriors, whether the scalp of the white man shall hang in the smoke of the council-chamber, or whether he shall be allowed to depart unharmed."

The warriors were then called upon to decide by vote.

Those who wished the death of Harwolf being instructed to thrust their knives in the earth at his feet, while those who wished the prisoner to be released were instructed to lay their tomahawks with the edges towards the door of the tent.

The assembled braves hastened to give their votes and in a few moments they had all resumed their seats.

The chief, Catahaga, then proceeded to sum up the chances of life or death.

At the feet of the prisoner were found seventeen knives.

At the door of the wigwam were five tomahawks.

Seventeen men desired the life of Andrew Harwolf, while only five were willing to give him a chance of amending his life.

The sentence was death by torture!

Preparations were at once made for carrying this sentence into effect.

Stout boys, who were not yet deemed old enough to go forth on the war-path, clashed their mimic weapons, and invented an extempore war-dance on the spot, when they heard the joyful news that the white prisoner was to be tortured.

Squaws, ugly, old, and yellow, screamed with weird, witch-like tongues as they thought how sweet an opportunity this would be to return on the pale-face all the injuries they had suffered by his race.

The warriors stood by, stern and uncompromising, painted in their usual colours, with the exception,

that every one had a black streak extending from the top of his forehead to the tip of his nose.

This signified in their rude heraldry—death!

A party of them now bore to the open space before the tents a pole, perhaps twelve feet high by four in diameter.

This they planted, with skill and care, deeply in the ground, treading in the earth tightly around it so that it seemed as firm as a rock.

The colour of this stake was black.

Around this they piled some few faggots of brushwood, and then returned to the wigwam which had served as a senate-house, in which Andrew Harwolf still sat in bondage.

"Pale-face dog!" cried one, "the fire waits you; come and burn for the Red man's sport."

"Burn!" shrieked Harwolf. "Burn! You cannot mean what you say—it is impossible!"

"White man burn, or cut to little pieces," said a second. "Choose which."

The wretched captive closed his eyes.

The possibility of either fate befalling him seemed too great, too appalling, too horrible to be realised.

Calling a sickly smile to his pallid lips, Harwolf in a few moments answered,

"You are joking, Indians, you are joking; but I'm not in the humour for fun. Let me go, and I promise you shall have many blankets, rifles and knives, with much powder and lead."

"White man coward—afraid to die," said the third Indian, in tones of the deepest contempt.

"You lie, Indian!" replied Harwolf, whom the taunt had in some measure restored to himself. He knew how highly valued by the Red tribes is animal courage, and how advantageous to occasionally give proofs of possessing it.

"White man sing good death song; but got no scalps to show though. Poor warrior—only a squaw."

Harwolf said nothing, and his captors raising him from his sitting position, led him forth to the spot where the stake was fixed, and the firewood piled.

Exasperated women loaded him with the most opprobrious epithets as he walked along.

Some spat in his face, others pinched him, while others again beat him with hickory rods, or pulled his hair and whiskers.

Some of the younger children even discharged their miniature arrows at him, which, piercing his clothes caused a stinging pain without making any dangerous wound.

His captors led him to the stake, and were about to fasten him to it.

But Harwolf perceiving how real and serious was his danger, began to struggle with amazing force and energy.

He threw himself on the ground, rolling over and over, screaming for help, and blaspheming with horrid oaths.

But the Indians were too strong for him, and his most strenuous endeavours only served to weaken him, while his enemies increased in numbers each minute.

They overpowered him, and bound him to the stake with thongs of raw hide, the material in their idea least likely to be affected by the flames.

We will leave him there a while, and return to follow the fortunes of his servant Miles, who, as our readers will recollect, was conveying one of his master's treasure caskets in the canoe to the willow island when Harwolf was seized by the Indians.

A STRUGGLE FOR LIFE.—See No. 74.

CHAPTER CCXLVIII.

THE HUT ON THE WILLOW ISLAND—ITS IN-
MATES—CAPTURE OF MILES—HE REJOINS
HIS MASTER—HARWOLF'S REPRIEVE.

MERRILY danced the little boat which contained
Miles Thornton and Andrew Harwolf's treasure over
the tiny sparkling waves of the broad and shining
river.

He neared the island, and though he had never
before set foot on it, yet from his master's directions
he experienced no apprehensions of difficulty in discovering the hut which was to become the resting-
place of so much wealth.

He moored the boat to the root of one of the
beautiful trees from which the island took its name,
and after first peering through the branches, threw
his treasure chest ashore.

No. 73.

Then awkwardly scrambled after it.

Taking the somewhat heavy burden on his
shoulder he began to stagger through bushes, bog,
fen and reeds, in the direction which Harwolf had
told him, occasionally anathematizing Silas Rye for
causing all this unwonted stir and labour.

"Cuss 'un; whoy couldn't thick chap stop at
home? A blamed ugly man he be, an' the pour
zquire, too, he be mortal cut up about it."

The heavy load began to oppress his shoulder, and
depositing his burden on the trunk of a tree he stood
still a moment to take breath.

"He'll be blamed cunnin' though if he gits over
we. Jest let we have two hours start o' 'un, zee
where he'll be."

With these words he took up the box once more
on his shoulders, and pursued his onward way.

At length he came in sight of the dense brake or thicket.

Here his work became much more laborious; so densely were the bushes and weeds interwoven that it was with the greatest difficulty he could make any progress at all.

However, he struggled on, and soon was rewarded by catching sight of the moss-grown log walls of the little hut.

"Well, that ere's a place as 'ud puzzle a stranger to vind out. Measter Harwolf knows a thing or two, he do."

So saying he threw his load on the ground and began to apply his whole strength to the task of opening the door.

At length it suddenly gave way, and Miles was thrown sprawling at full length on the floor of the hut.

A low laugh greeted this sudden and ludicrous entrance, and Miles looked round with astonishment.

In the hut he saw at least ten Indians in their war paint, while two others were standing at the door.

"White man, welcome," cried the chief; "long we waited for white man, now he come."

"Ya-as, but I'm blamed if I'ud a come though if I'd knowed your old painted pictur' mugs was here."

"White man, good, careful; bring here box with much gold for Redskin to take away."

"Not if I knows it, Measter Uglymug, that ain't to be touched by any o' your people, cos if ye do, there 'ill be a blamed row."

Miles was about to retreat from the hut to secure his charge, but the sight of two rifles levelled at his head, made him change his opinion and decide on remaining.

"White man stay here, no harm; if go, we shoot."

"Then I think as how I'll stop. Blamed if I zees the use o' getting a lot o' lead into my old carkiss all for nought."

"Good white man," said the chief, "my young men will take care of his treasure box. It is heavy, he cannot carry it alone."

"Don't ye make no mistake, Measter Jack in-t'-Green; I lay I'll carry that 'ere box further nor any a one o' your half-naked sweeps could."

"White man shall carry presently."

"No, I'm blamed if I do."

The Indian gently touched Miles with the edge of his tomahawk.

"Now then, old streaky; what is you up to? It hurts, ye know."

"White man will carry box when his red brother asks."

"Not a blamed step."

Again the tomahawk penetrated the somewhat tough skin of Miles, causing a very slight and gentle flow of blood to take place.

"Why, you darned old copper-coloured thief, carn't ye take a leetle care o' what you're doin'? You've b;en an' vetched the blood now, blame yer. You're about as ugly as old Scratch, and not half so perlite."

"White man must be good and carry box."

Miles, seeing that resistance was useless, and would probably lead to harsher measures on the part of his guards, sullenly obeyed their directions, and lifted the iron-bound box on his shoulder.

"I'm blamed," said he, "if this ain't too bad. They robs me fust o' measter's box, and then makes me carry 'un away to their houses wherever they mought be.

"White man go on," said the chieftain, again raising his tomahawk.

The sight of the glistening weapon worked so strongly on the nerves of poor Miles that he at once proceeded onwards without a word.

Between two Indians, closely watched, the poor man tottered onwards, but, to his surprise, found that his captors, instead of proceeding to the spot where he had left his canoe, urged him forward to a different part of the island.

"I'm blowed! they arn't goin' to drown me, be they?" muttered poor Miles.

But the Indians, to his great relief, he found showed no disposition to do anything of the kind.

Arrived at a point where a clump of huge willows totally concealed the banks of the island, he saw there three tolerably large canoes moored.

The whole party seated themselves in these and pushed off from the shore, poor Miles being made to paddle, now that he was relieved from his duties of bearing the treasure-box.

They steered straight for the spot where Miles had left Andrew Harwolf standing, but he now failed to see any trace of him, or the second box of treasure.

"White chief no wait for you," said one of the Indians, with a meaning smile. "Go away in woods."

They landed, and poor Miles was again compelled to shoulder his load, the bright tomahawk of the leader effectually quelling a slight attempt at mutiny.

Then forward into the woods for many a long mile, up hill, down hill, across streams and through ravines.

At length, Miles, weary and exhausted, stumbled and fell flat on the ground.

"White man, get up," said the chief, sternly.

"I carn't, I tell ye. I'm so tired I carn't wag a foot."

The tomahawk immediately descended, drawing blood.

But Miles refused to move.

"Kill me if you like. I tell ye, I'm tired, an' carn't move."

The Indians saw that what he said was true, and after a short consultation agreed to give him ten minutes' rest.

When this time was expired, they again set forward, but Miles was for a time relieved from carrying the box, which was suspended to a stout pole and borne on the shoulders of two stout Indians.

In this manner they proceeded for some time, and Miles, hoping his troubles were over, began to look about for some means of escape.

But he was disappointed, for a halt was called, and he was again compelled to carry the treasure.

In a few minutes more the opening through the trees gave the party a view of the camp which was their destination.

They could also see on the green sward before the wigwams a noisy crowd, which Miles felt some difficulty in accounting for, but which the Indians perfectly understood.

"White chief, Grey Wolf there. He very much burn, and you burn too."

This explanation did not tend to raise Miles's spirits very much, and he instinctively stopped, not wishing to become a victim while there was a single chance of putting off the evil for a minute.

But his captors obstinately refused to let him stop, and hurried the unfortunate man forward.

A smile of exultation played around the mouth of the chief, Catahaga, as he saw the second prisoner hurried forward into the camp.

"My warriors have hurried on their errand," he said, addressing the leader of the band which had captured Miles.

"Our steps have not been delayed, and the white prisoner travels quickly," replied the deputy.

On seeing the second prisoner brought into the camp, the whole party who had been about to commence the torture of Harwolf, left that individual, and crowded round the new arrival.

"Let both prisoners be carefully guarded till to-morrow," said Catahaga, turning to his warriors.

This order was received with a slight murmur, which, however, was instantly quelled when the chief waved his hand for silence.

"To-morrow," said he, "two white men shall be tied to the stake instead of one."

Then, with a loud shout, they untied the Grey Wolf from the stake, and in company with his servant, led him back to the council tent, where both were securely fastened.

It was now nearly dark, and after seeing the bonds of the prisoners secure, two young warriors stretched themselves across the doorway, and soon quietness reigned throughout the camp.

The red warriors slept, but when they arose in the morning, there was a terrible outcry.

The prisoners had escaped!

Their guards were dead!

Fearful cries of vengeance resounded through the forest as the warriors bounded off in pursuit.

For two whole days did the Indians scour the forest in every direction, but without success.

No trace of the fugitives could they find.

CHAPTER CCXLIX.

THE ESCAPE—NIGHT IN THE FOREST.

WHEN Andrew Harwolf, suddenly reprieved from torture, was bound up in the wigwam along with Miles, his first care was to ask the latter the success of his enterprise at the willow island

Miles related all that had occurred even to his being compelled to carry the chest so many miles.

"Curses on them!" muttered Harwolf, "the fruits of many years labours and crimes, are now wrested from me by these cursed redskin rascals!"

"Measter, dont'ee cuss zo," said Miles, "they savages be goin' to kill us, better zay a prayer or two."

"Prayer! I pray? Ha! ha! ha!" the man laughed, wildly. "Why, you fool! the words of a prayer would blister my tongue, and scorch my lips did I attempt to utter them!"

Nothing more was said on either side, and both the guards, without the tent, seeing that the prisoners were safe, stretched themselves out for another sleep.

But the prisoners slept not; the terrible fate which awaited them in the morning kept their eyes open and their senses fearfully awake.

The sentinels slumbered at their post, and heard not the slight noise made by some one in cutting away the skins which constituted the back part of the tent.

Harwolf heard and so did Miles.

"It can be no enemy," thought the ex-judge. "My foes would come in by the door of the tent."

They waited with anxiety, still listening.

They could see a little patch of faint light, where an opening had been already made close to the ground.

Rip, rip went the knife through the dry hides that composed the walls of the hut.

Andrew Harwolf uneasily turned his head towards the door where his two guards lay sleeping.

"Oh, that I had a knife," said he, half aloud.

As if by magic his wish became accomplished, for a knife in a sheath was thrown in such a manner as to fall between his legs, and within reach of his hands, which were fastened before him.

And then the noise of the unseen hand ceased, as though, having placed the means of escape in Harwolf's hands, there was nothing more to be done.

Andrew Harwolf clutched the knife eagerly, and cast a searching and anxious look towards his guards.

They slept, but lightly and uneasily, as though the slightest noise would awaken them to their duties.

Still they slept, and drawing forth the knife from its sheath, Andrew Harwolf slit the thongs which bound his wrists and ankles, severing at the same time the bonds which held his body to the post in the middle of the hut.

Miles was still in bondage.

Gently rising on his hands and knees, the "Grey Wolf," as the Indians called Harwolf, crawled with all the subtlety of the animal whose name he bore, and with knife uplifted gazed upon the faces of the two redskin guards.

Then, suddenly throwing himself upon the one nearest him, the keen, broad blade drank the warrior's heart's blood, and the sleeping sentinel expired without a groan or cry.

The other still slept.

Miles watched his master's proceedings with awe and anxiety, wondering much if the other sentinel was to be disposed of in the same manner.

Andrew Harwolf paused a moment, drew a deep

breath, and then crawling softly over the gory carcase, approached the second Indian, who lay at the distance of four or five feet from his dead companion.

The red warrior turned over and muttered some unintelligible words to himself in his sleep.

But Andrew Harwolf fancied that he was about to awake.

Therefore with a sudden dash he threw himself on the sleeping foe covering the warrior's mouth with his left hand, while with his right he plunged his knife into the Indian's chest.

For a moment there was a struggle with the unarmed and wounded Indian.

Harwolf had taken the precaution to remove his weapons from his reach.

But Harwolf kept his hand pressed over the Indian's mouth to prevent his giving the alarm, while he again and again repeated his stabs.

The deep red blood rolled down on the ground an ensanguined tide, the hands and face of Andrew Harwolf were tinged with the same fearful dye.

Presently the muscles of the struggling Indian relaxed.

There was a slight gurgling noise in his throat.
His eyes became fixed.
He was dead !

With a deep sigh of relief Harwolf again crawled back into the hut where he had left Miles bound, and with a few swift strokes of the knife set him at liberty.

"Get up and stretch your cramped limbs," said he.

Miles obeyed, and soon by a slight exertion restored the impeded circulation of his blood.

While so doing he watched with eager and curious eye the further actions of his master.

With knife in hand, Andrew Harwolf again approached the bodies of the Indian guards.

What could be his object ?

Was he about to repeat his deadly thrusts to make death doubly sure ?

Not so ; his object was a far more fiendish one. His object was to mutilate those senseless corpses.

Kneeling down beside one of them, he passed the keen point of his knife round the head of the Indian, cutting through to the skull-bone.

Then, twisting the long hair round his hand, a strong pull brought off the scalp, leaving a hideous bare and bleeding skull.

Miles shuddered.

Scalping was something new to him, and the operation gave him an unpleasant reminder of what might be his fate should he fail to make his escape, or if by any chance he again fell into the hands of the Indians.

But Harwolf's nerves were of iron.

Wiping his knife across the long lock of black hair, he tucked the scalp beneath his belt, and advanced towards the other corpse.

This he treated in the same manner as the former, then returned to Miles in the hut.

"Now, Miles, are you ready ?" he asked.

"Ees zquire, I be, and mortal glad to get away from here."

"Then follow me gently and silently."

The two men stepped out of the hut together over the bodies of the Indians, whom they robbed of their rifles and powder-horns.

Their first thought was to look round the wigwam together, and see, if possible, the unknown, whose gift of a knife had enabled them to escape.

Not a soul was there.

The whole camp was silent as death.

Being in no fear of any enemy, the Indians did not deem it necessary to place scouts or sentinels round their village.

Andrew Harwolf and his companion in captivity proceeded slowly and stealthily through the camp towards the spot where the horses of the tribe were enclosed in a kind of rude paddock.

Entering this, they managed without much difficulty to secure a steed each, which they carefully led out of the enclosure and beyond the confines of the camp.

Then they mounted and dashed wildly away through the woods, never stopping till they arrived at the place where the Indians had moored their canoes.

Into one of these they stepped, first driving the horses into the water.

The animals swam out into the stream a little way, but in a few minutes were devoured by alligators.

Then cutting the other canoes adrift they pulled out into the stream, and by daybreak were many miles away, drifting down the stream on the opposite side of the river.

While the Indians were yet weeping and mourning over the bodies of their dead warriors, Silas Rye, accompanied by Oiny Macarne, entered the camp.

They had heard from Nat Weatherfield, who became possessed of the information in some peculiar manner only known to back-wood trappers, that Harwolf and Miles were in the hands of Catahaga and his tribe.

Accordingly, they at once left their own encampment, and hurried to that of their Indian friends.

Great was the surprise of Silas on finding a party of Indians gathered about their council tent, saying the death dirge of the murdered braves in low, wailing, yet most pathetic tones.

Silas advanced towards the group, amongst whom he saw Catahaga.

Many vengeful glances were cast at them as they passed along.

The whole generation of whites were hateful to the Indians that morning, for had not two of their bravest and best warriors been sacrificed to aid the escape of the white prisoners ?

But Catahaga stilled all expressions of enmity on the part of his braves, and beckoned Silas to advance.

"My white brother is welcome," said the chief; "but the heart of Eagle Wing is very sad."

"What has happened ?" asked Silas.

Catahaga pointed in silence to the two bodies, which were now dressed in their best robes, and freshly painted.

"I see," said Silas. "Catahaga, you doubtlessly loved the brave warriors who have fallen by the hand of the enemy."

"Eagle Wing honoured and respected his braves."

"But what enemy has done this ?"

"The Grey Wolf was a captive in the hands of Catahaga. These warriors watched the tent in which he was bound. The judge of the white men slew the braves and escaped on the Indians' horses."

"Escaped !" cried Silas ; "then again are all my hopes defeated ! But know you which way they went ?"

"To the great river."

"And will you not follow them ?"

"We cannot ; they have taken our canoes with them."

This was sore news for Silas, who had fondly hoped to find himself once more face to face with Harwolf.

"Water leaves no trail," continued the chief, and my young men's eyes cannot see a day's journey ahead."

"You are right," replied Silas; "but I will not leave this part of the country yet. I have hope."

Who had helped the prisoners to escape was ever a mystery in the Indian camp.

But we, the writer, can tell our readers.

It was Owhwana, the "Lily Bell!"

An Indian maiden whose gentle heart loved not the scenes of blood and horror in which the stern warriors of her tribe delighted.

She it was who had opened the walls of the wigwam and thrown the knife with precision and dexterity to Harwolf's reach.

Then, when she saw him grasp it, she withdrew, fearing lest she should be seen by the sentinels.

She retired to her tent.

What use Harwolf made of the weapon thus conveyed to him we have seen; but had Owhwana known what was known to all the tribe at daybreak, the white man might have perished ere she would have stirred to save him.

Remorse and anguish struck her gentle soul.

She often and fervently prayed to the great Manitou for forgiveness.

But the load of her sin seemed to her unbearable.

So one fine summer evening she dressed herself in her best robes, and with slow footsteps ascended to the summit of a neighbouring precipice.

Calling on the Great Spirit to be merciful to her, she threw herself down headlong, seeking thus to expiate her sins.

So perished Owhwana.

And Indian maidens now tell of the fate of the Lily Bell, who, *for love,* as they suppose, threw herself from the top of the rock, which bears to this day the name of Love's Folly.

Meanwhile, Andrew Harwolf and Miles floated on down the broad and sparkling stream, keeping carefully on the opposite side to that on which Catahaga and his band of warriors were encamped.

They hardly dared use the fire-arms of which they had despoiled their foes, lest the report should alarm the watchful redskins.

If there had not been some old fish-hooks and tackle of the rudest Indian manufacture in the bottom of the canoe, hunger would have, indeed, proved a most severe foe.

But Miles baited one of the hooks, and soon had the satisfaction of pulling out a fine red fish which they landed and broiled on the coals of a fire which they ventured to light in the midst of a dense thicket.

Then they again embarked, and glided swiftly onwards over the silent highway till evening began to fall, and they found themselves between two high and rocky banks through which the river rushed with considerable rapidity.

"Look out for a cave in the bank, Miles, and let us take up our quarters there for the night," said Harwolf. "I am greatly in need of sleep."

"Zo be I, zur; but I thort I mought n't speak afore you, ye know, zquire."

"Then keep your eye on the bank."

In a few minutes they found a dark fissure in the rock, into which they unhesitatingly thrust the boat.

It was a complete cave, the extreme back of which could not by any means be seen from the outside, and around which was a rocky shelf, about a foot from the sandy bottom.

Here they landed, and having collected a quantity of drift wood from the shore, soon were enabled to light a fire.

The fish-hooks were then put in requisition again, and a supper was quickly hauled from the rapid stream.

Then they lit their pipes, of which their Indian captors had not deprived them, and were thankful in their rude blasphemous way for having escaped their almost certain death.

Presently they began to talk.

"Have you ever seen the ghost which glides about these parts, Miles?" said Harwolf.

"No, zur; an' I doan't want to."

"If you will listen to me I will tell you all about it."

Miles placed himself in an attitude of attention, and, after a few preliminary whiffs of his pipe, Andrew Harwolf began the following tale of

THE SPIRIT OF THE RAPID RIVER.

"It is about sixty years ago now, that a party of Indians of the Comanche tribe were seated about their fires, smoking their pipes and lasily conversing with each other.

"Their unpainted faces, and other appearances in their dress, showed that these warriors were on a hunting excursion, and not on a war path.

"They glanced lazily at the fire, and then at the quarters of venison which hung from the trees around; but they were all too indolent and too much at ease to think of roasting another rib.

"Presently some of the young men began to talk of the fair Indian maidens they would take to their wigwams when they returned from their hunt.

"Among the speakers was Calstagela, a young warrior, who spoke thus:—

"'I love the snowdrop of our tribe, and when I return to our wigwams she has promised to become the bride of Calstagela, and what maiden in the tribe so fair as she, or so light of foot?'

"A guttural 'ugh' was all that followed this speech, and one brave rose from his seat by the fire and walked away into the forest.

"Calstagela was a generous, warm-hearted young man, and when he saw this he followed his companion into the forest, thinking that perhaps *he* too had a love for 'the snowdrop,' and wishing, at all events, to explain his prior claim to the maiden's hand and heart.

"He overtook the 'Night Raven' as the other warror was called, standing in a gloomy attitude near the foot of a tree.

"'What ails my brother that he thus leaves the fire?' said Calstagela.

"'The Night Raven's heart is full—he loves the Lily Bell of the Comanches.'

"'But my brother has never told his love to the fair Lily.'

"'No.'

"'Would the Night Raven take away from his brother the bride on whom he has set his heart?'

"'While Calstagela lives, the Lily Bell is as nothing to the Night Raven.'

"'While Calstagela lives!' little thought the unfortunate young chief of the double meaning of treachery which those words contained within them.

"'Will the Night Raven return to the camp of the hunters?' asked Calstagela.

"'The Night Raven will walk by the river side to cool his hot head.'

"Kind, generous Calstagela walked away with his rival to the cliffs which overlook the river, hoping, by soft words of kindness, to help his friend to forget the helpless passion he had formed for the Lily Bell.

"They walked on and on, the Night Raven silent and reserved, while the young Calstagela poured into his ear words of hope and encouragement, speaking of other damsels of the tribe quite equal to the Lily Bell whom he might perchance woo and wed.

"At length they reached a spot where the cliffs receded inland a little.

"Here the Night Raven suddenly turned upon Calstagela, and, with one blow of his tomahawk, killed the kind, brave young warrior.

"Dragging the body of his victim for some distance along the cliffs, he rolled it over into the water

"Down it fell with a heavy splash, startling the fish-hawk from its perch in the bushes by the cliffs.

"It sank, and the Night Raven saw his rival no more.

"He returned to the fire, wrapped himself in his buffalo robe, and laid down to sleep.

"The other warriors began to grow anxious when they found that Calstagela did not return.

"Some of them questioned the Night Raven as to what had become of the young chieftain.

"'I know not,' was the reply.

"Like Cain, his hands were dyed with the blood of his nearest relative, for the young men were cousins.

"But next morning, the traces of his guilt were so evident that he was at once taken to the headquarters of the tribe, where, after a short and unceremonious trial, he was condemned to death.

"He was bound to the trunk of a tree, and a flight of arrows soon satisfied the requirements of earthly vengeance.

"But the Lily Bell of the Comanches long mourned for the loss of her brave and gallant Calstagela, who had been so suddenly snatched from her.

"The tribe remained in the neighbourhood, and the fair girl spent many a moonlight night in wandering along the cliff on which her lover had met his death.

"Her mind was turned, as said the Indian women, and she often spoke of seeing her beloved sailing in the clouds, or floating over the surface of the broad river.

"One night she repaired to her favourite promenade on the cliff.

"As she walked she thought she saw her beloved Calstagela skimming over the moonlit waves, and beckoning to her.

"'I come, dearest,' she cried, with accents of unfeigned love.

"Then, without pause for thought or reflection, threw herself down head foremost.

"Next morning her body was found, disfigured and mutilated, on the sharp-pointed rocks.

"They took up her poor, bruised remains gently, and laid her in the sepulchre of her fathers.

"And many an Indian maiden strewed garlands of the choicest flowers on the simple pile of stones which marks the last resting-place of the fair, the loving Lily Bell of the Comanches.

"And they say that now her spirit nightly haunts the river."

By the time Harwolf had finished this narrative he perceived that Miles was fast asleep, and that, consequently, all his eloquence had been wasted on the stone walls around him.

"Insensible brute!" muttered Harwolf. "He has no more taste for the sentimental than I have. I'll never again waste my time telling him Indian stories."

So saying, he laid himself down, and in a short time was, like his follower, in the land of dreams.

But we forbear to say what those dreams were.

CHAPTER CCL.

THE BUFFALO HUNT.

BUT to return to Silas Rye and Oiny Macarne.

After the grief of the Indian warriors for their murdered brethren was somewhat assuaged, and the braves had been interred with cheftains' honours, the two friends still remained some days with Catahaga and his band.

At length one day a buffalo hunt on a grand scale was proposed, and, being agreed to, the whole of the full-grown men of the tribe sallied forth for the chase.

The two white men were the only ones armed with fire-arms, for the Indians had left all their rifles behind, not caring to use so noisy a weapon.

Their arms were bows, arrows, and long, sharp-pointed lances.

They were all mounted on the fiery, swift mustangs of the south, and full of hope and excitement, they commenced their journey.

Every man carried two days' food before him on the saddle, for it was uncertain when or where they might fall in with the gigantic game they were in pursuit of.

They kept on their course in a westerly direction over the rolling prairies.

Now the use of their reserve of provisions became apparent.

Game was scarce, and, if it had not been for the jerked beef they brought with them, hunger would almost have prevented them from following the expedition on which they started.

And in this wild solitude Silas Rye began to observe and consider what a different creature is the Indian in the wilderness and the Indian who haunts cities.

In Washington or New York the red man is almost dumb, and much embarrassed; in the wigwam of the Comanches or Sioux, a white man feels the same; both for the same reason—they have no one to talk to.

A wild Indian, to reach the civilized world, must needs travel some thousands of miles in vehicles to which he is unaccustomed; through towns and villages which are new to him; through latitudes and longitudes of which he knows nothing; eating food to which he is unused; stared and gazed at by thousands and tens of thousands whom he is unable to bid mind their own business, because he cannot speak their language, sick at heart and grieved in spirit to see the exhibition of white wealth and luxury which are enjoyed in the land which was once his redskinned fathers, and over the spots which contain the bones of his revered ancestors.

Place the white man in a Delaware village, and see what position he stands in.

To reach the out-of-the-way collection of huts and wigwams the white man must travel first by steamboat, then by canoe; he must ride on horseback and walk on foot.

The white rover must also wade through quagmires, swim rivers; he must patch his mocassins over and over again as well as his breeches.

He must also be able to live on meat, and meat alone; to sleep on the bare ground must be thought no hardship, and dreams of home comforts and friends looked upon as effeminate and unmanly.

Well, when he arrives at this Indian village he is half naked, half starved, sick and homeless; compelled to beg for food, and a place to sleep in; he is the laughing stock of dozens of Indian boys and girls who flock about the stranger to look at and criticise his appearance.

They presume that no white man could come among them save to buy, sell, or barter, and pester him accordingly.

With Silas Rye and Oiny Macarne it was different.

They were the guests and friends of Catahaga the chief, and under his protection fared well in that great prairie wilderness or desert.

Water was what they wanted most, and, to avoid being entirely without this precious fluid, they kept as near as possible in a line with the river.

The third day of their journey they fell in with fresh tracks of the buffalo.

All hearts beat high, and expectation was at its greatest.

They urged their horses forward over the grass-grown plains, and soon had the satisfaction of seeing on the prairie at a long distance a number of black dots, which the experienced eye of the chief at once recognised.

"Buffalo!" said he, pointing towards the vast herd.

A halt was called, and a council held as to the best method of surrounding the animals.

It was deemed impossible to inclose the whole herd in a circle of Indian warriors, so they resolved to ride up against the wind, and when the herd should become alarmed every warrior would trust to his swift horse and unerring bow.

Up they crept quietly, and scattered at a distance from each other like a line of riflemen, till they came within about a hundred yards of the spot where the first of the herd was at his ease, lazily chewing the cud.

The gigantic beast snuffed danger.

He rose to his feet, shook his shaggy mane, and bellowed fiercely.

This challenge was the signal for the whole herd to rise and gallop off.

"Let each man choose his buffalo, and follow in the chace," shouted Catahaga, at the same time giving his steed the rein, and dashing off in pursuit of the bull who had given the alarm.

He soon came up with the gigantic adversary, and planted an arrow deep between his ribs.

With a roar the huge animal turned, and, with lowered head, rushed at his brave human foe.

Catahaga reined up his horse, and waited the shock.

Just as the bull was about to plant his horns in the horse's chest the rider pulled his steed sharply round, and the buffalo, unable to stop, went thundering past.

He received another arrow, however, and came up staggering.

The ponderous animal repeated the charge with the same result.

A minute he paused, lolling his big tongue out of his foaming mouth, and then again turned to attack the Indian chieftain.

But after running a dozen steps his knees tottered under him, he staggered, and fell bleeding on the prairie.

A loud shout proclaimed the victory of human skill and courage over brute strength.

Silas Rye's rifle had been heard more than once.

On proceeding towards him Catahaga perceived that a fine young bull had fallen victim to the white man's gun.

Meanwhile, Oiny Macarne was nowhere to be seen, and, with considerable alarm, Silas questioned the warriors who had returned from the chase whether they had seen his follower.

One Indian had seen him riding in pursuit of an immense bull, but had since lost sight of him.

Some of the warriors were still chasing the wild animals over the plain, and these groups were eagerly scanned by Silas, who also called to his assistance the eagle eye of Catahaga.

"He is not with my warriors," said the chief, gravely.

"Then where can he be?" muttered Silas.

At this moment, the keen vision of Catahaga caught sight of something moving in a grove of trees at some distance.

"Let us search in the wood yonder. Perhaps we may there find him whom you seek," said he.

They urged their horses forward towards the timber in question, but when within a few yards of it Catahaga pulled up his steed, and whispered Silas to proceed with great caution.

They at length were within the shadow of the grove, and on peering through the trees, Silas could see Oiny seated on the branch of a young tree, but a few inches above the horns of an immense buffalo bull, who, pawing the ground with his hoofs, seemed determined not to quit the spot till he had revenged himself on his adversary.

Oiny had dropped his gun, and had no weapon with which to put his enemy to flight.

But he had managed to cut himself a good stout stick, with which he occasionally aimed a blow at his adversary's head or horns when he came too close.

Oiny had handled the blackthorn at many a village fair and festival, therefore he thought that if he could only get a fair blow at his enemy, he would be able to floor him "as nately as a Skibbereen boy."

At that instant, however, a shot from Silas, who had approached unobserved, caused the huge brute to stagger and fall.

"Hurroo!" shouted Oiny. "Bejabers that's a foine shot, entoirely!"

With these words he scrambled down from the tree, and with his cudgel commenced an attack upon the body of his dying foe.

"Och! you grate thafe, an' ye'd be afther puttin' yer ugly horns into the body of an Oirishman, 'ud yez? Bad cess to ye for a blaygardly spalpeen!"

"Come away, Oiny; leave the poor beast alone now he is dead," cried Silas.

"An' ain't I to kill him afther he's been' keepin' me up in the tree for his own swate will an' plaisure?"

"You shall skin him if you like."

"Now is it a butcher you're afther taking me for, Misther Rye? Sure I niver skinned a bull in me life."

"Then some one else must do so. But come, if you will not skin him, leave him lying there."

After much persuasion Oiny walked away shaking his stick and muttering execration on the " thafe of the worruld," as he termed his late enemy.

It appeared that Oiny had chased the beast nearly up to the timber, and managed to give him a shot which took little effect.

The bull turned to charge, and the mustang Oiny rode endeavoured to perform the same evolution which his Indian masters had alway done.

However, Oiny, who was unprepared for anything of the kind, managed to lose his seat and fall between the legs of his steed, which immediately galloped off across the prairie.

Oiny managed to pick himself up before the bull had time to turn after his charge ; and, minus his gun, ran at full speed for the grove, where he hoped to find shelter.

But the buffalo soon found out his little game, and came thundering at his heels with a speed which m ore than doubled Oiny's pace.

For some time he dodged round about the trees, narrowly escaping the horns of the bull on several occasions.

At length he caught sight of a little tree, up which he climbed or rather jumped, and in which he was compelled to sit till the timely arrival of Silas and Catahaga ended his troubles.

The bodies of the slaughtered cattle were half-skinned, and the fine tender parts of the body cut out.

Such of this as was not required for immediate consumption was cut in thin strips and dried in the sun.

This jerked beef, as it is called, forms part of the food of the Indians at such times as game is scarce, and few wigwams are without it.

After the business of hanging this beef to dry, the whole party returned to a spot near the water where they encamped, and with the fresh meat they had brought with them made a famous supper.

Then pipes were lit, and many a strange tale of Indian warfare was told round the camp fires.

Silas Rye listened to all these stories with some attention, and so did Oiny; who, however, retaliated by inflicting on his hearers some little account of Donnybrook Fair, to which the Indians listened with the most polite attention.

They, however, knew no more of Irish when he had finished than before he opened his mouth.

After a time the Indians stretched themselves in their blankets, the fires was replenished, one or two scouts were appointed, and soon deep slumber reigned through the camp.

It was a strange weird scene.

The glowing embers threw their flickering rays on the bronze countenances of the sleeping warriors, casting deep shadows all around.

The tall trees among which their horses were tethered waved their branches, and whispered wild words to the night wind.

Silas Rye slept.

He lay beside the chieftain Catahaga.

But as he slept he dreamed a dream of strange import.

He thought he saw the figure of his friend Foxley, the detective, standing pointing with his finger towards the setting sun.

A smile wreathed the lips of the vision as it gazed.

But in another moment his face changed. The face of the setting sun seemed specked or dotted.

The specks grew larger and larger, and at length assumed human shapes.

The shapes were those of Harwolf and Miles.

"Follow them," cried the vision.

"But whither?" demanded Silas.

"To the west ; there you shall find them. Avenge me."

"I will," murmured Silas, and then the vision vanished.

CHAPTER CCLI.

ON THE TRACK.

GREATLY perturbed, in spirit Silas awoke.

Oiny was snoring by his side, and, with a shake, he woke him.

"Did you see anything?" demanded he, and, receiving an answer in the negative, allowed his companion to snore again.

But no more sleep visited the eyes of Silas Rye that night.

Early in the morning he related to Catahaga what he had seen.

"Let us travel towards the setting sun," replied the chief.

The camp was broken up and the whole party moved westward.

But they as yet saw no signs of what they sought.

But on the evening of the second day after the buffalo hunt above described, a warrior, who was riding apart from the band, suddenly stopped while crossing a stream.

He gave a peculiar cry which soon brought the chief to the spot.

"White men have been here," said he, pointing to the track of feet.

Catahaga eagerly leaped from his horse and gazed down on the marks. Two men had passed and left their foot-prints on the bank.

Catahaga at once summoned Silas to the spot, and pointing to the marks, exclaimed,

"The Grey Wolf has been here!"

Silas started. His dream seemed realized.

"But it is now more than six days since the white man passed through this water."

"We have horses," said Silas, "and will follow for six months if necessary."

THE DEATH OF CLARA AND HER CHILD.—*(See page 586.)*

The Indian chief perceived plainly by the trail that the two white men were unattended, and therefore dismissed his braves to their wigwams under the guidance of an old and experienced warrior.

He judged that himself and his two white comrades would be able to capture the Grey Wolf and his companion without any assistance.

In the afternoon of the day after leaving the warriors they passed through an open glade in the forest where several traces of former cultivation and civilization met their eye.

The charred remains of a log hut grimly peeped out of the mantle of verdure which had overgrown it.

A few broken and scattered rails proclaimed that a fence had once surrounded the little patch of corn and pumpkins, while stumps of trees showed plainly that the inhabitants had intended further progress in cultivation.

Who built the hut? Where are the inhabitants now?

Such were the questions which rose to the lips of Silas Rye as he beheld the remains of what had doubtless once been a happy home.

"Be japers, shure an' they're gone away to Californey, an' no fools either," ejaculated Oiny Macarne.

Silas smiled.

Catahaga frowned darkly and turned his eyes away from the scene.

"The Comanches are dogs!" he said.

"Then you know the story of this deserted settlement?" asked Silas.

"I do," replied the Indian.

"Then tell me. I feel anxious to know how this evidently once flourishing settlement fell into decay."

The Indian consented, and, drawing nearer to his companion, began to relate his tale.

This we will divest of all its Indian phrases and expressions, and lay before our readers in a more intelligible form.

Some six years ago a big, burly, good-humoured

Yankee, Bob Shirley by name, after wandering for some months through the woods on his mustang, happened to halt on this very spot.

He saw at once that it was a beautiful and fertile valley, and resolved here to make himself a home in the wilderness.

Backwood homes are easily managed. Bob needed no help; but at once set to work hacking and chopping at the tall trees around.

Soon four rude posts were erected, then the rough planks were fastened on one by one, and Bob began to look upon the structure as a little palace.

His admiration, however, did not cause him to cease from his labours. He worked on day after day, and soon a roof and a chimney arose over the weatherboard walls.

Then Bob laid down his axe, and entering the hut, lit a fire on the mud hearth, determined to have a jollification.

He cooked venison steaks and corn cakes out of the little packet of flour he had remaining, and brewed himself a stiff jorum of whisky and water from the flask which, for many days, had been untouched.

Then when the supper was finished, for lack of company, he sang " Hail Columbia," " Yankee Doodle," and other patriotic songs for the edification of his rough pony which cropped the short grass before the hut.

The building finished, Bob Shirley arose the next morning with a planting mania in his head, and after spending some hours in fashioning a few rude tools began to scratch and work at the earth around.

When this was sufficiently prepared to suit his fancy he dropped into it some grains of Indian corn and pumpkin seeds.

The backwoodsman's next care was to fence round his little field, and then to fell trees and prepare firewood for the winter.

This was done, and Bob Shirley looked around to behold himself lord and master of a house, *furnished* after his ideas, and a flourishing little farm.

And so he sat himself down to smoke his pipe, and enjoy himself.

But somehow or other Bob did not feel so completely happy in the midst of his prosperity.

Often he lay thinking at night what could it be that he lacked?—and, at length, one night an idea struck him.

Bob came to the conclusion that he wanted a companion—in fact, a wife.

" And that's jest what I du want, I reckon," he muttered, as he rose early in the morning, and saddled his steed.

Bob Shirley was none of your dallying fellows, who are for ever putting things off. He wanted a wife, and he rode straight off to the nearest settlement, a distance of about three hundred miles, determined to bring one back with him.

In due time Bob Shirley arrived at the flourishing town of New Babylon, on a branch of the Red River.

This town, consisting of six log huts, occupied by farmers, a store-house, and a meeting-house, was much enlivened by the appearance of Bob, who soon became a favourite, especially with the girls.

For he was not a bad-looking fellow, could tell most tremendous tales of adventures with bears, panthers, and snakes, danced very well (*for that part of the world*), and was immensely fond of frolics of every description.

But in the course of a fortnight a change seemed to come over the young hunter; he became fond of long walks and moonlight rambles.

Of course he had a companion, and that companion was Clara Barker, the minister's only daughter.

The grey-haired old man, finding that his daughter's heart was completely wrapped up in the young hunter, consented to their union, and himself performed the ceremony, though his heart was sad as he thus gave his darling to be the bride of a lonely dweller in the wilderness.

A week after the marriage Bob and his bride started off in a waggon for their home in the forest.

Many gifts and presents did they carry with them, but Bob prized none so much as the fair-haired girl who travelled with him.

He cheered her spirits by his songs and tales, and carefully guarded her when they encamped at night against all the dangers of the wild forest.

At length, after a long and weary journey, they arrived in sight of the log hut, and found everything as Bob had left it.

" It ain't a very big location, Clara, I guess, but it's big enough for us."

" I shall be very happy here with you, dear," replied she, though, if the truth must be told, the fair girl's heart sank when she beheld the wild forest around.

He kissed her, lifted her from the waggon, and was completely happy.

In due course a little boy was born, and the hunter's heart grew more fond than ever of the gentle, fragile mother.

When this infant was about two years old, Bob took his rifle one morning, and went forth into the woods to hunt.

Clara, who had been suffering from fever, and was still weak and ill, sat some time thinking of her old father, and then, placing her infant in its rude cot, went down to the spring near the house for water. She returned with her pitcher to find the house surrounded with Comanche Indians, who were busily appropriating various household articles.

No sooner was she observed than one, who appeared to be the chief, caught her by the arm, and pushing her aside, said,

" Stay; there is room in Medawah's wigwam for the white squaw."

Clara's heart sank within her, and she trembled violently, but at that moment her infant, aroused by the rude warriors, set up a feeble cry, and sprang towards her.

But she had barely clasped it in her arms, when a painted monster tore it from her, and with the most unparelleled brutality, drove his hatchet into its brains.

The act called forth more than human rage from the mother's breast.

Stepping back, she snatched a pistol from its resting place, and shot the Indian dead on the spot.

In a moment a tomahawk crashed through her skull.

She fell, and her long bright tresses were speedily dangling at the girdle of the chief.

Then a demon seemed to take possession of the whole band; pigs, ducks, fowls, were all sacrificed in mere wantoness by the Indians.

Dragging forth the two human bodies before the door they departed.

Day passed along, and then, when the sun had almost run its course, a merry song from the forest proclaimed the return of the hunter.

A song that should soon be hushed.

The unwonted silence seemed to strike him with a cold chill as he emerged from the wood, and casting to the ground the fat buck he had been carrying, the hunter sprang forward to his hut.

A single glance revealed to him the horrors of the scene.

He tenderly raised the mangled corpse of her he had loved so dearly, and spoke words of love and endearment, but in vain.

Then the hunter rose from his knees, and muttered one word,

"Vengeance!"

He dug a rude grave, in which he placed the bodies of those he loved, carefully arching it over with planks to keep the earth from pressing on that fair form, and piling a huge stone over all to mark the spot.

Then the strong man threw himself down by his wife's grave, and for one hour gave way to his mad agony of spirit.

But thoughts of vengeance stirred him up to action.

He arose, and re-entered the hut.

From beneath the floor he unearthed a keg of powder, another of bullets, and a third containing strong whisky.

Two large powder horns were filled, a large pouch was well stored with bullets, his bottle replenished with whisky.

The remainder he buried at his wife's feet, and then, with a loud cry of,

"Vengeance!" he plunged into the wild forest.

That was the last word he was ever known to speak, but the Comanches even to this day shudder when they hear the name of "the silent hunter" mentioned.

For he hung on their trail and cut off every straggler who chanced to lag on the path, and even now follows them whether they hunt the bison or go forth on the war-path.

Those who have seen him say that the stock of his rifle is covered with notches, and that every notch denotes the death of a Comanche warrior.

Such was the wild tale of backwood vengeance to which Silas Rye listened with fixed attention.

By the time the young Indian had finished his story the sun had almost disappeared behind the distant hills, and Silas, tired from being in the saddle all day, hinted at camping.

"Not here," said Catahaga; "no water, no shelter. Come further on."

He turned off to the left and led the party down some rough, uneven ground which soon brought them into a deep ravine.

They could hear the sound of a river at no great distance, and, in a few minutes, stood on its rocky bank.

"Surely you don't intend to camp here?" cried Silas.

"No! Cave up here."

So saying he led the way up a steep and winding path by the side of the river till they came to a deep chasm across which two rough planks had been thrown.

Urging their horses across this narrow and dangerous bridge they found the path continue for a yard or two and then terminate in a cave, the mouth of which was shielded by thick bushes.

Catahaga struck a light and soon revealed the extent and beauty of the cavern.

It was, perhaps, forty feet deep by twelve broad, and the arched roof seemed at least thirty feet above their heads.

Exploring it at the farther end Silas found a pool of limpid water which was constantly supplied from the roof overhead, while the surplus ran away in a little channel down the side of the cave and tumbled over the rocks into the big river.

The wayfarers picketed their horses near the mouth of the cave where they could browse on the shrubs and bushes.

They then lit a fire with the dead wood which was scattered about plentifully, and prepared their own supper from the ribs of a deer which the Indian had shot during the course of the day's ride.

This, washed down with a pannikin of whisky and water, of which Catahaga refused to partake, formed an excellent meal, after which they lit their pipes, and, stretching on their blankets, sought rest and sleep.

Catahaga assured them that they were in perfect safety, and that in his opinion no human footstep had visited the cavern since he himself made it his resting-place before he married Minna Wyotti.

But little was said.

Silas was reflecting on the strange chain of circumstances which had brought him there, while the Indian's thoughts were far away with his pale-faced wife.

Oiny Macarne, after in vain endeavouring to sing himself into cheerfulness with various snatches of Irish melodies, gave it up for a bad job and joined in the general dullness and silence.

Presently they all slept, wearied by their long day's ride.

Even Oiny, who had volunteered to watch, lay with his back against a stone, and facing the entrance to the cave, while his hand grasped a "twig of illigant dimensions."

His loud snore rivalling the grunt of the four-legged tenants of his native cabin, told plainly how sound were his slumbers.

After awhile, Silas rose, feeling heated and fevered by the somewhat hot and confined atmosphere of the cavern, and walked to the mouth of the cave to secure, if possible, a more cool and agreeable seat.

He had not left the fire long ere he heard the sound of stealthy footsteps ascending the pathway towards the cave.

He listened attentively, then crept back to the fire for his rifle.

Armed with this he took his place behind a thick bush, prepared to fire on the first foe he should see.

The moon, which had hitherto been hidden by clouds, now shone out, and he was enabled to see an immense panther, or "painter," as the Yankee backwoodsmen prefer to call the animal, standing within a few yards of the mouth of the cave.

To take hasty aim and fire was the work of a moment, and drawing his knife prepared to resist the attack of the wounded animal.

The panther with a fierce growl sprang upon Silas, but scarcely had the claws touched his shoulder when a gleam of light was seen and the beast sunk dead.

Its skull had been cleft in two by the sharp, unerring tomahawk of Catahaga.

Oiny, awakened by the noise, came rushing up, brandishing his stick and declaring himself able and willing to fight all the Indians in America.

"Och, bedad, an' it's a foine pussy cat, entirely, ye've kilt, Misther Rye!" he exclaimed, when he saw the dead animal. "An' axin' parding, sir, would the baste be afther aitin' us if he weren't dead?"

"You'd be but a mouthful to him, Oiny," answered Silas, with a light laugh.

"An, it's a tough mouthful he'd have if he swalleyed me and me stick."

Silas, meanwhile, was intently watching the Indian chief, who, with his his keen knife was skinning the beast with a swift dexterity that would have done honour to a professional butcher or slaughterman.

The tail he presented to Silas, to wear in memory of his escape, while the skin, by general consent, was handed over to Oiny, whose blanket was none of the best.

"And it's a 'Ottentoter you'll be makin' ov me, Misther Silas," cried Oiny, as he wrapped the trophy round his shoulders grandly.

We presume he meant Hottentot, but preferred giving his own term.

This interruption over, they rolled the body of the " painter " over into the ravine, where he was soon devoured by hungry wolves.

Then the whole party returned once more to the fire, which they replenished, and then slept soundly till the rising sun began to gild the sky.

CHAPTER CCLII.

THE RAFT—BREAKERS AHEAD—HARWOLF AND DIEGO—MAN OVERBOARD—THE ISLAND OF PALM TREES.

THE fragile raft which bore the senseless forms of Diego, the Spaniard, and Daniel Harwolf, sped swiftly over the foaming sea, impelled by the boisterous wind that filled the tattered sail.

The storm howled furiously, but the enemies heard it not.

The briny waves dashed over their senseless forms, wetting them to the skin, but they felt them not.

Were they dead ?

Any one who had seen them would almost have answered in the affirmative, so still and death-like were their limbs.

Yet the pulse of each beat feebly, and the scanty blood performed its accustomed course through their veins.

The raft hurried on, through the dark and raging sea, till at length a low, long, faint streak of pale light on the horizon proclaimed the coming dawn.

The wind seemed in some measure to still itself, or rather to have partly exhausted its fury.

The light grew stronger and stronger, each minute revealing the frightful danger to which the two senseless pirates were exposed.

Right before them, at the distance of about a mile, lay a long low range of rocks, over which the surf beat with a loud roaring, booming noise.

Unless the sleepers awoke, both must be dashed to pieces on those rugged points.

A slight tremour ran through the frame of Daniel Harwolf.

He opened his bloodshot eyes, and gazed feebly round him.

Diego stirred not.

Harwolf, with difficulty, raised himself on his elbow and gazed with a look of malignant hate at the motionless Spaniard.

With a muttered curse on his own weakness, the ruffian fell back again, to think—to plan—to accomplish, if possible, his fell purpose.

He felt in his belt for weapons. None could he find.

Both knife and pistol had been washed off the raft by the waves. He and his enemy were alike unarmed.

But in his coat pocket the ruffian felt what made his heart rejoice.

It was a flask of brandy which he had placed in his pocket in the treasure cave.

Harwolf drew this from its resting-place, and took a hearty draught.

The potent spirit revived his courage and his energy. He again raised himself.

This time he managed to stagger to his feet, and approach the Spaniard.

He laid his hand on the collar of Diego, huskily muttering,

" I will pitch him into the sea; the sharks and the rocks may fight for the honor of mangling his cursed bones."

But the grasp on his throat had aroused the wounded Diego.

He saw at once that he was in a position of great danger.

He had no hope of mercy.

Gathering all his strength he endeavoured to rise and wrestle with Harwolf.

But his weakness overcame him, and, after one brief struggle, he fell back, completely in the power of the savage pirate captain.

" Spanish dog !" muttered Harwolf, " had I a knife I would open your veins and bleed you to death and gloat over your prolonged agony ; or had I a handspike I would beat your brains out and eat them. But the sea must be your death-bed, and, I hope, the sharks your physicians."

" Hound !" cried Diego, " I did not ask or expect mercy at your hands ; but, if I die, I shall be most terribly avenged."

" You threaten me ; then take your fate, my bold Don !"

With these words Harwolf rolled the helpless Spaniard to the edge of the raft.

" A speedy voyage to Davy Jones, my friend," cried he, exultingly.

There was a splash.

The body sank, then rose again and floated onwards on the heaving waves.

Having thus disposed of his foe Harwolf turned his whole attention to the difficulties and dangers before him.

He was now within a hundred yards of the belt of rocks which surrounded a little coral island.

In the midst of the reef he saw an opening through which, if he could steer his clumsy craft, he might safely approach the shore.

The raft, under his guidance, slowly drifted towards the opening through which the tide ran like a mill-race.

He had ceased to bestow any thought on the Spaniard, whom he thought was, doubtless, torn to pieces by the sharks.

The wind shifted slightly, enabling him to use his little sail for a moment with great advantage, then dropped suddenly.

Big drops of perspiration stood on Harwolf's brow as he found himself thus suddenly becalmed while his raft drifted onwards, slowly yet surely towards the breakers.

Again the breeze sprung up, a mere catspaw, however, dying away as suddenly as it came.

But it saved the life of Daniel Harwolf.

Saved him for more crimes and bloodshed.

Saved him for vengeance !

That slight breeze had carried the pirate captain and his raft right into the midst of the stream which bore, with such terrific force, through the opening in the belt of rocks.

Harwolf furled his light sail and unshipped the rude mast.

This he held in his hands to guide the raft, if possible, and keep its frail timbers from rough contact with the rocks.

And now the raft began to toss and shake and quiver in every timber as it dashed over the foaming waves swift as lightning.

Harwolf, with clenched teeth, waited the crisis of the struggle.

The raft whirled round and round, now threatening to dash on a rock, now seemingly swallowed up by the waves.

It rocked violently, turned almost over, whirled rapidly round, and then floated calmy on smooth water.

Harwolf heaved a deep sigh of relief, and thrusting the pole which had served him for a mast down into the shallow water, urged his raft onwards to the sandy beach.

In a few minutes it grated on the shingle, and, with a joyous cry, Daniel Harwolf sprung ashore.

He lay a moment on the sand exhausted by the excitement and weakness.

But another draught from his flask revived him, and rising to his feet he looked around him eagerly.

A thick clump of palm trees stood a few yards distant from the shore beyond which a series of cliffs raised their heads.

There Daniel Harwolf resolved to make his abiding place till the chances of life should again remove him from the island.

His first care was to haul the raft as high up on the shore as possible, and remove from it his treasure, which he buried half way between two trees, marking well the spot in his mind.

His next care was to collect and eat a hearty meal of shell-fish and birds eggs, then dragging the tattered old sail up into the palm grove he spread it under him, and quickly fell asleep.

Meanwhile, Diego the Spaniard, after being thrown into the sea by Harwolf, managed, by dint of great exertions, to keep afloat, and soon found the cool water brace his shattered nerves.

But he was still weak, and unable to make headway against the tide.

Besides, Harwolf thought him dying, and to encourage the idea he allowed himself to be carried along by the waves.

He soon was drawn into a current which bore him away from the pirate captain, whose raft was soon hidden from him by a projecting rock towards which Diego swam.

He climbed up this, and cautiously watching Harwolf saw him land.

Then, after a few minutes' rest, the cautious Spaniard dropped again into the sea, and striking out as well as he was able, made for the other side of the island.

But the limbs of the bold swimmer were weak, and he had much ado to keep clear of the breakers.

At length, however, his task was accomplished, his foot touched the sandy shore.

Diego the Spaniard stood erect on the island on which his deadly foe had taken refuge.

They were the only human beings on that deserted coral rock.

CHAPTER CCLIII.

MARRIED LIFE—CHARLES RYE AT HOME—A LETTER—AND A DEBATE.

CHARLES RYE sat in the pleasant little drawing room of his pleasant little home, with his beautiful and beloved Emily by his side.

All thoughts of the beautiful *danseuse* had fled from his mind; he was sincerely happy in the possession of his wife.

"Charley, dear," said she, looking up in his face, "how much better and stronger you are than you were some time ago."

"I am, and I have to thank three people for the recovery of my health."

"And who are those three?"

"Yourself, in the first place," said he, giving her a kiss.

"And the others?"

"My brother and Lord Hawksbury."

"His lordship has, indeed, been a good friend to you."

"He has; for by his advice was it that I married you."

"Ah! then it was a conspiracy after all."

"Certainly; his lordship and myself being the chief conspirators, and you the victim."

The victim blushed, and withal did not look very unhappy.

There was a long pause, during which the thoughts of the young couple were busy, though they neither uttered a word.

They were too much entranced in their own happiness to pay attention to the outer world around them.

Presently came a thundering postman's knock at the door, arousing the lovers from their day dreams.

"A letter!" cried Charley; "from whom, I wonder?"

"Quite an event," said his wife; "your correspondents are not very numerous."

The servant at this instant brought the letter in question.

It bore many post-marks, and was addressed in a handwriting which Charles well remembered.

It was from Silas.

Dated from the log hut of Nat Weatherfield in the wilds of Arkansas, and posted at some little out-of-the-way place on the river, at which the few steam-boats which navigated that water usually stopped to take in wood and any chance passenger who might happen to be wandering in that direction.

Charles opened the precious missive eagerly, and read it aloud to his wife.

It detailed many of those adventures which have been already related to our readers, and concluded by assuring them that the writer was on the track of the man he sought.

"Send this letter to Lord Hawksbury," said the writer, in conclusion, "and let him know that though Foxley is dead, I am on the track of the fiend, and shall not leave him till I finally bring him to justice and vengeance."

"So far, all is well," said Charles, as he finished reading the letter, "but, as I don't know exactly where Lord Hawksbury is, how am I to send this to him?"

"We must wait a few days, and then, perhaps, you will hear."

"I hope so, indeed; but it seems a long time to wait when, perhaps, such news is precious and important."

"Suppose you wrote to Mr. Mortimer? Perhaps he could tell you where Lord Hawksbury is."

"A good idea, my dear wife, and one which I will act upon at once."

Charles Rye drew up to the table and wrote a short note to Lord Hawksbury's private secretary, stating that he had important news and wished to know his lordship's address.

This was dispatched, and then the young couple once more wound their arms round each other, and forgot the past in their present happiness.

CHAPTER CCLIV.

DEATH—VOYAGE HOME—THE BOY PIRATE IN ENGLAND—THE GRAVE—CONCEALMENT.

THE Boy Pirate remained standing on the deck of Lord Hawksbury's yacht, holding in his arms the mortal remains of her whom he had so often yearned and longed to see, and had only seen to receive her last breath.

Kneeling down by her side, he passionately wept, and kissed the cold clay.

"Mother," he cried, "was it for this I longed to see you? Come back, oh, come back to bless your son! For surely a mother's blessing will do somewhat to remove the heavy load of guilt from my heart. Guilt! Aye 'twas the knowledge of my crimes that slew her, and I am my mother's murderer!"

"Christopher," said Lord Hawksbury, touching him on the shoulder.

"What want you? Can you restore the breath of life to her body? Can you cause the blood to flow again through her veins? She is dead, and I have now no joy in life. I will die!"

So saying, the impetuous youth rushed to the side of the vessel and was about to cast himself overboard, when again Lord Hawksbury's hand was laid on his arm.

"Remember your wife—remember Lilia," he said, gently.

The Boy Pirate threw himself on the deck, and again shed a flood of bitter tears.

"My wife? Aye, I must live for her sake; she is all I have now to live for."

The physician now interposed.

"You can do no good here; go below and sleep, if possible."

"And my mother?"

"She was my sister," said Lord Hawksbury, in solemn tones.

They assisted the Boy Pirate into the cabin, where he flung himself on a couch.

"Dearest Christopher," whispered Lilia, while the tears rolled down her lovely cheeks, "do not grieve so, we shall meet her again."

"You will, but shall I?"

"Doubtlessly."

"With all my black crimes? No. I was doomed to be parted from her both here and hereafter."

"There is forgiveness for all," whispered Lilia, raising his head on her bosom.

The Boy Pirate said no more, but in a few minutes was fast asleep on the warm breast, and encircled by the soft, white arms of his lonely wife.

The body of Lady Edgeforth was, under the doctor's directions, placed in the saloon, under the careful watch of two of Lord Hawksbury's oldest and most faithful servants.

The nobleman himself passed the night beside the remains of his only and long-lost sister.

But in his inmost mind he thought of her only son—his nephew, the Boy Pirate.

The night passed heavily and gloomy.

The sailors felt an unusual oppression of spirits, and were dull as seamen will be when their cargo consists of a corpse.

As Lilia nestled beside her husband and held his hot head to her breast, a tinge of joy shot through her heart as she listened to the low muttered words he murmured in his restless and troubled sleep.

She now hoped that his career as a pirate and outlaw was finished, and that in some quiet unknown corner she might be enabled to settle down with her loved husband in peace and quietness far away from the reach of Daniel Harwolf or any of his ruffian comrades.

She forgot that he was completely beyond the pale of the law, and that in any land he was liable to a swift and violent death, dignified by the name of justice.

But Lilia looked only at the bright side of the picture, and almost smiled through all her present misery as she thought of a happy future.

Day broke, and still the yacht lay at anchor, though the top-sails were lowered, and the flag floated at only half its usual elevation.

The Boy Pirate awoke, and like one in a dream, walked on deck.

"What means this?" he said, with a stupified air; "where am I?"

The sailor touched his hat, but could find no words with which to answer our hero.

Then the remembrance of all his sorrow flashed upon the mind of the young sailor, and with a low wailing cry, he rushed below to seek comfort and sympathy from his sweet wife.

After awhile Lord Hawksbury entered and sat down beside his nephew.

"Christopher!" he said, "is your anguish sufficiently calmed down to allow you to talk of her?"

"Yes."

"It was ever her wish to be buried near Frontemore; do you consent?"

"I do."

"And will you, dare you accompany me to England to see the last sad rites performed?"

"I must—I will."

The Boy Pirate spoke these words with an energy and determination which convinced Lord Hawksbury that his nephew's mind was fully settled.

"But reflect on the dangers."

"What are dangers to me?"

"You must avoid them for the sake of her who sits by your side."

"True. Pardon me, Lilia, my grief has made me selfish and reckless."

"I will go with you, dearest," whispered the fair young wife.

"After all," continued Lord Hawksbury, "you do not run much risk, if you keep quiet. Andrew Harwolf is in America, and his son no one knows where."

"Risk or no risk, I go to England to see my own mother's remains committed to the earth."

"Then I will at once give orders to proceed homewards," replied Lord Hawksbury.

The Boy Pirate languidly nodded acquiesence and then slowly walked away to the spot where his mother's corpse lay.

To pray and weep.

To ask forgiveness for his black crimes, which he still imagined to be the cause of his mother's death.

Meanwhile, the good yacht glided onwards, and ere long came to anchor off the coast of Sussex, not far from Frontemore.

And then the hallowed remains were landed from the boat, and, followed by at least four sincere mourners, conveyed to the little burial ground.

Strangely those words sounded on Christopher's ears, "I am the Resurrection and the Life." But when the mould came rattling down on the coffin, the sound seemed to wake him to madness.

Had he not been held by strong hands he would have thrown himself into the grave with her.

One last long look and then they hurried him away.

Far away to a place of concealment; for many curious eyes had watched the young sailor's behaviour at the funeral, and many busy tongues had made it their business to talk of him.

Some there were of the Frontemore rustics who professed to trace a resemblance between the young mourner and Kit Foundling.

So, to hide the young sailor from these busy-bodies until such time as he could be morally cleansed, Lord Hawksbury took the Boy Pirate and his wife to London, and in the course of three or four days had the satisfaction of seeing them installed as inmates of the house in which Charles Rye and his charming wife dwelt.

This was an arrangement which gave satisfaction to every one.

Lilia had a friend and companion in whose ear she might whisper all her hopes, joys and sorrows.

The society of Charles, quiet Charles, began to have its effect on the mind of the rover.

He, too, began to sigh for the peace and quietness of home.

Lord Hawksbury would have taken his wild young nephew into his own house, but hardly deemed it prudent to bring him beneath the notice of so many gaping, chattering servants.

He, however, sat down and wrote a long letter to Silas Rye, telling him that the lost heir was found, and the truant's wings, in some measure, clipped; and, at the same time, urging him to follow up the trail of Andrew Harwolf to the last, and, if possible, bring the scoundrel to justice.

This done, his lordship sat himself down to think and plan the best way to relieve his young nephew from the heavy charges which might be brought against him.

CHAPTER CCLV.

IN THE BAY OF BISCAY OH!—NOTHING TO DO—A PROPOSAL—SOCK AND BUSKIN—OTHELLO UNDER DIFFICULTIES—GRAND TRANSFORMATION SCENE—THE FALL OF THE CURTAIN.

OUR readers will recollect that when the Boy Pirate was so suddenly summoned to his mother's side he gave his crew no notice of his intended absence.

The day passed away and still the pirates heard no news of their chief.

The night passed, too, and the morning sun broke over one of the loveliest scenes of mountain wood and wave that e'er the eye of man beheld.

Still their chief was absent.

The bold outlaws began to grow alarmed, lest some disaster should have happened to their gallant young captain.

As they still bore the assumed characters of merchantmen which they had brought with them from the Baltic, they had no hesitation with regard to the course they intended to pursue.

They made every possible inquiry both among the municipal authorities and the people who hung about jetties and landing-places.

But no trace, till Gomez made his appearance with the news that their young leader had gone on board Lord Hawksbury's yacht to visit his dying mother.

Much sympathy was evinced by the rough tars, who dearly loved the Boy Pirate.

But where was the little toy ship gone?

Whither had the nobleman conveyed their chief?

They had not noticed the departure of the death ship in the early morning, or, if they had, knew not whither it had sailed.

The question now arose, who was to command the fleet during the Boy Pirate's absence.

This question was discussed by all the officers, and after a little debate, it was agreed that the supreme command should be entrusted to a council, consisting of Black Ralph, Dick Caffyn, and Brierly.

"Now, men," cried the first-named worthy, "you are under the immediate eye of the Lords of the Admiralty, so do your duty nobly."

"But, Massa Ralph," interposed Zampa, "we's got nuffin to do."

"Silence, ebony ignoramus; listen to, and obey the voice of your leader."

"Dat's all berry fine, but dis 'ere chile no like to be cussed dat fashion."

"Zamp, come here!" cried Ralph.

The negro approached.

"I like that scowl on your face, and will make a great man of you, if you don't make a fool of yourself."

"How?"

"You shall be a great warrior, and I—I will be your wife."

Zampa started back in amazement.

His big eyes, opened to their widest extent, showed a white circle the size of a tea-cup, while his mouth—well, we refrain from describing the enormous extent of that cavity, lest we should be accused of exaggeration.

"Gor a'mighty, surely him gone and went clean out ob him's mind."

"Yes, Zamp," cried Ralph, taking no notice of the negro's astonishment, "I will be your blushing bride."

"Do you think you could blush if you tried?" asked Sam Cassidy, who had been a silent spectator of the scene.

"Yes; I promise you I will blush like a girl if I don't make that sable Apollo play Othello in fine style to-morrow night."

"Play Othello?"

"Certainly. My soul yearns once more for the mystic enchantments of the stage. I long to tread the boards and feel myself a hero without trouble, and—and I am determined to convert the main deck of this good ship into a patent portable theatre that Richardson himself might have envied."

"And the actors?"

"Myself, Zampa, Caffyn, Brierly, with a host of the jolly tars for supers."

No serious objection was made by any one to the proposed frolic, and, accordingly, Black Ralph set a party of the men to work preparing the stage and painting scenery.

Zampa, seated on a gun, was still rolling his eyes and muttering disjointed sentences, regarding the hopeless madness of Black Ralph.

Ralph Talbot's tyrannical overbearing nature enabled him to fill the important post of stage manager with all the dignity and importance which that functionary usually assumes towards the humbler portion of his company.

He raved and swore at supers and scene-shifters with a vehemence and versatility that would have done credit to a gentleman with whom the author was once connected in a provincial theatre.

In fact so engrossed was he with the minors of the drama, that he quite forgot till about an hour before the performance was to commence that the principal characters had no rehearsal.

He had every reason to believe that, with the exception of himself, not one of them had ever read a line of Shakspeare's immortal drama.

Black Ralph was not to be daunted by such difficulties as those.

A play he would have.

He gave the signal for the performers to retire to their dressing-room to robe themselves.

Then another and greater difficulty presented itself—there were no dresses!

"Then I will make them," cried the indefatigable manager.

So he did.

Zampa was compelled to turn his trousers up as far above his knees as possible; a red guernsey encased his body, while a couple of wide purple sashes crossed over his broad breast completed the costume of the warlike Moor.

The Ethiopian grinned with delight, mingled with a slight tinge of alarm at this new phase in Ralph's madness.

Poor old Brierly suddenly found his head and face covered with tow, which was the only substitute for the grey hairs of Desdemona's father that Ralph could procure.

The bold outlaw himself being compelled to "double" to a most alarming extent, assumed a variety of strange disguises as occasion required.

When all the arrangements were complete, the curtain was drawn up, and Ralph summoned Dick Caffyn to accompany him as Roderigo.

"What am I to do?" asked Dick.

"Anything you like."

"But I don't know what to say."

Ralph scratched his head in perplexity, bit his lip, and then crying "I have it," dragged his unfortunate comrade forward.

A loud laugh greeted their appearance, which increased when Black Ralph, waving his hand for silence, said,

"Ladies and gentlemen, this is a very foolish young nobleman, named Roderigo, who has gone mad for love and money. He thinks about drowning himself, but I, his mentor as well as tempter, advise him better, and bid him put money in his purse."

Loud and uproarious applause followed this speech, and then Ralph, wishing to get through his troubles as quickly as possible, gave the signal.

The scene changed, and behold the warlike Moor before the Doge, on a charge of child-stealing.

Black Ralph again had to do all the talk, for Zampa knew no more of the Swan of Avon than he did of comic sections.

"Most potent, grave and reverend signors—I mean the audience—it is quite true that this black thief has stolen that old man's daughter."

"Dam' lie!" shouted Zampa. "Dis ere nigger nebber stoled nobody's chile."

"Silence, rascal!" shouted Ralph, amid the roars of the audience.

"It is quite true, also," he continued, "that he married her, though we did not see the announcement in the Morning Post."

Zampa again interrupted the scene.

Striding across to the spot where Brierly stood, Zampa looked his supposed father-in-law full in the face, and exclaimed,

"Look'ee 'ere, Massa Brierly; if you is gwine to swar' to ebbery big lie dat ere madman tells, dere'ull be a jolly row."

The fun was becoming fast and furious.

Black Ralph, having primed himself with a couple of glasses of grog, enjoyed the scene as much as did the audience, and determined to continue the play in the same burlesque style in which he had commenced.

When Othello's rage had in some measure calmed, the ex-tragedian proceeded,

"He is rude in his speech, as you have just seen, for when those arms of his had seven year pith, he hunted monkeys in his native forests, and was afterwards transferred to an American cotton plantation, which is one reason why he has no grace in speaking for himself. He is, you must know, accused of using witchcraft in winning my affections, but in a few moments I shall appear in the character of that young lady, and bear witness that the only witchcraft he had used was telling most terrible yarns."

So saying he darted away to change his dress, leaving the audience convulsed with laughter, and the performers in a state of open-mouthed astonishment, wondering what new prank would be played by their manager.

In a few moments that worthy returned robed in a long white sheet, tied round his waist, and an old bonnet, which had once belonged to the fair Lilia, perched on the top of his raven hair.

Never, in the whole course of his theatrical experience, had Ralph earned such prolonged and unanimous applause.

But his triumph was doomed to end.

A smile stole over Zampa's broad face, as, putting his finger to his nose, he stepped behind the fair Desdemona, while the lady was in the act of bowing to the audience, and placed his broad foot on the skirt of her dress.

The result may easily be imagined.

On attempting to move, he fell forward on his face, while a sudden movement of the vessel rolled him against the table at which the Doge and his councillors were seated.

Over went the whole majesty and nobility of Venice in a confused heap, while, to add to the confusion, some pieces of scenery which had not been properly set, came clattering down upon the human mass.

A by-stander, seeing the state of affairs, let down the curtain, and so the tragedy came to an untimely conclusion.

As soon as order was in some measure restored, the whole company turned their attention to Black Ralph, who, still dressed in white, was chasing the unfortunate Othello round the deck of the vessel.

Brierly and Caffyn managed, after some difficulty, to seize the enraged actor, and forced him to a seat.

"Bring here every nigger you can lay your hands on!" cried he. "By the Bard of Avon, whom they have reviled, I'll hang them like onions, fifty on a rope!"

The offender, however, had hidden, and was seen no more till the wrath of the irate tragedian had cooled down.

A brief half hour was sufficient to bring Black Ralph once more to his senses, and then Cassidy, who had joined the group, began to intercede for Zampa.

"You know," said he, "Zampa has not had your theatrical experience, and thinking you had commenced joking, imagined no harm in putting a climax to the fun."

"I should have put a climax to his existence, if I had caught him."

"Lucky you did not."

"Well, let the rascal come and ask pardon; perhaps I may forgive him."

Cassidy went below to seek for the offender, and speedily reappeared on deck bringing the culprit with him.

Loud roars of laughter, in which Black Ralph joined heartily, greeted the appearance of Othello.

And well they might laugh, for the Moor was no longer black.

In the struggle beneath the falling scenery, a pail of whitewash had accidentally been overturned in such a manner that the contents flowed over Zampa's face.

Black was turned to white, and as he now stood before Black Ralph, grinning with all his might, the effect was ludicrous.

"I axes pardon, Massa Ralph, if you is recovered from your mad fit."

"Zampa," cried Ralph, "you will never be an actor; but it is a wonder you have no more reverence for the drama."

CHAPTER CCLVI.

THE ISLE OF PALM TREES—HARWOLF AGAIN—THE LOST TREASURE—THE THIEF—SAIL HO!—THE COMBAT—THE GOOD SHIP "WHITE DUCK."

WHEN Daniel Harwolf laid himself down to sleep on the coral island he little thought that his mortal foe Diego had escaped the jaws of death, and therefore fancied himself in complete security.

Diego, on landing, was so exhausted by fatigue and loss of blood that he was compelled to seek refuge under a shady tree to rest and regain his strength.

MARY MACALLISTER.

He knew well that Harwolf was on the island, for, as narrated in a previous chapter, he had seen him land.

Big thoughts of vengeance swelled his heart.

His wrongs were ever constant in his mind; even when struggling for life in the boiling surf he only hoped for safety that he might again face his foe.

Weakness overcame him.

He fell into a deep and death-like sleep.

Meanwhile, Harwolf, after some hours of slumber, woke refreshed and strengthened.

He strolled lazily along the shore without any object save to pass away the time.

Suddenly a thought struck him.

How long could he live on that little island? What chances were there of a ship passing and releasing him from his prison?

Big drops of perspiration broke out on the villain's brow as he thought of these things. The prospect of starving seemed so awful.

No. 75.

He knew well enough that he had no fire-arms with which to supply himself with those sea-birds that floated in the air above and around him.

Shell-fish and eggs must be his sole provision, and how soon would that store be exhausted?

He tore his hair and cursed; he even rose to his feet with the intention of ending his miseries in the waves.

But then the love of life became strong within him, and he again sat down to wail and bemoan his misfortunes.

And so the day passed till night again spread her sable mantle over the earth, shrouding isle and ocean in darkness.

Harwolf retired to the spot where he had left the sail of his raft, and, wrapping himself up in it, laid himself down to sleep.

And he slept soundly.

Just as the darkness commenced, Diego woke and gazed round him.

It was some little time before he could sufficiently recollect the events of the last two days to account for his being in such a strange situation.

Presently memory returned; he recollected that his deadly foe was with him on the island, and, rising to his feet, he determined to go in search of the pirate captain.

He armed himself with a thick branch of the tree beneath whose shade he had slept, and with cautious steps began to traverse the beach in the dim, uncertain twilight.

The Spaniard carefully looked along the waterside for any traces, but, for a time, found none.

"Can I be dreaming?" he muttered. "Is the villain not here?"

He could not convince himself that it was a dream, and so continued his toilsome search.

At length he reached the spot where Harwolf landed, and his eyes glittered with renewed hopes of revenge as he saw the raft, which had so nearly proved fatal to both of them, hauled upon the beach.

But where was the pirate captain?

He saw traces of his feet in every direction, and followed the tracks along the shore for some distance.

But he had to return again.

The moon began to shed a faint light from her gilded crescent, and by the feeble ray the young Spaniard saw other tracks which he had not before noticed.

These tracks led up to the interior of the island.

He followed them.

They took them towards the palm grove, and his eyes again sparkled with renewed hope.

He clutched his stick with a firmer grasp and hurried onwards.

In a few moments he stood within the grove, and then the light which had hitherto guided him ceased.

Still he wandered on, till, at length, his foot struck against a heap of earth, which much reminded him of a newly-made grave.

He started back in astonishment.

"Can there," he muttered, "be other people on the island besides us two?"

He stirred the soil lightly with his stick.

It yielded easily.

Then the thought struck him that he would uncover this grave, and, if possible, unravel the mystery.

He worked swiftly yet quietly for above a quarter of an hour, when his stick, which he had used as a spade, struck against some hard substance.

Diego stooped down, and with his hands removed more of the earth.

In a few minutes more he had unearthed the caskets which Harwolf had carried on board his raft, and had, on landing, hidden in the earth.

The Spaniard resolved to appropriate the spoil, and, tying them together, slung the precious boxes over his shoulders.

Harwolf, meanwhile, lay sleeping within twenty yards of the spot, alike unconscious of the presence of his enemy and the robbery of his precious treasures.

But though Diego searched in every conceivable manner, he failed to find his foe, and it was only when morning's grey light began to tinge the sky that he desisted and returned to his own side of the island.

"Can it be possible that a ship has taken him off while I slept?" he cried. "But no, he would hardly leave the treasure for which he risked so much. He must be hidden in some cavern, and I will do the same, lest he should come upon me unawares."

So saying, Diego searched along the shore, till at length he found a crevice in the rock in which he would be completely secure from observation.

To this he clambered, and placing the treasure near his head, sat down to think.

"I will not again venture out till dusk. The fiend is probably well armed, and as I know not where he lurks, it would be dangerous."

He began to revolve in his subtle mind numerous plans for discovering the hiding-place of his foe, and was nearly lost in thought when a distant speck on the blue ocean attracted his attention.

It came nearer and nearer, till at length he was plainly able to discern the sails of a ship.

Would it pass by, or did the mariners intend to revisit the palm-tree island?

The ship drew nearer and nearer, and Diego clambered up to the highest part of the little island.

A sight met his eye which at once drew his attention from the approaching vessel.

He saw Daniel Harwolf coming towards him, waving in his hands the old sail of the raft.

Presently the pirate captain caught sight of the Spaniard.

Dropping the sail, he rushed towards him.

"Rascally thief!" cried Harwolf. "So it is you who have stolen my treasure? I thought you were in the belly of a shark by this time; but you shall not escape me this time!"

"I am not doomed to die by your hands, Englishman," answered Diego.

"We will see, my bold Spaniard."

So saying, Harwolf rushed forward upon his antagonist.

He, too, was armed with a bludgeon, with which he made a furious blow at Diego's head.

The Spaniard parried it, and in return laid his stick heavily on the shoulder of Captain Harwolf.

Smarting with rage more than pain, Harwolf struck out furiously, and Diego was compelled to exercise great caution in avoiding the heavy blows.

"Ha! I have you at last," cried Harwolf, as he struck the Spaniard on the head.

Diego reeled and staggered, but recovered and continued the contest.

But the recent loss of blood and want of food had unnerved his arm.

He managed, however, to hit his foe on the head, and was about to grapple with him, when another blow from Harwolf's cudgel felled him to the ground.

"You shall die this time," cried Harwolf, striking him a second and a third blow as he lay on the ground. "Oh, for a knife to drink the life blood from your heart!"

He now noticed that the ship had hauled up before the wind, and that a boat was rapidly approaching the island.

"I must be quick," he muttered, "or they will be here before I have finished my job. But curse him, where did he hide my treasure?"

With these words he stooped down and lifting the body of the still senseless Diego in his arms, walked towards the edge of the cliffs on which the combat had taken place.

"If he lives after reaching the bottom of this precipice he must be the devil himself."

So saying he dropped the body of the luckless Spaniard over the rocks into the sea beneath.

He saw his foe disappear beneath the waves and watched.

Diego did not rise again to the sight of Harwolf.

Yet the Spaniard was not dead, as will be seen in our narrative.

Having thus disposed, as he thought, of his victim, Harwolf hurried down to meet the boat.

They neared the island and hailed him.

"What cheer, mate? Are you all alone on that little bit of sand and rock?"

"Aye, aye," replied the pirate, "but, for Heaven's sake, take me off. I have been here a fortnight without any food but the winkles and shell-fish."

A few more strokes of the oars, and the keel of the boat grated on the sandy shore.

Two seamen and an officer sprang on the beach and began to question Harwolf.

"How came you here, my friend?" asked the officer, a good-looking, weather-beaten middle-aged sailor.

"I belonged to the ship 'Richard' of Bristol, and we were homeward bound with a cargo of palm oil, when a strange sail hove in sight and chased us. We crowded every stitch of canvas, but in vain. Our pursuer, who proved to be a pirate called the Red Raven, tumbled over our mainmast with a twenty-eight pound shot and boarded us. The pirates began to kill every one of the crew, and I myself received a wound which you may see here."

Harwolf opened his shirt and displayed the stab he had received from Diego's knife on the raft.

"Thinking I was dead, they left me and began to pillage the vessel, and during the confusion I managed to slip overboard. I sunk beneath the water and managed to rise under an old hen-coop, which they had thrown overboard. In a very short time the pirates had finished their work of plunder, and after setting fire to the ship, sailed away. I was the only one of the crew who escaped. Well, I managed to make a raft from some spars, and even procured a small sail, which I hoisted, and sailed away beneath the shadow of the smoke which arose from the burning ship. Two days and nights passed wearily, till I reached this island, where I have remained, living, as I said, on shell-fish, and occasionally a few birds' eggs. If you will land me at any port I shall be most grateful."

"We are bound for Liverpool, and as we have been some time out, shall not touch at any port on the way," replied the stranger, who was first mate of the ship.

Harwolf winced a little. He had not much inclination to revisit England; but then he feared that if he refused the chance he might not so easily find another opportunity.

So he said, slowly,

"I would rather you were bound for some American port; but never mind, if I once get to Liverpool I can easily find a ship for the United States."

"Well, come on board, then. We will give you ship room, and in return you shall lend us a helping hand during the voyage; but you are not an ordinary seaman?"

"No, I was supercargo on board the 'Richard;' but, nevertheless, I can put my hand to a rope as well as any man."

They all stepped into the boat, and pushed off from the shore.

"But what is the name of your ship?" asked Harwolf.

"The 'White Duck,' of Liverpool," replied the officer, whose name was Henry Elliott, the first mate of the ship in question.

Harwolf said little more; but pretending hunger and fatigue relapsed into silence, thinking of the past, planning for the future.

The boat neared the ship, and at length reached the side.

Harwolf was assisted to the deck, received a hearty meal, and was then placed in a hammock.

He slept, and three hours after, when he awoke, the isle of palm trees was no longer visible.

"Diego is dead; but my treasure—" he muttered. "Well, I will have it yet, if I tear the whole island to pieces."

So saying he came on deck while the good ship "White Duck" bounded merrily over the waves, and the sailors sung gladsome songs, for which Daniel Harwolf in his heart cursed them.

They were homeward bound; but what was home to him?

————

CHAPTER CCLVII.

AMERICA AGAIN—MILES AND HIS MASTER—DREAMS—THE CATARACT—MEN WHO ARE BORN TO BE HANGED CAN'T DROWN—A WALK ACROSS THE PRAIRIE.

WE left Andrew Harwolf, the father of the fiend whose adventures we have just described, sleeping in a cavern by the side of the big river after his escape from the Indian encampment.

Both he and Miles slept long and soundly, for both were fatigued.

The sun was high in the heavens when they awoke, and Miles, when he saw the daylight streaming in through the opening of the cavern, began to bustle about with amazing energy preparing to continue their journey.

"Come, zquire, I be darned if we mustn't make haste away out o' this ere blessed diggins, or them tarnation savages 'ull be arter us like winkin.'"

"No hurry, Miles," responded the ex-judge, "recollect their canoes are all afloat, and we are on the other side of the river."

"Sure, zo we be, measter; but, then, they rascals can zwim like vishes."

"You don't think they would swim across the river do you?"

"Shouldn't wonder much if they did, blame 'em; they can do a'most anything they likes."

"Well, we'll have some breakfast before we start, so bait the hooks again."

Miles did as desired, and in a few minutes landed a fine salmon trout.

Andrew Harwolf, meanwhile, had kindled a fire, and prepared a rude gridiron for the fish by crossing two iron ramrods over the glowing coals.

The fish was soon cooked, and they sat down to eat.

"I'm blest if this bean't a zight better nor England, zquire. Now, if I'd a done this at Vronte-more, I'd a been pulled up and got a month for it," ejaculated Miles, with his mouth full.

A shudder visibly crept over the strong frame of Andrew Harwolf as that name was mentioned.

"Miles," he said, in a husky voice, "if you wish me not to do you an injury, don't mention that word again."

"I vorgot, zquire, I wont zay it again."

"It will be well for you if you don't."

"I promise 'ee, Measter Harwolf, I won't zay nothin' about Vrontemore, nor Lord Edgeforth, nor any o' the durned lot."

Harwolf started to his feet with anger and fury depicted on his countenance.

His right hand clutched the knife which he had lately wielded with such fatal effect.

But the look of blank amazement on the face of Miles convinced him that what had been said was merely a slip of the tongue, and, with a deep sigh, he sat down again.

"Why, what's the matter, zquire?—blame it all, you didn't think as how I meant anything by what I zaid? It come out all o' a heap like, afore I could stop it."

"Miles, I have dreamed dreams to-night that have made me unsettled and nervous."

"Well ye know, measter, they do zay as how dreams allus goes by contraireys."

To this intended piece of comfort Harwolf returned no answer; but proceeded to relate the vision which had produced such an impression on his mind.

"I thought, Miles, I was standing in the streets of London, gazing at a female figure which seemed familiar to me, though I could not see the face nor call to mind who it was like. Then two men came in sight—one a young man, dressed as a sailor, the other a gentleman, several years more advanced in age. The sailor stopped and pointed towards me, saying, 'Who is that man?—I know him to be an enemy.' The other replied, 'That is the man who murdered your father, and was the cause of your mother's madness.' The young man jumped towards me, and caught me by the throat. Then I saw that it was the son of—of——"

"Lord ——," said Miles.

"Lord Edgeforth," cried Harwolf, with a sudden energy. "And his companion was her brother, Lord Hawksbury."

"An' what did 'em do to 'ee?" asked Miles, with a sceptical smile, which showed that he did not believe in dreams.

"The young sailor threw me on the ground, and held his hand so tightly on my throat that my senses left me, and then I awoke."

Here Andrew Harwolf impatiently moved his neck-cloth as though to tear the Boy Pirate's fingers away, and revealed to the gaze of the astonished Miles a deep crimson mark on his throat.

Miles started, changed colour, but recovered himself ere the eye of Harwolf could notice his unusual agitation.

"And be that all, zquire?" demanded he, in a less confident tone than before.

"All! Miles, in those few moments I suffered over again all the pangs of remorse and stings of conscience that I ever felt in my life. Those moments were to me an age of mental terror and torture."

Miles said nothing in reply, and Harwolf continued,

"But this is not all; for when I slept again I fancied I saw Silas Rye standing before me with a smile of demoniacal joy and triumph, curling his lip. He bore a rifle in his hand, and while I was utterly powerless and unable to move, I saw him pass that bullet—you know the one I mean—into the barrel of his piece. He raised the weapon, fired, and I fell helpless, motionless, though conscious of all that took place. Then another form appeared, which I recognised as the cursed detective I shot the other day. I heard Silas Rye say, 'There lies your foe,' and then the pale shade of the officer stooped down and lifted me up in his arms. I felt myself borne away through the air to the top of a mountain, and then the spirit spoke, 'The murder of my brother and myself must be avenged.' He pointed down, and I beheld a horrible pool of burning brimstone, in which strange figures were standing, like the place I used, when a boy, to read of——"

"Hell you means, measter."

"With a shrill shriek the ghost of the detective hurled me from the top of the mountain into the blazing lake. I felt the fierce heat, my flesh was scorched, though my clothes were not singed. I looked up to behold him, his brother, and Silas Rye standing above me mocking my agonies. I cried, I struggled to escape, and at length again awoke."

Miles looked serious, and for some time spoke not. At length he jumped to his feet crying,

"Measter, if we be goin' to get away from all they devil's we'd better look alive."

Harwolf took the hint, and soon after both were seated in the canoe.

On they glided over the silver bosom of the river, little dreaming of danger, till, at length, Miles, who was paddling, dropped his oar in the deep water.

It sunk, but rose again, beyond the reach of either of them.

Miles muttered a curse on his own carelessness as he saw the oar glide rapidly down the stream.

"What ails you, Miles?" said Harwolf, now speaking for the first time since they had left the cavern.

"Don't know, zquire," replied Miles, gloomily.

"Well, it can't be helped; we must go with the stream now."

And they went with the stream, little thinking whither the rapid tide was hurrying them so swiftly.

On they went, the boat increasing its speed each moment, till, at length, a dull continuous roar met their ears.

Harwolf turned deadly pale, and stood up in the bottom of the boat.

"What's the matter, zur?" asked Miles.

"We are nearing a waterfall; we must be dashed to pieces."

Miles turned as pale as his master, and his voice trembled as he murmured,

"Lord help us!"

With a fierce oath, Harwolf bade him at his peril use those words again.

No reply. And Harwolf continued to gaze ahead.

"You fool!" he cried. "Would you sooner

escape from the water to be hanged than cheat the gallows like a brave man?"

"If we be born to be hung, d'ye zee, zquire, we carn't very well be drownded."

With this piece of philosophy, Miles again relapsed into silence.

"Miles," said the master rascal, after a long pause, during which they were rapidly nearing the cataract, "it is just possible that we may escape both the rope and the river."

"I be most mortal glad to hear'ee zay zo, measter," replied Miles.

"You can swim?"

"I reckon I can, jest a leetle."

"Then prepare yourself for a cold bath."

So saying, Andrew Harwolf stripped off his outer garments, rolling them into a compact bundle.

In the midst of this bundle he placed his powder flask, the mouth of which he closely stopped with a roll of linen torn from his pocket handkerchief.

Miles imitated him in every respect.

He then slung his rifle over his back in such a manner that it should not inconvenience him in swimming, and to the strap he attached his bundle of wearing apparel.

Then both men stood up in the canoe, awaiting the moment that was either to save or destroy them.

The little boat danced lightly over the rushing stream, while the roar of the cataract became more distinct and awful.

"Measter Harwolf," said Miles, "if we jumps out here, we can't zwim across, because, d'ye see, the water is a zight too powerful for us."

This was a circumstance which had escaped Andrew Harwolf's attention.

He nodded his head, and replied,

"Then we must go down in the boat, and take our chance."

With set teeth, and blanched faces, they approached the yawning watery gulf.

The boat spun round and round with the eddying tide.

"We are lost!" muttered Harwolf.

A moment the light canoe quivered at the top of the cataract as if hesitating to take the fatal leap.

Then plunged down some twenty feet or more into the roaring, boiling, foaming abyss, and in a moment was out of sight.

The fishing-eagle, perched on a blasted tree, screamed loudly, and winged his rapid flight away from the scene.

Still the proud river thundered on, seeming unconscious in its terrific might that two puny human beings had braved its power.

The canoe rose again some thirty yards below the fall, *bottom upwards!*

Then a dark spot was seen amid the hissing foam and another quickly appeared by its side.

Andrew Harwolf and his partner in crime had escaped the terrors of the fall; it remained to be seen whether they could reach the shore.

Miles struggled bravely, and soon neared the bank of the river.

He was uninjured.

A cry for help fell upon his ear faintly through the roaring of the cataract, and, turning his head, he beheld Harwolf borne away by the swift water.

A moment of hesitation, a moment of doubt whether or not he should leave his associate to his fate, and Miles turned to swim to his rescue.

He soon reached Harwolf's side, and, bidding him hold fast to the rifle on his back, struck out once more for the shore.

He reached it, and with some difficulty dragged his now insensible master beyond the reach of the water.

"Well, I'm durned, if that ere wern't about as near a touch as ever I know'd," he muttered, as he chafed Harwolf's chest and throat with his hands.

A long drawn respiration and the sometime master of Frontemore opened his eyes in a vague, dreamy manner.

"Do'ee feel better now, measter?"

Harwolf nodded.

"Then git up if ye can, an' let's vind a better place than this 'ere to dry ourselves."

"I fear I can't walk," replied Harwolf. "I'm much bruised, and fancy some of my ribs are broken."

"Don't'ee zay zo; try an' walk if ye can."

Harwolf did try, and, after several attempts, managed to stand on his feet.

But he staggered, and would have fallen had not the strong arm of Miles supported him. A few steps onwards then he struggled then sank down again.

Miles was almost at his wit's end to think how he could convey his master to a place of security.

"Stop here a minit, zur, an' I'll go and look out vor a good campin' place," he cried.

And, ere Harwolf could object, he was out of sight amid the rocks and bushes.

Strange, yet not unaccountable terror took possession of Harwolf's mind (soul he had none more than the rock on which he lay) when he found himself alone.

What if Miles had deserted him, and left him there to die alone in the wilderness? Such a death would be ten times more painful and terrible than drowning or hanging.

To lie there day after day, bruised and powerless, without food or drink, while the vultures wheeled their heavy flight over his head impatient for the feast, to be alone, to die alone, not suddenly, but by prolonged starvation, seemed to be his horrible fate.

But at that moment Miles once more returned, and he again knew hope.

"Well, Miles?"

"If 'ee can walk twenty yards there's a stunnin' place wi' a lot o' dry leaves to make 'ee a zoft bed."

"I'll try."

Once more, with the assistance of Miles, he moved onwards, and after several delays reached the spot alluded to.

It was a nook in the shape of an angle, formed by two rocks meeting, and completely concealed by bushes. But within two bushes was a small plat of soft turf, on which Harwolf wearily flung himself.

Miles collected a quantity of wood, and uncovering his powder flask, by its aid soon made a bright fire, before which both men stretched themselves.

The warmth seemed to impart some degree of comfort to Harwolf's bruised frame, and after a short time he began to converse.

"Well, Miles," he said, "I begin to believe your maxim, that water has no power over those who are destined to adorn a rope."

"I don't think as how he be goin' to do one nor t'other, measter," replied Miles, with a grin. "Mister Zilas Rye must be durned clever if he tracks we down that ere place."

"I don't think he would venture."

"No; nor yet a one o' them blamed painted rascals as we cut away from."

Harwolf grimly smiled.

"But, Miles, see if the powder is dry. We shall want something to eat presently."

Miles unrolled his bundle of clothes, and uncovered his powder flask.

Not a drop of water had penetrated to it, and Harwolf's was in the same condition.

"Zummut to eat, measter? Well, I be durned if that ain't jest what I was a thinkin' about."

"Then go and try your luck."

Miles took up his rifle and departed, while Harwolf continued to lie uneasily before the fire.

He was mistaken in thinking his ribs were broken, but he had received severe blows on the chest, sides, and shoulders from being thrown against the rocks at the bottom of the cataract.

In his own mind he felt certain that it would be at least two days before he could travel, and restless anxiety took possession of him.

Presently the thought of Silas Rye crossed his mind again, and he felt uneasy lest by any means his indefatigable pursuer should learn in which direction he had gone.

The loss of the papers and deeds of Frontemore, too, vexed him sorely.

He knew full well that they had been taken by Catahaga's warriors, and doubted not but that the chief had handed them over to Silas.

"Curse him, why did I not put a bullet through him while I had the chance, without letting him see who did the deed? That infernal Irish marplot, too, had better take care how he crosses my path if I recover."

He reflected a moment.

"If I recover, that is the question! Shall I recover? If not, why, then, I have committed all these crimes for nothing; all seems lost at present save life, and that——. Curses on them all; my evil destiny is in the ascendant! That bullet, too, is gone. Whither? I would give anything to have it once more in my possession."

At that moment he heard the sound of a rifle near, and, raising himself on his elbow, he anxiously waited the return of Miles.

"Rye was a traitor, the gipsy a fool; Miles is worth a dozen of either."

The last named gentleman now made his appearance bearing in his hand a large rabbit he shot.

"Here he is, zquire; there bean't no geame laws here, so I popped 'un off."

"Then we'll very quickly eat him, Miles."

"Aye, zur, I be blamed hungry."

"So am not I; but I must eat to restore my strength, if possible."

Miles was too busily engaged in skinning his prize to answer, and, after a pause, Harwolf said,

"We must remain here all day to-morrow, Miles, unless I feel very much better than I do at present."

"Very well, zur, I reckon we'll git plenty o' grub about here."

So saying he spitted the animal on his ramrod and placed it in such a position that it would cook quickly and well.

Then, feeling in his pockets, he pulled forth a short pipe.

He had forgotten, though, that his tobacco was reduced to a pulp by immersion in the water.

"Well, I'm durned, if this 'ere ain't a purty go; ne'er a smoke to be had now."

"Place it close to the fire, fool; and it will soon dry."

Miles did so, and then sat watching his cookery with earnestness.

At length he concluded that it was fit to eat, and, taking it down from the fire, both men began to devour their food with a ravenous eagerness more resembling famished wolves than human beings.

Leaving them to their supper and their fire we will change the scene, and again present to our reader's notice some of the other characters who have found places in our narrative.

CHAPTER CCLVIII.

RUSSIAN LIFE—A VAPOUR BATH—SCRAPING THE BEAR AND FINDING THE TARTER—IN THE WOODS—SMUGGLERS.

IF our readers have not totally forgotten the existence of Edward Leighton and the Polish girl, Katinka, they will recollect that at the town of Tobolsk they parted from the Prince and Princess Aronzow.

As before stated, they had assumed the character of fur dealers, and in their outlandish vehicle they drove swiftly from settlement to settlement in a southernly direction, purchasing skins occasionally of hunters and exiles who had permission to trade.

Some six or seven days after leaving Tobolsk, and when they had arrived at a distance where they imagined their escape and flight would be unknown, they determined on halting at a little village for a few days to rest both themselves and their tired horse.

With some little difficulty they procured a lodging in the house of one of the richest and most important peasants of the place.

They had not much choice in the matter, for, with the exception of the priest or pope, as the ministers of the Greek church are called, the entire population of the village was composed of peasant serfs, subject to a noble who lived at a distance, and graciously allowed them to cultivate the soil; in return for which condescension, he sent, twice each year, a steward or a collector, who usually wrung from them the whole of their hardly won earnings, and a tithe of their cattle and corn, under the title of tribute for his excellency.

The worthy serf, with whom Edward Leighton and his supposed sister took up their abode, being the cultivator of a larger tract of land than the others, possessed a more extensive house than his fellow villagers.

His name was Alexis Linsky, a big, jovial, but withal meek-looking man, with a large tawny beard descending to his breast.

His residence was constructed of pine logs, fastened together with wooden pegs instead of iron nails, and covered with plaster on the inside.

It consisted of three rooms, a rather unusual

number for the habitation of a Russian serf, who is generally content with one.

Of these rooms the largest was used as a general sitting-room, and contained the huge stove which gave warmth to the whole house.

A second and smaller room was used for a sleeping apartment by the serf and his wife, while the third was a kind of store-room for provisions and various agricultural implements.

On taking up their abode there, Edward Leighton arranged that this store-room should be fitted up as a sleeping apartment for Katinka, not caring that she should share the other room with good Alexis and his *nine* children, who all slept in the same apartment, for warmth probably, or else for mutual protection against the fleas, which swarm in every Russian village, and are both large and ferocious.

Edward Leighton himself preferred sleeping in the sitting-room, judging that the immense army of the pigmy enemy would be most likely to encamp where provisions were most plentiful.

These domestic arrangements were soon completed, and the amateur trader sallied forth among the rustics in search of merchandise.

As he could not speak Russian with anything like perfection he pretended to be a German, and having some papers with the custom house stamp upon them, gravely showed the bills of lading in lieu of passport.

The couple of ignorant Cossacks, to whom was entrusted the task of keeping order in the village, knew not the difference, and reverently pressed the spread eagle to their dirty lips in token of respect and submission to their father and master, the Emperor.

Withal they were bound in serfdom the peasants seemed happy and contented, though there was an air of listless indolence and carelessness in their every action.

Their food hardly suited the dainty civilized stomach of Leighton, who could not see much to admire in the cabbage soup and black rye bread, which formed the staple of their diet.

On returning to the hut of Alexis Linsky, the evening after his arrival in the village, Edward Leighton was much astonished to find the door fastened on the inside.

It, however, was opened hastily, and he was dragged in to find himself in the midst of a dense vapour.

The cause of this was soon made evident. A huge slab, covered with a blanket, had been placed on the top of the stove, and on this slab reclined the worthy host in a state of semi-nudity, while his good wife gently poured over him a trickling stream of water, which, descending on the heated slab, ascended again in dense clouds of steam.

The heat was almost unbearable (except to a Russian peasant), and Leighton was glad to escape to Katinka's room, where the atmosphere was a trifle cooler, leaving the worthy wife to scrub her husband's hide at her leisure.

The vapour bath is used in various other ways, but the Russian serf always manages to get one of some kind or other, and esteems it a great luxury.

The Polish girl was seated near the little window busily engaged with the needle.

"Well, Katinka," cried he, "and in what direction are we to travel next?"

"Wherever monsieur pleases," said she, gravely.

"Had I my will I would go back to Poland, and learn what has happened during our absence; but that journey would be attended with much danger and difficulty."

Tears come sparkling in the corners of Katinka's eyes when her friend and companion spoke of Poland.

"Ah! unhappy land!" she cried. "Will thy children ever be free?"

"Let us hope so," replied Leighton, "for slavery is fast disappearing from the face of the earth; and even the Czar, stern autocrat though he be, cannot always disobey the voice of the free and civilized world."

Let us hope that it may be so, and that Poland, once the pride of Europe, and the bulwark of civilised Christianity, may again take her place among the nations, and once more fulfil a glorious destiny. Her troubles and misfortunes have been great, and have lasted many years. May liberty, peace, and prosperity be showered down plentifully upon her sons and daughters, so that they may forget, in some measure, the misery and unhappiness of the past.

Is there a man with tongue unfettered, and who boasts himself free, that can for a moment uphold or defend the unparalleled audacity of the foreign powers, who, taking advantage of trivial internal dissensions in a neigbouring state, divided and reduced to a nonentity in the map of Europe one of the finest nations and bravest people that the eastern half of the globe could boast of?

But the day may come—let us hope at no great distance of time—when *might* shall no longer give a *right* to injustice, and when man, combining with his fellow man, shall form—not only in Poland, but over all the earth—a free sovereign and independent nation, over which neither king nor czar shall have any power.

Edward Leighton sat quietly regarding the form of the girl before him.

She seemed in his eye a type of her nation; physically weak, yet mentally strong and hopeful; crushed by adversity, yet springing up again from her former ruin, even as the fabled bird of Arabia rises from its own ashes.

"Katinka," said he, "you love your unfortunate land?"

"Much, monsieur; more than I can find words to tell. It was my home, and the home of my father."

"You shall some day revisit your home; perhaps not long hence."

"Oh, monsieur, each day will seem an age till I breathe my native air once more."

"I can well understand your feelings, Katinka, but it would, as I have said, be unsafe at present; we must wait."

Katinka made no reply, but the tears again added to the lustre of her bright eye.

After a long silence, however, she looked up and asked,

"How long will you stay in this village, monsieur?"

"Two days longer, and then we follow our journey again. But come, our worthy host has, I fancy by this time, finished boiling himself; we will adjourn to the next room and find a supper if we can."

They entered the common room and found their worthy host attired from head to foot in clean garments, it being his birth-day.

In general the Russian peasantry dispense with the ceremony of putting on clean clothing, except on three occasions—Easter, the fête day of their patron saint, and their birth-day.

On such occasions the moujik performs as a religious and social duty, what the London mechanic does at least once a week for his own comfort and satisfaction.

The worthy Alexis, with a profusion of bows, apologised for the inconvenience he had given his visitors, and then ordered the table to be spread.

The viands consisted of the eternal cabbage soup for the first course, after which came a dish of mutton swimming in its own tallow, and adorned with hard boiled eggs.

This was looked upon as the very acme of luxury, for your Russian seldom eats meat at any time *save when he changes his linen.*

A huge cake of flour, figs, and honey concluded the repast, after which a large supply of a coarse, fiery brandy was placed on the table, and the whole family, with the utmost complacency, began to intoxicate themselves with the stimulant.

In the course of half an hour they were all too far gone to notice the absence of the two guests.

Katinka had retired to her room to sleep, and dream of Poland, while Edward Leighton sauntered forth into the open air to breathe a cooler atmosphere than could be found within the walls of the peasant's house.

With his hands in his pockets, he sauntered round the house till he arrived at a kind of hovel which was used as a pig-stye, and which, at that moment, contained two fine fat young grunters.

There he paused a moment to rub his eyes, for, unless he was mistaken, he saw a man, probably a robber, climbing over the railings which formed one side of the stye.

Determined to save, if possible, his host's property, he seized a large hoe which lay at his feet, and struck the robber a heavy blow on the head.

The *robber* turned round with a deep growl, and discovered itself to be a brown bear.

With determined war in his looks and voice, he advanced towards Leighton, who at once dropped the hoe and drew a broad strong knife he had purchased at Tobolsk.

Another moment the bear was upon him; the huge paws were stretched forth for an embrace, which, in most cases, proves fatal.

Leighton lacked not courage, but his heart almost failed him. He struck his weapon at the brute's heart, and in a moment was in the bear's hug. The warm breath of the animal fell on his cheek, and he gave himself up for lost, though he repeated his fierce stabs.

Then, in a moment, there was a crushing sound; the brute's gripe relaxed, and it fell to the ground dead.

Its skull had been cloven in two by the broad axe of the Russian serf.

When he could recover breath, Leighton turned to thank his preserver, but Alexis was no longer visible: in another moment, however, his voice was heard within the stye, rejoicing over the escape of his darling porkers.

Leighton could hardly keep his countenance when the Russian reappeared, so profuse were his thanks for the stranger's bravery in defending his darlings.

Edward now began to inquire how it was that the peasant had arrived so luckily when his aid was most required.

Katinka, it was, who had heard the growl of the brute and given the alarm, which caused Alexis at once to sally forth in quest of the spoiler.

The Russian at once called for lights, and soon, amid the glare of half-a-dozen pine torches, tore the skin from the carcase of the disappointed bruin.

Some of the prime parts were removed to the hut, and the remainder left for the wolves.

They then all retired within the house, and shortly afterwards Morpheus held the whole company in his capacious elastic arms.

The second day after this awkward adventure of Leighton's, he and Katinka once more harnessed their horse to the sledge, and travelled towards the south.

For some little time there was a road, or rather beaten track, but after awhile this ceased, and the travellers were left to their own knowledge of the country to pursue their journey.

Their prospects were certainly rather gloomy, for it was long past noon, and, as yet, there was no sign of any human habitation.

A dull sombre forest of pines was before them, and towards it they urged their horse.

They had scarcely entered its shadows when they heard the noise of other horses approaching, and in a few minutes a company of ten sledges, all filled with armed men, made their appearance.

"Halt!" cried they to our run-aways. "Who and what are you?"

"We are fir merchants travelling to collect goods," replied Leighton.

By this time the strangers were close to them, and one of them, who appeared to be the leader, leaping from the sledge, approached them.

"You are not Russian," he said.

"No," replied Leighton, "I am German."

The man gave a light laugh, and said, in a low whisper,

"You look very much more like two of the escaped convicts, whose descriptions are in every large town."

Leighton's hand was on his knife, but the stranger continued,

"Fear nothing, we are smugglers, and have as much reason to avoid the Cossacks as you have. If they take us our fate will be worse than yours."

THE CONFLICT ON THE PRAIRIE.

CHAPTER CCLIX.

CHRISTOPHER AND LILIA—STORMS AND SUN-
SHINE—AN EXCURSION AND ITS RESULTS—
THE GIPSY TENT—PAST AND FUTURE.

IN the quiet home of Charles Rye, the Boy Pirate
gradually recovered from the deep and distressing
grief into which he had been thrown by the lamented
death of his parent.

His fair and amiable wife, too, by her tender love
and kindness, did much to banish the black shadow of
death from his heart.

But when grief departed there again arose
within his bosom the restless longing for change and
excitement which had characterized every action of
his life.

He had established a correspondence with his

No. 76.

comrades, who still remained off the coast of Spain,
and in his own mind had resolved ere long to rejoin
them.

The notion of resuming their old sea-faring life
was distasteful to Lilia, who did all in her power to
dissuade her husband from his purpose.

"Dearest Christopher," she said, one fine morning,
winding her arms round his neck as she spoke, "I
wish you would give up all your wild ideas, and try to
wean yourself from all those romantic notions which
have wrapped themselves around your mind."

"It is not romance, dearest Lilia," replied he,
kissing her fair brow; "it is stern necessity which
urges me on. My fate cannot be altered. I am an
outlaw, a worse than a felon, and my fate—if I remain here—a felon's death!"

"Nay, speak not so despondingly, my love; you

know Lord Hawksbury has both money and influence; he will use them freely in your behalf."

"With what result? It is useless."

"It may result in the moderation of your punishment."

The Boy Pirate laughed.

"Moderation! ha! ha! that means, I suppose, some ten years' penal servitude, after which the pirate may emerge from the hulks or the quarries, and assume the title of Lord Edgeforth! No, Lilia, I am too wild a raven to be ever chained or caged."

"But you might receive a free pardon."

"If so, I must retire into obscurity. Men would not take the pirate's hand in friendship even though he were a lord."

"Yes, good, noble-minded men would, forgetting your faults when they heard the long, black list of crimes that compelled you to be what you are."

"But, Lilia, you forget my bold comrades. Am I to desert, abandon them, leave them to be hanged or imprisoned at the mercy of stony-hearted judges?"

"If the *chief* is pardoned, who will care to injure or punish his followers?"

"You are hopeful, Lilia, but I fear your hopes are based on a very weak foundation."

"I am hopeful, indeed; wherefore should I be otherwise? But my chief hope is to lead you on to a brighter and better destiny than that of a rover."

The Boy Pirate was silent.

The hand which had held that of Lilia's seemed to relax its grasp.

The fair wife looked up in his face with an inquiring, loving glance.

"What ails you, dearest?" she said.

"You are weary of being the pirate's bride. Well, go, leave me to my fate."

Lilia threw her arms round his neck, and bursting into a flood of passionate tears, cried,

"Christopher, dearest, you wrong me. When did I ever repine or regret my union with you? But I would that my own brave husband were anything but a pirate."

She hid her face on his bosom, and sobbed violently.

The Boy Pirate saw in a moment that he had wronged her gentle heart, and repented his harshness.

"Come, Lilia," said he, "weep not, my love; I meant not what I said, and had I known the pain those words would cause they should never have passed my lips."

Reassured by these words the fair wife dried her tears, and sunshine soon replaced the shower.

"But, Lilia, dearest, why should we sit in melancholy mood within the walls of a house while the sun shines, and there are green fields and singing birds within a short distance?"

"Oh, yes; let us have a day's trip into the country, dearest," replied she.

"Agreed. Go, prepare yourself."

Lilia left the room, and in a few minutes returned arrayed for the journey.

Christopher again kissed his fair bride, and arm-in-arm they sallied forth.

Towards London Bridge they took their way, and an hour after leaving home were wandering beneath the noble trees which beautify the royal park at Greenwich.

Peace was totally restored, and they were both once more happy.

The delicious verdure and freshness of the scene sent a thrill of delight and enjoyment through their hearts.

But Lilia observed that her husband's eye was often turned towards the broad river, on whose bosom floated a forest of masts.

Was it possible? Did he expect to see the Red Raven on that shining stream?"

She dismissed the thought from her mind as idle and unworthy of her.

At length they had reached the remotest part of the park, and passed through the gates on to the wild common of Blackheath, the Boy Pirate laughingly proposing that Lilia should mount one of the shaggy donkeys that may always be seen there.

She, however, shook her head, and they wandered on till they reached a spot where a tent, a rude cart, and two rough horses marked the temporary home of one of those gipsy families which always hang on the outskirts of civilization.

Two brown-faced women, a dark, evil-looking man, and several very ragged children were reposing on the turf; but all started up when a dog, as savage-looking as his owner, gave notice of the approach of our hero and his bride.

The man quieted the surly animal, and again threw himself on his back to enjoy the pleasures of indolence and a short pipe.

The women and children, however, had a keen eye to business, and while the juveniles threw summersaults for halfpence the sybil of the family accosted our hero with the familiar question of,

"Shall I tell your fortune, my noble gentleman and lady?"

Christopher looked at Lilia, and she returned the look with an arch smile.

"I know my fortune well," he said.

"Then you will be able to tell whether I speak the truth," replied the gipsy.

Christopher held out the palm of his hand, which the woman examined closely.

She then looked earnestly into the depths of his dark eyes for some moments, and at last spoke.

"Before I reveal the future, I will show you that I am acquainted with the past.

"You are the son of a nobleman, who, in your infancy, met with a cruel and violent death. Am I not right?"

"You are, indeed," replied Christopher, in amazement. "But continue."

A curl of satirical triumph passed over the gipsy woman's lips as she proceeded,

"Adverse fate forced you at an early age to brave the dangers of the deep; cruelty and oppression drove you to madness, and you—— Shall I continue?"

"It is needless," replied Christopher, in a husky voice. "Now for the future."

"Dark clouds still hover o'er your destiny; there are yet dangers to be encountered. Amid those clouds the evil star which has followed you from your birth glows with a baleful light. Beware of your old enemy, who is nearer you than you think. But fear not; light breaks through the darkness, evil is overcome, and you will yet be victorious over all your foes."

She ceased, and dropped the hand, which, while speaking, she had continued to hold in her own.

The Boy Pirate placed two guineas in her hand, saying as he did so,

"You should have twenty if you would tell me whence you derived your information."

"From the stars and the lines in your palm," replied she, with a strange smile.

Christopher shook his head incredulously.

"But fear not, LORD EDGEFORTH," she continued; "we poor gipsies never betray those who harm us not. Our secrets are never revealed to strangers."

So saying, she returned to the tent, and seated herself in silence on the ground.

Christopher and his fair Lilia walked on in an equally solemn manner.

After a long pause the Boy Pirate, turning to his wife, said, with a kiss,

"You see, dearest, I was right; dangers do threaten me here. We must again make ourselves a home on the ocean."

"What dangers do you mean, dear Christopher?

Surely you do not place any faith in the prophecies of that gipsy woman?"

"She knows my secret; that in itself is a great danger."

Lilia's cheek blanched a little, but she quickly forced a smile, saying,

"But you know, dearest, you are to escape all dangers, and be victorious over all your enemies."

"I must escape the danger first, and I can only see one way of doing that."

Poor Lilia said no more; everything seemed to cross her plans of happiness.

The Boy Pirate was equally thoughtful, and after a slight refreshment they returned home.

CHAPTER CCLX.

THE "WHITE DUCK" AGAIN—DISCUSSIONS IN THE FORECASTLE—THE VOYAGE—LAND HO!— LIVERPOOL — FURTHER ADVENTURES OF DANIEL HARWOLF—A STRUGGLE FOR LIFE.

DANIEL HARWOLF worked his passage on board the "White Duck," though offered all the privileges of an officer.

His reason, he asserted, was that he had lost his everything in the vessel which had been taken by the pirates, and wished to earn money so that he might not be totally destitute on landing at Liverpool.

So he was allowed to have his way, and soon made himself as unpopular with the bold seamen who navigated the "White Duck" as ever he had been with his own outlaw crew.

They hated him, one and all, for he often forgot the fact that he was now an ordinary seaman, and bullied his comrades as though he were still on the quarter-deck of his own ship.

"If that 'ere cove sails with us next trip I'm blowed if I ships in the 'White Duck' again," said one of the jolly tars, with a frown.

"Nor I," said a second.

"I'd sooner sail with the Flying Dutchman than with such a fellow," cried a third.

"I don't believe his yarn about the pirates," said the first speaker, in a low whisper; "he looks a precious sight more like one hisself than ere a man I clapped my eyes on lately."

"You're right, Bill," responded No. 2.

"Didn't you see blood on his hands when he come aboard? Now, I should jest like to know, if he'd a been on that ere island so many days as he said, wouldn't he have washed his mawleys once in the while?"

The sailors nodded in a mysteriously knowing manner, and smoked their pipes in silence.

From that time Daniel Harwolf was looked upon with distrust and suspicion by the whole crew, who avoided him as much as possible.

The captain, who liked to see peace and harmony among his men, sent for Harwolf to his cabin and gave him some useful advice on the importance of being friendly and sociable with his chosen comrades.

"For," said the worthy skipper, "it is by your own choice that you are with them, therefore you should not assume any airs of superiority."

Harwolf hated advice of all kinds, more especially such as was calculated to do him good.

So he left the cabin, cursing and muttering imprecations on both captain, ship, and crew.

"If I ever sail beneath the black banner again look out for yourselves. The 'White Duck' shall share the fate that has befallen many a better craft."

After this, things went on a trifle more smoothly, and the captain calculated that, in about another week, he would be safe in harbour.

And so it was. The good ship escaped from all the dangers of the mighty Atlantic and was soon lying snugly in the Mersey.

The men were paid their wages, and so was Daniel Harwolf, who, with secret fear in his guilty heart, once more set foot on English soil.

His first care was to disguise himself, and, for this purpose, he purchased a dress such as is usually worn by mechanics and the labouring classes.

This done, he procured a lodging in a low part of the great town, and looked about for means of learning what was doing at Frontemore, ere he again sought a ship.

Daniel Harwolf now, for the first time in his life, knew what it was to be short of money.

"Curse it!" he muttered. "Without coin I can't stir. Yet how easy it would be to hoist the black flag again if I only had the contents of one of those boxes that cursed Diego robbed me of on the island."

He, however, had several valuable articles of jewellery about him, the sale of which enabled him to live in a kind of rude state of comfort.

Ever restless and uneasy while alone, he soon began to visit the low dens of vice and iniquity that disgrace Liverpool as all other large towns.

One of his favourite haunts was a kind of vault or cellar near the water-side, which was frequented by the lowest and most abandoned of both sexes.

The liquor was abominable, the company hideous, but Harwolf fancied himself more secure from observation there than in the more public haunts to which he might have found his way.

Guilt ever loves darkness and concealment, and so in this den, amid filthy outcasts, the son of the late master of Frontemore chose to spend his evenings.

One night, on repairing to this boozing-ken as usual, Harwolf noticed a man seated in one corner whom he had not seen in the house before.

"A stranger," muttered Harwolf. "Who can he be? I must keep my eye open."

With this sage reflection, he sat himself down in his accustomed place and called for brandy and a pipe.

The vile compound, which they dignified by the name of cognac, was brought, and with a self-satisfied air Daniel Harwolf began to sip the fiery beverage, still furtively glancing at the unknown in the corner.

"Who is that man?" he asked of the individual who sat next to him.

"No one knows," was the reply.

"How long has he been here?"

"About two hours. He came in, looked very carefully all round, and then sat down in that corner. He's been watching the door ever since he entered."

"Detective!" muttered Harwolf.

His companion, an absconding merchant's clerk, trembled and turned pale, as he nodded in assent to the suggestion.

"He can't be after me," thought Harwolf, "or he would have hoisted his colours by this time. I'll watch his little game."

The stranger still continued motionless and silent, never touching the beer which he had ordered on his first arrival.

Harwolf drank glass after glass, for he was excited.

His companion, the clerk, too, felt nervous to a certain extent.

A man cannot continue for a long time to drink spirits, especially bad spirits, without showing in his voice and manner the effects of his potations.

So it was with Daniel Harwolf.

His voice began to grow husky, and he talked in a more loud and rapid manner than when he entered the cellar.

The drunken observations he made use of, and attempts at wit, were principally directed against the unknown, who, for a time, took no notice whatever of the indirect insults of the pirate.

"It's the general custom for new comers to pay their footing," said Harwolf, looking towards the quiet stranger.

The unknown made no answer; but his keen, grey eyes were fixed for a moment full on the speaker's face.

"Some of you wake up the gentleman," he continued; "perhaps he's come to the wrong house."

"Mind your own business," was the reply, in stern, commanding tones, which for a moment cowed even the drunken boldness of Harwolf.

But having, as it were, thrown down the gauntlet the ruffian seemed to consider himself bound to continue the game he had commenced.

"Don't you know how—hic—to speak to a—hic—gentleman? Where's your manners—hic?"

"If you don't leave me alone," replied the stranger, "I shall be under the disagreeable necessity of making you."

"Make me!" cried Harwolf; "you make me? If you'll come out into the middle of the room I'll jump down your throat and turn you inside out, you fat-headed son of a swine!"

The stranger accepted the challenge, and stalked into the middle of the cellar, while Harwolf, with fury depicted on his countenance, advanced towards him.

Assuring himself of an easy victory, the drunken pirate aimed a heavy blow full at his antagonist's face; but he had made a slight mistake.

The stranger was in every respect a foeman worthy of a more respectable enemy.

Right and left he delivered his fists with crushing effects on Harwolf's face, sending him heavily to the floor.

Gazing a moment on the prostrate drunkard, the unknown turned, and was about to resume his seat when a cry made him half turn round; but ere he could have time to defend himself Harwolf's left arm was thrown round his neck, while the other brandished a broad shining knife.

"Rascal!" cried the stranger, catching the hand that held the knife in his own, "would you stab me?"

"Aye, with the greatest of pleasure," hissed the hoarse voice of the would-be assassin.

And he struggled violently to release his right arm, while he compressed the other more firmly round the stranger's neck.

But though taken at a disadvantage the man wrestled valiantly, though the tight pressure on his throat almost strangled him. Harwolf exerted all his strength to hurl his adversary to the ground.

The stranger's struggles grew weaker and weaker, till at length, with a sudden jerk, the pirate released the hand which held the knife, and with a curse struck it heavily between the stranger's ribs.

He then rushed from the room.

As he hurried up the stairs the shrill sound of a whistle fell upon his ear, and in a moment two other strangers made their appearance at the doorway.

Harwolf glided into a recess behind a door till they had descended into the cellar, then darted with lightning speed into the street, and rushed wildly away.

The quarrel, and the events of the last few minutes, had in some measure sobered him.

He knew full well that the good town of Liverpool would now be unsafe for him.

So hurrying to his lodgings, he hastily changed his dress, stuck a pair of false moustachoes on his upper lip, and made the best of his way to the railway station.

On arriving there he had not the least idea whither he should go, but the voice of an elderly gentleman asking for a second class ticket for London decided him.

"I shall be as safe there as anywhere, provided that confounded Jewess doesn't happen to see me."

So he too took a second-class ticket for London, and entering the same carriage with the old gentleman was soon rapidly borne away by the midnight express.

"I shall be nearer Frontemore, too," he thought, "and with a little additional disguise, might even venture down there myself, if I can't find a trusty agent."

So saying, he drew a pipe from his pocket, filled and lit it, and was soon lost in a train of gloomy thoughts.

CHAPTER CCLXI.

THE VULTURES—WARDLAW AND RAMSEY—PLANS—A CRUISE—"WHEN GREEK FIGHTS GREEK"—CAPTURE OF THE CHINESE JUNK.

AFTER Daniel Harwolf, and Johnson his deliverer, had escaped from the pirate vessel, as narrated in No. 70 of this tale, our readers will recollect the ship was consigned by the crew to the command of Wardlaw, the former lieutenant, who appointed Ramsey his second in command, and established a sort of rude discipline among the disorderly and somewhat mutinous seamen.

With one accord they demanded to sail for a new cruising ground, where they were comparatively unheard of, and where there was a chance of capturing rich prizes.

Wardlaw very readily consented to this, and proposed the Indian Archipelago and Chinese Sea, as a likely place to pick up a few rich merchantmen.

The proposition was received with shouts of approval, after which the men returned to their duty in a more orderly manner than they had done for many a day past.

"We must govern with a firm hand, Ramsey," said the new captain, as he stood on the quarterdeck, watching the helmsman.

"We must indeed; but with strictness justice must be mingled to a large degree."

"It is a difficult task."

"It is indeed," replied Ramsey, with a sigh; "and one that I should be most happy to have nothing to do, if such a course were at all possible."

"You do but speak my own ideas, Ramsey; I am as tired of this life as you are."

"Then why not leave it?"

"Because, my dear Ramsey, it is impossible to do so at present. But the time may come."

Both men heaved a weary sigh.

"I wonder," said Ramsey, "what has become of our late captain?"

"Gone to the sharks probably."

"Surely they would not devour one so much like themselves."

Wardlaw laughed bitterly.

"Yes; even wolves devour each other."

"Pray Heaven I may never see him again, the brute—the fiend."

"And we?"

"Bad enough, I grant, but not so foul as that black accursed villain."

"I hope not; but what means this?"

A party of men, apparently a deputation, approached the two officers.

"What is it, my brave men?" said Wardlaw.

"Why, cap'en," said the spokesman, "you see as how Cap'en Harwolf is gone. Now, what we wants is for you to say as how we ain't to obey his orders, if so be as how he should chance to come among us agen."

"Of course, Harwolf having deserted you, has forfeited all right to command the ship. You elected me your captain, and I shall expect my orders to be obeyed."

"Then, that's all settled; 'cos if he was to come aboard agen and you was to give up command to him, the chances is as how you'd have to walk the plank yourself."

Wardlaw's brow grew stern.

"No threats, my men," he said, "but return to your duty. Daniel Harwolf never more commands this ship."

The deputation retired somewhat over-awed by the sternness of his bearing, but withal in some measure pleased to find that they had one over them who would hold the reins of government with a tight hand for the general good.

A few minutes after, three ringing cheers for Captain Wardlaw resounded over the ocean, scaring the sea-birds that floated by on snowy pinions.

"So far good," said Wardlaw, "but if I make one mistake I shall never be forgiven."

"Rule impartially and you can make no mistake."

"So I will endeavour to do, *so long as I remain in command.*"

"What, you still think of——"

"Hush! Not so loud in our new dignity, we are watched more closely than of yore."

"They cannot hear."

"Still it looks suspicious. We will speak more of this another time."

So saying, Wardlaw descended to his cabin, leaving Ramsey on deck, with directions to change the ship's course to the southern oceans.

The men obeyed with a will, and soon the vessel was speeding away on a new tack.

The watches were appointed, and then, those who were not for immediate duty, began to eat, drink, and sleep, and all recollection of the past revolution seemed to have vanished from their minds.

Wardlaw was a thoroughly competent officer, one in whom the men knew they could trust, either in tempest or battle.

By nature of a mild and gentle disposition he had been steeled down in the rough school of piracy to a certain methodical sternness of speech and manners that deceived many people as to his real character.

Apparently a calculating, crafty and unrelenting pirate, he in reality loathed the life he was compelled to lead, and, earnestly longing to abandon his unhallowed calling, as yet saw no means of accomplishing his wish.

Ramsey, too, was far more warm-hearted, generous and really brave to see any glory or heroism beneath the buccaneering banner under which he at present sailed.

Like his chief he only sought a chance to quit the pirate ship, but, unlike Wardlaw, had not the calmness necessary to disguise his thoughts and intentions from others.

After giving the necessary directions for altering the ship's course he, too, went below to rejoin his superior officer.

He found Wardlaw lying on a couch intently studying a chart which was spread on the floor beside him.

The captain pointed to a seat, rolled up the chart, and handed his lieutenant a glass of wine.

"Now," cried Ramsey, "we can speak unreservedly of what we were talking just now."

"But we must not speak too loudly," replied cautious Wardlaw; "these partitions are not very thick, and there may be eaves-droppers. Come here; sit nearer me."

Ramsey moved his seat to the side of the couch on which the captain was reclining.

"And what are your plans, my bold captain?" he asked, sinking his voice to a whisper.

"Plans I have none, as yet, Ramsey, only some rough crude ideas floating through my brain, which must work and ferment till at length they become shaped into a definite and practicable scheme."

"Can I assist you in any way?"

"You can, and more than anything by wearing a mask over your heart, which at present appears to be pinned to your sleeve."

Ramsey blushed.

"I have not lived so long among these men as you or I might be better able to disguise my feelings."

The captain made no reply but again unrolled his chart.

"We are bound for the Indian Archipelago."

"So you say, but do you really intend to sail in that direction?"

"I do; it is, I fancy, our only hope."

"How so?"

"Most of our crew are unacquainted with that nest of islands; I know them each one. That must be our cruising ground for some considerable time, during which we shall be compelled to do our usual butcher's business."

Ramsey sighed deeply.

"Will there never be an end to this damned, accursed buccaneering?"

"There will; among these islands, if I mistake not; otherwise——"

"Otherwise where?"

"In the grave," replied Wardlaw, solemnly, covering his face with his hands.

There was a long and thoughtful silence on the part of both the officers.

And who can wonder at their thoughtfulness? Who can be surprised that remorse sometimes touched their hearts? For they were men of respectable birth and education, though driven by folly more than crime into the guilty course which, for some time past, they had followed.

Should their plans fail, they had little hope of mercy from the pirate crew, who, in all cases, confounded desertion with betrayal, and would take speedy and bloody vengeance on the supposed traitors. Who can wonder then that they were silent and thoughtful?

Ramsey was the first to recommence the broken conversation.

"But you have not yet told me, captain, what these Indian isles have to do with our giving up buccaneering?"

"Have I not?" replied Wardlaw, rousing from his reverie; "then I will do so. Among these islands are many European settlements, and to one of these we may escape."

"In what manner?"

"Either by one of the boats, or by running the ship aground. Then we place ourselves under the protection of the first European flags we meet with."

"But the crew will denounce us."

"They dare not, even if they discover our hiding place. It would be telling on themselves."

Ramsey drew a long breath, and filled himself another glass of wine.

"Your scheme is practicable I believe. Here's success to it, and us."

The men clinked their glasses together, and drank a full bumper each.

"I never drank a toast with greater relish," said Ramsey, setting down his empty glass.

"Nor I; but now we must go on deck and see if the men have any suspicion of our plans."

They ascended to the deck, and mixed in a familiar manner with two or three groups of the seamen, who were playing cards or telling yarns.

The men received their newly-elected captain with much more respect than they had ever shown the old one; but it was soon evident that none of them had the slightest doubt of Wardlaw's honesty.

After exhorting them to keep a good look-out for prizes, the captain again retired to his cabin, leaving Ramsey on deck.

Many days passed quiet enough, for harmony and unity appeared completely restored on board the pirate ship.

It is true the crew grumbled at meeting with no prizes; but, by report, they knew the sea to which they were bound was much frequented by merchant ships, and so continued to trust in their captain.

After a long and tedious voyage, they found themselves in the neighbourhood of the Spice Islands, and all hands were on the alert.

At last came the longed-for cry from the mast-head, "Sail ho!"

"Where away?" demanded Wardlaw.

"Bearing right down upon us on the starboard-bow."

"What do you make her out to be?"

"A square-rigged vessel."

Wardlaw seized a glass, and ascended the rigging to view the stranger.

In a few minutes he was able to discern that the strange sail was a Chinese junk, and that unlike the generality of that strange race, her captain was steering direct for the barbarian vessel.

"We must shorten sail," said Wardlaw to his lieutenant, "and allow the celestials to come up with us."

"Do you mean then, to sink, burn, and destroy?" asked Ramsey, in a whisper.

"We must; but I will do all I can to let the crew escape."

The pirates were in a state of high glee and ex-ultation at the prospect of clutching the dollars they doubted not the Chinese carried with them: and some of the more hardened ruffians openly boasted of the pleasure they hoped to experience when the orientals should be compelled to walk the plank.

But the captain soon discovered that the blood-thirsty were in a minority; and after some little conversation, said,

"Well, my boys, these Chinese never fight. I suppose we may let them run, provided they leave their ship behind?"

Three or four dissentient voices were heard, but the greater part of the crew, as before said, were in favour of showing mercy.

The junk drew nearer and nearer, the men clutched the weapons they had hidden beside the guns, and awaited with fierce eagerness the moment for the onslaught.

Wardlaw had hoisted the colours of the Dutch, and was standing near the mizzen-mast, when suddenly the Chinese craft became draped in a cloud of white smoke; the heavy boom of a gun was heard, and a ball hissed through the mainsail of Wardlaw's ship.

The Chinese, too, were pirates, and thought they had a prize!

A look of surprise passed over every face, and the men rushed to the guns.

Wardlaw, however, restrained them from firing, and calmly awaited the nearer approach of his foe.

At length the celestial freebooter hauled up within about two hundred yards of his supposed prize, and was about to deliver a second shot, when, as if by magic, the ports of the aforesaid prize flew open, and a crashing broadside whizzed through his rigging, bringing down the grass sails about his ears.

It was now the turn of John Chinaman to be surprised; but he was a tolerably brave fellow, and soon recovered his energy.

His long eighteen pounder was heard again, and splinters flew from the bulwarks of the brigantine.

But Wardlaw had well disciplined his men, and his voice was heard encouraging as well as commanding them.

"What, my boys, shall we allow rivals to exist on our cruising ground? Shall these oblique-eyed rascals share all the plunder of the South Seas with us? No, my brave lads, look to your cutlasses and pistols, for in five minutes you shall be on the deck of yon treacherous rascals."

Ramsey was at the helm, and bore right down on the junk.

In a minute the ships touched, and, without waiting to throw grappling irons, Wardlaw and his men rushed on to the deck of their strange enemy.

The Chinese fought well and bravely, but the discipline and weapons of their European antagonists at last overcame them.

They threw their spears and matchlocks on the deck, but not till two-thirds of their number were lying dead.

Wardlaw himself was engaged in an exciting and desperate contest with the Chinese leader, who, armed with a triple-pointed spear, made furious thrusts at the captain of the brigantine.

And, perhaps, it would have fared hard with the bold sailor, for his foot slipped on the gory planks, he stumbled, and in another moment would have been pinned to the deck with his antagonist's formidable weapon, but Ramsey saw Wardlaw's peril, and swift as thought a pistol-shot whistled through the Chinaman's brain, who fell lifeless.

With his fall all resistance ceased, and after gathering up the surrendered weapons, the bold buccaneers began to lay hands upon the spoil.

And a rich spoil it was too.

The plunder of many unfortunate trading ships of all nations which had fallen into the hands of the ferocious Chang Hayai.

"Bring everything on board the brigantine," cried Wardlaw. "The junk is sinking rapidly."

His commands were obeyed.

Chests of tea, boxes of specie, bags of spices, opium, and even mail bags were rapidly passed from one vessel to the other, and piled upon the deck of the brigantine.

"Look out for the Chinamen!" shouted one of the pirates.

And all eyes were turned towards the stern of the junk, where the survivors were, as hastily as their baggy trousers would permit, clambering over the side, and into a boat.

Wardlaw made a rush to prevent them, but was too late.

The Chinese cut themselves adrift, and rapidly paddled away.

"Give them a shot," cried one.

And ere the captain could interpose, a twelve-pound shot was fired at the crowded boat.

One of the escaping villains was killed, and then the missile passed through the bows of the boat, leaving a fair round hole through which the waves dashed.

However, they continued to paddle and bale, the pirates being too intent on their plunder to molest them any more.

At length everything deemed valuable was removed from the junk, and ranged in order on board the brigantine.

The men gave three hearty cheers for the black banner, three for Captain Wardlaw, and three for Lieutenant Ramsey.

"What are we to do with yon ugly-looking craft, captain?" asked the boatswain.

"I think we may waste a barrel of powder," was the laconic reply.

Th pirates took the hint.

A keg of gunpowder was placed in the hold of the junk, with a slow match attached to it.

All hands then hurried back to the brigantine, which slowly sailed away.

There was a cloud of smoke, a dull roar, and the junk was scattered in fragments over the sea.

CHAPTER CCLXII.

SAFETY OF DIEGO—HIS DISAPPOINTMENT AT THE ESCAPE OF DANIEL HARWOLF.

It is now time that we should return to the Palm-tree Island, or rather to the ocean that surrounds it, and see how it fared with Diego, the young Spaniard, after he was thrown by Daniel Harwolf, bleeding, senseless, and apparently dead, into the rolling tide.

The ex-captain of pirates did not see him rise to the surface of the water, for this reason : many rocks reared their black heads above the water at that place, and beneath one of these, which, at low water, showed the form of an arch, the body of the Spaniard passed.

The deep and thrilling plunge had, in some measure, restored his consciousness, though it did not bring back strength to his sinews, or blood to his exhausted veins.

On the further side of this arched rock he rose to the surface, and seeing a ledge or shelf nearly level with the surface of the water, clambered up, and laid himself down on it to die, as he thought.

His limbs were feeble, but his breast was full only of one thought—the villain, his enemy, his deadly foe, had escaped.

"Ah! what disappointment!" he muttered. "I must die here like a dog, with only the gulls and cormorants to bury me, while he, d—d villain, walks the deck of yon vessel, and, perhaps, even glories in my death."

The thought brought passionate tears to the eyes of the hot-blooded and resentful Spaniard.

Hope seemed hopeless, despair took possession of his soul, though, with the usual dignified bravery of his nation, he suppressed every outward sign of emotion.

"Oh ! why did I not be more cautious when I clambered on to the raft ? I might have stabbed the villain as he slept ; but now he laughs and exults in his victory. But," and a smile played round the Spaniard's mouth, "his treasure, for which he sold his soul, is wrested from him ; and I must die here, yon hungry bird is already impatient to commence the feast. Ah! I will sleep, and so shall life pass away without pain."

So saying the youth turned over on his side, and resting his head on his arm became still and motionless.

Many hours passed away, the sun set, darkness held sway, and again gave place to the bright rays of heaven's luminary, yet still the youth stirred not.

Was he dead? Had his prophetic words been fulfilled, and an earthly sleep lapsed into an eternal one?

Ah, no; for see, as the returning beams again give warmth, his pulses stir, a faint respiration is seen in his throat! a tinge of colour glows in his pale cheek, he lives and wakes!

"Where am I? how came I here?" he feebly muttered, raising himself on his elbow. "I thought I was dead. Can it be true, and is this bare rock the pirate's purgatory?"

He sighed wearily, and again reclined on the rock.

"But my senses wander. How came I here? How long have I been here ? I don't recollect anything. Surely I am going mad !"

He rolled about as if in agony at the thought of losing control over his brain.

At length, by a great effort, he calmed himself, and endeavoured to think.

Then the truth flashed across his brain.

"Yes, I recollect now. Harwolf killed me, as he thought, and threw me into the water, which, I suppose, washed me up here. But let me recollect—aye, there was a ship in sight which he was signalling. I will return to the island if possible."

The thought seemed to give him more strength ; he rose to his feet, though with difficulty, and peered over the top of the rock.

Not a sail was in sight, or any token of human life on the island.

"If I only had strength sufficient to swim ashore—but at present it is impossible, I fear, weak as I am."

He hesitated a moment, and then gently dropped down into the water.

"I can but try," he muttered, "and may succeed ; while, if I fail, it is no worse than dying by slow starvation on the rock."

He did succeed, with far greater ease than he had anticipated, though he was much exhausted on reaching the shore.

But once more on land his heart revived, while several bird's eggs which he sucked gave fresh strength to his body.

After a short rest, he walked slowly and painfully onwards towards the spot where he had hidden Harwolf's treasure.

The pirate captain had been unable to find it, though Diego walked to the place without the least hesitation.

He sat down on the rock, and attempted to open the chest, though want of any tool rendered the task a difficult one.

At length, however, he succeded in hammering the lock to pieces with a huge stone ; the hinges gave way, and the treasure was revealed to him.

The chest contained nine long bars or ingots of gold, a bag of Spanish doubloons, and, as though to guard the treasure, a knife, pistol, powder-flask, and bullet-flask, were laid on the top of all.

The young Spaniard prized the blade and the pistol as much, if not more, than the glittering gold.

He was now armed, and might boldly seek out Harwolf if he still remained on the island.

First burying the treasure, but in a more secure spot than Harwolf had done, he loaded the pistol and continued his search.

But he soon saw on the beach the marks of a boat's keel and tracks of several men, which convinced him that the pirate captain had been taken off by the ship he had seen.

"I must wait my time," said he, to himself, as he walked slowly back to his hidden treasure ; "surely, another ship will come some time or other."

He then looked out for a secure nook in which to sleep, lit a fire, and cooked himself a supper of shell-fish and eggs.

Then a long, hearty sleep.

Next morning he arose by times, and ascended to the highest part of the island. But not a sail passed that day.

The next day glided away with the like results, but the third morning a small spot on the horizon proclaimed that a ship was in sight.

Diego immediately applied fire to a huge pile of wood he had placed there, and in a few minutes had the satisfaction of seeing a dense cloud of smoke ascend slowly towards the clouds,

The sail approached nearer and nearer, while a sudden thought struck the brain of the Spaniard.

Suppose it should be Corderes and his ruffian crew? Well, he had pistol for his foe and knife for himself.

Those on board the ship had evidently seen the signal fire, for the helm was put up, and the direction of the vessel changed.

The young Spaniard concealed about his dress as much of the gold as possible, then carefully covered over the remainder, not forgetting to keep his pistol and knife in his belt.

By the time he had done so, the ship was within a mile of the island, and Diego saw with joy a boat lowered, in which were four men.

"Ha, ha!" he laughed in his glee. "I still live, and shall live to take a deep and deadly vengeance on my hated foe. This knife shall settle all scores!"

Then he was silent, for he could hear the measured strokes of the oars, and in a few minutes the boat grated on the beach.

The new comers, who were Danish sailors from the Baltic, hailed Diego in their native tongue, with which the Spaniard was totally unacquainted.

He replied in Spanish, at which they shook their heads, but motioned him to enter the boat. This he did without the least hesitation.

One of the men, seeing he looked pale and ill, offered him a brandy flask, the contents of which had a beneficial effect.

They pulled away then, and soon reached the ship, on the stern of which Diego read the characters, "Jonkörnik," which he endeavoured in vain to pronounce.

He was helped up the side, and found himself in the presence of a red-haired captain, who, in a few words of Spanish, demanded how he came on the Island.

Diego succeeded in making him understand that he had been on a raft, which the worthy Northman seemed to take for granted meant that he had been shipwrecked.

Then, giving some guttural orders to his sailors, he motioned the Spaniard below, where he was soon made comfortable by the hospitable Danes.

And on board the "Jonkörnik" we must leave him awhile, to follow the fortunes of our other friends.

CHAPTER CCLXIII.

RUSSIAN SMUGGLERS—THE CAMP FIRE—THE ALARM—THE SHOT IN THE DARK—A SHORT FIGHT—PRINCESS ARONZOW AGAIN.

THE chief of the band of smugglers, after quieting the natural alarm of Edward Leighton and Katinka, led them back to the vehicles occupied by his followers.

"Night is approaching," he said, "and, as we must all camp during the darkness, I think you will be safer with us than if you were alone."

"But how am I to know that ——"

"That I shall keep faith with you, you would say. Why, I will show you some of the contraband goods we carry with us, and you shall judge afterwards if I am likely to put my head in the lion's—or, rather, the bear's, jaws."

Still Leighton hesitated.

"The lady, too," continued the smuggler, "will be treated with every respect and civility. I am monarch of that band; see my insignia of royalty and authority."

As he spoke he threw back his overcoat and displayed a belt well furnished with pistols and daggers.

"I will go with you," replied Leighton.

In a few moments more they were in the midst of the band of smugglers, a party of rough-looking men whose faces wore an air of determined resolution very seldom met with among the Russian serfs.

The leader introduced the two strangers to the party, and then, assigning to their sledge a position next his own, the procession swept onwards.

"Whither are you taking us?" asked Leighton.

"We travel southwards, and, unless you wish to return to Tobolsk, you will do so also."

"But we are journeying from Tobolsk."

"Doubtless you thought you were, but it takes an experienced traveller to steer correctly across these plains without either compass or sun to point the path. When we met you your horse's head was turned to the north-east."

The smuggler spoke the truth.

Edward Leighton had been travelling, as many less fortunate travellers have done, in a circular direction, and would, in the course of time, have again reached the farm of Alexis Linsky.

The chief drew from his pocket a small compass, by the aid of which he convinced our friend of the truth of his assertion.

"I see my error," said Leighton, "and can only thank you for setting me right. But the night approaches, where is our halting place?"

"You see where yonder two or three leafless trees stretch their branches? Well, beyond that is a deep chasm or ravine in which are many caverns; there we will rest during the night."

"Suppose the Cossacks should be attracted by the light of your fire?"

"They would keep at the greater distance for the ravine is reputed among the ignorant peasantry, who are but thinly scattered over these plains, to be haunted."

They hurried their horses onwards, and, in a short time, arrived at the camping place.

Descending a steep, rocky pathway they reached the bottom of the ravine, as dark and dismal a place as could well be selected.

Looking upwards, Leighton saw that the sides, or rather the walls, of the glen were overhung with bushes, while at the bottom, as the smuggler had said, were several caves of different sizes.

Heaps of ashes in various places told that the bold outlaws of the steppes had oftentimes before found a home in the ravine.

The chief of the smugglers, and one who appeared to be second in importance, examined these remnants of the past with considerable care and attention.

"All is well," he cried, after he had finished his scrutiny. "No one has been here since we left. So now, my men, let us make ourselves comfortable."

Thus adjured, some of the smugglers began to collect firewood, while others, opening packages, produced cooking utensils, various articles of food, together with a packet of tea, which the chief assured Leighton was grown for the Chinese Emperor's own use.

Kettles and saucepans were soon in active employment, and in a very short space of time a smoking hot supper was served up.

When the remains of the meal had been cleared away, a flask of spirits was handed round, the sight of which caused the eyes of the outlaws to brighten. Leighton alone passed it by, and, rising from the group, examined the caverns one after another to choose a resting-place for the fair Katinka.

He selected one, and, after making it as comfortable as possible with cloaks and furs, led her to it, and then, wrapping himself in a sheep-skin garment, placed himself across the entrance to guard her from intrusion or annoyance.

Meanwhile, round the fires, the smugglers were giving themselves up to merriment, drinking and good humour. Toasts were drank, the custom-house authorities subjected to the most merciless sarcasm, when suddenly the leader gave a signal which produced instant silence.

The fires were partly quenched, and every man grasped his weapons.

Quick ears are a great treasure to the possessor, and these the chief possessed.

Far off on the bleak plain he had caught the sound of a human voice, and that too of some one evidently in danger or distress.

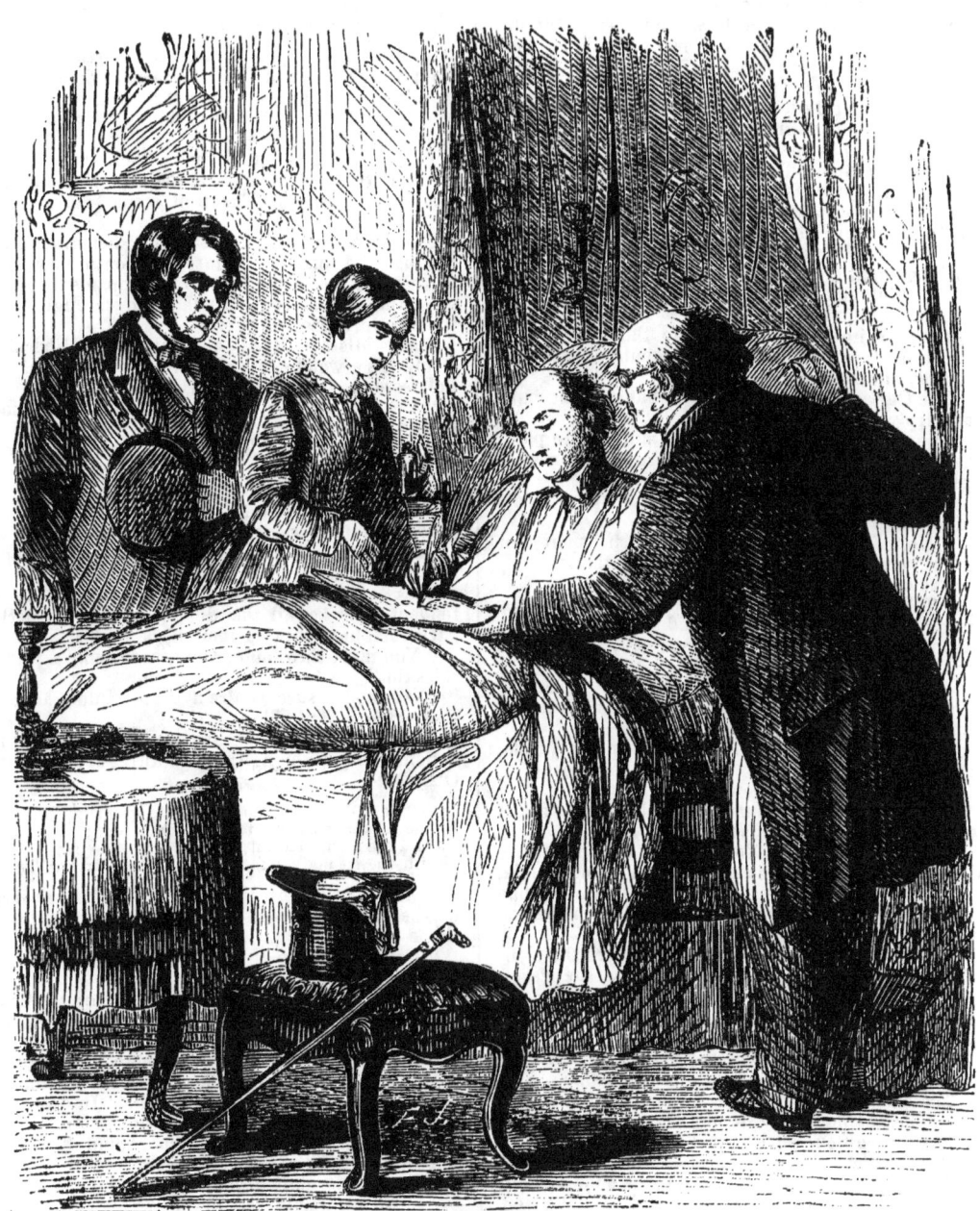

SIGNING THE WILL.

They all listened in dead silence.

The cry was repeated.

Bold yet cautious, quick in resolve yet thoughtful, the smuggler chief had in two minutes formed his plan.

Eight men, commanded by the lieutenant, were to guard the camp, while the chief himself, with four of his boldest, trustiest followers ascended to the plain to discover the cause of the disturbance.

By the faint light of the crescent moon he could discern forms apparently of men struggling in desperate combat. Then came a flash and the report of a pistol, followed by a shrill, prolonged female scream.

The instantaneous flash of the pistol had revealed to the quick eyes of the smuggler that two Cossack soldiers were combating with two apparently

unarmed men, while a lady knelt on the ground wringing her hands and filling the air with sobs and lamentations.

As soon as the bold smuggler caught sight of the Cossacks his eye blazed with glaring enmity.

Drawing two pistols he rushed forward, followed by his men, and springing into the midst of the combatants his powerful aid quickly turned the tide of victory.

The Cossacks, two in number, were disarmed and bound, while the chief himself devoted his attention to the lady, who was now sobbing in the arms of a stately old man—her father, apparently.

The servant or driver of the sledge had been killed by the pistol of the Cossack, his limbs were fast becoming stiff and rigid.

"Come, fair lady," said the smuggler, "and you,

sir, come with me. Travelling is unsafe at night; but in my camp you will be able to repose yourselves in peace and safety."

"Who are you?" demanded the old man.

"I and my men are outlaws, smugglers; but still we boast of more civilized manners than those savages."

With these words Ivan Urkitosky, for so the chief smuggler was called, pointed to the cowering, sullen Cossacks, who, with their arms tied behind them, stood guarded by the outlaw's four followers.

"I accept your offer," replied the old man; "but my daughter, will she be respected by your men?"

"My men would pay respect even to those Cossacks did I give the order. But tell me, noble sir, do you know if there are any more of these rascals lurking about?"

"I think not. Nay, I am almost certain they were travelling alone."

Ivan Urkitosky then turned to the captives, and addressed them in a barbarous, uncouth dialect, half Tartar, half Russian.

The Cossacks shook their heads, but did not make any reply.

The smuggler pressed the cold muzzle of a pistol against the forehead of each, and in stern tones repeated his question.

"Had you any comrades with you when you attacked this lady and gentleman?"

"No, no, no; but in mercy, good sir, spare our lives!" cried the trembling cowards together.

The outlaw smiled grimly.

"Take them to the camp," said he, addressing his men; "guard them well, and bid the cooks prepare supper for a noble lady and gentleman, who will be my guests."

Lifting the body of the driver into the sledge, Urkitosky then led his new guests towards the camping-place of the smugglers.

"Fear not, lady, if our lodging be somewhat rude, and my men uncouth; no one will dare insult or injure you while I am there."

"How far is your camp from this spot?" asked the lady, reassured by his words.

"Not many yards. You will not be alone there, lady, for this evening we encountered a young couple, who call themselves Germans, on the plain; they had evidently lost themselves, and accepted my invitation to camp with us."

By this time they had reached the top of the glen. The lady shuddered, and drew back as she gazed down the rocky hollow upon the glowing fires, and the strange, uncouth forms that clustered around them.

Faith in the outlaw, however, prevailed, and she followed her aged father down the steep defile.

The whole of the smugglers were waiting to receive their captain's guest, and amongst them stood Edward Leighton, curious to know the cause of all the commotion.

Judge his surprise when he saw the chief return, followed by the Prince Aronzow, and his daughter, the Princess Sophia.

He advanced from the circle of smugglers, and saluted them with a low bow, which the prince returned gracefully, while his daughter, the haughty princess, turned coldly away.

"Will your excellency tell me how I have offended the princess?" asked Leighton.

"I know not, save that she is angry with you for travelling about the country with that Polish girl, whom she asserts is your wife."

"Ha! if that is the case, Katinka herself shall undeceive her."

Supper was now placed before the new arrivals, after which the whole party retired to rest in various nooks and caverns.

The princess was shown to a cave, in which, by the dim light of her torch, she could see the recumbent figure of a female.

This was Katinka, who, rising, ran towards the haughty lady, and dropping on her knees, kissed her hands.

CHAPTER CCLXIV.

PURSUIT OF ANDREW HARWOLF AND MILES—DISCOVERY OF THE TRAIL BY CATAHAGA—SILAS RYE WOUNDED.

It is now necessary that we should return to Silas Rye, Catahaga, and Oiny Macarne, whom we left travelling westward, in hopes of finding some traces of Andrew Harwolf and his friend Miles Thornton, *alias* Joe Miles.

For three days after the adventure with the panther they were unrewarded by the slightest shadow of success. The trail seemed to be completely lost.

Oiny began to hint at returning homeward, but finding the others resolute in continuing their journey, he was compelled to accompany them, for only the Indian could guide them through those trackless prairies and forests.

"An' Mister Rye," ejaculated the Hibernian, "sure it's a woild goose chase inthirely, barrin' that the geese are follyon' the sportsmen."

"You mean to say, then, Oiny, that we are fools to go forward?"

"Och, sure, an' it's meself 'ud niver drame of sayin' thim words."

"You are getting tired, then?"

"Yer honour, it's fine exercise this ridin', but sure the cloth is worn out, an' then it'll be nothin' at all, at all, axin yer pardin, but leather upon leather."

Silas could not repress a laugh as he heard his attendant thus bewail the dilapidation of his nether garments, but checking himself, he replied,

"You must turn tailor, Oiny, and make a pair of the skin."

"Och hone! sure you're a grate janius, Misther Rye. Bedad, an' I'll do it."

With these words he commenced to sing a popular national ditty touching the adventures of Mr. Bryan O'Lynn :—

Sure Bryan O'Lynn had no breeches to wear,
An' he got him a catskin to make him a pair ;
Turned the fleshy side out, and the furry side in ;
'Faith, they're fine summer trowsers,' says Bryan O'Lynn.

"An' he was a great man intirely, Misther Rye; maybe you never heard how he got off hangin' for shape-stalin'?"

"Can't say that I did, Oiny; suppose you enlighten us on the matter."

"Well, yer hanner, Bryan had been on the drink for a grate time, and soold the pig an' the praties, an' everything the broker 'ud buy. An' so there was nothin' at all at all to ate in the cabin. What does the gossoon do but walks off an' stales a foine fat ram belongin' to Farmer Magrath. In coorse he killed the baste afore takin' him home to Judy; and as he was a walkin' along, who should be afther meetin' him but the farmer himself.

"'Good mornin,' Bryan,' says the farmer.

"'Sure ye kindly,' ses Bryan.

"'An' whats that ye are after carryin' away beyant me shape-fold?'

"Bryan was foorced to spake the truth for wanst in his life, and in coorse got locked up. He was fetched afore the justices an' sure enough condemned to be hung.

"'Wont yer hanner give a poor bhoy a chance?' says Bryan.

"'Divil a chance at all,' ses the judge.

"'Oh! be the Holy Vargin, yer hanner, sure yez wouldn't be afther disgracin' a gintleman by hangin' him 'pon the same gallies as Barney Ryan was hung what sthole the poor widdy's tay-caddy!'

"An' then the judge, after lookin' in his books, ses, 'Ye shall be hanged upon any tree ye like, Bryan; so be quick wid ye, an' give it a name.'

"'Sure then, yer hanner,' ses Bryan, 'I am afther thinkin' I'd die as aisy on a gooseberry bush as any tree I can think of.'

"'Goosebery bush!' roars the judge. 'Why, you tunderin' big blaygard, sure an' there isn't a gooseberry bush in all Oireland that's big enough to hang yez.'

" ' Och, be aisy, yer hanner, sure, an' I'll be waitin' the while it grows.' An' the judge was foorced to let him wait."

"That's a very good yarn, Oiny," cried Silas, breaking out in a cheery laugh. He then translated it into more intelligible language for the benefit of Catahaga ; and even that stern warrior smiled, evidently amused at the Irishman's wit.

" But, Oiny, though we laugh and joke, we must not neglect to look out for traces of Harwolf and Miles."

" Och, the murderin' villins !"

" My white brother has good eyes, yet he cannot see the trail on the grass," said the Indian.

" Trail ! where ?" cried Silas, almost leaping from his horse.

The Indian dismounted, and showed some marks which no one but a redskin would have noticed. A rotten stick, which lay before them, bore the impress of two hob nails, such as only a white man would wear. About a yard distant was another broken stick, but no marks of nails.

" The Grey Wolf and his mate have been here," said the Indian ; and then, as if further explanation were unnecessary, remounted his steed, and beckoned the white men to follow him.

And now in the distance Silas could dimly discern, what he at first imagined to be a dense mass of cloud resting on the bosom of the prairie, but which, he was told by the Indian, were the great Rocky Mountains.

" Then, you think that Harwolf will seek a refuge among its passes and cliffs ?" asked Silas.

" The Grey Wolf is too cunning to take refuge in a mountain. He will pass beyond to the land of the precious metal of the pale-faces."

" He will try to reach California you mean ?"

The Indian nodded assent.

" Californey !" shouted Oiny. " Hurroo ! Bedad, Misther Rye, it's a goose chase we're on afther all ; but it's the goose that's lyin' the goolden aigs."

" Then you don't want to turn back, now ?"

" Sure, an' I mane to have a rael han'ful o' goold, if iver I gits to Californey."

" How far ahead do you think those rascals are ?" asked Silas, turning to the Indian.

" Two days' journey," replied Catahaga.

" Then they will be in the mountains before we can reach them ?"

" They will. But the Grey Wolf has no horses to carry him up the steep places. *He is lame, too.*"

" Lame ! How know you that ?"

" He walks more on one leg than on the other," replied the observant Catahaga.

Silas grew each moment more and more surprised at the knowledge and tact shown by his guide, and for some time was silent.

" Catahaga," said he, at length. " Do you not regret having left your wife ?"

The warrior winced rather at this question.

He did regret, and his silence could be accounted for, by his thoughts being constantly with her.

" She is a warrior's bride, and knows that I am on the war path."

" Supposing she should be subject to insult during your absence ?"

" She has a rifle. And Catahaga will not show mercy to those who rob him of his wife."

The young chieftain's eyes glared with a light that told how fearfully he would avenge any insult or injury to his beloved Minna.

Silas would not speak any more on such a delicate subject, but turned his attention to Oiny, who was still in raptures at the prospect of paying a visit to " Californey."

Like many others, he fancied that in the El Dorado of the New World gold was quite as plentiful as pebbles are in less favoured spots.

" Be quiet, you noisy rascal !" cried Silas. " If you don't stop your chatter, we'll leave you."

" Sure, an' its a purty babe in the wood I'd be,

Misther Rye. But yer hanner 'ud never be so cruel."

" You must keep silence, then. And let me tell you, too, Master Oiny, that we shall have plenty to do in California, without searching for gold."

The Irishman's countenance became elongated, and he again commenced his favourite song of " Bryan O'Lynn."

" Sure there's no harm in a poor bhoy's singing, Misther Rye ?"

" No, so long as you don't sing too loud."

Oiny promised obedience, and for a long time his sonorous humming was the only sound that broke the stillness of the deserted prairie.

The next day at noon they were at the foot of the mountains, and their road, hitherto smooth and easy, became rough and precipitous.

But the strong hardy horses they rode then bore them bravely onwards up the steep path, which the keen eye of Catahaga assured him had been traversed by Harwolf.

Still on, and on along the edge of perpendicular cliffs, where one false step might hurl them all to destruction, underneath overhanging rocks which threatened each moment to fall and crush them, then through wild ravines, down which the mountain torrent dashed with a bewildering noise and resistless fury.

Not one of the party thought of turning back ; even Oiny managed to keep up his courage, allured by the golden land beyond.

At lenth they arrived at an almost perpendicular pass, up which it seemed impossible to force their steeds.

They dismounted, and held an earnest consultation as to the best means of surmounting the difficulty.

" The horses must stay," said Catahaga, in decisive tones ; " they can go no farther."

" An', axin yer pardin, who'll be lookin' afther the animals ?"

" They must look after themselves," cried Silas, " while we press onwards."

" My brother is right," said the Indian, " the ' Grey Wolf' is not far before us. No time must be lost."

" You are right, Catahaga ; the horses must shift for themselves. For my own part I vow never to rest till I have brought those villains——"

Silas was unable to finish the sentence, for the strong arm of the Indian threw both him and Oiny to the earth just as a couple of rifle bullets whizzed over their heads.

" Lie close," he whispered, " the Grey Wolf commands the pass. Be cautious !"

It was quite true ; Andrew Harwolf and Miles were above them, and Catahaga had caught sight of their rifle barrels just in time to save the lives of his two companions.

" Och, be japers, an' I'll make the thaves dance a jig to their own music !" cried Oiny, half rising.

Again the Indian pulled him back, not, however, till a third bullet had passed through his hat, slightly disarranging the short black curls.

" What is to be done ?" whispered Silas.

" We must remain here till the darkness hides us," was the calm reply.

" And then attack their stronghold ?"

Catahaga shook his head.

He had no notion of exposing himself to the fire of two good marksmen while there was a chance of gaining the victory by stratagem.

" When the great fire manitou hides his face we must find another path."

" But while we are waiting here they may escape us."

Again the Indian shook his head.

" If the Grey Wolf runs away from the hunters we shall know it."

So saying he took the circlet of feathers from his head and raised it an inch above the rock behind which they were lying.

Another bullet whizzed over them, and one of the plumes fell to the earth cut off by the swift missile.

Catahaga smiled grimly, and placed the circlet on his brow again.

Hour after hour passed, and by occasionally raising their hats or some article of clothing they ascertained that the two ruffians were still defending the path.

Catahaga prayed fervently to his god to hasten his departure, and at length that god dipped below the range of their sight.

There was a short half-hour's twilight, then darkness veiled the scene, and all was quiet, save the occasional scream of some night bird.

Silently did Catahaga, Silas and Oiny, retrace their steps for, perhaps, two hundred yards, and then as silently did they ascend by another path, which the Indian judged, and rightly too, would bring them to the summit of the elevation which the Grey Wolf and his comrade still defended.

All was well, and they reached the summit of the cliff, and began to peer carefully into the surrounding darkness.

Suddenly Oiny's foot slipped on a stone.

He stumbled and fell, uttering a loud oath as he did so.

A low, hissing laugh was heard, followed by two reports, and Silas Rye fell backwards, apparently dead.

The Indian crouched silently on the ground, hoping to catch sight of the enemy, but they were invisible.

He then turned his attention to Silas, who lay without sense or motion.

Whispering to Oiny to be more cautious, he lifted the helpless form of the white man in his arms and descended the slope with as much precaution as he had ascended.

Reaching what he deemed a secure place, he laid the inanimate Silas on a rude couch formed of the outer garments of the whole party, and bidding the Irishman keep a strict watch, again mounted to the crest of the rock.

Cautiously did the Indian glide from rock to rock, till at length he reached a spot within ten yards of the shelter from behind which the shot had been fired.

With all his Indian acuteness, he was unable to distinguish a sound for some time, but after waiting patiently, the fall of a footstep far up the pass convinced him that the enemy had fled.

He then returned to his white companions, and to his great joy found Silas sitting up, conversing, though feebly, with Oiny Macarne.

Harwolf's bullet had passed through the fleshy part of his leg, inflicting a deep though not dangerous wound, the pain of which caused him to faint.

Catahaga examined it with a critical glance by the light of a rude torch, and with a grave face pronounced that at least four days must elapse before they could follow the chase of the two ruffians.

With a muttered curse Silas dropped back on his couch, his heart full of rage at being thus again defeated.

CHAPTER CCLXV.

HYDE PARK AFTER DARK—MEETING OF DANIEL HARWOLF AND THE BOY PIRATE—CHRISTOPHER LEAVES ENGLAND—BLACK RALPH AGAIN—A FIGHT—ITS RESULTS.

THE prophesies of the gipsy-woman seemed to have great effect on the mind of the Boy Pirate.

Next day he again visited Blackheath; but the party of dark skins had left the neighbourhood.

Christopher became more gloomy and thoughtful than ever.

Lilia did all in her power to enliven him; she even proposed a visit to his fleet, and this, to her great surprise, he refused.

There was business to be attended to in London, he said, which would not allow of the least delay.

One evening, about a week after meeting the gipsy-woman, he took his hat, and after placing a pair of pistols in his belt, sallied forth alone.

Chance, more than intention or design, brought him to the gates of Hyde Park just as darkness had settled down over the face of the great and noisy city.

Christopher entered the park, and in deep thought slowly sauntered onwards.

He thought of his dead mother, and, in his disordered brain, fancied that he heard her calling on him to avenge her own wrongs as well as the murder of his father.

At length he arrived on the north bank of the Serpentine, and throwing himself on one of the benches, gave way to his bitter fancy.

Suddenly he fancied he heard a light step behind him, and turning suddenly, saw the dark form of a man, whose features he could not discern, hastily creeping away.

The man's movements were so silent and hasty, and he seemed so much bent on escaping observation, that Christopher could not help muttering to himself with a smile,

"Now I dare say that fellow thought to rob me. Rob me!—ha! ha! ha! That would be a joke, indeed, if some poor paltry footpad succeeded in accomplishing what powerful governments have failed to do."

He then dismissed the subject from his mind, and continued his airy castle building.

The topmost turret had been placed on the building, the work was finished, and in anticipation Christopher saw the Harwolfs—both father and son—dangling before the Old Bailey, when again he was startled.

This time it was a voice.

"Help! help! help!" it cried, growing weaker and fainter with each utterance.

Christopher rose from his seat.

"My friend, the footpad, has a victim, I suppose; but I must go and make him disgorge his prey."

So saying he ran hastily towards the spot from whence the sounds had proceeded.

He found a well-dressed man struggling in the grasp of a ruffian who was endeavouring to deprive his victim of watch and purse.

With a bound, Christopher sprang forward, and striking the robber between the eyes, knocked him backwards into the muddy road.

The ruffian rose with an oath and the Boy Pirate could plainly see the glitter of a long knife in his hand.

"Stand clear!" cried he, to the man he had rescued.

But his words were valueless, for the timorous citizen had vanished the instant the robber's grasp was relaxed.

"Now, ruffian! you had better quietly deliver yourself up. That long knife will not be of any use, for I have pistols."

The robber laughed, and, with a rush, threw himself upon our hero.

Christopher evaded the blow, and closing with the man, wrestled with him for possession of the knife.

Presently they both came heavily to the ground together.

At that moment the moon half showed herself through a dark cloud, and the antagonists recognised each other.

Harwolf saw that he was struggling with the Boy Pirate.

Christopher perceived that he was wrestling with his worst enemy.

"Ha! ha! Do we meet thus, my bold Boy Pirate? It is well. To-morrow all London shall hear that the Red Raven is dead!"

"Villain, you lie! If either of us remain on this ground, it is you!"

Again they struggled, and Harwolf succeeded in inflicting a slight wound on Christopher's shoulder.

"You have not got your crew here to help you, my bold Raven, therefore, as I said before, you must die!"

He attempted to repeat the stab, but Christopher by a sudden jerk wrested the knife from his grasp.

"No, rascal, it is you who must die! your lone career of crime is about to end!"

He raised the knife, and aimed a heavy blow at Harwolf's heart.

The broad blade descended, but only to find a bloodless sheath in the sand and gravel.

In the moment of triumph Christopher had relaxed his grasp, and the moment he did so Harwolf rolled over with a splash into the water.

The Boy Pirate hesitated a moment whether he should follow, but the night was so dark that he was unable to see his foe.

He therefore made the best of his way to the gates, and after looking cautiously round to see that he was not watched, jumped into a cab and drove rapidly home.

He arrived at Charles Rye's house pale with rage at the escape of his foe.

"What is the matter, dearest?" cried Lilia, in alarm, winding her arms around him.

"I have seen the fiend!"

"The fiend! What fiend?"

"Daniel Harwolf."

Lilia turned pale as her husband, but with fear, rather than with anger, lest that scoundel should harm her noble husband.

"Oh, Christopher, dearest! let us leave this place at once. I feel certain that he will do mischief in some way or another."

"He shall do you no harm while I am by your side, Lilia," murmured the Boy Pirate, to his wife.

"It is not for myself that I fear, dearest, but for you. The villain might betray you."

"He dare not!"

"Such men as he will dare anything for the sake of revenge."

"He shall feel the weight of my vengeance."

"But, dearest, you must not neglect to provide for your own safety."

"Then shall we pay a visit to the bold Avengers as you proposed?"

"Anything rather than remain near that fearful man, dearest," replied Lilia.

"Then we will start at once. Remain here while I go and inform our friends of our sudden departure."

He passed into another room in which Charles Rye and his wife were sitting.

"I must leave you," he said briefly.

"Leave us; why?"

"Because it is no longer safe for me to be in London."

"Surely no one knows——"

"Some one does know; more than one person."

"But no one who will betray you?"

"I, this evening, met and spoke to Daniel Harwolf."

There was a blank silence at this startling announcement. Charles Rye looked at his wife, and then at Christopher.

"You must have been dreaming," he said, "Daniel Harwolf would surely never venture his life in London."

"If men stab each other in dreams, their blows don't leave such marks as that," replied Christopher, throwing off his coat and exhibiting his wounded shoulder.

"You are wounded! You must have medical aid before you go."

The Boy Pirate shook his head.

"That would, indeed, be betraying me, Charles; if you wish me to escape the Old Bailey, you will not call in any chattering surgeons. I have had many worse wounds than this."

Poor gentle Emily looked almost fainting at the sight of human blood, so Christopher replaced his coat, and in brief terms, recounted his evening's adventure, concluding by repeating his intention to go at once.

"Farewell, Charley! Farewell, Mrs. Rye! It is not for myself I care, but for my gentle wife, who is more dear to me now than ever."

So saying, he rushed from the room and rejoined Lilia, who, in her eagerness, was already prepared for the journey.

A cab was called, in which the young couple seated themselves, and were driven off rapidly to the railway station.

As they stepped on the platform to take their places in the night express, a dark man in very tattered costume, touched our hero on the shoulder.

Christopher's hand at once grasped a pistol.

"I am a friend, fear not!" cried the stranger, revealing the features of the male companion of the Blackheath gipsy.

"What want you?"

"To give you information."

"Well—"

"Daniel Harwolf is fled to Bristol, but he first informed the police that you were in London. You must therefore keep quiet for a time."

"I am about to leave town," replied Christopher, reservedly.

"It is well. I will hunt the villain, hunt him to death!"

Christopher made no answer.

"But," continued the stranger, "I shall be able to communicate with the Boy Pirate when I have accomplished my task of vengeance."

"Who are you?"

The man laughed wildly.

"It matters not; but his father slew my only brother, and I have sworn to be revenged."

Christopher regarded the stranger for a moment in silence.

"You are poor," he said.

"Yes, but rich enough to accomplish all my plans."

"Nevertheless, gold may be useful to you. Take this purse, and if you know anything of me keep that knowledge a secret."

"Fear not, I never harm those who do me no injury."

So saying the man glided away, and in another moment the Boy Pirate and his bride were travelling rapidly towards Frontemore.

They intended to go to sea in Lord Hawksbury's yacht, which his lordship had placed at their disposal.

* * * * *

After the failure of Othello, Black Ralph could not succeed in getting up another dramatic performance, the men being afraid of his tricks and practical jokes.

So the fleet of the Avengers still lay in idleness in the little bay of San Sarolta.

The men were allowed plenty of liberty or shore, and as money was abundant they did not seem particularly discontented.

The strict supervision and watchfulness of Cassidy, Dick Caffyn, and Don Gomez prevented the slothful inhabitants of the town from forming any idea of the real character of the pretended merchantmen.

Black Ralph alone was restless, but even he was not unhappy, for the black-eyed senoritas of the town possessed many charms, and Ralph's heart was of the most inflammable material.

"Where are you going, Ralph?" asked Cassidy, one evening, seeing him prepare to go ashore.

"Cassidy, I love thee, but cannot let you into all my secrets."

"An appointment with a lady?" suggested Dick Caffyn.

Black Ralph nodded with a smile.

"And is your suit successful?" asked Cassidy.

"D—n it, no; no impression has been made on her hard heart yet; but I don't despair, although I cannot obtain an interview."

> "From love's weak childish bow she lives unarmed,
> She will not stay the siege of loving terms,
> Nor bide the encounter of assailing eyes,
> Nor ope her lap to saint seducing gold.
> Oh, she is rich in beauty."

Zampa, who had approached the group, started back in alarm at the sound of Shakspeare, and could, with difficulty, be persuaded to come within three yards of the tragedian pirate.

"De boat am ready, massa Ralph!" he cried, at length.

"Ready!" cried Ralph, "so am I." Then, striking an attitude, he shook his head and continued,

"Some consequence, yet hanging in the stars,
Shall bitterly begin his fearful date,
With this night's revels;
But he that hath the steerage of my course
Direct my sail! On, lusty gentlemen."

So saying, he descended into the boat, leaving his comrades leaning over the side watching him.

After about a quarter of an hour's rowing, the boat touched the beach, and, directing the men to wait at a wine-shop, Ralph Talbot rapidly ascended to the upper portion of the little town, where dwelt Don Gregorio Aminto, a retired merchant, and his only daughter the Senorita Rosalie.

On arriving before the house which held his goddess, Ralph's first care was to carefully survey the grounds, in order to be certain that no watchers or eaves-droppers were about.

Then he gave a long, low whistle, and waited with impatience.

In a few minutes a light was seen at a window, then it was extinguished, and a moment afterwards a richly-dressed lady stood on the balcony.

"Now for the second edition of Romeo and Juliet," muttered Ralph, hurrying forward; "and I fancy that balcony is not so dangerous to our necks as those usually erected by stage carpenters."

So saying, he swiftly clambered up the wooden pillars, and stood beside the lady.

"Dearest Henriquez," cried she, clasping his hand, "again you have braved my father's displeasure for my sake."

"Madame," replied Black Ralph, in his smoothest tones, "I would dare five thousand fathers to pass only a minute in your company."

"Holy Virgin!" cried the lady, in alarm. "What is this? Who are you? Speak!"

"Fair lady, fear not, I am a stranger—an Englishman, and have no other excuse for my conduct than that your beauty has proved irresistible."

"An Englishman! a heretic! Leave me!"

"Nay, fair lady; your loveliness shall convert me."

"But if Don Henriquez should come——"

"He surely will not be rude enough to intrude when he sees that you have a visitor?"

"My character will be defamed."

"I will cut out the tongue of any man who dares speak a word against you."

The lady was silenced, all her objections overruled by the impetuous Englishman.

"But how came you hither?" she asked, after a long silence.

"The magnet attracts steel, the sweet flower draws the bee towards it. You are my magnet, my sweet flower, in whose delicious sweetness I hope to rest."

"You must be careful of your sting, good Senor Bee."

"Ah, fair senorita, in your presence I shall be a humble bee—a veritable, stingless drone, whose only pleasure shall be to buzz and flit near you."

"Be cautious lest the angry wasp should catch you; he wears a long, sharp sting by his side."

"I defy wasps, hornets, and all such spiteful venomous insects. But if the wasp comes you will be as likely to suffer as I."

"True; therefore you must go. It would be death to be seen here with you."

Black Ralph rose to his feet and passed his arm round the lady's waist.

"Bid me remain and I defy any one to do you harm."

"It cannot be; go, go!"

"You are angry with me?"

"You have appeased my anger."

"And yet you bid me go?"

"Aye! it would be wise and prudent."

"When may I come again?"

"The third night from this. Now go."

"Thou wilt not leave me so unsatified," said Ralph, again quoting Shakespeare.

"How? I do not understand."

"Then I will teach you."

So saying the gallant rover pressed her palpitating form to his bosom, and, ere she could resist, printed a dozen burning kisses on her cherry lips.

"Senor, that is ungenerous."

"Then give them back, fair lady."

Again their lips met, this time without the least resistance on the part of the lady.

"Now go," she whispered, reclining her head on his shoulder; "but remember, three nights from this."

So saying she disengaged herself from his embrace and darted into her chamber, closing the window after her.

Ralph gazed a moment, but, seeing that she was really gone, leaped to the ground.

He passed through the grounds, and through the outer gate of the premises.

As he did so he ran against a man whom he had not seen approaching, so entirely was his mind with the fair senorita.

"Diavolos!" muttered the new-comer, drawing back, and half drawing his sword.

"Who the devil are you swearing at?" growled Ralph, "and what do you want?"

"I was about to ask that question, senor; know you that this house is the residence of the Senor Aminto and his daughter?"

"Aye! therefore I ask, what the devil do you want here?"

"Senor, this insolence must be atoned for."

"Don Henriquez, if it be you, I shall be most happy to give you satisfaction for any real or imaginary affront I may have put on you."

"Senor, if you be not a coward you will meet me in the morning——"

"Morning!" roared Ralph, "no, you degenerate son of the Cid! now or never!"

"It is dark, senor; in the morning."

"Draw, sir; or, by the bright eyes of the senorita, I will spit you like a frog."

"Ah! the senorita, say you? Then die!"

So saying the Spaniard drew his long sword, and made a furious lunge at Black Ralph's breast.

The pirate, however, parried, and returned the thrust without effect.

The combat grew furious; both men fought with skill, and, although there was scarcely any light, neither could for a long time touch the other.

"There's for you, my fine don," cried Ralph, at length, as by a dexterous thrust he pierced the Spaniard's sword arm, causing him to drop his weapon.

By this time the sound of the combat had alarmed the inmates of the house; lights began to appear, and the Senor Aminto, at the head of half a dozen servants, rushed forth.

Ralph saw the approaching posse, and after bestowing a hearty kick on the poor, discomfited Don Henriquez, took to his heels, and made towards the beach.

His men were waiting at the wine-shop. He called them, and leaping into the boat, was rapidly rowed off.

They quickly reached the spot where the vessel was at anchor, and leaped on the deck.

"Here comes poor Romeo without his roe, like a dried herring!" cried Cassidy.

Ralph gave him a look of supreme contempt and scorn.

"You miserable mutilator of Shakespeare! see, rather, the conquering hero comes, for I can indeed boast the title of conqueror, having won the lady, and pinked her don."

"Bravo, Ralph!" cried Caffyn.

"But will no mischief come of this?" asked cautious Cassidy.

"I know not, neither do I care," replied Ralph.

They then separated, and those not on the watch retired to rest.

With early dawn next morning a small boat was seen approaching, rowed by a lad of about fourteen.

He approached the vessel, and quickly climbing up the side, looked round with an inquiring gaze.

At that moment Black Ralph ascended to the deck, and seeing him, the boy's countenance brightened.

He ran forward, placed a letter in his hand, and quickly regained his skiff.

The letter was from the senorita, and ran as follows:—

Sweet senor, for the love of Heaven, take your ship away! Don Henriquez has denounced you as pirates, and in two hours' time a company of soldiers will be sent to capture you. Adieu.

ROSALIE AMINTO.

"The devil!" cried Ralph, showing the letter to Cassidy.

"We must weigh anchor at once, Ralph. Luckily all the men are on board."

"What, run from those pitiful, dancing, fandango-skipping Spaniards?"

"I care not to fight, unless by our chief's direction."

"Well, have your own way," growled Ralph.

Cassidy had his way; the signal to weigh anchor was hoisted, white sails were spread to the breeze, and in less than an hour the Avengers' fleet was gliding over the rolling billows of the Bay of Biscay.

Black Ralph remained below in a very sulky humour.

CHAPTER CCLXVI.

DANIEL HARWOLF'S ESCAPE FROM LONDON—A CHAPTER OF ACCIDENTS—THE HOSPITAL—THE TAP-ROOM—HARWOLF AT SEA—THE TWO TYRANTS.

FEAR is the inseparable companion of guilt, and experience goes far to show that the greatest cowards are the greatest rogues; not that we would deny the burglar or the highwayman the due amount of credit for their physical courage, which is merely a reliance in the strength of their muscles and bones, but they all lack the moral bravery of the honest man, who suffers rather than inflict suffering on the harmless, who denies himself rather than deprive the needy of a comfort or necessary.

So it was with Daniel Harwolf.

Though he was strong and stoutly built, yet when once deprived of his weapon, he feared to continue the contest with the Boy Pirate, but, as we have seen, plunged into that muddy duck-pool designated "ornamental water" in Hyde Park, and in a couple of minutes was lost sight of in the darkness.

Turning and floating on his back when a few yards from the shore, he could distinctly see the figure of his enemy, rendered visible by contrast with the white gravel on which he stood.

He saw the Boy Pirate move away towards the park gates, and then knowing he was safe, the scoundrel swam ashore.

"That was cursedly near a case," he muttered, while wringing the moisture from his garments.

He shivered with cold, and his teeth chattered together as he spoke.

At length, when so far dry that his appearance would excite no particular attention, he walked briskly towards the gates.

They were closed, and the church clocks chiming eleven, warned him that it would be unsafe to attempt to climb over the railing.

In doubt as to the propriety of such a proceeding, he wandered away towards the water once more.

Suddenly he saw a tall figure approaching, dressed in the uniform of a park constable.

"Ha! my little jail-bird, and wot might you're leetle game be 'ere?" cried the official.

"My little game is to get out, if I can."

"Get out! You'll be getting in to the station-'ouse."

"On what charge?"

"Bein' 'ere arfter 'ours for a himproper purpose."

"Nonsense; I fell asleep on one of the benches three hours ago, and only this minute awoke. You can prove nothing."

As he spoke, Daniel Harwolf slipped two half-crowns in the official's hand.

After this judicious administration of *palm* oil, the constable's tongue became as smooth as it had previously been rough.

"Beg pardon, sir; you see, sir, there is sich a lot o' roughs as mouches about 'ere after dark, an' at fust I took you for one, but I sees now you're a real gentleman."

"That's all very well, but I want to get out of this place."

"This way, sir. Hi've got a key."

So saying, the constable led the way to the gate, which he opened with a profusion of bows.

"Good night, sir."

"Good night," replied Harwolf, moodily.

The park-keeper gazed after him for a moment, with a grin, and exclaimed,

"Well, you may be a gentleman, but you doesn't look werry much like it. But I never likes to do anybody any 'arm, 'specially ven they behaves well."

And the worthy man retired to his lodge, well satisfied with himself.

Harwolf, on gaining the street, at once darted off to his lodgings, somewhere in the back streets of Westminster, and hastily changing his clothes, swallowed a huge draught of brandy, and started off at a rapid pace towards the Great Western Railway.

Both London and Liverpool were now, in his opinion, too hot to hold him.

Bristol, as a great sea-port, remained to be tried.

He knew not that a dark figure followed his footsteps and even entered the station with him.

Yet it was so.

Our readers will easily guess that this was the gipsy-man who had warned the Boy Pirate of Harwolf's departure.

Only a few minutes elapsed before the train was in motion, but each second seemed an hour.

He was afraid.

At length they started—no, a signal stops them! Can it be possible that already the officers of justice are after him?

Harwolf clutched his pistol, resolved to sell his life dearly, if such should be the case.

They move again, and once more the pirate breathes freely.

On, on, on! over high embankments, through gloomy tunnels and across slim bridges they rattled.

The clock struck one as they drew up at an intermediate station.

But Daniel Harwolf cared nothing for the time; he was flying from London, from his foe.

And, while he was travelling to the west, the Boy Pirate was rushing as rapidly to the south-east.

Mile after mile was rapidly traversed, and, at length, the train was running swiftly over a high embankment, rocking to and fro.

Suddenly there was a rumbling sound, a harsh grating; the carriages bumped and jolted; the whole train seemed to stand still a moment.

Then, with a shrill scream, that sounded almost like its death agony, the engine rolled off the embankment.

A horrid crash, and the foremost carriages followed it, while those above were torn from their couplings and thrown over on their sides.

Screams, shrieks and groans rent the air as victims were killed, crushed and disfigured.

Those of the passengers who preserved their senses and their bones unbroken leaped hastily from their seats and commenced to do all in their power to alleviate the sufferings of those who were unable to extricate themselves from the fearful ruin.

But it was dark, and their efforts were only partly successful.

Both engine-driver and fireman were dead, ki ed by the carriages falling on them.

And now, to heap horror on horror, tongues of flame began to creep out of the mass of timber, among which a few human beings are still imprisoned.

"Fire! fire! fire!"

In vain was the cry; not a drop of water was to be found to quench those flames, which increased every moment.

Still all who were able worked with an energy almost superhuman. Dead and wounded were dragged from the burning ruin, and laid side by side on the grass.

The flames burnt on, and shortly afterwards when day broke nothing was remaining but a mass of charred timber and hot iron.

Daniel Harwolf was among the wounded. The shock had thrown him against the side of the carriage, cutting his head open, and for a time depriving him of sense and motion.

When he recovered he found himself jolting in a rough cart through the streets of Bristol towards the hospital.

Weak and exhausted he lay back in the vehicle, and gave himself up to reflection.

Could it be possible that he was going to die, to face the grim king of terrors, who never releases any prisoner he once shut up in his strong hold—the grave?

"I am not fit to die," he moaned. "I must have time. I can't—I won't die!"

The cart reached the hospital, and the pirate—the murderer was lifted out with as much care and tenderness as if his life had been a model of goodness.

The surgeon examined the wound, dressed it, and, to Harwolf's intense delight, pronounced it not dangerous.

"You will be able to leave the hospital tomorrow," said the surgeon. "There are others who require much more attendance than you."

"I shall be very glad to do so," replied Harwolf. "there is nothing I hate so much as lying in bed."

The doctor's prophecy came true.

Next morning Harwolf left the charitable institution, with a white bandage round his head, and looking very ill.

He immediately sought a lodging in some back street near the water, and made inquiries for a ship.

For some time his endeavours were without success; but, entering a beer-house one night, he overheard two sea-faring men talking.

"Well, Bill," cried one, "have you got a berth?"

"No, dam'me; no luck yet."

"Why don't you ship aboard the 'Newport,' Captain Pickitt wants hands?"

"Captain Pickitt may want and be d——d, afore I ships with him," replied Bill.

"Well, mate, I must say as how he ain't a very pleasant skipper. I know well enough how two o' the boys went overboard last voyage."

"So do I. But if you've sailed with him afore why not ship again mate?"

"I shall."

"You will?"

"Yes. But hark ye, mate," and the speaker lowered his voice, "Captain Pickett must mind what he's up to."

"How so?"

"Why, Dan Keef and Jem Wallbrook ship with me, and two or three more nice boys."

The man addressed as Bill gave a low prolonged whistle.

"And," continued the speaker, "if he cuts any capers, why he walks the plank, and we runs up the black flag."

"Then I'll ship with you," cried Bill.

"And so will I," thought Harwolf to himself, though he did not give the thought expression. "Those are just the men for me, and it will be strange if I cannot manage to take the lead."

The conversation changed, and Harwolf shortly afterwards left the tap-room.

Early next morning, however, he sought out the captain of the "Newport," which he found to be a swift-sailing clipper, with sharp graceful lines, and tall tapering masts.

"Well, my man," cried Captain Pickett, in sharp, snapping tones, as Harwolf accosted him, "what do you want?"

The pirate briefly stated that he wished to ship as able seaman on board the "Newport," bound for New Orleans.

"Able seaman, eh? and what the devil does an able seaman want with a bandage round his head? Take it off, sir. I have no sick men on board my ship."

Daniel Harwolf tore off the bandage, and then the captain looked at him with a more approving air.

"Hum! well, the pay is three pound ten a month and small stores; if that suits you you can come on board at once."

"Aye, aye, sir," replied Harwolf, then a moment after he touched his hat.

Two hours after five other hands made their appearance, among whom he recognized the two sailors he had met the previous evening.

In the course of the day one or two other poor wretches, who knew nothing of the captain's character, also engaged themselves.

Then the skipper, considering he had sufficient hands, gave orders to weigh anchor, and soon the rays of the setting sun shone on the white sails of the clipper ship "Newport" as she skimmed swiftly and gracefully over the waves of the Bristol Channel.

Daniel Harwolf would have shouted for joy, but the harsh voice of the captain proclaimed silence.

"I'll have no d——d singing or fiddling on board the 'Newport.'"

The tables were now turned—tyrant was ruled by a tyrant.

At length the work on deck was completed, ropes were coiled down, the boats lashed to their davits, and then Harwolf, with the others, went below.

Captain Pickett remained pacing the deck, wondering in how short a space of time he could possibly make the voyage, and how many bales of cotton he could cram into the hold.

CHAPTER CCLXVII.

THE AVENGER'S FLEET—BLACK RALPH MORALIZES—SAIL HO!—THE BOY PIRATE.

WHEN the pirate fleet sailed away from the Spanish coast the seamen were delighted at the prospect of another cruise and rich prizes.

Still they wondered that their beloved chief was not with them, though all knew the reason of his absence.

But when the motive for their sailing was made known to them, disgust at what they considered unnecessary trouble filled their hearts.

"Why avoid a parcel of Spanish soldiers? Why, one ship's crew was sufficient to beat an army of them."

So reasoned the men, though many of them were of Spanish birth.

The foreigners, from having been so long in contact and companionship with the English portion of the crews, had imbibed something of their courage and daring.

Black Ralph, mean while, sat in his cabin in moody silence.

He was only aroused by the entrance of Zampa with a bottle of wine.

"So, Zamp, you are one of the runaways, are you? I thought you had more courage than to show your back to a pitiful, paltry set of Spanish curs."

"D—n all!" cried Zampa. "Dis ere nigger am good enuf for all de d——n lot; but, den, Massa Ralph, recollect dat de Boy Pirate am not here!"

DIEGO'S BATTLE WITH THE SHARK.—(See page 620.)

So saying the darkie withdrew.

Ralph rose to his feet and paced the cabin with uneasy strides.

"'The Boy Pirate is not here.' Now what is there in that name that should redouble the energy and courage of these fellows? One would think that a big man pirate, like myself, would inspire them with more confidence than a dozen boys. I can't make it out."

He walked about in deep thought, seeming determined to unravel the mystery of his self-elected chief's popularity.

"He is brave, very brave; but, then, Ralph Talbot is no coward, no, nor any one of his crew. It can't be, then, his courage; but I more than suspect that his generosity has something to do with it, for he shares like one of the common sailors."

No. 78.

Ralph paused, and drank a glass of wine.

"Well," he continued, "I'll give up every dollar I take and see if I can't be a popular hero. But, no, I won't take any advantage during his absence, for he once saved my life, and I am under his authority of my own accord."

Again he paused, and then a bright thought struck him.

"I have it! It's because he is a married man that he is so popular! Well, I'll marry too, if I can get a wife, and then see if Ralph Talbot the Vulture won't take the lead of the Boy Raven. But who can I have? There's Deborah the Jewess, she's handsome and rich. I marry! no, I won't just yet, for fear I should catch a tartar. Who else is there? Ah! Rosalie the Spanish maiden, the beloved of the long-sworded cavalier I kicked. But, damn it all, I can't go back and marry her, or else I should, most probably, be sentenced to swing on nothing. I'll get a ship and crew; I'll return and carry her off in spite of those cursed soldiers, who, I dare say, are glad enough that we are out of the way."

The report of a gun stopped his soliloquy, and hurrying on deck, he found that the shot had come from a vessel which had pursued them from the little harbour they had left.

The authorities at the port, thinking it incumbent on them to do something, had despatched a revenue boat armed with two twelve-pounders after the pirates, the captain receiving strict injunctions to avoid an engagement if the outlaws refused to strike their flag and surrender.

The shot had been fired to bring them to; but the prudent commander of the attacking force, not caring to venture too near, had discharged the gun before he was within two miles of the Avengers.

"Shall I send them back a shot?" asked old Brierly, laying his hand on a long thirty-two.

"Not yet; but load your gun."

The revenue-cutter seeing no signs of resistance on the part of the outlaws, came scudding on bravely, her captain almost imagining that there was a chance of making a seizure.

But he was doomed to bitter and great disappointment if he entertained any hope of capturing Brierly.

For the old tar allowed him to approach within range of his long gun, and then turning to Cassidy, said,

"I fancy I can pitch a shot through his rigging now."

"Blaze away, then," was the reply.

And Brierly did blaze away to some purpose, for the heavy shot, striking the mizzen-mast, snapped it like a twig, and brought it down with the standing rigging in a confused heap on the deck.

The cruise of the revenue-cutter was at an end, and the captain, to tell the truth, felt glad in his heart when he saw the pirate ships once more before the wind, and skimming rapidly over the water.

It might have been worse, he thought, had he come into close contact with them.

And visions of cut throats, smashed skulls, and a long plank on which people were compelled to walk blindfolded, presented themselves in such rapid succession to his mind, that he inwardly resolved to give up his commission as soon as possible after reaching the shore.

The Avengers, after a loud laugh at the consummate impudence of their foe, held on their course; the different captains having resolved to steer towards the British coast in order to learn, if possible, some tidings of their chief.

Black Ralph again resumed his speculations on matrimony and other subjects, while Cassidy after watching for some time the discomfiture of his foe, turned his glass in another direction.

A small craft was bearing down towards them rapidly.

All eyes were directed towards the little vessel, which seemed to seek rather than shun the long dreaded outlaws.

Nearer and nearer it drew, bowling along swiftly o'er the dancing waves, its rig and graceful outlines plainly showing that it was one of those toy ships with which the wealthy Englishman loves to amuse himself.

"See!" cried Dick Caffyn. "There is a signal."

He spoke the truth, and Cassidy, hurriedly snatching up the glass, examined the bright coloured bunting that fluttered in the breeze.

"The captain, by Jove!" he exclaimed.

Black Ralph snatched the glass from Cassidy's hand, and in turn examined the signal flag.

"You have managed to speak the truth for once in your life, Master Cassidy," he cried. "So now you can prepare yourself to be tried by court-martial for running away from those lubberly Spaniards."

A few minutes more and Lord Hawsbury's little

yacht was alongside the "Red Raven," and with a bound the Boy Pirate stood once more on the deck of his splendid ship.

A deafening cheer pealed over the waves, as the crews of the four ships once more beheld the lithe form and handsome features of their youthful commander.

With flushed face, Christoper briefly thanked the men, and then assisted the fair Lilia to reach the deck.

And then another cheer in honour of the rover's bride rent the air.

Lilia looked supremely happy as she saw the homage thus paid to her noble husband; in fact, she almost forgot that he was an outlawed rover. To her he was a hero.

"And now, my brave comrades," cried Christopher, "I am once more among you, and though I have resolved no more to hoist the black flag, my intention is to——"

"Pave a certain unmentionable place," interposed Black Ralph.

"You are wrong, Captain Ralph. I have not the slightest intention of becoming bricklayer in ordinary to the gentleman whom Captain Macallister designates 'Auld Clootie.' But, as I was about to observe when you interrupted me, we will sail to the Southern Seas and try if there are no riches to be gained in a honest way; and by that I mean, see if there are no slavers on the water. It is no piracy to stop those gentlemen."

"Bravo! Hurrah for the Avenger!" cried all the men in chorus.

"Well, after all, that's not so bad!" cried Black Ralph. "It will, at all events, keep us from growing lazy and fat. Besides, an occasional brush with those rascals, will keep us in mind of old times—times which, I suppose, are past."

"And, Ralph," whispered Cassidy, "you might meet with some sable Venus to console you for your past failures in the matrimonial line."

"Pshaw! I'd about as soon marry a blacking-bottle!"

"Say, my bold companions, do you assent to my proposition?" cried Christopher.

"Yes, yes!" was the reply.

"We agrees to anything as you proposes, cap'en," said Brierly.

"Then the sooner we change our course the better; for, to tell you the truth, England is yet too hot to hold me."

"As for the matter o' that why we'd burn down Newgate, and hang the lord mayor if he offered to lay a hand on you," replied the jolly old salt.

"I know you would try, Brierly; but such things are not so easily done in England."

So saying our hero led Lilia to the cabin, and when he again stood on the deck the compass showed him that they were rapidly speeding in a southerly direction.

CHAPTER CCLXVIII.

THE CAPTAIN AND THE CREW—PLOTS AND COUNTER-PLOTS—VERY LIKE A WHALE—THE ESCAPE OF WARDLAW AND RAMSEY—THE ISLAND.

OUR readers must not forget the existence of Messrs. Wardlaw and Ramsey, who had been unanimously elected to the command of Daniel Harwolf's vessel.

As these gentlemen have yet to influence the destinies of our characters, it will be well to follow their steps.

After the capture and burning of the Chinese pirate, an act which neither of the officers much regretted, they cruised about for some time amongst the Spice Islands of the Southern Seas, Wardlaw, the only one who knew anything about those latitudes, purposely keeping out of the track usually pursued by merchantmen.

His object was to find some little creek or harbour, into which he might run the ship under pretence of repairs, and then leave her and her crew to her fate.

"Well, captain," said Ramsey, "you see that it is a more difficult thing to get rid of the ship than you anticipated."

"Not at all, Ramsey, it only requires a little patience."

"A little; a great deal."

"Well, your patience will not be put to the test much longer."

"Ha! then——"

"Be ready as soon as it is well dusk to-night. We shall sight land before two hours are over our heads."

It was about noon when this conversation took place.

"I will be ready," replied Ramsey.

"And have one of the boats lowered on some pretext or other."

"For what purpose?"

"Anything you like—fishing, bathing, no matter what excuse; but remember to let it remain towing astern."

"Now I see your drift."

"By-the-bye, you had better discover some new species of gull, or something of that kind; there will, then, be an excuse for taking a couple of guns with you."

"It strikes me that the new species of gull will be the crew," said Ramsey, with a light laugh.

"Hush! never speak loud while we are by ourselves."

"You are right, captain; but I am so happy at the thought of escaping from these cut-throats that I can hardly contain myself."

"Now go on deck and prepare for action. Be cool and deliberate; above all, show no sign of impatience or anxiety."

"And you?"

"I have some preparations to make that will not take long. I will rejoin you in half an hour."

Ramsey ascended to the deck, and, after glancing at the compass, entered into friendly conversation with the men.

Presently he suggested bathing, and gave directions to lower a boat.

"There are sharks in these waters I expect, lieutenant. Keep a sharp look out," said one of the crew.

"Never fear, lad, I shall not go five yards from the boat."

He leaped into the little skiff, and leisurely commenced to undress himself.

At that instant Wardlaw made his appearance on deck and Ramsey had no fear.

Suddenly he cried in a loud voice,

"What is that yonder, captain? It seems to me like a strange bird."

"If you think so you had better go and shoot it," responded Wardlaw.

"Give me a gun, and I will."

The crew were, as both the officers had anticipated, completely *gulled*; the object in question being nothing more than a scrap of white paper which the crafty captain had dropped from his cabin window, and which now floated along on the top of the waves.

"Here's your gun," cried Wardlaw, handing him a double-barrelled one, together with a supply of ammunition. "Stay, you had better take another in case the first should miss."

In another moment Ramsey passed a second gun, and pulled away leisurely towards the object that had attracted his attention.

His object was to get far enough away from the ship to be enabled to hide the weapons.

As there was scarcely any wind, the crew, on seeing their officer start, once more retired to take their siesta, the man at the wheel soon being the only one who was not stretched on the deck or his hammock.

A double report was heard as Ramsey fired at the paper *decoy duck*, but few, if any, troubled themselves to raise their heads. The extreme heat of the weather had overcome them.

Then the boat returned, and Ramsey climbed to the deck flushed with his exertions.

The guns remained in the boat, which, according to his instructions, he allowed to tow alongside.

The crew took no notice of his return, and he descended to the cabin in which Wardlaw was seated.

"Well," cried the captain.

"Act the first has finished successfully."

"And we must wait for darkness to commence the second."

"But suppose, captain, any of the men should see the guns in the boat."

"Tell them that you forgot to remove them."

"And what's the next thing to be done?"

"Rest awhile."

"That's impossible in my excited state."

"Do so if you can. You will need all your strength and energy for the night."

"But, captain, where away is this land you spoke of?"

"It should be in sight. Go on deck, then, and look out for it, if you can't rest."

Full of impatience, the younger officer darted up, and seizing a glass, began to scan the horizon.

"Land ho!" shouted the look-out, awakening from a nap.

"Where away?" asked Wardlaw, coming on the scene.

"On the starboard bow, captain."

"This will be a good opportunity to take in water," said the captain, "we will anchor off the shore to-night. Send a man into the fore-chains, Mr. Ramsey, to see what water we have beneath us."

"Aye, aye, sir," responded the lieutenant, and in a moment all was activity.

"Just half a point more," cried the captain to the man at the wheel; "there, steady, keep her so."

There was deep water under their keel; but the lead was kept constantly going on account of the many coral reefs which abound in those seas.

But their course was uninterrupted and free from impediment, neither rock nor shoal barring their progress.

An hour and a half before sunset they cast anchor about half a mile from the shore of one of the numerous green islands that stud the Indian Ocean.

After seeing everything in order on deck, the two officers retired to the cabin.

"Well, captain, here we are at last; the next thing is to get ashore."

"Don't be impatient, Ramsey; how many times have I told you to wait till dark?"

Ramsey sat himself down on a chest and sighed deeply.

"You have your pistols, of course?" said Wardlaw.

"A whole pocket full of them, and ammunition to last a week."

"I hope we may not need to use them; but it is well to be prepared. Now, eat and drink heartily, and stow away as many biscuits as you can about you."

For some time they proceeded with their meal in silence, which was presently broken by a knock at the door.

"Come in," cried both.

Three of the men made their appearance, and requested permission to go ashore.

"Not to-night, my men," answered the captain; "to-morrow, you may, if you like."

"Thank ye, captain," they answered, and again withdrew.

Had Daniel Harwood been in command, probably *his* refusal would have caused a mutiny, or if not, at least moody discontent would have followed. But Wardlaw had, in addition to maintaining discipline, always treated the men justly and with civility; therefore they were satisfied with their promised leave of absence on the morrow.

This interruption over, the two officers waited with what patience they could, till at length the welcome dusk of evening spread its mantle of mist over the sea.

"Now is our time, Ramsey," whispered Wardlaw. "Just go and see what the men are doing."

The crew were gathered about the mainmast smoking, and listening with great attention to a wonderful yarn which one of them was relating for the amusement of his comrades.

Ramsey returned and reported the fact to his captain, who at once noiselessly threw open the cabin window.

The rope by which the boat was made fast to the ship was within his reach, and grasping it he crawled through the window, thus being able to slide down into the little craft which was his hope of escape.

All this was accomplished without the slightest noise, and Ramsey followed him quite as silently.

"Hist! Be quiet a moment, till we know whether we are missed or not."

The two men crouched silent and motionless in the bottom of the boat, but there was no sound to be heard save the laughter of the crew as they endeavoured to swallow the toughest portions of their comrade's story.

A moment more, and the rope that held them to the ship was severed.

"Use your oar gently, very gently," whispered Wardlaw, as they slowly, and without noise paddled away.

The speed was soon increased, however, and in a short time they landed under a thicket of bushes, into the midst of which they hauled their boat.

"Safe at last, captain," cried Ramsey.

"Safe at *present*; but I am no longer your captain, only your companion, so the sooner you drop that title the better."

"I don't think they'll venture ashore after us, do you?"

"On shore, yes, but not inland; therefore, as there is a considerable interval of space between acts two and three, we will make the best possible use of our time by putting those hills between us and the good ship which I heartily hope I may never see more."

"But do you know where we are?"

"Yes; this is the island of Sommorostro, belonging to the Spaniards, who have a small port on the further side."

"And we make our way to that port?"

"Not just yet. We must see what becomes of our late comrades, first. On the top of yon rock that looms up so darkly in the moonlight, we may keep a good look-out till danger is past."

"Then forward, for see, lights are moving about the deck, and I rather fancy that they have discovered our absence."

The two friends commenced walking at a swift pace, and speedily placed a long distance between them and the water's edge.

At length they arrived in the midst of a thick wood and choosing the shelter of a huge tree, laid themselves down to take a short rest.

CHAPTER CCLXIX.

THE JONKORNIK IN A CALM—THE SHARK—A FEARFUL COMBAT—THE HURRICANE—"A SAIL IN SIGHT APPEARS" — THE BOY PIRATE.

THE good ship "Jonkornik," with its crew of northmen and Diego the Spaniard, continued its homeward course with a fair breeze, till they had left Neptune's toll-gate—the equator—far behind.

Then came a calm.

The air was still, and almost suffocating in its sultry hotness.

The sea more resembled a huge sheet of glass, than the foaming tide to which we dwellers in northern latitudes are accustomed, while the sails hung down limp and empty.

The crew stretched themselves on their hammocks beneath a large awning which had been spread over the deck, and slept their time away during the hours of fierce sunlight, only rising to eat and drink during the somewhat cooler watches of the night.

Much did they resemble the barque described by the Ancient Mariner—

"————a painted ship
Upon a painted ocean."

Four days and nights this continued, and on the fifth an incident occurred which, in a slight measure, awoke the seamen from their listlessness.

This was the appearance of a huge shark alongside, floating calmly nearly on the surface of the water, through which his grey body and large fins might be plainly discerned.

A lump of pork was thrown to him by the cook, on seeing which, he gave a dart forward, turning belly upwards as he did so, and opening a huge mouth which exhibited six rows of strong sharp teeth, swallowed the tempting morsel, closing the dreadful jaws with a snap which caused many a stout northman to shudder.

The huge fish continued to float near the ship, and the sailors to watch him.

Suddenly there was a fearful cry,

"A man overboard!"

Instantly all was in commotion.

Ropes were thrown, and preparations were made to lower the boats.

The unfortunate man sunk to a considerable depth, and, on rising to the surface, was about halfway between the ship's side and the fearful shark.

He managed to keep himself floating, but was unable to clutch a rope.

The shark began slowly to glide towards the sailor, though those on deck knew not whether it had perceived the man or not.

Suddenly another actor appeared on the scene.

The young Spaniard, naked, with the exception of his light trowsers, which were rolled up to his thighs, leaped on the bulwarks brandishing a knife in his hand.

With a few expressive motions he made the crew understand that he would attack the shark, and deliver the half-drowned man.

Then grasping one of the ropes which had been thrown to the Dane, the bold young man dived swift as lightning in the water.

He rose between the Danish sailor and the shark, and handing the man the rope, swam towards the huge fish.

The fins of the monster began to move more rapidly, and like a flash of light, he darted full at Diego, who dived only in time to escape his jaws.

The Danish sailor, meanwhile, had neared the ship, and was already half out of water, when the shark dashed at him.

There was a scream of agony, and the poor man was hauled up on deck.

Both legs had been snapped off close to the body, and the poor sailor was placed on a layer of hammocks to wait for the grim hand of death to end his painful sufferings.

Disappointed and angry, the shark turned once more towards Diego, who, instead of avoiding the combat, calmly awaited his onslaught.

Again the shark, turning on his back, darted at the lithe, nimble Spaniard, who seemed almost as much at home in the water as any fish.

But a second time he avoided the aquatic monster by diving, and as he rose to the surface, great bubbles of blood told that one or other of the combatants was wounded.

But the fish was not inclined to give up his coveted dainty, and besides, the smart of his wound rendered him furiously savage.

Lashing the water into foam, he turned again, and darted at his opponent with such velocity that his sharp teeth grazed Diego's body as he dived.

Those on board the ship thought that the brave

young Spaniard had fallen a victim to his daring courage.

Both shark and man had dissappeared beneath the waves, but still the blood continued to rise to the surface, tinging the glassy waters with its roseate hues.

Every eye was strained to watch the re-appearance of either.

The Spaniard came to the surface first, almost breathless with his long dive.

" A rope !—A rope !" he cried.

Some few of those on the deck of the Jonkörnik understood, and a long coil splashed into the water near him.

Grasping the end of this in his hand, Diego waited for the shark, who soon rose, and again made for his foe, though feebly, for he was evidently severely wounded.

Diego easily avoided him, and again dived under his belly.

The shark followed, and there was another fight beneath the water, in which it was soon evident that the human combatant had the best of it.

For in a few minutes he rose to the surface of the sea again some yards distant from the shark, and by voice and motion incited those on the deck to haul in the line.

Half a dozen stout pair of arms obeyed the signal, though their efforts met with considerable resistance.

It soon became evident that Diego had fastened the rope tightly round the shark's body, and the monster was drawn, in spite of his rage, towards the ship's side.

He snapped at the vessel, he lashed the water with his tail, and by sudden jerks, endeavoured to break the rope.

But in vain : tail foremost, he was drawn to the ship's side, then a pair of grapnells were stuck in his body, and he was hauled up to the deck.

A blow from a hatchet, about two feet from his tail, rendered him incapable of doing mischief, and he lay gasping, quivering, and writhing on the blood-stained planks.

The young Spaniard then climbed on board to receive the unintelligible thanks and congratulations of the crew, who looked upon him as a hero, though some there were who regarded him as a kind of " Sea Devil," so superhuman appeared his courage and skill in the water.

After that the shark was opened, and in his capacious maw was discovered a whole magazine of articles, eatable and otherwise.

First the mangled limbs of the unfortunate dying sailor were brought to light; then, on further investigation, some articles of clothing that plainly showed master shark had tasted human flesh on some other occasion ; a revolver, some ten inches of iron chain, to the end of which a huge hook was attached, and several large stones, mingled with halves of fish and bodies of sea birds, made up the inventory of the contents of the sea monster's capacious stomach.

Although the poor mutilated seaman, to save whose life Diego had risked his own, received every attention the rough crew could think of, they were unable to staunch the fearful flow of blood from the severed limbs.

Within an hour after the shark was hoisted on board he breathed his last, keeping the hand of the young Spaniard clasped in his own.

His body was committed to the deep in the presence of his mourning shipmates, sewn in his hammock, with forty pounds weight of iron attached to keep the remains at the bottom beyond the reach of sharks.

The sailors returned to their duty, but every one remembered the bravery of Diego, and all showed their gratitude in some way.

Next day, a breeeze sprung up, and the sails filling out, the good ship began to move along the waters.

Still higher and higher rose the wind, black clouds began to make their appearance on the horizon.

The skipper, glass in hand, watched the messengers of coming storms, and quickly furled each stitch of canvas.

The sky rapidly became overcast, and, far away to windward, a long line of white foam showed the advance of the tornado. A hoarse hollow sound, something between a whistle and a roar, came along over the bosom of the waters.

Flash !

Forked lightning, so dazzlingly vivid that neither pen nor tongue can describe it, darted athwart the murky sky.

Then there was a silence in the gloomy air for a moment, as though the elements were gathering all their strength and energy for their attack on the poor ship.

Crash !—crash !—crash !

Thunder, wind, and wave at once dashed their forces on the vessel ; the seething waters swept the deck, bearing strong men away into the ocean ; the howling tempest raged through the rigging, tearing spars and shrouds to pieces.

The pealing thunder overhead kept up such a deafening stunning reverberation as though all earth's artillery had combined to fire one grand salvo in honour of Heaven's wrath and fury.

The men seemed to lose their courage, and, lashing themselves to masts or bulwarks, awaited their fate.

Only the skipper rushed to the wheel, which the steersman had abandoned ; but his unaided efforts were unavailing to direct the course of the ship.

Diego rushed to help him, and the pair, by keeping the ship's head before the wind, saved her from total wreck.

Though every rag of canvas had been blown away by the first fierce gust, the ship continued to dash through the foam at a most terrific speed.

The old skipper had thanked his stars that he had plenty of sea room.

Flash !—flash !

The tall mast seemed to be shrouded with fire, so dazzling was the light.

And now the rain began to pour, not in little drops, as we see it, but in a torrent, which dashed strong men to the deck, which was soon flooded full six inches deep. The darkness increased. The thunder continued its fearful roaring, and the vivid flashes swiftly following each other cast fitful glares of light on a scene of the most wild and desolate grandeur.

The planks of the stout ship creaked and groaned beneath the fearful strain, and men's hearts failed them as they thought of their fate if she should go to pieces in that fearful sea.

A ball of fire was seen to glide through the air ; it struck the mizen-mast, and in an instant the tall timber fell with a crash over the side of the ship.

One or two of the men had sufficient courage to rush and cut the fragments adrift, then, clinging once more for dear life to the bulwarks, they waited their fate, whether destruction or safety.

The darkness of night succeeded the darkness of the tornado, yet still the drenched mariners clung to their posts.

But the tempest had spent its fury, though the wind still blew with violence and the waves towered up to a height that seemed to threaten the ship and her crew with a watery grave.

Neither moon nor star shed the faintest light through the darkness.

Only the occasional vivid flashes of lightning assured them that they were still on the surface of the water.

A long, dreary, dismal night it was to them ; many a heart that had almost forgotten how to pray now offered a rude supplication for safety.

Daylight, at length, slowly broke, and with it the tempest abated its fury.

Then was seen the fearful amount of damage that the ship had sustained.

Of one mast only a splintered stump remained above the deck, while the foretop-mast had likewise fallen overboard.

The men gazed round at each other.

Many familiar faces were missed.

Of a crew of eighteen men only eleven remained—seven had been swept away.

Food and drink were necessary, and one by one they staggered below to refresh their weary bodies.

The sun rose, the clouds cleared away, and the sky looked so glad and smiling that one could scarcely believe that barely six hours ago such a horrible tempest had raged.

The sailors had enough to keep them employed without gazing abroad.

New spars and sails had to be fitted, while a new danger threatened them.

A plank had started !

The water was rapidly filling the hold !

A look of deep despair was on every face as the news passed from mouth to mouth.

But still they worked with a dogged perseverance that promised success if it were possible, and gang after gang relieved each other at the pumps with unabated energy.

"A sail in sight !"

The eyes of those on deck were directed towards the welcome sight.

Not one sail but *four* were plainly visible on the horizon.

The only serviceable gun on board the ship was hoisted up on deck, loaded with as heavy a charge of powder as it would bear, and a loud report went booming through the air

Five minutes elapsed, and then a white puff of smoke from one of the four vessels showed that the signal had been heard and answered.

But the captain of the "Jonkörnik" did not for a moment relax his efforts to clear his ship of the water.

All hands waited and looked with impatience for the approach of the strangers, who did not appear to have suffered much from the hurricane.

A long weary time did it seem before those four vessels neared the Danish ship; but while they were a great distance off Diego knew and recognised them.

He felt certain that they were the ships of the gallant Boy Pirate.

"Now," thought he, "I may have another chance of avenging myself on the villian Harwolf. The Boy Pirate, too, will give anything for a chance of meeting him, and I will show him where the treasure is hidden which so nearly cost me my life."

Nearer and nearer came the ships. A boat was lowered and pulled rapidly towards the Danish vessel.

In a few minutes it came alongside, and the Boy Pirate stood on the deck of the "Jonkörnik."

"Senor," cried Diego, "do you not remember me?"

"Aye, indeed; but how came you here?"

The Spaniard related all that had passed, the fight on the raft, his adventures on the island, the escape of Harwolf, and, finally, his own deliverance by the ship on which he now stood.

"And will you ship on board the 'Red Raven?'"

"Aye, most willingly, senor; but I pray you, if you can assist these kind people, do so, for I assure you they need it."

"Where is the captain?"

"He is here, senor," pointing to a sailor standing near.

Captain Christopher doffed his hat, and, addressing the gentleman in question in French, asked if he could render any service.

"Aye, sir," replied the Dane; "the help of half-a-dozen of your men for a couple of hours would be most welcome and beneficial."

"You shall have a dozen; but when we part company you must allow me to take this Spanish youth, who is an old friend of mine."

"Take anything you like, captain, but help me to get my ship righted."

A signal was quickly run up the shattered rigging, and boats were seen leaving the different vessels well manned with stout able seamen.

They boarded the half-wrecked "Jonkörnik," and set to work with true British energy under the direction and guidance of their commander.

In a short space of time the hold was so far cleared of water that the carpenters were able, in a great measure, to stop the leak, while aloft men were busily engaged bending new sails and splicing ropes.

Christopher continued asking information with regard to Harwolf's treasure, and Diego gave him every possible information.

Four hours passed away, the "Jonkörnik" floated once more lightly on the bosom of the heaving waves, while sufficient canvas had been spread to carry her on her way.

The rovers returned to their boats.

Diego accompanied them, and Christopher was about to follow when the Danish captain laid his hand on the Boy Pirate's arm.

"Accept my thanks, generous stranger," he said, "for your kind and welcome aid; I shall ever most gratefully remember it. But tell me your own name and that of your ship."

Christopher hesitated a moment.

"I am called," he at length replied, "the Boy Pirate, my ship is known as the 'Red Raven.'"

The hardy Dane changed colour.

"You are that bold outlaw?"

"I am; but fear not, I have no wish to molest you or your cargo."

He stepped into his boat, reached his ship, and left the captain of the "Jonkörnik" standing in a state of amazement at such unusual generosity on the part a man whom he had been taught to look upon as a bloodthirsty pirate.

CHAPTER CCLXX.

THE GIPSY AND HIS WIFE CHARGED WITH ROBBERY.

WHEN the strange man who had accosted the Boy Pirate at the railway station had seen our hero fairly off, he turned away, and walking swiftly sought his home, if the miserable attic to which he wended his way might be called home.

Down into the dirty purlieus of Kent Street, in the Borough, he turned his steps, and entering a dark court knocked at the door of the most dilapidated house of the block.

A light glimmered a moment at an upper window, and something fell with a metallic ring on the pavement.

It was a key which the man picked up, and after carefully wiping it from the mud, applied to the fastening of the door.

A dark passage was rendered visible by the lesser darkness of the court, then the door was closed.

In the dark passage aforesaid the man struck a lucifer match, and threw its blue rays on a steep flight of stairs, which would have proved dangerous to a stranger, for in some places the boards had been worn through, while in others, inmates, destitute of firewood, had carried away the planks bodily.

Sometimes taking three steps together, then treading as near the dirty wall as possible to avoid the numerous holes and pitfalls, the gipsy ascended till, at length, he could go no higher.

A faint gleam of light shone beneath a door, which the man immediately pushed open and entered.

The rays of the tallow candle revealed the features of the gipsy woman who had told our hero such strange things at Blackheath.

The man who had just entered was her husband.

"Well, Bertram," she cried, lifting her eyes from the fire, "what success?"

"They are running away from each other as fast as they can. They met in the park, had a quarrel, in which our friend Captain Christopher got the best of it; Harwolf bolted to Bristol, and the youngster, after packing up his traps, took his wife and started for Frontemore."

"What can he want there?"

"I fancy this: Lord Hawksbury's yacht is lying off the coast; she's a smart sailing boat, and he means to take a trip in her."

"You will go to Bristol to-night?"

"I can't."

"Then Harwolf will escape."

"Not he; Bertram Cooper, the gipsy, knows the use of telegraph wires as well as other folks. Peter Hawkins will be waiting for him at the station."

"But why did you not go in the same train with him?"

"Because I wanted to get Captain Christopher out of the way. You leave this affair to me, Rebecca, for though you are a first-rate fortune-teller you ain't much of a detective."

"Perhaps not; but still I want to learn. Why not send to the Bristol police instead of Hawkins?"

"I don't want to have anything more to do with the police than I can help. Peter Hawkins doesn't care for them."

"And what is the next move?"

"I shall stay here all day to-morrow, and if I don't hear from Hawkins, I go to Bristol myself the next day. You will have to let Lord Hawksbury know the news."

"Hist, hark! what noise is that?"

A sound as of the splintering of wood was heard, and voices in earnest conversation.

Then men were heard, evidently strangers to the house, stumbling up the steep and narrow stairs.

A knock was heard at the door, and the gipsy couple held their breath.

Again the knock was repeated.

"Open, or we force the door."

Hastily the gipsy threw off the upper portions of his dress, while the woman as quickly laid herself down on the bundle of rags in the corner which served as a bed.

Then, opening the door, he found himself face to face with two police officers; while a person, in the garb of a gentleman, stood behind them.

"He did it! That is the man," cried the *civilian*, as individuals not belonging to the *force* are sometimes designated by arrogant peelers.

"Young man," said the senior officer, with a stern countenance, "you are wanted."

"Who want's me?" growled the gipsy brother of Esau Cooper.

"The law wants yer, young man, for pickin' the pocket of this 'ere gentleman."

"That gentleman tells a thundering lie if he says I picked his pocket."

"Yes you did," screamed the *gentleman*, keeping carefully in the shadow of the police.

"I'll break your head in a minute," said Bertram Cooper, taking a step forward.

"I warns yer not to resist hus in the hexecution of hour hoffice, young man," said the principal bobby, lugging out his truncheon.

"I don't much care for your damned rolling pin," he answered, "but I know it would be against me."

The policeman produced a pair of handcuffs, and fastened them with a snap round the gipsy's wrists.

"There's the woman asleep in the corner, policeman," whispered the gent.

"Vell, wot hof it?"

"She was with him."

"Ho! ho! an accomplish then. Robert, guard carefully this prisoner while hi secures t'other one."

So saying, with a flourish of his baton, and a martial step, which almost sent him through the flooring, he advanced towards the fortune-teller.

"Now, then, young 'oman," cried he, shaking her by the arm; "this ere shammin' wont do, yer know. You must get up, and come along with me into yonder shady tree where I keeps a small bird or two; by vich I means the station 'ouse where I keeps my bird hin a cage."

"What want you, man?"

"Oh! come, come; this 'ere won't do at all, yer know well enough what yer wanted for."

"I do not. But I do know that I am not compelled to go with you unless you tell me the charge."

"Now, are yer comin' or not?"

With these words the valiant officer raised his truncheon, and would doubtless have struck her had not the husband bounded into the middle of the room.

"You dare strike her!" he shouted. "I'll dash your brains out with my fist!"

The constable turned round, regarded the gipsy with a stare of astonishment, and then pulling out a greasy pocket-book made a memorandum in it.

"Come along quietly, Rebecca," continued Bertram; "it will be much better for us."

Together the rude pair descended the stairs, the constables keeping close behind, while the accuser, being in less hurry, kept some distance in the rear of the officers.

A little crowd had assembled in the court to witness the unusual sight of two of the dwellers in the locality being forcibly removed by the police.

Deep sullen murmurs were heard from this body of law despisers, and more than once a movement was made as if to rescue the prisoners from the officers.

But the sudden glimmer of a bull's-eye at the entrance of the court made them hang back, and the two gipsies were conveyed to the station-house followed by the timid, stylishly-dressed prosecutor.

An inspector, with magnificent whiskers, was seated dozing at a desk, but opened his eyes wide with a pleasurable look when he saw two prisoners standing before him.

With a loud pompous "Ahem!" he dipped his pen in ink, and blandly asked the senior constable what was the matter.

The active intelligent officer stated that the prosecutor had called upon him to stop a man who had stolen his watch, and that after a desperate fight he had managed to capture both in a house in Kent Street."

"Is this true, young man?"

"Quite true, sir," responded Mr. Adolphus Sillyboy. "And I charge them with stealing my gold watch and chain, value £3 10s., at the London Bridge Station."

"And what have you got to say?" asked Mr. Inspector, turning to the prisoners.

"Nothing," replied Rebecca.

"Nothing—you have nothing to say? Mind, you are not bound to answer any questions; but you may speak if you like."

"I have nothing to say."

"And you?" turning to Bertram.

"I have only to say that you had best hold your tongue, and ask me no impertinent questions."

"You are insolent, young man. I shall enter that against you."

"Yes, sir," interposed the senior officer, "and hi furthermore charge the male prisoner with usin' thretnin' langwidge when hi took 'im into custody."

The inspector entered both charges, and the prisoners were conducted to a cell.

But the garret in Cooks Rents, Kent Street, was not completely empty.

As our readers may recollect, there were children in the camp on Blackheath, and three of those had been transferred to the attic.

One of these, a boy of about eight years of age, but precocious and sharp as such wild children usually are, had heard the conversation between his father and mother, and had seen both parents marched off to the police-station.

He well recollected the most important points of the conversation—that Harwolf had gone to Bristol, Captain Christopher to Frontemore, and also the injunction to his mother to tell Lord Hawksbury the news.

He resolved, now that both parents were in durance vile. to take upon himself the responsibility of finding Lord Hawksbury, and giving him the items of news.

The little fellow lay restlessly on his heap of straw and shavings till the first streak of dawn, then, first placing some food where his younger brothers could reach it, he crept silently down the stairs, and out into the almost deserted streets.

But how to find Lord Hawksbury perplexed his mind.

A policeman was standing by the stall of one of those coffee dealers who make their day out of the morning, and to him did the young gipsy address himself.

"Now, look 'ere, youngster, if you don't want a wipe aside the head, just 'ook it. None o' your little games 'ere."

With a yell of derision, the boy darted off, swift as an arrow, his flight accelerated by the noise which the policeman's heavy boots made as they clattered in pursuit.

The young gipsy soon managed to evade his pursuer, and continued his way without further interruption down through a maze of back streets, with which he seemed well acquainted, till he reached Westminster Bridge.

Here he again asked, but this time a labouring man.

"Go over the bridge and across the park, then ask again."

The boy did as he was directed, and soon stood in Piccadilly.

A groom was slowly walking two noble-looking horses along, and the boy put to him the question.

"What do you want with Lord Hawksbury?"

"I've got something partic'lar to tell him."

"Well, come with me, and I'll show you the house."

The young gipsy followed his guide for a few minutes.

"There," cried the groom, "that's it."

The boy darted across the road, and gave a smart pull at the bell.

CHAPTER CCLXXI.

THE PRINCESS ARONZOW—EXPLANATIONS—THE PARTING—ALONE ON THE STEPPE—A SNOW STORM—THE LONE HUT IN THE WOOD.

WHEN the proud and haughty Princess Aronzow beheld the Polish girl Katinka kneeling at her feet it was some moments ere she could collect her thoughts sufficiently to be able to speak.

The first thought was that Leighton had brought about the interview in order that the truth of the rumoured marriage might meet her ears; but on consideration she deemed it impossible that one apparently so noble-minded would thus shrink from speaking the truth.

"Welcome, excellency," said Katinka, "the poor couch is at your disposal."

"Rise, girl, and return to your bed; this is no place for me while your husband is in the camp."

"Husband!" cried Katinka. "What means your highness? I have no husband!"

"No husband? Is not the Englishman your husband?"

"He is not, excellency, nor has he been aught to me beyond a kind friend."

These words were spoken with a deep sigh, while the flush on the Polish girl's face, and the tear drop in her eye, showed that though she spoke the truth, yet that truth was a hardship to her gentle unsophisticated heart.

The heart of the haughty princess was moved at the sight of Katinka's emotion, and her language became more kind.

"You are speaking the truth, I feel certain, my

girl; but the falsehood told me by the sledge driver has caused me much unhappiness."

The poor Polish girl, who had lost her heart to the brave young Anglo Saxon, turned pale and gasped for breath.

"Ah! then you love him?" said the princess, hastily.

"Excellency, he is brave, and has been most kind to me," sobbed Katinka.

The princess said no more, but throwing herself on the rude couch endeavoured to sleep, while the Polish girl crouched down at a distance, shedding bitter tears.

After awhile the Princess Aronzow rose, and proceeding to Katinka passed her arm round the peasant girl's waist, and drew her towards the couch.

"At all events I must not wholly deprive you of your bed," she said.

And then the rivals in love nestled in each other's arms, while Leighton stretched himself by the camp fire, totally unconscious of the misery and heart-burnings of the two inmates of the cave.

Morning broke, and with its earliest dawn the smugglers were in motion, preparing a meal with which to fortify themselves against the fatigues and privations of the day's journey.

The guests partook of the savoury repast, and during the progress of the morning meal the princess studiously avoided the earnest gaze of Edward Leighton, conversing in low whispers with her father, by whose side she sat.

When every one was once more ready to start, Edward Leighton approached the haughty beauty, and thus addressed her,

"Am I to have the honour of the company of yourself and the prince, your father, for the remainder of my journey?"

"It cannot be, sir. We continue with the smugglers."

Leighton gazed at her earnestly for a moment, while she shunned his looks.

"Have I offended you in aught, princess?"

"You have not, sir; yet henceforth we must be as strangers to each other."

"Strangers! and wherefore?"

"You must be well aware what reasons there are. If you are generous you will not ask me for an explanation."

Leighton reflected a moment.

"It is that rumour which has doubtless reached your ears that I am wedded to the poor Polish girl yonder."

The flush on the princess's cheek told Leighton that he had guessed the truth, and the Russian lady did not deny it.

"That rumour is false, princess; I have never breathed one word of love in her ear."

"She loves you!"

Leighton started as if an arrow had pierced his heart.

"Loves me? Impossible!"

"I speak the truth, Mr. Leighton."

"Then she has told you."

"Nay; but when I questioned her she burst into tears and tried to evade answering me. In her troubled sleep, too, she continually murmured your name."

Edward Leighton, in perplexity, passed his hand slowly over his brow, and stood lost in thought. A movement on the part of the princess only aroused him from his reverie.

"I go now to rejoin my father, Mr. Leighton. Farewell, and if we meet again the past is forgotten, and we are strangers."

"Princess," cried Edward, starting. But she was already seated in the sledge.

"Farewell, Mr. Leighton," said the prince, waving his hand courteously, and the cavalcade again set in motion.

But Ivan Urkitosky, the smuggler chief, lingered till the others were out of hearing.

ZAMPA TRIES HIS SKILL IN HORSEMANSHIP.

"I must now bid you farewell, Sir *German trader*," said he, "but as you seem to have no very distinct notion of steppe travelling will you allow me to direct you?"

"Certainly; you will greatly oblige me."

"Then where do you intend to go?"

"My object is, if possible, to reach some port on the Black Sea, from which I can take ship to England."

"Then you can't do better than go direct to Odessa, not far from the mouth of the river Dniester."

"But how far might that be from this spot, my friend?"

"Somewhat over a thousand miles, English. I fancy you understand English measurement better than Russian versts. You will proceed nearly south-

No. 79.

east for about a hundred and fifty miles to the town of Orenburg, and after disposing of your furs there, continue in the same direction till you reach Saratov, on the river Volga, where I should advise you to make another halt, as the distance between the two towns is something like two hundred and fifty miles. Then direct your course a point more to the south-ward, and after a long journey of nearly five hundred miles you will reach Pultowa, which should be your last halting-place before you reach Odessa, from which you are then only a hundred and fifty miles distant."

"Thanks," replied Mark, but his heart sank within him as he heard the smuggler recount the weary way he had to travel ere he could be in safety.

The smuggler guessed his thoughts.

"Don't be down-hearted," he cried, "the way I have told you is much nearer than to St. Petersburg, to say nothing of being safer. By the way, have you passports?"

"I have not," replied Leighton, and he then related how he had imposed upon the Cossacks by means of the old bills of lading.

The smuggler laughed and produced from an inner pocket some blank forms, *stamped and signed*, which he had procured in some mysterious manner.

"You will be all the better for having these in your possession when you reach a more cultivated district," he said, and gravely proceeded to fill up the forms with the description and appearance of Leighton and Katinka, whom he certified to be Herr Presch and his wife, subjects of the Prussian kingdom, and requested all military and municipal authorities to render them aid and protection.

"There is your passport, and here is a pocket-compass to enable you to find your way, as well as ammunition for your pistols; in return I ask you to deliver this letter to the principal priest or papa at Saratov."

"I will do so," replied Leighton, "and again I thank you for your kindness."

"Farewell!" cried the smuggler, springing into his vehicle.

He passed away quickly, rejoined his band, and Leighton was left with Katinka alone on the wide steppe.

"We must also away," he said, after gazing at the departing cavalcade, in the midst of which was the Princess Aronzow. "But what ails you, Katinka, you have been weeping?"

"Oh, I wish I were at home in Poland once more, monsieur."

"Is that *all?*" asked he, with a searching look.

The poor girl made no reply beyond a sob.

They started, and, in a short time, had left the ravine far behind them.

Mile after mile of wild, desolate country they passed till noon came and they halted to breathe the horse and refresh themselves.

Katinka had been silent all the morning and even now kept her eyes fixed on the ground.

"She is very pretty," thought Leighton to himself, "and in temper worth a dozen of the Princess Aronzow."

And truly she did look lovely; the usual bright flush on her cheek being displaced by a paleness which greatly enhanced the sparkling brilliancy of her eyes, while beneath her tight-fitting dress the outlines of her full and rounded bosom could be seen rising and falling with every sigh the poor girl breathed.

"Why do you sigh, Katinka?" he asked.

She turned a tearful eye towards him ere she replied,

"Because I am friendless and an exile."

"Nay, you are not friendless. I am with you to be your friend and protector."

"I am very thankful to you, monsieur; but this morning I was unhappy because I thought that you would accompany the princess."

"Katinka?" said Leighton, in low tones, taking her hand, "the princess told me this morning that you love me; is that true?"

"Oh! I am betrayed," murmured the poor girl; and covering her face with her hands, gave way to the tears that had been waiting for the slightest provocation to spring forth.

"You were betrayed into a confession of love this morning, and now I confess I love you most dearly, Katinka; your goodness, purity, and patriotism, render you worthy of every one's love. I seek that love at your hands; shall I seek in vain?"

"Oh monsieur! I—I—"

What more she would have said we know not; but Leighton, taking the disjointed sentence for a favourable reply, caught her in his arms, and sealed her lips with kisses.

For some few moments Katinka appeared overcome with joy, then another dark and grave doubt crossed her mind.

"But, monsieur?" said she, partly withdrawing from his arms, "though I am only a poor peasant girl, I bear a stainless name which I must preserve unsullied."

"No act or word of mine, dear Katinka, shall cast a shadow of doubt or suspicion on your character. But," and he again drew her close to him, "at the next town we reach you must become my wife."

"Monsieur——" she whispered.

"Nay, be not so ceremonious; my name is Edward."

"Then, Edward, I will be yours."

"Heaven bless you for that word."

And still holding her closely in his arms, he poured into her willing ear an ardent tale of love, candidly confessing how he had doubted in his own mind whether he loved her most or the princess, till the cold haughty behaviour of the latter had caused him to seek for sympathising love in the heart of the dear girl he held in his arms.

"And now, dearest," he continued, "one more kiss to seal the contract, and then to the sledge."

Katinka, willing, reached up her rosy lips to him, though not one kiss but a good dozen were printed on them by the enraptured young man.

"But, Edward, dearest," she said, as he led her to the vehicle, "what will your friends say when they know that we travelled together by ourselves for so many weeks?"

"You, dearest, will never have occasion to say that I treated you otherwise than honourably; they may say what they please."

So saying, he placed her carefully in the sledge, wrapping her round with rugs to defend her beloved form from a keen north-east wind that had risen."

Elated by the discovery of his new-found treasure, the young man scarcely noticed the threatening aspect of the weather till a few large flakes of snow falling called his attention to the fact that a heavy storm was rapidly overtaking them.

"We must reach some shelter, and that quickly, too, my love," he said, "for with the snow, darkness will set in apace."

"Yon wood might prove better than the open plain," replied Katinka, pointing to another of the pine forests which are abundant in the Russian wilds.

"You have quick eyes, dearest; I had not noticed the trees, but if we have to camp there, we shall be in danger from the wolves."

"Not more so than here, for they roam about in every direction."

"Then the wood be it. There, at all events, we can have fires all round us."

So saying he urged the horse forward, and entered the wood just as the snow began to fall in good earnest.

A few yards within the wood, however, he saw a sight which gave him hope of comfort.

A clearing had been made, and a rude hut built apparently of the timber of the felled trees. The door of this rude specimen of architecture stood invitingly open.

Driving up towards it, Leighton jumped to the ground, and was about to lift Katinka from the sledge, when, with a snarling yell, a big she-wolf sprang out of the doorway, followed by three cubs.

Leighton sent a pistol bullet whistling after them, but it missed its aim, and the brutes disappeared in the forest.

First glancing within to be certain that there were no more of the tribe there, he lifted his love from the sledge, and placed her inside the hut, which, from its deserted look, seemed not to have been inhabited by human beings for many months.

A huge pile of dried wood was then collected, and a fire made beneath the rude chimney, after which the horse was unharnessed, and he, too, placed beneath the shelter of the hut, two or three large branches being placed so as to keep him to his proper side of the building.

Then, every article was removed from the sledge, and brought to the fireside. A stout pine log was cut out so as to bar the door, and with a smile of triumph, the young man turned to assist his betrothed in preparing the homely supper of tea, brown bread, and slices of bacon toasted at the fire.

Katinka seemed to have recovered her spirits, and as Leighton listened to her affectionate conversation, he quite forgot the proud and haughty Princess Aronzow.

Darkness quickly set in, and the boisterous storm howled through the forest, shaking the tall pine trees in its fury.

Presently a dismal, melancholy howl was heard without, and another answered it.

The wolves had already scented the horse, who trembled and moved uneasily at the hideous sound.

Katinka, too, drew nearer her lover, who, with a smile, assured her that there was no cause for fear.

"I know it, dear Edward," she replied, "but that dreadful sound always makes me afraid."

"They must devour me ere they touch you, my own love; but, at all events, I will load my pistols."

He did so, and, peering through a crevice, could discern eight or ten of the brutes standing not far from the hut, while another was stealthily joining them from the forest, the white snow rendering them distinctly visible.

Taking careful aim, he fired at the largest of the pack, and a fearful yell of agony told him that his aim had been true.

When the smoke had cleared away, the brute was struggling in the midst of his mates, who, in a few minutes more had devoured him.

Another pistol shot hissed into the midst of the mass, and another wolf, hard hit, slowly crawled away, followed by the remainder of the pack, who allowed the cripple to reach the wood ere they sprang upon him.

For some time after they were more cautious, keeping beneath the shadow of the trees, and Leighton once more returned to his seat.

"You must not be afraid, my love," he said, passing his arm round the waist of the fair girl, who now willingly allowed him to caress her; "these cowardly brutes will vanish when daylight comes."

"I am not afraid, dear Edward, I repeat, but their cries are so fearful."

"And you are not afraid to trust yourself alone with me in this hut?"

A blush mantled to her cheek as she replied,

"I have your promise that you would not abuse the confidence I place in you?"

"And, my own love, that promise shall be faithfully kept."

The flickering fire threw a dim light through the rude hut, the wolves at intervals joined in dismal chorus with the howling storm, but those warm young hearts heeded neither tempest nor brute.

Katinka's head was laid lovingly on Leighton's shoulder as they sat by the fire, a thick rug was wrapped round her body, and in happy silence they thought only of each other.

As he gazed on her innocent, confiding face the strength of Leighton's passions were disarmed of every evil intent and all idea of taking an unfair advantage of her defenceless position passed from his mind.

"The wolves will not trouble us much, dear, after all," he whispered, after a long silence.

She made no reply, and then, for the first time, he observed that her eyes were closed in slumber.

Gently laying her back on the skins he had arranged as a couch, he spread his cloak over her, and, heaping more wood on the fire, passed to the further side of the hut to spread his own rug for repose.

Lightly he slept with pistols ready to his hand, yet his dreams were of his fair Polish girl and of her alone.

CHAPTER CCLXXII.

THE "NEWPORT"—DANIEL HARWOLF FLOGGED —THE CABIN AND THE FORECASTLE—A CONSPIRACY, WHICH ENDS IN MUTINY—A BLOODY REVENGE.

Two days after Daniel Harwolf shipped on board the dashing clipper ship, which Captain Pickett commanded, he almost repented the step he had taken.

But it was too late to retreat now, for they were fairly out at sea.

The captain was a tyrant of the harshest kind; everything had to be performed with a celerity almost magical, and even then only curses greeted the ears of the crew as a reward.

Murmurs were heard amongst the sailors, but the captain took no notice of them, and when, during a stiff breeze in the Bay of Biscay, the mate reported, or rather hinted that the men were discontented, the only reply that that officer received for his pains was,

"Bring me no more reports of the kind, but flog the first one who mutinies either by word, deed, or look."

"But, sir——"

"But, sir, no more on that subject. We shall have a storm on us in a few minutes, see the hatches battened down."

"I see, sir, and if I might suggest an opinion it would be well to wear round——"

"You are right, Mr. Harper; give me the trumpet."

The second officer handed the instrument just as the full force of the storm struck the ship.

"Ready there, fore and aft!" shouted Captain Pickett.

The men scrambled along to their posts, holding by belaying pins. Daniel Harwolf was at the wheel.

"Up with the helm!" roared the captain, "slack off the main-sheet, brail up the main-sail, ease down the weather boom-guy!"

The rest of his command was unheard in the furious howl of the tempest, but the men knew their work, and the ship payed off before the wind, darting like lightning between two tremendous waves.

The brine swelled green over her larboard bulwark as she heeled over with a heavy lurch.

"Aft with the main-sail! Haul for your lives!"

The gallant vessel came trembling up in the long bight of the sea, and took the gale steadily on her other beam.

It blew harder than ever, and the scud of the sea almost rolled the ship bodily away as she met it on her weather bow, washing over the handrail; the gale heaving her down on the lee beam at every forward pitch, so that all hands were forced to keep crowded together aft.

Harwolf's unaided strength was not sufficient to keep the helm up, and a second hand was sent to the wheel.

But at length the storm spent its fury, the sullen winds hushed themselves, though the sea was still running in huge waves, which threatened each moment to overwhelm the gallant bark.

Officers and men drew a long breath when they saw the captain retire to his cabin, for they knew then that he deemed all danger over, and despite his harshness Captain Pickett was no despicable seaman.

Another man took Harwolf's place at the helm, and that worthy was about to go below, when the captain again made his appearance.

"Next time I tell you to put the helm up, you will obey my orders a little more quickly than you did but now."

"I did so as quickly as you could," replied Harwolf, forgetting for a moment that he was addressing his officer.

"Nothing of the kind. You are no seaman; but I will teach you ere long."

"Teach your grandmother!"

"What, mutiny!" cried Captain Pickett, presenting a pistol at Harwolf's head. "Here, seize this man, and put him in irons."

Ere he could have time to resist, the poor pirate was knocked down, handcuffed, and hurled down the companion ladder, to meditate on the probable consequences of his rash speech.

He was not kept long in suspense.

Two hours after he was again summoned to the deck. and the crew was called to witness punishment.

" Lash him up to the mainmast."

The order was quickly obeyed, and the boatswain made his appearance with the much-dreaded scourge in his hand.

"Give him two dozen!"

The lash swept through the air, and descending on Harwolf's naked shoulders, left nine red marks, or rather stripes.

He groaned, and moved his shoulders uneasily.

Again the cat set her nine claws on his back, and the marks of the first stroke became blurred and indistinct.

After the next stroke drops of blood were seen to trickle down the untouched part of his back.

Dismal groans were uttered by the victim of Captain Pickett's severity, but—though with great difficulty—he kept himself from screaming, which would have destroyed his reputation for courage in the eyes of the seamen, whom he wished to get under his influence.

At length the horrid torture was over, the fastenings which bound him up to the mainmast were cut, and he was at liberty to depart.

In grim silence he went below, and submitted himself to the rude doctoring of his messmates, who rubbed salt and vinegar on his mangled shoulders, thereby adding not a little to the smart.

"I'm blowed, if you ain't a plucky one, mate!" said Bill Green, one of the men whose conversation at the Bristol beer-shop had induced him to ship in the "Newport."

"That's nothing," responded Harwolf. "But I'll be even with the old ruffian yet."

"Damn my eyes! if he ain't a reg'lar devil."

"Then the sooner he's sent back to the hell he came from the better."

The men, called Keef and Wallbrook, overheard part of this sentence, and gathered closer round the flogged pirate.

Harwolf gave one glance in their faces, and saw at once that they were ripe for any scheme of mutiny had they but brains to form a plot.

"The thing is how to send him back," said Jem Wallbrook.

"There are plenty of ways."

"Well, tell us one or two of 'em."

"Hush! Not now. To-night when our watch turns in, come to my hammock, and bring all true-blue boys you know with you."

"All right," whispered the men, separating, for the mate was seen descending the ladder.

The day passed; night came, and Harwolf with his messmates kept their watch on deck.

No word of the conspiracy was breathed while there, but just as they were relieved a man whispered to two of the crew, who as yet knew nothing of the intended meeting.

"Come to Harwolf's hammock, when you get below. Silence!"

The captain in his cabin little thought that another storm, more fearful than that of the elements, was about to break over him.

With a bottle of wine and box of cigars by his bedside, he enjoyed himself, relying on his pistols in case of a disturbance.

And now the conspirators had assembled, in all six men; four only, and two officers remained to be arranged with.

"Before we begin to talk," said Harwolf, "let us see that no one is here."

And striking a match, he threw a ray of light all round him; but there was no one near save those

fierce, evil-minded men, who knew well what was about to be proposed.

"We're all safe, so now to business; we can see if any one comes down."

"Well, mate, what have you got to propose?" asked Keef.

"It's no use beating about the bush; what I have got to propose is that we put it out of the captain's power to do any more mischief."

"Aye, aye, mate!" they all murmured.

"He is a blasted tyrant," muttered Keef; "and I, for one, will not put up with it!"

"Nor I, nor I !" was heard all round.

"Then, mates, is it agreed we take the ship and hoist the black flag?"

"The black flag! Dam'me, you're a brick!" ejaculated Wallbrook.

"Hush! Not so loud."

"But who can we have to navigate if we don't let the mate do it?' said a cautious one.

"I can navigate this ship or any other on the ocean," replied Harwolf. "This is the first time I ever sailed in a vessel unless I at the same ;time commanded her."

"Then you shall be captain," proposed one of the conspirators.

The others readily agreed.

"But share alike as regards the swag," interposed Wallbrook.

"Share alike, of course."

"Well, how is the trick to be done, mate ?" asked Bill Green.

"It had better be done at once. You can creep softly up on deck, and as the night is dark you won't be noticed, until two of you collar Harper, gag him and take his pistols. Fling master Rattan, the bo'swain over the side. and then, into the cabin to the captain. But don't kill him; leave him to me, when you have his barkers and sword. I'll pay him back the two-dozen with interest."

"Then, here goes," muttered Wallbrook, moving off softly.

The other men followed him silently as shadows, and gliding on to the deck, armed themselves with any weapons they could lay their hands on.

Mr. Harper, the mate, was looking over the side of the vessel watching the sparkling waves as they danced by the ship and thinking of his fair wife and babe, whom those waves separated him from, when suddenly a man's arm was thrown tightly round his neck, compressing his throat till he was unable to breathe.

Struggling was useless, for his hands were seized at the same time and bound behind him ; a gag was placed in his mouth, and he was thrown on the deck.

Startled at the sound of the fall, old Rattan, the boatswain, came running up, and he too was treated in a similar manner.

The remaining four men were too much astonished to be able to resist the mutineers, and in obedience to a whispered command from Harwolf, they left the deck.

"Now for the captain," whispered Keef.

"How is it to be done?" inquired Wallbrook.

"Take up the capstan bars, run altogether against the cabin door, and be in on him before he has time to wake."

Such was Harwolf's advice, and the men prepared to act on it.

Crash went the slight wood-work of the cabin door, and the mutineers crowded through the opening thus made.

Captain Pickett snatched a pistol, and sent a bullet through the head of one of the pirates; but ere he could repeat the shot, the whole of them were on him, and he was bound hand and foot.

The three officers being thus disposed of, Harwolf called the four men who had not taken any part in the struggle, and in brief terms thus addressed them :

"My lads, this is no longer a trading vessel, but a pirate, and I am its commander. You have your choice of two things, obey me or go overboard ; which is it to be ?"

Of two evils a wise man chooseth the lesser ; and as piracy seemed preferable to death, they joined their former companions.

"Now bring the prisoners up to the mainmast," cried Harwolf, exercising his new authority with promptness.

The men were so accustomed to obey others, that they forgot that, but half-an-hour ago, this man Harwolf was no better than themselves.

So the captain, the mate, and the boatswain, were dragged to the position indicated, and securely bound to the mast.

" Let them remain there till morning, and then show them what it is to be flogged," cried Harwolf. " Now, lads, for a good glass of grog each."

The whole crew entered the cabin save two who were left to watch the helm ; but those two were land bubbers, and consequently in great terror of the fierce pirates.

Bottles were uncorked, wine and brandy flowed in profusion, and by break of dawn the whole of the party were considerably intoxicated.

" Lets—hic—go an' flog those damned rascals at the—hic—mainmast," cried Harwolf, rising to his feet.

" And put them in brine afterwards," said Keef, pointing, with a grim smile, to the dashing waves.

" Certainly ; come on."

They returned to the deck, and, in a few minutes, Captain Pickett was in the same position which Harwolf had occupied.

" Give me the cat," he cried.

The men stood by yelling and laughing, while Harwolf, with all the rage of a drunken fiend, laid the lash on the captain's shoulders till his arm was tired.

" Rascals !" said Harper, the mate, " you will all be hanged for this !"

" You will never live to see your prophecy fulfilled, fool !" roared Harwolf, dropping the cat and drawing a pistol.

There was a flash, and the ball hissed through the brain of the unfortunate man.

His head dropped forward on his breast ; he was dead.

" Throw him overboard," cried the monster.

His orders were obeyed.

" Now, Cap'n Pickett," said Wallbrook, coming up, " you an' me has a leetle bill to square off. So jest hand over the cat, Cap'n Harwolf."

" Certainly ; I am only too happy to see him get another good flogging."

" But I ain't a going to flog where your marks is though ; turn him round with his back to the mast, boys."

In this altered position the unfortunate Captain Pickett of course presented his face and chest to the ribald crew who surrounded him.

The man Wallbrook raised the cat, already stiff and dripping with blood, and with fiendish barbarity commenced lashing his victim about the face and neck.

" There," said he, throwing down the instrument of torture, and drawing a knife, " now I'll finish you, blast you."

With these words he drove the knife up to the very hilt in Captain Pickett's heart.

" Send him to join company with Harper," roared Harwolf, and, with many a ribald jest, the mangled corpse was cast into the sea.

There now only remained the boatswain.

" I suppose you can swim, old Rattan ?" cried the new captain. " Tie a twenty-four pounder to his ankles and send him alive to take care of the dead."

" Thank you for the merciful death you have ordered me," replied the old salt.

A kick in the stomach silenced him, and, a few minutes after, he too sunk beneath the green waves.

" Now, lads, wash the deck down, and then sew poor Smith up in his hammock."

That was the name of the man who had been shot

by Captain Pickett, and his body was still lying at the cabin door.

Three hours afterwards there was no trace of the recent bloody deeds to be seen on board the ship.

Three twenty-four pound guns were placed in position, the name of the ship was altered to the " Revenge," and the " Newport " of Bristol was never more heard of.

But about a fortnight afterwards a Danish ship, the " Jonkörnik," entered Waterford Harbour, and the captain reported to the authorities that in 25 deg. west and 38 deg. north, he had found the bodies of two men, apparently officers of an English ship, one of whom appeared to have been shot through the head, while the other was much mutilated and had a deep wound in the left side. The bodies were too much decomposed to be brought into port, but they had been stripped and sunk ; and the worthy Dane begged to hand over their clothing for identification.

CHAPTER CCLXXIII.

SILAS RYE ON THE TRACK AGAIN — OINY TURNS TAILOR AND "TAILER" — ACROSS THE MOUNTAINS — GENERAL JONES AND FAMILY — MEETING OF SILAS RYE AND ANDREW HARWOLF.

As Catabaga had prophesied, four days elapsed ere Silas Rye was able to mount his mustang, and proceed up the second pathway they had discovered over the Great Rocky Mountains.

During the interval he was kindly and carefully nursed by Oiny, who also in his leisure moments occupied himself in the manufacture of the proposed leather breeches.

And a curious garment it was when the amateur tailor had finished his task, for, to avoid trouble, Oiny had adapted the skin of the panther to his own form as nearly as possible, cutting it in two and encasing his own thighs in that portion of the hide which had once covered the sinewy hinder limbs of the American tiger.

But having turned the " fleshy side out " during the process of sewing up, he had neglected to cut off the long furry tail of the animal, and in consequence was much surprised on making his first appearance in them to see both Silas and the Indian burst into roars of laughter.

Such an unusual circumstance on the part of the grave warrior induced Oiny to make inquiries as to what ailed them both.

" It's lucky you are not in England, Oiny, or you would be locked up till the fifth of November to keep you safe for a guy."

" Shure an' I don't know what ails yez at all, at all."

" How much do you want for your tail, Oiny ?"

" Now, be aisy wid yez, an' haven't I been afther usin' it for a pocket-hankeycher for this two months agone."

He thought that Silas was alluding to the tail of the garment which is usually worn beneath all others.

" My white brother will frighten the horses if he approaches them like that," said Catabaga, giving himself up unrestrainedly to mirth.

" An' whin yez have done jokin', perhaps I'll be afther hearin' what's ticklin' yer narves ?"

" You tickle our nerves with your tail, Oiny. Cut it off, man, unless you wish us to die with laughter."

The second allusion to his tail caused Oiny to glance behind him, and then he at once saw the cause of their merriment.

Bursting into a hearty guffaw himself it was some minutes ere he could speak.

" Indade ; an' I'm not wonderin' ye laughed,

shure 'twould make ould Nick laugh to see such a
foine immitaytion of his latther end."

"Well, make haste, man, and off with it, for now
I am able to go I want to be off at once."

"But, sir," whispered Oiny, "sarvin' yer prisence
it'll not be dacent, for there 'ill be a big hole there!"

"Well, leave about six inches of it then to sew
over."

Oiny drew his knife, and grasping a good handful
close up to his person cut off all the remainder of the
tail below.

"That's right," cried Silas, "never mind about
stitching up now, but mount."

"An' ye'd not be in such a hurry yerself if yez had
the wind whistlin' through yez loike I have at the
prisent moment," muttered Oiny, mounting his
horse.

"Once more we are in motion, and now for revenge!" cried Silas, pressing onwards; "but can
you discover their trail on this stony pathway?"

"The Grey Wolf is cunning; but he leaves a large
trail."

"It may be large to you, Catahaga; but I cannot
see it."

"Look there, the Grey Wolf set his foot on that
stone," said the Indian, pointing to a huge flint
which had recently been moved from its bed; "there
too he rested the butt of his rifle," pointing to an
almost imperceptible mark on the ground.

"And do you think we shall overtake them?"

"Yes, before many suns are set."

"The Grey Wolf is cunning."

"I know it; but his eyes are blinded, he thinks
that you are dead; he will not hasten his steps."

"An' I'll be glad to meet that same gintleman;
I'll make him remember the stab in the back he
give me, the baste," interrupted Oiny.

"In the land of gold we shall find him," was the
reply of the Indian warrior.

They travelled on towards the aforesaid land of
gold, mounting up steep pathways, diving down
seemingly bottomless ravines, crossing yawning
chasms on rude pine-tree bridges, and skirting
tremendous perpendicular precipices, whose bottom
could scarcely be discerned in the awful depths
below.

After some days of severe hardship, during which
they progressed but at a very slow rate on account of
the ruggedness of the road, and the obstacles which
had to be surmounted, they descended from the
mountains into the wild forests and plains and hills
of California.

The track of the Grey Wolf and his companion
was more plainly visible, but at last was lost in a
beaten pathway which had apparently been trodden
by numerous other white men.

"What is to be done now?" demanded Silas, when
Catahaga reported that he could no longer distinguish the trail of the persons they sought.

The warrior shook his head in evident perplexity.

"We can but go forward to the settlement which
this pathway leads us to, and see if he be there,"
continued Silas, answering his own questions.

So on they went, and ere nightfall arrived at the
city of Jonesville, a flourishing community, on a
site which had been intended for a large town.

But the population had not increased very rapidly,
so that although it was on the direct route to the
gold-fields, the original settlers, some twenty in
number, were its only inhabitants at the time our
three travellers entered it.

In answer to the questions of Silas, General Jones,
after whom the city was named, informed them that
they could sleep in his barn, and take their supper at
his table.

"Have you seen two white men pass through here
on foot within the last week?"

"Wa-al, I kalkelate as how I did see two darned
Britishers come here, but I guess they was too early
to let me set eyes on 'em when they sloped, blast 'em!"

"You didn't like them?"

"Stranger, I guess two darneder thieves never
stole hossflesh!"

"But they had no horses."

"I reckon they did though, the skunks; they jest
tuk two o' my best nags, without as much as sayin'
thankye."

"Which way did they go?"

"They said as how they was goin' to Fitzroy
diggin's, but I guess they didn't go that way at
all."

"Where, then, do you think is their destination?"

"Stranger, I don't know nothin' about destynay-
tion, but I guess if you wants 'em you must go right
slick away to San Franciskay. But who air you,
stranger?"

"I am a man whom the grey-bearded one has
tried to murder two or three times. He has also
stabbed my Irish friend."

"Then I reckon you want to square up with
him?"

"Just so."

"Then come in and licker."

They accepted the invitation, and when the
"licker" was disposed of, a smoking hot supper
was placed on the board, to which the General, his
wife, seven sons and six daughters, with the three
strangers, sat down, while sundry huge dogs tried to
find a place to put their noses on the table.

"We air a noomerous fam'ly, I guess," cried the
General, looking round with an air of pride on the
assembly, "and that boy"—pointing to his eldest—
"air a credit to his country. Siree, he can whop
seven niggers, chalk a red, or lick a grizzly out of
his skin!"

The boy in question—a young man some two and
twenty years old, and over six feet in height—blushed
at this bounteous praise.

"Wa-all, I guess I air a screamer, stranger," said
he, and immediately helped himself to a shoulder of
venison, which he managed to dispose of about as
easily as the seven niggers or the grizzly.

At length the *large* family finished their *large*
meal, and the General proposed more whisky.

But both Silas and Catahaga declined, though
Oiny's eyes glistened as he sniffed the fragrant
potion.

A sound night's rest saw them once more on their
path, and after passing other settlements and towns
in which they generally heard tidings of the fugitive
Harwolf and Miles, they arrived at Claremont
Creek, a gold digging station on the road to San
Francisco.

"Have you had two strangers here from the eastward?" asked Silas of the store-keeper, of whom he
purchased some provisions.

"Britishers, you mean?"

"Yes."

"Strikes me, they're in the diggin's now. Two
fine hosses they've got—guess the coons stole 'em."

Silas Rye's eye blazed with hopes of vengeance,
and he proceeded carefully through the whole of the
canvas village.

At length he saw the object of his search in a hole
which had been recently excavated, watching Miles,
who was stirring the loose ground with a spade.

"Welcome to California!" he cried.

Both Harwolf and Miles gazed up in utter astonishment.

"Silas Rye!" groaned Miles, while his sterner
companion said nothing.

Oiny touched his battered hat, and, twirling his
stick round and round, cried out, in joyful tones,

"Och! good luck to yer honner. Sure an haven't
yez got a job o' work for a poor boy?"

"To the devil with you!" roared Harwolf. "But
I see you have him with you," he continued, pointing
to Catahaga.

The Indian warrior unslung his rifle, and taking
deadly aim at the Grey Wolf, would, in another
instant have shot him dead, had not his arm been
struck up from behind.

"Guess, Mister Redskin, you mustn't come any
o' them capers in our diggins. I belongs to the
perlice."

Turning, they beheld a tall Yankee, dressed in a rude attempt at the military style, with a belt well stocked with pistols.

"Say, stranger," he continued, turning to Silas, "what's all this ere about?"

"That man has tried to murder all three of us."

"Well, call him out and chalk the darned skunk; but fair play, mind."

"I also charge him and his mate with stealing two horses, the property of General Jones, of Jonesville," continued Silas, feeling convinced that an accusation of murder would not be listened to in the diggings.

"Now that charge air some purpose, I calkilate. Jest walk yerself out o' that hole, mister."

And blowing a whistle, four others in the same dress came up.

Harwolf saw that resistance was unavailing, and slowly came from his digging with Miles, trusting to find some means of escape.

CHAPTER CCLXXIV.

CAPE TOWN—BUMBOATS AND THEIR OWNERS—FLATTERING TESTIMONIALS—UNSHIPPING BALLAST—BLACK RALPH LISTENS TO A SERMON—AND THE BOY PIRATE APPOINTS A CHAPLAIN FOR HIS FLEET.

WITHOUT any adventure worth recording the fleet of the Avengers arrived at the Cape of Good Hope, and cast anchor in Table Bay.

As Captain Kit still assumed the character of a merchantman, and the men of war were all away cruising for slavers on the west coast of the African continent, he had not the least fear of detection or capture.

He took up a temporary abode with Lilia in Cape Town, while the water casks were being refilled, and sundry small, though necessary repairs executed.

Scarcely had the anchors been dropped ere the ships were surrounded by a crowd of bumboats, manned by negroes, Jews, and Dutch crews of all ages and sexes, anxious for the honour and profit of supplying the ships' crews with fresh provisions.

One of these craft was commanded by a very stout old lady, evidently of Dutch extraction, who sat in a stately manner beneath the shade of a white canvas umbrella, with the handle of which she occasionally belaboured the ribs of two Hottentot youths, who handled the oars in such a clumsy manner as to excite the laughter of every one.

By dint of swearing at her rowers she at length managed to get alongside the "Red Raven," and by the aid of a stout rope was hoisted to the deck in triumph, bearing three full-blown cabbages under each arm, while the knuckles of a couple of legs of mutton peered from the folds of her greasy dress.

"Ya, mynheer," she bawled, addressing the Boy Pirate, "goot cabbage, goot scheep lags. Puy, mynheer?"

"No, thank you," responded our hero.

Approaching still closer, she dropped her voice to a loud whisper,

"Got goot schapps, mynheer; goot bier and pranty. Puy some, mynheer?"

"No, I have no use for them."

"Wass ze schirts, mynheer; clean ze stocking. Very little pay. Got goot letters from mynheers of many schips."

"Let us see your testimonials, then."

The old lady produced a packet of letters, of various dates, all black and greasy.

The first our hero looked at was something in this style:—

"British Ship 'Goldilocks.'
"This is to certify that the bearer, Vrouw Drunkendroff, is a cheat of the worst description. I had two fowls and a dozen eggs of her; in the bill she charged me for two dozen eggs, four legs of mutton, a sack of potatoes, and five fowls. I paid her with a five-pound note, in expectation of receiving four pounds fifteen shillings change; I have never set eyes on her since. My advice to my countrymen is, hav no dealings with her if any other boat is in sight.
"J. WILCOCKS, First Mate.

"P.S.—Eight of the eggs might have been charged as fowls, for they contained perfectly-formed chickens."

"That's good," said Christopher, laughing. "Now let us have a look at the next."

The Dutch woman smiled, nodded, and handed him another paper.

To captains of vessels:—The bearer, Vrouw Drunkendroff is the biggest thief that ever hailed a ship at anchor. Take care of all the portable articles on your deck. Only respect for her sex prevented our captain from ordering the boatswain to pay her instead of the purser.
H. ST. CLAIR, H.M. Ship "Cambrian."

"That is still better," cried Christopher. "Have you any more of the same kind?"

"Ya! ya! mynheer, plenty goot letter."

So saying she handed him a third.

"The fat old thief who bears this received from me fourteen shirts to wash. She returned me six dilapidated garments, averring that they were all the clothes she had from me. If the ship had remained here twenty-four hours longer I would have drowned her in her own wash-tub.
"N. A. Bob, Deputy-Judge, Rajahpoorrie district."

The Boy Pirate handed back these flattering testimonials to their happy possessor with a smile, while he motioned her to the side.

"Madam, I cannot deal with you myself, nor will I allow my men to do so. Be kind enough to return to your boat."

"Vat for you no puy? Got goot everyting, plenty cheap."

"That may be, but you must go."

"Go! Yah! you got no money, dam no goot; yah! very great mynheer, but much Got for dam tief."

"Hoist her over the side, Brierly."

"Aye, aye, cap'en!" responded the old tar, and taking her by the shoulders he led her to the side, but was unable to make her move an inch further.

"Aloft there!" shouted old Brierly, hailing a couple of men who were tarring down the rigging, "send down a couple of purchase blocks and tackle to hoist the old lady overboard."

The men, who heartily entered into the fun of the joke, lowered the tackle, which, with the assistance of Zampa, he fastened round the waist of the fat Vrouw.

In a few moments all was ready, and giving the word "pull, hoy!" the old lady was speedily dangling at the height of five feet above the deck, screaming and swearing in jaw-breaking Dutch, while one hand flourished the umbrella and the other a leg of mutton.

"Shove her off with the boat hook, Zamp. Now then, my lads, pay out!"

The men let the rope run through the blocks with such velocity that ere they were aware that the boat was not immediately beneath her they allowed her to drop with a loud splash in the water.

"Hollo there!" exclaimed Brierly, "hoist up again, the old craft's afloat when she ought to be in the dry dock!"

"Eh! golly!" grinned Zamp. "Yes, ain't she heavy now, Massa Brierly? Oh, lor! couldn't help it nohow!" he exclaimed, as pretending to be unable to hoist the weight, he allowed the woman to drop a second time into the water.

"That's enough," cried the Boy Pirate, who had been an amused spectator of the scene. "Now lower the old lady into her boat."

This feat was at length accomplished, and old Brierly wiped the perspiration from his brow, saying,

"If you wants any ballast, cap'en, you only got to send a boat's crew ashore, and man-handle the old lady aboard, and lay her down in the hold."

The Vrouw meanwhile was standing up in her boat screaming and swearing, while the Hottentots endeavoured to recover the vegetables she had dropped during her removal from the deck of the "Red Raven" to her own boat.

"I don't think she'll come on board again," said Christopher to his wife.

"But what a shame to use her so roughly," whispered the gentle Queen of the Avengers.

The same afternoon Black Ralph determined on visiting the town for the 'purpose of trying his luck once more in the paths of love.

Of course, after landing, the first thing the jolly outlaw did was to prime himself for whatever adventures he might encounter with a stiff glass of grog.

For this purpose he entered an inn, which looked more English than any other, and, sitting himself down in a kind of parlour, lit his cigar.

A slow, stately step in the passage called his attention from pretty little ideal vrouws to the things of this world.

The door opened, and a tall, lath-looking American, dressed in a suit of very seedy black clothes, entered.

Sitting himself down on a chair opposite the pirate, he placed first his heels on the table, then, beside them, a tattered-looking hymn-book, and gravely expectorated on the floor.

"Friend," said he, addressing the bold outlaw with a nasal twang, "I guess thou art one o' them as goes down to the sea in ships?"

"I kalkilate you are about correct, stranger," replied Ralph, imitating the tones of the Yankee.

"Ungodly rapscalious is all them seamen, an' I reckon you air not any chalks above the rest."

"Guess you air damned impertinent, stranger. Who air you? Where the devil was you raised?"

"I guess you hadn't ought to swar an a minister a settin' by. Listen unto me while I expounds the word."

Without waiting to learn whether Ralph was in an agreeable mood to listen to his exhortation, the preacher commenced howling a most dismal hymn, first opening the book and handing it to his auditor, with an injunction to "jine in."

> "Come, listen, all you wicked sailors,
> An' unbelievin' sojers too:
> Likewise ye shoemakers an' tailors,
> I brings the gospel unto you——"

"Hold hard!" shouted Ralph. "None of your blasted yelling here."

"'Cussed air he what cusses,' says the prophet Zerubabub," bawled the preacher, "an' I kalkilate to sermonize jest a few from that ere identycle text."

"Well, heave ahead," cried Ralph, beginning to be amused; "but no singing, mind, and perhaps you would preach all the better if you stowed a glass of grog away in your hold."

"Stranger, I reckon as how you begin to speak more like a Christian man, for the prophet Esrediah says, 'Blessed air the man what opens his bowels upon his brother which air in need.' I guess I can jest tote off a drain o' rum hot."

Ralph gave the necessary directions, and sitting down endeavoured to compose his features to the requisite degree of gravity.

"As I were a saying, stranger," continued the missionary, "when I were interrupted by your benevolent offer to stand a licker, 'Cussed air he what cusses,' an' as you cussed, stranger—I kalkilate you air not a goin' to deny that fact—it air pritty evident that you will be cussed——"

"Don't you curse me, though," said Ralph, with a threatening look.

"I reckon not: but there air only one road to save yerself, stranger. That air to hand over a few dollars to help build a church and endow a chaplang among the one alightened Hottingtots what dwells in the intereyer parts o' this ere land."

"Now, stash that, or I'll hand you over *two fives* that 'twill puzzle you to get changed," growled Ralph. "Now, tell us a good story about these aforesaid Hottentots."

"Stranger, I air a missionary, and as sich it air onbecoming o' me to be settin' here a spinning yarns, as it air called by all you wicked sailors; but I hev been amongst them Hottingtots jest a few. I

guess it were considerable hard work tu hammer the gospel intu their thick heads, an' like the holy 'possals I were persecuted some. But, stranger, the gospel says as how you air to heap coals o' fire on the heads o' them as hates you, an' I kinder kalkilate as how, if I gits my church an' house which I air a raisin' funds for, when I returns onto that stiff-necked generaytion o' rattlesnakes, I guess I'll jest frizzle their darned woolley heads for 'em, blast 'em! But they air a sinful people an' their wavs shall fail, an' they shall be drove hence an' shall flee onto the mountains of Ypsilon, where the lion ro-o-o-areth an' the wang-doodle mourneth for his first-born——"

A loud peal of laughter outside the window, in which Ralph felt compelled to join, checked the onward progress of the Yankey sermon.

Turning his head, the outlaw saw some six or eight of the crew of the "Red Raven" who had been attracted by the preacher's eloquence.

On seeing that they had drawn the missionary's eyes towards them, the jolly tars commenced singing a song,

> "Oh, if I was a cassowary
> On the plains of Timbuctoo,
> I guess I'd eat a missionary,
> Hat and boots and hymn-book too."

The unseemly shouting seemed to disconcert the preacher, who after bestowing a backhanded blessing on them for a "set o' darned cusses," again deposited his heels on the table, and requested Ralph to "loan" him "a chaw."

The outlaw replied that he had no tobacco, but at the same time ordered the waiter to bring the preacher a cigar.

He then passed out, and joined the sailors outside.

"Ask your parding, Cap'n Ralph," said one; "but is that ere chap a holding forth without collectin' any custom-house dooties?"

"By no means, my lads; take care of your dollars when you fall foul of him."

At this moment the preacher issued from the inn, and beckoned Ralph aside.

"Now you air a Christian man, stranger, an' I kalkilate you won't let a poor devil starve for the bread what perishes, though he air only a missionary."

"I certainly don't wish my worst enemy to starve."

"Then hand over a dollar, stranger, an' I guess I'll give yer my blessin'."

"Your blessing isn't worth much, nor would the dollar last you a very long time; but if you are willing to work I fancy I can procure you a berth as chaplain on board a ship, or rather as chaplain to a fleet, I should have said," replied Ralph, determined, if possible, to have some fun with the strange character.

"I guess I'll ship with yer, stranger, and blast them darned Hottingtots; let go to hell their own way. An', stranger, I reckon I ain't proud at all, and air a pretty considerable good cook."

"Well, meet me here to-morrow morning at nine o'clock, and here is the dollar to spend mean while."

"Stranger, you air a downright screamer, let's licker."

"No, thank you," replied Ralph, who then departed, after whispering to the sailors to treat him with every respect.

At the bottom of the street he met Christopher and the fair Lilia, to whom he recounted his amusement, and also the hope which he had held out to the Yankee.

"Bring him on board the 'Raven;' but, Ralph, if you have any respect for our stomachs don't let him have anything to do with the cooking."

"Trust me for that; I'll tell old Brierly to give him the end of a rope if he goes anywhere near the galley. So for the present, farewell."

"Whither away, Ralph?"

"Listen, a lady is in the case."

"Well, I won't detain you; but don't make any disturbance if you can avoid it."

THE RAGE OF THE YANKEE PREACHER.—(*See page 642.*)

CHAPTER CCLXXV.

RAMSEY AND WARDLAW—THE ISLAND—TWO
CRUSOES—A LONG YARN—A WHITE MAN WHO
HAS BEEN A BLACK SLAVE.

WE left the temporary commanders of the ship
which had once called Daniel Harwolf her captain
sleeping under a tree after their escape to the
island.

When, however, the night had passed, and, refreshed by some four or five hours' sleep, they awoke,
the ship was no longer visible.

The noise and lights they had noticed had been
eated by the crew in their surprise at the desertion
cr heir officer .

No. 80.

Fearful lest they should be betrayed by the new
captain and his companion, the ruffians had heaved
the anchor, and stood out to sea.

"They are gone!" cried Wardlaw, after gazing
round.

"To the other side of the island, perhaps," replied
Ramsey.

"Not much fear of that. However, by scrambling
to the top of this rock we shall be able to see if they
are in sight."

After much hard work and perspiration, they
managed to reach the platform at the top of the cliff,
which happened to be the highest point of the
island.

No ship was in sight, and after carefully sweeping

the horizon with a glass which he had taken the precaution to bring with him, Wardlaw pronounced his opinion that the outlaws had departed.

"But, Ramsey," he continued, "this is not the island I fancied it to be."

"How so?"

"There should be a long line of breakers away out there to the nor'-east, and a little town down here on that mud-flat."

"Some error in our navigation."

"Most likely those rascals have altered the ship's course at times when we have not been watching them. However, here we are, and we must make the best of our position."

"Well, a Robinson Crusoe life is preferable to buccaneering, in my estimation."

"And in mine."

"But what is the best thing to do now, Gerald?"

"We'll have some breakfast first, then see if the rascals left us our boat."

"At all events, we are tolerably well provided as regards arms and ammunition."

"Yes, and you may put some of your ammunition to a good use, by shooting yon goat," replied Wardlaw, pointing to an animal that was browsing at a distance of some twenty yards to windward, seemingly unconscious of their presence.

Ramsey raised his gun, and fired.

The animal bounded some five feet into the air, and fell lifeless.

"There is breakfast and dinner too," said the late captain, as he proceeded to skin the animal.

"Why, I declare you seem quite a professional butcher, Gerald," cried Ramsey, laughing.

"It is not the first time I have skinned a goat; but make yourself useful and carry this haunch down to the beach, these ribs are for present use."

The two friends started off laughing and joking till they arrived at the outskirts of the wood, near which they had landed on the previous night.

"We'll just hang the meat on a branch of this tree for a moment. It is well to be cautious, and perhaps those fellows have placed an ambush near the boat and then sailed away out of sight to induce us to return and so fall into the trap."

With guns cocked the two friends advanced, peering cautiously into every bush and round each rock, but no enemy was in sight.

When they reached the shore they found the boat just as they had left it, and no sign of any one having landed save themselves.

"All right," cried Wardlaw, "so let us make ourselves comfortable."

"By all means," replied the lieutenant, "so here goes for cooking."

With these words he commenced to gather fuel, and, in a very few minutes, had made a roaring fire before which the goat's ribs were roasting.

It was yet early morning, and a hazy sort of mist pervaded the lower parts of the island, while the rock in the centre, and the blue ocean beyond, were clear and bright in the rays of the rising sun, who already began to make his powerful rays felt by the two seamen.

"Is the island inhabited think you, Gerald?" asked Ramsey, with his mouth full of goat's flesh.

"I don't really know, but if not I should imagine it was occasionally visited by Malays from other islands."

"Dangerous customers, are they not?"

"Rather! If we are captured by them it will be a toss-up between slavery or death."

"I think of the two I should prefer the latter."

"Life is sweet, but slavery is bitter—cruelly bitter. I was a slave once."

"Yes, under Daniel Harwolf's rule."

"No; long before I ever saw Daniel Harwolf I was a *black* slave."

"No! you are joking, Gerald. A black slave! Ha, ha! you might be a very brown one, though."

"I assure you I was a *black* slave, Ramsey, and if you will listen, I'll tell you how it happened."

"Fire away; I like a good yarn as well as any old tar."

"Well, some years ago I was mate aboard a sharp, long-nosed schooner engaged in the slave trade at the mouth of the Bonny river. Our skipper was a slab-sided 'cute Yankee, about as wide awake as a weazel, who made his fortune by the trade and built a large Methodist chapel somewhere in Massachussetts.

"In this schooner we felt quite safe from anything the British government had on the coast; in fact we used to lower our mainsail out of politeness before taking the wind of one old ten-gun brig who had honoured us with her particular attention for three years, off and on.

"She would chase us under a crowd of canvas till she saw it was no use, then after she had fired a gun of which we took no notice, haul her wind and jog back to the mouth of the river, from which, by that time, the other slavers had departed.

"Well one night we ran out of the river in the tail of a squall, and as soon as it cleared away, there was the brig, as we thought, rolling away after us and shaking out sheet after sheet, but Washington Jones—that was our skipper's name—never showed a stitch more canvas, because he had two friends just outside the bar at the mouth of the river, waiting to slip out when we had led the old brig away.

"However, the cruiser began to overhaul us, so we set one gaff-tops'l, then another, but still the brig was creeping up, till at length our flying-jib made us walk away from her, when bang went a gun, and before the sound had hardly reached our ears a round shot knocked the fore-topmast out of us. Then the moonlight came out and showed us our mistake, for instead of our old friend the brig, with her two masts, there were three raking masts in a fine new sloop of war. But, however, the schooner had the start, and we left her far behind, though the two unfortunate fellows who had been trusting to escape, were both picked up, one by the sloop, while the old brig overhauled the other.

"Well, the next trip we found the coast clear enough, and the common report was that both sloop and brig were up at Ascension, and that a young lieutenant had been left on the watch in a kind of lantern-rigged tender. However, in a day or two, the said tender made its appearance, and stood off the mouth of the river for some time. When we dropped anchor he sent a boat with a reefer on board, to ask whether we had any slaves in our hold. Our skipper retired into his cabin, first hoisting Portuguese colours, and supplying the Portuguese steward, who acted as captain for the occasion, with Portuguese papers. The most English looking portion of the crew were carefully kept below. All appeared right and straightforward, so after loitering about for a couple of days or so, the young navy swell departed, though if he had not, Washington Jones would have run out of the river, and risked the chances of a fight rather than lose the Cuba market, where slaves were very valuable just then.

"As soon as he was gone, of course we began to raft the niggers aboard, but before we had half our full cargo, a most terrific hurricane burst on us, and we were obliged to slip our cable and stand out to sea with barely a day's provisions or water on board."

"A pleasant situation, certainly," cried Ramsey.

"The next morning we were out of sight of land, but we got the sea breeze and stood in again under every inch of canvas we could spread, till we caught sight of the island of Fernando Po, about two leagues off, and a couple of brigs in the same line of trade as ourselves beating off in company.

"As our skipper knew the brigs he heaved to and pulled out to the nearest one, and presently came back in high glee, with word that the brigs had seen the man-of-war tender that morning bottom upwards, she having capsized in the hurricane.

"So we started away again for the Bonny, but in a short time the breeze dropped, and there we were becalmed all three of us.

"It was frightfully hot, and, as you may suppose, before long we had not a drop of water left, so a boat's crew pulled away to the nearest brig to beg or buy some, but being outward-bound they would not part with a drop.

"The captain himself then went aboard, taking with him eight of the negroes, and after a great deal of haggling obtained two casks in exchange for them. Then the breeze rose again for a short time, and we slowly made way to the river, when the calm again stopped our progress, and, of course, the two casks of water were soon exhausted, while the brigs were further off than ever.

"However, we boarded them; but not another drop would they part with for dollars or niggers either, and, as a matter of course, before morning broke again half those we had in our hold were dead.

"It was a sickening sight to see the sharks snap the poor devils up one after another—at one time I counted no less than twenty of them by the ship's side.

"By noon we had resolved to board one of the brigs and obtain what we wanted by force, when a breeze came off the island, and both the brigs set stun'sails and away, to the great wrath of Washington Jones, who gave orders to clear away the long gun amidships and after them.

"But ere that order could be obeyed we saw a craft rounding the island which we supposed to be a Bristol brig that had lost half her hands in the Gaboon river.

"Out went our boats, six men in each, with short cutlasses inside each man's trowsers, and without answering the repeated hails of the stranger we boarded her.

"The master and five or six men were on deck with a long-legged young fellow, who was sitting over the companion-hatch with a tumbler of grog in his hand.

"'What schooner's that?' says the youngster.

"'Never mind,' says our skipper; 'but give us a drink, for I guess we are considerable dry.'

"'Well,' replies the young fellow, super-cargo we thought him, 'we'll give you a pannikin each.'

"'A devil!' roared Washington Jones, feeling the handle of his cutlass. 'Nothing less than a couple of casks 'll suit me I reckon.'

"'Well,' replies the young fellow, 'I'll give you a couple of casks for a couple of niggers, as we are short of hands.'

"'I couldn't give ye a nigger's nail paring,' replies our skipper.

"'And yet,' says the youngster, 'you shipped a whole raft full.'

"'To the sharks with ye, you skunk!' roars our captain. 'If you won't give it we'll take it. Here, lads.'

"In a moment the tumbler of grog was in his face, and ere he could wipe it from his eyes, the young fellow knocks him down, while five and twenty man-of-war's men came rushing out of the cabin, and in less than ten minutes we were bound hand and foot.

"'I guess you are too 'cute to play jokes on,' says our skipper.

"'Yes, especially when that joke happens to be piracy,' replies the youngster, 'so I have you for that, even if you have no slaves on board.'

"Of course our skipper was very much down in the mouth about it, but ere we had time to think, we were stripped, and the man-of-war's men dressed up in our togs, the lieutenant of the cruiser, for he it was who had played us such a trick, assuming the skipper's garments. But hand the flask and the pannikin here, talking is dry work."

Ramsey did as desired, and after a draught, Wardlaw proceeded with his narrative, which, we hope, our readers will find as interesting as the listener did.

"We were all thrown down into the cabin, and away goes the lieutenant and his men to the schooner, and being near the stern window, I was able to see what passed. They boarded the schooner, and in less than five minutes the Union Jack was waving at the mast-head. Not satisfied with this, apparently, the lieutenant, finding the breeze continue, set sail and chased the two brigs. I reported this to our skipper, and for some time he said nothing, apparently endeavouring to fix some plan of escape.'

"But what has all this to do with your being a black slave?" asked Ramsey.

"I am coming to that part of my tale. While our skipper was thinking, a little black cabin-boy came in for something or other with a knife in his hand.

"'Come here, my lad,' says the captain, 'I'll thank you to give me a drink of water.'

"The boy came and held the pannikin to the skipper's lips, his hands being tied.

"'Now, look between my legs and you'll find a dollar.'

"The boy stooped down, and Washington Jones caught the poor devil's neck between his knees, and squeezed as hard as he could, till the nigger dropped down dead.

"'Now we are all right, I guess,' said he, and catching the knife in his teeth, he sawed away at the rope round my wrist, till he had severed it, when, of course, I quickly released all hands.

"'I calculate that cussed lieutenant has got my schooner, but this will, perhaps, pay expenses. At all events, as I've been called a pirate, I'll earn the name.'

"Well, we looked up the hatchway, and found no one on deck but a reefer, standing with his back towards us, watching the five or six men who had been left in charge, when our skipper slips off his shoes, and gliding softly up, caught hold of a capstan bar, and brought it down with a crash on the poor fellow's skull. The sight of the blood made us all blood-thirsty, and before we knew what we had done, all hands of them were dead and overboard. Heaven help me! That was the beginning of the fearful life I have led since.

"The end of it was that we crowded all sail, and by sunset had run down the brig up one of the creeks of the Camaroon river, where we intended to lie till all was forgotten. The lieutenant of the cruiser was back very shortly, and hunting about for us as sharp as a terrier after a rat, so that we durst not come down the river. What with the stink of the mud, weeds, mangroves, and other rank vegetation amongst which we were surrounded, it was not long before all hands died of the fever, with the exception of myself and Captain Washington Jones. Not knowing how soon it might be my own turn, I slipped into the gig one night and silently rowed away up the creek till near daybreak, when I jumped ashore and off into the bush never stopping till I ran right into the middle of a native village, not far from the mouth of the river. I had managed to lose my reckoning in the jungle, and had returned nearly to the sea-coast. But it is nearly time we thought of doing something for ourselves; so let us begin by stowing the boat away somewhere amongst these bushes. I'll finish my tale during the heat of the day when we can't work."

Ramsey assented, and the friends rose to prepare themselves for a sojourn in the island.

CHAPTER CCLXXVI.

THE YARN SPUN OUT — THE BLACK MAN
TURNED WHITE AGAIN.

WHEN Wardlaw and Ramsey had stowed their boat away, they commenced building a kind of hut of branches of trees interlaced, but before they had made much progress the sun was high in the heavens, and his powerful beams rendered labour almost impossible.

So, after a slight refreshment, the two friends reclined themselves beneath the most shady tree they could find to while away the time till the cool breeze should once more enable them to continue their necessary labours.

"Come, Gerald, let's have the remainder of your yarn," said Ramsey.

"Let me see—where did I leave off?"

"You had just arrived at a negro village."

"Yes, and on arriving there my appearance created no small stir, and it was full half an hour before any of the niggers would venture to come near me. At length I conciliated them by prostrating myself before their fetish, or idol, and after a short time they began to be more friendly; the fetish man himself taking me under his especial charge, and setting me to work telling fortunes with an old quadrant they had stolen. I had a hut and two wives given me, and every thing seemed to be going on comfortably when one morning there was the sloop of war in the mouth of the river. The sight set me in a terrible fright, for I had no doubt that I should be hung if caught; so I told the fetish man that I was reckoned a great man at home, and that the king of England had sent to kidnap me away, adding that I preferred remaining with the black men. Off starts the priest, but soon returns with some kind of oil with which he rubbed me all over. *In half an hour I was as black as any nigger among them!* A boat landed from the sloop with the very lieutenant who had captured our schooner, and searched the village for the white man they had heard was there. I sat before a hut all the while pounding away at some rice till the boat and crew departed.

"But in the course of a day or two I began to feel uneasy as the colour would not wash off, and hinted to the fetish man my desire to become white again. He pretended not to understand me, and I grew angry. Thinks I, 'I'll take your trade away, my boy,' so I set to work with my knife till I had carved an image twice as big and ugly as his, when of course I was the most popular of the two. At length my fame extended to the next village, in which the king of the tribe resided, and he sent for me, at which the fetish man looked very vexed.

"However, the king received me very graciously, though I could scarcely refrain from laughing at the queer look of royalty, dressed in a marine's old coat and top boots. The next day I met my rival in the woods, and he, pretending to be very friendly, induced me to take a walk with him. All of a sudden, however, he started off into the bush, comes back with a kind of red leaf in his hand, which he drew across my forehead. I had not the least idea what it meant till I got back to the town, where I found all the people staring at me. I looked in an old glass which the king had in his hut, and found a white streak where the leaf had touched.

"That day the king refused to see me, and at sunset I was dragged away and thrown into a filthy den in which a dozen niggers were confined. Thinks I, 'I am going to be killed, and my skull will no doubt occupy a prominent position over his majesty's throne.' But such was not the case, for about midnight we were all dragged out and carried away to the water-side where a fire was burning, by the light of which I could see a schooner anchored not many yards from shore. Hiss! went a red-hot iron

across my shoulders, and before I had time to cry out I was pushed head foremost into a large canoe which was then paddled off to the schooner.

"I was on board a slaver, amongst slaves, and treated as one of them, but amid all the thoughts that came crowding to my mind was one of joy when I saw the fetish man and the king not far from me. I managed to squeeze myself pretty close to an open port, so did not suffer so much as others did from the stifling heat. In fact, I slept for some time, and was only awakened by the sound of a gun, and looking out beheld the sloop in chase. Some two hours after the slaver was taken by the war ship, and I was thinking of proclaiming who and what I was, when I saw the very lieutenant who had taken the schooner commanded by Washington Jones. Then, as a matter of course, I held my tongue.

"Five days after we arrived at Sierra Leone, where we were put ashore and treated very tenderly, and I was tolerably comfortable, till one day I saw a printed bill posted against the church door, offering a reward for the apprehension of all concerned in the piracy, with my own name and description full-length. So I thought it high time to slope if possible, and watching my chance, went off one night to a Yankee brig that was on the point of sailing, and told the skipper some part of my story.

"'Well, my lad,' said he, 'there is freedom in the States, I reckon, and I'm your friend. But are there any more of you in the same fix?'

"'Not that I know,' I replied.

"The end of it was that I worked my passage in the ship till we reached New Orleans, when I, of course, expected to receive my wages, and leave the craft.

"Says the rascally Yankee,

"'My lad, have you got any friends here?'

"'No,' I replied, 'but there are plenty of ships wanting hands.'

"'Well,' said he, 'come into the city with me, and I'll introduce you to a gentleman who, I dare say, will employ you in some better berth than a forecastle hand.'

"Off we started, and at length reached a large house in the outskirts of the town, where I was left waiting in the verandah, while the captain and his friend were talking. After an hour's absence my friend, the skipper, returned, and told me I might remain, adding, that he would send my things up in a cart.

"No sooner was he gone than the master of the house made his appearance, and looked at me for some minutes without speaking.

"'Now, Pompey,' says he, 'though that was a pretty 'cute tale you told my friend, the captain, but it's no use.'

"'My name is not Pompey, sir,' I replied, 'and the tale I told the captain is true.'

"However, he refused to believe it, adding that he had *bought* me, and that free papers were the only things that could help me.

"'And,' he added, by way of caution, 'don't talk too much about those nuts and leaves, for my overseer is a rough customer, and sometimes cuts the niggers' tongues out when they are noisy.'

"Off he goes, leaving me in the verandah, thinking how to escape, but I could see no means, as the house was surrounded by a high wall. Presently comes the overseer and his black assistant, who stripped me, and made me put on a pair of cotton drawers and a broad hat, and marched me away to a plantation about ten miles away, where I was at once set to work hoeing sugar-cane with a gang of negroes."

"Is this all true, Gerald?" asked Ramsey, "or are you inventing for my amusement?"

"Perfectly true. There is one proof," said he, opening the neck of his shirt, and showing the brand on his shoulders.

"In about six months I was sent to another plantation a long way further up the river, where the work was harder, the sun hotter, and the overseer more ferocious. I grew home-sick, and many a night I spent in weeping and thinking of my mother and sister.

"Blows were plentiful though food was not, and I was making up my mind to do some desperate deed, when one day as I was chopping wood in the midst of a thick forest I saw a leaf—the leaf which alone could make me white. Of course, it was not long before I had my hat full of them, and most anxiously did I wait for darkness that I might try the experiment.

"About an hour after sunset I started off towards a town about ten miles distant down the river, and as soon as I thought half my journey over I sat down and rubbed myself all over with the leaves; then I dived into the water, after which I gave myself another rub with the leaf, and watched anxiously enough for the daylight.

"It came at length, and glancing at the reflection in the water, I saw that I was white once more after being black for upwards of eighteen months. But I knew it would not do to remain there, so I swam down the river for a couple of miles, and then concealed myself in a thick tree that hung over the water till noon when I heard the yell of bloodhounds on my track. So I dropped into the water again, after burying my slave's clothes in the mud, and swam on till I came to the landing-place near the little town where there were plenty of ships and boats.

"As I had no clothes my next thought was how to rig myself, so I began to shout out to the people on the landing-place to bring me my clothes; but no clothes were to be seen.

"'Then they must be stolen,' I cried, 'and I'll give ten dollars for the conviction of the thief. There were notes for a hundred and fifty dollars in the coat pocket,' and with that I began to describe the lost articles.

"'But I'm getting cold,' I continued, 'so I guess I'll come ashore and run to my hotel.'

"'Wait a minute,' says one, 'we'll lend you some togs,' and with that they brought me a dress very much like the one I had described, and, by way of gratitude for not shocking their modesty, the ladies subscribed a hundred and fifty dollars to make up my loss, as well as inviting me to a public dinner, where I was compelled to address the meeting on the glorious freedom of the United States."

"Which you could well do," interposed Ramsey.

"I assure you my emotion was so great that they set me down as a most earnest patriot. However, that same night I left them, and went down to New Orleans in a steam tug, where I wasn't long before I found a ship bound for Bristol, and, you may be sure, I was heartily glad to leave the land of freedom, as it is called, behind me. So hand the grog this way, as that is the end of my yarn."

CHAPTER CCLXXVII.

THE GIPSY BOY'S VISIT TO LORD HAWKSBURY —BERTRAM COOPER AND HIS WIFE BEFORE THE MAGISTRATE—THE FALSE CHARGE— THE ACQUITTAL.

WHEN the gipsy boy, the son of Bertram Cooper, knocked at the door of Lord Hawksbury's mansion, an elegant flunkey, who was rather sentimental in his habits, was the only one of the household astir.

"What his the matter, boy? What do yer want?" asked his elegance.

"I want to see Lord Hawksbury."

"Pooh! 'ook it, you young scamp, be hoff with yer," then, in a milder tone, he added, "I, too, must be hoff to meet the sun upon the hupland lawn of Hyde Park, where Mary Jane, the charmink cre'tur, comes tripping lightly o'er the mountain du."

"I don't know anything about Mary Jane, I wants to see Lord Hawksbury," cried the boy.

"'Is lordship's abed, and carn't be' distubbed for sich as you, so be hoff afore I fetches a perliceman."

At that moment a rubicund butler thrust his night-capped visage from the area window.

"What's the row, Jeames?"

"Ho, Mister Magnum, 'eres a small boy in rags as wants to see 'is lordship; did ye hever 'ear sich imperence?"

"What does he want?"

"I don't know, Mr. Magnum."

"Then you'd better hask, has it may be somethink of himportance."

"What do you want to see his lordship about, my boy?" asked Jeames.

"I'll tell him when I see him. It's a secret."

"Hit's a secret, Mr. Magnum; we'll send the boy about his business hif you 'as no hobjection."

"Send 'im down here, Jeames; you know 'is lordship 'as strange people sometimes to see 'im."

Jeames unlocked the area gate, and grandly motioned the boy to descend to the kitchen, where the young arab looked very ill at ease till the butler, who was a very liberal man (with his master's goods), placed some hot coffee and bread and butter before him, when he began to feel more at home.

Mr. Magnum tried all that he knew to draw the secret from the boy, and was beginning to feel very angry at the youngster's ingratitude when a bell rang.

"Ah! 'is lordship is awake, then I'll let 'im know you are 'ere."

So saying, the worthy man trotted off, and shortly returned with surprised looks to usher the gipsy boy into the nobleman's dressing-room.

"You can go now, Magnum," said Lord Hawksbury, observing that the butler lingered in the room.

"But, my lord, these fellers is orful rogues generally speakin', something might be missed afterwards."

"Go, I say; he is honest enough."

Magnum went—to the other side of the door—where he pressed his ear as closely as possible to the keyhole.

"Now, my lad," said Lord Hawksbury, "what do you want?"

"Dad and mam is locked up by the peelers——"

"And you want me to get them off? But who is your father?"

"Bertram Cooper."

"Ah! then I must see to this! What is he locked up for?"

"A bloke said as how he pinched his ticker."

"By which you mean that your father is accused of stealing a watch?"

"That ain't all, sir; last night I heard 'em talking, and they said as how Harwolt was gone to Bristol, and that mam must let you know to-day."

"Are you sure that was what they said?"

"Yes; they said somethin' else, but I can't mind what."

"And so because they are locked up you came to tell me?"

"Yes, sir; I thought you might get 'em off bein' lagged."

"I will if I can, my boy. Take this and run home; if you don't see your father to-night come here again to-morrow morning."

The kind-hearted nobleman gave the boy a sovereign and rang the bell.

Off ran the young gipsy, nearly throwing down the butler, who had been listening most attentively without being able to catch more than half-a-dozen words of the conversation.

Lord Hawksbury dressed himself, and wrote a couple of notes, which he gave to a servant to deliver immediately.

The effect of these missives was that when Bertram Cooper and his wife were placed before the magistrate, charged with felony, Mr. Ripson and Mr. Smith, two of the most celebrated Old Bailey lawyers of the present day, announced themselves as engaged for the defence.

Lord Hawksbury at that moment entered the court, and heard, with a smile, that the prosecution had no legal aid.

The first witness was the prosecutor, Mr. Adolphus Sillyboy, who stated that at the previous night he was at the London Bridge station when he saw the male prisoner standing near him, and on looking down discovered that his watch and chain were gone. He accused the prisoner, who pushed him on one side and left the station. The prosecutor stated that he gave information to the police, who followed the prisoner, and took him into custody in a house near Kent Street.

Mr. Ripson cross-examined the witness, asking him in the first place,

"How far was the prisoner from you when you first saw him?"

"Well—I don't—in fact he was pretty close to me."

"How many yards from you?"

"Well, perhaps four or five."

"Then he must have pretty long arms to pick your pocket at that distance. Was any one else near?"

"Yes, a lady and gentleman."

Mr. Ripson sat down, and his colleague rose to cross-examine.

"You would recognise the lady and gentleman again, and be able to identify your watch?"

"Yes, certainly."

"Is this your watch?"

The young man took the watch presented to him, and after stating that it was his, handed it back to the lawyer, who passed it to the magistrate.

"What was the name of the maker, and the number of your watch?"

Name, Candy; number 12065."

The magistrate opened the watch and after examining it, said,

"There can be no doubt this is your watch."

"Now," continued Mr. Smith, "how were the lady and gentleman dressed?"

"The gentleman in dark clothes with a light overcoat and white hat, and the lady in a blue silk dress with a large India shawl."

"Like those people?" asked the lawyer, pointing to a couple who stood near two policemen.

"Yes; why they are the very ones!"

"Good; you may stand down."

The important peeler was then sworn, and de-

posed that he was on duty at the station, when the prosecutor called him and said that *that* man had stolen his watch. Followed male prisoner, to a house in Kent Street, and captured him after considerable resistance.

The magistrate peered through his spectacles at the witness, and said,

"Why, you don't look much the worse for it. Did he strike or kick you?"

"No, yer wushup, but he used threatening langwidge and swore orful."

"Enough to make him, if you locked him up for nothing. Did you find the watch in his house?"

"No, yer wushup; but as the 'ooman was there I took her for being an accomplish."

"You ought to be locked up yourself. Is there any more evidence?"

There was no more for the prosecution, and the first witness for the prisoners, after being sworn, nodded very familiarly to many of the police in court, and gave evidence as follows.

"I am a detective officer, and last night was at the London Bridge Station watching two persons, who will presently be brought before your worship, on a charge of picking pockets, in fact the two who were identified by the prosecutor as the ones who stood by his side. I took them into custody after they had robbed an old lady of her purse, and on being searched, the watch and chain which the prosecutor identified as his, was found upon the *lady* as he called her, though she is better known to me and the police as Slippery Sal."

"That's enough," cried the magistrate, "the prisoners are discharged, and I only hope the prosecutor will be sued for damages. It is a most groundless charge."

"Hooray!" shouted two small voices in the court, and Bertram Cooper, turning round, beheld his children shouting with delight.

The couple left the dock together and proceeded to the place where the two lawyers were sitting,

"I am very thankful for what you have done for me. But tell me who sent you here?"

"A gentleman who is in the court, and wishes to speak to you."

Bertram looked round till his gaze fell on Lord Hawksbury, who nodded in a friendly manner.

"'Twas kind, indeed, my lord," said the gipsy, approaching the noble; "but I can't think how you knew it."

"A little bird told me, Cooper."

"Well, my lord, I have news to tell you."

"I know; Harwolf is gone to Bristol."

The gipsy stared with surprise.

"Then of course you know where Captain Christopher is?" he said, when he had recovered his speech.

"That I don't know, but I dare say you can tell me."

"He's gone to Frontemore; that's how I came to be at the station."

"Ah! for what is he gone there?"

"To go off in your yacht, my lord. Now as I've told you all I know, please tell me who let you know I was locked-up."

"Well, Bertram, it was your boy, and he it was who told me of Harwolf; he over-heard you and your wife talking last night."

"Then I didn't think he was so sharp. But I must be off to Bristol, my lord. I can't rest till both father and son are hanged—the Harwolfs I mean."

"Away with you, then, and never fear that your wife and children will want for any thing while you are away."

They parted. The gipsy to his home in Kent Street, and the nobleman to his mansion in the West End.

"Don't forget to let me know how you succeed," were Lord Hawksbury's last words.

CHAPTER CCLXXVIII.

RUSSIA AGAIN—THE OLD PRIEST—A MARRIAGE.

WE pass over the adventures of Edward Leighton and Katinka until they arrived at the town of Saratov, where, in accordance with the promise he had made the chief of the smugglers, the young man made inquiries with regard to the residence of the chief priest, pope, or papa of the church, leaving Katinka, meanwhile, at a little inn or post-house kept by a Jew.

Edward Leighton had not much difficulty in discovering the abode of the person he sought, for, with the exception of the church and the barracks, it was the only stone edifice in the town, the shops and dwellings being constructed of pine logs from the neighbouring forest.

A good-looking peasant girl opened the door, and, after explaining with some difficulty that he wished to see the priest, Leighton was ushered into the apartment occupied by that worthy man.

It was a large, tolerably well furnished room, lighted by a glass sash window, and carpeted.

One side of the room was occupied by a set of book shelves, near the window was a table covered with writing materials, while an earthenware stove stood in the centre.

The priest himself, a venerable-looking man dressed in a long caftan, was seated near the stove smoking a long Turkish pipe and drinking coffee.

On the entrance of his visitor the priest rose, and, with a graceful bow, motioned him to a chair.

"You bring a letter for me, I hear?" said he, in German.

"I do, sir. Here it is," replied Leighton, producing the packet.

The old man took the letter and read it through without speaking.

When he had finished perusing it he turned to Leighton and said,

"You, of course, know the writer of this missive?"

"Slightly," replied Leighton, and he then detailed the circumstances of their meeting and what occurred afterwards.

"He requests me to render you all the aid in my power," continued the priest. "How can I be of service to you?"

"Sir, you can render me the greatest service by giving, during the few days I remain in Saratov, a home to a young Polish girl who accompanies me."

"I will do so with pleasure; but say in what relation do you stand to this young lady?"

"I am her betrothed husband."

"And you are travelling together?"

"We are. Start not, good father, she is pure as the mountain snow."

"It would be better if you were married."

A sudden thought struck Leighton.

"I know it would, good father, and therefore I am bold enough to request that you would perform the ceremony which makes us one."

"My dear young friend, that I will do with pleasure, and as quickly as you like, for, believe me, nothing would give me greater pleasure than to see two lovers united by the Holy Church."

"Then to-morrow be it."

"To-morrow be it; and now allow me to offer you some refreshments."

"Thanks, holy sir, but I must now return to my love and prepare her for the all-important ceremony."

"Go then, but return again with her, for recollect this is to be her home until you have the right to take her to yours."

With a low bow Edward Leighton departed, and on entering the inn hastened to the apartment in which he had left his dear Katinka.

He found her sitting near the little lattice-window, and so engrossed was she in contemplation of the queer-looking streets and its mixed multitude of passengers, European and Asiatics, that she did not hear him enter, nor was she aware of his presence till he announced it by a kiss on the forehead.

"You are soon back, dear Edward," said she, holding out her hand.

"Yes, dearest," replied Edward; "such news as I bring would hasten the most slothful man in existence."

"What is your news? Is it good?"

"So good that it will cover your cheeks with blushes."

The blushes came before the news was told, for Katinka held down her head and forbore to question her lover further.

"My news is, dearest, that to-morrow a good old priest has consented to unite us in the bonds of matrimony."

The fair girl hung her head yet lower down on her heaving bosom but did not attempt to withdraw her hand from her lover.

"You have consented to be mine," continued Leighton. "You will not withdraw that consent now."

She did not reply, and bending down, the young man's lips sought her's as though he would kiss an answer from them.

"I am still yours, dear Edward," she whispered in his ear.

"Mine now, mine for ever!" cried the passionate young man, as he pressed her luxurious form in his arms and kissed her with an ardour that deepened the crimson on her cheeks and neck.

She did not attempt to repel his caresses, but with her arm round his waist whispered in his ear,

"Remember your promise, dear Edward; remember the promise you made on the day when I first confessed I loved you."

"Right, dear girl, you must pardon my haste. But now come with me to the house of this good priest, where you are to stay till I have a right to take you away."

Katinka rose, and, placing her hand on her lover's arm, walked forth with him.

In a short time they were at the priest's house, and the venerable churchman, coming forth to meet them, lifted his hands and pronounced a benediction as they entered the doorway.

"Welcome, my daughter, welcome," cried he, as he led the way to the room in which Leighton first found him.

"I have to thank you, good father, for your kindness, and entreat you to tell me if there is any way in which I can show my gratitude."

"You can best be thankful by becoming a kind, loving and faithful husband," replied the old priest, with a smile.

A smoking hot supper of much better materials than they had lately enjoyed was placed on the table, and the party fell to, the priest showing that, notwithstanding his age, he retained his appetite.

Then, after a cup of coffee, in obedience to a hint from Papa Petchorow, Edward Leighton returned to the inn, after promising to return early in the morning to make the blushing Polish girl his wife.

And punctually he did return, and, in a short time after, a small party of the servants of the old priest were assembled in the church as witnesses to the ceremony that made two loving hearts happy.

After another sumptuous repast, the young couple—Mrs. and Mr. Edward Leighton—again started forth on ther journey across the wild plains, full of hope, love and confidence.

———

CHAPTER CCLXXIX.

THE BOY PIRATE'S CHAPLAIN IS SHIPPED AS ORDINARY SEAMAN—A FORECASTLE FROLIC—ZAMPA'S HORSEMANSHIP.

ON the morning after his interview with Black Ralph the American missionary was punctually at the place appointed.

He smelt considerably strong of rum, and his clothes were very dusty and disordered, as though he had slept in them.

After waiting some few minutes and plentifully watering the road with tobacco saliva, he was about to depart when he saw the black-bearded Britisher advancing.

"Top o' the mornin', stranger," he shouted; "I kalkilate you air jest a trifle behind."

"Very good time," replied Ralph; "but are you ready to go on board?"

"Aye, stranger, I air; an' ready to do a good feed tu, I reckon."

"A good feed you shall have, so come along."

"But I kalkilate I hev some notions an' traps in this 'ere confounded old diggins, mister."

"Well, fetch them out and bring them down to the boat."

The Yankee obeyed, and, in a short space of time, was seated in the boat.

Black Ralph then gave the word, and the oars flashed merrily in the sunbeams, as the men pulled away towards the "Red Raven."

After pulling for about half an hour, the bows of the boat grated against the ship's side, and Black Ralph quickly stood on deck.

"Come on board, sir," said he, touching his hat gravely to the Boy Pirate, just as the long face of the preacher peered over the bulwarks.

"I am glad to see you, Captain Ralph; but who is that lubber?"

"That is the chaplain I told you of last night."

"Then bring him aft and introduce me to him; we must receive the holy man with all proper respect."

A smile passed over Ralph Talbot's face.

"I fancy I shall pretty quickly introduce him to a rope's end if I get him fairly under my hand."

The Boy Pirate laughed a little at this speech, and Ralph walked forward to where the Yankee was standing, peering about with a strange mixture of brazen-faced self-assurance and bashfulness.

With some difficulty, he persuaded the preacher to walk aft and be presented to the commander.

"I guess I ain't fixed up very spry, stranger."

"Never mind, you must come."

And Ralph hauled the bashful preacher to where Christopher was standing by the binnacle.

"This, sir," said Ralph, bowing, "is the clergyman I spoke of."

Christopher made a low bow, and with great difficulty preventing himself from laughing, asked,

"What name shall I have the pleasure of knowing you by, sir?"

"Wa-all, I guess my name is Jefferson Jeremiah Brown."

"This gentleman," continued Christopher, pointing to Ralph, "tells me you are desirous of engaging yourself as chaplain, Mr. Brown."

"So I do, I guess, though if so be as the vacancy is filled, I don't mind shippin' as second steward."

"I think the latter occupation would suit you best."

"Wall, it's fact, stranger, so do I."

"But that place is already filled."

"Then, I guess I'll be chapling as it was intended I should be."

"Better ship as ordinary seaman, I give good pay."

"Now you air a jokin', capting."

"No, indeed; I think that you would do better as a sailor than a preacher; besides, you can practice a little on the forecastle hands."

"Where air ye bound for, capting?"

"The Pacific most likely; I hardly know yet myself."

"Then I guess I'll go, though you'll have to put me down at San Franciskey, I guess."

"You shall land at that port if we touch there."

And with these words the Boy Pirate turned and walked away.

"Here, Zamp," cried Ralph, beckoning the negro forward, "introduce this gentleman to the forecastle."

"Berry proud to hab de honour ob seducin' de gemman to de hands. You come dis way, sir?"

"I say, you darned nigger, where the devil is my bed-room? I guess I'll jist turn in and have a snooze."

"Bed, sir! you want bed? Berry well now, s'pose you got knife?"

"Yes."

"Den look out for good soft plank; take dat for bed, and stick in de knife for pillow."

"Now, none o' yer darned jokes with me, you blasted woolley-headed cuss; I guess I'm a 'Merican."

THE INTERVIEW.—*See No.* 82.

"Berry sorry to hear it, sir, 'cause de nigger am quite as good as you am here, an' he hate de dam Yankees."

Jefferson Jeremiah Brown opened his eyes wide at the announcement, but the negro seemed in nowise scared by the stare with which he was honoured.

"Come along," said he, sharply, as the Yankee seemed inclined to lag behind, and in a few moments more the pair stood in the forecastle, where many of the men at once recognised the preacher who had so amused them on the previous evening.

"Hullo, mate, what cheer?" hailed one.

"Pipe all hands for church," cried a second.

"Good mornin', strangers," said the Yankee, with a low bow.

No. 81

"What bring ye here, mate? Going to give us a bit of a sarmon?"

"I were brought here by that black cuss to' be interdooced to yer, an' I kalkilate I air glad to see yer all pretty bobbish."

Very few of the tars understood this speech, and silence reigned till Zamp spoke.

"What you tink, lads, dis ere coon want to know where hims bed am?"

"What, have ye shipped, mate?"

"I kalkilate I hev."

"And do ye know——"

"He doesn't," said Caffyn, who at that moment walked up to the group, "and there is no reason why he should."

By which speech Dick meant to intimate that it was not necessary that the new hand should know all the history of the past.

"Stranger," said the Yankee, turning towards Dick, "air you anybody in partickler?"

"You will soon find I am," replied the young man.

"Then, for the love of Heaven, show me where I can have a snooze. I air jist considerable sleepy."

"You'll have a hammock given you presently, but for the present you can stow yourself away in that old mainsail," replied Dick, pointing to some old canvas."

"Then, good-night, strangers all," cried the Yankee, immediately burying himself in the folds of canvas till only his sallow face was visible; what became of his legs and body it is difficult to say, they were so long and thin that it was impossible to discover where they were located.

The men gazed in surprise and amusement at their strange new messmate, who was no sooner snugly ensconced than a succession of most dismal snores came pealing through his nose.

"Poor devil! he's sound enough. Now, I wonder if he'd sleep so sound if so be he knowed as how we was——"

"Hush!" whispered Caffyn.

"He sleep berry sound," said Zampa. "S'pose, now, we hab one damn spree when him wake up."

"What do ye mean, Zamp!"

"Why, him called me 'damn nigger,' cuss and swar' at me. S'pose, now, we make him nigger, an' swar' at him."

A low laugh from all around testified their willingness to join in the spree, as Zampa called it.

"What are ye goin' to paint his figure-head with?"

"You leave dis chile alone, he know a trick or two," and hastening away, proceeded towards the cabin in which Christopher kept a medicine-chest.

The owner was absent, and the negro, after looking carefully round, entered, and lifted the lid of the chest.

He could see nothing there that seemed suitable, and began to speculate on the result of painting the Yankee white.

While meditating on this subject Zampa took up a small stick of white substance, and after shutting the lid of the chest again, returned to the forecastle.

"Now, boys, dis chile am goin' to make a damn white nigger ob him!" cried Zampa.

Wetting the white substance with a camel's hair brush saturated with water, he then with much gravity proceeded to lay the colour on.

Judge the surprise of, not only the negro, but all the hands, when they saw the white paint gradually turn black as it dried on the face of the Yankee, who slept on unconscious of what was taking place.

At length the task was completed, and Zampa returned with the stick of caustic to the captain's cabin, where the owner was now sitting.

"What do you want, Zampa?"

"Oh, golly! Massa Christopher, tell dis poor nigger what dis am."

"That? Why it's caustic. Where did you get it?"

"Out ob dat chest, massa."

"Out of my medicine chest? Why what on earth could you want with it?"

"I tell you, massa. I come here to find black stuff to put on de dam Yankee's face, but dere ain't none, so I say I'll paint him white. Golly! massa, in ten minutes de white paint turn black, an he am now dark as dis darky—heigh! ha! ha!"

"It's all very well for you to laugh, but it will be a serious matter for the new-comer. All the skin will come off his face."

"Oh, lor! didn't know dat, massa."

"It won't hurt him much, though," said Christopher, more to himself than to Zampa, who, however, caught the words and treasured them up.

"Now go away you rascal and make friends with your new messmate, if you possibly can."

"All right, massa captain."

And black Zampa returned to the forecastle, where the black Yankee was snoring away in blessed unconsciousness of the change which had come upon him since he had closed his eyes.

Cautiously, for fear of disturbing his Yankee brother, Zampa slid between the folds of the sail which enclosed the body of J. J. Brown, and laid himself side by side by that worthy individual.

Still the Yankee slept, and Zampa, too, took a slight nap.

At length one of the men in moving struck his foot against a substance which soon proved to be the Rev. Mr. Brown's boot.

With a huge yawn the Yankee rubbed his eyes, opened them, but rubbed harder than ever when he saw the stolid countenance of his bedfellow.

"Now, Pompey, or what yer blasted name is, jest make tracks, ye darned nigger, will yer?"

"No more nigger dan yourself," replied Zampa.

"Did ye ever see sich impudence?" said Jefferson Brown, turning to the men, who were anxious to see the upshot of the spree.

"Well," replied one of them, "you are certainly black. I thought when you came aboard this morning you were rather dark."

"What do yer mean, stranger?"

"Look at yourself, mate," said the man, producing a small pocket looking-glass.

The ex-preacher did look, first at the front then at the back of the glass, to make certain that there was no optical delusion.

"The devil!" he exclaimed, at length, when fully convinced that he was really black. "Which o' you fellows were it which chalked my face black in this ere extrornary style?"

There was no answer.

"I guess it were you, ye darned impudent nigger, and, if it air, by the eternal General Jackson, I'll plug yer, I guess."

Zampa burst into a loud laugh, which so enraged the American that he drew a bowie-knife from his coat, and rushing forward would certainly have stabbed the negro had he not been tripped up behind and disarmed.

"What's all this about?" said a stern voice, and

in another moment Black Ralph appeared on the scene.

A glance at the face of the chaplain, which was just a trifle blacker than the faded battered hat above it, informed him the cause of the quarrel.

He too burst into a laugh, in which he was joined by the whole of the assembled party, while the Yankee looked sulkily from one to another.

"Wash your face, man," cried Ralph.

A pail of water was brought, but soap nor towel could remove the hue from his skin.

Brierly at that moment came forward, attracted by the noise and commotion, and having heard the whole history from the Boy Pirate, in a whisper explained to Black Ralph what had occurred.

"This is too bad. Zampa, I must report your conduct."

And he did report to the Boy Pirate what had happened, causing the young rover and his bride to laugh most heartily.

But Zampa was to be punished, though the utmost that Christopher could find it in his heart to inflict was to banish him from his presence for a fortnight.

So Zampa took up his quarters on board the "Avenger," for after his visit to England the Boy Pirate had removed his flag back to the "Red Raven" again, and appointed Cassidy to the steamer.

Ralph Talbot had no direct command, but passed from one ship to the other, quoting Shakespeare, giving help and advice, and making himself generally beloved by every one.

So when Zampa had been two days on board the steamer he was not at all surprised to hear the big voice of the big, black-bearded pirate hailing him.

Since the theatrical performance Zampa had been very shy of approaching Ralph, and therefore skulked below some time ere he answered the hail, and leisurely walked to the deck.

"Zampa, would you like to have a couple of days on shore?"

"Eh, Massa Ralph; but you isn't goin' to play any tricks?"

"No; I want you to see a young lady for me."

"White gal, Massa Ralph? Oh, lor! dis nigger am de chile to make lub!"

"I don't want you to make love to her; only to take this letter and give it to her when she is alone."

"How is I to know which is she?"

"I'll tell you if you'll listen, you confounded rascal."

And then Ralph, with great minuteness, described the lady and the situation of her father's house, which was about twenty-five miles from Cape Town in the interior of the country.

Ralph had chosen Zampa for the task, thinking that the African would best be able to encounter the dangers and difficulties of a journey in his own burning continent.

"You must change your clothes, though, Zampa, it will never do to go running through the bush in this man-o'-war dress."

"What am dis boy to wear, den, Massa Ralph?"

"Why here are some things will suit you exactly," replied Ralph, throwing him a bundle, which on being opened, was found to contain a coarse canvas jacket and trousers, such as are generally worn by the domesticated blacks in the Cape colony. A huge pair of coarse hide boots supplied the place of the light shoes, or bare feet in which Zampa had been accustomed to parade the deck.

These preparations being made, and armed with a revolver, Zampa dropped into a boat alongside, and was rowed to shore after receiving a repetition of the instructions.

Springing on to the wharf Zampa's first thought was to refresh and strengthen himself for his long journey.

For this purpose he entered a public-house, and speedily demolished two glasses of grog .

Then away through the town, skirting the base of Table Mountain, till, at length, he found himself alone on the hot arid road, or rather track that led to the house of the fair damsel he was to communicate with.

The road now led up an incline, and reaching the top of it the negro saw, to his intense delight, a farm house standing among a few scattered trees.

Something to eat and drink was all that the sight at first suggested to Zampa's mind.

He boldly entered the enclosure in which several cows and horses were feeding, and knocked at the door.

There was no reply, nor a sound of anything living within.

Zampa knocked again with the butt of his pistol; but still there was no response to his summons.

He went to the window, and peered through; but the big room which constituted the whole ground-floor of the house was empty.

He tried the upper windows with the same success.

Nobody at home, and he turned away from the door after a deep draught of water from the well beside it.

Returning to the road his eye fell on the three powerful horses that were quietly grazing.

"Oh, lor! golly! dis chile don't walk no more on de dam dusty road, borrow the white buckras horse, and return him when I comes back."

So saying he looked round, and felt in his pockets for something to serve as a bridle.

About three yards of stout rope were twisted round his body in case of any emergency, and unwinding this a halter was quickly formed.

"Now, massa pony, s'pose yo nebber hab nigger on your back afore, jes see if dis chile don't hold on."

With these words he approached the animal he judged to be swiftest and strongest, and by means of a little gentle coaxing managed to get near enough to lay his hand on the horse's neck.

Then in a minute the halter, which he had hitherto kept behind his back, was thrown over his head, and Zampa led the snorting, prancing animal towards the gate of the enclosure, which was only a few yards distant from the house.

There he intended to mount, and after several trials he succeeded.

"Oh, lor! ain't dis nigger berry grand?" he cried, in his exultation, but the words were scarcely out of his mouth when the animal threw its heels high in the air, and poor Zampa over its head.

Then, with a proud air, as though conscious of having done a clever thing, he trotted away to join his companions.

"Gor a mighty!" groaned Zampa, rising and rubbing himself, "here is my shoulders, but whar am my head?"

By dint of feeling he at last convinced himself that his head was really attached to his body, and then broke out in a torrent of invective against the horse.

"You damn white buckra horse, what for you fling me off? Reckon dis chile won't jes lay the cat 'bout you when he cotch you. Insult coloured gemman dat way, you big damn good-for-nothing tief."

The gallant steed paid no attention to this, but after a rapid canter round the field, as if to show off his paces to the unsuccessful jockey, recommenced grazing.

But Zampa was not to be done out of his ride.

Picking up the straw hat, which had flown from his head in the daring act of equestrianism, he ran to a shed by the side of the house, and returned with his hat full of oats.

Then he again approached the fiery and untamed steed, about whose head the rope was still fastened, and holding out the hat before him quickly enticed the animal within reach of his hand.

Then throwing the oats on the ground, he led his captive in triumph towards the gate a second time.

The sound of voices was heard just as he had succeeded in remounting, and a fat Dutch farmer vainly shouted after the negro as he urged his horse at full speed along the dusty road.

―――

CHAPTER CCLXXX.

A CALIFORNIAN PRISON—TORCHLIGHT PROCESSION—JUDGE LYNCH.

WHEN Andrew Harwolf and Miles surrendered themselves to the official head-constable at Claremont Creek, they had neither of them the least intention of remaining in the log-prison to which they were conveyed.

It was about two hours before sunset when they were taken to the little lock-up, and now, about an hour after the great luminary had departed, they heard voices and saw flashing pine-knot torches through the crevices in the rude walls of their prison.

"Durn it, zquire! what's the matter wi' the noisy houn's?" said Miles.

"Some other poor devil coming to keep us company, I suppose."

"Aye, zurly, do seem zo."

The Grey Wolf rose and applied his eye to the key-hole.

"I see many men, but no one who looks like a prisoner."

"Durned if I can make it out, measter," replied Miles.

"Perhaps, though, they are going to remove us to a safer place."

"Jist as they likes about that; but why couldna they do it afore, an' then I'd ne'er a took the trouble to draw them wooden pegs from the wall."

In fact, during the three hours which they had been confined, the two villains, the greater and the less, had been using every effort to escape, and it is a question whether the rude walls could have held out much longer against their determined attacks.

Suddenly the door was thrown open, and the head-constable summoned them to come forth.

"What reason can you have for removing us at this time of night?" asked Harwolf.

"You are to be tried immediately on a charge of horse-stealing."

"I never knew yet there was a court-house or a magistrate in this place."

"We want no court-house; but we have a judge, though, to try offenders."

"Yourself, I presume?" said Harwolf, with a sneer.

"No; he is called Judge Lynch!"

Harwolf, hardened as he was, and inured to danger, turned deadly pale, while Joe Miles, who knew nothing about the peculiar institutions of the country, stared at him in amazement.

"Dang it, zquire, what's the matter wi' ye? I never heard tell o' this cove afore," whispered he to his desponding master.

"We are doomed men, Miles," he whispered, hoarsely.

"Whoy, measter, pluck a leetle courage up; dang it all, doan't show the white veather, now."

"I am ready to accompany you," said Harwolf, and, with a constable on each side, and the mob in the rear, waving their glaring torches, the prisoners marched away from the lock-up towards the forest.

"Dang it, measter, there be jist a chance, now. We be goin' towards the woods, do 'ee zee?"

"Going there, because tall trees are plentiful, and no stunted bush will do for you and I to dangle from."

The possibility of such a thing happening seemed to strike Miles, too, at that moment, for he suddenly became pale, silent, and thoughtful, though his keen eyes roving on every side, showed that, if he had a chance, he would make an attempt to escape.

But there was no chance. They were too closely surrounded for anything of the kind, and in weird array the motly procession hurried onwards.

At length they arrived at an open glade, in the middle of which a huge tree had once stood erect, but now, prostrated by the woodman's axe, reclined his huge length along the ground.

The stump was covered with an old flag, and on it a thoughtful-looking man was seated, while along the trunk a row of twelve other men were seated.

The man on the stump, who wore a red flannel shirt and a wide-awake, and who, in common with the twelve jurymen on the stump, smoked vigorously, was the representative of Judge Lynch.

The two prisoners were placed so as to face the judge, and then the mob closed round in a circle, holding their pine knots aloft, so as to throw a lurid glare on the ghastly faces of the delinquents.

"Silence!" proclaimed the judge, in a loud voice.

The rough mob instantly became still and silent, save that, now and again, the dried grass and leaves crackled beneath the feet of those who moved their position.

"What is the charge against these men?" inquired the judge, gravely, at the same time opening a pocket-book.

"They stand accused of stealing two horses, the property of General Jones of Jonesville," replied the constable.

The judge entered the accusation in his pocket-book, and then asked the prisoners,

"Have you any objection to be tried by any one of the twelve jurymen now sitting?"

"I object to the whole assembly as unconstitutional and illegal," replied Harwolf.

"That we care nothing about," returned the judge, "but have you any personal objection to any one of the jurymen?"

"No."

"The first evidence I shall produce," said the chief constable, stepping forward, "will be two British subjects, Silas Rye and Oiny Macarne."

Silas stepped to a position in which he could see the prisoners' faces, and related his story, which was confirmed by Oiny.

There was some objection as to receiving the evidence of Catahaga, whom the prisoners denominated a heathen and outlaw.

"Is this all the evidence?" asked the judge.

"Yes," replied the constable.

"No, I say," cried a nasal voice in the crowd, "I kalkilate as how I can enlighten this 'ere honerable assembly something considerable about them hosses; and this 'ere boy too."

It was General Jones himself who spoke, and his boy was seen by his side, towering above the multitude.

CHAPTER CCLXXXI.

THE TRIAL OF ANDREW HARWOLF AND MILES BY LYNCH LAW—VERDICT AND SENTENCE.

JUDGE LYNCH looked pleased, and his jurymen astonished when General Jones thus announced himself to the court.

"Before you can give evidence you must be sworn," said the judge, checking the eager General.

"Swar away then, judge, I guess I can swar as much now as I cussed when them coons stul my hosses."

The oath was administered, by which the General was bound to speak the truth, the whole truth, and nothing but the truth; and though he considered it binding on the whole, yet it did not prevent the worthy man from indulging in occasional metaphors and figures of speech.

"What have you to say?" demanded the judge.

"Why, that them ere two cusses come to my location, an' 'arter gettin' a bellyful o' grub, makes tracks with two hosses."

"When did this happen?"

"It air only three days ago last Tuesday, I kalkilate."

"Have the horses been found?"

One of the rural police stepped forward and stated that two horses had been found hobbled and tethered to the tent occupied by the prisoners.

"Can you identify your horses, General?"

"Come now, judge, you air jokin'; can I 'dentify that ere boy which air a credit to his country an' his rearin'? I kalkilate I can identify them hosses jest a leetle."

"Describe them."

"One on 'em air a black hoss, fifteen hands high, with a white star on his forehead, an' two white feet, off foot afore an' near foot behind : t'other air a bay mare, marked J. J. on off shoulder."

"Does that descrption correspond with the horses you found tethered to the prisoners' tent?" asked the judge of the policeman.

"I guess it do, judge,"

"An', judge, if ye don't hang 'em, you arn't fit for yer office," bawled the General, "for two cusseder skunks never walked across these ere diggins, I guess; riglar ripstavers they air."

"Silence!" cried the judge, "have a proper respect for the court."

"I guess I have, judge; but it riles my feelin's to see them rogues a standin' there a grinnin' like 'possums, when the mighty eagle of Hail Columbiar air a settin' on the top o' that ere snow-capped rock a waitin' to swoop down an' fill his belly with the blood an' bones o' them ere blasted Britishers and all other varmin. I say, judge, it air a shame that rogues should live on the face o' this ere mighty land which I guess can whip all creation into a 'tarnal smash, an' then whip the bits together agin. I say, judge, that if you has any respect for the laws an' constitootion o' this ere great, free, an' enlightened country, you'll hist the stars and stripes to the top o' the tallest tree in these ere mighty forestes, an' hang them rapscallions beneath its glorious shadder as a warnin' that Uncle Sam air a rigler screamer."

This bit of bunkum to a great extent decided the fate of the prisoners.

The judge, perhaps, was the most cool and unimpassioned man in the whole assembly, and therefore best fitted for his office. He alone of the assembly was unmoved by the general's oratory, if we except Silas Rye and the Indian chief.

Briefly he summed up the evidence relating that the prisoners had been seen to steal horses from the last witness, which same horses had been found in their possession, and concluded by advising the gentlemen of the jury to consider their verdict calmly and dispassionately.

The gentlemen of the jury obeyed this injunction by springing to their feet, and shouting out in loud tones,

"Guilty, judge! there ain't the least doubt about it."

This announcement was followed by most uproarious shouts of applause from the great unwashed multitude, who threw their hats in the air, and considered—at least most of them did—that the prisoners were already as good as hanged.

Some, however, like the Scottish baron of old, resolved to "mak' sicker," and accordingly rushed into the arena with a tolerably stout piece of rope.

"Hold!" cried the judge, rising.

The men stopped short.

"I was elected by you to fill the office of judge, therefore I shall expect you to be satisfied with the sentence I am about to pass on the prisoners."

"They oughter be hung, judge," cried one or two voices.

"An' I guess I'll hang 'em, if Judge Lynch don't," cried General Jones.

"Silence!" cried the judge.

Silence was at length restored, and the judge then pronounced the following speech,

"Prisoners, you have been found guilty of horse stealing, for which crime the court passes the following sentence upon you: That you be taken hence one hundred yards in the forest, and there have a rope tied about your necks, and your hands tied behind your backs; the ends of the ropes round your necks are then to be firmly tied to a branch of a tree over your heads, and you are then to be placed, with your legs unbound, on the backs of the horses you have stolen, and there left, leaving it to the discretion of the animals whether you are hanged by the necks or not."

The applause which followed this sentence was terrific, and both the wretches to whom it was addressed gave themselves up as lost.

Miles threw himself on the ground, and in piteous accents begged for mercy.

It was in vain, however.

Harwolf spoke not, though his face was ghastly white, and he trembled in every limb.

He knew full well that nothing could set aside the sentence of Judge Lynch.

Preparations were at once made for carrying out the sentence. The horses were brought into the ring, and the whole procession moved away to a spot in the forest, where an immense tree, the monarch of the woods, spread his huge branches around over an open space, and beneath this they halted.

The condemned were then placed each on the back of a horse (their hands were already tied), a rope was tied round each of their necks, and the ends thrown over one of the branches, on which Olny Macarne was already seated, waiting to make fast.

And the Irishman did make them fast, too, in such a manner that if the horses moved a step forward both would be left dangling.

"An', be jabers, sure it's Jack Ketch hisself 'ud be puzzled to bate that. It's the natust gallus I iver set my eyes on, barrin the one Bryan O'Linn was sintenced to be hung on."

But what was the judge doing all this time, while his officers were so busy?

With his keen bowie knife he had been cutting away at the back of the tree, and when at length his task was finished he stepped back, and viewed with satisfaction these words, as they showed out sharp and white on the big brown trunk—

"JUDGE LYNCH."

This was the writ and the signature by whose authority wayfarers and strangers would understand that the act had been performed.

Then, with many sarcastic wishes of "good night," and "pleasant dreams" the mob dispersed, leaving the two wretches on the backs of the two spirited horses, whose first step would hurry them to eternity.

CHAPTER CCLXXXII.

THE "REVENGE"—A CHASE—THE DECK FIGHT.

ON board the "Revenge," late "Newport," things went well enough for a few days. The wind was fresh and steady, while the men, under the influence of plenty of grog and hopes of prizes, did what little work was absolutely necessary without grumbling.

But when a week had passed, and the excitement of their successful mutiny began to wear off, they grew moody and insolent.

Harwolf looked out, therefore, with increasing anxiety for a prize, or a storm, or, in fact, anything that would rouse the crew from their sullen humour.

The sky, at length, began to give indications of a coming storm, the wind having drawn round towards the east, and sombre-looking clouds gathering about that quarter.

Harwolf walked the deck briskly, and had succeeded in infusing some degree of energy into his crew, when a loud oath near at hand startled him.

"What's the matter?" he asked.

"I'll be damned if it ain't a sail, captain," replied the man addressed.

Harwolf levelled his glass at the object in question, and surely enough it was a ship under a crowd of canvas.

"Shake out every rag!" roared Harwolf, wild with excitement, and in a few minutes the gallant ship began to slip through the waves in glorious style.

The strange vessel, too, saw that she was pursued, and used every means her commander could think of to avoid the very suspicious-looking "Revenge."

But it was no use.

The light, sharp-bowed ship which Harwolf commanded gained fast on the object of her pursuit, and very quickly the order was given to clear away a gun and stand ready to pitch a shot into her.

Walbrook, who had *appointed himself* second officer, undertook this task, and had the gun slewed round and loaded, while he stood by blowing a match and waiting for the word "fire!"

"Are you ready?" demanded Harwolf.

"All right, captain."

"Then mind your eye and fire!"

The white smoke blew away to leeward, and the ball could be seen spinning across the waves towards the stranger's bows, and Harwolf was just beginning to think it had gone wide of the mark when all at once she luffed up in the wind, and the pirates could plainly see the spritsail yards hanging across the spars.

"Hurrah! she is ours!"

The shot had effectually crippled the strange vessel—a poor whaler returning from a very unsuccessful cruise in the Pacific.

So the "Revenge" easily bore down alongside her, and after giving another shot which made a huge rent in the mainsail, the grapnels were hooked on, and the pirates swarmed on the deck of the whaler.

A hand to hand contest ensued, and Harwolf was soon busily engaged, cut and thrust, with the skipper of the whaler.

The two crews were nearly equal in numbers, and both parties fought with energy and desperation. Two men only were left on board the "Revenge," but they were quite sufficient to take charge of the clipper; every man on board was engaged in the conflict.

The skipper was a bold and determined man, so were his crew; he knew that if he could once clear his deck of the enemy he had a chance of escape, for on the forecastle he had two long guns which he had just managed to load and get in position when the pirates first boarded him.

With these guns he could retaliate could he force the enemy back to his own ship and get once more under weigh.

To effect this end he rallied and encouraged his men both by word and action, and putting himself at their head made a furious charge, which, however, failed to expel the pirates.

Harwolf thought he had gained an advantage by thus withstanding and repelling their onslaught and was willing to take advantage of it. With a cheer he led his men forward, and after another desperate fight succeeded in driving the whalers to the after part of the vessel.

Some considerable time had been spent in these hitherto fruitless conflicts, which had made the whalers lose heart and confidence. The pirates too found that they had a more difficult task than they had anticipated.

So the two parties stood opposite each other muttering oaths and glaring with angry looks, though neither felt willing to make another attack.

But Harwolf knew well enough that defeat in the present instance would be attended with the most disastrous consequences to himself, so again he rushed on the hardy whalers, who resolutely stood their ground.

A wound in the arm fell to the share of the pirate leader in this attack, and at the head of his men he slowly retreated again.

But on arriving at the forecastle his eye caught sight of the two guns which the whaler had not been able to use, and the devil at the same time suggested to him that they might win the battle for him.

He whispered a word in the ears of two or three of his crew, who immediately wheeled the guns round and pointed them at the group of whalers aft, and then in addition to the ball in each began to stuff them with iron bolts, rails, or any old rubbish they could lay their hands on.

Then a man took up his position at the breech of each with a lighted match in hand.

These preparations being completed to his satisfaction, Harwolf stepped forward between the guns and hailed the skipper.

"Surrender instantly! Lay down your arms or I'll blow you all to bits."

It was an anxious moment, and the stout-hearted skipper gazed in the faces of his crew, but they were all evidently filled with dismay. Despair was plainly written on their countenances.

"Surrender, I say!" roared Harwolf, perceiving their irresolution and resolving to profit by it.

"Will you spare our lives?" cried the whaler, coming forward.

"Yes, of course."

The whaler held a whispered consultation with his men, the result of which was that in a few minutes he again advanced to inform the pirates that they yielded.

"Then throw down your arms, and stand where you are," said Harwolf.

This order was obeyed, but scarcely had they dropped their weapons when Harwolf seized the match from the man nearest him, and applied it to the breech of the gun. A roaring explosion shook the deck of the whaler, which, for a minute, was enveloped in smoke.

When it cleared away a horrible sight was seen.

Seven stout men lay on the deck, some dead, others dying, all fearfully mutilated; four only, of whom the captain was one, stood erect. The planks and wood-work of the ship were splintered to pieces by the terrific discharge.

Even the pirates looked on in dismay.

The captain of the whaler then stepped forward, and spoke,

"I see by this what I have to expect, but prefer to die my own way. But your end shall not be so easy."

So saying he sprang overboard between the two ships, and was seen no more, though Harwolf used every means to recover him.

He would have tortured the brave whaling captain.

The captain of the "Revenge" then hailed the three men who remained, and asked whether they would prefer to take service under him or die?

The first, a stern-looking old tar, squirted some tobacco juice towards the pirate, and said,

"I'll be damned if I serve under a blood-thirsty pirate."

With an oath Harwolf drew his revolver, and shot the old seaman through the heart.

The two others loved life, and promised obedience to the ruffian in whose power they found themselves.

"Now, heigh for plunder, lads!" cried Harwolf; "the ship is ours."

The men were already busily searching every nook and corner, but little that was valuable could they discover save provisions and gunpowder.

The two long guns, however, were a prize to Harwolf, who had them removed with the other valuables to the deck of his own smart ship.

"With these," thought he, "I could sail round the 'Red Raven' even, and do as I liked. So let the Boy Pirate be careful how he crosses my course."

"All the plunder is aboard, captain," said Walbrook, coming up; "there ain't nothing left but the stinkin' oil, and we can't find stowage room for that."

"Then get our men on board, and set the cursed ship on fire."

"But them fellers, captain?"

"Who?"

"The wounded men to be sure."

"Blast them! let them burn with the ship. You'll find I am none of your soft-hearted gentlemen rovers, but a regular devil."

The surly-looking lieutenant of the "Revenge" withdrew, and in a few minutes it was evident how well he had obeyed his captain's orders.

Faint wreaths of smoke began to curl from the port-holes and to darken the cabin windows. It grew thicker and whiter.

The grapnels were unhooked, and the "Revenge" sailed away without heeding the prayers and supplications of the poor maimed wretches who begged and implored to be taken on board or cast at once into the waves.

Any death seemed preferable to that to which the demon-like pirate captain had condemned them.

The only answer which he made to their prayers as he stood on his own deck was to laugh at their sufferings, and mockingly bid them jump overboard since they were so fond of the water.

Their curses sounded on his ear as the distance between the two ships increased, and he could see them writhing with bodily pain and mental agony as the fire crept nearer and nearer.

Harwolf turned away, and, descending to his cabin, drank a huge draught of brandy to quiet his somewhat shaken nerves.

On regaining the deck, he found his men already quarrelling about the division of the plunder.

"Give up everything at once," he cried. "I will see it properly divided, and, as this is our first prize, I give my share to increase yours."

And, with a certain kind of rude justice, he did so, with the exception of the guns, ammunition and stores, which were voted part of the ship's outfit, and, therefore, at the more immediate disposal of the captain.

The booty, though not much, was sufficient to make them all contented for a time, and when the grog had been served out, they gave way to their mirth in songs, dances, toasts and oaths.

Harwolf preferred to drink himself insensible in the cabin of the late Captain Pickett, but his absence was not much noticed by the crew, who were too intent on their own enjoyment.

Rum and brandy now flowed freely as blood had previously done, and the evening was brought to a close with the ceremony of swearing in the two new hands, which was done with a profusion of oaths, threats and curses.

Then the grog can passed round again and the men were in a state of the most digusting, beastly intoxication, when Harwolf, after about an hour's sleep, managed to stagger on deck.

"Wh-what —hic—the devil," cried he, gazing round with a drunken leer.

Before he could say anything more a can of grog was hurled in his face by some unseen hand, and, reeling back, he tumbled down the companion ladder, at the bottom of which he lay helpless, though fully sensible that he heard a loud laugh greet his disappearance.

When he was again able to reach his cabin he took the precaution to lock the door, and then pile every atom of furniture against it.

This was quite a needless precaution, for, even in their drunken madness, the men remembered that he alone of their number was capable of navigating the vessel.

The evening came, and luckily the wind ceased, and a perfect calm was on the ocean, for neither captain nor crew were capable of taking care of the ship, even in a moderate breeze.

The night was lovely as ever eye looked on even in those southern latitudes, the heavens cloudless, the full round moon shining high off the mast-head, the stars drawn up into her bright light, and trembling through her radiant brightness like dewdrops in gossamer on a summer's morn; the sea appeared to meet the sky on every side without a speck on the clear line of the horizon.

There was something pleasant in the air, which was cool and fresh, smelling of the brine.

The men—the pirates—lay scattered on the deck, each just as he fell after the drunken bout; some looked dead, so still and silent were they; others snored loudly and moved uneasily, while Walbrook,

being possessed of the hardest head in the company, was just rubbing his eyes and looking, or rather trying to look, around him, when suddenly a white figure appeared standing by him.

The first impression of the man was that it was a spirit, and he was about to mumble some words of rude prayer to it when his eye caught the features.

It was Daniel Harwolf.

"What, my bully captain," said the man, recovering from his fright, "so hot you're obliged to air yourself with nothin' but staysails on?"

The captain spoke not, but seemed to be gazing steadfastly at the bowsprit.

Then, rising to his feet, Walbrook gazed in his commander's face, and plainly saw that he was asleep.

Still he gazed with a scared wild look at the bowsprit, motioning Walbrook to keep perfect silence.

The man unconsciously followed his commander's gaze, but there was nothing save the huge timber, the taut ropes, and the flapping canvas, while the moonshine cast a halo of indistinctness over all, so dazzling was its brightness.

"See!" murmured Harwolf, in low tones. "There! there! Now he moves!"

"What moves, captain?" asked the man, unable to see any animate object.

"The Jew! I see him now, pointing towards me with bloodstained-finger! He comes! He comes!"

And the guilty wretch trembled violently, as he thus fancied he saw the father of Deborah, the Jewess.

"See, now, my foe has joined him, and together they mock and jeer at me!"

A dark shadow passed across the foresail, and to Walbrook's half drunken fancy it seemed like the outlines of a man's figure.

"It is passed—it is gone! But, why, oh! why did he beckon me here, unless it be to tell me that my doom is approaching? Fiend, I defy thee! My destiny is not given thee to rule, nor he who stands by thy side!"

The bright moonbeams shone on in their glory as the wretched man thus raved.

"Heaven, have mercy!" he cried. "She comes now to torment me!"

And the wretched man fell on the deck, his hands clenched with desperation, and his mouth foaming.

Walbrook dashed a pail of water over his face, and his apparent agony subsided into a hard quick heaving of the chest and a convulsive twitching about the mouth.

Another pail of water was thrown over him, and he sat up.

"Give me some brandy," he said.

The spirit was given him, and he drained it off.

"Did any one else see this?" he asked.

"Not a soul, captain."

Which was perfectly true, for the remainder of the pirates had not yet recovered from their debauch and were still sleeping.

"Say nothing about this to any one!" said Harwolf, "and I will be your friend for life."

Walbrook promised secrecy, and Harwolf re-entered his cabin.

THE WEDDING FESTIVITIES.—*See No.* 84.

CHAPTER CCLXXXIII.

FURTHER CAREER OF DANIEL HARWOLF—THE "EL DORADO"—PRIEST AND PIRATE—A WORK OF DESTRUCTION.

DANIEL HARWOLF and Walbrook, therefore, became much more closely connected, though, as the latter-named individual had been appointed second in command, the rest of the brutal unreasoning crew were not so much surprised.

"Captain," said Walbrook, about three days after the capture of the whaler, "if we cruise about here for a time we stand a good chance of picking up a Portuguese ship going out to their missionary settlements."

"A good plan; then we'll keep off and on about here. I suppose these Portuguese carry something besides parsons though?"

"Generally a pretty good supply of money, to No. 82.

say nothing of a few gold cups and candlesticks for their churches."

"Which shall deck our cabin-table if I fall in or fall out with them. Do they fight much, think you?"

"Not much, I fancy, from what I have seen of the nation, though they do generally carry a few short guns."

"We carry long ones, so let them look out."

"We can very easily outsail any ship that flies the Portuguese flag, I fancy, captain," said Walbrook, looking aloft at the light and graceful spars.

"We can; therefore all that remains is to keep a strict look out. Tell the men, will you, that more prizes may be expected, and keep them sober."

So saying, Harwolf retired to his cabin, where he certainly did not observe the sobriety he enjoined on deck.

From his half-drunken reverie he was aroused by

the entrance of a man who announced a sail in sight.

With an oath Harwolf buckled on his sword, and returned to the deck.

In a few minutes all was bustle and excitement on the deck of the " Revenge."

The blood-thirsty pirates stood with gleaming eyes, grasping their cutlasses, knives, pikes, and marlin-spikes.

The splendid ship raced forward after its prey, scarcely lifting on the rolling waves, but gliding along like a swallow.

They gained on the stranger every minute, for she was a heavy, square-rigged ship, though, in her own clumsy fashion, she was dashing and rolling along with commendable speed.

The men were eager for the fray, and Harwolf added not a little to their excitement by speculating aloud on the hoarded gold they might expect to find.

" No doubt they will fight, comrades," said he; " but we are English, and each a match for half a dozen of Portuguese."

" I think we are near enough to send her a message by one of these," said Walbrook, touching one of the long guns with his cutlass.

" Well, try your luck," responded Harwolf. " You proved not a bad gunner in the case of our late friend the whaler."

The gun was loaded, pointed, and, watching his opportunity as the ship rose on a wave, Walbrook applied the lighted match.

The ball spun away, but, badly aimed, fell some distance astern of the ship, which immediately hoisted the Portuguese colours.

" Then show them our ebony ensign," cried Harwolf, and a minute afterwards the black flag rolled out from the mast-head of the " Revenge."

" Hold on awhile till we get a better range, and then we'll see what they are made of," cried the disappointed gunner, rubbing his eyes.

And so the beautiful ship, which was manned by such an unlovely crew, continued to near the lumbering Portuguese till Harwolf judged that they were near enough to risk another shot.

A second time, therefore, did the long gun belch forth its flame and smoke, this time with better effect, as the shower of splinters from the deck of the Portuguese attested.

But scarcely had the dull roar of the gun ceased to reverberate ere the ports of the stranger opened, and a whole broadside from her six short guns came hissing about Harwolf's ears, while three of his stoutest men were hurled lifeless to the deck.

" Damn them !" roared Harwolf, stamping his foot with fury. " But they shall suffer for this."

" I didn't think they had so much pluck," said Walbrook, as he bound a handkerchief round his arm, which had been wounded slightly.

" Blood for blood ! They shall die, every one of them !"

" Well, at all events, we can pay them back in their own coin now. Our broadside guns would tell."

Let us take a look at the cabin and decks of the Portuguese ship, the " El Dorado," as she was not unaptly named.

The sailors armed themselves for the fight, so did the passengers, and then they all crowded round a venerable-looking man, whose silken cassock betrayed at once his sacred calling.

" Be brave, be valiant, my children, and resist unto the utmost these fearful and blood-thirsty men, and may all the saints bless you."

So saying the old priest dipped his fingers into a bowl of consecrated water, and sprinkled it upon all the company.

Then while the men, inspirited by the blessing, rushed away to their guns with loud shouts of defiance, he turned towards a fair young girl who stood at his elbow, and said,

" Retire to your cabin, dear Sophia. It is not meet for you to look on scenes of strife and bloodshed."

" And you, dear uncle ?"

" I must remain at my post to shrive and absolve the wounded men, who will doubtlessly soon encumber our decks."

" Then while you minister to their spiritual needs and necessities, I will attend to their bodily requirements."

The old man again objected to her thus exposing herself, but Sophia Vedras was determined to take such share in the conflict as a poor, weak woman might.

Barely eighteen years of age, and possessed of considerable wealth, the fair young girl had given up a home of ease and luxury to accompany her old uncle in his perilous enterprise to convert the wild inhabitants of southern Africa to a knowledge of Christianity.

Both father and mother had died in her infancy, and her sole remaining relative was the good Father Theodore, to whom she had ever been as a daughter.

And when the old man announced his intention of performing a vow he had made in his youth, nothing could induce the fair girl to remain behind.

And so now she stood on the deck of the " El Dorado," binding the wounds of those who were hurt, and refreshing their parched lips with the precious cup of water.

The rude sailors blessed her as they saw her light graceful form gliding about amid the smoke.

The pirates, however, after having been once subjected to the fire of the Portuguese broadside, had sheered off, for Harwolf had so few men under him that he dared not risk a close combat till he had first crippled his prey with the long guns.

This he did, sailing round the poor ship beyond the range of her short carronades, and raking her with those long range pieces.

Very soon the rigging of the " El Dorado," was so much cut up that they were unable to make any progress through the water.

" Our time is come," said Harwolf to Walbrook.

" Aye, so it is, and I'll soon pay those rascals out for my wounded arm."

And like a hawk swooping down upon a defenceless dove the " Revenge" bore down upon the Portuguese, answering her small guns with the roar of those terrible ones which had already done such execution.

Crash ! crash !

The two ships met, and the pirates poured like raging wolves from the deck of their own ship to that of the " El Dorado."

Short, desperate, and bloody was the fight, and it was only when half their number lay on the deck that the survivors threw down their arms.

" So at length ye surrender," hissed Harwolf; " but you shall dearly rue this obstinacy."

" Man of blood," said the old priest, " we defended our own lives as long as was in our power—"

" Silence !" roared the pirate captain. " Send your officers to me, and, Walbrook, place sentries to see that no one goes below."

Only one officer made his appearance, the others had all fallen in the fight.

Harwolf looked at his prisoner for a moment, and then struck him a heavy blow in the face.

The lieutenant said nothing, nor could he retaliate, for his hands were bound behind his back.

" Where is the money concealed, rascal ?" cried Harwolf.

" What money ?"

" The treasures you are known to have on board."

The officer was silent.

" Speak," said Harwolf, " or torture shall make you !"

" Torture cannot make me speak, scoundrel."

" We will see. Again I ask you, where is the money kept ?"

" You must find it."

Mad with rage Harwolf drew a pistol from his belt, and shot the poor helpless captive through the heart.

"To the sharks with him! Now bring all the passengers here."

Eight or ten trembling men and women were placed before the pirate.

"Who are you?" demanded Harwolf of the first.

"I am servant to his reverence, Father Theodore."

"Ah! and who is Father Theodore?"

"A holy father who is about to proceed on a missionary expedition into the interior of Africa."

"Place him on one side, and bring Father Theodore forward."

The order was obeyed, and with the lovely Sophia Vedras hanging on his arm, the priest stood before the pirate.

"Are you the priest?" demanded the brutal Harwolf, as he suffered his licentious gaze to fall upon the lovely form and features of the girl.

"I am a minister of the holy church," replied the old man.

"And as such you have a quantity of money and plate in your charge on board this vessel?"

"My son, the silver and the gold are not thine, so covet them not."

"No d——d preaching, but quickly tell where they are stowed away."

"That I refuse to do."

"Indeed! then I can perhaps extract the information by means that you had not thought of."

"You may try, but never shall my mouth reveal the secret."

"Here, you fellow," said Harwolf, turning towards the old priest's servant.

The man stepped forward trembling.

"You see that?" said the pirate, pointing to the water, in which half a dozen sharks were fiercely contending for the mangled remains of the murdered Portuguese officer.

The man nodded assent.

"Unless you wish to take part in that sport, I would advise you to inform me where the treasure is kept."

"Oh, mercy, senor!" cried the man. "I—I—the holy Father will curse me if I tell anyone."

"I shall kill you if you do not, so you have to choose."

"Oh, senor, for Heaven's sake——"

"Here, once more take a look at these beautiful fish."

The man cast a frightened look towards the sharks, and then fell on the deck.

All the while Father Theodore kept his stern glance on the face of his frightened servant.

"I give you one minute," cried Harwolf.

"Oh, have pity, senor!—have pity! The money is in the spirit——"

Ere he could finish his words, the poor wretch was rolling in convulsions on the deck.

"Over with him!" roared Harwolf.

There was another splash, and the ocean became tinged with blood as the ravenous sharks tore him limb from limb.

"Away there, idlers, hunt the spirit-room, and be quick, too."

Four men, headed by Walbrook, started on this errand, but quickly returned with blank faces.

"Well?" said Harwolf.

"Captain, the ship has been struck between wind and water, there is now five feet of water in the spirit-room."

It was perfectly true, the old ship was settling down slowly yet surely into the bosom of the waters.

"Old man," said Harwolf, "best tell me now where your treasures are."

"I refuse as firmly as ever."

"Do you? Then here, my lads, take this girl to do as you like with her—she is yours."

"Monstrous villain!" cried the priest, "thy atrocities shall yet be punished!"

With the fire of licentious lust in his eyes Walbrook advanced and laid hold of the beauteous girl.

Uttering a loud scream she broke from him, and, running to her uncle, threw her arms round his neck.

Again the ruffian advanced and bore her away.

But, ere two yards from the worthy priest, she again wrenched herself from his rude grasp, and, with a thrilling cry, leaped into the water.

Her fair limbs were soon the prey of the sharks.

"Now, old man, again I put the question, and methinks I have been very forbearing, your ship is sinking, and cannot be saved, why should all your treasures go with it?"

"I would rather every coin were at the bottom of the sea than that they should fall into your hands."

"I will spare your life, and give you half."

"No, pirate, in vain you tempt me; the gold of the holy church shall never fall into your blood-stained hands."

"Obstinate fool," roared Harwolf, and, with his sword, he cleft the old priest's skull.

"Throw him over; and now, my lads, throw every valuable you can lay your hands on into their boats, for the ship is sinking rapidly.

"And these lubbers, captain?" said Walbrook, pointing to the remainder of the passengers and crew.

"Lash them together, two and two, then throw them overboard."

The order was literally obeyed.

The ocean was soon dotted with human forms, while the busy sharks snapped off legs, arms and heads.

The waters assumed a red tinge, while many piercing shrieks were heard.

One poor fellow, in the desperate agony of his struggles, had managed to force his hands, and had laid hold of the gunwale of one of the boats at the moment Harwolf entered it.

With a brutal oath the ruffian drew a rope from his pocket, and, after passing one end of it round the poor wretch's arm, attached it to the bow of the cutter; then, taking an axe, he with a blow severed the hand from the arm.

At length all the valuables they could discover were placed in the boats of the Portuguese ship, and then the pirates pulled away to their own vessel.

"Not such a bad booty," thought Harwolf, as his eyes fell on three small chests, bound with iron and sealed, together with a couple of bags full of coin.

The poor Portuguese ship rocked to and fro for a minute, and then, with a terrific lurch, plunged head foremost to the bottom of the ocean.

CHAPTER CCLXXXIV.

CHARLES RYE IN AUSTRALIA—HIS HOUSE IS ENTERED BY BURGLARS—HE SHOOTS ONE OF THE ROBBERS—HE MEETS WITH HIS BROTHER SILAS.

RETURN we to England and take a peep into the private counting-house of Messrs. Bullion, the bankers.

Charles Rye stands before them with a beam of delight in his eye.

The worthy financiers had thoroughly regained confidence in him, had they not, they would hardly have proposed to him such an undertaking.

For to him they had just proposed a voyage to America—California, in fact—for the following purpose:

Though *gold* was plentiful at San Francisco, *coin* was scarce. The idea, therefore, had occurred to Messrs. Bullion to send out an agent well supplied with American currency, to exchange for the dust and nuggets of the miners.

Charles Rye was the first to whom they spoke on the subject.

Perhaps the thought that they owed him some reparation for their previous injustice prompted them to appoint him their agent.

For Charles Rye, though a steady business-like young man, was certainly not superior to many others employed in the same office.

" I thank you, gentlemen," said he, " but I have a wife with whom I must consult, ere I accept your kind offer."

" Oh, yes, certainly ask Mrs. Rye's opinion ; but at the same time, as we don't wish to deprive you of her company, we should have no objection to her being your fellow traveller."

With a bow, Charles left the room, and not long after was seated by the side of his beloved Emily.

" Well, dear, what do you say ?" he asked, after he had recounted to her the offer of his employers.

" I say, my dear Charles, that you must decide for yourself ; but if you go I go with you."

" I am not very ambitious to become a great traveller, but there is one reason why I should like to undertake this journey."

" And what is that ?"

" Why, you know, dear, my brother Silas is in America. I might hear something of him if I went, for, to speak truly, I begin to feel anxious, it is so long since I had a letter from him."

" I hope no mischief has happened," said Emily, nestling up closer than ever.

" So do I ; but in those wild woods of America there is no safety or security."

" And yet you wish to tempt those dangers," said Emily, reproachfully.

" Nay, my love ; the town of San Francisco to which I go, if I accept the offer of my employers, is a large and populous place, though certainly not so refined as London."

" And why do you think you will be able to hear news of your brother there ?"

" Because he has been following those rascals in a westerly direction during the whole time. I think it is very likely, therefore, that California will be the scene of their final capture."

" Dear Charlie, go if you like, but in any case I go with you."

" Then I will go, so you must make haste and prepare yourself, for in a week's time we sail."

So the die was cast, and the next morning Charles Rye told his employers that he had decided on accepting their offer, and that his wife would accompany him.

" Then you must be ready to sail on Monday next" (it was on a Tuesday morning that the conversation took place), " for the ship cannot be delayed, and if your wife is not ready, why you must give up the berth to some one else, who is not so much encumbered."

" She will be ready, sir, so shall I. But what ship do we sail in ?"

" The 'Uxbridge,' A 1, bound for New York. Now you had better go, for you will want some time to make your arrangements, so don't come here any more before Saturday next, when we will give you your final instructions. Good morning, Mr. Rye."

" Good morning, gentlemen."

A week afterwards the " Uxbridge," A 1, screw steamer, was speeding down the channel with a goodly muster of passengers on her deck, waving with their handkerchiefs adieu to the shores of old England.

Among these might be seen Charles Rye and his wife.

With the usual amount of sea-sickness and discomfort the voyage began and terminated, for in sixteen days after leaving the Thames the steamer cast anchor before the city of New York.

Charles and his wife were among the first to land, and then the young man despatched a letter to his employers, announcing his safe arrival in America.

His English notes and securities were quickly changed for American gold, and then, without a moment's delay, the young man, his wife, and two stout men sent with him by the bankers, commenced their long and difficult journey to California.

At the last military station on their route they obtained an escort of a dozen soldiers, for such protection was needful in the wild regions which they now had to traverse.

On and on over the Rocky Mountains, through forests, across prairies, till, at length, they reached a comparatively more civilized region.

But even there they halted not ; but still pressed onwards till, after many trials and hardships, they entered the great and wooden town of San Francisco.

Here all their troubles ceased, and after making his arrangements with the principal bankers of the place, the young man had time to look about and fix upon a residence for himself and wife in some more quiet spot than the second-floor of the immense hotel where they first stayed.

A little house near a small stream in the outskirts of the town was vacant, and this Charles Rye quickly secured.

It was a small wooden building, as were most of the houses in the town ; "but still," thought Charlie, " there is a feeling of independence in having one's own house, to say nothing of avoiding those mountains of stairs."

So into this little hut they removed, and for some few days were in peace and quietness.

One of the men who had accompanied him resided there while the other had charge of an office which Charles had opened in the heart of the city for the transaction of business.

One night, about three weeks after his arrival, the young couple had retired to rest, and everything seemed quiet save the wind, which howled dismally.

" Hark ! what is that noise, dear ?" said Emily.

" Only the wind rattling through the streets."

The quarter in which the house was situated could scarcely be called a street, for the houses were detached, and in many instances unfinished.

Emily seemed satisfied with the explanation her husband gave of the noise which had startled her, and nestling up close to his side was soon asleep.

And Charles, as he gazed on the fair face as revealed by the dim rays of a night-lamp, thought she had never looked so exquisitely beautiful.

" Lovely girl," he whispered, as he watched the rosy lips and heaving breast, " how earnest, how strong must be your love that for me you undertook to brave all the terrors of the trackless wilderness."

And bending over her till her warm breath fanned his cheek, he pressed a light but fervent kiss on her forehead.

Charles Rye fervently loved his fair Emily, the more so that she had that day whispered in his ear that in the natural course of events he would some day be a father.

But all his dreams of happiness were checked, and his thoughts drawn back to the present by a repetition of the sound which had alarmed Emily.

What could it be ?

The wind, perhaps ; but no, the wind does not often make a sound like a saw.

At all events, as there was a considerable sum of money in the house, it behoved him as its guardian to see into the cause of this strange unusual sound.

Quietly slipping from his bed he half dressed himself, and taking a couple of revolvers from his chest proceeded to the room occupied by his man.

The man was soundly sleeping, though he quickly started up when Charles shook him by the shoulder.

" What is it, sir ?" he asked.

" Hush ! listen ! do you hear any strange noise ?"

The man listened attentively for a moment, and then replied,

" I do, sir, and if I mistake not some thieves are breaking into the house."

And without another word he too jumped up and armed himself.

Turning down all the lights as much as possible they proceeded from room to room to discover, if possible, at what point the thieves were endeavouring to force an entrance.

The roof was evidently the object of their attack, and after waiting some time to find out what part of the roof, the servant proposed that he should quietly creep out at the front door to reconnoitre.

He was a bold, fearless fellow, and Charles acceded to his suggestion.

The door was unbarred, and he was about to creep out when a long and piercing scream almost froze the blood in Charlie's heart.

"Good heavens! it comes from her room!" he cried, and bounded away as fast as possible to the room in which he had left Emily sleeping.

Who can describe his horror when he saw his beloved wife struggling in the hands of a ruffian, who wore a crape mask over his face, while another man, similarly disguised, was hastily ransacking the chests and drawers?

Levelling his pistol at the man who held his wife, threatening her with instant death if she moved or spoke, Charlie pulled the trigger.

The room was in an instant filled with smoke, but through its sulphurous clouds Charles Rye could see the ruffian stagger back, clap his hands to his head, and then fall heavily on the floor.

Alarmed at the sudden and unexpected turn things had taken, the second robber dropped his plunder, and, leaping through the open window, ran off hastily down the street.

After soothing his wife, who was sobbing violently at the rudeness she had experienced, Charles removed her to another room, and then returned to the man he had shot.

The young man trembled violently, as well he might, for never before had his hand been lifted against a fellow-creature in anger.

His face turned ashy pale, too, as, raising the man's head, he saw that he was dead.

Meanwhile the police, alarmed at the sound of fire-arms, which, though frequent enough in the more populous part of the town, in the bars and gambling-rooms, was seldom heard in that quiet quarter, were loudly knocking for admittance.

They came up into the room, and heard the explanation which Charles and his man had to give of the affair, and then, after a short consultation, dispatched one of their number for assistance and a stretcher.

It was brought, and the unsightly corpse removed to the court-house.

Early next morning Charles had to attend before the judge for the purpose of deposing how the deceased met his death.

"Do you know anything of him?" asked the justice.

"I never before set eyes on him that I am aware of."

"Let the body be advertised for identification," said the justice, to the clerk of the court.

"I can identify him as one Joe Miles, *alias* Miles Thornton, an outlawed Englishman," said a voice.

Charlie turned, beheld his brother Silas, and, in a moment was clasped in his arms.

CHAPTER CCLXXXV.

ZAMPA'S FURTHER ADVENTURES—CHARLOTTE CARDROSS—THE DUTCHMAN SHOOTS HIS OWN HORSE—ZAMPA AND THE LION.

"STOP tiefs! You Got for dammed rascal, dat ish mine pony!" shouted the Dutch farmer, when he beheld Zampa riding away.

"Berry sorry dis chile can't 'blige," said Zampa, in reply.

"Dat ish mine horz! dat ish mine own peautiful horz!" the Dutchman continued to shout long after the negro was out of hearing.

Finding that the thief absolutely refused to return with the stolen property Mynheer lit his pipe and speedily enveloped himself in a thick cloud.

After smoking for two hours, two ideas suggested themselves to him. The first being to nail up the gate of the paddock, and the second that, being a justice of the peace, he would severely punish the thief if he caught him.

Providence did not suggest to his thick intellect any plan whereby the offender might be captured—two ideas at one time being properly considered a most unnecessary and unaccountable thing.

So Zampa rode on his way rejoicing while Mynheer Puffenbluff, after finishing his pipe proceeded to lock the stable, or rather the paddock gate, though the horse was stolen.

And we will leave him at that task to follow the fortunes of Zampa whom Black Ralph had chosen to be love's postman.

Laughing, grinning, rolling himself on the saddle, he hurried forward, and soon arrived at the house to which he had been dispatched, and which was known by the name of Bullockbourne Farm.

The owner of this out-of-the-way place was a man who had emigrated from the south of England with his wife some years before, and was about as ignorant, surly, ill-tempered a brute as you could find in the colony.

But he had a very pretty daughter though, and Black Ralph had seen her under peculiar circumstances.

Early on the day on which he first met the Yankee parson, Ralph's attention had been drawn towards the market-place, where had girl in question was weeping bitterly amid her poultry and eggs.

A few kind words from the rover soon opened her heart and her mouth, and she informed him that her father had been cruelly beating her.

Ralph sympathised with her, and after a little more conversation a meeting was arranged for the evening.

The appointment was punctually kept on both sides, and the result of the interview was that Charlotte Cardross consented to elope with the black-bearded mariner, and the escapade would have taken place there and then had not her father at that moment made his appearance.

She, however, managed to slip into his hand a scrap of paper, on which was written full directions how he might communicate with her.

Acting on these instructions he had sent Zampa to inform her that in a week's time his ship would sail, and therefore she must expect to receive a visit from him in the course of five days.

When Zampa arrived in sight of the farm-house, his first care was to reconnoitre, for he had heard the father's character from Black Ralph, and did not care to expose himself to any chance of failure in his errand.

Not a soul was to be seen in or about the homestead, but at the distance of three quarters of a mile or more he could see a horseman driving a flock of sheep up the mountain side, and he at once came to the conclusion that it must be the father.

So dismounting from his steed, he advanced to the door of the hut and knocked boldly.

A shrewish, withered-looking old woman responded to his summons.

"What do you want?" she demanded, in vinegar accents.

Zampa saw at once that this was not the person to whom the letter was addressed, and therefore to gain time till he could frame a discreet answer, the worthy black man puffed and panted and fanned himself with his straw hat as though he were completely out of breath through some violent exertion.

"Well, can't you answer, thick-head?" said the lady.

"Oh, gor——oh golly, missis! Dis nigger see de debbil!"

"Is that all you came to tell me?"

"No, missis, but you jes' wait till Zamp gits his breaf again."

And in order to do so he recommenced panting more vigorously than before.

"You stupid fool!" ejaculated Mrs. Cardross, beginning to grow angry. "Why the devil don't you say what you want, instead of standing there grinning like a black baboon?"

"Eh, missis? Dis nigger got somefin to say to Massa Cardross."

"Well, he isn't at home, so you must come again."

"Yah, now, you don't want to kill poor Zamp. S'pose you let poor nigger stop till massa come home."

"Very well; Charlotte, come and stay here while I go out, and see that this black rascal don't steal anything."

At this command Charlotte came tripping out of a back room, while at the same time her mother made her exit by the front door.

As soon as they were alone, Zampa laid his finger on his lips and made a variety of gestures to intimate that strict silence was to be observed.

The girl gazed on him with astonishment and surprise.

"What is the matter?" she asked.

"Hush-h!" whispered Zampa, at the same time just showing her the letter, which he immediately returned to his pocket.

"Give it me," said Charlotte, at once comprehending the meaning of his mysterious behaviour.

Zampa rolled his eyes frightfully, and made signs to intimate that it was dangerous to speak until the mother should be at a greater distance from them.

Charlotte rose from her seat, and humming a tune, walked carelessly to the door.

On looking out, she discovered that her mother was at least a quarter of a mile from the house.

"She is gone now, so give me the letter if it is for me."

"Yes, missy, it am for you, sure as dis nigger's black."

Charlotte eagerly broke the seal, and read the few lines which composed the letter.

"Tell him I will be ready; but stay, I will write him an answer so that there can be no mistake."

She returned to her room for a short time, and then returned with a letter and a small parcel, which apparently contained wearing apparel.

"Give this to your master," she said, "and here, take these two dollars for yourself."

"No, missy, Zampa don't want de money; but s'pose you gib me somefin to eat an' drink."

"Oh yes, I did not think of that."

And in a few minutes Zampa found himself face to face with a huge lump of cold beef, some white bread, and, what pleased him most, a foaming jug of British beer, which had somehow found its way to that remote region.

After surprising the eatables and drinkables to a considerable extent, Zampa took up his hat and made the best of his way homewards, or rather to Cape Town.

But now his troubles began again, for the mother of the fair one he had just left was rapidly approaching the house in company with her husband when Zampa mounted his horse.

"Here is Mr. Cardross, if you want to see him," screamed the woman, who was the first to cast eyes on the negro.

Zampa pretended not to hear, and hurried to climb to the back of his steed, which was, as we have seen before, a work of considerable difficulty.

"Do you hear?" screamed Mrs. Cardross, at the top of her voice.

Zampa still continued silent, and, having by good fortune gained his steed's back, hastened off as fast as possible.

The farmer, seeing this hurried departure, set his horse in swifter motion, and dashed away in pursuit, while his wife hastened to the cottage to inquire the reason of the black man's extraordinary behaviour.

But Charlotte had seen the whole scene, and by the time her mother reached the hut had a tale ready, feeling pretty certain that her father would not overtake the negro messenger.

Two silver spoons, on which a great value was set, were missing from the side table, and the girl, with the utmost assurance, informed her mother that the black had stolen them.

Poor Mrs. Cardross bitterly bewailed her hard fate, and cursed the day she left old England to be " robbed and murdered by them thieving savages. "

And, in the course of half an hour, things were not much improved, when the master of the house returned, leading his horse by the bridle, having broken both its knees in leaping a wide gully, over which Zampa had passed unharmed.

The two sour tempers together made such a little hell that Charlotte was really not sorry when her father angrily ordered her to remain in her chamber as a prisoner during his sovereign will and pleasure.

She retired with a light heart, and consoled herself by reading Ralph's letter, reflecting at the same time that ere many days he would come and take her away.

Whither he would take her the girl had not the slightest idea. Any place was preferable to home with a brutal father and a scolding mother.

Meanwhile, Zampa, having had a good laugh at his unlucky pursuer, leisurely continued his course towards Cape Town, refreshing himself with an occasional pull at the bottle, which he had cajoled Charlotte into giving him.

He had forgotten all about the Dutch farmer, from whom he had borrowed the horse, and was riding along in a very steady manner, when a harsh, guttural voice commanded him to stop. Instead of obeying this command, he urged his horse forward.

"Stop, or I schoots!" roared the voice, and, turning his head, Zampa beheld the very identical gentleman from whom he had so unceremoniously borrowed the horse, in the act of levelling a huge gun towards him.

Zampa closed his eyes, and gave himself up for a gone coon, riding all the while like the Wild Huntsman.

Bang! went the gun, and the gallant steed swerved from his course, recovered himself, staggered, and rolled over—dead!

The Dutchman had shot his own horse while the thief was unharmed.

With a profusion of the most guttural unpronounceable oaths in the Dutch vocabulary, the irate farmer threw down his large gun and waddled after the half-frightened Zampa, who, quickly regaining his feet, darted off with considerable swiftness.

The Dutchman made chase with all the energy in his lethargic nature, but lost ground at every step.

At length, he gave up in disgust, returning leisurely to smoke and weep by the side of his poor unfortunate horse.

Zampa still continued running with all his might till he reached a bushy tract of ground through which his path lay.

Suddenly he halted; his face became almost white with fear, while his limbs trembled under him.

And there was good cause for his emotion, for in the midst of his path lay an enormous lion, who quietly raised his head when Zampa approached.

"Oh, gorra! all up wid dis nigger!" he moaned, gazing at the huge beast, which at that moment opened its gigantic jaws to indulge in a yawn.

"Zampa am only a mouthful to dat 'ere big brute," he sighed, at the same time rolling his eyes around him to look out for some place of safety.

There was a tolerably large tree close at hand, and stealthily creeping to it Zampa commenced ascending the trunk and was already congratulating himself on his providential escape, when a rattling noise among the pebbles with which the place abounded arrested his attention.

Glancing downwards he perceived the lion moving towards the tree.

"Dam dat beast!" said Zampa. "Won't let poor nigger 'lone."

The fact was that the lion had sunned himself sufficiently, and now wished for a cooler retreat.

The tree offered him the same shelter that it did Zampa, and he was soon beneath the shadow of its wide-spreading branches.

The first thing his lionship did was to stretch himself at full length up the trunk of the tree, scratching the bark with his fearful nails and yawning to such an extent, that Zampa afterwards declared he could see right down into the brute's stomach.

Then he stretched himself at full length with his

head towards the trunk, and, resting his jaws on his paws, tried to sleep, while Zampa in the tree above did not feel at all somnolently disposed.

However, there was no help for it; the lion felt inclined to sleep, but the flies would not let him, and Zampa began to reflect on the nature of brutes in general, and of lions in particular.

The bent of his philosophic meditation was to think on some method by which he might drive his foe away.

Had the lion been capable of reasoning Zampa would have endeavoured to persuade him to depart and feast on the Dutchman's dead horse.

But lions are not logical, and the one with which Zampa had to do evidently seemed of opinion that a nigger in the bush was worth two dead horses elsewhere.

After a vast deal of thought—a rather laborious task for Zampa—he came to the conclusion that the only means to drive away his foe was by fire.

And acting on this suggestion he accordingly pulled off all the withered branches he could lay his hands on, binding them up in as large a bundle as possible with his handkerchief.

Then plucking some dry moss, he mixed with it a small quantity of gunpowder, thus making a kind of tinder.

Flint and steel were set to work, but at the first sound the lion raised himself on his haunches, and gazed up into the tree to discover the author of the noise.

His keen eyes soon discovered Zampa, and he gave a low growl.

"Never you mind, massa lion," replied Zampa. "You hab lark with dis nigger; my turn now."

In a few minutes he had thrust the burning moss into the midst of the bundle of sticks, and blew it with all his might.

Smoke began to ascend, and the lion grew uneasy.

At length a tiny tongue of flame rewarded Zampa's efforts, and then, with a malignant grin, he threw the bundle down before the lion, who gazed with surprise, and moved a step or two from it.

The breeze fanned the fire, and suddenly a bright flame shot forth, scaring the lion, who, with a loud roar, dashed away, while Zampa hastily descended, anxious to get clear away ere the beast should return.

But he saw no more of his foe, and after a long, weary walk reached Cape Town in safety.

After a thorough refreshment of the inner man at the first inn he came to, he made his way down towards the harbour.

Black Ralph was walking by the beach when Zampa neared the waterside, and started with surprise to see his messenger return so quickly.

Zampa related all his adventures, at which Ralph laughed heartily, and then both went on board the "Raven."

CHAPTER CCLXXXVI.

THE INTERVIEW—AN INSULTING PROPOSAL—
BLACK RALPH TO THE RESCUE—THE DUEL—
DEPARTURE OF THE AVENGERS FROM CAPE
TOWN.

FAIR LILIA, the queen of the Avengers, was sitting alone in her room in the hotel at which she resided with her husband during their stay at Cape Town.

She was thinking of the past, of the long period of love and happiness that had elapsed since she first surrendered herself to her husband.

Her fair face had all its old sunshine restored to it, yet there was an expression of anxiety, of nervousness about her mouth which was unpleasant to see in one so young and beautiful.

But how could she be otherwise than thoughtful when day and night the awful thought was before her that her beloved husband might at any time be snatched from her arms by the strong hand of the law, and consigned to a violent death?

Hope, however, was strong within her breast, and she trusted that the good fortune which had hitherto enabled him to defeat the ends of his foes would still continue to shield them both with its beneficent influence.

She was sitting, as I have said, in her room, when a knock was heard at the door.

"Come in," she said, in her gentlest accents.

"A gentleman wishes to see you, madam," said a waiter, making his appearance.

"A gentleman? Who is he?"

"I know not, I assure you, madam."

"Did he not give his name?"

"He did not, and when I asked it he replied it was of no consequence as you were not acquainted with it."

"Well, I suppose I must see him. Show him here."

The waiter retired and Lilia indulged in all kinds of conjectures as to who the stranger could be.

She was not long kept in doubt, however, for in a few minutes a gentleman, dressed in the height of fashion, entered the room, and made a low bow to the fair queen of the Avengers.

"Be seated, sir, and pray explain to me the object of your visit."

"Thanks, madam; the object of my intrusion is one for which I know you will thank me when you hear it."

Lilia started, the colour forsook her fair cheek, and her hand trembled.

"Your words are strange, sir, and as I have never had the pleasure of seeing you before, I cannot but feel slightly alarmed at being thus addressed by one whom I know not."

"Madam," replied the stranger, "there is not the slightest cause for fear or alarm."

"Then, in Heaven's name, who are you, and what do you want?"

"You are, madam, if I mistake not, the wife of the owner of those fine ships yonder?" said he, pointing to the bay.

"I am. Do you know my husband?"

"Slightly; in fact I almost expected to find him here."

"If you wish to see him I can easily send a message to him."

"Oh, no; I should be sorry to put you to so much trouble, madam."

"Then your business is with me?"

"It is; and, madam, surely you cannot be ignorant of what has brought me here?"

"I neither know why you came nor do I care how soon you leave," replied Lilia, for, to say the truth, she began to dislike the bold looks of the stranger.

"Madam, you are stern, you are cold, but I love you the more for it. Never, till this day, did I see you look so beautiful."

"Sir, how dare you address me so? Quit the room instantly, or——"

"Or you will be mine. Stay, do not attempt to ring the bell nor to scream for assistance, for, if you do, I at once denounce your husband."

"This is cruel!" murmured Lilia, bursting into tears. "Oh, that he were here, he would hurl you from the window to the pavement below."

"But he is not here. "No, I choose my times well, madam; and now I entreat you to hear what I have to say to you."

Lilia made no answer, and the wretch, who thus took advantage of her defenceless state, threw himself at her feet.

"Beautiful creature," he said, "I need not tell you how much I love you, it would be impossible; but I will rather tell you that to such a pitch has your beauty inflamed my passions that you must be mine."

"Never!" cried Lilia, rising to her feet with energy.

"Ever, you mean, fair creature. Reflect now on what I say. I offer you a house and a thousand pounds a year to be my mistress; accept these terms and you shall be happy; refuse, and your brave captain is hanged at the yard arm of yon frigate of which I am commander, while you yourself will be imprisoned for life as an accomplice."

"I refuse your offer with scorn, for you must be indeed a bad and base man to tempt a woman to leave her husband."

"You refuse, do you? Then I will put one portion of my threat in execution. I will hang your lover, but reserve you for myself."

"My husband is too brave and strong to fear you, vile man!"

"We shall see; meanwhile, in order to keep me in remembrance of you till we meet again, I must have one kiss."

And rising from his seat the ruffian threw his arm about her waist.

"Help! help!" she screamed, struggling with all her might.

"It is useless to shriek, my lovely one," said he, placing his hand over her fair mouth.

At that moment a knock was given at the door, and the ruffian desisted a moment in his attempts.

The knock was repeated.

"Help! help!" again screamed Lilia.

Crash went the panels of the door, and in rushed Black Ralph, Caffyn, and Brierly, who, having been roving about the town all the day, had resolved to call on their chief for orders ere they retired to the fleet for the night.

Quick as thought Caffyn leaped forward, and with a blow of his fist struck the ruffian prostrate.

The sudden revulsion from danger to safety was so great that Lilia fainted the moment she saw that she was rescued.

"You attend to the lady, Mister Talbot; I'll stop this cove's jaw," said old Brierly, taking out his handkerchief, and thrusting it into the stranger's mouth.

Ralph, by forcing her to swallow a few drops of water, at length restored Lilia to consciousness, and by that time Brierly, with Dick Caffyn's assistance, had completely gagged and bound the brutal ruffian.

"We must leave this place immediately," said Lilia, "that man knows all, and you are in danger."

"That man!" said Ralph Talbot, casting a contemptuous look on the helpless being on the floor. "Why, he no more deserves to be called a man than Zampa to be called white. He's an ape of humanity, madam, and I think the best thing we can do is to take him on board the 'Raven,' and chain him up to one of the masts."

Dick Caffyn laid his hand on a pistol, and, so great was his rage, would doubtlessly have shot the unmanly captain of the frigate had not the other two restrained him.

"Remember, Dick, we are on shore now, and we must be careful."

"But is he to escape punishment?"

"Certainly not," replied Ralph; "we will keep him here till dark, and then take him on board the 'Raven.' Captain Christopher shall decide his fate."

"Bravo, Ralph, that's just the thing," said Caffyn; "and if the lubber isn't hung to-morrow morning, why, I'll shoot him!"

"Then off you go, and report to the most noble captain."

"Nay, Ralph, you go and leave me sentinel!"

"Why, you don't mean to let the rascal run, do you?"

"Not I, Ralph, depend on it."

"Why, then, you shall e'en stay; for hang me if I like to be seen in the company of such a brute."

"You are going on board the 'Raven,' Captain Ralph?" said Lilia, raising her head.

"I am, madam; and my advise is that you go with me. Who knows but we may find ourselves in trouble ere long through that man?"

"I will accompany you, for I am not without my fears. Would my husband were here."

"He will be here fast enough, I warrant you, when he hears how you have been insulted."

"Shall I stay here, captain?" said old Brierly.

"Hum! well I hardly know, what say you Caffyn?"

"I leave it to your discretion, worthy senor."

"Then, Brierly, come with us, you may be wanted on board ere long."

So saying, with a bow, he offered his arm to Lilia, and followed by old Brierly, left the hotel.

The whole party quickly boarded the "Red Raven," where the Boy Pirate was watching his men as they bustled about preparing for the next voyage.

Lilia sprang towards him, and nestled lovingly in his encircling arms.

"What is the matter, darling?" said the rover, tenderly.

"Oh, Christopher! I have been so frightened and so rudely treated by a man."

"A man! What man dare insult my wife?"

"I know not his name, dear Christopher; but he said that he was commander of a ship of war, and that he would hang you unless I consented to be his."

"And what said you?"

"I refused of course; he then caught me by the waist. I screamed for help, and our three noble friends, Captain Ralph, Dick Caffyn, and Brierly, came to my assistance."

"I thank them from my heart; but where is this villain, assailant of defenceless women?"

"At the hotel; they tied his hands and legs, and left Dick to guard him."

"Ah, then I'll have a chat with the gentleman at once."

"Oh, Christopher dearest, don't imperil your safety, I implore you! What would become of me if you were taken from me?"

"Why, then you could marry Black Ralph, you know. But don't be alarmed, dearest. The man who can be such a coward cannot hurt me."

"But why go, dearest? Would it not be better at once to quit the place? He is a sailor, recollect, and in his ship can follow you."

"His ship must have good wings to overtake the 'Raven.' But, my darling, if he is at all dangerous, I will be on board and away ere he can reach his ship."

So saying, he gave orders to hoist the signal to prepare for sailing; and then lightly stepped into the boat alongside, Ralph Talbot following him with a belt full of pistols, and a bundle which appeared to contain swords.

Poor Lilia stood watching them with tearful eyes till the boat touched the beach.

She saw her husband and his companion leap ashore and hurry off towards the town.

Then, when they were no longer to be seen, she retired to her cabin, and prayed that her gallant husband might be once more restored to her arms.

Let us follow him, and be unseen witnesses of the interview between him and the man who had so grossly insulted his wife.

On arriving at the hotel they found Dick Caffyn standing with folded arms, with his back towards the door, watching the writhings and twistings of his captive.

Christopher gazed a moment in the man's face, and then bade Dick untie his bonds.

It was soon done, and the would-be seducer stood face to face with the angry husband.

"Your name, sir," said Christopher, sternly.

"Captain Adolphus Cowslip, of H.M. ship 'Stanmore,'" replied he.

"Then Captain Adolphus Cowslip, you are the most degraded ruffian beneath the British flag."

The naval officer said nothing.

"I should be perfectly justified," continued Christopher, "if I shot you through the heart, but as you bear the semblance of a man in your face, and wear the uniform of a brave nation, I will give you a chance in fair combat. You will fight me, I presume?"

THE CONSULTATION AT THE LAWYER'S.—*See No. 83.*

"You are an outlaw; I will not disgrace myself."

"Now, by the immortal bard," cried Ralph, "here is a conscientious ruffian who will disgrace himself while he is alone, and yet refuse a fair offer to retrieve his honour."

Captain Cowslip cast a look of disdain on Ralph.

"I struck you not long ago, my gallant master. Will you not take offence at it?"

"You are a companion of this outlaw."

"Aye, I am, and I feel proud of the honour."

"I repeat, I cannot degrade myself by taking part in a combat with either of you."

"Now, by all the devils in hell and out, I'll give you a most confounded thrashing if you dare link my name with the word degrade!"

"Silence, Ralph," said Christopher. "This is my quarrel."

No. 83.

"Then I only hope you will spare his worthless life for my sake, for I cannot rest till I have had satisfaction."

"We may be outlaws," said Christopher, "but we have never insulted defenceless women, and therefore I consider myself your equal in every respect."

"And I your better in many respects," growled Ralph.

Captain Cowslip hesitated.

He knew that every British officer must sustain his character for bravery, and he feared that if he refused the duel the affair would get wind to his disadvantage. If, on the other hand, he could succeed in killing the Boy Pirate, it would be something to brag of for ever afterwards.

"I will fight with either," he said, after a pause, "but not with both."

"If you conquer me you shall go."

"He must fight me first, though," thought Ralph.

"Bring the swords, Dick," said the Boy Pirate.

"What, do you mean to fight now?" said Captain Cowslip. "This is very irregular; we have no seconds, nor yet a surgeon."

"It must be now or never."

The swords were unfolded from the bundle, and Dick handed them to the officer for choice.

Captain Cowslip was not a bad swordsman, that is with foils, and he handled the weapons with the air of a professor of the noble art.

He chose his weapon, and handed the other back to Dick Caffyn, who presented it to our hero.

Both men threw off their coats, and advancing into the midst of the room, saluted gracefully.

The Boy Pirate seemed thoughtless for his own safety, but a bright spot on his cheek told how ardently he burned to avenge the insult done to his wife.

His antagonist, on the other hand, seemed collected enough. He evidently did not expect to find a pirate well skilled in the use of the small-sword.

He stood in silence, endeavouring in vain to read the countenance of his adversary.

There was a deep silence.

And then, each of the duellists advancing his foot, the swords crossed.

For a short time both feinted, to endeavour to discover the other's tactics and weak points.

Captain Cowslip soon found he had to deal with one quite as skilful as himself.

And the Boy Pirate had the advantage, too, of having often been engaged in real combat, whereas Captain Cowslip's practice had been confined to the fencing schools.

The grating and clinking of the blades was now heard, for the fight was becoming more vigorous.

The men were pretty evenly matched, and for some little time neither seemed to have any advantage.

"You have it!" cried Christopher, suddenly raising his arm, and the point of his weapon pierced his antagonist's right shoulder.

The naval officer shook his head, and although a faint streak of blood was visible, continued the combat.

Again the blades grated together or rang in the parry.

With foot advanced, Christopher was driving his foe backwards.

Suddenly Captain Cowslip made a rapid lunge, which almost reached our hero's bosom, but with a swift, dexterous turn of the wrist he put it aside.

"Have a care, captain," said Caffyn.

"All right, Dick," replied our hero.

And, in truth, he was all right, for, in reply, he made a fierce thrust forward, and his sword sank deeply into the breast of the naval captain.

"I am killed!" cried that worthy, throwing up his arms and then falling forward.

And so he was to all appearance, for he lay motionless on the floor, while the blood trickled from his wound to a pool on the boards.

"Come, captain," said Ralph Talbot, "we must cut and run ere the alarm be given."

"Wherefore?"

"Because that man knows us."

"But he is dead?"

"Not so; he still breathes, though slightly."

"Then I am with you," said Christopher, and, passing his arm through Dick's, the three friends left the house.

"Take care of that gentleman upstairs," said Ralph, as they passed out, "he is ill, I think."

In a few minutes more they had reached their boat, and pulled off swiftly towards the "Red Raven."

The signal he had hoisted before going ashore had been strictly obeyed, and all four ships were now ready for sea, riding only by a single anchor each.

Again a flag fluttered up the signal-halyard, and in obedience to it, capstans were manned, anchors were raised, and the whole fleet stood out to sea just as the sun dropped down beneath the ocean.

Christopher remained on deck some time, seeing everything made right for the night.

At length the deck was in complete order, and then the young commander gave orders to heave the log that he might know what progress they were making through the waves.

For the benefit of our non-nautical readers a short description of this instrument would not, perhaps, be out of place.

The log is a small, flat piece of timber of the form of a triangle or of a quarter of a circle. It is from a quarter to half an inch in thickness, and about five or six inches from the angular point to the base. A small plate of lead is nailed to the base or circular side, which balances the instrument so that it swims perpendicularly in the water.

A thin cord or line is fastened to the log by means of two legs, one of which passes through the apex or point of the instrument, and is knotted on the other side; while the other leg is attached to the arch by a pin which is moveable at pleasure.

The line thus attached is wound round a reel, and an estimate of the ship's speed is made by observing the length of line unwound in half a minute's time told by a half-minute glass.

The line itself is divided and marked by knots at the distance of fifty feet from each other, and for so many knots of line run out in the half minute, so many miles the ship is computed to sail in an hour.

Of course, the log is liable to slight errors; but it tells the rate of sailing near enough for all ordinary purposes.

The name of the inventor of this ingenious yet simple device is not known, being lost, like that of the inventors of many other useful things, in the darkness of ages; but the first mention of it on record occurs in the account of a voyage made to the East Indies by some of the Company's servants, published by a printer named Purchas, in the year 1614.

On the present occasion the log showed Christopher that his ship was ploughing the waves at the rate of nine miles an hour, and then after another look aloft at the sky and the sails he descended to the cabin which contained his treasure—his bride.

She was already in bed when he entered, but started up at the sound of his footstep.

"Thank Heaven you have returned safely, dearest," she whispered, throwing her arms round his neck.

"Sweet darling, be not alarmed for my safety. I told you he could not hurt me. But I have most terribly avenged the insult he offered to you."

"Have you killed him, Christopher?"

"Not killed, but severely wounded him; but say no more about it darling, for he is on shore while we are bounding over the waves."

CHAPTER CCLXXXVII.

PERILOUS SITUATION OF WARDLAW AND RAMSEY ON THE OCEAN IN A BOAT—A FEARFUL STORM—LAND IN SIGHT—THEY ARRIVE ON THE ISLAND OF DIOS LAGOS—THEY ARE TAKEN PRISONERS ON A CHARGE OF SMUGGLING.

WE left Messieurs Wardlaw and Ramsey on the island to which they fled after abandoning the pirate schooner.

At the conclusion of the late captain's strange story of his slaving adventures, they had another walk round their little domain, which was uninhabited save by themselves.

Ramsey looked at his companion, who returned the gaze.

"Well, Gerald, are we to remain here all our lives like two Crusoes?"

"By no means, we will take a voyage to-morrow, if you like."

"I should like amazingly, for, to tell the truth, I don't feel safe in this lonely spot; who knows but we may be carried off by the Malays some night?"

"That is the greatest danger to which we are exposed, certainly."

"Therefore, I shall be only too glad to be once more in a civilized community, be it Dutch, Spanish, English, French, or even Chinese."

This speech resolved the whole question, and it was decided that on the morrow they should depart towards the north, in the hopes there to fall in with some European settlement.

And so early the next day beheld our bold adventurers depart in their little boat, well stocked with provisions, such as cocoa-nuts, roasted goats' flesh, eggs boiled hard, and a plentiful supply of water.

An old sail, which had been lying in the bottom of the boat, was hoisted to a temporary mast, made of a cocoa sapling, and, with their guns and ammunition, away they sailed.

And merrily they sailed all that day, directing their course by a tiny compass, which Ramsey had attached to his watch chain.

Night came on, and the two bold sailors slept by turns, wrapping themselves in pieces of the old sail, and gazing, during their period of watching, on the bright and countless stars with which the southern sky is studded.

Morning broke and yet there was no sign of land, yet the sailors comforted themselves with the hope that it could not be far distant.

At mid-day a storm arose. The wind blew, the waves heaved themselves up like mountains, bearing the little boat on their summits, now up into the clouds, and then down fathoms deep into a foaming, green, yawning valley of waters.

The forked lightnings flashed, and the loud thunder tried to out-roar the furious ocean.

It was a trial of strength between Jove and Neptune, in which the ocean king held his own.

The great waves, at times, almost filled the little boat, and it was only by the most incessant exertions in baling that she was kept above the water.

Cold, wet, and hungry, the adventurous mariners held on their course till the sun, for a moment, showed herself, and then went down red as copper into the ocean.

Then the wind gave one furious howl, and a blast of more than ordinary strength, and was comparatively quiet.

But the ocean refused to be at rest.

Wind and storm had so ruffled his bosom that he heaved and swelled still with rage, rendering the utmost care necessary in navigating the little craft.

The two bold hearts in that cockle shell at last found time to eat a few morsels of food, and to warm their drenched and shivering bodies.

The morning broke, the sun arose, the sea subsided, and their bodies once more felt the genial warmth of day.

Still no sign of land.

"Gerald," said Ramsey, "the salt water has played havoc among our provisions."

"Yes, and we must economize them, for I know not when we shall get any more."

Ramsey looked aghast at this announcement.

"Do you consider our case so very bad, then?"

"I do."

"But you said that the island was one of a group."

"I thought so, and had the ship been steered according to my directions we should have reached a group; but I am now firmly convinced that the helm and compass both were tampered with, and that instead of being amongst the Spice Islands we have been resting ourselves on some unknown land far down in the Southern ocean."

"And when shall we reach land?"

"In a week, perhaps, if we escape the dangers of the sea. I calculate we have fully a thousand miles to sail ere we arrive at Java, to which we are as near as to any land."

"Small store of provisions for a week, Gerald; I could eat the lot myself in three days."

"I did not calculate on more than three days' sail when we left our island; but we must make the most of it. Let's see what we have."

They "took stock" of their provisions, and found they had eight small biscuits, twenty cocoa-nuts, and a piece of meat weighing about three or four pounds; their fresh water amounted to about five quarts.

"Then," said Gerald, "we will, if you have no objection, issue the stores in the following manner:— Quarter of a biscuit and a whole cocoa-nut for breakfast, a second quarter of biscuit and two ounces of meat for dinner, and I should strongly advise you to save part of your nut for supper, as I don't think I can venture to issue any."

"And how about the water?"

"Quarter of a pint with dinner and in the evening, cocoa-nut milk for your morning beverage."

"And the spirit we have in our flasks?"

"Why, I should strongly advise you not to touch it save on days such as we have just passed."

And so they sailed along across the trackless sea. Six days passed, and the seventh brought them no sign of land. They looked askance at their little remaining store, consisting of two days' provision, and resolved, though half starved already, to make it last them four days.

The weather was no longer stormy, but a brisk breeze blew, and the sun shone down with such hot fierceness that the want of water made their tongues swell in their mouths till talking became painful.

Had they not kept pistol balls constantly rolling about in their mouths they would have lost all their saliva and have miserably perished of thirst.

The morning of the eighth day rose in cloudless splendour, sea and sky were alike, beautiful; but oh, how eagerly did those two half-starved mariners long for green earth, for ripe fruits, and running streams of fresh and cool water.

Mid-day came, and their last biscuit was broken. Their goat's flesh had been devoured the previous day; but its place was supplied by a sea bird, which Ramsey had shot, and which, uncooked, formed the principal portion of their meal.

Few but those who have fasted long can understand the craving, the yearning which the hungry man has for animal food.

"Gerald," said Ramsey, laying down his food, "I cannot stand this long-protracted agony much longer. I must jump overboard, and let some shark end my worthless life."

"And I forbid you to do anything of the kind. I am captain here, and will have my commands obeyed; if you are mutinous I will tie your hands and feet, and lie you down in the bottom of the boat."

"Better to die at once."

"Pshaw! a young man like you talk of dying!"

"Aye; what have I to live for?"

"Live for an opportunity to amend the past. See," continued Wardlaw, "even as I speak land appears to bid us hope."

"Land! you are dreaming, Gerald!"

"Not so; look, right before us."

"Some bright mirage, which will fade away into thin air as we approach it."

The elder of the two officers made no reply to his despondent young friend's remark, but, carefully wiping the glasses of his telescope, surveyed the object which had attracted his attention earnestly.

"It is land, Ramsey, and we shall be saved."

"How far away?"

"Not more than five and twenty miles."

"How long will it take us to reach it with this wind?"

"About three hours."

The young man once more took up his rejected food, and began to eat ravenously.

"That's right, my friend," said Wardlaw, "and if you don't object, we'll have double rations."

Ramsey's only answer was to hold out his hand for the second allowance. His mouth and his heart were both too full to allow him to speak.

And when the meal was ended both felt twice as strong as before.

The land now began to loom up big and large before them, and the gallant little boat lightly breasted the waves as though eager to reach a haven.

Full two hours before sunset they ran the boat ashore near the mouth of a little stream, by the banks of which was a pathway leading into the interior of the island or continent, whichever it might be.

The two half-famished men first took a huge draught of water, and then, throwing the remainder of the food ashore, made a hearty meal.

"Well, what's the next thing to be done, Gerald?" said Ramsey, stretching himself.

"Remain here till morning, and then have a good look round to see where we are."

"I shall not be sorry to stretch myself at full length once more, for the brave old boat is at best but a very short bed."

In half an hour their arrangements were complete, their fire lit, and a slight shelter of boughs erected. Before the fire was a kind of spit, on which four delicious fat pigeons were cooking for supper.

"Now, then, Gerald," said the younger man, "come along, and quickly, too, or I shall eat these birds myself."

"Insatiable cormorant, will you never leave off eating?" replied Wardlaw.

"Not while I have plenty of food."

They both sat down, and the birds were withdrawn from the spit, when suddenly a sound of footsteps was heard, and the next minute they were surrounded by a party of Spanish soldiers.

"Surrender!" exclaimed the officer.

The two men at once laid down their guns, which they had snatched up on the first alarm, and bowed their heads.

Two men then stepped from the ranks for the purpose of placing manacles on the wrists of the captives.

"It is needless, senor," said Wardlaw to the officer, "I will go with you quietly."

"I must obey my instructions," said he.

The irons were fastened, the soldiers closed in round them, and the whole party marched away through the forest.

"It is all up with us now," said Ramsey.

"Don't be so desponding. You used not to be so easily discouraged. Trust me we shall yet find a way to overcome this trouble."

After a long walk they came to the walls of a fortified town, and passing the drawbridge, were conducted to a large square tower, erected on the side nearest the sea.

The door of this huge building yawned open at their approach, and the two prisoners found themselves in a large stone room, which seemed to occupy the whole of the basement of the edifice, with the exception of a small staircase.

The door was plated and studded with iron, the windows of which—there were two, overlooking the water—were crossed by strong iron bars, and, on the whole, it would not have been an uncomfortable dwelling had they but possessed the key and a small quantity of furniture.

It was just growing dusk when they were incarcerated, and about an hour afterwards, when it was quite dark, a man entered, bearing in his arms a lantern and a huge bundle of rush matting.

The matting he deposited in one corner of the room, and informed the prisoners that it was to be their bed.

"What are we imprisoned for?" said Wardlaw, in Spanish, of which he knew a very little.

"Quien sabe, senor," replied the man; "who knows?"

"Strange that we should be locked up for nothing."

"You will be tried to-morrow, perhaps."

"I hope so, for I am anxious to know what offence we have committed."

The man shook his head, and laid his finger to his lips, as much as to say that he dared not speak, and then departed.

The two friends heard the huge lock grate rustily and harshly as the bolt was thrown forward, and then for the first time did they really believe they were prisoners.

"Gerald," said Ramsey, "I do verily believe that our late captain, Harwolf, must be on the island. Surely they would not lock us up for merely landing on the coast of their island; and I don't know that we have been guilty of any other offence."

"Well, we shall see to-morrow; though I don't think that, even if Harwolf is here, he will dare to say anything against us, lest he too should be convicted."

Both were silent.

Though but recently escaped from the perils of the ocean, though only just recovered from the pangs of starvation, though prisoners for an unknown cause, those two men slept soundly in their dungeon on their coarse mat.

For they were happy for having escaped the fiendish crew of ruffians with whom they had previously been associated.

The morning broke, and the two prisoners anxiously awaited the escort which was to conduct them to their trial.

But the day wore on, and save the gaoler who brought them their food and drink, not a soul did they see.

The very ocean itself seemed deserted, though the fact of their being in a fortified place by the sea shore, they could not doubt but that a port or harbour of some kind was at hand.

The next morning broke, and on glancing from the barred window at the sparkling waves, on which the greater part of his life had been spent, four large ships were plainly visible to Wardlaw's eye, at anchor about a mile from the shore.

The sight gladdened his heart, and he was therefore smiling and happy when the guard came to summon them before the commandant of the fort, who united in himself both the civil and military authority of the island of Dios Lagos, as was named the land in which our two adventurers found themselves thus strangely situated.

The court was composed of the Commandant Senor Colonel Don Jucaro, and his Adjutant Senor Don Cardoverro, both of them high-blooded hidalgos, from Castille, who held in contempt all foreigners.

The drum-major officiated as usher of the court, while the lieutenant who commanded the capturing party was in attendance to give evidence.

"You are guilty, of course?" said the colonel, as soon as the prisoners were in his presence.

"Senor, pardon me, we do not know what crime we are charged with."

"Diavolos! what matters; you had better confess at once."

"What shall we confess, senor?"

"Confound these Yenglese; they are so obstinately stupid. Why, you know well enough you are smugglers."

It was certainly a great relief to hear this, for both prisoners fully expected to be tried as pirates, and the Spaniards, though they may overlook the failings of their own buccanners, certainly show no mercy to those of other nations who fall into their hands.

"Senor colonel," said Wardlaw, "we plead Not Guilty. Neither I nor my companion ever dealt in contraband goods."

"Give your evidence, lieutenant."

The lieutenant stepped forward, and being an officer and a gentleman, was allowed to give his testimony without being sworn.

He stated, that two nights ago he was ordered to proceed to a point on the coast about ten miles distant, where two men had been seen to land. He did so, and captured the prisoners, who were well-armed. From their general appearance and language he had no doubt that they were opium smugglers.

"That's quite sufficient," cried the colonel. "The

prisoners are guilty, and must be garotted according to our laws."

The two Englishmen heard this strange verdict and sentence with the utmost astonishment.

"But, colonel, will you not give me a chance of proving my innocence?" said Wardlaw.

"Not a chance!" replied the court.

"Surely a brave, noble soldier like yourself would never condemn an innocent man?"

This little bit of flattery did the work.

The colonel stroked his moustachios, and looked rather pleased.

"Well, you shall have a week to establish your innocence, to my satisfaction, mind, and no witnesses will be allowed to enter the fort. Pens, ink, and paper shall be allowed you, however, so now begone back to your dugeon."

The prisoners bowed low, and were taken back to the place from whence they came.

"Well, what do you think of our chances now, Gerald?" asked Ramsey.

"I think we were very lucky to get a week's grace; we can——"

"Reflect on the death that awaits us. No, I confess that if I am to be strangled, I would rather it should be done off hand."

"Why, Ramsey, you have taken leave of your senses. You forget that those lubbers forgot to search us, and that we still have our knives and our pistols. With the one we could almost cut our way out through these iron bars, which are only fixed with lead, while with the fire-arms I fancy we could drive Senor Colonel and his whole army out of the fort."

"Which shall we try?"

"Neither; but I will try pen and ink first."

"How?"

"You see those ships at anchor yonder?"

"Aye, I do."

"Well, I fancy they are English, and mean to send a letter on board."

"Ha, ha, ha! Why, it is you who have taken leave of your senses, Gerald. Why, where will you find your postman?"

"Our worthy gaoler, I fancy, will find means to forward it, for I have some gold left, Ramsey."

"That is good, but why not try and bribe our bold judge and jury?"

"I would if I could have a private interview with the noble warrior."

"The brave and noble soldier would doubtlessly be very glad to pocket a few pieces."

"Aye; well, I mean to send this letter to the captain of either of those ships, entreating them to see justice done to us. If it has no effect we must remove these bars, drop down to the beach, no very great distance, and look out for a boat."

"Good; write at once."

Wardlaw accordingly did write, as follows:—

"TO THE CAPTAIN OF THE SHIP.

"SIR,—Two prisoners in the castle of the fort venture to beg your aid and assistance in procuring justice. We are condemned to death for smuggling, an offence of which we have never been guilty, nor do we know what can be our offence, unless it be criminal for two ship-wrecked mariners, who had made a voyage of over a thousand miles in a boat, to land on this island. Your influence with the colonel commandant would doubtless procure our release, or a greater share of justice than has hitherto been meted out to us. And in procuring this we beg your help.

"GERALD WARDLAW.
"LIONEL RAMSEY."

"There," said the last-named officer, as he signed his name with a flourish. "If that don't do the business he's a hard-hearted Turk, that's all I can say."

"Yes, but I must first touch our worthy gaoler's heart with a piece of gold."

A few minutes after the individual alluded to made his appearance, bearing the prisoners' food and water.

"My friend," said Wardlaw, "have you been in your situation long?"

"Aye, senor, it is a good twenty years, come Christmas next."

"Then, doubtless, you are a rich man?"

"Nay, how should I be? If I squeezed a piece from a prisoner I should be removed."

"Your earnings are not great?"

"Madre de dios! no."

"And, my friend, a couple of gold pieces would be of service to you?"

"Aye, senor, but speak low."

"You shall have them on one condition."

"Name it."

"That you carry this letter to either of those ships you see yonder."

The gaoler took the letter in his hand, and turned it over two or three times.

"There's no treason in it, I hope?"

"No, my friend, it is only to inform my brave comrades yonder that I am here."

"Then I'll do it with pleasure, senor."

"Here is your gold, and now speed away."

The man took the money and withdrew, while the two prisoners sat down to their dinner with an evident increase of appetite.

CHAPTER CCLXXXVIII.

HARWOLF AND MILES SAVED FROM DEATH—THEIR BASE INGRATITUDE TO THEIR PRESERVER.

MUTUAL explanations followed fast upon the meeting of Charles Rye and his brother Silas; and our readers would, perhaps, like to be informed how it happened that Harwolf's bosom friend happened to be at liberty in San Francisco.

When the two culprits were left alone beneath the tree with the rope around their necks, their first words were those of blasphemy and wickedness.

"Damn them!" roared the ex-judge. "Steady, horse! do they mean to—woh! stand still, blast you! Do they mean to let us swing in this heathenish style?"

"Do 'ee be quiet, zquire; taint no use a runnin' on zo; but may I be blamed and cussed to all the devils out o' hell if I don't scarify their darned hides for 'em if ever I catches 'em."

So said Miles, and then a silence reigned for some minutes beneath the hoary old forest trees.

Both men were too much engaged with their own thoughts—their own ideas of death and judgment to make any effort at speech. Guilty cowards as they were, they had no hope in this world or the next.

"Steady, horse! stand still!" cried Harwolf, as the steed on which he was mounted moved half an inch forward as though to crop the short grass.

"It ain't no use, zquire. We'd better zwing ourzelves off at once," said Miles.

"Silence, fool! Don't you see your voice frightens the horses."

"Blamed if I wouldn't sooner be hanged right off than bide like this."

"Shut up your mouth, ill-omened croaker. Let others escape, even if you have no wish to."

Miles was silent, so was his master, and again the thoughts of those two black-minded men fell on all the ills that they had committed.

Who can paint the anguish of Andrew Harwolf's mind during those fearful moments, when the shadow of his murdered master seemed to rise up in judgment against him, while the pale-faced maniac lady pointed her white bony finger at the trembling wretch?

In the background, too, there seemed to be standing a whole group of figures, amongst whom might be seen Foxley the detective, Esau Cooper, his own faithless wife, and many others.

Anguish smote the sorrowful wretch's soul; repentance seemed impossible. Death seemed most awfully hideous.

"Mercy! mercy!" he groaned aloud; but there was no one to answer him.

"Measter," suddenly whispered Joe Miles, "do'ee zee that 'ere black thing a movin' about there?"

"Black thing! Aye, Miles," and here he sunk his voice to a whisper, "it is all over with us; yonder comes the fiend!"

"Now, do'ee try to keep up a leetle bit o' pluck."

"But, see, he comes!—he comes!"

And any one who had been standing by the side of the two condemned culprits might at that moment have seen a tall, giant-like man, dressed in a strange, outlandish costume of skins, approaching through the dark vistas of the wood.

By the side of this stranger a four-legged beast was ambling, which, in the darkness and obscurity of night, far more resembled a bear than any other animal.

"Ahoy!" cried a hoarse voice, "who are you who ride by night beneath the forest tree?"

"Jist you come and cut these 'ere ropes, an' I'll tell 'ee," responded Miles.

"Fool!" said Harwolf, in a hoarse whisper, "why have you called him?"

"'Cause I wants to get off this 'ere hosse's back, and I don't care if he be the devil, so long as he cuts these ropes."

The unknown came nearer and nearer, the animal by his side looming bigger and bigger, till their forms seemed immense.

Then suddenly they came more immediately within the limited range of vision, and the suppositious fiend with a bear proved to be a tall man with a shaggy dog by his side.

"What are you doing here?" said the stranger, as soon as he saw the very perilous situation in which the two Lynched men were placed.

"We be a tryin' to keep these 'ere hosses quiet," replied Miles.

"Then, I s'pose you don't want me about 'ere."

"Yes we do; jest cut these ropes for us."

"Who tied you up?"

"Now, I'm blowed if I can tell ye, friend."

"Then I can't think of cutting you down. He may be a friend of mine."

"Look on the trunk of the tree," said Harwolf, in dismal tones. "You will very soon see who tied us up."

"Ah!" said the stranger, as his eyes fell on the white letters on the tree. "So you want me to take the law out of Judge Lynch's hands, do you?"

"No, we only wants you to cut the ropes. Damn the law, and Judge Lynch too!"

"But you must have been guilty of some awful crime, or you would never have incurred such a punishment."

"Now, did we ever harm you?" said Harwolf, joining the conversation.

"I hardly know, but I cannot take the law out of the hands of its executors, or I should have to take your place."

"Then you will leave us here to die?" moaned Harwolf.

"That all depends on the horses, my friends. Two nice, likely-looking nags. Whose are they?"

"Heartless man, can you jest while we are in such a situation?"

"I s'pose the verdict is 'served you right.' However, I can't stand here talking all night, so good-bye."

And the stranger moved away a few paces into the forest.

"Stay! stay!" shrieked Harwolf, as he saw his only chance of life on the verge of departure. "I will give you anything if you will only remain here awhile."

"Why should I stay?"

"It is so awful to be alone," muttered the grey-bearded villain.

"Then there must be something the matter with your conscience, my friend, if solitude is so fearful. Now, I am not afraid to be alone for days and nights

together, but, then, I never committed any big crime, such as murder or——"

"Murder! who talks of murder? I—I—I protest I am innocent. I am condemned for stealing horses, not for murder."

"Indeed, then it only confirms me in my opinion that I ought not to interfere with the course of justice, especially when administered by such a stern judge."

"Then, may the curses of two dying men light on your head, if you do not help us!" replied Harwolf.

"My friend, so near death as you are, prayer would better become your lips. But, say now, what will you give me to release you?"

"All I have in the world. See here, I have gold, and I can get more. Take it all—take it all. Oh, I would give all the gold in the universe to be assured of twenty years more life!"

"Will you give me those horses if I cut you down?"

"Aye, most willingly," said Harwolf.

"And deuced glad to get rid on 'em," continued Miles.

"Then here goes," said the stranger, drawing a knife from his breast.

He was standing nearer Miles than Harwolf, and, as a matter of course, proceeded towards the first-named individual.

He seized the horse by the bridle with one hand, while with the other he severed the rope which bound the felon's hands.

"Now cut the rope round your neck," said the stranger, handing him the knife.

It was done almost as soon as the words were spoken, and delighted at being once more free, Miles leaped from the horse with such agility as to frighten the animal on which Harwolf was seated.

The horse made two steps forward, and Andrew Harwolf was suspended by the neck from the branch of the tree.

"Help, help!" he shrieked, as the horse moved from beneath him; then the rope tightened around his neck and speech became impossible.

The stranger at once saw how matters stood, and, rushing forward, seized Harwolf's legs, thus supporting him, and relieving the rope from his weight.

Miles quickly released his master, who, however, was for some moments unable to stand or speak from the fright he had received.

A few drops of strong whisky from the stranger's flask revived him, and he sat up and began to pour out his thanks, of which his deliverer took little notice, but, moving off, secured the two horses, and was preparing to mount.

"Miles," whispered Harwolf, "we must not let him have those beasts; we shall want them to carry us away."

"You be quite right, zquire. But how be we to stop 'im?"

"Why here is a big stick, I think with that we shall be able to master him. Come, let us try."

The two men rose from their seats on the grass and walked towards their deliverer.

"Sir," said Harwolf, "we hardly know how to express our thankfulness for the service you have rendered us."

"Well, I am pretty well paid for my share of the business, I have got the horses and am perfectly satisfied."

So saying he laid his hand on the neck of one of the animals and was about to spring on its back when Harwolf said,

"At all events accept this as a proof of our gratitude."

And then the stick descended with fearful force on the head of the stranger, felling him to the ground.

"Mount and away, Miles," said the master villain.

"Hadn't I better zettle this 'ere chap, first?"

"No more murder. He is safe, he dares not split on us."

Another minute and they were both galloping wildly through the forest, and, when out of sight, the stranger rose, rubbing his head.

"Well, that was a striking proof of their gratitude. I'll never interfere with the course of justice again," he said, and then, followed by his dog, disappeared into the gloomy woods.

Meanwhile Harwolf and Miles rode at the utmost speed of which their horses were capable for many miles.

They headed towards San Francisco, for Harwolf judged rightly that there was more safety in a crowded city than either forest or mining village.

The road to the great seaport was plainly and well defined; the horses were staunch and strong, and by the time daylight broke they had placed more than twenty miles between them and Claremont Creek.

Late in the day they passed along a precipitous ledge of rock about six miles from San Francisco. At the bottom of the cliff, a depth of fifty feet, a rapid river ran madly, foaming along.

"Miles," said Harwolf, "we must not take these horses into the town with us, or we shall be caught again."

"That be purty true, measter, but there bean't no hoss dealers here to zell 'em to," responded the man addressed.

"Then we must turn them loose."

"Better turn 'em over these 'ere rocks, measter."

"A good idea," replied Harwolf, and, dismounting, both men blindfolded their steeds, then urged them over the precipice. The poor helpless animals were mangled and bruised by the fall, but the torrents swept them away out of sight.

With a grim smile at the cruel manner in which they had hidden their trail, they walked forward until they reached the wooden city, San Francisco.

A hearty supper, copious supplies of drink, and a rude straw bed, restored them to something like their former spirits, but the following day they found their small supply of gold had grown still smaller through the previous night's debauch.

"Something must be done, Miles," said Harwolf, as they stood before a building over the door of which was a board with the inscription,

"Bullion and Money-Exchange."

"There's money there, zquire," whispered Miles; "why not have zome?"

Harwolf made no reply, he was evidently reckoning the chances of success.

At that moment the door opened and a young man came forth, bearing in his hand a bag which was evidently full of the precious metal.

Instinctively the two men followed him, and as instinctively whispered to each other their plans for robbing the young man when they reached a retired spot.

But he passed on quickly, and entered a house which was apparently his own ere the robbers could overtake him.

"Mark the house, Miles, and just look at the plate on the door. What name is it?"

"The name, zir—is—Charles Rye."

"Then Charles Rye's money must become ours. I know not whether he be any way related to my foe or not, but I hate the name, and it will go hard with him if I once find myself inside the house."

The two men moved away, but returned at midnight, and attempted their burglarious scheme, with what result the reader has already learned in a previous chapter.

CHAPTER CCLXXXIX.

EDWARD LEIGHTON AND HIS WIFE EMBARK FOR ENGLAND—THEY ARE SHIPWRECKED—PROVIDENTIAL ESCAPE FROM DEATH—THEY ARE TAKEN PRISONERS—THEIR ESCAPE!

IT is hardly necessary to follow step by step the travels of Edward Leighton and his young wife across the Russian plains, nor would such a narrative prove very interesting, as the journey was accomplished with swiftness and security, thanks to the good old priest.

In due course of time they arrived at Odessa, as had been planned, and, after waiting in that port—which has for these last twelve years been famous or infamous as the scene of one of the blackest pieces of treachery that ever the Russian government perpetrated—they found a passage in a ship bound for London, with a cargo of corn, hides, hemp and other bulky articles.

The passengers were few, the captain was a German, his crew were mostly Maltese and Greeks.

The gallant ship sailed easily on across the Euxine, through the Hellespont, past the beautiful city of Constantinople, and then along by the numerous islands which stud the eastern end of the Mediterranean.

Then the wind began to blow, seemingly from all quarters of the heavens at once! the sea ran with tempestuous fury through the narrow and rocky channels between the clusters of islets.

The captain lost heart, and the men stood together in groups, conversing in whispers, suffering the ship to drift at the pleasure of the wind and waves.

Presently with a crash came a mountainous wave sweeping over the deck, and carrying away into the foaming sea the captain and mate, who were exposed to its full violence.

A Greek sailor then rushed to the helm, and, shouting some directions in his own language, the ship was in some measure righted.

Still the hurricane bore them onwards, and still the helmsman seemed to cling to the more dangerous part of the sea, instead of seeking more open water.

The object was soon apparent, for a rocky isle on the summit of which frowned a ruined tower was quickly visible.

Towards this the ship's course was directed, but, unused to navigating such a large vessel, the helmsman steered for a passage which, though deep enough to admit the light boats of the islanders, was certain destruction to a ship of such heavy burden as the one in which Edward Leighton and his wife were passengers.

A harsh grating sound was heard;-a violent shock threw every one prostrate!

The ship was on the rocks!

The fearful sea beat with terrific force on the sides of the straining vessel, while some huge waves leaped right over her, sweeping away everything on the deck.

Katinka clung to her husband in alarm; she had never been to sea before, and the rude violence of the water alarmed her, as, indeed, it did strong men.

"We must take our chance of escape, darling, together."

"Edward, dearest, come life or death, I will not leave your side."

He pressed her closer to him, and anxiously awaited his fate.

The boats had been washed away, there was no means of escape save by swimming or by constructing a raft.

The sailors seemed to be inclined to the latter expedient for they pointed to a variety of broken spars which dangled loosely in the rigging. Some of them pointed to the inhabitants of the isle, who were assembled in groups watching the progress of the work of destruction.

At length the fatal moment came.

The whole of the ship's timbers groaned and creaked beneath the force of the wind and waters. Plank after plank gave way, the huge masts toppled and fell, and Edward Leighton, grasping his wife round the waist, found himself in the foaming sea.

A huge plank floated near him, he seized it, and with it formed a kind of support for Katinka, who was fainting with terror.

Swimming with one hand, and supporting her with the other, he was borne rapidly towards the rugged beach.

Just as he reached it a tall islander stretched forth

his hand, and drew him up on the shore beyond the reach of the waves, which would otherwise have carried him back again.

The young man took his wife up in his arms, and bore her to a place where a large fire burned beneath the rocks, and after chafing her hands and feet she revived sufficiently to thank him for his tenderness and love.

Most of the crew had escaped, and seemed on most intimate terms with the islanders. The two passengers seemed to be the object of their conversation, for as they conversed in their musical tongue they frequently pointed towards the spot where Edward Leighton and his wife were sitting.

Presently a tall, ruffianly-looking man, whose belt was well supplied with daggers and pistols, approached the young couple, and beckoned them to follow him.

At first Leighton hesitated, but the gesture being repeated in a more imperative manner, he rose, and passing his arm round Katinka's waist, followed in the footsteps of his strange guide.

Up a steep rock-hewn flight of steps they took their way, and, on arriving nearly at the summit, Leighton perceived for the first time that two men with long guns over their shoulders followed them.

" We are prisoners, no doubt, love," he whispered, " but be of good cheer."

" I fear nothing while you are with me, Edward," she replied.

They reached the old tower, which formed so conspicuous a land-mark, and then their conductor, opening a strong door, led them into a kind of vaulted chamber.

" Remain here," said the guide, in German, to Edward, "and you follow me," he continued, addressing Katinka.

" But she is my wife; she does not wish to leave me."

" I wish it, and my wish is law," replied the Greek.

" But I insist on her remaining with me," cried Leighton, rushing forward.

Ere, however, he could reach her side, a blow on the head from a gun stock stretched him senseless on the floor.

The tall guide caught Katinka in his arms, and, regardless of her prayers and entreaties, carried her away up a winding staircase into a room above the one in which her husband was.

Frantically she struggled with her rude captor, but her efforts were all unavailing.

The man placed her against the wall, bound her hands and then secured her to a pillar, which appeared to support the roof.

" When you have recovered your senses I will send you some food," he said, and then walked slowly from the room, locking the door after him.

She was then left alone bound in the gloomy chamber.

Hours seemed to pass, and still no one came. Katinka thought that she had been forgotten and left to starve when again the door opened.

A tall young Greek girl, with regular features and jet black hair, entered the room with a jug of water.

The new comer set the vessel down on the floor, and gazed earnestly in the face of the prisoner.

" What is your name?" presently she asked, in tolerable German.

" Katinka Leighton," replied the Polish girl.

" And you are the wife of the Englishman who is confined below?"

" I am. Pray tell me how he is?"

" He is well, but raves about you. Do you love him?"

" I do most dearly."

" And wish to be with him, I suppose?"

" You, who are a woman, can well imagine how much I long to be again with the only man I ever loved."

" The only man you ever loved, but he is not the only man who loves you?"

" How? What mean you?"

" Cornelius loves you."

" And who is Cornelius, I know him not?"

" He brought you here. Would the sea had drowned you!"

" Your words are strange. Wherefore should you wish me evil?"

" Because I hate you! Aye, and good cause have I for hatred!"

" But I never harmed you," said the gentle Katinka, who began to grow alarmed at the rage of her visitor.

" Never harmed me!" echoed the Greek girl, scornfully. " You are my rival, for before the accursed hour in which you came to our shores I was all in all to Cornelius, and his love made me happy. Now comes your pale face and he forgets all past vows of love, all past moments of ardent passion, and resolves to make you his."

" Oh, Heaven! protect me from him!" ejaculated Katinka, fervently.

" What, do you not love him, then?" said the Greek girl, who thought it impossible that any one of her sex should not be smitten with the manly graces of Cornelius.

" Love him? No! I would give anything to be able to escape from his power!"

" Ho, there, Myra, I say!" cried a voice without, " what a time you are staying. Are you helping the prisoner to escape?"

Myra made no answer, and a moment after Cornelius entered the room.

He glanced from one to the other with a look of suspicion, then turned to the door again, saying,

" I hold you responsible for her safety, so look well that her bonds be secure, and then join me on the beach—I have much to say to you."

Myra rose while he stood in the doorway, and under pretence of examining the cords which bound Katinka's wrists, slipped a knife and a key within the folds of her dress.

" The key will liberate your husband," she whispered, " and when he is free go both of you away by the top of the tower."

The door closed, and Katinka was once more alone. Her brave heart began to beat freely once more. She now had a double object in working for her freedom, to save her husband and at the same time escape from the loathsome embraces of the Greek fisherman.

Her heart throbbed wildly, however, as she struggled with the cords till the blood started from her wrists, for the knife had been placed in such a position that she could but just touch it with the tips of her fingers.

And now, horror of horrors, she felt it gradually slipping from her! Then all her hopes would be gone.

It fell, and by a great effort she caught it on her knees. She would be saved after all!

After several efforts she managed to clutch it firmly, and then was just about to commence cutting the ropes when a step was heard.

She hastily concealed the knife in her sleeve as Myra and Cornelius again stood at the door.

Strange to say, neither of them entered, but merely looked in, apparently to satisfy him that the prisoner was secure.

Then they went away again, and Katinka's heart leaped with joy as she heard them descend the echoing staircase.

She then renewed her battle with the cords, and contrived to get the edge of the knife against the rope, pressing it upwards with her knees.

Suddenly the rope gave way; she was free with the exception of the cord which bound her to the pillar.

But the exertion and excitement were almost too much for her; she felt faint and dizzy.

Luckily, however, Myra had left the jug of water, and a deep draught from it revived her.

Then taking the key, she boldly approached the door, the barrier between herself and liberty.

THE INTERRUPTION.

It was locked, and, at first, obstinately refused to yield.

Katinka bruised her soft fingers against the hard iron, she exerted her utmost strength, and at length the bolt rolled back with a harsh, grating sound, which filled her with alarm lest any of the outlaws—for such they undoubtedly were—should hear the unwonted sound.

She listened cautiously, but could hear nothing; then grasping the knife in her hand, to serve as a weapon in case of necessity, she carefully descended the gloom staircase.

The door of the room in which her husband had been confined was reached, it yielded to her key, the door flew open, and Katinka rushed forward.

The room was empty!

The poor girl stared around her with surprise, and rubbed her eyes to be certain that she saw plainly, and to keep down the tears as well.

"Where can he be?" she thought. "Can they have killed him in order that there may be no obstacle between me and poor Myra's faithless lover? Such men are capable of any atrocity, and they have no doubt——"

The poor girl almost swooned at the crowd of horrible thoughts which her imagination conjured up.

No. 84.

Scarcely six weeks wedded, it seemed doubly horrible to think of widowhood so soon, and with all the love of her young, ardent heart, burning in her breast, separation from him seemed to her a worse and more fearful punishment than any of those refined tortures fabled in olden tales and history.

A scrap of paper on the floor near the door met her eye, and stooping down she eagerly clutched at it. It might afford some clue to his mysterious disappearance. It contained these words:—

"He has been removed to the chamber immediately over the one in which you were confined. Escape by the battlements."

No name was signed to this document, but Katinka had no doubt but that Myra's hand had dropped the billet.

She gently closed the door, and then lightly tripped up the staircase past her own prison, till she reached the room above, and then she paused.

He heart beat so violently that she could scarcely stand, but by an effort she recovered herself, and applied the key to the lock, scarcely daring to hope that it would open the heavy door.

It did though, and the prisoner within started to his feet with the utmost amazement as he saw his beloved wife enter.

"My wife, my wife!" he cried, "how came you here? Have they released you, and restored you to my arms?"

"Nay, dear Edward, I have escaped, and am come to release you."

"Escaped! But where you not locked in a dungeon?"

"I was, but escaped through the kindness of a friend. But let me cut these cords that tie your hands."

So saying, she drew the knife across his bonds, and he too was free.

He clasped his wife to his breast, kissed her fervently, and said,

"Now, my darling, let us go hence."

"We must go to the roof though, for so my friend instructed me."

"Your friend! what friend?"

As they ascended the steep staircase together Katinka told her husband how and by whose agency she had escaped.

At length a door before them barred their progress, but that yielded as all the others had done to the influence of the key Katinka bore.

They emerged on to the flat roof of the tower, and were not a little surprised to see two small cannon mounted in such a position as to command the approach from the sea.

"But how are we to escape now, dearest? We are not birds, you know," said Edward Leighton, gazing around.

"There must be a descent somewhere," replied Katinka. "Let us search for it."

They gazed cautiously round the battlements, and on the further side found a rope ladder hanging.

Leighton gazed over and found that by it they could descend to a ruined wall, about four feet in thickness, which was apparently used as a footpath.

"Dare you venture?" he said, turning to his wife, who shuddered slightly.

"I dare venture anywhere with you," replied she, smiling away her fears.

"Then, come. Hold tight to my girdle, and look upwards."

The next moment both were suspended in mid air.

CHAPTER CCXC.

NEW ORLEANS—DICK CAFFYN IN LOVE—THE SLAVE MOTHER AND HER DAUGHTERS—DEATH, AND ITS PROBABLE RESULTS.

AFTER avenging the insult offered to his wife at Cape Town, the Boy Pirate, in his good ship, the "Red Raven," and accompanied by his fleet, pursued their way merrily across the Atlantic till they arrived within about two hundred miles of the island of Jamaica.

Then arose a fearful hurricane, the ships were tossed hither and thither by the waves, and Christopher had only time to signal for the fleet to rendezvous at New Orleans in case of dispersion ere they were separated by the angry winds, which roared most furiously.

But the good old "Raven" escaped the storm, and after cruising about for a day or two in hopes of falling in with either of the other vessels, Christopher directed his course towards the city which had been named as the point of meeting.

In due time they reached the entrance of the Mississippi river, and after proceeding up that noble river for a distance of over a hundred miles, arrived at the beautiful crescent city.

And here, after giving the necessary directions to old Brierly as to what was to be done in the event of his comrades making their appearance, our hero and his wife went ashore, and took up their residence in one of those beautiful villas embosomed in orange blossoms with which New Orleans abounds.

For a few days they were happy enough, especially Dick Caffyn, who always kept as near his foster-brother as possible.

Dick, therefore, was a constant guest at the Boy Pirate's residence, sometimes passing three or four days, or even a week, in the society of his gallant captain and the fair Lilia.

In fact, these visits became so frequent and so prolonged, that Christopher remarked it, and even, in a bantering tone, affected jealousy.

Lilia was, however, the first to discover the real cause of the young sailor's sudden love of dry land.

The next house to that in which the Boy Pirate resided was occupied by an old planter named Moore, his wife, and two daughters, who showed a little darker tinge in their skins than is consistent with pure Saxon blood.

In fact, the mother was a quadroon, and her two daughters, though fair, rich, and extremely beautiful, had too much of the taint of slavery in their veins to allow them to be received in the halls and society of the aristocracy of New Orleans.

Therefore the lovely sisters were rarely seen beyond the seclusion of their own beautiful garden, which was easily overlooked by that attached to the house in which the Boy Pirate and his wife resided.

Dick Caffyn had seen the youngest, and his heart had fallen a captive to her charms.

One day a pet lap-dog belonging to the lady strayed through the fence which separated the two gardens, and the restoration of the animal to its fair owner afforded the young man an opportunity of speaking to her.

"I thank you most sincerely, sir," said she, as Dick restored the truant; "Pompey is very roving in his disposition, and, I fear, will frequently trouble you, now that he has found an entrance to your garden."

"When I find him here, madam, I shall always most happily restore him to you," replied Dick.

"Thanks, sir; but, to avoid trouble, we will have the fence mended."

Dick heartily hoped in his heart that she would enlarge the opening rather, so that the dog might find his way through fifty times a day.

The fair one tripped away, and Dick saw no more of her that day.

Next morning he was watching early, and, at length, his patience was rewarded by seeing the two sisters coming arm in arm from their father's house.

The dog was with them, and, seeming resolved to explore the unknown region from which he had been so very quickly ousted the day before, again darted through the fence.

Again did Dick restore him, and, in so doing, his hand met that of the fair owner, and it seemed to him as though the soft fingers willingly remained in his.

"Really, sir, you will in time hate both me and my dog, we both give you so much trouble," said she.

"Never, I assure you, madam," replied Dick.

"At all events, pray come to our house, that I may be able to thank you more conveniently than over the fence."

"I will do so with the greatest pleasure this evening."

"Do not forget, for we shall expect you," cried the young lady, tripping lightly away.

Dick thought it would be very strange indeed if he forgot; he would as soon neglect an invitation from an angel.

Evening came, and Dick left his temporary home ere the light of the sun was hardly gone. He knocked at the door of his fair neighbour's dwelling, and was quickly introduced to Mrs. Moore and her two daughters, Jessie and Florence, the latter of whom was the one whose bright eyes had ensnared the young sailor's heart.

Gracefully bowing to them the young man looked around for the master of the house.

"Ah!" said Mrs. Moore, "you are looking for my

husband; but he very seldom spends his evening at home."

"Then I must accuse him of very bad taste to prefer any society to that of yourself and these young ladies," replied Dick.

Mrs. Moore sighed deeply.

"You are an Englishman, and know little of American life."

There was a long pause, and then Mrs. Moore continued, in low tones,

"You have doubtlessly remarked, Mr. Caffyn, that in the complexions of myself and those dear girls are some traces of African blood. Now, were my husband to spend his time at home, he would be not only sneered at by all his acquaintance, but neglected by those who now transact business with him."

"But you are free, madam; what difference can your parentage make in that case?"

"The taint of birth can never be removed—in this country."

It is too true, for though the recent mighty conflict which has convulsed the American continent has ended by proclaiming the slave free, yet does the unfortunate man upon whom the curse of slavery has ever sat continue to be despised and scorned by those very men who risked soul and body to rend his chains.

Dick was silent for some time, and in a few minutes Mrs. Moore contrived to form some excuse for sending both daughters from the room.

She then turned to the young sailor.

"To you I will confess what *they* know not," she said. "I dare not say to them what I am about to tell you lest the knowledge should drive them to madness. I am a slave, they are slaves!"

"Good Heavens!"

"You may well say so, though the fault rests not with my husband, who has always shown every kindness to me and my daughters; but still the horrid fact remains that we are his slaves, and that at his death we become the property of his next heir, who, I believe, is his only brother's son."

"But surely he—I mean Mr. Moore—will set you free? There is a legal process."

"But it is so expensive that he has not been able to do so hitherto. I have no doubt though that he will do so at some future time."

The girls at this moment returned, and the conversation was stopped.

The evening passed away pleasantly enough, and Caffyn was about to retire, when a loud knocking was heard at the front door.

Then heavy footsteps were heard ascending the stairs, and a black servant came rushing in with alarm and horror depicted on her face.

"Oh! missy! Massa am dead!"

Mrs. Moore almost fainted at the suddenness of this announcement, but a moment sufficed to carry away the faintness.

"You must be mistaken; remain here children. I will go to your father."

Florence and Jessie sat in the most anxious expectation. Half a minute elapsed, then their mother's voice was heard resounding through the house in a loud scream.

Both at once rushed from the room to the adjoining one, where they found their mother lying senseless by the side of their father's corpse.

It appeared from the statement of the persons who brought the body home, that a quarrel had taken place in the streets, in which revolvers were used, and several shots fired, one of which pierced Mr. Moore's forehead as he was quietly walking past the noisy crowd.

With the utmost melancholy in his heart, Dick Caffyn left the abode of death, and returned to the house of his friend and captain.

Lilia was reclining on a sofa, while her husband occupied a low stool by her side. She at once saw by Dick's face that something unusual had occurred.

"Have you seen a ghost," she asked, "you look almost as pale as a spectre yourself?"

"I have seen what appalled me more than a dozen spectres. I have seen two girls, ladies by manners and education, suddenly reduced to poverty and slavery, which is a million times worse."

He then related the events of the evening, and how his visit to Mrs. Moore's house terminated.

"This is awful!" said Lilia. "What will become of them?"

"It all depends on the next heir," replied Christopher, "if he has the feelings of a man in him he will treat them with honour and kindness until such time as they can be legally freed."

"Heaven protect them, then, for I fear the heir will do little to rescue them from a life of misery."

"You, Dick," said Christopher, "I fancy look with the eye of a lover on one of them."

"Aye; I do love her, though I have never told my love."

"Then I should advise you to do so as soon as their father's remains have been committed to earth."

"And I," said Lilia, "will visit them in the morning when the violence of their grief is somewhat abated."

The night passed, and Lilia was as good as her word.

She proceeded to the house occupied by Mrs. Moore, well knowing how valuable is a woman's love and sympathy to her distressed sisters.

It is almost needless to say how impatiently Dick Caffyn awaited her return that he might hear some news of his beloved Florence.

But anxious as he was he was hardly prepared to see the Boy Pirate's bride return within five minutes after she departed.

"What is the matter?" he cried. "Where are they? What does this mean?"

"Calm yourself, my friend," replied Lilia. "It may not be so bad as it appears at first sight."

"So bad! Explain yourself."

"I will endeavour to do so. The next of kin who has taken possession refuses to allow any one to see his *slaves!*"

"Villain! But are they well?"

"Aye; as well as children so suddenly bereft of father and mother can be."

"What! is Mrs. Moore, then, dead?"

"She is. The shock was more than she could bear, and within two hours after her husband was brought home, she breathed her last."

"Orphans and slaves! O curse of earth! when shall thy hateful chains be entirely destroyed? But still my heart hopes they shall yet be free."

"I will aid you, Dick," said our hero. "So be of good cheer."

"Thanks, thanks. With your sword at my disposal who can doubt the result?"

"My dear friend, my sword is a good one, and my arm is tolerably skilful in its use; but we are now in a land where other means must be used. Gold is more powerful than steel, Dick; my purse shall aid you first, and then, if that fails, we will boldly use our blades."

"But what do you mean? My head is in such confusion that I can scarcely understand you."

"I mean that you must legally purchase them of their owner."

———

CHAPTER CCXCI.

WARDLAW AND RAMSEY RECEIVE AN ANSWER TO THEIR NOTE—A DEBATE—THE DAY OF EXECUTION—FREEDOM AND EXPLANATION.

SOME three hours after Wardlaw and Ramsey had dispatched their note asking for aid the old turnkey once more made his appearance.

"Have you seen the captain of either of the ships?" asked Wardlaw.

"Si, senor, I have, and I have this note for you in reply."

"Heaven be thanked," ejaculated Ramsey, fervently, "we shall once more be——"

"Clothed in decent garments," said Wardlaw, taking the sentence out of his comrade's mouth; then, in a low tone, he whispered,

"Be cautious in your speech; I know not yet how far this man is our friend."

The note was as follows:—

"GENTLEMEN,—You shall be released if gold has influence to bribe, or steel to alarm, the tyrant by whom you are illegally imprisoned.   RALPH TALBOT."

"Black Ralph, by all that is damnable!" cried Ramsey, as he dropped the letter on the floor.

"Yes; and we know well that he will perform his promise."

Ramsey made no reply.

"So that we may already look upon ourselves as free," continued Wardlaw.

"But, Gerald, it will be a regular case of out of the frying-pan into the fire. You recollect, I suppose, how, where, and when we last met Black Ralph?"

"I do; but still I apprehend no injury at his hands, for Ralph Talbot, though a fierce, hot-tempered man, is not vindictive or revengeful."

"Rather a broken reed to trust in; but, still, we can but take our chance."

"And that chance is an extremely good one, I tell you, Ramsey, for the very wording of his letter proves that he harbours no enmity against us."

"He may be practising hypocrisy."

"I don't think so; he was always outspoken and honest in speech."

"But to obtain possession of us perhaps he is dissimulating."

"I think not; he says that gold shall be used if necessary. Surely he would never pay a large sum of money for the pleasure of killing us?"

There was no other method of settling the question but by awaiting the result of their letter, which they did with considerable impatience.

The day passed, darkness came, and, about an hour after sunset, the two prisoners were preparing for sleep when a stream of light flashed through the grating in the door of their prison, the key rumbled in the lock, and two persons entered, followed by the gaoler bearing a torch.

The visitors were Colonel Don Jucaro and Ralph Talbot.

"Well, villains," said the colonel, who was very drunk, "have you made up your mind yet to die in a Christian-like manner?"

"Senor, surely you don't mean to hang us until the week you granted us is expired?" replied Wardlaw.

"No, but I mean to sell you though, rascals."

"Of all evils a wise man chooseth the lesser, so slavery be it rather than the noose."

"This gentleman will buy you, and so you had better mind what you are about, for he is one who will not submit to any impertinence."

"Senor, have we ever been impertinent to you?"

"Yes, may the devil roast you? Did you not ask me for a week's respite?"

"Surely——"

"Surely you are both drunk!" roared the colonel, "though I know not how you could procure liquor. Come along, my gallant captain."

So saying, he staggered off, followed by Black Ralph, who had not spoken a word, but who, as he now left the cell, tossed a packet on the bed of the two prisoners.

The colonel was so drunk that he did not see that the gaoler, ere he locked the door, lighted a second torch, and placed it in the hands of the younger of the two prisoners.

They were no sooner left alone than Wardlaw eagerly tore open the packet to see what it contained.

There was a file, a strong chisel, and about twenty feet of strong cord. There was also a purse and a note.

The purse contained about thirty pounds in Spanish coin; the note contained the following words:—

"If you are not released before noon to-morrow cut through your window-bars, and meet me on the beach at midnight. Fear not; I am your friend.
          "RALPH TALBOT."

"Bravo, Ralph! I do believe he means well by us, so now let us to bed. But, stay, here is another visitor."

Again the door opened, and the gaoler made his appearance, bearing in his hand a basket.

"Here is some refreshment the Capitano Americano has sent you," said the man, setting down the basket.

"But, tell, me, my friend," said Wardlaw, "has the commandant——"

"Pardon, senor, I cannot stay to answer questions now; the adjutant is waiting for me."

The man hurried from the cell, and Ramsey proceeded to open the basket.

It contained a small loaf of white bread, a cold fowl, a couple of bottles of wine, and some fruits.

"Upon my word, Gerald, I begin to believe in Black Ralph after all. He would not send us such a supper if he intended to ill-treat us afterwards."

"Ramsey, the true way to obtain possession of your heart is, I see, to attack your stomach."

"Scandal, sir! But explain to me, wise comrade, what did our worthy gaoler mean by calling him El Capitano Americano?"

"I suppose Ralph has represented himself to be an American, the better to conceal his plans."

"How lucky the colonel was so much the worse for liquor. Had he not been sacrificing to Bacchus we should have been supperless and in the dark."

"Very true, Ramsey; therefore, if you would have your head clear for to-morrow's work, whatever it may be, leave the other bottle untouched."

Ramsey obeyed, and, after secreting their tools, the two men sought their hard couch, to dream of liberty, and of the strange friend and benefactor they had so suddenly and so strangely found.

The morning broke, and, with its earliest beams the two prisoners were awake and eagerly watching from the window to see if any movement on board either of the ships betokened approaching liberty.

For some time all was quiet, but, about three hours before noon, a boat put off from one of the vessels and approached the shore.

Wardlaw thought he could distinguish the figure of Black Ralph sitting in the stern sheets.

But three, four, five hours passed away, and the boat returned without the prisoners receiving their freedom.

"He has failed in his scheme of purchasing us, so we must set to work with the file," said Wardlaw.

"Better wait till dark," said Ramsey, "there is a sentinel posted on the beach about thirty yards to the right."

"It is almost dark and I have no fear of the sentinel; gold will, I fancy, stop his tongue."

So saying he commenced filing, and worked away vigorously.

Then, after a time, Ramsey took his place, and, ere he was fatigued, one of the bars was severed save a slight thickness of metal which might be torn asunder by their strong hands.

"Hush!" said Wardlaw, suddenly, "here comes some one."

The door of the dungeon was opened, and Colonel Don Jucaro entered, followed by his adjutant Don Cardoverro.

An official-looking paper was in the adjutant's hand, which, at a signal from the colonel, he unrolled and read.

It purported that the two prisoners—names unknown—having been duly tried and condemned, would be strangled on the following morning.

When Don Cardoverro had concluded the interesting document, the colonel demanded, in a pompous voice, whether either of the prisoners had any last request or communication to make.

"None at all," replied Wardlaw, and his words were echoed by Ramsey.

"Do you wish to see a priest?"

"No; we are not Catholics."

The colonel then faced about in military style, and left the cell, followed by his adjutant.

"I am afraid the worthy man will be disappointed of the pleasure of seeing us choked to-morrow morning," said Ramsey, with a laugh.

"Yes, but we must work away, though. Luckily it is dark now; we shall not be observed."

The file worked briskly, and in a short space of time all the bars were cut through so that they could be wrenched from their hold in a moment by a strong hand.

The rope was then uncoiled, and placed close at hand, after which the two friends waited for the stroke of midnight, amusing themselves in the meantime with the bottle of wine they had reserved from the previous night.

At length the hour came, the bars were wrenched from the window, the rope was secured and dropped through the window, and Ramsey was already half way between the dungeon and the beach when a tramp of armed men was heard, and about twenty soldiers came in sight, two of them bearing torches.

The sentinel at the corner of the fort challenged as the young sailor hastily climbed up the rope again.

It was the guard coming to relieve the man who challenged, and place another on his beat.

"Confound it!" cried Wardlaw, "here is a delay."

"Why a delay? All is quiet now; I will descend again."

"But the new sentry?"

"Is but one man. If he is at all unruly or rude I shall knock him on the head."

"You have quite recovered, it seems," said Wardlaw.

"Recovered what?"

"Your spirits and courage, which, I thought, had taken leave of you altogether, my friend."

Ramsey's only answer was to slide down the rope again, while Gerald Wardlaw prepared to follow him.

A minute afterwards both stood on the beach, gazing anxiously round for Black Ralph.

"Ah!" said Ramsey, bitterly, "he is unwilling to risk himself any more."

"Who is unwilling?" asked Wardlaw.

"Ralph Talbot. He is not here as he promised he would be."

"Ralph Talbot is here," whispered a voice, and the rover stepped forward.

"Sir," said Wardlaw, "I thank you for your kindness; but was unaware when I wrote that letter that it would fall into your hands."

"It did though, and as a proof that past events are forgotten I am here. Give me your hands."

Touched by this generous behaviour on the part of Black Ralph, the two companions extended their hands, which the outlaw grasped warmly.

"Now to the boat, and on board my ship we may laugh at your scarecrow-colonel with his Don Quixote of an adjutant."

So saying he led them off carefully towards the spot where his boat was waiting, with two hardy seamen at the oars.

But a slight noise caused by the displacement of a pebble attracted the attention of the sentinel.

"Who goes there?" rung out over the sandy space.

No answer was returned to the challenge, and the sentinel at once fired in the direction of the sound.

Black Ralph drew a pistol and would have returned the shot, but Wardlaw laid his hand on his arm.

"Do not fire," he said; "it will only reveal our whereabouts."

"Sensible as ever, Wardlaw: but here is the boat. Once in it, I defy your rusty old Spaniard and all his forces."

The three men stepped into the boat, and pushed off from the shore.

The noise attending this movement, however, drew another shot from the sentinel, which seemed to arouse the whole of the fort.

Lights were seen hither and thither.

A bell sounded noisily, and the hoarse voice of the adjutant was heard calling his troops together.

"The birds are flown, my friend," said Ralph. But, Wardlaw, what have you done with our old captain—Daniel Harwolf, I mean?"

"The crew revolted, and he was deposed from his command. I was elected captain in his stead; but grew disgusted with the continual bloodshed and rapine, so deserted along with Ramsey, and after many adventures found ourselves at Dios Lagos. But how happened you to be there?"

"My ship belongs to the Boy Pirate's fleet, and an accident having separated me from him for a short time, I came here in pursuit of two slaving vessels which seem to be in no hurry to quit their harbour of refuge."

"The Boy Pirate's fleet! Why, how many ships has he?"

"He has four good ships, all of them manned by daring seamen; but he is a pirate no longer, he lives only to aid the oppressed and free the slave."

CHAPTER CCXCII.

DICK CAFFYN AT A SLAVE AUCTION—HE PURCHASES THE TWO SISTERS AND MARRIES THE BEAUTIFUL FLORENCE.

POOR Dick Caffyn was in a most melancholy state, after the sudden death of Mr. and Mrs. Moore.

Florence and her sister were kept in great seclusion not being allowed even to follow their father's remains to the grave.

But the other mourners were whites, who, of course, could not tolerate the presence of slaves amongst them.

But Dick, the constant, thought that the sad ceremony once over, they would surely show themselves in the garden as usual.

He was doomed, however, to disappointment, for they still continued in the most strict retirement.

Several times both he and Lilia had gone forth with the intention of paying a visit to the two friendless girls, but on every occasion had they been refused an interview by the new proprietor.

But one day Dick came flying to the Boy Pirate's residence, with anger written in plain lines on his face.

"Well, what has happened?" said Christopher, who was, as usual, by the side of his fair Lilia.

"Happened! It is infamous—it is disgusting—I wonder the earth does not swallow them up!"

"Swallow who? and for what crimes?"

"Read that," said Dick, thrusting forward a paper folded so that an advertisement met the Boy Pirate's eye.

Christopher started to his feet, and a hearty oath fell from his lips.

"Damn them! this is too bad!"

The announcement was as follows:—

"NOTICE!

"IMPORTANT SALE BY ORDER OF THE EXECUTORS.

"Messrs Puffem beg to announce to their patrons and the public, that they will have the honour to submit to public auction on Wednesday next, the household furniture, pictures, plate, wines, and domestic servants of the late Mr. Moore. Among other lots, of which a printed catalogue is issued, the auctioneers deem the following worthy of especial notice.

"Florence, a female slave, aged eighteen, nearly white, and of great beauty and accomplishments.

"Jessie, sister to the above, aged nineteen years and a half.

"The above girls would make excellent ladies' maids

"Tom Brown, a mulatto groom and coachman, a steady lad, and careful driver.

"The pictures will be found perfect gems of art, many of them having been imported at great expense from Europe.

"The goods are on view at the auction rooms, and may be inspected between the hours of eleven and three."

The Boy Pirate swore another great oath when he had finished reading the advertisement, and throwing the paper on the floor, said,

"I should like to have Messrs. Puffem and the young heir on board the 'Raven' for six months, I'd give them a taste of slavery not in its mildest form; but, of course, you will attend the auction Dick, and bid for the poor girls."

"I shall, and I would like to see the man who out-bids me."

"I don't know the price of slaves; but I fancy our funds united would more than suffice to buy everything in the auction-room."

"Can we see them," asked Lilia, "before the day comes? It would, perhaps, ease their minds a little to know that friends were looking out for their safety."

"We can; so let's go at once."

They went accordingly, and though from the crowd who were assembled, they were unable to say much, yet Lilia managed to whisper a few words which cheered the heart of the afflicted.

The day came, and the two friends boldly walked to the auction mart, a kind of rotunda lit up by a beautiful coloured glass dome, in which no less than three sales were going on at the same time.

Elbowing their way through a motley throng of Yankees, Jews, and Spaniards, they approached the rostrum of the Messrs. Puffem just as Tom Brown the mulatto was placed on the table. Bidding was very flat, and in a few minutes he was knocked down for eight hundred dollars to a celebrated Jew attorney.

Dick's heart beat wildly as he then saw his beloved pushed forward, and exposed to the gaze of the mob.

Beautiful she looked, though tears were in her eyes, and the auctioneer had taken care that she should be arrayed in a dress well calculated to display her loveliness. Her dress was cut very low in front, revealing a round and swelling bosom heaving as it was with grief and indignation, while the petticoats were shortened so that her finely-formed leg was visible nearly to the knee.

"Now, who'll bid for this fine article, warranted possessed of every accomplishment? As to her good looks, why you can see 'em."

So spoke the auctioneer as he pushed her forward.

"Bid slowly," whispered the Boy Pirate, in his comrade's ear. "Don't appear too anxious."

"Thousand dollars!" cried a long-legged Yankee.

"Twelve hundred!" shouted a dirty-looking Jew.

"Fifteen hundred!" said Dick, in a loud voice.

"Really, gentlemen, your bids are not worth a rap. She cannot be sold under eighteen hundred dollars."

There was a pause, and then the Jew advanced fifty dollars beyond the price named by the auctioneer.

"Eighteen fifty. Going at——"

"Nineteen!" said the Yankee.

"Going at nineteen. Going——"

"Two thousand!" said Caffyn.

There was a long pause, and though the auctioneer tried to increase the bidding, for some time he was unsuccessful.

"Going at two thousand dollars. What a paltry price for such a fine girl?"

"Fifty!" said the Jew.

"One hundred!" said Caffyn.

The Israelite muttered the name of Moses, coupled with something that was not a blessing, and retired from the scene.

"Two thousand one hundred dollars, gentlemen. Going at two thousand one hundred. Going—going—gone!"

The hammer descended, and Florence Moore was pushed off the table, while Dick, walking up to the desk, said to the auctioneer,

"I will pay you in cash as soon as the sale is at an end."

Jessie Moore was then exposed to the competition of the crowd, and the bidding became more spirited.

But Dick Caffyn outbid them all, and the two sisters both became his property.

Lilia, the Queen of the Avengers, then led them to her own home, while the young sailor remained behind to pay for the goods he had purchased.

When seated in the light, airy apartment which Lilia most frequented the poor girls fell on their knees before her, and with tears thanked her for her kindness, for they fancied that she was the real mistress they now belonged to.

"Only let us be together, and we will work early and late for you, and endeavour to make some return for your kindness; but if you separate us we shall pine away and die."

"My dear girls, you must not talk of working for me," replied Lilia, "for you are my friends and guests, so dry your tears, and be happy."

"But, madam," said Florence, "we owe you our eternal gratitude, if it is only for the immense amount of money you expended to rescue us."

"Florence, dear, let me whisper a word in your ear. Mr. Caffyn loves you, and his money it was brought you hither; let me plead for him—can you return his love and become a loving wife to him?"

The rich warm blood rushed wildly over the beautiful girl's neck and bosom. She hid her face and made no reply; but Lilia interpreted her silence favourably.

"Your sister will always be near you, so that there will be no need of separation, unless, indeed, she should look favourably on some other bold sailor."

At this moment Christopher and Dick entered; and both the girls rose to greet their new master.

"My dear young ladies," said Dick, "you may rely on receiving your freedom in some way or other ere many days, until then you are my friends."

And when, a few moments afterwards, Lilia found an opportunity to whisper in his ear that his suit would be favourably accepted, the brave, true-hearted young fellow felt that the old saying, that "happiness cannot be bought with money," was untrue.

It is needless to pursue the whole narrative of Dick's wooing, suffice it to say that the next morning Florence consented to become his wife, and an early day was appointed for the wedding.

A long time it seemed though to Dick, but at length the happy morn arrived and a small yet happy party was assembled in the large drawing-room to witness the ceremony.

Old Brierly was in attendance to give the bride away, Christopher having pleaded his youth as an excuse. He himself stood by the side of his beloved Lilia, who looked supremely happy.

The minister produced his book, and the marriage ceremony, according to the church of England's ritual, was performed.

Documents were signed, and Florence for the first time wrote her name, "Florence Caffyn."

Then, to the dining room, where, under the supervision of two or three black servants, a repast was spread, which, for richness and delicacy, could not be surpassed.

Brierly, as bride's father, took the head of the table, and having been previously instructed a little with regard to etiquette, rose to propose the health of the bride in a foaming glass of champagne.

"Shipmates," said he, looking about as awkward as could be in the long shore togs he had donned for the occasion. "Shipmates and ladies, I ain't much of a chap for jaw crackin', but seein' as how I've been hauled on the quarter-deck, I'm bound to give orders, an' you likewise is bound to obey them orders. Now, what I've got to say is, that you'll all drink the health o' the young lady as our messmate has just got spliced to, and give three rousing good cheers."

"The health of the bride!" cried Christopher. "Hurrah!"

And the glasses jingled in a most musical manner, as the tribute of respect was paid her.

Florence blushed deeply, and laid her hand on her husband's arm, while the old minister who had just united them, in his confusion poured himself out three glasses one after another.

"Come, Dick," said Lilia, in a joking tone, "after Mr. Brierly has so highly complimented your bride it is your duty to return thanks in a long speech."

"I cannot speak much, my heart is too full," replied he; "but as this day has made me the happiest of men, I thank you all from the bottom of my heart for the kindness with which you have treated her who has made me happy!"

The champagne—a drink to which he was unaccustomed—began to operate on Brierly's brain, but its only effect was to make him much more talkative than usual.

"Now, gentlemen," said he, "you must obey the signal and drink a bumper to our gallant captain and his lady, and if you gave three cheers for Caffyn, why give thirty for Captain Christopher!"

It is needless to say how rapturously this toast was received.

The clergyman, who knew about as much of the Boy Pirate as he did of the Emperor of China, drank a glass to each cheer, and shortly afterwards was asleep beneath the table.

Having been removed from his quarters by the servants, the wedding festivities proceeded until Dick and his bride took their departure to a house which had been provided for them on the banks of the lake Pontchartrain.

Brierly returned to the "Red Raven," and Christopher was left alone with his fair Lilia.

CHAPTER CCXCIII.

ANDREW HARWOLF'S FLIGHT—THE GAMBLING HOUSE—A DESPERATE QUARREL IN THE DARK—HARWOLF'S NEW COMPANION.

WHEN Andrew Harwolf fled from the scene of his burglarious enterprise, and the spot where Miles had so suddenly met his doom, he ran like one pursued by fiends, without any fixed destination or object.

Taking the straight road before him away he scudded, till convinced by the silence, which was unbroken, save by his own footsteps and hard breathing, that he was not followed.

Then the run became a long, shuffling walk, till day suddenly broke, and Andrew Harwolf as suddenly stopped.

Stopped to the reflection that he was taking the most likely course to meet that detection he so much wished to avoid.

He thought of Silas Rye, of the keen-eyed Indian Catahaga, of the hot, impetuous Irishman, Oiny Macarne, and as he thought of them he knew full well that they were on the track.

Whither, then, should he go to escape from them? Well he knew that the keen eyes of the Indian chief would find his trail in the pathless forest or the rolling prairie. Silas Rye would be indefatigable in his searches if he sought civilized life.

So backwards and forwards he roamed in the gloomy forest without the town to which his steps had first been directed until daylight began to glimmer, and birds chirruped loudly in the leafy trees.

How he hated those feathered songsters. It seemed to him as though the thrush were continually screaming, "Here's Andrew Harwolf! here's Andrew Harwolf!" while the robin, in his gentle twitter, said, "Come here, good folks, and see the man who tried to commit the burglary last night!"

He cast his eyes with a baleful curse towards the branch on which they sat, while he exclaimed, "I wish in the devil's name there were no birds."

Fatigue began to assert itself in such a powerful manner that its claims could hardly be withstood; but there is no rest for the guilty, and Andrew Harwolf dared not rest, lest the minions of justice—Justice Lynch, should catch him napping.

A brief pause while he swallowed a huge draught of water from a little streamlet, and then the wretched man again resumed his desultory wanderings.

At length an idea crossed his brain that, after all, he would be safer in the densely populated town than in the forest.

Silas Rye in the city was not so much to be feared as Catahaga on the prairie.

So taking a wide circuit, he returned into San Francisco by a different route.

It was late in the evening when he again entered the city, and, without pausing, he hurried on, casting furtive and troubled looks over his shoulder to see if he was followed, till at length he reached one of the lowest quarters of the town, a conglomeration of drinking and gambling dens, with here and there a gaudily-painted concert hall.

Hither resorted the more wild and lawless of the diggers when, after three, four or six months' toil, they betook themselves to city life for *change* to enjoy their hardly won gold.

Men of all nations and in every variety of costume might be seen; the backwoodsman who had laid aside his rifle for the pickaxe, the absconding clerk from New York or Boston, the dashing Mexican in his picturesque costume, the Celestial with his pigtail and almond eyes, the fair-haired German, the swarthy Malay and the kilted Scot.

Cautiously glancing round he entered one of the establishments devoted to gambling, and calling for a drink, seated himself in a secluded corner where he would be tolerably free from observation.

The players were loud and noisy, a perfect Babel of tongues, among which the Anglo-Saxon was the predominating.

From his quiet nook Andrew Harwolf watched what was passing around him with a keen observant eye.

Solitary as he was, yet solitude had no charms for him; in that motley assembly he sought a comrade, a companion spirit.

Presently a quarrel arose at a table at which four men were seated.

"I guess you're a tarnation infernal liar!" cried a tall Yankee, addressing one of his associates.

"Bedad," said the man addressed, "an' ye're devil a bit better yerself."

The oath the American swore when he heard his words thus returned was too terrific to be recorded.

"An' ye may swear, ye grate big blatherin' hound; divil a bit will I be froightened of yez," continued Paddy, while his hand grasped his stick ready for action.

Placing his heels on the table the Yankee squirted a mouthful of tobacco juice full in the Irishman's face, at the same time drawing a revolver from his pocket.

"Tare an' blazes! Be the howly Saint Pathrick I'll be the death of yez, ye omadhaun!" shouted Paddy, leaping to his feet with such haste that he overturned the table and the chair on which his antagonist was seated.

"Shtand up loike a man," he continued, while the other players left their games in the excitement of a general row.

"I guess you're a gone coon," shouted the Yankee, and immediately two shots were heard from his revolver, one of which sent a harmless German to his last sleep, while the other slightly wounded a Mexican who stood near.

" Bad cess to ye !" shouted the Irishman, swinging his shillalah high in air.

There was a loud crash, and the chandelier, which gave light to the whole room, fell to the ground with a smash, leaving the room in darkness.

" Och ! howly soul ! I'm kilt ! I'm murdered in-toirely !" screamed Paddy, while shouts and oaths proclaimed that blows were being recklessly struck in the dark by more than one of the crowd.

Another shot was fired, and then another, which struck the wall a few inches over the head of Andrew Harwolf, who sat still in his corner, having no in-clination to become mixed up in this indiscriminate fight in the dark.

" Lights ! lights !" shouted a voice, and a few moments later the master of the establishment en-tered, bearing a lamp in one hand and a revolver in the other.

A mass of human beings now slowly separated themselves ; the dead, two in number, were carried into an adjoining room, and a surgeon arrived to look after the wounded.

The Irishman was severely wounded, not by the pistol shots, but by the long dagger of a Mexican digger, whom he had accidently struck with his stick in the dark ; two broken heads testified to the strength of his arm, and the toughness of his black-thorn, while two bullets had found their billets in the legs of a Chinaman.

The Yankee, whose rude conduct had been the cause of this disturbance, was nowhere to be seen, having made his escape after the last shot.

But the survivors swore a bitter vengeance against him should he fall into their power, and then re-sumed their gambling.

Andrew Harwolf rose from his seat, and left the house.

He knew, now, that if he could only find the flying Yankee, he should have a companion, one of the right sort—one whose hands were red with the blood of his fellow men—and, best of all, one over whom he could exercise controul by holding up to him the terrors of Judge Lynch.

In [such frame of mind, the Grey Wolf left the gambling-room, and passed out into the street.

Every grog-shop, singing-room, monte-table did he visit, but no glimpse of the tall assassin gladdened his eyes.

At length, he was compelled to seek repose in one of the numerous lodging-houses in the neighbour-hood, and after paying half a dollar, was shown a rude military bed in a large room, in which a dozen men were already assembled, some sleeping, others smoking or conversing in low tones as they reclined on their hard and not over clean pallets.

Andrew Harwolf had no friend to converse with, nor did he particularly wish to talk at that moment. His busy brain was plotting and scheming.

How to dispose of Silas Rye—how to recover the Frontemore papers and treasures which had been wrested from him by Catahaga—and finally, how to discover the whereabouts of the man he had fixed upon to be his tool and companion, were the problems which he endeavoured to solve.

At length he fell asleep, a deep, heavy slumber, produced by long continued fatigue ; nor did he wake till late the next morning, when he found that half of the previous night's company had departed, and others were actively preparing to go.

Andrew Harwolf rubbed his eyes, cast a glance round the room, and was about to commence dress-ing, when his gaze rested on a tall figure which lay in the next bed to him.

Though the head was nearly covered beneath the coarse brown rug, sufficient of it was visible to tell Andrew Harwolf that this could be none other than the man who had commenced the fatal affray at the gambling-house.

So he laid himself down once more, pretending to sleep, though he all the time kept his eye fixed on the sleeping individual.

At length all had departed save these two, and then the Yankee, after sundry yawns and stretches,

proceeded to insert his legs in the lengthy pantaloons which lay across his bed.

Andrew Harwolf, too, began to assume his raiment, convinced more than ever by the stealthy glance which the Yankee cast towards him that it was the man he sought.

" Fine morning," said he, breaking the silence.

" I reckon yes," was the reply.

" Quite calm after last night's storm ?" continued Harwolf.

" What do yer mean, stranger ?" cried the Yankee, while his hand sought his coat pocket for his re-volver.

" I mean the row at the gambling-house up the street," replied Harwolf, laying *his* revolver on the bed.

" What the devil do you know about it ?"

" I was there ; I saw you fire, and I saw a man fall, and I know that Judge Lynch is waiting for you."

" I guess them as wants me 'll have to wake up bright an' airly, an' not come anigh me while this 'ere six-shooter are in sportin' condition."

" Pooh ! put your pistol away, man," replied Harwolf. " I don't want to hurt you ; if I had thought of giving you up I should have done so an hour ago while you were asleep."

There was some reason in this, so the wrath of the American abated.

" P'raps you chalked out some coon yerself up thar, stranger ?"

" Whether I did or not matters nothing to you. You can prove nothing against me, while I, with a word, could send you to prison."

The Yankee rubbed his chin thoughtfully, looking all the while at his pistol.

" Now I s'pose you ain't a preaching all this 'ere sarmon for nothing, mister. What do yer want ?"

" I want your services in a matter I can't very well do myself."

" Fire away ; but stop, though, let me jump into my duds, and then we'll have a licker up below."

Acting on this suggestion, the two men clothed themselves, and proceeded to the dirty bar below, which was, to all intents and purposes, a private room, as no one was there save the negro barman.

Neat spirits were called for, and the new friends sat down in the remotest corner of the bar, carefully keeping their faces from the doorway.

This behaviour did not attract the notice of the barman, who was too well accustomed to such sus-picious actions and people to pay any attention to these in particular.

For some little time the men drank in silence.

" Wa-al," said the Yankee, at length, tired of waiting.

Harwolf looked fixedly at his companion for a moment.

" Can you keep a secret ?" he said.

" I guess I can, if you pay—"

" Don't talk to me about paying ; recollect I have your secret in my hands, my friend."

" Wa-al, I reckon that air true ; but don't drive a hard bargain mister."

" Then listen to me, and if you value your life, don't repeat a word of what you hear."

" Go ahead—guess I'm all ears and no tongue."

" There is a man in this place—this town I mean—whom I hate ; he once robbed me of some papers and money —"

" Mean skunk ! thar's the police ye know, mister."

" I don't love the police any more than you ; so don't interrupt. This man I fancy has the papers with him, if not, they are hidden somewhere by an Indian named Catahaga—"

" Jeru-sa-lem ! and air that Injen in Californey, mister ?" cried the Yankee, starting to his feet.

" He is. But it is not with him that you will have to do ; if this Silas Rye has not got the papers with him, they are hidden somewhere in Arkansas. I want you to watch this Silas Rye, to make him drunk if you can, to pump him, and rob him if he has the papers."

THE RESCUE.

"Ax yer pardon, mister ; but is this ere Silas Rye anyways o' kin to the young feller as had his house broke into t'other day ?"

"Harwolf changed colour slightly ; but regaining his self-possession, answered,

"I don't know ; but you can easily find out. And there's another thing, too. Come close : he has a bullet—*a pistol bullet attached to his chain*—if you can bring me that, I'll give you a hundred dollars."

"That's all very well, ye know, mister ; but I guess my phizmahogany is too well knowed about these ere diggins to allow o' my takin' all this ere out o' doors exercise."

"I can disguise you so that your own mother won't know you."

"Wa-al then, hand over a couple o' dollars to begin with, an' shout for another licker."

Harwolf gave him the coin, had the glasses replenished, and while they were drinking, briefly described Silas Rye's personal appearance.

"What's your name, my friend ?" he then asked.

"Byron Homer Penn. And what might yours be mister ?"

Andrew Harwolf hesitated a moment ere he replied,

"Henry Jarvis."

No. 85.

CHAPTER CCXCIV.

FAILURE OF BERTRAM COOPER'S SCHEME— CONSULTATION AT THE LAWYERS — MRS. DUSTYMAN'S REVELATIONS — SOME LIGHT ELICITED.

BERTRAM COOPER proceeded to Bristol, as he said he would do when he was released from the police constable's hands.

He made every inquiry for the absconding Harwolf, but without success, for the gipsy only entered the town just as the "Newport," with the pirate on board, sailed out of the harbour.

A week spent there without the slightest clue being obtained as to the whereabouts of him he sought convinced the gipsy that his search was hopeless, and with a heavy heart he returned to the Kent Street garret, where his wife, the fortune-teller, and the ragged children still resided, notwithstanding Lord Hawksbury had more than once urged them to seek a more respectable abode.

But the gipsies stuck to their tumbledown, ruinous abode in the filthy street, for there was more friendship and society for them there than in a cleaner and more airy neighbourhood.

Without being altogether criminal Bertram Cooper's life had been a very suspicious one. The police said, and said truly enough, that the few mats the swarthy couple made and hawked about the streets could not produce sufficient to keep them from starvation; but those astute gentlemen with the blue coats made no allowance for the comfortable sums of money which fell into the woman's hand when she officiated as fortune-teller. And now, having access to Lord Hawkbury's kitchen, and listening to the tattle of the numerous servants, the fortune-telling became much easier than before, and many a half crown did the wife of Bertram Cooper earn amongst the beaux and belles of Hyde Park.

In brief terms the gipsy told his wife of his failure, and then retired to his rude couch to repose.

In the morning, however, he was up betimes, and on his way to the residence of Lord Hawksbury.

"Well, Cooper," said his lordship, when the gipsy entered the room, "and have you succeeded?"

"I have not, my lord, nor could I hear any tidings of the villain; but I'll see him hanged yet."

"You hate that man?"

"Not more than I hate his father; the very name of Harwolf makes my blood boil."

"You told me once *why* you felt so revengeful, but I have forgotten."

"I told you, my lord," said the gipsy, grinding his teeth, and clenching his hands, "that my poor brother was ruined and murdered by that cursed villain, and I told you when I left the police court that I should never rest satisfied till I had seen them both hanged."

"No trace, you say, can be found; but do you think he is still in England?"

"I do not, my lord. I have no doubt he proceeded to Bristol, and obtained a berth on board some ship sailing at once. Had I not been locked up that night I fancy I should have been in time to stop him."

"Well, nothing can be done at present; we must wait the course of events, and look out for news. In the mean time, take this purse, and if you should hear anything, let me know at once."

Bertram Cooper took the purse, and with many thanks, withdrew to his lodgings.

The next day he and his family were miles away from London, on their way to a little country fair to be held not far from Frontemore.

It was merely a speculation on his part, but he thought that perhaps he might pick up some little bit of evidence that would form a link in the chain which was to bind the Harwolfs to the scaffold.

Lord Hawksbury, after his departure, finished perusing the paper, and then put on his hat to proceed to the office of Messrs. Tape and Pounce, two acute lawyers to whom he had entrusted the task of proving the Boy Pirate's right to the lordship of Frontemore.

While he is walking thither, let us take a peep into the office of the solicitors, and introduce the inmates.

Mr. Tape, the senior partner, having fallen into the hands of his old enemy, the gout, had given up the management of the business into the hands of young Pounce, keeping himself cosily in his private apartments, and drawing a nice sum of money per annum for the use of his name on the door-post.

Mr. Pounce was a keen, wide-awake young fellow, or, rather, a man who, by constantly shaving off every particle of hair from his face, kept up an appearance of perpetual youth. His nose was slightly hooked, and he wore his hat rather on one side, had a slight cast in the right eye, and a good-humoured smile perpetually on his mouth. He was rather a sporting character, but withal a sharp business man, for he never allowed his pleasures to interfere with office duties.

The office also contained Mr. Folyo, his clerk, a man who imitated his employer, wore large neckties and was very fond of beer, and with him were associated Bob Rabbit, a gamekeeper from the somewhat deserted Frontemore estates, and Mrs. Dustyman, the char-woman who had the care of the several suites of offices of which the building No. 14, Pump-handle Alley, Outer Temple, consisted.

Bob Rabbit, the keeper, was an ordinary man of his class, and wore a velveteen coat.

Mrs. Dustyman, on the other hand, was a remarkable woman.

Perhaps some official in the confidence of the honourable benchers of the Outer Temple could enlighten the reader as to the precise year in which Mrs. Dustyman entered on her present mode of life; suffice it to say that the author knows no more than that she was well remembered by the oldest tenant in the block of buildings, and he had held his chambers for forty-six consecutive years.

Mrs. Dustyman certainly did not look more than fifty-five, but then time, the great destroyer, deals more mercifully with some than with others.

As, when she took up her duties as housekeeper she stated her age to be thirty, we leave the reader to form his own opinion as to how many winters had in reality lent their aid to place that frosty crown upon her hairs.

But still she was strong and active, could sweep a floor and drink a glass of gin with any char-woman in the neighbourhood; her frame was upright, bony and muscular, while her voice had lost none of its bold masculine tones.

The dress in which this specimen of the fair sex was wont to appear in was of a coarse blue, similar in pattern and texture to that so much in vogue in workhouses and charity girls' schools, though why paupers and orphans should be condemned to walk this world in garments of the hue in which mythology clothes hope, is one of those unsolved problems which we leave to the antiquarian of future ages.

A coarse apron with a bib up to the chin preserved this precious fabric from contaminating substances, her head was adorned with a bonnet of the ancient and true coal-scuttle plan, while in lieu of staff she bore in her hand a long broom.

When Lord Hawksbury entered the old worm-eaten door which bore upon it the name of—

"TAPE AND POUNCE,
        "Solicitors,"

these worthies were engaged in a discussion of the affairs which had brought them together, and a pot of porter.

Lord Hawksbury knocked without obtaining any answer, and, then, gently opening the door, peeped in.

Mrs. Dustyman was vehemently engaged in laying down the law, accompanying her words with very appropriate gestures with the broom and an old key which she clutched in her left hand.

"Now what I says and maintains is—though why poor widows should be looked upon as a lorful prey by t'other sex which goes about like a roarin' lion, is one o' them things which Mr. Dustyman couldn't make out though he were a wise man, and went home in dew time—is that these 'ere ragamuffins which is allus a lookin' out for their wittuls should have the horderin' of sich as you and I."

"Hear, hear!" cried Mr. Pounce, who had his own reasons for humouring the old woman, whom at other times he voted a bore. "Mrs. Dustyman is quite right, or my name isn't Pounce."

"Which it may or may not be, accordin' as yer godfathers an' godmothers did promise and vow; but as I was a sayin' why a poor 'ooman which her only fortune is a dustpan should be made a prey of to them 'ere wampires in top boots which goes about a seekin' to devour unperfected females is a thing which Mr. Dustyman—"

"How long has he been dead, madam?" asked Mr. Folyo in tones which at once touched the widow's heart.

"Five an' thirty year next Lady-day, which I well remember, seeing as how my black silk gownd—Ah! they did make silk in them days though. Why the poor Spittlefelds weavers should always be out o' work when the frosty weather comes, poor dear Mr. Dustyman, which, as you are aware, gentlemen, was in the ham an' beef line, an' was sold up owin' to a bad cold which didn't allow of his seein' the gravy were properly made. an' if it hadn't a been for that, I'd a been a lady ridin' in my coach, with plenty o' boiled carrots, and you know the song they sings is simply disgustin', to say nothink of their bein' a himposition and a humbug; but them wagabones is what ought to be put down—a devouring of other folks rights, and if the young lord of Frontemore only knowed, why he'd—he'd——"

And Mrs. Dustyman, being rather perplexed in her own mind as to whether the young lord of Frontemore would vent his ire on the devouring lions, the boiled beef, the weavers, or the boiled carrots, took a huge gulp of beer to hide her indignation.

"How long is it since you comed away from Frontemore, mother?" asked the gamekeeper.

"Ah!" said she, with a melancholy wag of the head, "I were a young and giddy thing then, and knowed nothing about chambers nor poor dear Dustyman, which is now in heaven in a hearse with oysterish feathers and a marble tombstone, and haven't been there since but once in a carrier's wan which was a day and a night on the road, reckonin' the numerous publics where we was obliged to stop——"

"But let's hear how long ago it is since you were there last, Mrs. Dustyman," said Mr. Pounce, who had his ears wide open.

"Three years ago were my last visit, which my best gingham umbrellar can testify as how the weather were rainy, and cost three shillings second hand in a pawnbroker's shop, and the clerk cheated me by givin' of a bad half-crown in change."

"Did you see any one there in particular?" asked Lord Hawksbury, entering the room suddenly.

"Nobody in partickler, unless it were the clergyman a buryin' a new born child in his surplice an' bands, which died some time after havin' caught cold from the rain and never recovered; leastwise, I did see a young man there which they called Kit Foundling, though why he should be so named poor Mr. Dustyman could——"

"But he was dead years before Kit Foundling was born."

"Ah, poor dear! I think I sees him now in heaven just as ever I remember him in his top boots, and a long churhwarden pipe——"

The idea of the late Mr. Dustyman parading the abode of the Blessed in top boots and with a long pipe in his mouth, was too much for Lord Hawksbury's nerves. He laughed aloud.

"Never mind the pipe," said Folyo, grinning, "tell us about Kit Foundling."

"Though tobaccy might be an abomination to some of ye what isn't among the angels and a smokin' of segars which is the custom, yet, as I were a sayin', Kit Foundling were at Frontemore, and well I recollects him, even if it hadn't a been for running away with that bleessed gal as I never set eyes on, and give me a new bonnet into my own blessed hands——'

"Take a drop of porter, Mrs. Dustyman," said Lord Hawksbury; "it will clear your brains."

"Which I throwed into the dusthole, last Tuesday were a fortnight," continued Mrs. Dustyman, taking no heed of the interruption, "and people do say as how Mr. Harwolf done it though the hevidence is weak."

"What! Mr. Harwolf threw your bonnet into the dusthole?"

"No; but made away with his father, which Bob Rabbits here can testify to havin' been engaged by Mr. Harwolf just after he came into the property."

Lord Hawksbury whispered for a moment into the ear of Mr. Pounce, who, stilling his male auditors with a wave of the hand, proceeded to cross-examine Mrs. Dustyman.

"Do you know who this Christopher or Kit Foundling is, Mrs. Dustyman?"

"Not I, sir; though them as do can tell better."

"Better leave that question alone, Mr. Pounce," said Lord Hawksbury, "Silas Rye knows all about it."

"Still additional evidence is not to be despised; we must make a strong case. Mrs. Dustyman, were you at Frontemore Hall when Mr. Harwolf married the late lady Edgeforth?"

"Not I; lord bless you, what should I be a doin' among lords an' ladies at a grand weddin', though for the matter o' that, my husband's brothers wife's sister was head chamber-maid there at the time, and she did say as how it was very strange, though she is now in a almshouse, and nobody never took any notice of it except herself."

"What did she notice about it that appeared strange?"

"Why, she did say as how the lady Edgeforth as Mr. Harwolf married was not the same one as Lord Edgeforth brought home with him a twelvemonth before; but, then, you, know, she isn't very well off, and a trifle of tea and sugar—"

"I'll take care she never wants tea and sugar again as long as she lives," cried Lord Hawksbury, hurriedly, "but tell us where she resides,"

"Which is at Garden Row, close by Coldbath Fields, No. 3, in Simms's Almshouses, and ask for Mrs. Tester, knocking four times very hard, because as she had the misfortune to lose her hearin' nigh fifteen years ago."

"Pounce, you must go to this place at once, and find out Mrs. Tester. Bring her away from there if you like, but don't frighten her, or perhaps she won't tell anything."

So said Lord Hawksbury, and was about to leave the office, when his eye fell on Bob Rabbits.

"Nothin' to say to me, my lord?" cried the ex-poacher.

"Yes, a great deal; but I can't stop now, come to my house in two hours' time."

CHAPTER CCXCV.

PERILOUS SITUATION OF LEIGHTON AND HIS WIFE—THE ESCAPE FROM PRISON—THE PURSUIT—SHOCKING DEATH OF CORNELIUS—THEY TAKE REFUGE IN A CHAPEL, WHERE LEIGHTON TURNS SAINT.

WITH his wife clinging to him, and supporting her with one arm, Edward Leighton cautiously descended the rope ladder from the battlements of the tower in which he had been a prisoner.

The ladder was not secured at the bottom, and as their combined weight was brought upon the ropes it oscillated to and fro like a gigantic pendulum.

Still, however, the young man continued his descent as steadily as he could.

Suddenly a jerk caused him to look up, and he saw the ferocious countenance of the tall fisherman Cornelius peering over the battlements.

In his hand he had a crowbar, with which he was raising the rope preparatory to giving them another and harder jerk than before. His countenance wore a most villanous expression as he twisted the bar round the rope.

"Softly, fair sir," he shouted. "Don't trouble yourself, you shall both reach the ground without any more exertion on your part."

"Villain!" cried Leighton, clinging to the rope with all the tenacity his hands were capable of.

A sardonic smile played over the mouth of the fisherman, who united the calling of petty pirate with his more legitimate occupation, and, bending down, he exerted all his strength, and raised the ladder with the two human beings on it the height of a yard.

"Now!" he cried, as suddenly withdrawing the crowbar from its hold he let them drop.

The shock was terrific, but Edward Leighton's muscles were firm, and though the strain almost made him faint, he never relaxed his grip.

"Ha, ha! my bold birds," shouted he on the battlements, "if I can't dislodge you in one way I will another. So prepare yourselves."

Leighton glanced upwards, and saw the villain preparing to saw through the ropes with his dagger.

Then he glanced downwards, and saw that he was fully twenty feet from the wall on which the ladder terminated.

Doubling his speed he had already accomplished more than two-thirds of his progress when another shock caused him to halt.

Cornelius had severed one rope, and was now looking over to see whether the runaways had yet reached a place of safety.

Fatal look it was for him, for as he stretched himself over the low battlements, his foot gave way, and having nothing to support his vast weight, he fell over and over, striking Leighton in his descent, dashing with terrific force on the ruined wall, and rolling over into the dark and ruined cavernous vault that yawned some thirty feet beneath.

No cry was heard, nothing but the dull heavy thud of the body as it dropped upon the pavement below.

The Greek pirate was dead, and Leighton stepping on the wall, used every effort to revive his wife, who had fainted from very fright.

At length she revived, and then, still supporting her, Leighton carefully took his way along the ruined wall, which, as before said, showed signs of having been used as a footpath.

After walking about thirty feet or so, a tree, whose topmost branches were enshrouded in long festoons of ivy, hung over their path like an archway.

Creeping through this, they then reached a little doorway, and paused a moment for reflection ere they entered, as by so doing, they might put themselves again in the power of the islanders.

Voices on the battlements from whence they had just escaped aroused Leighton once more to action.

Peeping forth from the clustering ivy, he saw men on the roof of the tower in earnest conversation. Their gestures and looks convinced him that these men were searching for him, and with no good intent, for they handled their daggers in a way which seemed to express the pleasure they would feel in plunging them into the escaped prisoners' bodies.

After carefully examining the remaining rope, they crept over the roof of the turret, and with great caution commenced descending one after another.

But though the rope was strong enough to bear Leighton and his wife, the forms of three strong, robust men, proved too great a weight for it. The efforts of Cornelius to dislodge our friends, too, had chafed and frayed it where it hung over the battlements.

The leader of the party was hardly half-way down the rope when it gave way, hurling the three men with terrific violence into the vaults beneath.

There was a loud groan or two, and then the gloomy chasm was again silent.

Poor Katinka trembled as she breathed a prayer to Heaven for the souls of those four men, and thought how nearly she and her husband had met their fate.

"Come, dear," said Leighton, "we cannot retreat, let us advance boldly, and look our dangers in the face, whatever they may be."

"I fear we shall fare badly now if we fall into the hands of any of their associates," replied she.

"And we shall starve if we remain here, so forward, dear girl."

Thus urged, she again grasped her husband's girdle, and approached the little arched door beneath the ivy.

It was not fastened, and swung open at their approach.

A long, gloomy passage appeared dimly lighted by clefts in the solid rock, out of which it was hewn.

At the extreme end was another door, and this, too, yielded to their efforts.

They found themselves then in a small chapel, in which, no doubt, the cruel, piratical fishermen were wont to offer up thanks to Heaven on their safe return from an expedition, and invoke the protection of their saints for the next cruise.

In many respects it resembled a Catholic chapel, but instead of the crucifix a large picture was the only ornament over the altar, which was lit up by two tall candles, and bore on it a rich display of gold plate. A window of coloured glass gave light to the building, which appeared, like the passage leading to it, to be hewn out of the solid rock.

Hardly had Edward Leighton and his wife gazed round when again voices made themselves heard.

"They come, dear Edward, they come! Fly, for Heaven's sake!" cried Katinka, in great alarm.

"Whither, dearest? We should no doubt face our foes did we return by the way we came."

"Then we shall be killed!"

"Not so, dear; see, we will hide beneath the altar. If I mistake not, these islanders are superstitious, and would not dare lay a hand on this drapery, which will shroud us from their view.

As he spoke he darted up the steps leading to the sacred place, and gently forced his wife under the crimson and white hangings. Then, giving a last look round to see if there were any other outlet, he joined her in her concealment just as the door flew open and two men entered.

The conversation of the pursuers, which had before been loud and noisy, was instantly stilled when they entered the chapel.

"He is not here," said one.

"Then where can he be?" replied the other; "he can't scale the wall back to the tower again?"

"That's true; let's look behind the pillars, they may be hiding about here."

Accordingly they carefully searched every nook and corner with the exception of the place where the fugitives were concealed.

"Perhaps they are under the altar," said the first speaker.

"Not likely. Holy St. Constantine would strike them dead if they dared do such a thing."

"Well, that's true; so it's quite certain they ain't in the chapel. But, Conrad, they might be hiding among the ivy, or in the passage; we haven't searched this way yet."

"Haven't searched this way yet," thought Leighton; "then which way did they come? There must be another door to the chapel."

Cautiously peering forth he saw the men departing by the passage through which he and Katinka had entered, but, at the same time, he observed with joy another door exactly opposite, and by which it seemed certain that his pursuers had admitted themselves to the sacred edifice.

Just as he was whispering this joyful intelligence to Katinka the men returned from their unsuccessful hunt.

"Well, they must have flown away, or else they tumbled down into the vaults with poor Cornelius."

"But if they had they would have been killed, too, stupid. Well, after all, I ain't so sorry our bold captain broke his neck, I shall be lieutenant now."

"A pretty lieutenant you'll make. Come along."

Their footsteps echoed as they strode across the floor of the chapel, the door was closed, and Edward Leighton and his wife were once more alone.

But not for a long time, for scarcely had they crept from their hiding-place, when again they were compelled to resume it.

The door opened and the Greek girl, Myra, entered slowly and like one in a dream.

Her eyes bore traces of weeping, and her hair was disordered.

Advancing with tottering steps to the altar she cast herself before it, and earnestly invoked the patron saint of the building, before whose picture she was kneeling, to intercede for the guilty soul of her unfortunate lover.

It was indeed a touching sight, and Katinka, as she peeped out at the upturned face of poor Myra, could scarce restrain her own tears.

"Holy saint," she sobbed, "have pity on the soul

of Cornelius, and bear him to the home of the blessed; teach me what I must do to make atonement for his sins."

A sudden thought struck Edward, and though his heart inwardly revolted at such deception, yet it appeared to him necessary for his own safety.

In hollow and dismal tones as he could assume he uttered the girl's name. "Myra!"

She started and gazed earnestly at the picture of the saint, from which she supposed the sound proceeded.

"Myra," he said, "wouldst thou know what to do?"

"Holy saint, forgive a poor sinful woman's presumption, and guide me aright."

"If thou wouldst atone for the many sins committed by thy lover during his life thou must aid the prisoners still further to escape."

"Aid them to escape! What, with the blood of Cornelius on their hands?"

"His blood be on his own head, they are guiltless of it; but you must aid these prisoners to escape not only from the Tower, but from the island itself; you must provide them with a boat with provisions and wine if you would wish the soul of your Cornelius to be at rest."

"All this I will do, holy saint."

"Then place your hand on the shrine and swear."

Myra reached out her hand, and placed it on the altar, saying as she did so,

"I swear to help the two prisoners of Cornelius Barkytoris to escape from this island, and I will provide them a boat and needful provisions. But, holy saint, our best mountaineers have not been able to discover the hiding-place of the fugitives."

"Behold them!" cried the sham saint, as he crept forth from beneath the altar.

Myra's face flushed with anger as she saw at once the deception which had been practiced. Her hand sought the hilt of her dagger.

"Forgive me," said Leighton, "for this; but I saw no other means of escaping."

"I have sworn," said she, coldly, "and will keep my oath. Remain here till I return."

She passed out of the chapel, motioning Leighton and his wife back to their hiding-place.

———

CHAPTER CCXCVI.

THE "REVENGE" CHASED BY A STRANGE SCHOONER—A FRIGATE IN SIGHT—HARWOLF'S STRATAGEM—DISCONTENT ON BOARD THE "REVENGE."

AFTER capturing and destroying the Portuguese ship, the pirates, under the command of Daniel Harwolf, cruised for some time off the west coast of Africa without capturing any prizes.

One morning, however, about two hours after daybreak, the second officer reported a sail on the weather bow.

Harwolf immediately rushed on deck and surveyed the stranger through his glass; it was a very large schooner under full sail.

"She appears to be steering towards us," he murmured, "and there is a man-of-wars look about her that I don't like at all."

"What do you fancy she is, sir?" said Walbrook.

"One of the preventive squadron, I fancy."

Walbrook hitched up the waistband of his trowsers, took a fresh quid, and,

"Exclaimed, 'G—d d—n!'—those syllables intense, Nucleus of England's native eloquence."

Harwolf echoed his companion's words, and then considered what was to be done in the circumstances.

"Pity we're so short handed," he observed, after a pause.

"But ye know, captain, we don't really know that she is a government schooner; let's wait till she shows her colours."

The vessel in pursuit was then about five miles distant, steering for the "Revenge," which was on a wind.

A puff of smoke shot out from her side, and the British flag floated out boldly above her canvas.

"I thought so; one of those d——d cruisers," said Harwolf. "Ready about!" continued he, walking aft.

It now became evident that the stranger was in pursuit, for as soon as the "Revenge" tacked the schooner took in her topmast studding-sail, and hauled her wind. This brought her well on the weather quarter of the "Revenge," and Harwolf at once made all sail.

The pirates, who were moral cowards, as criminals generally are, finding they had to do with others than peaceful merchantmen, showed as much anxiety to avoid an encounter as they generally did to seek it.

At the first trial of sailing between the two vessels there was no perceptible difference; for half an hour they both continued on a wind, and when Daniel Harwolf examined his sextant a second time he could not perceive that he had gained a cable's length on the schooner.

The commander of the schooner kept his ship away half a point, and thus, still holding the weather gage, increased his speed. He neared the "Revenge" slowly.

Harwolf noticed the movement ere it had been executed ten minutes.

"They are nearing us," he said; "we must keep away a point."

Away went the "Revenge," and would have recovered her distance, but the schooner was again steered more off the wind.

And thus did they continue altering their course, until the studding-sails, both below and aloft, were set by both, and the position of the ships was changed, the schooner being now on the starboard quarter of the "Revenge."

The relative distance between the two was, however, about the same, that is, between four and five miles from each other, and there was every prospect of a long and weary day's work ere they could rid themselves of their troublesome and pertinacious pursuers.

Both vessels were now running east, and so they continued the whole day, during which the chase was kept up with undiminished ardour by the active schooner.

About an hour before it grew dark that night another sail hove in sight right ahead of the "Revenge," evidently a frigate. Harwolf did not at all relish his prospects, as there could be but little doubt that the new comer was also a British man-of-war.

Even if she was not, they had good reason to believe that she would assist in their capture, for she had evidently perceived the two smaller vessels, and kept tacking every quarter of an hour so as to keep her relative position.

The commander of the schooner had also observed the frigate, as was evident by his firing with a long gun, though not within range of the "Revenge" by a considerable distance.

"Damn that fellow!" cried Harwolf, as he paced the deck excitedly, "he is calling his mate. We shall be in an awkward position presently."

"It will be dark soon, captain," replied Walbrook. "That is our only chance."

Harwolf reflected for some minutes.

"Get the long gun ready, lads!" he cried, at last. "We will return her fire, and run up the Yankee flag. That will puzzle the frigate, at all events, and night may do the rest."

"Stop a minute, captain," said Walbrook. "If I were in your place I'd keep the long gun quiet, or else the frigate's people will think we're equally matched, and will want to know why we are running away. Now, if you were to fire one of the broadside guns, the difference of sound between that and the long one they are firing would make the frigate think we are Yankee traders."

"By Jove! A good idea!" replied Harwolf, "I'll do as you say, and as America is now at peace with all the world, of course they'll think the schooner is a pirate."

And he rubbed his hands with glee, as he anticipated an easy escape.

"Hold hard with the long gun, there!" he cried, "and unship the starboard ports. Walbrook, you just see the stars and stripes hoisted—see that the ensign blows out clear."

In a few moments his orders were obeyed, and the "Revenge" commenced firing an occasional gun from her broadside, the tiny report of which hardly reached the frigate, while the loud resonance of the schooner's long-gun reverberated over the water.

And such was the state of things when, after a long chase, the sun sank down suddenly in the waves, and the three vessels were hidden from each other's sight, except with the assistance of a night telescope.

Neither ship exhibited any lights, and their positions were only known to a few on board each vessel.

Harwolf and Walbrook descended together into the cabin, and each swallowed a draught of brandy.

"And what's the next dodge, captain?" asked Walbrook, as he set down his empty glass on the table.

Harwolf passed his hand thoughtfully across his brow, ere he replied,

"I tell you what it is, Walbrook, I have made up my mind to do a plucky thing, a dodge they'll never suspect. I mean to run down to the frigate, as if for protection, tell him that the schooner is a pirate, and ask him to shelter me."

"And then he'll want you to lay to close by him."

"He may want; the moon doesn't rise till past one o'clock, and trust me to escape somehow."

"It's rather rash, ain't it, to venture? Suppose the frigate suspects us when we are under her broadside?"

"Why, then, I'll show the frigate a clean pair of heels. I can easily slip away from her and her broadside."

After some other conversation the two returned on deck, and directed the helmsman to steer straight for the frigate.

The other hands were gradually shortening sail, as if there were but few men on board, and keeping as many of them as possible out of sight, Harwolf ran under the stern of the frigate.

"Ship ahoy!" hoarsely hailed a voice from the frigate. "What ship is that?"

"The 'Happy-go-Lucky' of Boston, from the Gaboon River," replied Harwolf. "That schooner in chase," he continued, "is a pirate. Shall I send a boat aboard?"

"No; keep company with us."

"Aye, aye, sir!" cried Harwolf, grinning at the success of the first part of his stratagem.

Meanwhile, the commander of the schooner, unable to fathom the deep designs of his supposed slaver, bore down upon the frigate, thinking, perhaps, that the "Revenge" had surrendered to the larger ship.

The captain of the frigate, too, was astonished at the cool impudence of the *supposed* pirate, and got ready his broadside in order to give the schooner a warm reception.

On came the lightly-built cruiser to seek an explanation of the frigate, when, bang! went a gun from the latter, and the schooner's topmast was cut in two.

"Ship, ahoy!" hailed the commander of the schooner; "what **frigate** is that?"

"Her Majesty's frigate 'Rattlesnake.' So surrender, you rascals, or I'll blow you out of the water!"

"Surrender? Why, this is the schooner 'Cecil!' Send a boat aboard if you don't believe me."

By this time the "Revenge" had gradually dropped off to the windward of the frigate to such a distance that the broadside of the latter could do her little or no harm.

The captain of the frigate was furious when he discovered how he had been gulled, but, finding that the "Revenge" was beyond the reach of his guns, he wisely forbore pursuit, and sent a boat load of carpenters and riggers on board the schooner to repair the damage done to the rigging. It was quite two days before every thing was in order again on the deck of the schooner, during which time the captain of the frigate did nothing but curse the credulity which had led him into such a mistake, while the commander of the schooner stalked about in the majesty of offended pride, vowing he would demand a court-martial as soon as he rejoined the squadron.

Harwolf slipped away easily from his crippled pursuer, and when once beyond fear gave way to his appetite for drink in a way that appalled the crew, if anything could appal ruffians with such case-hardened consciences.

Along with his friend and comrade, Walbrook, the debauched villain employed the remainder of the night in getting intoxicated scientifically.

In this they both succeeded long ere morning light shed its first glow over the ocean, when, issuing on the deck, Harwolf's first act was to hurl a half-empty bottle he had brought with him from the cabin at the helmsman's head.

Down fell the unfortunate man, bathed in blood, while a sudden lurch threw the captain and lieutenant on their faces.

The noise of the fall and the rattling of the broken glass aroused the watch, who were quietly snoring away their period of duty in one of the boats.

Hastily starting up, these men seized their arms, under the impression that the ship had been boarded, or had struck on a rock. A glance, however, was sufficient to show them the real state of affairs.

They were about to rush forward to aid the wounded helmsman when Harwolf stopped them.

"What!" said he, "open mutiny! Devil burn me, if I don't make examples of some of you drunken swabs!"

With these words he drew a pair of pistols from his pocket, and presented them at the astonished group of sailors.

Walbrook, too, flourished a huge cutlass in his hand, and with much drunken eloquence, and many oaths, expressed his determination to stand by the captain.

"Damned rascals! I'll shoot you, every mother's son, if you interfere, blast your livers!" roared the intoxicated Harwolf, standing unsteadily on his feet.

The helmsman by this time had managed to raise himself to a sitting posture, and was endeavouring to staunch the blood which flowed from two large cuts, one on his forehead, and the other on his cheek bone.

"What have I done to be served thus?" he asked, when his eyes fell upon the perpetrator of the outrage.

"Silence, sir! I'll teach you all about mutiny!" roared Harwolf, who was now perfectly mad with rage and brandy.

If he had been left to himself—if he had been quietly allowed to kill the steersman without any opposition, either from the victim himself or the rest of the crew, most probably Daniel Harwolf would then have retired to bed satisfied with his night's performance. But to be opposed by the watch on deck, and have his justice questioned by the very individual he had selected to be his victim, aroused the demon of bloodthirstiness within his soul.

He snatched the cutlass from Walbrook's hand, giving him a pistol in exchange, and staggering forward, aimed a heavy blow at the helmsman's head, which, however, from his excessive drunkenness, he missed, the point of the weapon grazing the man's ear, and falling with full force on his neck.

Again the man fell prone to the deck, and placing his foot on the chest of his victim, Harwolf thrust the cutlass through the poor fellow's stomach.

"Take that, you blackguard! and that!" shouted the madman, repeating his cruel thrusts.

The poor man could only breathe an answer in groans.

Enraged at the sight of this wanton cruelty, the men on deck rushed forward, but the pistols held by Walbrook were immediately discharged, while Harwolf, turning from the body of his first victim, glanced about him with bloodshot eyes for a second.

Only one man was wounded by the discharge of Walbrook's weapons, and he only so slightly that in a few minutes he was quite forgetful of the circumstance.

The shots fired on deck aroused the sleepers below, who came hurrying up, half clothed and half armed, to take part in the tumult whatever it might be.

A whisper from the sailor whose arm had been wounded by the pistol shot, and then in a compact body they rushed at the two drunken officers.

Harwolf and Walbrook were overthrown and secured in a moment, and a cutlass was at the throat of each, when one, more thoughtful than the rest, suggested to place them in confinement till morning.

"Good! throw 'em down into the hold!" cried one or two.

While another voice said, in audible tones, "Throw 'em overboard!"

There was a short whispered consultation between the seamen, then the hands of the two officers were tied, and they were lowered down the hatchway, care being first taken to deprive them of everything in the shape of weapon.

The dead body was then removed and covered with an old sail.

Another man took the helm, and the ship once more glided quietly over the ocean.

As soon as it was well light the crew assembled together, and consulted what should be done with Harwolf and Walbrook.

"Hang the pair on 'em," suggested one rough tar, handling a rope the while, as if anxious to commence the job at once, and finish off hand.

"Give 'em six dozen first," cried another man.

There was a silence of some minutes.

Neither of these plans of punishment seemed to find favour with the crew.

"Put 'em into a boat and send the damned thieves adrift," was the third suggestion.

"Can't spare the boat," said an old sailor, who had not yet spoken.

"Well, then, old salt, what does yer mean to do?"

"Put 'em ashore first land we makes."

"Aye, aye," murmured the men.

"But," continued the old man, "how are we going to make any land, seein' as how neither you, nor I, nor 'ere a one on us knows how to navygate this 'ere ship onless it's them two?"

There was a dead silence.

The men thoughtfully turned their quids in their mouths, revolving the question in their somewhat hazy brains.

As no one seemed to have an idea, they all looked towards the old man again, as though they expected him to speak.

"Come, old hand, you has got us into this here fix, an' you must get us out on it. What is we to do?"

"The only thing is to cut the lashings from their hands and feet, and put 'em on the quarter deck again."

"What! arter they killed poor Boston Bill?"

"Aye, mates."

"I say, old shipmate," said one of the men, "has you lost your top gear?"

"No; but if you'll listen I'll tell you all about it. Now, we can't navygate, consequintly must have

them fellers back again. Now, if we let's 'em know why they be released, why they'll play the devil and all, so we must talk wery big like a parson or lawyer about showin' mercy, and so forth, and wind up by makin' 'em swear never to strike 'ere a man of the crew while we sails together."

There was some little murmuring amongst the crew, but they were helpless.

Then, by direction of the old man, the captain and his companion in bondage were brought on deck, and firmly bound to the mast.

Four men then loaded their muskets, and bade the prisoners prepare for instant death.

Harwolf began to beg and pray for mercy, urging as a plea for forgiveness the frightfully intoxicated condition in which he was at the time.

"Silence!" cried the ringleader of the mutiny, "the time for mercy is past."

"Forgive me this once! I'll never be guilty of such an action again!—forgive me!"

The old man made a signal, and four musket-barrels were levelled towards the two culprits.

"One—two!" counted the commander for the time being: then followed the word of command—"Recover arms!"

Then advancing towards the captain, he spoke as follows:—

"Captain Harwolf, if I'd given the word 'fire,' there ain't a man here as would have blamed me. But we are more merciful than you, so we'll set you at liberty, on one condition."

"I promise—I promise—whatever it my be!" screamed Harwolf.

"The condition is that you never lift your hand against one of us any more. If any man does wrong why we'll try him by court martial."

Harwolf gave the requisite promise, his bonds were cut, and he was once more at liberty.

CHAPTER CCXCVII.

PARAMARIBO—A SCENE ON SHORE—ZAMPA TAKEN PRISONER—BIG THREATS—THE MAGISTRATE AND BLACK RALPH.

WHEN Black Ralph had the two escaped Englishmen—Wardlaw and Ramsey—on board his ship, he sailed away from the island of Dios Lagos, intending to join the Boy Pirate's fleet at New Orleans.

But again violent tempests interfered, and drove the vessel out of her course, at the same time damaging the ship and rigging to such an extent that the bold Ralph was obliged to make for the nearest land to repair and refit.

The nearest land, in this case, happened to be the coast of South America, and, in a short time, Captain Talbot anchored in the River Surinam, befor the town of Paramaribo, which is situated on the right side of the river, and about eighteen miles from its mouth.

Paramaribo is a very handsome town, when it is borne in mind that it was built by, and still belongs to the Dutch, who usually sacrifice elegance to usefulness.

It is founded on a kind of gravelly soil, and has none of those dykes and canals, in which the mynheers generally delight, both at home and abroad.

The streets are straight, and lined with orange and tamarind trees, which are always bearing either flowers or fruit, sometimes both at once.

It possesses a fort, a hospital, a church, a synagogue, and a court-house, which are the only buildings constructed of stone or brick, the dwelling-houses being of timber, roofed with shingles, without chimneys, for in this happy land they light no fires in their houses, all cooking being done in the garden behind the house.

But the court-house of Paramaribo is the building with which we and Black Ralph have most to do, if we except a little inn kept by a mild-looking, stout Dutch woman in the street at the back of the seat of justice.

Black Ralph, having anchored, and seen everything as it should be on board his ship, entered his boat and rowed off to the shore for the purpose of informing the Custom House authorities who he was, and his object in coming to Paramaribo.

He was directed by a sentry at the landing-place to proceed towards the court-house, in which the custom officers held state—indeed the magistrate was also principal collector of revenue.

His business was soon and easily arranged to the satisfaction of himself and the worthy Mynheer Stoutbragurt, the civil ruler of Paramaribo.

After leaving the town-hall or court-house Ralph then proceeded to make several contracts for the various repairs which his vessel needed, and then retired for the night.

The next day passed, and at eventime Ralph again set his foot on shore, taking with him Zampa as a kind of esquire or escort.

As they passed the town-hall a little crowd was collected, watching the soldiers as they conveyed a party of negroes to the cells beneath that building.

Just as the party passed the spot where Black Ralph and his still blacker companion were standing there was a loud shout, the crowd swayed violently to and fro, and a hundred voices cried out that the prisoners had escaped.

The soldiers charged hither and thither amongst the people, and in the confusion Zampa got separated from Ralph Talbot.

"Where is you, Massa Ralph?" said Zampa, who was not clad in his ordinary sailor's dress, but merely in canvas trowsers and check shirt, on account of the extreme heat.

Hardly had the words escaped his lips before a hand was laid on his collar, and a soldier with fixed bayonet appeared each side of him.

"Eh, golly! you buckras goin' to pertect dis nigger from dem d——d tieves," he cried, grinning.

A stern motion of the hand waved him away with his escort.

"What de debbil you doin'? You jist let Zamp alone."

His captors, though they heard, understood not, nor was their answer intelligible to the poor Ethiopian thus suddenly kidnapped.

So they dragged him away towards the prison cells, which, as before said, were under the court-house.

"Massa Ralph, Massa Ralph!" shouted the enraged Zampa, as he struggled with his captors, "dey got me by de troat, and is goin' to lock me up, an' dey keeps prickin' me with dere baynets. Come and help a poor nigger, Massa Ralph."

Ralph Talbot heard his follower's cry of distress, and rushed forward, unarmed as he was, to the rescue.

He was just in time to see the broad shoulders and woolly head of Zampa disappear, as the door of the prison closed with a bang.

"What has he done?" demanded Ralph, indignantly of the officer.

"They have been robbing a plantation in the forest, and murdered the owner."

"Impossible!" replied Ralph, "for that man only arrived in my ship yesterday, and never set his foot on this shore till this evening."

"Perhaps you were in the plot and received part of their booty, or the whole," said the Dutchman, turning away.

Ralph gazed after him a moment, then at the door through which Zampa had disappeared.

Two sentries were before it, and it appeared to be of immense strength; Ralph, too, was unarmed, there were a great many people about, and it would be unsafe to venture an open attack on the prison under such circumstances.

Such was the conclusion at which Ralph arrived, and he walked away, resolving to be in the court in the morning and claim his man.

Muffling a large cloak round him he walked away rapidly till he reached the little inn aforesaid kept by the stout, mild-looking Dutch woman.

Entering this hostel he called for a glass of schiedam, and, seating himself in a remote corner, watched the company in the room.

For some time nothing passed worthy of record; the men, worthy scions of old Amsterdam, puffed away at their pipes and drank their grog in solemn silence.

Black Ralph found the schiedam so excellent that he called for a second glass of it.

It had hardly been placed before him when a general bustle among the waiters, and a movement on the part of the company, heralded the arrival of some one, evidently an important personage in the town of Paramaribo.

A big, black servant placed an easy-chair by the side of the open window, and then a little stout person, with cheeks of a purple hue, and of a fatness which might make many a full-grown porker blush, entered.

In this pompous individual Ralph easily and readily recognised the magistrate with whom he had had an interview the previous day.

Everybody in the room bowed low when the illustrious Mynheer Stoutbragurt entered, and it was a sight worth seeing to behold the condescending manner in which the magnate of the law and the excise seated himself in his chair of state and gravely filled his pipe, while the officious waiter stood by, light in hand, awaiting the magistrate's pleasure.

Then the puffs of smoke began to arise and curl round the rubicund features of the law-giver, who, after unbuttoning his shirt collar, gave himself up for some minutes to reflection.

At length the voice of the oracle was heard.

"Mynheer Runtwick, has your good vrow got safely over her trouble yet?"

"Yah, mynheer," replied the individual addressed. "Two as fine boys as ever father clapped eyes on."

"Two!" ejaculated the magistrate, swallowing a mouthful of smoke in his hurry and surprise. "Beware, my dear sir, how you impoverish the state by thus rapidly increasing the population; but, at the same time, be careful and have them both duly registered within the period assigned by law."

After delivering this long speech, the Mynheer Stoutbragurt coughed in a vehement manner, and called for another glass of schiedam.

"Have your officers captured the prisoners yet, mynheer?" at length said one, more bold than the rest.

Mynheer Stoutbragurt cast a long look at the inquirer, took three long pulls at his pipe, and fixed his eyes intently on the ceiling ere he replied,

"They have—all save one."

"A very strange affair," said another of the company.

The worthy magistrate nodded in reply.

"But," continued the last speaker, "I hear the captain of this strange ship which has just entered the port under pretence of repairs has had something to do with the matter?"

"Yah!" said Mynheer Stoutbragurt, slowly puffing the smoke from his capacious mouth.

"Do you know, though, who this stranger is," continued the talkative man, "this pretended Englishman?"

"Nein," said Stoutbragurt.

"Then I will tell you," continued the man, who loved his own voice.

Mynheer looked as though he did not much care to hear; but the other edged his chair nearer to that in which the worthy magistrate was seated, and exclaimed in a whisper that could be heard by every one,

"He is a pirate!"

Of course Ralph's ears were wide open at hearing this announcement, and he reflected a moment on the best means of escape in case his enemies should be too numerous.

THE CONFESSION.

A fat, greasy chuckle from the throat of the magistrate reassured him.

"You fool!" said he. "Do you think any pirate would dare set his foot on this shore while I am magistrate?"

No answer was returned.

"What pirate do you think he is, blockhead?" demanded Stoutbragurt.

"Why one who went by the name of Black Ralph."

"If any pirate dared come within a hundred miles of this spot," said the magistrate, "I'd take him by the collar and put him along with those negroes."

CHAPTER CCXCVIII.

THE ISLAND OF CAVES—HARWOLF IN A TRAP—
HIDE AND SEEK—A PIRATE'S TRICK—THE
COMBAT, AND ITS RESULTS.

ABOUT two degrees, or, in other words, nearly one hundred and forty miles to the northward of the island of St. Domingo, is a little group of islands generally called the Cayques.

These islands are uninhabited at the present time, but in the days of Captain Kidd, Blackbeard, and

No. 86.

other notables, who infested those seas, they were much resorted to by the gentlemen who made piracy their trade.

And they were well adapted to become the homes of lawless men, being surrounded with reefs and shoals, which afforded them protection from their larger pursuers, while few pilots, save the buccaneers, knew the passages through this dangerous and intricate navigation.

The largest of this group forms a curve like a horse shoe towards the south, with a safe and good anchorage when once in the bay; but before reaching this harbour, it is necessary to conduct a vessel through the reefs for a distance of forty miles, by a very difficult and intricate passage.

The islands themselves, and the principal of the group in particular, are composed of coral, between the rocky interstices of which sufficient earth had accumulated to allow a few cocoa-nut trees to take root, while a scanty and stunted brushwood rose up in other spots.

But the chief peculiarity of the island, and that which rendered it such a convenient dwelling-place for lawless freebooters, was the numerous caves with which the rock was perforated, some above high water mark, but the majority of them with the sea water rushing in and out of them, in some cases merely entering at high water and leaving pools behind when the tide receded, while others at all times had quite sufficient depth of water at their mouths to allow a large boat to enter freely.

It was for this island that Daniel Harwolf steered after so successfully eluding the schooner and frigate. The men had demanded that he should take them to some place where their presence would not be expected, and having once before visited the Cayques, he bethought himself to turn his ship's course thither.

But he did not reach the island so soon as he had expected, for again the "Revenge" was chased by an English frigate, the captain of which, having unsuccessfully followed a Portuguese slaver for a couple of thousand miles, was in a particularly angry and pertinacious humour.

Harwolf, indeed, had a very narrow escape, for the frigate followed him three days before a brisk wind, when, just as he was congratulating himself on having left the new pursuer astern, the wind became light, shifted a couple of points, and subsided into a calm.

The boats of the frigate were then hoisted out to board the "Revenge" when again the fickle wind began to blow, and the fact of the pirate being to windward, together with the change of course, enabled them to leave the enemy far behind.

The scarcity of water was an evil which they now felt, and as there was not a sufficient supply to last till they reached the island, although the crew had been placed on half allowance, they were obliged to make for a little rocky isle, where was a spring, in order to obtain sufficient.

That done, they again made sail, but were so impeded by contrary winds and currents, that it was not till a fortnight after they were chased by the second frigate, that the Cayques islands greeted their sight.

Harwolf alone, of all the pirate crew, knew the narrow and intricate track leading to the anchorage, the slightest deviation from which would be the ship's destruction.

At the wheel, therefore, he stationed himself, while the crew at their various posts were in readiness at his word to assist by trimming and altering the disposition of the sails.

An anxious time it was for all, for the waves beat high over submerged rocks on each side; while others, more deeply sunk in the water, but all the more dangerous on that account, gave no sign of their presence.

The danger, however, was safely passed, and with a sigh of relief the pirate captain surrendered the helm to one of his crew, while stepping forward he gave orders to clew up the sails and drop anchor.

His commands were obeyed, and in a few minutes, the gallant ship was motionless on the surface of the blue mirror-like water.

By the time they had safely reached their anchoring ground it was almost night, and after carefully surveying the horizon with his glass, Harwolf retired to rest, and most of his crew did the same.

Very lax was the watch kept that night on the deck of the "Revenge;" the men were weary with long protracted toil and want of sleep, and though a portion of the crew went through the form of remaining on deck, it may be most emphatically said they did not keep a look out: in man-of-wars' language, they "caulked it," i. e. curled themselves up in corners, dozing when they should have been watching.

A surprise awaited them in the morning, for, at the first glimpse of day, the officer in charge glancing out to sea, discerned the topsails of a ship, which appeared to be carefully threading its way through the narrow channel.

Hastily running aloft, the man surveyed the stranger from his more elevated position.

No stranger either, though the look out rubbed first his eyes and then the glasses of his telescope in his anxiety to convince himself that he was not still dreaming.

There could be no mistake about it; it was the schooner which had first chased them off the African coast.

Descending as hastily as he had ascended, he darted into the captain's cabin.

Harwolf was in a half-sleeping, half-waking state when his subaltern entered.

Hastily starting up, however, he snatched his sword.

"What the devil is the matter?" he asked, in husky tones.

"Captain, there's a ship away in the channel."

"Then let her alone; she'll be certain to go on the rocks and go to pieces.

"She seems to be sounding her way through."

"The devil!"

"And, captain, it's none other than that d——d schooner."

"You lie!"

"It's true, as I'm a living man. Come and look, if you don't believe me; anybody who saw her once would know her amongst a thousand."

"A thousand infernal fire-ships burn the cursed craft!" exclaimed the captain of the pirates, turning pale with rage and fear.

But, nevertheless, he hastily dressed himself, and hurried on deck, where he found that his lieutenant had indeed spoken the truth.

"Well, captain, what do you think of this?" asked Walbrook.

"We're in an infernal pretty pickle; there is no way of getting out of this cul-de-sac," replied Harwolf.

The lieutenant looked blue as his own jacket at this piece of news.

"But what's to be done, captain?"

"Wait a bit, and, in the mean time, prepare all hands for action."

"That's all right; but, captain, I'd better keep the men out of sight as much as possible?"

"Certainly; never show the enemy our strength, and run a couple of those guns over this side."

He walked impatiently up and down the deck, while his commands were being executed.

"After all, it may not come to a fight," he said.

"Don't think that fellow means to go off afore he's overhauled us," replied Walbrook.

"He may get on the rocks, and then why, instead of being captured, we shall be able to make a pretty picking amongst his timbers."

"But look, he's got a couple of boats out sounding. He picks his road like a lady in a muddy street."

"Oh! for an hour of the fiercest gale that ever blew! We could ride it out well enough, but that fellow would be smashed into splinters."

The schooner was by this time about ten miles distant from the harbour in which the pirate ship was anchored.

Harwolf walked up and down in an excited manner, revolving in his mind scheme after scheme, but he could not concoct one that seemed to promise success.

"Walbrook, how many men do we muster altogether?"

"Twenty."

"And that schooner has——"

"Fifty at the least, and able men, too; they don't put any hospital sailors on board these special service ships."

"And how about his guns?"

"Why, you know, he's got a long twenty-four; ours is only an eighteen-pounder; the other metal is about equal, I guess."

"Blast him! he has every advantage. With his crew he could fire two shots to our one, and have plenty of men behind in reserve."

"What's to be done, then?"

"I don't know, curse me if I do, unless we leave the ship and take to the boats."

"Where should we go?"

"I don't know, d——n it! as if I hadn't enough to think about without your everlastingly bothering me."

"Well, captain, whatever you do, take my advice,

and don't show the white feather before these fellows, or else they'll surrender without even showing fight."

"Leave me alone a little while. I want to think."

Walbrook left his chief standing by the capstan buried in deep thought; and, in order to keep up appearances, bustled about as if preparing for a desperate action.

The schooner mean time advanced slowly, and was still eight miles from the "Revenge."

Harwolf kept his eye on the coming foe, and a sudden thought entered his head which filled his heart with hope as he once more dreamed of safety.

"Here, Walbrook," he cried.

In a moment the lieutenant was by his side.

"Just take another look at the schooner; she is not moving."

"No, by G—d! they are fast on the rocks," replied the man addressed.

Such, however, was not the case. The commander of the war ship, finding the passage so intricate and beset with rocks, had dropped his anchor, and proposed to attack the "Revenge" with his boats.

In fact, within ten minutes after Harwolf spoke, they were seen to prepare for the task of the assault.

"A thought strikes me, Walbrook," cried Harwolf.

"Then give it vent, my noble captain."

"They must have forty men in those four boats?"

"Yes, or more."

"And, consequently, can't have more than ten or a dozen left on board. Now, what I mean to do is this. Put all our men into the boats, well armed, of course; and then knock a big hole right through our ship's bottom, and make for the island."

"I see; and pepper their boats from behind the rocks?"

"Nothing of the kind, you fool. It's high tide nearly, and will be quite by the time they reach the shore. I mean to hide in one of the caves; they will be sure to land to capture us, and while they are hunting about all over the island, we'll row off and board the schooner, which is quite as good a vessel as the 'Revenge,' and better armed."

"Bravo! good idea."

"Then see about it at once."

Walbrook bustled forward, and in a few minutes had the boats launched. All the men were assembled on the deck, though the nature of the stratagem which Harwolf was about to put in execution was known only to two beside themselves—the two carpenters. Arms and ammunition were supplied in abundance, a light carronade was placed in the bows of the largest boat, and the men all embarked save the four above mentioned.

Harwolf did not deem it expedient to let the crew know that the "Revenge" was to be deserted until it was too late to save her.

Descending, therefore, with the two carpenters to the hold, a few minutes sufficed to do such damage to the ship that it was impossible she could remain more than an hour above water.

Then hastily entering the boat, they pulled towards the shore, taking care to keep the hulk of the "Revenge" between them and the schooner's boats, so that their movements might not be perceived.

Harwolf, who, as before stated, was acquainted with the island, pulled towards a cave which was always full, no matter what the state of the tide, though at high water the mouths—for there were two entrances—were such narrow openings and so hidden by masses of rock, that a man might pass by within two yards without being aware of the existence of any such hiding-place.

Within was a lofty vaulted roof, enclosing a pool of water, in which a line of battle ship might float at ease and safety.

A faint light glimmered through a crevice near the mouth of the cave, and ranging his boats one on each side of each entrance, Harwolf, by means of some rude steps, clambered up to this orifice, which was in the face of a perpendicular rock, and commanded a full view of the harbour and offing.

From the look out he could plainly see the schooner's boats advancing, the bright oar blades flashing in the sun.

They reached within half a mile of the "Revenge" and then a puff of smoke was seen to issue from the bows of the foremost boat, a shower of splinters flew up from the deck of the "Revenge," while the report of a carronade reached the ears of the pirates.

"Ha! Ha!" laughed Harwolf, "let them fire away, the old 'Revenge' will not answer."

The boats advanced a hundred yards nearer, then halted while another shot was fired.

Finding the enemy did not reply, like true British seamen, they bent again to their oars with hearty good will, and in a short time reached the pirate vessel.

Two boats' crews leaped on the deck with a cheer, but instant silence succeeded when they found that the birds were flown.

Cautiously they peered down the hatchway lest some surprise should be intended, but all was quiet save the movements of their own feet.

"They must be on the island!" cried the officer in command. "Follow, my lads! Stay, though," he continued, "we must provide against their return."

And twelve men were detailed to remain in charge of the prize.

The remainder regained their boats, and pulled towards the island.

At length they leaped on shore, and Harwolf, whispering his men to be still and quiet, continued his observations.

Though they landed within thirty feet of the mouth of the cave and not much further from the spot where Harwolf stood, the pirates' hiding-place escaped their observation.

Their conversation could be heard.

"They must be hidden somewhere amongst these caves," said a young man, wearing the uniform of a lieutenant.

"Or, perhaps, amongst those bushes higher up. It's a steep rock, and resolute men could make a desperate defence there," replied the midshipman addressed.

"Well, you take half the men and search round that side well as far as you can see. I will go along this side of the island, and we'll meet at the top of the hill in half an hour's time."

"And in case I find the rascals?"

"Summon them to surrender. If they refuse, I suppose you know what to do?"

"Certainly, sir."

"Away with you, then. If I hear any firing, I'll be with you."

The two parties separated and proceeded on their search; the one commanded by the lieutenant passing scarcely two yards over Harwolf's head.

When they had proceeded as nearly as the pirate captain could guess about half a mile from their landing place, and were, therefore, a mile from each other, Harwolf gave the word and his boats rowed swiftly and silently from under the natural archway where they had been concealed.

The boats of the schooner were lying on the beach unguarded, and a new thought entered Harwolf's fertile brain, which he at once hastened to put in practice.

Rowing towards them it took but a few minutes to tow them all out into the middle of the bay, so that the pirate hunters were on shore without the means of quitting.

The men who had been left on the deck of the prize at once saw and comprehended this trick, though, so listless had they been, that they had not noticed the rapidity with which the "Revenge" was settling down into the water.

But when they saw their comrades' boats thus taken away and sunk, they at once loaded a gun and fired at the advancing horde of pirates.

It was the last shot ever fired on the deck of the "Revenge," for the concussion of the heavy gun shook the damaged planks at the bottom of the vessel to such an extent that the timbers started from their places. An overpowering torrent of water rushed into the ill-fated vessel and the men on board had barely time to throw themselves into the sea before the ill-fated clipper toppled over to starboard, and then plunged head foremost in to the bosom of the blue waves.

The report of the gun called the attention of those on shore; but when they saw their prize disappear beneath the waves they at once comprehended the whole. The lieutenant and temporary commander of the schooner cursed and raved and tore his hair as he saw the pirates row past the spot where their vessel had sunk, and, with loud derisive cheers, thrust those of his men who were swimming, beneath the water with their oars and boat-hooks.

A man—a young man—begged earnestly of the pirate captain to save him from the sharks.

"Tell me exactly how many men there are on board your schooner?" said Harwolf.

"Ten and a midshipman."

"You are not telling me the truth, you rascal."

"I am—I swear I am!" replied the poor drowning wretch.

"Then give us your hand."

The man stretched out his hand, which Harwolf grasped, and was already half way over the gunwale of the boat.

Then the pirate's cutlass glittered in the bright sun, and the poor sailor slipped back into the water, his skull split open and his brains dashed to atoms by the force of the blow.

Dead! but the dead man's grip was strong, the fixed fingers clung to Harwolf's wrist, and, as he stood up in the boat to release himself, those fixed eyeballs glared at him, and he thought that their expression was changed from a look of earnest entreaty to undying hate and enmity.

"Cut it off! cut it off!" he cried, pointing to the dead man's hand.

But ere the order could be obeyed the ghastly corpse relaxed its hold, and sank down into the deep water.

Wiping the drops of perspiration from his face, the pirate captain took a draught of brandy from a flask with which he had taken care to provide himself ere he left the cabin of the "Revenge," and then continued his course towards the schooner.

The lieutenant and men on shore watched the proceedings of the pirates, as may be supposed, with anxiety.

The unfortunate officer could only hope that the midshipman in charge would raise the anchor, and stand out at sea.

But this was not done, as the men on board knew not how to steer through the passage.

They, however, saw the pirates advancing, and prepared for a most vigorous defence.

Guns were loaded with grape and canister, small arms were served out, and cutlasses buckled on.

Nearer and nearer drew the pirates, and the long gun on the deck of the schooner was discharged at the boats.

The ball whistled through the air, striking off the head of one man in the stern of the second boat, and plumping into the sea close by the side of the third.

"Pull, my lads, pull; let's get to close quarters," shouted Harwolf.

The men bent their broad backs and the boats dashed through the waves rapidly.

Another puff of smoke enveloped the schooner, and a hail of grape-shot agitated the surface of the water.

A moment the men in the boats ceased their labours, but the next moment they were again on their way though two of their number breathed no more.

Again the guns of the schooner belched forth a cloud of smoke, and two more of their crew had pulled their last stroke.

A dense white sulphurous cloud now hung about the decks of the schooner obscuring the view, nor did the bold sailors again catch sight of their foes

till, with a loud shout, the bearded pirates dashed up the vessel's side.

The bold tars answered their enemies' shouts, and returned their blows lustily.

Harwolf found himself actively engaged with the middy, a tall, active youth, who, while he gave the pirate captain no small amount of trouble and anxiety, encouraged his men by his voice to resist the treacherous foe to the utmost.

"No quarter!" he shouted. "Death to the pirates! Down with the rascals!"

"No quarter!" cried Walbrook, from behind, as he plunged his cutlass into the gallant youth's back.

The brave boy fell to the deck, and uttering a cheer, vented his last breath.

"On, my lads, on! The ship is ours!" cried Harwolf.

"Not if I knows it, you rascal!" cried the hoarse voice of a grizzle-haired boatswain's mate, as he discharged his pistol full in Harwolf's face.

The pirate could scarcely repress the cry which rose to his lips as the ball ploughed its way along his cheek like the searing of a hot iron.

"Down with you!" cried Walbrook, who kept close at his captain's elbow; and with the words he plunged his reeking cutlass into the old sailor's heart.

Of the eleven men who had been left in charge of the schooner only three kept their ground. Their bold comrades were dead, or too severely wounded to take part in the combat.

But with their backs to the mast these three defied the pirates, and still maintained the fight.

Of the pirates five had been killed in the boats and six of them lay on the schooner's deck.

Nine of them still remained, and in a close body they hurled themselves at the devoted little group.

They fell; and the ship was in the hands of the pirates.

CHAPTER CCXCIX.

A NIGHT-SCENE, IN WHICH A DEVIL APPEARS—LORD HAWKSBURY TO THE RESCUE—LADY HAUTAINE AT HOME—THE INTERRUPTION—AN ADDRESS WANTED.

THOSE who have wandered through the squares and streets of the western portion of the metropolis during the hours when simple, sober-minded people of the lower classes are eating their suppers—if they have any—and thinking of retiring to bed, have no doubt witnessed at the above-named hours, that is, from nine in the evening upwards, long lines of carriages setting down their loads of handsomely-dressed ladies and gentlemen at the door of an elegant mansion.

"Coming home from a spree, and going to bed," thinks the country cousin, who knows nothing of London life, manners, and customs.

No such thing, Cousin Green; in the opinion of those "curled darlings of the nation" the evening has hardly yet begun, their *spree* is to come, if spree it can be called, to stand for some hours in the midst of a hot, densely-crowded room, amongst a lot of people who will think you ill-bred and unmannerly if you cough or sneeze, or necessity compels you to blow your nose.

However, as these fashionable assemblies are kept up, and people resort to all kinds of dodges to obtain an invitation, we suppose there must be a certain amount of pleasure enjoyed by those who participate therein.

On the evening of the day after Lord Hawksbury's interview with "Messrs. Tape and Pounce, solicitors" (as represented by Mr. Pounce), such an assemblage of carriages rolled up to the door of an imposing mansion situated in Ossulton Square, Mayfair, the town residence of Lady Hautaine.

Lady Hautaine was "at home" that evening, and as that was rather an unusual circumstance, only occurring once a fortnight, her friends and acquaintance, as well as many ladies and gentlemen who were neither one nor the other, flocked together to see how her ladyship looked in her own saloons.

Outside quite a little crowd of the "lower orders" had gathered together to watch the proceedings, and speculate upon the probable cost of the rich dresses which *half* covered the forms of the fair ladies, dresses which represented, and had cost, more than some in that lowly fustian and moleskin clad group could earn by a twelve months' hard and constant labour.

Some of them murmured a little, and gave utterance to the bitter thoughts that filled their minds. Who can wonder? for bread is not to be obtained at all times, and the constant clamour of hungry children makes many an honest man's heart sore as he hears their cry, but is unable to appease their wants. One twentieth part of the value of the costly jewel that sparkles in yon lady's ear (why don't they ring their noses?) would make many a one happy, for would it not procure little Jane a new frock, get Bob's boots, and the new shawl which he promised the missis long ago, and pay the fortnight's rent for which the landlord has been dunning for these three days past, as well as release the best blanket from the pawnbroker?

But they sigh in vain, for they don't belong to any institution, and those ladies, as a rule, don't care to give charity unless they can see it advertised in the "Times" next day.

Of course there were plenty of boys in the crowd —regular London boys, full of fun and frolic, and they were very critical in their remarks and opinions.

The most prominent of the group was a young gentleman in his shirt-sleeves, whose smutty face was surmounted by a paper cap, the inky marks on which told the acute observer that the wearer was a regular devil—printer's devil, I mean.

From an airy and elevated position on the summit of a lamp-post this modern Mercury viewed the proceedings, and edified his more lowly companions with remarks original and select.

"Hooray! 'ere's the queen a-coming," shouted a small boy on the pavement as a very stout lady alighted from a carriage, on the panel of which a coronet was emblazoned.

"Wot a crammer!" responded the elevated devil. "You'd better keep yer tater-trap shut, young man, I know it's only one o' the beef-eaters in masquerade costoom."

A loud laugh burst from many a juvenile throat as the lady swept into the hall.

"'Ere's the King o' the Cannibal Islands! Holler boys!" shouted the impudent youngster, as a gorgeously attired Parsee merchant alighted from his carriage.

The boys did "holler," and the misguided Oriental, thinking that the lads were paying him homage, turned round, and, placing his hand on his heart, gravely salaamed three several times ere his English servant could induce him to enter the house.

A distinguished foreigner, whose name is well known in connection with Italy and freedom, was the next to run the gauntlet.

"Three cheers for the Hemperor of Rushiar!" cried Mercury, and the cheers were given, though nothing could have been more distasteful to the patriot than to be thus, as he imagined, mistaken for the aristocrat of the north.

Then came a distinguished statesman — if any member of the Conservative school of politics can be said to be distinguished.

"Ah, ma tear," said the young printer, mimicing the pronunciation affected by the Israelites, "got a goot vatsh to shell, Moshes? Vat'll yer bid for ma ole clo?"

"This is unbearable," muttered the statesman, "Where are the police?"

"Here, sir," replied an officer, coming forward, and touching his hat.

"I wish you would bring that rude boy down from the lamp-post, and give him a good thrashing."

As he spoke the words, he slipped five shillings into the policeman's hand.

"Mustn't thrash him, sir; lock the young rascal up if you like."

"Do what you like, but don't allow him to remain there, and annoy people."

The officer looked up at the lad, as the political gentleman disappeared.

"Now, then, young shaver, I'll just trouble you to come down out of that."

"Werry much obliged," responded the young shaver, "but I'm quite comfortable where I am."

"You'd better come down."

"Opinions differs, sometimes, yer know well enough, or else cookey 'ud stick to yer, instead of havin' the sojer in to tea on Sunday nights."

"If you don't come down, I'll give you such a hiding, my young gentleman."

"Shame! Shame! Let the boy alone," said several.

"What's the matter? What's the matter?" cried Lord Hawksbury, whose cab drew up at the door at that moment.

"Why, it's bribery an' corruption, an' stoppin' the liberty o' the press," responded he on the lamp-post.

"I don't understand you, my boy; explain yourself."

"Why a hold cove 'as just give the peeler a tanner to quod me."

"You may as well let the boy stay where he is, and enjoy himself," said his lordship, slipping a coin into the policeman's hand.

The officer touched his hat, and walked a few yards off, while Lord Hawksbury darted up the steps into the mansion.

With the reader's kind permission we will follow him.

In a long, lofty, brilliantly-lighted room, were all the rank and fashion of London assembled, staring at each other, or conversing in little groups.

Through all these Lord Hawksbury elbowed his way towards the upper end of the room, to pay his respects to Lady Hautaine.

This little ceremony over, he had time to look about him, and being, as the reader knows, a single man, was immediately pounced upon by a coterie of mammas, all of whom had eligible daughters for disposal.

But among these ladies his lordship tarried not long, nor did he ever cast more than a courteous glance on the fair maids themselves, though their faces were wreathed with smiles.

"Have you seen young Ponsonby?" he inquired, of an aristocratic-looking young man who had sought in vain the very society from which Lord Hawksbury had just quitted.

But the young man was a younger son, and those thoughtful mothers would not encourage the advances of a clever but poor peer, whose principal income was derived from his diplomatic appointment.

So the young viscount's accents were sorrowful and his mien sad, as he answered,

"What, Ponsonby of the guards? Yes, I saw him about ten minutes ago, with a dooced pretty girl on his arm. Ah, lucky dog!"

"Where is he now?"

"Now, my dear friend, you ask a question which I cannot answer. But, I suppose, he is somewhere in the house, unless he has bolted off to Gretna Green by the mail train."

Finding there was no information to be abstracted from the embryo embassador, Lord Hawksbury left him lamenting his hard fate and envying the happy Ponsonby, who, though only an ensign and a thorough muff, had six thousand a year, and was permitted to pick and choose amongst a bevy of belles.

At length, after a lengthened search, Lord Hawksbury found the young guardsman in full uniform, sitting with his chosen fair one in a recess where they were screened from observation by a mass of heavy drapery which fell from the richly gilded cornice above.

Advancing, Lord Hawksbury laid his hand on the shoulder of the youth, who at once started to his feet.

"Who's that?" he cried.

"I," replied Lord Hawksbury, showing himself.

"And what can I have the honour of doing for you?" asked the ensign, glancing at his interrupter.

"I want just five minutes conversation with you. Come. Pardon me, madam, but I have something important to say to Mr. Ponsonby."

"What the dooce is the matter?" asked the ensign, when they were beyond hearing.

"The matter is that your father's bank will never open again; it's utterly smashed."

The young man gazed in Lord Hawksbury's face with a stupefied air for a moment.

"No, you're joking, now!" he said, at length.

"I saw your father but half an hour ago. He was my informant, and requested me to ask you to go to him at once."

"But he lives in Wussell Square. Where the dooce is that?"

"Take a cab, my boy, and the driver will drive you there in less time than it would take me to make you understand."

"Then, I'm off," muttered the youth, as he moved towards the door.

"What, without one word of adieu to Miss Hautaine?"

"Yes; there's no need that she should know anything about it at present, so pray don't split."

"No fear, though I dare say I shall be in her company all the time I remain here. Farewell, if you are really going."

The youth moved off, and Lord Hawksbury returned to the place where he had left the lady, a daughter of the noble hostess.

Seating himself, with a bow, in the chair which the young guardsman had just vacated, he said,

"I am glad of an opportunity to say a few words with you in private, Miss Hautaine, for you have it in your power to do me an important favour."

"Consider the favour granted, my lord, for I shall only be too happy to oblige you. What is it, to accompany you to the review to-morrow?"

"Not so; a young soldier would be a much more fit companion for you, so, therefore, I will not deprive poor Ponsonby of the pleasure he anticipates."

"But what have you done with Mr. Ponsonby?"

"I brought him a message from his father, who wishes to see him at once."

"Is his father ill, then?"

"I fear very."

"I am sorry, indeed. But what is this favour you require of me, my lord?"

"I want you to give me the address of a young lady, who, I believe, does embroidery and other fancy work for you."

"A lady? Well, there is a young *person* who does such work for us sometimes. You mean——"

"Yes, I believe I recommended her to your notice."

"May be; I really don't recollect. But mamma will be able to tell you where she lives; I haven't the least idea."

"Then I will seek Lady Hautaine, and get the information from her if I can."

And with these words Lord Hawksbury rose, bowed, and walked away, much to the chagrin of the young lady, who had promised herself a nice quiet flirtation with the nobleman during the ensign's absence.

He found Lady Hautaine in the midst of a circle of admiring dowagers discussing the present state of the matrimonial market, which, in the opinion of most of them, was decidedly flat.

Of course such a peculiarly feminine topic was immediately dropped when the noble lord pushed rather hastily amongst them.

"Can I have a word with you, Lady Hautaine?" asked he.

"Yes, certainly. Why, gracious, what is the matter? You are actually impatient about something, I can tell by your manner."

"I wish you would be so kind as to tell me the address of a young person who does needlework for you. I mean——"

"My lord, I shall do nothing of the kind, and I should have thought you would have known better than to ask such an exceedingly indelicate question before the Countess of Baden-Baden and the Hon. Mrs. Robinson."

"I am very sorry indeed to have offended your ladyship, but I did not for a moment think the question would be considered indelicate. I am sure if you knew my motives you would not think so."

"I know not what your motives may be, but I think you should have more tact than to ask me to assist you in getting up an intrigue with a low needlewoman, and in the presence of the Countess of Baden-Baden and the——"

"Countess be ——!"

Lord Hawksbury was about to use strong language, such as is not generally used in the society of ladies, but he checked himself in time.

"Lady Hautaine, I am sorry you will not give me the information I require, since it compels me to seek it otherwise than in your very agreeable society. I have the honour to leave you now."

"*Au revoir*, my lord."

Indignant at the aspersions which had been thrown on him by Lady Hautaine, Lord Hawksbury was about to leave the house, when a thought struck him he might yet obtain the address of her he sought within the walls of Lady Hautaine's mansion.

Pausing in the hall, he beckoned one of the gorgeously-attired flunkeys towards him, and, slipping half a sovereign in his hand, bade him summon the housekeeper.

Jeames departed with a grin on his face, and a minute afterwards Mrs. Keyes made her appearance.

Briefly Lord Hawsbury told her why he had summoned her, and begged of her to give the required address.

"I really don't know where she lives, but I recollect the girl well—a pretty and well-behaved girl. I dare say, however, Miss Boddice, the lady's-maid, knows though, she had more to do with the girl than I."

"Then haste and call her, for I am in a hurry."

"Yes, my lord. But I hope your lordship doesn't mean any harm or mischief to the poor girl, for I think she is very respectable."

"Confound the women, they are all alike," muttered the young nobleman. "I mean her no harm, so haste and give me the address."

The good lady departed, and shortly returned with a slip of paper on which was written—

> JESSIE VERE,
> 6, Arabella Row,
> Cheyne Walk,
> Chelsea.

CHAPTER CCC.

ZAMPA IS SENTENCED TO BE HANGED—HE IS LIBERATED BY THE STRATEGY OF WARELAW—BLACK RALPH PUNISHES THE MAGISTRATE.

So Zampa remained all night in the prison cells of the court-house of Paramaribo, while Black Ralph, after listening awhile to the impotent threats of Mynheer Stoutbragurt, departed to the waterside and summoned his two new coadjutors, Ramsey and

Wardlaw, to counsel concerning the best means of procuring the black man's release.

"We had best go up to the court-house in the morning, and prove that he is one of my crew," said Ralph.

"A note to the British consul would probably be very effective," suggested Wardlaw.

"If I dared—but, to tell you the truth, I don't care about too many inquiries into the history of my vessel, though my papers are all right. I heard some of the fat paunches this evening whispering my name."

"Supposing he should be condemned?"

"Then we'll rescue him to-morrow night, if I have to burn the prison and the town to boot."

"We'll try stratagem, though, first, if you have no objection."

"I have no objection, in fact I should feel excessively grateful if you could plan some dodge in your dreams to-night."

"I'll try, though as I don't know the position of the court-house, I can hardly arrange the details of this cruise on shore. But good night, captain, I will turn in now."

They separated and turned in as proposed, after Black Ralph had first been on deck and exhorted the officer in charge to keep vigilant watch.

Morning came, and the three friends made their way to the court.

The trial was short, in fact, Mynheer Stoutbragurt seemed rather disgusted at having to try a lot of negroes at all. Why not punish them at once?

Those who had been recaptured, and Zampa along with them, were sentenced to be hanged the next morning.

Poor Zampa rolled his eyes piteously as he heard the sentence, but happening to catch sight of Black Ralph, who placed his finger by the side of his nose, he became more composed.

They were all led back to prison, while the three officers, after loitering about some time, and surveying the building and adjacent streets, departed.

A large gallows was erected in the centre of the public square, long ere dark, and the honest burghers retired to their beds in the full conviction that an edifying spectacle awaited them on the morrow.

But they were doomed to disappointment, as will be seen.

"Let me look at your medicine chest," said Wardlaw, when they were once more on board the "Defiance."

Ralph Talbot unlocked a side-board, and brought forth a tolerably large-sized chest, the key of which he handed to Wardlaw.

Carefully examining all the numerous phials arranged therein, the last-named officer selected one which he placed in his waistcoat pocket.

"Why," said Ralph, "surely you don't mean to go into the Borgia line of business, Wardlaw, and poison the whole province?"

"Not at all, though this phial contains the material for such a plan if it existed."

"I should not like that; but, however, I trust to you, so while you are culling your simples I'll go on deck for a few minutes so that all the responsibility may be off my shoulders."

"Don't be alarmed, I have all I want," replied Wardlaw.

"Then I'll return. Do you know, Wardlaw, that though I'd pass my sword through a dozen of their fat carcases without hesitation, I couldn't sleep for a month if I thought I had a hand in poisoning any one."

"But I'm not going to poison any one, Captain Ralph."

"Then pass the bottle, and let me get such thoughts out of my head—the whiskey bottle, I mean."

Ralph filled his glass, and the subject changed.

About midnight three figures might have been seen cautiously wending their way along a footpath which flanked the palisades of the fort and leads direct to the court-house.

Underneath the cloaks which enveloped their figures were seen pistols and swords. The leader—a tall man, with a black beard—carried a heavy stick in his hand, while one of the others wore thick woollen gloves. The whole party bore a suspicious resemblance to the three officers of the "Defiance," and the readers may as well know that it was indeed Black Ralph, Wardlaw and Ramsey.

Wardlaw being the gentleman from whose fertile brain the scheme proceeded, was really in command, though Ralph Talbot, with his usual impatience, took the lead.

The moon shone as she only shines between the tropics, and the party kept as much as possible in the shadow of the fence.

They arrived within sight of the court-house, and then paused awhile under the shadow of a tree.

Then came the heavy tramp of armed men. The sentry before the gateway challenged, and then the soldiers proceeded on their march.

"But how is this, Wardlaw?" said Ralph. "If we are to catch them sleeping surely we have come at the wrong time, for they are just relieving the sentries."

"Just as I wished it to be," replied Wardlaw. "We shall now have three good hours before us."

"Well, I don't yet understand. Pray explain."

A short whispered dialogue ensued, at the conclusion of which Black Ralph appeared perfectly satisfied with regard to Wardlaw's intentions.

Leaving his two companions under a tree, as soon as the patrol had passed the last-named officer stepped forward, and advanced towards the court-house, singing a merry song, and assuming the manner of a man three sheets in the wind.

The court-house, it must be understood, was fronted by a colonnade, from which steps ascended to the principal entrance, while beneath these steps was an archway leading to the prison cells in which Zampa was confined.

These cells were arranged on each side of a long passage, in which a sentry was always posted.

Advancing, then, with a careless gait, Wardlaw continued his singing.

The sentry, supposing him to be only a drunken sailor from one of the ships in the river, stood and looked at him with an air of amusement.

Pausing in front of the colonnade, the sailor took a flask from his pocket and raised it to his lips, the sentry watching this new movement more earnestly than ever.

"Have a drop?" said he, holding out the bottle towards the soldier.

The man looked carefully round, and, as no one was in sight, reached out his hand for the treat.

"Very goot," said the Dutchman, handing back the flask to its owner, after a deep draught.

"I believe you, my boy," replied Wardlaw. "Now, what do you say to a smoke?"

Of course such a proposal could but make the Dutchman's eyes glisten. He pulled out his pipe in anxious expectation.

"Smell that," cried Wardlaw, holding up a roll of tobacco in his gloved hand.

The sentry bent forward his head, and took a hearty sniff at the proffered weed.

"It's very goot," he murmured, and then had another smell.

Wardlaw leisurely filled his own pipe, keeping up a careless, nonsensical conversation the while.

Then handing the tobacco to the soldier, he struck a silent match and commenced smoking.

Before the sentry could follow his example, he felt drowsy, and, leaning his back against one of the pillars, became immediately insensible.

The gloves which Wardlaw wore on his hands were saturated with chloroform. The match with which Wardlaw lit his pipe was also a signal to his two companions to advance.

Their forms were seen gliding over the moonlit space, and in two minutes the sleeping sentry was bound and gagged.

"Good," cried Ralph, "Thus far into the bowels

of the land have we marched on without impediment."

"Silence!" cried Wardlaw. "Recollect that there is yet another foe to be overcome."

"Then on, bold warrior, and strike terror into the hearts of those Dutchmen."

Wardlaw crept cautiously round to the archway leading to the prison cells to ascertain the position of the second sentry.

He found the soldier walking carelessly up and down the passage, pipe in mouth, and with a bunch of keys dangling at his belt.

"Can you give me a light, soldier?" said the sailor, stepping forward. "Your comrade outside has not got one, but he allowed me to come in here and ask you."

The man was simple-minded and good-natured, as most of his countrymen are, and held the bowl of his pipe towards the tempter.

Wardlaw approached, and while in the act of lighting his own pipe managed to drop a little bit of opium into the bowl of that which the sentry was smoking, at the same time placing the gloved hand close to the man's face.

"Thanks," said he, when the task was completed, "I have a flask here which once contained Schiedam; try if your comrade has left any?"

The man nodded in reply; but was asleep ere Wardlaw could produce the flask from his pocket.

Disarming the second sentry, and laying him on his back, Wardlaw gently summoned his companions, who at once entered the archway.

"Bravo, Wardlaw!" cried Black Ralph. "You have, indeed, managed excellently!"

"But you must be quick and let us get away out of this place as soon as we can."

"All right; but how are we to open these doors? If we break them in the noise will certainly alarm the guard."

"Why here are the keys in the sentry's belt."

"Another success! Why it all works like a well-rehearsed melo-drama."

"We have no time for acting now, it must be action!"

"Then, thus I commence act the third of our drama!" replied Ralph, stooping down and removing the keys from the belt of the senseless sentry.

"Do you intend to release all the prisoners?" asked Ramsey.

"Every man; and if I should happen to see the worthy magistrate who was so valiant last night, why I'd clap him into one of the cells and lose the key."

So saying he approached the first door and fitted a key into the lock.

A thick darkness met his eyes, and it was only when Ramsey lighted a dark lantern with which they had provided themselves with, that he was able to discern the form of a huge negro stretched on the stone floor in a deep slumber.

Rousing the man with his foot, Ralph bade him depart quietly and go where he pleased.

Only too glad to obey, the poor fellow, who was really guiltless of the crime of which he was accused, started off at a rapid pace.

One after another the doors were opened and the prisoners released with a similar benediction.

Zampa was in the last cell, and his eyes glistened when he saw who it was who thus visited him in the dead of night.

"Bless you, Massa Ralph, I knowed you'd come," he said, in a low whisper.

"Zampa, you rascal, if ever you put me to such trouble again I'll take you back to the States, and sell you again."

"Hi! hi!" laughed the negro. "You wouldn't hurt poor Zamp no how, massa."

"Clear out, all you rascals, and make yourselves scarce," cried Ralph, addressing the men he had rescued, some of whom still lingered about the prison. "But stop, here's a dollar each for you. Now be off."

They instantly vanished, and the four rovers were alone with the sleeping sentinel.

"What shall we do with him?" asked Ramsey.

"Cut hims troat," suggested Zamp, remembering the aphorism that "dead men tell no tales."

"No, you rascal; we'll just lock the doors, give him back his keys, and leave him there."

"He will sleep for half an hour yet," said Wardlaw.

"Then by the time he awakes we shall be on board the 'Defiance.'"

So saying Ralph closed the cells, placed the keys in the sentry's belt, and, followed by his three friends, departed.

The soldier outside slept as soundly as he within, and after removing his bonds and the gag, they left him to finish his nap, shaping their course to that part of the river where the boat, in charge of two men, was waiting for them. Ten minutes afterwards they stood on the deck of the "Defiance."

The sentries finished their naps, shortly before it was time for them to be relieved, and suspected not that the prisoners were gone.

Early next morning quite a crowd might have been observed in the square and round the gallows, waiting for the sight of a party of their fellow men hanging by the neck. Strange it is that the most degrading and shameful sight can thus attract men professing to be Christians, and even draws them together in larger numbers than any other spectacle.

Presently a procession was seen advancing, consisting of the worthy Mynheer Stoutbragurt, and several other civil functionaries in their robes of state.

Bowing low to the assembled multitude, the pompous magistrate, in a loud tone of voice, ordered one of his officers to demand the bodies of the prisoners from those who had them in charge.

While the man was gone on his bootless errand, the good Mynheer made a short speech, in which he told the people that he hoped the sight they were about to see would be a lesson to them.

The shining bayonets of the soldiers were now seen glimmering in the morning sun as a party of them advanced from the court-house to the place of execution.

The face of Mynheer Stoutbragurt grew rather redder than usual with anger, as he perceived that the prisoners were not with them.

Could it be possible that the commandant of the garrison meant to dispute his authority? If such were the case, Mynheer Stoutbragurt told those near him in a whisper, he would hang the commandant and all his officers, as well as one out of every five of the private soldiers.

In a few minutes more the officer in command of the party was by the side of the magistrate, and to him communicated the astounding fact that the prisoners had escaped.

"Escaped! How?—where?—when?" roared the excited magistrate, who felt a certain amount of fear at hearing the news.

"No one knows," replied the officer. "They were safely locked up, and the keys never left the possession of the sentries."

"That's a lie!" said a deep, gruff voice in the crowd.

Both the magistrate and the officer looked hard to discover the speaker, but no one could tell whose lips had uttered those words.

"Escaped, have they? Then it must be the captain of that English ship who aided them. I'll hang him!"

"You will not," said the same strange voice, and Mynheer Stoutbragurt grew fairly pale with fear.

"Who spoke?" he asked.

There was no reply.

"Fellow citizens," said the magistrate, "the prisoners have escaped; though how no one knows. Return to your homes quietly and orderly."

Of course, being Dutchmen, they obeyed this order literally. Each man filled his pipe and departed, leaving such a cloud of smoke behind that the hideous instrument of death was, for a short time, quite obscured.

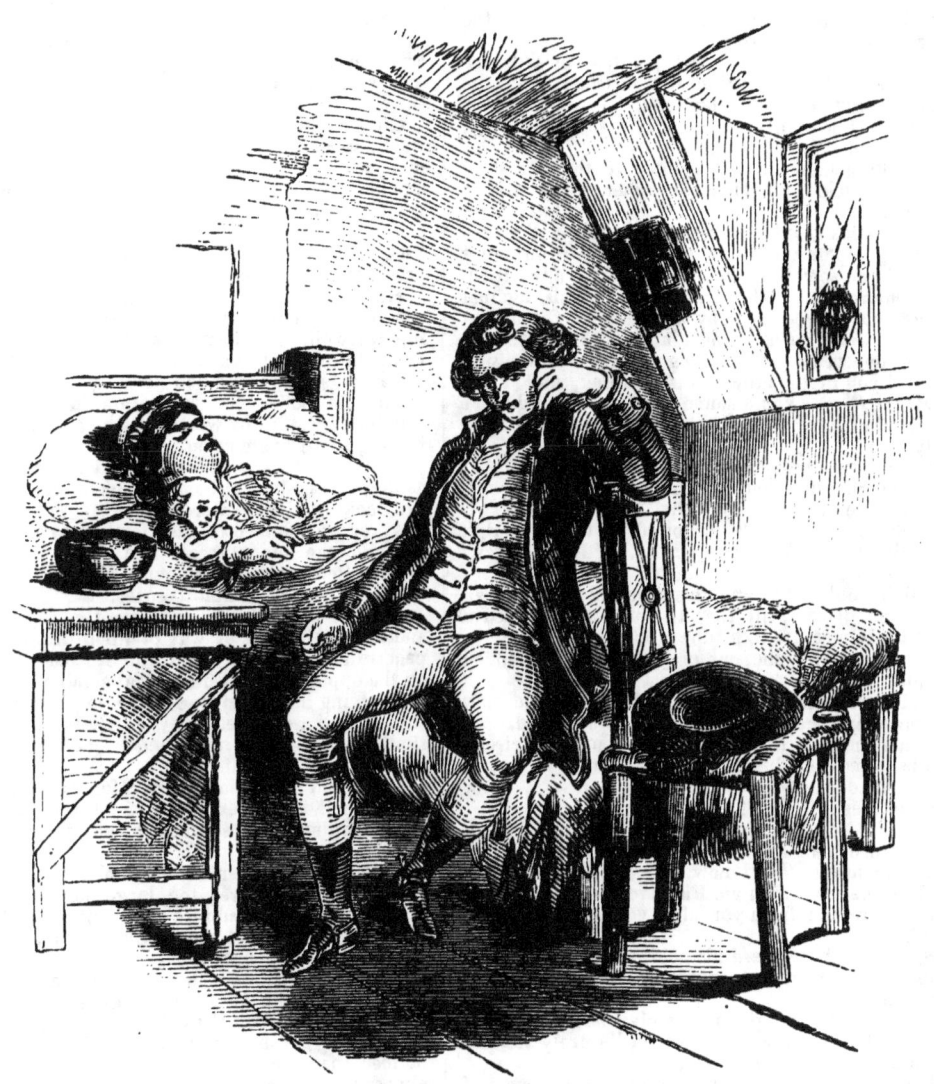

THE VISITOR.

The magistrate, too, hurried away to his private residence, which was some little distance from the town, mentally vowing never to leave it unless under the protection of a strong escort of soldiers.

By the time he had reached the outskirts of the town he had walked himself into a violent perspiration.

He paused a moment to wipe the heat drops from his brow ere he resumed his walk.

As he did so a man advanced towards him, and Mynheer Stoutbragurt saw, with considerable alarm, that it was the English captain whom he had but a short time before threatened to hang by the neck.

"Good morning, worshipful sir," said Black Ralph, raising his hat.

"Then he was not there?" thought the magistrate. "He doesn't know what I said."

And, summoning up a faint, sickly smile, he responded to the seaman's salutation.

"If you are going towards the town, mynheer, I will bear you company, for I wish to hear how those fellows met their fate, though I could not bear the idea of being present at their execution."

"They managed to escape," said the magistrate. "I wish I knew who helped them, I'd certainly swing him on the same gallows."

No. 87.

"Did your excellency never hear tell of a divining-rod ?"

"A what?"

"A divining-rod; that is, a stick cut under particular circumstances and in a particular manner, which will sometimes point out criminals and their aiders and abettors."

"I never heard of such a thing; but I wish I had one at the present moment."

"Then," replied Ralph, "as I learned the secret from a celebrated professor of the art, I will cut one from this hedge at once and present it to you."

So saying he selected a stout sapling of the thickness of his finger from a cluster of bushes, and with the thickest end traced a circle on the road, muttering to himself as he did so.

"But all this is witchcraft; it's illegal," cried the magistrate.

"It is not witchcraft, though I know not whether it is illegal," replied Ralph with a smile. "Stand in that circle while I proceed with the ceremony."

The magistrate obeyed, and Ralph Talbot trimmed the other end of the stick till it resembled a stout cane about a yard in length.

"Now," said Ralph, advancing into the circle,

and placing his hand on Mynheer Stoutbragurts' shoulder. "Ask the stick any questions you like."

"Where are the escaped prisoners?" said the magistrate in a loud voice.

The small end of the stick pointed towards the forest, and the magistrate was satisfied that the escaped negroes were in the wood.

"Who aided them to escape?" said Mynheer, more confidently than before.

As if by magic the stick pointed to the breast of him who held it, and the burgher grew rather frightened.

"The stick is quite correct," said Ralph, tightening his grasp on the Dutchman's collar, "and now I will tell you something that it cannot. Know, then, most valorous man, that I am Black Ralph, against whom you uttered so many and terrible threats at the inn two nights ago, and I am now come to give you an opportunity of fulfilling them. I it was who mocked you in the crowd this morning, and I am now here to give you a sound castigation, and drive the devil of lying and boasting out of your fat little body."

So saying he brought down the stick on that part of the magistrate's body which he usually sat on with all the force of his vigorous arm.

"Oh! oh! oh! oh!" bellowed mynheer, Ralph repeating the stroke at each outcry. "Have mercy! have mercy!"

Ralph's only reply was to shower his blows down faster than before, till the fat Dutchman danced a most lively measure to a tune of his own singing.

"Is the devil gone out of you yet?" demanded Ralph.

"Mercy! mercy!—oh! oh! oh!" was the only response, and again the castigation commenced.

Again the good Mynheer danced round the circle, and bellowed most lustily the whole time.

"Is the devil gone yet?" asked Ralph.

"Yes, yes! Mercy! mercy!"

"I think it must have been that last stroke, then, that banished him," said Ralph, dealing a harder cut than usual; "and now, Mynheer, if you will walk to the town with me I'll give you a good glass of Schiedam to refresh you after your unusual exercise."

So saying, he released his hold, and the frightened man darted off as fast as his short fat legs could carry him.

"He might have given me a civil answer," muttered Ralph, with a smile, as he leisurely stepped onwards towards Paramaribo.

The bold rover felt no fear for the consequences of his rash act, for he felt perfectly certain that Mynheer Stoutbragurt would not venture outside of his own door that day.

Sending his men on board, he gave orders to weigh anchor, and when Mynheer Stoutbragurt ventured to glance from his window that evening, the dreaded Englishman's ship was gone.

CHAPTER CCCI..

ANDREW HARWOLF AND HIS NEW FRIEND— HOLY JOE—THE SECRET HIDING-PLACE— BYRON HOMER PENN ON BUSINESS, AND HIS SUDDEN INTERVIEW WITH ONE HE WISHED TO AVOID.

ANDREW HARWOLF and his Yankee friend, Byron Homer Penn, left the liquor shop in which they had formed their acquaintance, and cautiously shrouding their faces from view, took their way to a quarter of the town of San Francisco still more low and degraded than that district in which they had passed the night.

Their object was to seek a place in which they might change dresses without attracting any particular attention.

To aid them in disguising themselves, Harwolf laid out a few coins as they passed through the street in cosmetics and chemicals, with which to alter the appearance of their faces.

The house to which the Yankee (who appeared to know every den of iniquity in the town) conducted him was situated in a most filthy street, and bore all the outward appearance of a drinking shop.

On entering, however, it was seen that the bar was deserted, save by a huge repulsive-looking man, who had all the appearance of a prize-fighter, and something of the air of a convicted felon.

He was one, having first passed through every prison in three of the principal states, ere he established himself in *business* in San Francisco, with the proceeds of a successful burglary.

Holy Joe, as he was called by his friends and customers, knew Byron Homer Penn well, and seeing Harwolf, *alias* Henry Jarvis, with him, extended to the latter worthy a cordial welcome.

"Now, stranger, ye ken lie snug here, as if there wasn't no police nor regulators in the whole of Californey," said the worthy, as he opened the door leading to a private room.

"Give us the key of No. 2," said Harwolf's friend, as they passed into a room, in which some half-dozen evil-looking villains were sitting.

A key was handed to him forthwith, and passing through the more frequented apartment, Byron Homer Penn opened the door of an inner room, and beckoned his companion to enter.

It was a bare-looking apartment, with only a table and two chairs in it by way of furniture. The light penetrated through a window of frosted glass, while on the opposite side were several small round holes.

Applying his eye to one of these, Harwolf found that he had a complete view of the street, while a similar orifice under the window gave him a wide prospect over the water.

Large and heavy bolts were attached to the door, which itself was of extraordinary thickness.

The two men first secured the entrance, and then changed clothes.

Harwolf had hitherto worn a tolerably respectable suit, though a degree too large for him. These fitted the Yankee admirably, while the shrunken garments of Byron Homer Penn appeared as if made for the Englishman.

This transformation having been accomplished, they were about to alter the appearance of their faces, or "make up," as theatrical people have it, but the sharp sound of a bell, which Harwolf had noticed hanging in one corner, caused his friend almost to jump out of the window with fright.

"The police, I guess," he said, laconically, when a second touch of the bell made him still more excited.

"Open that winder, will ye, mister," he whispered, "and put all these traps in yer pocket."

Harwolf swept the cosmetics and paints into his coat pocket, and hastily opened the window as desired.

He then perceived a rope ladder dangling from some upper region, and in obedience to a sign from his companion, hastily climbed up it.

Byron Homer Penn, after removing the fastenings of the door, protruded his long body from the window, stepped on to the ladder, and then lowered the sash through which the precious pair had effected their escape.

Harwolf ascended as high as he could, and was wondering where he should find himself, for the ladder appeared to be attached to the wall.

On arriving at the top of the steps, however, his friend whispered to him to push against the wall, which he did.

A small trap-door, painted so as to exactly resemble the remainder of the house, exhibited itself, and through it Harwolf crawled, finding himself in a kind of garret, which there was no other means of entering.

The long Yankee followed him, and when safely

landed pulled up the ladder into the loft and closed the trap-door.

When this was done, the most acute observer would not know that there was any such entrance or secret hiding-place, unless, as in the present instance, they were in the confidence of Holy Joe.

Scarcely had they thus ensconced themselves when a third stroke on the bell reached their ears.

The Yankee then pointed out to his companion a little hole through which he could observe what went on in the room beneath.

To those below this seemed merely a crack in the plastered ceiling, but Harwolf found he had a complete view of the apartment.

In a few minutes the door opened, and two men, in the uniform of policemen, entered, followed by the landlord.

A self-satisfied smile played over Holy Joe's features when he saw that the birds had flown.

The officers looked everywhere—under the table, under the chairs, up the chimney, and out of the window on to the water.

But they evidently found no trace of those they sought, and after a caution or two to the landlord, with regard to harbouring felons, which Joe took in very good part, they departed.

Harwolf thought it was time to descend, and told his companion so.

"I guess you carn't, mister," replied Byron Homer Penn. "We're both locked up, an' carn't move out till Holy Joe gives the word. Try the door, if you don't believe me."

Harwolf did so, and found the door as fast as the wall by its side.

The Yankee chuckled as he witnessed Harwolf's discomfiture, and said,

"The key is down in the cellar, and so is the key-hole, too. I'll show yer presently."

"But why cannot we depart?" asked Harwolf, impatiently.

"'Cos Joe han't got rid o' them precious wisitors of his'n yet. You don't know the ways of the house yet, mister."

There was no remedy for it save patience, and Andrew Harwolf was obliged to call all his into play to keep him quiet during the hour which elapsed before Holy Joe suffered them to descend.

At the expiration of that time, a sharp metallic snap was heard in the wall by the trap door, and on pushing, Harwolf found a ready entrance.

As if by magic, and without being touched by either of the confederates, the rope ladder tumbled through the opening, and the worthy couple once more descended to "No. 2."

Here they completed their disguises, and descended to the bar.

"Say, Joe," said the Yankee, "this 'ere Britisher 'ud like to see the lock and key o' that 'ere private apartment where we have a been amusin' ourselves this last hour."

A grin, intended for a smile, passed over the features of the ex-prize-fighter, and, opening a small door in his bar, he led the way down a steep flight of steps into a dark vault.

At first, Harwolf's eyes, unaccustomed to the gloom, could discern nothing.

Holy Joe, however, lit a taper, and exhibited an array of barrels of all sizes to his visitor's eye.

But where was the mysterious lock and key?

Joe anticipated this question by proceeding to one of the largest casks and removing the head.

Harwolf looked in and saw nothing, so he again turned to his guide.

"See them two nails?" said Joe, pointing to a couple which seemed driven about half their length into the side of the cask.

Harwolf did see, and said so.

"The top one locks you in when I presses it, and t'other one lets you out when all's square."

And removing the light to the back of the cask he showed the surprised Harwolf that the nails in question communicated with two wires which commanded the fastening of the secret door above.

Harwolf felt satisfied. He knew now that he had a secure hiding-place in case of necessity.

They then proceeded to the bar, where liquors were ordered, for which the Englishman was asked to pay.

"Two dollars," said Holy Joe.

Andrew Harwolf paid the money, thinking the knowledge cheap at the price.

Byron Homer Penn now began to complain of hunger, so the pair adjourned to a cheap boarding house opposite, much patronised by the frequenters of Holy Joe's establishment, and made a tolerable meal off very indifferent materials.

Then Harwolf and his friend separated; the latter going to seek an interview with Silas Rye, while the Grey Wolf purposed taking a few hours' recreation in the gambling dens of the neighbourhood.

It was about dusk that same evening, and Silas Rye was sitting in his brother's house conversing over things of the past, when Byron Homer Penn, Esq. took up a post of observation.

But he did not know that he himself was watched by a pair of the keenest eyes in the whole of the American continent.

Yet it was so; for Catahaga was but a few yards off, and keeping a calm steady gaze fixed on him.

The Indian knew something of the Yankee, and Penn himself held Catahaga in dread. Had he known that the famed chief was so near and so intently observant of his motions, he would have seen Andrew Harwolf at the bottom of the Pacific Ocean ere he undertook to play the spy upon Silas Rye or his brother Charles.

A light shone through a window, and the Yankee could plainly see reflected on the blind the forms of three persons, two male and one female.

"All right," thought he; "Mister Rye is here, I guess."

But he did not advance to the house at once, preferring to wait till the darkness of the evening should become more dense.

So for nearly an hour he waited till at length he was satisfied.

Then after a cautious glance round, he approached the door and gave a loud knock.

The man whom Charles Rye had chosen to reside with him, opened the door.

"Do Mister Rye live in this 'ere house, sir-ee?" said the Yankee.

"He does," replied the man.

"Then jist be kind enough to tell him as how I'd like to have about five minutes private talk."

"What name?"

"Ahem! Wa-al, tell him it's—General Horatio Northwood."

The man ascended the staircase, and in a few minutes Charles himself descended to do the honour to his illustrious visitor.

"Pray walk up stairs, general," said Charles; "it was really too bad to keep you waiting here at the door like a beggar."

"Don't apologise, it's all right, I guess it ain't the fust time."

Had not Charles already seen one or two specimens of the Yankee military, his visitor's queer language would have caused him to suspect that all was not right. But, then, when you find generals who never saw a regiment and colonels who can't spell, you soon get used to their trifling offences against the rules of speech.

The sham general, nothing loth, ascended the stairs and was ushered, with due respect, into the room in which Silas and Emily were seated.

"This is my wife, general," said Charles, by way of introduction, "and this is my brother, Silas Rye, Esquire."

"Now this air a honour I must confess I didn't look for, or else, by gum, I'd a come in u-niform! How air you, squire?" said he, holding out a huge and unclean hand towards Silas.

"Well, thank you," replied the person addressed, barely touching the extended fingers.

"Now, holy poker and General Jackson! if I didn't

ought to be whipped into streaks o' jerked beef; now' madam, will you forgive me?"

"I have nothing to forgive, general," replied Emily, to whom this last observation was addressed; "pray sit down and take your hat off."

The *general*, at another time, would have insisted on keeping his *chapeau* on his head, but as he had an object in view, he waived his Republican privilege, and deposited his tall form on a chair close by the side of Silas.

"D'ye chaw?" he said, by way of commencing a conversation.

Silas shook his head, and seemed loth to have anything to say to the general.

"I guess it's a healthy practice, and one t'would do you Britishers a power o' good to commence. Nothing like it, marm, it cleans yer teeth, an' kills all the worms in the stummick."

Emily laughed slightly.

"Then you take it in a medical point of view, general?"

"That's jest it. Now, I did a good sight o' business in the docterin' line afore I jined the army, in Varmont an' Kaintucky."

"Indeed, then you have been physician as well as soldier?"

"I reckon 'twould take a cute man to tell what I hain't been. Soger, lawyer, schoolmaster, shopkeeper, clergyman, sailor, an' doctor."

"But what is this business you have to speak about?" interposed Charles.

"Why, you're the indiwidwal as keeps the gold agency office up town, ain't yer?"

"Yes, certainly."

"Then I got a few nuggets down home as I wants coin for, an' I have heard as you gives more than them infarnel Jews does."

Charles named the price which he was authorised to give for bullion, and the general agreed that it was a fair and just one.

During the little conference that ensued relative to the business, which it is hardly necessary to say the visitor never intended to transact, Emily left the room, while Silas turned his head away from the Yankee.

This was exactly what Byron Homer Penn wanted, for, a few minutes afterwards, while Charles was busily engaged in looking for some paper or prospectus, the cute Yankee seized the opportunity to detach *the bullet* from the link by which it hung from Silas Rye's watch-chain.

He wore it there in example of Foxley, the detective, whose death he hoped, with it, to avenge if he should fail in bringing the murderer before a legal tribunal.

Harwolf's agent had it, however, and quietly transferred it to his trousers pocket, without the owner being aware of the theft.

Hardly had the act been accomplished ere another knock at the door was heard.

"Who can that be at this hour of the night?" said Charles.

"I can't think," replied his wife, who, at that moment, re-entered the room.

There was evidently some delay in opening the door, for the knock was repeated in a more peremptory manner.

"It is Catahaga!" ejaculated Silas, rousing from his fit of abstraction.

"Wa-al, I'll be off now. Good-night," cried the Yankee, rising suddenly, when he heard that name.

"Pray stay awhile longer, general," cried Charles, "it is only a friend of ours, an Indian chief."

"Now, I couldn't think o' stoppin'," ejaculated Byron Homer.

As he spoke the door was thrown open, and the Indian chief stood in the entrance.

It was too late for retreat now, and the Yankee dropped down into his chair again almost fainting with terror.

He had one hope, however, and that was that the dreaded red man would not recognise him.

But as Catahaga's eye fell on him Byron Homer Penn knew that he was detected. But still the Indian knew not the object of his visit.

"My friends have received a visit from a great warrior," said Catahaga, with a sneer on his face.

"What, do you know the general, then?" said Charles.

"Catahaga once dwelt in the great wilderness where there were but few white men. A band of robbers and thieves roved through the woods, plundering red and white indiscriminately. The tall white warrior yonder was one of them, though his beard no longer grows as it used."

"What mean you, Catahaga?" cried Silas, starting forward.

"The white man yonder was one of the band of Oswald Lamond."

"Then, general, or rascal, you stir not hence!" cried Silas.

The Yankee shivered with fear as he heard these words; but in a few minutes he plucked up a little courage, and said,

"Now, this is what I calls rig'lar down-right onhandsome usings, to take a feller like this an' make yerself into a gaoler at once."

"You know you are a scoundrel, and unfit to live," cried Silas.

"I know it's agen all law to shut a feller up in a room like this, an' so interfere with his liberty. If you got anything agen me put me in Court."

"I've a great mind to take you at your word," said Silas, but more quietly, for the Yankee's last speech had struck him forcibly.

"Then, I s'pose I may go now, squire?"

"Yes; but recollect if I catch you in the streets of San Francisco to-morrow, I'll give you into custody as a robber and an outlaw."

"You can't prove anything agen me," said the Yankee, with a grin. "You know they'll never take a Ingen's word afore a white man's in our courts."

Nevertheless, he did not intend to put the experiment to proof, for he knew that the affray at the gambling-house was still a topic of conversation, and cute Mr. Penn did not care to risk recognition by making a public appearance in the court-house of San Francisco.

So he left the house, resolving to get the hundred dollars from his employer for the bullet, and then make tracks for some more secluded and liberal-minded community.

Chuckling at the success which had attended him he was hastening along the dark street when a light footstep was heard behind, a hand was laid heavily on his shoulder, and the cold iron of a tomahawk was pressed to his forehead.

It was the Indian, Catahaga, who had thus arrested his steps.

"Come with me," said the chief, sternly pointing towards the house he had just left.

"What for?" cried Byron Homer Penn, in disgust.

"To answer questions that may be put to you; but, first of all, give me that bullet you stole from my white brother, and which is now in your left-hand pocket."

The Yankee saw that his aim was defeated, and drawing the bullet from his pocket placed it in the Indian's hand, saying,

"Who, in the 'tarnal name o' thunder, could a told yer, I don't know."

Catahaga had seen the Yankee's hand gradually moving towards the pocket in question, and so shrewdly guessed that the bullet was there.

Without another word he then proceeded by the side of the Indian to Charles Rye's house.

"Thief!" said Silas, "and why did you steal the bullet from my chain?"

The rascal was silent.

"You must have had some motive in so doing. Did any one employ you to do this?"

"Supposin' I splits, what 'll you stand?" said the culprit, resolved to make as good a bargain as he could.

"As much as you were to have for your trouble had you succeeded."

"Then I'll tell yer; it were a man named Henry Jarvis."

"Describe him," said Silas Ryc.

And the Yankee did so.

"Andrew Harwolf!" said Catahaga.

"Je-ru-salem!" exclaimed Byron Homer Penn.

CHAPTER CCCII.

LEIGHTON'S ESCAPE FROM THE PIRATES OF THE ISLAND—VOYAGE IN A BOAT—LA BELLE FRANCE—JEAN GROGNOIR—THE RESCUE—REVENGE.

EDWARD LEIGHTON and Katinka remained in the Greek chapel an hour and a half ere Myra returned. When the latter re-appeared she bore in her hands a large basket containing a quantity of flat loaves, some dried fish, and two bottles of wine.

"This is all the food I can procure you," she said. "There is a small cask of water in the boat. Follow me, and silently, too."

She led the way through the door of the church and underneath a long archway somewhat similar to that they had traversed on entering the chapel, and finally emerged into a thick bushy pathway, the opposite side of the island to that on which the two wanderers had been cast ashore.

"Be careful how you descend this path?" said Myra. "If we are discovered my life is forfeited as well as yours. "Though," she added, in a low tone, "I have little left to live for now, unless it be to offer up my prayers for his soul."

"Dear friend," said Katinka, throwing her arms round the Greek girl's neck, "you must live for the sake of those who love you. I love you!"

"Join us in our flight," said Edward. "In other lands you may yet be happy, and forget your misfortunes."

"There is no happiness in store for me on this earth; nor can I quit my native island. I love the home of my fathers."

"But, perhaps you will be suspected of aiding our escape, and will receive ill-treatment in consequence," said Leighton.

"I must bear with it patiently; but do not urge me, I cannot accede to your request."

"Then, at all events, take this ring as a remembrance of those you have made happy once more," continued the young man, drawing a jewel from his finger.

"Nay, keep it. I have no wish to remember you when forgetfulness will banish so many sad thoughts."

They proceeded on down the steep and rocky path in silence, and at length reached the shore.

The stormy wind had lulled itself to rest, and the little island lay calmly slumbering in the soft moonlight like a gem in the midst of the sea.

Leading the way to a pile of rocks Myra showed the young couple a small skiff that lay concealed there. The little light mast and sail were lying by its side, and in it was the cask of water of which Myra had spoken.

"One thing more," said she, as Leighton stepped into the boat, "here is a compass by which you may direct your course. And now I must away. May guardian angels protect you."

Ere Edward Leighton or Katinka could reply, she had darted up the steep path and was hidden from sight by a clump of bushes.

The young man gazed after her a moment; but she did not return, and then carefully lifting his wife into the bark, he hoisted the sail, and a light breeze bore them rapidly away from the island-home of the Greek pirates.

The next morning some of the fishermen going to their boats early found the body of poor Myra lying crushed at the bottom of a precipice.

Whether she had fallen over accidentally or had thrown herself down was never known.

But they buried her by the side of him she loved, and long after sung her fate in a pathetic ballad.

Meanwhile, Edward Leighton and his wife sailed onwards over the moonlit sea, and were far away from the group of islands ere day began to pale the deep blue night sky.

Katinka had long been asleep, wrapped carefully in an old cloak which the careful hand of the ill-fated Greek girl had thrown into the boat.

But when the sun began to rise, the wind also seemed to awake from its slumber.

The waves curled higher and higher, and the little boat was threatened with destruction.

The poor Polish girl was greatly alarmed, as well she might be, with the remembrance of their late shipwreck so vividly before her.

"Lie down in the bottom of the boat, dearest, and wrap yourself as much as possible in your old cloak," said her husband.

Katinka obeyed his injunctions, though both were in a few moments completely soaked by the showers of spray which were dashed from the top of each wave by the wind.

Yet the little boat breasted the seething waters gallantly, though, of course, driven much out of the course which Leighton had intended to take.

The whole sky was overcast with black clouds, and forked lightning played vividly in the distance.

The sound of the thunder, if there was any, was swallowed by the howling wind and roaring waves.

Presently a stronger gust than usual swept across the wilderness of waters, and with a snap their little mast was carried away.

Knife in hand, Leighton cut away the entangled cordage from the boat, and by most strenuous exertions managed to save both sail and spar.

Bending all his strength to the task, he so far managed to fix the slight stick in its socket again, and it was well he did so, for had he not been able, by spreading his canvas, to keep the boat before the wind, they must have infallibly been swallowed up by the mountainous waves.

Hour after hour they thus rode over the foaming sea, and about an hour before sunset caught sight of a rocky island, which Leighton supposed was Malta, at a distance, though from the extreme violence of the wind they were unable to direct their boat towards it.

When the sun went down the wind again ceased, and the two wet and weary mariners prepared themselves to pass another night on the bosom of the heaving sea.

They had provisions and drink luckily, so, therefore, did not suffer from hunger or thirst. But the cold produced by their wet garments was intense.

That night, while Katinka slept, Leighton employed himself in setting the rigging of his little boat to rights, in order to prepare for another day's hurricane if such should be their lot.

He judged that they were now some distance to the westward of the south point of the island of Sicily, and, such being the case, he proposed to sail boldly on till he reached some port on the French coast.

His task finished, he sat down in the bottom of the boat and slept, though not for a long time, and when he awoke felt much refreshed.

The morning of the second day of their voyage broke, and though the wind again blew, yet it was not with so much violence as before, and the boat proceeded swiftly onwards.

Another day passed and another night, but when the next morn arrived Leighton announced that their voyage was at an end, and pointed out the distant coast, on which might be seen a large town.

Two hours afterwards the little boat which had so bravely borne the fury of the ocean glided into the harbour of Marseilles, and there, for a time, the troubles of the young couple ended.

Considerable surprise was excited amongst the lively Frenchmen by the relation of their adventures, and for two days Edward Leighton was a hero. The third day they were forgotten in the excitement attendant on some new object of curiosity.

As there was no steamer about to start for England, Leighton suggested to his wife that they should travel over land to Paris, and thence to Boulogne or some other port on the west coast, and, in order that they might be able to perform the journey economically, he also suggested that they should attire themselves in the costume of the peasants of the country, and so be allowed to escape all the persecution and consequent expense to which an English " milord " would be subjected.

Behold, then, Katinka in short petticoats, with a bright-coloured scarf over her head, while Leighton assumed knee-breeches and a light jacket or blouse.

For three days they travelled by easy stages, and on the fourth reached the little town of Gironac, where an adventure befell Edward Leighton, which not only delayed their journey for a time but nearly cost him his life.

It was in this manner.

On arriving at Gironac the young couple took up their abode at a little quiet *auberge*, intending to depart on the morrow.

Early in the evening, before it was dark, in fact, Katinka retired to rest, and Edward sallied forth for a stroll through the quaint little streets of the quiet old town.

On returning, or rather on attempting to return, he found he had forgotten the way, and looked around for some one to direct him.

A dirty, ill-looking scoundrel, dressed in the garb of a labourer of the lowest class, hurried by, and turned down a narrow street in which several of the houses were uninhabited and propped up from falling by huge beams.

As no one else was in sight Leighton hurried after this man; but on turning the corner of the street above mentioned, he was surprised to see the man crouching in the doorway of one of the deserted houses.

" That fellow is up to no good," thought Leighton, " I will hide myself, and see what he does."

Accordingly he crept quietly down the street, and ensconced himself in the next doorway to the one in which the man was concealed.

He had not long to wait, for in a few minutes a little girl, apparently about twelve years of age, came running along the street, and Leighton could see the man drawing himself up like about to spring on his prey.

On came the young girl, unconscious of any danger, and, as if to tempt the cupidity of the concealed ruffian, rattling in her hand some few coins with which she had apparently been sent to make a purchase.

The young Saxon, however, did not stop to inquire whether the man meant robbery or a baser crime, and when he saw the man spring out of his hiding-place, he also leaped forth, and interposing himself between the girl and the Frenchman brought his fist down with considerable weight on the ruffian's chest.

He staggered but recovered, and again rushed forward, while the poor child, after looking from one to the other, clung to her protector, and burst into tears.

Again did Edward Leighton strike the ruffian, who, on receipt of the second blow, saw that he had a powerful adversary.

" Are you not ashamed, you villain, thus to assault a child ?" asked the young man.

" Blow for blow !" muttered the skulking rascal, as he shuffled off. " I will be revenged."

Turning to the girl he comforted her, and offered to accompany her home to her parents.

The offer was gratefully accepted.

" Do you know that man, my child ?" asked Leighton, as he walked by the side of the young girl.

" No, monsieur, but I have heard people say that he has twice been convicted and punished for assaulting and ill-using children. But here is my mother's house ; will you not come in ?"

" No, child, I must return, but tell me the way to the *Auberge Nationale*."

" You must pass through that street, again, monsieur, and turn to the left."

" Thanks," he said, and then turning round, walked rapidly past the scene of his late adventures, and had quite forgotten the scoundrelly ruffian from whom he had rescued the girl.

But hardly had he reached the top of the street when he heard a rapid step behind him, and ere he could turn, a knife was plunged twice into his side.

" Blow for blow !" hissed a voice in his ear, and as the young man fell, he saw the form of his late antagonist vanishing down the street.

" Help ! Murder !" cried Leighton, as he fell, and that fearful cry resounding through the quiet streets, soon brought aid.

While some started in pursuit of the assassin, others carefully lifted the young man and bore him to the inn.

Great was Katinka's alarm when her loved husband was thus brought home in a senseless state.

But she was by nature brave, and had perfect command over herself; so she stilled the beatings of her heart that she might attend to his wounds.

A surgeon was promptly sent for, and examined the wounded man.

He shook his head, gravely, and whispered to the landlord, who immediately quitted the room.

The surgeon continued his work of staunching the blood that flowed copiously from the wound, but had hardly finished when the landlord re-entered, ushering in the chief magistrate, and the chief of the gendarmes.

" Then you do not think your patient can live, Monsier Tourniquet ?" said the justice.

" I think not," replied the man of probes and lancets.

Then I will at once take his depositions.

This was done, and when Leighton described the manner in which he had received his wounds, and the person who inflicted them, the Frenchmen turned from one to another, and held up their hands in astonishment.

" Jean Grognoir, again !" said the chief of police, sententiously.

" We must catch him, and hang him !" cried the magistrate.

But the villain remained uncaught and unhung for more than a fortnight, during which time Edward Leighton tossed restlessly on his bed, attended by Katinka and the girl he had rescued from the clutches of Jean Grognoir.

───────

CHATER CCCIII.

THE " RED RAVEN " ON A CRUISE—MEETING OF CHRISTOPHER AND BLACK RALPH—THE CHASE OF HARWOLF'S SCHOONER — BALL PRACTICE.

THE " Red Raven " and the Boy Pirate still remained at New Orleans, where all his ships had met with the exception of the " Defiance," on board which were Black Ralph and Tom Garrod.

The non-arrival of the last named vessel occasioned Christopher no little uneasiness, for although he had no doubt that, being a good ship, she had weathered the gale—both her officers, he knew, were thorough seamen—he feared that Ralph Talbot's impetuous temper had hurried them into some scrape, from which not even his well-known courage had been able to extricate them.

After waiting with great anxiety for three weeks or more, during which time, as the reader knows,

Black Ralph visited Dios Lagos, Paramaribo, and other places, of which we shall have occasion to speak in another chapter, he resolved to put to sea again in the "Red Raven," leaving the other two vessels in harbour.

The best men were draughted from the crews of the other ships to serve on board the "Red Raven," and those thus selected felt highly delighted at the preference thus shown them by their young commander.

Lilia, of course, accompanied her beloved husband; to be separated from him for the space of one hour was a torture not easily endured.

With the good wishes of those they left behind, the anchor was raised from its bed of mud, the sails were hoisted to the wind, and the "Red Raven" soon once more breasted the waves of the Atlantic Ocean.

For three days they cruised, the Boy Pirate inquiring of every vessel they met whether they had seen anything of the "Defiance."

Nothing was to be heard of the lost ship, and Christopher began to fear that his gallant friends had perished.

Still hope clung to his soul, and he continued to cruise about those latitudes where the fleet was first dispersed by the gale.

One day, however, when Cristopher was lying on a sofa in his cabin, listening to the soft voice of Lilia, as she touchingly sung a song of home, a young sailor entered the apartment.

"Beg pardon, sir, but there's a sail away on the starboard bow, and Mr. Brierly says as how he thinks it's the 'Defiance.'"

"Thank Heaven!" exclaimed the Boy Pirate, "I'll be on deck in a minute."

So saying, he snatched up a powerful glass, and hastily imprinting a kiss on his wife's cheek, left the cabin.

As the man had said, there was a sail in sight, and apparently in the act of chasing another, for, as the young commander ascended to the mast-head to have a better view, a cloud of white smoke was distinctly visible as it rolled from the vessel's side, and presently the dull heavy boom of a gun solemnly reverberated across the intervening waters.

"Whether it's the 'Defiance' or not it's coming to blows," cried Christopher, as he descended. "So we will go and look on. Perhaps we may be called upon to take a hand in the game."

"Aye, aye, sir," responded Brierly. "The old 'Raven' hasn't lost her wings, and we shall soon be able to overhaul them."

"Then clap on all canvas, and call me again in half an hour; be alive, boys."

The boys were alive, and soon had such a crowd of canvas spread that the good old ship reeled like a drunkard as she bounded over the waves.

Christopher then returned to his cabin, and imparted the news to Lilia.

"I hope, dearest, that Black Ralph hasn't turned —traitor," she said. "I heard the sound of a gun."

"Fear not, my love," said Christopher, "I have his solemn promise, and I know Ralph Talbot, with all his crimes, is no perjurer."

Lilia was satisfied, and resumed her interrupted song.

Half an hour elapsed, and then, according to orders, Brierly entered the cabin to report.

"Well, how now, old friend?"

"Well, you see, captain, we're just walkin' over the ground hand over hand, and shall be within gun shot of her in another hour."

"Does she show any colours yet?"

"Not as I can make out, but my glass ain't so powerful as yours."

"Then take mine, Brierly; I can, I dare say, manage with yours, so we'll exchange."

Old Brierly took the proffered telescope, and, with many expressions of eternal fidelity, left the cabin.

In another hour Brierly returned.

"We ain't more nor a mile from her now, captain, and though she must have seen us, they don't show a bit of bunting."

"Do you think it is the 'Defiance?'"

"Certain on it as I be that this is the captain's cabin o' the 'Red Raven.'"

"Then fire a gun, and hoist a private signal. Stay, though, I will come on deck."

And acompanied by Brierly he left the cabin.

The gun was prepared and fired, and the signal fluttered up the halyards.

"See!" cried Christopher, "it is the 'Defiance.' She answers our signal, and shows the flag of the Avengers."

And such was the case, though, after responding to his chief, Black Ralph continued the chase as ardently as before.

The Boy Pirate could now see the object of his pursuit—a small schooner about three miles ahead—and speculation was rife as to the object which Ralph had in view.

"Run alongside, Brierly," said our hero, "and I will hail him."

This was easier said than done, for the "Defiance" was a good mile ahead, and Ralph had every inch of his canvas spread.

But there was not a sailing-ship on the ocean could match the "Red Raven," as Christopher well knew, so yard after yard the distance between the two was decreased until the Boy Pirate's ship glided along about forty yards to windward of the "Defiance," on the quarter-deck of which Ralph Talbot was seen with folded arms.

As the "Red Raven," however, ranged alongside, a word of command was given, and the yards were manned as though it were a ship of war, while the flag was lowered three times in token of respect.

Christopher returned the salute, and then hailed through his trumpet,

"'Defiance,' ahoy!"

"Aye, aye, sir!" responded Ralph, sending back his powerful voice without the aid of a tube.

"Where have you been?"

"I was driven a long way south, and had to put into port to repair."

"What schooner is that you are chasing?"

"It is called 'The Exchange,' and is commanded by Daniel Harwolf."

"What?" shouted the Boy Pirate, hardly trusting his ears.

"She is commanded by Daniel Harwolf, and has as pretty a crew of ruffians on board as you could find."

"Then, mine enemy, beware! The Avenger is at your heels!" cried the excited Christopher, as he hastily descended into the cabin for his sword and pistols.

"'Defiance,' ahoy!" he shouted, when he came on deck, "discontinue the chase, and leave Harwolf to me."

"I shall be compelled to mutiny, my gallant Raven, unless you countermand that order," replied Ralph; "I have chased him for two days, and don't feel disposed to be removed now that the affair is coming to a close."

"Then come on board the 'Raven' if you are anxious to be in at the death."

"Aye, aye, sir; Garrod doesn't mind taking command of the 'Defiance.'"

This was exactly what Garrod wished for; though he knew the Boy Pirate's commands were to capture Harwolf wherever he might be found, he did not care to take any part in the bloodshed that he foresaw must take place.

The course of the "Red Raven" was slackened the moment Christopher saw Black Ralph and his boat's crew quit the side of the "Defiance."

Ten minutes afterwards the ex-tragedian was on the deck exchanging hearty greetings with Christopher, Brierly, and his old comrades.

His boat was hoisted up, for the rowers were daredevil souls like himself, and anxious for the fight.

Zampa was amongst them, grinning with the whole extent of his capacious mouth. Jefferson

Jeremiah Brown was also there, for Black Ralph, having licked him into a tolerable sailor, had brought him to smell powder for the first time in his life.

"Zampa, you rascal, where have you been?" asked Christopher.

"He! he! dis poor nigger been in jail, goin' to be hunged," replied Zampa.

"Going to be hung! What do you mean, you rascal?"

"It's quite true, I assure you; and it cost me and two old friends I picked up on the voyage a great deal of trouble to get him away," said Black Ralph, who then explained the whole mystery.

"But who are these two friends of yours?"

"Two of Harwolf's old officers, who will be delighted to see him dangling from the yard-arm."

"Then they shall be gratified. But to your posts, men; see the decks cleared for action."

The order was obeyed with loud cheers, which the commander at once checked.

"Save your cheers, my lads, till you stand on the deck of yon vessel. We have lost way, Ralph, waiting for you, and must be careful, or night will come on ere we can board the villain."

"We are not more than three miles from them, captain," said Ralph, "suppose you fire a heavy gun and show them your old colours—the 'Raven' I mean. I fancy Harwolf doesn't like to see that banner hung out on your outward walls."

Christopher smiled, and then whispered a few words to Brierly.

Three minutes after the report of a heavy gun shook the deck of the good ship, and as the flag, so well remembered, floated out boldly in the breeze, three ringing cheers, which even Christopher could not check, rang through the air.

Harwolf, who had been intently watching the meeting between the vessel by which he was chased and the stranger, saw the "Raven" flag displayed, and his whole body shook with fear.

"Captain," said Walbrook, who had noticed it, "they have changed their bunting. Can you make out what it is?"

"Yes; it is the 'Red Raven,' my deadly enemy!"

"Then there'll be a fight, I expect. We'd better prepare. I have heard before now of that same 'Raven,' but never clapped eyes on her till now."

And he hurried away to prepare for the inevitable conflict, leaving his captain leaning over the bulwarks in a state of mind more easily imagined than described.

On the deck of the "Red Raven" all was bustle and activity as the men cheerfully prepared for action.

"I think we are near enough to try a shot in good earnest now," said Christopher, when they had gained upon the flying schooner.

"Then open the ball as soon as you please, for I am quite ready," cried Ralph, drawing his sword with a flourish.

The word was given, and a ball went whistling over the deep, falling with a splash into the water about twenty yards short of the schooner's stern.

"A good shot, but your gun was hardly elevated enough. Try again, Brierly."

The gun was loaded, and Brierly waiting a few minutes pitched a shot fairly into the low black hull of the schooner.

"Bravo! encore!" shouted Ralph, wild with glee, while the Boy Pirate paced the deck, impatiently waiting for the moment when he might face his foe sword in hand.

The schooner now returned the fire; but the shots fell half a mile short of the "Red Raven."

Brierly, on the contrary, kept pitching shot after shot through Daniel Harwolf's cabin-windows.

CHAPTER CCCIV.

LOST IN LONDON—THE MYSTERIOUS STEP—
THE CAB—LORD HAWKSBURY A PRISONER—
HIS ESCAPE—AND RE-CAPTURE.

WHEN Lord Hawksbury rushed away from Lady Hautaine's mansion after obtaining Jessie Vere's address his first thought was to proceed at once to Chelsea, and obtain an interview.

But when he passed by the doorway of a brightly-illuminated public-house not far from Cheyne Walk, he paused a moment to look at his watch, and the lateness of the hour told him that his motives would indeed be doubted if he disturbed the quiet little Chelsea home at such an unseasonable period.

He, therefore, entered the glaring public, wrote a note, requesting Jessie to call on him, and, after posting it, began to retrace his steps to the neighbourhood of Bond Street.

But his lordship was not very intimately acquainted with the region into which he had so venturously plunged, so it is not surprising that after traversing several quiet and narrow streets, he began to have a vague idea that he had lost himself.

Nothing very serious to a man with money in his pocket, and not pressed for time, so Lord Hawksbury walked quietly onwards, intending to make use of the knowledge of the first cabman he met with to extricate himself from his difficulties.

It was past midnight, and the inhabitants of the quiet district appeared to be asleep, for not a soul appeared in the somewhat gloomy lines of streets.

Even the police, those nocturnal guardians, whose midnight hours are supposed to be spent in guarding her Majesty's lieges, their homes and property, forebore to make an appearance.

Lord Hawksbury was no coward, but he certainly would have preferred to see a few people about, if it were only for the sake of company.

However, he lit a second cigar, and marched on, keeping a good look out for any stray cab that might have wandered into that desolate wilderness of bricks and mortar.

As he walked, however, it seemed to him as though another footstep behind him were re-echoing his own, or rather as if some one were following him keeping time with his steps.

Lord Hawksbury turned sharply, but could see no one, though he gazed up and down the street.

He proceeded on his walk, but with his ears wide open to catch the slightest sound.

For a minute all was quiet save his own feet; then came the mysterious echo, and, as Lord Hawksbury listened to it, he felt convinced that the ghost or unseen walker had iron-plates on its heels. His own boots, he knew well, were innocent of metal.

Again he halted, and gazed behind him, but, as in the first instance, no one was to be seen.

"It is very strange," muttered Lord Hawksbury, to himself, "who can be following me, I wonder? Well, they'll find me a difficult one to manage if robbery is meant."

He turned on his heel and proceeded on his walk; but ere he had gone a dozen steps, the same echoing noise was heard, and Lord Hawksbury buttoned up his coat, fixed his hat on his head, and prepared for the worst.

At that moment, however, a four-wheeled cab appeared at the end of the street, the effect of which was to cause the strange sound to cease at once.

Lord Hawksbury at once hailed the driver as he was about to turn down a yard.

"Just coming home," replied the man, in surly tones, "can't take you, my horse is too tired."

"Name your own price to take me into Regent Street," said the nobleman.

"I want to get home. Can't take you."

"I, too, wish to get home; but having lost my way, don't know where to go. If you will not drive me, at least direct me."

At that moment a man appeared walking towards them, and as soon as the cab-driver cast eyes on the new comer, a change at once came over him.

THE DUEL IN THE GAMBLING-HOUSE.

"Well, get in, sir; but I shall charge you five shillings."

"I don't care what you charge me; but make haste."

So saying, Lord Hawksbury stepped into the vehicle, and the man closed the door with a loud bang.

"What part of Regent Street, sir?"

"The Quadrant."

"You were walking away from it about as fast as you could," he said; and, mounting to his seat, he turned the horse's head, and drove off.

Lord Hawksbury caught sight of a man leaning against a lamp-post; but he did not observe that a signal passed between that man and the driver, nor, as the cab rolled along, did he imagine that the unknown was clinging to the back of the vehicle.

His lordship, lost in thought, took little note of the streets they passed; nor did he observe that the neighbourhood became more low and villanous-looking the further they proceeded. Yet it was so, and Lord Hawksbury was in the most depraved part of Westminster ere he knew it.

No. 88.

Cessation of motion re-called him to his senses, and he looked out to find himself in what appeared to be a kind of mews, though of the filthiest description. There was no lamp to shed a light on the scene; but in the gloom Lord Hawksbury plainly saw three men standing on each side of the cab, while a fourth was just opening a door in what appeared a dead wall.

Letting down the window, the young lord endeavoured to open the door by which he had entered the vehicle; but it would not yield to his efforts.

"What means this? Where am I?" he demanded.

"You are in a place where you must keep very quiet, or it will be the worse for you," said the driver.

"I care little for your threats, and insist upon being allowed to depart."

"You cannot depart as you wish, you must remain till we think proper to release you."

Lord Hawksbury immediately stepped from the cab, which the man now opened, and walked towards the gateway by which the vehicle had entered.

To his dismay he perceived that the ponderous

doors were fastened; but he put a bold face on the matter.

"You must follow me," said the driver, while three of his associates planted themselves immediately before the young nobleman.

"I refuse to do anything of the kind. Help! police! police!"

The men at once seized him, and a struggle ensued, in which, though Lord Hawksbury defended himself with the utmost desperation, he was thrown to the ground, and his arms pinioned by those about him.

"Help! help!" he shouted. "Police! help! murder!"

"The police never come this way," said the cabdriver, "though there will be murder done unless you keep quiet.

Seeing that he was completely in the hands of the ruffians he surrendered himself passively, though still keeping a sharp look out for any chance of escape.

Lifting him to his legs the men led Lord Hawksbury through a narrow low door into a kind of stable, at the further end of which was a staircase.

Up this he was compelled to proceed, through a kind of hay-loft along a dark passage, and then up more stairs to a great height.

At length his conductors opened a small door, apparently at the top of the house, and thrust him in.

"You may scream as long as you like," said the cab-driver, "your voice will never be heard."

Lord Hawksbury made no reply, and the men left him. The prisoner's heart failed him as he heard the door locked, and found himself in the dark, and he began to reflect on the object of his captors in thus confining him.

As he had not been robbed he very naturally felt puzzled to know what they could want with him, though he had little doubt that he had been kidnapped with a view to extortion.

Still, however, he resolved to defeat the villains if he could, and for that purpose looked round in the darkness to discover the window if there were any.

No opening of the kind was to be discovered, and Lord Hawksbury determined to grope his way round the wall in order to find if such an aperture existed.

But, with the exception of the doorway, the walls presented a smooth unbroken surface, and after, in vain, endeavouring to force the lock, the young noble sat himself down by the wall to think and plan.

Alone in the darkness, in the power of those ruffians who had already hinted at murder, yet Lord Hawksbury's courage failed him not.

He had no weapon of any kind, and his first thought was to construct one, which he did by emptying the contents of his purse into one corner of his silk pocket handkerchief, and tying the coins up in a hard and compact roll.

That done he lit a cigar, and quietly though impatiently waited for morning.

It came sooner than he had anticipated, and, by the slight light that now began to pervade his prison, Lord Hawksbury perceived that he was confined in a room about eight feet in height, lighted through a small square opening in the roof, which was barred with iron, while not a scrap of furniture was in the place.

The door, Lord Hawksbury knew, was of great strength and closely locked, though he again tried it. Escape seemed hopeless, and, though Lord Hawksbury tried to believe that all was right, yet he could not help in his own heart feeling that he was at the mercy of those who had brought him to his prison.

Hour after hour passed and it was near seven o'clock in the morning when a slight noise attracted the prisoner's attention; glancing towards the door he saw that a plank had been withdrawn, and that a dirty hand was in the act of thrusting a loaf, some butter and a teapot into the room.

"That's all you'll get till two o'clock, so take care of it," said a voice, which he at once recognised as having heard on the previous night.

Lord Hawksbury looked at the viands, and, although he certainly was hungry, yet he hardly dared eat for fear of poison.

Yet the more he looked the more hungry did he become, and at length the temptation could be no longer resisted, he poured himself a cup of tea, and broke a piece off the loaf, for he had no knife, saying as he did so,

"Surely they cannot mean to poison me; if my death had been desired they would have killed me during the night."

He made a tolerable meal, and then, lighting another cigar, of which he had a good supply, sat down to pass away the time till two o'clock, when he had been given to understand he would receive another visit from his unseen attendant.

As a matter of course his thoughts dwelt principally on some plan of escape and he endeavoured to recall to mind the manner in which Jack Sheppard escaped from Newgate.

But he was not well versed in Old Bailey literature, and could not trace any resemblance between his own case and that of the celebrated prison-breaker.

While still thinking he fell asleep, weary with the past night's watching, and, as he slept, he dreamed.

Dreamed that his captors were coming in a body to murder him while he lay helpless on the ground, unable to resist their blows which he felt all over his body, while the ruffian cab-driver was foremost in his fearful threats.

Lord Hawksbury awoke; awoke to consciousness, and to the knowledge that people were talking in an adjoining room.

He listened attentively, and ere long heard his own name mentioned.

The cab-driver was speaking, and apparently endeavouring to still the blood-thirsty propensities of the gang of ruffians with whom he was associated.

"Let him alone. What good can it do us to do anything now? If we keep him all right till Harwolf comes we are good for a clear hundred each."

"That's all very fine; but s'pose the bloke breaks loose, we not only lose the coin, but it's about three years each."

"He won't break out; he can't break out," replied the cab-driver. "I never knew any one break out of this crib."

"Won't I?" thought Lord Hawksbury to himself. "Just give me another twenty-four hours, and see if I dont circumvent you and the villain whom I see now is your employer."

The nobleman looked at his watch, it wanted five minutes to two, and he, therefore, judged that ere long he would again receive a visit from his mysterious, and, as yet, unknown gaoler.

Nor was he disappointed; for, as the clock of a neighbouring steeple struck the hour, he saw the slide open, and a dish containing a mutton chop and potatoes appeared through the opening.

While he was engaged in the demolition of the viands thus supplied, he again heard the voices which had awakened him from his dream.

"I must be off," said the cab-driver, who had been the main instrument in his captivity. "You know well I have other things to attend to beside the imperious orders of your Mr. Harwolf, who, by the way, does not pay so well as I could wish."

"Then go. What time shall you return?"

"Not before midnight."

"Then we shall be away. Are you not afraid to leave your prisoner unguarded?"

"No; it is impossible that he can escape. He will remain for the next three months in that room."

"Indeed!" thought Lord Hawksbury. "If you find me here to-morrow morning I shall be very much surprised."

The voices died away, and there was a sound as of footsteps descending the staircase.

When those sounds died away, Lord Hawksbury leaped to his feet, firmly determined that he would be outside those walls ere another morning's sun shone on the dingy walls of his prison-chamber.

Again he surveyed the garret cell in which he was confined, and again he resolved to escape, if escape were possible.

The only method appeared to be by the roof, and, therefore, did Lord Hawksbury determine to make his exit through the top of the house.

The bars of the skylight which gave light to the room were, as before said, about eight feet from the floor.

Now, as Lord Hawksbury stood about five feet eleven inches in his stockings, he could very nearly reach these impediments, and a sudden thought struck him—viz., that by throwing the end of his silk pocket handkerchief over one of the bars in question he might be able to obtain a firm grasp on one of the bars.

This he did, and had the satisfaction of finding the metal yield to his strength.

Scarcely five minutes had elapsed ere one of the bars gave way, then another, and in a quarter of an hour from the time of commencing his dangerous feat, Lord Hawksbury was in the act of forcing his way through the dirty panes of glass which were now the only barrier between him and freedom.

They yielded one by one, and although his lordship little cared what noise he made in thus forcing his way to liberty, yet his operations were undisturbed.

Pane after pane of glass was smashed, and at length the young nobleman stood on the roof of the old building a free man.

His next thought was, of course, to descend, and for that purpose he gazed over the parapet to find a means of lowering himself.

Sixty feet at least was he from the pavement, while not an inch of rope or even a friendly water-spout was within his reach.

While still debating within himself, a noise in the room which he had so recently quitted, aroused him.

Peering through the broken sky-light, the dirty unshaven face of one of the gang who had been instrumental in his capture, appeared before him in the act of climbing through the aperture which he had made.

With one of the bars of his prison window, Lord Hawksbury dealt the intruder such a blow on his head that he at once dropped back stunned and senseless into the room below.

Another man then made the attempt, and met a like fate; the other, for there were three of them, hung back, apparently not caring to have his head broken for the sake of recapturing the escaped prisoner.

Hastily stepping along the roof, he clambered over a parapet and had the satisfaction of seeing that he was now in view of a populous thoroughfare, in which both people and vehicles were passing.

However, to make sure of his escape, the young nobleman climbed over three or four more roofs, resolved not to hail those below till all chance of recapture was gone.

As he reached the last house in the street, which was flat roofed, an old woman, lean, withered, and dirty, stepped forth on the leads with some tattered garments she had been washing, in her hands.

On seeing Lord Hawksbury, she sat up a loud scream, and called to those in the house,

"Bill! Bill! here's a cove on the tiles; come up, quick!"

Bill made his appearance in the shape of the very cab-driver who had been the cause of his confinement.

On seeing that his prisoner had escaped, he rushed forward, as did two other men, and a fearful struggle took place on the house top.

Thrice did Lord Hawksbury, who felt most desperately savage at being thus thwarted, essay to hurl the man with whom he grappled over into the street, and was only prevented by the united strength of his foes.

He shouted aloud for help, but his voice was lost in the din of rolling wheels and the patter of feet.

At length, exhausted and breathless, he lay on the roof of the house, and his captors lost no time in securing his hands and legs. The young nobleman had a dim consciousness that he was carried along, and that the men were debating on the propriety of cutting his throat there and then, from which they were only restrained by the mention of the name of Harwolf.

Then came a period of oblivion, and, when the unfortunate young man recovered his senses, he found himself lying on a bundle of straw in a gloomy, damp, mouldy cellar, which received its only light through a strong iron grating high above his reach.

The bruises he had received ached painfully, and on attempting to rise to his feet he found that both hands and feet were securely fastened.

The most dismal forebodings took possession of his soul; but still one ray of comfort found its way to his heart along with the more gloomy images of despair.

He was not to be sacrificed till Harwolf returned!

CHAPTER CCCV.

A CIVIL CONVERSATION, AND A LEGAL CONSULTATION—OINY MACARNE'S CHALLENGE—THE DUEL—A TREACHEROUS SHOT—ALONE WITH THE VULTURES.

HOMER BYRON PENN was suffered to depart from Charles Rye's house after he had given the fullest information as to Andrew Harwolf's hiding-place, dress and appearance.

Once outside the door he rushed away to the docks, jumped on board a small craft that was on the point of sailing for a small settlement some miles distant, nor did he rest at ease till the little boat was out of sight of the harbour of San Francisco.

When gone, Silas, Charles, and the Indian held a long consultation as to the best means of entrapping the Grey Wolf.

"Best go at once to this house of which the man spoke, and demand to see him," said Charles.

"We should only find ourselves opposed by a party of the most desperate ruffians in the locality," replied his brother, "who, if they did us no injury, would, at all events, keep us away till he had time to escape."

"What, then, is to be done?"

"I hardly know," replied Silas. "The laws here are not strong enough to reach him for the crimes he has committed in this country, and I much doubt whether the authorities would take any notice of the evil deeds done in his own country on my information. I confess I know not how to act."

"What say you, Catahaga," cried Charles, looking to the Indian, "is the Grey Wolf to escape?"

"No," replied the chief. "If every other plan fails we will keep watch on him till he returns once more to the prairie when our hands will be unfettered and our rifles loaded. But my white brethren should consult some learned Sachem wise in the knowledge of the laws."

"You are right, Catahaga, and I will do so to-morrow," replied Silas.

"If our Irish friend were here, perhaps his quick wit could suggest some scheme," said Charles.

"Aye, and he shall go with us to the lawyer's to-morrow. By-the-bye, Charlie, can you recommend one?"

"I have not yet had occasion to employ one; but I was recommended in New York to entrust myself in the hands of a Mr. Napoleon Walker."

"What a rage these people have for grand names; only fancy that fellow who was here just now calling himself after two poets and a Quaker. However, Mr. Napoleon Walker it shall be, and if he can help me out of my difficulty he shall have something more than the usual fee."

The party then separated for the night, a meeting being appointed for an early hour in the morning.

All were punctual, and after a hasty breakfast the party proceeded towards the offices of Mr. Napoleon Walker, one of the most celebrated attorneys in San Francisco.

Oiny Macarne accompanied them, and cheered them on the road by several snatches of national melodies.

In due time they arrived at the offices of the great man, and found him sitting in an easy chair, picking his teeth with a quill, and occasionally spitting with dexterous aim into a plate of sawdust which stood behind the door.

"Top o' the mornin', sirs," said he, puckering up his lean and yellow visage into a smile. "What can I have the pleasure of doing for you?"

"We should like to have a few words in private, Mr. Walker," said Silas, glancing at the clerk, who was busily engaged at the desk.

"You, Josh, jest slope, will you, and come back in half an hour!" said the lawyer, aiming a mouthful of tobacco juice at a fly on the wall by the side of the clerk's face.

Josh stretched out his long legs, and took two steps through the doorway.

"Now, then, speak out, and make yourself sure; I'll do the best that can be done in this enlightened country——"

"Where the people have so much liberty that the law ——" cried Silas.

"Now, don't you interrupt me, young Britisher; you don't know anything about our laws."

Silas bowed his head, and acknowledged his ignorance.

"Well, now you tell me what's the matter," said Mr. Walker, "and I'll tell you what's the law."

Silas, first imposing a condition that what he heard should be in strict confidence, opened his case and briefly related the main incidents of the tragedy at Frontemore, the subsequent crimes of Andrew Harwolf, of his adventures in America, even to the Lynch law trial which so nearly cost the villain his life.

"Has this man robbed you at any time?" said the lawyer.

"No," replied Silas, "though he employed a man to make an unsuccessful attempt only last night."

"Has he ever done you any bodily injury?"

"He has."

"Under what circumstances?"

Silas related the history of the pursuit across the rocky mountains, and how he was wounded by the rifle bullet.

"Had you at that time anything in the shape of a warrant for the apprehension of this Harwolf?"

"Certainly not."

"Then, according to our laws, you had no right to follow him, and he was perfectly justified in firing at you."

"You mean to say that I have no right to follow him?" exclaimed Silas, in surprise.

"Certainly; unless you hold a warrant for his arrest."

"Then, I can only say that your laws are most extraordinary."

"This sir, is the land of liberty, where every man has a right to do as he likes."

"And where, as I was about to observe some time ago, liberty is so plentiful that the law has no power over the greatest criminal," said Silas. "Well, what can I do then, Mr. Napoleon Walker?"

"The only thing you can do, legally, is to call him out and shoot him. I shall be most happy to arrange a meeting."

"Hurroo!" shouted Oiny, who had hitherto remained silent; "an' be japers, it 'll come to a foight afther all. Masther, dear, sure, now, an' its meself ull stand afore the murtherin ruffian this time."

"The Grey Wolf is mine," said Catahaga, stepping forward.

"Hollo, what's all this? Can't you agree which is to fight him? Then trust it to me; I often arrange these matters for my clients. Come, now, we'll draw lots."

All assented, and three slips of paper of different lengths were prepared and arranged so that the ends were perfectly alike.

"Come, now," said the lawyer. "The drawer of the shortest slip has the first shot."

Silas reached forth his hand and took one of the slips from the lawyer's grasp.

Catahaga followed him, and then Oiny.

Charles was unanimously excluded from the affair.

The slips were then examined, and Oiny was found to be the holder of the shortest slip, Silas second, and Catahaga last.

"Hurroo! Old Oireland for ever!" shouted Oiny, waving his blackthorn round his head. "Sure, and the blissin of Saint Pathrick be upon me, and we'll banish the varmin."

"Hold your noise, Oiny; if you are going to fight there is no occasion to let every one in the street know it."

"Och! sure, an' it's not yer hanner 'ud hinder a poor bhoy from singin' a bit ov a song?—

"'Och! Paddy's the boy for frolic and fun,
  Paddy's the boy to foight,
With swoord or pistol, an' whin 'tis done,
  He'll dance with the girls all noight."

This stave finished he performed an Irish wardance, to the great delight of Catahaga, and then was about to rush forth to commence hostilities when a thought struck him.

"An' sure, though, we must do the thing dacently, so I'll just sind the divil a bit of a challenge, if ye'll koindly obleege me wid a bit ov paper."

The lawyer, much amused at this outbreak on the part of the Irishman, supplied him with the requisites, and Oiny sat down to send his hostile message.

After immense labour and sundry erasures, the following epistle was completed.

"MISTHER HARWOLF.—You're a dirthy scoundhrel, an' if ye'll koindly stand afore me for the space ov tin minits, I'll prove it to yer satisfacshun. My pistols is in good ordher, so sind a reply to your obaydient sirvint,
                    "OINY MACARNE."

The Irishman contemplated this challenge with the greatest delight, and handed it round for inspection ere he folded and sealed it.

On the outside he addressed it to—

"THE MURTHERIN' VILLAIN, HARWOLF."

and then handed it to the lawyer for transmission to his enemy.

"I'll send my clerk with it as soon as he returns, and bid him bring you the answer at once," said Mr. Walker.

"An' tell the blayguard it's meself 'ull be after pullin' his nose wid me blackthorn shtick if he don't come out loike a gintleman," said Oiny, as he followed Silas from the office.

Mr. Walker promised that both the letter and message should be delivered, and at once went out to look for his secretary, Josh, whom he at once started off on his hostile mission.

About three hours afterwards, Josh the clerk made his appearance with a tall Yankee, who announced himself as Mr. Harwolf's friend, and after some little conversation between him and the lawyer a meeting was arranged for the following morning.

Till that time came Oiny was restless, and at daybreak he started with Silas, Catahaga, and Mr. Walker towards the place of combat.

They reached a quiet, secluded spot in the forest, where a little stream ran purling and leaping through an open glade, and the song of the mocking-bird loudly resounded from the neighbouring tree tops.

As the enemy had not yet arrived, they all sat down on the grass, and gravely smoked their pipes.

"Oiny," said Silas, "you know it is just possible you may be killed in this encounter. Have you any friends in England or Ireland?"

"Divil a one, unless it is Lord Hawksbury, an' sure, he's forgot all about the poor Oirish bhoy afore now."

"Depend on it he has not forgotten, and if you have any relatives he will not forget them."

Oiny scratched his head thoughtfully for a moment.

"Niver a relaytion can I think on, 'cept my mother's first cousin, Mother Roach they calls her, as keeps a apple stall in Dhroory Lane whin she's not in the blissid walls of St. Goiles's Workhouse."

"Well, she shall know if anything happens to you."

"Divil a happen 'ull happen at all, at all. Now, do ye think, Misther Rye, that I'll be kilt be sich a smotherin' spalpeen as this same Andrew Harwolf, who niver fought an Oirishman in all his blissid loife?"

"There's no knowing," cried Silas. "But, see, here he comes."

"Then he'll foind Oiny ready," cried the Irishman, leaping to his feet, as Andrew Harwolf, accompanied by his second, came out of the forest into the open space.

"Stay where you are," cried Silas, as Oiny was about to rush forward. "The preliminaries are not yet settled."

"Shure, I thought it was all settled iver since yesterday."

Mr. Walker, acting as Oiny's friend, stepped forward, and saluted the new comers."

"Twelve paces, I suppose?" said he, addressing Harwolf's second.

"I guess that's about the ticket, an' each feller find his own shootin'-sticks."

"Certainly, although only one shot is to be fired from each pistol."

"All right; jest you chalk out the locations."

The ground was marked out, and the men placed back to back.

"At the word 'three,' you will both turn and fire one shot each."

The two men waited the signal, as it came slowly from the lawyer's mouth.

"One! two! three!!"

The two reports came so closely together that they could scarcely be distinguished, and a moment after Andrew Harwolf was seen lying on the grass.

Ere, however, his second could reach his side, he raised himself on his elbow and fired a second shot from his revolver at Oiny, who had remained standing.

"Och, I'm kilt by the murtherin thief," groaned the Irishman, as he fell heavily forward.

Silas bent down over him, and endeavoured to staunch the blood which flowed from a deep wound in his side, while the others rushed forward to the assassin.

When they reached him, however, the villain showed no signs of life.

"The dirtiest trick I ever saw in my life," said the lawyer.

"If I'd a know'd what a skunk he were, I guess I'd a seen him darned afore I'd comed out with him," said the Yankee second, spitting a stream of saliva on the face of the prostrate Harwolf.

"Well, you'd better see about burying him," said Walter.

"I guess them 'ull bury the cuss," replied the man, pointing to a flock of vultures that wheeled round in the air at a great height above them. "I won't show my face along side him again, if I knows it."

So saying, he departed, and the lawyer returned to Oiny's side.

Silas had succeeded in staunching the blood, and

they now bore him in their arms gently towards a kind of roadway, on arriving at which, Catahaga started off at great speed to procure a vehicle.

Andrew Harwolf was left senseless and apparently dead in the forest, while the unclean birds, scenting his blood, gathered closer and closer, till at length they alighted on the neighbouring trees.

Earnestly they regarded their prey, while their numbers were increased by fresh arrivals.

At length, one more bold than the rest, rose from his perch, and after wheeling round and round, dropped like a bullet on the dead man's chest.

It was a horrid sight, indeed, to see the foul bird, whose beak was already clotted with gore, standing on the breast of a human being, in whose veins the breath of life still ran, though feebly.

Another prepared to join him, and with a loud scream the first comer drove his beak into Harwolf's face.

CHAPTER CCCVI.

DANIEL HARWOLF AND HIS CREW CAPTURED BY THE AVENGERS—THE BOY PIRATE AND HIS MEN BLOWN UP ON BOARD HARWOLF'S SHIP.

BRIERLY, as master gunner on board the "Red Raven," continued to pitch shot after shot into the hull of Harwolf's schooner, and the Boy Pirate's ship was bearing down fast on its prey, though, as yet, they were at a considerable distance.

Harwolf walked up and down the deck of his vessel in an agitated state of mind; he knew that he had no chance of escaping from the "Red Raven," and he knew well enough that his doom was sealed if he fell into the hands of Black Ralph.

"What shall I do, Walbrook? what shall I do?" he cried.

"Why fight it out like a man, and then when it gets too hot jump overboard."

"No, I won't do that; the sharks, you know, I am afraid of them ever since we took the Portuguese ship."

"Then return their shot at all events, and try your best; our long gun will reach them now."

"Will it? Then we may yet escape, some lucky shot might cripple the 'Raven' while we have all our spars untouched as yet."

"That's right, rouse up, my captain, and show a bold face, if it's only for the sake of those who cruise with you."

But, as if to swamp all his hopes, at that moment a shot from the Avengers struck his fore-topmast, shivering it to pieces.

"Out boats!" cried Christopher, from the deck of the "Red Raven," when he saw the result of Brierly's artillery. "Out boats, and board them, my boys!"

"A boat, a boat! my kingdom for a trim-built wherry!" roared Ralph, "for Richard—I mean your captain—is himself again."

With a ringing cheer the men responded, for they delighted to see their loved young commander show some of his ancient spirit.

Five minutes elapsed, and the same number of boats, full of well-armed men, were swiftly cutting through the water towards the schooner.

Lilia stood watching with eager eye the danger into which her husband was about to thrust himself.

"Grape and cannister!" roared Walbrook, when he saw the boats approaching. "Load your guns to the muzzle, and swamp the rascals, captain," he whispered. "For Heaven's sake pluck up a little courage. Hurrah! fire away, lads, we'll soon show these cocks that the ocean doesn't belong to them entirely."

The guns discharged their awful contents, and many a brave man fell beneath the fire.

But the remainder pulled away with undaunted

courage, in spite of cannon and muskets, while the Boy Pirate standing erect, seemed to bear a charmed life, as the deadly missiles hissed past him.

The boats touched the schooner's side, and with a cheer the Avengers climbed to the deck.

"Down with them!" shouted Christopher. "Take the captain a prisoner!"

Harwolf heard the shout as he plunged sword in hand into the combat, outwardly brave, but inwardly fearful and trembling.

"Down, traitor, down, and beg our clemency!" shouted Ralph, as his sword crossed that of Walbrook, with a loud clang.

The faithless steel shivered at the hilt and left the gallant Talbot defenceless.

Ere, however, his adversary could take advantage of the accident, Ralph dealt him a blow on the cheek with the fragment of his blade which sent him staggering down the hatchway.

Ralph immediately caught another weapon from the hand of a dying man and rushed to where Harwolf was engaged in combat with one of the boarding party.

"What ho! prince of rat-catchers, turn and look upon thy death!" he shouted.

"Talbot!" cried Harwolf.

"Aye, the same, so lay on Macduffer, and damned be my sword if it doesn't pass through your craven heart!"

Daniel Harwolf would willingly have avoided a combat with the roaring champion whose prowess he so well knew.

But there was no means of escape, and he was compelled to guard himself against the furious thrust which Ralph made.

"Stay, Ralph!" cried the voice of the Boy Pirate. "This is my affair, you know."

"A d——d shame! but I obey orders," cried Ralph, as he turned his blade to seek some new adversary.

With fires of vengeance gleaming in his eye, the Boy Pirate engaged with his adversary.

Pass after pass was made, and the sword of Harwolf was beaten from his grasp.

But at that moment there was a roaring explosion, and both dead and dying, together with the furious combatants, were hurled through the air.

Walbrook had fired the powder magazine.

CHAPTER CCCVII.

ADELE PAON'S TALE — AN INTRODUCTION — FANCHETTE DEVIGNE AND HER PROPERTY —LEIGHTON TURNS LAWYER—AND GOES TO PARIS.

MANY anxious days and nights did Katinka watch by her husband's bedside, and fervently did she pray that he might be spared to her; for dark and dreary, indeed, would have been her lot had she been left a widow amongst strangers, and in a strange land.

But the turning point came, when, in spite of the worthy surgeon's ominous looks, he grew rapidly better, and three weeks after the occurrence, which had so nearly proved fatal, he was not only able to leave his bed, but to walk about the little town.

During his illness the girl whom he had saved from ill usage was a constant visitor, and Leighton was much struck by the numerous good qualities and intelligence of the child, whose appearance only denoted poverty.

One day, as he was sitting in an easy chair by the fireside, for the doctor had ordered artificial warmth to be kept up, she entered, and he then made some inquiries into her history.

Her name, it seemed, was Adele Paon, and her father had been—for the poor girl was now an orphan—a fisherman on the west coast of France, while her mother, who died of a broken heart soon after her father, was the daughter of an *aubergiste* in the same district.

Her father, she said, was descended from wealthy parents, who had discarded him on account of his reckless habits, which had on one or two occasions led him to band himself with smugglers, so that she had never seen any of them, though the aunt, with whom she resided, had told her that they were grand people, and had a fine chateau.

"But surely you know some of your mother's relations?" said Leighton, when the child had revealed thus much of her history.

"Oh, yes, monsieur, I live with my mother's sister, my Aunt Fanchette."

"And is she rich? I should fancy not."

"No, monsieur, her husband was one of the band of smugglers to which my father belonged; but he was killed in a skirmish with the gendarmes about two months after her marriage, and at the same time as my father. My mother's heart broke shortly after that, and then aunt took care of me, and brought me here."

"And how long is that ago?"

"Nearly two years, monsieur. She had some money—a little which she obtained in a strange manner—and with it she purchased the little shop and garden where we now reside."

"But how was it she thus strangely obtained the money. I feel interested in your tale."

"Why, monsieur, at the little town where they lived there arrived one day a strange ship, commanded by a handsome and gallant youth, who, when on shore, resided at the auberge. He was a good man, I believe, though men said he was very wicked, at all events he was kind and generous to my aunt. Well, one night, after a little merrymaking, when everybody was asleep, the house was attacked by English war sailors, who battered in the doors and windows, and attempted to capture the young stranger, saying that he was a pirate.

"However, the brave young man escaped after dressing himself in the garments of a priest, and my aunt Fanchette managed to convey him to the boat of my father, who carried him safely off. Some time after, when my father was dead, and she had almost forgotten about the young man, she received one day a letter containing money, and the best thanks of the Boy Pirate for aiding him to escape from his enemies."

"The Boy Pirate, say you?" ejaculated Leighton.

"That was what the sailors called him who came to take him, and that was the name signed to the letter. But, monsieur, I don't think he can be like the pirates we read about. My aunt says that he was generous, brave, and handsome; I always thought that pirates were ugly, wicked people, who killed everybody they met, and burned all the ships they could capture."

"There is truth in your remarks, Adele; the Boy Pirate is more sinned against than sinful in himself. I once met him, and he treated me very generously."

Leighton did not care to let the little gossip know the whole extent of his acquaintance with the renowned Boy Pirate, thinking, no doubt, that Adele would spread the news far and wide, and that he might perhance find himself in trouble in consequence.

"Then I will call on your aunt as soon as I am able, Adele, and thank her for having rendered a service to one who has befriended me."

"She will be delighted to see you, monsieur. Adieu!"

And the merry maiden skipped off, thinking that, in spite of past quarrels, the English were not such monsters as her countrymen represented them to be.

Those days of war and bloodshed are happily long since past, and instead of sending out hostile fleets to sink, burn, and destroy our brave sailors, pay friendly visits, and bombard their ancient enemies with champagne corks, while no powder is burnt except for purposes of festivity and rejoicing.

Albion has shaken hands with La Belle France, and may the well-cemented friendship outlive the odious memory of former strife, while a friendly rivalry exists as to which nation shall be foremost in the arts of peace. Such is our national wish, with all due deference to the prejudices of antiquated naval and millitary officers.

Some four days after the conversation above related, Edward Leighton walked to the abode of Adele Paon's aunt, who kept a small shop devoted to the sale of cheap confectionery.

Fanchette Devigne, though a widow, had lost none of that blooming beauty for which she was so remarkable when the Boy Pirate paid a visit to her father's auberge.

Though pale and care-worn, there still lingered about her face an expression of benevolent kindness and warmth of heart which was well borne out by the accounts he had heard of her from various of the townspeople.

In few and simple words Edward Leighton introduced himself to the young widow, who replied,

" I am glad you have paid me a visit, sir," said she, " for I wish to thank you from my heart for the kindness you have shown towards my niece."

" Madame Devigne," said Leighton, " if you speak of my rescuing your niece from the clutches of that villain, why it is nothing more than any man would think it his duty to do under the same circumstances."

" But you have suffered much by your generous action, therefore we are doubly beholden to you."

" Name it not, I pray you ; at any time I can do you a service, I will ; for you once befriended a friend of mine."

" I know to whom you allude, monsieur, and I assure you that I have never regretted the part I took in his escape. But I will take your offer of friendship and consult with you on a matter of importance, if you will allow me."

" Certainly, madame."

" It is relating to my husband's family, who have always refused to recognise me while his brothers lived. Gustave, my husband, you must know, was the youngest of three brothers, Henri and Julian being senior to him. His father, at an early age, took a dislike to him for some reason or other, and so, while the other two were petted and caressed, Gustave received nothing but hard words, difficult tasks, and oftentimes blows. From such cruel and unjust usage, his soul revolted, and he left his home to become a fisher boy at the little town where I resided. Perhaps he chose this course on account of a distant relationship existing between us ; at all events he was a frequent and welcome visitor at my father's house, and he always called me cousin till he had a right to use a more endearing term.

" Like most of our daring seamen, he became a contrabandist or smuggler ; but that did not alter the love I bore him, though his parents and brothers were highly incensed at it. He obtained command of a little sloop, and he it was who carried your friend, the Boy Pirate, as he is called, away from his enemies when they sought to capture and destroy him.

" Well, we were married, and—I lost him after a brief space of the most exquisite happiness ; but, though gone, I have never ceased to mourn him, and though far removed from the spot where the greater portion of his life was passed, his image is ever present in my heart.

" Now, but this morning, I received a letter informing me that his father, mother, and both brothers were dead, and that, consequently, the property which Gustave would have inherited on the death of Julian, had he survived the fatal encounter which widowed me, was mine, though it had been taken possession of by some cousins, who assert that my husband was a felon, and therefore could not lawfully inherit his father's estate. You, monsieur, I believe to be an Englishman, but still, as you speak our language well, I fancied that you might know sufficient of our laws to tell me if there is any hope of my gaining what is justly mine. Not that I have

any wish to be rich unless *he* were with me to share my wealth, but for the sake of Adele, who is dear to me as though she were my own child."

" Your husband, you say, was a smuggler ?" said Leighton, when he had heard the widow's tale to a patient conclusion. " Was he ever tried or convicted, or was any reward at any time offered for his arrest ?"

" Never," replied Madame Devigne. " Though well known amongst our fishers us a free-trader, the authorities never were certain of the fact until his death. His father knew it from the fact that Gustave wrote a letter giving him the information, and upbraiding him with the cruel conduct which had driven him to such a course of life."

" And in whose hands is that letter now ?"

" My husband's father returned it, and it was burnt."

" Then," said Leighton, " as your husband was never judicially convicted of crime, and as there exists no proof of his having committed any of the illegal actions which the holders of the property now accuse him of, I have no doubt that the property is legally yours. Do not, however, take my word for it, but place your case in the hands of some acute lawyer, one who will serve your interests without betraying any of your secrets."

" I will do so," replied Madame Devigne ; and, after some other trivial conversation, they parted.

The next day Leighton departed by easy stages towards Paris, where he expected to find a remittance of money, which he had written for from Marseilles.

They reached the gay city, and found that the banker, to whose office they proceeded, welcomed them with a smile.

CHAPTER CCCVIII.

LILIA'S SORROW—A FEARFUL SIGHT—BLACK RALPH'S· NEWS—THE MIDNIGHT SEARCH—DISAPPOINTMENT — HOPE REWARDED — WHERE IS DANIEL HARWOLF?

FROM the deck of the " Red Raven " Lilia the Queen of the Avengers eagerly watched the progress of the fight between her husband and Harwolf's crew.

Who can describe the agonising feelings that racked her soul when she saw the schooner blown to atoms, knowing, as she did that her husband, her brave, devoted Christopher, was on the deck of the ill-fated ship ?

A deadly paleness overspread her cheek, and, had she not received timely assistance from those near her, she would have fallen.

Carefully the rough tars bore her to her cabin and delivered her over to the care of her servant, who, by great exertions, at length succeeded in restoring her to consciousness.

She raised herself on her elbow, with glaring eyes and disordered locks, and, in hoarse tones demanded whether there were yet any tidings of her husband's fate.

" Not yet, madam," replied the attendant ; " the boats have not returned."

" Leave me," she said.

" And is this, then, to be his fate," she murmured, when alone ; " is this to be the sad end of that life which was more dear to me than my own? Oh, Christopher, Christopher, if thou art dead what is life worth ?"

Boat after boat returned to the side of the vessel bearing ghastly burdens of mangled bodies and writhing men in whom life was not yet extinct. Some were so torn and gashed as hardly to bear any resemblance to the human form divine, while others had hardly a look of anguish on their pale faces.

Side by side, friend and foe indiscriminately, they were laid upon the deck, and then the bold seamen again started to save, if possible, other sufferers.

With glazed, tearless eye Lilia gazed along the deck.

Her grief was too great to find relief in weeping.

Her husband was not there, and once more she staggered to her cabin, where, falling on her couch, she pressed her fevered brow to the pillow, giving forth sighs from her heaving bosom which seemed each to breathe a life's burden of anguish and unutterable woe.

"Fallen, fallen, fallen!" she moaned; "I have fallen from the height, the summit of happiness, to the lowest depths of misery and sorrow! The time has come when I must be alone in this great world, for he is gone! Never more will those bright eyes look lovingly in mine, for they are closed in death! Never again will those fond arms press me so lovingly to his heart! Never more will that Apollo-like head repose on this poor aching breast!"

Then again did she restlessly start up and hurry to the deck, to hear if any tidings of her husband had been heard.

"Best go below, marm," said Brierly. "You'll do yourself no good by worryin,' and I'll tell you as soon as he comes back."

"As soon as he comes back! Will he ever come back?"

"Lord bless yer, in course he will! So cheer up, marm. Arter passin' through all as he's done, d'ye think he's comin' to the end o' his yarn just through that 'ere little blow o' gunpowder? I warrant we'll find him cruising about somewheres on a bit of a spar, or such like, as merry as a cricket. So cheer up, cheer up. I haven't give up hopes yet by a long chalk!"

Lilia could not respond to the old sailor's encouraging speech, and as in her present state of mind she could be of no service to the rescued sufferers, she retired.

Old Brierly then gave directions to another party to proceed with the search for their missing commander, muttering, as he walked forward,

"Well, I hopes I may be forgiven for sayin' what I don't believe, but I pitied the poor young creetur' so. Howsover, we mustn't give up yet."

And drawing the sleeve of his jacket across his eyes, the old tar bustled about to keep down the sorrowful, hopeless feeling he had in his heart.

All that weary night the "Red Raven" cruised round and round the spot where Harwolf's schooner had gone to atoms, and where a buoy had been placed to mark the scene.

Bright lights were hung in the rigging, and boats' crews rowed over and over the place, while every eye peered out eagerly into the gloom.

Ever and anon one of the boats would return bearing some brave swimmer, or a shattered fragment of humanity.

About midnight Black Ralph was thus rescued, though the bold outlaw was fainting from loss of blood and long exposure to the waves.

But when he revived sufficiently to speak, a ray of hope shot through every heart on board that ship.

He had seen the Boy Pirate some time after the explosion clinging to a piece of one of the schooner's masts, but he was too weak to join him, and had been floating ever since that time.

Faithful to his promise, Brierly descended to Lilia's cabin.

The fair girl slept not, though hardly awake to anything save the great sorrow and grief that had come upon her.

She opened her eyes, when the old sailor entered; then wearily closed them again, as if there were no one worth seeing save the absent one whom she saw not.

"Cheer up, marm," he said, in low tones; "there is yet hope."

"What hope can there be save in Heaven above?"

"Well, that's true, marm; but, then, after the news——"

"What news?" cried Lilia, starting up eagerly, and clutching the old sailor's hand, while her eyes glistened with a new and more vivid lustre.

"Why, he was seen alive, and well"—the old sailor added the two last words on his own responsibility—"a long time after the blow up."

The young wife bent a most earnest gaze on the sailor's face.

"You are deceiving me," she said, "you are trying to buoy me up with false hopes."

"It's true."

"Who told you this?"

"Why, you see, marm, one of the boats has just come in, havin' picked up Captain Talbot; he said as how he seed him clinging to a bit o' timber, just as I said."

The latter part of this speech was addressed to the furniture in the cabin, for no sooner did Lilia hear Ralph Talbot's name mentioned than she bounded away to seek him.

"I know he will not deceive me," she thought, as she bounded to the deck with a gleam of renewed hope in her eye.

But she saw him not on the deck, and her heart was once more plunged into the depths of woe and despair.

"You're come to the wrong place, marm," said Brierly, "he's in his cabin."

A look of gratitude was all the answer Lilia made him ere she darted off to the little cabin occupied by Black Ralph.

The bold Talbot was in bed, propped up by pillows. Two of his ribs had been broken in the explosion, and his body otherwise bruised and injured. Nevertheless, he was perfectly sensible, and smiled when he saw Lilia.

"Oh, forgive this intrusion, Captain Talbot," said the Queen of the Avengers, "but you know not the anxiety of my heart. My husband, what know you of him? You have seen him?"

"Yes, fair lady," replied Ralph, "I have seen him, and expected to have found him here."

"Your words touch me like sharp needles. Was he well when you saw him?"

"Well? I can hardly say in truth, but he was clinging to the broken mast of the doomed ship with an energy that showed there was still life in him. I was too feeble to join him or even to hail him; but if I have managed to keep afloat so many hours why should not he? So do not despair."

"Oh, thanks for those words, Captain Talbot; I will not despair. But your hurts, can I do anything for you?" said Lilia, with a kind smile.

"Well," said Ralph, "you can do something for me. I begin to feel very hungry; I could eat a round of beef, a young elephant, or a nice pickled donkey; in fact, anything, provided you give me enough of it, so, if you will find me food, I will return you my most hearty thanks."

"I will, I will," replied Lilia, as she hastily left him.

In a short time she returned bearing a tray piled with sufficient provisions for three men in ordinary times; every delicacy that the "Red Raven" could produce was there.

Ralph, however, was recovering his appetite, and, when he had washed down the repast with a moderate quantity of wine, which Lilia carefully mixed with water, he announced himself satisfied.

"I must leave you now, Captain Talbot," said Lilia. "Sleep will refresh you; but I cannot sleep until I once more behold my husband."

Proceeding to the deck she inquired for Brierly.

"What can I do for you, marm?" said the old tar, touching his hat.

"Have you no further news?"

"Not yet, though I have no doubt we shall hear or see something before the morning."

"Are any boats out now?"

"Yes, two. The crews of the others are taking a couple of hours' rest before they again begin their search."

NOTICE TO OUR READERS.—"THE BOY PIRATE" will be completed in No. 92.

A DESPERATE LEAP.

"I must have a boat and go myself. My eyes can see where theirs cannot."

"But, marm, there is a high sea running. Boating is rather dangerous work now it's dark."

"I care not for danger; I must go. Men, who will accompany me?"

There was a moment's pause in which the men looked from one to the other, then, a minute after, twenty stout sailors stood by her side.

"Six only are wanted," said Brierly; and he then selected the steadiest and strongest of the volunteers.

The boat was lowered and in it the fair Lilia with her six devoted servants, each one of whom would have risked his life in her service.

The oars were dipped in the water and the little boat was borne away on the crests of the waves. Not a word was spoken. Those rude seamen, pirates, outlaws, felt too keenly the grief of their young mistress to intrude on her sorrow by words.

A lantern in the bows of the boat threw a bright light over the surrounding waste of waters, and, armed with a night-glass, Lilia anxiously surveyed the rolling ocean on every side.

No. 89.

"There, there!" she suddenly cried, pointing with her hand to an object which had caught her sight.

The men rowed towards the spot indicated merely to find—a lump of seaweed floating with the current.

The hot searing iron of disappointment again forced its burning passage through Lilia's breast as her hopes were once more damped.

"On, on men!" she cried, "while we tarry he suffers!"

Again a floating object met her view, and with renewed energy the hardy seamen pulled towards it.

Lilia's eyeballs were strained almost to bursting; but one thing was certain—it was a man clinging to a broken mast as Black Ralph had described.

"Pull away, men! 'tis he!" she cried.

The cheering news infused hope into every bosom, and the men bent to their oars with almost superhuman energy.

But while they were yet some yards distant Lilia saw the hands gradually relax their hold, and the body slipped down into the depths of the ocean.

With a low wailing cry she sank back, while the men strained every nerve and sinew to save the drowning mariner.

But he rose to the surface again, and feebly struck out towards the timber which had been his support apparently blind to the light which was now rapidly nearing him.

But what name is that which rings clearly yet feebly above the beating of the waves? It is the name of "Lilia!"

The Queen of the Avengers heard her husband's despairing cry, and would have leaped into the waters to join him had she not been forcibly withheld.

Two more strokes of the oars and they were beside him.

A brawny seaman reached forth his hand, and the Boy Pirate was dragged into the boat more dead than alive.

Lilia bent down over her regained treasure, and eagerly kissed his pale cheeks and lips, then nestling down beside him she raised his head to her bosom, and sought to impart the warmth of her own body to his icy frame.

But he spoke not, nor was any sign of life visible.

"Give him a drop o' this, marm," said one of the boatmen, pulling a little bottle of rum from his pocket.

Lilia forced the neck of the phial between her husband's clenched teeth, and poured a few drops of the spirit down his throat. It seemed not to take effect.

"Give him a little drop more, marm, in about five minutes," said the man, "an' if you was to take a sup yourself it wouldn't hurt."

She shook her head, and huskily bade them haste to the ship.

They did so, and in ten minutes afterwards the Boy Pirate and his wife were both hoisted up the side of the "Red Raven."

As yet not a spark of vitality was visible, but when he had been laid in warm blankets, and some brandy poured down his throat, he began to breathe gently, and Lilia shed tears of joy.

"I am glad he has survived," said Black Ralph, when the news was told him; "but does any one know what became of Harwolf?"

No one could tell, his fate was shrouded in mystery.

––––––––

CHAPTER CCCIX.

MRS. DUSTYMAN'S HUSBAND'S BROTHER'S WIFE'S SISTER — HER STORY — AND HER RELATIVE—THE VISITOR.

ALL the while that Lord Hawksbury was paying his visit to Lady Hautaine, and afterwards, when he was in the clutches of the ruffians whom Daniel Harwolf had appointed to capture him, Mr. Pounce, the lawyer, was engaged in prosecuting his inquiries with regard to the now almost forgotten occurrences by which the late lord of Frontemore lost his life.

After the information he had so unexpectedly gained from Mrs. Dustyman, the charwoman, or, rather, laundress, as she insisted on being called, of course his first act was to call upon the "husband's brother's wife's sister," who, as before stated, resided at Number 3, Simms's Almshouses, near Coldbath Fields, and bore the name of Mrs. Tester.

Mr. Pounce found Mrs. Tester at home—the inhabitants of almshouses generally are, in order to receive the visits of pious ladies, High Church curates, Scripture readers, and others, from whom they are in the habit of receiving sundry trifles over and above the almoner's weekly dole.

"Come in!" said an asthmatic voice, when the lawyer knocked at the door.

Mr. Pounce obeyed the invitation, and found himself in a little room, which evidently was used both as a parlour and sleeping apartment, while a slight suspicion of the kitchen still lingered about the fire-place.

Mrs. Tester was seated in an easy chair by the fireside; her hands were clasped upon her bosom, and she rocked herself to and fro in her chair like a person in deep distress, though Mr. Pounce could see no reason for anxiety, for the room was warm and comfortable, and the good lady's face had that placid expression which shows to best advantage after a plentiful dinner.

"Your servant, sir," said she. "Pray turn—that cat out—and sit down."

She made a pause between every two or three words, to recover breath, and had a very red nose, as if she were in the habit of taking a little drop of gin (and peppermint) to clear her throat and lungs.

Mr. Pounce had a good look at the lady to endeavour to read her character ere he opened the conversation.

"You must excuse this intrusion, Mrs. Tester," he began.

"Oh, don't mention it, sir; I am always glad—to see anybody. They always finds me—in a peaceful—state of mind—except when I am out of tea and sugar—and such trifles—which most visitors makes me a present of."

"Now, Mrs. Tester, I wish to ask you a few questions, and when you have answered them, I dare say we can find both sugar and tea in the neighbourhood."

"The best is at the big—shop at the corner, sir—and, you'll always find I've—got peace of mind."

Mr. Pounce, after asserting that tea and sugar were small articles in comparison with peace of mind, promised that she should have a supply that same evening, and continued,

"Your good relative, Mrs. Dustyman, who is my housekeeper, told me that you once lived at Frontemore Hall. Now, as the place is for sale, and I think of purchasing it, perhaps you could give me some information about it."

"Ah, sir, it's a long—long time—since I was there—I left soon after—Lord Edgeforth died—a long time before—my breath was—so bad—and for which—I'm obliged to take a little drop of cordial, sir."

"Do you know how Lord Edgeforth came to die? I mean, what complaint had he?"

"Well, you see, sir—'twas only a short time after—the birth of his son, that they said he—went on the continent again. Then, in three months came the news of his death—and then Mr. Harwolf married Lady Edgeforth. I left soon after that—and my breath—got so bad—that I'm obliged—to take a drop of cordial—sometimes, sir."

"What made you leave?"

"Well, sir—I didn't care much about living there—in consequence of what—the nurse-girl told me. Ah! she was a giddy girl—though she was but very young."

"And what did this girl tell you, Mrs. Tester?" asked Mr. Pounce.

"Well, she said as how—it was all a lie about Lord Edgeforth going abroad—she said that Mr. Harwolf killed him."

"Kill him! but how could he kill him without being discovered?"

"Oh! sir, I was too frightened to ask, and left the place at once—and my breath has—compelled me to—use a little—drop of cordial—ever since, sir."

" And do you know what has become of this girl, what's her name ?"

" Bless you, sir, she ain't a girl now—she must be six and thirty."

" Never mind her age ; can you tell me her name, and where she is to be found ?"

" Her name was Ann Lewis ; but where she's to be found ain't so easily to say. But her friends lived down in that neighbourhood, and do now."

" Thank you, Mrs. Tester, I will now wish you good day, and many thanks for the information you have given me."

" You're welcome, sir—welcome as my—cordial is—when my breath gets thick—and I'm quite out—of it, sir."

" Then, here is half a sovereign to buy more with, and I will send you tea and sugar."

With these words the lawyer started off at a rapid pace, and, after watching him out of sight, worthy Mrs. Tester put on her bonnet and sallied forth to replenish her cordial bottle. Tradition asserts that she did not return till nearly midnight when she was assisted home by a benevolent beadle, and scandal even goes so far as to say that he remained —to take care of her.

Early next morning Mr. Pounce was stirring, and a hansom cab deposited him at the railway station in time for the first passenger train.

His destination, of course, was Frontemore Hall, his object to seek out the Ann Lewis who had whispered into Mrs. Tester's ears a rumour that so much resembled truth.

In order to prevent suspicion as to his object he was dressed in a kind of agricultural costume, top-boots and striped waistcoat being the more prominent points, while his make-up would have done credit to a professional detective.

The train whirled along, and Mr. Pounce's brain whirled too, for he was on the high road to fortune, if not to fame.

Only once let him come before the public as a mover in the case of Lord Edgeforth v. Harwolf, and he would be a celebrated man ; aye, and rich too, for all the consultations, journeys, visits and cash expended would be reimbursed by some one or other.

And so he went merrily and gaily along thinking to himself that if rogues were not cowards how much less work there would be for the legal profession.

In due time he arrived at the platform where he was to alight, and, after leaving his little carpet bag in the cloak room, strolled out to have a look at the deserted hall, for it was deserted, save by an old couple who had resided in the house for thirty years and more.

The hall seemed going to decay ; the grounds and lawns were untrimmed, and full of weeds and rank grass ; windows were broken, marble fountains and statues smashed, the fish-pond choked up with bulrushes, fruit trees unpruned, while what had once been a choice conservatory was now a perfect wilderness of decayed exotic vegetation.

The same neglect and dirt were visible within the mansion. The grand staircase appeared not to have been swept since Andrew Harwolf departed, so thickly was it carpeted with dust and canopied with spider webs ; the pictures were covered with filth, mildew was everywhere apparent. In the library the books were damp and mouldy, in many places worm eaten, and certainly had not been dusted for many a long month.

" What part of the house do you reside in ?" said Mr. Pounce, to the old man who accompanied him.

" We lives in the butler's pantry," said the old servitor ; " it's about the warmest room in the house."

To the kitchen and offices next, pausing to take just a peep at the old man's quarters, and then Mr. Pounce requested to be shown the cellars.

The old man paused and looked confused ; but after some hesitation he complied with the request.

The reason of the old man's confusion and hesitation was then apparent : for the door of the wine cellar was found to be forced open, and some dozens of empty bottles lay scattered about the floor.

" So, ho !" thought the lawyer ; " then there is a reason why the old man finds the butler's pantry so snug and convenient."

" Now the beer cellar," he continued, after glancing around.

Again the old man's face assumed a look of dismay ; but Mr. Pounce was inexorable, and the poor old fellow was compelled to show the way.

Again the door showed tokens of violence, while empty bottles, bearing the labels of Messieurs Bass and Allsopp, showed plainly enough the reason.

A tap, too, in one of the numerous barrels, looked as if it had been used very lately.

" Is the ale good, my friend ?" asked Mr. Pounce, in a very mild voice.

" I—I know it used to be," replied the old guide.

" Then suppose you get a glass, and we'll try it."

A smile illumined the old man's features, and he hurried away out of the cellar to fetch the glasses.

It was good, Lawyer Pounce pronounced, when he had tasted it ; genuine ale.

" Don't drink too much of it, my friend," said, Mr. Pounce, " for you know Lord Edgeforth may return some of these days."

" Not likely, sir, I think," replied the old man.

" Bye-the-bye, can you tell me if a woman named Ann Lewis lives in the neighbourhood ? I believe she was a servant in the house at the time the late Lord Edgeforth died."

" Aye, indeed she was, though I don't know what has become of her, more than that she was seen about the neighbourhood just before Mr. Harwolf shut up the hall. She used to live at a little village called Deller, about four miles from here, and, for aught I know, may be living there now. She had just come from London then, and people said she had been living a very queer life ; but I never go far away, so I don't hear much."

" And which way do you go to reach this village of Deller ?"

" Take that road by the park, sir, and when you reach the ' Hedger's Arms,' turn off to the right, and go up the hill. When you reach the top you'll see the village down in a valley before you."

" Thanks, my friend. Take this for your trouble and show me out."

The old man took the proffered coin, and ushered his visitor to the gates with great respect.

The day was mild and pleasant, so Mr. Pounce walked along very comfortably, convinced that at last he was on the right track.

" It must be all right," he muttered. " If I can only worm out this woman's secret, and, even, if the Boy Pirate cannot take the property, I have no doubt it will fall into the hands of my Lord Hawksbury, who, I fancy, is the next heir, being a cousin of the late lord as well as sister to his wife."

The little public-house, once kept by Miles, was now tenanted by a much more respectable man, who had tidied up the place, and made it look quite a snug little roadside inn.

Here Mr. Pounce stopped to engage a bed, and drink a glass of ale ; but they could give him no information as to Ann Lewis, so he pursued his journey.

Deller was at length reached, and the lawyer

addressed himself to the first woman he met to aid him in his search.

"I don't know where she lives, sir," replied the woman; "but if you go right through the village you'll come to a nasty low beer shop; they can tell you, I've no doubt."

Lawyer Pounce was not the man to be disheartened by the length of his walk, and proceeded towards the beershop in question.

It was, as his informant had described it, a nasty, low, dirty-looking place, as if it were frequented by rural thieves, tramps, poachers, and such-like village offal.

Three or four lurching rascals were sitting on a bench before the house drinking, and they all stared with surprise at the appearance of the stranger.

The landlord was as suspicious-looking a party as his customers outside; but Pounce had come into contact with a good many shady characters in the course of his practice, and knew how to manage them.

A glass of muddy-looking ale was placed before him in obedience to his direction, and, after inviting the landlord to take a glass himself, he began a conversation with him about the weather, crops, and other matters of interest.

At length came the grand and important question,

"Do you know Ann Lewis?"

The landlord stared at his visitor in surprise for some seconds ere he replied,

"What might you want with her, master?"

"Well, it's about some money that is coming to her."

The landlord made no reply, but went into an inner room to consult with his wife, who, in her turn, peeped suspiciously at the stranger through the half-open door.

At length, when everything had been discussed between the worthy pair, the beer-seller returned.

"My missis thinks you'll find her in the first house you comes to up that lane there leading to the wood," he said.

"Thanks," said the lawyer, as he left the house, glad to get away from such a disreputable place.

The house to which he was directed hardly deserved the name, being a little hovel with mud walls, and a roof of tattered thatch.

The window panes were broken, the holes being stopped by means of old rag and pieces of paper; the chimney appeared in a state of indecision as to whether it should tumble forward into the road or backward into the garden. All the neglect and decay which made Frontemore Hall look so dismal were here on a smaller scale.

Lawyer Pounce knocked loudly at the broken door.

No answer was returned, so he knocked again, louder than before.

Still no answer, so the lawyer lifted the latch and walked into the miserable hut.

"How can human beings live in such a place?" thought Mr. Pounce, as he glanced round at the bare walls, at the wide, empty fire-place, at the few articles of furniture catalogued as a table, two wicker chairs, an iron candle-stick and a kettle, all of which stood on the floor, which the ingenious architect had formed of earth, and nothing else. In one corner was a steep rickety flight of steps leading to the upper regions.

Not a sign of anything living was visible, the hearth did not appear to have seen a fire for some days.

The lawyer knocked on the table with his stick, but with the same success that had attended his efforts on the door.

Thinking that the woman he sought was gone out on some errand Mr. Pounce sat himself down on one of the hard chairs to wait her return. He had not been there many minutes, however, before the feeble wailing cry of an infant struck his ear, followed by a moan, such as a human being makes when in agony or distress.

He listened attentively; it was repeated, and sounded as though over his head.

He darted up the rotten steps without pausing to consider, and found himself in a barely-furnished room, in which was a rude bed, a table, and a chair.

On this bed was a woman, and by her side a baby but a few days old.

"Is your name Ann Lewis?" asked the lawyer, regardless of the alarmed looks of the poor wretch, who appeared almost dying.

She made no reply, but continued to gaze on the face of her strange visitor till the lawyer, struck by her silence, saw that there was a reason for it.

"You are ill, are you not?" he asked, in milder tones.

A feeble nod signified assent.

"Then I think I have something here that will do you good," he continued, producing from his pocket a flask of port wine which he had provided himself with ere he started for London. A table-spoonful of this poured down the woman's throat revived her, and in a husky weak voice, she asked,

"What do you want?"

"I want to do you good if I can. Would you like some food?"

Again the head nodded, and the lawyer from another pocket produced a paper of sandwiches.

The poor woman devoured them ravenously, and while so engaged Mr. Pounce had time to observe her general appearance, and thereby gain some insight into her character, for the lawyer was an adept in the art of reading countenances.

She appeared about thirty six years of age, and had once been handsome, but time, care, and dissipation had left their marks on her face. The long black hair, once so carefully and smoothly combed, was now harsh and untidy, the marks of several bruises and scars were on her face and neck, her eyes were sunken, her cheeks sallow, while her mouth had lost two of its front teeth. She seemed like one who, having once fallen from the paths of virtue, had gone down, and down with the current without making an effort to turn aside from her evil courses.

"How came you to be left alone in this state?" asked the lawyer, who was at heart a generous good-natured man.

"Because I am not good enough for the proud folks in the village, so I've been alone ever since my master was took.

"Ah! then your husband is in trouble?"

"He isn't my husband."

"But what is he in trouble for? Don't fear to tell me, for I am a lawyer and could perhaps get him off."

"I don't think you could. He is tried and convicted of poaching, and beating the keepers, so I don't fancy you or any other lawyer could get him out of that scrape."

"But how long ago was this?"

"A fortnight ago."

"Doesn't the clergyman of your parish know of your destitute condition?"

The woman burst out into a wild hysterical laugh.

"Of course he knows. Ha! ha! Why it was he who prosecuted my master, and when I told him that if Bill was sent to gaol I should have no one to keep me, he said it served me right for living with such a rascal."

Now as Mr. Pounce lived by law it did not become him to say that the game laws are unjust or unnecessary; but he certainly did think that in this case they acted rather sharply upon persons who, in reality, were not the offenders. A sporting parson who preserves pheasants, and is a justice of the peace, has great influence, and is a most important personage on the local bench; but in this case the worthy magistrate seemed to have forgotten that he was also a minister of the gospel, and the consequence was that a poor sick woman, with a young babe, were condemned to slow starvation, because Bill had knocked down one of the reverend squire's hares, and then half killed a keeper.

Mr. Pounce resolved to amend the game laws when he should be a member of parliament.

CHAPTER CCCX.

DANIEL HARWOLF IN THE WATER—THE DESERTED BOAT — HARD FARE — BREAKERS AHEAD—"DROWNED! DROWNED!"

THOUGH the crew of the "Red Raven" had searched a long time for Daniel Harwolf amongst the timbers of the shattered ship, they could find no trace of him, and supposed that he had been killed and his body had sunk.

Such, however, was not the case, for though thrown into the air by the explosion, the ruffianly pirate was not yet doomed to perish.

Bruised and almost stunned he fell into the water, and by good fortune alighted close by a part of a broken yard to which a fragment of canvas was still attached.

For some time he clung to this, looking around with a kind of grim satisfaction on the scene, but, when he saw boats in the act of rescuing the dying men, he drew the canvas over his head to escape observation, preferring to perish alone at sea than to fall into the hands of an enemy from whom he knew he had no right to expect mercy.

Night closed around him, and partly supported by the timber he swam swiftly as possible away from the scene of destruction, for he saw plainly the lights in the boats which were searching for the Boy Pirate.

One of the boats came near—so near, that the bowman struck the log of timber with his boat-hook, though without discovering the man who clung to it.

Then, again, he was alone with the cold water splashing and dashing over him, still swimming away from his enemies, the Avengers.

Daylight came, and he was almost senseless with the long continued exposure to the water, but on raising himself up as high as possible he rejoiced to find that the "Red Raven" was no longer visible.

But soon other feelings began to take possession of his mind; he reflected that he was alone without provisions, and that, though in the midst of water, he dared not drink.

Without provisions, I said, but the expression is slightly erroneous, for, in the pocket of his jacket he had a flask containing nearly half a pint of rum, as well as a couple of biscuits which were now soaked most thoroughly by the salt water.

He managed to eat one of them, and then continued his strange career, trusting himself entirely to the waves and not attempting to guide the log to which he clung. The sun rose higher and higher in the heavens, and the burning heat became almost intolerable. He was glad to hide his head beneath the fragment of canvas that still flapped on the surface of the water.

About an hour after the time when he judged it to be midday, the spar to which Harwolf had lashed himself struck with great force against something.

Peeping forth from beneath the canvas he saw a small boat lying keel upwards.

The devil, his master, was helping him with a vengeance, he thought, and, without more ado, he set to work to right the boat and bale out the water that nearly filled her.

That was a long and tedious task; but, at length, he accomplished it, and had the satisfaction of beholding himself master of the little craft.

He tore the canvas from the spar on which he had so long floated, and drew it into the boat.

Then, after nibbling a bit of his second soaked biscuit, and taking a drain at his rum flask, he laid himself down and resigned himself to fate.

For some hours he slept, and when at last he awoke, it was night.

His heart almost failed him when, on rising, he saw his desolate condition.

He was alone in a little boat, without compass, or the means of existence, on the wide ocean, the wild and heaving waters shutting out everything from his sight, save the cloudy starless sky above him.

Then the folly and wickedness of his life struck him to the heart; he wished that he had never been born, or that he had died in infancy, ere he knew those crimes of his father's which first urged him onwards in the hellish path he had traversed.

He even shed bitter tears of anguish as he reflected on his desolate condition, in a boat without helm, and drifting at the mercy of the wind and waves.

Hunger for a long time kept his eyes open; however, at length, after another drop of rum, he again fell asleep, overcome by cold, toil, and long continued fasting.

His sleep was long and troubled; had any one been by his side they might have heard, by his broken, half-spoken words, that his conscience was ill at ease, and that the mind, burdened with crimes, cannot rest even when the body reposes.

It was nearly day-break when he again awoke, and the sky was clear. Harwolf felt slightly refreshed, though the pangs of hunger he endured were so great that he was compelled to eat half the biscuit which remained to stifle the gnawing feeling.

He then, by tearing up one of the seats of the boat, contrived to set up his fragment of canvas in such a manner that it would serve both as a sail and a shelter from the sun.

This done, he sat himself down, and endeavoured to think what course he was in.

South westerly, evidently, from the position of the sun; but the latitude and longitude were quite a different affair. However, he had no doubt that if he kept onwards he would, if he lived,—and the rascal's heart sank within him at the thought of death—reach some part of the coast of South America.

The breeze was fresh, and his little bark went swiftly through the dashing water. There was no vessel of any kind in sight.

Some hours afterwards, he found himself nibbling the remains of his biscuit, and began to think how he could recruit his store when that was gone.

He resolved to hold onwards on his course, and as the wind veered, so he shifted his sail.

The fear of starvation made him feel all its pangs already, and he could not help picturing to himself the agonies of those whom he had often left in the same condition in which he now found himself.

Yet, as the wind continued fresh, he knew he could not be long before he made land, or fell in with some vessel.

The question then resolved itself into this:—How many days could he support existence on an ounce of sodden biscuit, and a quarter of a pint of rum?

He was determined to run ashore at the first land he made, no matter what it might be, and continued to gaze ahead, hoping and expecting, till the shades of night obscured his vision.

Then another night of feverish and broken sleep,

succeeded by another day of hunger and mental torture, he felt sick and desponding.

The third day passed, and still no signs of land. At night he became wild and feverish; he started up in the boat, tore his hair, and cursed Heaven for having brought him to such a condition.

After a while the force of his frenzy was abated, and he sat sullenly in the stern of the boat.

The night was clear and cloudless, the silver moon giving almost as much light as day.

As Harwolf sat in moody silence there was a sudden splash, and something fell into the bottom of the boat.

He started up with eager haste, and joyously grasped his prize.

It was a glittering, silvery-scaled fish, weighing nearly a pound in weight. This, indeed, was a fortune, but his joy cooled on reflecting that he had no fire to cook it, nor even a knife to scale it, so ill was he provided for a voyage.

He threw it down in the bottom of the boat, and resumed his old seat in a greater despondency than ever. It seemed to his gloomy mind that the foul fiend was thus endeavouring to torture and wrack his mind.

Another hour passed, and then he saw a something dark floating on the surface of the water. He managed to steer the boat in that direction with a little plank, which served him for a rudder. He reached out his arms, and caught hold of what he supposed to be a log of wood, but which he immediately discovered to be a small turtle.

He threw it into the boat, and again sat down somewhat reassured by this lucky catch, which, at all events, would keep him from starvation for some few days.

Then, after eyeing them greedily for a time, he fell asleep.

But he was soon awakened by the water rushing over the gunwale of his boat, which had heeled over to the side he was lying. He had just recollection enough and presence of mind to strike his tattered sail, when the boat righted, though almost swamped by the quantity of water that had entered her, and which was almost up to the thwarts.

After securing the sail he had to set to work and bail with his cap. The wind had risen, the sea was increasing, and the weather looked loweringly, as if a storm threatened. Still the night was light, for the clouds had not accumulated in sufficient quantities to obscure the moon.

He reefed the sail, again set it; the boat scudded through the water at a great rate and he felt confident of seeing land by the morning.

Hunger was still raging in his stomach, and at length, unable to resist the temptation any longer, he caught hold of the fish which was lying at the bottom of the boat, and from biting a little bit out of the tail, he gradually proceeded upwards to the head.

It was deliciously refreshing; so far superior to anything he had ever eaten before, that Harwolf wondered how people could spoil them by cooking.

However, after eating ravenously for some time, he began to think of the morrow, and had forbearance sufficient to stop at the thick part, which he placed on one side.

The meal, however, had served rather to sharpen his appetite than to appease his hunger, and he began to look greedily at the turtle which was flapping about in a helpless manner, and recollecting how very nearly it escaped when the water came into the boat, he lashed it by the fins to the thwarts of the boat, with some strips torn from his ragged sail.

The remainder of the night was spent by Harwolf in thinking how he could open the shell of the animal to get at the meal beneath, and he cursed his thoughtlessness in not having carried a knife in his pocket or his belt.

With that and a quadrant, he felt as if he could navigate the globe in his little boat, for he felt full of confidence after his meal.

That night he ran a great distance in his boat.

As the day broke, he watched with the most intense anxiety to discover land ahead, but there was no sign.

There was a heavy sea running, almost as much as his little craft could live in, and he was obliged to keep constantly baling to prevent her from being swamped.

His life seemed to depend on making some land quickly, and his disappointment can hardly be described, as the partial darkness gave way to perfect light, and he discovered himself still on the wide ocean without a speck of land on the horizon to cheer his view.

The remainder of the fish was too tempting to be preserved longer, and he soon devoured it.

For some hours he thus continued in a state of hunger and suspense; at times he thought of hauling his wind, and endeavouring to find land in some other direction.

But his steering apparatus was so feeble, and his sail so bad that he was unable to do so, and had he not instantly again put the boat before the wind he would most certainly have been swamped by the high sea.

Notwithstanding all his endeavours to keep his eyes on the horizon ahead in order that he might catch the first appearance of land, and so shape his course as not to get to leeward of it, the fierce famine gnawing at the wretched Harwolf's stomach was such that, in spite of every endeavour to the contrary, his eye first began to wander, and then remained fixedly riveted on the poor turtle.

He could attend to nothing else; his thoughts were fixed.

If he exerted himself so as to turn his head another way, it was only like shaking a compass, the poor sprawling animal acting on his glaring eyeballs as the pole does on the magnetic needle, bringing it round again to the same point. His thoughts were absorbed in imagining and devising every possible means for opening its shell.

He unlashed it, brought it aft, and sat down to look at it.

He pored over the mazy lines, cracks and divisions marked on its iron-clad back, as though it had been a chart, which he was studying to avoid dangerous rocks and quicksands.

He, for a time, gave it up with a deep sigh of regret.

Never had he seen, it seemed to him, anything so well secured from attack, except the iron safe in a merchant's counting-house. To open either without some kind of iron tool seemed impossible.

He then began to study the structure of the boat till he knew every plank by heart, to discover whether a bolt or a nail might be abstracted with safety.

But in vain was his search.

The extremities of the animal, indeed, seemed to be more in his power, but they were almost impregnable; one end being locked securely by its horny head and bony fins, while the other end was secured by his hinder fins and a kind of skin much tougher than the sole of Harwolf's thick shoes.

As to its head, the beast seemed to be aware that it was invulnerable, and never even put it out of the case.

Harwolf then strove to crack the shell by hammering it against the gunwale of the boat, but the wood gave way in splinters, without the slightest fracture being made in the turtle's hard armour.

At length, after many fruitless attempts, he succeeded in grasping its head, which he secured with a little piece of rope-yarn, and killed it by the only expedient he could devise.

And a most murderous task it was, for to take its life he was compelled to gnaw through the skin of its throat, which he did, though his face was much bruised and scratched by its fins, which the poor creature flapped wildly about in its anguish.

He then thrust his fingers into the breast, forced off the flappers, and so got into it.

But in his haste or ignorance of such matters he burst the gall, and, on coming to eat the flesh, could hardly swallow it, so bitter it was.

In vain he washed it, the filthy taste still remained.

But there were a quantity of eggs in the animal, though they were but small, and these Harwolf found were the best part of his prey.

After satisfying his hunger he tore the remainder of the meat from the shell which he placed in such a position that it would catch the rain if any fell, of which he had hopes, for the sky was black and lowering.

An hour after it poured down in torrents and his tank was soon filled.

He took a deep draught and then a mere sip of rum, after which he felt much revived.

He then once more turned his attention to the ocean ahead, fearing to lose land unless he kept a sharp look out.

And it was well for him that he did, for, after the rain had continued two hours he saw land on the starboard bow.

The sight of this island, for such it was, revived his spirits.

The breeze was still freshening, indeed a fearful gale was coming on, and Daniel Harwolf strained every nerve to make the island quickly.

Although the boat almost flew through the water, driven by the old sail and one of the thwarts, which Harwolf used as a paddle, and the spray dashed over him, yet in his impatience it seemed that she lay like a log.

He saw several other islands to the south of this, so that if he missed one he still had a chance of making the other.

But the sun had nearly sunk below the horizon when he had approached near enough to the land to be able to see the surf breaking on the rocks that nearly surrounded it.

In his anxiety to reach the shore he heedlessly let the boat run on, neglecting to avoid the rocks and shoals or to seek a place where he might land easily.

When he saw what his impatience had brought him to it was too late to rectify the error.

The little boat scudded wildly on where the surf was highest and most furious, and Harwolf suddenly found himself embayed amidst rocks over which the waves were fiercely and unceasingly beating. In his too great eagerness to escape from other perils he was devoting himself to destruction on the far more dangerous rocks.

He let go the rope by which he had held the sail; it fluttered wildly in the wind.

The sea birds flew over him, screaming wildly.

The little barque, almost buried in the blinding spray which beat upon him like a hailstorm, was tossed and whirled about with the greatest violence, and she had shipped so much water that Harwolf hardly knew whether he still floated in her or the sea.

Just as the boat was borne by a high wave madly against a rock to be dashed to pieces, the wave, not breaking, bounded back like a ball, hurried her against the opposite rocks, and then again rebounded as if in sport.

The noise of the winds and waves breaking all about was deafening.

The space between Harwolf and the shore was white as milk, and frothy as a boiling cauldron; the land seemed close, yet he could not reach it.

Suddenly the boat disappeared from beneath Harwolf; it had been shaken to atoms by the fury of the elements.

Though he could swim his efforts appeared vain, for when he had, by expending all his strength, approached within an arm's length of one of the rocks, the swell would drive him back again mocking his exertions. He was bruised much, as tossed hither and thither he strove in vain to effect a landing. The timbers of the little boat which had hitherto done him such good service were dashing about in the foaming waters, and many a severe blow did he receive from these.

At length, worn out and bleeding at all parts from wounds inflicted all over his body by the sharp lancet-like points of the coral rocks against which he was driven, he felt himself going down.

He believed that it was all over with him, and the events of his past wicked life seemed to be sternly arraying themselves in judgment against him in this hour.

Bodily pain he felt not; the mere fact of death would not have been so dreadful it it were not for the fearful hereafter, which he could not but believe in, and which now seemed so near at hand.

Perhaps his previous exertions, hunger, fatigue and loss of blood rendered him more insensible to bodily feelings than another man would have been in his hopeless situation.

However that may be, the water closed over his head, and still he mechanically struggled on to avoid the doom which was so close. He seemed not to sink, but to be suspended in the water.

Then came a pang as if his heart had burst, and Daniel Harwolf's senses fled, leaving his body at the mercy of the waters.

CHAPTER CCCXI.

ANDREW HARWOLF'S FATE—THE LEPACOTAH INDIANS—AN IMPORTANT CONSULTATION—CATAHAGA GIVES THE CASTING VOTE.

WE left Andrew Harwolf, the father of the villain whose fortunes, or misfortunes, we have just been tracing, lying senseless in the forest glade after his duel with Oiny Macarne.

Silas Rye fully believed that his old enemy was dead or he would not have left him.

The Indian believed his spirit was gone to the hunting-ground of the blessed, or his scalping-knife would at once have put an end to the wretched man's life.

Oiny Macarne fancied that his enemy was "kilt entoirely," or, in spite of his wound, he would have returned to batter in Andrew Harwolf's skull with his sprig of shillalegh.

The lawyer, too, and the second of the senseless man, fancied all was over with him, and departed.

But when the unclean bird drove its sharp-pointed beak into his cheek, Andrew Harwolf once more returned to consciousness, and waved his arms wildly to scare away the feathered foe.

With a loud scream the bird flew away to rejoin its companions on the tree-tops, and wait for a more propitious moment to renew the attack.

Then Harwolf feebly endeavoured to sit up, but found himself unable to do so.

So, with eyes wide open, he lay just as he had fallen, watching the foul brood of vultures, and wondering whether it would be his fate to be their food.

Again and again the birds came swooping down to him, but a wave of the hand was sufficient to warn them that the time was not yet come, and they would then return to the tree tops, where lazily basking in the sun, they would wait patiently for hours.

The day passed slowly and wearily along. Harwolf's tongue was parched and his frame fevered; a stream ran at no great distance; he could hear it rattling along over its stony course; yet he had not strength enough to drag his limbs thither.

Not a sound was to be heard in the forest save the flapping of the wings of those patient watchers, as they shifted from one branch to another to obtain a better view of their expected feast.

Then the sun began to sink below the tall trees of the forest, which threw long shades across the face of the wounded man.

Night was coming, but not help or succour in this his fearful extremity.

The prairie wolf began to howl his mournful voice, echoing harshly beneath the lofty over-arching forest trees; the vultures wing their flight away to their roosting-places.

A feeling of utter loneliness and desertion came upon Andrew Harwolf's soul, as he thus lay helplessly in the great forest. He would have prayed for help and assistance, but instead of the humble petition nothing but curses and blasphemy could issue from his parched lips.

At length, when the shades of night had fallen upon him, he slept a deep and feverish sleep.

Strange indeed was his awakening, for he found himself in a strange place, in the midst of strange faces.

While he slept, a party of Red Indians had discovered him as they were returning from San Francisco, whither they had been to dispose of their skins, dried meat, and other commodities. Finding the white man alone in the woods, and sorely wounded, they lifted him to the back of one of their pack-horses, and conveyed him to the place where they intended to encamp, proposing to restore him to his friends when he should be well enough to travel.

So that when he opened his eyes once more, the scene was so striking, that he almost fancied himself in the infernal regions.

Three large fires surrounded him, and between these might be seen half-naked men and women, whose dark skins glowed almost like molten metal in the blazing light.

In a circle between the fires might be seen the tall, powerful forms of a dozen painted warriors, headed by a chieftain whose grey scalp-lock and wrinkled face told that age at least was one of his qualifications for command.

In this respect the Indians in some measure resemble our own enlightened military legislators, who, holding fast to the maxim that age begetteth experience, ignore the fact that it also produces decay of the powers, bodily and mental.

Standing at a respectful distance without the circle might be seen a few lads who had not yet attained the dignity of full-blown warriors, and a place in the council just as an ensign may take his seat at a council of war, though, of course, any suggestion he might make would not be listened to.

Women, children and dogs were grouped around in attitudes original and grotesque in the extreme.

A silence, only broken by occasional monosyllables, was maintained both within and without the circle; an old savage would occasionally grunt a remark to his neighbour, who would answer with a similar guttural brevity.

When Andrew Harwolf raised himself on his elbow and gazed curiously around every eye was fixed upon him, while every throat uttered the syllable,

"Ugh!"

Then, wrapping themselves in their blankets, the warriors sat in expectation for their chief to speak and open the parliament.

The Indians were dressed and painted variously, though all wore the colours by which they might be distinguished from another tribe, namely, a broad yellow stripe across the forehead just above the eyebrows, with another descending at right angles from it and reaching to the tip of the nose.

Beyond this there was no attempt at uniformity in their costume; for some of them were attired in blankets on which was worked the wearer's symbol or nickname by which he was known, while others wore skins of bears and buffaloes. Some sported moccassins, others travelled barefooted. Ornaments were very plentiful, especially in the way of beads and feathers.

Some few of the party carried rifles which they well knew how to use, while others were compelled to content themselves with bows and arrows. Every man, however, had a tomahawk and scalping knife at his girdle.

Exactly opposite the aged chief, who was called Walnahoshtehamtah, or Bird of Much Wisdom, was seated a youth of twenty or thereabouts, decked in a kind of hunter's shirt which was stitched all over with many colours.

This youth at a sign arose from his place and proceeding to the spot where their baggage had been piled, quickly returned with the camulet or pipe of peace.

This he reverently filled and presented to the chieftain, who took a few whiffs, then passed it to the man on his right hand who did the same, and so it travelled round the circle with the exception of the Indian who sat at the left hand of the aged chief.

This man alone passed it by with an air of disdain.

"A white prisoner was in their power," he said. "Why should they become squaws?"

This warrior was the medicine-man, priest, or wizard of the tribe, and with many of the warriors he had far more influence than the chief himself.

He was very fond of making very ambiguous prophesies, and then attributing any accident that befel any member of the band to a neglect of his advice or injunctions.

He was a short man, though he possessed a breadth of shoulders that betokened enormous strength. His arms were disproportionately long, and his head a full size too big for his body. The dress which this mysterious yellow dwarf assumed was of untanned beaver skin—a most costly material; on his legs and arms, which were bare, he had painted devices of snakes, toads, and other loathsome objects, while a necklace of rattlesnakes' fangs was suspended from his neck, while at his side he carried a bag filled with bones, teeth, stones, nuts, and other articles of *vertu*.

When he passed away the pipe without smoking, every eye was fixed upon his hideous face, while murmurs, some of dissent, some of approbation, were heard on all sides.

A moment afterwards he rose to his feet, performed some act of necromancy with the contents of his bag, then addressed the expectant and listening circle.

"Let the ears of the red man," he said, "be open to the words of Maratahnow, the medicine-man of the Lepacotahs. His words are true, and he tells no lies. Many years ago, the red men dwelt in peace in the shades of the thick woods, or on the bosom of the boundless prairie. The deer and the buffalo were plentiful, and the beavers lived only for the good of the red man—the favoured child of the great manitou. The war-hatchet was buried amongst all our tribes, while the smoke of the camulet ascended from the midst of the wigwams. Then came the white man from beyond the land of the rising sun; the white man came armed with fire-bow, with broad axe, and long knife. They killed the deer in the woods, and drove the buffalo to seek fresh pastures. Many of our young men were slain by their strange weapons, and many more died through the drinking of their fire-water which burnt their bellies, and dried up the blood in their veins. They said, 'Give us land that we may plant and reap, and grow corn.' Land was given them, yet, like hungry dogs as they are, they still cry, 'More! more!' Shall we give them more? Shall the great Lepacotahs be driven from their wigwams and their hunting-grounds to make room for these pale-faced

LORD HAWKESBURY ENTRAPPED.

squaws? No! let them return to their big canoes, to their land beyond the rising sun, and leave the red man to chase the buffalo, the deer, and the beaver, which the great manitou has given his children. Let them die if they remain in the land of the Lepacotahs! Let their scalps hang in our wigwams! And let the prisoner who is now in our midst be bound to the stake that the red men, the braves of the Lepacotah tribe, may bury their tomahawks in his flesh! I have spoken!"

Murmured grunts were heard on all sides as the speaker resumed his seat on the ground. Many were for commencing their refined torture at once, but as the chief rose to reply they remained still.

"Wahnahoshtehamtah," began the old chief, "is an aged man, his head is frosted with many winters. He remembers the time when the white man had not set foot in these forests, and when the buffalo knew not the sound of their fire-bows. But the white men are many in number like the leaves on

No. 90.

the white oak, and my young men, though brave, cannot contend against them. Let us leave the white man alone, and not dig up the war-hatchet which will cause so much bloodshed. Let the prisoner depart when his wounds are healed. It is good."

The old chieftain sat down, and it was evident from the quiet of the warriors that the numbers were nearly equally balanced for and against the prisoner.

Up started the young Indian who had performed the office of pipe-bearer to the old warrior.

"Let my fathers listen," he said. "Rapid River is like the branch of a tall pine rent away from the parent stem by the thunderbolt. I am the son of a chieftain who fell treacherously slain by the cowardly pale-faced Yengese. The white men are dogs; the blood of a red man is too precious to be spilled by them, and they must be driven from the land, for we cannot hunt in the same woods with these curs, and it is poison to drink of a stream where the white man has quenched his thirst. Let the prisoner die! my tomahawk thirsts for his blood."

"Ugh! it is good!" said several of the warriors, as the fiery young Indian once more resumed his seat.

Yet the prisoner had another orator to defend him, who rose for the purpose of delivering his speech.

"Let the white man live," said this warrior, who was a bloated-looking fellow with fat stomach and large fiery-looking nose that told tales of the firewater. "Let the white man live! Are the Lepacotahs too rich? Are skins so plentiful that they can afford to throw away their arrows? Let the pale-face be sent to his tribe, and we shall receive blankets and lead and much rum, which will rejoice the hearts of my brothers!"

And, thinking that after rum there was no other argument could be used, the fat warrior resumed his seat, having done some good for the prisoner by his harangue, for the Lepacotahs, like most Indians, were passionately fond of spirits.

The ancient chieftain then proceeded to recapitulate the evidence or opinions of the speakers, concluding by calling on the warriors to give their votes.

The manner of their voting was this. A long straight stick was laid in the midst of the circle, the old chief and the medicine man sitting on opposite sides as the heads of different factions.

The warriors one by one struck their knives into the ground on each side of the stick, those who desired the death of the prisoner burying their blades to the handle at the feet of the medicine man, while the rum-drinkers and peace-makers placed theirs in the turf on the side of the old chieftain.

The women and children all watched the process eagerly, for the torture of a prisoner was a luxury they could seldom indulge in.

The warriors, twelve in number, gave their votes in silence, and then the chief proceeded to count the numbers on both sides.

They were equal!

But as he announced the fact a long arm was stretched over into the circle, and a thirteenth knife was struck into the turf along with those of the peace party.

Every eye was turned towards the intruder, and they beheld a tall powerful young Indian in his paint, and carrying a rifle in his hand.

"My brother is welcome," said the ancient warrior, presenting the new comer with the pipe of peace, which he at once took a few puffs at then returned it.

The new comer sat down on the grass after performing a grave salutation to the company.

"Will not my brother reveal his name and his tribe?" continued the old warrior.

"I am Catahaga, the Eagle Wing of the Pawnee Loups," replied the new comer, and Andrew Harwolf, who had fallen into a slight doze, awoke at the sound of that dreaded name.

CHAPTER CCCXII.

LORD HAWKSBURY RESIGNS HIMSELF TO FATE—THE DANGERS OF SMOKING—"FIRE! FIRE!"—THE RESCUE—AND AN AWFUL DEATH.

WHEN Lord Hawksbury was hurled a second time into captivity by the ruffians who had entrapped him, he lay for a long time motionless.

When he at length recovered a sufficient degree of energy to look about him, he discovered that he was in a room which much resembled the one in which he had first been confined, except that the roof was at least a foot higher, and the door appeared much stronger.

All that evening and through the dark night he lay huddled up on the floor, having at heart the double object of deceiving his gaolers into the belief that he had given up all idea of escape as hopeless, and to give himself time to recover from the many bruises he had received in his fight on the tiles.

While struggling with his adversaries on the roofs he had an opportunity of observing that he was somewhere in Westminster, for the Abbey turret seemed hardly more than a quarter of a mile distant, while beyond he could see the top of the Nelson column in Trafalgar Square.

It was a low, wild, and lawless neighbourhood he well knew, and the villains who had so neatly entrapped him seemed to be in league with others equally at war with society. A man might be killed there without his cries attracting attention, and there could be no doubt but that such ruffians would have ready means at command for the disposal of the body.

Early in the morning the cabman who appeared to be at the head of the conspiracy, entered with a breakfast of muddy tea and coarse bread as before.

He had in his hand a heavy loaded stick which he flourished menacingly as if to warn the prisoner that any attempt to escape would be repelled with blows.

"I suppose you see by this time, my lord, that it's no use trying to get away from this comfortable little place where we have you?" he said.

"You will not dare keep me long; my friends will be on the search, aided by the best detectives in London."

The man winced slightly at the mention of detectives.

"Well, they are very clever, no doubt, but they don't find out everything."

This, alas! we know, is too true, for any one with a memory extending back only half a dozen years into the past, can doubtlessly call to mind many instances of fearful crimes being brought to light, the perpetrators of which have as yet evaded the hand of justice.

Lord Hawksbury thought of many such cases.

"I suppose, then, you mean to add my name to the long list of victims whose murderers are at large still?"

"Not at all, my lord. If you die, I don't suppose it will be by the hand of any one at present in the house. When our employer comes, you will be handed over to his custody, and he will determine your fate."

"Well, from Mr. Harwolf I can indeed expect little clemency."

The man started at hearing that his employer's name was known to the prisoner.

"Who told you? I suppose, though, that rascal Joe has been chattering. I shall be obliged to give him a tap on the head to keep him quiet."

"That rascal Joe—if that be the name of the fellow who brought me my food in the other room—has not been chattering or revealing any secrets. I gained my information in a very different manner," replied Lord Hawksbury. "But, as Mr. Harwolf does not happen to be in England at present, allow me to ask if it is his orders that I am to lay on bareboards till his return?"

"Certainly not; you shall have a bed and bedding to-night, though it will be spread on the floor."

"Well, then, I suppose I must resign myself to my fate, and make myself comfortable as long as I am allowed to do so."

"It is much the best plan, my lord; and just let

me remind you that, though I and my companions bear you no ill-will, yet we must obey the commands of our master. Any attempt to get away will at once be stopped with club, knife, or pistol bullet."

With these comfortable words, the man departed, leaving Lord Hawksbury to his reflections, which you may be assured were none of the pleasantest.

He knew not even what object Harwolf could have in keeping him thus immured, nor was he even aware which of them it was, though in his own mind he had fixed on the father of the apparent heir to Frontemore as the instigator of the ruffianly action.

The morning passed in a dull, heavy manner, during which the imprisoned nobleman devised several plans of escape, all of which were impracticable for want of implements.

His dinner consisted of a steak and a pint of porter, and about an hour afterwards one of the gang brought him a mattress and some blankets, which he spread on the floor of the room.

As soon as it grew dark, Lord Hawksbury undressed himself, and was soon buried in a sound sleep, not, however, before he had devised a plan which, though fraught with danger, seemed feasible.

The next day he rose with a light heart, resolved to put his plan into execution.

After breakfast, he requested his guardian gaoler to supply him with a pipe and tobacco or cigars, to pass away the time.

The man did so, and, thinking that his lordship might like to amuse himself with reading, brought several old copies of "Bell's Life," affirming that it was the only paper worth reading.

"But I want some matches to light my pipe," said Lord Hawksbury.

The man unthinkingly gave him a handful from his pocket, and then retired.

The whole day long Lord Hawksbury smoked and read his newspapers in a very contented manner, so that the man under whose charge he was thought that the prisoner had completely resigned himself to circumstances over which he had no controul.

But when it grew dark and he knew that he would be troubled with no more visits that night, then Lord Hawksbury began to prepare for his grand design.

He first examined the mattress which was stuffed with dry straw.

After a vigorous attack with fingers and teeth, he managed to tear it open, the contents he piled against the door.

The blankets were torn into three strips each, which, when twisted and tied together, formed a strong rope of considerable length.

When thus ready, he struck one of his lucifers, applied it to the heap of combustibles, and, retreating to the furthest corner of the room, watched the progress of the flames.

First a dense smoke filled the room, while the flickering flames crept hither and thither devouring the light straw, and licking the timber of the door with its hot forked tongue.

Taking good aim at the sky-light above, Lord Hawksbury threw his pipe at it and completely smashed one pane of glass, making an orifice through which the dense vapour poured in heavy columns.

Both the flooring and the door were now fairly on fire, and as Lord Hawksbury watched its rapid progress, he began to have some fears lest the spirit he had thus unceremoniously called up should devour him.

"Fire! fire! fire!" he shouted, with all the strength of his lungs.

"Fire! fire!" screamed a boy in the street below, whose quick young ears had caught the sound.

Men and women at once stopped to gaze round to see the locality of the conflagration, some fearing lest their own poor homes should be the prey of the devouring element.

The dense smoke soon told them where the fire was, and again that dread cry resounded through the streets as men rushed to hurry the engines to the scene of action.

By the time the inmates of the house could rush to their prisoner's room an impassable barrier of flame was between them.

A few pails of water were thrown on the roaring mass, but it had little effect, and then the next object of these men was to seek their own safety by instant flight.

As they passed out into the street one of them cried aloud,

"Make haste with the fire-escape! There is a man at the top of that house, and we can't get at him!"

A few minutes afterwards, the tall apparatus of ladders on wheels was seen coming round the corner, while at the same time an engine dashed in to the opposite side of the street at full gallop.

It was indeed a fine sight to see the splendid animals galloping madly forward as though conscious that life and death depended upon their swiftness and strength.

"Which room is he in?" cried the fireman. "Where shall we plant the escape?"

There was no answer, and when the bystanders looked about for the person who had told them that there was a human being in the house, he was gone from their sight.

Without wasting time in vain endeavours to discover the informant, the men placed the escape against the side of the house, and quickly ascended to the roof.

Another engine came tearing wildly along, and the water began to rush up in a torrent in the street, to the great delight of a multitude of small bare-footed boys, who dashed and dabbled their feet in it, splashing everybody but themselves.

A minute after the fire-escape was placed against the wall of the burning house Lord Hawksbury could hear footsteps on the roof.

"Help! help!" he shouted.

The firemen heard the cry, and rushed towards the spot.

With their axes they shivered the window to atoms and peering through, beheld the nobleman kneeling in one corner.

"Hold the end of this rope, Jem," said one of the men, detaching a cord from his waist.

Jem did as desired, and his companion, in a moment, slid down through the broken window into the burning room.

They were brave fellows those two firemen, and most of the brigade are, though a sneering misanthrope once stated that they were paid, and only did their duty in preserving life from death.

The man who entered the room found that Lord Hawksbury, though still sensible, was so distressed with the heat and smoke as to be unable to stand.

Not a moment was to be lost.

Quick as thought, the man lashed the end of the rope round the captive's body, just beneath the arms, and then called to his companion above.

"Haul away, Jem, and give us back the rope as quick as you can."

In less than a minute Lord Hawksbury was dangling over the flames, which had now nearly reached to the middle of the floor beneath the sky-light.

Then a stout hand grasped him by the collar, and dragged him up on the roof where he lay for a few minutes incapable of action.

Then the fireman on the roof lowered the rope, and Lord Hawksbury's preserver quickly clambered up it, and reached the roof in safety.

Just as they were about to descend the escape,

loud cries from another part of the roof fell on their ears—a female's voice in distress.

Hastening to the window which gave light to the room in which he had first been confined, Lord Hawksbury perceived the old woman who had given the alarm when he first tried to escape.

The fire had rapidly crossed the staircase, from one room to another, descending even to the floor below that which had first been ignited. The stairs had fallen in, so that it was impossible to escape by them.

It took but a short time to shiver the glass, as they had done in the case of Lord Hawksbury, but then the firemen found another and more difficult obstacle had to be overcome.

A double row of stout iron bars had been fixed across the opening since that young nobleman's escape, and to force these was a work of time with the bold men.

They laboured with pick, crowbar, and axe, but the irons were well and firmly fixed.

When it became known below that an old woman was imprisoned in the burning house, the excitement became tremendous.

Another escape was reared, and the men strove to force through the wall.

But the bricks were hard and well cemented together.

Meantime, within the fire stayed not its progress, though water was poured upon it in streams: it had too strong a hold on the building.

"Save me! Save me!" cried the woman, as the flames approached nearer and nearer.

"We will if we can!" replied those on the roof, as they strained every sinew to rescue her from the fearful situation in which she was placed.

The crowd beneath was immense, and though kept back by the police, their yells and shouts were so deafening that the words of the firemen on the roof could not be heard by their comrades below.

"Pass a hose up here!" shouted Lord Hawksbury. "By pouring a quantity of water down through the window we may prevent the fire from reaching her."

It was done, but ere the engine could play the flames caught hold of her tattered dress.

"Oh, save me! Help!" she screamed, fighting against the fierce burning flames with her hands and rushing wildly about the narrow space of flooring that still remained.

It was a fearful sight.

Lord Hawksbury, sick at heart, fainted away, and was lowered down the escape.

Even the firemen, inured as they were to such scenes, were compelled to avert their heads from the horrifying spectacle.

At length, urged on to madness by the flames, which now enveloped her, the poor wretch, with one last despairing shriek, plunged into the yawning gulf of fire, and was seen no more.

The smoke and flames shot up more briskly than before, and although the firemen worked with a will, they could not save the house or the adjoining one.

The fire had its will, and by sunrise the next morning nothing but a heap of smoking ruins was in the spot which had been the scene of Lord Hawksbury's strange imprisonment.

When he recovered his senses, the nobleman at once told his tale to the police, who heard it with wonder and astonishment.

The most expert detectives were set to hunt up this secret band of ruffians, and bring them to justice, but for a long time they were unsuccessful.

CHAPTER CCCXIII.

ANN LEWIS DIVULGES AN IMPORTANT SECRET TO MR. POUNCE RESPECTING THE MURDER OF LORD EDGEFORTH—THE LAWYER AND THE MAGISTRATE.

MR. POUNCE, the lawyer, as I have before said, resolved that if he ever reached the dignity of Member of Parliament he would devote a little of his leisure time to the amendment of the game laws, being moved to this little piece of reform by the consideration of the wretched object on the bed before him.

For some minutes there was a silence, in which the poor miserable woman intently gazed on the face of her visitor to endeavour to discover what kind of a heart beat beneath that striped waistcoat.

Lawyer Pounce's face was not so easily read, yet though the poor woman could not fathom its every expression, there was nothing of unkindness or cruelty visible in it.

"I know not who he may be or what he wants; but I will answer his questions, for he will do me no harm."

Such were her thoughts as she gazed upon the lawyer's countenance, and a few moments afterwards he recommenced the conversation.

"You know Mrs. Tester, I believe?" said the lawyer.

The woman shook her head; the name had escaped her memory.

"Who was formerly one of the upper-servants at Frontemore," continued Mr. Pounce.

Ann Lewis considered for a few seconds and then replied,

"Ah! I do remember; there was a person of that name there."

"I thought you would recollect if I gave you time. Now, were you not at the hall when the late Lord Edgeforth died?"

A wild look of alarm passed over the woman's face.

"Why do you ask?"

"Don't be alarmed, my good woman, you will do yourself no harm by telling me."

"Yes, I was there," replied Ann Lewis, gazing in a terrified manner at her questioner.

"You were there when the late Lord Edgeforth died?" repeated the lawyer, taking down her replies in his note-book.

The woman gave a nod of assent.

"And you saw him die?" continued the lawyer, fixing his keen eye full on her pale withered face.

"I!" shrieked the woman, covering her face with her hands. "No! no!"

"Think again," said the lawyer, "and recollect what I told you. You will meet with no harm through speaking the truth, whereas, by an ill-advised silence, you might be regarded as an accomplice in the fearful crime committed by Andrew Harwolf."

"Crime! aye, it was a crime, indeed!" said the woman, "but how came you to know aught of it?"

"A word escaped you soon after the occurrence, which Mrs. Tester treasured up in her mind."

"Then I will tell you all I know about it, sir. I was under nursery servant at the time, and I recollect well that on that fearful night I had occasion to go to the room in which that precious babe slept in his cot. The door was locked, but I peeped through the keyhole. I saw a sight I shall never forget. Lord Edgeforth was lying prostrate on the floor, and Mr. Harwolf was beating his brains out!"

"And why did you not at once give information of this hellish deed?"

"Because I feared he would kill me, he was such a bad and violent man."

"Oh! how many other crimes would have been

prevented if you had at once given the murderer up to justice," exclaimed the lawyer.

"But, sir, recollect I was a young girl then, barely fifteen years old."

"There is certainly some excuse to be made for you."

"And then when I grew older I feared to tell, lest I should be punished for not revealing the secret before; but it is off my mind now, and I shall be able to meet my punishment more boldly."

"Your punishment will be but a slight one, if indeed you receive any at all," replied the lawyer.

"Ah! sir, I have been punished sufficiently already. The terrors of mind, the fear of detection, and the horrible dreams which I endure at night have played havoc with my mind, and by driving me to seek refuge in drink ruined my body; but pray, good sir, tell me if you know what became of that sweet babe, the real heir to Frontemore? I know well enough that the lady Andrew Harwolf married was not Lady Edgeforth, nor was the young cub, whom he called the heir, the babe that I nursed."

"The real heir to Frontemore Hall lives, and it is to restore him to his rightful property that I am here making these inquiries."

"Then, sir, I will do all I can to atone for my past conduct by assisting you all that lies in my power."

"You can best do that by subscribing to the tale you have just told me in the presence of a magistrate," replied Mr. Pounce.

"A magistrate?" echoed the woman, something of her old alarm returning at the idea of coming face to face with the representative of justice.

"Even so. It is merely to sign a declaration, not to appear as a prisoner.

"But sir, I am ill, I cannot go to the magistrate's office."

"The magistrate will come to you then, so that there will be no difficulty."

The poor woman was silent for some few minutes. At length she continued,

"I suppose he will be hanged for it, sir?"

"Most certainly, if he is caught."

"And I shall have to give evidence against him?"

"Yes, undoubtedly."

"Well, it must be so, though I don't like to be the means of bringing any one to the gallows. It would seem to be as bad as putting the rope round his neck."

And certainly when we come to consider the horribly debasing and degrading nature of capital punishment, we can hardly feel surprised at the poor woman's scruples. Death in any shape exhibits terrors; but to the criminal condemned to die on the gallows it must be the most awful of all punishments, or no punishment at all.

To lie for days in the condemned cell, to be visited by the chaplain, to be summoned forth by the officers to meet the executioner, to walk on to the platform and be dimly conscious of a roaring scoffing crowd, who estimate a man according to the contempt he shows for the law and the law's punishment, will have such an effect on the mind that either the wretched criminal breaks down beneath the accumulated load of suffering, or inspires the beholders to emulate his deeds of darkness by "dying game."

Ann Lewis had been a spectator at more than one execution, and though she had scoffed and jeered at the sufferings of a stranger, yet it seemed to her mind most awful to be the means of meting out justice even to the most hardened and ferocious murderer, and such was Andrew Harwolf.

But having gone so far she could not now retract. The keen-eared lawyer had taken down every word of her statement.

While she was still thinking over the past and the prospective future the lawyer rose to take his leave.

"I shall return to-morrow with a magistrate to take an official deposition," he said, "in the meantime here is money to procure necessary articles for yourself and babe. When I return to the village I will send a woman to nurse you."

The woman clutched the money with an eager air.

"Recollect, no spirits allowed," said the lawyer, as he departed.

With a light heart he once more found himself on the high road again. A great link had been welded into the chain which, whether it bore the weight of a jury's opinion or not, would have to be paid for. It would be paid for Mr. Pounce knew right well.

The worthy lawyer was a queer compound of the generous and avaricious. Professionally he was as close-fisted a solicitor as ever charged six shillings and eightpence, or lent money at twelve and a half per cent., yet in private life or when the tale of poverty and woe was poured into his ear, he was a man, and an open-hearted one.

Reaching the village his first thought was to provide the nurse he had promised his odd pensioner. To effect this object he addressed himself to a member of the police, the only representative of the force to be found within a circuit of six miles.

"Well, sir," said he, of the oilskin hat, "I knows this ere Ann Lewis, and a queer 'un she is, mixed up wi' a lot o' rum c'rackters; but for a consideration I dare say my wife's sister would take charge of her."

"Good! I'll pay her what she likes, and then you can keep an eye on her, too, to see that she doesn't run away."

"Werry well, sir, I'll see to it."

"Now, tell me where the magistrate lives, my man?" continued the lawyer.

"Well, sir, our clergyman is the magistrate, leastwise, when I've got any charges I takes 'em before him."

"I suppose you don't have many cases down here?"

"Not many, sir. Sometimes boys steals turnips or apples, and once in a while there's a case of poaching. This 'ere ooman's man were a one o' that lot."

"Ah! What is the reverend gentleman's name, and where does he live?"

"It's the Reverend James Crofts, and he lives at the Vicarage close by the side of the church up yonder."

Mr. Pounce slipped a guinea into the hand of the officer, who certainly exhibited none of the activity and intelligence displayed by his London brethren, and then proceeded to the Vicarage.

The Reverend James Crofts was seated in his study composing a sermon on the text "Love one another," when the visitor was announced. Notwithstanding the holy nature of his employment, and the benevolent bearing of his text, the rural priest's heart was filled with bitterness and anger. A sturdy farmer had just issued a circular to his rate-paying brethren calling upon them to oppose the church-rate, and to abolish certain Puseyite ornaments and ceremonials which the Reverend James had introduced. No wonder, then, that his congregation stared, when, on the following Sunday, he delivered so sweet a subject, and then discoursed so sour a sermon.

"Sir, what can I have the honour to do for you?" said the reverend gentleman, as Mr. Pounce entered.

"You are a magistrate, I believe?" said Mr. Pounce.

"I am."

"Then, I wish you to take an official deposition."

"With pleasure; but who is it, and what about?"

"A parishioner of yours, named Ann Lewis."

"Sir, I can hear nothing more of that abandoned woman."

"But, sir——"

"But, sir, I am determined never to have anything to do with her any more. Kindness and threats alike have failed."

"Your duty as a magistrate must not be neglected. I am a solicitor."

"Well?"

"I will, therefore, call on you to-morrow morning, in order that we may go together to her house."

"It is perfectly abominable that a clergyman should be thus interrupted in the midst of his priestly duties to hear a tale told about that low woman. At what hour will you call?"

"At ten, precisely, sir. I will now wish you good evening."

"Good evening."

And the holy man again sat down to his sermon into which he infused an additional dash of sloe juice, while the lawyer proceeded towards the little roadside inn where he proposed to sleep, highly satisfied with himself and all the rest of his fellow creatures.

CHAPTER CCCXIV.

THE BOY PIRATE AND THE LITTLE OLD WOMAN —THE AVENGERS CAPTURE THE PIRATE SHIP "RED STAR,"

IT was many days ere the Boy Pirate recovered from the severe wounds and bruises he had received in the explosion; and it was only by the most careful nursing that he was once more restored to health and strength.

The two ships, after calling at New Orleans for their consorts, cruised for some little time about the Gulf of Mexico, at length came to anchor in a lagoon on the coast of Texas.

On the deck of the "Red Raven" was a boy, a stranger to most of the crew, and yet a favourite with every one on board the ship.

He had been found floating on a raft during the passage from New Orleans to their present anchorage, and though he seemed grateful to his preservers, yet he obstinately refused to give any account of himself.

The age of this youth could not be more than thirteen, and though very slightly built, the most casual observer could not fail to be attracted by his appearance, which betokened more than ordinary intelligence.

Finding him so obstinately reserved, the crew soon ceased questioning him, and he became known on board the "Raven" by the name of Peter.

Captain Christopher and Black Ralph were pacing the deck in the cool of the afternoon, when a boat was seen coming off from the shore.

Now, as the Avengers had supposed that part of the coast to be uninhabited, the circumstance excited some little surprise, inasmuch as all their own men were on board their respective vessels.

In the little craft was seated an old woman who apparently had a mixture of Indian and Saxon blood in her veins.

A few moments afterwards, she was alongside the "Red Raven," and, after inquiring for the captain both in Spanish and English, clambered up to the deck.

"One of Macbeth's witches," said Ralph Talbot, as he gazed on her curious costume and form.

The woman appeared to be nearly sixty years in age, quite small in frame and very much bowed down by disease or privation. Her hair was long and matted, and had once been jet black, but was now much interlaced with silvery lines; but her eyes were still bright, and glowed like coals of live fire with an intense brilliancy.

Her garb was very simple, consisting of the coloured blanket and skirt usually worn by the Indians of that part, who were half civilised, the only protection for the head being the folds of the blanket, which she could draw up at will. Her legs were shielded by untanned leggings, and on her feet she wore light boots of buffalo hide, such as are common amongst the Indians of Mexico and the adjoining coasts.

Take her all in all she was a curiosity of humanity, and, as she stood on the deck with her back bent, she looked like a dwarf with a huge hump, and reminded the beholder of one of those supernatural beings who so cunningly predicted the future to the Thane of Cawdor.

"I am the captain, my good woman," said Christopher. "What want you with me?"

"Why, Senor English," said she in a strange mixture of Spanish and English, "I see that your ships are well armed, and I would have you do me a service."

"Name it."

"I have heard of you, senor—no matter how—but I have heard that you are good and generous to the needy and oppressed. I have a daughter, senor, who is young and beautiful. She is a prisoner in the hands of pirates."

"What is the name of her captor?" demanded Christopher.

"He is called Jilok Tudel, and his ship is named the 'Red Star,' but my daughter is not on his ship, she is confined by him in a small but strong house about thirty miles from Vera Cruz."

"Then you wish me to rescue your daughter and restore her to you?" said the Boy Pirate.

"That is what I would ask of you," replied the woman, "and I will pray for you unceasingly."

"But, supposing I go in search of her, how am I to know the house in which she is imprisoned?"

"The house is the only one in the village which boasts of a height of two stories, the windows, too, are strongly barred. If you see such a house whistle the first bar of the tune 'Paciencia y barajar,' then pass on to the third and the fifth bars. She will answer you by singing the second, fourth and sixth strains of the tune."

"Good! and by what name shall I know your daughter?"

"She is called Irene St. Marc," replied the old woman, and, having said so, she once more stepped into her crazy-looking cockle-shell of a boat.

"Now, farewell, senor," she continued. "We shall meet again ere long."

As she spoke she dipped her paddle into the water, and was quickly lost to sight in the gloom, which now began to gather over both ocean and shore.

Nothing more was said on the subject till supper-time, when the youthful Boy Pirate imparted his plans to Black Ralph.

"I am ready and willing, though my arm is only a week out of the sling," said Ralph. "I like these stirring times, and, come blows or whacks, at least we'll die with jackets on our backs."

The following morning all hands were turned up at daybreak, and, having informed the principal officers of the object he had in view, Christopher ordered the anchors up and sail made; and ere the boatswain's whistle piped to breakfast, the "Red Raven" had cleared the lagoon, and entered the broad gulf.

The other vessels remained at anchor, forming a kind of rendezvous for the "Red Raven" in case of necessity.

The wind was moderate from the southward, and Christopher laid his course to the eastward, intending to take the track of vessels bound from New Orleans to Matamoras, having heard accidentally that the pirate of whom he was in search haunted that particular pathway of the ocean.

Thus he stood on till near night, and just as the sun was going down a sail was discovered to the eastward, which at length proved to be a brig standing in towards the coast.

Just as it grew dark Christopher spoke to her and found her to be a brig bound for Matamoras with a general cargo.

"Have you seen anything of a Mexican schooner?" inquired the Avenger, as he came up under the brig's quarter.

"Don't know," returned the commander of the merchantman; "but about three hours ago one of the men in the top saw a sail away to the south'ard and east'ard, but we lost sight of it."

"Could you make out which way she was standing?"

"I should think, from the way in which she went out of sight, that she was standing to the east'ard, and, perhaps, to the north'ard of that."

By this time the two vessels had fallen so far apart that it was difficult to understand more, and Christopher, squaring up his sails, stood on.

During the night a strict watch was kept up, but nothing was seen in the shape of a ship save their own shadow.

On the next morning, however, just as the men were getting up from their breakfasts, the lookout at the fore-topmast cross-trees reported a sail right ahead.

In half an hour more it was made out to be a brig standing to the southward.

All sail was put upon the "Red Raven," and at the end of an hour the stranger was found to be a vessel which aped the appearance of a man-of-war, her ports being plainly visible.

"She looks like a Mexican," said Christopher.

"And if she's not a Mexican man-of-war she must be our friend with the peculiar name—the pirate in fact," said Ralph Talbot, who was using his glass. "Look you, my bold captain, we'll stand on to the east'ard a few minutes, just to see what she'll do. They surely haven't time yet to tell that we've changed our course."

Accordingly the "Red Raven" was kept on, and in fifteen minutes more the stranger wore about and stood for her.

The wind was but very little south of west, and the brig had been standing on the starboard tack before she wore.

The guns of the "Red Raven" were all masked by sliding ports, though they were ready to run out at a minute's notice.

"She hopes to take us without a doubt," said Christopher, with a smile. "However, let her work awhile. We'll be certain who she is before we make any decided movement."

The "Red Raven" was now standing due east, and the brig was nearly abreast of her standing on a course across her forefoot.

Thus matters rested for half an hour more and then the brig was not over a mile distant.

She then hoisted the Mexican flag and fired a gun.

"That's rather cool, upon my word," said Ralph Talbot.

"It is; but if he knew whom he had fallen in with, I don't think he'd be quite so easy," said Christopher; "but we'll soon show him his mistake. Mr. Brierly, you may distribute small arms, and open the magazines. Have all hands turned up, and prepare for action. Work with a will, lads."

Thus speaking the Boy Pirate turned his glass once more and examined the brig; when he again spoke to his officers his face wore a gratified expression.

"It must be Tudel's vessel," he cried, closing his glass, "a man-of-war would never have her decks in such slovenly order. I think there can be no mistake, and, if he is not ours by the time the sun sets, the brave old 'Red Raven' must have lost half her good qualities."

By this time the brig was within half a mile and had fallen upon the "Red Raven's" quarter; all the men of the latter vessel had armed themselves and were standing by their guns ready for the command.

The Boy Pirate then ordered the French flag to be run up, and, the next minute, the tricolour folds were flapping out from the mast-head.

The sham Mexican then fired another shot which ploughed up the water under the "Red Raven's" stern.

"Stand by," cried Christopher, whose nether lip was now set, and whose step had become stern and emphatic as though he stood on impregnable ground. "All ready to take in the foretopsail!" he cried. "Aloft, and stand by to furl the sail!"

"Then, thank Heaven, we don't intend running to-day!" muttered Ralph Talbot, throwing out his chest, and giving a sigh of relief as he examined his pistols.

"I think our shot will reach her now," continued Christopher.

"No doubt o' that, sir," replied Brierly; "you might swear to that afore a justice."

"Then stand to your guns, lads, and we'll give 'em a taste of our starboard battery," continued the youthful commander. "Sheets there, fore and aft. Stand by to run out the guns."

This order was quickly obeyed, and, as soon as the guns had been run out, the priming was applied, the lighted matches were blown, and the captain was informed that everything was ready.

"Then return his compliments as quickly as possible. Helm a-port—easy. Round in on the sheets, so—steady."

This movement brought the "Red Raven" directly across the brig's bows, and the guns upon the starboard side having been well loaded with grape and round shot, old Brierly gave the order for the captain of each gun to fire as his piece was brought to bear on the enemy.

This was but the work of a minute, the reports following each other in rapid succession.

Without waiting to see the effects of the shot the "Red Raven" was kept on into the wind and put about in fine style, so that, in a few minutes, the larboard guns began to make their voices heard.

By this time the Mexican had begun to round in for luffing, but, ere she could turn her head away, the Avengers gave their second broadside.

When the smoke lifted it could be seen that the brig's fore-yard was carried away in the slings, some of the starboard fore rigging shot away, and the maintopsail cut to pieces.

"She's ours!" cried the excited Captain Talbot; "there goes her fore-yard, and round she goes into the wind."

"Shall we carry her by boarding?" asked the Boy Pirate, in clear, ringing tones as he glanced round at his expectant crew.

One simultaneous "yes" burst from the lips of the crew, and the next moment the order was given to bring the "Raven" to the wind.

The Mexican brig now lay stern to, and consequently could bring no guns to bear as the Avengers came up.

Christopher himself prepared to board in person, while old Brierly at the helm brought his vessel up under the pirate's quarter, and the grappling irons were thrown with such exact precision that the "Red Raven's" bows were stopped directly beneath the brig's main chains.

The Mexicans, who stood ready at their guns, had nothing to do but to drop their matches and seize their cutlasses.

Christopher was foremost on the deck of the pirate vessel, and, with the first sweep of his sword, Jilok Tudel's lieutenant fell.

It was but the work of a moment for the Avengers to gain the deck of the brig, and, when once there, they went to work with a power of purpose which was irresistible.

The Mexicans were bold men but they could not withstand the strange reckless bravery that met them now; for there are peculiarities of bravery other than the mere brute force and science of arms.

A knowledge of conscious right and of moral superiority, and the prestige of nationality, all have to do with the chances of the combat.

At all events the men of the "Red Raven" seemed almost like men inspired.

Where their blows fell death followed, and, ere long, the enemy began to give way.

From the commencement of the combat Black Ralph had endeavoured to find Jilok Tudel, and at length he met him; but, ere they could cross their swords, some of the Mexicans called out for quarter.

"Never!" shouted Tudel, in blind rage, "fight to the death every man of you! By the cross, the first man who flinches shall fall by my own hand! Now, senor."

This speech had the effect of bracing up the nerves of the Mexican pirates, but it also caused the Avengers to smite with new force in their arms.

As Tudel spoke the last sentence he crossed swords with Black Ralph; the pistols had all long since been fired and the combat was with cutlass alone.

At the second stroke Ralph struck up his antagonist's sword and would have passed his own through the pirate's body had not one of the Mexican men, who happened to stand near, beaten his weapon down.

That moment would have been the bold rover's last but for the timely assistance of the boy they had found on the raft.

He had been ordered to remain on board the schooner, but as the fight progressed his enthusiasm overcame every other consideration, and, seizing a sword and pistol, he rushed upon the deck of the brig.

He sprang upon the quarter-rail just in time to see the sword of Black Ralph beaten down, and an enemy's weapon at his breast. With quick motion, but steady nerve, the lad raised his pistol and shot the Mexican dead.

Ralph saw the movement, and, with a nod of gratitude to the boy, returned to the conflict.

Tudel had regained his guard, and his next blow was a downright cut at his antagonist's head. Quick as thought, Ralph sprung forward, and caught the coming blow upon his left arm, reaching far enough in to take the hilt upon his elbow, not the blade.

The movement was as unexpected as it was sudden, for the Mexican had never before thought of such a thing as warding a sword blow with the naked arm. The force of the blow staggered Ralph for a moment, but, with one smart blow from his fist, he felled the villain to the deck of his own vessel.

The downfall of their captain was the signal for renewed cries for quarter, and, at a word from the young commander of the "Raven," the combat ceased. Tudel had only been stunned by the effects of his blow, and, as soon as the master villain had been secured, Christopher turned his attention to the crew.

The conflict on the pirate's deck had been a sharp and severe one. Weapons of death had been used by those who meant death in every blow they dealt. The Avengers had only two men killed though seven or eight more were wounded.

The prisoners were all ironed and kept below, for the captor, as yet, hardly knew what to do with them.

The "Raven" then once more returned to the lagoon where she had left her consorts, but not until the Mexican ship had been fired in such a manner that nothing could save her from destruction.

It was nearly sunset when the Boy Pirate rejoined his fleet, and then he found waiting him a messenger, whom he had sent to procure all the local newspapers, in order to know whether his presence on the coast of Texas was known or expected.

After seeing that Jilok Tudel was safe, and that the sentry over him was wide awake, the young man went down into his cabin, and eagerly began to peruse his file of papers.

For some hours he sat, and had just finished an exciting article when he thought he heard a slight noise in the water.

Instantly he arose and threw open the cabin-windows.

It was nearly dark, for the moon was obscured behind a huge bank of misty vapour.

Yet, in the imperfect light, he fancied he saw a dark form gliding away over the waves.

"Who's there?" he cried.

No answer was vouchsafed.

"Speak, or I fire!"

Still the object, whatever it was, floated onwards without responding to his cry.

Christopher seized his pistols, and fired in the direction of the suspicious form.

KATINKA, THE POLISH MAIDEN.

The sound of the shots awakened those on deck, who, to tell the truth, had been sleeping instead of watching.

The sentinel at the top of the companion ladder challenged and then fired.

In an instant all was commotion on board the "Red Raven," though no one knew precisely the cause of the sudden alarm.

The men who had retired to rest came hastily up, half dressed and half armed.

"What is the matter, what is the matter?" they cried.

"Look to the prisoners!" cried the Boy Pirate.

The men below found themselves in perfect darkness when they were aroused, and mentioned the circumstance to their captain.

"Bring lights!"

Lights were brought, and a strong party descended to the berth deck.

No. 91,

All the prisoners were safe, with the exception of the pirate captain, Jilok Tudel.

His place was vacant, and by the side of a gun was stretched the sentry who had been placed in charge of the villain.

The guard, who was none other than the tall Yankee who had shipped at the Cape of Good Hope, was dead; a long, keen-pointed knife was driven quite through his head from one side to the other.

"Out with the boats!" cried the excited Boy Pirate, "the villain cannot be far off; his dress is so conspicuous that it is impossible for him to escape."

The boats were lowered, and about to put off when Zampa made his appearance in the most scanty clothing he could possibly wear, that is a shirt, and nothing else.

"Look'a here," cried the negro, holding forward a roll of something, "dat d——d rascal steal a nigga gemmen's clothes an' run away. What he leave dese ere for?"

And shaking open the bundle he displayed the picturesque costume which Jilok Tudel had hitherto worn.

"You must help to catch the thief, Zampa!" cried Black Ralph, who himself proposed to head the pursuing party.

"You trust dis 'ere nigger," said Zampa, "him won't 'scape me."

And he hastily jumped into the Mexican trousers, and then into the boat.

The shore was low, flat, and but scantily timbered, yet the fugitive was favoured by the darkness of the night, and quickly made away into the interior ere his pursuers reached land.

Black Ralph divided his forces, and spent several hours in the search, but unsuccessfully.

At length, an hour after daybreak, he returned to the ship, dispirited and out of temper.

CHAPTER CCCXV.

LORD HAWKSBURY FIGHTS A DUEL IN A GAMBLING HOUSE—HIS FLIGHT TO PARIS, WHERE HE MARRIES JESSIE VERE.

THOUGH Lord Hawksbury has, during the course of this narrative, performed many good actions, the reader must not therefore imagine he was faultless.

Like most men of wealth and rank he had follies, and his particular folly was gambling, downright straightforward gambling—that is to say, he would go to a room near Pall Mall, along with other noble swells, and there hazard hundreds of pounds on the turn-up of a card, or on the fall of a pair of dice.

So one evening, not long after his memorable escape from the hands of his enemies, he sauntered forth from his Belgravian mansion with the purpose and determination to play, in order that he might forget the screams of the old woman whom he had seen perish.

He entered the room where he was well-known exchanged a word or two with the snobbish proprietor, and then advanced to the centre table.

"Good evening, my lord," said a stylish-looking young fellow, apparently a foreigner both by his dress and speech.

"Good evening, Theodore," replied Lord Hawksbury.

The man was an Italian, who had suddenly appeared in the midst of the best society of London, though no one knew where he came from.

"Will you play with me, my lord?" asked Theodore di Vitelli.

"With pleasure."

"Ecartè, I presume?"

"Certainly."

"And the stakes?"

"Anything you like."

"Suppose, then, we say a pony on the game?"

"Agreed!"

A table was set, and the two friends commenced playing.

For some time all went well.

Lord Hawksbury won the first game; the Italian won the second, and the third was in progression, when Lord Hawksbury saw in a large mirror before him, the figure of the proprietor of the room making some signals to his adversary.

This little circumstance excited his attention, and though he saw no more communications pass, yet he resolved to keep a watch on the Italian, feeling pretty certain that he would cheat if an opportunity presented.

A fresh pack of cards was put upon the table, and Lord Hawksbury narrowly watched his adversary as he dealt them.

The Italian seemed to be aware that the Englishman's eyes were upon him, and was unable to perform any of the little tricks that he had hitherto been using to his own advantage.

But the habit of cheating had taken so strong a hold on him that he was unable to refrain from it for any great length of time, so that when four or five more games had been played, with varying success, and Lord Hawksbury's suspicions were lulled to a certain extent, he once more took advantage of a moment when the nobleman's eyes were averted, to conceal the four kings in his sleeve.

Again they commenced playing; but, unluckily for the Italian, he contrived to drop his prizes on the floor.

Lord Hawksbury saw the cards fall, and though he could not be certain from whence the cards came, yet he felt sure that foul play was the cause of such a mischance.

He rose from his seat, saying as he did so,

"I play no more."

"And wherefore, my lord?" demanded the Italian.

"I prefer to gamble with those who play fairly."

"What mean you, my lord? Do you mean to accuse me of cheating?"

"There needs no accusation when the proof is so evident," replied Lord Hawksbury.

"This is insolence unprecedented," cried the Italian.

"Yet not uncalled for," replied the Englishman.

"Weally this is funny!" exclaimed the Honourable Ensign Silverspurs. "We haven't had a wow for some time."

"This may explain how you managed to lose three thousand last week," whispered his friend, Lieutenant Royster.

"I see," said the Italian, "that an unlucky accident has caused the company to look upon me with suspicion. There is but one way to clear my character, and that is, to demand from you, Lord Hawksbury, such satisfaction as one gentleman can accord another."

"You wish me to fight, I presume?" said Lord Hawksbury.

"There can be no other interpretation placed upon my words."

"I might, without loss of caste or honour, refuse to meet one whom I pronounce a swindler, a cheat, a blackleg, yet I waive all those considerations. Name your time, place, and weapons."

"The time, now!—the place, here!—the weapons, rapiers!"

"Weally, my lord," cried the Honourable Ensign, "you must allow me—aw!—to be youaw fwiend in this mattaw."

"Willingly," replied Lord Hawksbury.

A half-pay captain volunteered to peform the same friendly offices for the Italian stranger, and the room was cleared for a combat.

Nor was it the first time such a scene had been enacted in that gaily decorated saloon. Human blood is naturally hot, and gambling is apt to provoke quarrelling.

The tables were cleared away, leaving an open space beneath the central chandelier, swords were brought, and then the doors were locked.

"But is there no way of settling this affair without fighting?" said one of the spectators, who was not quite so eager to see blood spilt as his companions.

The half-pay officer consulted a moment with his principal.

"The only remedy is an open and public apology from Lord Hawksbury," he then said.

"Which I do not choose to make," replied the young noble.

"Then the duel must take its course."

And with this sentence ended all attempts to bring about a reconciliation between the parties.

Both the principals then stripped, and rolled up their shirt sleeves, while the two seconds measured the weapons.

Lord Hawksbury, as the challenged person, had his first choice, and after trying the temper of both selected one.

The other having been handed to the Italian, the combatants advanced into the centre of the rooom, and crossed their weapons.

Lord Hawksbury had learnt and practised the noble art under the best Parisian masters, and was quite a match for his antagonist, who, like all his countrymen, was a skilful fencer.

It was evident that the Italian was bent on mischief, and that if a chance offered Lord Hawksbury's life would certainly be sacrificed to appease his vengeance.

But the Englishman would not give the chance, and, though the foreigner practised every art known in the fencing schools of his native land, he could make no impression.

Suddenly a piercing shriek was heard, a private door was thrown open, and a black-eyed, dark-haired girl rushed forward between the angry combatants.

"Oh! Theodore, Theodore, put up your sword! Monsieur, pray do him no injury; he is my husband!"

This unexpected apparition caused no slight sensation amongst the aristocratic frequenters of the gambling house.

"Peace!" cried the Italian, in harsh tones, "retire to your chamber."

And in an instant his weapon was again crossed with that of Lord Hawksbury.

But the gambler's eye was not so steady nor his wrist so firm, and in another moment Lord Hawksbury felt that the point of his sword had pierced his adversary's breast.

A piercing shriek burst from the lips of the dark-eyed girl as she saw her husband fall bathed in blood.

"Oh, my husband! my husband! Look once more upon me! Speak to me once again!"

A look of maddening sorrow passed across her brain as the Italian fixed his eyes on her for a moment with a baleful scowl, and then closed them in the sleep of death.

"You had better make yourself invisible for a time, my lord," said the gentleman who had tried to stop the quarrel. "This Italian was in partnership with our worthy host, if I mistake not."

And, to judge from the unamiable looks with which the ostensible proprietor of the gambling-house regarded the successful duelist, it might well be surmised that such was the case.

Prudence suggested the course, and Lord Hawksbury quickly quitted the apartment.

But instead of proceeding direct to the railway station to seek refuge on the continent, he once more turned his steps towards Chelsea.

Lord Hawsbury could not conceal from himself that he loved the pretty work-girl whom he had so strangely encountered in one of his nocturnal rambles about the west end of town.

On reaching the little house in Arabella Row, Chelsea—which Jessie Vere maintained by her earnings—he found that she was about to retire to rest.

She blushed when Lord Hawksbury entered, but yet seemed pleased to see him.

"You must forgive my negligence in not calling before, Miss Vere, but many circumstances have prevented me from so doing."

"I could hardly expect your lordship would honour us with a visit," replied Jessie.

"Yet I have often thought of you, and congratulated myself on the circumstance — disgraceful though it be to me—which first made us acquainted with each other."

"That circumstance caused you to form a bad opinion of me," said Jessie.

"Which subsequent events have entirely eradicated."

There was then a few moments silence, during which Lord Hawksbury's gaze was fixed admiringly on the blushing girl before him.

"Where is Mrs. Vere?" he inquired at length.

"She retired to her room some minutes before you knocked, and I was about to follow her."

After a few moments' hesitation Lord Hawksbury continued,

"Miss Vere, I proceed to Paris to-morrow morning, so that it will, probably, be some weeks ere I see you again. But may I have the privilege of writing to you during that interval?"

"My lord, I—I don't think——"

"Dear, Jessie," cried the nobleman, falling on his knees before her, "I love you more than words can tell—be mine—be my own wife, and thus give me an opportunity of leading a more respectable life than when I first met you."

Poor Jessie trembled in every limb, and was so agitated as scarcely to be able to reply.

"My lord, think what a difference between us; you a nobleman, I a poor seamstress."

"I think of nothing but your goodness and beauty, Jessie, dear; and when you are mine, the difference will be levelled."

What could she say in reply? She could not with truth say that she did not love him, for she knew, in her own heart, that she did.

She, therefore, remained silent.

Lord Hawksbury wound one arm round her waist, and again spoke the important question in a low whisper.

In faint accents came the trembling answer, "Yes!"

"Dearest, you are mine for ever," he whispered, as he printed kisses on her lips and forehead.

What more they said, it is unnecessary to repeat; but Jessie sat by his side with her fair head reclining on his shoulder till late in the night, and when, at length, they parted, it was with the distinct understanding that, within a week, they should be united to part no more.

The next day Lord Hawksbury occupied rooms in one of the most fashionable French hotels, while workmen were busily engaged in fitting up a superb mansion for the reception of a bride.

Such was the magic rapidity with which the Parisian upholsterers and decorators worked under the influence of English gold, that in four days the preparations were complete.

On the fifth day a marriage was solemnized at the chapel, and in the presence of the English ambassador, and Jessie Vere became Lady Hawksbury.

And right proud was the nobleman of his beautiful wife as he received the congratulations of a circle of admiring friends.

Jessie was happy; she had experienced bitter privations in early life, but now all was passed away.

Eagerly as Lord Hawksbury scanned the London newspapers, he could gain no tidings of the Italian whom he imagined he had killed in the gambling house.

At length he received a letter from his *friend*, Ensign Silver-purs, stating that the foreigner was not dead, but had been seen in Baden-Baden, along with his dark-eyed wife.

"Then we may return to England as soon as you please, my love," said he, drawing his wife towards him.

"When *you* please, my love," cried Jessie, throwing her white arms round him; "for my pleasure is to be always with you."

CHAPTER CCCXVI.

THE AVENGERS ATTEMPT THE RESCUE OF IRENE ST. MARC — JILOK TUDEL SHOOTS IRENE — THE BOY PIRATE AVENGES IRENE'S MURDER.

AFTER Black Ralph's unsuccessful search on the shores of the lagoon, for the pirate, Jilok Tudel, the Boy Pirate, or rather Avenger, as he now called himself, made sail towards that point of the coast where the old woman had informed him that the stronghold of the Mexican outlaw was situated, and where, therefore, the daughter of his informant was in confinement.

A day's sail it was from the spot where he had captured the Mexican vessel, and it was night when he cast anchor before the little tower, which, with its beacon light, was a likely object to attract the attention of the mariner.

For when Jilok Tudel was absent from his tower the light was kept constantly burning, in order that he might be able to run into a little creek or harbour on the banks of which his tower was placed.

In the present instance, as his ship had not returned, the light was burning in pursuance of orders.

But as Christopher knew not whether it was intended as a guide or a warning, he picked his way cautiously with the lead, till arrived within about five hundred yards of the shore, when finding that he had barely a fathom of water beneath his keel, he prudently dropped his anchor.

Not knowing what garrison the pirate might have in his stronghold, our hero observed the precaution of taking with him a well-armed party of eight men, whom he placed in readiness at the foot of the steep ascent, which on landing he found led up to the house.

And a queer-looking old place it appeared, by the dim and imperfect light.

Built perhaps a century ago, when the red men were masters of all the country, save some of the more important towns and villages, it presented a strong front to any party of men who were not provided with artillery.

A high wall surrounded the greater portion of the building, joining the hexagonal tower, so that three sides only of that structure were undefended.

The builder had employed the sun-burnt bricks, or *adobes*, used in Mexico, and the whole appeared to be of immense thickness.

No window appeared within ten feet of the ground, and then they were crossed with bars of iron.

Beneath one of these our hero halted, and in accordance with the old woman's instructions, whistled the first bar of a tune well known in the the regions of central America, called "*Paciencia y Barajar;*" then passing on to the third, and from that to the fifth bar.

A few moments elapsed, then a light which appeared to be shaded was seen at one of the windows of the tower.

Christopher waited a few moments, and then repeated his serenade.

A soft female voice was then heard in low tones singing the alternate bars of the melody.

A dark form came to the window and obscured the light, but the stars were sufficiently brilliant to enable him to see that it was the form of a female.

It could be no one but Irene St. Marc, and Christopher softly whispered her name.

"Holy Virgin, who calls?" said the young lady.

"A friend who comes from your mother, and

who will, if it be possible, deliver you from captivity."

"But, senor, it cannot be."

"Why not?"

"I am locked in this room, and the windows are barred."

"Both these obstacles may be overcome with patience and courage, senora. But how many men has the pirate left in charge of this tower?"

"Only five."

"And can you trust me?"

"Yes; any fate is preferable to that which the outlaw designs for me."

"Then, fasten this iron crook to the bar of your window, and then drop the end of the rope to me."

So saying, Christopher threw a coil of rope up with a good aim.

It passed through the bars and fell upon the floor of the room in which Irene St. Marc was confined.

The lady obeyed his directions to the letter, and in another minute the chief of the Avengers was at her window.

The bars were strong, and not to be wrenched from their sockets by his unaided efforts.

A file which he had brought with him was brought into active service, and in a few minutes the obstacle was removed.

Christopher then entered the room, and, by the light of the lamp, saw her whom he had come to rescue.

Irene St. Marc was a true child of the tropics. Though not more than sixteen years of age, she was a woman in appearance, for the fierce sunshine of her native land produces early maturity.

Tall and graceful in her movements, with hair glossy and jet black as the raven's wing, she moved with the majesty of a queen, her black eyes flashing like diamonds. Her cheek was flushed with mingled hope and excitement, and her full bosom heaved with emotion.

"Now, senora, where is this door through which it is necessary to pass?"

"Here. But surely, senor, you do not mean to undertake the task of facing all those fierce men without assistance?"

"Ah, I had forgotten that. But *my* men are not far off; I will call them if you have no objection."

"Your men? Who and what are you, senor?"

"I am the captain of a ship which was attacked by Jilok Tudel. I sunk his ship and captured him, but he contrived to kill his gaoler and escape."

"And your men hate him?"

"They do."

"Are they enough to overcome the pirates who remain here?"

"Eight well-armed Englishmen, should, I think, be enough to battle with five ruffianly robbers."

"You, then, are English, senor?"

"I am, senora; and, as an Eglishman, will I rescue you from this ruffian, who, I have no doubt, will soon return. My wife will be glad of a companion on board my ship."

"But you will restore me to my mother, senor?"

"Certainly; were I to do otherwise I should be worse than him whose actions I feel it my mission to punish."

With these words he advanced to the window and blew upon a small whistle the signal which would bring his men to his aid.

In less than five minutes they were heard beneath the tower.

The call at the same time had aroused Irene's guards, who kept not so good a watch as they ought to do.

They were heard in the passage outside the room; but the Boy Pirate had taken means to prevent their entrance by bolting the door inside.

When the men were grouped at the bottom of the tower, he held a consultation with Irene as to the best mode of exit—whether it should be by the door or window.

All this while the outlaws, whom Jilok Tudel had left in charge of his house and his captive, were hammering away at the door and endeavouring to force an entrance.

Others, too, from the top of the tower kept up a fire of musket bullets on the men of the Red Raven beneath, luckily without doing any serious injury.

"Do you know the way to the gates?" asked Christopher.

"I do not," replied Irene. "It was dark when I was brought here, and I have never since quitted these rooms."

"Then, I offer you your choice. Shall I lower you through the window, or shall my men come up here and so storm the tower?"

"Oh, senor, I cannot pretend to decide; you must act as you think fit."

"Then, I will call them up."

He did so, and the crew of his boat climbed swiftly up the rope one by one, and in a few minutes all were in the apartment.

"My lads, we will burn this place to the ground when we have rescued this lady," he said, "for this is the stronghold of that pirate whose ship you so gallantly conquered."

A suppressed cheer was the response, and without any more hesitation, the door was thrown open.

The pirates, who knew not the number of the attacking force, rushed boldly into the room, brandishing their weapons; but they were received with a volley from the Avengers' pistols, which killed three of their number, and the others, after a short struggle, were captured and bound.

"Hurrah! the fort is won!" they shouted; but in the midst of their rejoicing came the report of a pistol, and one of them fell dead.

Irene uttered a scream of terror as she saw in the doorway the form of Jilok Tudel the pirate.

Wih a most fearful oath the ruffian le.elled a second pistol and pulled the trigger.

Too well it had been aimed, for the deadly bullet pierced Irene's breast, and, with a groan, she sank down on the floor of the room.

"I die!" she moaned, faintly. "Kind senor, avenge me!"

"I will!" cried Christopher, as he bent over her, "by all I hold dear and sacred I will."

"Holy Virgin have——"

Ere she could complete the petition, breath had departed from her fair body.

"Now, sanguinary monster!" cried Christopher, "vengeance is at hand, and I am the Avenger of innocent blood!"

The only reply of Jilok Tudel was to aim a down-right blow at our hero's head, which, had it taken effect, would have laid him dead on the ground.

But the Boy Pirate was prepared, and as a good swordsman, much superior to the Mexican.

He received the stroke on the hilt of his weapon, and returned it with interest.

His men stood round, watching the progress of the fight, not interfering, from that love of fair play and equality which is the characteristic of the Briton, yet ready to protect him should he be hard pressed by the Mexican pirate.

But they had confidence in his skill, and, like spectators at a show, warmly applauded each stroke and thrust.

In five minutes Jilok Tudel received Christopher's sword through his body, and the wretch fell with a horrid imprecation on his lips.

"Carry out the body of this lady," said the Boy Pirate to his men, and pointing towards the corpse of Irene St. Marc.

Two of the crew of the "Red Raven" advanced for that purpose, while the remainder looked towards their commander for orders.

"You, my lads, search the place, turn out anyone that may be in it, and then fire the building. I am determined it shall harbour no more ruffians such as these."

"How about these bodies, captain?" asked one of the men.

"Leave them to be consumed in the flames."

He then followed the party who were carrying the body of Irene St. Marc.

A short distance from the house they dug a grave beneath a verdant, wide-spreading mahogany tree, and in it they laid the fair corpse of the murdered girl.

A short prayer was repeated while those rude sailors stood by with uncovered heads.

Then the earth was filled in, and a pile of huge stones placed upon the grave to mark the resting-place of one so young, so fair, and so virtuous.

While this ceremony was going on a different scene took place in the old tower, and its surrounding buildings.

Several females, wives of the pirate crew of Tudel were expelled from the old house.

Then bundles of straw and faggots of wood were heaped up in the ground floor, and a torch thrown on the pile.

Smoke drifted about in dense volumes, then a body of flame burst forth which served well to light the Avengers to their ship.

About half an hour afterwards there was a terrific explosion, the fire having reached a magazine of powder which Jilok Tudel had stored away in his tower.

Huge masses of masonry were thrown up into the

air, while the wall which surrounded the house was hurled flat to the ground.

Then the fire gradually died away, and shortly afterwards nothing but a mass of ruins, hot and smoking, with here and there a half-burnt beam of timber glowing redly in the midst of the confusion, marked the spot were Jilok Tudel had defied justice so oft.

With break of day Christopher set sail to report to the old Mexican woman the unfortunate death of her daughter.

CHAPTER CCCXVII.

EDWARD LEIGHTON RECEIVES INTELLIGENCE FROM AMERICA.

WHEN Edward Leighton opened the letters which had been left for him at the banker's office at Paris, he found one which informed him that all the other male branches of his family were dead, and that he was now the representative of the house of Leighton.

As he was not a selfish man he deeply regretted this news, though the event placed him in possession of considerable property in England as well as America.

The Parisian banker, who had undertaken the charge of affairs, condoled with him, but without avail. His heart was really and deeply wounded by the news.

With the letters were also some copies of American newspapers, in which were full details of the death of Mark Leighton.

The latter, it appeared by the newspaper accounts, had gone into Texas, and while there attempted to kidnap and carry away the wife of a man named Lamond, who, it was said, had once quarrelled with Leighton; the woman, too, was a relative of the deceased.

The husband, however, prevented the forcible abduction of his bride, and then challenged Mark Leighton to meet him with pistols. This invitation was accepted, and the hostile parties faced each other with revolvers.

Mark Leighton fired the first shot, and, ere his adversary returned it, a second, but it was his last act, for Lamond's bullet struck him fairly in the centre of the forehead, and penetrated to the brain.

The writer or reporter then went on to say that when this intelligence was communicated to the deceased's father, who lived and held property in one of the newly-settled districts of Arkansas, he was so affected that an effusion of blood to the brain carried him off suddenly.

Edward Leighton could not disbelieve these statements.

The rash attempt to carry Agnes off from her husband so well accorded with what he knew of Mark's character, while he had often heard of the wondrous skill with the pistol which Lamond *alias* Regan, the ex-bush-ranger, possessed.

That the news of Mark's death should hurry his father to the grave he could well understand, for he knew the old gentleman to be of a very nervous, ex-

citable temperament, while at the same time possessing a full habit of body rather inclining to stoutness.

After a decent period had elapsed Edward, with
his wife, set sail for America, whither he went to
dispose of his property, and provide for any of his
relations who needed such assistance.

But he did not intend to remain in the Backwoods,
for he would not for all the world expose his beloved
Katinka to such dangers as she would have to
encounter.

After all the privations and troubles she had
undergone he was resolved that her future life should
be one of ease and comfort if a husband's love and
wealth could produce such effects.

A short journey across the Atlantic, and a long
journey through fertile plains, under lofty mountains, across broad rivers, and through dense forests,
and he reached Larchville.

The old house was shut up, and the plantation
seemed going to ruin.

Nevertheless, he soon had several offers for it from
neighbouring planters, who desired to increase their
territory.

It was soon disposed of to his satisfaction, and then
he started for the western part of Texas, where
Agnes was living with her husband, who now
planted and hunted, instead of plundering others of
their goods and chattels.

Sorrowful as was the meeting between Edward
and Agnes, there was much to be said besides that
which had reference to the mournful event which
brought him to America.

"Edward," said she, when he had been seated in
her log hut for a few minutes, "you are not come
to quarrel with my husband?"

"No," replied he; "why should I?"

"Because of—Mark's—death," said she, while the
tears sprung to her eyes.

"Dear Agnes," said Edward, "though no one
can deplore Mark's untimely end more than I do,
yet I remember whose fault it was, and have no
wish to create any more unhappiness."

"Thanks, thanks, for those words; for he,
Oswald, is my husband, and my heart is so bound
up in his, that it would kill me were anything to
happen to him. See, here is the bond which unites
us so firmly."

And lifting the coverlet from the bed, she disclosed the infantine features and fingers of a babe
scarce three months old.

"And are you happy, Agnes?"

"Yes, Edward; for though we are poor, our
wants are few, and easily as well as honestly supplied."

"Then you have no wish to change your lot?"

"None, whatever."

"That I am truly glad to hear, my dear girl. But
lest you should ever come to want, take this paper.
On presenting this at the City bank at New York,
you will be paid three thousand dollars a year so long
as you live, and at your death, your children will
inherit."

"But, Edward, this is too generous; how can I
thank you?"

"By thinking of me when I am thousands of
miles away, and by keeping up a correspondence
with me."

"I will, I will. But here comes my husband."

And Agnes flew to the door to meet him.

Oswald Lamond frowned when he heard who was
inside his hut, and entering, glanced haughtily on
one whom he supposed had come to pick a quarrel
with him.

"Who have we here?" he said. "Another Leighton in the field?"

Edward extended his hand, and replied,

"Another Leighton, who is come to reconcile all
ill blood that ever existed between our families."

The young hunter liked the frank reply, and he
warmly grasped the extended hand.

"What could I do?" he said. "My wife's
honour was at stake?"

"Let the past be forgotten," replied Edward
Leighton, "and let us recur no more to that unhappy subject."

And the death of Mark was no more spoken of,
while the young hunter told all that had happened
since his marriage with Agnes, and with a father's
joy and pride he exhibited the beautiful boy with
which his wife had presented him.

"My only fear is," he whispered, "that some one
may recognise me as the bushranger, and so the law
may clutch me. Not that I fear death, but then
my wife would be alone in the world, and destitute."

"No," replied Edward, "I have provided for her
in case anything should happen to you."

"Thanks, thanks," said Oswald. "You have
indeed set my mind at rest. But here comes a party
of friends to see me."

The door of the cottage opened, and in stalked an
Indian chief, followed by a white woman, who
bore a babe in her bosom.

The Indian supported his wife tenderly, and
gazed on her handsome face with pride and affection.

They were, as the reader will have no difficulty in
guessing, Catahaga and his wife, Minna Wyotti.

How the Eagle-Wing returned to his bride from
California we need not relate, but when he did return
he brought news that the Grey Wolf was in the
hands of those who sought him.

By the influence of old Nat Weatherfield a reconciliation was effected between the white chief and
the red, so that the two young men lived near each
other.

But Edward could not stay long amongst them,
so he returned once more to Paris, where he passed
his time in happiness in the society of his wife.

What befel others of our characters will be found
in another chapter.

CHAPTER CCCXVIII.

ANDREW HARWOLF UNWILLINGLY BECOMES
THE PRISONER OF SILAS RYE—THEY TAKE
SHIP HOMEWARDS—HARWOLF'S DEATH.

WHEN Catahaga, the Indian chief, stepped into the

centre of the tribe of Lepacotahs, and demanded that the prisoner's life should be spared, there was only one redskin who felt anything like disappointment at the circumstance.

That was Maratahnow the ugly medicine man.

The hideous wretch was by nature and principle bloodthirsty, he hated the idea of extending clemency to any one.

The other members of the band were not cruel by disposition, so that when Catahaga offered powder, lead, and rum in abundance in exchange for their prisoner, nearly all were willing to accept the proposal.

After much delay it was therefore decided that the white prisoner should be given up to the Eagle-Wing, and Harwolf was condemned to be escorted to San Francisco by two braves of the Lepacotahs, who were to bring back the treasures for which the tribe had bargained.

And so the next morning they started on the return journey, though Harwolf was so weak with loss of blood as to be unable to walk. He was therefore lifted to the back of a mule, by the side of which marched the two Lepacotahs, while Catahaga, with his rifle in readiness, brought up the rear.

The Eagle-Wing was lost in deep thought, his thoughts were of his pale-faced wife, whom he had left some hundreds of miles away in the hut of Weatherfield the trapper.

What troubles or trials she had been compelled to meet since then he knew not, but in his own mind he resolved on a terrible revenge on the heads of those who had dared to molest her during his absence.

For Catahaga loved Miuna Wyotti deeply, truly, and tenderly, and though at times his conduct towards her might appear harsh it was more the influence of early habits and education than any lack of love or kindness.

The little party swiftly threaded the avenues between the grand primeval forest trees. Eagle-Wing alone of the three warriors bore no scalps in his girdle, but his reputation as a warrior was so great and so widely spread that this circumstance did not produce the least feeling of contempt or disrespect in the minds of his redskin comrades.

Harwolf was silent, partly from pain and weakness, partly because he knew neither his destination or his fate, and therefore knew not how to open a conversation.

"Eagle-Wing's trail is like the swift flight of a bird," at length said one of the Lepacotahs; "it passes through the air and leaves no mark."

"Ugh!" was the reply.

"What does my brother intend to do with his prisoner?"

"He is not my prisoner," replied Catahaga, "and he will be delivered over to the Sachems of the white men."

The two Lepacotahs seemed astonished at this news They fancied that at least the Eagle-Wing would reserve to himself the privilege of torturing a man for whom he was to pay so many kegs of rum and powder.

"And will not Eagle-Wing take the scalp of his prisoner?"

"Catahaga will take no more scalps; he has been amongst the pale faces, and has known the meaning of justice."

"Does the hunter show mercy to the venomous rattlesnake? And will the Grey Wolf be allowed to live?"

"He will not be allowed to live, but his blood will not redden the hands of Catahaga."

This was the first intimation that Andrew Harwolf had of what was intended to be done with him.

There could be no doubt but that he was in some way—how he knew not—to be delivered up to the strong hand of justice.

The thought was anything but pleasant to him.

He writhed about in his saddle, but his bonds were secure; he bit his lips till the blood came to drive away the spectral visions that arose before his eyes.

What were those visions?

A stately room in an English mansion—a man struggling on the floor whilst a murderer with heavy hand and cruel blows beat out his brains!—a vision of a black and hideous gallows, beneath which that murderer tottered, while the dense and raging mob greeted him with yells of execration and derision!

Again he writhed and struggled, but was powerless as a partridge in the jaws of a fox.

His senses reeled as he was thus dragged along, trees and bushes became in his eyes grinning gibing spectres conjured up by the demon of remorse.

At length his face fell forward on the back of the mule, and he became senseless.

After satisfying himself that his prisoner was not dead, Catahaga again proceeded on his journey, nor did he halt till within about two miles of San Francisco.

All day they had journeyed, and the shades of evening were beginning to fall darkly over the forest from which the cavalcade had just emerged.

A light waggon drawn by a powerful horse, and containing two men was drawn up by the roadside, and towards these Catahaga directed his course.

The men in the waggon were Silas Rye and Oiny Macarne, who bestowed a brief greeting to Eagle-Wing as he halted by their side.

"I am glad you have not disappointed us," said Silas. "What ransom is demanded for him?"

Catahaga briefly specified the articles which were to be given to the Lepacotahs, and the goods named were placed on the mule, from the back of which Harwolf was lifted to the waggon.

A dram of rum was then given to each of the strange warriors, who once more turned about and retraced their steps to the spot where they had left their tribe.

Catahaga and Silas Rye then jumped up into the waggon, taking their seats each side of the prisoner, while the Irishman, seizing the reins, drove off at a rapid pace.

The vehicle skirted the town for some distance and then took a road which led to the beach about six miles from the harbour.

It was dark when they reached their destination, but coloured lights showed that a ship was lying not far distant from the shore, while the rays of a lantern discovered a boat waiting on the beach.

Towards this spot Oiny guided his horse which he drew up within two yards of the boat.

"What! cheerily ho!" hailed a most unmistakably British voice as the waggon drove up, "what ship, mates?"

"The 'Western Star!'" replied Silas, in answer to this hail.

"All right, cast your anchor alongside here!"

The speaker, who appeared by his dress to be one of the principal officers of the vessel, advanced to the side of the vehicle and grasped Silas by the hand.

"So you've taken your deserter, then, my friend?" he said.

"Not I, but my Indian friend."

"But what's the matter? He seems very quiet."

"He is, no doubt; he lost a quantity of blood in his duel with Oiny."

"Well, bring him on board, we'll soon doctor him up with tar and salt."

"You are not afraid to go on with the enterprise, I suppose?" asked Silas.

"Not a bit. In less than two hours we shall be on the high seas, and, then, we've a right to apprehend him as being a criminal."

Two men at that moment came forward, and, with their aid, Harwolf was transferred from the waggon to the boat.

He was still insensible.

In a few minutes they reached the side of the "Western Star," and all the party ascended to the deck.

The prisoner was taken below and laid on a couch in one of the cabins which, by the enterprise of Silas Rye, had been prepared for his reception.

For Silas, to make certain that the villain had met the death he so richly deserved, had returned with Catahaga to the scene of the duel that same evening.

No trace of him was to be found, but the footprints of the Lepacotahs told plainly in which direction and in what manner he had disappeared.

"He still lives," said Catahaga; "I will follow the trail and bring him back."

A plan of action was then agreed on, and the Eagle-Wing, after being authorised to offer any quantity of goods to the strange tribe, departed.

With what success he performed his errand the reader already knows.

But, while Catahaga was thus absent, Silas Rye was not idle.

He bargained with an English captain, to whom he explained most of the circumstances, to provide a secure passage for the prisoner.

Captain Johnson readily agreed to wait a few days, and took his ship to the spot where she now ay, in order that Harwolf might be smuggled on board with greater facility.

When the last-named individual had been conveyed to his cabin, the captain passed the word to weigh anchor, and Catahaga took leave of his friends, returning home in the waggon which had been used for the conveyance of the murderer of Lord Edgeforth.

No. 92.

A few minutes more, and the "Western Star" was swiftly floating away towards the shores of England with a mad felon in her state cabin.

A watch was, of course, kept upon Harwolf, that is to say, a man was placed on guard before the door to prevent his issuing forth.

It was some hours ere the wretched man recovered his senses, and then he had some difficulty in coming to a consciousness of where he was.

But slowly recollection dawned upon him, and with it came again the agonising mental tortures to which he had been subjected for many days and nights past.

"And so all is over," he muttered, as, through an opening in the door, he saw the sentry pace up and down. "My career is, at length, run, and now comes retribution. Retribution means death!—death in its most hideous and revolting form! Better that I had died in the lone wilderness, had perished in the cataract, or fallen by the arrows of the Indians, than by the fearful hand of the hangman! I cannot, will not submit to such a destiny!"

The wretched man raised himself on his elbow, and glared fearfully round.

A lamp threw a faint glimmer through the skylight, and his face looked perfectly deathlike, so pale was it with fear and weakness.

He cast an eager glance towards the door, and saw that it was securely fastened.

Though disarmed he had not been searched, and now he drew from his pocket a small phial.

It contained prussic acid!

"Thus I defy fate, and cheat the hangman!" he muttered, with a low laugh, as he raised the phial to his lips.

But no sooner had the poison passed his lips than came regret for the rash act.

"Help! help!" he cried.

The sentry without gave the alarm, and Silas Rye, accompanied by the captain rushed into the room.

Harwolf was gasping for breath, and could scarcely speak.

"What's the matter? What have you done?" they demanded.

"Poison!" he muttered, hoarsely.

Silas took up the bottle from the place where it had fallen.

The smell was sufficient to tell him what deleterious liquid the unhappy wretch had swallowed.

"Why have you done this?" demanded Silas with alarm, lest justice should be defeated.

"Ha, ha! it was a swindle! I am not destined to make a spectacle for an English mob. Oh, heavens, help me! Damnation, it is eating into my bones! Water! water!"

A draught was given him, and then he continued,

"Lord Edgeforth died an easier death. I killed him in two blows; but I must burn in hell fire before my time."

"Take note of what he says," whispered Silas to the captain.

"The Boy Pirate will be a pretty peer to sit in the senate. You know that he is the heir! you, you! I killed him though, and now I burn! Hell's curses on you all! Why don't you take those dogs away, they tear my bowels out?"

The wretch fell back groaning with pain and writhing.

In a few seconds he started up again, and with a wild curse on his lips, fell down dead!

Whither had that spirit gone?

Such a sudden death greatly disappointed Silas Rye, who had hoped to have the unfaithful steward tried by an English jury.

But at all events his confession was witnessed by the captain of the ship, and that, with the papers which Catahaga had taken from Harwolf in Arkansas, would most probably suffice to set Christopher in his proper position.

For Silas Rye knew not how Mr. Pounce had been working for the benefit of his young friend.

The good ship "Western Star" was speedily rid

of the loathsome presence of the murderer's body, and then sailed swiftly over the waves with light hearts on board, till at length a safe anchorage was made in a British harbour.

Then Silas with his party hastened to London with his news and his documents, and learnt, with no small surprise and gratification, that son, as well as father, was dead.

The proofs of Christopher's identity, as well as of Harwolf's crime and perfidy, were placed in the hands of Mr. Pounce, who at once made an application to the House of Lords on behalf of Christopher Lord Edgeforth.

CHAPTER CCCXIX.

STRANGE COMPANY—THE SLAVER AND THE BOY PIRATE—DANIEL HARWOLF'S HIDING-PLACE—HIS DEATH.

WHEN Daniel Harwolf felt himself sinking down through the waves, he thought that his last hour was come, and then consciousness left him.

When he recovered he found himself on a sandy beach, surrounded by a group of sailors, who were pouring brandy down his throat, and endeavouring to recover him.

With a sigh he sat up and looked around him.

"Where am I? Who are you?" he asked.

"Yankee tars, my lad, so make yourself easy. But how came you here?"

"In a boat; but I was drowned, I believe."

"I guess not. But take another sup o' this stuff, that'll bring you to again."

The pirate did so, and soon after found himself able to sit up, and even to walk about a little.

He much wondered who his strange preservers could be, and what they were doing on a little unimportant island.

By listening to several expressions which fell from them, he at length came to the conclusion that they were slavers, and ventured to ask them if such were not the fact.

"You're correct, mister," replied the skipper. "Do yer fancy sailin' with us?"

"I do," replied Harwolf, and forthwith his name was enrolled in the ship's books.

It appeared that the slavers had been chased by a cruiser, from which they had some trouble to escape, and when at length they did so, found they were so short of water as to be compelled to make for this island.

Harwolf's body rolling on the beach at the mercy of the waves attracted their attention, and the result was his salvation from death.

The next day all their preparations for continuing the voyage were completed.

The anchor was dragged up from its sandy bed, the sails were set, and the ship speeded away with a cargo of living misery beneath the hatches.

Before they had lost sight of land another sail hove in sight.

"Another o' them blasted cruisers, I guess!" cried the Yankee captain.

He took another look through his glass, and repeated his opinion.

Daniel Harwolf had no telescope, or he would have known the vessel; as it was, he thought that the spars and canvas seemed familiar to him, distant and indistinct though they were.

"'Bout ship!" cried the skipper, and the order was quickly obeyed.

The slaver, on another course, sought to place the island between her and the stranger for concealment.

Strange trade of guilt was that which makes men shun their fellow men and hide like mice from a cat.

The stranger slightly altered her course. She had apparently seen the slaver, and wished a little closer acquaintance.

And the new-comer was a swift sailer, too; one from whom there was evidently no escaping, though the slaver could out-sail any of the preventative squadron.

"It ain't a man o' war, I guess," said the captain, "and yet it looks British build. Who the devil can she be?"

As she spoke Harwolf once more directed his eyes towards the stranger, and he recognised her, as well he might.

It was the Boy Pirate's ship.

It was the "Red Raven!"

Harwolf's strength forsook him as he recognised his foe.

"Hunted!" he cried, "I shall ever be hunted by that most implacable foe."

"What, d'ye make her out, mate?" asked the skipper, turning to his new hand.

"It is the celebrated Pirate, the Red Raven," answered Harwolf, while trembling in every limb.

"What are yer 'fraid on?" said the captain. "Why, you blasted fool, pirates don't prey on slavers."

"But this one—"

"May go to hell, I ain't goin' to alter my course any more."

Harwolf knew not what to say. If he told all his villanies, and why he feared the Boy Pirate, there would be witnesses in after life to convict him of his crime.

The slaver again neared the island, and at length reached within about a mile from the shore, standing off, and under a light spread of canvas.

As the pursuer came nearer and nearer, Harwolf, whose guilty soul was ill at ease, began to look about him for some means of escape.

A little boat was towing alongside, and he resolved to drop into this when he should find an opportunity, and hide underneath an old sail which was lying in its bottom.

On came the "Red Raven," and Harwolf could recognise the form of his mortal enemy as he paced the quarter-deck.

He prepared for his desperate enterprise.

Taking a coil of rope, he fastened one end of it to the bulwarks and tied the other in a running knot.

Then, when every eye was turned towards the stranger, he gently lowered himself over the ship's side, and crept beneath the folds of canvas, holding the coil of rope in his hand.

To hide himself, he was compelled to lie beneath the thwarts of the boat, and, in creeping to this position, he managed, unintentionally, to get the slip knot round his neck.

Meanwhile the Boy Pirate came on board the slaver, and, finding her real character, at once took possession.

When the slight dispute which arose between the two captains had been settled, and the freed negroes were scampering over the deck, Ralph Talbot called to two or three of them, and directed them to haul up the boat in which Harwolf was concealed.

Thinking that the rope which he held in his hand and round his neck was the one which kept it in tow, the blacks began to pull away with a will, six of them to the end of the rope, which immediately tightened round Harwolf's neck.

His body was squeezed underneath the thwarts, and he was utterly unable to make any sound or cry.

The black workmen pulled away, and half lifted the boat from the water, when they were ordered to desist by Black Ralph, who had no idea that his old enemy was concealed there.

And so half an hour afterwards, when a man descended to throw out the sail, Daniel Harwolf was a blackened corpse, with his neck firmly bound by the cord, and his head pressed against the seat of the boat.

"Dead!" cried Christopher. "And I not the cause of his death!"

"You should rejoice at that, dearest," said Lilia, who now accompanied her husband wherever he went. "It would have been no honour to have stained your hands with the blood of so base and worthless a man."

But Christopher could not be satisfied.

The thought that the son of his father's murderer had fallen a victim to any hands but his own was gall and wormwood to him.

"Search his pockets," cried he, as he stood by the side of the blackened corpse, whose features were distorted with the agony of death, and whose hands were clenched in a fruitless endeavour to loosen the fatal noose.

The order was obeyed, but nothing could be found to throw any light on his past life.

That was now among the mysteries which could not be unveiled save as we have feebly attempted in these pages.

Within two hours after death the corpse of Daniel Harwolf was thrown to the mercy of the waves, and speedily found a grave in the stomachs of those sharks which had refused to devour him during life.

The slaves were all released on the island, and weapons placed in their hands to defend themselves against any aggression of the Yankees, or any attempt to recapture them.

Then again the Boy Pirate set sail, and proceeded on his way towards the shores of Great Britain.

Nothing occurred for the space of several days during which time Lilia was happy as could be, for she now saw a chance of the fulfilment of her heart's wishes.

She fondly hoped that her husband would now be restored to that station which was his by right of birth, and that, at least, he would be allowed to live henceforth in peace and quietness.

CHAPTER CCCXX.

THE BOY PIRATE ON HIS VOYAGE HOME TO ENGLAND—A FEARFUL STORM—DESTRUCTION OF THE "RED RAVEN," AND LOSS OF ALL ON BOARD BUT THE BOY PIRATE AND LILIA.

THE "Red Raven," as I have said, floated easily over the ocean till within about a week's sail from the west coast of Ireland.

Then a storm arose, which buffeted about the brave old ship, and rent the sails and cordage from the masts

Lightnings, thunder, and rain, all did their utmost to sweep every vestige of humanity from the bosom of the ocean.

The sailors, men who had passed through hundreds of storms and tempests, huddled up together, and lashed themselves to the bulwarks fearing to be washed away.

Ralph Talbot alone stood at the wheel, and sought to direct the course of the vessel; but the labouring tempest-strained ship refused to obey the guidance of the helm.

Near him was Christopher, and clinging to him his fair wife, who refused to be separated from him.

Mast after mast went over, and timber after timber started in the bottom.

The water rushed into the hold, and rapidly filled the ship. It was evident that she could not hold together much longer, and all those helpless beings were thus staring death full in the face.

For what boat could live in that raging, furious sea? It would be folly to attempt to lower them.

And so they stood mutely, yet brave and obedient to their commander to the last.

At length the crisis came.

"Save yourselves all!" he cried, and the men sprang overboard. He followed them, still keeping his beloved wife in his arms.

There was a roar like that of a whirlpool, and in a second the "Red Raven" went down bows foremost with the flag that had so often led her crew on to victory floating at the stump of a mast that remained.

Few of those who plunged into the raging sea ever were seen again.

Christopher arose to the surface of a wave, and for a moment glanced around.

Here and there might be seen the head of some poor fellow struggling for life, but there was no chance of giving that assistance which he so much longed to bestow.

Clasping his left arm tightly around his wife's waist, he struck out so as to get as clear as possible of the floating timbers which strewed the ocean.

Poor Lilia was half dead with terror, but she clung to her husband with a loving confidence.

She knew well that he would not desert her while life remained.

A fragment of a mast came floating by, and, grasping a piece of cordage which was still attached to it, Christopher was enabled to secure his prize, and thus give Lilia additional support.

The Rover's bride still retained her consciousness in the midst of all these terrors, and thanked her husband with a feeble smile.

Then away they drifted on the bosom of the pathless ocean, whither they knew not.

For hours they thus floated till, at length, night began to shade the waters, and there seemed no hope of salvation.

But just as the sun, who showed his face for a short time after the storm, was about to dip down behind the waves, a strange form was seen to glide out into the midst of his coppery face.

After glancing at it with interest for a while, the Boy Pirate joyfully pronounced the words,

"A ship! a ship!"

And a sail it was rapidly approaching them on the still powerful breeze and sailing directly towards them.

Lilia heard the news, but was too exhausted to make any reply, and Christopher's only fear now was that his lovely wife would perish ere assistance could reach her.

He cheered her with words of love and tenderness, and, pressing her close to him, sought to impart warmth to her chilled frame by contact with his own.

How slowly that ship seemed to him to sail, though those on board of her fancied that they never had passed through the water at such a rapid rate.

Raising himself up, the gallant young fellow sought to attract their attention by waving his jacket in the air, and at length had the satisfaction of feeling certain that he had attracted their attention.

Down came the sail, a boat was lowered, and the half-dead pair speedily hoisted to the deck.

Christopher had a dim recollection of being surrounded by faces, and some of them familiar faces too.

Then recollection fled, and he became delirious.

It was two days ere he recovered his senses, and when he did, he found Silas and Charles Rye sitting by his bedside.

"What does this mean?" he cried, "I don't recollect—"

"My dear friend, be still, you are with those who love you," said Silas.

"And my wife—Lilia?"

The curtain was thrown aside, and the Queen of the Avengers entered.

An explanation was then volunteered by Silas, who simply stated the fact that they were homeward bound from California with all the proofs of Andrew Harwolf's treacherous villany on board, when they caught sight of him.

"Did you find any of my companions?" asked Christopher.

"Not one."

"Then all must have perished."

It was too true. Of all the souls who were on board the "Red Raven" when the storm struck her, not one save Christopher and Lilia escaped.

The young sailor shed many bitter tears at the fate of his comrades, yet, in the midst of his grief, thanked Heaven that he had disposed of his other ships ere he commenced his last sad voyage.

The good ship "Eagle" then held on her course, and at length safely anchored in the Mersey.

Christoper and Lilia were provided with a home in a secluded spot until the result of Lord Hawksbury's work could be known.

This decision was obtained after various delays, which, along with other obstacles, were at length overcome by the energy and perseverance of Lord Hawksbury and Mr. Pounce.

The dying confession of Andrew Harwolf, and the testimony of Ann Lewis cleared the way; and then Silas Rye stood forward, and while he confessed to a certain amount of complicity in the horrid deed, yet his evidence was accepted, and Christopher Foundling, the Boy Pirate, became Lord Edgeforth!

But before he could be entirely installed in his new title and estates he had to pass the ordeal of a British jury.

A charge of piracy was made against him by the counsel for the crown, and he was held to bail in the sum of five thousand pounds.

The day of trial came, and the prosecuting counsel made a long oration setting forth the enormity of the offence and the terrible punishment which should be awarded to pirates.

Mr. Pounce's reply was brief, but to the purpose.

He called upon the honourable gentleman to produce one jot of evidence to support the charge; and by so doing completely astounded the crown counsel who never for a moment imagined that the charge would be denied. As, however, there were no witnesses to prove anything against Christopher, Mr. Pounce simply remarked that he would leave the case in the hands of a British jury, who, he felt certain, would not convict a man on the bare assertion of a man who could not bring forward the least bit of proof to sustain the charge.

The jury, without leaving their box, returned a verdict of "Not Guilty," and Christopher walked from the dock to be congratulated as Lord Edgeforth.

Two days afterwards he took up his residence at Frontemore, and in less than a month after the trial Lilia gave birth to a son, in whose infantine smiles Lord Edgeforth forgot the chequered career he had passed as

THE BOY PIRATE!

CHAPTER CCCXXI.

THE TWO MERCHANTS OF NEW ORLEANS—A MEETING IN PARIS—ONCE MORE WE MEET.

WHEN the Boy Pirate started in pursuit of Daniel Harwolf, he left his two other ships in harbour, under the joint command of Sam Cassidy and Dick Caffyn, with instructions to sell the vessels and turn the money to the best account they could.

This, both the young men were perfectly willing to do, for they were tired of the roving, aimless, and lawless life which they had for some time been leading.

Both were, as our readers know, married, and they resided near each other, so that the wives might enjoy each other's company when the husbands were absent.

The vessels were thoroughly repaired, fresh painted and newly rigged, some of the guns were dismounted so that it was impossible to recognise them as the Brazilian war sloops, they looked so much more like peaceful traders.

And so they were, for the partners opened a regular trade between New Orleans and the northern cities of the United States, and in that capacity amassed an immense fortune.

It seemed as if peace was to be their portion for life.

But not so.

For when, after years of discontent, the mighty civil war broke out which has but so recently been ended, Cassidy and Caffyn, espousing the side of the state in which they resided, became blockade runners and in that capacity did good service to their adopted land.

With better success than some of those who espoused the same side they escaped to France with the remnants of their fortunes, and there do they reside to the present day.

And there, too, they were destined to meet an old friend.

As Dick Caffyn, who was now transformed from a rude seaman to a polished though manly-looking gentleman, was walking one day along the Rue de Banque he was accosted by a swell of the first magnitude.

"So you have turned up at last," said the swell, in good English; "come home and dine with me and tell me all about our old friends."

"Sir," replied Caffyn, "you have the advantage. I have not the honour of your acquaintance."

"What! forgotten me already, Mr. Caffyn? My name is Edward Leighton, and I saw some little service with you in Poland."

"Pardon me, pardon me, I should have remembered."

And a hearty shake of the hand convinced Edward that the lack of recollection was unintentional.

Of course a long after-dinner chat took place, and all the items of news were exchanged on both sides.

Dick had heard of his foster-brother's elevation to the peerage and proposed a visit to England for the purpose of seeing him.

And so they did, with perfect safety, for no one would dream of imagining that the elegant gentlemen who, unannounced, entered Frontemore Hall, were the companions of the once dreaded Boy Pirate.

A happy reunion was the immediate result, though the friends in the midst of their mirth did not forget to shed a tear to the memory of Black Ralph.

THE END.